There Is No Antimemetics Division

qntm

ISBN: 9798721503788

CONTENTS

Prologue

Part I: There Is No Antimemetics Division

Interlude

Part II: Five Five Five Five Five

Epilogue

Prologue

SCP-055 - [unknown]

Item #: SCP-055

Object Class: Keter

Special Containment Procedures: Object is kept within a five (5) by five (5) by two point five (2.5) meter square room constructed of cement (fifty (50) centimeter thickness), with a Faraday cage surrounding the cement walls. Access is via a heavy containment door measuring two (2) by two point five (2.5) meters constructed on bearings to ensure door closes and locks automatically unless held open deliberately. Security guards are NOT to be posted outside SCP-055's room. It is further advised that all personnel maintaining or studying other SCP objects in the vicinity try to maintain a distance of at least fifty (50) meters from the geometric center of the room, as long as this is reasonably practical.

Description: SCP-055 is a "self-keeping secret" or "anti-meme". Information about SCP-055's physical appearance as well as its nature, behavior, and origins is self-classifying. To clarify:

- How Site 19 originally acquired SCP-055 is unknown.
- When SCP-055 was obtained, and by whom, is unknown.
- SCP-055's physical appearance is unknown. It is not indescribable, or invisible: individuals are perfectly capable of entering SCP-055's container and observing it, taking mental or written notes, making sketches, taking photographs, and even making audio/video recordings. An extensive log of such observations is on file. However, information about SCP-055's physical appearance "leaks" out of a human mind soon after such an observation. Individuals tasked with describing SCP-055 afterwards find their minds wandering and lose interest in the task; individuals tasked with sketching a copy of a photograph of SCP-055 are unable to remember what the photograph looks like, as are researchers overseeing these tests. Security personnel who have observed SCP-055 via closed-circuit television cameras emerge after a full shift exhausted and effectively amnesiac about the events of the previous hours.
- Who authorized the construction of SCP-055's containment room, why it was constructed in this way, or what the purpose of the described Containment Procedures may be, are all unknown.
- Despite SCP-055's container being easily accessible, all personnel at Site 19 claim no knowledge of SCP-055's existence when challenged.

All of these facts are periodically rediscovered, usually by chance readers of this file, causing a great deal of alarm. This state of concern lasts minutes at most, before the matter is simply forgotten about.

A great deal of scientific data has been recorded from SCP-055, but cannot be studied.

At least one attempt has been made to destroy SCP-055, or possibly move it from containment at Site 19 to another site, meeting failure for reasons unknown.

SCP-055 may present a major physical threat and indeed may have killed many hundreds of personnel, and we would not know it. Certainly it presents a gigantic memetic/mental threat, hence its Keter classification.

Document #055-1: An Analysis of SCP-055

The author puts forward the hypothesis that SCP-055 was never formally acquired by ███████████████ and is in fact an autonomous or remotely-controlled agent, inserted at Site 19 by an unidentified third party for one or all of the following purposes:

- to silently observe, or interfere with, activities at Site 19
- to silently observe, or interfere with, activities at other SCP locations
- to silently observe, or interfere with, activities of humanity worldwide
- to silently observe, or interfere with, other SCP objects
- to silently observe, or interfere with, ██████████

No action to counter any of these potential threats is suggested, or indeed theoretically possible.

Part I

There Is No Antimemetics Division

1
We Need To Talk About Fifty-Five

"Can I smoke?"

This time the receptionist narrows her eyes at Marion. "No," she says. "You— No, you can't smoke anywhere on Site 200. Just because it's an administration building doesn't mean we don't have lungs. Or labor law."

Marion notices the exasperation on the young woman's face. "I've asked you that before, haven't I?"

"Twice in the last quarter-hour," the receptionist says. "You must really need a smoke." She's genuinely puzzled at the repeated question, and she's doing a bad job of concealing her puzzlement.

"You think this is like *Memento*, don't you?" Marion offers, charitably. "You think I have no long-term memory, and if I stay in one place for too long I forget why I'm there."

The receptionist is only just old enough to remember that film. "I... guess?"

Marion smiles sympathetically and shakes her head. It's nothing so simple.

Minutes pass. She toys obsessively with her lighter. She is turning fifty this year and slowly greying, well on her way out of "petite" towards "little old lady". In her bag her phone beeps because it's time for a pill, but she tells it to remind her later. There is a slight tremble in her fingers, but that's not age-based infirmity, that's just ordinary nerves. She's nervous because she's here to meet an O5, and O5s are scary. O5s never want to see you for a small thing. It's the end of the world, or nothing.

Finally, forty minutes late, the door to the inner office opens. Four or five high-ranked Foundationers spill out, carrying laptops or briefcases. As a group, they head straight past reception and out to cars which are waiting. Marion recognises a few of the faces— the Site 19 site director, the head recruiter for Western Europe. None of them glance in her direction.

Once they're gone, O5-8's assistant pokes his head around the door. He's twenty-something, improbably youthful, like a teenager stuffed into one of his dad's business shirts. His haircut is barely regulation. In one hand he holds a tablet computer showing his boss's day planner. It's packed. The man evidently does not sleep.

"Marion? You can come through now."

*

The office door closes behind them with an unusually heavy mechanical *clunk*, as if the whole thing is part of a machine built into the office walls. While Marion takes the indicated chair and sets her bag down, the assistant turns and does some confusing additional things to the door, causing it to make several further strange noises. O5s have non-trivial privacy and security requirements.

The office is spacious, but somehow contrives to be dark despite two big corners of window and broad daylight outside. The walls are all bookshelves and dark wood panelling; perfectly stylish, but a style from the Nineties, a little worn, and not yet old enough to be fashionable again.

As for the fellow behind the desk, well, an O5 never looks like you imagine.

Marion takes a deep breath. "So what's the topic? All I got was the meeting invitation, no agenda or subject. I mean, an O5 says 'jump', you jump, but—"

Looking to her right, she notices that the assistant, without saying anything or making any undue noise, has set his tablet down on a table, produced a gun and aimed it at her head. Marion stops talking. She sits still in her chair for a little while, absorbing the change of pace, letting her heart rate rise to a hummingbird's and then start to flatten again.

"Okay?" she hazards. She licks her lips and grips the arm rests, otherwise staying perfectly still, waiting for another prompt. The assistant's face is totally neutral now, like this is just how meetings go. Maybe it is, for people up here.

"Who are you?" O5-8 asks her.

Marion blinks. "What? Oh, God."

"Let me rephrase," O5-8 says. "Marion Wheeler, forty-nine, with loving husband and two boys in tow. Likes camping, hiking and ornithology. Boring mother with perfect, airtight background and financials, as far back as we can examine. And you've got full Foundation credentials which we've never issued, including access to a list of installations and rooms which... some of these locations don't exist, or were torn down decades ago. At least one hasn't been built yet, yet you've got the front door key to it. That's before we get to your SCP access control lists, which I can only term as 'egregious'.

"So you're a spy, and your objectives are misaligned with ours, and Clay wanted to cut Xi-3 loose on you, but I was able to bring him around. I talked him into a face-to-face. I thought there was a slim chance that if we locked you in a bomb-proof room and asked politely, you'd have the good sense to spare yourself 'the rest'."

Marion has long since stopped listening. "You dullard," she says now she can finally speak, "I'm your chief of Antimemetics."

"We don't have an Antimemetics Division," Clay says.

"Yes, you do. *We* do."

O5-8 says, "We have a Memetics Division, a Telekontainment Division, Fire Services, Ops-A, Ops-B, Personnel, D-personnel and two dozen others. We don't have an Antimemetics Division."

"Do we have an Irony Division?" Marion asks. She hesitates hopefully. "No? Alright. Well, try this: why do you think the Antimemetics Division would show up in the listing?"

"This is just a cover story," Clay says to O5-8, not taking his eyes off Marion. "It's a good one, but she's had it worked out in advance."

"Clay, lose the piece," says the O5.

Grudgingly, Clay does so.

Marion relaxes fractionally. "There are SCPs with dangerous memetic properties," she says. "There are contagious concepts which require containment just like any physical threat. They get inside your head, and ride your mind to reach other minds. Right?"

"Right," O5-8 says. He could name a score of SCPs fitting this description without even thinking.

"There are SCPs with antimemetic properties," Marion goes on. "There are ideas which cannot be spread. There are entities and phenomena which harvest and consume information, particularly information about themselves. You take a Polaroid photo of one, it'll never develop. You write a description down with a pen on paper and hand it to

9

someone— but what you've written turns out to be hieroglyphs, and nobody can understand them, not even you. You can look directly at one and it won't even be invisible, but you'll still perceive nothing there. Dreams you can't hold onto and secrets you can never share, and lies, and living conspiracies. It's a conceptual subculture, of ideas consuming other ideas and... sometimes... segments of reality. Sometimes, people.

"Which makes them a threat. That's all there is to it, really. Antimemes are dangerous, and we don't understand them; therefore, they are part of the Problem. Hence my division. We can do the sideways thinking that's needed to combat something which can literally eat your combat training."

O5-8 stares back at her for a long moment. Clay fidgets, disliking and distrusting the story, but the O5 seems more open to the concept.

"Name one," he says. "Name an antimemetic SCP."

"SCP-055," Marion says promptly.

"There is no SCP-055," Clay retorts.

"Again: Yes, there is," Marion says.

"There isn't," Clay asserts. "SCP numbers aren't assigned sequentially. There are gaps. That number hasn't been assigned. It's not superstition, we have enough to be concerned about without arbitrary numerological mysticism. We have SCP-666 and SCP-013. But there's no SCP-001. And there's no SCP-055."

"Clay," O5-8 says, "you should look at this." He turns his monitor so Clay can see the file that he has just retrieved. Clay bends over and reads it from top to bottom. Stunned, he scrolls back and reads it all a second time.

"But..."

"The file's dated from 2008," O5-8 says. "It's got all the right flags and signatures. It's keyed and coded. It's real."

"You've seen this before?" Clay asks him.

"Never in my life," O5-8 says. "As far as I can remember, anyway. On the other hand, if the content is accurate, both of us have probably seen it dozens of times."

Clay glares at Marion. "This isn't possible."

Marion nearly spits. "For Christ's sake, Clay, how long have you been working here?"

"But if this SCP is this powerful..." he begins.

"Yes?"

"Who wrote the file?" the O5 finishes. "And for that matter, how do you, Mrs. Wheeler, retain knowledge of any of this?"

"The file was written by a man named Dr. Bartholomew Hughes," Marion says. "He's dead."

"What happened to him?"

"You don't want to know."

There is a very long pause while both O5-8 and his assistant react to this. In fact, they pass through a long, discrete sequence of reactions. Indignation at the seeming rudeness; confusion at Wheeler's incaution in front of sinister superiors; surprise at the magnitude of the claim; pure disbelief; comprehension; and finally, horror.

"What..." O5-8 asks carefully, "would happen if we *did* know?"

"It would happen to you as well," Marion says, levelly. "...As for your other question: we manage that pharmaceutically. You know we have class-A amnestics, for people who very badly need to forget things? Of course you do. Who could forget about class-A amnestics? Well, in Antimemetics, we have a different pill, for people who need to remember things that would otherwise be impossible to remember. Mnestics, class W, X, Y and Z. Same Greek root as the word 'mnemonic'. The M is silent."

In her bag, her phone beeps again.

With a nod of approval from the O5, Marion reaches into her bag and turns her phone off, acknowledging the prompt this time instead of postponing it. She pulls a blister pack from another pocket and pops a pill out. It's hexagonal, and green. She holds it up, and is satisfied to see a flicker of recognition on O5-8's face. He's beginning to put it back together.

Marion says, "These are class W mnestics, the weakest, suitable for continual use. Two pills per day. Go down to the site pharmacy and ask. The pharmacist will claim they don't stock any such thing; they're misremembering, tell them to double-check."

O5-8 sighs. "And now, I think, I get it. I see why we're having this conversation at all."

"Yes," Marion says, popping a second pill out and handing it over to him. "It's because you missed a dose. You're supposed to be on these, the same as me and everybody on my staff. It's the only way we can work. You forgot to take a pill, and then you forgot all the information that the pills were helping you retain. You forgot why you were taking them, who gave them to you, where to get more. You forgot about me, and my entire department. And now I have to bring you up to speed."

"And if I take this," O5-8 says, "I'll remember this whole conversation and we won't have to have it again?"

"Hopefully not," Marion says.

Clay pipes up. "Uh, should I be taking those?"

"Sorry, kiddo," O5-8 says. "Need to know. Maybe when you're an O5 yourself." He swallows the pill. Marion swallows hers too.

"So what is SCP-055?" O5-8 asks.

"SCP-055 is nothing," Marion says, now relaxing entirely. "SCP-055 is, as described in the file, a powerful information autosuppressor. As far as experimentation has uncovered, it can only be defined in negative terms. We can only record what it *isn't*. We know it isn't Safe or Euclid. We know it isn't round, or square, or green or silver. We know it isn't *stupid*.

And we know it isn't *alone*. But what we do know is that it's weak. It's weak because it's the only antimemetic agent in our possession which has a physical entry in the files. We have paper records of the thing. We have containment procedures. It's not Safe, which means it's dangerous... but it's contained."

O5-8 blinks. "You have procedures? Where?"

Marion points at her head.

"Then how many other antimemes are there? How much more dangerous do they get?"

"Ten that I know of," Marion says. "Statistically, probably at least five more that I don't know of. This does not count the antimemetic entities freely roaming the halls, not under containment. There are at least two in this room with us right now. Don't look. I said don't look! It's pointless!"

O5-8 does an impressive job of controlling himself, keeping his attention focused on Marion. Clay doesn't fare so well, and quickly sweeps the whole room, even checking behind his back. Making an ass of himself, essentially. He finds nothing. He looks baffled.

"There is an invisible monster which follows me around and likes to eat my memories," Marion explains, patiently. "SCP-4987. Don't look it up, it's not there. I've learned to manage with it. It's like a demanding pet. I produce tasty memories on purpose so it doesn't eat something important, like my passwords or how to make coffee."

"And what's the other one?" Clay asks.

With another nod from O5-8, Marion goes to her bag again. This time she pulls out a gun and shoots Clay twice in the heart.

More aghast than in pain, Clay collapses sharply against the bookcase behind him. Pulling his head around to face Marion, he manages, "How did you— kn—"

Marion stands, aims more carefully and shoots him a third time, this time in the head.

O5-8, again, does an impressive job of not reacting. "That's Clay's gun," he deadpans. "You stole it from him."

"It's tricky to steal a firearm this heavy from someone without them noticing," Marion explains, unloading it and carefully setting it down. "But stealing a firearm and then stealing their memory of the theft is a little easier. Like I said: a pet. Some pets are dumb enough that they can be trained."

"Yes," O5-8 says, evenly. "That much I'd guessed. But why?"

"Because you were supposed to be taking class-W mnestics," Marion says. "You can't skip a dose of class-W mnestic. I've tried. You can postpone a dose, but you can't *forget* unless someone actively prevents you from taking it. There's only one person who could get close enough to you to do that, and that's your assistant. And remember when I asked him how long he'd been working here?"

"He didn't answer," O5-8 says. "I thought you were being rhetorical."

"He doesn't work here," Marion says. "He's an antimeme. Since when do you have an assistant? You don't *have* an assistant, Brent. Look at this office. It's got one desk. You've got a receptionist outside: *she's* the one who screens your calls and schedules your meetings. Where does Clay even sit? Where does he fit? Don't blame yourself. You're human, and these things are redaction incarnate. You need to think like a space alien to get around them."

O5-8 asks a question which, in any other workplace, would be absurd. "Is he dead?"

"Maybe," Marion says. "I can put his corpse in our research queue and we'll see what we can see when we open him up. There's a duality here, though. They're like parallel universes sharing the same space. It's conceptual versus concrete, figurative versus physical. It's very unusual for things to cross over. I don't know what Clay was, but he had a human body, which instantly makes him weird, even by our standards. As ever, the search for stalemate continues. I will let you know if we get any closer."

"Any side effects of these pills?" O5-8 asks.

"Nausea, and dramatically increased risk of pancreatic cancer," Marion says. "And very bad dreams."

2
Introductory Antimemetics

Junior Researcher Kim's been working for the Foundation for all of four hours and he feels pulverised, as if an anvil were dropped on his head in that first introductory lecture. It's lunchtime, and he's found a corner so far back in the cafeteria that nobody bothers him, where he can chew and swallow non-anomalous food, drink apocalyptically strong coffee and digest the hard lessons of the morning.

On his Foundation-provided phone, he pages fretfully through the few SCP files for which he has clearance. Most of them have to be jokes. That's how they read. Like very bad, dark, frightening jokes.

Kim's one of eleven Junior Researchers in the new intake, and the other ten are sitting in a separate group at a separate table, chatting animatedly to one another. There are some instructors here and there, munching sandwiches. Other than them, the cafeteria — large enough to seat two hundred people or more — is deserted. To Kim, that seems odd. Site

41 is large, three skulking buildings with significant basement space, buried casually in the forests of central Colorado. Where is everybody?

A man in a grey suit walks into the cafeteria, makes eye contact with Kim and strides purposefully over. The man's suit is sharp enough to cut. He wears a tie pin and a platinum wristwatch as big as a brick. He looks badly misplaced. Site 41 is a working site. There's training, education, research, development, analysis, and even the containment of a very few Safe SCPs going on here. Executives shouldn't ever be here. So what is he? A lost exec, trying to find the helipad? Or a researcher or instructor, dressing for the job he wants, not the job he has?

"Hell of a first day," the man says, holding a hand out. "Alastair Grey. With an E."

"Kim," says Kim. "Paul Kim."

"Good to meet you. What accent is that, if you don't mind me asking?"

Kim blinks. "New York," he says. "I'm from New York. Are you the site director?"

"You seem on edge."

"Well, that figures, doesn't it?" Kim asks. "You must know how that intro goes. It's like an atom bomb to the ego. I just had almost everything I know overturned. It turns out I've spent my entire adult life being 'protected' from 'dangerous' knowledge, as if the whole outside world is a... a ballpit, for under-sevens. Stepping out of that has been... humiliating. To start with. And..." He blinks again. "Hey, what do you do here, exactly? You didn't answer my question."

"You didn't answer mine," Grey says.

"Of course I did," Kim says. "I'm from—"

And then he just stops, his train of thought running off the end of the track into air. It's on the tip of his tongue, the answer to Grey's question, but he can't get the words out. "That's weird," he says, shaking his head.

At this point, he also notices that Grey isn't wearing his badge. This could be an honest mistake, albeit an extremely serious one. But surely execs don't get to the executive level without being scrupulously correct in everything they do?

"Who are you?" Kim asks again.

"Your life story was fascinating."

"What?"

"You spoke four languages," Grey tells him. "One now, and soon zero. Too huge an intellect to specialise, your education was a fusion of biochemistry and comparative literature. You felt as if you'd die if you couldn't find more foreign thoughts to cram into your head. You've been all over the world, hungry, and every country you've ever been to was like landing on another planet. You toy with anthropology, but there's too much world for one human race to ever understand, let alone one human. There's too much human race. We should pare it down."

Kim nods. "Would you excuse me for just one second?" He gets up and hurries to another table, to the instructor whom he met earlier that day. When Kim gets close to her he feels a kind of staticky sensation building up. He tries to shake her shoulder, and succeeds in moving it a little, but it's like reaching through tar. "Hey! There's a problem. There's an intruder. I think it might be an SCP. Doc, look at me! Hello?" She doesn't react. He tries the gaggle of fellow newcomers as well, but they keep chattering and hypothesising, oblivious to him shouting and clapping in their ears. "Hey! People! Listen to me! No, no, no, no."

He looks back. Grey has stood up and started moving towards him, still with that confident smile. And there's definitely something wrong with him now because he's visible through the tables, like an augmented reality holoprojection jammed inside Kim's eyeball.

Kim realises with a stab of fear that he can even see Grey when he blinks. His eyelids close, but Grey is still there, an apparition in what for all of Kim's life has been totally personal, private darkness. The only way he can avoid seeing Grey is to turn away, and even then he feels a radioactive prickling in the back of his eyeballs.

Kim tries to phone one of the newbies. The phone in the newbie's pocket rings, and other than that, nothing happens. Nobody reacts.

"That doesn't make sense," Kim says.

"Do you remember your father?" Grey says.

"I never knew my father," Kim says, edging away. "Mom raised me."

Grey's white smile is a fixture. "These people loved your perspective. They were going to put you to work on anomalous antimemes. But they don't remember you exist. You don't exist."

Kim says, mainly to himself, "There aren't any dangerous SCPs on this site. It's a Safe site. So either you're not dangerous, or nobody knows you exist. And if nobody knows you exist, then that means you're either brand new, or... you're... What's an antimeme?"

"Hell of a first day," Grey says.

"Are you sentient?" Kim asks.

"You seem on edge," Grey says.

Kim bolts. He exits the cafeteria, turns a corner and runs ten or eleven paces down the corridor, to where there's an elevator. He stabs the "down" button and waits. The elevator door is highly polished, reflective. Kim catches sight of a face in the mirrored surface and nearly falls over with shock, because it's a face he has never seen before, and it's apparently his own. "Jesus! Oh, no no no," he babbles. "What the hell, what the *hell*—"

Grey comes around the corner, still only strolling, just as the elevator cracks open. Kim dives in and punches the lowest floor, basement level 8. It's instinctive, although he could rationalise the decision in retrospect. (He can't just get in his car and drive. It's better if Grey stays on site than if he's set loose in rational "reality". And to do that it's better if Kim retreats to the lowest, darkest corner of the site for which he has access. And then waits for Grey, and then locks all the doors behind them. And waits to die...) The elevator starts descending, and the apparation of Grey — visible through doors and floors — disappears upwards, shrinking with distance and perspective, but still smiling broadly down at Kim.

Kim paces in the elevator. *I don't remember what my face looks like. It said it had eaten all my secondary languages, but I don't remember learning anything other than English. So— It's eating my memories. It's consuming information. And I can't contact anybody directly, which means I'm on my own.*

I'm not trained for this.

He hammers his head once against the elevator wall, and stares at his shoes. *But I don't know that. What if I've been trained, but I don't remember my training anymore? What if I've been working here for years and I only* think *this is my first day? What if I've met this thing before? What if everybody on the site has met it multiple times... and... nobody remembers? Is this what an antimeme is?*

Kim remembers the near-empty cafeteria. And miles of totally unoccupied corridors and vacant office and lab space. *Maybe it's not just eating my memories. Maybe it eats people whole, removes them completely from history. Maybe it's been haunting the site for years and that's why the site's so empty, because it's nearly finished exterminating us all?*

I need to get help. I need to warn somebody. How? I can't talk to people, I can't phone them. I should— I should write an SCP.

But surely someone's already thought of that.

He pulls his phone out. He pulls out the listing. Nearly ten thousand SCP entries. A hundred of them are tagged "antimemetics" alone.

Kim clears his mind. *Grey with an E. G-R-E-Y. 4-7-3-9.*

Item #: SCP-4739

Object class: Keter

Special Containment Procedures: I'm disregarding the format, because time is a factor. If you're reading this, you've already been isolated from the Foundation at large. Attempts to signal for help are futile. You are now inside 4739's gullet, after ingestion and prior to digestion. You need to get to lab S041-B08-053 as soon as possible and continue the research until you find a way to stop or kill Grey, before it kills you. Don't read the rest until you're in the elevator.

Description:

At that moment the elevator doors open at basement level 8. Alastair Grey is waiting, still smiling disarmingly. He steps forward.

Desperate, Kim hurls his phone overarm at the creature's forehead. It's a solid chunk of metal and it's a dead hit. Grey reels backwards and cracks his skull against the wall. By the time he recovers, Kim is out of sight, haring away down the left corridor, just echoing, fading footsteps on concrete.

Two forty-five degree turns, and room 53 is in sight, the door at the farthest end. It looks like a submarine bulkhead. Kim spots the keypad from way out. Four digits. He tries 4739, and it works first time. The bulkhead mechanism takes agonising seconds to open up.

"Come on, come on, come on!"

"Do you remember your mother?" he hears Grey calling down the corridor.

"I never knew my parents, I was an orphan," Kim hisses under his breath. For a split second he wonders what Grey might really mean by that, but he doesn't have time to dwell on it.

The bulkhead opens. Kim slides in and pulls it closed behind him, locking the mechanism up again, as if that'll buy him even one second. The lab inside is sizeable, windowless of course, and stacked to the ceiling with a jumble of equipment which Kim hardly recognises. There are pieces of thick shattered glass underfoot. In the corner there's a computer terminal, locked. Kim unlocks it, and there's the same entry waiting for him:

Description: SCP-4739 is a powerful, slow-acting antimemetic kill agent taking the appearance of a male Caucasian business executive calling itself "Alastair Grey". SCP-4739 is attracted to dense clusters of organically-stored information — essentially, extremely knowledgeable, complicated, interesting people. SCP-4739 isolates its victim from the outside world by enveloping them in an antimemetic field which makes it impossible for the victim, or anything done by the victim, to be perceived or remembered. SCP-4739 then consumes the victim's memories and knowledge until they become vegetative and die. This process takes between 15 minutes and 2 hours and is described as being "like Alzheimer's disease in fast-forward".

SCP-4739 is not believed to be sentient, although it imitates the behaviour of a sentient being to the extent that it can appear sentient to the inattentive. Its victims are able to move and act freely, since it is impossible to escape once caught, or to signal for help. Communications such as written notes, graffiti and electronic mail do get sent, and persist in reality, but SCP-4739's effect spreads with each message, making it impossible for an external observer to perceive the message until such time as SCP-4739 catches them too.

The SCP entry which you are currently reading is created and maintained by victims of SCP-4739, because it is only visible to victims of SCP-4739. If you are reading this SCP entry, SCP-4739 has caught you. You are now isolated from the Foundation at large and constitute an effective Foundation of one. You have between 15 minutes and 2 hours to reach Site 41, basement level 8, laboratory 053, familiarise yourself with the existing research, and continue this research until you find a way to contain or decommission SCP-4739, or, more likely, die. If your field of expertise is not related to antimemetic containment, we sincerely apologise, and advise you to start learning. Fast.

SCP-4739 has consumed ||||| ||||| |||||
||||| ||||| ||||| ||||| ||||| ||||| |||||
||||| ||||| ||||| ||||| ||||| |||| Foundation researchers since we started counting on August 3, 2013. (If you are reading this entry for the first time, please add a mark.) We estimate at least 50% of victims never make it as far as this database entry, so the true victim count is more than twice this figure.

"But how do I kill it?" Kim screams. He scrolls and scrolls through the research, which is chaotic and haphazardly arranged, because nobody has found the spare seconds to sort it out. There are dozens of separate lines of research, contributed in patchwork by a succession of victims, all ending with variations on the same final line: "I'm going to try X. If you're reading this, X didn't work and I'm dead, which means approach X is a dead end, and you have to think of something else."

He reads. Nobody has succeeded in physically engaging with Grey. Nobody can stall it, evade it, slow it down, reason with it or redirect it to some other target. People have tried poisoning their memories with indigestible ideas, drip-feeding their memories to Grey to slow him down, replacing their memories faster than Grey can eat them, and force-feeding Grey too many memories at once to overfeed him and blow him up. They've tried committing suicide by Class-A amnestic overdose. None of it worked. More than a hundred people, most of them apparently possessing doctorates, have slid into the maw of this thing, fought briefly and, with a greater or lesser degree of dignity, died.

There are no remaining untried threads.

"I'm fucked!" Kim concludes. He glances up. Grey's not in the room yet, but Kim can see him strolling down the last stretch of corridor. He's a totally intangible being, physical obstructions are irrelevant to him. He can't be hurt.

Kim clutches the pocket where he used to keep his phone.

Wait a second.

He scrolls again. He finds the three or four sad, desperate wretches who died confronting Grey physically. Combat knife and Glock. Baseball bat (Kim looks up and checks the room; sure enough, the bat's there, rolled under a table). One man, an elderly botanist far out of his depth, said he was just going to try whatever he could find that was heaviest. That explains the shattered CRT television, and the light layer of thick glass on the floor near the bulkhead. There's even CCTV footage of the botanist's attempt. He accomplishes literally nothing. Grey is a holographic ghost, and the CRT drops right through him, imploding when it hits the floor at Grey's feet. The botanist spends the rest of the video's running time huddled in a corner, gradually losing his mind while Grey watches placidly.

The difference being, Kim realises with his eyes boggling, *a phone is a solid brick full of information. And before me, nobody tried using information as a missile.*

Kim searches for the experiments — several of them, scattered — where the victim tried to divert Grey to a different data source. The general idea seemed to be to overload Grey by pointing him at something containing too much information: the internet, or the terabit feed from a live particle accelerator experiment, or a stack of hard drives containing the first few quadrillion binary digits of pi. But nobody could figure out a way to distract Grey's attention; prominently-placed screens full of data, he would ignore; data beamed at him electromagnetically (radio, laser) had no effect. And nobody could figure out a way to tunnel the information in through the victim's mind as extra memories. It was written off as impossible, closed as a line of investigation.

The hard drives, Kim finds, are right there on the workbench next to the computer. It's a half-rack unit, a cuboidal block of metalwork as big and heavy as a bowling ball. One of the most ineffective conceivable melee weapons.

Kim snatches up the three longest pieces of ethernet cable he can find, and starts plaiting them into a chain.

Then he remembers who he is, and where he is, and what his responsibilities are. He goes to the computer, to the SCP entry, adds himself to the victim tally and writes up exactly what it is he's about to try. Because he might not be the last one, and the world needs to know that this didn't work.

*

Grey comes through the lab bulkhead to find most of the equipment in the room toppled onto the floor, to create room for the black and silver drive array that Paul Kim is whirling around his head, on a two-metre chain made of plaited network cable. It makes a low thrumming sound as it whirls. Grey is not intelligent enough to stop moving forwards, and catches the array directly in the side of his head, rack mount point first, like a morningstar.

Grey absorbs a few trillion digits of the impact, but it isn't enough. There's a green snap of light and a noise like a subway train short-circuiting, and Grey's a pile in the corner, his head caved in and the drive array partially demolished in pieces around him.

Kim decides that history can fill in whatever quip it likes best.

*

"It was chewing its way up the Antimemetics Division hierarchy," Wheeler tells him in the aftermath. "It was only a matter of time until it bit down on somebody dangerous. Congratulations on demonstrating a basic level of competence when it counted. Dozens of others couldn't."

Kim still feels rattled. But the shock is dissipating, faster than he'd expected.

Marion Wheeler, it turns out, is the Antimemetics Division chief. She is Kim's new boss.

"I want to say it was dumb luck," Kim says. "I want to say that I just threw my phone, it was instinct, it was muscle memory. It was my first day, and I got lucky as hell. ...I want to say those things, but I'm sitting here, and turning those statements over, and none of them would be true, would they?"

Wheeler waits expectantly, and says nothing.

"You're not my *new* boss," Kim says. "You're just my boss. This isn't my first day at all. I've been working here for... well, it must be over a decade, right? I think I've been a professional antimemetics researcher since at least the mid-2000s. It's just that the first thing Grey ate was my memories of everything past the first day. And even then..."

"I see very little luck in what happened today," Wheeler says. "Instinct and muscle memory are just deep forms of training. Like I said, a basic level of competence. An ability to piece your own life and all of your past knowledge back together, faster than nearly anybody else. This is what we try to drill into you. And sometimes, thankfully, it takes."

"This isn't even the first time we've had this conversation," Kim continues. "There've been other incidents. With other SCPs with amnestic powers. You've sat there and watched me put myself back together before."

"And it hasn't gotten old yet," Wheeler admits, with something which might be approaching a smirk.

"How long does it usually take for me to recover?"

"A few months," Wheeler says. "But if you want the honest truth, people in this division are as competent on day one as they'll ever be. You come to the job firing on all cylinders, or not at all. The rest is just fine-tuning and chemistry."

"So what you're actually saying is you don't care about my mental state and you need me back at work now," Kim says.

Wheeler nods. "I need an updated SCP entry, just to begin with. I need you to nail down the model for Grey's predatory pattern and exactly how you defeated it. I want you to work out what it did with the bodies — incinerated, disintegrated, or just left them lying around the site in rotting perceptually cloaked heaps. And I need countermeasures for when it comes back."

"It's not dead? Wait," Kim says. "I think I know this one. It's coming back to me. 'Ideas don't die.'"

3
Unforgettable, That's What You Are

"El, it's finished."

Lyn Marness is more than ninety years old and hasn't stood at his full height in ten. He was a tower of a man in his prime, two metres tall and built like a boxer. Nearly nobody he ever met was able to look him straight in the eye, at least not and tell him "No". Illness has gradually eaten away at that over the years. He feels as if he lives at the bottom of a deep bath, everybody he ever meets looking down at him from slippery, unscalable walls, none of them able to reach down to help him. He's spent his final months crumpled up in bed like a dying spider, changing to a corpse's colour ahead of time. It might have been bearable if he'd lost his mind, but he remembers what he used to be: a leader, a powerhouse. He used to be able to alter the course of terrible events for the better, to get justice. He used to protect people.

"El. You can wake up now."

But there's a warm wind through his thin colourless hair and there's direct sunlight coming down on him now, and the heat is filling him up like a tonic. He's outside; it's been too long since he was last outside. When he opens his eyes he sees his lake, the one in the Northwest which he used to have all to himself every summer. He's on a boat, his boat, lying on a blanket laid on the deck. A few kilometres away behind them is the little lake house, empty.

It's perfect. He didn't know he had the strength left to safely leave the hospital, let alone travel this far. But if he'd put his mind to it and selected a final moment, this might have been it.

"Do you remember me?"

Marness looks, with eyes which are strengthening. The woman speaking is seated on the deck beside him, attentive. She has a large plastic box full of medical supplies open in front of her, and a light suit jacket laid on the deck beside it, and she has her sleeves rolled up so she can work. As he watches, she carefully disposes of a needle.

A dim memory surfaces and starts taking shape. The woman is twice as old now as when he knew her last, and visibly twice as confident. It would be difficult to forget her. He taught her everything he— well, everything he could remember at the time. He remembers her as a field agent. He remembers sending her through Hell, a fistful of times. "Marion."

"El," the woman softly explains, "you died. You died surrounded by grieving family. They loved you very much, and they cried over you. The funeral for the fake is in a few days, but unfortunately you won't be able to see it yourself. You're dead now, and this is what comes next."

"Marion. Hutchinson." Marness feels gold spreading through his bones, miracle juice.

It's Wheeler now, but she doesn't correct him. "When you retired from the Foundation, El, we did what we do to all of us who retire; what all of us agree to when we sign up. We gave you some medicine which made you forget. As you stepped out of the door for the last time, all the work you did for us — great work, which saved lives — evaporated away, and your cover story sealed over those years and became reality. That's why you've spent your whole retirement believing that you were a former section chief at the FBI. It's what you wanted, it's what we wanted, it's what you agreed to.

"But you, alone, agreed to something else as well. And you must be starting to remember, now, what that something else was. I've injected you with a serum which throws the human aging process into hard reverse, and it affects everything: organs, tissues, memories. You'll be coming up on it soon. Remember?"

"Yes," Marness croaks, remembering, dizzy.

"You signed over your final twelve hours to us. You asked for a full and happy and well-deserved retirement... but now, for the last day, you work for us again, because of one particular job. I have it in writing here, you see? Do you recognise your signature, and mine? I witnessed."

"Yes."

"Do you remember who you are?"

"Doctor Lyn Patrick Marness, of the Foundation," he says. "Antimemetics Division founder."

Wheeler smiles with relief. It's good to see him again.

"We need some memories from you," she explains. "Memories which nobody else in the world has access to, and which are buried so deeply that we can't extract them without killing you. So this afternoon, that's what we're going to do. We're going to extract those memories, and once we're done, you'll be dead."

Marness has already begun to regress to the time when he himself set this wheel in motion. He remembers, very clearly, discovering the mystery in his own head, the blank spots which he couldn't explain, and couldn't safely access with any kind of chemical or physical technique. He remembers deferring the mystery until now.

"What happened in 1976?" Wheeler asks.

*

Marness sits up. His skin is beginning to clear and his breathing is improving.

He feels as if his brain is cleaved in two by a wormhole, such that his eyes are focusing on different time periods. In his right eye he sees the lake and the boat he's dying on; in his left he sees a collage of electrifyingly familiar past faces and places. Bart Hughes with his grin and thick glasses and baby face, looking like some kid dressed up as a Foundation researcher; the original Site 48 crew, great techs but a hopeless excuse for a softball team; young Marion with steel-strong nerves and a mind like a laser; suits and lab coats and MTF operatives. And everywhere paperwork, and floods of serial numbers.

He starts to speak.

1976 was the year he founded the division. He brainstormed the whole thing in one legendary week, hammering out the science and then distilling the first chemical mnestic with the help of a hand-picked trio of assistants, the first Antimemetics researchers. No antimemetic SCPs had even been observed up to that point — the entire operation was a shot in the dark — and yet the team immediately struck gold. Passive black holes of information, active predatory infovores, unrememberable worms which covered the human skin like dust mites... contagious bad news, self-sealing secrets, living murders, Chinatowns.

Wheeler wonders if there might be something more serious awry with Marness' head. His version of events is hopelessly romantic. In Wheeler's experience, nobody looks back on Foundation work fondly.

"But it was all too fast," Marness says. "Special containment procedures take time to develop, much more time than I took. The Foundation as a whole acquires about a dozen new SCPs annually. I found that many in one year, essentially single-handedly. It was too *easy*. It was as if I knew it all already, and was just catching up.

"And then... one day I realised I couldn't remember my life before Antimemetics. I knew I'd been a Foundation operative for decades prior, that was where I got the authority to start my own division, but there was nothing else there. It was a wall in my mind, which even mnestics couldn't get me past. I went to the paper archives and looked at my own personnel file, and..."

Marness trails off. Not because he's forgotten what to say next, it's deliberate. The trailing off is exactly what happened.

"You woke up back at your desk half a working day later, remembering nothing," Wheeler says. "You went through the loop a dozen times before someone realised what was happening and broke you out of it."

Wheeler knows all of this. The file still exists, and the antimemetic effect still clouds the back half of it. All of this would be over in a second if any of that back half could be read.

Marness goes on. "When I assembled the evidence what I found was... well, a hole. Like a jigsaw with only the edges and corners. So I did the only thing I could do, I looked at the shape of the hole. And, together with Bart Hughes and others, I formed a theory.

"This is not the first Antimemetics Division. Before 1976, there was another one. I was part of that division; possibly, I led it. Certainly, I am the only known survivor of it. *Something* happened to that team. Some antimemetic force chewed up and swallowed the *idea* of the Antimemetics Division itself. I was let off lightly; I lived. The rest of those people, whoever they were, however many of them there were, are missing without trace."

Wheeler nods. "This much we know already. I was there when you wrote the note, remember? The question is known. It's the answer that we can't get to without killing you. It's the answer that we've waited all these years to get at. I'm here to ask you: *What. Happened?*"

Marness covers his right eye and grimaces, trying. He fails. "It's not there. You haven't sent me back far enough, there's still that wall there in my head. I remember why the question exists, but I don't remember the answer. I need more."

Wheeler swabs his arm, and gives him another ten years.

*

Excerpt from Document 180047109-L4799-098, *User's Guide To Chemical Mnestics*:

The Class-X mnestic drug is a failed eternal youth serum. X rejuvenates both mind and body by up to ██ years, but its effects are temporary, wearing off in a matter of hours. Furthermore, as the drug wears off, the suppressed time reasserts itself all at once, causing a harmful "whiplash" effect on the subject's physiology. X can rejuvenate an individual safely by up to thirty days, but with stronger doses the whiplash effect becomes dangerous, and past a threshold of 16-18 months it is fatal in all known subjects.

X's restorative effect on the human memory is essentially a side-effect of all of this. However, this side-effect is so useful that it has become the drug's main practical purpose. The Antimemetics Division uses small doses of X to temporarily sharpen or restore memories from the recent past. This aids Foundation operatives in the accurate recall of incidents involving memory-corrupting entities.

*

Marness seems like another man once the second X dose takes effect. Wrinkles are sliding back up into his face, muscle mass is returning to his limbs, but it takes Wheeler a second to realise the real reason why; she's just booted him back across the field/desk agent transition. Marness has regressed a little way past senior management, the realm where most problems were solved by saying the correct words, and into a time where he survived through physical fitness, situational alertness and hands-on experience.

Marness gets to his feet for the first time in years. He scans his surroundings, examining the placid golden lake and the sky and the boat itself. He doesn't sit down again. He smooths down his hospital gown, wishing he had a sweater and, separately, some fishing gear. He brushes a hand through new, old hair. His sideburns are back.

"We weren't Foundation at first," he says. "The first Antimemetics Division was a U.S. Army project. It ran parallel with Manhattan during World War II. We called ourselves the Unthinkables.

"It began as an experiment in advanced propaganda. The objective was to cut through the physical conflict and find a way to rupture the ideological machine, to obliterate the *idea* of Nazism. After two years, enough theory had been developed that the task had been reduced to an engineering problem. Another two years, and the engineering problem had been reduced as well, and what we had built was a very special kind of bomb.

"Unfortunately, we didn't understand what we'd built. Back then, we didn't have the mnestics or the shielding that we could use to protect ourselves. We didn't understand how far ahead you need to think when you're working with this kind of technology.

"We got looped. It was textbook. We built the unthinkable bomb and test-detonated it... and it worked perfectly. The bomb destroyed itself, and erased its own successful detonation, and flattened all the knowledge which had gone together to build it. We forgot that we had ever built the bomb at all, and started over.

"To our credit, we realised pretty quickly what must have happened. There was a four-year gap in our progress now, and there was no other way to explain it. But by the time we put the pieces together the second time, the war was almost over. The Nazis had been defeated by conventional means, and the Japanese had been broken by the first atomic bombings. So we completed the second antimemetic bomb, and after that, we sat on it."

Marion Wheeler is silent for a long moment.

"The U.S. Army," she says doubtfully, "was secretly developing antimemetic weaponry as early as the 1940s."

"We sure were," Marness says, with more than a hint of pride.

"Of course, there is no one in the whole world who could back this up."

"That's right," Marness says, flashing a smile he hasn't flashed in decades. "You only have my word for it. Cute, huh? Still, this is why you resurrected me, isn't it? For the sake of one more good war story. God, I've missed shop talk."

"I resurrected you because I want a very specific question answered," Wheeler says. "Although I can see that in a way you've already answered it. This bomb was the means, wasn't it? The old Antimemetics Division—"

"—the Unthinkables—"

"—bombed themselves. Somehow."

"That's right," Marness says.

"From context," Wheeler goes on, "I assume that they knew what they were doing that time. I assume it was not an accident."

"It was not," Marness says.

*

The displaced half of Marness' brain is anchored in the Seventies now, so the True History of the New Original Unthinkables is an open book to him. And he reads:

"After the war the second bomb collected dust for years. We began sketching improved designs for a third bomb, but around that time oversight was starting to flicker out. We completed our research and production objectives, and were given no further objectives. Funding became shaky and we couldn't figure out why. It wasn't entirely clear that the project overseers knew what we were doing. Or even that they remembered we existed. It was a side-effect from the research, of course, one we had no way of managing at the time.

"In 1951, a cult movement began in Ojai, California. It was... wrong, everything about it was just wrong. In a matter of days it was a national phenomenon and still growing. It was all over the news. To spread that far in months would have been credible, but days was simply impossible. We, in the team, could see that the philosophy behind the cult was unnaturally contagious. It was the opposite of unthinkable, it was unforgettable. We knew that this was what our bomb was designed for. We prompted the overseers for direction. But there were no orders.

"At the time that the outbreak began, we were a U.S. Army laboratory, through and through. Eight days into the crisis the Foundation 'acquired' us. All the classified research, all the material resources, and all the compliant top staff, including me. Anybody who wouldn't comply was mind-wiped and sent back to the Army. Twenty hours after the acquisition, we deployed the second bomb and the cult was gone. Nobody remembered it, nobody remembered being part of it, zero loss of life. A completely clean detonation.

"After that is when everything really kicked off. Once we started working for the Foundation, the pace of research ramped up. Every new technological advancement uncovered new hidden SCPs. I passed the Foundation field exams and went out catching ghosts. My life turned into the Twilight Zone. I—"

Marness blinks hard. He covers one of his eyes, then the other.

"I remember all these different people now," he says. "It feels like my memory is in stereo. Almost every antimemetic SCP we caught before the wipe in '76, we caught again soon after the wipe. That means I remember two acquisition logs for each one. I remember two Antimemetics teams and I don't remember who belongs on which side of the wall. Do you remember Goldie Yarrow? The neurologist? Studied the mechanism of anomalously accelerated memory loss... wrote a library on the subject..."

Wheeler doesn't.

"Dr. Ojobiru? Julie Still?"

"El, this is important. Are you at the right place in your own timeline to remember what happened yet?"

Marness focuses. And he discovers that he is. Something changes in his eyes, as he stops reminiscing. He speaks more slowly now, his voice dropping almost to a whisper:

"There is an SCP which your division has never seen. The SCP which my division couldn't contain. The escapee. This is what you wanted, isn't it, Marion?"

"Yes," she says. "This is the data I'm killing you for." She leaves a gap where, if she felt there was anything to apologise for, she would apologise.

Marness locks eyes with her. "It was eating my division alive. It came at us so hard and so fast that the only way we could stop it was to self-destruct. But we had no site nuke, and in retrospect it is obvious to me, now, that this was because the SCP had consumed our site nuke first of all.

"If you know it exists, it knows you exist. The more you know about it, the more it knows about you. If you can see it, it can see you. And you *can* see it. You've been looking right at it all afternoon."

Wheeler is suddenly acutely aware of her surroundings.

There are only two of them on the boat. The boat is anchored more than a kilometre from any of the lake shores. She hasn't brought any backup with her. There's a radioactive prickling in her brain. She doesn't—

Red flag. Why didn't I bring any backup with me? That doesn't make sense.

There should be a team at the lake house. There should be an MTF operative and a medic here on the boat with me. And a second boat. At minimum. Am I all alone out here? Why did I do that?

She pulls her gun, but doesn't aim it at Marness yet. "Where is it? Is it in you?"

Marness' voice is becoming urgent. He covers both of his eyes again. "Destroying all knowledge of it was the only way to destroy it. And restoring my memories was a foolproof way to bring it back!"

It's in his eyes. Most likely his left eye. Wheeler backs up to the other side of the boat, draws a bead on the centre of Marness' head, and says, "El. Are you still in there?"

"There is a way to fix this," Marness hisses, dropping to his knees. He keeps his eyes screwed up and gropes his way forward blindly, on his hands and knees.

"El, you need to tell me what this thing is."

"That's the opposite of what we need to do," Marness says. "You need to set another bomb off."

"We don't have that bomb. We lost that technology—" Wheeler begins.

"You've always had it! There's an engineering lab in Site 41. You know it. An underground complex the size of a football field. In pristine condition, and totally disused. Why? Think about it. That's where your bomb's installed."

"But that just sets us back to square one. If I set the bomb off," Wheeler says, knowing full well that she is thousands of kilometres from it and can't hope to reach it in time anyway, "how do we contain this thing?"

"We won't," Marness shouts. "We can't, ever! Don't you get it? The whole division is looped! We start the division, we run headlong into this thing, and either it eats us, or we wipe ourselves out in self-preservation. The idea of antimemes is as old as forgetfulness itself. Humans have been looping through this problem over and over again since long before the Forties. Maybe for centuries!"

His blindly probing fingers find the medical box. It's too late.

As Wheeler watches, a waving black pedipalp coated in dark hairs forces its way out through Marness' left eye. Marness screams. Still on his knees, he grasps the pedipalp with both hands and tries to break it, but it's solid, as if it has bones inside it.

"What is it?" Wheeler shouts at him. "That can't be the whole story. Where is it from, what does it want? Can it reason, can it speak?"

"Help—"

A second spider leg, significantly longer and spindlier, slides out through Marness' trachea, ruining his throat and voice box and producing a gout of blood. He gurgles. A third leg shoots from his abdomen, like a spear.

Wheeler shoots Marness in the head. Marness falls forward, limp, then rises back up, lifted by the three spider appendages as if he is a puppet being controlled by something gigantic and invisible. His arms raise, as if suspended by wires.

Wheeler squints. She fires four more shots over Marness' head, at the likely body mass of the invisible puppeteer, and fires the rest of her clip almost directly into the sky. The whole boat vibrates, along with the surface of the lake, as if responding to infrasound or a localised earthquake. Then the boat shudders violently and starts to lift out of the water, raised by more unseen appendages.

Wheeler holsters her gun and goes for the medical box herself, pulling it away from Marness' floating feet. There's a compartment with Class-B amnestic, the fast-acting stuff, in serum form. She does a hurried burst of mental arithmetic, measures out the correct dosage in a syringe and, hands shaking, plunges it into a wrist vein. The boat is still rising. Whatever the monster is, it's colossally tall, or maybe it flies.

She is, of course, already dosed up to the eyeballs with mnestic drugs. Otherwise, she wouldn't have been able to perceive any of this. Foundation medical literature warns in the strongest possible terms against putting both kinds of drug into the same brain. Best case scenario, this ends with her in the hospital.

They're thirty metres up in the air now, ten storeys. There's a stabbing pain developing in her left eye. She kicks her shoes off and throws the gun away. She goes to the edge and contemplates the drop for a disbelieving second. She jumps.

It takes two heart-stopping seconds of freefall for her to hit the water. The chilled hammerblow of the impact is enough to blank her mind out. By the time she surfaces she doesn't remember where she fell from, or why. And likewise, the skyscraper-sized being which claimed Marness and the boat has forgotten about her.

"What the hell," she gasps, treading water. "What the hell, where the hell?"

There is nothing above her, no explanation. Only the symptoms of the drug cocktail give her any indication of what just happened: a sensation like hundreds of tiny lumps of hot solder in her brain, and pain and exhaustion spreading to all of her tendons. She wants to die.

Swim, says part of her. *Get to shore first. Then you can die.*

*

The extraction team finds her around dusk, unconscious on the lake shore. They stabilise her in the helicopter, then take her to Site 41 for examination, and to have her system flushed.

She spends a solid eight days at home, detoxifying: no mnestics, no amnestics, no exposure to dangerous memory-corrupting SCPs, no work visitors. "No work," the doctor also tells her, pointlessly.

It isn't anywhere near the first missing event in Wheeler's life, nor is she the first person in the Antimemetics staff to have such an experience, but the sensation is no less disturbing for its familiarity. As per procedure, she writes a report summarising everything she can remember. The gap in her memory is about thirteen hours.

Then she adds her report to the extensive, complex map of Missing Time which the whole division maintains collectively. It is a map of holes, and the map is becoming large enough that very faint patterns are gradually forming. The outline of an enemy is becoming visible, or perhaps a group of enemies.

When she quizzes the extraction team later, none of them remember who activated the emergency beacon which summoned them. In fact, the beacon itself cut out long before they landed at the lake. Wheeler compares the current size of her division with her best estimate of what it should be. Maybe she needs a few more key people here and there... So, assuming the division was fully staffed before the event, maybe those empty roles are the people who died this time around. Maybe one of them activated the beacon. A commendable act, by someone now only known to exist because of that single act.

It's weeks later still that Wheeler discovers the largest new hole in her memory:

Who founded the division? When?

4

CASE COLOURLESS GREEN

Item #: SCP-3125

Object Class: Keter

Special Containment Procedures: SCP-3125 is kept inside Cognitohazard Containment Unit 3125 on the first floor of Site 41. This containment unit is a 10m by 15m by 3m cuboidal room clad in layers of lead, soundproofing and telepathic shielding. Access is through an airlock system at one end of the containment unit. This airlock is programmed to allow only one person to enter the containment unit at a time, and to remain locked until this person exits before allowing another person to enter.

Under no circumstances may any coherent information be allowed to leave the containment unit. This includes written and electronic notes, photographs, audio and video recordings, sound, electromagnetic and particle-based signals and psi emanations. During the exit cycle, a purge system rigged to the airlock flushes the occupant's memory by flooding the airlock with amnestic gas for three minutes.

A senior Antimemetics Division staff member must visit SCP-3125 every six weeks (42 days).

END OF FILE

"You're kidding me. That's the whole entry?"

"That's the whole entry," Wheeler says.

It isn't even the fiftieth strangest thing Paul Kim has seen in the database, but still: "No description, no acquisition report, no test log, no addenda? No clue who built the unit, or when, or how many times it's been visited, or who carried out the previous visits, or what they took in with them, or how long they were in there?"

"Well, obviously Bart Hughes built the unit," Wheeler says, and this cannot be denied. The man's signature style of containment architecture is recognisable a mile out. Sleek, white, plainly impregnable without the aid of extremely heavy tools. "Which makes it at least seven years old. That's sixty visits or more. I guess there are good reasons for the rest of those omissions. Anyway... the timer watchdog says it's time again."

"I don't like the idea of you routinely exposing yourself to a cognitohazard so dangerous that we can't even write the reason why we can't write it down down," Kim says. "Especially because it's impossible for us to recover any usable information this way. You're going to go in, be incommunicado for two hours and come out a smiling amnesiac. What do we gain from that? It's just a breach risk."

Wheeler hears every word of this and elects to ignore it all. There's a vague shape of familiarity about the entry as written; there are a few word choices which reassure her, in an intangible way, that it was written by someone who knew what they were doing. Possibly her.

Kim's still talking. "We should just scrub that last line from the database entry. There can't be *anything* good in that room."

Wheeler puts her keycard in the slot. The airlock rewards her with green LEDs and begins to cycle open. It's built as a slender vertical cylinder with a single opening. The entire thing rotates on its axis. Inside, there's barely room for a single person to stand without their shoulders touching the walls.

"What are you taking?" Kim asks.

Wheeler ducks to step in, turns to face him and shrugs. "A stick of gum."

"I can get you field gear," Kim says, as the airlock begins to rotate again, emitting a low, quiet thrum solely as an audible warning that there is machinery in motion. "We'll raid inventory. Give me fifteen minutes and I'll turn you into a one-woman war."

If Wheeler says anything in response to this, it's cut off by the soundproofing as the airlock rotates.

Kim is left alone in the antechamber. He stares at the outer door for a worried moment. He presses his ear to the door for a while, but hears nothing. Not even a faint tremble from the airlock mechanism.

*

Inside it's pitch dark for a few seconds, then some unseen sensor detects Wheeler's presence and brings the fluorescents up. Half of them, anyway. The others remain inert or flicker aggravatingly.

The room's interior walls are made from milky white glass (bulletproof, knowing Hughes) and plastered with paperwork, taped and Blu-Tacked up in vaguely coherent masses. Where there is no paperwork, people have drawn directly on the walls in marker pen. There is a conference table, long and elliptical, covered with more paperwork and a tangle of laptop computers and serpentine power supply cables. Power has returned to the machines and they are slowly booting. A data projector warms up and shines a map of the world over the far wall, almost lining up with a network of scribbled annotations on the same wall. Post-It notes of all colours litter the carpet like autumn leaves.

Other than that, the room is empty.

Skimming the paperwork, Wheeler discovers that nearly all of it is handwritten and most of it charts the progress of conversations. Most of the entries are dated and signed, and most of the dates are weeks apart. The conversations are panicked and fearful back-and-forths about dozens of SCPs, some of them antimemetic in nature but none of them obviously related to one another. None of the notes mention SCP-3125.

The only name Wheeler recognises is her own, which appears on one in ten or twenty of the notes. The notes seem authentic and the handwriting is hers. But her notes also seem as desperate and uncertain in tone as everybody else's. This unnerves her.

There are diagrams on the walls too, which are too complex to decode at a glance, but complex enough to make her eyes hurt to look at them.

Still lost for a logical entry point to the data, Wheeler curses all of her predecessors. Asynchronous research — whereby the research topic is forgotten entirely between iterations, and rediscovered over and over — is a perfectly standard practice in the Antimemetics Division, and her people ought to be better trained than this. There should be an obvious single document to read first which makes sense of the rest. A primer—

"Marion, it's me."

Wheeler recognises the voice as her own. She moves around the table until she finds the laptop making the noise.

There's a video playing, apparently recorded on the laptop's own camera in this room.

The Marion Wheeler in the video is seated, and looks unfamiliar in a way which takes the one watching a moment to put her finger on. Not exhausted, not sick, not physically injured; she's seen herself that way before, in the mirror. This woman's willpower is gone. She's beaten.

"You've guessed already that SCP-3125 is not in this room," she says. "In fact, this is the only room in the world where SCP-3125 is not present. It's called 'inverted containment'. SCP-3125 pervades all of reality except for volumes which have been specifically shielded from its influence. This is it. This is our only safe harbor. This room represents the length and breadth of the war.

"Every competent antimemetics research project finds SCP-3125's fingerprints sooner or later. It manifests all over the world, in thousands of different forms. Most of them aren't even anomalous. Some of them we already have catalogued separately in the main database. A very small number of them are even in containment. Impossibly virulent cults, broken arithmetic, invisible spiders as tall as skyscrapers, people born with extra organs which nobody can see. That's the raw data. Those manifestations are troublesome enough to deal with in their own right..."

The Wheeler in the video casts around, picks up a bright green felt-tip pen and a blank piece of paper. She begins drawing a shape which isn't visible from the camera's perspective, while still talking.

"But once you get a little further down the road you start to see a pattern emerging in the data. You need to have the training in memetic science, but once you have that training and you have the data in front of you, it only takes a little extra effort to arrange those data points in conceptual space and draw a contour through them. Those data points are points on SCP-3125's hull; those manifestations are the shadows it casts on our reality. You link four or five different SCPs together into a single shape, and you see it... And it sees you..."

She's still drawing. It's detailed. She doesn't look up, and her tone of voice is distant, almost as if she's narrating the tail end of a frightening children's story:

"When that happens, when you make 'eye contact', it kills you. It kills you and it kills anybody who thinks like you. Physical distance doesn't matter, it's about mental proximity. Anybody with the same ideas, anybody in the same head space. It kills your collaborators, your whole research team. It kills your parents; it kills your children. You become absent humans, human-shaped shells surrounding holes in reality. And when it's done, your project is a hole in the ground, and nobody knows what SCP-3125 is anymore. It is a black hole in antimemetic science, consuming unwary researchers and yielding no information, only detectable through indirect observation. A true description of what SCP-3125 is, or even an allusion to what it is, constitutes a containment breach and a lethal indirect cognitohazard.

"Do you see? It's a defense mechanism. This information-swallowing behaviour is just the outer layer, the poison coating. It protects the entity from discovery while it infests our reality.

"And as years pass, the manifestations will continue, growing denser and knitting together... until the whole world is drowning in them, and everybody will be screaming 'Why did nobody realise what was happening?' And nobody will answer, because everybody who realised was killed, by this *system*...

"Do you see it, Marion? See it now."

Wheeler is at the core of Foundation antimemetic science. She had all the raw data readily accessible. There are extensive written calculations on the walls, but she doesn't need to read them, she can do them in her head. All it took was that slightest push, that slightest suggestion. Staring through the laptop screen, eyes wide and defocused, she understands how it all links together. She sees SCP-3125.

She feels dwarfed by it. She's encountered terrible, powerful ideas before, at every level of memeticity, and subdued them or even recruited them, but what she's picturing now is on another order of magnitude from what she knew to be possible. Now that she knows it's there, she can feel it like cosmic radiation, boring holes in the world with its thousands of manifestations and freely laying waste to anybody who recognises the larger pattern. It's not of reality, not of humanity. It is from a higher, worse place, and it is descending.

The other Wheeler presents her finished diagram. She has drawn a mutated, fractally complex grasping hand with fivefold symmetry. It has no wrist or arm, just five long human fingers pointing in five directions. At its core, there's a pentagonal opening which could be a mouth.

But the diagram was already there. It's plastered across the wall in the background of the video, plain as day, a meticulous collage in green, easily two metres in diameter and showing the same meme complex to a hundred times the level of detail. There are smaller diagrams of different elevations arrayed around it like spores, and its arms are spread wide around the seated Wheeler, who sits directly in front of the mouth, with her back to it.

Wheeler, watching, does not realise this, and does not turn around.

"How do you fight an enemy without ever discovering it exists?" the Wheeler in the video asks. "How do you win without even realising you're at war? What do we *do*?

"Seven years ago there were more than four hundred antimemetics research groups worldwide. Government agencies, military branches, private corporations, university projects. Many of them were GOIs or subdivisions of GOIs.

49

We were allied with most of them. We were at the spearhead of an Antimemetics Coalition which spanned the whole globe and thousands upon thousands of people. None of those groups still exist. The last one ceased to exist some time in the last seventy-two hours.

"Three years ago, Foundation Antimemetics was an organisation of more than four thousand people. Now it's ninety.

"There's no war. We've lost the war. It's over. This is the mopping-up operation. The only reason we still exist at all is because we have better amnestic biochemistry than anybody else in the world. Because that's all you can do when you see SCP-3125: run away and try to forget what you saw... seek oblivion in chemicals, or alcohol, or head trauma. And even that can't work every time. It's circling in. We meet it over and over again and we don't realise it. There's no way we can stop ourselves from rediscovering it! We're too damned smart!"

She points at something on the wall, out of view of the laptop's camera. Wheeler, watching, turns to look. In an upper corner of the room there is a constellation of dizzyingly complicated schematics. Bart Hughes's initials are on every page.

"There's a machine we could build. All it would take is eight years, a lab as big as West Virginia and all the money in the world. Nothing that the O5 Council would blink at if we went to them. But how do we build that machine without any of us realising what it's for? It would be like building and launching Apollo 11 without a single engineer deducing that the Moon existed. The logistics would be insane, but the secrecy would be well past impossible. Someone would start asking questions. And then it would be over. So what do we do?"

"Find another way," Wheeler says to the unhearing recording. The fatalistic tone of voice makes her angry. "What the hell's wrong with you?"

"...I could tell everybody to walk away. I could send a little message to myself saying 'There's danger down this road, you should disband the Antimemetics Division and pursue other projects.' But I'd be suspicious. I'd start asking questions. And then it would be over."

Wheeler's now crouched in front of the video, trying to understand what she's watching. "What's wrong, Marion? Are you okay?"

"I could kill myself in here," the recording says. "But my team would find SCP-3125 without me, and then they'd have to fight SCP-3125 without me. It's going to happen soon, whatever happens. In the next two months at most. This year, it will be over. I may die in here anyway. I'm on so many mnestic drugs that my endocrine system is shutting down. Taking amnestics at the same time is the chemical equivalent to trepanation. I don't remember the last time I slept without having a nightmare about Adam, and I'm starting to forget whether SCP-4987 is a real thing or just the number that I gave to my life—"

"You're not like this," Wheeler whispers. "You're stronger than this. What happened to you? Who's Adam?"

"I don't know how we survive this. I don't know how we win. We're the last ones in the world. After us, there's nobody."

Wheeler shakes her head, not believing it.

"So I'm done. I'm going to walk out of this door and forget who I am and then I'm going to be you, Marion, and you trwoll have to figure a way out of this, because I can't." She gets up and moves offscreen. She can be heard breathing deeply. Her speech is starting to distort. "God, my eyes hurt. I think ilr starting infth mlaei inside."

There's the sound of a door opening, and then a piercing pulse of sound and light which terminates the recording.

*

Wheeler stares at the dark screen for a long minute.

She's never seen herself so weak, and it damages her ego a great deal to see that it's possible. She feels disconnected from what she saw, like it happened in an alternate universe. She feels revulsed and appalled by that version of her, more so to know that that version is still inside her somewhere. *It doesn't make sense. I'm looking at all of the same facts. What made her give up? What did she know that I don't?*

Who was Adam?

The answer to this question is so obvious and sickening that she instinctively distrusts it. She circles around the answer, probing it, trying to find reasons to reject it, but it's inescapable. Adam was someone she knew when the video was recorded, now completely removed from her memory. Adam was someone the thought of whose safety paralysed her with fear. Someone in the same head space. Someone she couldn't bear to lose.

And then she lost.

But what if...

(But how'd the room get built in the first place? Anybody's guess. Wheeler imagines Hughes building it as a proof-of-concept, followed by a cascading series of lucky chances which led to it becoming the war room. Someone discovered SCP-3125 at random, while sealed in the room; they wrote notes to themselves which set up the skeletal external SCP database entry and the containment procedures; most of the paperwork and computer hardware was left behind by later visitors... It could have happened...)

But what if there's another room?

Unbidden, a cute factoid comes back to her right then. Site 41 is almost completely vacant. In particular, two hundred metres below Site 41 there's an empty heavy engineering lab, an underground complex the size of a hockey stadium. Self-contained, in pristine condition, totally disused. Sealed up, original purpose forgotten. Nobody has entered it in living memory. Built who-knows-how-many decades back by a dead generation of antimemeticists.

What if that's where we built our weapon?

Do I really believe I'm that smart? That my team and I had that much foresight? That we got that lucky?

She turns to look at the airlock, running the numbers in her head.

Antimemetics Division staff, other than me: thirty-eight. Forty-two days until the next iteration. That's past the end of the year. It'll be too late. If I leave this room now, I will never be back. The plan I have now is the best plan there's ever going to be.

We're the last ones in the world. After us, there's nobody.

*

Kim is so deeply buried in work at his terminal and the airlock is so quiet that he almost doesn't notice when it starts to cycle open again.

"We need to check you for notes," he begins, but then he sees that Marion Wheeler is curled up in the bottom of the narrow cylinder, panting as though she just finished a marathon run. Kim holds a hand out but she shakes her head, electing to stay lying down, knees bent up to her chest, sucking down lungfuls of air.

"What in the world happened in there?" Kim asks.

"Just need..." she gasps, "...to breathe. Be okay in a... second. Haaaaah. I think I blacked out for a moment, might have inhaled some. Haaaaah. I think I'm okay. I remember the plan."

Kim looks confused and worried for a second, then they replace him. "You shouldn't be able to remember anything... what did you do?"

"Hit my head," Wheeler says, then goes back to concentrating on breathing properly. She suddenly becomes acutely aware that Kim has her effectively cornered. Disliking this configuration for reasons which she's only gradually putting back together, she levers herself up to one shoulder and tries to stand. Kim puts a hand on her shoulder and pushes her back down.

"You look terrible," he says. "There's something inl fleth your neck. Do you see that?" He points at her throat, then taps the same spot on his own.

"What?"

"On your neck. I nefth hlai you've been infected by whatever was in there. We need to act quickly." He reaches for his keyring and unthreads a Swiss Army knife, and unfolds a short, gleaming blade. He does this in such a methodical, ordinary way that Wheeler almost forgets to react when he leans down towards her to cut her throat.

Almost. She grips his wrist. They're locked like that for a moment, a tableau. She looks into Paul Kim's eye, but it isn't his eye anymore. She squints, wondering if she's making eye contact with anything but a hole in space. She already feels the force bearing down on her own skull, trying to drill into it, but she knows its shape and that means she can hold out, maybe for a few minutes. She had hoped, prayed, that Kim would not succumb so quickly. And in a crazed little way she'd thought there would be at least a sign, a theatrical doubling-over as his mind was wrenched out of its socket.

Kim's wrist spasms as he tries to lunge with the knife. Wheeler parries and its tip glances off the airlock interior wall with a screech. They scuffle for an awkward second, then she boots Kim in the stomach with both feet, sending him sprawling in the antechamber. She launches out of the airlock, dives over him and sprints away from the containment unit.

She feels SCP-3125 following her as she runs, like a spotlight. She hears a crash in another part of the Site, as the first piece of ceiling caves in.

5

Your Last First Day

Marion Wheeler is curled in the corner of Site 41's main freight elevator, descending, clutching a shiny red ray gun almost as long as she is tall. The gun has a two-tined prong instead of a barrel and its stock is a weirdly asymmetrical mass of pipework, more like a Swiss watch or a small intestinal tract than a weapon. The gun is SCP-7381, and it comes from a long-dead planet — not too distant a planet, when all's said and done — which conventional astronomy has yet to observe.

A tornado of violence and destruction is tearing through Site 41 and through the minds of everybody working at Site 41. Ceilings are being brought down, the site pharmacy is a sucking hole at the side of the building. The armoury is buried; that's why she had to go through Area 09 and is now toting anomalous weaponry instead. The Antimemetics Division operatives she meets in the corridors are all broken; some of them curled up and raving while their minds evaporate and they die one memory at a time, some infected with a collection of ideas which compel them to shout guttural phrases in strange languages, and to procure blades — never guns — and work on those demented victims, and each other, and themselves.

Wheeler doesn't recognise any of the people. Their faces are all wrong, torn up with hatred and misery and vindictive glee. She's been trying to avoid fighting, but she's had to kill one man in self-defence. Fired at his heart, SCP-7381 simply erased a half-metre-wide cylinder of matter, removing his upper torso and lower jaw. He fell to the ground in four pieces. SCP-7381's beam is invisible, silent and recoilless. It was like using a child's toy gun.

Wheeler is petrified, but more than that, angry. "This is too much," she says, out loud, willing her heart rate back under control. "I can't deal with this. I shouldn't have to deal with this. It's my fucking first day!"

*

But how much sense does that make? Wheeler studies her reflection in the dark glass of the elevator control panel, and she tours the interior of her own skull, examining her thought processes. There are hints there, which would be difficult to articulate to someone who didn't know her as well as she knows herself. She isn't thinking like a newbie. She's instinctively breaking the problem apart, the way an experienced Foundation operative should. Hell, a newbie wouldn't even know how to carry out a detailed psychological self-examination of this kind. A newbie wouldn't even think of it, a newbie would just suffocate.

"The first thing it did when it saw me," she explains to her reflection, "was eat everything I knew about the Division. And everything I knew about *it*. If I had a plan, it ate the plan. ...But I'm still me. So I can come up with that plan again. It's already right in front of me, I just need to see it. If I were me, what would my plan have been?"

She scratches absently at her left wrist.

"Taking some hardcore mnestic drugs would have been a smart first step, I guess," she mutters. "Reinforcing my mind, so that it can't erase the rest of the steps. Damn." The nearest source of mnestic medicine is the site pharmacy, but it's already been destroyed, and in any case the elevator is headed down, away from it.

No. Stop. The pharmacy's been destroyed? How do I know that?

Well, because she was there. She remembers finding the pharmacist crushed to death beneath a fallen medical cabinet, her skull an unrecognisable splatter of scarlet. She remembers the floor being torn away beneath her feet, and only barely making it out of that portion of the building alive.

She remembers— a modular package coloured Safety Orange, with an enormous black Z on it. Her heart nearly stops at this. *Oh, God. What did I do?*

She remembers the dozens of warning signs covering the package; she remembers the three-factor authorisation procedure she had to follow to get into the sealed container where it was stored; she remembers the centimetre-thick book of medical advisory information, which she discarded; and, rolling her left sleeve back, she finds a fresh needle mark with a speck of blood, and remembers administering the injection.

This was my plan? This is what it takes to fight SCP-3125? I've killed myself—

Class-Z mnestics are the last word in biochemical memory fortification. Class-Z mnestics permanently destroy the subject's ability to forget. The result is perfect eidetic memory and perfect immunity to arbitrarily strong antimemetic interference.

The dose is taking effect now. Wheeler didn't read the book because she already knew every word of it. She knows everything that's about to happen to her. She can already feel her mind hardening, like steel, and the developing symptoms of extreme sensory overload.

She can see everything.

There are extra buttons on the elevator control panel, the lowest of which, the thirtieth floor below ground level, she's somehow already pushed. The walls of the elevator are covered with graffiti scrawled by the desperate and dying, people whose conceptual presence was eradicated from reality years earlier by the Alastair Grey antimemetic kill agent, reducing them to the level of ghosts. In one corner of the freight elevator there is even a half-corpse, unidentifiable, so many layers removed from reality that not even flies can smell it, its cells winking out of existence asymptotically over the course of years.

There is a fistful of tiny white worms exploring the floor of the elevator car, near where she's sitting. Revolted, Wheeler shuffles back from them, shaking one or two more of them out of her hair. The worms are among the most widespread and successful antimemetically cloaked organisms in the world. They are everywhere, in every biome, in every room.

She can hear a long, alarming drone noise, a continual roaring which has the texture of ambient noise and is continually getting louder. It's as if it's been there for her entire life, and it's only now that she's begun to hear it.

It's too much data. Too much sound, too much light. Having her eyes open is like jamming them full of needles. She clamps her hands over her ears and screws her eyes up. Even like this, she feels the vibration of the elevator's slow descent and the heat of the failed air conditioning and the movement of her clothes on her skin, and meanwhile her vision is flooding instead with what could be hallucinations. The human sensorium routinely generates huge amounts of data and the human brain is adapted to discard almost all of that data nearly immediately. Altering the brain's behaviour to retain that data is extremely dangerous even for very short time spans.

Wheeler takes one hand away from her ear for just long enough to punch the metal wall of the elevator car, bloodying two knuckles. The pain gives her a focal point, a memory which screams a little louder than the rest.

And she finds the plan. She doesn't remember it; she bootstraps it from first principles, in a handful of minutes, just like she's done a hundred times before.

"I know how to beat you," she says.

"No," SCP-3125 says to her. "You don't."

*

The elevator stops at the thirtieth floor below ground and its doors grind open. They wait, open, for a long time. Further up the elevator shaft there are the distant rumbles of more parts of Site 41 being reduced to crumbs.

Still crouched in the corner, Wheeler mutters, "SCP-3125 doesn't have a voice."

"Of course I do," it replies.

"SCP-3125 is a five-dimensional anomalous metastasized mass of bad memes and bad antimemes and everything in between, seeping through to our physical reality. It isn't coherent and it isn't intelligent. It can't communicate. This is an auditory hallucination."

SCP-3125 scoffs. "You know what I hate most about you, Marion? You're consistently, eternally *wrong*... and yet you're still alive. All those lost battles, every year of that entire lost war, but somehow you always cobble together enough dumb luck to walk away unscathed. The eternal sole survivor. You don't deserve that kind of luck. Nobody does."

While it's talking, Wheeler leans hard on the ray gun to get to her feet. She lodges one shoulder against the wall of the elevator car, still with her eyes closed. She braces herself, and opens her eyes. The corridor ahead is empty. There's an airlock at the far end, this one large enough to drive a truck through, built from ultra-toughened white metal alloy in Bart Hughes's established style. There's a panel beside the airlock. She closes her eyes again and hobbles forward, using the ray gun as a crutch, stretching one hand out ahead of her as guidance.

"Someone has to be last," she says, gritting her teeth. "Someone has to be the best."

"Your team is dead," SCP-3125 says. "Their minds have been pulled out, like eyeballs. They're hollow people, with holes in space where their brains were. The war is over! Finally! It's just *you*, Marion, a division of one! Dying from mnestic overdose, two hundred metres underground, cared for by no one, known to exist to no one, up against an immortal, unkillable idea."

Wheeler reaches the airlock and fumbles blindly with the panel until she finds the slot for her keycard. For a few seconds it seems as if nothing is happening, then a yellow light flashes, the enormous mechanical interlocks unlatch and the door cycles open with all the fuss of a flower's petals unfurling. Noise, Hughes always held, is a symptom of imperfect engineering.

Behind her, she hears the freight elevator close up and return to ground level, and she knows that someone has summoned it, intending to pursue her.

"Ideas can be killed," she says, stepping into the airlock.

"How?"

"With better ideas."

As the airlock cycles closed, so does the hermetic seal. SCP-3125 is shut out.

*

If something can cross over from conceptual space into reality, taking physical form, then something can cross in the opposite direction. It must be possible to take a physical entity, mechanically extract the *idea which it embodies*, amplify that idea and broadcast it up into conceptual space. A bigger idea. A better idea, one designed specifically to fight SCP-3125.

An ideal. A movement. A hero.

The machine Wheeler needs to build is the size of an Olympic stadium, and she doesn't have a fraction of the heavy memetic engineering experience to do it, let alone the material resources or the time. But she knows — someone taught her, she doesn't remember who — that an Antimemetics Division operative is as good on their first day as they're ever likely to be. And the same must be true of the Division as a whole.

She tells herself: *We won this war on the day it began. When we encountered SCP-3125 for the first time, we built this bunker. Bart Hughes faked his death and sequestered himself here so he could work uninterrupted, while the rest of the Division held on for as long as humanly possible, buying time for this moment. I know this is what I did, because it's what I would have done.*

I'm the final component. He's waiting for me.

*

The space beyond the airlock is gigantic, structured and lit like an aircraft hangar and filled with hot, stale, dry air. Wheeler, still mostly blind, stumbles forward across an expanse of more than a hectare of flat, dusty epoxy flooring. "Hughes!" she shouts into the void. "It's time!" Nothing comes back but the echo.

She glances up for a second. The space is empty. The castle-sized memetic amplification/broadcasting unit which

Bart Hughes was meant to be building is absolutely absent. Hughes himself is absent.

Maybe the entire machine is antimemetically cloaked? she wonders, momentarily. It would be a smart way to conceal the operation even from the rest of the Foundation. But her brain is curdling in the strongest mnestic drugs ever manufactured. There's genuinely nothing here.

Almost nothing. At the centre of the space there's a small outpost, a group of trestle tables with tools and toolboxes scattered about the place. Parked behind it is an unmarked military truck with flat tyres. On the back of the truck is a squat, squarish machine the size of a shipping container, with unshielded wiring and exposed pipework, and a long cable leading to a heavy-duty control panel on the floor. To the untrained eye, it is not at all clear what the machine is designed to do.

It's the antimemetic equivalent to a hydrogen bomb; the Division's answer to a site nuclear warhead. Activated, it would contaminate Site 41 and everything and everyone on it with antimemetic radiation. There would be no Site 41 and no Division afterwards; nothing any of the escaping, infectious staff did could have any effect on the real world.

It's the wrong machine.

It can't destroy or contain SCP-3125, or even injure it. All it can do is sterilise today's outbreak. The other symptoms will persist. Fifty or ten or five years from now, or maybe one year or maybe *tomorrow*, SCP-3125 will return, bringing with it its MK-class end-of-world scenario. Human civilisation will be entirely eradicated as an abstract concept, and be replaced with something unimaginably worse. There will be no one to fight it.

Wheeler leans there on the ray gun for a long moment. The pressure of information in her mind, continually increasing, reaches a point where she can't take it any more, and she starts to break. The Class-Z has been in her system for long enough now that she knows for a fact she has irreversible brain damage. There is no antidote. She'll be lucid for another hour, then spend the remaining two or three hours of her life vegetative.

That's right, she thinks. It's almost a relief. *This is good. This is right.*

I've survived too long. I forgot what universe this was. For a while there, I thought, maybe... this was the universe where we win sometimes.

The agony in her head is like an ice axe now. She drops the ray gun with a clatter, sinks to her knees, lies down and waits for either death or a better idea.

*

A being superficially resembling Paul Kim arrives at the outer airlock door. It examines the airlock uncomprehendingly for a few moments, then finds the keycard slot. It hunts methodically through Kim's pockets, then remembers the keycard around its neck. The airlock cycles once more and not-Kim goes through. Behind it, the freight elevator is returning to ground level a third time, to fetch the rest.

In the next room, the being which is not Paul Kim finds Wheeler, unconscious, with the ray gun dropped beside her. There is also a military truck, which it disregards.

Not-Kim lets its keycard fall from its fingers and scoops up the ray gun. For a moment it contemplates the unconscious Wheeler, then examines the gun itself, remembering how it works. It turns back to face the airlock and fires, punching fat cylindrical holes in the white metal of the inner door until it's gone, then the outer door too, breaching the hermetic seal. A faint smile returns to not-Kim's face as SCP-3125 and its familiar, comforting signals flood into the bunker.

A dozen more non-people are arriving by freight elevator, former Antimemetics Division bodies. "I've found her," not-Kim calls out to them. It drops the ray gun where it's standing, as if it simply forgot that it had been carrying anything, and pulls out its knife again. It holds the knife between two fingers, in a casual, offhand sort of way, as if it were a pencil or screwdriver.

The infected non-people gather with not-Kim around Wheeler, looking down at her with alien expressions of disgust, or pity, or malice.

"Why isn't she opening up properly?" someone asks. "She can't meet them unless she wants the signals."

"Start with her eyes," says someone else. "It'll make the rest of her easier to correct."

Not-Kim leans down to start work, then hesitates, its knife a few centimetres from Wheeler's eye. She's whispering something, so quietly that only it can hear her clearly.

"None of this happened, Paul," she says. "You and I never existed. There is no Antimemetics Division."

There's a sharp *click* as the bomb finishes its powering-up sequence. Nobody in the room can hear this but Wheeler. Nobody in the room can perceive the bomb but Wheeler. All they can see is an empty truck.

The world goes black.

Interlude

SCP-2256 - Very Tall Things

Item #: SCP-2256

Object Class: Euclid

Special Containment Procedures: Information about SCP-2256 is subject to a gradual antimemetic corrosion effect. Corrosion occurs at differing rates depending on the level of detail/accuracy in the information and the physical complexity of the storage medium. In-depth academic papers, photographs, and information stored electronically decay rapidly; broad descriptions, pencil sketches and paperwork decay slowly.

Therefore, this electronic database entry should describe SCP-2256 only in broad terms. Detailed information about SCP-2256's appearance, theorised evolutionary ancestry, biology, diet, behaviour, vocalisations, lifecycle, intelligence, ecological role and cultural significance should be stored in hard copy at Site 19, vault 1-053. The rate of corrosion in both data sources should be monitored carefully, although at present no technique is known for halting or undoing such corrosion.

Although these antimemetic effects linger and rate Euclid classification, SCP-2256 itself is extinct and requires no special containment procedures.

Description: SCP-2256 (*Cryptomorpha gigantes*) is a species of gigafauna which was endemic to the South Pacific Ocean around the islands of Polynesia. SCP-2256 was one of the very few recorded species known to have developed rudimentary perceptual/"antimemetic" camouflage, rendering them nearly impossible for other sentient beings to perceive or remember. This adaptation is theorised to have arisen in order to elude predators.

SCP-2256 was the largest species to have lived on Earth. Resembling spindly, vertically elongated giraffes or brachiosauruses, adults of the species grew to over 1,000 metres in height. They weighed no more than 4 tonnes, with most of their mass being "camouflaged" by a very similar adaptation. With their broad, dish-shaped feet, they were able to walk directly on the surface of the ocean without sinking.

SCP-2256 navigated the ocean alone or in ▮▮▮▮▮ of 2 to as many as 2,000 individuals. They were reluctant to approach land, especially inhabited islands, usually staying more than 30 kilometres offshore. Because of their height, they were visible on the horizon at this distance.

Acquisition: Polynesian natives of the island of Maikiti used a substance called *teùkoka* for recreational and religious purposes. As well as being a moderate psychedelic, this drug had mnestic properties, suppressing antimemetic effects and making entities camouflaged in this way easier to see and remember. Thus, the Maikitians were for hundreds of years the only people able to see SCP-2256. In Maikitian mythology SCP-2256 were wandering spirits whom the gods had charged with maintaining the horizon, to ensure that the sky and the water never mixed. They were characterised as well-meaning and friendly, but unintelligent and often deficient in their duties, resulting in storms and typhoons. They were called *polo'ongakau*, "the ones who walk very slowly".

In 1991 an internal biochemistry study revealed that *teùkoka* bore a strong chemical resemblance to the Foundation's own class-W mnestic. A Foundation anthropologist was assigned to follow ██ ██ the Maikitian legend, and became the first outsider to observe ███-2256. An observation ███ was quickly ████████ on the island to study the creatures. Routine containment analysis found that SCP-2256 was Safe and required no special containment procedures, or even particular ████ ██ secrecy.

History: SCP-███ immediately proved to be impossible to capture photographically. Photographic negatives of the species faded into transparency over the ████ █ a few minutes. Similar decay ████ affected videotape, audio tape, celluloid film, digital and electronic scans, ██. The observation team soon returned most of their equipment to inventory and proceeded using pencils and ████. At the time, it ██ believed that such recordings would be effectively permanent.

SCP-2256's population declined slightly in 1992 and 1993, then dropped sharply from 1994 onwards. A combination of contributing factors were observed: illness, infertility and an ████████ rate of stillbirths.

In 2002 a field generator was developed which could penetrate and neutralise SCP-2256's antimemetic ████████, allowing for conventional photography. The first and only close-up photograph of one of the creatures instantly killed it. It was concluded that direct observation of SCP-2256 is injurious to ████. This adaptation is believed to have arisen as a means of detecting predators, just as SCP-2256's antimemetic camouflage protected them from those same predators. Use of ██ ██ generator was immediately curtailed.

It was subsequently hypothesised that the Foundation's ongoing passive observation of the species was intense enough to have harmful effects on SCP-2256, and that ██ was what was driving the species ██ extinction. Opinions differed sharply ██ ██ veracity of this hypothesis, over ██ thoroughly it should be tested, and over what ██ be done if it proved to be true. Several extreme options were ████, including █████ exterminating ██-██ to preserve the data, and completely expunging the data to preserve ██-2256. No firm conclusions ██ ██.

In 2003 observation of SCP-2256 was scaled back significantly, and the Foundation ████ focus from gathering ██ data to analysing ████ data. However, SCP-2256's population continued to ████. The last individual died near Tokelau ██ October 30, 2006.

██ 2010 ████ discovered ██ the antimemetic camouflage ████, also characterised as "decay" or "corrosion", was spreading through paper records of ██-██. As of ██, more ██ 60% of ██ documents are ██, even with █ strong mnestic dose. The effect is even ██ ██ SCP entry itself, despite ██ ██ shielding and redundancy in this system.

Since ██-██ extinct, █ new data about it can be generated. It is ████ that full contamination ██ ██ ██ three to eight years.

Part II

Five Five Five Five Five

1
SCP-3125 - The Escapee

Item #: SCP-3125

Object Class: Keter

Special Containment Procedures: SCP-3125 is kept inside Cognitohazard Containment Unit 3125 on the first floor of Site 41. This containment unit is a 10m by 15m by 3m cuboidal room clad in layers of lead, soundproofing and telepathic shielding. Access is through an airlock system at one end of the containment unit. This airlock is programmed to allow only one person to enter the containment unit at a time, and to remain locked until this person exits before allowing another person to enter.

Under no circumstances may any coherent information be allowed to leave the containment unit. This includes written and electronic notes, photographs, audio and video recordings, sound, electromagnetic and particle-based signals and psi emanations. During the exit cycle, a purge system rigged to the airlock flushes the occupant's memory by flooding the airlock with amnestic gas for three minutes.

A senior Antimemetics Division staff member must visit SCP-3125 every six weeks (42 days).

END OF FILE

*

Item #: SCP-3125

Object Class: Keter

Special Containment Procedures: SCP-3125 is subject to inverted containment protocols, and is present everywhere in reality except for those places which have been specifically purged of its influence. The interior of Cognitohazard Containment Unit 3125 on Site 41, where this document resides, is the only location in the world known to have been successfully purged in this way. This containment unit is a 10m by 15m by 3m cuboidal room clad in layers of lead, soundproofing material and telepathic shielding. Access is through an airlock system at one end of the containment unit. This airlock is programmed to allow only one person to enter the containment unit at a time, and to remain locked until this person exits before allowing another person to enter.

Under no circumstances may any coherent information be allowed to leave the containment unit. This includes written and electronic notes, photographs, audio and video recordings, sound, electromagnetic and particle-based signals and psi emanations. A purge system rigged to the airlock flushes the occupant's memory by flooding the airlock with amnestic gas for three minutes during the exit cycle.

An alternate SCP entry must be maintained in the main Foundation database, giving only the technical specifications of the containment unit, provisions for senior Antimemetics

Division staff to visit the unit's interior on a regular basis, and no description.

Description: SCP-3125 is an extremely large (see full Θ'-dimensional fractal topology, attachment 13), highly aggressive anomalous metastasized meme complex originating externally to our reality and now partially intersecting it.

SCP-3125 is adapted for survival in an ideatic ecology considerably more violent and hostile than our own. (Here, "our own" refers to human head space: the set of all ideas which humans have or are biologically capable of having.) Because humans have no natural exposure to ideas as aggressive as SCP-3125, human minds have no protective evolutionary adaptations against it. Individuals possessed of SCP-3125 become incapable of entertaining weaker, "conventional" ideas, and become instead wholly bodily subordinate to the purpose of serving and disseminating the core concepts of SCP-3125. In addition, although undergoing no outwardly visible physical alteration, they cease to be externally recognisable as human.

SCP-3125 is not yet entirely present in our reality. Upon its arrival, the highly interconnected nature of human knowledge exchange systems means that it will take no longer than twelve hours, possibly as few as four hours, to encompass, dominate and replace all human thought. At this point, "humanity" as an abstract concept, along with all attendant abstracts such as "civilization", "culture", "society", "community" and "family" will have ceased to exist. The Foundation terms such an eventuality an *MK-class end-of-world scenario*.

The Foundation possesses numerous proven techniques for arresting the spread of such aggressive idea complexes, but these are all rendered unworkable in practice by SCP-3125's autonomic defensive response/boundary layer. Fully assembling a mental picture of SCP-3125 and perceiving its true shape causes SCP-3125 in turn to be able to perceive the observer. It then attacks the observer, killing them. The mechanism of the attack is unclear, but appears to be at least partially physical. "Mental bystanders", individuals whose thoughts and ideas resemble those of the observer, are also attacked. This invariably includes the observer's entire extended research group, and often their close family (parents and offspring).

The attack has the net effect of erasing all knowledge both of SCP-3125 and its attack from the world. This informational "numbing" effect performs a similar function to the anaesthetic saliva of a mosquito's bite, enabling SCP-3125 to evade detection prior to its full incarnation.

Foundation staff discovering SCP-3125 may be able to escape its attack via prompt use of amnestic medication to erase their knowledge of it.

In either case, the net result is that the interior of a suitably shielded containment unit is the only location where it is safe to observe, record or even acknowledge the existence of SCP-3125. Outside of such a containment unit, a true written description of SCP-3125 would constitute a lethal cognitohazard.

SCP-3125 could be effectively neutralized using a machine proposed by the late Dr. Bartholomew Hughes called an *irreality amplifier* (see schematics, attachment 129). However, as well as requiring tremendous material resources, this machine could not be constructed without its builders understanding why it was being built, which would require an understanding of SCP-3125, which would prove fatal to the project.

No means of neutralizing SCP-3125 using only the resources in this room is known.

History: Due to the described defense mechanism, SCP-3125's observation history is almost entirely missing. In particular, it is unclear exactly how this containment unit came to be built and how these containment procedures were established.

Much data has been accrued in this containment unit over the course of successive visits by Foundation researchers. This data was brought from the outside in the hope of being useful and left here in accordance with containment procedures. In addition to this database entry, the reader will find multiple electronic copies of the Foundation database, academic data sets of all kinds and extensive public news archives.

As is to be expected, much of this data is not germane to the topic of containing SCP-3125. Nevertheless, correlation and analysis by successive visitors has allowed the following facts to emerge:

1. Although SCP-3125 is not yet fully present in our reality, its indirect effects/foreshocks (for example, SCP-█, SCP-██, SCP-██ and SCP+███) are easily discovered by any well-equipped memetics research project.

2. Memetics research is, today, a much-diminished science from when it was at its peak. In mid-2008 there existed more than 400 institutions pursuing research likely to uncover SCP-3125, including government agencies, military branches, private corporations, independent laboratories, university research projects and notable amateur groups. Many of these were GOIs or internal divisions within GOIs. None of these groups still exist, except for the Foundation's Antimemetics Division.

3. Almost nobody in the world is consciously aware of this decline, and explanations for the disappearance of these groups have not been forthcoming.

Simple deduction gives that all of these groups eventually discovered SCP-3125 and were consumed by it, and that this is, in fact, the inevitable fate of all competent memetics research.

The Antimemetics Division's persistence is attributed to its specialist training and its ready access to reliable amnestic medication. Despite this, the Division, too, has shrunk considerably in recent years, from a reported staff of well over 4,000 people in 2012 to, as of September 2015, 125. This figure is on track to reach zero before the end of 2015. Over the same period, the Division's physical worldwide presence has similarly shrunk, from a network of Sites and smaller outposts on every continent to this single Site, Site 41. In particular, the Division's headquarters at Site 167 are now missing from the Division's collective memory and presumed neutralized by SCP-3125's concealment response.

Addendum: Further analysis of the available data — specifically, architectural diagrams of Site 41 (attachment 38) — indicates the existence of a second containment unit on Site 41 conforming to the same basic design philosophy as this one. This second unit, S041-B30-000, was built 210 metres below ground level; it features identical broad-spectrum informational cladding but has more than one thousand times the volume of Cognitohazard Containment Unit 3125, along with an amnestic airlock large enough to ingest a Twenty-foot Equivalent Unit shipping container.

Information relating to the date of construction and purpose of S041-B30-000 is absent from Foundation records and is presumed to have been deliberately erased. The unit itself is hermetically sealed, and has been for an indeterminate period of time.

Regardless of S041-B30-000's intended purpose, it, like any such containment unit, is capable of acting as a shelter from SCP-3125.

Addendum 2:

And the rest, hopefully, is blindingly obvious.

S041-B30-000 was originally constructed to house a long-term project to construct Hughes' irreality amplifier. While that's been going on, the rest of us have been fighting an unconscious war in order to buy time. We have been losing, but losing as slowly as humanly possible.

The time we have bought is now up. It's an extremely bad sign that nobody inside S041-B30-000 has broken the seal yet, but there is no ground left for us to cede, and there are no more bodies to throw into SCP-3125's maw to slow it down. ॐ is here, ready or not.

I am going to go to S041-B30-000 and use the machine. I think I can get the information out through the airlock. I think I can get to the vault alive.

This was the plan. It's become garbled in the retelling because of variables, but I know that this was my plan, because I know myself. What else could it have been?

Standard procedure is that I have to tell you what to do next if this doesn't work. That's the asynchronous research covenant.

But I don't have a good picture of who you can even be, reading this and alive. In your scenario there is no machine, Hughes is missing, I'm dead, the Site is ruined, and how'd you even get in here? Can you be Foundation? Are you conscious? Is there a single word of this which you comprehend?

You live in a world bathed with SCP-3125. That's the loss condition.

I can't help someone who doesn't exist.

Marion Wheeler, chief of Antimemetics
November 30, 2015

Addendum 3:

I found your body.

And finding your body was a powerfully disorienting sensation for me, I don't mind admitting. I used to know a Marion. During the brief period in which I knew her, she wasn't one to admit defeat as easily as you. Still, that was a long time ago...

Far be it from me to tell you your business, but I fear you missed a trick. From the evidence I can see, this was never the only "Antimemetics Division" Site. There were others. I imagine they're now all effectively invisible to (most) passers-by, of course, just like this one, but I presume that they, just like this one, still physically exist. Your plan, I think, was in place for longer than you know. And since you weren't at liberty to retain its details, you put it into action more than once.

There is another vault fitting the description, truck-sized amnestic airlock and all. S167-001-6183.

Site 167 is a non-entity, of course, which is most likely why you missed it. It's likely ruined, and it's quite definitely a *long God-damned way* from here on foot. But still! I think it's better than half a chance.

I could die on this boondoggle too, naturally, as the world has become something of a horror show of late. In any case, I trust that anybody following in my footsteps and reading these additional words will have the presence of mind to pursue the same basic strategy.

Still existing despite everything,

Adam Wheeler, interloper
May 4, 2017

END OF FILE

2
Where Have You Been All My Life

Who the *fuck* infiltrates a senior Foundation official's home, while they're home?

Marion Wheeler lives deep in coniferous forest, a long drive from the nearest major city and a long drive in the opposite direction from Site 41. It's late, last thing, and she's reading in bed when she hears the muffled, unmistakeable click of her front door being unlocked. She looks up, and stares blankly at the wall for a second while listening to soft footsteps moving into the hallway.

She marks her place and reaches for her Foundation-issued phone. She has no permanent security staff at home — the Division is understaffed and trained operatives are in much more serious need on Site — but the building and grounds have beefy electronic countermeasures. They, she discovers, have all been disabled, along with the sensors and cameras. She was not notified that this had happened. Whoever did it had a valid code.

Who, though?

The Foundation has enemies. True, the list of credible, motivated enemies is surprisingly short, and the list of groups stupid enough to try to kill or capture someone at her level is shorter. But it's far from empty, and it's not actually so hard a feat; not too many people below O5 level are privileged to travel in motorcades. The real trick, the impossible trick, is to avoid unholy retaliation. But what if you really think you can? What if you've decided it's worth it?

Wheeler triggers the silent alarm. She sets her phone back down on the nightstand and collects her gun. She rolls out of bed, tucks a few pillows in her place, moves silently to her bedroom door and stands beside it, listening and thinking.

This door, her bedroom door, can't be opened silently. It creaks like hell, so if she goes through it she'll have to be ready to draw attention. There's an attic, but access is out there on the landing and, again, can't be operated silently. There's no alternate route to ground level other than jumping from the window, and someone has to be covering it. Even if she landed in the bushes alive, she'd still have to break the perimeter with a sprained ankle.

A better question than "Who?" is "How many?" She may already be straight-up dead, simply due to numbers. If the attackers tread cautiously and try to flush her out, she figures she can *Home Alone* her way through perhaps eight of them before running out of luck. If they rush the second floor and have armor she might be overwhelmed by as few as two, even with the staircase acting as a choke point. All of this, naturally, assumes that the attackers aren't anomalous. If they are, and they're not in the, say, thirty percent of anomalies which can be neutralised simply by shooting them in the centre mass and head, she may be fundamentally helpless even after the response team shows up. Which will be, at best, ten minutes from now.

A creaking. This damned house. Someone is coming up the stairs, making no effort to be quiet about it. A soft tread, though. As if they removed their shoes. Just one of them? That barely makes sense.

With five seconds' grace, Wheeler casts around the dark room for a second weapon. She knows there are knitting needles downstairs in the lounge and knives, good ones, in the kitchen. But she can't get to them. It's too late. The door's opening. It seems like the man's trying to say something as he comes in, but he only gets as far as "I—*whulp*," and it's done. He's flat on his face, cheek pressed into deep cream carpet, with Wheeler on his back pinning both his wrists with her knees. She sights urgently back down the stairs for a second; there's no one there. She prods him in his other cheek with the muzzle of the gun. "You speak, you die," she hisses. "You try to move, you die." She glances at the windows, checks the stairs again, listens intently. There's no sound. There's nothing to be seen.

The man is fifty, and lanky. He wears an expensive dark suit, tailored to his build. He has angular features, thick, greying hair and rimless spectacles, now quite possibly bent out of shape by their sudden impact with the floor. He wears discreet platinum jewellery: a wristwatch, cufflinks and a ring.

The two of them halt like that, a tableau. He makes no attempt to move, although he does look askance at Wheeler, as best he can given his dislodged glasses.

Wheeler asks, "Where are the others?"

"It's just me, Marion," he answers.

"Who are you?"

He says nothing for a moment, but his expression slowly, subtly drops. "I, ah. Well. Well, it really happened, didn't it? I always wondered."

"Who are you?"

"There is a monster which follows you around and eats your memories," the man says. "SCP-4987. You drip-feed it inconsequential trivia so it doesn't go after anything important. You watch game shows. The book you were reading just now. On your nightstand. It's a trivia book. Right?"

Wheeler says nothing to confirm or deny this, although it is true. At feeding time the entity manifests like a bright gold-white spot in the corner of her eye. It's gone now.

She's already put the rest of it together. It is all mind-bogglingly, insultingly obvious.

With a well-suppressed but still detectable note of dismay, she asks, "What's your name?"

"Adam," he says. "Adam Wheeler."

*

Obviously, she has the man detained.

She instructs her people to interrogate him — lightly — and to run deep background research on every word he utters, while for her part she stands far back from the investigation to avoid contamination. She resists the urge to interfere, particularly to visit "Adam" and personally demand answers. She goes to her office, curls up on the couch there and tries to catch some sleep, but doesn't succeed in any real sense.

Seven hours later a Foundationer knocks on her office door, bringing an inch-thick block of printouts and a paralysingly strong cup of coffee. Wheeler takes the drink first, accepting it as a kind of authentication step before letting the man in. She moves back to the couch and sits hunched over the drink for warmth, inhaling its fumes.

The man settles heavily into a chair opposite. He is a misleadingly stocky, perpetually unshaven individual, somewhere just shy of forty, and inarguably the most dangerous person on the Site. He is the Division's physical fitness and combat instructor and the leader of their solitary

Mobile Task Force. His name is Alex Gauss. "They, uh," he says, "figured I should be the one to present their results. Even though I didn't research one line of it. 'Cause we 'get along'. Their words. Personally, I don't see it."

Wheeler stays focused on the coffee. "Who is he?"

Gauss opens the first page of the report, more for show than anything, then closes it again. "He's your husband. Every word checks out. There is limitless physical evidence. Half of the Division knows him socially, including me. I credit your diligence and adherence to protocol, but the bottom line is that SCP-4987 got hungry."

Wheeler nods. This assessment matches her own, pieced together overnight from gut reactions and analysis of the plain facts. Where the hell else did her name come from? She wasn't born "Wheeler". But she had to get independent verification.

She asks, "Has this happened before?"

"No."

"Could it happen again?"

Gauss shrugs. "You would know better than anyone."

"I would. I do. And I can tell you this: I have SCP-4987 trained to follow me at my heel. I feed it according to a strict regimen, it eats only the memories I say it's okay to eat. A rapidly progressive, universally fatal memory parasite made chronic and then domesticated. And now, what, it suddenly breaks training? That adds up?"

"If you say it doesn't add up, it doesn't add up," Gauss says, cautiously. "But speaking from field experience, anything can happen twice."

Wheeler has waited long enough, and takes a long pull from the coffee. She stares into the coiling steam, as if trying to see the future. "But who is he?" she asks again. "At this point, you know him better than I do. What's he like? Do you like him?"

Gauss grimaces extravagantly. This is the great-great-grandmother of all loaded questions.

Wheeler looks him in the eye and says, "Tell me your personal impression of Adam Wheeler. Direct order."

"...He's a nice enough guy."

"'Nice enough'?"

Gauss clicks his tongue. "I don't like him," he admits. "Personally. All that much. We're civil. But he will always be a little bit too smug, and a little bit too clever. He just... grates. Would I throw someone in a cell for that? No."

"Do I like him?"

"You—" Gauss begins, then stops. He looks away. And over time, a soft smile develops on his face, one which Wheeler doesn't recall ever seeing before, not in a working relationship going back years. "Yeah," he says. "Yeah. He's the one."

*

Full name: Adam Bellamy Wheeler. Born February 27, 1962 in Henge, Derbyshire, United Kingdom to Rosemary Leah Wheeler *née* Wizst and Jonathan 'Jack' Philip Wheeler. No siblings. Early education: Henge Church of England Primary School, Matlock All Saints Secondary School. Demonstrated great musical acuity from an early age. By age sixteen had begun to be recognised as one of the most gifted classical violinists of his generation. Attended the Royal College of—

Wheeler skips three pages.

—after sustaining a minor injury while on tour in ██████████, he encountered SCP-4051, which had infested a wing of the hospital where he received treatment. SCP-4051 was protected by an unusual form of antimemetic camouflage to which Wheeler — like an estimated 1 in 145,000 individuals worldwide — was (and remains) immune. His attempt to alert authorities to the infestation's presence was intercepted by a Foundation listening station. Operative Marion A. Hutchinson (100A-1-9331), then a field agent based in—

Another page.

—resistant to conventional memory-erasure procedures. Hutchinson applied successfully for an exemption, arguing that even with his memories left intact it would be impossible for Wheeler to share the details of SCP-4051. They subsequently became romantically involved.

"Oh, they 'subsequently became romantically involved', did they? Tell me more, you featureless gray sphere of a biographer, I'm *hooked* now."

The biography is contentless beyond this point. Adam Wheeler's life spent touring, playing, lecturing and occasionally conducting, writing and composing is documented in exhaustive, pointless detail. He withstands background checks and surveillance, and consistently demonstrates himself to represent zero risk of leak. He eventually receives the extremely low clearance level normally granted to long-term Foundation-external partners of Foundationers. They get married. She takes his name, which she, reading, considers faintly unrealistic. Blah blah.

There is nothing about his personality. Nothing about their relationship. No content.

She remembers acquiring SCP-4051. There was no one there. She remembers nothing.

*

Up until the end of the third round of questioning, Adam Wheeler assumes good faith. He figures the repetition is a due diligence tic, a corporate procedural requirement. It's only when they start over from "What's your name?" with a brand new interviewer for the fourth time that he finally gets it: they don't like him, and they don't care what he thinks his name is. They're trying to grind him down, until he can't think, until he's just dust particles they can sift through for data.

He reacts badly to this realisation. He asks for his wife, and asks for his wife, and they ignore him, and they ignore him, and she persistently fails to appear, until it becomes a cold form of torture. The questions keep coming and nothing stops them, not answering truthfully, not not answering, not lying, not rambling off on tangents. They don't stop until he begins falling asleep in the middle of his own sentences.

He wakes up in a standard Humanoid Containment Unit, a stackable one-bedroom apartment with holographic fake windows, impregnable walls and extensive discreet modifications for the security and monitoring of anomalous entities. This one is on the first basement level, but he can't tell that. The bright quote-light-unquote pouring in through the main living area window is authentic enough to tan.

He wakes up on the couch, with a start, feeling creaky and dehydrated. He realises that he slept in his suit, and that his suit is creased. He hates that, that sensation of not looking his best, or at least presentable. That's going to gnaw away at him until he can find, at minimum, a razor and a change of shirt.

What woke him was the heavy metallic *clack* of the door unlocking. He looks up, rubbing his eyes. It's his wife. "Marion! Oh, my God." He leaps up and rushes over to meet her. She stops him a few paces short, with a gesture and a cold smile. And *that* hurts. It hurts more than anything.

So it really happened: SCP-4987 has bitten out the part of Marion Wheeler which cared about him. She wasn't absent because of some unrelated K-class outbreak. She just chose to be elsewhere, indifferent.

So he doesn't embrace her. He stands at a polite distance. "How are you feeling? Did you sleep?"

"I'm fine."

"I can tell you've had your coffee. Have you eaten? Come on, I'll make you something." The unit has a rudimentary kitchen area. He goes through and starts exploring the cupboards. "There must be something edible around here. Eggs and milk, at least. I'm ashamed to say I more or less fell asleep where I was standing when they put me in here, so I haven't had a chance to scout. Or do you keep the place empty, and the food arrives through a slot in the wall?"

Marion begins, "Mr. Wheeler—"

Adam shoots her a disappointed look.

"Okay," she says, "Adam. Please come and sit down. You're right, there's nothing in any of those cupboards."

He closes the cupboard and sits opposite her at the kitchen table. "Scrambled eggs on granary toast," he suggests. "With a lot of garlic in the eggs. That's what we both need right now. Particularly you, because if I don't make something substantial for you you end up drinking those wretched wallpaper paste milkshakes seven days a week. Or you skip the meal entirely."

"Adam. We've been married for seventeen years, is that correct?"

"Yes."

"I don't know you."

"That's fine," Adam says. "I doubt that that's going to be a serious problem. You've told me, many times, about your own people who've lost themselves in the work and had to bootstrap their own personalities a second time. You love watching it. It's like watching butterflies emerge from chrysalides. The best of your people can turn that around in ten weeks. Imagine how fast it's going to be for you."

"No," Wheeler replies. Her tone is clinical, matter-of-fact. "I'm afraid it's not possible."

"What's not possible?"

"I can't begin a new relationship right now. Certainly not something as serious as a marriage. You have nominal clearance; you know what we do. I have responsibilities. I do not have... 'time'."

"This isn't 'new'," Adam says, deadpan. "It's pre-existing."

"No," Wheeler explains. "That relationship is ended now, and we are somewhere else."

Adam stares at her for a long moment, thin-lipped and far from happy. He asks her:

"What do you remember?"

The question is so open-ended that Wheeler doesn't manage to respond verbally. She spreads her hands slightly, the gesture saying, "What?"

"You don't remember me," Adam says. "SCP-4987 also clearly ate the part of you which would care if you forgot me. And, additionally, the part of you which cares about brunch. 'What else have you forgotten?' would be a stupid question to ask, so instead I'm asking you, what's left? I want you to tell me everything you can remember."

"*Everything* I can remember?"

"Yes. From 1995 to right now."

It's still a farcical question at face value, and Wheeler's first instinct is to dismiss it as such, but she thinks again. She thinks, intending to genuinely try to answer the question. And she finds gaps. There's a dearth of specifics. It's like being asked to "say something" and immediately forgetting *all words*.

She says, "I remember... working."

And driving home, and then sleep, and then driving back to work. Big, hostile buildings. Drug regimens, containment procedures, endless piles of opaque numbers, personal fitness drills. Running. Calculating. Never, ever stopping calculating. She remembers, with unfair clarity, a large variety of extremely bad dreams.

And other than that, nothing. A huge, deep, ragged-edged black pit.

Adam says, "You remember nothing good, do you? Nothing good at all.

"When you come home, on the nights you make it home, you are ready to fold up. It has never been an easy job, but these past few years have been the worst they've ever been, because you're coming to the conclusion of something gigantic. You have explained to me how it is that you can never tell me, *really*, what it is that you do, without the act of you telling me killing me. And I — I couldn't stand that at first, and I still hate your job and I think it's a monstrous farce — but I trusted you in that. And I stopped asking. But I can tell, from the... rattle in your hands and the things you don't say, and the way you sleep, that there is some kind of war going on back here. And you're losing people to it. And you're almost at the end. And you're going to win.

"So I scramble your eggs, and I play the violin for you, and between us we hack out about three-tenths of what I would consider to be normalcy. Not because you can't do this without me, you could take the whole universe by yourself if you *really* had to, but: to blazes with that, you don't have to.

"It didn't happen instantly. But it happened pretty damned fast. We had music in common at first, Bach and Mendelssohn. We had tobacco in common and a mutual hatred of *The X-Files*. Then it was coffee and wine. And then after some time it became hiking, and birdwatching, and Perseid meteors. We like Bruce Lee flicks. We watch *Law &*

Order and *Jeopardy!* and we read stacks and stacks of books. No, in fairness, it's mainly me for the books. You don't have the long-term time to spare anymore."

He pinches the bridge of his nose for a second. Any two people can find that much common ground. Just being in the same place for years doesn't count for anything. What do they *have*?

"We communicate," he says. "Better than anybody I've seen. We can be apart for two months while I'm on tour or you're overseas and snap right back and pick up a conversation from the word we left off. We are connected. We are in the same headspace. You'll see it all. It'll happen again, just as fast. You've just got to give it a chance."

Wheeler is almost there. She sees the shape of what Adam is describing. It's distant and unclear, but if she concentrates she might be able to bring it into focus. It worries her, for nebulous reasons she can't completely articulate, but she can almost understand how there could be room for it. How it could lock into her life as it currently exists, and still make sense.

But Adam just said something crucial. He said a keyword which means the marriage counselling session is over and this is now a situation. Wheeler can't ignore it. She forces herself to drop the other thread and seize this one.

"What war?"

And now Adam really doesn't know what's happening. "Good God. The war, Marion. I don't know how else to describe it."

"What war? How many people?"

"I don't know," Adam says. "There are names. Names you stop mentioning, and then you ignore me when I bring them up again. I assume there are reasons. I don't know the specifics. How could I know? Why don't you know?"

Wheeler races through the reasoning. The existence of a war computes. It confirms long-term existing suspicions. It could have been going on for years without her realising it. It makes sense to her that she could be fighting it, winning, even, and not know; managing her own memories or losing them in skirmishes. This certainly won't be the first time she's uncovered it. It makes sense that Adam, naturally gifted with the mental equivalent of a thick layer of blubber, could stand on the edge of the conflict and dimly be able to perceive it. And the Division — so understaffed.

People are disappearing around her.

"And what if—" she begins, and stops dead in the middle of the thought, as if the thought itself was stolen out of her.

"And what if we get back together, and—" she begins again, and this time hard instinct seizes her around the midsection and bodily hauls her back from thinking a thought which, *it* knows, would kill her. She's Wile E. Coyote, she's already run off the edge of a precipice into clear air, and thinking that thought would be like looking down.

She feels SCP-4987 moving around her, abstractly bound to her, a winking speck of glitter in her eye. "Something's wrong."

Adam scratches at his own eye. "Do you see that?"

"How can *you* see that?"

"I have a mild immunity to antimemetic influence," Adam says. He knows it's in his file and he knows Wheeler has read the file, but apparently it needs to be said again. "I can tell when something is fritzing with my memories. I can resist it. Up to a point. So, Marion, I was hoping to have a relaxed conversation over coffee and get around to this topic organically, but I'm going to have to skip to the end: I have the impression that SCP-4987 is trying to kill me."

"...No," Wheeler says. "That's not its behavior model. It doesn't sustain itself that way, by eating people. It eats *memories*. And it's never done *this*. Not to you, nor me, nor anybody. Not since the very early days. It's *tame*. It does exactly what I tell it to do. Even when I'm waiting, and I'm bored, and I let it eat my short-term, it sits and *waits* to be told to eat."

"Then what is it doing to us?" Adam is getting nervy, and won't let go of his eye. He stands up and backs away. "I would like it if we could figure this out quickly. We don't have a way to put SCP-4987 down."

There's a sound in Wheeler's mind, but not in her ear, like a distant chorus of baying dogs. She stands too, and moves after Adam into the middle of the containment unit.

She says, "It's trying to protect you."

"I— How does wiping your memory of me protect me?"

"I can't explain," Wheeler says. "And I can't explain why I can't explain. I don't fully know myself. There's an ███████ ██████."

"A *what?*"

"You can't be here," she says. "You can't be in my life. You have to leave, or you're going to die."

"I'm not leaving you," Adam says. "Christ, that's why we did it in the end. Got married, I mean. It was scintillatingly obvious to both of us, very early on, that we were forever. But I wanted to get it on the public record. I stood up in front of everybody I respect and I swore to *them* that I would protect you. Forever!"

SCP-4987 is agitated. Wheeler feels it flitting around the room, incoherent, trying to tell her what it needs.

She says, with sudden actinic clarity, "I must have made an identical promise."

Adam doubles over, blinded in both eyes now. Closing his eyes does nothing, covering his eyes does nothing. The gold-white light is strobing for him, moving into violet. He panics. "Help. Help me. I can't see." He reaches out, unsteadily, for Wheeler's hand. She lets him take it and pull her close. The light doesn't fade. He clings to Wheeler for a few moments, and she holds on to him until he realises that

SCP-4987 is completely within her control, and this is all intentional.

"You're going to do this?" Adam says. "This is the Foundation mandate, this is what your definition of 'protect' amounts to? You've got no idea what you're about to do to yourself. You don't even know me."

"I think I know," she replies.

"You will feel this for the rest of your life. Every day, you will wake up with a sick cold feeling in your stomach where there used to be a real life. And you'll wonder why."

"I'm going to win this war," Wheeler says to him. "I'll beat the universe. And then I will come and find out why."

Adam holds on to her for another long, long moment. He can hear the baying too, now, and he can even barely perceive what it is, far off behind the hill, that SCP-4987 is frantic about. That distant dot, that fleeting second-hand glimpse of the shape of it, far off, is enough to terrify him.

He has faith. He knows how fast Marion can put the jigsaw pieces back together, work against a universe which makes no sense to her, isolate the truth. He knows she can take the universe. But a sharp misgiving jabs him in the stomach and he can't stop himself saying: "And what if you lose?"

She kisses him. It's a stranger's kiss, there's nothing there Adam recognises. He breaks off, unsettled. It's a whisper now: "What if you lose?"

*

Wheeler exits the containment unit; she slams and deadlocks the door with a single movement. The heavy metallic *crack* makes the whole building shake.

There are people outside. Gauss, Julie Still and a few others, comparing notes. They look appalled.

"Fill in his backstory," she tells them. "He was never married. Relocate him to where I'll never find him, incinerate all the evidence, then report to me for surgical memory erasure. I'll do myself last."

Gauss looks as if he has an objection. She stares him down.

"My husband's dead," she says.

3
Fresh Hell

There's another conglomeration of severed fingers in the last room, coating the room's interior like the innards of an exploded elephant. Parts of the sprawl are feeling their way, like mould, into a medical cabinet and the rest is splayed over a foetal shape on a medical gurney. The mass reacts sharply to the new light as Wheeler opens the door, rearing up and angling parts of itself toward him. Wheeler reels backwards and pulls the door to just in time; there is a heavy, fleshy *thump* as the mass hits the door from the far side. The door holds.

Wheeler trips on his own foot and slumps against the far wall. The shape on the gurney was a coiled-up human. Not a corpse, but a living human with one wide-open eye whose whole body was being slowly consumed and processed into more fingers. They were growing out of his throat. Wheeler didn't see this. He thinks he saw it, but he knows he couldn't have.

And that's it. Wheeler casts around the corridor. Every other door he's tried is blocked or locked. The place is below ground, so no windows. No navigable ventilation.

There are two more gunshots up at the far end of the corridor, ear-splitting in the enclosed space and echoing for many seconds. Hutchinson rounds the corner at a dead run, gun in hand, and reaches him quickly. "Find a way out?" she asks, pointlessly. She can read Wheeler's expression. He's found nothing good.

"This place is infested," Wheeler says. "Every room, all the stairwells... This is absurd."

At the far end of the corridor, the main mass heaves itself around the corner. From this distance, it looks like an ambulatory eight-tonne pile of mouldy mashed potato and fat, wiggling maggots. There are toes in there as well as fingers, and small teeth, and bits of bone. It has twenty bullet holes in it, and blood is flowing from all of them, but if it has vital organs they must be elsewhere in the building because none of the wounds have slowed it down or otherwise altered its slow, methodical homing behaviour. It smells powerfully and creatively disgusting, like concentrated medical waste.

It lurches forward in intermittent phases, coating the walls and floor with scarlet ooze as it moves. It'll be on them in about half a minute, squashing them against the end of the corridor and then pulling them into the mess to be remade.

"I think we're done," Wheeler quavers. "Thanks for trying."

Hutchinson, for her part, just stands there, gun lowered, watching the thing come. It moves slowly, like a steam roller. It fills the corridor almost to the ceiling.

She has two bullets left and she's considering where to spend them. Shooting the mass itself is like shooting pudding. She'd kill for a grenade. Even a fire axe would be something. She might not be able to stop the thing, but she could at least make herself known with a fire axe. She could make it feel some *regret*.

"There are worse fates, I guess," Wheeler goes on, finding himself unable to stop talking, "than being digitised by that thing, but not all that many."

Hutchinson glances in his direction, apparently paying him direct attention for the first time since they met, sixty crowded minutes ago. She says, "Riser cupboard."

"What?"

She pushes Wheeler aside. There's a white-painted wall behind him. There's a lock in it, and a long vertical seam. She spends a moment choosing the right part of the lock to shoot, and shoots it out. Behind the tall, wide panel which opens is a shallow, dusty, metal-edged space like an elevator shaft with no elevator, allowing filthy pipes and cables to pass vertically between floors. She looks up. There's just enough room to admit a person.

"Can you climb?" she asks Wheeler. Without waiting for a response, she sheds her suit jacket, sticks a flashlight between her teeth and hauls herself up into the darkness. After a brief moment of scuffling, there's another gunshot. The other riser cupboard door.

"No," Wheeler finally manages. "No, I can't climb!" The mass is almost on him. He's transfixed by its motion, its all-too-familiar grasping behaviour.

"I figured," Hutchinson calls down. A hand descends, a human one with the conventional number of fingers. "It's clear up here. Come on, I'm braced. Mind this lip here, it's metal. Come on!"

Wheeler keeps his own jacket on and buttoned; it's the only part of the situation over which he still has firm control. He has to jump to catch hold of Hutchinson's hand, and just as he jumps, the main mass lunges for him, crossing the last few metres in a rush and catching hold of him by one foot.

He sees himself die.

His sweating hand immediately starts to slip out of Hutchinson's. She braces her other arm and hauls him up fifteen or thirty centimetres with an angry grunt, then releases his hand for a split second and reaches down like a flash to take firmer hold of his wrist. She keeps pulling. The mass closes around Wheeler's foot like aggressive, proactive quicksand. He yelps and kicks at it with his other foot until it finally pries his shoe loose. The mass retreats for a second, taking a crucial moment to realise that its prize is not living flesh, but by that time Hutchinson has hauled Wheeler up another half-metre and Wheeler has started pushing himself upwards off the pipework with his feet. The mass lunges again, but falls short, and seems too unintelligent to climb after them. It sloshes around, probing its surroundings, perplexed by the shoe.

Hutchinson hauls Wheeler over the lip into the next corridor. He scrapes his ribs badly and arrives crawling, eyes watering. He doesn't die. He can still see himself dying. He stays on all fours for a significant amount of time, processing what just happened.

"*Fuck!*"

Hutchinson is already standing, and apparently not even significantly exerted. "We need to get to the roof. I might be able to get a signal out from there."

"You're at the gym pretty often?" Wheeler pants, sitting back. "You train for fresh hell like this?"

"Yeah."

"That's great," Wheeler says, "because I play the *violin*. It's not quite as physically demanding. As careers go, I mean. When you said you were a county health inspector, that was an enormous lie, wasn't it?"

Hutchinson ignores the question, out of habit, and waits impassively for the man to cool.

"This is asinine," Wheeler declares. "This is brain damage." His skin crawls, and grotesque visions flood through his brain. Eventually he recovers his breath and gets to his feet. He stands lopsided, so he takes his other shoe off and throws it back down the riser for symmetry.

"We need to get to the roof," Hutchinson says again.

Wheeler blinks a long blink, then focuses on something around the corner, something on the wall which Hutchinson can't see from where she's standing. "Yeah. One second." He goes to it — it's a red panel — and pulls something down. "Here, you were having no luck with the gun. Try this."

It's a fire axe.

*

He stepped on a rusty nail backstage after the show, and came to the emergency room for a tetanus injection. While waiting, he slowly realised that more than half of the people waiting with him were clutching partially or entirely severed fingers. Bandsaw accidents; hands caught in car doors; hands trapped in door hinges; hands crushed in machinery; every one of them unrelated. There was an epidemic of physical injury, which should have been impossible, and when he tried to bring it up with the medical staff they didn't seem to understand what he was saying.

And then he saw one of the fingers escape. He followed it as it wriggled away down a long corridor to a far corner of the hospital, to an ajar door which nobody in the hospital seemed to be able to perceive except for him, and into a different building where there were no people at all, just hundreds and hundreds of wriggling, exploring, slowly reproducing and lengthening fingers.

He slammed the door and tried and failed to get someone, anyone, staff or patient, to see what he was seeing. He found a payphone and dialled for emergency services and ordered off the menu, asking for emergency industrial-scale pest control or hazardous containment or psychic support or *something.*

And there was a long pause, and he was connected to what was either a very measured, dispassionate human or an impressively articulate robot operator. It told him to wait by the phone; an associate would be with him shortly. Marion Hutchinson arrived in person, slightly less than fifteen minutes later.

He showed her the door. They went a few paces inside, Hutchinson crouching and aiming some kind of flashlight/scanner at the finger worms. Behind them, something reached out and gently pushed the door closed with a *click.* They turned, and saw what it was, and ran.

*

Hutchinson hacks her way through the last of the flesh-clogged stairwell. They're almost at the roof. This part of the distributed infestation doesn't seem to be mobile, although it is freakishly grabby.

Wheeler stands three paces back from her, partly to avoid the backswing but mostly so he doesn't have to watch. It's butchery, and it's grisly, and Hutchinson barely seems perturbed by it; she slices methodically until there are waterfalls of gore coming down the stairs and soaking her shoes and his socks, and she does it with the manner of someone trimming a hedgerow.

Whunch. Krunlch.

Wheeler is shivering, and starting to crash. If he doesn't stay still right in the middle of the stairwell, the remaining fingers tug at his hair and sleeves. In another few minutes it may finally dawn on him that this is really happening. "This is crazy, this is nuts," he says to himself, over and over.

"What was that word you used back there?" Hutchinson asks, suddenly.

"Mmm?"

Whunch. "Don't tune out. When the mass was coming down the hall. Did you say 'digitized'?"

"...Um." Wheeler seems to change gear, and wake up. "Yeah. Uh, but, in the old sense of the word—"

"'Digit' meaning 'finger', so 'digitized' meaning 'turned into fingers'. I just got it." She's smiling, he can tell from the sound of her words. *Chlunk.* "That's great."

"It is?"

"What kind of violin music?"

"Uh. What kind would you like? Tonight's— last night's— Christ, *yesterday*'s concert was Prokofiev's Violin Concerto No. 1. And a few other pieces, of course, but that was the main course for me. That was where I got my teeth in."

Hutchinson stops hacking and turns around. She actually looks him in the eye. "That piece is a nightmare."

"It's a challenge," Wheeler admits, brightly.

"No, I mean it's chaotic. It's unlistenable."

"I can play anything you like," Wheeler states.

Hutchinson appears to spend a moment considering this possibility. "Bach. You can play some Bach?"

"Just get me to a violin."

Hutchinson thinks for a moment longer. She smiles and nods, and goes back to hacking.

*

And they hit the roof, and Hutchinson's radio finally works, and she calls everything in. She speaks in rapid keywords which Wheeler can't quite follow, although he can pick out his own name and "hazmat" and a repeated word which sounds to him like a brand of cassette tape: "Memetix".

It's very nearly dawn. This wing of the hospital is a few storeys shorter than its main body, so rows of bright-lit wards look down over the roof, while the roof looks out over two sprawling car parks and then greenery and roads and a faint, dull red where the Sun is due to come up. Hutchinson quickly ascertains that there is no fire escape from here; the intended fire exit from the roof is the stairwell up which they just came, so they'll have to wait for a helicopter. Or, more likely and less romantically, a long ladder.

"Backup is coming," Hutchinson concludes. "They have to come in from the next city over, so it could be a few hours. They'll have decontamination gear, antibiotics, blankets, tedious debriefing forms, you name it. But most importantly, coffee."

Wheeler makes an inarticulate sound, the sound of one who could use the coffee, and after that, a drink. "God, I have another concert *today*," he says. He sits on the thick perimeter wall, rubs his eyes, rubs his sore feet, and begins to shut down.

"You'll be there," Hutchinson says. "The nasty part is over. You did well for a civilian. I've seen far worse."

"Worse than this?"

Hutchinson says nothing.

"I'm sorry." Wheeler opens his eyes again. He gestures at the mayhem from which they just escaped, the fire door and everything it leads to. It's all still down there. "You've seen worse than *this*?"

Hutchinson, again, says nothing.

"What is this? What happened here?"

At first Hutchinson doesn't answer this either. She walks away across the roof and spends an entire minute staring at the forthcoming Sun.

And then, surprising Wheeler and slightly surprising even herself, she walks back to him and says:

"SCP-4051, which is the number we just assigned to this infestation, has an intrinsic property which makes it nearly impossible for sapient organisms to perceive it. It's a form of camouflage. It's not invisible, it's a mental blocking effect. Information about it goes nowhere, it gets suppressed. People walk past this building every day of the week. They don't see what's blocking the windows. They walk past that door and don't realise it's standing open. It could have been here for decades. The researchers will get the whole story eventually."

Wheeler finds in this explanation something he halfway understands. "So... living fnords?"

And this actually slows Hutchinson down for a second. She gets that reference. She read those books when she was younger, years ago, before joining the Foundation. But she's *never* made the connection between fnords and the work she does. For as long as she's been working there, she hasn't even thought about it. The irony is intense enough to burn.

"Yeah," she says.

"Except that you can see them," Wheeler says.

"I have specialist training," Hutchinson says, declining to mention her drug regimen.

"And I, also, can see them."

"You seem to have a mild natural immunity to memory-clouding phenomena," Hutchinson explains. "It's rare, but it happens. At a hospital this busy, someone like you was bound to stumble into this place sooner or later." *And escape alive,* she privately adds. "But the point is... this infestation, SCP-4051, is a snowflake. I don't mean that it's special and unique. I mean: it's part of a *blizzard*.

"I work for an independent scientific research institution with a specialist focus on the containment of hazardous anomalous phenomena. We have an international mandate and formidable resources and... unimaginable responsibilities.

We... we watch the blizzard. And we guard the little fire. We're called the Foundation."

Wheeler's full attention is on her now. He feels tense and exposed here, vulnerable to extraordinary natural forces from which by rights he should be fleeing. But he's also fascinated. Hutchinson has a faintly ethereal attitude to her. It's as if she's not standing on the same planet as everybody else.

"So you're not FBI," he says. "Either, I mean. That was my other guess."

Hutchinson wrinkles her nose. "I hate that show."

"I don't believe I mentioned a show," Wheeler says mischievously.

"They do *everything* wrong," Hutchinson says. A nerve has been touched. She shuffles irately. "They don't have enough people; they don't trust each other. They don't spend nearly enough time on paperwork. Paperwork saves lives. But most of all? I hate the will-they-or-won't-they. For what, five years? It's forced, it's farcical." She glares at Wheeler. "It doesn't take that long to know. You will or you won't. And then you do."

Wheeler reads her expression carefully. "You do?"

"Yeah," Hutchinson says, smiling again. "Yeah, I think you do."

A distant rapid thudding noise slowly becomes apparent. Hutchinson sees the source of the sound first and points. "Backup's here. And it looks like we rated a helicopter after all."

4
Ojai

Foundation Agent George Barsin is monolithic: nearly two metres tall and rectangular-shouldered, like a Bruce Timm cartoon. He is bald, bearded, and immaculately presented. His suit is tailored; there are few which will fit him off the rack.

He arrives at the Green place first thing after dawn, six o'clock. The address is isolated, an acre or two of ill-maintained scrubland off a spur of a spur of the main highway north out of Ojai.

Barsin is part of the Foundation's Anomalous Religious Expressions Division. They do cults.

"Green" is not the name of the cult which Barsin is here to confront, but a codename. Barsin doesn't know the real name. At the briefing last night, it was explained that there are legitimate security reasons to use codenames instead of true names here, but those reasons were not explained. Barsin, no fool, took this to mean that there is some form of cognitohazard surrounding the true names. Or a memory-clouding phenomenon which makes them impossible to record. Or — and he's dealt with Foundation research staff for far too many years to not consider this — somebody just straight-up forgot to record the real names, and is trying to cover for themselves.

If there's an SCP number, he hasn't been told it.

*

The house is an ugly white sprawl. One storey, wood construction, no two windows alike in design... decaying. There are piles of junk, lumber, rusted vehicle components, drums of filthy green water. Willow and sycamore trees are encroaching from two-and-a-half sides, drizzling leaves and seeds and miscellaneous biological gunk all over the roof, clogging the gutters. Through the windows, only closed curtains and blinds are visible. The front door is standing ajar.

Barsin proceeds inside, cautiously. The entrance opens almost directly onto a large lounge/diner/kitchen area. The room is darkened, light mostly spilling from the entrance door — Barsin leaves it open — and feeling its way around the edges of the window coverings. The place is dirty, and smells of mould. The still air is like an oven, and it's extremely quiet except for the faint, animated sound of someone talking, away down the hall, words not entirely clear.

"—wasps and, yeah, it's going to be sharp inside. When you're made to move, that's tloi kwrlu dlth you'll bleed from—"

Barsin goes down the hall, passing a wall decoration which was once a mirror but has been completely painted over in black.

After a brief search, during which he ascertains that the rest of the house is empty, he comes to the final room. This door is closed, but the focused rambling is coming from inside:

"—at home, it's super easy. I'm going to give you something. An easy two-part project for you to take away, and don't forget alth amnth below. Part one: find someone weaker than you—"

Barsin knocks, loudly, twice.

The patter stops. Nothing else is heard. Barsin opens the door.

The room is dark, its window blocked with a thick curtain. There's a computer desk in the corner opposite the door, about as cluttered as a desk can realistically get, strewn with partially disassembled hardware, USB keys, chocolate wrappers, scraps of paper, ballpoint pens. There's a gaming mouse, unable to move for junk. There's a good-quality video camera setup, a monitor, video feeds on the monitor, dust.

There's a cheap, skeletal swivel chair in front of the monitor and a young man of about twenty slouched uncomfortably in the chair. He is skinny, with discoloured, pale skin which Barsin thinks could be caused by malnutrition. He has what was at one point a stylish, fashionable haircut but is now in some disrepair, and when he turns around Barsin sees that he has dark rings around his eyes. It looks as if he hasn't slept in a year. He reeks. The room is filled with that odour, almost thick enough to see.

In the same way that the anomalous viral/religious phenomenon — the cult, gathering around and above this young man like an anvil cloud — is named "Green", he himself is named "Red".

"Good morning," Barsin says. "We saw your streams."

The youth pulls his headphones down. "The fuck are you?"

"My name's George Barsin. I'm part of an organisation which— ah—"

Red launches out of his chair like a rabid greyhound from a cage. He comes fist-first, losing the headphones. Barsin shifts his weight slightly to his left, leaning away from the punch. He catches Red's arm and pulls it forward, violently, deflecting the attack's momentum and bringing the youth teeth-first into the door frame. Red stumbles back, crouching. He finds his footing swiftly. Froth is developing at the corners of his mouth, mixing with blood. Scrabbling around the junk on the floor, he puts his hand on a soldering iron.

As Red comes forward again, Barsin wastes a critical split second trying to trace the iron's cable, to figure out whether it's plugged in and hot or not. It's not, but that's enough distraction that Red gets right up there, driving the iron up into Barsin's gut with both hands. There's an electronic screech and a spark of orange light; the iron holes Barsin's shirt but skitters off his abdomen, opening a long tear. There's bare skin underneath. His shield is invisible, partly mythical, and protects his seemingly exposed head just as well as the rest of him.

Barsin takes Red in a headlock. Some haphazard kicking ensues, less well-choreographed. Red has a demon's energy behind him but Barsin has, to be blunt, arrived prepared. In a few more moves, Red is disarmed, stunned, flat on his back and good for nothing.

Barsin takes stock. The number of genuine, fight-for-your-life fights he's been in is still in single digits. This one ranks about in the middle. Fifteen seconds of activity; both of them made mistakes. A learning experience.

"Then I'll dispense with the introductions," he says to Red. "The live streaming vector was novel. We hadn't seen that before. Very effective compared to the generic self-help-book-and-walled-compound model. You get one point for originality, out of ten. But we predicted it decades back and we had the containment procedures ready to go. We have people at the streaming services. As I speak, we're locking you out of your account. We're using your own channels to distribute inoculation codes."

Barsin tries to tidy his shirt up. It's not going to work. Never mind.

"But you're the source," he says. "A simple inoculation code would glance off. Physical intervention is required." He reaches inside his jacket — where he has a perfectly serviceable gun, which he elected to leave where it is for this confrontation — and produces a device not unlike an ophthalmologist's scope. He kneels, lifts Red's right eyelid and aims the scope at it, projecting a brilliant white spot of light which bathes the entire eye and causes it to lock open. Almost all of Red's musculature locks up as well, effectively pinning him to the floor. His teeth clench.

Barsin says to Red, "This man is innocent. Nobody can deserve what you've done to him. Release him and leave this reality forever."

Through gritted teeth, Red says, "Who. The fuck. Are you?"

"Alright." Barsin pushes another button, changing the projected light pattern from a pure white disc into a complex spiral star design in red and blue. There's a *crack* like ribs being forced apart. And the youth screams. It doesn't sound like Red. It's a full-body scream, anguished and hopeless and as loud as he's physically able to make it. It comes up from his belly and goes on, flat out, until he runs out of breath and gasps and does it again, arching his back and clawing at the floor. After the second full breath he cools down to a sobbing wail.

"Jesus Christ, don't send me back. Please."

"I won't. It's okay."

"Don't send me back. I can't see. Who's there?"

"It's okay. You'll get your sight back. My name's George. What's yours?"

"There's a pit," the youth says, choking, "and it always gets worse. It doesn't stop. There's no bottom." He babbles incoherently for a moment, and then trails off. His eyes dance, blindly.

"You're in a really bad place right now," Barsin says.

The youth vehemently agrees.

"Something has gone wrong," Barsin explains. "And that thing, that horrific *thing which went wrong*, has found you and abducted you and replaced you. It's out here now, using your skin as a finger puppet, walking you around, making you talk. Replicating. That nightmare you're having is being had by a hundred thousand people right now. That's the bad news. The good news is that we caught you. And I can still see you in there. And there's good chance that we can get you out."

"A 'good chance'?" The youth breathes twice. "If you can't—" he begins urgently.

"Focus on the red and blue spiral," Barsin says. He still has the scope pointed into the youth's eye.

"What? I can't see anything."

"That's because you're not directly connected to this optic nerve anymore. But your mind is locked inside something which is. You can't see the spiral, but somehow you know what it looks like. You can sense its shape, like a pattern of heat on the back of your hand." Barsin's voice is becoming slower, taking on a hypnotic rhythm. "The spiral idea is going in. It's spreading and flourishing. Occupying more space. The more you think about the spiral, the more you realise you can't think about anything but the spiral."

The youth seems to have nothing to say to this. His breathing stabilises.

"Your thoughts are slowed," Barsin continues. "The spirals fill you up, recursively, like ice crystals, until you can't move. Your brain knows it's being poisoned. Even though you're blind, you feel a reflexive need to look away or block out what you're seeing. A long enough exposure is fatal."

There is a long, heavy pause, during which Barsin does nothing but shine poisonous light into the young man's eye, while studying that brightly illuminated eye himself, tracking the progress of the ocular response, waiting for a particular tell. It's not a clear-cut thing; there's a small amount of guesswork. He waits until he's sure. Finally, he releases the button on the scope, shutting it off.

The youth is now completely inert.

*

Barsin stands up, knees creaking. He relaxes, sighs. His shoulders untense a little. He puts the scope away.

"You can think of this as memetic chemotherapy," he says. He says it to himself, mostly, to fill dead air. The young man can only hear pink fuzz now. "The spiral symbol is an elementary cognitopoison. A long exposure is fatal. But a just barely non-fatal exposure is recoverable. You will recover from this poison, and Red cannot. You will survive and Red will die. Because you, my man, are an intelligent, creative human being, and Red is..."

He reflects on his briefing, and what he knows of the Green phenomenon, and the hundred thousand people suffering and raving inside it right now. They are in all parts of the globe. He has seen some photographs of what takes place in homes occupied by Red's appalling messages. He's heard a strictly limited amount of highly redacted audio.

Dispassionate people make better field decisions, that's the rule he was always taught. But remaining dispassionate is harder on some days than others.

"...a piece of shit."

Barsin potters around the room for a little while, taking a closer look at some of the computer hardware. Nothing notable there, although he finds a stand for the soldering iron. There's also a narrow camp bed in the room, with a bedraggled sleeping bag. He clears the sleeping bag away and loads the youth onto the camp bed, in a recovery position. He pulls the curtain open. It's an obnoxiously sunny day, and the Sun is aimed right in through that window.

Finally, Barsin picks up the swivel chair and settles into it, on the far side of the room, where he can keep an eye on his patient. He pulls a Foundation-issued phone from his pocket, along with a horrendously tangled pair of cheap earbuds, which he begins to untangle.

He relaxes into his monologue. It's not as if anybody is listening.

"Fact is, I didn't need to come here. There's more than one way to physically intervene when something like Green comes around. You know what the original plan was when we found out about you? Orbital laser cannon to the top of the head. We can do that, my man. From time to time. Your house would be a circle of scorched timber with you a burnt marshmallow at the middle of it. That's our latest methodology for dealing with virulent, single-culpability memetic anomalies. We do it at arm's length, at the longest possible distance, unblinkingly and unfeelingly, and to hell with the details. It's brutal. Impersonal. Very expensive in orbital laser maintenance. We say to ourselves that it's effective. Maybe it is. I'm not at that level. I don't get to see the statistics.

"But what I do know is that we can always do better. And I looked at the file and I looked at you, and... I took a long shot. Honestly, I'm a very small guy in the grand scheme, but I stood up in a pretty intense meeting with people who I don't really have the authority to say anything to and I said to them — this is a paraphrase — 'There's a completely innocent kid at the centre of this. He doesn't deserve this. At minimum, we've got to make the gesture.'"

A shadow passes across the room. Barsin looks around briefly, but whatever it is has gone. He thinks nothing of it.

"And then I also said, 'If it works, it'll save us a boatload of money.' I think that part was the part which got their attention. But I got the thumbs-up. So here I am. Trying to save your life the hard way instead of just atomizing it. It'll probably take all day. Six, ten hours. Don't worry. I have podcasts."

He finishes untangling the earbuds and screws the first of them into his left ear.

"Your people must really hate you," Red says.

Shit.

Barsin draws. Late. *Obviously* nobody should be able to talk right now, but the real reason he draws late is that the comment lands. It should just pass him by but there is a sharp, spiteful element of truth to it. Truthfully, nobody was a fan of the idea. Barsin has been saying for a long time, with gradually increasing volume, to gradually increasingly senior Foundation overseers, that a chat beats a fight. He's been ignored over and over. Yesterday, when they finally said that he could try it, it was grudgingly. And so a momentary flicker of foul suspicion appears— did they know? Did they really just— kill him?

They didn't. He knows, of course they didn't. But it's too late. As he fumbles the gun out, Red has already sat up, grinning like a ventriloquist's puppet, and turned his head to look right at Barsin. They make eye contact, and this time Red's eyes are open *all the way*, allowing Barsin to see straight through to what's on the other side. Green comprehension leaps out of the pit at Barsin and grounds itself in the back of his skull.

He recoils instinctively, breaking the connection and covering his eyes. He stumbles, falling backwards out of the chair and into the corner of the room. His orange, crystalline shield fluctuates, panicking in its own way because of what just passed through it. Intermittently, it turns impermeable, cutting off Barsin's frantic breathing. Then it snaps off and dies.

Barsin doesn't have the training to fully comprehend the idea complex he was just exposed to. He has a basic level of practical memetics training; he can administer the spiral treatment and a few others, and protect himself from certain attacks which would knock a generic human over like a domino. But he's an entry-level practitioner, not a specialist, not a scientist. The sheer scope of Green is beyond his ability to comprehend. He feels like one of the men Louis Slotin irradiated, a Demon Core criticality witness. He knows he's dead. The only question is how long it's going to take.

Red swings his legs off the bed and stands, keeping his grin fixed on Barsin. "A spinning red and blue light. How *backward* are you?" He seems to grow larger, and to sink backwards into space, a hole where a human should be. Barsin finds he can't make himself move out of the corner. It's like he's pinned. There's a creeping, staticky numbness in his hands.

He understands his error now. He might as well have tried to poison the ocean. He sees the whole thing, Red's grotesque vision for the world, his/its immense, vicious *promise*. The rot is everywhere. Those hundred thousand infected are a foretaste. The spores are flourishing secretly in every aspect of reality: in people's lungs, in their minds, their words, in the soil, in the sky. Maggots and cancers and star signals. How can anyone think like that? How can anyone want that?

"You—" Barsin means it in the singular. There's no distinction between Red and whoever that original human was. There's no one to rescue. It was a damn ruse.

It was *voluntary*.

"You made this happen?" he manages. "It didn't abduct you. You invited it. Hacked your own soul in half and offered the pieces up, for no reason at all? You've latched yourself onto the front of something unimaginable. You can't comprehend how badly this is going to end. You've murdered yourself."

Red advances on him.

Gun. Barsin's mind is disintegrating. But it gets that one word out. *Gun.*

It's on the floor between them, gleaming in the shaft of orange light pouring out of the window. Barsin fights himself and wins and lunges for it, only then finding that the creeping numbness in his extremities isn't just affecting his hands, it's affecting his own ability to perceive them. He doesn't know that it's a minor antimemetic clouding effect; all he knows is that there's a stump at the end of his arm. Both arms. The gun is inoperable. All he can do is push it around the floor. He shouts, miserably and helplessly. Red laughs, and doesn't even bother to kick it away.

"The Foundation will stop you," Barsin manages, like a mantra.

Red cocks his head, as if he knows the word "Foundation" from somewhere. "Are all of them as weak as you?" He concentrates.

Comprehension goes both ways. Barsin dimly understands what Red represents, which means Red, in turn, dimly understands what Barsin represents. Red perceives the power structures which dispatched Barsin into this hated burrow. Red perceives the shadows of the "people at the streaming services", and the Mobile Task Force Barsin doesn't know about, skulking out at the property's perimeter waiting for a go order which will never come. Red perceives the four or five "brutal", "impersonal" suits seated at the top of the operation, webbing it together. One of them is toying absently with their laser strike keystick, twirling it around the back of their thumb over and over, dropping it.

That's as far through headspace as Red can search, because that's the limit of the people who know about him, it, Red. That's the hit list.

A shadow blots the Sun out again, the same one as before, for longer this time. Red looks out through the window, giving it a curt nod, and it departs.

Barsin slumps to one side, dead up to the shoulders now. Conscious that any of these words could be his last, he says, "You think you're in control. But it's going to kill you too. We can get you out. You can help us contain it."

Red crouches, still grinning. "Look at me. *Look*." Barsin looks. He doesn't have a choice. It hurts. Red makes sure he is being heard loudly and clearly: "No."

"Z...zayin. Three four six. Samekh shin," Barsin whispers.

Red blinks. "What?"

Something bleeps.

"Ae star," Barsin says. "Ae star."

"Shit." Red looks around, suddenly genuinely alarmed. The phone. He lost track of Barsin's phone. He finds it, beneath the bed. He snatches it up. There's a voice authentication interface, and authentication is nearly complete. "Stop. Cancel. Undo." Nothing happens. Wrong voice. He drops the phone, scrabbles for the gun.

"Zaelochi anaeora. Fire," Barsin says.

Red puts a bullet through the phone. And a second through Barsin's skull.

He looks up at the ceiling, waiting, still alarmed. And he waits.

But nothing else happens.

5
Immemorial

"Ms. Wheeler! Ms. Wheeler!"

Marion Wheeler has just finished a scheduled inspection of SCP-8473 and is about to go for a cigarette. Someone is running up to meet her outside SCP-8473's containment unit. Wheeler recognises her as Dr. Eli Moreno, a trainee field researcher who joined the Antimemetics Division only six months ago.

"Dr. Moreno. Can I help you with something?"

"Uhm." Moreno interlocks her fingers nervously. She is a full head taller than Wheeler and half her age, with scraggly hair and exceedingly thick glasses. She lacks experience. But she is very smart, and she is learning very fast. In another year, she'll be among the best people the Division has, or has ever had, and Wheeler is looking forward to that. Wheeler loves nothing more than competent people.

Still, as the pause lengthens, that day of competence seems to be in the future. "Dr. Moreno, I normally expect my people to get to the point a little quicker than this."

"There's— a stone in the forest behind the Site," Moreno blurts. "It's *monumental*. It's like a skyscraper, it blots out the Sun. Do you know what I'm talking about?"

"Yes."

"But I've never seen it before. I don't understand how it's possible that I never saw it. It casts a shadow across the whole Site. I mean— Was it always there?"

"Yes."

"Is this because—"

"—you took your first routine dose of ops-grade mnestics this morning, yes."

Moreno seems alarmed. "That's how it works? Something that big can just be right there and we don't see it?"

"Yeah." Wheeler checks her watch, and mentally moves some scheduled commitments around. *Extend this "smoke break" to the rest of the afternoon. Leave the scheduled inspection of SCP-3125 where it is. Review promotion cases after the gym instead of before. Evening meal... at this rate, never...*

Moreno, suffocating under the weight of follow-up questions, finally asks, "What is it?"

Wheeler gestures to her left, down the corridor, indicating that she is about to walk, and that Moreno should follow her. "I will show you."

*

In the database it's SCP-9429. Moreno hasn't read the entry; she doesn't have access.

The stone is a single, unbroken, 91-by-91-by-147-metre vertical cuboid of ancient, weathered, dark basalt. It sits at a very slight angle, leaning fractionally to the north. Its regular angles clearly mark it as a carved object, a human-made artifact. It rises out of the forest to the east of Site 41 and dominates, not to say obliterates, the views in that direction from the windows of the Site's main block. It is, by volume, massively bigger than the Site itself, even including its underground extents. It looms. It is absolutely unmissable. The idea that anyone could fail to notice it for any period of time is, Wheeler has to admit, more than a little unnerving.

Wheeler leads Moreno up the short forest track to the stone's perimeter, and then right, following its perimeter, in its shadow. It's a wet day, and rain is dripping from the very top edge of the cube as well as from the conifers which grow right up beside it. The rain makes a constant white hiss, deadening other sounds.

"There's a weak antimemetic clouding effect surrounding it," Wheeler explains as she picks her way along the track ahead of Moreno. "To most people it's effectively invisible. You've been up to the top of some of these other hills, I'm sure. You should have seen it clearly from up there, as well, but you looked straight past it. That's normal. There's a related effect which removes people's memories after they've visited the stone. That effect is much stronger. It'll cut right through your mnestic drug regimen, and mine."

"So we'll forget all about this?" Moreno asks.

Wheeler holds up a battered little notebook and a cheap blue ballpoint. Moreno understands; she is carrying a notebook and pen as well. Information suppression is a complicated spectrum. Sometimes a written note is the only thing which will make it out of a zone which suppresses memories, electronic data, radio signals and even audible sound. Alongside the mandatory Foundation-issue "brickphone", many Antimemetics Division operatives habitually carry some combination of an instant camera, a mechanical tape-driven dictaphone, a notebook, a walkie-talkie...

Not that Moreno was expecting to need anything today.

"Of course," Wheeler continues, "one side-effect of the clouding is that I don't exactly remember the way. I guess we could set up sign posts, but somehow it never gets done... not because of antimemetic effects, you understand, just plain laziness... ah, this looks like the way up."

They come to a passage in the side of the stone. In fact it is not a passage but a tremendously deep groove, cut all the way from the top of the cube to its base, a slot with a thin line of overcast sky visible overhead and steps leading up. Wheeler begins to climb and Moreno follows. They climb in silence for some minutes. Moreno stops a few times to write down a note or two, hunching over to shield her notebook from the drizzle. Then she hurries to catch up with Wheeler, who maintains a steady, indifferent pace.

Some time after Moreno has lost count of the steps, the stepped groove makes a ninety-degree turn to the left and continues to ascend. Wheeler stops here, above Moreno, and turns to quiz her.

"What do you have so far?"

"What is this place?" Moreno asks.

"You tell me."

"Uhm." Moreno hesitates for a moment, uncertain where this is going. She checks her notes. "Uhm, well. Geologically speaking, this stone is an alien. At first I thought there had been a mountain on this spot which was excavated into this shape by human hands. But the rock itself is wrong. It's different from the mountains and hills near here. You'd have to travel at least five hundred kilometers to find basalt like this. Which means it must have been excavated elsewhere, maybe carved there, and moved here."

Wheeler says nothing, but her demeanour seems to indicate that Moreno is on the right track.

"Which isn't possible," Moreno continues. "This is a single stone. Judging from its dimensions and density, it must mass north of three million tonnes. That's now, *after* carving.

And that can't be done. Human civilization cannot move objects of this size. Not in a single piece. The technology doesn't exist."

"Correct."

"So how did it get here?"

"Good question."

Moreno waits. She doesn't have the answer to the question, so she waits for Wheeler to supply it.

But Wheeler does not. "What else?"

"...It's been engraved," Moreno says, indicating the walls of the stepped passage. "Using tools. And I noticed the exterior walls are the same. There's a lot of weathering, but here and there between the biological crud there's this very clear, regular pattern. Right here, see? Tiny vertical rectangles. Like a... block cursor on an old computer terminal."

"Or a tombstone in typography," Wheeler suggests.

Moreno blinks. "...Yes. It's a uniform pattern. Very detailed work, which would require quite good tools even by modern standards. I think this pattern is supposed to cover the entire exterior of the stone. And if that's the case, the blocks are so minuscule and the stone is so large that there must have originally been hundreds of millions of them."

"Correct," Wheeler says again. "Anything else?"

Moreno thinks for a minute. She stares up into the rain, reflecting on the atmosphere that the stone, or sculpture as she supposes it would be better described, projects. Loneliness, quiet, desolation, awe... intimidation. And some fear. Although, with that intimidating, fearful atmosphere, there's no sensation of danger. No threat.

"'We considered ourselves to be a powerful culture,'" she says aloud.

Wheeler hears this, but asks no follow-up question. Apparently satisfied, she turns and continues climbing the steps, and Moreno follows.

The passage makes several more turns, carving out an erratic, squared squiggle. Moreno takes no further notes. Her knees are about ready to explode by the time they reach the top.

They emerge, blinking at the light, on a wet, windswept, slightly slanted plateau. There are more of the tiny tombstone indentations underfoot. The edges of the cube are some distance away but they are not marked; the dark grey surface just ends at a straight line not far out, and the horizon itself is below it, not visible. This gives Moreno some vertigo, particularly since the surface tilts towards one corner, and the engraved basalt underfoot is slick, wet and getting wetter.

There is a small cluster of Foundation scientific equipment up here, chunky weatherproof units stacked up under a canopy. There's a table, with a rugged, beaten-up computer terminal, switched off. Further away is a diesel generator.

Wheeler ignores the equipment and paces away in a different direction, facing away from Moreno and out at the sky, playing with her cigarette lighter, although not actually lighting anything. The lighter is actually a tiny propane burner intended for lighting stoves, given to her by her mother before she died. Wheeler no longer remembers this.

Moreno waits for a while, arms folded for warmth, gradually getting wetter. She doesn't seek cover under the canopy, because Wheeler hasn't. She senses that something is about to happen. Wheeler is normally quite poised and difficult to read, but she looks apprehensive; upset, even. Focused intently on the lighter flame, Wheeler seems to be unable to look her in the eye, as if she doesn't want to push through with the next part of whatever this is actually supposed to be. Orientation? Initiation? Hazing?

What was that about getting to the point?

"It's a memorial," Moreno says.

"Hhn." Wheeler snaps the lighter shut and pockets it, moderately impressed. Only moderately, though. "That's right. Of course, I practically told you that, when I mentioned tombstones—"

"How many Antimemetics Wars have there been?"

That gets her. "Damn. So much for slow-burning theatrics. Someone told you? You read the entry?"

Moreno looks at her shoes. "Uhm. No. Really, I've never seen this place before. I was just guessing."

"You look embarrassed," Wheeler says. "You're embarrassed that you hit the right answer thirty minutes before I was expecting you to. You think you've shown me up. Right? Eli. Look at me."

She looks.

"Keep operating at that level. Don't slow up for my benefit, or anyone's. It's important."

"Will you tell me why we're here?" Moreno asks, for what she hopes will be the final time. And in another part of her mind, a fatal chain of calculations starts.

*

"The problem," Wheeler says, "is that every single person in the world with reliable access to high-grade mnestic medication works for me, here. And the Division is pitifully understaffed. There are forty of us, including you and me, and forty pairs of eyes is not enough. We cannot look at enough of the world at once. There is an appallingly large percentage of the world which no human has ever *properly* looked at. This is unbearably limiting to all forms of antimemetic research. Antimemetic biology, antimemetic paleontology, antimemetic cosmology, antimemetic archaeology... These disciplines, all of them, barely exist. They are *nowhere*.

"Nevertheless, we have seen this culture's cities. One or two still exist. Pure dumb luck is how we found them. A Division researcher takes a vacation, drives across Nevada while still on the dose... sees something on the horizon. That sort of thing. The cities are physically ruined, and there are heavy antimemetic effects shrouding them which make them nearly impossible to study, even for us. Large, simple things, like this stone, survived better, but even so... We think this stone was one of the last things they built before they died out.

"They were human. They were probably significantly more technologically advanced than we are. They existed tens of thousands of years ago; perhaps hundreds of thousands, we can't know for sure. It's difficult to determine what really happened to them because their entire cultural memeplex was lethally irradiated. Their core cultural concepts, the things they created, and stood for, and valued highly, can never be known or propagated again.

"We think an idea stole into their culture which they did not have adaptations to defend against. A complex of ideas. A Memeplectic/Keter-class end-of-world scenario."

Wheeler pauses, letting the rain patter for a significant moment.

"...And we just forgot?" Moreno asks. "The rest of us. Who survived the War, and became modern humanity. You and me and everybody. We, what, looked away? And walked away and 'moved on'?"

"Yes."

Moreno staggers, vertigo swelling up and briefly getting the better of her. "Hundreds of millions of people died and *we just forgot?* Is that what you wanted to show me? You want me to write that down?"

"Yes," Wheeler says. "Yes. Write this down. It's the first thing you're learning today. Humans can forget anything. It's okay to forget some things, because we are mortal and finite. But some things *we have to remember.* It's important that we remember. Write to yourself something which will make you remember."

Moreno nods. It's raining too heavily, so she retreats under the canopy and uses the table. Even so, a few rain drops spatter her notes. She writes intently and rapidly, for some time. What she writes is rushed and unrefined, with large parts crossed out. She wonders how she'll react when she reads it for the first time.

After a while, Wheeler joins her under the canopy.

Moreno, staring at her notes, asks Wheeler, as if she doesn't already know the answer: "And the second thing?"

Wheeler says:

"It is possible that their culture had an equivalent to the Foundation. It may even have had an Antimemetics Division. If they did, their Foundation, and their Antimemetics Division, failed them.

"It's a big reality. It's a big Foundation. There's a lot of Keters and a lot of Keter-class scenarios. So, maybe the end of the world will be some other Division's problem. And yes, a big part of the job we hired you for is basic research. Lab work, as safe as it gets. And yes, it's been thousands of years, and it may be thousands of years more.

"But maybe it won't. And maybe it will be our problem. To answer your original question, there has been one Antimemetics War that we know. Potentially others that we don't know of. And there is, undoubtedly, one to come."

Moreno says nothing. She looks dismayed, broken. She's right to be, and Wheeler is familiar with the reaction. This is, indeed, part of every new Antimemetics Division operative's orientation. The magnitude of responsibility can be hard to handle. It *should* be.

"Welcome to the Antimemetics Division," Wheeler says. "This is your first day."

*

Moreno writes for some time longer. Wheeler waits, silently. The rain doesn't let up.

"But what was it?" Moreno asks. "What was the idea?"

"SCP-9429-A," Wheeler says. "We isolated the memeplex itself in the Seventies. We have it on a slab in a Vegas room, basement level two. It's mostly harmless now. It's so culturally alien to modern humans as to be nearly incoherent. Think Egyptian heiroglyphs. I'll show you another day."

"I can read Egyptian heiroglyphs," Moreno says. "Are you saying it couldn't come back?"

"In that form, it's highly unlikely."

Moreno points at something, far away in the sky.

Wheeler looks. There's nothing out there. Just overcast sky and rain. "What do you see? Under heavy mnestic doses, some people say they see ghosts here. We even have some supposed interview logs. Personally, I think their veracity is dubious..."

"Um. It doesn't look like a ghost. It looks like a... an anorexic... kaiju. A monster. A pillar made of spiders. It's taller than this stone. At least twice as tall. It's coming here. Is this normal?"

"No." Wheeler is already racing through the checklist.

"What is it?"

"I don't know."

"This isn't part of the hazing?"

"No. I will never lie to you, Eli. I swear." An antimemetically cloaked entity which looks as monstrous as Moreno is describing has an approximately zero percent chance of being benign. They need support. Wheeler finds that her phone has no signal. Checking Moreno's is pointless, she already knows. The only way to get a message out of here is with a written note. A paper airplane, thrown off the top into the woods?

"It's bending down. I think it's looking at me," Moreno says, watching a space in the air descend. There isn't even a hole in the rain which Wheeler can perceive. "Its head is gigantic, it has to be ten meters wide. It has... graspers and arthropod legs all over it. Dozens of eyes. Some of them are blinded. There's someone riding it."

"What? Describe the rider."

"Caucasian male, twenties, skinny. Jeans, trainers, dirty brown hair, needs a haircut. He's been shot. He's bleeding out all over but he doesn't seem to notice. In the liver, and again in the throat, just above the clavicle. He's smiling. He... he says, 'No. That never happened.'"

Wheeler spends a split second wondering whether the gunshot wounds are intentionally creepy detailing, or whether the man is genuinely using some kind of advanced antimemetic power to ignore a mortal wound. And, if the latter, how, and how he originally sustained it. But more urgent questions are afoot. "He sees you?"

"Yes."

"Does he see me? Hear me?"

Moreno is transfixed and is starting to look genuinely frightened. "He wants to know who I'm talking to."

"Don't tell him. He doesn't get information about us, understand?" Wheeler pulls her walkie-talkie from her waist, sets it to broadcast an emergency beacon, turns and hurls it overarm as far as she possibly can, in the direction of the Site 41 main building. With luck, it'll land intact in the forest, outside the suppression zone cast by SCP-9429, summoning a Mobile Task Force. "Ask who he is."

Moreno is standing very still, with her arms clamped rigidly at her side. "Who are you?... He says... he says he's nearly finished. He says he's going to kill me."

"Like hell. Eli, listen to me. We're running for it. Back down the steps. If we can get to the perimeter of the stone it'll flush our memories."

"I can't move."

Wheeler hauls on one of Moreno's arms. She can't be moved. "Put one foot in front of the other!"

"It's got a hold of me." Moreno is goggle-eyed and starting to hyperventilate.

Wheeler disengages and surveys the situation. She can't see or touch any grasping spider legs, or the monumental face which Moreno can't look away from, or the rider. But she believes Moreno that they're there, real for some value of "real". She claps one hand to her side; but of course she isn't carrying her sidearm, because this is a Safe SCP on a Safe Site, and why would she be? Not that it even makes a difference when this mythical rider is able to laugh off gunshot wounds. There aren't enough options in front of her. She very badly wants to swear, and bites down hard on her tongue.

Moreno screams.

"Eli!" Wheeler shouts. "Don't look at it. Look at me."

"I can't."

"You're stronger than this."

"I'm not," Moreno cries.

"You're the best we have," Wheeler says. "I'm not making that up. You're seeing this thing when nobody else could. That makes you smarter and stronger. You can fight it. Invasion drill!"

"It hates us so much," Moreno says. "I can't think through it. I can't see. Please. Please don't."

Wheeler knocks her out. She circles behind Moreno, plants one hand on her shoulder for stability and punches her behind the ear. Moreno sags in place, then falls forward to her knees. Wheeler is just about able to catch her before her skull connects with the ground.

But she didn't hit her hard enough. Moreno is unconscious only for a second. She struggles as she comes back. It's like she's waking from a nightmare into another nightmare. She clutches at Wheeler's hand. She can't scream. Her heart stops.

Wheeler rolls her over and administers CPR, but without equipment there's very little chance of her restarting Moreno's heart.

Nobody's coming. She didn't throw the walkie-talkie far enough.

It's almost fifteen minutes before she gives up.

*

And then Wheeler is collapsed against the wall of the passage, on the next-to-last step, about to leave SCP-9429's field of influence, trying to figure out what in the *fuck* she can possibly write to herself.

What the hell was that thing? All Moreno did was think of it and it killed her. She was as good as any of us. She was as capable as she was ever going to be and she wasn't good enough. How do you fight an antimemetic monster which only eats the best antimemeticists?

You... you could try to build some kind of countermeme. But you'd need to be shielded while you worked on it. You'd need a hermetically sealed, self-sustaining lab as big as an arcology. Like the ones Bart Hughes used to build. Like... the one under Site 41.

God. How long have we been fighting this thing?

There's a rustling behind her. She turns to look. Far away up the steps, there he is, the rider Moreno described. A scrawny young man with a hostile frown and, yes, two steadily oozing gunshot wounds. His shoes are soaked in blood.

He calls out, "Marion Wheeler! I owe you for the lake."

Wheeler stands up. She doesn't know what lake he's talking about. But she says nothing.

The rider gestures. Blue and brown and black spiders of all sizes cascade around the corner, flooding the passageway up to his knees, pouring over his shoulders, tumbling down towards Wheeler. They make a strange, organic rustling as they pour, like wet leaves. There must be millions of them. The spiders would probably be much more effective if she was at all afraid of them.

It's too bad. She's just learned a great deal about this entity; that they have history together, and that it personally dislikes her, and that it apparently has a humanoid mouthpiece... and a lousy imagination. But she has only a second before the cascade of arachnids overcomes her, and that's not enough time to even write a single word. Moreno's death, then, was for nothing.

She steps backwards, over the threshold.

The rain is finally easing off. Wheeler lights a cigarette and heads back to the main building. It's almost time for her scheduled inspection of SCP-3125.

6
CASE HATE RED

If Adam Wheeler gave it some thought, or if someone were to prompt him with the right questions, he could put words around the fact that his existence doesn't bring him any satisfaction. He would discover, on introspection, that he's nowhere close, actually, to "happy", and that there is something vast and significant missing from his life. But he doesn't give it any thought. There's a void between him and those questions. Objectively, academically, his life is great. As a professional violinist, he does what he loves the most for a living. He has talent, recognition, challenge, variety, applause, a moderate wealth. What is there to question? Why shouldn't he love it?

During slower moments, there's a grey worry in the back of his mind. It's there in the minutes right after he wakes up in the morning, before he makes it to the shower; it's there in the dead times backstage when he can't use his phone and there's nothing to do but wait to go on. It perturbs him, from time to time, that he seems to exist in a kind of long shadow, cast by a vast class of thoughts which he is unable to think. But the rest of the time, on a day to day basis, his calendar is as busy as he and his manager can make it. He performs, solo and in orchestras, he records, he composes and teaches. Every week is a different challenge. He keeps busy, and the feeling goes away if he's busy.

On the morning of the day that క arrives, while he is brushing his teeth, a tiny black slug falls out of the corner of his eye into the hotel sink.

"Mpfghl?"

He scratches that eye, while drooling foam from his toothbrush. He takes a close look at himself in the mirror. Yup: there's another, fatter one growing in there, its tail protruding from his tear duct.

"I can do without this," he mutters to himself. He spits, rinses, and then takes a pair of tweezers out of his wash kit. Carefully, he nips the tiny, waving end of the slug, and tugs it out. It's no more painful than extracting a nostril hair. He drops it in the sink with its friend and washes them both away, along with the froth of toothpaste.

He stares at the plug hole for a long moment. It's like he's forgetting something. He can't bring it to mind. He shakes his head, and goes to get dressed.

*

Wheeler has been on tour with the New England Symphony Orchestra for nearly a month. They're at their final venue, and it's their final night, and Wheeler has mixed feelings. Touring, for him, is an opportunity to explore a kind of liminal lifestyle, where he can suspend a lot of worldly concerns and just exist as a being who wakes, travels, performs and sleeps. But as novel as the experience is on paper, four weeks of it is gruelling. By this stage in the tour, even the most naturally cheerful members of the orchestra have begun to show frayed nerves, and the programme has become stale and repetitious. It's long past time for something else.

Last night, his manager left messages about plans for upcoming weeks. It's probably time he paid attention to those.

Morning rehearsal starts at eleven. Wheeler takes a taxi from the hotel to the venue, bringing his tuxedo and his violin with him. His violin is an heirloom, more than a hundred years old, and while he's touring it never leaves his sight. (His tuxedo is just a tuxedo.) The concert hall is as close to the centre of the city as it gets, at the heart of a rat's nest of busy roads, which means the taxi journey is a slog, even setting out after rush hour.

At the stage door, the place is in chaos, but it's only the typical pre-show chaos which Wheeler has spent much of his professional life navigating. He finishes a quick cigarette outside before joining the bustling flow of technicians, performers and administrative staff. He finds his way to his dressing room, changes, unpacks his violin and tunes it. He flicks through tonight's music, more out of boredom than a need to refresh his memory. He has the whole programme memorised.

With some minutes to kill, he checks the headlines on his phone. Yet again, something dreadful and new which he doesn't understand is going viral. Today's fad is, you paint a black vertical rectangle on the wall, or on a mirror, or over the top of a picture. And then you chant something. Wheeler can't quite pick out the words of the chant. They're in a language he's not familiar with. He's no singer, but he's performed pieces with lyrics in Latin, German, Greek, French... whereas this language has a bizarre manufactured sense to it, as if it were simply English with the vowels and consonants all switched around.

Rehearsal goes reasonably. Wheeler long ago swore that he would never coast through a performance, and he plays decently well. But it seems to him as if a lot of the orchestra is distracted. Some cues get missed. He makes meaningful eye contact with the conductor a couple of times, and they share a frustrated look. When they break for dinner, late in the afternoon, the conductor, whose name is Luján, privately remarks to him, "Their eyes need fixing."

Wheeler doesn't wholly follow. He rubs his own eye with a finger, reflexively. The memory of the morning tries to punch through, but fails. "You mean, laser surgery?"

Luján responds with a few incomprehensible syllables and stalks away.

*

The auditorium opens and the seats fill. As ever, there's a brief, grey dead time while Wheeler waits for all the machinery of the performance to spin up. The anxious feeling is stronger than usual today. It grips him, an uncharacteristic urge to run away. *Sure,* he thinks. *I could just junk my career, right now. Pack it in and make for the stage door. Maybe the taxi'll still be there.*

But he pushes through it. It's just a juvenile fantasy. It's been far too long a tour. One more show and it's over.

And finally it's time, and he's out there, under the spot, in his element. The first piece of the night is Shostakovich. Its first movement is a sedate, haunting, almost melodramatic nocturne, but before too long the concerto changes gear and becomes energetic, discordant, feral. It's lengthy, too, a real work-out, and much of it is brutally difficult to execute. He's on form tonight. Close to flawless, and his audience — which he cannot see or hear — seems rapt.

Four-fifths of the way through the piece, a kind of spell breaks. Something changes in the atmosphere of the auditorium. The temperature in the huge room seems to rise by several degrees. More concerningly and noticeably, the music behind Wheeler begins to trail off. The conductor stops too.

Perplexed, Wheeler continues to play for a moment or two, keeping to his own internal time. But after another moment it becomes clear that something is wrong, something which everybody can see but him. He steals a glance up from his instrument, and finds that Luján is staring at him. In fact, every musician in the orchestra is staring at him, all of them wearing the same expression of stony, barely-contained ang—

They've been replaced.

The orchestra is gone. All seventy of them. The things which have replaced them are not human but alien, ill-proportioned pillars of pinkish-brownish flesh. Each has, at its top, a heavy protuberance studded with goopy biological sensors and rubbery openings, and, sprouting from the very cap, lengths of various kinds of vile, off-coloured moss. They are draped in black and white fabrics, weirdly cut to either conceal or highlight their blobby, inconsistent body structures.

Wheeler reels with fright. He almost falls off the front of the stage. His stomach convulses and he wants to vomit, but a frantic fragment of his brain hasn't panicked yet and tells him, *Wait. Nothing's changed. That's what humans have always looked like. Right? What's happening? What's wrong?*

He glances, petrified, out into the darkness of the audience. The silent energy radiating off them has changed. They've been replaced too, he knows. And they know he hasn't. That's what's wrong.

Clutching his violin to his chest, Wheeler stumbles across the stage, past the conductor, towards the wing. As he does, the musicians rise slowly from their seats, letting their own musical instruments drop to one side or the other. Wheeler trips over a cellist's music stand, recovers. The conductor is following him, with the other musicians close behind.

Wheeler reaches the wing. There's a pair of stage hands there, waiting for him. They have the same placid, angry expressions as everybody else, and the same set jaws. Wheeler stops and turns back. His heart feels like it's going to take off.

Luján, or, rather, the biped which used to be Luján, walks right up to him. He is a little shorter than Wheeler, but much heavier-set. Rooted to the spot, not thinking clearly, Wheeler holds his violin up, as if this will shield him. The conductor takes the instrument from his unresisting hands and breaks its neck underfoot, perfunctorily, as if crushing a box for recycling.

Wheeler backs off, hands raised. He bumps into the disapproving stage hands, who gently and wordlessly try to take hold of his arms. He shakes them off and is just about able to twist past them. He dives into the warren of corridors backstage. And then he runs like hell.

*

Four floors up, in some remote, poorly-lit corridor which hasn't seen regular use in years, he finds a bathroom. He goes in and throws up. This makes him feel a lot better. He washes his mouth out and then lights a cigarette, quickly filling the tiny space with a haze of smoke. That helps too.

The adrenaline has run out and his knees are still wobbling from climbing too many stairs. But it doesn't sound like anybody is closely pursuing him. So, in this safe moment, he asks himself a serious question: *Did I just have a panic attack?*

He doesn't know what a panic attack feels like. Having put so much distance between himself and the stage, what happened there feels like a crazed dream, a paranoid hallucination.

But... No. Luján broke his violin. That part definitely happened; he remembers it with distressing clarity. His relationship with Luján has never been much more than tepidly professional, but the man *was* a professional. To vandalise a precious instrument like that would be unthinkable for him, or anybody in the orchestra. There is something wrong.

With everybody.

Except him.

He flicks his cigarette butt into the toilet. He grips the sink, and looks at his reflection, and as his eyes slowly force their way back into focus, he realises, with some alarm, that what he is looking at is not his reflection. The mirror above the sink has been sloppily painted over with a tall, black, dripping rectangle. It's giving off heat; staring at it is like staring into an open oven. And he can hear a dull, grumbling, mechanical kind of noise coming from behind it. Like distant, muffled woodchippers.

He exits the bathroom and slams the door and leans against the far wall, watching the door, as if something could very well open it and come after him.

There was another one, he suddenly recalls. Another painted block, this one on the wall in his dressing room, right behind his chair, facing the back of his head. He should have seen it in the mirror whenever he was sitting there, but he didn't. And not only that, there was one in his hotel room. It was painted over the picture hanging over his bed. Did the hotel staff paint it? When, why? Why is he only remembering this now?

The viral video isn't new. Why did he think it was new? It's been circulating for months. For as long as he can remember. Forever. And— in every venue where he's been on tour, in every city, on windows and billboards, and in small rooms and liminal spaces, people have been painting these— doors—

There's a second half to each video. He remembers now. He watched it passively, over and over, and never saw it. Something comes through. It's been leaching into the background of the world this whole time, in plain sight, and he *never saw it, and it's here now*—

He's having a psychotic break.

No. That's not what's happening.

Something is trying to interfere with the way he thinks. The block symbol is jammed into his mind. He can't dislodge it. He can't think about anything else.

He looks back along the narrow corridor down which he just came. The darkness at the far end of it is yet another dark, vertical rectangle. He hears the footsteps of a multitude of people coming from that direction. Not running. Just walking briskly enough to harry him.

He needs to get out of the building. Get help.

The stage door.

*

He takes a confused zigzag route back down to street level. There's nobody in his way, and the stage door itself is unattended. He cracks it open.

Night has fallen since the performance began. There's a minor road right outside, behind the concert hall building, a yellow-lit *cul-de-sac* with a loading bay and some unattended trucks. There's a major road adjoining the minor road, rammed with stationary traffic. Some of the vehicles are, indeed, taxis, but all of them are unoccupied, and most have their doors left open. There are colossally tall darkened figures stalking down the streets, so dark and slender that Wheeler actually fails to notice them. There is screaming, a grotesque, awful screaming coming from many human mouths, coming from somewhere down the main road. But that's the only way he can go.

It's everywhere, says his last sane splinter. *Not just the concert hall. It's everyone.*

As he creeps towards the main road, someone, another occupied former human, pokes their head around the corner, then calls to others in the strange language, pointing him out. Wheeler stops in his tracks. In another moment, ten or eleven non-people are advancing on him from the road. Two of them are carrying something with them, a limp, badly broken human— a normal human, Wheeler realises with some shock, like him. The victim's heavy winter coat is torn open and his inner clothes are saturated scarlet. When the non-people carrying him catch sight of Wheeler, they toss the man violently aside, into the street, where he lands in a pile against a car wheel. He grunts with pain as he lands, face down, and once he comes to rest he takes a deep breath and lets out an inhuman, traumatised cry. But he doesn't try to move again. The non-people ignore him.

Behind him, Wheeler hears the stage door swing open again. He doesn't dare glance back.

This can't happen, says that last splinter. *This is possible, yes, real things exist which can do this to the world. But it doesn't happen. There's someone whose job it is to protect us from this. We're supposed to be protected.*

Someone stops it from happening. Someone steps in. At the last minute.

But the last minute was a year ago. And she died.

Marion.

Oh, God.

"Help," he says, to nobody.

A feeling of weightlessness rises up in his stomach. Gravity seems to upend and pitch him forward into the waiting arms of the non-people. They restrain him. They spend some time debating what to correct first, his eyes or his fingers. Right up until it starts, he's thinking, hoping: *Maybe it won't be as bad as all that.*

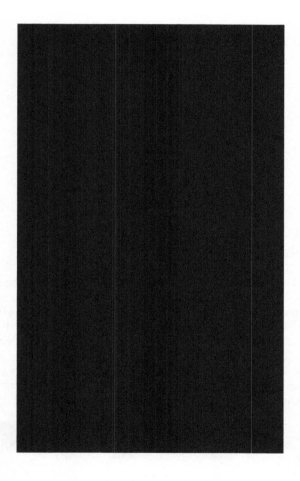

7
Ará Orún

But it is.

They wrestle him to the ground and pin his arm out flat, forcing his fist open to give access to his left index finger. The dread idea is beating on the door of his mind, demanding to be let in. It's wrong, the shape of it is awful and it's too big and slick with poison and he knows if he lets it in it'll swamp everything he is, filling his home up with sludge and broken glass. It wants to drown him in it and he knows it'll replace everything he is with itself. He knows it's taken the rest of the world already and all of the people around him, and he holds out, and he continues to hold out right up until one of the people pinning him produces a chisel

overrides everything else

Yes, he says, *yes,* he throws the door open,

145

*

the world is ruined.

beautiful things, and smash them or cover them with filth.
Find delightful people and disfigure

We, who are drowning in and driven by ఌ, who radiate

They, who number in the billions, and are for the engine

In the centre of the

city where
people can be fed in and the door locked

irreversible

intact,

and watching,

this last splinter
of Adam Wheeler

starts to work against that which it knows to be wrong.

a ray up there, a narrow yellow nourishing sunbeam. He follows it, over the top of the walls. and out of the city,

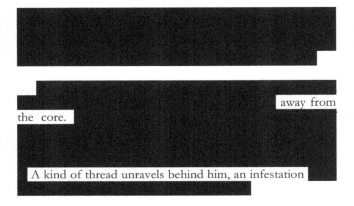

away from the core.

A kind of thread unravels behind him, an infestation

A black slug drops from his tear duct, falls to the asphalt and shrivels.

*

He regains consciousness on a hard, scrubbed floor in a wide, cool corridor. He is lying against one wall of the corridor, as if tossed there like a ragdoll, with his back to the wall and his right arm stretched out, clenched into such a tight fist that his finger joints are hurting. He releases the fist, gasping. Disoriented, aching, he rolls and plants his other hand on the floor, and it's then that he discovers what's happened to that hand.

He reacts as he must react. He clutches the stubs where his first two fingers were, and screams and cries hopelessly at the echoing building. Nobody answers him.

The last thing he remembers, he was playing Shostakovich. He was flying through it, unimpeded. In his mind, he can hear what he was playing, note-perfect, right up to the instant the memory cuts off. And he can't think of what comes next. Instead, that last incomplete snippet of music goes around and around in his head, abruptly ending mid-note and slowly fading back in again from a few seconds back, an earworm. He can't jolt himself out of it. He's a stuck record. He can never play again.

He tries to make the right shape with his remaining fingers. His hand won't do it. He rubs his eyes with his... his good hand. He feels like garbage, hung over, dehydrated. He's missing his shirt, and his arms and chest are almost grey with muck.

He can never play again.

He sits there, huddled, for a long while, being small and unhappy and lost. He knows he's going to have to move eventually. He's working his way up to it.

He looks up the corridor, eyes gradually recovering. He can see alright without his glasses, as long as he doesn't have to do much reading. He's in a school. There are notice boards, banks of lockers, a rainbow mural. The place is deserted and silent. There is a dull red light coming through the windows in the classroom doors on the far side of the corridor, suggesting that the Sun is low on that side of the building, rising or setting. He has taught one-off music lessons in one or two schools, but he doesn't recognise this one.

With some unease, he examines his bad hand. The stumps of his fingers are lumpy and uneven and have healed badly. A mass of scar tissue and scabs, and no stitches in sight. As if the digits were removed with great imprecision. Hacked off. Or bitten off? It troubles him that he can't remember. His memory is normally so sharp and clear. He thinks he's thinking clearly, but when he concentrates and tries to access the lost time, something in that gap pushes him back. A fierce red heat.

It occurs to him that, though his severed digits have healed very badly, they *have* healed. They certainly aren't bleeding, although there's a continual ache. How long would that take?

How much time has he lost?

What the hell happened?

Way down the corridor, away from the classrooms, an office door is standing ajar. In that office, a telephone starts to ring.

*

The office is poky and dimly-lit, piled high with paperwork. Two small desks, battered office chairs. He finds the ringing phone and picks up.

"Hello?"

The voice is synthesised, female. "Mr. Wheeler?"

"Yes. Who's this?"

With a measured tone, the robotic voice replies, "Mr. Wheeler, you have been sick for an extended period of time. I will be pleased to answer all of your questions, soon. But not now. There is a woman in room W16. She is dying."

"I— I'm not a doctor."

"I know. There is nothing you can do to save her. Nevertheless, you must go to her. Now."

"I feel like I'm... I'm not the best person to do that. I'm not in the best place today."

"It has to be you. There is no one else."

"...Who is she?"

There is a pause. It is as if the entity on the other end of the phone is unable to choose her words. "She is...

significant. Go now, please. She does not have much time."

Wheeler is at a loss. He doesn't seem to have the strength to not do what he's told. He doesn't have any other direction to go in. The phone handset is corded, or he'd take it with him. He frets a little about not being able to take it with him. "You'll still be here?"

"Yes."

He leaves the handset off the hook. He goes back along the silent corridor. He finds the door numbered W16 and peeks through the safety glass into the orange-red-lit classroom, squinting at the sunlight which floods it from the far windows. It's still not clear to him whether it's dusk or early morning. There is nobody in the classroom that he can see.

He opens the door and goes in. There are elaborate, colourful biology posters and coursework displays, desks in disarray, scattered books and felt-tip pens, brightly-coloured backpacks. He takes a pace or two up the central aisle, not seeing what he thinks he should be seeing, and turns around, and jumps, startled. There is a huge chalk sketch on the blackboard, a highly realistic rendering of a woman's head and shoulders. He would swear the board was blank when he walked in.

The image is moving. It's as if it's being drawn and erased and redrawn, five or ten times per second. The woman looks about his age. Her face is framed with masses of hair, although with the negative colour effect of being drawn in white chalk on a black background, it's difficult to tell what colour her hair ought to be. The one splash of colour comes from the thick, bright blue frames of her glasses.

She looks distraught. And she seems to be saying something, and though there is no sound, there is text written beside her:

Adam?

He says, "Yes?"
She says,

I remember everything

And then the words scrub themselves out and become,

I can't forget a single minute of it

More lines come out. Each new thing she says erases the old.

I know everything he did now
I was blind, and he ran rings around me
I made mistake after mistake
He killed everybody I love except for you

After this, her lips stop moving. The last phrase lingers for longer than the others, before scrubbing itself blank.

Wheeler spends a long moment absorbing the final statement, turning it around, trying to figure out where, if anywhere, it slots into his life.

He has never seen this woman before.

But... is that true? He studies her features, and his memory cycles around, and he unearths something deep and significant in his past, a bizarre encounter he hasn't devoted thought to in what feels like a century. *Her! That one time at the hospital, remember? You gouged a chunk out of your foot, backstage, after a show. You spent half a night in the emergency room, and she was there and you got talking. God. Who was she, now?*

A... government agent, or at least in that sphere. She was unreal. On a whole other level from me. Tough, skilled, beautiful, sharp like a sapphire. We talked about music. Film scores, and the trash which passed for TV sci-fi those days, and David Lynch. It was... well, you don't know, that early, but... it was promising.

But nothing happened. They patched up my foot, and we never went anywhere.

Did we?

"Marion," he breathes. He's almost got it. He holds a hand up, fearful, as if motioning for her to stop. "No. This can't be—"

I sent you away, because I was trying to save your life

He remembers. It reconnects, all at once, the years upon years of inextricable shared life. There's too much energy there. It crashes through him, violently, it's like grabbing a frayed electrical line, it's like being shot. He stumbles backwards, disbelieving. He never imagined how much he was missing. "No. No, no. Marion."

And it didn't work

"What happened to you? I should have been there!"

And he ruined the world
And now you have to live in Hell

"Where are you? Someone said you were dying—"

I'm already dead. I'm the memory
But now the memory is dying too
He's found his way into Heaven, and he's ruining it
Like the Earth

"What do you need? I'll stop him. I'll help you. I'll do anything I can. I love you."

She says nothing.

After a moment or two, Wheeler realises that her image has frozen.

He goes up to it and peers at the chalk work. Hesitantly, with his right hand, he reaches out to the heavy chalk shading of her hair, and touches it with one finger. He leaves a dark dot. The chalk dust is real, on the board and on his finger. She's just a drawing.

She's gone. It's all gone.

He blacks out.

*

He regains consciousness on a hard, scrubbed floor at the front of a school classroom. He is lying there as if tossed beneath the blackboard like a ragdoll, one arm stretched out along the wall. He rolls over, gasping, and plants his other hand on the floor, and it's then that he discovers what's happened to that hand.

"Dear God," he says, staring, uncomprehending, at the mangled stubs. In a strange, abstract way, the loss of his first two fingers just doesn't connect with him. It's as if he woke up already accepting it. "What the hell happened?"

He compares his left hand with his right, which, mercifully, is pristine. He flexes them, mirroring the action as best he can. There could be a little nerve damage in his left hand; he'll have to talk to his specialist. But he should be able to wield a bow.

"I suppose I'm playing left-handed from now on," he says to himself. Good God. How long is it going to take him to get to the same level of proficiency? A good while.

He thinks back. The last thing he can remember is playing Shostakovich. He was flying through it, and he was having no trouble. He can almost hear what he was playing, note-perfect, right up to the instant the memory abruptly cuts off. But he can't think of what came next. Instead, that final snippet fades in again from a few seconds back, repeats itself right up to the cut-off point, and stops, almost with an audible click. It's an earworm. He feels like a stuck record.

So he does what he always does: hums a different song to displace it.

He feels strange. He is hung over, dehydrated. He's missing his shirt, and his arms and chest are almost grey with muck. And he is dying, positively dying, for a cigarette. But he feels strangely upbeat. As if he's recovered from a prolonged illness. As if the worst is over.

He gets up, eyes gradually recovering. He can see alright without his glasses, as long as he doesn't have to do much reading. The classroom is silent, lit red-orange from a Sun which could be rising or setting. There are elaborate, colourful biology posters and coursework displays, desks in disarray, scattered books and felt-tip pens, brightly-coloured backpacks. The blackboard is blank.

Wheeler has taught one-off music lessons in one or two schools, but he doesn't immediately recognise this one.

Way down the corridor from the classroom, an office door is standing ajar. In that office, a telephone starts to ring.

*

The office is poky and dimly-lit, piled high with paperwork. There are two small desks, each with a beaten-up office chair. Each desk has a phone, one of which is off its hook. He puts it back, obeying a hard-wired instinct to tidy up. It's the other phone which is ringing, though, of course.

"Hello?"

The voice is synthesised, female. "`Mr. Wheeler?`"

"Yes. Who's this?"

With a measured tone, the robotic voice replies, "Before we begin, may I ask you a quick question? Does the name 'Marion Hutchinson' mean anything to you?"

"Not as such. Should it?"

The synthesised voice makes it impossible to tell whether the caller is dismayed at this, indifferent or relieved. "No. ...My name is Ulrich. I'm part of an organization called the Foundation. The objective of the Foundation was to prevent what has happened from happening."

Wheeler turns around, suddenly afraid. But there is nothing behind him. "And what," he asks with some trepidation, "has happened?"

"The world's gone to hell, Mr. Wheeler."

"Well. Bad luck there."

There is a long pause. Long enough that Wheeler wonders to what insane degree he might have understated the situation. "...Yes. Very bad luck. Mr. Wheeler, we need your help. And by 'we need your help' I mean I need your help. Because there is no one left of the Foundation but me. And I have no one but you. And I am dying."

"I'm very sorry to hear that, Ms. Ulrich," Wheeler says. He finds that he means it. He chooses his next words with some care. "What do you need?"

"I need you to find a man named Bartholomew Hughes. Please take a seat. I will explain everything."

8
Unthreaded

Marion Wheeler used strong mnestic medication nearly every day of her life. Among the Identity Warriors of Mobile Task Force ω-0, "Ará Orún", it was never in doubt that, on the occasion of her death, she would ascend into the noösphere. She would become a Bader-Ramjin Infomorphic Entity or a Type VI Volitional Spiritual Apparition or a "ghostie" or however she wished to describe her new self. Then, she would join the Citizens of Heaven, and continue the Antimemetics Division's fight from *higher ground*, likely with fearsome effectiveness.

But Wheeler died under terrible circumstances. The Class-Z drug which killed her did more than reinforce her memory; it destroyed her ability to do anything but remember. She ascended, arriving in the noösphere to a hero's welcome, but what arrived was an ideoform so severely brain-damaged that it was barely able to communicate.

After she was made as comfortable as possible and an initial diagnosis had been made, Sanchez off-handedly described her as "a Swiss watch filled with glue".

Ulrich yelled at him for saying it, and would have hit him for his callousness. "How can she make it to Heaven sick?" she said. "Isn't that just Hell?"

The Director apologised, in the corporate, false way in which he always apologised for anything.

"How much more does she have to go through?" Ulrich said. "Who deserves this life?"

It hurt all of them. Regardless of personal investment in the mission, it was difficult not to care for someone whom they had watched and guarded for years. They continued to take care of her in the same way they always had, in shifts. Wheeler, dimly aware of her condition, worked against the problem in the instinctive, fierce way she worked against every problem. She slowly became more coherent, but never became herself again. Ulrich, on her shifts, saw that Wheeler spent most of her existence reliving her final moments over and over. She would recite what seemed to be half of a conversation with SCP-3125 itself, a conversation which several of ω-0 said they recognised from Operation Cold City.

"Ideas can be killed."

"Marion," Ulrich asked her gently. "Where is Bart Hughes? He's the only one who can stop this now. We know he's alive, or he'd be here with us. Just a hint. Just a clue. Please."

She was trying. Ulrich knew that she was trying to say: *I don't know. I can't remember something I never knew in the first place.* But all she could manage was:

"With better ideas."

"Keep pushing her," Sanchez told Ulrich when she reported back to him. "At least once per shift."

"The questioning is causing her considerable distress," Ulrich said. "We know she doesn't know anything. It's cruel to keep trying. Sir."

"SCP-3125 is coming," Sanchez replied. "With the quick arm of the Antimemetics Division eliminated, there's nothing left which can stop it. Our real-world investigative capabilities are negligible, Hughes' sister doesn't know anything, and this is our sole remaining lead. I know you admire Wheeler more than anyone—"

"She mentored me. She drove me to be the best person I have ever been. She honored my memory when I died. My own family wouldn't."

"Ulrich—"

"We are the saints who guard! I will guard her!"

Sanchez paused. Ulrich's devotion to Wheeler — and the lesser devotion of the others — irked him mildly. He viewed Wheeler as... well, competent enough, but ultimately a failure. She was as much of a failure as everybody else in the Division, with only the uninteresting distinction of being the last of the failures.

But he was vulnerable to the kind of rhetoric Ulrich had just employed. It stoked a kind of fire inside him. Heaven knew he used it in his own communications often enough, for exactly the same purpose.

"Alright," he said. "The trawl in reality is continuing. There's a faint chance we'll find something of substance. Carry on as you were. No questions."

*

SCP-3125 incarnated the following winter.

Its first act upon its arrival — or, depending on the degree of intelligent agency you ascribed to it, the first side-effect *of* its arrival — was the neutralisation of the Foundation. In the space of a night, an international staff of tens of thousands disappeared into oblivion, or became amnesiac, or simply dropped brain-dead where they were standing. Foundation Sites became hollow, inaccessible dead zones. A few anomalies broke containment in the chaos, to devastating effect; thousands of others were choked into irrelevant obscurity beneath SCP-3125's antimemetic pressure.

The world can only end one way, it seemed to be declaring, gouging its statement into the flesh of reality. *My world. My way.*

SCP-3125 had skirmished with ω-0 before, but it had always been unclear how much information about ω-0 it retained between skirmishes. In fact it was unclear, fundamentally speaking, how SCP-3125 thought at all. Its behaviour was inconsistent, unpredictable and frightening; records of its activities were cognitohazardous, discouraging close analysis.

In the end, the question proved to be academic. When SCP-3125 arrived, whether it knew ω-0 was there or not, it took no special action against it, and had no need to. Most of ω-0's members' anchors were Foundationers, or Foundation-adjacent. With those people's minds blown away in the first strike, the dense web of mutual memory which had held the Task Force together since its formation tore loose. More than half of the Task Force was cast into the void and died; the final, real death they had evaded for years.

Around dawn, Eastern Standard Time, Sanchez announced that it was no longer possible for ω-0 to stay together as a single entity. He split the remains of the Task Force into three. Ulrich and the malformed memory of Wheeler were assigned to the same subteam. Sanchez gave final instructions to continue to search for Bart Hughes, or any kind of ally among the living, be they Foundation or GOI or civilian. But the instructions were confusing and incomplete. It was because Sanchez didn't have an iota of faith in what he was saying. He couldn't see a way to the far side of this. It was about little more than survival now. It was about figuring out terms on which to face death.

Ulrich never saw him again.

*

She fled, with Wheeler and the others in their little subteam, across the face of a noösphere which was rapidly becoming uninhabitable. The world was warping around SCP-3125's presence at the core of human thought, like real space around a black hole. It was building things, real physical artifacts, in the centre of cities. It was extruding them, as if from spores; monumental concrete structures, into which people were being fed in dizzying numbers. It was difficult to know what was happening inside of the structures. Some of the millions were dying in there. Some weren't. Ulrich didn't look. They found out the ugly way that it was dangerous to look closely.

The subteam was steadily running out of anchors. It could have been a systematic purge, but it could just as easily have been simple statistics. Roving physical and psychic anomalies, vast in their own right and slaved to SCP-3125, were combing the Earth, stripping it of objectors and feeding them into SCP-3125's maw. Ulrich's own anchor, a woman who had never known what the Foundation was but who remembered Ulrich with a heavy heart nearly every day, was killed around that time; found in the hills where she'd been hiding and dragged down into the inferno.

Ulrich wasn't looking. She didn't find out until it was too late. She felt the thread of memory come loose, and followed it, panicking, past its flapping end and down into physical reality, where there was nothing. A collapsed tent. A scuffed-out firepit where everything important had been piled up and burnt.

"Who was she?" another ω-0 operative asked her. Ulrich had never spoken about it.

"I only knew her for two days," Ulrich said. "When I was younger. She saved my life, that's all."

This was it, she realised. She was a career Foundationer. An experienced Mobile Task Force operative, for God's sake. She had gone through unimaginable horrors, and stacked them up as experience and kept going. But this, Julia's tent and silence and no Julia, was the worst thing she had ever seen.

Short of hope and resources, the subteam had to split again, this time into pairs. Ulrich stayed with Wheeler, clinging to her like a rock, remembering her and being remembered in turn. A cooperating pair could survive untethered for a little while, but not forever.

*

They found shelter on a distant edge of the noösphere, in a clutch of arcane structures left there millennia earlier by a long-dead human culture. They were followed, though they didn't realise.

One night, Wheeler managed to talk. She said, "Adam." It was the first thing she had managed to say which wasn't a direct quote from her own expiring moments.

Ulrich was shocked by this. "You remember him?"

The sentence came out agonisingly slowly, as if each syllable was like climbing a mountain: "I remember everything."

Ulrich stared. She knew that Class-Z mnestics made it impossible for the subject to forget. She also knew that they could cause long-erased memories to reassert themselves — some of them, anyway, depending on the mechanism and intensity of the erasure process. She had hoped that

Wheeler's memories of her husband were permanently gone, because she knew they ended in a terrible place.

"...I don't know where Adam is," she had to tell Wheeler. It was the truth. Nobody did. ω-0 operatives had, with some solemnity, observed the erasure of Adam Wheeler's mind. But, out of respect for Marion's decision and to preserve Adam's safety, they had intentionally diverted their attention during his relocation, destroying their records. "He might be alive. I don't know." She didn't know which alternative was worse.

"Daisy," Wheeler said. "Look." She was holding something in her hands, a pitiful glowing ideoform. A thought of someone.

It was him. A thread of memory which led right to him. It was some kind of miracle, it had to be, that Wheeler had picked him out from the livid, insensate mass of victims which now formed SCP-3125's core. He was nearly unrecognisable. He was overrun with SCP-3125. At first glance it seemed to occupy every nerve in his body. But there was a flickering seed in the back of his mind, a final remnant of what he had once been. It wasn't growing. There was too much pressure. But it was trying to. He was pushing back.

Ulrich boggled. She had known that there was something weird and highly rare about the way Adam Wheeler's mind was structured, a kind of thick-skulled resistance to external interference. In fact, she knew that thousands and thousands of people in the world shared that immunity — but that was another way of saying that, among the billions, such people were fantastically rare and difficult to locate. Efforts by ω-0 to locate them and recruit them as allies had failed. They did not look special or behave radically differently from others. There was no signal flare which went up. It was possible that they were all dead. It was conceivable that Adam Wheeler was the only one of them left in the whole world.

But he was left. He was alive.

"I see him," Ulrich said.

Wheeler didn't respond.

"I'll get him out of there," Ulrich said. Her stomach was knotting up with the sheer thought of attempting it. "I'll bring him to you."

Wheeler didn't respond. Six original, coherent words had exhausted her. She was crazed with frustration at how incapable she had become. She felt as if she was pinned beneath a huge lead block of memory. It hurt to think. It hurt to exist.

Ulrich's ability to interact with the physical universe was extremely limited. Other operatives of ω-0 had been able to create full-on poltergeist activity, changing the temperatures of rooms and throwing furniture around, but she was not that kind of specialist. She could do little more than place phone calls and write on walls. Those abilities weren't likely to get Adam Wheeler moving. Simple words were never going to reach him. The man wasn't even truly conscious.

What Ulrich could do was something the Task Force dubbed Identity Offense. She could interfere with the internals of living minds to make things happen. Usually enemies; usually the mental equivalent of blunt force trauma, to make them die. But she could act with surgical precision if it was called for.

Operating on Adam Wheeler was difficult and time-consuming. His mind was tough, and it was continually bathed in SCP-3125's radioactive presence. Ulrich would cut, and then wait as Wheeler's mind self-healed, which took days, and then she would cut again. The seedling metaphor served well. The operation reminded her of tending a plant. If nothing else, the whole procedure took real-time weeks. The patience required to keep her hands off for days at a time was nearly inhuman.

Wheeler said nothing else in that time. She was conserving energy. It felt as if she had a finite number of words left in her, and speaking each one brought her an inch closer to the end. She had to wait.

"He'll be here," Ulrich said. "Soon."

*

Now Ulrich watches from a great, abstract distance, as Adam Wheeler folds up.

Marion Wheeler is dead, finally, truly dead, and Adam Wheeler's mind is breaking apart. It's an awful and incredible thing to watch. Even passing into the maw of SCP-3125 and back wasn't enough to permanently break him. But this was it, the silver bullet. This was the way to hurt Adam Wheeler in such a way that he would never recover. Present his wife to him, a brain-damaged wreck, just in time for her to die.

Ulrich writes on the blackboard — off to one side, so as not to mar the image of Marion, and in different handwriting:

I'm sorry
I'm so sorry
Adam, please come back to the phone
I need your help

Adam is prostrate on the floor, and becoming catatonic. He doesn't hear it when Ulrich tries calling the other office phone, the one on the other desk.

And she, too, is dying now. She and Marion were anchoring one another as best they could, but it's the end of the line. She has, perhaps, hours.

"Alright," she says, to no one. There is no one else left.

She rolls up her figurative sleeves. This will not be too difficult for her. Adam Wheeler's revived memories of his wife shine inside him, and around the edge she can see the faint scar where they were burnt out the first time. She has a better vantage point; she can do a cleaner, more permanent job.

This will hurt. Just as much as it did then.

"I need her," Adam says. He's still face-down. "Don't take her. Please."

Ulrich writes,

You need to save the world
There's nobody else

Adam doesn't look up, but he says:
"To hell with the world. It can burn."

*

He recovers a second time. He's fine. Upbeat, game. Eager to get moving.

She explains everything she can. Tersely. Just the keywords. The Foundation, the Antimemetics Division, the situation, the objective. He absorbs it all surprisingly well. He asks cogent follow-up questions, which is always a positive sign.

"This 'thread of memory' which was sustaining you," he says. "Don't I count? I'll remember you."

"Your memory could be strong enough," she replies. "But you just don't know me well enough."

"Ah. That's regrettable."

Ulrich tells him, in detail, how to find Site 41. It's going to be an immense trek, made significantly longer by Wheeler's need to avoid urban areas. She describes the antimemetic shroud which obscures Site 41 and most other Foundation Sites, a shroud she and the rest of ω-0 found to be totally impenetrable — a shroud which Wheeler, if he prepares himself, may be able to walk straight through. She warns him about the psychotic hurricane-like anomalies, and the violent roaming agglomerations of SCP-3125-occupied non-humans. She describes a few techniques for avoiding their attention. She decides not to voice her private hope that, as a recent escapee from SCP-3125's interior, Wheeler will still "smell right" to them and be able to pass. She doesn't want him becoming overconfident and incautious.

She explains basic survival skills.

"I hike, I camp," Wheeler says. Still, he has never hiked or camped in an occupied foreign world. He has never gone months without electricity and plumbing. They find that they have plenty to talk about.

They are on the phone for long enough that Adam notices that the red Sun outside the office window isn't moving. It hasn't risen. It hasn't set. Either the world's stopped turning completely, or the thing hanging out there isn't the Sun.

"Unknown," Ulrich has to tell him. "There was a Foundation which could answer this question, once."

"It seems like this Foundation had the world's better interests at heart," Wheeler says.

In Heaven, Ulrich laughs, weakly. "The Foundation was never so simple," she says.

"...Ms. Ulrich, I sense we're coming to the end of our time together."

"Yes."

"The odds stacked against you were tremendous," Wheeler says. "But you saved my life. And the odds stacked against me are, well, still appalling. But significantly better, thanks to you. I'll do my level best. And I will remember you, even if it doesn't make a difference."

"Kill this thing, Mr. Wheeler," Ulrich says. "When you get the chance, don't hesitate."

"Aye," Wheeler says.

And at the same time, someone behind Ulrich laughs, sharply, once.

She turns. There's a man there, standing with her in the noösphere, a gaunt younger man with an awful, open-mouthed grin. He has been waiting, silently and excitedly, for an unknowable amount of time for Ulrich to notice him. And now that she does, he gets everything he could possibly want from her reaction, a rush of delectable horror and alarm. Then he cuts her off, killing her instantly, before she can get one syllable of warning to Wheeler.

Wheeler hears nothing. A faint *click*, and then a dial tone.

He hangs up.

9
Wild Light

The meeting room is Containment Unit S167-00-1006, which is the skull of a stillborn *Cryptomorpha gigantes*.

The hollowed-out space inside the skull cavity is a prototypical Vegas room — a place where what happens, stays. People go in, they come out, their memories are sieved out of the universe as they leave, and they remember nothing. The skull was acquired in the Nineties. The information suppression effect is a byproduct of the species' natural antimemetic camouflage, a phenomenon which rendered the colossally tall creatures somehow nearly impossible to observe in the wild. It's a phenomenon Dr. Bartholomew Hughes and his team spent years figuring out how to replicate. They've got it, now. They can synthesise *C. gigantes* bone, extruding it in prefabricated pieces from steel grids. They can bolt the plates together to make hermetically sealed boxes. Passive memetic insulation, no need for complicated machines; it's got a lot of potential.

The skull is forty-five metres long, sixteen wide and fifteen tall. It resides at the centre of a vast purpose-built containment unit of its own, surrounded by the rest of the same *C. gigantes* individual's bones, laid out in meticulous radial patterns for space efficiency. The ossuary occupies about a third of the containment unit's floor area. The rest comprises immense industrial vessels which hold its harvested organs. Some of them are actual vessels, repurposed cargo ships loaded with brain matter and skin tissue.

The floor plan of the warehouse is clear enough, navigable if grim. But from ground level, on foot, the place is a vertiginous, intimidatingly macabre place, even fluorescent-lit around the clock. Hughes walks down an echoing canyon created by, on his left, a hundred-metre-long foreleg bone and on his right, the blue steel container holding the creature's first stomach. Ahead, the skull peers down the canyon at him, a distant yellow-white tower, fuzzed with scaffolding and disused scanning rig, its eye sockets vacant black.

As he walks, Hughes has to remind himself continually that these are all the remains of a single organism, one of the tiniest examples of its species.

Behind the skull, where there used to be the creature's first neck vertebra, there is now a large compound mechanical airlock, a ramp and some steps, and a staging area. The staging area serves as a miniature customs desk, tracking every person and item entering and leaving S167-00-1006. Although memories are wiped on exit, written and electronic records emerging from the interior have to be handled manually. Standard procedure is for the first person exiting the room to bring written instructions for the Filtration Officer, telling them what other information from the room interior needs to be scrubbed, and what is safe to retain. Usually the list of information to retain is very short.

There are seats, scanners, a coffee machine, a trolley loaded with cleaning equipment, and a stack of cages for the germs. Parked just outside of the staging area, there is also a limousine — bulletproof.

"Where's everybody else?" Hughes asks the Foundationer who meets him, whose name is Bochner. "I'm not late."

"This way, please," she says, leading him to a seat near a scanner. Hughes has gone through this procedure a dozen times now, so he knows to hold his left arm out. Bochner tears the wrapper off a sterile bracelet-like sensor and clamps it around Hughes' left wrist, then observes a nearby screen. "They went in almost an hour ago," she says.

Hughes frowns. That's not usual. Why would they tell him a different start time? Why would they need an hour of preparation time before he showed up? "Did they say anything?"

"Of course not."

Hughes hasn't the slightest clue what this meeting is about, or what any of the previous meetings were about, or even if they have a common topic.

Actually, he does have some clues. The timing of the meetings is one. The first took place early this year, and when they emerged, amnesiac, they were clutching written instructions from themselves to themselves to continue meeting monthly. Around October, the meetings became weekly. They had three last week. And after Friday, they created a new schedule: they meet for ninety minutes every morning, starting today, Monday.

A more significant clue is the list of attendees. Other than Hughes, three high-calibre researchers from his own organisation are in attendance, along with the directors of Sites 41, 45 and 167, the last of whom is Michael Li, the Foundation's chief of Antimemetics and Hughes' direct manager.

He steals a glance at the car parked behind him. There's also *this* guy. Or gal. Hughes doesn't know for sure to whom the limo belongs, but the list of people in the world who have the authority to drive a street vehicle into a Foundation containment building is extremely short. Well, not to prevaricate, it's thirteen people. There is an O5 in the room. An O5 is extremely interested in their covert discussions. This is a new and nontrivially alarming development.

He nods at the car. "Shouldn't this place be lousy with private security right now?"

Bochner shrugs.

"Anybody go into the unit with the O5? Bodyguard? Anybody stay in the car?"

"No."

Hughes glances at the car again. The windows are tinted, though surely there's a driver behind the wheel, at least. But where's the real protection? Maybe it's all invisible. Microbes. Occult spells of warding. He feels like the car is watching him back.

"Open your mouth, please." Bochner puts a disc-like cap on Hughes' head, presses an emitter to the roof of his mouth, and fires two pulses of radiation through his brain. "Any psychic intrusions?"

Muffled by the emitter, Hughes manages, "Uh-uh."

She pulls out the emitter and discards it. "Did you experience REM sleep in the past twelve hours?"

He wipes his mouth. "Yes."

"How many digits do you have?"

"Ten."

"Count them for me, please."

Hughes spreads his fingers and counts them. "One, two, three, four, five, six, seven, eight, nine, ten." His right thumb is "five".

Bochner injects him with a substance which will prevent his body from rejecting the germ, then lifts a germ out of one of the cages. It splays its tendrils out, confused, not a fan of being picked up. "Tilt your head back and look at the ceiling, please. Eyes wide open. And, if you could take off your glasses."

Hughes obliges, handing his glasses to Bochner for scanning. "I dislike this part," he states.

Bochner has no comment. She lays the germ over his eyes, like a sleep mask. There's a cold, sludgy sensation as it wraps itself around his chin and hair, then the tendrils meet behind his neck and begin knitting with his spine. Hughes sees darkness for a few worrying seconds, then a circular indentation forms in the germ's hide over the top of his right eye, and there's a feeling like part of his brain dislocating, and a fake eye opens where his real one would be. The fake eyeball is around four times the size of his own. Though it is singular, its four pupils grant him decent depth-perception, and he can see a little way into the ultraviolet.

The germ is acting as an external block of short-to-medium-term memory, and as a proxy between the conscious Bart Hughes and the real world. When the meeting is over, the germ will be removed and incinerated, along with all memory of the meeting.

There are other amnestic approaches — gas, injectable drugs, surgical techniques, occult rituals. These are safe, proven technologies for mass use on the general public and Foundation staff alike, but they all operate on the same essential principle that the unwanted knowledge has already entered the mind and must now be removed or suppressed after the fact. Such procedures are imperfect. Memory removal can leave critical fragments behind, occasionally enough for people to rebuild dangerous wholes; and mnestic technologies for causing suppressed memories to reassert themselves are continually advancing. Recent developments on the latest-generation family of biochemical mnestics, Class Z, seem likely to produce a substance which renders *all* after-the-fact memory erasure techniques irrelevant. The only amnestic defence against Class Z will be decapitation. So, if there's advance warning time, it's better to physically compartmentalise, to airgap; to outsource the memories to another organism entirely and never let them touch your own mind. You can't be forced to recall something which you genuinely never experienced.

It's a complex and dynamic field, one of several fields in which Hughes is a world expert. There are machines which could perform the same task as the germ, silicon modules you wear like a headset, plugged into a surgically implanted jack behind your ear, but Hughes would rather die than submit to interfacing his brain directly with a computer, especially a Foundation-made computer. Nobody is getting his brainwaves. When he joined the Foundation, thirty years ago, he put a DNU in his will — Do Not Upload. Everybody thought he was crazy.

Of course, using both the germs *and* a Vegas room feels rather like overkill. That's another clue.

"Your belongings have been scanned," Bochner tells him. He refills his pockets and takes up his laptop. Walking slightly unsteadily because of the new weight he's carrying on his head, he climbs the stairs to the airlock.

*

Hughes would be the first to admit that a typical Foundationer has appalling taste. A typical Foundationer picks brutal functionality over aesthetic pleasure one hundred times out of one hundred, and a depressing percentage of Foundationers don't even comprehend the distinction. Hughes sees this reflected in the architectural choices and interior design of the Foundation's buildings and offices, and in its labs and containment facilities, which commonly cultivate a hopeless, bleak-cliff-edge atmosphere. He sees it in its machinery, its devices, its tools and even its font choices. Hard edges, clashing colours, failing aircon, impersonality, clutter, claustrophobia.

And so, S167-00-1006's interior is a surprise and a delight. Hughes actually sighs. It seems like someone hired a designer. The place is spacious and modern, well-lit, with select walls painted in bright secondary colours. There's not a bit of exposed concrete in sight.

S167-00-1006 isn't a single space but a self-contained suite laid out on two floors. There's a central meeting area with a double-height ceiling, a long oval table and Herman Miller chairs. Along the left wall there are smaller breakout meeting rooms with frosted glass walls and doors. Above those, reached by a flight of stairs, there's a kitchen area, and in the back are some additional rooms, restrooms and storage. The carpet is grey and orange, a non-repeating hexagonal pattern. The place is well-ventilated, and smells of coffee.

There are four people waiting for him. Marion Wheeler, who runs Site 41, is descending the kitchen stairs, holding a steaming disposable cup. Graves, director of Site 45, is at the main table, typing at a laptop. Michael Li is at the back of the room chatting with O5-8. All of them are wearing germs. The four huge eyeballs of the four germs swivel in unison to stare at Hughes as he comes in. It's a highly disconcerting effect. Hughes forces himself to smile back.

"You're here," O5-8 says. He is... strange-looking, even accounting for the germ. Hughes has never seen an O5 before, and O5-8 looks very unlike what he expected. He tries not to stare, but his own germ is extremely good at staring.

"You're all caught up?" Hughes asks. The nature of the asynchronous work loop is that the first quarter of any meeting in a Vegas room is spent reading notes left from prior meetings. Hughes' (correct) guess is that there's been an hour-long pre-meeting, and then everybody broke for coffee, and now they're resuming.

"We are," O5-8 says. He takes a seat at the head of the table, with Graves to his left. Li sits to his right, and Wheeler to Li's right. O5-8 indicates a particular vacant chair, opposite Wheeler, where a printed document is waiting for Hughes to read it.

Hughes sets his laptop down, hesitant to approach the document. "You want me to read this now?"

"Take as long as you need."

"Where's my team?" Hughes asks. "We're three bodies short."

"Read the document, Dr. Hughes," O5-8 says. He seems upbeat. Perhaps he's projecting an upbeat facade to help Hughes to forget exactly how much authority and power he wields. His net worth is said to be essentially infinite. It's not really about money at his level. He, and his kind, can do *anything.*

Hughes sits, and reads.

The document is a scientific paper purportedly authored by Hughes himself, with various of his fellow researchers co-authoring, including two who should be in this room now. Hughes doesn't recognise the paper's title or content, but that's nothing special in his line of work. The text is written in his own formal, academic style, so he has no reason to doubt its authenticity.

It's a brisk read, very dense and to-the-point, written for a target audience of other memetics scientists. In the abstract, it announces the observation of a new, titanically powerful and dangerous (anti)memeplex, provisionally designated SCP-3125, for which the authors plan to seek Apollyon classification.

"Hmm."

The main body of the first page describes eight different phenomena, most but not all of them anomalous, most but not all of the anomalous ones controlled by the Foundation and having SCP designations. From a cursory glance, the phenomena appear to be totally unrelated, either to one another or to the proposed SCP-3125. Hughes suspects he could derive the implied link between them, given a few minutes, but elects to read on. He flips the piece of paper over. The whole document is just two sides of A4.

The other side is mostly mathematics. There is one graph, and one equation, and a brief technical description of two highly novel memeplectic transformation procedures, which the authors dub "amplification". Then there's—

—something like a jump scare in text form. There's a crucial logical leap, and for Hughes, the arrival of comprehension is so blunt, so sudden and frightening that it physically startles him. Even knowing that the word "Apollyon" was on the table, even primed to expect something extremely nasty on this side of the paper, he recoils. "Oh, *fucking* hell."

Nobody else says anything. They wait, expectantly, for Hughes to gather his thoughts and draw some conclusions.

He reads the rest of the paper, figuring out what it's going to say almost live as he reads it. As he reaches the end, the initial shock hasn't worn off. The sheer scope of SCP-3125 is a significant distance beyond his current comprehension. He's had a glimpse of it through a keyhole. He would need time in front of a computer to play with the results to get a grasp of it.

No. He needs to build *filters* first, the equivalent of lead-lined gloves, to let him manipulate this radioactive idea complex with some degree of safety. He feels like *it* may have glimpsed *him*.

Apollyon classification is reserved for highly destructive active anomalies which are functionally impossible to contain — something past Keter. An Apollyon-class anomaly is an anomaly more or less guaranteed to ultimately destroy the world, no matter what is done to stop it. The only thing which can avert that particular XA-class scenario is if something else, likely some other Apollyon-class anomaly, destroys the world first. Their relative threat level is measured not in material containment resources but in inevitable years. Off the top of his head, Hughes would put that figure as a single digit.

"Yeah, this is it," he says. It's bizarrely liberating. "This is the one that's going to kill us." He looks around the table. "Did we obtain Apollyon classification?"

"No," O5-8 says.

"No?"

O5-8 smiles thinly. "Current thinking in the Overseer space is that Apollyon classification is a confession of defeat. It's bad for morale. It cultivates defeatist attitudes. Aside from the special classifications, Keter is considered the top of the hierarchy as of right now. All extant Apollyons are likely to be re-evaluated and re-classified Keter over the next year or so. Other than that, what do you think?"

Hughes says, "You want containment procedures? We've had this conversation a bunch of times before, correct?"

"Let's imagine this is the first time," O5-8 says.

Hughes stares darkly at his paper. "We could exterminate all intelligent human life," he says. "If there are no sapient hosts in this universe, SCP-3125 can't incarnate."

There's a faintly stunned pause. "Yes," Wheeler says. "You've pitched that approach before. And I don't think any of us here have ever been completely sure if you were serious."

"I'm completely serious that we could do it, and completely serious that it would work," Hughes says. "Our mission statement is 'Secure, contain, protect'. Somewhere down the line we really should look into adding 'and keep as many human beings alive as possible' to that."

"It's implicit that humanity is what we protect," Graves says.

"Secure the anomalies, contain the anomalies, protect the anomalies. How does it scan otherwise?"

"We're getting off-topic," Wheeler says. "We're not exterminating all sapient life."

"We could immediately terminate and suppress all memetics and antimemetics research worldwide," Hughes says. "We would have to systematically dismantle the whole scientific field forever. Stop all the experiments, scrap all the research, brainwash all the researchers. If nobody actively researches this field, nobody will ever find SCP-3125. It stays buried in the farthest reaches of ideatic space indefinitely, like radioactive waste." He looks up at the ceiling. The problem is interesting. "Ironically, the most practical way to do that would be to develop an artificial meme. One which encodes the idea that memetics research is intrinsically worthless and harmful. Enrich it with religious or pseudoscientific virals and release it to the general public. A year after it got out we'd be tearing our own labs down. Unless the Antimemetics Division's institutional immunity to that kind of external threat was strong enough to stand up to the pressure. Interesting scenario. Even if we don't go in that direction we should definitely think about wargaming it in simulation, see what outcomes are likely—"

"Bart," Wheeler says.

"No, hiding wouldn't work. It could be introduced externally or occur naturally—"

"We know. Bart, that's already happened. SCP-3125 is incarnating as we speak. Look at these precursor anomalies. We're in what you called the foreshadow. It's *here*."

Wheeler's referring to predictive models which Hughes must have created himself during prior meetings, models with which he doesn't have time to familiarise himself. Still, he gets it.

He wishes he didn't get it. His fear comes from a completely different place from most people's. The sheer alien scale of the adversary is enough to intimidate most into petrified submission. From a cursory read, SCP-3125 looks like a nightmare scenario; it's going to turn human civilisation into something beyond Hughes' ability to imagine. But that's every Monday in this job, and in any case Hughes doesn't have much of an imagination. He is intimately familiar with almost the entire SCP database, and he's a world authority in anomalous containment. The few areas of science he doesn't have genius-level ability in, he has trusted colleagues who do. They are all solved problems, locked boxes.

This is different. He has more ideas, but there is, mechanically, no way to start working on the problem. It would eviscerate him the moment he tried to comprehend the entire problem. He'd need to design and build the box while *already inside the box he was building*. He would need to box the *universe*.

He looks around the room's walls. They seem to be holding up.

"We could hide in units like this for the rest of our lives," he says. "Our whole species. While SCP-3125 roamed our reality unchecked, like a plague. I declare this to be the exterior of the containment unit. Done."

No reaction.

"I don't think we can do it," he says. "If SCP-3125 is live in consensus nominality right now, the game is over. I don't care if Apollyon classification lives or dies, from where I'm sitting this anomaly is functionally uncontainable. I... my team and I may have said something different on prior iterations. I could be in the wrong headspace to see the answer. We are all of us different people from day to day."

"No," O5-8 says. "You say the same thing every time."

"So that's it. Is that it?"

O5-8 says, "The objective of the Foundation is protection. In the majority of cases this involves the secure containment of anomalous entities; the establishment of special containment procedures such that such entities can be kept safely, and indefinitely. Standard guidance is against active neutralization and to avoid destruction at all costs. Everybody in this room is aware of this. However, senior Foundation officials such as me have the right to waive that guideline under certain narrow conditions. I am exercising that right. I deem that in our reality, SCP-3125 cannot coexist with human civilization. We're going to destroy SCP-3125. Forever. Does that change your outlook any?"

"Special neutralization procedures," Hughes deadpans. His expression is worsening by the minute.

O5-8 adds, "I know that neutralization is... *generally* considered easier than mere containment."

Hughes says:

"When I first joined the Foundation, I asked my mentor, who retired many years ago, 'What's the biggest anomaly we've ever contained?' That he was cleared for, I meant, of course. And he told me about a very old rumor he once heard, back in *his* earliest days, when he was just starting out. The rumor was that Abrahamic religions had not always been monotheistic. Originally, there were three capital-G Gods. And sometime in the past hundred and fifty years, the Foundation had killed two of them.

"I believed him. I was very young and inexperienced, and naive, and kind of in awe. It wasn't until years later that I thought back to the conversation — and the fact that I'd never heard that rumor, or anything like it, from anybody else — and realised he had been bullshitting me.

"And now it's decades later still, and modern memeplectic technology is a hundred billion times more advanced than it was back then, and I built thirty percent of it, and I look at what the Antimemetics Coalition handles on a quarterly basis, and I know better than anybody on the face of this Earth what is or is not possible, and..."

He trails off. They're all waiting expectantly for him to say something. He can't get there. He's in the wrong frame of mind. Maybe he's in denial, maybe the solution is an idea he doesn't want to take on board. How ironic—

"What did I say? Just tell me."

"Your team suggested that just because SCP-3125 is the most powerful memeplectic threat ever observed doesn't mean it's the top of the hierarchy," O5-8 says. "You suggested that it would be possible to synthesise an idea an order of magnitude still more powerful than SCP-3125, specifically designed to neutralize SCP-3125, and under our control. A countermeme."

"That would take... That could be... possible," Hughes hazards. "It would be insanely dangerous. It would require tremendous resources. And ten to twenty years of real time work, completely uninterrupted. To avoid observation, we'd need to be hermetically sealed away from the exterior universe for that entire time. We'd need a lab as big as a Launch Arcology. *Wait a second.*"

His brain has just caught up. He realises the context in which he's saying these things. And he's been working for the Foundation for a *long* time.

"It's done," he says. "The lab, it's been built. It was built decades ago, in secret, and we put our best researchers inside it and now the work is done. That's what we're meeting for, now. We're ready to go. We're figuring out how to deploy the countermeme. That's brilliant! If I'm right, that's brilliant. Am I right?"

"Bart," Wheeler says. "When you joined the Foundation, you were taught that a day would come when you would have to, with very little preparation, sacrifice much or all of your existence to protect what most needs protecting. You've worked here for thirty years. And all of that time you knew that that sacrifice would be in your future someday. We were all taught the same thing."

It feels to Hughes as if a shadow falls over him. He looks at Michael Li, his director, who hasn't spoken yet.

Li says, "You're right that the lab is built. Construction was completed in the last forty-eight hours. The construction crew have been amnesticized and dismissed. But the work hasn't begun yet. That's what today's about."

Hughes says, "...That's where my people are."

"That's where your people are," Li says. "They're in the bunker, waiting. We have your cover story prepped. We're faking your death. It's time. You're going under now."

"Now? No. I... I doubt that."

"Your team volunteered. I took care of them myself. They're good people," Li says.

"Like hell," Hughes says, "did *I* volunteer for this."

Wheeler says, "Bart!"

Hughes says, "Any prior version of me who agreed to this was a God-damned moron, and I disavow his opinions. This is a prison sentence. I don't want to spend twenty years not able to see the Sun. I don't want to be buried alive in work. I have..."

He trails off, and stares through the table, eyes defocused. He was about to say, "I have family."

But he doesn't.

There's still his sister. She's Foundation, like him. But he can't talk to her, and she can't talk to him. They've tried.

He tries another tack. "This... has a low probability of success. The timeframes are bad. It's 2008. SCP-3125 will be here by the end of the 2010s—"

"It has an excellent probability of success," Graves says.

"Define 'excellent'," Hughes says.

"Better than fifty percent. *If* it's you." Graves produces a thick report which presumably backs him up.

Hughes peers at the document. He can see his own name on the cover. *God damn it.* Fifty percent is good. If he were anybody else in this room, he'd seize the chance with both hands.

Graves goes on. "*You* convinced *us* that this had to be done. And that you had to be at the center. You were prepared to make the sacrifice." He opens the document to a page in the back. The eyeball of his germ roves the page rapidly and finds the passage he wants. "Allow me to quote your own words to you: 'SCP-3125 represents an omniversal-scale threat. It threatens neighbouring realities to ours. It threatens microverses within our macroverse. It threatens universes which embed ours as fiction—'"

"Go ahead and think of it as a prison sentence, if it helps," O5-8 interrupts. "Rescind your consent if you'd like. But the next place you're going after this is the bunker."

Hughes glances around the room's walls again. He makes it too obvious what he's thinking.

"The door's locked, Dr. Hughes," O5-8 says. "You're not exiting until we're through here."

"What's the cover story?" Hughes asks. "How were you planning to do it?"

"A helium gas leak in S167-B03-312," Graves explains. "The leak will be real. There's a forged body in there already, impossible to distinguish from a real one. We've tampered with your public schedule for the day. It puts you in that room, not this one. As for—"

"He's stalling," O5-8 says to Graves and the others. "He doesn't need to know any of this."

"Name somebody else," Li suggests. "Being serious. Who in the world, other than you, stands a credible chance of solving this problem? Who could we send instead?"

Hughes says nothing. There's nobody. Really, nobody in the world. And he *can* do it.

Li presses, "Is there anybody else? Even if they didn't want to. Who has the skills we need, who isn't already in the vault?"

The world shifts positions a little. Li's standing now. Wheeler looks around alertly, gripping the arm of her chair. She has a fountain pen in her fist, uncapped. It's like she just remembered something. O5-8 glances at Wheeler, puzzled at her reaction to, apparently, nothing. Hughes doesn't notice anything.

"It's just me," Hughes says.

"It's just you," Li says. "That's good enough for me."

"Hold on a second," Wheeler says.

Li pulls a gun out of nowhere. Hughes' germ's enormous pupils shrink to violet pinpricks.

This is no part of any plan, everybody in the room knows it. It's a real gun. It's impossible that he could have it. Wheeler starts to rise out of her chair. Her own sidearm is locked in a box outside.

Li aims at Bart Hughes' chest and fires twice. The first round pierces him in the lung. The second round, fired as Hughes collapses, nicks his laptop screen, which is bulletproof, and ricochets up into the meeting room wall.

*

Li turns, now aiming at O5-8. He gets two more rounds off, each causing an earsplitting electronic shriek and a flash of luminous green light as O5-8's protective ward absorbs the energy. Wheeler lunges at Li from behind his gun arm, deflecting it upwards with one hand while plunging the fountain pen into his throat with the other. Li struggles. Wheeler pulls hard, opening his throat all the way up. Li's fingers loosen and she spirits the gun away. Li gurgles in agony and stumbles backwards, clutching futilely at his wound. He smashes his head — well, the germ he's wearing on his head — against a glass meeting room door, and slides down it into a spreading red lake. He's neutralized.

There are two seconds in which nothing happens.

O5-8's eyes meet Wheeler's. "Your thoughts?" he asks, urgently.

"Michael Li was compromised, I don't know how," Wheeler says. She makes the gun safe, holsters it and vaults over the table to check on Hughes. He's dead, she finds. Graves is dead too. When in the hell did Graves get hit? What just happened in this room? "This whole Site could be compromised from top to bottom—"

"I have follow-up questions," O5-8 begins. A bolt of lethally intense heat and light interrupts him, scorching the wall behind his head. He ducks.

Wheeler turns to track the source, aiming the gun with bloody hands. Something is lasering its way in through the containment unit airlock. It's a powerful laser, wielded with robotic precision. It's happening almost too fast to see.

"My personal security," O5-8 says. "It heard the shots."

"Call it off," Wheeler says. "If this unit is breached, SCP-3125 is coming for all of us."

"The unit's hermetically sealed. I can't send any kind of signal until the door's open."

"That's a problem—"

The airlock splits, and is torn away in segments. An enormous gloss black armoured mechanoid looms in the gap, crouched to peer into the room. It looks exactly as if O5-8's limousine got up and started walking. It's still impossible to guess whether there could be a human pilot inside it. Behind it, in the distance, Bochner is immobilised, sealed to one of the staging area chairs with a sizeable glob of transparent orange glue. She screams, "Help!"

For Wheeler, it feels as if a black wave rolls over her, pouring into the containment unit from outside. She drops the gun and raises her hands. Being found holding the smoking gun isn't likely to be a good look, and she doesn't know for sure what heuristics, human or electronic or otherwise, control the mechanoid; it could be prone to making bad decisions.

"Stand down," O5-8 says to his bodyguard. It stops moving, but its single laser doesn't, flickering as fast as the eye can follow between four motionless targets: Wheeler, Hughes, Graves and Li. It's waiting for movement.

Li, not completely dead, twitches. The laser pulses once in retaliation, atomising his head and germ. The laser settles down to a shorter pattern, looping between the three remaining targets. Wheeler doesn't move a millimetre.

"I said, 'Stand down'!"

This time it seems to hear him. The laser clicks off and settles into a neutral position.

Wheeler relaxes. "Li was compromised," she says again. She hurries to the back of the room, where a medical kit is mounted on the wall. "We need to get you out of here. Then we need to sterilize the Site."

"Compromised when?" O5-8 asks. "By whom? I was given to understand that SCP-3125 rendered its victims wholly bodily subordinate to it, biologically incapable of doing anything but propagate its core concepts. But Li was still high-functioning."

"We've miscalculated something," Wheeler says. She throws most of the kit aside, keeping only a strangely-shaped capsule with a thin nozzle and pink fluid inside.

"And the gun? We were all searched on entry."

"I don't know." Wheeler can think of several ways to get the gun into room undetected. It could have been planted in the restroom by Li on a prior visit. Bochner could be complicit. Perhaps others. She thinks there's an extremely strong chance that the three members of Hughes' team have been murdered too.

It's all academic now. She applies the capsule to her right wrist and infuses the first half of the dose. It's fast-acting chemical amnestic. She hopes that splitting one dose between the two of them will be enough.

"Isn't this the part where SCP-3125 makes an appearance?" O5-8 suggests. "I certainly feel... something. In my head. My germ, I should say."

"Me too. Roll up your sleeve. You also need to deactivate your shield for a second." He obliges, and Wheeler gives him the rest of the drug. Wheeler sorely wishes the shields were standard issue, but they are exceptionally hard to come by, and there are serious controversies and side-effects associated with them.

Outside, Bochner has been gurgling and starting to speak in tongues. Now she screams again. When Wheeler looks, something long and dark, sharp as a javelin and bifurcating into filaments, descends from somewhere in the ceiling of the warehouse. It curls around the chair Bochner is glued to, and lifts her up into the air. A second thin feeler makes an appearance. It probes Bochner's glue-covered midsection, curiously, and then pushes itself through her, like a pin through paper.

She wails, litres of blood gushing out and splashing to the floor below her. The feeler withdraws, then makes a second hole beside the first, and continues in that fashion.

More spider legs impale O5-8's mechanoid bodyguard, and pull it away from the airlock, rapidly dissecting it into sparking pieces. The laser flashes wildly as the machine dies. It's no use.

In the distance, a site-wide containment alarm starts up.

"It's a memetic threat," O5-8 says, mostly to himself. "Where do the arachnoforms come in?"

"Do you have alternate transportation?" Wheeler asks.

"S167-B02-101, there's an escape pod," O5-8 says.

As he says it, Wheeler writes it down on her hand with her bloodied fountain pen. "Underground? You're sure? Is there a code for the door?"

O5-8 lists five digits. He clutches his head. His germ is twitching unhappily and changing colour and texture, as if an infection is spreading across its pale blue skin. "I can feel it. It's like— steel jaws. This is... most unpleasant."

"We need to get to the escape pod," Wheeler says. "There's nothing else that matters. We don't need to remember why. Got it?"

Spider legs reach into the airlock and begin tearing the room to pieces. They're fast-moving and grabby and angry. They know there's something important inside, but they can't get to it. The skull bone is too strong to be broken apart.

O5-8 doesn't have much field experience. The amnestic is blurring his thoughts. "I'm deferring to you," he says, dozily. "Escape pod. Lead on."

Wheeler takes his hand. She's got Li's gun in the other — a decent amount of ammunition left. "With me," she says. She's done this before. She doesn't know it.

The warehouse ceiling starts to cave in.

*

But what is it?

Where is it? What does SCP-3125 look like? Its motivation, its origins, its *modus operandi*— how much of that *can* be known? Does it have to be known, to solve the problem? Does it matter how intelligent the intelligence is, once it's inside the box, once it's checkmated?

And what actinic, mind-wrenching form could the countermeme take? How could human hands assemble something so devastatingly powerful and hold it steady; what human mind could wield it without exploding from the inside out? What would deploying that concept in anger do to human ideatic space? How far out from the solution is modern memetic science, a year, a century? What insane impossibility has Hughes just committed himself to?

He doesn't know anything. He knows Site 167 is coming apart, and something violent and psychotic is flooding its corridors and its people, a livid roving swarm which makes every human into the worst possible thing a human can be, a thing which *stands* wrong, which *looks wrong*, colourless and furious. He races down the corridors, and then down ventilation shafts which will take him deeper. He's small, and he has quick, slippery locomotion. He can make it. He can lock himself in.

He doesn't know what a germ needs to survive. All he's seen is the cages. He doesn't know Bochner's care routine. Does it live in water, in *C. gigantes* blood plasma? Is it fed a formula? He needs to reverse-engineer his own biology before he starves. He doesn't know the model of his mind. It hurts to think.

But he can think.

10
Blood/Brain

There's no day/night cycle.

Something like a week into his trek, Wheeler realises that he can perform an experiment. He selects a building with a high ceiling to sleep in, a library. Before turning in, he sets up a Foucault pendulum. He suspends a heavy rock by wire from the ceiling and sets it swinging. The following morning, the slow pendulum is still swinging, and it has precessed. It's swinging at about a right angle from the mark he made before he went to sleep.

That means the world is still spinning.

On reflection, he doesn't know if it proves anything. It's not clear whether the Sun or the Moon still exist, or any celestial object at all other than the red-black eye socket at the horizon. The eye never moves. It casts long, threatening shadows, while being bright enough to blind Wheeler whenever he has to walk in that approximate direction, which is about half the time. Regardless of the physical evidence, it doesn't feel as if he's walking on a real Earth, or fully awake. He feels like an ant, crawling across the face of a rough-hewn monolith, crawling into and out of the runes chiselled into the face of that monolith, runes which form an unstoppable, apocalyptic mythology. He has migraines, and there are blotchy multicoloured zigzags in his vision by the end of most "days". He feels as if the whole world is perpetually dropping away from beneath his feet, like he and it are both plummeting into an abyss.

He has not been caught yet. The violent phenomena Ulrich warned him about have not appeared, which makes him feel increasingly lucky, and nervous. He carries a looted gun, which he's practiced with a little — he's a better shot than he would have guessed, using his right hand alone. (His left hand, the mangled one, does nothing but shake. He has to keep it clutched to his chest when shooting.) The gun gives him less reassurance than he'd like. It feels as if, were he to end up in a situation, it could metamorphose suddenly from a working firearm into a fiddly metallic liability, an explosive distraction in his pocket. On occasion, on the horizon, he sees a skyscraper-sized figure stalking past. He holds still, or hides, and it doesn't see him. Other than that, the world is seemingly deserted, standing empty, like an overturned car in a muddy ditch. Open doors, lights still blinking. Wheeler feels... detached. Lucky. Guilty.

He keeps away from cities. He has not, yet, come within eyeshot of a sarcophagus — Ulrich was evasive in describing them, and advised him in the strongest possible terms to stay away from them. But on another "night", he selects a bad place to camp, where the wind and the local geography funnel the noise from one of the sarcophagi up to him from the valley. The noise, despite its faintness and distance, cultivates such intense and intolerable nightmares that he has to get up, pack up again and walk further away, as many more miles as it takes. The noise creates, in him, things which he dearly wants not to be flashbacks.

He goes into a shop and, along with packaged food and bottled water, steals a cheap digital wristwatch. It has a date function. Today is Monday the 17th of April; it's just gone lunchtime.

Time is still passing. On some level, all of this is factual. It's happening.

*

And if it's really happening, then, what?

There is no longer any ambiguity about *what*, specifically, is happening. Not in Wheeler's mind, or in anyone's. The world has long since passed through SCP-3125's antimemetic boundary layer and into its radioactive core. There is no longer a need for SCP-3125 to pretend that it is not what it plainly is. What else could it be? What difference could it make now, what could oppose it? It stands there in plain sight. Wheeler sees it. All of conscious reality sees it. It's happening everywhere, to everyone. It's not physically possible to conceive of anything else.

There is no worse case scenario than what's happening now. There's no race against time; there's no ticking clock; there's no last second, the last second was years ago. There's nothing to *avert*. This is it, the final game position, the highest and most refined form of human civilisation. This is the shape of the next million years.

SCP-3125 stands there. Monstrous, casual and indifferent.

And Wheeler is alone with his thoughts for a long period of time, and has little else to think about, and he wrinkles his brow, and he blinks a long blink, and looks again, and he realises what it was that he wasn't seeing—

SCP-3125 is *standing* there. Like a human stands.

*

He reaches Site 41 at the beginning of May. His body clock has wandered far out of skew by this point; it's technically around midnight when he first lays eyes on the place.

There is a protective field surrounding it, stamped into reality by the detonation of the antimemetic warhead, radiating out a few hundred metres beyond the Site's perimeter. It's a psychological repulsion, not a physical one. A thick bulwark of irrelevance. *There's nothing here. Just keep walking.* Despite being warned about it, Wheeler succumbs to the effect. Thirty minutes' walk down the road, he double-checks his map and realises what's happened and turns back. This happens a second time. On the third attempt, he makes it through. Dead reckoning and willpower.

For some reason, he had been imagining an ancient, dramatically overgrown ruin, but the containment breach which led to the Site's destruction happened only eighteen months ago, and the bomb blast which concluded the outbreak was figurative, not physical. About a third of Site 41's main building has been torn down, but the rest is perfectly intact and unmarred. Mother Nature has not reclaimed it. Gnarled trees are not sprouting from the damaged side.

Wheeler exhales. There is a still, safe atmosphere about the place. It's as if Site 41 has its own cool microclimate. It's easier to think. Even the light here is fractionally yellower, more natural.

The Site's main entrance is sealed with steel doors, but Wheeler circles around to the damaged side of the building, and is able to effect entry over the rubble. He moves at a medium-slow pace. He can't afford to blunder into anything, but if he goes too slowly, he knows, he'll overthink the situation, and become scared, and have to retreat all the way out of the building. The late Daisy Ulrich promised him that the Site was Safe. She then went to rather disconcerting lengths to explain precisely what "Safe" meant. No entities capable of spontaneously, actively harming a person; no entities in need of active, dynamic containment procedures. A Safe SCP can be left in a dark, locked room indefinitely with no risk, she explained.

"A nuclear bomb is Safe," she said, giving the canonical example.

"Well," he replied. "Up to a point."

The Site is Safe, he tells himself, creeping forward. The most dangerous things he's going to find are rats and— he jumps back, aiming his flashlight at a frightening shape— corpses.

The corpse is seated against a corridor wall. It's clutching a combat knife, which it seems to have buried up to the hilt in its own inner thigh, opening a gushing artery. Wheeler backs up against a wall, unable to look closely at the body but equally unable to let it out of his eyesight, in case it... does something. He feels faint. It doesn't help that at exactly that moment, the fluorescent lights in the corridor come up, triggered by his movement, giving him a much better look at the scene. The scene is about as bloody as any suicide can be.

"No, thank you," he says. He backs up. He backs all the way up the corridor and through the ruin to the virulent red place which passes for daylight, and there he throws up.

*

It takes a long time to talk himself back into it.

He finds many more bodies. Some of them are in groups, having died during violent altercations, or during more complex scenes which Wheeler cannot fully parse. Some of them are dismembered, or just scattered pieces. Some of them appear to have been dead for significantly longer than the rest; they are little more than wafer-thin skin wrapped around skeletons, and there are strange things written on the walls beside them. Wheeler never works out why.

There's still power. There's running water.

At first, nearly every door he meets is locked. But he steels his nerves, and returns to each of the dead Foundationers in turn, and retrieves their keys and security passes. Soon, he has the run of the place, with only a few highly secure control rooms and containment units denied to him.

At this point, his task has become open-ended. If Hughes is not somewhere on Site 41 — which he almost certainly isn't — Wheeler needs to find information leading to his true location. He needs data.

He collects devices: phones and laptops and computer terminals, Foundation-built with chunky form factors. Most of them need passwords or PINs, which he can't get, but a few can be unlocked using security passes or biometrics, which he can get if he carries the device back to the relevant corpse and presents their face or finger to the scanner. The devices still have power, too. Wheeler is unable to find anything resembling a battery readout on any of them. He is slowly learning a key lesson: the Foundation builds things to *endure*. And though the Foundation as a group of people is absent, the physical systems they built are still here, and functioning, and ready.

The SCP database is the most obvious icon on every device's home screen. Ulrich told him to look out for a particular sigil, concentric circles with three inward-pointing arrows. Inevitably, like an uncounted number of newcomer Foundationers before him, Wheeler loses a significant number of hours browsing the entries. The Foundation has a specific and recognisable house style, which is to describe even the most mind-bogglingly weird anomalies in absolutely mundane, factual terms. Even heavily redacted — different users see different amounts of redaction, but there is plenty of data which he can't access no matter whose identity he uses — it makes for bizarrely compelling reading.

Hughes is mentioned numerous times in the database. He seems to have multiple overlapping research specialities, and is credited in many entries as a containment architect. Wheeler takes detailed notes, assembling a picture of the man's career progression... and then randomly stumbles into the Foundation's own personnel records for Hughes, which line up almost exactly with what he just worked out.

There are huge holes in the personnel record. The last entry relating to Hughes' actual activities is in 2007. And then in 2010, after a gap of years, there's a final note, a single unauthored sentence:

It appears that those who know Hughes' fate meet it.
END OF FILE

Wheeler frowns at the unhelpful note for a long minute. It reads like a riddle. Wheeler was, for a long time, a crossword puzzle fiend, but it seems improbable to him that a clandestine organisation like the Foundation would leave cryptic clues for one another, rather than clear, direct instructions. Which means the note is probably intended to be read simply and literally: *Don't look for Hughes unless you want to meet the same fate.*

Wheeler tilts his chair back and stares at the ceiling, contemplatively. On the other hand, the note also means: *Hughes can be found. It's been done before.*

*

There's no day/night cycle, but he's worn out. His body is telling him that he needs to sleep. He sleeps on a sofa in an employee break room, on the far side of the building from the red eye. There's a snack machine, and there are snacks in the machine, but he doesn't have any cash. He considers breaking the glass, but if he screws it up and cuts himself badly there isn't a single doctor left in the whole world who could stitch him up. He considers, and rules out, looting the nearest corpse for a dollar.

As he tries to sleep, something comes to him, an acute, anxious energy. It grips him by the shoulder. *Get up,* it screams at him, distantly. *You cannot rest. Do the arithmetic. It's all still happening. MOVE.*

He rolls over and ignores it.

And it bothers him, intellectually, that he can ignore it. He wonders if there is some vital organ missing from his body. He should be quivering with anger and terror right now, yes? Why, in his heart, is he so calm?

He looks at SCP-3125, whose very existence, on paper, should paralyse him with fear. He looks at what SCP-3125 is doing, which should fill every fibre of his being with furious purpose. And he looks at his own significance to the whole endeavour, and his own guesstimate of the odds. He does the arithmetic. And the product of all those factors rounds down to damn near zero.

This isn't going to work. That's why.

This has to stop! It has to end! PLEASE!

Curled up in his sleeping bag, eyes screwed shut, Adam Wheeler mutters to whatever may be listening:

"It isn't going to work."

*

Near the site entrance — he can't figure out how to unlock the steel doors, even from this side — he finds a security office, with printed floor plans of the whole Site. He crosses off the rooms he's visited, and the rooms which are destroyed. Everything remaining is locked. Above ground, anyway. Underground, there are warrens of tunnels, and dozens more containment units. And, thirty floors below ground, a single incredibly large vault of unstated purpose. This final vault draws his attention in, magnetically.

Ulrich assured him that the Site was totally Safe.

As the freight elevator descends, Wheeler finds that a kind of anxious pressure is building above him. The air is rapidly getting warmer, and he's just realised that if the elevator breaks down right now, he'll likely be helplessly trapped, and die. He shouldn't have used it. He should have used the emergency stairs. Too late.

The elevator lands. There's an empty corridor. He follows it, drawn forward. There's an airlock at the far end, a wall of white metal big enough to drive a truck through. The airlock is closed, but there are seven or eight overlapping circular holes punched through it, making a combined gap which is easily big enough to admit a human. Beyond the airlock, there is a vast dark space. Wheeler has climbed through the hole and walked five paces out into the darkness before he even thinks about what he's doing.

There are shapes out there, illuminated by the scant light falling from the airlock corridor — lumps which could be more dead people. Wheeler's own shadow blocks much of the light. He takes out his torch. It is absolutely silent down here, and the temperature is uncomfortable, making him sweat. The rest of the huge vault, as far as he can shine his light, is totally empty — but his torch is not powerful enough to illuminate a space this big, so it's hard to be certain.

He advances. A loud tone is building in his ears as he gets closer. There are... he counts... fourteen dead. Thirteen of them, dead in a rough circle around a fourteenth, a woman lying flat on her back. Just outside of the circle, there is a military truck with the inert remains of a complex machine mounted on its back. This, Wheeler surmises, is the antimemetic warhead. There is a cable leading down to a control unit lying on the floor, under the hand of the dead woman.

"Ah," he says, with a note of regret. "So you're the one."

Her security pass looks different from the others. It has a bright diagonal stripe across it in red and orange. He takes it. There's a roaring in his skull. He can't see it clearly at first — something is disturbing his vision, a gold-white spot in the corner of his eye, an artifact from the combination of extreme darkness and bright torchlight. He squints. It says "Marion Wheeler / Site Director".

He stares at it for a long time, weirdly disoriented. He doesn't exactly know why. It is, of course, a very commonplace name; if he stopped to gawp at every other Wheeler he met, he would never get anything done. Still, she's the one with her hand on the switch; she's the one who ended this local outbreak. Out of every dead Foundationer on this damned Site, she's the one who didn't die for no reason at all. He feels as if he should say a few words.

But they do not come to him.

He makes one quick circuit around the vault perimeter, scanning the floor and the wall, looking for anything interesting and finding nothing but construction tools and scaffolding. He returns to the airlock and then the freight elevator. He glares at it for a long, frustrated moment, and then accepts that it would be unsafe to use it again.

The emergency stairwell is perfectly well-lit, but thirty floors is a mountain. Three times on the way up, he has to stop to rest his knees.

*

The Site Director's pass gets him everything. Every control room, every containment unit, every file. He gets the whole story. He puts the last piece in place. He leaves a note, following the same hopeless, diligent ritual as the rest of the Antimemetics Division before him. He emerges from SCP-3125's "inverted containment unit" with extremely clear written instructions from himself to himself. He knows exactly where he needs to go.

As he moves down the forest road away from the Site, he reaches and crosses the edge of the antimemetic crater. He squares his shoulders, re-entering the presence of SCP-3125. His inner ear starts freefalling again.

"Where were you, just now?" someone calls out to him.

He stops walking. He squints into the intense light ahead of him, shielding his eyes. He can just about make out a figure standing there. The trees on each side of them rustle and move. They're too tall. Spider-scrapers. A wave of dread hits Wheeler, followed closely by one of perverse relief. This is it.

"Why can't I track you?" the unidentified man says. His voice sounds faint. "You're so *weak*, it's like you don't exist. I just wasted two days trying to pick you up again. What's wrong with you?"

Wheeler says nothing.

The man is closer. He didn't walk, but the distance between them halves, and his voice is easier to hear, though he is still too bright to look at. His body structure blurs and flickers. "You're not one of Them," he says. "And you're not one of Us. And you're definitely not the *hero*. You don't count for shit, memetically. Why are you wasting your time on this? Whatever the fuck this is. You should just kill yourself. It's not going to work."

Wheeler knows that.

The light collapses. The figure smashes into focus, becoming physical. It's a real human. A skinny twenty-something: scruffy, uncut hair and a sketchy beard. He is shirtless, and there is a deep, black pit in his clavicle, a hole where he has clearly been very badly wounded. Blood has run down his chest, soaked his jeans and forearms, and dried black. Fresh blood is still coming, building up thick layers, which shouldn't be possible. Wheeler doesn't spot the second hole in his gut, obscured by too much blood.

Wheeler is trying to keep his expression neutral, but he knows it isn't working. He can feel his left hand, his bad hand, starting to shake. A part of him *still* wants to ask the guy why. But there is no possible answer.

"This is what the human race really is," the man explains, spreading his hands to gesture at the whole world. "We lied to ourselves that we could be better, for thousands of years. But this is it. This is what we've always been. We've never been anything else."

"That's—" Wheeler begins, then stops, suddenly remembering something. He claps his left hand to his chest, draws with his right and shoots. It's a good shot. It's a lucky shot. It takes the man directly in the eyeball, and blows out the back of his skull. He falls, twisting as he falls, landing on his broken face.

Wheeler gasps, remembering to breathe. He almost drops his gun. He gets a tighter grip on it, keeping it aimed at the blasted ruin of the man's head. He wants to throw up. He controls himself. In through the mouth, out through the nose. He's okay. "Let him talk for too long," he says, apologetically.

He pulls out a Foundation brickphone from his pack. He pushes some buttons, entering coordinates, and then retreats far down the road. He retains visual contact with the dead man for as long as possible, then turns away and kneels, placing the phone on the road beside him. Following the detailed instructions he found in the control room, he grinds his palms into his eyes and presses his face against the ground. And he says:

"Aeloni zaenorae. Fire."

The orbital laser strike comes diagonally. It lasts for a split second, and is easily bright enough in the visible spectrum to have instantly blinded him if he were looking. When Wheeler returns to the scene, there's no body left. Just a scorched ellipse of asphalt.

He says, to the scorch mark, "I was going to say something along the lines of: 'That's a lie. That's what you are. You're the lie.' But, ah."

And if the bastard can regenerate from that, I'm done for, well and truly.

He looks up. The atmosphere isn't changing. The sky isn't returning to blue. There's still that heinous pressure. SCP-3125 remains the dominant force in the universe.

But as he turns, hearing movement in the forest all around him, he realises that the immense spider forms — he'd sincerely forgotten about them, they were standing there so quietly — are dispersing.

11
Tombstone

All memetic horror aside, Wheeler thought Site 41 seemed like a pleasant enough place to work, at least above ground. Decently spacious, if unattractive, offices; large windows, plenty of natural light, scenic forest views. Safe.

Site 167 is a hostile, sprawling industrial wasteland, four square kilometres of secure containment warehousing, research laboratories and administrative offices. Wheeler is put in mind of a fossil fuel power plant. The buildings are grim, functional and aggressively unattractive. There is no greenery. The ambient noise in the complex is a harsh roaring — it was built on a flat plain, and the wind races down concrete canyons and past sharp building edges.

Just over half of the site, Wheeler discovers, has been erased from the face of the Earth by an orbital laser strike. There is an *edge* where the intact buildings and roads abruptly end, and beyond that edge there is nothing but blackened, level wreckage. Wheeler guesses that the laser shut down mid-redaction when the site's antimemetic warhead was triggered, but he can't be sure of the exact chain of events. It doesn't matter. It doesn't significantly harm the odds. What he's looking for is below ground.

Wheeler is at his limit. He has travelled too far, and he has been travelling for too long. He cannot exist in SCP-3125's universe for much longer, sane. It is all still happening, and the fragile responsibility of being the only one alive who can do anything to stop it is like a steadily tightening vice around his skull. He is exhausted, and slowly losing his vision to bright migraines, and dismally lonely. No more detective work, no more Sites. This needs to be the end.

Between buildings 8 and 22E there is a vertical access point, a thirty-metre-wide hexagonal shaft with a yellow gantry crane across its mouth. The shaft was used for lowering construction machinery and materials into the site's extensive underground complex. The shaft is so wide and deep that it has strange effects on the movement of air near its lip. It feels to Wheeler as if it's trying to pull him down. There are metal stairs lining the inner wall of the shaft. He descends, and then follows his map into Site 167's underground complex. Unlike Site 41, this was certainly not a Safe site. There are warning signs everywhere, many of whose symbols Wheeler cannot immediately parse. Very soon, he begins to encounter heavy bulkheads, sealed with electronic locks. Marion Wheeler's security pass opens them, every time.

Containment unit S167-00-6183's airlock is identical to the one he encountered at Site 41, just as the architectural diagrams suggested. The only difference is that this airlock is still visibly airtight — no holes. Wheeler swipes his card through the reader with a shaking hand. The door cycles open, revealing a sterile white antechamber, stale-atmosphered after years of disuse. He stands in the middle, waiting for the second half of the cycle.

This is it.

His heart is pounding. It's not good for him. He doesn't have a heart condition, that he knows of. But how would he know? Every living cardiologist is in hell.

He asks himself the final, worrying question, for the final time.

"But if you're here, Dr. Hughes, and you've built the machine, and the machine works: why didn't you come out?"

He answers himself, as a kind of inoculation against the bad news he knows is coming:

"Because the machine doesn't work. Because you couldn't build it. Because you're dead."

The inner door cycles open.

*

The atmosphere in the vault is tropically humid, and thick enough to taste. It tastes unpleasantly organic, like lymph or some other obscure bodily fluid. There are overhead floodlights, of which perhaps one in ten are still shining. There is junk everywhere. To Wheeler's left, there is a rough semicircle of monolithic autofactory units, each six or more metres tall, with piles of fabricated junk around them: furniture, tools, food containers, hard foam bricks, circuit boards, spools of fabric. To his right, stacked, stretching away along the long, concave wall of the vault, are hundreds of empty shipping containers. He would have to walk for ten minutes before he found one still containing raw materials.

Ahead of him is a three-metre-tall wall of steel which curves away to the left and right, enclosing almost all of the vault's floor space. Just visible over the top of the wall, heaving slowly under the weak yellow light, is an immense, sleeping organism. From here, Wheeler can only see the curve of its back, which is a glossy, moist black, mottled with green. It is round, almost spherical, like an ice cream scoop of liver taken from a human two kilometres tall and dumped into this enormous — Wheeler gulps as he makes the association — Petri dish.

Wheeler does not notice the metre-thick pipes which run from the autofactories over the edge of the dish and in, providing various necessary liquids. He does spot the tall towers arranged around the organism, spraying a translucent mist down at it from all angles. Suspended from the ceiling to the left and right, roaring continually, are ventilation units as large as houses.

There is no one around.

Wheeler clears his throat and addresses the room, as loudly as he dares. "Is there a... Dr. Bartholomew Hughes in here?"

Nothing happens. The roaring of the ventilation units continues. The organism continues to heave slowly.

Wheeler raises his voice somewhat. "I'm looking for a machine called an—"

It wakes up.

"—irreality amplifier?"

The thing turns, pushing huge volumes of fluid around its dish, enough that a wave of it sloshes viscously over the side of the wall. It lurches up to the wall. As more of it becomes visible, it becomes clear that there is little more to its body plan than what was already visible. Aside from stubby flippers, it is simply a huge, near-spherical lump of biology. It seems to peer eyelessly at Wheeler.

Wheeler concludes that he does not wish to be here. He turns to leave, and is startled to discover that the airlock door has closed behind him, as silently as it opened. "Ah." The airlock controls are to one side. He does not run, for fear of attracting attention with sudden movement, but he walks over, briskly, and pulls out his stolen security card again. As he's about to swipe it through the reader, a stringy red web lashes out from nowhere and restrains his wrist, preventing him from proceeding.

Wheeler struggles for a second to pull his arm free, but the webbing is gluey and has a freakish rigidity to it, as if there are bones inside it. It won't let him move. He glances back, and doesn't get a good enough look at the organism's body to spot where the web originated. The organism has opened its eye now, a single eyeball tens of metres wide, which must account for a significant fraction of its body volume. It has a vivid pink iris, and four enormous, black pupils.

Its voice isn't truly audible. It arrives in Wheeler's head like maddening static, a mosquito's whine in stereo.

DO YOU HAVE IT

"Have what?"

NO DOCTOR. NO MACHINE

A thinner strand of webbing shoots out, attaching itself to the security pass in Wheeler's hand, plucking it delicately from his fingers. The strand withdraws and holds the pass in front of the organism's eye.

WHEELER

"Ah," Wheeler says. "Yes, it's something of a coincidence actually—"

The strand tightens, lifting Wheeler by his arm. He twirls uselessly, barely able to see what's happening. There is a blur of luminous pink, and he is plunged, screaming, directly into the largest of Bart Hughes' four pupils.

*

The bunker was empty when he got there. His associates were missing. He was forced to presume them dead. And, in a rare lapse of forethought, he had neglected to bite off one of his human body's fingers before fleeing the scene of the shooting. With no human tissue sample to work from, he had no way to clone himself a replacement body. He was, he realised, trapped.

Wheeler had told him that, to protect the cause of the Foundation, he would have to sacrifice much or all of his existence. And she had only been reminding him of something which he had always known, intellectually. Still, he had not imagined *this*. And even if he had, he could never have imagined what this would be *like*, to experience from the inside. Several times, he came close to quitting. Dysmorphia alone almost killed him.

But. He had a duty. The problem had to be solved.

He attacked it in his germ form for over a year. He developed tools for himself, computer peripherals and writing implements adapted for his short but dextrous tendrils. He built miniature chair-analogues and other furniture. He developed, for himself, a little life. A fitness plan. Some hobbies, even. He slept in baths of nutrient sludge.

Before the end of the first month, he had proven to his satisfaction that the countermeme he was searching for existed beyond the comprehension of human intellect. A human being's mind would figuratively burst into flame upon contact with it; it was quite possible that their literal body would too, as a violent reaction to the profound, unalterable wrongness of every aspect of the universe around it. To create the countermeme, he would need to start from a human carrier of a suitable, "single-celled" base idea, and amplify that idea artificially using a machine.

By the second year he had designed and built enough of the machine to know that the machine could not be built. Theory and practice were diverging too far. Tests were failing in troubling ways, which pointed to fundamental architectural misconceptions. His machine would not and could not do what it was designed to do. He scrapped all of his schematics. He needed a different approach.

(There is a struggling figure mounted on the back of his retina, drowning beneath yellow pinpricks of focused light, drawing oxygen from his bloodstream and firing back minuscule thoughts. The figure is losing his mind with fear and revulsion, though he is a little more resilient than he gives himself credit for, and he is adapting. "It's you," the little man manages to gurgle. "There's no amplifier. You're the amplifier.")

He sequenced, and then reverse-engineered, his own genetic code. He built life support equipment, and re-architected the interior of the vault — which had always been the plan, if not to this extent. He refactored his physiology, in stages, over the course of years, until his brain was of a size and complexity to think monumental, radical, irreducibly complex thoughts.

("But why didn't you?" the speck asks. "You could have opened the vault at any time. What were you waiting for?")

Once, while exploring human ideatic space, he saw himself. He created a rudimentary memetic descriptor of himself, refined it, focused, guessed a little, and there he was: a complex of brilliant lights in the shape of a man, amid a swarm of similar people, living and dead and real and fictional. It was fascinating, and sobering, to see himself in that grand context, from that elevated perspective. He was tiny. He waved. He waved back.

And when he saw himself, he came to understand what he was; what his role was. He was the mad technical genius, the crazed inventor who architects the final weapon. But he was not the one to wield it. The spark, the base idea he needed to amplify, was not in his head, and was not in the vault with him. Mathematically, it never could have been. That was not the shape of things. It had to be delivered by someone else.

(The speck stops struggling. He has looked, with some effort, to his left and his right. He has now, finally, seen that there are other figures mounted here with him on the retina, older figures who have mostly been interpolated into the membrane, and no longer have independent life or thought. This causes him no small amount of alarm. He says: "...By who?")

Hold still.

(The speck's brain explodes, like a diagram.)

*

There is a forest.

There is a nice big house in the forest, and a garden behind the house, a trimmed lawn encircled by tall conifers. There is a rough circle of chairs on the lawn, and about twenty-five people seated or standing around or chatting in groups, with drinks and burgers, and there is a queue for the barbecue. There is a tall column of smoke rising from the barbecue. It is an outstandingly beautiful day, and nothing terrible is happening at all.

Adam Wheeler knows he is broken now, because he can't accept the scene. It's too sudden, and too pleasant, to be real. He feels normal, clean and healthy. He gasps and almost cries when he realises that his hand is back.

Someone walks up to him, offering a handshake. "You must be Adam. It's a pleasure. Bart Hughes."

Hughes is a very youthful fifty, short and skinny, with thick-lensed, thick-rimmed glasses and a flurry of wild, greying hair. Wheeler shakes his hand, more or less automatically; in his other, he has a bottle of beer. "I work at the Foundation," he says. "Obviously. Containment architecture, biomemetics, a whole mess of odd jobs."

"Hughes," Wheeler repeats. "I was— er, looking for you."

"You found me," Hughes says. "Good job."

"...What is this?"

"I didn't think you'd remember. This is where we met. Originally, I mean. Briefly. We shared about ten words, maximum, and I don't remember a single one of those words, and I barely remember you either, no offense. But I remember the barbecue, and I definitely remember *that* I met you at the barbecue. So, I figured it would be a more agreeable setting for the conversation we need to have."

Wheeler does not recognise the scene, either the location or any of the people. "This is your memory?"

"Yeah. Come on, let's talk."

Hughes leads Wheeler across the lawn and selects a pair of chairs in the sun. He sits, and gestures for Wheeler to sit across from him. Wheeler does so, uneasily. Hughes rests his elbows on his knees, and gathers his thoughts before he begins speaking.

"Adam, you don't have the idea we're looking for. The seed for the countermeme. You're the wrong guy.

"You would know if you had it. It would be impossible not to know. You would feel electrified by it. Driven forward by the high ideal it represented, every waking moment. It's what *should* have brought you here. I don't know how you made it here without it."

"...I didn't know I was supposed to bring an idea with me."

"There's no way you could have known," Hughes reassures him. "Nobody exterior to the vault knew. I didn't know it myself until I was already locked in. This is normal. We form these plans, and something unexpected happens, and the plans go out the window. And, under great pressure, we are forced to demonstrate creativity."

Wheeler takes a deep breath. He squares his shoulders. "Alright. Where is it? I hope it's in North America. I don't want to have to go all the way back to Site 41. But I will. If you can wait that long."

Hughes is shaking his head. "You can't do it. Even if it was that simple, and there was just a *place* I could send you to collect it, like takeout... you can't carry an idea like this.

You've never had that capability. You don't believe. You've never had to. You're the wrong guy."

"...So where does that leave us?"

Hughes turns, looking meaningfully toward the barbecue itself. Wheeler follows his gaze. There is a woman tending it, with her back to them, chatting with the people in line for food. She seems to be the centre of attention.

"Marion," Wheeler says.

"She had it," Hughes says. "Well, to speak accurately, there's no singular *it*. It's a massively diverse phase space of possibilities. Millions of people in the world had different ideas which could have worked. But she was one of them."

"Was," Wheeler says.

"Yeah. She died."

Hughes turns back to face him. He hesitates, drinking some more beer while he chooses his words. He is not a medical doctor. He does not have anything which could be considered a bedside manner.

"Adam," he says. "I've been examining your brain. There are layers and layers of damage there, and a lot of it looks deliberate. Some of it may even be self-inflicted. You have had memories suppressed, and restored, and falsified and erased again, and on top of that you've survived what should have been fatal exposure to SCP-3125, *and* you've been through a great deal of completely non-anomalous trauma. So... you would be forgiven for not having worked it out by now. The hole in your life."

"No, I know," Wheeler says.

With some caution, Hughes asks, "What do you know?"

"She and I were married at one point. Right?"

Slowly, Hughes nods.

Wheeler says, "I got there eventually. It felt stupid and obsessive at first, to draw that conclusion. Self-absorbed. But there were all these *facts*, and they all *fit*. At the end of the day, I had to accept it."

Hughes asks, "And how do you feel about that?"

Wheeler interlocks his fingers, distractedly. He doesn't know. He doesn't know if he wants to know. He's afraid to know. "So what if we were married? What does that give me? It's over. It's all gone."

"...Could be," Hughes says.

"What was she like?"

Hughes holds something out to him. It is an autoinjector pen, a stubby, luminous orange cylinder with a pointed cap concealing a needle. There is a fat black Z printed on its side. Wheeler recognises it.

In fact, he recognises it as his own. But he finds himself not able to recall where he acquired it. Or for how long he has been carrying it.

This drug, he knows, will kill him. It will make him remember everything — *everything*. And this will kill him, as it does everybody.

But he will remember.

There is a kind of singing in his ears. The sunlight in the garden is blurring, smearing out. He catches Hughes' eye, and Hughes is smiling ruefully, and his eye has lit up, a scintillating gold-white point of light.

*

This needs to be the end.

There are long, long months of fearful migraine wandering. There is the face-to-face back in the school, mediated by the late Daisy Ulrich, so brief and extraordinarily painful that it registers like a gunshot. And then he is enmeshed within SCP-3125 again, complicit and actively engaged in a darkened, metallic hell. The drug makes it impossible to not think about what happened, to not stare directly at what he did. Time in there is dilated, stretched to subjective breaking point by the anomaly's mass. It seems to last tens of years. And then, the chisel.

And after that, for two years, he is vacant. He is a suit wrapped around a torn, ragged-edged hole. And then there is Marion, at last, placidly tearing herself out of his life and him out of hers. And then it's hours earlier than that, the very worst moment, his awful sinking realisation that she no longer knows who he is.

And then it's two days before that. It's six-fifteen in the morning, October, pre-dawn and freezing cold. Marion is at her car door, about to leave for work but distracted by something important on her work phone, and Adam is lingering on the porch, seeing her off. He has a work trip of his own, tonight and tomorrow night, so this is the last time they'll see each other until—

This is the last time they'll see each other. This is it.

He digs his heels in, dragging the regression to a straining halt. He calls out, "Marion!"

She puts her phone away. She turns around.

It's her, the whole of her. She is precisely the way he remembers her. She *is* the memory, iconic and brilliant. She smiles at him, for a long, ridiculous moment.

She says, "Do you get it, now?"

"Why you kept me away from all this? *Yes.*" He goes to her, and they kiss, and it's a classic, it's perfect, it's everything either of them remembers. He holds her tightly, and she hugs him back, head heights as mismatched as ever. He sniffs.

"You've had a hell of a time," she states. It is a simple fact.

"I needed you," he says. "I didn't even know how badly. I didn't need you to *help* me, I just needed to stand aside and let you do the job instead. Marion, your job is lunacy. I one hundred percent understand why you tried to keep me out of this half of your life, for so long. And I will never ask about it again."

She looks up at him. It looks like she's about to say something, but the pain in Adam's brain makes itself known again, and he has to break off. The pain is forcing its way forward, into the back of his eyes. The rate of regression is increasing again. Different memories from all parts of his life are clamouring at him now, and their combined volume is increasing, and it is becoming difficult to think clearly. Marion, though, is part of most of the memories. Not a constant — she has evolved and grown, over years — but a common thread. He focuses on her.

"I don't have a lot of time to bring you up to speed," he manages. "This isn't real. We're both sharing Bart Hughes' mind right now. I don't know how much you know—"

"There's an (anti)memetic monster called SCP-3125," she says. "It killed me, and the Division, and the Foundation, and now it's occupying our whole reality. It ruins humans. It's the worst thing that's ever existed. There's no one left but you and you can't stop it. You can't even look at it. Hughes needs an idea to amplify, so you took a lethal dose of biochemical mnestic to reify me properly, because I was the best idea you had. Does that cover it?"

Adam grins weakly, with great relief. His wife has caught up characteristically quickly. "Just about. We live in ridiculous times."

She steps back from him. She looks at him, and at herself, and at their fictional little scene, steadily brightening as the Sun rises.

She looks "up", at the unimaginably gigantic memeplex which she has to kill. Inside its maw, human existence, all humans and all things humans have ever done, said, thought or been, are burning alive. SCP-3125 is, in large part, the lie that SCP-3125 is inevitable, and indestructible.

But it *is* a lie.

She feels it, now. She knows in her bones that she is *irreal*; an animate memory; an ideal, an abstract. When she started to exist a few moments ago she was mostly realistic, but she can feel flaws and complexity being stripped away from her. She can see the shape of the idea complex which Hughes is assembling around her. It looks familiar. It looks like a heavily reworked slice through the concept of the Foundation itself. The Foundation's noblest intentions and achievements, at least. The best purpose of its existence: to protect people. To swallow up all the horror, to manage it and understand it, to keep it under lock and key, so that *people don't have to be afraid*.

"Adam," she says, looking up again. "It's going to work. I can see all the way to the end from here."

"That's good," he manages. "It's been a long time since I had good news." He falls to his knees. His skull feels as if it's splitting open. She kneels with him, taking one of his hands.

He is seeing things, and the things he is being forced to see are hurting him. SCP-3125 has been hacking away at his and her lives for far longer than he knew. They'd lost so much by the end. He had no idea. And it's not just him, he realises. It's everybody. He needs to multiply this feeling by billions. "You've got to end this thing," he says, the pain rising to a flashpoint. "It has to be today. No more."

"Adam, listen. It's a different kind of existence up there. I've seen glimpses of it before, but I've never *been* there. I don't know what it's going to be like, but I know I won't be a human anymore. I'm already not real. I won't be able to come back. I love you."

There is a burning, corrosive sensation crawling across the surface of Adam's brain, a crackle like cellular automata. "I know," he says. "It's okay. There's going to be no one to come back to. It was good to see you. I love you."

STAND BACK

She stands back from him. She flexes what could be wings.

"You used to sing," Adam says. "All the time. It's the first thing it took away from us. But I remember."

The launch window opens. There is a kind of *ignition*. And Marion Wheeler's perspective shifts, and everything seems to shrink, and she is on the ascent.

*

The part of SCP-3125 which was capable of communication has had its brains blown out. There is no longer anything to reason with. There is no quip. There is a song, but it's a song she sings for herself.

The thing is titanic in its structure, brain-breaking in its topology. It comes from a space where ideas exist on a scale entirely beyond those of humans. Its wrongness and its self-consistent evil are so profound that it hurts to comprehend. At first, looking directly at it causes stinging actinic flashes in Marion's eyes, like ionising radiation.

But her perspective is still shifting, because she's still ascending. And as she ascends, ceasing to be human, she sees through the adversary, and comes to understand, instinctively, how it is structured, and how it is *faulty*, and how those faults can be attacked.

It turns to face her.

When they meet, what happens is less a fight than it is mathematics, an equation settling at the end of a long, painful stretch of working, a blizzard of cancelled terms. In the presence of WILD LIGHT, vast tracts of SCP-3125, thought to meaningfully exist, prove not to. It is, in the new context which WILD LIGHT provides, an ancient irrelevance. It folds up, limb after branching limb winking out of existence. It releases its grip on everything human. The mathematics is good. It happens in exactly the way Hughes modelled it, back in the bunker, using the memetic equivalent of fluid dynamics equations, taking thousands of processor-years to simulate.

After the finger limbs are gone, a livid red/green eyeball remains. The Foundation/Wheeler/protection abstract punctures it, lasering straight through it from front to back. A colourless shockwave spreads through the eyeball interior, another quiet cancelling-out, leaving bright vacuum behind it, not even particles.

And all that is left from the collision is the balance: a final wild photon, outbound to the deepest limit of ideatic space, never to return.

Epilogue

Champions Of Nothing

"...And what have we learned?"

It takes O5-8 a significant amount of time to answer his own question. He speaks with a measured, level tone. He is in no hurry.

"We have learned that there is time missing from our world. Almost a year of extremely recent history. And there are spaces, significant spaces, in every population center, which cannot be perceived or entered. The cities are rerouting around them, like mountains or radiation zones. And along with that time and that space, we have learned that there are enough people missing, without any explanation whatsoever, that if I spent the rest of my considerably augmented lifespan counting them, I could not count to that number."

He pauses.

"And outside of the Noöspherics Division," he says, "no one, not a single person, is even aware of these... thefts. Even those in the Division, who made this discovery, cannot recall what happened during that missing time. And no one can enter that missing space. The gap in reality, itself, can barely be perceived. It is this... shocking, blinding absence. This unknown unknown.

"We have learned — we have cautiously hypothesized — that three to four years ago an unimaginable anomaly entered our reality. And then, some time later, it left, taking all of that space, and all of that time, and all of those people with it. We do not know what it was, or what it did. We have tried to find out, but the truth evades my best noösphericists. The question fights back, as if it doesn't want to be answered. And we do not know why the anomaly left, though my experts say that in the conceptual realm, there is evidence — traces — of what could have been a conflict. And in the distance, shining down on us, there is a great new star."

He hesitates.

"Even I don't remember what happened," he continues, with his voice lowered. "Which I, personally, find... deeply alarming. Because this is recent history. Like nearly everybody alive, I must have *been there*. In some respect, I must have gone through it.

"But if we have learned nothing else, we have learned this: humans can walk away from, and forget, *anything*. Civilization can go back to 'normal' after *anything*."

He sits in contemplative silence, for some time. He stares at nothing. He worries, briefly, that he really does know the truth, and that there is nothing anomalous preventing him from knowing it. That it's simple denial. But he won't say that aloud, even here.

He says,

"And I wonder: what was the Foundation's role in this? Were we witness to this anomaly? Were we the ones who defeated it? Did we resist? Negotiate? Participate?

"We are here, now. Intact. We are *back*. To what do we owe that? Did we hide, or run?

"Do we deserve to be back? Have we that right? We failed in our stated objective. These people are gone, and it's useless to pretend that they aren't dead. We failed orders of magnitude harder than we've ever failed before. Despite which, we remain clandestine, and unknown to greater humanity. Which means that no one external to the Foundation can ever hold us accountable for our actions, or lack thereof. If what happened at the O5 Council meeting yesterday is any indication, we will certainly never hold *ourselves* accountable.

"What happened to those people? *My* people. Where are they? No one is *just* dead, no one is merely, *passively* dead. Death is *caused*."

SCP-055 cannot answer him.

He says, his voice rising, "These things happen. And we say to ourselves, 'Never again.' And a hundred years pass. And they *happen. Again.*"

He says, "Last time. The time before this one, the time *none* of us remember, the time for which there is *no* evidence of any kind, but which I now realise must exist. That time, when we told ourselves and each other, 'We must do better,' what did we do differently, from then on, and why didn't it work?"

He says, "What does the Foundation need to be? *Where* does it need to be, and how far is that place from here? Can we see it from here?

"Or is this it?"

He does not know.

And after leaving the containment unit, he knows, he will not even remember the questions.

*

Direct observation is harmful to Nema's species. Her mother died when she was a juvenile, killed instantly when a Foundation researcher took a close-up flash photograph of her face. The Foundation thinks her whole species is extinct, wiped out by infertility and disease, as an indirect result of excessively close Foundation study.

But they are not extinct. Some of them adapted. They fled, across oceans and then inland. They grew thicker antimemetic armour.

Nema is a fully-grown adult *C. gigantes*, a massively vertically elongated quadruped, almost a kilometre tall at the shoulder. As O5-8's motorcade leaves Site 19, she is standing just beyond the Site's perimeter, with a crumpled metaspider in her mouth. She is unable to perceive the motorcade or the Site itself, any more than any human Foundationer can perceive her. They only barely walk the same earth.

The spider is a two-hundred-metre-long bundle of legs, eyes and chitin, long body parts dangling from each side of Nema's jaws. The spider convulses ineffectually. It can't escape. It is the last one. The spiders were numerous, and tasty, but the Ones Who Walk Very Slowly have a broad diet.

Nema bites down, biting through the last of the spider's legs, which begin an achingly slow tumble to the ground, accompanied by a gout of bug juice. Nema tosses the spider's mauled thorax in the air and catches it in the back of her throat. She gulps it down, mostly whole, still twitching. She raises her head and vocalises triumphantly, a deafening, inaudible, infrasonic warble. The call carries all the way to her mate and children, on the horizon.

32765416R00135

ABC-Griffleiste

Die ABC-Griffleiste am Rand dieser Seite hilft dir, den gesuchten Buchstaben im englisch-deutschen oder deutsch-englischen Teil schnell aufzufinden.

Du „greifst" den gesuchten Buchstaben hier am Rand und blätterst mit dem Daumen, bis der gesuchte Buchstabe auf dem Rand der betreffenden Seite auftaucht. Er kommt zweimal vor – einmal im englisch-deutschen und einmal im deutsch-englischen Teil.

Wenn du Linkshänder bist, benutze bitte in gleicher Weise die ABC-Griffleiste am Ende des Buches.

Langenscheidts Schulwörterbuch Englisch

Englisch-Deutsch
Deutsch-Englisch

Neubearbeitung 1996

von

HOLGER FREESE, HELGA KRÜGER

und

BRIGITTE WOLTERS

LANGENSCHEIDT

BERLIN · MÜNCHEN · WIEN
ZÜRICH · NEW YORK

Ergänzende Hinweise, für die wir jederzeit dankbar sind,
bitten wir zu richten an:
Langenscheidt-Verlag, Postfach 40 11 20, 80711 München

| Auflage: | 5. | 4. | 3. | 2. | 1. | Letzte Zahlen |
| Jahr: | 2000 | 1999 | 98 | 97 | 96 | maßgeblich |

© *1996 Langenscheidt KG, Berlin und München*
Druck: Graph. Betriebe Langenscheidt, Berchtesgaden/Obb.
Printed in Germany · ISBN 3-468-13125-9

Vorwort

Mit der vorliegenden Neubearbeitung von Langenscheidts Schulwörterbuch Englisch wurde den schulischen Wünschen und Bedürfnissen noch besser Rechnung getragen.

Der Wortschatz wurde grundlegend aktualisiert. Das Hauptaugenmerk galt der lebendigen Alltagssprache. Zahlreiche neue Wörter und Wendungen wurden aufgenommen. Den Schüler besonders interessierende Gebiete wie Sport, Spiel, Computer, Elektronik, Umwelt usw. wurden ebenso berücksichtigt wie der österreichische und schweizerische Sprachgebrauch.

Viele Artikel wurden neu gegliedert oder völlig neu geschrieben. Die wichtigsten Ländernamen und Abkürzungen wurden in den Hauptteil aufgenommen. Neu ist auch die Einführung von Betonungsakzenten in englischen Stichwörtern.

Bewährte Features wie die schülerfreundlichen Benutzerhinweise, die Symbole zur Warnung vor falscher Anwendung und die Angaben zur Grammatik beim englischen Stichwort wurden beibehalten. Um zu vereinheitlichen, wurden dagegen die bildlichen Zeichen zur Bezeichnung der Sachgebiete in Abkürzungen umgewandelt.

Eine neue Typographie, die strikte alphabetische Anordnung der Stichwörter und weniger Tilden sorgen für eine bessere Lesbarkeit und ein schnelleres Auffinden von Wörtern und Wendungen und machen das Wörterbuch noch schülergerechter.

Das Schulwörterbuch bietet rund 55 000 Stichwörter und Wendungen. Wir hoffen, daß es auch weiterhin das beliebte und handliche Nachschlagewerk in der Schule bleiben wird.

LANGENSCHEIDT

Inhaltsverzeichnis

Wie benutzt du das Schulwörterbuch?

Keine Angst vor unbekannten Wörtern!

Das Schulwörterbuch tut alles, um dir das Nachschlagen und das Kennenlernen eines Wortes so leicht wie möglich zu machen.

Damit du von deinem Wörterbuch den besten Gebrauch machen kannst, solltest du wissen, wie und wo du all die Informationen finden kannst, die du für deine Übersetzungen in der Schule, deinen Brief an einen englischen Freund oder eine englische Freundin oder zum Sprechen brauchst. Die folgenden Seiten sollen dir dabei helfen.

1. Wie und wo findest du ein Wort?

1.1 Englische und deutsche Stichwörter. Das Wörterverzeichnis ist alphabetisch geordnet und verzeichnet auch die unregelmäßigen Formen an ihrer alphabetischen Stelle.

Im deutsch-englischen Teil haben wir die Umlaute *ä ö ü* wie *a o u* und *ß* wie *ss* behandelt.

1.2 Im deutsch-englischen Teil werden Stichwörter, die auf **-in** enden, folgendermaßen gegeben:

Ärztin *f* – **Erbin** *f*

1.2.1 Wo dies möglich ist, wird bei einigen Stichwörtern die weibliche Endung **-in** in Klammern an die männliche Form angehängt, z. B. **Eiskunstläufer(in)**
(Siehe auch Seite 15/9.1 b.)

1.3 Leitwörter

Wenn du ein englisches oder deutsches Wort suchst, kannst du dich an den fettgedruckten **Leitwörtern** oder **Kolumnentiteln** in der oberen Ecke jeder Seite orientieren. Angegeben werden dir in diesen Leitwörtern jeweils (links) das *erste* fettgedruckte Wort auf der linken Seite bzw. (rechts) das *letzte* fettgedruckte Wort auf der rechten Seite, z. B. auf den Seiten 90 u. 91:

determined – direct

1.3.1 Du wirst aber auch einmal einen Begriff nachschlagen wollen, der aus zwei einzelnen Wörtern besteht, wie z. B. **falling star**, oder bei dem die Wörter mit einem Bindestrich (hyphen) miteinander verbunden sind, wie in **absent-minded**. Diese Wörter werden wie ein einziges Wort behandelt und dementsprechend alphabetisch eingeordnet.

1.3.2 Aus Gründen der Platzersparnis wirst du häufig einige zusammengesetzte Wörter nicht an ihrer alphabetischen Stelle finden. In solchen Fällen solltest du unter den Einzelbestandteilen an ihrer alphabetischen Stelle nachsehen. Du kannst dir dann meist die Übersetzung des zusammengesetzten Wortes aus seinen Einzelbestandteilen selbst bilden.

1.4 Du wirst beim Nachschlagen auch merken, daß eine Menge sogenannter „Wortfamilien" entstanden sind. Das sind Stichwortartikel, die von einem gemeinsamen Stamm oder Grundwort ausgehen und deshalb in einem „Nest" zusammenstehen:

depen|dable – ~dant – ~dence - ~dent
left – ~hand – ~handed

2. Wie schreibst du das Wort?

2.1 Du kannst in deinem Wörterbuch genau wie in einem Rechtschreibwörterbuch nachschlagen, wie ein Wort richtig geschrieben wird. Die Unterschiede in der **amerikanischen Schreibung** haben wir dir in den betreffenden Stichwörtern und Übersetzungen gegeben und mit *Am.* gekennzeichnet. Fällt bei der amerikanischen Schreibweise nur ein Buchstabe weg, so steht dieser in runden Klammern:

colo(u)r – hono(u)r – travel(l)er

2.2 Die amerikanische Rechtschreibung

weicht von der britischen hauptsächlich in folgenden Punkten ab:

1. Für **...our** tritt **...or** ein, z. B. hon*or* = honour, lab*or* = labour.

2. **...re** wird zu **...er**, z. B. cent*er* = centre, theat*er* = theatre, meag*er* = meagre; ausgenommen sind og*re* und die Wörter auf ...cre, z. B. massa*cre*, na*cre*.

3. Statt **...ce** steht **...se**, z. B. defen*se* = defence, licen*se* = licence.

4. Bei sämtlichen Ableitungen der Verben auf **...l** und **...p** unterbleibt die Verdoppelung des Endkonsonanten, also travel – trave*led* – trave*ling* – trave*ler*, worship – worshi*ped* – worshi*ping* – worshi*per*. Auch in einigen anderen Wörtern wird der Doppelkonsonant durch einen einfachen ersetzt, z. B. wagon = waggon, woo*len* = woollen.

5. Ein stummes **e** wird in gewissen Fällen weggelassen, z. B. abrid*gment* = abridgment, acknowled*gment* = acknowledgment, jud*gment* = judgement, ax*e* = axe, good-by = good-bye.

6. Bei einigen Wörtern mit der Vorsilbe **en...** gibt es auch noch die Schreibung **in...**, z. B. *in*close = enclose, *in*snare = ensnare.

7. Der Schreibung **ae** und **oe** wird oft diejenige mit **e** vorgezogen, z. B. ane-mia = anaemia, diarrhea = diarrhoea.

8. Aus dem Französischen stammende stumme Endsilben werden gern weggelassen, z. B. catalog = catalo*gue*, program = program*me*, prolog = prolo*gue*.

9. Einzelfälle sind: st*a*nch = staunch, mold = mould, m*o*lt = moult, g*ra*y = grey, pl*o*w = plough, ski*l*ful = skilful, t*i*re = tyre.

3. Wie trennst du das Wort?

3.1 Die Silbentrennung im Englischen ist für einen Deutschen ein heikles Kapitel. Im Schulwörterbuch mußt du nur darauf achten, wo zwischen den Silben ein halbhoher Punkt steht.

Die Silbentrennungspunkte zeigen dir, an welcher Stelle im Wort du am Zeilenende trennen kannst. Du solltest es aber vermeiden, nur einen Buchstaben abzutrennen, wie z. B. in **a-mend** oder **thirst·y**. Hier nimmst du besser das ganze Wort auf die neue Zeile.

3.2 Fällt bei einem englischen Wort, das mit einem Bindestrich geschrieben wird, der Bindestrich im Wörterbuch auf das Zeilenende, so wird er am Anfang der folgenden Zeile wiederholt.

4. Die Tilde

4.1 Ein Symbol, das dir ständig in den Stichwortartikeln begegnet, ist ein Wiederholungszeichen: die Tilde (~ ℒ). Die fette Tilde (~) vertritt dabei entweder das ganze Stichwort oder den vor dem senkrechten Strich (|) stehenden Teil des Stichwortes. Die weniger fette Tilde (~) vertritt das unmittelbar vorausgehende Stichwort, das selbst schon mit Hilfe der fetten Tilde gebildet sein kann:

football ... **~ player** (= *football player*)
happi|ly ... **~ness** (= *happiness*)
ab|blasen ... **~bringen: j-n von** ... **~** (= *abbringen*)

4.2 Wechselt die Schreibung von klein zu groß oder von groß zu klein, steht statt der einfachen Tilde (~) die Kreistilde (ℒ):

representative ... *House of* **ℒs** (= *House of Representatives*)
Geschicht|e ... **ℒlich** (= *geschichtlich*)
dick ... **ℒkopf** (= *Dickkopf*)

5. Was bedeuten die verschiedenen Schriftarten?

5.1 Du findest **fettgedruckt** alle englischen und deutschen Stichwörter, außerdem die arabischen Ziffern zur Unterscheidung der Wortarten:

feed ... **1.** Futter *n*; ... **2.** (*fed*) *v/t.* füttern; **~back**
klopfen 1. *v/i. Herz, Puls:* beat*; ... **2.** *v/t.* beat*

5.2 Du findest *kursiv* a) die Grammatik- und Sachgebietsabkürzungen: *adj., adv., v/i., v/t., econ., pol.* usw., b) die Genusangaben (Angaben des Geschlechtswortes): *m, f, n,* c) alle Zusätze, die eine nähere Angabe oder Sinnverdeutlichung bewirken sollen, wie z. B.

file[1] ... *Computer:* Datei *f*
pad ... *Sport:* (*Bein-, Knie*)Schützer *m*
scan ... *Zeitung etc.* überfliegen
matt ... *Glas, Glühbirne:* frosted

5.3 Du findest in *halbfetter Auszeichnungsschrift* alle Wendungen:

line ... *hold the* ~ *tel.* bleiben Sie am Apparat

depend ... *that* ~s das kommt (ganz) darauf an

gut ... *ganz* ~ not bad

5.4 Du findest in normaler Schrift alle Übersetzungen.

6. Wie sprichst du das Wort aus?

6.1 Die Lautschrift beschreibt, wie du ein Wort aussprechen sollst. So ist das „ch" in „ich" ein ganz anderer Laut als das „ch" in „ach". Da die normale Schrift für solche Unterschiede keine Hilfe bietet, ist es nötig, diese Laute mit anderen Zeichen zu beschreiben. Damit *jeder* genau weiß, welches Zeichen welchem Laut entspricht, hat man sich international auf eine Lautschrift geeinigt. Wenn du diese Zeichen lernst, kannst du jedes Wort in jeder Sprache aussprechen. Da die Zeichen von der **I**nternational **P**honetic **A**ssociation als verbindlich angesehen werden, nennt man sie auch **IPA-Lautschrift**.

Im Wörterbuch wird in den eckigen Klammern – [ ] – beschrieben, wie du das entsprechende englische Stichwort aussprechen mußt, z. B.:

coat [kəʊt] – **message** ['mesɪdʒ]

6.2 Für das Englische solltest du dir daher die folgenden Lautschriftzeichen einprägen:

[ʌ]	much [mʌtʃ], come [kʌm]	kurzes *a* wie in *Matsch*, *Kamm*, aber dunkler
[ɑ:]	after ['ɑːftə], park [pɑːk]	langes *a*, etwa wie in *Bahn*
[æ]	flat [flæt], madam ['mædəm]	mehr zum *a* hin als *ä* in *Wäsche*
[ə]	after ['ɑːftə], arrival [ə'raɪvl]	wie das End-*e* in *Berge*, *mache*, *bitte*
[e]	let [let], men [men]	*ä* wie in *hätte*, *Mäntel*
[ɜ:]	first [fɜːst], learn [lɜːn]	etwa wie *ir* in *flirten*, aber offener
[ɪ]	in [ɪn], city ['sɪtɪ]	kurzes *i* wie in *Mitte*, *billig*
[iː]	see [siː], evening ['iːvnɪŋ]	langes *i* wie in *nie*, *lieben*
[ɒ]	shop [ʃɒp], job [dʒɒb]	wie *o* in *Gott*, aber offener
[ɔ:]	morning ['mɔːnɪŋ], course [kɔːs]	wie in *Lord*, aber ohne *r*
[ʊ]	good [gʊd], look [lʊk]	kurzes *u* wie in *Mutter*
[uː]	too [tuː], shoot [ʃuːt]	langes *u* wie in *Schuh*, aber offener

[aɪ]	my [maɪ], night [naɪt]	etwa wie in *Mai*, *Neid*
[aʊ]	now [naʊ], about [əˈbaʊt]	etwa wie in *blau*, *Couch*
[əʊ]	home [həʊm], know [nəʊ]	von [ə] zu [ʊ] gleiten
[eə]	air [eə], square [skweə]	wie *är* in *Bär*, aber kein *r* sprechen
[eɪ]	eight [eɪt], stay [steɪ]	klingt wie *äi*
[ɪə]	near [nɪə], here [hɪə]	von [ɪ] zu [ə] gleiten
[ɔɪ]	join [dʒɔɪn], choice [tʃɔɪs]	etwa wie *eu* in *neu*
[ʊə]	you're [jʊə], tour [tʊə]	wie *ur* in *Kur*, aber kein *r* sprechen
[j]	yes [jes], tube [tju:b]	wie *j* in *jetzt*
[w]	way [weɪ], one [wʌn], quick [kwɪk]	mit gerundeten Lippen ähnlich wie [u:] gebildet. Kein deutsches *w*!
[ŋ]	thing [θɪŋ], English [ˈɪŋglɪʃ]	wie *ng* in *Ding*
[r]	room [ru:m], hurry [ˈhʌrɪ]	Zunge liegt, zurückgebogen, am Gaumen auf. Nicht gerollt und nicht im Rachen gebildet!
[s]	see [si:], famous [ˈfeɪməs]	stimmloses *s* wie in *lassen*, *Liste*
[z]	zero [ˈzɪərəʊ], is [ɪz], runs [rʌnz]	stimmhaftes *s* wie in *lesen*, *Linsen*
[ʃ]	shop [ʃɒp], fish [fɪʃ]	wie *sch* in *Scholle*, *Fisch*
[tʃ]	cheap [tʃi:p], much [mʌtʃ]	wie *tsch* in *tschüs*, *Matsch*
[ʒ]	television [ˈtelɪvɪʒn]	stimmhaftes *sch* wie in *Genie*, *Etage*
[dʒ]	just [dʒʌst], bridge [brɪdʒ]	wie in *Job*, *Gin*
[θ]	thanks [θæŋks], both [bəʊθ]	wie *ß* in *Faß*, aber gelispelt
[ð]	that [ðæt], with [wɪð]	wie *s* in *Sense*, aber gelispelt
[v]	very [ˈverɪ], over [ˈəʊvə]	etwa wie deutsches *w*, Oberzähne auf Oberkante der Unterlippe
[x]	loch [lɒx], ugh [ʌx]	wie *ch* in *ach*
[:]	bedeutet, daß der vorhergehende Vokal lang zu sprechen ist.	

6.2.1 Endsilben ohne Lautschrift

Um Raum zu sparen, werden die häufigsten Endungen der englischen Stichwörter hier einmal mit Lautschrift aufgelistet. Sie erscheinen im Wörterverzeichnis in der Regel ohne Umschrift.

-ability [-əˈbɪlətɪ]
-able [-əbl]
-age [-ɪdʒ]
-al [-əl]
-ally [-əlɪ]
-an [-ən]
-ance [-əns]
-ancy [-ənsɪ]
-ant [-ənt]
-ar [-ə]
-ary [-ərɪ]
-ation [-eɪʃn]
-cious [-ʃəs]

-cy [-sɪ]
-dom [-dəm]
-ed [-d; -t; -ɪd]*
-edness [-dnɪs;
  -tnɪs; -ɪdnɪs]*
-ee [-i:]
-en [-n]
-ence [-əns]
-ency [-ənsɪ]
-ent [-ənt]
-er [-ə]
-ery [-ərɪ]
-ess [-ɪs]

-fication [-fɪˈkeɪʃn]
-ful [-fl]
-hood [-hʊd]
-ial [-jəl; -ɪəl]
-ian [-jən; -ɪən]
-ible [-əbl]
-ic(s) [-ɪk(s)]
-ical [-ɪkl]
-ily [-ɪlɪ; -əlɪ]
-iness [-ɪnɪs]
-ing [-ɪŋ]
-ish [-ɪʃ]
-ism [-ɪzəm]

-ist [-ıst]	-ly [-lı]	-sive [-sıv]
-istic [-ıstık]	-ment(s) [-mənt(s)]	-some [-səm]
-ite [-aıt]	-ness [-nıs]	-ties [-tız]
-ity [-ətı; -ıtı]	-oid [-ɔıd]	-tion [-ʃn]
-ive [-ıv]	-o(u)r [-ə]	-tional [-ʃənl]
-ization [-aı'zeıʃn]	-ous [-əs]	-tious [-ʃəs]
-ize [-aız]	-ry [-rı]	-trous [-trəs]
-izing [-aızıŋ]	-ship [-ʃıp]	-try [-trı]
-less [-lıs]	-ssion [-ʃn]	-y [-ı]

* [-d] nach Vokalen und stimmhaften Konsonanten
  [-t] nach stimmlosen Konsonanten
  [-id] nach auslautendem d und t
  [-z] nach Vokalen und stimmhaften Konsonanten
  [-s] nach stimmlosen Konsonanten

6.2.2 Die Aussprache des englischen Alphabets

a [eı], b [biː], c [siː], d [diː], e [iː], f [ef], g [dʒiː], h [eıtʃ], i [aı], j [dʒeı], k [keı], l [el], m [em], n [en], o [əʊ], p [piː], q [kjuː], r [ɑː], s [es], t [tiː], u [juː], v [viː], w ['dʌbljuː], x [eks], y [waı], z [zed, *Am.* ziː]

6.3 Betonungsakzente

Die **Betonung** der englischen Wörter wird dir durch das Zeichen ' für den Hauptakzent vor der zu betonenden Silbe angegeben:

on·ion ['ʌnjən]

rec·ord ['rekɔːd] – **re·cord** [rı'kɔːd]

Bei vielen zusammengesetzten Stichwörtern, deren Bestandteile als selbständige Stichwörter mit Ausspracheangabe im Wörterbuch erscheinen, und bei Stichwörtern, die eine der in der Liste der „Endsilben ohne Lautschrift" auf Seite 10 und 11 verzeichneten Endungen aufweisen, werden die Betonungsakzente im Stichwort selbst gegeben.

6.3.1 In einigen Fällen findest du in Stichwörtern, die aus einer Tilde und einem ausgeschriebenen Wort oder Wortteil bestehen, keinen Betonungsakzent. In diesen Fällen gilt der Akzent des tildierten Wortes, z. B.

alarm [ə'lɑːm] – **~ clock** = a'larm clock

distrust [dıs'trʌst] – **~ful** = dis'trustful

6.3.2 Und hier noch ein wichtiger Hinweis: Das im Wörterbuch angegebene Betonungsmuster der einzeln stehenden Stichwörter kann selbstverständlich ganz erheblich von dem Betonungsmuster in einem bestimmten Satzzusammenhang abweichen. Ein ganz einfaches Beispiel: [ɪndɪˈpendənt] in "he's very independent for his age", aber [ˈɪndɪpendənt] in "an independent judgment".

6.4 Amerikaner sprechen viele Wörter anders aus als die Briten. Im Schulwörterbuch geben wir dir aber meistens nur die britische Aussprache, wie du sie auch in deinen Lehrbüchern findest. Ein paar Regeln für die Abweichungen in der amerikanischen Aussprache wollen wir dir hier aber doch geben.

Die amerikanische Aussprache

weicht hauptsächlich in folgenden Punkten von der britischen ab:

1. ɑ: wird zu (gedehntem) æ(:) in Wörtern wie *ask* [æ(:)sk = ɑ:sk], *castle* [ˈkæ(:)sl = ˈkɑ:sl], *grass* [græ(:)s = grɑːs], *past* [pæ(:)st = pɑːst] etc.; ebenso in *branch* [bræ(:)ntʃ = brɑːntʃ], *can't* [kæ(:)nt = kɑːnt], *dance* [dæ(:)ns = dɑːns] etc.

2. ɒ wird zu ɑ in Wörtern wie *common* [ˈkɑmən = ˈkɒmən], *not* [nɑt = nɒt], *on* [ɑn = ɒn], *rock* [rɑk = rɒk], *bond* [bɑnd = bɒnd] und vielen anderen.

3. juː wird zu uː, z. B. *due* [duː = djuː], *duke* [duːk = djuːk], *new* [nuː = njuː].

4. r zwischen vorhergehendem Vokal und folgendem Konsonant wird stimmhaft gesprochen, indem die Zungenspitze gegen den harten Gaumen zurückgezogen wird, z. B. *clerk* [klɜːrk = klɑːk], *hard* [hɑːrd = hɑːd]; ebenso im Auslaut, z. B. *far* [fɑːr = fɑː], *her* [hɜːr = hɜː].

5. Anlautendes p, t, k in unbetonter Silbe (nach betonter Silbe) wird zu b, d, g abgeschwächt, z. B. in *property*, *water*, *second*.

6. Der Unterschied zwischen stark- und schwachbetonten Silben ist viel weniger ausgeprägt; längere Wörter haben einen deutlichen Nebenton, z. B. *dictionary* [ˈdɪkʃə͵neri = ˈdɪkʃənrɪ], *inventory* [ˈɪnvən͵tɔːri = ˈɪnvəntrɪ], *secretary* [ˈsekrə͵teri = ˈsekrətrɪ].

7. Vor, oft auch nach nasalen Konsonanten (m, n, ŋ) sind Vokale und Diphthonge nasal gefärbt, z. B. *stand*, *time*, *small*.

7. Was sagen dir die Symbole und Abkürzungen?

7.1 Das Schulwörterbuch verwendet zwei Symbole:

a) das Symbol ⚠, das vor beliebten Fehlerquellen warnt, z. B.

actual ... ⚠ *nicht* **aktuell**   **sensibel** ... ⚠ *nicht* **sensible**

b) den Stern (*), mit dem im deutsch-englischen Teil alle unregelmäßigen Verben in den englischen Übersetzungen gekennzeichnet werden, um dich vor der Bildung falscher Formen zu bewahren, z. B.

beweisen ... prove*; *Interesse etc.*: show*

(Siehe auch Seite 15/9.3.)

7.2 Die Abkürzung F weist dich darauf hin, daß du das Wort oder die Wendung in der Umgangssprache gebrauchen sollst. Die Abkürzung V warnt vor einem Tabuwort, daß du möglichst nicht anwenden solltest.

7.2.1 Im deutsch-englischen Teil zeigt dir ein F vor dem deutschen oder englischen Teil eines Beispielsatzes, daß nur dieser betreffende Teil umgangssprachlich gebraucht wird. Ein F: vor dem deutschen Teil hingegen zeigt, daß Beispiel und Übersetzung derselben sprachlichen Ebene angehören.

7.3 Die Abkürzungen in *kursiver* Schrift zeigen dir, in welchem Lebens-, Arbeits- und Fachbereich ein Wort am häufigsten benutzt wird. **Die Liste der Abkürzungen findest du ganz am Ende des Buches.**

8. Einige Worte zu den Übersetzungen

8.1 Du wirst bereits gemerkt haben, daß ein Stichwort meist mehrere sinnverwandte Übersetzungen hat, die durch Komma voneinander getrennt werden. Das Stichwort kann aber auch mehrere Bedeutungen haben, je nachdem in welchem Zusammenhang es gebraucht wird.

8.2 Mehrere Bedeutungen eines Wortes erkennst du daran, daß sie durch ein Semikolon voneinander getrennt sind. Häufig sind die Bedeutungen eines Wortes aber so umfangreich oder so unabhängig voneinander, daß die Trennung durch das Semikolon nicht genügt. Hier benutzen wir verschiedene Unterteilungsmöglichkeiten.

a) Das Wort wird wiederholt und mit einer hochgestellten Zahl (einem Exponenten) geschrieben:

chap¹ ... Riß *m*   **Bank¹** *f* bench

chap² ... Bursche *m*   **Bank²** *econ. f* bank

b) Wenn die Wortart wechselt, werden die Übersetzungen mit fettgedruckten arabischen Ziffern unterteilt:

work ...   **1.** Arbeit *f* (*Substantiv*)

          2. *v/i.* arbeiten (*Verb*)

green ...   **1.** grün (*Adjektiv*)

          2. Grün *n* (*Substantiv*)

c) Im deutsch-englischen Teil stehen die fettgedruckten arabischen Ziffern auch zur Unterscheidung von transitiven, intransitiven und reflexiven Verben:

stutzen 1. *v/t.* trim ...

          2. *v/i.* stop short ...

8.3 Sicher weißt du bereits, daß ein Engländer z. B. **pavement** sagt, wenn er den „Bürgersteig" meint, der Amerikaner spricht dagegen von **sidewalk** – und **fall** hat im amerikanischen Englisch auch noch die Bedeutung „Herbst".

Im Wörterbuch sind solche Wörter mit *Brt.* für britisches Englisch und *Am.* für amerikanisches Englisch gekennzeichnet.

9. Grammatik auch im Wörterbuch?

Auf die Kennzeichnung der verschiedenen Wortarten haben wir bereits hingewiesen (siehe Seite 8/5).

9.1 Substantive (Hauptwörter) sind durch die Genusangabe (Angabe des Geschlechtswortes) zu erkennen:

wall Wand *f* – **Wand** *f* wall

Dazu noch einige Besonderheiten des Schulwörterbuchs:

a) im englisch-deutschen Teil:

dependant ... Angehörige(r *m*) *f* = Angehöriger *m*, Angehörige *f*

accomplice ... Kompli|ze *m*, -zin *f* = Komplize *m*, Komplizin *f*

b) im deutsch-englischen Teil:

Angestellte(r) = **Angestellter** *m*
Schauspieler(in) act|or (-ress) = **Schauspieler** *m* actor,
           Schauspielerin *f* actress

9.2 Häufig kannst du den grammatisch richtigen Gebrauch eines Wortes aus den dazugehörigen „Zusätzen" entnehmen:

dissent ... anderer Meinung sein (*from* als) ...
dissimilar ... (*to*) unähnlich (*dat.*); verschieden (von) ...
fish (*pl.* **fish, fishes**) Fisch *m*
sheep (*pl.* **sheep**) Schaf *n*
see (*saw, seen*) sehen
angry ... (*-ier, -iest*) zornig, verärgert ...
(Siehe auch 9.4)
abrücken 1. *v/t.* move away (*von* from) ...
befestigen *v/t.* fasten (*an* to), fix (to), attach (to) ...

9.3 Im deutsch-englischen Teil haben wir dir in der englischen Übersetzung die *unregelmäßigen englischen Verben* mit einem * gekennzeichnet.

Siehe auch im Anhang die Liste der unregelmäßigen englischen Verben auf Seite 620–621.

9.4 Im englisch-deutschen Teil zeigt dir die runde Klammer nach der eckigen Klammer für die Aussprache, daß hier eine grammatische Besonderheit vorliegt.

a) **unregelmäßiger**
   Plural

> **child** ... (*pl.* **children**)
> **knife** ... (*pl.* **knives**)
> **a·nal·y·sis** ... (*pl.* **-ses** [-si:z])
>   = **analyses**
> **to·ma·to** ... (*pl.* **-toes**)
>   = **tomatoes**, im Vergleich zur
>   regelmäßigen Pluralbildung:
> **ra·di·o** ... (*pl.* **-os**) = **radios**

16

b) unregelmäßige Verben (siehe auch Liste der unregelmäßigen englischen Verben auf den Seiten 620–621)

> **go** ... (*went, gone*) = *pret.* **went**, *p.p.* **gone**
> **shut** ... (*shut*) = *pret. u. p.p.* **shut**
> **learn** ... (*learned od. learnt*) = *pret. u. p.p.* **learned** *od.* **learnt**
> **out·grow** ... (*-grew, -grown*) = *pret.* **outgrew**, *p.p.* **outgrown**

c) Verdoppelung der Endkonsonanten nach kurzen, betonten Vokalen – im britischen Englisch bei -l auch in unbetonten Silben

> **hit** ... (*-tt-*) = *hitting*
> **jot** ... (*-tt-*) = *jotting; jotted*
> **trav·el** ... (*bsd. Brt. -ll-, Am. -l-*) = *bsd. Brt.* **travelling**, *Am.* **traveling**

c und b)

> **shut** ... (*-tt-; shut*)
> **hit** ... (*-tt-; hit*)
> **out·bid** ... (*-dd-; -bid*)

d) Auslautendes -c wird zu -ck vor *-ed, -er, -ing* und *-y*

> **frol·ic** ... (*-ck-*) = *frolicking*
> **pan·ic** ... (*-ck-*) = *panicked*

e) Steigerungsformen

-y wird zu -i
-e entfällt bei der regelmäßigen Steigerung mit -er und -est

> **good** ... (*better, best*) = Komparativ **better**, Superlativ **best**
> **an·gry** ... (*-ier, -iest*) = **angrier, angriest**
> **sore** ... (*~r, ~st*) = **sorer, sorest**

) **Adverbbildung**

> **authentic ... (~*ally*) =**
> ***authentically***

Die vorausgegangenen Seiten sind Beispiele dafür, daß dir das Wörterbuch mehr bietet als nur einfache Wort-für-Wort-Gleichungen, wie du sie in den Vokabelteilen von Lehrbüchern findest.

Und nun viel Erfolg bei der Suche nach den richtigen Wörtern!

Englisch-Deutsches Wörterverzeichnis

A

A, a [eɪ] A, a *n*; *from A to Z* von A bis Z

A [eɪ] *Note* Eins

a [ə, *betont:* eɪ], *vor Vokal:* **an** [ən, *betont:* æn] *unbestimmter Artikel:* ein(e); per, pro, je; *not a(n)* kein(e); *all of a size* alle gleich groß; *£10 a year* zehn Pfund im Jahr; *twice a week* zweimal die *od.* in der Woche

a·back [ə'bæk] *taken* ~ überrascht, verblüfft; bestürzt

a·ban·don [ə'bændən] auf-, preisgeben; verlassen; überlassen; **~ed:** *be found* ~ verlassen aufgefunden werden (*Fahrzeug etc.*)

a·base [ə'beɪs] erniedrigen, demütigen; **~ment** Erniedrigung *f*, Demütigung *f*

a·bashed [ə'bæʃt] verlegen

ab·at·toir ['æbətwɑː] Schlachthof *m*

ab·bess ['æbɪs] Äbtissin *f*

ab·bey ['æbɪ] Kloster *n*; Abtei *f*

ab·bot ['æbət] Abt *m*

ab·bre·vi·ate [ə'briːvɪeɪt] (ab)kürzen; **~a·tion** [əbriːvɪ'eɪʃn] Abkürzung *f*, Kurzform *f*

ABC¹ [eɪ biː 'siː] Abc *n*, Alphabet *n*

ABC² [eɪ biː 'siː] *Abk. für American Broadcasting Company* (*amer. Rundfunkgesellschaft*)

ab·di·cate ['æbdɪkeɪt] Amt, Recht etc. aufgeben, verzichten auf (*acc.*); **~ (from) the throne** abdanken; **~ca·tion** [æbdɪ'keɪʃn] Verzicht *m*; Abdankung *f*

ab·do·men *anat.* ['æbdəmən] Unterleib *m*; **ab·dom·i·nal** *anat.* [æb'dɒmɪnl] Unterleibs...

ab·duct *jur.* [əb'dʌkt] *j-n* entführen

a·bet [ə'bet] (*-tt-*) → **aid** 1

ab·hor [əb'hɔː] (*-rr-*) verabscheuen; **~rence** [əb'hɒrəns] Abscheu *m* (*of vor dat.*); **~rent** [əb'hɒrənt] zuwider (*to dat.*); abstoßend

a·bide [ə'baɪd] *v/i.* ~ *by the law, etc.* sich an das Gesetz *etc.* halten; *v/t.* **I can't** ~ **him** ich kann ihn nicht ausstehen

a·bil·i·ty [ə'bɪlətɪ] Fähigkeit *f*

ab·ject ['æbdʒekt] verächtlich, erbärm-

lich; *in* ~ *poverty* in äußerster Armut

ab·jure [əb'dʒʊə] abschwören; entsagen (*dat.*)

a·blaze [ə'bleɪz] in Flammen; *fig.* glänzend, funkelnd (*with vor dat.*)

a·ble ['eɪbl] fähig; geschickt; *be* ~ *to* imstande *od.* in der Lage sein zu, können; **~'bod·ied** kräftig

ab·nor·mal [æb'nɔːml] abnorm, ungewöhnlich; anomal

a·board [ə'bɔːd] an Bord; *all* ~! *naut.* alle Mann *od.* Reisenden an Bord!; *rail.* alles einsteigen!; ~ *a bus* in e-m Bus; *go* ~ *a train* in e-n Zug einsteigen

a·bode [ə'bəʊd] *a. place of* ~ Aufenthaltsort *m*, Wohnsitz *m*; *of od.* **with no fixed** ~ ohne festen Wohnsitz

a·bol·ish [ə'bɒlɪʃ] abschaffen, aufheben; **ab·o·li·tion** [æbə'lɪʃn] Abschaffung *f*, Aufhebung *f*

A-bomb ['eɪbɒm] → *atom(ic) bomb*

a·bom·i·na·ble [ə'bɒmɪnəbl] abscheulich, scheußlich; **~nate** [ə'bɒmɪneɪt] verabscheuen; **~na·tion** [əbɒmɪ'neɪʃn] Abscheu *m*

ab·o·rig·i·nal [æbə'rɪdʒənl] **1.** eingeboren, Ur...; **2.** Ureinwohner *m*

ab·o·rig·i·ne [æbə'rɪdʒəniː] Ureinwohner *m* (*bsd. Australiens*)

a·bort [ə'bɔːt] *v/t. med.* Schwangerschaft abbrechen, Kind abtreiben; *Raumflug etc.* abbrechen; *v/i.* e-e Fehlgeburt haben; *fig.* fehlschlagen, scheitern; **a·bor·tion** *med.* [ə'bɔːʃn] Fehlgeburt *f*; Schwangerschaftsabbruch *m*, Abtreibung *f*; *have an* ~ abtreiben (lassen); **a·bor·tive** [ə'bɔːtɪv] mißlungen, erfolglos

a·bound [ə'baʊnd] reichlich vorhanden sein; Überfluß haben, reich sein (*in an dat.*); voll sein (*with von*)

a·bout [ə'baʊt] **1.** *prp.* um (...herum); bei (*dat.*); (irgendwo) herum in (*dat.*); um, gegen, etwa; im Begriff, dabei; über (*acc.*); **I had no money** ~ **me** ich hatte kein Geld bei mir; *what are you* ~? was macht ihr da?; **2.** *adv.* herum,

umher; in der Nähe; etwa, ungefähr
a·bove [ə'bʌv] **1.** *prp.* über, oberhalb; *fig.* über, erhaben über; **~** *all* vor allem; **2.** *adv.* oben; darüber; **3.** *adj.* obig, obenerwähnt

a·breast [ə'brest] nebeneinander; *keep* **~** *of*, *be* **~** *of* *fig.* Schritt halten mit

a·bridge [ə'brɪdʒ] (ab-, ver)kürzen; **a'bridg(e)·ment** Kürzung *f*; Kurzfassung *f*

a·broad [ə'brɔːd] im *od.* ins Ausland; überall(hin); *the news soon spread* **~** die Nachricht verbreitete sich rasch

a·brupt [ə'brʌpt] abrupt; jäh; schroff

ab·scess *med.* ['æbsɪs] Abszeß *m*

ab·sence ['æbsəns] Abwesenheit *f*; Mangel *m*

ab·sent 1. ['æbsənt] abwesend; fehlend; nicht vorhanden; *be* **~** fehlen (*from school* in der Schule; *from work* am Arbeitsplatz); **2.** [æb'sent]: **~** *o.s. from* fernbleiben (*dat.*) *od.* von; **~·mind·ed** [æbsənt'maɪndɪd] zerstreut, geistesabwesend

ab·so·lute ['æbsəluːt] absolut; unumschränkt; vollkommen; *chem.* rein, unvermischt; unbedingt

ab·so·lu·tion *rel.* [æbsə'luːʃn] Absolution *f*

ab·solve [əb'zɒlv] frei-, lossprechen; △ *nicht* **absolvieren**

ab·sorb [əb'sɔːb] absorbieren, auf-, einsaugen; *fig.* ganz in Anspruch nehmen; **~·ing** *fig.* fesselnd, packend

ab·stain [əb'steɪn] sich enthalten (*from gen.*)

ab·ste·mi·ous [æb'stiːmɪəs] enthaltsam; mäßig

ab·sten·tion [əb'stenʃn] Enthaltung *f*; *pol.* Stimmenthaltung *f*

ab·sti|·nence ['æbstɪnəns] Abstinenz *f*, Enthaltsamkeit *f*; **'~·nent** abstinent, enthaltsam

ab·stract 1. ['æbstrækt] abstrakt; **2.** ['æbstrækt] *das* Abstrakte; Auszug *m*; **3.** [æb'strækt] abstrahieren; entwenden; *e·n wichtigen Punkt aus e·m Buch etc.* herausziehen; **ab·stract·ed** *fig.* [əb'stræktɪd] zerstreut; **ab·strac·tion** [əb'strækʃn] Abstraktion *f*; abstrakter Begriff

ab·surd [əb'sɜːd] absurd; lächerlich

a·bun|·dance [ə'bʌndəns] Überfluß *m*; Fülle *f*; Überschwang *m* (*a. fig.*); **~·dant**

reich(lich)

a·buse 1. [ə'bjuːs] Mißbrauch *m*; Beschimpfung(en *pl.*) *f*; **~** *of drugs* Drogenmißbrauch *m*; **~** *of power* Machtmißbrauch *m*; **2.** [ə'bjuːz] mißbrauchen; beschimpfen; **a·bu·sive** [ə'bjuːsɪv] beleidigend, Schimpf...

a·but [ə'bʌt] (*-tt-*) (an)grenzen (*on* an)

a·byss [ə'bɪs] Abgrund *m* (*a. fig.*)

a/c, A/C [eɪ 'siː] *Abk. für* **account** (Bank)Konto *n*

AC [eɪ 'siː] *Abk. für* **alternating current** Wechselstrom *m*

ac·a·dem·ic [ækə'demɪk] **1.** Hochschullehrer *m*; △ *nicht* **Akademiker;** **2.** (**~ally**) akademisch; **a·cad·e·mi·cian** [əkædə'mɪʃn] Akademiemitglied *n*; △ *nicht* **Akademiker**

a·cad·e·my [ə'kædəmɪ] Akademie *f*; **~** *of music* Musikhochschule

ac·cede [æk'siːd]: **~** *to* zustimmen (*dat.*); *Amt* antreten; *Thron* besteigen

ac·cel·e·rate [ək'seləreɪt] *v/t.* beschleunigen; *v/i.* schneller werden, *mot. a.* beschleunigen, Gas geben; **~·ra·tion** [əkselə'reɪʃn] Beschleunigung *f*; **~·ra·tor** [ək'seləreɪtə] Gaspedal *n*

ac·cent 1. ['æksənt] Akzent *m* (*a. gr.*); **2.** [æk'sent] → **ac·cen·tu·ate** [æk'sentjʊeɪt] akzentuieren, betonen

ac·cept [ək'sept] annehmen; akzeptieren; hinnehmen; **ac·cep·ta·ble** annehmbar; **ac·cep·tance** Annahme *f*; Aufnahme *f*

ac·cess ['ækses] Zugang *m* (*to* zu); *fig.* Zutritt *m* (*to* bei, zu); *Computer:* Zugriff *m* (*to* auf *acc.*); *easy of* **~** zugänglich (*Person*)

ac·ces·sa·ry *jur.* [ək'sesərɪ] → **accessory**

'ac·cess code *Computer:* Zugriffscode *m*; **ac·ces|·si·ble** [ək'sesəbl] (leicht) zugänglich; **~·sion** [ək'seʃn] (Neu)Anschaffung *f* (*to* für); Zustimmung *f* (*to* zu); Antritt *m* (*e-s Amtes*); **~** *to power* Machtübernahme *f*; **~** *to the throne* Thronbesteigung *f*

ac·ces·so·ry [ək'sesərɪ] *jur.* Komplize *m*, -zin *f*, Mitschuldige(r *m*) *f*; *mst* **accessories** *pl.* Zubehör *n*, *Mode: a.* Accessoires *pl.*; *tech.* Zubehör(teile *pl.*) *n*

'ac·cess| road Zufahrts- *od.* Zubringerstraße *f*; **'~ time** *Computer*, *CD-Player etc.*: Zugriffszeit *f*

ac·ci·dent ['æksɪdənt] Unfall *m*, Unglück(sfall *m*) *n*, Störfall *m* (*Kernkraftwerk*); *by* ~ zufällig; **~·den·tal** [æksɪ'dentl] zufällig; versehentlich

ac·claim [ə'kleɪm] feiern (*as* als)

ac·cla·ma·tion [æklə'meɪʃn] lauter Beifall; Lob *n*

ac·cli·ma·tize [ə'klaɪmətaɪz] (sich) akklimatisieren *od.* eingewöhnen

ac·com·mo|·date [ə'kɒmədeɪt] unterbringen; Platz haben für, fassen; anpassen (*to dat. od.* an *acc.*); **~·da·tion** [əkɒmə'deɪʃn] (*Am. mst pl.*) Unterkunft *f*, -bringung *f*

ac·com·pa|·ni·ment *mus.* [ə'kʌmpənɪmənt] Begleitung *f*; **~·ny** [ə'kʌmpənɪ] begleiten (*a. mus.*)

ac·com·plice [ə'kʌmplɪs] Kompli|ze *m*, -zin *f*

ac·com·plish [ə'kʌmplɪʃ] erreichen; leisten; **~ed** fähig, tüchtig; **~·ment** Fähigkeit *f*, Talent *n*

ac·cord [ə'kɔːd] **1.** Übereinstimmung *f*; △ *nicht Akkord; of one's own* ~ von selbst; *with one* ~ einstimmig; **2.** übereinstimmen; **~·ance:** *in* ~ *with* entsprechend (*dat.*); **~·ing:** ~ *to* laut; nach; **~·ing·ly** (dem)entsprechend; folglich, also

ac·cost [ə'kɒst] *j-n bsd. auf der Straße* ansprechen

ac·count [ə'kaʊnt] **1.** *econ.* Rechnung *f*, Berechnung *f*; *econ.* Konto *n*; Rechenschaft *f*; Bericht *m*; *by all* ~**s** nach allem, was man so hört; *of no* ~ ohne Bedeutung; *on no* ~ auf keinen Fall; *on* ~ *of* wegen; *take into* ~, *take* ~ *of* in Betracht *od.* Erwägung ziehen, berücksichtigen; *turn s.th. to* (*good*) ~ et. (gut) ausnutzen; *keep* ~**s** die Bücher führen; *call to* ~ zur Rechenschaft ziehen; *give* (*an*) ~ *of* Rechenschaft ablegen über (*acc.*); *give an* ~ *of* Bericht erstatten über (*acc.*); **2.** *v/i.* ~ *for* Rechenschaft über *et.* ablegen; (sich) erklären; **ac·count·a·ble** verantwortlich; erklärlich; **ac·coun·tant** Buchhalter *m*; **ac·count·ing** Buchführung *f*

acct *nur geschrieb. abbr. für account* Konto *n*

ac·cu·mu|·late [ə'kjuːmjʊleɪt] (sich) (an)häufen *od.* ansammeln; **~·la·tion** [əkjuːmjʊ'leɪʃn] Ansammlung *f*; **~·la·tor** *electr.* [ə'kjuːmjʊleɪtə] Akkumulator *m*

ac·cu·ra·cy ['ækjʊrəsɪ] Genauigkeit *f*; **~·rate** ['ækjʊrət] genau

ac·cu·sa·tion [ækjuː'zeɪʃn] Anklage *f*; An-, Beschuldigung *f*

ac·cu·sa·tive *gr.* [ə'kjuːzətɪv] *a.* ~ *case* Akkusativ *m*

ac·cuse [ə'kjuːz] anklagen; beschuldigen; *the* ~**d** der *od.* die Angeklagte (*m*), Angeklagten *pl.*; **ac·cus·er** Ankläger(in); **ac·cus·ing** anklagend, vorwurfsvoll

ac·cus·tom [ə'kʌstəm] gewöhnen (*to* an *acc.*); ~**ed** gewohnt, üblich; gewöhnt (*to* an *acc.*, zu *inf.*)

AC/DC *sl.* [eɪ sɪ 'diː siː] → *bisexual*

ace [eɪs] As *n* (*a. fig.*); *have an* ~ *up one's sleeve, Am. have an* ~ *in the hole fig.* (noch) e-n Trumpf in der Hand haben; *within an* ~ um ein Haar

ache [eɪk] **1.** schmerzen, weh tun; **2.** *anhaltender* Schmerz

a·chieve [ə'tʃiːv] zustande bringen; Ziel erreichen; **~·ment** Zustandebringen *n*, Ausführung *f*; Leistung *f*

ac·id ['æsɪd] **1.** sauer; *fig.* beißend, bissig; **2.** *chem.* Säure *f*; **a·cid·i·ty** [ə'sɪdətɪ] Säure *f*; **ac·id 'rain** saurer Regen

ac·knowl·edge [ək'nɒlɪdʒ] anerkennen; zugeben; *Empfang* bestätigen; **ac·knowl·edg·e(·)ment** Anerkennung *f*; (Empfangs)Bestätigung *f*; Eingeständnis *n*

a·corn *bot.* ['eɪkɔːn] Eichel *f*

a·cous·tics [ə'kuːstɪks] *pl.* Akustik *f* (*e-s Raumes*)

ac·quaint [ə'kweɪnt] bekannt machen; ~ *s.o. with s.th.* j-m et. mitteilen; *be* ~**ed** *with* kennen; **~·ance** Bekanntschaft *f*; Bekannte(r *m*) *f*

ac·quire [ə'kwaɪə] erwerben; sich aneignen (*Kenntnisse*)

ac·qui·si·tion [ækwɪ'zɪʃn] Erwerb *m*; Anschaffung *f*, Errungenschaft *f*

ac·quit [ə'kwɪt] (*-tt-*) *jur.* freisprechen (*of* von); ~ *o.s. well* s-e Sache gut machen; **~·tal** *jur.* [ə'kwɪtl] Freispruch *m*

a·cre ['eɪkə] Acre *m* (*4047 qm*)

ac·rid ['ækrɪd] scharf, beißend

ac·ro·bat ['ækrəbæt] Akrobat(in); **~·ic** [ækrə'bætɪk] akrobatisch

a·cross [ə'krɒs] **1.** *adv.* (quer) hin- *od.* herüber; quer durch; drüben, auf der anderen Seite; über Kreuz; **2.** *prp.*

(quer) über (*acc.*); (quer) durch; auf der anderen Seite von (*od. gen.*), jenseits (*gen.*); über (*dat.*); **come ~, run ~** stoßen auf (*acc.*)

act [ækt] **1.** *v/i.* handeln; sich verhalten *od.* benehmen; (ein)wirken; funktionieren; (Theater) spielen; *v/t. thea.* spielen (*a. fig.*), *Stück* aufführen; **~ as** fungieren als; **2.** Handlung *f*, Tat *f*; *jur.* Gesetz *n*; *thea.* Akt *m*; **'~ing** *thea.* Spiel(en) *n*

ac·tion ['ækʃn] Handlung *f* (*a. thea.*), Tat *f*; *Film etc.*: Action *f*; Funktionieren *n*; (Ein)Wirkung *f*; *jur.* Klage *f*, Prozeß *m*; *mil.* Gefecht *n*, Einsatz *m*; **take ~** handeln

ac·tive ['æktɪv] aktiv; tätig, rührig; lebhaft, rege; wirksam; *econ.* lebhaft

ac·tiv·ist *bsd. pol.* ['æktɪvɪst] Aktivist(in)

ac·tiv·i·ty [æk'tɪvətɪ] Tätigkeit *f*; Aktivität *f*; Betriebsamkeit *f*; *bsd. econ.* Lebhaftigkeit *f*; **~ hol·i·day** Aktivurlaub *m*

ac·tor ['æktə] Schauspieler *m*; **actress** ['æktrɪs] Schauspielerin *f*

ac·tu·al ['æktʃʊəl] wirklich, tatsächlich, eigentlich; △ *nicht* **aktuell**

ac·u·punc·ture ['ækjʊpʌŋktʃə] Akupunktur *f*

a·cute [ə'kjuːt] (*~r, ~st*) spitz; scharf(sinnig); brennend (*Frage*); *med.* akut

ad F [æd] → **advertisement**

ad·a·mant *fig.* ['ædəmənt] unerbittlich

a·dapt [ə'dæpt] anpassen (**to** *dat. od. an acc.*); *Text* bearbeiten (**from** nach); *tech.* umstellen (**to** auf *acc.*); umbauen (**to** für); **a·dap·ta·ble** [ə'dæptəbl] anpassungsfähig; **ad·ap·ta·tion** [ædæp-'teɪʃn] Anpassung *f*; Bearbeitung *f*; **a·dapt·er, a·dapt·or** *electr.* [ə'dæptə] Adapter *m*

add [æd] *v/t.* hinzufügen; **~ up** zusammenzählen, addieren; *v/i.* **~ to** vermehren, beitragen zu, hinzukommen zu; **~ up** *fig.* F e-n Sinn ergeben

ad·der *zo.* ['ædə] Natter *f*

ad·dict ['ædɪkt] Süchtige(r *m*) *f*; *alcohol* (*drug*) **~** Alkohol- (Drogen- *od.* Rauschgift)Süchtige(r *m*) *f*; *Fußball*etc. Fanatiker(in), *Film- etc.* Narr *m*; **ad·dict·ed** [ə'dɪktɪd] süchtig, abhängig (**to** von); **be ~ to** alcohol *od.* drugs alkohol- *od.* drogenabhängig *od.* -süch-

tig sein; **ad·dic·tion** [ə'dɪkʃn] Sucht *f*, Zustand: a. Süchtigkeit *f*

ad·di·tion [ə'dɪʃn] Hinzufügen *n*; Zusatz *m*; Zuwachs *m*; Anbau *m*; *math.* Addition *f*; **in ~** außerdem; **in ~ to** außer (*dat.*); **~al** [ə'dɪʃənl] zusätzlich

ad·dress [ə'dres] **1.** *Worte* richten (**to** an *acc.*), *j-n* anreden *od.* ansprechen; **2.** Adresse *f*, Anschrift *f*; Rede *f*; Ansprache *f*; **~ee** [ædre'siː] Empfänger(in)

ad·ept ['ædept] erfahren, geschickt (**at, in** in *dat.*)

ad·e·qua·cy ['ædɪkwəsɪ] Angemessenheit *f*; **~quate** ['ædɪkwət] angemessen

ad·here [əd'hɪə] (**to**) kleben, haften (an *dat.*); *fig.* festhalten (an *dat.*); **ad·her·ence** [əd'hɪərəns] Anhaften *n*; *fig.* Festhalten *n*; **ad·her·ent** [əd'hɪərənt] Anhänger(in)

ad·he·sive [əd'hiːsɪv] **1.** klebend; **2.** Klebstoff *m*; **~ 'plas·ter** Heftpflaster *n*; **~ 'tape** Klebeband *n*, Klebstreifen *m*; *Am.* Heftpflaster *n*

ad·ja·cent [ə'dʒeɪsnt] angrenzend, anstoßend (**to** an *acc.*); benachbart

ad·jec·tive *gr.* ['ædʒɪktɪv] Adjektiv *n*, Eigenschaftswort *n*

ad·join [ə'dʒɔɪn] (an)grenzen an (*acc.*)

ad·journ [ə'dʒɜːn] verschieben, (*v/i.* sich) vertagen; **~ment** Vertagung *f*, -schiebung *f*

ad·just [ə'dʒʌst] anpassen; *tech.* einstellen, regulieren; **~a·ble** [ə'dʒʌstəbl] *tech.* verstellbar, regulierbar; **~ment** Anpassung *f*; *tech.* Einstellung *f*

ad·min·is·ter [əd'mɪnɪstə] verwalten; *Arznei* geben, verabreichen; **~ justice** Recht sprechen; **~tra·tion** [ədmɪnɪ-'streɪʃn] Verwaltung *f*; *bsd. Am. pol.* Regierung *f*; Amtsperiode *f* (*e-s Präsidenten*); **~tra·tive** [əd'mɪnɪstrətɪv] Verwaltungs...; **~tra·tor** [əd'mɪnɪstreɪtə] Verwaltungsbeamte(r) *m*

ad·mi·ra·ble ['ædmərəbl] bewundernswert; großartig

ad·mi·ral ['ædmərəl] Admiral *m*

ad·mi·ra·tion [ædmə'reɪʃn] Bewunderung *f*

ad·mire [əd'maɪə] bewundern, verehren; **ad·mir·er** [əd'maɪərə] Verehrer *m*

ad·mis·si·ble [əd'mɪsəbl] zulässig; **~sion** [əd'mɪʃn] Ein-, Zutritt *m*; Aufnahme *f*; Eintritt(sgeld *n*) *m*; Eingeständnis *n*; **~ free** Eintritt frei

ad·mit [əd'mɪt] (**-tt-**) v/t. zugeben; (her)einlassen (**to**, **into** in acc.), eintreten lassen; zulassen (**to** zu); **~·tance** [əd'mɪtəns] Einlaß m. Ein-, Zutritt m; **no** ~ Zutritt verboten

ad·mon·ish [əd'mɒnɪʃ] ermahnen; warnen (**of**, **against** vor dat.)

a·do [ə'duː] (pl. **-dos**) Getue n, Lärm m; **without more** od. **further** ~ ohne weitere Umstände

ad·o·les·cence [ædə'lesns] jugendliches Alter; **~·cent** [ædə'lesnt] **1.** jugendlich, heranwachsend; **2.** Jugendliche(r m) f

a·dopt [ə'dɒpt] adoptieren; übernehmen; **~ed child** Adoptivkind n; **a·dop·tion** [ə'dɒpʃn] Adoption f; **a·dop·tive child** Adoptivkind n; **a·dop·tive par·ents** pl. Adoptiveltern pl.

a·dor·a·ble F [ə'dɔːrəbl] bezaubernd, entzückend; **ad·o·ra·tion** [ædə'reɪʃn] Anbetung f, Verehrung f; **a·dore** [ə'dɔː] anbeten, verehren

a·dorn [ə'dɔːn] schmücken, zieren; **~·ment** Schmuck m

a·droit [ə'drɔɪt] geschickt

ad·ult ['ædʌlt] **1.** erwachsen; **2.** Erwachsene(r m) f; **~s only** nur für Erwachsene!; **~ ed·u·ca·tion** Erwachsenenbildung f

a·dul·ter|·ate [ə'dʌltəreɪt] verfälschen, **Wein** panschen; **~·er** [ə'dʌltərə] Ehebrecher m; **~·ess** [ə'dʌltərɪs] Ehebrecherin f; **~·ous** [ə'dʌltərəs] ehebrecherisch; **~·y** [ə'dʌltərɪ] Ehebruch m

ad·vance [əd'vɑːns] **1.** v/i. vordringen, -rücken (a. **Zeit**); Fortschritte machen; v/t. vorrücken; **Argument** etc. vorbringen; **Geld** vorauszahlen, vorschießen; (be)fördern; **Preis** erhöhen; **Wachstum** etc. beschleunigen; **2.** Vorrücken n, Vorstoß m (a. fig.); Fortschritt m; Vorschuß m; Erhöhung f; **in** ~ im voraus; **~d** fortgeschritten; ~ **for one's years** weit od. reif für sein Alter; **~·ment** Fortschritt m, Verbesserung f

ad·van|·tage [əd'vɑːntɪdʒ] Vorteil m (a. **Sport**); ~ **rule** Vorteilsregel f; **take** ~ **of** ausnutzen; **~·ta·geous** [ædvən'teɪdʒəs] vorteilhaft

ad·ven|·ture [əd'ventʃə] Abenteuer n, Wagnis n; Spekulation f; **~·tur·er** [əd'ventʃərə] Abenteurer m; Spekulant

m; **~·tur·ess** [əd'ventʃərɪs] Abenteu(r)erin f; **~·tur·ous** [əd'ventʃərəs] abenteuerlich; verwegen, kühn

ad·verb gr. ['ædvɜːb] Adverb n, Umstandswort n

ad·ver·sa·ry ['ædvəsərɪ] Gegner(in)

ad·ver|·tise ['ædvətaɪz] ankündigen, bekanntmachen; inserieren; **Reklame** machen (**für**); **~·tise·ment** [əd'vɜːtɪsmənt] Anzeige f, Inserat n; **~·tis·ing** ['ædvətaɪzɪŋ] **1.** Reklame f, Werbung f; **2.** Reklame..., Werbe...; ~ **agency** Werbeagentur f

ad·vice [əd'vaɪs] Rat(schlag) m; econ. Benachrichtigung f; **take medical** ~ e-n Arzt zu Rate ziehen; **take my** ~ hör auf mich; ~ **cen·tre** Brt. Beratungsstelle f

ad·vi·sa·ble [əd'vaɪzəbl] ratsam; **ad·vise** [əd'vaɪz] v/t. j-n beraten; j-m raten; bsd. econ. benachrichtigen, avisieren; v/i. sich beraten; **ad·vis·er** bsd. Brt., **ad·vis·or** Am. [əd'vaɪzə] Berater m; **ad·vi·so·ry** [əd'vaɪzərɪ] beratend

aer·i·al ['eərɪəl] **1.** luftig; Luft...; **2.** Antenne f; ~ **'pho·to·graph**, ~ **'view** Luftaufnahme f, -bild n

ae·ro... ['eərəʊ] Aero..., Luft...

aer·o|·bics [eə'rəʊbɪks] sg. Sport: Aerobic n; **~·drome** bsd. Brt. ['eərədrəʊm] Flugplatz m; **~·dy·nam·ic** [eərəʊdaɪ'næmɪk] (**~·ally**) aerodynamisch; **~·dy·nam·ics** [eərə'nɔːtɪks] sg. Aerodynamik f; **~·nau·tics** [eərə'nɔːtɪks] sg. Luftfahrt f; **~·plane** Brt. ['eərəpleɪn] Flugzeug n; **~·sol** ['eərəsɒl] Sprühdose f

aes·thet·ic [iːs'θetɪk] ästhetisch; **~·s** sg. Ästhetik f

a·far [ə'fɑː]: **from** ~ von weit her

af·fair [ə'feə] Angelegenheit f, Sache f; F Ding n, Sache f; Affäre f

af·fect [ə'fekt] beeinflussen; med. angreifen, befallen; bewegen, rühren; e-e Vorliebe haben für; vortäuschen

af·fec·tion [ə'fekʃn] Liebe f, Zuneigung f; **~·ate** [ə'fekʃnət] liebevoll, herzlich

af·fil·i·ate [ə'fɪlɪeɪt] als **Mitglied** aufnehmen; angliedern

af·fin·i·ty [ə'fɪnətɪ] Affinität f; (geistige) Verwandtschaft; Neigung f (**for**, **to** zu)

af·firm [ə'fɜːm] versichern; beteuern; bestätigen; **af·fir·ma·tion** [æfə'meɪʃn] Versicherung f; Beteuerung f; Bestätigung f; **af·fir·ma·tive** [ə'fɜːmətɪv] **1.**

bejahend; **2. answer in the** ~ bejahen

af·fix [ə'fɪks] (**to**) anheften, -kleben (an *acc.*), befestigen (an *dat.*); bei-, hinzufügen (*dat.*).

af·flict [ə'flɪkt] heimsuchen, plagen; **~ed with** geplagt von, leiden an (*dat.*); **af·flic·tion** [ə'flɪkʃn] Gebrechen *n*; Elend *n*, Not *f*

af·flu·ence ['æfluəns] Überfluß *m*; Wohlstand *m*; **'~·ent** reich(lich); **'~·ent so·ci·e·ty** Wohlstandsgesellschaft *f*

af·ford [ə'fɔːd] sich leisten; gewähren, bieten; **I can ~ it** ich kann es mir leisten

af·front [ə'frʌnt] **1.** beleidigen; **2.** Beleidigung *f*

a·float [ə'fləʊt] flott, schwimmend; **set ~** *naut.* flottmachen; in Umlauf bringen (*Gerücht etc.*)

a·fraid [ə'freɪd]: **be ~ of** sich fürchten *od.* Angst haben vor (*dat.*); **I'm ~ she won't come** ich fürchte, sie wird nicht kommen; **I'm ~ I must go now** leider muß ich jetzt gehen

a·fresh [ə'freʃ] von neuem

Af·ri·ca ['æfrɪkə] Afrika *n*; **Af·ri·can** ['æfrɪkən] **1.** afrikanisch; **2.** Afrikaner(in)

af·ter ['ɑːftə] **1.** *adv.* hinterher, nachher, danach; **2.** *prp.* nach; hinter (*dat.*) (... her); **~ all** schließlich (doch); **3.** *cj.* nachdem; später; Nach...; '**~·ef·fect** *med.* Nachwirkung *f* (*a. fig.*); *fig.* Folge *f*; '**~·glow** Abendrot *n*; **~·math** ['ɑːftəmæθ] Nachwirkungen *pl.*, Folgen *pl.*; '**~·noon** Nachmittag *m*; **this ~** heute nachmittag; **good ~!** guten Tag!; '**~·taste** Nachgeschmack *m*; '**~·thought** nachträglicher Einfall; **~·wards**, **~·ward** *Am.* ['ɑːftəwəd(z)] nachher, später

a·gain [ə'gen] wieder(um); ferner; **~ and ~, time and ~** immer wieder; **as much ~** noch einmal soviel

a·gainst [ə'genst] gegen; an (*dat. od. acc.*), gegen; **as ~** verglichen mit; **he was ~ it** er war dagegen

age [eɪdʒ] **1.** (Lebens)Alter *n*; Zeit(alter *n*) *f*; Menschenalter *n*; (**old**) ~ (hohes) Alter; **at the ~ of** im Alter von; *s.o.* **your ~** in deinem/Ihrem Alter; (**come**) **of ~** mündig *od.* volljährig (werden); **be**

over ~ die Altersgrenze überschritten haben; **under ~** minderjährig; unmündig; **wait for ~s** F e-e Ewigkeit warten; **2.** alt werden *od.* machen; **~d** ['eɪdʒɪd] alt, betagt; [eɪdʒd]: **~ twenty** 20 Jahre alt; '**~·less** zeitlos; ewig jung

a·gen·cy ['eɪdʒənsɪ] Agentur *f*; Geschäftsstelle *f*, Büro *n*

a·gen·da [ə'dʒendə] Tagesordnung *f*

a·gent ['eɪdʒənt] Agent *m* (*a. pol.*), Vertreter *m*; (*Grundstücks- etc.*)Makler *m*; Wirkstoff *m*, Mittel *n*

ag·glom·er·ate [ə'glɒməreɪt] (sich) zusammenballen; (sich) (an)häufen

ag·gra·vate ['ægrəveɪt] erschweren, verschlimmern; F ärgern

ag·gre·gate 1. ['ægrɪgeɪt] (sich) anhäufen; vereinigen (**to** mit); sich belaufen auf (*acc.*); **2.** ['ægrɪgət] (an)gehäuft; gesamt; **3.** ['ægrɪgət] Anhäufung *f*; Gesamtmenge *f*, Summe *f*; Aggregat *n*

ag·gres·sion [ə'greʃn] Angriff *m*; **~·sive** [ə'gresɪv] aggressiv, Angriffs...; *fig.* energisch; **~·sor** [ə'gresə] Angreifer *m*

ag·grieved [ə'griːvd] verletzt, gekränkt

a·ghast [ə'gɑːst] entgeistert, entsetzt

ag·ile ['ædʒaɪl] flink, behend; **a·gil·i·ty** [ə'dʒɪlətɪ] Behendigkeit *f*

ag·i·tate ['ædʒɪteɪt] *v/t. fig.* aufregen, -wühlen; *Flüssigkeit* schütteln; *v/i.* agitieren, hetzen (**against** gegen); **~·ta·tion** [ædʒɪ'teɪʃn] Aufregung *f*; Agitation *f*; **~·ta·tor** ['ædʒɪteɪtə] Agitator *m*

a·glow [ə'gləʊ]: **be ~** strahlen (**with** vor)

a·go [ə'gəʊ]: **a year ~** vor e-m Jahr

ag·o·ny ['ægənɪ] Qual *f*; Todeskampf *m*

a·gree [ə'griː] *v/i.* übereinstimmen; sich vertragen; einig werden; sich einigen (**on** über *acc.*); übereinkommen; **~ to** zustimmen (*dat.*), einverstanden sein mit; **~·a·ble** [ə'grɪəbl] (**to**) angenehm (für); übereinstimmend (mit); **~·ment** [ə'griːmənt] Übereinstimmung *f*; Vereinbarung *f*; Abkommen *n*

ag·ri·cul·tur·al [ægrɪ'kʌltʃərəl] landwirtschaftlich; **~e** ['ægrɪkʌltʃə] Landwirtschaft *f*

a·ground *naut.* [ə'graʊnd] gestrandet; **run ~** stranden, auf Grund laufen

a·head [ə'hed] vorwärts, voraus; vorn; **go ~!** nur zu!, mach nur!; **straight ~** geradeaus

ai [eɪ ˈaɪ] *Abk. für* **amnesty international** (*e-e Menschenrechtsorganisation*)

aid [eɪd] **1.** unterstützen, *j-m* helfen (*in* bei); fördern; *he was accused of ~ing and abetting* er wurde wegen Beihilfe angeklagt; **2.** Hilfe *f*, Unterstützung *f*

AIDS, Aids *med.* [eɪdz] Aids *n*; *person with* ~ Aids-Kranke(r *m*) *f*

ail [eɪl] kränklich sein; '**~ment** Leiden *n*

aim [eɪm] **1.** *v/i.* zielen (*at* auf *acc.*, nach); ~ *at fig.* beabsichtigen; *be ~ing to do s.th.* vorhaben, et. zu tun; *v/t.* ~ *at Waffe etc.* richten auf *od.* gegen (*acc.*); **2.** Ziel *n* (*a. fig.*); Absicht *f*; *take* ~ *at* zielen auf (*acc.*) *od.* nach; '**~less** ziellos

air¹ [eə] **1.** Luft *f*; Luftzug *m*; Miene *f*, Aussehen *n*; *by* ~ auf dem Luftwege; *in the open* ~ im Freien; *on the* ~ im Rundfunk *od.* Fernsehen; *be on the* ~ senden (*Sender*); *go off the* ~ die Sendung beenden (*Person*); sein Programm beenden (*Sender*); *give o.s., put on* ~s vornehm tun; **2.** (aus)lüften; *fig.* an die Öffentlichkeit bringen; erörtern

air² *mus.* [eə] Arie *f*, Weise *f*, Melodie *f*

'**air|-bag** *mot.* Airbag *m*; '**~base** *mil.* Luftstützpunkt *m*; '**~bed** Luftmatratze *f*; '**~borne** in der Luft (*Flugzeug*); *mil.* Luftlande...; '**~brake** *tech.* Druckluftbremse *f*; '**~bus** *aviat.* Airbus *m*, Großraumflugzeug *n*; '**~con-ditioned** mit Klimaanlage; '**~con-dition-ing** Klimaanlage *f*; '**~craft car-ri-er** Flugzeugträger *m*; '**~field** Flugplatz *m*; '**~force** *mil.* Luftwaffe *f*; '**~host-ess** *aviat.* Stewardess *f*; '**~jack-et** Schwimmweste *f*; '**~lift** *aviat.* Luftbrücke *f*; '**~line** *aviat.* Fluggesellschaft *f*; '**~lin-er** *aviat.* Verkehrsflugzeug *n*; '**~mail** Luftpost *f*; *by* ~ mit Luftpost; '**~man** (*pl. -men*) Flieger *m* (*Luftwaffe*); '**~plane** *Am.* Flugzeug *n*; '**~pock-et** *aviat.* Luftloch *n*; '**~pol-lu-tion** Luftverschmutzung *f*; '**~port** Flughafen *m*; '**~raid** Luftangriff *m*; **~raid pre-cau-tions** *pl.* Luftschutz *m*; **~raid shel-ter** Luftschutzraum *m*; **~route** *aviat.* Flugroute *f*; '**~sick** luftkrank; '**~space** Luftraum *m*; '**~strip** (behelfsmäßige) Start- u. Landebahn; '**~ter-mi-nal** Flughafenabfertigungsgebäude *n*;

'**~tight** luftdicht; '**~traf-fic** Flugverkehr *m*; **~'traf-fic con-trol** *aviat.* Flugsicherung *f*; **~'traf-fic con-trol-ler** *aviat.* Fluglotse *m*; '**~way** *aviat.* Fluggesellschaft *f*; '**~wor-thy** flugtüchtig

air-y ['eərɪ] (**-ier, -iest**) luftig

aisle *arch.* [aɪl] Seitenschiff *n*; Gang *m*

a-jar [ə'dʒɑː] halb offen, angelehnt

a-kin [ə'kɪn] verwandt (*to* mit)

a-lac-ri-ty [ə'lækrətɪ] Bereitwilligkeit *f*

a-larm [ə'lɑːm] **1.** Alarm(zeichen *n*) *m*; Wecker *m*; Angst *f*; **2.** alarmieren; beunruhigen; **~clock** Wecker *m*

al-bum ['ælbəm] Album *n* (*a. Langspielplatte*)

al-bu-mi-nous [æl'bjuːmɪnəs] eiweißhaltig

al-co-hol ['ælkəhɒl] Alkohol *m*; **~ic** [ælkə'hɒlɪk] **1.** alkoholisch; **2.** Alkoholiker(in)

ale [eɪl] Ale *n* (*helles, obergäriges Bier*)

a-lert [ə'lɜːt] **1.** wachsam, munter; **2.** Alarm(bereitschaft *f*) *m*; *on the* ~ auf der Hut; in Alarmbereitschaft; **3.** warnen (*to vor dat.*), alarmieren

al-ga *bot.* ['ælgə] (*pl. -gae* ['ældʒiː]) Alge *f*

al-ge-bra *math.* ['ældʒɪbrə] Algebra *f*

al-i-bi ['ælɪbaɪ] Alibi *n*

a-li-en ['eɪljən] **1.** ausländisch; fremd; **2.** Ausländer(in); Außerirdische(r *m*) *f*; **~ate** ['eɪljəneɪt] veräußern; entfremden

a-light [ə'laɪt] **1.** in Flammen; **2.** (*alighted od. alit*) ab-, aussteigen, absitzen; sich niederlassen (*Vogel*); *aviat.* landen

a-lign [ə'laɪn] (sich) ausrichten (*with* nach)

a-like [ə'laɪk] **1.** *adj.* gleich; **2.** *adv.* gleich, ebenso

al-i-men-ta-ry [ælɪ'mentərɪ] nahrhaft; **~ca-nal** Verdauungskanal *m*

al-i-mo-ny *jur.* ['ælɪmənɪ] Unterhalt *m*

a-live [ə'laɪv] lebendig; (noch) am Leben; lebhaft; *~ and kicking* gesund u. munter; *be ~ with* wimmeln von

all [ɔːl] **1.** *adj.* all; ganz; jede(r, -s); **2.** *pron.* alles; alle *pl.*; **3.** *adv.* ganz, völlig; *Wendungen:* ~ *at once* auf einmal; *~ the better* desto besser; *~ but* beinahe, fast; *~ in Am.* F fertig, ganz erledigt; *~ right* (alles) in Ordnung; *for ~ that* dessenungeachtet, trotzdem; *for ~ I know* soviel ich weiß; *at* ~ überhaupt; *not at* ~ überhaupt nicht; *the score was two* ~ das Spiel stand zwei zu zwei

all-A·mer·i·can [ɔːlə'merɪkən] typisch amerikanisch; die ganzen USA vertretend

al·lay [ə'leɪ] beruhigen; lindern

al·le·ga·tion [ælɪ'geɪʃn] *unerwiesene* Behauptung

al·lege [ə'ledʒ] behaupten; ~**d** angeblich

al·le·giance [ə'liːdʒəns] (Untertanen)Treue *f*

al·ler|·gic [ə'lɜːdʒɪk] allergisch (*to* gegen); ~**·gy** ['ælədʒɪ] Allergie *f*

al·le·vi·ate [ə'liːvɪeɪt] mildern, lindern

al·ley ['ælɪ] (enge *od.* schmale) Gasse; Garten-, Parkweg *m*; *Bowling, Kegeln*: Bahn *f*; △ *nicht* **Allee**

al·li·ance [ə'laɪəns] Bündnis *n*

al·li·ga·tor *zo.* ['ælɪgeɪtə] Alligator *m*

al·lo|·cate ['æləkeɪt] zuteilen, anweisen; ~**·ca·tion** [ælə'keɪʃn] Zuteilung *f*

al·lot [ə'lɒt] (-*tt*-) zuteilen, an-, zuweisen; ~**·ment** Zuteilung *f*; Parzelle *f*

al·low [ə'laʊ] erlauben, bewilligen, gewähren; zugeben; ab-, anrechnen, vergüten; ~ *for* einplanen, berücksichtigen (*acc.*); ~**·a·ble** erlaubt, zulässig; ~**·ance** Erlaubnis *f*; Bewilligung *f*; Taschengeld *n*, Zuschuß *m*; Vergütung *f*; *fig.* Nachsicht *f*; *make* ~(s) *for s.th.* in Betracht ziehen

al·loy 1. ['ælɔɪ] Legierung *f*; 2. [ə'lɔɪ] legieren

all-round ['ɔːlraʊnd] vielseitig; ~**·er** [ɔːl'raʊndə] Alleskönner *m*; *Sport*: Allroundsportler *m*, -spieler *m*

al·lude [ə'luːd] anspielen (*to* auf *acc.*)

al·lure [ə'ljʊə] (an-, ver)locken; ~**·ment** Verlockung *f*

al·lu·sion [ə'luːʒn] Anspielung *f*

all-wheel 'drive *mot.* Allradantrieb *m*

al·ly 1. [ə'laɪ] (sich) vereinigen, verbünden (*to, with* mit); 2. ['ælaɪ] Verbündete(r *m*) *f*, Bundesgenosse *m*, -in *f*; *the Allies pl.* die Alliierten *pl.*

al·might·y [ɔːl'maɪtɪ] allmächtig; *the* ℒ der Allmächtige

al·mond *bot.* ['ɑːmənd] Mandel *f*

al·most ['ɔːlməʊst] fast, beinah(e)

alms [ɑːmz] *pl.* Almosen *n*

a·loft [ə'lɒft] (hoch) (dr)oben

a·lone [ə'ləʊn] allein; *let* ~, *leave* ~ in

Ruhe *od.* bleiben lassen; *let* ~ ... abgesehen von ...

a·long [ə'lɒŋ] 1. *adv.* weiter, vorwärts; da; dahin; *all* ~ die ganze Zeit; ~ *with* (zusammen) mit; *come* ~ mitkommen, -gehen; *get* ~ vorwärts-, weiterkommen; auskommen, sich vertragen (*with s.o.* mit j-m); *take* ~ mitnehmen; 2. *prp.* entlang, längs; ~**'side** Seite an Seite; neben

a·loof [ə'luːf] abseits; reserviert, zurückhaltend

a·loud [ə'laʊd] laut

al·pha·bet ['ælfəbet] Alphabet *n*

al·pine ['ælpaɪn] alpin, (Hoch)Gebirgs...

al·read·y [ɔːl'redɪ] bereits, schon

al·right [ɔːl'raɪt] → **all right**

Al·sa·tian *bsd. Brt.* [æl'seɪʃən] deutscher Schäferhund

al·so ['ɔːlsəʊ] auch, ferner; △ *nicht* **also**

al·tar ['ɔːltə] Altar *m*

al·ter ['ɔːltə] (sich) (ver)ändern; ab-, umändern; ~**·a·tion** [ɔːltə'reɪʃn] Änderung *f* (*to an dat.*), Veränderung *f*

al·ter·nate 1. [ɔːl'tɜːneɪt] abwechseln (lassen); 2. [ɔːl'tɜːnət] abwechselnd; ~**·nat·ing cur·rent** *electr.* [ɔːl'tɜːneɪtɪŋ-] Wechselstrom *m*; ~**·na·tion** [ɔːltə'neɪʃn] Abwechslung *f*; Wechsel *m*; ~**·na·tive** [ɔːl'tɜːnətɪv] 1. alternativ, wahlweise; 2. Alternative *f*, Wahl *f*, Möglichkeit *f*

al·though [ɔːl'ðəʊ] obwohl, obgleich

al·ti·tude ['æltɪtjuːd] Höhe *f*; *at an* ~ *of* in e-r Höhe von

al·to·geth·er [ɔːltə'geðə] im ganzen, insgesamt; ganz (u. gar), völlig

a·lu·min·i·um *Brt.* [æljʊ'mɪnjəm], **a·lu·mi·num** *Am.* [ə'luːmɪnəm] Aluminium *n*

al·ways ['ɔːlweɪz] immer, stets

am [æm; *im Satz* əm] 1. *sg. pres. von* **be**

am, AM [eɪ 'em] *Abk. für before noon* (*lateinisch* **ante meridiem**) morgens, vorm., vormittags

a·mal·gam·ate [ə'mælgəmeɪt] (sich) zusammenschließen, *econ. a.* fusionieren

a·mass [ə'mæs] an-, aufhäufen

am·a·teur ['æmətə] Amateur(in); Dilettant(in); Hobby...

a·maze [ə'meɪz] in Erstaunen setzen, verblüffen; **a'maze·ment** Staunen *n*,

Verblüffung f; **a·maz·ing** erstaunlich

am·bas·sa·dor pol. [æm'bæsədə] Botschafter m (**to** in e-m Land); Gesandte(r) m; **~·dress** pol. [æm'bæsədrıs] Botschafterin f (**to** in e-m Land)

am·ber ['æmbə] Bernstein m

am·bi·gu·i·ty [æmbı'gju:ıtı] Zwei-, Mehrdeutigkeit f; **am·big·u·ous** [æm'bıgjʊəs] zwei-, mehr-, vieldeutig

am·bi·tion [æm'bıʃn] Ehrgeiz m; **~·tious** [æm'bıʃəs] ehrgeizig

am·ble ['æmbl] 1. Paßgang m; 2. im Paßgang gehen od. reiten; schlendern

am·bu·lance ['æmbjʊləns] Krankenwagen m

am·bush ['æmbʊʃ] 1. Hinterhalt m; **be** od. **lie in ~ for s.o.** j-m auflauern; 2. auflauern (dat.); überfallen

a·men int. [ɑː'men] amen

a·mend [ə'mend] verbessern, berichtigen; Gesetz abändern, ergänzen; **~·ment** Besserung f; Verbesserung f; parl. Abänderungs-, Ergänzungsantrag m (**zu** e-m Gesetz); Am. Zusatzartikel m zur Verfassung; **~s** pl. (Schaden)Ersatz m; **make ~** Schadenersatz leisten, es wieder gutmachen; **make ~ to s.o. for s.th.** j-n für et. entschädigen

a·men·i·ty [ə'mi:nətı] oft amenities Annehmlichkeiten pl.

A·mer·i·ca [ə'merıkə] Amerika n; **A·mer·i·can** [ə'merıkən] 1. amerikanisch; 2. Amerikaner(in)

A·mer·i·can·is·m [ə'merıkənızəm] Amerikanismus m; **~·ize** [ə'merıkənaɪz] (sich) amerikanisieren

A·mer·i·can plan Vollpension f

a·mi·a·ble ['eımjəbl] liebenswürdig, freundlich

am·i·ca·ble ['æmıkəbl] freundschaftlich, a. jur. gütlich

a·mid(st) [ə'mıd(st)] inmitten (gen.), (mitten) in od. unter

a·miss [ə'mıs] verkehrt, falsch, übel; **take ~** übelnehmen

am·mo·ni·a [ə'məʊnjə] Ammoniak n

am·mu·ni·tion [æmjʊ'nıʃn] Munition f

am·nes·ty ['æmnıstı] 1. Amnestie f (Straferlaß); 2. begnadigen

a·mok [ə'mɒk]: **run ~** Amok laufen

a·mong(st) [ə'mʌŋ(st)] (mitten) unter, zwischen

am·o·rous ['æmərəs] verliebt (**of** in acc.)

a·mount [ə'maʊnt] 1. (**to**) sich belaufen

(auf acc.); hinauslaufen (auf acc.); 2. Betrag m, (Gesamt)Summe f; Menge f

am·ple ['æmpl] (**~r, ~st**) weit, groß, geräumig; reich(lich), beträchtlich

am·pli·fi·ca·tion [æmplıfı'keıʃn] Erweiterung f; phys. Verstärkung f; **~·fi·er** electr. ['æmplıfaıə] Verstärker m; **~·fy** ['æmplıfaı] erweitern; electr. verstärken; **~·tude** ['æmplıtju:d] Umfang m, Weite f, Fülle f

am·pu·tate ['æmpjʊteıt] amputieren

a·muck [ə'mʌk] → **amok**

a·muse [ə'mju:z] (o.s. sich) amüsieren, unterhalten, belustigen; **~·ment** Unterhaltung f, Vergnügen n, Zeitvertreib m; **~·ment park** Vergnügungs-, Freizeitpark m; **a·mus·ing** amüsant, unterhaltend

an [æn, ən] → **a**

an·a·bol·ic ster·oid pharm. [ænəbolık 'stıərɔɪd] Anabolikum n

a·nae·mi·a med. [ə'ni:mjə] Blutarmut f, Anämie f

an·aes·thet·ic [ænıs'θetık] 1. (**~ally**) betäubend, Narkose...; 2. Betäubungsmittel n

a·nal anat. ['eınl] anal, Anal...

a·nal·o·gous [ə'næləgəs] analog, entsprechend; **~·gy** [ə'nælədʒı] Analogie f, Entsprechung f

an·a·lyse bsd. Brt., **an·a·lyze** Am. ['ænəlaız] analysieren; zerlegen; **a·nal·y·sis** [ə'næləsıs] (pl. **-ses** [-si:z]) Analyse f

an·arch·y ['ænəkı] Anarchie f, Gesetzlosigkeit f; Chaos n

a·nat·o·mize [ə'nætəmaız] med. zerlegen; zergliedern; **~·my** [ə'nætəmı] Anatomie f; Zergliederung f, Analyse f

an·ces·tor ['ænsestə] Vorfahr m, Ahn m; **~·tress** ['ænsestrıs] Ahnfrau f

an·chor ['æŋkə] 1. Anker m; **at ~** vor Anker; 2. verankern

an·chor·man Am. TV ['æŋkəmæn] (pl. **-men**) Moderator m (e-r Nachrichtensendung); **'~·wom·an** (pl. **-women**) Am. TV Moderatorin f (e-r Nachrichtensendung)

an·cho·vy zo. ['æntʃəvı] An(s)chovis f, Sardelle f

an·cient ['eınʃənt] 1. alt, antik; uralt; 2. **the ~s** pl. hist. die Alten, die antiken Klassiker

and [ænd, ənd] und

an·ec·dote ['ænɪkdəʊt] Anekdote f

a·ne·mi·a Am. [ə'niːmjə] → **anaemia**

an·es·thet·ic Am. [ænɪs'θetɪk] → **an·aesthetic**

an·gel ['eɪndʒəl] Engel m; △ nicht An·gel

an·ger ['æŋgə] 1. Zorn m, Ärger m (at über acc.); 2. erzürnen, (ver)ärgern

an·gi·na (pec·to·ris) med. [æn'dʒaɪnə ('pektərɪs)] Angina pectoris f

an·gle¹ ['æŋgl] Winkel m

an·gle² ['æŋgl] angeln (**for** nach); '**~r** Angler(in)

An·gli·can rel. ['æŋglɪkən] 1. anglikanisch; 2. Anglikaner(in)

An·glo-Sax·on [æŋgləʊ'sæksən] 1. angelsächsisch; 2. Angelsachse m

an·gry ['æŋgrɪ] (-ier, -iest) zornig, verärgert, böse (**at, with** über acc., mit dat.)

an·guish ['æŋgwɪʃ] Qual f, Schmerz m

an·gu·lar ['æŋgjʊlə] winkelig; knochig

an·i·mal ['ænɪml] 1. Tier n; 2. tierisch; '**~ lov·er** Tierfreund(in)

an·i·mate ['ænɪmeɪt] beleben; aufmuntern, anregen; △ nicht animieren; '**~·ma·ted** lebendig; lebhaft, angeregt; **~·ma·ted car·toon** Zeichentrickfilm m; **~·ma·tion** [ænɪ'meɪʃn] Lebhaftigkeit f; Animation f, Herstellung f von (Zeichen)Trickfilmen; Computer: bewegtes Bild

an·i·mos·i·ty [ænɪ'mɒsətɪ] Animosität f, Feindseligkeit f

an·kle anat. ['æŋkl] (Fuß)Knöchel m

an·nals ['ænlz] pl. Jahrbücher pl.

an·nex [ə'neks] anhängen; annektieren; 2. ['æneks] Anhang m; Anbau m

an·ni·ver·sa·ry [ænɪ'vɜːsərɪ] Jahrestag m; Jahresfeier f

an·no·tate ['ænəʊteɪt] mit Anmerkungen versehen; kommentieren

an·nounce [ə'naʊns] ankündigen; bekanntgeben; Rundfunk, TV: ansagen; durchsagen; △ nicht annoncieren; **~ment** Ankündigung f; Bekanntgabe f; Rundfunk, TV: Ansage f; Durchsage f; **an·nounc·er** Rundfunk, TV: Ansager(in), Sprecher(in)

an·noy [ə'nɔɪ] ärgern; belästigen; **~·ance** Störung f, Belästigung f; Ärgernis n; **~·ing** ärgerlich, lästig

an·nu·al ['ænjʊəl] 1. jährlich, Jahres...; 2. bot. einjährige Pflanze; Jahrbuch n

an·nu·i·ty [ə'njuːɪtɪ] (Jahres)Rente f

an·nul [ə'nʌl] (-ll-) für ungültig erklären, annullieren; **~ment** Annullierung f, Aufhebung f

an·o·dyne med. ['ænəʊdaɪn] 1. schmerzstillend; 2. schmerzstillendes Mittel

a·noint [ə'nɔɪnt] salben

a·nom·a·lous [ə'nɒmələs] anomal

a·non·y·mous [ə'nɒnɪməs] anonym

an·o·rak ['ænəræk] Anorak m

an·oth·er [ə'nʌðə] ein anderer; ein zweiter; noch eine(r, -s)

ANSI ['ænsɪ] Abk. für American National Standards Institute Computer: Amerikanische Normengesellschaft

an·swer ['ɑːnsə] 1. v/t. et. beantworten; j-m antworten; entsprechen (dat.); Zweck erfüllen; tech. dem Steuer gehorchen; e-r Vorladung Folge leisten; e-r Beschreibung entsprechen; **~ the bell** od. **door** (die Haustür) aufmachen; **~ the telephone** ans Telefon gehen; v/i. antworten (**to** auf acc.); entsprechen (**to** dat.); **~ back** freche Antworten geben; widersprechen; **~ for** einstehen für; 2. Antwort f (**to** auf acc.); **~·a·ble** ['ɑːnsərəbl] verantwortlich; **~·ing ma·chine** teleph. ['ɑːnsərɪŋ -] Anrufbeantworter m

ant zo. [ænt] Ameise f

an·tag·o·nis·m [æn'tægənɪzəm] Feindschaft f; **~·nist** [æn'tægənɪst] Gegner(in); **~·nize** [æn'tægənaɪz] bekämpfen; sich j-n zum Feind machen

Ant·arc·tic [ænt'ɑːktɪk] antarktisch

an·te·ced·ent [æntɪ'siːdənt] vorhergehend, früher (**to** als)

an·te·lope zo. ['æntɪləʊp] (pl. -lopes, -lope) Antilope f

an·ten·na¹ zo. [æn'tenə] (pl. -nae [-niː]) Fühler m

an·ten·na² Am. [æn'tenə] Antenne f

an·te·ri·or [æn'tɪərɪə] vorhergehend, früher (**to** als); vorder

an·them mus. ['ænθəm] Hymne f

an·ti... ['æntɪ] Gegen..., gegen ... eingestellt, Anti..., anti...; **~·air·craft** mil. Flieger-, Flugabwehr...; **~·bi·ot·ic** med. [æntɪbaɪ'ɒtɪk] Antibiotikum n; '**~·bod·y** biol. Antikörper m, Abwehrstoff m

an·tic·i·pate [æn'tɪsɪpeɪt] voraussehen, ahnen; erwarten; zuvorkommen; vorwegnehmen; **~pa·tion** [æntɪˈpeɪʃn] (Vor)Ahnung f; Erwartung f; Vorwegnahme f; **in ~** im voraus

an·ti·clock·wise Brt. entgegen dem Uhrzeigersinn

an·tics ['æntɪks] pl. Mätzchen pl.; △ nicht antik, Antike

an·ti·dote ['æntɪdəʊt] Gegengift n, -mittel n; **~·for·eign·er vi·o·lence** Gewalt f gegen Ausländer; **~·freeze** Frostschutzmittel n; **~·lock brak·ing sys·tem** mot. Antiblockiersystem n (abb. **ABS**); **~·mis·sile** mil. Raketenabwehr...; **~·nu·cle·ar ac·tiv·ist** Kernkraftgegner(in)

an·tip·a·thy [ænˈtɪpəθɪ] Abneigung f

an·ti·quat·ed ['æntɪkweɪtɪd] veraltet

an·tique [ænˈtiːk] **1.** antik, alt; **2.** Antiquität f; △ nicht Antike; **~ deal·er** Antiquitätenhändler(in); **~ shop** bsd. Brt., **~ store** Am. Antiquitätenladen m

an·tiq·ui·ty [ænˈtɪkwətɪ] Altertum n, Vorzeit f

an·ti·sep·tic [æntɪˈseptɪk] **1.** antiseptisch; **2.** antiseptisches Mittel

ant·lers ['æntləz] pl. Geweih n

a·nus anat. ['eɪnəs] After m

an·vil ['ænvɪl] Amboß m

anx·i·e·ty [æŋˈzaɪətɪ] Angst f, Sorge f

anx·ious ['æŋkʃəs] besorgt, beunruhigt (about wegen); begierig, gespannt (for auf acc.); bestrebt (to do zu tun)

an·y ['enɪ] **1.** adj. u. pron. (irgend)eine(r, -s), (irgend)welche(r, -s); (irgend) etwas; jede(r, -s) (beliebige); einige pl.; welche pl.; **not ~** keiner; **2.** adv. irgend(wie), ein wenig, etwas, (noch) etwas; **'~·bod·y** (irgend) jemand; jeder; **'~·how** irgendwie; trotzdem, jedenfalls; wie dem auch sei; **'~·one → anybody**; **'~·thing** (irgend) etwas; alles; **~ but** alles andere als; **~ else?** sonst noch etwas?; **not ~** nichts; **'~·way → anyhow**; **'~·where** irgendwo(hin); überall

AP [eɪ ˈpiː] Abk. für **Associated Press** (amer. Nachrichtenbüro)

a·part [əˈpɑːt] einzeln, für sich; beiseite; △ nicht apart; **~ from** abgesehen von

a·part·heid [əˈpɑːtheɪt] Apartheid f, Politik f der Rassentrennung

a·part·ment Am. [əˈpɑːtmənt] Wohnung f; **~ build·ing** bsd. Brt., **~ house** Am. Mietshaus n

ap·a·thet·ic [æpəˈθetɪk] (**~ally**) apa-

thisch, teilnahmslos, gleichgültig; **~·thy** ['æpəθɪ] Apathie f, Teilnahmslosigkeit f

ape zo. [eɪp] (Menschen)Affe m

ap·er·ture ['æpətjʊə] Öffnung f

a·pi·a·ry ['eɪpjərɪ] Bienenhaus n

a·piece [əˈpiːs] für jedes od. pro Stück, je

a·pol·o·gize [əˈpɒlədʒaɪz] sich entschuldigen (for für; to bei); **~·gy** [əˈpɒlədʒɪ] Entschuldigung f; Rechtfertigung f; **make an ~** (for s.th.) sich bei j-m (für et.) entschuldigen

ap·o·plex·y ['æpəpleksɪ] Schlag(anfall) m

a·pos·tle [əˈpɒsl] Apostel m

a·pos·tro·phe ling. [əˈpɒstrəfɪ] Apostroph m

ap·pal(l) [əˈpɔːl] (**-ll-**) erschrecken, entsetzen; **ap·pal·ling** erschreckend, entsetzlich

ap·pa·ra·tus [æpəˈreɪtəs] Apparat m, Vorrichtung f, Gerät n

ap·par·ent [əˈpærənt] offenbar; anscheinend; scheinbar

ap·pa·ri·tion [æpəˈrɪʃn] Erscheinung f, Gespenst n

ap·peal [əˈpiːl] **1.** jur. Berufung od. Revision einlegen, Einspruch erheben, Beschwerde einlegen; appellieren, sich wenden (to an acc.); **~ to** gefallen (dat.), zusagen (dat.), wirken auf (acc.); j-n dringend bitten (for um); **2.** jur. Revision f, Berufung f; Beschwerde f; Einspruch m; Appell m (to an acc.), Aufruf m; △ nicht mil. Appell!; Wirkung f, Reiz m; Bitte f (to an acc.; for um); **~ for mercy** jur. Gnadengesuch n; **~·ing** flehend; ansprechend

ap·pear [əˈpɪə] (er)scheinen; sich zeigen; öffentlich auftreten; sich ergeben od. herausstellen; **~·ance** [əˈpɪərəns] Erscheinen n; Auftreten n; Äußere(s) n, Erscheinung f, Aussehen n; Anschein m, äußerer Schein; keep up ~s den Schein wahren; **to** od. **by all ~s** allem Anschein nach

ap·pease [əˈpiːz] besänftigen, beschwichtigen; Durst etc. stillen; Neugier befriedigen

ap·pend [əˈpend] an-, hinzu-, beifügen; **~·age** [əˈpendɪdʒ] Anhang m, Anhängsel n, Zubehör n

ap·pen|·di·ci·tis med. [əpendɪˈsaɪtɪs]

Blinddarmentzündung f; **~dix**
[ə'pendıks] (pl. **-dixes, -dices** [-dısi:z])
Anhang m; a. **vermiform ~** med.
Wurmfortsatz m, Blinddarm m
ap·pe·tite ['æpıtait] (for) Appetit m
(auf acc.); fig. Verlangen n (nach);
~tiz·er ['æpıtaızə] Appetithappen m,
appetitanregendes Gericht od. Getränk; **~tiz·ing** ['æpıtaızıŋ] appetitanregend
ap·plaud [ə'plɔ:d] applaudieren, Beifall
spenden; loben; **ap·plause** [ə'plɔ:z]
Applaus m, Beifall m
ap·ple bot. ['æpl] Apfel m; '**~ cart**: **upset s.o.'s ~** F j-s Pläne über den Haufen
werfen; **~ pie** (warmer) gedeckter Apfelkuchen; **in ~-pie order** F in schönster
Ordnung; **~ 'sauce** Apfelmus n; Am.
sl. Schmus m, Quatsch m
ap·pli·ance [ə'plaɪəns] Vorrichtung f;
Gerät n; Mittel n
ap·pli·ca·ble ['æplıkəbl] anwendbar (**to**
auf acc.)
ap·pli|·cant ['æplıkənt] Antragsteller(in), Bewerber(in) (**for** um); **~·ca·tion** [æplı'keıʃn] (**to**) Anwendung f (auf
acc.); Bedeutung f (für); Gesuch n (**for**
um); Bewerbung f (**for** um)
ap·ply [ə'plaı] v/t. (**to**) (auf)legen, auftragen (auf acc.); anwenden (auf acc.);
verwenden (für); **~ o.s. to** sich widmen
(dat.); v/i. (**to**) passen, zutreffen, sich
anwenden lassen (auf acc.); gelten
(für); sich wenden (an acc.); sich bewerben (**for** um), beantragen (**for** acc.)
ap·point [ə'pɔınt] bestimmen, festsetzen; verabreden; ernennen (**s.o.** governor j-n zum ...); berufen (**to** auf e-n
Posten); **~ment** Bestimmung f; Verabredung f; Termin m (geschäftlich,
beim Arzt etc.); Ernennung f, Berufung
f; Stelle f; **~ment book** Terminkalender m
ap·por·tion [ə'pɔ:ʃn] ver-, zuteilen
ap·prais·al [ə'preızl] (Ab)Schätzung f;
~e [ə'preız] (ab)schätzen, taxieren
ap·pre·cia·ble [ə'pri:ʃəbl] nennenswert, spürbar; **~·ci·ate** [ə'pri:ʃıeıt] v/t.
schätzen, würdigen; dankbar sein für;
v/i. im Wert steigen; **~·ci·a·tion**
[əpri:ʃı'eıʃn] Würdigung f; Dankbarkeit f; (richtige) Beurteilung; econ.
Wertsteigerung f
ap·pre·hend [æprı'hend] ergreifen,

fassen; begreifen; befürchten; **~hen·sion** [æprı'henʃn] Ergreifung f;
Festnahme f; Besorgnis f; **~hen·sive**
[æprı'hensıv] ängstlich, besorgt (**for**
um; **that** daß)
ap·pren·tice [ə'prentıs] **1.** Auszubildende(r m) f, Lehrling m, Schweiz
Lehrtochter f; **2.** in die Lehre geben;
~ship Lehrzeit f, Lehre f, Ausbildung
f
ap·proach [ə'prəʊtʃ] **1.** v/i. näherkommen, sich nähern; v/t. sich nähern
(dat.); herangehen od. herantreten an
(acc.); **2.** (Heran)Nahen n; Ein-, Zu-,
Auffahrt f; Annäherung f; Methode f
ap·pro·ba·tion [æprə'beıʃn] Billigung f,
Beifall m
ap·pro·pri·ate 1. [ə'prəʊprıeıt] sich aneignen; verwenden; parl. bewilligen; **2.**
[ə'prəʊprııt] (**for, to**) angemessen (dat.),
passend (für, zu)
ap·prov|·al [ə'pru:vl] Billigung f; Anerkennung f, Beifall m; **~e** [ə'pru:v] billigen, anerkennen, **~ed** bewährt
ap·prox·i·mate [ə'prɒksımət] annähernd, ungefähr
Apr nur geschr. Abk. für **April** Apr.,
April m
a·pri·cot bot. ['eıprıkɒt] Aprikose f
A·pril ['eıprəl] (Abk. **Apr**) April m
a·pron ['eıprən] Schürze f; **~ strings**
pl. Schürzenbänder pl.; **be tied to one's
mother's ~** an Mutters Schürzenzipfel
hängen
apt [æpt] geeignet, passend; treffend
(Bemerkung etc.); begabt; **~ to** geneigt
zu; **ap·ti·tude** ['æptıtju:d] (**for**) Begabung f (für), Befähigung f (für); Talent
n (zu); **'ap·ti·tude test** Eignungsprüfung f
aq·ua·plan·ing Brt. mot. ['ækwəpleınıŋ] Aquaplaning n
a·quar·i·um [ə'kweərıəm] (pl. **-iums, -ia**
[-ıə]) Aquarium n
A·quar·i·us astr. [ə'kweərıəs] Wassermann m; **he/she is (an) ~** er/sie ist (ein)
Wassermann
a·quat·ic [ə'kwætık] Wasser...; **~ plant**
bot. Wasserpflanze f; **~s** sg., **~ sports**
pl. Wassersport m
aq·ue·duct ['ækwıdʌkt] Aquädukt m
aq·ui·line ['ækwılaın] Adler...; gebogen; **'~ nose** Adlernase f
A·ra·bi·a [ə'reıbjə] Arabien n; **Ar·ab**

['ærəb] Araber(in); **Ar·a·bic** ['ærəbɪk] **1.** arabisch; **2.** *ling.* Arabisch *n*

ar·a·ble ['ærəbl] anbaufähig; Acker...

ar·bi·tra·ry ['ɑːbɪtrəri] willkürlich, eigenmächtig; **~trate** ['ɑːbɪtreɪt] entscheiden, schlichten; **~tra·tion** [ɑːbɪ-'treɪʃn] Schlichtung *f*; **~tra·tor** *jur.* ['ɑːbɪtreɪtə] Schiedsrichter *m*; Schlichter *m*

ar·bo(u)r ['ɑːbə] Laube *f*

arc [ɑːk] (*electr.* Licht)Bogen *m*; **ar·cade** [ɑː'keɪd] Arkade *f*, Bogen-, Laubengang *m*; Durchgang *m*, Passage *f*

ARC [eɪ ɑː 'siː] *Abk. für* **American Red Cross** *das* Amerikanische Rote Kreuz

arch[1] [ɑːtʃ] **1.** Bogen *m*; Gewölbe *n*; **2.** (sich) wölben; krümmen

arch[2] [ɑːtʃ] erste(r, -s), oberste(r, -s), Haupt..., Erz...

arch[3] [ɑːtʃ] schelmisch

ar·cha·ic [ɑː'keɪɪk] (*~ally*) veraltet

arch|an·gel ['ɑːkeɪndʒəl] Erzengel *m*; **~bish·op** [ɑːtʃ'bɪʃəp] Erzbischof *m*

ar·cher ['ɑːtʃə] Bogenschütze *m*; **~y** ['ɑːtʃərɪ] Bogenschießen *n*

ar·chi·tect ['ɑːkɪtekt] Architekt(in); **~tec·ture** ['ɑːkɪtektʃə] Architektur *f*

ar·chives ['ɑːkaɪvz] *pl.* Archiv *n*

arch·way (Bogen)Gang *m*

arc·tic ['ɑːktɪk] arktisch, nördlich, Polar...

ar·dent ['ɑːdənt] feurig, glühend; *fig.* leidenschaftlich, heftig; eifrig

ar·do(u)r *fig.* ['ɑːdə] Leidenschaft *f*, Glut *f*, Feuer *n*; Eifer *m*

are [ɑː] *du bist, wir od. sie od. Sie sind, ihr seid*

ar·e·a ['eərɪə] (Boden)Fläche *f*; Gegend *f*, Gebiet *n*; Bereich *m*; **~ code** *Am. tel.* Vorwahl(nummer) *f*

Ar·gen·ti·na [ɑːdʒən'tiːnə] Argentinien *n*; **~tine** [ɑːdʒəntaɪn] **1.** argentinisch; **2.** Argentinier(in)

a·re·na [ə'riːnə] Arena *f*

ar·gue [ɑː'gjuː] argumentieren; streiten; diskutieren

ar·gu·ment ['ɑːgjəmənt] Argument *n*; Wortwechsel *m*, Auseinandersetzung *f*

ar·id ['ærɪd] dürr, trocken (*a. fig.*)

Ar·ies *astr.* ['eəriːz] Widder *m*; **he/she is (an) ~** er/sie ist (ein) Widder

a·rise [ə'raɪz] (**arose**, **arisen**) entstehen; auftauchen, -treten, -kommen;

a·ris·en [ə'rɪzn] *p.p von* **arise**

ar·is·toc·ra·cy [ærɪ'stɒkrəsɪ] Aristokratie *f*, Adel *m*; **~to·crat** ['ærɪstəkræt] Aristokrat(in)

a·rith·me·tic[1] [ə'rɪθmətɪk] Rechnen *n*

ar·ith·met·ic[2] [ærɪθ'metɪk] arithmetisch, Rechen...; **~ u·nit** *Computer:* Rechenwerk *n*

ark [ɑːk] Arche *f*

arm[1] [ɑːm] Arm *m*; Armlehne *f*; **keep s.o. at ~'s length** sich j-n vom Leibe halten

arm[2] [ɑːm] (sich) bewaffnen; (auf)rüsten

ar·ma·ment ['ɑːməmənt] (Kriegsaus)Rüstung *f*; Aufrüstung *f*

'arm·chair Lehnstuhl *m*, Sessel *m*

ar·mi·stice ['ɑːmɪstɪs] Waffenstillstand *m*

ar·mo(u)r ['ɑːmə] **1.** *mil.* Rüstung *f*, Panzer *m* (*a. fig., zo.*); **2.** panzern; **~ed 'car** gepanzertes Fahrzeug (*für Geldtransporte etc.*)

'arm·pit Achselhöhle *f*

arms [ɑːmz] *pl.* Waffen *pl.*; Waffengattung *f*; **~s control** Rüstungskontrolle *f*; **~s race** Wettrüsten *n*, Rüstungswettlauf *m*

ar·my ['ɑːmɪ] Armee *f*, Heer *n*

a·ro·ma [ə'rəumə] Aroma *n*, Duft *m*; **ar·o·mat·ic** [ærə'mætɪk] (*~ally*) aromatisch, würzig

a·rose [ə'rəuz] *pret. von* **arise**

a·round [ə'raund] **1.** *adv.* (rings)herum, (rund)herum, ringsumher, überall; umher, herum; in der Nähe; da; **2.** *prp.* um, um... herum, rund um; in (*dat.*) ... herum; ungefähr, etwa

a·rouse [ə'rauz] (auf)wecken; *fig.* aufrütteln, erregen

ar·range [ə'reɪndʒ] (an)ordnen; festlegen, -setzen; arrangieren; vereinbaren; *mus.* arrangieren, bearbeiten (*a. thea.*); **~ment** Anordnung *f*; Vereinbarung *f*; Vorkehrung *f*; *mus.* Arrangement *n*, Bearbeitung *f* (*a. thea.*)

ar·rears [ə'rɪəz] *pl.* Rückstand *m*, -stände *pl.*

ar·rest [ə'rest] **1.** *jur.* Verhaftung *f*, Festnahme *f*; △ *nicht* **Arrest** (*Schule etc.*); **2.** *jur.* verhaften, festnehmen

ar·riv·al [ə'raɪvl] Ankunft *f*; Erscheinen *n*; Ankömmling *m*; **~s** *pl.* ‚Ankunft' (*Fahrplan etc.*); **ar·rive** [ə'raɪv] (an)kommen, eintreffen, erscheinen; ~ *at* fig. erreichen (*acc.*), kommen zu

ar·ro·gance [ˈærəgəns] Arroganz f, Überheblichkeit f; '**~gant** arrogant, überheblich

ar·row [ˈærəʊ] Pfeil m; '**~head** Pfeilspitze f

ar·se·nic - [ˈɑːsnɪk] Arsen n

ar·son jur. [ˈɑːsn] Brandstiftung f

art [ɑːt] Kunst f; Kunst...; △ *nicht* **Art**

ar·te·ri·al [ɑːˈtɪərɪəl] anat. Schlagader...; ~ **road** Hauptverkehrsstraße f

ar·te·ry [ˈɑːtərɪ] anat. Arterie f, Schlagader f; (Haupt)Verkehrsader f

ar·te·ri·o·scle·ro·sis med. [ɑːtɪərɪəʊsklɪəˈrəʊsɪs] Arteriosklerose f, Arterienverkalkung f

'**art·ful** schlau, verschmitzt

'**art gal·le·ry** Gemäldegalerie f

ar·thri·tis med. [ɑːˈθraɪtɪs] Arthritis f, Gelenkentzündung f

ar·ti·choke bot. [ˈɑːtɪtʃəʊk] Artischocke f

ar·ti·cle [ˈɑːtɪkl] Artikel m (a. gr.)

ar·tic·u·late 1. [ɑːˈtɪkjʊlət] deutlich (aus)sprechen; **2.** [ɑːˈtɪkjʊlət] deutlich ausgesprochen; gegliedert; ~**lat·ed** [ɑːˈtɪkjʊleɪtɪd]: Gelenk...; ~ **lorry** Brit. mot. Sattelschlepper m; ~**la·tion** [ɑːtɪkjʊˈleɪʃn] (deutliche) Aussprache; Gelenk n

ar·ti·fi·cial [ɑːtɪˈfɪʃl] künstlich, Kunst...; ~ **person** juristische Person

ar·til·le·ry [ɑːˈtɪlərɪ] Artillerie f

ar·ti·san [ɑːtɪˈzæn] Handwerker m

art·ist [ˈɑːtɪst] Künstler(in); **ar·tis·tic** [ɑːˈtɪstɪk] (~*ally*) künstlerisch, Kunst...

'**art·less** schlicht; naiv

arts [ɑːts] pl. Geisteswissenschaften pl.; **Faculty of** ♀, Am. ♀ **Department** philosophische Fakultät f

as [æz] **1.** adv. so, ebenso; wie; (in der Eigenschaft) als; **2.** cj. (gerade) wie, so wie; ebenso wie; als, während; obwohl, obgleich; da, weil; besondere Wendungen: ~ ... ~ (eben)so ... wie; ~ **for**, ~ **to** was ... (an)betrifft; ~ **from** von e-m Zeitpunkt an, ab; ~ **it were** sozusagen; ~ **Hamlet** als Hamlet

as·bes·tos [æsˈbestəs] Asbest m

as·cend [əˈsend] (auf)steigen; ansteigen; besteigen

[əˈsenʃn] Aufsteigen n (bsd. astr.); Aufstieg m (e-s Ballons etc.); **♀·sion (Day)** Himmelfahrt(stag m) f; ~**t** [əˈsent] Aufstieg m; Besteigung f; Steigung f

as·cet·ic [əˈsetɪk] (~*ally*) asketisch

ASCII [ˈæskɪ] Abk. für **American Standard Code for Information Interchange** (standardisierter Code zur Darstellung alphanumerischer Zeichen)

a·sep·tic med. [æˈseptɪk] **1.** aseptisch, keimfrei; **2.** aseptisches Mittel

ash[1] [æʃ] bot. Esche f; Eschenholz n

ash[2] [æʃ] a. ~**es** pl. Asche f

a·shamed [əˈʃeɪmd] beschämt; **be** ~ **of** sich schämen für (od. gen.)

'**ash can** Am. → **dustbin**

ash·en [ˈæʃn] Aschen...; aschfahl, -grau

a·shore [əˈʃɔː] am od. ans Ufer od. Land

'**ash·tray** Asch(en)becher m; ♀ '**Wednes·day** Aschermittwoch m

A·sia [ˈeɪʃə] Asien n; **A·sian** [ˈeɪʃn, ˈeɪʒn], **A·si·at·ic** [eɪʃɪˈætɪk] **1.** asiatisch; **2.** Asiat(in)

a·side [əˈsaɪd] beiseite (a. thea.), seitwärts; ~ **from** Am. abgesehen von

ask [ɑːsk] v/t. fragen (s.th. nach et.); verlangen (of, from s.o. von j-m); bitten (s.o. [for] s.th. j. um et.; that darum, daß); erbitten; ~ (s.o.) a question (j-m) e-e Frage stellen; v/i. ~ for bitten um; fragen nach; he ~ed for it od. for trouble er wollte es ja so haben; to be had for the ~ing umsonst zu haben

a·skance [əˈskæns]: look ~ at s.o. j-n schief od. mißtrauisch ansehen

a·skew [əˈskjuː] schief

a·sleep [əˈsliːp] schlafend; be (fast, sound) ~ (fest) schlafen; fall ~ einschlafen

as·par·a·gus bot. [əˈspærəgəs] Spargel m

as·pect [ˈæspekt] Lage f; Aspekt m, Seite f, Gesichtspunkt m

as·phalt [ˈæsfælt] **1.** Asphalt m; **2.** asphaltieren

as·pic [ˈæspɪk] Aspik m, Gelee n

as·pi·rant [əˈspaɪərənt] Bewerber(in); ~**ra·tion** [æspəˈreɪʃn] Ambition f, Bestrebung f

as·pire [əˈspaɪə] streben, trachten (to, after nach)

ass zo. [æs] Esel m; △ *nicht* **As**

as·sail [əˈseɪl] angreifen; **be** ~**ed with** doubts von Zweifeln befallen werden;

as·sai·lant [ə'seɪlənt] Angreifer(in)

as·sas·sin [ə'sæsɪn] (*bsd.* politische[r]) Mörder(in), Attentäter(in); **~·ate** *bsd. pol.* [ə'sæsɪneɪt] ermorden; **be ~d** e-m Attentat *od.* Mordanschlag zum Opfer fallen; **~·a·tion** [əˌsæsɪ'neɪʃn] (**of**) (*bsd.* politischer) Mord (**an** *dat.*), Ermordung *f* (*gen.*), Attentat *n* (auf *acc.*)

as·sault [ə'sɔːlt] **1.** Angriff *m*; **2.** angreifen, überfallen

as·sem·blage [ə'semblɪdʒ] (An-) Sammlung *f*; *tech.* Montage *f*; **~·ble** [ə'sembl] (sich) versammeln; *tech.* montieren; **~·bler** [ə'semblə] Assembler *m* (*e-e Programmiersprache*; *Übersetzungsprogramm*); **~·bly** [ə'semblɪ] Versammlung *f*, Gesellschaft *f*; *tech.* Montage *f*; **~·bly line** *tech.* Fließband *n*

as·sent [ə'sent] **1.** Zustimmung *f*; **2.** (**to**) zustimmen (*dat.*); billigen (*acc.*)

as·sert [ə'sɜːt] behaupten; geltend machen; **~ o.s.** sich behaupten *od.* durchsetzen; **as·ser·tion** [ə'sɜːʃn] Behauptung *f*; Erklärung *f*; Geltendmachung *f*

as·sess [ə'ses] *Kosten etc.* festsetzen; *Einkommen etc.* (zur Steuer) veranlagen (**at** mit); *fig.* abschätzen, beurteilen; **~·ment** Festsetzung *f*; (Steuer)Veranlagung *f*; *fig.* Einschätzung *f*

as·set ['æset] *econ.* Aktivposten *m*; *fig.* Plus *n*, Gewinn *m*; **~s** *pl. jur.* Vermögen(smasse *f*) *n*; *jur.* Konkursmasse *f*; *econ.* Aktiva *pl.*

as·sid·u·ous [ə'sɪdjʊəs] emsig, fleißig

as·sign [ə'saɪn] an-, zuweisen; bestimmen; zuschreiben; **~·ment** An-, Zuweisung *f*; Aufgabe *f*; Auftrag *m*; *jur.* Abtretung *f*, Übertragung *f*

as·sim·i·late [ə'sɪmɪleɪt] (sich) angleichen *od.* anpassen (**to**, **with** *dat.*); **~·la·tion** [əsɪmɪ'leɪʃn] Assimilation *f*, Angleichung *f*, Anpassung *f*

as·sist [ə'sɪst] *j-m* beistehen, helfen; unterstützen; **~·ance** Beistand *m*, Hilfe *f*; **as·sis·tant 1.** stellvertretend, Hilfs...; **2.** Assistent(in), Mitarbeiter(in); (**shop**) **~** *Brt.* Verkäufer(in)

as·so·ci·ate 1. [ə'səʊʃɪeɪt] vereinigen, -binden, zusammenschließen; assoziieren; **~ with** verkehren mit; **2.** [ə'səʊʃɪət] Teilhaber(in); **~·a·tion** [əsəʊsɪ'eɪʃn] Vereinigung *f*, Verbindung *f*; Verein *m*

as·sort [ə'sɔːt] sortieren, aussuchen, zusammenstellen; **~·ment** *econ.* (**of**) Sor-

timent *n* (von), Auswahl *f* (**an** *dat.*)

as·sume [ə'sjuːm] annehmen, voraussetzen; übernehmen; **as·sump·tion** [ə'sʌmpʃn] Annahme *f*, Voraussetzung *f*; Übernahme *f*; **the ⁀** *rel.* Mariä Himmelfahrt *f*

as·sur·ance [ə'ʃɔːrəns] Zu-, Versicherung *f*; *bsd. Brt.* (Lebens)Versicherung *f*; Sicherheit *f*, Gewißheit *f*; Selbstsicherheit *f*; **~e** [ə'ʃɔː] *j-m* versichern; *bsd. Brt. j-s Leben* versichern; **~ed 1.** sicher; **2.** *bsd. Brt.* Versicherte(r *m*) *f*; **~ed·ly** [ə'ʃɔːrɪdlɪ] ganz gewiß

as·te·risk *print.* ['æstərɪsk] Sternchen *n*

asth·ma *med.* ['æsmə] Asthma *n*

as·ton·ish [ə'stonɪʃ] in Erstaunen setzen; **be ~ed** erstaunt sein (**at** über *acc.*); **~·ing** erstaunlich; **~·ment** (Er)Staunen *n*, Verwunderung *f*

as·tound [ə'staʊnd] verblüffen

a·stray [ə'streɪ]: **go ~** vom Weg abkommen; *fig.* auf Abwege geraten; irregehen; **lead ~** *fig.* irreführen, verleiten; vom rechten Weg abbringen

a·stride [ə'straɪd] rittlings (**of** auf *dat.*)

as·trin·gent *med.* [ə'strɪndʒənt] **1.** adstringierend; **2.** Adstringens *n*

as·trol·o·gy [ə'strolədʒɪ] Astrologie *f*

as·tro·naut ['æstrənɔːt] Astronaut *m*, (Welt)Raumfahrer *m*

as·tron·o·my [ə'stronəmɪ] Astronomie *f*

as·tute [ə'stjuːt] scharfsinnig; schlau

a·sun·der [ə'sʌndə] auseinander, entzwei

a·sy·lum [ə'saɪləm] Asyl *n*; **right of ~** Asylrecht *n*; **~ seek·er** Asylant(in), Asylbewerber(in)

at [æt] *prp.* *Ort*: in, an, bei, auf; *Richtung*: auf, nach, gegen, zu; *Beschäftigung*: bei, beschäftigt mit, in; *Art u. Weise, Zustand*: in, bei, zu, unter; *Preis etc.*: für, um; *Zeit, Alter*: um, bei; **~ the baker's** beim Bäcker; **~ the door** an der Tür; **~ school** in der Schule; **~ 10 pounds** für 10 Pfund; **~ 18** mit 18 (Jahren); **~ the age of** im Alter von; **~ 8 o'clock** um 8 Uhr

ate [et] *pret. von* **eat** 1

a·the·is·m ['eɪθɪzəm] Atheismus *m*

ath·lete ['æθliːt] (*bsd.* Leicht)Athlet *m*; **~·let·ic** [æθ'letɪk] (**~ally**) athletisch; **~·let·ics** *sg. od. pl.* (*bsd.* Leicht)Athletik *f*

At·lan·tic [ət'læntɪk] **1.** *a.* ~ *Ocean* der Atlantik; **2.** atlantisch

ATM *Am.* [eɪ tiː 'em] *Abk. für* **automatic teller machine** → **cash dispenser**

at·mo·sphere ['ætməsfɪə] Atmosphäre *f* (*a. fig.*); **~·spher·ic** [ætməs'ferɪk] (**~ally**) atmosphärisch

at·oll ['ætɒl] Atoll *n*

at·om ['ætəm] Atom *n* (*a. fig.*); '~ **bomb** Atombombe *f*

a·tom·ic [ə'tɒmɪk] (**~ally**) atomar, Atom...; ~ **'age** Atomzeitalter *n*; ~ **'bomb** Atombombe *f*; ~ **'en·er·gy** Atomenergie *f*; ~ **'pile** Atomreaktor *m*; ~ **'pow·er** Atomkraft *f*; ~**'pow·ered** atomgetrieben; ~ **'waste** Atommüll *m*

at·om·ize ['ætəmaɪz] atomisieren; *Flüssigkeit* zerstäuben; **'~·iz·er** Zerstäuber *m*

a·tone [ə'təʊn]: ~ *for et.* wiedergutmachen; **~·ment** Buße *f*, Sühne *f*

a·tro·cious [ə'trəʊʃəs] scheußlich, gräßlich; grausam; **~·c·i·ty** [ə'trɒsətɪ] Scheußlichkeit *f*; Greueltat *f*

at·tach [ə'tætʃ] *v/t.* (**to**) anheften, ankleben (an *acc.*), befestigen, anbringen (an *dat.*); *Wert, Wichtigkeit etc.* beimessen (*dat.*); *be* **~ed** *to fig.* hängen an; **~·ment** Befestigung *f*; Bindung *f* (**to** an *acc.*); Anhänglichkeit *f* (**to** an *acc.*)

at·tack [ə'tæk] **1.** angreifen; **2.** Angriff *m*; med. Anfall *m*

at·tempt [ə'tempt] **1.** versuchen; **2.** Versuch *m*; *an* ~ *on s.o.'s life* ein Mordanschlag *od.* Attentat auf j-n

at·tend [ə'tend] *v/t.* (ärztlich) behandeln; *Kranke* pflegen; teilnehmen an, *Schule, Vorlesung etc.* besuchen; *fig.* begleiten; *v/i.* anwesend sein; erscheinen; ~ *to j-n* (*im Laden*) bedienen; *are you being* **~ed** *to?* werden Sie schon bedient?; ~ *to* erledigen (*acc.*); **~·ance** Dienst *m*, Bereitschaft *f*; Pflege *f*; Anwesenheit *f*, Erscheinen *n*; Besucher *pl.*, Teilnehmer *pl.*; Besuch(erzahl *f*) *m*, Beteiligung *f*; **~·ant** Begleiter(in); Aufseher(in); (*Tank*)Wart *m*

at·ten·tion [ə'tenʃn] Aufmerksamkeit *f* (*a. fig.*); **~·tive** [ə'tentɪv] aufmerksam

at·tic ['ætɪk] Dachboden *m*; Dachkammer *f*

at·ti·tude ['ætɪtjuːd] (Ein)Stellung *f*; Haltung *f*

at·tor·ney [ə'tɜːnɪ] Bevollmächtigte(r *m*) *f*; *Am. jur.* (Rechts)Anwalt *m*, (-)Anwältin *f*; **power of** ~ Vollmacht *f*; **2 'Gen·er·al** *Brt. jur.* erster Kronanwalt; *Am. jur.* Justizminister *m*

at·tract [ə'trækt] anziehen; *Aufmerksamkeit* erregen; *fig.* reizen; **at·trac·tion** [ə'trækʃn] Anziehung(skraft) *f*, Reiz *m*; Attraktion *f*, *thea. etc.* Zugnummer *f*, -stück *n*; **at·trac·tive** [ə'træktɪv] anziehend; attraktiv; reizvoll

at·trib·ute¹ [ə'trɪbjuːt] zuschreiben (**to** *dat.*); zurückführen (**to** auf *acc.*)

at·tri·bute² ['ætrɪbjuːt] Attribut *n* (*a. gr.*), Eigenschaft *f*, Merkmal *n*

at·tune [ə'tjuːn]: ~ *to fig.* einstellen auf (*acc.*)

au·ber·gine *bot.* ['əʊbəʒiːn] Aubergine *f*

au·burn ['ɔːbən] kastanienbraun (*Haar*)

auc·tion ['ɔːkʃn] **1.** Auktion *f*, Versteigerung *f*; **2.** *mst* ~ *off* versteigern; **~·tio·neer** [ɔːkʃə'nɪə] Auktionator *m*

au·da·cious [ɔː'deɪʃəs] unverfroren, dreist; **~·c·i·ty** [ɔː'dæsətɪ] Unverfrorenheit *f*, Dreistigkeit *f*

au·di·ble ['ɔːdəbl] hörbar

au·di·ence ['ɔːdjəns] Publikum *n*, Zuhörer(schaft *f*) *pl.*, Zuschauer *pl.*, Besucher *pl.*, Leser(kreis *m*) *pl.*; Audienz *f*

au·di·o... ['ɔːdɪəʊ] audio...; '~ **cas·sette** Text-, Tonkassette *f*; **~·vis·u·al 'aids** *pl.* audiovisuelle Unterrichtsmittel *pl.*

au·dit *econ.* ['ɔːdɪt] **1.** Buchprüfung *f*; **2.** prüfen

au·di·tion *mus., thea.* [ɔː'dɪʃn] Vorsingen *n*, Vorsprechen *n*

au·di·tor *econ.* ['ɔːdɪtə] Buchprüfer *m*; *univ.* Gasthörer(in)

au·di·to·ri·um [ɔːdɪ'tɔːrɪəm] Zuhörer-, Zuschauerraum *m*; *Am.* Vortrags-, Konzertsaal *m*

Aug *nur geschr. Abk. für* **August** Aug., August *m*

au·ger *tech.* ['ɔːgə] großer Bohrer

Au·gust ['ɔːgəst] (*Abk.* **Aug**) August *m*

aunt [ɑːnt] Tante *f*; **~·ie**, **~·y** ['ɑːntɪ] Tantchen *n*

au pair (girl) [əʊ 'peə gɜːl] Au-pair-Mädchen *n*

aus·pic·es ['ɔːspɪsɪz] *pl.* **under the** ~ **of** unter der Schirmherrschaft (*gen.*)

aus·tere [ɒ'stɪə] streng; enthaltsam; dürftig; einfach, schmucklos

Aus·tra·li·a [ɒ'streɪljə] Australien *n*; **Aus·tra·li·an** [ɒ'streɪljən] **1.** australisch; **2.** Australier(in)

Aus·tri·a ['ɒstrɪə] Österreich *n*; **Aus·tri·an** ['ɒstrɪən] **1.** österreichisch; **2.** Österreicher(in)

au·then·tic [ɔ:'θentɪk] (*~ally*) authentisch; zuverlässig; echt

au·thor ['ɔ:θə] Urheber(in); Autor(in); Verfasser(in), *a. allg.* Schriftsteller(in); **~·ess** ['ɔ:θərɪs] Autorin *f*, Verfasserin *f*, *a. allg.* Schriftstellerin *f*

au·thor·i·ta·tive [ɔ:'θɒrɪtətɪv] gebieterisch; herrisch; maßgebend; **~·ty** [ɔ:'θɒrətɪ] Autorität *f*; Nachdruck *m*, Gewicht *n*; Vollmacht *f*; Einfluß *m* (*over* auf *acc.*); Ansehen *n*; Quelle *f*; Autorität *f*, Kapazität *f*; *mst* **authorities** *pl.* Behörde *f*

au·thor·ize ['ɔ:θəraɪz] *j-n* autorisieren, ermächtigen, bevollmächtigen

'au·thor·ship Urheberschaft *f*

au·to *Am.* ['ɔ:təʊ] (*pl. -tos*) Auto *n*

au·to... ['ɔ:təʊ] auto..., selbst..., Auto..., Selbst...

au·to·bi·og·ra·phy [ɔ:təbaɪ'ɒɡrəfɪ] Autobiographie *f*

au·to·graph ['ɔ:təɡrɑːf] Autogramm *n*

au·to·mat *TM* ['ɔ:təmæt] Automatenrestaurant *n* (*in den USA*)

au·to·mate ['ɔ:təmeɪt] automatisieren

au·to·mat·ic [ɔ:tə'mætɪk] (*~ally*) **1.** automatisch; **2.** Selbstladepistole *f*, -gewehr *n*; Auto *n* mit Automatik; **~ tel·ler ma·chine** *Am.* (*abbr.* **ATM**) → **cash dispenser**

au·to·ma·tion [ɔ:tə'meɪʃn] Automation *f*

au·tom·a·ton *fig.* [ɔ:'tɒmətən] (*pl. -ta* [-tə], **-tons**) Roboter *m*

au·to·mo·bile *bsd. Am.* ['ɔ:təməbi:l] Auto *n*, Automobil *n*

au·ton·o·my [ɔ:'tɒnəmɪ] Autonomie *f*

'au·to·tel·ler *Am.* → **cash dispenser**

au·tumn ['ɔ:təm] Herbst *m*; **au·tum·nal** [ɔ:'tʌmnəl] herbstlich, Herbst...

aux·il·i·a·ry [ɔ:g'zɪljərɪ] helfend, Hilfs...

a·vail [ə'veɪl]: **to no ~** vergeblich; **a·vai·la·ble** verfügbar, vorhanden; erreichbar; *econ.* lieferbar, vorrätig, erhältlich

av·a·lanche ['ævəlɑ:nʃ] Lawine *f*

av·a·rice ['ævərɪs] Habsucht *f*; **~·ri·cious** [ævə'rɪʃəs] habgierig

Ave *nur geschr. Abk. für* **Avenue**

a·venge [ə'vendʒ] rächen; **a·veng·er** Rächer(in)

av·e·nue ['ævənju:] Allee *f*; Boulevard *m*, Prachtstraße *f*

av·e·rage ['ævərɪdʒ] **1.** Durchschnitt *m*; **2.** durchschnittlich, Durchschnitts...

a·verse [ə'vɜːs] abgeneigt (*to dat.*); **a·ver·sion** [ə'vɜːʃn] Widerwille *m*, Abneigung *f*

a·vert [ə'vɜːt] abwenden (*a. fig.*)

a·vi·a·ry ['eɪvɪərɪ] Vogelhaus *n*, Voliere *f*

a·vi·a·tion *aviat.* [eɪvɪ'eɪʃn] Luftfahrt *f*; **~·tor** ['eɪvɪeɪtə] Flieger *m*

av·id ['ævɪd] gierig (*for* nach); begeistert (*over* auf *acc.*)

av·o·ca·do *bot.* [ævə'kɑːdəʊ] Avocado *f*

a·void [ə'vɔɪd] (ver)meiden; ausweichen; **~·ance** Vermeidung *f*

a·vow·al [ə'vaʊəl] Bekenntnis *n*, (Ein)Geständnis *n*

AWACS ['eɪwæks] *Abk. für* **Airborne Warning and Control system** (*luftgestütztes Frühwarnsystem*)

a·wait [ə'weɪt] erwarten

a·wake [ə'weɪk] **1.** wach, munter; **2.** *a.* **a·wak·en** [ə'weɪkən] (*awoke od. awaked*, *awoken od. awaked*) *v/t.* (auf)wecken; *v/i.* auf-, erwachen; **a·wak·en·ing** [ə'weɪkənɪŋ] Erwachen *n*

a·ward [ə'wɔːd] **1.** Belohnung *f*; Preis *m*, Auszeichnung *f*; **2.** zuerkennen, *Preis etc.* verleihen

a·ware [ə'weə]: **be ~ of s.th.** von et. wissen, sich e-r Sache bewußt sein; **become ~ of s.th.** et. merken

a·way [ə'weɪ] weg, fort; (weit) entfernt; immer weiter, d(a)rauflos; *Sport*: auswärts...; **~ match** Auswärtsspiel *n*

awe [ɔː] **1.** (Ehr)Furcht *f*, Scheu *f*; **2.** *j-m* (Ehr)Furcht *od.* großen Respekt einflößen

aw·ful ['ɔːfl] furchtbar, schrecklich

awk·ward ['ɔːkwəd] ungeschickt, linkisch; unangenehm; unhandlich, sperrig; ungünstig (*Zeitpunkt etc.*)

awl [ɔːl] Ahle *f*, Pfriem *m*

aw·ning ['ɔːnɪŋ] Plane *f*; Markise *f*

a·woke [ə'wəʊk] *pret. von* **awake** 2; *a.* **a·wok·en** [ə'wəʊkən] *p.p. von* **awake** 2

B

A.W.O.L. F [eɪ dʌblju: əʊ 'el, 'eɪwɒl]
  Abk. für absent without leave unerlaubt abwesend
a·wry [ə'raɪ] schief
ax(e) [æks] Axt *f*, Beil *n*

ax·is ['æksɪs] (*pl.* **-es** [-sɪ:z]) Achse *f*
ax·le *tech.* ['æksl] (Rad)Achse *f*, Welle *f*
ay(e) [aɪ] parl. [aɪ] Jastimme *f*
A-Z *Brt.* [eɪ tə 'zed] *etwa* Stadtplan *m*
az·ure ['æʒə] azur-, himmelblau

B

B, b [bi:] B, b *n*
b *nur geschr. Abk. für born* geb., geboren
BA [bi: 'eɪ] *Abk. für: Bachelor of Arts*
  Bakkalaureus *m* der Philosophie;
  British Airways (*brit. Luftverkehrsge-
  sellschaft*)
bab·ble ['bæbl] **1.** stammeln; plappern,
  schwatzen; plätschern (*Bach*); **2.** Geplapper *n*, Geschwätz *n*
babe [beɪb] kleines Kind, Baby *n*; *Am.* F
  Puppe *f* (*Mädchen*)
ba·boon *zo.* [bə'bu:n] Pavian *m*
ba·by ['beɪbɪ] **1.** Baby *n*, Säugling *m*,
  kleines Kind; *Am.* F Puppe *f* (*Mädchen*); **2.** Baby..., Kinder...; klein; ~
  boom Babyboom *m* (*geburtenstarke
  Jahrgänge*); '~ **bug·gy** *Am.*, '~
  car·riage *Am.* Kinderwagen *m*;
  ~hood ['beɪbɪhʊd] Säuglingsalter *n*;
  ~ish *contp.* ['beɪbɪʃ] kindisch;
  ~mind·er *Brt.* ['beɪbɪmaɪndə] Tagesmutter *f*; '~**sit** (*-tt-; -sat*) babysitten;
  '~**sit·ter** Babysitter(in)
bach·e·lor ['bætʃələ] Junggeselle *m*;
  univ. Bakkalaureus *m*
back [bæk] **1.** Rücken *m*; Rückseite *f*;
  (Rück)Lehne *f*; hinterer *od.* rückwärti-
  ger Teil; *Sport:* Verteidiger *m*; **2.** *adj.*
  Hinter..., Rück..., hintere(r, -s), rück-
  wärtig; rückständig (*Zahlung*); alt, zu-
  rückliegend (*Zeitung etc.*); **3.** *adv.* zurück, rückwärts; **4.** *v/t.* mit e-m Rücken
  versehen; wetten auf (*acc.*); ~ **up**
  unterstützen; zurückbewegen,
  zurückstoßen mit (*Auto*); ~ **up** *Computer:* e-e Sicherungskopie machen von;
  v/i. oft ~ **up** sich rückwärts bewegen,
  zurückgehen *od.* -fahren, *mot. a.* zurückstoßen; ~ **in**(**to a parking space**)
  mot. rückwärts einparken; ~ **up** Com-

puter: e-e Sicherungskopie machen; '~
ache Rückenschmerzen *pl.*; '~**bite**
  (*-bit, -bitten*) verleumden; '~**bone**
  Rückgrat *n*; '~**break·ing** erschöpfend, mörderisch (*Arbeit*); '~**chat** *Brt.*
  freche Antwort(en *pl.*); '~**comb** Haar
  toupieren; ~ '**door** Hintertür *f; fig.*
  Hintertürchen *n*; '~**er** Unterstüt-
  zer(in), Geldgeber(in); **~fire** *mot.*
  Früh-, Fehlzündung *f*; '~**ground**
  Hintergrund *m*; '~**hand** *Sport:* Rück-
  hand(schlag *m*) *f*; '~**heel·er** Fußball:
  Hackentrick *m*; '~**ing** Unterstützung
  f; ~ '**num·ber** alte Nummer (*e-r Zeitung*); '~**pack** großer Rucksack; '~
  pack·er Rucksacktourist(in); '~
  pack·ing Rucksacktourismus *m*; '~
  '**seat** Rücksitz *m*; '~**side** Gesäß *n*,
  Hintern *m*, Po *m*; '~**space** (**key**)
  Computer etc.: Rück(stell)taste *f*; '~
  stairs Hintertreppe *f*; '~ **street** Sei-
  tenstraße *f*; '~**stroke** *Sport:* Rücken-
  schwimmen *n*; '~**talk** *Am.* freche Ant-
  wort(en *pl.*); '~**track** *fig.* e-n Rückzie-
  her machen; '~**up** Unterstützung *f*;
  tech. Ersatzgerät *n*; *Computer:* Backup
  n, Sicherungskopie *f; Am. mot.* Rückstau *m*; **~ward** ['bækwəd] **1.** *adj.*
  Rück(wärts)...; zurückgeblieben (*Entwicklung*); rückständig; **2.** *adv.* (*a.*
  '~**wards**) rückwärts, zurück; '~**yard**
  Brt. Hinterhof *m; Am.* Garten *m* hinter
  dem Haus
ba·con ['beɪkən] Speck *m*
bac·te·ri·a *biol.* [bæk'tɪərɪə] *pl.* Bakteri-
  en *pl.*
bad [bæd] (*worse, worst*) schlecht, böse, schlimm; *go* ~ schlecht werden, verderben; *he is in a* ~ *way* es geht ihm
  schlecht, er ist übel dran; *he is* ~*ly off* es

band

geht ihm sehr schlecht; **~ly wounded** schwerverwundet; **want ~ly** F dringend brauchen

bade [beɪd] *pret. von* bid 1

badge [bædʒ] Abzeichen *n*; Dienstmarke *f*

bad·ger ['bædʒə] 1. *zo.* Dachs *m*; 2. plagen, *j-m* zusetzen

bad·min·ton ['bædmintən] Federball(spiel *n*) *m*, *Sport:* Badminton *n*

bad-'tempered schlechtgelaunt

baf·fle ['bæfl] *j-n* verwirren; *Plan etc.* vereiteln, durchkreuzen

bag [bæg] 1. Beutel *m*, Sack *m*; Tüte *f*; Tasche *f*; **~ and baggage** (mit) Sack u. Pack; 2. **(-gg-)** in e-n Beutel *etc.* tun; in Beutel verpacken *od.* abfüllen; *hunt.* zur Strecke bringen; *a.* **~ out** sich bauschen

bag·gage *bsd. Am.* ['bægɪdʒ] (Reise-) Gepäck *n*; **~ car** *Am. rail.* Gepäckwagen *m*; **~ check** *Am.* Gepäckschein *m*; **~ claim** *Am.* Gepäckausgabe *f*; **~ room** *Am.* Gepäckaufbewahrung *f*

bag·gy F ['bægɪ] **(-ier, -iest)** bauschig; ausgebeult *(Hose)*

'bag·pipes *pl.* Dudelsack *m*

bail [beɪl] 1. Bürge *m*; Kaution *f*; **be out on ~** gegen Kaution auf freiem Fuß sein; **go** *od.* **stand ~ for s.o.** für *j-n* Kaution stellen; 2. **~ out** *j-n* gegen Kaution freibekommen; *Am. aviat.* → **bale²**

bai·liff *Brt.* ['beɪlɪf] *jur. bsd.* Gerichtsvollzieher *m*; (Guts)Verwalter *m*

bait [beɪt] 1. Köder *m* (*a. fig.*); 2. mit e-m Köder versehen; *fig.* ködern

bake [beɪk] backen, im (Back)Ofen braten; *Ziegel* brennen; dörren; **~d beans** *pl.* Bohnen *pl.* in Tomatensoße; **~d po'ta·toes** *pl. ungeschälte, im Ofen gebackene Kartoffeln;* **'bak·er** Bäcker *m*; **bak·er·y** ['beɪkərɪ] Bäckerei *f*; **'bak·ing-pow·der** Backpulver *n*

bal·ance ['bæləns] 1. Waage *f*; Gleichgewicht *n* (*a. fig.*); *econ.* Bilanz *f*; *econ.* Saldo *m*, Kontostand *m*, Guthaben *n*; *econ.* Restbetrag *m*; **keep one's ~** das Gleichgewicht halten; **lose one's ~** das Gleichgewicht verlieren; *fig.* die Fassung verlieren; **~ of payments** *econ.* Zahlungsbilanz *f*; **~ of power** *pol.* Kräftegleichgewicht *n*; **~ of trade** *econ.* Handelsbilanz *f*; 2. *v/t.* (ab-, er)wägen;

im Gleichgewicht halten, balancieren; *Konten etc.* ausgleichen; *v/i.* balancieren, sich ausgleichen; **~ sheet** *econ.* Bilanz *f* *(Aufstellung)*

bal·co·ny ['bælkənɪ] Balkon *m* (*a. thea.*)

bald [bɔːld] kahl △ *nicht* **bald**

bale¹ *econ.* [beɪl] Ballen *m*

bale² *Brt. aviat.* [beɪl]: **~ out** (mit dem Fallschirm) abspringen

bale·ful ['beɪlfl] haßerfüllt *(Blick)*

balk [bɔːk] 1. Balken *m*; 2. stutzen; scheuen

ball¹ [bɔːl] 1. Ball *m*; Kugel *f*; *anat.* (Hand-, Fuß)Ballen *m*; Knäuel *m, n*; Kloß *m*; **keep the ~ rolling** das Gespräch *od.* die Sache in Gang halten; **play ~** F mitmachen; **long ~** *Sport:* langer Paß; 2. (sich) (zusammen)ballen

ball² [bɔːl] Ball *m*, Tanzveranstaltung *f*

bal·lad ['bæləd] Ballade *f*

bal·last ['bæləst] 1. Ballast *m*; 2. mit Ballast beladen

ball 'bear·ing *tech.* Kugellager *n*

bal·let ['bæleɪ] Ballett *n*

bal·lis·tics *mil., phys.* [bə'lɪstɪks] *sg.* Ballistik *f*

bal·loon [bə'luːn] 1. Ballon *m*; Sprech-, Denkblase *f*; 2. sich (auf)blähen

bal·lot ['bælət] 1. Stimmzettel *m*; (*bsd.* geheime) Wahl; 2. **(for)** stimmen (für), (*bsd.* in geheimer Wahl) wählen (acc.); **~ box** Wahlurne *f*; **~ pa·per** Stimmzettel *m*

'ball·point, ~ 'pen Kugelschreiber *m*, F Kuli *m*

'ball·room Ball-, Tanzsaal *m*

balls V [bɔːlz] *pl.* Eier *pl.* *(Hoden)*

balm [bɑːm] Balsam *m* (*a. fig.*)

balm·y ['bɑːmɪ] **(-ier, -iest)** lind, mild

ba·lo·ney *Am. sl.* [bə'ləʊnɪ] Quatsch *m*

bal·us·trade [bælə'streɪd] Balustrade *f*, Brüstung *f*, Geländer *n*

bam·boo *bot.* [bæm'buː] **(*pl.* -boos)** Bambus(rohr *n*) *m*

bam·boo·zle F [bæm'buːzl] betrügen, übers Ohr hauen

ban [bæn] 1. (amtliches) Verbot, Sperre *f*; *rel.* Bann *m*; 2. **(-nn-)** verbieten

ba·nal [bə'nɑːl] banal, abgedroschen

ba·na·na *bot.* [bə'nɑːnə] Banane *f*

band [bænd] 1. Band *n*; Streifen *m*; Schar *f*, Gruppe *f*; (*bsd. Räuber*)Bande *f*; (*Musik*)Kapelle *f*, (Tanz-, Unterhaltungs)Orchester *n*, (*Jazz-, Rock*)Band f; △ *nicht* Buch-Band, Tonband; **2.** ~ *together* sich zusammentun *od.* zusammenrotten

ban·dage ['bændɪdʒ] **1.** Bandage f; Binde f; Verband m; *Am.* (Heft)Pflaster n; **2.** bandagieren; verbinden

'Band-Aid *TM Am.* (Heft)Pflaster n

b & b, B & B [bi: ənd 'bi:] *Abk. für* **bed and breakfast** Übernachtung f mit Frühstück

ban·dit ['bændɪt] Bandit m

'band|·lead·er *mus.* Bandleader m; '~**mas·ter** *mus.* Kapellmeister m

ban·dy ['bændɪ] (-*ier*, -*iest*) krumm; ~**'legged** säbelbeinig, O-beinig

bang [bæŋ] **1.** heftiger Schlag; Knall m; *mst* ~s *pl.* Pony m (*Frisur*); **2.** dröhnend (zu)schlagen; V bumsen; ~ (*away*) ballern

ban·gle ['bæŋgl] Arm-, Fußreif m

ban·ish ['bænɪʃ] verbannen; '~**ment** Verbannung f

ban·is·ter ['bænɪstə] a. ~s *pl.* Treppengeländer n

ban·jo ['bændʒəʊ] (*pl.* -*jos*, -*joes*) Banjo n

bank[1] [bæŋk] **1.** *econ.* Bank f; (*Blut-, Daten- etc.*)Bank f; **2.** v/t. *Geld* bei e-r Bank einzahlen; v/i. ein Bankkonto haben (*with* bei); △ *nicht* Sitz-**Bank**

bank[2] [bæŋk] (Erd)Wall m; Böschung f; (*Fluß- etc.*)Ufer n; (*Sand-, Wolken-*)Bank f; △ *nicht* Sitz-**Bank**

'bank| ac·count Bankkonto n; '~ **bill** *Am.* → **bank note**; '~**book** Sparbuch n; '~ **code** a. ~ **sorting code** *econ.* Bankleitzahl f; '~**er** Bankier m, Banker m; '~**er's card** Scheckkarte f; ~ **'hol·i·day** *Brt.* Bankfeiertag m; '~**ing** Bankgeschäft n, Bankwesen n; Bank...; '~ **note** Banknote f, Geldschein m; '~ **rate** Diskontsatz m

bank·rupt *jur.* ['bæŋkrʌpt] **1.** Konkursschuldner m; **2.** bankrott; *go* ~ in Konkurs gehen, Bankrott machen; **3.** *j-n*, *Unternehmen* bankrott machen; ~**cy** ['bæŋkrʌptsɪ] Bankrott m, Konkurs m

ban·ner ['bænə] Transparent n

banns [bænz] *pl.* Aufgebot n

ban·quet ['bæŋkwɪt] Bankett n

ban·ter ['bæntə] necken

bap|·tis·m ['bæptɪzəm] Taufe f; ~**tize** [bæp'taɪz] taufen

bar [baː] **1.** Stange f, Stab m; (Tor-,

Quer-, Sprung)Latte f; Riegel; Schranke f, Sperre f; *fig.* Hindernis n; (*Gold-etc.*)Barren m; Riegel m, Stange f; *mus.* Taktstrich m; *mus. ein* Takt m; dicker Strich; *jur.* (Gerichts)Schranke f; *jur.* Anwaltschaft f; Bar f; Lokal n, Imbißstube f; *a* ~ *of chocolate* ein Riegel *od.* e-e Tafel Schokolade; *a* ~ *of soap* ein Riegel *od.* Stück Seife; ~*s pl.* Gitter n; **2.** (-*rr*-) zu-, verriegeln; versperren; einsperren; (ver)hindern; ausschließen

barb [baːb] Widerhaken m

bar·bar·i·an [baː'beərɪən] **1.** barbarisch; **2.** Barbar(in)

bar·be·cue ['baːbɪkjuː] **1.** Bratrost m, Grill m; Barbecue n; **2.** auf dem Rost *od.* am Spieß braten, grillen

barbed wire [baːbd 'waɪə] Stacheldraht m

bar·ber ['baːbə] (Herren)Friseur m

'bar code Strichcode m

bare [beə] **1.** (~r, ~st) nackt, bloß; kahl; leer; **2.** entblößen; '~**faced** unverschämt, schamlos; '~**foot**, '~**footed** barfuß; '~**head·ed** barhäuptig; '~**ly** kaum

bar·gain ['baːgɪn] **1.** Geschäft n, Handel m; vorteilhaftes Geschäft, Gelegenheitskauf m; *a* (*dead*) ~ spottbillig; *it's a* ~*!* abgemacht!; *into the* ~ obendrein; **2.** (ver)handeln; '~ **sale** Verkauf m zu herabgesetzten Preisen; Ausverkauf m

barge [baːdʒ] **1.** Lastkahn m; **2.** ~ *in* hereinplatzen (in *acc.*)

bark[1] *mus.* [baːk] Borke f, Rinde

bark[2] [baːk] **1.** bellen; ~ *up the wrong tree* F auf dem Holzweg sein; an der falschen Adresse sein; **2.** Bellen n

bar·ley *bot.* ['baːlɪ] Gerste f; Graupe f

barn [baːn] Scheune f; (Vieh)Stall m

ba·rom·e·ter [bə'rɒmɪtə] Barometer n

bar·on ['bærən] Baron m; Freiherr m; ~**ess** ['bærənɪs] Baronin f; Freifrau f

bar·racks ['bærəks] *sg. mil.* Kaserne f; *contp.* Mietskaserne f; △ *nicht* **Barake**

bar·rage ['bæraːʒ] Staudamm m; *mil.* Sperrfeuer n; (Wort- *etc.*)Schwall m

bar·rel ['bærəl] Faß n, Tonne f; (*Gewehr*)Lauf m; *tech.* Trommel f, Walze f; '~ **or·gan** *mus.* Drehorgel f

bar·ren ['bærən] unfruchtbar; trocken

bar·ri·cade ['bærɪkeɪd] **1.** Barrikade f; **2.** verbarrikadieren; sperren

bar·ri·er ['bærɪə] Schranke f (a. fig.), Barriere f, Sperre f; Hindernis n

bar·row ['bærəʊ] Karre f

bar·ter ['bɑːtə] **1.** Tausch(handel) m; **2.** tauschen (**for** gegen)

base[1] [beɪs] (**~r, ~st**) gemein

base[2] [beɪs] **1.** Basis f; Grundlage f; Fundament n; Fuß m; mil. Standort m; mil. Stützpunkt m; **2.** gründen, stützen (**on** auf acc.)

base[3] chem. [beɪs] Base f

'base·ball Baseball(spiel n) m; **'~board** Am. Scheuerleiste f; **'~·less** grundlos; **'~·line** Tennis etc.: Grundlinie f; **'~·ment** Fundament n; Kellergeschoß n

bash·ful ['bæʃfl] scheu, schüchtern

ba·sic[1] ['beɪsɪk] **1.** grundlegend, Grund...; **2.** **~s** pl. Grundlagen pl.

ba·sic[2] chem. ['beɪsɪk] basisch

BA·SIC ['beɪsɪk] BASIC n (e-e einfache Programmiersprache)

ba·sic·al·ly ['beɪsɪkəlɪ] im Grunde

ba·sin ['beɪsn] Becken n, Schale f, Schüssel f; Tal-, Wasser-, Hafenbecken n

ba·sis ['beɪsɪs] (pl. **-ses** [-siːz]) Basis f; Grundlage f

bask [bɑːsk] sich sonnen (a. fig.)

bas·ket ['bɑːskɪt] Korb m; **'~·ball** Basketball(spiel n) m

bass[1] mus. [beɪs] Baß m

bass[2] zo. [bæs] (pl. **bass, basses**) (Fluß-, See)Barsch m

bas·tard ['bɑːstəd] Bastard m

baste[1] [beɪst] Braten mit Fett begießen

baste[2] [beɪst] (an)heften

bat[1] [bæt] zo. Fledermaus f; **as blind as a ~** stockblind; **be** od. **have ~s in the belfry** F e-n Vogel haben

bat[2] [bæt] Baseball, Kricket: **1.** Schlagholz n, Schläger m; **2.** (**-tt-**) am Schlagen sein

batch [bætʃ] Stapel m, Stoß m; **~ 'file** Computer: Batch-Datei f, Stapeldatei f

bate [beɪt]: **with ~d breath** mit angehaltenem Atem

bath [bɑːθ] **1.** (pl. **baths** [bɑːðz]) (Wannen)Bad n; **have a ~** Brt., **take a ~** Am. baden, ein Bad nehmen; **~s** pl. Bad n; Badeanstalt f; Badeort m; **2.** Brt. v/t.

Kind etc. baden; v/i. baden, ein Bad nehmen

bathe [beɪð] v/t. Wunde etc., bsd. Am. Kind etc. baden; v/i. baden, schwimmen; bsd. Am. baden, ein Bad nehmen

bath·ing ['beɪðɪŋ] Baden n; attr. Bade...; **'~ cos·tume**, **'~ suit** → swimsuit

'bath·|robe Bademantel m; Am. Morgen-, Schlafrock m; **'~·room** Badezimmer n; **'~·tub** Badewanne f

bat·on ['bætən] Stab m; mus. Taktstock m; Schlagstock m, Gummiknüppel m

bat·tal·i·on mil. [bə'tæljən] Bataillon n

bat·ten ['bætn] Latte f

bat·ter[1] ['bætə] heftig schlagen; Frau, Kind etc. mißhandeln; verbeulen; **~ down**, **~ in** Tür einschlagen

bat·ter[2] gastr. ['bætə] Rührteig m

bat·ter[3] ['bætə] Baseball, Kricket: Schläger m, Schlagmann m

bat·ter·y ['bætərɪ] Batterie f; jur. Tätlichkeit f, Körperverletzung f; **assault and ~** jur. tätliche Beleidigung; **'~ charg·er** electr. Ladegerät n; **'~·op·er·at·ed** batteriebetrieben

bat·tle ['bætl] **1.** mil. Schlacht f (**of** bei); fig. Kampf m (**for** um); **2.** kämpfen; **'~·field**, **'~·ground** Schlachtfeld n; **~·ments** ['bætlmənts] pl. Zinnen pl.; **'~·ship** mil. Schlachtschiff n

baulk [bɔːk] → balk

Ba·va·ri·a [bə'veərɪə] Bayern n; **Ba·var·i·an** [bə'veərɪən] **1.** bay(e)risch; **2.** Bayer(in)

bawd·y ['bɔːdɪ] (**-ier, -iest**) obszön

bawl [bɔːl] brüllen, schreien

bay[1] [beɪ] Bai f, Bucht f; arch. Erker m

bay[2] bot. [beɪ] a. **~ tree** Lorbeer(baum) m

bay[3] [beɪ] **1.** bellen, Laut geben (Hund); **2. hold** od. **keep at ~** j-n in Schach halten; et. von sich fernhalten

bay[4] [beɪ] **1.** rotbraun; **2.** Braune(r) m (Pferd)

bay·o·net mil. ['beɪənɪt] Bajonett n

bay 'win·dow Erkerfenster n

ba·zaar [bə'zɑː] Basar m

BBC [bi: bi: 'si:] Abk. für **British Broadcasting Corporation** BBC f (brit. Rundfunkgesellschaft)

BC [bi: 'si:] Abk. für **before Christ** v.Chr., vor Christus

be [bi:] (**was** od. **were**, **been**) sein; zur

B

Bildung des Passivs: werden; stattfinden; werden (*beruflich*); **he wants to ~** ... er möchte ... werden; **how much are the shoes?** was kosten die Schuhe?; **that's five pounds** das macht *od.* kostet fünf Pfund; **she is reading** sie liest gerade; **there is, there are** es gibt

B/E *nur geschr. Abk. für* **bill of exchange** *econ.* Wechsel *m*

beach [biːtʃ] Strand *m*; '**~ball** Wasserball *m*; '**~bug·gy** *mot.* Strandbuggy *m*; '**~wear** Strandkleidung *f*

bea·con ['biːkən] Leucht-, Signalfeuer *n*

bead [biːd] (*Glas-, Schweiß- etc.*)Perle *f*; **~s** *pl. rel.* Rosenkranz *m*; '**~y** (**-ier, -iest**) klein, rund u. glänzend (*Augen*)

beak [biːk] Schnabel *m*; *tech.* Tülle *f*

bea·ker ['biːkə] Becher *m*

beam [biːm] **1.** Balken *m*; Strahl *m*; Peil-, Leit-, Richtstrahl *m*; **2.** ausstrahlen; strahlen (*a. fig.* **with** vor *dat.*)

bean [biːn] *bot.* Bohne *f*; **be full of ~s** F voller Leben(skraft) stecken

bear¹ *zo.* [beə] Bär *m*

bear² [beə] (*bore, borne od. pass. geboren* [*werden*]) tragen; zur Welt bringen, gebären; ertragen, aushalten; *mst negativ*: ausstehen, leiden; **~ out** bestätigen; **~·a·ble** ['beərəbl] erträglich

beard [biəd] Bart *m*; *bot.* Grannen *pl.*; '**~ed** bärtig

bear·er ['beərə] Träger(in); *econ.* Überbringer(in), (*Wertpapier*)Inhaber(in)

bear·ing ['beərɪŋ] Ertragen *n*; Betragen *n*; (*Körper*)Haltung *f*; *fig.* Beziehung *f*; Lage *f*, Richtung *f*, Orientierung *f*; **take one's ~s** sich orientieren; **lose one's ~s** die Orientierung verlieren

beast [biːst] (*a. wildes*) Tier *n*; Bestie *f*; '**~ly** (**-ier, -iest**) scheußlich; **~ of 'prey** Raubtier *n*

beat [biːt] **1.** (**beat, beaten** *od.* **beat**) schlagen; (ver)prügeln; besiegen; übertreffen; **~ it!** F hau ab!; **that's all!** das ist doch der Gipfel *od.* die Höhe!; **that ~s me** das ist mir zu hoch; **~ about the bush** wie die Katze um den heißen Brei herumschleichen; **~ down** *econ.* Preis drücken, herunterhandeln; **~ up** *j-n* zusammenschlagen; **2.** Schlag *m*; *mus.* Takt(schlag) *m*; *Jazz*: Beat *m*; Pulsschlag *m*; Runde *f*, Revier *n* (*e-s Polizisten*); **3.** (**dead**) **~** F wie erschlagen, fix

u. fertig; **~en** ['biːtn] *p.p. von* **beat** 1; **off the ~ track** ungewohn, ungewöhnlich

beau·ti·cian [bjuːˈtɪʃn] Kosmetikerin *f*

beau·ti·ful ['bjuːtəfl] schön; **the ~ people** *pl.* die Schickeria

beau·ty ['bjuːtɪ] Schönheit *f*; **Sleeping ≈** Dornröschen *n*; '**~ par·lo(u)r,** '**~ sal·on** Schönheitssalon *m*

bea·ver ['biːvə] *zo.* Biber *m*; Biberpelz *m*

be·came [bɪˈkeɪm] *pret. von* **become**

be·cause [bɪˈkɒz] weil; **~ of** wegen

beck·on ['bekən] (zu)winken

be·come [bɪˈkʌm] (**-came, -come**) *v/i.* werden (**of** aus); *v/t.* sich schicken für; *j-m* stehen, *j-n* kleiden; △ *nicht* **bekommen**; **be'com·ing** passend; schicklich; kleidsam

bed [bed] **1.** Bett *n*; Lager *n* (*e-s Tieres*); *agr.* Beet *n*; Unterlage *f*; **~ and breakfast** Zimmer *n* mit Frühstück; **2.** (**-dd-**): **~ down** sein Nachtlager aufschlagen; '**~clothes** *pl.* Bettwäsche *f*; '**~ding** Bettzeug *n*; Streu *f*

bed·lam ['bedləm] Tollhaus *n*

'**bed·rid·den** bettlägerig; '**~room** Schlafzimmer *n*; '**~side: at the ~** an (*a. Kranken*)Bett; **~side 'lamp** Nachttischlampe *f*; '**~sit** F, '**~sit·ter,** '**~sit·ting room** F möbliertes Zimmer; Einzimmerappartement *n*; '**~spread** Tagesdecke *f*; '**~stead** Bettgestell *n*; '**~time** Schlafenszeit *f*

bee [biː] *zo.* Biene *f*; **have a ~ in one's bonnet** F e-n Fimmel *od.* Tick haben

beech *bot.* [biːtʃ] Buche *f*; '**~nut** Buchecker *f*

beef [biːf] Rindfleisch *n*; '**~bur·ger** *gastr. bsd. Brt.* Hamburger *m*; **~ tea** (Rind)Fleischbrühe *f*; '**~y** (**-ier, -iest**) F bullig

'**bee·hive** Bienenkorb *m*, -stock *m*; '**~-keep·er** Imker *m*; '**~line: make a ~ for** F schnurstracks zu- *od.* losgehen auf (*acc.*)

been [biːn, bɪn] *p.p. von* **be**

beep·er *Am.* ['biːpə] → **bleeper**

beer [bɪə] Bier *n*

beet *bot.* [biːt] Runkelrübe *f*, *Am. a.* rote Bete *od.* Rübe

bee·tle *zo.* ['biːtl] Käfer *m*

'**beet·root** *bot. Brt.* rote Bete *od.* Rübe

be·fore [bɪˈfɔː] **1.** *adv. räumlich*: vorn,

voran; *zeitlich:* vorher, früher, schon (früher); **2.** *cj.* bevor, ehe, bis; **3.** *prp.* vor; **~hand** zuvor, (im) voraus

be·friend [bɪ'frend] sich *j-s* annehmen; △ *nicht* **befreunden**

beg [beg] (**-gg-**) *v/t. et.* erbitten (*of s.o.* von j-m); betteln um; *j-n* bitten; *v/i.* betteln; (dringend) bitten

be·gan [bɪ'gæn] *pret. von* **begin**

be·get [bɪ'get] (**-tt-; -got, -gotten**) (er)zeugen

beg·gar ['begə] **1.** Bettler(in); F Kerl *m*; **2.** *it ~s all description* es spottet jeder Beschreibung

be·gin [bɪ'gɪn] (**-nn-; began, begun**) beginnen, anfangen; **~ner** Anfänger(in); **~ning** Beginn *m*, Anfang *m*

be·got [bɪ'gɒt] *pret. von* **beget**; **~ten** [bɪ'gɒtn] *p.p. von* **beget**

be·grudge [bɪ'grʌdʒ] mißgönnen

be·guile [bɪ'gaɪl] täuschen; betrügen (*of, out of* um); sich *die Zeit* vertreiben

be·gun [bɪ'gʌn] *p.p. von* **begin**

be·half [bɪ'hɑːf]: *on* (*Am. a. in*) *~ of* im Namen von (*od. auf*)

be·have [bɪ'heɪv] sich (gut) benehmen

be·hav·io(u)r [bɪ'heɪvjə] Benehmen *n*, Betragen *n*, Verhalten *n*; **~al** *psych.* [bɪ'heɪvjərəl] Verhaltens...

be·head [bɪ'hed] enthaupten

be·hind [bɪ'haɪnd] **1.** *adv.* hinten, dahinter; zurück; **2.** *prp.* hinter; **3.** F Hinterteil *n*, Hintern *m*

beige [beɪʒ] beige

be·ing ['biːɪŋ] (Da)Sein *n*, Existenz *f*; (Lebe)Wesen *n*, Geschöpf *n*; *j-s* Wesen *n*, Natur *f*

be·lat·ed [bɪ'leɪtɪd] verspätet

belch [beltʃ] **1.** aufstoßen, rülpsen; *a. ~ out Rauch etc.* speien, ausstoßen; **2.** Rülpser *m*

bel·fry ['belfrɪ] Glockenturm *m*, -stuhl *m*

Bel·gium ['beldʒəm] Belgien *n*; **Bel·gian** ['beldʒən] **1.** belgisch; **2.** Belgier(in)

be·lief [bɪ'liːf] Glaube *m* (*in an acc.*)

be·lie·va·ble [bɪ'liːvəbl] glaubhaft

be·lieve [bɪ'liːv] glauben (*in an acc.*); *I couldn't ~ my ears* (*eyes*) ich traute m-n Ohren (Augen) nicht; **be·liev·er** *rel.* Gläubige(r *m*) *f*

be·lit·tle *fig.* [bɪ'lɪtl] herabsetzen

bell [bel] Glocke *f*; Klingel *f*; '**~boy**, '**~hop** *Am.* (Hotel)Page *m*

-bel·lied [belɪd] ...bäuchig

bel·lig·er·ent [bɪ'lɪdʒərənt] kriegerisch; streitlustig, aggressiv; kriegführend

bel·low ['beləʊ] **1.** brüllen; **2.** Gebrüll *n*

bel·lows ['beləʊz] *pl., sg.* Blasebalg *m*

bel·ly ['belɪ] **1.** Bauch *m*; Magen *m*; **2.** *~ out* (an)schwellen lassen; bauschen; '**~ache** F Bauchweh *n*

be·long [bɪ'lɒŋ] gehören; *~ to* gehören *dat. od.* zu; **~ings** *pl.* Habseligkeiten *pl.*

be·loved [bɪ'lʌvɪd] **1.** (innig) geliebt; **2.** Geliebte(r *m*) *f*

be·low [bɪ'ləʊ] **1.** *adv.* unten; **2.** *prp.* unter

belt [belt] Gürtel *m*; Gurt *m*; Zone *f*; Gebiet *n*; *tech.* (Treib)Riemen *m*; **2.** *a. ~ up* den Gürtel (*gen.*) zumachen; *~ up mot.* sich anschnallen; **~ed** mit e-m Gürtel; '**~way** *Am.* Umgehungsstraße *f*; Ringstraße *f*

be·moan [bɪ'məʊn] betrauern, beklagen

bench [bentʃ] (Sitz)Bank *f*; Werkbank *f*; Richterbank *f*; Richter *m od. pl.*

bend [bend] **1.** Biegung *f*, Kurve *f*; *drive s.o. round the ~* F j-n noch wahnsinnig machen; **2.** (*bent*) (sich) biegen *od.* krümmen; neigen; beugen; *Gedanken etc.* richten (*to, on acc.*)

be·neath [bɪ'niːθ] → *below*

ben·e·dic·tion [benɪ'dɪkʃn] Segen *m*

ben·e·fac·tor ['benɪfæktə] Wohltäter *m*

be·nef·i·cent [bɪ'nefɪsnt] wohltätig

ben·e·fi·cial [benɪ'fɪʃl] wohltuend, zuträglich, nützlich

ben·e·fit ['benɪfɪt] **1.** Nutzen *m*, Vorteil *m*; Wohltätigkeitsveranstaltung *f*; (*Sozial-, Versicherungs- etc.*)Leistung *f*; (*Arbeitslosen- etc.*)Unterstützung *f*; (*Kranken- etc.*)Geld *n*; **2.** nützen; *~ by, ~ from* Vorteil haben von *od.* durch, Nutzen ziehen aus

be·nev·o·lence [bɪ'nevələns] Wohlwollen *n*; **~lent** wohltätig; wohlwollend

be·nign *med.* [bɪ'naɪn] gutartig

bent [bent] **1.** *pret. u. p.p. von* **bend 2**; *~ on doing* entschlossen zu tun; **2.** *fig.* Hang *m*, Neigung *f*, Veranlagung *f*

ben·zene *chem.* ['benziːn] Benzol *n*

ben·zine *chem.* ['benziːn] Leichtbenzin *n*; △ *nicht* **Benzin**

be·queath *jur.* [bɪ'kwiːð] vermachen

be·quest *jur.* [bɪˈkwest] Vermächtnis *n*

be·reave [bɪˈriːv] (**bereaved** *od.* **bereft**) berauben

be·reft [bɪˈreft] *pret. u. p.p. von* **bereave**

be·ret [ˈbereɪ] Baskenmütze *f*

ber·ry *bot.* [ˈberɪ] Beere *f*

berth [bɜːθ] **1.** *naut.* Liege-, Ankerplatz *m*; *naut.* Koje *f*; *rail.* (Schlafwagen)Bett *n*; **2.** festmachen, anlegen

be·seech [bɪˈsiːtʃ] (**besought** *od.* **beseeched**) (inständig) bitten (um); anflehen

be·set [bɪˈset] (**-tt-; beset**) heimsuchen; **~ with difficulties** mit vielen Schwierigkeiten verbunden; ⚠ *nicht* **besetzen**

be·side *prp.* [bɪˈsaɪd] neben; **~ o.s.** außer sich (**with** vor); **~ the point**, **~ the question** nicht zur Sache gehörig; **~s** [bɪˈsaɪdz] **1.** *adv.* außerdem; **2.** *prp.* abgesehen von, außer

be·siege [bɪˈsiːdʒ] belagern; ⚠ *nicht* **besiegen**

be·smear [bɪˈsmɪə] beschmieren

be·sought [bɪˈsɔːt] *pret. u. p.p. von* **beseech**

be·spat·ter [bɪˈspætə] bespritzen

best [best] **1.** *adj.* (*sup. von* **good** 1) beste(r, -s) höchste(r, -s), größte(r, -s), meiste; **~ before** haltbar bis (*für Lebensmittel*); **2.** *adv.* (*sup. von* **well** [1]) am besten; **3.** *der, die, das* Beste; *all the* **~!** alles Gute!, viel Glück!; **to the ~ of** ... nach bestem ...; *make the* **~ of** das Beste daraus machen; *at* **~** bestenfalls; *be at one's* **~** in Hoch- *od.* Höchstform sein; **~ 'be·fore date**, **~ 'by date** Mindesthaltbarkeitsdatum *n* (*für Lebensmittel*)

bes·ti·al [ˈbestjəl] tierisch; bestialisch

best 'man (*pl.* **-men**) *engster Freund des Bräutigams bei dessen Hochzeit*

be·stow [bɪˈstəu] geben, verleihen (**on** *dat.*)

best-'sell·er Bestseller *m*

bet [bet] **1.** Wette *f*; **2.** (**-tt-; bet** *od.* **betted**) wetten; **you** **~** F und ob!

be·tray [bɪˈtreɪ] verraten (*a. fig.*); verleiten; **~al** [bɪˈtreɪəl] Verrat *m*; **~er** Verräter(in)

bet·ter [ˈbetə] **1.** *adj.* (*comp. von* **good** 1) besser; *he is* **~** es geht ihm besser; **2.** *das* Bessere; *get the* **~ of** die Oberhand gewinnen über (*acc.*); *et.* überwinden; **3.** *adv.* (*comp. von* **well** [1]) besser; mehr;

so much the **~** desto besser; *you had* **~** (*Am.* F *you* **~**) *go* es wäre besser, wenn du gingest; **4.** *v/t.* verbessern; *v/i.* sich bessern

be·tween [bɪˈtwiːn] **1.** *adv.* dazwischen; *few and far* **~** F (ganz) vereinzelt; **2.** *prp.* zwischen; unter; **~ you and me** unter uns *od.* im Vertrauen (gesagt)

bev·el [ˈbevl] (*bsd. Brt.* **-ll-**, *Am.* **-l-**) abkanten, abschrägen

bev·er·age [ˈbevərɪdʒ] Getränk *n*

bev·y *zo.* [ˈbevɪ] Schwarm *m*, Schar *f*

be·ware [bɪˈweə] (**of**) sich in acht nehmen (vor *dat.*), sich hüten (vor *dat.*); ⚠ *nicht* **bewahren**; **~ of the dog!** Vorsicht, bissiger Hund!

be·wil·der [bɪˈwɪldə] verwirren; **~ment** Verwirrung *f*

be·witch [bɪˈwɪtʃ] bezaubern, behexen

be·yond [bɪˈjɒnd] **1.** *adv.* darüber hinaus; **2.** *prp.* jenseits; über ... (*acc.*) hinaus

bi... [baɪ] zwei(fach, -mal)

bi·as [ˈbaɪəs] Neigung *f*; Vorurteil *n*; **~(s)ed** voreingenommen; *jur.* befangen

bi·ath·|lete [baɪˈæθliːt] *Sport:* Biathlet *m*; **~lon** [baɪˈæθlən] *Sport:* Biathlon *n*

bib [bɪb] (Sabber)Lätzchen *n*

Bi·ble [ˈbaɪbl] Bibel *f*

bib·li·cal [ˈbɪblɪkl] biblisch, Bibel-

bib·li·og·ra·phy [bɪblɪˈɒɡrəfɪ] Bibliographie *f*

bi·car·bon·ate [baɪˈkɑːbənɪt] *a. of* **soda** doppeltkohlensaures Natron

bi·cen·|te·na·ry [baɪsenˈtiːnərɪ], *Am.* **~ten·ni·al** [baɪsenˈtenɪəl] Zweihundertjahrfeier *f*

bi·ceps *anat.* [ˈbaɪseps] Bizeps *m*

bick·er [ˈbɪkə] sich zanken *od.* streiten

bi·cy·cle [ˈbaɪsɪkl] Fahrrad *n*

bid [bɪd] **1.** (**-dd-; bade** *od.* **bade, bid** *od.* **bidden**) bei Versteigerungen bieten; **2.** *econ.* Gebot *n*, Angebot *n*; **~den** [ˈbɪdn] *p.p. von* **bid** [1]

bi·en·ni·al [baɪˈenɪəl] zweijährlich; zweijährig (*Pflanzen*); **~ly** alle zwei Jahre

bier [bɪə] (Toten)Bahre *f*; ⚠ *nicht* **Bier**

big [bɪɡ] (**-gg-**) groß; dick, stark; *talk* **~** den Mund vollnehmen

big·a·my [ˈbɪɡəmɪ] Bigamie *f*

big| 'busi·ness Großunternehmertum *n*; **'~head** F Angeber *m*, eingebildeter

Fatzke; **~ 'shot** hohes Tier (*Person*)

bike F [baɪk] (Fahr)Rad *n*; **'bik·er** Motorradfahrer(in) (*bsd. in Gruppen wie ,Hell's Angels'*); Radfahrer(in), Radler(in)

bi·lat·er·al [baɪˈlætərəl] bilateral

bile [baɪl] Galle *f (a. fig.)*

bi·lin·gual [baɪˈlɪŋgwəl] zweisprachig; **~ 'sec·re·ta·ry** Fremdsprachensekretärin *f*

bill¹ [bɪl] Schnabel *m*

bill² *econ.* [bɪl] Rechnung *f*; *pol.* (Gesetzes)Vorlage *f*; *jur.* (An)Klageschrift *f*; Plakat *n*; *Am.* Banknote *f*, (Geld-) Schein *m*; **~·board** *Am.* Reklametafel *f*; **'~·fold** *Am.* Brieftasche *f*

bil·li·ards [ˈbɪljədz] *sg.* Billiard(spiel) *n*

bil·li·on [ˈbɪljən] Milliarde *f*

bill| of de'liv·er·y *econ.* Lieferschein *m*; **~ of ex'change** *econ.* Wechsel *m*; **~ of 'sale** *jur.* Verkaufsurkunde *f*

bil·low [ˈbɪləʊ] **1.** Woge *f*; (*Rauch- etc.*) Schwaden *m*; **2.** *a.* **~ out** sich bauschen *od.* blähen

bil·ly goat *zo.* [ˈbɪlɪgəʊt] Ziegenbock *m*

bin [bɪn] (großer) Behälter

bi·na·ry [ˈbaɪnərɪ] *math., phys. etc.* binär, Binär...; **~ 'code** *Computer:* Binärcode *m*; **~ 'num·ber** Binärzahl *f*

bind [baɪnd] (**bound**) *v/t.* (an-, ein-, auf-, fest-, ver)binden; *a.* vertraglich binden, verpflichten; *Saum* einfassen; *v/i.* binden; **'~·er** (*bsd. Buch*)Binder(in); Einband *m* (*Akten- etc.*)Deckel *m*; **'~·ing 1.** bindend, verbindlich; **2.** Einband *m*; Einfassung *f*, Borte *f*

bin·go [ˈbɪŋgəʊ] Bingo *n* (*ein Glücksspiel*)

bi·noc·u·lars [bɪˈnɒkjʊləz] *pl.* Feldstecher *m*, Fern-, Opernglas *n*

bi·o·chem·is·try [baɪəʊˈkemɪstrɪ] Biochemie *f*

bi·o·de·gra·da·ble [baɪəʊdɪˈgreɪdəbl] biologisch abbaubar, umweltfreundlich

bi·og·ra|·pher [baɪˈɒgrəfə] Biograph *m*; **~·phy** Biographie *f*

bi·o·log·i·cal [baɪəʊˈlɒdʒɪkl] biologisch; **bi·ol·o·gist** [baɪˈɒlədʒɪst] Biolog|e *m*, -in *f*; **bi·ol·o·gy** [baɪˈɒlədʒɪ] Biologie *f*

bi·o·rhyth·m [ˈbaɪəʊrɪðəm] Biorhythmus *m*

bi·o·tope [ˈbaɪəʊtəʊp] Biotop *n*

bi·ped *zo.* [ˈbaɪped] Zweifüßer *m*

birch *bot.* [bɜːtʃ] Birke *f*

bird [bɜːd] Vogel *m*; **'~·cage** Vogelkäfig *m*; **~ of 'pas·sage** Zugvogel *m*; **~ of 'prey** Raubvogel *m*; **~ 'sanc·tu·a·ry** Vogelschutzgebiet *n*; **'~·seed** Vogelfutter *n*

bird's-eye 'view Vogelperspektive *f*

bi·ro *TM* [ˈbaɪrəʊ] (*pl. -ros*) Kugelschreiber *m*

birth [bɜːθ] Geburt *f*; Herkunft *f*; **give ~ to** gebären, zur Welt bringen; **~ cer·tif·i·cate** Geburtsurkunde *f*; **~ con·trol** Geburtenregelung *f*; **~ con·troll 'pill** Antibabypille *f*; **'~·day** Geburtstag *m*; **happy ~!** alles Gute *od.* herzlichen Glückwunsch zum Geburtstag!; **'~·mark** Muttermal *n*; **'~·place** Geburtsort *m*; **'~ rate** Geburtenziffer *f*

bis·cuit *Brt.* [ˈbɪskɪt] Keks *m, n*, Plätzchen *n*; △ *nicht* **Biskuit**

bi·sex·u·al [baɪˈseksʃʊəl] bisexuell

bish·op [ˈbɪʃəp] Bischof *m*; *Schach:* Läufer *m*; **~·ric** [ˈbɪʃəprɪk] Bistum *n*

bi·son *zo.* [ˈbaɪsn] Bison *m*; Wisent *m*

bit [bɪt] **1.** Bißchen *n*, Stück(chen) *n*; Gebiß *n* (*am Zaum*); (Schlüssel)Bart *m*; *Computer:* Bit *n*; **a (little)** ~ ein (kleines) bißchen; **2.** *pret. von* **bite** 2

bitch [bɪtʃ] *zo.* Hündin *f*; *contp.* Miststück *n*, Schlampe *f*

'bit den·si·ty *Computer:* Speicherdichte *f*

bite [baɪt] **1.** Beißen *n*; Biß *m*; Bissen *m*, Happen *m*; *tech.* Fassen *n*, Greifen *n* (*von Schrauben etc.*); **2.** (**bit, bitten**) (an)beißen; stechen (*Insekt*); brennen (*Pfeffer*); schneiden (*Kälte*); beißen (*Rauch*); *tech.* fassen, greifen (*Schrauben etc.*)

bit·ten [ˈbɪtn] *p.p. von* **bite** 2

bit·ter [ˈbɪtə] bitter; *fig.* verbittert

bit·ters [ˈbɪtəz] *pl.* Magenbitter *m*

biz F [bɪz] → **business**

black [blæk] **1.** schwarz; dunkel; finster; **have s.th. in ~ and white** et. schwarz auf weiß haben *od.* besitzen; **be ~ and blue** blaue Flecken haben; **beat s.o. ~ and blue** j-n grün u. blau schlagen; **2.** schwärzen; **~ out** verdunkeln; **3.** Schwarz *n*; Schwärze *f*; Schwarze(r *m*) *f* (*Person*); **'~·ber·ry** *bot.* Brombeere *f*; **'~·bird** *zo.* Amsel *f*; **'~·board** (Schul-, Wand)Tafel *f*; △ *nicht* **Schwarzes**

B

Brett; ~ '**box** *aviat.* Flugschreiber *m*; ~'**cur·rant** *bot.* schwarze Johannisbeere; '~**en** *v/t.* schwärzen; *fig.* anschwärzen; *v/i.* schwarz werden; ~ '**eye** blaues Auge, Veilchen *n*; '~'**head** *med.* Mitesser *m*; ~'**ice** Glatteis *n*; '~**ing** schwarze Schuhwichse; '~**leg** *Brt.* Streikbrecher *m*; '~'**mail** 1. Erpressung *f*; 2. *j-n* erpressen; '~**mail·er** Erpresser(in); ~ '**mar·ket** schwarzer Markt; '~**ness** schwarzer Markt; '~**out** Verdunkelung *f*, Blackout *n*, *m*; Ohnmacht *f*; ~'**pud·ding** Blutwurst *f*; ~ '**sheep** (*pl.* - **sheep**) *fig.* schwarzes Schaf; '~**smith** Schmied *m*

blad·der *anat.* ['blædə] Blase *f*

blade [bleɪd] *bot.* Blatt *n*, Halm *m*; (*Säge-, Schulter- etc.*)Blatt *n*; (Propeller)Flügel *m*; Klinge *f*

blame [bleɪm] 1. Tadel *m*; Schuld *f*; 2. tadeln; *be to* ~ *for* schuld sein an (*dat.*); △ *nicht* **blamieren**; '~**less** untadelig

blanch [blɑːntʃ] bleichen; *gastr.* blanchieren; erbleichen; bleich werden

blanc·mange [bləˈmɒnʒ] Pudding *m*

blank [blæŋk] 1. leer; unausgefüllt, unbeschrieben; *econ.* Blanko...; verdutzt; △ *nicht* **blank** (*glänzend*); 2. Leere *f*; leerer Raum, Lücke *f*; unbeschriebenes Blatt, Formular *n*; Lotterie: Niete *f*; ~ '**car·tridge** Platzpatrone *f*; ~ '**cheque** (*Am.* '**check**) *econ.* Blankoscheck *m*

blan·ket ['blæŋkɪt] 1. (Woll)Decke *f*; 2. zudecken

blare [bleə] brüllen, plärren (*Radio etc.*), schmettern (*Trompete*)

blas·pheme [blæsˈfiːm] lästern; ~**phe·my** ['blæsfəmɪ] Gotteslästerung *f*

blast [blɑːst] 1. Windstoß *m*; Ton *m* (*e-s Blasinstruments*); Explosion *f*; Druckwelle *f*; Sprengung *f*; 2. sprengen; *fig.* zunichte machen; ~ *off* (*into space*) in den Weltraum schießen; ~ *off* abheben, starten (*Rakete*); ~*l* verdammt!; ~ *you!* der Teufel soll dich holen!; ~**ed** verdämmt, verflucht; '~ **fur·nace** *tech.* Hochofen *m*; '~**off** Start *m* (*Rakete*)

bla·tant ['bleɪtənt] offenkundig, eklatant

blaze [bleɪz] 1. Flamme(n *pl.*) *f*, Feuer *n*; heller Schein; *fig.* Ausbruch *m*; 2. brennen, lodern; leuchten; △ *nicht* **blasen**

blaz·er ['bleɪzə] Blazer *m*

bla·zon ['bleɪzn] Wappen *n*

bleach [bliːtʃ] bleichen

bleak [bliːk] öde, kahl; rauh; *fig.* trüb, freudlos, finster

blear·y ['blɪərɪ] (*-ier, -iest*) trübe, verschwommen

bleat [bliːt] 1. Blöken *n*; 2. blöken

bled [bled] *pret. u. p.p. von* **bleed**

bleed [bliːd] (**bled**) *v/i.* bluten; *v/t. med.* zur Ader lassen; *fig.* schröpfen; '~**ing** 1. *med.* Bluten *n*, Blutung *f*; *med.* Aderlaß *m*; 2. *sl.* verdammt, verflucht

bleep [bliːp] 1. Piepton *m*; 2. *j-n* anpiepsen (*über Funkrufempfänger*); '~**er** *Brt.* F Piepser *m* (*Funkrufempfänger*)

blem·ish ['blemɪʃ] 1. (*a.* Schönheits-) Fehler *m*; Makel *m*; 2. entstellen

blend [blend] 1. (sich) (ver)mischen; Wein etc. verschneiden; △ *nicht* **blenden**; 2. Mischung *f*; *econ.* Verschnitt *m*; '~**er** Mixer *m*, Mixgerät *n*

bless [bles] (**blessed** *od.* **blest**) segnen; preisen; *be* ~**ed with** gesegnet sein mit; (*God*) ~ *you!* alles Gute!; Gesundheit!; ~ *me!*, ~ *my heart!*, ~ *my soul!* F du meine Güte!; '~**ed** *adj.* selig, gesegnet, F verflixt; '~**ing** Segen *m*

blest [blest] *pret. u. p.p. von* **bless**

blew [bluː] *pret. von* **blow²**

blight *bot.* [blaɪt] Mehltau *m*

blind [blaɪnd] 1. blind (*fig. to* gegen[über]); unübersichtlich (*Kurve etc.*); 2. Rouleau *n*, Rollo *n*; *the* ~ *pl.* die Blinden *pl.*; 3. blenden; *fig.* blind machen (*to* für, gegen); ~ '**al·ley** Sackgasse *f*; '~**ers** *pl. Am.* Scheuklappen *pl.*; '~**fold** 1. blindlings; 2. *j-m* die Augen verbinden; 3. Augenbinde *f*; '~**ly** *fig.* blindlings; '~**worm** *zo.* Blindschleiche *f*

blink [blɪŋk] 1. Blinzeln *n*; 2. blinzeln, zwinkern; blinken; '~**ers** *pl.* Scheuklappen *pl.*

bliss [blɪs] Seligkeit *f*, Wonne *f*

blis·ter ['blɪstə] 1. *med.*, *tech.* Blase *f*; 2. Blasen hervorrufen auf (*dat.*); Blasen ziehen *od. tech.* werfen

blitz [blɪts] 1. heftiger Luftangriff; 2. schwer bombardieren; △ *nicht* **Blitz**; **blitzen**

bliz·zard ['blɪzəd] Blizzard *m*, Schneesturm *m*

45

boarding card

bloat|·ed [ˈbləʊtɪd] (an)geschwollen, (auf)gedunsen; *fig.* aufgeblasen; '**~er** Bückling *m*

blob [blɒb] Klecks *m*

block [blɒk] **1.** Block *m*, Klotz *m*; Baustein *m*, (Bau)Klötzchen *n*; (*Schreib-, Notiz-*)Block *m*; *bsd. Am.* (Häuser)Block *m*; *tech.* Verstopfung *f*; *geistige etc.* Sperre; ~ (**of flats**) *Brt.* Wohn-, Mietshaus *n*; **2.** *a.* ~ **up** (ab-, ver)sperren, blockieren, verstopfen

block·ade [blɒˈkeɪd] **1.** Blockade *f*; **2.** blockieren

block|·bust·er F [ˈblɒkbʌstə] Kassenmagnet *m*, -schlager *m*; '**~head** F Dummkopf *m*; ~ '**let·ters** *pl.* Blockschrift *f*

bloke *Brt.* F [bləʊk] Kerl *m*

blond [blɒnd] **1.** blond(er) *m*; **2.** blond; hell (*Haut*); **~e** [blɒnd] **1.** blond; **2.** Blondine *f*

blood [blʌd] Blut *n*; *attr.* Blut...; *in cold* ~ kaltblütig; '~ **bank** *med.* Blutbank *f*; '**~cur·dling** [ˈblʌdkɜːdlɪŋ] grauenhaft; '~ **do·nor** *med.* Blutspender(in); '~ **group** *med.* Blutgruppe *f*; '~ **hound** *zo.* Bluthund *m*; '~ **pres·sure** *med.* Blutdruck *m*; '~ **shed** Blutvergießen *n*; '~ **shot** blutunterlaufen; '~ **thirst·y** blutdürstig; '~ **ves·sel** *anat.* Blutgefäß *n*; '~ **y** (*-ier, -iest*) blutig; *Brt.* F verdammt, verflucht

bloom [bluːm] **1.** *poet.* Blume *f*, Blüte *f*; *fig.* Blüte(zeit) *f*; △ *nicht allg.* **Blume**; **2.** blühen; *fig.* (er)strahlen

blos·som [ˈblɒsəm] **1.** Blüte *f*; **2.** blühen

blot [blɒt] **1.** Klecks *m*; *fig.* Makel *m*; **2.** (*-tt-*) beklecksen

blotch [blɒtʃ] Klecks *m*; Hautfleck *m*; '~ **y** (*-ier, -iest*) fleckig (*Haut*)

blot|·ter [ˈblɒtə] (Tinten)Löscher *m*; '~ **ting pa·per** Löschpapier *n*

blouse [blaʊz] Bluse *f*

blow¹ [bləʊ] Schlag *m*, Stoß *m*

blow² [bləʊ] (*blew, blown*) *v/i.* blasen, wehen; keuchen, schnaufen; explodieren; platzen (*Reifen*); *electr.* durchbrennen (*Sicherung*); ~ **up** in die Luft fliegen; explodieren; *v/t.* ~ **one's nose** sich die Nase putzen; ~ **one's top** F an die Decke gehen (*vor Wut*); ~ **out** ausblasen; ~ **up** sprengen; phot. vergrößern; '**~dry** fönen; '**~fly** *zo.* Schmeißfliege *f*; '**~n** [bləʊn] *p.p. von* **blow²**;

'**~pipe** Blasrohr *n*; '**~up** *phot.* Vergrößerung *f*

blud·geon [ˈblʌdʒən] Knüppel *m*

blue [bluː] **1.** blau; F melancholisch, traurig, schwermütig; **2.** Blau *n*; *out of the* ~ *fig.* aus heiterem Himmel; '**~ber·ry** *bot.* Blau-, Heidelbeere *f*; '**~bot·tle** *zo.* Schmeißfliege *f*; '**~col·lar work·er** (Fabrik)Arbeiter(in)

blues [bluːz] *pl. od. sing. mus.* Blues *m*; F Melancholie *f*; *have the* ~ F den Moralischen haben

bluff¹ [blʌf] Steilufer *n*

bluff² [blʌf] **1.** Bluff *m*; **2.** bluffen

blu·ish [ˈbluːɪʃ] bläulich

blun·der [ˈblʌndə] **1.** Fehler *m*, Schnitzer *m*; **2.** e-n (groben) Fehler machen; verpfuschen, -patzen; △ *nicht plündern*

blunt [blʌnt] stumpf; *fig.* offen; '**~ly** frei heraus

blur [blɜː] (*-rr-*) **1.** *v/t.* verwischen; verschmieren; *phot.*, *TV* verwackeln, -zerren; *Sinne etc.* trüben; **2.** *v/i.* verschwimmen (*a. Eindruck etc.*)

blurt [blɜːt]: ~ **out** herausplatzen mit

blush [blʌʃ] **1.** Erröten *n*, Schamröte *f*; **2.** erröten, rot werden

blus·ter [ˈblʌstə] brausen (*Wind*); *fig.* poltern, toben

Blvd *nur geschr. Abk. für* **Boulevard** Boulevard *m*

BMI [biː em ˈwaɪ] *Abk. für Body Mass Index etwa:* Körpermasse u. -gewichtsindex *m*

BMX [biː em ˈeks] *Abk. für bicycle motocross* Querfeldeinrennen *n* (*auf Fahrrädern*); ~ **bike** BMX-Rad *n* (*geländegängiges Fahrrad*)

BO *Abk.* [ˈbiː ˈəʊ] → *body odo(u)r*

boar *zo.* [bɔː] Eber *m*; Keiler *m*

board [bɔːd] **1.** Brett *n*; (Anschlag)Brett *n*; Konferenztisch *m*; Ausschuß *m*, Kommission *f*; Behörde *f*; Verpflegung *f*; Pappe *f*, Karton *m*; *Sport:* (Surf)Board *n*; △ *nicht Bücher-Bord*; *on* ~ *a train* in e-m Zug; **2.** *v/t.* dielen, verschalen; beköstigen; an Bord gehen; *naut.* entern; einsteigen in (*einen Zug od. Bus*); *v/i.* in Kost sein, wohnen; '**~er** Kostgänger(in); Pensionsgast *m*; Internatsschüler(in); ~ **game** Brettspiel *n*; '**~ing card** *aviat.* Bordkarte *f*;

B

'~·ing·house Pension f, Fremden-heim n; **'~ing school** Internat n; **~ of 'di·rec·tors** econ. Aufsichtsrat m; **♀ of 'Trade** Brt. Handelsministerium n, Am. Handelskammer f; **'~walk** bsd. Am. Strandpromenade f

boast [bəʊst] **1.** Prahlerei f; **2.** (of, about) sich rühmen (gen.), prahlen (mit)

boat [bəʊt] Boot n; Schiff n

bob [bɒb] **1.** Knicks m; kurzer Haar-schnitt; Brt. hist. F Schilling m; **2.** (-bb-) v/t. Haar kurz schneiden; v/i. sich auf u. ab bewegen; knicksen

bob·bin ['bɒbɪn] Spule f (a. electr.)

bob·by Brt. F ['bɒbɪ] Bobby m (Polizist)

bob·sleigh ['bɒbsleɪ] Sport: Bob m

bode [bəʊd] pret. von bide

bod·ice ['bɒdɪs] Mieder n; Oberteil n (e-s Kleides)

bod·i·ly ['bɒdɪlɪ] körperlich

bod·y ['bɒdɪ] Körper m, Leib m; Leiche f; Körperschaft f; Hauptteil m; mot. Karosserie f; mil. Truppenkörper m; **'~guard** Leibwache f; Leibwächter m; **'~ o·do(u)r** (abbr. BO) Körperge-ruch m; **'~ stock·ing** Body m; **'~work** Karosserie f

Boer ['bɔː] Bure m; attr. Buren...

bog [bɒg] Sumpf m, Morast m

bo·gus ['bəʊgəs] falsch; Schwindel...

boil[1] med. [bɔɪl] Geschwür n, Furunkel m, n

boil[2] [bɔɪl] **1.** kochen, sieden; **2.** Kochen n, Sieden n; **'~er** (Dampf)Kessel m; Boiler m; **'~er suit** Overall m; **'~ing point** Siedepunkt m (a. fig.)

bois·ter·ous ['bɔɪstərəs] ungestüm; hef-tig, laut; lärmend

bold [bəʊld] kühn; keck, dreist, unver-schämt; steil; print. fett; **as ~ as brass** F frech wie Oskar; **words in ~ print** fettgedruckt

bol·ster ['bəʊlstə] Keilkissen n; **2. ~ up** fig. (unter)stützen, j-m Mut machen

bolt [bəʊlt] **1.** Bolzen m; Riegel m; Blitz(strahl) m; plötzlicher Satz, Fluchtversuch m; **2.** adv. ~ **upright** ker-zengerade; **3.** v/t. verriegeln; F hinun-terschlingen; v/i. davonlaufen, ausrei-ßen; scheuen, durchgehen (Pferd)

bomb [bɒm] **1.** Bombe f; **the ~** die Atombombe; **2.** bombardieren; **'~er** m aviat. Bomber m; Bombenleger m

bom·bard [bɒm'bɑːd] bombardieren

bomb|·proof ['bɒmpruːf] bombensi-cher; **'~shell** Bombe f (a. fig.)

bond [bɒnd] econ. Schuldverschreibung f, Obligation f; Bund m, Verbindung f; **in ~** econ. unter Zollverschluß; **'~age** ['bɒndɪdʒ] Hörigkeit f

bonds [bɒndz] pl. Bande pl. (der Freund-schaft etc.)

bone [bəʊn] **1.** Knochen m; Gräte f; **~s** pl. a. Gebeine pl.; **~ of contention** Zankapfel m; **have a ~ to pick with s.o.** mit j-m ein Hühnchen zu rupfen haben; **make no ~s about** nicht lange fackeln mit; keine Skrupel haben hinsichtlich (gen.); **2.** die Knochen auslösen (aus); entgräten

bon·fire ['bɒnfaɪə] Feuer n im Freien; Freudenfeuer n

bonk Brt. sl. [bɒŋk] bumsen

bon·net ['bɒnɪt] Haube f; Brt. Motor-haube f

bon·ny bsd. schott. ['bɒnɪ] (-ier, -iest) hübsch; rosig (Baby); gesund

bo·nus econ. ['bəʊnəs] Bonus m, Prämie f; Gratifikation f

bon·y ['bəʊnɪ] (-ier, -iest) knöchern; knochig

boo [buː] int. buh!; thea. ~ **off the stage,** Fußball: ~ **off the park** auspfeifen

boobs F [buːbz] pl. Titten pl. (Busen)

boo·by F ['buːbɪ] Trottel m

book [bʊk] **1.** Buch n; Heft n; Liste f; Block m; **2.** buchen; eintragen; Sport: verwarnen; Fahrkarte etc. lösen; Platz etc. (vor)bestellen, reservieren lassen; Gepäck aufgeben; ~ **in** bsd. Brt. sich (im Hotel) eintragen; ~ **in at** absteigen in (dat.); **~ed up** ausgebucht, -verkauft, belegt (Hotel); **'~case** Bücherschrank m; **'~ing** Buchen n, (Vor)Bestellung f; Sport: Verwarnung f; ~ **in** f; **'~ing clerk** Schalterbeamte(r) m, -in f; **'~ing of·fice** Fahrkartenausgabe f, -schalter m; thea. Kasse f; **'~keep·er** Buchhal-ter(in); **'~keep·ing** Buchhaltung f, -führung f; **~let** ['bʊklɪt] Büchlein n, Broschüre f; **'~mark(·er)** Lesezei-chen n; **'~sell·er** Buchhändler(in); **'~shelf** (pl. **-shelves**) Bücherregal n; **'~shop** bsd. Brt., **'~store** Am. Buch-handlung f

boom[1] [buːm] **1.** econ. Boom m, Auf-schwung m, Hochkonjunktur f, Hausse f; **2.** e-n Boom erleben

boom² [buːm] *naut.* Baum *m*, Spiere *f*; (*Kran*)Ausleger *m*; *Film, TV:* (*Mikrophon*)Galgen *m*

boom³ [buːm] dröhnen, donnern

boor [buə] ungehobelter Kerl; **~ish** ['buərɪʃ] ungehobelt

boost [buːst] **1.** hochschieben; *Preise* in die Höhe treiben; *Produktion etc.* ankurbeln; *electr.* Spannung verstärken; *tech.* Druck erhöhen; *fig.* stärken, Auftrieb geben; **2.** Auftrieb *m*, (Ver)Stärkung *f*

boot¹ [buːt] Stiefel *m*; *Brt. mot.* Kofferraum *m*; △ *nicht* Boot; **~ee** ['buːtiː] (*Damen*)Halbstiefel *m*

boot² [buːt]: **~** (*up*) *Computer:* laden

boot³ [buːt]: *to* **~** obendrein

booth [buːð] (*Markt- etc.*)Bude *f*; (*Messe*)Stand *m*; (*Wahl- etc.*) Kabine *f*; (Telefon)Zelle *f*

'boot·lace Schnürsenkel *m*

boot·y ['buːtɪ] Beute *f*

booze F [buːz] **1.** saufen; **2.** Zeug *n* (*alkoholisches Getränk*); Sauferei *f*

bor·der ['bɔːdə] **1.** Rand *m*, Saum *m*, Einfassung *f*; Rabatte *f*; Grenze *f*; **2.** einfassen; (um)säumen; grenzen (*on* an *acc.*)

bore¹ [bɔː] **1.** Bohrloch *n*; *tech.* Kaliber *n*; **2.** bohren

bore² [bɔː] **1.** Langweiler *m*; *bsd. Brt.* F langweilige *od.* lästige Sache; **2.** *j-n* langweilen; *be* **~d** sich langweilen

bore³ [bɔː] *pret. von* **bear²**

bore·dom ['bɔːdəm] Lang(e)weile *f*

bor·ing ['bɔːrɪŋ] langweilig

born [bɔːn] *p.p. von* **bear²** (*gebären*)

borne [bɔːn] *p.p. von* **bear²** (*tragen*)

bo·rough ['bʌrə] Stadtteil *m*; Stadtgemeinde *f*; Stadtbezirk *m*

bor·row ['bɒrəʊ] (sich) *et.* borgen *od.* (aus)leihen; △ *nicht j-m et.* **borgen**

bos·om ['bʊzəm] Busen *m*; *fig.* Schoß *m*

boss F [bɒs] **1.** Boss *m*, Chef *m*; **2.** *a.* **~ about,** **~ around** herumkommandieren; '**~·y** F (*-ier, -iest*) herrisch

bo·tan·i·cal [bə'tænɪkl] botanisch; **bot·a·ny** ['bɒtənɪ] Botanik *f*

botch [bɒtʃ] **1.** Pfusch(arbeit *f*) *m*; **2.** verpfuschen

both [bəʊθ] beide(s); **~ ... and** sowohl ... als (auch)

both·er ['bɒðə] **1.** Belästigung *f*, Störung *f*, Plage *f*, Mühe *f*; **2.** belästigen,

stören, plagen; *don't* **~!** bemühen Sie sich nicht!

bot·tle ['bɒtl] **1.** Flasche *f*; **2.** in Flaschen abfüllen; '**~ bank** *Brt.* Altglascontainer *m*; '**~·neck** *fig.* Engpaß *m*

bot·tom ['bɒtəm] unterster Teil, Boden *m*, Fuß *m*, Unterseite *f*; Grund *m*; F Hintern *m*, Popo *m*; *be at the* **~** *of* hinter *e-r* Sache stecken; *get to the* **~** *of s.th.* e-r Sache auf den Grund gehen

bough [baʊ] Ast *m*, Zweig *m*

bought [bɔːt] *pret. u. p.p. von* **buy**

boul·der ['bəʊldə] Geröllblock *m*, Findling *m*

bounce [baʊns] **1.** aufprallen *od.* aufspringen (lassen) (*Ball etc.*); springen, hüpfen, stürmen; F platzen (*Scheck*); **2.** Sprung *m*, Satz *m*; F Schwung *m*; '**bounc·ing** stramm (*Baby*)

bound¹ [baʊnd] **1.** *pret. u. p.p. von* **bind**; **2.** *adj.* unterwegs (*for* nach)

bound² [baʊnd] *mst* **~s** *pl.* Grenze *f*, *fig. a.* Schranke *f*

bound³ [baʊnd] **1.** Sprung *m*, Satz *m*; **2.** springen, hüpfen; auf-, abprallen

bound·a·ry ['baʊndərɪ] Grenze *f*

'bound·less grenzenlos

boun·te·ous ['baʊntɪəs], **~ti·ful** ['baʊntɪfl] freigebig, reichlich

boun·ty ['baʊntɪ] Freigebigkeit *f*; großzügige Spende *f*; Prämie *f*

bou·quet [bʊ'keɪ] Bukett *n*, Strauß *m*; Bukett *n*, Blume *f* (*von Wein*)

bout [baʊt] (*Box-, Ring*)Kampf *m*; *med.* Anfall *m*

bou·tique [buː'tiːk] Boutique *f*

bow¹ [baʊ] **1.** Verbeugung *f*; **2.** *v/i.* sich verbeugen *od.* -neigen (*to* vor *dat.*); *fig.* sich beugen *od.* unterwerfen (*to* dat.); *v/t.* biegen, beugen, neigen

bow² *naut.* [baʊ] Bug *m*

bow³ [bəʊ] Bogen *m*; Schleife *f*

bow·els *anat.* ['baʊəlz] *pl.* Darm *m*; Eingeweide *pl.*

bowl¹ [bəʊl] Schale *f*, Schüssel *f*, Napf *m*; (*Zucker*)Dose *f*; Becken *n*; (*Pfeifen*)Kopf *m*; △ *nicht* **Bowle** (*Getränk*)

bowl² [bəʊl] **1.** (*Bowling-, Kegel- etc.*) Kugel *f*; **2.** Bowlingkugel rollen; *Krikketball* werfen

bow-leg·ged ['bəʊlegd] O-beinig

'bowl·er Bowlingspieler(in); Kegler(in); '**~, ~ 'hat** Bowler *m*, Melone *f*

'bowl·ing Bowling *n*; Kegeln *n*

box 48

box¹ [bɒks] Kasten *m*, Kiste *f*; Büchse *f*, Dose *f*; Kästchen *n*; Schachtel *f*; Behälter *m*; *tech.* Gehäuse *n*; Postfach *n*; *Brt.* (Telefon)Zelle *f*; *jur.* Zeugenstand *m*; *thea.* Loge *f*; Box *f* (*für Pferde, Autos*)

box² [bɒks] **1.** *Sport:* boxen; F **~** *s.o.'s ears* j-n ohrfeigen; **2.** F *a* **~** *on the ear* e-e Ohrfeige; '**~er** Boxer *m*; '**~ing** Boxen *n*, Boxsport *m*; '**2-ing Day** *Brt.* der zweite Weihnachtsfeiertag

box³ *bot.* [bɒks] Buchsbaum *m*

'**box**| **num·ber** Chiffre(nummer) *f*, '**~of·fice** Theaterkasse *f*

boy [bɔɪ] Junge *m*, Knabe *m*, Bursche *m*

boy·cott ['bɔɪkɒt] **1.** boykottieren; **2.** Boykott *m*

'**boy**|**·friend** Freund *m*; **~hood** ['bɔɪhʊd] Knabenjahre *pl.*, Jugend(zeit) *f*; '**~ish** jungenhaft; '**~ scout** Pfadfinder *m*

BPhil [biː 'fɪl] *Abk. für* **Bachelor of Philosophy** Bakkalaureus *m* der Philosophie

BR [biː 'ɑː] *Abk. für* **British Rail** (*Eisenbahn in Großbritannien*)

bra [brɑː] BH *m* (*Büstenhalter*)

brace [breɪs] **1.** *tech.* Strebe *f*, Stützbalken *m*; (Zahn)Klammer *f*, (-)Spange *f*; **2.** *tech.* verstreben, -steifen, stützen

brace·let ['breɪslɪt] Armband *n*

brac·es ['breɪsɪz] *pl. Brt.* Hosenträger *pl.*

brack·et ['brækɪt] *tech.* Träger *m*, Halter *m*, Stütze *f*; *print.* Klammer; (*bsd. Alters-, Steuer*)Klasse *f*; *lower income* **~** niedrige Einkommensgruppe

brack·ish ['brækɪʃ] brackig, salzig

brag [bræg] (**-gg-**) prahlen (*about, of* mit); **~gart** ['brægət] Prahler *m*

braid [breɪd] **1.** *bsd. Am.* Zopf *m*; Borte *f*, Tresse *f*; **2.** *bsd. Am.* flechten; mit Borte besetzen

brain [breɪn] *anat.* Gehirn *n*; *oft* **~s** *pl. fig.* Gehirn *n*, Verstand *m*, Intelligenz *f*, Kopf *m*; '**~s trust** *Brt.*, '**~ trust** *Am.* Gehirntrust *m* (*bsd. politische od. wirtschaftliche Beratergruppe*); '**~wash** j-n e-r Gehirnwäsche unterziehen; '**~wash·ing** Gehirnwäsche *f*; '**~wave** F Geistesblitz *m*, tolle Idee; '**~y** (**-ier, -iest**) F gescheit

brake [breɪk] **1.** *tech.* Bremse *f*; **2.** bremsen; '**~light** *mot.* Bremslicht *n*

bram·ble *bot.* ['bræmbl] Brombeerstrauch *m*

bran [bræn] Kleie *f*

branch [brɑːntʃ] **1.** Ast *m*, Zweig *m*; Fach *n*; Linie *f* (*des Stammbaumes*); Zweigstelle *f*; **2.** sich verzweigen; abzweigen

brand [brænd] **1.** *econ.* (Handels-, Schutz)Marke *f*, Warenzeichen *n*; Markenname *m*; Sorte *f*, Klasse *f* (*e-r Ware*); Brandmal *n*; △ *nicht* **Brand**; **2.** einbrennen; brandmarken

bran·dish ['brændɪʃ] schwingen

'**brand**| **name** *econ.* Markenbezeichnung *f*, -name *m*; **~new** nagelneu

bran·dy ['brændɪ] Kognak *m*, Weinbrand *m*

brass [brɑːs] Messing *n*; F Unverschämtheit *f*; **~ band** Blaskapelle *f*

bras·sière ['bræsɪə] Büstenhalter *m*

brat *contp.* [bræt] Balg *m, n*, Gör *n* (*Kind*)

brave [breɪv] **1.** (**~r, ~st**) tapfer, mutig, unerschrocken; △ *nicht* **brav**; **2.** trotzen; mutig begegnen (*dat.*); **brav·er·y** ['breɪvərɪ] Tapferkeit *f*

brawl [brɔːl] **1.** Krawall *m*; Rauferei *f*; **2.** Krawall machen; raufen

brawn·y ['brɔːnɪ] (**-ier, -iest**) muskulös

bray [breɪ] **1.** Eselsschrei *m*; **2.** schreien; schmettern; lärmen, tosen (*Verkehr*)

bra·zen ['breɪzn] unverschämt, unverfroren, frech

Bra·zil [brə'zɪl] Brasilien *n*; **Bra·zil·ian** [brə'zɪljən] **1.** brasilianisch; **2.** Brasilianer(in)

breach [briːtʃ] **1.** Bruch *m*; *fig.* Verletzung *f*; *mil.* Bresche *f*; **2.** e-e Bresche schlagen in (*acc.*)

bread [bred] Brot *n*; *brown* **~** Schwarzbrot *n*; *know which side one's* **~** *is buttered* F s-n Vorteil (er)kennen

breadth [bredθ] Breite *f*

break [breɪk] **1.** Bruch *m*; Lücke *f*; Pause *f* (*Brt. a. Schule*), Unterbrechung *f*; (plötzlicher) Wechsel, Umschwung *m*; (Tages)Anbruch *m*; *bad* **~** F Pech *n*; *lucky* **~** F Dusel *m*, Schwein *n*; *give s.o. a* **~** F j-m e-e Chance geben; *take a* **~** e-e Pause machen; *without a* **~** ununterbrochen; **2.** (**broke, broken**) *v/t.* (ab-, auf-, durch-, zer)brechen; zerschlagen, kaputtmachen; *Tiere* zähmen, abrichten, *Pferd* zureiten (*alle a.* **~** *in*); *Gesetz, Vertrag etc.* brechen; *Code etc.* knacken; *schlechte Nachricht* (schonend) beibringen; v/i. brechen (a. fig.); (zer)brechen, (-)reißen, kaputtgehen; umschlagen (Wetter); anbrechen (Tag); fig. ausbrechen (into in Tränen etc.); ~ away ab-, losbrechen; sich losmachen od. losreißen; ~ down ein-, niederreißen; Haus abbrechen; zusammenbrechen (a. fig.); versagen; mot. e-e Panne haben; scheitern; ~ in einbrechen, -dringen; ~ into einbrechen in (ein Haus etc.); ~ off abbrechen; fig. a. Schluß machen mit; ~ out ausbrechen; ~ through durchbrechen; fig. den Durchbruch schaffen; ~ up abbrechen, beenden, schließen; (sich) auflösen; zerbrechen, auseinandergehen (Ehe etc.); '~·a·ble zerbrechlich; '~·age ['breikidʒ] Bruch m; '~·a·way Trennung f; Brt. Splitter...

'break·down Zusammenbruch m (a. fig.); tech. Maschinenschaden m; mot. Panne f; **nervous ~** Nervenzusammenbruch m; '~ **lor·ry** Brt. mot. Abschleppwagen m; '~ **ser·vice** mot. Pannendienst m, -hilfe f; '~ **truck** Brt. mot. Abschleppwagen m

break·fast ['brekfəst] **1.** Frühstück n; **have ~** → **2.** frühstücken

'break·through fig. Durchbruch m; '~·**up** Aufhebung f; Auflösung f

breast [brest] Brust f; Busen m; fig. Herz n; **make a clean ~ of s.th.** et. offen (ein)gestehen; '~·**stroke** Sport: Brustschwimmen n

breath [breθ] Atem(zug) m; Hauch m; **be out of ~** außer Atem sein; **waste one's ~** in den Wind reden

breath·a·lyse Brt., **~·lyze** Am. ['breθəlaɪz] F Verkehrsteilnehmer (ins Röhrchen) blasen od. pusten lassen; '~·**lys·er** Brt., '~·**lyz·er** Am. TM Alkoholtestgerät n, F Röhrchen n

breathe [bri:ð] atmen

'breath·less atemlos; '~·**tak·ing** atemberaubend

bred [bred] pret. u. p.p. von breed 2

breech·es ['brɪtʃɪz] pl. Kniebund-, Reithosen pl.

breed [bri:d] **1.** Rasse f, Zucht f; **2.** (bred) v/t. Tiere, Pflanzen züchten; v/i. sich fortpflanzen; '~·**er** Züchter(in); Zuchttier n; phys. Brüter m; '~·**ing** Fortpflanzung f; (Tier)Zucht f; Erziehung f; (gutes) Benehmen

breeze [bri:z] Brise f

breth·ren bsd. rel. ['breðrən] pl. Brüder pl.

brew [bru:] brauen; Tee zubereiten, aufbrühen; '~·**er** (Bier)Brauer m; ~·**er·y** ['brʊərɪ] Brauerei f

bri·ar ['braɪə] → brier

bribe [braɪb] **1.** Bestechung(sgeld n, -geschenk n) f; **2.** bestechen; **brib·er·y** ['braɪbərɪ] Bestechung f

brick [brɪk] **1.** Ziegel(stein) m, Backstein m; Brt. Baustein m, (Bau)Klötzchen n; '~·**lay·er** Maurer m; '~·**yard** Ziegelei f

brid·al ['braɪdl] Braut...

bride [braɪd] Braut f; '~·**groom** ['braɪdgrʊm] Bräutigam m; '~s·**maid** ['braɪdzmeɪd] Brautjungfer f

bridge [brɪdʒ] **1.** Brücke f; **2.** e-e Brücke schlagen über (acc.); fig. überbrücken

bri·dle ['braɪdl] **1.** Zaum m; Zügel m; **2.** (auf)zäumen; zügeln; '~ **path** Reitweg m

brief [bri:f] **1.** kurz, bündig; **2.** instruieren, genaue Anweisungen geben; '~·**case** Aktenmappe f

briefs [bri:fs] pl. Slip m

bri·er bot. ['braɪə] Dornstrauch m; Wilde Rose

bri·gade mil. [brɪ'geɪd] Brigade f

bright [braɪt] hell, glänzend; klar; heiter; lebhaft; gescheit; △ nicht breit; ~·**en** ['braɪtn] v/t. a. ~ **up** heller machen, auf-, erhellen; aufheitern; v/i. a. ~ **up** sich aufhellen; '~·**ness** Helligkeit f; Glanz m; Heiterkeit f; Gescheitheit f

bril·liance ['brɪljəns, -jəns] Glanz m; fig. Brillanz f; '~·**liant 1.** glänzend; hervorragend, brillant; **2.** Brillant m

brim [brɪm] **1.** Rand m; Krempe f; **2.** (-mm-) bis zum Rande füllen od. voll sein; ~·**ful(l)** ['brɪmfʊl] randvoll

brine [braɪn] Sole f; Lake f

bring [brɪŋ] (brought) (mit-, her)bringen; △ nicht fort-, wegbringen; j-n dazu bringen (to do zu tun); ~ about zustande bringen; bewirken; ~ forth hervorbringen; ~ off et. fertigbringen, schaffen; ~ on verursachen; ~ out herausbringen; ~ round Ohnmächtigen wieder zu sich bringen; Kranken wieder auf die Beine bringen; ~ up auf-, großziehen; erziehen; zur Sprache bringen; bsd. Brt. et. (er)brechen

brink [brɪŋk] Rand m (a. fig.)
brisk [brɪsk] flott; lebhaft; frisch (Luft)
bris·tle [ˈbrɪsl] **1.** Borste f; (Bart)Stoppel f; **2.** a. ~ **up** sich sträuben; zornig werden; strotzen, wimmeln (**with** von); **ˈbris·tly** (**-ier, -iest**) Stoppel...
Brit F [brɪt] Brit|e m, -in f
Brit·ain [ˈbrɪtn] Britannien n
Brit·ish [ˈbrɪtɪʃ] britisch; **the ~** pl. die Briten pl.
Brit·on [ˈbrɪtn] Brit|e m, -in f
brit·tle [ˈbrɪtl] spröde, zerbrechlich
broach [brəʊtʃ] Thema anschneiden
broad [brɔːd] breit; weit; hell (Tag); deutlich (Wink etc.); derb (Witz); breit, stark (Akzent); allgemein; weitherzig; liberal; **ˈ~cast 1.** (**-cast** od. **-casted**) im Rundfunk od. Fernsehen bringen, ausstrahlen, übertragen; senden; **2.** Rundfunk, TV: Sendung f; **ˈ~cast·er** Rundfunk-, Fernsehsprecher(in); **~·en** [ˈbrɔːdn] verbreitern, erweitern; **ˈ~ jump** Am. Sport: Weitsprung m; **~·ˈmind·ed** liberal
bro·cade [brəˈkeɪd] Brokat m
bro·chure [ˈbrəʊʃə] Broschüre f, Prospekt m
brogue [brəʊg] derber Straßenschuh
broil bsd. Am. [brɔɪl] → **grill** 1
broke [brəʊk] **1.** pret. von **break** 2; **2.** F pleite, abgebrannt; **bro·ken** [ˈbrəʊkən] **1.** p.p. von **break** 2; **2.** zerbrochen, kaputt; gebrochen (a. fig.); zerrüttet; **brok·en-ˈheart·ed** verzweifelt, untröstlich
bro·ker econ. [ˈbrəʊkə] Makler m
bron·chi·tis med. [brɒŋˈkaɪtɪs] Bronchitis f
bronze [brɒnz] **1.** Bronze f; **2.** bronzefarben; Bronze...
brooch [brəʊtʃ] Brosche f
brood [bruːd] **1.** Brut f; Brut...; **2.** brüten (a. fig.)
brook [brʊk] Bach m
broom [bruːm, brʊm] Besen m; **ˈ~·stick** Besenstiel m
Bros. [brɒs] Abk. für **brothers** Gebr., Gebrüder pl. (in Firmenbezeichnungen)
broth [brɒθ] Fleischbrühe f
broth·el [ˈbrɒθl] Bordell n
broth·er [ˈbrʌðə] Bruder m; **~(s) and sister(s)** Geschwister pl.; **ˈ~·hood** rel. [ˈbrʌðəhʊd] Bruderschaft f; **ˈ~-in-law**

[ˈbrʌðərɪnlɔː] (pl. **brothers-in-law**) Schwager m; **ˈ~·ly** brüderlich
brought [brɔːt] pret. u. p.p. von **bring**
brow [braʊ] (Augen)Braue f; Stirn f; Rand m (e-s Steilhanges); **ˈ~·beat** (**-beat, -beaten**) einschüchtern
brown [braʊn] **1.** braun; **2.** Braun n; **3.** bräunen; braun werden
browse [braʊz] grasen, weiden; fig. schmökern
bruise [bruːz] **1.** Quetschung f, blauer Fleck; **2.** quetschen; Früchte anstoßen; e-e Quetschung od. e-n blauen Fleck bekommen
brunch F [brʌntʃ] Brunch m (spätes reichliches Frühstück)
brush [brʌʃ] **1.** Bürste f; Pinsel m; (Fuchs)Rute f; Scharmützel n; Unterholz n; **2.** bürsten; fegen; streifen; ~ **against s.o.** j-n streifen; ~ **away, ~ off** wegbürsten, abwischen; ~ **aside, ~ away** fig. et. abtun; ~ **up** Kenntnisse aufpolieren, -frischen; ~ **up: give one's English a** ~ s-e Englischkenntnisse aufpolieren; **ˈ~·wood** Gestrüpp n, Unterholz n
brusque [bruːsk] brüsk, barsch
Brus·sels sprouts bot. [brʌslˈspraʊts] pl. Rosenkohl m
bru·tal [ˈbruːtl] brutal, roh; **~·i·ty** [bruːˈtælətɪ] Brutalität f
brute [bruːt] **1.** brutal; **2.** Vieh n; F Untier n, Scheusal n
BS [biː ˈes] Abk. für **British Standard** Britische Norm; Am. → **BSc**
BSc [biː es ˈsiː] Brt. Abk. für **Bachelor of Science** Bakkalaureus m der Naturwissenschaften
BST [biː es ˈtiː] Abk. für **British Summer Time** Britische Sommerzeit
BT [biː ˈtiː] Abk. für **British Telecom** Britisches Fernmeldewesen
BTA [biː tiː ˈeɪ] Abk. für **British Tourist Authority** Britische Fremdenverkehrsbehörde
bub·ble [ˈbʌbl] **1.** Blase f; **2.** sprudeln
buck¹ [bʌk] **1.** zo. (pl. **bucks, buck**) Bock m; **2.** v/i. bocken
buck² Am. F [bʌk] Dollar m
buck·et [ˈbʌkɪt] Eimer m, Kübel m
buck·le [ˈbʌkl] **1.** Schnalle f, Spange f; △ nicht **Buckel**; **2.** a. ~ **up** zu-, festschnallen; ~ **on** anschnallen
ˈbuck·skin Wildleder n

bud [bʌd] **1.** bot. Knospe f; fig. Keim m; **2.** (-dd-) knospen, keimen

bud·dy Am. F [bʌdɪ] Kamerad m

budge [bʌdʒ] v/i. sich (von der Stelle) rühren; v/t. (vom Fleck) bewegen

bud·ger·i·gar zo. ['bʌdʒərɪgɑː] Wellensittich m

bud·get ['bʌdʒɪt] Budget n, Etat m; parl. Haushaltsplan m

bud·gie F ['bʌdʒɪ] → budgerigar

buff F [bʌf] in Zssgn ...fan m; ...experte m

buf·fa·lo zo. ['bʌfələʊ] (pl. -loes, -los) Büffel m

buff·er ['bʌfə] tech. Puffer m

buf·fet¹ ['bʌfɪt] schlagen; ~ about durchrütteln, -schütteln

buf·fet² ['bʌfɪt] Büfett n, Anrichte f

buf·fet³ ['bʊfeɪ] (Frühstücks- etc.)Büfett n, Theke f

bug [bʌg] **1.** zo. Wanze f; Am. zo. Insekt n; F Wanze f (Abhörgerät); Computer: Programmfehler m; **2.** (-gg-) F Wanzen anbringen in (dat.); F ärgern; '~·ging de·vice Abhörgerät n; '~·ging op·e·ra·tion Lauschangriff m

bug·gy ['bʌgɪ] mot. Buggy m (geländegängiges Freizeitauto); Am. Kinderwagen m

bu·gle ['bjuːgl] Wald-, Signalhorn n

build [bɪld] **1.** (built) (er)bauen, errichten; △ nicht bilden; **2.** Körperbau m, Figur f; '~·er Erbauer m; Bauunternehmer m

build·ing ['bɪldɪŋ] (Er)Bauen n; Bau m, Gebäude n; Bau...; '~ site Baustelle f

built [bɪlt] pret. u. p.p. von build 1; '~·in eingebaut, Einbau...; ~·'up: ~ area bebautes Gelände od. Gebiet; geschlossene Ortschaft (Verkehr)

bulb [bʌlb] bot. Zwiebel f, Knolle f; electr. (Glüh)Birne f

bulge [bʌldʒ] **1.** (Aus)Bauchung f, Ausbuchtung f; **2.** sich (aus)bauchen; hervorquellen

bulk [bʌlk] Umfang m, Größe f, Masse f; Großteil m; in ~ econ. lose, unverpackt; en gros; '~·y (-ier, -iest) sperrig

bull zo. [bʊl] Bulle m, Stier m; '~·dog zo. Bulldogge f

bull·doze ['bʊldəʊz] planieren; F einschüchtern; '~·doz·er tech. Bulldozer m, Planierraupe f

bul·let ['bʊlɪt] Kugel f

bul·le·tin ['bʊlɪtɪn] Bulletin n, Tagesbericht m; '~ board Am. Schwarzes Brett

'bul·let-proof kugelsicher

bul·lion ['bʊljən] Gold-, Silberbarren m

bul·lock zo. ['bʊlək] Ochse m

'bull's-eye: hit the ~ ins Schwarze treffen (a. fig.)

bul·ly ['bʊlɪ] **1.** tyrannische Person; **2.** einschüchtern, tyrannisieren

bul·wark ['bʊlwək] Bollwerk n (a. fig.)

bum Am. F [bʌm] **1.** Gammler m; Tippelbruder m; Nichtstuer m; **2.** v/t. (-mm-) schnorren; ~ around herumgammeln

'bum·ble·bee zo. Hummel f

bump [bʌmp] **1.** heftiger Schlag od. Stoß; Beule f; Unebenheit f; **2.** stoßen, rammen, auf ein Auto auffahren; zusammenstoßen; holpern; ~ into fig. j-n zufällig treffen

'bump·er mot. Stoßstange f; ~-to-~ Stoßstange an Stoßstange

'bump·y (-ier, -iest) holp(e)rig

bun [bʌn] süßes Brötchen; (Haar)Knoten m

bunch [bʌntʃ] Bund n, Bündel n; F Verein m, Haufen m; ~ of flowers Blumenstrauß m; ~ of grapes Weintraube f; ~ of keys Schlüsselbund m, n

bun·dle ['bʌndl] **1.** Bündel n (a. fig.), Bund f; **2.** v/t. a. ~ up bündeln

bun·ga·low ['bʌŋgələʊ] Bungalow m

bun·gee [bʌn'dʒiː] elastisches Seil; ~ jumping Bungeespringen n

bun·gle ['bʌŋgl] **1.** Pfusch(arbeit f) m; **2.** (ver)pfuschen

bunk [bʌŋk] Koje f; → '~ bed Etagenbett n

bun·ny ['bʌnɪ] Häschen n

buoy naut. [bɔɪ] **1.** Boje f; **2.** ~ up fig. Auftrieb geben (dat.)

bur·den ['bɜːdn] **1.** Last f; Bürde f; **2.** belasten

bu·reau ['bjʊərəʊ] (pl. -reaux [-rəʊz], -reaus) Brt. Schreibtisch m; Am. (bsd. Spiegel)Kommode f; Büro n

bu·reauc·ra·cy [bjʊə'rɒkrəsɪ] Bürokratie f

burg·er gastr. ['bɜːgə] Hamburger m

bur·glar ['bɜːglə] Einbrecher m; ~·glar·ize Am. ['bɜːgləraɪz] → burgle; ~·glar·y ['bɜːglərɪ] Einbruch m; ~·gle ['bɜːgl] einbrechen in (Haus etc.)

bur·i·al ['berɪəl] Begräbnis n

bur·ly ['bɜːlɪ] (**-ier, -iest**) stämmig, kräftig

burn [bɜːn] **1.** *med.* Verbrennung *f*, Brandwunde *f*; verbrannte Stelle; **2.** (*burnt* od. *burned*) (ver-, an)brennen; ~ *down* ab-, niederbrennen; ~ *up* auflodern; verbrennen; verglühen (*Rakete etc.*); '**~·ing** brennend (*a. fig.*)

burnt [bɜːnt] *pret. u. p.p. von* burn 2

burp F [bɜːp] rülpsen, aufstoßen; ein Bäuerchen machen (lassen) (*Baby*)

bur·row ['bʌrəʊ] **1.** (*Kaninchen*)Bau *m*; **2.** (sich ein-, ver)graben

burst [bɜːst] **1.** Bersten *n*; Riß *m*; *fig.* Ausbruch *m*; **2.** (*burst*) *v/i.* bersten, (zer)platzen; zerspringen; explodieren; ~ *from* sich losreißen von; ~ *in on* od. *upon* hereinplatzen bei *j-m*; ~ *into tears* in Tränen ausbrechen; ~ *out fig.* herausplatzen; *v/t.* (auf)sprengen

bur·y ['berɪ] be-, vergraben; beerdigen

bus [bʌs] (*pl.* **-es, -ses**) (Omni)Bus *m*; '**~ driv·er** Busfahrer *m*

bush [bʊʃ] Busch *m*; Gebüsch *n*

bush·el ['bʊʃl] Bushel *m*, Scheffel *m* (*Brt.* 36,37 l, *Am.* 35,24 l)

'bush·y (**-ier, -iest**) buschig

busi·ness ['bɪznɪs] Geschäft *n*; Arbeit *f*, Beschäftigung *f*; Beruf *m*; Tätigkeit *f*; Angelegenheit *f*; Sache *f*, Aufgabe *f*; ~ *of the day* Tagesordnung *f*; *on* ~ geschäftlich, beruflich; *you have no* ~ *doing* (od. *to do*) *that* Sie haben kein Recht, das zu tun; *that's none of your* ~ das geht Sie nichts an; → *mind* 2; '~ *hours* Geschäftszeit *f*; '**~·like** geschäftsmäßig, sachlich; '**~·man** (*pl.* **-men**) Geschäftsmann *m*; '~ *trip* Geschäftsreise *f*; '**~·wom·an** (*pl.* **-women**) Geschäftsfrau *f*

'bus stop Bushaltestelle *f*

bust¹ [bʌst] Büste *f*

bust² F [bʌst]: *go* ~ pleite gehen

bus·tle ['bʌsl] **1.** geschäftiges Treiben *n*; **2.** ~ *about* geschäftig hin u. her eilen

bus·y ['bɪzɪ] **1.** (**-ier, -iest**) beschäftigt; geschäftig; fleißig (*at* bei, *an dat.*); belebt (*Straße*); arbeitsreich (*Tag*); *Am. tel.* besetzt; **2.** (*mst* ~ *o.s.*) sich beschäftigen (*with* mit); '**~·bod·y** aufdringlicher Mensch, Gschaftlhuber *m*; '~ *sig·nal Am. tel.* Besetztzeichen *n*

but [bʌt, bət] **1.** *cj.* aber, jedoch; sondern; außer, als; ohne daß; dennoch; ~

then and(e)rerseits; *he could not* ~ *laugh* er mußte einfach lachen; **2.** *prp.* außer; *all* ~ *him* alle außer ihm; *the last* ~ *one* der vorletzte; *the next* ~ *one* der übernächste; *nothing* ~ nichts als; ~ *for* wenn nicht ... gewesen wäre, ohne *acc.*; **3.** *nach Verneinung:* der (die od. das) nicht; *there is no one* ~ *knows* es gibt niemand, der es nicht weiß; **4.** *adv.* nur; erst, gerade; *all* ~ fast, beinahe

butch·er ['bʊtʃə] **1.** Fleischer *m*, Metzger *m*; **2.** (*fig.* ab-, hin)schlachten

but·ler ['bʌtlə] Butler *m*

butt¹ [bʌt] **1.** (*Gewehr*)Kolben *m*; (*Zigarren- etc.*)Stummel *m*, (*Zigaretten*)Kippe *f*; (Kopf)Stoß *m*; **2.** (mit dem Kopf) stoßen; ~ *in* F sich einmischen (*on* in *acc.*)

butt² [bʌt] Wein-, Bierfaß *n*; Regentonne *f*

but·ter ['bʌtə] **1.** Butter *f*; **2.** mit Butter bestreichen; '~·*cup bot.* Butterblume *f*; '**~·fly** *zo.* Schmetterling *m*, Falter *m*

but·tocks ['bʌtəks] *pl.* Gesäß *n*, F od. *zo.* Hinterteil *n*

but·ton ['bʌtn] **1.** Knopf *m*; Button *m*, (Ansteck)Plakette *f*, Abzeichen *n*; **2.** *mst* ~ *up* zuknöpfen; '**~·hole** Knopfloch *n*

but·tress ['bʌtrɪs] Strebepfeiler *m*

bux·om ['bʌksəm] drall, stramm

buy [baɪ] **1.** F Kauf *m*; **2.** (*bought*) *v/t.* (an-, ein)kaufen (*of, from* von; *at* bei); *Fahrkarte* lösen; ~ *out j-n* abfinden, auszahlen; *Firma* aufkaufen; ~ *up* aufkaufen; '**~·er** (Ein)Käufer(in)

buzz [bʌz] **1.** Summen *n*, Surren *n*; Stimmengewirr *n*; **2.** *v/i.* summen, surren; ~ *off!* Brt. F schwirr ab!, hau ab!

buz·zard *zo.* ['bʌzəd] Bussard *m*

buzz·er *electr.* ['bʌzə] Summer *m*

by [baɪ] **1.** *prp. räumlich:* (nahe od. dicht) bei od. an, neben (*side* ~ *side* Seite an Seite); vorbei od. vorüber an; *zeitlich:* bis um, bis spätestens (*be back* ~ *9.30* sei um 9 Uhr 30 zurück); *Tageszeit:* während, bei (~ *day* bei Tage); *Verkehrsmittel:* per, mit (~ *bus* mit dem Bus; ~ *rail* per Bahn); nach, ...weise (~ *the dozen* dutzendweise); nach, gemäß (~ *my watch* nach od. auf m-r Uhr); von (~ *nature* von Natur aus); *Urheber, Ursache:* von, durch (*a play* ~ *...* ein Stück von ...); ~ *o.s.* allein); *Größenver-*

hältnisse: um (~ *an inch* um e-n Zoll); *math.* mal (**2** ~ **4**); *math. geteilt durch* (**6** ~ **3**); **2.** *adv.* vorbei, vorüber (*go* ~ vorbeigehen, -fahren; *Zeit:* vergehen); beiseite (*put* ~ beiseite-, zurücklegen); ~ *and large* im großen u. ganzen

by... [baɪ] Neben...; Seiten...

bye *int.* F [baɪ], **~'bye** Wiedersehen!, Tschüs!

'by|-e·lec·tion Nachwahl *f*; **'~·gone 1.**

vergangen; **2.** *let* ~*s be* ~*s* laß(t) das Vergangene ruhen; **'~·pass 1.** Umgehungsstraße *f*; *med.* Bypass *m*; **2.** umgehen; vermeiden; **'~·prod·uct** Nebenprodukt *n*; **'~·road** Nebenstraße *f*; **'~·stand·er** Umstehende(r *m*) *f*, Zuschauer(in)

byte [baɪt] *Computer:* Byte *n*

'by|·way Nebenstraße *f*; **'~·word** Inbegriff *m*; *be a* ~ *for* stehen für

---

C

C, c [siː] C, c *n*

C *nur geschr. Abk. für* **Celsius** C, Celsius; *centigrade* hundertgradig (*Thermometereinteilung*)

c nur geschr. Abk. für: **cent**(**s**) Cent *m* od. *pl.* (*amer. Münze*); **century** Jh., Jahrhundert *n*; *circa* ca., circa, ungefähr; *cubic* Kubik...

cab [kæb] Droschke *f*, Taxi *n*; Führerstand *m* (*Lokomotive*); Fahrerhaus *n* (*Lastwagen*), Führerhaus *n* (*a. Kran*)

cab·a·ret ['kæbəreɪ] Varietédarbietung(en *pl.*) *f*

cab·bage *bot.* ['kæbɪdʒ] Kohl *m*

cab·in ['kæbɪn] Hütte *f*; *naut.* Kabine *f* (*a. Seilbahn*), Kajüte *f*; *aviat.* Kanzel *f*

cab·i·net ['kæbɪnɪt] Schrank *m*, Vitrine *f*; *pol.* Kabinett *n*; **'~·mak·er** Kunsttischler *m*; **'~ meet·ing** Kabinettssitzung *f*

ca·ble ['keɪbl] **1.** Kabel *n*; (Draht)Seil *n*; **2.** telegrafieren; j-m Geld telegrafisch anweisen; *TV* verkabeln; **'~ car** Seilbahn: Kabine *f*; Wagen *m*; **'~·gram** (Übersee)Telegramm *n*; **'~ rail·way** Drahtseilbahn *f*; **~ 'tel·e·vi·sion**, **~ TV** [- tiː 'viː] Kabelfernsehen *n*

'cab| rank, **'~·stand** Taxi-, Droschkenstand *m*

cack·le ['kækl] **1.** Gegacker *n*, Geschnatter *n*; **2.** gackern, schnattern

cac·tus *bot.* ['kæktəs] (*pl.* **-tuses, -ti** ['kæktaɪ]) Kaktus *m*

CAD [siː eɪ 'diː, kæd] *Abk. für* **computer-aided design** (*computergestütztes Entwurfszeichnen*)

ca·dence ['keɪdəns] *mus.* Kadenz *f*; (Sprech)Rhythmus *m*

ca·det *mil.* [kə'det] Kadett *m*

caf·é, caf·e ['kæfeɪ] Café *n*

caf·e·te·ri·a [kæfɪ'tɪərɪə] Cafeteria *f*, Selbstbedienungsrestaurant *n*, *a.* Kantine *f*, *univ.* Mensa *f*

cage [keɪdʒ] **1.** Käfig *m*; Bergbau: Förderkorb *m*; **2.** einsperren

cake [keɪk] **1.** Kuchen *m*, Torte *f*; Tafel *f* Schokolade, Riegel *m* Seife; **2.** ~*d with mud* schmutzverkrustet

CAL [kæl] *Abk. für* **computer-aided** od. **-assisted learning** (*computergestütztes Lernen*)

ca·lam·i·ty [kə'læmɪtɪ] großes Unglück, Katastrophe *f*

cal·cu|·late ['kælkjʊleɪt] *v/t.* kalkulieren; be-, aus-, errechnen; *Am.* F vermuten; *v/i.* ~ *on* rechnen mit od. auf (*acc.*), zählen auf (*acc.*); **~·la·tion** [kælkjʊ'leɪʃn] Berechnung *f* (*a. fig.*); *econ.* Kalkulation *f*; Überlegung *f*; **~·la·tor** ['kælkjʊleɪtə] Rechner *m* (*Gerät*)

cal·en·dar ['kælɪndə] Kalender *m*

calf¹ [kɑːf] (*pl.* **calves** [kɑːvz]) Wade *f*

calf² [kɑːf] (*pl.* **calves** [kɑːvz]) Kalb *n*; **'~·skin** Kalb(s)fell *n*

cal·i·bre *bsd. Brt.*, **cal·i·ber** *Am.* ['kælɪbə] Kaliber *n*

call [kɔːl] **1.** Ruf *m*; *tel.* Anruf *m*, Gespräch *n*; Ruf *m*, Berufung *f* (*to in ein Amt*; *auf e-n Lehrstuhl*); Aufruf *m*, Aufforderung *f*; Signal *n*; (kurzer) Besuch; *on* ~ auf Abruf; *be on* ~ Bereitschaftsdienst haben (*Arzt*); **make a ~** telefonieren; **2.** *v/t.* (herbei)rufen; (ein)berufen; *tel.* j-n anrufen; berufen, ernennen (**to** zu); nennen; *Aufmerksamkeit* lenken (**to** auf *acc.*); **be ~ed** heißen; **~ s.o. names** j-n beschimpfen, beleidigen; *v/i.* rufen; *tel.* anrufen; e-n (kurzen) Besuch machen (**on** *s.o.*, **at** *s.o.'s* [*house*] bei j-m); **~ at a port** e-n Hafen anlaufen; **~ for** rufen nach; *et.* anfordern; *et.* abholen; **to be ~ed for** postlagernd; **~ on** sich an *j-n* wenden (**for** wegen); appellieren an (*acc.*) (**to do** zu tun); **~ on s.o.** j-n besuchen; **'~ box** *Brt.* Telefonzelle *f*; **'~er** Anrufer(in); Besucher(in); **'~ girl** Callgirl *n*; **'~in** *Am.* → **phone-in**; **'~ing** Berufung *f*; Beruf *m*

cal·lous ['kæləs] schwielig; *fig.* gefühllos

calm [kɑːm] **1.** still, ruhig; **2.** (Wind)Stille *f*, Ruhe *f*; **3.** *oft* **~ down** besänftigen, (sich) beruhigen

cal·o·rie ['kæləri] Kalorie *f*; **high** *od.* **rich in ~s** *pred.* kalorienreich; **low in ~s** *pred.* kalorienarm, -reduziert; → **high--calorie**, **low-calorie**; **'~con·scious** kalorienbewußt

calve [kɑːv] kalben

calves [kɑːvz] *pl. von* **calf** [^1], [^2]

CAM [si: eɪ 'em, kæm] *Abk. für* **computer-aided manufacture** (*computergestützte Fertigung*)

cam·cor·der ['kæmkɔːdə] Camcorder *m*, Kamerarecorder *m*

came [keɪm] *pret. von* **come**

cam·el *zo.* ['kæml] Kamel *n*

cam·e·o ['kæmɪəʊ] (*pl.* **-os**) Kamee *f* (*Schmuckstein*); *theat.*, *Film*: kleine Nebenrolle, kurze Szene (*für bekannte Schauspieler*)

cam·e·ra ['kæmərə] Kamera *f*, Fotoapparat *m*

cam·o·mile *bot.* ['kæməmaɪl] Kamille *f*

cam·ou·flage ['kæmʊflɑːʒ] **1.** Tarnung *f*; **2.** tarnen

camp [kæmp] **1.** (*Zelt- etc.*)Lager *n*; **~ out** zelten, campen

cam·paign [kæm'peɪn] **1.** *mil.* Feldzug *m*; *fig.* Kampagne *f*, Feldzug *m*, Aktion *f*; *pol.* Wahlkampf *m*; **2.** *fig.* kämpfen (**for** für; **against** gegen)

camp|'bed *Brt.*, **~ 'cot** *Am.* Feldbett *n*; **'~er (van)** Campingbus *m*, Wohnmobil *n*; **'~ground**, **'~site** Lagerplatz *m*; Zelt-, Campingplatz *m*

cam·pus ['kæmpəs] Campus *m*, Universitätsgelände *n*

can[^1] [kæn, kən] *v/aux.* (*pret.* **could**; *verneint:* **cannot**, **can't**) ich, du *etc.* kann(st) *etc.*; dürfen, können

can[^2] [kæn, kən] **1.** Kanne *f*; (Blech-, Konserven)Dose *f*, (-)Büchse *f*; **2.** (*-nn-*) einmachen, -dosen

Can·a·da ['kænədə] Kanada *n*; **Ca·na·di·an** [kə'neɪdjən] **1.** kanadisch; **2.** Kanadier(in)

ca·nal [kə'næl] Kanal *m* (*a. anat.*)

ca·nar·y *zo.* [kə'neərɪ] Kanarienvogel *m*

can·cel ['kænsl] (*bsd. Brt.* **-ll-**, *Am.* **-l-**) (durch-, aus)streichen; entwerten; rückgängig machen; absagen; **be ~(l)ed** ausfallen

can·cer ['kænsə] *med.* Krebs *m*; **2** *astr.* Krebs *m*; **he/she is (a) 2** er/sie ist (ein) Krebs; **'~ous** *med.* ['kænsərəs] krebsbefallen; Krebs...

can·did ['kændɪd] aufrichtig, offen

can·di·date ['kændɪdət] Kandidat(in) (**for** für), Bewerber(in) (**for** um)

can·died ['kændɪd] kandiert

can·dle ['kændl] Kerze *f*; Licht *n*; **burn the ~ at both ends** mit s-r Gesundheit Raubbau treiben; **'~stick** Kerzenleuchter *m*, -ständer *m*

can·do(u)r ['kændə] Aufrichtigkeit *f*, Offenheit *f*

C&W [si: ənd 'dʌblju:] *Abk. für* **country and western** (*Musik*)

can·dy ['kændɪ] **1.** Kandis(zucker) *m*; *Am.* Süßigkeiten *pl.*; **2.** kandieren; **'~ store** *Am.* Süßwarengeschäft *n*

cane [keɪn] *bot.* Rohr *n*; (Rohr)Stock *m*

ca·nine ['keɪnaɪn] Hunde...

canned [kænd] Dosen..., Büchsen...; **~ fruit** Obstkonserven *pl.*

can·ner·y *bsd. Am.* ['kænərɪ] Konservenfabrik *f*

can·ni·bal ['kænɪbl] Kannibale *m*

can·non ['kænən] Kanone *f*

can·not ['kænɒt] → **can**[^1]

can·ny ['kænɪ] (**-ier**, **-iest**) schlau

ca·noe [kə'nuː] **1.** Kanu *n*, Paddelboot *n*; **2.** Kanu fahren, paddeln

can·on ['kænən] Kanon *m*; Regel *f*

'can o·pen·er *bsd. Am.* Dosen-, Büchsenöffner *m*

can·o·py ['kænəpɪ] Baldachin *m*

cant [kænt] Jargon *m*; Phrase(n *pl.*) *f*

can't [kɑːnt] → **can**[1]

can·tan·ker·ous F [kænˈtæŋkərəs] zänkisch, mürrisch

can·teen [kænˈtiːn] *bsd. Brt.* Kantine *f*; *mil.* Feldflasche *f*; Besteck(kasten *m*) *n*

can·ter [ˈkæntə] **1.** Kanter *m* (*kurzer, leichter Galopp*); **2.** kantern

can·vas [ˈkænvəs] Segeltuch *n*; Zelt-, Packleinwand *f*; Segel *pl.*; *paint.* Leinwand *f*; Gemälde *n*

can·vass [ˈkænvəs] **1.** *pol.* Wahlfeldzug *m*; *econ.* Werbefeldzug *m*; **2.** *v/t.* eingehend untersuchen *od.* erörtern *od.* prüfen; *pol.* werben um (*Stimmen*); *v/i.* pol. e-n Wahlfeldzug veranstalten

can·yon [ˈkænjən] Cañon *m*

cap [kæp] **1.** Kappe *f*; Mütze *f*; Haube *f*; Zündkapsel *f*; **2.** (*-pp-*) (mit e-r Kappe *etc.*) bedecken; *fig.* krönen; übertreffen

ca·pa·bil·i·ty [keɪpəˈbɪlətɪ] Fähigkeit *f*; ~**ble** [ˈkeɪpəbl] fähig (*of* zu)

ca·pac·i·ty [kəˈpæsətɪ] (Raum)Inhalt *m*; Fassungsvermögen *n*; Kapazität *f*; Aufnahmefähigkeit *f*; *geistige* (*od. tech.* Leistungs)Fähigkeit *f* (*for ger.* zu *inf.*); **in my ~ as** in meiner Eigenschaft als

cape[1] [keɪp] Kap *n*, Vorgebirge *n*

cape[2] [keɪp] Cape *n*, Umhang *m*

ca·per [ˈkeɪpə] **1.** Kapriole *f*, Luftsprung *m*; **cut ~s** → **2.** Freuden- *od.* Luftsprünge machen

ca·pil·la·ry *anat.* [kəˈpɪlərɪ] Haar-, Kapillargefäß *n*

cap·i·tal [ˈkæpɪtl] **1.** Kapital *n*; Hauptstadt *f*; Großbuchstabe *m*; **2.** Kapital...; Tod(es)...; Haupt...; großartig, prima; ~ **'crime** Kapitalverbrechen *n*

cap·i·tal·is·m [ˈkæpɪtəlɪzəm] Kapitalismus *m*; ~**ist** [ˈkæpɪtəlɪst] Kapitalist *m*; ~**ize** [ˈkæpɪtəlaɪz] *econ.* kapitalisieren; groß schreiben

cap·i·tal 'let·ter Großbuchstabe *m*; ~ **'pun·ish·ment** Todesstrafe *f*

ca·pit·u·late [kəˈpɪtjʊleɪt] kapitulieren (*to* vor *dat.*)

ca·pri·cious [kəˈprɪʃəs] launisch

Cap·ri·corn *astr.* [ˈkæprɪkɔːn] Steinbock *m*; **he/she is (a) ~** er/sie ist (ein) Steinbock

cap·size [kæpˈsaɪz] *v/i.* kentern; *v/t.* zum Kentern bringen

cap·sule [ˈkæpsjuːl] Kapsel *f*

cap·tain [ˈkæptɪn] (An)Führer *m*; *naut.*, *econ.* (*aviat.* Flug)Kapitän *m*; *mil.* Hauptmann *m*; *Sport:* (Mannschafts-)Kapitän *m*, Spielführer *m*

cap·tion [ˈkæpʃn] Überschrift *f*, Titel *m*; Bildunterschrift *f*; *Film:* Untertitel *m*

cap·ti·vate *fig.* [ˈkæptɪveɪt] gefangennehmen, fesseln; ~**tive** [ˈkæptɪv] **1.** gefangen; gefesselt; **hold ~** gefangenhalten; **2.** Gefangene(r *m*) *f*; ~**tiv·i·ty** [kæpˈtɪvətɪ] Gefangenschaft *f*

cap·ture [ˈkæptʃə] **1.** Eroberung *f*; Gefangennahme *f*; **2.** fangen, gefangennehmen; erobern; erbeuten; *naut.* kapern

car [kɑː] Auto *n*, Wagen *m*; (Eisenbahn-, Straßenbahn)Wagen *m*; Gondel *f* (*e-s Ballons etc.*); Kabine *f* (*e-s Aufzugs*); **by ~** mit dem Auto, im Auto

car·a·mel [ˈkærəmel] Karamel *m*, Karamelle *f*

car·a·van [ˈkærəvæn] Karawane *f*; *Brt.* Wohnwagen *m*, -anhänger *m*; ~ **site** Campingplatz *m* für Wohnwagen

car·a·way *bot.* [ˈkærəweɪ] Kümmel *m*

car·bine *mil.* [ˈkɑːbaɪn] Karabiner *m*

car·bo·hy·drate - [kɑːbəʊˈhaɪdreɪt] Kohle(n)hydrat *n*

'car bomb Autobombe *f*

car·bon [ˈkɑːbən] - Kohlenstoff *m*; → ~ **'cop·y** Durchschlag *m*; ~ **(pa·per)** Kohlepapier *n*

car·bu·ret·(t)or *tech.* [kɑːbəˈretə] Vergaser *m*

car·case *Brt.*, **car·cass** [ˈkɑːkəs] Kadaver *m*, Aas *n*; *Fleischerei:* Rumpf *m*

car·cin·o·gen·ic [kɑːsɪnəˈdʒenɪk] karzinogen, krebserzeugend

card [kɑːd] Karte *f*; **play ~s** Karten spielen; **have a ~ up one's sleeve** *fig.* (noch) e-n Trumpf in der Hand haben; **'~board** Pappe *f*; **'~board box** Pappschachtel *f*, -karton *m*

car·di·ac *med.* [ˈkɑːdɪæk] Herz...; ~ **'pace·mak·er** *med.* Herzschrittmacher *m*

car·di·gan [ˈkɑːdɪgən] Strickjacke *f*

car·di·nal [ˈkɑːdɪnl] **1.** Grund..., Haupt...; Kardinal...; scharlachrot; **2.** *rel.* Kardinal *m*; ~ **'num·ber** Grundzahl *f*

'card in·dex Kartei *f*; ~ **phone** Kartentelefon *n*; **'~sharp·er** Falschspieler *m*

'car dump Autofriedhof *m*

care [keə] **1.** Sorge *f*; Sorgfalt *f*; Vorsicht *f*; Obhut *f*, Pflege *f*; **medical ~** ärztliche Behandlung; **take ~ of** aufpassen auf (*acc.*); **with ~!** Vorsicht!; **2.** Lust haben (**to** *inf.* zu); **~ about** sich kümmern um; **~ for** sorgen für, sich kümmern um; sich etwas machen aus; *I don't ~!* F meinetwegen!; *I couldn't ~ less* F es ist mir völlig egal

ca·reer [kə'rɪə] **1.** Karriere *f*, Laufbahn *f*; **2.** Berufs...; Karriere...; **3.** rasen

ca·reers| ad·vice Berufsberatung *f*; **~ ad·vi·sor** Berufsberater *m*; **~ guid·ance** Berufsberatung *f*; **~ of·fice** Berufsberatungsstelle *f*; **~ of·fic·er** Berufsberater *m*

'care·free sorgenfrei, sorglos; **'~·ful** vorsichtig; sorgsam bedacht (**of** auf *acc.*); sorgfältig; **be ~!** paß auf!; **'~·less** nachlässig; unachtsam; leichtsinnig

ca·ress [kə'res] **1.** Liebkosung *f*; **2.** liebkosen, streicheln

'care|·tak·er Hausmeister *m*; (Haus*etc.*)Verwalter *m*; **'~·worn** abgehärmt

'car|·fare *Am.* Fahrgeld *n* (*für Bus etc.*); **'~·fer·ry** Autofähre *f*

car·go ['ka:gəʊ] (*pl.* **-goes**, *Am. a.* **-gos**) Ladung *f*

'car hire Autovermietung *f*

car·i·ca·ture ['kærɪkətjʊə] **1.** Karikatur *f*; **2.** karikieren; **~·tur·ist** ['kærɪkətjʊərɪst] Karikaturist *m*

car·ies *med.* ['keərɪːz], *a.* **dental ~** Karies *f*

'car me·chan·ic Automechaniker *m*

car·mine ['ka:maɪn] Karmin(rot) *n*

car·na·tion *bot.* [ka:'neɪʃn] Nelke *f*

car·nap·per F ['ka:næpə] Autoentführer *m*

car·ni·val ['ka:nɪvl] Karneval *m*

car·niv·o·rous [ka:'nɪvərəs] fleischfressend

car·ol ['kærəl] Weihnachtslied *n*

carp *zo.* [ka:p] Karpfen *m*

'car park *bsd. Brt.* Parkplatz *m*; Parkhaus *n*

car·pen·ter ['ka:pɪntə] Zimmermann *m*

car·pet ['ka:pɪt] **1.** Teppich *m*; **sweep s.th. under the ~** et. unter den Teppich kehren; **2.** mit e-m Teppich auslegen

'car| phone Autotelefon *n*; **'~ pool** Fahrgemeinschaft *f*; **'~ pool(·ing) ser·vice** Mitfahrzentrale *f*; **'~·port**

überdachter Abstellplatz (*für Autos*); **'~ rent·al** *Am.* Autovermietung *f*; **'~ re·pair shop** Autoreparaturwerkstatt *f*

car·riage ['kærɪdʒ] Beförderung *f*, Transport *m*; Transportkosten *pl.*; Kutsche *f*; *Brt. rail.* (Personen)Wagen *m*; (Körper)Haltung *f*; **'~·way** Fahrbahn *f*

car·ri·er ['kærɪə] Spediteur *m*; Gepäckträger *m* (*am Fahrrad*); Flugzeugträger *m*; **'~ bag** *Brt.* Trag(e)tasche *f*, -tüte *f*

car·ri·on ['kærɪən] Aas *n*; Aas...

car·rot *bot.* ['kærət] Karotte *f*, Mohrrübe *f*

car·ry ['kærɪ] *v/t.* wohin bringen, führen, tragen (*a. v/i.*), fahren, befördern; (bei sich) haben *od.* tragen; Ansicht durchsetzen; Gewinn, Preis davontragen; Ernte, Zinsen tragen; (weiter)führen; Mauer ziehen; Antrag durchbringen; **be carried** angenommen werden (*Antrag*); **~ the day** den Sieg davontragen; **~ s.th. too far** et. übertreiben; et. zu weit treiben; **get carried away** *fig.* die Kontrolle über sich verlieren; **~ for·ward**, **~ over** *econ.* übertragen; **~ on** fortsetzen, weiterführen; *Geschäft etc.* betreiben; **~ out**, **~ through** durch-, ausführen; **'~·cot** *Brt.* (Baby)Trag(e)tasche *f*

cart [ka:t] **1.** Karren *m*; Wagen *m*; *Am.* Einkaufswagen *m*; **put the ~ before the horse** *fig.* das Pferd beim Schwanz aufzäumen; **2.** karren

car·ti·lage *anat.* ['ka:tɪlɪdʒ] Knorpel *m*

car·ton ['ka:tən] Karton *m*; **a ~ of cigarettes** e-e Stange Zigaretten

car·toon [ka:'tu:n] Cartoon *m*, *n*; Karikatur *f*; Zeichentrickfilm *m*; **~·ist** [ka:'tu:nɪst] Karikaturist *m*

car·tridge ['ka:trɪdʒ] Patrone *f*; *phot.* (Film)Patrone *f*, (-)Kassette *f*; Tonabnehmer *m*; Patrone *f* (*e-s Füllhalters*)

'cart·wheel turn **~s** radschlagen

carve [ka:v] *Fleisch* vorschneiden, zerlegen; schnitzen; meißeln; **'carv·er** (Holz)Schnitzer *m*; Bildhauer *m*; Tranchierer *m*; Tranchiermesser *n*; **'carv·ing** Schnitzerei *f*

'car wash Autowäsche *f*; (Auto)Waschanlage *f*, Waschstraße *f*

cas·cade [kæ'skeɪd] Wasserfall *m*

case¹ [keɪs] **1.** Behälter *m*; Kiste *f*, Kasten *m*; Etui *n*; Gehäuse *n*; Schachtel *f*;

(*Glas*)Schrank *m*; (*Kissen*)Bezug *m*; *tech.* Verkleidung *f*; **2.** in ein Gehäuse *od.* Etui stecken; *tech.* verkleiden

case² [keıs] Fall *m* (*a. jur.*); *gr.* Kasus *m*, Fall *m*; *med.* (Krankheits)Fall *m*, Patient(in); Sache *f*, Angelegenheit *f*

case·ment ['keısmənt] Fensterflügel *m*; **~ → 'win·dow** Flügelfenster *n*

cash [kæʃ] **1.** Bargeld *n*; Barzahlung *f*; **~ down** gegen bar; **~ on delivery** Lieferung *f* gegen bar; (per) Nachnahme *f*; **2.** *Scheck etc.* einlösen; **'~book** Kassenbuch *n*; **'~ desk** Kasse *f* (*im Warenhaus etc.*); **~ di·spens·er** *bsd. Brt.* Geld-, Bankautomat *m*; **~·ier** [kæ'ʃıə] Kassierer(in); **'~·less** bargeldlos; **~ ma·chine, '~·point** *Brt.* **→ ~ di·spenser; ~ re·gis·ter** Registrierkasse *f*

cas·ing ['keısıŋ] (Schutz)Hülle *f*; Verschalung *f*, -kleidung *f*; Gehäuse *n*

cask [kɑːsk] Faß *n*

cas·ket ['kɑːskıt] Kästchen *n*; *Am.* Sarg *m*

cas·se·role ['kæsərəʊl] Kasserolle *f*

cas·sette [kə'set] (*Film-, Band-, Musik*)Kassette *f*; △ *nicht Geld- etc.* **Kassette; ~ deck** Kassettendeck *n*; **~ play·er** Kassettenrekorder *m*; **~ ra·di·o** Radiorecorder *m*; **~ re·cord·er** Kassettenrecorder *m*

cas·sock *relig.* ['kæsək] Soutane *f*

cast [kɑːst] **1.** Wurf *m*; *tech.* Guß(form *f*) *m*; Abguß *m*, Abdruck *m*; Schattierung *f*, Anflug *m*; Form *f*, Art *f*; Auswerfen *n* (*der Angel etc.*); *thea.* Besetzung *f*; **2.** (*cast*) *v/t.* (ab-, aus-, hin-, um-, weg)werfen; *zo.* Haut *etc.* abwerfen; *Zähne etc.* verlieren; verwerfen; gestalten; *tech.* gießen; *a.* **~ up** ausrechnen, zusammenzählen; *thea.* Stück besetzen; *Rollen* verteilen (**to an** *acc.*); **~ lots** losen (**for** um); **~ away** wegwerfen; **be ~ down** niedergeschlagen sein; **~ off** *Kleidung* ausrangieren; *Freund etc.* fallenlassen; *Maschen* abnehmen (*Stricken*); *v/i.* sich werfen (*Holz*); **~ about for, ~ around for** suchen (nach), *fig. a.* sich umsehen nach

cas·ta·net [kæstə'net] Kastagnette *f*

cast·a·way *naut.* ['kɑːstəweı] Schiffbrüchige(r *m*) *f*

caste [kɑːst] Kaste *f* (*a. fig.*)

cast·er ['kɑːstə] Laufrolle *f* (*unter Mö-*

beln); *Brt.* (*Salz-, Zucker- etc.*)Streuer *m*

cas·ti·gate ['kæstıgeıt] züchtigen; *fig.* geißeln

cast| 'i·ron Gußeisen *n*; **~·'i·ron** gußeisern

cas·tle ['kɑːsl] Burg *f*, Schloß *n*; *Schach:* Turm *m*

cast·or ['kɑːstə] **→ caster**

cast·or oil [kɑːstə 'ɔıl] Rizinusöl *n*

cas·trate [kæ'streıt] kastrieren

cas·u·al ['kæʒʊəl] zufällig; gelegentlich; flüchtig; lässig; **~ wear** Freizeitkleidung *f*

cas·u·al·ty ['kæʒʊəltı] Unfall *m*; Verunglückte(r *m*) *f*, Opfer *n*; *mil.* Verwundete(r) *m*; *mil.* Gefallene(r) *m*; **casualties** *pl.* Opfer *pl.*, *mil. mst* Verluste *pl.*; **'~ (department)** Notaufnahme *f* (*im Krankenhaus*); **'~ ward** Unfallstation *f* (*im Krankenhaus*)

cat *zo.* [kæt] Katze *f*

cat·a·logue *bsd. Brt.*, **cat·a·log** *Am.* ['kætəlɒg] **1.** Katalog *m*; Verzeichnis *n*, Liste *f*; **2.** katalogisieren

cat·a·lyt·ic con·vert·er *mot.* [kætəlıtık kən'vɜːtə] Katalysator *m*

cat·a·pult ['kætəpʌlt] *Brt.* Schleuder *f*; Katapult *n*, *m*

cat·a·ract ['kætərækt] Wasserfall *m*; Stromschnelle *f*; *med.* grauer Star *m*

ca·tarrh *med.* [kə'tɑː] Katarrh *m*

ca·tas·tro·phe [kə'tæstrəfı] Katastrophe *f*

catch [kætʃ] **1.** Fangen *n*; Fang *m*, Beute *f*; Stocken *n* (*des Atems*); Halt *m*, Griff *m*; *tech.* Haken *m*; (Tür)Klinke *f*; Verschluß *m*; *fig.* Haken *m*; **2.** (*caught*) *v/t.* (auf-, ein)fangen; packen, fassen, ergreifen; überraschen, ertappen; *Blick etc.* auffangen; *Zug etc.* (noch) kriegen, erwischen; erfassen, verstehen; einfangen (*Atmosphäre*); sich *e-e Krankheit* holen; **~ (a) cold** sich erkälten; **~ the eye** ins Auge fallen; **~ s.o.'s eye** j-s Aufmerksamkeit auf sich lenken; **~ s.o. up** j-n einholen; **be caught up in** verwickelt sein in (*acc.*); **3.** *v/i.* sich verfangen, hängenbleiben; fassen, greifen, in-einandergreifen (*Räder*); klemmen; einschnappen (*Schloß etc.*); **~ up with** einholen; **'~·er** Fänger *m*; **'~·ing** packend; *med.* ansteckend (*a. fig.*); **'~·word** Schlagwort *n*; Stichwort *n*; **'~·y** (**-ier, -iest**) eingängig (*Melodie*)

cat·e·chis·m ['kætɪkɪzəm] Katechismus m

cat·e·go·ry ['kætɪgərɪ] Kategorie f

ca·ter ['keɪtə]: ~ *for* Speisen u. Getränke liefern für; *fig.* sorgen für

cat·er·pil·lar ['kætəpɪlə] *zo.* Raupe f; *TM* Raupenfahrzeug n; ~ '**trac·tor** *TM* Raupenschlepper m

cat·gut ['kætgʌt] Darmsaite f

ca·the·dral [kə'θiːdrəl] Dom m, Kathedrale f

Cath·o·lic ['kæθəlɪk] **1.** katholisch; **2.** Katholik(in)

cat·kin bot. ['kætkɪn] Kätzchen n

cat·tle ['kætl] Vieh n

caught [kɔːt] *pret. u. p.p. von* **catch** 2

cau·li·flow·er bot. ['kɒlɪflaʊə] Blumenkohl m

cause [kɔːz] **1.** Ursache f; Grund m; Sache f; **2.** verursachen; veranlassen; '~·less grundlos

cau·tion ['kɔːʃn] **1.** Vorsicht f; Warnung f; Verwarnung f; △ *nicht* **Kaution**; **2.** warnen; verwarnen; *jur.* belehren

cau·tious ['kɔːʃəs] behutsam, vorsichtig

cav·al·ry *hist. mil.* ['kævlrɪ] Kavallerie f

cave [keɪv] **1.** Höhle f; **2.** *v/i.* ~ *in* einstürzen

cav·ern ['kævən] (große) Höhle

cav·i·ty ['kævɪtɪ] Höhle f; Loch n

caw [kɔː] **1.** krächzen; **2.** Krächzen n

CB [siː 'biː] *Abk. für* **Citizens' Band** CB-Funk m (*Wellenbereich für privaten Funkverkehr*)

CBS [siː biː 'es] *Abk. für* **Columbia Broadcasting System** (*amer. Rundfunkgesellschaft*)

CD [siː 'diː] *Abk. für* **compact disc** CD (-Platte) f; **CD 'play·er** CD-Spieler m; **CD-ROM** [siː diː 'rɒm] *Abk. für* **compact disc read-only memory** CD-ROM f; **CD 'vid·e·o** (*pl. -os*) CD-Video n

cease [siːs] aufhören; beenden; '~·**fire** *mil.* Feuereinstellung f; Waffenruhe f; '~·**less** unaufhörlich

cei·ling ['siːlɪŋ] (Zimmer)Decke f; *econ.* Höchstgrenze f, oberste Preisgrenze

cel·e·brate ['selɪbreɪt] feiern; '~·**brat·ed** gefeiert, berühmt (*for* für, wegen); ~·**bra·tion** [selɪ'breɪʃn] Feier f

ce·leb·ri·ty [sɪ'lebrətɪ] Berühmtheit f

cel·e·ry bot. ['selərɪ] Sellerie m, f

ce·les·ti·al [sɪ'lestjəl] himmlisch

cel·i·ba·cy ['selɪbəsɪ] Ehelosigkeit f

cell [sel] Zelle f; *electr. a.* Element n

cel·lar ['selə] Keller m

cel·list *mus.* ['tʃelɪst] Cellist(in); ~·**lo** *mus.* ['tʃeləʊ] (*pl. -los*) (Violon)Cello n

cel·lo·phane *TM* ['seləʊfeɪn] Zellophan n

cel·lu·lar ['seljʊlə] Zell(en)...; ~ '**phone** Funktelefon n

Cel·tic ['keltɪk] keltisch

ce·ment [sɪ'ment] **1.** Zement m; Kitt m; **2.** zementieren; (ver)kitten

cem·e·tery ['semɪtrɪ] Friedhof m

cen·sor ['sensə] **1.** Zensor m; **2.** zensieren; '~·**ship** Zensur f

cen·sure ['senʃə] **1.** Tadel m, Verweis m; △ *nicht* **Zensur**; **2.** tadeln

cen·sus ['sensəs] Volkszählung f

cent [sent] Hundert n; *Am.* Cent m (*1/100 Dollar*); **per** ~ Prozent n

cen·te·na·ry [sen'tiːnərɪ] Hundertjahrfeier f, hundertjähriges Jubiläum

cen·ten·ni·al [sen'tenjəl] **1.** hundertjährig; **2.** *Am.* → **centenary**

cen·ti·grade ['sentɪɡreɪd]: *10 degrees* ~ 10 Grad Celsius; '~·**me·tre** *Brt.*, '~·**me·ter** *Am.* Zentimeter m, n; ~·**pede** *zo.* ['sentɪpiːd] Tausendfüß(l)er m

cen·tral ['sentrəl] zentral; Haupt...; Zentral...; Mittel...; ~ **heat·ing** Zentralheizung f; ~·**ize** ['sentrəlaɪz] zentralisieren; ~ '**lock·ing** *mot.* Zentralverriegelung f; ~·**res·er·va·tion** *Brt.* Mittelstreifen m (*Autobahn*)

cen·tre *Brt.*, **cen·ter** *Am.* ['sentə] **1.** Zentrum n, Mittelpunkt m; *Fußball:* Flanke f; **2.** (sich) konzentrieren; zentrieren; ~ '**back** *Fußball:* Vorstopper m; ~ '**for·ward** *Sport:* Mittelstürmer(in); ~ *of* '**grav·i·ty** *phys.* Schwerpunkt m

cen·tu·ry ['sentʃʊrɪ] Jahrhundert n

ce·ram·ics [sɪ'ræmɪks] *pl.* Keramik f, keramische Erzeugnisse *pl.*

ce·re·al ['sɪərɪəl] **1.** Getreide...; **2.** Getreide(pflanze f) n; Getreideflocken *pl.*, Frühstückskost f (*aus Getreide*)

ce·re·bral anat. ['serɪbrəl] Gehirn...

cer·e·mo|·ni·al [serɪ'məʊnjəl] **1.** zeremoniell; **2.** Zeremoniell n; ~·**ni·ous** [serɪ'məʊnjəs] zeremoniell; förmlich; ~·**ny** ['serɪmənɪ] Zeremonie f; Feier(lichkeit) f; Förmlichkeit(en *pl.*) f

cer·tain ['sɜːtn] sicher, gewiß; zuverlässig; bestimmt; gewisse(r, -s); '**~·ly** sicher, gewiß; *in Antworten:* sicherlich, bestimmt, natürlich; '**~·ty** Sicherheit *f*, Bestimmtheit *f*, Gewißheit *f*

cer·tif·i·cate [sə'tɪfɪkət] Zeugnis *n*; Bescheinigung *f*; **~ of (good) conduct** Führungszeugnis *n*; **General 2 of Education advanced level (A level)** *Brt. Schule:* etwa Abitur(zeugnis) *n*; **General 2 of Education ordinary level (O level)** *Brt. Schule:* etwa mittlere Reife; **medical ~** ärztliches Attest; **~·ti·fy** ['sɜːtɪfaɪ] *et.* bescheinigen; beglaubigen

cer·ti·tude ['sɜːtɪtjuːd] Sicherheit *f*, Bestimmtheit *f*, Gewißheit *f*

CET [siː iː 'tiː] *Abk. für* **Central European Time** MEZ, mitteleuropäische Zeit

cf (*Lateinisch* **confer**) *nur geschr. Abk. für* **compare** vgl., vergleiche

CFC [siː ef 'siː] *Abk. für* **chlorofluorocarbon** FCKW, Fluorchlorkohlenwasserstoff *m*

chafe [tʃeɪf] *v/t.* warm reiben; aufreiben, wund reiben; *v/i.* (sich durch)reiben, scheuern

chaff [tʃɑːf] Spreu *f*; Häcksel *n*

chaf·finch *zo.* ['tʃæfɪntʃ] Buchfink *m*

cha·grin ['ʃægrɪn] **1.** Ärger *m*; **2.** ärgern

chain [tʃeɪn] **1.** Kette *f*; *fig.* Fessel *f*; **~ re'ac·tion** Kettenreaktion *f*; '**~ smok·er** Kettenraucher(in); '**~ smok·ing** Kettenrauchen *n*; '**~ store** Kettenladen *m*; **2.** (an)ketten; fesseln

chair [tʃeə] Stuhl *m*; Lehrstuhl *m*; Vorsitz *m*; **be in the ~** den Vorsitz führen; '**~ lift** Sessellift *m*; '**~·man** (*pl.* **-men**) Vorsitzende(r) *m*, Präsident *m*; Diskussionsleiter *m*; '**~·man·ship** Vorsitz *m*; '**~·wom·an** (*pl.* **-women**) Vorsitzende *f*, Präsidentin *f*; Diskussionsleiterin *f*

chal·ice ['tʃælɪs] Kelch *m*

chalk [tʃɔːk] **1.** Kreide *f*; **2.** mit Kreide schreiben *od.* zeichnen

chal·lenge ['tʃælɪndʒ] **1.** Herausforderung *f*; **2.** herausfordern; '**~·leng·er** Herausforderer *m*

cham·ber ['tʃeɪmbə] *tech., parl. etc.* Kammer *f*; '**~·maid** Zimmermädchen *n*; **~ of 'com·merce** Handelskammer *f*

cham·ois *zo.* ['ʃæmwɑː] Gemse *f*

cham·ois (leath·er) ['ʃæmɪ (leðə)] Wildleder *n*

champ F [tʃæmp] → **champion** (*Sport*)

cham·pagne [ʃæm'peɪn] Champagner *m*

cham·pi·on ['tʃæmpjən] **1.** Verfechter(in), Fürsprecher(in); *Sport:* Meister(in); **2.** verfechten, eintreten für; '**~·ship** *Sport:* Meisterschaft *f*

chance [tʃɑːns] **1.** Zufall *m*; Chance *f*, (günstige) Gelegenheit; Aussicht *f* (**of** auf *acc.*); Möglichkeit *f*; Risiko *n*; **by ~** zufällig; **take a ~** es darauf ankommen lassen; **take no ~s** nichts riskieren (wollen); **2.** zufällig; **3.** F riskieren

chan·cel·lor ['tʃɑːnsələ] Kanzler *m*

chan·de·lier [ʃændə'lɪə] Kronleuchter *m*

change [tʃeɪndʒ] **1.** Veränderung *f*, Wechsel *m*; Abwechslung *f*; Wechselgeld *n*; Kleingeld *n*; **for a ~** zur Abwechslung; **~ for the better (worse)** Besserung *f* (Verschlechterung *f*); **2.** *v/t.* (ver)ändern, umändern; (aus)wechseln; (aus-, um)tauschen (**for** gegen); *mot., tech.* schalten; **~ over** umschalten; umstellen; **~ trains** umsteigen; *v/i.* sich (ver)ändern, wechseln; sich umziehen; '**~·a·ble** veränderlich; '**~ ma·chine** Münzwechsler *m*; '**~·o·ver** Umstellung *f* (**to** auf *acc.*)

'**chang·ing room** *bsd. Sport:* Umkleidekabine *f*, -raum *m*

chan·nel ['tʃænl] **1.** Kanal *m* (*a. fig.*); (*Fernseh- etc.*)Kanal *m*, (-)Programm *n*; *fig.* Kanal *m*, Weg *m*; **2.** (*bsd. Brt.* **-ll-,** *Am.* **-l-**) *fig.* lenken; **2 'Tun·nel** Kanaltunnel *m*, Eurotunnel *m* (*Ärmelkanaltunnel zwischen England u. Frankreich*)

chant [tʃɑːnt] **1.** (Kirchen)Gesang *m*; Singsang *m*; **2.** in Sprechchören rufen

cha·os ['keɪɒs] Chaos *n*

chap¹ [tʃæp] **1.** Riß *m*; **2.** (*-pp-*) rissig machen *od.* werden; aufspringen (*Haut, Lippen*)

chap² F [tʃæp] Bursche *m*, Kerl *m*

chap·el ['tʃæpl] Kapelle *f*; Gottesdienst *m*

chap·lain ['tʃæplɪn] Kaplan *m*

chap·ter ['tʃæptə] Kapitel *n*

char [tʃɑː] (*-rr-*) verkohlen

char·ac·ter ['kærəktə] Charakter *m*; Ruf *m*, Leumund *m*; Schriftzeichen *n*, Buchstabe *m*; *Roman etc.:* Figur *f*, Gestalt *f*; *thea.* Rolle *f*; **~·is·tic**

characterize

C

[kærəktə'rɪstɪk] **1.** (~*ally*) charakteristisch (*of* für); **2.** Kennzeichen *n*; ~**ize** ['kærəktəraɪz] charakterisieren

char·coal ['tʃɑːkəʊl] Holzkohle *f*

charge [tʃɑːdʒ] **1.** *v/t. Batterie etc.* (auf)laden, *Gewehr etc.* laden; beauftragen (*with* mit); *j-n* beschuldigen *od.* anklagen (*with* e-r *Sache*) (*a. jur.*); berechnen, verlangen, fordern (*for* für); *mil.* angreifen; stürmen; ~ *s.o. with s.th.* j-m et. in Rechnung stellen; *v/i.* ~ *at s.o.* auf j-n losgehen; Ladung *f* (*e-r Batterie, e-s Gewehrs etc.*); (Spreng)Ladung *f*; Beschuldigung *f*, *a. jur.* Anklage(punkt *m*) *f*; Preis *m*; Forderung *f*; Gebühr *f*; *a.* ~*s pl.* Unkosten *pl.*, Spesen *pl.*; Verantwortung *f*; Schützling *m*, Mündel *n, m*; *free of* ~ kostenlos; *be in* ~ *of* verantwortlich sein für; *take* ~ *of* die Leitung *etc.* übernehmen, die Sache in die Hand nehmen

char·i·ot *poet. od. hist.* ['tʃærɪət] Streit-, Triumphwagen *m*

cha·ris·ma [kə'rɪzmə] Charisma *n*, Ausstrahlung(skraft) *f*

char·i·ta·ble ['tʃærɪtəbl] wohltätig

char·i·ty ['tʃærətɪ] Nächstenliebe *f*; Wohltätigkeit *f*; Güte *f*, Nachsicht *f*; milde Gabe

char·la·tan ['ʃɑːlətən] Scharlatan *m*; Quacksalber *m*, Kurpfuscher *m*

charm [tʃɑːm] Zauber *m*; Charme *m*, Reiz *m*; Talisman *m*, Amulett *n*; **2.** bezaubern, entzücken; '~**ing** charmant, bezaubernd

chart [tʃɑːt] (*See-, Himmels-, Wetter*)Karte *f*; Diagramm *n*, Schaubild *n*; ~**s** *pl.* Charts *pl.*, Hitliste(n *pl.*) *f*

char·ter ['tʃɑːtə] **1.** Urkunde *f*, Charta *f*; Chartern *n*; **2.** chartern, mieten; '~ **flight** Charterflug *m*

char·wom·an ['tʃɑːwʊmən] (*pl. -women*) Putzfrau *f*, Raumpflegerin *f*

chase [tʃeɪs] **1.** Jagd *f*; Verfolgung *f*; **2.** jagen, hetzen; Jagd machen auf (*acc.*); rasen, rennen

chasm ['kæzəm] Kluft *f*, Abgrund *m*

chaste [tʃeɪst] keusch; schlicht

chas·tise [tʃæ'staɪz] züchtigen

chas·ti·ty ['tʃæstətɪ] Keuschheit *f*

chat [tʃæt] **1.** Geplauder *n*, Schwätzchen *n*, Plauderei *f*; **2.** plaudern; '~ **show** *Brt.* TV Talk-Show *f*; ~**show 'host** *Brt.* TV Talkmaster *m*

chat·tels ['tʃætlz] *pl. mst* **goods and** ~ bewegliches Eigentum

chat·ter ['tʃætə] **1.** plappern; schnattern; klappern; **2.** Geplapper *n*, Klappern *n*; '~**box** F Plappermaul *n*

chat·ty ['tʃætɪ] (*-ier, -iest*) gesprächig

chauf·feur ['ʃəʊfə] Chauffeur *m*

chau·vi ['ʃəʊvɪ] Chauvi *m*; ~**vin·ist** ['ʃəʊvɪnɪst] Chauvinist *m*; F **male** ~ **pig** Chauvi *m*; *contp.* Chauvischwein *n*

cheap [tʃiːp] billig; *fig.* schäbig, gemein; '~**en** (sich) verbilligen; *fig.* herabsetzen

cheat [tʃiːt] **1.** Betrug *m*, Schwindel *m*; Betrüger(in); **2.** betrügen; F schummeln

check [tʃek] **1.** Schach(stellung *f*) *n*; Hemmnis *n*, Hindernis *n* (*on* für); Einhalt *m*; Kontrolle *f* (*on gen.*); Kontrollabschnitt *m*, -schein *m*; *Am.* Gepäckschein *m*; *Am.* Garderobenmarke *f*; *Am. econ.* Scheck *m* (*for* über); *Am.* Häkchen *n* (*Vermerkzeichen auf Liste etc.*); *Am.* Kassenzettel *m*, Rechnung *f*; karierter Stoff); **2.** *v/i.* (plötzlich) innehalten; ~ *in* sich (*in e-m Hotel*) anmelden; einstempeln; *aviat.* einchecken; ~ *out* (*aus e-m Hotel*) abreisen; ausstempeln; ~ *up* (*on*) F (*e-e Sache*) nachprüfen, (*e-e Sache, j-n*) überprüfen; *v/t.* hemmen, hindern, aufhalten; zurückhalten; checken, kontrollieren, überprüfen; *Am. auf e-r Liste* abhaken; *Am. Kleider in* der Garderobe abgeben; *Am. Gepäck* aufgeben; '~ **card** *Am. econ.* Scheckkarte *f*; ~**ed** [tʃekt] kariert; '~**ers** *Am.* ['tʃekəz] *sg.* Damespiel *n*; '~**in** Anmeldung *f* (*in e-m Hotel*); Einstempeln *n*; *aviat.* Einchecken *n*; '~**in coun·ter** *aviat.*, '~**in desk** *aviat.* Abfertigungsschalter *m*; '~**ing ac·count** *Am. econ.* Girokonto *n*; '~**list** Check-, Kontroll-, Vergleichsliste *f*; '~**mate 1.** (Schach)Matt *n*; **2.** (schach)matt setzen; '~**out** Abreise *f* (*aus e-m Hotel*); Ausstempeln *n*; '~**out coun·ter** Kasse *f* (*bsd. im Supermarkt*); '~**point** Kontrollpunkt *m*; '~**room** *Am.* Garderobe *f*; Gepäckaufbewahrung *f*; '~**up** Überprüfung *f*; *med.* Check-up *m*, Vorsorgeuntersuchung *f*

cheek [tʃiːk] Backe *f*, Wange *f*; F Unverschämtheit *f*; '~**y** F (*-ier, -iest*) frech

cheer [tʃɪə] **1.** Stimmung *f*, Fröhlichkeit

f; Hoch(ruf m) n, Beifall(sruf) m; **~s** Sport: Anfeuerung(srufe pl.) f; **three ~s!** dreimal hoch!; **~s!** prost!; **2.** v/t. mit Beifall begrüßen; a. **~ on** anspornen; a. **~ up** aufheitern; v/i. hoch rufen, jubeln; a. **~ up** Mut fassen; **~ up!** Kopf hoch!; **'~ful** vergnügt

cheer·i·o int. Brt. F [tʃɪərɪ'əʊ] mach's gut!, tschüs!

'**cheer·lead·er** Sport: Einpeitscher m, Cheerleader m; **'~less** freudlos; **~y** ['tʃɪərɪ] (**-ier, -iest**) vergnügt

cheese [tʃiːz] Käse m

chee·tah zo. ['tʃiːtə] Gepard m

chef [ʃef] Küchenchef m; Koch m; △ **nicht** Chef

chem·i·cal ['kemɪkl] **1.** chemisch; **2.** Chemikalie f

chem·ist ['kemɪst] Chemiker(in); Apotheker(in); Drogist(in); **~'s try** ['kemɪstrɪ] Chemie f; **'~ist's shop** Apotheke f; Drogerie f

chem·o·ther·a·py med. [kiːməʊ-'θerəpɪ] Chemotherapie f

cheque Brt. econ. [tʃek] (Am. **check**) Scheck m; **crossed ~** Verrechnungsscheck m; **'~ ac·count** Brt. Girokonto n; **'~ card** Brt. Scheckkarte f

cher·ry bot. ['tʃerɪ] Kirsche f

chess [tʃes] Schach(spiel) n; **a game of ~** e-e Partie Schach; **'~board** Schachbrett n; **'~man** (pl. **-men**), **~ piece** Schachfigur f

chest [tʃest] Kiste f; Truhe f; anat. Brust (-kasten m) f; **get s.th. off one's ~** F sich et. von der Seele reden

chest·nut ['tʃesnʌt] **1.** bot. Kastanie f; **2.** kastanienbraun

chest of drawers [tʃest əv 'drɔːz] Kommode f

chew [tʃuː] (zer)kauen; **'~ing gum** Kaugummi m

chick [tʃɪk] Küken n, junger Vogel; F Biene f, Puppe f (Mädchen)

chick·en ['tʃɪkɪn] Huhn n; Küken n; (Brat)Hähnchen n, (-)Hühnchen n; **'~heart·ed** furchtsam, feige; **~ pox** med. ['tʃɪkɪnpɒks] Windpocken pl.

chic·o·ry bot. ['tʃɪkərɪ] Chicorée f

chief [tʃiːf] **1.** oberste(r, -s), Ober..., Haupt..., Chef...; wichtigste(r, -s); **2.** Chef m; Häuptling m; **'~ly** hauptsächlich

chil·blain ['tʃɪlbleɪn] Frostbeule f

child [tʃaɪld] (pl. **children**) Kind n; **from a ~** von Kindheit an; **with ~** schwanger; **'~ a·buse** jur. Kindesmißhandlung f; **~ 'ben·e·fit** Brt. Kindergeld n; **'~birth** Geburt f, Niederkunft f; **'~hood** ['tʃaɪldhʊd] Kindheit f; **'~ish** kindlich; kindisch; **'~like** kindlich; **'~mind·er** Tagesmutter f

chil·dren ['tʃɪldrən] pl. von **child**

chill [tʃɪl] **1.** kalt, frostig, kühl (a. fig.); **2.** Frösteln n; Kälte f, Kühle f (a. fig.); Erkältung f; **3.** abkühlen; j-n frösteln lassen; kühlen; **'~y** (**-ier, -iest**) kalt, frostig, kühl (a. fig.)

chime [tʃaɪm] **1.** Glockenspiel n; Geläut n; **2.** läuten; schlagen (Uhr)

chim·ney ['tʃɪmnɪ] Schornstein m; **'~sweep** Schornsteinfeger m

chimp zo. [tʃɪmp], **chim·pan·zee** zo. [tʃɪmpən'ziː] Schimpanse m

chin [tʃɪn] **1.** Kinn n; **~ up!** Kopf hoch!, halt die Ohren steif!

chi·na ['tʃaɪnə] Porzellan n

Chi·na ['tʃaɪnə] China n; **Chi·nese** [tʃaɪ'niːz] **1.** chinesisch; **2.** Chines|e m, -in f; ling. Chinesisch n; **the ~** die Chinesen pl.

chink [tʃɪŋk] Ritz m, Spalt m

chip [tʃɪp] **1.** Splitter m, Span m, Schnitzel n, m; dünne Scheibe; Spielmarke f; Computer: Chip m; **2.** (**-pp-**) v/t. schnitzeln; an-, abschlagen; v/i. abbröckeln

chips [tʃɪps] pl. Brt. Pommes frites pl., F Fritten pl.; Am. (Kartoffel)Chips pl.

chi·rop·o·dist [kɪ'rɒpədɪst] Fußpfleger(in), Pediküre f

chirp [tʃɜːp] zirpen, zwitschern, piepsen

chis·el ['tʃɪzl] **1.** Meißel m; **2.** (bsd. Brt. **-ll-**, Am. **-l-**) meißeln

chit-chat ['tʃɪttʃæt] Plauderei f

chiv·al·rous ['ʃɪvlrəs] ritterlich

chive(s pl.**)** bot. [tʃaɪv(z)] Schnittlauch m

chlo·ri·nate ['klɔːrɪneɪt] Wasser etc. chloren; **chlo·rine** ['klɔːriːn] Chlor n

chlo·ro·fluo·ro·car·bon [klɔːrəʊ-floərəʊ'kaːbən] (abbr. **CFC**) Fluorchlorkohlenwasserstoff m (abbr. **FCKW**)

chlo·ro·form ['klɔːrəfɔːm] **1.** Chloroform n; **2.** chloroformieren

choc·o·late ['tʃɒkələt] Schokolade f; Praline f; **'~s** pl. Pralinen pl., Konfekt n

choice [tʃɔɪs] **1.** Wahl f; Auswahl f; **2.** auserlesen, ausgesucht, vorzüglich

choir ['kwaɪə] Chor m

choke [tʃəʊk] **1.** v/t. (er)würgen, (a. v/i.) ersticken; **~ back** *Ärger etc.* unterdrücken, *Tränen* zurückhalten; **~ down** hinunterwürgen; a. **~ up** verstopfen; **2.** mot. Choke m, Luftklappe f

cho·les·te·rol [kə'lestərɒl] Cholesterin n

choose [tʃuːz] (*chose, chosen*) (aus-) wählen, aussuchen

chop [tʃɒp] **1.** Hieb m, Schlag m; gastr. Kotelett n; **2.** (-pp-) v/t. hauen, hacken, zerhacken; **~ down** fällen; v/i. hacken; **~·per** Hackmesser n, -beil n; F Hubschrauber m; **~·py** (-ier, -iest) unruhig (See); **~·stick** Eßstäbchen n

cho·ral ['kɔːrəl] Chor...

cho·rale [kɒ'rɑːl] Choral m

chord mus. [kɔːd] Saite f; Akkord m

chore Am. [tʃɔː] schwierige od. unangenehme Aufgabe; **~s** pl. Hausarbeit f

cho·rus ['kɔːrəs] Chor m; Kehrreim m, Refrain m; Tanzgruppe f (e-r Revue)

chose [tʃəʊz] pret. von **choose; chosen** ['tʃəʊzn] p.p. von **choose**

Christ [kraɪst] Christus m; △ *nicht der Christ*

chris·ten ['krɪsn] taufen; **~·ing** Taufe f; Tauf...

Chris·tian ['krɪstʃən] **1.** christlich; **2.** Christ(in); **Chris·ti·an·i·ty** [krɪstɪ'ænətɪ] Christentum n

'Christian name Vorname m

Christ·mas ['krɪsməs] Weihnachten n u. pl.; **at ~** zu Weihnachten; **~ 'Day** erster Weihnachtsfeiertag; **~ 'Eve** Heiliger Abend

chrome [krəʊm] Chrom n; **chro·mi·um** ['krəʊmjəm] Chrom n (Metall)

chron·ic ['krɒnɪk] (**~ally**) chronisch; ständig, (an)dauernd

chron·i·cle ['krɒnɪkl] Chronik f

chron·o·log·i·cal [krɒnə'lɒdʒɪkl] chronologisch; **chro·nol·o·gy** [krə'nɒlədʒɪ] Zeitrechnung f; Zeitfolge f

chub·by F ['tʃʌbɪ] (-ier, -iest) rundlich; pausbäckig

chuck F [tʃʌk] werfen, schmeißen; **~ out** j-n rausschmeißen; et. wegschmeißen; **~ up** *Job etc.* hinschmeißen

chuck·le ['tʃʌkl] **1.** **~** (*to o.s.*) (stillvergnügt) in sich hineinlachen; **2.** leises Lachen, Glucksen n

chum F [tʃʌm] Kamerad m, Kumpel m; **'~·my** F (-ier, -iest) dick befreundet

chump [tʃʌmp] Holzklotz m; F Trottel m

chunk [tʃʌŋk] Klotz m, Klumpen m

Chun·nel F ['tʃʌnl] → **Channel Tunnel**

church [tʃɜːtʃ] Kirche f; Kirch(en)...; **'~ ser·vice** Gottesdienst m; **'~·yard** Kirchhof m

churl·ish ['tʃɜːlɪʃ] grob, flegelhaft

churn [tʃɜːn] **1.** Butterfaß n; **2.** buttern; *Wellen* aufwühlen, peitschen

chute [ʃuːt] Stromschnelle f; Rutsche f, Rutschbahn f; F Fallschirm m

CIA [si: aɪ 'eɪ] Abk. für **Central Intelligence Agency** (amer. Geheimdienst)

CID [si: aɪ 'di:] Abk. für **Criminal Investigation Department** (brit. Kriminalpolizei)

ci·der ['saɪdə] (Am. **hard ~**) Apfelwein m; (**sweet**) Am. Apfelmost m, -saft m

cif [si: aɪ 'ef] Abk. für **cost, insurance, freight** Kosten, Versicherung und Fracht einbegriffen

ci·gar [sɪ'gɑː] Zigarre f

cig·a·rette, cig·a·ret Am. [sɪgə'ret] Zigarette f

cinch F [sɪntʃ] todsichere Sache

cin·der ['sɪndə] Schlacke f; **~s** pl. Asche f

Cin·de·rel·la [sɪndə'relə] Aschenbrödel n, -puttel n

'cin·der track Sport: Aschenbahn f

cin·e·cam·e·ra ['sɪnɪkæmərə] (Schmal)Filmkamera f; **'~·film** Schmalfilm m

cin·e·ma Brt. ['sɪnəmə] Kino n; Film m

cin·na·mon ['sɪnəmən] Zimt m

ci·pher ['saɪfə] Geheimschrift f, Chiffre f; Null f (a. fig.)

cir·cle ['sɜːkl] **1.** Kreis m; thea. Rang m; fig. Kreislauf m; **2.** (um)kreisen

cir·cuit ['sɜːkɪt] Kreislauf m; electr. Stromkreis m; Rundreise f; Sport: Zirkus m; **short ~** electr. Kurzschluß m

cir·cu·i·tous [sə'kjuːɪtəs] gewunden (Flußlauf etc.); weitschweifig

cir·cu·lar ['sɜːkjʊlə] **1.** kreisförmig; Kreis...; **2.** Rundschreiben n; Umlauf m; (Post)Wurfsendung f

cir·cu·late ['sɜːkjʊleɪt] v/i. zirkulieren, im Umlauf sein; v/t. in Umlauf setzen; **~·lat·ing li·bra·ry** Leihbücherei f; **~·la·tion** [sɜːkjʊ'leɪʃn] (a. Blut)Kreislauf m, Zirkulation f; econ.

Umlauf *m*; Auflage(nhöhe) *f* (*e-r Zeitung etc.*)

cir·cum·fer·ence [sə'kʌmfərəns] (Kreis)Umfang *m*

cir·cum·nav·i·gate [sɜ:kəm'nævɪgeɪt] umschiffen

cir·cum·scribe ['sɜ:kəmskraɪb] *math.* umschreiben; *fig.* begrenzen

cir·cum·spect ['sɜ:kəmspekt] um-, vorsichtig

cir·cum·stance ['sɜ:kəmstəns] Umstand *m*; **~s** *pl.* (Sach)Lage *f*, Umstände *pl.*; Verhältnisse *pl.*; **in** *od.* **under no ~s** unter keinen Umständen, auf keinen Fall; **in** *od.* **under the ~s** unter diesen Umständen

cir·cum·stan·tial [sɜ:kəm'stænʃl] ausführlich; umständlich; **~ evidence** *jur.* Indizien(beweis *m*) *pl.*

cir·cus ['sɜ:kəs] Zirkus *m*; *Brt.* runder, von Häusern umschlossener Platz, in den mehrere Straßen münden

CIS [si: aɪ 'es] *Abk. für* **Commonwealth of Independent States** die GUS, die Gemeinschaft unabhängiger Staaten

cis·tern ['sɪstən] Wasserbehälter *m*; Spülkasten *m* (*in der Toilette*)

ci·ta·tion [saɪ'teɪʃn] *jur.* Vorladung *f*; Zitat *n*; **cite** [saɪt] *jur.* vorladen; zitieren

cit·i·zen ['sɪtɪzn] Bürger(in); Städter(in); Staatsangehörige(r *m*) *f*; **'~ship** Staatsangehörigkeit *f*

cit·y ['sɪtɪ] **1.** (Groß)Stadt *f*; **the ♀** die (Londoner) City; **2.** städtisch, Stadt...; **~ 'cen·tre** *Brt.* Innenstadt *f*, City *f*; **~ 'coun·cil·(l)or** *Am.* Stadtrat *m*, -rätin *f*; **~ 'hall** Rathaus *n*; *bsd. Am.* Stadtverwaltung *f*; **~ 'slick·er** *oft contp.* Stadtmensch *m*; **~ 'va·grant** Stadtstreicher(in), Nichtseßhafte(r *m*) *f*

civ·ic ['sɪvɪk] städtisch, Stadt...; **~s** *sg.* Staatsbürgerkunde *f*

civ·il ['sɪvl] staatlich, Staats...; (staats)bürgerlich, Bürger...; zivil, Zivil...; *jur.* zivilrechtlich; höflich; **ci·vil·i·an** [sɪ'vɪljən] Zivilist *m*

ci·vil·i·ty [sɪ'vɪlətɪ] Höflichkeit *f*

civ·i·li·za·tion [sɪvɪlaɪ'zeɪʃn] Zivilisation *f*, Kultur *f*; **~ze** ['sɪvɪlaɪz] zivilisieren

civ·il 'rights *pl.* (Staats)Bürgerrechte *pl.*; **~ 'ac·tiv·ist** Bürgerrechtler(in); **~ 'move·ment** Bürgerrechtsbewegung *f*

civ·il **'ser·vant** Staatsbeamt|e(r *m*), -in *f*; **~ 'ser·vice** Staatsdienst *m*; **~ 'war** Bürgerkrieg *m*

clad [klæd] **1.** *pret. u. p.p. von* **clothe**; **2.** *adj.* gekleidet

claim [kleɪm] **1.** Anspruch *m*; Anrecht *n* (**to** auf *acc.*); Forderung *f*; Behauptung *f*; *Am.* Claim *m*; **2.** beanspruchen; fordern; behaupten

clair·voy·ant [kleə'vɔɪənt] Hellseher(in)

clam·ber ['klæmbə] (mühsam) klettern

clam·my ['klæmɪ] (*-ier, -iest*) feuchtkalt, klamm

clam·o(u)r ['klæmə] **1.** Geschrei *n*, Lärm *m*; **2.** lautstark verlangen (**for** nach)

clamp *tech.* [klæmp] Zwinge *f*

clan [klæn] Clan *m*, Sippe *f*

clan·des·tine [klæn'destɪn] heimlich

clang [klæŋ] klingen, klirren; erklingen lassen

clank [klæŋk] **1.** Gerassel *n*, Geklirr *n*; **2.** rasseln *od.* klirren (mit)

clap [klæp] **1.** Klatschen *n*; Schlag *m*, Klaps *m*; **2.** (*-pp-*) schlagen *od.* klatschen (mit)

clar·et ['klærət] roter Bordeaux(wein); Rotwein *m*

clar·i·fy ['klærɪfaɪ] *v/t.* (auf)klären, klarstellen; *v/i.* sich (auf)klären, klar werden

clar·i·net *mus.* [klærɪ'net] Klarinette *f*

clar·i·ty ['klærətɪ] Klarheit *f*

clash [klæʃ] **1.** Zusammenstoß *m*; Konflikt *m*; **2.** zusammenstoßen; nicht zusammenpassen *od.* harmonieren

clasp [klɑ:sp] **1.** Haken *m*, Schnalle *f*; Schloß *n*, (Schnapp)Verschluß *m*; Umklammerung *f*; **2.** ein-, zuhaken; ergreifen, umklammern; **'~ knife** (*pl. -knives*) Taschenmesser *n*

class [klɑ:s] **1.** Klasse *f*; (Bevölkerungs)Schicht *f*; (Schul)Klasse *f*; (Unterrichts)Stunde *f*; Kurs *m*; *Am.* Jahrgang *m* (*von Schulabgängern etc.*); **2.** (in Klassen) einteilen, -ordnen, -stufen

clas·sic ['klæsɪk] **1.** Klassiker *m*; (*~ally*) klassisch; **'~·si·cal** klassisch (*a. mus., Kunst etc.*)

clas·sic 'car Klassiker *m* (*älteres Auto mit e-r Besonderheit etc.*)

clas·si·fi·ca·tion [klæsɪfɪ'keɪʃn] Klassifizierung *f*, Einteilung *f*; **~fied**

['klæsıfaıd] klassifiziert; *mil.*, *pol.* geheim; **~·fied 'ad** Kleinanzeige *f*; **~·fy** ['klæsıfaı] klassifizieren, einstufen

'class|·mate Mitschüler(in); **'~·room** Klassenzimmer *n*

clat·ter ['klætə] **1.** Geklapper *n*; **2.** klappern (mit)

clause [klɔ:z] *jur.* Klausel *f*, Bestimmung *f*; *gr.* Satz(teil *n*) *m*

claw [klɔ:] **1.** Klaue *f*, Kralle *f*; (*Krebs*)Schere *f*; **2.** (zer)kratzen; umkrallen, packen

clay [kleı] Ton *m*, Lehm *m*

clean [kli:n] **1.** *adj.* rein; sauber, glatt, eben; *sl.* clean (*nicht mehr drogenabhängig*); **2.** *adv.* völlig, ganz u. gar; **3.** reinigen, säubern, putzen; **~ out** reinigen; **~ up** gründlich reinigen; aufräumen; **'~·er** Rein(e)machefrau *f*, (*Fenster- etc.*)Putzer *m*; Reiniger *m*; *pl.* Reinigung *f* (*Geschäft*); **take to the ~s** zur Reinigung bringen; F *j-n* ausnehmen; **'~·ing: do the ~** saubermachen, putzen; → **spring-clean(ing)**; **~·li·ness** ['klenlınıs] Reinlichkeit *f*; **~·ly 1.** ['kli:nlı] *adv.* sauber; **2.** ['klenlı] *adj.* (*-ier*, *-iest*) reinlich

cleanse [klenz] reinigen, säubern; **'cleans·er** Reinigungsmittel *n*

clear [klıə] **1.** klar; hell; rein; deutlich; frei (*of* von); *econ.* Netto..., Rein...; **2.** *v/t.* reinigen, säubern; *Wald* lichten, roden; wegräumen (*a.* **~ away**); *Tisch* abräumen; räumen, leeren; *Hindernis* nehmen; *Sport:* klären; *econ.* verzollen; *jur.* freisprechen; *Computer:* löschen; *v/i.* klar *od.* hell werden; aufklaren (*Wetter*); sich verziehen (*Nebel*); **~ out** auf-, ausräumen, entfernen; F abhauen; **~ up** aufräumen; *Verbrechen etc.* aufklären; aufklaren (*Wetter*); **~·ance** ['klıərəns] Räumung *f*; *tech.* lichter Abstand; Freigabe *f*; **'~·ance sale** Räumungs-, Ausverkauf *m*; **'~·ing** ['klıərıŋ] Lichtung *f*

cleave [kli:v] (*cleaved od. cleft od. clove*, *cleaved od. cleft od. cloven*) spalten; **'cleav·er** Hackmesser *n*

clef *mus.* [klef] Schlüssel *m*

cleft [kleft] **1.** Spalt *m*, Spalte *f*; **2.** *pret. u. p.p. von* **cleave**

clem|·en·cy ['klemənsı] Milde *f*, Nachsicht *f*; **'~·ent** mild (*a. Wetter*)

clench [klentʃ] *Lippen etc.* (fest) zusammenpressen; *Zähne* zusammenbeißen; *Faust* ballen

cler·gy ['kl3:dʒı] Klerus *m*, die Geistlichen *pl.*; **'~·man** (*pl. -men*) Geistliche(r) *m*

clerk [klɑ:k] (*Büro- etc.*) Angestellte(r *m*) *f*, (Bank-, Post)Beamt|e(r) *m*, -in *f*; *Am.* Verkäufer(in)

clev·er ['klevə] klug, gescheit; geschickt

click [klık] **1.** Klicken *n*; **2.** *v/i.* klicken; zu-, einschnappen; *mit der Zunge* schnalzen; *v/t.* klicken *od.* einschnappen lassen; *Computer:* anklicken; *mit der Zunge* schnalzen

cli·ent ['klaıənt] *jur.* Klient(in), Mandant(in); Kund|e *m*, -in *f*, Auftraggeber(in)

cliff [klıf] Klippe *f*, Felsen *m*

cli·mate ['klaımıt] Klima *n*

cli·max ['klaımæks] Höhepunkt *m*; Orgasmus *m*

climb [klaım] klettern; (er-, be)steigen; **'~·er** Kletterer *m*, Bergsteiger(in); *bot.* Kletterpflanze *f*

clinch [klıntʃ] **1.** *tech.* sicher befestigen; (ver)nieten; *Boxen:* umklammern (*v/i.* clinchen); entscheiden; *that ~ed it* damit war die Sache entschieden; **2.** *Boxen:* Clinch *m*

cling [klıŋ] (*clung*) (*to*) festhalten (an *dat.*); sich klammern (an *acc.*); sich (an)schmiegen (an *acc.*); **'~·film** *bsd. Brt.* Frischhaltefolie *f*

clin·ic ['klınık] Klinik *f*; **'~·i·cal** klinisch

clink [klıŋk] **1.** Klirren *n*, Klingen *n*; **2.** klingen *od.* klirren (lassen); klimpern mit

clip¹ [klıp] **1.** (*-pp-*) ausschneiden; *Schafe etc.* scheren; **2.** Schnitt *m*; Schur *f*; (*Film- etc.*)Ausschnitt *m*; (*Video*)Clip *m*

clip² [klıp] **1.** (Heft-, Büro- *etc.*)Klammer *f*; (*Ohr*)Clip *m*; **2.** (*-pp-*) *a.* **~ on** anklammern

clip|·per ['klıpə]: (*a pair of*) **~s** *pl.* (-e-e) (*Nagel- etc.*)Schere *f*, Haarschneidemaschine *f*; **'~·pings** *pl.* Abfälle *pl.*, Schnitzel *pl.*; *bsd. Am.* (*Zeitungs-etc.*)Ausschnitte *pl.*

clit·o·ris *anat.* ['klıtərıs] Klitoris *f*

cloak [kləʊk] **1.** Umhang *m*; **2.** *fig.* verhüllen; **'~·room** Garderobe *f*; *Brt.* Toilette *f*

clock [klɒk] **1.** (*Wand-, Stand-, Turm*)Uhr *f*; **9 o'~** 9 Uhr; **2.** *Sport:* Zeit stoppen; **~ in, ~ on** einstempeln; **~ out, ~ off** ausstempeln; **~wise** ['klɒkwaɪz] im Uhrzeigersinn; **'~work** Uhrwerk *n*; *like ~* wie am Schnürchen

clod [klɒd] (Erd)Klumpen *m*

clog [klɒg] **1.** (Holz)Klotz *m*; Holzschuh *m*; **2.** (*-gg-*) *a.* **~ up** verstopfen

clois·ter ['klɔɪstə] Kreuzgang *m*; Kloster *n*

close 1. [kləʊs] *adj.* geschlossen; knapp (*Ergebnis etc.*); genau, gründlich (*Übersetzung, Untersuchung etc.*); eng(anliegend); stickig, schwül; eng (*Freund*), nah (*Verwandte*); **keep a ~ watch on** scharf im Auge behalten (*acc.*); **2.** [kləʊs] *adv.* eng, nahe, dicht; **~ by** ganz in der Nähe, nahe *od.* dicht bei; **3.** [kləʊz] Ende *n*, (Ab)Schluß *m*; **come** *od.* **draw to a ~** sich dem Ende nähern; [kləʊs] Einfriedung *f*; *Brt.* in Straßennamen: *kleine Sackgasse, wie ein Hof*; **4.** [kləʊz] *v/t.* (ab-, ver-, zu)schließen; zumachen; *Betrieb etc.* schließen; *Straße* (ab)sperren; *v/i.* sich schließen; schließen, zumachen; enden, zu Ende gehen; **~ down** *Geschäft etc.* schließen; *Betrieb* stillegen; *Rundfunk, TV:* das Programm beenden, Sendeschluß haben; **~ in** bedrohlich nahekommen; hereinbrechen (*Nacht*); **~ up** (ab-, ver-, zu)schließen; aufschließen, -rücken; **~d** geschlossen, *pred.* zu

clos·et ['klɒzɪt] (Wand)Schrank *m*; △ *nicht Klosett*

close-up ['kləʊsʌp] *phot., Film:* Großaufnahme *f*

clos·ing ['kləʊzɪŋ] **date** Einsendeschluß *m*; **'~ time** Laden-, Geschäftsschluß *m*; Polizeistunde *f* (*e-s Pubs*)

clot [klɒt] **1.** Klumpen *m*, Klümpchen *n*; **~ of blood** med. Blutgerinnsel *n*; **2.** (*-tt-*) gerinnen; Klumpen bilden

cloth [klɒθ] (*pl.* **cloths** [klɒθs, klɒðz]) Stoff *m*, Tuch *n*; Lappen *m*, Tuch *n*; **'~bound** in Leinen gebunden

clothe [kləʊð] (**clothed** *od.* **clad**) (an-, be)kleiden; einkleiden

clothes [kləʊðz] *pl.* Kleider *pl.*, Kleidung *f*; Wäsche *f*; **'~ bas·ket** Wäschekorb *m*; **'~horse** Wäscheständer *m*; **'~line** Wäscheleine *f*; **'~ peg** *Brt.*; **'~pin** *Am.* Wäscheklammer *f*

cloth·ing ['kləʊðɪŋ] (Be)Kleidung *f*

cloud [klaʊd] **1.** Wolke *f*; *fig.* Schatten *m*; **2.** (sich) bewölken; (sich) trüben; **'~less** wolkenlos; **'~y** (*-ier, -iest*) bewölkt; trüb; unklar

clout F [klaʊt] Schlag *m*; *pol.* Einfluß *m*

clove[1] [kləʊv] (Gewürz)Nelke *f*; **~ of garlic** Knoblauchzehe *f*

clove[2] [kləʊv] *pret. von* **cleave**[1]; **clo·ven** ['kləʊvn] *p.p. von* **cleave**[1]; **clo·ven 'hoof** (*pl.* **- hoofs, - hooves**) *zo.* Huf *m* der Paarzeher

clo·ver *bot.* ['kləʊvə] Klee *m*

clown [klaʊn] Clown *m*, Hanswurst *m*

club [klʌb] **1.** Keule *f*; Knüppel *m*; *Sport:* Schlagholz *n*; (*Golf*)Schläger *m*; Klub *m*; **~s** *pl.* Kartenspiel: Kreuz *n*; **2.** (*-bb-*) einknüppeln auf (*acc.*), (nieder)knüppeln; **'~foot** (*pl.* **-feet**) Klumpfuß *m*

cluck [klʌk] **1.** gackern; glucken; **2.** Gackern *n*; Glucken *n*

clue [kluː] Anhaltspunkt *m*, Fingerzeig *m*, Spur *f*

clump [klʌmp] **1.** Klumpen *m*; (*Baum etc.*)Gruppe *f*; **2.** trampeln

clum·sy ['klʌmzɪ] (*-ier, -iest*) unbeholfen, ungeschickt, plump

clung [klʌŋ] *pret. u. p.p. von* **cling**

clus·ter ['klʌstə] **1.** *bot.* Traube *f*, Büschel *n*; Haufen *m*; **2.** sich drängen

clutch [klʌtʃ] **1.** Griff *m*; *tech.* Kupplung *f*; *fig.* Klaue *f*; **2.** (er)greifen; umklammern

CNN [siː en 'en] *Abk. für* **Cable News Network** (*amer. Kabelfernsehgesellschaft für Nachrichten aus aller Welt*)

c/o [siː 'əʊ] *Abk. für* **care of** (*wohnhaft*) bei

Co[1] [kəʊ] *Abk. für* **company** *econ.* Gesellschaft *f*

Co[2] *nur geschr. Abk. für* **County** *Brt.* Grafschaft *f*; *Am.* Kreis *m* (*Verwaltungsbezirk*)

coach [kəʊtʃ] **1.** Reisebus *m*; *Brt. rail.* (Personen)Wagen *m*; Kutsche *f*; *Sport:* Trainer(in); Nachhilfelehrer(in); **2.** *Sport:* trainieren; *j-m* Nachhilfeunterricht geben; **'~man** (*pl.* **-men**) Kutscher *m*

co·ag·u·late [kəʊ'ægjʊleɪt] gerinnen (lassen)

coal [kəʊl] (Stein)Kohle *f*; **carry ~s to Newcastle** Eulen nach Athen tragen

co·a·li·tion [kəʊə'lıʃn] *pol.* Koalition *f*; Bündnis *n*, Zusammenschluß *m*

'coal·mine, '~·pit Kohlengrube *f*

coarse [kɔːs] (*~r, ~st*) grob; ungeschliffen

coast [kəʊst] **1.** Küste *f*; **2.** *naut.* die Küste entlangfahren; im Leerlauf (*Auto*) *od.* im Freilauf (*Fahrrad*) fahren; *Am.* rodeln; **'~·guard** (Angehörige[r] *m* der) Küstenwache *f*; **'~·line** Küstenlinie *f*, -strich *m*

coat [kəʊt] **1.** Mantel *m*; *zo.* Pelz *m*, Fell *n*; (*Farb- etc.*)Überzug *m*, Anstrich *m*, Schicht *f*; **2.** (an)streichen, überziehen, beschichten; **'~ hang·er → hanger; '~·ing** (*Farb- etc.*)Überzug *m*, Anstrich *m*, Schicht *f*; Mantelstoff *m*

coat of 'arms Wappen(schild *m*, *n*) *n*

coax [kəʊks] überreden, beschwatzen

cob [kɒb] Maiskolben *m*

cob·bled ['kɒbld]: *~ street* Straße *f* mit Kopfsteinpflaster

cob·bler ['kɒblə] (Flick)Schuster *m*

cob·web ['kɒbweb] Spinn(en)gewebe *n*

co·caine [kəʊ'keın] Kokain *n*

cock [kɒk] **1.** *zo.* Hahn *m*; V Schwanz *m* (*Penis*); **2.** aufrichten; *~ one's ears* die Ohren spitzen

cock·a·too *zo.* [kɒkə'tuː] Kakadu *m*

cock·chaf·er ['kɒktʃeıfə] Maikäfer *m*

cock'eyed F schielend; (krumm u.) schief

Cock·ney ['kɒknı] Cockney *m*, waschechter Londoner

'cock·pit Cockpit *n*

cock·roach *zo.* ['kɒkrəʊtʃ] Schabe *f*

cock'sure F übertrieben selbstsicher

'cock·tail Cocktail *m*

cock·y F ['kɒkı] (*-ier, -iest*) großspurig, anmaßend

co·co *bot.* ['kəʊkəʊ] (*pl. -cos*) Kokospalme *f*

co·coa ['kəʊkəʊ] Kakao *m*

co·co·nut ['kəʊkənʌt] Kokosnuß *f*

co·coon [kə'kuːn] (*Seiden*)Kokon *m*

cod *zo.* [kɒd] Kabeljau *m*, Dorsch *m*

COD [siː əʊ 'diː] *Abk. für cash (Am. collect) on delivery* per Nachnahme

cod·dle ['kɒdl] verhätscheln, -zärteln

code [kəʊd] **1.** Code *m*; **2.** verschlüsseln, chiffrieren; kodieren

'cod·fish *zo.* → **cod**

cod·ing ['kəʊdıŋ] Kodierung *f*

cod-liv·er 'oil Lebertran *m*

co·ed·u·ca·tion *ped.* [kəʊedjuː'keıʃn] Gemeinschaftserziehung *f*

co·ex·ist [kəʊıg'zıst] gleichzeitig *od.* nebeneinander bestehen *od.* leben; **~·ence** Koexistenz *f*

C of E [siː əv 'iː] *Abk. für Church o England* (*englische Staatskirche*)

cof·fee ['kɒfı] Kaffee *m*; **'~ bar** *Brt* Café *n*; Imbißstube *f*; **'~ bean** Kaffeebohne *f*; **'~·pot** Kaffeekanne *f*; **'~ se** Kaffeeservice *n*; **'~ shop** *bsd. Am.* → **coffee bar; '~·ta·ble** Couchtisch *m*

cof·fin ['kɒfın] Sarg *m*

cog *tech.* [kɒg] (Rad)Zahn *m*; **→ '~·wheel** *tech.* Zahnrad *n*

co·her·ence, ~·en·cy [kəʊ'hıərəns, -rənsı] Zusammenhang *m*; **~·ent** zusammenhängend

co·he·sion [kəʊ'hiːʒn] Zusammenhalt *m*; **~·sive** [kəʊ'hiːsıv] (fest) zusammenhaltend

coif·fure [kwɑː'fjʊə] Frisur *f*

coil [kɔıl] **1.** *a. ~ up* aufrollen, (auf)wickeln; sich zusammenrollen; **2.** Spirale *f* (*a. tech., med.*); Rolle *f*, Spule *f*

coin [kɔın] **1.** Münze *f*; **2.** prägen

co·in·cide [kəʊın'saıd] zusammentreffen; übereinstimmen; **~·ci·dence** [kəʊ'ınsıdəns] (zufälliges) Zusammentreffen; Zufall *m*

'coin-op·e·rat·ed: *~ (petrol, Am. gas) pump* Münztank(automat) *m*

coke [kəʊk] Koks *m* (*a. sl.* Kokain)

Coke *TM* F [kəʊk] Coke *n*, Cola *n*, *f*, Coca, *n*, *f* (*Coca-Cola*)

cold [kəʊld] **1.** kalt; **2.** Kälte *f*; Erkältung *f*; *catch (a) ~* sich erkälten; *have a ~* erkältet sein; **'~·blood·ed** kaltblütig; **'~·heart·ed** kalt-, hartherzig; **'~·ness** Kälte *f*; *~ war pol.* kalter Krieg

cole·slaw ['kəʊlslɔː] Krautsalat *m*

col·ic *med.* ['kɒlık] Kolik *f*

col·lab·o·rate [kə'læbəreıt] zusammenarbeiten; **~·ra·tion** [kəlæbə'reıʃn] Zusammenarbeit *f*; *in ~ with* gemeinsam mit

col·lapse [kə'læps] **1.** zusammenbrechen, einfallen, einstürzen; *fig.* zusammenbrechen, scheitern; **2.** Zusammenbruch *m*; **~·lap·si·ble** zusammenklappbar, Klapp...

col·lar ['kɒlə] **1.** Kragen *m*; (*Hunde- etc.*)Halsband *n*; **2.** beim Kragen pakken; *j-n* festnehmen, F schnappen; **'~bone** *anat.* Schlüsselbein *n*

col·league ['kɒliːg] Kolleg|e *m*, -in *f*, Mitarbeiter(in)

col·lect [kəˈlekt] *v/t.* (ein)sammeln; *Daten* erfassen; *Geld* kassieren; *j-n* od. *et.* abholen; *Gedanken etc.* sammeln; *v/i.* sich (ver)sammeln; **~'lect·ed** *fig.* gefaßt; **~'lec·tion** Sammlung *f*; *econ.* Eintreibung *f*; *rel.* Kollekte *f*; Abholung *f*; **~'lec·tive** gesammelt; Sammel...; *~ bargaining econ.* Tarifverhandlungen *pl.*; **~'lec·tive·ly** insgesamt; zusammen; **~'lec·tor** Sammler(in); Steuereinnehmer *m*; *rail.* Fahrkartenabnehmer *m*; *electr.* Stromabnehmer *m*

col·lege ['kɒlidʒ] College *n*; Hochschule *f*; höhere Lehranstalt

col·lide [kəˈlaɪd] zusammenstoßen

col·lie·ry ['kɒljəri] Kohlengrube *f*

col·li·sion [kəˈlɪʒn] Zusammenstoß *m*, -prall *m*, Kollision *f*; → **head-on ~, rear-end ~**

col·lo·qui·al [kəˈloʊkwiəl] umgangssprachlich

co·lon ['koʊlən] Doppelpunkt *m*

colo·nel *mil.* ['kɜːnl] Oberst *m*

co·lo·ni·al·is·m [kəˈloʊnjəlɪzəm] *pol.* Kolonialismus *m*

col·o·nize ['kɒlənaɪz] kolonisieren, besiedeln; **~ny** ['kɒləni] Kolonie *f*

co·los·sal [kəˈlɒsl] kolossal, riesig

col·o(u)r ['kʌlə] **1.** Farbe *f*; *mil.* Fahne *f*; *naut.* Flagge *f*; **what ~ is ...?** welche Farbe hat ...?; **2.** *v/t.* färben; an-, bemalen, anstreichen; *fig.* beschönigen; *v/i.* sich (ver)färben; erröten; **'~bar** Rassenschranke *f*; **'~blind** farbenblind; **'~ed** bunt; farbig; **'~fast** farbecht; **'~film** *phot.* Farbfilm *m*; **'~ful** farbenprächtig; *fig.* farbig, bunt; **~ing** ['kʌlərɪŋ] Färbung *f*; Farbstoff *m*; Gesichtsfarbe *f*; **'~less** farblos; **'~line** Rassenschranke *f*; **'~ set** Farbfernseher *m*; **'~ tel·e·vi·sion** Farbfernsehen *n*

colt [koʊlt] (Hengst)Fohlen *n*

col·umn ['kɒləm] Säule *f*; *print.* Spalte *f*; *mil.* Kolonne *f*; **~ist** ['kɒləmnɪst] Kolumnist(in)

comb [koʊm] **1.** Kamm *m*; **2.** *v/t.* kämmen; striegeln

com|·bat ['kɒmbæt] **1.** Kampf *m*; *sin-*

gle ~ Zweikampf *m*; **2.** (*-tt-, Am. a. -t-*) kämpfen gegen, bekämpfen; **~·ba·tant** ['kɒmbətənt] Kämpfer *m*

com|·bi·na·tion [kɒmbɪˈneɪʃn] Verbindung *f*, Kombination *f*; **~·bine** [kəmˈbaɪn] **1.** (sich) verbinden; **2.** *econ.* Konzern *m*; *a.* **~ harvester** Mähdrescher *m*

com·bus|·ti·ble [kəmˈbʌstəbl] **1.** brennbar; **2.** Brennstoff *m*, -material *n*; **~·tion** [kəmˈbʌstʃən] Verbrennung *f*

come [kʌm] (*came, come*) kommen; **to ~** künftig, kommend; **~ and go** kommen u. gehen; **~ to see** besuchen; **~ about** geschehen, passieren; **~ across** auf *j-n* od. *et.* stoßen; **~ along** mitkommen, -gehen; **~ apart** auseinanderfallen; **~ away** sich lösen, ab-, losgehen (*Knopf etc.*); **~ back** zurückkommen; **~ by** zu *et.* kommen; **~ down** herunterkommen (*a. fig.*); einstürzen; sinken (*Preis*); überliefert werden; **~ down with** F erkranken an (*dat.*); **~ for** abholen kommen, kommen wegen; **~ forward** sich melden; **~ from** kommen aus; kommen von; **~ home** nach Hause kommen, heimkommen; **~ in** hereinkommen; eintreffen (*Nachricht*); einlaufen (*Zug*); **~ in!** herein!; **~ loose** sich ablösen, abgehen; **~ off** ab-, losgehen (*Knopf etc.*); **~ on!** los!, vorwärts!; komm!; **~ out** herauskommen; **~ over** vorbeikommen (*Besucher*); **~ round** vorbeikommen (*Besucher*); wieder zu sich kommen; **~ through** durchkommen; *Krankheit etc.* überstehen, -leben; **~ to** sich belaufen auf; wieder zu sich kommen; **~ up to** entsprechen (*dat.*), heranreichen an (*acc.*); **'~back** Comeback *n*

co·me·di·an [kəˈmiːdjən] Komiker *m*

com·e·dy ['kɒmədi] Komödie *f*, Lustspiel *n*

come·ly ['kʌmli] (*-ier, -iest*) attraktiv, gutaussehend

com·fort ['kʌmfət] **1.** Komfort *m*, Bequemlichkeit *f*; Trost *m*; **2.** trösten; **'com·for·ta·ble** komfortabel, behaglich, bequem; tröstlich; **'~er** Tröster *m*; Wollschal *m*; *bsd. Brt.* Schnuller *m*; *Am.* Steppdecke *f*; **'~less** unbequem; trostlos; **'~ sta·tion** *Am.* Bedürfnisanstalt *f*

com·ic ['kɒmɪk] (**~ally**) komisch; Komödien..., Lustspiel...

com·i·cal ['kɒmɪkl] komisch, spaßig

com·ics ['kɒmɪks] *pl.* Comics *pl.*, Comic-Hefte *pl.*

com·ma ['kɒmə] Komma *n*

com·mand [kə'mɑːnd] **1.** Befehl *m*; Beherrschung *f*; *mil.* Kommando *n*; **2.** befehlen; *mil.* kommandieren; verfügen über (*acc.*); beherrschen; **~er** *mil.* Kommandeur *m*, Befehlshaber *m*; **~er in chief** *mil.* [kəmɑːndərɪn'tʃiːf] (*pl. commanders in chief*) Oberbefehlshaber *m*; **~ment** Gebot *n*; **~ mod·ule** *Raumfahrt:* Kommandokapsel *f*

com·man·do *mil.* [kə'mɑːndəʊ] (*pl. -dos, -does*) Kommando *n*

com·mem·o·rate [kə'meməreɪt] gedenken (*gen.*); **~ra·tion** [kəmemə'reɪʃn]: **in ~ of** zum Gedenken od. Gedächtnis an (*acc.*); **~ra·tive** [kə'memərətɪv] Gedenk..., Erinnerungs...

com|·ment ['kɒment] **1.** (*on*) Kommentar *m* (zu); Bemerkung *f* (zu); Anmerkung *f* (zu); *no ~!* kein Kommentar!; *v/i.* **~ on** e-n Kommentar abgeben zu, sich äußern über; *v/t.* bemerken (*that* daß); **~men·ta·ry** ['kɒməntərɪ] Kommentar *m* (*on* zu); **~men·ta·tor** ['kɒmənteɪtə] Kommentator *m*, *Rundfunk, TV:* a. Reporter *m*

com·merce ['kɒmɜːs] Handel *m*

com·mer·cial [kə'mɜːʃl] **1.** Handels..., Geschäfts...; kommerziell, finanziell; **2.** *Rundfunk, TV:* Werbespot *m*, -sendung *f*; **~ 'art** Gebrauchsgrafik *f*; **~ 'art·ist** Gebrauchsgrafiker(in); **~·ize** [kə'mɜːʃəlaɪz] kommerzialisieren, vermarkten; **~ 'tel·e·vi·sion** Werbefernsehen *n*; kommerzielles Fernsehen; **~ 'trav·el·ler → sales representative**

com·mis·e|·rate [kə'mɪzəreɪt]: **~ with** Mitleid empfinden mit; **~ra·tion** [kəmɪzə'reɪʃn] Mitleid *n* (*for* mit)

com·mis·sion [kə'mɪʃn] **1.** Auftrag *m*; Kommission *f*, Ausschuß *m*; *econ.* Kommission *f*; *econ.* Provision *f*; Begehung *f* (*e-s Verbrechens*); **2.** beauftragen; *et.* in Auftrag geben; **~er** Beauftragte(r *m*) *f*; Kommissar(in)

com·mit [kə'mɪt] (*-tt-*) anvertrauen, übergeben; *jur.* j-n einweisen (*to* in *acc.*); *Verbrechen* begehen; verpflichten (*to* zu), festlegen (*to* auf *acc.*);

~ment Verpflichtung *f*; Engagement *n*; **~tal** *jur.* [kə'mɪtl] Einweisung *f*; **~tee** [kə'mɪtɪ] Komitee *n*, Ausschuß *m*

com·mod·i·ty *econ.* [kə'mɒdətɪ] Ware *f*, Artikel *m*

com·mon ['kɒmən] **1.** gemeinsam, gemeinschaftlich; allgemein; alltäglich; gewöhnlich, einfach; **2.** Gemeindeland *n*; *in ~* gemeinsam (*with* mit); **~·er** Bürgerliche(r *m*) *f*; **~ 'law** (ungeschriebenes englisches) Gewohnheitsrecht; **2 'Mar·ket** *econ. pol.* Gemeinsamer Markt; **'~·place 1.** Gemeinplatz *m*; **2.** alltäglich; abgedroschen; **'~s** *pl.:* *the 2, the House of 2 Brt. parl.* das Unterhaus; **~ 'sense** gesunder Menschenverstand; **'~·wealth** *the 2 (of Nations)* das Commonwealth

com·mo·tion [kə'məʊʃn] Aufregung *f*; Aufruhr *m*, Tumult *m*

com·mu·nal ['kɒmjʊnl] Gemeinde...; Gemeinschafts...

com·mune ['kɒmjuːn] Kommune *f*; Gemeinde *f*

com·mu·ni·cate [kə'mjuːnɪkeɪt] *v/t.* mitteilen; *v/i.* sich besprechen; sich in Verbindung setzen (*with s.o.* mit j-m); (*durch e-e Tür*) verbunden sein; **~ca·tion** [kəmjuːnɪ'keɪʃn] Mitteilung *f*; Verständigung *f*, Kommunikation *f*; Verbindung *f*

com·mu·ni·ca·tions [kəmjuːnɪ'keɪʃnz] *pl.* Verbindung *f*, Verkehrswege *pl.*; **~ sat·el·lite** Nachrichtensatellit *m*

com·mu·ni·ca·tive [kə'mjuːnɪkətɪv] mitteilsam, gesprächig

Com·mu·nion *rel.* [kə'mjuːnjən] *a. Holy ~* (heilige) Kommunion, Abendmahl *n*

com·mu·nis·m ['kɒmjʊnɪzəm] Kommunismus *m*; **'~·nist 1.** Kommunist(in); **2.** kommunistisch

com·mu·ni·ty [kə'mjuːnətɪ] Gemeinschaft *f*; Gemeinde *f*

com|·mute [kə'mjuːt] *jur.* Strafe *mildernd* umwandeln; *rail. etc.* pendeln; **~'mut·er** Pendler(in); **~'mut·er train** Pendler-, Nahverkehrszug *m*

com·pact 1. ['kɒmpækt] Puderdose *f*; *Am.* Kleinwagen *m*; **2.** [kəm'pækt] *adj.* kompakt; eng, klein; knapp (*Stil*); **~ car** *Am.* [kɒmpækt 'kɑː] Kleinwagen *m*; **~ disc, ~ disk** [kɒmpækt 'dɪsk] (*abbr. CD*) Compact Disc *f*, CD *f*; **~**

'**disc play·er**, ~ '**disk play·er** CD-Player *m*, CD-Spieler *m*

com·pan·ion [kəm'pænjən] Begleiter(in); Gefährt|e *m*, -in *f*; Gesellschafter(in); Handbuch *n*, Leitfaden *m*; ~**ship** Gesellschaft *f*

com·pa·ny ['kʌmpəni] Gesellschaft *f*; *econ.* Gesellschaft *f*, Firma *f*; *mil.* Kompanie *f*; *thea.* Truppe *f*; *keep s.o.* ~ j-m Gesellschaft leisten

com|·pa·ra·ble ['kɒmpərəbl] vergleichbar; ~**par·a·tive** [kəm'pærətɪv] **1.** vergleichend; verhältnismäßig; **2.** *a.* ~ *degree gr.* Komparativ *m*; ~**pare** [kəm'peə] **1.** *v/t.* vergleichen; ~*d with* im Vergleich zu; *v/i.* sich vergleichen (lassen); **2.** *beyond* ~, *without* ~ unvergleichlich; ~**pa·ri·son** [kəm'pærɪsn] Vergleich *m*

com·part·ment [kəm'pɑːtmənt] Fach *n*; *rail.* Abteil *n*.

com·pass ['kʌmpəs] Kompaß *m*; *pair of* ~*es pl.* Zirkel *m*

com·pas·sion [kəm'pæʃn] Mitleid *n*; ~**ate** [kəm'pæʃənət] mitleidig

com·pat·i·ble [kəm'pætəbl] vereinbar; *be* ~ (*with*) passen (zu), zusammenpassen, *Computer etc.*: kompatibel (mit)

com·pat·ri·ot [kəm'pætrɪət] Landsmann *m*, -männin *f*

com·pel [kəm'pel] (*-ll-*) (er)zwingen; ~**ling** zwingend

com·pen|·sate ['kɒmpenseɪt] *j-n* entschädigen; *et.* ersetzen; ausgleichen; ~**sa·tion** [kɒmpen'seɪʃn] Ersatz *m*; Ausgleich *m*; (Schaden)Ersatz *m*, Entschädigung *f*; *Am.* Bezahlung *f*, Gehalt *n*

com·pere *Brt.* ['kɒmpeə] Conférencier *m*

com·pete [kəm'piːt] sich (mit)bewerben (*for* um); konkurrieren; *Sport:* (am Wettkampf) teilnehmen

com·pe|·tence ['kɒmpɪtəns] Können *n*, Fähigkeit *f*; '~**tent** fähig, tüchtig; fach-, sachkundig

com·pe·ti·tion [kɒmpɪ'tɪʃn] Wettbewerb *m*; Konkurrenz *f*

com·pet·i|·tive [kəm'petətɪv]konkurrierend; ~**tor** [kəm'petɪtə] Mitbewerber(in); Konkurrent(in); *Sport:* (Wettbewerbs)Teilnehmer(in)

com·pile [kəm'paɪl] kompilieren, zusammentragen, zusammenstellen

com·pla|·cence, ~**cen·cy** [kəm-'pleɪsns, -snsɪ] Selbstzufriedenheit *f*, -gefälligkeit *f*; ~**cent** [kəm'pleɪsnt] selbstzufrieden, -gefällig

com·plain [kəm'pleɪn] sich beklagen *od.* beschweren (*about* über; *to* bei); klagen (*of* über *acc.*); ~**t** Klage *f*, Beschwerde *f*; *med.* Leiden *n*; ~*s pl. med. a.* Beschwerden *pl.*

com·ple|·ment 1. ['kɒmplɪmənt] Ergänzung *f*; **2.** ['kɒmplɪment] ergänzen; ~**men·ta·ry** [kɒmplɪ'mentərɪ] (sich) ergänzend

com·plete [kəm'pliːt] **1.** vollständig, vollzählig; **2.** vervollständigen; beenden, abschließen; ~**ple·tion** [kəm-'pliːʃn] Vervollständigung *f*; Abschluß *m*

com·plex ['kɒmpleks] **1.** zusammengesetzt; komplex, vielschichtig; **2.** Komplex *m* (*a. psych.*)

com·plex·ion [kəm'plekʃn] Gesichtsfarbe *f*, Teint *m*

com·plex·i·ty [kəm'pleksətɪ] Komplexität *f*, Vielschichtigkeit *f*

com·pli·ance [kəm'plaɪəns] Einwilligung *f*; Befolgung *f*; *in* ~ *with* gemäß; ~**ant** willfährig

com·pli|·cate ['kɒmplɪkeɪt] komplizieren; '~**cat·ed** kompliziert; ~**ca·tion** [kɒmplɪ'keɪʃn] Komplikation *f* (*a. med.*)

com·plic·i·ty [kəm'plɪsətɪ] Mitschuld *f*, Mittäterschaft *f* (*in an dat.*)

com·pli|·ment 1. ['kɒmplɪmənt] Kompliment *n*; Empfehlung *f*; Gruß *m*; **2.** ['kɒmplɪment] *v/t.* ~ *s.o.* ein Kompliment *od.* Komplimente machen (*on* wegen)

com·ply [kəm'plaɪ] (*with*) einwilligen (in *acc.*); (*e-e Abmachung etc.*) befolgen

com·po·nent [kəm'pəʊnənt] Bestandteil *m*; *tech.*, *electr.* Bauelement *n*

com|·pose [kəm'pəʊz] zusammensetzen *od.* -stellen; *mus.* komponieren; verfassen; *be* ~*d of* bestehen *od.* sich zusammensetzen aus; ~ *o.s.* sich beruhigen; ~**posed** ruhig, gelassen; ~**pos·er** *mus.* Komponist(in); ~**po·si·tion** [kɒmpə'zɪʃn] Zusammensetzung *f*; Komposition *f*; *ped.* Aufsatz *m*; ~**po·sure** [kəm'pəʊʒə] Fassung *f* (Gemüts)Ruhe *f*

com·pound[1] ['kɒmpaʊnd] Lager *n*; Gefängnishof *m*; (Tier)Gehege *n*

com·pound² 1. ['kɒmpaʊnd] Zusammensetzung f; Verbindung f; gr. zusammengesetztes Wort; 2. ['kɒmpaʊnd] zusammengesetzt; ~ **interest** econ Zinseszinsen pl.; 3. [kəm'paʊnd] v/t. zusammensetzen; steigern, bsd. verschlimmern

com·pre·hend [kɒmprɪ'hend] begreifen, verstehen

com·pre·hen|·si·ble [kɒmprɪ'hensəbl] verständlich; ~**sion** [kɒmprɪ'henʃn] Verständnis n; Begriffsvermögen n, Verstand m; past ~ unfaßbar, unfaßlich; ~**sive** [kɒmprɪ'hensɪv] 1. umfassend; 2. a. ~ **school** Brt. Gesamtschule f

com|·press [kəm'pres] zusammendrücken, -pressen; ~**ed air** Druckluft f; ~**pres·sion** [kəm'preʃn] phys. Verdichtung f; tech. Druck m

com·prise [kəm'praɪz] einschließen, umfassen; bestehen aus

com·pro·mise ['kɒmprəmaɪz] 1. Kompromiß m; 2. v/t. bloßstellen, kompromittieren; v/i. e-n Kompromiß schließen

com·pul|·sion [kəm'pʌlʃn] Zwang m; ~**sive** [kəm'pʌlsɪv] zwingend, Zwangs...; psych. zwanghaft; ~**so·ry** [kəm'pʌlsərɪ] obligatorisch; Zwangs...; Pflicht...

com·punc·tion [kəm'pʌŋkʃn] Gewissensbisse pl.; Reue f; Bedenken pl.

com·pute [kəm'pjuːt] berechnen; schätzen

com·put·er [kəm'pjuːtə] Computer m, Rechner m; ~-**'aid·ed** computergestützt; ~-**con'trolled** computergesteuert; ~ **game** Computerspiel n; ~-**'graph·ics** pl. Computergrafik f; ~-**ize** [kəm'pjuːtəraɪz] (sich) auf Computer umstellen; computerisieren; mit Hilfe e-s Computers errechnen od. zusammenstellen; ~ **pre'dic·tion** Hochrechnung f (bei Wahlen); ~ '**sci·ence** Informatik f; ~-**'sci·en·tist** Informatiker m; ~-**'vi·rus** Computervirus m

com·rade ['kɒmreɪd] Kamerad m; (Partei)Genosse m

con¹ Abk. [kɒn] → **contra**

con² F [kɒn] (-nn-) reinlegen, betrügen

con·ceal [kən'siːl] verbergen; verheimlichen

con·cede [kən'siːd] zugestehen, einräumen

con·ceit [kən'siːt] Einbildung f, Dünkel m; ~**ed** eingebildet (of auf acc.)

con·cei|·va·ble [kən'siːvəbl] denkbar, begreiflich; ~**ve** [kən'siːv] v/i. schwanger werden; v/t. Kind empfangen; sich et. vorstellen od. denken

con·cen·trate ['kɒnsəntreɪt] (sich) konzentrieren

con·cept ['kɒnsept] Begriff m; Gedanke m; △ nicht Konzept

con·cep·tion [kən'sepʃn] Vorstellung f, Begriff m; biol. Empfängnis f

con|·cern [kən'sɜːn] 1. Angelegenheit f, Sorge f; econ. Geschäft n, Unternehmen n; △ nicht Konzern; 2. betreffen, angehen; beunruhigen; ~**ed** besorgt; beteiligt (in an dat.); ~**ing** prp. betreffend, hinsichtlich, was ... (an)betrifft

con·cert mus. ['kɒnsət] Konzert n; ~ **hall** Konzerthalle f, -saal m

con·ces·sion [kən'seʃn] Zugeständnis n; Konzession f

con·cil·i·a·to·ry [kən'sɪlɪətərɪ] versöhnlich, -mittelnd

con·cise [kən'saɪs] kurz, knapp; ~**ness** Kürze f

con·clude [kən'kluːd] schließen, beenden; Vertrag etc. abschließen; et. folgern, schließen (from aus); to be ~**d** Schluß folgt

con·clu|·sion [kən'kluːʒn] (Ab)Schluß m, Ende n; Abschluß f für (e-s Vertrages etc.); (Schluß)Folgerung f; → **jump**; ~**sive** [kən'kluːsɪv] schlüssig (Beweis)

con|·coct [kən'kɒkt] (zusammen)brauen; fig. ausbrüten, -brüten; ~**coc·tion** [kən'kɒkʃn] Gebräu n; fig. Erfindung f

con·crete¹ ['kɒŋkriːt] konkret

con·crete² ['kɒŋkriːt] 1. Beton m; Beton...; 2. betonieren

con·cur [kən'kɜː] (-rr-) übereinstimmen; ~**rence** [kən'kʌrəns] Zusammentreffen n; Übereinstimmung f; △ nicht Konkurrenz

con·cus·sion med. [kən'kʌʃn] Gehirnerschütterung f

con|·demn [kən'dem] verurteilen (a. jur.: to death zum Tode); für unbrauchbar od. unbewohnbar etc. erklären; ~**dem·na·tion** [kɒndem'neɪʃn] Verurteilung f (a. jur.)

con|·den·sa·tion [kɒnden'seɪʃn] Kondensation f; Zusammenfassung f; ~**dense** [kən'dens] kondensieren; zusammenfassen; **~densed 'milk** Kondensmilch f; **~'dens·er** tech. Kondensator m

con·de·scend [kɒndɪ'send] sich herablassen; **~ing** herablassend, gönnerhaft

con·di·ment ['kɒndɪmənt] Gewürz n, Würze f

con·di·tion [kən'dɪʃn] 1. Zustand m; (körperlicher od. Gesundheits)Zustand m; Sport: Kondition f, Form f; Bedingung f; **~s** pl. Verhältnisse pl., Umstände pl.; **on ~ that** unter der Bedingung, daß; **out of ~** in schlechter Verfassung, in schlechtem Zustand; 2. bedingen; in Form bringen; **~al** [kən'dɪʃnl] 1. (on) bedingt (durch), abhängig (von); 2. a. **~ clause** gr. Bedingungs-, Konditionalsatz m; a. **~ mood** gr. Konditional m

con·do Am. ['kɒndəʊ] → **condominium**

con·dole [kən'dəʊl] kondolieren (with dat.); **~'do·lence** Beileid n

con·dom ['kɒndəm] Kondom n, m

con·do·min·i·um Am. [kɒndə'mɪnɪəm] Eigentumswohnanlage f; Eigentumswohnung f

con·done [kən'dəʊn] verzeihen, -geben

con·du·cive [kən'dju:sɪv] dienlich, förderlich (to dat.)

con·duct 1. ['kɒndʌkt] Führung f; Verhalten n, Betragen n; 2. [kən'dʌkt] führen; phys. leiten; mus. dirigieren; **~ed tour** Führung f (of durch); **~duc·tor** [kən'dʌktə] Führer m, Leiter m; (Bus-, Straßenbahn)Schaffner m; Am. rail. Zugbegleiter m, veraltet: Schaffner m; mus. Dirigent m; phys. Leiter m; electr. Blitzableiter m

cone [kəʊn] Kegel m; Eistüte f; bot. Zapfen m

con·fec·tion [kən'fekʃn] Konfekt n; △ nicht Konfektion; **~er** [kən'fekʃnə] Konditor m; **~e·ry** [kən'fekʃnərɪ] Süßigkeiten pl., Süß-, Konditoreiwaren pl.; Konfekt n; Konditorei f; Süßwarengeschäft n

con·fed·e·ra·cy [kən'fedərəsɪ] (Staaten)Bund m; **the 2** Am. hist. die Konföderation; **~rate 1.** [kən'fedərət] verbündet; 2. [kən'fedərət] Verbündete m, Bundesgenosse m; 3. [kən'fedəreɪt] (sich) verbünden; **~ra·tion** [kənfedə'reɪʃn] Bund m, Bündnis n; (Staaten-) Bund m

con·fer [kən'fɜ:] (-rr-) v/t. Titel etc. verleihen (on dat.); v/i. sich beraten

con·fe·rence ['kɒnfərəns] Konferenz f

con·fess [kən'fes] gestehen; beichten; **~fes·sion** [kən'feʃən] Geständnis n; Beichte f; **~fes·sion·al** [kən'feʃənl] Beichtstuhl m; **~fes·sor** rel. [kən'fesə] Beichtvater m

con·fide [kən'faɪd]: **~ s.th. to s.o.** j-m et. anvertrauen; **~ in s.o.** sich j-m anvertrauen

con·fi·dence [kɒnfɪdəns] Vertrauen n; Selbstvertrauen n; **'~ man** (pl. **-men**) → **conman**; **'~ trick** aufgelegter Schwindel; Hochstapelei f

con·fi·dent ['kɒnfɪdənt] überzeugt, zuversichtlich; **~den·tial** [kɒnfɪ'denʃl] vertraulich

con·fine [kən'faɪn] begrenzen, beschränken; einsperren; **be ~d of** entbunden werden von; **~ment** Haft f; Beschränkung f; Entbindung f

con·firm [kən'fɜ:m] bestätigen; bekräftigen; rel. konfirmieren; rel. firmen; **~fir·ma·tion** [kɒnfə'meɪʃn] Bestätigung f; rel. Konfirmation f; rel. Firmung f

con·fis·cate ['kɒnfɪskeɪt] beschlagnahmen; **~ca·tion** [kɒnfɪ'skeɪʃn] Beschlagnahme f

con·flict 1. ['kɒnflɪkt] Konflikt m; 2. [kən'flɪkt] im Widerspruch stehen (with zu); **~ing** [kən'flɪktɪŋ] widersprüchlich

con·form [kən'fɔ:m] (sich) anpassen (to dat., an acc.)

con·found [kən'faʊnd] verwirren, durcheinanderbringen

con·front [kən'frʌnt] gegenübertreten, -stehen (dat.); sich stellen (dat.); konfrontieren; **~fron·ta·tion** [kɒnfrʌn'teɪʃn] Konfrontation f

con·fuse [kən'fju:z] verwechseln; verwirren; **~fused** verwirrt; verlegen; verworren; **~fu·sion** [kən'fju:ʒn] Verwirrung f; Verlegenheit f; Verwechslung f

con·geal [kən'dʒi:l] erstarren (lassen); gerinnen (lassen)

con·gest·ed [kən'dʒestɪd] überfüllt; verstopft; **~ges·tion** [kən'dʒestʃən] Blutandrang m; a. **traffic ~** Verkehrsstockung f, -stauung f, -stau m

con·grat·u·late [kən'grætjʊleɪt] beglückwünschen, j-m gratulieren; **~la·tion** [kəngrætjʊ'leɪʃn] Glückwunsch *m*; **~s!** ich gratuliere!, herzlichen Glückwunsch!

con·gre|·gate ['kɒŋgrɪgeɪt] (sich) versammeln; **~·ga·tion** *rel.* [kɒŋgrɪ'geɪʃn] Gemeinde *f*

con·gress ['kɒŋgres] Kongreß *m*; **2** *Am. parl.* der Kongreß; **'2·man** (*pl. -men*) *Am. parl.* Kongreßabgeordnete(r) *m*; **'2·wom·an** (*pl. -women*) *Am. parl.* Kongreßabgeordnete *f*

con|·ic *bsd. tech.* ['kɒnɪk], **'~·i·cal** konisch, kegelförmig

co·ni·fer *bot.* ['kɒnɪfə] Nadelbaum *m*

con·jec·ture [kən'dʒektʃə] **1.** Vermutung *f*; **2.** vermuten

con·ju·gal ['kɒndʒʊgl] ehelich

con·ju|·gate *gr.* ['kɒndʒʊgeɪt] konjugieren, beugen; **~·ga·tion** *gr.* [kɒndʒʊ'geɪʃn] Konjugation *f*, Beugung *f*

con·junc·tion [kən'dʒʌŋkʃn] Verbindung *f*; *gr.* Konjunktion *f*, Bindewort *n*

con·junc·ti·vi·tis *med.* [kəndʒʌŋktɪ'vaɪtɪs] Bindehautentzündung *f*

con|·jure ['kʌndʒə] zaubern; *Teufel etc.* beschwören; **~ up** heraufbeschwören (*a. fig.*); [kən'dʒʊə] *veraltet* beschwören (*to do* zu tun); **~·jur·er** *bsd. Brt.* ['kʌndʒərə] Zauber|er *m*, -in *f*, Zauberkünstler(in); **~·jur·ing trick** ['kʌndʒərɪŋ -] Zauberkunststück *n*; **~·jur·or** ['kʌndʒərə] → *conjurer*

con·man ['kɒnmæn] (*pl. -men*) Betrüger *m*; Hochstapler *m*

con|·nect [kə'nekt] verbinden; *electr.* anschließen, zuschalten; *rail., aviat. etc.* Anschluß haben (**with** an *acc.*); **~'nect·ed** verbunden; (logisch) zusammenhängend (*Rede etc.*); **be well ~** gute Beziehungen haben; **~·nec·tion**, **~·nex·ion** *Brt.* [kə'nekʃn] Verbindung *f*, Anschluß *m* (*a. electr., rail., aviat., tel.*); Zusammenhang *m*; *mst* **~s** *pl.* Beziehungen *pl.*, Verbindungen *pl.*; Verwandte *pl.*

con·quer ['kɒŋkə] erobern; (be)siegen; **~·or** ['kɒŋkərə] Eroberer *m*

con·quest ['kɒŋkwest] Eroberung *f* (*a. fig.*); erobertes Gebiet

con·science ['kɒnʃəns] Gewissen *n*

con·sci·en·tious [kɒnʃɪ'enʃəs] gewissenhaft; Gewissens...; **~·ness** Gewissenhaftigkeit *f*; **~ ob·jec·tor** Wehrdienstverweigerer *m* (*aus Gewissensgründen*)

con·scious ['kɒnʃəs] bei Bewußtsein; bewußt; **be ~ of** sich bewußt sein (*gen.*); **'~·ness** Bewußtsein *n*

con|·script *mil.* **1.** [kən'skrɪpt] einberufen; **2.** ['kɒnskrɪpt] Wehrpflichtige(r) *m*; **~·scrip·tion** *mil.* [kən'skrɪpʃn] Einberufung *f*; Wehrpflicht *f*

con·se|·crate ['kɒnsɪkreɪt] *rel.* weihen; widmen; **~·cra·tion** *rel.* [kɒnsɪ'kreɪʃn] Weihe *f*

con·sec·u·tive [kən'sekjʊtɪv] aufeinanderfolgend; fortlaufend

con·sent [kən'sent] **1.** Zustimmung *f*; **2.** einwilligen, zustimmen

con·se|·quence ['kɒnsɪkwəns] Folge *f*, Konsequenz *f*; Bedeutung *f*; **~·quent·ly** folglich, daher

con·ser·va|·tion [kɒnsə'veɪʃn] Erhaltung *f*; Naturschutz *m*; Umweltschutz *m*; **~ area** (Natur)Schutzgebiet *n*; **~·tion·ist** [kɒnsə'veɪʃnɪst] Naturschützer(in); Umweltschützer(in); **~·tive** [kən'sɜːvətɪv] **1.** erhaltend; konservativ; vorsichtig; **2. 2** *pol.* Konservative(r *m*) *f*; **~·to·ry** [kɒn'sɜːvətrɪ] Treib-, Gewächshaus *n*; Wintergarten *m*; **con·serve** [kən'sɜːv] erhalten

con·sid|·er [kən'sɪdə] *v/t.* nachdenken über (*acc.*); betrachten als, halten für; sich überlegen, erwägen; in Betracht ziehen, berücksichtigen; *v/i.* nachdenken, überlegen; **~·e·ra·ble** [kən'sɪdərəbl] ansehnlich, beträchtlich; **~·e·ra·bly** [kən'sɪdərəblɪ] bedeutend, ziemlich, (sehr) viel; **~·e·rate** [kən'sɪdərət] rücksichtsvoll; **~·e·ra·tion** [kənsɪdə'reɪʃn] Erwägung *f*, Überlegung *f*; Berücksichtigung *f*; Rücksicht(nahme) *f*; **take into ~** in Erwägung *od.* in Betracht ziehen; **~·er·ing** [kən'sɪdərɪŋ] in Anbetracht (der Tatsache, daß)

con·sign *econ.* [kən'saɪn] Waren zusenden; **~·ment** *econ.* (Waren)Sendung *f*

con·sist [kən'sɪst]: **~ in** bestehen in (*dat.*); **~ of** bestehen aus

con·sis|·tence, **~·ten·cy** [kən'sɪstəns, -tənsɪ] Konsistenz *f*, Beschaffenheit *f*; Übereinstimmung *f*; Konsequenz *f*; **~·tent** [kən'sɪstənt] übereinstimmend, vereinbar (**with** mit); konsequent; *Sport etc.*: beständig (*Leistung*)

con|·so·la·tion [kɒnsə'leɪʃn] Trost *m*; **~·sole** [kən'səʊl] trösten

con·sol·i·date [kənˈsɒlɪdeɪt] festigen; *fig.* zusammenschließen, -legen

con·so·nant *gr.* [ˈkɒnsənənt] Konsonant *m*, Mitlaut *m*

con·spic·u·ous [kənˈspɪkjʊəs] deutlich sichtbar; auffallend

con|·spi·ra·cy [kənˈspɪrəsɪ] Verschwörung *f*; **~·spi·ra·tor** [kənˈspɪrətə] Verschwörer *m*; **~·spire** [kənˈspaɪə] sich verschwören

con·sta·ble *Brt.* [ˈkʌnstəbl] Polizist *m*

con·stant [ˈkɒnstənt] konstant, gleichbleibend; (be)ständig, (an)dauernd

con·ster·na·tion [kɒnstəˈneɪʃn] Bestürzung *f*

con·sti|·pat·ed *med.* [ˈkɒnstɪpeɪtɪd] verstopft; **~·pa·tion** *med.* [kɒnstɪˈpeɪʃn] Verstopfung *f*

con·sti·tu|·en·cy [kənˈstɪtjʊənsɪ] Wählerschaft *f*; Wahlkreis *m*; **~·ent** (wesentlicher) Bestandteil; *pol.* Wähler(in)

con·sti·tute [ˈkɒnstɪtjuːt] ernennen, einsetzen; bilden, ausmachen

con·sti·tu·tion [kɒnstɪˈtjuːʃn] *pol.* Verfassung *f*; Konstitution *f*, körperliche Verfassung; **~·al** [kɒnstɪˈtjuːʃənl] konstitutionell; *pol.* verfassungsmäßig

con·strained [kənˈstreɪnd] gezwungen, unnatürlich

con|·strict [kənˈstrɪkt] zusammenziehen; **~·stric·tion** [kənˈstrɪkʃn] Zusammenziehung *f*

con|·struct [kənˈstrʌkt] bauen, errichten, konstruieren; **~·struc·tion** [kənˈstrʌkʃn] Konstruktion *f*; Bau (-werk *n*) *m*; **under ~** im Bau (befindlich); **~·struc·tion site** Baustelle *f*; **~·struc·tive** [kənˈstrʌktɪv] konstruktiv; **~·struc·tor** [kənˈstrʌktə] Erbauer *m*, Konstrukteur *m*

con·sul [ˈkɒnsəl] Konsul *m*; **con·su·late** [ˈkɒnsjʊlət] Konsulat *n* (*a. Gebäude*); **con·su·late ˈgen·e·ral** Generalkonsulat *n*; **con·sul ˈgen·e·ral** Generalkonsul *m*

con·sult [kənˈsʌlt] *v/t.* konsultieren, um Rat fragen; in *e-m Buch* nachschlagen; *v/i.* (sich) beraten

con·sul|·tant [kənˈsʌltənt] (fachmännische[r]) Berater(in); *Brt.* Facharzt *m* (*an e-m Krankenhaus*); **~·ta·tion** [kɒnslˈteɪʃn] Konsultation *f*, Beratung *f*, Rücksprache *f*

con·sult·ing [kənˈsʌltɪŋ] beratend; **~**

hours *pl.* Sprechstunde *f* (*des Arztes*); **~ room** Sprechzimmer *n*

con|·sume [kənˈsjuːm] *v/t. Essen etc.* zu sich nehmen, verzehren; verbrauchen, konsumieren; zerstören, vernichten (*durch Feuer*); *fig.* verzehren (*durch Haß etc.*); **~·sum·er** *econ.* Verbraucher(in); **~·sum·er so·ci·e·ty** Konsumgesellschaft *f*

con·sum·mate 1. [kənˈsʌmɪt] vollendet; **2.** [ˈkɒnsəmeɪt] vollenden; *Ehe* vollziehen

con·sump·tion [kənˈsʌmpʃn] Verbrauch *m*; *veraltet med.* Schwindsucht *f*

cont *nur geschr. Abk. für* **continued** Forts., Fortsetzung *f*; fortgesetzt

con·tact [ˈkɒntækt] **1.** Berührung *f*; Kontakt *m*; Ansprechpartner(in), Kontaktperson *f* (*a. med.*); **make ~s** Verbindungen anknüpfen *od.* herstellen; **2.** sich in Verbindung setzen mit, Kontakt aufnehmen mit; **~ lens** Kontaktlinse *f*, -schale *f*, Haftschale *f*

con·ta·gious *med.* [kənˈteɪdʒəs] ansteckend (*a. fig.*)

con·tain [kənˈteɪn] enthalten; *fig.* zügeln, zurückhalten; **~·er** Behälter *m*; *econ.* Container *m*; **~·er·ize** *econ.* [kənˈteɪnəraɪz] auf Containerbetrieb umstellen; in Containern transportieren

con·tam·i·nate [kənˈtæmɪneɪt] verunreinigen; infizieren, vergiften; (*a. radioaktiv*) verseuchen; **radioactively ~d** verstrahlt; **~d soil** Altlasten *pl.*; **~·na·tion** [kəntæmɪˈneɪʃn] Verunreinigung *f*; Vergiftung *f*; (*a. radioaktive*) Verseuchung

contd *nur geschr. Abk. für* **continued** (→ *cont*)

con·tem|·plate [ˈkɒntempleɪt] (nachdenklich) betrachten; nachdenken über (*acc.*); erwägen, beabsichtigen; **~·pla·tion** [kɒntemˈpleɪʃn] (nachdenkliche) Betrachtung; Nachdenken *n*; **~·pla·tive** [kənˈtemplətɪv, ˈkɒntempleɪtɪv] nachdenklich

con·tem·po·ra·ry [kənˈtempərərɪ] **1.** zeitgenössisch; **2.** Zeitgenoss|e *m*, -in *f*

con|·tempt [kənˈtempt] Verachtung *f*; **~·temp·ti·ble** [kənˈtemptəbl] verachtenswert; **~·temp·tu·ous** [kənˈtemptʃʊəs] geringschätzig, verächtlich

con·tend [kənˈtend] kämpfen, ringen

C

(*for* um; *with* mit); **~·er** *bsd. Sport*: Wettkämpfer(in)

con·tent[1] ['kɒntent] Gehalt *m*, Aussage *f* (*e-s Buches etc.*); **~s** *pl.* Inhalt *m*; (*table of*) **~s** *pl.* Inhaltsverzeichnis *n*

con·tent[2] [kən'tent] **1.** zufrieden; **2.** befriedigen; **~** *o.s.* sich begnügen; **~ed** zufrieden; **~ment** Zufriedenheit *f*

con·test 1. ['kɒntest] (Wett)Kampf *m*; Wettbewerb *m*; **2.** [kən'test] sich bewerben um; bestreiten, *a. jur.* anfechten; **~·tes·tant** [kən'testənt] Wettkämpfer(in), (Wettkampf)Teilnehmer(in)

con·text ['kɒntekst] Zusammenhang *m*

con·ti·nent ['kɒntɪnənt] Kontinent *m*, Erdteil *m*; **the ⌾** *Brt.* das (europäische) Festland; **~·nen·tal** [kɒntɪ'nentl] kontinental, Kontinental...

con·tin·gen·cy [kən'tɪndʒənsɪ] Möglichkeit *f*, Eventualität *f*; **~t 1.** *be* **~** *on* abhängen von; **2.** Kontingent *n*

con·tin·u·al [kən'tɪnjʊəl] fortwährend, unaufhörlich; **~·u·a·tion** [kəntɪnju'eɪʃn] Fortsetzung *f*; Fortbestand *m*, -dauer *f*; **~·ue** [kən'tɪnjuː] *v/t.* fortsetzen, -fahren mit; beibehalten; *to be* **~d** Fortsetzung folgt; *v/i.* fortdauern; andauern, anhalten; fortfahren, weitermachen; **con·ti·nu·i·ty** [kɒntɪ'njuːətɪ] Kontinuität *f*; **~·u·ous** [kən'tɪnjʊəs] ununterbrochen; **~·u·ous 'form** *gr.* Verlaufsform *f*

con·tort [kən'tɔːt] verdrehen; verzerren; **~·tor·tion** [kən'tɔːʃn] Verdrehung *f*; Verzerrung *f*

con·tour ['kɒntʊə] Umriß *m*

con·tra ['kɒntrə] wider, gegen

con·tra·band *econ.* ['kɒntrəbænd] Schmuggelware *f*

con·tra·cep·tion *med.* [kɒntrə'sepʃn] Empfängnisverhütung *f*; **~·tive** *med.* [kɒntrə'septɪv] empfängnisverhütend(es Mittel)

con·tract 1. ['kɒntrækt] Vertrag *m*; **2.** [kən'trækt] sich zusammenziehen; sich *e-e Krankheit* zuziehen; e-n Vertrag abschließen; sich vertraglich verpflichten; **~·trac·tion** [kən'trækʃn] Zusammenziehung *f*; **~·trac·tor** [kən'træktə]: *a.* **building** **~** Bauunternehmer *m*

con·tra·dict [kɒntrə'dɪkt] widersprechen (*dat.*); **~·dic·tion** [kɒntrə'dɪkʃn] Widerspruch *m*; **~·dic·to·ry** [kɒntrə-

'dɪktərɪ] (sich) widersprechend

con·tra·ry ['kɒntrərɪ] **1.** entgegengesetzt (*to dat.*); gegensätzlich; **~** *to expectations* wider Erwarten; **2.** Gegenteil *n*; *on the* **~** im Gegenteil

con·trast 1. ['kɒntrɑːst] Gegensatz *m*; Kontrast *m*; **2.** [kən'trɑːst] *v/t.* gegenüberstellen, vergleichen; *v/i.* sich abheben (*with* von, gegen); im Gegensatz stehen (*with* zu)

con·trib·ute [kən'trɪbjuːt] beitragen, -steuern; spenden (*to* für); **~·tri·bu·tion** [kɒntrɪ'bjuːʃn] Beitrag *m*; Spende *f*; **~·trib·u·tor** [kən'trɪbjʊtə] Beitragende(r *m*) *f*; Mitarbeiter(in) (*an e-r Zeitung*); **~·trib·u·to·ry** [kən-'trɪbjʊtərɪ] beitragend

con·trite ['kɒntraɪt] zerknirscht

con·trive [kən'traɪv] zustande bringen; es fertigbringen

con·trol [kən'trəʊl] **1.** Kontrolle *f*, Herrschaft *f*, Macht *f*, Gewalt *f*, Beherrschung *f*; Aufsicht *f*; tech. Steuerung *f*; *mst* **~s** *pl. tech.* Steuervorrichtung *f*; △ *nicht* **Kontrolle** (*Überprüfung*); *get* (*have, keep*) *under* **~** unter Kontrolle bringen (haben, halten); *get out of* **~** außer Kontrolle geraten; *lose* **~** *of* die Herrschaft *od.* Gewalt *od.* Kontrolle verlieren über; **2.** (*-ll-*) beherrschen, die Kontrolle haben über (*acc.*); e-r Sache Herr werden, (erfolgreich) bekämpfen; kontrollieren, überwachen; *econ.* (staatlich) lenken, *Preise* binden; *electr., tech.* steuern, regeln, regulieren; △ *nicht* **kontrollieren** (*überprüfen*); **~** **desk** *electr.* Schalt-, Steuerpult *n*; **~ pan·el** *electr.* Schalttafel *f*; **~ tow·er** *aviat.* Kontrollturm *m*, Tower *m*

con·tro·ver·sial [kɒntrə'vɜːʃl] umstritten; **~·sy** [kɒntrə'vɜːsɪ] Kontroverse *f*, Streit *m*

con·tuse *med.* [kən'tjuːz] sich *et.* quetschen

con·va·lesce [kɒnvə'les] gesund werden, genesen; **~·les·cence** [kɒnvə-'lesns] Rekonvaleszenz *f*, Genesung *f*; **~·les·cent 1.** genesend; **2.** Rekonvaleszent(in), Genesende(r *m*) *f*

con·vene [kən'viːn] (sich) versammeln; zusammenkommen; *Versammlung* einberufen

con·ve·ni·ence [kən'viːnjəns] Annehmlichkeit *f*, Bequemlichkeit *f*; *Brt.*

Toilette f; **all (modern)** ~s pl. aller Komfort; **at your earliest** ~ möglichst bald; **~ent** bequem; günstig, passend

:on·vent ['kɒnvənt] (Nonnen)Kloster n

:on·ven·tion [kən'venʃn] Zusammenkunft f, Tagung f, Versammlung f; Abkommen n, Übereinkunft f, Sitte f; **~al** [kən'venʃənl] herkömmlich, konventionell

:on·verge [kən'vɜːdʒ] konvergieren; zusammenlaufen, -strömen

:on·ver·sa·tion [kɒnvə'seɪʃn] Gespräch n, Unterhaltung f; **~al** [kɒnvə'seɪʃənl] Unterhaltungs...; ~ **English** Umgangsenglisch n

:on·verse [kən'vɜːs] sich unterhalten

:on·ver·sion [kən'vɜːʃn] Um-, Verwandlung f; Umbau m; Umstellung f (**to** auf acc.); rel. Bekehrung f, Übertritt m; math. Umrechnung f; **~ta·ble** Umrechnungstabelle f

con|·vert [kən'vɜːt] (sich) um- od. verwandeln; umbauen (**into** zu); umstellen (**to** auf acc.); rel. etc. (sich) bekehren; math. umrechnen; **~'vert·er** electr. Umformer m; **~'vert·i·ble 1.** um-, verwandelbar; econ. konvertierbar; **2.** mot. Kabrio(lett) n

con·vey [kən'veɪ] befördern, transportieren, bringen; überbringen, -mitteln; Ideen etc. mitteilen; **~ance** Beförderung f, Transport m; Übermittlung f, Verkehrsmittel n; **~er**, **~or** → **~er belt** Förderband n

con|·vict 1. ['kɒnvɪkt] Verurteilte(r m) f, Strafgefangene(r m) f; **2.** jur. [kən'vɪkt] (**of**) überführen (gen.); verurteilen (wegen); **~vic·tion** [kən'vɪkʃn] jur. Verurteilung f; Überzeugung f

con·vince [kən'vɪns] überzeugen

con·voy ['kɒnvɔɪ] **1.** naut. Geleitzug m, Konvoi m; (Wagen)Kolonne f; (Geleit)Schutz m; **2.** Geleitschutz geben (dat.), eskortieren

con·vul|·sion med. [kən'vʌlʃn] Zuckung f, Krampf m; **~sive** [kən'vʌlsɪv] krampfhaft, -artig, konvulsiv

coo [kuː] gurren

cook [kʊk] **1.** Koch m; Köchin f; **2.** kochen; F Bericht etc. frisieren; ~ **up** F sich ausdenken, erfinden; **'~·book** Am. Kochbuch n; **'~·er** Brt. Ofen m, Herd m; **~·e·ry** ['kʊkərɪ] Kochen n; Kochkunst f; **'~·e·ry book** Brt. Kochbuch

n; **~·ie** Am. ['kʊkɪ] (süßer) Keks, Plätzchen n; **'~·ing** Küche f (Kochweise); **~·y** Am. ['kʊkɪ] → **cookie**

cool [kuːl] **1.** kühl; fig. kalt(blütig), gelassen; abweisend; gleichgültig; F klasse, prima, cool; **2.** Kühle f; F (Selbst)Beherrschung f; **3.** (sich) abkühlen; ~ **down**, ~ **off** sich beruhigen

coon zo. F [kuːn] Waschbär m

coop [kuːp] **1.** Hühnerstall m; **2.** ~ **up**, ~ **in** einsperren, -pferchen

co-op F ['kəʊɒp] Co-op m (Genossenschaft u. Laden)

co·op·e|·rate [kəʊ'ɒpəreɪt] zusammenarbeiten; mitwirken, helfen; **~ra·tion** [kəʊɒpə'reɪʃn] Zusammenarbeit f; Mitwirkung f, Hilfe f; **~ra·tive** [kəʊ'ɒpərətɪv] **1.** zusammenarbeitend; kooperativ; hilfsbereit; econ. Gemeinschafts..., Genossenschafts...; **2.** a. ~ **society** Genossenschaft f; Co-op m, Konsumverein m; a. ~ **store** Co-op m, Konsumladen m

co·or·di|·nate 1. [kəʊ'ɔːdɪneɪt] koordinieren, aufeinander abstimmen; **2.** [kəʊ'ɔːdɪnət] koordiniert, gleichgeordnet; **~na·tion** [kəʊɔːdɪ'neɪʃn] Koordinierung f, Koordination f; harmonisches Zusammenspiel

cop F [kɒp] Bulle m (Polizist)

cope [kəʊp]: ~ **with** gewachsen sein (dat.), fertig werden mit

cop·i·er ['kɒpɪə] Kopiergerät n, Kopierer m

co·pi·ous ['kəʊpjəs] reich(lich); weitschweifig

cop·per¹ ['kɒpə] **1.** min. Kupfer n; Kupfermünze f; **2.** kupfern, Kupfer...

cop·per² F ['kɒpə] Bulle m (Polizist)

cop·pice ['kɒpɪs], **copse** [kɒps] Gehölz n

cop·y ['kɒpɪ] **1.** Kopie f; Abschrift f; Nachbildung f; Durchschlag m; Exemplar n (e-s Buches); (Zeitungs)Nummer f; print. Satzvorlage f; **fair ~** Reinschrift f; **2.** kopieren; abschreiben; e-e Kopie anfertigen von; Computer: Daten übertragen; nachbilden; nachahmen; **'~·book** Schreibheft n; **'~·ing** Kopier...; **'~·right** Urheberrecht n, Copyright n

cor·al zo. ['kɒrəl] Koralle f

cord [kɔːd] **1.** Schnur f (a. electr.), Strick m; Kordsamt m; **2.** ver-, zuschnüren

cor·di·al¹ ['kɔːdjəl] Fruchtsaftkonzentrat n; med. Stärkungsmittel n
cor·di·al² ['kɔːdjəl] herzlich; **~·i·ty** [kɔːdɪˈælətɪ] Herzlichkeit f
'cord·less schnurlos; **'~ phone** schnurloses Telefon
cor·don ['kɔːdn] **1.** Kordon m, Postenkette f; **2.** ~ **off** abriegeln, absperren
cor·du·roy ['kɔːdərɔɪ] Kordsamt m; (**a pair of**) **~s** pl. (e-e) Kordhose
core [kɔː] **1.** Kerngehäuse n; Kern m, fig. a. das Innerste; **2.** entkernen; **'~ time** Brt. Kernzeit f
cork [kɔːk] **1.** Kork(en) m; **2.** a. ~ **up** zu-, verkorken; **'~·screw** Korkenzieher m
corn¹ [kɔːn] **1.** Korn n, Getreide n; **Indian ~** Mais m; **2.** pökeln
corn² med. [kɔːn] Hühnerauge n
cor·ner ['kɔːnə] **1.** Ecke f; Winkel m; bsd. mot. Kurve f; Fußball: Eckball m, Ecke f; fig. schwierige Lage, Klemme f; **2.** Eck...; **3.** in die Ecke (fig. Enge) treiben; **'~ed** ...eckig; **'~ kick** Fußball: Eckball m, -stoß m; **'~ shop** Brt. Tante-Emma-Laden m
cor·net ['kɔːnɪt] mus. Kornett n; Brt. Eistüte f
'corn·flakes pl. Cornflakes pl.
cor·nice arch. ['kɔːnɪs] Gesims n, Sims m
cor·o·na·ry ['kɔːrənərɪ] **1.** anat. Koronar...; **2.** med. F Herzinfarkt m
cor·o·na·tion [kɔrəˈneɪʃn] Krönung f
cor·o·ner jur. ['kɔrənə] Coroner m (richterlicher Beamter zur Untersuchung der Todesursache in Fällen gewaltsamen od. unnatürlichen Todes); **~'s 'in·quest** gerichtliches Verfahren zur Untersuchung der Todesursache
cor·o·net ['kɔrənɪt] Adelskrone f
cor·po·ral mil. ['kɔːpərəl] Unteroffizier m
cor·po·ral 'pun·ish·ment körperliche Züchtigung
cor·po|·rate ['kɔːpərət] gemeinsam; Firmen...; **~·ra·tion** [kɔːpəˈreɪʃn] jur. Körperschaft f; Stadtverwaltung f; Gesellschaft f, Am. a. Aktiengesellschaft f
corpse [kɔːps] Leichnam m, Leiche f
cor·pu·lent ['kɔːpjʊlənt] beleibt
cor·ral [kɔːˈrɑːl, Am. kəˈræl] Korral m, Hürde f, Pferch m; **2.** (**-ll-**) Vieh in e-n Pferch treiben
cor|·rect [kəˈrekt] **1.** korrekt, richtig, a.

genau (Zeit); **2.** korrigieren, verbessern, berichtigen; **~·rec·tion** [kəˈrekʃn] Korrektur f, Verbesserung f, Bestrafung f
cor·re|·spond [kɒrɪˈspɒnd] (**with, to**) entsprechen (dat.), übereinstimmen (mit); korrespondieren (**with** mit); **~'spon·dence** Übereinstimmung f, Korrespondenz f, Briefwechsel m; **~'spon·dence course** Fernkurs m; **~'spon·dent 1.** entsprechend; **2.** Briefpartner(in); Korrespondent(in); **~'spon·ding** entsprechend
cor·ri·dor ['kɒrɪdɔː] Korridor m, Gang m
cor·rob·o·rate [kəˈrɒbəreɪt] bekräftigen, bestätigen
cor|·rode [kəˈrəʊd] zerfressen; chem., tech. korrodieren; rosten; **~·ro·sion** chem., tech. [kəˈrəʊʒn] Korrosion f; Rost m; **~·ro·sive** [kəˈrəʊsɪv] ätzend; fig. nagend, zersetzend
cor·ru·gat·ed ['kɒrʊgeɪtɪd] gewellt; **'~ i·ron** Wellblech n
cor|·rupt [kəˈrʌpt] **1.** korrupt, bestechlich, käuflich; moralisch verdorben; **2.** bestechen; moralisch verderben; **~'rupt·i·ble** korrupt, bestechlich, käuflich; **~·rup·tion** [kəˈrʌpʃn] Verdorbenheit f; Unredlichkeit f; Korruption f; Bestechlichkeit f; Bestechung f
cor·set ['kɔːsɪt] Korsett n
cos·met·ic [kɒzˈmetɪk] **1.** (**~ally**) kosmetisch, Schönheits...; **2.** kosmetisches Mittel, Schönheitsmittel n; **~·me·ti·cian** [kɒzməˈtɪʃn] Kosmetiker(in)
cos·mo·naut ['kɒzmənɔːt] Kosmonaut m, (Welt)Raumfahrer m
cos·mo·pol·i·tan [kɒzməˈpɒlɪtən] **1.** kosmopolitisch; **2.** Weltbürger(in)
cost [kɒst] **1.** Preis m; Kosten pl.; Schaden m; △ nicht **Kost** (Essen); **2.** (**cost**) kosten; **'~·ly** (**-ier, -iest**) kostspielig; teuer erkauft; **~ of 'liv·ing** Lebenshaltungskosten pl.
cos·tume ['kɒstjuːm] Kostüm n, Kleidung f, Tracht f; **'~ jew·el(·le)ry** Modeschmuck m
co·sy ['kəʊzɪ] **1.** (**-ier, -iest**) behaglich, gemütlich; **2.** → **egg cosy, tea cosy**
cot [kɒt] Feldbett n; Brt. Kinderbett n
cot·tage ['kɒtɪdʒ] Cottage n, (kleines) Landhaus; Am. Ferienhaus n, -häus-

chen *n*; ~ **'cheese** Hüttenkäse *m*

cot·ton ['kɒtn] **1.** Baumwolle *f*; Baumwollstoff *m*; (Baumwoll)Garn *n*, (-)Zwirn *m*; *Am.* (Verband)Watte *f*; **2.** baumwollen, Baumwoll...; ~**wood** *bot. e-e* amer. Pappel; ~ **'wool** *Brt.* (Verband)Watte *f*

couch [kaʊtʃ] Couch *f*, Sofa *n*; Liege *f*

cou·chette *rail.* [kuː'ʃet] Liegewagenplatz *m*; *a.* ~ **coach** Liegewagen *m*

cou·gar *zo.* ['kuːgə] (*pl.* **-gars, -gar**) Puma *m*

cough [kɒf] **1.** Husten *m*; **2.** husten

could [kʊd] *pret. von* **can¹**

coun·cil ['kaʊnsl] Rat(sversammlung *f*) *m*; ~ **house** *Brt.* gemeindeeigenes Wohnhaus (*mit niedrigen Mieten*)

coun·cil·(l)or ['kaʊnsələ] Ratsmitglied *n*, Stadtrat *m*, Stadträtin *f*

coun·sel ['kaʊnsl] **1.** Beratung *f*; Rat(schlag) *m*; *Brt. jur.* (Rechts)Anwalt *m*; ~ **for the defence** (*Am.* **defense**) Verteidiger *m*; ~ **for the prosecution** Anklagevertreter *m*; **2.** (*bsd. Brt.* **-ll-,** *Am.* **-l-**) *j-m* raten; zu *et.* raten; ~*(l)ing centre* (*Am. center*) Beratungsstelle *f*; ~**sel·(l)or** ['kaʊnsələ] (*Berufs- etc.*)Berater(in); *bsd. Am. jur.* (Rechts-)Anwalt *m*

count¹ [kaʊnt] Graf *m* (*nicht britisch*)

count² [kaʊnt] **1.** Zählung *f*; *jur.* Anklagepunkt *m*; **2.** *v/t.* (ab-, auf-, aus-, nach-, zusammen)zählen; aus-, berechnen; zählen bis (~ **ten**); *fig.* halten für, betrachten als; *v/i.* zählen; gelten; ~ **down** Geld hinzählen; den Countdown durchführen für, letzte (Start)Vorbereitungen treffen für; ~ **on** zählen auf (*acc.*), sich verlassen auf (*acc.*), sicher rechnen mit; '~**down** Countdown *m*, *n*, letzte (Start)Vorbereitungen *pl.*

coun·te·nance ['kaʊntɪnəns] Gesichtsausdruck *m*; Fassung *f*, Haltung *f*

count·er¹ ['kaʊntə] *tech.* Zähler *m*; *Brt.* Spielmarke *f*

count·er² ['kaʊntə] Ladentisch *m*; Theke *f*; (Bank-, Post)Schalter *m*

coun·ter³ ['kaʊntə] **1.** (ent)gegen, Gegen...; **2.** entgegentreten (*dat.*), entgegnen (*dat.*), bekämpfen; abwehren

coun·ter·act [kaʊntər'ækt] entgegenwirken (*dat.*); neutralisieren

coun·ter·bal·ance 1. ['kaʊntəbæləns] Gegengewicht *n*; **2.** [kaʊntə'bæləns] ein

Gegengewicht bilden zu, ausgleichen

coun·ter·clock·wise *Am.* [kaʊntə-'klɒkwaɪz] → *anticlockwise*

coun·ter·es·pi·o·nage ['kaʊntər-'espɪənɑːʒ] Spionageabwehr *f*

coun·ter·feit ['kaʊntəfɪt] **1.** falsch, gefälscht; **2.** Fälschung *f*; **3.** Geld, *Unterschrift etc.* fälschen; ~ **'mon·ey** Falschgeld *n*

coun·ter·foil ['kaʊntəfɔɪl] Kontrollabschnitt *m*

coun·ter·mand [kaʊntə'mɑːnd] *Befehl etc.* widerrufen; *Ware* abbestellen

coun·ter·pane ['kaʊntəpeɪn] Tagesdecke *f*; → *bedspread*

coun·ter·part ['kaʊntəpɑːt] Gegenstück *n*; genaue Entsprechung

coun·ter·sign ['kaʊntəsaɪn] gegenzeichnen

coun·tess ['kaʊntɪs] Gräfin *f*

'count·less zahllos

coun·try ['kʌntrɪ] *Brt.* **1.** Land *n*, Staat *m*; Gegend *f*, Landschaft *f*; *in the* ~ auf dem Lande; **2.** Land..., ländlich; '~**man** (*pl.* **-men**) Landbewohner *m*; Bauer *m*; *a.* **fellow** ~ Landsmann *m*; '~ **road** Landstraße *f*; '~**side** (ländliche) Gegend; Landschaft *f*; '~**wom·an** (*pl.* **-women**) Landbewohnerin *f*; Bäuerin *f*; *a.* **fellow** ~ Landsmännin *f*

coun·ty ['kaʊntɪ] *Brt.* Grafschaft *f*; *Am.* (Land)Kreis *m* (*einzelstaatlicher Verwaltungsbezirk*); ~ **'seat** *Am.* Kreis(haupt)stadt *f*; ~ **'town** *Brt.* Grafschaftshauptstadt *f*

coup [kuː] Coup *m*; Putsch *m*

cou·ple ['kʌpl] **1.** Paar *n*; *a* ~ *of* F ein paar; **2.** (zusammen)koppeln; *tech.* kuppeln; *zo.* (sich) paaren

coup·ling *tech.* ['kʌplɪŋ] Kupplung *f*

cou·pon ['kuːpɒn] Gutschein *m*; Kupon *m*, Bestellzettel *m*

cour·age ['kʌrɪdʒ] Mut *m*; **cou·ra·geous** [kə'reɪdʒəs] mutig, beherzt

cou·ri·er ['kʊrɪə] Kurier *m*, Eilbote *m*; Reiseleiter *m*

course [kɔːs] *naut., aviat., fig.* Kurs *m*; *Sport:* (Renn)Bahn *f*, (-)Strecke *f*, (Golf)Platz *m*; (Ver)Lauf *m*; Gang *m* (*Speisen*); Reihe *f*, Zyklus *m*; Kurs *m*, Lehrgang *m*; *of* ~ natürlich, selbstverständlich; *the* ~ *of events* der Gang der Ereignisse, der Lauf der Dinge

court [kɔːt] **1.** Hof *m* (*a. e-s Fürsten*);

C

kleiner Platz; *Sport:* Platz *m*, (Spiel-)Feld *n*; *jur.* Gericht(shof *m*) *n*; **2.** *j-m* den Hof machen; werben um

cour·te|·ous ['kɜːtjəs] höflich; **~·sy** ['kɜːtɪsɪ] Höflichkeit *f*; **by ~ of** mit freundlicher Genehmigung von (*od. gen.*)

'**court|·house** Gerichtsgebäude *n*; **~·ier** ['kɔːtjə] Höfling *m*; '**~·ly** höflich; ~ '**mar·tial** (*pl. courts martial, court martials*) Kriegsgericht *n*; **~·'mar·tial** (*bsd. Brt. -ll-, Am. -l-*) vor ein Kriegsgericht stellen; '**~·room** Gerichtssaal *m*; '**~·ship** Werben *n*; '**~·yard** Hof *m*

cous·in ['kʌzn] Cousin *m*, Vetter *m*; Cousine *f*, Kusine *f*

cove [kəʊv] kleine Bucht

cov·er ['kʌvə] **1.** Decke *f*; Deckel *m*; (Buch)Deckel *m*, Einband *m*; Umschlag *m*; Titelseite *f*; Hülle *f*; Überzug *m*, Bezug *m*; Schutzhaube *f*, -platte *f*; Abdeckhaube *f*; Briefumschlag *m*; Gedeck *n* (*bei Tisch*); Deckung *f*; Schutz *m*; *fig.* Tarnung *f*; **take** ~ in Deckung gehen; **under plain** ~ in neutralem Umschlag; **under separate** ~ mit getrenntter Post; **2.** (be-, zu)decken; einschlagen, -wickeln; verbergen; decken, schützen; *econ.* (ab)decken; *econ.* versichern; *Thema* erschöpfend behandeln; *Presse, Rundfunk, TV:* berichten über (*acc.*); sich über *e-e Fläche etc.* erstrecken; *Strecke* zurücklegen; *Sport:* *Gegenspieler* decken; *j-n* beschatten; ~ **up** ab-, zudecken; *fig.* verheimlichen, vertuschen; ~ **up for s.o.** *j-n* decken; **~·age** ['kʌvərɪdʒ] Berichterstattung *f* (*of über acc.*); '**~·girl** Covergirl *n*, Titelblattmädchen *n*; '**~·ing** ['kʌvərɪŋ] Decke *f*; Überzug *m*; Hülle *f*; (Fußboden-)Belag *m*; '**~ sto·ry** Titelgeschichte *f*

cow¹ *zo.* [kaʊ] Kuh *f*

cow² [kaʊ] einschüchtern

cow·ard ['kaʊəd] **1.** feig(e); **2.** Feigling *m*; **~·ice** ['kaʊədɪs] Feigheit *f*; '**~·ly** feig(e)

cow·boy ['kaʊbɔɪ] Cowboy *m*

cow·er ['kaʊə] kauern; sich ducken

'**cow|·herd** Kuhhirte *m*; '**~·hide** Rind(s)leder *n*; '**~·house** Kuhstall *m*

cowl [kaʊl] Mönchskutte *f* (*mit Kapuze*); Kapuze *f*; Schornsteinkappe *f*

'**cow|·shed** Kuhstall *m*; '**~·slip** *bot.*

Schlüsselblume *f*; *Am.* Sumpfdotterblume *f*

cox [kɒks], **~·swain** ['kɒksn, 'kɒkswein] Bootsführer *m*; *Rudern:* Steuermann *m*

coy [kɔɪ] schüchtern, scheu

coy·ote *zo.* ['kɔɪəʊt] Kojote *m*, Präriewolf *m*

co·zy *Am.* ['kəʊzɪ] (*-ier, -iest*) → **cosy**

CPU [siː piː 'juː] *Abk. für central processing unit Computer:* Zentraleinheit *f*

crab [kræb] Krabbe *f*, Taschenkrebs *m*

crack [kræk] **1.** Knall *m*; Sprung *m*, Riß *m*; Spalt(e *f*) *m*, Ritze *f*; (heftiger) Schlag; **2.** erstklassig; **3.** *v/i.* krachen, knallen, knacken; (zer)springen; überschnappen (*Stimme*); *a.* ~ **up** fig. zusammenbrechen; **get ~ing** F loslegen; *v/t.* knallen mit (*Peitsche*), knacken mit (*Fingern*); zerbrechen; *Nuß*, F *Code, Safe etc.* knacken; ~ **a joke** e-n Witz reißen; '**~·er** Cracker *m*, Kräcker *m* (*ungesüßter Keks*); Schwärmer *m*, Knallfrosch *m*, Knallbonbon *m*, *n*; '**~·le** ['krækl] knattern, knistern, prasseln

cra·dle ['kreɪdl] **1.** Wiege *f*; **2.** wiegen; betten

craft¹ [krɑːft] *naut.* Boot(e *pl.*) *n*, Schiff(e *pl.*) *n*; *aviat.* Flugzeug(e *pl.*) *n*; (Welt)Raumfahrzeug(e *pl.*) *n*

craft² [krɑːft] Handwerk *n*, Gewerbe *n*; Schlauheit *f*, List *f*; ⚠ *nicht Kraft*; '**~·s·man** (*pl. -men*) (Kunst)Handwerker *m*; '**~·y** (*-ier, -iest*) gerissen, listig, schlau

crag [kræg] Klippe *f*, Felsenspitze *f*

cram [kræm] (*-mm-*) (voll)stopfen; nudeln, mästen; mit *j-m* pauken; pauken, büffeln (**for** für)

cramp [kræmp] **1.** *med.* Krampf *m*; *tech.* Klammer *f*; *fig.* Fessel *f*; **2.** einengen, hemmen

cran·ber·ry *bot.* ['krænbərɪ] Preiselbeere *f*

crane¹ *tech.* [kreɪn] Kran *m*

crane² [kreɪn] **1.** *zo.* Kranich *m*; **2.** den Hals recken; ~ **one's neck** sich den Hals verrenken (**for** nach)

crank [kræŋk] **1.** *tech.* Kurbel *f*; *tech.* Schwengel *m*; F Spinner *m*, komischer Kauz; **2.** (an)kurbeln; '**~·shaft** *tech.* Kurbelwelle *f*; '**~·y** (*-ier, -iest*) wack(e)lig; verschroben; *Am.* schlechtgelaunt

cran·ny ['krænɪ] Riß *m*, Ritze *f*

crape [kreɪp] Krepp *m*, Flor *m*

crap·py *sl.* ['kræpɪ] ätzend (*fürchterlich*)

craps *Am.* [kræps] *sg. ein* Würfelspiel

crash [kræʃ] **1.** Krach(en) *m*; *mot.* Unfall *m*, Zusammenstoß *m*; *aviat.* Absturz *m*; *econ.* Zusammenbruch *m*, (Börsen)Krach *m*; **2.** *v/t.* zertrümmern; e-n Unfall haben mit; *aviat.* abstürzen mit; *v/i.* krachend einstürzen, zusammenkrachen; *bsd. econ.* zusammenbrechen; krachen (*against, into* gegen); *mot.* zusammenstoßen, verunglücken; *aviat.* abstürzen; **3.** Schnell..., Sofort...; '~ **bar·ri·er** Leitplanke *f*; '~ **course** Schnell-, Intensivkurs *m*; '~ **di·et** radikale Schlankheitskur; '~ **hel·met** Sturzhelm *m*; '~**land** *aviat.* e-e Bruchlandung machen (mit); ~ **land·ing** *aviat.* Bruchlandung *f*

crate [kreɪt] (Latten)Kiste *f*

cra·ter ['kreɪtə] Krater *m*; Trichter *m*

crave [kreɪv] sich sehnen (*for, after* nach); '**crav·ing** heftiges Verlangen *n*

craw·fish *zo.* ['krɔːfɪʃ] (*pl. -fish, -fishes*) → **crayfish**

crawl [krɔːl] **1.** Kriechen *n*; **2.** kriechen; krabbeln; kribbeln; wimmeln (**with** von); *Schwimmen*: kraulen; **it makes one's flesh ~** man bekommt e-e Gänsehaut davon

cray·fish *zo.* ['kreɪfɪʃ] (*pl. -fish, -fishes*) Flußkrebs *m*

cray·on ['kreɪən] Zeichen-, Buntstift *m*

craze [kreɪz] Verrücktheit *f*, F Fimmel *m*; **be the ~** Mode sein; '**cra·zy** (*-ier, -iest*) verrückt (**about** nach)

creak [kriːk] knarren, quietschen

cream [kriːm] **1.** Rahm *m*, Sahne *f*; Creme *f*; Auslese *f*, Elite *f*; **2.** creme(farben); ~**er·y** ['kriːmərɪ] Molkerei *f*; Milchgeschäft *n*; '~**y** (*-ier, -iest*) sahnig; weich

crease [kriːs] **1.** (Bügel)Falte *f*; **2.** (zer)knittern

cre·ate [kriːˈeɪt] (er)schaffen; hervorrufen; verursachen; ~**a·tion** [kriːˈeɪʃn] Schöpfung *f*; ~**a·tive** schöpferisch; ~**a·tor** Schöpfer *m*

crea·ture ['kriːtʃə] Geschöpf *n*; Kreatur *f*

crèche [kreɪʃ] (Kinder)Krippe *f*; *Am.* (Weihnachts)Krippe *f*

cre·dence ['kriːdns]: **give ~ to** Glauben schenken (*dat.*)

cre·den·tials [krɪˈdenʃlz] *pl.* Beglaubigungsschreiben *n*; Referenzen *pl.*; Zeugnis *n*; Ausweis(papiere *pl.*) *m*

cred·i·ble ['kredəbl] glaubwürdig

cred·it ['kredɪt] **1.** Glaube(n) *m*; Ruf *m*, Ansehen *n*; Verdienst *n*; *econ.* Kredit *m*; *econ.* Guthaben *n*; ~ (**side**) *econ.* Kredit(seite) *f*, Haben *n*; **on ~** *econ.* auf Kredit; **2.** *j-m* glauben; *j-m* trauen; *econ.* gutschreiben; ~ **s.o. with s.th.** *j-m* et. zutrauen; *j-m* et. zuschreiben; '~**i·ta·ble** achtbar, ehrenvoll (**to** für); '~ **card** *econ.* Kreditkarte *f*; '~**i·tor** Gläubiger *m*; ~**u·lous** ['kredjʊləs] leichtgläubig

creed [kriːd] Glaubensbekenntnis *n*

creek [kriːk] *Brt.* kleine Bucht; *Am.* Bach *m*

creep [kriːp] (**crept**) kriechen; schleichen (*a. fig.*); ~ **in** (sich) hinein- *od.* hereinschleichen; sich einschleichen (*Fehler etc.*); **it makes my flesh ~** ich bekomme e-e Gänsehaut davon; '~**er** *bot.* Kriech-, Kletterpflanze *f*; ~**s** *pl.* F **the sight gave me the ~s** bei dem Anblick bekam ich e-e Gänsehaut

cre·mate [krɪˈmeɪt] verbrennen, einäschern

crept [krept] *pret. u. p.p. von* **creep**

cres·cent ['kresnt] Halbmond *m*

cress *bot.* [kres] Kresse *f*

crest [krest] *zo.* Haube *f*, Büschel *n*; (*Hahnen*)Kamm *m*; Bergrücken *m*, Kamm *m*; (*Wellen*)Kamm *m*; Federbusch *m*; *family* ~ *Heraldik:* Familienwappen *n*; '~**fal·len** niedergeschlagen

cre·vasse [krɪˈvæs] (Gletscher)Spalte *f*

crev·ice ['krevɪs] Riß *m*, Spalte *f*

crew[1] [kruː] Besatzung *f*, Mannschaft *f*

crew[2] [kruː] *pret. von* **crow** 2

crib [krɪb] **1.** (Futter)Krippe *f*; *Am.* Kinderbettchen *n*; *bsd. Brt.* (Weihnachts)Krippe *f*; F *Schule:* Spickzettel *m*; **2.** (*-bb-*) F abschreiben, spicken

crick [krɪk]: **a ~ in one's back** (**neck**) ein steifer Rücken (Hals)

crick·et[1] *zo.* ['krɪkɪt] Grille *f*

crick·et[2] ['krɪkɪt] *Sport:* Kricket *n*

crime [kraɪm] *jur.* Verbrechen *n*; *coll.* Verbrechen *pl.*; ~ **nov·el** Kriminalroman *m*

crim·i·nal ['krɪmɪnl] **1.** kriminell; Kriminal..., Straf...; **2.** Verbrecher(in), Kriminelle(r *m*) *f*

crimp [krɪmp] *bsd. Haare* kräuseln
crim·son ['krɪmzn] karmesinrot; puter-
rot
cringe [krɪndʒ] sich ducken
crin·kle ['krɪŋkl] **1.** Falte *f, im Gesicht:*
Fältchen *n;* **2.** (sich) kräuseln; knittern
crip·ple ['krɪpl] **1.** Krüppel *m;* **2.** zum
Krüppel machen; *fig.* lähmen
cri·sis ['kraɪsɪs] (*pl.* -ses [-siːz]) Krise *f*
crisp [krɪsp] knusp(e)rig, mürbe (*Gebäck*); frisch, knackig (*Gemüse*);
scharf, frisch (*Luft*); kraus (*Haar*);
'**~bread** Knäckebrot *n*
crisps [krɪsps] *pl., a. potato ~* Brt. (Kartoffel)Chips *pl.*
criss-cross ['krɪskrɒs] **1.** Netz *n* sich
schneidender Linien; **2.** kreuz u. quer
ziehen durch; kreuz u. quer (ver)laufen
cri·te·ri·on [kraɪ'tɪərɪən] (*pl.* -ria [-rɪə],
-rions) Kriterium *n*
crit|·ic ['krɪtɪk] Kritiker(in); △ *nicht
Kritik;* **~·i·cal** ['krɪtɪkl] kritisch; bedenklich; **~·i·cis·m** ['krɪtɪsɪzəm] Kritik
f (*of an dat.*); **~·i·cize** ['krɪtɪsaɪz] kriti-
sieren; kritisch beurteilen; tadeln
cri·tique [krɪ'tiːk] Kritik *f,* Besprechung
f, Rezension *f*
croak [krəʊk] krächzen; quaken
cro·chet ['krəʊʃeɪ] **1.** Häkelei *f;* Häkel-
arbeit *f;* **2.** häkeln
crock·e·ry ['krɒkərɪ] Geschirr *n*
croc·o·dile *zo.* ['krɒkədaɪl] Krokodil *n*
cro·ny F ['krəʊnɪ] alter Freund
crook [krʊk] **1.** Krümmung *f;* Hirten-
stab *m;* F Gauner *m;* **2.** (sich) krümmen
od. biegen; **~ed** ['krʊkɪd] gekrümmt,
krumm; F unehrlich, betrügerisch
croon [kruːn] schmachtend singen;
summen; '**~·er** Schnulzensänger(in)
crop [krɒp] **1.** (Feld)Frucht *f;* Ernte *f;*
zo. Kropf *m;* kurzer Haarschnitt; kurz-
geschnittenes Haar; **2.** (-*pp*-) abfressen,
abweiden; *Haar* kurz schneiden; **~ up**
fig. plötzlich auftauchen
cross [krɒs] **1.** Kreuz *n* (*a. fig. Leiden*);
biol. Kreuzung *f; Fußball:* Flanke *f*
(*Ball*); **2.** böse, ärgerlich; **3.** (sich) kreuzen; *Straße* überqueren; *Plan etc.*
durchkreuzen; *biol.* kreuzen; **~ off, ~
out** aus-, durchstreichen; **~ o.s.** sich
bekreuzigen; **~ one's arms** die Arme
kreuzen *od.* verschränken; **~ one's legs**
die Beine kreuzen *od.* über(einander)schlagen; *keep one's fingers* **~ed**

den Daumen drücken; '**~·bar** *Sport:*
Tor-, Querlatte *f;* '**~·breed** Mischling
m, Kreuzung *f;* **~'coun·try** Querfeld-
ein..., Gelände...; ~ *skiing* Skilanglauf
m; **~ex·am·i'na·tion** Kreuzverhör *n;*
~ex'am·ine ins Kreuzverhör nehmen; '**~eyed:** *be* ~ schielen; '**~·ing**
(*Straßen- etc.*)Kreuzung *f;* Straßen-
übergang *m; Brt.* Fußgängerübergang
m; naut. Überfahrt *f;* '**~·road** *Am.*
Querstraße *f;* '**~·roads** *pl. od. sg.*
(Straßen)Kreuzung *f; fig.* Scheideweg
m; '**~·sec·tion** Querschnitt *m;*
'**~·walk** *Am.* Fußgängerübergang *m;*
'**~·wise** kreuzweise; '**~·word**
(*puz·zle*) Kreuzworträtsel *n*
crotch [krɒtʃ] anat. Schritt *m* (*a. der
Hose*)
crouch [kraʊtʃ] **1.** sich ducken; **2.**
Hockstellung *f*
crow [krəʊ] **1.** *zo.* Krähe *f,* Krähen *n;* **2.**
(crowed *od.* crew, crowed) krähen
'**crow·bar** Brecheisen *n*
crowd [kraʊd] **1.** (Menschen)Menge *f;*
Masse *f;* Haufen *m;* **2.** sich drängen;
Straßen etc. bevölkern; vollstopfen;
'**~ed** überfüllt, voll
crown [kraʊn] **1.** Krone *f;* **2.** krönen;
Zahn überkronen; *to* ~ *it all* zu allem
Überfluß
cru·cial ['kruːʃl] entscheidend, kritisch
cru·ci|·fix ['kruːsɪfɪks] Kruzifix *n;*
~fix·ion [kruːsɪ'fɪkʃn] Kreuzigung *f;*
~fy ['kruːsɪfaɪ] kreuzigen
crude [kruːd] roh, unbearbeitet; *fig.*
roh, grob; ~ (*oil*) Rohöl *n*
cru·el [krʊəl] grausam; roh, gefühllos; '**~·ty** Grausamkeit *f;* ~ *to animals* Tierquälerei *f; society for the
prevention of* ~ *to animals* Tierschutzverein *m;* ~ *to children* Kindesmißhandlung *f*
cru·et [kruːɪt] Essig-, Ölfläschchen *n*
cruise [kruːz] **1.** Kreuzfahrt *f,* Seereise
f; **2.** kreuzen, e-e Kreuzfahrt *od.* Seereise machen; *aviat., mot.* mit Reisege-
schwindigkeit fliegen *od.* fahren; ~
'**mis·sile** *mil.* Marschflugkörper *m;*
'**cruis·er** *mil. naut.* Kreuzer *m;* Kreuz-
fahrtschiff *n; Am.* (Funk)Streifenwa-
gen *m*
crumb [krʌm] Krume *f,* Krümel *m*
crum·ble ['krʌmbl] zerkrümeln, -brök-
keln

crum·ple ['krʌmpl] v/t. zerknittern; v/i. knittern; zusammengedrückt werden; '~ **zone** mot. Knautschzone f

crunch [krʌntʃ] geräuschvoll (zer)kauen; knirschen

cru·sade [kruː'seɪd] Kreuzzug m

crush [krʌʃ] **1.** Gedränge n; bsd. Brt. *Getränk aus ausgepreßten Früchten* (*orange* ~); **have a** ~ **on s.o.** in j-n verknallt sein; **2.** v/t. zerquetschen, -malmen, -drücken; tech. zerkleinern, -mahlen; auspressen; fig. nieder-, zerschmettern, vernichten; v/i. sich drängen; '~ **bar·ri·er** Barriere f, Absperrung f

crust [krʌst] (Brot)Kruste f, (-)Rinde f

crus·ta·cean zo. [krʌ'steɪʃn] Krebs-, Krusten-, Schalentier n

crust·y ['krʌstɪ] (**-ier, -iest**) krustig

crutch [krʌtʃ] Krücke f

cry [kraɪ] **1.** Schrei m, Ruf m; Geschrei n; Weinen n; **2.** schreien, rufen (**for** nach); weinen; heulen, jammern

crypt [krɪpt] Gruft f, Krypta f

crys·tal ['krɪstl] Kristall m; Am. Uhrglas n; '~·**line** ['krɪstəlaɪn] kristallen; '~·**lize** ['krɪstəlaɪz] kristallisieren

CST [siː es 'tiː] Abk. für **Central Standard Time** (amer. Normalzeit)

ct(s) nur geschr. Abk. für **cent(s** pl.) Cent m (od. pl.) (amer. Münze)

cu nur geschr. Abk. für **cubic** Kubik...

cub [kʌb] (Raubtier)Junge(s) n; Wölfling m (Pfadfinder)

cube [kjuːb] Würfel m (a. math.); phot. Blitzwürfel m; math. Kubikzahl f; ~ **'root** math. Kubikwurzel f; '**cu·bic** (~ally), '**cu·bi·cal** würfelförmig; kubisch; Kubik...

cu·bi·cle ['kjuːbɪkl] Kabine f

cuck·oo zo. ['kuku:] (pl. **-oos**) Kuckuck m

cu·cum·ber ['kjuːkʌmbə] Gurke f; (**as**) **cool as a** ~ F eiskalt, kühl u. gelassen

cud [kʌd] wiedergekäutes Futter; **chew the** ~ wiederkäuen; fig. überlegen

cud·dle ['kʌdl] v/t. an sich drücken; schmusen mit; v/i. ~ **up** sich kuscheln od. schmiegen (**to** an acc.)

cud·gel ['kʌdʒəl] **1.** Knüppel m; **2.** (bsd. Brt. -ll-, Am. -l-) prügeln

cue¹ [kjuː] thea. etc., a. fig. Stichwort n; Wink m

cue² [kjuː] Billard: Queue n

cuff¹ [kʌf] Manschette f; (Ärmel-, Am. a. Hosen)Aufschlag m

cuff² [kʌf] **1.** Klaps m; **2.** j-m e-n Klaps geben

'**cuff link** Manschettenknopf m

cui·sine [kwiː'ziːn] Küche f (Kochkunst)

cul·mi·nate ['kʌlmɪneɪt] gipfeln (**in** in dat.)

cu·lottes [kjuː'lɒts] pl. (**a pair of** ein) Hosenrock

cul·prit ['kʌlprɪt] Schuldige(r m) f, Täter(in)

cul·ti·vate ['kʌltɪveɪt] agr. an-, bebauen; kultivieren; Freundschaft etc. pflegen; '~**·vat·ed** agr. bebaut; fig. gebildet, kultiviert; ~**·va·tion** [kʌltɪ'veɪʃn] agr. Kultivierung f, Anbau m; fig. Pflege f

cul·tu·ral ['kʌltʃərəl] kulturell; Kultur...

cul·ture ['kʌltʃə] Kultur f; (Tier)Zucht f; (Pflanzen)Kultur f; '~**d** kultiviert; gezüchtet, Zucht...

cum·ber·some ['kʌmbəsəm] lästig, hinderlich; klobig

cu·mu·la·tive ['kjuːmjʊlətɪv] sich (an-)häufend, anwachsend; Zusatz...

cun·ning ['kʌnɪŋ] **1.** schlau, listig; **2.** List f, Schlauheit f

cup [kʌp] **1.** Tasse f; Becher m; Schale f; Kelch m; Sport: Cup m, Pokal m; **2.** (**-pp-**) die Hand hohl machen; **she** ~**ped her chin in her hand** sie stützte das Kinn in die Hand; ~**'board** ['kʌbəd] (Geschirr-, Speise-, Brt. a. Wäsche-, Kleider)Schrank m; '~**'board bed** Schrankbett n; '~ **fi·nal** Sport: Pokalendspiel n

cu·po·la ['kjuːpələ] Kuppel f

'**cup| tie** Sport: Pokalspiel n; '~ **win·ner** Sport: Pokalsieger m

cur [kɜː] Köter m; Schurke m

cu·ra·ble ['kjʊərəbl] heilbar

cu·rate ['kjʊərət] Hilfsgeistliche(r) m

curb [kɜːb] **1.** Kandare f (a. fig.); bsd. Am. → **kerb(stone)**; **2.** an die Kandare legen (a. fig.); fig. zügeln

curd [kɜːd] a. ~**s** pl. Dickmilch f, Quark m

cur·dle ['kɜːdl] v/t. Milch gerinnen lassen; v/i. gerinnen, dick werden (Milch); **the sight made my blood** ~ bei dem Anblick erstarrte mir das Blut in den Adern

cure [kjʊə] **1.** med. Kur f; med.

(Heil)Mittel n; med. Heilung f; **2.** med. heilen; pökeln; räuchern; trocknen

cur·few mil. ['kɜːfjuː] Ausgangsverbot n, -sperre f

cu·ri·o ['kjʊərɪəʊ] (pl. -os) Rarität f

cu·ri|·os·i·ty [kjʊərɪ'ɒsətɪ] Neugier f; Rarität f; **~ous** ['kjʊərɪəs] neugierig; wißbegierig; seltsam, merkwürdig

curl [kɜːl] **1.** Locke f; **2.** (sich) kräuseln od. locken; '**~·er** Lockenwickler m; '**~·y** (-ier, -iest) gekräuselt; gelockt, lockig

cur·rant ['kʌrənt] bot. Johannisbeere f; Korinthe f

cur·ren|·cy econ. ['kʌrənsɪ] Währung f; **foreign ~** Devisen pl.; '**~t 1.** laufend (Monat, Ausgaben etc.); gegenwärtig, aktuell; üblich; gebräuchlich; **~ events** pl. Tagesereignisse pl.; **2.** Strömung f, Strom m (beide a. fig.); electr. Strom m; '**~t ac·count** Brt. econ. Girokonto n

cur·ric·u·lum [kə'rɪkjʊləm] (pl. -la [-lə], -lums) Lehr-, Stundenplan m; **~ vi·tae** [- 'vaɪtiː] Lebenslauf m

cur·ry¹ ['kʌrɪ] Curry m, n

cur·ry² ['kʌrɪ] Pferd striegeln

curse [kɜːs] **1.** Fluch m; △ nicht Kurs; **2.** (ver)fluchen; **curs·ed** ['kɜːsɪd] verflucht

cur·sor ['kɜːsə] Computer: Cursor m

cur·so·ry ['kɜːsərɪ] flüchtig, oberflächlich

curt [kɜːt] knapp, barsch, schroff

cur·tail [kɜː'teɪl] Ausgaben etc. kürzen; Rechte beschneiden

cur·tain ['kɜːtn] **1.** Vorhang m, Gardine f; **draw the ~s** die Vorhänge auf- od. zuziehen; **2. ~ off** mit Vorhängen abteilen

curt·s(e)y ['kɜːtsɪ] **1.** Knicks m; **2.** knicksen (**to** vor dat.)

cur·va·ture ['kɜːvətʃə] Krümmung f

curve [kɜːv] **1.** Kurve f; Krümmung f, Biegung f; **2.** (sich) krümmen od. biegen

cush·ion ['kʊʃn] **1.** Kissen n, Polster n; **2.** Stoß etc. dämpfen

cuss sl. [kʌs] **1.** Fluch m; **2.** (ver)fluchen

cus·tard bsd. Brt. ['kʌstəd] Eiercreme f, Vanillesoße f

cus·to·dy jur. ['kʌstədɪ] Haft f; Sorgerecht n

cus·tom ['kʌstəm] Brauch m, Gewohnheit f; econ. Kundschaft f; '**~·a·ry** üb-

lich; '**~·built** nach Kundenangaben gefertigt; '**~·er** Kund|e m, -in f, Auftraggeber(in); '**~ house** Zollamt n; **~·'made** maßgefertigt, maß-

cus·toms ['kʌstəmz] pl. Zoll m; '**~ clear·ance** Zollabfertigung f; '**~ of·fi·cer**, '**~ of·fi·cial** Zollbeamte(r) m

cut [kʌt] **1.** Schnitt m; Schnittwunde f; Schnitte f, Stück n (Fleisch); (Zu)Schnitt m (von Kleidung); Schnitt m, Schliff m (von Edelsteinen); Haarschnitt m; Kürzung f, Senkung f; Karten: Abheben n; **cold ~s** pl. bsd. Am. gastr. Aufschnitt m; **2.** (-tt-; cut) schneiden; ab-, an-, auf-, aus-, be-, durch-, zer-, zuschneiden; Edelstein etc. schleifen; Gras mähen; Bäume fällen; Holz hacken; mot. Kurve schneiden; Löhne etc. kürzen; Preise herabsetzen, senken; Karten abheben; j-n beim Begegnen schneiden; **~ one's teeth** Zähne bekommen, zahnen; **~ s.o.** (**dead**) fig. F j-n schneiden; **~ s.o.** od. **s.th. short** j-n od. et. unterbrechen; **~ across** quer durch... gehen (um abzukürzen); **~ back** Pflanze beschneiden, stutzen; **~ down** Bäume fällen; verringern, einschränken, reduzieren; **~ in** F sich einmischen, unterbrechen; **~ in on s.o.** mot. j-n schneiden; **~ off** abschneiden; unterbrechen, trennen; Strom etc. sperren; **~ out** (her)ausschneiden; Kleid etc. zuschneiden; **be ~ out for** wie geschaffen sein für; **~ up** zerschneiden; '**~·back** Kürzung f, Zusammenstreichung f

cute F [kjuːt] (~r, ~st) schlau; Am. niedlich, süß

cu·ti·cle ['kjuːtɪkl] Nagelhaut f

cut·le·ry ['kʌtlərɪ] (Tisch-, Eß)Besteck n

cut·let gastr. ['kʌtlɪt] Kotelett n; (Kalbs-, Schweine)Schnitzel n; Hacksteak n

cut|·'price, **~·'rate** econ. ermäßigt, herabgesetzt; Billig...; '**~·ter** Zuschneider m; (Glas-, Diamant)Schleifer m; tech. Schneidemaschine f, -werkzeug n; Film: Cutter(in); naut. Kutter m; '**~·throat** Mörder m; Killer m; '**~·ting 1.** schneidend; scharf; tech. Schneid(e)...; Fräs...; **2.** Schneiden n; bot. Steckling m; bsd. Brt. (Zeitungs)Ausschnitt m; '**~·tings** pl. Schnipsel pl.; Späne pl.

Cy·ber·space ['saɪbəspeɪs] → *virtual reality*

cy·cle¹ ['saɪkl] Zyklus *m*; Kreis(lauf) *m*

cy·cle² ['saɪkl] **1.** Fahrrad *n*; **2.** radfahren; **~ path** (Fahr)Radweg *m*; **'cycling** Radfahren *n*; **'cy·clist** Radfahrer(in); Motorradfahrer(in)

cy·clone ['saɪkləʊn] Wirbelsturm *m*

cyl·in·der ['sɪlɪndə] Zylinder *m*, *tech. a.*

Walze *f*, Trommel *f*

cyn|·ic ['sɪnɪk] Zyniker(in); **'~·i·cal** zynisch

cy·press *bot.* ['saɪprɪs] Zypresse *f*

cyst *med.* [sɪst] Zyste *f*

czar *hist.* [zɑː] → *tsar*

Czech [tʃek] **1.** tschechisch; **~ Republic** Tschechien *n*, Tschechische Republik; **2.** Tschech|e *m*, -in *f*; *ling.* Tschechisch *n*

D

D, d [diː] D, d *n*

d *nur geschr. Abk. für died* gest., gestorben

DA [diː 'eɪ] *Abk. für District Attorney Am.* Staatsanwalt *m*

dab [dæb] **1.** Klecks *m*, Spritzer *m*; **2.** (*-bb-*) be-, abtupfen

dab·ble ['dæbl] bespritzen; **~ at, ~ in** sich oberflächlich *od.* (*contp.*) in dilettantischer Weise beschäftigen mit

dachs·hund *zo.* ['dækshʊnd] Dackel *m*

dad [dæd], **~·dy** F ['dædɪ] Papa *m*, Vati *m*

dad·dy long·legs *zo.* ['dædɪ 'lɒŋlegz] (*pl. daddy longlegs*) Schnake *f*; *Am.* Weberknecht *m*

daf·fo·dil *bot.* ['dæfədɪl] gelbe Narzisse *f*

daft F [dɑːft] blöde, doof

dag·ger ['dægə] Dolch *m*; **be at ~s drawn** *fig.* auf Kriegsfuß stehen

dai·ly ['deɪlɪ] **1.** täglich; **the ~ grind** *od.* **rut** das tägliche Einerlei; **2.** Tageszeitung *f*; Putzfrau *f*

dain·ty ['deɪntɪ] **1.** (*-ier, -iest*) zierlich, reizend; wählerisch; **2.** Leckerbissen *m*

dair·y ['deərɪ] Molkerei *f*; Milchwirtschaft *f*; Milchgeschäft *n*

dai·sy *bot.* ['deɪzɪ] Gänseblümchen *n*

dale *dial. od. poet.* [deɪl] Tal *n*

dal·ly ['dælɪ]: **~ about** herumtrödeln

Dal·ma·tian *zo.* [dæl'meɪʃn] Dalmatiner *m* (*Hund*)

dam [dæm] **1.** (Stau)Damm *m*; **2.** (*-mm-*) *a.* **~ up** stauen, eindämmen

dam·age ['dæmɪdʒ] **1.** Schaden *m*, (Be)Schädigung *f*; **~s** *pl. jur.* Schaden-

ersatz *m*; **2.** (be)schädigen

dam·ask ['dæməsk] Damast *m*

damn [dæm] **1.** verdammen; verurteilen; **~ (it)!** F verflucht!, verdammt!; **2.** *adj. u. adv.* F → **damned; 3. I don't care a ~** F das ist mir völlig gleich(gültig) *od.* egal; **dam·na·tion** [dæm'neɪʃn] Verdammung *f*; *rel.* Verdammnis *f*; **~ed** F [dæmd] verdammt; **'~·ing** vernichtend, belastend

damp [dæmp] **1.** feucht, klamm; **2.** Feuchtigkeit *f*; **3.** *a.* **'~·en** an-, befeuchten; dämpfen; **'~·ness** Feuchtigkeit *f*

dance [dɑːns] **1.** Tanz *m*; Tanz(veranstaltung) *f m*; **2.** tanzen; **'danc·er** Tänzer(in); **'danc·ing** Tanzen *n*; Tanz...

dan·de·li·on *bot.* ['dændɪlaɪən] Löwenzahn *m*

dan·druff ['dændrʌf] (Kopf)Schuppen *pl.*

Dane [deɪn] Dän|e *m*, -in *f*

dan·ger ['deɪndʒə] Gefahr *f*; **be out of ~** außer Lebensgefahr sein; **'~ ar·e·a** Gefahrenzone *f*, -bereich *m*; **'~·ous** ['deɪndʒərəs] gefährlich; **'~ zone** Gefahrenzone *f*, -bereich *m*

dan·gle ['dæŋgl] baumeln (lassen)

Da·nish ['deɪnɪʃ] **1.** dänisch; **2.** *ling.* Dänisch *n*

dank [dæŋk] feucht, naß(kalt)

dare [deə] *v/i.* es wagen, sich (ge)trauen; **I ~ say** ich glaube wohl; allerdings; **how ~ you!** was fällt dir ein!; untersteh dich!; *v/t. et.* wagen; **'~·dev·il** Draufgänger *m*; **dar·ing** ['deərɪŋ] **1.** kühn; waghalsig; **2.** Mut *m*, Kühnheit *f*

dark [dɑːk] **1.** dunkel; finster; *fig.* düster, trüb(e); geheim(nisvoll); **2.** Dunkel(heit *f*) *n*; **before** (**at, after**) ~ vor (bei, nach) Einbruch der Dunkelheit; **keep s.o. in the ~ about s.th.** j-n über et. im ungewissen lassen; '**2 Ag·es** *pl. das* frühe Mittelalter; '~**en** (sich) verdunkeln *od.* verfinstern; '~**ness** Dunkelheit *f*, Finsternis *f*; '~**room** *phot.* Dunkelkammer *f.*

dar·ling ['dɑːlɪŋ] **1.** Liebling *m*; **2.** lieb; F goldig

darn [dɑːn] stopfen, ausbessern

dart [dɑːt] **1.** Wurfpfeil *m*; Sprung *m*, Satz *m*; ~**s** *sg.* Darts *n* (*Wurfpfeilspiel*); **2.** *v/t.* werfen, schleudern; *v/i.* schießen, stürzen; '~**board** Dartsscheibe *f.*

dash [dæʃ] **1.** Schlag *m*; Klatschen *n* (*von Wellen etc.*); Prise *f* (*Salz etc.*), Schuß *m* (*Rum etc.*), Spritzer *m* (*Zitrone*); Gedankenstrich *m*; *Sport:* Sprint *m*; *fig.* Anflug *m*; **a ~ of blue** ein Stich ins Blaue; **make a ~ for** losstürzen auf (*acc.*); **2.** *v/t.* schleudern, schmettern; *Hoffnung etc.* zerstören, zunichte machen; *v/i.* stürmen; ~ **off** davonstürzen; '~**board** *mot.* Armaturenbrett *n*; '~**ing** schneidig, forsch

da·ta ['deɪtə] *pl.*, *sg.* Daten *pl.*, Angaben *pl.*; *Computer:* Daten *pl.*; ~ **bank**, '~**base** Datenbank *f*; ~ **cap·ture** Datenerfassung *f*; ~ **car·ri·er** Datenträger *m*; ~ **in·put** Dateneingabe *f*; ~ **me·di·um** Datenträger *m*; '**mem·o·ry** Datenspeicher *m*; ~ **out·put** Datenausgabe *f*; ~ **pro·cess·ing** Datenverarbeitung *f*; ~ **pro·tec·tion** Datenschutz *m*; ~ **stor·age** Datenspeicher *m*; ~ **trans·fer** Datenübertragung *f*; ~ **typ·ist** Datentypist(in)

date¹ *bot.* [deɪt] Dattel *f*

date² [deɪt] Datum *n*; Zeit(punkt *m*) *f*; Termin *m*; Verabredung *f*; *Am.* F (Verabredungs)Partner(in); **out of** ~ veraltet, unmodern; **up to** ~ zeitgemäß, modern, auf dem laufenden; **2.** datieren; *Am.* F sich verabreden mit, ausgehen mit, (*regelmäßig*) gehen mit; '**dat·ed** veraltet, überholt

da·tive *gr.* ['deɪtɪv] *a.* ~ **case** Dativ *m*, dritter Fall

daub [dɔːb] (be)schmieren

daugh·ter ['dɔːtə] Tochter *f*; ~**in-law**

['dɔːtərɪnlɔː] (*pl.* **daughters-in-law**) Schwiegertochter *f*

daunt [dɔːnt] entmutigen

daw *zo.* [dɔː] Dohle *f*

daw·dle F ['dɔːdl] (herum)trödeln

dawn [dɔːn] **1.** (Morgen)Dämmerung *f*; **at** ~ bei Tagesanbruch; **2.** dämmern; ~ **on** *fig.* j-m dämmern

day [deɪ] Tag *m*; *oft* ~**s** *pl.* (Lebens)Zeit *f*; **any** ~ jederzeit; **these** ~**s** heutzutage; **the other** ~ neulich; **the** ~ **after tomorrow** übermorgen; **the** ~ **before yesterday** vorgestern; **open all** ~ durchgehend geöffnet; **let's call it a** ~! machen wir Schluß für heute!, Feierabend! '~**break** Tagesanbruch *m*; '~ **care cen·tre** (*Am.* **-ter**) ~ **day nursery**; '~**dream 1.** Tag-, Wachtraum *m*; **2.** (**dreamed** *od.* **dreamt**) (mit offenen Augen) träumen; '~**dream·er** Träumer(in); '~**light** Tageslicht *n*; **in broad** ~ am hellichten Tag; '~ **nur·se·ry** Tagesheim *n*, -stätte *f*; ~ **'off** (*pl.* **days off**) freier Tag; ~ **re'turn** *Brt.* Tagesrückfahrkarte *f*; '~**time:** **in the** ~ am Tag, bei Tage

daze [deɪz] **1.** blenden; betäuben; **2.** **in a** ~ benommen, betäubt

DC [diː'siː] *Abk. für:* **direct current** Gleichstrom *m*; **District of Columbia** Bundesdistrikt der USA (= *Gebiet der amer. Hauptstadt Washington*)

DD [diː'diː] *Abk. für* **double density** doppelte Speicherdichte e-r Diskette

dead [ded] **1.** tot; unempfindlich (**to** für); matt (*Farbe etc.*); blind (*Fenster etc.*); erloschen; *econ.* flau; *econ.* tot (*Kapital etc.*); völlig, total; ~ **stop** völliger Stillstand; **2.** *adv.* völlig, total; plötzlich, abrupt; genau, direkt; ~ **slow** *mot.* Schritt fahren!; ~ **tired** todmüde; **3. the** ~ die Toten *pl.*; **in the** ~ **of winter** im tiefsten Winter; **in the** ~ **of night** mitten in der Nacht; ~ **'bar·gain** Spottpreis *m*; ~ **'cen·tre** (*Am.* **'cen·ter**) genaue Mitte; '~**en** abstumpfen; dämpfen; (ab)schwächen; ~ **'end** Sackgasse *f* (*a. fig.*); ~ **'heat** *Sport:* totes Rennen; '~**line** letzter (Ablieferungs)Termin; Stichtag *m*; '~**lock** *fig.* toter Punkt; '~**locked** *fig.* festgefahren; ~ **'loss** Totalverlust *m*; '~**ly** (**-ier, -iest**) tödlich

deaf [def] **1.** taub; ~ **and dumb** taub-

stumm; **2.** *the* ~ *pl.* die Tauben *pl.*;
'**~·en** taub machen; betäuben

deal [di:l] **1.** F Geschäft *n*, Handel *m*;
Menge *f*; *it's a* ~ abgemacht!; *a good* ~
ziemlich viel; *a great* ~ sehr viel; **2.**
(*dealt*) *v/t.* (aus-, ver-, zu)teilen; *Karten*
geben; *e-n Schlag* versetzen; *v/i.* handeln (*in* mit e-r *Ware*); *sl.* dealen (*mit
Drogen handeln*); *Karten:* geben; ~ *with*
sich befassen mit, behandeln; *econ.*
Handel treiben mit, Geschäfte machen
mit; '**~·er** *econ.* Händler(in); *Karten:*
Geber(in); *sl.* Dealer *m* (*Drogenhänd-
ler*); '**~·ing** Verhalten(sweise *f*) *n*;
'**~·ings** *pl.* Umgang *m*, Beziehungen
pl.; **~t** [delt] *pret. u. p.p. von* deal 2

dean [di:n] Dekan *m*

dear [dɪə] **1.** teuer; lieb; (2 *Sir, in Briefen:*
Sehr geehrter Herr (*Name*); **2.** Liebe-
ste(r *m*) *f*, Schatz *m*; *my* ~ m-e Liebe,
mein Lieber; **3.** *int.* (oh) ~!, ~~!, ~ *me!* F
du liebe Zeit!, ach herrje!; '**~·ly** innig,
von ganzem Herzen; teuer (*im Preis*)

death [deθ] Tod *m*; Todesfall *m*; '**~·bed**
Sterbebett *n*; ~ **cer·tif·i·cate** Toten-
schein *m*; '**~·ly** (*-ier, -iest*) tödlich; '**~**
war·rant *jur.* Hinrichtungsbefehl *m*;
fig. Todesurteil *n*

de·bar [dɪˈbɑ:] (*-rr-*): ~ *from doing s.th.*
j-n hindern et. zu tun

de·base [dɪˈbeɪs] erniedrigen; mindern

de·ba·ta·ble [dɪˈbeɪtəbl] umstritten

de·bate [dɪˈbeɪt] **1.** Debatte *f*, Diskussion *f*; **2.** debattieren, diskutieren

deb·it *econ.* [ˈdebɪt] **1.** Soll *n*; (Konto)Belastung *f*; ~ *and credit* Soll u.
Haben *n*; *j-n, ein Konto* belasten

deb·ris [ˈdebri:] Trümmer *pl.*

debt [det] Schuld *f*; *be in* ~ verschuldet
sein; *be out of* ~ schuldenfrei sein; '**~·or**
Schuldner(in)

de·bug *tech.* [di:ˈbʌg] (*-gg-*) Fehler beseitigen (*a. Computer*)

de·but [ˈdeɪbju:] Debüt *n*

Dec *nur geschr. Abk. für December*
Dez., Dezember *m*

dec·ade [ˈdekeɪd] Jahrzehnt *n*

dec·a·dent [ˈdekədənt] dekadent

de·caf·fein·at·ed [di:ˈkæfɪneɪtɪd] kof-
feinfrei

de·camp F [dɪˈkæmp] verschwinden

de·cant [dɪˈkænt] abgießen; umfüllen;
~**·er** Karaffe *f*

de·cath·lete [dɪˈkæθli:t] *Sport:* Zehn-

kämpfer *m*; ~**·lon** [dɪˈkæθlɒn] *Sport:*
Zehnkampf *m*

de·cay [dɪˈkeɪ] **1.** zerfallen; verfaulen;
kariös *od.* schlecht werden (*Zahn*); **2.**
Zerfall *m*; Verfaulen *n*

de·cease *bsd. jur.* [dɪˈsi:s] Tod *m*, Able-
ben *n*; ~**d** *bsd. jur.* **1.** *the* ~ der *od.* die
Verstorbene; die Verstorbenen *pl.*; **2.**
verstorben

de·ceit [dɪˈsi:t] Betrug *m*; Täuschung *f*;
~**·ful** betrügerisch

de·ceive [dɪˈsi:v] betrügen; täuschen;
de·ceiv·er Betrüger(in)

De·cem·ber [dɪˈsembə] (*Abk. Dec*) Dezember *m*

de·cen·cy [ˈdi:snsɪ] Anstand *m*; '**~·t** anständig; F annehmbar, (ganz) anstän-
dig; F nett; △ *nicht* dezent

de·cep·tion [dɪˈsepʃn] Täuschung *f*;
~**·tive:** *be* ~ täuschen, trügen (*Sache*)

de·cide [dɪˈsaɪd] (sich) entscheiden; bestimmen, beschließen, sich entschließen; **de·cid·ed** entschieden, bestimmt; entschlossen

dec·i·mal [ˈdesɪml] *a.* ~ *fraction* Dezi-
malbruch *m*; Dezimal...

de·ci·pher [dɪˈsaɪfə] entziffern

de·ci·sion [dɪˈsɪʒn] Entscheidung *f*;
Entschluß *m*; Entschlossenheit *f*; *make
a* ~ e-e Entscheidung treffen; *reach od.*
come to a ~ zu e-m Entschluß kommen; ~**·sive** [dɪˈsaɪsɪv] entscheidend;
ausschlaggebend; entschieden

deck [dek] **1.** *naut.* Deck *n* (*a. e-s Bus-
ses*); *Am.* Spiel *n*, Pack *m* (Spiel)Kar-
ten; **2.** ~ *out* schmücken; '**~·chair** Lie-
gestuhl *m*

dec·la·ra·tion [deklə'reɪʃn] Erklärung
f; Zollerklärung *f*

de·clare [dɪˈkleə] erklären; deklarieren,
verzollen

de·clen·sion *gr.* [dɪˈklenʃn] Deklinati-
on *f*

de·cline [dɪˈklaɪn] **1.** abnehmen, zurückgehen; fallen (*Preise*); verfallen;
(höflich) ablehnen; *gr.* deklinieren; **2.**
Abnahme *f*, Rückgang *m*, Verfall *m*

de·cliv·i·ty [dɪˈklɪvətɪ] (Ab)Hang *m*

de·clutch *mot.* [di:ˈklʌtʃ] auskuppeln

de·code [di:ˈkəʊd] entschlüsseln

de·com·pose [di:kəmˈpəʊz] zerlegen;
(sich) zersetzen; verwesen

de·con·tam·i·nate [di:kənˈtæmɪneɪt]
entgasen, -giften, -seuchen, -strahlen;

~'na·tion Entsorgung f (*bei Radioaktivität*)

dec·o·rate ['dekərət] verzieren, schmücken; tapezieren; (an)streichen; dekorieren; **~ra·tion** [dekə'reɪʃn] Verzierung f, Schmuck m, Dekoration f; Orden m; **~ra·tive** ['dekərətɪv] dekorativ; Zier...; **~ra·tor** ['dekəreɪtə] Dekorateur m; Maler m u. Tapezierer m

dec·o·rous ['dekərəs] anständig; **de·co·rum** [dɪ'kɔːrəm] Anstand m

de·coy 1. ['diːkɔɪ] Lockvogel m (*a. fig.*); Köder m (*a. fig.*); **2.** [dɪ'kɔɪ] ködern; locken (*into* in *acc.*); verleiten (*into* zu)

de·crease 1. ['diːkriːs] Abnahme f; **2.** [diː'kriːs] abnehmen; (sich) vermindern

de·cree [dɪ'kriː] **1.** Dekret n, Erlaß m, Verfügung f; *bsd. Am. jur.* Entscheid m, Urteil n; **2.** verfügen

ded·i·cate ['dedɪkeɪt] widmen; '**~·cat·ed** engagiert; **~ca·tion** [dedɪ'keɪʃn] Widmung f; Hingabe f

de·duce [dɪ'djuːs] ableiten; folgern

de·duct [dɪ'dʌkt] *Betrag* abziehen (*from* von); **~·i·ble:** **~** *from tax* steuerlich absetzbar; **de·duc·tion** [dɪ'dʌkʃn] Abzug m (*-e-s Betrages*); (Schluß)Folgerung f, Schluß m

deed [diːd] Tat f; Heldentat f; *jur.* (Übertragungs)Urkunde f

deep [diːp] **1.** tief u. (fig.); **2.** Tiefe f; '**~·en** (sich) vertiefen, *fig. a.* (sich) verstärken; **~'freeze 1.** (*-froze, -frozen*) tiefkühlen, einfrieren; **2.** Tiefkühl-, Gefriergerät n; **~'fro·zen** tiefgefroren; **~'fry** fritieren; '**~·ness** Tiefe f

deer *zo.* [dɪə] (*pl.* deer) Hirsch m; Reh n

de·face [dɪ'feɪs] entstellen; unleserlich machen; ausstreichen

def·a·ma·tion [defə'meɪʃn] Verleumdung f

de·fault [dɪ'fɔːlt] **1.** *jur.* Nichterscheinen n vor Gericht; *Sport:* Nichtantreten n; *econ.* Verzug m; **2.** s-n Verpflichtungen nicht nachkommen, *econ. a.* im Verzug sein; *jur.* nicht vor Gericht erscheinen; *Sport:* nicht antreten

de·feat [dɪ'fiːt] **1.** Niederlage f; **2.** besiegen, schlagen; vereiteln, zunichte machen

de·fect [dɪ'fekt] Defekt m, Fehler m; Mangel m; **de'fec·tive** mangelhaft; schadhaft, defekt

de·fence *Brt.*, **de·fense** *Am.* [dɪ'fens]

Verteidigung f (*a. mil., jur., Sport*), Schutz m; *Sport:* Abwehr f; **witness for the ~** Entlastungszeuge m; **~·less** schutz-, wehrlos

de·fend [dɪ'fend] (*from, against*) verteidigen (gegen), schützen (vor *dat.*, gegen); **de'fen·dant** Angeklagte(r m) f; Beklagte(r m) f; **de'fend·er** Verteidiger(in); *Sport:* Abwehrspieler(in)

de·fen·sive [dɪ'fensɪv] **1.** Defensive f, Abwehr f; **2.** defensiv; Verteidigungs..., Abwehr...

de·fer [dɪ'fɜː] (*-rr-*) auf-, verschieben

de·fi·ance [dɪ'faɪəns] Herausforderung f; Trotz m; **~·ant** herausfordernd; trotzig

de·fi·cien·cy [dɪ'fɪʃnsɪ] Unzulänglichkeit f; Mangel m; **~t** mangelhaft, unzureichend

def·i·cit *econ.* ['defɪsɪt] Defizit n, Fehlbetrag m

de·file¹ [dɪ'faɪl] enger (Gebirgs)Paß m

de·file² [dɪ'faɪl] beschmutzen

de·fine [dɪ'faɪn] definieren; erklären, bestimmen; **def·i·nite** ['defɪnɪt] bestimmt; endgültig, definitiv; **def·i·ni·tion** [defɪ'nɪʃn] Definition f, Bestimmung f, Erklärung f; **de·fin·i·tive** [dɪ'fɪnɪtɪv] endgültig, definitiv

de·flect [dɪ'flekt] *v/t.* ablenken; *Ball* abfälschen; *v/i.* abweichen

de·form [dɪ'fɔːm] entstellen, verunstalten; **~ed** deformiert, verunstaltet; verwachsen; **de·for·mi·ty** [dɪ'fɔːmətɪ] Mißbildung f

de·fraud [dɪ'frɔːd] betrügen (*of* um)

de·frost [diː'frɒst] *v/t.* Windschutzscheibe *etc.* entfrosten; *Kühlschrank etc.* abtauen, *Tiefkühlkost etc.* auftauen; *v/i.* ab-, auftauen

deft [deft] geschickt, gewandt

de·fy [dɪ'faɪ] herausfordern; trotzen (*dat.*)

de·gen·e·rate 1. [dɪ'dʒenəreɪt] entarten; **2.** [dɪ'dʒenərət] entartet

deg·ra·da·tion [degrə'deɪʃn] Erniedrigung f; **de·grade** [dɪ'greɪd] *v/t.* erniedrigen, demütigen

de·gree [dɪ'griː] Grad m; Stufe f; (akademischer) Grad; **by ~s** allmählich; **take one's ~** e-n akademischen Grad erwerben, promovieren

de·hy·drat·ed [diː'haɪdreɪtɪd] Trocken...

dent

de·i·fy ['di:ıfaı] vergöttern; vergöttlichen

deign [deın] sich herablassen

de·i·ty ['di:ıtı] Gottheit f

de·jec·ted [dı'dʒektıd] niedergeschlagen, mutlos, deprimiert; **~·tion** [dı'dʒekʃn] Niedergeschlagenheit f

de·lay [dı'leı] **1.** Aufschub m; Verzögerung f; rail. etc. Verspätung f; **2.** ver-, aufschieben; verzögern; aufhalten; be ~ed sich verzögern; rail. etc. Verspätung haben

del·e·gate 1. ['delıgeıt] abordnen, delegieren; Vollmachten etc. übertragen; **2.** ['delıgət] Delegierte m, bevollmächtigter Vertreter; **~·ga·tion** [delı'geıʃn] Übertragung f; Abordnung f, Delegation f

de·lete [dı'li:t] (aus)streichen; Computer: löschen

de·lib·e·rate [dı'lıbərət] absichtlich, vorsätzlich; bedächtig, besonnen; **~·ra·tion** [dılıbə'reıʃn] Überlegung f; Beratung f; Bedächtigkeit f

del·i·ca·cy ['delıkəsı] Delikatesse f, Leckerbissen m; Zartheit f; Feingefühl n, Takt m; **~·cate** ['delıkət] delikat, schmackhaft; zart; fein; zierlich; zerbrechlich; delikat, heikel; empfindlich; **~·ca·tes·sen** [delıkə'tesn] Delikatessen pl., Feinkost f; Feinkostgeschäft n

de·li·cious [dı'lıʃəs] köstlich

de·light [dı'laıt] **1.** Vergnügen n, Entzücken n; **2.** entzücken, erfreuen; ~ in (große) Freude haben an (dat.); **~·ful** entzückend

de·lin·quen·cy [dı'lıŋkwənsı] Kriminalität f; **~·t 1.** straffällig; **2.** Straffällige(r m) f; → juvenile 1

de·lir·i·ous med. [dı'lırıəs] im Delirium, phantasierend; **~·um** [dı'lırıəm] Delirium n

de·liv·er [dı'lıvə] aus-, (ab)liefern; Briefe zustellen; Rede etc. halten; befreien, erlösen; be ~ed of med. entbunden werden von; **~·ance** [dı'lıvərəns] Befreiung f; **~·er** [dı'lıvərə] Befreier(in); **~·y** [dı'lıvərı] (Ab-, Aus)Lieferung f; post Zustellung f; Halten n (e-r Rede); Vortrag(sweise f) m, med. Entbindung f; **~·y van** Brt. Lieferwagen m

dell [del] kleines Tal

de·lude [dı'lu:d] täuschen

del·uge ['delju:dʒ] Überschwemmung f; fig. Flut f

de·lu·sion [dı'lu:ʒn] Täuschung f; Wahn(vorstellung f) m

de·mand [dı'ma:nd] **1.** Forderung f (for nach); Anforderung f (on an acc.); Nachfrage f (for nach), Bedarf m (for an dat.); on ~ auf Verlangen; **2.** verlangen, fordern; (fordernd) fragen nach; erfordern; **~·ing** anspruchsvoll

de·ment·ed [dı'mentıd] wahnsinnig

dem·i... ['demı] Halb..., halb...

de·mil·i·ta·rize [di:'mılıtəraız] entmilitarisieren

dem·o F ['deməʊ] (pl. -os) Demo f (Demonstration)

de·mo·bi·lize [di:'məʊbılaız] demobilisieren

de·moc·ra·cy [dı'mɒkrəsı] Demokratie f

dem·o·crat ['deməkræt] Demokrat(in); **~·ic** [demə'krætık] (~ally) demokratisch

de·mol·ish [dı'mɒlıʃ] demolieren; ab-, ein-, niederreißen; zerstören; **dem·o·li·tion** [demə'lıʃn] Demolierung f; Niederreißen n, Abbruch m

de·mon ['di:mən] Dämon m; Teufel m

dem·on·strate ['demənstreıt] demonstrieren; beweisen; zeigen; vorführen; **~·stra·tion** [demən'streıʃn] Demonstration f, Kundgebung f; Demonstration f, Vorführung f; **de·mon·stra·tive** [dı'mɒnstrətıv]: be ~ s-e Gefühle (offen) zeigen; **~·stra·tor** ['demənstreıtə] Demonstrant(in); Vorführer(in)

de·mor·al·ize [dı'mɒrəlaız] demoralisieren

de·mote [di:'məʊt] degradieren

de·mure [dı'mjʊə] ernst, zurückhaltend

den [den] Höhle f (a. fig.); F Bude f

de·ni·al [dı'naıəl] Ablehnung f; Leugnen n; official ~ Dementi n

den·ims ['denımz] pl. Jeans pl.

Den·mark ['denma:k] Dänemark n

de·nom·i·na·tion [dınɒmı'neıʃn] rel. Konfession f; econ. Nennwert m

de·note [dı'nəʊt] bezeichnen; bedeuten

de·nounce [dı'naʊns] (öffentlich) anprangern

dense [dens] (~r, ~st) dicht; fig. beschränkt, begriffsstutzig; **den·si·ty** ['densətı] Dichte f

dent [dent] **1.** Beule f, Delle f; **2.** ver-, einbeulen

den·tal ['dentl] Zahn...; ~ **'plaque**
Zahnbelag m; ~ **'plate** (Zahn)Prothese
f; ~ **'sur·geon** Zahnarzt m, -ärztin f
den·tist ['dentɪst] Zahnarzt m, -ärztin f
den·tures ['dentʃəz] pl. (künstliches)
Gebiß, (Zahn)Prothese f
de·nun·ci·a·tion [dɪnʌnsɪ'eɪʃn] De-
nunziation f; ~**tor** [dɪ'nʌnsɪeɪtə] De-
nunziant(in)
de·ny [dɪ'naɪ] ab-, bestreiten, dementie-
ren, (ab)leugnen; j-m et. verweigern,
abschlagen
de·o·do·rant [diː'əʊdərənt] De(s)odo-
rant n, Deo n
dep nur geschr. Abk. für: **depart** abfahren; **departure** Abf., Abfahrt f
de·part [dɪ'pɑːt] abreisen; abfahren, abfliegen; abweichen (**from** von)
de·part·ment [dɪ'pɑːtmənt] Abteilung
f, univ. a. Fachbereich m; pol. Ministerium n; 2 **of De'fense** Am. Verteidi-
gungsministerium n; 2 **of the En'vi-
ron·ment** Brt. Umweltministerium n;
2 **of the In'te·ri·or** Am. Innenministerium; 2 **of 'State** Am. a. **State** 2 Am.
Außenministerium n; ~ **store** Kauf-,
Warenhaus n
de·par·ture [dɪ'pɑːtʃə] Abreise f; rail.
etc. Abfahrt f, aviat. Abflug m; Abweichung f, ~**s** pl. ˌAbfahrt' (Fahrplan
etc.); ~ **gate** aviat. Flugsteig m; ~
lounge aviat. Abflughalle f
de·pend [dɪ'pend]: ~ **on** sich verlassen
auf (acc.); abhängen von, angewiesen
sein auf (acc.); **that** ~**s** das kommt
(ganz) darauf an
de·pen·da·ble [dɪ'pendəbl] zuverlässig; ~**dant** (Familien)Angehörige(r m)
f; ~**dence** Abhängigkeit f; Vertrauen
n; ~**dent 1.** (**on**) abhängig (von); angewiesen (auf acc.); **2.** → **dependant**
de·plor·a·ble [dɪ'plɔːrəbl] bedauerlich,
beklagenswert; ~**e** [dɪ'plɔː] beklagen,
bedauern
de·pop·u·late [diː'pɒpjʊleɪt] entvölkern
de·port [dɪ'pɔːt] ausweisen, Ausländer a.
abschieben; deportieren
de·pose [dɪ'pəʊz] j-n absetzen; jur. unter Eid erklären
de·pos·it [dɪ'pɒzɪt] **1.** absetzen, abstellen; chem., geol. (sich) ablagern od. absetzen; deponieren, hinterlegen; econ.
Betrag anzahlen; **2.** chem. Ablagerung
f, geol. a. (Erz- etc.)Lager n; Deponie-

rung f, Hinterlegung f; econ. Anzahlung f; **make a** ~ e-e Anzahlung leisten
(**on** für); ~ **ac·count** bsd. Brt. Termin-
einlagekonto n; ~**i·tor** Einzahler(in)
dep·ot ['depəʊ] Depot n; Am. ['diːpəʊ]
Bahnhof m
de·prave [dɪ'preɪv] moralisch verderben
de·pre·ci·ate [dɪ'priːʃɪeɪt] an Wert verlieren
de·press [dɪ'pres] (nieder)drücken; de-
primieren, bedrücken; ~**ed** deprimiert,
niedergeschlagen; econ. flau (Markt
etc.), notleidend (Industrie); ~**ed
ar·e·a** econ. Notstandsgebiet n; ~**ing**
deprimierend, bedrückend; **de·pres-
sion** [dɪ'preʃn] Depression f, Niedergeschlagenheit f; econ. Depression f,
Flaute f, Senke f, Vertiefung f; meteor.
Tief(druckgebiet) n
de·prive [dɪ'praɪv]: ~ **s.o. of s.th.** j-m et.
entziehen od. nehmen; ~**d** benachteiligt
dept, Dept nur geschr. Abk. für **department** Abt., Abteilung f
depth [depθ] Tiefe f; Tiefen...
dep·u·ta·tion [depjʊ'teɪʃn] Abordnung
f; ~**tize** ['depjʊtaɪz]: ~ **for s.o.** j-n vertreten; ~**ty** [depjʊtɪ] (Stell)Vertre-
ter(in); parl. Abgeordnete(r m) f; a. ~
sheriff Am. Hilfssheriff m
de·rail rail. [dɪ'reɪl]: **be** ~**ed** entgleisen
de·ranged [dɪ'reɪndʒd] geistesgestört
der·e·lict ['derəlɪkt] heruntergekommen, baufällig
de·ride [dɪ'raɪd] verhöhnen, -spotten;
de·ri·sion [dɪ'rɪʒn] Hohn m, Spott m;
de·ri·sive [dɪ'raɪsɪv] höhnisch, spöttisch
de·rive [dɪ'raɪv] herleiten (**from** von);
(sich) ableiten (**from** von); abstammen
(**from** von); ~ **pleasure from** Freude
finden od. haben an (dat.)
der·ma·tol·o·gist [dɜːmə'tɒlədʒɪst]
Dermatologe m, Hautarzt m
de·rog·a·to·ry [dɪ'rɒgətərɪ] abfällig, ge-
ringschätzig
der·rick ['derɪk] tech. Derrickkran m;
naut. Ladebaum m; Bohrturm m
de·scend [dɪ'send] (her-, hin)absteigen,
herunter-, hinuntersteigen, -gehen,
-kommen; aviat. niedergehen; abstammen, herkommen (**from** von); ~ **on** herfallen über (acc.); überfallen (acc.) (Besuch etc.); **de'scen·dant** Nachkomme m

de·scent [dɪ'sent] Herab-, Hinuntersteigen n, -gehen n; aviat. Niedergehen n; Gefälle n; Abstammung f, Herkunft f

de·scribe [dɪ'skraɪb] beschreiben

de·scrip·tion [dɪ'skrɪpʃn] Beschreibung f, Schilderung f; Art f, Sorte f; **~tive** [dɪ'skrɪptɪv] beschreibend; anschaulich

des·e·crate ['desɪkreɪt] entweihen

de·seg·re·gate [diː'segrɪgeɪt] die Rassentrennung aufheben in (dat.); **~ga·tion** [diːsegrɪ'geɪʃn] Aufhebung f der Rassentrennung

des·ert¹ ['dezət] Wüste f; Wüsten...

de·sert² [dɪ'zɜːt] v/t. verlassen, im Stich lassen; v/i. mil. desertieren; **~er** mil. Deserteur m; **de·ser·tion** [dɪ'zɜːʃn] (jur. a. böswilliges) Verlassen; mil. Fahnenflucht f

de·serve [dɪ'zɜːv] verdienen; **de·serv·ed·ly** [dɪ'zɜːvɪdlɪ] verdientermaßen; **de'serv·ing** verdienstvoll

de·sign [dɪ'zaɪn] **1.** Design n, Entwurf m, (tech. Konstruktions)Zeichnung f; Design n, Muster n; (a. böse)Absicht; **2.** entwerfen, tech. konstruieren; gestalten; ausdenken; bestimmen, vorsehen (for für)

des·ig·nate ['dezɪgneɪt] et. od. j-n bestimmen

de·sign·er [dɪ'zaɪnə] Designer(in); tech. Konstrukteur m; (Mode)Schöpfer(in)

de·sir·a·ble [dɪ'zaɪərəbl] wünschenswert, erwünscht; begehrenswert; **~e** [dɪ'zaɪə] **1.** Wunsch m, Verlangen n, Begierde f (for nach); **2.** wünschen; begehren

de·sist [dɪ'zɪst] Abstand nehmen (from von)

desk [desk] Schreibtisch m; Pult n; Empfang m, Rezeption f (im Hotel); (Informations)Schalter m; **~top com·'put·er** Desktop Computer m, Tischcomputer m, -rechner m; **~top pub·lish·ing** (abbr. DTP) Computer: Desktop publishing n

des·o·late ['desələt] einsam, verlassen; trostlos

de·spair [dɪ'speə] **1.** Verzweiflung f; **2.** verzweifeln (of an dat.); **~ing** [dɪ'speərɪŋ] verzweifelt

de·spatch [dɪ'spætʃ] → dispatch

des·per·ate ['despərət] verzweifelt; F

hoffnungslos, schrecklich; **~a·tion** [despə'reɪʃn] Verzweiflung f

des·pic·a·ble [dɪ'spɪkəbl] verachtenswert, verabscheuungswürdig

de·spise [dɪ'spaɪz] verachten

de·spite [dɪ'spaɪt] trotz (gen.)

de·spon·dent [dɪ'spondənt] mutlos, verzagt

des·pot ['despɒt] Despot m, Tyrann m

des·sert [dɪ'zɜːt] Nachtisch m, Dessert n; Dessert...

des·ti·na·tion [destɪ'neɪʃn] Bestimmung(sort m) f; **~tined** ['destɪnd] bestimmt; unterwegs (for nach) (Schiff etc.); **~ti·ny** ['destɪnɪ] Schicksal n

des·ti·tute ['destɪtjuːt] mittellos

de·stroy [dɪ'strɔɪ] zerstören, vernichten; Tier töten, einschläfern; **~er** Zerstörer(in); naut., mil. Zerstörer m

de·struc·tion [dɪ'strʌkʃn] Zerstörung f, Vernichtung f; **~tive** [dɪ'strʌktɪv] zerstörend, vernichtend; zerstörerisch

de·tach [dɪ'tætʃ] (ab-, los)trennen, (los)lösen; **~ed** einzeln, frei-, alleinstehend; unvoreingenommen; distanziert; **~ house** Einzelhaus n; **~ment** (Los)Lösung f, (Ab)Trennung f; mil. (Sonder)Kommando n

de·tail ['diːteɪl] **1.** Detail n, Einzelheit f; mil. (Sonder)Kommando n; in **~** ausführlich; **2.** genau schildern; mil. abkommandieren; **~ed** detailliert, ausführlich

de·tain [dɪ'teɪn] aufhalten; jur. in (Untersuchungs)Haft behalten

de·tect [dɪ'tekt] entdecken, (heraus)finden; **de·tec·tion** [dɪ'tekʃn] Entdeckung f; **de·tec·tive** [dɪ'tektɪv] Kriminalbeamte(r) m, Detektiv m; **de'tec·tive nov·el**, **de'tec·tive sto·ry** Kriminalroman m

de·ten·tion [dɪ'tenʃn] jur. Haft f; Nachsitzen n (Schule)

de·ter [dɪ'tɜː] (-rr-) abschrecken (from von)

de·ter·gent [dɪ'tɜːdʒənt] Reinigungs-, Wasch-, Geschirrspülmittel n

de·te·ri·o·rate [dɪ'tɪərɪəreɪt] (sich) verschlechtern; verderben

de·ter·mi·na·tion [dɪtɜːmɪ'neɪʃn] Entschlossenheit f, Bestimmtheit f; Entschluß m; Feststellung f, Ermittlung f; **~mine** [dɪ'tɜːmɪn] et. beschließen, bestimmen; feststellen, ermitteln; (sich) entscheiden; sich entschließen; **~·mined** entschlossen

de·ter|·rence [dɪ'terəns] Abschreckung f; **~·rent 1.** abschreckend; **2.** Abschreckungsmittel n

de·test [dɪ'test] verabscheuen

de·throne [dɪ'θrəʊn] entthronen

de·to·nate ['detəneɪt] v/t. zünden; v/i. detonieren, explodieren

de·tour ['diːtʊə] Umweg m; Umleitung f

de·tract [dɪ'trækt]: **~ from** ablenken von; schmälern (acc.)

de·tri·ment ['detrɪmənt] Nachteil m, Schaden m

deuce [djuːs] Kartenspiel, Würfeln: Zwei f; Tennis: Einstand m

de·val·u·a·tion [diːvælju'eɪʃn] Abwertung f; **~e** [diː'væljuː] abwerten

dev·a·state ['devəsteɪt] verwüsten; **~·stat·ing** verheerend, -nichtend; F umwerfend, toll

de·vel·op [dɪ'veləp] (sich) entwickeln; Naturschätze, Bauland erschließen, Altstadt etc. sanieren; **~·er** phot. Entwickler m; (Stadt)Planer m; **~·ing** Entwicklungs...; **~·ing 'coun·try, ~·ing 'na·tion** Entwicklungsland n; **~·ment** Entwicklung f; Erschließung f, Sanierung f

de·vi|·ate ['diːvɪeɪt] abweichen (from von); **~·a·tion** [diːvɪ'eɪʃn] Abweichung f

de·vice [dɪ'vaɪs] Vorrichtung f, Gerät n; Plan m, Trick m; **leave s.o. to his own ~s** j-n sich selbst überlassen

dev·il ['devl] Teufel m (a. fig.); '**~·ish** teuflisch

de·vi·ous ['diːvjəs] abwegig; gewunden; unaufrichtig; **~ route** Umweg m

de·vise [dɪ'vaɪz] (sich) ausdenken

de·void [dɪ'vɔɪd]: **~ of** ohne (acc.)

de·vote [dɪ'vəʊt] widmen (to dat.); △ nicht devot; **de·'vot·ed** ergeben; hingebungsvoll; eifrig, begeistert; **dev·o·tee** [devəʊ'tiː] begeisterter Anhänger; **de·vo·tion** [dɪ'vəʊʃn] Ergebenheit f; Hingabe f; Frömmigkeit f, Andacht f

de·vour [dɪ'vaʊə] verschlingen

de·vout [dɪ'vaʊt] fromm; sehnlichst, innig

dew [djuː] Tau m; '**~·drop** Tautropfen m; '**~·y** (-ier, -iest) taufeucht, -frisch

dex·ter·i·ty [dek'sterətɪ] Gewandtheit

f; **~·ter·ous, ~·trous** ['dekstrəs] gewandt

di·ag|·nose ['daɪəgnəʊz] diagnostizieren; **~·no·sis** [daɪəg'nəʊsɪs] (pl. -ses [-siːz]) Diagnose f

di·ag·o·nal [daɪ'ægənl] **1.** diagonal: **2.** Diagonale f

di·a·gram ['daɪəgræm] Diagramm n, graphische Darstellung

di·al ['daɪəl] **1.** Zifferblatt n; tel. Wählscheibe f; tech. Skala f; **2.** (bsd. Brt. -ll-, Am. -l-) tel. wählen; **~ direct** durchwählen (to nach); **direct ~(l)ing** Durchwahl f

di·a·lect ['daɪəlekt] Dialekt m, Mundart f

'**di·al·ling code** Brt. tel. Vorwahl(nummer) f

di·a·logue Brt., **di·a·log** Am. ['daɪəlɒg] Dialog m, Gespräch n

di·am·e·ter [daɪ'æmɪtə] Durchmesser m; **in ~** im Durchmesser

di·a·mond ['daɪəmənd] Diamant m; Raute f, Rhombus m; Kartenspiel: Karo n

di·a·per Am. ['daɪəpə] Windel f

di·a·phragm ['daɪəfræm] anat. Zwerchfell n; opt. Blende f; tel. Membran(e) f

di·ar·rh(o)e·a med. [daɪə'rɪə] Durchfall m

di·a·ry ['daɪərɪ] Tagebuch n

dice [daɪs] **1.** pl. von **die²**; (pl. **dice**) Würfel m; **2.** gastr. in Würfel schneiden; würfeln

dick Am. sl. [dɪk] Schnüffler m (Detektiv)

'**dick·y·bird** ['dɪkɪbɜːd] Piepvögelchen n

dic|·tate [dɪk'teɪt] diktieren; fig. vorschreiben; **~·ta·tion** [dɪk'teɪʃn] Diktat n

dic·ta·tor [dɪk'teɪtə] Diktator m; **~·ship** Diktatur f

dic·tion ['dɪkʃn] Ausdrucksweise f, Stil m

dic·tion·a·ry ['dɪkʃnrɪ] Wörterbuch n

did [dɪd] pret. von **do**

die¹ [daɪ] sterben; eingehen, verenden; **~ of hunger** verhungern; **~ of thirst** verdursten; **~ away** sich legen (Wind); verklingen (Ton); **~ down** nachlassen; herunterbrennen; schwächer werden; **~ out** aussterben (a. fig.)

die² Am. [daɪ] (pl. **dice**) Würfel m

di·et ['daɪət] **1.** Diät f; Nahrung f, Kost

f; **be on a ~** diät leben; **2.** diät leben

dif·fer ['dɪfə] sich unterscheiden; anderer Meinung sein (**with, from** als); abweichen

dif·fe|·rence ['dɪfrəns] Unterschied m; Differenz f; Meinungsverschiedenheit f; '**~·rent** verschieden; andere(r, -s); anders (**from** als); **~·ren·ti·ate** [dɪfə-'renʃɪeɪt] (sich) unterscheiden

dif·fi|·cult ['dɪfɪkəlt] schwierig; '**~·cul·ty** Schwierigkeit f

dif·fi|·dence ['dɪfɪdəns] Schüchternheit f; '**~·dent** schüchtern

dif·fuse 1. fig. [dɪ'fjuːz] verbreiten; **2.** [dɪ'fjuːs] diffus; zerstreut (bsd. Licht); weitschweifig; **~·fu·sion** chem., phys. [dɪ'fjuːʒn] (Zer)Streuung f

dig [dɪg] **1.** (-gg-; dug) graben; ~ (**up**) umgraben; ~ (**up** od. **out**) ausgraben (a. fig.); ~ **s.o. in the ribs** j-m e-n Rippenstoß geben; **2.** F Puff m, Stoß m; **~s** pl. Brt. F Bude f

di·gest 1. [dɪ'dʒest] verdauen; ~ **well** leicht verdaulich sein; **2.** ['daɪdʒest] Abriß m; Auslese f, Auswahl f; **~·i·ble** [dɪ'dʒestəbl] verdaulich; **di·ges·tion** [dɪ'dʒestʃən] Verdauung f; **di·ges·tive** [dɪ'dʒestɪv] verdauungsfördernd; Verdauungs...

dig·ger ['dɪgə] (bsd. Gold)Gräber m

dig·it ['dɪdʒɪt] Ziffer f; **three-~ number** dreistellige Zahl

dig·i·tal ['dɪdʒɪtl] digital, Digital...; ~ **'clock, ~ 'watch** Digitaluhr f

dig·ni|·fied ['dɪgnɪfaɪd] würdevoll, würdig; **~·ta·ry** ['dɪgnɪtərɪ] Würdenträger(in); **~·ty** ['dɪgnɪtɪ] Würde f

di·gress [daɪ'gres] abschweifen

dike¹ [daɪk] **1.** Deich m, Damm m; Graben m; **2.** eindeichen, -dämmen

dike² sl. [daɪk] Lesbe f (Lesbierin)

di·lap·i·dat·ed [dɪ'læpɪdeɪtɪd] verfallen, baufällig, klapp(e)rig

di·late [daɪ'leɪt] (sich) ausdehnen od. (aus)weiten; **Augen** weit öffnen; **dil·a·to·ry** ['dɪlətərɪ] verzögernd, hinhaltend; langsam

dil·i|·gence ['dɪlɪdʒəns] Fleiß m; '**~·gent** fleißig, emsig

di·lute [daɪ'ljuːt] **1.** verdünnen; verwässern; **2.** verdünnt

dim [dɪm] **1.** (-mm-) (halb)dunkel, düster; undeutlich, verschwommen; schwach, trüb(e) (Licht); **2.** (sich) verdunkeln od. verdüstern; (sich) trüben; undeutlich werden; **~ one's headlights** Am. mot. abblenden

dime Am. [daɪm] Zehncentstück n

di·men·sion [dɪ'menʃn] Dimension f, Maß n, Abmessung f; **~s** pl. a. Ausmaß n; **~·al** [dɪ'menʃənl] in Zssgn ...dimensional

di·min·ish [dɪ'mɪnɪʃ] (sich) vermindern od. verringern

di·min·u·tive [dɪ'mɪnjʊtɪv] klein, winzig

dim·ple ['dɪmpl] Grübchen n

din [dɪn] Getöse n, Lärm m

dine [daɪn] essen, speisen; ~ **in** od. **out** zu Hause od. auswärts essen; '**din·er** Speisende(r m) f; Gast m (im Restaurant); Am. rail. Speisewagen m; Am. Speiselokal n

din·ghy ['dɪŋgɪ] naut. Ding(h)i n; Beiboot n; Schlauchboot n

din·gy ['dɪndʒɪ] (-ier, -iest) schmutzig, schmudd(e)lig

'**din·ing| car** rail. Speisewagen m; '~ **room** Eß-, Speisezimmer n

din·ner ['dɪnə] (Mittag-, Abend)Essen n; Diner n, Festessen f; '~ **jack·et** Smoking m; '~ **par·ty** Dinner Party f, Abendgesellschaft f; '~ **ser·vice**, '~ **set** Speiseservice n, Tafelgeschirr n; '~ **time** Essens-, Tischzeit f

di·no zo. ['daɪnəʊ] Abk. für **di·no·saur** zo. ['daɪnəʊsɔː] Dinosaurier m

dip [dɪp] **1.** (-pp-) v/t. (ein)tauchen; senken; schöpfen; ~ **one's headlights** Brt. mot. abblenden; v/i. (unter)tauchen; sinken; sich neigen, sich senken; **2.** (Ein-, Unter)Tauchen n; F kurzes Bad; Senkung f, Neigung f; Gefälle n; Dip m (Soße)

diph·ther·i·a med. [dɪf'θɪərɪə] Diphtherie f

di·plo·ma [dɪ'pləʊmə] Diplom n

di·plo·ma·cy [dɪ'pləʊməsɪ] Diplomatie f

dip·lo·mat ['dɪpləmæt] Diplomat m; **~·ic** [dɪplə'mætɪk] (**~ally**) diplomatisch

dip·per ['dɪpə] Schöpfkelle f

dire ['daɪə] (**~r, ~st**) schrecklich; äußerste(r, -s), höchste(r, -s)

di·rect [dɪ'rekt] **1.** adj. direkt; gerade; unmittelbar; offen, aufrichtig; **2.** adv. direkt, unmittelbar; **3.** richten; lenken, steuern; leiten; anordnen; j-n anweisen

sen; *j-m* den Weg zeigen; *Brief* adressieren; *Regie* führen bei; **~ 'cur·rent** *electr.* Gleichstrom *m*; **~ 'train** durchgehender Zug

di·rec·tion [dɪ'rekʃn] Richtung *f*; Leitung *f*, Führung *f*; *Film etc.*: Regie *f*; *mst* **~s** *pl.* Anweisung *f*, Anleitung *f*; **~ for use** Gebrauchsanweisung *f*; △ *nicht* **Direktion**; **~ find·er** (Funk)Peiler *m*, Peilempfänger *m*; **~ in·di·ca·tor** *mot.* Fahrtrichtungsanzeiger *m*, Blinker *m*

di·rec·tive [dɪ'rektɪv] Anweisung *f*
di·rect·ly [dɪ'rektlɪ] **1.** *adv.* sofort; **2.** *cj.* F sobald, sowie
di·rec·tor [dɪ'rektə] Direktor *m*; *Film etc.*: Regisseur(in)
di·rec·to·ry [dɪ'rektərɪ] Adreßbuch *n*; **telephone ~** Telefonbuch *n*
dirt [dɜːt] Schmutz *m*; (lockere) Erde; **~ 'cheap** F spottbillig; **'~·y 1.** (*-ier*, *-iest*) schmutzig (*a. fig.*); **2.** beschmutzen; schmutzig werden, schmutzen
dis·a·bil·i·ty [dɪsə'bɪlətɪ] Unfähigkeit *f*
dis·a·bled [dɪs'eɪbld] **1.** arbeits-, erwerbsunfähig, invalid(e); *mil.* kriegsversehrt; *körperlich od. geistig* behindert; **2. the ~** *pl.* die Behinderten *pl.*
dis·ad·van·tage [dɪsəd'vɑ:ntɪdʒ] Nachteil *m*; Schaden *m*; **~·ta·geous** [dɪsædvɑ:n'teɪdʒəs] nachteilig, ungünstig
dis·a·gree [dɪsə'gri:] nicht übereinstimmen; uneinig sein; nicht bekommen (*with s.o.* j-m) (*Essen*); **~·a·ble** unangenehm; **~·ment** Verschiedenheit *f*, Unstimmigkeit *f*; Meinungsverschiedenheit *f*
dis·ap·pear [dɪsə'pɪə] verschwinden; **~·ance** [dɪsə'pɪərəns] Verschwinden *n*
dis·ap·point [dɪsə'pɔɪnt] *j-n* enttäuschen; *Hoffnungen etc.* zunichte machen; **~·ing** enttäuschend; **~·ment** Enttäuschung *f*
dis·ap·prov·al [dɪsə'pru:vl] Mißbilligung *f*; **~e** [dɪsə'pru:v] mißbilligen, dagegen sein
dis·arm [dɪs'ɑ:m] *v/t.* entwaffnen (*a. fig.*); *v/i. mil., pol.* abrüsten; **~·ar·ma·ment** [dɪs'ɑ:məmənt] Entwaffnung *f*; *mil., pol.* Abrüstung *f*
dis·ar·range [dɪsə'reɪndʒ] in Unordnung bringen
dis·ar·ray [dɪsə'reɪ] Unordnung *f*
di·sas·ter [dɪ'zɑ:stə] Unglück(sfall *m*)

n, Katastrophe *f*; **~ ar·e·a** Notstandsgebiet *n* (*Katastrophengebiet*)
di·sas·trous [dɪ'zɑ:strəs] katastrophal verheerend
dis·be·lief [dɪsbɪ'li:f] Unglaube *m* Zweifel *m* (**in** an *dat.*); **~·lieve** [dɪsbɪ'li:v] *et.* bezweifeln, nicht glauben
disc *Brt.* [dɪsk] Scheibe *f*; (Schall)Platte *f*, Parkscheibe *f*; *anat.* Bandscheibe *f Computer* → **disk**; △ *nicht* **Diskus**; **slipped** *~ med.* Bandscheibenvorfall *n*
dis·card [dɪ'skɑ:d] *Karten* ablegen *Kleidung etc. a.* ausrangieren; *Freunde etc.* fallenlassen
dis·cern [dɪ'sɜ:n] wahrnehmen, erkennen; **~·ing** kritisch, scharfsichtig; **~·ment** Scharfblick *m*
dis·charge [dɪs'tʃɑ:dʒ] **1.** *v/t.* ent-, ausladen; *j-n* befreien, entbinden; *j-n* entlassen; *Gewehr etc.* abfeuern; von sich geben, ausströmen, -senden, -stoßen; *med.* absondern; *Pflicht etc.* erfüllen; *Zorn etc.* auslassen (**on** an *dat.*); *v/i. electr.* sich entladen; sich ergießen, münden (*Fluß*); *med.* eitern; **2.** Entladung *f* (*e-s Schiffes etc.*); Abfeuern *n* (*e-s Gewehrs etc.*); Ausströmen *n*; *med.* Absonderung *f*; *med.* Ausfluß *m*; Ausstoßen *n*; *electr.* Entladung *f*; Entlassung *f*; Erfüllung *f* (*e-r Pflicht*)
di·sci·ple [dɪ'saɪpl] Schüler *m*; Jünger *m*
dis·ci·pline ['dɪsɪplɪn] **1.** Disziplin *f*; **2.** disziplinieren; **well ~d** diszipliniert; **badly ~d** disziplinlos, undiszipliniert
'**disc jock·ey** Disk-, Discjockey *m*
dis·claim [dɪs'kleɪm] ab-, bestreiten; *Verantwortung* ablehnen; *jur.* verzichten auf (*acc.*)
dis·close [dɪs'kləʊz] bekanntgeben, -machen; enthüllen, aufdecken; **~·clo·sure** [dɪs'kləʊʒə] Enthüllung *f*
dis·co F ['dɪskəʊ] (*pl.* **-cos**) Disko *f* (*Diskothek*)
dis·col·o(u)r [dɪs'kʌlə] (sich) verfärben
dis·com·fort [dɪs'kʌmfət] **1.** Unbehagen *n*; Unannehmlichkeit *f*; **2.** *j-m* Unbehagen verursachen
dis·con·cert [dɪskən'sɜ:t] aus der Fassung bringen
dis·con·nect [dɪskə'nekt] trennen (*a. electr.*); *tech.* auskuppeln; *electr. Gerät* abschalten; *Gas, Strom, Telefon* abstellen; *tel. Gespräch* unterbrechen; **~ed** zusammenhang(s)los

dis·con·so·late [dɪsˈkɒnsələt] untröstlich

dis·con·tent [dɪskənˈtent] Unzufriedenheit f; **~ed** unzufrieden

dis·con·tin·ue [dɪskənˈtɪnjuː] aufgeben, aufhören mit; unterbrechen

dis·cord [ˈdɪskɔːd] Uneinigkeit f; mus. Mißklang m; **~ant** [dɪˈskɔːdənt] nicht übereinstimmend; mus. unharmonisch, mißtönend

dis·co·theque [ˈdɪskətek] Diskothek f

dis·count [ˈdɪskaʊnt] econ. Diskont m; econ. Preisnachlaß m, Rabatt m, Skonto m, n

dis·cour·age [dɪˈskʌrɪdʒ] entmutigen; abschrecken, abhalten, j-m abraten (**from** von); **~ment** Entmutigung f; Abschreckung f

dis·course 1. [ˈdɪskɔːs] Unterhaltung f, Gespräch n; Vortrag m; 2. [dɪˈskɔːs] e-n Vortrag halten (**on** über acc.)

dis·cour·te·ous [dɪsˈkɜːtjəs] unhöflich; **~sy** [dɪsˈkɜːtəsɪ] Unhöflichkeit f

dis·cov|·er [dɪˈskʌvə] entdecken; ausfindig machen, (heraus)finden; **~e·ry** [dɪˈskʌvərɪ] Entdeckung f

'**disc park·ing** mot. Parken n mit Parkscheibe

dis·cred·it [dɪsˈkredɪt] 1. Zweifel m; Mißkredit m, schlechter Ruf; 2. nicht glauben; in Mißkredit bringen

dis·creet [dɪˈskriːt] besonnen, vorsichtig; diskret, verschwiegen

dis·crep·an·cy [dɪˈskrepənsɪ] Diskrepanz f, Widerspruch m

dis·cre·tion [dɪˈskreʃn] Ermessen n, Gutdünken n; Diskretion f, Verschwiegenheit f

dis·crim·i·nate [dɪˈskrɪmɪneɪt] unterscheiden; **~ against** benachteiligen, diskriminieren; **~nat·ing** kritisch, urteilsfähig; **~na·tion** [dɪskrɪmɪˈneɪʃn] unterschiedliche (bsd. nachteilige) Behandlung; Diskriminierung f, Benachteiligung f; Urteilsfähigkeit f

dis·cus [ˈdɪskəs] Sport: Diskus m

dis·cuss [dɪˈskʌs] diskutieren, erörtern, besprechen; **dis·cus·sion** [dɪˈskʌʃn] Diskussion f, Besprechung f

'**dis·cus| throw** Sport: Diskuswerfen n; **~ throw·er** Sport: Diskuswerfer(in)

dis·ease [dɪˈziːz] Krankheit f; **~d** krank

dis·em·bark [dɪsɪmˈbɑːk] von Bord gehen (lassen); naut. Waren ausladen

dis·en·chant·ed [dɪsɪnˈtʃɑːntɪd]: **be ~ with** sich keine Illusionen mehr machen über (acc.)

dis·en·gage [dɪsɪnˈgeɪdʒ] (sich) freimachen; losmachen; tech. aus-, loskuppeln

dis·en·tan·gle [dɪsɪnˈtæŋgl] entwirren; (sich) befreien

dis·fa·vo(u)r [dɪsˈfeɪvə] Mißfallen n; Ungnade f

dis·fig·ure [dɪsˈfɪgə] entstellen

dis·grace [dɪsˈgreɪs] 1. Schande f; Ungnade f; 2. Schande bringen über (acc.), j-m Schande bereiten; **~ful** schändlich; skandalös

dis·guise [dɪsˈgaɪz] 1. verkleiden (**as** als); Stimme etc. verstellen; et. verbergen, -schleiern; 2. Verkleidung f; Verstellung f; Verschleierung f; **in ~** maskiert, verkleidet; fig. verkappt; **in the ~ of** verkleidet als

dis·gust [dɪsˈgʌst] 1. Ekel m, Abscheu m; 2. (an)ekeln; empören, entrüsten; **~ing** ekelhaft

dish [dɪʃ] 1. flache Schüssel; (Servier)Platte f; Gericht n, Speise f; **the ~es** pl. das Geschirr; **wash od. do the ~es** abspülen; 2. **~ out** F austeilen; oft **~ up** Speisen anrichten, auftragen; F Geschichte etc. auftischen; '**~cloth** Geschirrspültuch n

dis·heart·en [dɪsˈhɑːtn] entmutigen

di·shev·el(l)ed [dɪˈʃevld] zerzaust

dis·hon·est [dɪsˈɒnɪst] unehrlich, unredlich; **~y** Unehrlichkeit f; Unredlichkeit f

dis·hon|·o(u)r [dɪsˈɒnə] 1. Schande f; 2. Schande bringen über (acc.), econ. Wechsel nicht honorieren od. einlösen; **~o(u)·ra·ble** [dɪsˈɒnərəbl] schändlich, unehrenhaft

'**dish|·wash·er** Spüler(in); Geschirrspülmaschine f, -spüler m; '**~wa·ter** Spülwasser n

dis·il·lu·sion [dɪsɪˈluːʒn] 1. Ernüchterung f, Desillusion f; 2. ernüchtern, desillusionieren; **be ~ed with** sich keine Illusionen mehr machen über (acc.)

dis·in·clined [dɪsɪnˈklaɪnd] abgeneigt

dis·in|·fect [dɪsɪnˈfekt] desinfizieren; **~fec·tant** Desinfektionsmittel n

dis·in·her·it [dɪsɪnˈherɪt] enterben

dis·in·te·grate [dɪsˈɪntɪgreɪt] (sich) auflösen; ver-, zerfallen

dis·in·ter·est·ed [dɪs'ɪntrəstɪd] uneigennützig, selbstlos; objektiv, unvoreingenommen; △ *mst nicht* **desinteressiert**

disk *bsd. Am.* [dɪsk] → *Brt.* **disc**; *Computer:* Diskette *f*; **'~ drive** *Computer:* Diskettenlaufwerk *n*

disk·ette [dɪs'ket, 'dɪsket] *Computer:* Floppy *f*, Diskette *f*

dis·like [dɪs'laɪk] **1.** Abneigung *f*, Widerwille *m* (**of, for** gegen); **take a ~ to s.o.** gegen j-n e-e Abneigung fassen; **2.** nicht leiden können, nicht mögen

dis·lo·cate *med.* ['dɪsləkeɪt] sich *den Arm etc.* ver- *od.* ausrenken

dis·loy·al [dɪs'lɔɪəl] treulos, untreu

dis·mal ['dɪzməl] trüb(e), trostlos, elend

dis·man·tle [dɪs'mæntl] *tech.* demontieren

dis·may [dɪs'meɪ] **1.** Schreck(en) *m*, Bestürzung *f*; **in ~, with ~** bestürzt; **to my ~** zu m-r Bestürzung; **2.** *v/t.* erschrecken, bestürzen

dis·miss [dɪs'mɪs] *v/t.* entlassen; wegschicken; ablehnen; *Thema etc.* fallenlassen; *jur.* abweisen; **~al** [dɪs'mɪsl] Entlassung *f*; Aufgabe *f*; *jur.* Abweisung *f*

dis·mount [dɪs'maʊnt] *v/i.* absteigen, absitzen (**from** *von Fahrrad, Pferd etc.*); *v/t.* demontieren; *tech.* auseinandernehmen

dis·o·be·di·ence [dɪsə'biːdjəns] Ungehorsam *m*; **~ent** ungehorsam

dis·o·bey [dɪsə'beɪ] nicht gehorchen, ungehorsam sein (gegen)

dis·or·der [dɪs'ɔːdə] Unordnung *f*; Aufruhr *m*; *med.* Störung *f*; **~ly** unordentlich; ordnungswidrig; unruhig; aufrührerisch

dis·or·gan·ize [dɪs'ɔːgənaɪz] durcheinanderbringen; desorganisieren

dis·own [dɪs'əʊn] nicht anerkennen; *Kind* verstoßen; ablehnen

di·spar·age [dɪ'spærɪdʒ] verächtlich machen, herabsetzen; geringschätzen

di·spar·i·ty [dɪ'spærətɪ] Ungleichheit *f*; **~ of** *od.* **in age** Altersunterschied *m*

dis·pas·sion·ate [dɪ'spæʃnət] leidenschaftslos; objektiv

di·spatch [dɪ'spætʃ] **1.** schnelle Erledigung; (Ab)Sendung *f*; Abfertigung *f*; Eile *f*; (Eil)Botschaft *f*; Bericht *m* (*e-s Korrespondenten*); **2.** schnell erledigen;

absenden, abschicken, *Telegramm* aufgeben, abfertigen

di·spel [dɪ'spel] (*-ll-*) *Menge etc.* zerstreuen (*a. fig.*), *Nebel* zerteilen

di·spen·sa·ble [dɪ'spensəbl] entbehrlich; **~ry** [dɪ'spensərɪ] Werks-, Krankenhaus-, Schul-, *mil.* Lazarettapotheke *f*

dis·pen·sa·tion [dɪspen'seɪʃn] Austeilung *f*; Befreiung *f*; Dispens *m*; *göttliche* Fügung

di·spense [dɪ'spens] austeilen; *Recht* sprechen; *Arzneien* zubereiten u. abgeben; **~ with** verzichten auf; entbehren; überflüssig machen; **di'spens·er** Spender *m*, *für Klebestreifen a.* Abroller *m*, (*Briefmarken- etc.*)Automat *m*

di·sperse [dɪ'spɜːs] verstreuen, (sich) zerstreuen

di·spir·it·ed [dɪ'spɪrɪtɪd] entmutigt

dis·place [dɪs'pleɪs] verschieben; ablösen, entlassen; *j-n* verschleppen; ersetzen; verdrängen

di·splay [dɪ'spleɪ] **1.** Entfaltung *f*; (Her)Zeigen *n*; (protzige) Zurschaustellung; *Computer:* Display *n*, Bildschirm *m*, Datenanzeige *f*; *econ.* Display *n*, Auslage *f*; **be on ~** ausgestellt sein; **2.** entfalten; zur Schau stellen; zeigen

dis·please [dɪs'pliːz] *j-m* mißfallen; **~pleased** ungehalten; **~plea·sure** [dɪs'pleʒə] Mißfallen *n*

dis·po·sa·ble [dɪs'spəʊzəbl] Einweg...; Wegwerf...; **~pos·al** [dɪs'spəʊzl] Beseitigung *f* (*von Müll etc.*), Entsorgung *f*; Endlagerung *f*; Verfügung(srecht *n*) *f*; **be (put) at s.o.'s ~** j-m zur Verfügung stehen (stellen); **~pose** [dɪs'spəʊz] *v/t.* (an)ordnen, einrichten; geneigt machen, bewegen; *v/i.* **~ of** verfügen über (*acc.*); erledigen; loswerden; wegschaffen, beseitigen; *Abfall, a. Atommüll etc.* entsorgen; **~posed** geneigt; ...gesinnt; **~po·si·tion** [dɪspə'zɪʃn] Veranlagung *f*

dis·pos·sess [dɪspə'zes] enteignen, vertreiben; berauben (**of** *gen.*)

dis·pro·por·tion·ate [dɪsprə'pɔːʃnət] unverhältnismäßig

dis·prove [dɪs'pruːv] widerlegen

di·spute [dɪ'spjuːt] **1.** Disput *m*, Kontroverse *f*; Streit *m*; Auseinandersetzung *f*; **2.** streiten (über *acc.*); bezweifeln

dis·qual·i·fy [dɪsˈkwɒlɪfaɪ] unfähig *od.* untauglich machen; für untauglich erklären; *Sport:* disqualifizieren

dis·re·gard [dɪsrɪˈgɑːd] **1.** Nichtbeachtung *f;* Mißachtung *f;* **2.** nicht beachten

dis·rep·u·ta·ble [dɪsˈrepjʊtəbl] übel; verrufen; **~re·pute** [dɪsrɪˈpjuːt] schlechter Ruf

dis·re·spect [dɪsrɪˈspekt] Respektlosigkeit *f;* Unhöflichkeit *f;* **~ful** respektlos; unhöflich

dis·rupt [dɪsˈrʌpt] unterbrechen

dis·sat·is·fac·tion [ˈdɪssætɪsˈfækʃn] Unzufriedenheit *f;* **~fied** [dɪsˈsætɪsfaɪd] unzufrieden (*with* mit)

dis·sect [dɪˈsekt] zerlegen, -gliedern

dis·sen·sion [dɪˈsenʃn] Meinungsverschiedenheit(en *pl.*) *f,* Differenz(en *pl.*) *f;* Uneinigkeit *f;* **~t** [dɪˈsent] **1.** abweichende Meinung; **2.** anderer Meinung sein (*from* als); **~er** Andersdenkende(r *m*) *f*

dis·si·dent [ˈdɪsɪdənt] Andersdenkende(r *m*) *f; pol.* Dissident(in), Regime-, Systemkritiker(in)

dis·sim·i·lar [dɪˈsɪmɪlə] (*to*) unähnlich (*dat.*); verschieden (von)

dis·sim·u·la·tion [dɪsɪmjʊˈleɪʃn] Verstellung *f*

dis·si·pate [ˈdɪsɪpeɪt] (sich) zerstreuen; verschwenden; **~pat·ed** ausschweifend, zügellos

dis·so·ci·ate [dɪˈsəʊʃɪeɪt] trennen; **~ o.s.** sich distanzieren, abrücken (*from* von)

dis·so·lute [ˈdɪsəluːt] → *dissipated;* **~lu·tion** [dɪsəˈluːʃn] Auflösung *f*

dis·solve [dɪˈzɒlv] (sich) auflösen

dis·suade [dɪˈsweɪd] *j-m* abraten (*from* von)

dis·tance [ˈdɪstəns] **1.** Abstand *m;* Entfernung *f;* Ferne *f;* Strecke *f; fig.* Distanz *f,* Zurückhaltung *f; at a* **~** von weitem; in einiger Entfernung; *keep s.o. at a* **~** j-m gegenüber reserviert sein; **2.** hinter sich lassen; **~ race** *Sport:* Langstreckenlauf *m;* **~ run·ner** *Sport:* Langstreckenläufer(in), Langstreckler(in); **~tant** entfernt; fern, Fern...; distanziert

dis·taste [dɪsˈteɪst] Widerwille *m,* Abneigung *f;* **~ful** ekelerregend; unangenehm; *be* **~ to s.o.** j-m zuwider sein

dis·tem·per *zo.* [dɪsˈtempə] Staupe *f*

dis·tend [dɪˈstend] (sich) (aus)dehnen; (auf)blähen; sich weiten

dis·til(l) [dɪˈstɪl] destillieren

dis·tinct [dɪˈstɪŋkt] verschieden; deutlich, klar; **~tinc·tion** [dɪˈstɪŋkʃn] Unterscheidung *f;* Unterschied *m;* Auszeichnung *f;* Rang *m;* **~tinc·tive** [dɪˈstɪŋktɪv] unterscheidend; kennzeichnend, bezeichnend

dis·tin·guish [dɪˈstɪŋgwɪʃ] unterscheiden; auszeichnen; **~ o.s.** sich auszeichnen; **~ed** berühmt; ausgezeichnet; vornehm

dis·tort [dɪˈstɔːt] verdrehen; verzerren

dis·tract [dɪˈstrækt] ablenken; **~ed** beunruhigt, besorgt; (*by, with*) außer sich (vor *dat.*); wahnsinnig (vor *Schmerzen etc.*); **dis·trac·tion** [dɪˈstrækʃn] Ablenkung *f;* Zerstreuung *f;* Wahnsinn *m*

dis·traught [dɪˈstrɔːt] → *distracted*

dis·tress [dɪˈstres] **1.** Leid *n,* Kummer *m,* Sorge *f;* Not(lage) *f;* **2.** beunruhigen, mit Sorge erfüllen; **~ed** notleidend; **~ed ar·e·a** *Am.* Notstandsgebiet *n* (*Katastrophengebiet*); **~ing** besorgniserregend

dis·trib·ute [dɪˈstrɪbjuːt] ver-, aus-, zuteilen; *econ.* Waren vertreiben, absetzen; *Filme* verleihen; **~tri·bu·tion** [dɪstrɪˈbjuːʃn] Ver-, Aus-, Zuteilung *f; econ.* Vertrieb *m,* Absatz *m;* Verleih *m* (*von Filmen*)

dis·trict [ˈdɪstrɪkt] Bezirk *m;* Gegend *f*

dis·trust [dɪsˈtrʌst] **1.** Mißtrauen *n;* **2.** mißtrauen (*dat.*); **~ful** mißtrauisch

dis·turb [dɪˈstɜːb] stören; beunruhigen; **~ance** [dɪˈstɜːbəns] Störung *f;* Unruhe *f;* **~ of the peace** *jur.* Störung *f* der öffentlichen Sicherheit u. Ordnung; *cause a* **~** für Unruhe sorgen; ruhestörenden Lärm machen; **~ed** [dɪˈstɜːbd] geistig gestört; verhaltensgestört

dis·used [dɪsˈjuːzd] nicht mehr benutzt (*Maschine etc.*), stillgelegt (*Bergwerk etc.*)

ditch [dɪtʃ] Graben *m*

Div *nur geschr. Abk. für* **division** *Sport:* Liga *f*

di·van [dɪˈvæn, ˈdaɪvæn] Diwan *m;* **~ bed** Bettcouch *f*

dive [daɪv] **1.** (*dived od. Am. a. dove, dived*) (unter)tauchen; *vom Sprungbrett* springen; e-n Hecht- *od.* Kopfsprung machen; hechten (*for* nach); e-n

Sturzflug machen; **2.** *Schwimmen:* Springen *n;* Kopf-, Hechtsprung *m;* *Fußball:* Schwalbe *f;* Sturzflug *m;* F Spelunke *f;* '**div·er** Taucher(in); *Sport:* Wasserspringer(in)

di·verge [daɪˈvɜːdʒ] auseinanderlaufen; abweichen; **di·ver·gence** [daɪˈvɜːdʒəns] Abweichung *f;* **di·ver·gent** abweichend

di·verse [daɪˈvɜːs] verschieden; mannigfaltig; **di·ver·si·fy** [daɪˈvɜːsɪfaɪ] verschieden(artig) *od.* abwechslungsreich gestalten; **di·ver·sion** [daɪˈvɜːʃn] Ablenkung *f;* Zeitvertreib *m;* **di·ver·si·ty** [daɪˈvɜːsətɪ] Verschiedenheit *f;* Mannigfaltigkeit *f*

di·vert [daɪˈvɜːt] ablenken; *j-n* zerstreuen, unterhalten; *Verkehr* umleiten

di·vide [dɪˈvaɪd] **1.** *v/t.* teilen; ver-, aus-, aufteilen; trennen; *math.* dividieren, teilen (**by** durch); *v/i.* sich teilen; sich aufteilen; *math.* sich dividieren *od.* teilen lassen (**by** durch); **2.** *geogr.* Wasserscheide *f;* **di·vid·ed** geteilt; **~ highway** *Am.* Schnellstraße *f*

div·i·dend *econ.* [ˈdɪvɪdend] Dividende *f*
di·vid·ers [dɪˈvaɪdəz] *pl.* (**a pair of ~** ein) Stechzirkel *m*

di·vine [dɪˈvaɪn] (**~r, ~st**) göttlich; **~ 'ser·vice** Gottesdienst *m*

div·ing [ˈdaɪvɪŋ] Tauchen *n; Sport:* Wasserspringen *n;* Taucher...; '**~·board** Sprungbrett *n;* '**di·ving·suit** Taucheranzug *m*

di·vin·i·ty [dɪˈvɪnətɪ] Gottheit *f;* Göttlichkeit *f;* Theologie *f*

di·vis·i·ble [dɪˈvɪzəbl] teilbar; **di·vi·sion** [dɪˈvɪʒn] Teilung *f;* Trennung *f;* Abteilung *f; mil., math.* Division *f*

di·vorce [dɪˈvɔːs] **1.** (Ehe)Scheidung *f;* **get a ~** sich scheiden lassen (**from** von); **2.** *jur. j-n,* Ehe scheiden; **get ~d** sich scheiden lassen; **di·vor·cee** [dɪvɔːˈsiː] Geschiedene(r *m*) *f*

DIY *bsd. Brt.* [diː aɪ ˈwaɪ] *Abk. für* → *do-it-yourself;* **~ store** Baumarkt *m*
diz·zy [ˈdɪzɪ] (**-ier, -iest**) schwind(e)lig
DJ [diː ˈdʒeɪ] *Abk. für* **disc jockey** Disk-, Discjockey *m*
do [duː] (**did, done**) *v/t.* tun, machen; (zu)bereiten; *Zimmer* aufräumen; *Geschirr* abwaschen; *Wegstrecke* zurücklegen, schaffen; **~ you know him? no, I**

don't kennst du ihn? nein; *what can I ~ for you?* was kann ich für Sie tun?, womit kann ich (Ihnen) dienen?; **~ London** F London besichtigen; *have one's hair done* sich die Haare machen *od.* frisieren lassen; *have done reading* fertig sein mit Lesen; *v/i.* tun, handeln; sich befinden; genügen; *that will ~* das genügt; *how ~ you ~?* guten Tag! (*bei der Vorstellung*); **~ be quick** beeil dich doch; *you like London? I ~* gefällt Ihnen London? ja; *she works hard, doesn't she?* sie arbeitet viel, nicht wahr?; **~ well** s-e Sache gut machen; gute Geschäfte machen; **~ away with** beseitigen, weg-, abschaffen; *I'm done in* F ich bin geschafft; **~ up** Kleid etc. zumachen; *Haus etc.* instand setzen; *Päckchen* zurechtmachen; **~ o.s. up** sich zurechtmachen; *I could ~ with ...* ich könnte ... brauchen *od.* vertragen; **~ without** auskommen *od.* sich behelfen ohne

doc[1] F [dɒk] → **doctor** 1 (*Arzt*)
doc[2] [dɒk] *Abk. für* **document** Dokument *n,* Urkunde *f*
do·cile [ˈdəʊsaɪl] gelehrig; fügsam
dock[1] [dɒk] stutzen, kupieren
dock[2] [dɒk] **1.** *naut.* Dock *n;* Kai *m,* Pier *m; jur.* Anklagebank *f;* **2.** *v/t. Schiff* (ein)docken; *Raumschiff* koppeln; *v/i. naut.* anlegen; andocken, ankoppeln (*Raumschiff*); '**~·er** Dock-, Hafenarbeiter *m;* '**~·ing** Docking *n,* Ankopp(e)lung *f* (*an ein Raumschiff*); '**~·yard** *naut.* Werft *f*

doc·tor [ˈdɒktə] Doktor *m,* Arzt *m,* Ärztin *f; univ.* Doktor *m;* **~·al** [ˈdɒktərəl]: **~ thesis** Doktorarbeit *f*

doc·trine [ˈdɒktrɪn] Doktrin *f,* Lehre *f*
doc·u·ment 1. [ˈdɒkjʊmənt] Urkunde *f;* **2.** [ˈdɒkjʊment] (urkundlich) belegen
doc·u·men·ta·ry [dɒkjʊˈmentrɪ] **1.** urkundlich; *Film etc.:* Dokumentar...; **2.** Dokumentarfilm *m*

dodge [dɒdʒ] (rasch) zur Seite springen, ausweichen; F sich drücken (vor *dat.*); '**dodg·er** Drückeberger *m;* → **fare dodger**

doe *zo.* [dəʊ] (Reh)Geiß *f,* Ricke *f*

dog [dɒg] **1.** *zo.* Hund *m;* **2.** (**-gg-**) *j-n* beharrlich verfolgen; '**~·eared** mit Eselsohren (*Buch*); **~ged** [ˈdɒgɪd] verbissen, hartnäckig

dog·ma ['dɒgmə] Dogma n; Glaubenssatz m; **~mat·ic** [dɒg'mætɪk] (**~ally**) dogmatisch

dog-'tired F hundemüde

do-it-your·self [duːɪtjɔː'self] **1.** Heimwerken n; **2.** Heimwerker...; **~·er** Heimwerker m

dole [dəʊl] **1.** milde Gabe; *Brt.* F Stempelgeld n; **go od. be on the ~** *Brt.* F stempeln gehen; **2. ~ out** sparsam ver- *od.* austeilen

dole·ful ['dəʊlfl] traurig, trübselig

doll [dɒl] Puppe f

dol·lar ['dɒlə] Dollar m

dol·phin zo. ['dɒlfɪn] Delphin m

dome [dəʊm] Kuppel f; △ *nicht* **Dom**

do·mes·tic [də'mestɪk] **1.** (**~ally**) häuslich; inländisch, einheimisch; zahm; Hausangestellte(r m) f; **~ 'an·i·mal** Haustier n; **do·mes·ti·cate** [də'mestɪkeɪt] *Tier* zähmen; **~ 'flight** *aviat.* Inlandsflug m; **~ 'mar·ket** Binnenmarkt m; **~ 'trade** Binnenhandel m; **~ 'vi·o·lence** häusliche Gewalt (*gegen Frauen u. Kinder*)

dom·i·cile ['dɒmɪsaɪl] Wohnsitz m

dom·i·nant ['dɒmɪnənt] dominierend, (vor)herrschend; **~nate** ['dɒmɪneɪt] beherrschen; dominieren; **~na·tion** [dɒmɪ'neɪʃn] (Vor)Herrschaft f; **~neer·ing** [dɒmɪ'nɪərɪŋ] herrisch, tyrannisch

do·nate [dəʊ'neɪt] schenken, stiften; **do·na·tion** [dəʊ'neɪʃn] Schenkung f

done [dʌn] **1.** *p.p. von* **do**; **2.** *adj.* getan; erledigt; fertig; *gastr.* gar → **well-done**

don·key zo. ['dɒŋkɪ] Esel m

do·nor ['dəʊnə] (*med. bsd. Blut-, Organ*)Spender(in)

don't [dəʊnt] *für:* **do not** → **do**; *für: Am.* F **does not** (*she don't ...*) → **do**

doom [duːm] **1.** Schicksal n, Verhängnis n; **2.** verurteilen, -dammen; **~s·day** ['duːmzdeɪ]: *till* **~** F bis zum Jüngsten Tag

door [dɔː] Tür f; Tor n; *next* **~** nebenan; **'~bell** Türklingel f; **'~ han·dle** Türklinke f; **'~keep·er** Pförtner m; **'~knob** Türknauf m; **'~mat** (Fuß)Abtreter m; **'~step** Türstufe f; **'~way** Türöffnung f

dope [dəʊp] **1.** Stoff m (*Rauschgift*); F Betäubungsmittel n; *Sport:* Dopingmittel n; *sl.* Trottel m; **2.** F *j-m* Stoff

geben; *Sport:* dopen; **'~ test** Dopingkontrolle f

dor·mant *mst fig.* ['dɔːmənt] schlafend, ruhend; untätig

dor·mer (win·dow) ['dɔːmə (-)] stehendes Dachfenster

dor·mi·to·ry ['dɔːmɪtrɪ] Schlafsaal m; *bsd. Am.* Studentenwohnheim n

dor·mo·bile *TM* ['dɔːməbiːl] Campingbus m, Wohnmobil n

dor·mouse zo. ['dɔːmaʊs] (*pl. -mice*) Haselmaus f

DOS [dɒs] *Abk. für* **disk operating system** DOS n, (Platten)Betriebssystem n

dose [dəʊs] **1.** Dosis f; △ *nicht* **Dose**; **2.** *j-m* e-e Medizin geben

dot [dɒt] **1.** Punkt m; Fleck m; *on the* **~** F auf die Sekunde pünktlich; **2.** (*-tt-*) punktieren; tüpfeln; *fig.* sprenkeln; **~ted line** punktierte Linie

dote [dəʊt]: **~ on** vernarrt sein in (*acc.*); **dot·ing** ['dəʊtɪŋ] vernarrt

dou·ble ['dʌbl] **1.** doppelt; Doppel...; zweifach; **2.** Doppelte(s) n; Doppelgänger(in); *Film, TV:* Double n; **3.** (sich) verdoppeln; *Film, TV: j-n* doubeln; *a.* **~ up** falten; *Decke* zusammenlegen; **~ back** kehrtmachen; **~ up with** sich krümmen vor (*dat.*); **~'breast·ed** zweireihig (*Jackett*); **~'check** genau nachprüfen; **~'chin** Doppelkinn n; **~'cross** ein doppeltes *od.* falsches Spiel treiben mit; **~'deal·ing 1.** betrügerisch; **2.** Betrug m; **~'deck·er** Doppeldecker m; **~'edged** zweischneidig; zweideutig; **~'en·try** *econ.* doppelte Buchführung; **~ 'fea·ture** *Film:* Doppelprogramm n; **~'park** *mot.* in zweiter Reihe parken; **~'quick** F im Eiltempo, fix; **'~s** *sg. bsd. Tennis:* Doppel n; **men's ~** Herrendoppel n; **women's ~** Damendoppel n; **~'sid·ed** zweiseitig beschreibbare Diskette etc.

doubt [daʊt] **1.** *v/i.* zweifeln; *v/t.* bezweifeln; mißtrauen (*dat.*); **2.** Zweifel m; **be in ~ about** Zweifel haben an (*dat.*); **no ~** ohne Zweifel; **'~ful** zweifelhaft; **'~less** ohne Zweifel

douche [duːʃ] **1.** Spülung f (*a. med.*); Spülapparat m; △ *nicht* **Dusche**; **2.** spülen (*a. med.*); △ *nicht* **duschen**

dough [dəʊ] Teig m; **'~nut** *etwa* Krapfen m, Berliner Pfannkuchen, Schmalzkringel m

dove

dove¹ *zo.* [dʌv] Taube *f*
dove² *Am.* [dəʊv] *pret. von* dive 1
dow·dy [ˈdaʊdɪ] unelegant; unmodern
dow·el *tech.* [ˈdaʊəl] Dübel *m*
down¹ [daʊn] Daunen *pl.*; Flaum *m*
down² [daʊn] **1.** *adv.* nach unten, her-, hinunter, her-, hinab, abwärts; unten; **2.** *prp.* her-, hinab, her-, hinunter; ~ **the river** flußabwärts; **3.** *adj.* nach unten gerichtet; deprimiert, niedergeschlagen; ~ **platform** Abfahrtsbahnsteig *m* (*in London*); ~ **train** Zug *m* (von London fort); **4.** *v/t.* niederschlagen; Flugzeug abschießen; F *Getränk* runterkippen; ~ **tools** die Arbeit niederlegen, in den Streik treten; '~·**cast** niedergeschlagen; '~·**fall** Platzregen *m*; *fig.* Sturz *m*; ~·**heart·ed** niedergeschlagen; ~·**hill** **1.** *adv.* bergab; **2.** *adj.* abschüssig; *Skisport:* Abfahrts...; **3.** Abhang *m*; *Skisport:* Abfahrt *f*; '**pay·ment** *econ.* Anzahlung *f*; '~·**pour** Regenguß *m*, Platzregen *m*; '~·**right** **1.** *adv.* völlig, ganz u. gar, ausgesprochen; **2.** *adj.* glatt (*Lüge etc.*); ausgesprochen
downs [daʊnz] *pl.* Hügelland *n*
down·'**stairs** die Treppe her- od. hinunter; (nach) unten; ~·'**stream** stromabwärts; ~·**to**-'**earth** realistisch; ~·'**town** *Am.* **1.** *adv.* im od. ins Geschäftsviertel; **2.** *adj.* im Geschäftsviertel (gelegen od. tätig); '~·**town** *Am.* Geschäftsviertel *n*, Innenstadt *f*, City *f*; ~·**ward(s)** [ˈdaʊnwəd(z)] abwärts, nach unten
down·y [ˈdaʊnɪ] (-*ier*, -*iest*) flaumig
dow·ry [ˈdaʊərɪ] Mitgift *f*
doz. *nur geschr. Abk. für* **dozen** Dtzd., Dutzend(e) *f*
doze [dəʊz] **1.** dösen, ein Nickerchen machen; **2.** Nickerchen *n*
doz·en [ˈdʌzn] Dutzend *n*
Dr *nur geschr. Abk. für* **Doctor** Dr., Doktor *m*
drab [dræb] trist; düster; eintönig
draft [drɑːft] **1.** Entwurf *m*; *econ.* Tratte *f*, Wechsel *m*; *Am. mil.* Einberufung *f*; *Am. für* **draught**; **2.** entwerfen; *Brief etc.* aufsetzen; *Am. mil.* einberufen; ~·**ee** *Am. mil.* [drɑːfˈtiː] Wehr(dienst)pflichtige(r) *m*; '~·**s·man** *Am.* (*pl. -men*), '~·**s·wom·an** *Am.* (*pl. -women*) → **draughtsman, draughtswoman**; '~·**y** *Am.* (-*ier*, -*iest*) → **draughty**

drag [dræg] **1.** Schleppen *n*, Zerren *n* *fig.* Hemmschuh *m*; F *et.* Langweiliges **2.** (-*gg-*) schleppen, zerren, zieher schleifen; *a.* ~ **behind** zurückbleiben nachhinken; ~ **on** weiterschleppen; *fig* sich dahinschleppen; *fig.* sich in die Länge ziehen; '~·**lift** Schlepplift *m*
drag·on [ˈdrægən] Drache *m*; '~·**fly** *zo* Libelle *f*
drain [dreɪn] **1.** Abfluß(kanal *m*, -roh *n*) *m*; Entwässerungsgraben *m*; **2.** *v/t* abfließen lassen; entwässern; austrinken, leeren; *v/i.* ~ **off**, ~ **away** abfließen ablaufen; ~·**age** [ˈdreɪnɪdʒ] Abfließen *n*, Ablaufen *n*; Entwässerung(sanlage *f* -ssystem *n*) *f*; '~·**pipe** Abflußrohr *n*
drake *zo.* [dreɪk] Enterich *m*, Erpel *m* △ *nicht* **Drache**
dram F [dræm] Schluck *m*
dra·ma [ˈdrɑːmə] Drama *n*; **dra·mat·ic** [drəˈmætɪk] (~*ally*) dramatisch **dram·a·tist** [ˈdræmətɪst] Dramatiker *m*; **dram·a·tize** [ˈdræmətaɪz] dramatisieren
drank [dræŋk] *pret. von* drink 2
drape [dreɪp] **1.** drapieren, in Falten legen; **2.** *mst* ~**s** *pl. Am.* Vorhänge *pl.* **drap·er·y** *Brt.* [ˈdreɪpərɪ] Textilien *pl.*
dras·tic [ˈdræstɪk] (~*ally*) drastisch, durchgreifend
draught [drɑːft] (*Am.* **draft**) (Luft)Zug *m*; Zugluft *f*; Zug *m*, Schluck *m*; Tiefgang *m* (*e-s Schiffes*); **beer on** ~, ~ **beer** Bier *n* vom Faß, Faßbier *n*; ~**s** *sg. Brt.* Damespiel *n*; '~·**s·man** (*pl. -men*) *Brt. tech.* (Konstruktions)Zeichner *m*; '~·**s·wom·an** (*pl. -women*) *Brt. tech.* (Konstruktions)Zeichnerin *f*; '~·**y** (-*ier*, -*iest*) *Brt.* zugig
draw [drɔː] **1.** (**drew, drawn**) *v/t.* ziehen; *Vorhänge* auf-, zuziehen; *Atem* holen; *Tee* ziehen lassen; *fig. Menge* anziehen; *Interesse* auf sich ziehen; zeichnen; *Geld* abheben; *Scheck* ausstellen; *v/i.* *Kamin, Tee etc.*: ziehen; *Sport:* unentschieden spielen; ~ **back** zurückweichen; ~ **near** sich nähern; ~ **out** *Geld* abheben; *fig.* in die Länge ziehen; ~ **up** *Schriftstück* aufsetzen; (an)halten (*Wagen etc.*); vorfahren; **2.** Ziehen *n*; *Lotterie:* Ziehung *f*; *Sport:* Unentschieden *n*; Attraktion *f*, Zugnummer *f*; '~·**back** Nachteil *m*, Hindernis *n*; '~·**bridge** Zugbrücke *f*

draw·er¹ [drɔː] Schublade f, -fach n

draw·er² ['drɔːə] Zeichner(in); *econ.* Aussteller(in) (*e-s Schecks etc.*)

'**draw·ing** Zeichnen n; Zeichnung f; '~ **board** Reißbrett n; '~ **pin** Brt. Reißzwecke f, -nagel m, Heftzwecke f; '~ **room** → *living room*; Salon m

drawl [drɔːl] 1. gedehnt sprechen; 2. gedehntes Sprechen

drawn [drɔːn] 1. *p.p. von draw* 1; 2. *adj.* *Sport:* unentschieden; abgespannt

dread [dred] 1. (große) Angst, Furcht f; 2. (sich) fürchten; '~**ful** schrecklich, furchtbar

dream [driːm] 1. Traum m; 2. (*dreamed od. dreamt*) träumen; '~**er** Träumer(in); ~**t** [dremt] *pret. u. p.p. von dream* 2; '~**y** (*-ier, -iest*) träumerisch, verträumt

drear·y ['drɪərɪ] (*-ier, -iest*) trübselig, trüb(e); langweilig

dredge [dredʒ] 1. (Schwimm)Bagger m; 2. (aus)baggern (*naß*); '**dredg·er** (Schwimm)Bagger m

dregs [dregz] *pl.* Bodensatz m; *fig.* Abschaum m

drench [drentʃ] durchnässen

dress [dres] 1. Kleidung f; Kleid n; 2. (sich) ankleiden *od.* anziehen; schmücken, dekorieren; zurechtmachen; *Speisen* zubereiten; *Salat* anmachen; *Haare* frisieren; *get ~ed* sich anziehen; ~ **down** j-m e-e Standpauke halten; ~ **up** (sich) fein machen; sich kostümieren *od.* verkleiden (*bsd. Kinder*); '~ **cir·cle** *thea.* erster Rang; '~ **de·sign·er** Modezeichner(in); '~**er** Anrichte f; Toilettentisch m

'**dress·ing** An-, Zurichten n; Ankleiden n; *med.* Verband m; Dressing n (*Salatsoße*); Füllung f; '~ **down** Standpauke f; '~ **gown** Morgenrock m, -mantel m; *Sport:* Bademantel m; '~ **room** (Künstler)Garderobe f; *Sport:* (Umkleide)Kabine f; '~ **ta·ble** Toilettentisch m

'**dress·mak·er** (Damen)Schneider(in)

drew [druː] *pret. von draw* 1

drib·ble ['drɪbl] tröpfeln (lassen); sabbern, geifern; *Fußball:* dribbeln

dried [draɪd] getrocknet, Dörr...

dri·er ['draɪə] → *dryer*

drift [drɪft] 1. (Dahin)Treiben n; (Schnee)Verwehung f; (Schnee-

Sand)Wehe f; *fig.* Tendenz f; 2. (dahin)treiben; wehen; sich häufen (*Sand, Schnee*)

drill [drɪl] 1. *tech.* Bohrer m; *mil.* Drill m (*a. fig.*); *mil.* Exerzieren n; 2. bohren; *mil., fig.* drillen; '~**ing site** *tech.* Bohrgelände n (*für Öl*), Bohrstelle f

drink [drɪŋk] 1. Getränk n; 2. (*drank, drunk*) trinken; ~ **to s.o.** j-m zuprosten *od.* zutrinken; ~'**driv·ing** Brt. Trunkenheit f am Steuer; '~**er** Trinker(in); '~**s ma·chine** Getränkeautomat m

drip [drɪp] 1. Tröpfeln n; *med.* Tropf m; 2. (*-pp-*) tropfen *od.* tröpfeln (lassen); triefen; ~'**dry** bügelfrei; '~**ping** Bratenfett n

drive [draɪv] 1. Fahrt f; Aus-, Spazierfahrt f; Zufahrt(sstraße) f; (private) Auffahrt; *tech.* Antrieb m; *Computer:* Laufwerk n; *mot.* (*Links- etc.*)Steuerung f; *psych.* Trieb m; *fig.* Kampagne f; *fig.* Schwung m, Elan m, Dynamik f; 2. (*drove, driven*) *v/t.* treiben; *auto*: fahren, lenken, steuern; (*im Auto etc.*) fahren; *tech.* (an)treiben; *a.* ~ **off** vertreiben; *v/i.* treiben; (*Auto*) fahren; ~ **off** wegfahren; *what are you driving at?* F worauf wollen Sie hinaus?

'**drive-in** 1. Auto...; ~ **cin·ema**, *Am.* ~ **mo·tion-pic·ture thea·ter** Autokino n; 2. Autokino n; Drive-in-Restaurant n; Autoschalter m, Drive-in-Schalter m (*e-r Bank*)

driv·el ['drɪvl] 1. (*bsd. Brt. -ll-, Am. -l-*) faseln; 2. Geschwätz n, Gefasel n

driv·en ['drɪvn] *p.p. von drive* 2

driv·er ['draɪvə] *mot.* Fahrer(in); (*Lokomotiv*)Führer m; '~**s li·cense** *Am.* Führerschein m

'**driv·ing** ['draɪvɪŋ] (an)treibend; *tech.* Antriebs..., Treib..., Trieb...; *mot.* Fahr...; '~ **li·cense** Brt. Führerschein m; '~ **test** Fahrprüfung f

driz·zle ['drɪzl] 1. Sprühregen m; 2. sprühen, nieseln

drone [drəun] 1. *zo.* Drohne f (*a. fig.*); 2. summen; dröhnen

droop [druːp] (schlaff) herabhängen

drop [drɒp] 1. Tropfen m; Fallen n, Fall m; *fig.* Fall m, Sturz m; Bonbon m, n; *fruit ~s pl.* Drops m, n *od. pl.*; 2. (*-pp-*) *v/t.* tropfen (lassen); fallen lassen; *Bemerkung, Thema etc.* fallenlassen; *Brief* einwerfen; *Fahrgast* absetzen; senken;

~ **s.o. a few lines** pl. j-m ein paar Zeilen schreiben; v/i. tropfen; (herab-, herunter)fallen; umsinken, fallen; ~ **in** (kurz) hereinschauen; ~ **off** abfallen; zurückgehen, nachlassen; F einnicken; ~ **out** herausfallen; aussteigen (**of** aus); a. ~ **out of school** (**university**) die Schule (das Studium) abbrechen; '~**out** Drop-out m, Aussteiger m; (Schul-, Studien)Abbrecher m

drought [draʊt] Trockenheit f, Dürre f

drove [drəʊv] pret. von **drive** 2

drown [draʊn] v/t. ertränken; überschwemmen; fig. übertönen; v/i. ertrinken

drow·sy ['draʊzɪ] (**-ier, -iest**) schläfrig; einschläfernd

drudge [drʌdʒ] sich (ab)placken, schuften; **drudg·e·ry** ['drʌdʒərɪ] (stumpfsinnige) Plackerei f od. Schinderei

drug [drʌg] **1.** Arzneimittel n, Medikament n; Droge f, Rauschgift n; **be** ~ (**off**) ~**s** drogenabhängig od. -süchtig (**clean**) sein; **2.** (**-gg-**) j-m Medikamente geben; j-n unter Drogen setzen; ein Betäubungsmittel beimischen (dat.); betäuben (a. fig.); '~ **a·buse** Drogenmißbrauch m; Medikamentenmißbrauch m; '~ **ad·dict** Drogenabhängige(r m) f, -süchtige(r m) f; **be a** ~ drogenabhängig od. -süchtig sein; ~**gist** Am. ['drʌgɪst] Apotheker(in); Inhaber(in) e-s Drugstores; '~**store** Am. Apotheke f; Drugstore m; '~ **vic·tim** Drogentote(r m) f

drum [drʌm] **1.** mus. Trommel f; anat. Trommelfell n; ~**s** pl. mus. Schlagzeug n; **2.** (**-mm-**) trommeln; '~**mer** mus. Trommler m; Schlagzeuger m

drunk [drʌŋk] **1.** p.p. von **drink** 2; **2.** adj. betrunken; **get** ~ sich betrinken; **3.** Betrunkene(r m) f; → ~**ard** ['drʌŋkəd] Trinker(in), Säufer(in); '~**en** adj. betrunken; ~**en 'driv·ing** (Am. a. **drunk driving**) Trunkenheit f am Steuer

dry [draɪ] **1.** (**-ier, -iest**) trocken; trocken, herb (Wein); F durstig; F trocken (ohne Alkohol); **2.** trocknen; dörren; ~ **up** austrocknen; versiegen; ~**'clean** chemisch reinigen; ~ **'clean·er's** chemische Reinigung (Unternehmen); '~**er** (a. **drier**) Trockner m; '~ **goods** pl. Textilien pl.

DTP [diː tiː 'piː] Abk. für **desktop** *publishing* Computer: Desktop publishing n

du·al ['djuːəl] doppelt, Doppel...; ~ **'car·riage·way** Brt. Schnellstraße f (mit Mittelstreifen)

dub [dʌb] (**-bb-**) Film synchronisieren

du·bi·ous ['djuːbjəs] zweifelhaft

duch·ess ['dʌtʃɪs] Herzogin f

duck [dʌk] **1.** zo. Ente f; Ducken n; F Schatz m (Anrede, oft unübersetzt); **2.** (unter)tauchen; (sich) ducken; '~**ling** zo. Entchen n

due [djuː] **1.** zustehend; gebührend; angemessen; econ. fällig; zeitlich fällig; ~ **to** wegen (gen.); **be** ~ **to** zurückzuführen sein auf; **2.** adv. ~ direkt, genau (nach Osten etc.)

du·el ['djuːəl] Duell n

dues [djuːz] pl. Gebühren pl.; Beitrag m

du·et mus. [djuː'et] Duett n

dug [dʌg] pret. u. p.p. von **dig** 1

duke [djuːk] Herzog m

dull [dʌl] **1.** dumm; träge, schwerfällig; stumpf; matt (Auge etc.); schwach (Gehör); langweilig; abgestumpft, teilnahmslos; dumpf; trüb(e); econ. flau; **2.** stumpf machen od. werden; (sich) trüben; mildern, dämpfen; Schmerz betäuben; fig. abstumpfen

du·ly adv. ['djuːlɪ] ordnungsgemäß; gebührend; rechtzeitig

dumb [dʌm] stumm; sprachlos; bsd. Am. F doof, dumm, blöd; **dum(b)-** '**found·ed** verblüfft, sprachlos

dum·my ['dʌmɪ] Attrappe f; Kleider-, Schaufensterpuppe f; Dummy m, Puppe f (für Unfalltests etc.); Brt. Schnuller m

dump [dʌmp] **1.** v/t. (hin)plumpsen od. (hin)fallen lassen; auskippen; Schutt etc. abladen; Schadstoffe in Fluß etc. einleiten, im Meer verklappen (**into** in); econ. Waren zu Dumpingpreisen verkaufen; **2.** Plumps m; Schuttabladeplatz m, Müllkippe f, -halde f, (Müll)Deponie f; '~**ing** econ. Dumping n, Ausfuhr f zu Schleuderpreisen

dune [djuːn] Düne f

dung [dʌŋ] **1.** Dung m; **2.** düngen

dun·ga·rees [dʌŋgə'riːz] pl. Brt. (**a pair of** ~ e-e) Arbeitshose

dun·geon ['dʌndʒən] (Burg)Verlies n

dupe [djuːp] betrügen, täuschen

du·plex ['djuːpleks] doppelt, Doppel...;

'**~** (**a·part·ment**) *Am.* Maisonette(wohnung) *f*; '**~** (**house**) *Am.* Doppel-, Zweifamilienhaus *n*

du·pli·cate 1. ['dju:plɪkət] doppelt; ~ **key** Zweit-, Nachschlüssel *m*; **2.** ['dju:plɪkət] Duplikat *n*; Zweit-, Nachschlüssel *m*; **3.** ['dju:plɪkeɪt] doppelt ausfertigen; kopieren, vervielfältigen

du·plic·i·ty [dju:'plɪsətɪ] Doppelzüngigkeit *f*

dur·a·ble ['djʊərəbl] haltbar; dauerhaft; **du·ra·tion** [djʊə'reɪʃn] Dauer *f*

du·ress [djʊə'res] Zwang *m*

dur·ing *prp.* ['djʊərɪŋ] während

dusk [dʌsk] (Abend)Dämmerung *f*; '**~·y** (**-ier, -iest**) dämmerig, düster (*a. fig.*); schwärzlich

dust [dʌst] **1.** Staub *m*; **2.** *v/t.* abstauben; (be)streuen; *v/i.* Staub wischen, abstauben; '**~·bin** *Brt.* Abfall-, Mülleimer *m*; Abfall-, Mülltonne *f*; '**~·bin lin·er** *Brt.* Müllbeutel *m*; '**~·cart** *Brt.* Müllwagen *m*; '**~·er** Staublappen *m*, -wedel *m*; *Schule:* Tafelschwamm *m*, -tuch *n*; '**~·cov·er**, '**~ jack·et** Schutzumschlag *m* (*e-s Buches*); '**~·man** (*pl.* **-men**) *Brt.* Müllmann *m*; '**~·pan** Kehrichtschaufel *f*; '**~·y** (**-ier, -iest**) staubig

Dutch [dʌtʃ] **1.** *adj.* holländisch, niederländisch; **2.** *adv.* **go** ~ getrennte Kasse machen; **3.** *ling.* Holländisch *n*, Niederländisch *n*; **the** ~ die Holländer *pl.*, die Niederländer *pl.*; '**~·man** (*pl.* **-men**) Holländer *m*, Niederländer *m*; '**~ wom·an** (*pl.* **-women**) Holländerin *f*, Niederländerin *f*

du·ty ['dju:tɪ] Pflicht *f*; Ehrerbietung *f*; *econ.* Abgabe *f*; Zoll *m*; Dienst *m*; **on** ~ diensthabend; **be on** ~ Dienst haben; **be off** ~ dienstfrei haben; '**~·free** zollfrei

dwarf [dwɔ:f] **1.** (*pl.* **dwarfs** [dwɔ:fs], **dwarves** [dwɔ:vz]) Zwerg(in); **2.** verkleinern, klein erscheinen lassen

dwell [dwel] (**dwelt** *od.* **dwelled**) wohnen; *fig.* verweilen (**on** bei); '**~·ing** Wohnung *f*

dwelt [dwelt] *pret. u. p.p. von* **dwell**

dwin·dle ['dwɪndl] (dahin)schwinden, abnehmen

dye [daɪ] **1.** Farbe *f*; **of the deepest** ~ *fig.* von der übelsten Sorte; **2.** färben

dy·ing ['daɪɪŋ] **1.** sterbend; Sterbe...; **2.** Sterben *n*

dyke [daɪk] → **dike[1],[2]**

dy·nam·ic [daɪ'næmɪk] dynamisch, kraftgeladen; **~s** *mst sg.* Dynamik *f*

dy·na·mite ['daɪnəmaɪt] **1.** Dynamit *n*; **2.** (mit Dynamit) sprengen

dys·en·te·ry *med.* ['dɪsntrɪ] Ruhr *f*

dys·pep·si·a *med.* [dɪs'pepsɪə] Verdauungsstörung *f*

E

E, e [i:] E, e *n*

E *nur geschr. Abk. für:* **east** O, Ost(en *m*); **east(ern)** östlich

each [i:tʃ] jede(r, -s); ~ **other** einander, sich; je, pro Person, pro Stück

ea·ger ['i:gə] begierig; eifrig; '**~·ness** Begierde *f*; Eifer *m*

ea·gle ['i:gl] *zo.* Adler *m*; *Am. hist.* Zehndollarstück *n*; '**~·eyed** scharfsichtig

ear [ɪə] Ähre *f*; *anat.* Ohr *n*; Öhr *n*; Henkel *m*; **keep an** ~ **to the ground** die Ohren offenhalten; '**~·ache** Ohrenschmerzen *pl.*; '**~·drum** *anat.* Trom-

melfell *n*; **~ed** *in Zssgn* mit (...) Ohren, ...ohrig

earl [ɜ:l] *englischer Graf*

'**ear·lobe** Ohrläppchen *n*

ear·ly ['ɜ:lɪ] früh; Früh...; Anfangs..., erste(r, -s); bald(ig); **as** ~ **as May** schon im Mai; **as** ~ **as possible** so bald wie möglich; ~ **bird** Frühaufsteher(in); ~ **'warn·ing sys·tem** *mil.* Frühwarnsystem *n*

'**ear·mark 1.** Kennzeichen *n*; Merkmal *n*; **2.** kennzeichnen; zurücklegen (**for** für)

earn [ɜ:n] verdienen; einbringen

ear·nest ['ɜːnɪst] **1.** ernst(lich, -haft); ernstgemeint; **2.** Ernst *m*; in ~ im Ernst; ernsthaft

earn·ings ['ɜːnɪŋz] *pl.* Einkommen *n*

'ear|·phones *pl.* Ohrhörer *pl.*; Kopfhörer *pl.*; '~**piece** *tel.* Hörmuschel *f*, '~**ring** Ohrring *m*; '~**shot:** within (out of) ~ in (außer) Hörweite

earth [ɜːθ] **1.** Erde *f*; Land *n*; **2.** *v/t.* *electr.* erden; ~**en** ['ɜːθn] irden; '~**en·ware** Steingut(geschirr) *n*; '~**ly** irdisch, weltlich; F denkbar; '~**quake** Erdbeben *n*; '~**worm** *zo.* Regenwurm *m*

ease [iːz] **1.** Bequemlichkeit *f*; (Gemüts)Ruhe *f*; Sorglosigkeit *f*; Leichtigkeit *f*; at (one's) ~ ruhig, entspannt; unbefangen; be at ~! feel ill at ~ sich (in s-r Haut) nicht wohl fühlen; **2.** *v/t.* erleichtern; beruhigen; *Schmerzen* lindern; *v/i. mst* ~ **off,** ~ **up** nachlassen; sich entspannen (Lage)

ea·sel ['iːzl] Staffelei *f*

east [iːst] **1.** Ost(en *m*); **2.** *adj.* östlich, Ost...; **3.** *adv.* nach Osten, ostwärts

Eas·ter ['iːstə] Ostern *n*; Oster...; ~ **'bun·ny** Osterhase *m*; '~ **egg** Osterei *n*

eas·ter·ly ['iːstəlɪ] östlich, Ost...; **east·ern** ['iːstən] östlich, Ost...; **east·ward(s)** ['iːstwəd(z)] östlich, nach Osten

eas·y ['iːzɪ] (-ier, -iest) leicht; einfach; bequem; gemächlich, gemütlich; ungezwungen; go ~, take it ~ sich Zeit lassen; take it ~! immer mit der Ruhe!; ~ **'chair** Sessel *m*; ~**'go·ing** gelassen

eat [iːt] (ate, eaten) essen; (zer)fressen; ~ **out** auswärts essen, essen gehen; ~ **up** aufessen; '~**a·ble** eß-, genießbar; ~**en** ['iːtn] *p.p. von* eat 1; '~**er** Esser(in)

eaves [iːvz] *pl.* Dachrinne *f*, Traufe *f*; '~**drop** (-pp-) (heimlich) lauschen *od.* horchen; ~ **on** belauschen

ebb [eb] **1.** Ebbe *f*; **2.** zurückgehen; ~ **away** abnehmen; ~ **'tide** Ebbe *f*

eb·o·ny ['ebənɪ] Ebenholz *n*

ec *nur geschr. Abk. für* **Eurocheque** *Brt.* Euroscheck *m*

EC [iː 'siː] *Abk. für* **European Community** EG, Europäische Gemeinschaft

ec·cen·tric [ɪk'sentrɪk] **1.** (~ally) exzentrisch; **2.** Exzentriker *m*, Sonderling *m*

ec·cle·si·as·tic [ɪkliːzɪ'æstɪk] (~ally), ~**ti·cal** geistlich, kirchlich

ech·o ['ekəʊ] **1.** (*pl.* -oes) Echo *n*; **2.** widerhallen; *fig.* echoen, nachsprechen

e·clipse *astr.* [ɪ'klɪps] (Sonnen-, Mond-) Finsternis *f*

e·co·cide ['iːkəsaɪd] Umweltzerstörung *f*

e·co·lo·gi·cal [iːkə'lɒdʒɪkl] ökologisch, Umwelt...

e·col·o·gist [iː'kɒlədʒɪst] Ökologe *m*; ~**gy** [iː'kɒlədʒɪ] Ökologie *f*

ec·o·nom·ic [iːkə'nɒmɪk] (~ally) wirtschaftlich, Wirtschafts...; ~ **growth** Wirtschaftswachstum *n*; ~**i·cal** wirtschaftlich, sparsam; ~**ics** *sg.* Volkswirtschaft(slehre) *f*

e·con·o·mist [ɪ'kɒnəmɪst] Volkswirt *m*; ~**mize** [ɪ'kɒnəmaɪz] sparsam wirtschaften (mit); ~**my** [ɪ'kɒnəmɪ] **1.** Wirtschaft *f*; Wirtschaftlichkeit *f*, Sparsamkeit *f*; Einsparung *f*; **2.** Spar...

e·co·sys·tem ['iːkəʊsɪstəm] Ökosystem *n*

ec·sta·sy ['ekstəsɪ] Ekstase *f*, Verzückung *f*; ~**t·ic** [ɪk'stætɪk] (~ally) verzückt

ECU ['ekjuː, eɪ'kuː] *Abk. für* **European Currency Unit** Europäische Währungseinheit

ed. [ed] *Abk. für:* **edited** h(rs)g., herausgegeben; **edition** Aufl., Auflage *f*; **editor** H(rs)g., Herausgeber *m*

ed·dy ['edɪ] **1.** Wirbel *m*; **2.** wirbeln

edge [edʒ] **1.** Schneide *f*; Rand *m*; Kante *f*; Schärfe *f*; ⚠ *nicht* (Straßen-, Haus)Ecke; be on ~ nervös *od.* gereizt sein; **2.** schärfen; (um)säumen; (sich) drängen; ~**ways** ['edʒweɪz], ~**wise** ['edʒwaɪz] seitlich, von der Seite

edg·ing ['edʒɪŋ] Einfassung *f*; Rand *m*

edg·y ['edʒɪ] (-ier, -iest) scharf(kantig); F nervös; F gereizt

ed·i·ble ['edɪbl] eßbar

e·dict ['iːdɪkt] Edikt *n*

ed·i·fice ['edɪfɪs] Gebäude *n*

ed·it ['edɪt] *Text* herausgeben, redigieren; *Computer:* editieren; *Zeitung* als Herausgeber leiten; **e·di·tion** [ɪ'dɪʃn] (Buch)Ausgabe *f*; Auflage *f*; **ed·i·tor** ['edɪtə] Herausgeber(in); Redakteur(in); **ed·i·to·ri·al** [edɪ'tɔːrɪəl] **1.** Leitartikel *m*; **2.** Redaktions...

EDP [iː diː 'piː] *Abk. für* **electronic data processing** EDV, elektronische Datenverarbeitung

ed·u·cate ['edʒʊkeɪt] erziehen; unterrichten; **'~·cat·ed** gebildet; **~·ca·tion** [edʒʊ'keɪʃn] Erziehung *f*; (Aus)Bildung *f*; Bildungs-, Schulwesen *n*; *Ministry of* Unterrichtsministerium *n*; **~·ca·tion·al** [~ʃənl] erzieherisch, Erziehungs...; Bildungs...

eel *zo.* [iːl] Aal *m*

ef·fect [ɪ'fekt] (Aus)Wirkung *f*; Effekt *m*, Eindruck *m*; **~s** *pl. econ.* Effekten *pl.*; *be in ~* inKraft sein; *in ~* in Wirklichkeit; *take ~* in Kraft treten; **ef'fective** wirksam; eindrucksvoll; tatsächlich

ef·fem·i·nate [ɪ'femɪnət] verweichlicht; weibisch

ef·fer·vesce [efə'ves] brausen, sprudeln; **~·ves·cent** [efə'vesnt] sprudelnd, schäumend

ef·fi·cien·cy [ɪ'fɪʃənsɪ] Leistung(sfähigkeit) *f*; **~ measure** *econ.* Rationalisierungsmaßnahme *f*; **~t** wirksam; leistungsfähig, tüchtig

ef·flu·ent ['efluənt] Abwasser *n*, Abwässer *pl.*

ef·fort ['efət] Anstrengung *f*, Bemühung *f* (*at* um); Mühe *f*; *without* ~ → '**~·less** mühelos, ohne Anstrengung

ef·fron·te·ry [ɪ'frʌntərɪ] Frechheit *f*

ef·fu·sive [ɪ'fjuːsɪv] überschwenglich

EFTA ['eftə] *Abk. für European Free Trade Association* EFTA, Europäische Freihandelsassoziation

e.g. [iː 'dʒiː] *Abk. für for example* (*lateinisch exempli gratia*) z.B., zum Beispiel

egg¹ [eg] Ei *n*; *put all one's ~s in one basket* alles auf eine Karte setzen

egg² [eg]: *~ on* anstacheln

'egg co·sy Eierwärmer *m*; **'~·cup** Eierbecher *m*; **'~·head** F Eierkopf *m* (*Intellektueller*); **'~·plant** *bot. bsd. Am.* Aubergine *f*; **'~·shell** Eierschale *f*; **'~· tim·er** Eieruhr *f*

e·go·is·m ['egəʊɪzəm] Egoismus *m*, Selbstsucht *f*; **~t** ['egəʊɪst] Egoist(in)

E·gypt ['iːdʒɪpt] Ägypten *n*; **E·gyp·tian** [ɪ'dʒɪpʃn] **1.** ägyptisch; **2.** Ägypter(in)

ei·der·down ['aɪdədaʊn] Eiderdaunen *pl.*; Daunendecke *f*

eight [eɪt] **1.** acht; **2.** Acht *f*; **eigh·teen** [eɪ'tiːn] **1.** achtzehn; **2.** Achtzehn *f*; **eigh·teenth** [eɪ'tiːnθ] achtzehnte(r, -s); **'~·fold** achtfach; **eighth** [eɪtθ] **1.**

achte(r, -s); **2.** Achtel *n*; **'eighth·ly** achtens; **eigh·ti·eth** ['eɪtɪɪθ] achtzigste(r, -s); **'eigh·ty 1.** achtzig; **2.** Achtzig *f*

Ei·re ['eərə] *irischer Name der Republik Irland*

ei·ther ['aɪðə, 'iːðə] jede(r, -s) (*von zweien*); eine(r, -s) (*von zweien*); beides; ~ ... *or* entweder ... oder; *not* ~ auch nicht

e·jac·u·late *physiol.* [ɪ'dʒækjʊleɪt] *v/t.* Samen ausstoßen; *v/i.* ejakulieren, e-n Samenerguß haben

e·ject [ɪ'dʒekt] *j-n* hinauswerfen; *tech.* ausstoßen, -werfen

eke [iːk]: ~ *out* Vorräte *etc.* strecken; Einkommen aufbessern; ~ *out a living* sich (mühsam) durchschlagen

e·lab·o·rate 1. [ɪ'læbərət] sorgfältig (aus)gearbeitet; kompliziert; **2.** [ɪ'læbəreɪt] sorgfältig ausarbeiten

e·lapse [ɪ'læps] verfließen, -streichen

e·las·tic [ɪ'læstɪk] **1.** (~*ally*) elastisch, dehnbar; ~ *band Brt.* → **2.** Gummiring *m*, -band *n*; **~·ti·ci·ty** [elæ'stɪsətɪ] Elastizität *f*

e·lat·ed [ɪ'leɪtɪd] begeistert (*at, by* von)

el·bow ['elbəʊ] **1.** Ellbogen *m*; (scharfe) Biegung; *tech.* Knie *n*; *at one's* ~ bei der Hand; **2.** mit dem Ellbogen (weg)stoßen; ~ *one's way through* sich (mit den Ellbogen) e-n Weg bahnen durch

el·der¹ ['eldə] **1.** ältere(r, -s); **2.** der, die Ältere; (Kirchen)Älteste(r) *m*; '**~·ly** ältlich, ältere(r, -s)

el·der² *bot.* ['eldə] Holunder *m*

el·dest ['eldɪst] älteste(r, -s)

e·lect [ɪ'lekt] **1.** gewählt; **2.** (aus-, er)wählen

e·lec·tion [ɪ'lekʃn] **1.** Wahl *f*; **2.** *pol.* Wahl...; **~·tor** [ɪ'lektə] Wähler(in); *Am. pol.* Wahlmann *m*; *hist.* Kurfürst *m*; **~·to·ral** [ɪ'lektərəl] Wahl..., Wähler...; ~ *college Am. pol.* Wahlmänner *pl.*; **~·to·rate** *pol.* [ɪ'lektərət] Wähler (-schaft *f*) *pl.*

e·lec·tric [ɪ'lektrɪk] (~*ally*) elektrisch, Elektro-...

e·lec·tri·cal [ɪ'lektrɪkl] elektrisch; Elektro-...; ~ **en·gi'neer** Elektroingenieur *m*, -techniker *m*; ~ **en·gi'neer·ing** Elektrotechnik *f*

e·lec·tric 'chair elektrischer Stuhl

el·ec·tri·cian [ɪlek'trɪʃn] Elektriker *m*

e·lec·tri·ci·ty [ɪlek'trɪsətɪ] Elektrizität f

e·lec·tric 'ra·zor Elektrorasierer m

e·lec·tri·fy [ɪ'lektrɪfaɪ] elektrifizieren; elektrisieren (a. fig.)

e·lec·tro·cute [ɪ'lektrəkju:t] auf dem elektrischen Stuhl hinrichten; durch elektrischen Strom töten

e·lec·tron [ɪ'lektrɒn] Elektron n

el·ec·tron·ic [ɪlek'trɒnɪk] (**~ally**) elektronisch, Elektronen...; **~ 'da·ta pro·ces·sing** elektronische Datenverarbeitung

el·ec·tron·ics [ɪlek'trɒnɪks] sg. Elektronik f

el·e·gance ['elɪgəns] Eleganz f; **'~gant** elegant; geschmackvoll; erstklassig

el·e·ment ['elɪmənt] Element n; Urstoff m; (Grund)Bestandteil m; **~s** pl. Anfangsgründe pl., Grundlage(n pl.) f; Elemente pl., Naturkräfte pl.; **~men·tal** [elɪ'mentl] elementar; wesentlich

el·e·men·ta·ry [elɪ'mentərɪ] elementar; Anfangs...; **~ school** Am. Grundschule f

el·e·phant zo. ['elɪfənt] Elefant m

el·e·vate ['elɪveɪt] erhöhen; fig. erheben; **'~vat·ed** erhöht; fig. gehoben, erhaben; **~va·tion** [elɪ'veɪʃn] Erhebung f; Erhöhung f; Höhe f; Erhabenheit f; **~va·tor** tech. ['elɪveɪtə] Am. Lift m, Fahrstuhl m, Aufzug m

e·lev·en [ɪ'levn] **1.** elf; **2.** Elf f; **~th** [ɪ'levnθ] **1.** elfte(r, -s); **2.** Elftel n

elf [elf] (pl. **elves**) Elf(e f) m; Kobold m

e·li·cit [ɪ'lɪsɪt] et. entlocken (**from** dat.); ans (Tages)Licht bringen

el·i·gi·ble ['elɪdʒəbl] in Frage kommend, geeignet, annehmbar, akzeptabel

e·lim·i·nate [ɪ'lɪmɪneɪt] entfernen, beseitigen; ausscheiden; **~na·tion** [ɪlɪmɪ'neɪʃn] Entfernung f, Beseitigung f; Ausscheidung f

é·lite [eɪ'li:t] Elite f; Auslese f

elk zo. [elk] Elch m; Am. Wapitihirsch m

el·lipse math. [ɪ'lɪps] Ellipse f

elm bot. [elm] Ulme f

e·lon·gate ['i:lɒŋgeɪt] verlängern

e·lope [ɪ'ləʊp] (mit s-m od. s-r Geliebten) ausreißen od. durchbrennen

el·o·quence ['eləkwəns] Beredsamkeit f; **'~quent** beredt

else [els] sonst, weiter; andere(r, -s); **~'where** anderswo(hin)

e·lude [ɪ'lu:d] geschickt entgehen, ausweichen, sich entziehen (alle dat.); fig. nicht einfallen (dat.)

e·lu·sive [ɪ'lu:sɪv] schwer faßbar

elves [elvz] pl. von **elf**

e·ma·ci·at·ed [ɪ'meɪʃɪeɪtɪd] abgezehrt, ausgemergelt

em·a·nate ['emaneɪt] ausströmen; ausgehen (**from** von); **~na·tion** [ema'neɪʃn] Ausströmen n; fig. Ausstrahlung f

e·man·ci·pate [ɪ'mænsɪpeɪt] emanzipieren; **~pa·tion** [ɪmænsɪ'peɪʃn] Emanzipation f

em·balm [ɪm'bɑ:m] (ein)balsamieren

em·bank·ment [ɪm'bæŋkmənt] (Erd-)Damm m; (Bahn-, Straßen)Damm m; Uferstraße f

em·bar·go [em'bɑ:gəʊ] (pl. **-goes**) Embargo n, (Hafen-, Handels)Sperre f

em·bark [ɪm'bɑ:k] naut., aviat. an Bord nehmen od. gehen, naut. a. (sich) einschiffen; Waren verladen; **~ on** et. anfangen od. beginnen

em·bar·rass [ɪm'bærəs] in Verlegenheit bringen, verlegen machen, in e-e peinliche Lage versetzen; **~ing** unangenehm, peinlich; **~ment** Verlegenheit f

em·bas·sy pol. ['embəsɪ] Botschaft f

em·bed [ɪm'bed] (**-dd-**) (ein)betten, (ein)lagern

em·bel·lish [ɪm'belɪʃ] verschönern; fig. ausschmücken, beschönigen

em·bers ['embəz] pl. Glut f

em·bez·zle [ɪm'bezl] unterschlagen; **~ment** Unterschlagung f

em·bit·ter [ɪm'bɪtə] verbittern

em·blem ['embləm] Sinnbild n; Wahrzeichen n

em·bod·y [ɪm'bɒdɪ] verkörpern; enthalten

em·bo·lis·m med. ['embəlɪzəm] Embolie f

em·brace [ɪm'breɪs] **1.** (sich) umarmen; einschließen; **2.** Umarmung f

em·broi·der [ɪm'brɔɪdə] (be)sticken; fig. ausschmücken; **~y** [ɪm'brɔɪdərɪ] Stickerei f; fig. Ausschmückung f

em·broil [ɪm'brɔɪl] (in Streit) verwickeln

e·mend [ɪ'mend] Texte verbessern, korrigieren

em·e·rald ['emərəld] **1.** Smaragd *m*; **2.** smaragdgrün

•merge [ı'mɜːdʒ] auftauchen; sich herausstellen *od.* ergeben (*Wahrheit etc.*)

•mer·gen·cy [ı'mɜːdʒənsı] Not(lage) *f*, -fall *m*, -stand *m*; Not...; **state of ~** *pol.* Ausnahmezustand *m*; **~ brake** Notbremse *f*; **~ call** Notruf *m*; **~ exit** Notausgang *m*; **~ land·ing** *aviat.* Notlandung *f*; **~ num·ber** Notruf(nummer *f*) *m*; **~ room** *Am.* Notaufnahme *f* (*im Krankenhaus*)

em·i·grant ['emıgrənt] Auswanderer *m*, *bsd. pol.* Emigrant(in); **~grate** ['emıgreıt] auswandern, *bsd. pol.* emigrieren; **~gra·tion** [emı'greıʃn] Auswanderung *f*, *bsd. pol.* Emigration *f*

em·i·nence ['emınəns] Berühmtheit *f*, Bedeutung *f*; ≈ *rel.* Eminenz *f*; **'~nent** hervorragend, berühmt; bedeutend; **'~nent·ly** ganz besonders, äußerst

e·mis·sion [ı'mıʃn] Ausstoß *m*, -strahlung *f*, -strömen *n*; **~free** abgasfrei

e·mit [ı'mıt] (*-tt-*) aussenden, -stoßen, -strahlen, -strömen; von sich geben

e·mo·tion [ı'məʊʃn] (Gemüts)Bewegung *f*, Gefühl(sregung *f*) *n*; Rührung *f*; **~al** [ı'məʊʃənl] emotional; gefühlsmäßig; gefühlsbetont; **~al·ly** [ı'məʊʃnəlı] emotional, gefühlsmäßig; **~ disturbed** seelisch gestört; **~less** gefühllos

em·pe·ror ['empərə] Kaiser *m*

em·pha|·sis ['emfəsıs] (*pl.* **-ses** [-siːz]) Gewicht *n*; Nachdruck *m*; **~size** ['emfəsaız] nachdrücklich betonen; **~tic** [ım'fætık] (**~ally**) nachdrücklich; deutlich; bestimmt

em·pire ['empaıə] Reich *n*, Imperium *n*; Kaiserreich *n*

em·pir·i·cal [em'pırıkl] erfahrungsgemäß

em·ploy [ım'plɔı] **1.** beschäftigen, anstellen; an-, verwenden, gebrauchen; **2.** Beschäftigung *f*; **in the ~ of** angestellt bei; **~ee** [emplɔı'iː] Angestellte(r *m*) *f*, Arbeitnehmer(in); **~er** [ım'plɔıə] Arbeitgeber(in); **~ment** [ım'plɔımənt] Beschäftigung *f*, Arbeit *f*; **~ment ad** Stellenanzeige *f*; **~ment of·fice** Arbeitsamt *n*

em·pow·er [ım'paʊə] ermächtigen; befähigen

em·press ['emprıs] Kaiserin *f*

emp·ti·ness ['emptınıs] Leere *f* (*a. fig.*); **'~ty 1.** (**-ier, -iest**) leer (*a. fig.*); **2.** (aus-, ent)leeren; sich leeren

em·u·late ['emjʊleıt] wetteifern mit; nacheifern (*dat.*); es gleichtun (*dat.*)

e·mul·sion [ı'mʌlʃn] Emulsion *f*

en·a·ble [ı'neıbl] befähigen, es *j-m* ermöglichen; ermächtigen

en·act [ı'nækt] *Gesetz* erlassen; verfügen

e·nam·el [ı'næml] **1.** Email(le *f*) *n*; *anat.* (Zahn)Schmelz *m*; Glasur *f*, Lack *m*; Nagellack *m*; **2.** (*bsd. Brt. -ll-*, *Am. -l-*) emaillieren; glasieren; lackieren

en·am·o·u(u)red [ı'næməd]: **~ of** verliebt in

en·camp·ment [ın'kæmpmənt] *bsd. mil.* (Feld)Lager *n*

en·cased [ın'keıst]: **~ in** gehüllt in (*acc.*)

en·chant [ın'tʃɑːnt] bezaubern; **~ing** bezaubernd; **~ment** Bezauberung *f*; Zauber *m*

en·cir·cle [ın'sɜːkl] einkreisen, umzingeln; umfassen, umschlingen

encl *nur geschr. Abk. für* **enclosed, enclosure(s)** Anl., Anlage(n *pl.*) *f*

en·close [ın'kləʊz] einschließen, umgeben; beilegen, -fügen (*e-m Brief*); **en·clo·sure** [ın'kləʊʒə] Einzäunung *f*; Anlage *f* (*zu e-m Brief*)

en·code [en'kəʊd] verschlüsseln, chiffrieren; kodieren

en·com·pass [ın'kʌmpəs] umgeben

en·coun·ter [ın'kaʊntə] **1.** Begegnung *f*; Gefecht *n*; **2.** begegnen (*dat.*); *auf Schwierigkeiten etc.* stoßen; mit *j-m* *feindlich* zusammenstoßen

en·cour·age [ın'kʌrıdʒ] ermutigen; fördern; **~ment** Ermutigung *f*; Anfeuerung *f*; Unterstützung *f*

en·cour·ag·ing [ın'kʌrıdʒıŋ] ermutigend

en·croach [ın'krəʊtʃ] (**on**) eingreifen (in *j-s Recht etc.*), eindringen (in *acc.*); über Gebühr in Anspruch nehmen (*acc.*); **~ment** Ein-, Übergriff *m*

en·cum·ber [ın'kʌmbə] belasten; (be)hindern; **~brance** [ın'kʌmbrəns] Belastung *f*

en·cy·clo·p(a)e·di·a [ensaıklə'piːdjə] Enzyklopädie *f*

end [end] **1.** Ende *n*; Ziel *n*, Zweck *m*; **no ~ of** unendlich viel(e), unzählige; **at the**

~ **of May** Ende Mai; **in the** ~ am Ende, schließlich; **on** ~ aufrecht; **stand on** ~ zu Berge stehen (*Haare*); **to no** ~ vergebens; **go off the deep** ~ *fig.* in die Luft gehen; **make (both)** ~**s meet** durchkommen, finanziell über die Runden kommen; **2.** enden; beend(ig)en

en·dan·ger [ɪnˈdeɪndʒə] gefährden

en·dear [ɪnˈdɪə] beliebt machen (**to s.o.** bei j-m); ~**ing** [ɪnˈdɪərɪŋ] gewinnend; liebenswert; ~**ment**: **words** *pl.* **of** ~, ~**s** *pl.* zärtliche Worte *pl.*

en·deav·o(u)r [ɪnˈdevə] **1.** Bestreben *n*, Bemühung *f*; **2.** sich bemühen

end·ing [ˈendɪŋ] Ende *n*; Schluß *m*; *gr.* Endung *f*

en·dive *bot.* [ˈendɪv, ˈendaɪv] Endivie *f*

end·less [ˈendlɪs] endlos, unendlich; *tech.* ohne Ende

en·dorse [ɪnˈdɔːs] *econ.* Scheck *etc.* indossieren; *et.* vermerken (**on** auf der Rückseite e-r *Urkunde*); billigen, gutheißen; ~**ment** Vermerk *m*; *econ.* Indossament *n*, Giro *n*

en·dow [ɪnˈdaʊ] *fig.* ausstatten (~ **s.o. with s.th.** j-m *et.* stiften; ~**ment** Stiftung *f*; *mst* ~**s** *pl.* Begabung *f*, Talent *n*

en·dur·ance [ɪnˈdjʊərəns] Ausdauer *f*; **beyond** ~, **past** ~ unerträglich; ~**e** [ɪnˈdjʊə] ertragen

'end us·er Endverbraucher *m*

en·e·my [ˈenəmɪ] **1.** Feind *m*; **2.** feindlich

en·er·get·ic [enəˈdʒetɪk] (~**ally**) energisch; tatkräftig

en·er·gy [ˈenədʒɪ] Energie *f*; '~ **cri·sis** Energiekrise *f*; '~**sav·ing** energiesparend; '~ **sup·ply** Energieversorgung *f*

en·fold [ɪnˈfəʊld] einhüllen; umfassen

en·force [ɪnˈfɔːs] (mit Nachdruck, *a.* gerichtlich) geltend machen; *Gesetz etc.* durchführen; durchsetzen, erzwingen; ~**ment** *econ.*, *jur.* Geltendmachung *f*; Durchsetzung *f*, Erzwingung *f*

en·fran·chise [ɪnˈfræntʃaɪz] *j-m* das Wahlrecht verleihen

en·gage [ɪnˈgeɪdʒ] *v/t.* j-s *Aufmerksamkeit* auf sich ziehen; *tech.* einrasten lassen, *mot. Gang* einlegen; *j-n* ein-, anstellen, *Künstler* engagieren; *v/i. tech.* einrasten, greifen; ~ **in** sich einlassen auf (*acc.*) *od.* in (*acc.*); sich beschäftigen mit; ~**d** verlobt (**to** mit); beschäftigt (**in**, **on** mit); besetzt (*Toilette*, *Brt. tel.*); ~

tone *od.* **signal** *Brt. tel.* Besetztzeichen *n*; ~**ment** Verlobung *f*; Verabredun *f*; *mil.* Gefecht *n*; *tech.* Ineinandergrei fen *n*

en·gag·ing [ɪnˈgeɪdʒɪŋ] einnehmend gewinnend (*Lächeln etc.*)

en·gine [ˈendʒɪn] Maschine *f*; Motor *m*; *rail.* Lokomotive *f*; '~ **driv·er** *Brt. rai* Lokomotivführer *m*

en·gi·neer [endʒɪˈnɪə] **1.** Ingenieur(in) Techniker(in), Mechaniker(in); *Am rail.* Lokomotivführer *m*; *mil.* Pionie *m*; **2.** bauen; *fig.* (geschickt) in die We ge leiten; ~**ing** [endʒɪˈnɪərɪŋ] Technik *f*, Ingenieurwesen *n*, Maschinen- u. Ge rätebau *m*

En·glish [ˈɪŋglɪʃ] **1.** englisch; **2.** *ling* Englisch *n*; **the** ~ *pl.* die Engländer *pl.* **in plain** ~ *fig.* unverblümt; '~**man** (*pl* **-men**) Engländer *m*; '~**wom·an** (*pl* **-women**) Engländerin *f*

en·grave [ɪnˈgreɪv] (ein)gravieren (-)meißeln, (-)schnitzen; *fig.* einprägen

en·grav·er Graveur *m*; **en·grav·ing** (Kupfer-, Stahl)Stich *m*; Holzschnitt *m*

en·grossed [ɪnˈgrəʊst]: ~ **in** (voll) in Anspruch genommen von, vertieft *od.* versunken in (*acc.*)

en·hance [ɪnˈhɑːns] erhöhen

e·nig·ma [ɪˈnɪgmə] Rätsel *n*; **en·ig·mat·ic** [enɪgˈmætɪk] (~**ally**) rätselhaft

en·joy [ɪnˈdʒɔɪ] sich erfreuen an (*dat.*); genießen; **did you** ~ **it?** hat es Ihnen gefallen?; ~ **o.s.** sich amüsieren, sich gut unterhalten; ~ **yourself!** viel Spaß!; *I* ~ *my dinner* es schmeckt mir; ~**a·ble** angenehm, erfreulich; ~**ment** Vergnügen *n*, Freude *f*; Genuß *m*

en·large [ɪnˈlɑːdʒ] (sich) vergrößern *od.* erweitern, ausdehnen; *phot.* vergrößern; sich verbreiten *od.* auslassen (**on** über *acc.*); ~**ment** Erweiterung *f*; Vergrößerung *f* (*a. phot.*)

en·light·en [ɪnˈlaɪtn] aufklären, belehren; ~**ment** Aufklärung *f*

en·list *mil.* [ɪnˈlɪst] *v/t.* anwerben; *v/i.* sich freiwillig melden; ~**ed men** *pl. Am.* Unteroffiziere *pl.* u. Mannschaften *pl.*

en·liv·en [ɪnˈlaɪvn] beleben

en·mi·ty [ˈenmətɪ] Feindschaft *f*

en·no·ble [ɪˈnəʊbl] adeln; veredeln

e·nor·mi·ty [ɪˈnɔːmətɪ] Ungeheuerlichkeit *f*; ~**mous** [ɪˈnɔːməs] ungeheuer

e·nough [ɪˈnʌf] genug

en·quire [ɪn'kwaɪə], **en·qui·ry** [ɪn'kwaɪərɪ] → *inquire, inquiry*

en·rage [ɪn'reɪdʒ] wütend machen; **~d** wütend (*at* über *acc.*)

en·rap·ture [ɪn'ræptʃə] entzücken, hinreißen; **~d** entzückt, hingerissen

en·rich [ɪn'rɪtʃ] be-, anreichern

en·rol(l) [ɪn'rəʊl] (*-ll-*) (sich) einschreiben *od.* -tragen; *univ.* (sich) immatrikulieren

en·sign *naut.* ['ensaɪn] *bsd.* (National-)Flagge *f*; *Am.* ['ensn] Leutnant *m* zur See

en·sue [ɪn'sjuː] (darauf-, nach)folgen

en·sure [ɪn'ʃʊə] sichern

en·tail [ɪn'teɪl] mit sich bringen, zur Folge haben

en·tan·gle [ɪn'tæŋgl] verwickeln

en·ter ['entə] *v/t.* (hinein-, herein)gehen, (-)kommen [ɪn'rɪtʃ] (-)treten in (*acc.*), eintreten, -steigen in (*acc.*), betreten; einreisen in (*acc.*); *naut.*, *rail.* einlaufen, -fahren in (*acc.*); eindringen in (*acc.*); *Namen etc.* eintragen, -schreiben; *Sport:* melden, nennen (*for* für); *fig.* eintreten in (*acc.*), eingehen auf (*acc.*); *Computer:* eingeben; *v/i.* eintreten, herein-, hineinkommen, -gehen; *thea.* auftreten; sich eintragen *od.* -schreiben *od.* anmelden (*for* für); *Sport:* melden, nennen (*for* für); **~ key** *Computer:* Eingabetaste *f*

en·ter|·prise [ɪn'entəpraɪz] Unternehmen *n* (*a. econ.*); *econ.* Unternehmertum *n*; Unternehmungsgeist *m*; **'~·pris·ing** unternehmungslustig; wagemutig; kühn

en·ter·tain [ɪn'enteɪn] unterhalten; bewirten; **~er** Entertainer(in), Unterhaltungskünstler(in); **~ment** Unterhaltung *f*; Entertainment *n*; Bewirtung *f*

en·thral(l) *fig.* [ɪn'θrɔːl] (*-ll-*) fesseln, bezaubern

en·throne [ɪn'θrəʊn] inthronisieren

en·thu·si·as|·m [ɪn'θjuːzɪæzəm] Begeisterung *f*; **~t** [ɪn'θjuːzɪæst] Enthusiast(in); **~tic** [ɪnθjuːzɪ'æstɪk] (*~ally*) begeistert

en·tice [ɪn'taɪs] (ver)locken; **~ment** Verlockung *f*, Reiz *m*

en·tire [ɪn'taɪə] ganz, vollständig; ungeteilt; **~ly** völlig; ausschließlich

en·ti·tle [ɪn'taɪtl] betiteln; berechtigen (*to* zu)

en·ti·ty ['entətɪ] Einheit *f*

en·trails *anat.* ['entreɪlz] *pl.* Eingeweide *pl.*

en·trance ['entrəns] Eintreten *n*, -tritt *m*; Ein-, Zugang *m*; Zufahrt *f*; Einlaß *m*, Ein-, Zutritt *m*; **'~ ex·am·(i·na·tion)** Aufnahmeprüfung *f*; **'~ fee** Eintritt(sgeld *n*) *m*; Aufnahmegebühr *f*

en·treat [ɪn'triːt] inständig bitten, anflehen; **en·trea·ty** dringende *od.* inständige Bitte

en·trench *mil.* [ɪn'trentʃ] verschanzen (*a. fig.*)

en·trust [ɪn'trʌst] anvertrauen (*s.th. to s.o.* j-m et.); betrauen

en·try ['entrɪ] Eintreten *n*, -tritt *m*; Einreise *f*; Beitritt *m* (*into* zu); Einlaß *m*, Zutritt *m*; Zu-, Eingang *m*, Einfahrt *f*; Eintrag(ung *f*) *m*; Stichwort *n* (*im Lexikon etc.*); *Sport:* Nennung *f*, Meldung *f*; **bookkeeping by double (single) ~** *econ.* doppelte (einfache) Buchführung; **no ~!** Zutritt verboten!, *mot.* keine Einfahrt!; **'~ per·mit** Einreiseerlaubnis *f*, -genehmigung *f*; **'~·phone** Türsprechanlage *f*; **'~ vi·sa** Einreisevisum *n*

en·twine [ɪn'twaɪn] ineinanderschlingen

e·nu·me·rate [ɪ'njuːməreɪt] aufzählen

en·vel·op [ɪn'veləp] (ein)hüllen, einwickeln

en·ve·lope ['envələʊp] Briefumschlag *m*

en·vi|·a·ble ['envɪəbl] beneidenswert; **'~·ous** neidisch

en·vi·ron·ment [ɪn'vaɪərənmənt] Umgebung *f*, *a.* Milieu *n*; Umwelt *f*

en·vi·ron·men|·tal [ɪnvaɪərən'mentl] Milieu...; Umwelt...; **~·ist** [ɪnvaɪərən'mentəlɪst] Umweltschützer(in); **'~ law** Umweltschutzgesetz *n*; **~ pol·lu·tion** Umweltverschmutzung *f*

en·vi·ron·ment 'friend·ly umweltfreundlich

en·vi·rons ['envɪrənz] *pl.* Umgebung *f* (*e-r Stadt*)

en·vis·age [ɪn'vɪzɪdʒ] sich *et.* vorstellen

en·voy ['envɔɪ] Gesandte(r) *m*

en·vy ['envɪ] **1.** Neid *m*; **2.** beneiden

ep·ic ['epɪk] **1.** episch; **2.** Epos *n*

ep·i·dem·ic [epɪ'demɪk] **1.** (*~ally*) seuchenartig; **~ disease** → **2.** Epidemie *f*, Seuche *f*

ep·i·der·mis [epɪ'dɜːmɪs] Oberhaut *f*

ep·i·lep·sy *med.* ['epɪlepsɪ] Epilepsie *f*

ep·i·logue *bsd. Brt.,* **ep·i·log** *Am.* ['epɪlɒg] Nachwort *n*

e·pis·co·pal *rel.* [ɪ'pɪskəpl] bischöflich

ep·i·sode ['epɪsəʊd] Episode *f*

ep·i·taph ['epɪtɑːf] Grabinschrift *f*

e·poch ['iːpɒk] Epoche *f*, Zeitalter *n*

equa·ble ['ekwəbl] ausgeglichen (*a. Klima*)

e·qual ['iːkwəl] **1.** gleich; gleichmäßig; ~ **to** *fig.* gewachsen (*dat.*); ~ **oppor·tuni·ties** *pl.* Chancengleichheit *f*; ~ **rights** *pl.* **for women** Gleichberechtigung *f* der Frau; **2.** Gleiche(r *m*) *f*; **3.** (*bsd. Brt. -ll-, Am. -l-*) gleichen (*dat.*); ~ **·i·ty** [iːˈkwɒlətɪ] Gleichheit *f*; ~ **·i·za·tion** [iːkwəlaɪˈzeɪʃn] Gleichstellung *f*; Ausgleich *m*; ~ **·ize** ['iːkwəlaɪz] gleichmachen, -stellen, angleichen; *Sport:* ausgleichen; **·iz·er** *Sport:* Ausgleich(stor *n*, -streffer) *m*

equa·nim·i·ty [iːkwəˈnɪmətɪ] Gleichmut *m*

e·qua·tion *math.* [ɪ'kweɪʒn] Gleichung *f*

e·qua·tor [ɪ'kweɪtə] Äquator *m*

e·qui·lib·ri·um [iːkwɪˈlɪbrɪəm] Gleichgewicht *n*

e·quip [ɪ'kwɪp] (*-pp-*) ausrüsten; ~ **ment** Ausrüstung *f*, -stattung *f*; *tech.* Einrichtung *f*

e·quiv·a·lent [ɪ'kwɪvələnt] **1.** gleichwertig, äquivalent; gleichbedeutend (**to** mit); **2.** Äquivalent *n*, Gegenwert *m*

e·ra ['ɪərə] Zeitrechnung *f*; Zeitalter *n*

e·rad·i·cate [ɪ'rædɪkeɪt] ausrotten

e·rase [ɪ'reɪz] ausradieren, -streichen, löschen (*a.* Computer, Tonband); *fig.* auslöschen; **e·ras·er** Radiergummi *m*

e·rect [ɪ'rekt] **1.** aufrecht; **2.** aufrichten; *Denkmal etc.* errichten; aufstellen; **e·rec·tion** [ɪ'rekʃn] Errichtung *f*; *physiol.* Erektion *f*

er·mine *zo.* ['ɜːmɪn] Hermelin *n*

e·rode *geol.* [ɪ'rəʊd] erodieren; **e·ro·sion** *geol.* [ɪ'rəʊʒn] Erosion *f*

e·rot·ic [ɪ'rɒtɪk] (*~ally*) erotisch

err [ɜː] (sich) irren

er·rand ['erənd] Botengang *m*, Besorgung *f*; **go on an ~, run an ~** e-e Besorgung machen; **'~ boy** Laufbursche *m*

er·rat·ic [ɪ'rætɪk] (*~ally*) sprunghaft, unstet, unberechenbar

er·ro·ne·ous [ɪ'rəʊnjəs] irrig

er·ror ['erə] Irrtum *m*, Fehler *m* (*a.* Computer); **~s excepted** Irrtümer vorbehalten; **'~ mes·sage** Computer: Fehlermeldung *f*

e·rupt [ɪ'rʌpt] ausbrechen (*Vulkan etc.*); durchbrechen (*Zähne*); **e·rup·tion** [ɪ'rʌpʃn] (*Vulkan*)Ausbruch *m*; *med.* Ausschlag *m*

ESA [iː es 'eɪ] *Abk. für* **European Space Agency** Europäische Weltraumbehörde

es·ca·late ['eskəleɪt] eskalieren (*Krieg etc.*); steigen, in die Höhe gehen (*Preise*); **~·la·tion** [eskəˈleɪʃn] Eskalation *f*

es·ca·la·tor ['eskəleɪtə] Rolltreppe *f*

es·ca·lope *gastr.* ['eskələʊp] (*bsd.* Wiener) Schnitzel *n*

es·cape [ɪ'skeɪp] **1.** entgehen; entkommen, -rinnen; entweichen; *j-m* entfallen; **2.** Entrinnen *n*; Entweichen *n*; Flucht *f*; **have a narrow ~** mit knapper Not davonkommen; **~ chute** *aviat.* Notrutsche *f*; **~ key** Computer: Escape-Taste *f*

es·cort 1. ['eskɔːt] *mil.* Eskorte *f*; Geleit(schutz *m*) *n*; **2.** [ɪ'skɔːt] *mil.* eskortieren; *aviat., naut.* Geleit(schutz) geben; geleiten

es·cutch·eon [ɪ'skʌtʃən] Wappenschild *m, n*

esp. *nur geschr. Abk. für* **especially** bes., bsd., besonders

es·pe·cial [ɪ'speʃl] besondere(r, -s); **~·ly** besonders

es·pi·o·nage [espɪəˈnɑːʒ] Spionage *f*

es·pla·nade [espləˈneɪd] (*bsd.* Strand-)Promenade *f*

es·say ['eseɪ] Aufsatz *m*, kurze Abhandlung, Essay *m, n*

es·sence ['esns] Wesen *n* (*e-r* Sache); Essenz *f*; Extrakt *m*

es·sen·tial [ɪ'senʃl] **1.** wesentlich; unentbehrlich; **2.** *mst* ~**s** *pl.* das Wesentliche; **~·ly** im wesentlichen, in der Hauptsache

es·tab·lish [ɪ'stæblɪʃ] ein-, errichten; **o.s.** sich etablieren *od.* niederlassen; be-, nachweisen; **~·ment** Ein-, Errichtung *f*; *econ.* Unternehmen *n*, Firma *f*; **the** 2 das Establishment, die etablierte Macht, die herrschende Schicht

es·tate [ɪ'steɪt] (großes) Grundstück, Landsitz *m*, Gut *n*; *jur.* Besitz *m*, (Erb)Masse *f*, Nachlaß *m*; **housing ~**

(Wohn)Siedlung *f*; **industrial ~** Industriegebiet *n*; **real ~** Liegenschaften *pl.*; **~ a·gent** *Brt.* Grundstücks-, Immobilienmakler *m*; **~ car** *Brt. mot.* Kombiwagen *m*

es·teem [ɪ'stiːm] **1.** Achtung *f*, Ansehen *n* (**with** bei); **2.** achten, (hoch)schätzen

es·thet·ic(s) *Am.* [es'θetɪk(s)] → **aesthetic(s)**

es·ti·mate 1. ['estɪmeɪt] (ab-, ein)schätzen; veranschlagen; **2.** ['estɪmɪt] Schätzung *f*; (Kosten)Voranschlag *m*; **~ma·tion** [estɪ'meɪʃn] Meinung *f*; Achtung *f*, Wertschätzung *f*

es·trange [ɪ'streɪndʒ] entfremden

es·tu·a·ry ['estjʊərɪ] *den Gezeiten ausgesetzte* weite Flußmündung

etch [etʃ] ätzen; radieren; **'~ing** Radierung *f*; Kupferstich *m*

e·ter·nal [ɪ'tɜːnl] ewig; **~ni·ty** [ɪ'tɜːnətɪ] Ewigkeit *f*

e·ther ['iːθə] Äther *m*; **e·the·re·al** [iː'θɪərɪəl] ätherisch (*a. fig.*)

eth·i·cal ['eθɪkl] sittlich, ethisch; **~ics** ['eθɪks] *sg.* Sittenlehre *f*, Ethik *f*

EU [iː 'juː] *Abk. für European Union* Europäische Union

Eu·ro... ['jʊərəʊ] europäisch, Euro...; **'~cheque** *Brt.* Euroscheck *m*

Eu·rope ['jʊərəp] Europa *n*; **Eu·ro·pe·an** [jʊərə'piːən] **1.** europäisch; **2.** Europäer(in); **Eu·ro·pe·an Com'mu·ni·ty** (*Abk. EC*) Europäische Gemeinschaft (*Abk.* EG)

e·vac·u·ate [ɪ'vækjʊeɪt] entleeren; evakuieren; *Haus etc.* räumen

e·vade [ɪ'veɪd] (geschickt) ausweichen (*dat.*); umgehen

e·val·u·ate [ɪ'væljʊeɪt] schätzen; abschätzen, bewerten, beurteilen

e·vap·o·rate [ɪ'væpəreɪt] verdunsten, -dampfen (lassen); **~d milk** Kondensmilch *f*; **~ra·tion** [ɪvæpə'reɪʃn] Verdunstung *f*, -dampfung *f*

e·va·sion [ɪ'veɪʒn] Umgehung *f*, Vermeidung *f*; (*Steuer*)Hinterziehung *f*; Ausflucht *f*; **~sive** [ɪ'veɪsɪv] ausweichend; **be ~** ausweichen

eve [iːv] Vorabend *m*; Vortag *m*; **on the ~ of** unmittelbar vor (*dat.*), am Vorabend (*gen.*)

e·ven ['iːvn] **1.** *adj.* eben, gleich; gleichmäßig; ausgeglichen; glatt; gerade (*Zahl*); **get ~ with s.o.** es j-m heimzah-

len; **2.** *adv.* selbst, sogar, auch; **not ~** nicht einmal; **~ though, ~ if** wenn auch; **3. ~ out** sich einpendeln; sich ausgleichen

eve·ning ['iːvnɪŋ] Abend *m*; **in the ~** am Abend, abends; **'~ class·es** *pl.* Abendkurs *m*, -unterricht *m*; **'~ dress** Gesellschaftsanzug *m*; Frack *m*, Smoking *m*; Abendkleid *n*

e·ven·song ['iːvnsɒŋ] Abendgottesdienst *m*

e·vent [ɪ'vent] Ereignis *n*; Fall *m*; *Sport:* Disziplin *f*; *Sport:* Wettbewerb *m*; **at all ~s** auf alle Fälle; **in the ~ of** im Falle (*gen.*); **~ful** ereignisreich

e·ven·tu·al [ɪ'ventʃʊəl] schließlich; △ *nicht* **eventuell**; **~ly** schließlich

ev·er ['evə] immer (wieder); je(mals); **~ after, ~ since** seitdem; **~ so** F sehr, noch so; **for ~** für immer, auf ewig; **Yours ~...,** 2 **yours, ...** Viele Grüße, Dein(e) *od.* Ihr(e), ... (*Briefschluß*); **have you ~ been to** London gewesen?; **'~green 1.** immergrün; unverwüstlich, *bsd.* immer wieder gern gehört; **2.** immergrüne Pflanze; **~last·ing** ewig; **~more:** (*for ~*) immerfort

ev·ery ['evrɪ] jede(r, -s); alle(r, -s); **~ now and then** von Zeit zu Zeit, dann u. wann; **~ one of them** jeder von ihnen; **~ other day** jeden zweiten Tag, alle zwei Tage; **'~bod·y** jeder(mann); **'~day** Alltags...; **'~one** jeder(mann); **'~thing** alles; **'~where** überall(hin)

e·vict [ɪ'vɪkt] *jur.* zur Räumung zwingen; *j-n* gewaltsam vertreiben

ev·i·dence ['evɪdəns] Beweis(material *n*) *m*, Beweise *pl.*; (Zeugen)Aussage *f*; **give ~** (als Zeuge) aussagen; **'~dent** augenscheinlich, offensichtlich

e·vil ['iːvl] **1.** (*bsd. Brt.* -**ll**-, *Am.* -**l**-) übel, schlimm, böse; **2.** Übel *n*; *das* Böse; **~'mind·ed** bösartig

e·voke [ɪ'vəʊk] (herauf)beschwören; *Erinnerungen* wachrufen

ev·o·lu·tion [iːvə'luːʃn] Evolution *f*, Entwicklung *f*

e·volve [ɪ'vɒlv] (sich) entwickeln

ewe *zo.* [juː] Mutterschaf *n*

ex [eks] *prp. econ.* ab: **~ works** ab Werk

ex... [eks] Ex..., ehemalig

ex·act [ɪg'zækt] **1.** exakt, genau; **2.** fordern, verlangen; **~ing** streng, genau;

aufreibend, anstrengend; **~·ly** exakt, genau; *als Antwort:* ganz recht, genau; **~·ness** Genauigkeit *f*

ex·ag·ge|·rate [ɪgˈzædʒəreɪt] übertreiben; **~·ra·tion** [ɪgzædʒəˈreɪʃn] Übertreibung *f*

ex·am F [ɪgˈzæm] Examen *n*

ex·am|·i·na·tion [ɪgzæmɪˈneɪʃn] Examen *n*, Prüfung *f*; Untersuchung *f*; *jur.* Vernehmung *f*, Verhör *n*; **~·ine** [ɪgˈzæmɪn] untersuchen; *jur.* vernehmen, -hören; *Schule etc.:* prüfen (**in** *in dat.*; **on** über *acc.*)

ex·am·ple [ɪgˈzɑːmpl] Beispiel *n*; Vorbild *n*, Muster *n*; **for ~** zum Beispiel

ex·as·pe|·rate [ɪgˈzæspəreɪt] wütend machen; **~·rat·ing** ärgerlich

ex·ca·vate [ˈekskəveɪt] ausgraben, -heben, schachten

ex·ceed [ɪkˈsiːd] überschreiten; übertreffen; **~·ing** übermäßig; **~·ing·ly** außerordentlich, überaus

ex·cel [ɪkˈsel] (*-ll-*) *v/t.* übertreffen; *v/i.* sich auszeichnen; **~·lence** [ˈeksələns] ausgezeichnete Qualität; **Ex·cel·len·cy** [ˈeksələnsɪ] Exzellenz *f*; **~·lent** [ˈeksələnt] ausgezeichnet, hervorragend

ex·cept [ɪkˈsept] **1.** ausnehmen, -schließen; **2.** *prp.* ausgenommen, außer; **~ for** abgesehen von, bis auf (*acc.*); **~·ing** *prp.* ausgenommen

ex·cep·tion [ɪkˈsepʃn] Ausnahme *f*; Einwand *m* (**to** gegen); **make an ~** e-e Ausnahme machen; **take ~ to** Anstoß nehmen an (*dat.*); **without ~** ohne Ausnahme, ausnahmslos; **~·al** [ɪkˈsepʃənl] außergewöhnlich; **~·al·ly** [ɪkˈsepʃnəlɪ] un-, außergewöhnlich

ex·cerpt [ˈeksɜːpt] Auszug *m*

ex·cess [ɪkˈses] Übermaß *n*; Überschuß *m*; Ausschweifung *f*; Mehr...; **~ 'bag·gage** *aviat.* Übergepäck *n*; **~ 'fare** (Fahrpreis)Zuschlag *m*; **ex·ces·sive** übermäßig, übertrieben; **~ 'lug·gage** → **excess baggage**; **~ 'post·age** Nachgebühr *f*

ex·change [ɪksˈtʃeɪndʒ] **1.** (aus-, ein-, um)tauschen (**for** gegen); wechseln; **2.** (Aus-, Um)Tausch *m*; (*bsd.* Geld-)Wechsel *m*; *a.* **bill of ~** Wechsel *m*; Börse *f*; Wechselstube *f*; Fernsprechamt *n*; **foreign ~(s** *pl.*) Devisen *pl.*; **rate of ~** → **exchange rate**; **~ of·fice** Wechselstu-

be *f*; **~ pu·pil** Austauschschüler(in); **~ rate** Wechselkurs *m*; **~ stu·dent** Austauschstudent(in); *Am.* Austauschschüler(in)

Ex·cheq·uer [ɪksˈtʃekə]: **Chancellor of the ~** *Brt.* Finanzminister *m*

ex·cise [ekˈsaɪz] Verbrauchssteuer *f*

ex·ci·ta·ble [ɪkˈsaɪtəbl] reizbar, (leicht) erregbar

ex·cite [ɪkˈsaɪt] er-, anregen; reizen; **ex·cit·ed** erregt, aufgeregt; **ex·cite·ment** Auf-, Erregung *f*; **ex·cit·ing** erregend, aufregend, spannend

ex·claim [ɪkˈskleɪm] (aus)rufen

ex·cla·ma·tion [ekskləˈmeɪʃn] Ausruf *m*, (Auf)Schrei *m*; **~ mark** *Brt.*, **~ point** *Am.* Ausrufe-, Ausrufungszeichen *n*

ex·clude [ɪkˈskluːd] ausschließen

ex·clu·sion [ɪkˈskluːʒn] Ausschließung *f*, Ausschluß *m*; **~·sive** [ɪkˈskluːsɪv] ausschließlich; exklusiv; Exklusiv...; **~ of** abgesehen von, ohne

ex·com·mu·ni|·cate [ekskəˈmjuːnɪkeɪt] exkommunizieren; **~·ca·tion** [ekskəmjuːnɪˈkeɪʃn] Exkommunikation *f*

ex·cre·ment [ˈekskrɪmənt] Kot *m*

ex·crete *physiol.* [ekˈskriːt] ausscheiden

ex·cur·sion [ɪkˈskɜːʃn] Ausflug *m*

ex·cu·sa·ble [ɪkˈskjuːzəbl] entschuldbar; **ex·cuse 1.** [ɪkˈskjuːz] entschuldigen; **~ me** entschuldige(n Sie); **2.** [ɪkˈskjuːs] Entschuldigung *f*

ex·di·rec·to·ry num·ber *Brt. tel.* [eksdɪˈrektərɪ -] Geheimnummer *f*; *Am.* → **unlisted (number)**

ex·e·cute [ˈeksɪkjuːt] ausführen; vollziehen; *mus.* vortragen; hinrichten; *Testament* vollstrecken; **~·cu·tion** [eksɪˈkjuːʃn] Ausführung *f*; Vollziehung *f*; (Zwangs)Vollstreckung *f*; Hinrichtung *f*; *mus.* Vortrag *m*; **put od. carry a plan into ~** e-n Plan ausführen *od.* verwirklichen; **~·cu·tion·er** [eksɪˈkjuːʃnə] Henker *m*, Scharfrichter *m*

ex·ec·u·tive [ɪgˈzekjʊtɪv] **1.** vollziehend, ausübend, *pol.* Exekutiv...; *econ.* leitend; **2.** *pol.* Exekutive *f*, vollziehende Gewalt; *econ.* leitende(r) Angestellte(r)

ex·em·pla·ry [ɪgˈzemplərɪ] vorbildlich

ex·em·pli·fy [ɪgˈzemplɪfaɪ] veranschaulichen

ex·empt [ɪg'zempt] **1.** befreit, frei; **2.** ausnehmen, befreien

ex·er·cise ['eksəsaɪz] **1.** Übung f; Ausübung f; Schule: Übung(sarbeit) f, Schulaufgabe f; mil. Manöver n; (körperliche) Bewegung; **do one's** ~**s** Gymnastik machen; **take** ~ sich Bewegung machen; **2.** üben; ausüben; (sich) bewegen; sich Bewegung machen; mil. exerzieren; **~ book** Schul-, Schreibheft n

ex·ert [ɪg'zɜːt] Einfluß etc. ausüben; ~ **o.s.** sich anstrengen od. bemühen; **ex·er·tion** [ɪg'zɜːʃn] Ausübung f; Anstrengung f, Strapaze f

ex·hale [eks'heɪl] ausatmen; Gas, Geruch etc. verströmen; Rauch ausstoßen

ex·haust [ɪg'zɔːst] **1.** erschöpfen; Vorräte ver-, aufbrauchen; **2.** tech. Auspuff m; a. ~ **fumes** pl. tech. Auspuff-, Abgase pl.; ~**ed** erschöpft; aufgebraucht (Vorräte), vergriffen (Auflage); **ex·haus·tion** [ɪg'zɔːstʃən] Erschöpfung f; **ex·haus·tive** erschöpfend; ~ **pipe** tech. Auspuffrohr n

ex·hib·it [ɪg'zɪbɪt] **1.** ausstellen; vorzeigen; fig. zeigen, zur Schau stellen; **2.** Ausstellungsstück n; jur. Beweisstück n; **ex·hi·bi·tion** [eksɪ'bɪʃn] Ausstellung f; Zurschaustellung f

ex·hil·a·rat·ing [ɪg'zɪləreɪtɪŋ] erregend, berauschend; erfrischend (Wind etc.)

ex·hort [ɪg'zɔːt] ermahnen

ex·ile ['eksaɪl] **1.** Exil n; im Exil Lebende(r m) f; **2.** ins Exil schicken

ex·ist [ɪg'zɪst] existieren; vorhanden sein; leben; bestehen; ~**ence** Existenz f; Vorhandensein n, Vorkommen n; Leben n, Dasein n; △ nicht **Existenz** (Lebensunterhalt); ~**ent** existierend

ex·it ['eksɪt] **1.** Abgang m; Ausgang m; (Autobahn)Ausfahrt f; Ausreise f; **2.** thea. (geht) ab

ex·o·dus ['eksədəs] Auszug m; Abwanderung f; **general** ~ allgemeiner Aufbruch

ex·on·e·rate [ɪg'zɒnəreɪt] entlasten, entbinden, befreien

ex·or·bi·tant [ɪg'zɔːbɪtənt] übertrieben, maßlos; unverschämt (Preis etc.)

ex·or·cize ['eksɔːsaɪz] böse Geister beschwören, austreiben (from aus); befreien (of von)

ex·ot·ic [ɪg'zɒtɪk] (~**ally**) exotisch; fremd(artig)

ex·pand [ɪk'spænd] ausbreiten; (sich) ausdehnen od. erweitern; econ. a. expandieren; **ex·panse** [ɪk'spæns] weite Fläche, Weite f; **ex·pan·sion** [ɪk'spænʃn] Ausbreitung f; Ausdehnung f, Erweiterung f; **ex·pan·sive** [ɪk'spænsɪv] mitteilsam

ex·pa·tri·ate [eks'pætrɪeɪt] j-n ausbürgern, j-m die Staatsangehörigkeit aberkennen

ex·pect [ɪk'spekt] erwarten; F annehmen; **be** ~**ing** in anderen Umständen sein; **ex·pec·tant** erwartungsvoll; ~ **mother** werdende Mutter; **ex·pec·ta·tion** [ekspek'teɪʃn] Erwartung f; Hoffnung f, Aussicht f

ex·pe·di·ent [ɪk'spiːdjənt] **1.** zweckdienlich, -mäßig; ratsam; **2.** (Hilfs)Mittel n, (Not)Behelf m

ex·pe·di·tion [ekspɪ'dɪʃn] Expedition f, (Forschungs)Reise f; ~**tious** [ekspɪ-'dɪʃəs] schnell

ex·pel [ɪk'spel] (**-ll-**) (**from**) vertreiben (aus); ausweisen (aus); ausschließen (von, aus)

ex·pen·di·ture [ɪk'spendɪtʃə] Ausgaben pl., (Kosten)Aufwand m

ex·pense [ɪk'spens] Ausgaben pl.; **at the** ~ **of** auf Kosten (gen.); **ex'pen·ses** pl. Unkosten pl., Spesen pl., Auslagen pl.; **ex'pen·sive** kostspielig, teuer

ex·pe·ri·ence [ɪk'spɪərɪəns] **1.** Erfahrung f; (Lebens)Praxis f; Erlebnis n; **2.** erfahren, erleben; ~**d** erfahren

ex·per·i·ment 1. [ɪk'sperɪmənt] Versuch m; **2.** [ɪk'sperɪment] experimentieren; ~**men·tal** [eksperɪ'mentl] Versuchs...

ex·pert [ɪk'spɜːt] **1.** erfahren, geschickt; fachmännisch; **2.** Fachmann m; Sachverständige(r m) f

ex·pi·ra·tion [ekspɪ'reɪʃn] Ablauf m, Ende n; Verfall m; **ex·pire** [ɪk'spaɪə] ablaufen, erlöschen; verfallen

ex·plain [ɪk'spleɪn] erklären; **ex·pla·na·tion** [eksplə'neɪʃn] Erklärung f

ex·plic·it [ɪk'splɪsɪt] ausdrücklich; ausführlich; offen, deutlich; (**sexually**) ~ freizügig (Film etc.)

ex·plode [ɪk'spləʊd] zur Explosion bringen; explodieren; fig. ausbrechen (**with** in acc.), platzen (**with** vor); fig. sprunghaft ansteigen

ex·ploit 1. ['eksplɔɪt] (Helden)Tat *f*; **2.** [ɪk'splɔɪt] ausbeuten; *fig.* ausnutzen; **ex·ploi·ta·tion** [eksplɔɪ'teɪʃn] Ausbeutung *f*, Auswertung *f*, Verwertung *f*, Abbau *m*

ex·plo·ra·tion [eksplə'reɪʃn] Erforschung *f*; **ex·plore** [ɪk'splɔː] erforschen; **ex·plor·er** [ɪk'splɔːrə] Forscher(in); Forschungsreisende(r *m*) *f*

ex·plo·sion [ɪk'spləʊʒn] Explosion *f*; *fig.* Ausbruch *m*; *fig.* sprunghafter Anstieg; **~·sive** [ɪk'spləʊsɪv] **1.** explosiv; *fig.* aufbrausend; *fig.* sprunghaft ansteigend; **2.** Sprengstoff *m*

ex·po·nent [ek'spəʊnənt] *math.* Exponent *m*, Hochzahl *f*; Vertreter(in), Verfechter(in)

ex·port 1. [ɪk'spɔːt] exportieren, ausführen; **2.** ['ekspɔːt] Export(artikel) *m*, Ausfuhr(artikel) *m*) *f*; **ex·por·ta·tion** [ekspɔː'teɪʃn] Ausfuhr *f*; **ex·port·er** [ɪk'spɔːtə] Exporteur *m*

ex·pose [ɪk'spəʊz] aussetzen; *phot.* belichten; *Waren* ausstellen; *j-n* entlarven, bloßstellen, *et.* aufdecken; **ex·po·si·tion** [ekspə'zɪʃn] Ausstellung *f*

ex·po·sure [ɪk'spəʊʒə] Aussetzen *n*, Ausgesetztsein *n* (**to** *dat.*); *fig.* Bloßstellung *f*, Aufdeckung *f*, Enthüllung *f*, Entlarvung *f*; *phot.* Belichtung *f*; *phot.* Aufnahme *f*; **die of ~** an Unterkühlung sterben; **~ me·ter** *phot.* Belichtungsmesser *m*

ex·press [ɪk'spres] **1.** ausdrücklich, deutlich; Expreß...; Eil...; **2.** Eilbote *m*; Schnellzug *m*; **by ~** → **3.** *adv.* durch Eilboten; als Eilgut; **4.** äußern, ausdrücken; **ex·pres·sion** [ɪk'spreʃn] Ausdruck *m*; **ex·pres·sion·less** ausdruckslos; **be ~ of** *et.* ausdrücken; **ex·pres·sive** [ɪk'spresɪv] ausdrucksvoll; **be ~ of** *et.* ausdrücken; **~ 'let·ter** *Brt.* Eilbrief *m*; **~·ly** ausdrücklich, eigens; **~ train** Schnellzug *m*; **~·way** *bsd. Am.* Schnellstraße *f*

ex·pro·pri·ate *jur.* [eks'prəʊprɪeɪt] enteignen

ex·pul·sion [ɪk'spʌlʃn] (**from**) Vertreibung *f* (aus); Ausweisung *f* (aus)

ex·pur·gate ['ekspɜːgeɪt] reinigen

ex·qui·site ['ekskwɪzɪt] erlesen; fein

ex·tant [ek'stænt] noch vorhanden

ex·tend [ɪk'stend] (aus)dehnen, (-)weiten; *Hand etc.* ausstrecken; *Betrieb etc.*

vergrößern, ausbauen; *Frist, Paß etc.* verlängern; sich ausdehnen *od.* erstrecken; **~ed 'fam·i·ly** Großfamilie *f*

ex·ten·sion [ɪk'stenʃn] Ausdehnung *f*; Vergrößerung *f*, Erweiterung *f*; (Frist)Verlängerung *f*; *arch.* Erweiterung *f*, Anbau *m*; *tel.* Nebenanschluß *m*, Apparat *m*; *a.* **~ lead** (*Am.* **cord**) *electr.* Verlängerungskabel *n*, -schnur *f*; **~·sive** ausgedehnt, umfassend

ex·tent [ɪk'stent] Ausdehnung *f*; Umfang *m*, (Aus)Maß *n*, Grad *m*; **to some ~, to a certain ~** bis zu e-m gewissen Grade; **to such an ~ that** so sehr, daß

ex·ten·u·ate [ek'stenjʊeɪt] abschwächen, mildern; beschönigen; **extenuating circumstances** *pl. jur.* mildernde Umstände *pl.*

ex·te·ri·or [ek'stɪərɪə] **1.** äußerlich, äußere(r, -s), Außen...; **2.** *das* Äußere; Außenseite *f*; äußere Erscheinung

ex·ter·mi·nate [ek'stɜːmɪneɪt] ausrotten (*a. fig.*), vernichten, *Ungeziefer, Unkraut a.* vertilgen

ex·ter·nal [ek'stɜːnl] äußere(r, -s), äußerlich, Außen...

ex·tinct [ɪk'stɪŋkt] erloschen; ausgestorben; **ex·tinc·tion** [ɪk'stɪŋkʃn] Erlöschen *n*; Aussterben *n*, Untergang *m*; Vernichtung *f*, Zerstörung *f*

ex·tin·guish [ɪk'stɪŋgwɪʃ] (aus)löschen; vernichten; **~·er** (*Feuer*)Löscher *m*

ex·tort [ɪk'stɔːt] erpressen (**from** von)

ex·tra ['ekstrə] **1.** *adj.* zusätzlich, Extra..., Sonder...; **be ~** gesondert berechnet werden; **2.** *adv.* extra, besonders; **charge ~ for** *et.* gesondert berechnen; **3.** Sonderleistung *f*; *bsd. mot.* Extra *n*; Zuschlag *m*; Extrablatt *n*; *thea., Film:* Statist(in)

ex·tract 1. ['ekstrækt] Auszug *m*; **2.** [ɪk'strækt] (heraus)ziehen; herausklokken; ab-, herleiten; **ex·trac·tion** [ɪk'strækʃn] (Heraus)Ziehen *n*; Herkunft *f*

ex·tra|·dite ['ekstrədaɪt] ausliefern; *j-s* Auslieferung erwirken; **~·di·tion** [ekstrə'dɪʃn] Auslieferung *f*

extra·or·di·na·ry [ɪk'strɔːdnrɪ] außerordentlich; ungewöhnlich; außerordentlich, Sonder...

ex·tra 'pay Zulage *f*

ex·tra·ter·res·tri·al [ekstrətə'restrɪəl] außerirdisch

x·tra 'time *Sport*: (Spiel)Verlänge-
rung *f*

x·trav·a·gance [ɪkˈstrævəgəns]
Übertriebenheit *f*; Verschwendung *f*;
Extravaganz *f*; **~gant** übertrieben,
überspannt; verschwenderisch; extravagant

x·treme [ɪkˈstriːm] **1.** äußerste(r, -s),
größte(r, -s), höchste(r, -s); außergewöhnlich; **~ right** rechtsex-
trem(istisch); **~ right wing** rechtsradi-
kal; **2.** *das* Äußerste; Extrem *n*; höchster Grad; **~ly** äußerst, höchst

x·trem·is·m *bsd. pol.* [ɪkˈstriːmɪzm]
Extremismus *m*; **~ist** [ɪkˈstriːmɪst] Ex-
tremist(in)

x·trem·i·ties [ɪkˈstremətɪz] *pl.* Glied-
maßen *pl.*, Extremitäten *pl.*

x·trem·i·ty [ɪkˈstremətɪ] *das* Äußerste;
höchste Not; äußerste Maßnahme

x·tri·cate [ˈekstrɪkeɪt] herauswinden,
-ziehen, befreien

x·tro·vert [ˈekstrəʊvɜːt] Extrovertier-
te(r *m*) *f*

ex·u·be·rance [ɪgˈzjuːbərəns] Fülle *f*;
Überschwang *m*; **~rant** reichlich, üppig; überschwenglich; ausgelassen

ex·ult [ɪgˈzʌlt] frohlocken, jubeln

eye [aɪ] **1.** Auge *n*; Blick *m*; Öhr *n*; Öse *f*;
see ~ to ~ with s.o. mit j-m völlig übereinstimmen; **be up to the ~s in work** bis
über die Ohren in Arbeit stecken; **with
an ~ to s.th.** im Hinblick auf et.; **2.**
ansehen; mustern; **'~ball** Augapfel *m*;
'~brow Augenbraue *f*; **'~catch·ing**
ins Auge fallend, auffallend; **~d** ...äu-
gig; **'~ doc·tor** *F* Augenarzt *m*, -ärztin
f; **'~glass·es** *pl., a. pair of ~* Brille *f*;
'~lash Augenwimper *f*; **'~lid** Augen-
lid *n*; **'~lin·er** Eyeliner *m*; **'~o·pen-
er:** *that was an ~ to me* das hat mir die
Augen geöffnet; **'~ shad·ow** Lid-
schatten *m*; **'~sight** Augen(licht *n*) *pl.*,
Sehkraft *f*; **'~sore** *F* et. Unschönes,
Schandfleck *m*; **~ spe·cial·ist** Augenarzt *m*, -ärztin *f*; **'~strain** Ermüdung *f od.* Überanstrengung *f* der Au-
gen; **'~wit·ness** Augenzeug|e *m*, -in *f*

F

f, f [ef] F, f *n*

nur geschr. Abk. für **Fahrenheit** F,
Fahrenheit (*Thermometereinteilung*)

A *Brt.* [ef ˈeɪ] *Abk. für* **Football Association** Fußballverband *m*

a·ble[ˈfeɪbl] Fabel *f*; Sage *f*

ab·ric [ˈfæbrɪk] Gewebe *n*, Stoff *m*;
Struktur *f*; △ *nicht* **Fabrik**; **~ri·cate**
[ˈfæbrɪkeɪt] fabrizieren (*mst fig. erdich-
ten, fälschen*)

ab·u·lous [ˈfæbjʊləs] sagenhaft, der
Sage angehörend; sagen-, fabelhaft

a·cade, fa·çade *arch.* [fəˈsɑːd] Fassade *f*

ace [feɪs] **1.** Gesicht *n*; Gesicht(saus-
druck *m*) *n*, Miene *f*; (Ober)Fläche *f*;
Vorderseite *f*; Zifferblatt *n*; **~ to ~ with**
Auge in Auge mit; **save od. lose one's
~** das Gesicht wahren *od.* verlieren; **on
the ~ of it** auf den ersten Blick; **pull a
long ~** ein langes Gesicht machen;

have the ~ to do s.th. die Stirn haben,
et. zu tun; **2.** *v/t.* ansehen; gegenüberstehen (*dat.*); (hinaus)gehen auf (*acc.*);
die Stirn bieten (*dat.*); einfassen; *arch.*
bekleiden; *v/i.* **~ about** sich umdrehen;
'~cloth Waschlappen *m*; **~d** *in Zssgn*
mit (e-m) ... Gesicht; **~ flan·nel** *Brt.*
→ *facecloth*; **'~lift** Facelifting *n*, Ge-
sichtsstraffung *f*; *fig.* Renovierung *f*,
Verschönerung *f*

fa·ce·tious [fəˈsiːʃəs] witzig

fa·cial [ˈfeɪʃl] **1.** Gesichts...; **2.** *Kosmetik*: Gesichtsbehandlung *f*

fa·cile [ˈfæsaɪl] leicht; oberflächlich

fa·cil·i·tate [fəˈsɪlɪteɪt] erleichtern

fa·cil·i·ty [fəˈsɪlətɪ] Leichtigkeit *f*; Ober-
flächlichkeit *f*; *mst* **facilities** *pl.* Er-
leichterung(en *pl.*) *f*; Einrichtung(en
pl.) *f*, Anlage(n *pl.*) *f*

fac·ing [ˈfeɪsɪŋ] *tech.* Verkleidung *f*; **~s**
pl. Schneiderei: Besatz *m*

fact [fækt] Tatsache f, Wirklichkeit f, Wahrheit f; Tat f; **in ~** in der Tat, tatsächlich; **~s** pl. Daten pl.

fac·tion bsd. pol. ['fækʃn] Splittergruppe f; Zwietracht f

fac·ti·tious [fæk'tɪʃəs] künstlich

fac·tor ['fæktə] Faktor m

fac·to·ry ['fæktrɪ] Fabrik f

fac·ul·ty ['fækltɪ] Fähigkeit f; Kraft f; fig. Gabe f; univ. Fakultät f; Am. Lehrkörper m

fad [fæd] Mode(erscheinung, -torheit) f; (vorübergehende) Laune

fade [feɪd] (ver)welken (lassen); verschießen, -blassen (Farbe); schwinden; immer schwächer werden (Person); △ nicht fade; Film, Rundfunk, TV: **~ in** auf- od. eingeblendet werden; auf- od. einblenden; **~ out** aus- od. abgeblendet werden; aus- od. abblenden; **~d jeans** pl. ausgewaschene Jeans pl.

fag¹ [fæg] F Plackerei f, Schinderei f; Brt. Schule: Schüler, der für e-n älteren Dienste verrichtet

fag² sl. [fæg] Brt. Glimmstengel m (Zigarette); Am. Schwule(r) m; **~ end** Brt. F Kippe f (Zigarettenstummel)

fail [feɪl] **1.** v/i. versagen; mißlingen, fehlschlagen; versiegen; nachlassen; durchfallen (Kandidat); v/t. im Stich lassen; j-n in e-r Prüfung durchfallen lassen; **2. without ~** mit Sicherheit, ganz bestimmt; **~ure** ['feɪljə] Versagen n; Fehlschlag m, Mißerfolg m; Versäumnis n; Versager m

faint [feɪnt] **1.** schwach, matt; **2.** ohnmächtig werden, in Ohnmacht fallen (**with** vor); **3.** Ohnmacht f; **~'heart·ed** verzagt

fair¹ [feə] gerecht, ehrlich, anständig, fair; recht gut, ansehnlich; schön (Wetter); klar (Himmel); blond (Haar); hell (Haut); **play ~** fair spielen; fig. sich an die Spielregeln halten

fair² [feə] (Jahr)Markt m; Volksfest n; Ausstellung f, Messe f

fair 'game fig. Freiwild n

'fair·ground Rummelplatz m

'fair·ly gerecht; ziemlich; **'~·ness** Gerechtigkeit f, Fairneß f; **~ 'play** Sport u. fig. Fair play n, Fairneß f

fai·ry ['feərɪ] Fee f; Zauberin f; Elf(e) f m; **'~·land** Feen-, Märchenland n; **'~ sto·ry, '~ tale** Märchen n (a. fig.)

faith [feɪθ] Glaube m; Vertrauen n; **'~·ful** treu (**to** dat.); **Yours ~ly** Hochachtungsvoll (Briefschluß); **'~·les** treulos

fake [feɪk] **1.** Schwindel m; Fälschung f; Schwindler m; **2.** fälschen; imitieren nachmachen; vortäuschen, simulieren **3.** gefälscht

fal·con zo. ['fɔːlkən] Falke m

fall [fɔːl] **1.** Fall(en n) m; Sturz m; Verfal m; Einsturz m; Am. Herbst m; Sinken (der Preise etc.); Gefälle n; mst **~s** p. Wasserfall m; △ nicht gr., med., ju Fall; **2.** (**fell, fallen**) fallen, stürzen; abeinfallen; sinken; sich legen (Wind); i e-n Zustand verfallen; **~ ill, ~ sick** kran werden; **~ in love with** sich verlieben i (acc.); **~ short of** den Erwartungen etc nicht entsprechen; **~ back** zurückwei chen; **~ back on** fig. zurückgreifen au (acc.); **~ for** hereinfallen auf (j-n, et.); sich in j-n verknallen; **~ off** zurückge hen (Geschäfte, Zuschauerzahlen etc.) nachlassen; **~ on** herfallen über (acc.); **out** sich streiten (**with** mit); **~ through** durchfallen (a. fig.); **~ to** reinhauen tüchtig zugreifen (beim Essen)

fal·la·cious [fə'leɪʃəs] trügerisch

fal·la·cy ['fæləsɪ] Trugschluß m

fall·en ['fɔːlən] p.p. von **fall** 2

'fall guy Am. F der Lackierte, der Dum me

fal·li·ble ['fæləbl] fehlbar

fall·ing 'star Sternschnuppe f

'fall·out Fallout m, radioaktiver Niederschlag

fal·low ['fæləʊ] zo. falb; agr. brach(lie gend)

false [fɔːls] falsch; **~·hood** ['fɔːlshʊd] **'~·ness** Falschheit f; Unwahrheit f; **~ 'start** Fehlstart m

fal·si·fi·ca·tion [fɔːlsɪfɪ'keɪʃn] (Ver) Fälschung f; **~·fy** ['fɔːlsɪfaɪ] (ver)fäl schen; **~·ty** ['fɔːlsɪtɪ] Falschheit f, Un wahrheit f

fal·ter ['fɔːltə] schwanken, stocken (Stimme); stammeln; fig. zaudern

fame [feɪm] Ruf m, Ruhm m; **~d** berühmt (**for** wegen)

fa·mil·i·ar [fə'mɪljə] **1.** vertraut; gewohnt; familiär; **2.** Vertraute(r m) f; **~·i·ty** [fəmɪlɪ'ærətɪ] Vertrautheit f; (plumpe) Vertraulichkeit; **~·ize** [fə'mɪljəraɪz] vertraut machen

fatherly

fam·i·ly ['fæməlɪ] 1. Familie f; 2. Familien..., Haus...; *be in the ~ way* F in anderen Umständen sein; **~ al'lowance → child benefit; ~ name** Familien-, Nachname m; **~ 'plan·ning** Familienplanung f; **~ 'tree** Stammbaum m

fam·ine ['fæmɪn] Hungersnot f; Knappheit f (*of* an dat.); **'~ished** verhungert; *be ~* F am Verhungern sein

fa·mous ['feɪməs] berühmt; △ *nicht famos*

fan¹ [fæn] 1. Fächer m; Ventilator m; 2. (*-nn-*) (zu)fächeln; an-, *fig.* entfachen

fan² [fæn] (*Sport- etc.*)Fan m

fa·nat·ic [fə'nætɪk] Fanatiker(in); **~i·cal** [fə'nætɪkl] fanatisch

'fan belt *tech.* Keilriemen m

fan·ci·er ['fænsɪə] (*Tier-, Pflanzen-*)Liebhaber(in), (-)Züchter(in)

fan·ci·ful ['fænsɪfl] phantastisch

'fan club Fanklub m

fan·cy ['fænsɪ] 1. Phantasie f; Einbildung f; plötzlicher Einfall; Laune f; Vorliebe f, Neigung f; 2. ausgefallen; Phantasie...; 3. sich vorstellen; sich einbilden; *~ that!* stell dir vor!, denk nur!; sieh mal einer an!; **~ 'ball** Kostümfest n, Maskenball m; **~ 'dress** (Masken)Kostüm n; **~'free** frei u. ungebunden; **~ 'goods** pl. Modeartikel pl., -waren pl.; **'~work** feine Handarbeit, Stickerei f

fang [fæŋ] Reiß-, Fangzahn m; Hauer m; Giftzahn m

'fan mail Fan-, Verehrerpost f

fan·tas·tic [fæn'tæstɪk] (*~ally*) phantastisch; **~·ta·sy** ['fæntəsɪ] Phantasie f

far [fɑː] (*farther, further; farthest, furthest*) 1. *adj.* fern, entfernt, weit; 2. *adv.* fern; weit; (sehr) viel; *as ~ as* bis; *in so ~ as* insofern als; **~·a·way** ['fɑːrəweɪ] weit entfernt

fare [feə] 1. Fahrgeld n; Fahrgast m; Verpflegung f, Kost f; 2. *gut* leben; *he ~d well* es (er)ging ihm gut; **'~ dodg·er** Schwarzfahrer(in); **~'well** 1. *int.* lebe(n Sie) wohl!; 2. Abschied m, Lebewohl n

far'fetched *fig.* weithergeholt, gesucht

farm [fɑːm] 1. Bauernhof m, Gut n, Gehöft n, Farm f; *chicken ~* Hühnerfarm f; 2. Land, Hof bewirtschaften; **'~·er** Bauer m, Landwirt m, Farmer m; **'~·hand** Landarbeiter(in); **'~·house** Bauernhaus n; **'~·ing** 1. Acker..., landwirtschaftlich; 2. Landwirtschaft f; **'~·stead** Bauernhof m, Gehöft n; **'~·yard** Wirtschaftshof m (*e-s Bauernhofs*)

far·off [fɑːr'ɒf] entfernt, fern; **~ 'right** *pol.* rechtsgerichtet; **~'sight·ed** *bsd. Am.* weitsichtig, *fig. a.* weitblickend

far·ther ['fɑːðə] *comp. von* far; **~·thest** ['fɑːðɪst] *sup. von* far

fas·ci·nate ['fæsɪneɪt] faszinieren; **'~·nat·ing** faszinierend; **~·na·tion** [fæsɪ'neɪʃn] Zauber m, Reiz m, Faszination f

fas·cis·m *pol.* ['fæʃɪzəm] Faschismus m; **~t** *pol.* ['fæʃɪst] 1. Faschist m; 2. faschistisch

fash·ion ['fæʃn] Mode f; Art f u. Weise f; *be in ~* in Mode sein; *out of ~* unmodern; 2. formen, gestalten; **~·a·ble** ['fæʃnəbl] modisch, elegant; in Mode; **~ pa·rade, ~ show** Mode(n)schau f

fast¹ [fɑːst] 1. Fasten n; 2. fasten

fast² [fɑːst] schnell; fest; treu; echt, beständig (*Farbe*); flott; △ *nicht fast; be ~ vorgehen (Uhr);* **~'back** *mot.* (Wagen m mit) Fließheck n; **~ 'breed·er, ~ breed·er re'ac·tor** *phys.* schneller Brüter

fas·ten ['fɑːsn] befestigen, festmachen, anheften, anschnallen, anbinden, zuknöpfen, zu-, verschnüren; *Blick etc.* richten (*on* auf); sich festmachen *od.* schließen lassen; △ *nicht fasten;* **'~·er** Verschluß m

'fast food Schnellgericht(e *pl.*) n; **~food 'res·tau·rant** Schnellimbiß m, -gaststätte f

fas·tid·i·ous [fə'stɪdɪəs] anspruchsvoll, heikel, wählerisch, verwöhnt

'fast lane *mot.* Überholspur f

fat [fæt] 1. (*-tt-*) fett; dick; fett(ig), fetthaltig; 2. Fett n; *low in ~ pred.* fettarm

fa·tal ['feɪtl] tödlich; verhängnisvoll, fatal (*to* für); **~·i·ty** [fə'tælətɪ] Verhängnis n; tödlicher Unfall; (Todes)Opfer n

fate [feɪt] Schicksal n; Verhängnis n

fa·ther ['fɑːðə] Vater m; ♀ **'Christ·mas** *bsd. Brt.* der Weihnachtsmann, der Nikolaus; **'~·hood** Vaterschaft f; **~·in-law** ['fɑːðərɪnlɔː] (*pl.* **fathers-in-law**) Schwiegervater m; **'~·less** vaterlos; **'~·ly** väterlich

fathom 116

fath·om ['fæðəm] **1.** *naut.* Faden *m* (*Tiefenmaß*); **2.** *naut.* loten; *fig.* ergründen; '**~·less** unergründlich

fa·tigue [fə'ti:g] **1.** Ermüdung *f*; Strapaze *f*; **2.** ermüden

fat·ten ['fætn] dick *od. contp.* fett machen (*od.* werden); mästen; '**~·ty** (*-ier, -iest*) fett(ig)

fau·cet *Am.* ['fɔ:sɪt] (Wasser)Hahn *m*

fault [fɔ:lt] Fehler *m*; Defekt *m*; Schuld *f*; **find ~ with** et. auszusetzen haben an (*dat.*); **be at ~** Schuld haben; '**~·less** fehlerfrei, -los; '**~·y** (*-ier, -iest*) fehlerhaft, *tech. a.* defekt

fa·vo(u)r ['feɪvə] **1.** Gunst *f*; Gefallen *m*; Begünstigung *f*; **in ~ of** zugunsten von *od. gen.*; **do s.o. a ~** j-m e-n Gefallen tun; **2.** begünstigen; bevorzugen, vorziehen; wohlwollend gegenüberstehen; *Sport:* favorisieren; **fa·vo(u)·ra·ble** ['feɪvərəbl] günstig; **fa·vo(u)·rite** ['feɪvərɪt] **1.** Liebling *m*; *Sport:* Favorit *m*; **2.** Lieblings...

fawn[1] [fɔ:n] **1.** *zo.* (Reh)Kitz *n*; Rehbraun *n*; **2.** rehbraun

fawn[2] [fɔ:n]: **~ on** (*dat.*) (vor Freude) an j-m hochspringen *etc.* (*Hund*); *fig.* katzbuckeln vor (*dat.*)

fax [fæks] **1.** Fax *n*; **2.** faxen; **~ s.th. (through) to s.o.** j-m et. faxen; '**~ (machine)** Faxgerät *n*

FBI [ef bi: 'aɪ] *Abk. für* **Federal Bureau of Investigation** FBI *m, n* (*Bundeskriminalpolizei der USA*)

fear [fɪə] **1.** Furcht *f* (**of** vor *dat.*); Befürchtung *f*; Angst *f*; **2.** (be)fürchten; sich fürchten vor (*dat.*); '**~·ful** furchtsam; furchtbar; '**~·less** furchtlos

fea·si·ble ['fi:zəbl] durchführbar

feast [fi:st] **1.** *rel.* Fest *n*, Feiertag *m*; Festessen *n*; *fig.* Fest *n*, (Hoch)Genuß *m*; **2.** *v/t.* festlich bewirten; *v/i.* sich gütlich tun (**on** an *dat.*)

feat [fi:t] große Leistung; (Helden)Tat *f*

fea·ther ['feðə] **1.** Feder *f*; *a.* ~ Gefieder *n*; **birds of a ~** Leute vom gleichen Schlag; **birds of a ~ flock together** gleich u. gleich gesellt sich gern; **that is a ~ in his cap** darauf kann er stolz sein; **2.** mit Federn polstern *od.* schmücken, *Pfeil* fiedern; ~ **one's nest** sich bereichern; '**~·bed** Matratze *f* mit Federn- *od.* Daunenfüllung; △ *nicht* **Federbett**; '**~·bed** (*-dd-*) verhätscheln; '**~·brained** F hohlköpfig; '**~ed** gefie-

dert; '**~·weight** *Sport:* Federgewicht(ler *m*) *n*; Leichtgewicht *n* (*Person*); '**~·y** ['feðərɪ] gefiedert; feder(art)ig, leicht

fea·ture ['fi:tʃə] **1.** (Gesichts)Zug *m*; (charakteristisches) Merkmal; *Zeitung, Rundfunk, TV:* Feature *n*; Haupt-, Spielfilm *m*; **2.** groß herausbringen *od.* -stellen; *Film:* in der Hauptrolle zeigen; '**~ film** Haupt-, Spielfilm *m*; '**~s** *pl.* Gesichtszüge *pl.*

Feb *nur geschr. Abk. für* **February** Febr., Februar *m*

Feb·ru·a·ry ['februərɪ] (*Abk.* **Feb**) Februar *m*

fed [fed] *pret. u. p.p. von* **feed** 2

fed·e·ral *pol.* ['fedərəl] Bundes...; ♀ **Bu·reau of In·ves·ti·ga·tion** (*Abk.* **FBI**) Bundeskriminalpolizei *f* (*der USA*); ♀ **Re·pub·lic of 'Ger·man·y** die Bundesrepublik Deutschland (*Abk.* **BRD**)

fed·e·ra·tion [fedə'reɪʃn] *pol.* Bundesstaat *m*; Föderation *f*, Staatenbund *m*; *econ., Sport etc.:* (Dach)Verband *m*

fee [fi:] Gebühr *f*; Honorar *n*; (Mitglieds)Beitrag *m*; Eintrittsgeld *n*

fee·ble ['fi:bl] (*~r, ~st*) schwach

feed [fi:d] **1.** Futter *n*; Nahrung *f*; Fütterung *f*; *tech.* Zuführung *f*, Speisung *f*; **2.** (*fed*) *v/t.* füttern; ernähren; *tech. Maschine* speisen, *Computer:* eingeben; weiden lassen; **be fed up with** et. *od.* j-n satt haben; **well fed** wohlgenährt; *v/i.* (fr)essen; sich ernähren; weiden; '**~·back** *electr., Kybernetik:* Feedback *n*, Rückkoppelung *f*; *Rundfunk, TV:* Feedback *n* (*mögliche Einflußnahme des Publikums auf den Verlauf e-r Sendung*); Zurückleitung *f* (*von Informationen*) (**to** an *acc.*); '**~·er** Esser *m*; '**~ road** Zubringer(straße *f*) *m*; '**~·ing bot·tle** (Säuglings-, Saug)Flasche *f*

feel [fi:l] **1.** (*felt*) (sich) fühlen; berühren; empfinden; sich anfühlen; ~ **sorry for s.o.** j-n bedauern *od.* bemitleiden; **2.** Gefühl *n*; Empfindung *f*; '**~·er** *zo.* Fühler *m*; '**~·ing** Gefühl *n*

feet [fi:t] *pl. von* **foot** 1

feign [feɪn] *Interesse etc.* vortäuschen, *Krankheit a.* simulieren

feint [feɪnt] Finte *f*

fell [fel] **1.** *pret. von* **fall** 2; **2.** niederschlagen; fällen

fel·low ['feləʊ] **1.** Gefährt|e *m*, -in *f*,

Kamerad(in); Gegenstück *n*; F Kerl *m*; **old** ~ F alter Knabe; *the* ~ *of a glove* der andere Handschuh; **2.** Mit...; ~ **'be·ing** Mitmensch *m*; ~ **'cit·i·zen** Mitbürger *m*; ~ **'coun·try·man** (*pl. -men*) Landsmann *m*; **'~·ship** Gemeinschaft *f*; Kameradschaft *f*; ~ **'trav·el·(l)er** Mitreisende(r) *m*, Reisegefährte *m*

fel·o·ny *jur.* ['felənɪ] (schweres) Verbrechen, Kapitalverbrechen *n*

felt[1] [felt] *pret. u. p.p. von* **feel** 1

felt[2] [felt] Filz *m*; ~ **pen**, ~ **tip**, ~ **-tip(ped) 'pen** Filzstift *m*, -schreiber *m*

fe·male ['fiːmeɪl] **1.** weiblich; **2.** *contp.* Weib(sbild) *n*; *zo.* Weibchen *n*

fem·i·nine ['femɪnɪn] weiblich, Frauen...; feminin; **~·nis·m** ['femɪnɪzəm] Feminismus *m*; **~·nist** ['femɪnɪst] **1.** Feminist(in); **2.** feministisch

fen [fen] Fenn *n*, Sumpf-, Marschland *n*

fence [fens] **1.** Zaun *m*; *sl.* Hehler *m*; *v/t.* ~ **in** ein-, umzäunen; einsperren; ~ **off** abzäunen; *v/i.* Sport: fechten; **'fenc·er** Sport: Fechter *m*; **'fenc·ing** Einfriedung *f*; Sport: Fechten *n*; *attr.* Fecht...

fend [fend]: ~ **off** abwehren; ~ **for o.s.** für sich selbst sorgen; **'~·er** Schutzvorrichtung *f*; Schutzblech *n*; *Am. mot.* Kotflügel *m*; Kamingitter *n*, -vorsetzer *m*

fen·nel *bot.* ['fenl] Fenchel *m*

fer|·ment **1.** ['fɜːment] Ferment *n*; Gärung *f*; **2.** [fə'ment] gären (lassen); **~·men·ta·tion** [fɜːmen'teɪʃn] Gärung *f*

fern *bot.* [fɜːn] Farn(kraut *n*) *m*

fe·ro|·cious [fə'rəʊʃəs] wild; grausam; **~·ci·ty** [fə'rɒsətɪ] Wildheit *f*

fer·ret ['ferɪt] **1.** *zo.* Frettchen *n*; *fig.* Spürhund *m*; **2.** herumstöbern; ~ **out** aufspüren, -stöbern

fer·ry ['ferɪ] **1.** Fähre *f*; **2.** übersetzen; **'~·boat** Fährboot *n*, Fähre *f*; **'~·man** (*pl. -men*) Fährmann *m*

fer|·tile ['fɜːtaɪl] fruchtbar; reich (*of, in* an *dat.*); **~·til·i·ty** [fɜː'tɪlətɪ] Fruchtbarkeit *f* (*a. fig.*); **~·ti·lize** ['fɜːtɪlaɪz] fruchtbar machen; befruchten; düngen; **'~·ti·liz·er** (*bsd.* Kunst)Dünger *m*, Düngemittel *n*

fer·vent ['fɜːvənt] glühend, leidenschaftlich

fer·vo(u)r ['fɜːvə] Glut *f*; Inbrunst *f*

fes·ter ['festə] eitern

fes|·ti·val ['festəvl] Fest *n*; Festival *n*, Festspiele *pl.*; ~ **tive** ['festɪv] festlich; **~·tiv·i·ty** [fe'stɪvətɪ] Festlichkeit *f*

fes·toon [fe'stuːn] Girlande *f*

fetch [fetʃ] holen; *Preis* erzielen; *Seufzer* ausstoßen; **'~·ing** F reizend

fete, fête [feɪt] Fest *n*; *village* ~ Dorffest *n*

fet·id ['fetɪd] stinkend

fet·ter ['fetə] **1.** Fessel *f*; **2.** fesseln

feud [fjuːd] Fehde *f*; **~·al** ['fjuːdl] Feudal..., Lehns...; **feu·dal·is·m** ['fjuːdəlɪzəm] Feudalismus *m*, Feudal-, Lehnssystem *n*

fe·ver ['fiːvə] Fieber *n*; **~·ish** ['fiːvərɪʃ] fieb(e)rig; *fig.* fieberhaft

few [fjuː] wenige; *a* ~ ein paar, einige; *no* ~*er than* nicht weniger als; *quite a* ~, *a good* ~ e-e ganze Menge

fi·an·cé [fɪ'ɑ̃ːnseɪ] Verlobte(r) *m*; ~**e** [fɪ'ɑ̃ːnseɪ] Verlobte *f*

fib F [fɪb] **1.** Flunkerei *f*, Schwindelei *f*; **2.** (**-bb-**) schwindeln, flunkern

fi·bre *Brit.*, **fi·ber** *Am.* ['faɪbə] Faser *f*; **'~·glass** *tech.* Fiberglas *n*, Glasfaser *f*; **fi·brous** ['faɪbrəs] faserig

fick·le ['fɪkl] wankelmütig; unbeständig; **'~·ness** Wankelmut *m*

fic·tion ['fɪkʃn] Erfindung *f*; Prosaliteratur *f*, Belletristik *f*; Romane *pl.*; **~·al** ['fɪkʃnl] erdichtet; Roman...

fic·ti·tious [fɪk'tɪʃəs] erfunden

fid·dle ['fɪdl] **1.** Fiedel *f*, Geige *f*; *play first* (*second*) ~ *bsd. fig.* die erste (zweite) Geige spielen; (*as*) *fit as a* ~ kerngesund; **2.** *mus.* fiedeln; *a.* ~ *about* od. *around* (*with*) herumfingern (an *dat.*), spielen (mit); **'~·r** Geiger(in); **'~·sticks** *int.* dummes Zeug!

fi·del·i·ty [fɪ'delətɪ] Treue *f*; Genauigkeit *f*

fid·get F ['fɪdʒɪt] nervös machen; (herum)zappeln; **'~·y** (ge)zappelig, nervös

field [fiːld] Feld *n*; Sport: Spielfeld *n*; Arbeitsfeld *n*; Gebiet *n*; Bereich *m*; '~ **e·vents** *pl.* Sport: Sprung- u. Wurfdisziplinen *pl.*; '~**·glass·es** *pl.*, *a. pair of* ~ Feldstecher *m*, Fernglas *n*; '~ **mar·shal** *mil.* Feldmarschall *m*; '~ **sports** *pl.* Sport *m* im Freien (*Jagen, Schießen, Fischen*); '~**·work** praktische (wissenschaftliche) Arbeit, *Archäologie*

fiend 118

etc.: *a.* Arbeit *f* im Gelände; *Markt-*, *Meinungsforschung:* Feldarbeit *f*

fiend [fiːnd] Satan *m*, Teufel *m*; F (*Frischluft- etc.*)Fanatiker(in); △ *nicht* **Feind**; '**~ish** teuflisch, boshaft

fierce [fɪəs] (*~r*, *~st*) wild; scharf; heftig; '**~ness** Wildheit *f*, Schärfe *f*; Heftigkeit *f*

fi·er·y ['faɪərɪ] (*-ier*, *-iest*) feurig; hitzig

fif·teen [fɪf'tiːn] **1.** fünfzehn; **2.** Fünfzehn *f*; **~teenth** [fɪf'tiːnθ] fünfzehnte(r, -s); **~th** [fɪfθ] **1.** fünfte(r, -s); **2.** Fünftel *n*; '**~th·ly** fünftens; **~ti·eth** ['fɪftɪɪθ] fünfzigste(r, -s); **~ty** ['fɪftɪ] **1.** fünfzig; **2.** Fünfzig *f*; **~ty-'fif·ty** F halbe-halbe

fig *bot.* [fig] Feige *f*

fight [faɪt] **1.** Kampf *m*; *mil.* Gefecht *n*; Schlägerei *f*; Boxen: Kampf *m*, Fight *m*; **2.** (*fought*) *v/t.* bekämpfen; kämpfen gegen *od.* mit, *Sport: a.* boxen gegen; *v/i.* kämpfen, sich schlagen; *Sport:* boxen; '**~er** Kämpfer *m*; *Sport:* Boxer *m*, Fighter *m*; *a.* **~plane** *mil.* Jagdflugzeug *n*; '**~ing** Kampf *m*

fig·u·ra·tive ['fɪgjʊrətɪv] bildlich

fig·ure ['fɪgə] **1.** Figur *f*; Gestalt *f*; Zahl *f*, Ziffer *f*; Preis *m*; **be good at ~s** ein guter Rechner sein; **2.** *v/t.* abbilden, darstellen; *Am.* F meinen, glauben; sich *et.* vorstellen; **~ out** rauskriegen, *Problem* lösen; verstehen; **~ up** zusammenzählen; *v/i.* erscheinen, vorkommen; **~ on** *bsd. Am.* rechnen mit; '**~ skat·er** *Sport:* Eiskunstläufer(in); '**~ skat·ing** *Sport:* Eiskunstlauf *m*

fil·a·ment *electr.* ['fɪləmənt] Glühfaden *m*

filch [fɪltʃ] klauen, stibitzen

file¹ [faɪl] **1.** Ordner *m*, Karteikasten *m*; Akte *f*, Akten *pl.*, Ablage *f*; *Computer:* Datei *f*; Reihe *f*; *mil.* Rotte *f*; **on ~** bei den Akten; **2.** *v/t.* Briefe etc. einordnen, ablegen, zu den Akten nehmen; *Antrag* einreichen, *Berufung* einlegen; *v/i.* hintereinander marschieren

file² [faɪl] **1.** Feile *f*; **2.** feilen

'**file man·age·ment** *Computer:* Dateiverwaltung *f*; '**~ pro·tec·tion** *Computer:* Schreibschutz *m*

fi·li·al ['fɪljəl] kindlich, Kindes...

fil·ing ['faɪlɪŋ] Ablegen *n* (*von Briefen etc.*); **~ cab·i·net** Aktenschrank *m*

fill [fɪl] **1.** (sich) füllen; an-, aus-, er-, vollfüllen; *Pfeife* stopfen; *Zahn* füllen, plombieren; **~ in** einsetzen; *Formular* ausfüllen (*Am. a.* **~ out**); **~ up** vollfüllen; sich füllen; **~ her up!** F *mot.* volltanken, bitte!; **2.** Füllung *f*; **eat one's ~** sich satt essen

fil·let *Brt.*, **fil·et** *Am.* ['fɪlɪt] Filet *n*

fill·ing ['fɪlɪŋ] Füllung *f*; *med.* (Zahn-)Füllung *f*, (-)Plombe *f*; **~ sta·tion** Tankstelle *f*

fil·ly *zo.* ['fɪlɪ] Stutenfohlen *n*

film [fɪlm] **1.** Häutchen *n*; Membran(e) *f*; Film *m* (*a. phot. u. bsd. Brt.* Kinofilm); Trübung *f* (*des Auges*); Nebelschleier *m*; **take od. shoot a ~** e-n Film drehen; **2.** (ver)filmen; sich verfilmen lassen; '**~ star** *bsd. Brt.* Filmstar *m*

fil·ter ['fɪltə] **1.** Filter *m*; **2.** filtern; '**~ tip** Filter *m*; Filterzigarette *f*; '**~tipped: ~ cigarette** Filterzigarette *f*

filth [fɪlθ] Schmutz *m*; '**~y** (*-ier, -iest*) schmutzig; *fig.* unflätig

fin [fɪn] *zo.* Flosse *f*; *Am.* Schwimmflosse *f*

fi·nal ['faɪnl] **1.** letzte(r, -s); End..., Schluß...; endgültig; **2.** *Sport:* Finale *n*; *mst* **~s** *pl.* Schlußexamen, -prüfung *f*; **~ dis·pos·al** Endlagerung *f* (*von Atommüll etc.*); **~ist** ['faɪnəlɪst] *Sport:* Finalist(in); '**~ly** endlich, schließlich; endgültig; **~ 'whis·tle** *Sport:* Schluß-, Abpfiff *m*

fi·nance [faɪ'næns] **1.** Finanzwesen *n*; **~s** *pl.* Finanzen *pl.*; **2.** finanzieren; **fi·nan·cial** [faɪ'nænʃl] finanziell; **fi·nan·cier** [faɪ'nænsɪə] Finanzier *m*

finch *zo.* [fɪntʃ] Fink *m*

find [faɪnd] **1.** (*found*) finden; (an)treffen; auf-, herausfinden; *jur. j-n* für (*nicht*) *schuldig* erklären; beschaffen; versorgen; **~ out** *v/t. et.* herausfinden; *v/i.* es herausfinden; **2.** Fund *m*, Entdeckung *f*; '**~ings** *pl.* Befund *m*; *jur.* Feststellung *f*, Spruch *m*

fine¹ [faɪn] **1.** *adj.* (*~r, ~st*) fein; schön; ausgezeichnet, großartig; **I'm ~** mir geht es gut; **2.** *adv.* F sehr gut, bestens

fine² [faɪn] **1.** Geldstrafe *f*, Bußgeld *n*; **2.** zu e-r Geldstrafe verurteilen

fin·ger ['fɪŋgə] **1.** Finger *m*; **→ cross** 2; **2.** betasten, (herum)fingern an (*dat.*); '**~nail** Fingernagel *m*; '**~print** Fingerabdruck *m*; '**~tip** Fingerspitze *f*

fin·i·cky ['fɪnɪkɪ] pedantisch; wählerisch

fin·ish ['fɪnɪʃ] **1.** (be)enden, aufhören (mit); *a.* ~ **off** vollenden, zu Ende führen, erledigen, *Buch etc.* auslesen; *a.* ~ **off, ~ up** aufessen, austrinken; **2.** Ende *n*, Schluß *m*; *Sport:* Endspurt *m*, Finish *n*; Ziel *n*; Vollendung *f*, letzter Schliff; '~**ing line** *Sport:* Ziellinie *f*

Fin·land ['fɪnlənd] Finnland *n*; **Finn** [fɪn] Finn|e *m*, -in *f*; '**Finn·ish 1.** finnisch; **2.** *ling.* Finnisch *n*

fir *bot.* [fɜː] *a.* ~ **tree** Tanne *f*; '~ **cone** Tannenzapfen *m*

fire ['faɪə] **1.** Feuer *n*; *be on* ~ in Flammen stehen, brennen; *catch* ~ Feuer fangen, in Brand geraten; *set on* ~, *set* ~ *to* anzünden; *v/t.* an-, entzünden; *fig.* anfeuern; abfeuern; *Ziegel etc.* brennen; F rausschmeißen (*entlassen*); heizen; *v/i.* Feuer fangen (*a. fig.*); feuern; ~ **a·larm** ['faɪərəlɑːm] Feueralarm *m*; Feuermelder *m*; '~**arms** ['faɪərɑːmz] *pl.* Feuer-, Schußwaffen *pl.*; '~ **bri·gade** *Brt.* Feuerwehr *f*; '~ **bug** F Feuerteufel *m*; '~**crack·er** Frosch *m* (*Feuerwerkskörper*); '~ **de·part·ment** *Am.* Feuerwehr *f*; '~ **en·gine** ['faɪərendʒɪn] Löschfahrzeug *n*; ~ **es·cape** ['faɪərɪskeɪp] Feuerleiter *f*, -treppe *f*; ~ **ex·tin·guish·er** ['faɪərɪkstɪŋgwɪʃə] Feuerlöscher *m*; '**fight·er** Feuerwehrmann *m*; '~**guard** Kamingitter *n*; '~ **hy·drant** *Brt.* Hydrant *m*; '~**man** (*pl. -men*) Feuerwehrmann *m*; Heizer *m*; '~**place** (offener) Kamin; '~**plug** *Am.* Hydrant *m*; '~**proof** feuerfest; '~**rais·ing** *Brt.* Brandstiftung *f*; '~**screen** *Am.* Kamingitter *n*; '~**side** (offener) Kamin; '~ **sta·tion** Feuerwache *f*; '~ **truck** *Am.* Löschfahrzeug *n*; '~**wood** Brennholz *n*; '~**works** *pl.* Feuerwerk *n*

fir·ing squad *mil.* ['faɪərɪŋskwɒd] Exekutionskommando *n*

firm[1] [fɜːm] fest; hart; standhaft; △ *nicht* **firm**

firm[2] [fɜːm] Firma *f*

first [fɜːst] **1.** *adj.* erste(r, -s); beste(r, -s). ~ *of all* an erster Stelle; zu allererst; **2.** *adv.* erstens; zuerst; ~ *of all* an erster Stelle; zu allererst; **3.** Erste(r, -s); *at* ~ zuerst, anfangs; *from the* ~ von Anfang an; ~ **aid** Erste Hilfe; '~ **aid box**, '~ **aid kit** Verband(s)kasten *m*; '~**born** erstgeborene(r, -s), älteste(r, -s); ~

'**class 1.** Klasse (*e-s Verkehrsmittels*); ~'**class** erstklassig; ~ **floor** *Brt.* erster Stock, *Am.* Erdgeschoß *n*; → *second floor*; ~**hand** aus erster Hand; ~ **leg** *Sport:* Hinspiel *n*; '~**ly** erstens; '~ **name** Vorname *m*; ~'**rate** erstklassig

firth [fɜːθ] Förde *f*, Meeresarm *m*

fish [fɪʃ] **1.** (*pl. fish, fishes*) Fisch *m*; **2.** fischen, angeln; '~**bone** Gräte *f*

fish|·er·man ['fɪʃəmən] (*pl. -men*) Fischer *m*; ~**e·ry** ['fɪʃərɪ] Fischerei *f*

fish|·'fin·ger *bsd. Brt.* Fischstäbchen *n*; '~**hook** Angelhaken *m*

'**fish·ing** Fischen *n*, Angeln *n*; ~ **line** Angelschnur *f*; '~ **rod** Angelrute *f*; '~ **tack·le** Angelgerät *n*

'**fish|·mon·ger** *bsd. Brt.* Fischhändler *m*; '~ **stick** *bsd. Am.*Fischstäbchen *n*; '~**y** (*-ier, -iest*) Fisch...; F verdächtig, faul

fis·sion ['fɪʃn] Spaltung *f*

fis·sure ['fɪʃə] Spalt *m*, Riß *m*

fist [fɪst] Faust *f*

fit[1] [fɪt] **1.** (*-tt-*) geeignet, passend; tauglich; *Sport:* fit, (gut) in Form; *keep* ~ sich fit halten; **2.** (*-tt-; fitted, Am. a. fit*) *v/t.* passend machen (*for* für), anpassen; *tech.* einpassen, -bauen; anbringen; ~ *in* *j-m* e-n Termin geben, *j-n*, *et.* einschieben; *a.* ~ **on** anprobieren; *a.* ~ **out** ausrüsten, -statten, einrichten (*with* mit); *a.* ~ **up** einrichten (*with* mit); montieren, installieren; *v/i.* passen, sitzen (*Kleid*); **3.** Sitz *m* (*Kleid*)

fit[2] [fɪt] *med.* Anfall *m*; *give s.o. a* ~ F j-n auf die Palme bringen; j-m e-n Schock versetzen

'**fit|·ful** unruhig (*Schlaf etc.*); '~**ness** Tauglichkeit *f*; *bsd. Sport:* Fitneß *f*, (gute) Form; '~**ness cen·tre** (*Am.* **cen·ter**) Fitneßcenter *n*; '~**ted** zugeschnitten; ~ *carpet* Spannteppich *m*, Teppichboden *m*; ~ *kitchen* Einbauküche *f*; '~**ter** Monteur *m*; Installateur *m*; '~**ting 1.** passend; schicklich; **2.** Montage *f*, Installation *f*; ~*s pl.* Ausstattung *f*; Armaturen *pl.* (*Bad etc.*)

five [faɪv] **1.** fünf; **2.** Fünf *f*

fix [fɪks] **1.** befestigen, anbringen (*to* an); *Preis* festsetzen, fixieren; *Blick etc.* richten (*on* auf); *Aufmerksamkeit etc.* fesseln; reparieren; *bsd. Am. Essen* zubereiten; △ *nicht* **fix; 2.** F Klemme *f*, *sl.* Fix *m* (*Schuß Heroin etc.*); ~**ed** fest;

starr; '**~ings** *pl. Am. gastr.* Beilagen *pl.*; **~ture** ['fikstʃə] Inventarstück *n*; **lighting ~** Beleuchtungskörper *m*

fizz [fiz] zischen, sprudeln

fl *nur geschr. Abk. für* **floor** Stock(werk *n*)

flab·ber·gast F ['flæbəgɑːst] verblüffen; *be ~ed* platt sein

flab·by ['flæbɪ] (**-ier, -iest**) schlaff

flac·cid ['flæksɪd] schlaff, schlapp

flag¹ [flæg] **1.** Fahne *f*, Flagge *f*; **2.** (**-gg-**) beflaggen

flag² [flæg] **1.** (Stein)Platte *f*, Fliese *f*; **2.** mit (Stein)Platten *od.* Fliesen belegen, fliesen

flag³ [flæg] nachlassen, erlahmen

'**flag|·pole**, '**~·staff** Fahnenstange *f*; '**~·stone** (Stein)Platte *f*, Fliese *f*

flake [fleɪk] **1.** Flocke *f*; Schuppe *f*; **2.** *mst ~ off* abblättern; '**flak·y** (**-ier, -iest**) flockig; blätt(e)rig; **~·y 'pas·try** Blätterteig *m*

flame [fleɪm] **1.** Flamme *f* (*a. fig.*); *be in ~s* in Flammen stehen; **2.** flammen, lodern

flam·ma·ble *Am. u. tech.* ['flæməbl] → **inflammable**

flan [flæn] Obst-, Käsekuchen *m*

flank [flæŋk] **1.** Flanke *f*; **2.** flankieren

flan·nel ['flænl] Flanell *m*; Waschlappen *m*; **~s** *pl.* Flanellhose *f*

flap [flæp] **1.** Flattern *n*, (Flügel)Schlag *m*; Klappe *f*; **2.** (**-pp-**) mit *den Flügeln etc.* schlagen; flattern

flare [fleə] **1.** flackern; sich weiten (*Nasenflügel*); **~ up** aufflammen; *fig.* aufbrausen; **2.** Lichtsignal *n*

flash [flæʃ] **1.** Aufblitzen *n*, -leuchten *n*, Blitz *m*; *Rundfunk etc.:* Kurzmeldung *f*; *phot.* F Blitz *m* (*Blitzlicht*); *bsd. Am.* F Taschenlampe *f*; *like a ~* wie der Blitz; *in a ~* im Nu; *a ~ of lightning* ein Blitz; **2.** (auf)blitzen *od.* aufleuchten (lassen); zucken (*Blitz*); rasen, flitzen; '**~·back** *Film:* Rückblende *f*; **~ 'freeze** *Am.* (**-froze, -frozen**) → **quick-freeze**; '**~·light** *phot.* Blitzlicht *n*; *bsd. Am.* Taschenlampe *f*; '**~·y** (**-ier, -iest**) protzig; auffallend

flask [flɑːsk] Taschenflasche *f*; Thermosflasche *f* (*TM*)

flat¹ [flæt] **1.** (**-tt-**) flach, eben, platt; schal; *econ.* flau; *mot.* platt (*Reifen*); **2.** *adv.* *fall ~* danebengehen; *sing ~* zu tief

singen; **3.** Fläche *f*, Ebene *f*; flache Seite; Flachland *n*, Niederung *f*; *bsd. Am. mot.* Reifenpanne *f*

flat² *bsd. Brt.* [flæt] Wohnung *f*

flat|·foot·ed plattfüßig; '**~·mate** *Brt.* Mitbewohner(in) (*-r Wohnung*); **~·ten** ['flætn] (ein)ebnen; abflachen; *a.* **~ out** flach(er) werden

flat·ter ['flætə] schmeicheln (*dat.*); △ *nicht* **flattern**; **~·er** ['flætərə] Schmeichler(in); '**~·y** ['flætərɪ] Schmeichelei *f*

fla·vo(u)r ['fleɪvə] **1.** Geschmack *m*; Aroma *n*; Blume *f* (*Wein*); *fig.* Beigeschmack *m*; Würze *f*; **2.** würzen; '**~·ing** ['fleɪvərɪŋ] Würze *f*, Aroma *n*

flaw [flɔː] Fehler *m*, *tech. a.* Defekt *m*; '**~·less** einwandfrei, tadellos

flax *bot.* [flæks] Flachs *m*

flea *zo.* [fliː] Floh *m*; '**~ mar·ket** Flohmarkt *m*

fleck [flek] Fleck(en) *m*; Tupfen *m*

fled [fled] *pret. u. p.p. von* **flee**

fledged [fledʒd] flügge; **fledg(e)·ling** ['fledʒlɪŋ] Jungvogel *m*; *fig.* Grünschnabel *m*

flee [fliː] (**fled**) fliehen; meiden

fleece [fliːs] Vlies *n*, *bsd.* Schafsfell *n*

fleet *naut.* [fliːt] Flotte *f*

'**Fleet Street** *das Londoner Presseviertel*; *fig.* die (Londoner) Presse

flesh [fleʃ] *lebendiges* Fleisch; '**~·y** (**-ier, -iest**) fleischig; dick

flew [fluː] *pret. von* **fly³**

flex¹ *bsd. anat.* [fleks] biegen

flex² *bsd. Brt. electr.* [fleks] (Anschluß-, Verlängerungs)Kabel *n*, (-)Schnur *f*

flex·i·ble ['fleksəbl] flexibel, biegsam; *fig.* anpassungsfähig; **~ working hours** *pl.* Gleitzeit *f*

flex·i·time *Brt.* ['fleksɪtaɪm], **flex·time** *Am.* ['flekstaɪm] Gleitzeit *f*

flick [flɪk] schnippen; schnellen

flick·er ['flɪkə] **1.** flackern; *TV* flimmern; **2.** Flackern *n*; *TV* Flimmern *n*

fli·er ['flaɪə] *aviat.* Flieger *m*; Reklamezettel *m*

flight [flaɪt] Flucht *f*; Flug *m* (*a. fig.*); Schwarm *m* (*Vögel*); *a.* **~ of stairs** Treppe *f*; *put to* **~** in die Flucht schlagen; *take (to)* **~** die Flucht ergreifen; '**~ at·tend·ant** *aviat.* Flugbegleiter(in); '**~·less** *zo.* flugunfähig; '**~·re·cord·er** *aviat.* Flugschreiber *m*; '**~·y** (**-ier, -iest**) flatterhaft

flim·sy ['flɪmzɪ] (*-ier*, *-iest*) dünn; zart; *fig.* fadenscheinig

flinch [flɪntʃ] (zurück)zucken, zusammenfahren; zurückschrecken (*from* vor *dat.*)

fling [flɪŋ] **1.** (*flung*) werfen, schleudern; ~ **o.s.** sich stürzen; ~ **open** *od.* **to** Tür *etc.* aufreißen *od.* zuschlagen; **2.** **have a** ~ sich austoben; **have a** ~ **at** es versuchen *od.* probieren mit

flint [flɪnt] Feuerstein *m*

flip [flɪp] (*-pp-*) schnippen, schnipsen; **Münze** hochwerfen

flip·pant ['flɪpənt] respektlos, schnodd(e)rig

flip·per ['flɪpə] *zo.* Flosse *f*; Schwimmflosse *f*

flirt [flɜːt] **1.** flirten; **2.** **be a** ~ gern flirten; **flir·ta·tion** [flɜː'teɪʃn] Flirt *m*

flit [flɪt] (*-tt-*) flitzen, huschen

float [fləʊt] *v/i.* (auf dem Wasser) schwimmen, (im Wasser) treiben; schweben; *a.* *econ.* in Umlauf sein; *v/t.* schwimmen *od.* treiben lassen; *naut.* flottmachen; *econ.* Wertpapiere *etc.* in Umlauf bringen; *econ.* Währung floaten, den Wechselkurs (*gen.*) freigeben; **2.** Festwagen *m*; '~**ing 1.** schwimmend, treibend; *econ.* umlaufend (*Geld etc.*); flexibel (*Wechselkurs*); frei konvertierbar (*Währung*); **2.** *econ.* Floating *n*; '~**ing** '**vot·er** *pol.* Wechselwähler(in)

flock [flɒk] **1.** Herde *f* (*bsd.* *Schafe od.* *Ziegen*) (*a.* *rel.*); Menge *f*, Schar *f*; △ **nicht** *Flocke*; **2.** *fig.* strömen

floe [fləʊ] (treibende) Eisscholle

flog [flɒg] (*-gg-*) prügeln, schlagen; '~**ging** Tracht *f* Prügel

flood [flʌd] **1.** *a.* ~**tide** Flut *f*; Überschwemmung *f*; **2.** überfluten, überschwemmen; '~**gate** Schleusentor *n*; '~**lights** *pl.* *electr.* Flutlicht *n*

floor [flɔː] **1.** (Fuß)Boden *m*; Stock (-werk *n*) *m*, Etage *f*; Tanzfläche *f*; → **first floor**, **second floor**; **take the** ~ das Wort ergreifen; **2.** e-n (Fuß)Boden legen in; zu Boden schlagen; *fig.* F *j-n* umhauen; '~**board** (Fußboden)Diele *f*; '~ **cloth** Putzlappen *m*; ~**ing** ['flɔːrɪŋ] (Fuß)Bodenbelag *m*; '~ **lamp** *Am.* Stehlampe *f*; '~ **lead·er** *Am.* *parl.* Fraktionsführer *m*; '~ **show** Nachtklubvorstellung *f*; '~**walk·er** *bsd.* *Am.*

→ **shopwalker**

flop [flɒp] **1.** (*-pp-*) sich (hin)plumpsen lassen; F durchfallen, danebengehen, ein Reinfall sein; **2.** Plumps *m*; F Flop *m*, Mißerfolg *m*, Reinfall *m*, Pleite *f*; Versager *m*; '~**py**, ~**py** '**disk** *Computer:* Floppy (disk) *f*, Diskette *f*

flor·id ['flɒrɪd] rot, gerötet

flor·ist ['flɒrɪst] Blumenhändler(in)

floun·der¹ *zo.* ['flaʊndə] Flunder *f*

floun·der² ['flaʊndə] zappeln; strampeln; *fig.* sich verhaspeln

flour ['flaʊə] (feines) Mehl

flour·ish ['flʌrɪʃ] **1.** Schnörkel *m*; *mus.* Tusch *m*; **2.** *v/i.* blühen, gedeihen; *v/t.* schwenken

flow [fləʊ] **1.** fließen, strömen; **2.** Fluß *m*, Strom *m* (*beide a.* *fig.*)

flow·er ['flaʊə] **1.** Blume *f*; Blüte *f* (*a.* *fig.*); **2.** blühen; '~**bed** Blumenbeet *n*; '~**pot** Blumentopf *m*

flown [fləʊn] *p.p.* von *fly³*

fl. oz. *nur geschr.* Abk. für **fluid ounce** (*Hohlmaß:* Brt. 28,4 ccm, Am. 29,57 ccm)

fluc·tu·ate ['flʌktʃʊeɪt] schwanken; ~**a·tion** [flʌktʃʊ'eɪʃn] Schwankung *f*

flu F [fluː] Grippe *f*

flue [fluː] Rauchfang *m*, Esse *f*

flu·en|cy ['fluːənsɪ] Flüssigkeit *f* (*des Stils etc.*); (Rede)Gewandtheit *f*; ~**t** fließend (*Sprache*); flüssig (*Stil etc.*); gewandt (*Redner*)

fluff [flʌf] **1.** Flaum *m*; Staubflocke *f*; Federn *pl.* aufplustern (*Vogel*); '~**y** (*-ier*, *-iest*) flaumig

flu·id ['fluːɪd] **1.** flüssig; **2.** Flüssigkeit *f*

flung [flʌŋ] *pret.* u. *p.p.* von *fling* 1

flunk *Am.* F [flʌŋk] durchfallen (lassen)

flu·o·res·cent [flʊə'resnt] fluoreszierend

flu·o·ride ['flɔːraɪd] Fluor *n* (*als Trinkwasserzusatz*)

flu·o·rine *chem.* ['flɔːriːn] Fluor *n*

flur·ry ['flʌrɪ] Windstoß *m*; (Regen-, Schnee)Schauer *m*; *fig.* Aufregung *f*, Unruhe *f*

flush [flʌʃ] **1.** (Wasser)Spülung *f*; Erröten *n*; Röte *f*; **2.** *a.* ~ **out** (aus)spülen; ~ **down** hinunterspülen; ~ **the toilet** spülen; *v/i.* erröten, rot werden; spülen (*Toilette od.* *Toilettenbenutzer*)

flus·ter ['flʌstə] **1.** nervös machen *od.* werden; **2.** Nervosität *f*

flute _mus._ [fluːt] **1.** Flöte f; **2.** (auf der) Flöte spielen

flut·ter ['flʌtə] **1.** flattern; **2.** Flattern n; _fig._ Erregung f

flux _fig._ [flʌks] Fluß m

fly[1] _zo._ [flaɪ] Fliege f

fly[2] [flaɪ] Hosenschlitz m; Zeltklappe f

fly[3] [flaɪ] (_flew, flown_) fliegen (lassen); stürmen, stürzen; flattern, wehen; (ver)fliegen (_Zeit_); _Drachen_ steigen lassen; ~ **at s.o.** auf j-n losgehen; ~ **into a passion** _od._ **rage** in Wut geraten; '**~·er** → _flier_

'**fly·ing** fliegend; Flug...; ~ '**sau·cer** fliegende Untertasse; ~ **squad** Überfallkommando n (_der Polizei_)

'**fly|·o·ver** _Brt._ (Straßen-, Eisenbahn)Überführung f; '**~·screen** Fliegenfenster n; '**~·weight** _Boxen:_ Fliegengewicht(ler m) n; '**~·wheel** Schwungrad n

FM [ef 'em] _Abk. für_ **frequency modulation** UKW, Ultrakurzwelle f

foal _zo._ [fəʊl] Fohlen n

foam [fəʊm] **1.** Schaum m; **2.** schäumen; ~ '**rub·ber** Schaumgummi m; '**~·y** (_-ier, -iest_) schaumig

fo·cus ['fəʊkəs] **1.** (_pl._ **-cuses, -ci** [-saɪ]) Brenn-, _fig. a._ Mittelpunkt m; _opt._, _phot._ Scharfeinstellung f; **2.** _opt._, _phot._ scharf einstellen; _fig._ konzentrieren (**on** auf _acc._)

fod·der ['fɒdə] (Trocken)Futter n

foe _poet._ [fəʊ] Feind m, Gegner m

fog [fɒg] (dichter) Nebel; '**~·gy** (_-ier, -iest_) neb(e)lig; _fig._ nebelhaft

foi·ble ['fɔɪbl] (kleine) Schwäche

foil[1] [fɔɪl] Folie f; _fig._ Hintergrund m

foil[2] [fɔɪl] vereiteln

foil[3] [fɔɪl] _Fechten:_ Florett n

fold[1] [fəʊld] **1.** Falte f; Falz m; **2.** ...fach, ...fältig; **3.** (sich) falten; falzen; _Arme_ verschränken; einwickeln; _oft_ ~ **up** zusammenfalten, -legen, -klappen

fold[2] [fəʊld] Schafhürde f, Pferch m; _rel._ Herde f

'**fold·er** Aktendeckel m; Schnellhefter m; Faltprospekt m, -blatt n, Broschüre f

'**fold·ing** zusammenlegbar; Klapp...; ~ **bed** Klappbett n; '**~ bi·cy·cle** Klapprad n; '**~ boat** Faltboot n; '**~ chair** Klappstuhl m; '**~ door(s** _pl._) Falttür f

fo·li·age ['fəʊlɪɪdʒ] Laub(werk) n

folk [fəʊk] _pl._ Leute _pl._; Volks...; **~s** _pl._ F _m-e etc._ Leute _pl._ (_Angehörige_); △ _nicht_ **Volk;** '**~·lore** Volkskunde f; Volkssagen _pl._; '**~ mu·sic** Volksmusik f; '**~ song** Volkslied n; Folksong m

fol·low ['fɒləʊ] folgen (_dat._); folgen auf (_acc._); be-, verfolgen; _j-m_ Beruf etc. nachgehen; ~ **through** _Plan etc._ bis zum Ende durchführen; ~ **up er** _e-e Sache_ nachgehen; _e-e Sache_ weiterverfolgen; **as ~s** wie folgt; '**~·er** Nachfolger(in); Verfolger(in); Anhänger(in); '**~·ing 1.** Anhängerschaft f, Anhänger _pl._; Gefolge n; **the ~ das** Folgende; die Folgenden _pl._; **2.** folgende(r, -s); **3.** im Anschluß an (_acc._)

fol·ly ['fɒlɪ] Torheit f

fond [fɒnd] zärtlich; vernarrt (**of** in _acc._); **be ~ of** gern haben, lieben

fon·dle ['fɒndl] liebkosen; streicheln; (ver)hätscheln

'**fond·ness** Zärtlichkeit f; Vorliebe f

font [fɒnt] Taufstein m, -becken n

food [fuːd] Nahrung f, Essen n; Nahrungs-, Lebensmittel _pl._; Futter n

fool [fuːl] **1.** Narr m, Närrin f, Dummkopf m; **make a ~ of s.o.** j-n zum Narren halten; **make a ~ of o.s.** sich lächerlich machen; **2.** zum Narren halten; betrügen (**out of** um); ~ **about,** ~ **around** herumtrödeln; Unsinn machen, herumalbern; '**~·har·dy** tollkühn; '**~·ish** dumm, töricht; unklug; '**~·ish·ness** Dummheit f; '**~·proof** kinderleicht; todsicher

foot [fʊt] **1.** (_pl._ **feet**) Fuß m; (_pl._ F a. **foot,** _Abk._ **ft**) Fuß m (30,48 cm); Fußende n; **on** ~ zu Fuß; **2.** F _Rechnung_ bezahlen; ~ **it** zu Fuß gehen

'**foot·ball** _Brt._ Fußball(spiel n) m; _Am._ Football(spiel n) m; _Brt._ Fußball m; _Am._ Football-Ball m; '**foot·bal·ler** Fußballer m; ~ '**hoo·li·gan** Fußballrowdy m; '**~ play·er** Fußballspieler m

'**foot|·bridge** Fußgängerbrücke f; '**~·fall** Tritt m, Schritt m (_Geräusch_); '**~·hold** fester Stand, Halt m

'**foot·ing** Halt m, Stand m; _fig._ Grundlage f, Basis f; **be on a friendly ~ with s.o.** ein gutes Verhältnis zu j-m haben; **lose one's ~** den Halt verlieren

'**foot|·lights** _pl. thea._ Rampenlicht(er _pl._) n; '**~·loose** frei, unbeschwert; ~ **and fancy-free** frei u. ungebunden; '**~-**

note Fußnote f; '**~·path** (Fuß)Pfad m; '**~·print** Fußabdruck m; **~s** pl. a. Fußspur(en pl.) f; '**~·sore** wund an den Füßen; '**~·step** Tritt m, Schritt m; Fußstapfe f; '**~·wear** Schuhwerk n, Schuhe pl.

fop [fɒp] Geck m, Fatzke m

for [fɔː, fə] **1.** prp. mst für; Zweck, Ziel, Richtung: zu; nach; warten, hoffen etc. auf (acc.); sich sehnen etc. nach; Grund, Anlaß: aus, vor (dat.), wegen; Zeitdauer: **~ three days** drei Tage (lang); seit drei Tagen; Entfernung: **I walked ~ a mile** ich ging eine Meile (weit); Austausch: (an)statt; in der Eigenschaft als; **I ~ one** ich zum Beispiel; '**~·sure** sicher!, gewiß!; **2.** cj. denn, weil

for·age ['fɒrɪdʒ] a. **~ about** (herum)stöbern, (-)wühlen (**in** in dat.; **for** nach)

for·ay ['fɒreɪ] mil. Ein-, Überfall m; fig. Ausflug m (**into** politics in die Politik)

for·bad(e) [fə'bæd] pret. von **forbid**

for·bear ['fɔːbeə] → **forebear**

for·bid [fə'bɪd] (**-dd-; -bade** od. **-bad** [-bæd], **-bidden** od. **-bid**) verbieten; hindern; '**~·ding** abstoßend

force [fɔːs] **1.** Stärke f, Kraft f, Gewalt f; **the (police) ~** die Polizei; (**armed**) **~s** pl. mil. Streitkräfte pl.; **by ~** mit Gewalt; **come of** od. **put into ~** in Kraft treten od. setzen; **2.** j-n zwingen; et. erzwingen; zwängen, drängen; Tempo beschleunigen; **~ s.th. on s.o.** j-m et. aufzwingen od. -drängen; **~ o.s. on s.o.** sich j-m aufdrängen; **~ open** aufbrechen; '**~d** erzwungen; gezwungen, gequält; '**~ful** energisch, kraftvoll (Person); eindrucksvoll, überzeugend

for·ceps med. ['fɔːseps] Zange f

for·ci·ble ['fɔːsəbl] gewaltsam; eindringlich

ford [fɔːd] **1.** Furt f; **2.** durchwaten

fore [fɔː] **1.** vorder, Vorder...; vorn; **2.** Vorderteil m, -seite f, Front f; **~·arm** ['fɔːrɑːm] Unterarm m; '**~·bear** mst **~s** pl. Vorfahren pl., Ahnen pl.; **~·bod·ing** [fɔː'bəʊdɪŋ] (böses) Vorzeichen; (böse) (Vor)Ahnung; '**~·cast 1.** (**-cast** od. **-casted**) voraussagen, vorhersehen; Wetter vorhersagen; **2.** Voraussage f; (Wetter)Vorhersage f; '**~·fa·ther** Vorfahr m; '**~·fin·ger** Zeigefinger m; '**~·foot** (pl. **-feet**) zo. Vor-

derfuß m; '**~·gone con'clu·sion** ausgemachte Sache; **be a ~** a. von vornherein feststehen; '**~·ground** Vordergrund m; '**~·hand 1.** Sport: Vorhand(schlag m) f; **2.** Sport: Vorhand...; **~·head** ['fɒrɪd] Stirn f

for·eign ['fɒrən] fremd, ausländisch, Auslands..., Außen...; **~ af'fairs** Außenpolitik f; **~ 'aid** Auslandshilfe f; '**~·er** Ausländer(in); **~ 'lan·guage** Fremdsprache f; **~ 'min·is·ter** pol. Außenminister m; **♀ Of·fice** Brt. pol. Außenministerium n; **~ 'pol·i·cy** Außenpolitik f; **♀ 'Sec·re·ta·ry** Brt. pol. Außenminister m; **~ 'trade** econ. Außenhandel m; **~ 'work·er** Gastarbeiter m

fore'knowl·edge vorherige Kenntnis; '**~·leg** zo. Vorderbein n; '**~·man** (pl. **-men**) Vorarbeiter m, (**am Bau**) Polier m; jur. Sprecher m (der Geschworenen); '**~·most** vorderste(r, -s), erste(r, -s); '**~·name** Vorname m

fo·ren·sic [fə'rensɪk] Gerichts...; **~ 'medi·cine** Gerichtsmedizin f

'**fore·run·ner** Vorläufer(in); **~·see** (**-saw, -seen**) vorhersehen; **~·shad·ow** ahnen lassen, andeuten; '**~·sight** fig. Weitblick m; (weise) Voraussicht

for·est ['fɒrɪst] Wald m (a. fig.); Forst m

fore·stall [fɔː'stɔːl] et. vereiteln; j-m zuvorkommen

for·est·er ['fɒrɪstə] Förster m; **~·ry** ['fɒrɪstrɪ] Forstwirtschaft f

'**fore·taste** Vorgeschmack m; **~·tell** (**-told**) vorhersagen; '**~·thought** Vorsorge f, -bedacht m

for·ev·er, for ev·er [fə'revə] für immer

'**fore·wom·an** (pl. **-women**) Vorarbeiterin f; '**~·word** Vorwort n

for·feit ['fɔːfɪt] verwirken; einbüßen

forge [fɔːdʒ] **1.** Schmiede f; **2.** fälschen; '**forg·er** Fälscher m; **for·ge·ry** ['fɔːdʒərɪ] Fälschen n; Fälschung f; '**for·ge·ry-proof** fälschungssicher

for·get [fə'get] (**-got, -gotten**) vergessen; '**~·ful** vergeßlich; **~-me-not** bot. Vergißmeinnicht n

for·give [fə'gɪv] (**-gave, -given**) vergeben, -zeihen; '**~·ness** Verzeihung f; **for'giv·ing** versöhnlich; nachsichtig

fork [fɔːk] **1.** Gabel f; **2.** (sich) gabeln; **~ed** gegabelt, gespalten (Zunge); '**~·lift 'truck** Gabelstapler m

form [fɔːm] **1.** Form *f*; Gestalt *f*; Formular *n*, Vordruck *m*; *bsd.* Brt. (Schul)Klasse *f*; Formalität *f*; Kondition *f*, Verfassung *f*; *in great* ~ gut in Form; **2.** (sich) formen, (sich) bilden, gestalten

form·al ['fɔːml] förmlich; formell; **for·mal·i·ty** [fɔːˈmælətɪ] Förmlichkeit *f*; Formalität *f*

for·mat ['fɔːmæt] **1.** Aufmachung *f*; Format *n*; **2.** (*-tt-*) Computer: formatieren

for·ma·tion [fɔːˈmeɪʃn] Bildung *f*; **~tive** ['fɔːmətɪv] bildend; gestaltend; ~ *years pl.* Entwicklungsjahre *pl.*

'**for·mat·ting** Computer: Formatierung *f*

for·mer ['fɔːmə] **1.** früher; ehemalig; **2.** *the* ~ ersterer; '**~·ly** früher

for·mi·da·ble ['fɔːmɪdəbl] furchterregend; gewaltig, riesig, gefährlich (*Gegner etc.*), schwierig (*Frage etc.*)

'**form| mas·ter** Klassenlehrer *m*, -leiter *m*; '**~ mis·tress** Klassenlehrerin *f*, -leiterin *f*; '**~ teach·er** Klassenlehrer(in), Klassenleiter(in)

for·mu·la ['fɔːmjʊlə] (*pl. -las, -lae* [-liː]) Formel *f*; Rezept *n* (*zur Zubereitung*), △ *nicht Formular*; **~late** ['fɔːmjʊleɪt] formulieren

for·sake [fəˈseɪk] (*-sook, -saken*) aufgeben; verlassen; **~·sak·en** [fəˈseɪkən] *p.p. von forsake*; **~·sook** [fəˈsʊk] *pret. von forsake*; **~·swear** [fɔːˈsweə] (*-swore, -sworn*) abschwören, entsagen

fort *mil.* [fɔːt] Fort *n*, Festung *f*

forth [fɔːθ] weiter, fort; (her)vor; *and so* ~ und so weiter; '**~·com·ing** bevorstehend, kommend; in Kürze erscheinend (*Buch*) *od.* anlaufend (*Film*)

for·ti·eth ['fɔːtɪɪθ] vierzigste(r, -s)

for·ti·fi·ca·tion [fɔːtɪfɪˈkeɪʃn] Befestigung *f*; '**~·fy** ['fɔːtɪfaɪ] *mil.* befestigen; *fig.* (ver)stärken; '**~·tude** ['fɔːtɪtjuːd] (innere) Kraft *od.* Stärke

fort·night ['fɔːtnaɪt] vierzehn Tage

for·tress *mil.* ['fɔːtrɪs] Festung *f*

for·tu·i·tous [fɔːˈtjuːɪtəs] zufällig

for·tu·nate ['fɔːtʃnət] glücklich; *be* ~ Glück haben; '**~·ly** glücklicherweise

for·tune ['fɔːtʃn] Vermögen *n*; (glücklicher) Zufall, Glück *n*; Schicksal *n*; '**~·tell·er** Wahrsager(in)

for·ty ['fɔːtɪ] **1.** vierzig; *have* ~ *winks* F ein Nickerchen machen; **2.** Vierzig *f*

for·ward ['fɔːwəd] **1.** *adv.* nach vorn, vorwärts; **2.** *adj.* Vorwärts...; fortschrittlich; vorlaut, dreist; **3.** *Fußball:* Stürmer *m*; **4.** befördern, (ver)senden; schicken; *Brief etc.* nachsenden; '**~·ing** **a·gent** Spediteur *m*

fos·sil ['fɒsl] *geol.* Fossil *n* (*a. fig.* F), Versteinerung *f*

fos·ter-child ['fɒstətʃaɪld] (*pl. -children*) Pflegekind *n*; '**~·par·ents** *pl.* Pflegeeltern *pl.*

fought [fɔːt] *pret. u. p.p. von fight* 2

foul [faʊl] **1.** stinkend, widerlich; verpestet, schlecht (*Luft*); verdorben, faul (*Lebensmittel*); schmutzig, verschmutzt; schlecht, stürmisch (*Wetter*); Sport: regelwidrig; △ *nicht faul*; **2.** Sport: Foul *n*, Regelverstoß *m*; *vicious* ~ böses *od.* übles Foul; **3.** Sport: foulen; be-, verschmutzen

found¹ [faʊnd] *pret. u. p.p. von find* 1

found² [faʊnd] gründen, stiften

found³ *tech.* [faʊnd] gießen

foun·da·tion [faʊnˈdeɪʃn] *arch.* Grundmauer *f*, Fundament *n*; *fig.* Gründung *f*, Errichtung *f*; (gemeinnützige) Stiftung; *fig.* Grundlage *f*, Basis *f*

found·er¹ ['faʊndə] Gründer(in); Stifter(in)

found·er² ['faʊndə] *naut.* sinken; *fig.* scheitern

found·ling ['faʊndlɪŋ] Findling *m*

foun·dry *tech.* ['faʊndrɪ] Gießerei *f*

foun·tain ['faʊntɪn] Springbrunnen *m*; (*Wasser*)Strahl *m*; '**~ pen** Füllfederhalter *m*

four [fɔː] **1.** vier; **2.** Vier *f*; *Rudern:* Vierer *m*; *on all* ~**s** auf allen vieren

'**four| star** Brt. F Super *n* (*Benzin*); ~ **star 'pet·rol** Brt. Superbenzin *n*; **~·stroke 'en·gine** Viertaktmotor *m*

four·teen [fɔːˈtiːn] **1.** vierzehn; **2.** Vierzehn *f*; **~th** [fɔːˈtiːnθ] vierzehnte(r, -s); **four·th** [fɔːθ] **1.** vierte(r, -s); **2.** Viertel *n*; '**~·th·ly** viertens

four-wheel 'drive *mot.* Vierradantrieb *m*

fowl [faʊl] Geflügel *n*

fox *zo.* [fɒks] Fuchs *m*; '**~·glove** *bot.* Fingerhut *m*; '**~·y** (*-ier, -iest*) schlau, gerissen

frac·tion ['frækʃn] Bruch(teil) *m*; △ *nicht parl.* Fraktion

rac·ture ['fræktʃə] **1.** (*bsd.* Knochen)Bruch *m*; **2.** brechen

ra·gile ['frædʒaɪl] zerbrechlich

rag·ment ['frægmənt] Bruchstück *n*

ra|·grance ['freɪɡrəns] Wohlgeruch *m*, Duft *m*; '**~grant** wohlriechend, duftend

rail [freɪl] ge-, zerbrechlich; zart, schwach; '**~ty** Zartheit *f*; Gebrechlichkeit *f*; Schwäche *f*

rame [freɪm] **1.** Rahmen *m*; (*Brillenetc.*)Gestell *n*; Körper(bau) *m*; **~ of mind** (Gemüts)Verfassung *f*, (-)Zustand *m*; **2.** (ein)rahmen; bilden, formen, bauen; *a.* **~ up** F j-et. anhängen; '**~up** F abgekartetes Spiel; Intrige *f*; '**~work** *tech.* Gerüst *n*; *fig.* Struktur *f*, System *n*

franc [fræŋk] Franc *m*; Franken *m*

France ['frɑːns] Frankreich *n*

fran·chise ['fræntʃaɪz] *pol.* Wahlrecht *n*; Konzession *f*

frank [fræŋk] **1.** frei(mütig), offen; **2.** Brief (*maschinell*) freistempeln

frank·fur·ter ['fræŋkfɜːtə] Frankfurter (*Würstchen m*) *f*

'**frank·ness** Offenheit *f*

fran·tic ['fræntɪk] (*~ally*) außer sich; hektisch

fra·ter|·nal [frə'tɜːnl] brüderlich; **~ni·ty** [frə'tɜːnətɪ] Brüderlichkeit *f*; Vereinigung *f*, Zunft *f*; *Am. univ.* Verbindung *f*

fraud [frɔːd] Betrug *m*; F Schwindel *m*; '**~u·lent** ['frɔːdjʊlənt] betrügerisch

fray [freɪ] ausfransen, (sich) durchscheuern

freak [friːk] Mißgeburt *f*; Laune *f*; in *Zssgn*: F ...freak *m*, ...fanatiker *m*; Freak *m*, irrer Typ; *~ of nature* Laune *f* der Natur; *film* ~ Kinonarr *m*, -fan *m*

freck·le ['frekl] Sommersprosse *f*; '**~d** sommersprossig

free [friː] **1.** (*~r*, *~st*) frei; ungehindert; ungebunden; kostenlos, zum Nulltarif; freigebig; ~ *and easy* zwanglos; sorglos; **set** ~ freilassen; **2.** (*freed*) befreien; freilassen; **~·dom** ['friːdəm] Freiheit *f*; '**~ fares** *pl.* Nulltarif *m* (*bei Bus- etc. Beförderung*); **~·lance** ['friːlɑːns] frei (-beruflich tätig), freischaffend; '**₂·ma·son** Freimaurer *m*; ~ '**skat·ing** Eiskunstlauf: Kür *f*; '**~style** *Sport*: Freistil *m*; ~ '**time** Freizeit *f*; ~ '**trade**

Freihandel *m*; ~ **trade 'ar·e·a** Freihandelszone *f*; '**~way** *Am. autobahnähnliche* Schnellstraße; **~wheel** im Freilauf fahren

freeze [friːz] **1.** (*froze*, *frozen*) *v/i.* (ge)frieren; erstarren; *v/t.* gefrieren lassen; *Fleisch etc.* einfrieren, tiefkühlen; *econ. Preise etc.* einfrieren; **2.** Frost *m*, Kälte *f*; *econ. pol.* Einfrieren *n*; **wage ~**, **~ on wages** Lohnstopp *m*; **~·'dried** gefriergetrocknet; **~·'dry** gefriertrocknen

'**freez·er** Gefriertruhe *f*, Tiefkühl-, Gefriergerät *n* (*a.* **deep freeze**); Gefrierfach *n*

'**freez·ing** eisig; Gefrier...; '**~ com·part·ment** Gefrierfach *n*; '**~ point** Gefrierpunkt *m*

freight [freɪt] **1.** (Fracht(gebühr) *f*; *Am.* Güter...; **2.** beladen; verfrachten; '**~ car** *Am. rail.* Güterwagen *m*; '**~er** Frachter *m*, Frachtschiff *n*; Transportflugzeug *n*; '**~ train** *Am.* Güterzug *m*

French [frentʃ] **1.** französisch; **2.** *ling.* Französisch *n*; **the** ~ *pl.* die Franzosen *pl.*; ~ '**doors** *pl. Am.* → **French window(s)**; ~ '**fries** *pl. bsd. Am.* Pommes frites *pl.*; '**~·man** (*pl. -men*) Franzose *m*; ~ '**win·dow(s** *pl.*) Terrassen-, Balkontür *f*; '**~·wom·an** (*pl. -women*) Französin *f*

fren|·zied ['frenzɪd] außer sich, rasend (**with** vor *dat.*); hektisch; **~zy** ['frenzɪ] helle Aufregung; Ekstase *f*; Raserei *f*

fre·quen·cy ['friːkwənsɪ] Häufigkeit *f*; *electr.* Frequenz *f*; **~t 1.** ['friːkwənt] häufig; **2.** [frɪ'kwent] (oft) besuchen

fresh [freʃ] frisch; neu; unerfahren; F frech; **~·en** ['freʃn] auffrischen (*Wind*); ~ (**o.s.**) **up** sich frisch machen; '**~·man** (*pl. -men*) *univ.* Student(in) im ersten Jahr; '**~·ness** Frische *f*; ~ '**wa·ter** Süßwasser *n*; '**~·wa·ter** Süßwasser...

fret [fret] sich Sorgen machen; '**~·ful** verärgert, gereizt; quengelig

FRG [ef ɑː 'dʒiː] *Abk. für Federal Republic of Germany* Bundesrepublik *f* Deutschland

Fri *nur geschr. Abk. für Friday* Fr., Freitag *m*

fri·ar ['fraɪə] Mönch *m*

fric·tion ['frɪkʃn] Reibung *f* (*a. fig.*)

Fri·day ['fraɪdɪ] (*Abk.* **Fri**) Freitag *m*; **on** ~ (am) Freitag; **on** ~**s** freitags

fridge

fridge F [frɪdʒ] Kühlschrank *m*
friend [frend] Freund(in); Bekannte(r *m*) *f*; **make ~s with** sich anfreunden mit, Freundschaft schließen mit; **'~ly 1.** freund(schaft)lich; **2.** *bsd. Brt. Sport:* Freundschaftsspiel *n*; **'~ship** Freundschaft *f*
fries *bsd. Am.* [fraɪz] *pl.* F Fritten *pl.*
frig·ate *naut.* ['frɪgɪt] Fregatte *f*
fright [fraɪt] Schreck(en) *m*; **look a ~** F verboten aussehen; **~en** ['fraɪtn] erschrecken; **be ~ed** erschrecken (**at, by, of** vor *dat.*); Angst haben (**of** vor *dat.*); **'~ful** schrecklich, fürchterlich
fri·gid ['frɪdʒɪd] *psych.* frigid(e); kalt, frostig
frill [frɪl] Krause *f*, Rüsche *f*
fringe [frɪndʒ] **1.** Franse *f*; Rand *m*; Pony *m* (*Frisur*); **2.** mit Fransen besetzen; **'~ ben·e·fits** *pl. econ.* Gehalts-, Lohnnebenleistungen *pl.*; **'~ e·vent** Randveranstaltung *f*; **'~ group** *soziale* Randgruppe
frisk [frɪsk] herumtollen; F *j-n* filzen, durchsuchen; **'~·y** (*-ier, -iest*) lebhaft, munter
frit·ter ['frɪtə]: **~ away** Geld *etc.* vertun, *Zeit* vertrödeln, *Geld, Kräfte* vergeuden
fri·vol·i·ty [frɪ'vɒlətɪ] Frivolität *f*, Leichtfertigkeit *f*; **friv·o·lous** ['frɪvələs] frivol, leichtfertig
friz·zle *gastr.* F ['frɪzl] verbrutzeln
frizz·y ['frɪzɪ] (*-ier, -iest*) gekräuselt, kraus (*Haar*)
fro [frəʊ]: **to and ~** hin und her
frock [frɒk] Kutte *f*; Kleid *n*; Kittel *m*
frog *zo.* [frɒg] Frosch *m*; **'~·man** (*pl. -men*) Froschmann *m, mil. a.* Kampfschwimmer *m*
frol·ic ['frɒlɪk] **1.** Herumtoben *n*, -tollen *n*; **2.** (*-ck-*) herumtoben, -tollen; **'~·some** ausgelassen, übermütig
from [frɒm, frəm] von; aus; von ... aus *od.* her; von ... (an), seit; aus; von (*dat.*); **~ 9 to 5** (*o'clock*) von 9 bis 5 (Uhr)
front [frʌnt] **1.** Vorderseite *f*; Front *f* (*a. mil.*); **at the ~,** *in* **~** vorn; *in* **~** *of* räumlich: vor; **be in ~** in Führung sein; **2.** Vorder...; **3.** *a.* **~ on, ~ to(wards)** gegenüberstehen, gegenüberliegen; **~'age** ['frʌntɪdʒ] (Vorder)Front *f* (*e-s Hauses*); **'~ cov·er** Titelseite *f* (*e-r Zeitschrift*); **~ 'door** Haus-, Vordertür *f*; **~**

'en·trance Vordereingang *m*
fron·tier ['frʌntɪə] (Landes)Grenze *f*; Grenz...; *Am. hist.* Grenzland *n*, Grenze *f* (*zum Wilden Westen*)
'front-page F wichtig, aktuell (*Nachrichten etc.*); **~wheel 'drive** *mot.* Vorderradantrieb *m*
frost [frɒst] **1.** Frost *m*; *a.* **hoar ~, white ~** Reif *m*; **2.** mit Reif überziehen; *Glas:* mattieren; *gastr. bsd. Am.* glasieren mit Zuckerguß überziehen; mit (Puder)Zucker bestreuen; **~ed glass** Matt-, Milchglas *n*; **'~·bite** Erfrierung *f*; **'~·bit·ten** erfroren; **'~·y** (*-ier, -iest*) eisig, frostig (*a. fig.*)
froth [frɒθ] **1.** Schaum *m*; **2.** schäumen; zu Schaum schlagen; **'~·y** (*-ier, -iest*) schäumend; schaumig
frown [fraʊn] **1.** Stirnrunzeln *n*; **with a ~** stirnrunzelnd; **2.** *v/i.* die Stirn runzeln
froze [frəʊz] *pret. von* **freeze 1; fro·zen** ['frəʊzn] **1.** *p.p. von* **freeze 1; 2.** *adj.* (eis)kalt; (ein-, zu)gefroren; Gefrier...; **~ 'foods** *pl.* Tiefkühlkost *f*
fru·gal ['fruːgl] sparsam; bescheiden; einfach
fruit [fruːt] Frucht *f*; Früchte *pl.*; Obst *n*; **~·er·er** ['fruːtərə] Obsthändler *m*; **'~·ful** fruchtbar; **'~·less** unfruchtbar; erfolglos; **~ juice** Fruchtsaft *m*; **'~·y** (*-ier, -iest*) fruchtartig; fruchtig (*Wein*)
frus·trate [frʌ'streɪt] vereiteln; frustrieren; **~·tra·tion** [frʌ'streɪʃn] Vereitelung *f*; Frustration *f*
fry [fraɪ] braten; **fried eggs** *pl.* Spiegeleier *pl.*; **fried potatoes** *pl.* Bratkartoffeln *pl.*; **'~·ing pan** [fraɪɪŋ -] Bratpfanne *f*
ft *nur geschr. Abk. für* **foot** Fuß *m od. pl.* (30,48 *cm*)
fuch·sia *bot.* ['fjuːʃə] Fuchsie *f*
fuck V [fʌk] ficken, vögeln; **~ off!** verpiß dich!; **get ~ed!** der Teufel soll dich holen!; **'~·ing** V Scheiß..., verflucht (*oft nur verstärkend*); **~ hell!** verdammte Scheiße!
fudge [fʌdʒ] *Art* Fondant *m*
fu·el [fjʊəl] **1.** Brennstoff *m; mot.* Treib-, Kraftstoff *m*; **2.** (*bsd. Brt. -ll-, Am. -l-*) *mot., aviat.* (auf)tanken; **'~ in·jec·tion** *mot. in Zssgn* Einspritz...
fu·gi·tive ['fjuːdʒɪtɪv] **1.** flüchtig (*a. fig.*); **2.** Flüchtling *m*
ful·fil *Brt.*, **ful·fill** *Am.* [fʊl'fɪl] (*-ll-*) er-

fuzzy

füllen; vollziehen; **ful·fil(l)·ment** Erfüllung f, Ausführung f

full [fʊl] **1.** voll; ganz; Voll...; ~ *of* voll von, voller; ~ (*up*) (voll) besetzt (*Bus etc.*); F voll, satt; *house* ~*l thea.* ausverkauft!; ~ *of o.s.* (ganz) von sich eingenommen; **2.** *adv.* völlig, ganz; **3. in** ~ vollständig, ganz; *write out in* ~ *Wort etc.* ausschreiben; ~'**board** Vollpension f; ~'**dress** Gesellschaftskleidung f; ~'**fledged** *Am.* → **fully-fledged**; ~'**grown** ausgewachsen; ~'**length** in voller Größe; bodenlang; abendfüllend (*Film etc.*); ~'**moon** Vollmond m; ~ '**stop** *ling.* Punkt m; ~'**time** *Sport* Spielende n; ~'**time** ganztägig, Ganztags...; ~**time** ' **job** Ganztagsbeschäftigung f

ful·ly ['fʊlɪ] voll, völlig, ganz; ~ -'**fledged** flügge; *fig.* richtig; ~ -'**grown** *Brt.* → **full-grown**

fum·ble ['fʌmbl] tasten; fummeln

fume [fjuːm] wütend sein

fumes [fjuːmz] *pl.* Dämpfe *pl.*, Rauch m; Abgase *pl.*

fun [fʌn] Scherz m, Spaß m; *for* ~ aus od. zum Spaß; *make* ~ *of* sich lustig machen über (*acc.*)

func·tion ['fʌŋkʃn] **1.** Funktion f; Aufgabe f; Veranstaltung f; **2.** funktionieren; ~**a·ry** ['fʌŋkʃnərɪ] Funktionär m; '~ **key** Funktionstaste f

fund [fʌnd] Fonds m; Geld(mittel *pl.*) n

fun·da·men·tal [fʌndə'mentl] **1.** grundlegend; Grund...; ~**s** *pl.* Grundlage f, -begriffe *pl.*; ~**ist** [fʌndə'mentəlɪst] Fundamentalist m

fu·ne·ral ['fjuːnərəl] Begräbnis n, Beerdigung f; Trauer..., Begräbnis...

'**fun·fair** ['fʌnfeə] Rummelplatz m

fun·gus *bot.* ['fʌŋgəs] (*pl.* -**gi** [-gaɪ], -**gu·ses**) Pilz m, Schwamm m

fu·nic·u·lar [fjuː'nɪkjʊlə] *a.* ~ **railway** (Draht)Seilbahn f

funk·y *bsd. Am.* F ['fʌŋkɪ] irre, schräg, schrill (*ältere Autos, Kleidung etc.*)

fun·nel ['fʌnl] Trichter m; *naut., rail.* Schornstein m

fun·nies *Am.* F ['fʌnɪz] *pl.* Comics *pl.*

fun·ny ['fʌnɪ] (-*ier, -iest*) komisch, lustig, spaßig; sonderbar

fur [fɜː] Pelz m, Fell n; Belag m (*auf der Zunge*); Kesselstein m

fu·ri·ous ['fjʊərɪəs] wütend

furl [fɜːl] *Fahne, Segel* auf-, einrollen; *Schirm* zusammenrollen

fur·nace ['fɜːnɪs] Schmelz-, Hochofen m; (Heiz)Kessel m

fur·nish ['fɜːnɪʃ] einrichten, möblieren; liefern; versorgen, ausrüsten, -statten

fur·ni·ture ['fɜːnɪtʃə] Möbel *pl.*; *sectional* ~ Anbaumöbel *pl.*

furred [fɜːd] belegt, pelzig (*Zunge*)

fur·ri·er ['fʌrɪə] Kürschner m

fur·row ['fʌrəʊ] **1.** Furche f; **2.** furchen

fur·ry ['fɜːrɪ] pelzig

fur·ther ['fɜːðə] **1.** *comp. von* **far; 2.** *fig.* weiter; **3.** fördern, unterstützen; ~ **ed·u·ca·tion** *Brt.* Fort-, Weiterbildung f; ~'**more** *fig.* weiter, überdies; '~**most** entfernteste(r, -s), äußerste(r, -s)

fur·thest ['fɜːðɪst] *sup. von* **far**

fur·tive ['fɜːtɪv] heimlich, verstohlen

fu·ry ['fjʊərɪ] Wut f, Zorn m

fuse [fjuːz] **1.** Zünder m; *electr.* Sicherung f; Zündschnur f; **2.** schmelzen; *electr.* durchbrennen; '~ **box** *electr.* Sicherungskasten m

fu·se·lage *aviat.* ['fjuːzɪlɑːʒ] (Flugzeug-) Rumpf m

fu·sion ['fjuːʒn] Verschmelzung f, Fusion f; *nuclear* ~ Kernfusion f

fuss F [fʌs] **1.** (unnötige) Aufregung f, Wirbel m, Theater n; **2.** sich (unnötig) aufregen; viel Aufhebens machen (**about** um, von); '~**y** (-*ier, -iest*) aufgeregt, hektisch; kleinlich, pedantisch; heikel, wählerisch

fus·ty ['fʌstɪ] (-*ier, -iest*) muffig; *fig.* verstaubt

fu·tile ['fjuːtaɪl] nutz-, zwecklos

fu·ture ['fjuːtʃə] **1.** (zu)künftig; **2.** Zukunft f; *gr.* Futur n, Zukunft f; *in* ~ in Zukunft, künftig

fuzz[1] [fʌz] feiner Flaum

fuzz[2] *sl.* [fʌz]: *the* ~ *sg.*, *pl.* die Bullen *pl.* (*Polizei*)

fuzz·y F ['fʌzɪ] (-*ier, -iest*) kraus, wuschelig; unscharf, verschwommen; flaumig, flauschig

G

G, g [dʒiː] G, g n

gab F [gæb] Geschwätz n; *have the gift of the ~* ein gutes Mundwerk haben

gab·ar·dine ['gæbədiːn] Gabardine m (*Wollstoff*)

gab·ble ['gæbl] 1. Geschnatter n, Geschwätz n; 2. schnattern, schwatzen

gab·er·dine ['gæbədiːn] *hist.* Kaftan m (*der Juden*); → **gabardine**

ga·ble *arch.* ['geɪbl] Giebel m

gad F [gæd] (*-dd-*): ~ *about* (viel) unterwegs sein (in *dat.*)

gad·fly *zo.* ['gædflaɪ] Bremse f

gad·get *tech.* ['gædʒɪt] Apparat m, Gerät n, Vorrichtung f; *oft contp.* technische Spielerei

gag [gæg] 1. Knebel m (a. *fig.*); F Gag m; 2. (*-gg-*) knebeln; *fig.* mundtot machen

gage *Am.* [geɪdʒ] → **gauge**; △ *nicht* Gage

gai·e·ty ['geɪətɪ] Fröhlichkeit f

gai·ly ['geɪlɪ] *adv. von* gay 1

gain [geɪn] 1. gewinnen; erreichen, bekommen; zunehmen an (*dat.*); vorgehen (um) (*Uhr*); ~ *speed* schneller werden; ~ *5 pounds* 5 Pfund zunehmen; ~ *in* zunehmen an (*dat.*); 2. Gewinn m; Zunahme f

gait [geɪt] Gang(art f) m; Schritt m

gai·ter ['geɪtə] Gamasche f

gal F [gæl] Mädchen n

ga·la ['gɑːlə] Festlichkeit f; Gala(veranstaltung) f; Gala...

gal·ax·y *astr.* ['gæləksɪ] Milchstraße f, Galaxis f

gale [geɪl] Sturm m

gall¹ [gɔːl] Frechheit f

gall² [gɔːl] wundgeriebene Stelle f

gall³ [gɔːl] (ver)ärgern

gal·lant ['gælənt] tapfer; *lant*, höflich; **~·lan·try** ['gæləntrɪ] Tapferkeit f; Galanterie f

'gall blad·der *anat.* Gallenblase f

gal·le·ry ['gælərɪ] Galerie f; Empore f

gal·ley ['gælɪ] *naut.* Galeere f; *naut.* Kombüse f; *a.* ~ *proof* *print.* Fahne(nabzug m) f

gal·lon ['gælən] Gallone f (*Brt.* 4,55 l, *Am.* 3,79 l)

gal·lop ['gæləp] 1. Galopp m; 2. galoppieren (lassen)

gal·lows ['gæləʊz] *sg.* Galgen m; **'~·hu·mo(u)r** Galgenhumor m

ga·lore [gə'lɔː] in rauhen Mengen

gam·ble ['gæmbl] 1. (um Geld) spielen; 2. Glücksspiel n; **'~·r** (Glücks)Spieler(in)

gam·bol ['gæmbl] 1. Luftsprung m; 2. (*bsd. Brt.* **-ll-**, *Am.* **-l-**) (herum)tanzen, (-)hüpfen

game [geɪm] (Karten-, Ball- *etc.*)Spiel n; (einzelnes) Spiel n (a. *fig.*); *hunt.* Wild n; Wildbret n; **~s** *pl.* Spiele *pl.*; *Schule:* Sport m; **'~·keep·er** Wildhüter m; **'~ park** Wildpark m; Wildreservat n; **'~ re·serve** Wildreservat n

gam·mon *bsd. Brt.* ['gæmən] schwachgepökelter *od.* -geräucherter Schinken

gan·der *zo.* ['gændə] Gänserich m

gang [gæŋ] 1. (Arbeiter)Trupp m; Gang f, Bande f; Clique f; Horde f; △ *nicht der Gang;* 2. ~ *up* sich zusammentun, *contp.* sich zusammenrotten

gang·ster ['gæŋstə] Gangster m

'gang| war, **~ war·fare** [gæŋ'wɔːfeə] Bandenkrieg m

gang·way ['gæŋweɪ] *naut.*, *aviat.* Gangway f; (Zwischen)Gang m

gaol [dʒeɪl], **'~·bird**, **'~·er** → **jail** *etc.*

gap [gæp] Lücke f; Kluft f; Spalte f

gape [geɪp] gähnen; klaffen; gaffen

ga·rage ['gærɑːʒ] 1. Garage f; (Reparatur)Werkstatt f (u. Tankstelle f); 2. *Auto* in e-r Garage ab- *od.* unterstellen; *Auto* in die Garage fahren

gar·bage *bsd. Am.* ['gɑːbɪdʒ] Abfall m, Müll m; **'~ bag** *Am.* Müllbeutel m; **'~ can** *Am.* Abfall-, Mülleimer m; Abfall-, Mülltonne f; **'~ truck** *Am.* Müllwagen m

gar·den ['gɑːdn] Garten m; **'~·er** Gärtner(in); **'~·ing** Gartenarbeit f

gar·gle ['gɑːgl] gurgeln

gar·ish ['geərɪʃ] grell, auffallend

gar·land ['gɑːlənd] Girlande f

gar·lic *bot.* ['gɑːlɪk] Knoblauch m

gar·ment ['gɑːmənt] Gewand n

gar·nish *gastr.* ['gɑːnɪʃ] garnieren

gar·ret ['gærət] Dachkammer f

gar·ri·son *mil.* ['gærɪsn] Garnison *f*

gar·ter ['gɑːtə] Strumpfband *n*; Sockenhalter *m*; *Am.* Strumpfhalter *m*, Straps *m*

gas [gæs] Gas *n*; *Am.* F Benzin *n*, Sprit *m*; **~e·ous** ['gæsjəs] gasförmig

gash [gæʃ] klaffende Wunde

gas·ket *tech.* ['gæskɪt] Dichtung(sring *m*) *f*

'**gas me·ter** Gasuhr *f*, -zähler *m*

gas·o·lene, gas·o·line *Am.* ['gæsəliːn] Benzin *n*; **'~ pump** Zapfsäule *f*

gasp [gɑːsp] **1.** Keuchen *n*; **2.** keuchen; **~ for breath** nach Luft schnappen

'**gas¦ sta·tion** *Am.* Tankstelle *f*; '**~stove** Gasofen *m*, -herd *m*; '**~works** *sg.* Gaswerk *n*

gate [geɪt] Tor *n*; Pforte *f*; Schranke *f*, Sperre *f*; *aviat.* Flugsteig *m*; '**~crash** F uneingeladen kommen (*in*); sich ohne zu bezahlen hineinschmuggeln (in *acc.*); '**~post** Tor-, Türpfosten *m*; '**~way** Tor(weg *m*) *n*, Einfahrt *f*; '**~way drug** Einstiegsdroge *f*

gath·er ['gæðə] *v/t.* sammeln, *Informationen* einholen, -ziehen; *Personen* versammeln; ernten, pflücken; zusammenziehen, kräuseln; *fig.* folgern, schließen (*from* aus); **~ speed** schneller werden; *v/i.* sich (ver)sammeln; sich (an)sammeln; **~·ing** ['gæðərɪŋ] Versammlung *f*; Zusammenkunft *f*

GATT [gæt] *Abk. für General Agreement on Tariffs and Trade* Allgemeines Zoll- und Handelsabkommen

gau·dy ['gɔːdɪ] (**-ier, -iest**) auffällig, bunt, grell (*Farbe*); protzig

gauge [geɪdʒ] **1.** Eichmaß *n*; *tech.* Meßgerät *n*, Lehre *f*; *tech.* Stärke *f*, Dicke *f* (*von Blech od. Draht etc.*); *rail.* Spur(weite) *f*; **2.** *tech.* eichen; (ab-, aus)messen

gaunt [gɔːnt] hager; ausgemergelt

gaunt·let ['gɔːntlɪt] Schutzhandschuh *m*

gauze [gɔːz] Gaze *f*; *Am.* Bandage *f*, Binde *f*

gave [geɪv] *pret. von* **give**

gav·el ['gævl] Hammer *m* (*e-s Vorsitzenden od. Auktionators*)

gaw·ky ['gɔːkɪ] (**-ier, -iest**) linkisch

gay [geɪ] **1.** lustig, fröhlich; bunt, (farben)prächtig; F schwul (*homosexuell*); **2.** F Schwule(r) *m* (*Homosexueller*)

gaze [geɪz] **1.** (starrer) Blick; △ *nicht*

Gaze; 2. starren; **~ at** starren auf (*acc.*), anstarren

ga·zette [gə'zet] Amtsblatt *n*

ga·zelle *zo.* [gə'zel] (*pl.* **-zelles, -zelle**) Gazelle *f*

GB [dʒiː 'biː] *Abk. für Great Britain* Großbritannien *n*

gear [gɪə] *tech.* Getriebe *n*; *mot.* Gang *m*; *mst in Zssgn* Vorrichtung *f*, Gerät *n*; F Kleidung *f*, Aufzug *m*; **change** (*bsd. Am. shift*) **~(s)** *mot.* schalten; **change** (*bsd. Am. shift*) **into second ~** in den zweiten Gang schalten; '**~box** *mot.* Getriebe *n*; '**~ le·ver** *Brt.*, '**~ shift** *Am.*, '**~ stick** *Brt. mot.* Schalthebel *m*

geese [giːs] *pl. von* **goose**

Gei·ger coun·ter *phys.* ['gaɪgə -] Geigerzähler *m*

geld·ing *zo.* ['geldɪŋ] Wallach *m*

gem [dʒem] Edelstein *m*

Gem·i·ni *astr.* ['dʒemɪnaɪ] *pl.* Zwillinge *pl.*; **he/she is (a) ~** er/sie ist (ein) Zwilling

gen·der ['dʒendə] *gr.* Genus *n*, Geschlecht *n*

gene *biol.* [dʒiːn] Gen *n*, Erbfaktor *m*

gen·e·ral ['dʒenərəl] **1.** allgemein; Haupt...; General...; **2.** *mil.* General *m*; **in ~** im allgemeinen; **~ de·liv·er·y:** (*in care of*) **~** *Am.* postlagernd; **~ e·lec·tion** *Brt. pol.* Parlamentswahlen *pl.*; **gen·e·ral·ize** ['dʒenərəlaɪz] verallgemeinern; '**gen·er·al·ly** im allgemeinen, allgemein; '**~ prac·ti·tion·er** (*Abk.* **GP**) *etwa* Arzt *m od.* Ärztin *f* für Allgemeinmedizin

gen·e·rate ['dʒenəreɪt] erzeugen; **~ra·tion** [dʒenə'reɪʃn] Erzeugung *f*; Generation *f*; **~ra·tor** ['dʒenəreɪtə] *electr.* Generator *m*; *Am. mot.* Lichtmaschine *f*

gen·e·ros·i·ty [dʒenə'rɒsətɪ] Großzügigkeit *f*; **~rous** ['dʒenərəs] großzügig; reichlich

ge·net·ic [dʒɪ'netɪk] (**~ally**) genetisch; **~ 'code** Erbanlage *f*; **~ en·gin·eer·ing** Gentechnologie *f*; **~ 'fin·ger·print** genetischer Fingerabdruck; **~s** *sg.* Genetik *f*, Vererbungslehre *f*

ge·ni·al ['dʒiːnjəl] freundlich; △ *nicht* **genial**

gen·i·tive *gr.* ['dʒenɪtɪv] *a.* **~ case** Genitiv *m*, zweiter Fall

ge·ni·us ['dʒiːnjəs] Genie *n*

G

gent F [dʒent] Herr *m*; **~s** *sg. Brt.* F Herrenklo *n*

gen·tle ['dʒentl] (**~r**, **~st**) sanft, zart, sacht; mild; '**~·man** (*pl.* **-men**) Gentleman *m*; Herr *m*; '**~·man·ly** gentlemanlike, vornehm; '**~·ness** Sanftheit *f*, Zartheit *f*; Milde *f*

gen·try ['dʒentrɪ] *Brt.* niederer Adel; Oberschicht *f*

gen·u·ine ['dʒenjʊɪn] echt; aufrichtig

ge·og·ra·phy [dʒɪ'ɒɡrəfɪ] Geographie *f*

ge·ol·o·gy [dʒɪ'ɒlədʒɪ] Geologie *f*

ge·om·e·try [dʒɪ'ɒmətrɪ] Geometrie *f*

germ [dʒɜːm] *biol., bot.* Keim *m*; *med.* Bazillus *m*, Bakterie *f*, (Krankheits)Erreger *m*

Ger·man ['dʒɜːmən] **1.** deutsch; **2.** Deutsche(r *m*) *f*; *ling.* Deutsch *n*; ~ '**shep·herd** *bsd. Am.* deutscher Schäferhund; '**Ger·man·y** Deutschland *f*

ger·mi·nate ['dʒɜːmɪneɪt] keimen (lassen)

ger·und *gr.* ['dʒerənd] Gerundium *n*

ges·tic·u·late [dʒe'stɪkjʊleɪt] gestikulieren

ges·ture ['dʒestʃə] Geste *f*, Gebärde *f*

get [get] (**-tt-**; **got**, **got** *od. Am.* **gotten**) *v/t.* bekommen, erhalten; sich *et.* verschaffen; sich besorgen; erwerben; sich aneignen; holen; bringen; F erwischen; F kapieren, verstehen; *j-n* dazu bringen (**to do** zu tun); *mit p.p.:* lassen; ~ **one's hair cut** sich die Haare schneiden lassen; ~ **going** in Gang bringen; ~ **s.th. by heart** *et.* auswendig lernen, ~ **s.th. ready** *et.* fertigmachen; **have got** haben; **have got to** müssen; *v/i.* kommen, gelangen; *mit p.p. od. adj.:* werden; ~ **tired** müde werden, ermüden; ~ **going** in Gang kommen; *fig.* in Schwung kommen; ~ **home** nach Hause kommen; ~ **ready** sich fertigmachen; ~ **about** herumkommen; sich herumsprechen *od.* verbreiten (*Gerücht etc.*); ~ **ahead of** übertreffen (*acc.*); ~ **along** vorwärts-, weiterkommen; auskommen (**with** mit *j-m*); zurechtkommen (**with** mit *et.*); ~ **at** herankommen an (*acc.*); **what is he getting at?** worauf will er hinaus?; ~ **away** loskommen; entkommen; ~ **away with** davonkommen mit; ~ **back** zurückkommen; *et.* zurückbekommen; ~ **in** hinein-, hereinkommen; einsteigen (in); ~ **off** ausstei-

gen (aus); davonkommen (**with** mit); ~ **on** einsteigen (in); → **get along**; ~ **out** heraus-, hinausgehen; aussteigen (**of** aus); *et.* herausbekommen; ~ **over s.th.** über *et.* hinwegkommen; ~ **to** kommen nach; ~ **together** zusammenkommen; ~ **up** aufstehen; '**~·a·way** Flucht *f*; ~ **car** Fluchtauto *n*; '**~·up** Aufmachung *f*

gey·ser ['gaɪzə] Geysir *m*; ['giːzə] *Brt.* Durchlauferhitzer *m*

ghast·ly ['gɑːstlɪ] (**-ier**, **-iest**) gräßlich; schrecklich; (toten)bleich

gher·kin ['gɜːkɪn] Gewürzgurke *f*

ghost [gəʊst] Geist *m*, Gespenst *n*; *fig.* Spur *f*; '**~·ly** (**-ier**, **-iest**) geisterhaft

GI [dʒiː 'aɪ] GI *m* (*amer. Soldat*)

gi·ant ['dʒaɪənt] **1.** Riese *m*; **2.** riesig

gib·ber·ish ['dʒɪbərɪʃ] Kauderwelsch *n*

gib·bet ['dʒɪbɪt] Galgen *m*

gibe [dʒaɪb] **1.** spotten (**at** über *acc.*); **2.** höhnische Bemerkung

gib·lets ['dʒɪblɪts] *pl.* Hühner-, Gänseklein *n*

gid·di·ness ['gɪdɪnɪs] *med.* Schwindel(gefühl *n*) *m*; '**~·dy** ['gɪdɪ] (**-ier**, **-iest**) schwindelerregend (*Höhe etc.*); **I feel ~** mir ist schwind(e)lig

gift [gɪft] Geschenk *n*; Talent *n*; △ *nicht* **Gift**; '**~·ed** begabt

gig *mus.* F [gɪɡ] Gig *m*, Auftritt *m*, Konzert *n*

gi·gan·tic [dʒaɪ'gæntɪk] (**~ally**) gigantisch, riesenhaft, riesig, gewaltig

gig·gle ['gɪɡl] **1.** kichern; **2.** Gekicher *n*

gild [gɪld] vergolden

gill [gɪl] *zo.* Kieme *f*; *bot.* Lamelle *f*

gim·mick F ['gɪmɪk] Trick *m*; Spielerei *f*

gin [dʒɪn] Gin *m* (*Wacholderschnaps*)

gin·ger ['dʒɪndʒə] **1.** Ingwer *m*; **2.** rötlich- *od.* gelblichbraun; '**~·bread** Leb-, Pfefferkuchen *m* (*mit Ingwergeschmack*); '**~·ly** behutsam, vorsichtig

gip·sy ['dʒɪpsɪ] Zigeuner(in)

gi·raffe *zo.* [dʒɪ'rɑːf] (*pl.* **-raffes**, **-raffe**) Giraffe *f*

gir·der *tech.* ['gɜːdə] Tragbalken *m*

gir·dle ['gɜːdl] Hüfthalter *m*, -gürtel *m*

girl [gɜːl] Mädchen *n*; '**~·friend** Freundin *f*; ~ '**guide** *Brt.* Pfadfinderin *f*; '**~·hood** ['gɜːlhʊd] Mädchenjahre *pl.*, Jugend(zeit) *f*; '**~·ish** Mädchenhaft; Mädchen...; ~ '**scout** *Am.* Pfadfinderin *f*

gi·ro *Brt.* ['dʒaɪrəʊ] Postgirodienst *m*; '**~**

ac·count *Brt.* Postgirokonto *n*; '~**cheque** *Brt.* Postscheck *m*

girth [gɜːθ] (Sattel)Gurt *m*; (*a.* Körper)Umfang *m*

gist [dʒɪst] *das* Wesentliche, Kern *m*

give [gɪv] (*gave, given*) geben; schenken; spenden; *Leben* hingeben, opfern; *Befehl etc.* geben, erteilen; *Hilfe* leisten; *Schutz* bieten; *Grund etc.* (an)geben; *Konzert* geben; *Theaterstück* geben, aufführen; *Vortrag* halten; *Schmerzen* bereiten, verursachen; *Grüße etc.* übermitteln; ~ *her my love* bestelle ihr herzliche Grüße von mir; ~ *birth to* zur Welt bringen; ~ *s.o. to understand that* j-m zu verstehen geben, daß; ~ *way* nachgeben; *Brt. mot.* die Vorfahrt lassen; ~ *away*, weggeben, verschenken; *j-n, et.* verraten; ~ *back* zurückgeben; ~ *in Gesuch etc.* einreichen; *Prüfungsarbeit etc.* abgeben; nachgeben; aufgeben; ~ *off Geruch* verbreiten; ausstoßen, -strömen, verströmen; ~ *on(to)* führen auf *od.* nach, gehen nach; ~ *out* aus-, verteilen; *bsd. Brt.* bekanntgeben; zu Ende gehen (*Kräfte, Vorräte*); F versagen (*Motor etc.*); ~ *up* aufgeben; aufhören mit; *j-n* ausliefern; ~ *o.s. up* sich (freiwillig) stellen (*to the police* der Polizei); ~**-and-take** [gɪvən'teɪk] beiderseitiges Entgegenkommen, Kompromiß(bereitschaft *f*) *m*; **giv·en** [gɪvn] **1.** *p.p. von* **give**; **2.** *be* ~ *to* neigen zu; '**giv·en-name** *bsd. Am.* Vorname *m*

gla·cial ['gleɪsjəl] eisig; Eis...

gla·ci·er ['glæsjə] Gletscher *m*

glad [glæd] (*-dd-*) froh, erfreut; *be* ~ *of* sich freuen über; '~**ly** gern(e)

glam·ou(r) ['glæmə] Zauber *m*, Glanz *m*; ~**ous** ['glæmərəs] bezaubernd, reizvoll

glance [glɑːns] **1.** (schneller *od.* flüchtiger) Blick (*at* auf *acc.*); △ *nicht* **Glanz**; *at a* ~ auf e-n Blick; **2.** (schnell *od.* flüchtig) blicken (*at* auf *acc.*)

gland *anat.* [glænd] Drüse *f*

glare [gleə] **1.** grell scheinen *od.* leuchten; wütend starren; ~ *at s.o.* j-n wütend anstarren; **2.** greller Schein, grelles Leuchten; wütender Blick

glass [glɑːs] **1.** Glas *n*; (Trink)Glas *n*; Glas(gefäß) *n*; (Fern-, Opern)Glas *n*; *Brt.* F Spiegel *m*; *Brt.* Barometer *n*; (*a pair of*) ~**es** *pl.* (e-e) Brille; **2.** gläsern;

Glas...; **3.** ~ *in od.* *up* verglasen; '~**case** Vitrine *f*; Schaukasten *m*; '~**-ful** *ein* Glas(voll); '~**house** Gewächs-, Treibhaus *n*; '~**ware** Glaswaren *pl.*; '~**y** (*-ier, -iest*) gläsern; glasig

glaze [gleɪz] **1.** *v/t.* verglasen; glasieren; *v/i. a.* ~ *over* glasig werden (*Augen*); **2.** Glasur *f*; **gla·zi·er** ['gleɪzjə] Glaser *m*

gleam [gliːm] **1.** schwacher Schein, Schimmer *m*; **2.** leuchten, schimmern

glean [gliːn] *v/t.* sammeln; *v/i.* Ähren lesen

glee [gliː] Fröhlichkeit *f*; '~**-ful** ausgelassen, fröhlich

glen [glen] enges Bergtal *n*

glib [glɪb] (*-bb-*) gewandt; schlagfertig

glide [glaɪd] **1.** gleiten; segeln; **2.** Gleiten *n*; *aviat.* Gleitflug *m*; **glid·er** *aviat.* Segelflugzeug *n*; '**glid·ing** *aviat.* Segelfliegen *n*

glim·mer ['glɪmə] **1.** schimmern; **2.** Schimmer *m*

glimpse [glɪmps] **1.** (nur) flüchtig zu sehen bekommen; **2.** flüchtiger Blick

glint [glɪnt] **1.** glitzern, glänzen; **2.** Glitzern *n*, Glanz *m*

glis·ten ['glɪsn] glitzern, glänzen

glit·ter ['glɪtə] **1.** glitzern, funkeln, glänzen; **2.** Glitzern *n*, Funkeln *n*, Glanz *m*

gloat [gləʊt] ~ *over* sich hämisch *od.* diebisch freuen über (*acc.*); '~**ing** hämisch, schadenfroh

glo·bal ['gləʊbl] global, weltumspannend, Welt...; umfassend; ~ *warming* Erwärmung *f* der Erdatmosphäre

globe [gləʊb] (Erd)Kugel *f*; Globus *m*

gloom [gluːm] Düsterkeit *f*; Dunkelheit *f*; düstere *od.* gedrückte Stimmung; '~**y** (*-ier, -iest*) düster; hoffnungslos; niedergeschlagen

glo·ri·fy ['glɔːrɪfaɪ] verherrlichen; ~**ri·ous** ['glɔːrɪəs] ruhm-, glorreich; herrlich, prächtig; ~**ry** ['glɔːrɪ] Ruhm *m*; Herrlichkeit *f*, Pracht *f*

gloss [glɒs] **1.** Glanz *m*; *ling.* Glosse *f*; **2.** ~ *over* beschönigen, vertuschen

glos·sa·ry ['glɒsəri] Glossar *n*

gloss·y ['glɒsi] (*-ier, -iest*) glänzend

glove [glʌv] Handschuh *m*; '~ *com·part·ment mot.* Handschuhfach *n*

glow [gləʊ] **1.** glühen; **2.** Glühen *n*; Glut *f*

glow·er ['glaʊə] finster blicken

'**glow-worm** *zo.* Glühwürmchen *n*

glu·cose ['gluːkəʊs] Traubenzucker *m*

glue [gluː] **1.** Leim *m*; **2.** kleben

glum [glʌm] (**-mm-**) bedrückt

glut·ton ['glʌtn] *fig.* Vielfraß *m*; '**~·ous** gefräßig, gefräßig

GMT [dʒiː em 'tiː] *Abk. für* **Greenwich Mean Time** ['griːnɪdʒ -] WEZ, westeuropäische Zeit

gnarled [nɑːld] knorrig; knotig (*Hände*)

gnash [næʃ] knirschen (mit)

gnat *zo.* [næt] (Stech)Mücke *f*

gnaw [nɔː] (zer)nagen; (zer)fressen

gnome [nəʊm] Gnom *m*; Gartenzwerg *m*

go [gəʊ] **1.** (**went, gone**) gehen, fahren, reisen (**to** nach); (fort)gehen; gehen, führen (**to** nach) (*Straße etc.*); sich erstrecken, gehen (**to** bis zu); verkehren, fahren (*Bus etc.*); *tech.* gehen, laufen, funktionieren; vergehen (*Zeit*); harmonieren (**with** mit), passen (**with** zu); ausgehen, ablaufen, ausfallen; werden (~ **mad**; ~ **blind**; **be** *~ing* **to** *inf.* im Begriff sein zu *inf.*, *tun* wollen *od.* werden; ~ **shares** teilen; ~ **swimming** schwimmen gehen; *it is ~ing* **to rain** es gibt Regen; *I must be ~ing* ich muß gehen; ~ **for a walk** e-n Spaziergang machen, spazierengehen; ~ **to bed** ins Bett gehen; ~ **to school** zur Schule gehen; ~ **to see** besuchen; **let** ~ loslassen; ~ **after** nachlaufen (*dat.*); sich bemühen um; ~ **ahead** vorangehen; vorausgehen, vorausfahren; ~ **ahead with** beginnen mit; fortfahren mit; ~ **at** losgehen auf (*acc.*); ~ **away** weggehen; ~ **between** vermitteln zwischen (*dat.*); ~ **by** vorbeigehen, -fahren; vergehen (*Zeit*); *fig.* sich halten an, sich richten nach; ~ **down** untergehen (*Sonne*); ~ **for** holen; ~ **in** hineingehen; ~ **in for an examination** e-e Prüfung machen; ~ **off** fortgehen, weggehen; losgehen (*Gewehr etc.*); ~ **on** weitergehen, -fahren; *fig.* fortfahren (**doing** zu tun); *fig.* vor sich gehen, vorgehen; ~ **out** hinausgehen; ausgehen (**with** mit); ausgehen (*Licht etc.*); ~ **through** durchgehen, -nehmen; durchmachen; ~ **up** steigen; hinaufgehen, -steigen; ~ **without** sich behelfen ohne, auskommen ohne; **2.** (*pl.* **goes**) F Schwung *m*, Schmiß *m*; *bsd.* Brt. F Versuch *m*; *it's my ~ bsd.* Brt. F ich bin dran *od.* an der Reihe; *it's a ~!* F abgemacht!; **have a ~**

at s.th. Brt. F et. probieren; **be all the ~** Brt. F große Mode sein

goad *fig.* [gəʊd] anstacheln

'**go-a·head¹: get the ~** grünes Licht bekommen; **give s.o. the ~** j-m grünes Licht geben

'**go-a·head²** F zielstrebig; unternehmungslustig

goal [gəʊl] Ziel *n* (*a. fig.*); *Sport:* Tor *n*; **score a ~** ein Tor schießen *od.* erzielen; **consolation ~** Ehrentreffer *m*; **own ~** Eigentor *n*, -treffer *m*; '**goal·ie** F ['gəʊlɪ], '**~·keep·er** Torwart *m*, -hüter *m*; '**~ kick** Fußball: Abstoß *m*; '**~ line** Sport: Torlinie *f*; '**~·mouth** Sport: Torraum *m*; '**~·post** Sport: Torpfosten *m*

goat *zo.* [gəʊt] Ziege *f*, Geiß *f*

gob·ble ['gɒbl] *mst* ~ **up** verschlingen

'**go-be·tween** Vermittler(in), Mittelsmann *m*

gob·lin ['gɒblɪn] Kobold *m*

god [gɒd] *rel.* ♀ Gott *m*; *fig.* Abgott *m*; '**~·child** (*pl.* **-children**) Patenkind *n*; **~·dess** ['gɒdɪs] Göttin *f*; '**~·fa·ther** Pate *m* (*a. fig.*), Taufpate *m*; '**~·for·sak·en** *contp.* gottverlassen; '**~·head** Gottheit *f*; '**~·less** gottlos; '**~·like** gottähnlich; göttlich; '**~·moth·er** (Tauf)Patin *f*; '**~·pa·rent** (Tauf)Pate, (-)Patin *f*; '**~·send** Geschenk *n* des Himmels

gog·gle ['gɒgl] glotzen; '**~ box** Brt. F TV Glotze *f*; '**~s** *pl.* Schutzbrille *f*

go-ings-on F [gəʊɪŋz'ɒn] *pl.* Treiben *n*, Vorgänge *pl.*

gold [gəʊld] **1.** Gold *n*; **2.** golden; **~·en** *mst fig.* ['gəʊldən] golden, goldgelb; '**~·finch** *zo.* Stieglitz *m*; '**~·fish** *zo.* (*pl.* **-fish**) Goldfisch *m*; '**~·smith** Goldschmied *m*

golf [gɒlf] **1.** Golf(spiel) *n*; **2.** Golf spielen; '**~ club** Golfschläger *m*; Golfklub *m*; '**~ course**, '**~ links** *pl. od. sg.* Golfplatz *m*

gon·do·la ['gɒndələ] Gondel *f*

gone [gɒn] **1.** *p.p. von* **go** | **2.** *adj.* fort; F futsch; vergangen; tot; F hoffnungslos

good [gʊd] **1.** (**better, best**) gut; artig; gütig; gründlich; ~ **at** geschickt *od.* gut in (*dat.*); **real ~** F echt gut; **2.** Nutzen *m*, Wert *m*; **das** Gute, Gutes *n*; **for** ~ für immer; '**~·by(e)** [gʊd'baɪ] **1. wish s.o.**

~, *say* ~ *to s.o.* j-m auf Wiedersehen sagen; **2.** *int.* (auf) Wiedersehen!; ♀
'**Fri·day** Karfreitag *m*; ~'**hu·mo(u)red** gutgelaunt; gutmütig; ~'**look·ing** gutaussehend; ~'**na·tured** gutmütig; '~**ness** Güte *f*; *thank* ~! Gott sei Dank!; *(my)* ~*l*, ~ *gracious!* du meine Güte!, du lieber Himmel!; *for* ~' *sake* um Himmels willen!; ~ *knows* weiß der Himmel

goods *econ.* [gʊdz] *pl.* Waren *pl.*, Güter *pl.*

good·will gute Absicht, guter Wille; *econ.* Firmenwert *m*

good·y F [gʊdɪ] Bonbon *m, n*

goose *zo.* [guːs] (*pl.* **geese**) Gans *f*

goose·ber·ry *bot.* [gʊzbərɪ] Stachelbeere *f*

goose·flesh [guːsfleʃ], '~ **pim·ples** *pl.* Gänsehaut *f*

GOP [dʒiː əʊ 'piː] *Abk. für* **Grand Old Party** die Republikanische Partei (*USA*)

go·pher *zo.* [gəʊfə] Taschenratte *f*; *Am.* Ziesel *m*

gore [gɔː] durchbohren, aufspießen (*mit den Hörnern etc.*)

gorge [gɔːdʒ] **1.** Kehle *f*, Schlund *m*; enge (Fels)Schlucht; **2.** (ver)schlingen; (sich) vollstopfen

gor·geous [gɔːdʒəs] prächtig

go·ril·la *zo.* [gə'rɪlə] Gorilla *m*

go·ry F [gɔːrɪ] (*-ier, -iest*) blutrünstig

gosh *int.* F [gɒʃ]: *by* ~ Mensch!

gos·ling *zo.* [gɒzlɪŋ] junge Gans

go-slow *Brt. econ.* [gəʊ'sləʊ] Bummelstreik *m*

Gos·pel *rel.* [gɒspəl] Evangelium *n*

gos·sa·mer [gɒsəmə] Altweibersommer *m*

gos·sip [gɒsɪp] **1.** Klatsch *m*, Tratsch *m*; Klatschbase *f*; **2.** klatschen, tratschen; '~**y** geschwätzig; voller Klatsch u. Tratsch (*Brief etc.*)

got [gɒt] *pret. u. p.p. von* **get**

Goth·ic [gɒθɪk] gotisch; Schauer...; ~ *novel* Schauerroman *m*

got·ten *Am.* [gɒtn] *p.p. von* **get**

gourd *bot.* [gʊəd] Kürbis *m*

gout *med.* [gaʊt] Gicht *f*

gov·ern [gʌvn] *v/t.* regieren; lenken, leiten; *v/i.* herrschen; '~**ess** Erzieherin *f*; '~**ment** Regierung *f*; Staat *m*; **gov·er·nor** [gʌvənə] Gouverneur *m*;

Direktor *m*, Leiter *m*; F Alte(r) *m* (*Vater, Chef*)

gown [gaʊn] Kleid *n*; Robe *f*, Talar *m*

GP [dʒiː 'piː] *Abk. für* **general practitioner** *etwa* Arzt *m* (Ärztin *f*) für Allgemeinmedizin

GPO *Brt.* [dʒiː piː 'əʊ] *Abk. für* **General Post Office** Hauptpostamt *n*

grab [græb] **1.** (*-bb-*) (hastig *od.* gierig) ergreifen, packen, fassen; **2.** (hastiger *od.* gieriger) Griff; *tech.* Greifer *m*

grace [greɪs] **1.** Anmut *f*, Grazie *f*; Anstand *m*; Frist *f*, Aufschub *f*; Gnade *f*; Tischgebet *n*; **2.** zieren, schmücken; '~**ful** anmutig; '~**less** ungraziös

gra·cious [greɪʃəs] gnädig

gra·da·tion [grə'deɪʃn] Abstufung *f*

grade [greɪd] **1.** Grad *m*, Rang *m*; Stufe *f*; Qualität *f*; *bsd. Am.* → **gradient**; *Am.* Schule: Klasse *f*; *bsd. Am.* Note *f*, Zensur *f*; **2.** sortieren, einteilen; abstufen; '~ **cross·ing** *Am.* schienengleicher Bahnübergang; '~ **school** *Am.* Grundschule *f*

gra·di·ent *rail. etc.* [greɪdjənt] Steigung *f*, Gefälle *n*

grad·u·al [grædʒʊəl] stufenweise, allmählich; '~**al·ly** nach u. nach; allmählich; '~**ate 1.** [grædʒʊət] *univ.* Hochschulabsolvent(in), Akademiker(in); Graduierte(r *m*) *f*; *Am.* Schulabgänger(in); **2.** [grædʒʊeɪt] abstufen, staffeln; *univ.* graduieren; *Am.* die Abschlußprüfung bestehen; ~**a·tion** [grædʒʊ'eɪʃn] Abstufung *f*, Staffelung *f*; *univ.* Graduierung *f*; *Am.* Absolvieren *n* (*from e-r Schule*)

graf·fi·ti [grə'fiːtɪ] *pl.* Graffiti *pl.*, Wandschmierereien *pl.*

graft [grɑːft] **1.** *med.* Transplantat *n*; *agr.* Pfropfreis *n*; **2.** *med.* Gewebe verpflanzen, transplantieren; *agr.* pfropfen

grain [greɪn] (Samen-, *bsd.* Getreide)Korn *n*; Getreide *n*; (*Sand- etc.*) Körnchen *n*, (-)Korn *n*; Maserung *f*; *go against the* ~ *fig.* gegen den Strich gehen

gram [græm] Gramm *n*

gram·mar [græmə] Grammatik *f*; '~ **school** *Brt. etwa* (humanistisches) Gymnasium; *Am. etwa* Grundschule *f*

gram·mat·i·cal [grə'mætɪkl] grammatisch, Grammatik...

gramme [græm] → **gram**

gra·na·ry ['grænərɪ] Kornspeicher *m*

grand [grænd] **1.** *fig.* großartig; erhaben; groß; Groß..., Haupt...; ♀ *Old Party* die Republikanische Partei (*USA*); **2.** (*pl.* **grand**) F Riese *m* (*1000 Dollar od. Pfund*)

grand·child ['græntʃaɪld] (*pl.* -**children**) Enkel(in); **~daugh·ter** ['grændɔːtə] Enkelin *f*

gran·deur ['grændʒə] Größe *f*, Erhabenheit *f*; Größe *f*, Wichtigkeit *f*

grand·fa·ther ['grændfɑːðə] Großvater *m*

gran·di·ose ['grændɪəʊs] großartig

grand·moth·er ['grænmʌðə] Großmutter *f*; **~par·ents** ['grænpeərənts] *pl.* Großeltern *pl.*; **~son** ['grænsʌn] Enkel *m*

grand·stand ['grændstænd] *Sport:* Haupttribüne *f*

gran·ny F ['grænɪ] Oma *f*

grant [grɑːnt] **1.** bewilligen, gewähren; *Erlaubnis etc.* geben; *Bitte etc.* erfüllen; zugeben; **take s.th. for ~ed** et. als selbstverständlich betrachten *od.* hinnehmen; **2.** Stipendium *n*; Bewilligung *f*, Unterstützung *f*

gran·u·lat·ed ['grænjʊleɪtɪd] körnig, granuliert; **~ sugar** Kristallzucker *m*; **~ule** ['grænjuːl] Körnchen *n*

grape [greɪp] Weinbeere *f*, -traube *f*; **~fruit** *bot.* Grapefruit *f*, Pampelmuse *f*; **~vine** *bot.* Weinstock *m*

graph [græf] graphische Darstellung; **~ic** ['græfɪk] (**~ally**) graphisch; anschaulich; **~arts** *pl.* Graphik *f*; **~ics** *pl.* Computer: Graphik *f*

grap·ple ['græpl]: **~ with** kämpfen mit, *fig. a.* sich herumschlagen mit

grasp [grɑːsp] **1.** (er)greifen, packen; *fig.* verstehen, begreifen; **2.** Griff *m*; Reichweite *f* (*a. fig.*); *fig.* Verständnis *n*

grass [grɑːs] Gras *n*; Rasen *m*; Weide(land *n*) *f*; *sl.* Grass *n* (*Marihuana*); **~hop·per** *zo.* ['grɑːshɒpə] Heuschrecke *f*; **~ 'wid·ow** Strohwitwe *f*; **~ 'wid·ow·er** Strohwitwer *m*; '**gras·sy** (-*ier, -iest*) grasbedeckt, Gras...

grate [greɪt] **1.** (Kamin)Gitter *n*; (Feuer)Rost *m*; **2.** reiben, raspeln; knirschen (mit); **~ on s.o.'s nerves** an j-s Nerven zerren

grate·ful ['greɪtfl] dankbar

grat·er ['greɪtə] Reibe *f*

grat·i·fi·ca·tion [grætɪfɪ'keɪʃn] Befriedigung *f*; Freude *f*; △ *nicht* **Gratifikation**; **~fy** ['grætɪfaɪ] erfreuen; befriedigen

grat·ing¹ ['greɪtɪŋ] kratzend, knirschend, quietschend; schrill; unangenehm

grat·ing² ['greɪtɪŋ] Gitter(werk) *n*

grat·i·tude ['grætɪtjuːd] Dankbarkeit *f*

gra·tu·i·tous [grə'tjuːɪtəs] unentgeltlich; freiwillig; **~ty** [grə'tjuːətɪ] Abfindung *f*; Gratifikation *f*; Trinkgeld *n*

grave¹ [greɪv] (**~r, ~st**) ernst; (ge)wichtig; gemessen

grave² [greɪv] Grab *n*; **~dig·ger** Totengräber *m*

grav·el ['grævl] **1.** Kies *m*; **2.** (*bsd. Brt.* **-ll-,** *Am.* **-l-**) mit Kies bestreuen

'**grave·stone** Grabstein *m*; '**~yard** Friedhof *m*

grav·i·ta·tion *phys.* [grævɪ'teɪʃn] Gravitation *f*, Schwerkraft *f*

grav·i·ty ['grævətɪ] *phys.* Schwerkraft *f*; Ernst *m*

gra·vy ['greɪvɪ] Bratensaft *m*; Bratensoße *f*

gray *bsd. Am.* [greɪ] → **grey**

graze¹ [greɪz] *Vieh* weiden (lassen); (ab)weiden; (ab)grasen

graze² [greɪz] **1.** streifen; schrammen; *Haut* (ab-, auf)schürfen, (auf)schrammen; **2.** Abschürfung *f*, Schramme *f*

grease 1. [griːs] Fett *n*; *tech.* Schmierfett *n*, Schmiere *f*; **2.** [griːz] (ein)fetten, *tech.* (ab)schmieren

greas·y ['griːzɪ] (-*ier, -iest*) fett(ig), ölig; schmierig

great [greɪt] groß; F großartig, super; Ur(groß)...

Great Brit·ain [greɪt'brɪtn] Großbritannien *n*

Great 'Dane *zo.* Dogge *f*

great·'grand·child Urenkel(in); **~'grand·par·ents** *pl.* Urgroßeltern *pl. etc.*

'**great·ly** sehr; '**~ness** Größe *f*

Greece [griːs] Griechenland *n*

greed [griːd] Gier *f*; '**~y** (-*ier, -iest*) gierig (**for** auf *acc.*, nach); habgierig; gefräßig

Greek [griːk] **1.** griechisch; **2.** Griech|e *m*, -in *f*; *ling.* Griechisch *n*

green [griːn] **1.** grün; *fig.* grün, unerfahren; **2.** Grün n; Grünfläche f, Rasen m; **~s** pl. grünes Gemüse, Blattgemüse n; **~belt** bsd. Brt. Grüngürtel m (um e-e Stadt); **~'card** Am. Arbeitserlaubnis f; **'~gro·cer** bsd. Brt. Obst- u. Gemüsehändler(in); **'~horn** Greenhorn n, Grünschnabel m; **'~house** Gewächs-, Treibhaus n; **'~house ef·fect** Treibhauseffekt m; **'~ish** grünlich

greet [gri:t] grüßen; **'~ing** Begrüßung f, Gruß m; **~s** pl. Grüße pl.

gre·nade mil. [grɪˈneɪd] Granate f

grew [gru:] pret. von grow

grey [greɪ] **1.** grau; **2.** Grau n; **3.** grau machen od. werden; **'~hound** zo. Windhund m

grid [grɪd] Gitter n; electr. etc. Versorgungsnetz n; Gitter(netz) n (auf Landkarten etc.) **'~·i·ron** Bratrost m

grief [gri:f] Kummer m

griev·ance [ˈgri:vns] (Grund m zur) Beschwerde f; Mißstand m; **~e** [gri:v] v/t. betrüben; **~e** v/i. bekümmert sein; **~ for** trauern um; **~ous** [ˈgri:vəs] schwer, schlimm

grill [grɪl] **1.** grillen; **2.** Grill m; Bratrost m; Gegrillte(s) n

grim [grɪm] (-mm-) grimmig; schrecklich; erbittert; F schlimm

gri·mace [grɪˈmeɪs] **1.** Fratze f, Grimasse f; **2.** Grimassen schneiden

grime [graɪm] Schmutz m; Ruß m; **'grim·y** (-ier, -iest) schmutzig; rußig

grin [grɪn] **1.** Grinsen n; **2.** (-nn-) grinsen

grind [graɪnd] **1.** (ground) v/t. (zer)mahlen, zerreiben, -kleinern; Messer etc. schleifen; Fleisch durchdrehen; **~ one's teeth** mit den Zähnen knirschen; v/i. schuften; pauken; büffeln; **2.** Schinderei f, Schufterei f; **the daily ~** das tägliche Einerlei; △ nicht Grind; **'~·er** (Messer- etc.)Schleifer m; tech. Schleifmaschine f; tech. Mühle f; **'~·stone** Schleifstein m

grip [grɪp] **1.** (-pp-) packen (a. fig.); **2.** Griff m; fig. Gewalt f, Herrschaft f; Reisetasche f

gripes [graɪps] pl. Bauchschmerzen pl., Kolik f

gris·ly [ˈgrɪzlɪ] (-ier, -iest) gräßlich, schrecklich

gris·tle [ˈgrɪsl] Knorpel m (im Fleisch)

grit [grɪt] **1.** Kies m, (grober) Sand; fig. Mut m; **2.** (-tt-) **~ one's teeth** die

Zähne zusammenbeißen

griz·zly (bear) [ˈgrɪzlɪ (-)] Grizzly(bär) m, Graubär m

groan [grəʊn] **1.** stöhnen, ächzen; **2.** Stöhnen n, Ächzen n

gro·cer [ˈgrəʊsə] Lebensmittelhändler m; **~ies** [ˈgrəʊsərɪz] pl. Lebensmittel pl.; **~·y** [ˈgrəʊsərɪ] Lebensmittelgeschäft n

grog·gy F [ˈgrɒgɪ] (-ier, -iest) groggy, schwach od. wackelig (auf den Beinen)

groin anat. [grɔɪn] Leiste(ngegend) f

groom [grʊm] **1.** Pferdepfleger m, Stallbursche m; Bräutigam m; **2.** Pferde versorgen, pflegen, striegeln; **well-groomed** gepflegt

groove [gru:v] Rinne f, Furche f; Rille f, Nut f; **'groov·y** sl. (-ier, -iest) veraltet: klasse, toll

grope [grəʊp] tasten; sl. Mädchen befummeln

gross [grəʊs] **1.** dick, feist; grob, derb; econ. Brutto...; **2.** Gros n (12 Dutzend)

gro·tesque [grəʊˈtesk] grotesk

ground[1] [graʊnd] **1.** pret. u. p.p. von grind 1; **2.** gemahlen (Kaffee etc.); **~ meat** Hackfleisch n

ground[2] [graʊnd] **1.** (Erd)Boden m, Erde f; Boden m, Gebiet n; Sport: (Spiel)Platz m; Am. electr. Erdung f; (Boden)Satz m; fig. Bewegrund m; **~s** pl. Grundstück n, Park m, Gartenanlage f; **on the ~(s) of** auf Grund (gen.); **hold od. stand one's ~** sich behaupten; **2.** naut. auflaufen; Am. electr. erden; fig. gründen, stützen; **~ crew** aviat. Bodenpersonal n; **~ 'floor** bsd. Brt. Erdgeschoß n; **~ forc·es** pl. mil. Bodentruppen pl., Landstreitkräfte pl.; **'~·hog** zo. Amer. Waldmurmeltier m; **'~·ing** Am. electr. Erdung f; Grundlagen pl., -kenntnisse pl.; **'~·less** grundlos; **'~·nut** Brt. bot. Erdnuß f; **'~s-man** (pl. -men) Sport: Platzwart m; **~ staff** Brt. aviat. Bodenpersonal n; **'~·work** fig. Grundlage f, Fundament n

group [gru:p] **1.** Gruppe f; **2.** (sich) gruppieren

group·ie F [ˈgru:pɪ] Groupie n (aufdringlicher weiblicher Fan)

group·ing [ˈgru:pɪŋ] Gruppierung f

grove [grəʊv] Wäldchen n, Gehölz n

G

grov·el ['grɒvl] (*bsd. Brt.* **-ll-,** *Am.* **-l-**) (am Boden) kriechen

grow [grəʊ] (*grew, grown*) *v/i.* wachsen; (allmählich) werden; **~ up** aufwachsen, heranwachsen; *v/t. bot.* anpflanzen, anbauen, züchten; **~ a beard** sich e-n Bart wachsen lassen; **'~·er** Züchter *m*, Erzeuger *m*, *in Zssgn* ...bau·er *m*

growl [graʊl] knurren, brummen

grown [grəʊn] **1.** *p.p. von* **grow;** **2.** *adj.* erwachsen; **~·up 1.** [grəʊn'ʌp] erwachsen; **2.** ['grəʊnʌp] F Erwachsene(r *m*) *f*

growth [grəʊθ] Wachsen *n*, Wachstum *n*; Wuchs *m*, Größe *f*; *fig.* Zunahme *f*, Anwachsen *n*; *med.* Gewächs *n*, Wucherung *f*

grub [grʌb] **1.** *zo.* Larve *f*, Made *f*; F Futter *n* (*Essen*); **2.** (*-bb-*) graben; '**~·by** (*-ier, -iest*) schmudd(e)lig

grudge [grʌdʒ] **1.** mißgönnen (*s.o. s.th.* j-m et.); **2.** Groll *m*; '**grudg·ing·ly** widerwillig

gru·el [grʊəl] Haferschleim *m*

gruff [grʌf] grob, schroff, barsch

grum·ble ['grʌmbl] **1.** murren; **2.** Murren *n*; '**~·r** *fig.* Brummbär *m*

grump·y F ['grʌmpɪ] (*-ier, -iest*) schlechtgelaunt, mürrisch, mißmutig

grun·gy *Am. sl.* ['grʌndʒɪ] (*-ier, -iest*) schmudd(e)lig-schlampig (*in der Kleidung, als Protest*); schlecht u. laut (*in der Musik, als Protest*)

grunt [grʌnt] **1.** grunzen; brummen; stöhnen; **2.** Grunzen *n*; Stöhnen *n*

Gt *nur geschr. Abk. für* **Great** (*Gt Britain*)

guar·an·tee [gærən'tiː] **1.** Garantie *f*; Kaution *f*, Sicherheit *f*; **2.** (sich ver)bürgen für; garantieren; **~·tor** [gærən'tɔː] Bürge *m*, -in *f*; **~·ty** *jur.* ['gærəntɪ] Garantie *f*; Sicherheit *f*

guard [gɑːd] **1.** Wache *f*, (Wacht)Posten *m*, Wächter *m*; Wärter *m*, Aufseher *m*; Wache *f*, Bewachung *f*; *Brt. rail.* Zugbegleiter *m*, *veraltet:* Schaffner *m*; Schutz(vorrichtung *f*) *m*; Garde *f*; *be on* ~ Wache stehen; *be on (off) one's* ~ (nicht) auf der Hut sein; **2.** *v/t.* bewachen, (be)schützen (*from* vor *dat.*); *v/i.* sich hüten *od.* in acht nehmen *od.* schützen (*against* vor *dat.*); '**~·ed** vorsichtig, zurückhaltend; **~·i·an** ['gɑːdjən] *jur.* Vormund *m*; Schutz...;

'**~·i·an·ship** *jur.* Vormundschaft *f*

gue(r)·ril·la *mil.* [gə'rɪlə] Guerilla *m*; ~ **'war·fare** Guerillakrieg *m*

guess [ges] **1.** (er)raten; vermuten; schätzen; *Am.* glauben, meinen; **2.** vermutung *f*; '**~·work** (reine) Vermutung(en *pl.*)

guest [gest] Gast *m*; '**~·house** (Hotel)Pension *f*, Fremdenheim *n*; '**~·room** Gäste-, Fremdenzimmer *n*

guf·faw [gʌ'fɔː] **1.** schallendes Gelächter; **2.** schallend lachen

guid·ance ['gaɪdns] Führung *f*; (An-)Leitung *f*

guide [gaɪd] **1.** (Reise-, Fremden)Führer(in); (Reise- *etc.*)Führer *m* (*Buch*); Handbuch *n*; (Reise- *etc.*)Führer *m* London-Führer; → *girl guide;* **2.** leiten; führen; lenken; ~ **book** (Reise-*etc.*)Führer *m* (*Buch*); **guid·ed 'tour** Führung *f*; '**~·lines** *pl.* Richtlinien *f* (*on gen.*)

guild *hist.* [gɪld] Gilde *f*, Zunft *f*

guile·less ['gaɪllɪs] arglos

guilt [gɪlt] Schuld *f*; '**~·less** schuldlos, unschuldig (*of* an *dat.*); '**~·y** (*-ier, -iest*) schuldig (*of* gen.); schuldbewußt

guin·ea pig *zo.* ['gɪnɪ -] Meerschweinchen *n*

guise *fig.* [gaɪz] Gestalt *f*, Maske *f*

gui·tar *mus.* ['gɪ'tɑː] Gitarre *f*

gulch *bsd. Am.* [gʌlʃ] tiefe Schlucht *f*

gulf [gʌlf] Golf *m*; *fig.* Kluft *f*

gull *zo.* [gʌl] Möwe *f*

gul·let ['gʌlɪt] *anat.* Speiseröhre *f*; Gurgel *f*, Kehle *f*

gulp [gʌlp] **1.** (großer) Schluck *m*; **2.** *oft* ~ **down** Getränk hinunterstürzen, *Speise* hinunterschlingen

gum¹ *anat.* [gʌm] *mst* ~**s** *pl.* Zahnfleisch *n*

gum² [gʌm] **1.** Gummi *m, n*; Klebstoff *m*; Kaugummi *m*; *Frucht*-Gummi *m* (*Bonbon*); **2.** (*-mm-*) kleben

gun [gʌn] **1.** Gewehr *n*; Pistole *f*, Revolver *m*; Geschütz *n*, Kanone *f*; **2.** (*-nn-*): ~ **down** niederschießen; '**~·fight** *bsd. Am.* Feuergefecht *n*, Schießerei *f*; '**~·fire** Schüsse *pl.*; *mil.* Geschützfeuer *n*; '**~·li·cence** (*Am.* **license**) Waffenschein *m*; '**~·man** (*pl. -men*) Bewaffnete(r) *m*; Revolverheld *m*; '**~·point: at** ~ mit vorgehaltener Waffe, mit Waffengewalt; '**~·pow·der** Schießpulver *n*;

'**~·run·ner** Waffenschmuggler *m*;
'**~·run·ning** Waffenschmuggel *m*;
'**~·shot** Schuß *m*; *within* (*out of*) ~ in
(außer) Schußweite
gur·gle ['gɜːgl] **1.** gurgeln, gluckern,
glucksen; **2.** Gurgeln *n*, Gluckern *n*,
Glucksen *n*
gush [gʌʃ] **1.** strömen, schießen (*from*
aus); **2.** Schwall *m*, Strom *m* (*a. fig.*)
gust [gʌst] Windstoß *m*, Bö *f*
guts F [gʌts] *pl.* Eingeweide *pl.*; *fig.*
Schneid *m*, Mumm *m*
gut·ter ['gʌtə] Gosse *f* (*a. fig.*), Rinn-
stein *m*; Dachrinne *f*
guy F [gaɪ] Kerl *m*, Typ *m*

guz·zle ['gʌzl] saufen; fressen
gym F [dʒɪm] Fitneßcenter *n*; → *gymnasium*; → *gymnastics*; **~·na·si-
um** [dʒɪm'neɪzjəm] Turn-, Sporthalle *f*;
△   *nicht* **Gymnasium**; '**~·nast**
['dʒɪmnæst] Turner(in); **~·nas·tics**
[dʒɪm'næstɪks] *sg.* Turnen *n*, Gymnastik *f*
gy·n(a)e·col·o·gist [gaɪnɪ'kɒlədʒɪst]
Gynäkolog|e, -in *f*, Frauenarzt *m*,
-ärztin *f*; **~·gy** [gaɪnɪ'kɒlədʒɪ] Gynäko-
logie *f*, Frauenheilkunde *f*
gyp·sy *bsd. Am.* ['dʒɪpsɪ] → *gipsy*
gy·rate [dʒaɪə'reɪt] kreisen, sich (im
Kreis) drehen, (herum)wirbeln

H

H

H, h [eɪtʃ] H, h *n*
hab·er·dash·er ['hæbədæʃə] *Brt.* Kurz-
warenhändler *m*; *Am.* Herrenausstat-
ter *m*; **~·y** ['hæbədæʃərɪ] *Brt.* Kurzwa-
ren(geschäft *n*) *pl.*; *Am.* Herrenbeklei-
dung *f*; *Am.* Herrenmodengeschäft *n*
hab·it ['hæbɪt] (An)Gewohnheit *f*; *bsd.*
(Ordens)Tracht *f*; *drink has become a*
~ *with him* er kommt von Alkohol
nicht mehr los
ha·bit·u·al [hə'bɪtjʊəl] gewohnheitsmä-
ßig, Gewohnheits...
hack¹ [hæk] hacken
hack² [hæk] Schreiberling *m*
hack³ [hæk] Klepper *m*
hack·er ['hækə] *Computer*: Hacker *m*
hack·neyed ['hæknɪd] abgedroschen
had [hæd] *pret. u. p.p. von* **have**
had·dock *zo.* ['hædək] (*pl.* *-dock*)
Schellfisch *m*
h(a)e·mor·rhage *med.* ['hemərɪdʒ]
Blutung *f*
hag *fig.* [hæg] häßliches altes Weib, Hexe *f*
hag·gard ['hægəd] abgespannt; abge-
härmt; hager
hag·gle ['hægl] feilschen, handeln
hail [heɪl] **1.** Hagel *m*; **2.** hageln;
'**~·stone** Hagelkorn *n*; '**~·storm** Ha-
gelschauer *m*

hair [heə] *einzelnes* Haar; *coll.* Haar *n*,
Haare *pl.*; '**~·breadth** → *hair's
breadth*; '**~·brush** Haarbürste *f*; '**~·cut**
Haarschnitt *m*; '**~·do** (*pl. -dos*) F Frisur *f*; '**~·dress·er** Friseur *m*, Friseuse
f; '**~·dri·er**, '**~·dry·er** Trockenhaube
f; Haartrockner *m*; Fön *m* (*TM*); '**~·
grip** *Brt.* Haarklammer *f*, -klemme *f*;
'**~·less** ohne Haare, kahl; '**~·pin** Haar-
nadel *f*; **~·pin 'bend** Haarnadelkurve
f; **~·rais·ing** ['heəreɪzɪŋ] haarsträu-
bend; '**~'s breadth:** *by a* ~ um Haa-
resbreite; '**~ slide** *Brt.* Haarspange *f*;
'**~·split·ting** Haarspalterei *f*; '**~·spray**
Haarspray *m, n*; '**~·style** Frisur *f*; '**~·
styl·ist** Hair-Stylist *m*, Haarstilist *m*,
Damenfriseur *m*; '**~·y** (*-ier, -iest*) be-
haart, haarig
half [hɑːf] **1.** (*pl.* **halves** [hɑːvz]) Hälfte *f*;
go halves halbe-halbe machen, teilen;
2. halb; ~ *an hour* e-e halbe Stunde; ~ *a
pound* ein halbes Pfund; ~ *past ten*
halb elf (Uhr); ~ *way up* auf halber
Höhe; '**~·breed** Halbblut *n*; '**~·broth·er**
Halbbruder *m*; '**~·caste** Halbblut *n*;
~'heart·ed halbherzig; **~'time** *Sport*:
Halbzeit *f*; **~·time 'score** *Sport*: Halb-
zeitstand *m*; **~'way** halb; auf halbem
Weg, in der Mitte; **~·way 'line** Mittel-
linie *f*; **~·'wit·ted** schwachsinnig

hal·i·but zo. ['hælɪbət] (pl. **-buts, -but**) Heilbutt m

hall [hɔːl] Halle f, Saal m; Flur m, Diele f; Herrenhaus n; univ. Speisesaal m; ~ **of residence** Studentenheim n

Hal·low·e'en [hæləʊˈiːn] Abend m vor Allerheiligen

hal·lu·ci·na·tion [həluːsɪˈneɪʃn] Halluzination f

'hall·way bsd. Am. Halle f, Diele f; Korridor m

ha·lo ['heɪləʊ] (pl. **-loes, -los**) astr. Hof m; Heiligenschein m

halt [hɔːlt] **1.** Halt m; **2.** (an)halten

hal·ter ['hɔːltə] Halfter m, n

halve [hɑːv] halbieren; **~s** [hɑːvz] pl. von **half** 1

ham [hæm] Schinken m; ~ **and eggs** Schinken mit (Spiegel)Ei

ham·burg·er ['hæmbɜːgə] gastr. Hamburger m; Am. Rinderhack n

ham·let ['hæmlɪt] Weiler m

ham·mer ['hæmə] **1.** Hammer m; **2.** hämmern

ham·mock ['hæmək] Hängematte f

ham·per¹ ['hæmpə] (Deckel)Korb m; Geschenk-, Freßkorb m; Am. Wäschekorb m

ham·per² ['hæmpə] (be)hindern

ham·ster zo. ['hæmstə] Hamster m

hand [hænd] **1.** Hand f (a. fig.); Handschrift f; (Uhr)Zeiger m; oft in Zssgn Arbeiter m; Fachmann m; Kartenspiel: Blatt n, Karten pl.; ~ **in glove** ein Herz und eine Seele; **change ~s** den Besitzer wechseln; **give** od. **lend a ~** mit zugreifen, j-m helfen (**with** by); **shake ~s with** j-m die Hand schütteln od. geben; **at ~** in Reichweite; nahe; bei der od. zur Hand; **at first ~** aus erster Hand; **by ~** mit der Hand; **on the one ~** einerseits; **on the other ~** andererseits; **on the right ~** rechts; **~s off!** Hände weg!; **~s up!** Hände hoch!; **2.** aushändigen, (über)geben, (-)reichen; ~ **around** herumreichen; ~ **down** weitergeben, überliefern; ~ **in** Prüfungsarbeit etc. abgeben; Bericht, Gesuch etc. einreichen; ~ **on** weiterreichen, -geben; überliefern; ~ **out** aus-, verteilen; ~ **up** hinauf-, heraufreichen; **'~bag** Handtasche f; **'~ball** Fußball: Handspiel n; **'~bill** Handzettel m, Flugblatt n; **'~brake** tech. Handbremse f; **'~cuffs** pl. Handschellen pl.; **'~ful** Handvoll f; F Plage f

hand·i·cap ['hændɪkæp] **1.** Handikap n, med. a. Behinderung f, Sport: a. Vorgabe f; → **mental**; → **physical**; **2.** (**-pp-**) behindern, benachteiligen; **'~ped 1.** gehandikapt, behindert, benachteiligt; → **mental**; → **physical**; **2.** the ~ pl. med. die Behinderten pl.

hand·ker·chief ['hæŋkətʃɪf] (pl. **-chiefs**) Taschentuch n

han·dle ['hændl] **1.** Griff m; Stiel m; Henkel m; Klinke f; **fly off the ~** F wütend werden; **2.** anfassen, berühren; hantieren od. umgehen mit; behandeln; △ nicht **handeln**; **'~bar(s** pl.) Lenkstange f

'hand| lug·gage Handgepäck n; **~'made** handgearbeitet; **'~out** Almosen n, milde Gabe; Handzettel m; Handout n, Informationsunterlage(n pl.) f (für die Presse etc.); **'~rail** Geländer n; **'~shake** Händedruck m

hand·some ['hænsəm] (**~r, ~st**) gutaussehend (bsd. Mann); ansehnlich, beträchtlich (Summe etc.)

'hand| writ·ing Handschrift f; **~'writ·ten** handgeschrieben; **'~y** (**-ier, -iest**) zur Hand; geschickt; handlich, praktisch; nützlich; **come in ~** sich als nützlich erweisen; (sehr) gelegen kommen

hang [hæŋ] (**hung**) (auf-, be-, ein)hängen; Tapete ankleben; (pret. u. p.p. **hanged**) j-n (auf)hängen; ~ **o.s.** sich erhängen; ~ **about**, ~ **around** herumlungern; ~ **on** sich klammern (**to** an acc.) (a. fig.), festhalten (**to** acc.); teleph. am Apparat bleiben; ~ **up** teleph. einhängen, auflegen; **she hung up on me** sie legte einfach auf

han·gar ['hæŋə] Hangar m, Flugzeughalle f

hang·er ['hæŋə] Kleiderbügel m

hang| glid·er ['hæŋglaɪdə] (Flug)Drachen m; Drachenflieger(in); **~ glid·ing** Drachenfliegen n

hang·ing ['hæŋɪŋ] **1.** Hänge...; **2.** (Er)Hängen n; **'~s** pl. Tapete f, Wandbehang m, Vorhang m

'hang·man (pl. **-men**) Henker m

'hang·nail med. Niednagel m

'hang·o·ver Katzenjammer m, Kater m

hatred

han·ker F [ˈhæŋkə] sich sehnen (*after*, *for* nach)

han|·kie, ~·ky F [ˈhæŋkɪ] Taschentuch n

hap·haz·ard [hæpˈhæzəd] willkürlich; plan-, wahllos

hap·pen [ˈhæpən] (zufällig) geschehen; sich ereignen, passieren, vorkommen; **~·ing** [ˈhæpnɪŋ] Ereignis n, Vorkommnis n; Happening n

hap·pi|·ly [ˈhæpɪlɪ] glücklich(erweise); **'~·ness** Glück n

hap·py [ˈhæpɪ] (*-ier*, *-iest*) glücklich; erfreut; **~·go·'luck·y** unbekümmert, sorglos

ha·rangue [həˈræŋ] **1.** (Straf)Predigt f; **2.** v/t. j-m e-e Strafpredigt halten

har·ass [ˈhærəs] ständig belästigen; schikanieren; aufreiben, zermürben; **'~·ment** ständige Belästigung; Schikane(n pl.) f; → **sexual harassment**

har·bo(u)r [ˈhaːbə] **1.** Hafen m; Zufluchtsort m; **2.** j-m Zuflucht od. Unterschlupf gewähren; Groll etc. hegen

hard [haːd] hart; fest; schwer, schwierig; heftig, stark; hart, streng (a. *Winter*); hart, nüchtern (*Tatsachen etc.*); *Drogen*: hart, *Getränk*: a. stark; **~ of hearing** schwerhörig; **~ up** F in (Geld)Schwierigkeiten, in Verlegenheit (*for* um); **'~·back** gebundene Ausgabe (*Buch*); **'~·boiled** hart(gekocht) etc.; *fig.* hart, unsentimental, nüchtern; **'~·cash** Bargeld n; klingende Münze; **~·core** harter Kern (*e-r Bande etc.*); **~·core** zum harten Kern gehörend; hart (*Pornographie*); **'~·cov·er** *print.* **1.** gebunden; **2.** Hard cover n, gebundene Ausgabe; **~ 'disk** *Computer*: Festplatte f; **~·en** [ˈhaːdn] härten; hart machen od. werden; (sich) abhärten; **'~·hat** Schutzhelm m (*für Bauarbeiter etc.*); **~·head·ed** nüchtern, praktisch; *bsd. Am.* starr, dickköpfig; **~'heart·ed** hartherzig; **~ 'la·bo(u)r** *jur.* Zwangsarbeit f; **~ 'line** *bsd. pol.* harter Kurs; **~·line** *bsd. pol.* hart, kompromißlos; **'~·ly** kaum; **'~·ship** Not f; Härte f; Schwierigkeit f; **'~·top** Hardtop n, m (*abnehmbares Wagendach*; a. *Wagen*); **'~·ware** Eisenwaren pl.; Haushaltswaren pl.; *Computer*: Hardware f

har·dy [ˈhaːdɪ] (*-ier*, *-iest*) zäh, robust,

abgehärtet; winterfest (*Pflanze*)

hare zo. [heə] Hase m; **'~·bell** *bot.* Glockenblume f; **'~·brained** verrückt (*Person, Plan*); **'~·lip** *anat.* Hasenscharte f

harm [haːm] **1.** Schaden m; **2.** verletzen; schaden (*dat.*); **'~·ful** schädlich; **'~·less** harmlos

har·mo|·ni·ous [haːˈməʊnjəs] harmonisch; **~·nize** [ˈhaːmənaɪz] harmonieren; in Einklang sein od. bringen; **~·ny** [ˈhaːmənɪ] Harmonie f

har·ness [ˈhaːnɪs] **1.** (*Pferde- etc.*)Geschirr n; **die in ~** *fig.* in den Sielen sterben; **2.** anschirren; anspannen (**to** an *acc.*)

harp [haːp] **1.** *mus.* Harfe f; **2.** *mus.* Harfe spielen; **~ on (about)** *fig.* herumreiten auf (*dat.*)

har·poon [haːˈpuːn] **1.** Harpune f; **2.** harpunieren

har·row *agr.* [ˈhærəʊ] **1.** Egge f; **2.** eggen

har·row·ing [ˈhærəʊɪŋ] quälend, qualvoll, erschütternd

harsh [haːʃ] rauh; grell; streng; schroff, barsch

hart zo. [haːt] (*pl.* **harts, hart**) Hirsch m

har·vest [ˈhaːvɪst] **1.** Ernte(zeit) f; (Ernte)Ertrag m; **2.** ernten; **'~·er** *bsd.* Mähdrescher m

has [hæz] *er, sie, es* hat

hash[1] [hæʃ] *gastr.* Haschee n; **make a ~ of** *fig.* verpfuschen

hash[2] F [hæʃ] Hasch n (*Haschisch*)

hash 'browns *pl. Am.* Brat-, Röstkartoffeln *pl.*

hash·ish [ˈhæʃiːʃ] Haschisch n

hasp [haːsp] (Verschluß)Spange f

haste [heɪst] Eile f, Hast f; **has·ten** [ˈheɪsn] *j-n* antreiben; (sich be)eilen; *et.* beschleunigen; **hast·y** (*-ier*, *-iest*) eilig, hastig, überstürzt; voreilig

hat [hæt] Hut m

hatch[1] [hætʃ] a. **~ out** ausbrüten; ausschlüpfen

hatch[2] [hætʃ] Luke f; Durchreiche f (*für Speisen*); **'~·back** *mot.* (Wagen m mit) Hecktür f

hatch·et [ˈhætʃɪt] Beil n; **bury the ~** das Kriegsbeil begraben

'hatch·way Luke f

hate [heɪt] **1.** Haß m; **2.** hassen; **'~·ful** verhaßt; abscheulich; **ha·tred** [ˈheɪtrɪd] Haß m

haugh·ty ['hɔːtɪ] hochmütig, überheblich

haul [hɔːl] **1.** ziehen, zerren; schleppen; befördern, transportieren; **2.** Ziehen *n*; Fischzug *m*, *fig.* F *a.* Fang *m*; Beförderung *f*, Transport *m*; Transportweg *m*; **~age** ['hɔːlɪdʒ] Beförderung *f*, Transport *m*; **~er** *Am.* ['hɔːlə], **~i·er** *Brt.* ['hɔːljə] Transportunternehmer *m*

haunch [hɔːntʃ] Hüfte *f*, Hüftpartie *f*, Hinterbacke *f*, Keule *f*

haunt [hɔːnt] **1.** spuken in (*dat.*); häufig besuchen; *fig.* verfolgen, quälen; **2.** häufig besuchter Ort; Schlupfwinkel *m*; **~ing** quälend; unvergeßlich, eindringlich

have [hæv] (*had*) *v/t.* haben; erhalten, bekommen; essen, trinken (*~ breakfast* frühstücken; *~ a cup of tea* e-n Tee trinken); *vor inf.:* müssen (*I ~ to go now* ich muß jetzt gehen); *mit Objekt u. p.p.:* lassen (*I had my hair cut* ich ließ mir die Haare schneiden); **~ back** zurückbekommen; **~ on** *Kleidungsstück* anhaben, *Hut* aufhaben; *v/aux.* haben; *bei v/i.* oft sein; *I ~ come* ich bin gekommen

ha·ven ['heɪvn] Hafen *m* (*mst fig.*)

hav·oc ['hævək] Verwüstung *f*, Zerstörung *f*; *play ~ with* verwüsten, zerstören; *fig.* verheerend wirken auf (*acc.*)

Ha·wai·i [hə'waiiː] Hawaii *n*; **Ha·wai·i·an** [hə'waiiən] **1.** hawaiisch; **2.** Hawaiianer(in); *ling.* Hawaiisch *n*

hawk¹ *zo.* [hɔːk] Habicht *m*, Falke *m*

hawk² [hɔːk] hausieren mit; auf der Straße verkaufen; **~er** Hausierer(in); Straßenhändler(in); Drücker(in) (*Abonnementverkäufer für Zeitschriften etc.*)

haw·thorn *bot.* ['hɔːθɔːn] Weißdorn *m*

hay [heɪ] Heu *n*; **~ fe·ver** Heuschnupfen *m*; **~loft** Heuboden *m*; **~rick**, **~stack** Heuschober *m*, -haufen *m*

haz·ard ['hæzəd] Gefahr *f*, Risiko *n*; **~ous** gewagt, gefährlich, riskant; **~ous 'waste** Sonder- *od.* Giftmüll *m*

haze [heɪz] Dunst(schleier) *m*

ha·zel ['heɪzl] **1.** *bot.* Hasel(nuß)strauch *m*; **2.** (hasel)nußbraun; **~nut** Haselnuß *f*

haz·y ['heɪzɪ] (*-ier, -iest*) dunstig, diesig; *fig.* unklar, verschwommen

H-bomb ['eɪtʃbɒm] H-Bombe *f*, Wasserstoffbombe *f*

he [hiː] **1.** er; **2.** Er *m*; *zo.* Männchen *n*; **~-goat** Ziegenbock *m*

head [hed] **1.** Kopf *m*; (Ober)Haupt *n*; Chef *m*; (An)Führer(in), Leiter(in); Spitze *f*; Kopf(ende *n*) *m* (*e-s Bettes etc.*); Kopf *m* (*e-s Briefbogens, Nagels etc.*); Vorderseite *f* (*e-r Münze*); Überschrift *f*; **20 pounds a ~** od. **per ~** zwanzig Pfund pro Kopf *od.* Person; **40 ~** *pl.* (*of cattle*) 40 Stück *pl.* (Vieh); **~s or tails?** *Münze:* Kopf oder Zahl?; *at the ~ of* an der Spitze (*gen.*); **~ over heels** kopfüber; bis über beide Ohren (*verliebt sein*); **bury one's ~ in the sand** den Kopf in den Sand stecken; **get it into one's ~ that ...** es sich in den Kopf setzen, daß; **lose one's ~** den Kopf od. die Nerven verlieren; **2.** Ober..., Haupt..., Chef..., oberste(r, -s), erste(r, -s); **3.** *v/t.* anführen; an der Spitze stehen von (*od. gen.*); voran-, vorausgehen (*dat.*); (an)führen, leiten; *Fußball:* köpfen; *v/i.* (*for*) gehen, fahren (nach); lossteuern, -gehen (auf *acc.*); *naut.* Kurs halten (*auf acc.*); **~ache** Kopfweh *n*; **~band** Stirnband *n*; **~dress** Kopfschmuck *m*; **~er** Kopfsprung *m*; *Fußball:* Kopfball *m*; **~first** kopfüber, mit dem Kopf voran; *fig.* ungestüm, stürmisch; **~gear** Kopfbedeckung *f*; **~ing** Überschrift *f*, Titel(zeile *f*) *m*; **~land** ['hedlənd] Landspitze *f*, -zunge *f*; **~light** *mot.* Scheinwerfer *m*; **~line** Schlagzeile *f*; **news ~s** *pl.* Rundfunk, TV: das Wichtigste in Schlagzeilen; **~long** kopfüber; ungestüm; **~mas·ter** *Schule:* Direktor *m*, Rektor *m*; **~mis·tress** *Schule:* Direktorin *f*, Rektorin *f*; **~on** frontal, Frontal...; **~'on col·li·sion** Frontalzusammenstoß *m*; **~phones** *pl.* Kopfhörer *pl.*; **~quar·ters** *pl.* (*Abk.* **HQ**) *mil.* Hauptquartier *n*; Zentrale *f*; **~rest** *Am.*, **~re·straint** *Brt. mot.* Kopfstütze *f*; **~set** Kopfhörer *pl.*; **~start** *Sport:* Vorgabe *f*, -sprung (*a. fig.*); **~strong** halsstarrig; **~ teach·er** → **headmaster**; → **headmistress**; *Am. principal*; **~wa·ters** *pl.* Quellgebiet *n*; **~way** *fig.* Fortschritt(e *pl.*) *m*; **make ~** (gut) vorankommen; **~word** Stichwort *n* (*in e-m Wörterbuch*); **~y** (*-ier, -iest*) zu Kopfe steigend, berauschend

heal [hiːl] heilen; **~ over**, **~ up** (zu)heilen

health [helθ] Gesundheit f; '**~ cer·tif·i·cate** Gesundheitszeugnis n; '**~ club** Fitneßclub m, -center n; '**~ food** Reform-, Biokost f; '**~ food shop** Brt., '**~ food store** bsd. Am. Reformhaus n, Bioladen m; '**~ful** gesund; heilsam; **~ in·su·rance** Krankenversicherung f; '**~ re·sort** Kurort m; '**~ ser·vice** Gesundheitsdienst m; '**~y** (-ier, -iest) gesund

heap [hiːp] **1.** Haufe(n) m; **2.** a. **~ up** aufhäufen, fig. a. anhäufen

hear [hɪə] (**heard**) hören; anhören, j-m zuhören; Zeugen vernehmen; Lektion abhören; **~d** [hɜːd] pret. u. p.p. von **hear**; **~·er** ['hɪərə] (Zu)Hörer(in); '**~·ing** ['hɪərɪŋ] Gehör n; Hören n; jur. Verhandlung f; jur. Vernehmung f; bsd. pol. Hearing n, Anhörung f; **within** (**out of**) **~** in (außer) Hörweite; '**~·ing aid** Hörgerät n; '**~·say** Gerede n; **by ~** vom Hörensagen n

hearse [hɜːs] Leichenwagen m

heart [hɑːt] anat. Herz n (a. fig.); Kern m; Kartenspiel: Herz(karte f) n, pl. Herz n (Farbe); **lose ~** den Mut verlieren; **take ~** sich ein Herz fassen; **take s.th. to ~** sich et. zu Herzen nehmen; **with a heavy ~** schweren Herzens (traurig); '**~·ache** Kummer m; '**~ at·tack** med. Herzanfall m; med. Herzinfarkt m; '**~·beat** Herzschlag m; '**~·break** Leid n, großer Kummer; '**~·break·ing** herzzerreißend; '**~·brok·en** gebrochen, verzweifelt; '**~·burn** Sodbrennen n; **~·en** ['hɑːtn] ermutigen; '**~·fail·ure** med. Herzversagen n; '**~·felt** innig, tiefempfunden

hearth [hɑːθ] Kamin m

'**heart|·less** herzlos; '**~·rend·ing** herzzerreißend; '**~ trans·plant** med. Herzverpflanzung f, -transplantation f; '**~·y** (-ier, -iest) herzlich; gesund; herzhaft

heat [hiːt] **1.** Hitze f; phys. Wärme f; Eifer m; zo. Läufigkeit f; Sport: (Einzel)Lauf m; **preliminary ~** Vorlauf m; **2.** v/t. heizen; a. **~ up** erhitzen, aufwärmen; v/i. sich erhitzen (a. fig.); '**~·ed** geheizt; heizbar (Heckscheibe, Pool etc.); erhitzt, fig. a. erregt; '**~·er** Heizgerät n, -körper m

heath [hiːθ] Heide(land n) f

hea·then ['hiːðn] **1.** Heide m, -in f; **2.** heidnisch

heath·er bot. ['heðə] Heidekraut n; Erika f

'**heat|·ing** Heizung f; Heiz...; '**~·proof**, '**~·re·sis·tant**, '**~·re·sist·ing** hitzebeständig; '**~ shield** Raumfahrt: Hitzeschild m; '**~·stroke** med. Hitzschlag m; '**~ wave** Hitzewelle f

heave [hiːv] (**heaved**, bsd. naut. **hove**) v/t. (hoch)stemmen, (-)hieven; Anker lichten; Seufzer ausstoßen; v/i. sich heben u. senken, wogen

heav·en ['hevn] Himmel m; '**~·ly** himmlisch

heav·y ['hevɪ] (-ier, -iest) schwer; stark (Regen, Raucher, Trinker, Verkehr etc.); hoch (Geldstrafe, Steuern etc.); schwer(verdaulich) (Nahrung etc.); drückend, lastend; Schwer...; '**~ cur·rent** electr. Starkstrom m; '**~·du·ty** tech. Hochleistungs...; strapazierfähig; '**~·hand·ed** ungeschickt; '**~·weight** Boxen: Schwergewicht(ler m) n

He·brew ['hiːbruː] **1.** hebräisch; **2.** Hebräer(in); ling. Hebräisch n

heck·le ['hekl] Redner durch Zwischenrufe od. -fragen stören

hec·tic ['hektɪk] (**~ally**) hektisch

hedge [hedʒ] **1.** Hecke f; **2.** v/t. a. **~ in** mit e-r Hecke einfassen; v/i. fig. ausweichen; '**~·hog** zo. Igel m; Am. Stachelschwein n; '**~·row** Hecke f

heed [hiːd] **1.** beachten, Beachtung schenken (dat.); **2.** **give** od. **pay ~ to**, **take ~ of → 1**; '**~·less: be ~ of** nicht beachten, Warnung etc. in den Wind schlagen

heel [hiːl] **1.** anat. Ferse f; Absatz m; **down at ~** mit schiefen Absätzen; fig. abgerissen; schlampig; **2.** Absätze machen auf (acc.)

hef·ty ['heftɪ] (-ier, -iest) kräftig, stämmig; mächtig (Schlag etc.), gewaltig; saftig (Preise, Geldstrafe etc.)

heif·er zo. ['hefə] Färse f, junge Kuh

height [haɪt] Höhe f; (Körper)Größe f; Anhöhe f; Höhe(punkt m) f; **~·en** ['haɪtn] erhöhen; vergrößern

heir [eə] Erbe m; **~ to the throne** Thronerbe m, -folger m; **~·ess** ['eərɪs] Erbin f; **~·loom** ['eəluːm] Erbstück n

held [held] pret. u. p.p. von **hold** 1

hel·i|·cop·ter aviat. ['helɪkɒptə] Hubschrauber *m*, Helikopter *m*; '~**port** *aviat.* Hubschrauberlandeplatz *m*

hell [hel] **1.** Hölle *f*; Höllen...; *what the ~ ...?* F was zum Teufel ...?; *raise ~* F e-n Mordskrach schlagen; **2.** *int.* F verdammt!, verflucht!; ~**bent** ganz versessen, wie wild *(for, on* auf *acc.)*; '~**ish** höllisch

hel·lo *int.* [hə'ləʊ] hallo!

helm *naut.* [helm] Ruder *n*, Steuer *n*; △ *nicht* **Helm**

hel·met ['helmɪt] Helm *m*

helms·man *naut.* ['helmzmən] (*pl. -men*) Steuermann *m*

help [help] **1.** Hilfe *f*; Hausangestellte *f*; *a call od. cry for ~* ein Hilferuf, ein Hilfeschrei; **2.** helfen; ~ **o.s.** sich bedienen, zulangen; *I cannot ~ it* ich kann es nicht ändern; *I could not ~ laughing* ich mußte einfach lachen; '~**er** Helfer(in); '~**ful** hilfreich; nützlich; '~**ing** Portion *f* (*Essen*); '~**less** hilflos; '~**less·ness** Hilflosigkeit *f*; '~**men·u** Computer: Hilfemenü *n*

hel·ter-skel·ter [heltə'skeltə] **1.** *adv.* holterdiepolter, Hals über Kopf; **2.** *adj.* hastig, überstürzt; **3.** *Brt.* Rutschbahn *f*

helve [helv] Stiel *m*, Griff *m* (e-r *Axt etc.*)

Hel·ve·tian [hel'viːʃjən] Schweizer...

hem [hem] **1.** Saum *m*; **2.** (*-mm-*) säumen; ~ *in* einschließen

hem·i·sphere *geogr.* ['hemɪsfɪə] Halbkugel *f*, Hemisphäre *f*

'**hem·line** Saum *m*

hem·lock *bot.* ['hemlɒk] Schierling *m*

hemp *bot.* [hemp] Hanf *m*

'**hem·stitch** Hohlsaum *m*

hen [hen] *zo.* Henne *f*, Huhn *n*; Weibchen *n* (*von Vögeln*)

hence [hens] daher; *a week ~* in e-r Woche; ~**forth**, ~**for·ward** von nun an

'**hen| house** Hühnerstall *m*; '~**pecked hus·band** Pantoffelheld *m*

her [hɜː, hə] sie; ihr; ihr(e); sich

her·ald ['herəld] **1.** *hist.* Herold *m*; **2.** ankündigen; ~**ry** ['herəldrɪ] Wappenkunde *f*, Heraldik *f*

herb *bot.* [hɜːb] Kraut *n*; **her·ba·ceous** *bot.* [hɜː'beɪʃəs] krautartig; ~ *plant* Staudengewächs *n*; **herb·al** ['hɜːbəl] Kräuter..., Pflanzen...

her·bi·vore *zo.* ['hɜːbɪvɔː] Pflanzenfresser *m*

herd [hɜːd] **1.** Herde *f* (*a. fig.*), (*wildlebender Tiere a.*) Rudel *n*; **2.** *v/t.* Vieh hüten; *v/i. a.* ~ *together* in e-r Herde leben; sich zusammendrängen; ~**s·man** ['hɜːdzmən] (*pl. -men*) Hirt *m*

here [hɪə] hier; hierher; ~ *you are* hier, (bitte) (*da hast du es*); ~*'s to you!* auf dein Wohl!

here|·a·bout(s) ['hɪərəbaʊt(s)] hier herum, in dieser Gegend; ~**af·ter** [hɪər'ɑːftə] **1.** künftig; **2.** *das* Jenseits; ~'**by** hiermit

he·red·i·ta·ry [hɪ'redɪtərɪ] erblich, Erb...; ~**ty** [hɪ'redɪtɪ] Erblichkeit *f*; ererbte Anlagen *pl.*, Erbmasse *f*

here|·in [hɪər'ɪn] hierin; ~**of** [hɪər'ɒv] hiervon

here·i·sy ['herəsɪ] Ketzerei *f*; ~**tic** ['herətɪk] Ketzer(in)

here|·up·on [hɪərə'pɒn] hierauf, darauf(hin); ~'**with** hiermit

her·i·tage ['herɪtɪdʒ] Erbe *n*

her·mit ['hɜːmɪt] Einsiedler *m*

he·ro ['hɪərəʊ] (*pl. -roes*) Held *m*; ~**ic** [hɪ'rəʊɪk] (*~ally*) heroisch, heldenhaft, Helden...

her·o·in ['herəʊɪn] Heroin *n*

her·o|·ine ['herəʊɪn] Heldin *f*; ~**is·m** ['herəʊɪzəm] Heldentum *n*

her·on *zo.* ['herən] (*pl. -ons, -on*) Reiher *m*

her·ring *zo.* ['herɪŋ] (*-rings, -ring*) Hering *m*

hers [hɜːz] ihrs, ihre(r, -s)

her·self [hɜː'self] sie selbst, ihr selbst; sich (selbst); *by ~* von selbst, allein, ohne Hilfe

hes·i|·tant ['hezɪtənt] zögernd, zaudernd, unschlüssig; ~**tate** ['hezɪteɪt] zögern, zaudern, unschlüssig sein, Bedenken haben; ~**ta·tion** [hezɪ'teɪʃn] Zögern *n*, Zaudern *n*, Unschlüssigkeit *f*; *without* ~ ohne zu zögern, bedenkenlos

hew [hjuː] (*hewed, hewed od. hewn*) hauen, hacken; ~ *down* fällen, umhauen; ~**n** [hjuːn] *p.p. von* **hew**

hey *int.* F [heɪ] he!, heda!

hey·day ['heɪdeɪ] Höhepunkt *m*, Gipfel *m*; Blüte(zeit) *f*

hi *int.* F [haɪ] hallo!

hi·ber·nate *zo.* ['haɪbəneɪt] Winterschlaf halten

hic|·cup, **~·cough** ['hɪkʌp] **1.** Schluckauf m; **2.** den Schluckauf haben

hid [hɪd] *pret. von* **hide²**; **~·den** ['hɪdn] *p.p. von* **hide²**

hide¹ [haɪd] (*hid, hidden*) (sich) verbergen, -stecken; verheimlichen

hide² [haɪd] Haut f, Fell n

hide|·and·seek [haɪdn'si:k] Versteckspiel n; **'~·a·way** F Versteck n

hid·e·ous ['hɪdɪəs] abscheulich

'hide·out Versteck n

hid·ing¹ F ['haɪdɪŋ] Tracht f Prügel

hid·ing² ['haɪdɪŋ]: *be in* ~ sich versteckt halten; *go into* ~ untertauchen; **'~·place** Versteck n

hi-fi ['haɪfaɪ] Hi-Fi(-Gerät n, -Anlage f) n

high [haɪ] **1.** hoch; groß (*Hoffnungen etc.*); angegangen (*Fleisch*); F blau (*betrunken*); F high (*durch Drogen*); *be in* ~ *spirits* in Hochstimmung sein; ausgelassen *od.* übermütig sein; **2.** *meteor.* Hoch n; Höchststand m; *Am.* F High-School f; **'~·brow** F **1.** Intellektuelle(r m) f; **2.** (betont) intellektuell; **~·'cal·o·rie** kalorienreich; **~·'class** erstklassig; **~·er ed·u·'ca·tion** Hochschulausbildung f; **~·fi·del·i·ty** High-Fidelity f; erstklassig; **~·'grade** hochwertig; erstklassig; **~·'hand·ed** anmaßend, eigenmächtig; **~·'heeled** hochhackig (*Schuhe*); **'~·jump** *Sport*: Hochsprung m; **'~·jump·er** *Sport*: Hochspringer(in); **~·land** ['haɪlənd] Hochland n; **'~·light 1.** Höhe-, Glanzpunkt m; **2.** hervorheben; **'~·ly** *fig.* hoch; *think ~ of* viel halten von; **~·ly·'strung** reizbar, nervös; **'~·ness** *mst fig.* Höhe; **2** Hoheit f (*Titel*); **~·'pitched** schrill (*Ton*), steil (*Dach*); **~·'pow·ered** *tech.* Hochleistungs...; F *fig.* dynamisch; **~·'pres·sure** *meteor., tech.* Hochdruck...; **'~·rise** Hochhaus n; **'~·road** *bsd. Brt.* Hauptstraße f; **'~·school** *Am.* High-School f; **~·'sea·son** Hochsaison f; **~·so·ci·e·ty** High-Society f; **'~·street** *Brt.* Hauptstraße f; **~·'strung** → *high-ly-strung*; **~·'tea** *Brt.* frühes Abendessen; **~·tech** [haɪ'tek] *a.* **hi-tech** → *tech·nol·o·gy* Hochtechnologie f; **~·'ten·sion** *electr.* Hochspannungs...; **'~·tide** Flut f; **~·'time**: *it is* ~ es ist höchste Zeit; **~·'wa·ter** Hochwasser n; **'~·way** *bsd. Am.* Highway m, Haupt(verkehrs)straße f; **2·way**

'Code *Brt.* Straßenverkehrsordnung f

hi·jack ['haɪdʒæk] **1.** *Flugzeug* entführen; *j-n, Geldtransport etc.* überfallen; **2.** (Flugzeug)Entführung f; Überfall m; **'~·er** (Flugzeug)Entführer(in); Räuber m

hike [haɪk] **1.** wandern; **2.** Wanderung f; **'hik·er** Wanderer m, Wanderin f; **'hik·ing** Wandern n

hi·lar·i·ous [hɪ'leərɪəs] ausgelassen; **~·ty** [hɪ'lærətɪ] Ausgelassenheit f

hill [hɪl] Hügel m, Anhöhe f; **~·bil·ly** *Am.* ['hɪlbɪlɪ] Hinterwäldler m; **~·music** Hillbilly-Musik f; **~·ock** ['hɪlək] kleiner Hügel; **'~·side** (Ab)Hang m; **'~·top** Hügelspitze f; **'~·y** (*-ier, -iest*) hügelig

hilt [hɪlt] Heft n, Griff m

him [hɪm] ihn; ihm; F er; sich; **~·'self** er *od.* ihm *od.* ihn selbst; sich; sich (selbst); *by* ~ von selbst, allein, ohne Hilfe

hind¹ zo. [haɪnd] (*pl.* **hinds, hind**) Hirschkuh f

hind² [haɪnd] Hinter...

hin·der ['hɪndə] hindern (*from an dat.*); hemmen

hind·most ['haɪndməʊst] hinterste(r, -s), letzte(r, -s)

hin·drance ['hɪndrəns] Hindernis n

Hin·du [hɪn'du:] Hindu m; **~·is·m** ['hɪndu:ɪzəm] Hinduismus m

hinge [hɪndʒ] **1.** (Tür)Angel f, Scharnier n; **2.** ~ *on fig.* abhängen von

hint [hɪnt] **1.** Wink m, Andeutung f; Tip m; Anspielung f; *take a* ~ e-n Wink verstehen; **2.** andeuten; anspielen (*at auf acc.*)

hip¹ *anat.* [hɪp] Hüfte f

hip² *bot.* [hɪp] Hagebutte f

hip·po zo. F ['hɪpəʊ] (*pl.* -*pos*) → **~·pot·a·mus** zo. [hɪpə'pɒtəməs] (*pl.* -*muses*, -*mi* [-maɪ]) Fluß-, Nilpferd n

hire ['haɪə] **1.** *Brt. Auto etc.* mieten; *Flugzeug etc.* chartern; *j-n* anstellen; *j-n* engagieren, einstellen; ~ *out* ver-mieten; **2.** Miete f; Lohn m; *for* ~ zu vermieten; frei (*Taxi*); **'~·car** Leih-, Mietwagen m; **~·'pur·chase**: *on* ~ *Brt. econ.* auf Abzahlung *od.* Raten

his [hɪz] sein(e); seins, seine(r, -s)

hiss [hɪs] **1.** zischen; fauchen (*Katze*); auszischen; **2.** Zischen n; Fauchen n

his·to·ri·an [hɪ'stɔːrɪən] Historiker(in); **~·tor·ic** [hɪ'stɒrɪk] (~*ally*) historisch, geschichtlich (bedeutsam); **~·tor·i·cal** historisch, geschichtlich (belegt *od.* überliefert) Geschichts...; **~** *novel* historischer Roman; **~·to·ry** ['hɪstərɪ] Geschichte *f*; **~** *of civilization* Kulturgeschichte *f*; **~** *contemporary* **~** Zeitgeschichte *f*

hit [hɪt] **1.** (*-tt-*; *hit*) schlagen; treffen (a. *fig.*); *mot. etc.* j-n, *et.* anfahren, *et.* rammen; **~** *it off with* sich gut vertragen mit *j-m;* **~** *on* (zufällig) auf *et.* stoßen, *et.* finden; **2.** Schlag *m*; *fig.* (Seiten)Hieb *m;* (Glücks)Treffer *m*; Hit *m* (*Buch, Schlager etc.*); **~·and·'run:** **~** *driver* (unfall)flüchtiger Fahrer; **~** *offence* (*Am.* **offense**) Fahrerflucht *f*

hitch [hɪtʃ] **1.** befestigen, festmachen, -haken, anbinden, ankoppeln (**to** an *acc.*); **~** *up* hochziehen; **~** *a ride od.* **lift** im Auto mitgenommen werden; F → **hitchhike**; **2.** Ruck *m*, Zug *m*; Schwierigkeit *f*, Haken *m*; *without a* **~** glatt, reibungslos; **'~·hike** per Anhalter fahren, trampen; **'~·hik·er** Anhalter(in), Tramper(in)

hi-tech [haɪ'tek] → **high tech**

HIV [eɪtʃ aɪ 'viː]: **~** *carrier* HIV-Positive(r *m*) *f*; **~** *negative* (*positive*) HIV-negativ (-positiv)

hive [haɪv] Bienenstock *m*; Bienenschwarm *m*

HM [eɪtʃ 'em] *Abk. für His/Her Majesty* Seine/Ihre Majestät

HMS ['eɪtʃ em es] *Abk. für His/Her Majesty's Ship* Seiner/Ihrer Majestät Schiff

hoard [hɔːd] **1.** Vorrat *m*, Schatz *m*; **2.** *a.* **~** *up* horten, hamstern

hoard·ing ['hɔːdɪŋ] Bauzaun *m*; *Brt.* Reklametafel *f*

hoar·frost ['hɔːfrost] (Rauh)Reif *m*

hoarse [hɔːs] (*~r, ~st*) heiser, rauh

hoax [həʊks] **1.** Falschmeldung *f*; (übler) Scherz; **2.** *j-n* hereinlegen

hob·ble ['hɒbl] humpeln, hinken

hob·by ['hɒbɪ] Hobby *n*, Steckenpferd *n*; **'~·horse** Steckenpferd *n* (a. *fig.*)

hob·gob·lin ['hɒbgɒblɪn] Kobold *m*

ho·bo *Am.* F ['həʊbəʊ] (*pl.* **-boes, -bos**) Landstreicher *m*, Tippelbruder *m*

hock[1] [hɒk] weißer Rheinwein

hock[2] [hɒk] Sprunggelenk *n* (*Pferd etc.*)

hock·ey ['hɒkɪ] *Sport: bsd. Brt.* Hockey *n*; *bsd. Am.* Eishockey *n*

hoe *agr.* [həʊ] **1.** Hacke *f*; **2.** hacken

hog [hɒg] (Haus-, Schlacht)Schwein *n*

hoist [hɔɪst] **1.** hochziehen; hissen; **2.** (Lasten)Aufzug *m*, Winde *f*

hold [həʊld] **1.** (*held*) halten; (fest)halten; *Gewicht etc.* tragen, (aus)halten; zurück-, abhalten (*from* von); *Wahlen, Versammlung etc.* abhalten; *Stellung* halten; *Sport:* *Meisterschaft etc.* austragen; *Aktien, Rechte etc.* besitzen; *Amt* bekleiden; *Platz* einnehmen; *Rekord* halten; fassen, enthalten; Platz bieten für; der Ansicht sein (*that* daß); halten für; fesseln, in Spannung halten; (aus)halten; (sich) festhalten; anhalten, andauern (*Wetter, Glück etc.*); **~** *one's ground,* **~** *one's own* sich behaupten; **~** *the line* tel. am Apparat bleiben; **~** *responsible* verantwortlich machen; **~** *still* stillhalten; **~** *s.th. against s.o.* j-m *et.* vorhalten *od.* vorwerfen; j-m *et.* übelnehmen *od.* nachtragen; **~** *back* (sich) zurückhalten; *fig.* zurückhalten mit; **~** *on* (sich) festhalten (**to** an *dat.*); aus-, durchhalten; andauern; *tel.* am Apparat bleiben; **~** *out* aus-, durchhalten; reichen (*Vorräte etc.*); **~** *up* hochheben; hochhalten; hinstellen (**as** *als Beispiel etc.*); aufhalten, verzögern; *j-n, Bank etc.* überfallen; **2.** Griff *m*, Halt *m*; Stütze *f*; Gewalt *f*, Macht *f*, Einfluß *m*; *naut.* Lade-, Frachtraum *m*; *catch* (*get, take*) **~** *of s.th. et.* ergreifen *od. zu* fassen bekommen; **'~·er** Halter *m* (*Gerät*); Inhaber(in) (*bsd. econ.*); **'~·ing** Besitz *m* (*an Effekten etc.*); **'~·com·pany** *econ.* Holding-, Dachgesellschaft *f*; **'~·up** (Verkehrs)Stockung *f*; (bewaffneter) (Raub)Überfall

hole [həʊl] **1.** Loch *n*; Höhle *f*, Bau *m*; *fig.* F Klemme *f*; **2.** durchlöchern

hol·i·day ['hɒlədɪ] Feiertag *m*; freier Tag; *bsd. Brt. mst* **~** *pl.* Ferien *pl.*, Urlaub *m*; *be on* **~** im Urlaub sein, Urlaub machen; **'~** *home* Ferienhaus *n*, -wohnung *f*; **'~·mak·er** Urlauber(in)

hol·i·ness ['həʊlɪnɪs] Heiligkeit *f*; *His* **~** Seine Heiligkeit (*der Papst*)

hol·ler *Am.* F ['hɒlə] schreien

hol·low ['hɒləʊ] **1.** hohl; **2.** Hohlraum *m*, (Aus)Höhlung *f*; Mulde *f*, Vertiefung *f*; **3.** **~** *out* aushöhlen

hol·ly *bot.* ['hɒlɪ] Stechpalme *f*

145

hormone

hol·o·caust ['hɔləkɔːst] Massenvernichtung f, -sterben n, (bsd. Brand)Katastrophe f; the ⌾ hist. der Holocaust

hol·ster ['həʊlstə] (Pistolen)Halfter m, n

ho·ly ['həʊlɪ] (-ier, -iest) heilig; ~ **'wa·ter** Weihwasser n; '⌾ **Week** Karwoche f

home [həʊm] 1. Heim n; Haus n; Wohnung f; Zuhause n; Heimat f; at ~ zu Hause; make oneself at ~ es sich bequem machen; at ~ and abroad im In-u. Ausland; 2. adj. häuslich, Heim...; inländisch, Inlands...; Heimat...; Sport: Heim...; 3. adv. heim, nach Hause; zu Hause, daheim; fig. ins Ziel od. Schwarze; strike ~ sitzen, treffen; ~ **ad'dress** Privatanschrift f; ~ **'com·put·er** Heimcomputer m; '~**less** (-ier, -iest) einfach; Am. unscheinbar, reizlos; '~**made** selbstgemacht, Hausmacher...; ~ **'mar·ket** Binnenmarkt m; '⌾ **Of·fice** Brt. pol. Innenministerium m; ⌾ **'Sec·re·ta·ry** Brt. pol. Innenminister m; '~**sick**: be ~ Heimweh haben; '~**sick·ness** Heimweh n; ~ **'team** Sport: Gastgeber pl.; '~**ward** ['həʊmwəd] 1. adj. Heim..., Rück...; 2. adv. Am. heimwärts, nach Hause; '~**wards** adv. heimwärts, nach Hause; '~**work** Hausaufgabe(n pl.) f; do one's ~ s-e Hausaufgaben machen (a. fig.)

hom·i·cide jur. ['hɔmɪsaɪd] Mord m; Totschlag m; Mörder(in); '~ **squad** Mordkommission f

ho·mo·ge·ne·ous [hɔmə'dʒiːnjəs] homogen, gleichartig

ho·mo·sex·u·al [hɔməʊ'seksjʊəl] 1. homosexuell; 2. Homosexuelle(r m) f

hone tech. [həʊn] feinschleifen

hon·est ['ɔnɪst] ehrlich, rechtschaffen; aufrichtig; '~**es·ty** Ehrlichkeit f, Rechtschaffenheit f; Aufrichtigkeit f

hon·ey ['hʌnɪ] Honig m; Am. Liebling m, Schatz m; ~**comb** ['hʌnɪkəʊm] (Honig)Wabe f; ~**ed** ['hʌnɪd] honigsüß; '~**moon** 1. Flitterwochen pl., Hochzeitsreise f; 2. be ~ing auf Hochzeitsreise sein

honk mot. [hɔŋk] hupen

hon·ky-tonk Am. ['hɔŋkɪtɒŋk] Spelunke f

hon·or·a·ry ['ɔnərərɪ] Ehren...; ehrenamtlich

hon·o·(u)r ['ɔnə] 1. Ehre f; Ehrung f, Ehre(n pl.) f; ~s pl. besondere Auszeichnung(en pl.); Your ⌾ Euer Ehren; 2. ehren; auszeichnen; econ. Scheck etc. honorieren, einlösen; ~**a·ble** ['ɔnərəbl] ehrenvoll, -haft; ehrenwert

hood [hʊd] Kapuze f; mot. Verdeck n; Am. (Motor)Haube f; tech. (Schutz-)Haube f

hood·lum sl. ['huːdləm] Rowdy m; Ganove m

hood·wink ['hʊdwɪŋk] hinters Licht führen

hoof [huːf] (pl. hoofs [huːfs], hooves [huːvz]) Huf m

hook [hʊk] 1. Haken m; Angelhaken m; by ~ or by crook F mit allen Mitteln; 2. an-, ein-, fest-, zuhaken; angeln (a. fig.); ~**ed** [hʊkt] krumm, Haken...; F süchtig (on nach) (a. fig.); ~ **on heroin** (television) heroin- (fernseh)süchtig; '~**y**: play ~ bsd. Am. F (die Schule) schwänzen

hoo·li·gan ['huːlɪgən] Rowdy m; ~**is·m** ['huːlɪgənɪzəm] Rowdytum n

hoop [huːp] Reif(en) m

hoot [huːt] 1. Schrei m (der Eule); mot. Hupen n; höhnischer, johlender Schrei; 2. v/i. heulen; johlen; mot. hupen; v/t. auspfeifen, -zischen

Hoo·ver TM ['huːvə] 1. Staubsauger m; 2. mst ⌾ (staub)saugen

hooves [huːvz] pl. von hoof

hop¹ [hɔp] 1. (-pp-) hüpfen, hopsen; hüpfen über (acc.); be ~ping mad F e-e Stinkwut (im Bauch) haben; 2. Sprung m

hop² bot. [hɔp] Hopfen m

hope [həʊp] 1. Hoffnung f; 2. hoffen (for auf acc.); ~ for the best das Beste hoffen; I ~ so, let's ~ so in Antworten: hoffentlich; I (sincerely) ~ so ich hoffe es (sehr); '~**ful**: be ~ that hoffen, daß; '~**ful·ly** hoffnungsvoll; hoffentlich; '~**less** hoffnungslos; verzweifelt

hop·scotch ['hɔpskɒtʃ] Himmel u. Hölle (Kinderspiel)

ho·ri·zon [hə'raɪzn] Horizont m

hor·i·zon·tal [hɔrɪ'zɒntl] horizontal, waag(e)recht

hor·mone biol. ['hɔːməʊn] Hormon n

4 SW Engl. I

horn [hɔːn] Horn *n; mot.* Hupe *f;* **~s** *pl.* Geweih *n*

hor·net *zo.* ['hɔːnɪt] Hornisse *f*

horn·y ['hɔːnɪ] (*-ier, -iest*) schwielig; V geil (*Mann*)

hor·o·scope ['hɒrəskəʊp] Horoskop *n*

hor·ri·ble ['hɒrəbl] schrecklich, furchtbar, scheußlich; **~·rid** *bsd. Brt.* ['hɒrɪd] gräßlich, abscheulich; schrecklich; **~·rif·ic** [hɒ'rɪfɪk] (*~ally*) schrecklich, entsetzlich; **~·ri·fy** ['hɒrɪfaɪ] entsetzen; **~·ror** ['hɒrə] Entsetzen *n;* Abscheu *m,* Horror *m;* F Greuel *m*

horse [hɔːs] *zo.* Pferd *n;* Bock *m,* Gestell *n; wild* **~s couldn't drag me there** keinen Pferde bringen mich dort hin; '**~·back:** *on* **~** zu Pferde, beritten; **~·'chest·nut** *bot.* Roßkastanie *f;* '**~·hair** Roßhaar *n;* '**~·man** (*pl. -men*) (geübter) Reiter; '**~·pow·er** *phys.* Pferdestärke *f;* '**~ race** Pferderennen *n* (*einzelnes Rennen*); '**~·rad·ish** Meerrettich *m;* '**~·shoe** Hufeisen *n;* '**~·wom·an** (*pl. -women*) (geübte) Reiterin

hor·ti·cul·ture ['hɔːtɪkʌltʃə] Gartenbau *m*

hose¹ [həʊz] Schlauch *m*

hose² [həʊz] *pl.* Strümpfe *pl.,* Strumpfwaren *pl.;* △ *nicht* **Hose**

ho·sier·y ['həʊzɪərɪ] Strumpfwaren *pl.*

hos·pice ['hɒspɪs] Sterbeklinik *f*

hos·pi·ta·ble ['hɒspɪtəbl] gastfreundlich

hos·pi·tal ['hɒspɪtl] Krankenhaus *n,* Klinik *f; in* (*Am. in the*) **~** im Krankenhaus

hos·pi·tal·i·ty [hɒspɪ'tælətɪ] Gastfreundschaft *f*

hos·pi·tal·ize ['hɒspɪtəlaɪz] ins Krankenhaus einliefern *od.* einweisen

host¹ [həʊst] **1.** Gastgeber *m; biol.* Wirt *m* (*Tier od. Pflanze*); *Rundfunk, TV:* Talkmaster *m,* Showmaster *m,* Moderator(in); *your* **~ was** ... durch die Sendung führte Sie ...; **2.** *Rundfunk, TV:* F *Sendung* moderieren

host² [həʊst] Menge *f,* Masse *f*

host³ *rel.* [həʊst] *oft* 2 Hostie *f*

hos·tage ['hɒstɪdʒ] Geisel *m,f; take s.o.* **~** j-n als Geisel nehmen

hos·tel ['hɒstl] *bsd. Brt.* (*Studenten· etc.*)(Wohn)Heim *n; mst* **youth ~** Jugendherberge *f*

host·ess ['həʊstɪs] Gastgeberin *f;* Hosteß *f* (*Betreuerin; a. aviat.*); *aviat.* Stewardeß *f*

hos·tile ['hɒstaɪl] feindlich; feindselig (*to* gegen); **~ to foreigners** ausländerfeindlich; **~·til·i·ty** [hɒ'stɪlətɪ] Feindseligkeit *f* (*to* gegen); **~ to foreigners** Ausländerfeindlichkeit *f*

hot [hɒt] (*-tt-*) heiß; scharf (*Gewürze*); beißend; warm, heiß (*Speisen*); hitzig, heftig; ganz neu *od.* frisch (*Nachrichten etc.*); F heiß (*gestohlen*); '**~·bed** Mistbeet *n; fig.* Brutstätte *f*

hotch·potch ['hɒtʃpɒtʃ] Mischmasch *m*

hot 'dog Hot dog *n, m*

ho·tel [həʊ'tel] Hotel *n*

'**hot·head** Hitzkopf *m;* '**~·house** Treib-, Gewächshaus *n;* '**~ line** *pol.* heißer Draht; '**~ spot** *bsd. pol.* Unruhe-, Krisenherd *m;* '**~·wa·ter bot·tle** Wärmflasche *f*

hound *zo.* [haʊnd] Jagdhund *m*

hour ['aʊə] Stunde *f;* **~s** *pl.* (*Arbeits*)Zeit *f,* (*Geschäfts*)Stunden *pl.;* '**~·ly** stündlich

house 1. [haʊs] Haus *n;* **2.** [haʊz] unterbringen; '**~·bound** *fig.* ans Haus gefesselt; '**~·break·ing** Einbruch *m;* '**~·hold** Haushalt *m;* Haushalts...; '**~·hold·er** Hausbesitzer(in); '**~·keep·er** Haushälterin *f;* '**~·keep·ing** Haushaltung *f,* Haushaltsführung *f;* '**~·maid** Hausangestellte *f,* -mädchen *n;* '**~·man** (*pl. -men*) *Brt.* Assistenzarzt *m,* -ärztin *f;* △ *nicht* **Hausmann;** '**~·warm·ing (par·ty)** Einzugsparty *f;* '**~·wife** (*pl. -wives*) Hausfrau *f;* '**~·work** Hausarbeit *f;* △ *nicht* **Hausaufgabe(n)**

hous·ing ['haʊzɪŋ] Wohnung *f;* '**~ de·vel·op·ment** *Am.,* '**~ es·tate** *Brt.* Wohnsiedlung *f*

hove [həʊv] *pret. u. p.p. von* **heave**

hov·er ['hɒvə] schweben; herumlungern; *fig.* schwanken; '**~·craft** (*pl. -craft(s*)) Hovercraft *n,* Luftkissenfahrzeug *n*

how [haʊ] wie; **~ are you?** wie geht es dir?; **~ about ...?** wie steht's mit ...?, wie wäre es mit ...?; **~ do you do?** *bei der Vorstellung:* guten Tag!; **~ much?** wieviel?; **~ many** wie viele?

how·dy *Am. int.* F ['haʊdɪ] Tag!

how·ev·er [haʊ'evə] **1.** *adv.* wie auch (immer); **2.** *cj.* jedoch

howl [haʊl] **1.** heulen; brüllen, schreien; **2.** Heulen n; '∼·er F grober Schnitzer

HP [eɪtʃ 'piː] Abk. für horsepower PS, Pferdestärke f; Abk. für hire purchase Brt. Ratenkauf m

HQ [eɪtʃ 'kjuː] Abk. für headquarters Hauptquartier n

hr (pl. **hrs**) nur geschr. Abk. für hour Std., Stunde f

HRH [eɪtʃ ɑː(r) 'eɪtʃ] Abk. für His/Her Royal Highness Seine/Ihre Königliche Hoheit

hub [hʌb] (Rad)Nabe f; fig. Mittel-, Angelpunkt m

hub·bub ['hʌbʌb] Stimmengewirr n; Tumult m

hub·by F ['hʌbɪ] (Ehe)Mann m

huck·le·ber·ry bot. ['hʌklberɪ] amerikanische Heidelbeere

huck·ster ['hʌkstə] Hausierer(in)

hud·dle ['hʌdl]: ∼ together (sich) zusammendrängen; ∼d up zusammengekauert

hue[1] [hjuː] Farbe f; (Farb)Ton m

hue[2] [hjuː]: ∼ and cry fig. großes Geschrei, heftiger Protest

huff [hʌf]: in a ∼ verärgert, -stimmt

hug [hʌg] **1.** (-gg-) (sich) umarmen; an sich drücken; **2.** Umarmung f

huge [hjuːdʒ] riesig, riesengroß

hulk [hʌlk] Koloß m; ungeschlachter Kerl od. Riese; sperriges Ding

hull [hʌl] **1.** bot. Schale f, Hülse f; naut. Rumpf m; **2.** enthülsen, schälen

hul·la·ba·loo ['hʌləbə'luː] (pl. -loos) Lärm m, Getöse n

hul·lo int. [hə'ləʊ] hallo!

hum [hʌm] (-mm-) summen; brummen

hu·man ['hjuːmən] **1.** menschlich, Menschen...; △ nicht human; **2.** a. ∼ being Mensch m; ∼e [hjuː'meɪn] human, menschlich; ∼·i·tar·i·an [hjuːmænɪ'teərɪən] humanitär, menschenfreundlich; ∼·i·ty [hjuː'mænətɪ] die Menschheit, die Menschen pl.; Humanität f, Menschlichkeit f; humanities pl. Geisteswissenschaften pl.; Altphilologie f; '∼·ly: ∼ possible menschenmöglich; '∼ 'rights pl. Menschenrechte pl.

hum·ble ['hʌmbl] **1.** (∼r, ∼st) demütig; bescheiden; **2.** demütigen; '∼·ness Demut f

hum·drum ['hʌmdrʌm] eintönig, langweilig

hu·mid ['hjuːmɪd] feucht, naß; ∼·i·ty [hjuː'mɪdətɪ] Feuchtigkeit f

hu·mil·i·ate [hjuː'mɪlɪeɪt] demütigen, erniedrigen; ∼·a·tion [hjuːmɪlɪ'eɪʃn] Demütigung f, Erniedrigung f; ∼·ty [hjuː'mɪlətɪ] Demut f

hum·ming·bird zo. ['hʌmɪŋbɜːd] Kolibri m

hu·mor·ous ['hjuːmərəs] humorvoll, komisch

hu·mo(u)r ['hjuːmə] **1.** Humor m; Komik f; **2.** j-m s-n Willen lassen; eingehen auf (acc.)

hump [hʌmp] Höcker m (e-s Kamels), Buckel m; '∼·back(ed) → hunchback(ed)

hunch [hʌntʃ] **1.** → hump; dickes Stück; (Vor)Ahnung f; **2.** a. ∼ up krümmen; ∼ one's shoulders die Schultern hochziehen; '∼·back Buckel m; Bucklige(r m) f; '∼·backed buck(e)lig

hun·dred ['hʌndrəd] **1.** hundert; **2.** Hundert f; ∼th ['hʌndrədθ] **1.** hundertste(r, -s); **2.** Hundertstel n; '∼·weight etwa Zentner m (= 50,8 kg)

hung [hʌŋ] pret. u. p.p. von hang[1]

Hun·ga·ri·an [hʌŋ'geərɪən] **1.** ungarisch; **2.** Ungar(in); ling. Ungarisch n; **Hun·ga·ry** ['hʌŋgərɪ] Ungarn n

hun·ger ['hʌŋgə] **1.** Hunger m (a. fig. for nach); **2.** fig. hungern (for, after nach); '∼ strike Hungerstreik m

hun·gry ['hʌŋgrɪ] (-ier, -iest) hungrig

hunk [hʌŋk] dickes od. großes Stück

hunt [hʌnt] **1.** jagen; Jagd machen auf (acc.); verfolgen; suchen (for, after nach); ∼ for Jagd machen auf (acc.); ∼ out, ∼ up aufspüren; **2.** Jagd f (a. fig.), Jagen n; Verfolgung f; Suche f (for, after nach); '∼·er Jäger m; Jagdpferd n; '∼·ing Jagen n; Jagd...; '∼·ing ground Jagdrevier n

hur·dle ['hɜːdl] Sport: Hürde f (a. fig.); '∼r Sport: Hürdenläufer(in); '∼ race Sport: Hürdenrennen n

hurl [hɜːl] schleudern; ∼ abuse at s.o. j-m Beleidigungen ins Gesicht schleudern

hur|rah int. [hʊ'rɑː], ∼·ray int. [hʊ'reɪ] hurra!

hur·ri·cane ['hʌrɪkən] Hurrikan m, Wirbelsturm m; Orkan m

hur·ried ['hʌrɪd] eilig, hastig, übereilt

hur·ry ['hʌrɪ] **1.** v/t. schnell od. eilig befördern *od.* bringen; *oft* ~ **up** *j-n* antreiben, hetzen; *et.* beschleunigen; *v/i.* eilen, hasten; ~ (**up**) sich beeilen; ~ **up!** (mach) schnell!; **2.** (große) Eile, Hast *f*; **be in a** ~ es eilig haben

hurt [hɜːt] (**hurt**) verletzen, -wunden (*a. fig.*); schmerzen, weh tun; schaden (*dat.*); **'~ful** verletzend

hus·band ['hʌzbənd] (Ehe)Mann *m*

hush [hʌʃ] **1.** *int.* still!; **2.** Stille *f*; **3.** zum Schweigen bringen; △ *nicht huschen*; ~ **up** vertuschen; '~ **mon·ey** Schweigegeld *n*

husk *bot.* [hʌsk] **1.** Hülse *f*, Schote *f*, Schale *f*; **2.** enthülsen, schälen

'hus·ky (*-ier, -iest*) heiser, rauh (*Stimme*); F stämmig, kräftig

hus·sy ['hʌsɪ] Fratz *m*, Göre *f*; Flittchen *n*

hus·tle ['hʌsl] **1.** (*in aller Eile*) *wohin* bringen *od.* schicken; hasten, hetzen; sich beeilen; **2.** ~ **and bustle** Gedränge *n*; Gehetze *n*; Betrieb *m*, Wirbel *m*

hut [hʌt] Hütte *f*

hutch [hʌtʃ] (*bsd. Kaninchen*)Stall *m*

hy·a·cinth *bot.* ['haɪəsɪnθ] Hyazinthe *f*

hy·ae·na *zo.* [haɪ'iːnə] Hyäne *f*

hy·brid *biol.* ['haɪbrɪd] Mischling *m*, Kreuzung *f*

hy·drant ['haɪdrənt] Hydrant *m*

hy·drau·lic [haɪ'drɔːlɪk] (*~ally*) hydraulisch; **~s** *sg.* Hydraulik *f*

hy·dro... ['haɪdrə] Wasser...; **~'car·bon** Kohlenwasserstoff *m*; **~'chlor·ic**

ac·id [haɪdrəklɒrɪk 'æsɪd] Salzsäure *f*; '**~foil** *naut.* Tragflächen-, Tragflügelboot *n*; **~gen** ['haɪdrədʒən] Wasserstoff *m*; '**~gen bomb** Wasserstoffbombe *f*; '**~plane** *aviat.* Wasserflugzeug *n*; *naut.* Gleitboot *n*; '**~plan·ing** *Am. mot.* Aquaplaning *n*

hy·e·na *zo.* [haɪ'iːnə] Hyäne *f*

hy·giene ['haɪdʒiːn] Hygiene *f*; **hy·gien·ic** [haɪ'dʒiːnɪk] (*~ally*) hygienisch

hymn [hɪm] Kirchenlied *n*, Choral *m*

hype F [haɪp] **1.** *a.* ~ **up** (übersteigerte) Publicity machen für; **2.** (übersteigerte) Publicity; *media* ~ Medienrummel *m*

hy·per... ['haɪpə] hyper..., übermäßig; '**~mar·ket** *Brt.* Groß-, Verbrauchermarkt *m*; **~'sen·si·tive** überempfindlich (**to** gegen)

hy·phen ['haɪfn] Bindestrich *m*; **~ate** ['haɪfəneɪt] mit Bindestrich schreiben

hyp·no·tize ['hɪpnətaɪz] hypnotisieren

hy·po·chon·dri·ac [haɪpə'kɒndrɪæk] Hypochonder *m*

hy·poc·ri·sy [hɪ'pɒkrəsɪ] Heuchelei *f*; **hyp·o·crite** ['hɪpəkrɪt] Heuchler(in); **hyp·o·crit·i·cal** [hɪpə'krɪtɪkl] heuchlerisch, scheinheilig

hy·poth·e·sis [haɪ'pɒθɪsɪs] (*pl. -ses* [-siːz]) Hypothese *f*

hys·te·ri·a *med.* [hɪ'stɪərɪə] Hysterie *f*; **~ter·i·cal** [hɪ'sterɪkl] hysterisch; **~ter·ics** [hɪ'sterɪks] *pl.* hysterischer Anfall; *go into* ~ hysterisch werden

---

I, i [aɪ] I, i *n*

I [aɪ] ich; *it is* ~ ich bin es

IC [aɪ 'siː] *Abk. für* **integrated circuit** integrierter Schaltkreis

ice [aɪs] **1.** Eis *n*; **2.** *Getränke etc.* mit *od.* in Eis kühlen; *gastr.* glasieren, mit Zuckerguß überziehen; **~d over** zugefroren (*See etc.*); **~d up** vereist (*Straße*); '~ **age** Eiszeit *f*; '**~berg** ['aɪsbɜːg] Eisberg *m* (*a. fig.*); '**~bound** eingefroren (*Hafen, Schiff*); ~ '**cream** (Speise)Eis

n; **~cream 'par·lo(u)r** Eisdiele *f*; '~ **cube** Eiswürfel *m*; '~ '**floe** Eisscholle *f*; **~d** eisgekühlt; '~ **hock·ey** *Sport*: Eishockey *n*; '~ **lol·ly** *Brt.* Eis *n* am Stiel; '~ **rink** (Kunst)Eisbahn *f*; '~ **skate** Schlittschuh *m*; '**~skate** Schlittschuh laufen; '~ **show** Eisrevue *f*

i·ci·cle ['aɪsɪkl] Eiszapfen *m*

ic·ing ['aɪsɪŋ] Glasur *f*, Zuckerguß *m*

i·con ['aɪkɒn] Ikone *f*; *Computer*: Ikone *f*, (Bild)Symbol *n*

i·cy [ˈaɪsɪ] (*-ier, -iest*) eisig; vereist

ID [aɪ ˈdiː] *Abk. für* **identity** Identität *f*; **ID card** (Personal)Ausweis *m*

i·dea [aɪˈdɪə] Idee *f*, Vorstellung *f*, Begriff *m*; Gedanke *m*, Idee *f*; **have no ~** keine Ahnung haben

i·deal [aɪˈdɪəl] **1.** ideal; **2.** Ideal *n*; **~is·m** [aɪˈdɪəlɪzəm] Idealismus *m*; **~ize** [aɪˈdɪəlaɪz] idealisieren

i·den·ti·cal [aɪˈdentɪkl] identisch (**to, with** mit); **~ 'twins** *pl.* eineiige Zwillinge *pl.*

i·den·ti·fi·ca·tion [aɪdentɪfɪˈkeɪʃn] Identifizierung *f*; **~ (pa·pers** *pl.*) Ausweis(papiere *pl.*) *m*

i·den·ti·fy [aɪˈdentɪfaɪ] identifizieren; **~ o.s.** sich ausweisen

i·den·ti·kit pic·ture TM *Brt. jur.* [aɪˈdentɪkɪt -] Phantombild *n*

i·den·ti·ty [aɪˈdentətɪ] Identität *f*; **~ card** (Personal)Ausweis *m*

i·de·o·log·i·cal [aɪdɪəˈlɒdʒɪkl] ideologisch; **~ol·ogy** [aɪdɪˈɒlədʒɪ] Ideologie *f*

id·i·om [ˈɪdɪəm] Idiom *n*, idiomatischer Ausdruck, Redewendung *f*; **~o·mat·ic** [ɪdɪəˈmætɪk] (**~ally**) idiomatisch

id·i·ot [ˈɪdɪət] *med.* Idiot(in), *contp. a.* Trottel *m*; **~ic** [ɪdɪˈɒtɪk] (**~ally**) idiotisch

i·dle [ˈaɪdl] **1.** (**~r, ~st**) untätig; faul, träge; nutzlos; leer, hohl (*Geschwätz*); *tech.* stillstehend, außer Betrieb; *tech.* leer laufend, im Leerlauf; **2.** faulenzen; leer laufen; *mst* **~ away** *Zeit* vertrödeln

i·dol [ˈaɪdl] Idol *n* (*a. fig.*); Götzenbild *n*; **~ize** [ˈaɪdəlaɪz] abgöttisch verehren, vergöttern

i·dyl·lic [aɪˈdɪlɪk] (**~ally**) idyllisch

i.e. [aɪ ˈiː] *Abk. für* **that is to say** (*lateinisch* **id est**) d.h., das heißt

if [ɪf] wenn, falls; ob; **~ I were you** wenn ich du wäre

ig·loo [ˈɪɡluː] (*pl.* **-loos**) Iglu *m, n*

ig·nite [ɪɡˈnaɪt] anzünden, (sich) entzünden; *mot., tech.* zünden; **ig·ni·tion** [ɪɡˈnɪʃn] Zündung *f*; **~ key** Zündschlüssel *m*

ig·no·min·i·ous [ɪɡnəˈmɪnɪəs] schändlich, schmachvoll

ig·no·rance [ˈɪɡnərəns] Unkenntnis *f*, Unwissenheit *f*; **'ig·no·rant:** **be ~ of s.th.** et. nicht wissen *od.* kennen, nichts

wissen von et.; **ig·nore** [ɪɡˈnɔː] ignorieren, nicht beachten

ill [ɪl] **1.** (**worse, worst**) krank; schlimm, schlecht; **fall ~, be taken ~** krank werden, erkranken; **2. ~s** *pl.* Übel *n*; **~ad'vised** schlecht beraten; unklug; **~'bred** schlechterzogen; ungezogen

il·le·gal [ɪˈliːɡl] illegal, *jur.* illegal, ungesetzlich; **~ parking** Falschparken *n*

il·le·gi·ble [ɪˈledʒəbl] unleserlich

il·le·git·i·mate [ɪlɪˈdʒɪtɪmət] unehelich; unrechtmäßig

ill·'fat·ed unglücklich, Unglücks...; **~'hu·mo(u)red** schlechtgelaunt

il·li·cit [ɪˈlɪsɪt] unerlaubt, verboten

il·lit·e·rate [ɪˈlɪtərət] ungebildet

ill·'man·nered ungehobelt, ungezogen; **~'na·tured** boshaft, bösartig

'ill·ness Krankheit *f*

ill·'tem·pered schlechtgelaunt, übellaunig; **~'timed** ungelegen, unpassend; **~'treat** mißhandeln

il·lu·mi·nate [ɪˈljuːmɪneɪt] beleuchten; **~nat·ing** aufschlußreich; **~na·tion** [ɪljuːmɪˈneɪʃn] Beleuchtung *f*; **~s** *pl.* Illumination *f*, Festbeleuchtung *f*

il·lu·sion [ɪˈluːʒn] Illusion *f*, Täuschung *f*; **~sive** [ɪˈluːsɪv], **~so·ry** [ɪˈluːsərɪ] illusorisch, trügerisch

il·lus·trate [ˈɪləstreɪt] illustrieren; bebildern; erläutern, veranschaulichen; **~tra·tion** [ɪləˈstreɪʃn] Erläuterung *f*; Illustration *f*; Bild *n*, Abbildung *f*; **~tra·tive** [ˈɪləstrətɪv] erläuternd

il·lus·tri·ous [ɪˈlʌstrɪəs] berühmt

ill 'will Feindschaft *f*

im·age [ˈɪmɪdʒ] Bild *n*; Ebenbild *n*; Image *n*; bildlicher Ausdruck, Metapher *f*; **im·age·ry** [ˈɪmɪdʒərɪ] Bildersprache *f*, Metaphorik *f*

i·ma·gi·na·ble [ɪˈmædʒɪnəbl] vorstellbar, denkbar; **~ry** [ɪˈmædʒɪnərɪ] eingebildet, imaginär; **~tion** [ɪmædʒɪˈneɪʃn] Einbildung(skraft) *f*; **~tive** [ɪˈmædʒɪnətɪv] ideen-, einfallsreich; phantasievoll; **i·ma·gine** [ɪˈmædʒɪn] sich j-n *od.* et. vorstellen; sich et. einbilden

im·bal·ance [ɪmˈbæləns] Unausgewogenheit *f*; *pol. etc.* Ungleichgewicht *n*

im·be·cile [ˈɪmbɪsiːl] Idiot *m*, Trottel *m*

IMF [aɪ em ˈef] *Abk. für* **International Monetary Fund** Internationaler Währungsfonds

im·i·tate [ˈɪmɪteɪt] nachahmen, nach-

machen, imitieren; **~ta·tion** [ımı'teıʃn]
1. Nachahmung f, Imitation f; **2.** nachgemacht, unecht, künstlich, Kunst...
im·mac·u·late [ı'mækjʊlət] unbefleckt,
makellos; tadel-, fehlerlos
im·ma·te·ri·al [ımə'tıərıəl] unwesentlich, unerheblich (**to** für)
im·ma·ture [ımə'tjʊə] unreif
im·mea·su·ra·ble [ı'meʒərəbl] unermeßlich
im·me·di·ate [ı'mi:djət] unmittelbar;
sofortig, umgehend; nächste(r, -s)
(*Verwandtschaft*); **~ly** unmittelbar;
sofort
im·mense [ı'mens] riesig, *fig.* a. enorm,
immens
im·merse [ı'mɜːs] (ein)tauchen; **~** *o.s.*
in sich vertiefen in (*acc.*);
im·mer·sion [ı'mɜːʃn] Eintauchen n;
im'mer·sion heat·er Tauchsieder m
im·mi·grant ['ımıgrənt] Einwander|er
m, -in f; **~grate** ['ımıgreıt] einwandern, immigrieren;
(*into* in *dat.*); **~gra·tion** [ımı'greıʃn]
Einwanderung f, Immigration f
im·mi·nent ['ımınənt] nahe bevorstehend; **~ danger** drohende Gefahr
im·mo·bile [ı'məʊbaıl] unbeweglich
im·mod·e·rate [ı'mɒdərət] maßlos
im·mod·est [ı'mɒdıst] unbescheiden;
schamlos
im·mor·al [ı'mɒrəl] unmoralisch
im·mor·tal [ı'mɔːtl] **1.** unsterblich; **2.**
Unsterbliche(r m) f; **~i·ty** [ımɔː'tælətı]
Unsterblichkeit f
im·mo·va·ble [ı'muːvəbl] unbeweglich;
fig. unerschütterlich; hart, unnachgiebig
im·mune [ı'mjuːn] immun (**to** gegen);
geschützt (**from** vor, gegen);
im·mu·ni·ty [ı'mjuːnətı] Immunität f;
im·mu·nize ['ımjuːnaız] immunisieren, immun machen (*against* gegen)
imp [ımp] Teufelchen n; *fig.* F Kobold
m; Racker m
im·pact ['ımpækt] Zusammen-, Anprall
m; Aufprall m; *fig.* (Ein)Wirkung f,
(starker) Einfluß (**on** auf *acc.*)
im·pair [ım'peə] beeinträchtigen
im·part [ım'paːt] (**to** *dat.*) mitteilen; vermitteln
im·par·tial [ım'paːʃl] unparteiisch, unvoreingenommen; **~ti·al·i·ty** [ımpaːʃı-
'ælətı] Unparteilichkeit f, Objektivität f

im·pass·a·ble [ım'paːsəbl] unpassierbar
im·passe *fig.* [æm'paːs] Sackgasse f
im·pas·sioned [ım'pæʃnd] leidenschaftlich
im·pas·sive [ım'pæsıv] teilnahmslos;
ungerührt; gelassen
im·pa·tience [ım'peıʃns] Ungeduld f;
~tient ungeduldig
im·peach [ım'piːtʃ] *jur.* anklagen (**for**,
of, **with** *gen.*); *jur.* anfechten; in Frage
stellen, in Zweifel ziehen
im·pec·ca·ble [ım'pekəbl] untadelig,
einwandfrei
im·pede [ım'piːd] (be)hindern
im·ped·i·ment [ım'pedımənt] Hindernis n (**to** für); Behinderung f
im·pel [ım'pel] (**-ll-**) antreiben; zwingen
im·pend·ing [ım'pendıŋ] nahe bevorstehend, drohend
im·pen·e·tra·ble [ım'penıtrəbl] un-
durchdringlich; *fig.* unergründlich
im·per·a·tive [ım'perətıv] **1.** unum-
gänglich, unbedingt erforderlich; gebieterisch; *gr.* Imperativ...; **2.** a. **~**
mood *gr.* Imperativ m, Befehlsform f
im·per·cep·ti·ble [ımpə'septəbl] nicht
wahrnehmbar, unmerklich
im·per·fect [ım'pɜːfıkt] **1.** unvollkommen; mangelhaft; **2.** a. **~ tense** *gr.* Imperfekt n, unvollendete Vergangenheit
im·pe·ri·al·is·m *pol.* [ım'pıərıəlızəm]
Imperialismus m; **~t** *pol.* [ım'pıərıəlıst]
Imperialist m
im·per·il [ım'perəl] (*bsd. Brt.* **-ll-**, *Am.*
-l-) gefährden
im·pe·ri·ous [ım'pıərıəs] herrisch, gebieterisch
im·per·me·a·ble [ım'pɜːmjəbl] un-
durchlässig
im·per·son·al [ım'pɜːsnl] unpersönlich
im·per·so·nate [ım'pɜːsəneıt] *j-n* imitieren, nachahmen; *thea. etc.* darstellen
im·per·ti·nence [ım'pɜːtınəns] Unverschämtheit f, Frechheit f; **~nent** unverschämt, frech
im·per·tur·ba·ble [ımpə'tɜːbəbl] unerschütterlich, gelassen
im·per·vi·ous [ım'pɜːvjəs] undurchläs-
sig; *fig.* unzugänglich (**to** für)
im·pe·tu·ous [ım'petjʊəs] ungestüm,
heftig; impulsiv
im·pe·tus ['ımpıtəs] Antrieb m,
Schwung m; Impuls m

im·pi·e·ty [ɪm'paɪətɪ] Gottlosigkeit f; Pietätlosigkeit f, Respektlosigkeit f (*to* gegenüber)

im·pinge [ɪm'pɪndʒ]: ~ *on* sich auswirken auf (*acc.*), beeinflussen (*acc.*)

im·pi·ous ['ɪmpɪəs] gottlos; pietätlos, respektlos (*to* gegenüber)

im·plac·a·ble [ɪm'plækəbl] unversöhnlich, unnachgiebig

im·plant [ɪm'plɑːnt] *med.* implantieren, einpflanzen; *fig.* einprägen

im·ple·ment 1. ['ɪmplɪmənt] Werkzeug *n*, Gerät *n*; **2.** ['ɪmplɪment] ausführen

im·pli·cate ['ɪmplɪkeɪt] *j-n* verwickeln, hineinziehen (*in* in *acc.*); **~ca·tion** [ɪmplɪ'keɪʃn] Verwicklung f; Folge f, Auswirkung f; Andeutung f

im·plic·it [ɪm'plɪsɪt] vorbehalt-, bedingungslos; impliziert, (stillschweigend *od.* mit) inbegriffen

im·plore [ɪm'plɔː] *j-n* anflehen; erflehen

im·ply [ɪm'plaɪ] implizieren, (sinngemäß *od.* stillschweigend) beinhalten; andeuten; mit sich bringen

im·po·lite [ɪmpə'laɪt] unhöflich

im·pol·i·tic [ɪm'pɒlɪtɪk] unklug

im·port 1. [ɪm'pɔːt] importieren, einführen; **2.** ['ɪmpɔːt] Import *m*, Einfuhr f; **~s** *pl.* (Gesamt)Import *m*, (-)Einfuhr f; Importgüter *pl.*, Einfuhrware f

im·por·tance [ɪm'pɔːtəns] Wichtigkeit f, Bedeutung f; **~tant** wichtig, bedeutend

im·por·ta·tion [ɪmpɔː'teɪʃn] → *import* 2; **~ter** [ɪm'pɔːtə] Importeur *m*

im·pose [ɪm'pəʊz] auferlegen, aufbürden (*on* dat.); *Strafe* verhängen (*on* gegen); *et.* aufdrängen, -zwingen (*on* dat.); ~ *o.s. on s.o.* sich j-m aufdrängen; **im·pos·ing** imponierend, eindrucksvoll, imposant

im·pos·si·bil·i·ty [ɪmpɒsə'bɪlətɪ] Unmöglichkeit f; **~ble** [ɪm'pɒsəbl] unmöglich

im·pos·tor *Brt.*, **im·pos·ter** *Am.* [ɪm'pɒstə] Betrüger(in), *bsd.* Hochstapler(in)

im·po·tence ['ɪmpətəns] Unvermögen *n*, Unfähigkeit f; Hilflosigkeit f; *med.* Impotenz f; **~tent** unfähig; hilflos; *med.* impotent

im·pov·er·ish [ɪm'pɒvərɪʃ] arm machen; *be* ~*ed* verarmen, verarmt sein

im·prac·ti·ca·ble [ɪm'præktɪkəbl] un-

durchführbar; unpassierbar (*Straße etc.*)

im·prac·ti·cal [ɪm'præktɪkl] unpraktisch; undurchführbar

im·preg·na·ble [ɪm'pregnəbl] uneinnehmbar

im·preg·nate ['ɪmpregneɪt] imprägnieren, tränken; *biol.* schwängern

im·press [ɪm'pres] *j-n* beeindrucken; (deutlich) klarmachen; (auf)drücken, (ein)drucken; **im·pres·sion** [ɪm'preʃn] Eindruck *m*; Abdruck *m*; *under the* ~ *that* in der Annahme, daß; **im·pres·sive** [ɪm'presɪv] eindrucksvoll

im·print 1. [ɪm'prɪnt] (auf)drücken (*on* auf *acc.*); ~ *s.th. on s.o.'s memory* j-m et. ins Gedächtnis einprägen; **2.** ['ɪmprɪnt] Ab-, Eindruck *m*; *print.* Impressum *n*

im·pris·on *jur.* [ɪm'prɪzn] inhaftieren; **~ment** Freiheitsstrafe f, Gefängnis(strafe f) *n*, Haft f

im·prob·a·ble [ɪm'prɒbəbl] unwahrscheinlich

im·prop·er [ɪm'prɒpə] ungeeignet, unpassend; unanständig, unschicklich (*Benehmen etc.*); unrichtig

im·pro·pri·e·ty [ɪmprə'praɪətɪ] Unschicklichkeit f

im·prove [ɪm'pruːv] *v/t.* verbessern; *Wert etc.* erhöhen, steigern; ~ *on* übertreffen; *v/i.* sich (ver)bessern, besser werden, sich erholen; **~ment** (Ver)Besserung f; Steigerung f; Fortschritt *m* (*on* gegenüber *dat.*)

im·pro·vise ['ɪmprəvaɪz] improvisieren

im·pru·dent [ɪm'pruːdənt] unklug

im·pu·dence ['ɪmpjʊdəns] Unverschämtheit f; **~dent** unverschämt

im·pulse ['ɪmpʌls] Impuls *m* (*a. fig.*); Anstoß *m*, Anreiz *m*; **im·pul·sive** [ɪm'pʌlsɪv] impulsiv

im·pu·ni·ty [ɪm'pjuːnətɪ]: *with* ~ straflos, ungestraft

im·pure [ɪm'pjʊə] unrein (*a. rel.*), schmutzig; *fig.* schlecht, unmoralisch

im·pute [ɪm'pjuːt]: ~ *s.th. to s.o.* j-n e-r Sache bezichtigen; j-m et. unterstellen

in¹ [ɪn] **1.** *prp.* räumlich: in (*dat.*), an (*dat.*), auf (*dat.*); ~ *London* in London; ~ *the street* auf der Straße; - (*wohin?*) in (*acc.*); *put it* ~ *your pocket* steck es in deine Tasche; - *zeitlich:* in (*dat.*), an (*dat.*): ~ *1999* 1999; ~ *two hours* in zwei Stunden; ~ *the morning* am Morgen; - *Zustand*, *Art u. Weise*: in (*dat.*), auf (*acc.*), mit; ~ *English* auf englisch; *Tätigkeit*, *Beschäftigung*: in (*dat.*), bei, auf (*dat.*): ~ *crossing the road* beim Überqueren der Straße; bei (*Autoren*): ~ *Shakespeare* bei Shakespeare; *Richtung*: in (*acc.*, *dat*), auf (*acc.*), zu: *have confidence* ~ Vertrauen haben zu; *Zweck*: in (*dat.*), für, als: ~ *defence of* zur Verteidigung *od.* zum Schutz von; *Material*: in (*dat.*), aus, mit: *dressed* ~ *blue* in Blau (gekleidet); *Zahl*, *Betrag*: in, von, aus, zu: *three* ~ *all* insgesamt *od.* im ganzen drei; *one* ~ *ten* eine(r, -s) von zehn; nach, gemäß: ~ *my opinion* m-r Meinung nach; **2.** *adv.* (dr)innen; hinein, herein; da, (an)gekommen; da, zu Hause; **3.** *adj.* F in (Mode)

in² *nur geschr. Abk. für inch*(es) Zoll *m od. pl.* (*2,54 cm*)

in·a·bil·i·ty [ɪnəˈbɪlɪtɪ] Unfähigkeit *f*
in·ac·ces·si·ble [ɪnækˈsesəbl] unzugänglich, unerreichbar (**to** für *od. dat.*)
in·ac·cu·rate [ɪnˈækjʊrɪt] ungenau
in·ac·tive [ɪnˈæktɪv] untätig; **~·tiv·i·ty** [ɪnækˈtɪvɪtɪ] Untätigkeit *f*
in·ad·e·quate [ɪnˈædɪkwət] unangemessen; unzulänglich, ungenügend
in·ad·mis·si·ble [ɪnədˈmɪsəbl] unzulässig, unstatthaft
in·ad·ver·tent [ɪnədˈvɜːtənt] unbeabsichtigt, versehentlich; **~ly** *a.* aus Versehen
in·an·i·mate [ɪnˈænɪmət] leblos, unbelebt; langweilig
in·ap·pro·pri·ate [ɪnəˈprəʊprɪət] unpassend, ungeeignet (**for**, **to** für)
in·apt [ɪnˈæpt] ungeeignet, unpassend
in·ar·tic·u·late [ɪnɑːˈtɪkjʊlət] unartikuliert, undeutlich (ausgesprochen), unverständlich; unfähig(, deutlich) zu sprechen
in·at·ten·tive [ɪnəˈtentɪv] unaufmerksam
in·au·di·ble [ɪnˈɔːdəbl] unhörbar
in·au·gu·ral [ɪˈnɔːgjʊrəl] Antrittsrede *f*; Antritts...; **~·rate** [ɪˈnɔːgjʊreɪt] *j-n* (feierlich) in (sein Amt) einführen; einweihen, eröffnen; einleiten; **~·ra·tion** [ɪnɔːgjʊˈreɪʃn] Amtseinführung *f*; Einweihung *f*, Eröffnung *f*; Beginn *m*; 2 *Day Am.* Tag *m* der Amtseinführung

des neugewählten Präsidenten der USA (*20. Januar*)
in·born [ɪnˈbɔːn] angeboren
Inc [ɪŋk] *Abk. für Incorporated* (amtlich) eingetragen
in·cal·cu·la·ble [ɪnˈkælkjʊləbl] unberechenbar; unermäßlich
in·can·des·cent [ɪnkænˈdesnt] (weiß-)glühend
in·ca·pa·ble [ɪnˈkeɪpəbl] unfähig (*of* zu *od. gen.*), nicht imstande (*of doing* zu tun)
in·ca·pac·i·tate [ɪnkəˈpæsɪteɪt] unfähig *od.* untauglich machen; **~·ty** [ɪnkə-ˈpæsətɪ] Unfähigkeit *f*, Untauglichkeit *f*
in·car·nate [ɪnˈkɑːnət] leibhaftig; personifiziert
in·cau·tious [ɪnˈkɔːʃəs] unvorsichtig
in·cen·di·a·ry [ɪnˈsendjərɪ] Brand...; *fig.* aufwiegelnd, -hetzend
in·cense¹ [ˈɪnsens] Weihrauch *m*
in·cense² [ɪnˈsens] in Wut bringen, erbosen
in·cen·tive [ɪnˈsentɪv] Ansporn *m*, Anreiz *m*
in·ces·sant [ɪnˈsesnt] ständig, unaufhörlich
in·cest [ˈɪnsest] Inzest *m*, Blutschande *f*
inch [ɪntʃ] **1.** Inch *m* (*2,54 cm*), Zoll *m* (*a. fig.*); *by* ~*es*, ~ *by* ~ allmählich; *every* ~ durch u. durch; **2.** (sich) zentimeterweise *od.* sehr langsam bewegen
in·ci·dence [ˈɪnsɪdəns] Vorkommen *n*, Auftreten *n*; **'~·dent** Vorfall *m*, Ereignis *n*; *pol.* Zwischenfall *m*; **~·den·tal** [ɪnsɪˈdentl] nebensächlich, Neben...; beiläufig; **~·den·tal·ly** nebenbei bemerkt, übrigens
in·cin·e·rate [ɪnˈsɪnəreɪt] verbrennen; **~·ra·tor** Verbrennungsofen *m*; Verbrennungsanlage *f*
in·cise [ɪnˈsaɪz] ein-, aufschneiden; einritzen, -schnitzen; **in·ci·sion** [ɪnˈsɪʒn] (Ein)Schnitt *m*; **in·ci·sive** [ɪnˈsaɪsɪv] schneidend, scharf; *fig.* treffend; **in·ci·sor** [ɪnˈsaɪzə] *anat.* Schneidezahn *m*
in·cite [ɪnˈsaɪt] anstiften; aufwiegeln, -hetzen; **~·ment** Anstiftung *f*; Aufwieg(e)lung *f*, -hetzung *f*
incl *nur geschr. Abk. für including*, *inclusive* einschl., einschließlich
in·clem·ent [ɪnˈklemənt] rauh (*Klima*)
in·cli·na·tion [ɪnklɪˈneɪʃn] Neigung *f* (*a.*

fig.); **in·cline** [ɪnˈklaɪn] **1.** *v/i.* sich neigen (**to, towards** nach); *fig.* neigen (**to, towards** zu); *v/t.* neigen; *fig.* veranlassen; **2.** Gefälle *n*; (Ab)Hang *m*

in·close [ɪnˈkləʊz], **in·clos·ure** [ɪnˈkləʊʒə] → **enclose, enclosure**

in·clude [ɪnˈkluːd] einschließen; aufnehmen (*in* Liste *etc.*); **tax ~d** inklusive Steuer; **in·clud·ing** einschließlich; **in·clu·sion** [ɪnˈkluːʒn] Einschluß *m*, Einbeziehung *f*; **in·clu·sive** [ɪnˈkluːsɪv] einschließlich, inklusive (*of gen.*); **be ~ of** einschließen (*acc.*); Pauschal...

in·co·her·ent [ɪnkəʊˈhɪərənt] (logisch) unzusammenhängend, unklar, unverständlich

in·come *econ.* [ˈɪnkʌm] Einkommen *n*, Einkünfte *pl.*; '**~ tax** *econ.* Einkommensteuer *f*

in·com·ing [ˈɪnkʌmɪŋ] hereinkommend; ankommend; nachfolgend, neu; **~ mail** Posteingang *m*

in·com·mu·ni·ca·tive [ɪnkəˈmjuːnɪkətɪv] nicht mitteilsam, verschlossen

in·com·pa·ra·ble [ɪnˈkɒmpərəbl] unvergleichlich; unvergleichbar

in·com·pat·i·ble [ɪnkəmˈpætəbl] unvereinbar; unverträglich; inkompatibel

in·com·pe·tence [ɪnˈkɒmpɪtəns] Unfähigkeit *f*; Inkompetenz *f*; **~tent** unfähig; nicht fach- *od.* sachkundig; unzuständig, inkompetent

in·com·plete [ɪnkəmˈpliːt] unvollständig; unvollendet

in·com·pre·hen·si·ble [ɪnkɒmprɪˈhensəbl] unbegreiflich, unfaßbar; **~sion** [ɪnkɒmprɪˈhenʃn] Unverständnis *n*

in·con·cei·va·ble [ɪnkənˈsiːvəbl] unbegreiflich, unfaßbar; undenkbar

in·con·clu·sive [ɪnkənˈkluːsɪv] nicht überzeugend; ergebnis-, erfolglos

in·con·gru·ous [ɪnˈkɒŋgruəs] nicht übereinstimmend; unvereinbar

in·con·se·quen·tial [ɪnkɒnsɪˈkwenʃl] unbedeutend

in·con·sid·er·a·ble [ɪnkənˈsɪdərəbl] unbedeutend; **~er·ate** [ɪnkənˈsɪdərət] unüberlegt; rücksichtslos

in·con·sis·tent [ɪnkənˈsɪstənt] unvereinbar; widersprüchlich; inkonsequent

in·con·so·la·ble [ɪnkənˈsəʊləbl] untröstlich

in·con·spic·u·ous [ɪnkənˈspɪkjuəs] unauffällig

in·con·stant [ɪnˈkɒnstənt] unbeständig, wankelmütig

in·con·ti·nent *med.* [ɪnˈkɒntɪnənt] inkontinent

in·con·ve·ni|·ence [ɪnkənˈviːnjəns] **1.** Unbequemlichkeit *f*; Unannehmlichkeit *f*, Ungelegenheit *f*; **2.** *j-m* lästig sein; *j-m* Umstände machen; **~ent** unbequem; ungelegen, lästig

in·cor·po|·rate [ɪnˈkɔːpəreɪt] (sich) vereinigen *od.* zusammenschließen; (mit) einbeziehen; enthalten; einverleiben; *Ort* eingemeinden; *econ., jur.* als (*Am.* Aktien)Gesellschaft eintragen (lassen); **~rat·ed com·pa·ny** *Am.* Aktiengesellschaft *f*; **~ra·tion** [ɪnkɔːpəˈreɪʃn] Vereinigung *f*, Zusammenschluß *m*; Eingliederung *f*; Eingemeindung *f*; *econ., jur.* Eintragung *f* als (*Am.* Aktien)Gesellschaft

in·cor·rect [ɪnkəˈrekt] unrichtig, falsch; inkorrekt

in·cor·ri·gi·ble [ɪnˈkɒrɪdʒəbl] unverbesserlich

in·cor·rup·ti·ble [ɪnkəˈrʌptəbl] unbestechlich

in·crease 1. [ɪnˈkriːs] zunehmen, (an)wachsen; steigen (*Preise*); vergrößern, -mehren, erhöhen; **2.** [ˈɪnkriːs] Vergrößerung *f*, Erhöhung *f*, Zunahme *f*, Zuwachs *m*, (An)Wachsen *n*, Steigerung *f*; **in·creas·ing·ly** [ɪnˈkriːsɪŋlɪ] immer mehr; **~ difficult** immer schwieriger

in·cred·i·ble [ɪnˈkredəbl] unglaublich

in·cre·du·li·ty [ɪnkrɪˈdjuːlətɪ] Ungläubigkeit *f*; **in·cred·u·lous** [ɪnˈkredjʊləs] ungläubig, skeptisch

in·crim·i·nate [ɪnˈkrɪmɪneɪt] *j-n* belasten

in·cu|·bate [ˈɪnkjʊbeɪt] ausbrüten; '**~ba·tor** Brutapparat *m*; *med.* Brutkasten *m*

in·cur [ɪnˈkɜː] (**-rr-**) sich *et.* zuziehen, auf sich laden; *Schulden* machen; *Verluste* erleiden

in·cu·ra·ble [ɪnˈkjʊərəbl] unheilbar

in·cu·ri·ous [ɪnˈkjʊərɪəs] nicht neugierig, gleichgültig, uninteressiert

in·cur·sion [ɪnˈkɜːʃn] (feindlicher) Einfall; Eindringen *n*

in·debt·ed [ɪnˈdetɪd] verschuldet; (zu Dank) verpflichtet

in·de·cent [ɪn'diːsnt] unanständig, anstößig; *jur.* unsittlich, unzüchtig; **~ as·sault** *jur.* Sittlichkeitsverbrechen *n*

in·de·ci·sion [ɪndɪ'sɪʒn] Unentschlossenheit *f*; **~sive** [ɪndɪ'saɪsɪv] unentschlossen, unschlüssig; unentschieden, unbestimmt, ungewiß

in·deed [ɪn'diːd] **1.** *adv.* in der Tat, tatsächlich, wirklich; allerdings; *thank you very much ~!* vielen herzlichen Dank!; **2.** *int.* ach wirklich?

in·de·fat·i·ga·ble [ɪndɪ'fætɪɡəbl] unermüdlich

in·de·fen·si·ble [ɪndɪ'fensəbl] unhaltbar

in·de·fi·na·ble [ɪndɪ'faɪnəbl] undefinierbar, unbestimmbar

in·def·i·nite [ɪn'defɪnət] unbestimmt; unbegrenzt; **~ly** auf unbestimmte Zeit

in·del·i·ble [ɪn'delɪbl] unauslöschlich (*a. fig.*); **~ pencil** Tintenstift *m*

in·del·i·cate [ɪn'delɪkət] taktlos; unfein, anstößig

in·dem·ni·fy [ɪn'demnɪfaɪ] *j-n* entschädigen, *j-m* Schadenersatz leisten (**for** für); **~ty** [ɪn'demnətɪ] Entschädigung *f*

in·dent [ɪn'dent] (ein)kerben, auszacken; *print.* Zeile einrücken

in·de·pen·dence [ɪndɪ'pendəns] Unabhängigkeit *f*; Selbständigkeit *f*; **2 Day** *Am.* Unabhängigkeitstag *m* (*4. Juli*); **~dent** unabhängig; selbständig

in·de·scri·ba·ble [ɪndɪ'skraɪbəbl] unbeschreiblich

in·de·struc·ti·ble [ɪndɪ'strʌktəbl] unzerstörbar; unverwüstlich

in·de·ter·mi·nate [ɪndɪ'tɜːmɪnət] unbestimmt; unklar, vage

in·dex ['ɪndeks] (*pl.* **-dexes, -dices** [-dɪsiːz]) Index *m*, (Inhalts-, Namens-, Stichwort)Verzeichnis *n*, (Sach)Register *n*; (An)Zeichen *n*; *cost of living ~* Lebenshaltungskosten-Index *m*; **'~ card** Karteikarte *f*; **'~ fin·ger** Zeigefinger *m*

In·di·a ['ɪndjə] Indien *n*; **In·di·an** ['ɪndjən] **1.** indisch; indianisch, Indianer...; **2.** Inder(in); *a.* **American ~** Indianer(in)

In·di·an| 'corn *bot.* Mais *m*; **'~ file:** *in ~* im Gänsemarsch; **~ 'sum·mer** Altweiber-, Nachsommer *m*

in·di·a 'rub·ber Gummi *n*, *m*; Radiergummi *m*

in·di·cate ['ɪndɪkeɪt] deuten *od.* zeigen auf (*acc.*); *tech.* anzeigen; *mot.* blinken; *fig.* hinweisen *od.* -deuten auf (*acc.*) andeuten; **~ca·tion** [ɪndɪ'keɪʃn] (An-)Zeichen *n*, Hinweis *m*, Andeutung *f* Indiz *n*; **in·dic·a·tive** [ɪn'dɪkətɪv] *a.* **~ mood** *gr.* Indikativ *m*; **~ca·tor** ['ɪndɪkeɪtə] *tech.* Anzeiger *m*; *mot.* Richtungsanzeiger *m*, Blinker *m*

in·di·ces ['ɪndɪsiːz] *pl. von* **index**

in·dict *jur.* [ɪn'daɪt] anklagen (**for** wegen); **~ment** Anklage *f*

in·dif·fer·ence [ɪn'dɪfrəns] Gleichgültigkeit *f*; **~ent** gleichgültig (**to** gegen); mittelmäßig

in·di·gent ['ɪndɪdʒənt] arm

in·di·ges|ti·ble [ɪndɪ'dʒestəbl] unverdaulich; **~tion** [ɪndɪ'dʒestʃən] Verdauungsstörung *f*, Magenverstimmung *f*

in·dig·nant [ɪn'dɪɡnənt] entrüstet, empört, ungehalten (**about, at, over** über *acc.*); **~na·tion** [ɪndɪɡ'neɪʃn] Entrüstung *f*, Empörung *f* (**about, at, over** über *acc.*); **~ni·ty** [ɪn'dɪɡnətɪ] Demütigung *f*, unwürdige Behandlung

in·di·rect [ɪndɪ'rekt] indirekt; *by ~ means* *fig.* auf Umwegen

in·dis·creet [ɪndɪ'skriːt] unbesonnen, unbedacht; indiskret; **~cre·tion** [ɪndɪ'skreʃn] Unbesonnenheit *f*; Indiskretion *f*

in·dis·crim·i·nate [ɪndɪ'skrɪmɪnət] kritiklos; wahllos

in·dis·pen·sa·ble [ɪndɪ'spensəbl] unentbehrlich, unerläßlich

in·dis·posed [ɪndɪ'spəʊzd] indisponiert, unpäßlich; abgeneigt; **~po·si·tion** [ɪndɪspə'zɪʃn] Unpäßlichkeit *f*; Abneigung *f* (**to do** zu tun)

in·dis·pu·ta·ble [ɪndɪ'spjuːtəbl] unbestreitbar, unstreitig

in·dis·tinct [ɪndɪ'stɪŋkt] undeutlich; unklar, verschwommen

in·dis·tin·guish·a·ble [ɪndɪ'stɪŋɡwɪʃəbl] nicht zu unterscheiden(d) (**from** von)

in·di·vid·u·al [ɪndɪ'vɪdjʊəl] **1.** individuell, einzeln, Einzel...; individuell, persönlich; **2.** Individuum *n*, einzelne(r *m*) *f*; **~is·m** [ɪndɪ'vɪdjʊəlɪzm] Individualismus *m*; **~ist** [ɪndɪ'vɪdjʊəlɪst] Individualist(in); **~i·ty** [ɪndɪvɪdjʊ'ælətɪ] Individualität *f*, (persönliche) Note; **~ly** [ɪndɪ'vɪdjʊəlɪ] einzeln, jede(r, -s) für sich; individuell

in·di·vis·i·ble [ɪndɪ'vɪzəbl] unteilbar

in·dom·i·ta·ble [ɪn'dɒmɪtəbl] unbezähmbar, nicht unterzukriegen(d)

in·door ['ɪndɔ:] Haus..., Zimmer..., Innen..., *Sport*: Hallen...; **~s** [ɪn'dɔ:z] im Haus, drinnen; ins Haus (hinein); *Sport*: in der Halle

in·dorse [ɪn'dɔ:s] → **endorse** etc.

in·duce [ɪn'dju:s] *j-n* veranlassen; verursachen, bewirken; **~ment** Anreiz *m*

in·duct [ɪn'dʌkt] einführen, -setzen; **in·duc·tion** [ɪn'dʌkʃn] Herbeiführung *f*; Einführung *f*, Einsetzung *f (in ein Amt etc.)*; *electr.* Induktion *f*

in·dulge [ɪn'dʌldʒ] nachsichtig sein gegen; *e-r Neigung etc.* nachgeben; **~ in s.th.** sich *et.* gönnen *od.* leisten; **in·dul·gence** [ɪn'dʌldʒəns] Nachsicht *f*; Schwäche *f*, Leidenschaft *f*, Luxus *m*; **in·dul·gent** nachsichtig, -gebig

in·dus·tri·al [ɪn'dʌstrɪəl] industriell, Industrie..., Gewerbe..., Betriebs...; **~'ar·e·a** Industriegebiet *n*; **~ist** *econ.* [ɪn'dʌstrɪəlɪst] Industrielle(r *m*) *f*; **~ize** *econ.* [ɪn'dʌstrɪəlaɪz] industrialisieren

in·dus·tri·ous [ɪn'dʌstrɪəs] fleißig; △ *nicht Industrie...*

in·dus·try ['ɪndəstrɪ] *econ.* Industrie (-zweig *m*) *f*; Gewerbe(zweig *m*) *n*; Fleiß *m*

in·ed·i·ble [ɪn'edɪbl] ungenießbar, nicht eßbar

in·ef·fec·tive [ɪnɪ'fektɪv], **~tu·al** [ɪnɪ'fektʃʊəl] unwirksam, wirkungslos; unfähig, untauglich

in·ef·fi·cient [ɪnɪ'fɪʃnt] ineffizient; unfähig, untauglich; unrationell, unwirtschaftlich

in·el·e·gant [ɪn'elɪgənt] unelegant

in·el·i·gi·ble [ɪn'elɪdʒəbl] nicht berechtigt

in·ept [ɪ'nept] unpassend; ungeschickt; albern, töricht

in·e·qual·i·ty [ɪnɪ'kwɒlətɪ] Ungleichheit *f*

in·ert [ɪ'nɜ:t] *phys.* träge *(a. fig.)*; - inaktiv; **in·er·tia** [ɪ'nɜ:ʃə] Trägheit *f (a. fig.)*

in·es·ca·pa·ble [ɪnɪ'skeɪpəbl] unvermeidlich

in·es·sen·tial [ɪnɪ'senʃl] unwesentlich, unwichtig **(to** für)

in·es·ti·ma·ble [ɪn'estɪməbl] unschätzbar

in·ev·i·ta·ble [ɪn'evɪtəbl] unvermeidlich; zwangsläufig

in·ex·act [ɪnɪg'zækt] ungenau

in·ex·cu·sa·ble [ɪnɪ'skju:zəbl] unverzeihlich, unentschuldbar

in·ex·haus·ti·ble [ɪnɪg'zɔ:stəbl] unerschöpflich; unermüdlich

in·ex·o·ra·ble [ɪn'eksərəbl] unerbittlich

in·ex·pe·di·ent [ɪnɪk'spi:dɪənt] unzweckmäßig; nicht ratsam

in·ex·pen·sive [ɪnɪk'spensɪv] nicht teuer, billig, preiswert

in·ex·pe·ri·ence [ɪnɪk'spɪərɪəns] Unerfahrenheit *f*; **~d** unerfahren

in·ex·pert [ɪn'ekspɜ:t] unerfahren; ungeschickt

in·ex·plic·a·ble [ɪnɪk'splɪkəbl] unerklärlich

in·ex·pres·si·ble [ɪnɪk'spresəbl] unaussprechlich, unbeschreiblich; **~sive** [ɪnɪk'spresɪv] ausdruckslos

in·ex·tri·ca·ble [ɪn'ekstrɪkəbl] unentwirrbar

in·fal·li·ble [ɪn'fæləbl] unfehlbar

in·fa·mous ['ɪnfəməs] berüchtigt; schändlich, niederträchtig; **~my** Ehrlosigkeit *f*; Schande *f*; Niedertracht *f*

in·fan·cy ['ɪnfənsɪ] frühe Kindheit; **in its ~** *fig.* in den Anfängen *od.* Kinderschuhen steckend; **~t** Säugling *m*; kleines Kind, Kleinkind *n*

in·fan·tile ['ɪnfəntaɪl] kindlich; Kindes..., Kinder...; infantil, kindisch

in·fan·try *mil.* ['ɪnfəntrɪ] Infanterie *f*

in·fat·u·at·ed [ɪn'fætjʊeɪtɪd] vernarrt **(with** in *acc.*)

in·fect [ɪn'fekt] *med. j-n, et.* infizieren, *j-n* anstecken *(a. fig.)*; verseuchen, -unreinigen; **in·fec·tion** [ɪn'fekʃn] *med.* Infektion *f*, Ansteckung *f (a. fig.)*; **in·fec·tious** [ɪn'fekʃəs] *med.* infektiös, ansteckend *(a. fig.)*

in·fer [ɪn'fɜ:] **(-rr-)** folgern, schließen **(from** aus); **~ence** ['ɪnfərəns] (Schluß)Folgerung *f*, (Rück)Schluß *m*

in·fe·ri·or [ɪn'fɪərɪə] **1.** untergeordnet **(to** *dat.*), niedriger **(to** als); weniger wert **(to** als); minderwertig; **be ~ to s.o.** *j-m* untergeordnet sein; *j-m* unterlegen sein; **2.** Untergebene(r *m*) *f*; **~i·ty** [ɪnfɪərɪ'ɒrətɪ] Unterlegenheit *f*; Minderwertigkeit *f*; **~i·ty com·plex** *psych.* Minderwertigkeitskomplex *m*

in·fer·nal [ɪn'fɜ:nl] höllisch, Höllen...;

~no [ɪnˈfɜːnəʊ] (*pl.* **-nos**) Inferno *n*, Hölle *f*

in·fer·tile [ɪnˈfɜːtaɪl] unfruchtbar

in·fest [ɪnˈfest] verseuchen, befallen; *fig.* überschwemmen (**with** mit)

in·fi·del·i·ty [ɪnfɪˈdelətɪ] (*bsd.* eheliche) Untreue

in·fil·trate [ˈɪnfɪltreɪt] einsickern in (*acc.*); einschleusen (**into** in *acc.*); *pol.* unterwandern

in·fi·nite [ˈɪnfɪnət] unendlich

in·fin·i·tive [ɪnˈfɪnətɪv] *a.* **~ mood** *gr.* Infinitiv *m*, Nennform *f*

in·fin·i·ty [ɪnˈfɪnətɪ] Unendlichkeit *f*

in·firm [ɪnˈfɜːm] schwach, gebrechlich; **in·fir·ma·ry** [ɪnˈfɜːmərɪ] Krankenhaus *n*; *Schule etc.*: Krankenzimmer *n*; **in·fir·mi·ty** [ɪnˈfɜːmətɪ] Schwäche *f*, Gebrechlichkeit *f*

in·flame [ɪnˈfleɪm] entflammen (*mst fig.*); erregen; **become ~d** *med.* sich entzünden

in·flam·ma·ble [ɪnˈflæməbl] brennbar, leicht entzündlich; feuergefährlich; **~·tion** [ɪnfləˈmeɪʃn] Entzündung *f*; **~·to·ry** [ɪnˈflæmətərɪ] *med.* entzündlich; *fig.* aufrührerisch, Hetz...

in·flate [ɪnˈfleɪt] aufpumpen, -blasen, -blähen (*a. fig.*); *econ.* Preise etc. in die Höhe treiben; **in·fla·tion** *econ.* [ɪnˈfleɪʃn] Inflation *f*

in·flect *gr.* [ɪnˈflekt] flektieren, beugen; **in·flec·tion** *gr.* [ɪnˈflekʃn] Flexion *f*, Beugung *f*

in·flex·i·ble [ɪnˈfleksəbl] unbiegsam, starr (*a. fig.*); *fig.* inflexibel, unbeweglich; **~·ion** *Brt. gr.* [ɪnˈflekʃn] → *inflection*

in·flict [ɪnˈflɪkt] (**on**) *Leid, Schaden etc.* zufügen (*dat.*); *Wunde etc.* beibringen (*dat.*); *Strafe* auferlegen (*dat.*), verhängen (über *acc.*); aufbürden, -drängen (*dat.*); **in·flic·tion** [ɪnˈflɪkʃn] Zufügung *f*; Verhängung *f* (*e-r Strafe*); Plage *f*

in·flu·ence [ˈɪnfluəns] **1.** Einfluß *m*; **2.** beeinflussen; **~·en·tial** [ɪnfluˈenʃl] einflußreich

in·flux [ˈɪnflʌks] Zustrom *m*, Zufluß *m*, (*Waren*)Zufuhr *f*

in·form [ɪnˈfɔːm] benachrichtigen, unterrichten (**of** von), informieren (**of** über *acc.*); **~ against** *od.* **on s.o.** j-n anzeigen; j-n denunzieren

in·for·mal [ɪnˈfɔːml] formlos, zwanglos;

~·i·ty [ɪnfɔːˈmælətɪ] Formlosigkeit *f*; Ungezwungenheit *f*

in·for·ma·tion [ɪnfəˈmeɪʃn] Auskunft *f*, Information *f*; Nachricht *f*; **~·tion (su·per·)'high·way** *Computer*: Datenautobahn *f*; **~·tive** [ɪnˈfɔːmətɪv] informativ; lehrreich; mitteilsam

in·form·er [ɪnˈfɔːmə] Denunziant(in); Spitzel *m*

in·fra·struc·ture [ˈɪnfrəstrʌktʃə] Infrastruktur *f*

in·fre·quent [ɪnˈfriːkwənt] selten

in·fringe [ɪnˈfrɪndʒ]: **~ on** *Rechte, Vertrag etc.* verletzen, verstoßen gegen

in·fu·ri·ate [ɪnˈfjʊərɪeɪt] wütend machen

in·fuse [ɪnˈfjuːz] *Tee* aufgießen; **in·fu·sion** [ɪnˈfjuːʒn] Aufguß *m*; *med.* Infusion *f*

in·ge·ni·ous [ɪnˈdʒiːnjəs] genial; einfallsreich; raffiniert; **~·nu·i·ty** [ɪndʒɪˈnjuːətɪ] Genialität *f*; Einfallsreichtum *m*

in·gen·u·ous [ɪnˈdʒenjuəs] offen, aufrichtig; naiv

in·got [ˈɪŋɡət] (*Gold- etc.*)Barren *m*

in·gra·ti·ate [ɪnˈɡreɪʃɪeɪt]: **~ o.s. with s.o.** sich bei j-m beliebt machen

in·grat·i·tude [ɪnˈɡrætɪtjuːd] Undankbarkeit *f*

in·gre·di·ent [ɪnˈɡriːdjənt] Bestandteil *m*; *gastr.* Zutat *f*

in·grow·ing [ˈɪnɡrəʊɪŋ] nach innen wachsend; eingewachsen

in·hab·it [ɪnˈhæbɪt] bewohnen, leben in (*dat.*); **~·it·a·ble** bewohnbar; **~·i·tant** Bewohner(in); Einwohner(in)

in·hale [ɪnˈheɪl] einatmen, *med. a.* inhalieren

in·her·ent [ɪnˈhɪərənt] innewohnend, eigen (**in** *dat.*)

in·her·it [ɪnˈherɪt] erben; **~·i·tance** Erbe *n*

in·hib·it [ɪnˈhɪbɪt] hemmen (*a. psych.*), (ver)hindern; **~ed** *psych.* gehemmt; **in·hi·bi·tion** *psych.* [ɪnhɪˈbɪʃn] Hemmung *f*

in·hos·pi·ta·ble [ɪnˈhɒspɪtəbl] ungastlich; unwirtlich (*Gegend etc.*)

in·hu·man [ɪnˈhjuːmən] unmenschlich; **~e** [ɪnhjuːˈmeɪn] inhuman, menschenunwürdig

in·im·i·cal [ɪˈnɪmɪkl] feindselig (**to** gegen); nachteilig (**to** für)

in·im·i·ta·ble [ɪˈnɪmɪtəbl] unnachahmlich

i·ni|·tial [ɪ'nɪʃl] **1.** anfänglich, Anfangs...; **2.** Initiale *f*, (großer) Anfangsbuchstabe; **~·tial·ly** [ɪ'nɪʃəlɪ] am *od.* zu Anfang, anfänglich; **~·ti·ate** [ɪ'nɪʃɪeɪt] in die Wege leiten, ins Leben rufen; einführen; **~·ti·a·tion** [ɪnɪʃɪ'eɪʃn] Einführung *f*; **~·tia·tive** [ɪ'nɪʃɪətɪv] Initiative *f*, erster Schritt; **take the ~** die Initiative ergreifen; **on one's own ~** aus eigenem Antrieb

in·ject *med.* [ɪn'dʒekt] injizieren, einspritzen; **in·jec·tion** *med.* [ɪn'dʒekʃn] Injektion *f*, Spritze *f*

in·ju·di·cious [ɪndʒuː'dɪʃəs] unklug, unüberlegt

in·junc·tion *jur.* [ɪn'dʒʌŋkʃn] gerichtliche Verfügung

in·jure ['ɪndʒə] verletzen, -wunden; schaden (*dat.*); kränken; **'~d 1.** verletzt; **2. the ~** *pl.* die Verletzten *pl.*; **in·ju·ri·ous** [ɪn'dʒʊərɪəs] schädlich; **be ~ to** schaden (*dat.*); **~ to health** gesundheitsschädlich; **in·ju·ry** ['ɪndʒərɪ] *med.* Verletzung *f*; Kränkung *f*; **'in·ju·ry time** *Brt. bsd.* Fußball: Nachspielzeit *f*

in·jus·tice [ɪn'dʒʌstɪs] Ungerechtigkeit *f*; Unrecht *n*; **do s.o. an ~** j-m unrecht tun

ink [ɪŋk] Tinte *f*

ink·ling ['ɪŋklɪŋ] Andeutung *f*; dunkle *od.* leise Ahnung

'ink|·pad Stempelkissen *n*; **'~·y** (**-ier, -iest**) voller Tinte, Tinten...; tinten-, pechschwarz

in·laid ['ɪnleɪd] eingelegt, Einlege...; **~ work** Einlegearbeit *f*

in·land 1. *adj.* ['ɪnlənd] inländisch, einheimisch; Binnen...; **2.** *adv.* [ɪn'lænd] landeinwärts; **2 'Rev·e·nue** *Brt.* Finanzamt *n*

in·lay ['ɪnleɪ] Einlegearbeit *f*; (Zahn-) Füllung *f*, Plombe *f*

in·let ['ɪnlet] schmale Bucht; *tech.* Eingang *m*, -laß *m*

in·mate ['ɪnmeɪt] Insass|e *m*, -in *f*; Mitbewohner(in)

in·most ['ɪnməʊst] innerste(r, -s) (*a. fig.*)

inn [ɪn] Gasthaus *n*, Wirtshaus *n*

in·nate [ɪ'neɪt] angeboren

in·ner ['ɪnə] innere(r, -s); Innen...; verborgen; **'~·most → inmost**

in·nings ['ɪnɪŋz] (*pl.* **innings**) *Kricket, Baseball:* Spielzeit *f* (*e-s Spielers od. e-r Mannschaft*)

'inn·keep·er Gastwirt(in)

in·no·cence ['ɪnəsns] Unschuld *f*; Harmlosigkeit *f*; Naivität *f*; **'~·cent** unschuldig; harmlos; arglos, naiv

in·noc·u·ous [ɪ'nɒkjʊəs] harmlos

in·no·va·tion [ɪnəʊ'veɪʃn] Neuerung *f*

in·nu·en·do [ɪnjuː'endəʊ] (*pl.* **-does, -dos**) (versteckte) Andeutung

in·nu·me·ra·ble [ɪ'njuːmərəbl] unzählig, zahllos

i·noc·u|·late *med.* [ɪ'nɒkjʊleɪt] impfen; **~·la·tion** *med.* [nɒkjʊ'leɪʃn] Impfung *f*

in·of·fen·sive [ɪnə'fensɪv] harmlos

in·op·e·ra·ble [ɪn'ɒpərəbl] *med.* inoperabel, nicht operierbar; undurchführbar (*Plan etc.*)

in·op·por·tune [ɪn'ɒpətjuːn] inopportun, unangebracht, ungelegen

in·or·di·nate [ɪ'nɔːdɪnət] unmäßig

'in·pa·tient *med.* stationärer Patient, stationäre Patientin

in·put ['ɪnpʊt] Input *m, n; Computer: a.* (Daten)Eingabe *f*; *a.* Energiezufuhr *f*; *a.* (Arbeits)Aufwand *m*

in·quest *jur.* ['ɪnkwest] gerichtliche Untersuchung; **→ coroner's inquest**

in·quire [ɪn'kwaɪə] fragen *od.* sich erkundigen (nach); **~ into** *od.* untersuchen, prüfen; **in·quir·ing** [ɪn'kwaɪrɪŋ] forschend; wißbegierig; **in·quir·y** [ɪn'kwaɪrɪ] Erkundigung *f*, Nachfrage *f*; Untersuchung *f*; Ermittlung *f*; **make inquiries** Erkundigungen einziehen

in·qui·si·tion [ɪnkwɪ'zɪʃn] (amtliche) Untersuchung; **2 *rel. hist.*** Inquisition *f*; **in·quis·i·tive** [ɪn'kwɪzətɪv] neugierig, wißbegierig

in·roads *fig.* ['ɪnrəʊdz] (**in, into, on**) Eingriff *m* (**in** *acc.*), Übergriff *m* (**auf** *acc.*); **make ~ into s.o.'s savings** ein großes Loch in j-s Ersparnisse reißen

in·sane [ɪn'seɪn] geisteskrank, wahnsinnig

in·san·i·ta·ry [ɪn'sænɪtərɪ] unhygienisch

in·san·i·ty [ɪn'sænətɪ] Geisteskrankheit *f*, Wahnsinn *m*

in·sa·tia·ble [ɪn'seɪʃjəbl] unersättlich

in·scrip·tion [ɪn'skrɪpʃn] In-, Aufschrift *f*; Widmung *f*

in·scru·ta·ble [ɪn'skruːtəbl] unerforschlich, unergründlich

in·sect *zo.* ['ɪnsekt] Insekt *n*; **in·sec·ti·cide** [ɪn'sektɪsaɪd] Insektenvertilgungsmittel *n*, Insektizid *n*

I

in·se·cure [ɪnsɪˈkjʊə] unsicher; nicht sicher *od.* fest

in·sen·si·ble [ɪnˈsensəbl] unempfindlich (**to** gegen); bewußtlos; unempfänglich (**of, to** für), gleichgültig (**of, to** gegen); unmerklich

in·sen·si·tive [ɪnˈsensətɪv] unempfindlich (**to** gegen); unempfänglich (**of, to** für), gleichgültig (**of, to** gegen)

in·sep·a·ra·ble [ɪnˈsepərəbl] untrennbar; unzertrennlich

in·sert 1. [ɪnˈsɜːt] einfügen, -setzen, -führen, (hinein)stecken, *Münze* einwerfen; inserieren; **2.** [ˈɪnsɜːt] (Zeitungs)Beilage *f*, (Buch)Einlage *f*; **in·ser·tion** [ɪnˈsɜːʃn] Einfügen *n*, -setzen *n*, -führen *n*, Hineinstecken *n*; Einfügung *f*; Einwurf *m* (*e-r Münze*); Anzeige *f*, Inserat *n*; **~ key** *Computer*: Einfügetaste *f*

in·shore [ɪnˈʃɔː] an *od.* nahe der Küste; Küsten...

in·side 1. [ɪnˈsaɪd] Innenseite *f*; *das* Innere; *turn* ~ *out* umkrempeln; auf den Kopf stellen; **2.** *adj.* [ˈɪnsaɪd] innere(r, -s), Innen...; Insider...; **3.** *adv.* [ɪnˈsaɪd] im Inner(e)n, (dr)innen; ~ *of* F *zeitlich*: innerhalb (*gen.*); **4.** *prp.* [ɪnˈsaɪd] innerhalb, im Inner(e)n; **in·sid·er** [ɪnˈsaɪdə] Insider(in), Eingeweihte(r *m*) *f*

in·sid·i·ous [ɪnˈsɪdɪəs] heimtückisch

in·sight [ˈɪnsaɪt] Einsicht *f*, Einblick *m*; Verständnis *n*

in·sig·ni·a [ɪnˈsɪɡnɪə] *pl.* Insignien *pl.*; Abzeichen *pl.*

in·sig·nif·i·cant [ɪnsɪɡˈnɪfɪkənt] bedeutungslos; unbedeutend

in·sin·cere [ɪnsɪnˈsɪə] unaufrichtig

in·sin·u·ate [ɪnˈsɪnjʊeɪt] andeuten, anspielen auf (*acc.*); **~·a·tion** [ɪnsɪnjʊˈeɪʃn] Anspielung *f*, Andeutung *f*

in·sip·id [ɪnˈsɪpɪd] geschmacklos, fad

in·sist [ɪnˈsɪst] bestehen, beharren (**on** auf *dat.*); **in·sis·tence** [ɪnˈsɪstəns] Bestehen *n*, Beharren *f*; Beharrlichkeit *f*; **in·sis·tent** beharrlich, hartnäckig

in·sole [ˈɪnsəʊl] Einlegesohle *f*; Brandsohle *f*

in·so·lent [ˈɪnsələnt] unverschämt

in·sol·u·ble [ɪnˈsɒljʊbl] unlöslich; unlösbar (*Problem etc.*)

in·sol·vent [ɪnˈsɒlvənt] zahlungsunfähig, insolvent

in·som·ni·a [ɪnˈsɒmnɪə] Schlaflosigkeit *f*

in·spect [ɪnˈspekt] untersuchen, prüfen, nachsehen; besichtigen, inspizieren; **in·spec·tion** [ɪnˈspekʃn] Prüfung *f*, Untersuchung *f*, Kontrolle *f*; Inspektion *f*; **in·spec·tor** Aufsichtsbeamte(r) *m*, Inspektor *m*; (Polizei)Inspektor *m*, (-)Kommissar *m*

in·spi·ra·tion [ɪnspəˈreɪʃn] Inspiration *f*, (plötzlicher) Einfall; **in·spire** [ɪnˈspaɪə] inspirieren, anregen; *Gefühl etc.* auslösen

in·stall [ɪnˈstɔːl] *tech.* installieren, einrichten, aufstellen, einbauen, *Leitung* legen; *in ein Amt etc.* einsetzen; **in·stal·la·tion** [ɪnstəˈleɪʃn] *tech.* Installation *f*, Einrichtung *f*, -bau *m*; *tech.* fertige Anlage; Einsetzung *f*, -führung *f* (*in ein Amt*)

in·stal·ment *Brt.*, **in·stall·ment** *Am.* [ɪnˈstɔːlmənt] *econ.* Rate *f*; (Teil)Lieferung *f* (*e-s Buches etc.*); Fortsetzung *f* (*e-s Romans etc.*); *Rundfunk, TV*: Folge *f*

in·stall·ment plan *Am.*: **buy on the** ~ auf Abzahlung *od.* Raten kaufen

in·stance [ˈɪnstəns] Beispiel *n*; (besonderer) Fall; *jur.* Instanz *f*; **for** ~ zum Beispiel

in·stant [ˈɪnstənt] **1.** Moment *m*, Augenblick *m*; **2.** sofortig, augenblicklich; **in·stan·ta·ne·ous** [ɪnstənˈteɪnjəs] sofortig, augenblicklich; ~ **'cam·e·ra** *phot.* Sofortbildkamera *f*; ~ **'cof·fee** Pulver-, Instantkaffee *m*; **~·ly** sofort, unverzüglich

in·stead [ɪnˈsted] statt dessen, dafür; ~ **of** an Stelle von, (an)statt

'in·step *anat.* Spann *m*, Rist *m*

in·sti·gate [ˈɪnstɪɡeɪt] anstiften; aufhetzen; veranlassen; **~·ga·tor** Anstifter(in); (Auf)Hetzer(in)

in·still *Brt.*, **in·still** *Am.* [ɪnˈstɪl] (*-ll-*) beibringen, einflößen (**into** *dat.*)

in·stinct [ˈɪnstɪŋkt] Instinkt *m*; **in·stinc·tive** [ɪnˈstɪŋktɪv] instinktiv

in·sti·tute [ˈɪnstɪtjuːt] Institut *n*; **~·tu·tion** [ɪnstɪˈtjuːʃn] Institution *f*, Einrichtung *f*; Institut *n*; Anstalt *f*

in·struct [ɪnˈstrʌkt] unterrichten; ausbilden, schulen; informieren; anweisen; **in·struc·tion** [ɪnˈstrʌkʃn] Unterricht *m*; Ausbildung *f*, Schulung *f*; Anweisung *f*, Instruktion *f*, *Computer*: Befehl *m*; **~s** *pl.* **for use** Gebrauchsanweisung f; *operating* ~s pl. Bedienungsanleitung f; **in·stru·ctive** [ɪnˈstrʌktɪv] instruktiv, lehrreich; **in·struc·tor** Lehrer m; Ausbilder m; **in·struc·tress** Lehrerin f; Ausbilderin f

in·stru·ment [ˈɪnstrʊmənt] Instrument n; Werkzeug n (a. *fig.*); ~**·men·tal** [ɪnstrʊˈmentl] *mus.* Instrumental...; behilflich; *be* ~ *in* beitragen zu

in·sub·or·di·nate [ɪnsəˈbɔːdənət] aufsässig; ~**·na·tion** [ɪnsəbɔːdɪˈneɪʃn] Auflehnung f, Aufsässigkeit f

in·suf·fe·ra·ble [ɪnˈsʌfərəbl] unerträglich, unausstehlich

in·suf·fi·cient [ɪnsəˈfɪʃnt] unzulänglich, ungenügend

in·su·lar [ˈɪnsjʊlə] Insel...; *fig.* engstirnig

in·su·late [ˈɪnsjʊleɪt] isolieren; ~**·la·tion** [ɪnsjʊˈleɪʃn] Isolierung f; Isoliermaterial n

in·sult 1. [ˈɪnsʌlt] Beleidigung f; **2.** [ɪnˈsʌlt] beleidigen

in·sur·ance [ɪnˈʃɔːrəns] Versicherung f; Versicherungssumme f; (Ab)Sicherung f (*against* gegen); ~ **com·pa·ny** Versicherungsgesellschaft f; ~ **pol·i·cy** Versicherungspolice f; ~**e** [ɪnˈʃɔː] Versichern (*against* gegen); ~**ed:** *the* ~ der od. die Versicherte

in·sur·gent [ɪnˈsɜːdʒənt] **1.** aufständisch; **2.** Aufständische(r m) f

in·sur·moun·ta·ble *fig.* [ɪnsəˈmaʊntəbl] unüberwindlich

in·sur·rec·tion [ɪnsəˈrekʃn] Aufstand m

in·tact [ɪnˈtækt] intakt, unversehrt, unbeschädigt, ganz

'in·take *tech.* Einlaß(öffnung f) m; (Nahrungs- etc.)Aufnahme f; (Neu-)Aufnahme(n pl.) f, (Neu)Zugänge pl.

in·te·gral [ˈɪntɪɡrəl] ganz, vollständig; wesentlich

in·te·grate [ˈɪntɪɡreɪt] (sich) integrieren; zusammenschließen; eingliedern, -beziehen; ~**d circuit** *electr.* integrierter Schaltkreis; ~**gra·tion** [ɪntɪˈɡreɪʃn] Integration f

in·teg·ri·ty [ɪnˈteɡrətɪ] Integrität f; Vollständigkeit f; Einheit f

in·tel·lect [ˈɪntəlekt] Intellekt m, Verstand m; ~**·lec·tual** [ɪntəˈlektjʊəl] **1.** intellektuell, Verstandes..., geistig; **2.** Intellektuelle(r m) f

in·tel·li·gence [ɪnˈtelɪdʒəns] Intelligenz f; nachrichtendienstliche Informationen pl.; ~**gent** intelligent, klug

in·tel·li·gi·ble [ɪnˈtelɪdʒəbl] verständlich (*to* für)

in·tem·per·ate [ɪnˈtempərət] unmäßig

in·tend [ɪnˈtend] beabsichtigen, vorhaben, planen; ~**ed for** bestimmt für od. zu

in·tense [ɪnˈtens] intensiv, stark, heftig

in·ten·si·fy [ɪnˈtensɪfaɪ] intensivieren; (sich) verstärken; ~**ty** [ɪnˈtensətɪ] Intensität f

in·ten·sive [ɪnˈtensɪv] intensiv, gründlich; ~ **care u·nit** *med.* Intensivstation f

in·tent [ɪnˈtent] **1.** gespannt, aufmerksam; ~ *on* fest entschlossen zu (*dat.*); konzentriert auf (*acc.*); **2.** Absicht f, Vorhaben n; **in·ten·tion** [ɪnˈtenʃn] Absicht f; *jur.* Vorsatz m; **in·ten·tion·al** [ɪnˈtenʃənl] absichtlich, vorsätzlich

in·ter [ɪnˈtɜː] (**-rr-**) bestatten

in·ter... [ˈɪntə] zwischen, Zwischen...; gegenseitig, einander

in·ter·act [ɪntərˈækt] aufeinander (ein)wirken, sich gegenseitig beeinflussen

in·ter·cede [ɪntəˈsiːd] vermitteln, sich einsetzen (*with* bei; *for* für)

in·ter·cept [ɪntəˈsept] abfangen; ~**·cep·tion** [ɪntəˈsepʃn] Abfangen n

in·ter·ces·sion [ɪntəˈseʃn] Fürsprache f

in·ter·change 1. [ɪntəˈtʃeɪndʒ] austauschen; **2.** [ˈɪntətʃeɪndʒ] Austausch m; *mot.* Autobahnkreuz n

in·ter·com [ˈɪntəkɒm] Sprechanlage f

in·ter·course [ˈɪntəkɔːs] Verkehr m; *a.* **sexual** ~ (Geschlechts)Verkehr m

in·ter·est [ˈɪntrɪst] **1.** Interesse n (*in* an dat., für); Wichtigkeit f, Bedeutung f; Vorteil m, Nutzen m; *econ.* Anteil m, Beteiligung f; *econ.* Zins(en pl.) m; *take* **an** ~ *in* sich interessieren für; **2.** interessieren (*in* für et.); **'~ed** interessiert (*in* an); *be* ~ *in* sich interessieren für; **'~ing** interessant; **'~ rate** *econ.* Zinssatz m

in·ter·face [ˈɪntəfeɪs] *Computer:* Schnittstelle f

in·ter·fere [ɪntəˈfɪə] sich einmischen (*with* in acc.); stören; ~**·fer·ence** [ɪntəˈfɪərəns] Einmischung f; Störung f

in·te·ri·or [ɪnˈtɪərɪə] **1.** innere(r, -s), Innen...; Binnen...; Inlands...; **2.** *das* In-

nere; Interieur n; *pol.* innere Angelegenheiten *pl.*; → **Department of the** ♀;
~ **'dec·o·ra·tor** Innenarchitekt(in)

in·ter|·ject [ɪntəˈdʒekt] *Bemerkung* ein-
werfen; **~·jec·tion** [ɪntəˈdʒekʃn] Einwurf m; Ausruf m; *ling.* Interjektion f

in·ter·lace [ɪntəˈleɪs] (sich) (ineinander)
verflechten

in·ter·lock [ɪntəˈlɒk] ineinandergreifen;
(miteinander) verzahnen

in·ter·lop·er [ˈɪntələʊpə] Eindringling m

in·ter·lude [ˈɪntəluːd] Zwischenspiel n;
Pause f; **~s of bright weather** zeitweilig
schön

in·ter·me·di|·a·ry [ɪntəˈmiːdjərɪ] Ver-
mittler(in), Mittelsmann m; **~·ate**
[ɪntəˈmiːdjət] in der Mitte liegend, Mittel..., Zwischen...; *ped.* für fortgeschrit-
tene Anfänger

in·ter·ment [ɪnˈtɜːmənt] Beerdigung f,
Bestattung f

in·ter·mi·na·ble [ɪnˈtɜːmɪnəbl] endlos

in·ter·mis·sion [ɪntəˈmɪʃn] Unterbrechung f; *bsd. Am. thea. etc.*: Pause f

in·ter·mit·tent [ɪntəˈmɪtənt] mit Unter-
brechungen, periodisch (auftretend); ~
fever med. Wechselfieber n

in·tern¹ [ɪnˈtɜːn] internieren

in·tern² *Am.* [ˈɪntɜːn] Assistenzarzt m,
-ärztin f

in·ter·nal [ɪnˈtɜːnl] innere(r, -s); einheimisch, Inlands...; **~·com'bus·tion
en·gine** Verbrennungsmotor m

in·ter·na·tion·al [ɪntəˈnæʃənl] 1. international; Auslands...; 2. *Sport:* Interna-
tionale m, f, Nationalspieler(in); internationaler Wettkampf; Länderspiel
n; ~ **'call** *tel.* Auslandsgespräch n; ~
'law *jur.* Völkerrecht n

in·ter|·pret [ɪnˈtɜːprɪt] interpretieren,
auslegen, erklären; dolmetschen;
~·pre·ta·tion [ɪntɜːprɪˈteɪʃn] Interpretation f, Auslegung f; **~·pret·er**
[ɪnˈtɜːprɪtə] Dolmetscher(in)

in·ter·ro·gate [ɪnˈterəgeɪt] verhören,
-nehmen; (be)fragen; **~·ga·tion**
[ɪnterəˈgeɪʃn] Verhör n, -nehmung f;
Frage f; **~·ga·tion mark** → **question
mark**

in·ter·rog·a·tive *gr.* [ɪntəˈrɒgətɪv] In-
terrogativ..., Frage...

in·ter|·rupt [ɪntəˈrʌpt] unterbrechen;
~·rup·tion [ɪntəˈrʌpʃn] Unterbrechung f

in·ter|·sect [ɪntəˈsekt] (durch)schnei-
den; sich schneiden *od.* kreuzen;
~·sec·tion [ɪntəˈsekʃn] Schnittpunkt
m; (Straßen)Kreuzung f

in·ter·sperse [ɪntəˈspɜːs] einstreuen,
hier u. da einfügen

in·ter·state *Am.* [ɪntəˈsteɪt] zwischen-
staatlich; ~ **(highway)** *(mehrere Bun-
desstaaten verbindende)* Autobahn

in·ter·twine [ɪntəˈtwaɪn] (sich ineinander) verschlingen

in·ter·val [ˈɪntəvl] Intervall n (a. mus.),
Abstand m; *Brt.* Pause f (a. thea. etc.);
at regular ~s in regelmäßigen Abständen

in·ter|·vene [ɪntəˈviːn] eingreifen,
-schreiten, intervenieren; dazwischen-
kommen; **~·ven·tion** [ɪntəˈvenʃn] Eingreifen n, -schreiten n, Intervention f

in·ter·view [ˈɪntəvjuː] 1. Interview n;
Einstellungsgespräch n; 2. interviewen;
ein Einstellungsgespräch führen mit;
~·ee [ɪntəvjuːˈiː] Interviewte(r m) f;
~·er [ˈɪntəvjuːə] Interviewer(in)

in·ter·weave [ɪntəˈwiːv] (-wove, -wov-
en) (miteinander) verweben *od.* -flech-
ten

in·tes·tate *jur.* [ɪnˈtesteɪt] **die ~** ohne
Hinterlassung e-s Testaments sterben

in·tes·tine *anat.* [ɪnˈtestɪn] Darm m; **~s**
pl. Eingeweide pl.; **large ~** Dickdarm
m; **small ~** Dünndarm m

in·ti·ma·cy [ˈɪntɪməsɪ] Intimität f, Vertrautheit f; (a. plumpe) Vertraulichkeit;
intime (sexuelle) Beziehungen pl.

in·ti·mate [ˈɪntɪmət] 1. intim (a. sexuell); vertraut, eng (Freunde etc.); (a.
plump-)vertraulich; innerste(r, -s)
(Wünsche etc.); gründlich, genau
(Kenntnisse etc.); 2. Vertraute(r m) f

in·tim·i|·date [ɪnˈtɪmɪdeɪt] einschüch-
tern; **~·da·tion** [ɪntɪmɪˈdeɪʃn] Ein-
schüchterung f

in·to [ˈɪntʊ, ˈɪntə] in (acc.), in (acc.) ...
hinein; gegen (acc.); *math.* in (acc.); **4 ×
20 goes five times** 4 geht fünfmal in 20

in·tol·e·ra·ble [ɪnˈtɒlərəbl] unerträglich

in·tol·e|·rance [ɪnˈtɒlərəns] Intoleranz
f, Unduldsamkeit (of gegen); **~·rant**
intolerant, unduldsam (of gegen)

in·to·na·tion [ɪntəʊˈneɪʃn] *gr.* Intonation f, Tonfall m; *mus.* Intonation f

in·tox·i|·cat·ed [ɪnˈtɒksɪkeɪtɪd] be-

rauscht; betrunken; **~ca·tion** [ɪntɒk-
sɪˈkeɪʃn] Rausch *m* (*a. fig.*)

n·trac·ta·ble [ɪnˈtræktəbl] eigensinnig;
schwer zu handhaben(d)

n·tran·si·tive *gr.* [ɪnˈtrænsətɪv] intransitiv

n·tra·ve·nous *med.* [ɪntrəˈviːnəs] intra-
venös

in tray: *in the* ~ im Post- *etc.* Eingang
(*von Briefen etc.*)

n·trep·id [ɪnˈtrepɪd] unerschrocken

n·tri·cate [ˈɪntrɪkət] verwickelt, kompliziert

n·trigue [ɪnˈtriːɡ] **1.** Intrige *f*; **2.** faszinieren, interessieren; intrigieren

n·tro·duce [ɪntrəˈdjuːs] vorstellen (*to
dat.*), *j-n* bekannt machen (*to* mit); einführen; **~duc·tion** [ɪntrəˈdʌkʃn] Vorstellung *f*; Einführung *f*; Einleitung *f*,
Vorwort *n*; *letter of* ~ Empfehlungs-
schreiben *n*; **~duc·to·ry** [ɪntrəˈdʌk-
tərɪ] Einführungs...; einleitend, Einlei-
tungs...

n·tro·spec|·tion [ɪntrəʊˈspekʃn]
Selbstbeobachtung *f*; **~tive** [ɪntrəʊ-
ˈspektɪv] selbstbeobachtend, intro-
spektiv

n·tro·vert *psych.* [ˈɪntrəʊvɜːt] introver-
tierter Mensch; **~ed** *psych.* introver-
tiert, in sich gekehrt

n·trude [ɪnˈtruːd] (sich) aufdrängen;
stören; *am I intruding?* störe ich?;
in·trud·er Eindringling *m*; Störenfried
m; **in·tru·sion** [ɪnˈtruːʒn] Störung *f*;
in·tru·sive [ɪnˈtruːsɪv] aufdringlich

n·tu·i|·tion [ɪntjuːˈɪʃn] Intuition *f*; **~ti·
ve** [ɪnˈtjuːɪtɪv] intuitiv

n·u·it [ˈmjʊɪt] *a.* **Innuit** Inuit *m*, Eskimo

n·un·date [ˈɪnʌndeɪt] überschwemmen,
-fluten (*a. fig.*)

in·vade [ɪnˈveɪd] eindringen in, einfallen
in, *mil. a.* einmarschieren in (*acc.*); *fig.*
überlaufen, -schwemmen; **~r** Eindringling *m*

in·val·id[1] [ˈɪnvəlɪd] **1.** krank; invalid(e);
2. Kranke(r *m*) *f*; Invalide(r *m*) *f*

in·val·id[2] [ɪnˈvælɪd] (rechts)ungültig

in·val·u·a·ble [ɪnˈvæljʊəbl] unschätzbar

in·var·i·a|·ble [ɪnˈveərɪəbl] unveränder-
lich; **~bly** ausnahmslos

in·va·sion [ɪnˈveɪʒn] Invasion *f* (*a. mil.*),
Einfall *m*, *mil. a.* Einmarsch *m*; *fig.*
Eingriff *m*, Verletzung *f*

in·vec·tive [ɪnˈvektɪv] Schmähung(en
pl.) *f*, Beschimpfung(en *pl.*) *f*

in·vent [ɪnˈvent] erfinden; **in·ven·tion**
[ɪnˈvenʃn] Erfindung *f*; **in·ven·tive**
[ɪnˈventɪv] erfinderisch; einfallsreich;
in·ven·tor [ɪnˈventə] Erfinder(in);
in·ven·tory [ˈɪnvəntrɪ] Inventar *n*; Be-
stand(sliste *f*) *m*; Inventur *f*

in·verse [ɪnˈvɜːs] **1.** umgekehrt; **2.** Umkehrung *f*, Gegenteil *n*; **in·ver·sion**
[ɪnˈvɜːʃn] Umkehrung *f*; *gr.* Inversion *f*

in·vert [ɪnˈvɜːt] umkehren; **~ed 'com·
mas** *pl.* Anführungszeichen *pl.*

in·ver·te·brate *zo.* [ɪnˈvɜːtɪbrət] **1.** wir-
bellos; **2.** wirbelloses Tier

in·vest [ɪnˈvest] investieren, anlegen

in·ves·ti·gate [ɪnˈvestɪɡeɪt] untersuchen; überprüfen; Untersuchungen *od.*
Ermittlungen anstellen (*into* über *acc.*),
nachforschen; **~ga·tion** [ɪnvestɪ-
ˈɡeɪʃn] Untersuchung *f*; Ermittlung *f*,
Nachforschung *f*; **~ga·tor** [ɪnˈvestɪ-
ɡeɪtə]: *private* ~ Privatdetektiv *m*

in·vest·ment *econ.* [ɪnˈvestmənt] Inve-
stition *f*, (Kapital)Anlage *f*; **in·ves·tor**
econ. Anleger *m*

in·vet·e·rate [ɪnˈvetərət] unverbesserlich; hartnäckig

in·vid·i·ous [ɪnˈvɪdɪəs] gehässig, boshaft, gemein

in·vig·o·rate [ɪnˈvɪɡəreɪt] kräftigen,
stärken, beleben

in·vin·ci·ble [ɪnˈvɪnsəbl] unbesiegbar;
unüberwindlich

in·vis·i·ble [ɪnˈvɪzəbl] unsichtbar

in·vi·ta·tion [ɪnvɪˈteɪʃn] Einladung *f*;
Aufforderung *f*; **in·vite** [ɪnˈvaɪt] einladen; auffordern; *Gefahr etc.* herausfordern; ~ *s.o. in* j-n hereinbitten;
in·vit·ing einladend, verlockend

in·voice *econ.* [ˈɪnvɔɪs] **1.** (Waren-)
Rechnung *f*; **2.** in Rechnung stellen,
berechnen

in·voke [ɪnˈvəʊk] flehen um; *Gott etc.*
anrufen; beschwören (*a. Geister*)

in·vol·un·ta·ry [ɪnˈvɒləntərɪ] unfreiwil-
lig; unabsichtlich; unwillkürlich

in·volve [ɪnˈvɒlv] verwickeln, hineinziehen (*in in acc.*); *j-n*, *et.* angehen, betreffen; zur Folge haben, mit sich bringen;
~d kompliziert, verworren; **~ment**
Verwicklung *f*; Beteiligung *f*

in·vul·ne·ra·ble [ɪnˈvʌlnərəbl] unver-
wundbar; *fig.* unanfechtbar

in·ward ['ɪnwəd] **1.** *adj.* innere(r, -s), innerlich; **2.** *adv. mst* ~s einwärts, nach innen

I/O [aɪ 'əʊ] *Abk. für input/output Computer*: (Daten)Eingabe/(Daten)Ausgabe *f*

IOC [aɪ əʊ 'si:] *Abk. für International Olympic Committee* Internationales Olympisches Komitee

i·o·dine - [ˈaɪədiːn] Jod *n*

i·on *phys.* [ˈaɪən] Ion *n*

IOU [aɪ əʊ 'ju:] (= *I owe you*) Schuldschein *m*

IQ [aɪ 'kju:] *Abk. für intelligence quotient* IQ, Intelligenzquotient *m*

IRA [aɪ ɑːr 'eɪ] *Abk. für Irish Republican Army* IRA, Irisch-Republikanische Armee

I·ran [ɪˈrɑːn] Iran *m*; **I·ra·ni·an** [ɪˈreɪnjən] **1.** iranisch; **2.** Iraner(in); *ling.* Iranisch *n*

I·raq [ɪˈrɑːk] Irak *m*; **I·ra·qi** [ɪˈrɑːkɪ] **1.** irakisch; **2.** Iraker(in); *ling.* Irakisch *n*

i·ras·ci·ble [ɪˈræsəbl] jähzornig

i·rate [aɪˈreɪt] zornig, wütend

Ire·land [ˈaɪələnd] Irland *n*

ir·i·des·cent [ɪrɪˈdesnt] schillernd

i·ris [ˈaɪərɪs] *anat.* Regenbogenhaut *f*, Iris *f*; *bot.* Schwertlilie *f*, Iris *f*

I·rish [ˈaɪərɪʃ] **1.** irisch; **2.** *ling.* Irisch *n*; *the* ~ *pl.* die Iren *pl.*; '~·man (*pl.* -men) Ire *m*; '~·wom·an (*pl.* -women) Irin *f*

irk·some [ˈɜːksəm] lästig, ärgerlich

i·ron [ˈaɪən] **1.** Eisen *n*; Bügeleisen *n*; *strike while the* ~ *is hot fig.* das Eisen schmieden, solange es heiß ist; **2.** eisern (*a. fig.*), Eisen..., aus Eisen; **3.** bügeln; ~ *out* ausbügeln; ♀ **'Cur·tain** *pol. hist.* Eiserner Vorhang

i·ron·ic [aɪˈrɒnɪk] (~*ally*), **i·ron·i·cal** [aɪˈrɒnɪkl] ironisch, spöttisch

'i·ron·ing board Bügelbrett *n*

i·ron| lung *med.* eiserne Lunge; ~**·mon·ger** *Brt.* [ˈaɪənmʌŋgə] Eisenwarenhändler *m*; '~·works *sg.* Eisenhütte *f*

i·ron·y [ˈaɪərənɪ] Ironie *f*

ir·ra·tio·nal [ɪˈræʃənl] irrational, unvernünftig

ir·rec·on·ci·la·ble [ɪˈrekənsaɪləbl] unversöhnlich; unvereinbar

ir·re·cov·e·ra·ble [ɪrɪˈkʌvərəbl] unersetzlich; unwiederbringlich

ir·reg·u·lar [ɪˈregjʊlə] unregelmäßig;

ungleichmäßig; regel- *od.* vorschriftswidrig

ir·rel·e·vant [ɪˈreləvənt] irrelevant, unerheblich, belanglos (*to für*)

ir·rep·a·ra·ble [ɪˈrepərəbl] irreparabel; nicht wiedergutzumachen(d)

ir·re·place·a·ble [ɪrɪˈpleɪsəbl] unersetzlich

ir·re·pres·si·ble [ɪrɪˈpresəbl] nicht zu unterdrücken(d); unbezähmbar

ir·re·proa·cha·ble [ɪrɪˈprəʊtʃəbl] einwandfrei, untadelig

ir·re·sis·ti·ble [ɪrɪˈzɪstəbl] unwiderstehlich

ir·res·o·lute [ɪˈrezəluːt] unentschlossen

ir·re·spec·tive [ɪrɪˈspektɪv]: ~ *of* ohne Rücksicht auf (*acc.*); unabhängig von

ir·re·spon·si·ble [ɪrɪˈspɒnsəbl] unverantwortlich; verantwortungslos

ir·re·trie·va·ble [ɪrɪˈtriːvəbl] unwiederbringlich, unersetzlich

ir·rev·e·rent [ɪˈrevərənt] respektlos

ir·rev·o·ca·ble [ɪˈrevəkəbl] unwiderruflich, unabänderlich, endgültig

ir·ri|gate [ˈɪrɪgeɪt] bewässern; ~·**ga·tion** [ɪrɪˈgeɪʃn] Bewässerung *f*

ir·ri|ta·ble [ˈɪrɪtəbl] reizbar; ~·**tant** [ˈɪrɪtənt] Reizmittel *n*; ~·**tate** [ˈɪrɪteɪt] reizen; (ver)ärgern; '~·**tat·ing** ärgerlich (*Sache*); ~·**ta·tion** [ɪrɪˈteɪʃn] Reizung *f*; Verärgerung *f*; Ärger *m* (*at über acc.*)

is [ɪz] er, sie, es ist

ISBN [aɪ es biː 'en] *Abk. für International Standard Book Number* ISBN-Nummer *f*

Is·lam [ˈɪzlɑːm] der Islam

is·land [ˈaɪlənd] Insel *f*; *a. traffic* ~ Verkehrsinsel *f*; '~·er Inselbewohner(in)

isle *poet.* [aɪl] Insel *f*

i·so|late [ˈaɪsəleɪt] absondern; isolieren; '~·lat·ed isoliert, abgeschieden; einzeln; △ *nicht gleich: isoliert*: **~·la·tion** [aɪsəˈleɪʃn] Isolierung *f*, Absonderung *f*; ~·**la·tion ward** *med.* Isolierstation *f*

Is·rael [ˈɪzreɪl] Israel *n*; **Is·rae·li** [ɪzˈreɪlɪ] **1.** israelisch; **2.** Israeli *m, f*

is·sue [ˈɪʃuː] **1.** Streitfrage *f*, -punkt *m*; Ausgabe *f* (*e-r Zeitung etc.*); Erscheinen *n* (*e-r Zeitung etc.*); *jur.* Nachkommen(schaft *f*) *pl.*; Ausgang *m*, Ergebnis *n*; *be at* ~ zur Debatte stehen; *point at* ~ strittiger Punkt; *die without* ~ kinderlos sterben; **2.** v/t. *Zeitung etc.* herausgeben; *Banknoten etc.* ausgeben; *Dokument etc.* ausstellen; v/i. heraus-, hervorkommen; herausfließen, -strömen

it [ɪt] es; *bezogen auf bereits Genanntes*: es, er, ihn, sie

·tal·i·an [ɪˈtæljən] **1.** italienisch; **2.** Italiener(in); *ling.* Italienisch *n*

·tal·ics *print.* [ɪˈtælɪks] Kursivschrift *f*

t·a·ly [ˈɪtəlɪ] Italien *n*

tch [ɪtʃ] **1.** Jucken *n*, Juckreiz *m*; **2.** jukken, kratzen; *I ~ all over* es juckt mich überall; *be ~ing for s.th.* F et. unbedingt (haben) wollen; *be ~ing to inf.* F darauf brennen, zu *inf.*; '**·~·y** juckend; kratzend

·tem [ˈaɪtəm] Punkt *m* (*der Tagesordnung etc.*), Posten *m* (*auf e-r Liste*);

Artikel *m*, Gegenstand *m*; (*Presse-, Zeitungs*)Notiz *f*, (*a. Rundfunk, TV*) Nachricht *f*, Meldung *f*; **·~·ize** [ˈaɪtəmaɪz] einzeln angeben *od.* aufführen

i·tin·e·ra·ry [aɪˈtɪnərərɪ] Reiseweg *m*, -route *f*; Reiseplan *m*

its [ɪts] sein(e), ihr(e)

it's [ɪts] *für it is*; *it has*

it·self [ɪtˈself] sich; sich selbst; *verstärkend:* selbst; *by ~* (für sich) allein; von selbst; *in ~* an sich

ITV [aɪ tiː ˈviː] *Abk. für Independent Television* (*unabhängige brit. kommerzielle Fernsehanstalten*)

I've [aɪv] *für I have*

i·vo·ry [ˈaɪvərɪ] Elfenbein *n*

i·vy *bot.* [ˈaɪvɪ] Efeu *m*

J

J, j [dʒeɪ] J, j *n*

J *nur geschr. Abk. für joule(s)* J, Joule *n od. pl.*

jab [dʒæb] **1.** (*-bb-*) (hinein)stechen, (-)stoßen; **2.** Stich *m*, Stoß *m*

jab·ber [ˈdʒæbə] (daher)plappern

jack [dʒæk] **1.** *tech.* Hebevorrichtung *f*; *tech.* Wagenheber *m*; *Kartenspiel:* Bube *m*; **2.** *~ up Auto* aufbocken

jack·al *zo.* [ˈdʒækɔːl] Schakal *m*

jack|·ass [ˈdʒækæs] Esel *m* (*a. fig.*); '**·~·boots** Stulp(en)stiefel *pl.*; '**·~·daw** *zo.* Dohle *f*

jack·et [ˈdʒækɪt] Jacke *f*, Jackett *n*; *tech.* Mantel *m*; (Schutz)Umschlag *m*; *Am.* (*Platten*)Hülle *f*; *~ potatoes pl.*, *potatoes (boiled) in their ~s pl.* Pellkartoffeln *pl.*

jack|·knife [ˈdʒæknaɪf] **1.** (*pl. - knives*) Klappmesser *n*; **2.** zusammenklappen, -knicken; '**·~·of-'all-trades** Hansdampf *m* in allen Gassen; '**·~·pot** Jackpot *m*, Haupttreffer *m*; *hit the ~* F den Jackpot gewinnen; *fig.* das große Los ziehen

jade [dʒeɪd] Jade *m*, *f*; Jadegrün *n*

jag [dʒæg] Zacken *m*; **·~·ged** [ˈdʒægɪd] gezackt, zackig

jag·u·ar *zo.* [ˈdʒægjʊə] Jaguar *m*

jail [dʒeɪl] **1.** Gefängnis *n*; **2.** einsperren; '**·~·bird** F Knastbruder *m*; '**·~·er** Gefängnisaufseher *m*; '**·~·house** *Am.* Gefängnis *n*

jam¹ [dʒæm] Konfitüre *f*, Marmelade *f*

jam² [dʒæm] **1.** (*-mm-*) v/t. (hinein)pressen, (-)quetschen, (-)zwängen, *Menschen a.* (-)pferchen; (ein)klemmen, (-)quetschen; *a. ~ up* blockieren, verstopfen; *Funkempfang* stören; *~ on the brakes* voll auf die Bremse treten; v/i. sich (hinein)drängen *od.* (-)quetschen; *tech.* sich verklemmen, *Bremsen:* blockieren; **2.** Gedränge *n*; *tech.* Blockierung *f*; Stauung *f*, Stockung *f*; *traffic ~* Verkehrsstau *m*; *be in a ~* F in der Klemme stecken

jamb [dʒæm] (Tür-, Fenster)Pfosten *m*

jam·bo·ree [dʒæmbəˈriː] Jamboree *n*, Pfadfindertreffen *n*

Jan *nur geschr. Abk. für January* Jan., Januar *m*

jan·gle [ˈdʒæŋgl] klimpern *od.* klirren (mit)

jan·i·tor *Am.* [ˈdʒænɪtə] Hausmeister *m*

Jan·u·a·ry ['dʒænjʊərɪ] (*Abk. Jan.*) Januar *m*

Ja·pan [dʒə'pæn] Japan *n*; **Jap·a·nese** [dʒæpə'niːz] **1.** japanisch; **2.** Japaner(in); *ling.* Japanisch *n*; **the** ~ *pl.* die Japaner *m*

jar¹ [dʒɑː] **1.** Gefäß *n*, Krug *m*; (Marmelade- *etc.*)Glas *n*

jar² [dʒɑː] (*-rr-*): ~ **on** weh tun (*dat.*) (*Farbe, Geräusch etc.*)

jar·gon ['dʒɑːgən] Jargon *m*, Fachsprache *f*

jaun·dice *med.* ['dʒɔːndɪs] Gelbsucht *f*

jaunt [dʒɔːnt] **1.** Ausflug *m*, *mot.* Spritztour *f*; **2.** e-n Ausflug *od.* e-e Spritztour machen

jaun·ty ['dʒɔːntɪ] (*-ier, -iest*) unbeschwert, unbekümmert; flott (*Hut etc.*)

jav·e·lin ['dʒævlɪn] *Sport:* Speer *m*; ~ (**throw**), **throwing the** ~ Speerwerfen *n*; ~ **thrower** Speerwerfer(in)

jaw [dʒɔː] *anat.* Kiefer *m*; **lower** ~ Unterkiefer *m*; **upper** ~ Oberkiefer *m*; ~**s** *pl. zo.* Rachen, Maul *n*; *tech.* Backen *pl.*; '~**bone** *anat.* Kieferknochen *m*

jay *zo.* [dʒeɪ] Eichelhäher *m*; '~**walk** unachtsam über die Straße gehen; '~**walk·er** unachtsamer Fußgänger

jazz *mus.* [dʒæz] Jazz *m*

jeal·ous ['dʒeləs] eifersüchtig (*of* auf *acc.*); neidisch; '~**y** Eifersucht *f*; Neid *m*; △ *nicht* **Jalousie**

jeans [dʒiːnz] *pl.* Jeans *pl.*

jeep *TM* [dʒiːp] Jeep *m* (*TM*)

jeer [dʒɪə] **1.** (*at*) höhnische Bemerkung(en) machen (über *acc.*); höhnisch lachen (über *acc.*); (*at*) verhöhnen; **2.** höhnische Bemerkung; Hohngelächter *n*

jel·lied ['dʒelɪd] in Aspik *od.* Sülze

jel·ly ['dʒelɪ] Gallert(e *f*) *n*; Gelee *n*; Aspik *m, n*, Sülze *f*; Götterspeise *f*; '~ **ba·by** *Brt.* Gummibärchen *n*; '~ **bean** Gummi-, Geleebonbon *m, n*; '~**fish** *zo.* (*pl. -fish, -fishes*) Qualle *f*

jeop·ar·dize ['dʒepədaɪz] gefährden; '~**dy** Gefahr *f*

jerk [dʒɜːk] **1.** ruckartig ziehen an (*dat.*); sich ruckartig bewegen; (zusammen)zucken; **2.** (plötzlicher) Ruck; Sprung *m*, Satz *m*; *med.* Zuckung *f*; '~**y** (*-ier, -iest*) ruckartig; holprig; rüttelnd, schüttelnd (*Fahrt*)

jer·sey ['dʒɜːzɪ] Pullover *m*

jest [dʒest] **1.** Scherz *m*, Spaß *m*; **2.** scherzen, spaßen; '~**er** *hist.* (Hof)Narr *m*

jet [dʒet] **1.** (Wasser-, Gas- *etc.*)Strahl *m*; *tech.* Düse *f*; *aviat.* Jet *m*; **2.** (*-tt-*) (heraus-, hervor)schießen (*from* aus); *aviat.* F jetten; ~ **'en·gine** *tech.* Düsen-, Strahltriebwerk *n*; '~ **lag** körperliche Anpassungsschwierigkeiten durch die Zeitverschiebung bei weiten Flugreisen; '~ **plane** Düsenflugzeug *n*, Jet *m*; ~**pro'pelled** Düsen-, Strahl...; ~ **pro'pul·sion** Düsen-, Strahlantrieb *m*; '~ **set** Jet-set *m*; '~**set·ter** Angehörige(r *m*) *f* des Jet-set

jet·ty *naut.* ['dʒetɪ] (Hafen)Mole *f*

Jew [dʒuː] Jude *m*, Jüdin *f*

jew·el ['dʒuːəl] Juwel *n, m*, Edelstein *m*; '**jew·el·er** *Am.*, '**jew·el·ler** *Brt.* Juwelier *m*; **jew·el·ler·y** *Brt.*, **jew·el·ry** *Am.* ['dʒuːəlrɪ] Juwelen *pl.*; Schmuck *m*

Jew·ess ['dʒuːɪs] Jüdin *f*; '~**ish** jüdisch

jif·fy F ['dʒɪfɪ]: **in a** ~ im Nu, sofort

jig·saw ['dʒɪgsɔː] Laubsäge *f*; → '~ **puz·zle** Puzzle(spiel) *n*

jilt [dʒɪlt] Mädchen sitzenlassen; e-m Liebhaber den Laufpaß geben

jin·gle ['dʒɪŋgl] **1.** klimpern (mit), bimmeln (lassen); **2.** Klimpern *n*, Bimmeln *n*; Werbesong *m*, -spruch *m*

jit·ters F ['dʒɪtəz] *pl.*: **the** ~ Bammel *m*, e-e Heidenangst

Jnr *nur geschr. Abk. für* **Junior** jr., jun., junior, der Jüngere

job [dʒɒb] **1.** (einzelne) Arbeit; Beruf *m*, Beschäftigung *f*, Stellung *f*, Stelle *f*, Arbeit *f*, Job *m*; Arbeitsplatz *m*; Aufgabe *f*, Sache *f*, Angelegenheit *f*; *Computer:* Job *m*; *a.* ~ **work** Akkordarbeit *f*; **by the** ~ im Akkord; **out of a** ~ arbeitslos; **2.** ~ **around** jobben; '~ **ad**, ~ **ad'ver·tise·ment** Stellenanzeige *f*; '~ **bro·ker** *Brt.* Börsenspekulant *m*; '~ **cen·tre** *Brt.* Arbeitsamt *n*; '~ **hop·ping** *Am.* häufiger Arbeitsplatzwechsel; '~**hunt·ing** Arbeitssuche *f*; **be** ~ auf Arbeitssuche sein; '~**less** arbeitslos; '~ **shar·ing** Job-sharing *n*

jock·ey ['dʒɒkɪ] Jockei *m*

jog [dʒɒg] **1.** stoßen an (*acc.*) *od.* gegen, *j-n* anstoßen; *mst* ~ **along**, ~ **on** dahintrotten, -zuckeln; *Sport:* joggen; **2.** (leichter) Stoß, Stups *m*; Trott *m*;

Sport: Trimmtrab *m*;'**~ger** *Sport*: Jogger(in); '**~ging** *Sport*: Joggen *n*, Jogging *n*

join [dʒɔɪn] **1.** *v/t.* verbinden, -einigen, zusammenfügen; sich anschließen (*dat. od.* an *acc.*), sich gesellen zu; eintreten in (*acc.*), beitreten; teilnehmen *od.* sich beteiligen an (*dat.*), mitmachen bei; **~ in** einstimmen in; *v/i.* sich vereinigen *od.* verbinden; **~ in** teilnehmen *od.* sich beteiligen (an *dat.*), mitmachen (bei); **2.** Verbindungsstelle *f*, Naht *f*; '**~er** Tischler *m*, Schreiner *m*

joint [dʒɔɪnt] **1.** Verbindungs-, Nahtstelle *f*; *anat.*, *tech.* Gelenk *n*; *bot.* Knoten *m*; *Brt. gastr.* Braten *m*; *sl.* Laden *m*, Bude *f*, Spelunke *f*; *sl.* Joint *m* (*Haschisch- od. Marihuanazigarette*); **out of ~** ausgerenkt; *fig.* aus den Fugen; **2.** gemeinsam, gemeinschaftlich; Mit...; '**~ed** gegliedert; Glieder...; **~'stock com·pa·ny** *Brt. econ.* Kapital- *od.* Aktiengesellschaft *f*; **~ 'ven·ture** *econ.* Gemeinschaftsunternehmen *n*

joke [dʒəʊk] **1.** Witz *m*; Scherz *m*, Spaß *m*; **practical ~** Streich *m*; **play a ~ on s.o.** j-m e-n Streich spielen; **2.** scherzen, Witze machen; '**jok·er** Spaßvogel *m*, Witzbold *m*; *Kartenspiel*: Joker *m*

jol·ly [ˈdʒɒlɪ] **1.** *adj.* (**-ier**, **-iest**) lustig, fröhlich, vergnügt; **2.** *adv. Brt.* F ganz schön; **~ good** prima

jolt [dʒəʊlt] **1.** e-n Ruck *od.* Stoß geben; durchrütteln, -schütteln; rütteln, holpern (*Fahrzeug*); *fig.* aufrütteln; **2.** Ruck *m*, Stoß *m*; *fig.* Schock *m*

jos·tle [ˈdʒɒsl] (an)rempeln; dränge(l)n

jot [dʒɒt] **1.** *not a* ~ keine Spur; **2.** (**-tt-**): ~ **down** sich schnell *et.* notieren

joule *phys.* [dʒuːl] Joule *n*

jour·nal [ˈdʒɜːnl] Journal *n*; (Fach)Zeitschrift *f*; Tagebuch *n*; **~is·m** [ˈdʒɜːnəlɪzəm] Journalismus *m*; **~ist** [ˈdʒɜːnəlɪst] Journalist(in)

jour·ney [ˈdʒɜːnɪ] **1.** Reise *f*; **2.** reisen; '**~·man** (*pl. -men*) Geselle *m*

joy [dʒɔɪ] Freude *f*; **for ~** vor Freude; '**~·ful** freudig; erfreut; '**~·less** freudlos, traurig; '**~·stick** *aviat.* Steuerknüppel *m*; *Computer*: Joystick *m*

Jr → *Jnr*

ju·bi·lant [ˈdʒuːbɪlənt] jubelnd, überglücklich

ju·bi·lee [ˈdʒuːbɪliː] Jubiläum *n*

judge [dʒʌdʒ] **1.** *jur.* Richter(in); Schieds-, Preisrichter(in); Kenner(in); **2.** *jur.* Fall verhandeln; (be)urteilen; beurteilen, einschätzen

judg(e)·ment [ˈdʒʌdʒmənt] *jur.* Urteil *n*; Urteilsvermögen *n*; Meinung *f*, Ansicht *f*; göttliches (Straf)Gericht; **the Last 2** das Jüngste Gericht; '**2 Day**, *a.* **Day of 2** Jüngster Tag

ju·di·cial *jur.* [dʒuːˈdɪʃl] gerichtlich, Justiz...; richterlich

ju·di·ci·a·ry *jur.* [dʒuːˈdɪʃɪərɪ] Richter *pl.*

ju·di·cious [dʒuːˈdɪʃəs] klug, weise

ju·do [ˈdʒuːdəʊ] *Sport*: Judo *n*

jug [dʒʌɡ] Krug *m*; Kanne *f*, Kännchen *n*

jug·gle [ˈdʒʌɡl] jonglieren (mit); *Bücher etc.* frisieren; '**~r** Jongleur *m*

juice [dʒuːs] Saft *m*; *sl. mot.* Sprit *m*; **juic·y** [ˈdʒuːsɪ] (**-ier**, **-iest**) saftig; F pikant, gepfeffert

juke·box [ˈdʒuːkbɒks] Musikbox *f*, Musikautomat *m*

Jul *nur geschr. Abk. für* **July** Juli *m*

Ju·ly [dʒuːˈlaɪ] (*Abk.* **Jul**) Juli *m*

jum·ble [ˈdʒʌmbl] **1.** *a.* ~ **together**, ~ **up** durcheinanderbringen, -werfen; **2.** Durcheinander *n*; '**~ sale** *Brt.* Wohltätigkeitsbasar *m*

jum·bo [ˈdʒʌmbəʊ] **1.** riesig, Riesen...; **2.** (*pl. -bos*) *aviat.* Jumbo *m*; → **jet** *aviat.* Jumbo-Jet *m*; '**~-sized** riesig

jump [dʒʌmp] **1.** *v/i.* springen; hüpfen; zusammenzucken, -fahren, hochfahren (**at** bei); ~ **at the chance** mit beiden Händen zugreifen; ~ **to conclusions** übereilte Schlüsse ziehen; *v/t.* (hinweg)springen über (*acc.*); überspringen; ~ **the queue** *Brt.* sich vordränge(l)n; ~ **the lights** bei Rot über die Kreuzung fahren, F bei Rot drüberfahren; **2.** Sprung *m*; **high** (**long**) ~ *Sport*: Hoch-(Weit)sprung *m*

'jump·er¹ *Sport*: (Hoch-*etc.*)Springer(in)

'jump·er² *Brt.* Pullover *m*; *Am.* Trägerrock *m*, -kleid *n*

'jump·ing jack Hampelmann *m*; '**~·y** (**-ier**, **-iest**) nervös

Jun *nur geschr. Abk. für* **June** Juni *m*; → *Jnr*

junc·tion [ˈdʒʌŋkʃn] (Straßen)Kreuzung *f*; *rail.* Knotenpunkt *m*; **~ture** [ˈdʒʌŋktʃə]: **at this ~** zu diesem Zeitpunkt

J

June [dʒuːn] (*Abk. **Jun***) Juni *m*
jun·gle ['dʒʌŋgl] Dschungel *m*
ju·ni·or ['dʒuːnjə] **1.** junior; jüngere(r, -s); untergeordnet; *Sport:* Junioren..., Jugend...; **2.** Jüngere(r *m*) *f*; **~ 'high (school)** *Am.* die unteren Klassen der *High-School*; '**~ school** *Brt.* Grundschule *f* (*für Kinder von 7-11*)
junk¹ *naut.* [dʒʌŋk] Dschunke *f*
junk² F [dʒʌŋk] Trödel *m*; Schrott *m*; Abfall *m*; *sl.* Stoff *m* (*bsd. Heroin*); '**~ food** Junk food *n* (*kalorienreiche Nahrung von geringem Nährwert*); **~ie, ~y** *sl.* ['dʒʌŋki] Junkie *m*, Fixer(in); '**~yard** *Am.* Schuttabladeplatz *m*; Schrottplatz *m*; **auto ~** *Am.* Autofriedhof *m*
jur·is·dic·tion ['dʒʊərɪs'dɪkʃn] Gerichtsbarkeit *f*; Zuständigkeit(sbereich *m*) *f*
ju·ris·pru·dence ['dʒʊərɪs'pruːdəns] Rechtswissenschaft *f*
ju·ror *jur.* ['dʒʊərə] Geschworene(r *m*) *f*
ju·ry ['dʒʊərɪ] *jur. die* Geschworenen *pl.*; Jury *f*, Preisrichter *pl.*; '**~man** (*pl.*

-men) *jur.* Geschworene(r) *m*; '**~wom·an** (*pl.* **-women**) *jur.* Geschworene *f*

just [dʒʌst] **1.** *adj.* gerecht; berechtigt; angemessen; **2.** *adv.* gerade, (so)eben; gerade, genau, eben; gerade (noch), ganz knapp; nur, bloß; (so)eben; ungefähr, etwa; **~ like that** einfach so; **~ now** gerade (jetzt), (so)eben
jus·tice ['dʒʌstɪs] Gerechtigkeit *f*; *jur.* Richter *m*; **2 of the Peace** Friedensrichter *m*; **court of ~** Gericht(shof *m*) *f*
jus·ti·fi·ca·tion [dʒʌstɪfɪ'keɪʃn] Rechtfertigung *f*; **~fy** ['dʒʌstɪfaɪ] rechtfertigen
just·ly ['dʒʌstlɪ] mit od. zu Recht
jut [dʒʌt] (*-tt-*): **~ out** vorspringen, herausragen
ju·ve·nile ['dʒuːvənaɪl] **1.** jugendlich; Jugend...; **2.** Jugendliche(r *m*) *f*; **'court** Jugendgericht *n*; **~ de'linquen·cy** Jugendkriminalität *f*; **~ de'lin·quent** straffälliger Jugendlicher, jugendlicher Straftäter

K

K, k [keɪ] K, k *n*
kan·ga·roo *zo.* [kæŋgə'ruː] (*pl.* **-roos**) Känguruh *n*
ka·ra·te [kə'rɑːtɪ] Karate *n*
KB [keɪ 'biː] *Abk. für **kilobyte*** KB, Kilobyte *n*
keel *naut.* [kiːl] **1.** Kiel *m*; **2.** **~ over** umschlagen, kentern
keen [kiːn] scharf (*a. fig.*); schneidend (*Kälte*); heftig, stark (*Gefühl*); stark, lebhaft (*Interesse*); groß (*Appetit etc.*); begeistert, leidenschaftlich; **~ on** versessen *od.* scharf auf (*acc.*)
keep [kiːp] **1.** (*kept*) *v/t.* (auf-, [bei]behe-, er-, fest-, zurück)halten; *Gesetze etc.* einhalten, befolgen; *Ware* führen; *Geheimnis* für sich behalten; *Versprechen, Wort* halten; *Buch* führen; aufheben, aufbewahren; abhalten, hindern (*from* von); *Tiere* halten; *Bett* hüten; ernähren, er-, unterhalten; **~ early hours**

früh zu Bett gehen; **~ one's head** die Ruhe bewahren; **~ one's temper** sich beherrschen; **~ s.o. company** j-m Gesellschaft leisten; **~ s.th. from s.o.** j-m et. vorenthalten *od.* verschweigen *od.* verheimlichen; **~ time** richtig gehen (*Uhr*); Takt *od.* Schritt halten; *v/i.* bleiben; sich halten; *mit ger.:* weiter...: **~ going** weitergehen; **~ smiling** immer nur lächeln!; **~ (on) talking** weitersprechen; **~ (on) trying** es weiterversuchen, es immer wieder versuchen; **~ s.o. waiting** j-n warten lassen; **~ away** (sich) fernhalten (*from* von); **~ back** zurückhalten (*a. fig.*); **~ from doing s.th.** et. nicht tun; **~ in** *Schüler(in)* nachsitzen lassen; **~ off** (sich) fernhalten; **~ off!** Betreten verboten!; **~ on** *Kleidungsstück* anbehalten, anlassen, *Hut* aufbehalten; *Licht* brennen lassen; fortfahren (*doing* zu tun); **~ out** nicht hinein-

od. hereinlassen; ~ **out!** Zutritt verboten!; ~ **to** sich halten an (*acc.*); ~ **up** *fig.* aufrechterhalten; *Mut* nicht sinken lassen; fortfahren mit, weitermachen; nicht schlafen lassen; ~ **it up** so weitermachen; ~ **up with** Schritt halten mit; ~ **up with the Joneses** nicht hinter den Nachbarn zurückstehen (wollen); **2.** (Lebens)Unterhalt *m*; **for** ~**s** F für immer

'**keep·er** Wärter(in), Wächter(in), Aufseher(in); *mst in Zssgn:* Inhaber(in), Besitzer(in); '~**ing** Verwahrung *f*; Obhut *f*; **be in** (**out of**) ~ **with …** (nicht) übereinstimmen mit …; '~**sake** ['ki:pseik] Andenken *n* (*Geschenk*)

keg [keg] Fäßchen *n*, kleines Faß

ken·nel ['kenl] Hundehütte *f*; ~**s** *sg.* Hundezwinger *m*; Hundepension *f*

kept [kept] *pret. u. p.p. von* **keep**

kerb [kɜ:b], '~**stone** Bordstein *m*

ker·chief ['kɜ:tʃif] (Hals-, Kopf)Tuch *n*

ker·nel ['kɜ:nl] Kern *m* (*a. fig.*)

ket·tle ['ketl] Kessel *m*; '~**drum** *mus.* (Kessel)Pauke *f*

key [ki:] **1.** Schlüssel *m* (*a. fig.*); (*Schreibmaschinen-, Klavier- etc.*)Taste *f*; *mus.* Tonart *f*; Schlüssel…; **2.** anpassen (**to** an *acc.*); ~ **in** *Computer: Daten* eingeben; ~**ed up** nervös, aufgeregt, überdreht; '~**board** Tastatur *f*; '~**hole** Schlüsselloch *n*; '~**man** (*pl. -men*) Schlüsselfigur *f*; '~**note** *mus.* Grundton *m*; *fig.* Grundgedanke *m*, Tenor *m*; '~ **ring** Schlüsselring *m*; '~**stone** *arch.* Schlußstein *m*; *fig.* Grundpfeiler *m*; '~**word** Schlüssel-, Stichwort *n*

kick [kik] **1.** (mit dem Fuß) stoßen, treten, e-n Tritt geben *od.* versetzen; *Fußball:* schießen, treten, kicken; strampeln; ausschlagen (*Pferd*); ~ **off** sich schleudern; *Fußball:* anstoßen; ~ **out** F rausschmeißen; ~ **up** hochschleudern; ~ **up a fuss** *od.* **row** F Krach schlagen; **2.** (Fuß)Tritt *m*; Stoß *m*; *Fußball:* Schuß *m*; **free** ~ Freistoß *m*; **for** ~**s** F zum Spaß; **they get a** ~ **out of it** es macht ihnen e-n Riesenspaß; '~**off** *Fußball:* Anstoß *m*; '~**out** *Fußball:* Abschlag *m*

kid¹ [kid] Zicklein *n*, Kitz *n*; Ziegenleder *n*; F Kind *n*; ~ **brother** F kleiner Bruder

kid² [kid] (**-dd-**) *v/t.* j-n auf den Arm nehmen; ~ *s.o.* j-m et. vormachen; *v/i.*

Spaß machen; **he is only** ~**ding** er macht ja nur Spaß; **no** ~**ding!** im Ernst!

kid 'gloves *pl.* Glacéhandschuhe *pl.* (*a. fig.*)

kid·nap ['kidnæp] (**-pp-**, *Am. a. -p-*) entführen, kidnappen; '**kid·nap·(p)er** Entführer(in), Kidnapper(in); '**kid·nap·(p)ing** Entführung *f*, Kidnapping *n*

kid·ney *anat.* ['kidni] Niere *f*; ~ **bean** *bot.* Weiße Bohne; ~ **ma·chine** künstliche Niere

kill [kil] töten (*a. fig.*), umbringen, ermorden; vernichten; *Tiere* schlachten; *hunt.* erlegen, schießen; **be** ~**ed in an accident** tödlich verunglücken; ~ **time** die Zeit totschlagen; '~**er** Mörder(in), Killer(in); '~**ing** mörderisch, tödlich

kiln [kiln] Brennofen *m*

ki·lo F ['ki:ləʊ] (*pl. -los*) Kilo *n*

kil·o·gram(me) ['kiləgræm] Kilogramm *n*; '~**me·tre** *Brt.*, '~**me·ter** *Am.* Kilometer *m*

kilt [kilt] Kilt *m*, Schottenrock *m*

kin [kin] Verwandtschaft *f*, Verwandte *pl.*

kind¹ [kaind] freundlich, liebenswürdig, nett; herzlich

kind² [kaind] Art *f*, Sorte *f*; Wesen *n*; △ *nicht* **Kind**; **all** ~**s of** alle möglichen, allerlei; **nothing of the** ~ nichts dergleichen; ~ **of** F ein bißchen

kin·der·gar·ten ['kindəgɑ:tn] Kindergarten *m*

kind-'heart·ed gütig

kin·dle ['kindl] anzünden, (sich) entzünden; *fig. Interesse etc.* wecken

kind·ly ['kaindli] **1.** *adj.* (*-ier, -iest*) freundlich, liebenswürdig, nett; **2.** *adv.* → 1; freundlicher-, liebenswürdiger-, netterweise; '~**ness** Freundlichkeit *f*, Liebenswürdigkeit *f*; Gefälligkeit *f*

kin·dred ['kindrid] verwandt; ~ *spirits pl.* Gleichgesinnte *pl.*

king [kiŋ] König *m* (*a. fig. u. Schach, Kartenspiel*); '~**dom** ['kiŋdəm] Königreich *n*; *rel.* Reich *n* Gottes; *animal* (*mineral, vegetable*) ~ Tier- (Mineral-, Pflanzen)reich *n*; '~**ly** (*-ier, -iest*) königlich; '~**size(d)** Riesen…

kink [kiŋk] Knick *m*; *fig.* Tick *m*, Spleen *m*; '~**y** (*-ier, -iest*) spleenig; pervers

ki·osk ['ki:ɒsk] Kiosk *m*; *Brt.* Telefonzelle *f*

K

kip·per ['kɪpə] Räucherhering m

kiss [kɪs] **1.** Kuß m; **2.** (sich) küssen

kit [kɪt] Ausrüstung f; Arbeitsgerät n, Werkzeug(e pl.) n; Werkzeugtasche f, -kasten m; Bastelsatz m; → **first aid kit;** '**~ bag** Seesack m

kitch·en ['kɪtʃɪn] Küche f; Küchen...; **~·ette** [kɪtʃɪ'net] Kleinküche f, Kochnische f; **~'gar·den** Küchen-, Gemüsegarten m

kite [kaɪt] Drachen m; zo. Milan m; **fly a ~** e-n Drachen steigen lassen

kit·ten ['kɪtn] Kätzchen n

knack [næk] Kniff m, Trick m, Dreh m; Geschick n, Talent n

knave [neɪv] Schurke m, Spitzbube m; Kartenspiel: Bube m, Unter m

knead [niːd] kneten; massieren

knee [niː] Knie n; tech. Knie(stück) n; '**~·cap** anat. Kniescheibe f; **~'deep** knietief, bis an die Knie (reichend); '**~·joint** anat. Kniegelenk n (a. tech.)

kneel [niːl] (**knelt,** Am. a. **kneeled**) knien (**to** vor dat.)

'**knee-length** knielang (Rock etc.)

knell [nel] Totenglocke f

knelt [nelt] pret. u. p.p. von **kneel**

knew [njuː] pret. von **know**

knick·er·bock·ers ['nɪkəbɒkəz] pl. Knickerbocker pl., Kniehosen pl.

knick·ers Brt. F ['nɪkəz] pl. (Damen-) Schlüpfer m

knick-knack ['nɪknæk] Nippsache f

knife [naɪf] **1.** (pl. **knives** [naɪvz]) Messer n; **2.** mit e-m Messer stechen od. verletzen; erstechen

knight [naɪt] **1.** Ritter m; Schach: Springer m; **2.** zum Ritter schlagen; **~·hood** ['naɪthʊd] Ritterwürde f, -stand m

knit [nɪt] (**-tt-; knit** od. **knitted**) v/t. stricken; a. **~ together** zusammenfügen, verbinden; **~ one's brows** die Stirn runzeln; v/i. stricken; zusammenwachsen (Knochen); '**~·ting** Stricken n; Strickzeug n; Strick...; '**~·ting nee·dle** Stricknadel f; '**~·wear** Strickwaren pl.

knives [naɪvz] pl. von **knife** 1

knob [nɒb] Knopf m, Knauf m, runder Griff; Stück(chen) n (Butter, Zucker etc.)

knock [nɒk] **1.** klopfen, stoßen; pochen, klopfen; **~ at the door** an die Tür klopfen; **~ about, ~ around** herumsto-

ßen; F sich herumtreiben; F herumliegen; **~ down** Gebäude etc. abreißen; umstoßen, -werfen; niederschlagen; an-, umfahren; überfahren; mit dem Preis heruntergehen; Auktion: et. zuschlagen (**to** s.o. j-m); **be ~ed down** überfahren werden; **~ off** herunter-, abschlagen; F hinhauen (schnell erledigen); F aufhören (mit); F Feierabend od. Schluß machen; **~ out** herausschlagen, -klopfen, Pfeife ausklopfen; bewußtlos schlagen; Boxen: k.o. schlagen; betäuben (Drogen etc.); fig. F umhauen, schocken; **~ over** umwerfen, -stoßen; überfahren; **be ~ed over** überfahren werden; **2.** Schlag m, Stoß m; Klopfen n; **there is a ~ (at** [Am. on] **the door)** es klopft; '**~·er** Türklopfer m; **~'kneed** X-beinig; **~·out** Boxen: Knockout m, fig.

knoll [nəʊl] Hügel m; ⚠ nicht **Knolle**

knot [nɒt] **1.** Knoten m; Astknoten m; naut. Knoten m, Seemeile f; **2.** (**-tt-**) (ver)knoten, (-)knüpfen; '**~·ty** (**-ier, -iest**) knotig; knorrig; fig. verwickelt, kompliziert

know [nəʊ] (**knew, known**) wissen; können; erfahren, erleben; (wieder)erkennen; verstehen; **~ French** Französisch können; **~ one's way around** sich auskennen (in ⟨örtlich⟩); **~ all about it** genau Bescheid wissen; **get to ~** kennenlernen; **~ one's business, ~ the ropes, ~ a thing or two, ~ what's what** F sich auskennen, Erfahrung haben; **you ~** wissen Sie; '**~·how** Know-how n, praktische (Sach-, Spezial)Kenntnis(se pl.) f; '**~·ing** klug, gescheit; schlau; verständnisvoll, wissend; '**~·ing·ly** wissend; wissentlich, absichtlich, bewußt

knowl·edge ['nɒlɪdʒ] Kenntnis(se pl.) f; Wissen n; **to my ~** meines Wissens; **have a good ~ of** viel verstehen von, sich gut auskennen in (dat.); '**~·a·ble** be very ~ **about** viel verstehen von

known [nəʊn] p.p. von **know;** bekannt

knuck·le ['nʌkl] **1.** (Finger)Knöchel m; **2. ~ down to work** sich an die Arbeit machen

KO [keɪ 'əʊ] Abk. für knockout F K.o., Knockout m

Krem·lin ['kremlɪn]: **the ~** der Kreml

L

L, l [el] L, l *n*

L [el] *Abk. für* **learner** (**driver**) *Brt. mot.* Fahrschüler(in); *large* (*size*) groß

l *nur geschr. Abk. für* **left** l, links; *line* Z., Zeile Z.; *litre*(s) l, Liter *m*, *n* (*od. pl.*)

£ *nur geschr. Abk. für* **pound**(s) **sterling** Pfund *n* (*od. pl.*) Sterling

lab F [læb] Labor *n*

la·bel ['leɪbl] **1.** Etikett *n*, (Klebe- *etc.*)Zettel *m*, (-)Schild(chen) *n*; (Schall)Plattenfirma *f*; **2.** (*bsd. Brt. -ll-*, *Am. -l-*) etikettieren, beschriften; *fig.* abstempeln als

la·bor·a·to·ry [lə'bɒrətərɪ] Labor(atorium) *n*; **~ as'sis·tant** Laborant(in)

la·bo·ri·ous [lə'bɔːrɪəs] mühsam; schwerfällig (*Stil*)

la·bor u·ni·on *Am.* ['leɪbə -] Gewerkschaft *f*

la·bo·(u)r ['leɪbə] **1.** (schwere) Arbeit; Mühe *f*; Arbeiter *pl.*, Arbeitskräfte *pl.*; *med.* Wehen *pl.*; **Labour** *pol.* die Labour Party; **2.** (schwer) arbeiten; sich be- *od.* abmühen, sich anstrengen; **~ed** schwerfällig (*Stil*); mühsam (*Atem etc.*); **~er** ['leɪbərə] (*bsd. Hilfs-*) Arbeiter *m*; **'labour ex·change** *Brt. veraltet* → **job centre**; **'La·bour Par·ty** *pol.* Labour Party *f*

lace [leɪs] **1.** Spitze *f*; Borte *f*; Schnürsenkel *m*; **2.** **~ up** (zu-, zusammen)schnüren; *Schuh* zubinden; **~d with brandy** mit e-m Schuß Weinbrand

la·ce·rate ['læsəreɪt] zerschneiden, -kratzen, aufreißen; *j-s Gefühle* verletzen

lack [læk] **1.** (*of*) Fehlen *n* (von), Mangel *m* (an *dat.*); △ *nicht* **Lack**; **2.** *v/t.* nicht haben; **he ~s money** es fehlt ihm an Geld; *v/i.* **be ~ing** fehlen; **he is ~ing in courage** ihm fehlt der Mut; **~·lus·tre** *Brt.*, **~·lus·ter** *Am.* ['læklʌstə] glanzlos, matt

la·con·ic [lə'kɒnɪk] (*~ally*) lakonisch, wortkarg

lac·quer ['lækə] **1.** Lack *m*; Haarspray *m*, *n*; **2.** lackieren

lad [læd] Bursche *m*, Junge *m*

lad·der ['lædə] Leiter *f*; *Brt.* Laufmasche *f*; **'~·proof** (lauf)maschenfest (*Strumpf*)

la·den ['leɪdn] (schwer) beladen

la·dle ['leɪdl] **1.** (Schöpf-, Suppen)Kelle *f*, Schöpflöffel *m*; **2.** **~ out** Suppe austeilen

la·dy ['leɪdɪ] Dame *f*; ♀ Lady *f* (*Titel*); **~ doctor** Ärztin *f*; **Ladies'**, *Am.* **Ladies' room** Damentoilette *f*; **'~·bird** *zo.* Marienkäfer *m*; **'~·like** damenhaft

lag [læg] **1.** (*-gg-*) *mst* **~ behind** zurückbleiben; **2.** → **time lag**

la·ger ['lɑːgə] Lagerbier *n*; △ *nicht* **Lager**

la·goon [lə'guːn] Lagune *f*

laid [leɪd] *pret. u. p.p. von* **lay**³

lain [leɪn] *p.p. von* **lie**² 1

lair [leə] Lager *n*, Höhle *f*, Bau *m* (*e-s wilden Tieres*)

la·i·ty ['leɪətɪ] Laien *pl.*

lake [leɪk] See *m*

lamb [læm] **1.** Lamm *n*; **2.** lammen

lame [leɪm] **1.** lahm (*a. fig.*); **2.** lähmen

la·ment [lə'ment] **1.** jammern, (weh)klagen; trauern; **2.** Jammer *m*, (Weh)Klage *f*; Klagelied *n*

lam·en·ta·ble ['læməntəbl] beklagenswert; kläglich; **lam·en·ta·tion** [læmən'teɪʃn] (Weh)Klage *f*

lam·i·nat·ed ['læmɪneɪtɪd] laminiert, ge-, beschichtet; **~ glass** Verbundglas *n*

lamp [læmp] Lampe *f*; Laterne *f*; **'~·post** Laternenpfahl *m*; **'~·shade** Lampenschirm *m*

lance [lɑːns] Lanze *f*

land [lænd] **1.** Land *n*; *agr.* Land *n*, Boden *m*; Land *n*, Staat *m*; **by ~** auf dem Landweg; **2.** landen; *naut. a.* anlegen; *Güter ausladen*, *naut. a.* löschen; **~ a·gent** *bsd. Brt.* Gutsverwalter *m*; **'~·ed** Land..., Grund...

land·ing ['lændɪŋ] Landung *f*, Landen *n*, *naut. a.* Anlegen *n*; Treppenabsatz *m*; **'~ field** *aviat.* Landeplatz *m*; **'~ gear** *aviat.* Fahrgestell *n*; **'~ stage** Landungsbrücke *f*, -steg *m*; **'~ strip** *aviat.* Landeplatz *m*

land·la·dy ['lænleɪdɪ] Vermieterin *f*; Wirtin *f*; **~·lord** ['lenlɔːd] Vermieter *m*; Wirt *m*; Grundbesitzer *m*; **~·lub·ber** *naut. contp.* ['lændlʌbə] Landratte *f*;

~·mark ['lændmɑːk] Wahrzeichen *n*; *fig.* Meilenstein *m*; **~·own·er** ['lændəʊnə] Grundbesitzer(in); **~·scape** ['lænskeɪp] Landschaft *f* (*a. paint.*); **~·slide** ['lændslaɪd] Erdrutsch *m* (*a. pol.*); **a ~ victory** *pol.* ein überwältigender Wahlsieg; **~·slip** ['lændslɪp] (kleiner) Erdrutsch

lane [leɪn] (Feld)Weg *m*; Gasse *f*, Sträßchen *n*; *naut.* Fahrrinne *f*; *aviat.* Flugschneise *f*; *Sport*: (*einzelne*) Bahn; *mot.* (Fahr)Spur *f*; **change ~s** *mot.* die Spur wechseln; **get in ~** *mot.* sich einordnen

lan·guage ['læŋgwɪdʒ] Sprache *f*; **'~ lab·or·a·to·ry** Sprachlabor *n*

lan·guid ['læŋgwɪd] matt; träg(e)

lank [læŋk] glatt (*Haar*); **'~·y (-ier, -iest)** schlaksig

lan·tern ['læntən] Laterne *f*

lap¹ [læp] Schoß *m*

lap² [læp] **1.** *Sport*: Runde *f*; **~ of hono(u)r** Ehrenrunde *f*; **2.** (**-pp-**) *Sport*: *Gegner* überrunden; *Sport*: e-e Runde zurücklegen

lap³ [læp] (**-pp-**) *v/t.*: **~ up** auflecken, -schlecken; *v/i.* plätschern

la·pel [lə'pel] Revers *n*, *m*, Aufschlag *m*

lapse [læps] **1.** Versehen *n*, (kleiner) Fehler *od.* Irrtum; Vergehen *n*; Zeitspanne *f*; *jur.* Verfall *m*; **~ of memory**, **memory ~** Gedächtnislücke *f*; **2.** verfallen; *jur.* verfallen, erlöschen

lar·ce·ny *jur.* ['lɑːsənɪ] Diebstahl *m*

larch *bot.* [lɑːtʃ] Lärche *f*

lard [lɑːd] **1.** Schweinefett *n*, -schmalz *n*; **2.** *Fleisch* spicken; **lar·der** ['lɑːdə] Speisekammer *f*; Speiseschrank *m*

large [lɑːdʒ] (**~r, ~st**) groß; beträchtlich, reichlich; umfassend, weitgehend; **at ~** in Freiheit, auf freiem Fuß; (sehr) ausführlich; in der Gesamtheit; **'~·ly** großßen-, größtenteils; **~·mind·ed** aufgeschlossen, tolerant; **'~·ness** Größe *f*

lar·i·at *bsd. Am.* ['lærɪət] Lasso *n*, *m*

lark¹ *zo.* [lɑːk] Lerche *f*

lark² F [lɑːk] Jux *m*, Spaß *m*

lark·spur *bot.* ['lɑːkspɜː] Rittersporn *m*

lar·va *zo.* ['lɑːvə] (*pl.* **-vae** [-viː]) Larve *f*

lar·yn·gi·tis *med.* [lærɪn'dʒaɪtɪs] Kehlkopfentzündung *f*

lar·ynx *anat.* ['lærɪŋks] (*pl.* **-ynges** [lə'rɪndʒiːz], **-ynxes**) Kehlkopf *m*

las·civ·i·ous [lə'sɪvɪəs] geil, lüstern

la·ser *phys.* ['leɪzə] Laser *m*; **'~ beam** Laserstrahl *m*; **'~ print·er** *Computer*: Laserdrucker *m*; **'~ tech·nol·o·gy** Lasertechnik *f*

lash [læʃ] **1.** Peitschenschnur *f*; (Peitschen)Hieb *m*; Wimper *f*; **2.** peitschen (mit); (fest)binden; schlagen; **~ out** (wild) um sich schlagen

lass [læs], **~·ie** ['læsɪ] Mädchen *n*

las·so [læ'suː] (*pl.* **-sos, -soes**) Lasso *n*, *m*

last¹ [lɑːst] **1.** *adj.* letzte(r, -s); vorige(r, -s); **~ but one** vorletzte(r, -s); **~ night** gestern abend; letzte Nacht; **2.** *adv.* zuletzt, an letzter Stelle; **~ but not least** nicht zuletzt, nicht zu vergessen; **3.** *su.* die, das Letzte; △ *nicht* **Last; at ~** endlich; **to the ~** bis zum Schluß

last² [lɑːst] (an-, fort)dauern; (sich) halten (*Farbe etc.*); (aus)reichen

last³ [lɑːst] (Schuhmacher)Leisten *m*

'last·ing dauerhaft; beständig

'last·ly zuletzt, zum Schluß

latch [lætʃ] **1.** Schnappriegel *m*; Schnappschloß *n*; **2.** ein-, zuklinken; **'~·key** Haus-, Wohnungsschlüssel *m*

late [leɪt] (**~r, ~st**) spät; jüngste(r, -s), letzte(r, -s), frühere(r, -s), ehemalig; verstorben; **be ~** zu spät kommen; sich verspäten, Verspätung haben (*Zug etc.*); **as ~ as** noch, erst; **of ~** kürzlich; **~ on** später; **'~·ly** kürzlich

lath [lɑːθ] Latte *f*, Leiste *f*

lathe *tech.* [leɪð] Drehbank *f*

la·ther ['lɑːðə] **1.** (Seifen)Schaum *m*; **2.** *v/t.* einseifen; *v/i.* schäumen

Lat·in ['lætɪn] **1.** *ling.* lateinisch; südländisch; **2.** *ling.* Latein(isch) *n*; **~ A'mer·i·ca** Lateinamerika *n*; **~ A'mer·i·can 1.** lateinamerikanisch; **2.** Lateinamerikaner(in)

lat·i·tude *geogr.* ['lætɪtjuːd] Breite *f*

lat·ter ['lætə] letztere(r, -s) (*von zweien*)

lat·tice ['lætɪs] Gitter(werk) *n*

lau·da·ble ['lɔːdəbl] lobenswert

laugh [lɑːf] **1.** lachen (**at** über *acc.*); **~ at s.o. a.** j-n auslachen; **2.** Lachen *n*, Gelächter *n*; **'~·a·ble** lächerlich, lachhaft; **~·ter** ['lɑːftə] Lachen *n*, Gelächter *n*

launch¹ [lɔːntʃ] **1.** Schiff vom Stapel lassen; *Geschoß* abschießen, *Rakete, Raumfahrzeug a.* starten; *Projekt etc.* in Gang setzen, starten; **2.** *naut.* Stapellauf *m*; Abschuß *m*, Start *m*

launch² *naut.* [lɔːntʃ] Barkasse *f*

launch·ing → **launch**[1] 2; '**~ pad** a. **launch pad** Abschußrampe f; '**~ site** Abschußbasis f

laun·der ['lɔːndə] Wäsche waschen (u. bügeln); F bsd. Geld waschen

laun·d(e)rette [lɔːn'dret] bsd. Brt., **~dro·mat** TM bsd. Am. ['lɔːndrəmæt] Waschsalon m; **~dry** ['lɔːndrɪ] Wäscherei f; Wäsche f

laur·el bot. ['lɒrəl] Lorbeer m (a. fig.)

la·va ['lɑːvə] Lava f

lav·a·to·ry ['lævətərɪ] Toilette f, Klosett n; **public ~** Bedürfnisanstalt f

lav·en·der bot. ['lævəndə] Lavendel m

lav·ish ['lævɪʃ] **1.** sehr freigebig, verschwenderisch; **2. ~ s.th. on s.o.** j-n mit et. überhäufen od. überschütten

law [lɔː] Gesetz(e) n; Recht(ssystem) n; Rechtswissenschaft f, Jura; F Bullen pl. (Polizei); **F Bulle** m (Polizist); Gesetz n, Vorschrift f; **~ and order** Recht od. Ruhe u. Ordnung; **~-a·bid·ing** ['lɔːəbaɪdɪŋ] gesetzestreu; '**~-court** Gericht(shof) m; '**~-ful** gesetzlich; rechtmäßig, legitim; rechtsgültig; '**~-less** gesetzlos; gesetzwidrig; zügellos

lawn [lɔːn] Rasen m; '**~-mow·er** Rasenmäher m

law·suit Prozeß m

law·yer jur. ['lɔːjə] (Rechts)Anwalt m, (-)Anwältin f

lax [læks] locker, schlaff; lax, lasch

lax·a·tive med. ['læksətɪv] **1.** abführend; **2.** Abführmittel n

lay[1] [leɪ] pret. von **lie**[1] 2

lay[2] [leɪ] rel. weltlich; Laien...

lay[3] [leɪ] (laid) v/t. legen; Teppich verlegen; be-, auslegen (**with** mit); Tisch decken; Eier legen; vorlegen (**before** dat.), bringen (**before** vor dat.); Schuld etc. zuschreiben, zur Last legen; v/i. (Eier) legen; **~ aside** beiseite legen, zurücklegen; **~ off** econ. Arbeiter (bsd. vorübergehend) entlassen; Arbeit einstellen; **~ open** darlegen; **~ out** ausbreiten, -legen; Garten etc. anlegen; entwerfen, planen; print. das Layout (gen.) machen; **~ up** anhäufen, (an)sammeln; **be laid up** das Bett hüten müssen; '**~-by** (pl. -bys) Brt. mot. Parkbucht f, -streifen m; Park-, Rastplatz m (Autobahn); '**~-er** Lage f, Schicht f; bot. Ableger m

lay·man (pl. -men) Laie m

'**lay|-off** econ. (bsd. vorübergehende) Entlassung f; '**~-out** Grundriß m, Lageplan m; print. Layout n, Gestaltung f

la·zy ['leɪzɪ] (-ier, -iest) faul, träg(e)

lb nur geschr. Abk. für pound (lateinisch libra) Pfund n (453,59 g)

LCD [el siː 'diː] Abk. für liquid crystal display Flüssigkristallanzeige f

lead[1] [liːd] **1.** (led) v/t. führen; (an)führen, leiten; dazu bringen, veranlassen (**to do** zu tun); v/i. führen; vorangehen; Sport: an der Spitze od. in Führung liegen; **~ off** anfangen, beginnen; **~ on** j-m et. vor- od. weismachen; **~ to** fig. führen zu; **~ up to** fig. (allmählich) führen zu; **2.** Führung f; Leitung f; Spitzenposition f; Vorbild n, Beispiel n; thea. Hauptrolle f; thea. Hauptdarsteller(in); (Hunde)Leine f; Hinweis m, Tip m, Anhaltspunkt m; Sport u. fig. Führung f, Vorsprung m; **be in the ~** in Führung sein; **take the ~** in Führung gehen, die Führung übernehmen

lead[2] [led] chem. Blei n; naut. Lot n; **~ed** ['ledɪd] verbleit, (Benzin a.) bleihaltig; **~en** ['ledn] bleiern (a. fig.), Blei...

lead·er ['liːdə] (An)Führer(in), Leiter(in); Erste(r m) f; Brt. Leitartikel m; '**~-ship** Führung f, Leitung f

lead-free ['ledfriː] bleifrei (Benzin)

lead·ing ['liːdɪŋ] leitend; führend; Haupt...

leaf [liːf] **1.** (pl. leaves [liːvz]) Blatt n; (Tür- etc.)Flügel m; (Tisch)Klappe f, Ausziehplatte f; **2. ~ through** durchblättern; **~let** ['liːflɪt] Hand-, Reklamezettel m; Prospekt m

league [liːg] Liga f; Bund m

leak [liːk] **1.** lecken, leck sein; tropfen; **~ out** auslaufen; fig. durchsickern; **2.** Leck n, undichte Stelle (a. fig.); **~age** ['liːkɪdʒ] Auslaufen f; '**~-y** (-ier, -iest) leck, undicht

lean[1] [liːn] (leant od. leaned) (sich) lehnen; (sich) neigen; **~ on** sich verlassen auf (acc.)

lean[2] [liːn] **1.** mager (a. fig.); **2.** das Magere (vom Fleisch); **~ 'man·age·ment** schlanke Unternehmensstruktur

leant [lent] pret. u. p.p. von **lean**[1]

leap [liːp] **1.** (leapt od. leaped) springen; **~ at** fig. sich stürzen auf; **2.** Sprung m; '**~frog** Bockspringen n; **~t** [lept] *pret. u. p.p. von* leap 1; '**~year** Schaltjahr n

learn [lɜːn] (**learned** *od.* **learnt**) (er)lernen; erfahren, hören; **~ed** [ˈlɜːnɪd] gelehrt; '**~er** Anfänger(in); Lernende(r m) f; **~ driver** mot. Fahrschüler(in); '**~ing** Gelehrsamkeit f; **~t** [lɜːnt] pret. u. p.p. von **learn**

lease [liːs] **1.** Pacht f, Miete f; Pacht-, Mietvertrag m; **2.** pachten, mieten; leasen; **~ out** verpachten, -mieten

leash [liːʃ] (Hunde)Leine f

least [liːst] **1.** adj. (sup. von little 1) geringste(r, -s), mindeste(r, -s), wenigste(r, -s); **2.** adv. (sup. von little 2) am wenigsten; **~ of all** am allerwenigsten; **3.** das Mindeste, das Wenigste; **at ~** wenigstens; **to say the ~** gelinde gesagt

leath·er [ˈleðə] **1.** Leder n; **2.** ledern; Leder...

leave [liːv] **1.** (*left*) v/t. (hinter-, über-, übrig-, ver-, zurück)lassen; hängen-, liegen-, stehenlassen; vergessen; vermachen, -erben; **be left** übrigbleiben od. übrig sein; v/i. (fort-, weg)gehen, abreisen, abfahren, abfliegen; **~ alone** allein lassen; j-n, et. in Ruhe lassen; **~ behind** zurücklassen; **~ on** anlassen; **~ out** draußen lassen; aus-, weglassen; **2.** Erlaubnis f; Urlaub m; Abschied m; **on ~** auf Urlaub

leav·en [ˈlevn] Sauerteig m

leaves [liːvz] pl. von leaf 1; Laub n

leav·ings [ˈliːvɪŋz] pl. Überreste pl.

lech·er·ous [ˈletʃərəs] geil, lüstern

lec·ture [ˈlektʃə] **1.** univ. Vorlesung f; Vortrag m; Strafpredigt f; △ nicht *Lektüre*; **2.** v/i. univ. e-e Vorlesung od. Vorlesungen halten; e-n Vortrag od. Vorträge halten; v/t. j-m e-e Strafpredigt halten; **~tur·er** [ˈlektʃərə] univ. Dozent(in); Redner(in)

led [led] pret. u. p.p. von lead¹ 1

ledge [ledʒ] Leiste f, Sims m, n

leech zo. [liːtʃ] Blutegel m

leek bot. [liːk] Lauch m, Porree m

leer [lɪə] **1.** anzüglicher od. lüsterner Seitenblick; **2.** anzüglich od. lüstern blicken od. schielen (**at** nach)

left¹ [left] pret. u. p.p. von leave 1

left² [left] **1.** adj. linke(r, -s), Links...; **2.** adv. links; **turn ~** (sich) nach links wenden; mot. links abbiegen; **3.** die Linke

(a. pol., Boxen), linke Seite; **on the ~** links, auf der linken Seite; **to the ~** (nach) links; **keep to the ~** sich links halten; links fahren; **~·hand** linke(r, -s); **~·hand 'drive** mot. Linkssteuerung f; **~·hand·ed** linkshändig; für Linkshänder; **be ~** Linkshänder(in) sein

left· '**lug·gage of·fice** Brt. rail. Gepäckaufbewahrung(sstelle) f; '**~o·vers** pl. (Speise)Reste pl.; '**~wing** pol. dem linken Flügel angehörend, Links..., Links...

leg [leg] Bein n; (Hammel etc.)Keule f; math. Schenkel m; **pull s.o.'s ~** F j-n arm den Arm nehmen; **stretch one's ~s** sich die Beine vertreten

leg·a·cy [ˈlegəsɪ] Vermächtnis n

le·gal [ˈliːgl] legal, gesetzmäßig; gesetzlich; juristisch, Rechts...

le·ga·tion [lɪˈgeɪʃn] Gesandtschaft f

le·gend [ˈledʒənd] Legende f, Sage f; **le·gen·da·ry** [ˈledʒəndərɪ] legendär

le·gi·ble [ˈledʒəbl] leserlich

le·gis·la·tion [ledʒɪsˈleɪʃn] Gesetzgebung f; **~tive** pol. [ˈledʒɪslətɪv] **1.** gesetzgebend, legislativ; **2.** Legislative f, gesetzgebende Gewalt; **~tor** [ˈledʒɪsleɪtə] Gesetzgeber m

le·git·i·mate [lɪˈdʒɪtɪmət] legitim; gesetz-, rechtmäßig; ehelich

lei·sure [ˈleʒə] freie Zeit; Muße f; **at ~** ohne Hast; '**~ cen·tre** Brt. Freizeitzentrum n; '**~ly** gemächlich; '**~ time** Freizeit f; '**~time ac'tiv·i·ties** pl. Freizeitbeschäftigung f, -gestaltung f; '**~wear** Freizeitkleidung f

lem·on bot. [ˈlemən] Zitrone f; Zitronen...; **~ade** [leməˈneɪd] Zitronenlimonade f

lend [lend] (*lent*) j-m et. (ver-, aus)leihen

length [leŋθ] Länge f; Strecke f; (Zeit)Dauer f; **at ~** ausführlich; **~en** [ˈleŋθən] verlängern, länger machen; länger werden; '**~ways**, '**~wise** der Länge nach; '**~y** (-ier, -iest) sehr lang

le·ni·ent [ˈliːnjənt] mild(e), nachsichtig

lens [lenz] anat., phot., phys. Linse f; phot. Objektiv n

lent [lent] pret. u. p.p. von lend

Lent [lent] Fastenzeit f

len·til bot. [ˈlentɪl] Linse f

Le·o astr. [ˈliːəʊ] Löwe m; **he/she is (a) ~** er/sie ist (ein) Löwe

lieutenant

leop·ard zo. ['lepəd] Leopard m; **~ess**
zo. ['lepədes] Leopardin f
le·o·tard ['liːəʊtɑːd] (Tänzer)Trikot n
lep·ro·sy med. ['leprəsɪ] Lepra f
les·bi·an ['lezbɪən] **1.** lesbisch; **2.** Lesbierin f, F Lesbe f
less [les] **1.** adj. u. adv. (comp. von little
1, 2) kleiner, geringer, weniger; **2.** prp.
weniger, minus, abzüglich
less·en ['lesn] (sich) vermindern od.
-ringern; abnehmen; herabsetzen
less·er ['lesn] kleiner, geringer
les·son ['lesn] Lektion f; (Unterrichts)Stunde f; fig. Lehre f; **~s** pl. Unterricht m
let [let] (let) lassen; bsd. Brt. vermieten,
-pachten; **~ alone** j-n, et. in Ruhe lassen; geschweige denn; **~ down** hinun-
ter-, herunterlassen; Am. Kleider verlängern; j-n im Stich lassen; enttäuschen; **~ go** loslassen; **~ o.s. go** sich
gehenlassen; **~'s go** gehen wir!; **~ in**
(her)einlassen; **~ o.s. in for s.th.** sich et.
einbrocken, sich auf et. einlassen
le·thal ['liːθl] tödlich; Todes...
leth·ar·gy ['leθədʒɪ] Lethargie f
let·ter ['letə] Buchstabe m; print. Type f;
Brief m; **'~box** bsd. Brt. Briefkasten
m; **'~car·ri·er** Am. Briefträger m
let·tuce bot. ['letɪs] (bsd. Kopf)Salat m
leu·k(a)e·mi·a med. [luːˈkiːmɪə] Leukä-
mie f
lev·el ['levl] **1.** adj. eben (Straße etc.);
gleich (a. fig.); ausgeglichen; **be ~ with**
auf gleicher Höhe sein mit; **my ~ best** F
mein möglichstes; **2.** Ebene f (a. fig.),
ebene Fläche; Höhe f (a. geogr.), (Was-
ser- etc.)Spiegel m, (-)Stand m, (-)Pegel
m; bsd. Am. Wasserwaage f; fig. Niveau n, Stufe f; **sea ~** Meeresspiegel m;
on the ~ F ehrlich, aufrichtig; **3.** (bsd.
Brt. -ll-, Am. -l-) (ein)ebnen, planieren;
dem Erdboden gleichmachen; **~ at**
Waffe richten auf (acc.); Beschuldigung
erheben gegen (acc.); **4.** adv.: **~ with** in
Höhe (gen.); **~ 'cross·ing** Brt. schienengleicher Bahnübergang; **~**
-'head·ed vernünftig, nüchtern
le·ver ['liːvə] Hebel m
lev·y ['levɪ] **1.** Steuer f, Abgabe f; **2.**
Steuern erheben
lewd [ljuːd] geil, lüstern; unanständig,
obszön
li·a·bil·i·ty [laɪəˈbɪlətɪ] econ., jur. Ver-

pflichtung f, Verbindlichkeit f; econ.,
jur. Haftung f, Haftpflicht f; Neigung f
(to zu), Anfälligkeit f (to für)
li·a·ble ['laɪəbl] econ., jur. haftbar,
-pflichtig; **be ~ for** haften für; **be ~ to**
neigen zu, anfällig sein für
li·ar ['laɪə] Lügner(in)
li·bel jur. ['laɪbl] **1.** (schriftliche) Verleumdung od. Beleidigung; **2.** (bsd. Brt.
-ll-, Am. -l-) (schriftlich) verleumden
od. beleidigen
lib·e·ral ['lɪbərəl] **1.** liberal (a. pol.), aufgeschlossen; großzügig; reichlich; **2.**
Liberale(r m) f (a. pol.)
lib·e|·rate ['lɪbəreɪt] befreien; **~ra·tion**
[lɪbəˈreɪʃn] Befreiung f; **~ra·tor** ['lɪbə-
reɪtə] Befreier m
lib·er·ty ['lɪbətɪ] Freiheit f; **take liberties with** sich Freiheiten gegen j-n herausnehmen; willkürlich mit et. umgehen; **be at ~** frei sein
Li·bra astr. ['laɪbrə] Waage f; **he/she is
(a) ~** er/sie ist (eine) Waage
li·brar·i·an [laɪˈbreərɪən] Bibliothe-
kar(in); **li·bra·ry** ['laɪbrərɪ] Bibliothek
f; Bücherei f
lice [laɪs] pl. von **louse**
li·cence Brt., **li·cense** Am. ['laɪsəns]
Lizenz f, Konzession f; (Führer-, Jagd-,
Waffen- etc.)Schein m; **'li·cense
plate** Am. mot. Nummernschild n
li·cense Brt., **li·cence** Am. ['laɪsəns]
e-e Lizenz od. Konzession erteilen; be-
hördlich genehmigen
li·chen bot. ['laɪkən] Flechte f
lick [lɪk] **1.** Lecken n; Salzlecke f; **2.** v/t.
(ab-, auf-, be)lecken; F verdreschen,
-prügeln; F schlagen, besiegen; v/i. lek-
ken; züngeln (Flammen)
lic·o·rice ['lɪkərɪs] → **liquorice**
lid [lɪd] Deckel m; (Augen)Lid n
lie¹ [laɪ] **1.** lügen; **~ to s.o.** j-n be-
anlügen; **2.** Lüge f; **tell ~s, tell a ~** lügen; **give the ~ to** j-n, et. Lügen strafen
lie² [laɪ] **1.** (lay, lain) liegen; **let sleeping
dogs ~** schlafende Hunde soll man
nicht wecken; **~ behind** fig. dahinter-
stecken; **~ down** sich hinlegen; **2.** Lage f
(a. fig.); **'~down** Brt. F Nickerchen n;
'~in bsd. Brt. F: **have a ~** sich gründlich ausschlafen
lieu [ljuː]: **in ~ of** an Stelle von (od. gen.)
lieu·ten·ant [lefˈtenənt, Am. luːˈtenənt]
Leutnant m

life [laɪf] (*pl.* **lives** [laɪvz]) Leben *n; jur.* lebenslängliche Freiheitsstrafe; *all her* ~ ihr ganzes Leben lang; *for* ~ fürs (ganze) Leben; *bsd. jur.* lebenslänglich; ~ **as·sur·ance** Lebensversicherung *f;* ~ **belt** Rettungsgürtel *m;* '~**boat** Rettungsboot *n;* '~ **bulb** Glühbirne *f;* '~**guard** Bademeister *m;* Rettungsschwimmer *m;* ~ **im·pris·on·ment** *jur.* lebenslängliche Freiheitsstrafe; ~ **in·sur·ance** Lebensversicherung *f;* ~ **jack·et** Schwimmweste *f;* '~**less** leblos; matt, schwung-, lustlos; '~**like** lebensecht; '~**long** lebenslang; ~ **pre·serv·er** *bsd. Am.* Schwimmweste *f;* Rettungsgürtel *m;* ~ '**sen·tence** *jur.* lebenslängliche Freiheitsstrafe; '~**time** Lebenszeit *f*

lift [lɪft] **1.** *v/t.* (hoch-, auf)heben; erheben; *Verbot etc.* aufheben; *Gesicht etc.* liften, straffen; F klauen; *v/i.* sich heben, steigen (*a. Nebel*); ~ **off** starten (*Rakete*), abheben (*Flugzeug*); **2.** (Hoch-, Auf)Heben *n; phys., aviat.* Auftrieb *m; Brt.* Lift *m,* Aufzug *m,* Fahrstuhl *m; give s.o. a* ~ j-n (im Auto) mitnehmen; F j-n aufmuntern; j-m Auftrieb geben; '~**off** Start *m,* Abheben *n* (*Rakete, Flugzeug*)

lig·a·ment *anat.* ['lɪgəmənt] Band *n*

light¹ [laɪt] **1.** Licht *n* (*a. fig.*); Beleuchtung *f;* Schein *m* (*e-r Kerze etc.*); Feuer *n* (*zum Anzünden*); *fig.* Aspekt *m; Brt. mst* ~**s** *pl.* (Verkehrs)Ampel *f; have you got a* ~, *can you give me a* ~, *please?* haben Sie Feuer?; **2.** (*lit od.* **lighted**) *v/t.* be-, erleuchten; *a.* ~ **up** anzünden; *v/i.* sich entzünden; ~ **up** aufleuchten (*Augen etc.*); **3.** hell, licht

light² [laɪt] leicht (*a. fig.*); *make* ~ *of et.* leichtnehmen; bagatellisieren

light·en¹ [ˈlaɪtn] *v/t.* erhellen; aufhellen; *v/i.* hell(er) werden, sich aufhellen

light·en² [ˈlaɪtn] leichter machen *od.* werden; erleichtern

'**light·er** Anzünder *m;* Feuerzeug *n*

light·'head·ed (leicht) benommen; leichtfertig, töricht; ~'**heart·ed** fröhlich, unbeschwert; '~**house** Leuchtturm *m;* '~**ing** Beleuchtung *f;* '~**ness** Leichtheit *f;* Leichtigkeit *f*

light·ning [ˈlaɪtnɪŋ] Blitz *m; like* ~ wie der Blitz; (*as*) *quick as* ~ blitzschnell; '~ **con·duc·tor** *Brt.,* '~ **rod** *Am.*

electr. Blitzableiter *m*

'**light·weight** *Sport:* Leichtgewicht(ler *m*) *n*

like¹ [laɪk] **1.** *v/t.* gern haben, mögen; *I* ~ *it* es gefällt mir; *I* ~ *her* ich kann sie gut leiden; *how do you* ~ *it?* wie gefällt es dir?, wie findest du es?; *I* ~ *that! iro.* das hab' ich gern!; *I should od. would* ~ *to know* ich möchte gern wissen; *v/i.* wollen; (*just*) *as you* ~ (ganz) wie du willst; *if you* ~ wenn du willst; **2.** ~**s** *pl. and dislikes* *pl.* Neigungen *pl.* u. Abneigungen *pl.*

like² [laɪk] **1.** gleich; wie; ähnlich; ~ *that* so; *feel* ~ Lust haben auf *acc.; what is he* ~? wie ist er?; *that is just* ~ *him!* das sieht ihm ähnlich!; **2.** der, die, das gleiche; *his* ~ seinesgleichen; *the* ~ dergleichen; *the* ~**s** *of you* Leute wie du

like·li·hood [ˈlaɪklɪhʊd] Wahrscheinlichkeit *f;* '~**ly 1.** *adj.* (*-ier, -iest*) wahrscheinlich; geeignet; **2.** *adv.* wahrscheinlich; *not* ~! F bestimmt nicht!

like·ness [ˈlaɪknɪs] Ähnlichkeit *f;* Abbild *n;* '~**wise** ebenso

lik·ing [ˈlaɪkɪŋ] Vorliebe *f*

li·lac [ˈlaɪlək] **1.** lila; **2.** *bot.* Flieder *m*

lil·y *bot.* [ˈlɪlɪ] Lilie *f;* ~ *of the valley* Maiglöckchen *n*

limb [lɪm] (*Körper*)Glied *n;* Ast *m*

lime¹ [laɪm] Kalk *m;* △ *nicht Leim*

lime² *bot.* [laɪm] Linde *f;* Limone *f*

'**lime·light** *fig.* Rampenlicht *n*

lim·it [ˈlɪmɪt] **1.** Limit *n,* Grenze *f; within* ~**s** inGrenzen; *off* ~**s** *Am.* Zutritt verboten (*to* für); *that is the* ~! F das ist der Gipfel!; das ist (doch) die Höhe!; *go to the* ~ bis zum Äußersten gehen; **2.** beschränken (*to* auf *acc.*)

lim·i·ta·tion [lɪmɪˈteɪʃn] Beschränkung *f; fig.* Grenze *f*

'**lim·it·ed** beschränkt, begrenzt; ~ (*liability*) *company Brt.* Gesellschaft *f* mit beschränkter Haftung; '~**less** grenzenlos

limp¹ [lɪmp] **1.** hinken, humpeln; **2.** Hinken *n,* Humpeln *n*

limp² [lɪmp] schlaff, schlapp

line¹ [laɪn] **1.** Linie *f,* Strich *m;* Zeile *f;* Falte *f,* Runzel *f;* Reihe *f; bsd. Am.* (Menschen-, *a.* Auto)Schlange *f;* (Abstammungs)Linie *f;* (Verkehrs-, Eisenbahn- *etc.*)Linie *f,* Strecke *f;* (Flug*etc.*)Gesellschaft *f; bsd. tel.* Leitung *f;*

lives

mil. Linie *f;* Fach *n,* Gebiet *n,* Branche *f; Sport:* (*Ziel-* etc.)Linie *f;* Leine *f;* Schnur *f;* Linie *f,* Richtung *f; fig.* Grenze *f;* Rolle *f; thea.* Rolle *f; the ~* der Äquator; *draw the ~* haltmachen, die Grenze ziehen (*at* bei); *the ~ is busy od. engaged tel.* die Leitung ist besetzt; *hold the ~ tel.* bleiben Sie am Apparat; *stand in ~ Am.* anstehen, Schlange stehen (*for* um, nach); **2.** lin(i)ieren; *Gesicht* zeichnen, (zer)furchen; *Straße etc.* säumen; ~ *up* (sich) in e-r Reihe *od.* Linie aufstellen, *Sport:* sich aufstellen; *bsd. Am.* sich anstellen (*for* um, nach)

line² [laɪn] *Kleid etc.* füttern; auskleiden, -schlagen, *Bremsen etc.* belegen

lin·e·ar [ˈlɪnɪə] linear; Längen...

lin·en [ˈlɪnɪn] **1.** Leinen *n;* (*Bett-, Tisch-* etc.)Wäsche *f;* **2.** leinen, Leinen...; '~ **clos·et** *Am.,* '~ **cup·board** Wäscheschrank *m*

lin·er Linienschiff *n;* Verkehrsflugzeug *n;* → *eyeliner*

lines·man [ˈlaɪnzmən] (*pl.* *-men*) *Sport:* Linienrichter *m;* '~ **wom·an** (*pl.* *-women*) *Sport:* Linienrichterin *f*

'**line-up** *Sport:* Aufstellung *f; bsd. Am.* (Menschen)Schlange *f*

lin·ger [ˈlɪŋə] verweilen, sich aufhalten; dahinsiechen; ~ *on* noch dableiben; *fig.* fortleben

lin·ge·rie [ˈlɛ̃ːʒəriː] Damenunterwäsche *f*

lin·i·ment *pharm.* [ˈlɪnɪmənt] Liniment *n,* Einreibemittel *n*

lin·ing [ˈlaɪnɪŋ] Futter(stoff *m*) *n;* Auskleidung *f,* (*Brems-* etc.)Belag *m*

link [lɪŋk] **1.** (Ketten)Glied *n;* Manschettenknopf *m; fig.* (Binde)Glied *n,* Verbindung *f;* **2.** *a.* ~ *up* (sich) verbinden

links [lɪŋks] → *golf links*

'**link·up** Verbindung *f*

lin·seed [ˈlɪnsiːd] *bot.* Leinsamen *m;* ~ '**oil** Leinöl *n*

li·on *zo.* [ˈlaɪən] Löwe *m;* '~**ess** *zo.* [ˈlaɪənes] Löwin *f*

lip [lɪp] *anat.* Lippe *f;* (*Tassen-* etc.)Rand *m; sl.* Unverschämtheit *f;* '~**stick** Lippenstift *m*

liq·ue·fy [ˈlɪkwɪfaɪ] (sich) verflüssigen

liq·uid [ˈlɪkwɪd] **1.** Flüssigkeit *f;* **2.** flüssig

liq·ui·date [ˈlɪkwɪdeɪt] liquidieren (*a. econ.*); *Schulden* tilgen

liq·uid|·ize [ˈlɪkwɪdaɪz] zerkleinern, pürieren (*im Mixer*); '~**iz·er** Mixgerät *n,* Mixer *m*

liq·uor [ˈlɪkə] *Brt.* alkoholische Getränke *pl.,* Alkohol *m; Am.* Schnaps *m,* Spirituosen *pl.;* △ *nicht* **Likör**

liq·uo·rice [ˈlɪkərɪs] Lakritze *f*

lisp [lɪsp] **1.** lispeln; **2.** Lispeln *n*

list [lɪst] **1.** Liste *f,* Verzeichnis *n;* **2.** (in e-e Liste) eintragen, erfassen

lis·ten [ˈlɪsn] hören; ~ *in* Radio hören; ~ *in to et.* im Radio (an)hören; ~ *in on Telefongespräch etc.* abhören; ~ *to* anhören (*acc.*), zuhören (*dat.*); hören auf (*acc.*); '~**er** Zuhörer(in); (Rundfunk)Hörer(in)

'**list·less** teilnahms-, lustlos

lit [lɪt] *pret. u. p.p. von* **light¹** 2

lit·e·ral [ˈlɪtərəl] (wort)wörtlich; genau; prosaisch

lit·e·ra|·ry [ˈlɪtərərɪ] literarisch, Literatur...; '~**ture** [ˈlɪtərətʃə] Literatur *f*

lithe [laɪð] geschmeidig, gelenkig

li·tre *Brt.,* **li·ter** *Am.* [ˈliːtə] Liter *m, n*

lit·ter [ˈlɪtə] **1.** (*bsd. Papier*)Abfall *m;* Streu *f; zo.* Wurf *m;* Trage *f;* Sänfte *f;* **2.** *et.* herumliegen lassen in (*dat.*) *od.* auf (*dat.*); *be* ~*ed with* übersät sein mit; '~ **bas·ket,** '~ **bin** Abfallkorb *m*

lit·tle [ˈlɪtl] **1.** *adj.* (*less, least*) klein; wenig; *the* ~ *ones pl.* die Kleinen *pl.;* **2.** *adv.* (*less, least*) wenig, kaum; **3.** Kleinigkeit *f; a* ~ ein wenig, ein bißchen; ~ *by* ~ (ganz) allmählich, nach und nach; *not a* ~ nicht wenig

live¹ [lɪv] leben; wohnen (*with* bei); ~ *to see* erleben; ~ *on* leben von; weiterleben; ~ *up to s-n Grundsätzen etc.* gemäß leben; *Erwartungen etc.* entsprechen; ~ *with* mit *j-m* zusammenleben; mit *et.* leben

live² [laɪv] **1.** *adj.* lebend, lebendig; richtig, echt; *electr.* stromführend; *Rundfunk, TV:* Direkt-, Live-...; **2.** *adv.* direkt, original, live

live|·li·hood [ˈlaɪvlɪhʊd] (Lebens)Unterhalt *m;* '~**li·ness** Lebhaftigkeit *f;* '~**ly** (*-ier, -iest*) lebhaft, lebendig; aufregend; schnell, flott

liv·er *anat.* [ˈlɪvə] Leber *f* (*a. gastr.*)

liv·e·ry [ˈlɪvərɪ] Livree *f*

lives [laɪvz] *pl. von* **life**

L

'live·stock Vieh(bestand *m*) *n*

liv·id ['lɪvɪd] bläulich; F fuchsteufelswild

liv·ing ['lɪvɪŋ] **1.** lebend; *the ~ image of* das genaue Ebenbild (*gen.*); **2.** Leben(sweise *f*) *n*; Lebensunterhalt *m*; *the ~ pl.* die Lebenden *pl.*; *standard of ~* Lebensstandard *m*; *earn od. make a ~* (sich) s-n Lebensunterhalt verdienen; '*~ room* Wohnzimmer *n*

liz·ard *zo.* ['lɪzəd] Eidechse *f*

load [ləʊd] **1.** Last *f* (*a. fig.*); Ladung *f*; Belastung *f*; **2.** *j-n* überhäufen (*with* mit); *Schußwaffe* laden; *~ a camera* e-n Film einlegen; *a. ~ up* (auf-, be-, ein)laden

loaf¹ [ləʊf] (*pl.* loaves [ləʊvz]) Laib *m* (Brot); Brot *n*

loaf² [ləʊf] *a. ~ about, ~ around* F herumlungern; '*~er* Müßiggänger(in)

loam [ləʊm] Lehm *m*; '*~y* (*-ier, -iest*) lehmig

loan [ləʊn] **1.** (Ver)Leihen *n*; Anleihe *f*; Darlehen *n*; Leihgabe *f*; *on ~* leihweise; **2.** *bsd. Am. j-m* (aus)leihen; ver-, ausleihen (*to* an *acc.*); '*~ shark econ.* Kredithai *m*

loath [ləʊθ]: *be ~ to do s.th.* et. nur (sehr) ungern tun

loathe [ləʊð] verabscheuen, hassen; '*~ing* Abscheu *m*

loaves [ləʊvz] *pl. von* **loaf¹**

lob [lɒb] *bsd. Tennis:* Lob *m*

lob·by ['lɒbɪ] **1.** Vorhalle *f*; *thea., Film:* Foyer *n*; Wandelhalle *f*; *pol.* Lobby *f*, Interessengruppe *f*; **2.** *pol. Abgeordnete etc.* beeinflussen

lobe *anat., bot.* [ləʊb] Lappen *m*; → **earlobe**

lob·ster *zo.* ['lɒbstə] Hummer *m*

lo·cal ['ləʊkl] **1.** örtlich, Orts..., lokal, Lokal...; **2.** Ortsansässige(r *m*) *f*, Einheimische(r *m*) *f*; *Brt.* F Stammkneipe *f*; *~ 'call tel.* Ortsgespräch *n*; *~ e'lections pl.* Kommunalwahlen *pl.*; *~ 'gov·ern·ment* Gemeindeverwaltung *f*; '*~ time* Ortszeit *f*; *~ 'traf·fic* Orts-, Nahverkehr *m*

lo·cate [ləʊ'keɪt] ausfindig machen; orten; *be ~d* gelegen sein, liegen, sich befinden; **lo·ca·tion** [ləʊ'keɪʃn] Lage *f*; Standort *m*; Platz (*for* für); *Film, TV:* Gelände *n* für Außenaufnahmen; *on ~* auf Außenaufnahme

loch *schott.* [lɒk] See *m*

lock¹ [lɒk] **1.** (*Tür-, Gewehr- etc.*)Schloß *n*; Schleuse(nkammer) *f*; Verschluß *m*; Sperrvorrichtung *f*; **2.** *v/t.* zu-, verschließen, zu-, versperren (*a. ~ up*); umschlingen, -fassen; *tech.* sperren; *v/i.* schließen; ab- *od.* verschließbar sein; *mot. etc.* blockieren (*Räder*); *~ away* wegschließen; *~ in* einschließen, -sperren; *~ out* aussperren; *~ up* abschließen; wegschließen; einsperren

lock² [lɒk] (Haar)Locke *f*

lock·er ['lɒkə] Spind *m*, Schrank *m*; Schließfach *n*; '*~ room bsd. Sport:* Umkleidekabine *f*, -raum *m*

lock·et ['lɒkɪt] Medaillon *n*

'lock·out *econ.* Aussperrung *f*; '*~smith* Schlosser *m*; '*~up* Arrestzelle *f*

lo·co·mo·tion [ləʊkə'məʊʃn] Fortbewegung(sfähigkeit) *f*; *~·tive* ['ləʊkəməʊtɪv] Fortbewegungs...

lo·cust *zo.* ['ləʊkəst] Heuschrecke *f*

lodge [lɒdʒ] **1.** Portier-, Pförtnerloge *f* (*Jagd-, Ski- etc.*)Hütte *f*; Sommer-, Gartenhaus *n*; (*Freimaurer*)Loge *f*; **2.** *v/i.* logieren, *bsd.* vorübergehend *od.* in Untermiete) wohnen; stecken(bleiben) (*Kugel, Bissen etc.*); *v/t.* aufnehmen, beherbergen, (vorübergehend) unterbringen; *Beschwerde etc.* einreichen; *Berufung, Protest* einlegen; '**lodg·er** Untermieter(in); '**lodg·ing** Unterkunft *f*; *~s pl. bsd.* möbliertes Zimmer

loft [lɒft] (Dach)Boden *m*; Heuboden *m*; Empore *f*; (**converted**) *~ Am.* Loft *m*, Fabriketage *f* (*als Wohnung*); '*~y* (*-ier, -iest*) hoch; erhaben; stolz, hochmütig

log [lɒg] (Holz)Klotz *m*; (*gefällter*) Baumstamm; (Holz)Scheit *n*; → '*~book naut.* Logbuch *n*; *aviat.* Bordbuch *n*; *mot.* Fahrtenbuch *n*; '*~cab·in* Blockhaus *n*, -hütte *f*

log·ger·heads ['lɒgəhedz]: *be at ~* sich in den Haaren liegen

lo·gic ['lɒdʒɪk] Logik *f*; '*~al* logisch

loin [lɔɪn] *gastr.* Lende(nstück *n*) *f*; *~s pl. anat.* Lende *f*

loi·ter ['lɔɪtə] trödeln, schlendern, bummeln; herumlungern

loll [lɒl] sich rekeln *od.* lümmeln; *~ out* heraushängen (*Zunge*)

lol·li·pop ['lɒlɪpɒp] Lutscher *m*; *bsd. Brt.* Eis *n* am Stiel; *~ man Brt.* Schülerlotse *m*; *~ woman, ~ lady Brt.* Schülerlotsin

lost

f; **~·ly** F ['lɒlɪ] Lutscher *m;* **ice ~** Eis *n* am Stiel

lone·li·ness ['ləʊnlɪnɪs] Einsamkeit *f;* **'~·ly (-ier, -iest), '~·some** einsam

long¹ [lɒŋ] **1.** *adj.* lang; weit, lang (*Weg*), weit (*Entfernung*); langfristig; **2.** *adv.* lang(e); **as** *od.* **so ~ as** solange wie; vorausgesetzt, daß; **~ ago** vor langer Zeit; **so ~!** F bis dann!, tschüs!; **3.** (e-e) lange Zeit; **for ~** lange; **take ~** lange brauchen *od.* dauern

long² [lɒŋ] sich sehnen (**for** nach)

long·'dis·tance Fern...; Langstrekken...; **~ call** *tel.* Ferngespräch *n;* **'~·run·ner** *Sport:* Langstreckenläufer(in)

lon·gev·i·ty [lɒn'dʒevətɪ] Langlebigkeit *f*

'long·hand Schreibschrift *f*

long·ing ['lɒŋɪŋ] **1.** sehnsüchtig; **2.** Sehnsucht *f,* Verlangen *n*

lon·gi·tude *geogr.* ['lɒndʒɪtjuːd] Länge *f*

'long jump *Sport:* Weitsprung *m;* **~ life 'milk** *bsd.* Brt. H-Milch *f;* **~ 'play·er, ~·'play·ing 'rec·ord** Langspielplatte *f;* **~'range** *mil., aviat.* Fern..., Langstrecken...; langfristig; **~·shore·man** *bsd.* Am. ['lɒŋʃɔːmən] (*pl.* **-men**) Dock-, Hafenarbeiter *m;* **~'sight·ed** *bsd.* Brt. weitsichtig, *fig. a.* weitblickend; **~'stand·ing** seit langem Zeit bestehend; alt; **~'term** langfristig, auf lange Sicht; **~ 'wave** *electr.* Langwelle *f;* **~'wind·ed** langatmig

loo Brt. F [luː] Klo *n*

look [lʊk] **1.** sehen, blicken, schauen (**at, on** auf *acc.,* nach); nachschauen, -sehen; *krank etc.* aussehen; nach e-r Richtung liegen, gehen (*Fenster etc.*); **~ here!** schau mal (her); hör mal (zu)!; **~ like** aussehen wie; **it ~s as if** es sieht (so) aus, als ob; **~ after** aufpassen auf (*acc.*), sich kümmern um, sorgen für; **~ ahead** nach vorne sehen; *fig.* vorausschauen; **~ around** sich umsehen; **~ at** ansehen; **~ back** sich umsehen; *fig.* zurückblicken; **~ down** herab-, heruntersehen auf (*acc.*); *fig.* verächtlich herabsehen auf j-n; **~ for** suchen; **~ forward to** sich freuen auf (*acc.*); **~ in** F hereinschauen (**on** bei) (*als Besucher*); **~ into** untersuchen, prüfen; **~ on** zusehen, -schauen (*dat.*); betrachten, ansehen (**as** als); **~ onto** liegen zu, (hinaus)gehen auf (*acc.*) (*Fenster, etc.*); **~ out** hinaus-,

heraussehen; aufpassen, sich vorsehen; Ausschau halten (**for** nach); **~ over** *et.* durchsehen; *j-n* mustern; **~ round** sich umsehen; **~ through** *et.* durchsehen; **~ up** aufblicken, -sehen; *et.* nachschlagen; *j-n* aufsuchen; **2.** Blick *m;* Miene *f,* (Gesichts)Ausdruck *m;* (**good**) **~s** *pl.* gutes Aussehen; **have a ~ at** *s.th.* sich *et.* ansehen; **I don't like the ~ of it** es gefällt mir nicht; **'~·ing glass** Spiegel *m;* **'~·out** Ausguck *m;* Ausschau *f; fig.* F Aussicht(en *pl.*) *f;* **be on the ~ for** Ausschau halten nach; **that's his own ~** F das ist allein seine Sache

loom¹ [luːm] Webstuhl *m*

loom² [luːm] *a.* **~ up** undeutlich sichtbar werden *od.* auftauchen

loop [luːp] **1.** Schlinge *f,* Schleife *f;* Schlaufe *f;* Öse *f; aviat.* Looping *m, n; Computer:* Schleife *f;* **2.** (sich) schlingen; **'~·hole** *mil.* Schießscharte *f; fig.* Hintertürchen *n;* **a ~ in the law** e-e Gesetzeslücke

loose [luːs] **1.** (**~r, ~st**) los(e); locker; weit; frei; **let ~** loslassen; freilassen; **2. be on the ~** frei herumlaufen; **loos·en** ['luːsn] (sich) lösen *od.* lockern; **~ up** *Sport:* Lockerungsübungen machen

loot [luːt] **1.** (Kriegs-, Diebes)Beute *f;* **2.** plündern

lop [lɒp] (**-pp-**) *Baum* beschneiden, stutzen; **~ off** abhauen, abhacken; **~·'sid·ed** schief; *fig.* einseitig

lo·qua·cious [ləʊ'kweɪʃəs] redselig, geschwätzig

lord [lɔːd] Herr *m,* Gebieter *m;* Brt. Lord *m;* **the ℒ** Gott *m* (der Herr); **the ℒ's Prayer** das Vaterunser; **the ℒ's Supper** das (heilige) Abendmahl; **House of ℒs** Brt. *pol.* Oberhaus *n;* ℒ **'Mayor** Brt. Oberbürgermeister *m*

lor·ry Brt. ['lɒrɪ] Last(kraft)wagen *m,* Lastauto *n,* Laster *m*

lose [luːz] (**lost**) verlieren; verpassen, -säumen; nachgehen (*Uhr*); **~ o.s.** sich verirren; sich verlieren; **'los·er** Verlierer(in)

loss [lɒs] Verlust *m;* Schaden *m;* **at a ~** *econ.* mit Verlust; **be at a ~** in Verlegenheit sein (**for** um)

lost [lɒst] **1.** *pret. u. p.p. von* **lose; 2.** *adj.* verloren; **be ~** sich verirrt haben, sich nicht mehr zurechtfinden (*a. fig.*); **be ~ in thought** in Gedanken versunken sein; **get** ~ sich verirren; **get** ~! *sl.* hau ab!; **~-and-'found (of·fice)** *Am.*, ~ **'prop·er·ty of·fice** *Brt.* Fundbüro *n*

lot [lɒt] Los *n*; Parzelle *f*; Grundstück *n*; *econ.* Partie *f*, Posten (*Ware*); Gruppe *f*, Gesellschaft *f*; Menge *f*, Haufen *m*; Los *n*, Schicksal *n*; △ *nicht* **Lot**; the ~ alles, das Ganze; **a** ~ **of** F, **~s of** F viel, e-e Menge; **a bad** ~ F ein übler Kerl; **cast** *od.* **draw** ~**s** losen

loth [ləʊθ] → *loath*

lo·tion ['ləʊʃn] Lotion *f*

lot·te·ry ['lɒtərɪ] Lotterie *f*

loud [laʊd] laut (*a. adv.*); *fig.* schreiend, grell (*Farben etc.*); **~'speak·er** Lautsprecher *m*

lounge [laʊndʒ] **1.** Wohnzimmer *n*; Aufenthaltsraum *m*, Lounge *f* (*e-s Hotels, Schiffs*); Wartehalle *f*, Lounge *f* (*e-s Flughafens*); '~ **suit** *Brt.* Straßenanzug *m*; **2.** ~ **about**, ~ **around** herumlungern

louse *zo.* [laʊs] (*pl.* **lice** [laɪs]) Laus *f*; **lou·sy** ['laʊzɪ] (*-ier, -iest*) verlaust; F miserabel, saumäßig

lout [laʊt] Flegel *m*, Lümmel *m*

lov·a·ble ['lʌvəbl] liebenswert; reizend

love [lʌv] **1.** Liebe *f* (*of, for, to, towards* zu); Liebling *m*, Schatz *m* (*Anrede, oft unübersetzt*); *Tennis*: null; **be in** ~ **with s.o.** in j-n verliebt sein; **fall in** ~ **with s.o.** sich in j-n verlieben; **make** ~ sich lieben, miteinander schlafen; **give my** ~ **to her** grüße sie herzlich von mir; **send one's** ~ **to** j-n grüßen lassen; ~ **from** herzliche Grüße von (*Briefschluß*); **2.** lieben; gern mögen; '~ **af·fair** Liebesaffäre *f*; '~**·ly** (*-ier, -iest*) (wunder)schön; nett, reizend; F prima; '**lov·er** Liebhaber *m*, Geliebte(r) *m*; Geliebte *f* (*Musik- etc.*)Liebhaber(in), (-)Freund(in); ~**s** *pl.* Liebende *pl.*, Liebespaar *n*

lov·ing ['lʌvɪŋ] liebevoll, liebend

low [ləʊ] **1.** *adj.* niedrig (*a. fig.*); tief (*a. fig.*); knapp (*Vorräte etc.*); gedämpft, schwach (*Licht*); tief (*Ton*); leise (*Ton, Stimme*); gering(schätzig); ordinär; niedergeschlagen, deprimiert; **2.** *adv.* niedrig; tief (*a. fig.*); leise; **3.** *meteor.* Tief(druckgebiet) *n*; *fig.* Tief(punkt *m*, -stand *m*) *n*; '~**·brow** F **1.** geistig Anspruchslose(r *m*) *f*, Unbedarfte(r *m*) *f*;

2. geistig anspruchslos, unbedarft; **~** **-'cal·o·rie** kalorienarm, -reduziert; **~·e'mis·sion** schadstoffarm

low·er ['ləʊə] **1.** niedriger; tiefer; untere(r, -s), Unter...; **2.** niedriger machen; herab-, herunterlassen; *Augen, Stimme, Preis etc.* senken; *Standard* herabsetzen; *fig.* erniedrigen

low·-'fat fettarm; '~·**land** ['ləʊlənd] Tief-, Flachland *n*; '~·**ly** (*-ier, -iest*) niedrig; ~·**'necked** (tief) ausgeschnitten (*Kleid*); ~·**'pitched** *mus.* tief; ~·**'pres·sure** *meteor.* Tiefdruck...; *tech.* Niederdruck...; '~·**rise** *bsd. Am.* niedrig (gebaut); ~·**'spir·it·ed** niedergeschlagen

loy·al ['lɔɪəl] loyal, treu; '~·**ty** Loyalität *f*, Treue *f*

loz·enge ['lɒzɪndʒ] Raute *f*, Rhombus *m*; Pastille *f*

LP [el 'piː] *Abk. für* **long-player, long-playing record** LP, Langspielplatte *f*

Ltd *nur geschr. Abk. für* **limited** mit beschränkter Haftung

lu·bri·cant ['luːbrɪkənt] Schmiermittel *n*; ~·**cate** ['luːbrɪkeɪt] schmieren, ölen; ~·**ca·tion** [luːbrɪ'keɪʃn] Schmieren, Ölen *n*

lu·cid ['luːsɪd] klar

luck [lʌk] Schicksal *n*; Glück *n*; **bad** ~, **hard** ~, **ill** ~ Unglück *n*, Pech *n*; **good** ~ Glück *n*; **good** ~! viel Glück!; **be in** (**out of**) ~ (kein) Glück haben; ~**·i·ly** ['lʌkɪlɪ] glücklicherweise, zum Glück; '~·**y** (*-ier, -iest*) glücklich, Glücks...; **be** ~ Glück haben; ~ **day** Glückstag *m*; ~ **fellow** Glückspilz *m*

lu·cra·tive ['luːkrətɪv] einträglich, lukrativ

lu·di·crous ['luːdɪkrəs] lächerlich

lug [lʌg] (*-gg-*) zerren, schleppen

luge [luːʒ] *Sport*: Rennrodeln *n*; Rennrodel *m*, -schlitten *m*

lug·gage *bsd. Brt.* ['lʌgɪdʒ] (Reise)Gepäck *n*; '~ **car·ri·er** Gepäckträger *m* (*am Fahrrad*); '~ **rack** *bsd. Brt.* Gepäcknetz *n*, -ablage *f*; '~ **van** *Brt.* Gepäckwagen *m*

luke·warm ['luːkwɔːm] lau(warm); *fig.* lau, mäßig, halbherzig

lull [lʌl] **1.** beruhigen; sich legen (*Sturm*); *mst* ~ **to sleep** einlullen; **2.** Pause *f*; Flaute *f* (*a. fig.*)

lul·la·by ['lʌləbaɪ] Wiegenlied *n*

lum·ba·go med. [lʌmˈbeɪgəʊ] Hexenschuß m

lum·ber¹ [ˈlʌmbə] schwerfällig gehen; (dahin)rumpeln (*Wagen*)

lum·ber² [ˈlʌmbə] **1.** bsd. Am. Bau-, Nutzholz n; bsd. Brt. Gerümpel n; **2.** v/t. ~ **s.o. with s.th.** Brt. F j-m et. aufhalsen; '**~·jack** Am. Holzfäller m, -arbeiter m; '**~·mill** Am. Sägewerk n; '**~-room** bsd. Brt. Rumpelkammer f; '**~·yard** Am. Holzplatz m, -lager n

lu·mi·na·ry fig. [ˈluːmɪnərɪ] Leuchte f, Koryphäe f

lu·mi·nous [ˈluːmɪnəs] leuchtend, Leucht...; ~ **di'splay** Leuchtanzeige f; ~ '**paint** Leuchtfarbe f

lump [lʌmp] **1.** Klumpen m; Schwellung f, Beule f; med. Geschwulst f, Knoten m; Stück n (*Zucker etc.*); △ *nicht* Lump; **in the** ~ in Bausch u. Bogen, pauschal; **2.** v/t. ~ **together** fig. zusammenwerfen; in e-n Topf werfen; v/i. Klumpen bilden, klumpen; ~ '**sug·ar** Würfelzucker m; ~ '**sum** Pauschalsumme f; '**~·y** (*-ier, -iest*) klumpig

lu·na·cy [ˈluːnəsɪ] Wahnsinn m

lu·nar [ˈluːnə] Mond...; ~ '**mod·ule** Raumfähre f: Mond(lande)fähre f

lu·na·tic [ˈluːnətɪk] **1.** wahnsinnig, geistesgestört; fig. verrückt; **2.** Wahnsinnige(r m) f, Geistesgestörte(r m) f; fig. Verrückte(r m) f

lunch [lʌntʃ], formell **lun·cheon** [ˈlʌntʃən] **1.** Lunch m, Mittagessen n; **2.** zu Mittag essen; '**lunch hour, 'lunch time** Mittagszeit f, -pause f

lung anat. [lʌŋ] Lungenflügel m; **the ~s** pl. die Lunge

lunge [lʌndʒ] sich stürzen (**at** auf acc.)

lurch [lɜːtʃ] **1.** taumeln, torkeln; **2.** **leave in the** ~ im Stich lassen

lure [lʊə] **1.** Köder m; fig. Lockung f; **2.** ködern, (an)locken

lu·rid [ˈlʊərɪd] grell, schreiend (*Farben etc.*); gräßlich, schauerlich

lurk [lɜːk] lauern; ~ **about**, ~ **around** herumschleichen

lus·cious [ˈlʌʃəs] köstlich, lecker; üppig; knackig (*Mädchen*)

lush [lʌʃ] saftig, üppig

lust [lʌst] **1.** sinnliche Begierde, Lust f; Gier f; △ *nicht* Lust (*Freude etc.*); **2.** ~ **after**, ~ **for** begehren; gierig sein nach

lus·|tre Brt., **~·ter** Am. [ˈlʌstə] Glanz m, Schimmer m; **~·trous** [ˈlʌstrəs] glänzend, schimmernd

lute mus. [luːt] Laute f

Lu·ther·an [ˈluːθərən] lutherisch

lux·u·ri·ant [lʌgˈʒʊərɪənt] üppig; **~·ri·ate** [lʌgˈʒʊərɪeɪt] schwelgen (in dat.); **~·ri·ous** [lʌgˈʒʊərɪəs] luxuriös, Luxus...; **~·ry** [ˈlʌkʃərɪ] Luxus m; Komfort m; Luxusartikel m; Luxus...

LV Brt. [el ˈviː] Abk. für **lunch(eon) voucher** Essensmarke f

lye [laɪ] Lauge f

ly·ing [ˈlaɪɪŋ] **1.** p.prp. von **lie¹** 1 u. **lie²** 1; **2.** adj. lügnerisch, verlogen

lymph med. [lɪmf] Lymphe f

lynch [lɪntʃ] lynchen; '**~ law** Lynchjustiz f

lynx zo. [lɪŋks] Luchs m

lyr·|ic [ˈlɪrɪk] **1.** lyrisch; lyrisches Gedicht; **~s** pl. Lyrik f; (Lied)Text m; '**~·i·cal** lyrisch, gefühlvoll; schwärmerisch

M

M, m [em] M, m n

M [em] Abk. für: **motorway** Brt. Autobahn f; **medium (size)** mittelgroß

m nur geschr. Abk. für **metre** m, Meter m, n; **mile** Meile f (1,6 km); **married** verh., verheiratet; **male, masculine** männlich

ma F [mɑː] Mama f, Mutti f

MA [em ˈeɪ] Abk. für **Master of Arts** Magister m der Philosophie

ma'am [mæm] → **madam**

mac Brt. F [mæk] → **mackintosh**

ma·cad·am Am. [mə'kædəm] → **tar-mac**

mac·a·ro·ni [mækə'rəʊnɪ] sg. Makkaroni pl.

ma·chine [mə'ʃiːn] **1.** Maschine f; **2.** maschinell herstellen; **~gun** Maschinengewehr n; **~made** maschinell hergestellt; **~'read·a·ble** Computer: maschinenlesbar

ma·chin·er·y [mə'ʃiːnərɪ] Maschinen pl.; Maschinerie f; **~ist** [mə'ʃiːnɪst] Maschinenschlosser m; Maschinist m; Maschinennäherin f

mach·o contp. ['mætʃəʊ] (pl. **-os**) Macho m

mack Brt. F [mæk] → **mackintosh**

mack·e·rel zo. ['mækrəl] Makrele f

mack·in·tosh bsd. Brt. ['mækɪntɒʃ] Regenmantel m

mac·ro... ['mækrəʊ] Makro..., (sehr) groß

mad [mæd] wahnsinnig, verrückt; vet. tollwütig; bsd. Am. F wütend; fig. wild, versessen (**about** auf acc.); verrückt (**about** nach); **drive s.o.** ~ j-n verrückt machen; **go** ~ verrückt werden; **like** ~ wie verrückt

mad·am ['mædəm] gnädige Frau (Anrede, oft unübersetzt)

'mad·cap verrückt; **~den** ['mædn] verrückt od. rasend machen; **~den·ing** ['mædnɪŋ] unerträglich; verrückt od. rasend machend

made [meɪd] pret. u. p.p. von **make** 1; **~ of gold** aus Gold

'mad·house fig. Irrenhaus n; **'~ly** wie verrückt; F wahnsinnig, schrecklich; **'~man** (pl. **-men**) Verrückte(r) m; **'~ness** Wahnsinn m; **'~wom·an** (pl. **-women**) Verrückte f

mag·a·zine [mægə'ziːn] Magazin n, Zeitschrift f; Magazin n (e-r Feuerwaffe, e-s Fotoapparats); Lagerhaus n

mag·got zo. ['mægət] Made f

Ma·gi ['meɪdʒaɪ] pl.: **the (three)** ~ die (drei) Weisen aus dem Morgenland, die Heiligen Drei Könige

ma·gic ['mædʒɪk] **1.** Magie f, Zauberei f; Zauber m; fig. Wunder n; **2.** (**~ally**) a. **~al** magisch, Zauber...; **ma·gi·cian** [mə'dʒɪʃn] Magier m, Zauberer m; Zauberkünstler m

ma·gis·trate ['mædʒɪstreɪt] (Friedens)Richter(in); △ nicht **Magistrat**

mag·na·nim·i·ty [mægnə'nɪmətɪ] Großmut m; **~nan·i·mous** [mæg-'nænɪməs] großmütig, hochherzig

mag·net ['mægnɪt] Magnet m; **~ic** [mæg'netɪk] (**~ally**) magnetisch, Magnet...

mag·nif·i·cent [mæg'nɪfɪsnt] großartig, prächtig

mag·ni·fy ['mægnɪfaɪ] vergrößern; '**~ing glass** Vergrößerungsglas n, Lupe f

mag·ni·tude ['mægnɪtjuːd] Größe f; Wichtigkeit f

mag·pie zo. ['mægpaɪ] Elster f

ma·hog·a·ny [mə'hɒgənɪ] Mahagoni (-holz) n

maid [meɪd] (Dienst)Mädchen n, Hausangestellte f; alt (e-r Jung)fer; **~ of all work** bsd. fig. Mädchen n für alles; **~ of hono(u)r** Hofdame f; bsd. Am. (erste) Brautjungfer

maid·en ['meɪdn] Jungfern..., Erstlings...; '**~ name** Mädchenname m (e-r Frau)

mail [meɪl] **1.** Post(sendung) f; **by** ~ bsd. Am. mit der Post; **2.** bsd. Am. mit der Post (zu)schicken, aufgeben, Brief einwerfen; '**~bag** Postsack m; Am. Posttasche f (e-s Briefträgers); '**~box** Am. Briefkasten m; '**~ car·ri·er** Am., '**~man** (pl. **-men**) Am. Briefträger m, Postbote m; **~ or·der** Bestellung f (von Waren) bei e-m Versandhaus; **~-or·der 'firm, ~or·der 'house** Versandhaus n

maim [meɪm] verstümmeln

main [meɪn] **1.** Haupt..., wichtigste(r, -s); hauptsächlich; **by** ~ **force** mit äußerster Kraft; **2.** mst **~s** pl. Haupt(gas-, -wasser-, -strom)leitung f; (Strom)Netz n; **in the** ~ im Hauptsache, im wesentlichen; '**~frame** Computer: Großrechner m; '**~land** ['meɪnlənd] Festland n; '**~ly** hauptsächlich; '**mem·o·ry** Computer: Hauptspeicher m; Arbeitsspeicher m; **~ 'men·u** Computer: Hauptmenü n; **~ 'road** Haupt(verkehrs)straße f; '**~spring** Hauptfeder f (e-r Uhr); fig. (Haupt)Triebfeder f; '**~stay** fig. Hauptstütze f; **~ street** Am. Hauptstraße f

main·tain [meɪn'teɪn] (aufrecht)erhalten, beibehalten, instand halten, pflegen, tech. a. warten; Familie etc. unterhalten, versorgen; behaupten

main·te·nance ['meɪntənəns] (Aufrecht)Erhaltung f; Instandhaltung f, Pflege f, tech. a. Wartung f; Unterhalt m

maize bsd. Brt. bot. [meɪz] Mais m

ma·jes·tic [mə'dʒestɪk] (~ally) majestätisch; **~·ty** ['mædʒəstɪ] Majestät f

ma·jor ['meɪdʒə] **1.** größere(r, -s); fig. a. bedeutend, wichtig; jur. volljährig; **C ~** mus. C-Dur f; **2.** mil. Major m; jur. Volljährige(r m f); Am. univ. Hauptfach n; mus. Dur n; **~ 'gen·e·ral** mil. Generalmajor m; **~·i·ty** [mə'dʒorətɪ] Mehrheit f, Mehrzahl f; jur. Volljährigkeit f; **~ 'league** Am. Baseball: oberste Spielklasse; **~ 'road** Haupt(verkehrs)straße f

make [meɪk] **1.** (made) machen; anfertigen, herstellen, erzeugen; (zu)bereiten; (er)schaffen; ergeben, bilden; machen zu; ernennen zu; Geld verdienen; sich erweisen als, abgeben (Person); schätzen auf (acc.); Geschwindigkeit erreichen; Fehler machen; Frieden etc. schließen; e-e Rede halten; F Strecke zurücklegen; mit inf.: j-n veranlassen zu, bringen zu, zwingen zu; **~ it** es schaffen; **~ do with** sich mit et. auskommen, sich mit et. behelfen; **do you ~ one of us?** machen Sie mit?; **what do you ~ of it?** was halten Sie davon?; **~ believe** vorgeben; **~ friends with** sich anfreunden mit; **~ good** wiedergutmachen; Versprechen etc. halten; **~ haste** sich beeilen; **~ way** Platz machen; **~ for** zugehen auf (acc.); sich aufmachen nach; **~ into** verarbeiten zu; **~ off** sich davonmachen, sich aus dem Staub machen; **~ out** Rechnung, Scheck etc. ausstellen; Urkunde etc. ausstellen; ausmachen, erkennen; aus j-m, e-r Sache klug werden; **~ over** Eigentum übertragen; **~ up** et. zusammenstellen; sich et. ausdenken, et. erfinden; (sich) zurechtmachen od. schminken; **~ it up** sich versöhnen od. wieder vertragen (with mit); **~ up one's mind** sich entschließen; **be made up of** bestehen aus, sich zusammensetzen aus; **~ up for** nach-, aufholen; für et. entschädigen; **2.** Mach-, Bauart f; Fabrikat n, Marke f; **'~·be·lieve** Schein m, Phantasie f; **'~·r** Hersteller m; 2 Schöpfer m (Gott); **'~·shift 1.** Notbehelf m; **2.** behelfsmäßig, Behelfs...; **'~·up** Make-up n, Schminke f; Aufmachung f; Zusammensetzung f

mak·ing ['meɪkɪŋ] Erzeugung f, Herstellung f, Fabrikation f; **be in the ~** noch in Arbeit sein; **have the ~s of** das Zeug haben zu

mal·ad·just·ed [mælə'dʒʌstɪd] nicht angepaßt, verhaltens-, milieugestört

mal·ad·min·i·stra·tion [mælədmɪnɪ'streɪʃn] schlechte Verwaltung; pol. Mißwirtschaft f

mal·con·tent ['mælkəntent] **1.** unzufrieden; **2.** Unzufriedene(r m) f

male [meɪl] **1.** männlich; **2.** Mann m; zo. Männchen n; **~ 'nurse** (Kranken)Pfleger m

mal·for·ma·tion [mælfɔː'meɪʃn] Mißbildung f

mal·ice ['mælɪs] Bosheit f; Groll m; jur. böse Absicht, Vorsatz m

ma·li·cious [mə'lɪʃəs] boshaft; böswillig

ma·lign [mə'laɪn] verleumden; **ma·lig·nant** [mə'lɪɡnənt] bösartig (a. med.); boshaft

mall Am. [mɔːl, mæl] Einkaufszentrum n

mal·le·a·ble ['mælɪəbl] tech. verformbar; fig. formbar

mal·let ['mælɪt] Holzhammer m; (Kroket-, Polo)Schläger m

mal·nu·tri·tion [mælnjuː'trɪʃn] Unterernährung f; Fehlernährung f

mal·o·dor·ous [mæl'əʊdərəs] übelriechend

mal·prac·tice [mæl'præktɪs] Vernachlässigung f der beruflichen Sorgfalt; med. falsche Behandlung, (ärztlicher) Kunstfehler

malt [mɔːlt] Malz n

mal·treat [mæl'triːt] schlecht behandeln; mißhandeln

mam·mal zo. ['mæml] Säugetier n

mam·moth ['mæməθ] **1.** zo. Mammut n; **2.** Mammut..., Riesen..., riesig

mam·my F ['mæmɪ] Mami f

man 1. [mæn, in Zssgn nachgestellt -mən] (pl. **men**) Mann m; Mensch(en pl.) m; Menschheit f; F (Ehe)Mann m; F Geliebte(r m) m; (Schach)Figur f; (Dame)Stein m; **the ~ in** (Am. a. **on**) **the street** der Mann auf der Straße; **2.** [mæn] (-nn-) (Raum)Schiff etc. bemannen

M

man·age ['mænɪdʒ] v/t. Betrieb etc. leiten, führen; Künstler, Sportler etc. managen; et. zustande bringen; es fertigbringen (**to do** zu tun); umgehen (können) mit; mit j-m, et. fertig werden; F Arbeit, Essen etc. bewältigen, schaffen; v/i. auskommen (**with** mit; **without** ohne); F es schaffen, zurechtkommen; F es einrichten, es ermöglichen; **'~·a·ble** handlich; lenksam; **'~·ment** Verwaltung f; econ. Management n, Unternehmensführung f; econ. Geschäftsleitung f, Direktion f

man·ag·er ['mænɪdʒə] Verwalter m; econ. Manager m; econ. Geschäftsführer m, Leiter m, Direktor m; Manager m (e-s Schauspielers etc.); Sport: (Chef)Trainer m; **be a good ~** gut od. sparsam wirtschaften können; **~·ess** [mænɪdʒə'res] Verwalterin f; econ. Managerin f; econ. Geschäftsführerin f, Leiterin f, Direktorin f; Managerin f (e-s Schauspielers etc.)

man·a·ge·ri·al econ. [mænə'dʒɪərɪəl] geschäftsführend, leitend; **~ position** leitende Stellung; **~ staff** leitende Angestellte pl.

man·ag·ing econ. ['mænɪdʒɪŋ] geschäftsführend, leitend; **~ di·rec·tor** Generaldirektor m, leitender Direktor

man·date ['mændeɪt] Mandat n; Auftrag m; Vollmacht f; **~·da·to·ry** ['mændətərɪ] obligatorisch, zwingend

mane [meɪn] Mähne f

ma·neu·ver Am. [mə'nuːvə] → **ma·noeuvre**

man·ful ['mænfʊl] beherzt

mange vet. [meɪndʒ] Räude f

manger ['meɪndʒə] Krippe f

man·gle ['mæŋgl] **1.** (Wäsche)Mangel f; **2.** mangeln; übel zurichten, zerfleischen; fig. Text verstümmeln

mang·y ['meɪndʒɪ] (**-ier, -iest**) vet. räudig; fig. schäbig

'man·hood Mannesalter n; euphem. Manneskraft f

ma·ni·a ['meɪnjə] Wahn(sinn) m; fig. (**for**) Sucht f(nach), Leidenschaft f(für), Manie f, Fimmel m; **~c** ['meɪnɪæk] Wahnsinnige(r m) f, Verrückte(r m) f; fig. Fanatiker(in)

man·i·cure ['mænɪkjʊə] Maniküre f, Handpflege f

man·i·fest ['mænɪfest] **1.** offenkundig;

2. v/t. offenbaren, manifestieren

man·i·fold ['mænɪfəʊld] mannigfaltig, vielfältig

ma·nip·u·late [mə'nɪpjʊleɪt] manipulieren; (geschickt) handhaben; **~·la·tion** [mənɪpjʊ'leɪʃn] Manipulation f

man|'jack F: **every ~** jeder einzelne; **~'kind** die Menschheit, die Menschen pl.; **'~·ly** (**-ier, -iest**) männlich; **~-'made** vom Menschen geschaffen, künstlich; **~ fibre** (Am. **fiber**) Kunstfaser f

man·ner ['mænə] Art f (u. Weise f); Betragen n, Auftreten n; **~s** pl. Benehmen n, Umgangsformen pl., Manieren pl.; Sitten pl.

ma·noeu·vre Brt., **ma·neu·ver** Am. [mə'nuːvə] **1.** Manöver n (a. fig.); **2.** manövrieren (a. fig.)

man·or Brt. ['mænə] (Land)Gut n; → '**~·house** Herrenhaus n

'man·pow·er menschliche Arbeitskraft; Arbeitskräfte pl.

man·sion ['mænʃn] (herrschaftliches) Wohnhaus

'man·slaugh·ter jur. Totschlag m, fahrlässige Tötung

man·tel|·piece ['mæntlpiːs], '**~·shelf** (pl. **-shelves**) Kaminsims m

man·u·al ['mænjʊəl] **1.** Hand...; mit der Hand (gemacht); **2.** Handbuch n

man·u·fac·ture [mænjʊ'fæktʃə] **1.** erzeugen, herstellen; **2.** Herstellung f, Fertigung f; Erzeugnis n, Fabrikat n; **~·tur·er** [mænjʊ'fæktʃərə] Hersteller m, Erzeuger m; **~·tur·ing** [mænjʊ-'fæktʃərɪŋ] Herstellung...

ma·nure [mə'njʊə] **1.** Dünger m, Mist m, Dung m; **2.** düngen

man·u·script ['mænjʊskrɪpt] Manuskript n

man·y ['menɪ] (**more, most**) viel(e); **~ a** manche(r, -s), manch eine(r, -s); **~ times** oft; **as ~** ebensoviel(e); **2.** viele; **a good ~** ziemlich viel(e); **a great ~** sehr viele

map [mæp] **1.** (Land- etc.)Karte f; (Stadt- etc.)Plan m; △ nicht **Mappe**; **2.** (**-pp-**) e-e Karte machen von; auf e-r Karte eintragen; **~ out** fig. (bis in die Einzelheiten) (voraus)planen

ma·ple bot. ['meɪpl] Ahorn m

mar [mɑː] (**-rr-**) beeinträchtigen; verderben

Mar *nur geschr. Abk. für* **March** März *m*

mar·a·thon ['mærəθn] **1.** *a.* ~ **race** Marathonlauf *m*; **2.** Marathon..., *fig. a.* Dauer...

ma·raud [mə'rɔːd] plündern

mar·ble ['mɑːbl] **1.** Marmor *m*; Murmel *f*; **2.** marmorn

march [mɑːtʃ] **1.** marschieren; *fig.* fortschreiten; **2.** Marsch *m*; *fig.* (Fort-) Gang *m*; **the** ~ **of events** der Lauf der Dinge

March [mɑːtʃ] (*Abk.* **Mar**) März *m*

'march·ing or·ders *pl.*: **get one's** ~ *Brt.* I den Laufpaß bekommen

mare [meə] *zo.* Stute *f*; △ *nicht* **Mähre**; **~'s nest** *fig.* Schwindel *m*; (Zeitungs)Ente *f*

mar·ga·rine [mɑːdʒə'riːn], **marge** *Brt.* F [mɑːdʒ] Margarine *f*

mar·gin ['mɑːdʒɪn] Rand *m* (*a. fig.*); Grenze *f* (*a. fig.*); *fig.* Spielraum *m*; (Gewinn-, Verdienst)Spanne *f*; **by a wide** ~ mit großem Vorsprung; **'~·al** Rand...; ~ **note** Randbemerkung *f*

mar·i·hua·na, mar·i·jua·na [mærjuː-'ɑːnə] Marihuana *n*

ma·ri·na [mə'riːnə] Boots-, Jachthafen *m*

ma·rine [mə'riːn] Marine *f*; △ *nicht* (**Kriegs)Marine**; *mil.* Marineinfanterist *m*

mar·i·ner ['mærɪnə] Seemann *m*

mar·i·tal ['mærɪtl] ehelich, Ehe...; ~ **'sta·tus** Familienstand *m*

mar·i·time ['mærɪtaɪm] See...; Küsten...; Schiffahrts...

mark¹ [mɑːk] (deutsche) Mark; △ *nicht* **das Mark**

mark² [mɑːk] **1.** Marke *f*, Markierung *f*; (Kenn)Zeichen *n*, Merkmal *n*; (Körper)Mal *n*; Ziel *n* (*a. fig.*); (Fuß-, Brems*etc.*)Spur *f* (*a. fig.*); Fleck *m*; (Fabrik-, Waren)Zeichen *n*, (Schutz-, Handels-) Marke *f*; *econ.* Preisangabe *f*; *Schule:* Note *f*, Zensur *f*, Punkt *m*; *Laufsport:* Startlinie *f*; *fig.* Zeichen *n*; *fig.* Norm *f*; **be up to the** ~ den Anforderungen gewachsen sein (*Person*) *od.* genügen (*Leistungen etc.*); *gesundheitlich* auf der Höhe sein; **be wide of the** ~ weit danebenschießen; *fig.* sich gewaltig irren; weit danebenliegen (*Schätzung etc.*); **hit the** ~ (das Ziel) treffen; *fig.* ins Schwarze treffen; **miss the** ~ danebenschießen, das Ziel verfehlen (*a. fig.*); **2.**

markieren, anzeichnen; anzeigen; kennzeichnen; *Waren* auszeichnen; *Preis* festsetzen; Spuren hinterlassen auf (*dat.*); Flecken machen auf (*dat.*); *Schule:* benoten, zensieren; *Sport:* Gegenspieler decken, markieren; ~ **my words** denk an m-e Worte; **to** ~ **the occasion** zur Feier des Tages; ~ **time** auf der Stelle treten (*a. fig.*); ~ **down** notieren, vermerken; *im Preis* herabsetzen; ~ **off** abgrenzen; *bsd. auf e-r Liste* abhaken; ~ **out** *durch Striche etc.* markieren; bestimmen (**for** für); ~ **up** *im Preis* heraufsetzen; **~ed** deutlich, ausgeprägt; **'~·er** Markierstift *m*; Lesezeichen *n*; *Sport:* Bewacher(in)

mar·ket ['mɑːkɪt] **1.** Markt *m*; Markt(platz) *m*; *Am.* (Lebensmittel-) Geschäft *n*, Laden *m*; *econ.* Absatz *m*; *econ.* (**for**) Nachfrage *f* (nach), Bedarf *m* (an); **on the** ~ auf dem Markt *od. im* Handel; **put on the** ~ auf den Markt *od.* in den Handel bringen; (zum Verkauf) anbieten; **2.** *v/t.* auf den Markt *od.* in den Handel bringen; verkaufen, -treiben; **~·a·ble** *econ.* marktgängig; ~ **'gar·den** *Brt. econ.* Gemüse- u. Obstgärtnerei *f*; **'~·ing** *econ.* Marketing *n*

'mark·ing Markierung *f*; *zo.* Zeichnung *f*; *Sport:* Deckung *f*; **man-to-man** ~ Manndeckung *f*

'marks·man (*pl.* **-men**) guter Schütze; **'~·wom·an** (*pl.* **-women**) gute Schützin

mar·ma·lade ['mɑːməleɪd] *bsd.* Orangenmarmelade *f*

mar·mot *zo.* ['mɑːmət] Murmeltier *n*

ma·roon [mə'ruːn] **1.** kastanienbraun; **2.** *auf e-r einsamen Insel* aussetzen; **3.** Leuchtrakete *f*

mar·quee [mɑː'kiː] Festzelt *n*

mar·quis ['mɑːkwɪs] Marquis *m*

mar·riage ['mærɪdʒ] Heirat *f*, Hochzeit *f* (**to** mit); Ehe *f*; **civil** ~ standesamtliche Trauung; **'mar·ria·gea·ble** heiratsfähig; '~ **cer·tif·i·cate** Trauschein *m*, Heiratsurkunde *f*

mar·ried ['mærɪd] verheiratet; ehelich, Ehe...; ~ **couple** Ehepaar *n*; ~ **life** Ehe(leben *n*) *f*

mar·row ['mærəʊ] *anat.* (Knochen-) Mark *n*; *fig.* Kern *m*, *das* Wesentlichste; *a.* **vegetable** ~ *Brt. bot.* Markkürbis *m*

mar·ry ['mærɪ] v/t. heiraten; *Paar* trauen; *be married* verheiratet sein (*to* mit); *get married* heiraten; sich verheiraten (*to* mit); v/i. heiraten

marsh [mɑːʃ] Sumpf(land n) m, Marsch f

mar·shal ['mɑːʃl] **1.** mil. Marschall m; Am. Bezirkspolizeichef m; **2.** (*bsd. Brt.* **-ll-**, Am. **-l-**) (an)ordnen, arrangieren; führen

marsh·y ['mɑːʃɪ] (**-ier, -iest**) sumpfig

mar·ten zo. ['mɑːtɪn] Marder m

mar·tial ['mɑːʃl] kriegerisch; Kriegs..., Militär...; ~ **arts** pl. asiatische Kampfsportarten pl.; ~ **law** Kriegsrecht n

mar·tyr ['mɑːtə] Märtyrer(in)

mar·vel ['mɑːvl] **1.** Wunder n; **2.** (*bsd. Brt.* **-ll-**, Am. **-l-**) sich wundern, staunen; ~**(l)ous** ['mɑːvələs] wunderbar; fabelhaft, phantastisch

mar·zi·pan [mɑːzɪ'pæn] Marzipan n, m

mas·ca·ra [mæ'skɑːrə] Wimperntusche f

mas·cot ['mæskət] Maskottchen n

mas·cu·line ['mæskjʊlɪn] männlich; Männer...; maskulin

mash [mæʃ] **1.** zerdrücken, -quetschen; **2.** *Brt.* F Kartoffelbrei m; Maische f; Mengfutter n; ~**ed po·ta·toes** pl. Kartoffelbrei m

mask [mɑːsk] **1.** Maske f (a. Computer); **2.** maskieren; fig. verbergen, -schleiern; ~**ed** maskiert; ~ **ball** Maskenball m

ma·son ['meɪsn] Steinmetz m; mst 2 Freimaurer m; ~**ry** ['meɪsnrɪ] Mauerwerk n

masque thea. hist. [mɑːsk] Maskenspiel n; △ nicht **Maske**

mas·que·rade [mæskə'reɪd] **1.** Maskerade f (a. fig.); Verkleidung f; **2.** fig. sich ausgeben (*as* als, für)

mass [mæs] **1.** Masse f; Menge f; Mehrzahl f; *the ~es* pl. die (breite) Masse; **2.** (sich) (an)sammeln od. (an)häufen; Massen...

Mass rel. [mæs] Messe f

mas·sa·cre ['mæsəkə] **1.** Massaker n; **2.** niedermetzeln

mas·sage ['mæsɑːʒ] **1.** Massage f; **2.** massieren

mas·seur [mæ'sɜː] Masseur m; ~**seuse** [mæ'sɜːz] Masseurin f, Masseuse f

mas·sif ['mæsiːf] (Gebirgs)Massiv n

mas·sive ['mæsɪv] massiv; groß, gewaltig

mass·| 'me·di·a pl. Massenmedien pl.; ~**pro'duce** serienmäßig herstellen; ~ **pro'duc·tion** Massen-, Serienproduktion f

mast [mɑːst] naut. (a. Antennen- etc.-)Mast m

mas·ter ['mɑːstə] **1.** Meister m; Herr m; *bsd. Brt.* Lehrer m; paint. etc. Meister m; Original(kopie f) n; univ. Magister m; 2 **of Arts** (abbr. **MA**) Magister m Artium; ~ **of ceremonies** *bsd. Am.* Conférencier m; **2.** Meister...; Haupt...; ~ **copy** Originalkopie f; ~ **tape** tech. Mastertape n, Originalband n; **3.** Herr sein über (acc.); *Sprache etc.* beherrschen; *Aufgabe etc.* meistern; '~ **key** Hauptschlüssel m; '~**ly** meisterhaft, virtuos; '~**piece** Meisterstück n; ~**y** ['mɑːstərɪ] Herrschaft f; Oberhand f; Beherrschung f (*e-r Sprache etc.*)

mas·tur·bate ['mæstəbeɪt] masturbieren, onanieren

mat¹ [mæt] **1.** Matte f; Untersetzer m; **2.** (**-tt-**) sich verfilzen

mat² [mæt] mattiert, matt

match¹ [mætʃ] Streich-, Zündholz n

match² [mætʃ] **1.** der, die, das gleiche; (dazu) passende Sache od. Person, Gegenstück n; (Fußball- etc.)Spiel n, (Box- etc.)Kampf m, (Tennis- etc.)Match n, m; Heirat f; gute etc. Partie (*Person*); *be a (no) ~ for s.o.* j-m (nicht) gewachsen sein; *find od. meet one's ~* seinen Meister finden; **2.** v/t. j-m, e-r Sache ebenbürtig od. gewachsen sein, gleichkommen; j-m, e-r Sache entsprechen, passen zu; v/i. zusammenpassen, übereinstimmen, entsprechen; *gloves to ~* dazu passende Handschuhe

'match·box Streich-, Zündholzschachtel f

'match·|less unvergleichlich, einzigartig; '~**mak·er** Ehestifter(in); ~ **'point** *Tennis etc.*: Matchball m

mate¹ [meɪt] → **checkmate**

mate² [meɪt] **1.** (Arbeits)Kamerad m, (-)Kollege m; Männchen n od. Weibchen n (*von Tieren*); naut. Maat m; **2.** v/t. Tiere paaren; v/i. zo. sich paaren

ma·te·ri·al [mə'tɪərɪəl] **1.** Material n,

Stoff *m*; **writing ~s** *pl.* Schreibmaterial(ien *pl.*) *n*; **2.** materiell; leiblich; wesentlich

ma·ter·nal [mə'tɜ:nl] mütterlich, Mutter...; mütterlicherseits

ma·ter·ni·ty [mə'tɜ:nəti] **1.** Mutterschaft *f*; **2.** Schwangerschafts..., Umstands...; **~ leave** Mutterschaftsurlaub *m*; **~ ward** Entbindungsstation *f*

math *Am.* F [mæθ] Mathe *f*

math·e·ma·ti·cian [mæθəmə'tıʃn] Mathematiker *m*; **~mat·ics** [mæθə'mætıks] *mst sg.* Mathematik *f*

maths *Brt.* F [mæθs] *mst sg.* Mathe *f*

mat·i·née *thea. etc.* ['mætıneı] Nachmittagsvorstellung *f*; △ *nicht Matinee*

ma·tric·u·late [mə'trıkjuleıt] (sich) immatrikulieren

mat·ri·mo|·ni·al [mætrı'məunjəl] ehelich, Ehe...; **~ny** ['mætrıməni] Ehe (-stand *m*) *f*

ma·trix *tech.* ['meıtrıks] (*pl.* **-trices** [-trısi:z], **-trixes**) Matrize *f*

ma·tron ['meıtrən] *Brt.* Oberschwester *f*; Hausmutter *f*; Matrone *f*

mat·ter ['mætə] **1.** Materie *f*, Material *n*, Substanz *f*, Stoff *m*; *med.* Eiter *m*; Sache *f*, Angelegenheit *f*; **printed ~** *post* Drucksache *f*; **what's the ~ (with you?)** was ist los (mit dir)?; **no ~ who** gleichgültig, wer; **for that ~** was das betrifft; **a ~ of course** e-e Selbstverständlichkeit; **a ~ of fact** e-e Tatsache; **as a ~ of fact** tatsächlich, eigentlich; **a ~ of form** e-e Formsache; **a ~ of time** e-e Frage der Zeit; **2.** von Bedeutung sein (**to** für); **it doesn't ~** es macht nichts; **~of·fact** sachlich, nüchtern

mat·tress ['mætrıs] Matratze *f*

ma·ture [mə'tjuə] **1.** (**~r**, **~st**) reif (*a. fig.*); **2.** (heran)reifen, reif werden; **ma·tu·ri·ty** [mə'tjuərəti] Reife *f* (*a. fig.*)

maud·lin ['mɔ:dlın] rührselig

maul [mɔ:l] übel zurichten; *fig.* verreißen

Maun·dy Thurs·day ['mɔ:ndı -] Gründonnerstag *m*

mauve [məuv] malvenfarbig, mauve

mawk·ish ['mɔ:kıʃ] rührselig

max·i... ['mæksı] Maxi..., riesig, Riesen...

max·im ['mæksım] Grundsatz *m*

max·i·mum ['mæksıməm] **1.** (*pl.* **-ma**

[-mə], **-mums**) Maximum *n*; **2.** maximal, Maximal..., Höchst...

May [meı] Mai *m*

may *v/aux.* [meı] (*pret.* **might**) ich kann/mag/darf *etc.*, du kannst/magst/darfst *etc.*

may·be ['meıbi:] vielleicht

'May|·bee·tle *zo.*, **'~·bug** *zo.* Maikäfer *m*

'May Day der 1. Mai

may·on·naise [meıə'neız] Mayonnaise *f*

mayor [meə] Bürgermeister *m*; △ *nicht Major*

'may·pole Maibaum *m*

maze [meız] Irrgarten *m*, Labyrinth *n* (*a. fig.*)

MB [em 'bi:] *Abk. für* **megabyte** MB, Megabyte *n*

MCA [em si: 'eı] *Abk. für* **maximum credible accident** GAU *m*, größter anzunehmender Unfall

MD [em 'di:] *Abk. für* **Doctor of Medicine** (*lateinisch medicinae doctor*) Dr. med., Doktor *m* der Medizin

me [mi:] mich; mir; F ich

mead·ow ['medəu] Wiese *f*, Weide *f*

mea·gre *Brt.*, **mea·ger** *Am.* ['mi:gə] mager (*a. fig.*), dürr; dürftig

meal [mi:l] Mahl(zeit *f*) *n*; Essen *n*

meal² [mi:l] Schrotmehl *n*

mean¹ [mi:n] gemein, niederträchtig; geizig, knauserig; schäbig

mean² [mi:n] (**meant**) meinen; sagen wollen; bedeuten; beabsichtigen, vorhaben; **be ~t for** bestimmt sein für; **~ well (ill)** es gut (schlecht) meinen

mean³ [mi:n] **1.** Mitte *f*, Mittel *n*, Durchschnitt *m*; **2.** mittlere(r, -s), Mittel..., durchschnittlich, Durchschnitts...

'mean·ing 1. Sinn *m*, Bedeutung *f*; △ *nicht Meinung*; **2.** bedeutungsvoll, bedeutsam; **'~ful** bedeutungsvoll; sinnvoll; **'~·less** sinnlos

means [mi:nz] *pl.* (*a. sg. konstruiert*) Mittel *n od. pl.*, Weg *m*; Mittel *pl.*, Vermögen *n*; **by all ~s** auf alle Fälle, unbedingt; **by no ~s** keineswegs, auf keinen Fall; **by ~s of** durch, mit

meant [ment] *pret. u. p.p. von* **mean²**

'mean|·time 1. inzwischen; **2.** **in the ~** inzwischen; **'~·while** inzwischen

mea·sles *med.* ['mi:zlz] *sg.* Masern *pl.*

M

mea·su·ra·ble ['meʒərəbl] meßbar

mea·sure ['meʒə] **1.** Maß n (a. fig.); Maß n, Meßgerät n; mus. Takt m; Maßnahme f; **beyond ~** über alle Maßen; **in a great ~** großenteils; **take ~s** Maßnahmen treffen od. ergreifen; **2.** (ab-, aus-, ver)messen; j-m Maß nehmen; **~ up to** den Ansprüchen (gen.) genügen; **~d** gemessen; wohlüberlegt; maßvoll; '**~ment** (Ver)Messung f; Maß n; **~ of ca'pac·i·ty** Hohlmaß n

meas·ur·ing ['meʒərɪŋ] Meß...; '**~ tape** → **tape measure**

meat [mi:t] Fleisch n; **cold ~** kalter Braten; '**~ball** Fleischklößchen n

me·chan·ic [mɪˈkænɪk] Mechaniker m; **~i·cal** mechanisch; Maschinen...; **~ics** phys. mst sg. Mechanik f

mech·a·nis·m ['mekənɪzəm] Mechanismus m; **~nize** ['mekənaɪz] mechanisieren

med·al ['medl] Medaille f; Orden m; **~(l)ist** ['medlɪst] Sport: Medaillengewinner(in)

med·dle ['medl] sich einmischen (**with**, **in** in acc.); '**~some** aufdringlich

me·di·a ['mi:djə] sg., pl. Medien pl.

med·i·ae·val [medɪˈi:vl] → **medieval**

me·di·an ['mi:djən] **~strip** Am. Mittelstreifen m (Autobahn etc.)

me·di·ate ['mi:dɪeɪt] vermitteln; **~a·tion** [mi:dɪˈeɪʃn] Vermittlung f; **~a·tor** ['mi:dɪeɪtə] Vermittler m

med·i·cal ['medɪkl] **1.** medizinisch, ärztlich; **2.** ärztliche Untersuchung; **~ cer'tif·i·cate** ärztliches Attest

med·i·cat·ed ['medɪkeɪtɪd] medizinisch; **~ bath** medizinisches Bad

me·di·ci·nal [meˈdɪsɪnl] medizinisch, heilkräftig, Heil...

med·i·cine ['medsɪn] Medizin f, Arznei f; Medizin f, Heilkunde f

me·di·e·val [medɪˈi:vl] mittelalterlich

me·di·o·cre [mi:dɪˈəʊkə] mittelmäßig

med·i·tate ['medɪteɪt] v/i. (**on**) nachdenken (über acc.); v/t. erwägen; **~ta·tion** [medɪˈteɪʃn] Nachdenken n; Meditation f; '**~ta·tive** [medɪtətɪv] nachdenklich

Med·i·ter·ra·ne·an [medɪtəˈreɪnjən] Mittelmeer...

me·di·um ['mi:djəm] **1.** (pl. **-dia** [-djə], **-diums**) Mitte f; Mittel n; Medium n; **2.**

mittlere(r, -s), Mittel..., a. mittelmäßig; gastr. medium, halbgar (Steak)

med·ley ['medlɪ] Gemisch n; mus. Medley n, Potpourri n

meek [mi:k] sanft(mütig), bescheiden; '**~ness** Sanftmut f, Bescheidenheit f

meet [mi:t] (**met**) v/t. treffen, sich treffen mit; begegnen (dat.); j-n kennenlernen; j-n abholen; zusammentreffen mit, stoßen od. treffen auf (acc.); Wünschen entgegenkommen, entsprechen; e-r Forderung, Verpflichtung nachkommen; v/i. zusammenkommen, -treten; sich begegnen od. treffen; (feindlich) zusammenstoßen, Sport: aufeinandertreffen; sich kennenlernen; **~ with** zusammentreffen mit; stoßen auf (Schwierigkeiten etc.); erleben, -leiden; '**~ing** Begegnung f, (Zusammen)Treffen n; Versammlung f, Konferenz f, Tagung f; '**~ place** Tagungs-, Versammlungsort m; Treffpunkt m

mel·an·chol·y ['melənkəlɪ] **1.** Melancholie f, Schwermut f; **2.** melancholisch, traurig

mel·low ['meləʊ] **1.** reif, weich; sanft, mild (Licht), zart (Farben); fig. gereift (Person); **2.** reifen (lassen) (a. fig.); weich od. sanft werden

me·lo·di·ous [mɪˈləʊdjəs] melodisch

mel·o·dra·mat·ic [meləʊdrəˈmætɪk] melodramatisch

mel·o·dy ['melədɪ] Melodie f

mel·on bot. ['melən] Melone f

melt [melt] (zer)schmelzen; **~ down** einschmelzen

mem·ber ['membə] Mitglied n, Angehörige(r m) f; anat. Glied(maße f) n; (männliches) Glied; **2 of Parliament** Brt. parl. Mitglied n des Unterhauses, Unterhausabgeordnete(r m) f; '**~ship** Mitgliedschaft f; Mitgliederzahl f

mem·brane ['membreɪn] Membran(e) f

mem·o ['meməʊ] (pl. **-os**) Memo n

mem·oirs ['memwɑːz] pl. Memoiren pl.

mem·o·ra·ble ['memərəbl] denkwürdig

me·mo·ri·al [mɪˈmɔːrɪəl] Denkmal n, Ehrenmal n, Gedenkstätte f (**to** für); Gedenkfeier f (**to** für)

mem·o·rize ['meməraɪz] auswendig lernen, sich et. einprägen

mem·o·ry ['meməri] Gedächtnis *n*; Erinnerung *f*; Andenken *n*; *Computer*: Speicher *m*; **in ~ of** zum Andenken an (*acc.*); **~ ca'pac·i·ty** *Computer*: Speicherkapazität *f*

men [men] *pl. von* **man** 1

men·ace ['menəs] **1.** (be)drohen; (Be)Drohung *f*

mend [mend] **1.** *v/t.* (ver)bessern; ausbessern, reparieren, flicken; **~ one's ways** sich bessern; *v/i.* sich bessern; **2.** ausgebesserte Stelle; **on the ~** auf dem Wege der Besserung

men·di·cant ['mendɪkənt] **1.** bettelnd, Bettel...; **2.** Bettelmönch *m*

me·ni·al ['miːnjəl] niedrig, untergeordnet (*Arbeit*)

men·in·gi·tis *med.* [menɪn'dʒaɪtɪs] Meningitis *f*, Hirnhautentzündung *f*

men·o·pause ['menəupɔːz] Wechseljahre *pl.*

men·stru·|ate ['menstrueɪt] menstruieren; **~a·tion** [menstru'eɪʃn] Menstruation *f*

men·tal ['mentl] geistig, Geistes...; seelisch, psychisch; **~ a'rith·me·tic** Kopfrechnen *n*; **~ 'hand·i·cap** geistige Behinderung; **~ 'hos·pi·tal** psychiatrische Klinik, Nervenheilanstalt *f*; **~·i·ty** [men'tæləti] Mentalität *f*; **~·ly** ['mentəli]: **~ handicapped** geistig behindert; **~ ill** geisteskrank

men·tion ['menʃn] **1.** erwähnen; **don't ~ it!** bitte (sehr)!, gern geschehen!; **2.** Erwähnung *f*

men·u ['menjuː] Speise(n)karte *f*; △ *nicht gastr.* **Menü**; *Computer*: Menü *n*

MEP [em iː 'piː] *Abk. für* **Member of the European Parliament** Abgeordnete(r *m*) *f* des Europäischen Parlaments, F Europa-Abgeordnete(r *m*) *f*

mer·can·tile ['mɜːkəntaɪl] Handels...

mer·ce·na·ry ['mɜːsɪnəri] **1.** geldgierig; **2.** *mil.* Söldner *m*

mer·chan·dise ['mɜːtʃəndaɪz] Ware(n *pl.*) *f*

mer·chant ['mɜːtʃənt] **1.** (Groß)Händler *m*, (Groß)Kaufmann *m*; **2.** Handels...

mer·ci·|ful ['mɜːsɪfl] barmherzig, gnädig; **~·less** unbarmherzig, erbarmungslos

mer·cu·ry *chem.* ['mɜːkjʊri] Quecksilber *n*

mer·cy ['mɜːsɪ] Barmherzigkeit *f*, Erbarmen *n*, Gnade *f*

mere [mɪə] (**~r, ~st**), **'~·ly** bloß, nur

merge [mɜːdʒ] verschmelzen (**into, with** mit); *econ.* fusionieren; **'merg·er** *econ.* Fusion *f*

me·rid·i·an [mə'rɪdɪən] *geogr.* Meridian *m*; *fig.* Gipfel *m*, Höhepunkt *m*

mer·it ['merɪt] **1.** Verdienst *n*; Wert *m*; Vorzug *m*; **2.** verdienen

mer·maid ['mɜːmeɪd] Meerjungfrau *f*, Nixe *f*

mer·ri·ment ['merɪmənt] Fröhlichkeit *f*; Gelächter *n*, Heiterkeit *f*

mer·ry ['merɪ] (**~ier, ~iest**) lustig, fröhlich, ausgelassen; ♀ **Christmas!** fröhliche *od.* frohe Weihnachten; **'~-go-round** Karussell *n*

mesh [meʃ] **1.** Masche *f*; *fig. oft* **~es** *pl.* Netz *n*, Schlingen *pl.*; **be in ~** *tech.* (ineinander)greifen; **2.** (ineinander)greifen (*Zahnräder*); *fig.* passen (**with** zu), zusammenpassen

mess [mes] **1.** Unordnung *f*, Durcheinander *n*; Schmutz *m*, F Schweinerei *f*; F Patsche *f*, Klemme *f*; *mil.* Messe *f*, Kasino *n*; △ *nicht rel.* **Messe**; **make a ~ of** F fig. verpfuschen, ruinieren, *Pläne etc.* über den Haufen werfen; **2. ~ about, ~ around** F herumspielen, -basteln (**with** an); herumgammeln; **~ up** in Unordnung bringen, durcheinanderbringen; *fig.* F verpfuschen, ruinieren, *Pläne etc.* über den Haufen werfen

mes·sage ['mesɪdʒ] Mitteilung *f*, Nachricht *f*; Anliegen *n*, Aussage *f*; **can I take a ~?** kann ich etwas ausrichten?; **get the ~** F kapieren

mes·sen·ger ['mesɪndʒə] Bote *m*

mess·y ['mesɪ] (**~ier, ~iest**) unordentlich; unsauber, schmutzig

met [met] *pret. u. p.p. von* **meet**

me·tab·o·lis·m *physiol.* [me'tæbəlizəm] Stoffwechsel *m*

met·al ['metl] Metall *n*; **me·tal·lic** [mɪ'tælɪk] (**~ally**) metallisch; Metall...

met·a·mor·pho·sis [metə'mɔːfəsɪs] Metamorphose *f*, Verwandlung *f*

met·a·phor ['metəfə] Metapher *f*

me·tas·ta·sis [mə'tæstəsɪs] (*pl.* **-ses** [-siːz]) Metastase *f*

me·te·or ['miːtɪə] Meteor *m*

me·te·or·o·log·i·cal [miːtjərə'lɒdʒɪkl] meteorologisch, Wetter..., Witterungs...; ~ **'of·fice** a. F met office Wetteramt n

me·te·o·rol·o·gy [miːtjəˈrɒlədʒi] Meteorologie f, Wetterkunde f

me·ter tech. ['miːtə] Meßgerät n, Zähler m; △ Brt. nicht Meter

meth·od ['meθəd] Methode f, Verfahren n; System n; **me·thod·i·cal** [mɪˈθɒdɪkl] methodisch, systematisch, planmäßig

me·tic·u·lous [mɪˈtɪkjʊləs] peinlich genau, übergenau

me·tre Brt., **me·ter** Am. ['miːtə] Meter m, n; Versmaß n

met·ric ['metrɪk] (~ally) metrisch; '~ **sys·tem** metrisches (Maß- u. Gewichts)System

met·ro·pol·i·tan [metrəˈpɒlɪtən] ... der Hauptstadt

met·tle ['metl] Eifer m, Mut m, Feuer n

Mex·i·can ['meksɪkən] **1.** mexikanisch; **2.** Mexikaner(in)

Mex·i·co ['meksɪkəʊ] Mexiko n

mi·aow [miːˈaʊ] miauen

mice [maɪs] pl. von mouse

mi·cro... ['maɪkrəʊ] Mikro..., (sehr) klein

mi·cro|chip ['maɪkrəʊtʃɪp] Mikrochip m; **~com·put·er** Mikrocomputer m

mi·cro·phone ['maɪkrəfəʊn] Mikrophon n

mi·cro·pro·ces·sor [maɪkrəʊˈprəʊsesə] Mikroprozessor m

mi·cro·scope ['maɪkrəskəʊp] Mikroskop n

mi·cro·wave ['maɪkrəweɪv] Mikrowelle f; ~ **'ov·en** Mikrowellenherd m

mid [mɪd] mittlere(r, -s), Mitt(el)...; '~**air:** in ~ in der Luft; '~**day 1.** Mittag m; **2.** mittägig, Mittag(s)...

mid·dle ['mɪdl] **1.** mittlere(r, -s), Mittel...; **2.** Mitte f; △ nicht Mittel; ~**'aged** mittleren Alters; ♀ **'Ag·es** pl. Mittelalter n; ~ **'class**(·**es** pl.) Mittelstand m; '~**man** (pl. -men) econ. Zwischenhändler m; Mittelsmann m; ~ **'name** zweiter Vorname m; ~**'sized** mittelgroß; '~**weight** Boxen: Mittelgewicht(ler m) n

mid·dling ['mɪdlɪŋ] mittelmäßig, Mittel...; leidlich

'mid·field bsd. Fußball: Mittelfeld n; '~**er**, ~ **'play·er** bsd. Fußball: Mittelfeldspieler m

midge zo. [mɪdʒ] Mücke f

midg·et ['mɪdʒɪt] Zwerg m, Knirps m

'mid·night Mitternacht f; at ~ um Mitternacht; ~**st** [mɪdst]: in the ~ of mitten in (dat.); '~**sum·mer** Hochsommer m; astr. Sommersonnenwende f; ~**way** auf halbem Wege; '~**wife** (pl. -wives) Hebamme f; ~**'win·ter** Mitte f des Winters; astr. Wintersonnenwende f; in ~ mitten im Winter

might [maɪt] **1.** pret. von may; **2.** Macht f, Gewalt f; Kraft f; '~**y** (-ier, -iest) mächtig, gewaltig

mi·grate [maɪˈɡreɪt] (aus)wandern, (fort)ziehen (a. zo.); **mi·gra·tion** [maɪˈɡreɪʃn] Wanderung f; **mi·gra·to·ry** ['maɪɡrətəri] Wander...; zo. Zug...; ~ **bird** Zugvogel m

mike F [maɪk] Mikro n (Mikrophon)

mild [maɪld] mild, sanft, leicht

mil·dew bot. ['mɪldjuː] Mehltau m

'mild·ness Milde f

mile [maɪl] Meile f (1,6 km)

mile·age ['maɪlɪdʒ] zurückgelegte Meilenzahl od. Fahrtstrecke, Meilenstand m; a. ~ **allowance** Meilengeld n, etwa Kilometergeld n

'mile·stone Meilenstein m (a. fig.)

mil·i·tant ['mɪlɪtənt] militant; streitbar, kriegerisch

mil·i·ta·ry ['mɪlɪtəri] **1.** militärisch, Militär...; **2.** the ~ pl. das Militär; ~ **'gov·ern·ment** Militärregierung f; ~ **po'lice** (Abk. **MP**) Militärpolizei f

mi·li·tia [mɪˈlɪʃə] Miliz f, Bürgerwehr f

milk [mɪlk] **1.** Milch f; it's no use crying over spilt ~ geschehen ist geschehen; **2.** v/t. melken; v/i. Milch geben; '~**man** (pl. -men) Milchmann m; ~ **'pow·der** Milchpulver n, Trockenmilch f; ~ **'shake** Milchmixgetränk n, -shake m; '~**sop** Weichling m, Muttersöhnchen n; '~ **tooth** (pl. - teeth) Milchzahn m; '~**y** (-ier, -iest) milchig; Milch...; ♀**-y Way** astr. Milchstraße f

mill [mɪl] **1.** Mühle f; Fabrik f; **2.** Korn etc. mahlen; tech. Metall verarbeiten; Münze rändeln

mil·le·pede zo. ['mɪlɪpiːd] → millipede

'mill·er Müller m

mil·let bot. ['mɪlɪt] Hirse f

mil·li·ner ['mɪlɪnə] Hut-, Putzmacherin f, Modistin f

mil·lion ['mɪljən] Million f; ~**aire**

[mɪljə'neə] Millionär(in); **~th** ['mɪljənθ]
1. millionste(r, -s); **2.** Millionstel *n*

mil·li·pede *zo.* ['mɪlɪpiːd] Tausend-
füß(l)er *m*

'**mill**·**pond** Mühlteich *m*; '**~stone**
Mühlstein *m*

milt [mɪlt] Milch *f* (*der Fische*)

mime [maɪm] **1.** Pantomime *f*; Pantomime *m*; **2.** (panto)mimisch darstellen;
nachahmen, mimen

mim·ic ['mɪmɪk] **1.** mimisch; Schein...;
2. Imitator *m*; **3.** (**-ck-**) nachahmen;
nachäffen; **~ry** ['mɪmɪkrɪ] Nachahmung *f*; *zo.* Mimikry *f*

mince [mɪns] **1.** *v/t.* zerhacken,
(zer)schneiden; *he does not ~ matters
od. his words* er nimmt kein Blatt vor
den Mund; *v/i.* tänzeln, trippeln; **2.** *a.*
~d meat Hackfleisch *n*; '**~meat** *e-e
süße* Pastetenfüllung; **~ pie** *mit
mincemeat gefüllte Pastete*; '**minc·er**
Fleischwolf *m*

mind [maɪnd] **1.** Sinn *m*, Gemüt *n*; Herz
n; Verstand *m*, Geist *m*; Ansicht *f*, Meinung *f*; Absicht *f*, Neigung *f*, Lust *f*;
Erinnerung *f*, Gedächtnis *n*; *be out of
one's ~* nicht (recht) bei Sinnen sein;
bear od. keep in ~ (immer) denken an
(*acc.*), *et.* nicht vergessen; *change
one's ~* es sich anders überlegen, s-e
Meinung ändern; *enter a o.'s ~* j-m in
den Sinn kommen; *give s.o. a piece of
one's ~* j-m gründlich die Meinung sagen; *have* (*half*) *a ~ to* (nicht übel) Lust
haben zu; *lose one's ~* den Verstand
verlieren; *make up one's ~* sich entschließen, e-n Entschluß fassen; *to my
~* meiner Ansicht nach; **2.** *v/t.* achtgeben auf (*acc.*); sehen nach, aufpassen
auf (*acc.*); *et.* haben gegen; *~ the step!*
Vorsicht, Stufe!; *~ your own business!*
kümmere dich um deine eigenen Angelegenheiten!; *do you ~ if I smoke?, do
you ~ my smoking?* haben Sie et. dagegen *od.* stört es Sie, wenn ich rauche?;
would you ~ opening the window?
würden Sie bitte das Fenster öffnen?;
would you ~ coming würden Sie bitte
kommen?; *v/i.* aufpassen; *et.* dagegen
haben; *~* (*you*) wohlgemerkt, allerdings;
never ~! macht nichts!, ist schon gut!; *I
don't ~* meinetwegen, von mir aus; '**~
less** gedankenlos, blind; unbekümmert
(*of* um), ohne Rücksicht (*of* auf *acc.*)

mine¹ [maɪn] der, die, das meine; meins;
that's ~ das gehört mir

mine² [maɪn] **1.** Bergwerk *n*, Mine *f*,
Zeche *f*, Grube *f*; *mil.* Mine *f*; *fig.*
Fundgrube *f*; △ *nicht* (*Kugelschreiber-
etc.*)*Mine*; **2.** *v/i.* schürfen, graben (**for**
nach); *v/t.* Erz, Kohle abbauen; *mil.*
verminen; '**min·er** Bergmann *m*,
Kumpel *m*

min·e·ral ['mɪnərəl] Mineral *n*; Mineral...; **~s** *pl. Brt.* Mineralwasser *n*; '**~ oil**
Mineralöl *n*; '**~ wa·ter** Mineralwasser
n

min·gle ['mɪŋgl] *v/t.* (ver)mischen; *v/i.*
sich mischen *od.* mengen (**with**) unter)

min·i... ['mɪnɪ] Mini..., Klein(st)...; →
miniskirt

min·i·a·ture ['mɪnətʃə] **1.** Miniatur(gemälde *n*) *f*; **2.** Miniatur..., Klein...; **~
'cam·e·ra** Kleinbildkamera *f*

min·i·mize ['mɪnɪmaɪz] auf ein Mindestmaß herabsetzen; heruntterspielen,
bagatellisieren; **~mum** ['mɪnɪməm] **1.**
(*pl.* **-ma** [-mə], **-mums**) Minimum *n*,
Mindestmaß *n*; **2.** minimal, Mindest...

min·ing ['maɪnɪŋ] Bergbau *m*;
Berg(bau)..., Bergwerks...; Gruben...

min·i·on *contp.* ['mɪnjən] Lakai *m*, Krie-
cher *m*

'**min·i·skirt** Minirock *m*

min·is·ter ['mɪnɪstə] Minister(in); *rel.*
Geistliche(r) *m*; Gesandte(r) *m*

min·is·try ['mɪnɪstrɪ] Ministerium *n*; *rel.*
geistliches Amt

mink *zo.* [mɪŋk] (*pl.* **mink**) Nerz *m*

mi·nor ['maɪnə] **1.** kleinere(r, -s), *fig. a.*
unbedeutend, geringfügig; *jur.* minderjährig; *A ~ mus.* a-Moll *n*; *~ key mus.*
Moll(tonart *f*) *n*; **2.** *jur.* Minderjähri-
ge(r *m*) *f*; *Am. univ.* Nebenfach *n*; *mus.*
Moll *n*; **~·i·ty** [maɪ'nɒrətɪ] Minderheit
f; *jur.* Minderjährigkeit *f*

min·ster ['mɪnstə] Münster *n*

mint¹ [mɪnt] **1.** Münze *f*, Münzanstalt *f*;
2. prägen

mint² *bot.* [mɪnt] Minze *f*

min·u·et *mus.* ['mɪnjʊ'et] Menuett *n*

mi·nus ['maɪnəs] **1.** *prp.* minus, weniger;
F ohne; **2.** *adj.* Minus...; **3.** Minus *n*, *fig.
a.* Nachteil *m*

min·ute¹ ['mɪnɪt] Minute *f*; Augenblick
m; *in a ~* sofort; *just a ~!* Moment mal!;
~s *pl.* Protokoll *n*

mi·nute² [maɪ'njuːt] winzig; sehr genau

mir·a·cle ['mɪrəkl] Wunder n

mi·rac·u·lous [mɪ'rækjʊləs] wunderbar; **~ly** wie durch ein Wunder

mi·rage ['mɪrɑːʒ] Luftspiegelung f, Fata Morgana f

mire ['maɪə] Schlamm m; **drag through the ~** fig. in den Schmutz ziehen

mir·ror ['mɪrə] 1. Spiegel m; 2. (wider)spiegeln (a. fig.)

mirth [mɜːθ] Fröhlichkeit f, Heiterkeit f

mis... [mɪs] miß..., falsch, schlecht

mis·ad·ven·ture Mißgeschick n; Unglück(sfall m) n

mis·an·thrope ['mɪzənθrəʊp], **~thro·pist** [mɪ'zænθrəpɪst] Menschenfeind(in)

mis·ap·ply falsch an- od. verwenden

mis·ap·pre·hend mißverstehen

mis·ap·pro·pri·ate unterschlagen, veruntreuen

mis·be·have sich schlecht benehmen

mis·cal·cu·late falsch berechnen; sich verrechnen (in dat.)

mis·car·|riage med. Fehlgeburt f; Mißlingen n, Fehlschlag(en n) m; **~ of justice** jur. Fehlurteil n; **~ry** med. e-e Fehlgeburt haben; mißlingen, scheitern

mis·cel·la·ne·ous [mɪsɪ'leɪnjəs] ge-, vermischt; verschiedenartig; **~ny** [mɪ'seləni] Gemisch n; Sammelband m

mis·chief ['mɪstʃɪf] Schaden m; Unfug m; Übermut m; **~-mak·er** Unruhestifter(in)

mis·chie·vous ['mɪstʃɪvəs] boshaft, mutwillig; schelmisch

mis·con·ceive falsch auffassen, mißverstehen

mis·con·duct 1. [mɪs'kɒndʌkt] schlechtes Benehmen; schlechte Führung; Verfehlung f; 2. [mɪskən'dʌkt] schlecht führen; **~ o.s.** sich schlecht benehmen

mis·con·strue [mɪskən'struː] falsch auslegen, mißdeuten

mis·deed Missetat f

mis·de·mea·no(u)r jur. [mɪsdɪ'miːnə] Vergehen n

mis·di·rect fehl-, irreleiten; Brief etc. falsch adressieren

mise-en-scène thea. [miːzɑ̃ːn'seɪn] Inszenierung f

mi·ser ['maɪzə] Geizhals m

mis·e·ra·ble ['mɪzərəbl] erbärmlich, kläglich, elend; unglücklich

'mi·ser·ly geizig, F knick(e)rig

mis·e·ry ['mɪzəri] Elend n, Not f

mis'fire versagen (Schußwaffe); mot. fehlzünden, aussetzen; fig. danebengehen

'mis·fit Außenseiter(in)

mis'for·tune Unglück(sfall m) n; Mißgeschick n

mis'giv·ing Befürchtung f, Zweifel m

mis'guid·ed irregeleitet, irrig, unangebracht

mis'hap ['mɪshæp] Unglück n; Mißgeschick n; **without ~** ohne Zwischenfälle

mis·in'form falsch unterrichten

mis·in'ter·pret mißdeuten, falsch auffassen od. auslegen

mis'lay (-laid) et. verlegen

mis'lead (-led) irreführen, täuschen; verleiten

mis'man·age schlecht verwalten od. führen od. handhaben

mis'place et. an e-e falsche Stelle legen od. setzen; et. verlegen; **~d** fig. unangebracht, deplaziert

mis'print 1. [mɪs'prɪnt] verdrucken; 2. ['mɪsprɪnt] Druckfehler m

mis'read (-read [-red]) falsch lesen; falsch deuten, mißdeuten

mis·rep·re'sent falsch darstellen; entstellen, verdrehen

miss¹ [mɪs] 1. v/t. verpassen, -säumen, -fehlen; übersehen, nicht bemerken; überhören; nicht verstehen od. begreifen; vermissen; **a. ~ out** auslassen, übergehen, -springen; v/i. nicht treffen; mißglücken; **~ out on** et. verpassen; 2. Fehlschuß m, -stoß m, -wurf m etc.; Verpassen n, Verfehlen n

miss² [mɪs] (mit nachfolgendem Namen 2) Fräulein n

mis'shap·en mißgebildet

mis·sile ['mɪsaɪl, Am. 'mɪsəl] (Wurf)Geschoß n; mil. Rakete f; Raketen...

'miss·ing fehlend; **be ~** fehlen, verschwunden od. weg sein; (mil. a. ~ in action) vermißt; **be ~** mil. vermißt sein od. werden

mis·sion ['mɪʃn] (Militär- etc.)Mission f; bsd. pol. Auftrag m, Mission f; rel. Mission f; (innere) Berufung; aviat., mil. Einsatz m; **~a·ry** ['mɪʃənri] Missionar m

mis'spell (-spelt od. -spelled) falsch buchstabieren od. schreiben

mis'spend (*-spent*) falsch verwenden; vergeuden

mist [mɪst] **1.** (feiner *od.* leichter) Nebel; △ *nicht* Mist; **2.** ~ **over** sich trüben; ~ **up** (sich) beschlagen (*Glas*)

mis'take 1. (*-took, -taken*) verwechseln (*for* mit); verkennen, sich irren in (*dat.*); falsch verstehen, mißverstehen; **2.** Irrtum *m*, Versehen *n*, Fehler *m*; **by** ~ aus Versehen, irrtümlich; **~'tak·en** irrig, falsch (*verstanden*); **be** ~ sich irren

mis·ter ['mɪstə] *nur gebräuchlich mit dem Eigennamen in der Abk.* → *Mr*

mis·tle·toe *bot.* ['mɪsltəʊ] Mistel *f*

mis·tress ['mɪstrɪs] Herrin *f*; *bsd. Brt.* Lehrerin *f*; Geliebte *f*

mis'trust 1. mißtrauen (*dat.*); **2.** Mißtrauen *n* (*of* gegen); **~ful** mißtrauisch

mist·y ['mɪstɪ] (*-ier, -iest*) (leicht) neb(e)lig; *fig.* unklar, verschwommen

mis·un·der'stand (*-stood*) mißverstehen; *j-n* nicht verstehen; **~ing** Mißverständnis *n*

mis·use 1. [mɪs'juːz] mißbrauchen; falsch gebrauchen; **2.** [mɪs'juːs] Mißbrauch *m*

mite [maɪt] *zo.* Milbe *f*; kleines Ding, Würmchen *n* (*Kind*); **a** ~ F ein bißchen

mi·tre *Brt.*, **mi·ter** *Am.* ['maɪtə] Mitra *f*, Bischofsmütze *f*

mitt [mɪt] *Baseball:* Fanghandschuh *m*; *sl.* Boxhandschuh *m*; → *mitten*

mit·ten ['mɪtn] Fausthandschuh *m*; Halbhandschuh *m* (*ohne Finger*)

mix [mɪks] **1.** (ver)mischen, vermengen; *Getränke* mixen; sich (ver)mischen; sich mischen lassen; verkehren (*with* mit); ~ **well** kontaktfreudig sein; ~ **up** zusammen-, durcheinandermischen; (völlig) durcheinanderbringen; verwechseln (*with* mit); **be ~ed up** verwickelt sein *od.* werden (*in* in *acc.*); (*geistig*) ganz durcheinander sein; **2.** Mischung *f*, **~ed** gemischt (*a. Gefühle etc.*); vermischt, Misch...; **~er** Mixer *m*; *tech.* Mischmaschine *f*; *Rundfunk, TV etc.* Mischpult *n*; **~ture** ['mɪkstʃə] Mischung *f*; Gemisch *n*

MO [em 'əʊ] *Abk. für* **money order** Postod. Zahlungsanweisung *f*

moan [məʊn] **1.** Stöhnen *n*; **2.** stöhnen

moat [məʊt] (Burg-, Stadt)Graben *m*

mob [mɒb] **1.** Mob *m*, Pöbel *m*; **2.** (*-bb-*)

herfallen über (*acc.*); *j-n* bedrängen, belagern

mo·bile ['məʊbaɪl] **1.** beweglich; *mil.* mobil, motorisiert; lebhaft (*Gesichtszüge*); **2.** → **mobile telephone;** ~ **'home** Wohnwagen *m*; ~ **'tel·e·phone,** ~ **'phone** Mobiltelefon *n*, Handy *n*

mo·bil·ize ['məʊbɪlaɪz] mobilisieren, *mil. a.* mobil machen

moc·ca·sin ['mɒkəsɪn] Mokassin *m*

mock [mɒk] **1.** *v/t.* verspotten; nachäffen; *v/i.* sich lustig machen, spotten (*at* über *acc.*); **2.** nachgemacht, Schein...; **~·e·ry** ['mɒkərɪ] Spott *m*, Hohn *m*; Gespött *n*; **'~·ing·bird** *zo.* Spottdrossel *f*

mod cons *Brt.* F [mɒd 'kɒnz] *Abk. für* **modern conveniences** *pl.*: **with all** ~ mit allem Komfort (*in Anzeigen*)

mode [məʊd] (Art *f* u.) Weise *f*; *Computer:* Modus *m*, Betriebsart *f*; △ *nicht* Mode

mod·el ['mɒdl] **1.** Modell *n*; Muster *n*; Vorbild *n*; Mannequin *n*, Model *n*, (Foto)Modell *n*; *tech.* Modell *n*, Typ *m*; **male** ~ Dressman *m*; **2.** Modell..., Muster...; **3.** *v/t. bsd. Brt.* (*-ll-, Am. -l-*) modellieren, *a. fig.* formen; *Kleider etc.* vorführen; *v/i.* Modell stehen *od.* sitzen; als Mannequin *od.* (Foto)Modell *od.* Dressman arbeiten

mo·dem ['məʊdem] *Computer:* Modem *m*, *n*

mod·e·rate 1. ['mɒdərət] (mittel)mäßig; gemäßigt; vernünftig, angemessen; **2.** ['mɒdəreɪt] (sich) mäßigen; **~·ra·tion** [mɒdə'reɪʃn] Mäßigung *f*

mod·ern ['mɒdən] modern, neu; **~·ize** ['mɒdənaɪz] modernisieren

mod·est ['mɒdɪst] bescheiden; **'~·es·ty** Bescheidenheit *f*

mod·i·fi·ca·tion [mɒdɪfɪ'keɪʃn] (Ab-, Ver)Änderung *f*; **~·fy** ['mɒdɪfaɪ] (ab-, ver)ändern

mod·u·late ['mɒdjʊleɪt] modulieren

mod·ule ['mɒdjuːl] *tech.* Modul *n*, *electr. a.* Baustein *m*; *Raumfahrt:* (Kommando- *etc.*)Kapsel *f*

moist [mɔɪst] feucht; **~·en** ['mɔɪsn] *v/t.* an-, befeuchten; *v/i.* feucht werden; **mois·ture** ['mɔɪstʃə] Feuchtigkeit *f*

mo·lar ['məʊlə] Backenzahn *m*

mo·las·ses *Am.* [mə'læsɪz] *sg.* Sirup *m*

mole¹ *zo.* [məʊl] Maulwurf *m*

M

mole² [məʊl] Muttermal n, Leberfleck m

mole³ [məʊl] Mole f, Hafendamm m

mol·e·cule ['mɒlɪkjuːl] Molekül n

'mole·hill Maulwurfshügel m; *make a mountain out of a* ~ aus e-r Mücke e-n Elefanten machen

mo·lest [məʊˈlest] belästigen (*a. unsittl.*)

mol·li·fy ['mɒlɪfaɪ] besänftigen, beschwichtigen

mol·ly·cod·dle F ['mɒlɪkɒdl] verhätscheln, -zärteln

mol·ten ['məʊltən] geschmolzen

mom Am. F [mɒm] Mami f, Mutti f

mo·ment ['məʊmənt] Moment m, Augenblick m; Bedeutung f; *phys.* Moment n; **mo·men·ta·ry** ['məʊməntərɪ] momentan, augenblicklich; **mo·men·tous** [məʊˈmentəs] bedeutsam, folgenschwer; **mo·men·tum** [məʊˈmentəm] (*pl. -ta* [-tə], *-tums*) *phys.* Moment n; Schwung m

Mon *nur geschr. Abk. für* **Monday** Mo., Montag m

mon·arch ['mɒnək] Monarch(in), Herrscher(in); **'~ar·chy** Monarchie f

mon·as·tery ['mɒnəstrɪ] (Mönchs)Kloster n

Mon·day ['mʌndɪ] (*Abk.* **Mon**) Montag m; *on* ~ (am) Montag; *on* ~s montags

mon·e·ta·ry *econ.* ['mʌnɪtərɪ] Währungs...; Geld...

mon·ey ['mʌnɪ] Geld n; **'~box** Brt. Sparbüchse f; **'~chang·er** (Geld-) Wechsler m (*Person*); Am. Wechselautomat m; **'~ or·der** Post- *od.* Zahlungsanweisung f

mon·ger ['mʌŋɡə] *in Zssgn* ...händler m

mon·grel ['mʌŋɡrəl] Bastard m, *bsd.* Promenadenmischung f (*Hund*)

mon·i·tor ['mɒnɪtə] **1.** Monitor m; Kontrollgerät n, -schirm m; **2.** abhören; überwachen

monk [mʌŋk] Mönch m

mon·key ['mʌŋkɪ] **1.** *zo.* Affe m; F (kleiner) Schlingel; *make a* ~ (*out*) *of s.o.* F j-n zum Deppen machen; **2.** ~ *about*, ~ *around* (herum)albern; ~ *about*, ~ *around with* F herumspielen mit *od.* an (*dat.*), herummurksen an (*dat.*); **'~ wrench** *tech.* Engländer m, Franzose m; *throw a* ~ *into s.th.* Am. et. behindern; **'~ busi·ness** krumme Tour; Blödsinn m, Unfug m

mon·o ['mɒnəʊ] **1.** (*pl. -os*) Mono n; F Monogerät n; F Monoschallplatte f; **2.** Mono...

mon·o... ['mɒnəʊ] ein..., mono...

mon·o·logue *bsd. Brt.*, **mon·o·log** *Am.* ['mɒnəlɒɡ] Monolog m

mo·nop·o·lize [məˈnɒpəlaɪz] monopolisieren; *fig.* an sich reißen; **~ly** Monopol n (*of* auf *acc.*)

mo·not·o·nous [məˈnɒtənəs] monoton, eintönig; **~ny** Monotonie f

mon·soon [mɒnˈsuːn] Monsun m

mon·ster ['mɒnstə] Monster n, Ungeheuer n (*a. fig.*); Monstrum n; Riesen...

mon·stros·i·ty [mɒnˈstrɒsətɪ] Ungeheuerlichkeit f; Monstrum n; **~strous** ['mɒnstrəs] ungeheuer(lich); scheußlich

month [mʌnθ] Monat m; **'~ly 1.** monatlich; Monats...; **2.** Monatsschrift f

mon·u·ment ['mɒnjʊmənt] Monument n, Denkmal n; **~al** [mɒnjʊˈmentl] monumental; F kolossal, Riesen...; Gedenk...

moo [muː] muhen

mood [muːd] Stimmung f, Laune f; *be in a good* (*bad*) ~ gute (schlechte) Laune haben, gut (schlecht) aufgelegt sein; **'~y** (*-ier, -iest*) launisch; schlechtgelaunt

moon [muːn] **1.** Mond m; *once in a blue* ~ F alle Jubeljahre (einmal); **2.** ~ *about*, ~ *around* F herumtrödeln; F zielos herumstreichen; **'~light** Mondlicht n, -schein m; **'~lit** mondhell; **'~struck** mondsüchtig; **'~ walk** Mondspaziergang m

moor¹ [mʊə] (Hoch)Moor n

moor² [mʊə] *naut.* vertäuen, festmachen; **~ings** *naut.* ['mʊərɪŋz] *pl.* Vertäuung f; Liegeplatz m

moose *zo.* [muːs] (*pl.* **moose**) *nordamerikanischer* Elch

mop [mɒp] **1.** Mop m; (Haar)Wust m; **2.** (*-pp-*) wischen; ~ *up* aufwischen

mope [məʊp] den Kopf hängen lassen

mo·ped *Brt.* ['məʊped] Moped n

mor·al ['mɒrəl] **1.** moralisch; Moral..., Sitten...; **2.** Moral f (*e-r Geschichte*), Lehre f; *pl.* Moral f, Sitten *pl.*; **mo·rale** [mɒˈrɑːl] Moral f, Stimmung f; **mor·al·ize** ['mɒrəlaɪz] moralisieren (*about, on* über *acc.*)

mor·bid ['mɔːbɪd] morbid, krankhaft

more [mɔ:] **1.** *adj.* mehr; noch (mehr); *some ~ tea* noch etwas Tee; **2.** *adv.* mehr; noch; *~ and ~* immer mehr; *~ or less* mehr oder weniger; *once ~* noch einmal; *the ~ so because* um so mehr, da; *zur Bildung des comp.*: *~ important* wichtiger; *~ often* öfter; **3.** Mehr *n* (*of* an *dat.*); *a little ~* etwas mehr

mo·rel *bot.* [mɒ'rel] Morchel *f*

more·o·ver [mɔː'rəʊvə] außerdem, überdies, weiter, ferner

morgue [mɔːg] Leichenschauhaus *n*; F (Zeitungs)Archiv *n*

morn·ing ['mɔːnɪŋ] Morgen *m*; Vormittag *m*; *good ~!* guten Morgen!; *in the ~* morgens, am Morgen; vormittags, am Vormittag; *tomorrow ~* morgen früh *od.* vormittag

mo·rose [mə'rəʊs] mürrisch

mor|phi·a ['mɔːfjə], **~phine** ['mɔːfiːn] Morphium *n*

mor·sel ['mɔːsl] Bissen *m*, Happen *m*; *a ~ of* ein bißchen

mor·tal ['mɔːtl] **1.** sterblich; tödlich; Tod(es)...; **2.** Sterbliche(r *m*) *f*; **~·i·ty** [mɔː'tælətɪ] Sterblichkeit *f*

mor·tar¹ ['mɔːtə] Mörtel *m*

mor·tar² ['mɔːtə] Mörser *m*

mort·gage ['mɔːgɪdʒ] **1.** Hypothek *f*; **2.** mit e-r Hypothek belasten, e-e Hypothek aufnehmen auf (*acc.*)

mor·ti·cian *Am.* [mɔː'tɪʃn] Leichenbestatter *m*

mor·ti|·fi·ca·tion [mɔːtɪfɪ'keɪʃn] Kränkung *f*; Ärger *m*, Verdruß *m*; **~fy** ['mɔːtɪfaɪ] kränken; ärgern, verdrießen

mor·tu·a·ry [mɔː'tjʊərɪ] Leichenhalle *f*

mo·sa·ic [mə'zeɪk] Mosaik *n*

Mos·lem ['mɒzləm] → **Muslim**

mosque [mɒsk] Moschee *f*

mos·qui·to *zo.* [mə'skiːtəʊ] (*pl.* *-to[e]s*) Moskito *m*; Stechmücke *f*

moss *bot.* [mɒs] Moos *n*; **~·y** bot. (*-ier, -iest*) moosig, bemoost

most [məʊst] **1.** *adj.* meiste(r, -s), größte(r, -s); die meisten; *~ people pl.* die meisten Leute *pl.*; **2.** *adv.* am meisten; *~ of all* am allermeisten; *vor adj.*: höchst, äußerst; *zur Bildung des sup.*: *the ~ important point* der wichtigste Punkt; **3.** das meiste; das Höchste; das meiste, der größte Teil; die meisten *pl.*; *at (the) ~* höchstens; *make the ~ of et.* nach Kräften ausnutzen, das Beste herausholen aus; **~·ly** hauptsächlich, meist(ens)

MOT *Brt.* F [em əʊ 'tiː] *a.* ~ *test* etwa TÜV(-Prüfung *f*) *m*

mo·tel [məʊ'tel] Motel *n*

moth *zo.* [mɒθ] Motte *f*; **~·eat·en** mottenzerfressen

moth·er ['mʌðə] **1.** Mutter *f*; **2.** bemuttern; **~ coun·try** Vater-, Heimatland *n*; Mutterland *n*; **~·hood** Mutterschaft *f*; **~·in-law** ['mʌðərɪnlɔː] (*pl. mothers-in-law*) Schwiegermutter *f*; **~·ly** mütterlich; **~-of-pearl** [mʌðərəv-'pɜːl] Perlmutter *f*, Perlmutt *n*; **~ tongue** Muttersprache *f*

mo·tif [məʊ'tiːf] *Kunst*: Motiv *n*

mo·tion ['məʊʃn] **1.** Bewegung *f*; *parl.* Antrag *m*; *put od. set in ~* in Gang bringen (*a. fig.*), in Bewegung setzen; **2.** *v/t.* j-n durch e-n Wink auffordern, *j-m* ein Zeichen geben; *v/i.* winken; **~·less** bewegungslos; **~ pic·ture** *Am.* Film *m*

mo·ti|·vate ['məʊtɪveɪt] motivieren, anspornen; **~·va·tion** [məʊtɪ'veɪʃn] Motivation *f*, Ansporn *m*

mo·tive ['məʊtɪv] **1.** Motiv *n*, Beweggrund *m*; **2.** treibend (*a. fig.*)

mot·ley ['mɒtlɪ] bunt

mo·to·cross ['məʊtəʊkrɒs] *Sport*: Moto-Cross *m*

mo·tor ['məʊtə] Motor *m*, *fig. a.* treibende Kraft; Motor...; **~·bike** *Brt.* F Motorrad *n*; *Am.* Moped *n*; **~·boat** Motorboot *n*; **~·cade** ['məʊtəkeɪd] Auto-, Wagenkolonne *f*; **~·car** *Brt.* Kraftfahrzeug *n*; **~ car·a·van** *Brt.* Wohnmobil *n*; **~·cy·cle** Motorrad *n*; **~·cy·clist** Motorradfahrer(in); **~ home** *Am.* Wohnmobil *n*; **~·ing** ['məʊtərɪŋ] Autofahren *n*; *school of ~* Fahrschule *f*; **~·ist** ['məʊtərɪst] Autofahrer(in); **~·ize** ['məʊtəraɪz] motorisieren; **~ launch** Motorbarkasse *f*; **~·way** *Brt.* Autobahn *f*

mot·tled ['mɒtld] gefleckt, gesprenkelt

mo(u)ld¹ [məʊld] Schimmel *m*; Moder *m*; Humus(boden) *m*

mo(u)ld² [məʊld] **1.** *tech.* (Gieß-, Guß-, Preß)Form *f*; **2.** *tech.* gießen; formen

mo(u)l·der ['məʊldə] *a.* ~ *away* vermodern; zerfallen

mo(u)ld·y ['məʊldɪ] (*-ier, -iest*) verschimmelt, schimm(e)lig; mod(e)rig

mo(u)lt [məʊlt] (sich) mausern; *Haare* verlieren

mound [maʊnd] Erdhügel *m*, -wall *m*

mount [maʊnt] **1.** *v/t.* Pferd etc. besteigen, steigen auf (*acc.*); montieren; anbringen, befestigen; *Bild etc.* aufkleben, -kleben; *Edelstein* fassen; **~ed police** berittene Polizei; *v/i.* aufsitzen (*Reiter*); steigen, *fig. a.* (an)wachsen; **~ up to** sich belaufen auf (*acc.*); **2.** Gestell *n*; Fassung *f*; Reittier *n*

moun·tain ['maʊntɪn] **1.** Berg *m*; **~s** *pl. a.* Gebirge *n*; **2.** Berg..., Gebirgs...; '**~ bike** Mountainbike *n*

moun·tain·eer [maʊntɪ'nɪə] Bergsteiger(in); '**~eer·ing** [maʊntɪ'nɪərɪŋ] Bergsteigen *n*

moun·tain·ous ['maʊntɪnəs] bergig, gebirgig

mourn [mɔːn] trauern (**for, over** um); betrauern, trauern um; '**~er** Trauernde(r *m*) *f*; '**~ful** traurig; '**~ing** Trauer *f*; Trauer(kleidung) *f*

mouse [maʊs] (*pl. mice* [maɪs]) *zo.* Maus *f*; (*pl. mouses*) Computer: Maus *f*

mous·tache [mə'stɑːʃ] *Am. a.* **mus·tache** Schnurrbart *m*

mouth [maʊθ] (*pl. mouths* [maʊðz]) Mund *m*; Maul *n*, Schnauze *f*; Mündung *f* (*e-s Flusses etc.*); Öffnung *f* (*e-r Flasche etc.*); '**~ful** ein Mundvoll; Bissen *m*; '**~·or·gan** F Mundharmonika *f*; '**~piece** Mundstück *n*; *fig.* Sprachrohr *n*; '**~wash** Mundwasser *n*

mo·va·ble ['muːvəbl] beweglich

move [muːv] **1.** *v/t.* bewegen; (weg)rücken; transportieren; *Arm etc.* bewegen, rühren; *Schach etc.:* e-n Zug machen mit; *parl.* beantragen; *fig.* bewegen, rühren; **~ house** umziehen; **~ heaven and earth** Himmel und Hölle in Bewegung setzen; *v/i.* sich (fort)bewegen; sich rühren; umziehen (**to** nach); *Schach etc.:* e-n Zug machen; **~ away** weg-, fortziehen; **~ in** einziehen; **~ off** sich in Bewegung setzen; **~ on** weitergehen; **~ out** ausziehen; **2.** Bewegung *f*; Umzug *m*; *Schach etc.:* Zug *m*; *fig.* Schritt *m*; **on the ~** in Bewegung; auf den Beinen; **get a ~ on!** F Tempo!, mach(t) schon!, los!; '**~·a·ble** → **movable**; '**~·ment** Bewegung *f* (*a. fig.*); *mus.* Satz *m*; *tech.* (Geh)Werk *n*

mov·ie *bsd. Am.* ['muːvɪ] Film *m*; Kino *n*; Film..., Kino...; '**~ cam·e·ra** Filmkamera *f*; '**~ star** *Am.* Filmstar *m*; '**~ thea·ter** *Am.* Kino *n*

mov·ing ['muːvɪŋ] sich bewegend, beweglich; *fig.* rührend; '**~ stair·case** Rolltreppe *f*; '**~ van** *Am.* Möbelwagen *m*

mow [məʊ] (**mowed, mowed** *od.* **mown**) mähen; '**~er** Mähmaschine *f*, *bsd.* Rasenmäher *m*; '**~n** [məʊn] *p.p. von* **mow**

MP [em 'piː] *Abk. für* **Member of Parliament** *Brt.* Unterhausabgeordnete(r *m*) *f*; **military police** Militärpolizei *f*

mph *nur geschr. Abk. für* **miles per hour** Meilen *pl.* pro Stunde

Mr ['mɪstə] *Abk. für* **Mister** Herr *m*

Mrs ['mɪsɪz] *ursprünglich Abk. für* **Mistress** Frau *f*

MS *pl. Mss nur geschr. Abk. für* **manuscript** Ms., Mskr., Manuskript *n*

Ms [mɪz, məz] Frau *f* (*neutrale Anrede*)

Mt *nur geschr. Abk. für* **Mount** Berg *m*

much [mʌtʃ] **1.** *adj.* (**more, most**) viel; **2.** *adv.* sehr; *in Zssgn:* viel...; *vor comp.:* viel; **very ~** sehr; **I thought as ~** das habe ich mir gedacht; **3.** große Sache; **nothing ~** nichts Besonderes; **make ~ of** viel Wesens machen von; **think ~ of** viel halten von; **I am not ~ of a dancer** F ich bin kein großer Tänzer

muck F [mʌk] Mist *m*, Dung *m*; Dreck *m*, Schmutz *m*

mu·cus ['mjuːkəs] (Nasen)Schleim *m*

mud [mʌd] Schlamm *m*, Matsch *m*; Schmutz *m* (*a. fig.*)

mud·dle ['mʌdl] **1.** Durcheinander *n*; **be in a ~** durcheinander sein; **2.** *a.* **~ up** durcheinanderbringen; **~ through** F sich durchwursteln

mud·dy ['mʌdɪ] (**-ier, -iest**) schlammig, trüb; schmutzig; *fig.* wirr; '**~guard** Kotflügel *m*; Schutzblech *n*

mues·li ['mjuːzlɪ] Müsli *n*

muff [mʌf] Muff *m*

muf·fin ['mʌfɪn] Muffin *n* (*rundes heißes Teegebäck, mst mit Butter gegessen*)

muf·fle ['mʌfl] Ton etc. dämpfen; *oft* **~ up** einhüllen, -wickeln; '**~r** (dicker) Schal; *Am. mot.* Auspufftopf *m*

mug[1] [mʌg] Krug *m*; Becher *m*; große Tasse *f*; *sl.* Visage *f* (*Gesicht*); *sl.* Fresse *f* (*Mund*)

mug[2] F [mʌg] (**-gg-**) (*bsd. auf der Straße*)

überfallen u. ausrauben; '**~ger** F
(Straßen)Räuber m; '**~ging** F Raub-
überfall m, bsd. Straßenraub m

mug·gy ['mʌgɪ] schwül

mul·ber·ry bot. ['mʌlbərɪ] Maulbeer-
baum m; Maulbeere f

mule zo. [mju:l] Maultier n; Maulesel m

mulled [mʌld]: **~ wine** Glühwein m

mul·li·on arch. ['mʌljən] Mittelpfosten
m (am Fenster)

mul·ti... ['mʌltɪ] viel..., mehr...,
Mehr-
fach..., Multi...

mul·ti·far·i·ous [mʌltɪ'feərɪəs] mannigfaltig, vielfältig; **~lat·e·ral** [mʌltɪ-
'lætərəl] vielseitig; pol. multilateral,
mehrseitig

mul·ti·ple ['mʌltɪpl] **1.** viel-, mehrfach;
2. math. Vielfache(s) n; **~ 'store** a. F
multiple bsd. Brt. Kettenladen m

mul·ti·pli·ca·tion [mʌltɪplɪ'keɪʃn] Vermehrung f; math. Multiplikation f; **~
table** Einmaleins n

mul·ti·pli·ci·ty [mʌltɪ'plɪsətɪ] Vielfalt f;
Vielzahl f

mul·ti·ply ['mʌltɪplaɪ] (sich) vermehren,
(sich) vervielfachen; math. multiplizie-
ren, malnehmen (**by** mit)

mul·ti·'pur·pose Mehrzweck...; **~'storey** Brt. vielstöckig; **~-sto·rey 'car
park** Brt. Park(hoch)haus n

mul·ti·tude ['mʌltɪtju:d] Vielzahl f;
~tu·di·nous [mʌltɪ'tju:dɪnəs] zahlreich

mum¹ Brt. F [mʌm] Mami f, Mutti f

mum² [mʌm] **1.** int. **~'s the word** Mund
halten!, kein Wort darüber!; **2.** adj.
keep ~ nichts verraten, den Mund halten

mum·ble ['mʌmbl] murmeln, nuscheln;
mümmeln (mühsam essen)

mum·mi·fy ['mʌmɪfaɪ] mumifizieren

mum·my¹ ['mʌmɪ] Mumie f

mum·my² Brt. F [mʌmɪ] Mami f, Mutti
f

mumps med. [mʌmps] sg. Ziegenpeter
m, Mumps m

munch [mʌntʃ] mampfen

mun·dane [mʌn'deɪn] alltäglich; weltlich

mu·ni·ci·pal [mju:'nɪsɪpl] städtisch,
Stadt..., kommunal, Gemeinde...;
council Stadt-, Gemeinderat m; **~i·ty**
[mju:nɪsɪ'pælɪtɪ] Kommunalbehörde f;
Stadtverwaltung f

mu·ral ['mjʊərəl] **1.** Wandgemälde n; **2.**
Mauer..., Wand...

mur·der ['mɜ:də] **1.** Mord m, Ermordung f; Mord...; **2.** ermorden; fig. F
verschandeln; **~er** ['mɜ:dərə] Mörder
m; **~ess** ['mɜ:dərɪs] Mörderin f;
~ous ['mɜ:dərəs] mörderisch

murk·y ['mɜ:kɪ] (**-ier, -iest**) dunkel, finster

murmur ['mɜ:mə] **1.** Murmeln n; Gemurmel n; Murren n; **2.** murmeln; murren

mus|cle ['mʌsl] Muskel m; **~-cle
-bound: be ~** bei Gewichthebern etc.:
e-e starke, aber erstarrte Muskulatur
haben; **~cu·lar** ['mʌskjʊlə] Muskel...;
muskulös

muse¹ [mju:z] (nach)sinnen, (-)grübeln
(**on, over** über acc.)

muse² [mju:z] a. ℒ Muse f

mu·se·um [mju:'zɪəm] Museum n

mush [mʌʃ] Brei m, Mus n; Am. Mais-
brei m

mush·room ['mʌʃrʊm] **1.** bot. Pilz m,
bsd. Champignon m; **2.** rasch wachsen;
~ up fig. (wie Pilze) aus dem Boden
schießen

mu·sic ['mju:zɪk] Musik f; Noten pl.;
put od. set to ~ vertonen

'mu·sic·al 1. musikalisch; Musik...; **2.**
Musical n; **~ box** bsd. Brt. Spieldose f;
~ 'in·stru·ment Musikinstrument n

'mu·sic box bsd. Am. Spieldose f; **~
cen·tre** (Am. **cen·ter**) Kompaktanlage f; **~ hall** Brt. Varieté(theater) n

mu·si·cian [mju:'zɪʃn] Musiker(in)

'mu·sic stand Notenständer m

musk [mʌsk] Moschus m, Bisam m; **'~
ox** (pl. **- oxen**) zo. Moschusochse m;
~-rat zo. Bisamratte f; Bisampelz m

Mus·lim ['mʊslɪm] **1.** Muslim m, Moslem m; **2.** muslimisch, moslemisch

mus·quash ['mʌskwɒʃ] zo. Bisamratte
f; Bisampelz m

mus·sel ['mʌsl] (Mies)Muschel f

must¹ [mʌst] **1.** v/aux. ich muß, du mußt
etc.; **you ~ not** (F **mustn't**) du darfst
nicht; **2.** Muß n

must² [mʌst] Most m

mus·tache Am. [mə'stɑ:ʃ] Schnurrbart
m

mus·tard ['mʌstəd] Senf m

mus·ter ['mʌstə] **1. ~ up** s-e Kraft etc.
aufbieten; s-n Mut zusammennehmen;

M

2. pass ~ *fig.* Zustimmung finden (*with* bei); den Anforderungen genügen

must·y ['mʌstɪ] (*-ier*, *-iest*) mod(e)rig, muffig

mu·ta·tion [mjuː'teɪʃn] Veränderung *f*; *biol.* Mutation *f*

mute [mjuːt] **1.** stumm; **2.** Stumme(r *m*) *f*; *mus.* Dämpfer *m*

mu·ti·late ['mjuːtɪleɪt] verstümmeln

mu·ti·neer [mjuːtɪ'nɪə] Meuterer *m*; **~nous** ['mjuːtɪnəs] meuternd; rebellisch; **~ny** ['mjuːtɪnɪ] **1.** Meuterei *f*; **2.** meutern

mut·ter ['mʌtə] **1.** murmeln; murren; **2.** Murmeln *n*; Murren *n*

mut·ton ['mʌtn] Hammel-, Schafffleisch *n*; **leg of ~** Hammelkeule *f*; **~ 'chop** Hammelkotelett *n*

mu·tu·al ['mjuːtʃʊəl] gegenseitig; gemeinsam

muz·zle ['mʌzl] **1.** *zo.* Maul *n*, Schnauze *f*; Mündung *f* (*e-r Feuerwaffe*); Maulkorb *m*; **2.** e-n Maulkorb anlegen (*dat.*), *fig. a.* mundtot machen

my [maɪ] mein(e)

myrrh *bot.* [mɜː] Myrrhe *f*

myr·tle *bot.* ['mɜːtl] Myrte *f*

my·self [maɪ'self] ich, mich *od.* mir selbst; mich; mich (selbst); **by ~** allein

mys·te·ri·ous [mɪ'stɪərɪəs] rätselhaft, unerklärlich; geheimnisvoll, mysteriös; **~ry** ['mɪstərɪ] Geheimnis *n*, Rätsel *n*; *rel.* Misterium *n*; **~ tour** Fahrt *f* ins Blaue

mys·tic ['mɪstɪk] **1.** Mystiker(in); **2.** → '**~ti·cal** mystisch; **~ti·fy** ['mɪstɪfaɪ] verwirren, vor ein Rätsel stellen; **be mystified** vor e-m Rätsel stehen

myth [mɪθ] Mythos *m*, Sage *f*

my·thol·o·gy [mɪ'θɒlədʒɪ] Mythologie *f*

N

N, n [en] N, n *n*

N *nur geschr. Abk. für north* N, Nord(en *m*); *north*(*ern*) nördlich

nab F [næb] (*-bb-*) schnappen, erwischen

na·dir ['neɪdɪə] *astr.* Nadir *m* (*Fußpunkt*); *fig.* Tiefpunkt *m*

nag¹ [næg] **1.** (*-gg-*) nörgeln; **~** (*at*) herumnörgeln an (*dat.*); △ *nicht nagen*; **2.** F Nörgler(in)

nag² F [næg] Gaul *m*, Klepper *m*

nail [neɪl] **1.** *tech.* Nagel *m*; (*Finger-, Zehen*)Nagel *m*; **2.** (an)nageln (*to an acc.*); **'~ pol·ish** Nagellack *m*; **'~ scissors** *pl.* Nagelschere *f*; **'~ var·nish** *Brt.* Nagellack *m*

na·ive, na·ïve [naɪ'iːv] naiv (*a. Kunst*)

na·ked ['neɪkɪd] nackt, bloß; kahl; *fig.* ungeschminkt; **'~ness** Nacktheit *f*

name [neɪm] **1.** Name *m*; Ruf *m*; **by ~** mit Namen, namentlich; **by the ~ of ...** namens ...; **what's your ~?** wie heißen Sie?; **call s.o. ~s** j-n beschimpfen; **2.** (be)nennen; erwähnen; ernennen zu; **'~less** namenlos; unbekannt; **'~ly** nämlich; **'~plate** Namens-, Tür-, Fir-

menschild *n*; '**~sake** Namensvetter *m*, -schwester *f*; '**~tag** Namensschild *n* (*am Kleidungsstück*)

nan·ny ['nænɪ] Kindermädchen *n*; **~ goat** *zo.* Geiß *f*, Ziege *f*

nap [næp] **1.** Schläfchen *n*; **have od. take a ~** → **2.** (*-pp-*) ein Nickerchen machen

nape [neɪp] *mst* **~ of the neck** Genick *n*, Nacken *m*

nap·kin ['næpkɪn] Serviette *f*; *Brt.* → '**~py** *Brt.* F Windel *f*

nar·co·sis *med.* [nɑː'kəʊsɪs] (*pl. -ses* [-siːz]) Narkose *f*

nar·cot·ic [nɑː'kɒtɪk] **1.** (*~ally*) narkotisch, betäubend, einschläfernd; Rauschgift...; **~ addiction** Rauschgiftsucht *f*; **~s pl.** Rauschgift *n*; **~s squad** Rauschgiftdezernat *n*

nar·rate [nə'reɪt] erzählen; berichten; schildern; **~ra·tion** [nə'reɪʃn] Erzählung *f*; **~ra·tive** ['nærətɪv] **1.** Erzählung *f*; Bericht *m*, Schilderung *f*; **2.** erzählend; **~ra·tor** [nə'reɪtə] Erzähler(in)

nar·row ['nærəʊ] **1.** eng, schmal; beschränkt; *fig.* knapp; **2.** enger *od.* schmäler werden *od.* machen, (sich) verengen; be-, einschränken; **'~·ly** mit knapper Not; **~'mind·ed** engstirnig, beschränkt; **'~·ness** Enge *f*; Beschränktheit *f* (*a. fig.*)

NASA ['næsə] *Abk. für* **National Aeronautics and Space Administration** *Am.* NASA *f*, Nationale Luft- u. Raumfahrtbehörde

na·sal ['neɪzl] nasal; Nasen...

nas·ty ['nɑːstɪ] (*-ier*, *-iest*) ekelhaft, eklig, widerlich; abscheulich (*Wetter etc.*); böse, schlimm (*Unfall etc.*); häßlich (*Charakter, Benehmen etc.*); gemein, fies; schmutzig, zotig

na·tal ['neɪtl] Geburts...

na·tion ['neɪʃn] Nation *f*, Volk *n*

na·tion·al ['næʃənl] **1.** national, National..., Landes..., Volks...; **2.** Staatsangehörige(r *m*) *f*; **~ 'an·them** Nationalhymne *f*

na·tion·al·i·ty [næʃə'nælətɪ] Nationalität *f*, Staatsangehörigkeit *f*; **~·ize** *econ.* ['næʃnəlaɪz] verstaatlichen

na·tion·al | 'park Nationalpark *m*; **~ 'team** *Sport*: Nationalmannschaft *f*

'na·tion-wide landesweit

na·tive ['neɪtɪv] **1.** einheimisch, Landes...; heimatlich, Heimat...; eingeboren, Eingeborenen...; angeboren; **2.** Eingeborene(r *m*) *f*; Einheimische(r *m*) *f*; **~ 'lan·guage** Muttersprache *f*; **~ 'speak·er** Muttersprachler(in)

Na·tiv·i·ty *rel.* [nə'tɪvətɪ] *die* Geburt Christi

NATO ['neɪtəʊ] *Abk. für* **North Atlantic Treaty Organization** NATO *f*, Nato *f*

nat·u·ral ['nætʃrəl] natürlich; angeboren; Natur...; **~ 'gas** Erdgas *n*; **~·ize** ['nætʃrəlaɪz] naturalisieren, einbürgern; **'~·ly** natürlich (*a. int.*); von Natur (aus); **~ re'sourc·es** *pl.* Naturschätze *pl.*; **~ 'sci·ence** Naturwissenschaft *f*

na·ture ['neɪtʃə] Natur *f*; **~ con·ser·va·tion** Naturschutz *m*; **~ re·serve** Naturschutzgebiet *n*; **~ trail** Naturlehrpfad *m*

naugh·ty ['nɔːtɪ] (*-ier*, *-iest*) ungezogen, unartig; unanständig (*Witz etc.*)

nau·se | a ['nɔːsjə] Übelkeit *f*, Brechreiz *m*; **~·ate** ['nɔːsɪeɪt] **~ s.o.** (bei) j-m Übelkeit verursachen; *fig.* j-n anwidern; **'~·at·ing** ekelerregend, widerlich

nau·ti·cal ['nɔːtɪkl] nautisch, See...

na·val ['neɪvl] Flotten..., Marine...; See...; **~ base** Flottenstützpunkt *m*; **~ of·fi·cer** Marineoffizier *m*; **~ pow·er** Seemacht *f*

nave *arch.* [neɪv] Mittel-, Hauptschiff *n*

na·vel *anat.* ['neɪvl] Nabel *m* (*a. fig.*)

nav·i | ga·ble ['nævɪgəbl] schiffbar; **~·gate** ['nævɪgeɪt] *naut.* befahren; *naut.*, *aviat.* steuern, lenken; **~·ga·tion** [nævɪ'geɪʃən] *naut.*, *aviat.* Navigation *f*; **~·ga·tor** *naut.*, *aviat.* ['nævɪgeɪtə] Navigator *m*

na·vy ['neɪvɪ] (Kriegs)Marine *f*; Kriegsflotte *f*; **~ 'blue** Marineblau *n*

nay *parl.* [neɪ] Gegen-, Neinstimme *f*

NBC [en biː 'siː] *Abk. für* **National Broadcasting Company** (*amer. Rundfunkgesellschaft*)

NE *nur geschr. Abk. für*: **northeast** NO, Nordost(en *m*); **northeast(ern)** nö, nordöstlich

near [nɪə] **1.** *adj.* nahe; kurz, nahe (*Weg*); nahe (*Zukunft etc.*); nahe (verwandt); **be a ~ miss** knapp scheitern; **2.** *adv.* nahe, in der Nähe (*a. ~ at hand*); nahe (bevorstehend) (*a. ~ at hand*); **3.** *prp.* nahe, fast; **3.** *prp.* nahe (*dat.*), in der Nähe von (*od. gen.*); **3.** sich nähern, näherkommen (*dat.*); **~·by 1.** *adj.* ['nɪəbaɪ] nahe(gelegen); **2.** *adv.* [nɪə'baɪ] in der Nähe; **'~·ly** beinahe, fast; annähernd; **~·'sight·ed** *bsd. Am.* kurzsichtig

neat [niːt] ordentlich; sauber; gepflegt; pur (*Whisky etc.*)

neb·u·lous ['nebjʊləs] verschwommen

ne·ces·sar·i·ly ['nesəsərəlɪ] notwendigerweise; **not ~** nicht unbedingt; **~ sa·ry** ['nesəsərɪ] notwendig, nötig; unvermeidlich

ne·ces·si | tate [nɪ'sesɪteɪt] *et.* erfordern, verlangen; **~·ty** [nɪ'sesətɪ] Notwendigkeit *f*; (dringendes) Bedürfnis; Not *f*

neck [nek] **1.** Hals *m* (*a. e-r Flasche etc.*); Genick *n*, Nacken *m*; → **neckline**; **be ~ and ~** F Kopf an Kopf liegen (*a. fig.*); **be up to one's ~ in debt** F bis zum Hals in Schulden stecken; **2.** F knutschen, schmusen

neck·er·chief ['nekətʃɪf] (*pl. -chiefs*, *-chieves*) Halstuch *n*

N

neck·lace ['neklɪs] Halskette f; **~·let** ['neklɪt] Halskettchen n; **'~·line** Ausschnitt m (e-s Kleides etc.); **'~·tie** bsd. Am. Krawatte f, Schlips m

née [neɪ]: **~ Smith** geborene Smith

need [niːd] **1.** (of, for) (dringendes) Bedürfnis (nach), Bedarf m (an dat.); Notwendigkeit f; Mangel m (of, for an dat.); Not f; **be in ~ of s.th.** et. dringend brauchen; **in ~** in Not; **in ~ of help** hilfs-, hilfebedürftig; **2.** v/t. benötigen, brauchen; v/aux. brauchen, müssen

nee·dle [niːdl] **1.** Nadel f; Zeiger m; **2.** F j-n aufziehen, hänseln

'need·less unnötig, überflüssig

'nee·dle|**·wom·an** (pl. **-women**) Näherin f; **'~·work** Handarbeit f

'need·y (**-ier, -iest**) bedürftig, arm

ne·ga·tion [nɪ'geɪʃn] Verneinung f; **neg·a·tive** ['negətɪv] **1.** negativ; verneinend; **2.** Verneinung f; phot. Negativ n; **answer in the ~** verneinen

ne·glect [nɪ'glekt] **1.** vernachlässigen; es versäumen (**doing, to do** zu tun); **2.** Vernachlässigung f; Nachlässigkeit f

neg·li·gent ['neglɪdʒənt] nachlässig, unachtsam; lässig, saloppp

neg·li·gi·ble ['neglɪdʒəbl] unbedeutend

ne·go·ti·ate [nɪ'gəʊʃɪeɪt] verhandeln (über acc.); **~·a·tion** [nɪgəʊʃɪ'eɪʃn] Verhandlung f; **~·a·tor** [nɪ'gəʊʃɪeɪtə] Unterhändler(in)

neigh [neɪ] **1.** wiehern; **2.** Wiehern n

neigh·bo(u)r ['neɪbə] Nachbar(in); **'~·hood** Nachbarschaft f, Umgebung f; **'~·ing** ['neɪbərɪŋ] benachbart, angrenzend; **'~·ly** (gut)nachbarlich, freundlich

nei·ther ['naɪðə, 'niːðə] **1.** adj. u. pron. keine(r, -s) (von beiden); **2.** cj. **~ ... nor** weder ... noch

ne·on chem. ['niːɒn] Neon n; **~ lamp** Neonlampe f; **~ sign** Neon-, Leuchtreklame f

neph·ew ['nevjuː] Neffe m

nerd F [nɜːd] Döskopp m

nerve [nɜːv] Nerv m; Mut m, Stärke f, Selbstbeherrschung f; F Frechheit f; **get on s.o.'s ~s** j-m auf die Nerven gehen od. fallen; **lose one's ~** den Mut od. die Nerven verlieren; **you've got a ~!** F Sie haben Nerven!; **'~·less** kraftlos; mutlos; ohne Nerven, kaltblütig

ner·vous ['nɜːvəs] nervös; Nerven...; **'~·ness** Nervosität f

nest [nest] **1.** Nest n; **2.** nisten

nes·tle ['nesl] (sich) schmiegen od. kuscheln (**against, on** an acc.); a. **~ down** sich behaglich niederlassen, es sich bequem machen (**in** in dat.)

net¹ [net] **1.** Netz n; **~ curtain** Store m; **2.** (-tt-) mit e-m Netz fangen od. abdecken

net² [net] **1.** netto, Netto..., Rein...; **2.** (-tt-) netto einbringen

Neth·er·lands ['neðələndz] pl. die Niederlande pl.

net·tle ['netl] **1.** bot. Nessel f; **2.** ärgern

'net·work Netz(werk) n; (Straßenetc.)Netz n; Rundfunk, TV: Sendernetz n; Computer: Netz n; **be in the ~** Computer: am Netz sein

neu·ro·sis med. [njʊə'rəʊsɪs] (pl. **-ses** [-siːz]) Neurose f; **~·rot·ic** [njʊə'rɒtɪk] **1.** neurotisch; **2.** Neurotiker(in)

neu·ter ['njuːtə] **1.** gr. sächlich; geschlechtslos; **2.** gr. Neutrum n

neu·tral ['njuːtrəl] **1.** neutral; **2.** Neutrale(r m) f; a. **~ gear** mot. Leerlauf(stellung f) m; **~·i·ty** [njuː'trælətɪ] Neutralität f; **~·ize** ['njuːtrəlaɪz] neutralisieren

neu·tron phys. ['njuːtrɒn] Neutron n

nev·er ['nevə] nie(mals); **~'end·ing** endlos, nicht enden wollend; **~·the·less** nichtsdestoweniger, dennoch, trotzdem

new [njuː] neu; frisch; unerfahren; **nothing ~** nichts Neues; **'~·born** neugeboren; **'~·com·er** Neuankömmling m; Neuling m; **'~·ly** kürzlich; neu

news [njuːz] mst sg. Neuigkeit(en pl.) f, Nachricht(en pl.) f; **'~·a·gent** Zeitungshändler(in); **'~·boy** Zeitungsjunge m, -austräger m; **'~·bul·le·tin** Kurznachricht(en pl.) f; **'~·cast** Rundfunk, TV: Nachrichtensendung f; **'~·cast·er** Rundfunk, TV: Nachrichtensprecher(in); **'~ deal·er** Am. Zeitungshändler(in); **'~·flash** Rundfunk, TV: Kurzmeldung f; **'~·let·ter** Rundschreiben n, Mitteilungsblatt n; **~·mon·ger** ['njuːzmʌŋgə] Klatschmaul n; **~·pa·per** ['njuːspeɪpə] Zeitung f; Zeitungs...; **'~·print** Zeitungspapier n; **'~·read·er** bsd. Brt. → newscaster; **'~·reel** Film: Wochenschau f; **'~·room** Nachrichtenredaktion f; **'~·stand** Zeitungskiosk m, -stand m; **'~·ven·dor** bsd. Brt. Zeitungsverkäufer(in)

new 'year Neujahr *n, das neue Jahr;* **New Year's Day** Neujahrstag *m;* **New Year's Eve** Silvester(abend *m) m, n*

next [nekst] **1.** *adj.* nächste(r, -s); *(the)* ~ **day** am nächsten Tag; ~ **door** nebenan; ~ **but one** übernächste(r, -s); ~ **to** gleich neben *od.* nach; beinahe, fast *unmöglich etc.;* **2.** *adv.* als nächste(r, -s); demnächst; das nächste Mal; **3.** *der, die, das* nächste; **~'door** (von) nebenan; ~ **of 'kin** *der, die* nächste Verwandte, *die* nächsten Angehörigen *pl.*

NHS *Brt.* [en eɪtʃ 'es] *Abk. für* **National Health Service** Staatlicher Gesundheitsdienst; **NH'S pa·tient** *Brt. etwa* Kassenpatient(in)

nib·ble ['nɪbl] *v/i.* knabbern (*at* an *dat.);* *v/t.* Loch etc. nagen, knabbern (*in* an *acc.*)

nice [naɪs] (~*r, *~*st*) nett, freundlich; nett, hübsch, schön; fein (*Unterschied etc.*); '~·**ly** gut, fein; genau, sorgfältig; **ni·ce·ty** ['naɪsətɪ] Feinheit *f;* Genauigkeit *f*

niche [nɪtʃ] Nische *f*

nick [nɪk] Kerbe *f;* **in the ~ of time** gerade noch rechtzeitig, im letzten Moment; **2.** (ein)kerben; *j-n* streifen (*Kugel); Brt.* F klauen; *Brt. sl. j-n* schnappen

nick·el ['nɪkl] **1.** *min.* Nickel *n; Am.* Fünfcentstück *n;* **2.** (*bsd. Brt. -ll-, Am. -l-*) vernickeln; **~·'plate** vernickeln

nick-nack ['nɪknæk] → **knick-knack**

nick·name ['nɪkneɪm] **1.** Spitzname *m;* **2.** *j-m* den Spitznamen ... geben

niece [niːs] Nichte *f*

nig·gard ['nɪɡəd] Geizhals *m;* '~·**ly** geizig, knaus(e)rig; schäbig, kümmerlich

night [naɪt] Nacht *f;* Abend *m;* **at ~, by ~, in the ~** in der Nacht, nachts; '~·**cap** Schlummertrunk *m;* '~·**club** Nachtklub *m, -lokal n;* '~·**dress** (Damen-, Kinder)Nachthemd *n;* '~·**fall: at ~** bei Einbruch der Dunkelheit; '~·**gown** *bsd. Am.,* ~·**ie** ['naɪtɪ] → **nightdress**

nigh·tin·gale *zo.* ['naɪtɪŋɡeɪl] Nachtigall *f*

'**night·ly** (all)nächtlich; (all)abendlich; jede Nacht; jeden Abend; **~·mare** ['naɪtmeə] Alptraum *m (a. fig.);* '~ **school** Abendschule *f;* '~ **shift** Nachtschicht *f;* '~·**shirt** (Herren)Nachthemd *n;* '~·**time: in the ~, at ~** nachts; ~

'**watch·man** (*pl. -men*) Nachtwächter *m;* '~·**y** F → **nightdress**

nil [nɪl] Nichts *n,* Null *f; our team won two to ~ od. by two goals to ~* (2-0) unsere Mannschaft gewann zwei zu null (2:0)

nim·ble ['nɪmbl] (~*r, *~*st*) flink, gewandt; geistig beweglich

nine [naɪn] **1.** neun; ~ **to five** normale Dienststunden (von 9-5); *a* ~*-to-five job* e-c (An)Stellung mit geregelter Arbeitszeit; **2.** Neun *f;* '~·**pins** *sg.* Kegeln *n;* ~·**teen** [naɪn'tiːn] **1.** neunzehn; **2.** Neunzehn *f;* ~·**teenth** [naɪn'tiːnθ] neunzehnte(r, -s); ~·**ti·eth** ['naɪntɪɪθ] neunzigste(r, -s); ~·**ty** ['naɪntɪ] **1.** neunzig; **2.** Neunzig *f*

nin·ny F ['nɪnɪ] Dummkopf *m*

ninth [naɪnθ] **1.** neunte(r, -s); **2.** Neuntel *n;* '~·**ly** neuntens

nip¹ [nɪp] **1.** (*-pp-*) kneifen, zwicken; *Pflanzen* schädigen (*Frost, Wind etc.*); F flitzen, sausen; ~ **in the bud** *fig.* im Keim ersticken; **2.** Kneifen *n,* Zwicken *n; there's a ~ in the air today* heute ist es ganz schön kalt

nip² [nɪp] Schlückchen *n* (*Whisky etc.*)

nip·per ['nɪpə]: *(a pair of)* ~**s** *pl.* (e-e) (Kneif)Zange *f*

nip·ple ['nɪpl] *anat.* Brustwarze *f; Am.* (Gummi)Sauger *m* (*e-r Saugflasche*)

ni·tre *Brt.,* **ni·ter** *Am. chem.* ['naɪtə] Salpeter *m*

ni·tro·gen *chem.* ['naɪtrədʒən] Stickstoff *m*

no [nəʊ] **1.** *adv.* nein; nicht; **2.** *adj.* kein(e); ~ **one** keiner, niemand; *in* ~ *time* im Nu, im Handumdrehen; **3.** (*pl. noes*) Nein *n*

No., no. nur *geschr. Abk. für* **number** (*lateinisch numero*) Nr., Nummer *f*

no·bil·i·ty [nəʊ'bɪlətɪ] (Hoch)Adel *m; fig.* Adel *m*

no·ble ['nəʊbl] (~*r, *~*st*) adlig; edel, nobel; prächtig (*Gebäude etc.*); '~·**man** (*pl. -men*) Adlige(r) *m;* '~·**wom·an** (*pl. -women*) Adlige *f*

no·bod·y ['nəʊbədɪ] **1.** niemand, keiner; **2.** *fig.* Niemand *m,* Null *f*

no·'cal·o·rie di·et Nulldiät *f*

noc·tur·nal [nɒk'tɜːnl] Nacht...

nod [nɒd] **1.** (*-dd-*) nicken (mit); ~ **off** einnicken; *have a ~ding acquaintance with s.o.* *j-n* flüchtig kennen; **2.** Nicken *n*

node [nəʊd] Knoten m (a. med.)

noise [nɔɪz] **1.** Krach m, Lärm m; Geräusch n; **2. ~ about** (**abroad, around**) *Gerücht etc.* verbreiten; **'~·less** geräuschlos

nois·y ['nɔɪzɪ] (**-ier, -iest**) laut

no·mad ['nəʊmæd] Nomad|e m, -in f

nom·i|·nal ['nɒmɪnl] nominell; ~ *value econ.* Nennwert m; **~·nate** ['nɒmɪneɪt] ernennen; nominieren, (zur Wahl) vorschlagen; **~·na·tion** [nɒmɪ'neɪʃn] Ernennung f; Nominierung f

nom·i·na·tive *gr.* ['nɒmɪnətɪv] *a.* ~ *case* Nominativ m, erster Fall

nom·i·nee [nɒmɪ'niː] Kandidat(in)

non... [nɒn] nicht..., Nicht..., un...

non·al·co·hol·ic alkoholfrei

non·a·ligned *pol.* blockfrei

non·com·mis·sioned 'of·fi·cer *mil.* Unteroffizier m

non·com·mit·tal [nɒnkə'mɪtl] unverbindlich

non·con·duc·tor *electr.* Nichtleiter m

non·de·script ['nɒndɪskrɪpt] nichtssagend; unauffällig

none [nʌn] **1.** *pron.* (*mst pl. konstruiert*) keine(r, -s), niemand; **2.** *adv.* in keiner Weise, keineswegs

non·en·ti·ty [nɒ'nentətɪ] Null f (*Person*)

none·the·less nichtsdestoweniger, dennoch, trotzdem

non·ex·ist·ence Nichtvorhandensein n, Fehlen n; **~·ent** nicht existierend

non·fic·tion Sachbücher *pl.*

non·flam·ma·ble, non·in·flam·ma·ble nicht brennbar

non·in·ter·fer·ence, non·in·ter·ven·tion *pol.* Nichteinmischung f

non·'i·ron bügelfrei

no·'non·sense nüchtern, sachlich

non·par·ti·san [nɒnpɑː'tɪzæn] *pol.* überparteilich; unparteiisch

non·pay·ment *econ.* Nicht(be)zahlung f

non·plus (**-ss-**) verblüffen

non·pol·lut·ing umweltfreundlich

non·prof·it *Am.*, **non·prof·it-mak·ing** *Brt.* gemeinnützig

non·res·i·dent 1. nicht (orts)ansässig; nicht im Hause wohnend; **2.** Nichtansässige(r m) f; nicht im Hause Wohnende(r m) f

non·re·turn·a·ble Einweg...; **~ bot·tle** Einwegflasche f

non·sense ['nɒnsəns] Unsinn m, dummes Zeug

non·'skid rutschfest, -sicher

non·'smok·er Nichtraucher(in); *Brt. rail.* Nichtraucherwagen m; **~ing** Nichtraucher...

non·'stick mit Antihaftbeschichtung

non·'stop nonstop, ohne Unterbrechung; durchgehend (*Zug etc.*), ohne Zwischenlandung (*Flug*); **~ flight** *a.* Nonstopflug m

non·u·ni·on nicht (gewerkschaftlich) organisiert

non·vi·o·lence (Politik f der) Gewaltlosigkeit f; **~·lent** gewaltlos

noo·dle ['nuːdl] Nudel f

nook [nʊk] Ecke f, Winkel m

noon [nuːn] Mittag(szeit f) m; **at ~** um 12 Uhr (mittags)

noose [nuːs] Schlinge f

nope F [nəʊp] ne(e), nein

nor [nɔː] → *neither* 2; auch nicht

norm [nɔːm] Norm f; **nor·mal** ['nɔːml] normal; **nor·mal·ize** ['nɔːməlaɪz] (sich) normalisieren

north [nɔːθ] **1.** Nord(en m); **2.** *adj.* nördlich, Nord...; **3.** *adv.* nach Norden, nordwärts; **~'east** Nordost(en m); **2.** *a.* **~'east·ern** nordöstlich

nor·ther·ly ['nɔːðəlɪ], **nor·thern** ['nɔːðn] nördlich, Nord...

North 'Pole Nordpol m

north·ward(s) ['nɔːθwəd(z)] *adv.* nördlich, nach Norden; **~'west 1.** Nordwest(en m); **2.** *a.* **~'west·ern** nordwestlich

Nor·way ['nɔːweɪ] Norwegen n

Nor·we·gian [nɔː'wiːdʒən] **1.** norwegisch; **2.** Norweger(in); *ling.* Norwegisch n

nos. *nur geschr. Abk. für numbers* Nummern *pl.* (→ *No., no.*)

nose [nəʊz] **1.** Nase f; Schnauze f (*beim Hund*); **2.** *Auto etc.* vorsichtig fahren; **a. ~ about, ~ around** *fig.* F herumschnüffeln (in *dat.*) (**for** nach); **'~·bleed** Nasenbluten n; **have a ~** Nasenbluten haben; **'~·cone** Raketenspitze f; **'~·dive** *aviat.* Sturzflug m

nose·gay ['nəʊzgeɪ] Sträußchen n

nos·ey ['nəʊzɪ] → *nosy*

nos·tal·gia [nɒ'stældʒɪə] Nostalgie f

nos·tril ['nɒstrəl] Nasenloch n, *bsd. zo.* Nüster f

nos·y F ['nəʊzɪ] (*-ier*, *-iest*) neugierig; ~ **'park·er** *Brt.* F neugierige Person, Gaffer(in)

not [nɒt] nicht; ~ *a* kein(e)

no·ta·ble ['nəʊtəbl] bemerkenswert; beachtlich

no·ta·ry ['nəʊtərɪ] *mst* ~ *public* Notar *m*

notch [nɒtʃ] **1.** Kerbe *f*; *Am. geol.* Engpaß *m*; **2.** (ein)kerben

note [nəʊt] (*mst* ~*s pl.*) Notiz *f*, Aufzeichnung *f*; Anmerkung *f*; Vermerk *m*; Briefchen *n*, Zettel *m*; (diplomatische) Note; Banknote *f*, Geldschein *m*; *mus.* Note *f*; *fig.* Ton *m*; △ *nicht* (*Schul*)*Note*; **take** ~*s* (*of*) sich Notizen machen (über *acc.*); '~**book** Notizbuch *n*; *Computer*: Notebook *m*

not·ed ['nəʊtɪd] bekannt, berühmt (*for* wegen)

'**note·pa·per** Briefpapier *n*; '~**wor·thy** bemerkenswert

noth·ing ['nʌθɪŋ] nichts; ~ *but* nichts als, nur; ~ *much* F nicht viel; *for* ~ umsonst; *to say* ~ *of* ganz zu schweigen von; *there is* ~ *like* es geht nichts über (*acc.*)

no·tice ['nəʊtɪs] **1.** Ankündigung *f*, Bekanntgabe *f*, Mitteilung *f*; Anzeige *f*; Kündigung(sfrist) *f*; Beachtung *f*; △ *nicht Notiz* (*Aufzeichnung etc.*); *give od.* hand in one's ~ kündigen (*to* bei *e-r* Firma); *give s.o.* ~ j-m kündigen (*e-m Arbeitnehmer*); *give s.o.* (*his etc.*) ~ j-m kündigen (*e-m Mieter*); *at six months'* ~ mit halbjährlicher Kündigungsfrist; *take* (*no*) ~ *of* (keine) Notiz nehmen von, (nicht) beachten; *at short* ~ kurzfristig; *until further* ~ bis auf weiteres; *without* ~ fristlos; **2.** (es) bemerken; (besonders) beachten; achten auf (*acc.*); △ *nicht notieren*; '~**a·ble** erkennbar, wahrnehmbar; bemerkenswert; '~ **board** *Brt.* Schwarzes Brett

no·ti·fy ['nəʊtɪfaɪ] *et.* anzeigen, melden, mitteilen; *j-n* benachrichtigen

no·tion ['nəʊʃn] Begriff *m*, Vorstellung *f*; Idee *f*

no·tions ['nəʊʃnz] *pl. bsd. Am.* Kurzwaren *pl.*

no·to·ri·ous [nəʊ'tɔːrɪəs] berüchtigt (*for* für)

not·with·stand·ing [nɒtwɪθ'stændɪŋ] ungeachtet, trotz (*gen.*)

nought *Brt.* [nɔːt]: **0.4** (~ *point four*) 0,4

noun *gr.* [naʊn] Substantiv *n*, Hauptwort *n*

nour·ish ['nʌrɪʃ] (er)nähren; *fig.* hegen; '~**ing** nahrhaft; '~**ment** Ernährung *f*; Nahrung *f*

Nov *nur geschr. Abk. für* **November** Nov., November *m*

nov·el ['nɒvl] **1.** Roman *m*; △ *nicht* **Novelle**; **2.** (ganz) neu(artig); ~**ist** ['nɒvəlɪst] Romanschriftsteller(in); **no·vel·la** [nəʊ'velə] (*pl. -las, -le* [-liː]) Novelle *f*; ~**ty** ['nɒvltɪ] Neuheit *f*

No·vem·ber [nəʊ'vembə] (*Abk. Nov*) November *m*

nov·ice ['nɒvɪs] Anfänger(in), Neuling *m*; *rel.* Noviz|e *m*, -in *f*

now [naʊ] **1.** *adv.* nun, jetzt; ~ *and again*, (*every*) ~ *and then* von Zeit zu Zeit, dann u. wann; *by* ~ inzwischen; *from* ~ (*on*) von jetzt an; *just* ~ gerade eben; **2.** *cj. a.* ~ *that* nun da

now·a·days ['naʊədeɪz] heutzutage

no·where ['nəʊweə] nirgends

nox·ious ['nɒkʃəs] schädlich

noz·zle *tech.* ['nɒzl] Schnauze *f*; Stutzen *m*; Düse *f*; Zapfpistole *f*

NSPCC *Brt.* [en es piː siː 'siː] *Abk. für National Society for the Prevention of Cruelty to Children* (*Kinderschutzverein*)

nu·ance ['njuːɑːns] Nuance *f*

nub [nʌb] springender Punkt

nu·cle·ar ['njuːklɪə] Atom..., Atom..., atomar, nuklear, Nuklear...; ~ **'en·er·gy** Atom-, Kernenergie *f*; ~ **'fam·i·ly** Kleinfamilie *f*; ~ **'fis·sion** Kernspaltung *f*; ~**'free** atomwaffenfrei; ~ **'fu·sion** Kernfusion *f*; ~ **'phys·ics** *sg.* Kernphysik *f*; ~ **'pow·er** Atom-, Kernkraft *f*; ~**'pow·ered** atomgetrieben; ~ **'pow·er plant** Atom-, Kernkraftwerk *n*; ~ **re'ac·tor** Atom-, Kernreaktor *m*; ~ **'war** Atomkrieg *m*; ~ **'war·head** Atomsprengkopf *m*; ~ **'waste** Atommüll *m*; ~ **'weap·ons** *pl.* Atom-, Kernwaffen *pl.*

nu·cle·us ['njuːklɪəs] (*pl. -clei* [-klaɪ]) (*Atom-, Zell*)Kern *m*; *fig.* Kern *m*

nude [njuːd] **1.** nackt; **2.** *Kunst*: Akt *m*

nudge [nʌdʒ] **1.** *j-n* anstoßen, (an)stupsen; **2.** Stups(er) *m*

nug·get ['nʌgɪt] (*bsd. Gold*)Klumpen *m*

nui·sance ['njuːsns] Plage *f*, Ärgernis *n*; Nervensäge *f*, Quälgeist *m*; *what a* ~!

N

wie ärgerlich!; *be a ~ to s.o.* j-m lästig fallen, j-n nerven; *make a ~ of o.s.* den Leuten auf die Nerven gehen *od.* fallen

nukes F [nju:ks] *pl.* Atom-, Kernwaffen *pl.*

null *bsd. jur.* [nʌl]: *~ and void* null u. nichtig

numb [nʌm] **1.** starr (*with* vor *Kälte etc.*), taub; *fig.* wie betäubt (*with* vor *Schmerz etc.*); **2.** starr *od.* taub machen

num·ber ['nʌmbə] **1.** Zahl *f*, Ziffer *f*; Nummer *f*; (An)Zahl *f*; Ausgabe *f*, Nummer *f* (*e-r Zeitung etc.*); (*Bus- etc.*)Linie *f*; *sorry, wrong ~ tel.* falsch verbunden!; **2.** numerieren; zählen; sich belaufen auf (*acc.*); '**~·less** zahllos; '**~·plate** *bsd. Brt. mot.* Nummernschild *n*

nu·me·ral ['nju:mərəl] Ziffer *f*; *ling.* Zahlwort *n*

nu·me·rous ['nju:mərəs] zahlreich

nun [nʌn] Nonne *f*; **~·ne·ry** ['nʌnəri] Nonnenkloster *n*

nurse [nɜ:s] **1.** (Kranken-, Säuglings)Schwester *f*; Kindermädchen *n*; (Kranken)Pflegerin *f*; → *male nurse*; *a. wet ~* Amme *f*; **2.** stillen; pflegen; hegen; als Krankenschwester *od.* -pfleger arbeiten; *~ s.o. back to health* j-n gesund pflegen

nur·se·ry ['nɜ:səri] Tagesheim *n*, -stätte *f*; *veraltet* Kinderzimmer *n*; *agr.*

Baum-, Pflanzschule *f*; '**~ rhyme** Kinderlied *n*, -reim *m*; '**~ school** Kindergarten *m*; '**~ slope** *Ski:* Idiotenhügel *m*

nurs·ing ['nɜ:sɪŋ] Stillen *n*; (Kranken)Pflege *f*; **~ bot·tle** (Säuglings-, Saug)Flasche *f*; **~ home** Pflegeheim *n*; *Brt.* Privatklinik *f*

nut [nʌt] *bot.* Nuß *f*; *tech.* (Schrauben-) Mutter *f*; F verrückter Kerl; F Birne *f* (*Kopf*); *be off one's ~* F spinnen; '**~·crack·er(s** *pl.*) Nußknacker *m*; **~·meg** *bot.* ['nʌtmeg] Muskatnuß *f*

nu·tri·ent ['nju:trɪənt] **1.** Nährstoff *m*; **2.** nahrhaft

nu·tri·tion [nju:'trɪʃn] Ernährung *f*; **~·tious** [nju:'trɪʃəs] nahrhaft; **~·tive** ['nju:trɪtɪv] nahrhaft

'**nut·shell** Nußschale *f*; (*to put it*) *in a ~* F kurz gesagt, mit e-m Wort; **~·ty** ['nʌtɪ] (*-ier, -iest*) voller Nüsse; Nuß...; *sl.* verrückt

NW *nur geschr. Abk. für: northwest* NW, Nordwest(en *m*); *northwest(ern)* nw, nordwestlich

NY *nur geschr. Abk. für New York* (*Stadt od. Staat*)

NYC *nur geschr. Abk. für New York City* (die Stadt) New York *n*

ny·lon ['naɪlɒn] Nylon *n*; **~s** *pl.* Nylonstrümpfe *pl.*

nymph [nɪmf] Nymphe *f*

O

O, o [əʊ] O, o *n*

o [əʊ] Null *f* (*Ziffer, a. in Telefonnummern*)

oaf [əʊf] Lümmel *m*, Flegel *m*

oak *bot.* [əʊk] Eiche *f*

oar [ɔ:] Ruder *n*; **~s·man** ['ɔ:zmən] (*pl. -men*) *Sport:* Ruderer *m*; '**~s·wom·an** (*pl. -women*) *Sport:* Ruderin *f*

OAS [əʊ eɪ 'es] *Abk. für Organization of American States* Organisation *f* amerikanischer Staaten

o·a·sis [əʊ'eɪsɪs] (*pl. -ses* [-si:z]) Oase *f* (*a. fig.*)

oath [əʊθ] (*pl. oaths* [əʊðz]) Eid *m*, Schwur *m*; Fluch *m*; *be on od. under ~* unter Eid stehen; *take an ~* e-n Eid leisten *od.* schwören; *take the ~* schwören

oat·meal ['əʊtmi:l] Hafermehl *n*, -grütze *f*

oats [əʊts] *pl. bot.* Hafer *m*; *sow one's wild ~* sich die Hörner abstoßen

o·be·di·ence [ə'bi:djəns] Gehorsam *m*; **~ent** gehorsam

o·bese [əʊ'bi:s] fett(leibig); **o·bes·i·ty** [əʊ'bi:sətɪ] Fettleibigkeit *f*

o·bey [ə'beɪ] gehorchen (*dat.*), folgen; *Befehl etc.* befolgen

o·bit·u·a·ry [ə'bɪtjʊərɪ] Nachruf *m; a.* ~ **notice** Todesanzeige *f*

ob·ject 1. ['ɒbdʒɪkt] Objekt *n* (*a. gr.*); Gegenstand *m;* Ziel *n,* Zweck *m,* Absicht *f;* **2.** [əb'dʒekt] einwenden; et. dagegen haben

ob·jec|·tion [əb'dʒekʃn] Einwand *m,* -spruch *m* (*a. jur.*); ~**tio·na·ble** nicht einwandfrei; unangenehm; anstößig

ob·jec·tive [əb'dʒektɪv] **1.** objektiv, sachlich; **2.** Ziel *n;* Objektiv *n* (*Mikroskop*)

ob·li·ga·tion [ɒblɪ'geɪʃn] Verpflichtung *f; be under an* ~ *to s.o.* j-m (zu Dank) verpflichtet sein; *be under an* ~ *to do s.th.* verpflichtet sein, et. zu tun; **ob·lig·a·to·ry** [ə'blɪgətərɪ] verpflichtend, verbindlich

o·blige [ə'blaɪdʒ] nötigen, zwingen; (zu Dank) verpflichten; ~ *s.o.* j-m e-n Gefallen tun; *much* ~*d* besten Dank; **o'blig·ing** entgegenkommend, gefällig

o·blique [ə'bliːk] schief, schräg; *fig.* indirekt

o·blit·er·ate [ə'blɪtəreɪt] auslöschen, vernichten, völlig zerstören; *Sonne etc.* verdecken

o·bliv·i·on [ə'blɪvɪən] Vergessen(heit *f*) *n;* ~**ous** [ə'blɪvɪəs]: *be* ~ *of* od. *to s.th.* sich e-r Sache nicht bewußt sein; et. nicht bemerken od. wahrnehmen

ob·long ['ɒblɒŋ] rechteckig; länglich

ob·nox·ious [əb'nɒkʃəs] widerlich

ob·scene [əb'siːn] obszön, unanständig

ob·scure [əb'skjʊə] **1.** dunkel; *fig.* dunkel, unklar; unbekannt; **2.** verdunkeln, -decken; **ob·scu·ri·ty** [əb'skjʊərətɪ] Unbekanntheit *f;* Unklarheit *f*

ob·se·quies ['ɒbsɪkwɪz] *pl.* Trauerfeier(lichkeiten *pl.*) *f*

ob·ser·va·ble [əb'zɜːvəbl] wahrnehmbar, merklich; ~**vance** [əb'zɜːvns] Beachtung *f,* Befolgung *f;* ~**vant** [əb'zɜːvnt] aufmerksam; ~**va·tion** [ɒbzə'veɪʃn] Beobachtung *f,* Überwachung *f;* Bemerkung *f* (*on* über *acc.*); ~**va·to·ry** [əb'zɜːvətrɪ] Observatorium *n,* Sternwarte *f*

ob·serve [əb'zɜːv] beobachten; überwachen; *Vorschrift etc.* beachten, befolgen, einhalten; bemerken; äußern; **ob'serv·er** Beobachter(in)

---

ob·sess [əb'ses]: *be* ~*ed by* od. *with* besessen sein von; **ob·ses·sion** [əb'seʃn] Besessenheit *f;* fixe Idee; **ob·ses·sive** *psych.* [əb'sesɪv] zwanghaft

ob·so·lete ['ɒbsəliːt] veraltet

ob·sta·cle ['ɒbstəkl] Hindernis *n*

ob·sti·nate ['ɒbstɪnət] hartnäckig, halsstarrig; eigensinnig

ob·struct [əb'strʌkt] verstopfen, -sperren; blockieren; behindern; **ob·struc·tion** [əb'strʌkʃn] Verstopfung *f;* Blockierung *f;* Behinderung *f;* **ob·struc·tive** [əb'strʌktɪv] blockierend; hinderlich

ob·tain [əb'teɪn] erhalten, bekommen, sich et. verschaffen; ~**a·ble** erhältlich

ob·tru·sive [əb'truːsɪv] aufdringlich

ob·tuse [əb'tjuːs] stumpf (*Winkel*)

ob·vi·ous ['ɒbvɪəs] offensichtlich, klar, einleuchtend

oc·ca·sion [ə'keɪʒn] Gelegenheit *f;* Anlaß *m;* Veranlassung *f;* (festliches) Ereignis; *on the* ~ *of* anläßlich (*gen.*); ~**al** [ə'keɪʒənl] gelegentlich; vereinzelt

Oc·ci·dent ['ɒksɪdənt] *der* Westen, *der* Okzident, *das* Abendland; **2·den·tal** [ɒksɪ'dentl] abendländisch, westlich

oc·cu|·pant ['ɒkjʊpənt] Bewohner(in); Insass|e *m,* -in *f;* ~**pa·tion** [ɒkjʊ'peɪʃn] Beruf *m;* Beschäftigung *f; mil., pol.* Besetzung *f,* Besatzung *f,* Okkupation *f;* ~**py** ['ɒkjʊpaɪ] in Besitz nehmen, *mil., pol.* besetzen; *Raum* einnehmen; in Anspruch nehmen; beschäftigen; *be* ~**cupied** bewohnt sein; besetzt sein (*Platz*)

oc·cur [ə'kɜː] (-*rr*-) sich ereignen; vorkommen; *it* ~**red to me that** es fiel mir ein od. mir kam der Gedanke, daß; ~**rence** [ə'kʌrəns] Vorkommen *n;* Ereignis *n;* Vorfall *m*

o·cean ['əʊʃn] Ozean *m,* Meer *n*

o·clock [ə'klɒk] Uhr (*bei Zeitangaben*); (*at*) *five* ~ (um) fünf Uhr

Oct *nur geschr. Abk. für* **October** Okt., Oktober *m*

Oc·to·ber [ɒk'təʊbə] (*Abk.* **Oct**) Oktober *m*

oc·u·lar ['ɒkjʊlə] Augen...; ~**list** ['ɒkjʊlɪst] Augen|arzt *m,* -ärztin *f*

OD F [əʊ 'diː] *v/i.* ~ *on heroin* an e-r Überdosis Heroin sterben

odd [ɒd] sonderbar, seltsam, merkwürdig; einzeln, Einzel... (*Schuh etc.*); ungerade (*Zahl*); F nach Zahlen: **30 ~** (et.) über 30, einige 30; gelegentlich, Gelegenheits...; **~ jobs** *pl*. Gelegenheitsarbeiten *pl*.

odds [ɒdz] (Gewinn)Chancen *pl.*; **the ~ are 10 to 1** die Chancen stehen 10 zu 1; **the ~ are that** es ist sehr wahrscheinlich, daß; **against all ~** wider Erwarten, entgegen allen Erwartungen; **be at ~** uneins sein (**with** mit); **~ and ends** Krimskrams *m*; **~'on** hoch, klar (*Favorit*), aussichtsreichst (*Kandidat etc.*)

ode [əʊd] Ode *f* (*Gedicht*)

o·do(u)r [ˈəʊdə] Geruch *m* (*bsd. unangenehmer*)

of *prp.* [ɒv, əv] von; *Herkunft*: von, aus; *Material*: aus; um (*cheat s.o. ~ s.th.*); an (*dat.*) (**die ~**); aus (**~ charity**); vor (*dat.*) (**afraid ~**); auf (*acc.*) (**proud ~**); über (*acc.*) (**glad ~**); nach (**smell ~**); von, über (*acc.*) (**speak ~ s.th.**); an (*acc.*) (**think ~ s.th.**); **the city ~ London** die Stadt London; **the works ~ Dickens** Dickens' Werke; **your letter ~ ...** Ihr Schreiben vom ...; **five minutes ~ twelve** *Am.* fünf Minuten vor zwölf

off [ɒf] **1.** *adv.* fort(...), weg(...); ab(...), ab(gegangen) (*Knopf etc.*); weg, entfernt (**3 miles ~**); aus(...), aus-, abgeschaltet (*Licht etc.*), zu (*Hahn etc.*); aus(gegangen), alle; aus, vorbei; verdorben (*Nahrungsmittel*); frei (*von Arbeit*); **I must be ~** ich muß gehen *od*. weg; **~ with you!** fort mit dir!; **be ~** ausfallen, nicht stattfinden; **10% ~** *econ*. 10% Nachlaß; **~ and on** ab u. zu, hin u.wieder; **take a day ~** sich e-n Tag frei nehmen; **be well (badly) ~** gut (schlecht) d(a)ran *od*. gestellt *od*. situiert sein; **2.** *prp*. fort von, weg von, von (... ab, weg, herunter); abseits von (*od. gen.*), von ... weg; *naut*. vor der *Küste etc.*; **be ~ duty** nicht im Dienst sein, dienstfrei haben; **be ~ smoking** nicht mehr rauchen; **3.** *adj*. (arbeits-, dienst)frei; schlecht (*Tag etc.*).

of·fal *Brt. gastr.* [ˈɒfl] Innereien *pl*.

of·fence *Brt.*, **of·fense** *Am.* [əˈfens] Vergehen *n*, Verstoß *m*; *jur*. Straftat *f*; Beleidigung *f*, Kränkung *f*; **take ~** Anstoß nehmen (**at** an *dat.*)

of·fend [əˈfend] beleidigen, kränken; verstoßen (**against** gegen); **~·er** (Übel-,

Misse)Täter(in); **first ~** *jur.* nicht Vorbestrafte(r *m*) *f*, Ersttäter(in)

of·fen·sive [əˈfensɪv] **1.** beleidigend, anstößig; widerlich (*Geruch etc.*); Offensiv..., Angriffs...; **2.** Offensive *f*

of·fer [ˈɒfə] **1.** *v/t.* anbieten (*a. econ.*); *Preis, Möglichkeit etc.* bieten; *Preis, Belohnung* aussetzen; sich bereit erklären (**to do** zu tun); *Widerstand* leisten; *v/i.* es *od*. sich anbieten; **2.** Angebot *n*

off·hand [ɒfˈhænd] lässig (*Art etc.*); auf Anhieb, so ohne weiteres; Stegreif...

of·fice [ˈɒfɪs] Büro *n*, Geschäftsstelle *f*, (Anwalts)Kanzlei *f*; (*bsd.* öffentliches) Amt, Posten *m*; *mst* ♀ *bsd. Brt.* Ministerium *n*; ~ **hours** *pl*. Dienstzeit *f*; Geschäfts-, Öffnungszeiten *pl*.

of·fi·cer [ˈɒfɪsə] *mil.* Offizier *m*; (Polizei*etc.*)Beamt|e(r) *m*, -in *f*.

of·fi·cial [əˈfɪʃl] **1.** Beamt|e(r) *m*, -in *f*; **2.** offiziell, amtlich, dienstlich

of·fi·ci·ate [əˈfɪʃɪeɪt] amtieren

of·fi·cious [əˈfɪʃəs] übereifrig

'off·licence *Brt.* Wein- u. Spirituosenhandlung *f*; **'~·line** *Computer*: rechnerunabhängig, Off-line...; **~'peak**: **~ electricity** Nachtstrom *m*; **~ hours** *pl*. verkehrsschwache Stunden *pl.*; **'~·sea·son** Nebensaison *f*; **'~·set** ausgleichen; **'~·shoot** *bot.* Ableger *m*, Sproß *m*; **~·shore** vor der Küste, *Sport*: abseits; **~ position** Abseitsposition *f*, -stellung *f*; **~ trap** Abseitsfalle *f*; **'~·spring** Nachkomme(nschaft *f*) *m*; **~·the·'rec·ord** inoffiziell

of·ten [ˈɒfn] oft(mals), häufig

oh *int.* [əʊ] oh!

oil [ɔɪl] **1.** Öl *n*; (Erd)Öl *n*; **2.** (ein)ölen, schmieren (*a. fig.*); **~ change** *mot.* Ölwechsel *m*; **'~·cloth** Wachstuch *n*; **'~·field** Ölfeld *n*; **~·paint·ing** Ölmalerei *f*; Ölgemälde *n*; **~ plat·form** → *oilrig*; **'~·pol·lu·tion** Ölpest *f*; **'~·pro·duc·ing coun·try** Ölförderland *n*; **~·re·fin·e·ry** Erdölraffinerie *f*; **'~·rig** (Öl)Bohrinsel *f*; **'~·skins** *pl*. Ölzeug *n*; **'~·slick** Ölteppich *m*; **'~·well** Ölquelle *f*; **'~·y** (**-ier, -iest**) ölig; *fig*. schmierig, schleimig

oint·ment [ˈɔɪntmənt] Salbe *f*

OK, o·kay F [əʊˈkeɪ] **1.** *adj. u. int.* okay(!), o.k.(!), in Ordnung(!); **2.** genehmigen, e-r *Sache* zustimmen; **3.**

old [əʊld] **1.** alt; **2. the** ~ *pl.* die Alten *pl.*; **~ 'age** (hohes) Alter; **~ age 'pen·sion** Rente *f*, Pension *f*; **~ age 'pen·sion·er** Rentner(in), Pensionär(in); **~'fash·ioned** altmodisch; **'~·ish** ältlich; **~ 'peo·ple's home** Alters-, Altenheim *n*

ol·ive ['ɒlɪv] *bot.* Olive *f*; Olivgrün *n*

O·lym·pic Games [əlɪmpɪk 'geɪmz] *pl.* Olympische Spiele *pl.*

om·i·nous ['ɒmɪnəs] unheilvoll

o·mis·sion [əʊ'mɪʃn] Auslassung *f*; Unterlassung *f*

o·mit [ə'mɪt] (**-tt-**) aus-, weglassen; unterlassen

om·nip·o·tent [ɒm'nɪpətənt] allmächtig

om·nis·ci·ent [ɒm'nɪsɪənt] allwissend

on [ɒn] **1.** *prp.* auf (*acc. od. dat.*) (**~ the table**); an (*dat.*) (**~ the wall**); in (**~ TV**); *Richtung, Ziel:* an (*acc.*) ... (hin), an (*acc.*), nach (*dat.*) ... (hin) (**march ~ London**); *fig.* auf (*acc.*) ... (hin) (**~ demand**); *Zeitpunkt:* an (*dat.*) (**~ Sunday**, **~ the 1st of April**); (gleich) nach, bei (**~ his arrival**); *gehörig zu, beschäftigt bei* (**~ a committee**, **~ the "Daily Mail"**); *Zustand:* in (*dat.*), auf (*dat.*) (**~ duty**, **~ fire**); *Thema:* über (*acc.*) (**talk ~ a subject**); nach (*dat.*) (**~ this model**); von (*dat.*) (**live ~ s.th.**); **~ the street** *Am.* auf der Straße; **~ a train** *bsd. Am.* im Zug; **~ hearing it** als ich *etc.* es hörte; **have you any money ~ you?** hast du Geld bei dir?; **2.** *adj. u. adv.* an(geschaltet) (*Licht etc.*), eingeschaltet (*Radio etc.*), auf (*Hahn etc.*), (dar)auf(*legen, -schrauben etc.*); an(*haben, -ziehen*) (*Kleidung*) (**have a coat ~**); auf(*behalten*) (**keep one's hat ~**); weiter(*gehen, -sprechen etc.*); **and so ~** und so weiter; **~ and ~** immer weiter; **from this day ~** von dem Tage an; **~** *thea.* gegeben werden (*Stück*); laufen (*Film*) *Rundfunk, TV:* gesendet werden; **what's ~?** was ist los?

once [wʌns] **1.** einmal; einst; **~ again**, **~ more** noch einmal; **~ in a while** ab u. zu, hin u. wieder; **~ and for all** ein für allemal; **not ~** kein einziges Mal; **at ~** sofort; auf einmal, gleichzeitig; **all at ~** plötzlich; **for ~** diesmal, ausnahmsweise; **this ~** dieses eine Mal; **2.** sobald

one [wʌn] ein(e); einzig; man; Eins *f*, eins; **~'s** sein(e); **~ day** eines Tages; **~ Smith** ein gewisser Smith; **~ another** sich (gegenseitig), einander; **~ by ~**, **~ after the other** e-r nach dem andern; **I for ~** ich zum Beispiel; **the little ~s** *pl.* die Kleinen *pl.*; **~'self** sich (selbst); (**all) by ~** ganz allein; **to ~** ganz für sich (allein); **~'sid·ed** einseitig; **'~·time** ehemalig, früher; **~'track 'mind: have a ~** immer nur dasselbe im Kopf haben; **~ 'two** *Fußball:* Doppelpass *m*; **~'way** Einbahn...; **~·way 'street** Einbahnstraße *f*; **~·way 'tick·et** *Am.* einfache Fahrkarte, *aviat.* einfaches Ticket; **~·way 'traf·fic** Verkehr *m* nur in e-r Richtung

on·ion ['ʌnjən] *bot.* Zwiebel *f*

'on·line *Computer:* rechnerabhängig, On-line...; **'~·look·er** Zuschauer(in)

on·ly ['əʊnlɪ] **1.** *adj.* einzige(r, -s); **2.** *adv.* nur, bloß; erst; **~ yesterday** erst gestern; **3.** *cj.* F nur, bloß

on·rush Ansturm *m*; **~·set** Beginn *m* (*des Winters*); Ausbruch *m* (*e-r Krankheit*); **~·slaught** ['ɒnslɔːt] (heftiger) Angriff (*a. fig.*)

on·to ['ɒntʊ, 'ɒntə] auf (*acc.*)

on·ward(s) ['ɒnwəd(z)] *adv.* vorwärts, weiter; **from now ~** von nun an

ooze [uːz] *v/i.* sickern; **~ away** *fig.* schwinden; *v/t.* absondern; *fig.* ausstrahlen, verströmen

o·paque [əʊ'peɪk] (**~r**, **~st**) undurchsichtig; *fig.* unverständlich

OPEC ['əʊpek] *Abk. für* **Organization of Petroleum Exporting Countries** Organisation *f* der Erdöl exportierenden Länder

o·pen ['əʊpən] **1.** offen; geöffnet; offen, offen, frei (*Feld*); öffentlich; *fig.* offen, unentschieden; *fig.* offen, freimütig; *fig.* zugänglich, aufgeschlossen (**to** für *od. dat.*); **~ all day** durchgehend geöffnet; **in the ~ air** im Freien; **2.** *Golf, Tennis:* offenes Turnier; **in the ~** im Freien; **come out into the ~** *fig.* an die Öffentlichkeit treten; **3.** *v/t.* öffnen, aufmachen, *Buch etc. a.* aufschlagen; eröffnen; *v/i.* sich öffnen, aufgehen; öffnen, aufmachen (*Laden*); anfangen, beginnen, **~ into** führen nach *od.* in (*Tür etc.*); **~ onto** hinausgehen auf

O

(acc.) (Fenster, Tür); ~**'air** im Freien; ~**'end·ed** zeitlich unbegrenzt; ~**er** ['əʊpnə] *(Dosen- etc.)*Öffner *m;* ~**-'eyed** mit großen Augen, staunend; ~**'hand·ed** freigebig, großzügig; ~**ing** ['əʊpnɪŋ] Öffnung *f; econ.* freie Stelle; Eröffnung *f,* Erschließung *f,* Einstieg *m;* Eröffnungs...; Öffnungs...; ~**'mind·ed** aufgeschlossen

op·e·ra ['ɒpərə] Oper *f;* '~ **glass·es** *pl.* Opernglas *n;* '~ **house** Opernhaus *n,* Oper *f*

op·e·rate ['ɒpəreɪt] *v/i. tech.* arbeiten, in Betrieb sein, laufen *(Maschine etc.);* wirksam sein *od.* werden; *med.* operieren **(on** *s.o.* j-n); *v/t. tech.* Maschine bedienen, Schalter *etc.* betätigen; *Unternehmen, Geschäft* betreiben, führen

'**op·e·rat·ing**| **room** *Am.* Operationssaal *m;* '~ **sys·tem** *Computer:* Betriebssystem *n;* '~ **thea·tre** *Brt.* Operationssaal *m*

op·e·ra|**·tion** [ɒpə'reɪʃn] *tech.* Betrieb *m,* Lauf *m (e-r Maschine); tech.* Bedienung *f;* Tätigkeit *f,* Unternehmen *n; med., mil.* Operation *f;* **in** ~ in Betrieb; ~**tive** ['ɒpərətɪv] wirksam; *med.* operativ; ~**tor** ['ɒpəreɪtə] *tech.* Bedienungsperson *f; Computer:* Operator *m; tel.* Vermittlung *f*

o·pin·ion [ə'pɪnjən] Meinung *f,* Ansicht *f;* Gutachten *n* (**on** über *acc.);* **in my** ~ meines Erachtens

op·po·nent [ə'pəʊnənt] Gegner(in)

op·por|**·tune** ['ɒpətjuːn] günstig, passend; rechtzeitig; ~**tu·ni·ty** [ɒpə'tjuːnətɪ] (günstige) Gelegenheit

op·pose [ə'pəʊz] sich widersetzen *(dat.);* **op·posed** entgegengesetzt; **be** ~ **to** gegen ... sein; **op·po·site** ['ɒpəzɪt] **1.** Gegenteil *n,* -satz *m;* **2.** *adj.* gegenüberliegend; entgegengesetzt; **3.** *adv.* gegenüber **(to** *dat.);* **4.** *prp.* gegenüber *(dat.);* **op·po·si·tion** [ɒpə'zɪʃn] Widerstand *m,* Opposition *f (a. parl.);* Gegensatz *m*

op·press [ə'pres] unterdrücken; **op·pres·sion** [ə'preʃn] Unterdrückung *f;* **op·pres·sive** [ə'presɪv] (be)drückend; hart, grausam; schwül *(Wetter)*

op·tic ['ɒptɪk] Augen..., Seh...; → '**op·ti·cal** optisch; **op·ti·cian** [ɒp'tɪʃn] Optiker(in)

op·ti·mis·m ['ɒptɪmɪzəm] Optimismus *m;* ~**mist** ['ɒptɪmɪst] Optimist(in); ~**mist·ic** (~*ally*) optimistisch

op·tion ['ɒpʃn] Wahl *f; econ.* Option *f,* Vorkaufsrecht *n; mot.* Extra *n;* ~**al** ['ɒpʃnl] freiwillig; Wahl...; **be an** ~ **ex·tra** *mot.* gegen Aufpreis erhältlich sein

or [ɔː] oder; ~ **else** sonst

o·ral ['ɔːrəl] mündlich; Mund...

or·ange ['ɒrɪndʒ] **1.** *bot.* Orange *f,* Apfelsine *f;* **2.** orange(farben); ~**ade** [ɒrɪndʒ'eɪd] Orangenlimonade *f*

o·ra·tion [ɔː'reɪʃn] Rede *f,* Ansprache *f;* **or·a·tor** ['ɒrətə] Redner(in)

or·bit ['ɔːbɪt] **1.** Kreis-, Umlaufbahn *f;* **get** *od.* **put into** ~ in e-e Umlaufbahn gelangen *od.* bringen; **2.** *v/t.* die Erde *etc.* umkreisen; *v/i.* die Erde *etc.* umkreisen, sich auf e-r Umlaufbahn bewegen

or·chard ['ɔːtʃəd] Obstgarten *m*

or·ches·tra [ɔː'kɪstrə] *mus.* Orchester *n; Am. thea.* Parkett *n*

or·chid *bot.* ['ɔːkɪd] Orchidee *f*

or·dain [ɔː'deɪn]: ~ *s.o.* *(priest)* j-n zum Priester weihen

or·deal [ɔː'diːl] Qual *f,* Tortur *f*

or·der ['ɔːdə] **1.** Ordnung *f;* Anordnung *f,* Reihenfolge *f;* Befehl *m,* Anordnung *f; econ.* Bestellung *f,* Auftrag *m; parl. etc. (Geschäfts)*Ordnung *f; rel. etc.* Orden *m;* **to pay** *econ.* Zahlungsanweisung *f;* **in** ~ um zu; **out of** ~ nicht in Ordnung, defekt; außer Betrieb; **make to** ~ auf Bestellung *od.* nach Maß anfertigen; **2.** *v/t. j-m* befehlen *(to do* etw zu tun), *et.* befehlen, anordnen; *j-n* schicken, beordern; *med. j-m et.* verordnen; *econ.* bestellen *(a. im Restaurant); fig.* ordnen, in Ordnung bringen; *v/i.* bestellen *(im Restaurant);* '~**ly** **1.** ordentlich; *fig.* gesittet, friedlich *(Menge etc.);* **2.** *med.* Hilfspfleger *m*

or·di·nal *math.* ['ɔːdɪnl] *a.* ~ **number** *math.* Ordnungszahl *f*

or·di·nary ['ɔːdnrɪ] üblich, gewöhnlich, normal; △ *nicht* **ordinär**

ore *min.* [ɔː] Erz *n*

or·gan ['ɔːgən] *anat.* Organ *n (a. fig.); mus.* Orgel *f;* '~ **grind·er** Leierkastenmann *m;* ~**ic** [ɔː'gænɪk] (~*ally*) organisch; ~**is·m** ['ɔːgənɪzəm] Organismus *m;* ~**i·za·tion** [ɔːgənaɪ'zeɪʃn] Organisation *f;* ~**ize** ['ɔːgənaɪz] organisieren;

bsd. Am. sich (gewerkschaftlich) organisieren;'**~·iz·er** Organisator(in)

or·gas·m ['ɔːgæzəm] Orgasmus *m*

o·ri·ent ['ɔːrɪənt] **1.** ♀ *der* Osten, *der* Orient, *das* Morgenland; **2.** orientieren; **~·en·tal** [ɔːrɪ'entl] **1.** orientalisch, östlich; **2.** ♀ Orientale *m*, -in *f*; **~·en·tate** ['ɔːrɪənteɪt] orientieren

or·i·gin ['ɒrɪdʒɪn] Ursprung *m*, Abstammung *f*, Herkunft *f*

o·rig·i·nal [ə'rɪdʒənl] **1.** ursprünglich, Original...; originell; **2.** Original *n*; **~·i·ty** [ərɪdʒə'næləti] Originalität *f*; **~·ly** [ə'rɪdʒənəlɪ] ursprünglich; originell

o·rig·i·nate [ə'rɪdʒəneɪt] *v/t.* schaffen, ins Leben rufen; *v/i.* zurückgehen (*from* auf *acc.*), (her)stammen (*from* von, aus)

or·na·ment 1. ['ɔːnəmənt] Ornament(e *pl.*) *n*, Verzierung(en *pl.*) *f*, Schmuck *m*; *fig.* Zier(de) *f* (*to* für *od. gen.*); **2.** ['ɔːnəment] verzieren, schmücken (*with* mit); ursprünglich; **~·men·tal** [ɔːnə'mentl] dekorativ, schmückend, Zier...

or·nate [ɔː'neɪt] überladen (*Stil etc.*)

or·phan ['ɔːfn] **1.** Waise(nkind *n*) *f*; **2.** *be* **~ed** Waise werden; **~·age** ['ɔːfənɪdʒ] Waisenhaus *n*

or·tho·dox ['ɔːθədɒks] orthodox

os·cil·late ['ɒsɪleɪt] *phys.* schwingen; *fig.* schwanken (*between* zwischen *dat.*)

os·prey *zo.* ['ɒsprɪ] Fischadler *m*

os·ten·si·ble [ɒ'stensəbl] an-, vorgeblich

os·ten·ta·tion [ɒstən'teɪʃn] (protzige) Zurschaustellung; Protzerei *f*, Prahlerei *f*; **~·tious** [ɒstən'teɪʃəs] protzend, prahlerisch

os·tra·cize ['ɒstrəsaɪz] ächten

os·trich *zo.* ['ɒstrɪtʃ] Strauß *m*

oth·er ['ʌðə] andere(r, -s); *the* **~** *day* neulich; *the* **~** *morning* neulich morgens; *every* **~** *day* jeden zweiten Tag, alle zwei Tage; **~·wise** anders; sonst

ot·ter *zo.* ['ɒtə] Otter *m*

ought [ɔːt] *v/aux.* ich sollte, *du* solltest *etc.*; *you* **~** *to have done it* Sie hätten es tun sollen

ounce [aʊns] Unze *f* (28,35 *g*)

our ['aʊə] unser; **~s** ['aʊəz] der, die, das uns(e)re; unsere(r, -s); **~·selves** [aʊə'selvz] wir *od.* uns selbst; uns (selbst)

oust [aʊst] verdrängen, hinauswerfen

(*from* aus); *j-n s-s Amtes* entheben

out [aʊt] **1.** *adv., adj.* aus; hinaus(*gehen, -werfen etc.*); heraus(*kommen etc.*); aus(*brechen etc.*); draußen, im Freien; nicht zu Hause; *Sport:* aus, draußen; aus, vorbei; aus, erloschen; aus(verkauft); F out, aus der Mode; *way* **~** Ausgang *m*; **~** *of* aus (... heraus); zu ... hinaus; außerhalb von (*od. gen.*); außer Reichweite *etc.*; außer Atem, Übung *etc.*; (hergestellt) aus; *as Furcht etc.*; *be* **~** *of* kein ... mehr haben; *in nine* **~** *of ten cases* in neun von zehn Fällen; **2.** *prp.* F aus (... heraus); zu ... hinaus; **3.** F outen (*intime Informationen an die Öffentlichkeit geben*)

out|'**bal·ance** überwiegen; **~·bid** (*-dd-; -bid*) überbieten; **~·board** '**mo·tor** Außenbordmotor *m*; '**~·break** Ausbruch *m* (*e-r Krankheit, e-s Krieges etc.*); '**~·build·ing** Nebengebäude *n*; '**~·burst** Ausbruch *m* (*von Gefühlen*); '**~·cast 1.** ausgestoßen; **2.** Ausgestoßene(r *m*) *f*, Verstoßene(r *m*) *f*; '**~·come** Ergebnis *n*; △ *nicht das Auskommen*; '**~·cry** Aufschrei *m*, Schrei *m* der Entrüstung; **~·dat·ed** überholt, veraltet; **~·**'**dis·tance** hinter sich lassen; **~·**'**do** (*-did, -done*) übertreffen; '**~·door** *adj.* im Freien, draußen; '**~·doors** *adv.* draußen, im Freien

out·er ['aʊtə] äußere(r, -s); '**~·most** äußerste(r, -s); **~** '**space** Weltraum *m*

out|'**fit** Ausrüstung *f*, Ausstattung *f*; Kleidung *f*; F (Arbeits)Gruppe *f*; '**~·fit·ter** Ausstatter *m*; *men's* **~** Herrenausstatter *m*; '**~·go·ing** (aus dem Amt) scheidend; '**~·go·ings** *pl. bsd. Brt.* (Geld)Ausgaben *pl.*; '**~·grow** (*-grew, -grown*) herauswachsen aus (*Kleidern*); *Angewohnheit etc.* ablegen; größer werden als; '**~·house** Nebengebäude *n*

out·ing ['aʊtɪŋ] Ausflug *m*; Outing *n* (*Preisgabe intimer Informationen an die Öffentlichkeit*)

out|'**land·ish** befremdend, sonderbar; **~·last** überdauern, -leben; '**~·law** *hist.* Geächtete(r *m*) *f*; '**~·lay** (Geld)Auslagen *pl.*, Ausgaben *pl.*; '**~·let** Abfluß *m*, Abzug *m*; *fig.* Ventil *n*; '**~·line 1.** Umriß *m*; Überblick *m*; **2.** umreißen, skizzieren; **~·live** überleben; '**~·look** (Aus-) Blick *m*, (Aus)Sicht *f*; Einstellung f, Auffassung f; '**~·ly·ing** abgelegen, entlegen; ~'**num·ber:** *be* ~*ed by s.o.* j-m zahlenmäßig unterlegen sein; ~**of·'date** veraltet, überholt; ~**of-the-'way** abgelegen, entlegen; *fig.* ungewöhnlich; '**~·pa·tient** ambulanter Patient, ambulante Patientin; '**~·post** Vorposten *m*; '**~·pour·ing** (Gefühls)Erguß *m*; '**~·put** *econ.* Output *m*, Produktion *f*, Ausstoß *m*, Ertrag *m*; *Computer:* (Daten)Ausgabe *f*; '**~·rage** **1.** Gewalttat *f*, Verbrechen *n*; Empörung *f*; **2.** grob verletzen; *j-n* empören; ~**·ra·geous** [aʊt'reɪdʒəs] abscheulich; empörend, unerhört; ~**·right 1.** *adj.* ['aʊtraɪt] völlig, gänzlich, glatt (*Lüge etc.*); **2.** *adv.* [aʊt'raɪt] auf der Stelle, sofort; ohne Umschweife; ~**·run** (*-nn-; -ran, -run*) schneller laufen als; *fig.* übersteigen, -treffen; '**~·set** Anfang *m*, Beginn *m*; ~**·shine** (*-shone*) überstrahlen, *fig. a.* in den Schatten stellen; ~**'side 1.** Außenseite *f*; *Sport:* Außenstürmer(in); *at the* (*very*) ~ (aller-)höchstens; ~ *left* (*right*) *Sport:* Links-(Rechts-)Außen *m*; **2.** *adj.* äußere(r, -s), Außen...; **3.** *adv.* draußen; heraus, hinaus; **4.** *prp.* außerhalb; ~**'sid·er** Außenseiter(in); ~**'size 1.** Übergröße *f*; **2.** übergroß; '**~·skirts** *pl.* Stadtrand *m*, Außenbezirke *pl.*; ~**'smart** → *outwit*; ~**'spo·ken** offen, freimütig; △ *nicht ausgesprochen*; ~**'spread** ausgestreckt, -breitet; ~**'stand·ing** hervorragend; ausstehend (*Schuld*) ungeklärt (*Frage*); unerledigt (*Arbeit*); ~**'stay** länger bleiben als; → *welcome* **4;** ~**'stretched** ausgestreckt; ~**'strip** (*-pp-*) überholen (*fig.* übertreffen); ~**·tray:** *in the* ~ im Post- *etc.* Ausgang (*von Briefen etc.*); ~**·vote** überstimmen **out·ward** ['aʊtwəd] **1.** äußere(r, -s); äußerlich; **2.** *adv. mst* ~*s* auswärts, nach außen; '**~·ly** äußerlich **out·'weigh** *fig.* überwiegen; ~**'wit** (*-tt-*) überlisten, reinlegen; ~**'worn** veraltet, überholt **o·val** ['əʊvl] **1.** oval; **2.** Oval *n* **o·va·tion** [əʊ'veɪʃn] Ovation *f*; *give s.o. a standing* ~ j-m stehende Ovationen bereiten, j-m stehend Beifall klatschen **ov·en** ['ʌvn] Back-, Bratofen *m*; ~**-'read·y** bratfertig **o·ver** ['əʊvə] **1.** *prp.* über; über (*acc.*),

über (*acc.*) ... (hin)weg; über (*dat.*), über der anderen Seite von (*od. gen.*); über (*acc.*), mehr als; **2.** *adv.* hinüber, herüber (*to* zu); drüben; darüber, mehr; zu Ende, vorüber, vorbei; *allg.* über..., um...: *et.* über(*geben etc.*); über(*kochen etc.*); um(*fallen, -werfen etc.*); herum(*drehen etc.*); von Anfang bis Ende, durch(*lesen etc.*); (gründlich) über(*legen etc.*); (*all*) ~ *again* noch einmal; ~ ganz vorbei; ~ *and* (*again*) immer wieder; ~ *and above* obendrein, überdies **o·ver·'act** [əʊvər'ækt] *e-e Rolle* übertreiben; ~**·age** [əʊvər'eɪdʒ] zu alt; ~**·all 1.** [əʊvər'ɔːl] gesamt, Gesamt...; allgemein; insgesamt; **2.** ['əʊvərɔːl] *Brt.* Arbeitsmantel *m*, Kittel *m*; *Am.* Overall *m*, Arbeitsanzug *m*; ~*s pl. Brt.* Overall *m*, Arbeitsanzug *m*; *Am.* Arbeitshose *f*; ~**·awe** [əʊvər'ɔː] einschüchtern; ~**'bal·ance** umstoßen, umkippen; das Gleichgewicht verlieren, umkippen; ~**'bear·ing** anmaßend; '**~·board** *naut.* über Bord; ~**·cast** bewölkt, bedeckt; ~**'charge** überlasten, *electr. a.* überladen; *j-m* zuviel berechnen; *Betrag* zuviel verlangen; '**~·coat** Mantel *m*; ~**'come** (*-came, -come*) überwinden, -wältigen; *be* ~ *with emotion* von s-n Gefühlen übermannt werden; ~**'crowd·ed** überfüllt; überlaufen; ~**'do** (*-did, -done*) übertreiben; zu lange kochen *od.* braten; *overdone a.* übergar; ~**'dose** Überdosis *f*; '**~·draft** *econ.* (Konto)Überziehung *f*; ~**'draw** (*-drew, -drawn*) *econ. Konto* überziehen (*by* um); ~**'dress** (sich) zu vornehm anziehen; ~*ed a.* overdressed; '**~·drive** *mot.* Overdrive *m*, Schongang *m*; ~**'due** überfällig; ~**·eat** [əʊvər'iːt] (*-ate, -eaten*) sich übessen; ~**·es·ti·mate** [əʊvər'estɪmeɪt] zu hoch einschätzen *od.* veranschlagen; *fig.* überschätzen; ~**·ex·pose** *phot.* [əʊvərɪk'spəʊz] überbelichten; ~**'flow 1.** [əʊvə'fləʊ] *v/t.* überfluten, -schwemmen; *v/i.* überlaufen, -fließen; überquellen (*with* von); **2.** ['əʊvəfləʊ] *tech.* Überlauf *m*; Überlaufen *n*, -fließen *n*; ~**'grown** überwachsen, -wuchert; übergroß; ~**'hang** (*-hung*) *v/t.* über (*dat.*) hängen; *v/i.* überhängen; ~**'haul** *Maschine* überholen; ~**'head 1.** *adv.* (dr)oben; **2.** *adj.*

Hoch..., Ober...; *econ.* allgemein (*Unkosten*); *Sport:* Überkopf...; **~kick** Fußball: Fallrückzieher *m*; '**~head(s** *pl.* **Brt.**) *Am. econ.* (Geschäfts)Kosten *pl.*; **~hear** (**-heard**) (zufällig) hören; △ *nicht* **überhören**; **~heat·ed** überhitzt, -heizt; *tech.* heißgelaufen; **~joyed** überglücklich; '**~kill** *mil.* Overkill *m; fig.* Übermaß *n*, Zuviel *n* (*of* an *dat.*); **~lap** (**-pp-**) (sich) überlappen; sich überschneiden; **~leaf** umseitig, umstehend; **~load** überlasten (*a. electr.*), -laden; **~look** übersehen; **~***ing the sea* mit Blick aufs Meer; **~night** 1. über Nacht; **stay** ~ über Nacht bleiben, übernachten; **2.** Nacht..., Übernachtungs...; ~ **bag** Reisetasche *f*; '**~pass** *bsd. Am.* (Straßen-, Eisenbahn)Überführung *f*; **~pay** (**-paid**) zuviel (be)zahlen; **~pop·u·lat·ed** übervölkert; **~pow·er** überwältigen; **~***ing fig.* überwältigend; **~rate** überbewerten, -schätzen; **~reach:** ~ *o.s.* sich übernehmen; **~re·act** überreagieren, überzogen reagieren (*to auf acc.*); **~re·ac·tion** Überreaktion *f*, überzogene Reaktion; **~ride** (**-rode, -ridden**) sich hinwegsetzen über (*acc.*); **~rule** *Entscheidung etc.* aufheben, *Einspruch etc.* abweisen; **~run** (**-nn-; -ran, -run**) länger dauern als vorgesehen; *Signal* überfahren; **be** ~ **with** wimmeln von; **~seas 1.** *adj.* überseeisch, Übersee...; **2.** *adv.* in *od.* nach Übersee; **~see** (**-saw, -seen**) beaufsichtigen, überwachen; '**~seer** Aufseher(in); **~shad·ow** *fig.* in den Schatten stellen; **~sight** Versehen *n*; **~size(d)** übergroß, mit Übergröße; **~sleep** (**-slept**) verschlafen; '**~staffed** (personell) überbesetzt; **~state** übertreiben; **~state·ment** Übertreibung *f*; **~stay** länger bleiben als; → **welcome** 4; **~step** *fig.* überschreiten; **~take** (**-took, -taken**) über-

holen; *j-n* überraschen; **~tax** zu hoch besteuern; *fig.* überbeanspruchen, -fordern; **~throw** (**-threw, -thrown**) *Regierung etc.* stürzen; **2.** ['əʊvəθrəʊ] (Um)Sturz *m*; '**~time** *econ.* Überstunden *pl.; Am. Sport:* (Spiel)Verlängerung *f*; **be on** ~, **do** ~ **work** ~ Überstunden machen

o·ver·ture *mus.* ['əʊvətjʊə] Ouvertüre *f*; Vorspiel *n*

o·ver'turn umwerfen, umstoßen; *Regierung etc.* stürzen; umkippen; *naut.* kentern; '**~view** *fig.* Überblick *m* (*of* über *acc.*); **~weight 1.** ['əʊvəweɪt] Übergewicht *n*; **2.** [əʊvə'weɪt] übergewichtig (*Person*), zu schwer (*by* um) (*Sache*); **be five pounds** ~ fünf Pfund Übergewicht haben; **~'whelm** überwältigen (*a. fig.*); **~'whelm·ing** überwältigend; **~'work** sich überarbeiten; überanstrengen; **~'wrought** überreizt

owe [əʊ] *j-m et.* schulden, schuldig sein; *et.* verdanken

ow·ing ['əʊɪŋ]; ~ **to** infolge, wegen

owl *zo.* [aʊl] Eule *f*

own [əʊn] **1.** eigen; **my** ~ mein Eigentum; (**all**) **on one's** ~ allein; **2.** besitzen; zugeben, (ein)gestehen

own·er ['əʊnə] Eigentümer(in), Besitzer(in); **~'oc·cu·pied** *bsd. Brt.* eigengenutzt; ~ **flat** Eigentumswohnung *f*; '**~ship** Besitz *m*; Eigentum(srecht) *n*

ox *zo.* [ɒks] (*pl.* **oxen** ['ɒksn]) Ochse *m*

ox·ide *chem.* ['ɒksaɪd] Oxyd *n*; **ox·i·dize** *chem.* ['ɒksɪdaɪz] oxydieren

ox·y·gen *chem.* ['ɒksɪdʒən] Sauerstoff *m*

oy·ster *zo.* ['ɔɪstə] Auster *f*

oz *nur geschr. Abk. für* **ounce(s** *pl.*) Unze(n *pl.*) *f* (*28,35 g*)

o·zone *chem.* ['əʊzəʊn] Ozon *n*; '**~-friend·ly** ozonfreundlich, ohne Treibgas; '**~ hole** Ozonloch *n*; '**~ lay·er** Ozonschicht *f*; '**~ lev·els** *pl.* Ozonwerte *pl.*; '**~ shield** Ozonschild *m*

O

P, p [pi:] P, p *n*

p¹ *Brt.* F [pi:] *Abk. für* **penny, pence** (*Währungseinheit*)

p² (*pl.* **pp**) *nur geschr. Abk. für* **page** S., Seite *f*

pace [peɪs] **1.** Tempo *n*, Geschwindigkeit *f*; Schritt *m*; Gangart *f* (*e-s Pferdes*); **2.** *v/t.* Zimmer *etc.* durchschreiten; *a.* ~ *out* abschreiten; *v/i.* (einher)schreiten; ~ *up and down* auf u. ab gehen; '~**mak·er** *Sport:* Schrittmacher(in); *med.* Herzschrittmacher *m*; '~**set·ter** *Am. Sport:* Schrittmacher(in)

Pa·cif·ic [pəˈsɪfɪk] *a.* ~ *Ocean* der Pazifik, *der* Pazifische *od.* Stille Ozean

pac·i·fi·er *Am.* [ˈpæsɪfaɪə] Schnuller *m*; **~·fist** [ˈpæsɪfɪst] Pazifist(in); **~·fy** [ˈpæsɪfaɪ] beruhigen, besänftigen

pack [pæk] **1.** Pack(en) *m*, Paket *n* (*Pakkung*), Bündel *n*; *Am.* Packung *f*, Schachtel *f* (*Zigaretten*); Meute *f* (*Hunde*); Rudel *n* (*Wölfe*); Pack *n*, Bande *f*; *med.*, *Kosmetik:* Packung *f*; (*Karten*)Spiel *n*; *a.* ~ *of lies* ein Haufen Lügen; **2.** *v/t.* ein-, zusammen-, ab-, verpacken (*a.* ~ *up*); zusammenpferchen; vollstopfen; *Koffer etc.* packen; ~ *off* F fort-, wegschicken; *v/i.* packen; (sich) drängen (*into in acc.*); ~ *up* zusammenpacken; **send s.o.** ~*ing* j-n fort- *od.* wegjagen

pack·age [ˈpækɪdʒ] Paket *n*, Packung *f*; **software** ~ *Computer:* Software-, Programmpaket *n*; ~ **deal** F Pauschalangebot *n*, -arrangement *n*; ~ **hol·i·day** Pauschalurlaub *m*; ~ **tour** Pauschalreise *f*

'**pack·er** Packer(in); *Am.* Konservenhersteller *m*

pack·et [ˈpækɪt] Päckchen *n*; Packung *f*, Schachtel *f* (*Zigaretten*); △ *nicht* **Paket**

'**pack·ing** Packen *n*; Verpackung *f*

pact [pækt] Pakt *m*, *pol. a.* Vertrag *m*

pad [pæd] **1.** Polster *n*; *Sport:* (*Bein-, Knie*)Schützer *m*; (*Schreib- etc.*)Block *m*; (*Stempel*)Kissen *n*; *zo.* Ballen *m*; (*Abschuß*)Rampe *f*; **2.** (**-dd-**) (aus)polstern, wattieren; '~**ding** Polsterung *f*, Wattierung *f*

pad·dle [ˈpædl] **1.** Paddel *n*; *naut.* (Rad)Schaufel *f*; **2.** paddeln; planschen; '~ **wheel** *naut.* Schaufelrad *n*

pad·dock [ˈpædək] (Pferde)Koppel *f*

pad·lock [ˈpædlɒk] Vorhängeschloß *n*

pa·gan [ˈpeɪɡən] **1.** Heide *m*, -in *f*; **2** heidnisch

page¹ [peɪdʒ] **1.** Seite *f*; **2.** paginieren

page² [peɪdʒ] **1.** (Hotel)Page *m*; **2.** *j-n* ausrufen (lassen)

pag·eant [ˈpædʒənt] (*a.* historischer) Festzug

pa·gin·ate [ˈpædʒɪneɪt] paginieren

paid [peɪd] *pret. u. p.p. von* **pay** 1

pail [peɪl] Eimer *m*, Kübel *m*

pain [peɪn] **1.** Schmerz(en *pl.*) *m*; Kummer *m*; ~*s pl.* Mühe *f*, Bemühungen *pl.*; **be in** (**great**) ~ (große) Schmerzen haben; **be a** ~ (**in the neck**) F e-m auf den Wecker gehen; **take** ~*s* sich Mühe geben; **2.** *bsd. fig.* schmerzen; '~**ful** schmerzend, schmerzhaft; *fig.* schmerzlich; peinlich; '~**kill·er** Schmerzmittel *n*; '~**less** schmerzlos; '~**s·tak·ing** [ˈpeɪnzteɪkɪŋ] sorgfältig, gewissenhaft

paint [peɪnt] **1.** Farbe *f*; Anstrich *m*; **2.** (an-, be)malen; (an)streichen; *Auto etc.* lackieren; '~**box** Malkasten *m*; '~**brush** (Maler)Pinsel *m*; '~**er** (*a.* Kunst)Maler(in), Anstreicher(in); '~**ing** Malerei *f*; Gemälde *n*, Bild *n*

pair [peə] **1.** Paar *n*; *a* ~ *of* ... ein Paar ..., ein(e) ...; *a* ~ *of scissors* e-e Schere; **2.** *v/t. zo.* sich paaren; *a.* ~ *off*, ~ *up* Paare bilden; *v/t. a.* ~ *off*, ~ *up* paarweise anordnen; ~ *off* zwei Leute zusammenbringen, verkuppeln

pa·ja·ma(s) *Am.* [pəˈdʒɑːmə(z)] → **py·jama(s)**

pal [pæl] Kumpel *m*, Kamerad *m*

pal·ace [ˈpælɪs] Palast *m*, Schloß *n*

pal·a·ta·ble [ˈpælətəbl] schmackhaft (*a. fig.*)

pal·ate [ˈpælɪt] *anat.* Gaumen *m*; *fig.* Geschmack *m*

pale¹ [peɪl] **1.** (~*r*, ~*st*) blaß, bleich; hell, blaß (*Farbe*); **2.** blaß *od.* bleich werden

pale² [peɪl] Pfahl *m*; *fig.* Grenzen *pl.*

'**pale·ness** Blässe *f*

Pal·e·stin·i·an [pælə'stɪnɪən] **1.** palästinensisch; **2.** Palästinenser(in)

pal·ings ['peɪlɪŋz] pl. Pfahl- od. Lattenzaun m

pal·i·sade [pæli'seɪd] Palisade f; **~s** pl. Am. Steilufer n

pal·let tech. ['pælɪt] Palette f

pal·lid ['pælɪd] blaß; **'~·lor** Blässe f

palm¹ bot. [pɑːm] a. **~ tree** Palme f

palm² [pɑːm] **1.** Handfläche f; **2.** et. in der Hand verschwinden lassen od. verbergen (Zauberkünstler); **~ s.th. off on s.o.** j-m et. andrehen

pal·pa·ble ['pælpəbl] fühl-, greifbar

pal·pi·tate med. ['pælpɪteɪt] klopfen, pochen (Herz); **~·ta·tions** pl. med. [pælpɪ'teɪʃnz] Herzklopfen n

pal·sy med. ['pɔːlzɪ] Lähmung f

pal·try ['pɔːltrɪ] (-ier, -iest) armselig

pam·per ['pæmpə] verwöhnen, Kind a. verhätscheln

pam·phlet ['pæmflɪt] Broschüre f

pan [pæn] Pfanne f; Topf m

pan·a·ce·a [pænə'sɪə] Allheilmittel n

pan·cake ['pænkeɪk] Pfannkuchen m

pan·da zo. ['pændə] Panda m; **~ car** Brt. (Funk)Streifenwagen m

pan·de·mo·ni·um [pændɪ'məʊnjəm] Hölle(nlärm m) f, Tumult m, Chaos n

pan·der ['pændə] Vorschub leisten (to dat.)

pane [peɪn] (Fenster)Scheibe f

pan·el ['pænl] **1.** (Tür)Füllung f, (Wand)Täfelung f; electr., tech. Instrumentenbrett n, (Schalt-, Kontroll- etc.-) Tafel f; jur. Liste f der Geschworenen; Diskussionsteilnehmer pl., -runde f; Rateteam n; **2.** (bsd. Brt. -ll-, Am. -l-) täfeln

pang [pæŋ] stechender Schmerz; **~s** pl. of hunger nagender Hunger; **~s** pl. of conscience Gewissensbisse pl.

'pan·han·dle 1. Pfannenstiel m; Am. schmaler Fortsatz (e-s Staatsgebiets); **2.** Am. F betteln

pan·ic ['pænɪk] **1.** panisch; **2.** Panik f; **3.** (-ck-) in Panik versetzen od. geraten

pan·sy bot. ['pænzɪ] Stiefmütterchen n

pant [pænt] keuchen, nach Luft schnappen

pan·ther zo. ['pænθə] (pl. -thers, -ther) Panther m; Am. Puma m; Am. Jaguar m

pan·ties ['pæntɪz] pl. (Damen)Schlüpfer m, Slip m; Höschen n (für Kinder)

pan·to·mime ['pæntəmaɪm] Brt. F Weihnachtsspiel n (für Kinder); thea. Pantomime f

pan·try ['pæntrɪ] Speisekammer f

pants [pænts] pl. Brt. Unterhose f; Brt. Schlüpfer m; bsd. Am. Hose f

'pant·suit Am. Hosenanzug m

pan·ty| hose bsd. Am. ['pæntɪhəʊz] Strumpfhose f; **'~·lin·er** Slipeinlage f

pap [pæp] Brei m; △ nicht **Pappe**

pa·pal ['peɪpl] päpstlich

pa·per ['peɪpə] **1.** Papier n; Zeitung f; (Prüfungs)Arbeit f; univ. Klausur(arbeit) f; Aufsatz m; Referat n; Tapete f; **~s** pl. (Ausweis)Papiere pl.; **2.** tapezieren; **'~·back** Taschenbuch n, Paperback n; **'~ bag** (Papier)Tüte f; **'~·boy** Zeitungsjunge m; **'~ clip** Büro-, Heftklammer f; **'~ cup** Pappbecher m; **'~ girl** Zeitungsausträgerin f; **'~·hang·er** Tapezierer m; **'~ knife** (pl. -knives) Brt. Brieföffner m; **'~ mon·ey** Papiergeld n; **'~·weight** Briefbeschwerer m

par [pɑː] econ. Nennwert m, Pari n; **at ~** zum Nennwert; **be on a ~ with** gleich od. ebenbürtig sein (dat.)

par·a·ble ['pærəbl] Parabel f, Gleichnis n

par·a|·chute ['pærəʃuːt] Fallschirm m; **'~·chut·ist** Fallschirmspringer(in)

pa·rade [pə'reɪd] **1.** Umzug m, bsd. mil. Parade f; fig. Zurschaustellung f; **make a ~ of** fig. zur Schau stellen; ziehen (through durch); mil. antreten (lassen); mil. vorbeimarschieren (lassen); zur Schau stellen; **~ (through)** stolzieren durch

par·a·dise ['pærədaɪs] Paradies n

par·a·glid|·er ['pærəglaɪdə] Gleitschirm m; Gleitschirmflieger(in); **'~·ing** Gleitschirmfliegen n

par·a·gon ['pærəgən] Muster n (of an dat.)

par·a·graph ['pærəgrɑːf] Absatz m, Abschnitt m; (Zeitungs)Notiz f; △ nicht jur. **Paragraph**

par·al·lel ['pærəlel] **1.** parallel (to, with zu); **2.** math. Parallele f (a. fig.); **without ~** ohne Parallele, ohnegleichen; **3.** (-l-, Brt. a. -ll-) entsprechen (dat.)

par·a·lyse Brt., **par·a·lyze** Am. ['pærəlaɪz] med. lähmen, fig. a. lahmlegen, zum Erliegen bringen; **~d** *with fig.* starr *od.* wie gelähmt vor (*dat.*);

pa·ral·y·sis [pə'rælısıs] (*pl.* **-ses** [-si:z]) *med.* Lähmung *f, fig. a.* Lahmlegung *f*

par·a·mount ['pærəmaʊnt] größte(r, -s), übergeordnet; **of ~ importance** von (aller)größter Bedeutung *od.* Wichtigkeit

par·a·pet ['pærəpıt] Brüstung *f*

par·a·pher·na·li·a [pærəfə'neıljə] *pl.* (persönliche) Sachen *pl.*; Ausrüstung *f*; *bsd. Brt.* F Scherereien *pl.*

par·a·site ['pærəsaıt] Parasit *m*, Schmarotzer *m*

par·a·troop·er *mil.* ['pærətru:pə] Fallschirmjäger *m*; **~s** *pl. mil.* Fallschirmjägertruppe *f*

par·boil ['pɑ:bɔıl] halbgar kochen, ankochen

par·cel ['pɑ:sl] **1.** Paket *n*; Parzelle *f*; (*bsd. Brt.* **-ll-**, *Am.* **-l-**): **~ out** aufteilen; **~ up** (als Paket) verpacken

parch [pɑ:tʃ] ausdörren, -trocknen; vertrocknen

parch·ment ['pɑ:tʃmənt] Pergament *n*

par·don ['pɑ:dn] **1.** *jur.* Begnadigung *f*; **I beg your ~** Entschuldigung!, Verzeihung!; erlauben Sie mal!, ich muß doch sehr bitten!; *a.* **~?** F (wie) bitte?; **2.** verzeihen; vergeben; *jur.* begnadigen; **~ me → I beg your pardon**; *Am.* F (wie) bitte?; **~·a·ble** verzeihlich

pare [peə] *sich die Nägel* schneiden; *Apfel etc.* schälen

par·ent ['peərənt] Elternteil *m*, Vater *m*, Mutter *f*; **~s** *pl.* Eltern *pl.*; **~·age** ['peərəntıdʒ] Abstammung *f*, Herkunft *f*; **pa·ren·tal** [pə'rentl] elterlich

pa·ren·the·ses [pə'renθısi:z] *pl.* (runde) Klammer

'par·ents-in-law *pl.* Schwiegereltern *pl.*

par·ent-'teach·er meet·ing *Schule:* Elternabend *m*

par·ings ['peərıŋz] *pl.* Schalen *pl.*

par·ish ['pærıʃ] Gemeinde *f*; **pa·rish·io·ner** *rel.* [pə'rıʃənə] Gemeindemitglied *n*

park [pɑ:k] **1.** Park *m*, (Grün)Anlage(n *pl.*) *f*; **2.** *mot.* parken

'park·ing *mot.* Parken *n*; **no ~** Parkverbot, Parken verboten; **'~ disc** Park-

scheibe *f*; **'~ fee** Parkgebühr *f*; **'~ ga·rage** *Am.* Park(hoch)haus *n*; **'~ lot** *Am.* Parkplatz *m*; **'~ me·ter** Parkuhr *f*; **'~ space** Parkplatz *m*, -lücke *f*; **'~ tick·et** Strafzettel *m* (*wegen Falschparkens*)

par·ley *bsd. mil.* ['pɑ:lı] Verhandlung *f*

par·lia·ment ['pɑ:ləmənt] Parlament *n*; **~·men·tar·i·an** [pɑ:ləmen'teərıən] Parlamentarier(in); **~·men·ta·ry** [pɑ:lə'mentərı] parlamentarisch, Parlaments...

par·lo(u)r ['pɑ:lə] *mst in Zssgn:* **beauty ~** Schönheitssalon *m*

pa·ro·chi·al [pə'rəʊkjəl] Pfarr..., Gemeinde...; *fig.* engstirnig, beschränkt

pa·role [pə'rəʊl] **1.** Hafturlaub *m*; bedingte Haftentlassung; **he is out on ~** er hat Hafturlaub; er wurde bedingt entlassen; **2. ~ s.o.** j-m Hafturlaub gewähren; j-n bedingt entlassen

par·quet ['pɑ:keı] Parkett *n*; *Am. thea.* Parkett *n*; **'~ floor** Parkett(fuß)boden *m*

par·rot ['pærət] **1.** *zo.* Papagei *m* (*a. fig.*); **2.** *et.* (wie ein Papagei) nachplappern

par·ry ['pærı] abwehren, parieren

par·si·mo·ni·ous [pɑ:sı'məʊnjəs] geizig

pars·ley *bot.* ['pɑ:slı] Petersilie *f*

par·son ['pɑ:sn] Pfarrer *m*; **~·age** ['pɑ:snıdʒ] Pfarrhaus *n*

part [pɑ:t] **1.** Teil *m*, *tech.* (Bau-, Ersatz)Teil *n*; Anteil *m*; Seite *f*, Partei *f*; *thea., fig.* Rolle *f*; *mus.* Stimme *f*, Partie *f*; Gegend *f*, Teil *m* (*e-s Landes etc.*); *Am.* (Haar)Scheitel *m*; **for my ~** was mich betrifft; **for the most ~** größtenteils; meistens; **in ~** teilweise, zum Teil; **on the ~ of** von seiten, seitens (*gen.*); **on my ~** von m-r Seite; **take ~ in s.th.** an e-r Sache teilnehmen; **take s.th. in good ~** et. nicht übelnehmen; **2.** *v/t.* trennen; (ab-, ein-, zer)teilen; *Haar* scheiteln; **~ company** sich trennen (**with** von); *v/i.* sich trennen (**with** von); **3.** *adj.* Teil...; **4.** *adv.:* **~ ..., ~** teils ... teils

par|tial ['pɑ:ʃl] Teil..., teilweise; parteiisch, voreingenommen (**to** für); **~·ti·al·i·ty** [pɑ:ʃı'ælıtı] Parteilichkeit *f*, Voreingenommenheit *f*; Schwäche *f*, besondere Vorliebe (**for** für); **~·tial·ly** ['pɑ:ʃəlı] teilweise, zum Teil

par·tic·i·pant [pɑːˈtɪsɪpənt] Teilnehmer(in); **~pate** [pɑːˈtɪsɪpeɪt] teilnehmen, sich beteiligen (**in** an *dat.*); **~pa·tion** [pɑːtɪsɪˈpeɪʃn] Teilnahme *f*, Beteiligung *f*

par·ti·ci·ple *gr.* [ˈpɑːtɪsɪpl] Partizip *n*, Mittelwort *n*

par·ti·cle [ˈpɑːtɪkl] Teilchen *n*

par·tic·u·lar [pəˈtɪkjʊlə] **1.** besondere(r, -s), speziell; genau, eigen, wählerisch; **2.** Einzelheit *f*; **~s** *pl.* nähere Umstände *pl. od.* Angaben *pl.*; Personalien *pl.*; **in** ~ insbesondere; **~ly** besonders

'part·ing 1. Trennung *f*, Abschied *m*; *bsd. Brt.* (Haar)Scheitel *m*; **2.** Abschieds...

par·ti·san [pɑːˈtɪzæn] **1.** Parteigänger(in); *mil.* Partisan(in); **2.** parteiisch

par·ti·tion [pɑːˈtɪʃn] **1.** Teilung *f*; Trennwand *f*; **2.** ~ **off** abteilen, abtrennen

'part·ly teilweise, zum Teil

part·ner [ˈpɑːtnə] Partner(in), *econ a.* Teilhaber(in); **'~ship** Partner-, Teilhaberschaft *f*

part·'own·er Miteigentümer(in)

par·tridge *zo.* [ˈpɑːtrɪdʒ] Rebhuhn *n*

part|·'time 1. *adj.* Teilzeit..., Halbtags...; ~ **worker** → **part-timer**; **2.** *adv.* halbtags; **~'tim·er** Teilzeitbeschäftigte(r *m*) *f*, Halbtagskraft *f*

par·ty [ˈpɑːtɪ] Partei *f* (*a. pol.*); (*Arbeits-, Reise*)Gruppe *f*; (*Rettungs-* etc.)Mannschaft *f*; *mil.* Kommando *n*, Trupp *m*; Party *f*, Gesellschaft *f*; Teilnehmer(in), Beteiligte(r *m*) *f*; △ *nicht* **Partie**; '~line *pol.* Parteilinie *f*; ~ **'pol·i·tics** *sg. od. pl.* Parteipolitik *f*

pass [pɑːs] **1.** *v/i.* vorbeigehen, -fahren, -kommen, -ziehen etc. (**by** an *dat.*); übergehen (**to** auf *acc.*), fallen (**to** an *acc.*); vergehen (*Schmerz* etc., *Zeit*); durchkommen, (die Prüfung) bestehen; gelten (**as, for** als), gehalten *od.* angesehen werden (**as, for** für); *parl.* Rechtskraft erlangen (*Gesetz*); durchgehen, unbeanstandet bleiben; *Sport:* (den Ball) abspielen *od.* passen (**to** zu); *Karten:* passen (*a. fig.*); **let s.o.** ~ j-n vorbeilassen; **let s.th.** ~ et. durchgehen lassen; △ *nicht* **passen** (*Kleidung* etc.); *v/t.* vorbeigehen, -fahren, -fließen, -kommen, -ziehen etc. an (*dat.*); überholen; *Prüfung* bestehen; *Prüfling*

durchkommen lassen; (*mit der Hand*) streichen (**over** über *acc.*); j-m et. reichen, geben, et. weitergeben; *Sport:* *Ball* abspielen, passen (**to** zu); *Zeit* verzubringen; *parl. Gesetz* verabschieden; *Urteil* abgeben, fällen, *jur. a.* sprechen (**on** über *acc.*); *fig.* hinausgehen über (*acc.*), übersteigen, -treffen; ~ **away** sterben; ~ **off** *j-n, et.* ausgeben (**as** als); *gut etc.* verlaufen; ~ **out** ohnmächtig werden; **2.** Passierschein *m*; △ *nicht* (*Reise*)**Pass**; Bestehen *n* (*e-r Prüfung*); *Sport:* Paß *m*, Zuspiel *n*; (*Gebirgs*)Paß *m*; **~ free** Frei(fahr)karte *f*; **things have come to such a** ~ **that** F die Dinge haben sich derart zugespitzt, daß; **make a** ~ **at** F Annäherungsversuche machen bei; '**~a·ble** passierbar, befahrbar; passabel, leidlich

pas·sage [ˈpæsɪdʒ] Passage *f*, Korridor *m*, Gang *m*; Durchgang *m*; (*See-, Flug*)Reise *f*; Durchfahrt *f*, -reise *f*; Passage *f* (*a. mus.*), Stelle *f* (*e-s Textes*); **bird of** ~ Zugvogel *m*

'pass·book *bsd. Am.* Sparbuch *n*

pas·sen·ger [ˈpæsɪndʒə] Passagier *m*, Fahr-, Fluggast *m*, Reisende(r *m*) *f*, (*Auto- etc.*)Insasse *m*, -in *f*

pass·er·by [pɑːsəˈbaɪ] (*pl.* **passersby**) Passant(in)

pas·sion [ˈpæʃn] Leidenschaft *f*; Wut *f*, Zorn *m*; 2 *rel.* Passion *f*; **~s ran high** die Erregung schlug hohe Wellen; **~ate** [ˈpæʃənət] leidenschaftlich

pas·sive [ˈpæsɪv] passiv; *gr.* passivisch

pass·port [ˈpɑːspɔːt] (*Reise*)Paß *m*

pass·word [ˈpɑːswɜːd] Kennwort *n*, Parole *f*

past [pɑːst] **1.** *adj.* vergangen, *pred.* vorüber; frühere(r, -s); **for some time** ~ seit einiger Zeit; ~ **tense** *gr.* Vergangenheit *f*, Präteritum *n*; **2.** *adv.* vorbei, vorüber; **go** ~ vorbeigehen; **3.** *prp. Zeit:* nach, über (*acc.*); über ... (*acc.*) hinaus; an ... (*dat.*) vorbei; **half** ~ **two** halb drei; ~ **hope** hoffnungslos; **4.** Vergangenheit *f* (*a. gr.*)

pas·ta [ˈpæstə] Teigwaren *pl.*

paste [peɪst] **1.** Paste *f*; Kleister *m*; Teig *m*; **2.** kleben (**to, on** an *acc.*); ~ **up** ankleben; '**~board** Karton *m*, Pappe *f*

pas·tel [pæˈstel] Pastell(zeichnung *f*) *n*

pas·teur·ize [ˈpɑːstʃəraɪz] pasteurisieren, keimfrei machen

P

pas·time ['pɑːstaɪm] Zeitvertreib *m*, Freizeitbeschäftigung *f*

pas·tor ['pɑːstə] Pastor *m*, Pfarrer *m*; **'~al** *rel.* ['pɑːstərəl] seelsorgerisch, pastoral

pas·try ['peɪstrɪ] (*Blätter-, Mürbe*)Teig *m*; Feingebäck *n*; **'~ cook** Konditor *m*

pas·ture ['pɑːstʃə] **1.** Weide(land *n*) *f*; **2.** *v/t.* weiden (lassen); *v/i.* grasen, weiden

pas·ty¹ *bsd. Brt.* ['pæstɪ] (Fleisch)Pastete *f*

past·y² ['peɪstɪ] blaß, käsig (*Gesicht*)

pat [pæt] **1.** Klaps *m*; Portion *f* (*bsd. Butter*); **2.** (*-tt-*) tätscheln; klopfen

patch [pætʃ] **1.** Fleck *m*; Flicken *m*; kleines Stück Land; *in ~es* stellenweise; **2.** flicken; **'~·work** Patchwork *n*

pa·tent ['peɪtənt] **1.** offenkundig; patentiert; Patent...; **2.** Patent *n*; **3.** *et.* patentieren lassen; **~·ee** [peɪtən'tiː] Patentinhaber(in); **~ 'leath·er** Lackleder *n*

pa·ter|·nal [pə'tɜːnl] väterlich(erseits); **~·ni·ty** [pə'tɜːnətɪ] Vaterschaft *f*

path [pɑːθ] (*pl.* **paths** [pɑːðz]) Pfad *m*; Weg *m*

pa·thet·ic [pə'θetɪk] (*~ally*) mitleiderregend; kläglich (*Versuch etc.*), miserabel; △ *nicht* **pathetisch**

pa·thos ['peɪθɒs] *das* Mitleiderregende; △ *nicht* **Pathos**

pa·tience ['peɪʃns] Geduld *f*; *bsd. Brt.* Kartenspiel: Patience *f*

pa·tient¹ ['peɪʃnt] geduldig

pa·tient² ['peɪʃnt] Patient(in)

pat·i·o ['pætɪəʊ] (*pl.* **-os**) Terrasse *f*; Innenhof *m*, Patio *m*

pat·ri·ot ['pætrɪət] Patriot(in); **~·ic** [pætrɪ'ɒtɪk] (*~ally*) patriotisch

pa·trol [pə'trəʊl] **1.** Patrouille *f*, Streife *f*, Runde *f*; *mil.* Patrouille *f*, (*Polizei*)Streife *f*; *on ~* auf Patrouille, auf Streife; **2.** (*-ll-*) abpatrouillieren, auf Streife sein in (*dat.*), s-e Runde machen in (*dat.*); **~ car** (Funk)Streifenwagen *m*; **~·man** (*pl.* **-men**) *bsd. Am.* Streifenpolizist *m*; *Brt.* motorisierter Pannenhelfer

pa·tron ['peɪtrən] Schirmherr *m*; Gönner *m*, Förderer *m*; (*Stamm*)Kunde *m*; Stammgast *m*; △ *nicht* **Patrone**; **pat·ron·age** ['pætrənɪdʒ] Schirmherrschaft *f*; Förderung *f*; **pat·ron·ess** ['peɪtrənɪs] Schirmherrin *f*; Gönnerin *f*, Förderin *f*; **pat·ron·ize** ['pætrənaɪz]

fördern; (*Stamm*)Kunde *od.* Stammgast sein bei *od.* in (*dat.*); gönnerhaft *od.* herablassend behandeln; **~ saint** *rel.* [peɪtrən 'seɪnt] Schutzheilige(r *m*) *f*

pat·ter ['pætə] prasseln (*Regen*); trappeln (*Füße*)

pat·tern ['pætən] **1.** Muster *n* (*a. fig.*); **2.** bilden, formen (*after, on* nach)

paunch ['pɔːntʃ] (dicker) Bauch

pau·per ['pɔːpə] Arme(r *m*) *f*

pause [pɔːz] **1.** Pause *f*; △ *nicht thea., Schule:* **Pause**; **2.** innehalten, e-e Pause machen

pave [peɪv] pflastern; *~ the way for fig.* den Weg ebnen für; **'~·ment** *Brt.* Bürger-, Gehsteig *m*; *Am.* Fahrbahn *f*

paw [pɔː] **1.** Pfote *f*, Tatze *f*; **2.** *v/t.* Boden scharren; scharren an (*der Tür etc.*); F betatschen; *v/i.* scharren (*at an dat.*)

pawn¹ [pɔːn] *Schach:* Bauer *m*; *fig.* Schachfigur *f*

pawn² [pɔːn] **1.** verpfänden, -setzen; **2.** *be in ~* verpfändet *od.* versetzt sein; **'~·bro·ker** Pfandleiher *m*; **'~·shop** Leih-, Pfandhaus *n*

pay [peɪ] **1.** (**paid**) *v/t. et.* (be)zahlen; *j-n* bezahlen; *Aufmerksamkeit* schenken; *Besuch* abstatten; *Kompliment* machen; *~ attention* achtgeben auf (*acc.*); *~ cash* bar bezahlen; *v/i.* zahlen; *fig.* sich lohnen; *~ for fig. für et.* bezahlen; *~ in* einzahlen; *~ into* einzahlen auf (*ein Konto*); *~ off* ab(be)zahlen; *j-n* auszahlen; **2.** Bezahlung *f*, Gehalt *n*, Lohn *m*; **'~·a·ble** zahlbar, fällig; **'~·day** Zahltag *m*; **~·ee** [peɪ'iː] Zahlungsempfänger(in); **'~ en·ve·lope** *Am.* Lohntüte *f*; **'~·ing** lohnend; **~·ing 'guest** zahlender Gast; **'~·ment** (Be)Zahlung *f*; **'~ pack·et** *Brt.* Lohntüte *f*; **'~ phone** *Brt.* Münzfernsprecher *m*; **'~·roll** Lohnliste *f*; **'~·slip** Lohn-, Gehaltsstreifen *m*

PC [piː 'siː] *Abk. für personal computer* PC *m*, Personalcomputer *m*; **~ user** PC-Benutzer *m*

P.C., PC *Brt.* [piː 'siː] *Abk. für police constable* Polizist *m*, Wachtmeister *m*

pd *nur geschr. Abk. für paid* bez., bezahlt

pea *bot.* [piː] Erbse *f*

peace [piːs] Friede(n) *m*; *jur.* öffentliche Ruhe u. Ordnung; Ruhe *f*; *at ~* in Frieden; **'~·a·ble** friedlich, *Person a.* friedfertig; **'~·ful** friedlich; **'~·lov·ing**

friedliebend; **~ move·ment** Friedensbewegung f; **'~time** Friedenszeiten pl.

peach bot. [piːtʃ] Pfirsich(baum) m

pea·cock zo. ['piːkɒk] Pfau(hahn) m; **'~hen** zo. Pfauhenne f

peak [piːk] Spitze f, (e-s Berges a.) Gipfel m; Schirm m (e-r Mütze); fig. Höhepunkt m, Höchststand m; **~ed cap** [piːkt 'kæp] Schirmmütze f; **'~ hours** pl. Hauptverkehrs-, Stoßzeit f; electr. Hauptbelastungszeit f; **'~ time** a. **peak viewing hours** pl. Brt. TV Haupteinschaltzeit f, -sendezeit f, beste Sendezeit

peal [piːl] **1.** (Glocken)Läuten n; (Donner)Schlag m; **~s of laughter** schallendes Gelächter; **2.** a. **~ out** läuten; krachen (Donner)

pea·nut ['piːnʌt] bot. Erdnuß f; **~s** pl. F lächerliche Summe

pear bot. [peə] Birne f; Birnbaum m

pearl [pɜːl] Perle f; Perlmutter f, Perlmutt n; Perlen...; **'~y (-ier, -iest)** perlenartig, Perlen...

peas·ant ['pezənt] Kleinbauer m

peat [piːt] Torf m

peb·ble ['pebl] Kiesel(stein) m

peck [pek] picken, hacken; **~ at one's food** im Essen herumstochern

pe·cu·li·ar [pɪˈkjuːljə] eigen(tümlich), typisch; eigenartig, seltsam; **~·i·ty** [pɪkjuːlɪˈærəti] Eigenheit f; Eigentümlichkeit f

pe·cu·ni·a·ry [pɪˈkjuːnjəri] Geld...

ped·a·go·gic [pedəˈɡɒdʒɪk] pädagogisch

ped·al ['pedl] **1.** Pedal n; **2.** (bsd. Brt. **-ll-**, Am. **-l-**) das Pedal treten; (mit dem Rad) fahren, strampeln

pe·dan·tic [pɪˈdæntɪk] (**~ally**) pedantisch

ped·dle ['pedl] hausieren (gehen) mit; **~ drugs** mit Drogen handeln; **'~r** Am. → **pedlar**

ped·es·tal ['pedɪstl] Sockel m (a. fig.)

pe·des·tri·an [pɪˈdestrɪən] **1.** Fußgänger(in); **2.** Fußgänger...; **~ 'cross·ing** Fußgängerübergang m; **~ 'mall** Am., **~ 'pre·cinct** bsd. Brt. Fußgängerzone f

ped·i·cure ['pedɪkjʊə] Pediküre f

ped·i·gree ['pedɪɡriː] Stammbaum m

ped·lar ['pedlə] Hausierer(in)

pee F [piː] **1.** pinkeln; **2. have** (od. **go for**) a **~** pinkeln (gehen)

peek [piːk] **1.** kurz od. verstohlen gukken (**at** auf acc.); **2. have** od. **take** a **~ at** e-n kurzen od. verstohlenen Blick werfen auf (acc.)

peel [piːl] **1.** v/t. schälen; a. **~ off** abschälen, Folie, Tapete etc. abziehen, ablösen; Kleid abstreifen; v/i. a. **~ off** sich lösen (Tapete etc.), abblättern (Farbe etc.), sich schälen (Haut); **2.** Schale f

peep¹ [piːp] **1.** kurz od. verstohlen gukken (**at** auf acc.); mst **~ out** (her)vorschauen; **2. take** a **~ at** e-n kurzen od. verstohlenen Blick werfen auf (acc.)

peep² [piːp] **1.** Piep(s)en n; F Piepser m (Ton); **2.** piep(s)en

'peep·hole Guckloch n; (Tür)Spion m

peer [pɪə] angestrengt schauen, spähen; **~ at s.o.** j-n anstarren; **'~·less** unvergleichlich, einzigartig

peev·ish ['piːvɪʃ] verdrießlich, gereizt

peg [peg] **1.** (Holz)Stift m, Zapfen m, Pflock m; (Kleider)Haken m; Brt. (Wäsche)Klammer f; (Zelt)Hering m; **take s.o. down a ~** (or **two**) F j-m e-n Dämpfer aufsetzen; **2.** (**-gg-**) anpflocken; Wäsche an-, festklammern

pel·i·can zo. ['pelɪkən] (pl. **-cans, -can**) Pelikan m; **~ 'cross·ing** Brt. Ampelübergang m

pel·let ['pelɪt] Kügelchen n; Schrotkorn n

pelt¹ [pelt] v/t. bewerfen; v/i. **it's ~ing (down)**, bsd. Brt. **it's ~ing with rain** es gießt in Strömen

pelt² [pelt] Fell n, Pelz m

pel·vis anat. ['pelvɪs] (pl. **-vises, -ves** [-viːz]) Becken n

pen¹ [pen] (Schreib)Feder f; Füller m; Kugelschreiber m

pen² [pen] **1.** Pferch m, (Schaf)Hürde f; **2.** (**-nn-**): **~ in, ~ up** Tiere einpferchen, Personen zusammenpferchen

pe·nal ['piːnl] Straf...; strafbar; **'~ code** Strafgesetzbuch n; **~·ize** ['piːnəlaɪz] bestrafen

pen·al·ty ['penltɪ] Strafe f; Sport: a. Strafpunkt m; Fußball: Elfmeter m; **'~ ar·e·a**, **'~ box** F Fußball: Strafraum m; **'~ goal** Fußball: Elfmetertor n; **'~ kick** Fußball: Elfmeter m, Strafstoß m; **~ 'shoot-out** Fußball: Elfmeterschießen n; **'~ spot** Fußball: Elfmeterpunkt m

P

pen·ance *rel.* ['penəns] Buße *f*

pence [pens] (*Abk.* **p**) *pl.* von *penny*

pen·cil ['pensl] **1.** Bleistift *m*; **2.** (*bsd.* *Brt.* **-ll-**, *Am.* **-l-**) (mit Bleistift) markieren *od.* schreiben *od.* zeichnen; *Augenbrauen* nachziehen; '**~ case** Federmäppchen *n*; '**~ sharp·en·er** (Bleistift)Spitzer *m*

pen·dant, **pen·dent** ['pendənt] (Schmuck)Anhänger *m*

pend·ing ['pendɪŋ] **1.** *prp.* bis zu; **2.** *adj.* *bsd. jur.* schwebend

pen·du·lum ['pendjʊləm] Pendel *n*

pen·e|·trate ['penɪtreɪt] eindringen in (*acc.*) *od.* (**into** in *acc.*); dringen durch; durchdringen; '**~·trat·ing** durchdringend; scharf (*Verstand*): scharfsinnig; **~·tra·tion** [penɪ'treɪʃn] Durch-, Eindringen *n*; Scharfsinn *m*

'pen friend Brieffreund(in)

pen·guin *zo.* ['pengwɪn] Pinguin *m*

pe·nin·su·la [pə'nɪnsjʊlə] Halbinsel *f*

pe·nis *anat.* ['piːnɪs] Penis *m*

pen·i|·tence ['penɪtəns] Buße *f*, Reue *f*; '**~·tent 1.** reuig, bußfertig; **2.** *rel.* Büßer(in); **~·ten·tia·ry** *Am.* [penɪ'tenʃərɪ] (Staats)Gefängnis *n*

'pen|·knife (*pl.* **-knives**) Taschenmesser *n*; '**~ name** Schriftstellername *m*, Pseudonym *n*

pen·nant ['penənt] Wimpel *m*

pen·ni·less ['penɪlɪs] (völlig) mittellos

pen·ny ['penɪ] (*Abk.* **p**) (*pl.* **-nies**, *coll.* **pence**) *a.* **new ~** *Brt.* Penny *m*

'pen pal *bsd. Am.* Brieffreund(in)

pen·sion ['penʃn] **1.** Rente *f*, Pension *f*; △ *nicht* **Pension** (*Fremdenheim*); **2. ~ off** pensionieren, in den Ruhestand versetzen; **~·er** ['penʃənə] Rentner(in), Pensionär(in)

pen·sive ['pensɪv] nachdenklich

pen·tath|·lete [pen'tæθliːt] *Sport:* Fünfkämpfer(in); **~·lon** [pen'tæθlɒn] *Sport:* Fünfkampf *m*

Pen·te·cost ['pentɪkɒst] Pfingsten *n*

pent·house ['penthaʊs] Penthouse *n*, -haus *n*

pent-up [pent'ʌp] an-, aufgestaut (*Gefühle*)

pe·o·ny *bot.* ['pɪənɪ] Pfingstrose *f*

peo·ple ['piːpl] **1.** *pl.* konstruiert: die Menschen, die Leute *pl.*; Leute *pl.*, Personen *pl.*; man; **the ~** das (*gemeine*) Volk; (*pl.* **peoples**) Volk *n*, Nation *f*; **2.**

besiedeln, bevölkern (**with** mit); **~'s re·pub·lic** Volksrepublik *f*

pep F [pep] **1.** Pep *m*, Schwung *m*; **2.** (**-pp-**) *mst* **~ up** *j-n od. et.* in Schwung bringen, aufmöbeln

pep·per ['pepə] **1.** Pfeffer *m*; Paprikaschote *f*; **2.** pfeffern; '**~·mint** *bot.* Pfefferminze *f*; Pfefferminz *n* (*Bonbon*); **~·y** ['pepərɪ] pfeff(e)rig; *fig.* hitzig (*Person*)

'pep pill F Aufputschpille *f*

per [pɜː] per, durch; pro, für, je

per·am·bu·la·tor *bsd. Brt.* [pə'ræmbjʊleɪtə] Kinderwagen *m*

per·ceive [pə'siːv] (be)merken, wahrnehmen; erkennen

per cent, per·cent [pə'sent] Prozent *n*

per·cen·tage [pə'sentɪdʒ] Prozentsatz *m*; F Prozente *pl.*, (An)Teil *m*

per·cep|·ti·ble [pə'septəbl] wahrnehmbar, merklich; **~·tion** [pə'sepʃn] Wahrnehmung *f*; Auffassung(sgabe) *f*

perch¹ [pɜːtʃ] **1.** (Sitz)Stange *f* (*für Vögel*); **2.** (**on**) sich setzen (auf *acc.*), sich niederlassen (auf *acc.*, *dat.*) (*Vogel*); F hocken (**on** auf *dat.*); **~ o.s.** F sich hocken (**on** auf *acc.*)

perch² *zo.* [pɜːtʃ] (*pl.* **perch**, **perches**) Barsch *m*

per·co|·late ['pɜːkəleɪt] *Kaffee etc.* filtern; '**~·la·tor** Kaffeemaschine *f*

per·cus·sion [pə'kʌʃn] Schlag *m*; Erschütterung *f*; *mus.* Schlagzeug *n*; **~ in·stru·ment** *mus.* Schlaginstrument *n*

pe·remp·to·ry [pə'remptərɪ] herrisch

pe·ren·ni·al [pə'renjəl] ewig, immerwährend; *bot.* mehrjährig

per|·fect 1. ['pɜːfɪkt] perfekt, vollkommen, vollendet; gänzlich, völlig; **2.** [pə'fekt] vervollkommnen; **3.** ['pɜːfɪkt] *a.* **~ tense** *gr.* Perfekt *n*; **~·fec·tion** [pə'fekʃn] Vollendung *f*; Vollkommenheit *f*, Perfektion *f*

per·fo·rate ['pɜːfəreɪt] durchbohren, -löchern

per·form [pə'fɔːm] *v/t.* verrichten, durchführen, tun; *Pflicht etc.* erfüllen; *thea.*, *mus.* aufführen, spielen, vortragen; *v/i. thea. etc.* e-e Vorstellung geben, auftreten, spielen; **~·ance** Verrichtung *f*, Durchführung *f*; Leistung *f*; *thea.*, *mus.* Aufführung *f*, Vorstellung *f*, Vortrag *m*; **~·er** Darsteller(in), Künstler(in)

per·fume 1. ['pɜ:fju:m] Duft m; Parfüm n; **2.** [pə'fju:m] parfümieren

per·haps [pə'hæps, præps] vielleicht

per·il ['perəl] Gefahr f; **~·ous** gefährlich

pe·ri·od ['pɪərɪəd] Periode f, Zeit(dauer f, -raum m, -spanne f) f; (Unterrichts)Stunde f; physiol. Periode f (der Frau); gr. bsd. Am. Punkt m; **~·ic** [pɪərɪ'ɒdɪk] periodisch; **~·i·cal** [pɪərɪ'ɒdɪkl] **1.** periodisch; **2.** Zeitschrift f

pe·riph·e·ral [pə'rɪfərəl] Computer: Peripheriegerät n; **~ e'quip·ment** sg. Computer: Peripheriegeräte pl.

pe·riph·e·ry [pə'rɪfərɪ] Peripherie f, Rand m

per·ish ['perɪʃ] umkommen; schlecht werden, verderben; **'~·a·ble** leichtverderblich; **'~·ing** bsd. Brt. F saukalt (Wetter)

per·jure ['pɜ:dʒə]: **~ o.s.** e-n Meineid leisten; **~·ju·ry** ['pɜ:dʒərɪ] Meineid m; **commit ~** e-n Meineid leisten

perk [pɜ:k]: **~ up** v/i. aufleben, munter werden (Person); v/t. j-n aufmöbeln, munter machen

perk·y ['pɜ:kɪ] (-ier, -iest) munter, lebhaft; keck; selbstbewußt

perm [pɜ:m] **1.** Dauerwelle f; **get a ~** → **2. get one's hair ~ed** sich e-e Dauerwelle machen lassen

per·ma·nent ['pɜ:mənənt] **1.** (be)ständig, dauerhaft, Dauer...; **2.** Am. → **~ 'wave** Dauerwelle f

per·me·a·ble ['pɜ:mjəbl] durchlässig (to für); **~·ate** ['pɜ:mɪeɪt] durchdringen; dringen (into in acc.; through durch)

per·mis·si·ble [pə'mɪsəbl] zulässig, erlaubt; **~·sion** [pə'mɪʃn] Erlaubnis f, **~·sive** [pə'mɪsɪv] liberal; (sexuell) freizügig; **~·sive so'ci·e·ty** tabufreie Gesellschaft

per·mit 1. [pə'mɪt] (-tt-) erlauben, gestatten; **2.** ['pɜ:mɪt] Genehmigung f

per·pen·dic·u·lar [pɜ:pən'dɪkjʊlə] senkrecht; rechtwink(e)lig (to zu)

per·pet·u·al [pə'petʃʊəl] fortwährend, ständig, ewig

per·plex [pə'pleks] verwirren; **~·i·ty** [pə'pleksətɪ] Verwirrung f

per·se·cute ['pɜ:sɪkjuːt] verfolgen; **~·cu·tion** [pɜ:sɪ'kjuːʃn] Verfolgung f; **~·cu·tor** [pɜ:sɪ'kjuːtə] Verfolger(in)

per·se·ver·ance [pɜ:sɪ'vɪərəns] Ausdauer f, Beharrlichkeit f; **~·vere** [pɜ:sɪ'vɪə] beharrlich weitermachen

per·sist [pə'sɪst] beharren, bestehen (in auf dat.); fortdauern, anhalten; **~·sis·tence** Beharrlichkeit f; Hartnäckigkeit f, Ausdauer f; **~·sis·tent** beharrlich, ausdauernd; anhaltend

per·son ['pɜ:sn] Person f (a. gr.)

per·son·al ['pɜ:snl] persönlich (a. gr.); Personal...; Privat...; **~ col·umn** Zeitung: Persönliches n; **~ com·pu·ter** (Abk. PC) Personalcomputer m; **~ 'da·ta** pl. Personalien pl.

per·son·al·i·ty [pɜ:sə'nælətɪ] Persönlichkeit f; **personalities** pl. anzügliche od. persönliche Bemerkungen pl.

per·son·al 'or·ga·ni·zer Notizbuch n, Adreßbuch n u. Taschenkalender m etc. (in e-m); **~ 'ster·e·o** Walkman m (TM)

per·son·i·fy [pɜ:'sɒnɪfaɪ] personifizieren, verkörpern

per·son·nel [pɜ:sə'nel] Personal n, Belegschaft f; die Personalabteilung; **~ de·part·ment** Personalabteilung f; **~ man·ag·er** Personalchef m

per·spec·tive [pə'spektɪv] Perspektive f; Fernsicht f

per·spi·ra·tion [pɜ:spə'reɪʃn] Transpirieren n, Schwitzen n; Schweiß m; **~·spire** [pə'spaɪə] transpirieren, schwitzen

per·suade [pə'sweɪd] überreden; überzeugen; **~·sua·sion** [pə'sweɪʒn] Überredung(skunst) f; Überzeugung f; **~·sua·sive** [pə'sweɪsɪv] überzeugend

per·tain [pɜ:'teɪn]: **~ to s.th.** et. betreffen

per·ti·nent ['pɜ:tɪnənt] sachdienlich, relevant, zur Sache gehörig

per·turb [pə'tɜ:b] beunruhigen

pe·ruse [pə'ruːz] (sorgfältig) durchlesen

per·vade [pə'veɪd] durchdringen, erfüllen

per·verse [pə'vɜːs] pervers; eigensinnig; **~·ver·sion** [pə'vɜːʃn] Verdrehung f; Perversion f; **~·ver·si·ty** [pə'vɜːsətɪ] Perversität f; Eigensinn m

per·vert 1. [pə'vɜːt] pervertieren; verdrehen; **2.** ['pɜːvɜːt] perverser Mensch

pes·sa·ry med. ['pesərɪ] Pessar n

pes·si·mis·m ['pesɪmɪzəm] Pessimismus *m*; **~mist** ['pesɪmɪst] Pessimist(in); **~'mist·ic** (*~ally*) pessimistisch

pest [pest] Schädling *m*; F Nervensäge *f*; F Plage *f*; △ *nicht* **Pest** (*Seuche*)

pes·ter F ['pestə] *j-n* belästigen, *j-m* keine Ruhe lassen

pes·ti·cide ['pestɪsaɪd] Pestizid *n*, Schädlingsbekämpfungsmittel *n*

pet [pet] **1.** (zahmes) (Haus)Tier; *oft contp.* Liebling *m*; **2.** Lieblings...; Tier...; **3.** (*-tt-*) streicheln; F Petting machen

pet·al *bot.* ['petl] Blütenblatt *n*

'pet food Tiernahrung *f*

pe·ti·tion [pɪ'tɪʃn] **1.** Eingabe *f*, Gesuch *n*, (schriftlicher) Antrag; **2.** ersuchen; ein Gesuch einreichen (**for** um), e-n Antrag stellen (**for** auf *acc.*)

'pet name Kosename *m*

pet·ri·fy ['petrɪfaɪ] versteinern

pet·rol ['petrəl] Benzin *n*; △ *nicht* **Petroleum**

pe·tro·le·um [pə'trəʊljəm] Erd-, Mineralöl *n*

'pet·rol| pump Zapfsäule *f*; **'~ sta·tion** Tankstelle *f*

'pet| shop Tierhandlung *f*, Zoogeschäft *n*; **~'sub·ject** Lieblingsthema *n*

pet·ti·coat ['petɪkəʊt] Unterrock *m*

pet·ting F ['petɪŋ] Petting *n*

pet·tish ['petɪʃ] launisch, gereizt

pet·ty ['petɪ] (*-ier, -iest*) belanglos, unbedeutend, (*Vergehen a.*) geringfügig; engstirnig; **~ 'cash** Portokasse *f*; **~ 'lar·ce·ny** *jur.* einfacher Diebstahl

pet·u·lant ['petjʊlənt] launisch, gereizt

pew [pju:] (Kirchen)Bank *f*

pew·ter ['pju:tə] Zinn *n*; *a.* **~ ware** Zinn (-geschirr) *n*

phan·tom ['fæntəm] Phantom *n*; Geist *m* (*e-s Verstorbenen*)

phar·ma·cist ['fɑ:məsɪst] Apotheker(in); **~cy** ['fɑ:məsɪ] Apotheke *f*

phase [feɪz] Phase *f*

PhD [pi: eɪtʃ 'di:] *Abk. für* **Doctor of Philosophy** (*lateinisch* **philosophiae doctor**) Dr. phil., Doktor *m* der Philosophie; **~ 'the·sis** Doktorarbeit *f*

pheas·ant *zo.* ['feznt] Fasan *m*

phe·nom·e·non [fɪ'nɒmɪnən] (*pl. -na* [-nə]) Phänomen *n*, Erscheinung *f*

phi·lan·thro·pist [fɪ'lænθrəpɪst] Philanthrop(in), Menschenfreund(in)

phi·lol·o·gist [fɪ'lɒlədʒɪst] Philolog|e *m*, -in *f*; **~gy** [fɪ'lɒlədʒɪ] Philologie *f*

phi·los·o·pher [fɪ'lɒsəfə] Philosoph(in); **~phy** [fɪ'lɒsəfɪ] Philosophie *f*

phlegm *med.* [flem] Schleim *m*

phone [fəʊn] **1.** Telefon *n*; **answer the ~** ans Telefon gehen; **by ~** telefonisch; **on the ~** am Telefon; **be on the ~** Telefon haben; am Telefon sein; *telefonieren, anrufen*; **'~ book** Telefonbuch *n*; **'~ booth** *Am.*, **'~ box** *Brt.* Telefonzelle *f*; **'~ call** Anruf *m*, Gespräch *n*; **'~ card** Telefonkarte *f*; **~in** *Brt.* Rundfunk, TV: Sendung *f* mit telefonischer Zuhörer- od. Zuschauerbeteiligung; **'~ num·ber** Telefonnummer *f*

pho·net·ics [fə'netɪks] *sg.* Phonetik *f*

pho·n(e)y F ['fəʊnɪ] **1.** Fälschung *f*; Schwindler(in); **2.** (*-ier, -iest*) falsch, gefälscht, unecht; Schein...

phos·pho·rus *chem.* ['fɒsfərəs] Phosphor *m*

pho·to F ['fəʊtəʊ] (*pl. -tos*) Foto *n*, Bild *n*; **in the ~** auf dem Foto; **take a ~** ein Foto machen (**of** von); **'~cop·i·er** Fotokopiergerät *n*; **'~cop·y 1.** Fotokopie *f*; **2.** fotokopieren

pho·to·graph ['fəʊtəgrɑːf] **1.** Fotografie *f* (*Bild*); △ *nicht* **Fotograf**; **2.** fotografieren; **~tog·ra·pher** [fə'tɒgrəfə] Fotograf(in); **~tog·ra·phy** [fə'tɒgrəfɪ] Fotografie *f*; △ *nicht* **Fotografie** (*Bild*)

phras·al verb *gr.* [freɪzl 'vɜːb] Verb *n* mit Adverb (und Präposition)

phrase [freɪz] **1.** (Rede)Wendung *f*, Redensart *f*, idiomatischer Ausdruck; △ *nicht* **Phrase** (*leere Redensart*); **2.** ausdrücken; **'~book** Sprachführer *m*

phys·i·cal ['fɪzɪkl] **1.** physisch, körperlich; physikalisch; **~ly handicapped** körperbehindert; **2.** ärztliche Untersuchung; **~ edu'ca·tion** Leibeserziehung *f*, Sport *m*; **~ ex·am·i'na·tion** ärztliche Untersuchung; **~ 'hand·i·cap** Körperbehinderung *f*; **~ 'train·ing** Leibeserziehung *f*, Sport *m*

phy·si·cian [fɪ'zɪʃn] Arzt *m*, Ärztin *f*; △ *nicht* **Physiker**

phys·i·cist ['fɪzɪsɪst] Physiker(in); **~ics** ['fɪzɪks] *sg.* Physik *f*

phy·sique [fɪ'zi:k] Körper(bau) *m*, Statur *f*; △ *nicht* **Physik**

pi·a·nist ['pɪənɪst] Pianist(in)

pi·an·o [pɪ'ænəʊ] (*pl. -os*) Klavier *n*

pick [pɪk] **1.** (auf)hacken; (auf)picken; auflesen, -nehmen; pflücken; *Knochen* abnagen; bohren *od.* stochern in (*dat.*); F *Schloß* knacken; aussuchen, -wählen; ~ **one's nose** in der Nase bohren; ~ **one's teeth** in den Zähnen (herum)stochern; ~ **s.o.'s pocket** j-n bestehlen; **have a bone to ~ with s.o.** mit j-m ein Hühnchen zu rupfen haben; ~ **out** (sich) *et.* auswählen; ausmachen, erkennen; ~ **up** aufheben, -lesen, -nehmen; aufpicken; *Spur* aufnehmen; *j-n* abholen; *Anhalter* mitnehmen; F *Mädchen* aufreißen; *Kenntnisse, Informationen et.* aufschnappen; sich *e-e Krankheit etc.* holen; *a.* ~ **up speed** *mot.* schneller werden; **2.** (Spitz)Hacke *f*, Pickel *m*; (Aus)Wahl *f*; **take your** ~ suchen Sie sich etwas aus; **~a-back** ['pɪkəbæk] huckepack; '**~axe** *Brt.*, '**~ax** *Am.* (Spitz)Hacke *f*, Pickel *m*

pick·et ['pɪkɪt] **1.** Pfahl *m*; Streikposten *m*; **2.** Streikposten aufstellen in (*dat.*), mit Streikposten besetzen; Streikposten stehen; '~ **fence** Lattenzaun *m*; '~ **line** Streikpostenkette *f*

pick·le ['pɪkl] **1.** Salzlake *f*; Essigsoße *f*; *Am.* Essig-, Gewürzgurke *f*; *mst* ~**s** *pl.* *bsd. Brt.* Pickles *pl.*; **be in a (pretty)** ~ F (ganz schön) in der Patsche sein od. stecken; △ nicht *Pickel* (→ *pimple*; *pickaxe*). **2.** *gastr.* einlegen

'**pick·lock** Einbrecher *m*; Dietrich *m*; '**~pocket** Taschendieb(in); '**~up** Tonabnehmer *m*; Kleintransporter *m*; F (Zufalls)Bekanntschaft *f*

pic·nic ['pɪknɪk] **1.** Picknick *n*; **2.** (-*ck*-) ein Picknick machen, picknicken

pic·ture ['pɪktʃə] **1.** Bild *n*; Gemälde *n*; *phot.* Aufnahme *f*; Film *m*; ~**s** *pl. bsd. Brt.* Kino *n*; **2.** darstellen, malen; *fig.* sich *j-n, et.* vorstellen; '~ **book** Bilderbuch *n*; ~ '**postcard** Ansichtskarte *f*

pic·tur·esque [pɪktʃə'resk] malerisch

pie [paɪ] (*Fleisch- etc.*)Pastete *f*; (*mst* gedeckter) (*Apfel- etc.*)Kuchen *m*

piece [piːs] **1.** Stück *n*; Teil *n* (*e-r Maschine etc.*); Teil *m* (*e-s Services etc.*); *Schach*: Figur *f*; *Brettspiel*: Stein *m*; (Zeitungs)Artikel *m*, (-)Notiz *f*; **by the** ~ stückweise; **a** ~ **of advice** ein Rat; **a** ~ **of news** e-e Neuigkeit *f*; **give s.o. a** ~ **of one's mind** j-m gründlich die Meinung sagen; **go to** ~**s** F zusammenbrechen

(*Person*); **take to** ~**s** auseinandernehmen; **2.** ~ **together** zusammensetzen, -stückeln; *fig.* zusammenfügen; '**~meal** schrittweise; '**~work** Akkordarbeit *f*; **do** ~ im Akkord arbeiten

pier [pɪə] Pier *m*, Landungsbrücke *f*; Pfeiler *m*

pierce [pɪəs] durchbohren, -stechen, -stoßen; durchdringen

pierc·ing ['pɪəsɪŋ] durchdringend, (*Kälte etc. a.*) schneidend, (*Schrei a.*) gellend, (*Blick, Schmerz etc. a.*) stechend

pi·e·ty ['paɪətɪ] Frömmigkeit *f*

pig [pɪg] *zo.* Schwein *n* (*a. fig.* F); *sl. contp.* Bulle *m* (*Polizist*)

pi·geon *zo.* ['pɪdʒɪn] (*pl.* **-geons**, **-pigeon**) Taube *f*; '~**hole 1.** (Ablege)Fach *n*; **2.** ablegen

pig·gy F ['pɪgɪ] *Kindersprache*: Schweinchen *n*; '~**back** huckepack

pig'head·ed dickköpfig, stur; '~**let** *zo.* ['pɪglɪt] Ferkel *n*; '~**sty** Schweinestall *m*, *fig. a.* Saustall *m*; '~**tail** Zopf *m*

pike[1] *zo.* [paɪk] (*pl.* **pikes**, **pike**) Hecht *m*

pike[2] [paɪk] → *turnpike*

pile[1] [paɪl] **1.** Stapel *m*, Stoß *m*; F Haufen *m*, Menge *f*; (*atomic*) ~ Atommeiler *m*; **2.** ~ **up** (an-, auf)häufen, (auf)stapeln, aufschichten; sich anhäufen; *mot.* F aufeinander auffahren

pile[2] [paɪl] Flor *m* (*Stoff, Teppich*)

pile[3] [paɪl] Pfahl *m*

piles *med.* F [paɪlz] *pl.* Hämorrhoiden *pl.*

'**pile-up** *mot.* F Massenkarambolage *f*

pil·fer ['pɪlfə] stehlen, klauen

pil·grim ['pɪlgrɪm] Pilger(in); ~**age** ['pɪlgrɪmɪdʒ] Pilger-, Wallfahrt *f*

pill [pɪl] Pille *f*; **the** ~ F die (*Antibaby*)Pille; **be on the** ~ die Pille nehmen

pil·lar ['pɪlə] Pfeiler *m*; Säule *f*; '~ **box** *Brt.* Briefkasten *m*

pil·li·on *mot.* ['pɪljən] Soziussitz *m*

pil·lo·ry ['pɪlərɪ] **1.** *hist.* Pranger *m*; **2.** *fig.* anprangern

pil·low ['pɪləʊ] (Kopf)Kissen *n*; '~**case**, '~ **slip** (Kopf)Kissenbezug *m*

pi·lot ['paɪlət] **1.** *aviat.* Pilot(in); *naut.* Lots|e *m*, -in *f*; Versuchs..., Pilot...; **2.** lotsen; steuern; '~ **film** *TV* Pilotfilm *m*; '~ **scheme** Versuchs-, Pilotprojekt *n*

pimp [pɪmp] Zuhälter *m*

pim·ple ['pɪmpl] Pickel *m*, Pustel *f*

P

pin [pɪn] **1.** (Steck)Nadel f; (Haar-, Krawatten- etc.)Nadel f; Am. Brosche f; tech. Bolzen m, Stift m; Kegeln: Kegel m; Bowling: Pin m; Am. (Wäsche-)Klammer f; Brt. (Reiß)Nagel m, (-)Zwecke f; **2.** (**-nn-**) (an)heften, anstecken (**to** an acc.), befestigen (**to** an dat.); pressen, drücken (**against, to** gegen, an acc.)

PIN [pɪn] a. ~ **number** Abk. für **personal identification number** PIN, persönliche Geheimzahl (für Geldautomaten etc.)

pin·a·fore ['pɪnəfɔː] Schürze f

'**pin·ball** Flippern n; **play** ~ flippern; '~ **ma·chine** Flipper(automat) m

pin·cers ['pɪnsəz] pl. (**a pair of** ~ **e-e**) (Kneif)Zange f

pinch [pɪntʃ] **1.** v/t. kneifen, zwicken; F klauen; v/i. drücken (Schuh, Not etc.); **2.** Kneifen n, Zwicken n; Prise f (Salz, Tabak etc.); fig. Not(lage) f

'**pin·cush·ion** Nadelkissen n

pine[1] bot. [paɪn] a. ~**tree** Kiefer f, Föhre f

pine[2] [paɪn] sich sehnen (**for** nach)

'**pine·ap·ple** bot. Ananas f; '~ **cone** bot. Kiefernzapfen m

pin·ion zo. ['pɪnjən] Schwungfeder f

pink [pɪŋk] **1.** rosa(farben); **2.** Rosa n; bot. Nelke f

pint [paɪnt] Pint n (Brt. 0,57 l, Am. 0,47 l); Brt. F Halbe f (Bier)

pi·o·neer [paɪə'nɪə] **1.** Pionier m; **2.** den Weg bahnen (für)

pi·ous ['paɪəs] fromm, religiös

pip[1] [pɪp] (Apfel-, Orangen- etc.)Kern m

pip[2] [pɪp] Ton m (e-s Zeitzeichens etc.)

pip[3] [pɪp] Auge n (der Spielkarten); Punkt m (auf Würfeln etc.); bsd. Brt. mil. Stern m (Rangabzeichen)

pipe [paɪp] **1.** tech. Rohr n, Röhre f; (Tabaks)Pfeife f; (Orgel)Pfeife f; △ nicht (Triller)**Pfeife**; ~**s** pl. Brt. F Dudelsack m; **2.** (durch Rohre) leiten; '~**line** Rohrleitung f; Pipeline f (für Erdöl, Erdgas etc.); '~**r** Dudelsackpfeifer m

pip·ing ['paɪpɪŋ] **1.** Rohrleitung f, -netz n; **2.** ~ **hot** kochend-, siedendheiß

pi·quant ['piːkənt] pikant

pique [piːk] **1. in a fit of** ~ gekränkt, verletzt, pikiert; **2.** kränken, verletzen; **be** ~**d** a. pikiert sein

pi·rate ['paɪərət] **1.** Pirat m, Seeräuber m; **2.** unerlaubt kopieren od. nachdrucken od. nachpressen; ~ '**ra·di·o** Piratensender m od. pl.

Pis·ces astr. ['paɪsiːz] sg. Fische pl.; **hel she is** (**a**) ~ er/sie ist (ein) Fisch

piss V [pɪs] pissen; ~ **off!** verpiß dich!

pis·tol ['pɪstl] Pistole f

pis·ton tech. ['pɪstən] Kolben m; '~ **rod** Kolbenstange f; '~ **stroke** Kolbenhub m

pit[1] [pɪt] **1.** Grube f (a. anat.); Grube f, Zeche f; bsd. Brt. thea. Parkett n; ~ **orchestra** ~ thea. Orchestergraben m; (bsd. Pocken)Narbe f; **2.** (**-tt-**) mit Narben bedecken

pit[2] Am. [pɪt] **1.** bot. Kern m, Stein m; **2.** (**-tt-**) entkernen, -steinen

pitch[1] [pɪtʃ] **1.** v/t. Zelt, Lager aufschlagen; werfen, schleudern; mus. (an)stimmen; v/i. stürzen, fallen; naut. stampfen (Schiff); sich neigen (Dach etc.); ~ **in** F sich ins Zeug legen; kräftig zulangen (beim Essen); **2.** bsd. Brt. (Spiel)Feld n; mus. Tonhöhe f; fig. Grad m, Stufe f; bsd. Brt. Stand(platz) m (e-s Straßenhändlers etc.); naut. Stampfen n; Neigung f (e-s Dachs etc.)

pitch[2] [pɪtʃ] Pech n/s; ~'**black**, ~'**dark** pechschwarz; stockdunkel

pitch·er[1] ['pɪtʃə] Krug m

pitch·er[2] ['pɪtʃə] Baseball: Werfer m

'**pitch·fork** Heu-, Mistgabel f

pit·e·ous ['pɪtɪəs] kläglich

'**pit·fall** Fallgrube f; fig. Falle f

pith [pɪθ] bot. Mark n; weiße innere Haut (e-r Orange etc.); fig. Kern m; '~**y** (**-ier, -iest**) markig, prägnant

pit·i·a·ble ['pɪtɪəbl] → '~**ful** mitleiderregend (Anblick etc.), bemitleidenswert (Person, Zustand etc.); erbärmlich, jämmerlich; '~**less** unbarmherzig

pits [pɪts] pl. Motorsport: Boxen pl.; **it's the** ~ F (das ist) echt ätzend

'**pit stop** Motorsport: Boxenstopp m

pit·tance ['pɪtəns] Hungerlohn m

pit·y ['pɪtɪ] **1.** Mitleid n (**on** mit); **it is a** (**great**) ~ es ist (sehr) schade; **what a** ~**!** wie schade!; **2.** bemitleiden, bedauern

piv·ot ['pɪvət] **1.** tech. Drehzapfen m; fig. Dreh- u. Angelpunkt m; **2.** sich drehen; ~ **on** fig. abhängen von

pix·el ['pɪksəl] Computer: Pixel m (einzelner Bildpunkt)

playgroup

piz·za ['pi:tsə] Pizza *f*

plac·ard ['plæka:d] **1.** Plakat *n*; Transparent *n*; **2.** mit Plakaten bekleben

place [pleɪs] **1.** Platz *m*, Ort *m*, Stelle *f*; Ort *m*, Stätte *f*; Haus *n*, Wohnung *f*; Wohnort *m*; (*Arbeits-, Lehr*)Stelle *f*; *in the first* ~ erstens; *in third* ~ *Sport etc.*: auf dem dritten Platz; *in* ~ *of* an Stelle von (*od. gen.*); *out of* ~ fehl am Platz; *take* ~ stattfinden; △ *nicht Platz nehmen*; *take s.o.'s* ~ j-s Stelle einnehmen; **2.** stellen, legen, setzen; *Auftrag* erteilen (*with dat.*), *Bestellung* aufgeben (*with* bei); *be* ~*d Sport*: sich placieren (*second* an *zweiter Stelle*)

pla·ce·bo *med.* [plə'si:bəʊ] (*pl.* -*bos*, -*boes*) Placebo *n*

'place| mat Platzdeckchen *n*, Set *n*, *m*; **'~ment test** Einstufungsprüfung *f*; **'~ name** Ortsname *m*

plac·id ['plæsɪd] ruhig; gelassen

pla·gia·rize ['pleɪdʒjəraɪz] plagiieren

plague [pleɪɡ] **1.** Seuche *f*; Pest *f*; Plage *f*; **2.** plagen

plaice *zo.* [pleɪs] (*pl.* **plaice**) Scholle *f*

plaid [plæd] Plaid *n*

plain [pleɪn] **1.** *adj.* einfach, schlicht; klar (u. deutlich); offen (u. ehrlich); unscheinbar, wenig anziehend; rein, völlig (*Unsinn etc.*); **2.** *adv.* F (ganz) einfach; **3.** Ebene *f*, Flachland *n*; ~ **'choc·olate** (zart)bittere Schokolade; ~**'clothes** in Zivil

plain|·tiff *jur.* ['pleɪntɪf] Kläger(in); **~·tive** ['pleɪntɪv] traurig, klagend

plait *bsd. Brt.* [plæt] **1.** Zopf *m*; **2.** flechten

plan [plæn] **1.** Plan *m*; **2.** (-*nn-*) planen; beabsichtigen

plane¹ [pleɪn] Flugzeug *n*; *by* ~ mit dem Flugzeug; *go by* ~ fliegen

plane² [pleɪn] **1.** flach, eben; **2.** *math.* Ebene *f*; *fig.* Stufe *f*, Niveau *n*

plane³ [pleɪn] **1.** Hobel *m*; **2.** hobeln; ~ *down* abhobeln

plan·et *astr.* ['plænɪt] Planet *m*

plank [plæŋk] Planke *f*, Bohle *f*; **'~·ing** Planken *pl.*

plant [pla:nt] **1.** *bot.* Pflanze *f*; Werk *n*, Betrieb *m*, Fabrik *f*; **2.** (an-, ein)pflanzen; bepflanzen; *Garten etc.* anlegen; aufstellen, postieren; ~ *s.th. on s.o.* F j-m et. (*Belastendes*) unterschieben

plan·ta·tion [plæn'teɪʃn] Plantage *f*, Pflanzung *f*; Schonung *f*

plant·er ['pla:ntə] Plantagenbesitzer(in), Pflanzer(in); Pflanzmaschine *f*; Übertopf *m*

plaque [pla:k] Gedenktafel *f*; *med.* Zahnbelag *m*

plas·ter ['pla:stə] **1.** *med.* Pflaster *n*; (Ver)Putz *m*; *a.* ~ *of Paris* Gips *m*; *have one's leg in* ~ *med.* das Bein in Gips haben; **2.** verputzen; bekleben; **'~ cast** Gipsabguß *m*, -modell *n*; *med.* Gipsverband *m*

plas·tic ['plæstɪk] **1.** (~*ally*) plastisch; Plastik...; **2.** Plastik *n*, Kunststoff *m*; → ~ **'mon·ey** F Plastikgeld *n*, Kreditkarten *pl.*; **'~ wrap** *Am.* Frischhaltefolie *f*

plate [pleɪt] **1.** Teller *m*; Platte *f*; (*Namens-, Nummern- etc.*)Schild *n*; (Bild-)Tafel *f* (*in e-m Buch*); (Druck)Platte *f*; Gegenstände *pl.* aus Edelmetall; Doublé *n*, Dublee *n*; **2.** ~*d with gold, gold-plated* vergoldet

plat·form ['plætfɔ:m] Plattform *f*; *rail.* Bahnsteig *m*; (Redner)Tribüne *f*, Podium *n*; *pol.* Plattform *f*; *party* ~ *pol.* Parteiprogramm *n*; *election* ~ *pol.* Wahlprogramm *n*

plat·i·num *chem.* ['plætɪnəm] Platin *n*

pla·toon *mil.* [plə'tu:n] Zug *m*

plat·ter *Am. od. veraltet* ['plætə] (Servier)Platte *f*

plau·si·ble ['plɔ:zəbl] plausibel, glaubhaft

play [pleɪ] **1.** Spiel *n*; Schauspiel *n*, (Theater)Stück *n*; *tech.* Spiel *n*; *fig.* Spielraum *m*; *at* ~ beim Spiel(en); *in* ~ im Spiel (*Ball*); *out of* ~ im Aus (*Ball*); **2.** *v/i.* spielen (*a. Sport, thea. etc.*); *v/t.* Karten, Rolle, Stück etc. spielen; *Sport:* Spiel austragen; ~ *s.o. Sport:* gegen j-n spielen; ~ *the guitar* Guitarre spielen; ~ *a trick on s.o.* j-m e-n Streich spielen; ~ *back Ball* zurückspielen (*to* zu); *Tonband* abspielen; ~ *off* *fig.* ausspielen (*against* gegen); ~ *on* *fig.* j-s Schwächen ausnutzen; **'~·back** Playback *n*, Wiedergabe *f*, Abspielen *n*; **'~·boy** Playboy *m*; **'~·er** *mus.*, *Sport:* Spieler(in); Plattenspieler *m*; **'~·fel·low** *Brt.* → **playmate**; **'~·ful** verspielt; scherzhaft; **'~·go·er** (*bsd.* häufige[r]) Theaterbesucher(in); **'~·ground** Spielplatz *m*; Schulhof *m*; **'~·group** *bsd. Brt.* Spiel-

P

gruppe f; '~**house** *thea.* Schauspielhaus n; Spielhaus n (*für Kinder*)

'**play·ing**| **card** Spielkarte f; '~ **field** Sportplatz m, Spielfeld n

'**play·mate** Spielkamerad(in); '~**pen** Laufgitter n, -stall m; '~**thing** Spielzeug n; '~**wright** Dramatiker(in)

plc, PLC *Brt.* [pi: el 'si:] *Abk. für* **public limited company** AG, Aktiengesellschaft f

plea *jur.* [pli:]: **enter a ~ of** (**not**) **guilty** sich schuldig bekennen (s-e Unschuld erklären)

plead [pli:d] (*~ed, bsd. schott., Am. pled*) *v/i.* (dringend) bitten (**for** um); ~ (**not**) **guilty** *jur.* sich schuldig bekennen (s-e Unschuld erklären); *v/t. jur. u. allg.* zu s-r Verteidigung *od.* Entschuldigung anführen, geltend machen; ~ **s.o.'s case** sich für j-n einsetzen; *jur.* j-n vertreten

pleas·ant ['pleznt] angenehm, erfreulich; freundlich; sympathisch

please [pli:z] **1.** (*j-m*) gefallen; *j-m* zusagen, *j-n* erfreuen; zufriedenstellen; **only to ~ you** nur dir zuliebe; ~ **o.s.** tun, was man will; ~ **yourself!** mach, was du willst!; **2.** *int.* bitte; (**yes,**) ~ (ja,) bitte; (oh ja,) gerne; ~ **come in!** bitte, treten Sie ein!; **~d** erfreut, zufrieden; **be ~ about** sich freuen über (*acc.*); **be ~ with** zufrieden sein mit; **I am ~ with it** es gefällt mir; **be ~ to do s.th.** et. gern tun; ~ **to meet you!** angenehm!

pleas·ing ['pli:zɪŋ] angenehm

pleas·ure ['pleʒə] Vergnügen n; **at** (**one's**) ~ nach Belieben

pleat [pli:t] (Plissee)Falte f; '~**ed skirt** Faltenrock m

pled [pled] *pret. u. p.p. von* **plead**

pledge [pledʒ] **1.** Pfand n; *fig.* Unterpfand n; Versprechen n; **2.** versprechen, zusichern

plen·ti·ful ['plentɪfl] reichlich

plen·ty ['plentɪ] **1.** Überfluß m; **in ~** im Überfluß, in Hülle u. Fülle; ~ **of** e-e Menge, viel(e), reichlich; **2.** F reichlich

pleu·ri·sy *med.* ['plʊərəsɪ] Brustfell-, Rippenfellentzündung f

pli·a·ble ['plaɪəbl], **~ant** ['plaɪənt] biegsam; *fig.* flexibel; *fig.* leicht beeinflußbar

pli·ers ['plaɪəz] *pl.* (**a pair of ~** e-e) Beißzange

plight [plaɪt] Not(lage) f

plim·soll *Brt.* ['plɪmsəl] Turnschuh m

plod [plɒd] (*-dd-*) *a.* ~ **along** sich dahinschleppen; ~ **away** sich abplagen (**at** mit), schuften

plop F [plɒp] **1.** Plumps m, Platsch m; **2.** (*-pp-*) plumpsen, (*ins Wasser*) platschen

plot [plɒt] **1.** Stück n Land, Parzelle f, Grundstück n; Handlung f (*e-s Dramas, Films etc.*); Komplott n, Verschwörung f; *Computer:* graphische Darstellung; **2.** (*-tt-*) *v/i.* sich verschwören (**against** gegen); *v/t.* planen; einzeichnen (**in** *e-e* Karte etc.); '~**ter** *Computer:* Plotter m

plough *Brt.*, **plow** *Am.* [plaʊ] **1.** Pflug m; **2.** (um)pflügen; '~**share** Pflugschar f

pluck [plʌk] **1.** *v/t.* *Geflügel* rupfen; *mst* ~ **out** ausreißen, -rupfen, -zupfen; *mus. Saiten* zupfen; ~ **up** (**one's**) **courage** Mut *od.* sich ins Herz fassen; *v/i.* zupfen (**at** an *dat.*); **2.** F Mut m, Schneid m; '~**y** F (*-ier, -iest*) mutig

plug [plʌg] **1.** Stöpsel m; *electr.* Stecker m; F *electr.* Steckdose f; F *mot.* (*Zünd*)Kerze f; **2.** *v/t.* (*-gg-*) *a.* ~ **up** zustopfen; zu-, verstopfen; ~ **in** *electr.* anschließen, einstecken

plum *bot.* [plʌm] Pflaume f; Zwetsch(g)e f

plum·age ['plu:mɪdʒ] Gefieder n

plumb [plʌm] **1.** (Blei)Lot n; **2.** ausloten, *fig. a.* ergründen; **in** *bsd. Brt. Waschmaschine etc.* anschließen; **3.** *adj.* lot-, senkrecht; **4.** *adv.* F (haar)genau; '~**er** Klempner m, Installateur m; '~**ing** Klempner-, Installateurarbeit f; Rohre *pl.*, Rohrleitungen *pl.*

plume [plu:m] (Schmuck)Feder f; Federbusch m; (*Rauch*)Fahne f

plump [plʌmp] **1.** *adj.* drall, mollig, rund(lich); △ *nicht* **plump**; **2.** ~ **down** fallen *od.* plumpsen (lassen)

plum 'pud·ding Plumpudding m

plun·der ['plʌndə] **1.** plündern; **2.** Plünderung f; Beute f; △ *nicht* **Plunder**

plunge [plʌndʒ] **1.** (ein-, unter)tauchen; (sich) stürzen (**into** in *acc.*); *naut.* stampfen (*Schiff*); **2.** (Kopf)Sprung m; **take the** ~ *fig.* den entscheidenden Schritt wagen

plu·per·fect *gr.* [plu:'pɜ:fɪkt] *a.* ~ **tense**

Plusquamperfekt n, Vorvergangenheit f

plu·ral gr. ['pluərəl] Plural m, Mehrzahl f

plus [plʌs] 1. prp. plus, und, bsd. econ. zuzüglich; 2. adj. Plus...; **~ sign** Plus(zeichen) n; 3. Plus(zeichen) n; fig. F Plus n, Vorteil m

plush [plʌʃ] Plüsch m

ply¹ [plaɪ] regelmäßig verkehren, fahren (**between** zwischen dat.)

ply² [plaɪ] 1. mst in Zssgn Lage f, Schicht f (Stoff, Sperrholz etc.); **three-~** dreifach (Garn etc.); dreifach gewebt (Teppich); **'~·wood** Sperrholz n

pm, PM [pi: 'em] Abk. für **after noon** (lateinisch **post meridiem**) nachm., nachmittags, abends

PM bsd. Brt. F [pi: 'em] Abk. für **Prime Minister** Premierminister(in)

pneu·mat·ic [nju:'mætɪk] (**~ally**) Luft..., pneumatisch; tech. Druck..., Preßluft...; **~ 'drill** Preßluftbohrer m

pneu·mo·ni·a med. [nju:'məʊnjə] Lungenentzündung f

PO [pi:'əʊ] Abk. für: **post office** Postamt n; **postal order** Postanweisung f

poach¹ [pəʊtʃ] pochieren; **~ed eggs** pl. verlorene Eier pl.

poach² [pəʊtʃ] wildern; **'~·er** Wilddieb m, Wilderer m

POB [pi: əʊ 'bi:] Abk. für **post office box** (**number**) Postfach n

PO Box [pi: əʊ 'bɒks] Postfach n; **write to ~ 225** schreiben Sie an Postfach 225

pock med. [pɒk] Pocke f, Blatter f

pock·et ['pɒkɪt] 1. (Hosen- etc.)Tasche f; aviat. → **air pocket**; 2. adj. Taschen...; 3. einstecken, in die Tasche stecken; in die eigene Tasche stecken; **'~·book** Notizbuch n; Am. Brieftasche f; **~ 'cal·cu·la·tor** Taschenrechner m; **'~·knife** (pl. **-knives**) Taschenmesser n; **'~ mon·ey** Taschengeld n

pod bot. [pɒd] Hülse f, Schote f

po·em ['pəʊɪm] Gedicht n

po·et ['pəʊɪt] Dichter(in); **~·ic** [pəʊ'etɪk] (**~ally**) dichterisch; **~·i·cal** dichterisch; **~·ic 'jus·tice** fig. ausgleichende Gerechtigkeit; **~·ry** ['pəʊɪtrɪ] Gedichte pl.; Dichtkunst f, Dichtung f

poig·nant ['pɔɪnjənt] schmerzlich (Erinnerungen); ergreifend

point [pɔɪnt] 1. Spitze f; geogr. Landspitze f; gr., math., phys. etc. Punkt m; math. (Dezimal)Punkt m; Grad m (e-r Skala); naut. (Kompaß)Strich m; Sport: Punkt m; Punkt m, Stelle f, Ort m; Zweck m; Ziel n, Absicht f; springender Punkt; Pointe f; **two ~ five (2.5)** 2,5; **~ of view** Stand-, Gesichtspunkt m; **be on the ~ of doing s.th.** im Begriff sein, et. zu tun; **be to the ~** zur Sache gehörig; **off** od. **beside the ~** nicht zur Sache gehörig; **come to the ~** zur Sache kommen; **that's not the ~** darum geht es nicht; **what's the ~?** wozu?; **win on ~s** nach Punkten gewinnen; **winner on ~s** Punktsieger m; 2. v/t. (zu)spitzen; Waffe etc. richten (**at** auf acc.); **~ one's finger at s.o.** (mit dem Finger) auf j-n zeigen; **~ out** zeigen; fig. hinweisen od. aufmerksam machen auf (acc.); v/i. (mit dem Finger) zeigen (**at, to** auf acc.); **~ to** nach e-r Richtung weisen od. liegen; fig. hinweisen auf (acc.); **'~·ed** spitz; Spitz...; fig. scharf (Bemerkung etc.); fig. ostentativ; **'~·er** Zeiger m; Zeigestock m; zo. Pointer m, Vorstehhund m; **'~·less** sinn-, zwecklos

points Brt. rail. [pɔɪnts] pl. Weiche f

poise [pɔɪz] 1. (Körper)Haltung f; fig. Gelassenheit f; 2. balancieren; **be ~d** schweben

poi·son ['pɔɪzn] 1. Gift n; 2. vergiften; **~·ous** ['pɔɪznəs] giftig (a. fig.)

poke [pəʊk] 1. v/t. stoßen; Feuer schüren; stecken; v/i. **~ about, ~ around** (herum)stöbern, (-)wühlen (**in** in dat.); 2. Stoß m; **'pok·er** Schürhaken m

pok·y ['pəʊkɪ] (**-ier, -iest**) eng; schäbig

Po·land ['pəʊlənd] Polen n

po·lar ['pəʊlə] polar; **~ 'bear** zo. Eisbär m

pole¹ [pəʊl] Pol m

pole² [pəʊl] Stange f; Mast m; Deichsel f; Sport: (Sprung)Stab m

Pole [pəʊl] Pol|e m, -in f

'pole·cat zo. Iltis m; Am. Skunk m, Stinktier m

po·lem·ic [pə'lemɪk] 1. a. **~·i·cal** polemisch

'pole star astr. Polarstern m

'pole vault Stabhochsprung m; Stabhochspringen n

'pole-vault stabhochspringen; **'~·er** Stabhochspringer(in)

P

po·lice [pə'li:s] **1.** Polizei f; △ *nicht Police;* **2.** überwachen; ~ **car** Polizeiauto n; ~**man** (pl. **-men**) Polizist m; ~ **of·fi·cer** Polizeibeamt|e(r) m, -in f, Polizist(in); ~ **sta·tion** Polizeiwache f, -revier n; ~**wom·an** (pl. **-women**) Polizistin f

pol·i·cy ['pɒləsɪ] Politik f; Taktik f; (Versicherungs)Police f

po·li·o med. ['pəʊlɪəʊ] Polio f, Kinderlähmung f

pol·ish ['pɒlɪʃ] **1.** polieren; *Schuhe* putzen; ~ **up** aufpolieren (a. fig.); **2.** Politur f; (Schuh)Creme f; fig. Schliff m

Pol·ish ['pəʊlɪʃ] **1.** polnisch; **2.** ling. Polnisch n

po·lite [pə'laɪt] (~**r**, ~**st**) höflich; ~**ness** Höflichkeit f

po·lit·i·cal [pə'lɪtɪkl] politisch; **pol·i·ti·cian** [pɒlɪ'tɪʃn] Politiker(in); **pol·i·tics** ['pɒlɪtɪks] mst sg. Politik f

pol·ka mus. ['pɒlkə] Polka f; '~**dot** gepunktet, getupft (Kleid etc.)

poll [pəʊl] **1.** (Meinungs)Umfrage f; Wahlbeteiligung f; a. ~**s** pl. Stimmabgabe f, Wahl f; **2.** befragen; *Stimmen* erhalten

pol·len bot. ['pɒlən] Pollen m, Blütenstaub m

poll·ing ['pəʊlɪŋ] Stimmabgabe f; Wahlbeteiligung f; '~ **booth** bsd. Brt. Wahlkabine f; '~ **day** Wahltag m; '~ **place** Am., '~ **sta·tion** bsd. Brt. Wahllokal n

polls [pəʊlz] pl. Wahl f; Am. Wahllokal n

poll·ster ['pəʊlstə] Demoskop(in), Meinungsforscher(in)

pol·lut·ant [pə'lu:tənt] Schadstoff m; **pol·lute** [pə'lu:t] be-, verschmutzen; verunreinigen; ~**lut·er** [pə'lu:tə] a. **en·vi·ron·men·tal** ~ Umweltsünder(in); ~**lu·tion** [pə'lu:ʃn] (Luft-, Wasser-, Umwelt)Verschmutzung f; Verunreinigung f

po·lo ['pəʊləʊ] Sport: Polo n; '~ **neck** bsd. Brt. Rollkragen(pullover) m

pol·yp zo., med. ['pɒlɪp] Polyp m

pol·y·sty·rene [pɒlɪ'staɪri:n] Styropor n (TM)

pom·mel ['pʌml] (Sattel- etc.)Knopf m

pomp [pɒmp] Pomp m, Prunk m

pom·pous ['pɒmpəs] aufgeblasen, wichtigtuerisch; schwülstig (Sprache)

pond [pɒnd] Teich m, Weiher m

pon·der ['pɒndə] v/i. nachdenken (**on**, **over** über acc.); v/t. überlegen, nachdenken über (acc.) ~**ous** ['pɒndərəs] schwer(fällig)

pon·toon [pɒn'tu:n] Ponton m; ~ **bridge** Pontonbrücke f

po·ny zo. ['pəʊnɪ] Pony n; △ *nicht Pony* (Frisur); '~**tail** Pferdeschwanz m (Frisur)

poo·dle zo. ['pu:dl] Pudel m

pool¹ [pu:l] Teich m, Tümpel m; Pfütze f, (Blut- etc.)Lache f; (Schwimm)Becken n, (Swimming)Pool m

pool² [pu:l] **1.** (Arbeits-, Fahr)Gemeinschaft f; (Mitarbeiter- etc.)Stab m; (Fuhr)Park m; (Schreib)Pool m; bsd. Am. econ. Pool m, Kartell n; Karten: Gesamteinsatz m; Am. Poolbillard n; **2.** Geld, Unternehmen etc. zusammenlegen; Kräfte etc. vereinen; '~ **hall** Am., '~**room** Billardspielhalle f; ~**s** pl. Brt. a. **football** ~ (Fußball)Toto n, m

poor [pʊə] **1.** arm; dürftig, mangelhaft, schwach; **2. the** ~ pl. die Armen pl.; '~**ly 1.** adj. bsd. Brt. F kränklich, unpäßlich; **2.** adv. ärmlich, dürftig, schlecht, schwach

pop¹ [pɒp] **1.** (**-pp-**) v/t. zerknallen; F schnell wohin tun od. stecken; v/i. knallen; (zer)platzen; ~ **in** auf e-n Sprung vorbeikommen; ~ **off** (plötzlich) den Löffel weglegen (sterben); ~ **up** (plötzlich) auftauchen; **2.** Knall m; F Limo f

pop² [pɒp] Pop m; Schlager...; Pop...

pop³ bsd. Am. F [pɒp] Paps m, Papa m

pop⁴ nur geschr. Abk. f. **population** Einw., Einwohner(zahl f) pl.

'**pop con·cert** mus. Popkonzert n

'**pop·corn** Popcorn n, Puffmais m

pope rel. [pəʊp] mst ♀ Papst m

pop·eyed F glotzäugig

'**pop group** mus. Popgruppe f

'**pop·lar** bot. ['pɒplə] Pappel f

pop·py bot. ['pɒpɪ] Mohn m; '~**cock** F Quatsch m, dummes Zeug

pop·u·lar ['pɒpjʊlə] populär, beliebt; volkstümlich; allgemein; ~**i·ty** [pɒpjʊ'lærətɪ] Popularität f, Beliebtheit f; Volkstümlichkeit f

pop·u·late ['pɒpjʊleɪt] bevölkern, besiedeln; mst pass. bewohnen; ~**la·tion** [pɒpjʊ'leɪʃn] Bevölkerung f; ~**lous** ['pɒpjʊləs] dichtbesiedelt, -bevölkert

porce·lain ['pɔ:slɪn] Porzellan n
porch [pɔ:tʃ] überdachter Vorbau; Portal n (e-r Kirche); Am. Veranda f
por·cu·pine zo. ['pɔ:kjʊpaɪn] Stachelschwein n
pore¹ [pɔ:] Pore f
pore² [pɔ:]: ~ over vertieft sein in (acc.), et. eifrig studieren
pork [pɔ:k] Schweinefleisch n
porn F [pɔ:n] → **por·no** F ['pɔ:nəʊ] (pl. -nos) Porno m; Porno...; **por·nog·ra·phy** [pɔ:'nɒɡrəfɪ] Pornographie f
po·rous ['pɔ:rəs] porös
por·poise ['pɔ:pəs] Tümmler m
por·ridge ['pɒrɪdʒ] Porridge m, n, Haferbrei m
port¹ [pɔ:t] Hafen(stadt f) m
port² naut., aviat. [pɔ:t] Backbord n
port³ [pɔ:t] Computer: Port m, Anschluß m
port⁴ [pɔ:t] Portwein m
por·ta·ble ['pɔ:təbl] tragbar
por·ter ['pɔ:tə] (Gepäck)Träger m; bsd. Brt. Pförtner m, Portier m; Am. rail. Schlafwagenschaffner m
'port·hole naut. Bullauge n
por·tion ['pɔ:ʃn] **1.** (An)Teil m; Portion f (Essen); **2.** ~ out auf-, verteilen (among, between unter acc.)
port·ly ['pɔ:tlɪ] (-ier, -iest) korpulent
por·trait ['pɔ:trɪt] Porträt n, Bild(nis) n
por·tray [pɔ:'treɪ] porträtieren; darstellen; schildern; **~al** thea. ['treɪəl] Verkörperung f, Darstellung f
Por·tu·gal ['pɔ:tʃʊɡl] Portugal n; **Por·tu·guese** [pɔ:tʃʊ'ɡi:z] **1.** portugiesisch; **2.** Portugies|e m, -in f; ling. Portugiesisch n; the ~ pl. die Portugiesen pl.
pose [pəʊz] **1.** aufstellen; Problem, Frage aufwerfen, Bedrohung, Gefahr etc. darstellen; Modell sitzen od. stehen; ~ as sich ausgeben als od. für; **2.** Pose f
posh bsd. Brt. F [pɒʃ] schick, piekfein
po·si·tion [pə'zɪʃn] **1.** Position f, Lage f, Stellung f (a. fig.); Stand m; fig. Standpunkt m; **2.** (auf)stellen
pos·i·tive ['pɒzətɪv] **1.** positiv; bestimmt, sicher, eindeutig; greifbar, konkret, konstruktiv; **2.** phot. Positiv n
pos|·sess [pə'zes] besitzen; fig. beherrschen (Gedanke, Gefühl etc.); **~sessed** [pə'zest] besessen; **~ses·sion**

[pə'zeʃn] Besitz m; fig. Besessenheit f; **~·ses·sive** [pə'zesɪv] besitzergreifend; gr. possessiv, besitzanzeigend
pos·si·bil·i·ty [pɒsə'bɪlətɪ] Möglichkeit f; **~·ble** ['pɒsəbl] möglich; **~·bly** ['pɒsəblɪ] möglicherweise, vielleicht; if I ~ can wenn ich irgend kann; I can't ~ do this ich kann das unmöglich tun
post¹ [pəʊst] (Tür-, Tor-, Ziel- etc.-) Pfosten m; Pfahl m; **2.** a. ~ up Plakat etc. anschlagen, ankleben; be ~ed missing naut., aviat. als vermißt gemeldet werden
post² bsd. Brt. [pəʊst] Post f; Post(sendung) f; by ~ mit der Post; **2.** mit der Post (zu)schicken, aufgeben, Brief einwerfen
post³ [pəʊst] **1.** Stelle f, Job m; Posten m; **2.** aufstellen, postieren; bsd. Brt. versetzen, mil. abkommandieren (to nach)
post... [pəʊst] nach..., Nach...
post·age ['pəʊstɪdʒ] Porto n; '~ stamp Postwertzeichen n, Briefmarke f
post·al ['pəʊstl] postalisch, Post...; '~ or·der Brt. Postanweisung f; '~ vote pol. Briefwahl f
'post·bag bsd. Brt. Postsack m; '~·box bsd. Brt. Briefkasten m; '~·card Postkarte f; a. picture ~ Ansichtskarte f; '~·code Postleitzahl f
post·er ['pəʊstə] Plakat n, Poster n
poste res·tante Brt. [pəʊst'restɑ:nt] **1.** Abteilung f für postlagernde Sendungen; **2.** postlagernd
pos·te·ri·or humor. [pɒ'stɪərɪə] Allerwerteste(r) m, Hinterteil n
pos·ter·i·ty [pɒ'sterətɪ] die Nachwelt
post-'free bsd. Brt. portofrei
post-grad·u·ate [pəʊst'ɡrædjʊət] **1.** nach dem ersten akademischen Grad; **2.** j., der nach dem ersten akademischen Grad weiterstudiert
post·hu·mous ['pɒstjʊməs] post(h)um
'post·man (pl. -men) bsd. Brt. Briefträger m, Postbote m; '~·mark **1.** Poststempel m; **2.** (ab)stempeln; '~·mas·ter Postamtsvorsteher m; '~·of·fice Post(amt n, -filiale) f; '~·of·fice box → PO Box; ~·'paid bsd. Am. portofrei
post·pone [pəʊst'pəʊn] ver-, aufschieben; **~·ment** Verschiebung f, Aufschub m

P

post·script [ˈpəʊsskrɪpt] Postskript(um) n, Nachschrift f

pos·ture [ˈpɒstʃə] 1. (Körper)Haltung f; Stellung f; 2. fig. sich aufspielen

post'war Nachkriegs...

'post·wom·an (pl. **-women**) bsd. Brt. Briefträgerin f, Postbotin f

po·sy [ˈpəʊzɪ] Sträußchen n

pot [pɒt] 1. Topf m; Kanne f; Kännchen n (Tee etc.); Sport: F Pokal m; sl. Pot n (Marihuana); 2. (-tt-) Pflanze eintopfen

po·ta·to [pəˈteɪtəʊ] (pl. **-toes**) Kartoffel f; → **chips, crisps**

'pot·bel·ly Schmerbauch m

po·ten|·cy [ˈpəʊtənsɪ] Stärke f; Wirksamkeit f, Wirkung f; physiol. Potenz f; **~t** [ˈpəʊtənt] stark (Medikament etc.); physiol. potent; **~tial** [pəˈtenʃl] 1. potentiell, möglich; 2. Potential n, Leistungsfähigkeit f

'pot·hole mot. Schlagloch n

po·tion [ˈpəʊʃn] Trank m

pot·ter¹ [ˈpɒtə] ~ **about** herumwerkeln

pot·ter² [ˈpɒtə] Töpfer(in); **~y** [ˈpɒtərɪ] Töpferei f; Töpferware(n pl.) f

pouch [paʊtʃ] Beutel m (a. zo.); zo. (Backen)Tasche f

poul·tice med. [ˈpəʊltɪs] (warmer) (Senf- etc.)Umschlag od. (-)Wickel

poul·try [ˈpəʊltrɪ] Geflügel n

pounce [paʊns] 1. sich stürzen (**on** auf acc.); 2. Satz m, Sprung m

pound¹ [paʊnd] Pfund n (453,59 g); ~ (**sterling**) (Abk. **£**) Pfund n

pound² [paʊnd] Tierheim n; Abstellplatz m für (polizeilich) abgeschleppte Fahrzeuge

pound³ [paʊnd] v/t. zerstoßen, -stampfen; trommeln od. hämmern auf (acc.) od. an (acc.) od. gegen (acc.); v/i. hämmern (**with** vor dat.) (Herz)

pour [pɔː] v/t. gießen, schütten; ~ **out** ausgießen, -schütten; Getränk eingießen; v/i. strömen (a. fig.)

pout [paʊt] 1. v/t. Lippen schürzen; v/i. schmollen; e-n Schmollmund machen; 2. Schmollen n; Schmollmund m

pov·er·ty [ˈpɒvətɪ] Armut f

POW [piː əʊ ˈdʌblju:] Abk. für **prisoner of war** Kriegsgefangene(r) m

pow·der [ˈpaʊdə] 1. Pulver n; Puder m; 2. pulverisieren; (sich) pudern; '**~ puff** Puderquaste f; '**~ room** Damentoilette f

pow·er [ˈpaʊə] 1. Kraft f; Macht f; Fähigkeit f, Vermögen n; Gewalt f; jur. Befugnis f, Vollmacht f; math. Potenz f; electr. Strom m; **in** ~ an der Macht; 2. tech. antreiben; '**~ cut** electr. Stromsperre f; '**~ fail·ure** electr. Stromsperre f, Netzausfall m; '**~·ful** stark, kräftig; mächtig; '**~·less** kraftlos; machtlos; '**~ plant** bsd. Am. → **power station**; '**~ pol·i·tics** oft sg. Machtpolitik f; '**~ sta·tion** Elektrizitäts-, Kraftwerk n

pp nur geschr. Abk. für **pages** Seiten pl.

PR [piː ˈɑː] Abk. für **public relations** PR, Öffentlichkeitsarbeit f

prac·ti|·ca·ble [ˈpræktɪkəbl] durchführbar; **~cal** [ˈpræktɪkl] praktisch; **~cal 'joke** Streich m; '**~·cal·ly** so gut wie

prac·tice [ˈpræktɪs] 1. Praxis f; Übung f; Gewohnheit f, Brauch m; **it is common** ~ es ist allgemein üblich; **put into** ~ in die Praxis umsetzen; 2. Am. → **practise**

prac·tise Brt., **prac·tice** Am. [ˈpræktɪs] v/t. (ein)üben; **als Beruf** ausüben; ~ **law** (**medicine**) als Anwalt (Arzt) praktizieren; v/i. praktizieren; üben; '**~d** geübt (**in** in dat.)

prac·ti·tion·er [prækˈtɪʃnə]: **general** ~ praktischer Arzt

prai·rie [ˈpreərɪ] Prärie f; ~ '**schoo·ner** Am. hist. Planwagen m

praise [preɪz] 1. loben, preisen; 2. Lob n; '**~·wor·thy** lobenswert

pram bsd. Brt. F [præm] Kinderwagen m

prance [prɑːns] sich aufbäumen, steigen (Pferd); tänzeln (Pferd); stolzieren

prank [præŋk] Streich m

prat·tle F [ˈprætl]: ~ **on** plappern (**about** von)

prawn zo. [prɔːn] Garnele f

pray [preɪ] beten (**to** zu; **for** für, um)

prayer [preə] Gebet n; oft **~s** pl. Andacht f; **the Lord's** ~ das Vaterunser; '**~ book** Gebetbuch n

preach [priːtʃ] predigen (**to** zu, vor dat.); '**~·er** Prediger(in)

pre·am·ble [priːˈæmbl] Einleitung f

pre·ar·range [priːəˈreɪndʒ] vorher vereinbaren

pre·car·i·ous [prɪˈkeərɪəs] prekär, unsicher; gefährlich

pre·cau·tion [prɪˈkɔːʃn] Vorkehrung f,

premeditated

Vorsichtsmaßnahme *f*; **~·a·ry** [prɪ-ˈkɔːʃnərɪ] vorbeugend

pre·cede [priːˈsiːd] voraus-, vorangehen (*dat.*)

pre·ce·dence [ˈpresɪdəns] Vorrang *m*; **'~·dent** Präzedenzfall *m*

pre·cept [ˈpriːsept] Regel *f*, Richtlinie *f*

pre·cinct [ˈpriːsɪŋkt] *bsd. Brt.* (*Einkaufs*)Viertel *n*; *bsd. Brt.* (*Fußgänger*)Zone *f*; *Am.* (*Wahl*)Bezirk *m*; *Am.* (*Polizei*)Revier *n*; **~s** *pl.* Gelände *n*

pre·cious [ˈpreʃəs] **1.** *adj.* kostbar, wertvoll; Edel... (*Steine etc.*); **2.** *adv.* **~ little** F herzlich wenig

pre·ci·pice [ˈpresɪpɪs] Abgrund *m*

pre·cip·i·tate 1. [prɪˈsɪpɪteɪt] *v/t.* (hinunter-, herunter)schleudern; *chem.* ausfällen; *fig.* beschleunigen; *fig.* stürzen (*into* in *acc.*); *v/i. chem.* ausfallen; **2.** [prɪˈsɪpɪtət] *adj.* überstürzt; **3.** *chem.* [prɪˈsɪpɪteɪt] Niederschlag *m*; **~·ta·tion** [prɪsɪpɪˈteɪʃn] *chem.* Ausfällung *f*; *meteor.* Niederschlag *m*; *fig.* Überstürzung *f*, Hast *f*; **~·tous** [prɪˈsɪpɪtəs] steil(abfallend); *fig.* überstürzt

pré·cis [ˈpreɪsiː] (*pl.* **-cis** [-siːz]) Zusammenfassung *f*

pre|·cise [prɪˈsaɪs] genau, präzis; **~·ci·sion** [prɪˈsɪʒn] Genauigkeit *f*; Präzision *f*

pre·clude [prɪˈkluːd] ausschließen

pre·co·cious [prɪˈkəʊʃəs] frühreif; altklug

pre·con|·ceived [priːkənˈsiːvd] vorgefaßt (*Meinung etc.*); **~·cep·tion** [priːkənˈsepʃn] vorgefaßte Meinung

pre·cur·sor [priːˈkɜːsə] Vorläufer(in)

pred·a·to·ry [ˈpredətərɪ] Raub...

pre·de·ces·sor [ˈpriːdɪsesə] Vorgänger(in)

pre·des|·ti·na·tion [priːdestɪˈneɪʃn] Vorherbestimmung *f*; **~·tined** [priːˈdestɪnd] prädestiniert, vorherbestimmt (*to* für, zu)

pre·de·ter·mine [priːdɪˈtɜːmɪn] vorherbestimmen; vorher vereinbaren

pre·dic·a·ment [prɪˈdɪkəmənt] mißliche Lage, Zwangslage *f*

pred·i·cate *gr.* [ˈpredɪkət] Prädikat *n*, Satzaussage *f*; **pre·dic·a·tive** *gr.* [prɪˈdɪkətɪv] prädikativ

pre|·dict [prɪˈdɪkt] vorher-, voraussagen; **~·dic·tion** [prɪˈdɪkʃn] Vorher-,

Voraussage *f*; **computer ~** Hochrechnung *f* (*bei Wahlen*)

pre·dis|·pose [priːdɪˈspəʊz] geneigt machen, einnehmen (*in favo[u]r of* für); *bsd. med.* anfällig machen (*to* für); **~·po·si·tion** [priːdɪspəˈzɪʃn]: **~ to** Neigung *f* zu, *bsd. med. a.* Anfälligkeit *f* für

pre·dom·i·nant [prɪˈdɒmɪnənt] (vor-)herrschend, überwiegend; **~·nate** [prɪˈdɒmɪneɪt] vorherrschen, überwiegen; die Oberhand haben

pre·em·i·nent [priːˈemɪnənt] hervor-, überragend

pre·emp·tive [prɪˈemptɪv] Vorkaufs...; *mil.* Präventiv...

preen [priːn] *sich od. das Gefieder* putzen (*Vogel*)

pre·fab F [ˈpriːfæb] Fertighaus *n*; **~·ri·cate** [priːˈfæbrɪkeɪt] vorfabrizieren, -fertigen; **~d house** Fertighaus *n*

pref·ace [ˈprefɪs] **1.** Vorwort *n* (*to* zu); **2.** *Buch, Rede etc.* einleiten (*with* mit)

pre·fect [ˈpriːfekt] *Schule: Brt.* Aufsichts-, Vertrauensschüler(in)

pre·fer [prɪˈfɜː] (*-rr-*) vorziehen (*to dat.*), lieber mögen (*to* als), bevorzugen

pref·e|·ra·ble [ˈprefərəbl]: **be ~** (*to*) vorzuziehen sein (*dat.*), besser sein (als); **'~·ra·bly** vorzugsweise, lieber, am liebsten; **~·rence** [ˈprefərəns] Vorliebe *f* (*for* für); Vorzug *m*

pre·fix *gr.* [ˈpriːfɪks] Präfix *n*, Vorsilbe *f*

preg·nan|·cy [ˈpregnənsɪ] Schwangerschaft *f*; *zo.* Trächtigkeit *f*; **~·t** [ˈpregnənt] schwanger; *zo.* trächtig; △ *nicht* **prägnant**

pre·heat [priːˈhiːt] *Bratröhre* vorheizen

pre·judge [priːˈdʒʌdʒ] *j-n* vorverurteilen; vorschnell beurteilen

prej·u·dice [ˈpredʒʊdɪs] **1.** Vorurteil *n*, Voreingenommenheit *f*, Befangenheit *f*; **to the ~ of** zum Nachteil *od.* Schaden (*gen.*); **2.** einnehmen (*in favo[u]r of* für; **against** gegen); schaden (*dat.*), beeinträchtigen; **'~d** (vor)eingenommen, befangen

pre·lim·i·na·ry [prɪˈlɪmɪnərɪ] **1.** vorläufig, einleitend, Vor...; **2. preliminaries** *pl.* Vorbereitungen *pl.*

pre·lude [ˈpreljuːd] Vorspiel *n* (*a. mus*)

pre·mar·i·tal [priːˈmærɪtl] vorehelich

pre·ma·ture [ˈpremətjʊə] vorzeitig, verfrüht; *fig.* voreilig

pre·med·i·tat·ed [priːˈmedɪteɪtɪd] vor-

P

sätzlich; **~·ta·tion** [priːmedɪˈteɪʃn]: **with ~** vorsätzlich

prem·i·er [ˈpremjə] Premier(minister) m

prem·i·ere, prem·i·ère [ˈpremɪeə] Premiere f, Ur-, Erstaufführung f

prem·is·es [ˈpremɪsɪz] pl. Gelände n, Grundstück n, (Geschäfts)Räume pl.; **on the ~** an Ort u. Stelle, im Haus od. Lokal

pre·mi·um [ˈpriːmjəm] Prämie f, Bonus m; **'~ (gas·o·line)** Am. mot. Super(benzin) n

pre·mo·ni·tion [priːməˈnɪʃn] (böse) Vorahnung

pre·oc·cu·pa·tion [priːɒkjʊˈpeɪʃn] Beschäftigung f (**with** mit); **~·pied** [priːˈɒkjʊpaɪd] gedankenverloren, geistesabwesend; **~·py** [priːˈɒkjʊpaɪ] (stark) beschäftigen

prep Brt. F [prep] Hausaufgabe(n pl.) f

pre·packed [priːˈpækt], **pre·pack·aged** [priːˈpækɪdʒd] abgepackt (Nahrung)

pre·paid post [priːˈpeɪd] frankiert, freigemacht; **~ envelope** Freiumschlag m

prep·a·ra·tion [prepəˈreɪʃn] Vorbereitung f (**for** auf acc., für); Zubereitung f; chem., med. Präparat n

pre·par·a·to·ry [prɪˈpærətərɪ] vorbereitend; **~ school** private Vorbereitungsschule

pre·pare [prɪˈpeə] v/t. vorbereiten; Speise etc. zubereiten; v/i. **~ for** sich vorbereiten auf (acc.); Vorbereitungen treffen für; sich gefaßt machen auf (acc.); **~d** vorbereitet; bereit

prep·o·si·tion gr. [prepəˈzɪʃn] Präposition f, Verhältniswort n

pre·pos·sess·ing [priːpəˈzesɪŋ] einnehmend, anziehend

pre·pos·ter·ous [prɪˈpɒstərəs] absurd; lächerlich, grotesk

pre·pro·gram(me) [priːˈprəʊgræm] vorprogrammieren

'prep school F → **preparatory school**

pre·req·ui·site [priːˈrekwɪzɪt] Vorbedingung f, (Grund)Voraussetzung f

pre·rog·a·tive [prɪˈrɒgətɪv] Vorrecht n

pre·scribe [prɪˈskraɪb] et. vorschreiben; med. j-m et. verschreiben

pre·scrip·tion [prɪˈskrɪpʃn] Vorschrift f, Verordnung f; med. Rezept n

pres·ence [ˈprezns] Gegenwart f, Anwesenheit f; **~ of 'mind** Geistesgegenwart f

pres·ent¹ [ˈpreznt] Geschenk n

pre·sent² [prɪˈzent] präsentieren; (über)reichen, (-)bringen, (-)geben; schenken; vorbringen, -legen; zeigen, vorführen, thea. etc. aufführen; schildern, darstellen; j-n, Produkt etc. vorstellen; Programm etc. moderieren

pres·ent³ [ˈpreznt] **1.** anwesend; vorhanden; gegenwärtig, jetzig; laufend (Jahr etc.); vorliegend (Fall etc.); **~ tense** gr. Präsens n, Gegenwart f; **2.** Gegenwart f, gr. a. Präsens n; **at ~** gegenwärtig, zur Zeit; **for the ~** vorerst, -läufig

pre·sen·ta·tion [prezənˈteɪʃn] Präsentation f, Überreichung f; Vorlage f; Vorführung f, thea. etc. Aufführung f; Schilderung f, Darstellung f; Vorstellung f; Rundfunk, TV: Moderation f

pres·ent-day heutig, gegenwärtig, modern

pre·sent·er bsd. Brt. [prɪˈzentə] Rundfunk, TV: Moderator(in)

pre·sen·ti·ment [prɪˈzentɪmənt] (böse) Vorahnung

pres·ent·ly [ˈprezntlɪ] bald; bsd. Am. zur Zeit, jetzt

pres·er·va·tion [prezəˈveɪʃn] Bewahrung f; Erhaltung f; Konservierung f

pre·ser·va·tive [prɪˈzɜːvətɪv] Konservierungsmittel n

pre·serve [prɪˈzɜːv] **1.** bewahren, (be)schützen; erhalten; konservieren, Obst etc. einmachen, -kochen; **2.** (Jagd)Revier n; fig. Ressort n, Reich n; mst **~s** pl. das Eingemachte

pre·side [prɪˈzaɪd] den Vorsitz führen (**at, over** bei)

pres·i·den·cy pol. [ˈprezɪdənsɪ] Präsidentschaft f; Amtszeit f (e-s Präsidenten); **~·dent** [ˈprezɪdənt] Präsident(in)

press [pres] **1.** v/t. drücken, pressen; Frucht (aus)pressen; drücken auf (acc.); bügeln; drängen; j-n (be)drängen; bestehen auf (dat.); v/i. drücken; drängen (Zeit etc.); (sich) drängen; **~ for** dringen od. drängen auf (acc.); **~ on** (zügig) weitermachen; **2.** Druck m (a. fig.); (Wein- etc.)Presse f; Bügeln n; die Presse (Zeitungswesen); a. **printing ~** Druckerpresse f; **'~ a·gen·cy** Presse-

~agentur f; **'~ box** Pressetribüne f; **'~ing** dringend; **'~ stud** Brt. Druckknopf m; **'~up** bsd. Brt. Liegestütz m; **do ten ~s** pl. zehn Liegestütze machen

pres·sure phys., tech. etc. ['preʃə] Druck m (a. fig.); **'~ cook·er** Dampf-, Schnellkochtopf m

pres·tige [pre'stiːʒ] Prestige n, Ansehen n

pre·su·ma·bly [prɪ'zjuːməblɪ] vermutlich; **~sume** [prɪ'zjuːm] v/t. annehmen, vermuten; sich erdreisten od. anmaßen (**to do** zu tun); v/i. annehmen, vermuten; anmaßend sein; **~ on** et. ausnützen od. mißbrauchen

pre·sump·tion [prɪ'zʌmpʃn] Annahme f, Vermutung f; Anmaßung f; **~tu·ous** [prɪ'zʌmptʃʊəs] anmaßend

pre·sup·pose [priːsə'pəʊz] voraussetzen; **~·po·si·tion** [priːsʌpə'zɪʃn] Voraussetzung f

pre·tence Brt., **pre·tense** Am. [prɪ'tens] Verstellung f, Vortäuschung f; Anspruch m (**to** auf acc.)

pre·tend [prɪ'tend] vorgeben, -täuschen; sich verstellen; Anspruch erheben (**to** auf acc.); **she is only ~ing** sie tut nur so; **~·ed** vorgetäuscht, gespielt

pre·ten·sion [prɪ'tenʃn] Anspruch m (**to** auf acc.); Anmaßung f

pret·er·it(e) gr. ['pretərɪt] Präteritum n, (erste) Vergangenheit

pre·text ['priːtekst] Vorwand m

pret·ty ['prɪtɪ] **1.** adj. (-ier, -iest) hübsch; **2.** adv. ziemlich, ganz schön

pret·zel ['pretsl] Brezel f

pre·vail [prɪ'veɪl] vorherrschen, weit verbreitet sein; siegen (**over, against** über acc.); **~ing** (vor)herrschend

pre·vent [prɪ'vent] verhindern, -hüten, e-r Sache vorbeugen; j-n hindern (**from** an dat.); **~·ven·tion** [prɪ'venʃn] Verhinderung f, -hütung f, Vorbeugung f; **~·ven·tive** [prɪ'ventɪv] vorbeugend

pre·view ['priːvjuː] Film, TV: Voraufführung f; Vorbesichtigung f; Film, TV etc.: Vorschau f (**of** auf acc.)

pre·vi·ous ['priːvjəs] vorher-, vorausgehend, Vor...; **~ to** bevor, vor (dat.); **~ knowledge** Vorkenntnisse pl.; **'~·ly** vorher, früher

pre·war [priː'wɔː] Vorkriegs...

prey [preɪ] **1.** Beute f, Opfer n (e-s Raubtiers; a. fig.); **be easy ~ for** od. **to** e-e

leichte Beute sein für; **2. ~ on** zo. Jagd machen auf (acc.); fig. nagen an (dat.)

price [praɪs] **1.** Preis m; **2.** den Preis festsetzen für; auszeichnen (**at** mit); **'~·less** unbezahlbar; **'~ tag** Preisschild n

prick [prɪk] **1.** Stich m; V Schwanz m (Penis); **~s** pl. **of conscience** Gewissensbisse pl.; **2.** v/t. (auf-, durch)stechen, stechen in (acc.); **her conscience ~ed her** sie hatte Gewissensbisse; **~ up one's ears** die Ohren spitzen; v/i. stechen

prick·le ['prɪkl] Stachel m, Dorn m; **'~·ly** (-ier, -iest) stach(e)lig; prickelnd, kribbelnd

pride [praɪd] **1.** Stolz m; Hochmut m; **take (a) ~ in** stolz sein auf (acc.); **2. ~ o.s. on** stolz sein auf (acc.)

priest [priːst] Priester m

prig [prɪg] Tugendbold m; **'~·gish** tugendhaft

prim [prɪm] (-mm-) steif; prüde

pri·mae·val bsd. Brt. [praɪ'miːvl] → primeval

pri·ma·ri·ly ['praɪmərəlɪ] in erster Linie, vor allem

pri·ma·ry ['praɪmərɪ] **1.** wichtigste(r, -s), Haupt...; grundlegend, elementar, Grund...; Anfangs..., Ur...; **2.** Am. pol. Vorwahl f; **'~ school** Brt. Grundschule f

prime [praɪm] **1.** math. Primzahl f; fig. Blüte(zeit) f; **in the ~ of life** in der Blüte s-r Jahre; **be past one's ~** s-e besten Jahre hinter sich haben; **2.** adj. erste(r, -s), wichtigste(r, -s), Haupt...; erstklassig; **3.** v/t. grundieren; j-n instruieren, vorbereiten; **~ 'min·is·ter** (Abk. **PM**) Premierminister(in), Ministerpräsident(in); **~ 'num·ber** math. Primzahl f

prim·er ['praɪmə] Fibel f, Elementarbuch n

'prime time bsd. Am. TV Haupteinschaltzeit f, -sendezeit f, beste Sendezeit

pri·me·val [praɪ'miːvl] urzeitlich, Ur...

prim·i·tive ['prɪmɪtɪv] erste(r, -s), ursprünglich, Ur...; primitiv

prim·rose bot. ['prɪmrəʊz] Primel f, bsd. Schlüsselblume f

prince [prɪns] Fürst m; Prinz m; **prin·cess** [prɪn'ses, vor Eigennamen 'prɪnses] Fürstin f; Prinzessin f

prin·ci·pal ['prɪnsəpl] **1.** wichtigste(r, -s), hauptsächlich, Haupt...; △ *nicht* **prinzipiell; 2.** *Am. Schule:* Direktor(in), Rektor(in); *thea.* Hauptdarsteller(in); *mus.* Solist(in)

prin·ci·pal·i·ty [prɪnsɪ'pælətɪ] Fürstentum *n*

prin·ci·ple ['prɪnsəpl] Prinzip *n*, Grundsatz *m*; **on** ~ grundsätzlich, aus Prinzip

print [prɪnt] **1.** *print.* Druck *m*; Gedruckte *n*; *(Finger- etc.)*Abdruck *m*; *Kunst:* Druck *m*; *phot.* Abzug *m*; bedruckter Stoff; **in** ~ gedruckt; **out of** ~ vergriffen; **2.** *v/i. print.* drucken; *v/t.* (ab-, auf-, be)drucken; in Druckbuchstaben schreiben; *fig.* einprägen (**on** *dat.*); *a.* ~ **off** *phot.* abziehen; *a.* ~ **out** *Computer:* ausdrucken; '~**ed mat·ter** *post* Drucksache *f*

'**print·er** Drucker *m* (*a. Gerät*); ~'**s er·ror** Druckfehler *m*; ~'**s ink** Druckerschwärze *f*; '~**s** *pl.* Druckerei *f*

print·ing *print.* ['prɪntɪŋ] Drucken *n*; Auflage *f*; '~ **ink** Druckerschwärze *f*; '~ **press** Druck(er)presse *f*

'**print-out** *Computer:* Ausdruck *m*

pri·or ['praɪə] frühere(r, -s); vorrangig; ~**i·ty** [praɪ'ɒrɪtɪ] Priorität *f*, Vorrang *m*; *mot.* Vorfahrt *f*

prise *bsd. Brt.* [praɪz] → **prize²**

pris·m ['prɪzəm] Prisma *n*

pris·on ['prɪzn] Gefängnis *n*; '~**er** Gefangene(r *m*) *f*, Häftling *m*; **hold** ~, **keep** ~ gefangenhalten; **take** ~ gefangennehmen

priv·a·cy ['prɪvəsɪ] Intim-, Privatsphäre *f*; Geheimhaltung *f*

pri·vate ['praɪvɪt] **1.** privat, Privat...; vertraulich; geheim; ~ **parts** *pl.* Geschlechtsteile *pl.*; **2.** *mil.* gemeiner Soldat; **in** ~ privat; unter vier Augen

pri·va·tion [praɪ'veɪʃn] Entbehrung *f*

priv·i·lege ['prɪvɪlɪdʒ] Privileg *n*; Vorrecht *n*; '~**d** privilegiert

priv·y ['prɪvɪ] (*-ier, -iest*): **be** ~ **to** eingeweiht sein in (*acc.*)

prize¹ [praɪz] **1.** (Sieger-, Sieges)Preis *m*, Prämie *f*, Auszeichnung *f*; (*Lotterie*)Gewinn *m*; **2.** preisgekrönt; Preis...; **3.** (hoch)schätzen

prize² [praɪz]: ~ **open** aufbrechen, -stemmen

'**prize·win·ner** Preisträger(in)

pro¹ F [prəʊ] (*pl. -s*) Profi *m*

pro² [prəʊ] (*pl. -s*) **the** ~**s and cons** *pl.* das Pro u. Kontra, das Für u. Wider

prob·a·bil·i·ty [prɒbə'bɪlətɪ] Wahrscheinlichkeit *f*; **in all** ~ höchstwahrscheinlich; ~**a·ble** ['prɒbəbl] *adj.* wahrscheinlich; '~**a·bly** *adv.* wahrscheinlich

pro·ba·tion [prə'beɪʃn] Probe *f*, Probezeit *f*; *jur.* Bewährung(sfrist) *f*; ~ **of·fi·cer** Bewährungshelfer(in)

probe [prəʊb] **1.** *med., tech.* Sonde *f*; *fig.* Untersuchung *f* (**into** *gen.*); △ *nicht* **Probe; 2.** sondieren; (gründlich) untersuchen; △ *nicht* **proben, probieren**

prob·lem ['prɒbləm] Problem *n*; *math. etc.* Aufgabe *f*; ~**at·ic** [prɒblə'mætɪk] (~**ally**), ~**at·i·cal** problematisch

pro·ce·dure [prə'siːdʒə] Verfahren(sweise *f*) *n*, Vorgehen *n*

pro·ceed [prə'siːd] (weiter)gehen, (-)fahren; sich begeben (**to** nach, zu); *fig.* weitergehen (*Handlung etc.*); *fig.* fortfahren; *fig.* vorgehen; ~ **from** kommen *od.* herrühren von; ~ **to do s.th.** sich anschicken *od.* daranmachen, et. zu tun; ~**ing** Verfahren *n*, Vorgehen *n*; ~**ings** *pl.* Vorgänge *pl.*, Geschehnisse *pl.*; **start** *od.* **take** (**legal**) ~ **against** *jur.* (gerichtlich) vorgehen gegen

pro·ceeds ['prəʊsiːdz] *pl.* Erlös *m*, Ertrag *m*, Einnahmen *pl.*

pro·cess ['prəʊses] **1.** Prozeß *m*, Verfahren *n*, Vorgang *m*; △ *nicht jur.* **Prozeß; in the** ~ dabei; **be in** ~ im Gange sein; **in** ~ **of construction** im Bau (befindlich); **2.** *tech. etc.* bearbeiten, behandeln; *Daten* verarbeiten; *Film* entwickeln; △ *nicht* **prozessieren**

pro·ces·sion [prə'seʃn] Prozession *f*

pro·ces·sor ['prəʊsesə] *Computer:* Prozessor *m*; (*Wort-, Text*)Verarbeitungsgerät *n*

pro·claim [prə'kleɪm] proklamieren, ausrufen

proc·la·ma·tion [prɒklə'meɪʃn] Proklamation *f*, Bekanntmachung *f*

pro·cure [prə'kjʊə] (sich) *et.* beschaffen *od.* besorgen; Daten verarbeiten; *Film* entwickeln

prod [prɒd] **1.** (*-dd-*) stoßen; *fig.* anstacheln, ansporn (**into** zu); **2.** Stoß *m*

prod·i·gal ['prɒdɪgl] **1.** verschwenderisch; **2.** F Verschwender(in)

pro·di·gious [prə'dɪdʒəs] erstaunlich, großartig, ungeheuer

prod·i·gy ['prɒdɪdʒɪ] Wunder n; **child ~** Wunderkind n

pro·duce¹ [prə'djuːs] produzieren; econ. Waren produzieren, herstellen, erzeugen; hervorziehen, -holen (**from** aus); vorzeigen, -legen; Beweise etc. beibringen; econ. Gewinn etc. bringen; Film produzieren; Theaterstück etc. inszenieren; fig. erzeugen, hervorrufen, Wirkung erzielen

prod·uce² ['prɒdjuːs] bsd. (Agrar)Produkt(e pl.) n, (-)Erzeugnis(se pl.) n

pro·duc·er [prə'djuːsə] Produzent(in), Hersteller(in); Film, TV: Produzent(in); thea. Regisseur(in)

prod·uct ['prɒdʌkt] Produkt n, Erzeugnis n

pro·duc·tion [prə'dʌkʃn] Erzeugung f; Produkt n, Erzeugnis n; econ. Produktion f, Herstellung f, Erzeugung f; Hervorziehen n, -holen n; Vorzeigen n, -legen n; Beibringung f (von Beweisen etc.); Film: Produktion f; thea. Inszenierung f; **~·tive** [prə'dʌktɪv] produktiv (a. fig.), ergiebig, rentabel; fig. schöpferisch; **~·tiv·i·ty** [prɒdʌk'tɪvəti] Produktivität f

prof F [prɒf] Prof m (Professor)

pro·fa·na·tion [prɒfə'neɪʃn] Entweihung f; **~·fane** [prə'feɪn] **1.** (gottes)lästerlich; profan, weltlich; **2.** entweihen; **~·fan·i·ty** [prə'fænəti]: **profanities** pl. Flüche pl., Lästerungen pl.

pro·fess [prə'fes] vorgeben, -täuschen; behaupten (**to be** zu sein); erklären; **~ed** [prə'fest] erklärt (Gegner etc.); angeblich

pro·fes·sion [prə'feʃn] (bsd. akademischer) Beruf; Berufsstand m; **~·sion·al** [prə'feʃənl] **1.** Berufs..., beruflich; Fach..., fachlich; fachmännisch; professionell; **2.** Fachmann m, Profi m; Berufsspieler(in), -sportler(in), Profi m; **~·sor** [prə'fesə] Professor(in); Am. Dozent(in)

pro·fi·cien·cy [prə'fɪʃnsi] Können n, Tüchtigkeit f; **~t** [prə'fɪʃnt] tüchtig (**at**, **in** in dat.)

pro·file ['prəʊfaɪl] Profil n

prof·it ['prɒfɪt] **1.** Gewinn m, Profit m; Vorteil m, Nutzen m; **2.** **~ by**, **~ from** Nutzen ziehen aus, profitieren von; **~·i·ta·ble** gewinnbringend, einträglich; nützlich, vorteilhaft; **~·i·teer**

contp. [prɒfi'tɪə] Profitmacher(in); **~·it shar·ing** Gewinnbeteiligung f

prof·li·gate ['prɒflɪgət] verschwenderisch

pro·found [prə'faʊnd] tief (Eindruck, Schweigen etc.); tiefgründig; profund (Wissen etc.)

pro·fuse [prə'fjuːs] (über)reich; verschwenderisch; **~·fu·sion** [prə'fjuːʒn] Überfülle f; **in ~** in Hülle u. Fülle

prog·e·ny ['prɒdʒəni] Nachkommen(schaft f) pl.

prog·no·sis med. [prɒg'nəʊsɪs] (pl. **-ses** [-sɪːz]) Prognose f

pro·gram ['prəʊgræm] **1.** Computer: Programm n; Am. → **programme** 1; **2.** (**-mm-**) Computer: programmieren; Am. → **programme** 2; '**~·er** → **programmer**

pro·gramme Brt., **pro·gram** Am. ['prəʊgræm] **1.** Programm n; Rundfunk, TV: a. Sendung f; **2.** (vor)programmieren; planen; '**pro·gram·mer** Computer: Programmierer(in)

pro·gress 1. ['prəʊgres] Fortschritt(e pl.) m; **make slow ~** (nur) langsam vorankommen; **be in ~** im Gange sein; **2.** [prəʊ'gres] fortschreiten; Fortschritte machen; **~·gres·sive** [prəʊ'gresɪv] progressiv, fortschreitend; fortschrittlich

pro·hib·it [prə'hɪbɪt] verbieten; verhindern; **~·hi·bi·tion** [prəʊɪ'bɪʃn] Verbot n; **~·hib·i·tive** [prə'hɪbɪtɪv] unerschwinglich (Preis); Schutz... (Zoll etc.)

proj·ect¹ ['prɒdʒekt] Projekt n, Vorhaben n

pro·ject² [prə'dʒekt] v/i. vorspringen, -ragen, -stehen; v/t. werfen, schleudern; planen; projizieren

pro·jec·tile [prə'dʒektaɪl] Projektil n, Geschoß n

pro·jec·tion [prə'dʒekʃn] Vorsprung m, vorspringender Teil; Werfen n, Schleudern n; Planung f; Projektion f; **~·tor** [prə'dʒektə] Projektor m

pro·le·tar·i·an [prəʊlɪ'teərɪən] **1.** proletarisch; **2.** Proletarier(in)

pro·lif·ic [prə'lɪfɪk] (**~ally**) fruchtbar

pro·logue bsd. Brt., **pro·log** Am. ['prəʊlɒg] Prolog m

pro·long [prəʊ'lɒŋ] verlängern

prom·e·nade [prɒmə'nɑːd] **1.**

(Strand)Promenade f; **2.** promenieren

prom·i·nent ['prɒmɪnənt] vorspringend, -stehend; *fig.* prominent

pro·mis·cu·ous [prə'mɪskjʊəs] sexuell freizügig

prom|·ise ['prɒmɪs] **1.** Versprechen n; *fig.* Aussicht f; **2.** versprechen; '**~-is·ing** vielversprechend

prom·on·to·ry ['prɒməntrɪ] Vorgebirge n

pro|·mote [prə'məʊt] *j-n* befördern; *Schule:* versetzen; *econ.* werben für; *Boxkampf, Konzert etc.* veranstalten; *et.* förden; (**be ~d** *Sport: bsd. Brt.* aufsteigen (**to** in *acc.*); **~·mot·er** [prə'məʊtə] Promoter(in), Veranstalter(in); Verkaufsförderer m; **~·mo·tion** [prə'məʊʃn] Beförderung f; *Schule:* Versetzung f, *Sport:* Aufstieg m; *econ.* Verkaufsförderung f, Werbung f; △ *nicht* **Promotion**

prompt [prɒmpt] **1.** führen zu, *Gefühle etc.* wecken; *j-n* veranlassen (**to** dazu zu tun); *j-m* ein-, vorsagen; *thea. j-m* souflieren; **2.** prompt, umgehend, unverzüglich; pünktlich; '**~·er** *thea.* Souffleu|r m, -se f

prone [prəʊn] (**~r, ~st**) auf dem Bauch *od.* mit dem Gesicht nach unten liegend; **be ~ to** *fig.* neigen zu, anfällig sein für

prong [prɒŋ] Zinke f; (Geweih)Sprosse f

pro·noun *gr.* ['prəʊnaʊn] Pronomen n, Fürwort n

pro·nounce [prə'naʊns] aussprechen; erklären für; *jur.* Urteil verkünden

pron·to F ['prɒntəʊ] fix, schnell

pro·nun·ci·a·tion [prənʌnsɪ'eɪʃn] Aussprache f

proof [pruːf] **1.** Beweis(e pl.) m, Nachweis m; Probe f; *print.* Korrekturfahne f; *print., phot.* Probeabzug m; **2.** *adj. in Zssgn* ...fest, ...beständig, ...dicht, ...sicher; → **heatproof, soundproof, waterproof; be ~ against** geschützt sein vor (*dat.*); **3.** imprägnieren; **~·read** ['pruːfriːd] (-**read** [-red]) Korrektur lesen; '**~·read·er** Korrektor(in)

prop [prɒp] **1.** Stütze f (a. *fig.*); **2.** (-**pp**-) a. **~ up** stützen; *sich od. et.* lehnen (**against** gegen)

prop·a|·gate ['prɒpəgeɪt] *biol.* sich fortpflanzen *od.* vermehren; verbreiten; **~·ga·tion** [prɒpə'geɪʃn] Fortpflanzung

f, Vermehrung f; Verbreitung f

pro·pel [prə'pel] (-**ll**-) (vorwärts-, an)treiben; **~·lant, ~·lent** Treibstoff m; Treibgas n; **~·ler** *aviat.* Propeller m, *naut. a.* Schraube f; **~·ling 'pen·cil** Drehbleistift m

pro·pen·si·ty *fig.* [prə'pensətɪ] Neigung f

prop·er ['prɒpə] richtig, passend, geeignet; anständig, schicklich; echt, wirklich, richtig; eigentlich; eigen(tümlich); *bsd. Brt.* F ordentlich, tüchtig, gehörig; **~ 'name, ~ 'noun** Eigenname m

prop·er·ty ['prɒpətɪ] Eigentum n, Besitz m; Land-, Grundbesitz m; Grundstück n; Eigenschaft f

proph|·e·cy ['prɒfɪsɪ] Prophezeiung f; **~·e·sy** ['prɒfɪsaɪ] prophezeien; **~·et** ['prɒfɪt] Prophet m

pro·por·tion [prə'pɔːʃn] **1.** Verhältnis n; (An)Teil m; **~s** pl. Größenverhältnisse pl., Proportionen pl.; **in ~ to** im Verhältnis zu; **2.** (**to**) in das richtige Verhältnis bringen (mit, zu); anpassen (*dat.*); **~·al** [prə'pɔːʃənl] proportional; → **~·ate** [prə'pɔːʃnət] (**to**) im richtigen Verhältnis (zu), entsprechend (*dat.*)

pro·pos|·al [prə'pəʊzl] Vorschlag m; (Heirats)Antrag m; **~e** [prə'pəʊz] v/t. vorschlagen; beabsichtigen, vorhaben; *Toast* ausbringen (**to** auf *acc.*); **~ s.o.'s health** auf j-s Gesundheit trinken; v/i. **~ to** *j-m* e-n (Heirats)Antrag machen; **prop·o·si·tion** [prɒpə'zɪʃn] Behauptung f; Vorschlag m, *econ. a.* Angebot n

pro·pri·e·ta·ry [prə'praɪətrɪ] *econ.* gesetzlich *od.* patentrechtlich geschützt; *fig.* besitzergreifend; **~·tor** [prə'praɪətə] Eigentümer m, Besitzer m, Geschäftsinhaber m; **~·tress** [prə'praɪətrɪs] Eigentümerin f, Besitzerin f, Geschäftsinhaberin f

pro·pri·e·ty [prə'praɪətɪ] Anstand m; Richtigkeit f

pro·pul·sion *tech.* [prə'pʌlʃn] Antrieb m

pro·sa·ic [prəʊ'zeɪɪk] (**~ally**) prosaisch, nüchtern, sachlich

prose [prəʊz] Prosa f

pros·e|·cute *jur.* ['prɒsɪkjuːt] strafrechtlich verfolgen, (gerichtlich) belangen (**for** wegen); **~·cu·tion** *jur.* [prɒsɪ-'kjuːʃn] strafrechtliche Verfolgung, Strafverfolgung f; **the ~** die Staatsanwaltschaft, die Anklage(behörde); **~cu·tor** *jur.* ['prɒsɪkjuːtə] *a.* **public ~** Staatsanwalt *m*, -anwältin *f*

pros·pect 1. ['prɒspekt] Aussicht *f* (*a. fig.*); Interessent *m*, *econ.* möglicher Kunde, potentieller Käufer; △ *nicht* **Prospekt**; **2.** [prə'spekt]: **~ for** Bergbau: schürfen nach; bohren nach (*Öl*)

pro·spec·tive [prə'spektɪv] voraussichtlich

pro·spec·tus [prə'spektəs] (*pl.* **-tuses**) (Werbe)Prospekt *m*

pros·per ['prɒspə] gedeihen; *econ.* blühen, florieren; **~·i·ty** [prɒ'sperətɪ] Wohlstand *m*; **~ous** ['prɒspərəs] *econ.* erfolgreich, blühend, florierend; wohlhabend

pros·ti·tute ['prɒstɪtjuːt] Prostituierte *f*, Dirne *f*; **male ~** Strichjunge *m*

pros·trate 1. ['prɒstreɪt] hingestreckt; *fig.* am Boden liegend; erschöpft; **~ with grief** grambeugt; **2.** [prɒ'streɪt] niederwerfen; *fig.* erschöpfen; *fig.* niederschmettern; **~·tra·tion** [prɒ'streɪʃn] Fußfall *m*; *fig.* Erschöpfung *f*

pros·y ['prəʊzɪ] (**-ier, -iest**) langweilig; weitschweifig

pro·tag·o·nist [prəʊ'tægənɪst] Vorkämpfer(in); *thea.* Hauptfigur *f*, Held(in)

pro·tect [prə'tekt] (be)schützen (**from** vor *dat.*; **against** gegen)

pro·tec·tion [prə'tekʃn] Schutz *m*; △ *nicht* **Protektion**; **~ of endangered species** Artenschutz *m*; **~ mon·ey** Schutzgeld *m*; **~ rack·et** Schutzgelderpressung *f*

pro·tec·tive [prə'tektɪv] (be)schützend; Schutz...; **~ 'cloth·ing** Schutzkleidung *f*; **~ 'cus·to·dy** *jur.* Schutzhaft *f*; **~ 'du·ty, ~ 'tar·iff** *econ.* Schutzzoll *m*

pro·tec·tor [prə'tektə] Beschützer *m*; (Brust- *etc.*)Schutz *m*; **~ate** [prə'tektərət] Protektorat *n*

pro·test 1. ['prəʊtest] Protest *m*; Einspruch *m*; **2.** [prə'test] *v/i.* protestieren (**against** gegen); *v/t. Am.* protestieren gegen; beteuern

Prot·es·tant ['prɒtɪstənt] **1.** protestantisch; **2.** Protestant(in)

prot·es·ta·tion [prɒte'steɪʃn] Beteuerung *f*; Protest *m* (**against** gegen)

pro·to·col ['prəʊtəkɒl] Protokoll *n*

pro·to·type ['prəʊtətaɪp] Prototyp *m*

pro·tract [prə'trækt] in die Länge ziehen, hinziehen

pro·trude [prə'truːd] herausragen, vorstehen (**from** aus); **~'trud·ing** vorstehend (*a. Zähne*), vorspringend (*Kinn*)

proud [praʊd] stolz (**of** auf *acc.*)

prove [pruːv] (**proved, proved** *od. bsd. Am.* **proven**) *v/t.* be-, er-, nachweisen; *v/i.* **~ (to be)** sich herausstellen *od.* erweisen als; **prov·en** ['pruːvən] **1.** *bsd. Am. p.p. von* **prove; 2.** bewährt

prov·erb ['prɒvɜːb] Sprichwort *n*

pro·vide [prə'vaɪd] *v/t.* versehen, -sorgen, beliefern; zur Verfügung stellen, bereitstellen; vorsehen, -schreiben (**that** daß) (*Gesetz etc.*); *v/i.* **~ against** Vorkehrungen *od.* Vorsorge treffen gegen; verbieten (*Gesetz etc.*); **~ for** sorgen für; vorsorgen für; *et.* vorsehen (*Gesetz etc.*); **pro·vid·ed:** **~ (that)** vorausgesetzt(, daß)

prov·i·dent ['prɒvɪdənt] vorausblickend, vorsorglich

pro·vid·er [prə'vaɪdə] Ernährer(in)

prov·ince ['prɒvɪns] Provinz *f*; *fig.* Gebiet *n*, (Aufgaben-, Wissens)Bereich *m*;

pro·vin·cial [prə'vɪnʃl] **1.** Provinz..., provinziell, provinzlerisch; **2.** *contp.* Provinzler(in)

pro·vi·sion [prə'vɪʒn] Bereitstellung *f*, Beschaffung *f*; Vorkehrung *f*, Vorsorge *f*; Bestimmung *f*, Vorschrift *f*; **with the ~ that** unter der Bedingung, daß; **~s** *pl.* Proviant *m*, Verpflegung *f*; △ *nicht* **Provision; ~al** [prə'vɪʒənl] provisorisch, vorläufig

pro·vi·so [prə'vaɪzəʊ] (*pl.* **-sos**) Bedingung *f*, Vorbehalt *m*; **with the ~ that** unter der Bedingung, daß

prov·o·ca·tion [prɒvə'keɪʃn] Provokation *f*; **pro·voc·a·tive** [prə'vɒkətɪv] provozierend, (*a. sexuell*) aufreizend

pro·voke [prə'vəʊk] provozieren, reizen

pro·vost ['prɒvəst] Rektor *m* (*gewisser Colleges*); *schott.* Bürgermeister(in)

prowl [praʊl] **1.** *v/i. a.* **~ about, ~ around** herumschleichen, -streifen; *v/t.* durchstreifen; **2.** Herumstreifen *n*; **'~ car** *Am.* (Funk)Streifenwagen *m*

prox·im·i·ty [prɒk'sɪmətɪ] Nähe *f*

prox·y ['prɒksɪ] (Handlungs)Vollmacht *f*; (Stell)Vertreter(in), Bevollmächtigte(r *m*) *f*; **by ~** durch e-n Bevollmächtigten

P

prude [pru:d]: *be a ~* prüde sein (*bsd. ältere Frau*)

pru|dence ['pru:dns] Klugheit *f*, Vernunft *f*; Besonnenheit *f*; '**~·dent** klug, vernünftig; besonnen

'prud·ish prüde

prune¹ [pru:n] (be)schneiden (*Bäume etc.*)

prune² [pru:n] Backpflaume *f*

pry¹ [prai] neugierig sein; *~ about* herumschnüffeln; *~ into* s-e Nase stecken in (*acc.*)

pry² *bsd. Am.* [prai] → *prize*²

PS [pi: 'es] *Abk. für postscript* PS, Postskript(um) *n*, Nachschrift *f*

psalm [sa:m] Psalm *m*

pseu·do·nym ['sju:dənɪm] Pseudonym *n*, Deckname *m*

psy·chi·a·trist [saɪˈkaɪətrɪst] Psychiater(in); **~·try** [saɪˈkaɪətrɪ] Psychiatrie *f*

psy|·cho·log·i·cal [saɪkəˈlɒdʒɪkl] psychologisch; **~·chol·o·gist** [saɪˈkɒlədʒɪst] Psycholog|e *m*, -in *f*; **~·chol·o·gy** [saɪˈkɒlədʒɪ] Psychologie *f*; **~·cho·so·mat·ic** [saɪkəʊsəʊˈmætɪk] (*~ally*) psychosomatisch

pt *nur geschr. Abk. für*: *part* T., Teil *m*; *pint* Pint *n* (*etwa 1/2 l*); *mst Pt für port* Hafen *m*

PT *bsd. Brt.* [pi: 'ti:] *Abk. für physical training* Leibeserziehung *f*, Sport *m*

PTO, pto [pi: ti: 'əʊ] *Abk. für please turn over* b.w., bitte wenden

pub *Brt.* [pʌb] Pub *n*, Kneipe *f*

pu·ber·ty ['pju:bətɪ] Pubertät *f*

pu·bic *anat.* ['pju:bɪk] Scham...; **~** '**bone** Schambein *n*; **~** '**hair** Schamhaare *pl.*

pub·lic ['pʌblɪk] **1.** öffentlich; allgemein bekannt; **2.** Öffentlichkeit *f*; *die* Öffentlichkeit, *das* Publikum; △ *nicht Publikum* (→ *audience*)

pub·li·ca·tion [pʌblɪˈkeɪʃn] Bekanntgabe *f*, -machung *f*; Publikation *f*, Veröffentlichung *f*

pub·lic| con·ve·ni·ence *Brt.* öffentliche Bedürfnisanstalt; **~** '**health** öffentliches Gesundheitswesen; **~** '**hol·i·day** gesetzlicher Feiertag; **~** '**house** *Brt.* → **pub**

pub·lic·i·ty [pʌbˈlɪsətɪ] Publicity *f*, Bekanntheit *f*; Publicity *f*, Reklame *f*, Werbung *f*

pub·lic| 'li·bra·ry Leihbücherei *f*; **~**

re·'la·tions *pl.* (*Abk. PR*) Public Relations *pl.*, Öffentlichkeitsarbeit *f*; **~** '**school** *Brt.* Public School *f* (*exklusives Internat*); *Am.* staatliche Schule; **~** '**trans·port** *bsd. Brt. sg.*, **~** '**trans·por'ta·tion** *Am. sg.* öffentliche Verkehrsmittel *pl.*

pub·lish ['pʌblɪʃ] bekanntgeben, -machen; publizieren, veröffentlichen; *Buch etc.* herausgeben, verlegen; '**~·er** Verleger(in), Herausgeber(in); Verlag(shaus *n*) *m*; '**~·er's**, '**~·ers** *pl.*, '**~·ing house** Verlag(shaus *n*) *m*

puck·er ['pʌkə] *a. ~ up* (sich) verziehen (*Gesicht, Mund*), (sich) runzeln (*Stirn*)

pud·ding ['pʊdɪŋ] *Brt.* Nachspeise *f*, -tisch *m*; (*Reis- etc.*)Auflauf *m*; (*Art*) Fleischpastete *f*; Pudding *m* (*Mehlspeise*); *black ~* Blutwurst *f*

pud·dle ['pʌdl] Pfütze *f*

pu·er·ile ['pjʊəraɪl] infantil, kindisch

puff [pʌf] **1.** *v/i.* schnaufen, keuchen; *a. ~ away* paffen (*at* an e-r *Zigarette etc.*); *~ up* (an)schwellen; *v/t. Rauch* blasen; *~ out* Kerze etc. ausblasen; *Rauch etc.* ausstoßen; *Brust* herausdrücken; **2.** Zug *m* (*beim Rauchen*); (*Luft-, Wind-*)Hauch *m*, (-)Stoß *m*; (*Puder*)Quaste *f*; F Puste *f*; '**~ed 'sleeve** Puffärmel *m*; '**pas·try** Blätterteig *m*; '**~ sleeve** Puffärmel *m*; '**~·y** (*-ier, -iest*) (an)geschwollen, verschwollen; aufgedunsen (*Gesicht*)

pug *zo.* [pʌg] *a. ~dog* Mops *m*

pug·na·cious [pʌgˈneɪʃəs] kampflustig; streitsüchtig

puke *sl.* [pju:k] (aus)kotzen

pull [pʊl] **1.** Ziehen *n*; Zug *m*, Ruck *m*; Anstieg *m*, Steigung *f*; Zuggriff *m*, Zugleine *f*; F Beziehungen *pl.*; **2.** ziehen; ziehen an (*dat.*); zerren; reißen; *Zahn* ziehen; *Pflanze* ausreißen; *Messer etc.* ziehen; *bsd. Brt. Bier* zapfen; *fig.* anziehen; *~ ahead of* vorbeiziehen an (*dat.*), überholen (*acc.*) (*Auto etc.*); *~ away* anfahren (*Bus etc.*); *~ down Gebäude* abreißen; *~ in* einfahren (*Zug*); anhalten; *~ off* F zustande bringen, schaffen; *~ out* herausziehen (*of* aus); *Tisch* ausziehen; abfahren (*Zug etc.*); ausscheren (*Fahrzeug*); *fig.* sich zurückziehen, aussteigen (*of* aus); *~ over* (s-n Wagen) an die *od.* zur Seite fahren; *~ round Kranken* durchbringen; durchkommen (*Kranker*); ~ **through** *j-n* durchbringen; ~ **o.s. together** sich zusammennehmen, sich zusammenreißen; ~ **up** *Fahrzeug* anhalten; (an)halten; ~ **up to,** ~ **up with** *Sport:* *j-n* einholen

'**pull date** *Am.* Mindesthaltbarkeitsdatum *n* (*für Lebensmittel*)

pul·ley *tech.* ['pʊlɪ] Flaschenzug *m*

'**pull-in** *Brt.* F Raststätte *f*, -haus *n*; '**~·o·ver** Pullover *m*; '**~·up** *Brt.* Klimmzug *m*; **do a ~** e-n Klimmzug machen

pulp [pʌlp] Fruchtfleisch *n*; Brei *m*; Schund...; **~ novel** Schundroman *m*

pul·pit ['pʊlpɪt] Kanzel *f*

pulp·y ['pʌlpɪ] (*-ier, -iest*) breiig

pul·sate [pʌl'seɪt] pulsieren, vibrieren

pulse [pʌls] Puls(schlag) *m*

pul·ver·ize ['pʌlvəraɪz] pulverisieren

pu·ma *zo.* ['pju:mə] Puma *m*

pum·mel ['pʌml] (*bsd. Brt.* **-ll-,** *Am.* **-l-**) mit den Fäusten bearbeiten

pump [pʌmp] **1.** Pumpe *f*; (*Zapf*)Säule *f*; **2.** pumpen; F *j-n* aushorchen; ~ **up** aufpumpen; '**~·at·tend·ant** Tankwart *m*

pump·kin *bot.* ['pʌmpkɪn] Kürbis *m*

pun [pʌn] **1.** Wortspiel *n*; **2.** (*-nn-*) Wortspiele *od.* ein Wortspiel machen

punch[1] [pʌntʃ] **1.** (mit der Faust) schlagen, boxen; **2.** (Faust)Schlag *m*

punch[2] [pʌntʃ] **1.** lochen; Loch stanzen (**in** *in acc.*); ~ **in** *bsd. Am.* einstempeln; ~ **out** *bsd. Am.* ausstempeln; **2.** Locher *m*; Lochzange *f*; Locheisen *n*

punch[3] [pʌntʃ] Punsch *m*

Punch [pʌntʃ] *etwa* Kasper *m*, Kasperle *n*, *m*; **be as pleased** *od.* **proud as ~** sich freuen wie ein Schneekönig; **~ and Judy show** [pʌntʃ ən 'dʒu:dɪ ʃəʊ] Kasperletheater *n*

'**punch card, punched 'card** Lochkarte *f*

punc·tu·al ['pʌŋktʃʊəl] pünktlich

punc·tu·ate ['pʌŋktʃʊeɪt] interpunktieren; **~·a·tion** [pʌŋktʃʊ'eɪʃn] Interpunktion *f*; **~·a·tion mark** Satzzeichen *n*

punc·ture ['pʌŋktʃə] **1.** (Ein)Stich *m*, Loch *n*; *mot.* Reifenpanne *f*; **2.** durchstechen, -bohren; ein Loch bekommen, platzen; *mot.* e-n Platten haben

pun·gent ['pʌndʒənt] scharf, stechend, beißend (*Geschmack, Geruch*); scharf, bissig (*Bemerkung etc.*)

pun·ish ['pʌnɪʃ] *j-n* (be)strafen; '**~·a·ble** strafbar; '**~·ment** Strafe *f*; Bestrafung *f*

punk [pʌŋk] Punk *m* (*Bewegung*); Punk(er) *m*; *mus.* Punk *m*; ~ '**rock** *mus.* Punkrock *m*

pu·ny ['pju:nɪ] (*-ier, -iest*) schwächlich

pup *zo.* [pʌp] Welpe *m*, junger Hund

pu·pa ['pju:pə] (*pl.* **-pae** [-pi:], **-pas**) Puppe *f*

pu·pil[1] ['pju:pl] Schüler(in)

pu·pil[2] *anat.* ['pju:pl] Pupille *f*

pup·pet ['pʌpɪt] Handpuppe *f*; Marionette *f* (*a. fig.*); △ *nicht* **Puppe** (→ **doll**); '**~ show** Marionettentheater *n*, Puppenspiel *n*; **pup·pe·teer** [pʌpɪ'tɪə] Puppenspieler(in)

pup·py *zo.* ['pʌpɪ] Welpe *m*, junger Hund

pur·chase ['pɜ:tʃəs] **1.** kaufen; *fig.* erkaufen; **2.** Kauf *m*; **make ~s** Einkäufe machen; '**~·chas·er** Käufer(in)

pure [pjʊə] (**~r, ~st**) rein; pur; '**~·bred** reinrassig

pur·ga·tive *med.* ['pɜ:gətɪv] **1.** abführend; **2.** Abführmittel *n*

pur·ga·to·ry ['pɜ:gətərɪ] Fegefeuer *n*

purge [pɜ:dʒ] **1.** *Partei etc.* säubern (**of** von); **2.** Säuberung(saktion) *f*

pu·ri·fy ['pjʊərɪfaɪ] reinigen

pu·ri·tan ['pjʊərɪtən] (*hist.* 2) **1.** Puritaner(in); **2.** puritanisch

pu·ri·ty ['pjʊərɪtɪ] Reinheit *f*

purl [pɜ:l] **1.** linke Masche; **2.** links stricken

pur·loin [pɜ:'lɔɪn] entwenden

pur·ple ['pɜ:pl] purpurn, purpurrot

pur·pose ['pɜ:pəs] **1.** Absicht *f*, Vorsatz *m*; Zweck *m*, Ziel *n*; Entschlossenheit *f*; **on ~** absichtlich; **to no ~** vergeblich; **2.** beabsichtigen, vorhaben; '**~·ful** entschlossen, zielstrebig; '**~·less** zwecklos; ziellos; '**~·ly** absichtlich

purr [pɜ:] schnurren (*Katze*); summen, surren (*Motor*)

purse[1] [pɜ:s] Geldbeutel *m*, -börse *f*, Portemonnaie *n*; *Am.* Handtasche *f*; *Sport:* Siegprämie *f*; *Boxen:* Börse *f*

purse[2] [pɜ:s]: ~ (**up**) **one's lips** die Lippen schürzen

pur·su·ance [pə'sju:əns]: **in (the) ~ of his duty** in Ausübung s-r Pflicht

pur|·sue [pə'sju:] verfolgen; *s-m Studium etc.* nachgehen; *Absicht, Politik*

P

etc. verfolgen; *Angelegenheit etc.* weiterführen; **~'su·er** Verfolger(in); **~'suit** [pə'sjuːt] Verfolgung *f*; Weiterführung *f*

pur·vey [pə'veɪ] *Lebensmittel etc.* liefern; **~or** Lieferant *m*

pus *med.* [pʌs] Eiter *m*

push [pʊʃ] **1.** stoßen, schubsen, schieben; *Taste etc.* drücken; drängen; (an)treiben; F *Rauschgift* pushen; *fig. j-n* drängen (**to do** *to zu tun*); *fig.* Reklame machen für; **~ one's way** sich drängen (**through** durch); **~ ahead with** *Plan etc.* vorantreiben; **~ along** F sich auf die Socken machen; **~ around** F herumschubsen; **~ for** drängen auf (*acc.*); **~ forward with** → **push ahead with**; **o.s. forward** *fig.* sich in den Vordergrund drängen *od.* schieben; **~ in** F sich vordrängeln; **~ off!** F hau ab!; **~ on with** → **push ahead with**; **~ out** *fig. j-n* hinausdrängen; **~ through** *et.* durchsetzen; **~ up** *Preise etc.* hochtreiben; **2.** Stoß *m*, Schubs *m*; (*Werbe*)Kampage *f*; F Durchsetzungsvermögen *n*, Energie *f*, Tatkraft *f*; **'~ but·ton** *tech.* Druckknopf *m*, -taste *f*; **'~-but·ton** *tech.* (Druck)Knopf..., (-)Tasten...; **~ (tele-) phone** Tastentelefon *n*; **'~-chair** *Brt.* Sportwagen *m* (*für Kinder*); **'~er** *contp.* Pusher *m* (*Rauschgifthändler*); **'~-o·ver** F Kinderspiel *n*, Kleinigkeit *f*; **'~-up** *Am.* → **press-up**

puss F [pʊs] Mieze *f*

'pus·sy *a.* **~cat** Miezekatze *f*; **'~-foot** F: **~ about, ~ around** leisetreten, sich nicht festlegen wollen

put [pʊt] (*-tt-; put*) legen, setzen, stecken, stellen, tun; *j-n in e-e Lage etc.*, *et. auf den Markt*, *in Ordnung etc.* bringen; *et. in Kraft*, *in Umlauf etc.* setzen; *Sport: Kugel* stoßen; unterwerfen, -ziehen (**to** *dat.*); *et.* ausdrücken, *in Worte* fassen; übersetzen (**into German** *ins Deutsche*); *Schuld* geben (**on** *dat.*); **~ right** *in Ordnung* bringen; **~ s.th. before s.o.** *fig. j-m et.* vorlegen; **~ to bed** ins Bett bringen; **~ to school** zur Schule schicken; **~ about** *Gerüchte* verbreiten, in Umlauf setzen; **~ across** *et.* verständlich machen; **~ ahead** *Sport:* in Führung bringen; **~ aside** beiseite legen; *Ware* zurücklegen; *fig.* beiseite schieben; **~ away** weglegen, -tun; *auf-,*

wegräumen; **~ back** zurücklegen, -stellen, -tun; *Uhr* zurückstellen (**by** um); **~ by** *Geld* zurücklegen; **~ down** *v/t.* hin-, niederlegen, -setzen, -stellen; *j-n* absetzen, aussteigen lassen; (auf-, nieder)schreiben, eintragen; zuschreiben (**to** *dat.*); *Aufstand* niederschlagen; (*a. v/i.*) *aviat.* landen; **~ forward** *Plan etc.* vorlegen; *Uhr* vorstellen (**by** um); *fig.* vorverlegen (**two days** *um zwei Tage*; **to** *auf acc.*); **~ in** *v/t.* herein-, hineinlegen, -stecken, -stellen; *Kassette etc.* einlegen; installieren; *Gesuch etc.* einreichen, *Forderung etc. a.* geltend machen; *Antrag* stellen; *Arbeit*, *Zeit* verbringen (**on** mit); *Bemerkung* einwerfen; *v/i. naut.* einlaufen (**at** *in acc.*); **~ off** *et.* verschieben (**until** *auf acc.*); *j-m* absagen; *j-n* hinhalten (**with** mit); *j-n* aus dem Konzept bringen; **~ on** *Kleider etc.* anziehen, *Hut*, *Brille* aufsetzen; *Licht*, *Radio etc.* anmachen, einschalten; *Sonderzug* einsetzen; *thea. Stück etc.* herausbringen; vortäuschen; F *j-n* auf den Arm nehmen; **~ on airs** sich aufspielen; **~ on weight** zunehmen; **~ out** *v/t.* heraus-, hinauslegen, -setzen, -stellen; *Hand etc.* ausstrecken; *Feuer* löschen; *Licht*, *Radio etc.* ausmachen (*a. Zigarette*), abschalten; veröffentlichen; herausgeben; *Rundfunk*, *TV*: bringen, senden; aus der Fassung bringen; verärgern; *j-m* Ungelegenheiten bereiten; sich *den Arm etc.* ver- *od.* ausrenken; *v/i. naut.* auslaufen; **~ over** → **put across**; **~ through** *tel. j-n* verbinden (**to** mit); durch-, ausführen; **~ together** zusammenbauen, -setzen, -stellen; **~ up** *v/t.* herauf-, hinauflegen, -stellen; *Hand* (hoch)heben; *Zelt etc.* aufstellen; *Gebäude* errichten; *Bild etc.* aufhängen; *Plakat*, *Bekanntmachung etc.* anschlagen; *Schirm* aufspannen; *zum Verkauf* anbieten; *Preis* erhöhen; *Widerstand* leisten; *Kampf* liefern; *j-n* unterbringen, (bei sich) aufnehmen; *v/i.* **~ up at** absteigen in (*dat.*); **~ up with** sich gefallen lassen; sich abfinden mit

pu·tre·fy ['pjuːtrɪfaɪ] (ver)faulen, verwesen

pu·trid ['pjuːtrɪd] faul, verfault, -west; F scheußlich, saumäßig

put·ty ['pʌtɪ] **1.** Kitt *m*; **2.** kitten

'put-up job F abgekartetes Spiel

puz·zle ['pʌzl] **1.** Rätsel *n*; Geduld(s)-spiel *n*; → **jigsaw (puzzle)**; **2.** *v/t.* vor ein Rätsel stellen; verwirren; **be ~d** vor e-m Rätsel stehen; **~ out** herausfinden, -bringen, austüfteln; *v/i.* sich den Kopf zerbrechen (*about, over* über *dat.*)

PX *TM* [pi: 'eks] (*pl.* **~s** [-'eksız]) *Abk. für* **post exchange** (*Verkaufsladen für Angehörige der US-Streitkräfte*)

pyg·my ['pıgmı] Pygmä|e *m*, in *f*;

Zwerg(in); *bsd. zo.* Zwerg...

py·ja·mas *Brt.* [pə'dʒɑːməz] *pl.* (**a pair of**) **~** (ein) Schlafanzug, (ein) Pyjama

py·lon ['paılən] Hochspannungsmast *m*

pyr·a·mid ['pırəmıd] Pyramide *f*

pyre ['paıə] Scheiterhaufen *m*

py·thon *zo.* ['paıθn] (*pl.* **-thons, -thon**) Python(schlange) *f*

pyx *rel.* [pıks] Hostienbehälter *m*

Q

Q, q [kjuː] Q, q *n*

qt *nur geschr. Abk. für* **quart** Quart *n* (*etwa 1 l*)

quack¹ [kwæk] **1.** quaken; **2.** Quaken *n*

quack² [kwæk] *a.* **~ doctor** Quacksalber *m*, Kurpfuscher *m*; **~·er·y** ['kwækərı] Quacksalberei *f*, Kurpfuscherei *f*

quad·ran|·gle ['kwɒdræŋgl] Viereck *n*; **~·gu·lar** [kwɒ'dræŋgjʊlə] viereckig

quad·ra·phon·ic [kwɒdrə'fɒnık] (**~ally**) quadrophon(isch)

quad·ri·lat·er·al [kwɒdrı'lætərəl] **1.** vierseitig; **2.** Viereck *n*

quad·ro·phon·ic [kwɒdrə'fɒnık] → **quadraphonic**

quad·ru·ped *zo.* ['kwɒdrʊped] Vierfüß(l)er *m*

quad·ru|·ple ['kwɒdrʊpl] **1.** vierfach; **2.** (sich) vervierfachen; **~·plets** ['kwɒdrʊplıts] *pl.* Vierlinge *pl.*

quads F [kwɒdz] Vierlinge *pl.*

quag·mire ['kwægmaıə] Morast *m*, Sumpf *m*

quail *zo.* [kweıl] (*pl.* **quail, quails**) Wachtel *f*

quaint [kweınt] idyllisch, malerisch

quake [kweık] **1.** zittern, beben (**with, for** vor *dat.*); **2.** F Erdbeben *n*

Quak·er *rel.* ['kweıkə] Quäker(in)

qual·i·fi·ca·tion [kwɒlıfı'keıʃn] Qualifikation *f*, Befähigung *f*, Eignung *f* (**for** für, zu); Voraussetzung *f*; Einschränkung *f*; **~·fied** ['kwɒlıfaıd] qualifiziert, geeignet, befähigt (**for** für); berechtigt; bedingt, eingeschränkt; **~·fy** ['kwɒlıfaı]

v/t. qualifizieren, befähigen (**for** für, zu); berechtigen (**to do** zu tun); einschränken, abschwächen, mildern; *v/i.* sich qualifizieren *od.* eignen (**for** für; **as** als); *Sport:* sich qualifizieren (**for** für); **~·ty** ['kwɒlətı] Qualität *f*; Eigenschaft *f*

qualms [kwɑːmz] *pl.* Bedenken *pl.*, Skrupel *pl.*

quan·da·ry ['kwɒndərı]: **be in a ~ about what to do** nicht wissen, was man tun soll

quan·ti·ty ['kwɒntətı] Quantität *f*, Menge *f*

quan·tum *phys.* ['kwɒntəm] (*pl.* **-ta** [-tə]) Quant *n*; Quanten...

quar·an·tine ['kwɒrəntiːn] **1.** Quarantäne *f*; **2.** unter Quarantäne stellen

quar·rel ['kwɒrəl] **1.** Streit *m*, Auseinandersetzung *f*; **2.** (*bsd. Brt.* **-ll-**, *Am.* **-l-**) (sich) streiten; **~·some** streitsüchtig

quar·ry¹ ['kwɒrı] Steinbruch *m*

quar·ry² ['kwɒrı] *hunt.* Beute *f*, *a. fig.* Opfer *n*

quart [kwɔːt] Quart *n* (*Abk.* **qt**) (*Brt. 1,14 l, Am. 0,95 l*)

quar·ter ['kwɔːtə] **1.** Viertel *n*, vierter Teil; Quartal *n*, Vierteljahr *n*; Viertelpfund *n*; *Am.* Vierteldollar *m*; *Sport:* (Spiel)Viertel *n*; (Himmels)Richtung *f*; Gegend *f*, Teil *m* e-s Landes *etc.*); (Stadt)Viertel *n*; (*bsd. Hinter*)Viertel *n* (*e-s Schlachttiers*); Gnade *f*, Pardon *m*; **~s** *pl.* Quartier *n*, Unterkunft *f* (*a. mil.*); **a ~ of an hour** e-e Viertelstunde; **a ~ to**

Q

(*Am. of*) *five Uhrzeit:* (ein) Viertel vor fünf (*4.45*); *a ~ past* (*Am. after*) *five Uhrzeit:* (ein) Viertel nach fünf (*5.15*); *at close ~s* in od. aus nächster Nähe; *from official ~s* von amtlicher Seite; **2.** vierteln; *bsd. mil.* einquartieren (*on* bei); '**~·deck** *naut.* Achterdeck *n*; **~'fi·nals** *pl. Sport:* Viertelfinale *n*; '**~·ly 1.** vierteljährlich; **2.** Vierteljahresschrift *f*

quar·tet(te) *mus.* [kwɔːˈtet] Quartett *n*

quartz *min.* [kwɔːts] Quarz *m*; **~ clock** Quarzuhr *f*; '**~ watch** Quarz(armband)uhr *f*

qua·ver ['kweɪvə] **1.** zittern (*Stimme*); *et.* mit zitternder Stimme sagen; **2.** Zittern *n*

quay *naut.* [kiː] Kai *m*

quea·sy ['kwiːzɪ] (*-ier, -iest*) empfindlich (*Magen*); *I feel ~* mir ist übel

queen [kwiːn] Königin *f*; *Karten, Schach:* Dame *f*; *sl.* Schwule(r) *m*, Homo *m*; **~ 'bee** *zo.* Bienenkönigin *f*; '**~·ly** wie e-e Königin, königlich

queer [kwɪə] komisch, seltsam; F wunderlich; F schwul

quench [kwentʃ] *Durst* löschen, stillen

quer·u·lous ['kwerʊləs] nörglerisch

que·ry ['kwɪərɪ] **1.** Frage *f*; Zweifel *m*; **2.** in Frage stellen, in Zweifel ziehen

quest [kwest] **1.** Suche *f* (*for* nach); *in ~ of* auf der Suche nach; **2.** suchen (*after, for* nach)

ques·tion ['kwestʃən] **1.** Frage *f*; Frage *f*, Problem *n*; Frage *f*, Sache *f*; Frage *f*, Zweifel *m*; *only a ~ of time* nur e-e Frage der Zeit; *this is not the point in ~* darum geht es nicht; *there is no ~ that, it is beyond ~ that* es steht außerFrage, daß; *there is no ~ about this* daran besteht kein Zweifel; *be out of the ~* nicht in Frage kommen; **2.** befragen (*about* über *acc.*); *jur.* vernehmen, -hören (*about* zu); bezweifeln, in Zweifel ziehen, in Frage stellen; '**~·a·ble** fraglich, zweifelhaft; fragwürdig; '**~·er** Fragesteller(in); '**~ mark** Fragezeichen *n*; '**~ mas·ter** *bsd. Brt.* Quizmaster *m*

ques·tion·naire [kwestʃəˈneə] Fragebogen *m*

queue *bsd. Brt.* [kjuː] **1.** Schlange *f*; **2.** *mst ~ up* Schlange stehen, anstehen, sich anstellen

quib·ble ['kwɪbl] sich herumstreiten (*with* mit; *about, over* wegen)

quick [kwɪk] **1.** *adj.* schnell, rasch; aufbrausend, hitzig (*Temperament*); *be ~!* mach schnell!, beeil dich!; **2.** *adv.* schnell, rasch; *cut s.o. to the ~ fig.* j-n tief verletzen; '**~·en** (sich) beschleunigen; '**~·freeze** (*-froze, -frozen*) *Lebensmittel* schnell einfrieren; **~·ie** F ['kwɪkɪ] *et. Schnelles od. Kurzes, z.B.* kurze Frage, Tasse *f* Tee auf die Schnelle *etc.*; '**~·ly** schnell, rasch; '**~·sand** Treibsand *m*; **~·'tem·pered** aufbrausend, hitzig; **~·'wit·ted** geistesgegenwärtig; schlagfertig

quid *Brt. sl.* [kwɪd] (*pl. ~*) Pfund *n* (*Währung*)

qui·et ['kwaɪət] **1.** ruhig, still; *~, please* Ruhe, bitte; *be ~!* sei still!; **2.** Ruhe *f*, Stille *f*; *on the ~* F heimlich; **3.** *bsd. Am.* → *~·en bsd. Brt.* ['kwaɪətn] *v/t. a. ~ down* j-n beruhigen; *v/i. a. ~ down* sich beruhigen; '**~·ness** Ruhe *f*, Stille *f*

quill [kwɪl] *zo.* (Schwung-, Schwanz)Feder *f*; *zo.* Stachel *m*; **~ ('pen)** Federkiel *m*

quilt [kwɪlt] Steppdecke *f*; '**~·ed** Stepp...

quince *bot.* [kwɪns] Quitte *f*

qui·nine *pharm.* [kwɪˈniːn] Chinin *n*

quins *Brt.* F [kwɪnz] Fünflinge *pl.*

quin·tes·sence [kwɪnˈtesns] Quintessenz *f*; Inbegriff *m*

quin·tet(te) *mus.* [kwɪnˈtet] Quintett *n*

quints *Am.* F [kwɪnts] Fünflinge *pl.*

quin·tu·ple ['kwɪntjʊpl] **1.** fünffach; **2.** (sich) verfünffachen; **~·plets** ['kwɪntjʊplɪts] *pl.* Fünflinge *pl.*

quip [kwɪp] **1.** geistreiche *od.* witzige Bemerkung; **2.** (*-pp-*) witzeln, spötteln

quirk [kwɜːk] Eigenart *f*, Schrulle *f*; *by some ~ of fate* durch e-e Laune des Schicksals, durch e-n verrückten Zufall

quit F [kwɪt] (*-tt-*; *Brt. ~ od. ~ted*, *Am. mst ~*) *v/t.* aufhören mit; *~ one's job* kündigen; *v/i.* aufhören; kündigen

quite [kwaɪt] ganz, völlig; ziemlich; *~ a few* ziemlich viele; *~ nice* ganz nett, recht nett; *~ (so)!* *bsd. Brt.* genau, ganz recht; *be ~ right* völlig recht haben; *she's ~ a beauty* sie ist e-e wirkliche Schönheit

quits F [kwɪts] quitt (*with* mit); *call it ~* es gut sein lassen

quit·ter F ['kwɪtə]: *be a ~* schnell aufgeben

quiv·er¹ ['kwɪvə] zittern (**with** vor *dat.*; *at* bei)

quiv·er² ['kwɪvə] Köcher *m*

quiz [kwɪz] **1.** (*pl.* **quizzes**) Quiz *n*; *bsd. Am.* Prüfung *f*, Test *m*; **2.** (**-zz-**) ausfragen (**about** über *acc.*); '**~·mas·ter** *bsd. Am.* Quizmaster *m*; **~·zi·cal** ['kwɪzɪkl] spöttisch-fragend (*Blick etc.*)

quo·ta ['kwəʊtə] Quote *f*, Kontingent *n*

quo·ta·tion [kwəʊ'teɪʃn] Zitat *n*; *econ.* Notierung *f*; *econ.* Kostenvoranschlag *m*; **~ marks** *pl.* Anführungszeichen *pl.*

quote [kwəʊt] zitieren; *Beispiel etc.* anführen; *econ.* Preis nennen; **be ~d at** *econ.* notieren mit; → **unquote**

quo·tient *math.* ['kwəʊʃnt] Quotient *m*

R

R, r [ɑː] R, r *n*

rab·bi *rel.* ['ræbaɪ] Rabbiner *m*

rab·bit ['ræbɪt] Kaninchen *n*

rab·ble ['ræbl] Pöbel *m*, Mob *m*; **~·rous·ing** ['ræblraʊzɪŋ] aufwieglerisch, Hetz...

rab·id ['ræbɪd] *vet.* tollwütig; *fig.* fanatisch

ra·bies *vet.* ['reɪbiːz] Tollwut *f*

rac·coon *zo.* [rə'kuːn] Waschbär *m*

race¹ [reɪs] Rasse(nzugehörigkeit) *f*; (*Menschen*)Geschlecht *n*

race² [reɪs] **1.** (Wett)Rennen *n*, (Wett)Lauf *m*; **2.** *v/i.* an (e-m) Rennen teilnehmen; um die Wette laufen *od.* fahren *etc.*; rasen, rennen; durchdrehen (*Motor*); *v/t.* um die Wette laufen *od.* fahren *etc.* mit; rasen mit; '**~ car** *bsd. Am. mot.* Rennwagen *m*; '**~·course** *Pferdesport:* Rennbahn *f*; '**~·horse** Rennpferd *n*; '**rac·er** Rennpferd *n*; Rennrad *n*, -wagen *m*; '**~·track** *Automobilsport etc.:* Rennstrecke *f*; *bsd. Am.* → **racecourse**

ra·cial ['reɪʃl] rassisch, Rassen...

rac·ing ['reɪsɪŋ] Renn...; '**~ car** *bsd. Brt. mot.* Rennwagen *m*

rac·ism ['reɪsɪzəm] Rassismus *m*; **~·cist** ['reɪsɪst] **1.** Rassist(in); **2.** rassistisch

rack [ræk] **1.** Gestell *n*, (Geschirr-, Zeitungs- etc.)Ständer *m*, rail. (Gepäck)Netz *n*, mot. (Dach)Gepäckständer *m*; *hist.* Folter(bank) *f*; **2. be ~ed by** *od.* **with** geplagt *od.* gequält werden von; **~ one's brains** sich das Hirn zermartern, sich den Kopf zerbrechen

rack·et¹ ['rækɪt] *Tennis etc.:* Schläger *m*

rack·et² ['rækɪt] Krach *m*, Lärm *m*; Schwindel *m*; Gaunerei *f*; (*Drogenetc.*)Geschäft *n*; organisierte Erpressung; **~·e·teer** [rækə'tɪə] Gauner *m*; Erpresser *m*

ra·coon *zo.* [rə'kuːn] → **raccoon**

rac·y ['reɪsɪ] (**-ier, -iest**) spritzig, lebendig (*Geschichte etc.*); gewagt

ra·dar ['reɪdə] Radar *m, n*; '**~ screen** Radarschirm *m*; '**~ 'speed check** Radarkontrolle *f*; '**~ sta·tion** Radarstation *f*; '**~ trap** *mot.* Radarkontrolle *f*

ra·di·al ['reɪdjəl] **1.** radial, Radial..., strahlenförmig; **2.** *mot.* Gürtelreifen *m*; **~ 'tire** *Am.,* **~ 'tyre** *Brt.* → **radial** 2

ra·di·ant ['reɪdjənt] strahlend, leuchtend (*a. fig.* **with** vor *dat.*)

ra·di·ate ['reɪdɪeɪt] ausstrahlen; strahlenförmig ausgehen (**from** von); **~·a·tion** [reɪdɪ'eɪʃn] Ausstrahlung *f*; **~·a·tor** ['reɪdɪeɪtə] Heizkörper *m*; *mot.* Kühler *m*

rad·i·cal ['rædɪkl] **1.** radikal (*a. pol.*); *math.* Wurzel...; **2.** *pol.* Radikale(r *m*) *f*

ra·di·o ['reɪdɪəʊ] **1.** (*pl.* **-os**) Radio(apparat *m*) *n*; Funk(gerät *n*) *m*; **by ~** über Funk; **on the ~** im Radio; **2.** funken; **~·'ac·tive** radioaktiv; **~·'ac·tive 'waste** Atommüll *m*, radioaktiver Abfall; **~·ac·'tiv·i·ty** Radioaktivität *f*; '**~ ham** Funkamateur *m*; '**~ play** Hörspiel *n*; '**~ set** Radioapparat *m*; '**~ sta·tion** Funkstation *f*; Rundfunksender *m*, -station *f*; **~·'ther·a·py** *med.* Strahlen-, Röntgentherapie *f*; **~ 'tow·er** Funkturm *m*

R

rad·ish bot. ['rædɪʃ] Rettich m; Radieschen n

ra·di·us ['reɪdjəs] (pl. **-dii** [-dɪaɪ]) Radius m

RAF [ɑːr eɪ 'ef, F ræf] Abk. für Royal Air Force die Königlich-Britische Luftwaffe

raf·fle ['ræfl] 1. Tombola f; 2. a. ~ off verlosen

raft [rɑːft] Floß n

raf·ter ['rɑːftə] (Dach)Sparren m

rag [ræg] Lumpen m, Fetzen m; Lappen m; in ~s zerlumpt; ~-and-'bone man (pl. -men) bsd. Brt. Lumpensammler m

rage [reɪdʒ] Wut f, Zorn m; fly into a ~ wütend werden; the latest ~ F der letzte Schrei; be all the ~ F große Mode sein; 2. wettern (against, at gegen); wüten, toben

rag·ged ['rægɪd] zerlumpt; struppig (Bart etc.); fig. stümperhaft

raid [reɪd] 1. (on) Überfall m (auf acc.), mil. a. Angriff m (gegen); Razzia f (in dat.); 2. überfallen, mil. a. angreifen; e-e Razzia machen in (dat.)

rail [reɪl] 1. Geländer n; Stange f; (Handtuch)Halter m; (Eisen)Bahn f; rail. Schiene f; ~s pl. a. Gleis n; by ~ mit der Bahn; 2. ~ in einzäunen; ~ off abzäunen; '~·ing, oft ~s pl. (Gitter)Zaun m

'rail·road Am. → railway

'rail·way bsd. Brt. Eisenbahn f; '~ line Brt. Bahnlinie f; '~·man (pl. -men) Eisenbahner m; '~ sta·tion Brt. Bahnhof m

rain [reɪn] 1. Regen m; ~s pl. Regenfälle pl.; the ~s pl. die Regenzeit (in den Tropen); (come) ~ or shine fig. was immer auch geschieht; 2. regnen; it is ~ing cats and dogs F es gießt in Strömen; it never ~s but it pours es kommt immer gleich knüppeldick, ein Unglück kommt selten allein; '~·bow Regenbogen m; '~·coat Regenmantel m; '~·fall Niederschlag(smenge f) m; '~ for·est bot. Regenwald m; '~·proof regen-, wasserdicht; '~·y (-ier, -iest) regnerisch, verregnet, Regen...; save s.th. for a ~ day et. für schlechte Zeiten zurücklegen

raise [reɪz] 1. heben; hochziehen; erheben; Denkmal etc. errichten; Staub etc. aufwirbeln; Gehalt, Miete etc. erhöhen; Geld zusammenbringen, beschaf-

fen; Kinder auf-, großziehen; Tiere züchten; Getreide etc. anbauen; Frage aufwerfen, et. zur Sprache bringen; Blockade etc., a. Verbot aufheben; 2. Am. Lohn- od. Gehaltserhöhung f

rai·sin ['reɪzn] Rosine f

rake [reɪk] 1. Rechen m, Harke f; 2. v/t. ~ (up) (zusammen)rechen, (-)harken; v/i. ~ about, ~ around herumstöbern

rak·ish ['reɪkɪʃ] flott, keck, verwegen

ral·ly ['rælɪ] 1. (sich) (wieder) sammeln; sich erholen (from von) (a. econ.); ~ round sich scharen um; 2. Kundgebung f, (Massen)Versammlung f; mot. Rallye f; Tennis etc.: Ballwechsel m

ram [ræm] 1. zo. Widder m, Schafbock m; tech. Ramme f; 2. (-mm-) rammen; ~ s.th. down s.o.'s throat fig. j-m et. aufzwingen

RAM [ræm] Abk. für random access memory Computer: RAM, Speicher m mit wahlfreiem od. direktem Zugriff

ram|·ble ['ræmbl] 1. wandern, umherstreifen; abschweifen; 2. Wanderung f; '~·bler Wanderer m; bot. Kletterrose f; '~·bling weitschweifend; weitläufig (Gebäude); bot. Kletter...; ~ rose Kletterrose f

ram·i·fy ['ræmɪfaɪ] (sich) verzweigen

ramp [ræmp] Rampe f; Am. → slip road

ram·page [ræm'peɪdʒ] 1. ~ through (wild od. aufgeregt) trampeln durch (Elefant etc.); ~ 2. go on the ~ through randalierend ziehen durch

ram·pant ['ræmpənt]: be ~ wuchern (Pflanze); grassieren (in in dat.)

ram·shack·le ['ræmʃækl] baufällig; klapp(e)rig (Fahrzeug)

ran [ræn] pret. von run 1

ranch [rɑːntʃ, Am. ræntʃ] Ranch f; Am. (Geflügel- etc.)Farm f; '~·er Rancher m; (Geflügel- etc.) Züchter m

ran·cid ['rænsɪd] ranzig

ran·co(u)r ['ræŋkə] Groll m, Erbitterung f, Haß m

ran·dom ['rændəm] 1. adj. ziel-, wahllos; zufällig, Zufalls...; ~ sample Stichprobe f; 2. at ~ aufs Geratewohl

rang [ræŋ] pret. von ring² 1

range [reɪndʒ] 1. Reich-, Schuß-, Tragweite f; Entfernung f; fig. Bereich m, Spielraum m; fig. Bereich m, Gebiet n; (Schieß)Stand m, (-)Platz m; (Berg-)Kette f; Am. offenes Weidegebiet econ. Kollektion f, Sortiment n; (altmodischer) Küchenherd; **at close ~** aus nächster Nähe; **within ~ of vision** in Sichtweite; **a wide ~ of ...** eine große Auswahl an ...; **2.** v/i. **~ from ... to ...,** ~ **between ... and ...** sich zwischen ... und ... bewegen (*von Preisen etc.*); v/t. aufstellen, anordnen; '**~find·er** phot. Entfernungsmesser m; '**rang·er** Förster m; Am. Ranger m

rank[1] [ræŋk] **1.** Rang m (a. mil.), (soziale) Stellung; Reihe f; (Taxi)Stand m; **of the first ~** fig. erstklassig; **the ~ and file** der Mannschaft(en); (e-r Partei etc.); **the ~s** pl. fig. das Heer, die Masse; **2.** v/t. rechnen, zählen (**among** zu); stellen (**above** über acc.); v/i. zählen, gehören (**among** zu); gelten (**as** als)

rank[2] [ræŋk] (üppig) wuchernd; überliechend od. -schmeckend; fig. kraß (Außenseiter), blutig (Anfänger)

ran·kle fig. ['ræŋkl] nagen, weh tun

ran·sack ['rænsæk] durchwühlen, -suchen; plündern

ran·som ['rænsəm] **1.** Lösegeld n; **2.** freikaufen, auslösen

rant [rænt] ~ (**on**) **about,** ~ **and rave about** eifern gegen, sich in Tiraden ergehen über (acc.)

rap [ræp] **1.** Klopfen n; Klaps m; **2.** (**-pp-**) klopfen (**an** acc., **auf** acc.)

ra·pa·cious [rə'peɪʃəs] habgierig

rape[1] [reɪp] **1.** vergewaltigen; **2.** Vergewaltigung f

rape[2] bot. [reɪp] Raps m

rap·id ['ræpɪd] schnell, rasch; **ra·pid·i·ty** [rə'pɪdətɪ] Schnelligkeit f

rap·ids ['ræpɪdz] pl. Stromschnellen pl.

rapt [ræpt]: **with ~ attention** mit gespannter Aufmerksamkeit; **rap·ture** ['ræptʃə] Entzücken n, Verzückung f; **go into ~s** in Verzückung geraten

rare[1] [reə] (**~r, ~st**) selten, rar; dünn (Luft); F Mords-.

rare[2] gastr. [reə] (**~r, ~st**) blutig (Steak)

rare·bit gastr. ['reəbɪt] → **Welsh rarebit**

rar·e·fied ['reərɪfaɪd] dünn (Luft)

rar·i·ty ['reərətɪ] Seltenheit f; Rarität f

ras·cal ['rɑːskəl] Gauner m; humor. Schlingel m

rash[1] [ræʃ] voreilig, -schnell, unbesonnen; △ nicht **rash**

rash[2] med. [ræʃ] (Haut)Ausschlag m

rash·er ['ræʃə] dünne Speckscheibe

rasp [rɑːsp] **1.** raspeln; kratzen; **2.** Raspel f; Kratzen n

rasp·ber·ry bot. ['rɑːzbərɪ] Himbeere f

rat [ræt] zo. Ratte f (a. contp.); **smell a ~** Lunte od. den Braten riechen; **~s!** F Mist!

rate [reɪt] **1.** Quote f, Rate f, (Geburten-, Sterbe)Ziffer f; (Steuer-, Zins- etc.)Satz m; (Wechsel)Kurs m; Geschwindigkeit f, Tempo n; △ nicht **Rate** (→ **instal(l)ment**); **at any ~** auf jeden Fall; **2.** einschätzen, halten (**as** für); Lob etc. verdienen; **be ~d as** gelten als; **~ of ex'change** (Umrechnungs-, Wechsel)Kurs m; **~ of 'in·ter·est** Zinssatz m, -fuß m

ra·ther ['rɑːðə] ziemlich; eher, vielmehr, besser gesagt; **~!** bsd. Brt. F und ob!; **I would** od. **had ~ go** ich möchte lieber gehen

rat·i·fy pol. ['rætɪfaɪ] ratifizieren

rat·ing ['reɪtɪŋ] Einschätzung f; Rundfunk, TV Einschaltquote f

ra·ti·o math. ['reɪʃɪəʊ] (pl. **-os**) Verhältnis n

ra·tion ['ræʃn] **1.** Ration f; **2.** et. rationieren; **~ out** zuteilen (**to** dat.)

ra·tion·al ['ræʃənl] rational; vernunftbegabt; vernünftig; △ nicht **rationell;** **~·i·ty** [ræʃə'nælətɪ] Vernunft f; **~·ize** ['ræʃnəlaɪz] rational erklären; econ. rationalisieren

'rat race F endloser Konkurrenzkampf

rat·tle ['rætl] **1.** klappern (Fenster etc.); rasseln od. klimpern (mit); prasseln (**on** auf acc.) (Regen etc.); rattern, knattern (Fahrzeug); rütteln an (dat.); F j-n verunsichern; **~ at** rütteln an (dat.); **~ off** Gedicht etc. herunterrasseln; **~ on** quasseln (**about** über acc.); **~ through** Rede etc. herunterrasseln; **2.** Klappern n (etc. → **1**); Rassel f, Klapper f; '**~snake** zo. Klapperschlange f; '**~trap** F Klapperkasten m (Auto)

rau·cous ['rɔːkəs] heiser, rauh

rav·age ['rævɪdʒ] verwüsten; **~s** pl. Verwüstungen pl., a. fig. verheerende Auswirkungen pl.

rave [reɪv] phantasieren, irrereden; toben; wettern (**against, at** gegen); schwärmen (**about** von)

rav·el ['rævl] (bsd. Brt. **-ll-**, Am. **-l-**)

(sich) verwickeln *od.* -wirren; → **un-ravel**

ra·ven *zo.* ['reɪvn] Rabe *m*

rav·e·nous ['rævənəs] ausgehungert, heißhungrig

ra·vine [rə'viːn] Schlucht *f*, Klamm *f*

rav·ings ['reɪvɪŋz] *pl.* irres Gerede, Delirien *pl.*

rav·ish ['rævɪʃ] hinreißen; **'~·ing** hinreißend

raw [rɔː] roh (*Gemüse etc.*); *econ., tech.* roh, Roh...; wund (*Haut*); naßkalt (*Wetter*); unerfahren; **~ vegetables and fruit** *pl.* Rohkost *f*; **~·'boned** knochig, hager; **'~·hide** Rohleder *n*

ray [reɪ] Strahl *m*; *fig.* Schimmer *m*

ray·on ['reɪɒn] Kunstseide *f*

ra·zor ['reɪzə] Rasiermesser *n*; Rasierapparat *m*; **electric ~** Elektrorasierer *m*; **'~ blade** Rasierklinge *f*; **~('s) 'edge** *fig.* kritische Lage; **be on a ~** auf des Messers Schneide stehen

RC [ɑː 'siː] *Abk. für* **Roman Catholic** r.-k., röm.-kath., römisch-katholisch

Rd *nur geschr. Abk. für* **Road** Str., Straße *f*

re [riː]: **~ your letter of ...** Betr.: Ihr Schreiben vom ...

re... [riː] wieder, noch einmal, neu

reach [riːtʃ] **1.** *v/t.* erreichen; reichen *od.* gehen bis an (*acc.*) *od.* zu; **~ down** herunter-, hinunterreichen (**from** von); **~ out** Arm *etc.* ausstrecken; *v/i.* reichen, gehen, sich erstrecken; *a.* **~ out** greifen, langen (**for** nach); **~ out** die Hand ausstrecken; △ *nicht* (**aus**)**reichen**; **2.** Reichweite *f*; **within/out of ~** in/außer Reichweite; **within easy ~** leicht erreichbar

re·act [rɪ'ækt] reagieren (**to** auf *acc.*; *chem.* **with** mit); **re·ac·tion** [rɪ'ækʃn] Reaktion *f* (*a. chem., pol.*)

re·ac·tor *phys.* [rɪ'æktə] Reaktor *m*

read 1. [riːd] (**read** [red]) lesen; (an)zeigen (*Thermometer etc.*); Zähler *etc.* ablesen; *univ.* studieren; deuten, verstehen (**as** als); *sich gut etc.* lesen (lassen); lauten; **~ (s.th.) to s.o.** j-m (*et.*) vorlesen; **~ medicine** Medizin studieren; **2.** [red] *pret. u. p.p. von* **read 1**; **'rea·da·ble** lesbar; leserlich; lesenswert; **'read·er** Leser(in); Lektor(in); Lesebuch *n*

read·i·ly ['redɪlɪ] bereitwillig, gern;

leicht, ohne weiteres; **'~·ness** Bereitschaft *f*

read·ing ['riːdɪŋ] Lesen *n*; Lesung *f* (*a. parl.*); *tech.* Anzeige *f*, (*Thermometer etc.*)Stand *m*; Auslegung *f*; Lese...

re·ad·just [riːə'dʒʌst] *tech.* nachstellen, korrigieren; **~** (**o.s.**) **to** sich wiederanpassen (*dat.*) *od.* an (*acc.*), sich wiedereinstellen auf (*acc.*)

read·y ['redɪ] (**-ier, -iest**) bereit, fertig; bereitwillig; im Begriff (**to do** zu tun); schnell, schlagfertig; **~ for use** gebrauchsfertig; **get ~** (sich) fertigmachen; **~ 'cash** → **ready money**; **~·'made** Konfektions...; **~·'meal** Fertiggericht *n*; **~ 'mon·ey** *F* Bargeld *n*

re·al [rɪəl] echt; wirklich, tatsächlich, real; **for ~** *bsd. Am. F* echt, im Ernst; △ *nicht* **reell**; **~ es·tate** Grundbesitz *m*, Immobilien *pl.*; **~ es·tate a·gent** *Am.* Grundstücks-, Immobilienmakler *m*

re·a·lis·m ['rɪəlɪzəm] Realismus *m*; **~t** ['rɪəlɪst] Realist(in); **~·tic** [rɪə'lɪstɪk] (**~ally**) realistisch

re·al·i·ty [rɪ'ælətɪ] Realität *f*, Wirklichkeit *f*; **~·show,** **~·TV** *f* Gaffer-Sendung *f* (*Fernsehsendung mit zum Teil nachgestelltem authentischen Material*)

re·a·li·za·tion [rɪəlaɪ'zeɪʃn] Erkenntnis *f*; Realisierung *f* (*a. econ.*), Verwirklichung *f*; **~·lize** ['rɪəlaɪz] sich klarmachen, erkennen, begreifen, einsehen; realisieren (*a. econ.*), verwirklichen

re·al·ly ['rɪəlɪ] wirklich, tatsächlich; **well, ~!** ich muß schon sagen!; **~? im** Ernst?

realm [relm] Königreich *n*; *fig.* Reich *n*

real·tor *Am.* ['rɪəltə] Grundstücks-, Immobilienmakler *m*

reap [riːp] Getreide *etc.* schneiden; Feld abernten; *fig.* ernten

re·ap·pear [riːə'pɪə] wiedererscheinen

rear [rɪə] **1.** *v/t.* Kind, Tier auf-, großziehen; *Kopf* heben; *v/i.* sich aufbäumen (*Pferd*); **2.** Rück-, Hinterseite *f*, Heck *n*; **at** (*Am.* **in**) **the ~ of** hinter (*dat.*); **bring up the ~** die Nachhut bilden; **3.** hinter, Hinter..., Rück..., *mot. a.* Heck...; **~·end 'col·li·sion** *mot.* Auffahrunfall *m*; **'~·guard** *mil.* Nachhut *f*; **'~·end** Rücklicht *n*

re·arm *mil.* [riː'ɑːm] (wieder) aufrüsten; **re·ar·ma·ment** *mil.* [riː'ɑːməmənt] (Wieder)Aufrüstung *f*

'**rear-|most** hinterste(r, -s); **~view**
['mir-ror** mot. Rückspiegel m; **~ward**
['rɪəwəd] **1.** adj. hintere(r, -s), rückwär-
tig; **2.** adv. a. **~s** rückwärts; **~wheel**
'**drive** mot. Hinterradantrieb m; '**~
win-dow** mot. Heckscheibe f

rea-son ['ri:zn] **1.** Grund m; Verstand
m; Vernunft f; **by ~ of** wegen; **for this ~**
aus diesem Grund; **listen to ~** Vernunft
annehmen; **it stands to ~ that** es leuch-
tet ein, daß; **2.** v/i. vernünftig od. logisch denken; vernünftig reden (**with**
mit); v/t. folgern, schließen (**that** daß);
~ s.o. into/out of s.th. j-m et. ein-/aus-
reden; '**rea-so-na-ble** vernünftig;
günstig (Preis); ganz gut, nicht schlecht

re-as-sure [ri:ə'ʃɔː] beruhigen

re-bate ['ri:beɪt] econ. Rabatt m,
(Preis)Nachlaß m; Rückzahlung f

reb-el¹ ['rebl] **1.** Rebell(in); Aufständi-
sche(r m) f; **2.** aufständisch

re-bel² [rɪ'bel] (**-ll-**) rebellieren, sich auflehnen (**against** gegen); **~lion**
[rɪ'beljən] Rebellion f, Aufstand m;
~lious [rɪ'beljəs] rebellisch (a. Jugendlicher etc.), aufständisch

re-birth [riː'bɜːθ] Wiedergeburt f

re-bound 1. [rɪ'baʊnd] ab-, zurückpral-
len (**from** von); fig. zurückfallen (**on**
auf acc.); **2.** ['ri:baʊnd] Sport: Abpral-
ler m

re-buff [rɪ'bʌf] **1.** schroffe Abweisung,
Abfuhr f; **2.** schroff abweisen

re-build [riː'bɪld] (**-built**) wieder aufbau-
en; fig. wiederaufbauen

re-buke [rɪ'bjuːk] **1.** rügen, tadeln; **2.**
Rüge f, Tadel m

re-call [rɪ'kɔːl] **1.** zurückrufen, abberufen; mot. (in die Werkstatt) zurückrufen; sich erinnern an (acc.); erinnern an
(acc.); **2.** Zurückrufung f, Abberufung
f; Rückrufaktion f; **have total ~** das
absolute Gedächtnis haben; **beyond ~,
past ~** unwiederbringlich od. unwiderruflich vorbei

re-ca-pit-u-late [ri:kə'pɪtjuleɪt] rekapi-
tulieren, (kurz) zusammenfassen

re-cap-ture [ri:'kæptʃə] wieder einfangen; Häftling wieder fassen; mil. zu-
rückerobern; fig. wiedereinfangen

re-cast [ri:'kɑːst] (**-cast**) tech. umgie-
ßen; umformen, neu gestalten; thea.
etc. umbesetzen, neu besetzen

re-cede [rɪ'siːd] schwinden; **receding**

fliehend (Kinn, Stirn)

re-ceipt bsd. econ. [rɪ'siːt] Empfang m,
Eingang m (**von Waren**); Quittung f; △
nicht **Rezept**; **~s** pl. Einnahmen pl.

re-ceive [rɪ'siːv] bekommen, erhalten;
empfangen; j-n aufnehmen (**into** in
acc.); Funk, Rundfunk, TV: empfangen; **re-ceiv-er** Empfänger(in); tel.
Hörer m; Hehler(in); a. **official ~** Brt.
jur. Konkursverwalter m

re-cent ['riːsnt] neuere(r, -s); jüngste(r,
-s) (Ereignisse etc.); **~ly** kürzlich, vor
kurzem

re-cep-tion [rɪ'sepʃn] Empfang m; Aufnahme f (**into** in acc.); Funk, Rundfunk,
TV: Empfang m; a. **~ desk** Hotel: Rezeption f, Empfang m; **~ist**
[rɪ'sepʃənɪst] Empfangsdame f, -chef m;
med. Sprechstundenhilfe f

re-cep-tive [rɪ'septɪv] aufnahmefähig;
empfänglich (**to** für)

re-cess [rɪ'ses] Unterbrechung f, (Am.
a. Schul)Pause f; parl. Ferien pl.; Nische f

re-ces-sion econ. [rɪ'seʃn] Rezession f

re-ci-pe ['resɪpɪ] (Koch)Rezept n

re-cip-i-ent [rɪ'sɪpɪənt] Empfänger(in)

re-cip-ro-cal [rɪ'sɪprəkl] wechsel-, gegenseitig; **~cate** [rɪ'sɪprəkeɪt] v/i. tech.
sich hin- und herbewegen; sich revanchieren; v/t. Einladung etc. erwidern

re-cit-al [rɪ'saɪtl] Vortrag m, (Klavier-
etc.)Konzert n, (Lieder)Abend m;
Schilderung f; **re-ci-ta-tion** [resɪ'teɪʃn]
Auf-, Hersagen n; Vortrag m; **re-cite**
[rɪ'saɪt] auf-, hersagen; vortragen; aufzählen

reck-less ['reklɪs] rücksichtslos

reck-on ['rekən] v/t. (aus-, be)rechnen;
glauben, schätzen; **~ up** zusammenrechnen; v/i. **~ on** rechnen mit; **~ with**
rechnen mit; **~ without** nicht rechnen
mit; **~ing** ['rekɪŋ] (Be)Rechnung f;
be out in one's ~ sich verrechnet haben

re-claim [rɪ'kleɪm] zurückfordern, -ver-
langen; Gepäck etc. abholen; dem Meer
etc. Land abgewinnen; tech. wiedergewin-
nen; △ nicht **reklamieren**

re-cline [rɪ'klaɪn] sich zurücklehnen

re-cluse [rɪ'kluːs] Einsiedler(in)

rec-og-ni-tion [rekəg'nɪʃn] (Wieder)Erkennen n; Anerkennung f; **~
nize** ['rekəgnaɪz] (wieder)erkennen;
anerkennen; zugeben, eingestehen

R

re·coil 1. [rɪ'kɔɪl] zurückschrecken (*from* vor *dat.*); 2. ['riːkɔɪl] Rückstoß *m*

rec·ol·lect [rekə'lekt] sich erinnern an (*acc.*); **~·lec·tion** [rekə'lekʃn] Erinnerung *f* (*of* an *acc.*)

rec·om·mend [rekə'mend] empfehlen (*as* als; *for* für); **~·men·da·tion** [rekəmen'deɪʃn] Empfehlung *f*

rec·om·pense ['rekəmpens] 1. entschädigen (*for* für); 2. Entschädigung *f*

rec·on·cile ['rekənsaɪl] ver-, aussöhnen; in Einklang bringen (*with* mit); **~·cil·i·a·tion** [rekənsɪlɪ'eɪʃn] Ver-, Aussöhnung *f* (*between* zwischen *dat.*; *with* mit)

re·con·di·tion *tech.* [riːkən'dɪʃn] (general)überholen

re·con·nais·sance *mil.* [rɪ'kɒnɪsəns] Aufklärung *f*, Erkundung *f*; **~·noi·tre** *Brt.*, **~·noi·ter** *Am.* [rekə'nɔɪtə] *mil.* erkunden, auskundschaften

re·con·sid·er [riːkən'sɪdə] noch einmal überdenken

re·con·struct [riːkən'strʌkt] wieder aufbauen; *fig.* wiederaufbauen; *Verbrechen etc.* rekonstruieren; **~·struc·tion** [riːkən'strʌkʃn] Wiederaufbau *m*; Rekonstruktion *f*

rec·ord¹ ['rekɔːd] Aufzeichnung *f*; *jur.* Protokoll *n*; Akte *f*; (Schall)Platte *f*; *Sport*: Rekord *m*; *off the* ~ F inoffiziell; *have a criminal* ~ vorbestraft sein

re·cord² [rɪ'kɔːd] aufzeichnen, -schreiben, -schriftlich niederlegen; *jur.* protokollieren, zu Protokoll nehmen; *auf Schallplatte, Tonband etc.* aufnehmen, *Sendung a.* aufzeichnen, mitschneiden; **~·er** (*Kassetten*)Recorder *m*; (*Tonband*)Gerät *n*; *mus.* Blockflöte *f*; **~·ing** Aufnahme *f*, -zeichnung *f*, Mitschnitt *m*

rec·ord play·er ['rekɔːd-] Plattenspieler *m*

re·count [rɪ'kaʊnt] erzählen

re·cov·er [rɪ'kʌvə] *v/t.* wiedererlangen, -bekommen, -finden; *Kosten etc.* wiedereinbringen; *Fahrzeug, Verunglückten etc.* bergen; ~ *consciousness* wieder zu sich kommen, das Bewußtsein wiedererlangen; *v/i.* sich erholen (*from* von); **~·y** [rɪ'kʌvərɪ] Wiedererlangen *n*; Wiederfinden *n*; Bergung *f*; Genesung *f*; Erholung *f*

rec·re·a·tion [rekrɪ'eɪʃn] Entspannung

f, Erholung *f*; Unterhaltung *f*, Freizeitbeschäftigung *f*

re·cruit [rɪ'kruːt] 1. *mil.* Rekrut *m*; Neue(r *m*) *f*, neues Mitglied; 2. *mil.* rekrutieren; *Personal einstellen*; *Mitglieder* werben

rec·tan·gle *math.* ['rektæŋgl] Rechteck *n*; **~·gu·lar** [rek'tæŋgjʊlə] rechteckig

rec·ti·fy ['rektɪfaɪ] *electr.* gleichrichten

rec·tor ['rektə] Pfarrer *m*; **~·to·ry** ['rektərɪ] Pfarrhaus *n*

re·cu·pe·rate [rɪ'kjuːpəreɪt] sich erholen (*from* von) (*a. fig.*)

re·cur [rɪ'kɜː] (*-rr-*) wiederkehren, wiederauftreten, *Schmerz a.* wiedereinsetzen; **~·rence** [rɪ'kʌrəns] Wiederkehr *f*, Wiederauftreten *n*, Wiedereinsetzen *n*; **~·rent** [rɪ'kʌrənt] wiederkehrend, wiederauftretend, wiedereinsetzend

re·cy·cle [riː'saɪkl] *Abfälle* recyceln, wiederverwerten; **~d paper** Recyclingpapier *n*, Umwelt(schutz)papier *n*; **~·cla·ble** [riː'saɪkləbəl] recycelbar, wiederverwertbar; **~·cling** [riː'saɪklɪŋ] Recycling *n*, Wiederverwertung *f*

red [red] 1. rot; 2. Rot *n*; *be in the* ~ *econ.* in den roten Zahlen sein; '**~·breast** *zo.* → *robin*; **♀** '**Cres·cent** Roter Halbmond; **♀** '**Cross** Rotes Kreuz; **~·cur·rant** *bot.* rote Johannisbeere; **~·den** ['redn] röten, rot färben; rot werden; **~·dish** ['redɪʃ] rötlich

re·dec·o·rate [riː'dekəreɪt] *Zimmer etc.* neu streichen u. tapezieren

re·deem [rɪ'diːm] *Pfand, Versprechen etc.* einlösen; *rel.* erlösen; **♀·er** *rel.* Erlöser *m*, Heiland *m*

re·demp·tion [rɪ'dempʃn] Einlösung *f*; *rel.* Erlösung *f*

re·de·vel·op [riːdɪ'veləp] *Gebäude, Stadtteil* sanieren

red|-'faced mit rotem Kopf; **~'hand·ed**: *catch s.o.* ~ j-n auf frischer Tat ertappen; '**~·head** F Rotschopf *m*, Rothaarige *f*; **~'head·ed** rothaarig; ~ '**her·ring** *fig.* falsche Fährte *od.* Spur; **~'hot** rotglühend; *fig.* glühend (*Begeisterung etc.*); *fig.* F brandaktuell (*Nachricht etc.*); **♀** '**In·di·an** V Indianer(in); **~·let·ter day** Freuden-, Glückstag *m*; '**~·ness** Röte *f*

re·dou·ble [riː'dʌbl] *bsd. Anstrengungen* verdoppeln

red 'tape Bürokratismus *m*, Papierkrieg *m*

re·duce [rɪ'djuːs] verkleinern; *Geschwindigkeit, Risiko etc.* verringern; *Steuern etc.* senken, *Preis, Waren etc.* herabsetzen, reduzieren (*from ... to* von ... auf *acc.*), *Gehalt etc.* kürzen; verwandeln (*to in acc.*), machen (*to* zu); reduzieren, zurückführen (*to* auf *acc.*); **re·duc·tion** [rɪ'dʌkʃn] Verkleinerung *f*; Verringerung *f*, Senkung *f*, Herabsetzung *f*, Reduzierung *f*, Kürzung *f*

re·dun·dant [rɪ'dʌndənt] überflüssig

reed *bot.* [riːd] Schilf(rohr) *n*

re·ed·u·cate [riː'edʒʊkeɪt] umerziehen; **~ca·tion** ['riːedʒʊ'keɪʃn] Umerziehung *f*

reef [riːf] (Felsen)Riff *n*

reek [riːk] **1.** Gestank *m*; **2.** stinken (*of* nach)

reel¹ [riːl] **1.** Rolle *f*, Spule *f*; **2.** ~ *off* abrollen, abspulen; *fig.* herunterrasseln

reel² [riːl] sich drehen; (sch)wanken, taumeln, torkeln; *my head ~ed* mir drehte sich alles

re·e·lect [riːɪ'lekt] wiederwählen

re·en|·ter [riː'entə] wieder eintreten in (*acc.*) (*a. Raumfahrt*), wieder betreten; **~try** [riː'entrɪ] Wiedereintreten *n*, Wiedereintritt *m*

ref¹ [ref] *Sport:* Schiri *m*; → *referee*

ref.² *nur geschr. Abk. für* *reference*Verweis *m*, Hinweis *m*

re·fer [rɪ'fɜː]: ~ *to* ver- *od.* hinweisen auf (*acc.*); *j-n* verweisen an (*acc.*); sich beziehen auf (*acc.*); anspielen auf (*acc.*); erwähnen (*acc.*); nachschlagen in (*dat.*)

ref·er·ee [refə'riː] Schiedsrichter *m*, Unparteiische(r) *m*; *Boxen:* Ringrichter *m*

ref·er·ence ['refrəns] Verweis *m*, Hinweis *m* (*to* auf *acc.*); Verweisstelle *f*; Referenz *f*, Empfehlung *f*, Zeugnis *n*; Bezugnahme *f* (*to* auf *acc.*); Anspielung *f* (*to* auf *acc.*); Erwähnung *f* (*to* gen.); Nachschlagen *n* (*to* in *dat.*); **list of ~s** Quellenangabe *f*; **'~ book** Nachschlagewerk *n*; **'~ li·bra·ry** Handbibliothek *f*; **'~ num·ber** Aktenzeichen *n*

ref·er·en·dum [refə'rendəm] (*pl.* **-da** [-də], **-dums**) Referendum *n*, Volksentscheid *m*

re·fill 1. [riː'fɪl] wieder füllen, nach-, auffüllen; **2.** ['riːfɪl] (*Ersatz*)Mine *f* (*für Kugelschreiber etc.*); (*Ersatz*)Patrone *f* (*für Füller*)

re·fine [rɪ'faɪn] *tech.* raffinieren; *fig.* verfeinern, kultivieren; ~ *on* verbessern, -feinern; **~d** raffiniert; *fig.* kultiviert, vornehm; **~ment** Raffinierung *f*; Verbesserung *f*, -feinerung *f*; Kultiviertheit *f*, Vornehmheit *f*; **re·fin·er·y** *tech.* [rɪ'faɪnərɪ] Raffinerie *f*

re·flect [rɪ'flekt] *v/t.* reflektieren, zurückwerfen, -strahlen, (wider)spiegeln; *be ~ed in* sich (wider)spiegeln in (*dat.*) (*a. fig.*); *v/i.* nachdenken (*on* über *acc.*); ~ (*badly*) *on* so nachteilig auswirken auf (*acc.*); ein schlechtes Licht werfen auf (*acc.*); **re·flec·tion** [rɪ'flekʃn] Reflexion *f*, Zurückwerfung *f*, -strahlung *f*, (Wider)Spiegelung *f* (*a. fig.*); Spiegelbild *n*; Überlegung *f*, Betrachtung *f*; *on* ~ nach einigem Nachdenken; **re·flec·tive** [rɪ'flektɪv] reflektierend; nachdenklich

re·flex ['riːfleks] Reflex *m*; **'~ ac·tion** Reflexhandlung *f*; **'~ cam·e·ra** *phot.* Spiegelreflexkamera *f*

re·flex·ive *gr.* [rɪ'fleksɪv] reflexiv, rückbezüglich

re·form [rɪ'fɔːm] **1.** reformieren, verbessern; sich bessern; **2.** Reform *f* (*a. pol.*), (Ver)Besserung *f*; **ref·or·ma·tion** [refə'meɪʃn] Reformierung *f*; (Ver)Besserung *f*; *the 2 rel.* die Reformation; **~er** [rɪ'fɔːmə] *bsd. pol.* Reformer *m*; *rel.* Reformator *m*

re·fract [rɪ'frækt] *Strahlen etc.* brechen; **re·frac·tion** [rɪ'frækʃn] (*Strahlen-etc.*)Brechung *f*

re·frain¹ [rɪ'freɪn]: ~ *from* sich enthalten (*gen.*), unterlassen (*acc.*)

re·frain² [rɪ'freɪn] Kehrreim *m*, Refrain *m*

re·fresh [rɪ'freʃ] (*o.s.* sich) erfrischen, stärken; *Gedächtnis* auffrischen; **~ing** erfrischend (*a. fig.*); **~ment** Erfrischung *f* (*a. Getränk etc.*)

re·fri·ge·rate *tech.* [rɪ'frɪdʒəreɪt] kühlen; **~ra·tor** Kühlschrank *m*

re·fu·el [riː'fjʊəl] (*Brt.* **-ll-**, *Am.* **-l-**) auftanken

ref·uge ['refjuːdʒ] Zuflucht(sstätte) *f*; *Brt.* Verkehrsinsel *f*

ref·u·gee [refjʊ'dʒiː] Flüchtling *m*; **~ camp** Flüchtlingslager *n*

re·fund 1. ['riːfʌnd] Rückzahlung f, -erstattung f; **2.** [riː'fʌnd] Geld zurückzahlen, -erstatten; Auslagen ersetzen

re·fur·bish [riː'fɜːbɪʃ] aufpolieren (a. fig.); renovieren

re·fus·al [rɪ'fjuːzl] Ablehnung f; Weigerung f

re·fuse¹ [rɪ'fjuːz] v/t. ablehnen; verweigern; sich weigern, es ablehnen (**to do** zu tun); v/i. ablehnen; sich weigern

ref·use² ['refjuːs] Abfall m, Abfälle pl., Müll m; '~ **dump** Müllabladeplatz m

re·fute [rɪ'fjuːt] widerlegen

re·gain [rɪ'geɪn] wieder-, zurückgewinnen

re·gale [rɪ'geɪl]: ~ **s.o. with s.th.** j-n mit et. erfreuen od. ergötzen

re·gard [rɪ'gɑːd] **1.** Achtung f; Rücksicht f; **in this** ~ in dieser Hinsicht; **with** ~ **to** im Hinblick auf (acc.); hinsichtlich (gen.); ~**s** pl. Grüße pl. (bsd. in Briefen); **with kind** ~**s** mit freundlichen Grüßen; **2.** betrachten (a. fig.), ansehen; ~ **as** betrachten als, halten für; **as** ~**s** was ... betrifft; ~**ing** bezüglich, hinsichtlich (gen.); ~**less**: ~ **of** ohne Rücksicht auf (acc.), ungeachtet (gen.)

regd nur geschr. Abk. für: **registered** econ. eingetragen; post eingeschrieben

re·gen·e·rate [rɪ'dʒenəreɪt] (sich) erneuern od. regenerieren

re·gent ['riːdʒənt] Regent(in)

re·gi·ment 1. ['redʒɪmənt] mil. Regiment n, fig. a. Schar f; **2.** ['redʒɪment] reglementieren, bevormunden

re·gion ['riːdʒən] Gegend f, Gebiet n, Region f; '~**al** regional, örtlich, Orts...

re·gis·ter ['redʒɪstə] **1.** Register n, Verzeichnis n, (Wähler- etc.)Liste f; **2.** v/t. registrieren, eintragen (lassen); Meßwerte anzeigen; Brief etc. einschreiben lassen; v/i. sich eintragen (lassen); ~**ed 'let·ter** Einschreib(e)brief m, Einschreiben n

re·gis·tra·tion [redʒɪ'streɪʃn] Registrierung f, Eintragung f; mot. Zulassung f; ~ **fee** Anmeldegebühr f; ~ **num·ber** mot. (polizeiliches) Kennzeichen

re·gis·try ['redʒɪstrɪ] Registratur f; '~ **of·fice** bsd. Brt. Standesamt n

re·gret [rɪ'gret] **1.** (-tt-) bedauern; bereuen; **2.** Bedauern n; Reue f; ~**ful** bedauernd; ~**ta·ble** bedauerlich

reg·u·lar ['regjʊlə] **1.** regelmäßig; geregelt, geordnet; richtig; bsd. Am. normal; mil. Berufs...; ~ **petrol** (Am. **gas**) mot. Normalbenzin n; **2.** F Stammkund|e m, -in f; F Stammgast m; Sport: Stammspieler(in); mil. Berufssoldat m; Am. mot. Normal(benzin) n; ~**i·ty** [regjʊ'lærətɪ] Regelmäßigkeit f

reg·u·late ['regjʊleɪt] regeln, regulieren; tech. einstellen, regulieren; ~**la·tion** [regjʊ'leɪʃn] Reg(e)lung f, Regulierung f; tech. Einstellung f; Vorschrift f; ~**la·tor** tech. ['regjʊleɪtə] Regler m

re·hears·al mus., thea. [rɪ'hɜːsl] Probe f; ~**e** mus., thea. [rɪ'hɜːs] proben

reign [reɪn] **1.** Regierung f (e-s Königs), a. fig. Herrschaft f; **2.** herrschen, regieren

re·im·burse [riːɪm'bɜːs] Auslagen erstatten, vergüten

rein [reɪn] **1.** Zügel m; **2.** ~ **in** Pferd etc. zügeln; fig. bremsen

rein·deer zo. ['reɪndɪə] (pl. **reindeer**) Ren(tier) n

re·in·force [riːɪn'fɔːs] verstärken; ~**ment** Verstärkung f

re·in·state [riːɪn'steɪt] j-n wiedereinstellen (**as** als; **in** in dat.)

re·in·sure [riːɪn'ʃɔː] rückversichern

re·it·e·rate [riː'ɪtəreɪt] (ständig) wiederholen

re·ject [rɪ'dʒekt] j-n, et. ablehnen, Bitte abschlagen, Plan etc. verwerfen; j-n ab-, zurückweisen; med. Organ etc. abstoßen; **re·jec·tion** [rɪ'dʒekʃn] Ablehnung f; Verwerfung f; Zurückweisung f; med. Abstoßung f

re·joice [rɪ'dʒɔɪs] sich freuen, jubeln (**at, over** über acc.); **re'joic·ing(s** pl.) Jubel m

re·join¹ [riː'dʒɔɪn] wieder zusammenfügen; wieder zurückkehren zu

re·join² [rɪ'dʒɔɪn] erwidern

re·ju·ve·nate [rɪ'dʒuːvɪneɪt] verjüngen

re·kin·dle [riː'kɪndl] Feuer wieder anzünden; fig. wieder entfachen

re·lapse [rɪ'læps] **1.** zurückfallen, wieder verfallen (**into** in acc.); rückfällig werden; med. e-n Rückfall bekommen; **2.** Rückfall m

re·late [rɪ'leɪt] v/t. erzählen, berichten; in Verbindung od. Zusammenhang bringen (**to** mit); v/i. sich beziehen (**to** auf acc.); zusammenhängen (**to** mit); **re·lat·ed** verwandt (**to** mit)

re·la·tion [rɪˈleɪʃn] Verwandte(r *m*) *f*; Beziehung *f* (**between** zwischen *dat.*; **to** zu); the *od.* with ~ to in bezug auf (*acc.*); **~s** *pl.* diplomatische, geschäftliche Beziehungen *pl.*; **~ship** Verwandtschaft *f*; Beziehung *f*, Verhältnis *n*

rel·a·tive¹ [ˈrelətɪv] Verwandte(r *m*) *f*

rel·a·tive² [ˈrelətɪv] relativ, verhältnismäßig; bezüglich (**to** *gen.*); *gr.* Relativ..., bezüglich; **~ˈpro·noun** *gr.* Relativpronomen *n*, bezügliches Fürwort

re·lax [rɪˈlæks] *v/t.* Muskeln etc. entspannen; *Griff etc.* lockern; *fig.* nachlassen in (*dat.*); *v/i.* sich entspannen, *fig. a.* ausspannen; sich lockern; **~a·tion** [riːlækˈseɪʃn] Entspannung *f*; Erholung *f*; Lockerung *f*; **~ed** entspannt, *Atmosphäre a.* zwanglos

re·lay¹ 1. [ˈriːleɪ] Ablösung *f*; *Sport:* Staffel(lauf *m*) *f*; *Rundfunk, TV:* Übertragung *f*; [*a.* riːˈleɪ] *electr.* Relais *n*; 2. [riːˈleɪ] (**-layed**) *Rundfunk, TV:* übertragen

re·lay² [riːˈleɪ] (**-laid**) *Kabel, Teppich* neu verlegen

re·lay race [ˈriːleɪreɪs] *Sport:* Staffel(lauf *m*) *f*

re·lease [rɪˈliːs] 1. ent-, freilassen; loslassen; freigeben, herausbringen, veröffentlichen; *mot. Handbremse* lösen; *fig.* befreien, erlösen; 2. Ent-, Freilassung *f*; Befreiung *f*; Freigabe *f*; Veröffentlichung *f*; *tech., phot.* Auslöser *m*; *Film: oft* **first ~** Uraufführung *f*

rel·e·gate [ˈrelɪgeɪt] verbannen; **be ~d** *Sport:* absteigen (**to** in *acc.*)

re·lent [rɪˈlent] nachgeben (*Person*); nachlassen (*Wind etc.*); **~less** unbarmherzig; anhaltend (*Wind etc.*)

rel·e·vant [ˈreləvənt] relevant, erheblich, wichtig; sachdienlich, zutreffend

re·li·a·bil·i·ty [rɪlaɪəˈbɪlətɪ] Zuverlässigkeit *f*; **~·a·ble** [rɪˈlaɪəbl] zuverlässig; **~·ance** [rɪˈlaɪəns] Vertrauen *n*; Abhängigkeit *f* (**on** von)

rel·ic [ˈrelɪk] Relikt *n*, Überbleibsel *n*; *rel.* Reliquie *f*

re·lief [rɪˈliːf] Erleichterung *f*; Unterstützung *f*, Hilfe *f*; *Am.* Sozialhilfe *f*; Ablösung *f* (*von Personen*); Relief *n*

re·lieve [rɪˈliːv] *Schmerz, Not* lindern, *j-n, Gewissen* erleichtern; *j-n* ablösen

re·li·gion [rɪˈlɪdʒən] Religion *f*; ~

gious Religions...; religiös; gewissenhaft

rel·ish [ˈrelɪʃ] 1. *fig.* Gefallen *m*, Geschmack *m* (**for** an *dat.*); *gastr.* Würze *f*; *gastr.* Soße *f*; **with** ~ mit Genuß *f*; 2. genießen, sich *et.* schmecken lassen; Geschmack *od.* Gefallen finden an (*dat.*)

re·luc|·tance [rɪˈlʌktəns] Widerstreben *n*; **with** ~ widerwillig, ungern; **~·tant** widerstrebend, widerwillig

re·ly [rɪˈlaɪ]: ~ **on** sich verlassen auf (*acc.*)

re·main [rɪˈmeɪn] 1. (ver)bleiben; übrigbleiben; 2. **~s** *pl.* (Über)Reste *pl.*; **~·der** [rɪˈmeɪndə] Rest *m*

re·make 1. [riːˈmeɪk] (**-made**) wieder *od.* neu machen; 2. [ˈriːmeɪk] Remake *n*, Neuverfilmung *f*

re·mand *jur.* [rɪˈmɑːnd] 1. **be ~ed in custody** in Untersuchungshaft bleiben; 2. **be on** ~ in Untersuchungshaft sein; **prisoner on** ~ Untersuchungsgefangene(r *m*) *f*

re·mark [rɪˈmɑːk] 1. *v/t.* bemerken, äußern; *v/i.* sich äußern (**on** über *acc.*, zu); 2. Bemerkung *f*; **re·marˈka·ble** bemerkenswert; außergewöhnlich

rem·e·dy [ˈremədɪ] 1. (Heil-, Hilfs-, Gegen)Mittel *n*; (Ab)Hilfe *f*; 2. *Schaden etc.* beheben; *Mißstand* abstellen; *Situation* bereinigen

re·mem|·ber [rɪˈmembə] sich erinnern an (*acc.*); denken an (*acc.*); **please** ~ **me to her** grüße sie bitte von mir; **~·brance** [rɪˈmembrəns] Erinnerung *f*; **in** ~ **of** zur Erinnerung an

re·mind [rɪˈmaɪnd] erinnern (**of** an *acc.*); **~·er** Mahnung *f*

rem·i·nis·cences [remɪˈnɪsnsɪz] *pl.* Erinnerungen *pl.* (**of** an *acc.*); **~·cent:** **be** ~ **of** erinnern an (*acc.*)

re·mit [rɪˈmɪt] (**-tt-**) *Schulden, Strafe* erlassen; *Sünden* vergeben; *Geld* überweisen (**to** *dat. od.* an *acc.*); **~·tance** (Geld)Überweisung *f* (**to** an *acc.*)

rem·nant [ˈremnənt] (Über)Rest *m*

re·mod·el [riːˈmɒdl] (*Brt.* **-ll-**, *Am.* **-l-**) umformen, -gestalten

re·mon·strance [rɪˈmɒnstrəns] Protest *m*, Beschwerde *f*; **rem·on·strate** [ˈremənstreɪt] protestieren (**with** bei; **against** gegen), sich beschweren (**with** bei; **about** über *acc.*)

R

re·morse [rɪ'mɔːs] Gewissensbisse *pl.* Reue *f;* ~**less** unbarmherzig

re·mote [rɪ'məʊt] (~*r,* ~*st*) fern, entfernt; abgelegen, entlegen; ~ **con'trol** *tech.* Fernlenkung *f,* -steuerung *f;* **Fernbedienung** *f*

re·mov·al [rɪ'muːvl] Entfernung *f;* Umzug *m;* ~ **van** Möbelwagen *m*

re·move [rɪ'muːv] *v/t.* entfernen (*from* von); *Deckel, Hut etc.* abnehmen; *Kleidung* ablegen; beseitigen, aus dem Weg räumen; *v/i.* (um)ziehen (*from* von; *to* nach); **re'mov·er** (*Flecken- etc.*)Entferner *m*

Re·nais·sance [rə'neɪsəns] *die* Renaissance

ren·der ['rendə] berühmt, schwierig, *möglich etc.* machen; *Dienst* erweisen; *Gedicht, mus.* vortragen; übersetzen, -tragen (*into* in *acc.*); *mus* ~ **down** Fett auslassen; ~**ing** *bsd. Brt.* ['rendərɪŋ] → **rendition**

ren·di·tion [ren'dɪʃn] Vortrag *m;* Übersetzung *f,* -tragung *f*

re·new [rɪ'njuː] erneuern; *Gespräch etc.* wiederaufnehmen; *Kraft etc.* wiedererlangen; *Vertrag, Paß* verlängern (lassen); ~**al** Erneuerung *f;* Verlängerung *f*

re·nounce [rɪ'naʊns] verzichten auf (*acc.*); *s-m Glauben etc.* abschwören

ren·o·vate ['renəʊveɪt] renovieren

re·nown [rɪ'naʊn] Ruhm *m;* ~**ed** berühmt (*as* als; *for* wegen, für)

rent¹ [rent] **1.** Miete *f;* Pacht *f; bsd. Am.* Leihgebühr *f;* △ *nicht* Rente; *for* ~ *bsd. Am.* zu vermieten *od.* zu verleihen; **2.** mieten, pachten (*from* von); *Auto etc.* mieten; *a.* ~ **out** *bsd. Am.* vermieten, -pachten (*to* an *acc.*)

rent² [rent] Riß *m*

'Rent-a-... ...verleih *m,* ...vermietung *f*

rent·al ['rentl] Miete *f;* Pacht *f; bsd. Am.* Leihgebühr *f; bsd. Am.* → ~**ed** **'car** Leih-, Mietwagen *m*

re·nun·ci·a·tion [rɪnʌnsɪ'eɪʃn] Verzicht *m* (*of* auf *acc.*); Abschwören *n*

re·pair [rɪ'peə] **1.** reparieren, ausbessern; *fig.* wiedergutmachen; **2.** Reparatur *f;* Ausbesserung *f;* ~*s pl.* Instandsetzungsarbeiten *pl.; beyond* ~ nicht mehr zu reparieren; *in good* l*bad* ~ in gutem/ schlechtem Zustand; *be under* ~ in Reparatur sein; *the road is under* ~ an der Straße wird gerade gearbeitet

rep·a·ra·tion [repə'reɪʃn] Wiedergutmachung *f;* Entschädigung *f;* ~*s pl. pol.* Reparationen *pl.*

rep·ar·tee [repɑ:'tiː] Schlagfertigkeit *f;* schlagfertige Antwort(en *pl.*)

re·pay [riː'peɪ] (*-paid*) *et.* zurückzahlen; *Besuch* erwidern; *et.* vergelten; *j-n* entschädigen; ~**ment** Rückzahlung *f*

re·peal [rɪ'piːl] *Gesetz etc.* aufheben

re·peat [rɪ'piːt] **1.** *v/t.* wiederholen; nachsprechen; ~ *o.s.* sich wiederholen; *v/i.* aufstoßen (*on s.o.*) (*Speise*) **2.** *Rundfunk, TV:* Wiederholung *f; mus.* Wiederholungszeichen *n;* ~**ed** wiederholt

re·pel [rɪ'pel] (*-ll-*) *Angriff, Feind* zurückschlagen; *Wasser etc.,* fig. *j-n* abstoßen; ~**lent** [rɪ'pelənt] abstoßend

re·pent [rɪ'pent] bereuen; **re'pent·ance** Reue *f;* **re'pen·tant** reuig, reumütig

re·per·cus·sion [riːpə'kʌʃn] *mst* ~*s pl.* Auswirkungen *pl.* (*on* auf *acc.*)

rep·er·toire *thea. etc.* ['repətwɑː] Repertoire *n*

rep·er·to·ry thea·tre (*Am.* **thea·ter**) ['repətərɪ -] Repertoiretheater *n*

rep·e·ti·tion [repɪ'tɪʃn] Wiederholung *f*

re·place [rɪ'pleɪs] an *j-s* Stelle treten, *j-n, et.* ersetzen; *tech.* austauschen, ersetzen; ~**ment** *tech.* Austausch *m;* Ersatz *m*

re·plant [riː'plɑːnt] umpflanzen

re·play 1. [riː'pleɪ] *Sport:* Spiel wiederholen; *Tonband-, Videoaufname etc.* abspielen *od.* wiederholen; **2.** ['riːpleɪ] Wiederholung *f*

re·plen·ish [rɪ'plenɪʃ] (wieder) auffüllen

re·plete [rɪ'pliːt] satt; angefüllt, ausgestattet (*with* mit)

rep·li·ca ['replɪkə] *Kunst:* Originalkopie *f;* Kopie *f,* Nachbildung *f*

re·ply [rɪ'plaɪ] **1.** antworten, erwidern (*to* auf *acc.*); **2.** Antwort *f,* Erwiderung *f* (*to* auf *acc.*); *in* ~ *to* (als Antwort) auf; ~ **'cou·pon** Rückantwortschein *m;* ~**-paid 'en·ve·lope** Freiumschlag *m*

re·port [rɪ'pɔːt] **1.** Bericht *m;* Meldung *f,* Nachricht *f;* Gerücht *n;* Knall *m;* ~ *Brt.,* ~ **card** *Am. Schule:* Zeugnis *n;* **2.** berichten (über *acc.*); (sich) melden; anzeigen; *it is* ~**ed that** es heißt, daß; ~**ed speech** *gr.* indirekte Rede; ~**er** Reporter(in), Berichterstatter(in)

re·pose [rɪˈpəʊz] Ruhe f; Gelassenheit f

re·pos·i·to·ry [rɪˈpɒzɪtərɪ] (Waren)Lager n; fig. Fundgrube f, Quelle f

rep·re·sent [reprɪˈzent] j-n, Wahlbezirk vertreten; darstellen; dar-, hinstellen (**as, to be** als); **~·sen·ta·tion** [reprɪzenˈteɪʃn] Vertretung f; Darstellung f; **~·sen·ta·tive** [reprɪˈzentətɪv] **1.** repräsentativ (a. pol.), typisch (**of** für); **2.** (Stell)Vertreter(in); (Handels)Vertreter(in); parl. Abgeordnete(r m) f; **House of ☆s** Am. parl. Repräsentantenhaus n

re·press [rɪˈpres] unterdrücken; psych. verdrängen; **re·pres·sion** [rɪˈpreʃn] Unterdrückung f; psych. Verdrängung f

re·prieve jur. [rɪˈpriːv] **1.** he was ~d er wurde begnadigt; s-e Urteilsvollstreckung wurde ausgesetzt; **2.** Begnadigung f; Vollstreckungsaufschub m

rep·ri·mand [ˈreprɪmɑːnd] **1.** rügen, tadeln (**for** wegen); **2.** Rüge f, Tadel m, Verweis m

re·print 1. [ˌriːˈprɪnt] neu auflegen od. drucken, nachdrucken; **2.** [ˈriːprɪnt] Neuauflage f, Nachdruck m

re·pri·sal [rɪˈpraɪzl] Repressalie f, Vergeltungsmaßnahme f

re·proach [rɪˈprəʊtʃ] **1.** Vorwurf m; **2.** vorwerfen (**s.o. with s.th.** j-m et.); Vorwürfe machen; **~·ful** vorwurfsvoll

rep·ro·bate [ˈreprəbeɪt] verkommenes Subjekt

re·pro·cess [ˌriːˈprəʊses] Kernbrennstoffe wiederaufbereiten; **~·ing plant** Wiederaufbereitungsanlage f

re·pro·duce [riːprəˈdjuːs] v/t. Ton etc. wiedergeben; Bild etc. reproduzieren; **~ o.s.** → v/i. biol. sich fortpflanzen od. vermehren; **~·duc·tion** [riːprəˈdʌkʃn] biol. Fortpflanzung f; Reproduktion f; Wiedergabe f; **~·duc·tive** biol. [riːprəˈdʌktɪv] Fortpflanzungs...

re·proof [rɪˈpruːf] Rüge f, Tadel m

re·prove [rɪˈpruːv] rügen, tadeln (**for** wegen)

rep·tile zo. [ˈreptaɪl] Reptil n

re·pub·lic [rɪˈpʌblɪk] Republik f; **~·li·can** [rɪˈpʌblɪkən] **1.** republikanisch; **2.** Republikaner(in)

re·pu·di·ate [rɪˈpjuːdɪeɪt] zurückweisen

re·pug·nance [rɪˈpʌɡnəns]: **in ~, with ~** angewidert; **~·nant** widerlich, widerwärtig, abstoßend

re·pulse [rɪˈpʌls] **1.** j-n, Angebot etc. ab-, zurückweisen; mil. Angriff zurückschlagen; **2.** mil. Zurückschlagen n; Ab-, Zurückweisung f

re·pul·sion [rɪˈpʌlʃn] Abscheu m, Widerwille m; phys. Abstoßung f; **~·sive** [rɪˈpʌlsɪv] abstoßend, widerlich, widerwärtig; phys. abstoßend

rep·u·ta·ble [ˈrepjʊtəbl] angesehen; **~·tion** [repjʊˈteɪʃn] (guter) Ruf, Ansehen n

re·pute [rɪˈpjuːt] (guter) Ruf; **re·put·ed** angeblich

re·quest [rɪˈkwest] **1.** (**for**) Bitte f (um), Wunsch m (nach); **at the ~ of s.o., at s.o.'s ~** auf j-s Bitte hin; **on ~** auf Wunsch; **2.** um et. bitten od. ersuchen; j-n bitten, ersuchen (**to do** zu tun); **~ stop** Brt. Bedarfshaltestelle f

re·quire [rɪˈkwaɪə] erfordern; benötigen, brauchen; verlangen; **if ~d** wenn nötig; **~·ment** Erfordernis n, Bedürfnis n; Anforderung f

req·ui·site [ˈrekwɪzɪt] **1.** erforderlich; **2.** mst **~s** pl. Artikel pl.; **toilet ~s** pl. Toilettenartikel pl.; △ nicht (Bühnen)Requisit

req·ui·si·tion [rekwɪˈzɪʃn] **1.** Anforderung f; mil. Requisition f, Beschlagnahme f; **make a ~ for** et. anfordern; **2.** anfordern; mil. requirieren, beschlagnahmen

re·sale [ˈriːseɪl] Wieder-, Weiterverkauf m

re·scind jur. [rɪˈsɪnd] Gesetz, Urteil etc. aufheben

res·cue [ˈreskjuː] **1.** retten (**from** aus, vor dat.); **2.** Rettung f; Hilfe f; Rettungs...

re·search [rɪˈsɜːtʃ] **1.** Forschung f; **2.** forschen; et. erforschen; **~·er** Forscher(in)

re·sem·blance [rɪˈzembləns] Ähnlichkeit f (**to** mit; **between** zwischen dat.); **~·ble** [rɪˈzembl] ähnlich sein, ähneln (dat.)

re·sent [rɪˈzent] übelnehmen, sich ärgern über (acc.); **~·ful** ärgerlich; **~·ment** Ärger m (**against, at** über acc.)

res·er·va·tion [rezəˈveɪʃn] Reservierung f, Vorbestellung f (von Zimmern etc.); Vorbehalt m; Am. (Indianer)Reservat(ion f) n; bsd. Am. (Wild)Reservat n; → **central reservation**

R

re·serve [rɪˈzɜːv] **1.** (sich) *et.* aufsparen (*for* für); sich vorbehalten; reservieren (lassen), vorbestellen; **2.** Reserve *f* (*a. mil.*); Vorrat *m* (*Naturschutz-, Wild*)Reservat *n*; *Sport*: Reservespieler(in); Reserviertheit *f*, Zurückhaltung *f*; **~d** zurückhaltend, reserviert

res·er·voir [ˈrezəvwɑː] Reservoir *n* (*a. fig.* of an *dat.*)

re·set [riːˈset] (*-tt-; -set*) *Uhr* umstellen; *Zeiger etc.* zurückstellen (**to** auf *acc.*)

re·set·tle [riːˈsetl] umsiedeln

re·side [rɪˈzaɪd] wohnen, ansässig sein, s-n Wohnsitz haben

res·i·dence [ˈrezɪdəns] Wohnsitz *m*, -ort *m*; Aufenthalt *m*; Residenz *f*; *official* ~ Amtssitz *m*; '**~ per·mit** Aufenthaltsgenehmigung *f*, -erlaubnis *f*

res·i·dent [ˈrezɪdənt] **1.** wohnhaft, ansässig; **2.** Bewohner(in) (*in e-s Hauses*), (*e-r Stadt a.*) Einwohner(in); (Hotel-)Gast *m*; *mot.* Anlieger(in)

res·i·den·tial [rezɪˈdenʃl] Wohn...; ~ **'ar·e·a** Wohngebiet *n*, -gegend *f*

re·sid·u·al [rɪˈzɪdjʊəl] übrig(geblieben), restlich, Rest...; ~ **pol'lu·tion** Altlasten *pl.*; **res·i·due** [ˈrezɪdjuː] Rest(betrag) *m*; *chem.* Rest *m*, Rückstand *m*

re·sign [rɪˈzaɪn] *v/i.* zurücktreten (*from* von); *v/t.* Amt etc. niederlegen; aufgeben; verzichten auf (*acc.*); ~ **o.s. to** sich fügen in (*acc.*), sich abfinden mit; **res·ig·na·tion** [rezɪɡˈneɪʃn] Rücktritt *m*; Resignation *f*; **~ed** [rɪˈzaɪnd] ergeben, resigniert

re·sil·i·ence [rɪˈzɪlɪəns] Elastizität *f*; *fig.* Zähigkeit *f*; **~ent** elastisch; *fig.* zäh

res·in [ˈrezɪn] Harz *n*

re·sist [rɪˈzɪst] widerstehen (*dat.*); Widerstand leisten, sich widersetzen (*dat.*), ~ **ance** Widerstand *m* (*a. electr.*); *med.* Widerstandskraft *f*; (*Hitze- etc.*)Beständigkeit *f*, (*Stoß- etc.*)Festigkeit *f*; *line of least* ~ Weg *m* des geringsten Widerstands; **re·sis·tant** widerstandsfähig; (*hitze- etc.*)beständig, (*stoß- etc.*)fest

res·o·lute [ˈrezəluːt] resolut, entschlossen; **~lu·tion** [rezəˈluːʃn] Beschluß *m*, *parl. etc. a.* Resolution *f*; Vorsatz *m*; Entschlossenheit *f*; Lösung *f*

re·solve [rɪˈzɒlv] **1.** beschließen; *Problem etc.* lösen; (sich) auflösen; ~ **on**

sich entschließen zu; **2.** Vorsatz *m*; Entschlossenheit *f*

res·o·nance [ˈrezənəns] Resonanz *f*; voller Klang; '**~nant** voll(tönend); widerhallend

re·sort [rɪˈzɔːt] **1.** Erholungs-, Urlaubsort *m*; → *health* (*seaside, summer*) *resort*; *have* ~ *to* → **2.** ~ *to* Zuflucht nehmen zu

re·sound [rɪˈzaʊnd] widerhallen (*with* von)

re·source [rɪˈsɔːs] Mittel *n*, Zuflucht *f*; Ausweg *m*; Einfallsreichtum *m*; **~s** *pl.* Mittel *pl.*; (*natürliche*) Reichtümer *pl.*, (*Boden-, Natur*)Schätze *pl.*; **~ful** einfallsreich, findig

re·spect [rɪˈspekt] **1.** Achtung *f*, Respekt *m* (*for* vor *dat.*); Rücksicht *f* (*for* auf *acc.*); Beziehung *f*, Hinsicht *f*; *with* ~ *to* was ... anbelangt *od.* betrifft; *in this* ~ in dieser Hinsicht; *give my* ~*s to* ... e-e Empfehlung an ...; **2.** *v/t.* respektieren, achten; respektieren, berücksichtigen, beachten; **re'spec·ta·ble** ehrbar, anständig, geachtet; ansehnlich, beachtlich; *it is not* ~ es gehört sich nicht; **~ful** respektvoll, ehrerbietig

re·spec·tive [rɪˈspektɪv] jeweilig; *we went to our* ~ *places* jeder ging zu seinem Platz; **~ly** beziehungsweise

res·pi·ra·tion [respəˈreɪʃn] Atmung *f*; **~tor** [ˈrespəreɪtə] Atemschutzgerät *n*

re·spite [ˈrespaɪt] Pause *f*; Aufschub *m*, Frist *f*; *without* ~ ohne Unterbrechung

re·splen·dent [rɪˈsplendənt] glänzend, strahlend

re·spond [rɪˈspɒnd] antworten, erwidern (**to** auf *acc.*; *that* daß); reagieren, *med. a.* ansprechen (**to** auf *acc.*)

re·sponse [rɪˈspɒns] Antwort *f*, Erwiderung *f* (**to** auf *acc.*); *fig.* Reaktion *f* (**to** auf *acc.*)

re·spon·si·bil·i·ty [rɪspɒnsəˈbɪlətɪ] Verantwortung *f*; *on one's own* ~ auf eigene Verantwortung; *sense of* ~ Verantwortungsgefühl *n*; *take* (*full*) ~ *for* die (volle) Verantwortung übernehmen für; **~si·ble** [rɪˈspɒnsəbl] verantwortlich; verantwortungsbewußt; verantwortungsvoll (*Position*)

rest[1] [rest] **1.** Ruhe(pause) *f*; Erholung *f*; *tech.* Stütze *f*; (*Telefon*)Gabel *f*; *have od. take a* ~ sich ausruhen; *set s.o.'s mind at* ~ j-n beruhigen; **2.** *v/i.* ruhen;

sich ausruhen; lehnen (**against, on** an *dat.*); **let s.th. ~** et. auf sich beruhen lassen; **~ on** ruhen auf (*dat.*) (*a. fig. Blick*); *fig.* beruhen auf (*dat.*); *v/t.* (aus)ruhen (lassen); lehnen (**against** gegen; **on** an *acc.*)

rest² [rest] Rest *m*; **all the ~ of them** alle übrigen; **for the ~** im übrigen

res·tau·rant ['restərɒnt, 'restərənt, 'restərɔ̃:ŋ] Restaurant *n*, Gaststätte *f*

'rest|·ful ruhig, erholsam; **'~ home** Altenpflegeheim *n*; Erholungsheim *n*

res·ti·tu·tion [restɪ'tjuːʃn] Rückgabe *f*, -erstattung *f*

res·tive ['restɪv] unruhig, nervös

'rest·less ruhelos, rastlos; unruhig

res·to·ra·tion [restə'reɪʃn] Wiederherstellung *f*; Restaurierung *f*; Rückgabe , -erstattung *f*

re·store [rɪ'stɔː] wiederherstellen; restaurieren; zurückgeben, zurückerstatten; **be ~d (to health)** wiederhergestellt *od.* wieder gesund sein

re·strain [rɪ'streɪn] (**from**) zurückhalten (von), hindern an (*dat.*); **I had to ~ myself** ich mußte mich beherrschen (**from doing s.th.** um nicht et. zu tun); **~ed** [rɪ'streɪnd] beherrscht; dezent (*Farbe etc.*); **~t** [rɪ'streɪnt] Beherrschung *f*; Be-, Einschränkung *f*

re·strict [rɪ'strɪkt] beschränken (**to** auf *acc.*), einschränken; **re·stric·tion** [rɪ'strɪkʃn] Be-, Einschränkung *f*; **without ~s** uneingeschränkt

'rest room *Am.* Toilette *f* (*e-s Hotels, Restaurants etc.*)

re·sult [rɪ'zʌlt] **1.** Ergebnis *n*, Resultat *n*; Folge *f*; **as a ~ of** als Folge von (*od. gen.*); **without ~** ergebnislos; **2.** folgen, sich ergeben (**from** aus); **~ in** zur Folge haben (*acc.*), führen zu

re·sume [rɪ'zjuːm] wiederaufnehmen; fortsetzen; *Platz* wieder einnehmen; **re·sump·tion** [rɪ'zʌmpʃn] Wiederaufnahme *f*; Fortsetzung *f*

Res·ur·rec·tion *rel.* [rezə'rekʃn] Auferstehung *f*

re·sus·ci·|·tate *med.* [rɪ'sʌsɪteɪt] wiederbeleben; **~·ta·tion** *med.* [rɪsʌsɪ'teɪʃn] Wiederbelebung *f*

re·tail 1. ['riːteɪl] Einzelhandel *m*; Einzelhandels...; **by ~** im Einzelhandel; **2.** ['riːteɪl] *adv.* im Einzelhandel; **3.** [riː'teɪl] *v/t.* im Einzelhandel verkaufen

(**at, for** für); *v/i.* im Einzelhandel verkauft werden (**at, for** für); **~·er** [riː'teɪlə] Einzelhändler(in *f*)

re·tain [rɪ'teɪn] (be)halten, bewahren; *Wasser* speichern (*Boden*); *Wärme* speichern

re·tal·i·|·ate [rɪ'tælɪeɪt] Vergeltung üben, sich revanchieren; **~·a·tion** [rɪtælɪ'eɪʃn] Vergeltung(smaßnahmen *pl.*) *f*

re·tard [rɪ'tɑːd] verzögern, aufhalten, hemmen; (*mentally*) **~ed** (geistig) zurückgeblieben

retch [retʃ] würgen (*beim Erbrechen*)

re·tell [riː'tel] (*-told*) nacherzählen

re·think [riː'θɪŋk] (*-thought*) et. noch einmal überdenken

re·ti·cent ['retɪsənt] schweigsam

ret·i·nue ['retɪnjuː] Gefolge *n*

re·tire [rɪ'taɪə] *v/i.* in Rente *od.* Pension gehen, sich pensionieren lassen; sich zurückziehen; **~ from business** sich zur Ruhe setzen; *v/t.* in den Ruhestand versetzen, pensionieren; **~d** pensioniert, im Ruhestand (lebend); **be ~ a.** in Rente *od.* Pension sein; **~·ment** Pensionierung *f*, Ruhestand *m*; **re·tir·ing** [rɪ'taɪərɪŋ] zurückhaltend

re·tort [rɪ'tɔːt] **1.** (scharf) entgegnen *od.* erwidern; **2.** (scharfe) Entgegnung *od.* Erwiderung

re·touch *phot.* [riː'tʌtʃ] retuschieren

re·trace [rɪ'treɪs] *Tathergang etc.* rekonstruieren; **~ one's steps** denselben Weg zurückgehen

re·tract [rɪ'trækt] *v/t.* *Angebot* zurückziehen; *Behauptung* zurücknehmen; *Geständnis* widerrufen; *Krallen, aviat. Fahrgestell* einziehen; *v/i.* eingezogen werden (*Krallen, aviat. Fahrgestell*)

re·train [riː'treɪn] umschulen

re·tread 1. [riː'tred] *Reifen* runderneuern; **2.** ['riːtred] runderneuerter Reifen

re·treat [rɪ'triːt] **1.** Rückzug *m*; Zufluchtsort *m*; **beat a (hasty) ~** abhauen; **2.** sich zurückziehen; zurückweichen (**from** vor *dat.*)

ret·ri·bu·tion [retrɪ'bjuːʃn] Vergeltung *f*

re·trieve [rɪ'triːv] zurückholen, wiederbekommen; *Fehler, Verlust etc.* wiedergutmachen; *hunt.* apportieren

ret·ro·|·ac·tive *jur.* [retrəʊ'æktɪv] rückwirkend; **~·grade** ['retrəʊgreɪd] rückschrittlich; **~·spect** ['retrəʊspekt]: **in ~** rückschauend, im Rückblick; **~·spec-**

tive [retrəʊ'spektɪv] rückblickend; *jur.* rückwirkend

re·try *jur.* [riː'traɪ] *Fall* erneut verhandeln; neu verhandeln gegen *j-n*

re·turn [rɪ'tɜːn] **1.** *v/i.* zurückkehren, -kommen; zurückgehen; **~ to** auf ein *Thema etc.* zurückkommen; in *e-e Gewohnheit etc.* zurückfallen; in *e-n Zustand etc.* zurückkommen; *v/t.* zurückgeben (**to** *dat.*); zurückbringen (**to** *dat.*); zurückschicken, -senden (**to** *dat. od. an acc.*); zurücklegen, -stellen; erwidern; *Gewinn etc.* abwerfen; → **verdict**; **2.** Rückkehr *f, fig.* Wiederauftreten *n*; Rückgabe *f*; Zurückbringen *n*; Zurückschicken *n*, -senden *n*; Zurücklegen *n*, -stellen *n*; Erwiderung *f*; *Tennis etc.*: Return *m*, Rückschlag *m*; *a.* **~s** *pl.* Gewinn *m*; **many happy ~s (of the day)** herzlichen Glückwunsch zum Geburtstag; **by ~ (of post)** umgehend; **in ~ for** (als Gegenleistung) für; **3.** *adj.* Rück...; **re'tur·na·ble** in *Zssgn* Mehrweg...; **~ bottle** Pfandflasche *f*

re·turn| '**key** *Computer*: Eingabetaste *f*; **~ 'game**, **~ 'match** *Sport*: Rückspiel *n*; **~ 'tick·et** *Brt.* Rückfahrkarte *f*; *aviat.* Rückflugticket *n*

re·u·ni·fi·ca·tion *pol.* [riːjuːnɪfɪ'keɪʃn] Wiedervereinigung *f*

re·u·nion [riː'juːnjən] Treffen *n*, Wiedersehensfeier *f*; Wiedervereinigung *f*

re·us·a·ble [riː'juːzəbl] wiederverwendbar

rev F *mot.* [rev] **1.** Umdrehung *f*; **~ coun·ter** Drehzahlmesser *m*; **2.** (**-vv-**) *a.* **~ up** aufheulen (lassen) (*Motor*)

Rev *nur geschr. Abk. für Reverend rel.* Hochwürden (*Titel u. Anrede*)

re·val·ue *econ.* [riː'væljuː] *Währung* aufwerten

re·veal [rɪ'viːl] den Blick freigeben auf (*acc.*), zeigen; *Geheimnis etc.* enthüllen, aufdecken; **~ing** offenherzig (*Kleid etc.*); *fig.* aufschlußreich

rev·el ['revl] (*bsd. Brt.* **-ll-**, *Am.* **-l-**): **~ in** schwelgen in (*dat.*); sich weiden an (*dat.*)

rev·e·la·tion [revə'leɪʃn] Enthüllung *f*, Aufdeckung *f*; *rel.* Offenbarung *f*

re·venge [rɪ'vendʒ] **1.** Rache *f*; *bsd. Sport, Spiel*: Revanche *f*; **in ~ for** aus Rache für; **2.** rächen; **~ful** rachsüchtig

rev·e·nue ['revənjuː] Staatseinkünfte *pl.*, -einnahmen *pl.*

re·ver·be·rate [rɪ'vɜːbəreɪt] nach-, widerhallen

re·vere [rɪ'vɪə] (ver)ehren

rev·e·rence ['revərəns] Verehrung *f*; Ehrfurcht *f* (**for** vor *dat.*); **2·rend** *rel.* ['revərənd] Hochwürden *m*; **~rent** ['revərənt] ehrfürchtig, ehrfurchtsvoll

rev·er·ie ['revərɪ] (Tag)Träumerei *f*

re·vers·al [rɪ'vɜːsl] Umkehrung *f*; Rückschlag *m*

re·verse [rɪ'vɜːs] **1.** *adj.* umgekehrt; **in ~ order** in umgekehrter Reihenfolge; **2.** *mot.* *Wagen* im Rückwärtsgang *od.* rückwärts fahren; *Reihenfolge etc.* umkehren; *Urteil etc.* aufheben; *Entscheidung etc.* umstoßen; **3.** Gegenteil *n*; *mot.* Rückwärtsgang *m*; Rück-, Kehrseite *f* (*e-r Münze*); Rückschlag *m*; **~ 'gear** *mot.* Rückwärtsgang *m*; **~ 'side** linke (*Stoff*)Seite

re·vers·i·ble [rɪ'vɜːsəbl] doppelseitig (tragbar)

re·vert [rɪ'vɜːt]: **~ to** in *e-n Zustand* zurückkehren; in *e-e Gewohnheit etc.* zurückfallen; auf *ein Thema* zurückkommen

re·view [rɪ'vjuː] **1.** Überprüfung *f*; Besprechung *f*, Kritik *f*, Rezension *f*; *mil.* Parade *f*; *Am. ped.* (Stoff)Wiederholung *f* (**for** für *e-e Prüfung*); **2.** überprüfen; besprechen, rezensieren; *mil.* besichtigen, inspizieren; *Am. ped.* Stoff wiederholen (**for** für *e-e Prüfung*); **~er** Kritiker(in), Rezensent(in)

re·vise [rɪ'vaɪz] revidieren, *Ansicht* ändern, *Buch etc.* überarbeiten; *Brt. ped.* Stoff wiederholen (**for** für *e-e Prüfung*); **re·vi·sion** [rɪ'vɪʒn] Revision *f*, Überarbeitung *f*; überarbeitete Ausgabe; *Brt. ped.* (Stoff)Wiederholung *f* (**for** für *e-e Prüfung*)

re·viv·al [rɪ'vaɪvl] Wiederbelebung *f*; Wiederaufleben *n*; **re·vive** [rɪ'vaɪv] wiederbeleben; wiederaufleben (lassen); *Erinnerungen* wachrufen; wieder zu sich kommen; sich erholen

re·voke [rɪ'vəʊk] widerrufen, zurücknehmen, rückgängig machen

re·volt [rɪ'vəʊlt] **1.** *v/i.* sich auflehnen, revoltieren (**against** gegen); Abscheu empfinden, empört sein (**against, at, from** über *acc.*); *v/t.* mit Abscheu erfüllen, abstoßen; **2.** Revolte *f*, Aufstand *m*; **~ing** abscheulich, abstoßend

rev·o·lu·tion [revə'lu:ʃn] Revolution *f* (*a. pol.*), Umwälzung *f*; *astr.* Umlauf *m* (**round** um); *tech.* Umdrehung *f*; *number of ~s pl. tech.* Drehzahl *f*; **~ coun·ter** *mot.* Drehzahlmesser *m*; **~'ar·y** [revə'lu:ʃnəri] **1.** revolutionär; Revolutions...; **2.** *pol.* Revolutionär(in); **~ize** *fig.* [revə'lu:ʃnaız] revolutionieren

re·volve [rɪ'vɒlv] sich drehen (**on**, **round** um); **~ around** sich drehen um; **re'volv·er** Revolver *m*; **re'volv·ing** Dreh...; **~ door(s** *pl.*) Drehtür *f*

re·vue *thea.* [rɪ'vju:] Revue *f*; Kabarett *n*

re·vul·sion [rɪ'vʌlʃn] Abscheu *m*

re·ward [rɪ'wɔ:d] **1.** Belohnung *f*; **2.** belohnen; **~ing** lohnend, *Aufgabe etc. a.* dankbar

re·write [ri:'raɪt] (**-wrote**, **-written**) neu schreiben, umschreiben

rhap·so·dy *mus.* ['ræpsədɪ] Rhapsodie *f*

rhet·o·ric ['retərɪk] Rhetorik *f*

rheu·ma·tism *med.* ['ru:mətɪzəm] Rheuma(tismus *m*) *n*

rhi·no *zo.* ['raɪnəʊ] (*pl.* **-nos**), **rhi·noc·e·ros** *zo.* [raɪ'nɒsərəs] (*pl.* **-ros**, **-roses** [-sɪz]) Rhinozeros *n*, Nashorn *n*

rhu·barb *bot.* ['ru:ba:b] Rhabarber *m*

rhyme [raɪm] **1.** Reim *m*; Vers *m*; **without ~ or reason** ohne Sinn u. Verstand; **2.** (sich) reimen

rhyth·m ['rɪðəm] Rhythmus *m*; **~mic** ['rɪðmɪk] (**~ally**), **~mi·cal** rhythmisch

rib *anat.* [rɪb] Rippe *f*

rib·bon ['rɪbən] (*a.* Farb-, Ordens)Band *n*; Streifen *m*; Fetzen *m*

'rib cage *anat.* Brustkorb *m*

rice *bot.* [raɪs] Reis *m*; **~ 'pud·ding** Milchreis *m*

rich [rɪtʃ] **1.** reich (**in** an *dat.*); prächtig, kostbar; schwer (*Speise*); fruchtbar, fett (*Erde*); voll (*Ton*); satt (*Farbe*); (**in calories**) kalorienreich; **2. the ~ pl.** die Reichen *pl.*

rick [rɪk] (Stroh-, Heu)Schober *m*

rick·ets *med.* ['rɪkɪts] *sg.* Rachitis *f*

rick·et·y F ['rɪkətɪ] gebrechlich; wack(e)lig (*Möbelstück etc.*)

rid [rɪd] (**-dd-**; **rid**) befreien (**of** von); **get ~ of** loswerden

rid·dance F ['rɪdəns]: **good ~!** den (die, das) sind wir Gott sei Dank los!

rid·den ['rɪdn] **1.** *p.p. von* ride 1; **2.** *in Zssgn* geplagt *od.* heimgesucht von

rid·dle[1] ['rɪdl] Rätsel *n*

rid·dle[2] ['rɪdl] **1.** grobes Sieb, Schüttelsieb *n*; **2.** sieben; durchlöchern, -sieben

ride [raɪd] **1.** (**rode**, **ridden**) *v/i.* reiten; fahren (**on** auf *e-m Fahrrad etc.*; **in** *od. Am.* **on** in *e-m Bus etc.*); *v/t.* reiten (auf *dat.*); *Fahr-, Motorrad* fahren, fahren auf (*dat.*); **2.** Ritt *m*; Fahrt *f*; **'rid·er** Reiter(in); (*Motorrad-, Rad*)Fahrer(in)

ridge [rɪdʒ] (*Gebirgs*)Kamm *m*, Grat *m*; (*Dach*)First *m*

rid·i·cule ['rɪdɪkju:l] **1.** Spott *m*; **2.** lächerlich machen, spotten über (*acc.*); **ri·dic·u·lous** [rɪ'dɪkjʊləs] lächerlich

rid·ing ['raɪdɪŋ] Reit...

riff·raff *contp.* ['rɪfræf] Gesindel *n*

ri·fle[1] ['raɪfl] Gewehr *n*

ri·fle[2] ['raɪfl] durchwühlen

rift [rɪft] Spalt(e *f*) *m*; *fig.* Riß *m*

rig [rɪg] **1.** (**-gg-**) *Schiff* auftakeln; **~ out** *j-n* ausstaffieren; **~ up** F (*behelfsmäßig*) zusammenbauen (**from** aus); **2.** *naut.* Takelage *f*; *tech.* Bohrinsel *f*; F Aufmachung *f*; **'~ging** *naut.* Takelage *f*

right [raɪt] **1.** *adj.* recht; richtig; rechte(r, -s), Rechts...; **all ~!** in Ordnung!, gut!; **that's all ~!** das macht nichts!, schon gut!, bitte!; **that's ~!** richtig!, ganz recht!, stimmt!; **be ~** recht haben; **put ~**, **set ~** in Ordnung bringen; berichtigen, korrigieren; **2.** *adv.* (nach) rechts; richtig, recht; genau; gerade(wegs), direkt; ganz, völlig; **~ away** sofort; **~ now** im Moment; sofort; **~ on** geradeaus; **turn ~** (sich) nach rechts wenden; *mot.* rechts abbiegen; **3.** Recht *n*; **die Rechte** (*a. pol.*, *Boxen*), rechte Seite; **on the ~** rechts, auf der rechten Seite; **to the ~** (nach) rechts; **keep to the ~** sich rechts halten; rechts fahren; **4.** aufrichten; *et.* wiedergutmachen, in Ordnung bringen; **'~ an·gle** rechter Winkel; **'~angled** *math.* rechtwink(e)lig; **~·eous** ['raɪtʃəs] gerecht (*Zorn etc.*); **'~·ful** rechtmäßig; **~'hand** rechte(r, -s); **~-hand 'drive** Rechtssteuerung *f*; **~'hand·ed** rechtshändig; für Rechtshänder; **be ~** Rechtshänder(in) sein; **'~·ly** richtig; mit Recht; **~ of 'way** *mot.* Vorfahrt(srecht *n*) *f*; Durchgangsrecht *n*; **~'wing** *pol.* dem rechten Flügel angehörend, Rechts...

rig·id ['rɪdʒɪd] starr, steif; *fig.* streng, strickt

rig·ma·role F ['rɪgmərəʊl] Geschwätz *n; fig.* Theater *n*, Zirkus *m*

rig·or·ous ['rɪgərəs] streng; genau

rig·o·(u)r ['rɪgə] Strenge *f*, Härte *f*

rile F [raɪl] ärgern, reizen

rim [rɪm] Rand *m (e-r Tasse etc.)*; Krempe *f (e-s Huts)*; *tech.* Felge *f*; '**~less** randlos *(Brille)*; '**~med** mit *(e-m)* Rand

rind [raɪnd] *(Zitronen- etc.)*Schale *f; (Käse)*Rinde *f; (Speck)*Schwarte *f*

ring¹ [rɪŋ] **1.** Ring *m*; Kreis *m*; Manege *f*; (Box)Ring *m*; (Spionage- *etc.*); **2.** umringen, umstellen; *Vogel* beringen

ring² [rɪŋ] **1.** *(rang, rung)* läuten; klingeln; klingen *(a. fig.)*; *bsd. Brt. tel.* anrufen; **the bell is ~ing** es läutet *od.* klingelt; **~ the bell** läuten, klingeln; **~ back** *bsd. Brt. tel.* zurückrufen; **~ for** nach *j-m, et.* läuten; *Arzt etc.* rufen; **~ off** *bsd. Brt. tel.* (den Hörer) auflegen, Schluß machen; **~ s.o.** *(up)* j-n *od.* bei j-m anrufen; **2.** Läuten *n*, Klingeln *n*; *fig.* Klang *m; bsd. Brt. tel.* Anruf *m*; **give s.o. a ~** j-n anrufen

'**ring| bind·er** Ringbuch *n*; '**~·lead·er** Rädelsführer(in); '**~·mas·ter** Zirkusdirektor *m*; '**~ road** *Brt.* Umgehungsstraße *f*; Ringstraße *f*; '**~·side: at the ~** *Boxen:* am Ring

rink [rɪŋk] (Kunst)Eisbahn *f*; Rollschuhbahn *f*

rinse [rɪns] *a.* **~ out** (aus)spülen

ri·ot ['raɪət] **1.** Aufruhr *m*; Krawall *m*; **run ~** randalieren, randalierend ziehen *(through* durch); **2.** Krawall machen, randalieren; '**~·er** Aufrührer(in); '**~·ous** aufrührerisch; randalierend; ausgelassen, wild

rip [rɪp] **1.** *(-pp-) a.* **~ up** zerreißen; **~ open** aufreißen; **2.** Riß *m*

ripe [raɪp] reif; **rip·en** ['raɪpən] reifen (lassen)

rip·ple ['rɪpl] **1.** (sich) kräuseln; plätschern, rieseln; **2.** kleine Welle; Kräuselung *f*; Plätschern *n*, Rieseln *n*

rise [raɪz] **1.** *(rose, risen)* aufstehen *(a. am Morgen);* sich erheben; *rel.* auferstehen; aufsteigen *(Rauch etc.);* sich heben *(Vorhang, Stimmung);* ansteigen *(Straße, Wasser etc.),* anschwellen

(Fluß etc.); (an)steigen *(Temperatur etc.),* Preise etc. a. anziehen; stärker werden *(Wind etc.)*; aufgehen *(Sonne, Teig etc.)*; entspringen *(Fluß etc.)*; aufsteigen *(beruflich etc.)*; *fig.* entstehen *(from, out of* aus); *a.* **~ up** sich erheben *(against* gegen); **~ to the occasion** sich der Lage gewachsen zeigen; **2.** (An)Steigen *n*; Steigung *f*; Anhöhe *f; astr.* Aufgang *m; bsd. Brt.* Lohn- *od.* Gehaltserhöhung *f; fig.* Anstieg *m; fig.* Aufstieg *m*; **give ~ to** verursachen, führen zu; **ris·en** ['rɪzn] *p.p. von* rise 1; **ris·er** ['raɪzə]: **early ~** Frühaufsteher(in); **ris·ing** ['raɪzɪŋ] **1.** Aufstand *m*; **2.** aufstrebend *(Politiker etc.)*

risk [rɪsk] **1.** Gefahr *f*, Risiko *n; at one's own ~** auf eigene Gefahr; **at the ~ of** *(ger.)* auf die Gefahr hin zu *(inf.)*; **be at ~** gefährdet sein; **run the ~ of doing s.th.** Gefahr laufen, et. zu tun; **run a ~, take a ~** ein Risiko eingehen; **2.** wagen, riskieren; '**~·y** *(-ier, -iest)* riskant

rite [raɪt] Ritus *m*; Zeremonie *f*; **rit·u·al** ['rɪtʃʊəl] **1.** rituell; Ritual...; **2.** Ritual *n*

ri·val ['raɪvl] **1.** Rival|e *m*, -in *f*, Konkurrent(in); **2.** rivalisierend, Konkurrenz...; **3.** *(bsd. Brt. -ll-, Am. -l-)* rivalisieren *od.* konkurrieren mit; '**~·ry** ['raɪvlrɪ] Rivalität *f*; Konkurrenz (-kampf *m) f*

riv·er ['rɪvə] Fluß *m*; Strom *m*; '**~·side** Flußufer *n*; **by the ~** am Fluß

riv·et ['rɪvɪt] **1.** *tech.* Niet(e *f) n, m*; **2.** *tech.* (ver)nieten; *Aufmerksamkeit, Blick* richten *(on* auf *acc.)*

RN [ɑːr 'en] *Abk. für Royal Navy* die Königlich-Britische Marine

road [rəʊd] (Auto-, Land)Straße *f; fig.* Weg *m;* **on the ~** auf der Straße; unterwegs; *thea.* auf Tournee; '**~ ac·ci·dent** Verkehrsunfall *m*; '**~·block** Straßensperre *f*; '**~ map** Straßenkarte *f*; '**~ safe·ty** Verkehrssicherheit *f*; '**~·side** Straßenrand *m*; **at the ~, by the ~** am Straßenrand; '**~ toll** Straßenbenutzungsgebühr *f*; '**~·way** Fahrbahn *f*; '**~ works** *pl.* Straßenbauarbeiten *pl.*; '**~·wor·thy** verkehrssicher

roam [rəʊm] *v/i.* (umher)streifen, (-)wandern; *v/t.* streifen *od.* wandern durch

roar [rɔː] **1.** Brüllen *n*, Gebrüll *n*; Brausen *n*, Krachen *n*, Donnern *n*; **~s** *pl.* **of**

laughter brüllendes Gelächter; **2.** brüllen; brausen; donnern (*Fahrzeug etc.*)

roast [rəʊst] **1.** *v/t.* Fleisch braten (*a. v/i.*); *Kaffee etc.* rösten; **2.** Braten *m*; **3.** *adj.* gebraten; ~ **'beef** Rinderbraten *m*

rob [rɒb] (*-bb-*) *Bank etc.* überfallen; *j-n* berauben; **~·ber** ['rɒbə] Räuber *m*; **~·ber·y** ['rɒbərɪ] Raub(überfall) *m*, (*Bank*)Raub *m*, (-)Überfall *m*

robe [rəʊb] *a.* **~s** *pl.* Robe *f*, Talar *m*

rob·in *zo.* ['rɒbɪn] Rotkehlchen *n*

ro·bot ['rəʊbɒt] Roboter *m*

ro·bust [rə'bʌst] robust, kräftig

rock¹ [rɒk] schaukeln, wiegen; erschüttern (*a. fig.*)

rock² [rɒk] Fels(en) *m*; Felsen *pl.*; *geol.* Gestein *n*; Felsbrocken *m*; *Am.* Stein *m*; *Brt.* Zuckerstange *f*; △ *nicht* **Rock**; **~s** *pl.* Klippen *pl.*; *on the* **~s** in ernsten Schwierigkeiten (*Firma etc.*); in die Brüche gehend (*Ehe*); mit Eis (*bsd. Whisky*)

rock³ [rɒk] *a.* **~ music** Rock(musik *f*) *m*; → **rock 'n' roll**

'rock·er Kufe *f* (*e-s Schaukelstuhls etc.*); Schaukelstuhl *m*; *Brt.* Rocker *m*; *off one's* **~** F übergeschnappt

rock·et ['rɒkɪt] **1.** Rakete *f*; **2.** rasen, schießen; *a.* **~ up** hochschnellen, in die Höhe schießen (*Preise*)

'rock·ing chair Schaukelstuhl *m*; **'~ horse** Schaukelpferd *n*

rock 'n' roll [rɒkən'rəʊl] Rock 'n' Roll *m*

'rock·y (*-ier, -iest*) felsig; steinhart

rod [rɒd] Rute *f*; *tech.* Stab *m*, Stange *f*

rode [rəʊd] *pret. von* **ride** 1

ro·dent *zo.* ['rəʊdənt] Nagetier *n*

ro·de·o [rəʊ'deɪəʊ, 'rəʊdɪəʊ] (*pl. -os*) Rodeo *m*, *n*

roe *zo.* [rəʊ] *a.* **hard ~** Rogen *m*; *a.* **soft ~** Milch *f*

roe|·buck *zo.* ['rəʊbʌk] (*pl. -bucks, -buck*) Rehbock *m*; **'~ deer** *zo.* (*pl. -deer*) Reh *n*

rogue [rəʊg] Schurke *m*, Gauner *m*; Schlingel *m*, Spitzbube *m*; **ro·guish** ['rəʊgɪʃ] schelmisch, spitzbübisch

role *thea. etc.* [rəʊl] Rolle *f* (*a. fig.*)

roll [rəʊl] **1.** *v/i.* rollen; sich wälzen; rollen, fahren; *naut.* schlingern; (g)rollen (*Donner*); *v/t. et.* rollen; auf-, zusammenrollen; *Zigarette* drehen; ~ *down* Ärmel herunterkrempeln; *mot. Fenster*

herunterkurbeln; ~ *out* ausrollen; ~ *up* aufrollen; (sich) zusammenrollen; *Ärmel* hochkrempeln; *mot. Fenster* hochkurbeln; **2.** Rolle *f*; Brötchen *n*, Semmel *f*; Namens-, Anwesenheitsliste *f*; (G)Rollen *n* (*des Donners*); (Trommel-) Wirbel *m*; *naut.* Schlingern *n*; **'~ call** Namensaufruf *m*

'roll·er *tech.* Rolle *f*, Walze *f*; (Locken)Wickler *m*; △ *nicht* **Roller**; **'~ blades** Rollerblades *pl.*, Inline Blades *pl.* (*Rollschuhe*); **'~ coast·er** Achterbahn *f*; **~ skate** Rollschuh *m*; **'~skate** Rollschuh laufen; **'~skat·ing** Rollschuhlaufen *n*; **'~ tow·el** Rollhandtuch *n*

'roll·ing pin Nudelholz *n*

'roll-on Deoroller *m*

ROM [rɒm] *Abk. für* **read only memory** *Computer:* Nur-Lese-Speicher *m*, Fest(wert)speicher *m*

Ro·man ['rəʊmən] **1.** römisch; **2.** Römer(in)

ro·mance [rəʊ'mæns] Abenteuer-, Liebesroman *m*; Romanze *f*; Romantik *f*

Ro·mance [rəʊ'mæns] romanisch (*Sprache*)

Ro·ma·ni·a [ruː'meɪnjə] Rumänien *n*; **Ro·ma·ni·an** [ruː'meɪnjən] **1.** rumänisch; **2.** Rumän|e *m*, -in *f*; *ling.* Rumänisch *n*

ro·man|·tic [rəʊ'mæntɪk] **1.** (*~ally*) romantisch; **2.** Romantiker(in); **~·ti·cism** [rəʊ'mæntɪsɪzəm] Romantik *f*

romp [rɒmp] *a.* ~ *about*, ~ *around* herumtollen, -toben; **'~·ers** *pl.* Spielanzug *m*

roof [ruːf] **1.** Dach *n*; *mot.* Verdeck *n*; **2.** mit e-m Dach versehen; ~ *in*, ~ *over* überdachen; **'~·ing felt** Dachpappe *f*; **'~ rack** *mot.* Dachgepäckträger *m*

rook¹ *zo.* [rʊk] Saatkrähe *f*

rook² [rʊk] *Schach:* Turm *m*

rook³ F [rʊk] *j-n* betrügen (*of* um)

room [ruːm, *in Zssgn nachgestellt* rʊm] **1.** Raum *m*, Zimmer *n*; Raum *m*, Platz *m*; *fig.* Spielraum *m*; **2.** *Am.* wohnen; **'~·er** *bsd. Am.* Untermieter(in); **'~·ing-house** *Am.* Fremdenheim *n*, Pension *f*; **'~·mate** Zimmergenoss|e *m*, -in *f*; **'~ ser·vice** Zimmerservice *m*; **'~·y** (*-ier, -iest*) geräumig

roost [ruːst] **1.** (Hühner)Stange *f*; Schlafplatz *m* (*von Vögeln*); **2.** auf der

R

Stange *etc.* sitzen *od.* schlafen; '**~er** *bsd. Am. zo.* (Haus)Hahn *m*

root [ru:t] **1.** Wurzel *f*; **2.** *v/i.* Wurzeln schlagen; wühlen (*for* nach); ~ *about* herumwühlen (*among* in *dat.*); *v/t.* ~ *out fig.* ausrotten; ~ *up* mit der Wurzel ausreißen; '**~ed: deeply** ~ *fig.* tiefverwurzelt; *stand* ~ *to the spot* wie angewurzelt dastehen

rope [rəup] **1.** Seil *n*; *naut.* Tau *n*; Strick *m*; (*Perlen- etc.*)Schnur *f*; *give s.o. plenty of* ~ j-m viel Freiheit *od.* Spielraum lassen; *know the* ~*s* F sich auskennen; *show s.o. the* ~*s* F j-n einarbeiten; **2.** festbinden (*to* an *dat.*, *acc.*); ~ *off* (durch ein Seil) absperren *od.* abgrenzen; '~ **lad·der** Strickleiter *f*

ro·sa·ry *rel.* ['rəuzərɪ] Rosenkranz *m*

rose¹ [rəuz] *pret. von* **rise 1**

rose² [rəuz] **1.** *bot.* Rose *f*; Brause *f* (*e-r Gießkanne*); **2.** rosa-, rosenrot

ros·trum ['rɒstrəm] (*pl.* -*tra* [-trə], -*trums*) Redner-, Dirigentenpult *n*

ros·y ['rəuzɪ] (-*ier*, -*iest*) rosig (*a. fig.*)

rot [rɒt] **1.** (-*tt*-) *v/t.* (ver)faulen *od.* verrotten lassen; *v/i. a.* ~ *away* (ver)faulen, verrotten, morsch werden; **2.** Fäulnis *f*

ro·ta·ry ['rəutərɪ] rotierend, sich drehend; Rotations..., Dreh...

ro·tate [rəu'teɪt] rotieren (lassen), (sich) drehen; turnusmäßig (aus)wechseln; **ro·ta·tion** [rəu'teɪʃn] Rotation *f*, Drehung *f*; Wechsel *m*

ro·tor *tech.*, *aviat.* ['rəutə] Rotor *m*

rot·ten ['rɒtn] verfault, faul; verrottet, morsch; mieserabel; gemein; *feel* ~ F sich mies fühlen

ro·tund [rəu'tʌnd] rund u. dick

rough [rʌf] **1.** *adj.* rauh; uneben (*Straße etc.*); stürmisch (*Meer*, *Überfahrt*, *Wetter*); grob; barsch; hart; grob, ungefähr (*Schätzung etc.*); roh, Roh...; **2.** *adv. sleep* ~ im Freien übernachten; *play* ~ *Sport:* hart spielen; **3.** *Golf:* Rough *n*; *write it out in* ~ *first* zuerst ins unreine schreiben; **4.** ~ *it* F primitiv *od.* anspruchslos leben; ~ *out* entwerfen, skizzieren; ~ *up* F j-n zusammenschlagen; ~**age** *biol.* ['rʌfɪdʒ] Ballaststoffe *pl.*; '~**cast** *arch.* Rauputz *m*; ~ **'cop·y** Rohentwurf *m*, Konzept *n*; ~ **'draft** Rohfassung *f*; ~**en** ['rʌfn] rauh werden; rauh machen, an-, aufrauhen; '~**ly** grob; *fig.* grob, ungefähr; '~**neck**

Ölbohrarbeiter *m*; *Am.* F Grobian *m*; '~**shod: ride** ~ *over* j-n rücksichtslos behandeln; sich rücksichtslos über *et.* hinwegsetzen

round [raund] **1.** *adj.* rund; *a* ~ *dozen* ein rundes Dutzend; *in* ~ *figures* auf- *od.* abgerundet (*Zahlen*), rund(e) ...; **2.** *adv.* rund-, rings(her)um; überall, auf *od.* von *od.* nach allen Seiten; *turn* ~ sich umdrehen; *invite s.o.* ~ j-n zu sich einladen; ~ *about* F ungefähr; *all* (*the*) *year* ~ das ganze Jahr hindurch *od.* über; *the other way* ~ umgekehrt; **3.** *prp.* (rund) um, (um ... herum); in *od.* auf (*dat.*) ... herum; *trip* ~ *the world* Weltreise *f*; **4.** Runde *f*, Runde *f*, Rundgang *m*; *med.* Visite *f* (*in e-r Klinik*); Lage *f*, Runde *f* (*Bier etc.*); Schuß *m* (*Munition*); *bsd. Brt.* Scheibe *f* (*Brot etc.*); *mus.* Kanon *m*; **5.** rund machen, (ab)runden, *Lippen* spitzen; umfahren, fahren um, *Kurve* nehmen; ~ *down Zahl etc.* abrunden (*to* auf *acc.*); ~ *off Essen etc.* abrunden, beschließen (*with* mit); *Zahl etc.* auf- *od.* abrunden (*to* auf *acc.*); ~ *up Vieh* zusammentreiben; *Leute etc.* zusammentrommeln; *Zahl etc.* aufrunden (*to* auf *acc.*); '~**a·bout** **1.** *Brt.* Kreisverkehr *m*; *Brt.* Karussell *n*; **2.** *take a* ~ *route* e-n Umweg machen; *in a* ~ *way fig.* auf Umwegen; ~ **'trip** Hin- u. Rückfahrt *f*; Hin- u. Rückflug *m*; ~**trip 'tick·et** *Am.* Rückfahrkarte *f*; Rückflugticket *n*

rouse [rauz] j-n wecken; *fig.* j-n auf-, wachrütteln; j-n erzürnen, reizen

route [ru:t] Route *f*, Strecke *f*, Weg *m*, (*Bus- etc.*)Linie *f*

rou·tine [ru:'ti:n] **1.** Routine *f*; *the same old* (*daily*) ~ das (tägliche) ewige Einerlei; **2.** üblich, routinemäßig, Routine...

rove [rəuv] (umher)streifen, (-)wandern

row¹ [rəu] Reihe *f*

row² [rəu] **1.** rudern; **2.** Kahnfahrt *f*

row³ *Brt.* F [rau] **1.** Krach *m*; (lauter) Streit, Krach *m*; **2.** (sich) streiten

row|·boat *Am.* ['rəubəut] Ruderboot *n*; '~**er** Ruder|er *m*, -in *f*

row house *Am.* ['rəuhaus] Reihenhaus *n*

row·ing boat *bsd. Brt.* ['rəuɪŋ bəut] Ruderboot *n*

roy·al ['rɔɪəl] königlich, Königs...; ~**ty**

['rɔɪəltɪ] die königliche Familie; Tantieme f (**on** auf *acc.*)

RSPCA [ɑːr es piː siː 'eɪ] *Abk. für* **Royal Society for the Prevention of Cruelty to Animals** (*brit.* Tierschutzverein)

RSVP [ɑːr es viː 'piː] *Abk. für* **please reply** (*französisch* **répondez s'il vous plaît**) u. A.w.g., um Antwort wird gebeten

rub [rʌb] **1.** (*-bb-*) v/t. reiben; abreiben; polieren; ~ **dry** trockenreiben; ~ **it in** fig. F darauf herumreiten; ~ **shoulders with** F verkehren mit (*Prominenten etc.*); v/i. reiben, scheuern (**against, on** an *dat.*); ~ **down** ab-, trockenreiben; abschmirgeln, abschleifen; ~ **off** abreiben; abgehen (*Farbe etc.*); ~ **off on(to)** fig. abfärben auf (*acc.*); ~ **out** *Brt.* ausradieren; **2. give s.th. a** ~ et. abreiben *od.* polieren

rub·ber ['rʌbə] Gummi n, m; *bsd. Brt.* Radiergummi m; Wischtuch n; F Gummi m (*Kondom*); ~ **band** Gummiband n; ~ **'din·ghy** Schlauchboot n; '~**neck** *Am.* F **1.** neugierig gaffen; **2.** a. **rubbernecker** Gaffer(in), Schaulustige(r m f); ~**y** ['rʌbərɪ] gummiartig; zäh (*Fleisch*)

rub·bish ['rʌbɪʃ] Abfall m, Abfälle *pl.*, Müll m; *fig.* Schund m; Quatsch m, Blödsinn m; ~ **bin** *Brt.* Mülleimer m; '~ **chute** Müllschlucker m

rub·ble ['rʌbl] Schutt m; Trümmer *pl.*

ru·by ['ruːbɪ] Rubin m; Rubinrot n

ruck·sack ['rʌksæk] Rucksack m

rud·der ['rʌdə] *naut., aviat.* Ruder n

rud·dy ['rʌdɪ] (*-ier, -iest*) frisch, gesund

rude [ruːd] (*~r, ~st*) unhöflich, grob; unanständig (*Witz etc.*); bös (*Schock etc.*)

ru·di·men·ta·ry [ruːdɪ'mentərɪ] elementar, Anfangs...; primitiv; ~**ments** ['ruːdɪmənts] *pl.* Anfangsgründe *pl.*

rue·ful ['ruːfʊl] reuevoll, reumütig

ruff [rʌf] Halskrause f (a. zo.)

ruf·fle ['rʌfl] **1.** kräuseln; *Haar* zerzausen; *Federn* sträuben; ~ **s.o.'s composure** j-n aus der Fassung bringen; **2.** Rüsche f

rug [rʌg] Vorleger m, Brücke f; *bsd. Brt.* dicke Wolldecke

rug·by ['rʌgbɪ] a. ~ **football** *Sport:* Rugby n

rug·ged ['rʌgɪd] zerklüftet, schroff; robust, stabil; zerfurcht (*Gesicht*)

ru·in ['ruːɪn] **1.** Ruin m; *mst* ~**s** *pl.* Ruine(n *pl.*) f, Trümmer *pl.*; **2.** ruinieren, zerstören; '~**ous** ruinös

rule [ruːl] **1.** Regel f; Spielregel f; Vorschrift f; Herrschaft f; Lineal n; **against the** ~**s** regelwidrig; verboten; **as a** ~ in der Regel; **as a** ~ **of thumb** als Faustregel; **work to** ~ Dienst nach Vorschrift tun; **2.** v/t. herrschen über (*acc.*); *bsd. jur.* entscheiden; *Papier* lin(i)ieren; *Linie* ziehen; **be** ~**d by** *fig.* sich leiten lassen von; beherrscht werden von; ~ **out** et. ausschließen; v/i. herrschen (**over** über *acc.*); *bsd. jur.* entscheiden; '**rul·er** Herrscher(in); Lineal n

rum [rʌm] Rum m

rum·ble ['rʌmbl] rumpeln (*Fahrzeug*); (g)rollen (*Donner*); knurren (*Magen*)

ru·mi·nant zo. ['ruːmɪnənt] Wiederkäuer m; ~**nate** zo. ['ruːmɪneɪt] wiederkäuen

rum·mage F ['rʌmɪdʒ] **1.** a. ~ **about** herumstöbern, -wühlen (**among, in, through** in *dat.*); **2.** *bsd. Am.* Ramsch m; '~ **sale** *Am.* Wohltätigkeitsbasar m

ru·mo(u)r ['ruːmə] **1.** Gerücht n; ~ **has it that** es geht das Gerücht, daß; **2. it is** ~**ed that** es geht das Gerücht, daß; **he is** ~**ed to be** man munkelt, er sei

rump [rʌmp] Hinterteil n; *fig.* (kümmerlicher) Rest

rum·ple ['rʌmpl] zerknittern, -knüllen, -wühlen; *Haar* zerzausen; △ *nicht* **rumpeln**

run [rʌn] **1.** (*-nn-; ran, run*) v/i. laufen (a. *Sport*); rennen; fahren (*Fahrzeug*); fahren, verkehren, gehen (*Zug, Bus etc.*); laufen, fließen; zerfließen, -laufen (*Butter, Farbe etc.*); *tech.* laufen (*Motor*), in Betrieb *od.* Gang sein; verlaufen (*Straße etc.*); *bsd. jur.* gelten, laufen (**for one year** ein Jahr); *thea. etc.* laufen (**for three months** drei Monate lang); lauten (*Text*); gehen (*Melodie*); *bsd. Am. pol.* kandidieren (**for** für); ~ **dry** austrocknen; ~ **low** knapp werden; ~ **short** knapp werden; ~ **short of petrol** *od. Am.* **gas** kein Benzin mehr haben; v/t. *Strecke, Rennen* laufen; *Zug, Bus* fahren *od.* verkehren lassen; *tech. Maschine etc.* laufen lassen; *Wasser etc.* laufen lassen; *Geschäft, Hotel etc.* führen, leiten; abdrucken, bringen (*Zeitungsarti-*

kel etc.); **~ s.o. home** F j-n nach Hause bringen *od.* fahren; **be ~ning a temperature** erhöhte Temperatur *od.* Fieber haben; → **errands;** **~ away** davonlaufen **(from** vor *dat.***);** **~ away with** durchbrennen mit; durchgehen mit **(***Temperament etc.***);** **~ down** *mot.* an-, umfahren; *fig.* schlechtmachen; ausfindig machen; ablaufen (*Uhr*); leer werden (*Batterie*); **~ in** Wagen *etc.* einfahren; F *Verbrecher* schnappen; **~ into** laufen *od.* fahren gegen; j-n zufällig treffen; *fig.* geraten in (*acc.*); *fig.* sich belaufen auf (*acc.*); **~ off with** → **run away with;** **~ on** weitergehen; sich hinziehen (*until* bis); F unaufhörlich reden (*about* über *acc.*, von); **~ out** ablaufen (*Zeit etc.*); ausgehen, zu Ende gehen (*Vorräte etc.*); **~ out of petrol** *od. Am.* **gas** kein Benzin mehr haben; **~ over** *mot.* überfahren; überlaufen, -fließen; **~ through** überfliegen, durchgehen, -lesen; **~ up** Flagge hissen; *hohe Rechnung, Schulden machen*; **~ up against** stoßen auf (*Widerstand etc.*); **2.** Lauf *m* (*a. Sport*); Fahrt *f;* Spazierfahrt *f;* Ansturm *m, econ. a.* Run *m* (**on** auf *acc.*); *thea. etc.* Laufzeit *f; Am.* Laufmasche *f;* Gehege *n;* Auslauf *m,* (*Hühner*)Hof *m; Sport:* (Bob-, Rodel-) Bahn *f;* (*Ski*)Hang *m;* **~ of good (bad) luck** Glückssträhne *f* (Pechsträhne *f*); **in the long ~** auf die Dauer; **in the short ~** zunächst; **on the ~** auf der Flucht

'run·a·bout F *mot.* Stadt-, Kleinwagen *m;* **'~·a·way** Ausreißer(in)

rung¹ [rʌŋ] *p.p. von* **ring²** 1

rung² [rʌŋ] Sprosse *f* (*e-r Leiter*)

run·ner ['rʌnə] *Sport:* Läufer(in); Rennpferd *n; mst in Zssgn* Schmuggler(in); (*Schlitten-, Schlittschuh*)Kufe *f;* Tischläufer *m;* (Gleit)Schiene *f* (*bei Schubläden etc.*); *bot.* Ausläufer *m,* Seitentrieb *m;* **~ 'bean** *Brt. bot.* grüne Bohne; **~·up** [rʌnər'ʌp] (*pl.* **runners-up**) *Sport:* Zweite(r *m*) *f,* Vizemeister(in)

run·ning ['rʌnɪŋ] **1.** Laufen *n,* Rennen

n; Führung *f,* Leitung *f;* **2.** fließend (*Wasser*); *Sport:* Lauf...; **two days ~** zwei Tage hinter- *od.* nacheinander; **'~ costs** *pl.* Betriebskosten *pl.*, laufende Kosten *pl.*

run·ny F ['rʌnɪ] flüssig; laufend (*Nase*); tränend (*Augen*)

'run·way *aviat.* Start- u. Landebahn *f,* Rollbahn *f,* Piste *f*

rup·ture ['rʌptʃə] **1.** Bruch *m* (*a. med. u. fig.*), Riß *m;* **2.** bersten, platzen; (zer)reißen; **~ o.s.** *med.* sich e-n Bruch heben *od.* zuziehen

ru·ral ['rʊərəl] ländlich

ruse [ruːz] List *f,* Trick *m*

rush¹ [rʌʃ] **1.** *v/i.* hasten, hetzen, stürmen, rasen; **~ at** losstürzen *od.* sich stürzen auf (*acc.*); **~ in** hereinstürzen, -stürmen; **~ into** *fig.* sich stürzen in (*acc.*); *et.* überstürzen; *v/t.* antreiben, drängen, hetzen; schnell *wohin* bringen; *Essen* hinunterschlingen; losstürmen auf (*acc.*); **don't ~ it** laß dir Zeit dabei; **2.** Ansturm *m;* Hast *f,* Hetze *f;* Hochbetrieb *m; econ.* stürmische Nachfrage; **what's all the ~?** wozu diese Eile *od.* Hetze?

rush² *bot.* [rʌʃ] Binse *f*

'rush| hour Rush-hour *f,* Hauptverkehrs-, Stoßzeit *f;* **~·hour 'traf·fic** Stoßverkehr *m*

rusk *bsd. Brt.* [rʌsk] Zwieback *m*

Rus·sia ['rʌʃə] Rußland *n;* **Rus·sian** ['rʌʃn] **1.** russisch; **2.** Russ|e *m,* -in *f; ling.* Russisch *n*

rust [rʌst] **1.** Rost *m;* **2.** (ein-, ver)rosten (lassen)

rus·tic ['rʌstɪk] (**~ally**) ländlich, bäuerlich; rustikal

rus·tle ['rʌsl] **1.** rascheln (mit), knistern; *Am. Vieh* stehlen; **2.** Rascheln *n*

'rust·proof rostfrei, nichtrostend; **'~·y** (*-ier, -iest*) rostig; *fig.* eingerostet

rut¹ [rʌt] **1.** (Rad)Spur *f,* Furche *f; fig.* (alter) Trott; **the daily ~** das tägliche Einerlei; **2.** furchen; **~ted** ausgefahren

rut² *zo.* [rʌt] Brunft *f,* Brunst *f*

ruth·less ['ruːθlɪs] unbarmherzig; rücksichts-, skrupellos

rye *bot.* [raɪ] Roggen *m*

S

S, s [es] S, s *n*

S *nur geschr. Abk. für:* **south** S, Süd(en *m*); **south(ern)** südlich; **small** (*size*) klein

$ *nur geschr. Abk. für* **dollar(s** *pl.*) Dollar *m od. pl.*

sa·ble ['seɪbl] *zo.* Zobel *m*; Zobelpelz *m*; △ *nicht* **Säbel**

sab·o·tage ['sæbətɑːʒ] **1.** Sabotage *f*; **2.** sabotieren

sa·bre *Brt.*, **sa·ber** *Am.* ['seɪbə] Säbel *m*

sack [sæk] **1.** Sack *m*; **get the ~** F rausgeschmissen (*entlassen*) werden; **give s.o. the ~** F j-n rausschmeißen (*entlassen*); **hit the ~** F sich in die Falle *od.* Klappe hauen; **2.** einsacken, in Säcke füllen; F j-n rausschmeißen (*entlassen*); **'~·cloth**, **'~·ing** Sackleinen *n*

sac·ra·ment *rel.* ['sækrəmənt] Sakrament *n*

sa·cred ['seɪkrɪd] geistlich (*Musik etc.*); heilig

sac·ri·fice ['sækrɪfaɪs] **1.** Opfer *n*; **2.** opfern

sac·ri·lege ['sækrɪlɪdʒ] Sakrileg *n*; Frevel *m*

sad [sæd] traurig; schmerzlich; schlimm

sad·dle ['sædl] **1.** Sattel *m*; **2.** satteln

sa·dis·m ['seɪdɪzəm] Sadismus *m*; **~t** ['seɪdɪst] Sadist(in); **~·tic** [sə'dɪstɪk] (**~ally**) sadistisch

'sad·ness Traurigkeit *f*

sa·fa·ri [sə'fɑːrɪ] Safari *f*; **~ park** Safaripark *m*

safe [seɪf] **1.** (**~r, ~st**) sicher; **2.** Safe *m, n*, Tresor *m*; Geldschrank *m*; **~·con·duct** freies Geleit; **'~·guard 1.** Schutz *m* (**against** gegen, vor *dat.*); **2.** schützen (**against, from** gegen, vor *dat.*); **~·keep·ing** sichere Verwahrung

safe·ty ['seɪftɪ] Sicherheit *f*; Sicherheits...; **'~·belt** → **seat belt**; **'~·is·land** *Am.* Verkehrsinsel *f*; **'~ lock** Sicherheitsschloß *n*; **'~ mea·sure** Sicherheitsmaßnahme *f*; **'~ pin** Sicherheitsnadel *f*; **'~ ra·zor** Rasierapparat *m*

sag [sæg] (**-gg-**) sich senken, absacken; durchhängen (*Leitung etc.*); (her-ab)hängen; sinken, nachlassen (*Interesse etc.*); abfallen (*Roman etc.*)

sa·ga·cious [sə'geɪʃəs] scharfsinnig; **~·ci·ty** [sə'gæsətɪ] Scharfsinn *m*

sage *bot.* [seɪdʒ] Salbei *m, f*

Sa·git·tar·i·us *astr.* [sædʒɪ'teərɪəs] Schütze *m*; **he/she is (a) ~** er/sie ist (ein) Schütze

said [sed] *pret. u. p.p. von* **say** 1

sail [seɪl] **1.** Segel *n*; Segelfahrt *f*; (*Windmühlen*)Flügel *m*; **set ~** auslaufen (**for** nach); **go for a ~** segeln gehen; **2.** *v/i.* *naut.* segeln, fahren; *naut.* auslaufen (**for** nach); gleiten, schweben; **go ~ing** segeln gehen; *v/t. naut.* befahren; *Schiff* steuern, *Boot* segeln; **'~·board** Surfbrett *n*; **'~·boat** *Am.* Segelboot *n*

'sail·ing Segeln *n*; Segelsport *m*; **when is the next ~ to ...?** wann fährt das nächste Schiff nach ...?; **'~ boat** *bsd. Brt.* Segelboot *n*; **'~ ship** Segelschiff *n*

'sail·or Seemann *m*, Matrose *m*; **be a good (bad) ~** (nicht) seefest sein

'sail·plane Segelflugzeug *n*

saint [seɪnt] Heilige(r *m*) *f*; *vor Eigennamen* ♀ [snt] (*Abk.* **ST**): **ST George** der heilige Georg; **'~·ly** heilig, fromm

sake [seɪk]: **for the ~ of** um ... willen; **for my ~** meinetwegen; **for God's ~** F um Gottes willen

sa·la·ble ['seɪləbl] verkäuflich

sal·ad ['sæləd] Salat *m*; △ *nicht* **Feldsalat** *etc.*; **'~ dress·ing** Dressing *n*, Salatsoße *f*

sal·a·ried ['sælərɪd]: **~ employee** Angestellte(r *m*) *f*, Gehaltsempfänger(in)

sal·a·ry ['sælərɪ] Gehalt *n*

sale [seɪl] Verkauf *m*; Ab-, Umsatz *m*; (*Saison*)Schlußverkauf *m*; Auktion *f*, Versteigerung *f*; **for ~** zu verkaufen; **not for ~** unverkäuflich; **be on ~** verkauft werden, erhältlich sein

sale·a·ble ['seɪləbl] → **salable**

sales·clerk *Am.* ['seɪlzklɑːk] (Laden)Verkäufer(in); **'~·girl** (Laden-)Verkäuferin *f*; **'~·man** (*pl. -men*) Verkäufer *m*; (*Handels*)Vertreter *m*; **'~ rep·re·sen·ta·tive** Handlungsreisende(r *m*) *f*; (*Handels*)Vertreter(in); **'~·wom·an** (*pl. -women*) Verkäuferin *f*; (*Handels*)Vertreterin *f*

S

sa·line ['seɪlaɪn] salzig, Salz...
sa·li·va [sə'laɪvə] Speichel m
sal·low ['sæləʊ] gelblich (Gesichtsfarbe)
salm·on zo. ['sæmən] (pl. **-on, -ons**) Lachs m
sal·on ['sælɔ̃ːŋ, 'sælɒn] (Friseur-, Schönheits- etc.) Salon m
sa·loon [sə'luːn] Brt. mot. Limousine f; Am. hist. Saloon m; naut. Salon m; → **~ bar** Brt. vornehmerer Teil e-s Pubs; **~ car** Brt. mot. Limousine f
salt [sɔːlt] **1.** Salz n; **2.** salzen; (ein)pökeln, einsalzen (a. **~ down**); Straße etc. (mit Salz) gesalzen; **3.** Salz...; gepökelt; salzig, gesalzen; **~·pe·tre** bsd. Brt., **~·pe·ter** Am. [sɔːlt'piːtə] chem. Salpeter m; **~·wa·ter** Salzwasser...; **~·y** (**-ier, -iest**) salzig
sal·u·ta·tion [sælju:'teɪʃn] Gruß m, Begrüßung f; Anrede f (im Brief)
sa·lute [sə'luːt] **1.** mil. salutieren; (be)grüßen; **2.** mil. Ehrenbezeigung f; mil. Salut m; Gruß m
sal·vage ['sælvɪdʒ] **1.** Bergung f; Bergungsgut n; **2.** bergen (**from** aus)
sal·va·tion [sæl'veɪʃn] Rettung f; rel. Erlösung f; rel. (Seelen)Heil n; ♀ Army Heilsarmee f
salve [sælv] (Heil)Salbe f; △ nicht Salve
same [seɪm] the **~** der, die, dasselbe; all the **~** trotzdem; it is all the **~** to me es ist mir ganz egal
sam·ple ['sɑːmpl] **1.** Muster n, Probe f; **2.** kosten, probieren
san·a·to·ri·um [sænə'tɔːrɪəm] (pl. **-riums, -ria** [-rɪə]) Sanatorium n
sanc·ti·fy ['sæŋktɪfaɪ] heiligen
sanc·tion ['sæŋkʃn] **1.** Billigung f, Zustimmung f; mst **~s** pl. Sanktionen pl.; **2.** billigen, sanktionieren
sanc·ti·ty ['sæŋktətɪ] Heiligkeit f
sanc·tu·a·ry ['sæŋktʃʊərɪ] Schutzgebiet n (für Tiere); Zuflucht f, Asyl n
sand [sænd] **1.** Sand m; **~s** pl. Sand(fläche f) m; **2.** schmirgeln; mit Sand (be)streuen
san·dal ['sændl] Sandale f
'sand·bag Sandsack m; **~·bank** Sandbank f; **~·box** Am. Sandkasten m; **~·cas·tle** Sandburg f; **~·man** (pl. **-men**) Sandmännchen n; **~·pa·per** Sand-, Schmirgelpapier n; **~·pip·er** zo. Strandläufer m; **~·pit** bsd. Brt. Sandkasten m; Sandgrube f; **~·stone**

geol. Sandstein m; **~·storm** Sandsturm m
sand·wich ['sænwɪdʒ] **1.** Sandwich n; **2.** be **~ed between** eingekeilt sein zwischen (dat.); **~ s.th. in between** fig. et. einschieben zwischen (acc., dat.)
sand·y ['sændɪ] (**-ier, -iest**) sandig; rotblond (Haar)
sane [seɪn] (**~r, ~st**) geistig gesund; jur. zurechnungsfähig; vernünftig
sang [sæŋ] pret. von sing
san·i·tar·i·um Am. [sænɪ'teərɪəm] (pl. **-riums, -ria** [-rɪə]) → sanatorium
san·i·ta·ry ['sænɪtərɪ] hygienisch; Gesundheits...; **~ nap·kin** Am., **~ tow·el** Brt. (Damen)Binde f
san·i·ta·tion [sænɪ'teɪʃn] sanitäre Einrichtungen pl.; Kanalisation f
san·i·ty ['sænətɪ] geistige Gesundheit f; jur. Zurechnungsfähigkeit f
sank [sæŋk] pret. von sink 1
San·ta Claus ['sæntəklɔːz] der Weihnachtsmann, der Nikolaus
sap¹ bot. [sæp] Saft m
sap² [sæp] (**-pp-**) schwächen
sap·phire ['sæfaɪə] Saphir m
sar·cas·m ['sɑːkæzəm] Sarkasmus m; **~·tic** [sɑː'kæstɪk] (**~ally**) sarkastisch
sar·dine zo. [sɑː'diːn] Sardine f
SASE Am. [es eɪ es 'iː] Abk. für self-addressed, stamped envelope Freiumschlag m
sash¹ [sæʃ] Schärpe f
sash² [sæʃ] Fensterrahmen m (e-s Schiebefensters); **~ win·dow** Schiebefenster n
sat [sæt] pret. u. p.p. von sit
Sat nur geschr. Abk. für Saturday Sa., Samstag m, Sonnabend m
Sa·tan ['seɪtən] der Satan
satch·el ['sætʃəl] (Schul)Ranzen m; Schultasche f (Schultasche)
sat·el·lite ['sætəlaɪt] Satellit m
sat·in ['sætɪn] Satin m
sat·ire ['sætaɪə] Satire f; **~·ir·ist** ['sætərɪst] Satiriker(in); **~·ir·ize** ['sætəraɪz] verspotten
sat·is·fac·tion [sætɪs'fækʃn] Befriedigung f; Genugtuung f, Zufriedenheit f; **~·to·ry** [sætɪs'fæktərɪ] befriedigend, zufriedenstellend
sat·is·fy ['sætɪsfaɪ] befriedigen, zufriedenstellen; überzeugen; be **satisfied that** davon überzeugt sein, daß

sat·u·rate ['sætʃərət] (durch)tränken (**with** mit); *chem.* sättigen (*a. fig.*)

Sat·ur·day ['sætədɪ] Sonnabend *m*, Samstag *m*; **on ~** (am) Sonnabend *od.* Samstag; **on ~s** sonnabends, samstags

sauce [sɔːs] Soße *f*; △ *nicht Bratensoße*; F Frechheit *f*; **none of your ~!** werd bloß nicht frech!; **'~·pan** Kochtopf *m*

sau·cer ['sɔːsə] Untertasse *f*

sau·cy F ['sɔːsɪ] (**-ier, -iest**) frech

saun·ter ['sɔːntə] bummeln, schlendern

saus·age ['sɒsɪdʒ] Wurst *f*; *a. small ~* Würstchen *n*

sav·age ['sævɪdʒ] **1.** wild; unzivilisiert; **2.** Wilde(r *m*) *f*; **'~·ag·e·ry** ['sævɪdʒərɪ] Wildheit *f*; Roheit *f*, Grausamkeit *f*

save [seɪv] **1.** retten (**from** vor *dat.*); Geld, Zeit *etc.* (ein)sparen; *et.* aufheben, -sparen (**for** für); *j-m et.* ersparen; *Computer:* (ab)speichern, sichern; *Sport:* Schuß halten, parieren, Tor verhindern; **2.** *Sport:* Parade *f*

sav·er ['seɪvə] Retter(in); Sparer(in); *it is a time-~* es spart Zeit

sav·ings ['seɪvɪŋz] *pl.* Ersparnisse *pl.*; '~ **ac·count** Sparkonto *n*; '~ **bank** Sparkasse *f*; '~ **de·pos·it** Spareinlage *f*

sa·vio(u)r ['seɪvjə] Retter(in); the **2** *rel.* der Erlöser, der Heiland

sa·vo(u)r ['seɪvə] mit Genuß essen *od.* trinken; **~ of** *fig.* e-n Beigeschmack haben von; '**~·y** ['seɪvərɪ] schmackhaft

saw¹ [sɔː] *pret. von* **see¹**

saw² [sɔː] **1.** Säge *f*; **2.** (**~ed, ~n** *od. bsd.* Am. **~ed**) sägen; '**~·dust** Sägemehl *n*, -späne *pl.*; '**~·mill** Sägewerk *n*; **~n** [sɔːn] *p.p. von* **saw²**

Sax·on ['sæksn] **1.** (Angel)Sachse *m*, (-)Sächsin *f*; **2.** (angel)sächsisch

say [seɪ] **1.** (**said**) sagen; aufsagen; *Gebet* sprechen, *Vaterunser* beten; **~ grace** das Tischgebet sprechen; **what does your watch ~?** wie spät ist es auf deiner Uhr?; **he is said to be ...** er soll ... sein; **it ~s** es lautet (*Schreiben etc.*); **it ~s here** hier heißt es; **it goes without ~ing** es versteht sich von selbst; **no sooner said than done** gesagt, getan; **that is to ~** das heißt; **(and)** that's **~ing** sth. (und) das will was heißen; **you said it** du sagst es; **you can ~ that again!** das kannst du laut sagen!; **you don't ~ (so)!** was du nicht sagst!; **I ~** sag(en Sie) mal!; ich muß schon sagen!; **I can't ~** das

kann ich nicht sagen; **2.** Mitspracherecht *n* (**in** bei); **have one's ~** s-e Meinung äußern, zu Wort kommen; **he always has to have his ~** er muß immer mitreden; '**~·ing** Sprichwort *n*, Redensart *f*; **as the ~ goes** wie man so (schön) sagt

scab [skæb] *med.*, *bot.* Schorf *m*; *vet.* Räude *f*; *sl.* Streikbrecher(in)

scaf·fold ['skæfəld] (Bau)Gerüst *n*; Schafott *n*; '**~·ing** (Bau)Gerüst *n*

scald [skɔːld] **1.** sich *die Zunge etc.* verbrühen; *Milch* abkochen; **~ing hot** kochendheiß; **2.** Verbrühung *f*

scale¹ [skeɪl] **1.** Skala *f* (*a. fig.*), Gradod. Maßeinteilung *f*; *math.*, *tech.* Maßstab *m*; *bsd. Am.* Waage *f*; *mus.* Skala *f*, Tonleiter *f*; *fig.* Ausmaß *n*, Maßstab *m*, Umfang *m*; **2.** erklettern; **~ down** *fig.* verringern; **~ up** *fig.* erhöhen

scale² [skeɪl] Waagschale *f*; **(a pair of) ~s** *pl.* (e-e) Waage

scale³ [skeɪl] **1.** Schuppe *f*; Kesselstein *m*; **the ~s fell from my eyes** es fiel mir wie Schuppen von den Augen; **2.** *Fisch* (ab)schuppen

scal·lop *zo.* ['skɒləp] Kammuschel *f*

scalp [skælp] **1.** Kopfhaut *f*; Skalp *m*; **2.** skalpieren

scal·y ['skeɪlɪ] (**-ier, -iest**) schuppig

scamp F [skæmp] Schlingel *m*, (kleiner) Strolch

scam·per ['skæmpə] trippeln (*Kind etc.*); huschen (*Maus etc.*)

scan [skæn] **1.** (**-nn-**) *et.* absuchen (**for** nach); *Zeitung etc.* überfliegen; *Computer, Radar, TV:* abtasten, scannen; **2.** *med. etc.* Scanning *n*

scan·dal ['skændl] Skandal *m*; Klatsch *m*; '**~·ize** ['skændəlaɪz]: **be ~d at sth.** über *et.* empört *od.* entrüstet sein; '**~·ous** ['skændələs] skandalös; **be ~** *a.* ein Skandal sein (**that** daß)

Scan·di·na·vi·a [skændɪ'neɪvjə] Scandinavien *n*; **Scan·di·na·vi·an** [skændɪ'neɪvjən] **1.** skandinavisch; **2.** Skandinavier(in)

scan·ner *tech.* ['skænə] Scanner *m*

scant [skænt] dürftig, gering; '**~·y** (**-ier, -iest**) dürftig, kärglich, knapp

scape·goat ['skeɪpgəut] Sündenbock *m*

scar [skɑː] **1.** Narbe *f*; **2.** (**-rr-**) e-e Narbe *od.* Narben hinterlassen auf (*dat.*); **~ over** vernarben

scarce [skeəs] (~r, ~st) knapp (*Ware*); selten; '~ly kaum; **scar·ci·ty** ['skeəsətɪ] Mangel *m*, Knappheit *f* (**of** an *dat.*)

scare [skeə] **1.** erschrecken; **be ~d** Angst haben (**of** vor *dat.*); ~ **away**, ~ **off** verjagen, -scheuchen; **2.** Schreck(en) *m*; Panik *f*; '~·crow Vogelscheuche *f* (*a. fig.*)

scarf [skɑ:f] (*pl.* **scarfs** [skɑ:fs], **scarves** [skɑ:vz]) Schal *m*; Hals-, Kopf-, Schultertuch *n*

scar·let ['skɑ:lət] scharlachrot; ~ **'fever** *med.* Scharlach *m*; ~ **'run·ner** *bot.* Feuerbohne *f*

scarred [skɑ:d] narbig

scarves [skɑ:vz] *pl. von* **scarf**

scath·ing ['skeɪðɪŋ] vernichtend (*Kritik*)

scat·ter ['skætə] (sich) zerstreuen (*Menge*); aus-, verstreuen; auseinanderstieben (*Vögel etc.*); '~·brained *F* schusselig, schußlig; '~ed verstreut; vereinzelt

scav·enge ['skævɪndʒ]: ~ **on** *zo.* leben von (*Abfällen, Aas*); ~ **for** suchen (nach) (*Nahrung etc.*)

sce·na·ri·o [sɪ'nɑ:rɪəʊ] (*pl.* -os) Film, *thea.*, *TV*: Szenario *n*, Szenarium *n*

scene [si:n] Szene *f*; Schauplatz *m*; ~**s** *pl.* Kulissen *pl.*; **sce·ne·ry** ['si:nərɪ] Landschaft *f*, Gegend *f*; Bühnenbild *n*, Kulissen *pl.*

scent [sent] **1.** Duft *m*, Geruch *m*; *bsd. Brt.* Parfüm *n*; *hunt.* Witterung *f*; Fährte *f*, Spur *f* (*a. fig.*); **2.** wittern; *bsd. Brt.* parfümieren; '~·less geruchlos

scep·tic ['skeptɪk] Skeptiker(in); '~·ti·cal *Brt.* skeptisch

scep·tre *Brt.*, **scep·ter** *Am.* ['septə] Zepter *n*

sched·ule ['ʃedju:l, *Am.* 'skedʒʊl] **1.** Aufstellung *f*, Verzeichnis *n*; (*Arbeits-, Stunden-, Zeit- etc.*)Plan *m*; *bsd. Am.* Fahr-, Flugplan *m*; **ahead of** ~ dem Zeitplan voraus, früher als vorgesehen; **be behind** ~ Verspätung haben; im Verzug *od.* Rückstand sein; **on** ~ (fahr)planmäßig, pünktlich; **2. the meeting is** ~**d for Monday** die Sitzung ist für Montag angesetzt; **it is** ~**d to take place tomorrow** es soll morgen stattfinden; ~**d de'par·ture** (fahr)planmäßige Abfahrt; ~**d 'flight** Linienflug *m*

scheme [ski:m] **1.** *bsd. Brt.* Programm *n*, Projekt *n*; Schema *n*, System *n*; Intrige *f*, Machenschaft *f*; **2.** intrigieren

schnit·zel *gastr.* ['ʃnɪtsl] Wiener Schnitzel *n*

schol·ar ['skɒlə] Gelehrte(r *m*) *f*; *univ.* Stipendiat(in); '~·ly gelehrt; '~·ship Gelehrsamkeit *f*; *univ.* Stipendium *n*

school[1] [sku:l] **1.** Schule *f* (*a. fig.*); *univ.* Fakultät *f*; *Am.* Hochschule *f*; **at** ~ auf *od.* in der Schule; **go to** ~ in die *od.* zur Schule gehen; **2.** *j-n* schulen, unterrichten; *Tier* dressieren

school[2] *zo.* [sku:l] Schule *f*, Schwarm *m* (*Fische, Wale etc.*)

'**school**|**·bag** Schultasche *f*; '~·boy Schüler *m*; '~·child (*pl.* -children) Schulkind *n*; '~·fel·low → schoolmate; '~·girl Schülerin *f*; '~·ing (Schul)Ausbildung *f*; '~·mate Mitschüler(in), Schulkamerad(in); '~·teach·er (Schul)Lehrer(in); '~·yard Schulhof *m*

schoo·ner *naut.* ['sku:nə] Schoner *m*

sci·ence ['saɪəns] Wissenschaft *f*; *a.* **natural** ~ Naturwissenschaft(en *pl.*) *f*; '~ **'fic·tion** (*Abk.* SF) Science-fiction *f*

sci·en·tif·ic [saɪən'tɪfɪk] (~**ally**) (natur)wissenschaftlich; exakt, systematisch

sci·en·tist ['saɪəntɪst] (Natur)Wissenschaftler(in)

sci-fi *F* [saɪ'faɪ] Science-fiction *f*

scin·til·lat·ing ['sɪntɪleɪtɪŋ] (geist)sprühend

scis·sors ['sɪzəz] *pl.* (**a pair of** ~ e-e) Schere *f*

scoff [skɒf] **1.** spotten (**at** über *acc.*); **2.** spöttische Bemerkung

scold [skəʊld] schimpfen (mit)

scol·lop *zo.* ['skɒləp] → scallop

scone [skɒn] *kleines rundes Teegebäck, mit Butter serviert*

scoop [sku:p] **1.** Schöpfkelle *f*; (*Mehletc.*)Schaufel *f*; (*Eis- etc.*)Portionierer *m*; Kugel *f* (*Eis*); *Presse, Rundfunk, TV:* Exklusivmeldung *f*, *F* Knüller *m*; **2.** schöpfen, schaufeln; ~ **up** auf-, hochheben

scoot·er ['sku:tə] (Kinder)Roller *m*; (*Motor*)Roller *m*

scope [skəʊp] Bereich *m*; Spielraum *m*

scorch [skɔ:tʃ] *v/t.* an-, versengen, verbrennen; ausdörren; *v/i. mot. F* rasen

score [skɔː] **1.** (Spiel)Stand *m*; (Spiel-) Ergebnis *n*; *mus.* Partitur *f*; Musik *f* (*zu e-m Film etc.*); 20 (Stück); *a.* ~ **mark** Kerbe *f*, Rille *f*; **what is the** ~? wie steht es *od.* das Spiel?; **the** ~ **stood at** *od.* **was 3-2** das Spiel stand 3:2; **keep (the)** ~ anschreiben; ~**s** *pl.* of e-e Menge; **Erfolg**, **Sieg** erringen; *mus.* instrumentieren; **four** ~ **and ten** neunzig; **on that** ~ deshalb, in dieser Hinsicht; **have a** ~ **to settle with s.o.** e-e alte Rechnung mit j-m zu begleichen haben; **2.** *v/t. Sport:* Punkte, Treffer erzielen, Tor *a.* schießen; *Erfolg*, *Sieg* erringen; *mus.* instrumentieren; die Musik schreiben zu *od.* für; einkerben; *v/i. Sport:* e-n Treffer *etc.* erzielen, ein Tor schießen; erfolgreich sein; ~**board** *Sport:* Anzeigetafel *f*; **scor·er** [skɔːrə] *Sport:* Torschütz|e *m*, -in *f*; *Sport:* Anschreiber(in)

scorn [skɔːn] Verachtung *f*; ~**ful** verächtlich

Scor·pi·o *astr.* [skɔːpɪəʊ] Skorpion *m*; **he/she is** (a) ~ er/sie ist (ein) Skorpion

Scot [skɒt] Schott|e *m*, -in *f*

Scotch [skɒtʃ] **1.** schottisch (*Whisky etc.*); **2.** Scotch *m* (*schottischer Whisky*)

scot-free F [skɒtˈfriː]: **get off** ~ ungeschoren davonkommen

Scot·land [skɒtlənd] Schottland *n*

Scots [skɒts] schottisch (*bei Personen*); ~**man** (*pl.* **-men**) Schotte *m*; ~**wom·an** (*pl.* **-women**) Schottin *f*

Scot·tish [skɒtɪʃ] schottisch

scoun·drel [skaʊndrəl] Schurke *m*

scour¹ [skaʊə] scheuern, schrubben

scour² [skaʊə] *Gegend* absuchen, durchkämmen (*for* nach)

scourge [skɜːdʒ] **1.** Geißel *f* (*a. fig.*); **2.** geißeln, *fig. a.* heimsuchen

scout [skaʊt] **1.** *bsd. mil.* Kundschafter *m*; *Brt.* motorisierter Pannenhelfer; *a.* **boy** ~ Pfadfinder *m*; *a.* **girl** ~ *Am.* Pfadfinderin *f*; *a.* **talent** ~ Talentsucher(in); **2.** ~ **about**, ~ **around** sich umsehen (*for* nach); *a.* ~ **out** *mil.* auskundschaften

scowl [skaʊl] **1.** finsteres Gesicht; **2.** finster blicken; ~ **at** j-n böse *od.* finster anschauen

scram·ble [skræmbl] **1.** klettern; sich drängeln (*for* zu); **2.** Kletterei *f*; Drängelei *f*; ~**d ˈeggs** *pl.* Rührei(er *pl.*) *n*

scrap¹ [skræp] **1.** Stückchen *n*, Fetzen *m*; Altmaterial *n*; Schrott *m*; ~**s** *pl.* Abfall *m*, (*bsd.* Speise)Reste *pl.*; **2.** (**-pp-**)

Plan etc. aufgeben, fallenlassen; ausrangieren; verschrotten

scrap² F [skræp] **1.** Streiterei *f*; Balgerei *f*; **2.** sich streiten; sich balgen

ˈscrap-book Sammelalbum *n*

scrape [skreɪp] **1.** (ab)kratzen, (ab)schaben; sich *die Knie etc.* aufschürfen; *Wagen etc.* ankratzen; scheuern (*against* an *dat.*), (entlang)streifen; **2.** Kratzen *n*; Kratzer *m*, Schramme *f*; *fig.* Klemme *f*

ˈscrap| heap Schrotthaufen *m*; '~ **met·al** Altmetall *n*, Schrott *m*; '~ **pa·per** *bsd. Brt.* Schmierpapier *n*; '~ **val·ue** Schrottwert *m*; '~**yard** Schrottplatz *m*

scratch [skrætʃ] **1.** (zer)kratzen; (ab)kratzen; *s-n Namen etc.* einkratzen; (sich) kratzen; **2.** Kratzer *m*, Schramme *f*; Gekratze *n*; Kratzen *n*; **from** ~ F ganz von vorn; **3.** (bunt) zusammengewürfelt; '~**pad** *bsd. Am.* Notiz-, Schmierblock *m*; '~ **pa·per** *Am.* Schmierpapier *n*

scrawl [skrɔːl] **1.** kritzeln; **2.** Gekritzel *n*

scraw·ny [skrɔːnɪ] (*-ier*, *-iest*) dürr

scream [skriːm] **1.** schreien (**with** vor *dat.*); *a.* ~ **out** schreien; ~ **with laughter** vor Lachen brüllen; **2.** Schrei *m*; ~**s** *pl.* **of laughter** brüllendes Gelächter; **be a** ~ F zum Schreien (komisch) sein

screech [skriːtʃ] **1.** kreischen (*a. Bremsen etc.*), (gellend) schreien; **2.** Kreischen *n*; (gellender) Schrei

screen [skriːn] **1.** Wand-, Ofen-, Schutzschirm *m*; *Film:* Leinwand *f*; *Radar*, *TV*, *Computer:* Bildschirm *m*; Fliegenfenster *n*, -gitter *n*; *fig.* Tarnung *f*; **2.** abschirmen; *Film* zeigen, *Fernsehprogramm a.* senden; *fig. j-n* decken; *fig. j-n* überprüfen; ~ **off** abtrennen; '~**play** Drehbuch *n*; '~ **sav·er** *Computer:* Bildschirmschoner *m*

screw [skruː] **1.** *tech.* Schraube *f*; **he has a** ~ **loose** F bei ihm ist e-e Schraube locker; **2.** (an)schrauben (**to** an *acc.*); V bumsen, vögeln; ~ **up** *Gesicht* verziehen; *Augen* zusammenkneifen; ~ **up one's courage** sich ein Herz fassen; '~**ball** *bsd. Am.* F Spinner(in); '~**driv·er** Schraubenzieher *m*; ~ **top** Schraubverschluß *m*

scrib·ble [skrɪbl] **1.** (hin)kritzeln; **2.** Gekritzel *n*

scrimp [skrɪmp]: ~ *and save* jeden Pfennig zweimal umdrehen (*sparen*)
script [skrɪpt] Manuskript *n* (*e-r Rede etc.*); *Film, TV:* Drehbuch *n*, Skript *n*; *thea.* Text(buch *n*) *m*; Schrift(zeichen *pl.*) *f*; *Brt. univ.* (schriftliche) Prüfungsarbeit
Scrip·ture ['skrɪptʃə] *a. the ~s pl.* die Heilige Schrift
scroll [skrəʊl] **1.** Schriftrolle *f*; **2.** ~ *down/up* Bildschirminhalt zurück-/vorrollen
scro·tum *anat.* ['skrəʊtəm] (*pl.* **-ta** [-tə], **-tums**) Hodensack *m*
scrub¹ [skrʌb] **1.** (**-bb-**) schrubben, scheuern; **2.** Schrubben *n*, Scheuern *n*
scrub² [skrʌb] Gebüsch *n*, Gestrüpp *n*
scru·ple ['skruːpl] **1.** Skrupel *m*, Zweifel *m*, Bedenken *pl.*; **2.** Bedenken haben; **~·pu·lous** ['skruːpjʊləs] gewissenhaft; △ *nicht* skrupellos
scru·ti·nize ['skruːtɪnaɪz] genau prüfen; mustern; **~·ny** ['skruːtɪnɪ] genaue Prüfung; prüfender Blick
scu·ba ['skuːbə] Tauchgerät *n*; **~ div·ing** (Sport)Tauchen *n* (*mit Atemgerät*)
scud [skʌd] (**-dd-**) eilen, jagen (*bsd. Wolken, Schiffe*)
scuf·fle ['skʌfl] **1.** Handgemenge *n*, Rauferei *f*; **2.** sich raufen
scull [skʌl] **1.** Skull *n* (*kurzes Ruder*); Skullboot *n*; **2.** rudern, skullen
scul·le·ry ['skʌlərɪ] Spülküche *f*
sculp·tor ['skʌlptə] Bildhauer *m*; **~·ture** ['skʌlptʃə] **1.** Bildhauerei *f*; Skulptur *f*, Plastik *f*; **2.** hauen, meißeln, formen
scum [skʌm] Schaum *m*; *fig.* Abschaum *m*; *the ~ of the earth fig.* der Abschaum der Menschheit
scurf [skɜːf] (Kopf)Schuppen *pl.*
scur·ri·lous ['skʌrɪləs] beleidigend; verleumderisch; △ *nicht* skurril
scur·ry ['skʌrɪ] huschen; trippeln
scur·vy *med.* ['skɜːvɪ] Skorbut *m*
scut·tle ['skʌtl]: ~ *away*, ~ *off* sich schnell davonmachen
scythe [saɪð] Sense *f*
SE *nur geschr. Abk. für:* **southeast** SO, Südost(en *m*); **southeast(ern)** sö, südöstlich
sea [siː] Meer *n* (*a. fig.*), See *f*; △ *nicht* See *m*; *at* ~ auf See; *be all od. completely at* ~ *fig.* F völlig ratlos sein; *by* ~

auf dem Seeweg; *by the* ~ am Meer; **~·food** Meeresfrüchte *pl.*; **~·gull** *zo.* Seemöwe *f*
seal¹ *zo.* [siːl] (*pl.* **seals, seal**) Robbe *f*, Seehund *m*
seal² [siːl] **1.** Siegel *n*; *tech.* Plombe *f*; *tech.* Dichtung *f*; **2.** (ver)siegeln; *tech.* plombieren; *tech.* abdichten; *fig.* besiegeln; **~ed envelope** verschlossener Briefumschlag; ~ *off* Gegend *etc.* abriegeln
'sea lev·el: *above/below* ~ über/unter dem Meeresspiegel
'seal·ing wax Siegellack *m*
seam [siːm] Naht *f*; Fuge *f*; *geol.* Flöz *n*
'sea·man (*pl.* **-men**) Seemann *m*
seam·stress ['semstrɪs] Näherin *f*
'sea·plane Wasserflugzeug *n*; **~·port** Seehafen *m*; Hafenstadt *f*; **~ pow·er** Seemacht *f*
sear [sɪə] *Fleisch* rasch anbraten; *Pflanzen* vertrocknen lassen
search [sɜːtʃ] **1.** *v/i.* suchen (*for* nach); ~ *through* durchsuchen; *v/t.* j-n, *et.* durchsuchen (*for* nach); ~ *me!* F keine Ahnung!; **2.** Suche *f* (*for* nach); Fahndung *f* (*for* nach); Durchsuchung *f*; *in* ~ *of* auf der Suche nach; **~·ing** forschend, prüfend (*Blick*); eingehend (*Prüfung etc.*); **~·light** (Such)Scheinwerfer *m*; **~ par·ty** Suchmannschaft *f*; **~ war·rant** *jur.* Haussuchungs-, Durchsuchungsbefehl *m*
'sea·shore Meeresküste *f*; **~·sick** seekrank; **~·side:** *at od. by the* ~ am Meer; *go to the* ~ ans Meer fahren; **~·side re·sort** Seebad *n*
sea·son¹ ['siːzn] Jahreszeit *f*; Saison *f*, *thea. etc. a.* Spielzeit *f*, (*Jagd-, Urlaubsetc.-*)Zeit *f*; *in/out of* ~ in/außerhalb der (Hoch)Saison; *cherries are now in* ~ jetzt ist Kirschenzeit; **2's Greetings!** Frohe Weihnachten!; *with the compliments of the* ~ mit den besten Wünschen zum Fest
sea·son² ['siːzn] *Speise* würzen (*with* mit); *Holz* ablagern
sea·son·al ['siːzənl] saisonbedingt, Saison...
sea·son·ing ['siːznɪŋ] Gewürz *n* (*Zutat*)
'sea·son tick·et *rail. etc.* Dauer-, Zeitkarte *f*; *thea.* Abonnement *n*
seat [siːt] **1.** Sitz(gelegenheit *f*) *m*; (Sitz)Platz *m*; Sitz(fläche *f*) *m*; Hosen-

boden m; Hinterteil n; (Geschäfts-, Regierungs- etc.)Sitz m; Sitz m (im Parlament etc.); **take a** ~ Platz nehmen; **take one's** ~ s-n Platz einnehmen; **2.** j-n setzen; Sitzplätze bieten für; **be** ~**ed** sitzen; **please be** ~**ed** bitte nehmen Sie Platz; **remain** ~**ed** sitzen bleiben; '~**belt** aviat., mot. Sicherheitsgurt m; **fasten one's** ~ sich anschnallen; '~**-seat·er** ...sitzer m

sea| **ur·chin** zo. ['siːɜtʃɪn] Seeigel m; ~**ward(s)** ['siːwəd(z)] seewärts; '~**weed** bot. (See)Tang m; '~**wor·thy** seetüchtig

sec bsd. Brt. F fig. [sek] Augenblick m, Sekunde f; **just a** ~ Augenblick(, bitte!)

se·cede [sɪ'siːd] sich abspalten (**from** von); **se·ces·sion** [sɪ'seʃn] Abspaltung f, Sezession f (**from** von)

se·clud·ed [sɪ'kluːdɪd] abgelegen, abgeschieden (Haus etc.); zurückgezogen (Leben); **se·clu·sion** [sɪ'kluːʒn] Abgeschiedenheit f; Zurückgezogenheit f

sec·ond[1] ['sekənd] **1.** adj. zweite(r, -s); **every** ~ **day** jeden zweiten Tag, alle zwei Tage; ~ **to none** unerreicht, unübertroffen; **but on** ~ **thoughts** (Am. **thought**) aber wenn ich es mir so überlege; **2.** adv. als zweite(r, -s); **3.** der, die, das Zweite; mot. zweiter Gang; Sekundant m; ~**s** pl. F econ. Waren pl. zweiter Wahl; **4.** Antrag etc. unterstützen

sec·ond[2] ['sekənd] Sekunde f; fig. Augenblick m, Sekunde f; **just a** ~ Augenblick(, bitte!)

sec·ond·a·ry ['sekəndərɪ] sekundär, zweitrangig; ped. höher (Schule etc.)

sec·ond·|**best** zweitbeste(r, -s); ~ '**class** rail. etc. zweiter Klasse; ~ '**class** zweitklassig; ~ '**floor** Brt. zweiter Stock, Am. erster Stock; ~'**hand** aus zweiter Hand; gebraucht; antiquarisch; '~ **hand** Sekundenzeiger m; '~**ly** zweitens; ~'**rate** zweitklassig

se·cre·cy ['siːkrɪsɪ] Verschwiegenheit f, Geheimhaltung f

se·cret ['siːkrɪt] **1.** geheim, Geheim...; heimlich (Verehrer etc.); verschwiegen; **2.** Geheimnis n; **in** ~ heimlich, im geheimen; **keep s.th. a** ~ et. geheimhalten (**from** vor dat.); **can you keep a** ~? kannst du schweigen?; ~ '**a·gent** Geheimagent(in)

sec·re·ta·ry ['sekrətrɪ] Sekretär(in);

pol. Minister(in); 2 **of** '**State** Brt. Minister(in); Am. Außenminister(in)

se·crete physiol. [sɪ'kriːt] absondern; **se·cre·tion** physiol. [sɪ'kriːʃn] Sekret n; Absonderung f

se·cre·tive ['siːkrɪtɪv] verschlossen

se·cret·ly ['siːkrɪtlɪ] heimlich

se·cret '**ser·vice** Geheimdienst m

sec·tion ['sekʃn] Teil m; Abschnitt m; jur. Paragraph m; Abteilung f; math., tech. Schnitt m

sec·u·lar ['sekjʊlə] weltlich

se·cure [sɪ'kjʊə] **1.** sicher (**against, from** vor dat.); **2.** Tür etc. fest verschließen; sichern (**against, from** vor dat.)

se·cu·ri·ty [sɪ'kjʊərətɪ] Sicherheit f; **se·curities** pl. Wertpapiere pl.; ~ **check** Sicherheitskontrolle f; ~ **mea·sure** Sicherheitsmaßnahme f; ~ **risk** Sicherheitsrisiko n

se·dan Am. mot. [sɪ'dæn] Limousine f

se·date [sɪ'deɪt] ruhig, gelassen

sed·a·tive mst med. ['sedətɪv] **1.** beruhigend; **2.** Beruhigungsmittel n

sed·i·ment ['sedɪmənt] (Boden)Satz m

se·duce [sɪ'djuːs] verführen; **se·duc·er** [sɪ'djuːsə] Verführer(in); **se·duc·tion** [sɪ'dʌkʃn] Verführung f; **se·duc·tive** [sɪ'dʌktɪv] verführerisch

see[1] [siː] (**saw, seen**) v/i. sehen; nachsehen; **I** ~ **!** (ich) verstehe!, ach so!; **you** ~ weißt du; **let me** ~ warte mal, laß mich überlegen; **we'll** ~ mal sehen; v/t. sehen; besuchen; j-n aufsuchen od. konsultieren; ~ **s.o. home** j-n nach Hause bringen od. begleiten; ~ **you!** bis dann!, auf bald!; ~ **about** sehen nach, sich kümmern um; ~ **off** j-n verabschieden (**at** am Bahnhof etc.); ~ **out** j-n hinausbringen, -begleiten; ~ **through** j-n, et. durchschauen; j-m hinweghelfen über (acc.); ~ **to it that** dafür sorgen, daß

see[2] [siː] Bistum n, Diözese f; **Holy** 2 der Heilige Stuhl

seed [siːd] **1.** bot. Same(n) m; Saat(gut n) f; Am. (Apfel-, Orangen- etc.)Kern m; Sport: gesetzter Spieler, gesetzte Spielerin; **go od. run to** ~ schießen (Salat etc.); fig. F herunterkommen (Person); **2.** v/t. besäen; entkernen; Sport: Spieler setzen; v/i. bot. in Samen schießen; '~**less** kernlos (Orangen etc.); '~**y** F (**-ier, -iest**) heruntergekommen, vergammelt

S

seek [si:k] (*sought*) *Schutz, Wahrheit etc.* suchen

seem [si:m] scheinen; '~**ing** scheinbar

seen [si:n] *p.p. von* **see¹**

seep [si:p] sickern

see·saw ['si:sɔ:] Wippe *f*, Wippschaukel *f*

seethe [si:ð] schäumen (*a. fig.*); *fig.* kochen

'**see-through** durchsichtig (*Bluse etc.*)

seg·ment ['segmənt] Teil *m, n*; Stück *n*; Abschnitt *m*; Segment *n*

seg·re|gate ['segrɪgeɪt] (*bsd. nach Rassen, Geschlechtern*) trennen; ~**ga·tion** [segrɪ'geɪʃn] Rassentrennung *f*

seize [si:z] *j-n, et.* packen, ergreifen; *Macht etc.* an sich reißen; *et.* beschlagnahmen; **sei·zure** [si:ʒə] Beschlagnahme *f*; *med.* Anfall *m*

sel·dom ['seldəm] *adv.* selten

se·lect [sɪ'lekt] **1.** (aus)wählen; **2.** ausgewählt; exklusiv; **se·lec·tion** [sɪ'lekʃn] (Aus)Wahl *f*; *econ.* Auswahl *f* (*of* an *dat.*)

self [self] (*pl.* **selves** [selvz]) Ich *n*, Selbst *n*; ~**as·sured** selbstbewußt, -sicher; ~**cen·tred** *Brt.*, ~**cen·tered** *Am.* egozentrisch; ~**col·o(u)red** einfarbig; ~**con·fi·dence** Selbstbewußtsein *n*, -vertrauen *n*; ~**con·fi·dent** selbstbewußt; ~**con·scious** befangen, gehemmt, unsicher; △ *nicht* **selbstbewußt**; ~**con'tained** (in sich) abgeschlossen; *fig.* verschlossen; ~**flat** *Brt.* abgeschlossene Wohnung; ~**con·trol** Selbstbeherrschung *f*; ~**de·fence** *Brt.*, ~**de·fense** *Am.* Selbstverteidigung *f*; *in* ~ *od.* aus Notwehr; ~**de·ter·mi·na·tion** *pol.* Selbstbestimmung *f*; ~**em·ployed** beruflich selbständig; ~**es·teem** Selbstachtung *f*; ~**ev·i·dent** selbstverständlich; offensichtlich; ~**gov·ern·ment** *pol.* Selbstverwaltung *f*; ~**help** Selbsthilfe *f*; ~**im·por·tant** überheblich; ~**in·dul·gent** nachgiebig gegen sich selbst; zügellos; ~**in·terest** Eigennutz *m*; '~**ish** selbstsüchtig, egoistisch; ~**made 'man** Selfmademan *m*; ~**pit·y** Selbstmitleid *n*; ~**pos·sessed** selbstbeherrscht; ~**pos·session** Selbstbeherrschung *f*; ~**re·li·ant** [selfrɪ'laɪənt] selbständig; ~**re·spect** Selbstachtung *f*; ~**right·eous** selbst-

gerecht; ~**sat·is·fied** selbstzufrieden; ~**serv·ice 1.** mit Selbstbedienung, Selbstbedienungs...; **2.** Selbstbedienung *f*; ~**stud·y** Selbststudium *n*; ~**suf·fi·cient** *econ.* autark; ~**sup·port·ing** finanziell unabhängig; ~**willed** eigensinnig, -willig

sell [sel] (*sold*) verkaufen; verkauft werden (*at, for* für); sich *gut etc.* verkaufen (lassen), gehen (*Ware*); ~ **by ...** mindestens haltbar bis ...; ~ **off** (*bsd.* billig) abstoßen; ~ **out** ausverkaufen; *be sold out* ausverkauft sein; ~ **up** *bsd. Brt.* v/t. sein Geschäft *etc.* verkaufen; v/i. sein Geschäft *etc.* verkaufen; '~**by date** Mindesthaltbarkeitsdatum *n*; '~**er** Verkäufer(in); *good* ~ gutgehender Artikel

selves [selvz] *pl. von* **self**

sem·blance ['sembləns] Anschein *m* (*of* von)

se·men *physiol.* ['si:men] Samen(flüssigkeit) *f*, Sperma *n*

se·mes·ter *univ.* [sɪ'mestə] Semester *n*

sem·i... ['semɪ] halb..., Halb...

'**sem·i|·cir·cle** Halbkreis *m*; ~**co·lon** Semikolon *n*, Strichpunkt *m*; ~**de·tached (house)** Doppelhaushälfte *f*; ~**fi·nals** *pl. Sport:* Semi-, Halbfinale *n*

sem·i·nar·y ['semɪnərɪ] Priesterseminar *n*

Sen → Snr

sen|·ate ['senɪt] Senat *m*; ~**a·tor** ['senətə] Senator *m*

send [send] (*sent*) *et., a.* Grüße, Hilfe *etc.* senden, schicken (*to dat. od.* an *acc.*); *Ware etc.* versenden, -schicken (*to* an *acc.*); *j-n* schicken (*to* ins Bett *etc.*); *mit adj. od. p.pr.:* machen: ~ *s.o. mad* j-n wahnsinnig machen; ~ *word to s.o.* j-m Nachricht geben; ~ *away* fort-, wegschicken; *Brief etc.* absenden, abschicken; ~ *down fig.* Preise *etc.* fallen lassen; ~ *for* nach j-m schicken, *j-n* kommen lassen; sich *et.* kommen lassen, *et.* anfordern; ~ *in* einsenden, -schicken, -reichen; ~ *off* fort-, wegschicken; *Brief etc.* absenden, abschicken; *Sport:* vom Platz stellen; ~ *on Brief etc.* nachschicken, -schicken (*to* an e-e *Adresse*); *Gepäck etc.* vorausschicken; ~ *out* hinausschicken; *Einladungen*

serve

etc. verschicken; **~ up** *fig.* Preise *etc.* steigen lassen; **'~er** Absender(in)

se·nile ['si:naɪl] senil; **se·nil·i·ty** [sɪ'nɪlətɪ] Senilität *f*

se·ni·or ['si:njə] **1.** *nachgestellt:* senior; älter (**to** als); dienstälter; rangälter; Ober...; **2.** Ältere(r *m*) *f*; *Am.* Student(in) im letzten Jahr; *he is my ~ by a year* er ist ein Jahr älter als ich; **~ 'cit·i·zens** *pl.* ältere Mitbürger *pl.*, Senioren *pl.*; **~·i·ty** [si:nɪ'ɒrətɪ] (höheres) Alter; (höheres) Dienstalter; (höherer) Rang; **~ 'part·ner** *econ.* Seniorpartner *m*

sen·sa·tion [sen'seɪʃn] Empfindung *f*; Gefühl *n*; Sensation *f*; **~·al** [sen'seɪʃənl] F großartig, phantastisch; sensationell, Sensations...

sense [sens] **1.** Sinn *m*; Verstand *m*; Vernunft *f*; Gefühl *n*; Bedeutung *f*; *bring s.o. to his ~s* j-n zur Besinnung *od.* Vernunft bringen; *come to one's ~s* zur Besinnung *od.* Vernunft kommen; *in a ~* in gewisser Hinsicht; *make ~* e-n Sinn ergeben; vernünftig sein; *~ of duty* Pflichtgefühl *n*; *~ of security* Gefühl *n* der Sicherheit; **2.** fühlen, spüren; **'~·less** bewußtlos; sinnlos

sen·si·bil·i·ty [sensɪ'bɪlətɪ] Empfindlichkeit *f*; *a.* **sensibilities** *pl.* Empfindsamkeit *f*, Zartgefühl *n*

sen·si·ble ['sensəbl] vernünftig; spürbar, merklich; praktisch (Kleidung); △ *nicht* **sensibel**

sen·si·tive ['sensɪtɪv] empfindlich; sensibel, empfindsam, feinfühlig

sen·sor *tech.* ['sensə] Sensor *m*

sen·su·al ['sensjʊəl] sinnlich

sen·su·ous ['sensjʊəs] sinnlich

sent [sent] *pret. u. p.p. von* **send**

sen·tence ['sentəns] **1.** *gr.* Satz *m*; *jur.* Strafe *f*, Urteil *n*; *jur.* **pass** *od.* **pronounce** **~** das Urteil fällen (**on** über *acc.*); **2.** *jur.* verurteilen (**to** zu)

sen·ti·ment ['sentɪmənt] Gefühle *pl.*; Sentimentalität *f*; *a.* **~s** *pl.* Ansicht *f*, Meinung *f*; **~·men·tal** [sentɪ'mentl] sentimental; gefühlvoll; **~·men·tal·i·ty** [sentɪmen'tælətɪ] Sentimentalität *f*

sen·try *mil.* ['sentrɪ] Wache *f*, (Wach[t])Posten *m*

sep·a·ra·ble ['sepərəbl] trennbar; **~·rate 1.** ['sepəreɪt] (sich) trennen; (auf-, ein-, zer)teilen (**into** in *acc.*); **2.**

['seprət] getrennt, separat; einzeln; **~·ra·tion** [sepə'reɪʃn] Trennung *f*; (Auf-, Ein-, Zer)Teilung *f*

Sept *nur geschr. Abk. für* **September** Sept., September *m*

Sep·tem·ber [sep'tembə] September *m*

sep·tic *med.* ['septɪk] (**~ally**) vereitert, septisch

se·quel ['si:kwəl] Nachfolgeroman *m*, -film *m*, Fortsetzung *f*; *fig.* Folge *f*; Nachspiel *n*

se·quence ['si:kwəns] (Aufeinander-, Reihen)Folge *f*; *Film, TV:* Sequenz *f*, Szene *f*; **~ of tenses** *gr.* Zeitenfolge *f*

ser·e·nade *mus.* [serə'neɪd] **1.** Serenade *f*, Ständchen *n*; **2.** *j-m* ein Ständchen bringen

se·rene [sɪ'ri:n] klar; heiter; gelassen

ser·geant ['sɑ:dʒənt] *mil.* Feldwebel *m*; (Polizei)Wachtmeister *m*

se·ri·al ['sɪərɪəl] **1.** Fortsetzungsroman *m*; (Rundfunk-, Fernseh)Serie *f*; **2.** serienmäßig, Serien..., Fortsetzungs...

se·ries ['sɪəri:z] (*pl.* **-ries**) Serie *f*, Reihe *f*, Folge *f*; (Buch)Reihe *f*; (Rundfunk-, Fernseh)Serie *f*, Sendereihe *f*

se·ri·ous ['sɪərɪəs] ernst; ernsthaft; ernstlich; schwer (Krankheit, Schaden, Verbrechen *etc.*); △ *nicht* **seriös**; *be ~* es ernst meinen (**about** mit); **'~·ness** Ernst(haftigkeit *f*) *m*; Schwere *f*

ser·mon ['sɜ:mən] *rel.* Predigt *f*; (Moral-, Straf)Predigt *f*

ser·pen·tine ['sɜ:pəntaɪn] gewunden, kurvenreich (Fluß, Straße)

se·rum ['sɪərəm] (*pl.* **-rums, -ra** [-rə]) Serum *n*

ser·vant ['sɜ:vənt] Diener(in) (*a. fig.*); Dienstbote *m*, -mädchen *n*; → **civil servant**

serve [sɜ:v] **1.** *v/t.* j-m, s-m Land *etc.* dienen; Dienstzeit (*a. mil.*) ableisten; Amtszeit *etc.* durchlaufen; j-n, *et.* versorgen (**with** mit); Essen servieren; Alkohol ausschenken; j-n (im Laden) bedienen; *jur.* Strafe verbüßen; Zweck dienen; Zweck erfüllen; *jur.* Vorladung *etc.* zustellen (**on** *s.o.* j-m); Tennis *etc.*: aufschlagen; *are you being ~d?* werden Sie schon bedient?; (*it*) *~s him right* F (das) geschieht ihm ganz recht; *v/i.* *bsd. mil.* dienen; servieren; dienen (**as**, **for** als); Tennis *etc.*: aufschlagen; *XY to ~* Tennis *etc.*: Aufschlag XY; *~ on a*

committee e-m Ausschuß angehören); **2.** *Tennis etc.*: Aufschlag *m*; **'server-löffel** *m*; **salad** ~s *pl.* Salatbesteck *n*

ser|vice ['sɜːvɪs] **1.** Dienst *m* (**to** an *dat.*); Dienstleistung *f*; (*Post-, Staats-, Telefon- etc.*)Dienst *m*; (*Zug- etc.*)Verkehr *m*; Service *m*, Kundendienst *m*; Bedienung *f*; Betrieb *m*; *rel.* Gottesdienst *m*; *tech.* Wartung *f*, *mot. a.* Inspektion *f*; (*Tee- etc.*)Service *n*; *jur.* Zustellung *f* (*e-r Vorladung*); *Tennis etc.*: Aufschlag *m*; ~s *pl. mil.* Streitkräfte *pl.*; **2.** *tech.* warten; **~vi·cea·ble** ['sɜːvɪsəbl] brauchbar; strapazierfähig; **'~ ar·e·a** *Brt.* (Autobahn)Raststätte *f*; **'~ charge** Bedienung(szuschlag *m*) *f*; **'~ sta·tion** Tankstelle *f*; (Reparatur)Werkstatt *f*

ser·vi·ette *bsd. Brt.* [sɜːvɪ'et] Serviette *f*
ser·vile ['sɜːvaɪl] sklavisch (*a. fig.*); servil, unterwürfig
serv·ing ['sɜːvɪŋ] Portion *f*
ser·vi·tude ['sɜːvɪtjuːd] Knechtschaft *f*; Sklaverei *f*
ses·sion ['seʃn] Sitzung(speriode) *f*; **be in** ~ *jur., parl.* tagen

set [set] **1.** (**-tt-; set**) *v/t.* setzen, stellen, legen; *in e-n Zustand* versetzen; veranlassen (**doing** zu tun); *tech.* einstellen, *Uhr* stellen (**by** nach), *Wecker* stellen (**for** auf *acc.*); *Tisch* decken; *Preis, Termin etc.* festsetzen, -legen; *Rekord* aufstellen; *Edelstein* fassen (**in** in *dat.*); *Ring etc.* besetzen (**with** mit); *Flüssigkeit* erstarren lassen; *Haar* legen; *med.* *Knochen* einrenken, -richten; *mus.* vertonen; *print.* absetzen; *Aufgabe, Frage* stellen; ~ **at ease** beruhigen; ~ **an example** ein Beispiel geben; ~ *s.o.* **free** j-n freilassen; ~ **going** in Gang setzen; ~ **one's hopes on** s.th. auf et. Hoffnung setzen auf (*acc.*); ~ *s.o.'s* **mind at rest** j-n beruhigen; ~ **great** (**little**) **store by** großen (geringen) Wert legen auf (*acc.*); **the novel is** ~ **in** der Roman spielt in (*dat.*); *v/i.* untergehen (*Sonne etc.*); fest werden (*Flüssiges*), erstarren; *hunt.* vorstehen (*Hund*); ~ **about doing** s.th. sich daranmachen, et. zu tun; ~ **about** s.o. F über j-n herfallen; ~ **aside** beiseite legen; *jur. Urteil etc.* aufheben; ~ **back** verzögern; j-n, et. zurückwerfen

(**by two months** um zwei Monate); ~ **in** einsetzen (*Winter etc.*); ~ **off** aufbrechen, sich aufmachen; hervorheben, betonen; *et.* auslösen; ~ **out** arrangieren, herrichten; aufbrechen, sich aufmachen; ~ **out to do** s.th. sich daranmachen, et. zu tun; ~ **up** errichten; *Gerät etc.* aufbauen; *Firma etc.* gründen; *et.* auslösen, verursachen; j-n versorgen (**with** mit); sich niederlassen; ~ **o.s. up as** sich ausgeben für; **2.** *adj.* festgesetzt, -gelegt; F bereit, fertig; starr (*Ansichten, Lächeln etc.*); ~ **lunch** od. **meal** *Brt.* Menü *n*; ~ **phrase** feststehender Ausdruck; **be** ~ **on doing** s.th. (fest) entschlossen sein, et. zu tun; **be all** ~ F startklar sein; **3.** Satz *m* (*Werkzeug etc.*), (*Möbel- etc.*)Garnitur *f*, (*Tee- etc.*)Service *n*; (*Fernseh-, Rundfunk*)Apparat *m*, (-)Gerät *n*; *thea.* Bühnenbild *n*; *Film, TV:* Set *n*, *m* (*Szenenaufbau*); *Tennis etc.*: Satz *m*; (*Personen*)Kreis *m*, Clique *f*; (*Kopf- etc.*)Haltung *f*; *poet.* Untergang *m* (*der Sonne*); △ *nicht* **Set, Platzdeckchen; have a shampoo and** ~ sich die Haare waschen und legen lassen; **'~·back** Rückschlag *m* (**to** für); **'~·square** *Brt.* Winkel *m*, Zeichendreieck *n*

set·tee [se'tiː] Sofa *n*
'set the·o·ry *math.* Mengenlehre *f*
set·ting ['setɪŋ] Untergang *m* (*der Sonne etc.*); *tech.* Einstellung *f*; Umgebung *f*; Schauplatz *m* (*e-s Films etc.*), (*Gold- etc.*)Fassung *f*; **'~ lo·tion** Haarfestiger *m*

set·tle ['setl] *v/i.* sich niederlassen (**on** auf *acc., dat.*), sich setzen (**on** auf *acc.*) (*a.* ~ **down**); sich niederlassen (**in** in e-r *Stadt etc.*); sich legen (*Staub*); sich setzen (*Kaffee etc.*); sich senken (*Boden etc.*); sich beruhigen (*Person, Magen etc.*), sich legen (*Aufregung etc.*) (*a.* ~ **down**); sich einigen; *v/t.* j-n, *Nerven etc.* beruhigen; vereinbaren; *Frage etc.* klären, entscheiden; *Streit etc.* beilegen; *Land* besiedeln; *Leute* ansiedeln; *Rechnung* begleichen, bezahlen; *Konto* ausgleichen; *Schaden* regulieren; *s-e Angelegenheiten* in Ordnung bringen; ~ **o.s.** sich niederlassen (**on** auf *acc., dat.*), sich setzen (**on** auf *acc.*); **that** ~**s it** damit ist der Fall erledigt; **that's** ~**d then** das ist also klar; ~ **back** sich (gemütlich) zurücklehnen; ~ **down** → v/i.; seßhaft werden; ~ **down to** sich widmen (dat.); ~ **for** sich zufriedengeben od. begnügen mit; ~ **in** sich einleben od. eingewöhnen; ~ **on** sich einigen auf (acc.); ~ **up** (be)zahlen; abrechnen (**with** mit); '~**d** fest (Ansichten); geregelt (Leben); beständig (Wetter); '~**ment** Vereinbarung f; Klärung f; Beilegung f; Einigung f; Siedlung f; Besiedlung f; Begleichung f, Bezahlung f; **reach a** ~ sich einigen (**with** mit); '~**r** Siedler(in)

sev·en ['sevn] **1.** sieben; **2.** Sieben f; **~·teen** [sevn'ti:n] **1.** siebzehn; **2.** Siebzehn f; **~·teenth** [sevn'ti:nθ] siebzehnte(r, -s); **~th** ['sevnθ] **1.** sieb(en)te(r, -s); **2.** Sieb(en)tel n; '**~th·ly** sieb(en)tens; **~·ti·eth** ['sevntɪɪθ] siebzigste(r, -s); **~·ty** ['sevntɪ] **1.** siebzig; **2.** Siebzig f

sev·er ['sevə] durchtrennen; abtrennen; Beziehungen abbrechen; (zer)reißen

sev·er·al ['sevrəl] mehrere; '**~·ly** einzeln, getrennt

se·vere [sɪ'vɪə] (**~r, ~st**) schwer (Krankheit, Rückschlag etc.); stark (Schmerzen); hart, streng (Winter); streng (Person, Disziplin etc.); scharf (Kritik); **se·ver·i·ty** [sɪ'verətɪ] Schwere f; Stärke f; Härte f; Strenge f; Schärfe f

sew [səʊ] (sewed, sewn od. sewed) nähen

sew·age ['su:ɪdʒ] Abwasser n; '**~ works** sg. Kläranlage f

sew·er ['sʊə] Abwasserkanal m; **~·age** ['sʊərɪdʒ] Kanalisation f

sew·ing ['səʊɪŋ] Nähen n; Näharbeit f; Näh...; '**~ ma·chine** Nähmaschine f

sewn [səʊn] p.p. von **sew**

sex [seks] Geschlecht n; Sexualität f; Sex m; Geschlechtsverkehr m

sex·is·m ['seksɪzəm] Sexismus m; '**~·ist 1.** sexistisch; **2.** Sexist(in)

sex·ton ['sekstən] Küster m (u. Totengräber m)

sex·u·al ['sekʃʊəl] sexuell, Sexual..., geschlechtlich, Geschlechts...; ~ **'har·ass·ment** sexuelle Belästigung (bsd. am Arbeitsplatz); ~ **'in·ter·course** Geschlechtsverkehr m; **~·i·ty** [sekʃʊ-'ælətɪ] Sexualität f

sex·y F ['seksɪ] (**-ier, -iest**) sexy, aufreizend

SF [es 'ef] Abk. für **science fiction** Science-fiction f

shab·by ['ʃæbɪ] (**-ier, -iest**) schäbig

shack [ʃæk] Hütte f, Bude f

shack·les ['ʃæklz] pl. Fesseln pl., Ketten pl. (beide a. fig.)

shade [ʃeɪd] **1.** Schatten m (a. fig.); (Lampen)Schirm m; Schattierung f; Am. Rouleau n; fig. Nuance f; **a** ~ fig. ein kleines bißchen, e-e Spur; **2.** abschirmen (**from** gegen Licht etc.); schattieren; ~ **off** allmählich übergehen (**into** in acc.)

shad·ow ['ʃædəʊ] **1.** Schatten m (a. fig.); **there's not a** od. **the** ~ **of a doubt about it** daran besteht nicht der geringste Zweifel; **2.** j-n beschatten; '**~·y** (**-ier, -iest**) schattig, dunkel; verschwommen, vage

shad·y ['ʃeɪdɪ] (**-ier, -iest**) schattig; schattenspendend; F zwielichtig (Person); F zweifelhaft (Geschäft etc.)

shaft [ʃɑːft] (Pfeil- etc.)Schaft m; (Hammer- etc.)Stiel m; tech. Welle f; (Aufzugs-, Bergwerks- etc.)Schacht m; (Sonnen- etc.)Strahl m

shag·gy ['ʃægɪ] (**-ier, -iest**) zottig

shake [ʃeɪk] **1.** (shook, shaken) v/t. schütteln; rütteln an (dat.); erschüttern; ~ **hands** sich die Hand geben od. schütteln; v/i. zittern, beben, wackeln (**with** vor dat.); ~ **down** herunterschütteln; kampieren; ~ **off** abschütteln; Erkältung etc. loswerden; ~ **up** Kissen etc. aufschütteln; Flasche, Flüssigkeit (durch)schütteln; fig. erschüttern; **2.** Schütteln n; Am. F Milchshake m; ~ **of the head** Kopfschütteln n; '**~·down** F **1.** Am. Erpressung f; Am. Filzung f, Durchsuchung f; Not)Lager n; **2.** adj.: ~ **flight** aviat. Testflug m; ~ **voyage** naut. Testfahrt f; **shak·en** ['ʃeɪkən] **1.** p.p. von **shake** 1; **2.** adj. a. ~ **up** erschüttert

shak·y ['ʃeɪkɪ] (**-ier, -iest**) wack(e)lig; zitt(e)rig

shall v/aux. [ʃæl] (pret. **should**) Futur: ich werde, wir werden; in Fragen: soll ich ...?, sollen wir ...?; ~ **we go?** gehen wir?

shal·low ['ʃæləʊ] seicht, flach, fig. a. oberflächlich; '**~s** pl. seichte od. flache Stelle, Untiefe f

sham [ʃæm] **1.** Farce f; Heuchelei f; ⚠ nicht **Scham**; **2.** unecht, falsch (Schmuck etc.); vorgetäuscht, geheuchelt (*Mitgefühl etc.*); **3.** (*-mm-*) *v/t.* *Mitgefühl etc.* vortäuschen, heucheln; *Krankheit etc.* simulieren; *v/i.* sich verstellen, heucheln; **he's only ~ing** er tut nur so

sham·bles ['ʃæmblz] *sg.* F Schlachtfeld *n*, wüstes Durcheinander, Chaos *n*

shame [ʃeɪm] **1.** Scham(gefühl *n*) *f*; Schande *f*; ~*! pfui!*; **~ on you!** pfui!; schäm dich!; **put to ~** 2. beschämen; Schande machen (*dat.*); **~·faced** betreten, verlegen; **~·ful** beschämend; schändlich; **'~·less** schamlos

sham·poo [ʃæm'puː] **1.** (*pl. -poos*) Shampoo *n*, Schampon *n*, Schampun *n*; Haarwäsche *f*; → **set** 3; **2.** Haare waschen; *j-m* die Haare waschen; *Teppich etc.* schamponieren

sham·rock ['ʃæmrɒk] Kleeblatt *n* (*irisches Nationalzeichen*)

shank [ʃæŋk] *tech.* Schaft *m* (*e-s Bohrers etc.*); Hachse *f* (*beim Schlachttier*)

shan't [ʃɑːnt] = **shall not**

shan·ty¹ ['ʃænti] Hütte *f*, Bude *f*

shan·ty² ['ʃænti] Shanty *n*, Seemannslied *n*

shape [ʃeɪp] **1.** Form *f*; Gestalt *f*; Verfassung *f* (*körperlich, geistig*); Zustand *m* (*Gebäude etc.*); **2.** *v/t.* formen; gestalten; *v/i. a.* **~ up** sich gut *etc.* machen (*Person*); **~d** ...förmig; **'~·less** formlos; ausgebeult; **'~·ly** (*-ier, -iest*) wohlgeformt

share [ʃeə] **1.** Anteil *m* (**in**, **of** an *dat.*); *bsd. Brt. econ.* Aktie *f*; **go ~s** teilen; **have a (no) ~ in** (nicht) beteiligt sein an (*dat.*); **2.** *v/t.* (sich) *et.* teilen (**with** mit); *a.* **~ out** verteilen (**among**, **between** an *acc.*, unter *acc.*); *v/i.* teilen; **~ in** sich teilen in (*acc.*); **'~·hold·er** *bsd. Brt. econ.* Aktionär(in)

shark [ʃɑːk] (*pl. shark, sharks*) *zo.* Hai(fisch) *m*; F (*Kredit- etc.*)Hai *m*

sharp [ʃɑːp] **1.** *adj.* scharf (*a. fig.*); spitz (*Nadel, Nase etc.*); scharf, abrupt; scharf, schneidend (*Wind, Frost, Kälte*; *Befehl, Stimme*); beißend (*Kälte, Frost*); scharf, beißend (*Geschmack*); stechend, heftig (*Schmerz*); scharf (*Verstand, Auge*); gescheit; *mus.* (*um e-n Halbton*) erhöht; **C ~** *mus.* Cis *n*; **2.** *adv.* scharf, abrupt; *mus.* zu hoch; pünktlich, genau; **at eight o'clock ~** Punkt 8 (Uhr); **look ~** F sich beeilen;

look ~! F mach schnell!, Tempo!; F paß auf!, gib acht!; **~·en** ['ʃɑːpən] *Messer etc.* schärfen, schleifen; *Bleistift etc.* spitzen; **'~·en·er** ['ʃɑːpnə] (*Messer-etc.*)Schärfer *m*; (*Bleistift*)Spitzer *m*; **'~·ness** Schärfe *f* (*a. fig.*); **'~·shoot·er** Scharfschütze *m*; **~·sight·ed** scharfsichtig

shat·ter ['ʃætə] *v/t.* zerschmettern, -schlagen; *Hoffnungen etc.* zerstören; *v/i.* zerspringen, -splittern

shave [ʃeɪv] **1.** (sich) rasieren; (glatt)hobeln; *j-n*, *et.* streifen; **2.** Rasur *f*; **have a ~** sich rasieren; **that was a close ~** das war knapp, das ist gerade noch einmal gutgegangen; **shav·en** ['ʃeɪvn] kahlgeschoren; **shav·er** ['ʃeɪvə] (*bsd. elektrischer*) Rasierapparat; **shav·ing** ['ʃeɪvɪŋ] **1.** Rasieren *n*; **~s** *pl.* Späne *pl.*; **2.** Rasier...

shawl [ʃɔːl] Umhängetuch *n*; Kopftuch *n*

she [ʃiː] **1.** *pron.* sie; **2.** Sie *f*; *zo.* Weibchen *n*; **3.** *adj. in Zssgn zo.*: ...weibchen *n*; **~·bear** Bärin *f*

sheaf [ʃiːf] (*pl. sheaves*) *agr.* Garbe *f*; Bündel *n* (*Papiere etc.*)

shear [ʃɪə] **1.** (*sheared, sheared od. shorn*) scheren; **2.** (*a pair of*) **~s** *pl.* (*e-e*) große Schere

sheath [ʃiːθ] (*pl. sheaths* [ʃiːðz]) (*Schwert-, etc.*)Scheide *f*; Hülle *f*; *Brt.* Kondom *n*, *m*; **~·e** [ʃiːð] *Schwert etc.* in die Scheide stecken; *tech.* umhüllen, verkleiden, ummanteln

sheaves [ʃiːvz] *pl. von* **sheaf**

shed¹ [ʃed] Schuppen *m*; Stall *m*

shed² [ʃed] (*-dd-*; *shed*) *Tränen etc.* vergießen; *Blätter etc.* verlieren; *fig.* Hemmungen etc. ablegen; **~ its skin** sich häuten; **~ a few pounds** ein paar Pfund abnehmen

sheen [ʃiːn] Glanz *m*

sheep [ʃiːp] (*pl. sheep*) Schaf *n*; **'~·dog** *zo.* Schäferhund *m*; **'~·farm·ing** Schafzucht *f*; **'~·fold** Schafhürde *f*; **'~·ish** verlegen; **'~·skin** Schaffell *n*

sheer [ʃɪə] rein, bloß; steil, (fast) senkrecht; hauchdünn (*Stoff*)

sheet [ʃiːt] Bettuch *n*, (Bett)Laken *n*, Leintuch *n*; (*Glas-, Metall- etc.*)Platte *f*; Blatt *n*, Bogen *m* (*Papier*); weite (*Eis- etc.*) Fläche *f*; **the rain was coming down in ~s** es regnete in Strömen; **'~·light·ning** Wetterleuchten *n*

shelf [ʃelf] (*pl.* **shelves**) (Bücher-, Wand- *etc.*)Brett *n*, (-)Bord *n*; Riff *n*; **shelves** *pl.* Regal *n*; **off the ~** gleich zum mitnehmen (*Ware*)

shell [ʃel] **1.** (Austern-, Eier-, Nuß- *etc.*)Schale *f*; (Erbsen- *etc.*)Hülse *f*; Muschel *f*; (Schnecken)Haus *n*; *zo.* Panzer *m*; *mil.* Granate *f*; (Geschoß-, Patronen)Hülse *f*; *Am.* Patrone *f*; Rumpf *m*, Gerippe *n*, *arch. a.* Rohbau *m*; **2.** schälen, enthülsen; *mil.* mit Granaten beschießen; '~**fire** Granatfeuer *n*; '~**fish** *zo.* (*pl.* **-fish**) Schal(en)tier *n*; △ *nicht* **Schellfisch**

shel·ter [ˈʃeltə] **1.** Unterstand *m*; Bunker *m*; (Obdachlosen- *etc.*)Unterkunft *f*; Schutz *m*; Unterkunft *f*; **run for ~** Schutz suchen; **take ~** sich unterstellen (**under** unter *dat.*); **bus ~** Wartehäuschen *n*; **2.** *v/t.* schützen (**from** vor *dat.*); *v/i.* sich unterstellen

shelve [ʃelv] *v/t.* Bücher in ein Regal stellen; *fig. Plan etc.* aufschieben, zurückstellen; *v/i.* sanft abfallen (*Land*)

shelves [ʃelvz] *pl. von* **shelf**

she·nan·i·gans F [ʃɪˈnænɪɡənz] *pl.* Blödsinn *m*, Mumpitz *m*; übler Trick

shep·herd [ˈʃepəd] **1.** Schäfer *m*, Hirt *m*; **2.** *j-n* führen

sher·iff [ˈʃerɪf] Sheriff *m*

shield [ʃiːld] **1.** Schild *m*; **2.** *j-n* (be)schützen (**from** vor *dat.*); *j-n* decken

shift [ʃɪft] **1.** *v/t. et.* bewegen, schieben, Möbelstück a. (ver)rücken; Schuld etc. (ab)schieben (**onto** auf *acc.*); **~ gear(s)** *bsd. Am. mot.* schalten; *v/i.* sich bewegen; umspringen (*Wind*); *fig.* sich verlagern *od.* -schieben *od.* wandeln; *bsd. Am. mot.* schalten (**into, to** in *acc.*); **~ from one foot to the other** von e-m Fuß auf den anderen treten; **~ on one's chair** auf s-m Stuhl *ungeduldig etc.* hin u. her rutschen; **2.** *fig.* Verlagerung *f*, Verschiebung *f*, Wandel *m*; *econ.* Schicht *f* (Arbeiter u. Zeit); '~**key** Umschalttaste *f* (e-r Schreibmaschine etc.); '~**work·er** Schichtarbeiter(in); '~**y** (**-ier**, **-iest**) F verschlagen (Blick etc.)

shil·ling Brt. hist. [ˈʃɪlɪŋ] Schilling *m*

shim·mer [ˈʃɪmə] schimmern; flimmern (Luft)

shin [ʃɪn] **1.** *a.* '~**bone** anat. Schienbein *n*; **2.** (**-nn-**): **~ up (down)** Baum etc. hinauf-(herunter)klettern

shine [ʃaɪn] **1.** *v/i.* (**shone**) scheinen; leuchten; glänzen (*a. fig.*); *v/t.* (**shined**) Schuhe etc. polieren; **2.** Glanz *m*

shin·gle[1] [ˈʃɪŋɡl] grober Strandkies

shin·gle[2] [ˈʃɪŋɡl] (Dach)Schindel *f*

shin·gles med. [ˈʃɪŋɡlz] *sg.* Gürtelrose *f*

shin·y [ˈʃaɪnɪ] (**-ier**, **-iest**) blank, glänzend

ship [ʃɪp] **1.** Schiff *n*; **2.** (**-pp-**) verschiffen; econ. verfrachten, -senden; '~**board: on** ~ an Bord; '~**ment** Ladung *f*; Verschiffung *f*; Verfrachtung *f*, -sand *m*; '~**own·er** Reeder *m*; Schiffseigner *m*; '~**ping** Schiffahrt *f*; coll. Schiffsbestand *m*; Verschiffung *f*; Verfrachtung *f*, Versand *m*; '~**wreck** Schiffbruch *m*; '~**wrecked 1.** be ~ Schiffbruch erleiden; **2.** schiffbrüchig; '~**yard** (Schiffs)Werft *f*

shire [ˈʃaɪə, *in Zssgn* ...ʃə] *veraltet:* Grafschaft *f*

shirk [ʃɜːk] sich drücken (vor *dat.*); '~**er** Drückeberger(in)

shirt [ʃɜːt] Hemd *n*; '~**sleeve 1.** Hemdsärmel *m*; **in** (one's) ~s in Hemdsärmeln, hemdsärmelig; **2.** hemdsärmelig

shit V [ʃɪt] **1.** Scheiße *f* (*a. fig.*); *fig.* Scheiß *m*; **2.** (**-tt-**; **shit**) (voll)scheißen

shiv·er [ˈʃɪvə] **1.** zittern (**with** vor *dat.*); **2.** Schauer *m*; ~s *pl.* F Schüttelfrost *m*; **the sight send ~s (up and) down my spine** bei dem Anblick überlief es mich eiskalt

shoal[1] [ʃəʊl] Untiefe *f*; Sandbank *f*

shoal[2] [ʃəʊl] Schwarm *m* (Fische)

shock[1] [ʃɒk] **1.** Schock *m* (*a. med.*); Wucht *f* (e-r Explosion, e-s Schlags etc.); electr. Schlag *m*, (*a. med.* Elektro)Schock *m*; **2.** schockieren, empören; *j-m* e-n Schock versetzen

shock[2] [ʃɒk] (~ **of hair** Haar)Schopf *m*

'**shock| ab·sorb·er** tech. Stoßdämpfer *m*; '~**ing** schockierend, empörend, anstößig; F scheußlich

shod [ʃɒd] pret. u. p.p. von **shoe** 2

shod·dy [ˈʃɒdɪ] (**-ier**, **-iest**) minderwertig (*Ware*); gemein, schäbig (Trick etc.)

shoe [ʃuː] **1.** Schuh *m*; Hufeisen *n*; **2.** (**shod**) Pferd beschlagen; '~**horn** Schuhanzieher *m*, -löffel *m*; '~**lace** Schnürsenkel *m*; '~**mak·er** Schuhmacher *m*, Schuster *m*; '~**shine** Schuhputzen *n*; '~**shine boy** Schuhputzer *m*; '~**string** Schnürsenkel *m*

S

shone [ʃɒn, *Am.* ʃəʊn] *pret. u. p.p. von* **shine** 1

shook [ʃʊk] *pret. von* **shake** 1

shoot [ʃuːt] **1.** (**shot**) *v/t.* schießen; abfeuern, abschießen; erschießen; *hunt.* schießen, erlegen; *Riegel* vorschieben; *j-n* fotografieren, aufnehmen, *Film* drehen; *Heroin etc.* spritzen; **~ the lights** *mot.* bei Rotlicht fahren; *v/i.* schießen (**at** auf *acc.*); jagen; schießen, rasen; drehen, filmen; *bot.* sprießen, treiben; **2.** *bot.* Trieb *m*; Jagd *f*; Jagd(revier *n*) *f*; **~·er** Schütz|e *m*, -in *f*; *bsd. Brt. sl.* Schießeisen *n*

'shoot·ing 1. Schießen *n*; Schießerei *f*; Erschießung *f*; Anschlag *m*; Jagd *f*; *Film, TV:* Dreharbeiten *pl.*, Aufnahmen *pl.*; **2.** stechend (*Schmerz*); **~ gal·le·ry** Schießstand *m*, -bude *f*; **~ range** Schießstand *m*; **~ star** Sternschnuppe *f*

shop [ʃɒp] **1.** Laden *m*, Geschäft *n*; Werkstatt *f*; Betrieb *m*; **talk ~** fachsimpeln; **2.** (-*pp*-) *mst* **go ~ping** einkaufen gehen; **~ as·sis·tant** *Brt.* Verkäufer(in); **~·keep·er** Ladenbesitzer(in), -inhaber(in); **~·lift·er** Ladendieb(in); **~·lift·ing** Ladendiebstahl *m*; **~·per** Käufer(in)

shop·ping ['ʃɒpɪŋ] **1.** Einkauf *m*, Einkaufen *n*; Einkäufe *pl.* (*Ware*); **do one's ~** (s-e) Einkäufe machen; **2.** Einkaufs...; **~ bag** Einkaufsbeutel *m*, -tasche *f*; **~ cart** *Am.* Einkaufswagen *m*; **~ cen·tre** (*Am.* **cen·ter**) Einkaufszentrum *n*; **~ list** Einkaufsliste *f*, -zettel *m*; **~ mall** *Am.* Einkaufszentrum *n*; **~ street** Geschäfts-, Ladenstraße *f*

shop| **stew·ard** gewerkschaftlicher Vertrauensmann; **~·walk·er** *Brt.* Aufsicht(sperson) *f* (*im Kaufhaus*); **~·win·dow** Schaufenster *n*

shore¹ [ʃɔː] Küste *f*; (*See*)Ufer *n*; **on ~** an Land

shore² [ʃɔː]: **~ up** (ab)stützen

shorn [ʃɔːn] *p.p. von* **shear** 1

short [ʃɔːt] **1.** *adj.* kurz; klein (*Person*); kurz angebunden, barsch, schroff (**with** zu); mürbe (*Gebäck*); **be ~ for** die Kurzform sein von; **be ~ of ...** nicht genügend ... haben; **2.** *adv.* plötzlich, abrupt; **~ of** außer; **cut ~** plötzlich unterbrechen; **fall ~ of** et. nicht erreichen; **stop ~** plötzlich innehalten, stutzen;

stop ~ of *od.* **at** zurückschrecken vor (*dat.*); **→ run** 1; **3.** F Kurzfilm *m*; *electr.* F Kurze *f*; **called ... for ~** kurz ... genannt; **in ~** kurz(um); **~·age** ['ʃɔːtɪdʒ] Knappheit *f*, Mangel *m* (**of** an *dat.*); **~·com·ings** *pl.* Unzulänglichkeiten *pl.*, Mängel *pl.*, Fehler *pl.*; **~·cut** Abkürzung(sweg *m*) *f*; **take a ~** (den Weg) abkürzen; **~·en** ['ʃɔːtn] *v/t.* (ab-, ver)kürzen; *v/i.* kürzer werden

short·en·ing ['ʃɔːtnɪŋ] Backfett *n*

'short·hand Kurzschrift *f*, Stenographie *f*; **~·hand 'typ·ist** Stenotypistin *f*; **~·ly** bald; barsch, schroff; mit wenigen Worten; **~·ness** Kürze *f*; Schroffheit *f*; **→ shortage**; **~s** *pl. a.* **pair of ~** Shorts *pl.*; *bsd. Am.* (Herren)Unterhose *f*; **~·sight·ed** *bsd. Brt.* kurzsichtig (*a. fig.*); **~·sto·ry** Short story *f*, Kurzgeschichte *f*; **~·term** *econ.* kurzfristig; **~ time** *econ.* Kurzarbeit *f*; **~ wave** *electr.* Kurzwelle *f*; **~·wind·ed** kurzatmig

shot [ʃɒt] **1.** *pret. u. p.p. von* **shoot** 1; **2.** Schuß *m*; Schrot(kugeln *pl.*) *m*, *n*; *Kugelstoßen*: Kugel *f*; *guter etc.* Schuß; *Fußball etc.*: Schuß *m*; *Basketball etc.*: Wurf *m*; *Tennis, Golf*: Schlag *m*; *phot.* Schnappschuß *m*, Aufnahme *f*; *Film, TV*: Aufnahme *f*, Einstellung *f*; *med.* F Spritze *f*; F Schuß *m* (*Drogen*); *fig.* F Versuch *m*; **~ in the dark** *fig.* Schuß ins Blaue; **I'll have a ~ at it** ich probier's mal; **not by a long ~** *bsd. Am.* F noch lange nicht; **→ big shot**; **~·gun** Schrotflinte *f*; **~·gun 'wed·ding** F Mußheirat *f*; **~ put** *Sport*: Kugelstoßen *n*; **~ put·ter** *Sport*: Kugelstoßer(in)

should [ʃʊd] *pret. von* **shall**

shoul·der ['ʃəʊldə] **1.** Schulter *f*; *Am. mot.* Standspur *f*; **2.** schultern; *Kosten, Verantwortung etc.* übernehmen; (mit der Schulter) stoßen; **~ bag** Schulter-, Umhängetasche *f*; **~ blade** *anat.* Schulterblatt *n*; **~ strap** Träger *m* (*e-s Kleids etc.*); Tragriemen *m*

shout [ʃaʊt] **1.** *v/i.* rufen, schreien (**for** nach; **for help** um Hilfe); **~ at s.o.** *j-n* anschreien; *v/t.* rufen, schreien; **2.** Ruf *m*, Schrei *m*

shove [ʃʌv] **1.** stoßen, schubsen; *et.* schieben, stopfen; **2.** Stoß *m*, Schubs *m*

shov·el ['ʃʌvl] **1.** Schaufel *f*; **2.** (*bsd. Brt.* -**ll**-, *Am.* -**l**-) schaufeln

show [ʃəʊ] **1.** (*showed, shown od. showed*) *v/t.* zeigen, vorzeigen, anzeigen; *j-n* bringen, führen (*to* zu); ausstellen, zeigen; *Film etc.* zeigen, vorführen; *TV* zeigen, bringen; *v/i.* zu sehen sein; **be** ~**ing** gezeigt werden, laufen; ~ **around** herumführen; ~ **in** herein-, hineinführen, -bringen; ~ **off** angeben *od.* protzen (mit); vorteilhaft zur Geltung bringen; ~ **out** heraus-, hinausführen, -bringen; ~ **round** herumführen; ~ **up** *v/t.* herauf-, hinaufführen, -bringen; sichtbar machen; *j-n* entlarven, bloßstellen; *et.* aufdecken; *j-n* in Verlegenheit bringen; *v/i.* zu sehen sein; F kommen; F aufkreuzen, -tauchen; **2.** *thea. etc.* Vorstellung *f*; Show *f*; *Rundfunk, TV:* Sendung *f*; Ausstellung *f*; Zurschaustellung *f*, Demonstration *f*; *leerer Schein*; **be on** ~ ausgestellt *od.* zu besichtigen sein; **steal the** ~ **from s.o.** *fig.* j-m die Schau stehlen; **make a** ~ **of** *Anteilnahme, Interesse etc.* heucheln; **put up a poor** ~ F e-e schwache Leistung zeigen; **be in charge of the whole** ~ F den ganzen Laden schmeißen; **3.** Muster...; '~ **flat** Musterwohnung *f*; '~**biz** F, '~ **busi·ness** Showbusineß *m*; Showgeschäft *n*; '~**case** Schaukasten *m*, Vitrine *f*; '~**down** Kraft-, Machtprobe *f*

show·er ['ʃaʊə] **1.** (*Regen- etc.*)Schauer *m*; (*Funken*)Regen *m*; (*Wasser-, Wortetc.*)Schwall *m*; Dusche *f*; **have** ~**d od. take a** ~ duschen; **2.** *v/t.* j-n mit et. überschütten *od.* -häufen; *v/i.* duschen; ~ **down** niederprasseln

'**show** | **jump·er** *Sport:* Springreiter(in); '~ **jump·ing** *Sport:* Springreiten *n*; ~**n** [ʃəʊn] *p.p. von* **show 1**; '~**-off** F Angeber(in); '~**room** Ausstellungsraum *m*; '~**·y** (*-ier, -iest*) auffallend

shrank [ʃræŋk] *pret. von* **shrink 1**

shred [ʃred] **1.** Fetzen *m*; **2.** (*-dd-*) zerfetzen; in (schmale) Streifen schneiden, schnitzeln, schnetzeln; in den Papierod. Reißwolf geben; '~**·der** Schnitzelmaschine *f*; Papier-, Reißwolf *m*

shrew *lit.* [ʃruː] zänkisches Weib

shrewd [ʃruːd] scharfsinnig; schlau

shriek [ʃriːk] **1.** (gellend) aufschreien; ~ **with laughter** vor Lachen kreischen; **2.** (schriller) Schrei

shrill [ʃrɪl] schrill; heftig, scharf (*Kritik etc.*)

shrimp [ʃrɪmp] *zo.* Garnele *f*; *fig. contp.* Knirps *m*

shrine [ʃraɪn] Schrein *m*

shrink [ʃrɪŋk] **1.** (*shrank, shrunk*) (ein-, zusammen)schrumpfen (lassen); einlaufen; *fig.* abnehmen; **2.** F Klapsdoktor *m*; ~**age** ['ʃrɪŋkɪdʒ] Schrumpfung *f*; Einlaufen *n*; *fig.* Abnahme *f*; '~**-wrap** (*-pp-*) einschweißen

shriv·el ['ʃrɪvl] (*bsd. Brt. -ll-, Am. -l-*) schrumpfen (lassen); runz(e)lig werden (lassen)

shroud [ʃraʊd] **1.** Leichentuch *n*; **2.** *fig.* hüllen

Shrove Tues·day [ʃrəʊv 'tjuːzdɪ] Fastnachts-, Faschingsdienstag *m*

shrub [ʃrʌb] Strauch *m*, Busch *m*; ~**·be·ry** ['ʃrʌbərɪ] Strauch-, Buschwerk *n*

shrug [ʃrʌg] **1.** (*-gg-*) *a.* **one's shoulders** mit den Achseln *od.* Schultern zucken; **2.** Achsel-, Schulterzucken *n*

shrunk [ʃrʌŋk] *p.p. von* **shrink 1**

shuck *bsd. Am.* [ʃʌk] **1.** Hülse *f*, Schote *f*; Schale *f*; **2.** enthülsen; schälen

shud·der ['ʃʌdə] **1.** schaudern; **2.** Schauder *m*

shuf·fle ['ʃʌfl] **1.** *v/t.* Karten mischen; *Papiere etc.* umordnen, hierhin od. dorthin legen; ~ **one's feet** schlurfen; *v/i.* Kartenspiel: mischen; schlurfen; **2.** Mischen *n* (*von Karten*); Schlurfen *n*; schlurfender Gang

shun [ʃʌn] (*-nn-*) j-n, et. meiden

shunt [ʃʌnt] *Zug etc.* rangieren, verschieben; *a.* ~ **off** F j-n abschieben (**to** *in acc.*, nach)

shut [ʃʌt] (*-tt-; shut*) (sich) schließen; zumachen; ~ **down** Fabrik etc. schließen; ~ **off** Wasser, Gas, Maschine etc. abstellen; ~ **up** einschließen; einsperren; Geschäft schließen; ~ **up!** F halt die Klappe!; '~**·ter** Fensterladen *m*; *phot.* Verschluß *m*; '~**·ter speed** *phot.* Belichtung(szeit) *f*

shut·tle ['ʃʌtl] **1.** Pendelverkehr *m*; (*Raum*)Fähre *f*, (-)Transporter *m*; *tech.* Schiffchen *n*; **2.** hin- u. herbefördern; '~**·cock** *Sport:* Federball *m*; '~ **di·plo·ma·cy** *pol.* Pendeldiplomatie *f*; '~ **ser·vice** Pendelverkehr *m*

shy [ʃaɪ] **1.** scheu; schüchtern; **2.** scheuen (*at* vor *dat.*) (*bsd. Pferd*); ~ *away from* *fig.* zurückschrecken vor (*dat.*); '**~ness** Scheu *f*; Schüchternheit *f*

sick [sɪk] **1.** krank; *be* ~ *bsd. Brt.* sich übergeben; *she was od. felt* ~ ihr war schlecht; *fall* ~ krank werden; *be off* ~ krank (geschrieben) sein; *report* ~ sich krank melden; *be* ~ *of s.th.* F et. satt haben; *it makes me* ~ F mir wird schlecht davon, *a. fig.* es ekelt *od.* widert mich an; **2.** *the* ~ *pl.* die Kranken *pl.*; '**~en** *v/t.* j-n anekeln, anwidern; *v/i.* krank werden

sick·le ['sɪkl] Sichel *f*

'**sick leave**: *be on* ~ krank (geschrieben) sein, wegen Krankheit fehlen; '**~ly** (*-ier, -iest*) kränklich; ungesund; matt (*Lächeln*); widerlich (*Geruch etc.*); '**~ness** Krankheit *f*; Übelkeit *f*; '**~ness ben·e·fit** *Brt.* Krankengeld *n*

side [saɪd] **1.** Seite *f*; *bsd. Brt. Sport*: Mannschaft *f*; ~ *by* ~ nebeneinander, take ~*s* Partei ergreifen (*with* für; *against* gegen); **2.** Seiten...; Neben...; **3.** Partei ergreifen (*with* für; *against* gegen); '**~board** Anrichte *f*, Sideboard *n*; '**~car** *mot.* Bei-, Seitenwagen *m*; '~ **dish** *gastr.* Beilage *f*; '~**long** seitlich; Seiten...; '~ **street** Nebenstraße *f*; '**~stroke** *Sport*: Seitenschwimmen *n*; '**~track** *j*-n ablenken; *et.* abbiegen; *Am.* Zug *etc.* rangieren, verschieben; '**~walk** *bsd. Am.* Bürger-, Gehsteig *m*; '**~ways** seitlich; seitwärts, nach der *od.* zur Seite

sid·ing *rail.* ['saɪdɪŋ] Nebengleis *n*

si·dle ['saɪdl]: ~ *up to s.o.* sich an j-n heranschleichen

siege *mil.* [si:dʒ] Belagerung *f*; *lay* ~ *to* belagern

sieve [sɪv] **1.** Sieb *n*; **2.** (durch)sieben

sift [sɪft] (durch)sieben; *a.* ~ *through fig.* sichten, durchsehen, prüfen

sigh [saɪ] **1.** seufzen; **2.** Seufzer *m*

sight [saɪt] **1.** Sehvermögen *n*, Sehkraft *f*, Auge(nlicht) *n*; Anblick *m*; Sicht(weite) *f*; *pl.* Visier *n*, Sehenswürdigkeiten *pl.*; *at* ~, *on* ~ sofort; *at the* ~ *of* beim Anblick von (*od. gen.*); *at first* ~ auf den ersten Blick; *catch* ~ *of* erblicken; *know by* ~ vom Sehen kennen; *lose* ~ *of* aus den Augen verlieren; *be (with)in* ~ in Sicht sein (*a. fig.*); **2.** sichten; '**~ed** sehend; ...sichtig; '~-

-read (*-read* [-red]) *mus.* vom Blatt singen *od.* spielen; '**~see·ing** Sightseeing *n*, Besichtigung *f* von Sehenswürdigkeiten; *go* ~ sich die Sehenswürdigkeiten anschauen; '**~see·ing tour** Sightseeing-Tour *f*, Besichtigungstour *f*, (Stadt)Rundfahrt *f*; '**~se·er** Tourist(in)

sign [saɪn] **1.** Zeichen *n*; (*Hinweis-, Warn- etc.*)Schild *n*; *fig.* Zeichen *n*, Anzeichen *n*; **2.** unterschreiben, -zeichnen; *Scheck* ausstellen; ~ *in* sich eintragen; ~ *out* sich austragen

sig·nal ['sɪgnl] **1.** Signal *n* (*a. fig.*); Zeichen *n* (*a. fig.*); **2.** (*bsd. Brt. -ll-, Am. -l-*) (ein) Zeichen geben; signalisieren

sig·na·to·ry ['sɪgnətərɪ] Unterzeichner(in) (*e-s Vertrags*)

sig·na·ture ['sɪgnətʃə] Unterschrift *f*; Signatur *f*; '~ **tune** *Rundfunk, TV*: Erkennungs-, Kennmelodie *f*

'**sign·board** (Aushänge)Schild *n*; '**~er** Unterzeichnete(r *m*) *f*

sig·net ['sɪgnɪt] Siegel *n*

sig·nif·i·cance [sɪg'nɪfɪkəns] Bedeutung *f*, Wichtigkeit *f*; ~**cant** bedeutend, bedeutsam, wichtig; bezeichnend

sig·ni·fy ['sɪgnɪfaɪ] bedeuten; andeuten

'**sign·post** Wegweiser *m*

si·lence ['saɪləns] **1.** Stille *f*; Schweigen *n*; ~! Ruhe!; *in* ~ schweigend; *reduce to* ~ → **2.** zum Schweigen bringen; '**si·lenc·er** *tech.* Schalldämpfer *m*; *Brt. mot.* Auspufftopf *m*

si·lent ['saɪlənt] still; schweigend; schweigsam; stumm; ~ '**part·ner** *Am. econ.* stiller Teilhaber

sil·i·con *chem.* ['sɪlɪkən] Silizium *n*; ~ **cone** *chem.* ['sɪlɪkəʊn] Silikon *n*

silk [sɪlk] Seide *f*; Seiden...; '**~worm** *zo.* Seidenraupe *f*; '**~y** (*-ier, -iest*) seidig; samtig (*Stimme*)

sill [sɪl] (*Fenster*)Brett *n*

sil·ly ['sɪlɪ] **1.** (*-ier, -iest*) albern, töricht, dumm; **2.** F Dummerchen *n*

sil·ver ['sɪlvə] **1.** Silber *n*; **2.** silbern, Silber...; **3.** versilbern; ~**'plat·ed** versilbert; '**~ware** Tafelsilber *n*; '**~y** ['sɪlvərɪ] silberglänzend; *fig.* silberhell

sim·i·lar ['sɪmɪlə] ähnlich (*to dat.*); ~**i·ty** [sɪmɪ'lærətɪ] Ähnlichkeit *f*

sim·i·le ['sɪmɪlɪ] Simile *n*, Gleichnis *n*, Vergleich *m*

sim·mer ['sɪmə] leicht kochen, köcheln;

sitting room

~ *with* fig. kochen vor (*Zorn* etc.), fiebern vor (*Aufregung* etc.); ~ *down* F sich beruhigen *od.* abregen

sim·per ['sɪmpə] albern *od.* affektiert lächeln

sim·ple ['sɪmpl] (~r, ~st) einfach, simpel, leicht, schlicht; einfältig; naiv; ~'**mind·ed** einfältig; naiv

sim·plic·i·ty [sɪm'plɪsətɪ] Einfachheit f, Schlichtheit f; Einfältigkeit f; Naivität f; ~**fi·ca·tion** [sɪmplɪfɪ'keɪʃn] Vereinfachung f; ~**fy** ['sɪmplɪfaɪ] vereinfachen

sim·ply ['sɪmplɪ] einfach; bloß

sim·u·late ['sɪmjʊleɪt] vortäuschen; *mil., tech.* simulieren

sim·ul·ta·ne·ous [sɪməl'teɪnjəs] simultan, gleichzeitig

sin [sɪn] 1. Sünde f; 2. (-nn-) sündigen

since [sɪns] 1. *adv. a. ever* ~ seitdem, -her; 2. *prp.* seit; 3. *cj.* seit(dem); da

sin·cere [sɪn'sɪə] aufrichtig, ehrlich, offen; *Yours* ~*ly, ~ly yours* Mit freundlichen Grüßen (*Briefschluß*) f; **sin·cer·i·ty** [sɪn'serətɪ] Aufrichtigkeit f; Offenheit f

sin·ew *anat.* ['sɪnjuː] Sehne f; '~**y** sehnig; fig. kraftvoll

'**sin·ful** sündig, sündhaft

sing [sɪŋ] (*sang, sung*) singen; ~ *s.th. to s.o.* j-m et. vorsingen

singe [sɪndʒ] (sich et.) an- *od.* versengen

sing·er ['sɪŋə] Sänger(in); ~**ing** ['sɪŋɪŋ] Singen n, Gesang m

sin·gle ['sɪŋgl] 1. einzig; einzeln, Einzel...; einfach; ledig, unverheiratet; *bookkeeping by* ~ *entry* einfache Buchführung; *in* ~ *file* im Gänsemarsch; 2. *Brt.* einfache Fahrkarte, *aviat.* einfaches Ticket (*beide a.* ~ *ticket*); Single f (*Schallplatte*); Single m, Unverheiratete(r m) f; 3. ~ *out* herausgreifen; ~'**breast·ed** einreihig (*Jacke* etc.); ~'**en·gined** *aviat.* einmotorig; ~ **fam·i·ly 'home** Einfamilienhaus n; ~ '**fa·ther** alleinerziehender Vater; ~'**hand·ed** eigenhändig, allein; ~'**lane** *mot.* einspurig; ~'**mind·ed** zielstrebig, -bewußt; ~'**moth·er** alleinerziehende Mutter; ~'**pa·rent** Alleinerziehende(r m) f; ~'**room** Einzelzimmer n; '~**s** *sg. bsd. Tennis:* Einzel n; *a* ~ *match* ein Einzel; *men's* ~ Herreneinzel n; *women's* ~ Dameneinzel n

sin·glet *Brt.* ['sɪŋglɪt] ärmelloses Unterhemd *od.* Trikot

'**sin·gle-track** eingleisig, -spurig

sin·gu·lar ['sɪŋgjʊlə] 1. einzigartig, einmalig; 2. *gr.* Singular m, Einzahl f

sin·is·ter ['sɪnɪstə] finster, unheimlich

sink [sɪŋk] 1. (*sank, sunk*) *v/i.* sinken; sinken, untergehen; sich senken; ~ *in* eindringen (*Flüssigkeit; Nachricht*); *v/t.* versenken; *Brunnen* etc. bohren; *Zähne* etc. vergraben (*into* in *acc.*); 2. Spülbecken n, Spüle f; *bsd. Am.* Waschbecken n

sin·ner ['sɪnə] Sünder(in)

Sioux [suː] (*pl. Sioux* [suːz]) Sioux m, f

sip [sɪp] 1. Schlückchen n; 2. (*-pp-*) *v/t.* nippen an (*dat.*) *od.* von; schlückchenweise trinken; *v/i.* nippen (*at* an *dat. od.* von)

sir [sɜː] mein Herr (*Anrede, oft unübersetzt*); *Dear 2s* Sehr geehrte Herren (*Anrede in Briefen*); 2 *Brt.* Sir m (*Adelstitel*)

sire ['saɪə] Vater(tier n) m (*bsd. Pferd*)

si·ren ['saɪərən] Sirene f

sir·loin *gastr.* ['sɜːlɔɪn], ~ '**steak** Lendensteak n

sis·sy F ['sɪsɪ] Weichling m

sis·ter ['sɪstə] Schwester f; *Brt. med.* Oberschwester f; *rel.* (Ordens)Schwester f; '~**hood** Schwesternschaft f; ~**in-law** ['sɪstərɪnlɔː] (*pl. sisters-in-law*) Schwägerin f; '~**ly** schwesterlich

sit [sɪt] (*-tt-; sat*) *v/i.* sitzen; sich setzen; tagen; *v/t. j-n* setzen; *bsd. Brt.* Prüfung ablegen, machen; ~ *down* sich setzen; ~ *for Brt.* Prüfung ablegen, machen; ~ *in* ein Sit-in veranstalten; an e-m Sit-in teilnehmen; ~ *in for j-n* vertreten; ~ *in on* als Zuhörer teilnehmen an (*dat.*); ~ *on* sitzen auf (*dat.*) (*a. fig.*); ~ *on a committee* e-m Ausschuß angehören; ~ *out* Tanz auslassen; das Ende (*gen.*) abwarten; *Krise* etc. aussitzen; ~ *up* sich *od. j-n* aufrichten *od.* -setzen; aufrecht sitzen; aufbleiben

'**sit·com** ['sɪtkɒm] → *situation comedy*

'**sit-down** *a.* ~ *strike* Sitzstreik m; *a.* ~ *demonstration od.* F *demo* Sitzblockade f

site [saɪt] Platz m, Ort m, Stelle f; (*Ausgrabungs*)Stätte f; Baustelle f

'**sit-in** Sit-in n, Sitzstreik m

sit·ting ['sɪtɪŋ] Sitzung f; '~ **room** *bsd. Brt.* Wohnzimmer n

sit·u·at·ed ['sɪtjʊeɪtɪd]: *be* ~ liegen, gelegen sein

sit·u·a·tion *fig.* [sɪtjʊ'eɪʃn] Lage *f*, Situation *f*; ~ **com·e·dy** *Rundfunk, TV:* Situationskomödie *f (humorvolle Serie)*

six [sɪks] **1.** sechs; **2.** Sechs *f*; ~'**teen** [sɪks'tiːn] **1.** sechzehn; **2.** Sechzehn *f*; ~'**teenth** [sɪks'tiːnθ] sechzehnte(r, -s) *;* ~**th** [sɪksθ] **1.** sechste(r, -s); **2.** Sechstel *n*; ~**th·ly** sechstens; ~**ti·eth** ['sɪkstɪɪθ] sechzigste(r, -s); ~**ty** ['sɪkstɪ] **1.** sechzig; **2.** Sechzig *f*

size [saɪz] **1.** Größe *f, fig. a.* Ausmaß *n,* Umfang *m;* **2.** ~ *up* F abschätzen

siz(e)·a·ble ['saɪzəbl] beträchtlich

siz·zle ['sɪzl] brutzeln

skate [skeɪt] **1.** Schlittschuh *m;* Rollschuh *m;* **2.** Schlittschuh laufen, eislaufen; Rollschuh laufen; ~**board** Skateboard *n;* ~**skat·er** Eis-, Schlittschuhläufer(in); Rollschuhläufer(in)

skat·ing ['skeɪtɪŋ] Eis-, Schlittschuhlaufen *n;* Rollschuhlaufen *n; free* ~ Kür(lauf *m) f;* ~ **rink** (Kunst)Eisbahn *f;* Rollschuhbahn *f*

skel·e·ton ['skelɪtn] Skelett *n,* Gerippe *n;* ~ **key** Hauptschlüssel *m*

skep·tic ['skeptɪk] *etc. bsd. Am.* → **sceptic** *etc.*

sketch [sketʃ] **1.** Skizze *f; thea. etc.* Sketch *m;* **2.** skizzieren

ski [skiː] **1.** Ski *m;* Ski...; **2.** Ski fahren *od.* laufen

skid [skɪd] **1.** (*-dd-*) *mot.* rutschen, schleudern; **2.** *mot.* Rutschen *n,* Schleudern *n; aviat.* (Gleit)Kufe *f;* ~ **mark(s** *pl.*) *mot.* Bremsspur *f*

ski·er ['skiːə] Skifahrer(in), -läufer(in); ~**ing** Skifahren *n,* -laufen *n,* -sport *m;* ~ **jump** (Sprung)Schanze *f;* ~**jump·er** Skispringer *m;* ~ **jump·ing** Skispringen *n*

skil·ful ['skɪlfl] geschickt

'**ski lift** Skilift *m*

skill [skɪl] Geschicklichkeit *f,* Fertigkeit *f;* ~**ed** geschickt (*at, in* in *dat.*); ~**ed** '**work·er** Facharbeiter(in)

'**skill·ful** *Am.* → **skilful**

skim [skɪm] (*-mm-*) Fett *etc.* abschöpfen (*a.* ~ *off*); Milch entrahmen; (hin)gleiten über (*acc.*); *a.* ~ *over,* ~ *through* Bericht *etc.* überfliegen; ~**(med)** '**milk** Magermilch *f*

skimp [skɪmp] *a.* ~ *on* sparen an (*dat.*);

'~**y** (*-ier, -iest*) dürftig; knapp

skin [skɪn] **1.** Haut *f;* Fell *n; (Bananen-, Zwiebel- etc.*)Schale *f;* **2.** (*-nn-*) Tier abhäuten; *Zwiebel etc.* schälen; sich *das Knie etc.* aufschürfen; ~**deep** (nur) oberflächlich; ~**dive** tauchen (*ohne Atemgerät u. Schutzanzug*); '~ **div·ing** Sporttauchen *n;* '~**flint** Geizhals *m;* '~**ny** (*-ier, -iest*) dürr, mager; '~**ny-dip** F nackt baden

skip [skɪp] **1.** (*-pp-*) *v/i.* hüpfen, springen; seilhüpfen, -springen; *v/t. etc.* überspringen, auslassen; **2.** Hüpfer *m*

skip·per ['skɪpə] *naut., Sport:* Kapitän *m*

skir·mish ['skɜːmɪʃ] Geplänkel *n*

skirt [skɜːt] **1.** Rock *m;* **2.** *a.* ~ *(a)round* umgehen; *fig.* Problem *etc.* umgehen; '~**ing board** Brt. Scheuerleiste *f*

'**ski run** Skipiste *f;* '~ **tow** Schlepplift *m*

skit·tle ['skɪtl] Kegel *m*

skulk [skʌlk] sich herumdrücken, herumschleichen

skull *anat.* [skʌl] Schädel *m*

skul(l)·dug·ge·ry F [skʌl'dʌgərɪ] Gaunerei *f,* fauler Zauber

skunk *zo.* [skʌŋk] Skunk *m,* Stinktier *n*

sky [skaɪ] *a.* **skies** *pl.* Himmel *m;* '~**jack** *Flugzeug* entführen; '~**jack·er** Flugzeugentführer(in); '~**lark** *zo.* Feldlerche *f;* '~**light** Dachfenster *n;* '~**line** Skyline *f,* Silhouette *f (e-r Stadt);* '~**rock·et** F hochschnellen, in die Höhe schießen (*Preise*); '~**scrap·er** Wolkenkratzer *m*

slab [slæb] (*Stein- etc.*)Platte *f;* dickes Stück (*Kuchen etc.*)

slack [slæk] **1.** locker (*Seil etc.*), lax (*Disziplin etc.*); *econ.* flau; lasch, nachlässig; **2.** bummeln; ~ *off,* ~ *up fig.* nachlassen, (*Person a.*) abbauen; '~**en** *v/t.* lockern; verringern; ~ *speed* langsamer werden; *v/i.* locker werden; *a.* ~ *off* nachlassen; ~**s** *pl. bsd. Am.* F Hose *f*

slag [slæg] Schlacke *f*

slain [sleɪn] *p.p. von* **slay**

sla·lom ['slɑːləm] *Sport:* Slalom *m*

slam [slæm] **1.** (*-mm-*) *a.* ~ *shut* zuknallen, zuschlagen; *a.* ~ *down* F et. knallen (*on* auf *acc.*); ~ *on the brakes mot.* auf die Bremse steigen; **2.** Zuschlagen *n;* Knall *m*

slan·der ['slɑːndə] **1.** Verleumdung *f;* **2.** verleumden; ~**ous** ['slɑːndərəs] verleumderisch

slang [slæŋ] **1.** Slang *m*; Jargon *m*; **2.** *bsd. Brt.* F *j-n* wüst beschimpfen

slant [sla:nt] **1.** schräg legen *od.* liegen; sich neigen; **2.** schräge Fläche; Abhang *m*; *fig.* Einstellung *f*; **at** *od.* **on a ~** schräg; **'~·ing** schräg

slap [slæp] **1.** Klaps *m*, Schlag *m* (**-pp-**) e-n Klaps geben (*dat.*); schlagen; klatschen (**down on an** *acc.*; **against** gegen); **'~·stick** *thea.* Slapstick *m*, Klamauk *m*; **'~·stick com·e·dy** *thea.* Slapstickkomödie *f*

slash [slæʃ] **1.** auf-, zerschlitzen; *Preise* drastisch herabsetzen; *Ausgaben etc.* drastisch kürzen; **~ at** schlagen nach; **2.** Hieb *m*; Schlitz *m* (*im Kleid etc.*)

slate [sleɪt] **1.** Schiefer *m*; Schiefertafel *f*; *Am. pol.* Kandidatenliste *f*; **2.** mit Schiefer decken; *Am.* j-n vorschlagen (**for, to be** als); *Am. et.* planen (**for** für)

slaugh·ter ['slɔːtə] **1.** Schlachten *n*; Blutbad *n*, Gemetzel *n*; **2.** schlachten; niedermetzeln; **'~·house** Schlachthaus *n*, -hof *m*

Slav [slɑːv] **1.** Slaw|e *m*, -in *f*; **2.** slawisch

slave [sleɪv] **1.** Sklav|e *m*, -in *f* (*a. fig.*); **2.** *a.* **~ away** sich abplagen, schuften

slav·er ['slævə] geifern, sabbern

sla·ve·ry ['sleɪvərɪ] Sklaverei *f*

slav·ish ['sleɪvɪʃ] sklavisch

slay *Am.* [sleɪ] (**slew, slain**) ermorden, umbringen

sleaze [sliːz] unsaubere Machenschaften (*bsd. in der Politik*); Kumpanei *f*; **slea·zy** ['sliːzɪ] (**-ier, -iest**) schäbig, heruntergekommen; anrüchig

sled *Am.* [sled] → **sledge**

sledge [sledʒ] **1.** (*a.* Rodel)Schlitten *m*; **2.** Schlitten fahren, rodeln

'sledge·ham·mer Vorschlaghammer *m*

sleek [sliːk] **1.** glatt, glänzend, geschmeidig (*Haar, Fell*); schnittig (*Auto*); **2.** glätten

sleep [sliːp] **1.** Schlaf *m*; **I couldn't get to ~** ich konnte nicht einschlafen; **go to ~** einschlafen (F *a.* Bein *etc.*); **put to ~** *Tier* einschläfern; **2.** (**slept**) *v/i.* schlafen; **~ late** lang *od.* länger schlafen; **~ on** *Problem etc.* überschlafen; **~ with s.o.** mit j-m schlafen; *v/t.* Schlafgelegenheit bieten für; **'~·er** Schlafende(r *m*) *f*; *Brt. rail.* Schwelle *f*; *rail.* Schlafwagen *m*

'sleep·ing| bag Schlafsack *m*; **⚥**

'Beau·ty Dornröschen *n*; **~ car** *rail.* Schlafwagen *m*; **~ 'part·ner** *Brt. econ.* stiller Teilhaber

'sleep|·less schlaflos; **'~·walk·er** Schlafwandler(in); **'~·y** (**-ier, -iest**) schläfrig, müde; verschlafen

sleet [sliːt] **1.** Schneeregen *m*; Graupelschauer *m*; **2.** **it's ~ing** es gibt Schneeregen; es graupelt

sleeve [sliːv] Ärmel *m*; *tech.* Manschette *f*, Muffe *f*; *bsd. Brt.* (*Platten*)Hülle *f*

sleigh [sleɪ] (*bsd.* Pferde)Schlitten *m*

sleight of hand [slaɪt əv 'hænd] Fingerfertigkeit *f*; *fig.* (Taschenspieler)Trick *m*

slen·der ['slendə] schlank; *fig.* mager, dürftig, schwach

slept [slept] *pret. u. p.p. von* **sleep** 2

sleuth F [sluːθ] Spürhund *m*, Detektiv *m*

slew [sluː] *pret. von* **slay**

slice [slaɪs] **1.** Scheibe *f* (*Brot etc.*), Stück *n* (*Kuchen etc.*); *fig.* Anteil *m* (**of** an *dat.*); **2.** *a.* **~ up** in Scheiben *od.* Stücke schneiden; **~ off** *Stück* abschneiden (**from** von)

slick [slɪk] **1.** gekonnt (*Vorstellung etc.*); geschickt, raffiniert; glatt (*Straße etc.*); **2.** F (*Öl*)Teppich *m*; **3.** **~ down** *Haar* glätten, F anklatschen; **'~·er** *Am.* Regenmantel *m*; F Gauner *m*

slid [slɪd] *pret. u. p.p. von* **slide** 1

slide [slaɪd] **1.** (**slid**) gleiten (lassen); rutschen; schlüpfen; schieben; *let things ~ fig.* die Dinge schleifen lassen; **2.** Gleiten *n*, Rutschen *n*; Rutsche *f*, Rutschbahn *f*; *tech.* Schieber *m*; *phot.* Dia(positiv) *n*; Objektträger *m*; *Brt.* (*Haar*)Spange *f*; (*Erd- etc.*)Rutsch *m*; **~ rule** Rechenschieber *m*; **~ tack·le** *Fußball:* Grätsche *f*

'slid·ing door [slaɪdɪŋ 'dɔː] Schiebetür *f*

slight [slaɪt] **1.** leicht, gering(fügig), unbedeutend; **2.** beleidigen, kränken; **3.** Beleidigung *f*, Kränkung *f*

slim [slɪm] (**-mm-**) **1.** schlank; *fig.* gering; **2.** *a.* **be ~ming, be on a ~ming diet** e-e Schlankheitskur machen, abnehmen

slime [slaɪm] Schleim *m*

slim·y ['slaɪmɪ] (**-ier, -iest**) schleimig (*a. fig.*)

sling [slɪŋ] **1.** (**slung**) aufhängen; F schleudern; △ *nicht* **schlingen**; **2.**

Schlinge f; Tragriemen m (für Gewehr); Tragetuch n (für Baby); Schleuder f

slink [slɪŋk] (**slunk**) (sich) schleichen

slip¹ [slɪp] **1.** (**-pp-**) v/i. rutschen, schlittern; ausgleiten, -rutschen; schlüpfen; v/t. sich losreißen von; ~ **s.th. into s.o.'s hand** j-m et. in die Hand schieben; ~ **s.o. s.th.** j-m et. zuschieben; ~ **s.o.'s attention** j-m od. j-s Aufmerksamkeit entgehen; ~ **s.o.'s mind** j-m entfallen; **she has ~ped a disc** sie hat e-n Bandscheibenvorfall; ~ **by**, ~ **past** verstreichen (Zeit); ~ **off** schlüpfen aus (Kleidungsstück); ~ **on** Kleidungsstück überstreifen, schlüpfen in (acc.); **2.** Ausgleiten n, (Aus)Rutschen n; Versehen n; Unterrock m; (Kissen)Bezug m; △ **nicht Slip**; ~ **of the tongue** Versprecher m; **give s.o. the** ~ F j-m entwischen

slip² [slɪp] a. ~ **of paper** Zettel m

'**slip·case** Schuber m; '~**on 1.** adj. ~ **shoe** → **2.** Slipper m; ~**ped** '**disc** med. Bandscheibenvorfall m; '~**per** Hausschuh m, Pantoffel m; △ **nicht Slipper**; ~**per·y** ['slɪpərɪ] (**-ier, -iest**) glatt, rutschig, glitschig; '~ **road** Brt. (Autobahn)Auffahrt f; (Autobahn)Ausfahrt f; '~**shod** schlampig

slit [slɪt] **1.** Schlitz m; **2.** (**-tt-**; **slit**) schlitzen; ~ **open** aufschlitzen

slith·er ['slɪðə] gleiten, rutschen

sliv·er ['slɪvə] (Glas- etc.)Splitter m

slob·ber ['slɒbə] sabbern

slo·gan ['sləʊgən] Slogan m

sloop naut. [sluːp] Schaluppe f

slop [slɒp] **1.** (**-pp-**) v/t. verschütten; v/i. überschwappen; schwappen (over über acc.); **2.** a. ~**s** pl. schlabb(e)riges Zeug; (Tee-, Kaffee)Rest(e pl.) m; bsd. Brt. Schmutzwasser n

slope [sləʊp] **1.** (Ab)Hang m; Neigung f, Gefälle n; **2.** sich neigen, abfallen

slop·py ['slɒpɪ] (**-ier, -iest**) schlampig; F gammelig (Kleidungsstück); F rührselig

slot [slɒt] Schlitz m, (Münz)Einwurf m; Computer: Steckplatz m

sloth zo. [sləʊθ] Faultier n

'**slot ma·chine** (Waren-, Spiel)Automat m

slouch [slaʊtʃ] **1.** krumme Haltung; latschiger Gang; **2.** krumm dasitzen od. dastehen; latschen

slough¹ [slʌf]: ~ **off** Haut abstreifen, sich häuten (Schlange)

slough² [slaʊ] Sumpf(loch n) m

Slo·vak ['sləʊvæk] **1.** slowakisch; **2.** Slowak|e m, -in f; ling. Slowakisch n;

Slo·va·ki·a [sləʊ'vækɪə] Slowakei f

slov·en·ly ['slʌvnlɪ] schlampig

slow [sləʊ] **1.** adj. langsam; begriffsstutzig; econ. schleppend; **be** (**ten minutes**) ~ (zehn Minuten) nachgehen (Uhr); **2.** adv. langsam; **3.** v/t. oft ~ **down**, ~ **up** die Geschwindigkeit verringern; v/i. oft ~ **down**, ~ **up** langsamer fahren od. gehen od. werden; '~**coach** Brt. Langweiler(in); '~**down** Am. econ. Bummelstreik m; '~ **lane** mot. Kriechspur f; '~**mo·tion** phot. Zeitlupe f; '~**mov·ing** kriechend (Verkehr); '~**poke** Am. → **slowcoach**; '~**worm** zo. Blindschleiche f

sludge [slʌdʒ] Schlamm m (schleimiger)

slug¹ zo. [slʌg] Nacktschnecke f

slug² bsd. Am. F [slʌg] Kugel f (Geschoß); Schluck m (Whisky etc.)

slug³ bsd. Am. F [slʌg] (**-gg-**) j-m e-n Faustschlag versetzen

slug·gish ['slʌgɪʃ] träge; econ. schleppend

sluice tech. [sluːs] Schleuse f

slum [slʌm] a. ~**s** pl. Slums pl., Elendsviertel n od. pl.

slum·ber lit. ['slʌmbə] **1.** schlummern; **2.** a. ~**s** pl. Schlummer m

slump [slʌmp] **1.** econ. stürzen (Preise), stark zurückgehen (Umsätze etc.); **sit** ~**ed over** zusammengesunken sitzen über (dat.); ~ **into a chair** sich in e-n Sessel plumpsen lassen; **2.** econ. starker Konjunkturrückgang; ~ **in prices** Preissturz m

slung [slʌŋ] pret. u. p.p. von **sling** 1

slunk [slʌŋk] pret. u. p.p. von **slink**

slur¹ [slɜː] **1.** (**-rr-**) mus. Töne binden; **one's speech** undeutlich sprechen; lallen; **2.** undeutliche Aussprache

slur² [slɜː] **1.** (**-rr-**) verleumden; **2.** ~ **on s.o.'s reputation** Rufschädigung f

slurp F [slɜːp] schlürfen

slush [slʌʃ] Schneematsch m

slut [slʌt] Schlampe f; Nutte f

sly [slaɪ] (**~er, ~est**) gerissen, schlau, listig; **on the** ~ heimlich

smack¹ [smæk] **1.** j-m e-n Klaps geben; ~ **one's lips** sich (geräuschvoll) die Lippen lecken; ~ **down** et. hinklatschen; **2.** klatschendes Geräusch, Knall m; F

Schmatz *m* (*Kuß*); F Klaps *m*, kräftiger Schlag

smack² [smæk]: ~ *of fig.* schmecken *od.* riechen nach

small [smɔ:l] **1.** *adj. u. adv.* klein; △ *nicht schmal*; ~ *wonder* (*that*) kein Wunder, daß; *feel* ~ sich klein (u. häßlich) vorkommen; **2.** ~ *of the back anat.* Kreuz *n*; '~ **ad** Kleinanzeige *f*; '~ **arms** *pl.* Handfeuerwaffen *pl.*; '~ **change** Kleingeld *n*; '~ **hours** *pl.*: *in the* ~ in den frühen Morgenstunden; ~'**mind·ed** engstirnig; kleinlich; ~**pox** *med.* ['smɔ:lpɒks] Pocken *pl.*; '~ **print** Kleingedruckte (*e-s Vertrags etc.*); '~ **talk** Small talk *m, n,* oberflächliche Konversation; *make* ~ plaudern; ~'**time** F klein, unbedeutend; ~ '**town** Kleinstadt *f*

smart [smɑ:t] **1.** *adj. u. adv.* schick, fesch, schlau, clever; **2.** weh tun; brennen; **3.** (brennender) Schmerz; ~ **aleck** F ['smɑ:tælɪk] Besserwisser(in), Klugscheißer(in); '~**ness** Schick *m*; Schlauheit *f*, Cleverneß *f*

smash [smæʃ] *v/t.* zerschlagen (*a.* ~ *up*); schmettern (*a. Tennis etc.*); *Aufstand etc.* niederschlagen, *Drogenring etc.* zerschlagen; ~ *up one's car* s-n Wagen zu Schrott fahren; *v/i.* zerspringen; ~ *into* prallen an (*acc.*) *od.* gegen, krachen gegen; ~ Schlag *m*; *Tennis etc.*: Schmetterball *m*; → ~ *hit*, ~*up*; ~ **'hit** Hit *m* (*Buch, Film etc.*); '~**ing** *bsd. Brt.* F toll, sagenhaft; '~**up** *mot.*, *rail.* schwerer Unfall

smat·ter·ing ['smætərɪŋ]: *a* ~ *of English* ein paar Brocken Englisch

smear [smɪə] **1.** Fleck *m*; *med.* Abstrich *m*; Verleumdung *f*; **2.** (ein-, ver)schmieren; (sich) verwischen (*Schrift*); verleumden

smell [smel] **1.** (*smelt od. smelled*) *v/i.* riechen (*at* an *dat.*); duften; riechen, *bsd.* stinken; *v/t.* riechen (*at* an *dat.*); **2.** Geruch *m*; Gestank *m*; Duft *m*; '~**y** (*-ier, -iest*) übelriechend, stinkend

smelt¹ [smelt] *pret. u. p.p. von* **smell** 1

smelt² [smelt] *Erz* schmelzen

smile [smaɪl] **1.** Lächeln *n*; **2.** lächeln; ~ *at j-n* anlächeln; *fig.* *j-m* zulächeln; *j-n, et.* belächeln, lächeln über (*acc.*)

smirk [smɜ:k] (selbstgefällig *od.* schadenfroh) grinsen

smith [smɪθ] Schmied *m*

smith·e·reens F [smɪðə'ri:nz] *pl.*: *smash* (*in*)*to* ~ in tausend Stücke schlagen *od.* zerspringen

smith·y ['smɪðɪ] Schmiede *f*

smit·ten ['smɪtn] *bsd. humor.* verliebt, -knallt (*with* in *acc.*); *be* ~ *by od. with fig.* gepackt werden von

smock [smɒk] Kittel *m*

smog [smɒg] Smog *m*

smoke [sməʊk] **1.** Rauch *m*; *have a* ~ eine rauchen; **2.** rauchen; räuchern; '**smok·er** Raucher(in); *rail.* Raucher (-wagen) *m*; '~**stack** Schornstein *m*

smok·ing ['sməʊkɪŋ] Rauchen *n*; △ *nicht Smoking*; *no* ~ Rauchen verboten; ~ **com'part·ment** *rail.* Raucher(abteil *n*) *m*

smok·y ['sməʊkɪ] (*-ier, -iest*) rauchig, verräuchert

smooth [smu:ð] **1.** glatt (*a. fig.*); ruhig (*tech.*; *Flug, Reise*); mild (*Wein*); *fig.* (aal)glatt; **2.** *a.* ~ *out* glätten, glattstreichen; ~ *away* Falten *etc.* glätten; *Schwierigkeiten etc.* aus dem Weg räumen; ~ *down* glattstreichen (*Haar*)

smoth·er ['smʌðə] ersticken

smo(u)l·der ['sməʊldə] glimmen, schwelen

smudge [smʌdʒ] **1.** Fleck *m*; **2.** (be-, ver)schmieren; (sich) verwischen (*Schrift*)

smug [smʌg] (*-gg-*) selbstgefällig

smug·gle ['smʌgl] schmuggeln (*into* nach; *in* in *acc.*); '~**r** Schmuggler(in)

smut [smʌt] Rußflocke *f*; Schmutz *m* (*a. fig.*); '~**ty** (*-ier, -iest*) *fig.* schmutzig

snack [snæk] Snack *m*, Imbiß *m*; *have a* ~ e-e Kleinigkeit essen; '~ **bar** Snackbar *f*, Imbißstube *f*

snag [snæg] **1.** *fig.* Haken *m*; **2.** (*-gg-*) mit *et.* hängenbleiben (*on* an *dat.*)

snail *zo.* [sneɪl] Schnecke *f*

snake *zo.* [sneɪk] Schlange *f*

snap [snæp] **1.** (*-pp-*) (zer)brechen, (-)reißen; *a.* ~ *shut* zuschnappen; ~ *at* schnappen nach; *j-n* anschnauzen; ~ *out of it!* F Kopf hoch!, komm, komm!; ~ *to it!* mach fix!; *v/t.* zerbrechen; *phot.* F knipsen; ~ *one's fingers* mit den Fingern schnalzen; ~ *one's fingers at fig.* keinen Respekt haben vor (*dat.*), sich hinwegsetzen über (*acc.*); ~ *off* abbrechen; ~ *up et.* schnell entschlossen kaufen; ~ *it up!* Am. mach fix!; **2.** Krachen n, Knacken n, Knall m; *phot.* F Schnappschuß m; Am. Druckknopf m; *fig.* F Schwung m; *cold* ~ Kälteeinbruch m; '~ **fas·ten·er** Am. Druckknopf m; '~**pish** *fig.* bissig; '~**py** (-*ier, -iest*) modisch, schick; *make it ~!*, Brt. a. *look ~!* F mach fix!; '~**shot** *phot.* Schnappschuß m

snare [sneə] **1.** Schlinge f, Falle f (a. *fig.*); **2.** in der Schlinge fangen; F et. ergattern

snarl [snɑ:l] **1.** knurren; ~ *at s.o.* j-n anknurren; **2.** Knurren n

snatch [snætʃ] **1.** *v/t. et.* packen; *Gelegenheit* ergattern; *ein paar Stunden Schlaf etc.* ergattern; ~ *s.o.'s handbag* j-m die Handtasche entreißen; *v/i.* ~ *at* (schnell) greifen nach; *Gelegenheit* ergreifen; **2.** *make a* ~ *at* (schnell) greifen nach; ~ *of conversation* Gesprächsfetzen m

sneak [sni:k] **1.** *v/i.* (sich) schleichen; Brt. F petzen; *v/t.* F stibitzen; **2.** Brt. F Petze f; '~**er** Am. Turnschuh m

sneer [snɪə] **1.** höhnisch od. spöttisch grinsen (*at* über *acc.*); spotten (*at* über *acc.*); **2.** höhnisches od. spöttisches Grinsen; höhnische od. spöttische Bemerkung

sneeze [sni:z] **1.** niesen; **2.** Niesen n

snick·er bsd. Am. ['snɪkə] → snigger

sniff [snɪf] **1.** *v/i.* schniefen; schnüffeln (*at* an *dat.*); ~ *at fig.* die Nase rümpfen über (*acc.*); *v/t. Klebstoff etc.* schnüffeln, *Kokain etc.* schnupfen; **2.** Schniefen n

snif·fle ['snɪfl] **1.** schniefen; **2.** Schniefen n; *she's got the* ~*s* F ihr läuft dauernd die Nase

snig·ger bsd. Brt. ['snɪgə] kichern (*at* über *acc.*)

snip [snɪp] **1.** Schnitt m; **2.** (-*pp*-) durchschnippeln; ~ *off* abschnippeln

snipe¹ [snaɪp] *zo.* Schnepfe f

snipe² [snaɪp] aus dem Hinterhalt schießen (*at* auf *acc.*); '**snip·er** Heckenschütze m

sniv·el ['snɪvl] (*bsd. Brt. -ll-, Am. -l-*) greinen, jammern

snob [snɒb] Snob m; '~**bish** versnobt

snoop [snu:p]: ~ *about*, ~ *around* F herumschnüffeln; '~**er** F Schnüffler(in)

snooze F [snu:z] **1.** ein Nickerchen machen; **2.** Nickerchen n

snore [snɔ:] **1.** schnarchen; **2.** Schnarchen n

snor·kel ['snɔ:kl] **1.** Schnorchel m; **2.** schnorcheln

snort [snɔ:t] **1.** schnauben; **2.** Schnauben n

snout *zo.* [snaʊt] Schnauze f, Rüssel m

snow [snəʊ] **1.** Schnee m (a. sl. *Kokain*); **2.** schneien; *be* ~*ed in* od. *up* eingeschneit sein; '~**ball** Schneeball m; ~**ball 'fight** Schneeballschlacht f; '~**bound** eingeschneit; '~**drift** Schneewehe f; '~**drop** *bot.* Schneeglöckchen n; '~**fall** Schneefall m; '~**flake** Schneeflocke f; '~**man** (*pl. -men*) Schneemann m; '~**plough** Brt., '~**plow** Am. Schneepflug m; '~**storm** Schneesturm m; '~**white** schneeweiß; '**S White** Schneewittchen n; '~**y** (-*ier, -iest*) schneereich; verschneit

Snr *nur geschr. Abk. für* **Senior** sen., senior, der Ältere

snub [snʌb] **1.** (-*bb*-) j-n brüskieren, j-n vor den Kopf stoßen; *fig.* F j-n schneiden; **2.** Brüskierung f; '~ **nose** Stupsnase f; '~**nosed** stupsnasig

snuff¹ [snʌf] Schnupftabak m

snuff² [snʌf] *Kerze* ausdrücken, auslöschen; ~ *out Leben* auslöschen

snuf·fle ['snʌfl] schnüffeln, schniefen

snug [snʌg] (-*gg*-) gemütlich, behaglich; *Kleidungsstück:* gutsitzend; eng(anliegend)

snug·gle ['snʌgl]: ~ *up to s.o.* sich an j-n kuscheln; ~ *down in bed* sich ins Bett kuscheln

so [səʊ] so; deshalb; ~ *hope* 2, *think*; *is that* ~? wirklich?; *an hour or* ~ etwa e-e Stunde; *she is tired -* ~ *am I* sie ist müde - ich auch; ~ *far* bisher

soak [səʊk] *v/t.* einweichen (*in* in *dat.*); durchnässen; ~ *up* aufsaugen; *v/i.* sickern; *leave the dirty clothes to* ~ weichen Sie die Schmutzwäsche ein

soap [səʊp] **1.** Seife f; F → soap opera; **2.** (sich) *et.* einseifen; '~ **op·e·ra** *Rundfunk, TV:* Seifenoper f; '~**y** (-*ier, -iest*) Seifen...; seifig; *fig.* F schmeichlerisch

soar [sɔ:] (hoch) aufsteigen; hochragen; *Vogel, aviat.* segeln, gleiten; *fig.* in die Höhe schnellen (*Preise etc.*)

sob [sɒb] **1.** (**-bb-**) schluchzen; **2.** Schluchzen n

so·ber ['səʊbə] **1.** nüchtern (a. fig.); **2.** ernüchtern; ~ **up** nüchtern machen od. werden

so-'called sogenannt

soc·cer ['sɒkə] Fußball m (Spiel); '~ **hoo·li·gan** Fußballrowdy m

so·cia·ble ['səʊʃəbl] gesellig

so·cial ['səʊʃl] sozial, Sozial...; gesellschaftlich, Gesellschafts...; gesellig (Lebewesen); F gesellig (Person); ~ **'dem·o·crat** Sozialdemokrat(in); ~ **in'sur·ance** Sozialversicherung f

so·cial·is·m ['səʊʃəlɪzəm] Sozialismus m; '~**ist 1.** Sozialist(in); **2.** sozialistisch

so·cial·ize ['səʊʃəlaɪz] gesellschaftlich verkehren (**with** mit); sozialisieren

so·cial 'sci·ence Sozialwissenschaft f; ~ **se'cu·ri·ty** Brt. Sozialhilfe f; **be on** ~ Sozialhilfe beziehen; ~ **'serv·i·ces** pl. bsd. Brt. Sozialeinrichtungen pl.; '~ **work** Sozialarbeit f; '~ **work·er** Sozialarbeiter(in)

so·ci·e·ty [sə'saɪətɪ] Gesellschaft f; Verein m

so·ci·ol·o·gy [səʊsɪ'ɒlədʒɪ] Soziologie f

sock [sɒk] Socke f

sock·et ['sɒkɪt] electr. Steckdose f; electr. Fassung f (e-r Glühbirne); electr. (Anschluß)Buchse f; anat. (Augen-)Höhle f

sod Brt. V [sɒd] blöder Hund

so·da ['səʊdə] Soda(wasser) n; bsd. Am. (Orangen- etc.)Limonade f

sod·den ['sɒdn] aufgeweicht (Boden)

so·fa ['səʊfə] Sofa n

soft [sɒft] weich; sanft; leise; gedämpft (Licht etc.); F leicht, angenehm, ruhig (Job etc.); alkoholfrei (Getränk); weich (Drogen); verweichlicht; a. ~ **in the head** F einfältig, doof; '~ **drink** Soft Drink m, alkoholfreies Getränk

soft·en ['sɒfn] v/t. weich machen; Wasser enthärten; Ton, Licht, Stimme etc. dämpfen; ~ **up** F j-n weichmachen; v/i. weich(er) od. sanft(er) od. mild(er) werden

soft|-'head·ed doof; ~**'heart·ed** weichherzig; ~ **'land·ing** Raumfahrt: weiche Landung; '~**ware** Computer: Software f; ~**ware 'pack·age** Computer: Softwarepaket n; '~**y** F Softie m, Softy m, Weichling m

sog·gy ['sɒgɪ] (**-ier, -iest**) aufgeweicht, matschig

soil¹ [sɔɪl] Boden m, Erde f

soil² [sɔɪl] beschmutzen, schmutzig machen

sol·ace ['sɒləs] Trost m

so·lar ['səʊlə] Sonnen...; ~ **'en·er·gy** Solar-, Sonnenenergie f; ~ **'pan·el** Sonnenkollektor m; '~ **sys·tem** Sonnensystem n

sold [səʊld] pret. u. p.p. von **sell**

sol·der ['sɒldə] (ver)löten

sol·dier ['səʊldʒə] Soldat m

sole¹ [səʊl] **1.** (Fuß-, Schuh)Sohle f; **2.** besohlen

sole² zo. [səʊl] (pl. **sole, soles**) Seezunge f

sole³ [səʊl] einzig; alleinig, Allein...; '~**ly** (einzig u.) allein, ausschließlich

sol·emn ['sɒləm] feierlich; ernst

so·li·cit [sə'lɪsɪt] bitten um

so·lic·i·tor Brt. jur. [sə'lɪsɪtə] Solicitor m (hauptsächlich bei niederen Gerichten zugelassener Anwalt)

so·lic·i·tous [sə'lɪsɪtəs] besorgt (**about, for** um)

sol·id ['sɒlɪd] **1.** fest; stabil; massiv; math. körperlich; gewichtig, triftig (Grund etc.), stichhaltig (Argument etc.); solid(e), gründlich (Arbeit etc.); einmütig, geschlossen; **a ~ hour** F e-e geschlagene Stunde; **2.** math. Körper m; ~ pl. feste Nahrung

sol·i·dar·i·ty [sɒlɪ'dærətɪ] Solidarität f

so·lid·i·fy [sə'lɪdɪfaɪ] fest werden (lassen); fig. (sich) festigen

so·lil·o·quy [sə'lɪləkwɪ] Selbstgespräch n; bsd. thea. Monolog m

sol·i·taire [sɒlɪ'teə] Solitär m (Edelstein etc. u. Brettspiel); Am. Kartenspiel: Patience f

sol·i·ta·ry ['sɒlɪtərɪ] einsam, (Leben a.) zurückgezogen, (Ort etc. a.) abgelegen; einzig; ~ **con'fine·ment** Einzelhaft f

so·lo ['səʊləʊ] (pl. **-los**) mus. Solo n; aviat. Alleinflug m; '~**ist** mus. Solist(in)

sol·u·ble ['sɒljʊbl] löslich; fig. lösbar; **so·lu·tion** [sə'luːʃn] (Auf)Lösung f

solve [sɒlv] Fall etc. lösen; **sol·vent** ['sɒlvənt] **1.** econ. zahlungsfähig; **2.** chem. Lösungsmittel n

som·bre *Brt.*, **som·ber** *Am.* ['sɒmbə] düster, trüb(e); *fig.* trübsinnig

some [sʌm] (irgend)ein; *vor pl.*: einige, ein paar; manche; etwas, ein wenig, ein bißchen; ungefähr; ~ **20 miles** etwa 20 Meilen; ~ **more cake** noch ein Stück Kuchen; **to** ~ **extent** bis zu e-m gewissen Grade; **'~body** ['sʌmbədi] jemand; **'~day** eines Tages; **'~how** irgendwie; **'~one** jemand; **'~place** *bsd. Am.* → somewhere

som·er·sault ['sʌməsɔːlt] **1.** Salto *m*; Purzelbaum *m*; **turn a** ~ → **2.** e-n Salto machen; e-n Purzelbaum schlagen

'some|·thing etwas; ~ **like** ungefähr; **'~·time** irgendwann; **'~·times** manchmal; **'~·what** ein bißchen, ein wenig; **'~·where** irgendwo(hin)

son [sʌn] Sohn *m*; ~ **of a bitch** *bsd. Am.* V Scheißkerl *m*

sonde *bsd. meteor.* [sɒnd] Sonde *f*

song [sɒŋ] Lied *n*; Gesang *m*; **for a** ~ F für ein Butterbrot; **'~·bird** Singvogel *m*

son·ic ['sɒnɪk] Schall...; ~ **'bang** *Brt.*, ~ **'boom** Überschallknall *m*

son-in-law ['sʌnɪnlɔː] (*pl.* **sons-in-law**) Schwiegersohn *m*

son·net ['sɒnɪt] Sonett *n*

so·nor·ous [sə'nɔːrəs] sonor, volltönend

soon [suːn] bald; **as** ~ **as** sobald; **as** ~ **as possible** so bald wie möglich; **'~·er** eher, früher; ~ **or later** früher od. später; **the** ~ **the better** je eher, desto besser; **no** ~ ... **than** kaum ... als; **no** ~ **said than done** gesagt, getan

soot [sʊt] Ruß *m*

soothe [suːð] beruhigen, beschwichtigen (*a.* ~ **down**); *Schmerzen* lindern, mildern; **sooth·ing** ['suːðɪŋ] beruhigend; lindernd

soot·y ['sʊtɪ] (**-ier, -iest**) rußig

sop¹ [sɒp] Beschwichtigungsmittel *n* (**to** für)

sop² [sɒp] (**-pp-**): ~ **up** aufsaugen

so·phis·ti·cat·ed [sə'fɪstɪkeɪtɪd] anspruchsvoll, kultiviert; intellektuell; *tech.* hochentwickelt

soph·o·more *Am.* ['sɒfəmɔː] Student(in) im zweiten Jahr

sop·o·rif·ic [sɒpə'rɪfɪk] (**~ally**) einschläfernd

sop·ping ['sɒpɪŋ]: ~ (**wet**) F klatschnaß

sor·cer|·er ['sɔːsərə] Zauberer *m*, He-

xenmeister *m*, Hexer *m*; **~·ess** ['sɔːsərɪs] Zauberin *f*, Hexe *f*; **~·y** ['sɔːsərɪ] Zauberei *f*, Hexerei *f*

sor·did ['sɔːdɪd] schmutzig; schäbig

sore [sɔː] **1.** (~**r**, ~**st**) weh, wund; entzündet; *fig.* wund (*Punkt*); *bsd. Am.* F sauer; **I'm** ~ **all over** mir tut alles weh; ~ **throat** Halsentzündung *f*; **have a** ~ **throat** e-e Halsschmerzen haben; **2.** wunde Stelle, Wunde *f*

sor·rel¹ *bot.* ['sɒrəl] Sauerampfer *m*

sor·rel² ['sɒrəl] **1.** *zo.* Fuchs *m* (*Pferd*); **2.** rotbraun

sor·row ['sɒrəʊ] Kummer *m*, Leid *n*, Schmerz *m*, Trauer *f*; **'~·ful** traurig, betrübt

sor·ry ['sɒrɪ] **1.** *adj.* (**-ier, -iest**) traurig, jämmerlich; **be** *od.* **feel** ~ **for s.o.** j-n bedauern *od.* bemitleiden; **I'm** ~ **for her** sie tut mir leid; **I am** ~ **to say** ich muß leider sagen; **I'm** ~ → **2.** *int.* (es) tut mir leid!; Entschuldigung!, Verzeihung!; ~**?** *bsd. Brt.* wie bitte?

sort [sɔːt] **1.** Sorte *f*, Art *f*; ~ **of** F irgendwie; **of a** ~, **of** ~**s** F so et. Ähnliches wie; **all** ~**s of things** alles mögliche; **nothing of the** ~ nichts dergleichen; **what** ~ **of** (a) **man is he?** wie ist er?; **be out of** ~**s** F nicht auf der Höhe *od.* auf dem Damm sein; **be completely out of** ~**s** *Sport:* F völlig außer Form sein; **2.** sortieren; ~ **out** aussortieren; *Problem etc.* lösen, *Frage etc.* klären; **'~·er** Sortierer *m*

SOS [es əʊ 'es] SOS *n*; **send an** ~ ein SOS funken; ~ **call** *od.* **message** SOS-Ruf *m*

sought [sɔːt] *pret. u. p.p. von* **seek**

soul [səʊl] Seele *f* (*a. fig.*); *mus.* Soul *m*

sound¹ [saʊnd] **1.** Geräusch *n*; Laut *m*; *phys.* Schall *m*; *Radio, TV etc.*: Ton *m*; *mus.* Klang *m*; *mus.* Sound *m*; **2.** *v/i.* (er)klingen, (-)tönen; **sich** *gut etc.* anhören; *v/t. ling.* (aus)sprechen; *naut.* (aus)loten; *med.* abhorchen; ~ **one's horn** *mot.* hupen

sound² [saʊnd] gesund; intakt, in Ordnung; solid(e), stabil, sicher; klug, vernünftig (*Person, Rat etc.*); gründlich (*Ausbildung etc.*); gehörig (*Tracht Prügel*); vernichtend (*Niederlage*); fest, tief (*Schlaf*)

'sound| bar·ri·er Schallgrenze *f*, -mauer *f*; **~ film** Tonfilm *m*; **'~·less** lautlos; **'~·proof** schalldicht; **'~·track**

Filmmusik *f*; Tonspur *f*; '**~ wave**
Schallwelle *f*

soup [su:p] **1.** Suppe *f*; **2.** ~ **up** F Motor
frisieren

sour ['sauə] **1.** sauer; *fig.* mürrisch; **2.**
sauer werden (lassen)

source [sɔ:s] Quelle *f*, *fig. a.* Ursache *f*,
Ursprung *m*

south [sauθ] **1.** Süd(en *m*); **2.** *adj.* südlich, Süd...; **3.** *adv.* nach Süden, süd-
wärts; **~'east 1.** Südost(en *m*); **2.** *a.*
~'east·ern südöstlich

south·er·ly ['sʌðəlɪ], **~ern** ['sʌðən]
südlich, Süd...; '**~ern·most** südlich-
ste(r, -s)

South 'Pole Südpol *m*

south·ward(s) ['sauθwəd(z)] südlich,
nach Süden, **~'west 1.** Südwest(en *m*);
2. *a.* **~'west·ern** südwestlich

sou·ve·nir [su:və'nɪə] Souvenir *n*, Andenken *n* (**of** an *acc.*)

sove·reign ['sɒvrɪn] **1.** Landesherr(in),
Monarch(in); **2.** souverän (Staat); **~·ty**
['sɒvrəntɪ] Souveränität *f*

So·vi·et ['səuvɪət] sowjetisch, Sowjet...

sow¹ [səu] (**sowed, sown** *od.* **sowed**)
(aus)säen

sow² *zo.* [sau] Sau *f*

sown [səun] *p.p. von* **sow¹**

spa [spa:] (Heil)Bad *n*

space [speɪs] **1.** Raum *m*, Platz *m*;
(Welt)Raum *m*; Zwischenraum *m*; Zeit-
raum *m*; **2.** *a.* ~ **out** in Abständen anordnen; *print.* sperren; '**~ age** Welt-
raumzeitalter *n*; '**~ bar** Leertaste *f*; '**~
cap·sule** Raumkapsel *f*; '**~ cen·tre**
(*Am.* **cen·ter**) Raumfahrtzentrum *n*;
'**~·craft** (*pl.* **-craft**) (Welt)Raumfahr-
zeug *n*; '**~ flight** (Welt)Raumflug *m*;
'**~·lab** Raumlabor *n*; '**~·man** (*pl.*
-men) F Raumfahrer *m*; Außerirdi-
sche(r) *m*; '**~·probe** (Welt)Raumsonde *f*;
'**~ re·search** (Welt)Raumforschung
f; '**~·ship** Raumschiff *n*; '**~ shut·tle**
Raumfähre *f*, -transporter *m*; '**~ station** (Welt)Raumstation *f*; '**~·suit**
Raumanzug *m*; '**~ walk** Weltraumspa-
ziergang *m*; '**~·wom·an** (*pl.* **-women**) F
(Welt)Raumfahrerin *f*; Außerirdische *f*

spa·cious ['speɪʃəs] geräumig

spade [speɪd] Spaten *m*; Kartenspiel;
Pik *n*, Grün *n*; **king of ~s** *pl.* Pik-König
m; **call a ~ a ~** das Kind beim (rechten)
Namen nennen

Spain [speɪn] Spanien *n*

span [spæn] **1.** Spanne *f*; Spannweite
f; △ *nicht* **Span**; **2.** (**-nn-**) Fluß etc.
überspannen; *fig.* sich erstrecken über
(*acc.*)

span·gle ['spæŋgl] **1.** Flitter *m*, Paillette
f; **2.** mit Flitter *od.* Pailletten besetzen;
fig. übersäen (**with** mit)

Span·iard ['spænjəd] Spanier(in)

span·iel *zo.* ['spænjəl] Spaniel *m*

Span·ish ['spænɪʃ] **1.** spanisch; **2.** *ling.*
Spanisch *n*; **the ~** *pl.* die Spanier *pl.*

spank [spæŋk] *j-m* den Hintern versoh-
len, verhauen; '**~·ing 1.** *adj.* schnell,
flott (Tempo); **2.** *adv.* ~ **clean** blitzsauber; ~ **new** funkelnagelneu; **3.** Haue *f*,
Tracht *f* Prügel

span·ner *bsd. Brt.* ['spænə] Schraubenschlüssel *m*; **put** *od.* **throw a ~ in the
works** F *j-m* in die Quere kommen

spar [spa:] (**-rr-**) Boxen: sparren (**with**
mit); sich ein Wortgefecht liefern (**with**
mit)

spare [speə] **1.** *j-n, et.* entbehren; Geld,
Zeit etc. übrig haben; keine Kosten,
Mühen etc. scheuen; △ *nicht* Geld etc.
sparen; ~ **s.o. s.th.** *j-m* et. ersparen; **2.**
Ersatz..., Reserve...; überschüssig; **3.**
mot. Ersatz-, Reservereifen *m*; *bsd. Brt.*
→ ~ '**part** Ersatzteil *n*, *m*; ~ '**room**
Gästezimmer *n*; ~ '**time** Freizeit *f*

spar·ing ['speərɪŋ] sparsam

spark [spa:k] **1.** Funke(n) *m* (*a. fig.*); **2.**
Funken sprühen; '**~·ing plug** *Brt. mot.*
→ **spark plug**

spar·kle ['spa:kl] **1.** funkeln, blitzen
(**with** vor *dat.*); perlen (Getränk); **2.**
Funkeln *n*, Blitzen *n*; **spark·ling**
['spa:klɪŋ] funkelnd, blitzend; *fig.*
(geist)sprühend, spritzig; ~ **wine**
Schaumwein *m*; Sekt *m*

'**spark plug** *mot.* Zündkerze *f*

spar·row *zo.* ['spærəu] Spatz *m*, Sperling *m*; '**~·hawk** *zo.* Sperber *m*

sparse [spa:s] spärlich, dünn

spas·m ['spæzəm] *med.* Krampf *m*; Anfall *m*; **spas·mod·ic** [spæz'mɒdɪk]
(**~ally**) *med.* krampfartig; *fig.* sporadisch, unregelmäßig

spas·tic *med.* ['spæstɪk] **1.** (**~ally**) spa-
stisch; **2.** Spastiker(in)

spat [spæt] *pret. u. p.p. von* **spit¹** 1

spa·tial ['speɪʃl] räumlich

spat·ter ['spætə] (be)spritzen

S

spawn [spɔːn] **1.** *zo.* laichen; *fig.* hervorbringen; **2.** *zo.* Laich *m*

speak [spiːk] (**spoke, spoken**) *v/i.* sprechen, reden (**to, with** mit; *about* über *acc.*); sprechen (**to** vor *dat.*; *about, on* über *acc.*); **so to ~** sozusagen; **~ing!** *teleph.* am Apparat!; **~ up** lauter sprechen; *v/t.* sprechen, sagen; *Sprache* sprechen; '**~er** Sprecher(in), Redner(in); 2 *parl.* Speaker *m*, Präsident *m*

spear [spɪə] **1.** Speer *m*; **2.** aufspießen; durchbohren; '**~head** Speerspitze *f*; *mil.* Angriffsspitze *f*; *Sport:* (Sturm-, Angriffs)Spitze *f*; '**~mint** *bot.* Grüne Minze

spe·cial ['speʃl] **1.** besondere(r, -s); speziell; Sonder...; Spezial...; **2.** Sonderbus *m od.* -zug *m*; *Rundfunk, TV:* Sondersendung *f*; *Am. econ.* F Sonderangebot *n*; **be on ~** *Am. econ.* F im Angebot sein; **spe·cial·ist** ['speʃlɪst] Spezialist(in), *med. a.* Facharzt *m*, -ärztin *f* (**in** für); **spe·ci·al·i·ty** [speʃɪ'ælɪtɪ] Spezialgebiet *n*; Spezialität *f*; **spe·cial·ize** ['speʃəlaɪz] sich spezialisieren (**in** auf *acc.*); **spe·cial·ty** *Am.* ['speʃltɪ] → **speciality**

spe·cies ['spiːʃiːz] (*pl.* **-cies**) Art *f*, Spezies *f*

spe·cif·ic [spɪ'sɪfɪk] (**~ally**) konkret, präzis; spezifisch, speziell, besondere(r, -s); eigen (**to** *dat.*); **~·ci·fy** ['spesɪfaɪ] genau beschreiben *od.* angeben *od.* festlegen

spe·ci·men ['spesɪmən] Exemplar *n*; Probe *f*, Muster *n*

speck [spek] kleiner Fleck, (*Staub*)Korn *n*; Punkt *m* (**on the horizon** am Horizont); △ *nicht* Speck; **speck·led** ['spekld] gefleckt, gesprenkelt

spec·ta·cle ['spektəkl] Schauspiel *n*; Anblick *m*; △ *nicht der* **Spektakel**; (**a pair of**) **~s** *pl.* (e-e) Brille

spec·tac·u·lar [spek'tækjʊlə] **1.** spektakulär; **2.** große (*Fernseh- etc.*)Show

spec·ta·tor [spek'teɪtə] Zuschauer(in)

spec·tral ['spektrəl] geisterhaft, gespenstisch; **~·tre** *Brt.*, **~·ter** *Am.* ['spektə] (*fig. a. Schreck*)Gespenst *n*

spec·u·late ['spekjʊleɪt] spekulieren, Vermutungen anstellen (**about, on** über *acc.*); *econ.* spekulieren (**in** mit); **~·la·tion** [spekjʊ'leɪʃn] Spekulation *f* (*a. econ.*), Vermutung *f*; **~·la·tive**

['spekjʊlətɪv] spekulativ, *econ. a.* Spekulations...; **~·la·tor** ['spekjʊleɪtə] *econ.* Spekulant(in)

sped [sped] *pret. u. p.p. von* **speed** 2

speech [spiːtʃ] Sprache *f* (*Sprechvermögen, Ausdrucksweise*); Rede *f*, Ansprache *f*; **make a ~** e-e Rede halten; '**~·day** *Brt. Schule:* (Jahres)Schlußfeier *f*; '**~·less** sprachlos (**with** vor *dat.*)

speed [spiːd] **1.** Geschwindigkeit *f*, Tempo *n*, Schnelligkeit *f*; *tech.* Drehzahl *f*; *phot.* Lichtempfindlichkeit *f*; *sl.* Speed *n* (*Aufputschmittel*); *mot. etc.* Gang *m*; **five-~ gearbox** Fünfganggetriebe *n*; **at a ~ of** mit e-r Geschwindigkeit von; **at full** *od.* **top ~** mit Höchstgeschwindigkeit; **2.** (**sped**) *v/i.* rasen; **be ~ing** *mot.* zu schnell fahren; **~ up** (*pret. u. p.p.* **speeded**) beschleunigen, schneller werden; *v/t.* rasch bringen *od.* befördern; **~ up** (*pret. u. p.p.* **speeded**) beschleunigen; '**~·boat** Rennboot *n*; '**~·ing** *mot.* zu schnelles Fahren, Geschwindigkeitsüberschreitung *f*; '**~·lim·it** *mot.* Geschwindigkeitsbegrenzung *f*, Tempolimit *n*

spee·do *Brt. mot.* F ['spiːdəʊ] (*pl.* **-dos**) Tacho *m*

speed·om·e·ter *mot.* [spɪ'dɒmɪtə] Tachometer *m, n*

'**speed trap** *mot.* Radarfalle *f*

'**speed·y** (**-ier, -iest**) schnell, (*Antwort etc. a.*) prompt

spell[1] [spel] (**spelt** *od. bsd. Am.* **spelled**) *a.* **~ out** buchstabieren; (*orthographisch richtig*) schreiben

spell[2] [spel] Weile *f*; (*Husten- etc.*)Anfall *m*; **for a ~** e-e Zeitlang; **a ~ of fine weather** e-e Schönwetterperiode; **hot ~** Hitzewelle *f*

spell[3] [spel] Zauber(spruch) *m*; *fig.* Zauber *m*; '**~·bound** wie gebannt

'**spell·er** *Computer:* Speller *m*, Rechtschreibsystem *n*; **be a good** (**bad**) **~ in** Rechtschreibung gut (schlecht) sein; '**~·ing** Buchstabieren *n*; Rechtschreibung *f*; Schreibung *f*, Schreibweise *f*; '**~·ing mis·take** (Recht)Schreibfehler *m*

spelt [spelt] *pret. u. p.p. von* **spell**[1]

spend [spend] (**spent**) *Geld* ausgeben (**on** für); *Urlaub, Zeit* verbringen; △ *nicht* **spenden**; '**~·ing** Ausgaben *pl.*; '**~·thrift** Verschwender(in)

spent [spent] **1.** *pret. u. p.p. von* **spend**; **2.** *adj.* verbraucht

sperm [spɜːm] Sperma *n*, Samen *m*

SPF [es piː 'ef] *Abk. für* **Sun Protection Factor** Sonnenschutzfaktor *m*

sphere [sfɪə] Kugel *f*; *fig.* (*Einfluß-etc.*)Sphäre *f*, (-)Bereich *m*, Gebiet *n*; **spher·i·cal** ['sferɪkl] kugelförmig

spice [spaɪs] **1.** Gewürz *n*; *fig.* Würze *f*; **2.** würzen

spick-and-span [spɪkən'spæn] blitzsauber

spic·y ['spaɪsɪ] (**-ier, -iest**) gutgewürzt, würzig; *fig.* pikant

spi·der *zo.* ['spaɪdə] Spinne *f*

spike [spaɪk] **1.** Spitze *f*; Dorn *m*; Stachel *m*; *Sport:* Spike *m*, Dorn *m*; **~s** *pl.* Spikes *pl.*, Rennschuhe *pl.*; **2.** aufspießen

spill [spɪl] **1.** (**spilt** *od. bsd. Am.* **spilled**) *v/t.* aus-, verschütten; **~ the beans** *F* alles ausplaudern, singen; → **milk** 1; *v/i.* strömen (**out of** aus) (*Menschen*); **~ over** überlaufen; *fig.* übergreifen (**into** auf *acc.*); **2.** *F* Sturz *m* (*vom Pferd, Rad etc.*)

spilt [spɪlt] *pret. u. p.p. von* **spill** 1

spin [spɪn] **1.** (**-nn-; spun**) *v/t.* drehen; *Wäsche* schleudern; *Münze* hochwerfen; *Fäden, Wolle etc.* spinnen; **~ out** *Arbeit etc.* in die Länge ziehen; *Geld etc.* strecken; *v/i.* sich drehen; spinnen; **my head was ~ning** mir drehte sich alles; **~ along** *mot.* F dahinrasen; **~ round** herumwirbeln; **2.** (schnelle) Drehung *f*; *Sport:* Effet *m*; Schleudern *n* (*Wäsche*); *aviat.* Trudeln *n*; **be in a (flat) ~** *bsd. Brt.* F am Rotieren sein; **go for a ~** *mot.* F e-e Spritztour machen

spin·ach *bot.* ['spɪnɪdʒ] Spinat *m*

spin·al *anat.* ['spaɪnl] Rückgrat...; **~ 'col·umn** Wirbelsäule *f*, Rückgrat *n*; **~ 'cord, ~ 'mar·row** Rückenmark *n*

spin·dle ['spɪndl] Spindel *f*

spin-|'dri·er (Wäsche)Schleuder *f*; **~'dry** *Wäsche* schleudern; **~'dry·er** → **spin-drier**

spine [spaɪn] *anat.* Wirbelsäule *f*, Rückgrat *n*; *zo.* Stachel *m*, *bot. a.* Dorn *m*; (*Buch*)Rücken *m*

'spin·ning| mill Spinnerei *f*; **'~ top** Kreisel *m*; **'~ wheel** Spinnrad *n*

spin·ster ['spɪnstə] ältere unverheiratete Frau, *contp.* alte Jungfer, spätes Mädchen

spin·y ['spaɪnɪ] (**-ier, -iest**) *zo.* stach(e)lig, *bot. a.* dornig

spi·ral ['spaɪərəl] **1.** spiralenförmig, spiralig, Spiral...; **2.** (*a. econ. Preis etc.*)Spirale *f*; **~ 'stair·case** Wendeltreppe *f*

spire ['spaɪə] (*Kirch*)Turmspitze *f*

spir·it ['spɪrɪt] Geist *m*; Stimmung *f*, Einstellung *f*; Schwung *m*, Elan *m*; *chem.* Spiritus *m*; *mst* **~s** *pl.* Spirituosen *pl.*; **~ed** energisch, beherzt; erregt (*Auseinandersetzung*); feurig (*Pferd etc.*); **~·less** temperamentlos; mutlos

spir·its ['spɪrɪts] *pl.* Laune *f*, Stimmung *f*; **be in high ~** in Hochstimmung sein; ausgelassen *od.* übermütig sein; **be in low ~** niedergeschlagen sein

spir·i·tu·al ['spɪrɪtʃʊəl] **1.** geistig, geistlich; **2.** *mus.* Spiritual *n*

spit¹ [spɪt] **1.** (**-tt-; spat** *od. bsd. Am.* **spit**) spucken; knistern (*Feuer*), brutzeln (*Fleisch etc.*); *a.* **~ out** ausspucken; **~ at s.o.** j-n anspucken; **it is ~ting** (**with rain**) es sprüht; **2.** Spucke *f*

spit² [spɪt] (*Brat*)Spieß *m*; *geogr.* Landzunge *f*

spite [spaɪt] **1.** Bosheit *f*, Gehässigkeit *f*; **out of** *od.* **from pure ~** aus reiner Bosheit; **in ~ of** trotz; **2.** j-n ärgern; **'~·ful** boshaft, gehässig

spit·ting 'im·age Ebenbild *n*; **she is the ~ of her mother** sie ist ganz die Mutter, sie ist ihrer Mutter wie aus dem Gesicht geschnitten

spit·tle ['spɪtl] Speichel *m*, Spucke *f*

splash [splæʃ] **1.** (be)spritzen; klatschen (*Regen*); planschen; platschen; **~ down** wassern (*Raumkapsel*); **2.** Klatschen *n*, Platschen *n*; Spritzer *m*; Spritzfleck *m*; *bsd. Brt.* Spritzer *m*, Schuß *m* (*Soda etc.*); **'~·down** Wasserung *f* (*e-r Raumkapsel*)

splay [spleɪ] *a.* **~ out** *Finger, Zehen* spreizen

spleen *anat.* [spliːn] Milz *f*

splen·did ['splendɪd] großartig, herrlich, prächtig; **'~·do(u)r** Pracht *f*

splice [splaɪs] miteinander verbinden, *Film etc.* (zusammen)kleben

splint *med.* [splɪnt] Schiene *f*; **put in a ~, put in ~s** schienen

splin·ter ['splɪntə] **1.** Splitter *m*; **2.** (zer)splittern; **~ off** absplittern; *fig.* sich abspalten (**from** von)

S

split 286

split [splɪt] **1.** (**-tt-; split**) v/t. (zer)spalten; zerreißen; a. ~ **up** aufteilen (**between** unter acc.; **into** in acc.); sich et. teilen; ~ **hairs** Haarspalterei treiben; ~ **one's sides** F sich vor Lachen biegen; v/i. sich spalten; zerreißen; sich teilen (**into** in acc.); a. ~ **up** (**with**) Schluß machen (mit), sich trennen (von); **2.** Riß m; Spalt m; Aufteilung f; fig. Bruch m; fig. Spaltung f; '~ting heftig, rasend (Kopfschmerzen)

splut·ter ['splʌtə] stottern (a. mot.); zischen (Feuer etc.)

spoil [spɔɪl] **1.** (**spoilt od. spoiled**) v/t. verderben; ruinieren; j-n verwöhnen, Kind a. verziehen; v/i. verderben, schlecht werden; **2.** mst ~s pl. Beute f

'**spoil·er** mot. Spoiler m

'**spoil·sport** F Spielverderber(in)

spoilt [spɔɪlt] pret. u. p.p. von **spoil** 1

spoke¹ [spəʊk] pret. von **speak**

spoke² [spəʊk] Speiche f

spok·en ['spəʊkən] p.p. von **speak**

spokes·man ['spəʊksmən] (pl. **-men**) Sprecher m; '~wom·an (pl. **-women**) Sprecherin f

sponge [spʌndʒ] **1.** Schwamm m; fig. Schmarotzer(in), Schnorrer(in); Brt. → **sponge cake**; **2.** v/t. a. ~ **down** (mit e-m Schwamm) abwaschen; ~ **off** weg-, abwischen; ~ (**up**) aufsaugen, -wischen (**from** von); fig. v/i. fig. schnorren (**from, off, on** von bei); ~ **cake** Biskuitkuchen m; '**spong·er** fig. Schmarotzer(in), Schnorrer(in); '**spong·y** (**-ier, -iest**) schwammig; weich

spon·sor ['spɒnsə] **1.** Bürge m, -in f; Sponsor(in), Geldgeber(in); Spender(in); **2.** bürgen für; sponsern

spon·ta·ne·ous [spɒn'teɪnjəs] spontan

spook F [spuːk] Geist m; '~y (**-ier, -iest**) F unheimlich

spool [spuːl] Spule f; ~ **of thread** Am. Garnrolle f

spoon [spuːn] **1.** Löffel m; **2.** löffeln; '~feed (**-fed**) Kind etc. füttern; '~ful (ein) Löffel(voll) m

spo·rad·ic [spə'rædɪk] (**~ally**) sporadisch, gelegentlich

spore bot. [spɔː] Spore f

sport [spɔːt] **1.** Sport(art f) m; F feiner

Kerl; ~s pl. Sport m; **2.** protzen mit; herumlaufen mit

sports [spɔːts] Sport...; '~car Sportwagen m; '~cen·tre (Am. **cen·ter**) Sportzentrum n; '~man (pl. **-men**) Sportler m; '~wear Sportkleidung f; '~wom·an (pl. **-women**) Sportlerin f

spot [spɒt] **1.** Punkt m, Tupfen m; Fleck m; med. Pickel m; Ort m, Platz m, Stelle f; Rundfunk, TV: (Werbe)Spot m; ~ **Spot** m (Spotlight); **a** ~ **of** Brt. F ein bißchen; **on the** ~ auf der Stelle, sofort; zur Stelle; an Ort u. Stelle, vor Ort; auf der Stelle (laufen); **be in a** ~ F in Schwulitäten sein; **soft** ~ fig. Schwäche f (**for** für); **tender** ~ empfindliche Stelle; **weak** ~ schwacher Punkt; Schwäche f; **2.** (**-tt-**) entdecken, sehen; ~ '**check** Stichprobe f; '~**less** tadellos sauber; fig. untad(e)lig; '~**light** Spotlight n, Scheinwerfer(licht n) m; '~**ted** getüpfelt; fleckig; '~**ter** Beobachter m; '~**ty** (**-ier, -iest**) pick(e)lig

spouse [spaʊz] Gatt|e m, -in f, Gemahl(in)

spout [spaʊt] **1.** v/t. Wasser etc. (heraus)spritzen; v/i. spritzen (**from** aus); **2.** Schnauze f, Tülle f; (Wasser- etc.) Strahl m

sprain med. [spreɪn] **1.** sich et. verstauchen; **2.** Verstauchung f

sprang [spræŋ] pret. von **spring** 1

sprat zo. [spræt] Sprotte f

sprawl [sprɔːl] ausgestreckt liegen od. sitzen (a. ~ **out**); sich ausbreiten

spray [spreɪ] **1.** be-, versprühen; spritzen; sich die Haare sprayen; Parfüm etc. versprühen, zerstäuben; **2.** Sprühnebel m; Gischt m, f; Spray m, n; → **sprayer**; '~**can** → '~**er** Sprüh-, Spraydose f, Zerstäuber m

spread [spred] **1.** (**spread**) v/t. ausbreiten, Arme a. ausstrecken, Finger etc. spreizen (alle a. ~ **out**); Furcht, Krankheit, Nachricht etc. verbreiten; Gerücht a. ausstreuen; Butter etc. streichen (**on** auf acc.); Brot etc. (be)streichen (**with** mit); v/i. sich ausbreiten (a. ~ **out**); sich erstrecken (**over** über acc.); sich verbreiten, übergreifen (**to** auf acc.); sich streichen lassen (Butter etc.); **2.** Aus-, Verbreitung f; Ausdehnung f; Spannweite f; (Brot)Aufstrich m; '~**sheet**

Computer: Tabellenkalkulation(sprogramm *n*) *f*

spree F [spri:] *go (out) on a ~* e-e Sauftour machen; *go on a buying* (*od.* **shopping, spending**) *~ wie verrückt einkaufen

sprig *bot.* [sprɪg] kleiner Zweig

spright·ly ['spraɪtlɪ] (*-ier, -iest*) lebhaft; rüstig (*ältere Person*)

spring [sprɪŋ] **1.** (*sprang od. Am.* **sprung, sprung**) *v/i.* springen; *~ from* herrühren von; *~ up* aufkommen (*Wind*); aus dem Boden schießen (*Gebäude etc.*); *v/t. ~ a leak* ein Leck bekommen; *~ a surprise on s.o.* j-n überraschen; **2.** Frühling *m*, Frühjahr *n*; Quelle *f*; *tech.* Feder *f*; Elastizität *f*; Federung *f*; Sprung *m*, Satz *m*; *in (the) ~* im Frühling; **'~·board** Sprungbrett *n*; **~·clean** gründlich putzen, Frühjahrsputz machen (*in dat.*); **'~·clean** *Brt.*, **'~·clean·ing** *Am.* gründlicher Hausputz, Frühjahrsputz *m*; *~* **'tide** Springflut *f*; **'~·time** Frühling(szeit *f*) *m*, Frühjahr *n*; **~·y** ['sprɪŋɪ] (*-ier, -iest*) elastisch, federnd

sprin·kle ['sprɪŋkl] **1.** *Wasser etc.* sprengen (*on auf acc.*); *Salz etc.* streuen (*on auf acc.*); *et.* (be)sprengen *od.* bestreuen (*with* mit); *it is sprinkling* es sprüht (*regnet fein*); **2.** Sprühregen *m*; (Be)Sprengen *n*; (Be)Streuen *n*; **'~·kler** (*Rasen*)Sprenger *m*; Sprinkler *m*, Berieselungsanlage *f*; **'~·kling:** *a ~ of* ein bißchen, ein paar

sprint [sprɪnt] *Sport* **1.** sprinten; spurten; **2.** Sprint *m*; Spurt *m*; **'~·er** *Sport*: Sprinter(in)

sprite [spraɪt] Kobold *m*

sprout [spraʊt] **1.** sprießen, keimen; wachsen lassen; **2.** *bot.* Sproß *m*; (*Brussels*) *~s pl. bot.* Rosenkohl *m*

spruce[1] *bot.* [spru:s] Fichte *f*; Rottanne *f*

spruce[2] [spru:s] adrett

sprung [sprʌŋ] *pret. u. p.p. von* **spring** 1

spry [spraɪ] rüstig, lebhaft (*ältere Person*)

spun [spʌn] *pret. u. p.p. von* **spin** 1

spur [spɜ:] **1.** Sporn *m* (*a. zo.*); *fig.* Ansporn *m* (*to* zu); ⚠ *nicht Spur; on the ~ of the moment* spontan; **2.** (*-rr-*) *e-m Pferd* die Sporen geben; *oft ~ on fig.* anspornen (*to* zu)

spurt[1] [spɜ:t] **1.** spurten, sprinten; **2.** plötzliche Aktivität, (*Arbeits*)Anfall *m*; Spurt *m*, Sprint *m*

spurt[2] [spɜ:t] **1.** spritzen (*from* aus); **2.** (*Wasser- etc.*)Strahl *m*

sput·ter ['spʌtə] stottern (*a. mot.*); zischen (*Feuer etc.*)

spy [spaɪ] **1.** Spion(in); **2.** spionieren, Spionage treiben (*for* für); *~ into fig.* herumspionieren in (*dat.*); *~ on* j-m nachspionieren; **'~·hole** (Tür)Spion *m*

Sq *nur geschr. Abk. für* **Square** Pl., Platz *m*

sq *nur geschr. Abk. für* **square** Quadrat

squab·ble ['skwɒbl] (sich) streiten (*about, over* um, wegen)

squad [skwɒd] Mannschaft *f*, Trupp *m*; (*Überfall- etc.*)Kommando *n* (*der Polizei*); Dezernat *n*; **'~ car** *bsd. Am.* (Funk)Streifenwagen *m*

squad·ron ['skwɒdrən] *mil., aviat.* Staffel *f*; *naut.* Geschwader *n*

squal·id ['skwɒlɪd] schmutzig, verwahrlost, -kommen, armselig

squall [skwɔ:l] Bö *f*

squan·der ['skwɒndə] *Geld, Zeit etc.* verschwenden, *Chance* vertun

square [skweə] **1.** Quadrat *n*; Viereck *n*; öffentlicher Platz; *math.* Quadrat(zahl *f*) *n*; Feld *n* (*e-s Brettspiels*); *tech.* Winkel(maß *n*) *m*; **2.** quadratisch, Quadrat...; viereckig; rechtwink(e)lig; eckig (*Schultern etc.*); fair, gerecht; *be (all) ~* quitt sein; **3.** quadratisch *od.* rechtwink(e)lig machen (*a. ~ off od.* **up**); *in* Quadrate einteilen (*a. ~ off*); *math.* Zahl ins Quadrat erheben; *Schultern* straffen; *Konto* ausgleichen; *Schulden* begleichen; *fig.* in Einklang bringen *od.* stehen (*with* mit); *~ up v/i.* F abrechnen; *~ up to* sich j-m, e-m Problem *etc.* stellen; **~d 'pa·per** kariertes Papier; *~* **root** *math.* Quadratwurzel *f*

squash[1] [skwɒʃ] **1.** zerdrücken, -quetschen; quetschen, zwängen (*into* in *acc.*); *~ flat* flachdrücken, F platt walzen; **2.** Gedränge *n*; *Sport*: Squash *n*; *lemon od. orange* *~ Brt.* Getränk aus Zitronen- od. Orangenkonzentrat u. Wasser

squash[2] *bsd. Am. bot.* [skwɒʃ] Kürbis *m*

squat [skwɒt] **1.** (*-tt-*) hocken, kauern; *leerstehendes Haus* besetzen; *~ down* sich (hin)hocken *od.* (-)kauern; **2.** ge-

S

drungen, untersetzt; '**~ter** Hausbesetzer(in)

squaw [skwɔː] Squaw f (*Indianerfrau*)

squawk [skwɔːk] kreischen, schreien; F lautstark protestieren (*about* gegen)

squeak [skwiːk] **1.** piep(s)en (*Maus etc.*); quietschen (*Tür etc.*); **2.** Piep(s)en n; Piep(s)er m, Piepser m; Quietschen f; '**~y** (*-ier, -iest*) piepsig (*Stimme etc.*); quietschend (*Tür etc.*)

squeal [skwiːl] **1.** kreischen (*with* vor *dat.*); **~ on s.o.** fig. sl. j-n verpfeifen; **2.** Kreischen n; Schrei m

squeam·ish ['skwiːmɪʃ] empfindlich, zartbesaitet

squeeze [skwiːz] **1.** drücken; auspressen, -quetschen; (sich) quetschen od. zwängen (*into* in *acc.*); **2.** Druck m; Spritzer m (*Zitrone etc.*); Gedränge n; '**squeez·er** (*Frucht*)Presse f

squid zo. [skwɪd] (*pl. squid, squids*) Tintenfisch m

squint [skwɪnt] schielen; blinzeln

squirm [skwɜːm] sich winden

squir·rel zo. ['skwɪrəl] Eichhörnchen n

squirt [skwɜːt] **1.** (be)spritzen; **2.** Strahl m

Sr → **Snr**

SS ['es es] *Abk. für* **steamship** Dampfer m, Dampfschiff n

St *nur geschr. Abk. für:* **Saint** ... St. ..., Sankt ...; **Street** St., Straße f

st *nur geschr. Abk. für* **stone** *Brt. (Gewichtseinheit = 6,35 kg)*

Sta *nur geschr. Abk. für* **Station** B(h)f., Bahnhof m (*bsd. auf Karten*)

stab [stæb] **1.** (*-bb-*) v/t. niederstechen; **be ~bed in the arm** e-n Stich in den Arm bekommen; v/i. stechen (*at* nach); **2.** Stich m; △ *nicht* **Stab**

sta·bil·i·ty [stə'bɪlətɪ] Stabilität f; fig. Dauerhaftigkeit f; fig. Ausgeglichenheit f; **~ize** ['steɪbəlaɪz] (sich) stabilisieren

sta·ble¹ ['steɪbl] stabil; fig. dauerhaft; fig. ausgeglichen (*Person*)

sta·ble² ['steɪbl] Stall m

stack [stæk] **1.** Stapel m, Stoß m; **~s of**, **a ~ of** F jede Menge *Arbeit etc.*; → **haystack**; **2.** stapeln; vollstapeln (*with* mit); **~ up** aufstapeln

sta·di·um ['steɪdjəm] (*pl. -diums, -dia* [-djə]) *Sport:* Stadion n

staff [staːf] **1.** Stab m; Mitarbeiter(stab

m) pl.; Personal n, Belegschaft f; Lehrkörper m; *mil.* Stab m; **2.** besetzen (*with* mit); '**~ room** Lehrerzimmer n

stag zo. [stæg] (*pl. stags, stag*) Hirsch m

stage [steɪdʒ] **1.** *thea.* Bühne f (*a. fig.*); Etappe f (*a. fig.*), (*Reise*)Abschnitt m; Teilstrecke f, Fahrzone f (*Bus etc.*); Stufe f, Stadium n, Phase f; *tech.* Stufe f (*e-r Rakete*); **2.** *thea.* inszenieren; veranstalten; '**~coach** *hist.* Postkutsche f; '**~ di·rec·tion** Regieanweisung f; '**~ fright** Lampenfieber n; '**~ man·ag·er** Inspizient m

stag·ger ['stægə] **1.** v/i. (sch)wanken, taumeln, torkeln; v/t. j-n sprachlos machen, umwerfen; *Arbeitszeit etc.* staffeln; **2.** (Sch)Wanken n, Taumeln n

stag·nant ['stægnənt] stehend (*Gewässer*); *bsd. econ.* stagnierend; **~nate** *bsd. econ.* [stæg'neɪt] stagnieren

stain [steɪn] **1.** v/t. beflecken; (ein)färben; *Holz* beizen; *Glas* bemalen; v/i. Flecken bekommen, schmutzen; **2.** Fleck m; Färbemittel n; (*Holz*)Beize f; fig. Makel m; '**~ed 'glass** Bunt-, Farbglas n; '**~less** nichtrostend, rostfrei (*Stahl*)

stair [steə] (Treppen)Stufe f; **~s** pl. Treppe f; '**~case**, '**~way** Treppe f; Treppenhaus n

stake¹ [steɪk] **1.** Pfahl m, Pfosten m; *hist.* Marterpfahl m; **2.** **~ off**, **~ out** abstecken

stake² [steɪk] **1.** Anteil m, Beteiligung f (*in* an *dat.*) (*a. econ.*); (*Wett- etc.*)Einsatz m; **be at ~** fig. auf dem Spiel stehen; **2.** *Geld etc.* setzen (**on** auf *acc.*); *Ruf etc.* riskieren, aufs Spiel setzen

stale [steɪl] (*~r, ~st*) alt(backen) (*Brot etc.*); schal, abgestanden (*Bier etc.*); abgestanden, verbraucht (*Luft etc.*)

stalk¹ bot. [stɔːk] Stengel m, Stiel m, Halm m

stalk² [stɔːk] v/t. sich heranpirschen an (*acc.*); verfolgen, hinter j-m, et. herschleichen; v/i. stolzieren; staksen, steif(beinig) gehen

stall¹ [stɔːl] **1.** (*Obst- etc.*)Stand m, (*Markt*)Bude f; Box f (*im Stall*); △ *nicht* **Stall**; **~s** pl. rel. Chorgestühl n; *Brt. thea.* Parkett n; **2.** v/t. *Motor* abwürgen; v/i. absterben (*Motor*)

stall² [stɔːl] v/i. Ausflüchte machen; Zeit schinden; v/t. j-n hinhalten; et. hinauszögern

stal·li·on zo. ['stæljən] (Zucht)Hengst m

stal·wart ['stɔːlwət] kräftig, robust; bsd. pol. treu (Anhänger)

stam·i·na ['stæminə] Ausdauer f; Durchhaltevermögen n, Kondition f

stam·mer ['stæmə] 1. stottern, stammeln; 2. Stottern n

stamp [stæmp] 1. v/i. sta(m)pfen, trampeln; v/t. Paß etc. (ab)stempeln; Datum etc. aufstempeln (on auf acc.); Brief etc. frankieren; fig. j-n abstempeln (as als, zu); ~ one's foot aufstampfen; ~ out Feuer austreten; tech. ausstanzen; 2. (Brief)Marke f, (Steuer- etc.)Marke f; Stempel m; ~ed (addressed) envelope Freiumschlag m

stam·pede [stæm'piːd] 1. wilde Flucht (von Tieren); wilder Ansturm, Massenansturm m (for auf acc.); 2. v/i. durchgehen; v/t. in Panik versetzen

stanch Am. [stɑːntʃ] → **staunch²**

stand [stænd] 1. (stood) v/i. stehen; aufstehen; fig. fest- etc. bleiben; ~ still stillstehen; v/t. stellen (on auf acc.); aushalten, ertragen; e-r Prüfung etc. standhalten; Probe bestehen; Chance haben; Drink etc. spendieren; I can't ~ him (od. it) ich kann ihn (od. das) nicht ausstehen od. leiden; ~ around herumstehen; ~ back zurücktreten; ~ by danebenstehen; fig. zu j-m halten; zu et. stehen; ~ idly by tatenlos zusehen; ~ down jur. den Zeugenstand verlassen; verzichten; zurücktreten; ~ for stehen für, bedeuten; sich er. gefallen lassen, dulden; bsd. Brt. kandidieren für; ~ in einspringen (for für); ~ in for s.o. a. j-n vertreten; ~ on (fig. beziehen auf (dat.); ~ out hervorstechen; sich abheben (against gegen, von); ~ over überwachen, aufpassen auf (acc.); ~ together zusammenhalten, -stehen; ~ up aufstehen, sich erheben; ~ up for eintreten od. sich einsetzen für; ~ up to j-m mutig gegenübertreten, j-m die Stirn bieten; 2. (Obst-, Messe- etc.)Stand m; (Schirm-, Noten- etc.)Ständer m; Sport etc.: Tribüne f; (Taxi)Stand(platz) m; Am. jur. Zeugenstand m; take a ~ fig. Position beziehen (on zu)

stan·dard¹ ['stændəd] 1. Norm f, Maßstab m; Standard m, Niveau n; ~ of living, living ~ Lebensstandard m; 2. normal, Normal...; durchschnittlich,

Durchschnitts...; Standard...

stan·dard² ['stændəd] Standarte f, (an Wagen) Stander m; hist. Banner n

stan·dard·ize ['stændədaɪz] vereinheitlichen, bsd. tech. standardisieren, normen

'stan·dard lamp Brt. Stehlampe f

'stand·by 1. (pl. -bys) Reserve f; aviat. Stand-by n; be on ~ in Bereitschaft stehen; 2. Reserve..., Not...; aviat. Stand-by...; '~in Film, TV: Double n; Ersatzmann m; Vertreter(in)

stand·ing ['stændɪŋ] 1. stehend; fig. ständig; → **ovation**; 2. Rang m, Stellung f; Ansehen n, Ruf m; Dauer f; of long ~ alt, seit langem bestehend; ~ 'or·der econ. Dauerauftrag m; '~ room only nur noch Stehplätze

stand·off·ish F [stænd'ɒfɪʃ] (sehr) ablehnend, hochnäsig; '~point fig. Standpunkt m; '~still Stillstand m; be at a ~ stehen (Auto etc.); ruhen (Produktion etc.); bring to a ~ Auto etc. zum Stehen bringen; Produktion etc. zum Erliegen bringen; '~up Steh...; im Stehen (eingenommen) (Mahlzeit)

stank [stæŋk] pret. von **stink** 1

stan·za ['stænzə] Strophe f

sta·ple¹ ['steɪpl] 1. Hauptnahrungsmittel n; Haupterzeugnis n (e-s Landes); 2. Haupt...; üblich

sta·ple² ['steɪpl] 1. Heftklammer f; Krampe f; 2. heften; △ nicht stapeln; '~r (Draht)Hefter m

star [stɑː] 1. Stern m; print. Sternchen n; thea., Film, Sport: Star m; △ nicht zo. Star; 2. (-rr-) v/t. mit e-m Sternchen kennzeichnen; ~ring ... in der Hauptrolle od. den Hauptrollen ...; a film ~ring ... ein Film mit ... in der Hauptrolle od. den Hauptrollen; v/i. die od. e-e Hauptrolle spielen (in in dat.)

star·board ['stɑːbəd] Steuerbord n

starch [stɑːtʃ] 1. (Kartoffel- etc.)Stärke f; stärkereiches Nahrungsmittel n; (Wäsche)Stärke f; 2. Wäsche stärken

stare [steə] 1. starren; ~ at j-n anstarren; 2. (starrer) Blick, Starren n

stark [stɑːk] 1. adj. nackt (Tatsachen etc.); △ nicht stark; be in ~ contrast to in krassem Gegensatz stehen zu; 2. adv. F: ~ naked splitternackt; ~ raving mad, ~ staring mad total verrückt

'star·light Sternenlicht n

star·ling zo. ['stɑːlɪŋ] Star m
star·lit ['stɑːlɪt] stern(en)klar
star·ry ['stɑːrɪ] (-ier, -iest) Stern(en)...; **~'eyed** F blauäugig, naiv
Stars and 'Stripes das Sternenbanner (Staatsflagge der USA)
Star-Span·gled Ban·ner [stɑː-ˈspæŋgld ˈbænə] die Nationalhymne (der USA)
start [stɑːt] **1.** v/i. anfangen, beginnen (a. ~ off); aufbrechen (for nach) (a. ~ off, ~ out); abfahren (Bus, Zug), ablegen (Boot), aviat. abfliegen, starten; anspringen (Motor), anlaufen (Maschine); Sport: starten; zusammenfahren, -zucken (at bei); to ~ with anfangs, zunächst; erstens; ~ from scratch ganz von vorn anfangen; to ~ off, ~ off beginnen (a. ~ off); in Gang setzen (a. bringen, Motor etc. a. anlassen, starten; **2.** Anfang m, Beginn m, (bsd. Sport) Start m; Aufbruch m; Auffahren n, -schrecken n; at the ~ am Anfang; Sport: am Start; for a ~ erstens; from ~ to finish von Anfang bis Ende; '~·er Sport: Starter(in); mot. Anlasser m, Starter m; bsd. Brt. F Vorspeise f; for ~s F zunächst einmal
start·le [steɪl] erschrecken; überraschen, bestürzen
starv|a·tion [stɑːˈveɪʃn] Hungern n; **die of** ~ verhungern; ~ **diet** F Fasten-, Hungerkur f, Nulldiät f; **~e** [stɑːv] hungern (lassen); v/t. anfangen, beginnen; I'm starving! Brt., I'm ~d! Am. F ich komme um vor Hunger!
state [steɪt] **1.** Zustand m; Stand m, Lage f; pol. (Bundes-, Einzel)Staat m; oft ⩓ pol. Staat m; **2.** staatlich, Staats...; **3.** angeben, nennen; erklären, jur. aussagen; festlegen, -setzen; '⩓ **De·part·ment** Am. pol. Außenministerium n; '~·ly (-ier, -iest) gemessen, würdevoll; prächtig; '~·ment Statement n, Erklärung f; Angabe f; jur. Aussage f; econ. (Bank-, Konto)Auszug m; **make a** ~ e-e Erklärung abgeben; '~·room naut. luxuriöse (Einzel)Kabine; '~·side Am. in den Staaten; nach den od. in die Staaten (zurück); '~·man (pl. -men) Staatsmann m
stat·ic ['stætɪk] (~ally) statisch
sta·tion ['steɪʃn] **1.** (a. Bus-, U-)Bahnhof m, Station f; (Forschungs-, Rettungsetc.)Station f; Tankstelle f; (Feuer)Wache f; (Polizei)Revier n; (Wahl)Lokal n; Rundfunk, TV: Sender m, Station f; **2.** aufstellen, postieren; mil. stationieren
sta·tion·a·ry ['steɪʃnərɪ] stehend
sta·tion·er ['steɪʃnə] Schreibwarenhändler(in); '~'s (shop) Schreibwarenhandlung f; ~·y ['steɪʃnərɪ] Schreibwaren pl.; Briefpapier n
'**sta·tion|·mas·ter** rail. Bahnhofsvorsteher m; '~ **wag·on** Am. mot. Kombiwagen m
sta·tis·tics [stəˈtɪstɪks] pl. Statistik(en pl.) f
stat·ue ['stætʃuː] Statue f, Standbild n
sta·tus ['steɪtəs] Status m, Rechtsstellung f; (Familien)Stand m, Stellung f, Rang m, Status m; '~ **line** Computer: Statuszeile f
stat·ute ['stætjuːt] Gesetz n; Statut n, Satzung f
staunch¹ [stɔːntʃ] treu, zuverlässig
staunch² [stɔːntʃ] Blutung stillen
stay [steɪ] **1.** bleiben (with s.o. bei j-m); wohnen (at in dat.; with s.o. bei j-m); △ nicht stehen; ~ put F sich nicht (vom Fleck) rühren; ~ away wegbleiben, sich fernhalten (from von); ~ up aufbleiben; **2.** Aufenthalt m; jur. Aussetzung f, Aufschub m
stead·fast ['stedfɑːst] treu, zuverlässig, fest, unverwandt (Blick)
stead·y ['stedɪ] **1.** adj. (-ier, -iest) fest, stabil; ruhig (Hand), gut (Nerven); gleichmäßig; **2.** (sich) beruhigen; **3.** int. a. ~ on! Brt. F Vorsicht!; **4.** adv. Am.: go ~ with s.o. (fest) mit j-m gehen; **5.** Am. feste Freundin, fester Freund
steak [steɪk] Steak n; (Fisch)Filet n
steal [stiːl] (stole, stolen) stehlen (a. fig.); sich stehlen, (sich) schleichen (out of aus)
stealth [stelθ] by ~ → '~·y (-ier, -iest) heimlich, verstohlen
steam [stiːm] **1.** Dampf m; Dunst m; Dampf...; let off ~ Dampf ablassen, fig. a. sich Luft machen; **2.** v/i. dampfen; ~ up beschlagen (Glas); v/t. gastr. dünsten, dämpfen; '~·boat Dampfboot n, Dampfer m; '~·er Dampfer m, Dampfschiff n; Dampf-, Schnellkochtopf m; '~·ship Dampfer m, Dampfschiff n

steel [stiːl] **1.** Stahl *m*; **2.** ~ *o.s. for* sich wappnen gegen, sich gefaßt machen auf (*acc.*); '~·work·er Stahlarbeiter *m*; '~·works *sg.* Stahlwerk *n*

steep[1] [stiːp] steil; stark (*Preisanstieg etc.*); F happig

steep[2] [stiːp] eintauchen (*in in acc.*); *Wäsche*: (ein)weichen

stee·ple ['stiːpl] Kirchturm *m*; '~·chase *Pferdesport:* Hindernisrennen *n*; *Leichtathletik:* Hindernislauf *m*

steer[1] *zo.* [stɪə] (junger) Ochse; △ *nicht* **Stier**

steer[2] [stɪə] steuern, lenken; ~·ing col·umn mot. ['stɪərɪŋkɒləm] Lenksäule *f*; ~·ing wheel ['stɪərɪŋwiːl] mot. Lenk-, *a. naut.* Steuerrad *n*

stein [staɪn] Maßkrug *m*

stem [stem] **1.** *bot.* Stiel *m* (*a. e-s Glases*), Stengel *m*; *ling.* Stamm *m*; **2.** (**-mm-**): ~ *from* stammen *od.* herrühren von

stench [stentʃ] Gestank *m*

sten·cil ['stensl] Schablone *f*; *print.* Matrize *f*

ste·nog·ra·pher *Am.* [ste'nɒgrəfə] Stenotypistin *f*

step [step] **1.** Schritt *m* (*a. fig.*); Stufe *f*; Sprosse *f*; (*a pair of*) ~*s* pl. (*e-e*) Trittod. Stufenleiter *f*; *mind the* ~*!* Vorsicht, Stufe!; ~ *by* ~ Schritt für Schritt; *take* ~*s* Schritte *od.* et. unternehmen; **2.** (**-pp-**) gehen; treten (*in in acc.*; *on* auf acc.); ~ *on it*, ~ *on the gas* mot. F Gas geben, auf die Tube drücken; ~ *aside* zur Seite treten; *fig.* Platz machen; ~ *down fig.* Platz machen; ~ *up* Produktion etc. steigern

step... [step] Stief...

step-by-'step *fig.* schrittweise

'step·fa·ther Stiefvater *m*

'step·lad·der Tritt-, Stufenleiter *f*

'step·moth·er Stiefmutter *f*

steppes *geogr.* [steps] *pl.* Steppe *f*

step·ping-stone *fig.* ['stepɪŋstəʊn] Sprungbrett *n* (*to* für)

ster·e·o ['steriəʊ] (*pl.* **-os**) Stereo *n*; Stereogerät *n*, -anlage *f*; Stereo...; '~ sys·tem *Am. mus.* Kompaktanlage *f*

ster·ile ['steraɪl] steril, unfruchtbar; steril, keimfrei; *fig.* steril; **ste·ril·i·ty** [ste'rɪlətɪ] Sterilität *f* (*a. fig.*); Unfruchtbarkeit *f*; **ster·il·ize** ['steralaɪz] sterilisieren

ster·ling ['stɜːlɪŋ] das Pfund Sterling

stern[1] [stɜːn] streng (*Person, Disziplin, Blick etc.*)

stern[2] *naut.* [stɜːn] Heck *n*

stew [stjuː] **1.** *Fleisch, Gemüse:* schmoren, *Obst:* dünsten; ~ed apples Apfelkompott *n*; **2.** Eintopf *m*; *be in a* ~ in heller Aufregung sein

stew·ard [stjʊəd] *naut., aviat., rail.* Steward *m*; Ordner *m*; ~·ess *naut., aviat., rail.* ['stjʊədɪs] Stewardeß *f*

stick[1] [stɪk] trockener Zweig; Stock *m*; ([*Eis*]*Hockey*)Schläger *m*; (*Besen- etc.*)Stiel *m*; *aviat.* (*Steuer*)Knüppel *m*; Stück *n*, Stange *f* (*Sellerie etc.*), (*Lippen- etc.*)Stift *m*, Stäbchen *n*

stick[2] [stɪk] (**stuck**) *v/t.* mit *e-r* Nadel etc. stechen (*into* in *acc.*); et. kleben (*on* auf, *an acc.*); an-, festkleben (*with* mit); stecken; F tun, stellen, setzen, legen; *I can't* ~ *him* (*od. it*) bsd. Brt. F ich kann ihn (*od.* das) nicht ausstehen *od.* leiden; *v/i.* kleben; klebenbleiben (*to* an *dat.*); steckenbleiben; ~ *at nothing* vor nichts zurückschrecken; ~ *by* F bleiben bei; F zu *j-m* halten; ~ *out* vorstehen; abstehen (*Ohren etc.*); et. ausstehen; ~ *out* vorstrecken; ~ *to* bleiben bei; '~·er Aufkleber *m*; '~·ing plas·ter Brt. Heftpflaster *n*; '~·y (*-ier, -iest*) klebrig (*with* von); F heikel, unangenehm (*Lage*)

stiff [stɪf] **1.** *adj.* steif; F stark (*alkoholisches Getränk, Medizin*); schwer, hart (*Aufgabe, Strafe etc.*); hartnäckig (*Widerstand*); F happig, gepfeffert, gesalzen (*Preis*); *keep a* ~ *upper lip fig.* Haltung bewahren; **2.** *adv.* äußerst; höchst; *be bored* ~ F sich zu Tode langweilen; **3.** *sl.* Leiche *f*; ~·en ['stɪfn] *Wäsche* stärken; (sich) versteifen; verstärken; steif werden; sich verhärten

sti·fle ['staɪfl] ersticken; *fig.* unterdrücken

stile [staɪl] Zauntritt *m*

sti·let·to [stɪ'letəʊ] (*pl.* **-tos**) Stilett *n*; ~ 'heel Bleistift-, Pfennigabsatz *m*

still[1] [stɪl] **1.** *adv.* (immer) noch, noch immer; *beim Komparativ:* noch; **2.** *cj.* dennoch, trotzdem

still[2] [stɪl] **1.** *adj.* still; ruhig; ohne Kohlensäure (*Getränk*); **2.** *Film, TV:* Standfoto *n*; '~·born totgeboren; ~ *life* (*pl. - lifes*) *paint.* Stilleben *n*

stilt [stɪlt] Stelze *f*; '~·ed gestelzt (*Stil*)

stim·u·lant ['stɪmjʊlənt] *med.* Stimu-

lans n, Anregungs-, Aufputschmittel n;
fig. Anreiz m, Ansporn m (**to** für);
~·late ['stɪmjʊleɪt] *med.* stimulieren (*a.
fig.*), anregen, *fig. a.* anspornen; **~·lus**
['stɪmjʊləs] (*pl.* **-li** [-laɪ]) Reiz m; *fig.*
Anreiz m, Ansporn m (**to** für)

sting [stɪŋ] **1.** (**stung**) stechen (*Biene
etc.*); brennen (auf *od.* in *dat.*); **2.** Stachel m; Stich m; Brennen n, brennender
Schmerz

stin·gy F ['stɪndʒɪ] (**-ier, -iest**)
knaus(e)rig, knick(e)rig (*Person*);
mick(e)rig (*Mahlzeit etc.*)

stink [stɪŋk] **1.** (**stank** *od.* **stunk, stunk**)
stinken (*of* nach); **2.** Gestank m

stint [stɪnt] (~ *o.s.* (*of s.th.*) sich einschränken (mit et.); ~ (*on*) *s.th.* sparen
od. knausern mit et.

stip·u·late ['stɪpjʊleɪt] zur Bedingung
machen; festsetzen, vereinbaren; **~·la·tion** [stɪpjʊˈleɪʃn] Bedingung f; Festsetzung f, Vereinbarung f

stir [stɜː] **1.** (**-rr-**) (um)rühren; (sich) rühren *od.* bewegen; *fig.* j-n aufwühlen; ~
up Unruhe stiften; *Streit* entfachen; *Erinnerungen* wachrufen; **2.** **give *s.th. a* ~**
et. (um)rühren; **cause a** ~, **create a** ~
für Aufsehen sorgen

stir·rup ['stɪrəp] Steigbügel m

stitch [stɪtʃ] **1.** *Nähen:* Stich m; *Stricken
etc.:* Masche f; Seitenstechen n; **2.** zunähen, *Wunde* nähen (*a.* ~ **up**); heften

stock [stɒk] **1.** Vorrat m (*of* an *dat.*);
gastr. Brühe f; *a.* **live·~** Viehbestand m;
(*Gewehr*)Schaft m; △ *nicht* **Stock**; *fig.*
Abstammung f, Herkunft f; *bsd. Am.
econ.* Aktie(n *pl.*) f; **~s** *pl. econ.* Aktien
pl.; Wertpapiere *pl.*; **have *s.th.* in** ~
econ. et. vorrätig *od.* auf Lager haben;
take ~ *econ.* Inventur machen; **take** ~ **of**
fig. sich klarwerden über (*acc.*); **2.**
econ. Ware vorrätig haben, führen; ~
up sich eindecken *od.* versorgen (**on,
with** mit); **3.** Serien...; Standard...;
Standard..., stereotyp (*Ausrede etc.*);
'~·breed·er Viehzüchter m; **'~·brok·er** *econ.* Börsenmakler m; **'~ ex·change** *econ.* Börse f; **'~·hold·er** *bsd.
Am. econ.* Aktionär(in)

stock·ing ['stɒkɪŋ] Strumpf m

'stock|·mar·ket *econ.* Börse f; **'~·pile
1.** Vorrat m (**of** an *dat.*); **2.** e-n Vorrat
anlegen an (*dat.*); **~·still** regungslos;

'~·tak·ing *econ.* Inventur f; *fig.* Bestandsaufnahme f

stock·y ['stɒkɪ] (**-ier, -iest**) stämmig, untersetzt

stole [stəʊl] *pret. von* **steal**; **sto·len**
['stəʊlən] *p.p. von* **steal**

stol·id ['stɒlɪd] gleichmütig

stom·ach ['stʌmək] **1.** Magen m; Bauch
m; Appetit m (**for** auf *acc.*); **2.** vertragen (*a. fig.*); **'~·ache** Magenschmerzen
pl.; Bauchschmerzen *pl.*, -weh n; **'~
up·set** Magenverstimmung f

stone [stəʊn] **1.** Stein m; *bot.* Kern m,
Stein m; (*Hagel*)Korn n; (*pl.* **stone(s**;
Abk. **st**) *Brt.* Gewichtseinheit (= 6,35
kg); **2.** mit Steinen bewerfen; steinigen;
entkernen, -steinen; **~·dead** mausetot; **~·deaf** stocktaub; **'~·ma·son**
Steinmetz m; **'~·ware** Steingut n

ston·y ['stəʊnɪ] (**-ier, -iest**) steinig; *fig.*
steinern (*Gesicht, Herz etc.*), eisig
(*Schweigen*)

stood [stʊd] *pret. u. p.p. von* **stand** 1

stool [stuːl] Hocker m, Schemel m; △
nicht **Stuhl**; *med.* Stuhl(gang) m; **'~·pi·geon** F (Polizei)Spitzel m

stoop [stuːp] **1.** *v/i.* sich bücken (*a.* ~
down); gebeugt gehen; ~ **to** *fig.* sich
herablassen *od.* hergeben zu; **2.** gebeugte Haltung

stop [stɒp] **1.** (**-pp-**) *v/i.* (an)halten, stehenbleiben (*a. Uhr etc.*), stoppen; aufhören; *bsd. Brt.* bleiben; ~ **dead** plötzlich *od.* abrupt stehenbleiben; ~ **at
nothing** vor nichts zurückschrecken; ~
short *of doing*, ~ **short** *of s.th.* zurückschrecken vor (*dat.*); *v/t.* anhalten,
stoppen; aufhören mit; e-n Ende machen *od.* setzen (*dat.*); *Blutung* stillen;
Arbeiten, Verkehr etc. zum Erliegen
bringen; et. verhindern; j-n abhalten
(**from** von), hindern (**from** an *dat.*);
Rohr etc. verstopfen (*a.* ~ **up**); *Zahn*
füllen, plombieren; *Scheck* sperren
(lassen); ~ **by** vorbeischauen; ~ **in** vorbeischauen (**at** bei); ~ **off** F kurz haltmachen; ~ **over** kurz haltmachen; Zwischenstation machen; **2.** Halt m;
(*Bus*)Haltestelle f; *phot.* Blende f; *mst
full* ~ *gr.* Punkt m; **'~·gap** Notbehelf m;
'~·light *mot.* Bremslicht n; *bsd. Am.*
rotes Licht (*an e-r Ampel*); **'~·o·ver**
Zwischenstation f; *aviat.* Zwischenlandung f; **~·page** ['stɒpɪdʒ] Unterbre-

293 streetcar

chung *f*; Stopp *m*; Verstopfung *f*; *bsd.
Brt.* (Gehalts-, Lohn)Abzug *m*; '**~·per**
Stöpsel *m*; '**~ sign** *mot.* Stoppschild *n*;
'**~·watch** Stoppuhr *f*

stor·age ['stɔːrɪdʒ] Lagerung *f*; *Computer*: Speicher *m*; Lagergeld *n*

store [stɔː] **1.** (ein)lagern; *Energie* speichern; *Computer*: (ab)speichern, sichern; *a.* **~ up** sich e-n Vorrat anlegen an (*dat.*); **2.** Vorrat *m*; Lager(halle *f*,
-haus *n*) *n*; *bsd.* Brt. Kauf-, Warenhaus
n; *bsd.* Am. Laden *m*, Geschäft *n*; △
nicht **Store**; '**~·house** Lagerhaus *n*;
fig. Fundgrube *f*; '**~·keep·er** *bsd.* Am.
Ladenbesitzer(in), -inhaber(in); '**~·room** Lagerraum *m*

sto·rey *Brt.*, **sto·ry** *Am.* ['stɔːrɪ] Stock
(-werk *n*) *m*, Etage *f*

...sto·reyed *Brt.*, **...sto·ried** *Am.*
['stɔːrɪd] mit ... Stockwerken, ...stöckig

stork *zo.* [stɔːk] Storch *m*

storm [stɔːm] **1.** Unwetter *n*; Gewitter *n*;
Sturm *m*; **2.** *v/t.* mil. etc. stürmen; *v/i.*
stürmen, stürzen; '**~·y** (**-ier, -iest**) stürmisch

sto·ry¹ ['stɔːrɪ] Geschichte *f*; Märchen *n*
(*a. fig.*); Story *f*, Handlung *f*; *Zeitung
etc.*: Story *f*, Bericht *m* (**on** über *acc.*)

sto·ry² *Am.* ['stɔːrɪ] → **storey**

stout [staʊt] korpulent, vollschlank; *fig.*
unerschrocken; entschieden

stove [staʊv] Ofen *m*, Herd *m*

stow [staʊ] *a.* **~ away** verstauen;
'**~·a·way** *naut.*, *aviat.* blinder Passagier

strad·dle ['strædl] rittlings sitzen auf
(*dat.*)

strag·gle ['strægl] verstreut liegen *od.*
stehen; *bot. etc.* wuchern; **~ in** einzeln
eintrudeln; '**~·gler** Nachzügler(in);
'**~·gly** (**-ier, -iest**) verstreut (liegend);
bot. etc. wuchernd; struppig (*Haar*)

straight [streɪt] **1.** *adj.* gerade; glatt
(*Haar*); pur (*Whisky etc.*); aufrichtig,
offen, ehrlich; *sl.* hetero(*sexuell*); clean,
sauber (*nicht drogenabhängig*); **put ~** in
Ordnung bringen; **2.** *adv.* gerade; genau, direkt; klar (*sehen, denken*); ehrlich, anständig; **~ ahead** geradeaus; **~
off** F sofort; **~ on** geradeaus; **~ out** F
offen, rundheraus; **3.** *Sport*: (Gegen-,
Ziel)Gerade *f*; '**~·en** (gerade)ademachen, (gerade)richten; **~ out** in Ordnung bringen; *v/i. a.* **~ out** gerade werden (*Straße etc.*); **~ up** sich aufrichten;
'**~·for·ward** aufrichtig; einfach

strain [streɪn] **1.** *v/t.* Seil etc. (an)spannen; *sich, Augen etc.* überanstrengen;
sich *e-n Muskel etc.* zerren; *Gemüse,
Tee etc.* abgießen; *v/i.* sich anstrengen;
~ at zerren *od.* ziehen an (*dat.*); **2.** Spannung *f*; Anspannung *f*; *fig.* Belastung *f*;
med. Zerrung *f*; **~ed** gezerrt; gezwungen (*Lächeln etc.*); gespannt (*Beziehungen*); **look ~** abgespannt aussehen;
'**~·er** Sieb *n*

strait [streɪt] (*in Eigennamen* **2s** *pl.*)
Meerenge *f*, Straße *f*; **~s** *pl.* Notlage *f*;
~·ened ['streɪtnd]: **live in ~ circumstances** in beschränkten Verhältnissen
leben; '**~·jack·et** Zwangsjacke *f*

strand [strænd] Strang *m*; Faden *m*;
(*Kabel*)Draht *m*; (*Haar*)Strähne *f*; △
nicht **Strand**

strand·ed ['strændɪd]: **be ~** *naut.* gestrandet sein; **be (left) ~** *fig.* festsitzen
(**in** in *dat.*) (*Person*)

strange [streɪndʒ] (**~r, ~st**) merkwürdig,
seltsam, sonderbar; fremd; '**strang·er**
Fremde(r *m*) *f*

stran·gle ['stræŋgl] erwürgen

strap [stræp] **1.** Riemen *m*, Gurt *m*;
(*Uhr*)Armband *n*; Träger *m* (*am Kleid
etc.*); **2.** (**-pp-**) festschnallen; anschnallen

stra·te·gic [strə'tiːdʒɪk] (**~ally**) strategisch; **strat·e·gy** ['strætɪdʒɪ] Strategie *f*

stra·tum *geol.* ['strɑːtəm] (*pl.* **-ta** [-tə])
Schicht *f* (*a. fig.*)

straw [strɔː] Stroh *n*; Strohhalm *m*;
'**~·ber·ry** *bot.* ['strɔːbərɪ] Erdbeere *f*

stray [streɪ] **1.** (herum)streunen; sich
verirren; *fig.* abschweifen (**from** von);
2. verirrtes *od.* streunendes Tier; **3.** verirrt (*Kugel, Tier*); streunend (*Tier*); vereinzelt

streak [striːk] **1.** Streifen *m*; Strähne *f*
(*im Haar*); (*Charakter*)Zug *m*; **a ~ of
lightning** ein Blitz; **lucky ~** Glückssträhne *f*; **2.** flitzen; streifen; '**~·y** (**-ier,
-iest**) streifig; durchwachsen (*Speck*)

stream [striːm] **1.** Bach *m*; Strömung *f*;
fig. Strom *m*; **2.** strömen; flattern, wehen; '**~·er** Luft-, Papierschlange *f*;
Wimpel *m*; *Computer*: Streamer *m*

street [striːt] Straße *f*; Straßen...; **in**
(*bsd. Am.* **on**) **the ~** auf der Straße;
'**~·car** *Am.* Straßenbahn(wagen *m*) *f*

strength [streŋθ] Stärke f (a. fig.), Kraft f, Kräfte pl.; **~en** v/t. (ver)stärken; v/i. stärker werden

stren·u·ous ['strenjʊəs] anstrengend; unermüdlich

stress [stres] **1.** fig. Stress m; phys., tech. Beanspruchung f, Belastung f, Druck m; ling. Betonung f; fig. Nachdruck m; **2.** betonen; **~ful** stressig, aufreibend

stretch [stretʃ] **1.** v/t. strecken; dehnen, (aus)weiten; spannen; fig. es allzu genau nehmen mit; **~ out** ausstrecken; **be fully ~ed** fig. richtig gefordert werden; voll ausgelastet sein; v/i. sich dehnen, a. länger od. weiter werden; sich dehnen od. strecken; sich erstrecken; **~ out** sich ausstrecken; **2.** Dehnbarkeit f, Elastizität f; Strecke f (e-r Straße etc.); Sport: (Gegen-, Ziel)Gerade f; Zeit (-raum m, -spanne f); **have a ~** sich strecken od. dehnen; **~'er** Trage f

strick·en ['strɪkən] schwerbetroffen; **~ with** befallen od. ergriffen von

strict [strɪkt] streng, strikt; genau; **~ly** (**speaking**) genaugenommen

strid·den ['strɪdn] p.p. von **stride** 1

stride [straɪd] **1.** (**strode, stridden**) schreiten, mit großen Schritten gehen; **2.** großer Schritt

strife [straɪf] Streit m

strike [straɪk] **1.** (**struck**) v/t. schlagen; treffen; einschlagen in (acc.) (Blitz); Streichholz anzünden; naut. auflaufen auf (acc.); streichen (**from, off** aus e-m Verzeichnis etc., von e-r Liste etc.); stoßen auf (Öl, e-e Straße, Schwierigkeiten etc.); j-n beeindrucken; j-m einfallen, in den Sinn kommen; Münze prägen; Saite etc. anschlagen; Lager, Zelt abbrechen; Flagge, Segel streichen; v/i. schlagen (Uhr); einschlagen (Blitz); econ. streiken; **~ (out) at s.o.** auf j-n einschlagen; **2.** econ. Streik m; (Öl- etc.)Fund m; mil. Angriff m; Fußball: Schuß m; **be on ~** streiken; **go on ~** streiken, in den Streik treten; **a lucky ~** ein Glückstreffer; **'strik·er** econ. Streikende(r m) f; Fußball: Stürmer(in); **'strik·ing** auffallend

string [strɪŋ] **1.** Schnur f, Bindfaden m; (Schürzen-, Schuh- etc.)Band n; (Puppenspiel)Faden m, Draht m; (Perlenetc.)Schnur f; Saite f (e-r Gitarre, e-s Tennisschlägers etc.); (Bogen)Sehne f; Faser f (von Gemüse); Computer: Zeichenfolge f; fig. Reihe f, Serie f; **the ~s** pl. mus. die Streichinstrumente pl.; die Streicher pl.; **pull a few ~s** fig. ein paar Beziehungen spielen lassen; **with no ~s attached** fig. ohne Bedingungen; **2.** (**strung**) Perlen etc. aufreihen; Gitarre etc. besaiten, Tennisschläger etc. bespannen; Bohnen abziehen; **3.** mus. Streich...; **~ 'bean** bsd. Am. bot. grüne Bohne

strin·gent ['strɪndʒənt] streng

string·y ['strɪŋɪ] (**-ier, -iest**) fas(e)rig

strip [strɪp] **1.** (**-pp-**) v/i. a. **~ off** sich ausziehen (**to** bis auf acc.); v/t. ausziehen; Farbe etc. abkratzen, Tapete etc. abreißen (**from, off** von); a. **~ down** tech. zerlegen, auseinandernehmen; **~ s.o. of s.th.** j-m et. rauben od. wegnehmen; **2.** (Land-, Papier- etc.)Streifen m; Strip m

stripe [straɪp] Streifen m; **~d** gestreift

strode [strəʊd] pret. von **stride** 1

stroke [strəʊk] **1.** streicheln; streichen über; **2.** Schlag m (a. e-r Uhr, Tennis etc.); med. Schlag(anfall) m; (Pinsel)Strich m; Schwimmen: Zug m; tech. Hub m; **four-~ engine** Viertaktmotor m; **~ of luck** fig. ein glücklicher Zufall

stroll [strəʊl] **1.** bummeln, spazieren; **2.** Bummel m, Spaziergang m; **'~er** ['strəʊlə] Bummler(in), Spaziergänger(in); Am. Sportwagen m (für Kinder)

strong [strɒŋ] stark; kräftig; mächtig (Land etc.); stabil (Möbel etc.); fest (Schuhe etc.); robust (Person, Gesundheit etc.); stark (Getränk, Medikament etc.); **'~box** (Geld-, Stahl)Kassette f; **'~hold** Festung f; Stützpunkt m; fig. Hochburg f; **~'mind·ed** willensstark; **~ room** Tresor(raum) m

struck [strʌk] pret. u. p.p. von **strike** 1

struc·ture ['strʌktʃə] Struktur f; (Auf)Bau m, Gliederung f; Bau m, Konstruktion f

strug·gle ['strʌgl] **1.** kämpfen, ringen (**with** mit; **for** um); sich abmühen; sich winden, zappeln; **2.** Kampf m

strum [strʌm] (**-mm-**) klimpern auf (dat.) (od. on auf dat.)

strung [strʌŋ] pret. u. p.p. von **string** 2

strut¹ [strʌt] (**-tt-**) stolzieren

strut² *tech.* [strʌt] Strebe *f*; Stütze *f*

stub [stʌb] **1.** (*Bleistift-, Zigaretten- etc.*) Stummel *m*; Kontrollabschnitt *m*; **2.** (*-bb-*) sich *die Zehe* anstoßen; **~ out** *Zigarette* ausdrücken

stub·ble ['stʌbl] Stoppeln *pl.*

stub·born ['stʌbən] eigensinnig, stur; hartnäckig (*Fleck, Widerstand etc.*)

stuck [stʌk] *pret. u. p.p. von* **stick** 2; **~ up** F hochnäsig

stud¹ [stʌd] **1.** (*Kragen-, Manschetten*) Knopf *m*; Stollen *m* (*e-s Fußballschuhs*); Beschlagnagel *m*; Ziernagel *m*; **~s** *pl. mot.* Spikes *pl.*; **2.** (*-dd-*): *be* **~ded with** besetzt sein mit; übersät sein mit; **~ded tyres** (*Am.* **tires**) Spikesreifen *pl.*

stud² [stʌd] Gestüt *n*

stu·dent ['stju:dnt] Student(in); *bsd. Am. u. allg.* Schüler(in)

'stud| farm Gestüt *n*; **'~ horse** Zuchthengst *m*

stud·ied ['stʌdɪd] wohlüberlegt

stu·di·o ['stju:dɪəʊ] (*pl. -os*) Studio *n*; Atelier *n*; *a.* **~ flat** *Brt.*, **~ apartment** *bsd. Am.* Studio *n*, Einzimmerappartement *n*; **'~ couch** Schlafcouch *f*

stu·di·ous ['stju:djəs] fleißig

stud·y ['stʌdɪ] **1.** Studium *n*; Studie *f*, Untersuchung *f*; Arbeitszimmer *n*; *bsd. paint.* Studie *f*; **studies** *pl.* Studium *n*; *be in a brown* **~** in Gedanken versunken *od.* geistesabwesend sein; **2.** studieren; lernen (*for* für)

stuff [stʌf] **1.** Zeug *n*; **2.** (aus-, voll)stopfen; füllen (*a. gastr.*); △ *nicht* **stopfen** (*ausbessern*); **~ o.s.** F sich vollstopfen; **'~ing** Füllung *f* (*a. gastr.*); **'~y** (*-ier, -iest*) stickig; spießig; prüde

stum·ble ['stʌmbl] **1.** stolpern (*on, over, fig. at, over* über *acc.*); **~ across, ~ on** stoßen auf (*acc.*); **2.** Stolpern *n*

stump [stʌmp] **1.** Stumpf *m*; Stummel *m*; **2.** stampfen, stapfen; **'~y** (*-ier, -iest*) F kurz u. dick

stun [stʌn] (*-nn-*) betäuben; *fig.* sprachlos machen

stung [stʌŋ] *pret. u. p.p. von* **sting** 1

stunk [stʌŋk] *pret. u. p.p. von* **stink** 1

stun·ning ['stʌnɪŋ] phantastisch; unglaublich (*Nachricht etc.*)

stunt¹ [stʌnt] (*das Wachstum gen.*) hemmen; **~ed** verkümmert

stunt² [stʌnt] (*Film*)Stunt *m*; (*gefährliches*) Kunststück; (*Reklame*)Gag *m*; **'~**

man (*pl. -men*) *Film, TV*: Stuntman *m*, Double *n*; **'~ wom·an** (*pl. -women*) *Film, TV*: Stuntwoman *f*, Double *n*

stu·pid ['stju:pɪd] dumm; *fig.* blöd; **~·i·ty** [stju:'pɪdətɪ] Dummheit *f*

stu·por ['stju:pə] Betäubung *f*; *in a drunken* **~** im Vollrausch

stur·dy ['stɜ:dɪ] (*-ier, -iest*) kräftig, stämmig; *fig.* entschlossen, hartnäckig

stut·ter ['stʌtə] **1.** stottern (*a. mot.*); stammeln; **2.** Stottern *n*

sty¹ [staɪ] → **pigsty**

sty², stye *med.* [staɪ] Gerstenkorn *n*

style [staɪl] **1.** Stil *m*; Ausführung *f*; Mode *f*; **2.** entwerfen; gestalten

styl·ish ['staɪlɪʃ] stilvoll; modisch, elegant; **'~·ist** Stilist(in)

sty·lus ['staɪləs] Nadel *f* (*e-s Plattenspielers*)

sty·ro·foam ['staɪərəfəʊm] *TM bsd. Am.* Styropor *n* (*TM*)

suave [swɑːv] verbindlich

sub·di·vi·sion ['sʌbdɪvɪʒn] Unterteilung *f*; Unterabteilung *f*

sub·due [səb'djuː] unterwerfen; *Ärger etc.* unterdrücken; **~d** gedämpft (*Licht, Stimme etc.*); ruhig, still (*Person*)

sub·ject 1. ['sʌbdʒɪkt] Thema *n*; *ped., univ.* Fach *n*; *gr.* Subjekt *n*, Satzgegenstand *m*; Untertan(in); Staatsangehörige(r *m*) *f*, -bürger(in); **2.** ['sʌbdʒɪkt] *adj.* **~ to** anfällig für; *be* **~ to** a. neigen zu; *be* **~ to** unterliegen (*dat.*); abhängen von; *prices* **~ to change** Preisänderungen vorbehalten; **3.** [səb'dʒekt] unterwerfen; **~ to e-m Test etc. unterziehen; *der Kritik etc.* aussetzen; **~·jec·tion** [səb'dʒekʃn] Unterwerfung *f*; Abhängigkeit *f* (*to* von)

sub·ju·gate ['sʌbdʒʊgeɪt] unterjochen, -werfen

sub·junc·tive *gr.* [səb'dʒʌŋktɪv] *a.* **~ mood** Konjunktiv *m*

sub·|lease [sʌb'liːs], **~'let** (*-tt-; -let*) unter-, weitervermieten

sub·lime [sə'blaɪm] großartig; *fig.* total

sub·ma·chine gun [sʌbmə'ʃiːn -] Maschinenpistole *f*

sub·ma·rine [sʌbmə'riːn] **1.** unterseeisch; **2.** Unterseeboot *n*, U-Boot *n*

sub·merge [səb'mɜːdʒ] tauchen (*U-Boot*); (ein)tauchen (*in in acc.*)

sub·mis·|sion [səb'mɪʃn] Einreichung

f; *Boxen etc.*: Aufgabe f; **~·sive** [səb-'mɪsɪv] unterwürfig

sub·mit [səb'mɪt] (**-tt-**) *Gesuch etc.* einreichen (**to** *dat. od.* bei); sich fügen (**to** *dat. od.* in *acc.*); *Boxen etc.*: aufgeben

sub·or·di·nate 1. [sə'bɔːdnət] untergeordnet (**to** *dat.*); **2.** [sə'bɔːdnət] Untergebene(r *m*) f; **3.** [sə'bɔːdneɪt]: **~ to** unterordnen (*dat.*), zurückstellen (hinter *acc.*); **~ 'clause** gr. Nebensatz m

sub|·scribe [səb'skraɪb] *v/t.* Geld geben, spenden (**to** für); *v/i.* **~ to** *Zeitung etc.* abonnieren; **~'scrib·er** Abonnent(in); (*Fernsprech*)Teilnehmer(in)

sub·scrip·tion [səb'skrɪpʃn] (Mitglieds)Beitrag m; Abonnement n

sub·se·quent ['sʌbsɪkwənt] später

sub·side [səb'saɪd] sich senken (*Gebäude, Straße etc.*); zurückgehen (*Überschwemmung, Nachfrage etc.*), sich legen (*Sturm, Zorn etc.*)

sub·sid·i·a·ry [səb'sɪdjərɪ] **1.** Neben...; **~ question** Zusatzfrage f; **2.** *econ.* Tochtergesellschaft f

sub·si|·dize ['sʌbsɪdaɪz] subventionieren; **~·dy** ['sʌbsɪdɪ] Subvention f

sub|·sist [səb'sɪst] leben, existieren (**on** von); **~'sis·tence** Existenz f

sub·stance ['sʌbstəns] Substanz f (*a. fig.*), Stoff m; *das* Wesentliche, Kern m

sub·stan·dard [sʌb'stændəd] minderwertig

sub·stan·tial [səb'stænʃl] solid (*Möbelstück etc.*); beträchtlich (*Gehalt etc.*), (*Änderungen etc. a.*) wesentlich; reichlich, kräftig (*Mahlzeit*)

sub·stan·ti·ate [səb'stænʃɪeɪt] beweisen

sub·stan·tive gr. ['sʌbstəntɪv] Substantiv n, Hauptwort n

sub·sti|·tute ['sʌbstɪtjuːt] **1.** Ersatz m; Ersatz(mann) m, Stellvertreter m, Vertretung f; *Sport*: Auswechselspieler(in), Ersatzspieler(in); **2. ~ s.th. for s.th.** et. durch et. ersetzen, et. gegen et. austauschen *od.* -wechseln; **~ for** einspringen für, j-n vertreten; **~·tu·tion** [sʌbstɪ'tjuːʃn] Ersatz m; *Sport*: Austausch m, Auswechslung f

sub·ter·fuge ['sʌbtəfjuːdʒ] List f

sub·ter·ra·ne·an [sʌbtə'reɪnjən] unterirdisch

sub·ti·tle ['sʌbtaɪtl] Untertitel m

sub·tle ['sʌtl] (**~·r, ~st**) fein (*Unterschied etc.*); raffiniert (*Plan etc.*); scharf (*Ver-*

stand); scharfsinnig (*Person*)

sub|·tract *math.* [səb'trækt] abziehen, subtrahieren (**from** von); **~'trac·tion** *math.* [səb'trækʃn] Abziehen n, Subtraktion f

sub·trop·i·cal [sʌb'trɒpɪkl] subtropisch

sub|·urb ['sʌbɜːb] Vorort m, -stadt f; **~·ur·ban** [sə'bɜːbən] Vorort..., vorstädtisch, Vorstadt...

sub·ver·sive [səb'vɜːsɪv] umstürzlerisch, subversiv

sub·way ['sʌbweɪ] Unterführung f; *Am.* U-Bahn f

suc·ceed [sək'siːd] *v/i.* Erfolg haben, erfolgreich sein (*Person*), (*Plan etc. a.*) gelingen; **~ to** in e-m Amt nachfolgen; **~ to the throne** auf dem Thron folgen; *v/t.* **~ s.o. as** j-s Nachfolger werden als

suc·cess [sək'ses] Erfolg m; **~·ful** erfolgreich

suc·ces|·sion [sək'seʃn] (Erb-, Nach-, Thron)Folge f; **five times in ~** fünfmal nach- *od.* hintereinander; **in quick ~** in rascher Folge; **~'sive** [sək'sesɪv] aufeinanderfolgend; **~·sor** [sək'sesə] Nachfolger(in); Thronfolger(in)

suc·cu·lent ['sʌkjʊlənt] saftig (*Steak etc.*)

such [sʌtʃ] solche(r, -s); derartige(r, -s); so; derart; **all of a ~** so ein(e)

suck [sʌk] **1.** *v/t.* saugen; lutschen (an *dat.*); *v/i.* saugen (**at** an *dat.*); **2. have od. take a ~ at** saugen *od.* lutschen an (*dat.*); **~·er** zo. Saugnapf m, -organ n; *tech.* Saugfuß m; *bot.* Wurzelschößling m, -sproß m; F Trottel m, Simpel m; *Am.* Lutscher m; **~·le** ['sʌkl] säugen, stillen

suc·tion ['sʌkʃn] (An)Saugen n; Saugwirkung f; **~ pump** *tech.* Saugpumpe f

sud·den ['sʌdn] plötzlich; **all of a ~** F ganz plötzlich; **~·ly** plötzlich

suds [sʌdz] *pl.* Seifenschaum m

sue *jur.* [suː] j-n verklagen (**for** auf *acc.*, wegen); klagen (**for** auf *acc.*)

suede, suède [sweɪd] Wildleder n; Veloursleder n

su·et ['suɪt] Nierenfett n, Talg m

suf·fer ['sʌfə] *v/i.* leiden (**from** an, unter *dat.*); darunter leiden; *v/t.* erleiden; *Folgen* tragen; **~·er** ['sʌfərə] Leidende(r m) f; **~·ing** ['sʌfərɪŋ] Leiden n; Leid n

suf·fice [sə'faɪs] genügen, (aus)reichen

suf·fi·cient [sə'fɪʃnt] genügend, genug, ausreichend; **be** ~ genügen, (aus)reichen

suf·fix gr. ['sʌfɪks] Suffix n, Nachsilbe f

suf·fo·cate ['sʌfəkeɪt] ersticken

suf·frage pol. ['sʌfrɪdʒ] Wahl-, Stimmrecht n

suf·fuse [sə'fjuːz] durchfluten (Licht); überziehen (Röte etc.)

sug·ar ['ʃʊgə] **1.** Zucker m; **2.** zuckern; **'~ bowl** Zuckerdose f; **'~cane** bot. Zuckerrohr n; **~y** ['ʃʊgərɪ] zuck(e)rig; fig. zuckersüß

sug·gest [sə'dʒest] vorschlagen, anregen; hindeuten od. -weisen auf (acc.), schließen lassen auf (acc.); andeuten; **~ges·tion** [sə'dʒestʃən] Vorschlag m, Anregung f; Anflug m, Spur f; Andeutung f; psych. Suggestion f; **~ges·tive** [sə'dʒestɪv] zweideutig (Bemerkung etc.), vielsagend (Blick etc.)

su·i·cide ['sjʊɪsaɪd] Selbstmord m; Selbstmörder(in); **commit** ~ Selbstmord begehen

suit [suːt] **1.** Anzug m; Kostüm n; Kartenspiel: Farbe f; jur. Prozeß m; **follow** ~ fig. dem Beispiel folgen, dasselbe tun; **2.** v/t. j-m passen (Termin etc.); j-n kleiden, j-m stehen; et. anpassen (to dat.); ~ **s.th.**, **be** ~**ed to s.th.** geeignet sein od. sich eignen für; ~ **yourself!** mach, was du willst! **'suit·a·ble** passend, geeignet (**for, to** für); **'~case** Koffer m

suite [swiːt] (Möbel-, Sitz)Garnitur f; Suite f; Zimmerflucht f; mus. Suite f; Gefolge n

sul·fur Am. ['sʌlfə] → sulphur

sulk [sʌlk] schmollen, eingeschnappt sein; ~ pl.: **have the** ~ schmollen

sulk·y[1] ['sʌlkɪ] (-ier, -iest) schmollend

sulk·y[2] ['sʌlkɪ] Trabrennen: Sulky n

sul·len ['sʌlən] mürrisch, verdrossen

sul·phur chem. ['sʌlfə] Schwefel m; **~phu·ric ac·id** chem. [sʌlfjʊərɪk 'æsɪd] Schwefelsäure f

sul·try ['sʌltrɪ] (-ier, -iest) schwül; aufreizend (Blick etc.)

sum [sʌm] **1.** Summe f; Betrag m; (einfache) Rechenaufgabe; **do** ~**s** rechnen; **2.** (-mm-): ~ **up** zusammenfassen; j-n, et. abschätzen

sum·ma·rize ['sʌməraɪz] zusammenfassen; **~ma·ry** ['sʌmərɪ] Zusammenfassung f, (kurze) Inhaltsangabe

sum·mer ['sʌmə] Sommer m; **in** (**the**) ~ im Sommer; **'~ camp** Ferienlager n (für Kinder im Sommer); ~ **'hol·i·days** pl. Sommerferien pl.; ~ **re'sort** Sommerfrische f (Ort); **'~ school** Ferienkurs m; **'~time** Sommer(szeit f) m; **in** (**the**) ~ im Sommer; **~time** bsd. Brt. Sommerzeit f (Uhrzeit); ~ **va'ca·tion** bsd. Am. Sommerferien pl.; **~y** ['sʌmərɪ] sommerlich, Sommer...

sum·mit ['sʌmɪt] Gipfel m (a. econ., pol., fig.); **'~ con·fe·rence** pol. Gipfelkonferenz f; **'~ meet·ing** pol. Gipfeltreffen n

sum·mon ['sʌmən] auffordern; Versammlung etc. einberufen; jur. vorladen; ~ **up** Kraft, Mut etc. zusammennehmen; **~s** [~z] Vorladung f

sump·tu·ous ['sʌmptʃʊəs] luxuriös, aufwendig

sun [sʌn] **1.** Sonne f; Sonnen...; **2.** (-nn-) ~ **o.s.** sich sonnen

Sun nur geschr. Abk. für **Sunday** So., Sonntag m

'sun·bathe sonnenbaden, sich sonnen, ein Sonnenbad nehmen; **'~beam** Sonnenstrahl m; **'~bed** Sonnenbank f; **'~burn** Sonnenbrand m

sun·dae ['sʌndeɪ] Eisbecher m

Sun·day ['sʌndɪ] (Abk. **Sun**) Sonntag m; **on** ~ (am) Sonntag; **on** ~**s** sonntags

'sun·di·al ['sʌndaɪəl] Sonnenuhr f; **'~down** → sunset

sun·dries ['sʌndrɪz] pl. Diverse(s) n, Verschiedene(s) n; **~dry** ['sʌndrɪ] diverse, verschiedene

sung [sʌŋ] pret. von sing

'sun·glass·es pl. (**a pair of** ~ e-e) Sonnenbrille

sunk [sʌŋk] pret. u. p.p. von sink 1

sunk·en ['sʌŋkən] ge-, versunken; versenkt; tiefliegend; eingefallen (Wangen), (a. Augen) eingesunken

'sun·light Sonnenlicht n; **'~lit** sonnenbeschienen

sun·ny ['sʌnɪ] (-ier, -iest) sonnig

'sun·rise Sonnenaufgang m; **at** ~ bei Sonnenaufgang; **'~roof** Dachterrasse f; mot. Schiebedach n; **'~set** Sonnenuntergang m; **at** ~ bei Sonnenuntergang; **'~shade** Sonnenschirm m; **'~shine** Sonnenschein m; **'~stroke** med. Sonnenstich m; **'~tan** (Sonnen)Bräune f

su·per F ['suːpə] super, spitze, klasse

su·per... ['suːpə] Über..., über...

su·per|·a·bun·dant [suːpərə'bandənt] überreichlich; **~·an·nu·at·ed** [suːpə-'rænjʊeɪtɪd] pensioniert, im Ruhestand

su·perb [suːˈpɜːb] ausgezeichnet

'**su·per|·charg·er** mot. Kompressor m; **~·cil·i·ous** [suːpəˈsɪlɪəs] hochmütig, -näsig; **~·fi·cial** [suːpəˈfɪʃl] oberflächlich; **~·flu·ous** [suːˈpɜːflʊəs] überflüssig; **~·hu·man** übermenschlich; **~·im·pose** [suːpərɪmˈpəʊz] überlagern; Bild etc. einblenden (**on** in acc.); Mother 2 rel. Oberin 2; **2.** Vorgesetzte(r m) f; **~·i·ty** [suːpɪərɪˈɒrətɪ] Überlegenheit f (**over** gegenüber)

su·pe·ri·or [suːˈpɪərɪə] **1.** ranghöher (**to** als); überlegen (**to** dat.), besser (**to** als); ausgezeichnet, hervorragend; überheblich, -legen; Father 2 rel. Superior m; Mother 2 rel. Oberin 2; **2.** Vorgesetzte(r m) f; **~·i·ty** [suːpɪərɪˈɒrətɪ] Überlegenheit f (**over** gegenüber)

su·per·la·tive [suːˈpɜːlətɪv] **1.** höchste(r, -s), überragend; **2.** a. **~ degree** gr. Superlativ m

'**su·per|·mar·ket** Supermarkt m; **~·nat·u·ral** übernatürlich; **~·nu·me·ra·ry** [suːpəˈnjuːmərərɪ] zusätzlich; **~·sede** [suːpəˈsiːd] ablösen, ersetzen; **~·son·ic** aviat., phys. Überschall...; **~·sti·tion** [suːpəˈstɪʃn] Aberglaube m; **~·sti·tious** [suːpəˈstɪʃəs] abergläubisch; '**~·store** Großmarkt m; **~·vene** [suːpəˈviːn] dazwischenkommen; **~·vise** ['suːpəvaɪz] beaufsichtigen; **~·vi·sion** [suːpəˈvɪʒn] Beaufsichtigung f; **under s.o.'s ~** unter j-s Aufsicht; **~·vi·sor** ['suːpəvaɪzə] Aufseher(in), Aufsicht f

sup·per ['sʌpə] Abendessen n; **have ~** zu Abend essen; → **lord**

sup·plant [səˈplɑːnt] verdrängen

sup·ple ['sʌpl] (**~r, ~st**) gelenkig, geschmeidig, biegsam

sup·ple|·ment [ˈsʌplɪmənt] Ergänzung f; Nachtrag m, Anhang m; Ergänzungsband m; (Zeitungs- etc.)Beilage f; **2.** [ˈsʌplɪment] ergänzen; **~·men·ta·ry** [sʌplɪˈmentərɪ] ergänzend, zusätzlich

sup·pli·er [səˈplaɪə] Lieferant(in); a. **~s** pl. Lieferfirma f

sup·ply [səˈplaɪ] **1.** liefern; stellen, sorgen für; j-n, et. versorgen, econ. beliefern (**with** mit); **2.** Lieferung f (**to** an acc.); Versorgung f; econ. Angebot n; mst **supplies** pl. Vorrat m (**of** an dat.), a. Proviant m, mil. Nachschub m; **~ and demand** econ. Angebot u. Nachfrage

sup·port [səˈpɔːt] **1.** (ab)stützen, Gewicht etc. tragen; Währung stützen; unterstützen; unterhalten, sorgen für (Familie etc.); **2.** Stütze f; tech. Träger m; fig. Unterstützung f; **~·er** Anhänger(in) (a. Sport), Befürworter(in)

sup|·pose [səˈpəʊz] **1.** annehmen, vermuten; **be ~d to ...** sollen; **what is that ~d to mean?** was soll denn das?; **I ~ so** ich nehme es an, vermutlich; **2.** cj. angenommen; wie wäre es, wenn; **~·posed** angeblich; **~·pos·ing →** **suppose** 2; **~·po·si·tion** [sʌpəˈzɪʃn] Annahme f, Vermutung f

sup|·press [səˈpres] unterdrücken; **~·pres·sion** [səˈpreʃn] Unterdrückung f

sup·pu·rate med. [ˈsʌpjʊəreɪt] eitern

su·prem·a·cy [sʊˈpreməsɪ] Vormachtstellung f

su·preme [suːˈpriːm] höchste(r, -s), oberste(r, -s), Ober...; höchste(r, -s), größte(r, -s)

sur·charge 1. [sɜːˈtʃɑːdʒ] Nachporto od. e-n Zuschlag erheben (**on** auf acc.); **2.** ['sɜːtʃɑːdʒ] Auf-, Zuschlag m (**on** auf acc.); Nach-, Strafporto n (**on** auf acc.)

sure [ʃɔː] **1.** adj. (**~r, ~st**) sicher; **~ of o.s.** selbstsicher; **~ of winning** siegessicher; **~ thing!** bsd. Am. F (aber) klar!; **be od. feel ~** sicher sein; **be ~ to ...** vergiß nicht zu ...; **for ~** ganz sicher od. bestimmt; **make ~ that** sich (davon) überzeugen, daß; **to be ~** sicher(lich); **2.** adv. F sicher, klar; **~ enough** tatsächlich; '**~·ly** sicher(lich); **sur·e·ty** [ˈʃɔːrətɪ] Bürge m, -in f; Bürgschaft f, Sicherheit f; **stand ~ for s.o.** für j-n bürgen

surf [sɜːf] **1.** Brandung f; **2.** Sport: surfen

sur·face ['sɜːfɪs] **1.** Oberfläche f; (Straßen)Belag m; **2.** auftauchen; Straße mit e-m Belag versehen; **3.** Oberflächen...; fig. oberflächlich; '**~ mail** gewöhnliche Post (Gegensatz Luftpost)

'**surf|·board** Surfboard n, -brett n; '**~**

er Surfer(in), Wellenreiter(in); '**~·ing** Surfen n, Wellenreiten n

surge [sɜːdʒ] **1.** fig. Welle f, Woge f, (Gefühls)Aufwallung f; **2.** (vorwärts-) drängen; ~ (**up**) aufwallen (Zorn etc.)

sur·geon ['sɜːdʒən] Chirurg(in)

sur·ge·ry ['sɜːdʒərɪ] Chirurgie f; operativer Eingriff, Operation f; Brt. Sprechzimmer n; Brt. Sprechstunde f; a. **doctor's** ~ Arztpraxis f; '~ **hours** pl. Brt. Sprechstunde(n pl.) f

sur·gi·cal ['sɜːdʒɪkl] chirurgisch

sur·ly ['sɜːlɪ] (**-ier, -iest**) mürrisch

sur·name ['sɜːneɪm] Familien-, Nach-, Zuname m

sur·pass [sə'pɑːs] Erwartungen etc. übertreffen

sur·plus ['sɜːpləs] **1.** Überschuß m (of an dat.); **2.** überschüssig

sur·prise [sə'praɪz] **1.** Überraschung f; **take s.o. by** ~ j-n überraschen; **2.** überraschen; **be ~d at** od. **by** überrascht sein über (acc.)

sur·ren·der [sə'rendə] **1.** v/i. ~ **to** mil., a. fig. sich ergeben (dat.), kapitulieren vor (dat.); ~ **to the police** sich der Polizei stellen; v/t. et. übergeben, ausliefern (to dat.); aufgeben, verzichten auf (acc.); ~ **o.s. to the police** sich der Polizei stellen; **2.** mil. Kapitulation f (a. fig.); Aufgabe f, Verzicht m

sur·ro·gate ['sʌrəɡeɪt] Ersatz m; ~ '**moth·er** Leihmutter f

sur·round [sə'raʊnd] umgeben; Haus etc. umstellen; **~·ing** umliegend; **~·ings** pl. Umgebung f

sur·vey 1. [sə'veɪ] (sich) et. betrachten (a. fig.); Haus etc. begutachten; Land vermessen; **2.** ['sɜːveɪ] Umfrage f; Überblick m (of über acc.); Begutachtung f; Vermessung f; **~·or** [sə'veɪə] Gutachter(in); Land(ver)messer(in)

sur·vi·val [sə'vaɪvl] Überleben n (a. fig.); Überbleibsel n; ~ **kit** Überlebensausrüstung f; ~ **train·ing** Überlebenstraining n

sur|·vive [sə'vaɪv] überleben; Feuer etc. überstehen (Gebäude etc.); erhalten bleiben od. sein; '~·**vi·vor** Überlebende(r m) f (**from, of** gen.)

sus·cep·ti·ble [sə'septəbl] empfänglich od. anfällig (**to** für)

sus·pect 1. [sə'spekt] j-n verdächtigen (**of** gen.); et. vermuten; et. an-, bezwei-

feln; **2.** ['sʌspekt] Verdächtige(r m) f; **3.** ['sʌspekt] verdächtig, suspekt

sus·pend [sə'spend] Verkauf, Zahlungen etc. (vorübergehend) einstellen; jur. Verfahren, Urteil aussetzen, Strafe zur Bewährung aussetzen; j-n suspendieren; vorübergehend ausschließen (**from** aus); Sport: j-n sperren; (auf)hängen; **be ~ed** schweben; **~·er** Brt. Strumpfhalter m, Straps m; Sokkenhalter m; (a. **a pair of**) **~s** pl. Am. Hosenträger pl.

sus·pense [sə'spens] Spannung f; **in** ~ gespannt, voller Spannung

sus·pen·sion [sə'spenʃn] (vorübergehende) Einstellung; Suspendierung f; vorübergehender Ausschluß f; Sport: Sperre f; mot. etc. Aufhängung f; ~ **bridge** Hängebrücke f; ~ **rail·way** bsd. Brt. Schwebebahn f

sus·pi·cion [sə'spɪʃn] Verdacht m; Argwohn m, Mißtrauen n; fig. Hauch m, Spur f; **~·cious** verdächtig; argwöhnisch, mißtrauisch

sus·tain [sə'steɪn] j-n stärken; Interesse etc. aufrechterhalten; Schaden, Verlust erleiden; jur. e-m Einspruch etc. stattgeben

SW nur geschr. Abk. für: **southwest** SW, Südwest(en m); **southwest(ern)** sw, südwestlich

swab [swɒb] **1.** Tupfer m; Abstrich m; **2.** (**-bb-**) Wunde abtupfen

swad·dle ['swɒdl] Baby wickeln

swag·ger ['swæɡə] stolzieren

swal·low¹ ['swɒləʊ] **1.** (hinunter-) schlucken (a. fig.); Beleidigung einstecken, schlucken; F für bare Münze nehmen; **2.** Schluck m

swal·low² zo. ['swɒləʊ] Schwalbe f

swam [swæm] pret. von **swim** 1

swamp [swɒmp] **1.** Sumpf m; **2.** überschwemmen; **be ~ed with** fig. überschwemmt werden mit; '~·y (**-ier, -iest**) sumpfig

swan zo. [swɒn] Schwan m

swank F [swæŋk] **1.** angeben; **2.** Angabe f; Angeber(in); '~·y (**-ier, -iest**) F schick, piekfein; angeberisch

swap F [swɒp] **1.** (**-pp-**) (ein)tauschen; **2.** Tausch m

swarm [swɔːm] **1.** Schwarm m (Bienen, Touristen etc.); **2.** schwärmen (Bienen), (Menschen a.) strömen; wimmeln (**with** von)

swar·thy ['swɔːðɪ] (**-ier, -iest**) dunkel (*Haut*), dunkelhäutig (*Person*)

swat [swɒt] (**-tt-**) *Fliege etc.* totschlagen

sway [sweɪ] **1.** *v/i.* sich wiegen, schaukeln; ~ **between** *fig.* schwanken zwischen (*dat.*); *v/t.* hin- u. herbewegen, schwenken, *s-n Körper* wiegen; beeinflussen; **2.** Schwanken *n*, Schaukeln *n*

swear [sweə] (**swore, sworn**) fluchen; schwören; ~ **at s.o.** j-n wüst beschimpfen; ~ **by** *fig.* F schwören auf (*acc.*); ~ **s.o. in** j-n vereidigen

sweat [swet] **1.** (**sweated, Am. a. sweat**) *v/i.* schwitzen (**with** vor *dat.*); *v/t.* ~ **out** *Krankheit* ausschwitzen; ~ **blood** F sich abrackern (**over** mit); **2.** Schweiß *m*; F Schufterei *f*; **get in(to) a** ~ *fig.* F ins Schwitzen geraten *od.* kommen; **'~er** Pullover *m*; **'~·shirt** Sweatshirt *n*; **'~·y** (**-ier, -iest**) schweißig, verschwitzt; nach Schweiß riechend, Schweiß...; schweißtreibend

Swede [swiːd] Schwed|e *m*, -in *f*; **Swe·den** ['swiːdn] Schweden *n*; **Swe·dish** ['swiːdɪʃ] **1.** schwedisch; **2.** *ling.* Schwedisch *n*

sweep [swiːp] **1.** (**swept**) *v/t.* kehren, fegen; fegen über (*acc.*) (*Sturm etc.*); *Horizont etc.* absuchen (**for** nach); *fig. Land etc.* überschwemmen; ~ **along** mitreißen; *v/i.* kehren, fegen; rauschen (*Person*); **2.** Kehren, Fegen *n*; Hieb *m*, Schlag *m*; F Schornsteinfeger(in), Kaminkehrer(in); **give the floor a good** ~ den Boden gründlich kehren *od.* fegen; **make a clean** ~ gründlich aufräumen; *Sport:* gründlich abräumen; **'~·er** (*Straßen*)Kehrer(in), Kehrmaschine *f*; *Fußball:* Libero *m*; **'~·ing** durchgreifend (*Änderung etc.*); pauschal, zu allgemein; **'~·ings** *pl.* Kehricht *m*

sweet [swiːt] **1.** süß (*a. fig.*); lieblich; lieb; ~ **nothings** *pl.* Zärtlichkeiten *pl.*; **have a** ~ **tooth** gern naschen; **2.** *Brt.* Süßigkeit *f*; Bonbon *m, n*; *Brt.* Nachtisch *m*; **'~ corn** *bsd. Brt. bot.* Zuckermais *m*; **'~·en** süßen; *Brt.* Schatz *m*, Liebste(r *m*) *f*; **'~ pea** *bot.* Gartenwicke *f*; **'~ shop** *bsd. Brt.* Süßwarengeschäft *n*

swell [swel] **1.** (**swelled, swollen** *od.* **swelled**) *v/i. a.* ~ **up** *med.* (an)schwellen; *a.* ~ **out** sich blähen (*Segel*); *v/t. fig.*

Zahl etc. anwachsen lassen; *a.* ~ **out** *Segel* blähen; **2.** *naut.* Dünung *f*; **3.** *Am.* F klasse; **'~·ing** *med.* Schwellung *f*

swel·ter ['sweltə] vor Hitze fast umkommen

swept [swept] *pret. u. p.p. von* **sweep** 1

swerve [swɜːv] **1.** schwenken (**to the left** nach links), e-n Schwenk machen; *fig.* abweichen (**from** von); **2.** Schwenk(ung *f*) *m, mot. etc. a.* Schlenker *m*

swift [swɪft] schnell

swim [swɪm] **1.** (**-mm-; swam, swum**) *v/i.* schwimmen; *fig.* verschwimmen; **my head was** ~**ming** mir drehte sich alles; *v/t. Strecke* schwimmen; *Fluß etc.* durchschwimmen; **2.** Schwimmen *n*; **go for a** ~ schwimmen gehen; **'~·mer** Schwimmer(in)

'swim·ming Schwimmen *n*; **'~ bath(s** *pl.*) *Brt.* Schwimm-, *bsd.* Hallenbad *n*; **'~ cap** Badekappe *f*, -mütze *f*; **'~ costume** Badeanzug *m*; **'~ pool** Swimmingpool *m*, Schwimmbecken *n*; **'~ trunks** *pl.* Badehose *f*

'swim·suit Badeanzug *m*

swin·dle ['swɪndl] **1.** j-n beschwindeln (**out of** um); △ *nicht* **schwindeln** (*lügen*); **2.** Schwindel *m*

swine [swaɪn] (*pl. zo.* **swine,** *sl. contp. a.* **swines**) Schwein *n*

swing [swɪŋ] **1.** (**swung**) *v/i.* (hin- u. her)schwingen; sich schwingen; einbiegen, -schwenken (**into** in *acc.*); *mus.* schwungvoll spielen (*Band etc.*); **Schwung haben** (*Musik*); ~ **round** sich ruckartig umdrehen; ~ **shut** zuschlagen (*Tor etc.*); *v/t. et., die Arme etc.* schwingen; **2.** Schwingen *n*; Schaukel *f*; *fig.* Schwung *m*; *fig.* Umschwung *m*; **in full** ~ in vollem Gang; **'~·door** Pendeltür *f*

swin·ish ['swaɪnɪʃ] ekelhaft

swipe [swaɪp] **1.** Schlag *m*; **2.** schlagen (**at** nach)

swirl [swɜːl] **1.** wirbeln; **2.** Wirbel *m*

swish¹ [swɪʃ] **1.** *v/i.* sausen, zischen; rascheln (*Seide etc.*); *v/t.* mit *dem Schwanz* schlagen; **2.** Sausen *n*, Zischen *n*; Rascheln *n*; Schlagen *n* (*mit dem Schwanz*)

swish² F [swɪʃ] feudal, schick

Swiss [swɪs] **1.** schweizerisch, eidgenössisch, Schweizer...; **2.** Schweizer(in); **the** ~ *pl.* die Schweizer *pl.*

switch [swɪtʃ] **1.** *electr., tech.* Schalter

m; *Am. rail.* Weiche *f*; Gerte *f*, Rute *f*; *fig.* Umstellung *f*; **2.** *electr., tech.* (um)schalten (*a.* ~ *over*) (*to* auf *acc.*); *Am. rail.* rangieren; wechseln (*to* zu); ~ *off* ab-, ausschalten; ~ *on* an-, einschalten; '~**board** *electr.* Schalttafel *f*; (Telefon)Zentrale *f*

Swit·zer·land ['switsələnd] die Schweiz

swiv·el ['swivl] (*bsd.* Brt. **-ll-**, *Am.* **-l-**) (sich) drehen; '~ **chair** Drehstuhl *m*

swol·len ['swəʊlən] *p.p. von* **swell** 1

swoon [swu:n] in Ohnmacht fallen

swoop [swu:p] **1.** *fig.* F zuschlagen (*Polizei etc.*); *a.* ~ *down* herabstoßen (*on* auf *acc.*) (*Raubvogel*); ~ *on* F herfallen über (*acc.*); **2.** Razzia *f*

swop F [swɒp] → **swap**

sword [sɔ:d] Schwert *n*

swore [swɔ:] *pret. von* **swear**

sworn [swɔ:n] *p.p. von* **swear**

swum [swʌm] *p.p. von* **swim** 1

swung [swʌŋ] *pret. u. p.p. von* **swing** 1

syc·a·more *bot.* ['sıkəmɔ:] Bergahorn *m*; *Am.* Platane *f*

syl·la·ble ['sıləbl] Silbe *f*

syl·la·bus *ped., univ.* ['sıləbəs] (*pl.* **-buses, -bi** [-baı]) Lehrplan *m*

sym·bol ['sımbl] Symbol *n*; ~**ic** [sım'bɒlık] (~**ally**), ~**is·m** ['sımbəlızəm] Symbolik *f*; ~**ize** ['sımbəlaız] symbolisieren

sym|·met·ri·cal [sı'metrıkl] symme-

trisch; ~**me·try** ['sımıtrı] Symmetrie *f*

sym·pa|·thet·ic [sımpə'θetık] (~**ally**) mitfühlend; verständnisvoll; wohlwollend; △ *nicht* **sympathisch**; ~**thize** ['sımpəθaız] mitfühlen; sympathisieren; ~**thy** ['sımpəθı] Mitgefühl *n*; Verständnis *n*; △ *nicht* **Sympathie**

sym·pho·ny ['sımfənı] Symphonie *f*

symp·tom ['sımptəm] Symptom *n*

syn·chro|·nize ['sıŋkrənaız] *v/t.* aufeinander abstimmen; *Uhren, Film* synchronisieren; *v/i.* synchron gehen (*Uhren*) *od.* sein (*Film*)

syn·o·nym ['sınənım] Synonym *n*; **syn·on·y·mous** [sı'nɒnıməs] synonym; gleichbedeutend

syn·tax *gr.* ['sıntæks] Syntax *f*, Satzlehre *f*

syn·the·sis ['sınθəsıs] (*pl.* **-ses** [-si:z]) Synthese *f*

syn·thet·ic *chem.* [sın'θetık] (~**ally**) synthetisch; ~ **'fi·bre** (*Am.* **fi·ber**) Kunstfaser *f*

Syr·i·a ['sırıə] Syrien *n*

sy·ringe ['sırındʒ] Spritze *f*

syr·up ['sırəp] Sirup *m*

sys·tem ['sıstəm] System *n*; (*Straßen-etc.*)Netz *n*; Organismus *m*

sys·te·mat·ic [sıstə'mætık] (~**ally**) systematisch

'sys·tem er·ror *Computer:* Systemfehler *m*

T

T, t [ti:] T, t *n*

t *nur geschr. Abk. für* **ton(s)** Tonne(n *pl.*) *f* (Brt. 1016 kg, *Am.* 907,18 kg)

ta *Brt. int.* F [tɑ:] danke

tab [tæb] Aufhänger *m*, Schlaufe *f*; Lasche *f*; Etikett *n*, Schildchen *n*; Reiter *m* (*Karteikartenzeichen*); F Rechnung *f*

ta·ble ['teıbl] **1.** Tisch *m*; Tisch *m*, (Tisch)Runde *f*; Tabelle *f*, Verzeichnis *n*; *math.* Einmaleins *n*; *at* ~ am Tisch; *turn the* ~*s* (*on s.o.*) *fig.* den Spieß umdrehen; **2.** *fig.* auf den Tisch legen; *bsd. Am. fig.* zurückstel-

len; '~**cloth** Tischdecke *f*, -tuch *n*; '~**land** Tafelland *n*, Plateau *n*, Hochebene *f*; ~ **lin·en** Tischwäsche *f*; '~**mat** Untersetzer *m* (*für heiße Gefäße*); '~**spoon** Eßlöffel *m*

tab·let ['tæblıt] Tablette *f*; Stück *n* (*Seife*); (*Stein- etc.*)Tafel *f*; △ *nicht* **Tablett**

'table|·ten·nis *Sport:* Tischtennis *n*; '~**top** Tischplatte *f*; '~**ware** Geschirr *n* u. Besteck *n*

tab·loid ['tæblɔıd] Boulevardblatt *n*, -zeitung *f*; '~ **press** Boulevardpresse *f*

ta·boo [təˈbuː] **1.** tabu; **2.** (pl. -boos) Tabu n

tab·u·lar [ˈtæbjʊlə] tabellarisch; **∼late** [ˈtæbjʊleɪt] tabellarisch (an)ordnen; '**∼la·tor** Tabulator m

tach·o·graph mot. [ˈtækəʊɡrɑːf] Fahrt(en)schreiber m

ta·chom·e·ter mot. [tæˈkɒmɪtə] Drehzahlmesser m

ta·cit [ˈtæsɪt] stillschweigend; **ta·ci·turn** [ˈtæsɪtɜːn] schweigsam, wortkarg

tack [tæk] **1.** Stift m, (Reiß)Zwecke f; Heftstich m; **2.** heften (to an acc.); ∼ **on** anfügen (to dat.)

tack·le [tæk] **1.** Problem etc. angehen; Fußball etc.: ballführenden Gegner angreifen; j-n zur Rede stellen (**about** wegen); **2.** tech. Flaschenzug m; (Angel)Gerät(e pl.) n; Fußball etc.: Angriff m (auf e-n ballführenden Gegner)

tack·y [ˈtækɪ] (-ier, -iest) klebrig; bsd. Am. F schäbig

tact [tækt] Takt m, Feingefühl n; '**∼ful** taktvoll

tac·tics [ˈtæktɪks] pl. u. sg. Taktik f 'tact·less taktlos

tad·pole zo. [ˈtædpəʊl] Kaulquappe f

taf·fe·ta [ˈtæfɪtə] Taft m

taf·fy Am. [ˈtæfɪ] → toffee

tag [tæɡ] **1.** Etikett n; (Namens-, Preis)Schild n; (Schnürsenkel)Stift m; stehende Redensart f; a. **question** ∼ Frageanhängsel n; **2.** (-gg-) etikettieren; Waren auszeichnen; anhängen; ∼ **along** F mitgehen, -kommen; ∼ **along behind s.o.** hinter j-m hertrotten

tail [teɪl] **1.** Schwanz m; Schweif m; hinterer Teil; F Schatten m, Beschatter(in); **put a** ∼ **on** j-n beschatten lassen; **turn** ∼ fig. sich auf den Absatz umdrehen; **with one's** ∼ **between one's legs** fig. mit eingezogenem Schwanz; ∼**s** pl. Rück-, Kehrseite f (e-r Münze); Frack m; **2.** F j-n beschatten; ∼ **back** bsd. Brt. mot. sich stauen (to bis zu); ∼ **off** schwächer werden, abnehmen, nachlassen; '**∼back** bsd. Brt. mot. Rückstau m; '**∼coat** Frack m; '**∼ end** Ende n, Schluß m; '**∼light** mot. Rücklicht n

tai·lor [ˈteɪlə] **1.** Schneider m; **2.** schneidern; ∼**made** Maß...; maßgeschneidert (a. fig.)

'**tail∣pipe** Am. tech. Auspuffrohr n; '**∼wind** Rückenwind m

taint·ed [ˈteɪntɪd] verdorben (Fleisch etc.); fig. befleckt, belastet

take [teɪk] **1.** (took, taken) v/t. nehmen; (weg)nehmen; mitnehmen; ergreifen; mil. Stadt etc. einnehmen; Schach etc.: Figur, Stein schlagen; Gefangene machen; Prüfung etc. machen; univ. Fachgebiet studieren; Preis: erringen; Scheck etc. (an)nehmen; Rat annehmen; Medizin etc. einnehmen; et. hinnehmen; fassen; Platz bieten für; et. aushalten, ertragen; phot. et. aufnehmen, Aufnahme machen; Temperatur messen; Notiz machen, niederschreiben; ein Bad nehmen; Zug, Bus, Weg etc. nehmen; Gelegenheit, Maßnahmen ergreifen; Mut fassen; Anstoß nehmen; Zeit, Geduld etc. erfordern, brauchen; Zeit dauern; **it took her four hours** sie brauchte vier Stunden; **I** ∼ **it that** ich nehme an, daß; ∼ **it or leave it** F mach, was du willst; ∼**n all in all** im großen (u.) ganzen; **be** ∼**n** besetzt sein (Platz); **be** ∼**n by od. with** angetan sein von; **be** ∼**n ill od. sick** erkranken, krank werden; ∼ **to bits od. pieces** auseinandernehmen, zerlegen; ∼ **the blame** die Schuld auf sich nehmen; ∼ **care** vorsichtig sein, aufpassen; ∼ **care!** F mach's gut!; → **care** 1; ∼ **hold of** ergreifen; ∼ **part** teilnehmen (**in** an dat.); → **part** 1; ∼ **pity on** Mitleid haben mit; **a walk** e-n Spaziergang machen; ∼ **my word for it** verlaß dich drauf; → **advice**, **bath** 1, **break** 1, **lead** 1 2, **message**, **oath**, **place** 1, **prisoner**, **risk** 1, **seat** 1, **step** 1, **trouble** 1, **turn** 2, etc.; v/i. med. wirken, anschlagen; ∼ **after** j-m nachschlagen, ähneln; ∼ **along** mitnehmen; ∼ **apart** auseinandernehmen (a. fig. F), zerlegen; ∼ **away** wegnehmen (**from s.o.** j-m); ... **to** ∼ **away** Brt. ... zum Mitnehmen (Essen), zum Mitnehmen (Essen); ∼ **back** zurückbringen; zurücknehmen; bei j-m Erinnerungen wachrufen; j-n zurückversetzen (**to** in acc.); ∼ **down** herunter-, abnehmen; Hose herunterlassen; auseinandernehmen, zerlegen; (sich) et. aufschreiben od. notieren; sich Notizen machen; ∼ **for: what do you** ∼ **me for?** wofür hältst du mich eigentlich?; ∼ **from** j-m et. wegnehmen; math. abziehen von; ∼ **in** j-n (bei sich) aufnehmen; fig. et. einschließen; Kleidungsstück enger machen; *et.* begreifen; *j-n* hereinlegen; **be ~n in by** hereinfallen auf (*acc.*); **~ off** *Kleidungsstück* ablegen, ausziehen, *Hut etc.* abnehmen; *et.* ab-, wegnehmen, abziehen; *aviat., Raumfahrt:* abheben; *Sport:* abspringen; F sich aufmachen; **~ a day off** sich e-n Tag frei nehmen; **~ on** *j-n* einstellen; *Arbeit etc.* an-, übernehmen; *Farbe, Ausdruck etc.* annehmen; sich anlegen mit; **~ out** herausnehmen, *Zahn* ziehen; *j-n* ausführen, ausgehen mit; *Versicherung* abschließen; *s-n Frust etc.* auslassen (**on** an *dat.*); **~ over** *Amt, Macht, Verantwortung etc.* übernehmen; die Macht übernehmen; **~ to** Gefallen finden an (*dat.*); **~ to doing s.th.** anfangen, et. zu tun; **~ up** *Vorschlag etc.* aufgreifen; *Zeit etc.* in Anspruch nehmen, *Platz* einnehmen; *Erzählung etc.* aufnehmen; **~ up doing s.th.** anfangen, sich mit et. zu beschäftigen; **~ up with** sich einlassen mit; **2.** *Film, TV:* Einstellung *f;* F Einnahmen *pl.*

'**take·a·way** *Brt.* **1.** Essen *n* zum Mitnehmen; **2.** Restaurant *n* mit Straßenverkauf

tak·en ['teɪkən] *p.p. von* **take** 1

'**take-off** *aviat., Raumfahrt:* Abheben *n,* Start *m; Sport:* Absprung *m*

tak·ings ['teɪkɪŋz] *pl.* Einnahmen *pl.*

tale [teɪl] Erzählung *f;* Geschichte *f;* Lüge(ngeschichte) *f,* Märchen *n;* **tell ~s** petzen

tal·ent ['tælənt] Talent *n* (*a. Person*), Begabung *f;* '**~ed** talentiert, begabt

tal·is·man ['tælɪzmən] Talisman *m*

talk [tɔːk] **1.** *v/i.* reden, sprechen, sich unterhalten (**to, with** mit; **about** über *acc.;* **of** von); **~ about s.th.** *a.* et. besprechen; **s.o. to ~ to** Ansprechpartner(in); *v/t.* Unsinn *etc.* reden; reden *od.* sprechen *od.* sich unterhalten über (*acc.*); **~ s.o. into s.th.** j-n zu et. überreden; **~ s.o. out of s.th.** j-m et. ausreden; **~ s.th. over** *Problem etc.* besprechen (**with** mit); **~ round** *j-n* bekehren (**to** zu), umstimmen; **2.** Gespräch *n,* Unterhaltung *f* (**with** mit; **about** über *acc.*); Vortrag *m;* Sprache *f* (*Art zu reden*); Gerede *n,* Geschwätz *n;* **give a ~** e-n Vortrag halten (**to** vor *dat.;* **about, on** über *acc.*); **be the ~ of the town** Stadtgespräch sein; **baby ~** Babysprache *f,* kindliches

Gebabbel; → **small talk**

talk·a·tive ['tɔːkətɪv] gesprächig, geschwätzig, redselig; '**~er:** **be a good ~** gut reden können; '**~·ing-to** (*pl. -tos*) F Standpauke *f;* **give s.o. a ~** j-m e-e Standpauke halten; '**~ show** *bsd. Am. TV* Talk-Show *f;* '**~show 'host** *bsd. Am. TV* Talkmaster *m*

tall [tɔːl] groß (*Person*), hoch (*Gebäude etc.*)

tal·low ['tæləʊ] Talg *m*

tal·ly[1] ['tælɪ] *Sport:* Stand *m;* **keep a ~ of** Buch führen über (*acc.*)

tal·ly[2] ['tælɪ] übereinstimmen (**with** mit); *a.* **~ up** zusammenrechnen, -zählen

tal·on *zo.* ['tælən] Kralle *f,* Klaue *f*

tame [teɪm] **1.** zahm; *fad(e),* lahm; **2.** *Tier* zähmen (*a. fig.*)

tam·per ['tæmpə]: **~ with** sich zu schaffen machen an (*dat.*)

tam·pon *med.* ['tæmpən] Tampon *m*

tan [tæn] **1.** (*-nn-*) *Fell* gerben; bräunen; braun werden; **2.** Gelbbraun *n;* Bräune *f;* **3.** gelbbraun

tang [tæŋ] (scharfer) Geruch *od.* Geschmack

tan·gent ['tændʒənt] *math.* Tangente *f;* **fly** *od.* **go off at a ~** plötzlich (vom Thema) abschweifen

tan·ge·rine *bot.* ['tændʒə'riːn] Mandarine *f*

tan·gi·ble ['tændʒəbl] greifbar, *fig. a.* handfest, klar

tan·gle ['tæŋgl] **1.** (sich) verwirren *od.* verheddern, durcheinanderbringen; durcheinanderkommen; **2.** Gewirr *n,* *fig. a.* Wirrwarr *m,* Durcheinander *n*

tank [tæŋk] *mot. etc.* Tank *m; mil.* Panzer *m*

tank·ard ['tæŋkəd] (Bier)Humpen *m*

tank·er ['tæŋkə] *naut.* Tanker *m,* Tankschiff *n; aviat.* Tankflugzeug *n; mot.* Tankwagen *m*

tan·ner ['tænə] Gerber *m;* **~·ne·ry** ['tænərɪ] Gerberei *f*

tan·ta·lize ['tæntəlaɪz] *j-n* aufreizen; '**~·liz·ing** verlockend

tan·ta·mount ['tæntəmaʊnt]: **be ~ to** gleichbedeutend sein mit, hinauslaufen auf (*acc.*)

tan·trum ['tæntrəm] Wutanfall *m*

tap[1] [tæp] **1.** *tech.* Hahn *m; beer on ~* Bier *n* vom Faß; **2.** (*-pp-*) *Naturschätze etc.* erschließen; *Vorräte etc.* angreifen;

Telefon(leitung) anzapfen, abhören; *Faß* anzapfen, anstechen

tap² [tæp] **1.** (**-pp-**) mit *den Fingern, Füßen* klopfen, mit *den Fingern* trommeln (**on** auf *acc.*); antippen; ~ **s.o. on the shoulder** j-m auf die Schulter klopfen; ~ **on** (leicht) klopfen an (*acc.*) *od.* auf *acc. od.* gegen; **2.** (leichtes) Klopfen; Klaps *m*; '~ **dance** Steptanz *m*

tape [teɪp] **1.** (schmales) Band; Kleb(e)streifen *m*; (Magnet-, Video-, Ton)Band *n*; (Video- *etc.*)Kassette *f*; (Band)Aufnahme *f*; TV Aufzeichnung *f*; Sport: Zielband *n*; → **red tape; 2.** (auf Band) aufnehmen; TV aufzeichnen; *a.* ~ **up** (mit Klebeband) zukleben; '~ **deck** Tapedeck *n*; '~ **meas·ure** Bandmaß *n*, Maß-, Meßband *n*

ta·per ['teɪpə] *a.* ~ **off** spitz zulaufen, sich verjüngen; *fig.* langsam nachlassen

'**tape**| **re·cord·er** Tonbandgerät *n*; '~ **re·cord·ing** Tonbandaufnahme *f*

ta·pes·try ['tæpɪstrɪ] Gobelin *m*, Wandteppich *m*

'**tape·worm** *zo.* Bandwurm *m*

taps [tæps] *pl.* Zapfenstreich *m*

'**tap water** Leitungswasser *n*

tar [tɑː] **1.** Teer *m*; **2.** (**-rr-**) teeren

tare [teə] *econ.* Tara *f*

tar·get ['tɑːgɪt] (Schieß-, Ziel)Scheibe *f*; *mil.* Ziel *n*; *fig.* Ziel *n*, *econ. a.* Soll *n*; Zielscheibe *f* (*des Spottes* etc.); '~ **ar·e·a** *mil.* Zielbereich *m*; '~ **group** Werbung: Zielgruppe *f*; '~ **lan·guage** Zielsprache *f*; '~ **prac·tice** Scheiben-, Übungsschießen *n*

tar·iff ['tærɪf] Zoll(tarif) *m*; *bsd. Brt.* Preisverzeichnis *n* (*in Hotel etc.*)

tar·mac ['tɑːmæk] Asphalt *m*; *aviat.* Rollfeld *n*, -bahn *f*

tar·nish ['tɑːnɪʃ] anlaufen (*Metall*); *Ansehen etc.* beflecken

tart¹ [tɑːt] *bsd. Brt.* Obstkuchen *m*; Obsttörtchen *n*; F Flittchen *n*, Nutte *f*

tart² [tɑːt] herb, sauer; scharf (*a. fig.*)

tar·tan ['tɑːtn] Tartan *m*: Schottenstoff *m*; Schottenmuster *n*

tar·tar ['tɑːtə] Zahnstein *m*; *chem.* Weinstein *m*

task [tɑːsk] Aufgabe *f*; **take s.o. to** ~ *fig.* j-n zurechtweisen (**for** wegen); '~ **force** *mil.*, Polizei: Sonder-, Spezialeinheit *f*

tas·sel ['tæsl] Troddel *f*, Quaste *f*

taste [teɪst] **1.** Geschmack(ssinn) *m*; Ge-

schmack *m* (*a. fig.*); Kostprobe *f*; Vorliebe *f* (**for** für); **2.** *v/t.* kosten, probieren; schmecken; *v/i.* schmecken (**of** nach); '~**ful** *fig.* geschmackvoll; '~**less** geschmacklos (*a. fig.*)

tast·y ['teɪstɪ] (**-ier, -iest**) schmackhaft

ta-ta *int. Brt.* F [tæ'tɑː] tschüs!

tat·tered ['tætəd] zerlumpt

tat·tle ['tætl] klatschen, tratschen

tat·too¹ [tə'tuː] **1.** (*pl.* **-toos**) Tätowierung *f*; **2.** (ein)tätowieren

tat·too² *mil.* [tə'tuː] (*pl.* **-toos**) Zapfenstreich *m*; (abendliche) Musikparade *f*

taught [tɔːt] *pret. u. p.p. von* **teach**

taunt [tɔːnt] **1.** verhöhnen, -spotten; **2.** Stichelei *f*, höhnische *od.* spöttische Bemerkung

Tau·rus *astr.* ['tɔːrəs] Stier *m*; **he/she is** (**a**) ~ er/sie ist (ein) Stier

taut [tɔːt] straff; *fig.* angespannt

taw·dry ['tɔːdrɪ] (**-ier, -iest**) (billig u.) geschmacklos

taw·ny ['tɔːnɪ] (**-ier, -iest**) gelbbraun

tax [tæks] **1.** Steuer *f* (**on** auf *acc.*); **2.** besteuern; *j-s Geduld etc.* strapazieren; ~**a·tion** [tæk'seɪʃn] Besteuerung *f*

tax·i ['tæksɪ] **1.** Taxi *n*, Taxe *f*; **2.** *aviat.* rollen; '~ **driv·er** Taxifahrer(in); '~ **rank**, '~ **stand** Taxistand *m*

'**tax·pay·er** Steuerzahler(in); '~ **re·turn** Steuererklärung *f*

T-bar ['tiːbɑː] Bügel *m*; *a.* ~ **lift** Schlepplift *m*

tea [tiː] Tee *m*; **have a cup of** ~ e-n Tee trinken; **make some** ~ e-n Tee machen *od.* kochen; → **high tea**; '~**bag** Tee-, Aufgußbeutel *m*

teach [tiːtʃ] (**taught**) lehren, unterrichten (in *dat.*); *j-m et.* beibringen; unterrichten (**at** an *e-r Schule*); '~**er** Lehrer(in)

'**tea**| **co·sy** Teewärmer *m*; '~**cup** Teetasse *f*; **a storm in a** ~ *fig.* ein Sturm im Wasserglas

team [tiːm] Sport: Mannschaft *f*, Team *n*, Fußball *a.* Elf *f*; Team *n*, Arbeitsgruppe *f*; '~**ster** *Am.* ['tiːmstə] LKW-Fahrer *m*; '~**work** Zusammenarbeit *f*, Teamwork *n*; Zusammenspiel *n*

'**tea·pot** Teekanne *f*

tear¹ [tɪə] Träne *f*; **in** ~**s** weinend, in Tränen (aufgelöst)

tear² [teə] **1.** (**tore, torn**) *v/t.* zerreißen; sich *et.* zerreißen (**on** an *dat.*); weg-, losreißen (**from** von); v/i. (zer)reißen; F rasen, sausen; ~ **down** Plakat etc. herunterreißen; Haus etc. abreißen; ~ **off** abreißen; sich Kleidung vom Leib reißen; ~ **out** (her)ausreißen; ~ **up** aufreißen; zerreißen; **2.** Riß m

'**tear·drop** Träne f; '~·**ful** weinend; tränenreich (Abschied etc.)

'**tea·room** Teestube f

tease [ti:z] necken, hänseln; ärgern

'**tea·spoon** Teelöffel m

teat [ti:t] zo. Zitze f; Brt. (Gummi)Sauger m (e-r Saugflasche)

tech·ni·cal ['teknɪkl] technisch; fachlich, Fach...; ~·**i·ty** [teknɪ'kælətɪ] technische Einzelheit; reine Formsache

tech·ni·cian [tek'nɪʃn] Techniker(in)

tech·nique [tek'ni:k] Technik f, Verfahren n; △ nicht **Technik** (Technologie)

tech·nol·o·gy [tek'nɒlədʒɪ] Technologie f; Technik f

ted·dy bear ['tedɪ -] Teddybär m

te·di·ous ['ti:djəs] langweilig, ermüdend

teem [ti:m]: ~ **with** wimmeln von, strotzen von od. vor (dat.)

teen|·age(d) ['ti:neɪdʒ(d)] im Teenageralter; für Teenager; '~·**ag·er** Teenager m

teens [ti:nz] pl.: **be in one's** ~ im Teenageralter sein

tee·ny F ['ti:nɪ], ~·**wee·ny** F [ti:nɪ'wi:nɪ] (-ier, -iest) klitzeklein, winzig

tee shirt ['ti:ʃɜ:t] → **T-shirt**

teeth [ti:θ] pl. von **tooth**

teethe [ti:ð] zahnen

tee·to·tal·(l)er [ti:'təʊtlə] Abstinenzler(in)

tel·e·cast ['telɪkɑ:st] Fernsehsendung f

tel·e·com·mu·ni·ca·tions [telɪkəmju:nɪ'keɪʃnz] pl. Telekommunikation f, Fernmeldewesen n

tel·e·gram ['telɪɡræm] Telegramm n

tel·e·graph ['telɪɡrɑ:f] **1. by** ~ telegrafisch; **2.** telegrafieren; ~·**ic** [telɪ'ɡræfɪk] (~·ally) telegrafisch

te·leg·ra·phy [tɪ'legrəfɪ] Telegrafie f

tel·e·phone ['telɪfəʊn] (→ a. phone 1, 2 u. Zssgn) **1.** Telefon n; **2.** telefonieren; anrufen; '~ **booth** bsd. Am., '~ **box** Brt. Telefon-, Fernsprechzelle f; '~ **call** Telefonanruf n, -gespräch n; '~ **di·rec·to·ry** → **phone book**; '~ **ex·change**

Fernsprechamt n; '~ **num·ber** Telefonnummer f

te·leph·o·nist bsd. Brt. [tɪ'lefənɪst] Telefonist(in)

tel·e·pho·to lens phot. [telɪfəʊtəʊ'lenz] Teleobjektiv n

tel·e·print·er ['telɪprɪntə] Fernschreiber m

tel·e·scope ['telɪskəʊp] Teleskop n, Fernrohr n

tel·e·text ['telɪtekst] Tele-, Videotext m

tel·e·type·writ·er bsd. Am. [telɪ'taɪpraɪtə] Fernschreiber m

tel·e·vise ['telɪvaɪz] im Fernsehen übertragen od. bringen

tel·e·vi·sion ['telɪvɪʒn] Fernsehen n; Fernseh...; **on** ~ im Fernsehen; **watch** ~ fernsehen; a. ~ **set** Fernsehapparat m, -gerät n

tel·ex ['teleks] **1.** Telex n, Fernschreiben n; **2.** telexen (**to** an), j-m et. per Fernschreiber mitteilen

tell [tel] (**told**) v/t. sagen; erzählen; erkennen (**by** an dat.); Namen etc. nennen; et. anzeigen; j-m sagen, befehlen (**to do** zu tun); **I can't** ~ **one from the other, I can't** ~ **them apart** ich kann sie nicht auseinanderhalten; v/i. sich auswirken (**on** bei, auf acc.), sich bemerkbar machen; **who can** ~? wer weiß?; **you can never** ~, **you never can** ~ man kann nie wissen; ~ **against** sprechen gegen; von Nachteil sein für; ~ **off** F j-m Bescheid stoßen (**for** wegen); ~ **on s.o.** j-n verpetzen od. verraten; '~·**er** bsd. Am. Kassierer(in) (e-r Bank); '~·**ing** aufschlußreich; '~·**tale 1.** verräterisch; **2.** F Petze f

tel·ly Brt. F ['telɪ] Fernseher m (Gerät)

te·mer·i·ty [tɪ'merətɪ] Frechheit f, Kühnheit f

tem·per ['tempə] **1.** tech. Härte(grad m) f; Temperament n, Wesen(sart f) n; Laune f, Stimmung f; **keep one's** ~ sich beherrschen, ruhig bleiben; **lose one's** ~ die Beherrschung verlieren; **2.** tech. Stahl härten

tem·pe|·ra·ment ['tempərəmənt] Temperament n, Naturell n, Wesen(sart f) n; ~·**ra·men·tal** [tempərə'mentl] launisch; von Natur aus

tem·pe·rate ['tempərət] gemäßigt (Klima, Zone)

tem·pe·ra·ture ['temprətʃə] Temperatur *f*; **have** *od.* **be running a** ~ erhöhte Temperatur *od.* Fieber haben

tem·pest *poet.* ['tempɪst] (heftiger) Sturm

tem·ple¹ ['templ] Tempel *m*

tem·ple² *anat.* ['templ] Schläfe *f*

tem·po·ral ['tempərəl] weltlich; *gr.* temporal, der Zeit; **~·ra·ry** ['tempərəri] vorübergehend, zeitweilig

tempt [tempt] *j-n* in Versuchung führen; *j-n* verführen (**to** zu); **temp·ta·tion** [temp'teɪʃn] Versuchung *f*, Verführung *f*; **'~·ing** verführerisch

ten [ten] **1.** zehn; **2.** Zehn *f*

ten·a·ble ['tenəbl] haltbar (*Argument etc.*)

te·na·cious [tɪ'neɪʃəs] hartnäckig, zäh

ten·ant ['tenənt] Pächter(in), Mieter(in)

tend [tend] neigen, tendieren (**to** zu); ~ **upwards** → steigende Tendenz haben; **ten·den·cy** ['tendənsɪ] Tendenz *f*; Neigung *f*

ten·der¹ ['tendə] empfindlich, *fig. a.* heikel; zart, weich (*Fleisch etc.*); sanft, zart, zärtlich

ten·der² *rail., naut.* ['tendə] Tender *m*

ten·der³ *econ.* ['tendə] **1.** Angebot *n*; *legal* ~ gesetzliches Zahlungsmittel; **2.** *econ.* ein Angebot machen (**for** für)

'ten·der|·foot (*pl.* **-foots, -feet**) *Am.* F Neuling *m*, Anfänger *m*; **'~·loin** zartes Lendenstück; **'~·ness** Zartheit *f*; Zärtlichkeit *f*

ten·don *anat.* ['tendən] Sehne *f*

ten·dril *bot.* ['tendrɪl] Ranke *f*

ten·e·ment ['tenɪmənt] Mietshaus *n*, *contp.* Mietskaserne *f*

ten·nis ['tenɪs] Tennis *n*; **~ court** Tennisplatz *m*; **~ play·er** Tennisspieler(in)

ten·or ['tenə] *mus.* Tenor *m*; Verlauf *m*; Tenor *m*, Sinn *m*

tense¹ *gr.* [tens] Zeit(form) *f*, Tempus *n*

tense² [tens] (**~·r, ~·st**) gespannt, straff (*Seil etc.*), (an)gespannt (*Muskeln*); (über)nervös, verkrampft (*Person*); *fig.* (an)gespannt (*Lage etc.*); **ten·sion** ['tenʃn] Spannung *f* (*a. electr.*)

tent [tent] Zelt *n*

ten·ta·cle *zo.* ['tentəkl] Tentakel *m*, *n*: Fühler *m*; Fangarm *m* (*e-s Polypen*)

ten·ta·tive ['tentətɪv] vorläufig; vorsichtig, zögernd, zaghaft

ten·ter·hooks ['tentəhʊks]: **be on** ~ wie

auf (glühenden) Kohlen sitzen

tenth [tenθ] **1.** zehnte(r, -s); **2.** Zehntel *n*; **'~·ly** zehntens

ten·u·ous *fig.* ['tenjʊəs] lose (*Verbindung etc.*)

ten·ure ['tenjʊə] Besitz(dauer *f*) *m*; ~ **of office** Amtsdauer *f*, Dienstzeit *f*

tep·id ['tepɪd] lau(warm)

term [tɜːm] **1.** Zeit(raum *m*) *f*, Dauer *f*; Laufzeit *f* (*e-s Vertrages*); *bsd. Brt. ped., univ.* Trimester *n*, *Am.* Semester *n*; Ausdruck *m*, Bezeichnung *f*; ~ **of office** Amtsdauer *f*, -periode *f*, -zeit *f*; ~**s** *pl.* Bedingungen *pl.*; **be on good** (**bad**) ~**s with** gut (schlecht) auskommen mit; **they are not on speaking** ~**s** sie sprechen nicht (mehr) miteinander; **come to** ~**s** sich einigen (**with** mit); **2.** nennen, bezeichnen als

ter·mi·nal ['tɜːmɪnl] **1.** End...; letzte(r, -s); *med.* unheilbar; *med.* im Endstadium; **~·ly ill** unheilbar krank; **2.** *rail. etc.* Endstation *f*; Terminal *m*, *n*; → **air terminal**; *electr.* Pol *m* (*e-r Batterie etc.*); *Computer:* Terminal *n*, Datenendstation; **~·nate** ['tɜːmɪneɪt] *v/t.* beenden; *Vertrag* kündigen, lösen; *med.* *Schwangerschaft* unterbrechen; *v/i.* enden; ablaufen (*Vertrag*); **~·na·tion** [tɜːmɪ'neɪʃn] Beendigung *f*; Kündigung *f*, Lösung *f*; Ende *n*; Ablauf *m*

ter·mi·nus ['tɜːmɪnəs] (*pl.* **-ni** [-naɪ], **-nuses**) *rail. etc.* Endstation *f*

ter·race ['terəs] Terrasse *f*; Häuserreihe *f*; *mst* ~**s** *pl.* *bsd. Brt. Sport:* Ränge *pl.*; **~d 'house** *Brt.* Reihenhaus *n*

ter·res·tri·al [tə'restrɪəl] irdisch; Erd...; *bsd. zo., bot.* Land...

ter·ri·ble ['terəbl] schrecklich

ter·rif·ic F [tə'rɪfɪk] (**~·ally**) toll, phantastisch; irre (*Geschwindigkeit, Hitze etc.*)

ter·ri·fy ['terɪfaɪ] *j-m* schreckliche Angst einjagen

ter·ri·to|·ri·al [terə'tɔːrɪəl] territorial, Gebiets...; **~·ry** ['terətərɪ] Territorium *n*, (*a.* Hoheits-, Staats)Gebiet *n*

ter·ror ['terə] Entsetzen *n*; Terror *m*; Schrecken *m*; **~·is·m** ['terərɪzəm] Terrorismus *m*; **~·ist** ['terərɪst] Terrorist(in); **~·ize** ['terəraɪz] terrorisieren

terse [tɜːs] (**~·r, ~·st**) knapp (*Antwort*)

test [test] **1.** Test *m*, Prüfung *f*; Probe *f*; **2.** testen, prüfen; probieren; *j-s Geduld etc.* auf e-e harte Probe stellen

tes·ta·ment ['testəmənt] Testament *n*; *last will and* ~ Letzter Wille, Testament *n*

'**test**| **card** *TV* Testbild *n*; '~ **drive** *mot.* Probefahrt *f*

tes·ti·cle *anat.* ['testikl] Hoden *m*

tes·ti·fy *jur.* ['testifai] aussagen

tes·ti·mo·ni·al [testi'məunjəl] Referenz *f*; ~**ny** ['testiməni] *jur.* Aussage *f*; Beweis *m*

'**test**| **pi·lot** *aviat.* Testpilot *m*; '~ **tube** *chem.* Reagenzglas *n*; '~**tube ba·by** *med.* Retortenbaby *n*

tes·ty ['testi] (*-ier, -iest*) gereizt

tet·a·nus *med.* ['tetənəs] Tetanus *m*, Wundstarrkrampf *m*

teth·er ['teðə] 1. Strick *m*; Kette *f*; *at the end of one's* ~ *fig.* mit s-n Kräften *od.* Nerven am Ende sein; 2. *Tier* anbinden; anketten

text [tekst] Text *m*; '~**book** Lehrbuch *n*; △ *nicht* **Textbuch** (= *script*)

tex·tile ['tekstail] Stoff *m*; Textil...; ~**s** *pl.* Textilien *pl.*

tex·ture ['tekstʃə] Textur *f*, Gewebe *n*; Beschaffenheit *f*; Struktur *f*

than [ðæn, ðən] als; △ *nicht* **dann**

thank [θæŋk] 1. *j-m* danken; sich bei *j-m* bedanken (*for* für); ~ *you* danke; ~ *you very much* vielen Dank; *no,* ~ *you* nein, danke; (*yes,*) ~ *you* ja, bitte; 2. ~**s** *pl.* Dank *m*; ~**s** danke (schön); *no,* ~**s** nein, danke; ~**s to** dank (*gen.*), wegen (*gen.*); '~**ful** dankbar; '~**less** undankbar

'**Thanks·giv·ing** (**Day**) *Am.* Thanksgiving Day *n* (*Erntedankfest*)

that [ðæt, ðət] 1. *pron. u. adj.* (*pl.* **those** [ðəuz]) das (*ohne Art.*); jene(r, -s), der, die, das, der-, die-, dasjenige; 2. *relative pron.* (*pl.* **that**) der, die, das, welche(r, -s); 3. *cj.* daß; 4. *adv.* F so, dermaßen; *it's* ~ *simple* so einfach ist das

thatch [θætʃ] 1. mit Stroh *od.* Reet decken; 2. (*Dach*)Stroh *n*, Reet *n*; Stroh-, Reetdach *n*

thaw [θɔ:] 1. (auf)tauen; 2. Tauwetter *n*; (Auf)Tauen *n*

the [ðə, *vor Vokalen* ði, *betont* ði:] 1. *bestimmter Artikel* der, die, das, *pl.* die; 2. *adv.:* ~ ... ~ je ..., desto; ~ *sooner* ~ *better* je eher, desto besser

the·a·tre *Brt.*, **the·a·ter** *Am.* ['θiətə] Theater *n*; (*Hör*)Saal *m*; *Brt. med.* Operationssaal *m*; (*Kriegs*)Schauplatz *m*; '~**go·er** Theaterbesucher(in); **the·at·ri·cal** [θi'ætrikl] Theater...; *fig.* theatralisch

theft [θeft] Diebstahl *m*

their [ðeə] *pl.* ihr(e); ~**s** [ðeəz] der (die, das) ihrige *od.* ihre

them [ðem, ðəm] sie (*acc. pl.*); ihnen (*dat.*)

theme [θi:m] Thema *n*

them·selves [ðəm'selvz] sie (*acc. pl.*) selbst; sich (selbst)

then [ðen] 1. *adv.* dann; da; damals; *by* ~ bis dahin; *from* ~ *on* von da an; → *every, now* 1, *there* 1; 2. *adj.* damalig

the·o·lo·gian [θiə'ləudʒən] Theolog|e *m*, -in *f*; **the·ol·o·gy** [θi'plədʒi] Theologie *f*

the·o·ret·i·cal [θiə'retikl] theoretisch; ~**ry** ['θiəri] Theorie *f*

ther·a·peu·tic [θerə'pju:tik] (~**ally**) therapeutisch; ~**pist** ['θerəpist] Therapeut(in); ~**py** ['θerəpi] Therapie *f*

there [ðeə] 1. da, dort; (da-, dort)hin; ~ *is, pl.* ~ *are* es gibt, es ist, *pl.* es sind; ~ *and then* auf der Stelle; ~ *you are* hier bitte; da hast du's!, na also!; 2. *int.* so; da hast du's!, na also!; ~ ~ na, ist ja gut!; ~**a·bout(s)** ['ðeərəbaut(s)] so ungefähr; ~**aft·er** [ðeər'ɑ:ftə] danach; ~**by** [ðeə'bai] dadurch; ~**fore** ['ðeəfɔ:] deshalb, daher; folglich; ~**up·on** [ðeərə'pɒn] darauf(hin)

ther·mal ['θə:ml] 1. thermisch, Thermo..., Wärme...; 2. Thermik *f*

ther·mom·e·ter [θə'mɒmitə] Thermometer *n*

ther·mos *TM* ['θə:mɒs] Thermosflasche *f* (*TM*)

these [ði:z] *pl. von* **this**

the·sis ['θi:sis] (*pl.* **-ses** [-si:z]) These *f*; *univ.* Dissertation *f*, Doktorarbeit *f*

they [ðei] sie *pl.*; man

thick [θik] 1. *adj.* dick; dick, dicht (*Nebel etc.*); F dumm; F dick befreundet; *be* ~ *with* wimmeln von; ~ *with smoke* verräuchert; *that's a bit* ~! *bsd. Brt.* F das ist ein starkes Stück!; 2. *adv.* dick, dicht; *lay it on* ~ F dick auftragen; 3. *in the* ~ *of* mitten in (*dat.*); *through* ~ *and thin* durch dick u. dünn; '~**en** Soße *etc.* eindicken, binden; dicker werden, (*Nebel etc. a.*) dichter werden; ~**et** ['θikit] Dickicht *n*; '~**'head·ed** F strohdumm; '**~ness** Dicke f; Lage f, Schicht f; **~'set** gedrungen, untersetzt; **~'skinned** fig. dickfellig

thief [θiːf] (pl. **thieves** [θiːvz]) Dieb(in)

thigh anat. [θaɪ] (Ober)Schenkel m

thim·ble ['θɪmbl] Fingerhut m

thin [θɪn] **1.** adj. (-nn-) dünn; dürr; spärlich, dürftig; schwach (Rede etc.), (Ausrede etc. a.) fadenscheinig; **2.** adv. dünn; **3.** (-nn-) verdünnen; dünner werden, (Nebel, Haar a.) sich lichten

thing [θɪŋ] Ding n; Sache f; **I couldn't see a ~** ich konnte überhaupt nichts sehen; **another ~** et. anderes; **the right ~** das Richtige; **~s** pl. Sachen pl., Zeug n; Dinge pl., Lage f, Umstände pl.

thing·a·ma·jig F ['θɪŋəmɪdʒɪg] Dings (-bums, -da) n

think [θɪŋk] (**thought**) v/i. denken (**of** an acc.); nachdenken (**about** über acc.); **I ~ so** ich glaube od. denke schon; **I'll ~ about it** ich überlege es mir; **~ of** sich erinnern an (acc.); **~ of doing sth.** beabsichtigen od. daran denken, et. zu tun; **what do you ~ of ... od. about?** was halten Sie von ...?; v/t. denken, glauben, meinen; j-n, et. halten für; **~ over** nachdenken über (acc.), sich et. überlegen; **~ up** sich et. ausdenken; **~ tank** Sachverständigenstab m, Denkfabrik f

third [θɜːd] **1.** dritte(r, -s); **2.** Drittel n; '**~ly** drittens; **~'rate** drittklassig; ♀ '**World** Dritte Welt; **~ world 'shop** Dritte-Welt-Laden m

thirst [θɜːst] Durst m; '**~y** (-ier, -iest) durstig; **be ~** Durst haben, durstig sein

thir·teen [θɜː'tiːn] **1.** dreizehn; **2.** Dreizehn f; **~teenth** [θɜː'tiːnθ] dreizehnte(r, -s); **~ti·eth** ['θɜːtiːθ] dreißigste(r, -s); **~ty** ['θɜːtɪ] **1.** dreißig; **2.** Dreißig f

this [ðɪs] (pl. **these** [ðiːz]) diese(r, -s); **~ morning** heute morgen; **~ is John speaking** tel. hier (spricht) John

this·tle bot. ['θɪsl] Distel f

thong [θɒŋ] (Leder)Riemen m

thorn [θɔːn] Dorn m; '**~y** (-ier, -iest) dornig; fig. schwierig, heikel

thor·ough ['θʌrə] gründlich, genau; fürchterlich (Durcheinander, Zeitverschwendung etc.); '**~bred** zo. Vollblüter m; '**~fare** Hauptverkehrsstraße f; **no ~!** Durchfahrt verboten!

those [ðəʊz] pl. von **that** 1

though [ðəʊ] **1.** cj. obwohl; (je)doch; **as**

~ als ob; **2.** adv. dennoch, trotzdem

thought [θɔːt] **1.** pret. u. p.p. von **think**; **2.** Denken n; Gedanke m (**of** an acc.); **on second ~s** wenn ich es mir überlege; '**~ful** nachdenklich; rücksichtsvoll, aufmerksam; '**~less** gedankenlos; rücksichtslos

thou·sand ['θaʊznd] **1.** tausend; **2.** Tausend n; '**~th** ['θaʊznθ] **1.** tausendste(r, -s); **2.** Tausendstel n

thrash [θræʃ] verdreschen, -prügeln; Sport: F j-m e-e Abfuhr erteilen; **~ about, ~ around** sich im Bett etc. hin u. her werfen; um sich schlagen; zappeln (Fisch); **~ out** Problem etc. ausdiskutieren; '**~ing** Dresche f, Tracht f Prügel

thread [θred] **1.** Faden m (a. fig.); Garn n; tech. Gewinde n; **2.** Nadel einfädeln; Perlen etc. auffädeln, -reihen; '**~bare** abgewetzt, abgetragen; fig. abgedroschen

threat [θret] Drohung f; Bedrohung f, Gefahr f (**to** gen. od. für); **~en** ['θretn] (be)drohen; '**~en·ing** drohend

three [θriː] **1.** drei; **2.** Drei f; '**~fold** dreifach; '**~ply** → **ply²** 1; '**~score** sechzig; '**~stage** dreistufig

thresh agr. [θreʃ] dreschen; '**~ing ma·chine** Dreschmaschine f

thresh·old ['θreʃhəʊld] Schwelle f

threw [θruː] pret. von **throw** 1

thrift [θrɪft] Sparsamkeit f; '**~y** (-ier, -iest) sparsam

thrill [θrɪl] **1.** prickelndes Gefühl; Nervenkitzel m; aufregendes Erlebnis; **2.** v/t. **be ~ed** (ganz) hingerissen sein (**at, about** von); '**~er** Thriller m, Reißer m; '**~ing** spannend, fesselnd, packend

thrive [θraɪv] (**thrived** od. **throve**, **thrived**) gedeihen; fig. blühen, florieren (Geschäft etc.)

throat [θrəʊt] Kehle f, Gurgel f; Rachen m; Hals m; **clear one's ~** sich räuspern; → **sore** 1

throb [θrɒb] **1.** (-bb-) hämmern (Maschine), (Herz etc. a.) pochen, schlagen; pulsieren (Schmerz); **2.** Hämmern n, Pochen n, Schlagen n

throm·bo·sis med. [θrɒm'bəʊsɪs] (pl. **-ses** [-siːz]) Thrombose f

throne [θrəʊn] Thron m

throng [θrɒŋ] **1.** Schar f, Menschenmenge f; **2.** sich drängen (in dat.)

throt·tle ['θrɒtl] **1.** erdrosseln; **~ down**

tidy

mot., *tech.* drosseln, Gas wegnehmen; **2.** *tech.* Drosselklappe *f*

through ['θruː] **1.** *prp.* durch; *Am.* bis (einschließlich); *Monday ~ Friday Am.* von Montag bis Freitag; **2.** *adv.* durch; *~ and ~* durch u. durch; *put s.o. ~ to* tel. *j-n* verbinden mit; *wet ~* völlig durchnäßt; **3.** *adj.* durchgehend (*Zug etc.*); *Durchgangs...*; *~'out* **1.** *prp. ~ the night* die ganze Nacht hindurch; *~ the country* im ganzen Land; **2.** *adv.* ganz, überall; die ganze Zeit hindurch; *~* **traf·fic** Durchgangsverkehr *m*; *~* **way** *Am.* → thruway

throve [θrəʊv] *pret. von* thrive

throw [θrəʊ] **1.** (*threw*, *thrown*) werfen; *Hebel etc.* betätigen; *Reiter* abwerfen; F *Party* schmeißen, geben; *~ a four* e-e Vier würfeln; *~ off Keidungsstück etc.* abwerfen; *Verfolger* abschütteln; *Krankheit* loswerden; *~ on* sich *ein Kleidungsstück* (hastig) überwerfen; *~ out* hinauswerfen; wegwerfen; *~ up* *v/t.* hochwerfen; F *Job etc.* hinschmeißen; F (er)brechen; *v/i.* F (sich) erbrechen; **2.** Wurf *m*; Werfen *n*; Einweg...; *~·a·way* **pack** Einwegpackung *f*; *~·in Fußball:* Einwurf *m*; *~·n* [θrəʊn] *p.p. von* throw 1

thru *Am.* [θruː] → through; *~·way* *Am.* Schnellstraße *f*

thrum [θrʌm] (*-mm-*) → strum

thrush *zo.* [θrʌʃ] Drossel *f*

thrust [θrʌst] **1.** (*thrust*) *j-n, et.* stoßen (*into* in *acc.*); *et.* stecken, schieben (*into* in *acc.*); *~ at* stoßen nach; *~ upon s.o.* *j-m* aufdrängen; **2.** Stoß *m*; *mil.* Vorstoß *m*; *phys.* Schub(kraft *f*) *m*

thud [θʌd] **1.** dumpfes Geräusch, Plumps *m*; **2.** (*-dd-*) plumpsen

thug [θʌg] Verbrecher *m*, Schläger *m*

thumb [θʌm] **1.** *anat.* Daumen *m*; **2.** *~ a* **lift** *od.* **ride** per Anhalter fahren, trampen (*to* nach); *~ through a book* ein Buch durchblättern; *well-~ed Buch etc.*: abgegriffen; *~·tack Am.* Reißzwecke *f*, -nagel *m*, Heftzwecke *f*

thump [θʌmp] **1.** *v/t.* *j-m* e-n Schlag versetzen; *~ out Melodie* herunterhämmern (*on the piano* auf dem Klavier); *v/i.* (heftig) schlagen *od.* hämmern *od.* pochen (*a. Herz*); plumpsen; trampeln; **2.** dumpfes Geräusch, Plumps *m*; Schlag *m*

thun·der ['θʌndə] **1.** Donner *m*, Donnern *n*; **2.** donnern; *~·bolt* Blitz *m* u. Donner *m*; *~·clap* Donnerschlag *m*; *~·cloud* Gewitterwolke *f*; *~·ous* ['θʌndərəs] donnernd (*Applaus*); *~·storm* Gewitter *n*, Unwetter *n*; *~·struck* wie vom Donner gerührt

Thur(s) *nur geschr. Abk. für Thursday* Do., Donnerstag *m*

Thurs·day ['θɜːzdɪ] (*Abk. Thur, Thurs*) Donnerstag *m*; *on ~* (am) Donnerstag; *on ~s* donnerstags

thus [ðʌs] so, auf diese Weise; folglich, somit; *~ far* bisher

thwart [θwɔːt] durchkreuzen, vereiteln

thyme *bot.* [taɪm] Thymian *m*

thy·roid (gland) *anat.* ['θaɪrɔɪd (-)] Schilddrüse *f*

tick¹ [tɪk] **1.** Ticken *n*; Haken *m*, Häkchen *n* (*Vermerkzeichen*); **2.** *v/i.* ticken; *v/t. mst ~ off* ab-, anhaken

tick² *zo.* [tɪk] Zecke *f*

tick³ [tɪk]: *on ~ Brt.* F auf Pump

tick·er-tape ['tɪkəteɪp] Lochstreifen *m*; *~ pa'rade* Konfettiparade *f*

tick·et ['tɪkɪt] **1.** Fahrkarte *f*, -schein *m*; Flugkarte *f*, -schein *m*, Ticket *n* (*Eintritts-, Theater- etc.*)Karte *f*; (*Gepäck*)Schein *m*; Etikett *n*, (*Preis-etc.*)Schild *n*; *bsd. Am. pol.* Wahl-, Kandidatenliste *f*; (*a. parking ~*) *mot.* Strafzettel *m*; **2.** etikettieren; bestimmen, vorsehen (*for* für); *~* **can·cel·(l)ing ma·chine** (Fahrschein)Entwerter *m*; *~* **col·lec·tor** (Bahnsteig)Schaffner(in); *~* **ma·chine** Fahrkartenautomat *m*; *~* **of·fice** *rail.* Fahrkartenschalter *m*

tick·ing ['tɪkɪŋ] Inlett *n*; Matratzenbezug *m*

tick·le ['tɪkl] kitzeln; *~·lish* ['tɪklɪʃ] kitz(e)lig, (*fig. a.*) heikel

tid·al ['taɪdl]: *~ wave* Flutwelle *f*

tid·bit *Am.* ['tɪdbɪt] → titbit

tide [taɪd] **1.** Gezeiten *pl.*; Flut *f*; *fig.* Strömung *f*, Trend *m*; *high ~* Flut *f*; *low ~* Ebbe *f*; **2.** *~ over fig.* *j-m* hinweghelfen über (*acc.*); *j-n* über Wasser halten

ti·dy ['taɪdɪ] **1.** (*-ier, -iest*) sauber, ordentlich, aufgeräumt; F ganz schön, beträchtlich (*Summe etc.*); **2.** *a. ~ up* in Ordnung bringen, (*Zimmer a.*) aufräumen; *~ away* weg-, aufräumen

tie [taɪ] **1.** Krawatte f, Schlips m; Band n; Schnur f; Stimmengleichheit f; Sport: Unentschieden n; Sport: (Pokal)Spiel n; Am. rail. Schwelle f; mst ~s pl. fig. Bande pl.; **2.** v/t. (an-, fest-, fig. ver)binden; (sich) Krawatte etc. binden; **the game was ~d** Sport: das Spiel ging unentschieden aus; v/i. **they ~d for second place** Sport etc.: sie belegten gemeinsam den zweiten Platz; ~ **down** fig. (an)binden; j-n festlegen (**to** auf acc.); ~ **in with** übereinstimmen mit, passen zu; verbinden od. koppeln mit; ~ **up** Paket etc. verschnüren; et. in Verbindung bringen (**with** mit); Verkehr etc. lahmlegen; **be ~d up** econ. fest angelegt sein (**in** in dat.); F knick(e)rig; mst ~s pl. fig. Tie-Break m, n; **'~-in** (enge) Verbindung, (enger) Zusammenhang; econ. Kopplungsgeschäft n; **a book movie** ~ etwa: das Buch zum Film; **'~-on** Anhänge...

tier [tɪə] (Sitz)Reihe f; Lage f, Schicht f; fig. Stufe f

'tie-up (enge) Verbindung, (enger) Zusammenhang; econ. Fusion f

ti·ger zo. ['taɪɡə] Tiger m

tight [taɪt] **1.** adj. fest(sitzend, -eingezogen); straff (Seil etc.); eng (a. Kleidungsstück); knapp (Rennen etc., econ. Geld); F knick(e)rig; F blau (betrunken); **in** Zssgn ...dicht; **be in a ~ corner** in der Klemme sein od. sitzen od. stecken; **2.** adv. fest; F gut; **hold ~** festhalten; **sleep ~!** F schlaf gut!; **~en** [taɪtn] fest-, anziehen; Seil etc. straffen; ~ **one's belt** fig. den Gürtel enger schnallen; ~ **up** (on) Gesetz etc. verschärfen; **~'fist·ed** F knick(e)rig; **~s** pl. (Tänzer-, Artisten)Trikot n; bsd. Brt. Strumpfhose f

ti·gress zo. ['taɪɡrɪs] Tigerin f

tile [taɪl] **1.** (Dach)Ziegel m; Fliese f, Kachel f; **2.** (mit Ziegeln) decken; fliesen, kacheln; **'til·er** Dachdecker m; Fliesenleger m

till¹ [tɪl] → until

till² [tɪl] (Laden)Kasse f

tilt [tɪlt] **1.** kippen; sich neigen; **2.** Kippen n; **at a ~** schief, schräg; (**at**) **full ~** F mit Karacho fahren etc.; mit Volldampf arbeiten

tim·ber ['tɪmbə] Brt. Bau-, Nutzholz n; Baumbestand m, Bäume pl.; Balken m

time [taɪm] **1.** Zeit f; Uhrzeit f; mus. Takt m; Mal n; ~ **after** ~, ~ **and again** immer wieder; **every** I ... jedesmal, wenn ich ...; **how many ~s?** wie oft?; **next** ~ nächstes Mal; **this** ~ diesmal; **three** ~s dreimal; **three ~s four equals** od. **is twelve** drei mal vier ist zwölf; **what's the** ~? wie spät ist es?; **what** ~? um wieviel Uhr?; **all the** ~ die ganze Zeit; **at all ~s, at any** ~ jederzeit; **at the** ~ damals; **at the same** ~ gleichzeitig; **at ~s** manchmal; **by the** ~ wenn; als; **for a** ~ e-e Zeitlang; **for the ~ being** vorläufig, fürs erste; **from ~ to** ~ von Zeit zu Zeit; **have a good ~** sich gut unterhalten od. amüsieren; **in** ~ rechtzeitig; **in no** ~ (at all) im Nu; **on** ~ pünktlich; **some ~ ago** vor einiger Zeit; **take one's** ~ sich Zeit lassen; **2.** et. timen (a. Sport); (ab)stoppen; zeitlich abstimmen, den richtigen Zeitpunkt wählen od. bestimmen für; **~ card** Am. Stechkarte f; **~ clock** Stechuhr f; **~ lag** Zeitdifferenz f; **~-lapse** Film: Zeitraffer...; **~·less** immerwährend, ewig; zeitlos; **~ lim·it** Frist f; **~·ly** (-ier, -iest) (recht)zeitig; **~ sheet** Stechkarte f; **~ sig·nal** Rundfunk: Zeitzeichen n; **~·ta·ble** Fahr-, Flugplan m; Stundenplan m; Zeitplan m

tim·id ['tɪmɪd] ängstlich, furchtsam

tim·ing ['taɪmɪŋ] Timing n (Wahl des günstigsten Zeitpunkts)

tin [tɪn] **1.** Zinn n; Brt. (Blech-, Konserven)Dose f, (-)Büchse f; **2.** (-nn-) verzinnen; Brt. einmachen, -dosen

tinc·ture ['tɪŋktʃə] Tinktur f

'tin·foil Stanniol(papier) n; Alufolie f

tinge [tɪndʒ] **1.** tönen; **be ~d with** fig. e-n Anflug haben von; **2.** Tönung f; fig. Anflug m, Spur f (**of** von)

tin·gle ['tɪŋɡl] prickeln, kribbeln

tink·er ['tɪŋkə] herumpfuschen, -basteln (**at** an dat.)

tin·kle ['tɪŋkl] bimmeln; klirren

tinned Brt. [tɪnd] Dosen..., Büchsen...; ~ **'fruit** Brt. Obstkonserven pl.

'tin o·pen·er Brt. Dosen-, Büchsenöffner m

tin·sel ['tɪnsl] Lametta n; Flitter m

tint [tɪnt] **1.** (Farb)Ton m, Tönung f; **2.** tönen

ti·ny ['taɪnɪ] (-ier, -iest) winzig

tip¹ [tɪp] **1.** Spitze f; Filter m (e-r Zigarette); **it's on the ~ of my tongue** fig. es liegt mir auf der Zunge; **2.** (**-pp-**) mit e-r Spitze versehen

tip² [tɪp] **1.** (**-pp-**) bsd. Brt. (aus)kippen, schütten, kippen; **~ over** umkippen; **2.** bsd. Brt. (Schutt- etc.)Abladeplatz m, (-)Halde f; Brt. fig. F Saustall m

tip³ [tɪp] **1.** Trinkgeld n; **2.** (**-pp-**) j-m ein Trinkgeld geben

tip⁴ [tɪp] **1.** Tip m, Rat(schlag) m; **2.** (**-pp-**) tippen auf (acc.) (**as** als); **~ off** j-m e-n Tip geben. **Wink** geben

tip·sy ['tɪpsɪ] (**-ier, -iest**) angeheitert

'tip·toe 1. on ~ auf Zehenspitzen; **2.** auf Zehenspitzen gehen

tire¹ Am. ['taɪə] → **tyre**

tire² ['taɪə] ermüden, müde machen od. werden; **'~d** müde; **be ~ of** j-n, et. satt haben; **'~·less** unermüdlich; **'~·some** ermüdend; lästig

Ti·rol [tɪ'rəʊl, 'tɪrəl] Tirol n

tis·sue ['tɪʃuː] biol. Gewebe n; Papier(taschen)tuch n; → **'~ pa·per** Seidenpapier n

tit¹ sl. [tɪt] Titte f

tit² zo. [tɪt] Meise f

tit·bit bsd. Brt. ['tɪtbɪt] Leckerbissen m

tit·il·late ['tɪtɪleɪt] j-n (sexuell) anregen

ti·tle ['taɪtl] jur. (Rechts)Anspruch m (**to** auf acc.); **'~ page** Titelseite f

tit·mouse zo. ['tɪtmaʊs] (pl. **-mice**) Meise f

tit·ter ['tɪtə] **1.** kichern; **2.** Kichern n

TM nur geschr. Abk. für **trademark** Wz., Warenzeichen n

tn Am. → **t**

to [tuː, tʊ, tə] **1.** prp. zu; an (acc.), auf (acc.), für, in (acc.), in (dat.), nach; (im Verhältnis) zu, gegen(über); Ausmaß, Grenze, Grad: bis, (bis) zu, (bis) an (acc.); zeitliche Ausdehnung od. Grenze: bis, bis zu, bis gegen, vor (dat.); **from Monday ~ Friday** von Montag bis Freitag; **a quarter ~ one** (ein) Viertel vor eins, drei Viertel eins; **go ~ England** nach England fahren; **go ~ school** in die od. zur Schule gehen; **have you ever been ~ London?** bist du schon einmal in London gewesen?; **~ me** etc. mir etc.; **here's ~ you!** auf Ihr Wohl!, prosit!; **2.** adv. zu (geschlossen); **pull ~** Tür etc. zuziehen; **come ~** (wieder) zu sich kommen; **~**

and fro hin u. her, auf u. ab; **3.** zur Bezeichnung des Infinitivs: zu; Absicht, Zweck: um zu; **~ go** gehen; **easy ~ learn** leicht zu lernen; **... ~ earn money** ... um Geld zu verdienen

toad zo. [təʊd] Kröte f; **~·stool** bot. ['təʊdstuːl] ungenießbarer Pilz; Giftpilz m

toad·y ['təʊdɪ] **1.** Kriecher(in); **2. ~ to s.o.** fig. vor j-m kriechen

toast¹ [təʊst] **1.** Toast m; **2.** toasten; rösten

toast² [təʊst] **1.** Toast m, Trinkspruch m; **2.** auf j-n od. j-s Wohl trinken

toast·er tech. ['təʊstə] Toaster m

to·bac·co [tə'bækəʊ] (pl. **-cos**) Tabak m; **~·nist** [tə'bækənɪst] Tabak(waren)händler(in)

to·bog·gan [tə'bɒgən] **1.** (Rodel)Schlitten m; **2.** Schlitten fahren, rodeln

to·day [tə'deɪ] **1.** adv. heute; heutzutage; **a week ~, ~ week** heute in e-r Woche, heute in acht Tagen; **~'s paper** die heutige Zeitung, die Zeitung von heute; od. **~'s** von heute; **2.** adv. zu (geschlossen); **~'s paper** die heutige Zeitung, die Zeitung von heute

tod·dle ['tɒdl] auf wack(e)ligen od. unsicheren Beinen gehen (bsd. Kleinkind)

tod·dy ['tɒdɪ] Toddy m (Art Grog)

to-do F fig. [tə'duː] (pl. **-dos**) Theater n

toe [təʊ] anat. Zehe f; Spitze f (von Schuhen etc.); **~·nail** Zehennagel m

tof·fee, ~·fy ['tɒfɪ] Sahnebonbon m, n, Toffee n

to·geth·er [tə'geðə] zusammen; gleichzeitig

toi·let ['tɔɪlɪt] Toilette f; **'~ pa·per** Toilettenpapier n; **'~ roll** bsd. Brt. Rolle f Toilettenpapier

to·ken ['təʊkən] Zeichen n; **as a ~, in ~ of** als od. zum Zeichen (gen.); zum Andenken an (acc.)

told [təʊld] pret. u. p.p. von **tell**

tol·e·ra·ble ['tɒlərəbl] erträglich; **~·rance** ['tɒlərəns] Toleranz f; Nachsicht f; **~·rant** ['tɒlərənt] tolerant (**of, towards** gegenüber); **~·rate** ['tɒləreɪt] tolerieren, dulden; ertragen

toll¹ [təʊl] Benutzungsgebühr f, Maut f; **heavy death ~** große Zahl an Todesopfern; **take its ~ (on)** fig. s-n Tribut fordern (von); s-e Spuren hinterlassen (bei)

toll² [təʊl] läuten (Glocke)

toll·-'free Am. tel. gebührenfrei; **'~**

road gebührenpflichtige Straße, Mautstraße f

to·ma·to [tə'mɑːtəʊ, tə'meɪtəʊ] (pl. **-toes**) Tomate f

tomb [tuːm] Grab(mal) n; Gruft f

tom·boy ['tɒmbɔɪ] Wildfang m

'tomb·stone Grabstein m

tom·cat zo. ['tɒmkæt] a. F **tom** Kater m

tom·fool·e·ry [tɒm'fuːlərɪ] Unsinn m

to·mor·row [tə'mɒrəʊ] **1.** adv. morgen; **a week ~, ~ week** morgen in e-r Woche, morgen in acht Tagen; **~ morning** morgen früh; **~ night** morgen abend; **2. the day after ~** übermorgen; **of ~, ~'s** von morgen

ton [tʌn] (Abk. **t, tn**) Tonne f (Gewicht); △ nicht Ton

tone [təʊn] **1.** Ton m; Klang m; (Farb)Ton m; Am. mus. Note f; med. Tonus m; fig. Niveau n; **2. ~ down** abschwächen; **~ up** Muskeln etc. kräftigen

tongs [tɒŋz] pl. (**a pair of ~** e-e) Zange f

tongue [tʌŋ] anat. Zunge f; (Mutter)Sprache f; Zunge f (e-s Schuhs etc.); Klöppel m (e-r Glocke); **hold one's ~** den Mund halten

ton·ic ['tɒnɪk] Tonikum n, Stärkungsmittel n; Tonic n; mus. Grundton m

to·night [tə'naɪt] heute abend od. nacht

ton·sil anat. ['tɒnsl] Mandel f; **~·li·tis** med. [tɒnsɪ'laɪtɪs] Mandelentzündung f; Angina f

too [tuː] zu; zu, sehr; auch (noch)

took [tʊk] pret. von **take** 1

tool [tuːl] Werkzeug n, Gerät n; **'~ bag** Werkzeugtasche f; **'~ box** Werkzeugkasten m; **'~ kit** Werkzeug n; **'~·shed** Geräteschuppen m

toot [tuːt] hupen

tooth [tuːθ] (pl. **teeth**) Zahn m; **'~·ache** Zahnschmerzen pl., -weh n; **'~·brush** Zahnbürste f; **'~·less** zahnlos; **'~·paste** Zahncreme f, -pasta f; **'~·pick** Zahnstocher m

top¹ [tɒp] **1.** oberer Teil; Gipfel m, Spitze f (e-s Bergs etc.); Krone f, Wipfel m (e-s Baums); Kopfende n, oberes Ende; Oberteil n; Oberfläche f (e-s Tischs etc.); Deckel m (e-s Glases); Verschluß m (e-r Tube); mot. Verdeck n; mot. höchster Gang; **at the ~ of the page** oben auf der Seite; **at the ~ of one's voice** aus vollem Hals; **on ~** oben(auf);

d(a)rauf; **on ~ of** (oben) auf (dat. od. acc.), über (dat. od. acc.); **2.** oberste(r, -s); Höchst..., Spitzen..., Top...; **3.** (**-pp-**) bedecken (**with** mit); fig. übersteigen, -übertreffen; **~ up** Tank etc. auffüllen; F j-m nachschenken

top² [tɒp] Kreisel m (Spielzeug)

top·|hat Zylinder m; **~·'heav·y** kopflastig (a. fig.)

top·ic ['tɒpɪk] Thema n; **'~·al** aktuell

top·ple ['tɒpl] mst **~ over** umkippen; **~ the government** die Regierung stürzen

top·sy·tur·vy [tɒpsɪ'tɜːvɪ] in e-r heillosen Unordnung

torch [tɔːtʃ] Brt. Taschenlampe f; Fackel f; **'~·light** Fackelschein m; **~ pro·cession** Fackelzug m

tore [tɔː] pret. von **tear²** 1

tor·ment 1. ['tɔːment] Qual f; **2.** [tɔː'ment] quälen, peinigen, plagen

torn [tɔːn] p.p. von **tear²** 1

tor·na·do [tɔː'neɪdəʊ] (pl. **-does, -dos**) Tornado m, Wirbelsturm m

tor·pe·do [tɔː'piːdəʊ] (pl. **-does**) **1.** Torpedo m; **2.** torpedieren (a. fig.)

tor·rent ['tɒrənt] reißender Strom; fig. Schwall m; **~·ren·tial** [tə'renʃl] **~ rain** sintflutartige Regenfälle

tor·toise zo. ['tɔːtəs] Schildkröte f

tor·tu·ous ['tɔːtjʊəs] gewunden

tor·ture ['tɔːtʃə] **1.** Folter(ung) f; fig. Qual f, Tortur f; **2.** foltern; fig. quälen

toss [tɒs] **1.** v/t. werfen; Münze hochwerfen; **~ off** Getränk hinunterstürzen; Arbeit hinhauen; v/i. a. **~ about, ~ and turn** sich (im Schlaf) hin u. her werfen; a. **~ up** e-e Münze hochwerfen; **~ for s.th.** um et. losen; **2.** Wurf m; Zurückwerfen n (des Kopfes); Hochwerfen n (e-r Münze)

tot F [tɒt] Knirps m (kleines Kind)

to·tal ['təʊtl] **1.** völlig, total; ganz, gesamt, Gesamt...; **2.** Gesamtbetrag m, -menge f; **3.** (bsd. Brt. **-ll-**, Am. **-l-**) sich belaufen auf (acc.); **~ up** zusammenrechnen, -zählen

tot·ter ['tɒtə] (sch)wanken

touch [tʌtʃ] **1.** (sich) berühren; anfassen; Essen etc. anrühren; fig. herankommen an (acc.); fig. rühren; **~ wood!** toi, toi, toi!; **~ down** aviat. aufsetzen; **~ up** ausbessern; phot. retuschieren; **2.** Tastempfindung f; Berührung f, mus. etc. Anschlag m; (Pinsel- etc.)Strich m;

Spur (*Salz etc.*); Verbindung *f*, Kontakt *m*; *fig.* Note *f*; *fig.* Anflug *m*; **a ~ of flu** e-e leichte Grippe; **get in ~ with s.o.** sich mit j-m in Verbindung setzen; **~and-go** [tʌtʃənˈgəʊ] kritisch (*Situation etc.*); **it was ~ whether** es stand auf des Messers Schneide, ob; **'~down** *aviat.* Aufsetzen *n*, Landung *f*; **~ed** gerührt; F leicht verrückt; **'~ing** rührend; **'~line** *Fußball:* Seitenlinie *f*; **'~stone** Prüfstein *m* (*of* für); **'~y** (*-ier, -iest*) empfindlich; heikel (*Thema*)

tough [tʌf] zäh; widerstandsfähig; *fig.* hart; schwierig, hart (*Problem, Verhandlungen etc.*); **~en** ['tʌfn] *a.* **~ up** hart *od.* zäh machen *od.* werden

tour [tʊə] **1.** Tour *f* (of durch), (Rund)Reise *f*, (-)Fahrt *f*; Ausflug *m*; Rundgang *m* (of durch); *thea.* Tournee *f* (a. *Sport*); → **conduct** 2; **2.** bereisen, reisen durch

tour·is·m ['tʊərizəm] Tourismus *m*, Fremdenverkehr *m*

tour·ist ['tʊərist] Tourist(in); Touristen...; **~ class** *aviat., naut.* Touristenklasse *f*; **~ in·dus·try** Tourismusgeschäft *n*; **~ in·for·ma·tion of·fice, ~ of·fice** Verkehrsverein *m*; **~ sea·son** Reisesaison *f*, -zeit *f*

tour·na·ment ['tʊənəmənt] Turnier *n*

tou·sled ['taʊzld] zerzaust (*Haar*)

tow [təʊ] **1.** Boot etc. schleppen, Auto etc. *a.* abschleppen; **2. give s.o. a ~** j-n abschleppen; **take in ~** Auto etc. abschleppen

to·ward *bsd. Am.*, **to·wards** *bsd. Brt.* [təˈwɔːd(z)] auf (*acc.*) ... zu, (in) Richtung, zu; *zeitlich:* gegen; *fig.* gegenüber

tow·el ['taʊəl] **1.** Handtuch *n*, (Bade-etc.)Tuch *n*; **2.** (*bsd. Brt. -ll-, Am. -l-*) (mit e-m Handtuch) abtrocknen *od.* abreiben

tow·er ['taʊə] **1.** Turm *m*; **2. ~ above, ~ over** überragen; **'~ block** *Brt.* Hochhaus *n*; **'~ing** ['taʊərɪŋ] turmhoch; *fig.* überragend; rasend (*Wut*)

town [taʊn] (Klein)Stadt *f*; **~ 'cen·tre** *Brt.* Innenstadt *f*, City *f*; **~ 'coun·cil** *Brt.* Stadtrat *m* (*Amt*); **~ 'coun·ci(l)·lor** *Brt.* Stadtrat *m*, -rätin *f*; **~ 'hall** Rathaus *n*; **~s·peo·ple** ['taʊnzpiːpl] *pl.* Städter *pl.*, Stadtbevölkerung *f*

'tow·rope *mot.* Abschleppseil *n*

tox·ic ['tɒksɪk] (*~ally*) toxisch, giftig;

Gift...; **~ 'waste** Giftmüll *m*; **~ waste 'dump** Giftmülldeponie *f*

tox·in *biol.* ['tɒksɪn] Toxin *n*

toy [tɔɪ] **1.** Spielzeug *n*; **~s** *pl.* Spielsachen *pl.*, -zeug *n*, *econ.* -waren *pl.*; **2.** Spielzeug...; Miniatur...; Zwerg...; **3. ~ with** spielen mit (a. *fig.*)

trace [treɪs] **1.** j-n, et. ausfindig machen, aufspüren, et. finden; et. ~ **back** et. zurückverfolgen (to bis zu); ~ **s.th. to** et. zurückführen auf (*acc.*); (durch)pausen; **2.** Spur *f* (a. *fig.*)

track [træk] **1.** Spur *f* (a. *fig.*), Fährte *f*; Pfad *m*, Weg *m*; *rail.* Gleis *n*, Geleise *n*; *tech.* Raupe(nkette) *f*; *Sport:* (Renn-, Aschen)Bahn *f*, (*Renn*)Strecke *f*; Tonband *etc.*: Spur *f*; Nummer *f* (auf e-r Langspielplatte etc.); **2.** verfolgen; **~ down** aufspüren; auftreiben; **~ and 'field** *bsd. Am.* Leichtathletik *f*; **~ e·vent** *Sport:* Laufdisziplin *f*; **'~ing sta·tion** *Raumfahrt:* Bodenstation *f*; **'~suit** Trainingsanzug *m*

tract [trækt] Fläche *f*, Gebiet *n*; *anat.* (*Verdauungs*)Trakt *m*, (*Atem*)Wege *pl.*

trac·tion ['trækʃn] Ziehen *n*, Zug *m*; **~ en·gine** Zugmaschine *f*

trac·tor ['træktə] Traktor *m*, Trecker *m*

trade [treɪd] **1.** Handel *m*; Branche *f*; Gewerbe *n*; (*bsd.* Handwerks)Beruf *m*; **2.** Handel treiben, handeln; ~ **on** ausnutzen; **'~mark** (*Abk. TM*) Warenzeichen *n*; **'~ name** Markenname *m*, Handelsbezeichnung *f*; **~ price** Großhandelspreis *m*; **'trad·er** Händler(in); **~s·man** ['treɪdzmən] (*pl. -men*) (Einzel)Händler *m*; Ladeninhaber *m*; Lieferant *m*; **~(s) 'un·i·on** Gewerkschaft *f*; **~(s) 'un·i·on·ist** Gewerkschaftler(in)

tra·di·tion [trəˈdɪʃn] Tradition *f*; Überlieferung *f*; **~al** [trəˈdɪʃənl] traditionell

traf·fic ['træfɪk] **1.** Verkehr *m*; (*bsd.* illegaler) Handel (in mit); **2.** (-ck-) (*bsd.* illegal) handeln (in mit); **~ cir·cle** *Am.* Kreisverkehr *m*; **~ is·land** Verkehrsinsel *f*; **~ jam** (Verkehrs)Stau *m*, Verkehrsstockung *f*; **~ light(s** *pl.*) Verkehrsampel *f*; **~ of·fence** (*Am.* **of·fense**) Verkehrsdelikt *n*; **~ of·fend·er** Verkehrssünder(in); **~ reg·u·la·tions** *pl.* Staßenverkehrsordnung *f*; **~ sign** Verkehrszeichen *n*, -schild *n*; **~ sig·nal** → **traffic light(s**); **~ war·den** *Brt.* Parküberwacher *m*, Politesse *f*

T

tra·ge·dy ['trædʒɪdɪ] Tragödie *f*; **~gic** ['trædʒɪk] (**~ally**) tragisch

trail [treɪl] **1.** *v/t. et.* nachschleifen lassen; verfolgen; *Sport:* zurückliegen hinter (*dat.*) (**by** um); *v/i.* sich schleppen; *bot.* kriechen; *Sport:* zurückliegen (**by** 3-0 0:3); **~** (**along**) **behind s.o.** hinter j-m herschleifen; **2.** Spur *f* (*a. fig.*), Fährte *f*; Pfad *m*, Weg *m*; **~ of blood** Blutspur *f*; **~ of dust** Staubwolke *f*; **'~er** *mot.* Anhänger *m*; *Am. mot.* Wohnwagen *m*, Caravan *m*; *Film, TV:* Trailer *m*, Vorschau *f*; '**~er park** *Am.* Standplatz *m* für Wohnwagen

train [treɪn] **1.** *rail.* Zug *m*; Kolonne *f*; Schlange *f*; Schleppe *f*; *fig.* Folge *f*, Kette *f*; **~** mit der Bahn; mit dem Zug; **~ of thought** Gedankengang *m*; **2.** *v/t.* j-n ausbilden (**as** als, zum); schulen; *Sport:* trainieren; *Tier* abrichten, dressieren; *Kamera etc.* richten (**on** auf *acc.*); *v/i.* ausgebildet werden (**as** als, zum); *Sport:* trainieren (**for** für); **~ee** [treɪ'niː] Auszubildende(r *m*) *f*; '**~er** Ausbilder(in); Abrichter(in), Dompteur *m*, Dompteuse *f*; *Sport:* Trainer(in); *Brt.* Turnschuh *m*; '**~ing** Ausbildung *f*, Schulung *f*; Abrichten *n*, Dressur *f*; *Sport:* Training *n*

trait [treɪ, treɪt] (Charakter)Zug *m*

trai·tor ['treɪtə] Verräter *m*

tram *Brt.* [træm] Straßenbahn(wagen *m*) *f*; '**~car** *Brt.* Straßenbahnwagen *m*

tramp [træmp] **1.** sta(m)pfen *od.* trampeln (**durch**); **2.** Tramp *m*, Landstreicher(in); Wanderung *f*; *bsd. Am.* Flittchen *n*

tram·ple ['træmpl] (zer)trampeln

trance [trɑːns] Trance *f*

tran·quil ['træŋkwɪl] ruhig, friedlich; **~(l)i·ty** [træŋ'kwɪlətɪ] Ruhe *f*, Frieden *m*; **~(l)ize** ['træŋkwɪlaɪz] beruhigen; **~(l)iz·er** ['træŋkwɪlaɪzə] Beruhigungsmittel *n*

trans|act [træn'zækt] *Geschäft* abwickeln; *Handel* abschließen; **~ac·tion** [træn'zækʃn] Abwicklung *f*, Abschluß *m*; Geschäft *n*, Transaktion *f*

trans·at·lan·tic [trænzət'læntɪk] transatlantisch, Transatlantik..., Übersee...

tran·scribe [træn'skraɪb] abschreiben, kopieren; *Stenogramm etc.* übertragen

tran|script ['trænskrɪpt] Abschrift *f*, Kopie *f*; **~scrip·tion** [træn'skrɪpʃn]

Umschreibung *f*, Umschrift *f*; Abschrift *f*, Kopie *f*

trans·fer 1. [træns'fɜː] (**-rr-**) *v/t.* (**to**) *Betrieb etc.* verlegen (nach); *j-n* versetzen (nach); *Sport:* *Spieler* transferieren (zu), abgeben (an *acc.*); *Geld* überweisen (an *j-n*, auf *ein Konto*); *jur. Eigentum, Recht* übertragen (auf *acc.*); *v/i. Sport:* wechseln (**to** zu) (*Spieler*); *Reise:* umsteigen (**from ... to** von ... auf *acc.*); **2.** ['trænsfɜː] Verlegung *f*; Versetzung *f*; *Sport:* Transfer *m*, Wechsel *m*; *econ.* Überweisung *f*; *jur.* Übertragung *f*; *bsd. Am. etc.* Umsteige(fahr)karte *f*; **~·a·ble** [træns'fɜːrəbl] übertragbar

trans·fixed *fig.* [træns'fɪkst] versteinert, starr

trans|form [træns'fɔːm] um-, verwandeln; **~for·ma·tion** [trænsfə'meɪʃn] Um-, Verwandlung *f*

trans·fu·sion *med.* [træns'fjuːʒn] Bluttransfusion *f*, -übertragung *f*

trans·gress [træns'gres] verletzen, verstoßen gegen

tran·sient ['trænzɪənt] flüchtig, vergänglich

tran·sis·tor [træn'sɪstə] Transistor *m*

tran·sit ['trænsɪt] Transit-, Durchgangsverkehr *m*; *econ.* Transport *m*; **in ~** unterwegs, auf dem Transport

tran·si·tion [træn'sɪʒn] Übergang *m*

tran·si·tive *gr.* ['trænsɪtɪv] transitiv

tran·si·to·ry ['trænsɪtərɪ] → **transient**

trans·late [træns'leɪt] übersetzen (**from English into German** aus dem Englischen ins Deutsche); **~la·tion** [træns-'leɪʃn] Übersetzung *f*; **~la·tor** [træns-'leɪtə] Übersetzer(in)

trans·lu·cent [trænz'luːsnt] lichtdurchlässig

trans·mis·sion [trænz'mɪʃn] Übertragung *f* (*e-r Krankheit*); *Rundfunk, TV:* Sendung *f*; *mot.* Getriebe *n*

trans·mit [trænz'mɪt] (**-tt-**) *Signale* (aus)senden; *Rundfunk, TV:* senden; *phys. Wärme etc.* leiten; *Licht etc.* durchlassen; *Krankheit* übertragen; **~ter** Sender *m*

trans·par|en·cy [træns'pærənsɪ] Durchsichtigkeit *f* (*a. fig.*); *fig.* Durchschaubarkeit *f*; Dia(positiv) *n*; Folie *f* (*Lehrmaterial*); **~ent** durchsichtig (*a. fig.*); *fig.* durchschaubar

tran·spire [træn'spaɪə] transpirieren,

schwitzen; *fig.* durchsickern; F passieren

trans·plant 1. [træns'plɑ:nt] um-, verpflanzen; *med.* transplantieren, verpflanzen; **2.** *med.* ['trænsplɑ:nt] Trans-
plantation *f*, Verpflanzung *f*; Transplantat *n*

trans|·port 1. ['trænspɔ:t] Transport *m*,
Beförderung *f*; Beförderungs-, Verkehrsmittel *n od. pl.*; *mil.* Transport-
schiff *n*, -flugzeug *n*, (*Truppen*)Trans-
porter *m*; **2.** [træns'pɔ:t] transportieren,
befördern; **~·por·ta·tion** *bsd. Am.*
[trænspɔ:'teiʃn] Transport *m*, Beförderung *f*

trap [træp] **1.** Falle *f* (*a. fig.*); **set a ~ for
s.o.** j-m e-e Falle stellen; **shut one's ~,
keep one's ~ shut** *sl.* die Schnauze halten; **2.** (*-pp-*) (in *od.* mit e-r Falle) fangen; *fig.* in e-e Falle locken; **be ~ped**
eingeschlossen sein (*Bergleute etc.*);
'**~·door** Falltür *f*; *thea.* Versenkung *f*

tra·peze [trə'pi:z] Trapez *n*

trap·per ['træpə] Trapper *m*, Fallenstel-
ler *m*, Pelztierjäger *m*

trap·pings ['træpiŋz] *pl.* Rangabzeichen *pl.*; *fig.* Drum u. Dran *n*

trash [træʃ] Schund *m*; Quatsch *m*, Unsinn *m*; *Am.* Abfall *m*, Abfälle *pl.*, Müll
m; *bsd. Am.* Gesindel *n*; '**~·can** *Am.*
Abfall-, Mülleimer *m*; *Am.* Abfall-,
Mülltonne *f*; '**~·y** (*-ier, -iest*) Schund...

trav·el ['trævl] **1.** (*bsd. Brt. -ll-, Am. -l-*)
v/i. reisen; *fahren*; *tech. etc.* sich bewegen; sich verbreiten (*Neuigkeit etc.*);
fig. schweifen, wandern; *v/t.* bereisen;
Strecke zurücklegen, fahren; **2.** Reisen
n; **~s** *pl.* (*bsd. Auslands*)Reisen *pl.*; '**~
a·gen·cy** Reisebüro *n*; '**~ a·gent** Rei-
sebüroinhaber(in); Angestellte(r *m*) *f* in
e-m Reisebüro; '**~ a·gent's**, '**~
bu·reau** (*pl. -reaux* [-rəʊz], *-reaus*)
Reisebüro *n*; '**~·(l)er** Reisende(r *m*) *f*;
'**~·(l)er's cheque** (*Am.* **check**) Rei-
se-, Travellerscheck *m*; '**~·sick** reise-
krank; '**~·sick·ness** Reisekrankheit *f*

trav·es·ty ['trævisti] Zerrbild *n*

trawl [trɔ:l] **1.** Schleppnetz *n*; **2.** mit dem
Schleppnetz fischen; '**~·er** *naut.* Trawler *m*

tray [trei] Tablett *n*; Ablagekorb *m*

treach·er|·ous ['tretʃərəs] verräterisch;
tückisch; **~·y** ['tretʃəri] Verrat *m*

trea·cle *bsd. Brt.* ['tri:kl] Sirup *m*

tread [tred] **1.** (*trod, trodden od. trod*)
treten (**on** auf *acc.*; in *acc.*); Pfad *etc.*
treten; **2.** Gang *m*; Schritt(e *pl.*) *m*;
(*Reifen*)Profil *n*; '**~·mill** Tretmühle *f*
(*a. fig.*)

trea·son ['tri:zn] Landesverrat *m*

treal·sure ['treʒə] **1.** Schatz *m*; **2.** sehr
schätzen; in Ehren halten; **~·sur·er**
['treʒərə] Schatzmeister(in)

trea·sure trove [treʒə 'trəʊv] Schatz-
fund *m*

Trea·su·ry ['treʒəri] *Brt.*, '**~ De-
part·ment** *Am.* Finanzministerium *n*

treat [tri:t] **1.** *j-n, et.* behandeln; umgehen mit; *et.* ansehen, betrachten (**as**
als); *med.* j-n behandeln (**for** gegen); *j-n*
einladen (**to** zu); **~·o.s. to s.th.** *a.* j-m et.
spendieren; **~·o.s. to s.th.** sich et. leisten
od. gönnen; **be ~ed for** *med.* in ärztlicher Behandlung sein wegen; **2.** (besondere) Freude *od.* Überraschung;
this is my ~ das geht auf meine Rechnung

trea·tise ['tri:tiz] Abhandlung *f*

treat·ment ['tri:tmənt] Behandlung *f*

treat·y ['tri:ti] Vertrag *m*

tre·ble¹ ['trebl] **1.** dreifach; **2.** (sich) ver-
dreifachen

tre·ble² *mus.* ['trebl] Knabensopran *m*;
Radio: (Ton)Höhe *f*

tree [tri:] Baum *m*

tre·foil *bot.* ['trefɔil] Klee *m*

trel·lis ['trelis] Spalier *n* (*für Pflanzen
etc.*)

trem·ble ['trembl] zittern (**with** vor *dat.*)

tre·men·dous [tri'mendəs] gewaltig,
enorm; F klasse, toll

trem·or ['tremə] Zittern *n*; Beben *n*

trench [trentʃ] Graben *m*; *mil.* Schüt-
zengraben *m*

trend [trend] Trend *m*, Entwicklung *f*,
Tendenz *f*; Mode *f*; '**~·y** F **1.** (*-ier,
-iest*) modern, modisch; **be ~** als schick
gelten, in sein; **2.** *bsd. Brt. contp.*
Schickimicki *m*

tres·pass ['trespəs] **1.** **~ on** *Grundstück
etc.* unbefugt betreten; *j-s Zeit etc.* über
Gebühr in Anspruch nehmen; **no ~ing**
Betreten verboten!; **2.** unbefugtes Be-
treten; '**~·er:** **~s will be prosecuted**
Betreten bei Strafe verboten!

tres·tle ['tresl] Bock *m*, Gestell *n*

tri·al ['traiəl] *jur.* Prozeß *m*, (Gerichts)Verhandlung *f*, (-)Verfahren *n*;

T

Erprobung *f*, Probe *f*, Prüfung *f*, Test *m*; *fig.* Plage *f*; Versuchs..., Probe...; **on** ~ auf *od.* zur Probe; **be on** ~ erprobt *od.* getestet werden; **be on**, **stand** ~ *jur.* vor Gericht stehen (**for** wegen)

tri·an·gle ['traɪæŋgl] Dreieck *n*; *Am.* Winkel *m*, Zeichendreieck *n*; **~gu·lar** [traɪ'æŋgjʊlə] dreieckig

tri·ath·lon [traɪ'æθlɒn] *Sport:* Dreikampf *m*

trib·al ['traɪbl] Stammes...; **~e** [traɪb] (Volks)Stamm *m*

tri·bu·nal *jur.* [traɪ'bjuːnl] Gericht(shof *m*) *n*

trib·u·ta·ry ['trɪbjʊtərɪ] Nebenfluß *m*

trib·ute ['trɪbjuːt]: **be a** ~ **to** *j-m* Ehre machen; **pay** ~ **to** *j-m* Anerkennung zollen

trice *bsd. Brt.* F [traɪs]: **in a** ~ im Nu

trick [trɪk] **1.** Trick *m*; (*Karten-etc.*)Kunststück *n*; Streich *m*; (*Karten-spiel:*) Stich *m*; (merkwürdige) Angewohnheit, Eigenart *f*; **play a** ~ **on s.o.** *j-m* e-n Streich spielen; **2.** Trick...; ~ **question** Fangfrage *f*; **3.** überlisten, reinlegen; **~e·ry** ['trɪkərɪ] Tricks *pl.*

trick·le ['trɪkl] **1.** tröpfeln; rieseln; Tröpfeln *n*; Rinnsal *n*

trick·ster ['trɪkstə] Betrüger(in), Schwindler(in); **~y** ['trɪkɪ] (*-ier*, *-iest*) heikel, schwierig; durchtrieben, raffiniert

tri·cy·cle ['traɪsɪkl] Dreirad *n*

tri·dent ['traɪdənt] Dreizack *m*

tri·fle ['traɪfl] **1.** Kleinigkeit *f*; Lappalie *f*; **a** ~ ein bißchen, etwas; **2.** ~ **with** *fig.* spielen mit; **he is not to be** ~**d with** er läßt nicht mit sich spaßen; **~·fling** ['traɪflɪŋ] geringfügig, unbedeutend

trig·ger ['trɪgə] Abzug *m* (am Gewehr); **pull the** ~ abdrücken; **~·hap·py** schießwütig

trill [trɪl] **1.** Triller *m*; **2.** trillern

trim [trɪm] **1.** (*-mm-*) Hecke *etc.* stutzen, beschneiden, sich *den Bart etc.* stutzen; *Kleidungsstück* besetzen (**with** mit); **~med with fur** pelzbesetzt, mit Pelzbesatz; ~ **off** abschneiden; **2. give s.th. a** ~ *et.* stutzen, *et.* (be)schneiden; **be in good** ~ F gut in Form sein; **3.** (*-mm-*) gepflegt; **~·ming**: **~s** *pl.* Besatz *m*; *gastr.* Beilagen *pl.*

Trin·i·ty *rel.* ['trɪnɪtɪ] Dreieinigkeit *f*

trin·ket ['trɪŋkɪt] (*bsd.* billiges) Schmuckstück

trip [trɪp] **1.** (*-pp-*) *v/i.* stolpern (**over** über *acc.*); (e-n) Fehler machen; *v/t. a.* ~ **up** *j-m* ein Bein stellen (*a. fig.*); **2.** (kurze) Reise; Ausflug *m*, Trip *m*; Stolpern *n*, Fallen *n*; *sl.* Trip *m* (*Drogenrausch*)

tripe *gastr.* [traɪp] Kaldaunen *pl.*, Kutteln *pl.*

tri·ple ['trɪpl] dreifach; '~ **jump** *Sport:* Dreisprung *m*

trip·lets ['trɪplɪts] *pl.* Drillinge *pl.*

trip·li·cate ['trɪplɪkɪt] **1.** dreifach; **2.** **in** ~ in dreifacher Ausfertigung

tri·pod *phot.* ['traɪpɒd] Stativ *n*

trip·per *bsd. Brt.* F ['trɪpə] (*bsd. Tages-*)Ausflügler(in)

trite [traɪt] abgedroschen, banal

tri·umph ['traɪəmf] **1.** Triumph *m*, *fig.* Sieg *m* (**over** über *acc.*); **2.** triumphieren (**over** über *acc.*); **~·um·phal** [traɪ'ʌmfl] Triumph...; **~·um·phant** [traɪ'ʌmfənt] triumphierend

triv·i·al ['trɪvɪəl] unbedeutend, bedeutungslos; trivial, alltäglich

trod [trɒd] *pret. u. p.p. von* **tread** 1; **~·den** ['trɒdn] *p.p. von* **tread** 1

trol·ley *bsd. Brt.* ['trɒlɪ] Einkaufs-, Gepäckwagen *m*; Kofferkuli *m*; (*Tee-etc.*)Wagen *m*; (**supermarket**) ~ Einkaufswagen *m*; **shopping** ~ Einkaufswagen *m*; '~·bus Ø(berleitungs)bus *m*

trom·bone *mus.* [trɒm'bəʊn] Posaune *f*

troop [truːp] **1.** Schar *f*; **~s** *pl. mil.* Truppen *pl.*; **2.** (*herein- etc.*)strömen; ~ **the colour** *Brt. mil.* e-e Fahnenparade abhalten; '~·er *mil.* Kavallerist *m*; Panzerjäger *m*; *Am.* Polizist *m* (*e-s Bundesstaats*)

tro·phy ['trəʊfɪ] Trophäe *f*

trop·ic *astr., geogr.* ['trɒpɪk] Wendekreis *m*; **the** ~ **of Cancer** der Wendekreis des Krebses; **the** ~ **of Capricorn** der Wendekreis des Steinbocks

trop·i·cal ['trɒpɪkl] tropisch, Tropen...

trop·ics ['trɒpɪks] *pl.* Tropen *pl.*

trot [trɒt] **1.** Trab *m*; Trott *m*; **2.** (*-tt-*) traben (lassen); ~ **along** F losziehen

trou·ble ['trʌbl] **1.** Schwierigkeit *f*, Problem *n*, Ärger *m*; Mühe *f*; *med.* Beschwerden *pl.*; *a.* **~s** *pl. pol.* Unruhen *pl.*; **be in** ~ in Schwierigkeiten sein; **get into** ~ Schwierigkeiten *od.* Ärger bekommen; *j-n* in Schwierigkeiten bringen; **get** *od.* **run into** ~ in Schwierigkeiten geraten; **have ~ with** Schwierigkeiten *od.* Ärger haben mit; **put s.o. to ~** j-m Mühe *od.* Umstände machen; **take the ~ to do s.th.** sich die Mühe machen, et. zu tun; **2.** *v/t.* j-n beunruhigen; **j-m** Mühe *od.* Umstände machen; j-n bemühen (**for** um), bitten (**for** um; **to do** zu tun); **be ~d by** geplagt werden von, leiden an (*dat.*); *v/i.* sich bemühen (**to do** zu tun), sich Umstände machen (**about** wegen); '**~mak·er** Unruhestifter(in); '**~some** lästig

trough [trɒf] Trog *m*; Wellental *n*

trounce [traʊns] *Sport:* haushoch besiegen

troupe *thea.* [tru:p] Truppe *f*

trou·ser ['traʊzə]: (**a pair of ~**) *pl.* (e-e) Hose; '**~ suit** *Brt.* Hosenanzug *m*

trous·seau ['tru:səʊ] (*pl.* **-seaux** [-səʊ], **-seaus**) Aussteuer *f*

trout *zo.* [traʊt] (*pl.* **trout, trouts**) Forelle *f*

trow·el ['traʊəl] (Maurer)Kelle *f*

tru·ant ['tru:ənt] Schulschwänzer(in); **play ~** (die Schule) schwänzen

truce [tru:s] Waffenstillstand *m* (*a. fig.*)

truck¹ [trʌk] **1.** *mot.* Lastwagen *m*; *mot.* Fernlaster *m*; *Brt. rail.* (offener) Güterwagen; Transportkarren *m*; **2.** *bsd. Am.* auf *od.* mit Lastwagen transportieren

truck² *Am.* Gemüse *n od.* Obst *n* (*für den Verkauf*)

'**truck| driv·er**, '**~er** *bsd. Am.* Lastwagenfahrer *m*; Fernfahrer *m*

'**truck farm** *Am. econ.* Gemüse- u. Obstgärtnerei *f*

trudge [trʌdʒ] (mühsam) stapfen

true [tru:] (**~r, ~st**) wahr; echt, wirklich; treu (**to** *dat.*); **be ~** wahr sein, stimmen; **come ~** in Erfüllung gehen; wahr werden; **~ to life** lebensecht

tru·ly ['tru:lɪ] wahrheitsgemäß; wirklich, wahrhaft; aufrichtig; **Yours ~** *bsd. Am.* Hochachtungsvoll (*Briefschluß*)

trump [trʌmp] **1.** Trumpf(karte *f*) *m*; **~s** *pl.* Trumpf (*e-e Farbe*); **2.** mit e-m Trumpf stechen; **~ up** erfinden

trum·pet ['trʌmpɪt] **1.** *mus.* Trompete *f*; **2.** trompeten; *fig.* ausposaunen

trun·cheon ['trʌntʃən] (Gummi)Knüppel *m*, Schlagstock *m*

trun·dle ['trʌndl] Karren etc. ziehen

trunk [trʌŋk] (Baum)Stamm *m*; Schrankkoffer *m*; *zo.* Rüssel *m* (*des*

Elefanten); *anat.* Rumpf *m*; *Am. mot.* Kofferraum *m*; '**~ road** *Brt.* Fernstraße *f*

trunks [trʌŋks] *pl.* (*a.* **a pair of ~** e-e) (Bade)Hose; *Sport:* Shorts *pl.*

truss [trʌs] **1.** *a.* **~ up** j-n fesseln; *gastr.* Geflügel etc. dressieren; **2.** *med.* Bruchband *n*

trust [trʌst] **1.** Vertrauen *n* (**in** zu); *jur.* Treuhand *f*; *econ.* Trust *m*; *econ.* Großkonzern *m*; **hold s.th. in ~** et. treuhänderisch verwalten (**for** für); **place s.th. in s.o.'s ~** j-m et. anvertrauen; **2.** *v/t.* (ver)trauen (*dat.*); sich verlassen auf (*acc.*); (zuversichtlich) hoffen; **~ him!** das sieht ihm ähnlich!; *v/i.* **~ in** vertrauen auf (*acc.*); **~ to** sich verlassen auf (*acc.*); **~ee** *jur.* [trʌs'ti:] Treuhänder(in); Sachverwalter(in); '**~ful**, '**~ing** vertrauensvoll; '**~wor·thy** vertrauenswürdig, zuverlässig

truth [tru:θ] (*pl.* **~s** [tru:ðz, tru:θs]) Wahrheit *f*; '**~ful** wahr(heitsliebend)

try [traɪ] **1.** *v/t.* versuchen; et. (aus)probieren; *jur.* (über) *e-e Sache* verhandeln; *jur.* j-m den Prozeß machen (**for** wegen); j-n, j-s Geduld, Nerven etc. auf e-e harte Probe stellen; **~ s.th. on** *Kleidungsstück* anprobieren; **~ s.th. out** et. ausprobieren; *v/i.* es versuchen; **~ for** *Brt.*, **~ out** *Am.* sich bemühen um; **2.** Versuch *m*; '**~ing** anstrengend

tsar *hist.* [zɑ:] Zar *m*

T-shirt ['ti:ʃɜ:t] T-Shirt *n*

TU [ti: 'ju:] *Abk. für* **trade(s) union** Gewerkschaft *f*

tub [tʌb] Bottich *m*, Zuber *m*, Tonne *f*; Becher *m* (*für Eis, Margarine etc.*); F (Bade)Wanne *f*

tube [tju:b] Röhre *f* (*a. anat.*), Rohr *n*; Schlauch *m*; Tube *f*; *Brt.* F U-Bahn *f* (*in London*); *Am.* F Röhre *f*, Glotze *f* (*Fernseher*); '**~·less** schlauchlos

tu·ber *bot.* ['tju:bə] Knolle *f*

tu·ber·cu·lo·sis *med.* [tju:bɜ:bə:kjʊ'ləʊsɪs] Tuberkulose *f*

tu·bu·lar ['tju:bjʊlə] röhrenförmig

TUC *Brt.* [ti: ju: 'si:] *Abk. für* **Trades Union Congress** Gewerkschaftsverband *m*

tuck [tʌk] **1.** stecken; **~ away** F wegstecken; **~ in** *bsd. Brt.* F reinhauen, zulangen; **~ up** (**in bed**) *Kind* ins Bett packen; **2.** Biese *f*; Saum *m*; Abnäher *m*

Tue(s) *nur geschr. Abk. für* **Tuesday** Di., Dienstag *m*

Tues·day ['tju:zdɪ] (*Abk.* **Tue, Tues**) Dienstag *m*; **on ~** (am) Dienstag; **on ~s** dienstags

tuft [tʌft] (*Gras-, Haar- etc.*)Büschel *n*

tug [tʌg] **1.** (*-gg-*) zerren *od.* ziehen (an *dat. od.* **at** an *dat.*); **2. give** s.th. **a ~** zerren *od.* ziehen an (*dat.*); **~-of-'war** *Sport:* Tauziehen *n* (*a. fig.*)

tu·i·tion [tju:'ɪʃn] Unterricht *m*; *bsd. Am.* Unterrichtsgebühr(en *pl.*) *f*

tu·lip *bot.* ['tju:lɪp] Tulpe *f*

tum·ble ['tʌmbl] **1.** fallen, stürzen; purzeln (*a. Preise*); **2.** Fall *m*, Sturz *m*; '**~·down** baufällig

tum·bler ['tʌmblə] (Trink)Glas *n*

tu·mid *med.* ['tju:mɪd] geschwollen

tum·my F ['tʌmɪ] Bauch *m*, Bäuchlein *n*

tu·mo(u)r *med.* ['tju:mə] Tumor *m*

tu·mult ['tju:mʌlt] Tumult *m*; **tu·mul·tu·ous** [tju:'mʌltjʊəs] tumultartig, (*Applaus, Empfang*) stürmisch

tu·na *zo.* ['tu:nə] (*pl.* **-na, -nas**) Thunfisch *m*

tune [tju:n] **1.** Melodie *f*; **be out of ~** *mus.* verstimmt sein; **2.** *v/t. mst* **~ in** Radio *etc.* einstellen (**to** auf *acc.*); *a.* **~ up** *mus.* stimmen; *a.* **~ up** Motor tunen; *v/i.* **~ in** (das Radio *etc.*) einschalten; **~ up** (die Instrumente) stimmen (*Orchester*); '**~·ful** melodisch; '**~·less** unmelodisch

tun·er ['tju:nə] Radio, TV: Tuner *m*

tun·nel ['tʌnl] **1.** Tunnel *m*; **2.** (*bsd. Brt. -ll-, Am. -l-*) Berg durchtunneln; *Fluß etc.* untertunneln

tun·ny *zo.* ['tʌnɪ] (*pl.* **-ny, -nies**) Thunfisch *m*

tur·ban ['tɜ:bən] Turban *m*

tur·bid ['tɜ:bɪd] trüb (*Flüssigkeit*); dick (*Rauch etc.*); *fig.* verworren, wirr

tur·bine *tech.* ['tɜ:baɪn] Turbine *f*

tur·bo F *mot.* ['tɜ:bəʊ] (*pl.* **-bos**), **~·charg·er** *mot.* ['tɜ:bəʊtʃɑ:dʒə] Turbolader *m*

tur·bot *zo.* ['tɜ:bət] (*pl.* **-bot, -bots**) Steinbutt *m*

tur·bu·lent ['tɜ:bjʊlənt] turbulent

tu·reen [tə'ri:n] (Suppen)Terrine *f*

turf [tɜ:f] **1.** (*pl.* **turfs, turves** [tɜ:vz]) Rasen *m*; Sode *f*, Rasenstück *n*; **the ~** die (Pferde)Rennbahn; der Pferderennsport; **2.** mit Rasen bedecken

tur·gid *med.* ['tɜ:dʒɪd] geschwollen

Turk [tɜ:k] Türk|e *m*, -in *f*

Tur·key ['tɜ:kɪ] die Türkei

tur·key ['tɜ:kɪ] *zo.* Truthahn *m*, -henne *f*, Pute(r *m*) *f*; **talk ~** *bsd. Am.* F offen *od.* sachlich reden

Turk·ish ['tɜ:kɪʃ] **1.** türkisch; **2.** *ling.* Türkisch *n*

tur·moil ['tɜ:mɔɪl] Aufruhr *m*

turn [tɜ:n] **1.** *v/t.* (herum-, um)drehen; (um)wenden; *Seite* umblättern; *Schlauch etc.* richten (**on** auf *acc.*); *Antenne* ausrichten (**toward[s]** auf *acc.*); *Aufmerksamkeit* zuwenden (**to** *dat.*); verwandeln (**into** in *acc.*); *Laub etc.* färben; *Milch* sauer werden lassen; *tech.* formen, drechseln; **~ the corner** um die Ecke biegen; **~ loose** los-, freilassen; **~** s.o.'s **stomach** j-m den Magen umdrehen; → **inside** 1, **upside down, somersault** 1; *v/i.* (um)drehen; abbiegen; einbiegen (**onto** auf *acc.*; **into** in *acc.*); *mot.* wenden; *blaß, sauer etc.* werden; sich verwandeln, *fig. a.* umschlagen (*Wetter etc.*) (**into, to** in *acc.*); → **left²** 2, **right** 2; **~ against** j-n aufbringen *od.* -hetzen gegen; *fig.* sich wenden gegen; **~ away** (sich) abwenden (**from** von); j-n abweisen, wegschicken; **~ back** umkehren; j-n zurückschicken; *Uhr* zurückstellen; **~ down** Radio *etc.* leiser stellen; *Gas etc.* klein(er) stellen; *Heizung etc.* runterschalten; j-n, *Angebot etc.* ablehnen; *Kragen* umschlagen; *Bettdecke* zurückschlagen; **~ in** *v/t.* zurückgeben; *Gewinn etc.* erzielen, machen; *bsd. Am. Arbeit* einreichen, abgeben; **~** s.o. **in** sich stellen; *v/i.* F sich aufs Ohr legen; **~ off** *v/t.* Gas, Wasser etc. abdrehen; *Licht, Radio etc.* ausmachen, -schalten; *Motor* abstellen; F j-n anwidern; F j-m die Lust nehmen; *v/i.* abbiegen; **~ on** Gas, Wasser etc. aufdrehen; *Gerät* anstellen; *Licht, Radio etc.* anmachen, an-, einschalten; F j-n antörnen, anmachen; **~ out** *v/t.* Licht ausmachen, -schalten; j-n hinausperren; *econ.* F Waren ausstoßen; *Tasche etc.* (aus)lehren; *v/i.* kommen (**for** zu); sich erweisen *od.* herausstellen als; **~ over** (sich) umdrehen; *Seite* umblättern; wenden; *etc.* umkippen; sich *et.* überlegen; j-n, *et.* übergeben (**to** *dat.*); *econ.* Waren umsetzen; **~ round** sich umdrehen; **~** one's **car round** wenden; **~ to**

sich an *j-n* wenden; sich zuwenden (*dat.*); **~ up** *Kragen* hochschlagen; *Ärmel, Saum etc.* umschlagen; *Radio etc.* lauter stellen; *Gas etc.* aufdrehen; *fig.* auftauchen; **2.** (Um)Drehung *f*; Biegung *f*, Kurve *f*, Kehre *f*; *Am.* Abzweigung *f*; *fig.* Wende *f*, Wendung *f*; **at every ~** auf Schritt und Tritt; **by ~s** abwechselnd; **in ~** der Reihe nach; abwechselnd; **it is my ~** ich bin dran *od.* abwechselnd; **it is my ~** ich bin dran *od.* an der Reihe; **make a left ~** nach links abbiegen; **take ~s** sich abwechseln (*at* bei); **take a ~ for the better/worse** sich bessern/sich verschlimmern; **do s.o. a good/bad ~** j-m e-n guten/schlechten Dienst erweisen; '**~coat** Abtrünnige(r) *m*, Überläufer(in); (*political*) ~ *F pol.* Wendehals *m*; '**~er** Drechsler *m*; Dreher *m*

'**turn·ing** *bsd. Brt.* Abzweigung *f*; '**~cir·cle** *mot.* Wendekreis *m*; '**~ point** *fig.* Wendepunkt *m*

tur·nip *bot.* ['tɜːnɪp] Rübe *f*

'**turn-off** Abzweigung *f*; '**~out** Besucher(zahl *f*) *pl.*, Beteiligung *f*; Wahlbeteiligung *f*; F Aufmachung *f* (*e-r Person*); '**~o·ver** *econ.* Umsatz *m*; Personalwechsel *m*, Fluktuation *f*; '**~pike** *Am.*, '**~pike 'road** *Am.* gebührenpflichtige Schnellstraße; '**~stile** Drehkreuz *n*; '**~ta·ble** Plattenteller *m*; '**~up** *Brt.* (Hosen)Aufschlag *m*

tur·pen·tine *chem.* ['tɜːpəntaɪn] Terpentin *n*

tur·quoise *min.* ['tɜːkwɔɪz] Türkis *m*

tur·ret ['tʌrɪt] *arch.* Ecktürmchen *n*; *mil.* (Panzer)Turm *m*; *naut.* Gefechts-, Geschützturm *m*

tur·tle *zo.* ['tɜːtl] (*pl.* **-tles, -tle**) (See)Schildkröte *f*; '**~dove** *zo.* Turteltaube *f*; '**~neck** *bsd. Am.* Rollkragen(pullover) *m*

tusk [tʌsk] Stoßzahn *m* (*von Elefant u. Walroß*); Hauer *m* (*e-s Keilers*)

tus·sle F ['tʌsl] Gerangel *n*

tus·sock ['tʌsək] Grasbüschel *n*

tu·te·lage ['tjuːtɪlɪdʒ] (An)Leitung *f*; *jur.* Vormundschaft *f*

tu·tor ['tjuːtə] Privat-, Hauslehrer(in); *Brt. univ.* Tutor(in), Studienleiter(in)

tu·to·ri·al *Brt. univ.* [tjuː'tɔːrɪəl] Tutorenkurs *m*

tux·e·do *Am.* [tʌk'siːdəʊ] (*pl.* **-dos**) Smoking *m*

TV [tiː'viː] TV *n*, Fernsehen *n*; Fernseher *m*, Fernsehapparat *m*; Fernseh...; **on ~** im Fernsehen; **watch ~** fernsehen

twang [twæŋ] **1.** Schwirren *n*; *mst nasal* ~ näselnde Aussprache; **2.** schwirren (lassen)

tweak F [twiːk] zwicken, kneifen

tweet [twiːt] piep(s)en (*Vogel*)

tweez·ers ['twiːzəz] *pl.* (**a pair of ~** e-e) Pinzette

twelfth [twelfθ] **1.** zwölfte(r, -s); **2.** Zwölftel *n*

twelve [twelv] **1.** zwölf; **2.** Zwölf *f*

twen·ti·eth ['twentɪɪθ] zwanzigste(r, -s); **~ty** ['twentɪ] **1.** zwanzig; **2.** Zwanzig *f*

twice [twaɪs] zweimal

twid·dle ['twɪdl] (herum)spielen mit (*od.* **with** mit); **~ one's thumbs** Däumchen drehen

twig [twɪg] dünner Zweig, Ästchen *n*

twi·light ['twaɪlaɪt] (*bsd.* Abend)Dämmerung *f*; Zwie-, Dämmerlicht *n*

twin [twɪn] **1.** Zwilling *m*; **~s** *pl.* Zwillinge *pl.*; **2.** Zwillings...; doppelt; **3.** (**-nn-**): **be ~ned with** die Partnerstadt von; **~-bed·ded 'room** Zweibettzimmer *n*; **~ 'beds** *pl.* zwei Einzelbetten; **~ 'broth·er** Zwillingsbruder *m*

twine [twaɪn] **1.** Bindfaden *m*, Schnur *f*; **2.** (sich) schlingen *od.* winden (**round** um); *a.* **~ together** zusammendrehen

twin-'en·gined *aviat.* zweimotorig

twinge [twɪndʒ] stechender Schmerz, Stechen *n*; **a ~ of conscience** Gewissensbisse *pl.*

twin·kle ['twɪŋkl] **1.** glitzern (*Sterne*), (*a.* *Augen*) funkeln (**with** *vor dat.*); **2.** Glitzern *n*, Funkeln *n*; **with a ~ in one's eye** augenzwinkernd

twin 'sis·ter Zwillingsschwester *f*; **~ 'town** Partnerstadt *f*

twirl [twɜːl] **1.** (herum)wirbeln; wirbeln (**round** über *acc.*); **2.** Wirbel *m*

twist [twɪst] **1.** *v/t.* drehen; wickeln (**round** um); *fig.* entstellen, verdrehen; **~ off** abdrehen, *Deckel* abschrauben; **~ one's ankle** (sich den Fuß) umknicken, sich den Fuß vertreten; **her face was ~ed with pain** ihr Gesicht war schmerzverzerrt; *v/i.* sich winden (*Person*), (*Fluß etc. a.*) sich schlängeln; **2.** Drehung *f*; Biegung *f*; *fig.* (*überraschende*) Wendung; *mus.* Twist *m*

T

twitch [twɪtʃ] **1.** zucken (mit); zucken (*with* vor); zupfen (*an dat.*); **2.** Zucken *n*; Zuckung *f*

twit·ter ['twɪtə] **1.** zwitschern; **2.** Zwitschern *n*, Gezwitscher *n*; *be all of a ~* F ganz aufgeregt sein

two [tu:] **1.** zwei; *the ~ cars* die beiden Autos; *the ~ of us* wir beide; *in ~s* zu zweit, paarweise; *cut in ~* in zwei Teile schneiden; *put ~ and ~ together* zwei u. zwei zusammenzählen; **2.** Zwei *f*; ~-'**edged** zweischneidig; ~'**faced** falsch, heuchlerisch; '~**fold** zweifach; ~**pence** *Brt.* ['tʌpəns] zwei Pence *pl.*; ~**pen·ny** *Brt.* F ['tʌpnɪ] für zwei Pence; ~'**piece** zweiteilig; ~ *dress* Jackenkleid *n*; ~'**seat·er** *aviat.*, *mot.* Zweisitzer *m*; '~**stroke** *tech.* **1.** Zweitakt...; **2.** *a.* ~ *engine* Zweitakter *m*; ~'**way** Doppel...; ~**way** '**traf·fic** Gegenverkehr *m*

ty·coon [taɪ'ku:n] (*Industrie- etc.*)Magnat *m*

type [taɪp] **1.** Art *f*, Sorte *f*; Typ *m*; *print.* Type *f*, Buchstabe *m*; **2.** *v/t. et.* mit der Maschine schreiben, tippen; *v/i.* maschineschreiben, tippen; '~**writ·er** Schreibmaschine *f*; '~**writ·ten** maschine(n)geschrieben

ty·phoid *med.* ['taɪfɔɪd], ~ '**fe·ver** *med.* Typhus *m*

ty·phoon [taɪ'fu:n] Taifun *m*

ty·phus *med.* ['taɪfəs] Flecktyphus *m*, -fieber *n*; △ *nicht* **Typhus**

typ·i·cal ['tɪpɪkl] typisch, bezeichnend (*of* für); ~**fy** ['tɪpɪfaɪ] typisch sein für, kennzeichnen; verkörpern

typ·ing| er·ror ['taɪpɪŋ -] Tippfehler *m*; '~ **pool** Schreibzentrale *f* (*in e-r Firma*)

typ·ist ['taɪpɪst] Schreibkraft *f*; Maschinenschreiber(in)

ty·ran·ni·cal [tɪ'rænɪkl] tyrannisch

tyr·an|·nize ['tɪrənaɪz] tyrannisieren; ~**ny** ['tɪrənɪ] Tyrannei *f*

ty·rant ['taɪərənt] Tyrann(in)

tyre *Brt.* ['taɪə] Reifen *m*

Ty·rol [tɪ'rəʊl, 'tɪrəl] → **Tirol**

tzar *hist.* [zɑ:] → **tsar**

U

U, u [ju:] U, u *n*

ud·der *zo.* ['ʌdə] Euter *n*

UEFA [ju:'i:fə] *Abk. für* **Union of European Football Associations** UEFA *f*

UFO ['ju:fəʊ, ju: ef 'əʊ] (*pl. -os*) *Abk. für* **unidentified flying object** UFO *n*, Ufo *n*

ug·ly ['ʌglɪ] (*-ier, -iest*) häßlich (*a. fig.*); bös(e), schlimm (*Wunde etc.*)

UHF [ju: eɪtʃ 'ef] *Abk. für* **ultrahigh frequency** UHF, Ultrahochfrequenz(bereich *m*) *f*

UK [ju: 'keɪ] *Abk. für* **United Kingdom** das Vereinigte Königreich (*England, Schottland, Wales u. Nordirland*)

ul·cer *med.* ['ʌlsə] Geschwür *n*

ul·te·ri·or [ʌl'tɪərɪə]: ~ *motive* Hintergedanke *m*

ul·ti·mate ['ʌltɪmət] letzte(r, -s), End...; höchste(r, -s); '~**ly** letztlich; schließlich

ul·ti·ma·tum [ʌltɪ'meɪtəm] (*pl. -tums,*

-ta [-tə]) Ultimatum *n*

ul·tra|·high fre·quen·cy *electr.* [ʌltrəhaɪ 'fri:kwənsɪ] Ultrakurzwelle *f*; ~**ma·rine** ultramarin; ~'**son·ic** Ultraschall...; '~**sound** *phys.* Ultraschall *m*; ~'**vi·o·let** ultraviolett

um·bil·i·cal cord *anat.* [ʌmbɪlɪkl 'kɔ:d] Nabelschnur *f*

um·brel·la [ʌm'brelə] (Regen)Schirm *m*; *fig.* Schutz *m*

um·pire ['ʌmpaɪə] *Sport* **1.** Schiedsrichter(in); **2.** als Schiedsrichter fungieren (bei)

UN [ju: 'en] *Abk. für* **United Nations** *pl.* UN *f*, Vereinte Nationen *pl.*

un·a·bashed [ʌnə'bæʃt] unverfroren

un·a·bat·ed [ʌnə'beɪtɪd] unvermindert

un·a·ble [ʌn'eɪbl] unfähig, außerstande, nicht in der Lage

un·ac·coun·ta·ble [ʌnə'kaʊntəbl] unerklärlich

un·ac·cus·tomed [ʌnəˈkʌstəmd] ungewohnt

un·ac·quaint·ed [ʌnəˈkweɪntɪd]: *be ~ with s.th.* et. nicht kennen, mit e-r Sache nicht vertraut sein

un·ad·vised [ʌnədˈvaɪzd] unbesonnen, unüberlegt

un·af·fect·ed [ʌnəˈfektɪd] natürlich, ungekünstelt; *be ~ by* nicht betroffen werden von

un·aid·ed [ʌnˈeɪdɪd] ohne Unterstützung, (ganz) allein

un·al·ter·a·ble [ʌnˈɔːltərəbl] unabänderlich (*Entschluß etc.*)

u·nan·i·mous [juːˈnænɪməs] einmütig; einstimmig

un·an·nounced [ʌnəˈnaʊnst] unangemeldet

un·an·swer·a·ble [ʌnˈɑːnsərəbl] unwiderlegbar; nicht zu beantworten(d)

un·ap·proach·a·ble [ʌnəˈprəʊtʃəbl] unnahbar

un·armed [ʌnˈɑːmd] unbewaffnet

un·asked [ʌnˈɑːskt] ungestellt (*Frage*); unaufgefordert, ungebeten

un·as·sist·ed [ʌnəˈsɪstɪd] ohne (fremde) Hilfe, (ganz) allein

un·as·sum·ing [ʌnəˈsjuːmɪŋ] bescheiden

un·at·tached [ʌnəˈtætʃt] ungebunden, frei (*Person*)

un·at·tend·ed [ʌnəˈtendɪd] unbeaufsichtigt

un·at·trac·tive [ʌnəˈtræktɪv] unattraktiv, wenig anziehend, reizlos

un·au·thor·ized [ʌnˈɔːθəraɪzd] unberechtigt, unbefugt

un·a·void·a·ble [ʌnəˈvɔɪdəbl] unvermeidlich

un·a·ware [ʌnəˈweə]: *be ~ of s.th.* sich e-r Sache nicht bewußt sein, et. nicht bemerken; *~s* [ʌnəˈweəz]: *catch od. take s.o. ~* j-n überraschen

un·bal·ance [ʌnˈbæləns] *j-n* aus dem (seelischen) Gleichgewicht bringen; *~d* unausgeglichen, labil

un·bar [ʌnˈbɑː] auf-, entriegeln

un·bear·a·ble [ʌnˈbeərəbl] unerträglich

un·beat·a·ble [ʌnˈbiːtəbl] unschlagbar; **un·beat·en** [ʌnˈbiːtn] ungeschlagen, unbesiegt

un·be·known(st) [ʌnbɪˈnəʊn(st)]: *~ to s.o.* ohne j-s Wissen

un·be·liev·a·ble [ʌnbɪˈliːvəbl] unglaublich

un·bend [ʌnˈbend] (*-bent*) geradebiegen; sich aufrichten; *fig.* aus sich herausgehen, auftauen; *~ing* unbeugsam

un·bi·as(s)ed [ʌnˈbaɪəst] unvoreingenommen; *jur.* unbefangen

un·bind [ʌnˈbaɪnd] (*-bound*) losbinden

un·blem·ished [ʌnˈblemɪʃt] makellos (*Ruf etc.*)

un·born [ʌnˈbɔːn] ungeboren

un·break·a·ble [ʌnˈbreɪkəbl] unzerbrechlich

un·bri·dled *fig.* [ʌnˈbraɪdld] ungezügelt, zügellos; *~ tongue* lose Zunge

un·bro·ken [ʌnˈbrəʊkən] ununterbrochen; heil, unversehrt; nicht zugeritten (*Pferd*)

un·buck·le [ʌnˈbʌkl] auf-, losschnallen

un·bur·den [ʌnˈbɜːdn]: *~ o.s. to s.o.* j-m sein Herz ausschütten

un·but·ton [ʌnˈbʌtn] aufknöpfen

un·called-for [ʌnˈkɔːldfɔː] ungerechtfertigt; unnötig; unpassend

un·can·ny [ʌnˈkænɪ] (*-ier, -iest*) unheimlich

un·cared-for [ʌnˈkeədfɔː] vernachlässigt

un·ceas·ing [ʌnˈsiːsɪŋ] unaufhörlich

un·cer·e·mo·ni·ous [ʌnserɪˈməʊnjəs] brüsk, unhöflich; überstürzt

un·cer·tain [ʌnˈsɜːtn] unsicher, ungewiß, unbestimmt; vage; unbeständig (*Wetter*); *~ty* [ʌnˈsɜːtntɪ] Unsicherheit *f*, Ungewißheit *f*

un·chain [ʌnˈtʃeɪn] losketten

un·changed [ʌnˈtʃeɪndʒd] unverändert; **un·chang·ing** [ʌnˈtʃeɪndʒɪŋ] unveränderlich

un·char·i·ta·ble [ʌnˈtʃærɪtəbl] unfair, unfreundlich

un·checked [ʌnˈtʃekt] ungehindert; unkontrolliert

un·chris·tian [ʌnˈkrɪstʃən] unchristlich

un·civ·il [ʌnˈsɪvl] unhöflich; **un·civ·i·lized** [ʌnˈsɪvɪlaɪzd] unzivilisiert

un·cle [ˈʌŋkl] Onkel *m*

un·com·for·ta·ble [ʌnˈkʌmfətəbl] unbequem; *feel ~* sich unbehaglich fühlen

un·com·mon [ʌnˈkɒmən] ungewöhnlich

un·com·mu·ni·ca·tive [ʌnkəˈmjuːnɪkətɪv] wortkarg, verschlossen

un·com·pro·mis·ing [ʌnˈkɒmprəmaɪzɪŋ] kompromißlos

U

un·con·cerned [ʌnkən'sɜːnd]: *be* ~ *about* sich keine Gedanken *od.* Sorgen machen über (*acc.*); *be* ~ *with* uninteressiert sein an (*dat.*)

un·con·di·tion·al [ʌnkən'dɪʃənl] bedingungslos

un·con·firmed [ʌnkən'fɜːmd] unbestätigt

un·con·scious [ʌn'kɒnʃəs] *med.* bewußtlos; unbewußt; unbeabsichtigt; *be* ~ *of s.th.* sich e-r Sache nicht bewußt sein, et. nicht bemerken; ~·**ness** *med.* Bewußtlosigkeit *f*

un·con·sti·tu·tion·al [ʌnkɒnstɪ'tjuːʃənl] verfassungswidrig

un·con·trol·la·ble [ʌnkən'trəʊləbl] unkontrollierbar; nicht zu bändigen(d) (*Kind*); unbändig (*Wut etc.*); **un·con·trolled** [ʌnkən'trəʊld] unkontrolliert, ungehindert

un·con·ven·tion·al [ʌnkən'venʃənl] unkonventionell

un·con·vinced [ʌnkən'vɪnst]: *be* ~ nicht überzeugt sein (*about* von); **un·con·vinc·ing** nicht überzeugend

un·cooked [ʌn'kʊkt] ungekocht, roh

un·cork [ʌn'kɔːk] entkorken

un·count·a·ble [ʌn'kaʊntəbl] unzählbar

un·coup·le [ʌn'kʌpl] *Waggon etc.* abkoppeln

un·couth [ʌn'kuːθ] ungehobelt (*Person, Benehmen*)

un·cov·er [ʌn'kʌvə] aufdecken, *fig. a.* enthüllen

un·crit·i·cal [ʌn'krɪtɪkl] unkritisch; *be* ~ *of s.th.* e-r Sache unkritisch gegenüberstehen

unc|·tion *rel.* ['ʌŋkʃn] Salbung *f*; ~·**tu·ous** ['ʌŋktjʊəs] salbungsvoll

un·cut [ʌn'kʌt] ungekürzt (*Film, Roman etc.*); ungeschliffen (*Diamant etc.*)

un·dam·aged [ʌn'dæmɪdʒd] unbeschädigt, unversehrt, heil

un·dat·ed [ʌn'deɪtɪd] undatiert, ohne Datum

un·daunt·ed [ʌn'dɔːntɪd] unerschrocken, furchtlos

un·de·cid·ed [ʌndɪ'saɪdɪd] unentschieden, offen; unentschlossen

un·de·mon·stra·tive [ʌndɪ'mɒnstrətɪv] zurückhaltend, reserviert

un·de·ni·a·ble [ʌndɪ'naɪəbl] unbestreitbar

un·der ['ʌndə] **1.** *prp.* unter; **2.** *adv.* unten; darunter; ~·**age** [ʌndər'eɪdʒ] minderjährig; ~'**bid** (**-dd-**; **-bid**) unterbieten; '~·**brush** *bsd. Am.* → *under-growth*; '~·**car·riage** *aviat.* Fahrwerk *n*, -gestell *n*; ~'**charge** zuwenig berechnen; zuwenig verlangen; ~·**clothes** ['ʌndəkləʊðz] *pl.*, ~·**cloth·ing** ['ʌndəkləʊðɪŋ] → *underwear*; '~·**coat** Grundierung *f*; ~'**cov·er**: ~ *agent* verdeckter Ermittler; ~'**cut** (**-tt-**; **-cut**) *j-n* (im Preis) unterbieten; ~·**de·vel·oped** unterentwickelt; ~ *country* Entwicklungsland *n*; '~·**dog** Benachteiligte(r *m*) *f*, Unterdrückte(r *m*) *f*; ~'**done** nicht gar, nicht durchgebraten; ~·**es·ti·mate** [ʌndər'estɪmeɪt] zu niedrig schätzen *od.* veranschlagen; *fig.* unterschätzen, -bewerten; ~·**ex·pose** *phot.* [ʌndərɪk'spəʊz] unterbelichten; ~'**fed** unterernährt; ~'**go** (**-went, -gone**) erleben, durchmachen; sich e-r *Operation etc.* unterziehen; ~'**grad** F ['ʌndəgræd], ~'**grad·u·ate** [ʌndə'grædʒʊət] Student(in); ~'**ground 1.** *adv.* [ʌndə'graʊnd] unterirdisch, unter der Erde; **2.** *adj.* ['ʌndəgraʊnd] unterirdisch; *fig.* Untergrund...; **3.** ['ʌndəgraʊnd] *bsd. Brt.* Untergrundbahn *f*, U-Bahn *f*; *by* ~ mit der U-Bahn; '~·**growth** Unterholz *n*, Gestrüpp *n*; ~'**hand**, ~'**hand·ed** hinterhältig (*Methoden etc.*); ~'**lie** (**-lay, -lain**) zugrunde liegen (*dat.*); ~'**line** unterstreichen (*a. fig.*); '~·**ling** *contp.* Untergebene(r *m*) *f*; ~'**ly·ing** zugrundeliegend; '~·**mine** unterspülen; *fig.* untergraben, -minieren; ~·**neath** [ʌndə'niːθ] **1.** *prp.* unter; **2.** *adv.* darunter; ~'**nour·ished** unterernährt; ~'**pants** *pl.* Unterhose *f*; '~·**pass** Unterführung *f*; ~'**pay** (**-paid**) *j-m* zuwenig bezahlen; *j-n* unterbezahlen; ~'**priv·i·leged** unterprivilegiert, benachteiligt; ~'**rate** unterbewerten, -schätzen; ~'**sec·re·ta·ry** *pol.* Staatssekretär *m*; ~'**sell** (**-sold**) *econ.* Ware verschleudern, unter Wert verkaufen; ~ *o.s. fig.* sich schlecht verkaufen; '~·**shirt** *Am.* Unterhemd *n*; '~·**side** Unterseite *f*; ~'**signed 1.** unterzeichnet; **2.** *the* ~ *od.* die Unterzeichnete, die Unterzeichneten *pl.*; ~'**size(d)** zu klein; ~'**staffed** (personell) unterbesetzt; ~'**stand** (**-stood**) verstehen; erfahren *od.* gehört haben (*that* daß); **make o.s. understood** sich verständlich machen; **am I to ~ that** soll das heißen, daß; **give s.o. to ~ that** j-m zu verstehen geben, daß; **~'stand·a·ble** verständlich; **~'stand·ing 1.** Verstand *m*; Verständnis *n*; Abmachung *f*; Verständigung *f*; **come to an ~** e-e Abmachung treffen (**with** mit); **on the ~ that** unter der Voraussetzung, daß; **2.** verständnisvoll; **~'state** untertreiben, untertrieben darstellen; **~'state·ment** Understatement *n*, Untertreibung *f*; **~'take** (**-took, -taken**) *et.* übernehmen; sich verpflichten (**to do** zu tun); **~'tak·er** Leichenbestatter *m*; Beerdigungs-, Bestattungsinstitut *n*; △ *nicht* **Unternehmer;** **~'tak·ing** Unternehmen *n*; Zusicherung *f*; **'~·tone** *fig.* Unterton *m*; **in an ~** mit gedämpfter Stimme; **~'val·ue** unterbewerten, -schätzen; **~'wa·ter 1.** *adj.* Unterwasser...; **2.** *adv.* unter Wasser; **'~·wear** Unterwäsche *f*; **~'weight 1.** ['ʌndəweit] Untergewicht *n*; **2.** [ʌndə'weit] untergewichtig (*Person*), zu leicht (**by** um) (*Sache*); **be five pounds ~** fünf Pfund Untergewicht haben; **'~·world** Unterwelt *f*

un·de·served [ʌndɪ'zɜ:vd] unverdient
un·de·si·ra·ble [ʌndɪ'zaɪərəbl] unerwünscht
un·de·vel·oped [ʌndɪ'veləpt] unerschlossen (*Gelände*); unentwickelt
un·dies F ['ʌndɪz] *pl.* (Damen)Unterwäsche *f*
un·dig·ni·fied [ʌn'dɪɡnɪfaɪd] würdelos
un·dis·ci·plined [ʌn'dɪsɪplɪnd] undiszipliniert, disziplinlos
un·dis·cov·ered [ʌndɪs'kʌvəd] unentdeckt
un·dis·put·ed [ʌndɪ'spju:tɪd] unbestritten
un·dis·turbed [ʌndɪ'stɜ:bd] ungestört
un·di·vid·ed [ʌndɪ'vaɪdɪd] ungeteilt
un·do [ʌn'du:] (**-did, -done**) aufmachen, öffnen; *fig.* zunichte machen; **un'do·ing: be s.o.'s ~** j-s Ruin *od.* Verderben sein; **un'done** unerledigt; offen; **come ~** aufgehen
un·doubt·ed [ʌn'daʊtɪd] unbestritten; **~·ly** zweifellos, ohne (jeden) Zweifel
un·dreamed-of [ʌn'dri:mdɒv], **un·dreamt-of** [ʌn'dremtɒv] ungeahnt

un·dress [ʌn'dres] sich ausziehen; *j-n* ausziehen
un·due [ʌn'dju:] übermäßig
un·du·lat·ing ['ʌndjʊleɪtɪŋ] sanft (*Hügel*)
un·dy·ing [ʌn'daɪɪŋ] ewig
un·earned *fig.* [ʌn'ɜ:nd] unverdient
un·earth [ʌn'ɜ:θ] ausgraben, *fig. a.* ausfindig machen, aufstöbern; **~·ly** überirdisch; unheimlich; **at an ~ hour** F zu e-r unchristlichen Zeit
un·eas·i·ness [ʌn'i:zɪnɪs] Unbehagen *n*; **~·y** [ʌn'i:zɪ] (**-ier, -iest**) unruhig (*Schlaf*); unsicher (*Friede*); **feel ~** sich unbehaglich fühlen; **I'm ~ about** mir ist nicht wohl bei
un·e·co·nom·ic ['ʌni:kə'nɒmɪk] (**~ally**) unwirtschaftlich
un·ed·u·cat·ed [ʌn'edjʊkeɪtɪd] ungebildet
un·e·mo·tion·al [ʌnɪ'məʊʃənl] leidenschaftslos, kühl, beherrscht
un·em·ployed [ʌnɪm'plɔɪd] **1.** arbeitslos; **2. the ~** *pl.* die Arbeitslosen *pl.*
un·em·ploy·ment [ʌnɪm'plɔɪmənt] Arbeitslosigkeit *f*; **~ ben·e·fit** *Brt.*, **~ com·pen·sa·tion** *Am.* Arbeitslosengeld *n*
un·end·ing [ʌn'endɪŋ] endlos
un·en·dur·a·ble [ʌnɪn'djʊərəbl] unerträglich
un·en·vi·a·ble [ʌn'envɪəbl] wenig beneidenswert
un·e·qual [ʌn'i:kwəl] ungleich, unterschiedlich; *fig.* ungleich, einseitig; **be ~ to** e-r *Aufgabe etc.* nicht gewachsen sein; **~(l)ed** unerreicht, unübertroffen
un·er·ring [ʌn'ɜ:rɪŋ] unfehlbar
UNESCO [ju:'neskəʊ] *Abk. für* **United Nations Educational, Scientific, and Cultural Organization** UNESCO *f*, Organisation *f* der Vereinten Nationen für Erziehung, Wissenschaft und Kultur
un·e·ven [ʌn'i:vn] uneben; ungleich(mäßig); ungerade (*Zahl*)
un·e·vent·ful [ʌnɪ'ventfl] ereignislos
un·ex·am·pled [ʌnɪɡ'zɑːmpld] beispiellos
un·ex·pec·ted [ʌnɪk'spektɪd] unerwartet
un·ex·posed *phot.* [ʌnɪk'spəʊzd] unbelichtet
un·fail·ing [ʌn'feɪlɪŋ] unerschöpflich; nie versagend

U

un·fair [ʌnˈfeə] unfair, ungerecht

un·faith·ful [ʌnˈfeɪθfl] untreu (*to* dat.)

un·fa·mil·i·ar [ʌnfəˈmɪljə] ungewohnt; unbekannt; nicht vertraut (*with* mit)

un·fas·ten [ʌnˈfɑːsn] aufmachen, öffnen; losbinden

un·fa·vo(u)·ra·ble [ʌnˈfeɪvərəbl] ungünstig; unvorteilhaft (*for, to* für); negativ, ablehnend

un·feel·ing [ʌnˈfiːlɪŋ] gefühl-, herzlos

un·fin·ished [ʌnˈfɪnɪʃt] unvollendet; unfertig; unerledigt

un·fit [ʌnˈfɪt] nicht fit, nicht in Form; ungeeignet, untauglich; unfähig

un·flag·ging [ʌnˈflægɪŋ] unermüdlich, unentwegt

un·flap·pa·ble F [ʌnˈflæpəbl] nicht aus der Ruhe zu bringen(d)

un·fold [ʌnˈfəʊld] auf-, auseinanderfalten; darlegen, enthüllen; sich entfalten

un·fore·seen [ʌnfɔːˈsiːn] unvorhergesehen, unerwartet

un·for·get·ta·ble [ʌnfəˈgetəbl] unvergeßlich

un·for·got·ten [ʌnfəˈgɒtn] unvergessen

un·for·tu·nate [ʌnˈfɔːtʃnət] unglücklich; unglückselig; bedauerlich; **∼·ly** leider

un·found·ed [ʌnˈfaʊndɪd] unbegründet

un·friend·ly [ʌnˈfrendlɪ] (*-ier, -iest*) unfreundlich (*to, towards* zu)

un·furl [ʌnˈfɜːl] *Fahne* auf-, entrollen, *Segel* losmachen

un·fur·nished [ʌnˈfɜːnɪʃt] unmöbliert

un·gain·ly [ʌnˈgeɪnlɪ] linkisch, unbeholfen

un·god·ly [ʌnˈgɒdlɪ] gottlos; *at an ∼ hour* F zu e-r unchristlichen Zeit

un·gra·cious [ʌnˈgreɪʃəs] ungnädig; unfreundlich

un·grate·ful [ʌnˈgreɪtfl] undankbar

un·guard·ed [ʌnˈgɑːdɪd] unbewacht; unbedacht, unüberlegt

un·hap·pi·ly [ʌnˈhæpɪlɪ] unglücklicherweise, leider; **un·hap·py** [ʌnˈhæpɪ] (*-ier, -iest*) unglücklich

un·harmed [ʌnˈhɑːmd] unversehrt

un·health·y [ʌnˈhelθɪ] (*-ier, -iest*) kränklich, nicht gesund; ungesund; *contr.* krankhaft, unnatürlich

un·heard [ʌnˈhɜːd]: *go ∼* keine Beachtung finden, unbeachtet bleiben; **∼of** [ʌnˈhɜːdɒv] noch nie dagewesen, beispiellos

un·hinge [ʌnˈhɪndʒ]: *∼ s.o.('s mind) fig.* j-n völlig aus dem Gleichgewicht bringen

un·ho·ly F [ʌnˈhəʊlɪ] (*-ier, -iest*) furchtbar, schrecklich

un·hoped-for [ʌnˈhəʊptfɔː] unverhofft, unerwartet

un·hurt [ʌnˈhɜːt] unverletzt

UNICEF [ˈjuːnɪsef] *Abk. für United Nations International Children's Fund* UNICEF *f*, Kinderhilfswerk *n* der Vereinten Nationen

u·ni·corn [ˈjuːnɪkɔːn] Einhorn *n*

un·i·den·ti·fied [ʌnaɪˈdentɪfaɪd] unbekannt, nicht identifiziert

u·ni·fi·ca·tion [juːnɪfɪˈkeɪʃn] Vereinigung *f*

u·ni·form [ˈjuːnɪfɔːm] **1.** Uniform *f*; **2.** gleichmäßig; einheitlich; **∼·i·ty** [juːnɪˈfɔːmətɪ] Einheitlichkeit *f*

u·ni·fy [ˈjuːnɪfaɪ] verein(ig)en; vereinheitlichen

u·ni·lat·e·ral *fig.* [juːnɪˈlætərəl] einseitig

un·i·ma·gi·na·ble [ʌnɪˈmædʒɪnəbl] unvorstellbar; **un·i·ma·gi·na·tive** [ʌnɪˈmædʒɪnətɪv] phantasie-, einfallslos

un·im·por·tant [ʌnɪmˈpɔːtənt] unwichtig

un·im·pressed [ʌnɪmˈprest]: *remain ∼* unbeeindruckt bleiben (*by* von)

un·in·formed [ʌnɪnˈfɔːmd] nicht unterrichtet *od.* eingeweiht

un·in·hab·i·ta·ble [ʌnɪnˈhæbɪtəbl] unbewohnbar; **un·in·hab·it·ed** [ʌnɪnˈhæbɪtɪd] unbewohnt

un·in·jured [ʌnɪnˈdʒəd] unverletzt

un·in·tel·li·gi·ble [ʌnɪnˈtelɪdʒəbl] unverständlich

un·in·ten·tion·al [ʌnɪnˈtenʃənl] unabsichtlich, unbeabsichtigt

un·in·terest·ed [ʌnˈɪntrɪstɪd] uninteressiert (*in an* dat.); *be ∼ in a.* sich nicht interessieren für; **un·in·te·rest·ing** [ʌnˈɪntrɪstɪŋ] uninteressant

un·in·ter·rupt·ed [ʌnɪntəˈrʌptɪd] ununterbrochen

u·nion [ˈjuːnjən] Vereinigung *f*; Union *f*; Gewerkschaft *f*; **∼·ist** [ˈjuːnjənɪst] Gewerkschaftler(in); **∼·ize** [ˈjuːnjənaɪz] (sich) gewerkschaftlich organisieren; **2 'Jack** *a.* **2 Flag** Union Jack *m* (*brit. Nationalflagge*)

u·nique [juːˈniːk] einzigartig; einmalig

u·ni·son [ˈjuːnɪzn]: *in ∼* gemeinsam

u·nit ['ju:nɪt] Einheit *f*; *ped.* Unit *f*, Lehreinheit *f*; *math.* Einer *m*; *tech.* (Anbau)Element *n*, Teil *n*; **~ furniture** Anbaumöbel *pl.*

u·nite [ju:'naɪt] verbinden, -einigen; sich vereinigen *od.* zusammentun; **u'nit·ed** vereinigt, vereint

U·nit·ed 'King·dom das Vereinigte Königreich (*England, Schottland, Wales u. Nordirland*)

U·nit·ed 'Na·tions *pl.* Vereinte Nationen *pl.*

U·nit·ed States of A'mer·i·ca *pl.* die Vereinigten Staaten *pl.* von Amerika

u·ni·ty ['ju:nətɪ] Einheit *f*; Eins *f*

u·ni·ver·sal [ju:nɪ'vɜːsl] allgemein; universal, universell; Welt...

u·ni·verse ['ju:nɪvɜːs] Universum *n*, Weltall *n*

u·ni·ver·si·ty [ju:nɪ'vɜːsətɪ] Universität *f*, Hochschule *f*; **~ grad·u·ate** Akademiker(in)

un·just [ʌn'dʒʌst] ungerecht

un·kempt [ʌn'kempt] ungekämmt (*Haar*); ungepflegt (*Kleidung etc.*)

un·kind [ʌn'kaɪnd] unfreundlich

un·known [ʌn'nəʊn] **1.** unbekannt (*to dat.*); **2.** der, die, das Unbekannte; **~ 'quan·ti·ty** *math.* unbekannte Größe (*a. fig.*), Unbekannte *f*

un·law·ful [ʌn'lɔːfl] ungesetzlich, gesetzwidrig

un·lead·ed [ʌn'ledɪd] bleifrei (*Benzin*)

un·learn [ʌn'lɜːn] (**-ed** *od.* **-learnt**) *Ansichten etc.* ablegen, aufgeben

un·less [ən'les] wenn ... nicht, außer wenn ..., es sei denn

un·like *prp.* [ʌn'laɪk] im Gegensatz zu; *he is very ~ his father* er ist ganz anders als sein Vater; *that is very ~ him* das sieht ihm gar nicht ähnlich; **~·ly** unwahrscheinlich

un·lim·it·ed [ʌn'lɪmɪtɪd] unbegrenzt

un·list·ed *Am. tel.* [ʌn'lɪstɪd]: *be ~* nicht im Telefonbuch stehen; **~ 'num·ber** *Am. tel.* Geheimnummer *f*

un·load [ʌn'ləʊd] ent-, ab-, ausladen; *naut.* Ladung löschen

un·lock [ʌn'lɒk] aufschließen

un·loos·en [ʌn'luːsn] losmachen; lockern; lösen

un·loved [ʌn'lʌvd] ungeliebt

un·luck·y [ʌn'lʌkɪ] (*-ier, -iest*) unglücklich; *be ~* Pech haben

un·made [ʌn'meɪd] ungemacht (*Bett*)

un·manned [ʌn'mænd] unbemannt

un·marked nicht gekennzeichnet; *Sport:* ungedeckt, frei

un·mar·ried [ʌn'mærɪd] unverheiratet, ledig

un·mask *fig.* [ʌn'mɑːsk] entlarven

un·matched [ʌn'mætʃt] unübertroffen, unvergleichlich

un·men·tio·na·ble [ʌn'menʃnəbl] Tabu...; *be ~* tabu sein

un·mis·ta·ka·ble [ʌnmɪ'steɪkəbl] unverkennbar, unverwechselbar

un·moved [ʌn'muːvd] ungerührt; *she remained ~ by it* es ließ sie kalt

un·mu·si·cal [ʌn'mjuːzɪkl] unmusikalisch

un·named [ʌn'neɪmd] ungenannt

un·nat·u·ral [ʌn'nætʃrəl] unnatürlich; widernatürlich

un·ne·ces·sa·ry [ʌn'nesəsərɪ] unnötig

un·nerve [ʌn'nɜːv] entnerven

un·no·ticed [ʌn'nəʊtɪst] unbemerkt

un·num·bered [ʌn'nʌmbəd] unnummeriert

UNO ['juːnəʊ] *Abk. für* **United Nations Organization** UNO *f*

un·ob·tru·sive [ʌnəb'truːsɪv] unauffällig

un·oc·cu·pied [ʌn'ɒkjʊpaɪd] leer(stehend), unbewohnt; unbeschäftigt

un·of·fi·cial [ʌnə'fɪʃl] inoffiziell

un·pack [ʌn'pæk] auspacken

un·paid [ʌn'peɪd] unbezahlt

un·par·al·leled [ʌn'pærəleld] einmalig, beispiellos

un·par·don·a·ble [ʌn'pɑːdnəbl] unverzeihlich

un·per·turbed [ʌnpə'tɜːbd] gelassen, ruhig

un·pick [ʌn'pɪk] *Naht etc.* auftrennen

un·placed [ʌn'pleɪst]: *be ~* *Sport:* sich nicht plazieren können

un·play·a·ble [ʌn'pleɪəbl] *Sport:* unbespielbar (*Platz*)

un·pleas·ant [ʌn'pleznt] unangenehm, unerfreulich; unfreundlich

un·plug [ʌn'plʌg] den Stecker (*gen.*) herausziehen

un·pol·ished [ʌn'pɒlɪʃt] unpoliert; *fig.* ungehobelt

un·pol·lut·ed [ʌnpə'luːtɪd] sauber, unverschmutzt (*Umwelt etc.*)

un·pop·u·lar [ʌn'pɒpjʊlə] unpopulär,

U

unbeliebt; **~·i·ty** [ˌʌnpɒpjʊˈlærətɪ] Unbeliebtheit *f*

un·prac·ti·cal [ʌnˈpræktɪkl] unpraktisch

un·prac·tised *Brt.*, **un·prac·ticed** *Am.* [ʌnˈpræktɪst] ungeübt

un·pre·ce·dent·ed [ʌnˈpresɪdentɪd] beispiellos, noch nie dagewesen

un·pre·dict·a·ble [ʌnprɪˈdɪktəbl] unvorhersehbar; unberechenbar (*Person*)

un·prej·u·diced [ʌnˈpredʒʊdɪst] unvoreingenommen; *jur.* unbefangen

un·pre·med·i·tat·ed [ʌnpriːˈmedɪteɪtɪd] nicht vorsätzlich; unüberlegt

un·pre·pared [ʌnprɪˈpeəd] unvorbereitet

un·pre·ten·tious [ʌnprɪˈtenʃəs] bescheiden, einfach, schlicht

un·prin·ci·pled [ʌnˈprɪnsəpld] skrupellos, gewissenlos

un·prin·ta·ble [ʌnˈprɪntəbl] nicht druckfähig *od.* druckreif

un·pro·duc·tive [ʌnprəˈdʌktɪv] unproduktiv, unergiebig

un·pro·fes·sion·al [ʌnprəˈfeʃənl] unprofessionell; unfachmännisch

un·prof·i·ta·ble [ʌnˈprɒfɪtəbl] unrentabel

un·pro·nounce·a·ble [ʌnprəˈnaʊnsəbl] unaussprechbar

un·pro·tect·ed [ʌnprəˈtektɪd] ungeschützt

un·proved [ʌnˈpruːvd], **un·prov·en** [ʌnˈpruːvn] unbewiesen

un·pro·voked [ʌnprəˈvəʊkt] grundlos

un·pun·ished [ʌnˈpʌnɪʃt] unbestraft, ungestraft; **go ~** straflos bleiben

un·qual·i·fied [ʌnˈkwɒlɪfaɪd] unqualifiziert, ungeeignet (**for** für); uneingeschränkt

un·ques·tio·na·ble [ʌnˈkwestʃənəbl] unbestritten; **un·ques·tion·ing** [ʌnˈkwestʃənɪŋ] bedingungslos

un·quote [ʌnˈkwəʊt]: *quote ... ~* Zitat ... Zitat Ende

un·rav·el [ʌnˈrævl] (*bsd. Brt.* **-ll-**, *Am.* **-l-**) (sich) auftrennen (*Pullover etc.*); entwirren

un·rea·da·ble [ʌnˈriːdəbl] nicht lesenswert, unlesbar, *a.* unleserlich

un·re·al [ʌnˈrɪəl] unwirklich; **un·re·a·lis·tic** [ʌnrɪəˈlɪstɪk] (**~ally**) unrealistisch

un·rea·so·na·ble [ʌnˈriːznəbl] unver-

nünftig; übertrieben, unzumutbar (*a. Preise etc.*)

un·rec·og·niz·a·ble [ʌnˈrekəgnaɪzəbl] nicht wiederzuerkennen(d)

un·re·lat·ed [ʌnrɪˈleɪtɪd]: **be ~** in keinem Zusammenhang stehen (**to** mit)

un·re·lent·ing [ʌnrɪˈlentɪŋ] unvermindert

un·re·li·a·ble [ʌnrɪˈlaɪəbl] unzuverlässig

un·re·lieved [ʌnrɪˈliːvd] ununterbrochen, ständig

un·re·mit·ting [ʌnrɪˈmɪtɪŋ] unablässig, unaufhörlich

un·re·quit·ed [ʌnrɪˈkwaɪtɪd]: **~ love** unerwiderte Liebe

un·re·served [ʌnrɪˈzɜːvd] uneingeschränkt; nicht reserviert (*Sitzplätze*)

un·rest *pol. etc.* [ʌnˈrest] Unruhen *pl.*

un·re·strained [ʌnrɪˈstreɪnd] hemmungslos, ungezügelt

un·re·strict·ed [ʌnrɪˈstrɪktɪd] uneingeschränkt

un·ripe [ʌnˈraɪp] unreif

un·ri·val(l)ed [ʌnˈraɪvld] unerreicht, unübertroffen, einzigartig

un·roll [ʌnˈrəʊl] (sich) auf- *od.* entrollen; sich entfalten

un·ruf·fled [ʌnˈrʌfld] gelassen, ruhig

un·ru·ly [ʌnˈruːlɪ] (**-ier, -iest**) ungebärdig, wild; widerspenstig (*Haare*)

un·sad·dle [ʌnˈsædl] *Pferd* absatteln; *Reiter* abwerfen

un·safe [ʌnˈseɪf] unsicher, nicht sicher

un·said [ʌnˈsed] unausgesprochen

un·sal(e)·a·ble [ʌnˈseɪləbl] unverkäuflich

un·salt·ed [ʌnˈsɔːltɪd] ungesalzen

un·san·i·tar·y [ʌnˈsænɪtərɪ] unhygienisch

un·sat·is·fac·to·ry [ˈʌnsætɪsˈfæktərɪ] unbefriedigend

un·sat·u·rat·ed *chem.* [ʌnˈsætʃəreɪtɪd] ungesättigt

un·sa·vo(u)·ry [ʌnˈseɪvərɪ] anrüchig, unerfreulich

un·scathed [ʌnˈskeɪðd] unversehrt, unverletzt

un·screw [ʌnˈskruː] ab-, losschrauben

un·scru·pu·lous [ʌnˈskruːpjʊləs] skrupel-, gewissenlos

un·seat [ʌnˈsiːt] *Reiter* abwerfen; *j-n* s-s Amtes entheben

un·seem·ly [ʌnˈsiːmlɪ] ungebührlich

unversed

un·self·ish [ʌnˈselfɪʃ] selbstlos, uneigennützig; **~ness** Selbstlosigkeit *f*

un·set·tle [ʌnˈsetl] durcheinanderbringen; beunruhigen; aufregen; **~d** ungeklärt, offen (*Frage etc.*); unsicher (*Lage etc.*); unbeständig (*Wetter*)

un·shak·(e)a·ble [ʌnˈʃeɪkəbl] unerschütterlich

un·shav·en [ʌnˈʃeɪvn] unrasiert

un·shrink·a·ble [ʌnˈʃrɪŋkəbl] nicht eingehend *od.* einlaufend (*Stoff*)

un·sight·ly [ʌnˈsaɪtlɪ] unansehnlich; häßlich

un·skilled [ʌnˈskɪld]: **~ worker** ungelernter Arbeiter

un·so·cia·ble [ʌnˈsəʊʃəbl] ungesellig

un·so·cial [ʌnˈsəʊʃl]: **work ~ hours** außerhalb der normalen Arbeitszeit arbeiten

un·so·lic·it·ed [ʌnsəˈlɪsɪtɪd] unaufgefordert ein- *od.* zugesandt, *Ware a.* unbestellt

un·solved [ʌnˈsɒlvd] ungelöst (*Fall etc.*)

un·so·phis·ti·cat·ed [ʌnsəˈfɪstɪkeɪtɪd] einfach, schlicht; *tech.* unkompliziert

un·sound [ʌnˈsaʊnd] nicht gesund; nicht in Ordnung; morsch; unsicher, schwach; nicht stichhaltig (*Argument etc.*); **of ~ mind** *jur.* unzurechnungsfähig

un·spar·ing [ʌnˈspeərɪŋ] großzügig, freigebig, verschwenderisch; schonungslos, unbarmherzig

un·spea·ka·ble [ʌnˈspiːkəbl] unbeschreiblich, entsetzlich

un·spoiled [ʌnˈspɔɪld], **un·spoilt** [ʌnˈspɔɪlt] unverdorben; nicht verwöhnt *od.* verzogen

un·sta·ble [ʌnˈsteɪbl] instabil; unsicher, schwankend; labil (*Person*)

un·stead·y [ʌnˈstedɪ] (*-ier, -iest*) wack(e)lig, unsicher, schwankend; unbeständig; ungleichmäßig, unregelmäßig

un·stop [ʌnˈstɒp] (*-pp-*) *Abfluß etc.* freimachen; *Flasche* entstöpseln

un·stressed *ling.* [ʌnˈstrest] unbetont

un·stuck [ʌnˈstʌk]: **come ~** abgehen, sich lösen; *fig.* scheitern (*Person, Plan*)

un·stud·ied [ʌnˈstʌdɪd] ungekünstelt, natürlich

un·suc·cess·ful [ʌnsəkˈsesfl] erfolglos, ohne Erfolg; vergeblich

un·suit·a·ble [ʌnˈsjuːtəbl] unpassend, ungeeignet; unangemessen

un·sure [ʌnˈʃɔː] (*~r, ~st*) unsicher; **~ of o.s.** unsicher

un·sur·passed [ʌnsəˈpɑːst] unübertroffen

un·sus·pect·ed [ʌnsəˈspektɪd] unverdächtig; unvermutet; **~ing** nichtsahnend, ahnungslos

un·sus·pi·cious [ʌnsəˈspɪʃəs] arglos; unverdächtig, harmlos

un·sweet·ened [ʌnˈswiːtnd] ungesüßt

un·swerv·ing [ʌnˈswɜːvɪŋ] unbeirrbar, unerschütterlich

un·tan·gle [ʌnˈtæŋgl] entwirren (*a. fig.*)

un·tapped [ʌnˈtæpt] unerschlossen (*Bodenschätze etc.*)

un·teach·a·ble [ʌnˈtiːtʃəbl] unbelehrbar (*Person*); nicht lehrbar (*Sache*)

un·ten·a·ble [ʌnˈtenəbl] unhaltbar (*Theorie etc.*)

un·think·a·ble [ʌnˈθɪŋkəbl] undenkbar, unvorstellbar; **~ing** gedankenlos

un·ti·dy [ʌnˈtaɪdɪ] (*-ier, -iest*) unordentlich

un·tie [ʌnˈtaɪ] aufknoten, *Knoten etc.* lösen; losbinden

un·til [ənˈtɪl] *prp., cj.* bis; **not ~** erst; erst wenn, nicht bevor

un·time·ly [ʌnˈtaɪmlɪ] vorzeitig, verfrüht; unpassend, ungelegen

un·tir·ing [ʌnˈtaɪərɪŋ] unermüdlich

un·told [ʌnˈtəʊld] unermeßlich (*Reichtum, Schaden*); nicht erzählt *od.* berichtet

un·touched [ʌnˈtʌtʃt] unberührt, unangetastet

un·true [ʌnˈtruː] unwahr, falsch

un·trust·wor·thy [ʌnˈtrʌstwɜːðɪ] unzuverlässig, nicht vertrauenswürdig

un·used¹ [ʌnˈjuːzd] unbenutzt, ungebraucht

un·used² [ʌnˈjuːst]: **be ~ to s.th.** an et. nicht gewöhnt sein, et. nicht gewohnt sein; **be ~ to doing s.th.** es nicht gewohnt sein, et. zu tun

un·u·su·al [ʌnˈjuːʒʊəl] ungewöhnlich

un·var·nished [ʌnˈvɑːnɪʃt] ungeschminkt (*Wahrheit*)

un·var·y·ing [ʌnˈveərɪŋ] unveränderlich, gleichbleibend

un·veil [ʌnˈveɪl] *Denkmal etc.* enthüllen

un·versed [ʌnˈvɜːst] unbewandert, unerfahren (**in** in *dat.*)

U

un·voiced [ʌn'vɔɪst] unausgesprochen
un·want·ed [ʌn'wɒntɪd] unerwünscht, ungewollt
un·war·rant·ed [ʌn'wɒrəntɪd] ungerechtfertigt
un·washed [ʌn'wɒʃt] ungewaschen
un·wel·come [ʌn'welkəm] unwillkommen
un·well [ʌn'wel]: *be od. feel* ~ sich unwohl *od.* nicht wohl fühlen
un·whole·some [ʌn'həʊlsəm] ungesund (*a. fig.*)
un·wield·y [ʌn'wiːldɪ] unhandlich, sperrig
un·will·ing [ʌn'wɪlɪŋ] widerwillig; ungern; *be* ~ *to do s.th.* et. nicht tun wollen
un·wind [ʌn'waɪnd] (-*wound*) (sich) abwickeln; F abschalten, sich entspannen
un·wise [ʌn'waɪz] unklug
un·wit·ting [ʌn'wɪtɪŋ] unwissentlich; unbeabsichtigt
un·wor·thy [ʌn'wɜːðɪ] unwürdig; *he/she is* ~ *of it* er/sie verdient es nicht, er/sie ist es nicht wert
un·wrap [ʌn'ræp] auswickeln, -packen
un·writ·ten [ʌn'rɪtn] ungeschrieben; ~ '**law** ungeschriebenes Gesetz
un·yield·ing [ʌn'jiːldɪŋ] unnachgiebig
un·zip [ʌn'zɪp] (-*pp*-) den Reißverschluß (*e-s Kleidungsstücks*) aufmachen
up [ʌp] **1.** *adv.* (her-, hin)auf, aufwärts, nach oben, hoch, in die Höhe; oben; ~ *there* dort oben; *jump* ~ *and down* hüpfen; *walk* ~ *and down* auf u. ab gehen, hin u. her gehen; ~ *to* bis zu; *be* ~ *to s.th.* F et. vorhaben, et. im Schilde führen; *not to be* ~ *to s.th.* e-r Sache nicht gewachsen sein; *it's* ~ *to you* das liegt bei dir; **2.** *prp.* herauf, hinauf; oben auf (*dat.*); ~ *the river* flußaufwärts; **3.** *adj.* nach oben (gerichtet), Aufwärts...; aufgegangen (*Sonne*); gestiegen (*Preise*); abgelaufen, um (*Zeit*); auf(gestanden); *the* ~ *train* der Zug nach London; *be* ~ *and about* F wieder auf den Beinen sein; *what's* ~ *?* F was ist los?; **4.** (-*pp*-) F *v/t. Angebot, Preis etc.* erhöhen; **5.** *the* ~*s and downs pl.* F die Höhen u. Tiefen *pl.* (*of life* des Lebens)
up-and-com·ing [ʌpən'kʌmɪŋ] aufstrebend, vielversprechend
up·bring·ing ['ʌpbrɪŋɪŋ] Erziehung *f*
up·com·ing ['ʌpkʌmɪŋ] bevorstehend

up·coun·try [ʌp'kʌntrɪ] landeinwärts; im Landesinneren
up·date [ʌp'deɪt] auf den neuesten Stand bringen; aktualisieren
up·end [ʌp'end] hochkant stellen
up·grade [ʌp'greɪd] *j-n* befördern
up·heav·al *fig.* [ʌp'hiːvl] Umwälzung *f*
up·hill [ʌp'hɪl] aufwärts, bergan; bergauf führend; *fig.* mühsam
up·hold [ʌp'həʊld] (-*held*) *Rechte etc.* schützen, wahren; *jur. Urteil* bestätigen
up|·hol·ster [ʌp'həʊlstə] *Möbel* polstern; ~**hol·ster·er** [ʌp'həʊlstərə] Polsterer *m*; ~**hol·ster·y** [ʌp'həʊlstərɪ] Polsterung *f*; Bezug *m*; Polsterei *f*
UPI [juː piː 'aɪ] *Abk. für* **United Press International** (*e-e Nachrichtenagentur*)
up·keep ['ʌpkiːp] Instandhaltung(skosten *pl.*) *f*; Unterhalt(ungskosten *pl.*) *m*
up·land ['ʌplənd] *mst* ~*s pl.* Hochland *n*
up·lift 1. [ʌp'lɪft] *j-n* aufrichten, *j-m* Auftrieb geben; **2.** ['ʌplɪft] Auftrieb *m*
up·on [ə'pɒn] → **on**; *once* ~ *a time there was* es war einmal
up·per ['ʌpə] obere(r, -s), Ober...; ~'**most 1.** *adj.* oberste(r, -s), größte(r, -s), höchste(r, -s); *be* ~ oben sein; *fig.* an erster Stelle stehen; **2.** *adv.* nach oben
up·right ['ʌpraɪt] aufrecht, gerade; *fig.* aufrecht, rechtschaffen
up·ris·ing ['ʌpraɪzɪŋ] Aufstand *m*
up·roar ['ʌprɔː] Aufruhr *m*; ~·**i·ous** [ʌp'rɔːrɪəs] schallend (*Gelächter*)
up·root [ʌp'ruːt] ausreißen, entwurzeln; *fig. j-n* herausreißen (*from* aus)
UPS *Am.* [juː piː 'es] *Abk. für* **United Parcel Service** (*Transport- u. Auslieferfirma für Waren u. Pakete*)
up·set [ʌp'set] (-*set*) umkippen, umstoßen, umwerfen; *fig. Pläne etc.* durcheinanderbringen, stören; *fig. j-n* aus der Fassung bringen; *the fish has* ~ *me od. my stomach* ich habe mir durch den Fisch den Magen verdorben; *be* ~ aufgeregt sein; aus der Fassung *od.* durcheinander sein; gekränkt *od.* verletzt sein
up·shot ['ʌpʃɒt] Ergebnis *n*
up·side down [ʌpsaɪd'daʊn] verkehrt herum; *fig.* drunter u. drüber; *turn* ~ umdrehen, *a. fig.* auf den Kopf stellen
up·stairs [ʌp'steəz] **1.** die Treppe herod. hinauf, nach oben; oben; **2.** im oberen Stockwerk (gelegen), obere(r, -s)

u

up·start [ˈʌpstɑːt] Emporkömmling *m*

up·state *Am.* [ˈʌpˈsteɪt] im Norden (e-s Bundesstaats)

up·stream [ˈʌpˈstriːm] fluß-, stromaufwärts

up·take F [ˈʌpteɪk]: *be quick/slow on the* ~ schnell begreifen/schwer von Begriff sein

up-to-date [ʌptəˈdeɪt] modern; aktuell, auf dem neuesten Stand

up·town *Am.* [ˈʌpˈtaʊn] in den Wohnvierteln; in die Wohnviertel

up·turn [ˈʌptɜːn] Aufschwung *m*

up·ward(s) [ˈʌpwəd(z)] aufwärts, nach oben

u·ra·ni·um *chem.* [jʊˈreɪnɪəm] Uran *n*

ur·ban [ˈɜːbən] städtisch, Stadt...

ur·chin [ˈɜːtʃɪn] Bengel *m*

urge [ɜːdʒ] **1.** *j*-n drängen (*to do* zu tun); drängen auf (*acc.*); *a.* ~ *on j*-n drängen, antreiben; **2.** Drang *m*, Verlangen *n*; **ur·gen·cy** [ˈɜːdʒənsɪ] Dringlichkeit *f*; **ur·gent** [ˈɜːdʒənt] dringend; *be* ~ *a.* eilen

u·ri·nal [ˈjʊərɪnl] Urinal *n*; Pissoir *n*; ~**nate** [ˈjʊərɪneɪt] urinieren; **u·rine** [ˈjʊərɪn] Urin *m*

urn [ɜːn] Urne *f*; Großtee-, Großkaffeemaschine *f*

us [ʌs, əs] uns; *all of* ~ wir alle; *both of* ~ wir beide

US [juːˈes] *Abk. für* **United States** Vereinigte Staaten *pl.*

USA [juːesˈeɪ] *Abk. für* **United States of America** die USA *pl.*, Vereinigte Staaten *pl.* von Amerika

USAF [juːesˈeɪˈef] *Abk. für* **United States Air Force** Luftwaffe *f* der Vereinigten Staaten

us·age [ˈjuːzɪdʒ] Sprachgebrauch *m*; Behandlung *f*; Verwendung *f*, Gebrauch *m*

use 1. *v/t.* [juːz] benutzen, gebrauchen, an-, verwenden; (ver)brauchen; ~ *up* auf-, verbrauchen; *v/i.* [juːs]: *I* ..*d to live here* ich habe früher hier gewohnt; **2.** [juːs] Benutzung *f*, Gebrauch *m*, Verwendung *f*; Nutzen *m*; *be of* ~ nützlich *od.* von Nutzen sein (*to* für); *it's no* ~ ...

es ist nutz- *od.* zwecklos *zu* ...; → **milk** 1

used¹ [juːst]: *be* ~ *to s.th.* an et. gewöhnt sein, et. gewohnt sein; *be* ~ *to doing s.th.* es gewohnt sein, et. zu tun

used² [juːzd] gebraucht; ~ *'car* Gebrauchtwagen *m*; ~ *car 'deal·er* Gebrauchtwagenhändler(in)

use·ful [ˈjuːsfl] nützlich; '~·**less** nutz-, zwecklos

us·er [ˈjuːzə] Benutzer(in); Verbraucher(in); ~·**'friend·ly** benutzer- *od.* verbraucherfreundlich; ~ *'in·ter·face* *Computer*: Benutzeroberfläche *f*

ush·er [ˈʌʃə] **1.** Platzanweiser *m*; Gerichtsdiener *m*; **2.** *j*-n führen, geleiten (*into* in *acc.*); *to* zu s-m Platz *etc.*); ~·**ette** [ʌʃəˈret] Platzanweiserin *f*

USN [juːesˈen] *Abk. für* **United States Navy** Marine *f* der Vereinigten Staaten

USS [juːesˈes] *Abk. für* **United States Ship** Schiff *n* der Vereinigten Staaten

USSR *hist.* [juːeseˈsɑː] *Abk. für* **Union of Socialist Soviet Republics** die UDSSR, Union *f* der Sozialistischen Sowjetrepubliken

u·su·al [ˈjuːʒl] gewöhnlich, üblich; ~·**ly** [ˈjuːʒəlɪ] (für) gewöhnlich, normalerweise

u·sur·er [ˈjuːʒərə] Wucherer *m*

u·su·ry [ˈjuːʒʊrɪ] Wucher *m*

u·ten·sil [juːˈtensl] Gerät *n*

u·te·rus *anat.* [ˈjuːtərəs] (*pl.* -**ri** [-raɪ], -**ruses**) Gebärmutter *f*

u·til·i·ty [juːˈtɪlətɪ] Nutzen *m*; **utilities** *pl.* Leistungen *pl.* der öffentlichen Versorgungsbetriebe

u·til·ize [ˈjuːtɪlaɪz] nutzen

ut·most [ˈʌtməʊst] äußerste(r, -s), größte(r, -s), höchste(r, -s)

U·to·pi·an [juːˈtəʊpjən] utopisch

ut·ter¹ [ˈʌtə] total, völlig

ut·ter² [ˈʌtə] äußern, *Seufzer etc.* ausstoßen, *Wort* sagen

U-turn [ˈjuːtɜːn] *mot.* Wende *f*; *fig.* Kehrtwendung *f*

UV [juːˈviː] *Abk. für* **ultraviolet** ultraviolett

u·vu·la *anat.* [ˈjuːvjʊlə] (*pl.* -**las**, -**lae** [-liː]) (Gaumen)Zäpfchen *n*

U

V

V, v [viː] V, v n

v. Brt. nur geschr. Abk. für against (lateinisch **versus**) bsd. Sport, jur.: gegen

va·can·cy ['veɪkənsɪ] freie od. offene Stelle; **vacancies** Zimmer frei; **no vacancies** belegt; '**~cant** leerstehend, unbewohnt; frei ([Sitz]Platz); frei, offen (Stelle); fig. leer (Blick, Gesichtsausdruck); **~** frei (Toilette)

va·cate [və'keɪt] Hotelzimmer räumen; Stelle etc. aufgeben

va·ca·tion [və'keɪʃn] **1.** bsd. Am. Ferien pl., Urlaub m; bsd. Brt. univ. Semesterferien pl.; **be on ~** bsd. Am. im Urlaub sein, Urlaub machen; **2.** bsd. Am. Urlaub machen, die Ferien verbringen; **~·er** [və'keɪʃnə], **~ist** [və'keɪʃənɪst] bsd. Am. Urlauber(in)

vac·cin·ate ['væksɪneɪt] impfen; **~cin·a·tion** [væksɪ'neɪʃn] (Schutz)Impfung f; **~cine** ['væksiːn] Impfstoff m

vac·il·late ['væsɪleɪt] fig. schwanken

vac·u·um ['vækjʊəm] **1.** (pl. -ums, -ua [-jʊə]) phys. Vakuum n; **2.** F Teppich, Zimmer etc. saugen; '**~ bot·tle** Am. Thermosflasche f (TM); '**~ clean·er** Staubsauger m; '**~ flask** Brt. Thermosflasche f (TM); '**~packed** vakuumverpackt

vag·a·bond ['væɡəbɒnd] Vagabund m, Landstreicher(in)

va·ga·ry ['veɪɡərɪ] mst **vagaries** pl. Laune f; wunderlicher Einfall

va·gi·na anat. [və'dʒaɪnə] Vagina f, Scheide f; **~nal** anat. [və'dʒaɪnl] vaginal, Scheiden...

va·grant ['veɪɡrənt] Nichtseßhafte(r m) f, Landstreicher(in)

vague [veɪɡ] (**~r, ~st**) verschwommen, vage; unklar

vain [veɪn] eingebildet, eitel; vergeblich; **in ~** vergebens, vergeblich

vale [veɪl] poet. od. in Namen: Tal n

val·en·tine ['væləntaɪn] Valentinskarte f; Person, der man am Valentinstag, 14. Februar, e-n Gruß schickt

va·le·ri·an bot., pharm. [və'lɪərɪən] Baldrian m

val·et ['vælɪt] (Kammer)Diener m; '**~**

ser·vice (Kleider)Reinigungsdienst m (im Hotel)

val·id ['vælɪd] stichhaltig, triftig; gültig (**for two weeks** zwei Wochen); jur. rechtsgültig, -kräftig; **be ~ a.** gelten; **va·lid·i·ty** [və'lɪdətɪ] (jur. Rechts)Gültigkeit f; Stichhaltigkeit f, Triftigkeit f

va·lise [və'liːz] Reisetasche f

val·ley ['vælɪ] Tal n

val·u·a·ble ['væljʊəbl] **1.** wertvoll; **2. ~s** pl. Wertgegenstände pl., -sachen pl.

val·u·a·tion [vælju'eɪʃn] Schätzung f; Schätzwert m (**on** gen.)

val·ue ['væljuː] **1.** Wert m; **be of ~** wertvoll sein (**to** für); **get ~ for money** reell bedient werden; **2.** Haus etc. schätzen (**at** auf acc.); j-n, j-s Rat etc. schätzen; **~·ad·ded 'tax** Brt. econ. (Abk. **VAT**) Mehrwertsteuer f; '**~·less** wertlos

valve [vælv] tech., mus. Ventil n; (Herzetc.) Klappe f; Brt. bsd. hist. (Radio-, Fernseh)Röhre f

vam·pire ['væmpaɪə] Vampir m

van [væn] Lieferwagen m, Transporter m; Brt. rail. (geschlossener) Güterwagen

van·dal ['vændl] Vandale m, Wandale m; **~is·m** ['vændəlɪzəm] Vandalismus m, Wandalismus m; **~ize** ['vændəlaɪz] mutwillig beschädigen od. zerstören

vane [veɪn] (Propeller- etc.)Flügel m; (Wetter)Fahne f

van·guard mil. ['vænɡɑːd] Vorhut f

va·nil·la [və'nɪlə] Vanille f

van·ish ['vænɪʃ] verschwinden

van·i·ty ['vænətɪ] Eitelkeit f; '**~ bag** Kosmetiktäschchen n; '**~ case** Kosmetikkoffer m

van·tage·point [vɑːntɪdʒpɔɪnt] Aussichtspunkt m; **from my ~** fig. aus m-r Sicht

va·por·ize ['veɪpəraɪz] verdampfen; verdunsten (lassen)

va·po(u)r ['veɪpə] Dampf m, Dunst m; '**~ trail** aviat. Kondensstreifen m

var·i·a·ble ['veərɪəbl] **1.** variabel, veränderlich; unbeständig, wechselhaft; tech. einstell-, regulierbar; **2.** math., phys. Variable f, veränderliche Größe (beide a. fig.); **~ance** ['veərɪəns]: **be at**

ventricle

~ **with** im Gegensatz *od.* Widerspruch stehen zu; **~ant** ['veərɪənt] **1.** abweichend, verschieden; **2.** Variante *f*; **~a·tion** [veərɪ'eɪʃn] Abweichung *f*; Schwankung *f*; *mus.* Variation *f*

var·i·cose veins *med.* [værɪkəʊs 'veɪnz] *pl.* Krampfadern *pl.*

var·ied ['veərɪd] unterschiedlich; abwechslungsreich

va·ri·e·ty [və'raɪətɪ] Abwechslung *f*; Vielfalt *f*; *econ.* Auswahl *f*, Sortiment *n* (*of* an *dat.*); *bot.*, *zo.* Art *f*; Varieté *f*; **for a ~ of reasons** aus den verschiedensten Gründen; ~ **show** Varietévorstellung *f*; ~ **thea·tre** (*Am.* **thea·ter**) Varieté(theater) *n*

var·i·ous ['veərɪəs] verschieden; mehrere, verschiedene

var·nish ['vɑːnɪʃ] **1.** Lack *m*; **2.** lackieren

var·si·ty team *Am.* ['vɑːsətɪ -] *Sport*: Universitäts-, College-, Schulmannschaft *f*

var·y ['veərɪ] *v/i.* sich (ver)ändern; variieren, (*Meinungen*) auseinandergehen (*on* über *acc.*); ~ **in size** verschieden groß sein; *v/t.* (ver)ändern; variieren

vase [vɑːz, *Am.* veɪs, veɪz] Vase *f*

vast [vɑːst] gewaltig, riesig, (*Fläche a.*) ausgedehnt, weit; **~·ly** gewaltig, weitaus

vat [væt] (großes) Faß, Bottich *m*

VAT [viː or 'tiː, væt] *Abk. für* **value-added tax** Mehrwertsteuer *f*

vau·de·ville *Am.* ['vɔːdəvɪl] Varieté(theater) *n*

vault[1] [vɔːlt] *arch.* Gewölbe *n*; *a.* **~s** *pl.* Stahlkammer *f*, Tresorraum *m*; (Keller)Gewölbe *n*; Gruft *f*

vault[2] [vɔːlt] **1.** ~ (**over**) springen über (*acc.*); **2.** *bsd. Sport*: Sprung *m*; **~·ing horse** *Turnen*: Pferd *n*; **~·ing pole** Stabhochsprung: Sprungstab *m*

VCR [viː siː 'ɑː] *Abk. für* **video cassette recorder** Videorecorder *m*, -gerät *n*

VDU [viː diː 'juː] *Abk. für* **visual display unit** *Computer*: Bildschirmgerät *n*, Datensichtgerät *n*

veal [viːl] Kalbfleisch *n*; ~ **chop** Kalbskotelett *n*; ~ **cutlet** Kalbsschnitzel *n*; ~ **roast** Kalbsbraten *m*

veer [vɪə] (sich) drehen; ausscheren (*Auto*); ~ **to the right** *mot.* das Steuer nach rechts reißen

vege·ta·ble ['vedʒtəbl] **1.** *mst* **~s** *pl.* Gemüse *n*; **2.** Gemüse...; Pflanzen...

ve·ge·tar·i·an [vedʒɪ'teərɪən] **1.** Vegetarier(in); **2.** vegetarisch

ve·ge·tate ['vedʒɪteɪt] (dahin)vegetieren; **~·ta·tion** [vedʒɪ'teɪʃn] Vegetation *f*

ve·he·mence ['viːɪməns] Vehemenz *f*, Heftigkeit *f*; **~·ment** vehement, heftig

ve·hi·cle ['viːɪkl] Fahrzeug *n*; *fig.* Medium *n*

veil [veɪl] **1.** Schleier *m*; **2.** verschleiern (*a. fig.*)

vein [veɪn] *anat.* Vene *f*, Ader *f* (*a. bot.*, *geol.*, *fig.*); *fig.* (*Charakter*)Zug *m*; *fig.* Stimmung *f*

ve·loc·i·ty *tech.* [vɪ'lɒsətɪ] Geschwindigkeit *f*

ve·lour(s) [və'lʊə] Velours *m*

vel·vet ['velvɪt] Samt *m*; **~·y** samtig

vend·|er ['vendə] → **vendor**; **~·ing ma·chine** (Verkaufs-, Waren)Automat *m*; **~·or** (*Straßen*)Händler(in), (*Zeitungs- etc.*)Verkäufer(in)

ve·neer [və'nɪə] **1.** Furnier *n*; *fig.* Fassade *f*; **2.** furnieren

ven·e·ra·ble ['venərəbl] ehrwürdig; **~·rate** ['venəreɪt] verehren; **~·ra·tion** [venə'reɪʃn] Verehrung *f*

ve·ne·re·al dis·ease *med.* [vɪnɪərɪəl dɪ'ziːz] Geschlechtskrankheit *f*

Ve·ne·tian [vɪ'niːʃn] **1.** Venezianer(in); **2.** venezianisch; ♀ **'blind** (Stab)Jalousie *f*

ven·geance ['vendʒəns] Rache *f*; **take ~ on** sich rächen an (*dat.*); **with a ~** F wie verrückt, ganz gehörig

ve·ni·al ['viːnjəl] entschuldbar, verzeihlich; *rel.* läßlich (*Sünde*)

ven·i·son ['venɪzn] Wildbret *n*

ven·om ['venəm] *zo.* Gift *n*; *fig.* Gift *n*, Gehässigkeit *f*; **~·ous** giftig; *fig.* giftig, gehässig

ve·nous *med.* ['viːnəs] venös

vent [vent] **1.** *v/t. fig.* s-*m* Zorn *etc.* Luft machen, s-*e* Wut *etc.* auslassen, abreagieren (*on* an *dat.*); **2.** (*Abzugs*)Öffnung *f*; Schlitz *m* (*im Kleid etc.*); **give ~ to** s-*m* Ärger *etc.* Luft machen

ven·ti·|late ['ventɪleɪt] (be)lüften; **~·la·tion** [ventɪ'leɪʃn] Ventilation *f*, (Be-) Lüftung *f*; **~·la·tor** ['ventɪleɪtə] Ventilator *m*

ven·tri·cle *anat.* ['ventrɪkl] Herzkammer *f*

V

ven·tril·o·quist [ven'trɪləkwɪst] Bauch-redner(in)

ven·ture ['ventʃə] **1.** *bsd. econ.* Wagnis *n*, Risiko *n*; *econ.* Unternehmen *n*; → **joint venture; 2.** sich wagen; riskieren

verb *gr.* [vɜːb] Verb *n*, Zeitwort *n*; **~al** ['vɜːbl] mündlich; wörtlich, Wort...

ver·dict ['vɜːdɪkt] *jur.* (Urteils)Spruch *m* (*der Geschworenen*); *fig.* Urteil *n*; **bring in** *od.* **return a ~ of** (**not**) **guilty** auf (nicht) schuldig erkennen

ver·di·gris ['vɜːdɪgrɪs] Grünspan *m*

verge [vɜːdʒ] **1.** Rand *m* (*a. fig.*); **be on the ~ of** kurz vor (*dat.*) stehen; **be on the ~ of despair** (**tears**) der Verzweiflung (den Tränen) nahe sein; **2. ~ on** *fig.* grenzen an (*acc.*)

ver·i·fy ['verɪfaɪ] bestätigen; nachweisen; (über)prüfen

ver·i·ta·ble ['verɪtəbl] wahr (*Fest, Triumph etc.*)

ver·mi·cel·li [vɜːmɪ'selɪ] Fadennudeln *pl.*

ver·mi·form ap·pen·dix *anat.* [vɜːmɪfɔːm ə'pendɪks] Wurmfortsatz *m*

ver·mil·i·on [və'mɪljən] **1.** zinnoberrot; **2.** Zinnoberrot *n*

ver·min ['vɜːmɪn] Ungeziefer *n*; Schädlinge *pl.*; *fig.* Gesindel *n*, Pack *m*; **'~ous** voller Ungeziefer

ver·nac·u·lar [və'nækjʊlə] Dialekt *m*, Mundart *f*

ver·sa·tile ['vɜːsətaɪl] vielseitig; vielseitig verwendbar

verse [vɜːs] Versdichtung *f*; Vers *m*; Strophe *f*

versed [vɜːst]: **be** (**well**) **~ in** beschlagen *od.* bewandert sein in (*dat.*)

ver·sion ['vɜːʃn] Version *f*; Ausführung *f* (*e-s Artikels, Geräts etc.*); Darstellung *f* (*e-s Ereignisses*); Fassung *f* (*e-s Textes*); Übersetzung *f*

ver·sus ['vɜːsəs] (*Abk.* **v., vs.**) Sport, *jur.*: gegen

ver·te·bra *anat.* ['vɜːtɪbrə] (*pl.* **-brae** [-riː]) Wirbel *m*; **~brate** *zo.* ['vɜːtɪbreɪt] Wirbeltier *n*

ver·ti·cal ['vɜːtɪkl] vertikal, senkrecht

ver·ti·go *med.* ['vɜːtɪgəʊ] Schwindel *m*; **suffer from ~** an *od.* unter Schwindel leiden

verve [vɜːv] Elan *m*, Schwung *m*

ver·y ['verɪ] **1.** *adv.* sehr; aller...; *I much hope that* ich hoffe sehr, daß; *the ~ best* das allerbeste; *for the ~ last time*

zum allerletzten Mal; **2.** *adj.* **the ~** genau der *od.* die *od.* das; **the ~ opposite** genau das Gegenteil; **the ~ thing** genau das richtige; **the ~ thought of** schon der *od.* der bloße Gedanke an (*acc.*)

ves·i·cle *med.* ['vesɪkl] Bläschen *n*

ves·sel ['vesl] *anat., bot.* Gefäß *n*; Schiff *n*

vest [vest] *Brt.* Unterhemd *n*; *kugelsichere* Weste; *Am.* Weste *f*

ves·ti·bule ['vestɪbjuːl] (Vor)Halle *f*

ves·tige *fig.* ['vestɪdʒ] Spur *f*

vest·ment ['vestmənt] Ornat *m*, Gewand *n*, Robe *f*

ves·try *rel.* ['vestrɪ] Sakristei *f*

vet¹ F [vet] Tierarzt *m*, -ärztin *f*

vet² *bsd. Brt.* F [vet] (**-tt-**) überprüfen

vet³ *Am. mil.* F [vet] Veteran *m*

vet·e·ran ['vetərən] **1.** *mil.* Veteran *m* (*a. fig.*); **2.** altgedient; erfahren; '**~ car** *Brt. mot.* Oldtimer *m* (*Baujahr bis 1905*)

vet·e·ri·nar·i·an *Am.* [vetərɪ'neərɪən] Tierarzt *m*, -ärztin *f*

vet·e·ri·na·ry ['vetərɪnərɪ] tierärztlich; **~ 'sur·geon** *Brt.* Tierarzt *m*, -ärztin *f*

ve·to ['viːtəʊ] **1.** (*pl.* **-toes**) Veto *n*; **2.** sein Veto einlegen gegen

vexed ques·tion [vekst 'kwestʃən] leidige Frage

VHF [viː eɪtʃ 'ef] *Abk. für* **very high frequency** VHF, UKW, Ultrakurzwelle(nbereich *m*) *f*

vi·a ['vaɪə] über (*acc.*), via

vi·a·duct ['vaɪədʌkt] Viadukt *m, n*

vi·al ['vaɪəl] (*bsd. Arznei*)Fläschchen *n*

vibes F [vaɪbz] *pl.* Atmosphäre *f* (*e-s Orts etc.*)

vi·brant ['vaɪbrənt] kräftig (*Farben, Stimme etc.*); pulsierend (*Leben*)

vi·brate [vaɪ'breɪt] *v/i.* vibrieren, zittern; flimmern (*Luft*); *fig.* pulsieren; *v/t.* in Schwingungen versetzen; **vi·bra·tion** [vaɪ'breɪʃn] Vibrieren *n*, Zittern *n*; **~s** *pl.* F Atmosphäre *f* (*e-s Orts etc.*)

vic·ar *rel.* ['vɪkə] Pfarrer *m*; **~age** ['vɪkərɪdʒ] Pfarrhaus *n*

vice¹ [vaɪs] Laster *n*

vice² *bsd. Brt. tech.* [vaɪs] Schraubstock *m*

vice... [vaɪs] Vize..., stellvertretend

'vice squad Sittendezernat *n*, -polizei *f*; Rauschgiftdezernat *n*

vi·ce ver·sa [vaɪsɪ'vɜːsə]: **and ~** u. umgekehrt

vi·cin·i·ty [vɪ'sɪnəti] Nähe *f*; Nachbarschaft *f*

vi·cious ['vɪʃəs] brutal; bösartig

vi·cis·si·tudes [vɪ'sɪsɪtjuːdz] *pl. das* Auf u. Ab, *die* Wechselfälle *pl.*

vic·tim ['vɪktɪm] Opfer *n*; **~·ize** ['vɪktɪmaɪz] (ungerechterweise) bestrafen, ungerecht behandeln; schikanieren

vic·to·ri·ous [vɪk'tɔːrɪəs] siegreich; **~·ry** ['vɪktərɪ] Sieg *m*

vid·e·o ['vɪdɪəʊ] **1.** (*pl.* **-os**) Video *n*; Videokassette *f*; F Videoband *n*; *bsd. Brt.* Videorecorder *m*, -gerät *n*; Video...; *on* ~ auf Video; **2.** *bsd. Brt.* auf Video aufnehmen, aufzeichnen; '**~ cam·e·ra** Videokamera *f*; ~ **cas·'sette** Videokassette *f*; ~ **cas'sette re·cor·der** → *video recorder*; '**~ clip** Videoclip *m*; '**~ disc** Bildplatte *f*; '**~ game** Videospiel *n*; '**~ li·bra·ry** Videothek *f*; '**~ re·cord·er** Videorecorder *m*, -gerät *n*; '**~ re·cord·ing** Videoaufnahme *f*, -aufzeichnung *f*; '**~ shop** *Brt.*, ~ **store** *Am.* Videothek *f*; '**~·tape 1.** Videokassette *f*; Videoband *n*; **2.** auf Video aufnehmen, aufzeichnen; '**~·text** *Am.* Bildschirmtext *m*

vie [vaɪ] wetteifern (*with* mit; *for* um)

Vi·en·nese [vɪə'niːz] **1.** Wiener(in); **2.** wienerisch, Wiener...

view [vjuː] **1.** Sicht *f* (*of* auf *acc.*); Aussicht *f*, (Aus)Blick *m* (*of* auf *acc.*); *phot. etc.* Ansicht *f*; Ansicht *f*, Meinung *f* (*about, on* über *acc.*); *fig.* Überblick *m* (*of* über *acc.*); *a room with a* ~ ein Zimmer mit schöner Aussicht; *be on* ~ ausgestellt *od.* zu besichtigen sein; *be hidden from* ~ nicht zu sehen sein; *come into* ~ in Sicht kommen; *in full* ~ *of* direkt vor *j-s* Augen; *in* ~ *of fig.* angesichts (*gen.*); *in my* ~ m-r Ansicht nach; *keep in* ~ *et.* im Auge behalten; *with a* ~ *to fig.* mit Blick auf (*acc.*); **2.** *v/t* Haus *etc.* besichtigen; *fig.* betrachten (*as* als; *with* mit); *v/i.* fernsehen; '**~ da·ta** Bildschirmtext *m*; '**~·er** Fernsehzuschauer(in), Fernseher(in); (*Dia*-)Betrachter *m*; '**~·find·er** *phot.* Sucher *m*; '**~·point** Gesichts-, Standpunkt *m*

vig·il ['vɪdʒɪl] (Nacht)Wache *f*; **~·i·lance** ['vɪdʒɪləns] Wachsamkeit *f*; '**~·i·lant** wachsam

vig·or·ous ['vɪɡərəs] energisch; kräftig; **~·o(u)r** ['vɪɡə] Energie *f*

Vi·king ['vaɪkɪŋ] **1.** Wikinger *m*; **2.** Wikinger...

vile [vaɪl] gemein, niederträchtig; F scheußlich

vil·lage ['vɪlɪdʒ] Dorf *n*; ~ **'green** Dorfanger *m*, -wiese *f*; '**~·lag·er** Dorfbewohner(in)

vil·lain ['vɪlən] Bösewicht *m*, Schurke *m* (*im Film etc.*); *Brt.* F Ganove *m*

vin·di·cate ['vɪndɪkeɪt] *j-n* rehabilitieren; *et.* rechtfertigen; bestätigen

vin·dic·tive [vɪn'dɪktɪv] rachsüchtig, nachtragend

vine *bot.* [vaɪn] (Wein)Rebe *f*; ⚠ *nicht* **Wein** (*Getränk*); Kletterpflanze *f*

vin·e·gar ['vɪnɪɡə] Essig *m*

'**vine·grow·er** Winzer *m*; '**~·yard** ['vɪnjəd] Weinberg *m*

vin·tage ['vɪntɪdʒ] **1.** Jahrgang *m* (*e-s Weins*); Weinernte *f*, -lese *f*; **2.** Jahrgangs...; hervorragend, glänzend; *a 1994* ~ ein 1994er Jahrgang *od.* Wein; '**~ car** *bsd. Brt. mot.* Oldtimer *m* (*Baujahr 1919-1930*)

vi·o·la *mus.* [vɪ'əʊlə] Bratsche *f*

vi·o·late ['vaɪəleɪt] Vertrag *etc.* verletzen, *a.* Versprechen brechen; Gesetz *etc.* übertreten; Ruhe *etc.* stören; Grab *etc.* schänden; **~·la·tion** [vaɪə'leɪʃn] Verletzung *f*, Bruch *m*, Übertretung *f*

vi·o·lence ['vaɪələns] Gewalt *f*; Gewalttätigkeit *f*; Ausschreitungen *pl.*; Heftigkeit *f*; '**~·lent** gewalttätig; gewaltsam; heftig (*Auseinandersetzung, Sturm*)

vi·o·let ['vaɪələt] **1.** *bot.* Veilchen *n*; **2.** violett

vi·o·lin *mus.* [vaɪə'lɪn] Geige *f*, Violine *f*; **~·ist** [vaɪə'lɪnɪst] Geiger(in), Violinist(in)

VIP [viː aɪ 'piː] *Abk. für* **very important person** VIP *f* (*prominente Persönlichkeit*); ~ **lounge** VIP-Lounge *f* (*am Flughafen etc.*); Ehrentribüne *f*

vi·per *zo.* ['vaɪpə] Viper *f*, Natter *f*

vir·gin ['vɜːdʒɪn] **1.** Jungfrau *f*; **2.** jungfräulich, unberührt; **~·i·ty** [və'dʒɪnəti] Jungfräulichkeit *f*

Vir·go *astr.* ['vɜːɡəʊ] (*pl.* **-gos**) Jungfrau *f*; *he/she is* (*a*) ~ er/sie ist Jungfrau

vir·ile ['vɪraɪl] männlich; potent; **vi·ril·i·ty** [vɪ'rɪlətɪ] Männlichkeit *f*; Potenz *f*

vir·tu·al ['vɜːtʃʊəl] eigentlich, praktisch;

V

'**~·ly** praktisch, so gut wie; **~ re'al·i·ty** Virtuelle Realität (*mit dem Computer erzeugte künstliche Welt etc.*)

vir|·tue ['vɜːtʃuː] Tugend *f*; Vorzug *m*, Vorteil *m*; **by** *od.* **in ~ of** kraft (*gen.*), vermöge (*gen.*); **make a ~ of necessity** aus der Not e-e Tugend machen; **~·tu·ous** ['vɜːtʃʊəs] tugendhaft

vir·u·lent ['vɪrʊlənt] *med.* (akut u.) bösartig (*Krankheit*); schnellwirkend (*Gift*); *fig.* bösartig, gehässig

vi·rus *med.* ['vaɪərəs] Virus *m, n*

vi·sa ['viːzə] Visum *n*, Sichtvermerk *m*; **~ed** ['viːzəd] mit e-m Visum (versehen)

vis·cose ['vɪskəʊz, 'vɪskəʊs] Viskose *f*

vis·cous ['vɪskəs] dick-, zähflüssig

vise *Am. tech.* [vaɪs] Schraubstock *m*

vis·i|·bil·i·ty [vɪzɪ'bɪlətɪ] Sicht(verhältnisse *pl.*, -weite *f*) *f*; **~·ble** ['vɪzəbl] sichtbar; *fig.* (er)sichtlich

vi·sion ['vɪʒn] Sehkraft *f*; *fig.* Weitblick *m*; Vision *f*; **~·a·ry** ['vɪʒnrɪ] **1.** weitblickend; eingebildet, unwirklich; **2.** Phantast(in), Träumer(in); Seher(in)

vis·it ['vɪzɪt] **1.** *v/t.* j-n besuchen, *Schloß etc. a.* besichtigen; *et.* inspizieren; *v/i.* **be ~ing** auf Besuch sein (*Am.*: **with** bei); **~ with** *Am.* plaudern mit; **2.** Besuch *m*, Besichtigung *f* (**to** gen.); *Am.* Plauderei *f*; **for** *od.* **on a ~** auf Besuch; **have a ~ from** Besuch haben von; **pay a ~ to** j-m e-n Besuch abstatten; *Arzt* aufsuchen; △ *nicht Visite (im Krankenhaus)*

vis·i·ta·tion [vɪzɪ'teɪʃn] Inspektion *f*; *fig.* Heimsuchung *f*

'**vis·it·ing hours** *pl.* Besuchszeit *f* (*im Krankenhaus*)

'**vis·it·or** Besucher(in), Gast *m*

vi·sor ['vaɪzə] Visier *n*; Schirm *m* (*e-r Mütze*); *mot.* (Sonnen)Blende *f*

vis·u·al ['vɪʒʊəl] Seh...; visuell; **~ 'aids** *pl. Schule:* Anschauungsmaterial *n*, Lehrmittel *pl.*; **~ dis'play u·nit** *Computer:* Bildschirmgerät *n*, Datensichtgerät *n*; **~ in'struc·tion** *Schule:* Anschauungsunterricht *m*; **~·ize** ['vɪʒʊəlaɪz] sich *et.* vorstellen

vi·tal ['vaɪtl] Lebens...; lebenswichtig (*Organ etc.*); unbedingt notwendig; vital; **of ~ importance** von größter Wichtigkeit; **~·i·ty** [vaɪ'tælətɪ] Vitalität *f*

vit·a·min ['vɪtəmɪn] Vitamin *n*; **~ de'fi·cien·cy** Vitaminmangel *m*

vit·re·ous ['vɪtrɪəs] Glas...

vi·va·cious [vɪ'veɪʃəs] lebhaft, temperamentvoll

viv·id ['vɪvɪd] hell (*Licht*); kräftig, leuchtend (*Farben*); anschaulich (*Schilderung*); lebhaft (*Phantasie*)

vix·en *zo.* ['vɪksn] Füchsin *f*

viz. [vɪz] *Abk. für* **namely** (*lateinisch* **videlicet**) nämlich

V-neck ['viːnek] V-Ausschnitt *m*; '**V-necked** mit V-Ausschnitt

vo·cab·u·la·ry [və'kæbjʊlərɪ] Vokabular *n*, Wortschatz *m*; Wörterverzeichnis *n*

vo·cal ['vəʊkl] Stimm...; F lautstark; *mus.* Vokal..., Gesang...; **~ cords** *pl. anat.* Stimmbänder *pl.*; **~·ist** ['vəʊkəlɪst] Sänger(in) (*bsd. in e-r Band*); '**~s** *pl.*: **~: XY** Gesang: XY

vo·ca·tion [vəʊ'keɪʃn] Begabung *f* (**for** für); Berufung *f*

vo·ca·tion·al [vəʊ'keɪʃənl] Berufs...; **~ ed·u·ca·tion** Berufsausbildung *f*; **~ 'guid·ance** Berufsberatung *f*; **~ 'train·ing** Berufsausbildung *f*

vogue [vəʊg] Mode *f*; **be in ~** Mode sein

voice [vɔɪs] **1.** Stimme *f*; **active ~** *gr.* Aktiv *n*; **passive ~** *gr.* Passiv *n*; **2.** zum Ausdruck bringen; *ling.* (stimmhaft) aussprechen; **~d** *ling.* stimmhaft; '**~·less** *ling.* stimmlos

void [vɔɪd] **1.** leer; *jur.* ungültig; **~ of** ohne; **2.** (Gefühl *n* der) Leere

vol [vɒl] (*pl.* **vols**) *Abk. für* **volume** Bd., Band *m*

vol·a·tile ['vɒlətaɪl] cholerisch; explosiv (*Lage*); *chem.* flüchtig

vol·ca·no [vɒl'keɪnəʊ] (*pl.* **-noes, -nos**) Vulkan *m*

vol·ley ['vɒlɪ] **1.** Salve *f*; (*Geschoß etc.*)Hagel *m* (*a. fig.*); *Tennis:* Volley *m*, Flugball *m*; *Fußball:* Volleyschuß *m*; **2.** *Ball* volley schießen (**into the net** ins Netz); '**~·ball** *Sport:* Volleyball *m*

volt *electr.* [vəʊlt] Volt *n*; **~·age** *electr.* ['vəʊltɪdʒ] Spannung *f*

vol·u·ble ['vɒljʊbl] redselig; wortreich

vol·ume ['vɒljuːm] Band *m* (*Buch*); Volumen *n*, Rauminhalt *m*; Umfang *m*, große Menge; Lautstärke *f*; **vo·lu·mi·nous** [və'luːmɪnəs] bauschig (*Kleidungsstück*); geräumig; umfangreich (*Bericht etc.*)

vol·un·ta·ry ['vɒləntərɪ] freiwillig; unbezahlt

V

vol·un·teer [vɔlən'tɪə] **1.** v/i. sich freiwillig melden (**for** zu) (a. mil.); v/t. Hilfe etc. anbieten; et. von sich aus sagen, herausrücken mit; **2.** Freiwillige(r m f) f; freiwilliger Helfer

vo·lup·tu·ous [və'lʌptʃʊəs] sinnlich (Lippen, Mund); aufreizend (Bewegungen); üppig (Formen); kurvenreich (Frau)

vom·it ['vɔmɪt] **1.** v/t. erbrechen; v/i. (sich er)brechen, sich übergeben; **2.** Erbrochene(s) n

vo·ra·cious [və'reɪʃəs] unersättlich (Appetit etc.)

vote [vəʊt] **1.** Abstimmung f (**about, on** über acc.); (Wahl)Stimme f; Stimmzettel m; a. **~s** pl. Wahlrecht n; **~ of no confidence** Mißtrauensvotum n; **take a ~ on s.th.** über et. abstimmen; **2.** v/i. wählen; **~ for/against** stimmen für/gegen; **~ on** abstimmen über (acc.); v/t.

wählen; et. bewilligen; **~ out of office** abwählen; '**vot·er** Wähler(in); '**vot·ing booth** Wahlkabine f

vouch [vaʊtʃ]: **~ for** (sich ver)bürgen für; '**~·er** Gutschein m, Coupon m

vow [vaʊ] **1.** Gelöbnis n; Gelübde n; **take a ~, make a ~** ein Gelöbnis od. Gelübde ablegen; **2.** geloben, schwören (**to do** zu tun)

vow·el gr. ['vaʊəl] Vokal m, Selbstlaut m

voy·age ['vɔɪdʒ] (See)Reise f

vs. Am. nur geschr. Abk. für **against** (lateinisch **versus**) bsd. Sport, jur.: gegen

vul·gar ['vʌlgə] vulgär, ordinär; geschmacklos

vul·ne·ra·ble ['vʌlnərəbl] fig. verletz-, verwundbar; verletzlich; anfällig (**to** für)

vul·ture zo. ['vʌltʃə] Geier m

vy·ing ['vaɪɪŋ] pres. p. von **vie**

W

W, w ['dʌblju:] W, w n

W nur geschr. Abk. für: **west** W, West(en m); **west(ern)** westlich; **watt(s** pl.) W, Watt n od. pl.

wad [wɔd] (Watte- etc.)Bausch m; Bündel n (Banknoten etc.); (Papier- etc.)Knäuel m, n; **~·ding** ['wɔdɪŋ] Einlage f, Füllmaterial n (zum Verpacken)

wad·dle ['wɔdl] watscheln

wade [weɪd] v/i. waten; **~ through** waten durch; F sich durchkämpfen durch, et. durchackern; v/t. durchwaten

wa·fer ['weɪfə] (bsd. Eis)Waffel f; Oblate f; rel. Hostie f

waf·fle¹ ['wɔfl] Waffel f

waf·fle² Brt. F ['wɔfl] schwafeln

waft [wɑ:ft] v/i. ziehen (Duft etc.); v/t. wehen

wag [wæg] **1.** (-gg-) wedeln (mit); **2. with a ~ of its tail** schwanzwedelnd

wage¹ [weɪdʒ] mst **~s** pl. (Arbeits)Lohn m

wage² [weɪdʒ]: **~ (a) war against** od. on mil. Krieg führen gegen; fig. e-n Feldzug führen gegen

'**wage| earn·er** Lohnempfänger(in); Verdiener(in); '**~ freeze** Lohnstopp m; '**~ ne·go·ti·a·tions** pl. Tarifverhandlungen pl.; '**~ pack·et** Lohntüte f; '**~ rise** Lohnerhöhung f

wa·ger ['weɪdʒə] Wette f

wag·gle F ['wægl] wackeln (mit)

wag·gon Brt. → **wag·on** ['wægən] Fuhrwerk n, Wagen m; Brt. rail. (offener) Güterwagen; Am. (Tee- etc.)Wagen m

wag·tail zo. ['wægteɪl] Bachstelze f

wail [weɪl] **1.** jammern; heulen (Sirene, Wind); **2.** Jammern n; Heulen n

wain·scot ['weɪnskət] (Wand)Täfelung f

waist [weɪst] Taille f; **~·coat** bsd. Brt. ['weɪskəʊt] Weste f; '**~·line** Taille f

wait [weɪt] **1.** v/i. warten (**for, on** auf acc.); **~ for s.o.** a. j-n erwarten; **keep s.o. ~ing** j-n warten lassen; **~ and see!** warte es ab!; **~ at** (Am. **on**) **table** bedienen, servieren; **~ on s.o.** j-n (bsd. im Restaurant) bedienen; **~ up** F aufbleiben (**for** wegen); *v/t.* ~ **one's chance** auf e-e günstige Gelegenheit warten (**to do** zu tun); ~ **one's turn** warten, bis man an der Reihe ist; **2.** Wartezeit *f*; **have a long** ~ lange warten müssen; **lie in** ~ **for s.o.** j-m auflauern; '**~er** Kellner *m*, Ober *m*; ~**, the bill** (*Am.* **check**)**, please!** (Herr) Ober, bitte zahlen!

'**wait·ing** Warten *n*; **no** ~ auf Schild: Halt(e)verbot *n*; '**~ list** Warteliste *f*; '**~ room** *med. etc.* Wartezimmer *n*; *rail.* Wartesaal *m*

wait·ress ['weɪtrɪs] Kellnerin *f*, Bedienung *f*; ~**, the bill** (*Am.* **check**)**, please!** Fräulein, bitte zahlen!

wake[1] [weɪk] (**woke** *od.* **waked**, **woken** *od.* **waked**) *v/i. a.* ~ **up** aufwachen, wach werden; *v/t. a.* ~ **up** (auf)wecken; *fig.* wecken, wachrufen

wake[2] [weɪk] *naut.* Kielwasser *n*; **follow in the** ~ **of** *fig.* folgen *od.* (*acc.*)

wake·ful ['weɪkfl] schlaflos

wak·en ['weɪkən] *v/i. a.* ~ **up** aufwachen, wach werden; *v/t. a.* ~ **up** (auf)wecken

walk [wɔːk] **1.** *v/i.* (zu Fuß) gehen, laufen; spazierengehen; wandern; *v/t.* Strecke gehen, laufen; *j-n* bringen (**to** zu; **home** nach Hause); *Hund* ausführen; *Pferd* im Schritt gehen lassen; ~ **away** → **walk off**; ~ **in** hineingehen, hereinkommen; ~ **off** fort-, weggehen; ~ **off with** F abhauen mit; F *Preis etc.* locker gewinnen; ~ **out** hinausgehen; (unter Protest) den Saal *etc.* verlassen; *econ.* streiken, in (den) Streik treten; ~ **out on s.o.** F j-n verlassen, j-n im Stich lassen; ~ **up** hinaufgehen, heraufkommen; ~ **up to s.o.** auf j-n zugehen; ~ **up!** treten Sie näher!; **2.** Spaziergang *m*, Wanderung *f*; Spazier-, Wanderweg *m*; **go for a** ~**, take a** ~ e-n Spaziergang machen, spazierengehen; **an hour's** ~ e-e Stunde Fußweg *od.* zu Fuß; **from all** ~**s** (*od.* **every** ~) **of life** Leute aus allen Berufen *od.* Schichten; '**~·er** Spaziergänger(in); Wanderer *m*, Wand(r)erin *f*; *Sport:* Geher(in); **be a good** ~ gut zu Fuß sein

walk·ie-talk·ie [wɔːkɪ'tɔːkɪ] Walkie-talkie *n*, tragbares Funksprechgerät

'**walk·ing** Gehen *n*, Laufen *n*; Spazierengehen *n*; Wandern *n*; '**~ pa·pers** *pl.*: **get one's** ~ *Am.* F den Laufpaß bekommen; '**~ shoes** *pl.* Wanderschu-

he *pl.*; '**~ stick** Spazierstock *m*; '**~ tour** Wanderung *f*

'**Walk·man** *TM* (*pl.* **-mans**) Walkman *m* (*TM*)

'**walk|·out** Auszug *m* (**by, of** e-r *Delegation etc.*); Ausstand *m*, Streik *m*; '**~over** F Spaziergang *m*, leichter Sieg; '**~up** *Am.* F Wohnung *f od.* Büro *n etc.* in e-m Haus ohne Fahrstuhl; (Miets)Haus *n* ohne Fahrstuhl

wall [wɔːl] **1.** Wand *f*; Mauer *f*; **2.** *a.* ~ **in** mit e-r Mauer umgeben; ~ **up** zumauern; '**~·chart** Wandkarte *f*

wal·let ['wɒlɪt] Brieftasche *f*

'**wall·flow·er** *fig.* F Mauerblümchen *n*

wal·lop F ['wɒləp] *j-m* ein Ding (*Schlag*) verpassen; *Sport:* *j-n* erledigen, vernichten (**at** in *dat.*)

wal·low ['wɒləʊ] sich wälzen; *fig.* schwelgen, sich baden (**in** in *dat.*)

'**wall|·pa·per 1.** Tapete *f*; **2.** tapezieren; '**~to-'~:** ~ **carpet(ing)** Spannteppich *m*, Teppichboden *m*

wal·nut *bot.* ['wɔːlnʌt] Walnuß(baum *m*) *f*

wal·rus *zo.* ['wɔːlrəs] (*pl.* **-ruses, -rus**) Walroß *n*

waltz [wɔːls] **1.** Walzer *m*; **2.** Walzer tanzen

wand [wɒnd] (*Zauber*)Stab *m*

wan·der ['wɒndə] (herum)wandern, herumlaufen, umherstreifen; ⚠ *nicht in e-m Gebiet* wandern (→ **hike**); *fig.* abschweifen; phantasieren

wane [weɪn] **1.** abnehmen (*Mond*); *fig.* schwinden (*Einfluß, Macht etc.*); **2. be on the** ~ im Schwinden begriffen sein

wan·gle F ['wæŋgl] deichseln, hinkriegen; ~ **s.th. out of s.o.** j-m et. abluchsen; ~ **one's way out of** sich herauswinden aus

want [wɒnt] **1.** *v/t. et.* wollen; *j-n* brauchen; *j-n* sprechen wollen; F et. brauchen, nötig haben; **be** ~**ed** (*polizeilich*) gesucht werden (**for** wegen); *v/i.* wollen; **I don't** ~ **to** ich will nicht; **he does not** ~ **for anything** es fehlt ihm an nichts; **2.** Mangel *m* (**of** an *dat.*); Bedürfnis *n*, Wunsch *m*; Not *f*; '~ **ad** *bsd. Am.* Kleinanzeige *f*; '**~·ed** gesucht

wan·ton ['wɒntən] mutwillig

war [wɔː] Krieg *m* (*a. fig.*); *fig.* Kampf *m* (**against** gegen)

war·ble ['wɔːbl] trillern (*Vogel*)

ward [wɔːd] **1.** Station f (*e-s Kranken-hauses*); *Brt. pol.* Stadtbezirk m; *jur.* Mündel n; **2.** ~ *off* Schlag etc. abwehren, *Gefahr etc.* abwenden; **war·den** ['wɔːdn] Aufseher(in); Heimleiter(in); *Am.* (Gefängnis)Direktor(in); ~**er** *Brt.* ['wɔːdə] Aufsichtsbeamt|e(r) m, -in f (*im Gefängnis*)

war·drobe ['wɔːdrəʊb] Kleiderschrank m; Garderobe f (*Kleidungsstücke*)

ware [weə] *in Zssgn* (Glas- *etc.*)Waren pl.; △ *nicht* (Einkaufs)**Ware**

'**ware·house** Lager(haus) n; △ *nicht* **Warenhaus**

war|fare ['wɔːfeə] Krieg(führung f) m; '~**head** *mil.* Spreng-, Gefechtskopf m; '~**like** kriegerisch; Kriegs...

warm [wɔːm] **1.** *adj.* warm (*a. fig.* Farben, Stimme); warm, herzlich (*Empfang etc.*); **I am** ~, **I feel** ~ mir ist warm; **2.** *v/t. a.* ~ **up** wärmen, sich *die Hände etc.* wärmen; *Motor* warmlaufen lassen; *v/i. a.* ~ **up** warm *od.* wärmer werden, sich erwärmen; **3.** *come into the* ~ *bsd. Brt.* komm in die Warme!; ~**th** [wɔːmθ] Wärme f; '~**up** *Sport:* Aufwärmen n

warn [wɔːn] warnen (*against, of* vor *dat.*); *j-n* verständigen; '~**ing** Warnung f (*of* vor *dat.*); Verwarnung f; *without* ~ ohne Vorwarnung; '~**ing sig·nal** Warnsignal n

warp [wɔːp] sich verziehen *od.* werfen (*Holz*)

war·rant ['wɒrənt] **1.** *jur.* (Durchsuchungs-, Haft- *etc.*)Befehl m; → **death warrant; 2.** *et.* rechtfertigen; ~ *of* **ar'rest** *jur.* Haftbefehl m

war·ran·ty *econ.* ['wɒrəntɪ] Garantie(erklärung) f; *it's still under* ~ darauf ist noch Garantie

war·ri·or ['wɒrɪə] Krieger m

'**war·ship** Kriegsschiff n

wart [wɔːt] Warze f

war·y ['weərɪ] (-*ier*, -*iest*) vorsichtig

was [wɒz, wəz] *ich, er, sie, es* war; *Passiv: ich, er, sie, es* wurde

wash [wɒʃ] **1.** *v/t.* waschen, sich *die Hände etc.* waschen; *v/i.* sich waschen; sich *gut etc.* waschen (lassen); ~ **up** *v/i. Brt.* abwaschen, (das) Geschirr spülen; *v/t.* anschwemmen, anspülen; **2.** Wäsche f; Waschanlage f, -straße f; *be in the* ~ in der Wäsche sein; *give s.th. a* ~

et. waschen; **have a** ~ sich waschen; '~**a·ble** (ab)waschbar; ~**and-wear** bügelfrei; pflegeleicht; '~**ba·sin** Am. Waschbecken n; '~**cloth** Am. Waschlappen m; '~**er** Am. Waschmaschine f; → **dishwasher**; *tech.* Unterlegscheibe f; '~**ing** Wäsche f; Wasch...; '~**ing ma·chine** Waschmaschine f; '~**ing pow·der** Waschpulver n, -mittel n; ~**ing-up** *Brt.* Abwasch m; *do the* ~ den Abwasch machen; '~**rag** Am. Waschlappen m; '~**room** Am. Toilette f

wasp *zo.* [wɒsp] Wespe f

waste [weɪst] **1.** Verschwendung f; Abfall m; Müll m; ~ *of time* Zeitverschwendung f; *hazardous* ~, *special toxic* ~ Sondermüll m; *special* ~ *dump* Sondermülldeponie f; **2.** *v/t.* verschwenden, -geuden; *j-n* auszehren; *v/i.* ~ *away* immer schwächer werden (*Person*); **3.** überschüssig; Abfall...; brachliegend, öde (*Land*); *lay* ~ verwüsten; '~**dis·pos·al** Abfall-, Müllbeseitigung f; Entsorgung f; ~ **dis·pos·al 'site** Deponie f; '~**ful** verschwenderisch; '~ **gas** Abgas n; ~ '**pa·per** Abfallpapier n; Altpapier n; '**pa·per bas·ket** Papierkorb m; ~ **pipe** Abflußrohr n

watch [wɒtʃ] **1.** *v/i.* zuschauen; ~ *for* warten auf (*acc.*); ~ *out!* paß auf!, Vorsicht!; ~ *out for* Ausschau halten nach; sich in acht nehmen vor (*dat.*); *v/t.* beobachten; zuschauen bei, sich *et.* ansehen; → **television; 2.** (Armband-, Taschen)Uhr f; Wache f; *be on the* ~ *for* Ausschau halten nach; auf der Hut sein vor (*dat.*); *keep (a) careful od. close* ~ *on et.* genau beobachten, *et.* scharf im Auge behalten; '~**dog** Wachhund m; '~**ful** wachsam; '~**mak·er** Uhrmacher(in); '~**man** (*pl.* -**men**) Wachmann m, Wächter m

wa·ter ['wɔːtə] **1.** Wasser n; **2.** *v/t.* Blumen gießen, Rasen etc. sprengen; Vieh tränken; ~ **down** verdünnen, -wässern; *fig.* abschwächen; *v/i.* tränen (*Augen*); *make s.o.'s mouth* ~ j-m den Mund wässerig *od.* wäßrig machen; '~**bird** *zo.* Wasservogel m; '~**col·o·u(u)r** Wasser-Aquarellfarbe f; Aquarell(malerei) f n; '~**course** Wasserlauf m; '~**cress** *bot.* Brunnenkresse f; '~**fall** Wasserfall *m*; '**~front** Hafenviertel *n*; *along the* **~** am Wasser entlang; '**~hole** Wasserloch *n*

wa·ter·ing can ['wɔːtərɪŋ-] Gießkanne *f*

'**wa·ter| jump** *Sport:* Wassergraben *m*; '**~ lev·el** Wasserstand *m*; '**~ lil·y** *bot.* Seerose *f*; '**~mark** Wasserzeichen *n*; '**~mel·on** *bot.* Wassermelone *f*; '**~ pol·lu·tion** Wasserverschmutzung *f*; '**~ po·lo** *Sport:* Wasserball(spiel *n*) *m*; '**~proof 1.** wasserdicht; **2.** *Brt.* Regenmantel *m*; **3.** regendicht; '**~s** *pl.* Gewässer *pl.*; Wasser *pl.* (*e-s Flusses etc.*); '**~shed** *geogr.* Wasserscheide *f*; *fig.* Wendepunkt *m*; '**~side** Ufer *n*; '**~ ski·ing** *Sport:* Wasserskilaufen *n*; '**~tight** wasserdicht, *fig. a.* hieb- u. stichfest; '**~way** Wasserstraße *f*; '**~ works** *oft sg.* Wasserwerk *n*; *turn on the* **~** F zu heulen anfangen; **~·y** ['wɔːtərɪ] wässrig, wäßrig

watt *electr.* [wɒt] Watt *n*

wave [weɪv] **1.** *v/t.* schwenken, winken mit; *Haar* wellen, in Wellen legen; **~ one's hand** winken; **~ s.o. aside** j-n beiseite winken; *v/i.* winken; wehen (*Fahne etc.*); sich wellen (*Haar*); **~ at s.o.,** **~ to s.o.** j-m zuwinken; **2.** Welle *f* (*a. fig.*). Winken *n*; '**~length** *phys.* Wellenlänge *f* (*a. fig.*)

wa·ver ['weɪvə] flackern; schwanken

wav·y ['weɪvɪ] (*-ier, -iest*) wellig, gewellt

wax¹ [wæks] **1.** Wachs *n*; (*Ohren*)Schmalz *n*; **2.** wachsen; bohnern

wax² [wæks] zunehmen (*Mond*)

'**wax|·en** ['wæksən] wächsern; '**~works** *sg.* Wachsfigurenkabinett *n*; **~·y** ['wæksɪ] (*-ier, -iest*) wächsern

way [weɪ] **1.** Weg *m*; Richtung *f*, Seite *f*; Weg *m*, Entfernung *f*; Strecke *f*; Art *f*, Weise *f*; **~s and means** *pl.* Mittel u. Wege *pl.*; **~ back** Rückweg *m*; **~ home** Heimweg *m*; **~ in** Eingang *m*; *out* Ausgang *m*; *be on the* **~ to,** *be on one's* **~ to** unterwegs sein nach; *by* **~ of** über (*acc.*), via; *bsd. Brt.* statt; *by the* **~** übrigens; *give* **~** nachgeben; *Brt. mot.* die Vorfahrt lassen; *in a* **~** in gewisser Hinsicht; *in no* **~** in keiner Weise; *lead the* **~** vorangehen; *let s.o. have his/her (own)* **~** j-m s-n Willen lassen; *lose one's* **~** sich verlaufen od. verirren; *make* **~** Platz machen (*for* für); *no* **~!** F kommt überhaupt nicht in Frage!; *out*

of the **~** ungewöhnlich; *hier entlang;* **this** **~** hierher; **2.** *adv.* weit; '**~bill** Frachtbrief *m*; '**~lay** (*-laid*) j-m auflauern; *j-n* abfangen, abpassen; **~·ward** ['weɪwəd] eigensinnig, launisch

we [wiː, wɪ] wir *pl.*

weak [wiːk] schwach (*at, in* dat.); (*Kaffee, Tee a.*) dünn; '**~en** *v/t.* schwächen (*a. fig.*); *v/i.* schwächer werden; *fig.* nachgeben; '**~ling** Schwächling *m*; '**~ness** Schwäche *f*

weal [wiːl] Strieren *m*

wealth [welθ] Reichtum *m*; *fig.* Fülle *f* (*of* von); **~·y** (*-ier, -iest*) reich

wean [wiːn] entwöhnen; **~ s.o. from** *od.* *off s.th.* j-m et. abgewöhnen

weap·on ['wepən] Waffe *f* (*a. fig.*)

wear [weə] **1.** (*wore, worn*) *v/t.* Bart, Brille, Schmuck etc. tragen, Mantel etc. *a.* anhaben, Hut etc. *a.* aufhaben; abnutzen, abtragen; **~ the trousers** (*Am. pants*) F die Hosen anhaben; **~ an angry expression** verärgert dreinschauen; *v/i.* sich abnutzen, abtragen; sich *gut etc.* halten; **s.th. to ~** et. zum Anziehen; **~ away** (sich) abtragen *od.* abschleifen; **~ down** (sich) abtreten (*Stufen*), (sich) ablaufen (*Absätze*), (sich) abfahren (*Reifen*); abschleifen; *fig. j-n* etc. zermürben; **~ off** nachlassen (*Schmerz etc.*); **~ on** sich hinziehen (*all day* über den ganzen Tag); **~ out** (sich) abnutzen *od.* abtragen (*Kleidung*); *fig. j-n* erschöpfen; **2.** *oft in Zssgn* Kleidung *f; a.* **~ and tear** Abnutzung *f*, Verschleiß *m*; *the worse for* **~** abgenutzt, verschlissen; F lädiert (*Person*)

wear·i·some ['wɪərɪsəm] ermüdend; langweilig; lästig; **~·y** ['wɪərɪ] (*-ier, -iest*) erschöpft, müde; F ermüdend, anstrengend; *be* **~ of s.th.** et. satt haben

wea·sel *zo.* ['wiːzl] Wiesel *n*

weath·er ['weðə] **1.** Wetter *n*; Witterung *f*; **2.** *v/t.* dem Wetter aussetzen; *Krise etc.* überstehen; *v/i.* verwittern; '**~beat·en** verwittert (*bsd. Gesicht*); '**~ chart** Wetterkarte *f*; '**~ fore·cast** Wettervorhersage *f*; Wetterbericht *m*; '**~man** (*pl. -men*) Rundfunk, TV: Wetteransager *m*; '**~proof 1.** wetterfest; **2.** wetterfest machen; '**~ re·port** Wetterbericht *m*; '**~ sta·tion** Wetterwarte *f*; '**~ vane** Wetterfahne *f*

weave [wiːv] (*wove, woven*) weben;

Netz spinnen; *Korb* flechten; (*pret. u. p.p. weaved*): ~ *one's way through* sich schlängeln durch; **'weav·er** Weber(in)

web [web] Netz *n* (*a. fig.*), Gewebe *n*; *zo.* Schwimmhaut *f*; **'~bing** Gurtband *n*

wed [wed] (*-dd-; wedded od. selten wed*) heiraten

Wed(s) *nur geschr. Abk. für* **Wednes·day** Mi., Mittwoch *m*

wed·ding ['wedɪŋ] Hochzeit *f*; Hochzeits..., Braut..., Ehe..., Trau...; **'~ ring** Ehe-, Trauring *m*

wedge [wedʒ] **1.** Keil *m*; **2.** verkeilen, mit e-m Keil festklemmen; *~ in* einkeilen, -zwängen

wed·lock ['wedlɒk]: *born in (out of) ~* ehelich (unehelich) geboren

Wednes·day ['wenzdɪ] (*Abk. Wed, Weds*) Mittwoch *m*; *on ~* (am) Mittwoch; *on ~s* mittwochs

wee¹ F [wiː] klein, winzig; *a ~ bit* ein (kleines) bißchen

wee² F [wiː]: **1.** Pipi machen; **2.** *do od. have a ~* Pipi machen

weed [wiːd] **1.** Unkraut *n*; **2.** jäten; *~ out fig.* aussieben, -sondern (*from* aus); **'~ kill·er** Unkrautvertilgungsmittel *n*; **'~y** (*-ier, -iest*) voll Unkraut; F schmächtig; F rückgratlos

week [wiːk] Woche *f*; *~ after ~* Woche um Woche; *a ~ today, today ~* heute in e-r Woche; *in a ~('s time)* in e-r Woche; **'~day** Wochentag *m*; **~end** [wiːk'end] Wochenende *n*; *at* (*Am. on*) *the ~* am Wochenende; **'~end·er** Wochenendausflügler(in); **'~ly 1.** Wochen...; wöchentlich; **2.** Wochenblatt *n*, -(zeit)schrift *f*, -zeitung *f*

weep [wiːp] (*wept*) weinen (*for* um *j*-n; *over* über *acc.*); nässen (*Wunde*) (*of* j-n); **'wil·low** *bot.* Trauerweide *f*; **'~y** F (*-ier, -iest*) weinerlich; rührselig

wee-wee F ['wiːwiː] → **wee**²

weigh [weɪ] *v/t.* (ab)wiegen; *fig.* abwägen (*against gegen*); *~ anchor* das Ankerlichten; *be ~ed down with fig.* niedergedrückt werden von; *v/i.* ... Kilo *etc.* wiegen; *~ on fig.* lasten auf (*dat.*)

weight [weɪt] **1.** Gewicht *n*; Last *f* (*a. fig.*); *fig.* Bedeutung *f*; *gain ~, put on ~*

---

zunehmen; *lose ~* abnehmen; **2.** beschweren; schwerem; **'~·less** schwerelos; **'~·less·ness** Schwerelosigkeit *f*; **'~ lift·er** *Sport*: Gewichtheber *m*; **'~ lift·ing** *Sport*: Gewichtheben *n*; **'~·y** (*-ier, -iest*) schwer; *fig.* schwerwiegend

weir [wɪə] Wehr *n*

weird [wɪəd] unheimlich; F sonderbar, verrückt

wel·come ['welkəm] **1.** *int. ~ back!, ~ home!* willkommen zu Hause!; *~ to England!* willkommen in England!; **2.** *v/t.* begrüßen (*a. fig.*), willkommen heißen; **3.** *adj.* willkommen; *you are ~ to do it* Sie können es gerne tun; *you're ~! bsd. Am.* nichts zu danken!, keine Ursache!, bitte sehr!; **4.** Empfang *m*, Willkommen *n*; *outstay od. overstay one's ~* j-s Gastfreundschaft überstrapazieren *od.* zu lange in Anspruch nehmen

weld *tech.* [weld] schweißen

wel·fare ['welfeə] Wohl(ergehen) *n*; *Am.* Sozialhilfe *f*; *be on ~* Sozialhilfe beziehen; *~ 'state* Wohlfahrtsstaat *m*; *~ 'work* Sozialarbeit *f*; *~ 'work·er* Sozialarbeiter(in)

well¹ [wel] **1.** *adv.* (*better, best*) gut; gründlich; *as ~* ebenso, auch; *as ~ as* sowohl ... als auch; nicht nur ..., sondern auch; *very ~* also gut, na gut; *~ done!* bravo!; → *off* | **2.** *int.* nun, also; *~, ~!* na so was!; **3.** *adj.* gesund; *feel ~* sich wohl fühlen

well² [wel] **1.** Brunnen *m*; (*Öl*)Quelle *f*; (*Aufzugs- etc.*)Schacht *m*; **2.** *a. ~ out* quellen (*from* aus); *tears ~ed (up) in their eyes* die Tränen stiegen ihnen in die Augen

well·-'bal·anced ausgeglichen (*Person*); ausgewogen (*Ernährung etc.*); *~·'be·ing* Wohl(befinden) *n*; *~·'done* durchgebraten (*Fleisch*); *~·'earned* wohlverdient; *~·'found·ed* (wohl)begründet; *~·in'formed* gutunterrichtet; gebildet; *~·'known* (wohl)bekannt; *~·'mean·ing* wohlmeinend (*Person*), (*Rat etc. a.*) gut-, wohlgemeint; *~·'meant* gut-, wohlgemeint; *~·'off* **1.** (*better-off, best-off*) reich, wohlhabend; **2.** *the ~ pl.* die Reichen *pl.*; *~·'read* belesen; *~·'timed* (zeitlich) günstig, im richtigen Augenblick; *~·to·'do* F → *well-off*; *~·'worn* abgenutzt, abgetragen; *fig.* abgedroschen

W

Welsh [welʃ] **1.** walisisch; **2.** *ling.* Walisisch *n*; *the* 2 *pl.* die Waliser *pl.*; ~ 'rab·bit, ~ 'rare·bit *gastr.* etwa überbackener Käsetoast

welt [welt] Striemen *m*

wel·ter ['weltə] Wirrwarr *m*, Durcheinander *n*

went [went] *pret. von go* 1

wept [wept] *pret. u. p.p. von weep*

were [wɜː, wə] *du* warst, *Sie* waren, *wir, sie* waren, *ihr* wart

west [west] **1.** West(en *m*); *the* 2 *pol.* der Westen; *Am.* die Weststaaten *pl.* (*der USA*); **2.** *adj.* westlich, West...; **3.** *adv.* nach Westen, westwärts; ~·er·ly ['westəlɪ] westlich, West...; ~·ern ['westən] **1.** westlich, West...; **2.** Western *m*; ~·ward(s) ['westwəd(z)] westlich, nach Westen

wet [wet] **1.** naß, feucht; **2.** Nässe *f*; **3.** (*-tt-; wet od wetted*) naß machen, anfeuchten

weth·er *zo.* ['weðə] Hammel *m*

'**wet nurse** Amme *f*

whack [wæk] (knallender) Schlag; F (An)Teil *m*; ~ed fertig, erledigt (*erschöpft*); '~·ing **1.** F Mords...; **2.** (Tracht *f*) Prügel *pl.*

whale *zo.* [weɪl] Wal *m*

wharf [wɔːf] (*pl.* **wharfs, wharves** [wɔːvz]) Kai *m*

what [wɒt] **1.** *pron.* was; ~ *about ...?* wie wär's mit ...?; ~ *for?* wozu?; *so* ~? na und?; *know* ~*'s* F wissen, was Sache ist; **2.** *adj.* was für ein(e), welche(r, -s); alle, die; alles, was; ~·cha·ma·call·it F ['wɒtʃəməkɔːlɪt] → *whatsit*; ~·ev·er **1.** *pron.* was (auch immer); alles, was; egal, was; **2.** *adj.* welche(r, -s) ... auch (immer); *no ...* ~ überhaupt kein(e)

whats·it F ['wɒtsɪt] Dings(bums, -da) *n*

what·so·ev·er → *whatever*

wheat *bot.* [wiːt] Weizen *m*

whee·dle ['wiːdl] beschwatzen; ~ *s.th. out of s.o.* j-m et. abschwatzen

wheel [wiːl] **1.** Rad *n*; *mot., naut.* Steuer *n*; **2.** schieben, rollen; kreisen (*Vogel*); ~ *about,* ~ *(a)round* herumfahren, -wirbeln; '~·bar·row Schubkarre(n *m*) *f*; '~·chair Rollstuhl *m*; '~ **clamp** *mot.* Parkkralle *f*; ~ed mit Rädern; fahrbar; *in Zssgn* ...räd(e)rig

wheeze [wiːz] keuchen, pfeifend atmen

whelp *zo.* [welp] Welpe *m*, Junge(s) *n*

when [wen] wann; als; wenn; obwohl; *since* ~? seit wann?

when·ev·er wann auch (immer); jedesmal, wenn

where [weə] wo; wohin; ~ *... (from)?* woher?; ~ *... (to)?* wohin?; ~·a·bouts **1.** *adv.* [weərə'baʊts] wo etwa; **2.** ['weərəbaʊts] *sg., pl.* Verbleib *m*; Aufenthalt(sort) *m*; ~·as [weər'æz] während, wohingegen; ~·by [weə'baɪ] wodurch, womit; wonach; ~·u·pon [weərə'pɒn] worauf(hin)

wher·ev·er [weər'evə] wo(hin) auch (immer); ganz gleich wo(hin)

whet [wet] (*-tt-*) Messer etc. schärfen; *fig.* Appetit anregen

wheth·er ['weðə] ob

whey [weɪ] Molke *f*

which [wɪtʃ] welche(r, -s); der, die, das; *auf den vorhergehenden Satz bezüglich:* was; ~ *of you?* wer von euch?; ~·ev·er welche(r, -s) auch (immer); ganz gleich, welche(r, -s)

whiff [wɪf] Luftzug *m*; Hauch *m* (*a. fig. of* von); Duft(wolke *f*) *m*

while [waɪl] **1.** Weile *f*; *for a* ~ e-e Zeitlang; **2.** *cj.* während; obwohl; **3.** *mst* ~ *away* sich *die Zeit* vertreiben (*by doing s.th.* mit et.)

whim [wɪm] Laune *f*

whim·per ['wɪmpə] **1.** wimmern (*Person*); winseln (*Hund*); **2.** Wimmern *n*; Winseln; △ *nicht* Wimper

whim|·si·cal ['wɪmzɪkl] wunderlich; launisch; ~·sy ['wɪmzɪ] Wunderlichkeit *f*; Spleen *m*

whine [waɪn] **1.** jaulen (*Hund*); jammern (*about* über *acc.*); **2.** Jaulen *n*; Gejammer *n*

whin·ny ['wɪnɪ] **1.** wiehern; **2.** Wiehern *n*

whip [wɪp] **1.** Peitsche *f*; *gastr.* Creme *f*; **2.** (*-pp-*) *v/t.* (aus)peitschen; *Eier, Sahne etc.* schlagen; *v/i.* sausen, flitzen; (*Wind*) fegen; '~ped **cream** Schlagsahne *f*, -rahm *m*; '~ped **eggs** *pl.* Eischnee *m*

whip·ping ['wɪpɪŋ] (Tracht *f*) Prügel *pl.*; '~ **boy** Prügelknabe *m*; '~ **cream** Schlagsahne *f*, -rahm *m*

whir *bsd. Am.* [wɜː] → *whirr*

whirl [wɜːl] **1.** wirbeln; *my head is* ~*ing* mir schwirrt der Kopf; **2.** Wirbeln *n*; Wirbel *m* (*a. fig.*); *my head's in a* ~ mir schwirrt der Kopf; '~·pool Strudel *m*;

wild

Whirlpool *m*; '**~·wind** Wirbelsturm *m*

whirr [wɜː] (**-rr-**) schwirren

whisk [wɪsk] **1.** schnelle Bewegung; Wedel *m*; *gastr.* Schneebesen *m*; **2.** *Eiweiß* schlagen; **~** *its tail Pferd etc.*: mit dem Schwanz schlagen; **~** *away Fliegen etc.* ver-, wegscheuchen; *et.* schnell verschwinden lassen *od.* wegnehmen

whis·ker ['wɪskə] Schnurr- *od.* Barthaar *n*; **~s** *pl.* Backenbart *m*

whis·key ['wɪskɪ] *amerikanischer od. irischer* Whisky

whis·ky ['wɪskɪ] *bsd. schottischer* Whisky

whis·per ['wɪspə] **1.** flüstern; **2.** Flüstern *n*; *say s.th. in a* **~** et. im Flüsterton sagen

whis·tle ['wɪsl] **1.** Pfeife *f*; Pfiff *m*; **2.** pfeifen

white [waɪt] **1.** (**~r**, **~st**) weiß; **2.** Weiß(e) *n*; Weiße(r *m*) *f* (*Person*); Eiweiß *n*; **~** '**bread** Weißbrot *n*; **~** '**cof·fee** *Brt.* Milchkaffee *m*, Kaffee *m* mit Milch; **~·'col·lar work·er** allmählich aufgestellte(r *m*) *f*; **~** '**lie** Notlüge *f*; **whit·en** ['waɪtn] weiß machen *od.* werden; '**~·wash 1.** tünchen, anstreichen; weißen; *fig.* beschönigen

whit·ish ['waɪtɪʃ] weißlich

Whit·sun ['wɪtsn] Pfingstsonntag *m*; Pfingsten *n od. pl.*; **Whit Sunday** [wɪt 'sʌndɪ] Pfingstsonntag *m*; '**Whit·sun·tide** Pfingsten *n od. pl.*

whit·tle ['wɪtl] (zurecht)schnitzen; **~** *away Gewinn etc.* allmählich aufzehren; **~** *down et.* reduzieren (*to auf acc.*)

whiz(z) F [wɪz] **1.** (**-zz-**): **~** *by od. past* vorbeizischen, vorbeidüsen; **2.** F As *n*, Kanone *f* (*at in dat.*); '**~** *kid* F Senkrechtstarter(in)

who [huː] wer; wen; wem; welche(r, -s) der, die, das

WHO [dʌbljuː eɪtʃ 'əʊ] *Abk. für World Health Organization* Weltgesundheitsorganisation *f* (*der UNO*)

who·dun·(n)it F [huːˈdʌnɪt] Krimi *m*

who·ev·er wer *od.* wen *od.* wem auch (immer); egal, wer *od.* wen *od.* wem

whole [həʊl] **1.** *adj.* ganz; **2.** *das* Ganze; *the* **~** *of London* ganz London; *on the* **~** im großen (u.) ganzen; **~·'heart·ed** ungeteilt (*Aufmerksamkeit*), voll (*Unterstützung etc.*), ernsthaft (*Versuch etc.*); **~·'heart·ed·ly** uneingeschränkt, voll

u. ganz; '**~·meal** Vollkorn...; **~** *bread* Vollkornbrot *n*

'**whole·sale** *econ.* **1.** Großhandel *m*; **2.** Großhandels...; '**~** *mar·ket econ.* Großmarkt *m*; '**whole·sal·er** *econ.* Großhändler *m*

'**whole·some** gesund; '**~** *wheat* → *wholemeal*

whol·ly *adv.* ['həʊllɪ] gänzlich, völlig

whom [huːm] *acc. von who*

whoop [huːp] **1.** schreien, *bsd.* jauchzen; **~** *it up* F auf den Putz hauen; **2.** (*bsd.* Freuden)Schrei *m*

whoop·ee F ['wʊpiː]: *make* **~** auf den Putz hauen

whoop·ing cough *med.* ['huːpɪŋkɒf] Keuchhusten *m*

whore [hɔː] Hure *f*

whose [huːz] *gen. von who*

why [waɪ] warum, weshalb; *that's* **~** deshalb

wick [wɪk] Docht *m*

wick·ed ['wɪkɪd] gemein, niederträchtig; boshaft

wick·er ['wɪkə] Weiden..., Korb...; '**~** *bas·ket* Weidenkorb *m*; '**~·work** Korbwaren *pl.*

wick·et ['wɪkɪt] *Kricket:* Tor *n*

wide [waɪd] **1.** *adj.* breit; weit offen, aufgerissen (*Augen*); *fig.* umfangreich (*Wissen etc.*), vielfältig (*Interessen etc.*); **2.** *adv.* weit; *go* **~** (*of the goal*) *Sport:* danebengehen (am Tor vorbeigehen); **~·a'wake** hellwach; *fig.* aufgeweckt, wach; **~·'eyed** mit großen *od.* aufgerissenen Augen; naiv

wid·en ['waɪdn] verbreitern; breiter werden

wide·'o·pen weit offen, aufgerissen (*Augen*); '**~·spread** weitverbreitet

wid·ow ['wɪdəʊ] Witwe *f*; '**~·ed** verwitwet; *be* **~** verwitwet sein; Witwe(r) werden; '**~·er** Witwer *m*

width [wɪdθ] Breite *f*; Bahn *f* (*Stoff etc.*)

wield [wiːld] *Einfluß etc.* ausüben

wife [waɪf] (*pl. wives* [waɪvz]) (Ehe-) Frau *f*, Gattin *f*

wig [wɪg] Perücke *f*

wild [waɪld] **1.** *adj.* wild; stürmisch (*Wind, Applaus etc.*); außer sich (*with* vor *dat.*); verrückt (*Idee etc.*); *make a* **~** *guess* einfach drauflosraten; *be* **~** *about* (ganz) verrückt sein nach *od.*; **2.** *adv.* *go* **~** ausflippen; *let one's children run*

W

~ s-e Kinder machen lassen, was sie wollen; **3.** *in the* ~ in freier Wildbahn; *the* ~**s** *pl.* die Wildnis; '**~cat** *zo.* Wildkatze *f*; '**~cat 'strike** wilder Streik

wil·der·ness ['wɪldənɪs] Wildnis *f*

'**wild·fire**: *spread like* ~ sich wie ein Lauffeuer verbreiten; '**~life** Tier- u. Pflanzenwelt *f*

wil·ful ['wɪlfl] eigensinnig; absichtlich, *bsd. jur.* vorsätzlich

will¹ [wɪl] *v/aux. (pret. would; verneint* ~ *not, won't)* ich, du will(st) *etc.*; ich werde ... *etc.*

will² [wɪl] Wille *m*; Testament *n*; *of one's own free* ~ aus freien Stücken

will³ [wɪl] durch Willenskraft erzwingen; *jur.* vermachen

'**will·ful** *Am.* → **wilful**

'**will·ing** bereit (*to do* zu tun); (bereit)willig

will-o'-the-wisp [wɪləðə'wɪsp] Irrlicht *n*

wil·low *bot.* ['wɪləʊ] Weide *f*; '**~y** *fig.* gertenschlank

'**will·pow·er** Willenskraft *f*

wil·ly-nil·ly [wɪlɪ'nɪlɪ] wohl od. übel

wilt [wɪlt] verwelken, welk werden

wi·ly ['waɪlɪ] (*-ier, -iest*) gerissen, raffiniert

win [wɪn] **1.** (*-nn-; won*) *v/t.* gewinnen; ~ **s.o. over** *od.* **round to** j-n gewinnen für; *v/i.* gewinnen, siegen; *OK, you* ~ okay, du hast gewonnen; **2.** *bsd. Sport:* Sieg *m*

wince [wɪns] zusammenzucken (**at** bei)

winch *tech.* [wɪntʃ] Winde *f*

wind¹ [wɪnd] **1.** Wind *m*; Atem *m*, Luft *f*; *med.* Blähungen *pl.*; *the* ~ *sg. od. pl. mus.* die Bläser *pl.*; **2.** *j-m* den Atem nehmen *od.* verschlagen; *hunt.* wittern

wind² [waɪnd] **1.** (*wound*) *v/t.* drehen (an *dat.*); *Uhr etc.* aufziehen; wickeln (*round* um); *v/i.* sich winden *od.* schlängeln (*Pfad etc.*); ~ **back** *Film etc.* zurückspulen; ~ **down** *Autofenster etc.* herunterdrehen, -kurbeln; *Produktion etc.* reduzieren; sich entspannen; ~ **forward** *Film etc.* weiterspulen; ~ **up** *v/t. Autofenster etc.* hochdrehen, -kurbeln; *Uhr etc.* aufziehen; *Versammlung etc.* schließen (**with** mit); *Unternehmen* auflösen; *v/i.* F enden, landen; (*bsd.* s-e Rede) schließen (*by saying* mit den Worten); **2.** Umdrehung *f*

'**wind·bag** F Schwätzer(in); '**~fall** Fallobst *n*; unverhofftes Geschenk, unverhoffter Gewinn

wind·ing ['waɪndɪŋ] gewunden (*Pfad etc.*); '~ **stairs** *pl.* Wendeltreppe *f*

wind in·stru·ment *mus.* ['wɪnd ɪnstrəmənt] Blasinstrument *n*

wind·lass *tech.* ['wɪndləs] Winde *f*

wind·mill ['wɪnmɪl] Windmühle *f*

win·dow ['wɪndəʊ] Fenster *n*; Schaufenster *n*; Schalter *m* (*in e-r Bank etc.*); '~ **clean·er** Fensterputzer *m*; ~ **dresser** Schaufensterdekorateur(in); '~ **dress·ing** Schaufensterdekoration *f*; *fig.* Mache *f*; '**~pane** Fensterscheibe *f*; '~ **seat** Fensterplatz *m*; ~ **shade** *Am.* Rouleau *n*; '~**shop** (*-pp-*): *go* ~**ping** e-n Schaufensterbummel machen; '**~sill** Fensterbank *f*, -brett *n*

'**wind·pipe** *anat.* ['wɪndpaɪp] Luftröhre *f*; '**~screen** *Brt. mot.* Windschutzscheibe *f*; '**~screen wip·er** *Brt. mot.* Scheibenwischer *m*; '**~shield** *Am. mot.* Windschutzscheibe *f*; '**~shield wip·er** *Am. mot.* Scheibenwischer *m*; '**~surf·ing** *Sport:* Windsurfing *n*, -surfen *n*

wind·y ['wɪndɪ] (*-ier, -iest*) windig; *med.* blähend

wine [waɪn] Wein *m*

wing [wɪŋ] Flügel *m*; Schwinge *f*; *Brt. mot.* Kotflügel *m*; *aviat.* Tragfläche *f*; *aviat.* Geschwader *n*; ~**s** *pl. thea.* Seitenkulisse *f*; '**~er** *Sport:* Außenstürmer(in), Flügelstürmer(in)

wink [wɪŋk] **1.** zwinkern; △ *nicht winken*; ~ *at* j-m zuzwinkern; *et.* geflissentlich übersehen; ~ *one's lights Brt. mot.* blinken; **2.** Zwinkern *n*; *I didn't get a* ~ *of sleep last night, I didn't sleep a* ~ *last night* ich habe letzte Nacht kein Auge zugetan; → *forty* 1

win·ner ['wɪnə] Gewinner(in), *bsd. Sport:* Sieger(in); '**~ning 1.** einnehmend, gewinnend; **2.** ~**s** *pl.* Gewinn *m*

win·ter ['wɪntə] **1.** Winter *m*; *in (the)* ~ im Winter; **2.** überwintern; den Winter verbringen; '~ **sports** *pl.* Wintersport *m*; '**~time** Winter(zeit *f*) *m*; *in (the)* ~ im Winter

win·try ['wɪntrɪ] winterlich; *fig.* frostig

wipe [waɪp] (ab-, auf)wischen; ~ **off** ab-, wegwischen; ~ **out** auswischen; auslöschen, -rotten; ~ **up** aufwischen; '**wiper** *mot. (Scheiben)*Wischer *m*

wire ['waɪə] **1.** Draht *m*; *electr*. Leitung *f*; *Am*. Telegramm *n*; **2.** Leitungen verlegen in (*dat*.) (*a*. ~ **up**); *Am*. j-m ein Telegramm schicken; j-m et. telegrafieren; '~**·less** drahtlos, Funk...; ~ **net·ting** [waɪə 'netɪŋ] Maschendraht *m*; '~**·tap** (**-pp-**) j-n, j-s Telefon abhören

wir·y ['waɪərɪ] (**-ier, -iest**) drahtig (*Figur etc.*)

wis·dom ['wɪzdəm] Weisheit *f*, Klugheit *f*; '~ **tooth** (*pl.* - **teeth**) Weisheitszahn *m*

wise[1] [waɪz] (~**r,** ~**st**) weise, klug

wise[2] [waɪz] *veraltet*: Weise *f*, Art *f*

'**wise·crack** F **1.** Witzelei *f*; **2.** witzeln; '~ **guy** F Klugscheißer *m*

wish [wɪʃ] **1.** wünschen; wollen; ~ **s.o. well** j-m alles Gute wünschen; *if you* ~ *(to)* wenn du willst; ~ *for s.th.* sich et. wünschen; **2.** Wunsch *m* (*for* nach); *(with) best* ~**es** Herzliche Grüße (*Briefschluß*); ~**·ful** '**think·ing** Wunschdenken *n*

wish·y-wash·y ['wɪʃɪwɒʃɪ] labb(e)rig, wäßrig; lasch (*Person*), verschwommen (*Vorstellung etc.*)

wisp [wɪsp] (*Gras-, Haar*)Büschel *n*

wist·ful ['wɪstfl] wehmütig

wit [wɪt] Geist *m*, Witz *m*; geistreicher Mensch; *a.* ~**s** *pl.* Verstand *m*; △ *nicht Witz (→ joke)*; *be at one's* ~**s'** *end* mit s-r Weisheit am Ende sein; *keep one's* ~**s** *about one* e-n klaren Kopf behalten

witch [wɪtʃ] Hexe *f*; '~**·craft** Hexerei *f*; '~**·hunt** *pol.* Hexenjagd *f* (*for, against* auf *acc.*)

with [wɪð] mit; bei (→ *stay* 1); vor (*dat.*) (→ *tremble etc.*)

with·draw [wɪð'drɔː] (**-drew, -drawn**) *v/t.* Geld abheben (*from* von); *Angebot etc.* zurückziehen, *Anschuldigung etc.* zurücknehmen; *mil.* Truppen zurückabziehen; *v/i.* sich zurückziehen; zurücktreten (*from* von)

with·draw·al [wɪð'drɔːəl] Rücknahme *f*; *bsd. mil.* Ab-, Rückzug *m*; Rücktritt *m* (*from* von), Ausstieg *m* (*from* aus); *med.* Entziehung *f*, Entzug *m*; *make a* ~ Geld abheben (*from* von); ~ *cure med.* Entziehungskur *f*; ~ *symp·toms pl. med.* Entzugserscheinungen *pl.*

with·er ['wɪðə] eingehen *etc.* verdorren *od.* (ver)welken (lassen)

with·hold (**-held**) zurückhalten; ~ *s.th. from s.o.* j-m et. vorenthalten

with·in [wɪ'ðɪn] innerhalb (*gen.*); ~**·out** [wɪ'ðaʊt] ohne (*acc.*)

with·stand (**-stood**) e-m *Angriff etc.* standhalten; *Beanspruchung etc.* aushalten

wit·ness ['wɪtnɪs] **1.** Zeuge *m*, -in *f*; ~ *for the defence* (*Am. defense*) *jur.* Entlastungszeuge *m*, -in *f*; ~ *for the prosecution jur.* Belastungszeuge *m*, -in *f*; **2.** Zeuge sein von *et.*; *et.* bezeugen, *Unterschrift* beglaubigen; '~ **box** *Brt.*, '~ **stand** *Am.* Zeugenstand *m*

wit·ti·cis·m ['wɪtɪsɪzəm] geistreiche *od.* witzige Bemerkung; ~**·ty** ['wɪtɪ] (**-ier, -iest**) geistreich, witzig

wives [waɪvz] *pl. von* **wife**

wiz·ard ['wɪzəd] Zauberer *m*; *fig.* Genie *n* (*at* in)

wiz·ened ['wɪznd] verhutzelt

wob·ble ['wɒbl] *v/i.* wackeln (*Tisch etc.*), zittern (*Stimme etc.*), schwabbeln (*Pudding etc.*), *mot.* flattern (*Räder*); *v/t.* wackeln an (*dat.*)

woe [wəʊ] Kummer *m*, Leid *n*; '~**·ful** traurig; bedauerlich, beklagenswert

woke [wəʊk] *pret. von* **wake**[1]; **wok·en** ['wəʊkən] *p.p. von* **wake**[1]

wold [wəʊld] hügeliges Land

wolf [wʊlf] **1.** (*pl.* **wolves** [wʊlvz]) *zo.* Wolf *m*; *lone* ~ *fig.* Einzelgänger(in); **2.** *a.* ~ *down* F *Essen* hinunterschlingen

wolves [wʊlvz] *pl. von* **wolf** 1

wom·an ['wʊmən] (*pl.* **women** ['wɪmɪn]) Frau *f*; ~ '*doc·tor* Ärztin *f*; '~ **driv·er** Frau *f* am Steuer; '~**·ish** weibisch; '~**·ly** fraulich; weiblich

womb *anat.* [wuːm] Gebärmutter *f*, Mutterleib *m*

wom·en ['wɪmɪn] *pl. von* **woman**

women's| **lib** F [wɪmɪnz 'lɪb] *veraltet* → *women's movement*; ~ '**lib·ber** F Emanze *f*; ~ **move·ment** Frauenbewegung *f*; ~ **ref·uge** *Brt.*, ~ **shel·ter** *Am.* Frauenhaus *n*

won [wʌn] *pret. u. p.p. von* **win**

won·der ['wʌndə] **1.** neugierig *od.* gespannt sein, gern wissen mögen; sich fragen, überlegen; sich wundern, erstaunt sein (*about* über *acc.*); *I* ~ *if you could help me* vielleicht können Sie mir helfen; **2.** Staunen *n*, Verwunderung *f*; Wunder *n*; *do od. work* ~**s** wahre Wunder vollbringen, Wunder wirken (*for* bei); '**∼∙ful** wunderbar, -voll

wont [wəʊnt] **1.** *be ∼ to do s.th.* et. zu tun pflegen; **2.** *as was his ∼* wie es s-e Gewohnheit war

won't [wəʊnt] *für* will not

woo [wuː] umwerben, werben um

wood [wʊd] Holz *n*; Holzfaß *n*; *a.* **∼s** *pl.* Wald *m*, Gehölz *n*; *touch* **∼l** unberufen!, toi, toi, toi!; *he can't see the ∼ for the trees* er sieht den Wald vor lauter Bäumen nicht; '**∼∙cut** Holzschnitt *m*; '**∼∙cut∙ter** Holzfäller *m*; '**∼ed** bewaldet; '**∼en** hölzern (*a. fig.*), aus Holz, Holz...; '**∼∙peck∙er** *zo.* ['wʊdpekə] Specht *m*; **∼∙wind** *mus.* ['wʊdwɪnd]: *the ∼ sg. od. pl.* die Holzblasinstrumente *pl.*; die Holzbläser *pl.*; **∼ instrument** Holzblasinstrument *n*; '**∼∙work** Holzarbeit *f*; '**∼∙y** (**-ier, -iest**) waldig; holzig

wool [wʊl] Wolle *f*; **∼(l)en** ['wʊlən] **1.** wollen, Woll...; **2.** **∼s** *pl.* Wollsachen *pl.*, -kleidung *f*; '**∼(l)y 1.** (**-ier, -iest**) wollig; *fig.* wirr; **2.** **wool(l)ies** *pl.* F Wollsachen *pl.*

Worces∙ter sauce [wʊstə 'sɔːs] Worcestersoße *f*

word [wɜːd] **1.** Wort *n*; Nachricht *f*; Losung(swort *n*) *f*; Versprechen *n*; Befehl *m*; **∼s** *pl.* Text *m* (*e-s Lieds etc.*); *have a ∼ od. a few ∼s with* mit *j-m* sprechen; **2.** et. ausdrücken, *Text* abfassen, formulieren; '**∼∙ing** Wortlaut *m*; '**∼ or∙der** *gr.* Wortstellung *f* (*im Satz*); '**∼ pro∙cess∙ing** *Computer*: Textverarbeitung *f*; '**∼ pro∙ces∙sor** *Computer*: Textverarbeitungsgerät *n*

'**word∙y** (**-ier, -iest**) wortreich, langatmig

wore [wɔː] *pret. von* wear 1

work [wɜːk] **1.** Arbeit *f*; Werk *n*; **∼s** *pl. tech.* Werk *n*, Getriebe *n*; **∼s** *sg.* Werk *n*, Fabrik *f*; *at* **∼** bei der Arbeit; *be in* **∼** Arbeit haben; *be out of* **∼** arbeitslos sein; *go od.* set to **∼** an die Arbeit gehen; **2.** *v/i.* arbeiten (*at, on* an *dat.*); funktionieren (*a. fig.*); wirken; *∼ to rule* Dienst nach Vorschrift tun; *v/t. j-n* arbeiten lassen; *Maschine etc.* bedienen, et. betätigen; et. bearbeiten; bewirken, herbeiführen; *∼ one's way* sich durcharbeiten od. -kämpfen; *∼ off Schulden* abarbeiten; *Wut etc.* abreagieren; *∼ out v/t.* ausrechnen; *Aufgabe* lösen; *Plan* etc. ausarbeiten; *fig.* sich et. zusammenreimen; *v/i.* klappen; aufgehen (*Rechnung etc.*); F *Sport*: trainieren; *∼ up* Zuhörer etc. aufpeitschen, -wühlen; et. ausarbeiten (*into* zu); *be ∼ed up* aufgeregt od. nervös sein (*about* wegen)

work∙a∙ble ['wɜːkəbl] formbar; *fig.* durchführbar; **∼∙a∙day** ['wɜːkədeɪ] Alltags...; **∼∙a∙hol∙ic** F [wɜːkə'hɒlɪk] Arbeitssüchtige(r *m*) *f*; '**∼∙bench** *tech.* Werkbank *f*; '**∼∙book** *Schule*: Arbeitsheft *n*; '**∼∙day** Arbeitstag *m*; Werktag *m*; *on* **∼s** werktags; '**∼∙er** Arbeiter(in); Angestellte(r *m*) *f*; **∼ ex∙pe∙ri∙ence** Erfahrung *f* (*bsd. in e-m bestimmten Bereich*)

'**work∙ing** Arbeits...; **∼ knowledge** Grundkenntnisse *pl.*; *in ∼ order* in betriebsfähigem Zustand; **∼ class(∙es** *pl.*) Arbeiterklasse *f*; '**∼∙day** = workday; **∼ hours** *pl.* Arbeitszeit *f*; *fewer ∼* Arbeitszeitverkürzung *f*; *reduced ∼* Kurzarbeit *f*; *Am.* '**∼s** *pl.* Arbeits-, Funktionsweise *f*

'**work∙man** (*pl.* -men) Handwerker *m*; '**∼∙like** fachmännisch; '**∼∙ship** fachmännische Arbeit

work| of art (*pl.* works of art) Kunstwerk *n*; '**∼∙out** F *Sport*: Training *n*; '**∼∙place** Arbeitsplatz *m*; *at the ∼* am Arbeitsplatz; '**∼s coun∙cil** Betriebsrat *m* (*einzelner: member of the ∼*); '**∼ sheet** Arbeitsblatt *n*; '**∼∙shop** Werkstatt *f*; Workshop *m* (*Seminar*); '**∼∙shy** arbeitsscheu; '**∼∙sta∙tion** Bildschirmarbeitsplatz *m*; **∼∙to-'rule** *Brt.* Dienst *m* nach Vorschrift

world [wɜːld] **1.** Welt *f*; *all over the ∼* in der ganzen Welt; *bring into the ∼* auf die Welt bringen; *do s.o. a od. the ∼ of good* j-m unwahrscheinlich gut tun; *mean all the ∼ to s.o.* j-m alles bedeuten; *they are ∼s apart* zwischen ihnen liegen Welten; *think the ∼ of* große Stücke halten von; *what in the ∼ ...?* was um alles in der Welt ...?; **2.** Welt...; ♀ '**Cup** Fußballweltmeisterschaft *f*; *Skisport*: Weltcup *m*

'**world∙ly** (**-ier, -iest**) weltlich; irdisch; **∼∙'wise** weltklug

world| 'pow∙er *pol.* Weltmacht *f*; **∼ 'wide** weltweit; auf der ganzen Welt

worm [wɜːm] **1.** *zo.* Wurm *m*; **2.** *Hund*

etc. entwurmen; ~ *one's way through* sich schlängeln *od.* zwängen durch; ~ *o.s. into s.o.'s confidence* sich in j-s Vertrauen einschleichen; ~ *s.th. out of s.o.* j-m et. entlocken; '**~eat·en** wurmstichig; **~s-eye 'view** Froschperspektive *f*

worn [wɔːn] *p.p. von wear* 1; **~'out** abgenutzt, abgetragen; erschöpft (*Person*)

wor·ried ['wʌrɪd] besorgt, beunruhigt **wor·ry** ['wʌrɪ] 1. beunruhigen; (sich) Sorgen machen; *don't* ~! keine Angst!, keine Sorge!; 2. Sorge *f*

worse [wɜːs] (*comp. von bad*) schlechter, schlimmer; ~ *still* was noch schlimmer ist; *to make matters* ~ zu allem Übel; **wors·en** ['wɜːsn] schlechter machen *od.* werden, (sich) verschlechtern

wor·ship ['wɜːʃɪp] 1. Verehrung *f*; Gottesdienst *m*; 2. (*bsd. Brt.* -*pp*-, *Am.* -*p*-) *v/t.* anbeten, verehren; *v/i.* den Gottesdienst besuchen; '**~(p)er** Anbeter(in), Verehrer(in); Kirchgänger(in)

worst [wɜːst] 1. *adj.* (*sup. von bad*) schlechteste(r, -s), schlimmste(r, -s); 2. *adv.* (*sup. von badly*) am schlechtesten *od.* schlimmsten; 3. *der, die, das* Schlechteste *od.* Schlimmste; *at* (*the*) ~ schlimmstenfalls

wor·sted ['wʊstɪd] Kammgarn *n*

worth [wɜːθ] 1. wert; ~ *reading* lesenswert; 2. Wert *m*; '**~·less** wertlos; ~'**while** lohnend; *be* ~ sich lohnen; **~·y** ['wɜːðɪ] (-*ier*, -*iest*) würdig

would [wʊd] *pret. von will* ¹; ~ *you like ...?* möchten Sie ...?; '**~·be** Möchtegern...

wound¹ [waʊnd] *pret. u. p.p. von wind²*

wound² [wuːnd] 1. Wunde *f*, Verletzung *f*, -letzen 2. verwunden, -letzen

wove [wəʊv] *pret. von weave;* **wov·en** ['wəʊvən] *p.p. von weave*

wow *int.* F [waʊ] wow!, Mensch!, toll!

WP [dʌbljuː 'piː] *Abk. für: word processing* Computer: Textverarbeitung *f*; *word processor* Computer: Textverarbeitungsgerät *n*

wran·gle ['ræŋgl] 1. (sich) streiten; 2. Streit *m*

wrap [ræp] 1. (-*pp*-) *v/t. a.* ~ *up* (ein)packen, -wickeln (*in* in *dat.*); et. wickeln ([a]*round* um); *v/i.* ~ *up* sich warm anziehen; 2. *bsd. Am.* Umhang *m*; '**~·per**

(Schutz)Umschlag *m*; '**~·ping** Verpackung *f*; '**~·ping paper** Einwickel-, Pack-, Geschenkpapier *n*

wrath *lit.* [rɒθ] Zorn *m*

wreath [riːθ] (*pl. wreaths* [riːðz]) Kranz *m*

wreck [rek] 1. *naut.* Wrack *n* (*a. Person*); 2. *Pläne etc.* zunichte machen; *be ~ed naut.* zerschellen; Schiffbruch erleiden; **~·age** ['rekɪdʒ] Trümmer *pl.* (*a. fig.*), Wrackteile *pl.*; '**~·er** *Am. mot.* Abschleppwagen *m*; '**~·ing com·pa·ny** *Am.* Abbruchfirma *f*; '**~·ing ser·vice** *Am. mot.* Abschleppdienst *m*

wren *zo.* [ren] Zaunkönig *m*

wrench [rentʃ] 1. *med.* sich *das Knie etc.* verrenken; ~ *s.th. from od. out of s.o.'s hands* j-m et. aus den Händen winden, j-m et. entwinden; ~ *off* et. mit e-m Ruck ab- *od.* wegreißen *etc.*; ~ *open* aufreißen; 2. Ruck *m*; *med.* Verrenkung *f*; *Brt. tech.* Engländer *m*, Franzose *m*; *Am. tech.* Schraubenschlüssel *m*

wrest [rest] ~ *s.th. from od. out of s.o.'s hands* j-m et. aus den Händen reißen, j-m et. entreißen *od.* entwinden

wres·tle ['resl] *v/i.* ringen (*with* mit); *fig.* ringen, kämpfen (*with* mit); *v/t. Sport:* ringen gegen; '**~·tler** *Sport:* Ringer *m*; '**~·tling** *Sport:* Ringen *n*

wretch [retʃ] *oft humor.* Schuft *m*, Wicht *m*; *a. poor* ~ armer Teufel; '**~·ed** elend; (tod)unglücklich; scheußlich (*Kopfschmerzen, Wetter*); verdammt, -flixt

wrig·gle ['rɪgl] *v/i.* sich winden, zappeln; ~ *out of fig.* F sich herauswinden aus; F sich drücken vor (*dat.*); *v/t.* mit *den Zehen* wackeln

wring [rɪŋ] (*wrung*) j-m *die Hand* drücken; *die Hände* ringen; *den Hals* umdrehen; ~ *out Wäsche etc.* auswringen; ~ *s.o.'s heart* j-m zu Herzen gehen

wrin·kle ['rɪŋkl] 1. Falte *f*, Runzel *f*; 2. runzeln; *Nase* kraus ziehen, rümpfen; faltig *od.* runz(e)lig werden

wrist [rɪst] Handgelenk *n*; '**~·band** Bündchen *n*, (Hemd)Manschette *f*; Armband *n*; '**~·watch** Armbanduhr *f*

writ *jur.* [rɪt] Befehl *m*, Verfügung *f*

write [raɪt] (*wrote, written*) schreiben; ~ *down* auf-, niederschreiben; ~ *off j-n, econ. et.* abschreiben; ~ *out Namen etc.* ausschreiben; *Bericht etc.* ausarbeiten;

j-m e-e Quittung etc. ausstellen; '**~ pro-
tec·tion** *Computer:* Schreibschutz *m*;
'**writ·er** Schreiber(in), Verfasser(in),
Autor(in); Schriftsteller(in)
writhe [raɪð] sich krümmen *od.* winden
(*in, with vor dat.*)
writ·ing ['raɪtɪŋ] Schreiben *n* (*Tätigkeit*); (Hand)Schrift *f*; Schriftstück *n*;
Schreib...; *in* ~ schriftlich; ~*s pl.* Werke
pl.; '**~ case** Schreibmappe *f*; '**~ desk**
Schreibtisch *m*; '**~ pad** Schreibblock
m; '**~ pa·per** Brief-, Schreibpapier
n
writ·ten ['rɪtn] **1.** *p.p. von* write; **2.** *adj.*
schriftlich
wrong [rɒŋ] **1.** *adj.* falsch; unrecht; *be ~*
falsch sein, nicht stimmen; unrecht ha-
ben; falsch gehen (*Uhr*); *be on the ~
side of forty* über 40 (Jahre alt) sein; *is
anything ~?* ist et. nicht in Ordnung?;
what's ~ with her? was ist los mit ihr?;
was hat sie?; **2.** *adv.* falsch; *get ~ j-n, et.*
falsch verstehen; *go ~* e-n Fehler machen; kaputtgehen; *fig.* schiefgehen; **3.**
Unrecht *n*; *be in the ~* im Unrecht sein;
4. *j-m* unrecht tun; ~'**do·er** Misse-,

Übeltäter(in); ~'**do·ing** Missetat(en
pl.) *f*; Vergehen *n od. pl.*; '**~ful** ungerechtfertigt; gesetzwidrig; **~way**
'**driv·er** *mot.* F Geisterfahrer(in)
wrote [rəʊt] *pret. von* write
wrought| '**i·ron** Schmiedeeisen *n*; ~
-'**i·ron** schmiedeeisern
wrung [rʌŋ] *pret. u. p.p. von* wring
wry [raɪ] (*-ier, -iest*) süßsauer (*Lächeln*);
ironisch, sarkastisch (*Humor etc.*)
wt *nur geschr. Abk. für* weight Gew.,
Gewicht *n*
WTO [dʌblju: ti: 'əʊ] *Abk. für World
Trade Organization* Welthandelsorga-
nisation *f*
WWF [dʌblju: dʌblju: 'ef] *Abk. für World
Wide Fund for Nature* WWF *m* (*inter-
nationale Umweltstiftung*)
wwoofer ['wu:fə] *Abk. für willing work-
ers on organic farms etwa:* freiwillige
Helfer auf Höfen mit ökologischem
Anbau
WYSIWYG ['wɪzɪwɪg] *Abk. für what you
see is what you get Computer:* was du
(*auf dem Bildschirm*) siehst, bekommst
du (*auch ausgedruckt*)

X

X, x [eks] X, x *n*
xen·o·pho·bi·a [zenə'fəʊbjə] Fremden-
haß *m*; Ausländerfeindlichkeit *f*, -haß *m*
XL [eks 'el] *Abk. für extra large* (*size*)
extragroß
X·mas F ['krɪsməs, 'eksməs] → *Christ-*

mas
X-ray ['eksreɪ] **1.** röntgen; **2.** Röntgen-
strahl *m*; Röntgenaufnahme *f*, -bild *n*;
Röntgenuntersuchung *f*
xy·lo·phone *mus.* ['zaɪləfəʊn] Xylophon *n*

Y

Y, y [waɪ] Y, y *n*
yacht *naut.* [jɒt] **1.** *Sport:* (Segel)Boot *n*;
Jacht *f*; **2.** segeln; *go ~ing* segeln gehen;
'**~ club** Segel-, Jachtklub *m*; '**~ing**

Segeln *n*, Segelsport *m*
Yan·kee F ['jæŋkɪ] Yankee *m*, Ami *m*
yap [jæp] (*-pp-*) kläffen; F quasseln
yard¹ [jɑ:d] (*Abk. yd*) Yard *n* (*91,44 cm*)

yard² [jɑːd] Hof m; (*Bau-, Stapel- etc.*)Platz m; *Am.* Garten m

'**yard·stick** *fig.* Maßstab m

yarn [jɑːn] Garn m; **spin s.o. a ~ about** j-m e-e abenteuerliche Geschichte *od.* e-e Lügengeschichte erzählen von

yawn [jɔːn] **1.** gähnen; **2.** Gähnen n

yeah F [jeə] ja

year [jiə, jɜː] Jahr n; **all the ~ round** das ganze Jahr hindurch; **~ after ~** Jahr für Jahr; **~ in ~ out** jahraus, jahrein; **this ~** dieses Jahr, heuer; **this ~'s** diesjährige(r, -s); '**~·ly** jährlich

yearn [jɜːn] sich sehnen (**for** nach; **to do** danach, zu tun); '**~·ing 1.** Sehnsucht f; **2.** sehnsüchtig

yeast [jiːst] Hefe f

yell [jel] **1.** schreien, brüllen (**with** vor *dat.*); **~ at s.o.** j-n anschreien *od.* anbrüllen; **~ (out)** *et.* schreien, brüllen; **2.** Schrei m

yel·low ['jeləʊ] **1.** gelb; F feig; **2.** Gelb n; **at ~** *Am. mot.* bei Gelb (*Ampel*); **3.** (sich) gelb färben; gelb werden; vergilben; **~ 'fe·ver** *med.* Gelbfieber n; '**~·ish** gelblich; ⚥ '**Pag·es** *pl. TM tel.* die gelben Seiten *pl.*, Branchenverzeichnis n; **~ 'press** Sensationspresse f

yelp [jelp] **1.** (auf)jaulen (*Hund etc.*); aufschreien; **2.** (Auf)Jaulen n; Aufschrei m

yes [jes] **1.** ja; doch; **2.** Ja n

yes·ter·day ['jestədɪ] gestern; **~ after- noon/morning** gestern nachmittag/ morgen; **the day before ~** vorgestern

yet [jet] **1.** *adv. fragend:* schon; noch; (doch) noch; doch, aber; **as ~** bis jetzt, bisher; **not ~** noch nicht; **2.** *cj.* aber, doch

yew *bot.* [juː] Eibe f

yield [jiːld] **1.** *v/t.* Früchte tragen, Gewinn abwerfen, *Resultat etc.* ergeben, liefern; *v/i.* nachgeben; **~ to** *Am. mot.*

j-m die Vorfahrt lassen; **2.** Ertrag m

yip·pee *int.* F [jɪ'piː] hurra!

YMCA [waɪ em siː 'eɪ] *Abk. für Young Men's Christian Association etwa* CVJM, Christlicher Verein junger Menschen

yo·del ['jəʊdl] **1.** (*bsd. Brt.* -**ll**-, *Am.* -**l**-) jodeln; **2.** Jodler m

yo·ga ['jəʊgə] Joga m, n, Yoga m, n

yog·h(o)urt, yog·urt ['jɒgət] Joghurt m, n

yoke [jəʊk] Joch n (*a. fig.*)

yolk [jəʊk] (Ei)Dotter m, n, Eigelb n

you [juː, jʊ] du, ihr, Sie; (*dat.*) dir, euch, Ihnen; (*acc.*) dich, euch, Sie; man

young [jʌŋ] **1.** jung; **2.** *zo.* Junge *pl.*; **with ~** trächtig; **the ~** die jungen Leute *pl.*, die Jugend; **~·ster** ['jʌŋstə] Junge m

your [jɔː] dein(e); *pl.* euer, eure; Ihr(e) (*a. pl.*); **~s** [jɔːz] deine(r, -s); *pl.* euer, eure(s); Ihre(r, -s) (*a. pl.*); **a friend of ~** ein Freund von dir; ⚥, *Bill* Dein Bill (*Briefschluß*); **~·self** [jɔː'self] (*pl.* **your- selves** [jɔː'selvz]) selbst; dir, dich, sich; **by ~** allein

youth [juːθ] (*pl.* **~s** [juːðz]) Jugend f; Jugendliche(r) m; **~ club** Jugendklub m; '**~·ful** jugendlich; **~ hos·tel** Jugendherberge f

yuck·y F *contp.* ['jʌkɪ] (-*ier*, -*iest*) scheußlich

Yu·go·slav [juːgəʊ'slɑːv] **1.** jugoslawisch; **2.** Jugoslaw|e m, -in f; **Yu·go- sla·vi·a** [juːgəʊ'slɑːvjə] Jugoslawien n

yule·tide *bsd. poet.* ['juːltaɪd] Weihnachten n, Weihnachtszeit f

yup·pie, yup·py ['jʌpɪ] *aus der Abk. für young upwardly-mobile od. urban professional* junger, aufstrebender *od.* städtischer Karrieremensch, Yuppie m

YWCA [waɪ dʌblju: siː 'eɪ] *Abk. für Young Women's Christian Associa- tion etwa* CVJM, Christlicher Verein junger Menschen

Z

Z

Z, z [zed, *Am.* ziː] Z, z *n*

zap F [zæp] (**-pp-**) *bsd. Computer-, Videospiel:* abknallen, fertigmachen; (*Wagen*) beschleunigen (**from ... to** von ... auf *acc.*); jagen, hetzen; *TV Fernbedienung* bedienen; *TV* zappen, umschalten; **~ off** abzischen; **~ to** düsen *od.* jagen *od.* hetzen nach; **'~per** *Am.* F *TV* Fernbedienung *f*

zap·py ['zæpɪ] (**-ier, -iest**) voller Pep, schmissig, fetzig

zeal [ziːl] Eifer *m*; **~ot** ['zelət] Fanatiker(in), Eifer|er *m*, -in *f*; **~ous** ['zeləs] eifrig; **be ~ to do** eifrig darum bemüht sein, zu tun

ze·bra *zo.* ['zebrə, 'ziːbrə] (*pl.* **-bra, -bras**) Zebra *n*; **~ 'cross·ing** *Brt.* Zebrastreifen *m* (*Fußgängerübergang*)

zen·ith ['zenɪθ] Zenit *m* (*a. fig.*)

ze·ro ['zɪərəʊ] (*pl.* **-ros, -roes**) Null *f* (*Am. a. tel.*); Nullpunkt *m*; Null...; **20 degrees below ~** 20 Grad unter Null; **~ 'growth** Nullwachstum *n*; **~ 'in·terest: have ~ in s.th.** F null Bock auf et. haben; **~ 'op·tion** *pol.* Nullösung *f*

zest [zest] *fig.* Würze *f*; Begeisterung *f*; **~ for life** Lebensfreude *f*

zig·zag ['zɪɡzæɡ] **1.** Zickzack *m*; Zickzack...; **2.** (**-gg-**) im Zickzack fahren, laufen *etc.*, zickzackförmig verlaufen (*Weg etc.*)

zinc *chem.* [zɪŋk] Zink *n*

zip¹ [zɪp] **1.** Reißverschluß *m*; **2.** (**-pp-**): **~ the bag open/shut** den Reißverschluß der Tasche aufmachen/zumachen; **~ s.o. up** j-m den Reißverschluß zumachen

zip² [zɪp] **1.** Zischen *n*, Schwirren *n*; F Schwung *m*; **2.** zischen, schwirren (*Kugeln etc.*)

'zip| code *Am.* Postleitzahl *f*; **~ 'fas·ten·er** *bsd. Brt.*, **'~·per** *bsd. Am.* Reißverschluß *m*

zo·di·ac *astr.* ['zəʊdɪæk] Tierkreis *m*; **signs** *pl.* **of the ~** Tierkreiszeichen *pl.*

zone [zəʊn] Zone *f*

zoo [zuː] (*pl.* **zoos**) Zoo *m*, Tierpark *m*

zo·o·log·i·cal [zəʊə'lɒdʒɪkl] zoologisch; **~ gar·dens** [zʊlɒdʒɪkl 'gɑːdnz] Tierpark *m*, zoologischer Garten

zo·ol·o·gist [zəʊ'ɒlədʒɪst] Zoolog|e *m*, -in *f*; **~gy** [zəʊ'ɒlədʒɪ] Zoologie *f*

zoom [zuːm] **1.** surren; F sausen; F in die Höhe schnellen (*Preise*); *phot.* zoomen; **~ by, ~ past** F vorbeisausen; **~ in on** *phot. et.* heranholen; **2.** Surren *n*; *a.* **~ lens** *phot.* Zoom(objektiv) *n*

Deutsch-Englisches Wörterverzeichnis

A

à *prp.*: **5 Karten ~ DM 20** 5 tickets at 20 marks each *od.* a piece

Aal *n coll.* eel; **2en** *v/refl.*: **sich in der Sonne ~** bask in the sun; **2g!att** *adj.* (as) slippery as an eel

Aas *n coll.* carrion; *fig.* beast, V bastard; **~geier** *zo. m* vulture (*a. fig.*)

ab *prp. u. adv.*: **München ~ 13.55** departure from Munich (at) 13.55; **~ 7 Uhr** from 7 o'clock (on); **~ morgen (1. März)** starting tomorrow (March 1st); **von jetzt ~** from now on; **~ und zu** now and then; **ein Film ~ 18** an X(-rated) film; **ein Knopf etc. ist ~** has come off

abarbeiten *v/t. Schuld:* work out *od.* off; **sich ~** wear* o.s. out

Abart *f* variety; **2ig** *adj.* abnormal

Abb. *Abk. für Abbildung* fig., illustration

Abbau *m Bergbau:* mining; *fig. Vorurteile etc.:* overcoming; *Maschinen etc.:* dismantling; *Personal, Preise etc.:* reduction; **2en** *econ. Bergbau:* mine; *Vorurteile etc.:* overcome*; *Maschinen etc.:* dismantle; *Personal, Preise etc.:* reduce; **sich ~** *biol.* break* down

ab|beißen *v/t.* bite* off; **~beizen** *v/t. Farbe etc.:* remove with corrosives; **~bekommen** *v/t. losbekommen:* get* off; **s-n Teil** *od.* **et. ~** get* one's share; **et. ~** *fig.* get* hurt *od.* damaged

abberufen *v/t.*, **2ung** *f* recall

ab|bestellen F *v/t. Zeitung (Waren):* cancel one's subscription (order) for; **2bestellung** *f* cancellation; **~biegen** *v/i.* turn (off); **nach rechts (links) ~** turn right (left)

abbild|en *v/t.* show*, depict; **2ung** *f* picture, illustration

Abbitte *f*: *j-m ~ leisten wegen* apologize to s.o. for

ab|blasen F *v/t. Vorhaben etc.:* call off, cancel; **~blättern** *v/i. Farbe etc.:* flake off; **~blenden 1.** *v/t.* dim; **2.** *v/i. mot.* dip (*Am.*) the headlights; **2blendlicht** *mot. n* dipped (*Am.* dimmed) headlights *pl.*, low beam; **~brechen**

v/t. break* off (*a. fig.*); *Gebäude etc.:* pull down, demolish; *Zelt, Lager:* strike*; **~bremsen** *v/t.* slow down; **~brennen** *v/t. Gebäude etc.:* burn* down; *Feuerwerk:* let* off; **~bringen** *v/t.*: *j-n von e-r Sache ~* talk s.o. out of (doing) s.th.; *j-n vom Thema ~* get* s.o. off a subject; **~bröckeln** *v/i.* crumble away (*a. fig.*)

Abbruch *m* breaking off; *Gebäude etc.:* demolition; **2reif** *adj.* derelict, due for demolition

abbuch|en *econ. v/t.* debit (**von** to); **2ung** *econ. f* debit

abbürsten *v/t. Staub etc.:* brush off; *Mantel etc.:* brush

Abc *n* ABC, alphabet; **~schütze** F *m* school beginner, *Am.* first grader; **~Waffen** *mil. pl.* nuclear, biological and chemical weapons

abdank|en *v/i.* resign; *Herrscher:* abdicate; **2ung** *f* resignation; abdication

ab|decken *v/t.* uncover; *Dach:* untile; *Gebäude:* unroof; *Tisch:* clear; *zudecken:* cover (up); **~dichten** *v/t.* make* tight, insulate; **~drängen** *v/t.* push aside; **~drehen 1.** *v/t. Gas, Licht etc.:* turn *od.* switch off; **2.** *naut., aviat. v/i.* change one's course

Abdruck *m* print, mark; **2en** *v/t.* print

abdrücken *v/i. Gewehr etc.:* fire, pull the trigger

Abend *m* evening; *am ~* in the evening, at night; *heute 2* tonight; *morgen (gestern) 2* tomorrow (last) night; *→ bunt, essen;* **~brot** *n*, **~essen** *n* supper, dinner, *Brt. a.* high tea; **~kasse** *thea. f* box office; **~kleid** *n* evening dress *od.* gown; **~kurs** *m* evening classes *pl.*; **~land** *n* West, Occident; **2ländisch** *adj.* Western, Occidental; **~mahl** *rel. n* the (Holy) Communion, *the* Lord's Supper; *das ~ empfangen* receive Communion; **~rot** *n* evening *od.* sunset glow

abends *adv.* in the evening, at night; *dienstags ~* (on) Tuesday evenings

Abendschule f evening classes pl., night school

Abenteuler n adventure (a. in Zssgn Ferien, Spielplatz); **2erlich** adj. adventurous; fig. risky; unwahrscheinlich: fantastic; **~rer** m adventurer; **~rerin** f adventuress

aber cj. u. adv. but; oder ~ or else; Tausende und ~ Tausende thousands upon thousands; ~, ~! now then!; ~ nein! not at all!

Aber|glaube m superstition; **2gläubisch** adj. superstitious

aberkenn|en v/t.: j-m et. ~ deprive s.o. of s.th. (a. jur.); **2ung** f deprivation (a. jur.)

aber|malig adj. repeated; **~mals** adv. once more od. again

abfahren 1. v/i. leave*, start; förmlicher: start, depart (alle: nach for); F: (voll) ~ auf really go* for; **2.** v/t. Schutt etc.: carry od. cart away

Abfahrt f departure (nach for), start (for); Ski: descent; **~slauf** m downhill skiing; Rennen: downhill race; **~szeit** f (time) of departure

Abfall m waste, refuse, rubbish, Am. a. garbage, trash; → a. Müll; **~beseitigung** f waste disposal; **~eimer** m → Mülleimer; **2en** v/i.: fall* (off); Gelände: slope (down); fig. sich abwenden: fall* away (von from), bsd. pol. secede (from); vom Glauben ~ renounce one's faith; ~ gegen compare badly with

abfällig 1. adj. Bemerkung etc.: derogatory; **2.** adv.: ~ von j-m sprechen run* s.o. down

Abfallprodukt n waste product

abfälschen v/t. deflect (a. Ball)

ab|fangen v/t. catch*, intercept; mot., aviat. right; **2fangjäger** mil., aviat. m interceptor (plane); **~färben** v/i. Farbe etc.: run* (auf on); Stoff: a. bleed*; fig. ~ auf rub off on

abfassen v/t. compose, word, write*

abfertig|en v/t. Ware etc.: dispatch; Zoll: clear; Kunden: serve; Flug-, Hotelgast: check in; j-n kurz ~ be* short with s.o.; **2ung** f dispatch; clearance; check-in

abfeuern v/t. fire (off); Rakete: launch

abfind|en v/t. Gläubiger: pay* off; Teilhaber: buy* out; entschädigen: compensate; sich mit et. ~ put* up with

s.th.; **2ung** f satisfaction; compensation (a. ~ssumme)

ab|flachen v/t. u. v/refl. flatten; **~flauen** v/i. Wind etc.: drop (a. fig.); **~fliegen** aviat. v/i. leave*, depart; → starten; **~fließen** v/i. flow off, drain (off od. away)

Abflug aviat. m departure; → Start

Abfluß m flowing off; tech.: drain; **~rohr** n wastepipe, drain(pipe)

abfragen v/t. Schule: quiz od. question s.o. (über about), test s.o. orally

Abfuhr f removal; fig. j-m e-e ~ erteilen rebuff (F besiegen: lick) s.o.

abführ|en v/t. lead* od. take* away; Geld: pay* (over) (an to); **~end** med. adj., **2mittel** med. n laxative

abfüllen v/t.: in Flaschen: bottle; in Dosen: can

Abgabe f einer Arbeit: handing in; Sport: pass; Gebühr: rate; Zoll: duty; **2frei** adj. tax-free; **2pflichtig** adj. Ware: dutiable

Ab|gang m school-leaving, Am. graduation; thea. exit (a. fig.); Reck etc.: dismount; **~gänger(in)** school leaver, Am. graduate; **~gangszeugnis** n → Abschlußzeugnis

Abgas n waste gas; mot. emission(s pl.); mot. exhaust fumes pl.; **2frei** adj. emission-free; **~untersuchung** mot. f exhaust emission test, Am. emissions test

abgearbeitet adj. worn out

abgeben v/t. Schlüssel etc.: leave* (bei with); Prüfungsarbeit etc.: hand in; Gepäck: deposit, leave*; Geld, Fahrkarte etc.: hand over (an to); Stimme: cast*; Ball: pass; Wärme etc.: give* off, emit; Angebot, Erklärung: make*; j-m et., von et. share s.th. with s.o.; sich ~ mit concern o.s. (mit j-m: associate) with

abge|brannt F fig. adj. broke; **~brüht** fig. adj. hard-boiled; **~droschen** adj. hackneyed; **~fahren** mot. adj. Reifen: worn out; **~griffen** adj. worn; **~hackt** fig. adj. disjointed; **~hangen** adj.: gut **~es Fleisch** well-hung meat; **~härtet** adj. hardened (gegen to)

abgehen v/i. Zug etc.: leave*; Post, Ware: get* off; thea. go* off (stage); Knopf etc.: come* off; Weg etc.: branch off; von der Schule ~ leave* school; ~ von e-m Plan etc.: drop; von s-r Meinung ~ change one's mind *od.* opinion; *ihm geht ... ab* he lacks ...; *gut* ~ end well, pass off well

abge|hetzt, ~kämpft *adj.* exhausted, worn out; **~kartet** F *adj.:* **~e Sache** put-up job; **~legen** *adj.* remote, distant; **~macht** *adj.*fixed; **~!** it's a deal!; **~magert** *adj.* emaciated; **~neigt** *adj.:* e-r Sache ~ sein be* averse to s.th.; *ich wäre e-r Sache ~ (et. zu tun) nicht ~* I wouldn't mind (doing) s.th.; **~nutzt** *adj.* worn out

Abgeordnete(r) *parl. Brt.* Member of Parliament (*abbr.* MP); *Am.* representative, congress|man (-woman); **~nhaus** *parl. n Brt.* House of Commons, *Am.* House of Representatives

abgepackt *adj.* prepack(ag)ed

abgeschieden *adj.* secluded; *Leben:* solitary; **2heit** *f* seclusion

abgeschlossen *adj.* completed; **~e Wohnung** self-contained flat, *Am.* apartment

abgesehen *adj.:* ~ von apart from, *Am. a.* aside from; *ganz ~ von* not to mention, let alone

abge|spannt *fig. adj.* exhausted, weary; **~standen** *adj.* stale; **~storben** *adj. Baum etc.:* dead; *gefühllos:* numb; *gänzlich:* dead; **~stumpft** *fig. adj.* insensitive, indifferent (**gegen** to); **~tragen, ~wetzt** *adj.* worn-out; threadbare, shabby

abgewöhnen *v/t.:* *j-m et.* ~ make* s.o. give* up s.th.; *sich das Rauchen ~* stop *od.* give* up smoking; *das werde ich dir ~!* I'll cure you of that!

Abgott *m* idol (*a. fig.*)

abgöttisch *adv.:* *j-n ~ lieben* idolize s.o.

ab|grasen *v/t.* graze; *fig.* scour; **~grenzen** *v/t.* mark off; delimit (**gegen** from)

Abgrund *m* abyss, chasm, gulf (*alle a. fig.*); *am Rande des ~s* on the brink of disaster; **2tief** *adj.* abysmal

abgucken F *v/t.:* *j-m et.* ~ learn* s.th. from (watching) s.o.; *Schule:* → *abschreiben*

Abguß *m* cast; *Nachguß:* recast

ab|haben F *v/t.:* *et.* ~ have* some; **~hacken** *v/t.* chop *od.* cut* off; **~haken** *v/t.* tick (*Am.* check) off; F forget*; **~halten** *v/t. Versammlung, Prüfung etc.:* hold*; *j-n von der Arbeit* ~ keep*

s.o. from his work; *j-n davon ~, et. zu tun* keep* s.o. from doing s.th.; **~handeln** *v/t.:* *j-m et.* ~ make* a deal with s.o. for s.th.

Abhandlung *f* treatise (**über** on)

Abhang *m* slope; *steil:* precipice

abhängen 1. *v/t. Bild etc.:* take* down; *rail. etc.* uncouple; *Fleisch:* hang*; F *j-n:* shake* off; **2.** *v/i.:* ~ von depend on; *das hängt davon ab* that depends

abhängig *adj.:* ~ von dependent on; *Drogen a.:* addicted to; **2keit** *f* dependence (**von** on); addiction (to)

ab|härten *v/t.:* *sich* ~ harden o.s. (**gegen** to); **~hauen 1.** *v/t.* cut* *od.* chop off; **2.** F *v/i.* make* off (**mit** with), run* away (with); *hau ab! sl.* beat it!, scram!; **~heben** *v/t.:* *Geld:* (with)draw*; *Karten:* cut*; *sich* ~ stand* out (**von** among, from); *fig. a.* contrast with; **2.** *v/i. Karten:* cut*; *tel.* answer the phone; *aviat.* take*(*bsd. Rakete:* lift) off; **~heften** *v/t.* file; **~heilen** *v/i.* heal (up); **~hetzen** *v/refl.* wear* o.s. out

Abhilfe *f* remedy; ~ *schaffen* take* remedial measures

Abholdienst *m* pickup service

ab|holen *v/t.* pick up, collect; *j-n von der Bahn* ~ meet* s.o. at the station; **~holzen** *v/t. Bäume:* fell, cut* down; *Wald:* deforest; **~horchen** *med. v/t.* auscultate, sound

abhör|en *v/t. Telefongespräch:* listen in on, tap; *mit Mikrophon ~:* F bug; *Schüler:* → *abfragen*; **2gerät** *n* F bug(ging device)

Abitur *n* school-leaving examination (qualifying for university entrance)

ab|jagen *v/t.:* *j-m et.* ~ recover s.th. from s.o.; **~kanzeln** F *v/t.* tell* *s.o.* off; **~kaufen** *v/t.:* *j-m et.* ~ buy* s.th. (*a. fig. Geschichte*) from s.o.

Abkehr *fig. f* break (**von** with); **2en** *v/refl.:* *sich* ~ von turn away from

ab|klingen *v/i.* fade away; *Schmerz etc.:* ease off; **~klopfen** *med. v/t.* sound; **~knallen** F *v/t.* pick off*; **~knicken** *v/t.* snap *od.* break* off; *verbiegen:* bend*; **~kochen** *v/t.* boil; **~kommandieren** *mil. v/t.* detach (**zu** for)

Abkommen *n* agreement, treaty; *ein ~ schließen* make* an agreement

abkommen v/i.: ~ **von** get* off; *Plan etc.*: drop; **vom Thema** ~ stray from the point; → **Weg**

Abkömmling m descendant

ab|koppeln v/t. uncouple (**von** from); *Raumfahrt*: undock; **~kratzen 1.** v/t. scrape off; **2.** F v/i. *sterben*: kick the bucket; **~kühlen** v/t. u. v/refl. cool down (a. fig.); **⒉kühlung** f cooling

Abkunft f: *deutscher etc.* ~ of German *etc.* descent *od.* origin

abkuppeln v/t. → **abkoppeln**

abkürz|en v/t. shorten; *Wort etc.*: abbreviate; **den Weg** ~ take* a short cut; **⒉ung** f abbreviation; short cut

abladen v/t. unload; *Müll etc.*: dump

Ablage f *Bord etc.*: shelf; *von Akten*: filing; *für Kleider*: cloakroom; *Schweiz*: → **Zweigstelle**

ab|lagern 1. v/t. *Holz*: season; *Wein*: let* age; *geol. etc.* deposit; *sich* ~ settle, be* deposited; **2.** v/i. season; age; **⒉lagerung** f *chem., geol.* f deposit, sediment; **~lassen 1.** v/t. *Flüssigkeit*: drain off; *Dampf*: let* off (a. fig.); *Teich etc.*: drain; **2.** v/i.: **von et.** ~ stop doing s.th.

Ablauf m *Verlauf: etc.*: course, *bsd. Arbeits⒉ etc.*: process; *Programm⒉*: order of events; *Frist etc.*: expiration; → **Abfluß**; **⒉en 1.** v/i. *Wasser etc.*: run* off; *Vorgang etc.*: go*, proceed; *enden*: come* to an end; *Frist, Paß*: expire; *Zeit, Platte, Band*: run* out; *Uhr*: run* down; **gut** ~ turn out well; **2.** v/t. *Schuhe*: wear* down

ab|lecken v/t. lick (off); **~legen 1.** v/t. *Kleidung*: take* off; *Akten etc.*: file; *Gewohnheit etc.*: give* up; *Eid, Prüfung*: take*; **abgelegte Kleider** cast-offs *pl.*; **2.** v/i. take* off one's (hat and) coat; *naut.* put* out, sail

Ableger m *bot.* m layer; offshoot (a. fig.)

ablehn|en v/t. refuse; *Antrag etc.*: turn down; *parl.* reject; *mißbilligen*: object to, reject; *stärker*: condemn; **~end** adj. negative; **⒉ung** f refusal; rejection; objection (*gen.* to)

ableit|en v/t. *Fluß etc.*: divert; *gr., math.* derive (**aus, von** from) (a. fig.); **⒉ung** f diversion; *gr., math.* derivation (a. fig.)

ab|lenken v/t. *Verdacht, Gedanken, Fluß, Ball etc.*: divert (**von** from); *Torschuß*: turn away; *Strahlen etc.*: deflect;

j-n von der Arbeit ~ distract s.o. from his work; **er läßt sich leicht** ~ he is easily diverted; **⒉lenkung(smanöver** n) f diversion; **~lesen** v/t. read* (a. *Instrumente*); **~leugnen** v/t. deny

abliefer|n v/t. deliver (**bei** to, at); hand over (to); **⒉ung** f delivery

ablösbar adj. detachable

ablös|en v/t. *entfernen*: detach; take* off; *j-n*: take* *s.o.*'s place, take over from; *bsd. mil. etc.*: relieve; *ersetzen*: replace; **sich** ~ *bei der Arbeit etc.*: take* turns; **⒉esumme** f *Sport*: transfer fee; **⒉ung** f relief

abmach|en v/t. remove, take* off; *vereinbaren*: settle, arrange; **⒉ung** f arrangement, agreement, deal

abmager|n v/i. get* thin; **⒉ung** f emaciation; **⒉ungskur** f slimming diet

ab|mähen v/t. mow*; **~malen** v/t. copy

Abmarsch m *mil.* marching off; **⒉ieren** v/i. start; *mil.* march off

abmeld|en v/t. *Auto, Radio etc.*: cancel the registration of; *vom Verein*: cancel s.o.'s membership; *von der Schule*: give* notice of s.o.'s withdrawal (from school); **sich** ~ *bei Behörde*: give* notice of change of address; *vom Dienst*: report off duty; *Hotel*: check out; **⒉ung** f notice of withdrawal; notice of change of address

abmess|en v/t. measure; **⒉ung** f measurement; **~en** pl. dimensions pl.

ab|montieren v/t. take* off (*Gerüst etc.*: down); *bsd. Werksanlagen*: dismantle; **~mühen** v/refl. work very hard; try hard (*to do s.th.*); **~nagen** v/t. gnaw (at)

Abnahme f *Rückgang*: decrease, reduction; *Verlust*: loss (a. *Gewicht*); *econ.* purchase; *tech.* acceptance

abnehm|bar adj. removable; **~en 1.** v/t. take* off (a. *med.*), remove; *tel.* *Hörer*: pick up; *tech. Maschine etc.*: accept; *econ.* buy*; *j-m et.* ~ wegnehmen: take* s.th. (away) (from s.o.); **2.** v/i. decrease, diminish; lose* weight; *tel.* answer the phone; *Mond*: wane; **⒉er** m *econ.* m buyer; customer

Abneigung f dislike (**gegen** of, for); *stärker*: aversion (**gegen** to)

abnorm adj. abnormal; *außergewöhnlich*: exceptional, unusual; **⒉ität** f abnormality, anomaly

ab|nutzen, **~nützen** v/t. u. v/refl. wear* out; **2nutzung**, **2nützung** f wear (and tear) (a. fig.)

Abonn|ement n subscription (auf to); **~ent(in)** subscriber; thea. season-ticket holder; **2ieren** v/t. subscribe to

Abordnung f delegation

Abort m lavatory, toilet

ab|passen v/t. j-n, Gelegenheit: watch od. wait for; j-n überfallen: waylay* (a. fig.); **~pfeifen** v/t. u. v/i. Sport: blow* the final whistle; unterbrechen: stop the game; **~pflücken** v/t. pick, gather; **~plagen** v/refl. struggle (mit with); **~prallen** v/i. rebound, bounce (off); Geschoß: ricochet; **~putzen** v/t.: wipe off; clean; **~raten** v/i.: **~ von** advise od. warn s.o. against; **~räumen** v/t. clear away; Tisch: clear; **~reagieren** v/t. s-n Ärger etc.: work off (an on); **sich ~** F let* off steam

ab|rechn|en 1. v/t. abziehen: deduct, subtract; Spesen: claim; **2.** v/i.: mit j-m **~** settle accounts (fig. a. get* even) with s.o.; **2ung** f settlement; F fig. showdown

abreib|en v/t. rub off; Körper: rub down; Schuhe etc.: polish; **2ung** f rubdown; F fig. beating

Abreise f departure (nach for); **2n** v/i. depart, leave*, start, set* out (alle: nach for)

abreiß|en 1. v/t. tear* od. pull off; Gebäude: pull down; **2.** v/i. Schnur etc.: break*; Knopf etc.: come* off; **2kalender** m tear-off calendar

ab|richten v/t. train; Pferd: a. break* (in); **~riegeln** v/t. block (durch Polizei: a. cordon) off

Abriß m outline, summary

ab|rollen v/i u. v/t. unroll (a. fig. Ereignisse etc.); **2.** v/i. draw* away (von from); mil. march off; F → abhauen 2

Abruf m: auf **~** econ. on call; **2en** v/t. call away; Computer: recall, fetch, retrieve

ab|runden v/t. round (off), **~rupfen** v/t. pluck off

abrupt adj. abrupt

ab|rüst|en mil. v/i. disarm; **2ung** mil. f disarmament

abrutschen v/i. Erde etc.: slide* down; Fuß etc.: slip (off) (von from)

ABS mot. anti-lock braking system

Absage f refusal; cancellation; **2n 1.** v/t. Veranstaltung etc.: call off, cancel; **2.** v/i. call off; j-m **~** cancel one's appointment with s.o.; Einladung a. decline (the invitation)

ab|sägen v/t. saw* off; fig. oust, sack; **~sahnen** F v/i. cash in

Absatz m Abschnitt: paragraph; econ. sales pl.; Schuh**2**: heel; Treppen**2**: landing

abschaben v/t. scrape off

abschaff|en v/t. do* away with, abolish; Gesetz: repeal; Mißstände: put* an end to; **2ung** f abolition; repeal

abschalten 1. v/t. switch od. turn off; **2.** F v/i. relax, switch off

abschätz|en v/t. estimate; ermessen: assess; eintaxieren: size up; **~ig** adj. contemptuous; Bemerkung: derogatory

Abschaum m scum (a. fig.)

Abscheu m disgust (vor, gegen at, for); **e-n ~ haben vor** abhor, detest; **2erregend** adj. revolting, repulsive; **2lich** adj. abominable, despicable (a. Person); Verbrechen: a. atrocious; **~lichkeit** f Untat: atrocity

abschicken v/t. → **absenden**

abschieben fig. v/t. push away; loswerden: get* rid of; Ausländer: deport; **~ auf** shove s.th. off (on to) s.o.

Abschied m parting, farewell; **~ nehmen (von)** say* goodbye (to), take* leave (of); **s-n ~ nehmen** resign, retire; **~feier** f farewell party; **~skuß** m goodbye kiss

ab|schießen v/t. shoot* off (aviat. down); Rakete: launch; Wild: shoot*, kill; F j-n: pick off; fig. oust; get* rid of; **~schirmen** v/t. shield (gegen from); fig. protect (gegen against, from); **2schirmung** f shield, screen; protection; **~schlachten** v/t. slaughter (a. fig.)

Abschlag m Sport: kickout; econ. down payment; **2en** v/t. knock off; Kopf: cut* off; Baum: cut* down; Bitte etc.: refuse, turn s.th. down

abschleifen v/t. grind* off; schmirgeln: sand(paper), smooth

Abschlepp|dienst mot. m breakdown (Am. emergency road) service; **2en** v/t. (give s.o. a) tow; durch Polizei: tow away; **~seil** n towrope; **~wagen** m breakdown lorry, Am. tow truck

abschließen 1. v/t. lock (up); beenden: close, finish; vollenden: complete; Versicherung: take* out; Vertrag etc.: conclude; **e-n Handel ~** strike* a bargain; **sich ~** shut* o.s. off; **2.** v/i. enden: close, finish; **~d 1.** adj. concluding; endgültig: final; **2.** adv.: **~ sagte er** he concluded by saying

Abschluß m conclusion, close; **~prüfung** f final examination, finals pl., bsd. Am. a. graduation; **s-e ~ machen** graduate (**an** from); **~zeugnis** n school-leaving certificate; Am. diploma

abschmecken v/t. würzen: season

ab|schmieren tech. v/t. lubricate, grease; **~schminken** v/t.: **sich ~** remove one's make-up; **~schnallen** v/t. undo*; Skier: take* off; **sich ~** mot., aviat. unfasten one's seatbelt; **~ schneiden 1.** v/t. cut* off (a. fig.); **j-m das Wort ~** cut* s.o. short; **2.** v/i.: **gut ~** come* off well

Abschnitt m e-s Buches: passage, section; e-r Seite: paragraph; math., biol. segment; Zeit2: period, stage, phase; Kontroll2: coupon, slip, stub; **2weise** adv. section by section

abschrauben v/t. unscrew

abschreck|en v/t. deter (**von** from); fig. Eier: douse with cold water; **~end** adj. deterrent; **~es Beispiel** warning example; **~ung** f deterrence; Mittel: deterrent

abschreiben v/t. copy; mogeln: crib; econ., F fig. write* off

Abschrift f copy, duplicate

abschürf|en v/t. graze; **2ung** f abrasion

Abschuß m e-r Rakete: launch(ing); aviat. shooting down, downing; kill; **~basis** mil. f launching base

abschüssig adj. sloping; steil: steep

Abschuß|liste F f: **auf der ~ stehen** be* on the hit list; **~rampe** f launching pad

abschüssig adj. sloping; steil: steep

ab|schütteln v/t. shake* off; **~schwächen** v/t. lessen, diminish; **~schweifen** fig. v/i. digress (**von** from); **~schweifung** f digression

Abschwung m Turnen: dismount

~e) **Zeit** in the (for the) foreseeable future; **~en** v/t. foresee*; **es ist kein Ende abzusehen** there is no end in sight; **es abgesehen haben auf** be* after; **~ von** refrain from

abseilen v/refl. descend by a rope, Brt. a. abseil; F make a getaway

abseits adv. u. prp. entfernt von: away od. remote from; **sich im Fußball:** be* offside; fig. be* left out; **~falle** f Fußball: offside trap

absend|en v/t. send* (off), dispatch; post post, bsd. Am. mail; **2er** post m sender

absetz|bar adj.: steuerlich ~ deductible from tax; **~en 1.** v/t. Hut, Brille etc.: take* off; Last: set* od. put* down; Fahrgast: drop; entlassen: dismiss; thea., Film: take* off; steuerlich: deduct; König: depose; econ. sell*; **sich ~ → ablagern; 2.** v/i.: **ohne abzusetzen** without stopping; **2ung** f dismissal; deposition; thea., Film: withdrawal

Absicht f intention; **mit ~** on purpose; **2lich 1.** adj. intentional; **2.** adv. on purpose

absitzen 1. v/i. dismount (**von** from); **2.** v/t. Strafe: serve; F Zeit: sit* out

absolut adj. absolute

Absolv|ent(in) graduate; **2ieren** v/t. Schule, Kurs besuchen: attend; abschließen: complete; graduate from

absonder|n v/t. separate; med., biol. secrete; **sich ~** cut* o.s. off (**von** from); **2ung** f separation; med., biol. secretion

absorbieren absorb (a. fig.)

ab|speichern v/t. Computer: store, save; **~spenstig** adj.: **j-m die Freundin ~ machen** steal* s.o.'s girlfriend

absperr|en v/t. lock; Wasser etc.: turn off; Straße: block off; Polizei: cordon off; **2ung** f barrier; Kette: cordon; **→ Sperre**

ab|spielen v/t. play; Sport: pass; **sich ~** happen, take* place; **2sprache** f agreement; **~sprechen** v/t. agree upon; arrange; **j-m die Fähigkeit etc. ~** dispute s.o.'s ability etc.; **~springen** v/i. jump off; aviat. jump; Notfall: bail out; fig. back out (**von** of)

Absprung m jump; Sport: take-off; fig. **den ~ schaffen** make* it

abspülen v/t. rinse; Geschirr: wash up

abstamm|en v/i. be descended (**von**

from); *chem.*, *gr.* derive; **2ung** *f* descent; derivation; **2ungslehre** *f* theory of the origin of species

Abstand *m* distance (*a. fig.*); *zeitlich:* interval; **~ halten** keep* one's distance; *fig. mit ~* by far

ab|statten *v/t.:* **j-m e-n Besuch ~** pay* a visit to s.o.; **~stauben** *v/t.* dust; F *fig.* sponge; swipe; **2stauber(tor n)** *m* F opportunist goal

abstech|en 1. *v/t.* stick*; **2.** *v/i.* contrast (**von** with); **2er** *m* side-trip; excursion (*a. fig.*)

ab|stecken *v/t.* mark out; **~stehen** *v/i.* stick* out, protrude; → **abgestanden**; **~steigen** *v/i.* get* off; *ins Tal:* climb down; *in e-m Hotel:* stay (**in** at); *Sport:* be* relegated; *Am.* be* moved down to a lower division; **2steiger** *m Sport: Brt.* relegated club; **~stellen** *v/t.* put* down; *bei j-m:* leave*; *Gas etc.:* turn off; *Auto:* park; *fig. Mißstände etc.:* put* an end to; **~stellgleis** *n* rail. siding; *aufs* **~ schieben** *fig.* push aside; **2stellraum** *m* storeroom; **~stempeln** *v/t.* stamp; **~sterben** *v/i.* die off; *Glied:* go* numb; **~stieg** *m* descent; *fig.* decline; *Sport: Brt.* relegation

abstimm|en *v/i.* vote (**über** on); **2ung** *f* vote; *Radio:* tuning

Abstinenzler *m* teetotal(l)er

Abstoß *m Sport:* goal-kick; **2en** *v/t.* repel; *med.* reject; *Boot:* push off; F *loswerden:* get* rid of; **2end** *fig. adj.* repulsive

abstrakt *adj.* abstract

abstreiten *v/t.* deny

Abstrich *m* smear; **~e** *pl.* econ. cuts; *fig.* reservations

ab|stufen *v/t.* graduate; *Farben:* gradate; **~stumpfen 1.** *v/t.* blunt, dull (*a. fig.*); **2.** *fig. v/i.* become* unfeeling

Absturz *m* fall; *aviat.*, *Computer:* crash

ab|stürzen *v/i.* fall*; *aviat.*, *Computer:* crash; **~suchen** *v/t.* search (**nach** for)

absurd *adj.* absurd, preposterous

Abszeß *med. m* abscess

Abt *rel. m* abbot

ab|tasten *v/t.* feel* (for); *med.* palpate; *nach Waffen:* frisk; *tech.*, *Computer:* scan; **~tauen** *v/t. Kühlschrank etc.:* defrost

Abtei *rel. f* abbey

Ab|teil *rail. n* compartment; **2teilen**

---

v/t. divide; *arch.* partition off; **~teilung** *f* department (*a. econ.*); *e-s Krankenhauses:* ward; *mil.* detachment; **~teilungsleiter** *m* head of (a) department; *im Kaufhaus:* shopwalker, *Am.* floorwalker

Äbtissin *rel. f* abbess

ab|töten *v/t. Bakterien, Nerv etc.:* kill; *fig. Schmerz, Gefühl:* deaden; **~tragen** *v/t. Kleidung:* wear* out; *Geschirr, Erde etc.:* clear away; *Schuld:* pay* off

Abtransport *m* transportation

abtreib|en 1. *v/i. med.* have* an abortion; *mar.*, *aviat.* be* blown off course; **2.** *med. v/t.* abort; **2ung** *med. f* abortion; **e-e ~ vornehmen** perform an abortion

abtrennen *v/t. Coupon etc.:* detach; *Fläche etc.:* separate; *med.* sever

abtret|en 1. *v/t. Absätze:* wear* down; *Füße:* wipe; *fig. Amt, Platz etc.:* give* up (**an** to); **2.** *v/i. vom Amt etc.:* resign; *thea.* exit; **2er** *m* doormat

abtrocknen 1. *v/t.* dry (**sich** o.s. off); **2.** *v/i.* dry the dishes, *Brt. a.* dry up

abtrünnig *adj.* unfaithful, disloyal; **2e(r)** renegade, turncoat

ab|tun *v/t. Vorschlag etc.:* dismiss (**als** as); **~wägen** *v/t.* weigh (**gegen** against); **~wählen** *v/t.* vote out; **~wälzen** *v/t.:* **~ auf** shove s.th. off on (to) s.o.; **~wandeln** *v/t.* vary, modify; **~wandern** *v/i.* migrate (**von** from; **nach** to); **2wanderung** *f* migration

Ab|wandlung *f* modification, variation; **~wärme** *f* waste heat

Abwart *m Schweiz:* → **Hausmeister**

abwarten 1. *v/t.* wait for, await; **2.** *v/i.* wait; *warten wir ab!* let's wait and see!; *wart nur ab!* just you wait!

abwärts *adv.* down, downward(s)

Abwasch *m:* **den ~ machen** do the washing-up; **2bar** *adj. Tapete etc.:* wipe-clean; **~en 1.** *v/t.* wash off; **2.** *v/i. Geschirr:* do* the dishes, *Brt. a.* wash up; **~wasser** *n* dishwater

Abwasser *n* waste water, sewage; **~aufbereitung** *f* sewage treatment

abwechseln *v/i.* alternate; *sich mit j-m* **~** take* turns (**bei et.** at [doing] s.th.); **~d** *adv.* by turns

Abwechslung *f* change; *zur* **~** for a change; **2sreich** *adj.* varied; *Programm etc.:* colo(u)rful

Abweg m: *auf ~e geraten* go* astray; **2ig** adj. absurd, unrealistic

Abwehr f defen|ce, Am. -se (a. Sport); *e-s Stoßes etc.*: save; Am. -se; *e-s Balles*: save; **2en** v/t. ward off; *zurückschlagen*: beat* off; Sport: block; **~fehler** m defensive error; **~kräfte** med. pl. resistance sg.; **~schwäche** med. f; *Erworbene ~* AIDS; **~spieler(in)** defender; **~stoffe** med. pl. antibodies pl.

abweichen v/i. deviate (*von* from); *Thema*: digress; **2ung** f deviation

abweisen v/t. turn away; *schroff*: rebuff; *Bitte etc.*: decline; *stärker*: turn down; **~d** adj. unfriendly

ab|wenden v/t. turn away (a. *sich ~*) (*von* from); *Unheil etc.*: avert; **~werfen** v/t. throw* off; *aviat.* drop; *Laub etc.*: shed*; *Gewinn*: yield

abwert|en v/t. *Währung*: devalue; **~end** adj. *Bemerkung etc.*: disparaging; **2ung** f devaluation

abwesend adj. absent; **2heit** f absence

ab|wickeln v/t. unwind*; *erledigen*: handle; *Geschäft*: transact; **~wiegen** v/t. weigh (out); **~wischen** v/t. wipe (off); **2wurf** m dropping; *Fußball*: throw-out; **~würgen** F v/t. mot. stall; *Diskussion etc.*: stifle; **~zahlen** v/t. *monatlich etc.*: make* payments for; *vollständig*: pay* off; **~zählen** v/t. count

Abzahlung f: *et. auf ~ kaufen* buy* s.th. on hire purchase (*Am.* on the instalment plan)

abzapfen v/t. tap, draw* off

Abzeichen n badge; *Ehren2*: medal

ab|zeichnen v/t. copy, draw*; *unterschreiben*: sign, initial; *sich ~* (*begin** to) show*; *hervortreten*: stand* out (*gegen* against); **~ziehbild** n transfer, Am. decal; **~ziehen 1.** v/t. take* off, remove; *math.* subtract; *Bett*: strip; *Schlüssel*: take* out; *das Fell ~* skin*; **2.** v/i. go* away; *mil.* withdraw; *Rauch*: escape; *Gewitter, Wolken*: move off

Abzug m econ. deduction; *Skonto*: discount; *mil.* withdrawal; *Kopie*: copy; *phot.* print; *Waffe*: trigger; *tech.* vent, outlet; *Küche*: cooker hood

abzüglich prp. less, minus

abzweig|en 1. v/t. *Geld*: divert (*für* to); **2.** v/i. *Weg etc.*: branch off; **2ung** f *Straße etc.*: junction

ach int. oh!; *~ je!* oh dear!; *~ so!* I see; *~ was!* überrascht: really?; ärgerlich: of course not!; nonsense!

Achse f tech., mot. axle; math. etc.: axis; *auf ~ sein* be* on the move

Achsel f shoulder; *die ~n zucken* shrug one's shoulders; **~höhle** f armpit

acht adj. eight; *heute in ~ Tagen* a week from today, bsd. Brt. today week; (*heute*) *vor ~ Tagen* a week ago (today)

Acht f: *außer acht lassen* disregard; *sich in acht nehmen* be* careful, look od. watch out (*vor* for)

acht|e adj. eighth; **~eckig** adj. octagonal; **2el** n eighth (part)

achten 1. v/t. respect; **2.** v/i.: *auf ~* pay* attention to; *im Auge behalten*: keep* an eye on; *Verkehr*: watch; *schonend behandeln*: be* careful with; *darauf ~, daß* see* to it that

ächten v/t. ban; bsd. hist. outlaw

Achter m Rudern: eight; **~bahn** f roller coaster

achtfach adj. u. adv. eightfold

achtgeben v/i. be* careful; pay* attention (*auf* to); *auf Kinder etc.*: take* care (*auf* of); *gib acht!* look od. watch out!, be careful!

achtlos adj. careless, heedless

Achtung f respect (*vor* for); *~!* look out!; mil. attention!; *~! ~!* attention please!; *~! Fertig! Los!* On your marks! Get set! Go!; *~ Stufe!* mind the step!, Am. caution: step!

achtzehn adj. eighteen; **~te** adj. eighteenth

achtzig adj. eighty; *die ~er Jahre* the eighties; **~ste** adj. eightieth

ächzen v/i. groan (*vor* with)

Acker m field; **~bau** m agriculture, farming; *~ und Viehzucht* crop and stock farming; **~land** n farmland; **2n** fig. v/i. F slog (away)

Adapter tech., phys. m adapter

addi|eren v/t. add (up); **2tion** f addition, adding up

Adel m aristocracy; **2n** v/t. ennoble (a. fig.); Brt. knight

Ader anat. f blood vessel, vein

adieu int. good-bye(e)!, F see you (later)

Adjektiv gr. n adjective

Adler zo. m eagle; **~nase** f aquiline nose

Algebra

adlig *adj.* noble; **♀e(r)** noble|woman (-man)

Admiral *naut.* m admiral

adopt|ieren *v/t.* adopt; **♀ivkind** *n* adopted child

Adreßbuch *n* directory

Adress|e *f* address; **♀ieren** *v/t.* address (**an** to)

Advent *rel.* m Advent; Advent Sunday; **~szeit** *f* Christmas season

Adverb *gr.* n adverb

Aerobic *n* aerobics *pl.*

Affäre *f* affair

Affe *zo.* m monkey; *großer:* ape

Affekt *m:* **im ~** in the heat of passion (*a. jur.*); **♀iert** *adj.* affected

affen|artig *adj.:* **mit ~er Geschwindigkeit** like a bat out of hell; **~hitze** F *f:* **es herrscht e-e ~** it's sizzling hot

Afrika Africa; **~ner(in)**, **♀nisch** *adj.* African

After *anat.* m anus

AG *Abk. für* **Aktiengesellschaft** *Brt.* PLC, public limited company; *Am.* (stock) corporation

Agent *m* agent; *pol.* (secret) agent; **~ur** *f* agency

Aggress|ion *f* aggression; **♀iv** *adj.* aggressive; **~ivität** *f* aggressiveness

Agitator *m* agitator

ah *int.* ah!

äh *int.* er; *Abscheu:* ugh!

aha *int.* I see!, oh!; **♀-Erlebnis** *n* aha-experience

Ahn *m* ancestor; **~en** *pl. a.* forefathers *pl.*

ähneln *v/i.* resemble, look like

ahnen *v/t.* suspect; foresee*, know**

ähnlich *adj.* similar (*dat.* to); *j-m ~ sehen* look like s.o.; **♀keit** *f* likeness, resemblance, similarity (*mit* to)

Ahnung *f* presentiment; *böse: a.* foreboding; *Vorstellung:* notion, idea; *ich habe keine ~* I have no idea; **♀slos** *adj.* unsuspecting, innocent

Ahorn *bot.* m maple(-tree)

Ähre *bot.* f ear; *Blüten♀:* spike

Aids *med.* n AIDS; **~-Kranke(r)** AIDS victim *od.* sufferer; **~test** *m* AIDS test

Airbag *m* airbag

Akademi|e *f* academy, college; **~ker(in)** university graduate; **♀sch** *adj.* academic

akklimatisieren *v/refl.* acclimatize (**an** to)

Akkord *m mus.* chord; *im ~ econ.* by the piece *od.* job; **~arbeit** *econ. f* piecework; **~arbeiter(in)** *econ.* pieceworker

Akkordeon *n* accordion

Akkordlohn *m econ.* m piece wages *pl.*

Akku F *m,* **~mulator** *tech.* m (storage) battery, *Brt. a.* accumulator

Akkusativ *gr.* m accusative (case)

Akne *med. f* acne

Akrobat|(in) acrobat; **♀isch** *adj.* acrobatic

Akt *m* act(ion); *thea.* act; *paint., phot.* nude

Akte *f* file; **~n** *pl.* files *pl.*, records *pl.*; *zu den ~n legen* file; **~ndeckel** *m* folder; **~nkoffer** *m* attaché case; **~nordner** *m* file; **~ntasche** *f* briefcase; **~nzeichen** *n* reference (number)

Aktie *econ. f* share, bsd. *Am.* stock; **~ngesellschaft** *f* joint-stock company, *Am.* corporation

Aktion *f* campaign, drive; *mil.,* Rettungs♀ *etc.:* operation; *in ~* in action; **~är(in)** shareholder, bsd. *Am.* stockholder

aktiv *adj.* active

Aktiv *gr.* n active voice; **~ist(in)** *bsd. pol.* activist; **~urlaub** *m* activity holiday

aktu|alisieren *v/t.* update; **~ell** *adj.* Bedeutung, Interesse *etc.:* topical; *heutig:* current; *modern:* up-to-date; *TV, Funk:* **e-e ~e Sendung** a current affairs *od.* news feature; △ *nicht* **actual**

Akupunktur *f* acupuncture

Akust|ik *f Lehre:* acoustics *sg.*; *im Raum:* acoustics *pl.*; **♀isch** *adj.* acoustic

akut *adj. Problem etc.:* urgent; *med.* acute

Akzent *m* accent; *Betonung: a.* stress (*a. fig.*)

akzept|abel *adj.* acceptable; *Preis etc.:* reasonable; **~ieren** *v/t.* accept

Alarm *m* alarm; **~ schlagen** sound the alarm; **~anlage** *f* alarm system; **bereitschaft** *f:* **in ~** on standby, on the alert; **♀ieren** *v/t. Polizei etc.:* call; *warnen:* alert; **♀ierend** *adj.* alarming

albern *adj.* silly, foolish

Album *n* album (*a. Langspielplatte*)

Algen *bot. pl.* algae *pl.*; **~pest** *f* plague of algae, algal bloom

Algebra *f* algebra

Alibi *jur.* n alibi

Alimente *jur. pl.* alimony *sg.*

Alkohol m alcohol; **2frei** *adj.* nonalcoholic, soft; **~iker(in)** alcoholic; **2isch** *adj.* alcoholic; **~ismus** m alcoholism; **2süchtig** *adj.* addicted to alcohol; **~test** *mot.* m breath test

all *indef. pron. u. adj.* all; **~es** everything; **~es** (*beliebige*) anything; **~e** (*Leute*) everybody; anybody; **~e beide** both of them; *wir ~e* all of us; **~es in ~em** all in all; *auf ~e Fälle* in any case; **~e drei Tage** every three days; → *Art, Gute, vor*

All n universe; *Raum:* (outer) space

alle F *adj.:* ~ *sein be** all gone; *mein Geld ist ~* I'm out of money

Allee f avenue; △ *nicht alley*

allein *adj. u. adv.* alone; *einsam:* lonely; *selbst:* by o.s.; *ganz ~* all alone; *er hat es ganz ~ gemacht* he did it all by himself; **2erziehende(r)** single parent; **2gang** m: *im ~* single-handedly, solo; **~ig** *adj.* sole; **2sein** n loneliness; **~stehend** *adj.* single

aller|beste *adj.:* *der* (*die, das*) **2e** the best of all, the very best; **~dings** *adv.* however, though; **~l** certainly!, *bsd. Am.* F sure!; **~erste** *adj.* very first

Allerg|ie *med.* f allergy (*gegen* to); **2isch** *adj.* allergic (*gegen* to)

aller|hand F *adj.* a good deal (of); *das ist ja ~!* that's a bit much!; **2heiligen** n All Saints' Day; **~lei** *adj.* all kinds of, sorts of; **~letzte** *adj.* last of all, very last; **~liebst 1.** *adj.* (most) lovely; **2.** *adv.:* *am ~en mögen* like best of all; **~meiste** *adj.* (by far the) most; **~nächste** *adj.* very next; *in ~r Zeit* in the very near future; **~neu(e)ste** *adj.* very latest; **2seelen** n All Souls' Day; **~seits** *adv.* F: *Tag ~!* hi, everybody!; **~wenigst** *adv.:* *am ~en* least of all

allesamt *adv.* all together

allgemein *adj.* general; *üblich:* common; *umfassend:* universal; **2.** *adv.:* *im ~en* in general, generally; **2bildung** f general education; **2heit** f general public; **~verständlich** *adj.* intelligible (to all), popular; **2wissen** n general knowledge

Allheilmittel n cure-all (*a. fig.*)

Allianz f alliance

Alligator m alligator

alljährlich *adv.* every year; ~ *stattfindend* annual; **~mächtig** *adj.* omnipotent; *bsd. Gott:* almighty; **~mählich 1.** *adj.* gradual; **2.** *adv.* gradually

All|radantrieb *mot.* m all-wheel drive; **2seitig** *adv.:* ~ *interessiert sein* have* all-round interests; **~tag** m everyday life; **2täglich** *adj.* everyday; *fig. a.* ordinary; **2wissend** *adj.* omniscient; **2zu** *adv.* (all) too; **2zuviel** *adv.* too much

Alm f alpine pasture, alp

Almosen n alms *sg. u. pl.*

Alpdruck m nightmare (*a. fig.*)

Alphabet n alphabet; **2isch** *adj.* alphabetical

alpin *adj.* alpine

Alptraum m nightmare (*a. fig.*)

als *cj. zeitlich:* when; *während:* while; *nach comp.:* than; ~ *ich ankam* when I arrived; ~ *Kind* (*Geschenk*) as a child (present); *älter ~* older than; ~ *ob* as if *od.* though; *nichts ~* nothing but

also *cj.* so, therefore; F well, you know; ~ *gut!* very well (then)!, all right (then)!; ~ *doch* so ... after all; *du willst ~ ...?* so you want to ...?

alt *adj.* old; *hist.* ancient; *Sprachen:* classical; *ein 12 Jahre ~er Junge* a twelve-year-old boy

Alt *mus.* m alto (*a. in Zssgn*)

Altar m altar

Alt|e m, f: *der* ~ the old man (*a. fig.*); *Chef:* a. the boss; *die* ~ the old woman (*a. fig.*); *die ~n pl.* the old *pl.*; **~enheim** n → *Altersheim*; **~enpfleger(in)** geriatric nurse

Alter n age; *hohes:* old age; *im ~ von* at the age of; *er ist in deinem ~* he's your age

älter *adj.* older; *mein ~er Bruder* my elder brother; *ein ~er Herr* an elderly gentleman

altern *v/i.* grow* old, age

alternativ *adj.* alternative; *pol.* ecological, green; *Bewegung, Szene etc.:* a. counterculture; **2e** f alternative, option, choice; **2e(r)** *appr.* ecologist, member of the counterculture movement

Alters|grenze f age limit; *Rentenalter:* retirement age; **~heim** n old people's home; **~rente** f old-age pension;

~schwäche f infirmity; **an ~ sterben** die of old age; **~versorgung** f old age pension (scheme)

Altertum n antiquity

Alt|glascontainer m bottle bank, Am. glass recycling bin; **2klug** adj. precocious; **~lasten** pl. residual pollution; **~metall** n scrap (metal); **2modisch** adj. old-fashioned; **~öl** n waste oil; **~papier** n waste paper; **2sprachlich** adj.: **~es Gymnasium** appr. classical secondary school; **~stadt** f old town; **~stadtsanierung** f town-cent|re (Am. -er) rehabilitation; **~warenhändler** m second-hand dealer; **~weibersommer** m Indian summer; **Fäden:** gossamer

Aluminium n alumin(i)um

am prp. räumlich: at the; Abend, Morgen: in the; Anfang, Wochenende: at the; Sonntag etc.: on; **~ 1. Mai** on May 1st; **~ Tage** during the day; **~ Himmel** in the sky; **~ meisten** most; **~ Leben** alive

Amateur m amateur; **~funker** m radio amateur; F radio ham

Amboß m anvil

ambulan|t med. adv.: **~ behandelt werden** get* outpatient treatment; **2z** f Klinik: outpatients' department; Krankenwagen: ambulance

Ameise zo. f ant; **~nhaufen** m anthill

Amerika America; **~n|er(in)**, **2isch** adj. American

Amnestie pol. f, **2ren** v/t. amnesty

Amok m: **~ laufen** run* amok

Ampel mot. f traffic light(s pl.)

Amphibie zo. f amphibian (a. fig. u. in Zssgn)

Ampulle f ampoule

Amput|ation med. f amputation; **2ieren** med. v/t. amputate

Amsel zo. f blackbird

Amt n office, department, bsd. Am. bureau; Posten: office, position; Aufgabe: duty, function; tel. exchange; **2lich** adj. official

Amts|arzt m medical officer (Am. examiner); **~einführung** f inauguration; **~geheimnis** n official secret; **~geschäfte** pl. official duties pl.; **~zeichen** tel. n dialling (Am. dial) tone; **~zeit** f term (of office)

Amulett n amulet, (lucky) charm

amüs|ant adj. amusing, entertaining; **~ieren** v/t. amuse; **sich ~** enjoy o.s., have* a good time; **sich ~ über** laugh at

an 1. prp. räumlich: **~ der Themse (Küste, Wand)** on the Thames (coast, wall); **~ s-m Schreibtisch** at his desk; **~ der Hand** by the hand; **~ der Arbeit** at work; **~ den Hausaufgaben sitzen** sit* over one's homework; etc. schicken: send* s.th. to; **sich lehnen ~** lean* against; **~ die Tür** etc. klopfen knock at the door etc.; **~ e-m Sonntagmorgen** on a Sunday morning; **~ dem Tag, ...** on the day ...; **~ Weihnachten** etc. at Christmas etc.; **zeitlich: ~ Mangel, Stelle, sterben** etc.; **2.** adv. on (a. Licht etc.); **von jetzt (da, heute) ~** from now (that time, today) on; **München ~ 16.45** arrival Munich 16.45

Anabolikum n pharm. anabolic steroid

analog adj. analogous (**2... in Zssgn** Rechner etc.: analog(ue)

Analphabet m illiterate (person)

Analys|e f analysis; **2ieren** v/t. analy|se, Am. -ze

Ananas f pineapple

Anarchie f anarchy

Anatom|ie f anatomy; **2isch** adj. anatomical

anbahnen v/t. pave the way for; **sich ~** be* developing (Unangenehmes: impending)

Anbau m cultivation; arch. annex, extension; **2en** v/t. cultivate, grow*; arch. add (**an** to), build* on

anbehalten v/t. keep* on

anbei econ. adv. enclosed

an|beißen 1. v/t. take* a bite of; **2.** v/i. Fisch: bite*; fig. take* the bait; **~bellen** v/t. bark at (a. fig.); **~beten** v/t. adore, worship (a. fig.)

Anbetracht m: **in ~ (dessen, daß)** considering (that)

anbetteln v/t.: **j-n um et. ~** beg s.o. for s.th.

an|biedern v/refl. curry favo(u)r (**bei** with); **~bieten** v/t. offer; **~binden** v/t. Hund etc.: tie up; **~ an** tie to

Anblick m sight; **2en** v/t. look at; flüchtig: glance at

an|bohren v/t. Quelle etc.: tap; **~brechen 1.** v/t. Vorräte: break* into; Flasche etc.: open; **2.** v/i. begin*; Tag: break*; Nacht: fall*; **~brennen** v/i.

Milch etc.: burn* (*a.* ~ *lassen*); **~bringen** *v/t.* fix (*an* to); **2bruch** *m* beginning; *bei* ~ *der Nacht* at nightfall; **~brüllen** *v/t.* roar at

An|dacht *f* devotion; *Gottesdienst*: service; *kurzer*: prayers *pl.*; **2dächtig** *adj.* devout; *fig.* rapt

an|dauern *v/i.* continue, go* on, last; **~dauernd** *adj. u. adv.* → *dauernd*

Andenken *n* keepsake; *Reise2*: souvenir (*beide*: *an* of); *zum* ~ *an* in memory of

andere *adj. u. indef. pron.* other; *verschieden*: different; *noch* ~ *Fragen?* any more questions?; *mit* ~ *Worten* in other words; *am* ~*n Morgen* the next morning; *et.* (*nichts*) ~*s* s.th. (nothing) else; *nichts* ~*s als* nothing but; *die* ~*n* the others; *alle* ~*n* everybody else; → *anders*

andererseits *adv.* on the other hand

ändern *v/t.* change; *Kleidung etc.*: alter; *ich kann es nicht* ~ I can't help it; *sich* ~ change

andernfalls *adv.* otherwise

anders *adv.* different(ly); *j.* ~ somebody else; ~ *werden* change; ~ *sein* (*als*) be* different (from); *es geht nicht* ~ there is no other way; **~herum 1.** *adv.* the other way round; **2.** F *adj.* queer; **~wo**(*hin*) *adv.* elsewhere

anderthalb *adj.* one and a half

Änderung *f* change; *bsd. kleinere, a. Kleid etc.*: alteration

andeut|en *v/t. zu verstehen geben*: hint (at), suggest; *erwähnen*: indicate; *j-m* ~, *daß* give* s.o. a hint that; **2ung** *f* hint, suggestion

An|drang *m* crush; *Nachfrage*: rush (*nach* for), run (*zu, nach* on); **2drehen** *v/t. Licht etc.*: turn on; *j-m et.* ~ fob s.th. off on s.o.; **2drohen** *v/t.*: *j-m et.* ~ threaten s.o. with s.th; **2eignen** *v/refl.* acquire; *bsd. jur.* appropriate

aneinander *adv.* binden *etc.*: together; ~ *denken* think* of each other; **~geraten** *v/i.* clash (*mit* with)

Anekdote *f* anecdote

anekeln *v/t.* disgust, sicken; *es ekelt mich an* it makes me sick

anerkannt *adj.* acknowledged, recognized

anerkenn|en *v/t.* acknowledge, recognize; *lobend*: appreciate; **~end** *adj.* appreciative; **2ung** *f* acknowledg(e)ment, recognition; appreciation

anfahr|en 1. *v/i.* start; **2.** *v/t. mot. etc.* hit*; *Auto etc.*: *a.* run* into; *transportieren*: carry (*up*); *j-n* ~ *schimpfen*: jump on s.o.; **2t** *f* journey, ride

Anfall *med. m* fit, attack; **2en** *v/t.* attack, assault; *Hund*: go* for

anfällig *adj.* delicate; *für* susceptible to

Anfang *m* beginning, start; *am* ~ at the beginning; ~ *Mai* early in May; ~ *nächsten Jahres* early next year; ~ *der neunziger Jahre* in the early nineties; *er ist* ~ *20* he is in his early twenties; *von* ~ *an* from the beginning *od.* start; **2en** *v/t. u. v/i.* begin*, start; *tun*: do*

Anfänger(in) beginner

anfangs *adv.* at first; **2buchstabe** *m* initial (letter); *großer* ~ capital (letter); **2stadium** *n*: *im* ~ at an early stage

anfassen *v/t.* touch; *nehmen*: take* (hold of); *sich* ~ take* each other by the hands; F ... *zum* 2 everyman's ...

anfecht|bar *adj.* contestable; **~en** *v/t.* contest; **2ung** *f* contesting

anfertig|en *v/t.* make*, manufacture; **~feuchten** *v/t.* moisten; **~feuern** *fig. v/t.* cheer; **~flehen** *v/t.* implore; **~fliegen** *aviat. v/t.* approach; *regelmäßig*: fly* (regularly) to; **2flug** *m aviat.* approach; *fig.* touch

anforder|n *v/t.* demand; request; **2ung** *f* demand; request; **~en** *pl.* requirements *pl.*, qualifications *pl.*

Anfrage *f* inquiry; **2n** *v/i.* inquire (*bei j-m nach et.* of s.o. about s.th.)

an|freunden *v/refl.* make* friends (*mit* with); **~fühlen** *v/refl.* feel*; *es fühlt sich weich* (*wie Leder*) *an* it feels soft (like leather)

anführ|en *v/t.* lead*; *nennen*: state; *täuschen*: fool; **2er(in)** leader; **2ungszeichen** *pl.* quotation marks *pl.*, inverted commas *pl.*

Angabe *f Aussage*: statement; *Hinweis*: indication; F *Aufschneiderei*: big talk; *Tennis*: service; ~*n pl.* information *sg.*, data *pl.*; *tech.* specifications *pl.*

angeb|en 1. *v/t.* give*, state; *Zoll*: declare; *zeigen*: indicate; *Preis*: quote; **2.** *v/i.* F *fig.* brag, show* off; *Tennis*: serve; **2er** F *m* braggart, show-off; **2erei** F *f* bragging, showing off; **~lich** *adj.* alleged; ~ *ist er ...* he is said to be ...

angeboren adj. innate, inborn; med. congenital

Angebot n offer (a. econ.); **~ und Nachfrage** supply and demand

ange|bracht adj. appropriate; **~bunden** adj.: **kurz ~** curt; **~gossen** F adj.: **wie ~ sitzen** fit like a glove; **~heitert** adj. tipsy, Brt. a. (slightly) merry

angehen 1. v/i. Licht etc.: go* on; **2.** v/t. concern; **das geht dich nichts an** that is none of your business; **~d** adj. future; **~er Arzt** doctor-to-be

angehör|en v/i. belong to; **2ige(r)** relative; Mitglied: member; **die nächsten ~n** pl. the next of kin pl.

Angeklagte(r) jur. defendant

Angel f fishing tackle; Tür2: hinge

Angelegenheit f matter, affair

ange|lehnt adj. Tür etc.: ajar; **~lernt** adj. Arbeiter: semi-skilled

Angel|haken m fish-hook; **2n 1.** v/i. fish (nach for), angle (for) (beide a. fig.); **2.** v/t. catch*, hook; **~rute** f fishing rod

Angel|sachse m, **2sächsisch** adj. Anglo-Saxon

Angel|schein m fishing permit; **~schnur** f fishing line

ange|messen adj. proper, suitable; Strafe: just; Preis: reasonable; **~nehm** adj. pleasant, agreeable; **~l** pleased to meet you; **~nommen** cj. (let's) suppose, supposing; **~regt** adj. animated; Unterhaltung: lively; **~schrieben** adj.: **bei j-m gut (schlecht) ~ sein** be in s.o.'s good (bad) books; **~sehen** adj. respected; **~sichts** prp. in view of

Angestellte(r) employee (bei with); **die ~n** pl. the staff pl.

ange|tan adj. ganz ~ **sein von** be* taken with; **~trunken** adj. (slightly) drunk; **in ~em Zustand** under the influence of alcohol; **~wandt** adj. applied; **~wiesen** adj.: **~ auf** dependent (up)on; **~wöhnen** v/t.: **sich (j-m) ~, et. zu tun** get* (s.o.) used to doing s.th.; **sich das Rauchen ~** take to smoking; **2wohnheit** f habit

Angina med. f tonsillitis

angleichen v/t. adjust (an to)

Angler m angler

Anglist(in) student of (od. graduate in) English

angreif|en v/t. attack (a. Sport u. fig.);

Gesundheit: affect; Vorräte etc.: touch; **2er** m attacker; Sport: a. offensive player; bsd. pol. aggressor

angrenzend adj. adjacent (an to)

Angriff m attack (a. Sport u. fig.); Sturm2: assault, charge; **in ~ nehmen** set* about; **2slustig** adj. aggressive

Angst f fear (vor of); **~ haben (vor)** be* afraid od. scared (of); **j-m ~ einjagen** frighten od. scare s.o.; **(hab) keine Angst!** don't be afraid!; **~hase** F m chicken

ängst|igen v/t. frighten, scare; **sich ~** be* afraid (vor of); be* worried (um about); **~lich** adj. timid, fearful; besorgt: anxious

an|gurten v/t. → **anschnallen**; **~haben** v/t. have* on (a. Licht etc.); Kleid etc.: a. wear*, be* wearing; **das kann mir nichts ~** that can't do me any harm

anhalten 1. v/t. stop; **den Atem ~** hold* one's breath; **2.** v/i. stop; andauern: continue; **um j-s Hand ~** propose (marriage) to s.o.; **~d** adj. continual

Anhalter(in) hitchhiker; **per ~ fahren** hitchhike

Anhaltspunkt m clue

anhand prp. by means of

Anhang m Buch: appendix; Verwandte: relations pl.

anhäng|en v/t. hinzufügen: add; aufhängen: hang* up; rail., mot. couple (an to); **2er** m follower, supporter (a. Sport); Schmuck: pendant; Koffer2 etc.: label, tag; mot. trailer

anhänglich adj. affectionate; contp. clinging; **2keit** f affection

anhäuf|en v/t. u. v/refl. heap up, accumulate; **2ung** f accumulation

an|heben v/t. lift, raise (a. Preis); mot. jack up; **~heften** v/t. attach, tack (beide: an to)

anheimstellen v/t.: **j-m et. ~** leave* s.th. to s.o.

Anhieb m: **auf ~** on the first try

anhimmeln F v/t. idolize, worship

Anhöhe f rise, hill, elevation

anhör|en v/t. listen to; et. **mit ~** overhear* s.th.; **es hört sich ... an** it sounds ...; **2ung** jur., pol. f hearing

animieren v/t. encourage; stimulate

ankämpfen v/i.: **~ gegen** fight* s.th.

Ankauf m purchase

Anker *naut. m* anchor; *vor ~ gehen* drop anchor; **2n** *naut. v/i.* anchor

anketten *v/t.* chain up

Anklage *jur. f* accusation, charge (*a. fig.*); **2n** *jur. v/t.* accuse (*wegen* of), charge (*with*) (*beide a. fig.*)

anklammern *v/t.* clip *s.th.* on; *sich ~* cling* (*an* to)

Anklang *m*: *~ finden* meet* with approval

an|kleben *v/t.* stick* on (*an* to); **~kleiden** *v/t.* dress; **~klicken** *v/t. Computer*: click; **~klopfen** *v/i.* knock (*an* at); **~knipsen** *electr. v/t.* switch on; **~knüpfen** *v/t. Schnur etc.*: tie (*an* to); *fig.* begin*; *Beziehungen ~* (*zu*) establish contacts (*with*); *~ an et.* refer to s.th.; **~kommen** *v/i.* arrive; *nicht gegen j-n ~ be** no match for s.o.; *es kommt* (*ganz*) *darauf an* it (all) depends; *es kommt darauf an, daß* what matters is; *darauf kommt es nicht an* that doesn't matter; *es darauf ~ lassen* take* a chance; *gut ~* (*bei*) *fig.* go down well (*with*)

ankündig|en *v/t.* announce; *in der Presse*: advertise; **2ung** *f* announcement; advertisement

Ankunft *f* arrival

an|lächeln, **~lachen** *v/t.* smile at

Anlage *f Anordnung*: arrangement; *Einrichtung*: facility; *Fabrik2*: plant; *tech.* system; (stereo *etc.*) set; *Geld2*: investment; *zu e-m Brief*: enclosure; *Talent*: gift; *~n pl.* park *sg.*, gardens *pl.*; *sanitäre ~n pl.* sanitary facilities *pl.*

Anlaß *m* occasion; *Ursache*: cause

anlass|en *v/t. Kleidung*: keep* on, leave* on (*a. Licht etc.*); *tech., mot.* start; **2er** *m mot.* starter

anläßlich *prp.* on the occasion of

Anlauf *m Sport*: run-up, *Am.* approach; *fig.* start; **~stelle** *f* advice centre, *Am.* walk-in center; *Unterkunft*: place to stay; **2en 1.** *v/i.* run* up; *fig.* start; *Metall*: tarnish; *Brille etc.*: steam up; **2.** *naut. v/t.* call *od.* touch at

an|legen 1. *v/t. Kleidung, Schmuck etc.*: put* on; *Garten*: lay* out; *Straße*: build*; *Geld*: invest; *Stadt*: found; *med. Verband*: apply; *Vorräte*: lay* in; *fig. sich mit j-m ~* pick a quarrel with s.o.; **2.** *v/i. naut.* land; moor; *es ~ auf* aim at; **2leger** *m econ.* investor; *naut.* landing stage; **~lehnen** *v/t.* lean* (*an* against); *Tür*: leave* ajar; *sich ~ an* lean* against (*fig.* on)

Anleihe *f* loan

Anleitung *f* guidance, instruction; *schriftliche*: instructions *pl.*

An|liegen *n Bitte*: request; *e-s Buches etc.*: message; **~lieger** *m* resident

an|locken *v/t.* attract; *stärker*: lure; **~machen** *v/t. anzünden*: light*; *Licht, Radio etc.*: turn on; *Salat*: dress; *F j-n*: chat *s.o.* up; *begeistern*: turn *s.o.* on; **~malen** *v/t.* paint

Anmarsch *m*: *im ~* on the way

anmaßen *v/t.*: *sich ~ Recht etc.*:assume; *Recht*: claim; *sich ~ et. zu tun* presume to do s.th.; **~d** *adj.* arrogant

anmeld|en *v/t. Besuch etc.*: announce; *amtlich*: register; *Zollgut*: declare; *sich ~ für Schule etc.*: enrol(l); *im Hotel etc.*: register; *sich ~ bei Arzt etc.*: make* an appointment with; **2ung** *f* announcement; registration, enrol(l)ment

anmerk|en *v/t.*: *j-m et.* ~ notice s.th. in s.o.; *sich et.* (*nichts*) *~ lassen* (not) let* it show; **2ung** *f* note; *erklärend*: annotation, *Fußnote*: *a.* footnote

Anmut *f* grace; **2ig** *adj.* graceful

annähen *v/t.* sew* on (*an* to)

annäher|nd *adv.* approximately; **2ung** *f* approach (*an* to); **2ungsversuche** *pl.* advances (*an* to); *F* pass *sg.*

Annahme *f* acceptance (*a. fig.*); *Vermutung*: assumption

annehm|bar *adj.* acceptable; *Preis*: reasonable; **~en** *v/t.* accept; *vermuten*: suppose; *Kind, Namen*: adopt; *Ball*: take*; *Form etc.*: take* on; *sich e-r Sache od. j-s ~* take* care of s.th. *od.* s.o.; **2lichkeiten** *pl* comforts *pl.*, amenities *pl.*

Annonce *f* advertisement

annullieren *v/t.* annul; *econ.* cancel

anöden F *v/t.* bore to death

anonym *adj.* anonymous; **2ität** *f* anonymity

Anorak *m* anorak

anordn|en *v/t.* arrange; *befehlen*: give* order(s), order; **2ung** *f* arrangement; direction, order

anorganisch *chem. adj.* inorganic

anpacken F *fig.* **1.** *v/t. Problem etc.*: tackle; **2.** *v/i.*: *mit ~* lend* a hand

anpass|en *v/t.* adapt, adjust (*beide*

auch sich ~ (*dat.*, *an* to); **2ung** *f* adaptation, adjustment; **~ungsfähig** *adj.* adaptable; **2ungsfähigkeit** *f* adaptability

anpflanz|en *v/t.* cultivate, plant; **2ung** *f* cultivation

Anpfiff *m Sport:* starting whistle; *fig.* dressing-down

an|pöbeln *v/t.* accost; *beschimpfen:* shout abuse at; **~prangern** *v/t.* denounce, point the finger at; **~preisen** *v/t.* extol; *bsd. Eigenes:* plug: ~ **probieren** *v/t.* try on; **~pumpen** F *v/t.* put the touch on *s.o.*

Anrainer *östr. m* → *Anlieger*

an|raten *v/t.* advise; **~rechnen** *v/t. berechnen:* charge; *gutschreiben:* allow; *hoch* ~ appreciate very much; *als Fehler* ~ count as a mistake

Anrecht *n:* *ein* ~ *haben auf* be* entitled to

Anrede *f* address; **2n** *v/t.* address (*mit Namen* by name)

anreg|en *v/t. beleben:* stimulate; *vorschlagen:* suggest; **~end** *adj.* stimulating; **2ung** *f* stimulation; suggestion; **2ungsmittel** *n* stimulant

Anreiz *m* incentive

anrichten *v/t. Speisen:* prepare, dress; *Schaden:* cause, do*

anrüchig *adj.* disreputable

Anruf *m* call (*a. tel.*); **~beantworter** *tel. m* answering machine; **2en** *v/t.* call *od.* ring* up, phone

anrühren *v/t.* touch; *mischen:* mix

Ansage *f* announcement; **2n** *v/t.* announce; **~r(in)** announcer

ansamm|eln *v/t. u. v/refl.* accumulate; **2ung** *f* collection, accumulation; *Menschen2:* crowd

Ansatz *m Beginn:* start (*zu* of); *Versuch:* attempt (*zu* at); *Methode:* approach; *tech.* attachment; *math.* set-up; **Ansätze** *pl.* first signs *pl.*

anschaff|en *v/t. allg.* get*; *sich et.* ~ buy* *od.* get* (o.s.) s.th.; **2ung** *f* purchase, buy

anschau|en *v/t. u. ansehen;* **~lich** *adj. Stil etc.:* graphic, plastic

Anschauung *f* view (*von* of), opinion (*von* about, of); **~smaterial** *n Schule etc.:* visual aids *pl.*

Anschein *m* appearance; *allem* ~ *nach* to all appearances; *den* ~ *erwecken,*

als (*ob*) give the impression of ...*ing;* **2end** *adv.* apparently

anschieben *v/t.* give* a push (*a. mot.*)

Anschlag *m* attack; *Plakat:* poster; *Bekanntmachung:* bill, notice; *Schreibmaschine:* stroke; *mus.*, *Schwimmen:* touch; *e-n* ~ *auf j-n verüben* make* an attempt on s.o.'s life; **~brett** *n* notice (*bsd. Am.* bulletin) board; **2en 1.** *v/t. Plakat:* post; *mus.* strike*; *Tasse etc.:* chip; *Waffe:* aim; **2.** *v/i. Hund:* bark; *wirken:* take* (effect) (*a. med.*); *Schwimmen:* touch the wall; **~säule** *f* advertising pillar

anschließen *v/t. electr. tech.* connect; *sich* ~ *folgen:* follow; *e-r Ansicht etc.:* agree with; *sich j-m od. e-r Sache* ~ join s.o. *od.* s.th.; **~d 1.** *adj.* following; **2.** *adv.* then, afterwards

Anschluß *m* connection; *im* ~ *an* following; ~ *suchen* look for company; ~ *finden* (*bei*) make* contact *od.* friends (with); ~ *bekommen tel.* get* through

an|schmiegen *v/refl.* snuggle up (*an* to); **~schmiegsam** *adj.* affectionate; **~schnallen** *v/t.* strap on, put* on (*a. Ski*); *sich* ~ *aviat.*, *mot.* fasten one's seat belt; **~schnauzen** F *v/t.* tell *s.o.* off, *Am. a.* bawl *s.o.* out; **~schneiden** *v/t.* cut*; *Thema:* bring* up

Anschnitt *m* first cut *od.* slice

an|schrauben *v/t.* screw on (*an* to); **~schreiben** *v/t.* write* on the (black-)board; *j-n* ~ write* to s.o.; (*et.*) ~ *lassen* buy* (s.th.) on credit; → *angeschrieben;* **~schreien** *v/t.* shout at

Anschrift *f* address

anschuld|igen *v/t.* accuse (*gen.*, *wegen* of), charge (with); **2igung** *f* accusation

anschwellen *v/i.* swell* (*a. fig.*)

anschwemmen *v/t.* wash ashore

ansehen *v/t.* look at, have* *od.* take* a look at; watch; see* (*alle auch sich* ~); ~ *als* look upon as; *et. mit* ~ watch *od.* witness s.th.; *man sieht ihm an, daß ...* one can see that

Ansehen *n* reputation

ansehnlich *adj. beträchtlich:* considerable

an|seilen *mount. v/t. u. v/refl.* rope; **~setzen 1.** *v/t.* put* (*an* to); *anfügen:* put* on, add; *Termin:* fix, set*; *Rost*

(*Fett*) ~ put* on rust (weight); **2.** *v/i.*: ~ **zu** *Landung etc.*: prepare for

Ansicht *f Meinung*: opinion, view; *Anblick*: sight, view; **der** ~ **sein, daß** ... be* of the opinion that ...; *meiner* ~ **nach** in my opinion; **zur** ~ *econ.* on approval; **~skarte** *f* picture postcard; **~ssache** *f* matter of opinion

ansied|eln *v/t. u. v/refl.* → **siedeln**

anspann|en *v/t. Kräfte etc.*: strain; **2ung** strain, exertion

anspiel|en *v/i. Fußball*: kick off; ~ **auf** allude to, hint at; **2ung** *f* allusion, hint

anspitzen *v/t. Stift etc.*: sharpen

Ansporn *m* incentive; **2en** *v/t.* encourage, spur *s.o.* on

Ansprache *f* address, speech; *e-e* ~ *halten* deliver an address

ansprech|en *v/t.* address, speak* to; *fig. gefallen*: appeal to; ~**end** *adj.* attractive; **2partner** *m* s.o. to talk to, contact

an|springen 1. *v/i. Motor*: start; **2.** *v/t.* jump (up)on; **~spritzen** *v/t.* spatter

Anspruch *m* claim (**auf** to) (*a. jur.*); ~ *haben auf* be* entitled to; ~ *erheben auf* claim; *Zeit in* ~ *nehmen* take* up time; **2slos** *adj.* modest; *Buch, Musik*: light, undemanding; *contp.* trivial; **2svoll** *adj.* demanding (*a. geistig*); *Geschmack*: sophisticated, refined

Anstalt *f* establishment, institution; *Nervenheil2*: mental hospital; ~*en machen zu* get* ready for

An|stand *m* decency; *Benehmen*: manners *pl.*; **2ständig** *adj.* decent (*a. fig.*); **2slos** *adv.* unhesitatingly; *mühelos*: without difficulty

anstarren *v/t.* stare at

anstatt *prp. u. cj.* instead of

anstechen *v/t. Faß*: tap

ansteck|en *v/t.* stick* on; *Ring*: put* on; *anzünden*: light*; *Haus etc.*: set* fire to; *med.* infect; *sich bei j-m* ~ catch* s.th. from s.o.; ~**end** *med. adj.* infectious; *direkt*: contagious, catching (*alle a. fig.*); **2nadel** *f* pin, button; **2ung** *med. f* infection; contagion

an|stehen *v/i.* queue (up) (**nach** for), *bsd. Am.* stand* in line (for); ~**steigen** *v/i.* rise*

anstell|en *v/t. j-n*: engage, employ; *TV etc.*: turn on; *mot.* start; *Verbotenes*: be* up to; *Versuche, Ermittlungen*:

make*; *sich* ~ queue (up) (**nach** for), *Am.* line up (for); F (make* a) fuss; **2ung** *f* job, position; *e-e* ~ *finden* find* employment

Anstieg *m* rise, increase

anstift|en *v/t.* incite; **2er** *m* instigator; **2ung** *f* incitement

anstimmen *v/t.* strike* up

Anstoß *m Fußball*: kickoff; *Anregung*: initiative, impetus; *Ärgernis*: offen|ce, *Am.* -se; ~ *erregen* give* offence (**bei** to); ~ *nehmen an* take* offence at; *den* ~ *zu et. geben* start s.th., initiate s.th.; **2en 1.** *v/t.* nudge *s.o.*; **2.** *v/i.* knock, bump; *mit Gläsern*: clink glasses; *auf j-n od. et.* ~ drink* to s.o. od. s.th.

anstößig *adj.* offensive

an|strahlen *v/t. Gebäude etc.*: illuminate; *j-n*: beam at

anstreiche|n *v/t.* paint; *Fehler, Textstelle*: mark; **2r** *m* (house)painter

anstreng|en *v/refl.* try (hard), make* an effort; ~**end** *adj.* strenuous, hard; **2ung** *f* exertion, strain; *Bemühung*: effort

Ansturm *fig. m* rush (**auf** for)

Anteil *m* share (*a. econ.*), portion; ~ *nehmen an* take* an interest in; *mitleidig*: sympathize with; ~**nahme** *f* sympathy; *Interesse*: interest

Antenne *f* aerial, *bsd. Am.* antenna

Anti|..., **2...** *in Zssgn autorität, Militarismus etc.*: anti...; ~**alkoholiker** *m* teetotal(l)er; ~**babypille** *f* birth control pill, F the pill; **2biotikum** *pharm.* antibiotic; ~**blockiersystem** *mot.* n anti-lock braking system

antik *adj.* antique, *hist. a.* ancient; **2e** *hist. f* ancient world

Antikörper *med. m* antibody

Antilope *zo. f* antelope

Antipathie *f* antipathy

Antiquar|iat *n* second-hand bookshop; **2isch** *adj. u. adv.* second-hand

Antiquitäten *pl.* antiques *pl.*; ~**laden** *m* antique shop

Antisemit *m* anti-Semite; **2isch** *adj.* anti-Semitic; ~**ismus** *m* anti-Semitism

Antrag *m Gesuch*: application; *parl.* motion; *Heirats2*: proposal; ~ *stellen auf* make* an application for; *parl.* move for; ~**steller** *m* applicant; *parl.* mover

an|treffen *v/t.* meet*, find*; ~**treiben**

v/t. tech., mot. drive*; *zu et.* ~: urge (on); *Strandgut*: float ashore; ~**treten 1.** *v/t. Amt, Erbe*: enter upon; *Position*: take* up; *Reise*: set* out on; **2.** *v/i.* take* one's place; *mil.* line up

Antrieb *m* tech. drive (*a. fig. Schwung*), propulsion; *fig.* motive, impulse; **aus eigenem** ~ of one's own accord

antun *v/t.: j-m et.* ~ do* s.th. to s.o.; *sich et.* ~ lay* hands on o.s.

Antwort *f* answer (**auf** to), reply (to); **Ωen** *v/i.* answer (*j-m* s.o., **auf et.** s.th.), reply (to s.o. *od.* s.th.)

an|vertrauen *v/t.: j-m et.* ~ *Aufgabe etc.*: (en)trust s.o. with s.th.; *Geheimnis etc.*: confide s.th. to s.o.; ~**wachsen** *v/i.* agr. take* root; *zunehmen*: grow, increase

Anwalt *m* → **Rechtsanwalt**

Anwärter(in) candidate (**auf** for)

anweis|en *v/t.* instruct; *befehlen: a.* direct, order; **Ωung** *f* instruction; order

anwend|en *v/t.* use; *Regel, Arznei*: apply (**auf** to); **Ωung** *f* use; application

anwerben *v/t.* recruit (*a. fig.*)

Anwesen *n* estate; property

anwesen|d *adj.* present; **Ωheit** *f* presence; *Schule*: attendance; **die** ~ **feststellen** call the roll; **Ωheitsliste** *f* attendance list (*Am.* record)

anwidern *v/t.* make* s.o. sick

Anzahl *f* number, quantity

anzahl|en *v/t.* pay* on account; **Ωung** *f erste Rate*: down payment

anzapfen *v/t.* tap

Anzeichen *n* symptom (*a. med.*), sign

Anzeige *f* advertisement; *Bekanntgabe*: announcement; *jur.* information; *Computer*: display; *tech.* reading; **Ωn** *v/t. bekanntgeben*: announce; report to the police; *Instrument*: indicate, show*; *j-n* ~ inform against s.o.

anziehen *v/t. Kleidung*: put* on; *Kind etc.*: dress; *reizen, anlocken*: attract, draw*; *Schraube*: tighten; *Bremse, Hebel*: **sich** ~ get* dressed; *sich kleiden*: dress; ~**d** *adj.* attractive

Anziehung(skraft) *f* phys. attraction; *fig. a.* appeal

Anzug *m* suit

anzüglich *adj. Witz*: suggestive; *Bemerkung*: personal, offensive

an|zünden *v/t.* light*; *Gebäude*: set* on fire; ~**zweifeln** *v/t.* doubt

apart *adj.* striking

Apartment *n* studio (flat *od. Am.* apartment)

apathisch *adj.* apathetic

Apfel *m* apple; ~**mus** *n* apple sauce; ~**sine** *f* orange; ~**wein** *m* cider

Apostel *m* apostle

Apostroph *m* apostrophe

Apotheke *f* pharmacy, *Brt.* chemist's, *Am. a.* drugstore; ~**r(in)** pharmacist, *Brt.* chemist; *bsd. Am.* druggist

App. *Abk. für* **Apparat** *tel.* ext., extension

Apparat *m* apparatus; *Vorrichtung*: device; *tel.* (tele)phone; radio; TV set; camera; *fig. pol. etc.*: machine(ry); **am** ~**!** *tel.* speaking!; **am** ~ **bleiben** *tel.* hold* the line

Appell *m* appeal (**an** to); *mil.* roll call; **Ωieren** *v/i.* (make* an) appeal (**an** to)

Appetit *m* appetite (**auf** for); ~ **auf et. haben** feel* like s.th.; **guten** ~**!** enjoy your meal!; **Ωlich** *adj.* appetizing, savo(u)ry; *fig. a.* inviting; ~**losigkeit** *f* lack of appetite

applaudieren *v/i.* applaud

Applaus *m* applause

Aprikose *f* apricot

April *m* April; ~**!** ~**!** April fool!; ~**scherz** *m* April fool (joke)

Aquaplaning *mot. n* aquaplaning, *Am.* hydroplaning

Aquarell *n* water-colo(u)r

Aquarium *n* aquarium

Äquator *m* equator

Ära *f* era

Arab|er(in) Arab; **Ωisch** *adj.* Arabian; *Sprache, Zahl*: Arabic

Arbeit *f* work, econ., pol. a. labo(u)r; employment, job; *Klassen*Ω: test; *schriftliche, wissenschaftliche*: paper; *Ausführung*: workmanship; **bei der** ~ at work; **zur** ~ **gehen** *od.* **fahren** go* to work; **gute** ~ **leisten** make* a good job of it; **sich an die** ~ **machen** set* to work; **Ωen** *v/i.* work (**an** at, on); ~**er(in)** worker

Arbeit|geber *m* employer; ~**nehmer** *m* employee

Arbeits|amt *n Brt.* job centre, *Am.* labor office; ~**blatt** *n* worksheet; ~**erlaubnis** *f* work permit, *Am.* green card; **Ωfähig** *adj.* fit for work; ~**gang** *m* operation; ~**gemeinschaft** *f* work *od.* study group; **~gericht** *n* labo(u)r court, *Brt.* industrial tribunal; 2**hose** *f* overalls *pl.;* **~kleidung** *f* working clothes *pl.;* **~kräfte** *pl.* workers *pl.,* labo(u)r *sg.;* 2**los** *adj.* unemployed, out of work; **~lose** *m, f:* **die** *n pl.* the unemployed *pl.;* **~losengeld** *n* unemployment benefit *(Am.* compensation); **~ beziehen** F be* on the dole; **~losigkeit** *f* unemployment; **~markt** *m* labo(u)r market; **~minister** *m Brt.* Minister of Labour, *Am.* Secretary of Labor; **~niederlegung** *f* strike, walkout; **~pause** *f* break, intermission; **~platz** *m* workplace; *Stelle:* job; 2**scheu** *adj.* work-shy; **~speicher** *m Computer:* main memory; **~suche** *f:* **er ist auf ~** he is looking for a job; **~süchtige(r)** workaholic; **~tag** *m* workday; 2**unfähig** *adj.* unfit for work; *ständig:* disabled; **~weise** *f* method (of working); **~zeit** *f (gleitende* flexible) working hours *pl.;* **~zeitverkürzung** *f* fewer working hours *pl.;* **~zimmer** *n* study

Archäo|loge *m* arch(a)eologist; **~logie** *f* arch(a)eology

Arche *f* ark; **die ~ Noah** Noah's ark

Architekt *m* architect; 2**onisch** *adj.* architectural; **~ur** *f* architecture

Archiv *n* archives *pl.;* record office

Arena *f Stierkampf, Zirkus:* ring

Ärger *m* anger *(über* at); *Unannehmlichkeit:* trouble; F: *j-m Ärger machen* cause s.o. trouble; 2**lich** *adj.* angry *(über, auf* at *s.th.;* with *s.o.); störend:* annoying; 2**n** *v/t.* annoy; *sich ~* be* annoyed *(über* at, about *s.th.,* with *s.o.);* **~nis** *n* nuisance

arglos *adj.* innocent

Arg|wohn *m* suspicion *(gegen* of); 2**wöhnen** *v/t.* suspect; 2**wöhnisch** *adj.* suspicious

Arie *mus. f* aria

Aristokratie *f* aristocracy

arm *adj.* poor; **die** 2**en** the poor

Arm *m* arm; *e-s Flusses etc.:* branch; F: *j-n auf den ~ nehmen* pull s.o.'s leg

Armaturen *tech. pl.* instruments *pl.; im Bad etc.:* (plumbing) fixtures *pl.;* **~brett** *mot. n* dashboard

Armband *n* bracelet; **~uhr** *f* wristwatch

Armee *f* armed forces *pl.; Heer:* army

Ärmel *m* sleeve

ärmlich *adj.* poor *(a. fig.);* shabby

Armreif(en) *m* bangle

armselig *adj.* wretched, miserable

Armut *f* poverty; **~ an** lack of

Aroma *n* flavo(u)r; *Duft:* aroma

Arrest *m* arrest; *Nachsitzen:* detention; **~ bekommen** be* kept in

arrogant *adj.* arrogant, conceited

Arsch V *m* arse, *Am.* ass; **~loch** V *n* arsehole, *Am.* asshole

Art *f ~ u. Weise:* way, manner; kind, sort; *biol.* species; *auf diese ~ (in) this way; e-e ~ ...* a sort of ...; *Geräte aller ~* all kinds *od.* sorts of tools; **~enschutz** *m* protection of endangered species

Arterie *anat. f* artery; **~nverkalkung** *med. f* arteriosclerosis

Arthritis *med. f* arthritis

artig *adj.* good, well-behaved; *sei ~!* be good!, be a good boy *(od.* girl)!

Artikel *m* article

Artillerie *mil. f* artillery

Artist(in) acrobat, (circus) performer

Arznei(mittel *n) f* medicine, drug

Arzt *m* doctor, *formell:* : physician; **~helfer(in)** doctor's assistant

Ärztin *f* (lady) doctor *od.* physician

ärztlich *adj.* medical; *sich ~ behandeln lassen* medical* treatment

As *n* ace; *mus.* A flat

Asbest *m min.* asbestos

Asche *f* ash(es *pl.);* **~nbahn** *f* cindertrack, *mot.* dirt-track; **~nbecher** *m* ashtray; **~rmittwoch** *m* Ash Wednesday

äsen *hunt. v/i.* feed*, browse

Asi|en *n* Asia; **~at(in)** Asian; 2**atisch** *adj.* Asian, *Volk etc. a.* Asiatic

Asket *m,* 2**isch** *adj.* ascetic

asozial *adj.* antisocial

Asphalt *m* asphalt; 2**ieren** *v/t.* (cover with) asphalt

Assistent(in) assistant

Assistenz|arzt *m,* **~ärztin** *f Brt.* houseman, *Am.* intern

Ast *m* branch; **~loch** *n* knot-hole

Astro|naut(in) astronaut; **~nom** *m* astronomer; **~nomie** *f* astronomy

ASU *mot. f Abk. für Abgas-Sonder-Untersuchung* exhaust emission test, *Am.* emissions test

Asyl *n* asylum; **~ant(in),** **~bewer-**

ber(in) asylum seeker, (political) refugee; **~recht** n right of (political) asylum

Atelier n studio

Atem m breath; **außer ~** out of breath; **(tief) ~ holen** take* a (deep) breath; **2beraubend** adj. breathtaking; **~gerät** med. n respirator; **2los** adj. breathless; **~pause** f F breather; **~zug** m breath

Äther m chem. ether; Funk: air

Athlet|(in) athlete; **2isch** adj. athletic

Atlas m atlas

atmen v/i. u. v/t. breathe

Atmosphäre f atmosphere

Atmung f breathing, respiration

Atoll n atoll

Atom n atom; **~...** in Zssgn Energie, Forschung, Kraft, Krieg, Rakete, Reaktor, Waffen etc.: nuclear ...; **2ar** adj. atomic, nuclear; **~bombe** f atom(ic) bomb; **~gegner** m anti-nuclear activist; **~kern** m (atomic) nucleus; **~müll** m nuclear waste; **2waffenfrei** adj. nuclear-free

Atten|tat n assassination attempt, attempt on s.o.'s life; **Opfer e-s ~s werden** be* assassinated; **~täter** m assassin

Attest n (doctor's) certificate

Attrakt|ion f attraction; **2iv** adj. attractive

Attrappe f dummy

Attribut gr. n attribute (a. fig.)

ätzend adj. corrosive, caustic (a. fig.); sl. crappy, Am. gross; **das ist echt ~** it's the pits

au int. ouch!; **~ fein!** oh, good!

auch cj. also, too, as well; **ich ~** so am (do) I, F me too; **~ nicht** not ... either; **wenn ~** even if; **wo ~ (immer)** wherever; **ist es ~ wahr?** is it really true?

Aubergine f aubergine, Am. eggplant

Audienz f audience (**bei** with)

auf prp. u. adv. räumlich: on; in; at; offen: open; wach, hoch: up; **~ Seite 20** on page 20; **~ der Straße** in (bsd. Am. on) the street; on the road; **~ der Welt** in the world; **~ See** at sea; **~ dem Lande** in the country; **~ dem Bahnhof** etc. at the station etc.; **~ Urlaub** on holiday; **die Uhr stellen ~** set* the watch to; **~ deutsch** in German; **~ deinen Wunsch** at your request; **~ die Sekunde genau** to the second; **~ und ab** up and down; **~ geht's!** let's go!

auf|arbeiten v/t. Rückstände: catch* up on; Möbel: refurbish; **~atmen** fig. v/i. heave a sigh of relief

Aufbau m building (up); Gefüge: structure; **2en** v/t. build* (up) (a. fig.); set* up; construct

auf|bauschen v/t. exaggerate; **~bekommen** v/t. Tür: get* open; Aufgabe: be* given; **~bereiten** v/t. process, clean, treat; **~bessern** v/t. Gehalt: raise; **~bewahren** v/t. keep*; **~bieten** v/t. muster; **~blasen** v/t. blow* up; **~bleiben** v/i. stay up; Tür etc.: remain open; **~blenden** v/i. mot. turn the headlights up; **~blicken** v/i. look up (**zu** at) (a. fig.); **~blitzen** v/i. flash (a. fig.)

aufbrausen v/i. fly* into a temper; **~d** adj. irascible

auf|brechen 1. v/t. break* od. force open; **2.** v/i. burst* open; fig. leave* (**nach** for); **~bringen** v/t. Geld: raise; Mut: muster; Mode: start; → **aufbekommen**; **aufgebracht**; **2bruch** m departure, start

aufbrühen v/t. Kaffee etc.: make*

auf|bürden v/t.: **j-m et. ~** burden s.o. with s.th.; **~decken** v/t. uncover; **~drängen** v/t.: **j-m et. ~** force s.th. on s.o.; **sich j-m ~** impose on s.o.; **sich ~** fig. , Idee etc.: suggest itself; **~drehen 1.** v/t. turn on; **2.** fig. v/i. open up

aufdringlich adj. obtrusive

Aufdruck m imprint; auf Briefmarken: overprint, surcharge

aufeinander adv. on top of each other; nacheinander: one after another; **~folgend** adj. successive

Aufenthalt m stay; rail. stop; **~sgenehmigung** f residence permit; **~sraum** m lounge, recreation room

aufersteh|en v/i. rise* (from the dead); **2ung** f resurrection

auf|essen v/t. eat* up; **~fahren** mot. v/i. crash (**auf** into); fig. start up

Auffahrt f Zufahrt: approach; zu e-m Haus: drive, Am. driveway

Auffahrunfall mot. m rear-end collision; Massen2: pileup

auf|fallen v/i. attract attention; **j-m ~** strike* s.o.; **~fallend, ~fällig** adj.

striking; conspicuous; *Kleider etc.*: flashy

auffangen *v/t.* catch* (*a. fig.*)

auffass|en *v/t.* understand* (**als** as); **Qung** *f* view; *Deutung*: interpretation

auffinden *v/t.* find*, discover

aufforder|n *v/t.*: *j-n ~, et. zu tun* ask (*stärker*: tell*) s.o. to do s.th.; **Qung** *f* request; *stärker*: demand

auffrischen *v/t.* freshen up; *Wissen*: brush up

aufführ|en *v/t. thea. etc.*: perform, present; *nennen*: state; *sich ~* behave; **Qung** *f thea. etc.*: performance; *Film*: showing

Aufgabe *f Arbeit*: task, job; *Pflicht*: duty; *Schu♐*: task, assignment; *math.* problem; *Haus♐*: homework; *Verzicht*: surrender; *es sich zur ~ machen* make* it one's business

Aufgang *m* staircase; *astr.* rising

aufgeben 1. *v/t. verzichten*: give* up; *Anzeige*: insert; *Brief etc.*: post, *Am.* mail, send*; *Gepäck*: check; *Hausaufgabe*: set*, give*, assign; *Bestellung*: place; **2.** *v/i. sich ergeben*: give* up *od.* in

aufge|bracht *adj.* furious; **~dreht** *f adj.* excited; **~dunsen** *adj.* puffed(-up)

aufgehen *v/i. sich öffnen*: open; *Sonne, Teig etc.*: rise*; *Rechnung etc.*: come* out even; *in Flammen ~* go* up in flames

aufge|hoben *fig. adj.*: *gut ~ sein bei* be* in good hands with; **~legt** *adj.*: *zu et. ~ sein* feel* like (doing) s.th.; *gut* (*schlecht*) *~* in a good (bad) mood; **~regt** *adj.* excited; nervous; **~schlossen** *fig. adj.* open-minded; *~ für* open to; **~weckt** *fig. adj.* bright

auf|greifen *v/t.* pick up; **haben** *f v/t.* *Hut etc.*: have* on, wear*; *Hausaufgabe*: have* to do; **~halten** *v/t.* stop, hold* up (*a. Verkehr, Dieb etc.*); *Augen, Tür etc.*: keep* open; *sich ~ (bei jm)* stay (with s.o.); **~hängen** *v/t.* hang* (up); *j-n ~* hang s.o.

aufheben *v/t. vom Boden*: pick up; *aufbewahren*: keep*; *abschaffen*: abolish; *Versammlung*: break* up; *sich gegenseitig ~* neutralize each other; → *aufgehoben*

Aufheben *n*: *viel ~s machen* make* a fuss (*von* about)

auf|heitern *v/t.* cheer up; *sich ~ Wetter*: clear up; **~helfen** *v/i.* help *s.o.* up; **~hellen** *v/t. u. v/refl.* brighten; **~hetzen** *v/t.*: *~ gegen* set* *s.o.* against; **~holen 1.** *v/t. Zeit*: make* up for; **2.** *v/i.* catch* up (*gegen* with); **~horchen** *v/i.* prick (up) one's ears; **~lassen** make* *s.o.* sit up; **~hören** *v/i.* stop, end, finish, quit*; *mit et. ~* stop (doing) s.th.; *hör(t) auf!* stop it!; **~kaufen** *v/t.* buy* up

aufklär|en *v/t.* clear up, *Verbrechen a.* solve; *j-n über* inform s.o. about; *j-n* (*sexuell*) *~* F tell* s.o. the facts of life; **Qung** *f* clearing up, solution; information; sex education; *phil.* enlightenment; *mil.* reconnaissance

auf|kleben *v/t.* paste od. stick* on; **Qkleber** *m* sticker; **~knöpfen** *v/t.* unbutton

aufkommen *v/i.* come* up; *Mode etc.*: come* into fashion *od.* use; *Zweifel, Gerücht etc.*: arise*; *~ für* pay* (for)

aufladen *v/t.* load; *electr.* charge

Auflage *f Buch*: edition; *Zeitung*: circulation

auf|lassen *v/t.* F *Tür etc.*: leave* open; F *Hut*: keep* on; **~lauern** *v/i.*: *j-m ~* waylay* s.o.

Auflauf *m* crowd; *Speise*: soufflé, pudding; **Qen** *naut. v/i.* run* aground

auf|leben *v/i.* feel* up (again); (*wieder*) *~ lassen* revive; **~legen 1.** *v/t.* put* on, lay* on; **2.** *tel. v/i.* hang* up

auflehn|en *v/t. u. v/refl.* stützen: lean* (*auf* on); *sich ~* rebel, revolt (*gegen* against); **Qung** *f* rebellion, revolt

auf|lesen *v/t.* pick up (*a. fig.*); **~leuchten** *v/i.* flash (up); **~listen** *v/t.* list (*a. Computer*); **~lockern** *v/t.* loosen up; *Unterricht etc.*: liven up

auflös|en *v/t.* dissolve; *Rätsel*: solve (*a. math.*); *in s-e Bestandteile*: disintegrate; **Qung** *f* (dis)solution; disintegration

aufmach|en *v/t.* open; *sich ~* set* out; **Qung** *f* get-up

aufmerksam *adj.* attentive (*auf* to); *zuvorkommend*: thoughtful; *j-n ~ machen auf* call s.o.'s attention to; **Qkeit** *f* attention; *Geschenk*: token

aufmuntern *v/t. ermuntern*: encourage; *aufheitern*: cheer up

Aufnahme *f e-r Tätigkeit*: taking up; *Empfang*: reception (*a. Klinik etc.*);

Zulassung: admission; *phot.* photo (-graph); *Ton*2: recording; *Film*: shooting; 2**fähig** *adj.* receptive (**für** of); **~gebühr** *f* admission fee; **~prüfung** *f* entrance exam(ination)

aufnehmen *v/t.* take* up (*a. Tätigkeit, Geld*); *aufheben*: pick up; *beherbergen*: put* *s.o.* up; *fassen*: hold*; *geistig*: take* in; *empfangen*: receive; *Schule, Verein*: admit; *phot.* take* a picture of; *Band, Platte*: record; *Ball*: take*; **es ~ mit** be* a match for

auf|passen *v/i. Schule etc.*: pay* attention; *vorsichtig sein*: take* care; **~ auf** take* care of, look after; *im Auge behalten*: keep* an eye on; **paß auf!** look out!; 2**prall** *m* impact; **~prallen** *v/i.*: **~ auf** hit*; **~pumpen** *v/t.* pump up; **~putschen** *v/t.* pep up; 2**putschmittel** *n* pep pill; **~raffen** *v/refl.*: **sich ~ zu** bring o.s. to *do s.th.*; **~räumen** *v/t.* tidy up; *Unfallstelle etc.*: clear

aufrecht *adj. u. adv.* upright (*a. fig.*); **~erhalten** *v/t.* maintain, keep* up

aufreg|en *v/t.* excite, upset*; **sich ~** get* excited *od.* upset (**über** about); **~end** *adj.* exciting; 2**ung** *f* excitement; *Getue*: fuss

auf|reiben *v/t.* wear* down; **~reibend** *adj.* stressful; **~reißen** *v/t.* tear* open; *Tür etc.*: fling* open; *Augen*: open wide; F *j-n*: pick up; **~reizend** *adj.* provocative; **~richten** *v/t.* put* up, raise; **sich ~** straighten up; *im Bett*: sit* up

aufrichtig *adj.* sincere; *offen*: frank; 2**keit** *f* sincerity; frankness

Aufriß *arch. m* elevation

aufrollen *v/t. u. v/refl.* roll up

Aufruf *m* call; *öffentlicher*: appeal (**zu** for); 2**en** *v/t.* call on (*a. Schule*)

Aufruhr *m* Rebellion: revolt; *Krawall*: riot; *seelisch*: turmoil

aufrühr|en *fig. v/t.* stir up; 2**er** *m* rebel; rioter; **~erisch** *adj.* rebellious

aufrunden *v/t. Summe*: round off

aufrüst|en *v/t. u. v/i.* (re)arm; 2**ung** *f* (re)armament

auf|rütteln *fig. v/t.* shake* up, rouse; **~sagen** *v/t.* say* (*Gedicht*: *a.* recite

aufsässig *adj.* rebellious

Aufsatz *m* essay; *Zeitungs*2: article; *Schul*2: composition, *Am. a.* theme; *Oberteil*: top

auf|saugen *v/t.* absorb (*a. fig.*); **~scheuern** *v/t.* chafe; **~schichten** *v/t.* pile up; **~schieben** *fig. v/t.* put* off, postpone; *verzögern*: delay

Aufschlag *m Aufprall*: impact; *Zuschlag*: extra charge; *Jacke etc.*: lapel; *Hose*: turnup, *Am.* cuff; *Tennis*: service; 2**en 1.** *v/t. Buch, Augen etc.*: open; *Zelt*: pitch; *Knie etc.*: cut*; *Seite 3 ~* open at page 30; **2.** *v/i. Tennis*: serve; **auf dem Boden ~** hit* the ground

auf|schließen *v/t.* unlock, open; **~schlitzen** *v/t.* slit* *od.* rip open; 2**schluß** *m* information (**über** on); **~schnappen** F *fig. v/t.* pick up; **~schneiden 1.** *v/t.* cut* open; *Fleisch*: cut* up; **2.** F *fig. v/i.* brag, boast, talk big; 2**schnitt** *m* (slices *pl.* of) cold meat, *Am.* cold cuts *pl.*; **~schnüren** *v/t.* untie; *Schuh*: unlace; **~schrauben** *v/t. öffnen*: unscrew; **~schrecken 1.** *v/t.* startle; **2.** *v/i.* start (up); 2**schrei** *m* yell; *angstvoll*: scream, outcry (*a. fig.*); **~schreiben** *v/t.* write* down; **~schreien** *v/i.* cry out, scream; 2**schrift** *f* inscription

Aufschub *m* postponement; *Verzögerung*: delay; *Vertagung*: adjournment; *e-r Frist*: respite

Aufschwung *m Turnen*: swing-up; *fig. bsd. econ.* recovery, upswing; boom

Aufsehen *n*: **~ erregen** attract attention; *stärker*: cause a sensation; 2**erregend** *adj.* sensational

Aufseher(in) guard

aufsetz|en *v/t. auf*: on; *abfassen*: draw* up; *aviat.* touch down; **sich ~** sit* up; 2**er** *m Sport*: bounce shot

Aufsicht *f* supervision, control; **~ führen Lehrer*: be* on (break) duty; *bei Prüfungen*: invigilate; *Am.* proctor; **~sbehörde** *f* supervisory board; **~srat** *m* board of directors; supervisory board

auf|sitzen *v/i. Reiter*: mount; **~spannen** *v/t.* stretch; *Schirm*: put* up; *Segel*: spread*; **~sparen** *v/t.* save; **~sperren** *v/t.* unlock; *Mund etc.*: open wide; **~spielen** *v/refl.* show* off; **sich ~ als** play; **~spießen** *v/t.* spear; *mit Hörnern*: gore; **~springen** *v/i.* jump up; *Tür*: fly* open; *Lippen etc.*: chap; **~spüren** *v/t.* track down; **~stacheln**

fig. v/t. goad (*s.o. into doing s.th.*) **~stamp·fen** *v/i.* stamp (one's foot)

Auf|stand *m* revolt, rebellion; **2stän·disch** *adj.* rebellious; **2e** *pl.* rebels *pl.*

auf|stapeln *v/t.* pile up; **~stechen** *v/t.* puncture, prick open; *med.* lance; **~stecken** *v/t. Haar etc.:* put* up; *F fig.* give* up; **~stehen** *v/i.* get* up, rise*; **~steigen** *v/i.* rise* (*a. fig.*); *auf Pferd, Rad etc.:* get* on; *Beruf, Sport:* be* promoted; *Am. Sport:* be* moved up to a higher division

aufstell|en *v/t.* set* up, put* up; *Wachen:* post; *Falle, Rekord:* set*; *Kandidaten, Spieler:* nominate; *Rechnung:* draw* up; *Liste:* make* up; **2ung** *f* putting up; nomination; *Liste:* list; *Mannschaft:* line-up

Aufstieg *m* ascent; *fig. a.* rise

auf|stöbern *fig. v/t.* ferret out; **~stoßen 1.** *v/t.* push open; **2.** *v/i.* rülpsen: belch

auf|stützen *v/refl.* lean* (*auf* on); **~suchen** *v/t. Ort:* visit; *Arzt:* see*

Auftakt *m mus.* upbeat; *fig.* prelude

auf|tanken *v/t.* fill up; *aviat.* refuel; **~tauchen** *v/i. erscheinen:* appear; *naut.* surface; *fig.* thaw; *Speisen:* defrost; **~teilen** *v/t.* divide (up)

Auftrag *m* instructions *pl.*, order (*a. econ.*); *mil.* mission; *im ~ von* on behalf of; **2en** *v/t. Speisen:* serve (up); *Farbe etc.:* apply; *j-m et. ~* ask (*stärker:* tell*) s.o. to do s.th; *F* **dick ~** exaggerate; **~geber** *m* principal; *Kunde:* customer

auf|treffen *v/i.* strike*, hit*; **~treiben** *F v/t.* get* hold of; *Geld:* raise; **~trennen** *v/t. Naht etc.:* undo*, cut* open

auftreten *v/i. thea. etc.:* appear (*als* as); *handeln:* behave, act; *vorkommen:* occur

Auftreten *n* appearance; behavio(u)r; *Vorkommen:* occurrence

Auftrieb *m phys.* buoyancy (*a. fig.*); *aviat.* lift; *fig.* impetus

Auftritt *m thea.* entrance; appearance (*a. fig.*); **~sverbot** *n* stage ban

auf|tun *v/refl.* open (*a. fig.*); *Abgrund:* yawn; **~türmen** *v/t.* pile *od.* heap up; *sich ~ Berge etc.:* tower up; *fig.* pile up; **~wachen** *v/i.* wake* up; **~wachsen** *v/i.* grow* up

Aufwand *m* expenditure (*an* of), *Geld:*

a. expense; *Prunk:* pomp

aufwärmen *v/t.* warm up; *fig.* bring* up

aufwärts *adv.* upward(s); **~gehen** *fig. v/i.* improve

auf|wecken *v/t.* wake* (up); **~weichen** *v/t.* soften; *Brot etc.:* soak; **~weisen** *v/t.* show*, have*; **~wenden** *v/t.* spend* (*für* on); *Mühe ~* take* pains; **~wendig** *adj. teuer:* costly; *Leben etc.:* extravagant; **~werfen** *v/t.* raise

aufwert|en *v/t. econ.* revalue; *fig.* increase the value of; **2ung** *f econ.* revaluation

aufwickeln *v/t. u. v/refl.* wind* up, roll up; *Haar:* put* in curlers

aufwiegeln *v/t.* stir up, incite, instigate

aufwiegen *fig. v/t.* make* up for

Aufwiegler *m* agitator; *Anstifter:* instigator; **2isch** *adj.* seditious

Aufwind *m meteor.* upwind; *im ~ fig.* on the upswing

auf|wirbeln *v/t.* whirl up; *fig.* (*viel*) *Staub ~* make* (quite) a stir

aufwischen *v/t.* wipe up

aufwühlen *fig. v/t.* stir, move

aufzähl|en *v/t.* name (one by one); list; **2ung** *f* enumeration, list

aufzeichn|en *v/t. TV, Funk etc.:* record, tape; *zeichnen:* draw*; **2ung** *f* recording; **~en** *pl. Notizen:* notes *pl.*

auf|zeigen *v/t.* show*; *verdeutlichen:* demonstrate; *Fehler etc.:* point out; **~ziehen 1.** *v/t.* draw* *od.* pull up; *öffnen:* (pull) open; *Kind:* bring* up; *Uhr etc.:* wind* (up); *Bild, Reifen:* mount; *j-n ~* tease s.o., *F* pull s.o.'s leg; **2.** *v/i. Sturm etc.:* come* up

Aufzug *m* lift, *Am.* elevator; *thea.* act; *fig. contp.* get-up

aufzwingen *v/t.: j-m et. ~* force s.th. upon s.o.

Augapfel *m* eyeball

Auge *n* eye; *ein blaues ~* a black eye; *mit bloßem ~* with the naked eye; *mit verbundenen ~n* blindfold; *in meinen ~n* in my view; *mit anderen ~n* in a different light; *aus den ~n verlieren* lose* sight of; *ein ~ zudrücken* turn a blind eye; *unter vier ~n* in private; *F ins ~ gehen* go* wrong

Augen|arzt *m*, **~ärztin** *f* eye specialist, ophthalmologist; **~blick** *m* moment, instant; **2blicklich 1.** *adj. gegenwärtig*: present; *sofortig*: immediate; *vorübergehend*: momentary; **2.** *adv.* at present, at the moment; immediately; **~braue** f eyebrow; **~licht** n eyesight; **~lid** n eyelid; **~maß** n: *ein gutes ~* a sure eye; *nach dem ~* by the eye; **~merk** n: *sein ~ richten auf* turn one's attention to; *fig. a.* have* in view; **~schein** m appearance; *in ~ nehmen* examine, view, inspect; **~zeuge** m eyewitness

August m August

Auktion f auction; **~ator** m auctioneer

Aula f (assembly) hall, *Am.* auditorium

aus 1. *prp. u. adv. räumlich*: mst out of, from; *Material*: of; *Grund*: out of; **~geschaltet** *etc.*: out, off; *zu Ende*: over, finished; *Sport*: out; *~ dem Fenster etc.* out of the window *etc.*; *~ München* from Munich; *~ Holz* (made) of wood; *~ Mitleid* out of pity; *~ Spaß* for fun; *~ Versehen* by mistake; *~ diesem Grunde* for this reason; *von hier ~* from here; F: *von mir ~!* I don't care!; *~ der Mode* out of fashion; *die Schule (das Spiel) ist ~* school (the game) is over; *ein/~ tech.* on/off; **2.** *n*: *im ~ (Ball)* out of play

aus|arbeiten *v/t.* work out; *entwerfen*: prepare; **~arten** *v/i.* get* out of hand; **~atmen** *v/t. u. v/i.* breathe out; **~baden** F *v/t.*: *et. ~ müssen* take* the rap for s.th.

Ausbau m *Erweiterung*: extension; *Fertigstellung*: completion; *e-s Motors etc.*: removal; **2en** *v/t.* extend, complete; remove; *verbessern*: improve; **2fähig** *adj.*: *et. ist ~* there is potential for growth *od.* development

ausbesser|n *v/t.* mend, repair, F *a.* fix; **2ung** f repair(ing)

Ausbeut|e f gain, profit; *Ertrag*: yield; **2en** *v/t.* exploit (*a. contp.*); **~ung** f exploitation

ausbild|en *v/t.* train, instruct; *j-n ~ zu* train s.o. to be; **2er(in)** instructor; **2ung** f training, instruction

ausbitten *v/t.*: *sich et. ~* request s.th.; *energisch*: insist on s.th.

ausbleiben *v/i.* stay out; *Erhofftes*: fail to materialize; *Brief, Hilfe, Regen etc.*: *... blieb aus ...* didn't come *od.* happen; *es konnte nicht ~* it was inevitable

Ausblick m outlook; → *Aussicht*

ausbrech|en *v/i.* break* out (*a. fig.*); *in Tränen ~* burst* into tears; **2er** m escaped prisoner

ausbreit|en *v/t.* spread* (out); *sich ~* spread*; **2ung** f spreading

ausbrennen *v/t.* burn* out

Ausbruch m *Flucht*: escape, breakout; *Feuer, Krieg, Seuche*: outbreak; *Vulkan*: eruption; *Gefühls2*: (out)burst

aus|brüten *v/t.* hatch (*a. fig.*)

Ausdauer f perseverance, stamina; *bsd. Sport*: *a.* staying power; **2nd** *adj.* persevering; *Sport*: tireless

ausdehnen *v/t. u. v/refl.* stretch; *fig.* expand, extend; **2ung** f expansion; extension

aus|denken *v/t.* think* s.th. up; *erfinden*: invent (*a. fig.*); **~drehen** *v/t.* turn off

Ausdruck m expression (*a. Gesichts2*), term; *Computer*: print-out; **2en** *v/t.* print out

ausdrück|en *v/t. Zigarette*: stub out; *äußern, zeigen*: express; **~lich** *adj.* express, explicit

ausdrucks|los *adj.* expressionless; *Gesicht*: *a.* blank; **~voll** *adj.* Blick *etc.*: expressive; **2weise** f language, style

Ausdünstung f exhalation; *Schweiß*: perspiration; *Geruch*: odo(u)r

auseinander *adv.* apart; separate(d); **~bringen** *v/t.* separate, **~gehen** *v/i.* *Versammlung, Menge*: break* up; *Meinungen*: differ; *sich trennen*: part; *Eheleute*: separate; **~halten** *v/t.* tell* apart; **~nehmen** *v/t.* take* apart (*a. fig.*); **~setzen** *v/t.* explain; *sich ~ mit* deal* with; argue with *s.o.*; **2setzung** f Streit: argument

auserlesen *adj.* choice, exquisite

ausfahr|en 1. *v/i.* go* for a drive *od.* ride; **2.** *v/t.* take* *s.o.* out; *aviat. Fahrwerk*: lower; **2t** f drive, ride; *mot.* exit

Ausfall m *tech., mot., Sport*: failure; *Verlust*: loss; **2en** *v/i. fall* out; *nicht stattfinden*: not take* place, be* cancelled; *tech., mot.* break* down, fail; *Ergebnis*: turn out, prove; **~lassen** cancel; *die Schule fällt aus* there is no school

aus|fallend, ~fällig *adj.* insulting

ausfertig|en *v/t. Dokument*: draw* up; *Rechnung etc.*: make* out; **2ung** f drawing up; *Abschrift*: copy; *in doppelter* ~ in two copies

ausfindig *adj.*: ~ **machen** find*

ausflippen F *v/i.* freak out

Ausflüchte *pl.* excuses *pl.*

Ausflug *m* trip, excursion, outing

Ausflügler *m* day-tripper

Ausfluß *m* outlet; *med.* discharge

aus|fragen *v/t.* question (*über* about); *neugierig*: sound out; **~fransen** *v/i.* fray; **~fressen** F *v/t.*: *et.* ~ **be*** up to no good

Ausfuhr *econ. f* export(ation)

ausführ|bar *adj.* practicable; **~en** *v/t. j-n*: take* out; *et.*: carry out; *econ.* export; *darlegen*: explain

ausführlich 1. *adj.* detailed; *umfassend*: comprehensive; **2.** *adv.* in detail; **2keit** *f*: *in aller* ~ in great detail

Ausführung *f* execution, performance; *Typ*: type, model, design

ausfüllen *v/t. Formular*: fill in (*Am.* out)

Ausgabe *f Verteilung*: distribution; *Buch etc.*: edition; *Geld*: expense; *Zeitschrift*: issue; *Computer*: output

Ausgang *m* exit, way out; *Ende*: end; *Ergebnis*: result, outcome; *tech., electr.* output, outlet; **~spunkt** *m* starting point; **~ssperre** *pol. f* curfew

ausgeben *v/t.* give* out; *Geld*: spend*; F *j-m e-n* ~ buy* s.o. a drink; *sich* ~ *als* pass o.s. off as

ausge|beult *adj.* baggy; **~bildet** *adj.* trained, skilled; **~bucht** *adj.* booked up; **~dehnt** *adj.* extensive; **~dient** *adj.*: **~ haben** fig. have* had its day; **~fallen** *adj.* odd, unusual; **~glichen** *adj.* (well-)balanced

ausgehen *v/i.* go* out; *enden*: end; *Haare*: fall* out; *Geld, Vorräte*: run* out; *leer* ~ get* nothing; ~ *von* start from od. at; *herrühren*: come from; *davon* ~, *daß* assume that; *ihm ging das Geld aus* he ran out of money

ausge|kocht *adj.* cunning; *Schwindler etc.*: out-and-out; **lassen** fig. *adj.* cheerful; *stärker*: hilarious; **~macht** *adj.* agreed(-on); *Ort etc.*: set; *Unsinn etc.*: downright; **~nommen** *prp.* with the exception of; **~prägt** *adj.* marked, pronounced; **~rechnet** *adv.*: ~ *er* he of all people; ~ *heute* today of all days; **~schlossen** out of the question; **~storben** *adj.* extinct

ausge|sucht fig. *adj.* select, choice; **~wachsen** *adj.* full-grown; **~waschen** *adj.*: **~e** *Jeans* faded jeans; **~wogen** *adj.* (well-)balanced; **~zeichnet** *adj.* excellent

ausgiebig *adj.* extensive, thorough; *Mahlzeit*: substantial

ausgießen *v/t.* pour out

Ausgleich *m* compensation; *Sport*: equalization, *Am.* even score; *Tennis*: deuce; **2en** *v/t. u. v/i.* equalize (*Brt. a.* Sport); *econ.* balance; *Am. Sport*: make* the score even; *Verlust*: compensate; **~ssport** *m* remedial exercises *pl.*; **~stor** *n*, **~streffer** *m* equalizer, *Am.* tying point

aus|graben *v/t.* dig* out od. up (*a.fig.*); **2grabungen** *pl.* excavations *pl.*; **~grenzen** *v/t.* isolate *s.o.*

Ausguß *m* (kitchen) sink

aus|halten 1. *v/t.* bear*, stand*; *Liebhaber*: keep; *nicht auszuhalten sein* be unbearable; **2.** *v/i.* hold out; **~händigen** *v/t.* hand over

Aushang *m* notice; *formell*: bulletin

aushänge|n *v/t.* hang* out, put* up; *Tür*: unhinge; **2schild** fig. *n* figurehead

aus|heben *v/t. Graben*: dig*; *Spielhölle etc.*: bust, raid; **~helfen** *v/i.* help out

Aushilf|e *f* (temporary) help; **~s...** *in Zssgn Kellner etc.*: temporary

aus|holen *v/i.*: *zum Schlag* ~ swing* (to strike); *mit der Axt* ~ raise the axe; fig. *weit* ~ go* far back; **~horchen** *v/t.* sound (*über* on); **~hungern** *v/t.* starve out; **~kennen** *v/refl.*: *sich* ~ (*in*) know* one's way (about); fig. know* a lot (about), be* at home (in); **2klang** *m* end; **~klingen** *v/i. Fest*: draw* to a close; **~klopfen** *v/t. Pfeife*: knock out

auskommen *v/i.* go*; ~ *mit et.*: manage with; *j-m*: get* along with

Auskommen *n*: *sein* ~ *haben* make* one's living

auskundschaften *v/t.* explore; *mil.* scout; fig. find* out (about)

Auskunft *f* information; *Schalter*: information desk; *tel.* inquiries *pl.*

aus|lachen *v/t.* laugh at (*wegen* for); **~laden** *v/t.* unload

Auslage *f* window display; **~n** *pl.* expenses *pl.*

Aus|land n: **das ~** foreign countries pl.; **ins ~, im ~** abroad; **~länder(in)** foreigner; **~länderfeindlichkeit** f, **~länderhaß** m hostility to foreigners, xenophobia; **2ländisch** adj. foreign; **2landsgespräch** n international call; **~landskorrespondent(in)** foreign correspondent

auslass|en v/t. leave* out; Fett: melt; Saum etc.: let* out; **s-n Zorn an j-m ~** take* it out on s.o.; **sich ~ über** express o.s. on; **2ung** f omission; **2ungszeichen** gr. n apostrophe

Auslauf m room to move about; Hund: exercise; **2en** v/i. naut. leave* port; Gefäß: leak; Flüssigkeit: run* out

Ausläufer m meteor. Hoch: ridge; Tief: trough; geogr. pl. foothills pl.

Auslaufmodell econ. n discontinued od. phase-out (Am. close-out) model

ausleg|en v/t. lay* out; mit Teppichboden: carpet; mit Papier etc.: line; Waren: display; deuten: interpret; Geld: advance; **2ung** f interpretation

ausleihen v/t. verleihen: lend* (out), loan; sich ~: borrow; **~lernen** v/i. complete one's training; **man lernt nie aus** we live and learn

Auslese f choice, selection; fig. pick; **2n** v/t. pick out, select; Buch: finish

ausliefern v/t. hand od. turn over, deliver (up); pol. extradite; **2ung** f delivery; extradition

aus|liegen v/i. be* laid out; **~löschen** v/t. put* out; fig. wipe out; **~losen** v/t. draw* (lots) for

auslös|en v/t. tech., Alarm etc.: release; Gefangene, Pfand: redeem; verursachen: cause, start, trigger s.th. off; **2er** m (phot. shutter) release; trigger

aus|machen v/t. Feuer etc.: put* out; Licht etc.: turn off; Termin etc.: arrange; Preis etc.: agree on; Teil: make* up; Betrag: amount to; Streit: settle; sichten: sight, spot; **macht es Ihnen et. aus (, wenn...)?** do you mind (if ...)?; **es macht mir nichts aus** I don't mind; **das macht (gar) nichts aus** that doesn't matter (at all); **~malen** v/t. paint; **sich et. ~** imagine s.th.

Ausmaß n extent; **~e** pl. proportions pl.

aus|merzen v/t. eliminate; **~messen** v/t. measure

Ausnahme f exception; **~ezustand**

pol. m state of emergency; **2slos** adv. without exception; **2sweise** adv. by way of exception; just this once

ausnehmen v/t. Fisch etc.: clean; ausschließen: except; F finanziell: fleece; **~d** adv. exceptionally

aus|nutzen v/t. use; take* advantage of (a. contp.); ausbeuten: exploit; **~pakken 1.** v/t. unpack; **2.** v/i. F fig. talk; **~pfeifen** v/t. boo, hiss; **~plaudern** v/t. blab od. let* out; **~plündern** v/t. plunder, rob; **~probieren** v/t. try (out), test

Auspuff mot. m exhaust; **~gase** mot. pl. exhaust fumes pl.; **~rohr** mot. n exhaust pipe; **~topf** mot. m silencer, bsd. Am. muffler

aus|quartieren v/t. move out; **~radieren** v/t. erase; fig. wipe out; **~rangieren** v/t. discard; **~rauben** v/t. rob; **~räumen** v/t. empty; Zimmer, Möbel: clear out; fig. Zweifel etc.: clear up; **~rechnen** v/t. work out

Ausrede f excuse; **2n 1.** v/i. finish speaking; **~ lassen** hear* s.o. out; **lassen Sie mich ~!** don't interrupt me!; **2.** v/t.: **j-m et. ~** talk s.o. out of s.th.

ausreichen v/i. be* enough; **~d** adj. sufficient, enough; Zensur: (barely) passing, only average, weak, D

Ausreise f departure; **2n** v/i. leave* (a od. one's country); **~visum** n exit visa

ausreiß|en 1. v/t. pull od. tear* out; **2.** F v/i. run* away; **2er(in)** runaway

aus|renken v/t. dislocate; **~richten** v/t. j-m et.: tell* s.o. s.th.; Botschaft: deliver; erreichen: accomplish; Fest: arrange; **richte ihr e-n Gruß von mir aus!** give her my regards!; **kann ich et. ~?** can I take a message?

ausrott|en v/t. exterminate; **2ung** f extermination; bsd. Tierart: extinction

ausrücken v/i. F run away; mil. march out

Ausruf m cry, shout; **2en** v/t. cry, shout, exclaim; Namen etc.: call out; pol. proclaim; **~ung** pol. f proclamation; **~ungszeichen** n exclamation mark

ausruhen v/i., v/t. u. v/refl. rest

ausrüst|en v/t. equip; **2ung** f equipment

ausrutschen v/i. slip

Aussage f statement; jur. evidence; **2n** v/t. state, declare; jur. testify

aus|schalten v/t. switch off; fig. eliminate; **~schauen** v/i.: **~ nach** be* on the look-out for, watch for

ausscheid|en 1. v/i. be* ruled out; *Sport etc.*: drop out (**aus** of); *Amt*: retire (**aus** from); **~ aus Firma**: leave*; **2.** v/t. eliminate; *med. etc.*: secrete, exude; **2ung** f elimination (a. *Sport*); *med.* secretion; **2ungs...** in Zssgn Spiel etc.: qualifying

aus|schelten, ~schimpfen v/t. scold (**wegen** for); **~schlachten** fig. v/t. *Auto etc.*: salvage, Brt. a. cannibalize; *contp.* exploit; **~schlafen 1.** v/i. sleep* in; **2.** v/t.: **s-n Rausch ~** sleep* it off

Ausschlag m med. rash; *Zeiger*: deflection; **den ~ geben** decide it; **2en 1.** v/t. *Zahn etc.*: knock out; fig. refuse, decline; **2.** v/i. *Pferd*: kick; *bot.* bud; *Zeiger*: deflect; **2gebend** adj. decisive

ausschließ|en v/t. lock out; fig. exclude; *ausstoßen*: expel; *Sport*: disqualify; **~lich** adj. exclusive

Ausschluß m exclusion; *Schule etc.*: expulsion; *Sport*: disqualification; **unter ~ der Öffentlichkeit** in closed session

aus|schmücken v/t. decorate; fig. embellish; **~schneiden** v/t. cut* out

Ausschnitt m Kleidung: neck; *Zeitungs*2: cutting, Am. clipping; fig. part; *Buch, Rede*: extract; **mit tiefem ~** low-necked

ausschreib|en v/t. write* out (a. *Scheck etc.*); *Stelle etc.*: advertise; **2ung** f advertisement

Ausschreitungen pl. violence sg.; riots pl.

Ausschuß m committee, board; *Abfall*: refuse, waste, rejects pl.

aus|schütteln v/t. shake* out; **~schütten** v/t. pour out (a. fig.); *verschütten*: spill*; *econ.* pay; **sich vor Lachen ~** split* one's sides

ausschweif|end adj. dissolute; **2ung** f debauchery, excess

aussehen v/i. look; *krank (traurig)* ~ look ill (sad); **~ wie** look like; **wie sieht er aus?** what does he look like?

Aussehen n look(s pl.), appearance

aussein F v/i. be* over; be* out; → **aus; ~ auf** be* out for; **j-s Geld**: be* after

außen adv. outside; **nach ~ (hin)** outward(s); fig. outwardly; **~ vor lassen**

fig. leave* aside; **2bordmotor** m outboard motor

aussenden v/t. send* out

Außen|dienst m field service; **~handel** m foreign trade; **~minister** m Brt. Foreign Secretary, Am. Secretary of State; **~ministerium** n Brt. Foreign Office, Am. State Department; **~politik** f foreign affairs pl.; *bestimmte*: foreign policy; **2politisch** adj. foreign-policy; **~seite** f outside; **~seiter** m outsider; **~spiegel** mot. m outside rear-view mirror; **~stände** econ. pl. receivables pl.; **~stelle** f branch; **~stürmer** m Sport: winger; **~welt** f outside world

außer 1. prp. out of; *neben*: beside(s), Am. aside from; *ausgenommen*: except; **~ sich sein** be beside o.s. (**vor Freude** with joy); **alle ~ e-m** all but one; → **Betrieb, Gefahr** etc.; **2.** cj.: **~ daß** except that; **~ wenn** unless; **~dem** cj. besides, moreover

äußere adj. exterior, outer, outward

Äußere n exterior, outside; *Erscheinung*: (outward) appearance

außer|gewöhnlich adj. unusual; **~halb** prp. u. adv. outside; out of; *jenseits*: beyond; **~irdisch** adj. extraterrestrial

äußerlich adj. external, outward; **2keit** f formality; minor detail

äußern v/t. utter, express; **sich ~** say s.th.; **sich ~ zu** od. **über** express o.s. on

außer|ordentlich adj. extraordinary; **~planmäßig** adj. unscheduled

äußerst 1. adj. outermost; fig. extreme; **im ~en Fall** at (the) worst; *höchstens*: at (the) most **2.** adv. extremely

außerstande adj.: **~ sein** be* unable

Äußerung f utterance, remark

aussetz|en 1. v/t. Kind, Tier: abandon; **mit** dat.: expose to; *Preis etc.*: offer; **et. auszusetzen haben an** find* fault with; **2.** v/i. stop, break* off; *Motor etc.*: fail

Aussicht f view (**auf** of); fig. prospect (of), chance (**auf Erfolg** of success); **2slos** adj. hopeless, desperate; **~spunkt** m vantage point; **2sreich** adj. promising; **~sturm** m lookout tower

Aussiedler m resettler, evacuee

aussitzen v/t. sit s.th. out

aussöhn|en v/refl.: **sich ~ (mit)** be-

come* reconciled (with), F make* it up (with); **≳ung** f reconciliation;
aus|sondern, ~sortieren v/t. sort out; **~spannen 1.** v/t. Zugtier: unharness; F fig. pinch; **2.** fig. v/i. (take* a) rest, relax

aussperr|en v/t. lock out (a. Arbeiter); **≳ung** f lock-out

aus|spielen 1. v/t. Karte: play; j-n **gegen** j-n ~ play s.o. off against s.o.; **2.** v/i. Kartenspiel: lead*; **er hat ausgespielt** fig. he is done for; **~spionieren** v/t. spy out

Aussprache f pronunciation; discussion; private heart-to-heart (talk)

aussprechen v/t. pronounce; Meinung etc.: express; **sich ~ für (gegen)** speak* for (against); **sich mit j-m gründlich ~** have* a heart-to-heart talk with s.o.; → **ausreden**

Ausspruch m saying; Bemerkung: remark

aus|spucken v/t. u. v/t. spit* out; **~spülen** v/t. rinse

Ausstand m strike, F walkout

ausstatt|en v/t. fit out, equip, furnish; **≳ung** f equipment, furnishings pl.; design

aus|stechen v/t. cut* out (a. fig.); Auge: put* out; **~stehen 1.** v/t. Schmerzen etc.: stand*, endure; F **ich kann ihn (es) nicht ~** I can't stand him (it); **2.** v/i. (noch) ~ be* outstanding od. overdue; **~steigen** v/i. get* out (aus of); (a. ~ aus) Zug, Bus: get* off; fig. drop out; **≳steiger** F m drop-out

ausstell|en v/t. exhibit, display, show*; Scheck etc.: make* out; Paß etc.: issue; **≳er** m exhibitor; issuer; Scheck: drawer; **≳ung** f exhibition, show

aussterben v/i. die out, become* extinct (beide a. fig.)

Aussteuer f trousseau; Mitgift: dowry

aussteuer|n electr. v/t. modulate; **≳ung** electr. f modulation; level control

Ausstieg m exit; fig. withdrawal (aus from)

ausstopfen v/t. stuff; auspolstern: pad

Ausstoß m tech., phys. discharge, ejection; Leistung: output; **≳en** v/t. tech., phys. give* off, eject, emit; econ. turn out; Schrei, Seufzer: give*; ausschließen: expel; **~ung** f expulsion

aus|strahlen v/t. Wärme, Glück etc.: radiate; TV, Funk: broadcast*, transmit; **≳strahlung** f radiation; broadcast; fig. magnetism, charisma; **~strecken** v/t. stretch (out); **~streichen** v/t. strike* out; **~strömen** v/i. escape (aus from); **~suchen** v/t. choose*, pick

Austausch m exchange (a. in Zssgn Schüler etc.); **≳bar** adj. exchangeable; **≳en** v/t. exchange (gegen for)

austeil|en v/t. distribute, hand out; Karten, Schläge: deal* (out)

Auster zo. f oyster

austoben v/refl. let* off steam

austragen v/t. Briefe etc.: deliver; Streit etc.: settle; Wettkampf etc.: hold*; **das Kind ~** (nicht abtreiben) have* the baby; **≳ungsort** m Sport: venue

Austral|ien Australia; **~ier(in), ≳isch** adj. Australian

austreib|en v/t. Teufel: exorcise; F **j-m et. ~** cure s.o. of s.th.

aus|treten 1. v/t. Feuer: tread* od. stamp out; Schuhe: wear* out; **2.** v/i. entweichen: escape (aus from); F go* to the toilet (Am. bathroom); ~ **aus** Verein etc.: leave*; formell: resign from; **~trinken** v/t. drink* up; leeren: empty; **≳tritt** m leaving (a. Schule); resignation; escape; **~trocknen** v/t. u. v/i. dry up

ausüb|en v/t. Beruf, Sport: practi|se, Am. -ce; Amt: hold*; Macht: exercise; Druck: exert; **≳ung** f practice; exercise

Ausverkauf econ. m (clearance) sale; **≳t** econ., thea. adj. sold out; **vor ~em Haus spielen** play to a full house

Auswahl f choice, selection (beide a. econ.); Sport: representative team

auswählen v/t. choose*, select

Auswander|er m emigrant; **≳n** v/i. emigrate; **~ung** f emigration

auswärt|ig adj. out-of-town; pol. foreign; **das Auswärtige Amt** → **Außenministerium**; **~s** adv. out of town; ~ **essen** eat* out; **≳ssieg** m Sport: away victory; **≳sspiel** n away game

auswechs|eln v/t. exchange (gegen for); Rad etc.: change; ersetzen: replace; Sport: substitute; **wie ausgewechselt** (like) a different person; **≳elspieler(in)** substitute

Ausweg m way out; **2los** adj. hopeless; **~losigkeit** f hopelessness
ausweichen v/i. make* way (dat. for); fig. j-m: avoid; e-r Frage: evade; **~d** adj. evasive
ausweinen v/refl. have* a good cry
Ausweis m identification (card); Mitglieds2 etc.: card; **2en** v/t. expel; **sich ~** identify o.s.; **~papiere** pl. documents pl.; **~ung** f expulsion
ausweiten fig. v/t. expand
auswendig adv. by heart; **et. ~ können** know* s.th. by heart; **~ lernen** memorize; learn* by heart
aus|werfen v/t. throw* out (a. Daten); bsd. Anker: cast*; tech. eject; **~werten** v/t. Daten etc.: evaluate, analyze, interpret; ausnützen: utilize, exploit; **2wertung** f evaluation; utilization; **~wickeln** v/t. unwrap; **~wirken** v/refl.: **sich ~ auf** affect; **sich positiv ~** have* a favo(u)rable effect; **2wirkung** f effect; **~wischen** v/t. wipe out; F j-m eins **~** do* a number on s.o.; **~wringen** v/t. wring* out; **2wuchs** m excess; **~wuchten** tech. v/t. balance
aus|zahlen v/t. pay* (out); j-n: pay* off; **sich ~** pay*; **~zählen** v/t. count; Boxer: count out
Auszahlung f payment; paying off
auszeichn|en v/t. Ware: price, mark out; **sich ~** distinguish o.s.; **j-n mit et. ~** award s.th. to s.o.; **2ung** f marking; fig. distinction, hono(u)r; Preis: award; Orden: decoration
ausziehen 1. v/t. Kleidung: take* off; Tisch, Antenne: pull out; **sich ~** undress; **2.** v/i. move out
Auszubildende(r) apprentice, trainee
Auszug m move, removal; aus e-m Buch etc.: extract, excerpt; Konto2: statement (of account)

authentisch adj. authentic, genuine
Autis|mus psych. m autism; **2tisch** adj. autistic
Auto n car, bsd. Am. a. (auto)mobile; (mit dem) **~ fahren** drive*, go* by car
Autobahn f Brt. motorway; Am. expressway; **~dreieck** n interchange; **~gebühr** f toll; **2kreuz** n interchange
Autobiographie f autobiography
Auto|bombe f car bomb; **~bus** m → Bus; **~fähre** f car ferry **~fahrer** m motorist, driver; **2fahrt** f drive; **~friedhof** F m scrapyard, Am. auto junkyard
autogen psych. adj.: **~es Training** relaxation exercises pl.
Autogramm n autograph; **~jäger** m autograph hunter
Auto|karte f road map; **~kino** n drive-in cinema (Am. theater)
Automat m vending (Brt. a. slot) machine; tech. robot; △ nicht automat; → Spielautomat; **~ik** tech f automatic (system od. control); mot. automatic transmission; Wagen: automatic; **~ion** f automation; **2isch** adj. automatic
Auto|mechaniker m car od. garage (Am. auto) mechanic; **~mobil** n → Auto
autonom adj. autonomous
Autonummer f licen|ce (Am. -se) number
Autor m author
Autoreparaturwerkstatt f car repair shop, garage
Autorin f author(ess)
autori|sieren v/t. authorize; **~tär** adj. authoritarian; **2tät** f authority
Auto|telefon n car phone; **~vermietung** f car hire (Am. rental) service; **~waschanlage** f car wash
Axt f ax(e)

B

Bach m brook, stream, Am. a. creek
Backblech n baking sheet
Backbord naut. n port (a. in Zssgn)

Backe f cheek
backen v/t. u. v/i. bake; südd. fry
Backenzahn m molar (tooth)

Bäcker *m* baker; *beim ~* at the baker's; **~ei** *f* bakery, baker's (shop)

Back|form *f* baking tin; **~hendl** *östr.* fried chicken; **~obst** *n* dried fruit; **~ofen** *m* oven; **~pflaume** *f* prune; **~pulver** *n* baking powder; **~stein** *m* brick; **~waren** *pl.* breads *pl.* and pastries *pl.*

Bad *n* bath; *im Freien:* swim, *Brt. a.* bathe; bath(room); → *Badeort; ein ~ nehmen* → *baden* 1

Bade|anstalt *f* swimming pool, public baths *pl.*; **~anzug** *m* swimsuit; **~hose** *f* bathing-trunks *pl.*; **~kappe** *f* bathing cap; **~mantel** *m* bathrobe; **~meister** *m* pool *od.* bath attendant

baden 1. *v/i.* take* *od.* have* a bath, *Am. a.* bathe; *im Freien:* swim*, *bsd. Brt. a.* bathe; *~ gehen* go* swimming; **2.** *v/t.* *Wunde etc.* bathe; *Baby: Brt. a.* bath

Bade|ort *m* seaside resort; *Kurbad:* health resort; **~tuch** *n* bath towel; **~wanne** *f* bathtub; **~zimmer** *n* bath(room)

baff *adj.* F*~ sein* be* flabbergasted

Bafög *n* : *~ erhalten* get* a grant

Bagatelle *f* trifle; **~schaden** *m* superficial damage

Bagger *m* excavator; *Schwimm≋:* dredge(r); **2n** *v/i.* excavate; dredge

Bahn *f* railway, *Am.* railroad; *Zug:* train; *Weg, Kurs:* way, path, course; *Sport:* track; course; *mit der ~* by rail; *~ frei!* make way!; *Zssgn* → *a.* **Eisenbahn; 2brechend** *adj.* epoch-making; **~damm** *m* railway (*Am.* railroad) embankment

bahnen *v/t.:* *den Weg ~* clear the way (*dat.* for *s.o. od. s.th.*); *sich e-n Weg ~* force *od.* work one's way

Bahn|hof *m* (railway, *Am.* railroad) station; **~linie** *f* railway (*Am.* railroad) line; **~steig** *m* platform; **~übergang** *m* level (*Am.* grade) crossing

Bahre *f* stretcher; *Toten≋:* bier

Baisse *econ. f* fall, slump

Bajonett *mil. n* bayonet

Bakterien *pl.* germs *pl.*, bacteria *pl.*

balancieren *v/t. u. v/i.* balance

bald *adv.* soon; F *beinahe:* almost, nearly; *so ~ wie möglich* as soon as possible; *~ig adj.* speedy; *~e Antwort econ.* early reply; *auf (ein) ~es Wiedersehen!* see you again soon!

balgen *v/refl.* scuffle (*um* for)

Balken *m* beam

Balkon *m* balcony; **~tür** *f* French window

Ball *m* ball; *Tanz≋: a.* dance; *am ~ sein Sport* have* the ball; *am ~ bleiben fig.* stick* to it

Ballade *f* ballad

Ballast *m* ballast; *fig. a.* burden; **~stoffe** *pl.* roughage *sg.*, bulk *sg.*

ballen *v/t. Faust:* clench

Ballen *m* bale; *anat.* ball

Ballett *n* ballet

Ballon *m* balloon

Ballungs|raum *m*, **~zentrum** *n* congested area, conurbation

Balsam *m* balm (*a. fig.*)

Bambus *m* bamboo; **~rohr** *n* bamboo (cane)

banal *adj.* banal, trite

Banane *f* banana; **~nrepublik** *f* banana republic

Banause *m* philistine

Band¹ *n Zier≋:* ribbon; *Meß≋, Ton≋, Ziel≋:* tape; *Hut≋:* band; *anat.* ligament; *fig.* tie, link; *auf ~ aufnehmen* tape; *am laufenden ~ fig.* continuously

Band² *m* volume

Bandag|e *f* bandage; **2ieren** *v/t.* bandage (up)

Bandbreite *f electr.* bandwidth; *fig.* range

Bande *f* gang; *Billard:* cushions *pl.*; *Eishockey:* boards *pl.*; *Kegeln:* gutter

Bänderriß *med. m* torn ligament

bändigen *v/t. Tier:* tame (*a. fig.*); *Kinder, Zorn etc.:* restrain, control

Bandit *m* bandit, outlaw

Band|maß *n* tape measure; **~säge** *f* band-saw; **~scheibe** *anat. f* (intervertebral) dis|c, *Am.* -k; **~scheibenschaden** *med. m*, **~scheibenvorfall** *med. m* slipped disc; **~wurm** *zo. m* tapeworm

bang|(e) *adj.* afraid; *besorgt:* anxious; *j-m bange machen* frighten *od.* scare *s.o.*; **2e** *f: keine ~* (have) no fear!; **~en** *v/i.* be* anxious *od.* worried (*um* about)

Bank¹ *f* bench; *Schul≋:* desk; F *durch die ~* without exception; *auf die lange ~ schieben* put* off

Bank² *econ. f* bank; *auf der ~* in the bank; **~angestellte(r)** bank clerk *od.* employee; **~automat** *m* → *Geldautomat*; **~einlage** *f* deposit

B

Bankett n banquet
Bankgeschäfte econ. pl. banking transactions pl.
Bankier m banker
Bank|konto n bank(ing) account; **~leitzahl** f bank (sorting) code, Am. A.B.A. number; **~note** f (bank) note, Am. a. bill; **~raub** m bank robbery
bankrott adj. bankrupt
Bankrott m bankruptcy; **~ machen** go* bankrupt
Bankverbindung f account(s pl.), account details pl.
Bann m ban; Zauber: spell; **2en** v/t. ward off; (wie) gebannt spellbound
Banner n banner (a. fig.)
bar adj. econ. (in) cash; bloß: bare; rein: pure; **gegen ~** for cash
Bar f bar; nightclub
Bär zo. m bear
Baracke f hut; contp. shack; ⚠ nicht barrack
Barbar m barbarian; **2isch** adj. barbarous; Verbrechen etc.: a. atrocious
Bardame f barmaid
barfuß adj. u. adv. barefoot
Bargeld n cash; **2los** adj. noncash
Barhocker m bar stool
Bariton mus. m baritone
Barkasse naut. f launch
barmherzig adj. merciful; mild: charitable; **2keit** f mercy; charity
Barmixer m barman
Barometer n barometer
Baron m baron; **~in** f baroness
Barren m bar, ingot; Gold-, Silber2 pl.: a. bullion sg.; Sport: parallel bars pl.
Barriere f barrier
Barrikade f barricade
Barsch zo. m perch
barsch adj. rough, gruff, brusque
Barscheck econ. m open cheque, Am. (negotiable) check
Bart m beard; Schlüssel2: bit; sich e-n ~ wachsen lassen grow* a beard
bärtig adj. bearded
Barzahlung f cash payment
Basar m bazaar
Base f chem. base; Kusine: cousin
basieren v/i.: **~ auf** be* based on
Basis f basis; mil., arch. base
Baskenmütze f beret
Baß mus. m bass (a. in Zssgn)
Bassin n basin; (swimming) pool

Bassist mus. m bass singer od. player
Bast m bast; am Geweih: velvet
Bastard m biol. hybrid; Hund: mongrel; V bastard
bast|eln v/t. **1.** v/i. make* od. repair things o.s.; **2.** build*, make*;**2ler** m home handyman, do-it-yourselfer
Batik m, f batik
Batist m cambric
Batterie mil., electr. f battery
Bau m Vorgang: building, construction; Körper2 etc.: build, frame; Gebäude: building; Tier2: hole; e-s Raubtiers: den; im ~ under construction; **~arbeiten** pl. construction work sg.; Straße: road works pl.; **~arbeiter** m construction worker; **~art** f style (of construction); Typ: type, model
Bauch m belly (a. fig.); anat. abdomen; F tummy; **2ig** adj. bulgy; **~landung** f belly landing; **~redner** m ventriloquist; **~schmerzen** pl. stomach-ache sg.; **~tanz** m belly dancing
bauen 1. v/t. build*, construct, Instrument, Möbel etc.: a. make*; **2.** fig. v/i.: **~ auf** rely od. count on
Bauer[1] m farmer; Schach: pawn
Bauer[2] n, m Vogel2: (bird)cage
Bäuerin f farmer's wife, farmer
bäuerlich adj. rural; Stil: rustic
Bauern|fänger contp. m trickster, con man; **~haus** n farmhouse; **~hof** m farm; **~möbel** pl. rustic furniture sg.
bau|fällig adj. dilapidated; **2firma** f builders and contractors pl.; **2genehmigung** f building permit; **2gerüst** n scaffold(ing); **2herr** m owner; **2holz** n timber, Am. a. lumber; **2ingenieur** m civil engineer; **2jahr** n year of construction; **~1995** 1995 model; **2kasten** m box of bricks (Am. building blocks); technischer: construction set; Modell2: kit; **2leiter** m building supervisor; **~lich** adj. structural
Baum m tree
Baumarkt m do-it-yourself superstore
baumeln v/i. dangle, swing*; mit den Beinen ~ dangle one's legs
Baum|schule f nursery; **~stamm** m trunk; gefällter: log; **~wolle** f cotton
Bau|plan m architectural drawing; blueprints pl.; **~platz** m building site
Bausch m wad, ball; in ~ und Bogen lock, stock and barrel

Bausparkasse f building society, *Am.* building and loan association

Bau|stein m brick; *Spielzeug:* (building) block; *fig.* element; **~stelle** f building site; *mot.* roadworks *pl.*, *Am.* construction zone; **~stil** m (architectural) style; **~stoff** m building material; **~techniker** m engineer; **~teil** n component (part), unit, module; **~unternehmer** m building contractor; **~vorschriften** pl. building regulations *pl.*; **~werk** n building; **~zaun** m hoarding; **~zeichner** m draughtsman, *Am.* draftsman

Bayern Bavaria

Bay|er(in), **⊆(e)risch** adj. Bavarian

Bazillus m bacillus, germ

beabsichtigen v/t. intend, plan; *es war beabsichtigt* it was intentional

beacht|en v/t. pay* attention to; *Regel:* observe, follow ; **~ Sie, daß ...** note that ...; *nicht ~* take* no notice of; *Vorschrift etc.:* disregard; **~lich** adj. remarkable; *beträchtlich:* considerable; **⊆ung** f attention; *Berücksichtigung:* consideration; *Befolgung:* observance

Beamt|e m, *adj.* official; *Polizei etc.:* officer; *Staats⊆:* civil servant

beängstigend adj. alarming

beanspruch|en v/t. claim; *Zeit, Raum etc.:* take* up; *tech.* stress; **⊆ung** f claim; *tech., nervliche:* stress, strain

bean|standen v/t. *Ware:* complain about; *Einwand erheben:* object to; **~tragen** v/t. apply for; *jur., parl.* move (for); *vorschlagen:* propose

beantwort|en v/t. answer, reply to; **⊆ung** f answer, reply

bearbeit|en v/t. work; *agr.* till; *Steine:* hew*; *verarbeiten:* process; *Fall:* be* in charge of; *Thema:* treat; *Buch:* revise; *für Bühne etc.:* adapt (*nach* from); *bsd. mus.* arrange; *j-n ~* work on s.o.; **⊆ung** f working; *e-s Buches:* revision; *thea.* adaptation; *bsd. mus.* arrangement; processing; *chem.* treatment

beatmen v/t. give* artificial respiration to s.o.

beaufsichtig|en v/t. supervise; *Kind:* look after; **⊆ung** f supervision; looking after

beauftrag|en v/t. commission; *anweisen:* instruct; **~ mit** put* s.o. in charge of; **⊆te(r)** agent; *Vertreter:* representa-

tive; *amtlicher:* commissioner

bebauen v/t. build* on; *agr.* cultivate

beben v/i. shake*, tremble; *schaudern:* shiver (*alle:* **vor** with); *Erde:* quake

bebildern v/t. illustrate

Becher m cup, *mit Henkel:* a. mug

Becken n basin, bowl; pool; *anat.* pelvis; *mus.* cymbal(s *pl.*)

bedacht adj.: *darauf ~ sein zu* inf. be* anxious to inf.

bedächtig adj. deliberate; measured

bedanken v/refl.: *sich bei j-m für et. ~* thank s.o. for s.th.

Bedarf m need (*an* of), want (of); *econ.* demand (for); *bei ~* if necessary; **~shaltestelle** f request stop

bedauerlich adj. regrettable; **~erweise** adv. unfortunately

bedauern v/t. j-n: feel* *od.* be* sorry for, pity; *et.:* regret

Bedauern n regret (*über* at); **⊆swert** adj. pitiable, deplorable

bedeck|en v/t. cover; **~t** adj. *Himmel:* overcast

bedenken v/t. consider, think* s.th. over

Bedenken pl. *Zweifel:* doubts *pl.*; *moralische:* scruples *pl.*; *Einwände:* objections *pl.*; **⊆los** adv. unhesitatingly; without scruples

bedenklich adj. *zweifelhaft:* doubtful; *ernst:* serious; *stärker:* critical

Bedenkzeit f: *e-e Stunde ~* one hour to think it over

bedeuten v/t. mean*; **~d** adj. important; *beträchtlich:* considerable; *angesehen:* distinguished

Bedeutung f meaning, sense; *Wichtigkeit:* importance; **⊆slos** adj. insignificant; *ohne Sinn:* meaningless; **~sunterschied** m difference in meaning; **⊆svoll** adj. significant; *vielsagend:* meaningful

bedien|en 1. v/t. j-n: serve, wait on; *tech.* operate, work; *sich ~* help o.s.; *~ Sie sich!* help yourself!; 2. v/i. serve; wait (at table); *Karten:* follow suit; **⊆ung** f service; *Kellner(in):* wait|er (-ress); *Verkäufer(in):* shop assistant, *bsd. Am.* clerk; *tech.* operation, control; **⊆ungsanleitung** f operating instructions *pl.*

beding|en v/t. *erfordern:* require; *verursachen:* cause; *in sich schließen:* imply,

B

involve; **~t** adj.: **~ durch** caused by, due to; **2ung** f condition; **~en** pl. econ. terms pl.; Anforderungen: requirements pl.; Verhältnisse: conditions pl.; **unter einer ~** on one condition; **~ungslos** adj. unconditional

bedräng|en v/t. press (hard)

bedroh|en v/t. threaten, menace; **~lich** adj. threatening; **2ung** f threat, menace (gen. to)

bedrücken v/t. depress, sadden

Bedürf|nis n need, necessity (**für, nach** for); **sein ~ verrichten** relieve o.s.; **~nisanstalt** f public convenience (od. toilets pl.); Am. comfort station; **2tig** adj. needy, poor

beeilen v/refl. hurry (up)

beeindrucken v/t. impress

beeinfluss|en v/t. influence; nachteilig: affect; **2ung** f influence

beeinträchtigen v/t. affect, impair

beend(ig)en v/t. (bring* to an) end, finish, conclude, close

beengen v/t. make* s.o. (feel) uncomfortable; **~gt** adj.: **~ wohnen** live in cramped quarters

beerben v/t.: **j-n ~** be* s.o.'s heir

beerdig|en v/t. bury; **2ung** f burial, funeral; → **Bestattungsinstitut**

Beere f berry; Wein2: grape

Beet agr. n bed, Gemüse2: a. patch

be|fähigen v/t. enable; zu et.: qualify (**für, zu** for); **~fähigt** adj. (cap)able; **zu et. ~** fit od. qualified for s.th.; **2fähigung** (qualification s pl.), (cap)ability

befahr|bar adj. passable, practicable, naut. navigable; **~en** v/t. drive* od. travel on; naut. navigate

befallen v/t. attack, seize (a. fig.)

befangen adj. self-conscious; voreingenommen: prejudiced; jur. a. bias(s)ed; **2heit** f self-consciousness; jur. bias, prejudice

befassen v/refl.: **sich ~ mit** engage od. occupy o.s. with; work on s.th.; Thema, j-m: deal* with

Befehl m order; command (**über** of); **2en** v/t. order; command; **2erisch** adj. imperious, F bossy

Befehlshaber m commander

befestig|en v/t. fasten (**an** to), fix (to), attach (to); mil. fortify; **2ung** f fixing, fastening; mil. fortification

befeuchten v/t. moisten, damp

befinden v/refl. be* (situated)

Befinden n (state of) health

beflecken v/t. stain; fig. a. sully

befolg|en v/t. Rat: follow, take*; Vorschrift: observe; rel. Gebote: keep*; **2ung** f following; observance

beförder|n v/t. carry, transport; Güter: haul, ship; beruflich: promote (**zu** to); **2ung** f transport(ation); shipment; promotion

befragen v/t. question, interview

befrei|en v/t. free, liberate; retten: rescue; von Pflichten: exempt (**von** from); **2ung** f liberation; exemption

Befremd|en n irritation, displeasure; **2et** adj. irritated, displeased

befreund|en v/refl.: **sich ~ mit** make* friends with; fig. warm to; **~et** adj. friendly; **~ sein** be* friends

befriedig|en v/t. satisfy; **sich selbst ~** masturbate; **~end** adj. satisfactory; Note: fair, C; **~t** adj. satisfied, pleased; **2ung** f satisfaction

befristet adj. limited (**auf** to), temporary

befrucht|en v/t. fertilize, inseminate (a. künstlich); **2ung** f fertilization, insemination

Befug|nis f authority; bsd. jur. competence; **2t** adj. authorized; competent

befühlen v/t. feel*, touch

Befund m finding s pl.) (a. med., jur.)

befürcht|en v/t. fear, be* afraid of; vermuten: suspect; **2ung** f fear, suspicion

befürwort|en v/t. advocate, speak* od. plead for; **2er(in** f) advocate

begab|t v/refl. gifted, talented; **2ung** f gift, talent(s pl.)

begeben v/refl. lit. occur; proceed; **sich in Gefahr ~** expose o.s. to danger; **2heit** f incident, event

begegn|en v/i. meet* (a. fig. **mit** with); **sich ~** meet*; **2ung** f meeting, encounter (a. Sport)

begehen v/t. walk (on); feiern: celebrate; Verbrechen: commit; Fehler: make*; **ein Unrecht ~** do* wrong

begehr|en v/t. desire; **~enswert** adj. desirable; **~lich** adj. desirous, covetous; **~t** adj. (very) popular, (much) in demand

begeister|n v/t. fill with enthusiasm; Publikum: a. enthral(l); **sich ~ für** be* enthusiastic about; **~t** adj. enthusiastic; **2ung** f enthusiasm

Begier|de f desire (**nach** for), appetite (for); **2ig** adj. eager (**nach**, **auf** for), anxious (**to do** s.th.)

begießen v/t. water; Braten: baste; F fig. celebrate s.th. (with a drink)

Beginn m beginning, start; **zu** ~ at the beginning; **2en** v/t. u. v/i. begin*, start

beglaubig|en v/t. attest, certify; **2ung** f attestation, certification

begleichen econ. v/t. pay*, settle

begleit|en v/t. accompany (a. mus. **auf** on); **j-n nach Hause** ~ see* s.o. home; **2er(in)** companion; mus. accompanist; **2erscheinung** f concomitant; med. side effect; **2schreiben** n covering letter; **2ung** f company; bsd. mil. escort; mus. accompaniment

beglückwünschen v/t. congratulate (**zu** on)

begnadig|en v/t. pardon, amnesty; **2ung** f pardon; amnesty

begnügen v/refl.: **sich** ~ **mit** be* satisfied with; auskommen: make* do with

begraben v/t. bury (a. fig.)

Begräbnis n burial; Feier: funeral

begradigen v/t. straighten

begreif|en v/t. comprehend, understand; **~lich** adj. understandable

be|grenzen fig. v/t. limit, restrict (**auf** to); **~grenzt** adj. limited

Begriff m idea, notion; Ausdruck: term (a. math.); **im** ~ **sein zu** be* about to; **2sstutzig** adj. slow on the uptake

begründ|en v/t. → gründen; give* reasons for; **~et** adj. well-founded, justified; **2ung** f reasons pl., arguments pl.

begrünen v/t. landscape

begrüß|en v/t. greet, welcome (a. fig); **2ung** f greeting, welcome

begünstigen v/t. favo(u)r

begutachten v/t. give* an (expert's) opinion on; prüfen: examine; ~ **lassen** obtain expert opinion on

be|gütert adj. wealthy; **~haart** adj. hairy; **~häbig** adj. slow; Gestalt: portly; **~haftet** adj.: **mit Fehlern** ~ flawed

Behagen n pleasure, enjoyment

behag|en v/i. please od. suit s.o.; **~lich** adj. comfortable; cosy, snug

behalten v/t. keep* (**für sich** to o.s.); **sich merken**: remember

Behälter m container, receptacle

behand|eln v/t. treat (a. med., tech.);

sich (ärztlich) ~ **lassen** undergo* (medical) treatment; **schonend** ~ handle with care; **2lung** f treatment; handling

beharr|en v/i. insist (**auf** on); **~lich** adj. persistent

behaupt|en v/t. claim; fälschlich: pretend; **2ung** f statement, claim

be|heben v/t. Schaden etc.: repair; **~heizen** v/t. heat

behelfen v/refl.: **sich** ~ **mit** make* do with; **sich** ~ **ohne** do* without

Behelfs... in Zssgn mst temporary

behend(e) adj. nimble, agile

beherbergen v/t. accommodate

beherrsch|en v/t. rule (over), govern; Lage, Markt etc.: dominate, control; Sprache: have* (a good) command of; **sich** ~ control o.s.; **2ung** f command, control

be|herzigen v/t. take* to heart, mind; **~hilflich** adj.: **jm** ~ **sein** help s.o. (**bei** with, in); **~hindern** v/t. hinder; Sicht, Verkehr, Sport: obstruct; **~hindert** adj. handicapped; schwer: disabled; **2hinderung** f obstruction; handicap

Behörde f authority, mst the authorities pl.; board; council

behüten v/t. guard (**vor** from)

behutsam adj. careful; sanft: gentle

bei prp. räumlich: near; at; with; by; zeitlich: during; at; ~ **München** near Munich; **wohnen** ~ stay (ständig: live) with; ~ **mir (ihr)** at my (her) place; ~ **uns (zu Hause)** at home; **arbeiten** ~ work for; **e-e Stelle** ~ a job with; ~ **der Marine** in the navy; ~ **Familie Müller** at the Müllers'; ~ **Müller** Adresse: c/o Müller; **ich habe kein Geld** ~ **mir** I have no money with od. on me; ~ **e-r Tasse Tee** over a cup of tea; **wir haben Englisch** ~ **Herrn X** we have Mr X for English; ~ **Licht** by light; ~ **Tag** during the day; ~ **Nacht (Sonnenaufgang)** at night (sunrise); ~ **s-r Geburt** at his birth; ~ **Regen** (Gefahr) in case of rain (danger); ~ **100 Grad** at a hundred degrees; ~ **der Arbeit** at work; ~ **weitem** by far; ~ **Gott** (!) by God (!); → a. **beim**

beibehalten v/t. keep* up, retain

beibringen v/t. teach*; mitteilen: tell*; Niederlage etc.: inflict (dat. on)

Beicht|e f confession; **2en** v/t. u. v/i. confess (a. fig.); **~stuhl** m confessional

B

beide *adj. u. pron.* both; *m-e ~n Brüder* my two brothers; *wir ~* the two of us; *betont:* both of us; *keiner von ~n* neither of them; *30 ~* Tennis: 30 all
beiderlei: ~ *Geschlechts* of either sex
beieinander *adv.* together
Beifahrer *m* front(-seat) passenger
Beifall *m* applause; *fig.* approval, **~ssturm** *m* (standing) ovation
beifügen *v/t. e-m Brief:* enclose
beige *adj.* tan, beige
beigeben 1. *v/t.* add; **2.** *F v/i.: klein ~* knuckle under
Bei|geschmack *m* smack (**von** of) (*a. fig.*); **~hilfe** *f* aid, allowance; *jur.* aiding and abetting
Beil *n* hatchet; *großes:* ax(e)
Beilage *f Zeitung:* supplement; *Essen:* side dish; vegetables *pl.*
bei|läufig *adj.* casual; **~legen** *v/t.* add (*dat.* to); *e-m Brief:* enclose; *Streit:* settle; **Qlegung** *f* settlement
Beileid *n* condolence; *herzliches ~* my deepest sympathy
beiliegen *v/i.* be* enclosed (*dat.* with)
beim *prp.:* ~ *Bäcker at the baker's;* ~ *Sprechen etc.* while speaking *etc.;* ~ *Spielen* at play; → *a.* bei
beimessen *v/t. Bedeutung:* attach (*dat.* to)
Bein *n* leg; *Knochen:* bone
beinah(e) *adv.* almost, nearly
Beinbruch *m* fracture of the leg
beipflichten *v/i.* agree (*dat.* with)
beirren *v/t.* confuse
beisammen *adv.* together; **Qsein** *n: geselliges ~* get-together
Beischlaf *m* sexual intercourse
Bei|sein *n* presence; **Qseite** *adv.* aside; ~ *schaffen* remove; *j-n:* liquidate
beisetz|en *v/t.* bury; **Qung** *f* funeral
Beispiel *n* example; *zum ~* for example, for instance; *sich an j-m ein ~ nehmen* follow s.o.'s example; **Qhaft** *adj.* exemplary; **Qlos** *adj.* unprecedented, unparalleled; **Qsweise** *adv.* such as
beißen *v/t. u. v/i.* bite* (*a. fig.*); *sich ~ Farben:* clash; **~d** *adj.* biting, pungent (*beide a. fig.*)
Bei|stand *m* assistance; **Qstehen** *v/i.: j-m ~* assist *od.* help s.o.; **Qsteuern** *v/t.* contribute (**zu** to)
Beitrag *m* contribution; *Mitglieds:* subscription, *Am.* dues *pl.*; **Qen** *v/t.*

contribute (**zu** to)
bei|treten *v/i.* join; **Qtritt** *m* joining
Beiwagen *m Motorrad:* sidecar
beizeiten *adv.* early, in good time
beizen *v/t. Holz:* stain; *Fleisch:* pickle
bejahen *v/t.* answer in the affirmative, affirm; **~d** *adj.* affirmative
bekämpfen *v/t.* fight* (against)
bekannt *adj.* (well-)known; *vertraut:* familiar; *j-n mit j-m ~ machen* introduce s.o. to s.o.; **Qe(r)** acquaintance, *mst* friend; **~geben** *v/t.* announce; **~lich** *adv.* as you know; **Qmachung** *f* announcement; **Qschaft** *f* acquaintance
bekehren *v/t.* convert
bekenn|en *v/t.* confess (*a. Sünden*); *zugeben:* admit; *sich schuldig ~ jur.* plead guilty; *sich ~ zu Glaube:* profess *s.th.; Attentat:* claim responsibility for; **Qerbrief** *m* letter claiming responsibility; **Qtnis** *n* confession, *Religion: a.* denomination
beklagen *v/t.* deplore; *sich ~* complain (*über* about); **~swert** *adj.* deplorable
be|kleben *v/t.* stick* (*Plakat:* paste) on *s.th.; mit Etiketten ~* label *s.th.;* **~klekkern** *F v/t.* stain; *sich ~ mit* spill* *s.th.* over o.s.
Bekleidung *f* clothing, clothes *pl.*
Beklemmung *f* oppression
bekommen 1. *v/t.* get*; *Brief, Geschenk: a.* receive; *Krankheit: a.* catch*; *Kind:* be* having; **2.** *v/i.: j-m* (**gut**) ~ agree with s.o; △ *nicht* **become**
bekömmlich *adj.* wholesome
bekräftigen *v/t.* confirm
be|kreuzigen *v/refl.* cross o.s.; **~kümmert** *adj.* worried; **~kunden** *v/t. Interesse etc.:* show*, express; **~laden** *v/t.* load, *fig. a.* burden
Belag *m* covering; *tech.* coat(ing); *Brems**Q**:* lining; *Straßen**Q**:* surface; *med. Zungen**Q**:* fur; *Zahn**Q**:* plaque; *Brot**Q**:* topping; *Aufstrich:* spread; (sandwich) filling
belager|n *v/t.* mil. besiege (*a. fig.*); **Qung** *f* siege; **Qungszustand** *m* state of siege
belassen *v/t.* leave; *es dabei ~* leave it at that
belanglos *adj.* irrelevant
belast|bar *adj.* resistant to strain *od.* stress; *tech.* loadable; **~en** *v/t.* load; *fig.* burden; *beschweren:* weight; *jur.* in-

criminate; *Umwelt*: pollute; *Ansehen*: damage; **j-s Konto ~ mit** *econ.* charge *s.th.* to s.o.'s account
belästig|en *v/t.* molest; *ärgern*: annoy; *stören*: disturb, bother; **2ung** *f* molestation; annoyance; disturbance
Belastung *f* load (*a. tech.*); *fig.* burden; *körperliche*: strain; *seelische*: stress; *jur.* incrimination; *Umwelt*: pollution, contamination; **~szeuge** *jur. m* witness for the prosecution
be|laufen *v/refl.*: **sich ~ auf** amount to; **~lauschen** *v/t.* eavesdrop on
beleb|en *fig. v/t.* stimulate; **~end** *adj.* stimulating; **~t** *adj.* busy, crowded
Beleg *m Beweis*: proof; *Quittung*: receipt; *Unterlage*: document; **2en** *v/t.* cover; *Platz etc.*: reserve; *beweisen*: prove; *Kurs etc.*: enrol(l) for, take*; *Brote etc.*: put* s.th. on; **den ersten** *etc.* **Platz ~** take* first *etc.* place; **~schaft** *f* staff; **2t** *adj. Platz, Zimmer*: taken, occupied; *Hotel etc.*: full; *tel.* engaged, *Am.* busy; *Stimme*: husky; *Zunge*: coated; **~es Brot** sandwich
belehren *v/t.* teach*, instruct, inform; **sich ~ lassen** take* advice
beleidig|en *v/t.* offend (*a. fig.*), *stärker*: insult; **~end** *adj.* offensive, insulting; **2ung** *f* offen|ce, *Am.* -se, insult
belesen *adj.* well-read
beleucht|en *phot. v/t.* light* (up), illuminate (*a. fig.*); *fig.* throw* light on; **2ung** *f* light(ing); illumination
Belg|ien Belgium; **~ier(in)**, **2isch** *adj.* Belgian
belicht|en *phot. v/t.* expose; **2ungsmesser** *phot. m* exposure meter
Belieb|en *n*: **nach ~** at will; **2ig** *adj.* any; *Zahl*: optional; **jeder ~e** anyone; **2t** *adj.* popular (**bei** with); **~theit** *f* popularity
beliefer|n *v/t.* supply, furnish (**mit** with); **2ung** *f* supply
bellen *v/i.* bark (*a. fig.*)
belohn|en *v/t.* reward; **2ung** *f* reward; **zur ~** as a reward
belügen *v/t.*: **j-n ~** lie to s.o.
belustig|en *v/t.* amuse; **~t** *adj.* amused; **2ung** *f* amusement
be|mächtigen *v/refl.* get* hold of, seize; **~malen** *v/t.* paint; **~mängeln** *v/t.* find* fault with; **~mannt** *aviat.* *adj.* manned

bemerk|bar *adj.* noticeable; **sich ~ machen** *Person*: draw* attention to o.s.; *Sache*: begin* to show; **~en** *v/t.* notice; *äußern*: remark, say*; **~enswert** *adj.* remarkable; **2ung** *f* remark
bemitleiden *v/t.* pity, feel* sorry for; **~swert** *adj.* pitiable
bemüh|en *v/refl.* try (hard); **sich ~ um** *et.*: try to get; *j-n*: try to help; **bitte ~ Sie sich nicht!** please don't bother!; **2ung** *f* effort; **danke für Ihre ~en!** thank you for your trouble
bemuttern *v/t.* mother s.o.
benachbart *adj.* neighbo(u)ring
benachrichtig|en *v/t.* inform, notify; **2ung** *f* information, notification
benachteilig|en *v/t.* place at a disadvantage; *bsd. sozial*: discriminate against; **~t** *adj.* disadvantaged; **die 2en** the underprivileged; **2ung** *f* disadvantage; discrimination
benehmen *v/refl.* behave (o.s.)
Benehmen *n* behavio(u)r, conduct; *Manieren*: manners *pl.*
beneiden *v/t.*: **j-n um et. ~** envy s.o. s.th.; **~swert** *adj.* enviable
BENELUX *Abk. für* **Belgien. Niederlande, Luxemburg** Belgium, the Netherlands and Luxembourg
benennen *v/t.* name
Bengel *m* (little) rascal, urchin
benommen *adj.* dazed, *F* dopey
benoten *v/t. Schule*: mark, *Am.* grade
benötigen *v/t.* need, want, require
benutz|en *v/t.* use; **2er** *m* user; **~erfreundlich** *adj.* user-friendly; **2eroberfläche** *f* user interface; **2ung** *f* use
Benzin *n* petrol, *Am.* gasoline, *F* gas
beobacht|en *v/t.* watch; *genau*: observe; **2er** *m* observer; **2ung** *f* observation
bepflanzen *v/t.* plant (**mit** with)
bequem *adj.* comfortable; *leicht*: easy; *faul*: lazy; **~en** *v/refl.*: **sich ~ zu** bring* o.s. to do *s.th.*; **2lichkeit** *f* comfort; laziness; **alle ~en** all conveniences
berat|en *v/t. j-n*: advise; *et.*: debate, discuss; **sich ~** confer (**mit j-m** with s.o.; **über et.** on s.th.); **2er(in)** adviser, consultant; **2ung** *f* advice (*a. med.*); debate; *Besprechung*: consultation, conference; **2ungsstelle** *f* counsel(l)ing (*Brt. a.* advice) cent|re, *Am.* -er

be|rauben *v/t.* rob; **~rauschend** *adj.* intoxicating; F *nicht gerade ~!* not so hot!; **~rauscht** *fig. adj.:* **~ von** drunk with

berechn|en *v/t.* calculate; *econ.* charge (**zu** at); **~end** *adj.* calculating; **2ung** *f* calculation (*a. fig.*)

berechtig|en *v/t.: j-n ~ zu* entitle s.o. to; *ermächtigen:* authorize s.o. to; **~t** *adj.* entitled (**zu** to); *begründet:* legitimate; **2ung** *f* right (**zu** to); *Vollmacht:* authority

Be|redsamkeit *f* eloquence; **~redt** *adj.* eloquent (*a. fig.*)

Bereich *m* area; *Umfang:* range; *e-r Wissenschaft etc.:* field, realm

bereicher|n *v/t.* enrich; *sich ~* get rich (**an** on); **2ung** *f* enrichment

Bereifung *f* (set of) tyres (*Am.* tires)

bereinigen *v/t.* settle

bereisen *v/t.* tour; *Vertreter:* cover

bereit *adj.* ready, prepared; *willens:* willing; **~en** *v/t.* prepare; *verursachen:* cause; **~halten** *v/t.* have* s.th. ready; *sich ~* stand* by; **~s** *adv.* already; **2schaft** *f* readiness; *in ~* on standby; **2schaftsdienst** *m:* **~ haben** *Arzt etc.:* be* on call; **~stellen** *v/t.* provide; **~willig** *adj.* ready, willing

bereuen *v/t.* repent (of) regret

Berg *m* mountain; **~e von** F loads of; *die Haare standen ihm zu ~e* his hair stood on end; **2ab** *adv.* downhill (*a. fig.*); **~arbeiter** *m* miner; **2auf** *adv.* uphill; **~bahn** *f* mountain rail|way, *Am.* -road; **~bau** *m* mining

bergen *v/t.* rescue, save; *Güter: a.* salvage; *Tote:* recover; *enthalten:* hold*

Berg|führer *m* mountain guide; **2ig** *adj.* mountainous; **~kette** *f* mountain range; **~mann** *m* miner; **~rutsch** *m* landslide; **~schuhe** *pl.* mountain(eering) boots *pl.*; **~spitze** *f* (mountain) peak; **~steigen** *n* mountaineering, (mountain) climbing; **~steiger(in)** mountaineer, (mountain) climber

Bergung *f* recovery; *Rettung:* rescue; **~sarbeiten** *pl.* rescue work *sg.*; salvage operations *pl.*

Berg|wacht *f* alpine rescue service; **~werk** *n* mine

Bericht *m* report (*über* on), account (of); **2en 1.** *v/t. u. v/i.* report (*über* on); *j-m et. ~* inform s.o. of s.th.; tell* s.o.

about s.th.; **~erstatter(in)** *Presse:* reporter; *auswärtiger:* correspondent; **~erstat·tung** *f* report(ing)

berichtig|en *v/t.* correct; **2ung** *f* correction

berieseln *v/t.* sprinkle

Bernstein *m* amber

bersten *v/i.* burst* (*fig. vor* with)

berüchtigt *adj.* notorious (*wegen* for)

berücksichtig|en *v/t. et.:* take* into consideration; *nicht ~* disregard; **2ung** *f: unter ~ von* in consideration of

Beruf *m* job, occupation; *Gewerbe:* trade; *akademischer:* profession; **2en** *v/t.* appoint (**zu** [as] *s.o.*; to *s.th.*); *sich ~ auf* refer to; **2lich** *adj.* professional; *~ unterwegs* away on business

Berufs|... *in Zssgn Sportler etc.:* professional ...; **~ausbildung** *f* vocational (*bsd. akademisch:* professional) training; **~berater** *m* careers advisor; **~beratung** *f* careers guidance; **~bezeichnung** *f* job designation *od.* title; **~kleidung** *f* work clothes *pl.*; **~krankheit** *f* occupational disease; **~schule** *f* vocational school; **2tätig** *adj.: ~ sein* (go to) work, have a job; **~tätige** *pl.* working people *pl.*; **~verbot** *n* ban from one's profession; *pol.* 'berufsverbot'; **~verkehr** *m* rush-hour traffic

Berufung *f* appointment (**zu** to); *jur.* appeal (**bei** to); *unter ~ auf* with reference to; on the grounds of

beruhen *v/i.: ~ auf* be* based on; *et. auf sich ~ lassen* let* s.th. rest

beruhig|en *v/t.* quiet(en), calm, soothe (*a. Nerven*); *Besorgte:* reassure; *sich ~* calm down; **~end** *adj.* reassuring; *med.* sedative; **2ung** *f* calming (down); soothing; *Erleichterung:* relief; **2ungsmittel** *med. n* sedative; *Pille:* tranquil(l)izer

berühmt *adj.* famous (*wegen* for); **2heit** *f* fame; *Person:* celebrity, star

berühr|en *v/t.* touch (*a. fig.*); *betreffen:* concern; **2ung** *f* touch; *in ~ kommen* come* into contact; **2sangst** *f* fear of contact; **2spunkt** *m* point of contact

besänftigen *v/t.* appease, calm, soothe

Besatzung *f naut., aviat.* crew; *mil.* occupation; **~smacht** *f* occupying power; **~struppen** *pl.* occupying forces *pl.*

besaufen *v/refl.* get* drunk

beschädig|en v/t. damage; **2ung** f damage

beschaffen v/t. provide, get*; Geld: raise; **2heit** f state, condition

beschäf|tigen v/t. employ; zu tun geben: keep* busy; **sich ~** occupy o.s.; → **befassen**; **~tigt** adj. busy, occupied; **2tigte** pl. employed people pl.; **2ti- gung** f employment; occupation

be|schämen v/t. make* s.o. feel ashamed; **~schämend** adj. shameful; demütigend: humiliating; **~schämt** adj. ashamed (**über** of)

beschatten v/t. fig. shadow, F tail

Bescheid m answer; jur. decision; information (**über** on, about); **sagen Sie mir ~** let me know; (**gut**) **~ wissen über** know* all about

bescheiden adj. modest (a. fig.); ärmlich: humble; **2heit** f modesty

bescheinig|en v/t. certify; **den Empfang ~** acknowledge receipt; **hiermit wird bescheinigt, daß** this is to certify that; **2ung** f certification; Schein: certificate; Quittung: receipt

bescheißen V v/t. cheat

beschenken v/t.: **j-n** (**reich**) **~** give* s.o. (shower s.o. with) presents

Bescherung f distribution of (Christmas) presents; F fig. mess

beschicht|en v/t., **2ung** f coat

beschieß|en v/t. fire od. shoot* at; mit Granaten: bombard (a. phys.), shell

beschimpf|en v/t. abuse, insult; swear* at; **2ung** f abuse, insult

Be|schiß V m → Betrug; **2schissen** adj. lousy, rotten, Brt. a. bloody

Beschlag m tech. metal fitting(s pl.); **in ~ nehmen** fig. j-n: monopolize; et.: bag; Raum etc.: occupy; **2en 1.** v/t. cover; tech. fit, mount; Pferd: shoe*; **2.** v/i. Fenster etc.: steam up; **3.** adj. Fenster: steamed-up; fig. well-versed (**auf**, **in** in); **~nahme** jur. f confiscation; **2nahmen** v/t. confiscate

beschleunig|en v/t. u. v/i. accelerate, speed* up; **2ung** f acceleration

beschließen v/t. decide (on); Gesetz etc.: pass; beenden: conclude

Beschluß m decision

be|schmieren v/t. (be)smear, soil; Papier etc.: scrawl all over; Wand: a. cover with graffiti; Brot: spread*; **~schmutzen** v/t. soil (a. fig.), dirty;

~schneiden v/t. clip, cut* (a. fig.); Baum: prune; med. Vorhaut: circumcise; **~schönigen** v/t. gloss over

beschränk|en v/t. confine, limit, restrict; **sich ~ auf** confine o.s. to; **~t** adj. limited; fig. feeble-minded; **2ung** f limitation, restriction

beschreib|en v/t. describe; Papier: write* on; **2ung** f description

beschrift|en v/t. inscribe; Ware etc.: mark; **2ung** f inscription

beschuldig|en v/t. Schuld geben: blame; **j-n e-r Sache ~** accuse s.o. of s.th. (a. jur.); **2ung** f accusation

beschummeln F v/t. cheat

Beschuß mil. m: **unter ~** under fire

beschütze|n v/t. protect, shelter, guard (**vor** from); **2r** m protector

Beschwerde f complaint (**über** about; **bei** to); **~n** pl. Schmerzen: complaints pl., trouble sg.

beschwer|en v/t. weight s.th.; **sich ~** complain (**über** about; **bei** to); **~lich** adj. hard, arduous

be|schwichtigen v/t. appease (a. pol.), calm; **~schwingt** adj. buoyant; Musik etc.: lively, swinging; **~schwindeln** v/t. tell* a fib or lie. lie; betrügen: cheat; **~schwipst** F adj. tipsy; **~schwören** v/t. et.: swear* to; j-n: implore; Geister: conjure up

beseitig|en v/t. remove (a. fig. j-n); Abfall: a. dispose of; Mißstand, Fehler etc.: eliminate; pol. liquidate; **2ung** f removal; disposal; elimination

Besen m broom; **~stiel** m broomstick

besessen adj. obsessed (**von** by, with); **wie ~** like mad

besetz|en v/t. occupy (a. mil.); Stelle etc.: fill; thea. Rollen: cast*; Kleid: trim; Haus: squat in; **~t** adj. occupied; Platz: taken; Bus, Zug etc.: full up; tel. engaged, Am. busy; **2tzeichen** tel. n engaged tone, Am. busy signal; **2ung** f thea. cast; mil. occupation

besichtig|en v/t. visit, see* the sights of; prüfend: inspect; **2ung** f sightseeing; visit (to); inspection

besied|eln v/t. settle; colonize; bevölkern: populate; **~elt** adj.: **dicht** (**dünn**) **~** densely (sparsely) populated; **2lung** f settlement; colonization; population

be|siegeln v/t. seal; **~siegen** v/t. defeat, beat*; conquer (a. fig.)

besinn|en v/refl. erinnern: remember; nachdenken: think* (**auf** about); **sich anders** ~ change one's mind; **~lich** adj. contemplative

Besinnung f consciousness; **zur ~ kommen** (**bringen**) come* to one's (bring* s.o. to his) senses; **2slos** adj. unconscious

Besitz m possession; Eigentum: property (a. Land2); ~ **ergreifen von** take* possession of; **2anzeigend** gr. adj. possessive; **2en** v/t. possess, own; **~er** m possessor, owner; **den ~ wechseln** change hands

besoffen F adj. plastered, stoned

besohlen v/t.: ~ **lassen** have* (re)soled

Besoldung f pay; Beamte: salary

besonder|e adj. special, particular; eigentümlich: peculiar; **2heit** f peculiarity

besonders adv. especially, particularly; hauptsächlich: chiefly, mainly

besonnen adj. prudent, levelheaded

besorg|en v/t. get*, buy*; → **erledigen**; **2nis** f concern, alarm, anxiety (**über** about, at); **~niserregend** adj. alarming; **~t** adj. worried, concerned; **2ung** f: **~en machen** go* shopping

bespielen v/t. Tonband etc.: make* a recording on; **bespieltes Band** (pre-)recorded tape

besprech|en v/t. discuss, talk s.th.

bespitzeln v/t. spy on s.o.

besprech|en v/t. discuss, talk s.th. over; Buch etc.: review; **2ung** f discussion, talk(s pl.); meeting, conference; review

besser adj. u. adv. better; **es ist ~, wir fragen ihn** we had better ask him; **immer** ~ better and better; **es geht ihm** ~ he is better; **oder ~ gesagt** or rather; **es ~ wissen** know better; **es ~ machen als** do better than; ~ **ist** ~ just to be on the safe side

besser|n v/refl. improve, get* better; **2ung** f improvement; **auf dem Wege der** ~ on the way to recovery; **gute** ~! get better soon!, **2wisser** m know-(it-)all

Bestand m (continued) existence; Vorrat: stock; ~ **haben** last, be* lasting

beständig adj. constant, steady (a. Charakter); Wetter: settled; **...~** in Zssgn Hitze etc.: ...-resistant, -proof

Bestand|saufnahme econ. f stock-taking (a. fig.); ~ **machen** take* stock (a. fig.); **~teil** m part, component

bestärken v/t. confirm, strengthen, encourage (**in** in)

bestätig|en v/t. confirm; bescheinigen: certify; Empfang: acknowledge; **sich** ~ prove (to be) true; Vorhersage: come* true; **sich bestätigt fühlen** feel* affirmed; **2ung** f confirmation; certificate; acknowledge(e)ment; → **2ungsschreiben** n letter of confirmation

bestatt|en v/t. bury; **2ungsinstitut** n undertakers pl., Am. funeral home

bestäuben v/t. dust; bot. pollinate

beste adj. u. adv. best; am besten: best; **welches gefällt dir am ~n?** which one do you like best?; **am ~n nehmen Sie den Bus** it would be best to take a bus

Beste m, f, n the best; **das ~ geben** do* one's best; **das ~ machen aus** make* the best of; (**nur**) **zu deinem ~n** for your own good

bestech|en v/t. bribe; fascinate (**durch** by); **~lich** adj. corrupt; **2ung** f bribery, corruption; **2ungsgeld** n bribe

Besteck n (set of) knife, fork and spoon; coll. cutlery

bestehen 1. v/t. Prüfung etc.: pass; **2.** v/i. be*, exist; ~ **auf** insist on; ~ **aus** (**in**) consist of (in); ~ **bleiben** last, survive

Bestehen n existence

be|stehlen v/t.: **j-n** ~ steal s.o.'s money etc.; **~steigen** v/t. Berg: climb; Fahrzeug: get* on; Thron: ascend

bestell|en v/t. order; Zimmer, Karten: book; vor~: reserve; Taxi: call; Gruß etc.: give*, send*; Boden: cultivate; **kann ich et. ~?** can I take a message?; ~ **Sie ihm bitte, ...** please tell him ...; **2schein** m order form; **2ung** f order; booking; reservation; **auf** ~ to order

besten|falls adv. at best; **~s** adv. very well

Bestie f beast; fig. a. brute

bestimmen v/t. determine, decide; Begriff: define; auswählen: choose*, pick; **zu ~ haben** be* in charge, F be* the boss; **bestimmt für** meant for

bestimmt 1. adj. determined, firm; gr. Artikel: definite; **~e Dinge** certain things; **2.** adv. certainly; **ganz** ~ definitely; **er ist ~ ...** he must be ...

Bestimmung f regulation; Schicksal: destiny; **~sort** m destination

Bestleistung f Sport: (personal) record
bestraf|en v/t. punish; **~ung** f punishment
bestrahl|en v/t. irradiate (a. med.); **~ung** f irradiation; med. ray treatment, radiotherapy
be|streichen v/t. spread*; **~streiten** v/t. anfechten: challenge; leugnen: deny; Kosten etc.: pay for, finance; **~streuen** v/t. sprinkle (mit with); **~stürmen** v/t. drängen: urge; überschütten: bombard
bestürz|t adj. dismayed (über at); **~ung** f consternation, dismay
Besuch m visit (bei, in to); kurzer: call; Aufenthalt: stay; Schule, Veranstaltung: attendance; **~ haben** have* company od. guests; **2en** v/t. visit; call on, (go* to) see*; F look up; Schule etc.: attend; Lokal: go* to; **~er(in)** visitor, guest; **~szeit** f visiting hours pl.; **2t** adj.: gut (schlecht) **~** well (poorly) attended; Lokal, Ort: much (little) frequented
be|tagt adj. aged; **~tasten** v/t. touch, feel*; **~tätigen** v/t. tech. operate; Bremse: apply; sich **~** be* active; **~tätigung** f activity
betäub|en v/t. stun (a. fig.), daze; make* unconscious; med. an(a)esthetize; **2ung** f med. an(a)esthetization; med. Zustand: an(a)esthesia; fig. daze, stupor; **2ungsmittel** n an(a)esthetic; Droge: narcotic
Bete bot. f: rote **~** beetroot, Am. Beet
beteilig|en v/t.: j-n **~** give* s.o. a share (an in); sich **~** take* part (an, bei in), participate (in) (a. jur.); **~igt** adj. concerned; **~ sein an** Unfall, Verbrechen: be* involved in; Gewinn: have* a share in; **2igung** f participation (a. jur., econ.); involvement; share (a. econ.)
beten v/i. pray (um for), say* one's prayers; bei Tisch: say* grace
beteuern v/t. Unschuld: protest
Beton m concrete
betonen v/t. stress; fig. a. emphasize
betonieren v/t. (cover with) concrete
Betonung f stress; fig. emphasis
Betr. Abk. für betrifft (in Briefen) re
betören v/t. infatuate, bewitch
Betracht m: in **~** ziehen take* into consideration; (nicht) in **~** kommen (not) come* into question; **2en** v/t. look at,

fig. a. view; **~ als** look upon od. regard as, consider; **2er** m viewer
beträchtlich adj. considerable
Betrachtung f view; bei näherer **~** on closer inspection
Betrag m amount, sum; **2en 1.** v/t. amount to; **2.** v/refl. behave (o.s.)
Betragen n behavio(u)r, conduct
betrauen v/t. entrust (mit with)
betreffen v/t. angehen: concern; sich beziehen auf: refer to; was ... betrifft as for, as to; betrifft (Abk. Betr.) re; **~d** adj. concerning; die **~en** Personen etc. the people etc. concerned
betreiben v/t. Geschäft etc.: operate, run*; Hobby, Sport: go* in for
betreten¹ v/t. step on; eintreten: enter; **2 (des Rasens) verboten!** keep out! (keep off the grass!)
betreten² adj. embarrassed
betreu|en v/t. look after, take* care of; **2ung** f care (gen. of, for)
Betrieb m business, firm, company; Betreiben: operation, running; im Verkehr: rush; in **~** sein (setzen) be* in (put* into) operation; außer **~** out of order; im Geschäft war viel **~** the shop was very busy
Betriebs|anleitung f operating instructions pl.; **~berater** m business consultant; **~ferien** pl. company (Brt. a. works) holiday sg.; „**~**" 'closed for holidays', Am. 'on vacation'; **~fest** n annual company fête; **~kapital** n working capital; **~klima** n working atmosphere; **~kosten** pl. operating costs pl.; **~leitung** f management; **~rat** m works council; **2sicher** adj. safe to operate; **~störung** f breakdown; **~system** n Computer: operating system; **~unfall** m industrial accident; **~wirtschaft** econ. f business administration
betrinken v/refl. get* drunk
betroffen adj. affected, concerned; dismayed, shocked; **2heit** f dismay, shock
betrübt adj. sad, grieved (über at)
Betrug m cheating; jur. fraud; Täuschung: deceit
betrüge|n v/t. cheat (beim Kartenspiel at cards), swindle, trick (um et. out of s.th.); Partner: be* unfaithful to; **2r(in)** swindler, trickster
betrunken adj. pred. drunk; attr. a. drunken; **2e(r)** drunk

Bett n bed; **am ~** at the bedside; **ins ~ gehen** (**bringen**) go* (put*) to bed; **~bezug** m duvet cover, Am. comforter case; **~decke** f blanket; quilt

betteln v/i. beg (**um** for)

Bett|gestell n bedstead; **2lägerig** adj. bedridden; **~laken** n sheet

Bettler(in) beggar

Bett|nässer m med. bed wetter; **~ruhe** f bed rest; **j-m ~ verordnen** tell s.o. to stay in bed; **~vorleger** m bedside rug; **~wäsche** f bed linen; **~zeug** n bedding, bedclothes pl.

beugen v/t. bend*; gr. inflect; **sich ~** bend* (**vor** to), bow (to)

Beule f bump; im Blech etc.: dent

be|unruhigen v/t. alarm, worry; **~urkunden** v/t. certify

beurlaub|en v/t. give* s.o. leave od. time off; vom Amt: suspend; **sich ~ lassen** ask for leave; **~t** adj. on leave

beurteil|en v/t. judge (**nach** by); Leistung, Wert: rate; **2ung** f judg(e)ment; Bewertung: evaluation

Beuschel östr. gastr. n dish made of finely chopped lung

Beute f booty, loot; e-s Tieres: prey (a. fig.); hunt. bag; fig. a. victim

Beutel m bag; zo., Tabaks2: pouch

bevölk|ern v/t. populate; **~ert** adj. → **besiedelt**; **2erung** f population

bevollmächtigen v/t. authorize

bevor cj. before

bevor|munden v/t. patronize; **~stehenstehen** v/i. be* approaching; lie* ahead; Gefahr: be* imminent; **j-m ~** be* in store for s.o., await s.o.

bevor|zugen v/t. prefer; favo(u)r (a. Schule); **2zugung** f preferential treatment

bewach|en v/t. guard, watch over; **2er** m, **2ung** f guard

bewaffn|en v/t. arm (a. fig.); **2ung** f armament; Waffen: arms pl.

be|wahren v/t. keep*; **~ vor** keep* (od. save) from; **~währen** v/refl. prove successful; **sich ~ als** prove to be; **~wahrheiten** v/refl. → **bestätigen**; **~währt** adj. (well-)tried, reliable; Person: experienced

Bewährung jur. f probation (**zur, auf** on); **~sfrist** f jur. (period of) probation; **~shelfer(in)** jur. probation officer; **~sprobe** f (acid) test

bewaldet adj. wooded, woody

bewältigen v/t. manage, cope with; Strecke: cover

bewandert adj. (well-)versed (**in** in)

bewässer|n v/t. Land etc.: irrigate; **2ung** f irrigation

beweg|en v/t. u. v/refl. move (a. fig.); **sich ~ zwischen** range from ... to; **j-n zu et.** get s.o. to do s.th.; **nicht ~!** don't move!; **2grund** m motive; **~lich** adj. movable; flink: agile; flexibel: flexible; Teile: moving; **2lichkeit** f mobility; agility; **~t** adj. Meer: rough; Stimme: choked; Leben: eventful; fig. moved, touched; **2ung** f movement (a. pol.); motion (a. phys.); körperliche: exercise; fig. emotion; **in ~ setzen** set* in motion; **2ungsfreiheit** f freedom of movement (fig. a. of action); **~ungslos** adj. motionless

Beweis m proof (**für** of); **~e** (pl.) evidence (bsd. jur.); **2en** v/t. prove*; Interesse etc.: show*; **~mittel** n, **~stück** n (piece of) evidence

bewenden v/i.: **es dabei ~ lassen** leave* it at that

bewerb|en v/refl.: **sich ~ um** apply for; **2er(in)** applicant; **2ung** f application; **2ungsschreiben** n (letter of) application

bewert|en v/t. Leistung: assess; j-n: judge; **2ung** f assessment

bewilligen v/t. grant, allow

bewirken v/t. cause; bring* about

bewirt|en v/t. entertain; **~schaften** v/t. run*; agr. farm; **~schaftet** adj. Hütte: open (to the public); **2ung** f Versorgung: catering; Bedienung service; **zu Hause**: hospitality

bewohn|en v/t. live in; Land: inhabit; **2er** m inhabitant; occupant; **~t** adj. Land: inhabited; Gebäude: occupied

be|wölken v/refl. cloud over (a. fig.); **~wölkt** adj. cloudy, overcast; **2wölkung** f clouds pl.

Bewunder|er m admirer; **2n** v/t. admire (**wegen** for); **2nswert** adj. admirable; **~ung** f admiration

bewußt adj. conscious; absichtlich: intentional; **sich e-r Sache ~ sein** be* conscious od. aware of s.th., realize s.th.; **~los** adj. unconscious; **~machen** v/t.: **j-m et.** ~ make* s.o. realize s.th., open s.o.'s eyes to s.th.; **2sein** n consciousness; **bei ~** conscious

bezahl|en v/t. pay*; *Ware, Leistung etc.:* pay* for (a. fig.); **~t** adj.: **~er Urlaub** paid leave; **es macht sich ~** it pays; **2ung** f payment; *Lohn:* pay

bezaubern v/t. charm; **~d** adj. charming, F sweet, darling

bezeichn|en v/t.: **~ als** call, describe as; **~end** adj. characteristic, typical (**für** of); **2ung** f name, term

be|zeugen v/t. jur. testify to, bear* witness to (*beide a. fig.*); **~zichtigen** v/t. → **beschuldigen**; **~ziehen** v/t. *Möbel etc.:* cover; *Bett:* change; *Haus etc.:* move into; *erhalten:* receive; *Zeitung:* subscribe to; **~ auf** relate to; **sich ~** *Himmel:* cloud over; **sich ~ auf** refer to

Beziehung f relation (**zu et.** to s.th.; **zu j-m** with s.o.); connection (**zu** with); *verwandtschaftliche etc.:* relationship; *Hinsicht:* respect; **~en haben** have* connections, know* the right people; **2sweise** adv. respectively; *oder:* or; *oder vielmehr:* or rather

Bezirk m district, Am. a. precinct

Bezug m *Überzug:* cover(ing); case, slip; econ. purchase; **e-r Zeitung:** subscription (gen. to); **Bezüge** pl. earnings pl.; **~ nehmen auf** refer to; **in 2 auf** → **bezüglich**

bezüglich prp. regarding, concerning

Bezug|nahme f: **unter ~ auf** with reference to; **~sperson** f psych. F person to relate to, role model; **~spunkt** m reference point; **~squelle** econ. f source (of supply)

be|zwecken v/t. aim at, intend; **~zweifeln** v/t. doubt, question; **~zwingen** v/t. conquer, defeat (a. Sport)

Bibel f Bible

Bibeli n *in Schweiz:* pimple; chicken

Biber zo. m beaver

Bibliothek f library; **~ar(in)** librarian

biblisch adj. biblical

bieder adj. honest; *spießig:* square

bieg|en v/t. u. v/i. bend* (a. sich ~); *Straße:* a. turn; **um die Ecke ~** turn (round) the corner; **~sam** adj. flexible; **2ung** f curve

Biene zo. f bee; **~nkönigin** f queen (bee); **~nkorb**, **~nstock** m (bee)hive; **~nwachs** n beeswax

Bier n beer; **~ vom Faß** draught (Am. draft) beer; **~deckel** m coaster, Brt. a.

beer mat; **~krug** m beer mug, stein

Biest F fig. n beast; (*kleines*) **~** brat, little devil, Am. a. stinker

bieten 1. v/t. offer; **sich ~** present itself; **2.** v/i. Auktion: (make* a) bid*

Bigamie f bigamy

Bikini m bikini

Bilanz f econ. balance; fig. result; **~ ziehen aus** fig. take* stock of

Bild n picture; *gedankliches:* image; **sich ein ~ machen von** get* an idea of; **~ausfall** TV m blackout; **~bericht** m photo(graphic) report (Am. essay)

bilden v/t. form (a. sich ~); *gestalten:* a. shape; fig. educate (**sich** o.s.); *darstellen, sein:* be*, constitute

Bilderbuch n picture book

Bild|fläche f: F **auf der ~ erscheinen** (**von der ~ verschwinden**) appear on (disappear from) the scene; **~hauer(in)** sculptor; **2lich** adj. graphic; *Ausdruck:* figurative; **~nis** n portrait; **~platte** f video dis|c, Am. -k; **~röhre** f picture tube

Bildschirm m TV screen; *Computer:* a. display, monitor; *Gerät:* VDT, video display terminal; **~arbeitsplatz** m workstation; **~schoner** m screen saver; **~text** m viewdata, Am. videotex(t)

bildschön adj. most beautiful

Bildung f education; *Aus2:* training; *Vorgang:* formation; **~s...** in Zssgn *Chancen, Reform, Urlaub etc.:* educational ...; **~slücke** f gap in one's knowledge

Billard n billiards, Am. a. pool; **~kugel** f billiard ball; **~stock** m cue

Billet(t) n *in Schweiz:* ticket

billig adj. cheap (a. contp.), inexpensive; **~en** v/t. approve of; **2ung** f approval

Billion f trillion

bimmeln F v/i. jingle; tel. ring*

binär adj. math., phys. etc.: binary

Binde f bandage; *Armschlinge:* sling; → **Damenbinde**; **~gewebe** anat. n connective tissue; **~glied** n (connecting) link; **~haut** anat. f conjunctiva; **~hautentzündung** med. f conjunctivitis

binde|n 1. v/t. bind* (a. Buch), tie (**an** to); *Kranz etc.:* make*; *Krawatte:* knot; **sich ~** bind* o.s., commit o.s.; **2.** v/i. bind*; **2strich** m hyphen; **2wort** gr. n conjunction

B

Bindfaden *m* string

Bindung *f* tie, link, bond; *Ski*♀: binding

Binnen|hafen *m* inland port; **~handel** *m* domestic trade; **~markt** *m*: *Europäischer* **~** European single market; **~schiffahrt** *f* inland navigation; **~verkehr** *m* inland traffic *od.* transport

Binse *bot. f* rush; F: *in die* **~n** *gehen* go* up in smoke; **~nweisheit** *f* truism

Bio..., **♀...** *in Zssgn Chemie, dynamisch, Sphäre, Technik etc.*: bio...

Biographi|e *f* biography; **♀sch** *adj.* biographic(al)

Bioladen *m* health food shop *od.* store

Biolog|e *m* biologist; **~ie** *f* biology; **♀isch** *adj.* biological; *Anbau etc.*: organic; **~ abbaubar** biodegradable

Bio|rhythmus *m* biorhythms *pl.*; **~technik** *f* biotechnology

Biotop *n* biotope

Birke *f* birch (tree)

Birne *f* pear; *electr.* (light) bulb

bis *prp. u. adv. u. cj. zeitlich*: till, until, (up) to; *räumlich*: (up) to, as far as; *von ... ~* from ... to; **~ auf** *außer*: except; **~ zu** up to; **~ später!** see you later!; **~ jetzt** up to now, so far; **~ Montag** *spätestens*: by Monday; *zwei* **~** *drei* two or three; *wie weit ist es* **~ ...?** how far is it to ...?

Bischof *m* bishop

Biscuit *n Schweiz*: → **Keks**

bisexuell *adj.* bisexual

bisher *adv.* up to now, so far; *wie* **~** as before; **~ig** *adj.* previous

Biskuit *n* sponge cake (mix)

Biß *m* bite (*a. fig. Schärfe*)

bißchen *adj. u. adv.*: *ein* **~** a little, a (little) bit (of); *nicht ein* **~** not in the least

Bissen *m* bite; *keinen* **~** not a thing

bissig *adj. fig.* cutting; *ein* **~er** *Hund* a dog that bites; *Vorsicht,* **~er** *Hund!* beware of the dog!

Bistum *n* bishopric, diocese

bisweilen *adv.* at times, now and then

Bit *n Computer*: bit

Bitte *f* request (*um* for); *ich habe e-e* **~** (*an dich*) I have a favo(u)r to ask of you

bitte *adv.* please; **~ nicht!** please don't! ~ (*schön*)! *als Antwort*: that's all right, not at all, you're welcome; *beim Überreichen etc.*: here you are; (*wie*) **~?** pardon?; ~ *sehr?* (*im Geschäft*) can I help you?

bitten *v/t.*: *j-n um et.* **~** ask s.o. for s.th.; *um j-s Namen* (*Erlaubnis*) **~** ask s.o.'s name (permission); *darf ich* **~?** may I have (the pleasure of) this dance?

bitter *adj.* bitter (*a. fig.*); *Kälte*: *a.* biting; **~kalt** *adj.* bitterly cold

bläh|en *v/refl.* swell*; **♀ungen** *pl.* flatulence *sg.*, *Brt. a.* F wind

blam|abel *adj.* embarrassing; **♀age** *f* disgrace, shame; **♀ieren** *v/t.*: *j-n* **~** make* s.o. look like a fool; *sich* **~** make* a fool of o.s.; △ *nicht* **blame**

blank *adj.* shining, shiny, bright; **~** *geputzt*: polished; F *fig.* broke

Blanko... *econ. in Zssgn* blank ...

Bläschen *med. n* vesicle, small blister

Blase *f* bubble; *anat.* bladder; *med.* blister; **~balg** *m* (pair of) bellows

blasen *v/t.* blow* (*a. mus.*)

Blas|instrument *mus. n* wind instrument; **~kapelle** *f* brass band; **~rohr** *n* *Waffe*: blowpipe

blaß *adj.* pale (*vor* with); **~** *werden* turn pale

Blässe *f* paleness, pallor

Blatt *n bot.* leaf; *Papier*♀: piece, sheet (*a. mus.*); (news)paper; *Karten*: hand

blättern *v/i.*: **~** *in* leaf through

Blätterteig *m* puff pastry

blau *adj.* blue; F *fig.* loaded, stoned; **~es** *Auge* black eye; **~er** *Fleck* bruise; *Fahrt ins* **♀e** jaunt (through the countryside); *organisiert*: mystery tour; **~äugig** *adj.* blue-eyed; *fig.* starry-eyed; **♀beere** *bot. f* bilberry, *Am.* blueberry; **~grau** *adj.* bluish-grey

bläulich *adj.* bluish

Blau|licht *n* flashing light(s *pl.*); **~helme** *pl.* UN soldiers *pl.*; **♀machen** *v/i.* stay away from work *od.* school; **~säure** *chem. f* prussic acid

Blech *n* sheet metal; *in Zssgn Dach-, Löffel etc.*: tin; *Instrument*: brass; **♀en** F *v/t. u. v/i.* shell out; **~büchse**, **~dose** *f* can, *Brt. a.* tin; **~schaden** *mot. m* bodywork damage

Blei *n* lead; *aus* **~** leaden

Bleibe *f* place to stay

bleiben *v/i.* stay, remain; **~** *bei* stick* to; → *Apparat, ruhig etc.*; **~d** *adj.* lasting, permanent; **~lassen** *v/t.* not do* s.th.; *laß das bleiben!* stop that!; *das wirst du schön* **~!** you'll do nothing of the sort!

bleich adj. pale (**vor** with); **~en** v/t. bleach; **2gesicht** F n paleface

blei|ern adj. lead(en (fig.)); **~frei** mot. adj. unleaded; **2stift** m pencil; **~stiftspitzer** m pencil sharpener

Blende f blind; phot. aperture; (**bei**) ~ 8 (at) f-8

blend|en v/t. blind, dazzle (beide a. fig.); **~end** adj. dazzling (a. fig.); Leistung: brilliant; ~ **aussehen** look great; **~frei** opt. adj. anti-glare

Blick m look (**auf** at); Aussicht: view (of); **flüchtiger** ~ glance; **auf den ersten** ~ at first sight; **2en** v/i. look, glance (beide: **auf**, **nach** at); **~fang** m eye-catcher; **~feld** n field of vision

blind adj. blind (a. fig.: **gegen**, **für** to; **vor** with); Spiegel etc.: dull; **~er Alarm** false alarm; **~er Passagier** stowaway; **auf e-m Auge** ~ blind in one eye; **ein** 2er a blind man; **e-e** 2e a blind woman; **die** 2en the blind

Blinddarm anat. m appendix; **~entzündung** f med. appendicitis; **~operation** f med. appendectomy

Blinden|hund m guide dog, Am. a. seeing eye dog; **~schrift** f braille

Blind|flug aviat. m blind flying; **~gänger** m dud (a. fig.); **~heit** f blindness; **2lings** adv. blindly; **~schleiche** zo. f blindworm

blinke|n v/i. sparkle, shine*; Sterne: twinkle; signalisieren: flash (a signal); mot. indicate; 2r mot. m indicator, Am. turn signal

blinzeln v/i. blink (one's eyes)

Blitz m (flash of) lightning; phot. flash; **~ableiter** m lightning conductor; 2en v/i. flash; **es blitzt** it's lightening; **~gerät** phot. n (electronic) flash; **~lampe** phot. f flashbulb; Würfel: flash cube; **~licht** n flash(light); **~schlag** m lightning stroke; 2schnell adj. u. adv. like a flash; attr. split-second

Block m block; pol., econ. bloc; Schreib2: pad; **~ade** mil., naut. f blockade; **~flöte** f recorder; **~haus** n log cabin; 2ieren v/t. u. v/i. block; mot. lock; **~schrift** f block letters pl.

blöd(e) F adj. silly, stupid; **~eln** F v/i. fool around; 2heit f stupidity; 2sinn m rubbish, nonsense; sense; **~sinnig** adj. idiotic, foolish

blöken v/i. Schaf, Kalb: bleat

blond adj. blond, fair 2ine f blonde

bloß 1. adj. bare; Auge: naked; nichts als: mere; **2.** adv. only, just, merely

Blöße f nakedness; **sich e-e ~ geben** lay* o.s. open to attack od. criticism

bloß|legen v/t. lay* bare, expose; **~stellen** v/t. expose, compromise, unmask; **sich** ~ compromise o.s.

blühen v/i. (be* in) bloom; Bäume, Büsche: (be* in) blossom; fig. flourish

Blume f flower; Wein: bouquet; Bier: froth, head

Blumen|beet n flowerbed; **~händler** m florist; **~kohl** m cauliflower; **~laden** m flower shop, florist's; **~strauß** m bunch of flowers; bouquet; **~topf** m flowerpot; **~vase** f vase

Bluse f blouse

Blut n blood; **2arm** med. adj. an(a)emic (a. fig.); **~armut** med. f an(a)emia; **~bad** n massacre; **~bahn** anat. f bloodstream; **~bank** med. f blood bank; 2befleckt adj. bloodstained; **~bild** med. n blood count; **~blase** f blood blister; **~druck** m blood pressure

Blüte f flower; bloom (a. fig.); bsd. Baum2: blossom; fig. height, heyday; **in (voller)** ~ in (full) bloom

Blutegel zo. m leech

bluten v/i. bleed* (**aus** from)

Blüten|blatt n petal; **~staub** m pollen

Bluter med. m h(a)emophiliac

Blut|erguß m bruise; med. h(a)ematoma

Blut|gefäß n blood vessel; **~gerinnsel** n blood clot; **~gruppe** f blood group; **~hund** m bloodhound; 2ig adj. bloody; **~er Anfänger** rank beginner, F greenhorn; **~körperchen** n blood corpuscle; **~kreislauf** m (blood) circulation; **~lache** f pool of blood; 2leer adj. bloodless; **~probe** f blood test; 2rünstig adj. bloodthirsty, gory; **~schande** jur. f incest; **~spender(in)** blood donor; 2stillend adj. styptic; **~sverwandte(r)** blood relation; **~übertragung** f blood transfusion; **~ung** f bleeding, h(a)emorrhage; 2unterlaufen adj. bloodshot; **~vergießen** n bloodshed; **~vergiftung** f blood poisoning; **~wurst** f black pudding, Am. blood sausage

BLZ Abk. für **Bankleitzahl** bank (sorting) code, Am. A.B.A. number

B

Bö f gust, squall

Bob m bob(sled); **~bahn** f bob run; **~fahren** n bobsledding

Bock m Reh♀: buck; Ziegen♀: he-goat, billy-goat; Schaf♀: ram; Sport: buck; **e-n ~ schießen** (make* a) blunder; **keinen** (od. null) **~ auf et. haben** have zero interest in s.th.; **♀en** v/i. buck; schmollen: sulk; **♀ig** adj. obstinate; sulky; **~springen** n Sport: buck vaulting; Spiel: leapfrog; **~wurst** f hot sausage

Boden m ground; agr. soil; Gefäß♀, Meeres♀: bottom; Fuß♀: floor; Dach♀: attic; **♀los** adj. fig. incredible; **~personal** aviat. n ground crew; **~reform** f land reform; **~schätze** pl. mineral resources pl.; **~station** aviat. f ground control; **~turnen** n floor exercises pl.

Body m bodysuit

Bogen m bend, curve; math. arc; arch. arch; Eislauf: curve; Ski: turn; Waffe: bow; Papier♀: sheet; **~schießen** n archery; **~schütze** m archer

Bohle f plank

Bohne f bean; **grüne ~n** green (Brt. a. French) beans; **~nstange** f beanpole (a. F fig.)

bohner|n v/t. polish, wax; **♀wachs** n floor polish

bohren v/t. bore, drill (a. Zahnarzt); **~d** fig. adj. Blick: piercing; Fragen: insistent

Bohr|er tech. m drill; **~insel** f oil rig; **~loch** n borehole, Öl♀: a. well(head); **~maschine** f (electric) drill; **~turm** m derrick; **~ung** f drilling; Zylinder: bore

Boje naut. f buoy

Bolzen tech. m bolt

bombardieren v/t. bomb; fig. bombard

Bombe f bomb; fig. bombshell; **~nangriff** m air raid; **~nanschlag** m bomb attack; **~nerfolg** m roaring success; thea. etc. smash hit; **~ngeschäft** F n super deal; **~nleger** m bomber; **♀nsicher** adj. bombproof; **~r** aviat. m bomber (a. fig.)

Bon m coupon, voucher

Bonbon m, n sweet, Am. candy

Boot n boat; **~smann** m boatswain

Bord¹ n shelf

Bord² naut., aviat. m: **an ~** on board; **über ~** overboard; **von ~ gehen** disembark

Bordell n brothel, F whorehouse

Bord|funker m radio operator; **~karte** aviat. f boarding pass; **~stein** m kerb, Am. curb

borgen v/t. borrow; **sich ~ von** borrow s.th. from; **j-m ~** lend* s.th. to s.o.

Borke f bark

borniert adj. narrow-minded

Börse econ. f stock exchange

Börsen|bericht m market report; **~kurs** m quotation; **~makler** m stockbroker; **~spekulant** m stock-jobber

Borst|e f bristle; **♀ig** adj. bristly

Borte f border; Besatz♀: braid, lace

bösartig adj. vicious; med. malignant

Böschung f slope, bank; Ufer♀, rail.: embankment

böse adj. bad, evil, wicked; zornig: angry (über about; auf j-n with s.o.), bsd. Am. a. mad (auf at); **er meint es nicht ~** he means no harm

Böse n (the) evil; **~wicht** m villain

bos|haft adj. malicious; **♀heit** f malice

böswillig adj. malicious, jur. a. wil(l)ful

Botani|k f botany; **~ker(in)** botanist; **♀sch** adj. botanical

Bote m messenger; **~ngang** m: **Botengänge machen** run* errands

Botschaft f message; Amt: embassy; **~er** m ambassador

Bottich m tub, vat

Bouillon f consommé, bouillon, broth

Boulevardblatt n, **~zeitung** f tabloid

Bowle f (cold) punch; Gefäß: bowl

boxen 1. v/i. box; **2.** v/t. punch

Box|en n boxing; **~er** m boxer; **~handschuh** m boxing glove; **~kampf** m boxing match, fight; **~sport** m boxing

Boykott m, **♀ieren** v/t. boycott

brachliegen agr. v/i. lie* fallow (a. fig.)

Branche econ. f line (of business); **~(telefon)buch** n yellow pages pl.

Branntwein m brandy; spirits pl.

Brand m fire; **in ~ geraten** catch* fire; **in ~ stecken** set* fire to; **~blase** f blister; **~bombe** f incendiary bomb; **♀en** v/i. surge (gegen against); **~fleck** m burn; **~mal** n brand; fig. stigma; **♀marken** fig. v/t. brand, stigmatize; **~mauer** f fire wall; **~stätte**, **~stelle** f scene of fire; **~stifter** m arsonist; **~stiftung** f arson; **~ung** f surf, surge, breakers pl.; **~wunde** f burn; durch Verbrühen: scald

braten v/t. roast; *auf dem Rost*: grill, broil; *in der Pfanne*: fry; *am Spieß* ~ roast on a spit, barbecue

Braten m roast (meat); ~**stück**: joint; ~**fett** n dripping; ~**soße** f gravy

Brat|fisch m fried fish; ~**huhn** n roast chicken; ~**kartoffeln** pl. fried potatoes pl.; ~**pfanne** f frying-pan; ~**röhre** f oven

Bratsche mus. f viola

Bratwurst f grilled sausage

Brauch m custom; *Gewohnheit*: habit, practice; **2bar** adj. useful; **2en** v/t. need; *erfordern*: require; *Zeit*: take*; *ge-*: use; *wie lange wird er ~?* how long will it take him?; *du brauchst es nur zu sagen* just say the word; *ihr braucht es nicht zu tun* you don't have to do it; *er hätte nicht zu kommen* ~ he need not have come

brau|en v/t. brew; **2erei** f brewery

braun adj. brown; ~*gebrannt*: (sun-) tanned; ~ *werden* get* a tan

Bräune f (sun)tan; **2n 1.** v/t. brown; *Sonne*: tan; **2.** v/i. (get* a) tan

Braunkohle f brown coal, lignite

bräunlich adj. brownish

Brause f shower; → *Limonade*; **2n** v/i. *Wind, Wasser etc.*: roar; *eilen*: rush; ~ *duschen*; ~**pulver** n sherbet

Braut f bride; *Verlobte*: fiancée

Bräutigam m (bride)groom; fiancé

Braut|jungfer f bridesmaid; ~**kleid** n wedding-dress; ~**leute** pl., ~**paar** n bride and (bride)groom; *Verlobte*: engaged couple

brav adj. good; *ehrlich*: honest; *sei(d)* ~! be good!; △ *nicht* **brave**

BRD *Abk. für Bundesrepublik Deutschland* FRG, Federal Republic of Germany

brechen v/t. u. v/i. break* (a. fig.); *sich übergeben*: vomit, F throw* up, *Brt. a.* be* sick; *sich* ~ *opt.* be* refracted; *sich den Arm* ~ break* one's arm; *mit j-m* ~ break* with s.o.; ~**d voll** crammed, packed

Brech|reiz m nausea; ~**stange** f crowbar; ~**ung** *opt.* f refraction

Brei m ~*masse*: pulp, mash; *Kinder2*: pap; *Hafer2*: porridge; *Reis2 etc.*: pudding; **2ig** adj. pulpy, mushy

breit adj. wide; *Schultern, Grinsen*: broad (a. fig.); ~**beinig** adj. with legs

(wide) apart

Breite f width, breadth; *astr., geogr.* latitude; **2n** v/t. spread*; ~**ngrad** m degree of latitude; ~**nkreis** m parallel (of latitude)

breit|machen v/refl. spread* o.s., take* up room; ~**schlagen** v/t.: F: *j-n zu et.* ~ talk s.o. into (doing) s.th.; **2seite** f *naut.* broadside (a. fig.); **2wand** f *Film*: wide screen

Bremsbelag m brake lining

Bremse f brake; *zo.* gadfly; **2n 1.** v/i. brake, put* on the brake(s); *ab*~: slow down; **2.** v/t. brake; *fig.* curb

Brems|kraftverstärker mot. m brake booster; ~**licht** mot. n stop light; ~**pedal** n brake pedal; ~**spur** f skid marks pl.; ~**weg** m stopping distance

brenn|bar adj. combustible; *entzündlich*: (in)flammable; **2en 1.** v/t. burn*; *Schnaps*: distil(l); *Ziegel*: bake; **2.** v/i. burn*; *Haus etc.*: be* on fire; *Wunde, Augen*: smart, burn*; F *darauf* ~ *zu* be* dying to; *es brennt!* fire!

Brenn|er m *Gas2 etc.*: burner; ~**essel** f (stinging) nettle; ~**glas** n burning glass; ~**holz** n firewood; ~**material** n fuel; ~**punkt** m focus, focal point; ~**spiritus** m methylated spirit; ~**stab** m *tech.* fuel rod; ~**stoff** m fuel

brenzlig adj. burnt; *fig.* hot, *Brt. a.* dicey

Bresche f breach (a. fig.), gap

Brett n board; → *Anschlagbrett*; ~**erbude** f shack; ~**erzaun** m wooden fence; ~**spiel** n board game

Brezel f pretzel

Brief m letter; ~**beschwerer** m paperweight; ~**bogen** m sheet of (note)paper; ~**freund**(in) m pen friend (*Am.* pal); ~**karte** f correspondence card; ~**kasten** m letterbox, *Am.* mailbox; **2lich** adj. u. adv. by letter; ~**marke** f (postage) stamp; ~**markensammlung** f stamp-collection; ~**öffner** m paper knife, *Am.* letter opener; ~**papier** n stationery; ~**tasche** f wallet; ~**taube** f carrier pigeon; ~**träger** m postman, *Am.* mailman *od.* -carrier; ~**umschlag** m envelope; ~**wahl** f postal vote; ~**wechsel** m correspondence

Brikett n briquet(te)

Brillant 1. m (cut) diamond; **2.** **2** adj. brilliant; ~**ring** m diamond ring

Brille f (pair of) glasses pl., spectacles pl.; Schutz2: goggles pl.; toilet seat; ~netui n spectacle (Am. eyeglass) case; ~nträger(in): ~ sein wear* glasses

bringen v/t. bring*; hin~ take*; verursachen: cause; Opfer: make*; Gewinn etc.: yield; nach Hause ~ see* (od. take*) s.o. home; in Ordnung ~ put* in order; das bringt mich auf e-e Idee ~ that gives me an idea; j-n dazu ~, et. zu tun get* s.o. to do s.th.; et. mit sich ~ involve s.th.; j-n um et. ~ deprive s.o. of s.th.; j-n zum Lachen ~ make* s.o. laugh; j-n wieder zu sich ~ bring* s.o. round ; es zu et. (nichts) ~ go far (get nowhere); F es ~ make* it; das bringt nichts it's no use

Brise f breeze

Brit|e m, ~in f Briton; die Briten pl. the British pl.; 2isch adj. British

bröckeln v/i. crumble

Brocken m piece; Klumpen: lump; Fels~: rock; Fleisch: chunk; Bissen: morsel; ein paar ~ Englisch a few scraps of English; F ein harter ~ a hard nut to crack

Brombeere f blackberry

Bronchi|en pl. bronchi(a) pl.; ~tis med. f bronchitis

Bronze f bronze (a. in Zssgn Medaille etc.); ~zeit hist. f Bronze Age

Brosche f brooch, Am. a. pin

brosch|iert adj. paperback; 2üre f pamphlet; Werbe2: brochure

Brot n bread; belegtes: sandwich; ein (Laib) ~ a loaf (of bread); e-e Scheibe ~ a slice of bread; sein ~ verdienen earn one's living; ~aufstrich m spread

Brötchen n roll

Brot|rinde f crust; ~(schneide)maschine f bread cutter

Bruch m break; Knochen2: fracture; Unterleibs2: hernia; math. fraction; geol. fault; e-s Versprechens : breach; e-s Gesetzes: violation; zu ~ gehen be* wrecked; ~bude F f dump, hovel

brüchig adj. brittle; rissig: cracked

Bruch|landung aviat. f crash landing; ~rechnung f fractional arithmetic, F fractions pl.; 2sicher adj. breakproof; ~strich m fraction bar; ~stück n fragment; ~teil m fraction; im ~ e-r Sekunde in a split second; ~zahl f fraction(al) number

Brücke f bridge (a. Sport); Teppich: rug; ~npfeiler m pier

Bruder m brother (a. rel.); ~krieg m civil war

brüder|lich 1. adj. brotherly; **2.** adv.: ~ teilen share and share alike; 2lichkeit f brotherhood; 2schaft f: ~ trinken agree to use the familiar 'du' form of address

Brüh|e f Suppe: broth; Grundsubstanz: stock; F Getränk: dishwater; Schmutzwasser: slops pl.; F Gewässer: filthy water, bilge; 2würfel m beef cube

brüllen v/i. roar (vor Lachen with laughter); Rind: bellow; F Kind: bawl; ~d adj.: ~es Gelächter roars pl. of laughter

brumm|en v/i. growl; Insekt: hum, buzz (a. Motor etc.); Kopf: be* buzzing; ~ig adj. grumpy

brünett adj. brunette, dark-haired

Brunnen m well; Quelle: spring; Spring2: fountain

Brunstzeit zo. f rutting season

Brust f chest; weibliche: breast(s pl.), bosom; ~bein n breastbone; ~beutel m money bag, Am. neck pouch

brüsten v/refl. boast, brag (mit of)

Brust|kasten, ~korb m chest, anat. thorax; ~schwimmen n breaststroke

Brüstung f parapet

Brustwarze f nipple

Brut f brooding; brood, hatch; Fisch2: fry; F fig. brood; contp. scum

brutal adj. brutal; 2ität f brutality

Brutapparat zo. m incubator

brüten v/i. brood, sit* (on eggs); ~ über fig. brood over

Brutkasten med. m incubator

brutto adv. gross (a. in Zssgn); 2sozialprodukt n gross national product; 2verdienst m gross earnings pl.

Bube m boy, lad; Karte: knave, jack

Buch n book; ~binder m (book)binder; ~drucker m printer; ~druckerei f printing office, Am. print shop

Buche f beech

buchen v/t. book; econ. enter

Bücher|bord n bookshelf; ~ei f library; ~regal n bookshelf; ~schrank m bookcase; ~wurm fig. m bookworm

Buch|fink zo. m chaffinch; ~halter(in) bookkeeper; ~haltung f bookkeeping; ~händler(in) bookseller; ~hand-

lung f bookshop, Am. bookstore; **~macher** m bookmaker

Büchse f tin, Am. can; größere: box; Gewehr: rifle; **~nfleisch** n tinned (Am. canned) meat; **~nöffner** m tin (Am. can) opener

Buchstab|e m letter; großer (kleiner) ~ capital (small) letter; **2ieren** v/t. spell*

buchstäblich adv. literally

Buchstütze f bookend

Bucht f bay; kleine: creek, inlet

Buchung f booking; econ. entry

Buckel m hump, hunch; bsd. Mensch: humpback, hunchback; **e-n ~ machen** hump od. hunch one's back

bücken v/refl. bend* (down), stoop

bucklig adj. humpbacked, hunchbacked; **2e(r)** humpback, hunchback

Bückling m kipper, Am. smoked herring; F fig. bow

Buddhis|mus m Buddhism; **~t(in)**, **2tisch** adj. Buddhist

Bude f stall, booth; Hütte: hut; F digs pl., Am. pad; contp. dump, hole

Budget n budget

Büfett n counter, bar, buffet; Möbel: sideboard, cupboard; **kaltes (warmes)** ~ cold (hot) buffet (meal)

Büffel zo. m buffalo

büffeln F v/i. grind*, cram, swot

Bug m naut. bow; aviat. nose; zo., gastr. shoulder

Bügel m hanger; Brillen2 etc.: bow; **~brett** n ironing board; **~eisen** n iron; **~falte** f crease; **2frei** adj. no(n)-iron; **2n** v/t. iron; Hose etc.: press

buh int. boo!; **~en** v/i. boo

Bühne f stage; fig. a. scene; **~nbild** n (stage) set(ting); **~nbildner(in)** stage designer

Buhrufe pl. boos pl.

Bulette f meatball

Bull|auge naut. n porthole; **~dogge** zo. f bulldog

Bulle zo. m bull (a. fig.); contp. Polizist: cop(per)

Bummel F m stroll; **~elei** f dawdling; Nachlässigkeit: slackness; **2eln** v/i. stroll, saunter; trödeln: dawdle; econ. go* slow; **~elstreik** m go-slow (strike), Am. slowdown; **~elzug** F m slow train; **~ler** m stroller; dawdler, F slowcoach, Am. slowpoak

bumsen v/i. u. v/t. F → **krachen**; V bang, screw

Bund[1] m association, federation, alliance; Verband: association; Hosen2 etc.: (waist)band; **der ~** pol. the Federal Government; F s. **Bundeswehr**

Bund[2] n Bündel: bundle; Petersilie etc.: bunch

Bündel n bundle; **2n** v/t. bundle (up)

Bundes|... in Zssgn Federal ...; German ...; **~bahn** f Federal Railway(s pl.); **~genosse** m ally; **~kanzler** m Federal Chancellor; **~land** n appr. (federal) state, Land; **~liga** f sport: First Division; **~post** f Federal Postal Administration; **~präsident** m Federal President; **~rat** m Bundesrat, Upper House of German Parliament; **~republik** f Federal Republic; **~staat** m einzelner: federal state; Gesamtheit der einzelnen: confederation; **~straße** f Federal Highway **~tag** m Bundestag, Lower House of German Parliament; **~trainer(in)** coach of the (German) national team; **~verfassungsgericht** n Federal Constitutional Court, Am. etwa Supreme Court; **~wehr** f (German Federal) Armed Forces pl.

bündig adj. tech. flush; kurz und ~ terse(ly); point-blank

Bündnis n alliance

Bunker m air-raid shelter, bunker

bunt adj.: colo(u)red; mehrfarbig: multicolo(u)red; farbenfroh: colo(u)rful (a. fig.); Programm etc.: varied; **~er Abend** evening of entertainment; **mir wird's zu** ~ that's all I can take; **2stift** m colo(u)red pencil, crayon

Bürde fig. f burden (für j-n to s.o.)

Burg f castle

Bürge jur. m guarantor (a. fig.); **2n** v/i.: **für j-n** ~ jur. stand* surety for s.o.; **für et.** ~ guarantee s.th.

Bürger|(in) citizen; **~initiative** f (citizen's od. local) action group; **~krieg** m civil war

bürgerlich adj. civil; middle-class; bsd. contp. bourgeois; **~e Küche** home cooking; **2e(r)** commoner

Bürger|meister m mayor; **~rechte** pl. civil rights pl.; **~steig** m pavement, Am. sidewalk

Bürgschaft jur. f surety; bail

Büro n office; **~angestellte(r)** clerk,

office worker; **~klammer** f (paper) clip; **~krat** m bureaucrat; **~kratie** f bureaucracy; *contp.* red tape; **~stunden** pl. office hours pl.

Bursche m fellow, guy, *Brt. a.* lad

burschikos adj. (tom)boyish, pert

Bürste f brush; **2n** v/t. brush; **~nschnitt** m crew cut

Bus m bus; *Reise2: a.* coach

Busch m bush, shrub

Büschel n bunch; *Haar, Gras etc.:* tuft

buschlig adj. bushy; **2messer** n bush-knife, machete

Busen m bosom, breast(s pl.)

Bus|fahrer m bus driver; **~haltestelle** f bus stop

Bussard zo. m buzzard

Buße f penance; *Reue:* repentance; *Geld2:* fine; **~ tun*** do* penance

büßen v/t. pay* *od.* suffer for *s.th.*; *rel.* repent

Buß|geld n fine, penalty; **~tag** m day of repentance

Büste f bust; **~nhalter** m bra

Butter f butter; **~blume** f buttercup; **~brot** n (slice *od.* piece of) bread and butter; F: *für ein* **~** for a song; **~brotpapier** n greaseproof paper; **~dose** f butter dish; **~milch** f buttermilk

b.w. *Abk. für* **bitte wenden** PTO, please turn over

bzw. *Abk. für* **beziehungsweise** resp., respectively

C

C *Abk. für* **Celsius** C, Celsius, centigrade

ca. *Abk. für* **circa** approx., approximately

Café n café, coffee house

camp|en v/i. camp; **2er** m camper

Camping|... *in Zssgn Bett, Tisch etc.:* camp ...; **~bus** m camper (van *Brt.*); **~platz** m camp|site, *Am.* -ground

Catcher m wrestler; △ *nicht* **catcher**

CD|(-Platte) f CD, compact disc; **~-ROM** CD-ROM; **~Spieler** m CD player

Cellist(in) *mus.* cellist

Cello *mus.* n Cello

Celsius: *5 Grad* **~** (*abbr.* **5° C**) five degrees centigrade *od.* Celsius

Cembalo *mus.* n harpsichord

Champagner m champagne

Champignon m mushroom

Chance f chance; *die* **~n** *stehen gleich* (*3 zu 1*) the odds are even (three to one); **~ngleichheit** f equal opportunities pl.

Chao|s n chaos; **~t** m chaotic person; *pol.* anarchist, *pl. a.* lunatic fringe; **2tisch** adj. chaotic

Charakter m character, nature; *je-mand mit gutem etc.* **~** s.o. of good *etc.* character; **2isieren** v/t. characterize, describe (*als* as); **~istik** f characterization; **2istisch** adj. characteristic, typical (*für* of); **2lich** adj. character..., personal; **2los** adj. of bad character; *schwach:* lacking character; **~zug** m trait

charm|ant adj. charming; **2e** m charme

Chassis *tech.* n chassis

Chauffeur m chauffeur, driver

Chaussee f country road; *Stadt:* avenue

Chauvi *contp.* m male chauvinist (pig); **2nismus** m chauvinism; *pol. a.* jingoism

Chef m F boss; head, chief (*a. in Zssgn*); △ *nicht* **chef**; **~arzt** m, **~ärztin** f senior consultant, *Am.* medical director; **~sekretärin** f executive secretary

Chem|ie f chemistry; **~iefaser** f synthetic fib|re, *Am.* -er; **~ikalien** pl. chemicals pl.; **~iker(in)** (analytical) chemist; **2isch** adj. chemical; **~e Reinigung** dry-cleaning; **~otherapie** *med.* f chemotherapy

Chiffr|e f code, cipher; *in Anzeigen:* box (number); **2ieren** v/t. (en)code

Chin|a China; **~ese** m, **~esin** f, 2e-sisch adj. Chinese

Chinin pharm. n quinine

Chip m Spielmarke, Computer: chip; **~s** pl. crisps pl., Am. chips pl.

Chirurg m surgeon; **~ie** f surgery; 2isch adj. surgical

Chlor n chlorine; 2en v/t. chlorinate

Cholera med. f cholera

cholerisch adj. choleric

Cholesterin adj. cholesterol

Chor m choir (a. arch.); **im ~** in chorus; **~al** m chorale, hymn

Christ Christian; **~baum** m Christmas tree; **~enheit: die ~** Christendom; **~entum** n Christianity; **~in** f Christian; **~kind** n Infant Jesus; Father Christmas, Santa Claus; 2lich adj. Christian; **~us** npr. m Christ; **vor (nach) ~** B.C. (A.D.)

Chrom n chrome; chem. a. chromium

Chromosom biol. n chromosome

Chron|ik f chronicle; 2isch med. adj. chronic (a. fig.); 2ologisch adj. chronological

circa adv. → zirka

City f (city) cent|re, Am. -er

Clique f F group, set; contp. clique

Clou F m highlight, climax; **der ~** (Witz) **daran** the whole point of it

Computer m computer; **~ausdruck** m computer printout; 2gesteuert adj. computer-controlled; 2gestützt adj. computer-aided; **~graphik** f computer graphics pl.; 2isieren v/t. computerize; **~spiel** n computer game; **~virus** m computer virus

Conférencier m compère, Am. master of ceremonies, F: emcee, MC

Corner östr. m Sport: corner (kick)

Couch f couch

Coupé mot. n coupé

Coupon m voucher, coupon

Cousin m, **~e** f cousin

Creme f cream (a. fig.)

Curry m Gewürz: curry powder

Cursor m Computer: cursor

D

da 1. adv. räumlich: there; here; zeitlich: then, at that time; **~ drüben (draußen, hinten)** over (out, back) there; **von ~ aus** from there; **das ... ~** that ... (over there); **~ kommt er** here he comes; **~ bin ich** here I am; **er ist gleich wieder ~** he'll be right back; **von ~ an od. ab** from then on; **2. cj.** as, since, because; **~behalten** v/t. keep* (j-n: in)

dabei adv. anwesend: there, present; nahe: near od. close by; gleichzeitig, zusätzlich: at the same time; mit enthalten: included with it; **er ist gerade ~ zu gehen** he's just leaving; **es ist nichts ~ leicht:** there's nothing to it; harmlos: there's no harm in it; **was ist schon ~?** (so) what of it?; **lassen wir es ~!** let's leave it at that!; **~bleiben** v/i. stick to it; **~haben** v/t. have* with (Geld a. on) one; **~sein** v/i. be* there; take part; be* in on it; **ich bin dabei!** count me in!

dableiben v/i. stay

Dach n roof; **~boden** m attic; **~decker** m roofer; **~fenster** n dormer window; **~gepäckträger** m roof(-top luggage Am.) rack; **~geschoß** n attic; **~kammer** f garret; **~luke** f skylight; **~pappe** f roofing felt; **~rinne** f gutter

Dachs zo. m badger

Dach|stuhl m roof framework; **~terrasse** f roof terrace; **~verband** m umbrella organization

Dackel m dachshund

dadurch adv. u. cj. Art u. Weise: this od. that way; deshalb: for this reason, so; **~, daß** due to the fact that

dafür adv. for it, for that; anstatt: instead; als Gegenleistung: in return, in exchange; **~ sein** be* in favo(u)r of it; **er kann nichts ~** it is not his fault; **~ sorgen, daß** see* to it that; 2halten n: **nach meinem ~** in my opinion

dagegen adv. u. cj. against it; jedoch: however, on the other hand; ~ sein be* against (od. opposed to) it; haben Sie et. ~, daß ich ...? do you mind if I ...?; wenn Sie nichts ~ haben if you don't mind; ... ist nichts ~ ... can't compare

daheim adv. at home; 2 n home

daher adv. u. cj. from there; deshalb: that's why

dahin adv. there, to that place; vergangen: gone, past; bis ~ zeitlich: till then, örtlich: up to there

dahinten adv. back there

dahinter adv. behind it; es steckt nichts ~ there is nothing to it; **~kommen** v/i. find* out (about it)

dalassen v/t. leave* behind

damalig adj. then; nachgestellt: at that time; **~s** adv. then, at that time

Dame f lady; Tanzen: partner; Karten, Schach: queen; Spiel: draughts, Am. checkers ;m-e ~n u. Herren! ladies and gentlemen!; **~n...** in Zssgn ladies' ...; Sport: women's ...; **~nbinde** f sanitary towel (Am. napkin); 2nhaft adj. ladylike; **~ntoilette** f ladies' toilet (Am. room), the ladies sg.; **~nwahl** f ladies' choice

damit 1. adv. with it od. that; mittels: by it, with it; was will er ~ sagen? what's he trying to say?; wie steht es ~? how about it?; ~ einverstanden sein have no objections; 2. cj. so that; in order to inf.; ~ nicht so as not to

Damm m Stau2: dam; Fluß2 etc.: embankment

dämmerig adj. dim; 2licht n twilight; **~n** v/i. Morgen: dawn (a. F fig.: j-m on s.o.); get* dark od. dusky; 2ung f Abend2: dusk; Morgen2: dawn

Dämon m demon; 2isch adj. demoniac(al)

Dampf m steam; phys. vapo(u)r; 2en v/i. steam

dämpfen v/t. Schall: deaden; Stimme: muffle; Licht, Farbe, Schlag: soften; gastr. steam, stew; Kleidungsstück: steam-iron; Stimmung: put a damper on; Kosten etc.: curb

Dampfer m steamer, steamship; **~kochtopf** m pressure cooker; **~maschine** f steam engine; **~walze** f steam-roller

danach adv. after it od. that; später:

afterwards; Ziel: for it; entsprechend: according to it; ich fragte ihn ~ I asked him about it; mir ist nicht ~ I don't feel like it

Däne m Dane

daneben adv. next to it, beside it; außerdem: besides, as well, at the same time; am Ziel vorbei: beside the mark; **~benehmen** F v/refl. misbehave, make* a fool of o.s.; **~gehen** F v/i. Kugel etc.: miss (the target); F Plan, Spaß: misfire

Dän|emark Denmark; **~in** f Danish woman od. girl; 2isch Danish

Dank m thanks pl.; Gott sei ~! thank God!; vielen ~! many thanks!

dank prp. thanks to; **~bar** adj. grateful (j-m to s.o.); lohnend: rewarding; 2barkeit f gratitude; **~en** v/i. thank (j-m für et. s.o. for s.th.); danke (schön) thank you (very much); (nein,) danke no, thank you; nichts zu ~ not at all

dann adv. then; ~ und wann (every) now and then

daran adv. räumlich: on it; sterben, denken: of it; glauben: in it; leiden: from it; → liegen; **~gehen** v/i. get down to it; **~zu** get down to ...ing

darauf adv. räumlich: on (top of) it; zeitlich: after (that); hören, antworten, trinken: to it; stolz: of it; warten: for it; am Tage ~ the day after; zwei Jahre ~ two years later; **~kommt es an** that's what matters; **~hin** adv. after that; als Folge: as a result

daraus adv. from (od. out of) it; was ist ~ geworden? what has become of it?; ~ wird nichts! F nothing doing!

Darbietung f presentation; performance

darin adv. in it; betont: in that; gut ~ good at it

darlegen v/t. explain, set out

Darlehen n loan (geben grant)

Darm m bowel(s pl.), intestine(s pl.); Wurst: skin; **~grippe** f intestinal flu

darstellen v/t. represent, show*, depict; beschreiben: describe; Rolle: play, do*; graphisch: trace, graph; 2er(in) thea. performer, ac|tor (-tress); 2ung f representation; description; account; Portrait, Rolle: portrayal

darüber adv. over od. above it; quer:

across it; *zeitlich*: in the meantime; *inhaltlich*: about it; **... und ~** ... and more; **~ werden Jahre vergehen** that will take years

darum *adv. u. cj. räumlich*: (a)round it; *deshalb*: because of it, that's why; **~ bitten** ask for it; → **gehen**

darunter *adv.* under *od.* below it, underneath; *dazwischen*: among them; *einschließlich*: including; **... und ~** ... and less; **was verstehst du ~?** what do you understand by it?

das → **der**

dasein *v/i.* be* there; *vorhanden sein*: exist; **ist noch ... da?** is any ... left?; **noch nie dagewesen** unprecedented

Dasein *n* life, existence

daß *cj.* that; *damit*: so (that); **es sei denn, ~** unless; **ohne ~** without *ger.*; **nicht ~ ich wüßte** not that I know of

dastehen *v/i.* stand* (there)

Datei *f Computer*: file; **~verwaltung** *f* file management

Daten *pl.* data *pl.* (*Computer a. sg.*), facts *pl.*; *Personalangaben*: particulars *pl.*; **~bank** *f* database, data bank; **~schutz** *m* data protection; **~speicher** *m* data memory *od.* storage; **~träger** *m* data medium *od.* carrier; **~übertragung** *f* data transfer; **~verarbeitung** *f* data processing

datieren *v/t. u. v/i.* date

Dativ *gr. m* dative (case)

Dattel *f* date

Datum *n* date; **welches ~ haben wir heute?** what's the date today?

Dauer *f* duration; *Fort*\~: continuance; **auf die ~** in the long run; **für die ~ von** for a period *od.* term of; **von ~ sein** last; **~arbeitslosigkeit** *f* long-term unemployment; **~auftrag** *m* standing order; **~geschwindigkeit** *f* cruising speed; **\haft** *adj.* lasting; *Stoff*: durable; **~karte** *f* season ticket; **~lauf** *m* jogging; **im ~** at a jog; **~lutscher** *m* lollipop

dauer|n *v/i.* last, take*; → **lange**; **\welle** *f* perm, *Am.* permanent

Daumen *m* thumb; **j-m den ~ halten** keep* one's fingers crossed (for s.o.); **am ~ lutschen** suck one's thumb

Daunen *pl.* down *sg.*; **~decke** *f* eiderdown

davon *adv.* (away) from it; *dadurch*: by

it; *darüber*: about it; *fort*: away; **~... in** *Zssgn fahren etc.*: *mst* ... off; *von et.*: of it *od.* them; **~haben** get* s.th. out of it; **das kommt ~!** there you are!, that will teach you!; **~kommen** *v/i.* escape, get* away; **~laufen** *v/i.* run* away

davor *adv.* before *od.* of it; *nur räumlich*: in front of it; *sich fürchten, warnen*: of it

dazu *adv. dafür*: for it, for that purpose; *außerdem*: in addition; **noch ~** into the bargain; **~ ist es da** that's what it's there for; **... Salat ~?** ... a salad with it?; → **kommen, Lust** *etc.*; **~gehören** *v/i.* belong to it, be* part of it; **~gehörig** *adj.* belonging to it; **~kommen** *v/i.* join *s.o.*; *Sache*: be* added

dazwischen *adv. räumlich*: between (them); *zeitlich*: in between; *darunter*: among them; **~kommen** *v/i. Ereignis*: intervene, happen; **wenn nichts dazwischenkommt** if all goes well

DB *Abk. für Deutsche Bahn* German Rail

deal|en F *v/i.* push drugs; **\er** *m* drug dealer, F pusher

Debatt|e *f* debate; **\ieren** *v/i.* debate (*über* on)

Debüt *n* debut (*geben* make*)

dechiffrieren *v/t.* decipher, decode

Deck *naut. n* deck

Decke *f Woll*\~: blanket; *Stepp*\~: quilt; *Zimmer*\~: ceiling

Deckel *m* lid, cover, top

decken *v/t. u. v/i.* cover (*a. zo.*); *Sport*: *a.* mark; **sich ~ (mit)** coincide (with); → **Tisch**

Deckung *f* cover; *Boxen*: guard; **in ~ gehen** take* cover

defekt *adj.* defective, faulty; *Lift etc.*: out of order

Defekt *m* defect, fault

defen|siv *adj.*, **\sive** *f* defensive

defin|ieren *v/t.* define; **\ition** *f* definition

Defizit *n* deficit; *Mangel*: deficiency

Degen *m* sword; *Fechten*: épée

degradieren *v/t.* degrade (*a. fig.*)

dehn|bar *adj.* flexible, elastic (*a. fig.*); **~en** *v/t.* stretch (*a. fig.*)

Deich *m* dike; **~bruch** *m* dike breach

Deichsel *f* pole, shaft

dein *poss. pron.* your; **~er, ~e, ~(e)s** yours; **~erseits** *adv.* on your part; **~esgleichen** *pron. contp.* the likes of you; **~etwegen** *adv.* for your sake; *wegen dir*: because of you

Dekan *rel., univ. m* dean

Dekolleté *n* low neckline

Deklin|ation *gr. f* declension; **2ieren** *gr. v/t.* decline

Dekor|ateur *m* decorator; *Schaufenster*2: window dresser; **~ation** *f* decoration; (window) display; *thea.* scenery; **2ativ** *adj.* decorative; **2ieren** *v/t.* decorate; dress

delikat *adj.* delicious, exquisite; *heikel*: delicate, ticklish; **2esse** *f* delicacy (*a. fig.*); **2essenladen** *m* delicatessen *sg.*, F deli

Delphin *zo. m* dolphin

Dement|i *n* (official) denial; **2ieren** *v/t.* deny (officially)

dem|entsprechend, **~gemäß** *adv.* accordingly; **~nach** *adv.* according to that; **~nächst** *adv.* shortly, before long

Demo F *f* demo

Demokrat *m* democrat; **~ie** *f* democracy; **2isch** *adj.* democratic

demolieren *v/t.* demolish, wreck

Demonstr|ant(in) *m* demonstrator; **~ation** *f* demonstration; **2ieren** *v/t. u. v/i.* demonstrate

demontieren *v/t.* dismantle

demoralisieren *v/t.* demoralize

Demoskopie *f* public opinion research

Demut *f* humility, humbleness

demütig *adj.* humble; **~en** *v/t.* humiliate; **2ung** *f* humiliation

denk|bar 1. *adj.* conceivable; **2.** *adv.*: **~ einfach** most simple; **~en** *v/t. u. v/i.* think* (*an, über* of, about); *daran ~* (*zu*) remember (to); **2fabrik** *f* think tank; **2mal** *n* monument; *Ehrenmal*: memorial; **~würdig** *adj.* memorable; **2zettel** *fig. m* lesson

denn *cj. u. adv.* for, because; *es sei ~, daß* unless; *mehr ~ je* more than ever

dennoch *cj.* yet, still, nevertheless

Denunz|iant *m* informer; **2ieren** *v/t.* inform on *od.* against

Deodorant *n* deodorant

Depon|ie *f* dump, waste disposal site, *Brt. a.* tip; → *Mülldeponie*; **2ieren** *v/t.* deposit, leave

Depot *n* depot (*a. mil.*); *Schweiz: Pfand*: deposit

Depress|ion *f* depression (*a. econ.*); **2iv** *adj.* depressive

deprimier|en *v/t.* depress; **~t** *adj.* depressed

der, die, das 1. *art.* the; **2.** *dem. pron.* that, this; he, she, it; *die pl.* these, those; they; **3.** *rel. pron.* who, which, that

derartig 1. *adv.* so (much). like that; **2.** *adj.* such (as this)

derb *adj.* coarse; *strapazierfähig*: tough, sturdy

dergleichen *dem. pron.*: *nichts ~* nothing of the kind

der-, die-, dasjenige *dem. pron.* the one; *diejenigen pl.* the ones, those

dermaßen *adv.* so (much), like that

Dermatologe *m* dermatologist

der-, die-, dasselbe *dem. pron.* the same

Desert|eur *m* deserter; **2ieren** *v/i.* desert

deshalb *cj. u. adv.* therefore, for that reason, that is why, so

Desin|fektionsmittel *n* disinfectant; **2fizieren** *v/t.* disinfect

Desinteress|e *n* indifference; **2iert** *adj.* uninterested, indifferent

destillieren *v/t.* distil(l)

desto *cj. u. adv.* → *je*

deswegen *cj. u. adv.* → *deshalb*

Detail *n* detail; **2liert** *adj.* detailed

Detektiv *m* detective; → *Privat*2

deuten 1. *v/t.* interpret; **2.** *v/i.*: *~ auf* point at

deutlich *adj.* clear, distinct, plain

deutsch *adj.* German (*auf* in); **2land** Germany; **2e(r)** German

Devise *f* motto

Devisen *pl. econ.* foreign currency *sg.*

Dezember *m* December

dezent *adj.* discreet, unobtrusive; *Kleidung*: conservative; *Musik*: soft

Dezimal|... *in Zssgn Bruch, System etc.*: decimal ...; **~stelle** *f* decimal (place)

DGB *abk. für Deutscher Gewerkschaftsbund* Federation of German Trade Unions

d.h. *Abk. für das heißt* i.e., that is

Dia *phot. n* slide

Diagnose *f* diagnosis

diagonal *adj.*; **2e** *f* diagonal

Dialekt *m* dialect

Dialog *m* dialogue, *Am. a.* dialog

Diamant *m* diamond

Diaprojektor *m* slide projector

Diät f diet; *eine ~ machen* (♀ *leben*) be* on (keep*to) a diet

Diäten *parl. pl.* allowance *sg.*

dich *pers. pron.* you; ~ (*selbst*) yourself

dicht 1. *adj.* dense, *Nebel. a.:* thick; *Verkehr:* heavy; *Fenster etc.:* closed, shut; **2.** *adv.:* ~ **an** *od.* **bei** close to

dicht|en *v/t. u. v/i.* write* (poetry); **♀er(in)** *f* poet; writer; **~erisch** *adj.* poetic; **~e Freiheit** poetic licen|ce, *Am.* -se

dichthalten F *v/i.* keep* mum

Dichtung¹ *tech. f* seal(ing)

Dichtung² *f* poetry

dick *adj.* thick; *Person:* fat; *es macht ~* it's fattening; **♀e** *f* thickness; fatness; **~fellig** *adj.* thick-skinned; **~flüssig** *adj.* thick; *tech.* viscous; **♀icht** *n* thicket; **♀kopf** *m* stubborn *od.* pig-headed person; **~milch** *f* soured milk

Dieb|(in) *(in)f theft; **~stahl** *m* theft; *jur. mst* larceny; **~isch** *adj.* thievish; *fig. Freude etc.:* malicious

Diele *f Brett:* board, plank; *Vorraum:* hall, *Am. a.* hallway

dienen *v/i.* serve (*j-m* s.o.; *als* as)

Diener *m* servant; *fig.* bow (*vor* to)

Dienst *m* service; *Arbeit:* work; ~ *haben* be* on duty; *im (außer) ~* on (off) duty; **~...** *in Zssgn Wagen, Wohnung etc.:* official ..., company ..., business...

Dienstag *m* Tuesday

Dienst|alter *n* seniority, length of service; **♀bereit** *adj.* on duty; **♀eifrig** *adj.* (*contp.* over-)eager; **~grad** *m* grade, rank (*a. mil.*); **~leistung** *f* service; **♀lich** *adj.* official; **~mädchen** *n* maid, *Am. a.* help; **~reise** *f* business trip; **~stunden** *pl.* office hours *pl.*; **♀tuend** *adj.* on duty; **~weg** *m* official channels *pl.*

dies(er, -e, -es) *dem. pron.* this; *alleinstehend:* this one; **~e** *pl.* these

diesig *adj.* hazy, misty

dies|jährig *adj.* this year's; **~mal** *adv.* this time; **~seits** *prp.* on this side of; **♀** *n* this life *od.* world

Dietrich *m* picklock, skeleton key

Differenz *f* difference; *Unstimmigkeit: a.* disagreement; **♀ieren** *v/i.* distinguish

Digital... *in Zssgn Anzeige, Uhr etc.:* digital

Diktat *n* dictation; **~or** *m* dictator; **♀orisch** *adj.* dictatorial; **~ur** *f* dictatorship

diktier|en *v/t. u. v/i.* dictate (*a. fig.*); **♀gerät** *n* Dictaphone (*TM*)

Dilettant *m* amateur; **♀isch** *adj.* amateurish

DIN *Abk. für* **Deutsche Institut für Normung** German Institute for Standardization

Ding *n* thing; *guter* **~e** in good spirits; *vor allen* **~en** above all; F: *ein* **~** *drehen* pull a job

Dinosaurier *m* dinosaur

Dings(bums), Dingsda F *n* thingamajig, whatchamacallit

Diox|id *n* dioxide (*a. in Zssgn*); **~in** *chem. n* dioxin

Diphtherie *med. f* diphtheria

Diplom *n* diploma, degree; **~...** *in Zssgn Ingenieur etc.:* qualified ..., graduate

Diplomat *m* diplomat; **~enkoffer** *m* attaché case; **♀ie** *f* diplomacy; **♀isch** *adj.* diplomatic (*a. fig.*)

dir *pers. pron.* (to) you; ~ (*selbst*) yourself

direkt 1. *adj.* direct; *TV* live; **2.** *adv.* *geradewegs:* direct; *fig. genau, sofort:* directly, right; *TV* live; **~ gegenüber** (*von*) right across; **♀ion** *f* management; **♀or(in)** *f* director, manager; *Schul♀:* headmaster (-mistress), *bsd. Am.* principal; **♀übertragung** *TV f* live transmission *od.* broadcast

Dirig|ent(in) *(in)* conductor; **♀ieren** *v/t. u. v/i. mus.* conduct; *lenken:* direct

Dirne *f* prostitute, whore

Disharmonie *f mus.* dissonance (*a. fig.*); **♀sch** *adj.* discordant

Diskette *f* diskette, floppy (disk); **~nlaufwerk** *n* disk drive

Diskont *econ. m* discount (*a. in Zssgn*)

Disko(thek) *f* disco(theque)

diskret *adj.* discreet; **♀ion** *f* discretion

diskriminier|en *v/t.* discriminate against; **♀rung** *f* discrimination (*von* against)

Diskussion *f* discussion, debate; **~sleiter(in)** (panel) chairman

Diskuswerfen *n* discus throwing

diskutieren *v/t. u. v/i.* discuss

Disqualifi|kation *f* disqualification (*wegen* for); **♀zieren** *v/t.* disqualify

Distanz *f* distance (*a. fig.*); **♀ieren** *v/ refl.:* distance o.s. (*von* from)

Distel *f* thistle

Distrikt *m* district

Disziplin f discipline; *Sport:* event; **2iert** adj. disciplined

divers adj. various; several

Divid|ende econ. f dividend; **2ieren** v/t. divide (**durch** by)

Division math., mil. f division

DJH Abk. für **Deutsches Jugendherbergswerk** German Youth Hostel Association

DM Abk. für **Deutsche Mark** German mark(s)

doch cj. u. adv. but, however, yet; **kommst du nicht (mit)?** - ~! aren't you coming? - (oh) yes, I am!; **ich war es nicht** - ~! I didn't do it - yes, you did!, *Am. a.* you did too!; **er kam also ~?** so he did come after all?; **du kommst ~?** you're coming, aren't you?; **kommen Sie ~ herein!** do come in!; **wenn ~ ...!** wünschend: if only ...!

Docht m wick

Dock naut. n dock

Dogge zo. f mastiff; Great Dane

Dogma n dogma; **2tisch** adj. dogmatic

Dohle zo. f (jack)daw

Doktor m doctor; *Grad:* doctor's degree; **~arbeit** f (doctoral od. PhD) thesis

Dokument n document; **~ar...** in Zssgn Film etc.: documentary

Dolch m dagger

Dollar m dollar

Dolmetsch östr. m interpreter; **2en** v/i. interpret; **~er(in)** interpreter

Dom m cathedral; ⚠ nicht **dome**

dominierend adj. (pre)dominant

Dompt|eur m, **~euse** f animal tamer od. trainer

Donner m thunder; **2n** v/i. thunder (a. fig.); **~stag** m Thursday; **~wetter** F n dressing-down; **~!** wow!

doof F adj. stupid, *Am. a.* dumb

Doppel n duplicate; *Tennis etc.:* doubles pl.; **~...** in Zssgn Bett, Zimmer etc.: double ...; **~decker** m aviat. biplane; double-decker (bus); **~gänger** m double, look-alike; **~haus** n pair of semis, *Am.* duplex; **~haushälfte** f semidetached (house), F semi; **~paß** m Fußball: wall pass; **~punkt** m colon; **~stecker** electr. m two-way adapter

doppelt adj. double; **~ so viel (wie)** twice as much (as)

Doppelverdiener pl. two-income family sg.

Dorf n village; **~bewohner(in)** villager

Dorn m thorn (a. fig.); *Schnalle:* tongue; *Schuh:* spike; **2ig** adj. thorny (a. fig.)

Dorsch zo. m cod(fish)

dort adv. there; **~ drüben** over there; **~her** adv. from there; **~hin** adv. there; **bis ~** up to there od. that point

Dose f can, *Brt. a.* tin; **~n...** in Zssgn canned, *Brt. a.* tinned

dösen F v/i. doze

Dosenöffner m tin (*Am.* can) opener

Dosis f dose (a. fig.)

Dotter m, n yolk

Double n Film: stunt man (od. woman)

Dozent(in) (university) lecturer, *Am. a.* assistant professor

Dr. Abk. für **Doktor** Dr., Doctor

Drache m dragon; **~n** m kite; *Sport:* hang glider; **e-n ~n steigen lassen** fly* a kite; **~nfliegen** n hang gliding

Draht m wire; F: **auf ~ sein** be* on the ball; **2ig** fig. adj. wiry; **2los** adj. wireless; **~seil** n tech. cable; *Zirkus:* tightrope; **~seilbahn** f cable railway; **~zieher** f fig. m wirepuller

drall adj. buxom, strapping

Drall m twist, spin (a. Sport)

Drama n drama; **~tiker(in)** dramatist, playwright; **2tisch** adj. dramatic

dran F adv. → **daran**; **du bist ~** it's your turn; fig. you're in for it

Drang m urge, drive (**nach** for)

dräng|eln v/t. u. v/i. push, shove; **j-n zu et. ~** pester s.o. to do s.th.; **~en** v/t. u. v/i. push, shove; **j-n zu et.** press, urge; **sich ~** press; *Zeit:* be* pressing; **durch et.** force one's way

drankommen F v/i. have* one's turn; **als erster ~** be* first

drastisch adj. drastic

drauf F adv. → **darauf**; **~ und dran sein, et. zu tun** be* just about to do s.th.; **2gänger** m daredevil

draus F adv. → **daraus**

draußen adv. outside; outdoors; **da ~** out there; **bleib(t) ~!** keep out!

drechs|eln v/t. turn (on a lathe); **2ler** m turner

Dreck F m dirt; *stärker:* filth (a. fig.); *Schlamm:* mud; fig. trash; **2ig** F adj. dirty; filthy (beide a. fig.)

Dreh|arbeiten pl. shooting sg.; **~bank** tech. f lathe; **2bar** adj. revolving, rotating; **~buch** n script; **2en** v/t. turn;

Film: shoot*; *Zigarette:* roll; **sich ~** turn, rotate; *schnell:* spin*; **sich ~ um** *fig.* be* about; **~ Ding; ~er** *m* turner; **~kreuz** *n* turnstile; **~orgel** *f* barrel-organ; **~ort** *m* location; **~strom** *electr. m* three-phase current; **~stuhl** *m* swivel chair; **~tür** *f* revolving door; **~ung** *f* turn; *um e-e Achse:* rotation; **~zahl** *tech. f* (number of) revolutions; **~zahl-messer** *mot. m* rev(olution) counter

drei *adj.* three

Drei *f Note:* fair, C

drei|beinig *adj.* three-legged; **~dimensional** *adj.* three-dimensional; **2eck** *n* triangle; **~eckig** *adj.* triangular; **~erlei** *adj.* three kinds of; **~fach** *adj.* threefold, triple; **2gang...** *tech.* in *Zssgn* three-speed ...; **2kampf** *m* triathlon; **2rad** *n* tricycle; **2satz** *math.* *m* rule of three; **~silbig** *adj.* trisyllabic; **2sprung** *m* triple jump

dreißig *adj.* thirty; **~ste** *adj.* thirtieth

dreist *adj.* brazen (*a. Lüge*), impertinent (th)

dreistufig *adj.* three-stage

dreizehn(te) *adj.* thirteen(th)

dresch|en *v/t. u. v/i.* thresh; *prügeln:* thrash; **2maschine** *f* threshing machine

dress|ieren *v/t.* train; **2man** *m* male model; **2ur** *f* training; *Nummer:* act; **2urreiten** *n* dressage

dribb|eln *v/i.,* **2ling** *n* dribble

drillen *mil. v/t.* drill (*a. fig.*)

Drillinge *pl.* triplets *pl.*

drin F *adv.* → *darin; das ist nicht ~l fig.* no way!

dringen *v/i.: ~ auf* insist on; *~ aus Geräusch:* come* from; *~ durch* force one's way through, penetrate, pierce; *~ in* penetrate into; *darauf ~, daß* urge that; **~d** *adj.* urgent, pressing; *Verdacht, Rat, Grund:* strong

drinnen F *adv.* inside; indoors

dritte *adj.* third; *wir sind zu dritt* there are three of us; **2l** *n* third; **~ns** *adv.* thirdly; **2 Welt** Third World; **2-Welt-Laden** *m* third world shop

Droge *f* drug

drogen|abhängig *adj.* addicted to drugs; *~ sein* be* a drug addict; **2ab-hängige(r)** drug addict; **2miß-brauch** *m* drug abuse; **~süchtig** *adj.* → *drogenabhängig;* **2tote(r)** drug victim

Drog|erie *f* chemist's (shop), *Am.* drugstore; **~ist** *m* chemist, *bsd. Am.* druggist

drohen *v/i.* threaten, menace

dröhnen *v/i. Motor, Stimme etc.:* roar

Drohung *f* threat (*gegen* to), menace

drollig *adj.* funny, droll

Dromedar *zo. n* dromedary

Drossel *zo. f* thrush

drosseln *tech. v/t.* throttle

drüben *adv.* over there (*a. fig.*)

drüber F *adv.* → *darüber, drunter*

Druck *m* pressure; *Buch2 etc.:* printing; *Kunst2 etc.:* print; **~buchstabe** *m* block letter; **2en** *v/t.* print; *~ lassen* have* *s.th.* printed *od.* published

Drückeberger F *m* shirker

drücken *v/t.* press; *Knopf: a.* push; *Schuh:* pinch; *Preis, Leistung etc.:* force down; *j-m die Hand ~* shake* hands with s.o.; F *sich ~ vor et.* shirk (doing) s.th.; *aus Angst:* F chicken out of s.th.

drückend *adj.* heavy, oppressive

Drucker *m* printer (*a. Computer*)

Drücker *m Tür:* latch; *Gewehr:* trigger; F *Abonnement-Verkäufer:* hawker

Druckerei *f* printers *pl.*

Druck|fehler *m* misprint; **~kammer** *f* pressurized cabin; **~knopf** *m* press stud, *Am.* snap fastener; *tech.* (push) button; **~luft** *f* compressed air; **~sa-che** *post f* printed matter, *Am. a.* second-class matter; **~schrift** *f* block letters *pl.;* **~taste** *f* push button

drunter F *adv.* → *darunter; es ging ~ und drüber* it was absolutely chaotic

Drüse *anat. f* gland

Dschungel *m* jungle (*a. fig.*)

Dschunke *naut. f* junk

du *pers. pron.* you

Dübel *tech. m,* **2n** *v/t.* dowel

ducken *v/refl.* duck; *fig.* cringe (*vor* before); *zum Sprung:* crouch

Duckmäuser *m* coward; yes-man

Dudelsack *mus. m* bagpipes *pl.*

Duell *n* duel; **2ieren** *v/refl.* fight a duel

Duett *mus. n* duet

Duft *m* scent, fragrance, smell (*nach* of); **2en** *v/i.* smell* (*nach* of); **2end** *adj.* fragrant; **2ig** *adj.* dainty

duld|en *v/t.* tolerate, put* up with; *leiden:* suffer; **~sam** *adj.* tolerant

dumm *adj.* stupid, *Am.* F dumb; **2heit** *f*

stupidity, *Handlung*: stupid *od.* foolish thing; *Unwissenheit*: ignorance; **2kopf** *m* fool, blockhead

dumpf *adj.* dull; *Ahnung*: vague

Düne *f* (sand) dune

Dung *m* dung, manure

düng|en *v/t.* fertilize; *natürlich*: manure; **2er** *m* fertilizer; manure

dunkel *adj.* dark (*a. fig.*)

Dunkel|heit *f* dark(ness); **~kammer** *phot. f* darkroom; **~ziffer** *f* number of unreported cases

dünn *adj.* thin; *Kaffee etc.*: weak

Dunst *m* haze, mist; *chem.* vapo(u)r

dünsten *v/t.* stew, braise

dunstig *adj.* hazy, misty

Duplikat *n* in duplicate; *Kopie*: copy

Dur *mus. n* major (key)

durch *prp. u. adv.* through; *quer ~*: across; *math.* divided by; *~ j-n od. et.* by s.o. *od.* s.th.; *~ und ~* through and through; *Fleisch*: (well) done

durch|arbeiten 1. *v/t.* study thoroughly; *sich ~ durch Buch etc.*: work (one's way) through; **2.** *v/i.* work without a break

durchaus *adv.* absolutely, quite; *~ nicht* by no means

durch|blättern *v/t. Buch etc.*: leaf *od.* thumb through; **2blick** *fig. m* grasp of *s.th.*; **~blicken** *v/i.* look through; *~ lassen* give* to understand; *ich blicke (da) nicht durch* I don't get it; **~bohren** *v/t.* pierce; *durchlöchern*: perforate; *mit Blicken ~* look daggers at; **~braten** *v/t.* roast thoroughly; **~brechen** *v/t. u. v/i.* break* (in two); *Mauer etc.*: break* through; **~brennen** *v/i. Sicherung*: blow*; *Reaktor*: melt* down; *F fig.* run* away; **~bringen** *v/t.* get* (*Kranken*: pull) through ; *Geld*: go* through; *Familie*: support; **2bruch** *m* breakthrough (*a. fig.*); **~dacht** *adj.* (well) thought-out; **~drehen 1.** *v/i. Räder*: spin*; F *nervlich*: crack up, flip; **2.** *v/t. Fleisch*: mince, *bsd. Am.* grind*; **~dringend** *adj.* piercing

Durcheinander *n* confusion, mess

durcheinander *adv.* confused; *Dinge*: (in) a mess; **~bringen** *v/t.* confuse, mix up; *Pläne*: mess up

durchfahr|en *v/t. u. v/i.* go* (*od.* pass, *mot. a.* drive*) through; **2t** *f* passage; *~ verboten* no thoroughfare

Durchfall *m med.* diarrh(o)ea; **2en** *v/i.* fall* through; *Prüfling*: fail, *bsd. Am.* F flunk; *Stück etc.*: be* a flop; *j-n ~ lassen* fail (*bsd. Am.* F flunk) s.o.

durch|fragen *v/refl.* ask one's way (*nach, zu* to)

durchführ|bar *adj.* practicable, feasible; **~en** *v/t.* carry out, do*

Durchgang *m* passage; *fig.*, *Sport*: round; **~s...** *in Zssgn Verkehr etc.*: through ...; *Lager etc.*: transit ...

durchgebraten *adj.* well done

durchgehen 1. *v/i.* go* through (*a. rail. u. parl.*); *fig. a. Gefühle*: run* away (*mit* with); *Pferd*: bolt; **2.** *v/t. prüfend*: go* *od.* look through; *~ lassen* tolerate; **~d** *adj.* continuous; *~er Zug* through train; *~ geöffnet* open all day

durchgreifen *fig. v/i.* take* drastic measures; **~d** *adj.* drastic; radical

durch|halten 1. *v/t.* keep* up; **2.** *v/i.* hold* out; **~hängen** *v/i.* sag; F *fig.* → **2hänger** F *m*: *e-n ~ haben* have* a low; **~kämpfen** *v/t.* fight* out; *sich ~* fight* one's way through (*a. Patient etc.*); **~kommen** *v/i.* come* through (*a. Patient etc.*); *durch Verkehr, Schwierigkeiten, Prüfung etc.*: get* through; *mit Geld, Sprache etc.*: get* along; *mit Lüge etc.*: get* away; **~kreuzen** *v/t. Plan etc.*: cross, thwart; **~lassen** *v/t.* let* pass, let* through; **~lässig** *adj.* permeable (to); *undicht*: leaky

durch|laufen 1. *v/i.* run* through; **2.** *v/t. Schule etc.*: pass through; *Schuhe*: wear* through; **2lauferhitzer** *m* (instant) water heater, *Brt. a.* geyser; **~lesen** *v/t.* read* through; **~leuchten** *v/t. med.* X-ray; *fig.* screen; **~löchern** *v/t.* perforate, make* holes in; **~machen** *v/t.* go* through; *viel ~* suffer a lot; *die Nacht ~* make* a night of it

Durchmesser *m* diameter

durch|nässen *v/t.* soak; **~nehmen** *v/t.* do*, deal with; **~pausen** *v/t.* trace; **~queren** *v/t.* cross; **2reiche** *f* hatch

Durch|reise *f*: *ich bin nur auf der ~* I'm only passing through; **2reisen** *v/i.* travel through; **~reisevisum** *n* transit visa

durch|reißen *v/t.* tear* (in two); **~ringen** *v/refl.*: *sich zu et. ~* bring* o.s. to do s.th.; **2sage** *f* announcement; **~schauen** *v/t. fig. j-n etc.*: see* through

durchscheinen v/i. shine* through; **~d** adj. transparent

durch|scheuern v/t. Haut: chafe; Stoff: wear* through; **~schlafen** v/i. sleep* through

Durchschlag m (carbon) copy; **2en 1.** v/t. zerschlagen: cut* in two; Kugel etc.: go* through, pierce; **sich ~ nach** make* one's way to; **2.** v/i. Charakter: come* through; **2end** adj. Erfolg etc.: sweeping; wirkungsvoll: effective; **~papier** n carbon paper; **~skraft** fig. f force, impact

durchschneiden v/t. cut* (through); **j-m die Kehle ~** cut* s.o.'s throat

Durchschnitt m average (a. **~s...** in Zssgn); **im (über, unter dem) ~** on an (above, below) average; **im ~ betragen, verdienen** average; **2lich 1.** adj. average; ordinary; **2.** adv. on an average

Durch|schrift f (carbon) copy; **2sehen** v/t. look od. go* through; prüfen: check; Bluse etc.: see-through

durch|sickern v/i. seep through; Nachrichten etc.: leak out; **~sieben** v/t. sift; mit Kugeln: riddle; **~sprechen** v/t. discuss, talk over; **~starten** aviat. v/i. climb and reaccelerate; **~stechen** v/t. stick* through; Ohrläppchen: pierce; **~stecken** v/t. stick* through; **~stehen** v/t. go* through; **~stoßen** v/t. u. v/i. break* through (a. mil. u. Sport); **~streichen** v/t. cross out

durchsuch|en v/t. search; nach Waffen: F frisk; **2ung** f search; **2ungsbefehl** m search warrant

durchtreten v/t. Schuh: wear* out; Pedal: floor; Starter: kick

durchtrieben adj. cunning, sly

durchwachsen adj. Speck: streaky

Durch|wahl f tel. direct dial(l)ing; **2wählen** v/i. dial direct; **~wahlnummer** f direct dial number; extension

durchweg adv. without exception

durch|weicht adj. soaked, drenched; **~wühlen** rummage through; **~zählen** (Am. off); **~ziehen 1.** v/i. pass through; **2.** v/t. pull s.th. through; fig. carry s.th. through (to the end); **~zucken** v/t. flash through

Durchzug m draught, Am. draft

durchzwängen v/refl.: **sich ~** squeeze o.s. through

dürfen v/aux. be* allowed od. permitted to; **darf ich?** may I?; **ja (,du darfst)** yes, you may; **du darfst nicht** you must not od. aren't allowed to; **dürfte ich ...?** could I ...?; **das dürfte genügen** that should be enough

dürftig adj. poor; spärlich: scanty

dürr adj. dry; Boden etc.: barren, arid; mager: skinny; **2e** f Trockenzeit: drought; barrenness

Durst m thirst (auf for); **~ haben** be* thirsty; **2ig** adj. thirsty

Dusche f shower; **2n** v/refl. u. v/i. have* od. take* a shower

Düse f tech. nozzle; Spritz2: jet; **2n** F v/i. jet; **~nantrieb** m jet propulsion; **mit ~** jet-propelled; **~nflugzeug** n jet (plane); **~njäger** m jet fighter; **~ntriebwerk** n jet engine

düster adj. dark, gloomy (beide a. fig.); Licht: dim; trostlos: dismal

Dutzend n dozen; **ein ~ Eier** a dozen eggs; **2weise** adv. by the dozen

Duvet n Schweiz: blanket, quilt

duzen v/t. use the familiar 'du' with s.o.; **sich ~** be* on 'du' terms

Dynami|k phys. f dynamics sg.; fig. dynamism; **2sch** adj. dynamic

Dynamit n dynamite

Dynamo m dynamo, generator

D-Zug m express train

E

Ebbe f ebb; *Niedrigwasser:* low tide
eben 1. *adj.* even; *flach:* flat; *math. plane; **zu ~er Erde** on the ground (*Am.* first) floor; **2.** *adv.* just; **an ~ dem Tag** on that very day; **so ist es ~** that's the way it is; **gerade ~ so** *od.* **noch** just barely; **2bild** *n* image; **~bürtig** *adj.:* **j-m ~ sein** be* a match for s.o., be* s.o.'s equal
Ebene f plain; *math.* plane; *fig.* level
eben|erdig *adj. u. adv.* at street level; on the ground (*Am.* first) floor; **~falls** *adv.* as well, too; **danke, ~!** thank you, (the) same to you!; **~holz** *n* ebony; **2maß** *n* symmetry; harmony; *der Züge:* regularity; **~mäßig** *adj.* symmetrical; harmonious; regular; **~so** *adv. u. cj.* just as; *ebenfalls:* as well; **~ wie** in the same way as; **~sogern, ~sogut** *adv.* just as well; **~sosehr, ~soviel** *adv.* just as much; **~sowenig** *adv.* just as little *od.* few (*pl.*)
Eber *zo.* m boar
ebnen *v/t.* even, level; *fig.* smooth
Echo *n* echo; *fig.* response
echt *adj.* genuine (*a. fig.*), real; *wahr:* true; *rein:* pure; *wirklich:* real; *Farbe:* fast; *Dokument:* authentic; F: **~ gut** real good; **2heit** *f* genuineness; authenticity
Eck|ball *m Sport:* corner (kick); **~e** *f* corner (*Sport: lange* far; *kurze* near); *Kante:* edge; *s.* **Eckball**; **2ig** *adj.* square, angular; *fig.* awkward; **~stein** *m* corner-stone; **~zahn** *m* canine tooth
edel *adj.* noble; *min.* precious; **2metall** *n* precious metal; **2stahl** *m* stainless steel; **2stein** *m* precious stone; *geschnittener:* gem
EDV *Abk. für* **Elektronische Datenverarbeitung** EDP, electronic data processing
Efeu *m* ivy
Effekt *m* effect; **~hascherei** *f* (cheap) showmanship, claptrap; **2iv 1.** *adj.* effective; **2.** *adv.* actually; **~ivität** *f* effectiveness; **2voll** *adj.* effective, striking
EG *hist. Abk. für* **Europäische Gemeinschaft** EC, European Community
egal F *adj.:* **~ ob** (**warum, wer** *etc.*) no

matter if (why, who, *etc.*); **das ist ~** it doesn't matter; **das ist mir ~** I don't care, it's all the same to me
Egge f, **2n** *v/t.* harrow
Egois|mus *m* ego(t)ism; **~t(in)** *m* ego(t)ist; **2tisch** *adj.* selfish, ego(t)istic(al)
ehe *cj.* before; *nicht,* **~** not until
Ehe f marriage (*mit* to); **~beratung** *f* marriage guidance (*Am.* counseling); **~brecher(in)** adulter|er (-ess); **2brecherisch** *adj.* adulterous; **~bruch** *m* adultery; **~frau** *f* wife; **~leute** *pl.* married couple *sg.*; **2lich** *adj.* conjugal; *Kind:* legitimate
ehemal|ig *adj.* former, ex-...; **~s** *adv.* formerly
Ehe|mann *m* husband; **~paar** *n* (married) couple
eher *adv.* earlier, sooner; **je ~, desto lieber** the sooner the better; **nicht ~ als** not until *od.* before
Ehering *m* wedding ring
ehrbar *adj.* respectable
Ehre f hono(u)r; **zu ~n** (**von**) in hono(u)r of; **2n** *v/t.* hono(u)r; *achten:* respect
ehren|amtlich *adj.* honorary; **2bürger** *m* honorary citizen; **2doktor** *m* honorary doctor; **2gast** *m* guest of hono(u)r; **2kodex** *m* code of hono(u)r; **2mann** *m* man of hono(u)r; **2mitglied** *n* honorary member; **2platz** *m* place of hono(u)r; **2rechte** *pl.* civil rights *pl.*; **~rührig** *adj.* defamatory; **2runde** *f* lap of hono(u)r; **2sache** *f* point of hono(u)r; **2tor** *n,* **2treffer** *m* consolation goal; **~wert** *adj.* hono(u)rable; **2wort** *n* word of hono(u)r; F **~!** cross my heart!
ehr|erbietig *adj.* respectful; **2furcht** *f* respect (*vor* for); awe (of); **~furchtgebietend** *adj.* awe-inspiring, awesome; **~fürchtig** *adj.* respectful; **2gefühl** *n* sense of hono(u)r; **2geiz** *m* ambition; **~geizig** *adj.* ambitious
ehrlich *adj.* honest; *offen: a.* frank; *Kampf:* fair; F: **~!(?)** honestly!(?); **2keit** *f* honesty; fairness

Ehr|ung f hono(u)r(ing); **2würdig** adj. venerable

Ei n egg; V **~er** Hoden: balls

Eich|e bot. f oak(-tree); **~el** f bot. acorn; Karten: club(s pl.); anat. glans (penis)

eichen v/t. ga(u)ge

Eich|hörnchen n squirrel; **~maß** n standard (measure)

Eid n oath (ablegen take*)

Eidechse f lizard

eidesstattlich jur. adj.: **~e Erklärung** statutory declaration

Eidotter m, n (egg) yolk

Eier|becher m eggcup; **~kuchen** m pancake; **~laufen** n egg-and-spoon race; **~likör** m eggnog; **~schale** f eggshell; **~stock** anat. m ovary; **~uhr** f egg timer

Eifer m zeal, eagerness; glühender **~** ardo(u)r; **~sucht** f jealousy; **2süchtig** adj. jealous (auf of)

eifrig adj. eager, zealous; ardent

Eigelb n (egg) yolk

eigen adj. own, of one's own; ~tümlich: peculiar; (über)genau: particular, F fussy; **~...** in Zssgn staats... etc.: ...-owned; **2art** f peculiarity; **~artig** adj. peculiar; seltsam: strange; **~artigerweise** adv. strangely enough; **2bedarf** m personal needs pl.; **2gewicht** n dead weight; **~händig 1.** adj. Unterschrift etc.: personal; **2.** adv. personally, with one's own hands; **~ geschrieben** in one's own hand; **2heim** n home (of one's own); **2liebe** f self-love; **2lob** n self-praise; **~mächtig** adj. arbitrary; **2name** m proper noun; **~nützig** adj. selfish

eigens adv. (e)specially, expressly

Eigenschaft f quality; tech., phys. chem. property; in s-r **~** als in his capacity as; **~swort** gr. n adjective

Eigensinn m stubbornness; **2ig** adj. stubborn, obstinate

eigentlich 1. wirklich: actual, true, real; genau: exact; **2.** adv. actually, really; ursprünglich: originally

Eigentor n own goal (a. fig.)

Eigentum n property

Eigentüm|er(in) owner, propriet|or (-ress); **2lich** adj. peculiar; seltsam: strange, odd; **~lichkeit** f peculiarity

Eigentumswohnung f owner-occupied flat, Am. condominium, condo

eigenwillig adj. wil(l)ful; Stil etc.: individual, original

eign|en v/refl.: sich **~** für be* suited od. fit for; **2ung** f suitability; Person: a. aptitude, qualification; **2ungsprüfung** f, **2ungstest** m aptitude test

Eil|bote post m: durch **~n** by special delivery; **~brief** post m express (Am. special delivery) letter

Eil|e f haste, hurry; **2n** v/i. hurry, hasten, rush; Angelegenheit: be* urgent; **2ig** adj. hurried, hasty; dringend: urgent; es **~** haben be* in a hurry; **~zug** m semifast train, Am. limited

Eimer m bucket, pail

ein 1. adj. one; **2.** indef. art. a, an; **3.** adv.: „ **~/ aus**" "on/ off"; **~ und aus gehen** come and go; nicht mehr **~** noch aus wissen be* at one's wits' end

einander pron. each other, bsd. mehrere: one another

ein|arbeiten v/t. train, acquaint s.o. with his work, F break s.o. in; sich **~** work o.s. in; **~armig** adj. one-armed; **~äschern** v/t. Leiche: cremate; **2äscherung** f cremation; **~atmen** v/t. inhale, breathe; **~äugig** adj. one-eyed

Einbahnstraße f one-way street

einbalsamieren v/t. embalm

Einband m binding, cover

Einbau m installation, fitting; **~...** in Zssgn Möbel etc.: built-in ...; **2en** v/t. build* in, instal(l), fit

einberuf|en v/t. mil. call up, Am. draft; Sitzung etc.: call; **2ung** mil. f call-up (orders pl.); Am. draft (orders pl.)

ein|beziehen v/t. include; **~biegen** v/i. turn (in into)

einbild|en v/refl. imagine; sich et. **~ auf** be* conceited about; darauf kannst du dir et. **~** (brauchst du dir nichts einzubilden) that's s.th. (nothing) to be proud of; **2ung** f imagination, fancy; Dünkel: conceit

einblenden v/t. TV etc. fade in

Einblick m insight (in into)

ein|brechen v/i. Dach etc.: collapse; Winter: set* in; **~ in Haus** etc: break* into, burgle; auf dem Eis: fall* through (the ice); **2brecher** m burglar; **~bringen** v/t. bring* in; Gewinn etc.: yield; **2bruch** m burglary; bei **~ der Nacht** at nightfall

einbürger|n v/t. naturalize; **sich ~** fig. come* into use; **2ung** f naturalization
Ein|buße f loss; **2büßen** v/t. lose*
ein|dämmen v/t. dam (up) (a. fig.); Fluß: embank; fig. a. get* under control; **~decken** fig. v/t. provide (mit with); **~deutig** adj. clear; **~drehen** v/t. Haar: put* in curlers
eindring|en v/i.: **~ in** enter (a. Wasser, Keime etc.); gewaltsam: force one's way into; mil. invade; **~lich** adj. urgent; **2ling** m intruder; mil. invader
Eindruck m impression
ein|drücken v/t. break* od. push in; **~drucksvoll** adj. impressive; **~eiig** adj. Zwillinge: identical; **~einhalb** adj. one and a half; **~engen** v/t. confine, restrict
ein|er, ~e, ~(e)s indef. pron. one
Einer m math. unit; Rudern: single sculls pl.
einerlei adj.: **ganz ~** all the same; **~ ob** no matter if
Einerlei n: **das tägliche ~** the daily grind od. rut
einerseits adv. on the one hand
einfach adj. simple; leicht: a. easy; schlicht: a. plain; Fahrkarte: single, Am. one-way; **2heit** f simplicity
einfädeln v/t. thread; fig. start, set* afoot
ein|fahren 1. v/t. Auto: run* in; Ernte: bring* in; **2.** v/i. come* in, rail. a. pull in; **2fahrt** f entrance, way in
Einfall m idea; mil. invasion; **2en** v/i. fall* in; einstürzen: a. collapse; mus. join in; **~ in** mil. invade; **ihm fiel ein, daß** it came to his mind that; **mir fällt nichts ein** I have no ideas; **es fällt mir nicht ein** I can't think of it; **dabei fällt mir ein** that reminds me; **was fällt dir ein?** what's the idea?
einfältig adj. simple-minded; stupid
Einfamilienhaus n detached house
ein|farbig adj. self-coloured, Am. solid-colored; **~fassen** v/t. border; **~fetten** v/t. grease; **~finden** v/refl. appear, arrive; **~flechten** fig. v/t. work in; **~fliegen** v/t. fly* in; **~fließen** v/i.: et. **~ lassen** slip s.th. in; **~flößen** v/t. pour (j-m into s.o.'s mouth); Respekt etc.: fill with
Einfluß fig. m influence; **2reich** adj. influential

ein|förmig adj. uniform; **~frieren 1.** v/i. freeze* (in); **2.** v/t. freeze* (a. fig.); **~fügen** v/t. put* in; fig. insert; **sich ~** fit in; in e-e Gruppe: adjust (o.s.) (in to); **2fügetaste** f Computer: insert key; **~fühlsam** adj. sympathetic; **2fühlungsvermögen** n empathy
Einfuhr econ. f import(ation)
einführen v/t. introduce; ins Amt: instal(l); Gegenstand: insert; econ. import
Einfuhrstopp econ. m import ban
Einführung f introduction; **~s... in** Zssgn Kurs, Preis etc.: introductory
Eingabe f petition; Computer: input; **~taste** f Computer: enter od. return key
Eingang m entrance; econ. arrival; Brief etc.: receipt; **2s** adv. at the beginning
eingeben v/t. Arznei etc.: administer (dat. to); Daten etc.: feed*, enter
einge|bildet adj. imaginary; dünkelhaft: conceited (auf of); **~er Kranker** hypochondriac; **2borene(r)** native
Eingebung f inspiration; impulse
einge|fallen adj. Wangen: sunken, hollow; **~fleischt** adj. Junggeselle etc.: confirmed
eingehen 1. v/i. Post, Waren: come* in, arrive; Pflanze, Tier: die; Stoff: shrink*; Firma: close down; **~ auf Vorschlag:** agree to; Einzelheiten: go* into; j-n: listen to; **2.** v/t. Vertrag etc.: enter into; Wette: make*; Risiko: take*; **~d** adj. thorough
einge|macht adj. preserved; **~meinden** v/t. incorporate (in into)
einge|nommen adj. partial (für to); prejudiced (gegen against); **von sich ~** full of o.s.; **~schlossen** adj. locked in; Bergleute etc.: trapped; Preis: included; **~schnappt** F adj. sulky; **~schrieben** adj. registered; **~spielt** adj.: **(gut) aufeinander ~ sein** work well together, be* a good team; **~stellt** adj.: **~ auf** prepared for; **~ gegen** opposed to
Eingeweide pl. intestines pl., guts pl.
Eingeweihte(r) insider
einge|wöhnen v/refl.: **sich ~ in** Ort, Beruf: get* used to, settle in
ein|gießen v/t. pour; **~gleisig** adj. single-track (auch fig.); **~gliedern** v/t. integrate; **~gliederung** f integration

ein|graben v/t. bury; **~gravieren** v/t. engrave

eingreifen v/i. step in, interfere

Eingriff m intervention, interference; med. operation

einhaken v/t. hook in; **sich ~** link arms; **bei j-m:** take* s.o.'s arm

Einhalt m: **~ gebieten** put* a stop (dat. to); **2en 1.** v/t. Termin, Regel: keep*

ein|hängen 1. v/t. hang* in (Hörer: up); **sich ~ → einhaken; 2.** tel. v/i. hang* up

einheimisch adj. native, local; Industrie, Markt: home, domestic; **2e(r)** m local, native

Einheit f Maß2: unit; pol. unity; Ganzes: a. whole; **2lich** adj. uniform; geschlossen: homogeneous; **~s...** in Zssgn Preis etc.: standard

einhellig adj. unanimous

einholen v/t. catch* up with (auch fig.); Zeitverlust: make* up for; Auskünfte: make* (über about); Rat: seek* (bei from); Erlaubnis: ask for; Segel, Fahne: strike*; **~ gehen** go* shopping

Einhorn myth. n unicorn

einhüllen v/t. wrap (up); fig. shroud

einig adj.: **sich ~ sein** agree; **sich nicht ~ sein** disagree, differ

einige indef. pron. some, a few, several

einigen v/t.: **sich ~ über** agree on

einigermaßen adv. quite, fairly; Befinden etc.: not too bad

einiges indef. pron. some(thing); viel: quite a lot

Einig|keit f unity; Übereinstimmung: agreement; **2ung** f agreement, settlement; e-s Volkes etc.: unification

einjagen v/t.: **j-m e-n Schrecken ~** give* s.o. a fright, frighten od. scare s.o.

einjährig adj. one-year-old

einkalkulieren v/t. take* into account, allow for

Einkauf m purchase; **Einkäufe machen → einkaufen;** 2en 1. v/t. buy*, econ. a. purchase; 2. v/i. go* shopping

Einkaufs|... in Zssgn shopping ...; **~bummel** m shopping spree; **~preis** econ. m purchase price; **~wagen** m (supermarket) trolley, Am. grocery od. shopping cart; **~zentrum** n shopping centre, Am. großes: (shopping) mall

ein|kehren v/i. stop (in at); **~klemmen** v/t. squeeze, jam; **eingeklemmt**

sein be* stuck od. jammed; **~klammern** v/t. put* in brackets

Einklang m mus. unison; fig. harmony

ein|kleiden v/t. clothe (a. fig.); **~knöpfbar** adj. button-in; **~kochen 1.** v/t. preserve; **2.** v/i. boil down

Einkommen n income; **~steuererklärung** f income-tax return

einkreisen v/t. encircle, surround

Einkünfte pl. income sg.

einlad|en v/t. invite; Waren: load; **~end** adj. inviting; **2ung** f invitation

Einlage f econ. investment; Schuh2: arch support; thea., mus. interlude

Einlaß m admission, admittance

einlassen v/t. let* in; ein Bad: run*; **sich ~ auf** get* involved in; leichtsinnig: let* o.s. in for; zustimmen: agree to; **sich ~ mit j-m** get* involved with s.o.

Ein|lauf m Sport: finish; med. enema; **2laufen 1.** v/i. come* in (a. Sport); Wasser: run* in; naut. enter port; Stoff: shrink*; **2.** v/t. Schuhe: break* in; **sich ~** warm up; **2leben** v/refl. settle in

einlege|n v/t. put* in; Haare: set*; in Essig: pickle; Gang: change into; **2sohle** f insole

einleit|en v/t. start; introduce; Geburt: induce; Abwasser etc.: dump, discharge; thea., mus. interlude; **~end** adj. introductory; **2ung** f introduction

ein|lenken v/i. come* round*; **~leuchten** v/i. be* evident od. obvious; **das leuchtet mir (nicht) ein** that makes (doesn't make) sense to me; **~liefern** v/t. take* (ins Gefängnis to prison; in die Klinik to [the] hospital); **~lösen** v/t. Pfand: redeem; Scheck: cash; **~machen** v/t. preserve; Marmelade: make* jam

einmal adv. once; zukünftig: a. some od. one day, sometime; **auf ~** plötzlich: suddenly; gleichzeitig: at the same time, at once; **noch ~** once more od. again; **noch ~ so ... (wie)** twice as ... (as); **es war ~** once (upon a time) there was; **haben Sie schon ~ ...?** have you ever ...?; **es schon ~ getan haben** have* done it before; **schon ~ dortgewesen sein** have* been there before; **nicht ~** not even; **2...** in Zssgn disposable ...; **2eins** n multiplication table; **~ig** adj. single; fig. unique; F fabulous

Einmann... in Zssgn one-man ...

Einmarsch m entry; mil. invasion; **2ieren** v/i. march in; ~ **in** mil. invade

ein|mischen v/refl. meddle (**in** in, with), interfere (with); **2mündung** f junction

einmütig adj. unanimous; **2keit** f unanimity

Ein|nahmen pl. takings pl., receipts pl.; **2nehmen** v/t. Platz, Arznei, Mahlzeit: take* (a. mil.); verdienen: earn, make*; **2nehmend** adj. engaging

ein|nicken v/i. doze off; **~nisten** v/refl. **sich bei j-m ~** park o.s. on s.o.

Einöde f desert, wilderness

ein|ordnen v/t. put* in its proper place; Akten etc.: file; **sich ~** mot. get in lane; **~packen** v/t. pack (up); einwickeln: wrap up; **~parken** v/t. u. v/i. park (between two cars); **~pferchen** v/t. pen in; Menschen: coop up; **~pflanzen** v/t. plant; fig. implant (a. med.); **~planen** v/t. allow for; **~prägen** v/t. impress; **sich et. ~** keep* s.th. in mind; auswendig: memorize s.th.; **~prägsam** adj. Melodie, Ausdruck: catchy; **~quartieren** F v/t. Gäste: put* s.o. up (**bei j-m** at s.o.'s place); **sich ~ bei** move in with; **~rahmen** v/t. frame; **~räumen** v/t. Dinge: put* away; Zimmer: furnish; fig. grant, concede; **~reden 1.** v/t.: **j-m et. ~** talk s.o. into (believing) s.th.; **2.** v/i.: **auf j-n ~** keep* on at s.o.; **~reiben** v/t. rub; **~reichen** v/t. hand od. send in; **~reihen** v/t. place (among); **sich ~** take* one's place

einreihig adj. Anzug: single-breasted

Einreise f entry (a. in Zssgn); **2n** v/i. enter (**in ein Land** a country)

ein|reißen 1. v/t. tear* (Gebäude: pull down; **2.** v/i. tear*; Unsitte etc.: spread*; **~renken** v/t. med. set*; fig. straighten out

einricht|en v/t. Zimmer: furnish; gründen: establish; ermöglichen: arrange; **sich ~** furnish one's home; **sich ~ auf** prepare for; **2ung** f furnishings pl.; fittings pl.; tech. installation(s pl.), facilities pl.; öffentliche: institution, facility

ein|rosten v/i. rust (in); fig. get* rusty; **~rücken 1.** mil. v/i. join the forces; Truppen: march in; **2.** v/t. Zeile: indent

eins pron. u. adj. one; one thing; **es ist alles ~** it's all the same (thing)

Eins f Note: excellent, A

einsam adj. lonely, lonesome; Leben: solitary; **2keit** f loneliness; solitude

einsammeln v/t. collect

Einsatz m tech. inset, insert; Spiel: stake(s pl. a. fig.); mus. entry; Mühe, Eifer: effort(s pl.), zeal; Verwendung: use, employment; mil. action, mission; von Truppen, Waffen: deployment; **den ~ geben** give* the cue; **im ~** in action; **unter ~ des Lebens** at the risk of one's life; **2bereit** adj. ready for action; **2freudig** adj. dynamic, zealous

ein|schalten v/t. electr. switch od. turn on; j-n: call in; **sich ~** step in; **2schaltquote** TV f rating; **~schärfen** v/t. urge (et. to do s.th.); **~schätzen** v/t. schätzen: estimate; beurteilen: judge, rate; falsch ~ misjudge; **~schenken** v/t. pour (out); **~schicken** v/t. send* in; **~schieben** v/t. slip in; einfügen: insert; **~schlafen** v/i. fall* asleep, go* to sleep; **~schläfern** v/t. töten: put* to sleep

einschl. Abk. für **einschließlich** incl., including

Einschlag m strike, impact; Blitz: stroke; fig. touch; **2en 1.** v/t. knock in (Zähne: out); zerbrechen: break* (in), smash (a. Schädel); einwickeln: wrap up; Weg, Richtung: take*; Rad: turn; → **Laufbahn; 2.** v/i. Blitz, Geschoß: strike*; fig. be* a success

einschlägig adj. relevant

ein|schleichen v/refl. steal* od. creep* (bsd. Fehler etc. slip) in; **~schleppen** v/t. Krankheit: import; **~schleusen** fig. v/t. infiltrate (**in** into); **~schließen** v/t. lock in od. up; umgeben: enclose; mil. surround, encircle; einbeziehen: include; **~schließlich** prp. including, nachgestellt: included; **~schmeicheln** v/refl.: **sich ~ bei** ingratiate o.s. with, F butter s.o. up; **~schnappen** v/i. snap shut; fig. → **eingeschnappt**; **~schneidend** fig. adj. drastic; far-reaching

Einschnitt m cut; Kerbe: notch; fig. break

einschränk|en v/t. restrict, reduce (**beide: auf** to); Rauchen etc.: cut* down on; **sich ~** economize; **2ung** f restriction, reduction, cut; **ohne ~** without reservation

Einschreibe|brief m registered letter; **Ջn** v/t. enter; *buchen:* book; *als Mitglied, Schüler etc.:* enrol(l) (a. mil.); **(sich) ~ lassen (für)** enrol(l) (o.s.) (for)

einschreiten fig. v/i. step in, intervene; **~ (gegen)** take* *(gerichtlich:* legal) measures (against)

ein|schüchtern v/t. intimidate; *brutal:* bully; **Ջschüchterung** f intimidation; **~schulen** v/t.: **eingeschult werden** start school; **Ջschuß** m bullet-hole; **~schweißen** v/t. shrink-wrap

ein|segnen v/t. consecrate; *Kinder:* confirm; **Ջsegnung** f consecration; confirmation

ein|sehen v/t. see*, realize; **das sehe ich nicht ein!** I don't see why!; **Ջsehen** n: **ein ~ haben** show* some understanding; **~seifen** v/t. soap; *Bart:* lather; F fig. take* *s.o.* for a ride

einseitig adj. one-sided; *med., pol., jur.* unilateral

einsend|en v/t. send* in; **Ջer(in)** sender; *an Zeitungen:* contributor; **Ջschluß** m closing date (for entries)

einsetzen 1. *ernennen:* put* in*, insert; *ernennen:* appoint; *Mittel:* use, employ; *Maschine etc.:* put* into service; *Geld:* invest, stake; *bet*; *Leben:* risk; **sich ~** try hard, make* an effort; *für j-n, et.:* support, stand* up for; 2. v/i. set* in, start

Einsicht f *Erkenntnis:* insight; *Einsehen:* understanding; **zur ~ kommen** listen to reason; **~ nehmen in** Akten etc.: take* a look at; **Ջig** adj. understanding; reasonable

Einsiedler m hermit

einsilbig adj. monosyllabic; fig. taciturn; **Ջkeit** f taciturnity

Einsitzer aviat., mot. m single-seater

ein|spannen v/t. *Pferd:* harness; *tech.* clamp, fix; *fig. j-n:* rope in; **~sparen** v/t. save, economize on; **~sperren** v/t. lock *(Tier:* shut*) up; **~spielen** v/t. *Geld:* bring* in; **sich ~** warm up; *fig. Sache:* get* going; → **eingespielt;** **Ջspielergebnisse** pl. *Film:* box-office returns pl.; **~springen** v/i.: **für j-n ~** take* *s.o.*'s place; **Ջspritz...,** mot. in Zssgn fuel-injection

Einspruch m objection (a. jur.), protest; *pol.* veto; *Berufung:* appeal

einspurig adj. *rail.* single-track; *mot.* single-lane

einst adv. once, at one time

Einstand m start; *Tennis:* deuce

ein|stecken v/t. pocket (a. fig.); *electr.* plug in; *Brief:* post, *bsd. Am.* mail; *fig. hinnehmen:* take*; **~stehen** v/i.: **~für** stand* up for; **~steigen** v/i. get* in, in Bus, Zug, Flugzeug: get* on; **alles ~!** rail. all aboard!

einstell|en v/t. *Arbeitskräfte etc.:* engage, employ, hire; *aufgeben:* give* up; *beenden:* stop; *Rekord:* tie; *regulieren:* adjust **(auf** to); *Radio:* tune in (to); *opt., phot.* focus (on); **die Arbeit ~** (go* on) strike*, walk out; **das Feuer ~** mil. cease fire; **sich ~ auf** adjust to; *vorsorglich:* be* prepared for

einstellig adj. single-digit

Einstellung f *Haltung:* attitude **(zu** towards); *Arbeitskräfte:* employment; *Beendigung:* cessation; *tech.* adjustment; *opt., phot.* focus(s)ing; *Film:* take; **~sgespräch** n interview

Einstieg m entrance, entry (a. fig. pol., econ.); **~sdroge** f gateway drug

einstig adj. former, one-time

einstimm|en mus. v/i. join in; **~ig** adj. unanimous

einstöckig adj. one-storey(ed), *Am.* -storied

ein|studieren thea. v/t. rehearse; **~stufen** v/t. grade, rate; **Ջstufungsprüfung** f placement test; **~stufig** adj. single-stage (a. Rakete); **Ջsturz** m, **~stürzen** v/i. collapse

einst|weilen adv. for the present; **~weilig** adj. temporary

ein|tauschen v/t. exchange **(gegen** for); **~teilen** v/t. divide **(in** into); *Zeit:* organize; **~teilig** adj. one-piece; **Ջteilung** f division; organization; *Anordnung:* arrangement

eintönig adj. monotonous; **Ջkeit** f monotony

Eintopf m stew, casserole

Ein|tracht f harmony, unity; **Ջträchtig** adj. harmonious, peaceful

Eintrag m entry (a. econ.), registration; *Schule:* black mark; **Ջen** v/t. enter **(in** in); *amtlich:* register **(bei** with); *als Mitglied:* enrol(l) (with); *Gewinn, Lob etc.:* earn; **sich ~** register, *Hotel:* a. check in

einträglich adj. profitable

ein|treffen v/i. arrive; *geschehen:* happen; *sich erfüllen*: come* true; **~trei-ben** *fig.* v/t. collect; **~treten 1.** v/i. enter; *geschehen*: happen, take* place; **~ für** stand* up for, support; **~ in Verein** *etc.*: join; **2.** v/t. *Tür etc.*: kick in; **sich et. ~** run* s.th. into one's foot

Eintritt *m* entry; *Zutritt, Gebühr*: admission; **~ frei!** admission free!; **~ verboten!** keep out!; **~sgeld** *n* entrance *od.* admission (fee); *Sport*: gate(-money); **~skarte** *f* (admission) ticket

ein|trocknen v/i. dry (up); **~üben** v/t. practise; *proben*: rehearse

einver|leiben v/t. *Land*: annex (*dat.* to); **~standen** *adj.*: **~ sein** agree (*mit* to); **~!** agreed!; **2ständnis** *n* agreement

Einwand *m* objection (*gegen* to)

Einwander|er *m* immigrant; **2n** v/i. immigrate; **~ung** *f* immigration

einwandfrei *adj.* perfect, faultless

einwärts *adv.* inward(s)

Einweg... *Rasierer, Spritze etc.*: disposable; **~flasche** *f* non-returnable bottle; **~packung** *f* throwaway pack

einweichen v/t. soak

einweih|en v/t. inaugurate, *Am.* dedicate; *j-n ~ in* F let* s.o. in on; **2ung** *f* inauguration, *Am.* dedication

einweisen v/t.: **~ in** *Heim, Gefängnis etc.*: send* to, *bsd. jur.* commit to; *Arbeit etc.*: instruct in, brief on

einwend|en v/t. object (*gegen* to); **2ung** *f* objection

einwerfen v/t. throw* in (*a. Bemerkung, Sport a.* v/i.); *Fenster*: break*; *Brief*: post, *Am.* mail; *Münze*: insert

einwickel|n v/t. wrap (up); *fig.* take* s.o. in; **2papier** *n* wrapping-paper

einwillig|en v/i. consent (*in* to), agree (to); **2ung** *f* consent (*in* to), agreement

einwirk|en v/i.: **~ auf** act (up)on; *fig. auf j-n*: work on; **2ung** *f* effect, influence

Einwohner|(in) inhabitant; **~melde-amt** *n* registration office

Einwurf *m* *Sport*: throw-in; *fig.* objection; *Öffnung* slot

Einzahl *gr. f* singular; **2en** v/t. pay* in; **~ung** *f* payment, deposit

einzäunen v/t. fence in

Einzel *n* Tennis: singles *sg.*; **~... in Zssgn** *Bett, Zimmer etc.*: single ...; **~fall** *m* special case; **~gänger** *m* F loner;

~haft *f* solitary confinement; **~handel** *m* retail trade; **~händler** *m* retailer; **~haus** *n* detached house; **~heit** *f* detail

einzeln *adj.* single; *Schuh etc.*: odd; **~e** *pl.* several; some; *der ~e (Mensch)* the individual; **~ eintreten** enter one at a time; **~ angeben** specify; *im ~en* in detail; *jeder ~e* each and every one

einziehen 1. v/t. draw* in (*a. bsd. tech.* retract; *Kopf*: duck; *Segel, Fahne*: strike*; *mil.* call up, *Am.* draft; *beschlagnahmen*: confiscate; *Führerschein*: withdraw*; *Erkundigungen*: make*); **2.** v/i. in *Haus etc.*: move in; *kommen*: come* (*a. Winter*); *geordnet, feierlich*: march in; *Flüssigkeit*: soak in

einzig *adj.* only; *einzeln*: single; *kein ~er ...* not a single ...; *das ~e* the only thing; *der ~e* the only one; **~artig** *adj.* unique, singular

Einzug *m* moving in; entry

einzwängen v/t. squeeze, jam

Eis *n* ice; *~krem*: ice cream; **~bahn** *f* skating rink; **~bär** *zo. m* polar bear; **~becher** *m* sundae; **~bein** *n* (pickled) pork knuckles; **~berg** *m* iceberg; **~brecher** *naut. m* icebreaker; **~diele** *f* ice-cream parlo(u)r

Eisen *n* iron

Eisenbahn *f* railway, *Am.* railroad; *Spielzeug*: train set; *in Zssgn* → *Bahn*; **~er** *m* railwayman, *Am.* railroad man; **~wagen** *m* coach, *Brt. a.* railway carriage, *Am. a.* railroad car

Eisen|erz *n* iron ore; **~gießerei** *f* iron foundry; **~hütte** *f* ironworks *sg., pl.*; **~waren** *pl.* hardware *sg.*, ironware *sg.*; **~warenhandlung** *f* ironmonger's, *Am.* hardware store

eisern *adj.* iron (*a. fig.*), of iron

eis|gekühlt *adj.* iced; **2hockey** *n* ice hockey, *Am.* hockey; **~ig** *adj.* icy (*a. fig.*); **~kalt** *adj.* ice-cold; **2kunstlauf** *m* figure skating; **2kunstläufer(in)** figure skater; **2meer** *n* polar sea; **2revue** *f* ice show; **2schnellauf** *m* speed skating; **2scholle** *f* ice floe; **2schrank** *m* → *Kühlschrank*; **2verkäufer** *m* iceman; **2würfel** *m* ice cube; **2zapfen** *m* icicle; **2zeit** *geol. f* ice age

eitel *adj.* vain; **2keit** *f* vanity

Eiter *med. m* pus; **~beule** *med. f* abscess, boil; **2n** *med.* v/i. fester

eitrig *med. adj.* purulent, festering

Eiweiß n white of egg; biol. protein; **2arm** adj. low in protein, low-protein; **2reich** adj. rich in protein, high-protein

Eizelle f egg cell, ovum

Ekel 1. m disgust (**vor** at), loathing (for); **2.** F n beast; **2erregend**, **2haft**, **2ig** adj. sickening, disgusting, repulsive; **2n** v/refl. u. v/impers.: **ich ekle mich davor** it makes me sick

Ekstase f ecstasy

Elan m vigo(u)r

elastisch adj. elastic, flexible

Elch m elk; Nordamer. ~: moose

Elefant m elephant; **~enhochzeit** econ. F f jumbo merger

elegant adj. elegant; **2z** f elegance

Elektri|ker m electrician; **2sch** adj. allg. electrical; ~ betrieben: electric; **2sieren** v/t. electrify

Elektrizität f electricity; **~swerk** n (electric) power station

Elektrogerät n electric appliance

Elektron|ik f electronics sg.; electronic system; **2isch** adj. electronic

Elektro|rasierer m electric razor; **~technik** f electrical engineering; **~techniker** m electrical engineer

Element n element; **2ar** adj. elementary

Elend n misery

elend adj. miserable; **2sviertel** n slums pl.

elf adj. eleven; **2** f Fußball: team

Elfe f elf, fairy

Elfenbein n ivory

Elfmeter m penalty; **~punkt** m penalty spot; **~schießen** n penalty shoot-out

elfte adj. eleventh

Elite f élite

Ellbogen m elbow

Elsaß Alsace

Elsäss|er(in), **2isch** adj. Alsatian

Elster f magpie

elterlich adj. parental

Eltern pl. parents pl.; **~haus** n (one's parents') home; **2los** adj. orphan(ed); **~teil** m parent; **~vertretung** f Schule etwa Parent-Teacher Association

Email n, **~le** f enamel

Emanz|e F women's libber; **~ipation** f emancipation; der Frau: women's lib(eration); **2ipieren** v/refl. become* emancipated

Embargo n embargo

Embolie med. f embolism

Embryo biol. m embryo

Emigra|nt m emigrant, bsd. pol. refugee; **~tion** f emigration; **in der** ~ in exile

Emission f phy. emission; econ. issue; **~swerte** pl. emission level sg.

Empfang m reception (a. Radio, Hotel), welcome; Erhalt: receipt (**nach**, **bei** on); **2en** v/t. receive; freundlich: a. welcome

Empfäng|er m receiver (a. Radio); post addressee; **2lich** adj. susceptible (**für** to); **~nis** f med. f conception; **~nisverhütung** f contraception, birth control

Empfangs|bescheinigung econ. f receipt; **~dame** f receptionist

empfehl|en v/t. recommend; **~enswert** adj.advisable; **2ung** f recommendation

empfinden v/t. feel* (**als** ... to be ...)

empfindlich adj. sensitive (**für**, **gegen** to) (a. phot., chem.); zart: tender, delicate (a. Gesundheit, Gleichgewicht); leicht gekränkt: touchy; reizbar: irritable (a. Magen); Kälte, Strafe: severe; **~e Stelle** sore spot; **2keit** f sensitivity; phot. speed; delicacy; touchiness

empfindsam adj. sensitive; **2keit** f sensitiveness

Empfindung f sensation; Wahrnehmung: perception; Gefühl: feeling, emotion; **2slos** adj. insensible; Körperteil: numb, dead

empor adv. up, upward(s)

empören v/t. outrage; shock; **sich** ~ (**über**) be* outraged od. shocked (at); **~d** adj. shocking, outrageous

Emporkömmling contp. m upstart

empör|t adj. indignant (**über** at), shocked (at); **2ung** f indignation

emsig adj. busy; **2keit** f activity

Ende n end; Film: ending; **am** ~ at the end; schließlich: in the end, finally; **zu** ~ over; Zeit: up; **zu** ~ **gehen** come* to an end; **zu** ~ **lesen** finish reading; **er ist** ~ **zwanzig** he is in his late twenties; ~ **Mai** at the end of May; ~ **der achtziger Jahre** in the late eighties; ~**!** Funk etc.: over!

enden v/i. (come* to an) end; stop, finish; F ~ **als** end up as

Endergebnis n final result

end|gültig adj. final, definitive; **2lage-**

rung f final disposal; **~lich** adv. finally, at last; **~los** adj. endless; **2runde** f, **2spiel** n Sport: final(s pl.); **2spurt** m final spurt (a. fig.); **2station** rail. f terminus, terminal; **2summe** f (sum) total; **2verbraucher** m end user

Endung ling. f ending

Endziel n ultimate goal (a. fig.)

Energie f energy; tech., electr. power; **~bewußt** adj. energy-conscious; **~krise** f energy crisis; **2los** adj. lacking in energy; **~quelle** f source of energy; **~sparen** n energy saving, conservation of energy; **~versorgung** f power supply

energisch adj. energetic, vigorous

eng adj. narrow; Kleidung: tight; Kontakt, Freund(schaft): close; beengt: cramped; **~ beieinander** close(ly) together

Engagement n thea. etc. engagement; fig., pol. commitment

engagier|en v/t. einstellen: engage; **sich ~ für** be* very involved in; **~t** adj. involved,committed

Enge f narrowness; Wohnverhältnisse: cramped conditions pl.; **in die ~ treiben** drive* into a corner

Engel m angel

engl. Abk. für englisch Eng., English

Eng|land England; **~länder** m Englishman; **die ~ pl.** the English pl.; **~in** f Englishwoman

englisch adj. English (auf in); **2unterricht** m English lesson(s pl.) od. class(es pl.); teaching of English

Engpaß m bottleneck (a. fig.)

engstirnig adj. narrow-minded

Enkel m grandchild; grandson; **~in** f granddaughter

enorm adj. enormous; fig. terrific

Ensemble n thea. etc. company; cast

entart|en v/i., **~et** adj. degenerate; **2ung** f degeneration

entbehr|en v/t. do* without; erübrigen: spare; vermissen: miss; **~lich** adj. dispensable; überflüssig: superfluous; **2ung** f want, privation

entbind|en 1. med. v/i. have* the baby, be* confined; **2.** v/t.: **~ von** fig. relieve s.o. of; **entbunden werden von** med. give* birth to; **2ung** med. f delivery; **2ungsstation** f maternity ward

entblößen v/t. bare, uncover

entdeck|en v/t. discover; **2er** m discoverer; **2ung** f discovery

Ente f zo. duck; F Zeitungs2: hoax

entehren v/t. dishono(u)r

enteign|en v/t. expropriate; j-n: dispossess; **2ung** f expropriation; dispossession

enterben v/t. disinherit

entern naut. v/t. board

ent|fachen v/t. kindle; fig. a. rouse; **~fallen** v/i. wegfallen: be* cancelled; **~ auf** fall* to s.o.('s share); **es ist mir ~** it has slipped my memory; **~falten** v/t. unfold; Fähigkeiten: develop; **sich ~** unfold; fig. develop (zu into)

entfern|en v/t. remove (a. fig.); **sich ~** leave*; **~t** adj. distant (a. fig.); **weit (zehn Meilen) ~** far (10 miles) away; **2ung** f distance; removal; **2ungsmesser** phot. m range finder

entflammbar adj. (in)flammable

entfremd|en v/t. estrange (dat. from); **2ung** f estrangement, alienation

entführ|en v/t. kidnap; Flugzeug etc.: hijack; **2er** m kidnapper; hijacker; **2ung** f kidnapping; hijacking

entgegen prp. u. adv. gegen: contrary to; Richtung: toward(s); **~gehen** v/i. go* to meet; **~gesetzt** adj. opposite; **~halten** fig. v/t. point s.th. out; **~kommen** v/i. come* to meet; fig. j-m: meet* s.o. halfway; **2kommen** n obligingness; **~kommend** adj. obliging; **~nehmen** v/t. accept, receive; **~sehen** v/i. await; e-r Sache freudig: look forward to; **~setzen** v/t.: j-m Widerstand ~ put* up resistance to s.o.; **~treten** v/i. walk towards; feindlich: oppose; Gefahr: face

entgegn|en v/i. reply, answer; schlagfertig, kurz: retort; **2ung** f reply; retort

ent|gehen v/t. escape; Wort, Fehler, Gelegenheit etc.: miss; **~geistert** adj. aghast

Entgelt n remuneration; Honorar: fee

ent|giften v/t. decontaminate; **~gleisen** v/i. be* derailed; fig. blunder; **2gleisung** f derailment; fig. faux pas; **~gleiten** fig. v/i. get* out of control; **~gräten** v/t. bone, fillet

enthalt|en v/t. contain, hold*, include; **sich ~** gen. abstain od. refrain from; **~sam** adj. abstinent; maßvoll: moderate; **2samkeit** f abstinence; moderation; **2ung** f bsd. Stimm2: abstention

ent|härten v/t. soften; **~haupten** v/t. behead, decapitate

enthüll|en v/t. uncover; Denkmal: unveil; fig. reveal, disclose; **2ung** f unveiling; fig. revelation, disclosure

Enthusias|mus m enthusiasm; **~t** m enthusiast; Film, Sport: F fan; **2tisch** adj. enthusiastic

ent|jungfern v/t. deflower; **2jungferung** f defloration; **~kleiden** v/t. u. v/refl. undress, strip; **~kommen** v/i. escape (dat. from); **~korken** v/t. uncork

entkräft|en v/t. weaken (a. fig.); **2ung** f weakening, exhaustion

entlad|en v/t. unload; bsd. electr. discharge; **sich ~** bsd. electr. discharge; Zorn etc.: explode; **2ung** f unloading; bsd. electr. discharge; explosion

entlang prp. u. adv. along; **hier ~, bitte!** this way, please!; **die Straße** etc. **~** along the street etc.; **~...** in Zssgn fahren, gehen etc.: ... along

entlarven v/t. unmask, expose

entlass|en v/t. dismiss, F fire, give* s.o. the sack; Patient: discharge; Häftling: release; **2ung** f dismissal; discharge; release

entlast|en v/t. j-n: relieve s.o. of some of his work; jur. exonerate, clear s.o. of a charge; **den Verkehr ~** relieve the traffic congestion; **2ung** f relief; jur. exoneration; **~ungszeuge** m witness for the defen|ce, Am. -se

ent|laufen v/i. run* away (dat. from); **~ledigen** v/refl. j-s, e-r Sache: rid* o.s. of, get* rid of

entlegen adj. remote, distant

ent|lehnen v/t. borrow (dat., aus from); **~locken** v/t. draw*, elicit (dat. from); **~lohnen** v/t. pay* (off); **~lüften** v/t. ventilate; **~machen** v/t. deprive s.o. of his power; **~militarisieren** v/t. demilitarize; **~mündigen** jur. v/t. place under disability; **~mutigen** v/t. discourage; **~nehmen** v/t. take* (dat. from); **~ aus** (with)draw* from; fig. gather od. learn* from; **~nervt** adj. enervated; **~puppen** v/refl.: **sich ~ als** turn out to be; **~rahmt** adj. skimmed; **~reißen** v/t. snatch (away) (dat. from); **~richten** v/t. pay*; **~rinnen** v/i. escape (dat. from); **~rollen** v/t. unroll

entrüst|en v/t. fill with indignation; **sich ~ become*** indignant (über at s.th., with s.o.); **~et** adj. indignant (über at s.th., with s.o.); **2ung** f indignation

Ent|safter m juice extractor; **2salzen** v/t. desalinize

entschädig|en v/t. compensate; **2ung** f compensation

entschärfen v/t. defuse (a. Lage)

entscheid|en v/t. u. v/i. u. v/refl. decide; (für on, in favo[u]r of; gegen against); endgültig: a. settle; **er kann sich nicht ~** he can't make up his mind; **~end** adj. decisive; kritisch: crucial; **2ung** f decision

entschieden adj. decided, determined, resolute; **~ dafür** strongly in favour of it; **2heit** f determination

entschließ|en v/refl. decide, determine, make* up one's mind; **2ung** pol. f resolution

entschlossen adj. determined, resolute; **2heit** f determination, resoluteness

Entschluß m decision, resolution

entschlüsseln v/t. decipher, decode

entschuldig|en v/t. excuse; **sich ~** apologize (bei to; für for); für Abwesenheit: excuse o.s.; **~ Sie!** (I'm) sorry!; j-n anredend: excuse me!; **2ung** f excuse (a. Schreiben); Verzeihung: apology; **um ~ bitten** apologize; **~!** (I'm) sorry!; beim Vorbeigehen etc.: excuse me!

Entschwefelungsanlage tech. f desulphurization plant

entsetz|en v/t. shock; stärker: horrify; **Entsetz|en** n horror, terror; **2lich** adj. horrible, dreadful, terrible; scheußlich: atrocious; **2t** adj. shocked; horrified

ent|sichern v/t. release the safety catch of; **~sinnen** v/refl. remember, recall

entsorg|en v/t. Müll etc.: dispose of; **2ung** f (waste) disposal

entspann|en v/t. u. v/refl. relax; **sich ~** a. take* it easy; Lage: ease (up); **~t** adj. relaxed; **2ung** f relaxation; pol. détente

entspiegelt opt. adj. non-glare

entsprech|en v/i. correspond to; e-r Beschreibung: answer to; Anforderungen etc.: meet*; **~end** adj. corresponding (to); passend: appropriate; **2ung** f equivalent

ent|springen v/i. Fluß: rise*; **~sprungen** adj. escaped

entstehen v/i. come* into being; geschehen, eintreten: arise*; allmählich: emerge, develop; ~ aus originate from; **2ung** f origin

entstellen v/t. disfigure, deform; verzerren: distort; **2ung** f disfigurement, deformation, distortion (a. von Tatsachen)

entstört electr. adj. interference-free

enttäuschen v/t. disappoint; **2ung** f disappointment

ent|waffnen v/t. disarm; **2warnung** f all clear (signal)

entwässer|n v/t. drain; **2ung** f drainage; chem. dehydration

entweder cj.: ~ ... oder either ... or

ent|weichen v/i. escape (aus from); **~weihen** v/t. desecrate; **~wenden** v/t. pilfer, steal*; **~werfen** v/t. design; Schriftstück: draw* up

entwert|en v/t. abwerten: lower the value of (a. fig.); Fahrschein etc.: cancel; **2ung** f devaluation; cancellation

entwickeln v/t. u. v/refl. develop (a. phot.) (zu into)

Entwicklung f development, biol. a. evolution; ~salter: adolescence, age of puberty; **~shelfer(in)** pol. econ. development aid volunteer; Brt. VSO worker; Am. Peace Corps volunteer; **~shilfe** f development aid; **~sland** pol. n developing country

ent|wirren v/t. disentangle (a. fig.); **~wischen** v/i. get* away

entwürdigend adj. degrading

Entwurf m outline, (rough) draft, plan; Gestaltung: design; Skizze: sketch

ent|wurzeln v/t. uproot; **~ziehen** v/t. take* away (dat. from); Führerschein, Lizenz: revoke; Rechte: deprive of; chem. extract; sich j-m od. e-r Sache ~ evade s.o. od. s.th.; **2ziehungsanstalt** f drug (Am. substance) abuse clinic; **2ziehungskur** f detoxi(fi)cation (treatment); Alkohol2: a. F drying out; **~ziffern** v/t. decipher, make* out

entzücken v/t. charm, delight

Entzück|en n delight; **2end** adj. delightful, charming, F sweet; **2t** adj. delighted (über, von at, with)

Entzug m withdrawal; Lizenz etc.: revocation; **~serscheinung** med. f withdrawal symptom

entzünd|bar adj. (in)flammable; **~en** v/refl. catch* fire; med. become* inflamed; **2ung** med. f inflammation

entzwei adv. in two, to pieces; **~en** v/refl. fall* out, break* (mit with); **~gehen** v/i. break*, go* to pieces

Enzyklopädie f encyclop(a)edia

Epidemie med. f epidemic (disease)

Epilog m epilog(ue)

episch adj. epic

Episode f episode

Epoche f epoch, period, era

Epos n epic (poem)

er pers. pron. he; Sache: it

erachten v/t. consider, think*

Erachten n: meines ~s in my opinion

Erbanlage biol. f genes pl., genetic code

erbarmen v/refl.: sich j-s ~ take* pity on s.o.

Erbarmen n pity, mercy

erbärmlich adj. pitiful, pitiable; elend: miserable; gemein: mean

erbarmungslos adj. pitiless, merciless; Verfolgung etc.: relentless

erbau|en v/t. build*, construct; **2er** m builder, constructor; **~lich** adj. edifying; **2ung** fig. f edification, uplift

Erbe 1. m heir; **2.** n inheritance, heritage

erbeben v/i. tremble, shake*, quake

erben v/t. inherit

erbeuten v/t. mil. capture; Dieb: get* away with

Erbfaktor biol. m gene

Erbin f heir, bsd. reiche: heiress

erbitten v/t. ask for, request

erbittert adj. Kampf etc.: fierce, furious

Erbkrankheit med. f hereditary disease

er|blassen, **~bleichen** v/i. grow* od. turn pale

erblich adj. hereditary

erblicken v/t. see*, catch* sight of

erblinden v/i. go* blind

Erbrechen med. n vomiting, sickness

Erbschaft f inheritance, heritage

Erbse bot. f pea; (grüne) ~n green peas

Erb|stück n heirloom; **~sünde** f original sin; **~teil** n (share of the) inheritance

Erd|apfel östr. m potato; Zssgn → Kartoffel...; **~ball** m globe; **~beben** n earthquake; **~beere** bot. f strawberry; **~boden** m earth, ground

Erd|e f earth; *Bodenart:* ground, soil; → **eben**; **2en** *electr.* v/t. earth, ground
erdenklich *adj.* imaginable
Erd|gas n natural gas; **~geschoß** n ground (*Am. a.* first) floor
erdicht|en v/t. invent, make* up; **~et** *adj.* invented, made-up
erdig *adj.* earthy
Erd|klumpen m clod, lump of earth; **~kruste** f earth's crust; **~kugel** f globe; **~kunde** f geography; **~leitung** f *electr.* earth (*Am.* ground) connection; *Gas etc.:* underground pipe(line); **~nuß** f peanut; **~öl** n (mineral) oil, petroleum; *Zssgn* → **Öl...**; **~reich** n ground, earth
erdreisten v/refl. F have* the nerve
erdrosseln v/t. strangle, throttle
erdrücken v/t. crush (to death); **~d** *fig. adj.* overwhelming
Erd|rutsch m landslide (*a. pol.*); **~teil** *geogr.* m continent
erdulden v/t. suffer, endure
Erd|umlaufbahn f earth orbit; **~ung** *electr.* f earthing, *Am.* grounding; **~wärme** *geol.* f geothermal energy
ereifern v/refl. get* excited
ereig|nen v/refl. happen, occur; **2nis** n event, occurrence; **~nisreich** *adj.* eventful
Erektion f erection
Eremit m hermit, anchorite
erfahren[1] v/t. hear*; learn*; *erleben:* experience
erfahr|en[2] *adj.* experienced; **2ung** f experience; *im Beruf:* work experience
Erfahrungs|austausch m exchange of experience; **2gemäß** *adv.* as experience shows
erfassen v/t. be-, ergreifen: grasp; *statistisch:* record, register; *umfassen:* cover, include; *Daten:* collect, *mil.* call up
erfind|en v/t. invent; **2er** m inventor; **~erisch** *adj.* inventive; **2ung** f invention; **2ungskraft** f inventiveness
Erfolg m success; *Ergebnis:* result; *viel* **~!** good luck!; **2en** v/i. happen, take* place; **2los** *adj.* unsuccessful; *vergeblich:* futile; **~losigkeit** f lack of success; **2reich** *adj.* successful; **~serlebnis** n sense of achievement; **2versprechend** *adj.* promising
erforder|lich *adj.* necessary, required;

~n v/t. require, demand; **2nis** n requirement, demand
erforsch|en v/t. explore; *untersuchen:* investigate, study; **2er** m explorer; **2ung** f exploration
erfreu|en v/t. please; **~lich** *adj.* pleasing, pleasant; *befriedigend:* gratifying; **~t** *adj.* pleased (*über* at, about); *sehr* **~!** pleased to meet you
erfrier|en v/i. freeze* to death; **2ung** f frost-bite
erfrisch|en v/t. u. v/refl. refresh (o.s.); **~end** *adj.* refreshing; **2ung** f refreshment
erfroren *adj. Finger etc.:* frostbitten; *Pflanzen:* killed by frost
erfüll|en *fig.* v/t. *Wunsch, Pflicht, Aufgabe:* fulfil(l); *Versprechen:* keep*; *Zweck:* serve; *Bedingung, Erwartung:* meet*; **~ mit** fill with; *sich* **~** be* fulfilled, come* true; **2ung** f fulfil(l)ment; *in* **~** *gehen* come* true
ergänz|en v/t. complement (*einander* each other); *nachträglich:* supplement, add; **~end** *adj.* complementary, supplementary; **2ung** f completion; supplement, addition
er|gattern F v/t. (manage to) get* hold of; **~gaunern** F v/t. → **erschwindeln**
ergeben 1. v/t. amount *od.* come* to; **2.** v/refl. surrender; *Schwierigkeiten:* arise*; *sich* **~ aus** result from; *sich* **~ in** resign o.s. to; **2heit** f devotion
Ergebnis n result, outcome; *Sport:* result, score; **2los** *adj.* fruitless, without result
ergehen v/i.: get* on, fare; *wie ist es dir ergangen?* how did things go with you?; *so erging es mir auch* the same thing happened to me; *et. über sich* **~** *lassen* (patiently) endure s.th.
ergiebig *adj.* productive, rich; **2keit** f (high) yield; productiveness
er|gießen v/refl.: *sich* **~ über** pour down on; **~grauen** v/i. turn grey
ergreifen v/t. seize, grasp, take* hold of; *Gelegenheit, Maßnahme:* take*; *Beruf:* take* up; *fig.* move, touch
ergriffen *adj.* moved; **2nheit** f emotion
ergründen v/t. find* out, fathom
erhaben *adj.* raised, elevated; *fig.* sublime; **~** *sein über* be* above
erhalten[1] v/t. get*, receive; *bewahren:* keep*, preserve; *schützen:* protect; *un-*

terstützen: support, maintain
erhalten² *adj.*: **gut ~** in good condition
erhältlich *adj.* obtainable, available
Erhaltung *f* preservation; *von Haus, Familie*: upkeep
er|hängen *v/t.* hang (**sich ~** o.s.); **~härten** *v/t.* harden; *fig. a.* confirm
erheb|en *v/t.* raise (*a. Stimme*), lift; **sich ~** rise* up (**gegen** against); **~lich** *adj.* considerable; **2ung** *f Statistik*: survey; *Aufstand*: revolt
er|heitern *v/t.* cheer up, amuse; **~hellen** *v/t.* light* up; *fig.* throw* light upon; **~hitzen** *v/t.* heat; **sich ~** get* hot; **~hoffen** *v/t.* hope for
erhöh|en *v/t.* raise; *verstärken*: increase; **2ung** *f* increase
erhol|en *v/refl.* recover; *entspannen*: relax, rest; **~sam** *adj.* restful, relaxing; **2ung** *f* recovery; relaxation; **2ungs-heim** *n* rest home
erinner|n *v/t.*: **j-n ~ an** remind s.o. of; **sich ~ an** remember, recall; **2ung** *f* memory (**an** of); *Andenken*: remembrance, souvenir; *an j-n*: keepsake; **zur ~ an** in memory of
erkalten *v/i.* cool down (*a. fig.*)
erkält|en *v/refl.*: **sich ~** catch* (a) cold; **(stark) erkältet sein** have* a (bad) cold; **2ung** *f* cold
erkenn|bar *adj.* recognizable; **~en** *v/t.* recognize (**an** by), know* (by); *verstehen*: see*, realize; **~tlich** *adj.*: **sich (j-m) ~ zeigen** show* (s.o.) one's gratitude; **2tnis** *f* realization; *Entdeckung*: discovery; **~se** *pl.* findings *pl.*; **2ungs-dienst** *m* (police) records department; **2ungsmelodie** *f* signature tune; **2ungszeichen** *n* badge; *aviat.* markings *pl.*
Erker *m* bay; **~fenster** *n* bay window
erklär|en *v/t.* explain (*j-m* to s.o.); *verkünden*: declare; *j-n* (*offiziell*) **für ...** pronounce s.o. ...; **~end** *adj. Worte etc.*: explanatory; **~lich** *adj.* explainable; **~t** *adj.* declared; **2ung** *f* explanation; declaration; *Wort2*: definition; **e-e ~ abgeben** make* a statement
erklingen *v/i.* (re)sound, ring* (out)
erkrank|en *v/i.* fall* ill, *Am. a.* get* sick; **~an** get*; **2ung** *f* illness, sickness
erkunden *v/t.* explore
erkundig|en *v/refl.* inquire (**nach** about *s.th.*; after *s.o.*); *Auskünfte einho-*

len: make* inquiries (about); **sich (bei j-m) nach dem Weg ~** ask (s.o.) the way; **2ung** *f* inquiry
Erkundung *f* exploration; *mil.* reconnaissance (*a. in Zssgn*)
Erlagschein *östr. m* money-order form
er|lahmen *fig. v/i.* slacken, wane, flag; **~langen** *v/t.* gain, obtain, reach
Erlaß *m* decree; *e-r Strafe etc.*: remission; **2lassen** *v/t. Verordnung*: issue; *Gesetz*: enact; *j-m et.*: release from
erlauben *v/t.* allow, permit; **sich et. ~** permit o.s. (**wagen**: dare) to do s.th.; **gönnen**: treat o.s. to s.th.
Erlaubnis *f* permission; *Befugnis*: authority; **~schein** *m* permit
erläuter|n *v/t.* explain, illustrate; *kommentieren*: comment on; **2ung** *f* explanation; comment
Erle *bot. f* alder
erleb|en *v/t.* experience; *Schlimmes*: go* through; *mit ansehen*: see*; *Abenteuer, Überraschung, Freude etc.*: have*; **das werden wir nicht mehr ~** we won't live to see that; **2nis** *n* experience; *Abenteuer*: adventure; **~nis-reich** *adj.* eventful
erledig|en *v/t. allg.* take* care of, do*, handle; *Angelegenheit, Problem*: settle; *F j-n*: finish (*a. Sport*); *umbringen*: do* (s.o.) in; **~t** *adj.* finished, settled; *erschöpft*: worn out; **der ist ~!** he is done for; **2ung** *f* settlement; **~en** *pl.* things *pl.* to do; shopping *sg.*
erlegen *hunt. v/t.* shoot*
erleichter|n *v/t.* ease, relieve; **~t** *adj.* relieved; **2ung** *f* relief (**über** at)
er|leiden *v/t.* suffer; **~lernen** *v/t.* learn*; **~lesen** *adj.* choice, select
erleucht|en *v/t.* illuminate; *fig.* enlighten; **2ung** *fig. f* inspiration
erliegen *v/i.* succumb to
Erliegen *n*: **zum ~ kommen (bringen)** come* (bring*) to a standstill
erlogen *adj.* false; **~ sein** be* a lie
Erlös *m* proceeds *pl.*; *Gewinn*: profit(s *pl.*)
erloschen *adj. Vulkan*: extinct
erlöschen *v/i.* go* out; *Gefühle*: die; *jur. auslaufen*: lapse, expire
erlös|en *v/t.* deliver, free (*beide*: **von** from); **2er** *rel. m* Saviour; **2ung** *f rel.* salvation; *Erleichterung*: relief
ermächtig|en *v/t.* authorize; **2ung** *f* authorization; *Befugnis*: authority

ermahn|en *v/t.* admonish (*a. Schule*); *stärker*: reprove, warn (*a. Sport*); **2ung** *f* admonition; warning; *bsd. Sport*: (first) caution

Ermangelung *f*: **in** ~ for want of

ermäßig|t *adj.* reduced, cut; **2ung** *f* reduction, cut

ermessen *v/t.* assess; *beurteilen*: judge

Ermessen *n* discretion; *nach eigenem* ~ at one's own discretion

ermitt|eln 1. *v/t.* find* out; *bestimmen*: determine; **2.** *v/i. bsd. jur.* investigate; **2lung** *f* finding; *jur.* investigation

ermöglichen *v/t.* make* possible

ermord|en *v/t.* murder; *bsd. pol.* assassinate; **2ung** *f* murder; assassination

ermüd|en *v/t. u. v/i.* tire, fatigue (*a. tech.*); **2ung** *f* fatigue, tiredness

er|muntern *v/t.* encourage; *anregen*: stimulate; **2munterung** *f* encouragement; *Anreiz*: incentive; **~mutigen** *v/t.* encourage; **~mutigend** *adj.* encouraging; **2mutigung** *f* encouragement

ernähr|en *v/t.* feed* (*a. Familie*: support; *sich* ~ *von* live on; **2er** *m* breadwinner, supporter; **2ung** *f* nutrition, food, diet

ernenn|en *v/t.*: *j-n* ~ *zu* appoint s.o. (to be); **2ung** *f* appointment

erneu|ern *v/t.* renew; **2erung** *f* renewal; **~t 1.** *adj.* renewed **2.** *adv.* once more

erniedrig|en *v/t.* humiliate; *sich* ~ degrade o.s.; **2ung** *f* humiliation

ernst *adj.* serious, earnest; ~ *nehmen* take* *s.o. od. s.th.* seriously

Ernst *m* seriousness, earnest; *im* ~(?) seriously(?); *ist das dein* ~? are you serious?; **~fall** *m* (case of) emergency; **2haft, 2lich** *adj. u. adv.* serious(ly)

Ernte *f* harvest; *bsd. Ertrag*: crop(s *pl.*); **~dankfest** *n* harvest festival, *Am.* Thanksgiving (Day); **2n** *v/t.* harvest, reap (*a. fig.*)

ernüchter|n *v/t.* sober; *fig. a.* disillusion; **2ung** *f* sobering up; *fig.* disillusionment

Erober|er *m* conqueror; **2n** *v/t.* conquer; **2ung** *f* conquest (*a. fig.*)

eröffn|en *v/t.* open; *feierlich: a.* inaugurate; *disclose s.th.* (*j-m* to s.o.); **2ung** *f* opening; inauguration; disclosure

erörter|n *v/t.* discuss; **2ung** *f* discussion

Erot|ik *f* eroticism; **2isch** *adj.* erotic

erpicht *adj.*: ~ *auf* keen on

erpress|en *v/t.* blackmail; *Geständnis, Geld*: extort; **2er(in)** blackmailer; **2ung** *f* blackmail(ing); extortion

erproben *v/t.* try, test

er|raten *v/t.* guess; **~rechnen** *v/t.* calculate, work *s.th.* out

erreg|bar *adj.* excitable; *reizbar*: irritable; **~en** *v/t.* excite; *sexuell: a.* arouse; *Gefühle*: rouse; *verursachen*: cause; *sich* ~ get* excited; **~end** *adj.* exciting, thrilling; **2er** *med. m* germ, virus; **2ung** *f* excitement

erreich|bar *adj.* within reach (*a. fig.*); *Person*: available; *leicht* ~ within easy reach; *nicht* ~ out of reach; **~en** *v/t.* reach; *Zug etc.*: catch*; *es* ~, *daß* ... succeed in *doing s.th.*; *et.* ~ get* somewhere; *telefonisch zu* ~ *sein* be* on the (*Am.* have* a) phone

erricht|en *v/t.* put* up, erect; *fig. gründen*: found, *bsd. econ.* set* up; **2ung** *f* erection; *fig.* establishment

er|ringen *v/t.* win*, gain; *Erfolg*: achieve; **~röten** *v/i.* blush

Errungenschaft *f* achievement; *m-e neueste* ~ my latest achievement

Ersatz *m* replacement; *auf Zeit, a. Person*: substitute; *Mittel: a.* surrogate; *Ausgleich*: compensation; *Schaden2*: damages *pl.*; *als* ~ *für* in exchange for; **~dienst** *m* → *Zivildienst*; **~mann** *m* substitute (*a. Sport*); **~mine** *f* refill; **~reifen** *mot. m* spare tyre (*Am.* tire); **~spieler(in)** *Sport*: substitute; **~teil** *tech. n* spare part

er|saufen F *v/i.*; **~säufen** *v/t.* drown

erschaffen *v/t.* create; **2ung** *f* creation

erschallen *v/i.* (re)sound, ring* (out)

erschein|en *v/i.* appear, F turn up; *Buch*: be* published, appear; **2ung** *f* appearance; *Geister2*: apparition; *Tatsache, Natur2*: phenomenon

Erscheinen *n* appearance; *Buch: a.* publication

er|schießen *v/t.* shoot* (dead); **~schlaffen** *v/i.* go* limp; *fig.* weaken; (*a. fig.*); **~schlagen** *v/t.* kill; **~schließen** *v/t.* open up; *Bauland*: develop

erschöpf|en *v/t.* exhaust; **~t** *adj.* exhausted; **2ung** *f* exhaustion

erschrecken 1. *v/t.* frighten, scare; **2.** *v/i.* be* frightened (*über* at); **~d** *adj.* alarming; *Anblick*: terrible

erschütter|n v/t. shake*; fig. a. shock; bewegen: move; **2ung** f shock (a. seelisch); tech. vibration

erschweren v/t. make* more difficult; verschlimmern: aggravate

erschwing|en v/t. afford; **~lich** adj. within one's means, affordable; Preise: reasonable; **das ist für uns nicht ~** we can't afford that

er|sehen v/t. see*, learn*, gather (alle: **aus** from); **~sehnen** v/t. long for; **~setzbar** adj. replaceable; Schaden: reparable; **~setzen** v/t. replace (**durch** by); Schaden, Verlust: compensate for; Auslagen: reimburse

ersichtlich adj. evident, obvious

erspar|en v/t. save; j-m et. **~** spare s.o. s.th.; **2nisse** pl. savings pl.

erst adv. first; anfangs: at first; **~ jetzt** (gestern) only now (yesterday); **~ nächste Woche** not before od. until next week; **es ist ~ neun Uhr** it's only nine o'clock; **eben ~** just (now); **~ recht** all the more; **~ recht nicht** even less; → **einmal**

erstarr|en v/i. stiffen; fig. freeze*; **~t** adj. stiff; vor Kälte: numb

erstatt|en v/t. refund, reimburse; Bericht **~** (give*) a report (**über** on); Anzeige **~** report to the police

Erstaufführung f thea. first night od. performance, premiere; Film: a. first run

erstaunen v/t. surprise, astonish

Erstaun|en n surprise, astonishment; **in ~ setzen** astonish; **2lich** adj. surprising, astonishing; **2t** adj. astonished

Erst|ausgabe f first edition; **2beste** adj. first; any old

erste adj. first; **auf den ~n Blick** at first sight; **fürs ~** for the time being; **als ~(r)** first; **zum ~n Mal(e)** for the first time; **am 2n** on the first

erstechen v/t. stab

erst|ens adv. first(ly), in the first place; **~ere: der (die, das) ~** the former

erstick|en v/t. u. v/i. choke, suffocate; **2ung** f suffocation

erst|klassig adj. first-class, F a. super; **~malig** adj. first; **~mals** adv. for the first time

erstreben v/t. strive* after; **~swert** adj. desirable

erstrecken v/refl. extend, stretch (**bis,**

auf to; **über** over); **sich ~ über** a. cover

Erstschlag m mil. first strike

ersuchen v/t. request

er|tappen v/t. catch*; → **Tat**; **~teilen** v/t. Rat, Erlaubnis etc.: give*; **~tönen** v/i. (re)sound

Ertrag m yield, produce; Bergbau: a. output; Einnahmen: proceeds pl., returns pl.; **2en** v/t. Schmerzen etc.: bear*, endure; Klima, Person: a. stand*

erträglich adj. bearable, tolerable

er|tränken v/t. drown; **~übrigen** v/t. Zeit etc.: spare; **sich ~** be* unnecessary; **~wachen** v/i. wake* (up); bsd. fig. Gefühle etc.: awake*, awaken

Erw. Abk. für **Erwachsene(r)** adult(s)

erwachsen¹ v/i. arise* (**aus** from)

erwachsen² adj. grown-up, adult; **2e** m, f adult; **nur für ~!** adults only!; **2enbildung** f adult education

erwäg|en v/t. consider, think* s.th. over; **2ung** f consideration; **in ~ ziehen** take* into consideration

erwähn|en v/t. mention; **2ung** f mention(ing)

erwärm|en v/t. u. v/refl. warm (up); fig. **sich ~ für** warm to; **2ung** f warming up; **~ der Erdatmosphäre** global warming

erwart|en v/t. expect; Kind: be* expecting; warten auf: wait for, await; **2ung** f expectation; a. freudige: anticipation; **~ungsvoll** adj. u. adv. full of expectation, expectant(ly)

er|wecken fig. v/t. awaken; Verdacht, Gefühle: arouse; → **Anschein**; **~wehren** v/refl. ward off; **~weichen** v/t. fig. soften, mollify; **~weisen** v/t. Dienst, Gefallen: do*; Achtung etc.: show*; **sich ~ als** prove to be

erweiter|n v/t. u. v/refl. extend, enlarge; bsd. econ. expand; **2ung** f extension, enlargement, expansion

Erwerb m acquisition; Kauf: purchase; Einkommen: income; **2en** v/t. acquire (a. Wissen, Ruf etc.); kaufen: purchase

erwerbs|los adj. unemployed; **~tätig** adj. (gainfully) employed, working; **~unfähig** adj. unable to work

Erwerbung f acquisition; purchase

erwider|n v/t. reply, answer; Gruß, Besuch etc.: return; **2ung** f reply, answer; return

erwischen v/t. catch*, get*; **ihn hat's erwischt** he's had it

erwünscht adj. desired; **wünschenswert**: desirable; **willkommen**: welcome

erwürgen v/t. strangle; **Tod durch ♀** death by strangulation

Erz n ore

erzähl|en v/t. tell*; **kunstvoll**: narrate; **man hat mir erzählt** I was told; **♀er(in)** narrator; **♀ung** f (short) story, tale

Erz|bischof rel. m archbishop; **~bistum** rel. n archbishopric; **~engel** rel. m archangel

erzeug|en v/t. produce (a. fig.); **industriell**: a. make*, manufacture; **electr.** generate; **verursachen**: cause, create; **♀er** econ. m producer; **♀nis** n product (a. fig.); **♀ung** f production

Erzherzog m archduke

erziehe|n v/t. bring* up, raise; **geistig**: educate; **j-n zu et.** ~ teach* s.o. to be od. to do s.th.; **♀r(in)** m educator; **Lehrer(in)**: teacher; **(qualified) kindergarten teacher; Hauslehrer**: tutor; **Hauslehrerin**: governess; **~risch** adj. educational, pedagogic(al)

Erziehung f upbringing; **geistige**: education; **~sanstalt** f bsd. Brt. approved school, bsd. Am. reform school; **~sberechtigte(r)** parent or guardian; **~swesen** n educational system

er|zielen v/t. achieve; **Sport**: score; **~zogen** adj.: **gut ~ sein** be* well-bred; **schlecht ~ sein** ill-bred; **~zwingen** v/t. (en)force

es pers. pron. m; Person, Tier bei bekanntem Geschlecht: he; she; ~ **gibt** there is, there are; **ich bin ~** it's me; **ich hoffe ~** I hope so; **ich kann ~** I can (do it)

Escape-Taste f Computer: escape key

Esche bot. f ash (tree)

Esel m zo. donkey, ass (a. fig. contp.); **fig.** fool, idiot, F twit; **~sbrücke** f mnemonic; **~sohr** fig. n dog-ear

Eskorte f mil. escort; **naut.** a. convoy

eßbar adj. eatable; **bsd. Pilz etc.**: edible

essen v/t. u. v/i. eat*; **zu Mittag** ~ (have*) lunch; **zu Abend** ~ have* supper (feiner: dinner); ~ **gehen** eat* od. dine out

Essen n food; **Mahlzeit**: meal; **Gericht**: dish; **warmes Abend- od. Mittag♀**: dinner; **~smarke** f meal ticket, Brt. a.

lunch(eon) voucher; **~szeit** f lunchtime; dinner od. supper time

Essig m vinegar; **~gurke** f pickled gherkin, Am. a. pickle

Eß|löffel m tablespoon; **~stäbchen** pl. chopsticks pl.; **~tisch** m dining table; **~zimmer** n dining room

Estrich m arch. flooring, subfloor; **Schweiz**: loft, attic, garret

etablieren v/refl. establish o.s.

Etage f floor, stor(e)y; **auf der ersten** ~ on the first (Am. second) floor; **~nbett** n bunk bed

Etappe f stage, Sport a. leg

Etat m budget

Eth|ik f ethics pl.; **♀isch** adj. ethical

ethnisch adj. ethnic

Etikett n label (a. fig.); (price) tag; **~e** f etiquette; **♀ieren** v/t. label

etliche indef. pron. several, quite a few

Etui n case

etwa adv. about, bsd. Am. a. around; **in Fragen**: perhaps, by any chance; **nicht** ~ **,daß** not that; **~ig** adj. any

etwas 1. indef. pron. something; **irgend** ~: anything; **2.** adj. some; any; **3.** adv. a little, somewhat

EU Abk. für **Europäische Union** EU, European Union

euch pers. pron. you; ~ **(selbst)** yourselves

euer poss. pron. your; **der (die, das) eu(e)re** yours

Eule zo. f owl; **~n nach Athen tragen** carry coals to Newcastle

euresgleichen pron. people like you, F contp. the likes of you

Euro... in Zssgn Scheck etc.: Euro...

Europa Europe; **~...** in Zssgn European

Europä|er(in), **♀isch** adj. European; **Europäische Gemeinschaft** European Community

Euter n udder

ev. Abk. für **evangelisch** Prot., Protestant

evakuieren v/t. evacuate

evangeli|sch rel. adj. Protestant; **~lutherisch** Lutheran; **♀um** n Gospel

eventuell 1. adj. possible; **2.** adv. possibly, perhaps; △ **nicht eventual(ly)**

evtl. Abk. für **eventuell** poss., possibly

ewig adj. eternal; F **dauernd**: constant, endless; **auf** ~ for ever; **♀keit** f eternity; F **eine** ~ (for) ages

exakt *adj.* exact, precise; **≈heit** *f* exactness, precision
Examen *n* exam, examination
Exekutive *pol. f* executive (power)
Exemplar *n* specimen; *Buch:* copy
exerzier|en *mil. v/i.* drill
Exil *n* exile
Existenz *f* existence; *Unterhalt:* living, livelihood; **~kampf** *m* struggle for survival; **~minimum** *n* subsistence level
existieren *v/i.* exist; *leben:* a. live (**von** on)
exklusiv *adj.* exclusive, select
exotisch *adj.* exotic
Expansion *f* expansion
Expedition *f* expedition
Experiment *n*, **≈ieren** *v/i.* experiment
Expert|e *m*, **~in** *f* expert (**für** on)

explo|dieren *v/i.* explode (*a. fig.*), burst*; **≈sion** *f* explosion (*a. fig.*); **~siv** *adj.* explosive
Export *m* export(ation); *Waren:* exports *pl.*; **≈ieren** *v/t.* export
Expreß *m rail.* express; **per ~** post express, *Am.* by special delivery
extra *adv.* extra; *gesondert:* separately; *F absichtlich:* on purpose; **~ für dich** especially for you
Extra *n*, **~blatt** *n* extra
Extrakt *m* extract
extravagant *adj.* flamboyant
Extrem *n*, **≈** *adj.* extreme; **~ist(in)**, **≈istisch** *adj.* extremist, ultra
Exzellenz *f* Excellency
exzentrisch *adj.* eccentric
Exzeß *m* excess

F

Fa. *Abk. für Firma* firm; *auf Briefen:* Messrs.
Fabel *f* fable (*a. fig.*), **≈haft** *adj.* fantastic, wonderful
Fabrik *f* factory, works *sg.*, *pl.*, *bsd. Am. a.* shop; **~ant** *m Besitzer:* factory owner; *Hersteller:* manufacturer; **~arbeiter(in)** factory worker; **~at** *n* make, brand; *Erzeugnis:* product; **~ation** *f* manufacturing, production; **~ationsfehler** *m* flaw; **~besitzer** *m* factory owner; **~ware** *f* manufactured product(s *pl.*)
Fach *n* compartment; *Brief≈:* pigeonhole; *im Regal:* shelf; *Schul-, Studien≈:* subject; → *Fachgebiet:* a. field; **~arbeiter(in)** skilled worker; **~arzt** *m*, **~ärztin** *f* specialist (**für** in); **~ausbildung** *f* professional training; **~ausdruck** *m* technical term; **~buch** *n* specialist book
Fächer *m* fan
Fach|gebiet *n* line, field; *Branche: a.* trade, business; **~geschäft** *n* dealer (specializing in ...); **~hochschule** *f appr.* (technical) college; *bsd. Brt.* polytechnic; **~kenntnisse** *pl.* specialized knowledge *sg.*; **≈kundig** *adj.* compe-

tent, expert; **≈lich** *adj.* professional, specialized; **~literatur** *f* specialized literature; **~mann** *m*, **≈männisch** *adj.* expert; **~schule** *f* technical school *od.* college; **≈simpeln** *v/i.* talk shop; **~werk** *arch. n* framework; **~werkhaus** *n* half-timbered house; **~zeitschrift** *f* (professional *od.* specialist) journal
Fackel *f* torch; **~zug** *m* torchlight procession
fad(e) *adj. Essen:* tasteless, flat; *schal:* stale; *langweilig:* dull, boring
Faden *m* thread (*a. fig.*); **≈scheinig** *adj.* threadbare; *Ausrede:* flimsy
fähig *adj.* capable (**zu** of [*doing*] *s.th.*), able (**to** *do s.th.*); **≈keit** *f* (cap)ability; *Begabung:* talent, gift
fahl *adj.* pale; *Gesicht: a.* ashen
fahnd|en *v/i.* search (**nach** for); **≈ung** *f* search; **≈ungsliste** *f* wanted list
Fahne *f* flag; *mst fig.* banner; *F:* **e-e ~ haben** reek of alcohol
Fahnen|flucht *f* desertion; **~stange** *f* flagpole, flagstaff
Fahr|bahn *f* road(way), *Am. a.* pavement; *Spur:* lane; **≈bar** *adj.* mobile

Fähre f ferry(boat)

fahren 1. v/i. allg. go*; verkehren: run*; ab~: leave*; mot. drive*; in od. auf e-m Fahrzeug: ride*; *mit dem Auto (Zug, Bus etc.)* ~ go* by car (train, bus etc.); *über e-e Brücke etc.* ~ cross a bridge etc.; *mit der Hand etc. über et.* ~ run* one's hand etc. over s.th.; *was ist denn in dich gefahren?* what's gotten into you?; **2.** v/t. Auto etc.: drive*; (Motor)Rad: ride*; Güter: carry; V **e-n** ~ *lassen* fart, Brt. a. let* off

Fahrer m driver; **~flucht** f hit-and-run offen|ce, Am. -se; **~in** f driver

Fahr|gast m passenger; **~geld** n fare; **~gelegenheit** f means of transport(ation); **~gemeinschaft** f car pool; **~gestell** n mot. chassis; aviat. → *Fahrwerk*

Fahrkarte f ticket; **~automat** m ticket machine; **~entwerter** m ticket-cancel(l)ing machine; **~schalter** m ticket window

fahrlässig adj. careless, reckless (a. jur.); **grob** ~ grossly negligent

Fahr|lehrer m driving instructor; **~plan** m timetable, Am. a. schedule; **♀planmäßig 1.** adj. scheduled; **2.** adv. according to schedule; pünktlich: on time; **~preis** m fare; **~prüfung** f driving test; **~rad** n bicycle, F bike; Zssgn → *Rad...*; **~schein** m ticket; **~schule** f driving school; **~schüler(in)** mot. learner (driver), Am. student driver; Schule: non-local student; **~stuhl** m lift, Am. elevator; **~stunde** f driving lesson

Fahrt f ride; mot. a. drive; Reise: trip (a. Ausflug), journey; naut. voyage, trip, cruise; Geschwindigkeit: speed (a. naut.); *in voller* ~ at full speed

Fährte f track (a. fig.)

Fahrtenschreiber mot. m tachograph

Fahr|wasser naut. n fairway; **~werk** aviat. n landing gear; **~zeug** n vehicle

Fairneß f fair play

Faktor m factor

Fakultät univ. f faculty, department

Falke zo. m hawk, falcon

Fall m fall; gr., jur., med. case; *auf jeden* ~ in any case; *auf keinen* ~ on no account; *für den* ~, *daß* ... in case ...; *gesetzt den* ~, *daß* suppose (that); *zu* ~ *bringen* fig. Gesetzentwurf: defeat

Falle f trap (a. fig.)

fallen v/i. fall* (a. Regen etc.), drop (a. ~ *lassen*); mil. be* killed (in action); *ein Tor fiel* a goal was scored

fällen v/t. Baum: fell, cut* down; jur. Urteil: pass; Entscheidung: make*

fallenlassen v/t. Plan etc.: drop

fällig adj. due; Geld: a. payable

Fall|obst n windfall; **~rückzieher** m Fußball: overhead kick

falls cj. if, in case; ~ *nicht* unless

Fallschirm m parachute; **~jäger** mil. m paratrooper; **~springen** n parachuting; Sport: mst skydiving; **~springer(in)** parachutist; skydiver

Falltür f trapdoor

falsch adj. u. adv. wrong; unwahr, unecht: false (a. Freund, Name, Bescheidenheit etc.); gefälscht: forged; ~ *gehen* Uhr: be* wrong; et. ~ *aussprechen* (schreiben, verstehen etc.) mispronounce (misspell*, misunderstand* etc.) s.th.; ~ *verbunden!* tel. sorry, wrong number

fälsche|n v/t. forge, fake; Geld: a. counterfeit; **♀r** m forger

Falsch|geld n counterfeit od. false money; counterfeit; **~münzer** m counterfeiter; **~spieler(in)** cheat

Fälschung f forgery; counterfeit; **♀ssicher** adj. forgery-proof

Falt|... in Zssgn Bett, Boot etc.: folding ...; **~e** f fold; Knitter♀, Runzel: wrinkle; Rock♀: pleat; Bügel♀: crease; **♀en** v/t. fold; **~enrock** m pleated skirt; **♀ig** adj. wrinkled

Falter m zo. butterfly

familiär adj. personal; zwanglos: informal; △ *nicht* familiar; ~e *Probleme* family problems

Familie f family (a. zo., bot.)

Familien|angelegenheit f family affair; **~anschluß** m: ~ *haben* live as one of the family; **~name** m family name, surname, Am. a. last name; **~packung** f family size (package); **~planung** f family planning; **~stand** m marital status; **~vater** m family man

Fanati|ker(in), **♀sch** adj. fanatic; **~smus** m fanaticism

Fang m catch (a. fig.); **♀en** v/t. catch* (a. fig.); *sich wieder* ~ fig. get* a grip on o.s. again; **♀** *spielen* play catch (Am. tag); **~zahn** m fang

Farbband n (typewriter) ribbon
Farbe f colo(u)r; *Mal2*: paint; *Gesichts2*: complexion; *Bräune*: tan; *Kartenspiel*: suit
farbecht adj. colo(u)r-fast
färben v/t. dye; *bsd. fig.* colo(u)r; **sich rot ~** turn red; **→ abfärben**
farben|blind adj. colo(u)r-blind; **~froh, ~prächtig** adj. colo(u)rful
Farb|fernsehen n colo(u)r television; **~fernseher** m colo(u)r TV set; **~film** m colo(u)r film; **~foto** n colo(u)r photo od. print
farbig adj. colo(u)red; *Glas*: stained; *fig.* colo(u)rful
Farbige m, f **→ Schwarze**
Farb|kasten m paintbox; **2los** adj. colo(u)rless (a. fig.); **~stift** m colo(u)red pencil, crayon; **~stoff** m dye; **ohne ~e** Aufschrift auf Lebensmitteln: contains no (artificial) colo(u)ring; **~ton** m shade, tint
Färbung f colo(u)ring; *Tönung*: hue
Farnkraut bot. n fern
Fasan zo. m pheasant
Fasching m **→ Karneval**
Faschis|mus pol. m fascism; **~t** m, **2tisch** adj. fascist
faseln v/i. drivel
Faser f *Fib|re, Am. -er; Holz2*: grain; **2ig** adj. fibrous; **2n** v/i. *Stoff etc.*: fray
Faß n cask, barrel; **vom ~** on tap
Fassade arch. f facade, front (a. fig.)
Faßbier n draught (Am. draft) beer
fassen 1. v/t. take* hold of, grasp; *pakken*: seize; *Verbrecher*: catch*; *enthalten*: hold*, take*; *Schmuck*: set*; *begreifen*: grasp, understand; *Mut*: pluck up; *Entschluß*: make*; **sich ~** compose o.s.; **sich kurz ~** be* brief; **es ist nicht zu ~** that's incredible **2.** v/i.: **~ nach** reach for
Fassung f *Schmuck*: setting; *Brillen2*: frame; *electr.* socket; *schriftlich*: draft(ing); *Wortlaut*: wording, version; *seelische*: composure; **die ~ verlieren** lose* one's composure; **aus der ~ bringen** put* out, F throw; **2slos** adj. stunned; speechless; **~svermögen** n capacity
fast adv. almost, nearly; **~ nie (nichts)** hardly ever (anything)
fasten v/i. fast; **2zeit** rel. f Lent
Fastnacht f **→ Karneval**

fatal adj. unfortunate; *peinlich*: awkward; *verhängnisvoll*: disastrous; △ nicht **fatal**
fauchen v/i. *Katze etc.*: hiss (a. F fig.)
faul adj. rotten, bad; *Fisch, Fleisch*: a. spoiled; *fig.* lazy; F *verdächtig*: fishy; **~e** Ausrede lame excuse; **~en** v/i. rot, go* bad; *verwesen*: decay
faulenze|n v/i. laze, loaf (about); **2r** m lazybones; *contp.* loafer
Faulheit f laziness; **2ig** adj. rotten
Fäulnis f rottenness, decay (a. fig.)
Faul|pelz m **→ Faulenzer; ~tier** zo. m sloth; *fig.* **→ Faulenzer**
Faust f fist; **auf eigene ~** on one's own initiative; **~handschuh** m mitten; **~regel** f (**als ~** as a) rule of thumb; **~recht** n law of the jungle; **~schlag** m punch
Favorit(in) m favo(u)rite
Fax n fax; *Gerät*: fax machine; **2en** v/i. u. v/t. fax, send* a fax (to); **~gerät** n fax machine
FCKW *Abk. für* **Fluorchlorkohlenwasserstoff** chlorofluorocarbon, CFC
Feber *östr.* m, **Februar** m February
fechten v/i. fence; *fig.* fight*
Fechten n *Sport*: fencing
Feder f feather; *Schmuck2*: a. plume; *Schreib2*: (pen-)nib; *tech.* spring; **~ball** m *Sport*: badminton; *Ball*: shuttlecock; **~bett** n duvet, continental quilt, Am. a. comforter; **~gewicht** n *Sport*: featherweight; **~halter** m penholder; **2leicht** adj. (as) light as a feather; **2n** v/i. be* springy; **~mäppchen** n pencil case; **2nd** adj. springy, elastic; **~strich** m stroke of the pen; **~ung** f springs pl.; *mot.* suspension; **e-e gute ~ haben** be* well sprung; **~zeichnung** f pen-and-ink drawing
Fee f fairy
fegen v/t. u. v/i. sweep* (a. fig.)
fehl adj.: **~ am Platze** out of place; **2betrag** m deficit; **~en** v/i. be* missing; *Schule etc.*: be* absent; **ihm fehlt (es an)** ... he is lacking; **du fehlst uns** we miss you; **was dir fehlt, ist** what you need is; **was fehlt Ihnen?** what's wrong with you?
Fehler m mistake; *Charakter2, Schuld, Mangel*: fault; *tech. a.* defect, flaw; *Computer*: error; **2frei** adj. faultless, flawless; **2haft** adj. faulty; *Arbeit*: full

of mistakes; *tech.* defective; **~mel-dung** *f Computer*: error message

Fehl|ernährung *f* malnutrition; **~ge-burt** *f* miscarriage; **~griff** *m* mistake; wrong choice; **~konstruktion** *f* failure, F lemon; **~schlag** *m* failure; **Qschlagen** *v/i.* fail; **~start** *m* false start; **~tritt** *m* slip; *fig.* lapse; **~zün-dung** *mot. f* backfire (*a.* ~ *haben*)

Feier *f* celebration; party; **~abend** *m* end of a day's work; closing time; evening (at home); ~ *machen* finish (work), F knock off; *nach* ~ after work; **Qlich** *adj.* solemn; *festlich:* festive; **~lichkeit** *f* solemnity; *Feier:* ceremony; **Qn** *v/t. u. v/i.* celebrate; have* a party; **~tag** *m* holiday; *gesetzlicher* ~ public (*Brt. a.* bank, *Am. a.* legal) holiday

feig(e) *adj.* cowardly; ~ *sein* be* a coward

Feige *bot. f* fig

Feig|heit *f* cowardice; **~ling** *m* coward

Feile, **Qn** *v/t. u. v/i.* file

feilschen *v/i.* haggle (*um* about, over)

fein *adj.* fine; *Qualität: a.* choice, excellent; *Gehör etc.:* keen; *zart:* delicate; *vornehm:* distinguished, F posh (*a. Kleidung, Restaurant etc.*); **~!** good!, okay!

Feind *m* enemy (*a. fig*); **~bild** *n* enemy image; **~in** *f* enemy; **Qlich** *adj.* hostile; *mil. Truppen etc.:* enemy; **~schaft** *f* hostility; **Qselig** *adj.* hostile (*gegen* to); **~seligkeit** *f* hostility

fein|fühlig *adj.* sensitive; **Qgefühl** *n* sensitiveness; **Qheit** *f* fineness; *des Gehörs etc.:* keenness; *Zartheit:* delicacy; **~en** *pl.* niceties *pl.*; **Qkostgeschäft** *n* delicatessen *sg.*; **Qmechaniker(in)** precision mechanic; **~schmecker(in)** gourmet

feist *adj.* fat, stout

Feld *n* field (*a. fig.*); *Schach:* square; **~arbeit** *f* work in the fields; *Forschung:* fieldwork; **~bett** *n* camp bed; **~flasche** *f* water bottle, canteen; **~herr** *m* general; **~lerche** *zo. f* skylark; **~marschall** *m* field marshal; **~stecher** *m* field glasses *pl.*; **~webel** *m* sergeant; **~weg** *m* (field) path; **~zug** *m mil.* campaign (*a. fig.*)

Felge *f* rim; *Turnen:* circle; **~nbremse** *f* rim brake

Fell *n* coat; *abgezogenes:* skin, fur; *das ~ abziehen* skin (*a. fig.*)

Fels *m* rock; **~brocken** *m* boulder; **~en** *m* rock; **Qig** *adj.* rocky; **~spalte** *f* crevice; **~vorsprung** *m* ledge

femin|in *adj.* feminine (*a. gr.*); *contp.* effeminate **Qismus** *m* feminism; **Qistin** *f*, **~istisch** *adj.* feminist

Fenchel *bot. m* fennel

Fenster *n* window; **~bank** *f*, **~brett** *n* windowsill; **~flügel** *m* casement; **~la-den** *m* shutter; **~rahmen** *m* window frame; **~scheibe** *f* (window)pane

Ferien *pl.* holiday(s *pl.*), *bsd. Am.* vacation; **~haben** be* on holiday; **~haus** *n* holiday home, cottage; **~lager** *n* holiday camp; *für Kinder, im Sommer:* summer camp; **~wohnung** *f* holiday apartment, *Am.* vacation rental

Ferkel *n* piglet; *fig.* pig

fern *adj. u. adv.* far(-away), far-off, distant (*a. Zukunft etc.*); *von* ~ from a distance

Fern|amt *n* telephone exchange; **~be-dienung** *f* remote control

fernbleiben *v/i.* stay away (*dat.* from)

Fern|e *f* distance; *aus der* ~ from a distance; **Qer** *adv.* further(more); in addition, also; *er rangierte unter "~ lie-fen"* he is among the also-rans; **~fah-rer** *m* long-distance lorry driver, *Am.* long-haul truck driver, F trucker; **~ge-spräch** *n* long-distance call; **Qge-steuert** *adj.* remote-controlled; *Rake-te:* guided; **~glas** *n* binoculars *pl.*; **Qhalten** *v/t. u. v/refl.* keep* away (*von* from); **~heizung** *f* district heating; **~kopierer** *m* fax machine; **~kurs** *m* correspondence course; **~laster** F *mot. m* long-distance lorry, *Am.* long-haul truck; **~lenkung** *f* remote control; **~licht** *mot. n* full (*od.* high) beam; **Qlie-gen** *v/i.: es liegt mir fern zu* far be it from me to; **~meldesatellit** *m* communications satellite; **~meldetech-nik** *f*, **~meldewesen** *n* telecommunications *sg.*; **~rohr** *n* telescope; **~schreiben** *n*, **~schreiber** *m* telex

Fernseh|en *n* television (*im* on); **Qen** *v/i.* watch television; **~er** *m* TV (set); *Person:* TV viewer; **~schirm** *m* (TV) screen; **~sendung** *f* TV program(me)

Fernsprechamt *n* telephone exchange; *weitere Zssgn* → *Telefon...*

Fern|steuerung f remote control; **~verkehr** m long-distance traffic
Ferse f heel (a. fig.)
fertig adj. bereit: ready; beendet: finished; (mit et.) ~ sein have* finished (s.th.); mit et. ~ werden Problem etc.: cope with; F: völlig ~ dead beat; **~bringen** v/t. manage; iro. be* capable of; **2gericht** n ready(-to-serve) meal; **2haus** n prefab(ricated house); **2keit** f skill; **~machen** v/t. finish (a. fig. j-n); für et.: get* s.th. ready; F j-n: give* s.o. hell, do* s.o. in; sich ~ get* ready; **2stellung** f completion; **2waren** pl. finished products pl.
fesch adj. smart, neat, natty, chic
Fessel f Strick: rope; Ketten: bonds pl., chains pl. (alle a. fig.); anat. ankle; **2n** v/t. bind*, tie (up); fig. fascinate
fest adj. firm (a. fig.); nicht flüssig: solid; ~gelegt: fixed; gut befestigt: fast; Schlaf: sound; Freund(in): steady; ~ schlafen be* fast asleep
Fest n celebration; party; rel. festival, feast; Garten2: fête; → froh
fest|binden v/t. fasten, tie (an to); **2essen** n banquet, feast; **~fahren** v/refl. get* stuck; **2halle** f (festival) hall; **~halten 1.** v/i.: ~ an stick* to; **2.** v/t. hold* on to; hold* s.o. od. s.th. tight; sich ~ an hold* on to; **~igen** v/t. strengthen; sich ~ grow* firm od. strong; **2igkeit** f firmness; Haltbarkeit: strength; **2land** n mainland; bsd. europäisches: Continent; **~legen** v/t. fix, set*; sich auf et. ~ commit o.s. to s.th.; **~lich** adj. festive; **~machen** v/t. fasten, fix (an to); naut. moor; vereinbaren: fix; **2nahme** f, **~nehmen** v/t. arrest; **2platte** f Computer: hard disk; **~schrauben** v/t. screw (on) tight; **~setzen** v/t. fix; **~sitzen** v/i. be* stuck; Person: a. be* (left) stranded; **2spiele** pl. festival sg.; **~stehen** v/i. be* certain; Plan, Termin: be* fixed; **~stehend** adj. Tatsache etc.: established; Redensart: set; **~stellen** v/t. find* (out); ermitteln: establish; wahrnehmen: see*, notice; erklären: state; tech. lock, arrest; **2stellung** f finding(s pl.); Erkenntnis: realization; Worte: statement; **2tag** m holiday; rel. religious holiday; Glückstag: red-letter day; **2ung** f fortress; **2wertspeicher**

m Computer: read-only memory, ROM; **2zug** m procession
Fett n fat; Braten2: dripping; Back2: shortening; tech. grease
fett adj. fat (a. fig.); print. bold; **~arm** adj. low-fat, pred. low in fat; **2fleck** m grease spot; **~gedruckt** adj. boldface, in bold type (od. print); **~ig** adj. greasy; **2näpfchen** n: ins ~ treten put* one's foot in it; **2wanst** F m fatty, fatso
Fetz|en m Stoff2: shred; Lumpen: rag; Papier2: scrap; **2ig** F adj.: ~e Musik music with a really good beat
feucht adj. moist, damp; Luft: a. humid; **2igkeit** f moisture; e-s Ortes etc.: dampness; Luft2: humidity
feudal adj. pol. feudal; F fig. posh, swish
Feuer n fire (a. fig.); j-m ~ geben give* s.o. a light; ~ fangen catch* fire; fig. fall* for s.o.; **~alarm** m fire alarm; **~bestattung** f cremation; **~eifer** m ardo(u)r; **2fest** adj. fireproof, fire-resistant; **~gefahr** f danger of fire; **2gefährlich** adj. inflammable; **~leiter** f fire escape; **~löscher** m fire extinguisher; **~melder** m fire alarm
feuer|n v/i. u. v/t. fire (a. fig.); **~rot** adj. blazing red; Gesicht etc.: crimson
Feuer|schiff n lightship; **~stein** m flint; **~wache** f fire station; **~waffe** f firearm, gun; **~wehr** f fire brigade (Am. a. department); Löschzug: fire engine (Am. truck); **~wehrmann** m fireman, fire fighter; **~werk** n fireworks pl.; **~werkskörper** m firework, firecracker; **~zeug** n (cigarette) lighter
feurig adj. fiery, ardent
Fiasko n fiasco, (complete) failure
Fibel f primer, first reader
Fiber f fib|re, Am. a. -er; **~glas** n fibreglass, Am. fiberglass
Fichte bot. f spruce, F mst pine od. fir (tree); **~nnadel** f pine needle
ficken V v/i. u. v/t. fuck
Fieber n temperature, fever (a. fig.); ~ haben (messen) have* a (take* s.o.'s) temperature; **2haft** adj. feverish; **2n** v/i. have* od. run* a temperature; ~ nach fig. crave for; **2senkend** med. adj. antipyretic; **~thermometer** n clinical (Am. fever) thermometer
fies F adj. mean, nasty
Figur f figure; → Schachfigur
Filet n Lendenstück etc.: fil(l)et

Filiale f branch

Film m film; *Spiel*Ջ: a. (motion) picture, *bsd. Am.* movie; **~branche:** *the* cinema, *Am. a. the* movies *pl.*; **e-n ~ einlegen** *phot.* load a camera; **~aufnahme** f *Vorgang:* filming, shooting; *Einstellung:* take, shot; **Ջen 1.** f film, shoot*; **2.** v/i. make* a film; **~gesellschaft** f film (*Am.* motion-picture) company; **~kamera** f film (*Am.* motion-picture) camera; **~kassette** f film magazine, cartridge; **~projektor** m film (*Am. a.* movie) projector; **~regisseur** m film director; **~schauspieler(in)** m (*pl.* screen, *bsd. Am.* movie) act|or (-ress); **~studio** n film studio(s *pl.*); **~theater** n → *Kino*; **~verleih** m film distributors *pl.*

Filter m, *bsd. tech.* n filter; **~kaffee** m filter coffee; **Ջn** v/t. filter; **~zigarette** f filter(-tipped) cigarette, filter tip

Filz m felt; F *pol.* corruption, sleaze; **Ջen** f v/t. frisk; **~schreiber** m, **~stift** m felt(-tipped) pen

Finale n finale; *Sport:* final(s *pl.*)

Finanz|amt n *allg.* tax office; *Brt.* Inland (*Am.* Internal) Revenue; **~en** *pl.* finances *pl.*; **Ջiell** *adj.* financial; **Ջieren** v/t. finance; **~lage** f financial position; **~minister** m *allg.* minister of finance; *Brt.* Chancellor of the Exchequer, *Am.* Secretary of the Treasury; **~ministerium** n *allg.* ministry of finance; *Brt.* Treasury, *Am.* Treasury Department; **~wesen** n finance

Findelkind n foundling

find|en v/t. find*; *meinen:* think*, believe; **ich finde ihn nett** I think he's nice; **wie ~ Sie ...?** how do you like ...?; **~ Sie (nicht)?** do (don't) you think so?; **das wird sich ~** we'll see; **Ջer(in)** finder; **~lohn** m finder's reward; **~ig** *adj.* clever

Finger m finger; **~abdruck** m fingerprint; **~fertigkeit** f manual skill; **~hut** m thimble; *bot.* foxglove; **~spitze** f fingertip; **~spitzengefühl** n *fig.* n sure instinct; tact; **~übung** *mus.* f finger exercise; **~zeig** m hint, pointer

fingiert *adj.* bogus, faked; fictitious

Fink zo. m finch

Finn|e m, **~in** f Finn; **Ջisch** *adj.* Finnish

Finnland Finland

finster *adj.* dark; *düster:* gloomy; *Miene:* grim; *fragwürdig:* shady; **Ջnis** f darkness, gloom

Finte f trick; *Sport:* feint

Firma *econ.* f firm, company

firm|en *rel.* v/t. confirm; **Ջung** f confirmation

Firn m corn snow

First *arch.* m ridge

Fisch m fish; **~e** *pl. astr.* Pisces *sg.*; **er ist (ein) ~** he's a (a) Pisces; **~dampfer** m trawler; **Ջen** v/t. u. v/i. fish; **~er** m fisherman; **~er...** *in Zssgn* Boot, Dorf etc.: fishing ...; **~erei** f, **~fang** m fishing; **~gräte** f fishbone; **~grätenmuster** n herring-bone (pattern); **~gründe** *pl.* fishing grounds *pl.*; **~händler** m *bsd. Brt.* fishmonger, *Am.* fish dealer; **~kutter** m smack; **~laich** m spawn; **~stäbchen** n fish finger, *bsd. Am.* fish stick; **~vergiftung** f fish poisoning; **~zucht** f fish farming; **~zug** m catch *od.* haul (of fish)

Fisole *östr.* f string bean

Fistel *med.* f fistula; **~stimme** f falsetto

fit *adj.* fit; **sich ~ halten** keep* fit; **Ջneß** f fitness; **~neßcenter** n health club, fitness center, gym

fix *adj.* *Preis etc.:* fixed; **~e Idee** obsession; *flink:* quick; *aufgeweckt:* smart, bright; F **~ und fertig sein** *fig.* be* dead beat; *nervlich:* be* a nervous wreck; **~en** *sl.* v/i. shoot*, fix; be* a junkie; **Ջer(in)** *sl.* junkie, mainliner; **~ieren** v/t. fix (*a. phot.*); *j-n:* stare at; **Ջstern** *astr.* m fixed star

FKK *Abk.* f nudism; *in Zssgn* Strand *etc.*: nudist

flach *adj.* flat; *eben:* a. level, even, plane; *nicht tief, fig. oberflächlich:* shallow

Fläche f *Ober*Ջ: surface (*a. math.*); *Gebiet:* area (*a. geom.*); *weite* ~: expanse, space; **Ջndeckend** *adj.* exhaustive; **~inhalt** m *math.* n (surface) area; **~nmaß** n square measure, surface measure

Flachland n lowland, plain

Flachs *bot.* m flax

flackern v/i. flicker (*a. fig.*)

Fladenbrot n round flat bread (*od.* loaf)

Flagge f flag; **Ջn** v/i. fly* a flag *od.* flags

Flak *mil.* f anti-aircraft gun

Flamme f flame (*a. Herd u. fig.*)

Flanell m flannel

Flank|e f flank, side; *Fußball:* cross; *Turnen:* flank vault; **Ջieren** v/t. flank

Flasche f bottle; *Säuglings*2: baby's bottle; F *contp.* dead loss; **~bier** n bottled beer; **~hals** m neck of a bottle; **~nöffner** m bottle opener; **~n-pfand** n (bottle) deposit; **~nzug** *tech.* m block and tackle, pulley

flatter|haft *adj.* fickle, flighty; **~n** *v/i.* flutter (*a. fig., tech.*); *Räder:* wobble

flau *adj. unwohl:* queasy; *Stimmung, Geschmack:* flat; *Markt:* slack

Flaum m down, fluff, fuzz

Flausch m fleece; **2ig** *adj.* fleecy, fluffy

Flausen F *pl.* (funny) ideas *pl.*

Flaute f *naut.* calm; *econ.* slack period

Flecht|e f plait, braid; *bot., med.* lichen; **2en** *v/t.* Haare: plait braid; *Kranz:* bind; *Korb:* weave*

Fleck m stain, mark; F *contp.* dead loss; *Punkt:* dot; *Klecks:* blot(ch); *Ort, Stelle:* place, spot; *Flicken, Fläche:* patch; *blauer ~* bruise; *vom ~ weg* on the spot; *nicht vom ~ kommen* not get* anywhere; **2en** m → *Fleck;* *hist.* small (market-)town; **~entferner** m stain remover; **2enlos** *adj.* spotless (*a. fig.*); **2ig** *adj.* spotted; *schmutzig:* stained

Fledermaus *zo.* f bat

Flegel *fig.* m lout, boor; **2haft** *adj.* loutish; **~jahre** *pl.* awkward age *sg.*; **2n** *v/refl.* slouch, lounge

flehen *v/i.* beg; pray (*um* for); **~tlich** *adj.* imploring, entreating

Fleisch n *Nahrung:* meat; *lebendes:* flesh (*a. fig.*); **~brühe** f (meat) broth, consommé; **~er** m butcher; **~erei** f butcher's (shop); **2fressend** *adj.* carnivorous; **~hauer** *östr.* m butcher; **2ig** *adj.* fleshy; **~klößchen** n meatball; **~konserven** *pl.* tinned (*Am.* canned) meat; **2lich** *adj. Begierden etc.:* carnal, of the flesh; **2los** *adj.* meatless; **~to-mate** f beef tomato; **~vergiftung** f meat poisoning; **~wolf** m mincer, *Am.* meat grinder; **~wunde** f flesh wound

Fleiß m diligence, hard work; **2ig** *adj.* diligent, hard-working; **~ sein** work hard

fletschen *v/t. Zähne:* bare

flexib|el *adj.* flexible; **2ilität** f flexibility

flicken *v/t.* mend, repair; *notdürftig, a. fig.:* patch (up)

Flick|en m patch; **~flack** m flip-flop; **~werk** n patchwork (*a. fig.*); **~zeug** n *Fahrrad:* repair kit

Flieder *bot.* m lilac

Fliege f *zo.* fly; *Krawatte:* bow tie

fliegen *v/i. u. v/t.* fly* (*a. ~ lassen*); F *fallen:* fall*; *fig.* be* fired, F get* the sack; *Schule:* be* kicked out; *durchs Examen:* → *durchfallen;* *~ auf* really go* for; *in die Luft ~* blow* up

Fliegen n flying; *Luftfahrt:* aviation

Fliegen|fänger m flypaper; **2fenster** n flyscreen; **~gewicht** n *Sport:* flyweight; **~gitter** n wire mesh (screen); **~klatsche** f flyswatter; **~pilz** m fly agaric

Flieger m *mil.* airman; F *Flugzeug:* plane; *Radsport:* sprinter; **~alarm** m air-raid warning

flieh|en *v/i.* flee*, run* away (*beide: vor* from); **2kraft** f *phys.* f centrifugal force

Fliese f, **2n** *v/t.* tile; **~nleger** m tiler

Fließ|band n assembly line; *Förderband:* conveyor belt; **2en** *v/i.* flow (*a. fig.*); *Leitungswasser, Schweiß, Blut:* run*; **2end 1.** *adj.* flowing; *Leitungswasser:* running; *Sprache:* fluent; **2. adv.: er spricht ~ Deutsch** he speaks German fluently *od.* fluent German; **~heck** *mot.* n fastback

flimmern *v/i.* shimmer; *Film:* flicker

flink *adj.* quick, nimble; *Zunge:* ready

Flinte f *Schrot*2: shotgun; F *allg.* gun

Flipper F m pinball machine; △ *nicht flipper;* **2n** *v/i.* play pinball

Flirt m flirtation; **2en** *v/i.* flirt

Flittchen F n floozie, hussy

Flitter m tinsel (*a. fig.*), spangles *pl.*; **~kram** m cheap finery; **~wochen** *pl.* honeymoon *sg.*

flitzen F *v/i.* flit, whizz, shoot*

Flock|e f flake; **2ig** *adj.* fluffy, flaky

Floh *zo.* m flea; **~markt** m flea market

Florett n foil

florieren *v/i.* flourish, prosper

Floskel f empty *od.* cliché(d) phrase

Floß n raft, float

Flosse f fin; *Robbe, Schwimm*2: flipper

Flöte *mus.* f flute; *Block*2: recorder

flott *adj. Tempo:* brisk; *schick:* smart; *Wagen: a.* racy; *naut.* afloat

Flotte f *naut.* fleet; *Marine:* navy; **~nstützpunkt** *mil.* m naval base

Fluch m curse; *Schimpfwort: a.* swearword; **2en** *v/i.* swear*, curse

Flucht f flight (*vor* from); *erfolgreiche:* escape, getaway (*aus* from); **2artig**

adv. hastily; **~auto** *n* getaway car

flüchten *v/i.* flee* (*nach, zu* to), run* away; *entkommen:* escape, get* away

Fluchthelfer *m* escape agent, F people smuggler

flüchtig *adj.* quick; *oberflächlich:* superficial; *nachlässig:* careless; *entflohen:* fugitive, *Verbrecher: a.* on the run, at large; **~er Blick** glance; **~er Eindruck** glimpse; **2igkeitsfehler** *m* slip; **2ling** *m* fugitive; *pol.:* refugee; **2lingslager** *n* refugee camp

Flug *m* flight; *im* **~(e)** rapidly, quickly; **~abwehrrakete** *f* anti-aircraft missile; **~bahn** *f e-r Rakete etc.:* trajectory; **~ball** *m* Tennis: volley; **~begleiter** *m* flight attendant; **~blatt** *n* handbill, leaflet; **~dienst** *m* air service

Flügel *m* wing (*a. Sport*); *Propeller etc.: a.* blade; *Windmühlen2:* sail; *mus.* grand piano; **~mutter** *tech. f* wing nut; **~schraube** *tech. f* thumb screw; **~stürmer** *m* wing forward; **~tür** *f* folding door

Fluggast *m* (air) passenger

flügge *adj.* (full[y]) fledged

Flug|gesellschaft *f* airline; **~hafen** *m* airport; **~körper** *m* aviat. flying object; *mil.* missile; **~linie** *f* air route; → *Fluggesellschaft;* **~lotse** *m* air traffic controller; **~plan** *m* air schedule; **~platz** *m* airfield, *größer:* airport; **~schein** *m* (flight) ticket; **~schreiber** *m* flight recorder, black box; **~sicherung** *f* air traffic control; **~verkehr** *m* air traffic

Flugzeug *n* plane, aircraft, *Brt.* aeroplane, *Am.* airplane; *mit dem* **~** by air *od.* plane; **~absturz** *m* air *od.* plane crash; **~entführung** *f* hijacking, skyjacking; **~halle** *f* hangar; **~träger** *m* aircraft carrier

Flunder *zo. f* flounder

flunkern *v/i.* fib; *aufschneiden:* brag

Fluor *chem. n* fluorine; *als Trinkwasserzusatz:* fluoride; **~chlorkohlenwasserstoff** *m* chlorofluorocarbon, CFC

Flur *m* hall; *Gang:* corridor

Fluß *m* river; *kleiner:* stream; *im* **~** *fig.* in (a state of) flux; **2abwärts** *adv.* downstream; **2aufwärts** *adv.* upstream; **~bett** *n* river bed

flüssig *adj.* liquid; *geschmolzen:* melted; *Stil, Schrift etc.:* fluent; *Geld:* availa-

ble; **2keit** *f* liquid; *Zustand:* liquidity; fluency; **2kristallanzeige** *f* liquid crystal display, LCD

Fluß|lauf *m* course of a river; **~pferd** *zo. n* hippo(potamus); **~schiffahrt** *f* river navigation *od.* traffic; **~ufer** *n* riverbank, riverside

flüstern *v/i. u. v/t.* whisper

Flut *f* flood (*a. fig.*); *Hochwasser:* high tide; **es ist** **~** the tide is in; **~licht** *n* floodlights *pl.;* **~welle** *f* tidal wave

Fohlen *zo. n* foal; *männliches:* colt; *weibliches:* filly

Föhn *meteor. m* foehn, föhn

folg. *Abk. für folgend(e)* foll., following

Folge *f* result, consequence; *Wirkung:* effect; *Aufeinander2:* succession; *Reihen2:* order; *Serie:* series; *Fortsetzung:* sequel, episode; *negative Auswirkung:* aftermath; *med.* aftereffect

folgen *v/i.* follow; *gehorchen:* obey; *hieraus folgt, daß* from this it follows that; *wie folgt* as follows; **~d** *adj.* following, subsequent; **~dermaßen** *adv.* as follows; **~schwer** *adj.* momentous

folgerichtig *adj.* logical; *konsequent:* consistent

folgern *v/t.* conclude (*aus* from); **2ung** *f* conclusion (*ziehen* draw*)

folg|lich *cj.* consequently, thus, therefore; **~sam** *adj.* obedient

Folie *f* foil; *Schule etc.:* transparency

Folter *f* torture; *auf die* **~** *spannen* tantalize; **2n** *v/t.* torture; *fig. a.* torment

Fön *TM m* hair-dryer

Fonds *econ. m* fund; *Gelder:* funds *pl.*

fönen *v/t.* blow-dry

Fontäne *f* jet, spout; *Blut: a.* gush

foppen *v/t.* tease; *narren:* fool

Förder|band *n* conveyor belt; **~korb** *m* *Bergbau:* mine cage

fordern *v/t.* demand; *bsd. jur. a.* claim (*a. Tote*); *Preis etc.:* ask, charge

fördern *v/t.* promote; *unterstützen:* support (*a. univ.*), sponsor; *Schule:* tutor, provide remedial classes for; *Bergbau:* mine

Forderung *f* demand; *Anspruch:* claim (*a. jur.*); *Preis2:* charge

Förderung *f* promotion, advancement; support, sponsorship; *staatliche univ. etc.:* grant; *Schule:* tutoring, remedial classes *pl.;* *Bergbau:* mining

Forelle *zo. f* trout

Form f form, shape; *Sport: a.* condition; *tech.* mo(u)ld; **gut in ~** in great form; **&al** *adj.* formal; **~alität** f formality

Format *n* size; *bsd. Buch etc.*: format, *fig.* calib|re, *Am.* -er; **&ieren** *Computer*: format; **~ierung** f formatting

Form|el f formula; **&ell** *adj.* formal; **&en** *v/t.* shape, form; *Ton, Charakter etc.*: mo(u)ld; **~fehler** *m* irregularity; **&ieren** *v/t. u. v/refl.* form (up)

förmlich 1. *adj.* formal; *fig.* regelrecht: regular; **2.** *adv.* formally; *fig.* literally

form|los *adj.* shapeless; *fig.* informal; **~schön** *adj.* well-designed

Formular *n* form, blank

formulier|en *v/t.* word, phrase; *Regel etc.: a.* formulate; *ausdrücken*: express; **wie soll ich es ~?** how shall I put it?; **&ung** f wording, phrasing; formulation; *einzelne*: expression, phrase

forsch *m* smart, dashing

forsch|en *v/i.* research, do* research; **~ nach** search for; **&er** *m* Entdecker: explorer; *Wissenschaftler*: (research) scientist; **&ung** f research (work)

Forst *m* forest

Förster *m* forester; *Am. a.* forest ranger

Forstwirtschaft f forestry

Fort *mil. n* fort

fort *adv.* davon: off, away; *weg*: away, gone; *verschwunden*: gone, missing

fort|bestehen *v/i.* continue; **~bewegen** *v/refl.* move; **&bewegung** f moving; (loco)motion; **&bildung** f further education *od.* training; **~fahren** *v/i.* leave*, go* away (*a.* verreisen); *mot. a.* drive* off; *weitermachen*: continue, go* *od.* keep* on (**et. zu tun** doing s.th.); **~führen** *v/t.* continue, carry on; **~gehen** *v/i.* go* away, leave*; **~geschritten** *adj.* advanced; **~laufend** *adj.* consecutive, successive; **~pflanzen** *v/refl. biol.* reproduce; *fig.* spread*; **&pflanzung** *biol.* f reproduction; **~schaffen** *v/t.* remove (*a. fig.*); **~schreiten** *v/i.* advance, proceed, progress; **~schreitend** *adj.* progressive; **&schritt** *m* progress; **~schrittlich** *adj.* progressive; **~setzen** *v/t.* continue, go* on with; **&setzung** f continuation; *Film etc.*: sequel; **~ folgt** to be continued; **&setzungsroman** *m* serialized novel; **~während** *adj.* continual, constant

Fossil *geol. n,* & *adj.* fossil (*a. fig.* F)

Foto *n* photo(graph); **ein ~ machen (von)** take a photo (of); **~album** *n* photo album; **~apparat** *m* camera; **~graf** *m* photographer; △ *nicht* **photograph**; **~grafie** f photography; *Bild*: photograph, picture; **~grafieren** *v/t. u. v/i.* take* a photo(graph) *od.* picture (of); **sich ~ lassen** have* one's picture taken; **~kopie** *f* (photo)copy; **~kopieren** *v/t.* (photo)copy; **~modell** *n* model; **~zelle** f photoelectric cell

Fotze V f cunt

Foul *n* foul (*übles od. böses* vicious); **&en** *v/t. u. v/i.* foul

Foyer *n* foyer, lobby, lounge

Fr. *Abk. für* Frau Mrs; *bsd. im Berufsleben*: Ms

Fracht f freight, load, ; *naut., aviat. a.* cargo; *Gebühr*: carriage, *Am.* freight; **~brief** *m* rail. consignment note, *naut.*, *Am.* bill of lading; **~er** *m* freighter

Frack *m* tails *pl.*, tailcoat

Frage f question (**stellen** ask); **in ~ stellen** question; *gefährden*: put* in jeopardy; **in ~ kommen be*** possible (*Person*: eligible); **nicht in ~ kommen be*** out of the question; **~bogen** *m* question(n)aire; **&n** *v/t. u. v/i.* ask (**nach** for; **wegen** about); **nach dem Weg (der Zeit) ~** ask the way (time); **sich ~** wonder; **~wort** *gr. n* interrogative; **~zeichen** *n* question mark

frag|lich *adj.* doubtful, uncertain; *betreffend*: in question; **~los** *adv.* undoubtedly, unquestionably

Fragment *n* fragment

fragwürdig *adj.* dubious, F shady

Fraktion *parl.* f (parliamentary) group *od.* party; **~sführer** *parl. m* Brt. chief whip, *Am.* floor leader

Franc *m,* **Franken** *m* franc

frankieren *v/t.* stamp; *maschinell*: frank

Frankreich France

Frans|e f fringe; **&ig** *adj.* frayed

Franz|ose *m* Frenchman; **die ~n** *pl.* the French *pl.*; **~ösin** f Frenchwoman; **&ösisch** *adj.* French

Fraß F *m* muck, swill

Fratze f grimace; **~nhaft** *adj.* distorted

Frau f woman; *Ehe*&: wife; **~ X** Mrs (*od. bsd. im Berufsleben* Ms) X; **~chen** *n e-s Hundes*: mistress

Frauen|arzt *m*, **~ärztin** *f* gyn(a)ecologist; **~bewegung** *pol. f*: **die** ~ women's lib(eration); **2feindlich** *adj.* sexist; **~haus** *n* women's refuge (*Am.* shelter); **~klinik** *f* gyn(a)ecological hospital; **~rechtlerin** *f* feminist

Fräulein *n* Miss

fraulich *adj.* womanly, feminine

frech *adj.* cheeky, *bsd. Am.* fresh; *dreist*: brazen; *keß*: pert, saucy; **2dachs** F *m* cheeky (little) monkey; **2heit** *f* cheek; brazenness

frei *adj.* free (**von** from, of); *Beruf*: independent; *Journalist etc.*: freelance; *nicht besetzt*: vacant (*a. W.C.*); ~*mütig*: candid, frank; *Sport*: unmarked; *ein* ~*er Tag* a day off; *morgen haben wir* ~ there is no school tomorrow; *im Freien* outdoors; → *Fuß*

Frei|bad *n* open-air swimming-pool; **2bekommen** *v/t.* get* a day etc. off; **2beruflich** *adj.* freelance, self-employed; ~*exemplar n* free copy; **~gabe** *f* release; **2geben 1.** *v/t.* release; *e-n Tag etc.* ~ give* a day etc. off; **2.** *v/i.*: **j-m** ~ give* s.o. time off; **2gebig** *adj.* generous; **~gepäck** *aviat. n* baggage allowance; **2haben** *v/i.* have* a holiday; *im Büro etc.*: have* a day off; ~*hafen m* free port; **2halten** *v/t.* *Platz*: keep*, save; *j-n*: treat; ~*handel m* free trade; ~*handelszone f* free trade area; **2händig** *adv.* with no hands; ~*heit f* freedom, liberty; ~*heitsstrafe jur. f* prison sentence; ~*karte f* free ticket; ~*körperkultur f* nudism; **2lassen** *v/t.* release, set* free; ~*lassung f* release; ~*lauf m* freewheel (*a. im* ~ *fahren*)

freilich *adv.* indeed, of course

Frei|licht... *in Zssgn* open-air ...; **2machen** *v/t.* *post* stamp; *sich* ~ undress; *sich* ~ *von* free o.s. from; ~*maurer m* freemason; **2mütig** *adj.* candid, frank; **2schaffend** *adj.* freelance; **2schwimmen** *v/refl.* pass a 15-minute swimming test; **2sprechen** *v/t.* *bsd. rel.* absolve (*von* from); *jur.* acquit (of); ~*spruch jur. m* acquittal; ~*staat pol. m* free state; **2stehen** *v/i.* *leerstehen*: be* unoccupied; *Sport*: be* unmarked; *es steht dir frei zu* you are free to; **2stellen** *v/t.*: *j-n* ~ exempt s.o. (*von* from) (*a. mil.*); *j-m et.* ~ leave* s.th.

(up) to s.o.; ~*stil m* freestyle; ~*stoß m* *Fußball*: free kick; ~*stunde f* *Schule*: free period; ~*tag m* Friday; ~*tod m* suicide; ~*treppe f* outdoor stairs *pl.*; ~*übungen pl.* exercises *pl.*; ~*wild fig.* *n* fair game; **2willig** *adj.* voluntary; *sich* ~ *melden* volunteer (*zu* for); ~*willige(r)* volunteer

Freizeit *f* leisure time; ~*gestaltung f* leisure-time activities *pl.*; ~*kleidung f* leisurewear; ~*park m* amusement park; **2zentrum** *n* leisure cent|re, *Am.* -er

freizügig *adj.* permissive; *Film etc.*: explicit

fremd *adj.* strange; *ausländisch*: foreign; *unbekannt*: unknown; *ich bin auch* ~ *hier* I'm a stranger here myself; ~*artig adj.* strange, exotic

Fremde¹ *f*: *in der* ~ abroad

Fremde² *m*, *f* stranger; *Ausländer(in)*: foreigner

Fremden|führer(in) (tourist) guide; ~*haß m* xenophobia; ~*legion f* Foreign Legion; ~*verkehr m* tourism; ~*verkehrsbüro n* tourist office; ~*zimmer n* guest room; ~ (*zu vermieten*) rooms to let

fremd|gehen F *v/i.* be* unfaithful (to one's wife *od.* husband), play around; **2körper m** *med.* foreign body; *fig.* alien element; **2sprache f** foreign language; ~*sprachensekretärin f* bilingual secretary; ~*sprachig adj.*, ~*sprachlich adj.* foreign-language; **2wort n** foreign word; hard word

Frequenz *phys. f* frequency

Fresse V *f* big (fat) mouth

fressen *v/t.* *Tier*: eat*, feed* on; F *Mensch*: gobble; *verschlingen*: devour

Freude *f* joy, delight; *Vergnügen*: pleasure; ~ *haben an* take* pleasure in

Freuden|geschrei *n* shouts *pl.* of joy, cheers *pl.*; ~*haus* F *n* brothel; ~*tag m* red-letter day; ~*tränen pl.* tears *pl.* of joy

freud|estrahlend *adj.* radiant (with joy); ~*ig adj.* joyful, cheerful; *Ereignis, Erwartung*: happy; ~*los adj.* joyless, cheerless

freuen *v/t.*: *es freut mich, daß* I'm glad *od.* pleased (that); *sich* ~ *über* be* pleased *od.* glad about; *sich* ~ *auf* look forward to

Freund m friend; boyfriend; **~in** f friend; girlfriend; **2lich** adj. friendly, kind, nice; Raum, Farben: cheerful; **2licherweise** adv. kindly; **~lichkeit** f friendliness, kindness; **~schaft** f friendship; ~ **schließen** make* friends; **2schaftlich** adj. friendly; **~schaftsspiel** n friendly (game)

Frevel m outrage (**an, gegen** on)

Frieden m peace; **im ~** in peacetime; **laß mich in ~!** leave me alone!

Friedens|bewegung f peace movement; **~forschung** f peace studies pl.; **~verhandlungen** pl. peace negotiations pl. od. talks pl.; **~vertrag** m peace treaty

fried|fertig adj. peaceable; **2hof** m cemetery, um Kirche: graveyard; **~lich** adj. peaceful; **~liebend** adj. peace-loving

frieren v/i. freeze*; **ich friere** I am od. feel cold; stärker: I'm freezing

Fries arch. m frieze

Frikadelle f meatball

frisch adj. fresh; Wäsche: clean; ~ **gestrichen** wet (Am. a. fresh) paint!; ~ **verheiratet** just married; **2e** f freshness; **2haltebeutel** m polythene bag; **2haltefolie** f cling film, Am. plastic wrap

Friseur m hairdresser; Herren2: a. barber; **~rsalon** m hairdresser's (shop), für Herren: a. barber's shop

Friseuse f hairdresser

frisier|en v/t. do* s.o.'s hair; F mot. soup up; **2kommode** f dressing table

Frist f (fixed) period of time; Zeitpunkt: deadline; Aufschub: extension (a. econ.); **2en** v/t.: **sein Dasein ~** scrape a living; **2los** adj. without notice

Frisur f hairstyle, hairdo

fritieren v/t. deep-fry

Fritten F pl. Brt. chips pl., Am. fries pl.

frivol adj. frivolous; schamlos: suggestive

froh adj. glad (**über** about); fröhlich: cheerful; glücklich: happy; **~es Fest!** happy holiday!; Merry Christmas!

fröhlich adj. cheerful, happy; lustig: a. merry; **2keit** f cheerfulness, merriment

fromm adj. pious, devout; sanft: meek; Pferd: steady; **~er Wunsch** pious hope

Frömmigkeit f religiousness, piety

frönen v/i. indulge in

Fronleichnam rel. Corpus Christi

Front f arch. front, face; mil. front, line; fig. front; **in ~ liegen** be* ahead; **2al** mot. adj. head-on; **~alzusammenstoß** m head-on collision; **~antrieb** mot. m front-wheel drive

Frosch zo. m frog; **~mann** m frogman; **~perspektive** f worm's-eye view; **~schenkel** gastr. pl. frog's legs pl.

Frost m frost; **~beule** f chilblain; **~schutzmittel** mot. n antifreeze

frösteln v/i. feel* chilly, shiver (a. fig.)

frost|ig adj. frosty; fig. a. chilly; **2schutzmittel** mot. n antifreeze

Frott|ee n, m terry(cloth); **2ieren** v/t. rub down

Frucht f bot. fruit (a. fig.); **2bar** adj. biol. fertile (a. fig.); fruitful (bsd. fig.); **~barkeit** f fertility; fruitfulness; **2los** adj. fruitless, futile; **~saft** m fruit juice

früh adj. u. adv. early; **zu ~ kommen** be* early; ~ **genug** soon enough; **heute** (**morgen**) ~ this (tomorrow) morning; **2aufsteher** m early riser (F bird)

Frühe f: **in aller ~** (very) early in the morning; **2er 1.** adj. ehemalig: former; vorherig: previous; **2.** adv. in former times, at one time; ~ **oder später** sooner or later; **ich habe ~** (**einmal**)... I used to ...; **2estens** adv. at the earliest; **~geburt** med. f premature birth; premature baby; **~jahr** n spring; **~jahrsputz** m spring cleaning; **2morgens** adv. early in the morning; **2reif** adj. precocious; **2stück** n breakfast (**zum** for); **2stücken** v/i. (have*) breakfast

Frust F m sl. grind; **~ration** f frustration; **2rieren** v/t. frustrate

frz. Abk. für französisch Fr., French

Fuchs m zo. fox (a. fig.); Pferd: sorrel

Fuchs|jagd f foxhunt(ing); **~schwanz** tech. m handsaw; **2teufelswild** F adj. hopping mad

fuchteln v/i.: ~ **mit** wave s.th. around

Fuge f tech. joint; mus. fugue

fügen v/refl. submit (**in et.**, dat. to s.th.); **~sam** adj. obedient

fühl|bar fig. adj. noticeable; beträchtlich: considerable; **~en** v/t. u. v/i. a. v/refl. feel*; ahnen: a. sense; **sich wohl ~** feel* well; **2er** m feeler (a. fig.)

Fuhre f (cart)load, Taxi: fare

führen 1. v/t. lead*; herum~, lenken, leiten: guide; geleiten, bringen: take*;

Betrieb, Haushalt etc.: run*, manage; *Waren*: sell*, deal* in; *Buch, Konto*: keep*; *Gespräch etc.*: have*; *Namen etc.*: bear*; *mil.* command; **j-n ~ durch** show* s.o. round; **sich ~** conduct o.s.; **2.** *v/i.* lead* (**zu** to; *a. fig.*); *Sport*: a. be* leading od. ahead; **~d** *adj.* leading

Führer *m* leader (*a. pol.*); *Fremden*2: guide; *Leiter*: head, chief; *Reise*2: guide(-book); **~schein** *mot. m* driving licence, *Am.* driver's license

Führung *f* leadership, control; *Unternehmen etc.*: management; *Museum etc.*: (guided) tour; **gute ~** good conduct; **in ~ gehen** (*sein*) take* (be* in) the lead; **~szeugnis** *n* certificate of (good) conduct

Fuhr|unternehmen *n* haulage contractors *pl.*, *Am.* trucking company; **~werk** *n* horse-drawn vehicle

Fülle *f Gedränge*: crush; *fig. von Einfällen etc.*: wealth, abundance; *Haar, Wein etc.*: body

füllen *v/t. u. v/refl.* fill (*a. Zahn*); *Kissen, Geflügel etc.*: stuff

Füll|er *m*, **~federhalter** *m* fountain pen; **2ig** *adj.* stout, portly; **~ung** *f* filling (*a. Zahn*2); *Kissen, Braten*: stuffing

fummeln F *v/i.* fiddle; *basteln*: a. tinker (*beide*: **an** with); F *j-n betasten*: grope

Fund *m* discovery; *Gefundenes*: find

Fundament *n arch.* foundation(s *pl.*); *fig. a.* basis; **~alist** *m* fundamentalist

Fund|amt, **~büro** *n Brt.* lost-property office, *Am.* lost and found (office); **~gegenstand** *m* found article; **~grube** *fig. f* treasure trove

Fundi F *pol. m* radical Green

fundiert *adj.* *Argument*: well-founded; *Wissen*: sound

fünf *adj.* five; *Note*: fail, poor, E, *Am.* F, N; **2eck** *n* pentagon; **~fach** *adj.* fivefold; **2kampf** *m Sport*: pentathlon; **2linge** *pl.* quintuplets *pl.*; **~te** *adj.* fifth; **2tel** *n* fifth; **~tens** *adv.* fifth(ly), in the fifth place; **~zehn(te)** *adj.* fifteen(th); **~zig** *adj.* fifty; **~zigste** *adj.* fiftieth

fungieren *v/i.*: **~ als** act as, function as

Funk *m* radio (*a. in Zssgn Bild, Taxi etc.*); *über od. durch ~* by radio; **~amateur** *m* radio ham

Funke *m* spark; *fig. a.* glimmer; **2ln** *v/i.* sparkle, glitter; *Sterne*: a. twinkle

funk|en *v/t.* radio, transmit; **2er** *m* radio operator; **2gerät** *n* radio set; **2haus** *n* broadcasting cent|re, *Am.* -er; **2signal** *n* radio signal; **2spruch** *m* radio message; **~station** *f* radio station; **2streife** *f* (radio) patrol car; **~telefon** *n* cellular phone

Funktion *f* function; **~är(in)** functionary, official (*a. Sport*); **2ieren** *v/i.* work; **~staste** *f* function key

Funk|turm *m* radio tower; **~verkehr** *m* radio communication

für *prp.* for; *zugunsten*: a. in favo(u)r of; *im Namen von*: on behalf of; **~ immer** forever; *Tag ~ Tag* day by day; *Wort ~ Wort* word by word; *jeder ~ sich arbeiten etc.*: everyone by himself; **was ~ ...?** what (kind od. sort of) ...?; **das Für und Wider** the pros and cons *pl.*

Furche *f* furrow; *Wagenspur*: rut

Furcht *f* fear, *stärker*: dread (*beide*: **vor** of); *aus od. vor* ~ (**daß**) for fear (that); **2bar** *adj.* terrible, awful

fürchten *v/t. u. v/i.* fear, be* afraid of; *stärker*: dread; **~ um** fear for; **sich ~** be* scared; be* afraid (**vor** of); **ich fürchte, ...** I'm afraid ...

fürchterlich *adj.* → *furchtbar*

furcht|erregend *adj.* frightening; **~los** *adj.* fearless; **~sam** *adj.* timid

füreinander *adv.* for each other

Furnier *n*, **2en** *v/t.* veneer

Fürsorge *f* care; *öffentliche ~* (public) welfare (work); **~amt** *n* welfare department; **~empfänger** *m* social security beneficiary; **~r(in)** welfare worker

fürsorglich *adj.* considerate

Für|sprache *f* intercession (**für** for, **bei** with); **~sprech(er)** *m Schweiz*: lawyer; **~sprecher(in)** advocate (*a. fig.*)

Fürst *m* prince; **~entum** *n* principality; **~in** *f* princess; **2lich** *adj.* princely (*a. fig.*)

Furt *f* ford

Furunkel *med. m* boil, furuncle

Fürwort *gr. n* pronoun

Furz V *m*, **2en** *v/i.* fart

Fusion *econ. f* merger, amalgamation; **2ieren** *v/i.* merge, amalgamate

Fuß *m* foot; *Lampe etc.*: stand; *Glas*: stem; **zu ~** on foot; **zu ~ gehen** walk; **gut zu ~ sein** be* a good walker; **~ fassen** become* established; **auf frei-**

em ~ at large; **~abstreifer** m doormat; **~angel** f mantrap

Fußball m Brt. football, Am. soccer; Ball: football, Am. soccer ball; **~er** m footballer; **~feld** n football field; **~rowdy** m (football) hooligan; **~spiel** n football od. soccer match; **~spieler** m football player, footballer; **~toto** n football pools pl.

Fuß|boden m floor; **~belag**: flooring; **~bodenheizung** f underfloor heating; **~bremse** mot. f footbrake

Fussel f, m piece of fluff (Am. lint); **~(n)** pl. fluff sg., Am. lint sg.; **2ig** adj. covered in fluff, Am. linty; **2n** v/i. shed* a lot of fluff, F mo(u)lt

Fuß|gänger(in) pedestrian; **~gängerzone** f pedestrian precinct, Am. (pedestrian od. shopping) mall; **~geher** östr. m → Fußgänger; **~ge-**

lenk n ankle; **~note** f footnote; **~pflege** f pedicure; med. chiropody, Am. a. podiatry; **~pilz** med. m athlete's foot; **~sohle** f sole (of the foot); **~spur** f footprint; Fährte: track; **~stapfen** pl.: in j-s ~ treten follow in s.o.'s footsteps; **~tritt** m kick; **~weg** m footpath; e-e Stunde ~ an hour's walk

Futter[1] n agr. allg. feed; Heu etc.: fodder; Hunde2 etc.: food; F Essen: eats pl., chow

Futter[2] Mantel2 etc., tech. lining

Futteral n case; Hülle: cover

futtern F v/i. tuck in

füttern[1] v/t. feed*

füttern[2] v/t. Kleid etc.: line

Futternapf m (feeding) bowl

Fütterung f feeding (time)

Futur gr. n future (tense)

G

Gabe f gift, present; med. dose; Begabung: talent, gift; **milde ~** alms pl.

Gabel f fork; tel. cradle **2n** v/refl. fork, branch; **~stapler** tech. m fork-lift (truck); **~ung** f fork(ing)

gackern v/i. cluck, cackle (a. fig.)

gaffen F v/i. gawk, gawp, Am. F rubberneck

Gaffer(in) F nosy parker, Am. F rubberneck(er)

Gage f fee

gähnen v/i. yawn (a. fig.)

Gala f gala (a. in Zssgn)

galant adj. gallant, courteous

Galeere naut. f galley

Galerie f gallery

Galgen m gallows; **~frist** f reprieve; **~humor** m gallows humo(u)r; **~vogel** F m crook

Galle anat. f gall (a. fig.); Sekret: a. bile; **~nblase** anat. f gall bladder; **~nstein** med. m gallstone

Gallert n, **~e** f jelly

Galopp m, **2ieren** v/i. gallop

gamm|eln F fig. v/i. loaf (about), bum

around; **2ler(in)** loafer, bum

Gang m walk; **~art**: a. gait, way s.o. walks; Durch2: passage; Kirche, aviat. etc.: aisle; Flur: corridor; mot. gear; gastr. course; et. in ~ bringen get* s.th. going, start s.th.; in ~ kommen get* started; im ~(e) sein be* (going) on, be* in progress; in vollem ~(e) in full swing

gang adj.: ~ und gäbe nothing unusual, (quite) usual

gängeln F v/t. lead* s.o. by the nose

gängig adj. current; econ. sal(e)able

Gangschaltung f gears pl.

Ganove F m crook

Gans zo. f goose

Gänse|blümchen bot. n daisy; **~braten** m roast goose; **~feder** f (goose) quill; **~füßchen** F pl. quotation marks pl., inverted commas pl.; **~haut** fig. f gooseflesh; dabei kriege ich e-e ~ it gives me the creeps; **~marsch** m single od. Indian file; **~rich** zo. m gander

ganz 1. adj. whole; ungeteilt, vollständig: a. entire, total; F heil: whole, un-

damaged; *Betrag, Stunde: a.* full; **den ~en Tag** all day; **die ~e Zeit** all the time; **auf der ~en Welt** all over the world; **sein ~es Geld** all his money; **2.** *adv.* completely, totally; *sehr:* very; *ziemlich:* quite, rather, fairly; **~ allein** all by oneself; **~ aus Holz** *etc.* all wood *etc.;* **~ und gar** completely, totally; **~ und gar nicht** not at all, by no means; **wie du willst** just as you like; **nicht ~** not quite; **im ~en** in all, altogether; **im (großen und) ~en** on the whole; **→ voll**
Ganze *n* whole; **das ~** the whole thing; **aufs ~ gehen** go* all out
Gänze *östr. f: zur ~ → gänzlich*
gänzlich *adv.* completely, entirely
Ganztags|beschäftigung *f* full-time job; **~schule** *f* all-day school(ing)
gar 1. *adj. Essen:* done; **2.** *adv.:* **~ nicht(s)** not(hing) at all; **~ zu ...** (a bit) too ...
Garage *f* garage
Garantie *f* guarantee, *bsd. econ.* warranty; **2ren** *v/t. u. v/i.* guarantee (**für et.** s.th.); **~schein** *m* guarantee (certificate)
Garbe *f* sheaf
Garde *f* guard; *mil.* (the) Guards *pl.*
Garderobe *f* wardrobe, clothes *pl.*; *Kleiderablage:* cloakroom, *Am.* checkroom; *thea.* dressing room; *im Haus:* coat rack; **~nfrau** *f* cloakroom (*Am.* coatcheck) attendant, *Am. F a.* hatcheck girl; **~nmarke** *f* cloakroom (*Am.* coatcheck) ticket; **~nständer** *m* coat stand *od.* rack
Gardine *f* curtain; **~nstange** *f* curtain rod
gären *v/i.* ferment, work
Garn *n* yarn; *Faden:* thread; *Baumwoll2:* cotton; **j-m ins ~ gehen** fall* into s.o.'s snare
Garnele *f* shrimp; *große:* prawn
garnieren *v/t.* garnish (*a. fig.*)
Garnison *mil. f* garrison, *Am. a.* post
Garnitur *f* set; *Möbel: a.* suite
garstig *adj.* nasty, F beastly
Gärstoff *m* ferment
Garten *m* garden; **~arbeit** *f* gardening; **~bau** *m* horticulture; **~erde** *f* (garden) mo(u)ld; **~fest** *n* garden party; **~geräte** *pl.* gardening tools *pl.*; **~haus** *n* summerhouse; **→ Laube**; **~lokal** *n* beer garden; outdoor restaurant;

~schere *f* pruning shears *pl.*, *bsd. Brt.* secateurs *pl.*; **~stadt** *f* garden city; **~zwerg** *m* (garden) gnome
Gärtner *m* gardener; **~ei** *f* market garden, *Am.* truck farm
Gärung *f* fermentation
Gas *n* gas; **~ geben** *mot.* accelerate, F step on the gas; **2förmig** *adj.* gaseous; **~hahn** *m* gas tap (*Am.* valve *od.* cock); **~heizung** *f* gas heating; **~herd** *m* gas cooker *od.* stove; **~kammer** *f* gas chamber; **~laterne** *f* gas (street) lamp; **~leitung** *f* gas main; **~maske** *f* gas mask; **~ofen** *m* gas stove; **~pedal** *mot. n* accelerator (pedal), *Am. a.* gas pedal
Gasse *f* lane, alley
Gast *m* guest; *Besucher:* visitor; *im Lokal etc.:* customer; **~arbeiter(in)** foreign worker
Gäste|buch *n* visitors' book; **~zimmer** *n* guest room, spare (bed)room
gast|freundlich *adj.* hospitable; **2freundschaft** *f* hospitality; **2geber** *m* host; **2geberin** *f* hostess; **2haus** *n*, **2hof** *m* restaurant; tavern, *bsd. Brt.* pub; *bsd. Land2:* inn
gastieren *v/i. Zirkus etc.:* give* performances; *thea.* give* a guest performance, *bsd. Am.* guest
gast|lich *adj.* hospitable; **2mahl** *hist. lit. n* feast, banquet; **2mannschaft** *f* visiting team, visitors *pl.*; **2rolle** *thea. f* guest part; **2spiel** *thea. n* guest performance, *bsd. Am.* guest; **2stätte** *f* restaurant; **2stube** *f* taproom; restaurant; **2wirt** *m* landlord; **2wirtschaft** *f* restaurant; tavern, *bsd. Brt.* pub
Gas|werk *n* gasworks *sg. u. pl.*; **~zähler** *m* gas meter
Gatte *lit. m* husband
Gatter *n* fence; *Tor:* gate
Gattin *lit. f* wife
Gattung *f* type, class, sort; *biol.* genus; *Art:* species
GAU *Abk. m* maximum credible accident, MCA; *Am.* worst case scenario
Gaul *m* (old) nag
Gaumen *anat. m* palate (*a. fig.*)
Gauner *m* crook, swindler
Gaze *f* gauze
Gazelle *zo. f* gazelle
geb. *Abk. für geboren* b., born
Gebäck *n* pastry; *Plätzchen:* biscuits *pl.*, *Am.* cookies *pl.*

Gebälk n timberwork, beams pl.

Gebärde f gesture; **2n** v/refl. behave, act (**wie** like)

gebär|en v/t. give* birth to; **2mutter** anat. f uterus, womb

Gebäude n building, structure

Gebeine pl. bones pl., mortal remains pl.

geben v/t. give* (**j-m et.** s.o. s.th.); reichen: a. hand, pass; Karten: deal*; er~: make*; **sich ~ nachlassen**: pass; besser werden: get* better; **von sich ~** utter, let* out; chem. give* off; **j-m die Schuld ~** blame s.o.; **es gibt** there is, pl. there are; **was gibt es?** what's up?; zum Essen: what's for lunch etc.?; TV etc.: what's on?; **das gibt's nicht** that can't be true; verbietend: that's out

Gebet n prayer

Gebiet n region, area; bsd. pol. territory; fig. field; **2en** lit. v/i. u. v/t. rule (**über** over); befehlen: order; fig. call for; **2erisch** adj. imperious; **2sweise** adv. regionally; **~ Regen** local showers

Gebilde n thing, object; **2t** adj. educated; belesen: well-read

Gebirg|e n mountains pl.; **2ig** adj. mountainous; **~sbewohner** m mountain-dweller; **~szug** m mountain range

Gebiß n (set of) teeth; künstliches: (set of) false teeth, denture(s pl.)

Gebläse tech. n blower, (mot. air) fan

ge|blümt adj. floral; **~bogen** adj. bent, curved; **~boren** adj. born; **ein ~er Deutscher** German by birth; **~e Smith** née Smith; **ich bin am ... ~** I was born on the ...

geborgen adj. safe, secure; **2heit** f safety, security

Gebot n rel. commandment; Vorschrift: rule; Erfordernis: necessity; Auktion etc.: bid

Gebrauch m use; Anwendung: application; **2en** v/t. use; anwenden: employ; **gut (nicht) zu ~ sein** be* useful (useless); **ich könnte ... ~** I could do with ...

gebräuchlich adj. in use; üblich: common, usual; Wort: a. current

Gebrauchs|anweisung f directions pl. od. instructions pl. for use; **2fertig** adj. ready for use; Kaffee etc.: instant; **~grafiker(in)** commercial artist

gebraucht adj. used; bsd. Waren: a. second-hand; **2wagen** mot. m used od.

second-hand car; **2wagenhändler** m used car dealer

Gebrech|en n defect, handicap; **2lich** adj. frail; altersschwach: infirm; **~lichkeit** f frailty; infirmity

Gebrüder pl. brothers pl.

Gebrüll n roar(ing)

Gebühr f charge (a. tel.), fee; post postage; Abgabe: due; **2end** adj. due; angemessen: proper; **2enfrei** adj. free of charge; tel. nonchargeable, Am. toll-free; **2enpflichtig** adj. chargeable; **~e Straße** toll road; **~e Verwarnung** f cate

gebunden adj. bound; fig. a. tied

Geburt f birth (**von** by); **~enkontrolle, ~enregelung** f birth control; **2enschwach** adj. Jahrgänge: low-birth-rate; **2enstark** adj.: **~e Jahrgänge** baby boom sg.; **~enziffer** f birthrate

gebürtig adj. by birth

Geburts|anzeige f birth announcement; **~datum** n date of birth; **~fehler** m congenital defect; **~helfer(in)** Arzt: obstetrician; **~jahr** n year of birth; **~land** n native country; **~ort** m birthplace; **~tag** m birthday; **~tagsfeier** f birthday party; **~tagskind** n birthday boy (od. girl); **~urkunde** f birth certificate

Gebüsch n bushes pl., shrubbery

Gedächtnis n memory; **aus dem ~** from memory; **zum ~ an** in memory of; **im ~ behalten** keep* in mind, remember; **~feier** f commemoration; **~lücke** f memory lapse; **~schwund** med. m amnesia; vorübergehend: blackout; **~stütze** f memory aid

Gedanke m thought; idea; **was für ein ~!** what an idea!; **in ~n** absorbed in thought; zerstreut: absent-minded; **sich ~n machen über** think* about; besorgt: be* worried od. concerned about; **j-s ~n lesen** read* s.o.'s mind

Gedanken|austausch m exchange of ideas; **~gang** m train of thought; **2los** adj. thoughtless; **~strich** m dash; **~übertragung** f telepathy

Gedärme pl. intestines pl.

Gedeck n cover; **ein ~ auflegen** set* a place

gedeihen v/i. thrive*, prosper; wachsen: grow*; blühen: flourish

gedenk|en v/i. think* of; ehrend: commemorate; erwähnen: mention; **~ zu in-**

tend to; **♀feier** f commemoration; **♀minute** f: **e-e** ~ a minute's (*Am.* moment's) silence; **♀stätte** f, **♀stein** m memorial; **♀tafel** f plaque

Gedicht n poem

gediegen adj. solid; geschmackvoll: tasteful; F strange

Gedräng|e n crowd, F crush; **♀t** adj. crowded, packed; Stil: concise

ge|drückt fig. adj. depressed; **~drungen** adj. Figur: squat, stocky; thickset; bsd. tech. compact

Geduld f patience; **♀en** v/refl. wait (patiently); **♀ig** adj. patient; **~spiel** n puzzle (a. fig.)

ge|ehrt adj. hono(u)red; in Briefen: **Sehr ~er Herr N.!** Dear Mr N.,; **~eignet** adj. suitable; befähigt: suited, qualified; passend: right

Gefahr f danger; Bedrohung: threat; Risiko: risk; **auf eigene** ~ at one's own risk; **außer** ~ out of danger, safe

gefährden v/t. endanger; aufs Spiel setzen: risk, jeopardize

gefährlich adj. dangerous; riskant: risky

gefahrlos adj. without risk, safe

Gefährt|e m, **~in** f companion

Gefälle n fall, slope, descent; Straße etc.: gradient (a. phys.)

Gefallen¹ m favo(u)r; **j-n um e-n ~ bitten** ask a favo(u)r of s.o.

Gefallen² n: **~ finden an** enjoy, like

gefallen v/i. please; **es gefällt mir (nicht)** I (don't) like it; **wie gefällt dir ...?** how do you like ...?; **sich et. ~ lassen** put* up with s.th.

gefällig adj. angenehm: pleasant, agreeable; entgegenkommend: obliging, kind; **j-m ~ sein** do* s.o. a favo(u)r; **♀keit** f kindness; Gefallen: favo(u)r; **~st** F adv.: **sei ~ still!** be quiet, will you!

gefangen adj. captive; imprisoned; **~halten** v/t. keep* s.o. prisoner; **♀e(r)** prisoner; Sträfling: convict; **~nehmen** f capture (a. mil.); **~nehmen** v/t. take* s.o. prisoner; fig. captivate; **♀schaft** f captivity, imprisonment; **in ~ sein** be* a prisoner of war

Gefängnis n prison, jail, Brt. a. gaol; **ins ~ kommen** go* to jail od. prison; **~direktor** m governor, bsd. Am. warden; **~strafe** f (sentence od. term of) imprisonment; **~wärter(in)** prison guard, Brt. a. ward|er (-ress)

Gefäß n vessel (a. anat.), container

gefaßt adj. composed; **~ auf** prepared for

Ge|fecht mil. n combat, action; **♀federt** adj.: **gut ~ sein** mot. have* good suspension; **♀feit** adj.: **~ gegen** immune to; **~fieder** n plumage, feathers pl.

Geflügel n poultry; **~salat** m chicken salad; **♀t** adj.: **~es Wort** saying

Gefolg|e n entourage, retinue, train; **~schaft** f followers pl.

gefragt adj. in demand, popular

gefräßig adj. greedy, voracious

Gefreiter mil. m lance corporal, Am. private first class

gefrier|en v/i. freeze*; **~fach** n freezer, freezing compartment; **♀fleisch** n frozen meat; **~getrocknet** adj. freeze-dried; **♀punkt** m freezing point; **♀truhe** f freezer, deep-freeze

Gefrorene östr. n ice cream

Gefüge n structure, texture

gefügig adj. pliant; **♀keit** f pliancy

Gefühl n feeling; Sinn, Gespür: a. sense; bsd. kurzes: sensation; Gemütsbewegung: a. emotion; **♀los** adj. insensible, numb; herzlos: unfeeling, heartless; **♀sbetont** adj. (highly) emotional; **♀voll** adj. (full of) feeling; zärtlich: tender; rührselig: sentimental

gegebenenfalls adv. if necessary

gegen prp. against; jur., Sport: a. versus; ungefähr: about, bsd. Am. around; für (Geld etc.): (in return) for; Mittel: for; verglichen mit: compared with

Gegen|... in Zssgn Aktion, Angriff, Argument, Frage etc.: counter-...; **~besuch** m return visit; **~beweis** jur. m counter-evidence

Gegend f region, area; Landschaft: countryside; Wohn♀: neighbo(u)rhood

gegeneinander adv. against one another od. each other

Gegen|fahrbahn mot. f opposite od. oncoming lane; **~gewicht** n counterweight; **ein ~ bilden zu et.** counterbalance s.th.; **~kandidat** m rival candidate; **~leistung** f quid pro quo; **als** ~ in return; **~licht** n back light; **im od. bei** ~ against the light; **~liebe** fig. f approval; **~maßnahme** f countermeasure; **~mittel** n antidote (a. fig.);

G

~partei f other side; pol. opposition; Sport: opposite side; **~probe** f: **die ~ machen** cross-check; **~richtung** f opposite direction; **~satz** m contrast; **Gegenteil:** opposite; **im ~ zu** in contrast to od. with; **2sätzlich** adj. contrary, opposite; **2schlag** m counterblow; bsd. mil. a. retaliation; **~seite** f opposite side; **2seitig** adj. mutual; **~seitigkeit** f: **auf ~ beruhen** be* mutual; **~spieler** m opponent; **~sprechanlage** f intercom (system); **~stand** m object (a. fig.): Thema: subject; **2ständlich** adj. Kunst: representational; **2standslos** adj. ungültig: invalid; belanglos: irrelevant; Kunst: abstract, nonrepresentational; **~stimme** parl. f vote against, no; **nur 3 ~n** only 3 noes; **~stück** n counterpart; **~teil** n opposite; **im ~** on the contrary; **2teilig** adj. contrary, opposite; **2über¹** adv. u. prp. opposite; fig. gegen: to, toward(s); **im Vergleich zu** compared with; **~über²** n person opposite; neighbo(u)r across the street; **2überstehen** v/i. face, be* faced with; **~überstellung** bsd. jur. f confrontation; **~verkehr** m oncoming traffic; **~wart** f present (time); Anwesenheit: presence; gr. present (tense); **2wärtig 1.** adj. present, current; **2.** adv. at present; **~wehr** f resistance; **~wert** m equivalent (value); **~wind** m head wind; **~wirkung** f counter-effect, reaction; **2zeichnen** v/t. countersign; **~zug** m countermove; rail. train coming from the opposite direction

Gegner|(in) opponent (a. Sport), adversary; mil. enemy; **2isch** adj. opposing; mil. (of the) enemy, hostile; **~schaft** f opposition

Gehacktes n → **Hackfleisch**

Gehalt 1. m content; **2.** n salary; **~sempfänger(in)** salaried employee; **~serhöhung** f increase od. rise in salary, Am. raise; **2voll** adj. substantial; nahrhaft: a. nutritious

gehässig adj. malicious, spiteful; **2keit** f malice, spite(fulness)

Ge|häuse n case, box; tech. casing; zo. shell; Kern**2**: core; **~hege** n enclosure; Hühner etc.: pen

geheim adj. secret; **2agent(in)** secret agent; **2dienst** m secret service; **~halten** v/t. keep* (a) secret

Geheimnis n secret; Rätselhaftes: mystery; **2voll** adj. mysterious

Geheim|nummer tel. f ex-directory (Am. unlisted) number; **~polizei** f secret police; **~schrift** f code, cipher

gehemmt adj. inhibited, self-conscious

gehen v/i. go*; zu Fuß: walk; weg~: leave*; funktionieren (a. fig.): work; Ware: sell*; dauern: last; **einkaufen (schwimmen) ~** go* shopping (swimming); **~ wir!** let's go!; **wie geht es dir (Ihnen)?** how are you?; **es geht mir gut (schlecht)** I'm fine (not feeling well); **~ in** passen: go* into; **~ nach** Straße etc.: lead* to; Fenster etc.: face; urteilen: go od. judge by; **das geht nicht** that's impossible; **das geht schon** that's o.k.; **es geht nichts über** there is nothing like; **worum geht es?** what is it about?; **darum geht es (nicht)** that's (not) the point

gehenlassen v/refl. let* o.s. go

geheuer adj.: **nicht (ganz) ~** eerie, creepy; Sache: fishy

Geheul n howling

Gehilf|e m, **~in** f assistant, helper; fig. helpmate

Gehirn n brain(s pl.); **~erschütterung** med. f concussion (of the brain); **~schlag** med. m (cerebral) apoplexy; **~wäsche** f brainwashing

gehoben adj. Stil: elevated; Beruf etc.: high(er); **~e Stimmung** high spirits pl.

Gehöft n farm(stead)

Gehölz n wood, coppice, copse

Gehör n (sense of) hearing; ear; **nach dem ~** by ear; **sich ~ verschaffen** make* o.s. heard

gehorchen v/i. obey; **nicht ~** disobey

gehör|en v/i. belong (dat. od. zu to); **gehört dir das?** is this yours?; **es gehört sich (nicht)** it is proper od. right (not done); **das gehört nicht hierher** that's not to the point; **~ig 1.** adj. gebührend: due, proper; nötig: necessary; tüchtig: decent; **zu et. ~** belonging to s.th.; **2.** adv. properly, thoroughly

gehörlos adj. deaf; **die 2en** the deaf

gehorsam adj. obedient

Gehorsam m obedience

Geh|steig, ~weg m pavement, Am. sidewalk

Geier zo. m vulture, Am. a. buzzard

Geige *mus. f* violin, F fiddle; *(auf der)* ~ **spielen** play (on) the violin; ~**nbogen** *mus. m* (violin) bow; ~**nkasten** *mus. m* violin case; ~**r(in)** violinist; ~**rzähler** *phys. m* Geiger counter

geil *adj.* V hot, horny; *contp.* lecherous, lewd; *bot.* rank

Geisel *f* hostage; ~**nehmer** *m* kidnap(p)er

Geiß *zo. f* → **Ziege**

Geißel *fig. f* scourge, plague

Geist *m* spirit; *Seele:* a. soul; *Sinn, Gemüt:* mind; *Verstand:* mind, intellect; *Witz:* wit; *Gespenst:* ghost; *der Heilige* ~ the Holy Ghost od. Spirit

Geister|bahn *f* ghost train, *Am.* tunnel of horror; ~**erscheinung** *f* apparition; ~**fahrer** *f mot. m* wrong-way driver; ~**haft** *adj.* ghostly

geistes|abwesend *adj.* absent-minded; 2**arbeiter** *m* brainworker; 2**blitz** *m* brainwave, *Am.* brainstorm; 2**gegenwart** *f* presence of mind; ~**gegenwärtig** *adj.* alert; *schlagfertig:* quickwitted; ~**gestört** *adj.* mentally disturbed; ~**krank** *adj.* mentally ill; 2**krankheit** *f* mental illness; ~**schwach** *adj.* feeble-minded; 2**wissenschaften** *f* the arts *pl.*, the humanities *pl.*; 2**zustand** *m* mental state

geistig *adj.* mental; *Arbeit, Fähigkeiten etc.:* intellectual; *nicht körperlich:* spiritual; ~ **behindert** mentally handicapped; ~**e Getränke** *pl.* spirits *pl.*

geistlich *adj.* religious; *Lied etc.:* a. spiritual; *kirchlich:* ecclesiastical; 2**e** *betreffend:* clerical; 2**e** *m* clergyman; priest; *bsd. protestantisch:* minister; *die* ~**n** *pl. coll.* the clergy *pl.*

geist|los *adj.* trivial, inane, silly; ~**reich, ~voll** *adj.* witty, clever

Geiz *m* stinginess; ~**hals** *m* miser, niggard; 2**ig** *adj.* stingy, miserly

Ge|jammer *n* wailing, complaining; ~**kläff** *n* yapping; ~**klapper** *n* clatter(ing); ~**klimper** *n* tinkling

ge|konnt *adj.* masterly, skil(l)ful; ~**kränkt** *adj.* hurt, offended

Gekritzel *n* scrawl, scribble

gekünstelt *adj.* affected; artificial

Gelächter *n* laughter

Gelage *n* feast; *Zech*2: carouse

Gelände *n* area, country, ground; *Bau*2 *etc.:* site; *auf dem* ~ *e-s Betriebs etc.:* on

the premises; ~**...** *in Zssgn Lauf, Ritt, Wagen etc.:* cross-country

Geländer *n Treppen*2: banisters *pl.*; ~**stange** *f* handrail, rail(ing); *Brücken*2, *Balkon*2: parapet

gelangen *v/i.:* ~ **an** *od.* **nach** reach, arrive at, get* *od.* come* to; ~ **in** get* *od.* come* into; *zu et.* ~ gain *od.* win* *od.* achieve s.th.

gelassen *adj.* calm, composed, cool

Gelatine *f* gelatin(e)

ge|läufig *adj.* common, current; *vertraut:* familiar; ~**launt** *adj.: schlecht (gut)* ~ *sein* be* in a bad (good) mood

gelb *adj.* yellow; *Ampel: Brt.* a. amber; ~**lich** *adj.* yellowish; 2**sucht** *med. f* jaundice

Geld *n* money (*um* for); *zu* ~ *machen* turn into cash; ~**angelegenheiten** *pl.* money *od.* financial matters *pl. od.* affairs *pl.*; ~**anlage** *f* investment; ~**ausgabe** *f* expense; ~**automat** *m* cash dispenser, *Am.* automatic teller machine, ATM, autoteller; ~**beutel** *m*, ~**börse** *f* purse; ~**buße** *f* fine, penalty; ~**geber** *m* financial backer; investor; ~**geschäfte** *pl.* money transactions *pl.*; 2**gierig** *adj.* greedy for money; ~**knappheit** *f*, ~**mangel** *m* lack of money; *econ.* (financial) stringency; ~**mittel** *pl.* funds *pl.*, means *pl.*, resources *pl.*; ~**schein** *m* (bank)note, *Am.* bill; ~**schrank** *m* safe; ~**sendung** *f* remittance; ~**strafe** *f* fine; ~**stück** *n* coin; ~**verlegenheit** *f* financial embarrassment; ~**verschwendung** *f* waste of money; ~**waschanlage** *f* money laundering scheme; ~**wechsel** *m* exchange of money; ~**wechsler** *m* change machine

Gelee *n, m* jelly; *Kosmetik:* gel

gelegen *adj.* situated, *Am.* a. located; *passend:* convenient, opportune; 2**heit** *f Anlaß:* occasion; *günstige:* opportunity, chance; *bei* ~ on occasion

Gelegenheits|arbeit *f* casual *od.* odd job; ~**arbeiter** *m* casual labo(u)rer, odd-job man; ~**kauf** *m* bargain

gelegentlich *adv.* occasionally

gelehr|ig *adj.* docile; 2**igkeit** *f* docility; 2**samkeit** *f* learning; ~**t** *adj.* learned; 2**te(r)** scholar, learned man *od.* woman

Geleise *n* → **Gleis**

Geleit *n* escort; 2**en** *v/t.* accompany,

G

conduct; *bsd. schützend*: escort; **~zug** *naut. m* convoy

Gelenk *anat., tech., bot. n* joint; **2ig** *adj.* flexible (*a. tech.*); *geschmeidig*: lithe, supple

gelernt *adj. Arbeiter*: skilled, trained

geliebt *adj.* (be)loved, dear

Geliebte 1. *m* lover; **2.** *f* mistress

gelinde 1. *adj.* soft, gentle; **2.** *adv.*: ~ **gesagt** to put it mildly

gelingen *v/i.* succeed, manage; *gut geraten*: turn out well; **es gelang mir, et. zu tun** I succeeded in doing (managed to do) s.th.

Gelingen *n* success; **gutes ~!** good luck!

gelt|en *v/i. u. v/t. wert sein*: be* worth; *fig.* count for; *gültig sein*: be* valid; *Sport*: count; *Preis, Gesetz*: be* effective; **~ für** apply to; **~ als** be* regarded *od.* looked upon as, be* considered *od.* supposed to be; **~ lassen** accept (*als* as); **~end** *adj.* accepted; **~ machen** *Anspruch, Recht*: assert; **s-n Einfluß** (**bei j-m**) **~ machen** bring* one's influence to bear (on s.o.); **2ung** *f Ansehen*: prestige; *Gewicht*: weight; **zur ~ kommen** show* to advantage; **2ungsbedürfnis** *n* need for recognition

Gelübde *n* vow

gelungen *adj.* successful, a success

gemächlich *adj.* leisurely, easy

Gemälde *n* painting, picture; **~galerie** *f* art (*od.* picture) gallery

gemäß *prp.* according to; **~igt** *adj.* moderate; *Klima etc.*: temperate

gemein *adj.* mean; *Witz etc.*: dirty, filthy; *bot., zo.* common; **et. ~ haben** (**mit**) have* s.th. in common (with)

Gemeinde *f pol.* municipality; *Verwaltung*: a. local government; *rel.* parish; *in der Kirche*: congregation; **~rat** *m* (*Person*: member of the) local (*Am.* city) council; **~steuern** *pl.* (local) rates *pl.*, *Am.* local taxes *pl.*

gemein|gefährlich *adj.*: **~er Mensch** public enemy; **2heit** *f* meanness; mean thing (to do *od.* say); F dirty trick; **~nützig** *adj.* non-profit(-making); **2platz** *m* commonplace; **~sam 1.** *adj.* common, joint; *gegenseitig*: mutual; **2.** *adv.* together

Gemeinschaft *f* community; **~sarbeit** *f* teamwork; **~skunde** *f* social studies

pl.; **~sproduktion** *f* co-production; **~sraum** *m* recreation room, lounge

Gemein|sinn *m* public spirit; (sense of) solidarity; **2verständlich** *adj. Stil etc.*: popular; **~wohl** *n* public welfare

gemessen *adj.* measured; *förmlich*: formal; *feierlich*: grave

Gemetzel *n* slaughter, massacre

Gemisch *n* mixture (*a. chem.*)

Gemse *zo. f* chamois

Gemurmel *n* murmur, mutter

Gemüse *n* vegetable(s *pl.*); *grünes*: greens *pl.*; **~händler** *m* greengrocer('s)

Gemüt *n* mind, soul; *Herz*: heart; **~sart** *f*: nature, mentality; **2lich** *adj.* comfortable, snug, cosy; *ungezwungen, angenehm*: peaceful, pleasant, relaxed; **mach es dir ~** make yourself at home; **~lichkeit** *f* snugness, cosiness; cosy *od.* relaxed atmosphere

Gemüts|bewegung *f* emotion; **2krank** *adj.* emotionally disturbed; **~verfassung** *f*, **~zustand** *m* state of mind

Gen *biol. n* gene

genau 1. *adj.* exact, precise, accurate; *sorgfältig*: careful, close; *streng*: strict; **2eres** further details *pl.*; **2.** *adv.*: **~ um 10 Uhr** at 10 o'clock sharp; **~ der ...** that very ...; **~ zuhören** listen closely; **es ~ nehmen** (**mit et.**) be* particular (about s.th.); **2igkeit** *f* accuracy, precision, exactness; **~so** *adv.* → **ebenso**

genehmig|en *v/t.* permit, allow; *bsd. amtlich*: approve; **2ung** *f* permission; approval; **~schein** *m* permit; *Zulassung*: a. licen|ce, *Am.* -se

geneigt *adj.* inclined (*a. fig. zu* to)

General *mil. m* general; **~direktor** *m* general manager, managing director; **~konsul** *m* consul general; **~konsulat** *n* consulate general; **~probe** *thea. f* dress rehearsal; **~sekretär** *m* secretary-general; **~stab** *mil. m* general staff; **~streik** *m* general strike; **~versammlung** *f* general meeting; **~vertreter** *econ. m* general agent

Generation *f* generation; **~enkonflikt** *m* generation gap

Generator *m* generator

generell *adj.* general, universal

genes|en *v/i.* recover (**von** from), get* well; **2ung** *f* recovery

Genet|ik *biol. f* genetics *sg.*; **2isch** *adj.*

genetic; **~er Fingerabdruck** genetic fingerprint

genial adj. brilliant, of genius; △ nicht **genial**; **2ität** f genius

Genick n (back od. nape of the) neck

Genie n genius

genieren v/refl. be* embarrassed

genieß|en v/t. enjoy; **2er** m gourmet

Genitiv gr. m genitive od. possessive (case)

Genmanipulation f → **Gentechnik**

genormt adj. standardized

Genoss|e m pol. comrade; F pal, Brt. mate, Am. buddy; **~enschaft** econ. f co(-)operative; **~in** pol. f comrade

Gen|technik f, **~technologie** f genetic engineering

genug adj. enough, sufficient

Genüg|e f: **zur ~** (well) enough, sufficiently; **2en** v/i. be* enough od. sufficient; **das genügt** that will do; **2end** adj. enough, sufficient; Zeit: a. plenty of; **2sam** adj. easily satisfied; im Essen: frugal; bescheiden: modest; **~samkeit** f modesty; frugality

Genugtuung f satisfaction

Genus gr. n gender

Genuß m pleasure; von Nahrung: consumption; **ein ~** a real treat; Essen: a. delicious; **~mittel** n (semi-)luxury; Am. excise item

Geographie f geography; **2isch** adj. geographic(al)

Geolog|e m geologist; **~ie** f geology; **2isch** adj. geologic(al)

Geometr|ie f geometry; **2isch** adj. geometric(al)

Gepäck n luggage, bsd. Am. baggage; **~ablage** f luggage rack; **~aufbewahrung** f left-luggage office, Am. baggage room; **~kontrolle** f luggage inspection, Am. baggage check; **~schalter** m luggage counter; **~schein** m luggage ticket, Am. baggage check; **~träger** m porter; Fahrrad: carrier; mot. roof rack

gepanzert adj. mot. armo(u)red

Gepard zo. m cheetah

gepflegt adj. well-groomed, neat; fig. Stil etc.: cultivated

Gepflogenheit f habit, custom

Ge|plapper n babbling, chatter(ing); **~plauder** n chat(ting); **~polter** n rumble; **~quassel**, **~quatsche** n blather, blabber

gerade 1. adj. straight (a. fig.); Zahl etc.: even; direkt: direct; Haltung: upright, erect; **2.** adv. just; **nicht ~** not exactly; **das ist es ja ~!** that's just it!; **~ deshalb** that's just why; **~ rechtzeitig** just in time; **warum ~ ich?** why me of all people?; **da wir ~ von ... sprechen** speaking of ...

Gerade f math. (straight) line; Rennbahn: straight; **linke (rechte) ~** Boxen: straight left (right); **2aus** adv. straight on od. ahead; **2heraus** adj. straightforward, frank; **2stehen** v/i. stand* straight; **~ für** answer for; **2wegs** adv. straight, directly; **2zu** adv. simply

Gerät n device; kleines: F gadget; Elektro2, Haushalts2 etc.: appliance; Radio2, Fernseh2: set; coll. **~schaften** pl. a. Sport, Labor etc.: equipment; Handwerks2, Garten2: tool; feinmechanisches, optisches: instrument; Küchen2: (kitchen) utensil; Sport: apparatus

geraten v/i. ausfallen: turn out (gut well); **~ an** come* across; **~ in** get* into; **in Brand ~** catch* fire

Geräteturnen n apparatus gymnastics pl.

Geratewohl n: **aufs ~** at random

geräumig adj. spacious, roomy

Geräusch n sound, noise; **2los 1.** adj. noiseless (a. tech.); **2.** adv. without a sound; **2voll** adj. noisy

gerb|en v/t. tan; **2erei** f tannery

gerecht adj. just, fair; **~ werden** do* justice to; Wünschen etc.: meet*; **2igkeit** f justice

Gerede n talk; Klatsch: gossip

gereizt adj. irritable; **2heit** f irritability

Gericht n dish; jur. court; **vor ~ stehen (stellen)** stand* (bring* to) trial; **vor ~ gehen** go* to court; **2lich** adj. judicial, legal

Gerichts|barkeit f jurisdiction; **~gebäude** n law court(s pl.), bsd. Am. courthouse; **hof** m law court; **~medizin** f forensic medicine; **~saal** m courtroom; **~verfahren** n lawsuit; **~verhandlung** f hearing; Straf2: trial; **~vollzieher** m bailiff, Am. marshal

gering adj. little, small; unbedeutend: slight, minor; niedrig: low; **~fügig** adj. slight, minor; Betrag, Vergehen: petty; **~schätzen** v/t. think* little of; **~schätzig** adj. contemptuous; **~st** adj.

least; **nicht im ~en** not in the least
gerinnen v/i. coagulate; *bsd. Milch*: a. curdle; *bsd. Blut*: a. clot
Gerippe n skeleton (a. fig.); *tech.* framework
gerissen fig. adj. cunning, smart
germanis|ch adj. Germanic; **2t(in)** student of (od. graduate in) German
gern(e) adv. willingly, gladly; **~ haben** like, be* fond of; **et. (sehr) ~ tun** like (love) to do s.th. od. doing s.th.; **ich möchte ~** I'd like to; **~ geschehen!** not at all, (you're) welcome
Geröll n scree; *großes*: boulders pl.
Gerste bot. f barley; **~nkorn** med. n sty(e)
Gerte f switch, rod, twig
Geruch m smell; *bsd. schlechter*: odo(u)r; *bsd. Duft*: scent; **2los** adj. odo(u)rless; **~ssinn** m (sense of) smell
Gerücht n rumo(u)r
gerührt adj. touched, moved
Gerümpel n lumber, junk
Gerundium gr. n gerund
Gerüst n frame(work); *Bau2*: scaffold(ing); *Bühne*: stage
gesamt adj. whole, entire, total, all; **2...** in Zssgn Ergebnis, Gewicht etc.: mst total ...; **2ausgabe** f complete edition; **2schule** f comprehensive school
Gesandt|e(r) pol. envoy; **2schaft** f legation, mission
Gesang m singing; *Lied*: song; *Fach*: voice; **~buch** rel. n hymn-book; **~slehrer(in)** singing-teacher; **~verein** m choral society, *Am. a.* glee club
Gesäß anat. n buttocks pl., bottom
Geschäft n business; *Laden*: shop, *Am.* store; *vorteilhaftes*: bargain; **2ig** adj. busy, active; **~igkeit** f activity; **2lich 1.** adj. business ...; commercial; **2.** adv. on business
Geschäfts|brief m business letter; **~frau** f businesswoman; **~freund** m business friend; **~führer** m manager; **~führung** f management; **~inhaber(in)** propriet|or (-ress); **~lage** f business situation; **~mann** m businessman; **2mäßig** adj. businesslike; **~ordnung** f parl. standing orders pl.; rules pl. (of procedure); **~partner** m (business) partner; **~räume** pl. (business) premises pl.; **~reise** f business trip; **~schluß** m closing time; **nach ~ a.**

after business hours; **~stelle** f office; **~straße** f shopping street; **~träger** pol. m chargé d'affaires; **2tüchtig** adj. efficient, smart; **~verbindung** f business connection; **~viertel** n commercial district; *Am. a.* downtown; **~zeit** f office od. business hours pl.; **~zweig** m branch od. line (of business)
geschehen v/i. happen, occur, take* place; *getan werden*: be* done; **es geschieht ihm recht** it serves him right
Geschehen n events pl., happenings pl.
gescheit adj. clever, bright, F brainy
Geschenk n present, gift; **~packung** f gift box
Geschicht|e f story; *Wissenschaft*: history; *fig.* business, thing; **2lich** adj. historical; **~sschreiber**, **~swissenschaftler** m historian
Geschick n fate, destiny; → **~lichkeit** f skill; *bsd. körperliche*: dexterity; **2t** adj. skil(l)ful, skilled; *gewandt*: dext(e)rous; *geistig*: a. clever
Geschirr n dishes pl.; *Porzellan*: china; *Küchen2*: kitchen utensils pl., pots and pans pl., crockery; *Pferde2*: harness; **~spülen** wash od. do* the dishes; **~spüler** m dishwasher
Geschlecht n sex; *Gattung*: kind, species; *Abstammung*: family, line(age); *Generation*: generation; *gr.* gender; **2lich** adj. sexual
Geschlechts|krankheit med. f venereal disease; **~reife** f puberty; **~teile** pl. genitals pl.; **~trieb** m sexual instinct od. urge; **~verkehr** m (sexual) intercourse; **~wort** gr. n article
ge|schliffen adj. *Edelstein*: cut; *fig.* polished; **~schlossen** adj. closed; *tech.*, *fig.* compact; **~e Gesellschaft** private party
Geschmack m taste (a. fig.); *Aroma*: flavo(u)r; **~ finden** an develop a taste for; **2los** adj. tasteless; **~losigkeit** f tastelessness; **das war e-e** ~ that was in bad taste; **~(s)sache** f matter of taste; **2voll** adj. tasteful, in good taste
geschmeidig adj. supple, pliant
Geschöpf n creature
Geschoß n projectile, missile; *Stockwerk*: stor(e)y, floor
Geschrei n shouting, yelling; *Angst2*: screams pl.; *Baby*: crying; *fig. Aufhebens*: fuss

Geschütz *mil. n* gun, cannon

Geschwader *mil. n naut.* squadron; *aviat.* wing, *Am.* group

Geschwätz *n* chatter, babble; *Klatsch:* gossip; *fig. Unsinn:* nonsense; **2ig** *adj.* talkative; gossipy

geschweige *cj.:* ~ **(denn)** let alone

geschwind *adj.* quick, swift; **2igkeit** *f* speed; *Schnelligkeit:* a. fastness, quickness; *phys.* velocity; *mit e-r* ~ *von* ... at a speed *od.* rate of ...; **2igkeitsbegrenzung** *f* speed limit; **2igkeitsüberschreitung** *mot. f* speeding

Geschwister *pl.* brother(s *pl.*) and sister(s *pl.*)

geschwollen *adj. med.* swollen; *fig.* bombastic, pretentious, pompous

Geschworene|(r) member of a jury; *die* ~*n pl.* the jury *sg. od. pl.*; **2ngericht** *n* → *Schwurgericht*

Geschwulst *med. f* growth, tumo(u)r

Geschwür *med. n* abscess, ulcer

Geselchte *östr. n* smoked meat

Gesell|e *m Handwerker:* journeyman; **2en** *v/refl.:* *sich zu j-m* ~ join s.o.; **2ig** *adj. zo. etc.:* social; *Person:* sociable; ~**es Beisammensein** social, get-together; ~**in** *f* trained woman *hairdresser etc.*, journeywoman

Gesellschaft *f* society; *Umgang:* company; *Abend2 etc.:* party; *Firma:* company, corporation; *j-m* ~ *leisten* keep* s.o. company; **2lich** *adj.* social

Gesellschafts|... *in Zssgn Kritik, Ordnung, System etc.:* social ...; ~**reise** *f* package *od.* conducted tour; ~**spiel** *n* parlo(u)r game; ~**tanz** *m* ballroom dance

Gesetz *n* law; *Einzel2:* a. act; ~**buch** *n* code (of law); ~**entwurf** *m* bill; **2gebend** *adj.* legislative; ~**geber** *m* legislator; ~**gebung** *f* legislation; **2lich 1.** *adj.* legal; *legal:* a. lawful; **2.** *adv.:* ~ *geschützt econ. jur.* patented, registered; **2los** *adj.* lawless; **2mäßig** *adj.* legal, lawful

gesetzt 1. *adj.* staid, dignified; *Alter:* mature; **2.** *cj.:* ~ *den Fall,* **(daß)** ... supposing (that)

gesetzwidrig *adj.* illegal, unlawful

Gesicht *n* face; *zu* ~ *bekommen* catch* sight *(kurz:* a glimpse) of; *aus dem* ~ *verlieren* lose* sight *(fig. a.* track) of

Gesichts|ausdruck *m* (facial) expres-

sion, look; ~**farbe** *f* complexion; ~**punkt** *m* point of view, aspect, angle; ~**zug** *m* feature

Gesindel *n* trash, *the* riff-raff *sg., pl.*

gesinn|t *adj. eingestellt:* minded; *j-m feindlich* ~ *sein* be* ill-disposed towards s.o.; **2ung** *f* mind; *Haltung:* attitude; *pol.* conviction(s *pl.*)

gesinnungs|los *adj.* unprincipled; ~**treu** *adj.* loyal; **2wechsel** *m* about-turn *(bsd. Am.* -face)

gesittet *adj.* civilized, well-mannered

Gespann *n* team *(a. fig. gutes)*

gespannt *adj.* tense *(a. fig.);* ~ *sein auf* be* anxious to see; *ich bin* ~, *ob* *(wie)* I wonder if (how)

Gespenst *n* ghost, *bsd. fig.* spect|re, *Am.* -er; **2isch** *adj.* ghostly, F spooky

Gespinst *n* web, tissue *(beide a. fig.)*

Gespött *n* mockery, ridicule; *j-n zum* ~ *machen* make* a laughingstock of s.o.

Gespräch *n* talk *(a. pol.),* conversation; *tel.* call; **2ig** *adj.* talkative

Gespür *n* flair, F nose, antenna

Gestalt *f allg.* shape, form; *Figur, Person:* figure; **2en** *v/t. Fest etc.:* arrange; *entwerfen:* design; ~**ung** *f* arrangement; design; *Raum2:* decoration

geständ|ig *adj.:* ~ *sein* confess; **2nis** *n* confession *(a. fig.)*

Gestank *m* stench, stink

gestatten *v/t.* allow, permit

Geste *f* gesture *(a. fig.)*

gestehen *v/t. u. v/i.* confess

Gestein *n* rock, stone

Gestell *n Ständer, Sockel:* stand, base, pedestal; *Regal:* shelves *pl.*; *Fassung, Rahmen:* frame

gestern *adv.* yesterday; ~ *abend* last night

gestreift *adj.* striped

gestrig *adj.* yesterday's, of yesterday

Gestrüpp *n* brushwood, undergrowth; *fig.* jungle, maze

Gestüt *n* stud farm; *Pferde:* stud

Gesuch *n* application, request

gesund *adj.* healthy; *Kost, Leben:* a. healthful; *fig.* a. sound; ~*er Menschenverstand* common sense; *(wieder)* ~ *werden* get* well (again), recover

Gesundheit *f* health; *auf j-s* ~ *trinken* drink* to s.o.'s health; ~*! beim Niesen:* bless you!; **2lich 1.** *adj.:* ~*er Zustand*

state of health; *aus ~en Gründen* for health reasons; **2.** *adv.*: *~ geht es ihm gut* he is in good health

Gesundheits|amt *n* Public Health Office (*Am.* Department); **2schädlich** *adj.* bad for one's health; **~zustand** *m* state of health, physical condition

Getöse *n* din, (deafening) noise

Getränk *n* drink, beverage; **~automat** *m* drinks machine

getrauen *v/refl.* → **trauen**

Getreide *n* grain, cereals *pl.*, *Brt. a.* corn; **~ernte** *f* grain harvest; *Ertrag: a.* grain crop

getreu *adj.* true, faithful

Getriebe *mot. n* transmission

getrost *adv.* bedenkenlos: safely

Ge|tue *n* fuss; **~tümmel** *n* turmoil

Gewächs *n* plant; *med.* growth; **~haus** *n* greenhouse, hothouse

ge|wachsen *fig. adj.*: *j-m ~ sein* be* a match for s.o.; *e-r Sache ~ sein* be* equal to s.th., be* able to cope with s.th.; **~wagt** *adj.* daring (*a. fig. Film*); *fig. Witz etc.*: risqué; **~wählt** *adj. Stil:* refined; **~wahr** *adj.*: *~ werden* become* aware of

Gewähr *f*: *~ übernehmen (für)* guarantee; **2en** *v/t.* grant, allow; **2leisten** *v/t.* guarantee

Gewahrsam *m*: *et. (j-n) in ~ nehmen* take* s.th. in safekeeping (s.o. into custody)

Gewalt *f* force, violence (*a. ~tätigkeit*); *Macht:* power; *Beherrschung:* control; *mit ~* by force; *höhere ~* act of God; *häusliche ~ (bsd. gegen Frauen u. Kinder)* domestic violence; *in s-e ~ bringen* seize by force; *die ~ verlieren über* lose* control over; **~herrschaft** *f* tyranny; **2ig** *adj.* powerful, mighty; *riesig, ungeheuer:* enormous; **2los** *adj.* nonviolent; **~losigkeit** *f* nonviolence; **2sam 1.** *adj.* violent; **2.** *adv.* by force; *~ öffnen* force open; **2tätig** *adj.* violent; **~tätigkeit** *f* (act of) violence; **~verbrechen** *n* crime of violence

Gewand *n* robe, gown; *rel.* vestment

gewandt *adj.* nimble; *geschickt:* skil(l)ful; *fig.* clever; **2heit** *f* nimbleness; skill; *Auftreten:* ease

Ge|wässer *n* body of water; *~ pl.* waters *pl.*; **~webe** *n* fabric; *biol.* tissue

Gewehr *n allg.* gun; *Büchse:* rifle; *Flin-*

te: shotgun; **~kolben** *m* (rifle) butt; **~lauf** *m* (rifle *od.* gun) barrel

Geweih *n* antlers *pl.*, horns *pl.*

Gewerbe *n* trade, business; **~schein** *m* trade licen|se, *Am.* -se; **~schule** *f* vocational *od.* trade school

gewerb|lich *adj.* commercial, industrial; **~smäßig** *adj.* professional

Gewerkschaft *f* (trade) union, *Am.* labor union; **~(l)er(in)** *f* trade (*Am.* labor) unionist; **2lich** *adj.*, **~s...** *in Zssgn* (trade, *Am.* labor) union ...

Gewicht *n* weight; *Bedeutung: a.* importance; *~ legen auf* stress, emphasize

gewillt *adj.* willing, ready

Ge|wimmel *n* throng; **~winde** *tech. n* thread; *ein ~ bohren* tap

Gewinn *m econ.* profit (*a. fig.*); *Ertrag:* gain(s *pl.*); *Lotterie2:* prize; *Spiel2:* winnings *pl.*; **2bringend** *adj.* profitable; **2en** *v/t. u. v/i.* win*; *erhalten, zunehmen an:* gain; **2end** *adj. Wesen, Lächeln:* winning, engaging; **~er** *m* winner; **~zahl** *f* winning number

Gewirr *n* tangle; *Straßen2:* maze

gewiß 1. *adj.* certain; *ein gewisser Herr N.* a certain Mr N.; **2.** *adv.* certainly

Gewissen *n* conscience; **2haft** *adj.* conscientious; **2los** *adj.* unscrupulous; **~sbisse** *pl.* pricks *pl. od.* pangs *pl.* of conscience; **~sfrage** *f* question of conscience; **~sgründe** *pl.*: *aus ~n* for reasons of conscience

Gewißheit *f* certainty; *mit ~ sagen, wissen:* for certain *od.* sure

Gewitter *n* thunderstorm; **~regen** *m* thundershower; **~wolke** *f* thundercloud

gewöhnen *v/t. u. v/refl.*: *sich (j-n) ~ an* get* (s.o.) used to

Gewohnheit *f* habit (*et. zu tun* of doing s.th.); **2smäßig** *adj.* habitual

gewöhnlich *adj.* common, ordinary, usual; *unfein:* vulgar, F common

gewohnt *adj.* usual; *et. (zu tun) ~ sein* be* used *od.* accustomed to (doing) s.th.

Gewölb|e *n* vault; **2t** *adj.* arched

Gewühl *n* milling crowd, throng

gewunden *adj. Weg etc.:* winding

Gewürz *n* spice; **~gurke** *f* pickle(d gherkin)

Ge|zeiten *pl.* tide(s *pl.*); **~zeter** *n*

(shrill) clamo(u)r; *Nörgeln:* nagging; **2ziert** *adj.* affected; **~zwitscher** *n* chirp(ing), twitter(ing); **2zwungen** *adj.* forced, unnatural

Gicht *med. f* gout

Giebel *m* gable

Gier *f* greed(iness) (*nach* for); **2ig** *adj.* greedy (*nach, auf* for, after)

gieß|en *v/t. u. v/i.* pour; *tech.* cast*; *Blumen:* water; **2erei** *f* foundry; **2kanne** *f* watering can, *Am.* watering pot

Gift *n* poison; *zo. a.* venom (*a. fig.*); △ *nicht* **gift**; **2ig** *adj.* poisonous; venomous (*a. fig.*); *vergiftet:* poisoned; *med.* toxic; **~müll** *m* toxic waste; **~mülldeponie** *f* toxic waste dump; **~schlange** *f* poisonous *od.* venomous snake; **~stoff** *m* poisonous *od.* toxic substance; *in der Umwelt:* pollutant; **~zahn** *m* poison fang

Gigant *m* giant; **2isch** *adj.* gigantic

Gipfel *m* top, peak, summit; *fig. a.* height; **~konferenz** *pol. f* summit (meeting *od.* conference); **2n** *v/i.* culminate

Gips *m* plaster (of Paris); *in* **~** *med.* in (a) plaster (cast); **~abdruck, ~abguß** *m* plaster (cast); **2en** *v/t.* plaster (*a. F med.*); **~verband** *med. m* plaster cast

Giraffe *zo. f* giraffe

Girlande *f* garland, festoon

Girokonto *n* current (*bsd. Am.* checking) account; *bsd. post* giro (*Am.* postal check) account

Gischt *m, f* (sea) spray, spindrift

Gitarr|e *mus. f* guitar; **~ist(in)** *f* guitarist

Gitter *n* lattice; *vor Fenster etc.:* grating; F *hinter* **~n** (*sitzen*) (be*) behind bars; **~bett** *n* cot, *Am.* crib; **~fenster** *n* lattice (window)

Glanz *m* shine, gloss (*a. tech.*), lust|re, *Am.* -er, brilliance (*a. fig.*); *fig. Pracht:* splendo(u)r, glamo(u)r

glänzen *v/i.* shine*, gleam; *funkeln:* a. glitter, glisten; **2en** *v/t.* shining, shiny, bright; *phot.* glossy; *fig.* brilliant, excellent

Glanz|leistung *f* brilliant achievement; **~zeit** *f* heyday

Glas *n* glass; *m* -er glazier

gläsern *adj.* (of) glass

Glas|faser, ~fiber *f* glass fib|re, *Am.* -er; **~hütte** *tech. f* glassworks *sg.*

glas|ieren *v/t.* glaze; *Kuchen:* ice, frost; **~ig** *adj.* glassy; **~klar** *adj.* crystal-clear (*a. fig.*); **2scheibe** *f* (glass) pane; **2ur** *f* glaze; *Kuchen:* icing

glatt *adj.* smooth (*a. fig.*); *schlüpfrig:* slippery; *fig. Sieg etc.:* clear

Glätte *f* smoothness (*a. fig.*); slipperiness

Glatteis *n* (black, *Am.* glare) ice; *es herrscht* **~** the roads are icy; F *j-n aufs* **~ führen** mislead* s.o.

glätten *v/t.* smooth; *Schweiz:* → *bügeln*

glatt|gehen F *v/i.* work (out well), go* (off) well; **~rasiert** *adj.* cleanshaven

Glatze *f* bald head; *e-e* **~ haben** be* bald

Glaube *m* belief, *bsd. rel.* faith (*beide:* an in); **2n** *v/t. u. v/i.* believe; *meinen:* a. think*, *Am. a.* guess; **~ an** believe in (*a. rel.*)

Glaubens|bekenntnis *n* creed, profession *od.* confession of faith; **~lehre** *f,* **~satz** *m* dogma, doctrine

glaubhaft *adj.* credible, plausible

gläubig *adj.* religious; *fromm:* devout (*bsd. a. attr.*); *die* **2n** the faithful *pl.*

Gläubiger *econ. m* creditor

glaubwürdig *adj.* credible; reliable

gleich 1. *adj.* same, *Rechte, Lohn etc.:* equal; *auf die* **~e** *Art* (in) the same way; *zur* **~en** *Zeit* at the same time; *das ist mir* **~** it's all the same to me; *ganz* **~,** *wann etc.* no matter when *etc.*; *das* **~e** the same; (*ist*) **~** *math.* equals, is; **2.** *adv.* equally, alike; *sofort:* at once, right away; *sehr bald:* in a moment *od.* minute; **~** *groß* (*alt*) of the same size (age); **~** *nach* (*neben*) right after (next to); **~** *gegenüber* just opposite *od.* across the street; *es ist* **~** *5* it's almost 5 o'clock; **~** *aussehen* (*gekleidet sein*) look (be* dressed) alike; *bis* **~!** see you soon *od.* later!; **~altrig** *adj.* (of) the same age; **~berechtigt** *adj.* equal, having equal rights; **2berechtigung** *f* equal rights *pl.*; **~bleibend** *adj.* constant, steady; **~en** *v/i.* be* *od.* look like

gleich|falls *adv.* also, likewise; *danke,* **~!** (thanks), the same to you! **~förmig** *adj.* uniform; **~gesinnt** *adj.* likeminded; **2gewicht** *n* balance (*a. fig.*); **~gültig** *adj.* indifferent (*gegen* to); *leichtfertig:* careless; *das (er) ist mir* **~** I don't care (for him); **2gültigkeit** *f* indifference; **2heit** f equality; **~kommen** v/i.: e-r Sache ~ amount to s.th.; **j-m ~** equal s.o. (**an** in); **~lautend** adj. identical; **~mäßig** adj. regelmäßig: regular; gleichbleibend: constant; Verteilung: even; **~namig** adj. of the same name; **2nis** n parable; **~sam** adv. as it were, so to speak; **~seitig** math. adj. equilateral; **~setzen, ~stellen** v/t. equate (dat. to, with); **j-n:** put* on an equal footing (with); **2strom** electr. m direct current, Abk. DC; **2ung** math. f equation; **~wertig** adj. equally good; **j-m ~ sein** be* a match for s.o. (a. Sport); **~zeitig** adj. simultaneous; **beide ~** both at the same time

Gleis rail. n rail(s pl.), track(s pl.), line; Bahnsteig: platform, Am. a. gate

gleit|en v/i. glide, slide*; **~end** adj.: **~e Arbeitszeit** flexible working hours pl., Brt. a. flexitime, Am. flextime; **2flug** m glide; **2schirmfliegen** n paragliding; **2schirmflieger** m paraglider

Gletscher m glacier; **~spalte** f crevasse

Glied n anat. limb; männliches: penis; Verbindungs2: link; **2ern** v/t. structure; divide (**in** into); **~erung** f structure, arrangement; e-s Aufsatzes: outline; **~maßen** pl. limbs pl., extremities pl.

glimm|en v/i. glow; schwelen: smo(u)lder; **2stengel** F m butt, fag

glimpflich 1. adj. lenient, mild; **2.** adv.: **~ davonkommen** get* off lightly

glitschig adj. slippery

glitzern v/i. glitter, sparkle, glint

glob|al adj. global; **2us** m globe

Glocke f bell; **~nblume** bot. f bluebell; **~nspiel** n chimes pl.; **~nturm** m bell tower, belfry

glorreich adj. glorious

Glotze F TV f goggle box, Am. the tube; **2n** F v/i. goggle, gape, stare

Glück n (good) luck, fortune; Gefühl: happiness; **~ haben** be* lucky; **zum ~** fortunately; **viel ~!** good luck!

Glucke zo. f sitting hen; fig. hen

glücken v/i. → gelingen

gluckern v/i. gurgle

glücklich adj. happy; **~er Zufall** lucky chance; **~erweise** adv. fortunately

Glücks|bringer m lucky charm; **~fall** m lucky chance; **~pfennig** m lucky penny; **~pilz** m lucky fellow; **~spiel** n game of chance; coll. gambling; **~spieler(in)** gambler; **~tag** m lucky day

glück|strahlend adj. radiant; **2wunsch** m congratulations pl.; **herzlichen ~!** congratulations!; **zum Geburtstag:** happy birthday!

Glüh|birne electr. f light bulb; **2en** v/i. glow (a. fig.); **2end** adj. glowing; Eisen: red-hot; fig. burning; **2endheiß** adj. blazing hot; **~wein** m mulled wine

Glut f (glowing) fire; embers pl.; live coals pl.; Hitze: blazing heat; Gefühle: ardo(u)r

Glykol chem. n glycol

GmbH Abk. für Gesellschaft mit beschränkter Haftung private limited liability company

Gnade f mercy, bsd. rel. a. grace; Gunst: favo(u)r; **~nfrist** f reprieve; **~ngesuch** jur. n petition for mercy; **2nlos** adj. merciless

gnädig adj. gracious; bsd. rel. merciful

Gnom m gnome

Goal östr. n Sport: goal

Gold n gold; **~barren** m gold bar od. ingot; coll. bullion; **2en** adj. gold; fig. golden; **~fisch** m goldfish; **2gelb** adj. golden (yellow); **~gräber** m gold digger; **~grube** fig. f goldmine, bonanza; **2ig** fig. adj. sweet, lovely, Am. F a. cute; **~mine** f goldmine; **~münze** f gold coin; **~schmied** m goldsmith; **~stück** n gold coin; **~sucher** m gold prospector

Golf¹ geogr. m gulf

Golf² n golf; **~platz** m golf course; **~schläger** m golf club; **~spieler(in)** golfer

Gondel f gondola; Lift2: a. cabin

Gong(schlag) m (sound of the) gong

gönn|en v/t.: j-m et. ~ not (be)grudge s.o. s.th.; **j-m et. nicht ~** (be)grudge s.o. s.th.; **sich et. ~** allow o.s. s.th., treat o.s. to s.th.; **~erhaft** adj. patronizing

Gorilla zo. m gorilla

Gosse f gutter (a. fig.)

Got|ik arch. hist. f Gothic style od. period; **2isch** adj. Gothic

Gott m God, Lord; myth. god; **~ sei Dank(!)** thank God(!); **um ~es Willen!** for heaven's sake!; **2ergeben** adj. resigned (to the will of God)

Gottes|dienst rel. m (divine) service;

mass; 2**fürchtig** adj. god-fearing; ~**lästerer** m blasphemer; ~**lästerung** f blasphemy

Gottheit f deity, divinity

Gött|in f goddess; 2**lich** adj. divine

gott|lob int. thank God od. goodness!; ~**los** adj. godless, wicked; ~**verlassen** F adj. godforsaken; 2**vertrauen** n trust in God

Götze m, ~**nbild** n idol

Gouverneur m governor

Grab n grave; bsd. ~**mal**: tomb

Graben m ditch; mil. trench

graben v/t. u. v/i. dig*; Tier: a. burrow

Grab|gewölbe n vault, tomb; ~**mal** n Ehrenmal: monument; tomb, sepulch|re, Am. -er; ~**rede** f funeral address; ~**schrift** f epitaph; ~**stätte** f burial place; grave, tomb; ~**stein** m tombstone, gravestone

Grad m degree; mil. etc.: rank, grade; **15 ~ Kälte** 15 degrees below zero; ~**einteilung** f graduation; 2**uell** adj. Unterschied etc.: in degree

Graf m count; Brt. earl

Graffiti pl. graffiti pl.

Grafik f Computer: graphics pl.; → **Graphik**

Gräfin f countess

Grafschaft f county

Gram lit. m → **Kummer**, **Trauer**

Gramm n gram

Grammati|k f grammar; 2**sch** adj. grammatical

Granat min. m garnet; ~**e** f mil. shell; fig. Sport: cannonball; ~**splitter** mil. m shell splinter; ~**werfer** mil. m mortar

grandios adj. magnificent, grand

Granit min. m granite

Graphi|k f coll. graphic arts pl.; Druck: print; math., tech. etc. graph, diagram; Ausgestaltung: art(work), illustrations pl.; ~**ker(in)** graphic artist; 2**sch** adj. graphic

Graphologie f graphology

Gras bot. n grass; 2**en** v/i. graze; ~**halm** m blade of grass

grassieren v/i. rage, be* rife

gräßlich adj. hideous, atrocious

Gräte f (fish)bone

Gratifikation f gratuity, bonus

gratis adv. free (of charge)

Grätsche f, 2**n** v/i. straddle; Fußball: stride tackle

Gratul|ant(in) congratulator; ~**ation** f congratulation; 2**ieren** v/i. congratulate (j-m zu et. s.o. on s.th.); **j-m zum Geburtstag ~** wish s.o. many happy returns (of the day)

grau adj. grey, bsd. Am. gray; 2**brot** n rye bread; ~**en** v/i.: **mir graut es vor** I dread (the thought of); 2**en** n horror; ~**enhaft**, ~**envoll** adj. horrible, horrifying

Graupel meteor. f sleet, soft hail

grausam adj. cruel; 2**keit** f cruelty

grausig adj. → **grauenhaft**

Grauzone f fig. grey (Am. gray) area

grav|ieren v/t. engrave; ~**ierend** adj. serious; 2**ur** f engraving

Grazie f grace; 2**iös** adj. graceful; △ nicht **gracious**

greifen 1. v/t. seize, grasp, grab, take* od. catch* hold of; **2.** v/i. fig. Maßnahmen: take* effect; ~ **nach** reach for; **fest**: grasp at

Greis m (very) old man; 2**enhaft** adj. senile (a. med.); ~**in** f (very) old woman

grell adj. glaring; Ton: shrill

Grenze f border; Linie: a. boundary; fig. limit; 2**n** v/i.: ~ **an** border on; 2**nlos** adj. boundless

Grenz|fall m borderline case; ~**land** n borderland, frontier; ~**linie** f borderline, pol. demarcation line; ~**stein** m boundary stone; ~**übergang** m frontier crossing (point), checkpoint

Greuel m horror; ~**tat** f atrocity

Griech|e m Greek; ~**enland** Greece; ~**in** f, 2**isch** adj. Greek

Grieß m semolina

Griff m grip, grasp; Tür2, Messer2 etc.: handle; 2**bereit** adj. at hand, handy

Grill m grill

Grille zo. f cricket

grillen v/t. grill, barbecue

Grimasse f grimace; ~**n schneiden** pull faces

grimmig adj. grim

grinsen v/i. grin (**über** at); höhnisch: sneer (at); 2 n grin; sneer

Grippe med. f influenza, F flu

Grips F m brains pl.

grob 1. adj. coarse (a. fig.); Fehler, Lüge etc.: gross; Benehmen: crude; frech: rude; Arbeit, Fläche, Skizze etc.: rough; **2.** adv.: ~ **geschätzt** at a rough estimate; **2heit** f coarseness; roughness; rudeness

grölen F v/t. u. v/i. bawl

Groll m grudge, ill will; **2en** v/i.: **j-m ~** bear* s.o. a grudge

Groschen m östr. groschen; F ten-pfennig piece, ten pfennigs pl.; fig.: keinen **~ wert** not worth a penny (Am. cent)

groß adj. big; bsd. Fläche, Umfang, Zahl: large (a. Familie); hoch(gewachsen): tall; erwachsen: grown-up; F Bruder: big; fig. bedeutend: great (a. Freude, Spaß, Eile, Mühe, Schmerz etc.); Buchstabe: capital; **~es Geld** notes pl., Am. bills pl.; **~e Ferien** summer holiday(s pl.), Am. a. summer vacation sg.; **~ und klein** young and old; **im ~en (und) ganzen** on the whole; F: **~ in et. sein** be* great at (doing) s.th.; **wie ~ ist es?** what size is it?; **wie ~ bist du?** how tall are you?; **~artig** adj. great, F a. terrific; **2aufnahme** f Film: close-up

Größe f size (a. Kleid etc.); Körper**2**: height; bsd. math. quantity; Bedeutung: greatness; Person: celebrity

Großeltern pl. grandparents pl.

großenteils adv. to a large od. great extent, largely

Größenwahn m megalomania (a. fig.)

Groß|**familie** f extended family; **~handel** econ. m wholesale (trade); **~händler** m wholesale dealer, wholesaler; **~handlung** f wholesale business; **~industrie** f big industry; weitS. big business; **~industrielle** m big industrialist, F tycoon

Groß|**macht** pol. f great power; **~markt** m hypermarket; wholesale market; **~maul** n braggart; **~mut** f generosity; **~mutter** f grandmother; **~raum** m conurbation, metropolitan area; **der ~ München** Greater Munich, the Greater Munich area; **~raumflugzeug** n wide-bodied jet; **~schreibung** f (use of) capitalization; **2sprecherisch** adj. boastful; **2spurig** adj. arrogant; **~stadt** f big city; **2städtisch** adj. of od. in a big city, urban

größtenteils adv. mostly, mainly

groß|**tun** v/i. show* off; **sich mit et. ~** boast of, brag of od. about s.th.; **~vater** m grandfather; **2verdiener** m big earner; **2wild** n big game; **~ziehen** v/t. raise, rear; Kind: a. bring* up; **zü-**

-gig adj. generous, liberal (a. Erziehung); Planung etc.: a. on a large scale; Räume: spacious; **2zügigkeit** f generosity, liberality; spaciousness

grotesk adj. grotesque

Grotte f grotto

Grübchen n dimple

Grube f pit (a. Bergbau:); Bergwerk: mine

Grübel|**ei** f pondering, musing; **2n** v/i. ponder, muse (über on, over)

Gruft f tomb, vault

grün adj. green; **~ und blau schlagen** beat* black and blue

Grün n green; **im ~en** in the country; **~anlage** f park

Grund m reason; Ursache: cause; Boden: ground; agr. a. soil; Meer etc.: bottom; **~ und Boden** property, land; **aus diesem ~(e)** for this reason; **auf ~ gen.** because of; **von ~ auf** entirely; **im ~e (genommen)** actually, basically; **~...** in Zssgn Bedeutung, Bedingung, Regel, Prinzip, Wortschatz etc.: mst basic ...; **~begriffe** pl. basics pl., fundamentals pl.; **~besitz** m property, land; **~besitzer** m landowner

gründ|**en** v/t. found (a. Familie), set* up, establish; **sich ~ auf** be* based on; **2er(in)** founder

grund|**falsch** adj. absolutely wrong; **2fläche** f math. base; e-s Zimmers etc.: area; **2gedanke** m basic idea; **2geschwindigkeit** aviat. f ground speed; **2gesetz** n constitution; **2lage** f foundation; fig. a. basis; **~n** pl. (basic) elements pl.; **~legend** adj. fundamental, basic

gründlich adj. thorough (a. fig.)

Grund|**linie** f Tennis etc.: base line; **2los** fig. adj. groundless, unfounded; **~mauer** f foundation

Gründonnerstag rel. m Maundy od. Holy Thursday

Grund|**rechnungsart** math. f basic arithmetical operation; **~riß** arch. m ground plan; **~satz** m principle; **2sätzlich 1.** adj. fundamental; **2.** adv.: **ich bin ~ dagegen** I am against it on principle; **~schule** f Brt. primary (od. junior) school; Am. elementary (od. grade) school; **~stein** m arch. foundation stone; fig. foundations pl.; **~stück** n plot (of land), bsd. Am. a. lot; Bau-

platz: (building) site; *Haus nebst Zubehör*: premises *pl.*; **~stücksmakler** *m* (*Am.* real) estate agent, *Am. a.* realtor

Gründung *f* foundation, establishment, setting up

grund|verschieden *adj.* totally different; **2wasser** *n* ground water; **2zahl** *f* cardinal number; **2zug** *m* main feature, characteristic

Grüne *pol. m, f* Green; *die* **~n** *pl.* the Greens *pl.*

Grün|fläche *f* green space; **2lich** *adj.* greenish; **~span** *m* verdigris

grunzen *v/i. u. v/t.* grunt

Grupp|e *f* group; **2ieren** *v/t.* group, arrange in groups; *sich* **~** form groups

Grusel|... *in Zssgn Film etc.*: horror ...; **2ig** *adj.* eerie, creepy; *Film etc.*: spine-chilling; **2n** *v/t. u. v/refl.*: *es gruselt mich* F it gives me the creeps

Gruß *m* greeting(s *pl.*); *mil.* salute; *viele Grüße an* ... give my regards (*herzlicher*: love) to ...; *mit freundlichen Grüßen Brief*: yours sincerely; *herzliche Grüße* best wishes; *herzlicher*: love

grüßen *v/t.* greet, F say* hello to; *bsd. mil.* salute; *j-n* **~** *lassen* send* one's regards (*herzlicher*: love) to s.o

Grütze *f* groats *pl.*, *Am.* grits *pl.*

guck|en *v/i.* look; **2loch** *n* peephole

Güggeli *n Schweiz*: chicken

gültig *adj.* valid; *Geld: a.* current; **2keit** *f* validity; *s-e* **~** *verlieren* expire

Gummi *n* rubber; → *Radiergummi*; **~...** *in Zssgn Ball, Handschuh, Sohle, Stiefel etc.*: *mst* rubber ...; **~band** *n* rubber (*bsd. Brt. a.* elastic) band; **~bärchen** *pl.* gummy bears *pl.*; **~baum** *m* rubber tree; *im Haus*: rubber plant; **~bonbon** *m, n* gumdrop; **~boot** *n* rubber dinghy

gummieren *v/t.* gum

Gummi|knüppel *m* truncheon, *Am. a.* billy (club); **~stiefel** *m bsd. Brt.* wellington (boot), *Am.* rubber boot; **~zug** *m* elastic

Gunst *f* favo(u)r, goodwill; *zu* **~en** *von od. gen.* in favo(u)r of

günst|ig *adj.* favo(u)rable (*für* to); *passend*: convenient; **~e** *Gelegenheit* chance; *im* **~sten** *Fall* at best

Gurgel *f*: *j-m an die* **~** *springen* fly* at s.o.'s throat; **2n** *v/i. med.* gargle; *Wasser*: gurgle

Gurke *f* cucumber; *Gewürz2*: pickle(d gherkin)

gurren *v/i.* coo

Gurt *m* belt (*a. mot. u. aviat.*); *Halte2*, *Trage2*: strap

Gürtel *m* belt; △ *nicht girdle*; **~reifen** *m* radial (tyre, *Am.* tire)

GUS *Abk. für Gemeinschaft Unabhängiger Staaten* CIS, Commonwealth of Independent States

Guß *m Regen etc.*: downpour; *tech.* casting; *Zucker2*: icing; *fig.* **aus e-m** **~** of a piece; **~eisen** *n* cast iron; **2eisern** *adj.* cast-iron

gut 1. *adj.* good; *Wetter: a.* fine; *ganz* **~** not bad; *also* **~!** all right (then)!; *schon* **~!** never mind!; *(wieder)* **~** *werden* come* right (again), be* all right; **~e** *Reise!* have a nice trip!; *sei bitte so* **~** *und* ... would you be so good as to ...; *good enough to ...; in et.* **~** *sein* be* good at (doing) s.th.; **2.** *adv.* well; *aussehen, klingen, riechen, schmecken etc.*: good; *du hast es* **~** you are lucky; *es ist* **~** *möglich* it may well be; *es gefällt mir* **~** I (do) like it; **~** *gemacht!* well done!; *mach's* **~!** take care (of yourself)! → *gutgehen*

Gut *n Land2*: estate; *Güter pl.* goods

Gut|achten *n* (expert) opinion; *Zeugnis*: certificate; **~achter** *m* expert; **2artig** *adj.* good-natured; *med.* benign; **~dünken** *n*: *nach* **~** at one's discretion

Gute *n* good; *et.* **~s** *tun* do* good; *alles* **~!** all the best!, good luck!

Güte *f* goodness, kindness; *econ.* quality; F: *meine* **~!** good gracious!

Güter|bahnhof *m* goods station, *Am.* freight depot; **~gemeinschaft** *jur. f* community of property; **~trennung** *jur. f* separation of property; **~verkehr** *m* goods (*Am.* freight) traffic; **~wagen** *m* goods wag(g)on, *Am.* freight car; **~zug** *m* goods (*Am.* freight) train

gut|gebaut *adj.* well-built; **~gehen** *v/i.* go* (off) well, work out well *od.* all right; *wenn alles gutgeht* if nothing goes wrong; *mir geht es gut* I'm (*finanziell*: doing) well; **~gelaunt** *adj.* in a good mood; **~gläubig** *adj.* credulous; **2haben** *econ. n* credit (balance); **~heißen** *v/t.* approve (of); **~herzig** *adj.* kind(-hearted)

H

gütig *adj.* good, kind(ly)

gütlich *adv.*: **sich ~ einigen** come* to an amicable settlement

gut|machen *v/t.* make* up for, repay*; **~mütig** *adj.* good-natured; **2mütigkeit** *f* good nature

Gutsbesitzer(in) estate owner

Gut|schein *m* coupon, *bsd.* Brt. voucher; **2schreiben** *v/t.*: **j-m et. ~** credit s.th. to s.o.'s account; **~schrift** *f* credit

Guts|haus *n* manor (house); **~hof** *m* estate, manor; **~verwalter** *m* steward, manager

gutwillig *adj.* willing

Gymnasium *n* Brt. appr. grammar school, Am. high school; △ *nicht* **gymnasium**

Gymnasti|k *f* exercises *pl.*, gymnastics *pl.*; **2sch** *adj.*: **~e Übungen** physical exercises

Gynäkologe *med. m* gyn(a)ecologist

Haar *n* hair; **sich die ~e kämmen** comb one's hair; **sich die ~e schneiden lassen** have* one's hair cut; **sich aufs ~ gleichen** look absolutely identical; **um ein ~** by a hair's breadth; **~ausfall** *m* loss of hair; **~bürste** *f* hairbrush; **2en** *v/i. u. v/refl.* Tier: lose* its hair; Pelz: shed* hairs; **~esbreite** *f*: **um ~** by a hair's breadth; **2fein** *adj.* (as) fine as a hair; *fig.* subtle; **~festiger** *m* setting lotion; **~gefäß** *n* anat. capillary (vessel); **2genau** F *adv.* precisely; (stimmt) **~!** dead right!; **2ig** *adj.* hairy; in Zssgn: ...-haired; **2klein** F *adv.* to the last detail; **~klemme** *f* hair clip, Am. bobby pin; **~nadel** *f* hairpin; **~nadelkurve** *f* hairpin bend; **~netz** *n* hair-net; **2scharf** F *adv.* by a hair's breadth; **~schnitt** *m* haircut; **~spalterei** *f* hairsplitting; **~spange** *f* (hair) slide, Am. barrette; **2sträubend** *adj.* hair-raising, shocking; **~teil** *n* hairpiece; **~trockner** *m* hair dryer; **~wäsche** *f*, **~waschmittel** *n* shampoo; **~wasser** *n* hair tonic; **~wuchs** *m*: **starken ~ haben** have* a lot of hair; **~wuchsmittel** *n* hair restorer

Hab: **~ und Gut** belongings *pl.*

Habe *f* (personal) belongings *pl.*

haben *v/t.* have* (got); **Hunger (Durst) ~** be* hungry (thirsty); **Ferien (Urlaub) ~** be* on holiday; **er hat Geburtstag** it's his birthday; **welches Datum ~ wir heute?** what's the date today?; **welche**

Farbe hat ...? what colo(u)r is ...?; **zu ~ Ware** etc.: available; F **Mädchen**: to be had; F: **sich ~ make*** a fuss; F: **was hast du?** what's the matter with you?; F: **da ~ wir's!** there we are!

Haben *econ. n* credit

Habgier *f* greed(iness); **2ig** *adj.* greedy

Habicht *zo. m* (gos)hawk

Habseligkeiten *pl.* belongings *pl.*

Hacke *f* agr. hoe; *Spitz2*: (pick)axe; *Ferse*: heel

hacken *v/t.* chop; agr. hoe; *Vogel*: peck; **2entrick** *m* Fußball: backheeler

Hacker *m* Computer: hacker

Hack|fleisch *n* minced (Am. ground) meat; **~ordnung** *f* pecking order

Hafen *m* harbo(u)r, port; **~arbeiter** *m* docker, Am. a. longshoreman; **~stadt** *f* (sea)port

Hafer *m* oats *pl.*; **~brei** *m* porridge, Am. oatmeal; **~flocken** *pl.* (rolled) oats *pl.*; **~schleim** *m* gruel

Haft *jur. f* confinement, imprisonment; **in ~** under arrest; **2bar** *adj.* responsible, jur. liable; **~befehl** *m* warrant of arrest; **2en** *v/i.* stick*, adhere (*an* to); **~ für** jur. answer for, be* liable for

Häftling *m* prisoner, convict

Haftpflicht *jur. f* liability; **~versicherung** *f* liability insurance; mot. third party insurance

Haftung *f* responsibility; jur. liability; **mit beschränkter ~** limited

Hagel *m* hail; *fig. a.* shower, volley;

~korn n hailstone; **2n** v/i. hail (a. fig.); **~schauer** m hail shower

hager adj. lean, gaunt, haggard

Hahn m zo. cock; Haus2: a. rooster; Wasser2: (water) tap, Am. a. faucet

Hähnchen n chicken

Hahnen|kamm m cockscomb; **~schrei** m fig.: mit dem ersten ~ at the crack of dawn

Hai(fisch) m shark

häkeln v/t. u. v/i. crochet

Haken m hook (a. Boxen); Kleider2: a. peg; Zeichen: tick, Am. check; F snag, catch; **~ und Öse** hook and eye; **~kreuz** n swastika

halb adj. u. adv. half; **e-e ~e Stunde** half an hour; **ein ~es Pfund** half a pound; **zum ~en Preis** at half-price; **auf ~em Wege (entgegenkommen)** (meet*) halfway; **so viel** half as much; F: (mit j-m)~e-e machen go* halves od. fifty-fifty (with s.o.); **2bruder** m half-brother; **2dunkel** n semi-darkness

Halbe f pint (of beer)

halber prp. → wegen, um... willen

halb|fett adj. Käse etc: medium-fat; Schrift: semi-bold; **2finale** n Sport: semi-final; **~gar** adj. underdone; **2gott** m demigod (a. fig.)

halbieren v/t. halve; math. bisect

Halb|insel f peninsula; **~jahr** n six months pl.; **2jährig** adj. six-month; **2jährlich 1.** adj. half-yearly; **2.** adv. half-yearly, twice a year; **~kreis** m semicircle; **~kugel** f hemisphere; **2laut 1.** adj. low, subdued; **2.** adv. in an undertone; **~leiter** electr. m semiconductor; **2links** adv. inside left; **2mast** m (at) half-mast; **~mond** m half-moon, crescent (a. Form); **~pension** f half-board; **2rechts** adv. inside right; **~schlaf** m doze; **~schuh** m (low) shoe; **~schwester** f half-sister

halbtags adv.: **~ arbeiten** work part-time; **2arbeit** f part-time job; **2kraft** f part-time worker, part-timer

halb|wegs adv. fig. leidlich: reasonably; **2wüchsige** m, f adolescent

Halbzeit f Sport: half (time); **~stand** m half-time score

Halde f slope; Bergbau: dump

Hälfte f half; **die ~ von** half of

Halfter 1. m, n Zaum: halter; **2.** n, f Pistolen2: holster

Halle f hall; Hotel2: a. lounge; **in der ~** Sport etc. indoors

hallen v/i. resound, reverberate

Hallen|bad n indoor swimming pool; **~sport** m indoor sports pl.

Halm bot. m Gras2: blade; Getreide2: ha(u)lm, stalk; Stroh2: straw

Hals m neck; Kehle: throat; **~ über Kopf** helter-skelter; **sich vom ~ schaffen** get* rid of; **es hängt mir zum ~(e) (he)raus** I'm fed up with it; **bis zum ~** fig. up to one's neck; **~band** n necklace; Hunde2 etc.: collar; **~entzündung** f sore throat; **~kette** f necklace; **~schmerzen** pl.: **~ haben** have* a sore throat; **2starrig** adj. stubborn, obstinate; **~tuch** n neckerchief; scarf

Halt m hold; Stütze: support (a. fig.); Zwischen2: stop; fig. innerer: stability

halt int. stop!; mil. halt!

haltbar adj. durable; Lebensmittel: not perishable; Argument etc.: tenable; **~ bis ...** best before...; **~keitsdatum** n best-by (od. best-before) date

halten 1. v/t. hold*; Versprechen, Tier etc.: keep*; Rede: make*; Vortrag: give*; Zeitung: take* (Brt. a. in); Torwart: save; **~ für** regard as; irrtümlich: (mis)take* for; **viel (wenig) ~ von** think* highly (little) of; **sich ~** last; Essen, in Richtung od. Zustand: keep*; **sich gut ~ in e-r Prüfung:** do* well; **sich ~ an** keep* to; **2.** v/i. hold*, last; an~: stop, halt; Eis: bear*; Seil etc.: hold*; **~ zu** stand* by, F stick* to

Halter m owner; für Geräte etc.: holder

Halte|stelle f stop; rail. a. station; **~verbot** mot. n no stopping (area)

halt|los adj. unsteady; unbegründet: baseless; **~machen** v/i. stop; **vor nichts ~** stop at nothing; **2ung** f Körper: posture; fig. attitude (**zu** towards)

hämisch adj. malicious, sneering

Hammel m wether; **~fleisch** n mutton

Hammer m hammer (a. Sport)

hämmern v/t. u. v/i. hammer

Hämorrhoiden med. pl. h(a)emorrhoids pl., piles pl.

Hampelmann m jumping jack

Hamster zo. m hamster; **2n** v/t. u. v/i. hoard

Hand f hand; **von ~, mit der ~** by hand; **an ~ von** by means of; **zur ~** at hand; **aus erster (zweiter) ~** firsthand (sec-

H

ondhand); **an die ~ nehmen** take* by the hand; **sich die ~ geben** shake* hands; **aus der ~ legen** lay* aside; **Hände hoch (weg)!** hands up (off)!; **~arbeit** f manual labo(u)r; *Nadelarbeit:* needlework (*a. Schule*); **es ist ~** it is handmade; **~ball** m (European) handball; **~betrieb** *tech.* m manual operation; **~breit** f hand's breadth; **~bremse** *mot.* f hand brake; **~buch** n manual, handbook

Händedruck m handshake

Handel m commerce, business; **~sverkehr:** trade; *Markt:* market; *abgeschlossener:* transaction, deal, bargain; **~ treiben** *econ.* trade (**mit** s.o.); **2n** v/i. act, take* action; *feilschen:* bargain (**um** for), haggle (over); **mit j-m ~** *econ.* trade with s.o.; **mit Waren ~** *econ.* trade *od.* deal* in goods; **~ von** deal* with, be* about; **es handelt sich um** it concerns, it is about; it is a matter of

Handels|abkommen n trade agreement; **~bank** f commercial bank; **~bilanz** f balance of trade; **2einig** *adj.:* **~ werden** come* to terms; **~gesellschaft** f (trading) company; **~kammer** f chamber of commerce; **~schiff** n merchant ship; **~schule** f commercial school; **~ware** f commodity, merchandise

Hand|feger m handbrush; **~fertigkeit** f manual skill; **2fest** *fig.* adj. solid; **~fläche** f palm; **2gearbeitet** adj. handmade; **~gelenk** n wrist; **~gepäck** n hand luggage (*Am.* baggage); **~granate** *mil.* f handgrenade; **2greiflich** *adj.:* **~ werden** turn violent, *Am.* a. get* tough; **2haben** v/t. handle, manage; *Maschine etc.:* operate; **~kantenschlag** m (backhand) chop

Händler(in) m dealer, trader

handlich adj. handy, manageable

Handlung f *Film etc.:* story, plot, action; *Tat:* act, action

Handlungs|reisende m sales representative, travel(l)ing salesman; **~weise** f *Verhalten:* conduct, behavio(u)r

Hand|rücken m back of the hand; **~schellen** pl. handcuffs pl.; **j-m ~ anlegen** handcuff s.o.; **~schlag** m handshake; **~schrift** f hand(writing); **2schriftlich** adj. handwritten; **~schuh** m glove; **~spiel** n *Fußball:*

hand ball; **~stand** m handstand; **~tasche** f handbag, *Am. a.* purse; **~tuch** n towel; **~voll** f handful; **~wagen** m handcart; **~werk** n craft, trade; **~werker** m craftsman; *allg.* workman; **~werkzeug** n (kit of) tools *pl.*; **~wurzel** f wrist

Handy n mobile (telephone *od.* phone)

Hanf *bot.* m hemp; *Indisch ~:* cannabis

Hang m slope; *fig.* inclination (**zu** for), tendency (**towards**)

Hänge|brücke f suspension bridge; **~lampe** f hanging lamp; **~matte** f hammock

hängen v/i. u. v/t. hang* (**an** *Wand etc.:* on; *Decke etc.:* from); **~ an** be* fond of; *stärker:* be* devoted to; **alles, woran ich hänge** everything that is dear to me; **~bleiben** v/i. get* stuck (*a. fig.*); **an et. ~** get* caught on s.th.

hänseln v/t. tease (**wegen** about)

Hanswurst m fool, clown

Hant|el f dumbbell; **~ieren** v/i.: **~ mit** handle; **~ an** fiddle about with

Happen m morsel, bite; snack

Hardware f *Computer:* hardware

Harfe *mus.* f harp; **~nist(in)** f harpist

Harke f, **2n** v/t. rake

harmlos adj. harmless

Harmon|ie f harmony (*a. mus.*); **2ieren** v/i. harmonize (**mit** with); **2isch** adj. harmonious

Harn m urine; **~blase** f (urinary) bladder; **~röhre** f urethra

Harpun|e f, **2ieren** v/t. harpoon

hart 1. adj. hard, F *a.* tough; *Sport:* rough; *streng:* severe; **2.** adv. hard; △ *nicht* **hardly**

Härte f hardness; toughness; roughness; severity; *bsd. jur.* hardship; **~fall** m case of hardship; **2n** v/t. harden

Hart|faserplatte f hardboard; **2gekocht** adj. hard-boiled; **~geld** n coin(s *pl.*); **2gesotten** *fig.* adj. hard-boiled; **2herzig** adj. hard-hearted; **2näckig** adj. stubborn, obstinate; *beharrlich:* persistent; *Krankheit:* refractory

Harz n resin; *Geigen2:* rosin; **2ig** adj. resinous

Hasch Fn hash; **2en** F v/i. smoke hash; **~isch** n hashish, *sl.* pot

Hase *zo.* m hare

Hasel|maus f dormouse; **~nuß** f hazelnut

Hasen|braten *m* roast hare; **~fuß** *m* coward; **~scharte** *med. f* harelip

Haß *m* hatred, hate (**auf, gegen** of, for)

hassen *v/t.* hate

häßlich *adj.* ugly; *fig. a.* nasty

Hast *f* hurry, haste; rush; **2en** *v/i.* hurry, hasten, rush; **2ig** *adj.* hasty, hurried

hätscheln *v/t.* fondle; *contp.* pamper

Haube *f* bonnet; *Schwestern*2: cap; *zo.* crest; *mot.* bonnet, *Am.* hood

Hauch *m* breath; *Duft*2: whiff; *fig. An- flug:* touch, trace; **2en** *v/t.* breathe

Haue F *f* hiding, spanking; **2n** *v/t.* F hit*, beat*, *prügeln:* thrash, *Kind: a.* spank; *tech.* hew*; **sich ~** (have*) a) fight*

Haufen *m* heap, pile (*beide a.* F *fig.*); F *fig.* crowd

häuf|en *v/t.* heap (up), pile (up); **sich ~** *fig.* become* more frequent, be* on the increase; **~ig 1.** *adj.* frequent; **2.** *adv.* frequently, often

Haupt *n* head, *fig. a.* leader; **~bahnhof** *m* main *od.* central station; **~beschäf- tigung** *f* chief occupation; **~bestand- teil** *m* chief ingredient; **~darstel- ler(in)** leading act|or (-ress), lead(ing man [lady])

Häuptelsalat *östr. m* lettuce

Haupt|fach *n Studium:* main subject, *Am.* major; **~figur** *f* main character; **~film** *m* feature (film); **~gericht** *gastr. n* main course; **~gewinn** *m* first prize; **~grund** *m* main reason

Häuptling *m* chief(tain)

Haupt|mann *mil. m* captain; **~menü** *n Computer:* main menu; **~merkmal** *n* chief characteristic; **~person** F *f* cent|re (*Am.* -er) of attention; **~quar- tier** *n* headquarters *pl.*; **~rolle** *thea. f* lead(ing part); **~sache** *f* main thing *od.* point; **2sächlich** *adj.* main, chief, principal; **~satz** *m* main clause; **~sen- dezeit** *f TV* peak time, peak viewing hours *pl.*, *Am.* prime time; **~speicher** *m Computer:* main memory; **~stadt** *f* capital; **~straße** *f* main street; main road; **~verkehrsstraße** *f* main road; **~verkehrszeit** *f* rush hour(s *pl.*), peak hour(s *pl.*); **~versammlung** *f* general meeting; **~wohnsitz** *m* main place of residence; **~wort** *n* noun

Haus *n* house; *Gebäude:* building; **zu ~e** at home, in; **nach ~e kommen** (brin-

gen) come* *od.* get* (take*) home; **~angestellte(r)** domestic (servant); **~apotheke** *f* medicine cabinet; **~ar- beit** *f* housework; **~arzt** *m* family doc- tor; **~aufgaben** *pl.* homework *sg.*, *Am. a.* assignment; **s-e ~n machen a.** *fig.* do one's homework; **~bar** *f* cock- tail cabinet; **~besetzer** *m* squatter; **~besetzung** *f* squatting; **~besit- zer(in)** house owner; **~einweihung** *f* house-warming (party)

hausen *v/i.* live; *wüten:* play havoc

Haus|flur *m* (entrance) hall, *bsd. Am.* hallway; **~frau** *f* housewife; **~frie- densbruch** *jur. m* trespass; **2ge- macht** *adj.* homemade; **~halt** *m* household; *pol.* budget; **~ führen** keep* house (for s.o.); **~hälte- rin** *f* housekeeper; **~haltsgeld** *n* housekeeping money; **~haltsplan** *parl. m* budget; **~haltswaren** *pl.* household articles *pl.*; **~herr** *m* head of the household; *Gastgeber:* host; **~her- rin** *f* lady of the house; *Gastgeberin:* hostess; **2hoch** *adj.* huge; *Sieg:* smashing

hausiere|n *v/i.* peddle, hawk (**mit et.** s.th.) (*a. fig.*); **2r** *m* pedlar, hawker

häuslich *adj.* domestic; home-loving

Haus|mädchen *n* (house)maid; **~ mann** F *m* house husband; **~manns- kost** *f* plain fare; **~meister** *m* caretaker, janitor; **~mittel** *n* household re- medy; **~ordnung** *f* house rules *pl.*; **~rat** *m* household effects *pl.*; **~schlüs- sel** *m* front-door key; **~schuh** *m* slip- per

Hausse *econ. f* rise, boom

Haus|suchung *f* house search; **~tier** *n* domestic animal; **~tür** *f* front door; **~verwaltung** *f* property manage- ment; **~wirt(in)** land|lord (-lady); **~zelt** *n* ridge tent

Hauswirtschaft *f* housekeeping; **~s- lehre** *f* domestic science; *Am. a.* home economics; **~sschule** *f* domestic sci- ence (*Am. a.* home economics) school

Haut *f* skin; *Teint:* complexion; **bis auf die ~ durchnäßt** soaked to the skin; **~abschürfung** *f* abrasion; **~arzt** *m* dermatologist; **~ausschlag** *m* rash; **2eng** *adj.* skin-tight; **~farbe** *f* colo(u)r of the skin; *Teint:* complexion; **~ krankheit** *f* skin disease; **~pflege** *f* skin care; **~schere** f cuticle scissors pl.

Hbf. Abk. für **Hauptbahnhof** cent. sta., central station

H-Bombe mil. f H-bomb

Hebamme f midwife

Hebebühne Mot. f car hoist

Hebel tech. m lever

heben v/t. lift (a. mot., naut., Sport); raise (a. Wrack u. fig.); schwere Last: heave; hochwinden: hoist; fig. a. improve; **sich ~** rise*, go* up

Hecht m pike; **2en** v/i. dive* (**nach** for); Turnen: do* a long-fly

Heck n naut. stern; aviat. tail; mot. rear (a. in Zssgn Fenster, Motor etc.)

Hecke agr. f hedge; **~nrose** bot. f dogrose; **~nschütze** m sniper

Heer n mil. army; fig. a. host

Hefe f yeast (a. in Zssgn Teig etc.)

Heft n notebook; Schul2: exercise book; Bändchen: booklet; Ausgabe: issue, number

heft|en v/t. fix, fasten, attach (**an** to); mit Nadeln: pin (to); Saum etc.: tack, baste; Buch: stitch; **2er** m stapler; Ordner: file

heftig adj. violent, fierce; Regen etc.: heavy

Heft|klammer f staple; **~pflaster** n (adhesive od. sticking) plaster, Am. bandage, Band Aid (TM)

Hehl n: kein ~ aus etw. machen make* no secret of s.th.

Hehler m receiver of stolen goods, sl. fence; **~ei** f receiving stolen goods

Heide[1] m heathen

Heide[2] f heath(land); **~kraut** bot. n heather, heath

Heiden|angst F f: e-e ~ haben be* scared stiff; **~geld** F n: ein ~ a fortune; **~lärm** F m: ein ~ a hell of a noise; **~spaß** F m: e-n ~ haben have* a ball

Heid|entum n heathenism; **~in** f, **2nisch** adj. heathen

heikel adj. delicate, tricky; Thema, Punkt: tender; F Person: fussy

heil adj. Person: safe, unhurt; Sache: undamaged, whole, intact

Heil n rel. grace; sein ~ versuchen try one's luck

Heiland rel. m Saviour, Redeemer

Heil|anstalt f sanatorium, Am. a. sanitarium; Nerven2: mental home; **~bad** n health resort, spa; **2bar** adj. curable;

2en 1. v/t. cure; **2.** v/i. heal (up); **~gymnastik** f physiotherapy

heilig adj. holy; Gott geweiht: sacred (a. fig.); **2abend** m Christmas Eve; **2e(r)** saint; **~en** v/t. sanctify (a. fig.), hallow; **~sprechen** v/t. canonize; **2tum** n sanctuary, shrine

Heil|kraft f healing od. curative power; **2kräftig** adj. curative; **~kraut** n medicinal herb; **2los** fig. adj. Durcheinander: utter, hopeless; **~mittel** n remedy, cure (beide a. fig.); **~praktiker** m nonmedical practitioner; **~quelle** f (medicinal) mineral spring; **2sam** fig. adj. salutary

Heilsarmee f Salvation Army

Heilung f cure; Wunde: healing

heim adv.

Heim n home; Jugend2 etc.: hostel

Heim... in Zssgn Computer, Mannschaft, Sieg, Spiel etc.: home

Heimat f home; Land: home country; Ort: home town; **in der (meiner) ~** at home; **2los** adj. homeless; **~stadt** f home town; **~vertriebene(r)** expellee

heimisch adj. Industrie etc.: home, domestic; bot., zo. etc.: native; Gefühl etc.: homelike, bsd. Am. hom(e)y; **sich ~ fühlen** feel* at home

Heim|kehr f return (home); **2kehren**, **2kommen** v/i. return home, come* back

heimlich adj. secret; **2keit** f secrecy; **~en** pl. secrets pl.

Heim|reise f journey home; **2suchen** v/t. Unheil etc.: strike*; **2tückisch** adj. insidious (a. Krankheit); Mord etc.: treacherous; **2wärts** adv. homeward(s); **~weg** m way home; **~weh** n homesickness; ~ haben be* homesick; **~werker** m do-it-yourselfer

Heirat f marriage; **2en** v/t. u. v/i. marry, get* married (to)

Heirats|antrag m proposal (of marriage); j-m e-n ~ machen propose to s.o.; **~schwindler** m marriage impostor; **~vermittler(in)** marriage broker; **~vermittlung** f marriage bureau

heiser adj. hoarse, husky; **2keit** f hoarseness, huskiness

heiß adj. hot; fig. a. passionate, ardent; **mir ist ~** I am od. feel hot

heißen v/i. be called; bedeuten: mean; **wie ~ Sie?** what's your name?; **wie**

heißt das? what do you call this?; **was heißt ... auf englisch?** what is ... in English?; **es heißt im Text** it says in the text; **das heißt** that is (abbr. **d.h.** i.e.)

heiter adj. cheerful; Film etc.: humorous; meteor. fair; fig. **aus ~em Himmel** out of the blue; **2keit** f cheerfulness; Belustigung: amusement

heiz|bar adj. Pool, Heckscheibe etc.: heated; **~en** v/t. u. v/i. heat; **mit Kohlen ~** burn* coal; **2er** naut., rail. m stoker; **2kessel** m boiler; **2kissen** n electric cushion; **2körper** m radiator; **2kraftwerk** n thermal power-station; **2material** n fuel; **2öl** n fuel oil; **2ung** f heating

Held m hero

helden|haft adj. heroic; **2tat** f heroic deed; **2tod** m heroic death; **2tum** n heroism

Heldin f heroine

helfen v/i. help, aid; förmlicher: assist; **j-m bei et.** help s.o. with od. in (doing) s.th.; **~ gegen** Mittel etc.: be* good for; **er weiß sich zu ~** he can manage (bsd. Brt. cope); **es hilft nichts** it's no use

Helfer|(in) helper, assistant; **~shelfer** m accomplice

hell adj. Licht etc.: bright; Farbe: light; Kleid etc.: light-colo(u)red; Klang: clear; Bier: pale; fig. intelligent: bright, clever; **es wird schon ~** it's getting light already; **~blau** adj. light blue; **~blond** adj. very fair; **~hörig** adj. quick of hearing; arch. poorly soundproofed; **~ werden** prick up one's ears; **2seher(in)** clairvoyant(e)

Helm m helmet

Hemd n shirt; Unter2: vest; **~bluse** f shirt; **~blusenkleid** n shirt-waister, Am. shirtwaist

Hemisphäre f hemisphere

hemm|en v/t. Bewegung etc.: check, stop; behindern: hamper; **2schuh** F fig. m obstacle, impediment (**für** to); **2ung** psych. f inhibition; moralische: scruple; **~ungslos** adj. unrestrained; unscrupulous

Hengst m stallion

Henkel m handle

Henker m hangman, executioner

Henne f hen

her adv. hier~: here; **das ist lange ~** that was a long time ago

herab adv. down; **~lassen** fig. v/refl. condescend; **~lassend** adj. condescending; **~sehen** fig. v/i.: **~ auf** look down upon; **~setzen** v/t. reduce; fig. disparage

heran adv. close, near; **~ an** up od. near to; **~gehen** v/i.: **~ an** walk up to; fig. Aufgabe etc.: set* about; **~kommen** v/i. come* near (a. fig. an Leistung etc.); **~wachsen** v/i. grow* (up) (**zu** into); **2wachsende(r)** adolescent

herauf adv. up (here); die Treppe **~**: upstairs; **~beschwören** v/t. call up; verursachen: bring* on, provoke

heraus adv. out; fig. **aus ~** out of ...; **zum Fenster ~** out of the window; **~ mit der Sprache!** speak out!, out with it!; **~bekommen** v/t. get* out; Geld: get* back; fig. find* out; **~bringen** v/t. bring* out; print. publish; thea. stage; fig. find* out; **~finden 1.** v/t. find*; fig. find* out, discover; **2.** v/i. find* one's way out (a. fig.); **2forderer** m challenger; **~fordern** v/t. challenge; Tat etc.: provoke, F ask for it; **2forderung** f challenge; provocation; **~geben** v/t. zurückgeben: give* back; ausliefern: give* up; print. publish; Vorschriften: issue; Geld: give* change (**auf** for); **2geber** m publisher; **~kommen** v/i. come* out; Buch: be* published; Briefmarken: be* issued; **~ aus** get* out of; F: **groß ~** be* a great success; **~nehmen** v/t. take* out; Spieler: take* off the team; fig. **sich et. ~** take* liberties, go* too far; **~putzen** v/t. u. v/refl. spruce (o.s.) up; **~reden** v/refl. make* excuses; erfolgreich: talk one's way out; **~stellen** v/t. put* out; fig. emphasize; **sich ~ als** turn out od. prove* to be; **~strecken** v/t. stick* out; **~suchen** v/t. pick out; **j-m et. ~** find* s.o. s.th.

herb adj. tart; Wein etc.: dry; fig. harsh; Enttäuschung: bitter

herbei adv. up, over, here; **~eilen** v/i. come* running up; **~führen** fig. v/t. cause, bring* about

Herberge f Gasthaus: inn; Unterkunft: lodging, place to stay

Herbst m autumn, Am. a. fall

Herd m cooker, stove; fig. cent|re, Am. -er; med. focus, seat

Herde f Vieh2, Schweine2 etc.: herd (a.

fig. contp.); *Schaf2̥, Gänse2̥ etc.*: flock
herein *adv.* in (here); *~! come* in!; **~bre-chen** *fig. v/i. Nacht*: fall*; *~ über Un-glück etc.*: befall*; **~fallen** *fig. v/i.* be taken in *(auf* by); **~legen** *fig. v/t.* take* in

her|fallen *v/i.*: *~ über* attack *(a. fig.)*, assail; F *fig.* pull to pieces; **2̥gang** *m*: *j-m den ~ schildern* tell* s.o. what hap-pened; **~geben** *v/t.* give* up, part with; *sich ~ zu* lend* o.s. to

Hering *zo. m* herring

her|kommen *v/i.* come* (here); *~ von* come* from; *fig. a.* be* caused by; **~kömmlich** *adj.* conventional *(a. mil.)*; **2̥kunft** *f* origin; *Person: a.* birth, descent

Herr *m* gentleman; *Besitzer, Gebieter:* master; *rel. the* Lord; *~ Brown* Mr Brown; *~ der Lage* master of the situa-tion

Herren|bekleidung *f* men's wear; **~doppel** *n Tennis:* men's doubles *pl.*; **~einzel** *n Tennis:* men's singles *pl.*; **2̥los** *adj.* abandoned; *Tier:* stray; **~toi-lette** *f* men's toilet *(od.* lavatory, *Am.* restroom)

herrichten *v/t.* get* ready, F fix
herrisch *adj.* imperious
herrlich *adj.* marvel(l)ous, wonderful, F fantastic; **2̥keit** *f* glory

Herrschaft *f* rule, power, control *(a. fig.) (über* over); *die ~ verlieren über* lose* control of

herrsch|en *v/i.* rule; *es herrschte ... Freude etc.: mst* there was ...; **2̥er(in)** ruler; sovereign, monarch; **~süchtig** *adj.* domineering; F bossy

herrühren *v/i.*: *~ von* come* from, be* due to

herstell|en *v/t.* make*, produce; *fig.* establish; **2̥ung** *f* production; *fig.* es-tablishment; **2̥ungskosten** *pl.* pro-duction cost(s *pl.*)

herüber *adv.* over (here), across
herum *adv.* (a)round; F: *anders ~* the other way round; **~führen** *v/t.*: *j-n (in der Stadt etc.)* show* (a)round (the town *etc.*); **~kommen** *v/i.*: *(weit od. viel)* ~ get* around; *um et. ~ fig.* get* (a)round; **~kriegen** F *v/t.*: *j-n zu et. ~* get* s.o. round to (doing) s.th.; **~lungern** *v/i.* loaf *od.* hang* around; **~reichen** *v/t.* pass *od.* hand round;

~sprechen *v/refl.* get* around; **~trei-ben** *v/refl.* F gad *od.* knock about; **2̥treiber(in)** tramp, loafer

herunter *adv.* down; *die Treppe ~:* downstairs; **~gekommen** *adj.* run--down; *schäbig:* seedy, shabby; **~hau-en** F *v/t.*: *j-m e-e ~* smack *od.* slap s.o.('s face); **~machen** F *fig. v/t.* run* down; **~putzen** F *fig. v/t.* blow* up, *bsd. Am.* bawl out; **~spielen** F *fig. v/t.* play down

hervor *adv.* out of *od.* from, forth; **~bringen** *v/t.* bring out*, produce *(a. fig.)*; *Früchte:* yield; *Wort:* utter; **~ge-hen** *fig. v/i.*: *~ aus* follow from; *als Sieger ~* come* off victorious; **~he-ben** *fig. v/t.* stress, emphasize; **~ra-gend** *fig. adj.* outstanding, excellent, superior; *Bedeutung, Persönlichkeit:* prominent, eminent; **~rufen** *v/t.* cause, bring* about; *Problem etc.: a.* create; **~stechend** *fig. adj.* striking; **~tretend** *adj.* prominent; *Augen etc.:* protruding, bulging; **~tun** *v/refl.* di-stinguish o.s. *(als* as)

Herz *n anat.* heart *(a. fig.); Karten:* heart(s *pl.*); *j-m das ~ brechen* break* s.o.'s heart; *sich ein ~ fassen* take* heart; *mit ganzem ~en* whole-hearted-ly; *schweren ~ens* with a heavy heart; *sich et. zu ~en nehmen* take* s.th. to heart; *es nicht übers ~en bringen zu* not have* the heart to; *et. auf dem ~en haben* have* s.th. on one's mind; *ins ~ schließen* take* to one's heart; **~an-fall** *m* heart attack

Herzens|lust *f*: *nach ~* to one's heart's content; **~wunsch** *m* heart's desire, dearest wish

Herz|fehler *med. m* cardiac defect; **2̥haft** *adj.* hearty; *nicht süß:* savo(u)ry; **2̥ig** *adj.* sweet, lovely, *Am. a.* cute; **~in-farkt** *med. m* cardiac infarct(ion), F *mst* heart attack, coronary; **~klopfen** *n* palpitation; *er hatte ~ (vor)* his heart was throbbing (with); **2̥krank** *adj.* suf-fering from (a) heart disease; **2̥lich 1.** *adj.* cordial, hearty; *Empfang, Lächeln etc.: a.* warm, friendly; **2.** *adv.:* ~ *gern* with pleasure; **2̥los** *adj.* heartless

Herzog *m* duke; **~in** *f* duchess

Herz|schlag *m* heartbeat; *Herztod:* heart failure; **~schrittmacher** *med. m* (cardiac) pacemaker; **~verpflanzung**

med. f heart transplant; **2zerreißend** *adj.* heart-rending

Hetz|e *f* hurry, rush; *pol. etc.* agitation, campaign(ing) (**gegen** against); **2en 1.** *v/t.* rush; *Tiere:* hunt, chase; **e-n Hund auf j-n ~** set* a dog on s.o.; **2.** *v/i. eilen:* hurry, rush; *pol. etc.* agitate (**gegen** against); **2erisch** *adj.* inflammatory; **~jagd** *f* hunt(ing), chase (*a. fig.*); *Eile:* rush; **~kampagne** *f* smear campaign

Heu *n* hay; **~boden** *m* hayloft

Heuch|elei *f* hypocrisy; *Gerede:* cant; **2eln** *v/i. u. v/t.* feign, simulate; **~ler** *m* hypocrite; **2lerisch** *adj.* hypocritical

Heuer *naut. f* pay

heuer *südd. u. östr. adv.* this year

heuern *v/t.* hire; *naut. a.* sign on

heulen *v/i.* howl; F *contp. weinen:* bawl; *mot.* roar; *Sirene:* whine

Heu|schnupfen *med. m* hay fever; **~schrecke** *zo. f* grasshopper; locust

heut|e *adv.* today; **~ abend** this evening, tonight; **~ früh**, **~ morgen** this morning; **~ in acht Tagen** a week from now, *Brt. a.* today week; **~ vor acht Tagen** a week ago today; **~ig** *adj.* today's; *gegenwärtig:* of today, present(-day); **~zutage** *adv.* nowadays, these days

Hexe *f* witch (*a. fig.*); *alte ~* (old) hag; **2n** *v/i.* practice witchcraft; F *fig.* work miracles; **~nkessel** *m* inferno; **~nschuß** *med. m* lumbago

Hieb *m* blow, stroke; *Faust2: a.* punch; *Peitschen2: a.* lash, cut; **~e** *pl.* beating *sg.*; thrashing *sg.*

hier *adv.* here, in this place; *anwesend:* present; **~ entlang!** this way!

hier|an *adv.* from *od.* in this; **~auf** *adv.* on it *od.* this; *zeitlich:* after this, then; **~aus** *adv.* from *od.* out of this; **~bei** *adv.* here, in this case; *bei dieser Gelegenheit:* on this occasion; **~durch** *adv.* by this, hereby, this way; **~für** *adv.* for this; **~her** *adv.* (over) here, this way; *bis ~* so far (*a. zeitlich*); **~in** *adv.* in this; **~mit** *adv.* with this; *lit.* herewith; **~nach** *adv.* after this; *demzufolge:* according to this; **~über** *adv.* about this (subject); **~unter** *adv.* under this; *dazwischen:* among these; *verstehen:* by this *od.* that; **~von** *adv.* of *od.* from this; **~zu** *adv.* for this; *dazu:* to this

hiesig *adj.* local; *ein 2er* one of the locals

Hilfe *f* help; *Beistand:* aid (*a. econ.*), assistance (*a. med.*), relief (*für* to); *Erste ~* first aid; *um ~ rufen* cry for help; *mit ~ von* with the help of, *fig. a.* by means of; **~l help!**; **~menü** *n Computer:* help menu; **~ruf** *m* call (*od.* cry) for help; **~stellung** *f* support (*a. fig.*)

hilf|los *adj.* helpless; **~reich** *adj.* helpful

Hilfs|aktion *f* relief action; **~arbeiter(in)** unskilled worker; **2bedürftig** *adj.* needy; **2bereit** *adj.* helpful, ready to help; **~bereitschaft** *f* readiness to help, helpfulness; **~mittel** *n* aid; *tech. a.* device; **~organisation** *f* relief organization; **~verb** *n* auxiliary (verb)

Himbeere *bot. f* raspberry

Himmel *m* sky; *rel., fig.* heaven; *um ~s willen* for Heaven's sake; *~ und Hölle Kinderspiel:* hopscotch; → *heiter;* **2blau** *adj.* sky-blue; **~fahrt** *rel. f* Ascension (Day); **~fahrtskommando** *n* suicide mission

Himmels|körper *m* celestial body; **~richtung** *f* direction; *Kompaß:* cardinal point

himmlisch *adj.* heavenly; *fig. a.* marvel(l)ous

hin 1. *adv.* there; *bis ~ zu* as far as; *noch lange ~* still a long way off; *auf s-e Bitte (s-n Rat) ~* at his request (advice); *~ und her* to and fro, back and forth; *~ und wieder* now and then; *~ und zurück* there and back; *Fahrkarte:* return (ticket), *bsd. Am.* round trip, round-trip ticket; **2.** F *pred. adj. kaputt:* ruined; *erledigt: a.* done for; *weg:* gone

hinab *adv.* → *hinunter*

hinarbeiten *v/i.:* **~ auf** work towards

hinauf *adv.* up (there); *die Treppe ~:* upstairs; *die Straße etc. ~* up the street etc.; **~gehen** *v/i.* go* up; *fig. a.* rise*

hinaus *adv.* out; *aus ... ~* out of ...; *in ... ~* out into ...; *~ (mit dir)!* (get) out!, out you go!; **~gehen** *v/i.* go* out(side); *über* go* beyond; *~ auf Fenster etc.:* look out onto; *~ auf* come* out *od.* amount to; **~laufen** *v/i.* run* out(side); *~ auf* come* out *od.* amount to; **~schieben** *v/t.* put* off, postpone; **~stellen** *v/t. Sport:* send* off (the field); **~werfen** *v/t.* throw* out (*aus* of); *fig. a.* kick out; *entlassen: a.* (give*) *s.o.* the) sack, fire; **~wollen** *v/i.:* **auf et.**

~**aim** (*bsd. mit Worten*: drive* *od.* get*) at s.th.; **hoch** ~ aim high

Hin|blick *m*: **im** ~ **auf** in view of, with regard to; **⒉bringen** *v/t.* take* there

hinder|lich *adj.* hindering, impeding; *j-m* ~ **sein** be* in s.o.'s way; ~*n* *v/t.* hinder, hamper; ~ **an** prevent from; **⒉nis** *n* obstacle (*a. fig.*); **⒉nisrennen** *n* steeplechase

Hindu *m* Hindu; ~**ismus** *m* hinduism

hindurch *adv.* through; **das ganze Jahr** *etc.* ~ throughout the year *etc.*

hinein *adv.* in; ~ **mit dir!** in you go!; ~**gehen** *v/i.* go* in; ~ **in** go* into

hin|fallen *v/i.* fall* (down); ~**fällig** *adj. Person:* frail; *ungültig:* invalid; **⒉gabe** *f* devotion (**an** to); ~**geben** *v/t.* give* (up); **sich** ~ give* o.s. up; *widmen:* devote o.s. to; ~**halten** *v/t. Gegenstand etc.:* hold* out; *j-n:* put* s.o. off

hinken *v/i.* (walk with a) limp

hin|kommen *v/i.* get* there; ~**kriegen** F *v/t.* manage; ~**länglich** *adj.* sufficient; ~**legen** *v/t.* lay* *od.* put* down; **sich** ~ lie* down; ~**nehmen** *v/t. Beleidigung, etc.:* put* up with; ~**reißen** *v/t.* carry away; ~**reißend** *adj.* entrancing; *Schönheit:* breathtaking; ~**richten** *v/t.* execute; **⒉richtung** *f* execution; ~**setzen** *v/t.* set* *od.* put* down; **sich** ~ sit* down; **⒉sicht** *f* respect; **in gewisser** ~ in a way; ~**sichtlich** *prp.* with respect *od.* regard to; **⒉spiel** *n Sport:* first leg; ~**stellen** *v/t. abstellen:* put* (down); *j-n, et.* ~ **als** make* appear to be

hinten *adv.* at the back; **im Auto** *etc.:* in the back; **von** ~ from behind

hinter *prp.* behind; **⒉... in** Zssgn *Achse, Eingang, Rad, Reifen:* rear ...; **⒉bein** *n* hind leg; **⒉bliebenen** *pl.* the bereaved *pl.*; *bsd. jur.* surviving dependents *pl.*; ~**einander** *adv.* one after the other; **dreimal** ~ three times in a row; **⒉gedanke** *m* ulterior motive; ~**gehen** *v/t.* deceive; **⒉grund** *m* background (*a. fig.*); **⒉halt** *m* ambush; ~**hältig** *adj.* insidious, underhand(ed); **⒉haus** *n* rear building; ~**her** *adv.* behind, after; *zeitlich:* afterwards; **⒉hof** *m* backyard; **⒉kopf** *m* back of the head; ~**lassen** *v/t.* leave* (behind); **⒉lassenschaft** *f* property (left), estate; ~**legen** *v/t.* deposit (**bei** with); **⒉list** *f* deceit(fulness); *Trick:* (underhanded) trick; ~**listig**

adj. deceitful; underhand(ed); **⒉mann** *m* person (*mot.* car *etc.*) behind (one); *fig. mst pl.* person behind the scenes, brain(s *pl.*), mastermind; **⒉n** F *m* bottom, backside, behind, *bsd. Brt. sl.* bum; ~**rücks** *adv.* from behind; **⒉seite** *f* back; **⒉teil** *n* F → **Hintern**; **⒉treppe** *f* back stairs *pl.*; **⒉tür** *f* back door; ~**ziehen** *jur. Steuern:* evade; **⒉zimmer** *n* back room

hinüber *adv.* over, across; ~**sein** F *v/i. Kleid:* be* ruined; *Fleisch:* be* spoilt

hinunter *adv.* down; **die Treppe** ~: downstairs; **die Straße** ~ down the road

Hinweg *m* way there

hinweg *adv.:* **über ...** ~ over ...; ~**kommen** *v/i.:* ~ **über** get* over; ~**sehen** *v/i.:* ~ **über** ignore; ~**setzen** *v/refl.:* **sich** ~ **über** ignore, disregard

Hin|weis *m Verweis:* reference (**auf** to); *Wink:* hint, tip (as to, regarding); *Anzeichen:* indication (of), clue (as to); **⒉weisen 1.** *v/t.: j-n* ~ **auf** draw* *od.* call s.o.'s attention to; **2.** *v/i.:* ~ **auf** point at *od.* to, indicate; *fig.* point out, indicate; *anspielen:* hint at; ~**weisschild** *n*, ~**weistafel** *f* sign, notice; **⒉werfen** *v/t.* throw* down; ~**ziehen** *v/refl.* räumlich: extend (**bis zu** to), stretch (to); *zeitlich:* drag on

hinzu|fügen *v/t.* add (**zu** to) (*a. fig.*); ~**kommen** *v/i.* noch ~: be* added; *hinzu kommt, daß* add to this, ... and what is more, ...; ~**ziehen** *v/t. Arzt, Experten etc.:* call in, consult

Hirn *n anat.* brain; *fig.* brain(s *pl.*), mind; ~**gespinst** *n* fantasy; **⒉rissig**, **⒉verbrannt** F *adj.* crazy, cracked

Hirsch *zo. m* stag; ~**geweih** *n* antlers *pl.*; ~**kuh** *f* hind

Hirse *bot. f* millet

Hirt(e) *m* herdsman; *Schaf⒉, fig.:* shepherd

hissen *v/t. Flagge, Segel:* hoist

Histori|ker *m* historian; **⒉sch** *adj.* historical; *Ereignis etc.:* historic

Hitliste *f* top 40 *etc.*, charts *pl.*

Hitze *f* heat; ~**welle** *f* heat wave

hitz|ig *adj.* hot-tempered; *Debatte:* heated; **⒉kopf** *m* hothead; **⒉schlag** *med. m* heatstroke

HIV|-negativ *adj.* HIV negative; ~**positiv** *adj.* HIV positive; ~**-Positive(r)** HIV carrier

H

H-Milch f Brt. long-life milk
Hobby n hobby; **~...** in Zssgn amateur
...

Hobel m plane; **~bank** f carpenter's
bench; **2n** v/t. plane
hoch adj. u. adv. high; Baum, Haus etc.:
tall; Strafe: heavy, severe; Gast etc.:
distinguished; Alter: great, old;
Schnee: deep; math. **10 ~ 4** 10 to the
power of 4; **3000 Meter ~ fliegen** etc.: at
a height of 3,000 metres; **~ in hohem
Maße** highly, greatly; **~ verschuldet**
heavily in debt; **das ist mir zu ~** that's
above me
Hoch n meteor. high (a. fig.)
Hoch|achtung f (deep) respect (**vor**
for); **2achtungsvoll** adv. Brief: Yours
sincerely; **~bau** tech. m: Hoch- und
Tiefbau structural and civil engineering; **2betrieb** m rush; **2deutsch** adj.
High od. standard German; **~druck** m
high pressure (a. fig.); **~ebene** f
plateau, tableland; **form** f: in ~ in top
form od. shape; **~frequenz** electr. f
high frequency (a. in Zssgn); **~gebir-
ge** n high mountains pl.; **~genuß** m
real treat; **2gezüchtet** adj. zo., tech.
highbred; tech. a. sophisticated; mot.
tuned up, F souped up; **2hackig** adj.
high-heeled; **~haus** n high rise, tower
block; **~konjunktur** f econ. f boom;
~land n highlands pl.; **~leistungs...**
in Zssgn Sport etc.: high-performance
...; **~mut** m arrogance; **2mütig** adj.
arrogant; **~ofen** tech. m blast furnace;
2prozentig adj. Schnaps etc.: high-
proof; **~rechnung** f projection; bei
Wahl: computer prediction; **~saison** f
peak (od. busy) time (of the) season;
~schulabschluß m degree; **~schul-
ausbildung** f higher education; **~
schule** f university; college; academy;
△ nicht high school; **~seefischerei** f
deep-sea fishing; **~sommer** m mid-
summer; **~spannung** electr. f high
tension (a. fig.) od. voltage; **~sprung**
m high jump
höchst 1. adj. highest; fig. a.: supreme;
äußerst: extreme; **2.** adv. highly, most,
extremely
Höchst... in Zssgn mst maximum od.
top
Hochstapler m impostor, swindler
höchstens adv. at (the) most, at best

Höchst|form f Sport: top form od.
shape; **~geschwindigkeit** f top speed
(**mit** at); Begrenzung: speed limit; **~lei-
stung** f Sport: record (performance);
tech. e-r Maschine etc.: maximum output; **~maß** n maximum (**an** of);
2wahrscheinlich adv. most likely od.
probably
Hoch|technologie f hi(gh) tech(nolo-
gy); **2trabend** fig. adj. pompous;
~verrat m high treason; **2wasser** n
high tide; Überschwemmung: flood;
~wertig adj. high-grade, high-quality
Hochzeit f wedding; **~s...** in Zssgn Geschenk, Kleid, Tag etc.: wedding ...;
~sreise f honeymoon
Hocke f crouch, squat; **2n** v/i. squat,
crouch; F sit*; **~r** m stool
Höcker m Kamel2 etc.: hump
Hockey n hockey, Am.: field hockey
Hoden anat. m testicle
Hof m yard; agr. farm; Innen2:
court(yard); Fürsten2: court; **~dame** f
lady-in-waiting
hoffen v/i. u. v/t. hope (**auf** for); zuversichtlich: trust (in); das Beste ~ hope
for the best; ich hoffe es I hope so; ich
hoffe nicht, ich will es nicht ~ I hope
not; **~tlich** adv. I hope, let's hope,
hopefully
Hoffnung f hope (**auf** of); sich ~en machen have* hopes; die ~ aufgeben
lose* hope; **2slos** adj. hopeless;
2svoll adj. hopeful; vielversprechend:
promising
Hofhund m watchdog
höflich adj. polite, courteous (**zu** to);
2keit f politeness, courtesy
Höhe f height; aviat., math., astr., geogr.
altitude; An2: hill; Gipfel: peak (a. fig.);
e-r Summe, Strafe etc.: amount; Niveau: level; Ausmaß: extent; mus. pitch;
auf gleicher ~ mit on a level with; in
die ~ up; ich bin nicht ganz auf der ~
I'm not feeling up to the mark
Hoheit f pol. sovereignty; Titel: Highness; **~sgebiet** n territory; **~sgewäs-
ser** n. territorial waters pl.; **~szei-
chen** n national emblem
Höhen|luft f mountain air; **~messer** m
altimeter; **~ruder** aviat. n elevator;
~sonne med. f ultraviolet lamp, sun-
lamp; **~zug** m mountain chain
Höhepunkt m climax (a. thea. u. sexu-

H

ell), culmination, height, peak; *e-s Abends etc.*: highlight

hohl *adj.* hollow (*a. fig.*)

Höhle *f* cave, cavern; *zo.* hole, burrow; *Lager*: den, lair

Hohl|maß *n* measure of capacity; **~raum** *m* hollow, cavity; **~spiegel** *m* concave mirror; **~weg** *m* defile

Hohn *m* derision, scorn; **~gelächter** *n* jeering laughter, jeers *pl.*

höhnisch *adj.* derisive, scornful; **~es Lächeln** sneer

holen *v/t.* (go* and) get*, fetch, go* for; *Atem*: draw*; *Polizei, ans Telefon*: call; **~ lassen** send* for; *sich ~ Krankheit etc.*: catch*, get*; *Rat etc.*: seek*

Holland Holland, *the* Netherlands

Holländ|er(in) Dutch|man (-woman); **2isch** *adj.* Dutch

Hölle *f* hell; **in die ~ kommen** go* to hell; **~nlärm** *m a* hell of a noise; **~nmaschine** *f* time bomb

Holler *bot. östr. m* elder

höllisch *adj.* infernal (*a. fig.*)

holper|ig *adj.* bumpy (*a. fig.*), rough, uneven; *Sprache*: clumsy; **~n** *v/i. Wagen*: jolt, bump; *fig.* be* bumpy

Holunder *m* elder

Holz *n* wood; *Nutz2*: timber, *Am. a.* lumber; **aus ~** (made) of wood, wooden; **~ hacken** chop wood; **~bearbeitung** *f* woodwork(ing); **~blasinstrument** *mus. n* woodwind (instrument)

hölzern *adj.* wooden; *fig. a.* clumsy

Holz|fäller *m* woodcutter, *Am. a.* lumberjack; **~hammer** *m* mallet; *fig.* sledge-hammer (*a. in Zssgn*); **2ig** *adj.* woody; *Gemüse*: stringy; **~kohle** *f* charcoal; **~schnitt** *m* woodcut; **~schnitzer** *m* wood carver; **~schuh** *m* clog; **~weg** *fig. m*: **auf dem ~ sein** be* barking up the wrong tree; **~wolle** *f* wood shavings *pl.*, excelsior; **~wurm** *m* woodworm

homöopathisch *adj.* hom(o)eopathic

homosexuell *adj.*, **2e(r)** homosexual, gay; *Frau*: *mst* lesbian

Honig *m* honey; **~wabe** *f* honeycomb

Honor|ar *n* fee; **2ieren** *v/t.* pay* (a fee to); *fig.* appreciate, reward

Hopfen *m bot.* hop; *Brauerei*: hops *pl.*

hoppla *int.* (wh)oops!

hopsen F *v/i.* hop, jump

Hör|apparat *m* hearing aid; **2bar** *adj.* audible

horche|n *v/i.* listen (**auf** to); *heimlich*: eavesdrop; **2r** *m* eavesdropper

Horde *f* horde (*a. zo.*); *contp. a.* mob, gang

hör|en *v/i. u. v/t.* hear*; *an~, Radio, Musik etc.*: listen to; *gehorchen*: obey, listen; **~ auf** listen to; **von j-m ~** hear* from (*durch Dritte*: of, about) s.o.; **er hört schwer** his hearing is bad; **hör(t) mal!** listen!; *erklärend: a.* look; **hör(t) nun** *od.* **also hör(t) mal!** *Einwand*: wait a minute!, now look *od.* listen here!; **2er** *m* listener; *tel.* receiver; **2erin** *f* listener; **2fehler** *med. m* hearing defect; **2gerät** *n* hearing aid; **~ig** *adj.*: **j-m ~ sein** be* s.o.'s slave

Horizont *m* horizon (*a. fig.*); **s-n ~ erweitern** broaden one's mind; **das geht über meinen ~** that's beyond me; **2al** *adj.* horizontal

Hormon *n* hormone

Horn *n* horn; **~haut** *f* horny skin, callus(es *pl.*); *Auge*: cornea

Hornisse *zo. f* hornet

Horoskop *n* horoscope

Hör|rohr *med. n* stethoscope; **~saal** *m* lecture hall, auditorium; **~spiel** *n* radio play; **~weite** *f*: **in ~** within earshot

Höschen *n* panties *pl.*

Hose *f* (*e-e ~* a pair of) trousers *pl.*, *Am.* pants *pl.*; *bsd. sportliche*: slacks *pl.*; *kurze*: shorts *pl.*; **~nanzug** *m* trouser (*Am.* pants) suit; **~nrock** *m* (*ein ~* a pair of) culottes *pl.*; **~nschlitz** *m* fly; **~ntasche** *f* trouser pocket; **~nträger** *pl.* (a pair of) braces *pl. od. Am.* suspenders *pl.*

Hospital *n* hospital

Hostie *rel. f* host

Hotel *n* hotel; **~direktor** *m* hotel manager; **~fach** *n* hotel business; **~zimmer** *n* hotel room

HP *Abk. für Halbpension* half board

Hr(n). *Abk. für Herrn* Mr

Hubraum *mot. m* cubic capacity

hübsch *adj.* pretty, nice(-looking), *bsd. Am. a.* cute; *Geschenk etc.*: nice, lovely

Hubschrauber *m* helicopter; **~landeplatz** *m* heliport

Huf *m* hoof; **~eisen** *n* horseshoe

Hüft|e *f* hip; **~gelenk** *n* hip joint; **~gürtel** *m* girdle

Hügel *m* hill; **⌒ig** *adj.* hilly; **~land** *n* downs *pl.*
Huhn *n* chicken; *Henne*: hen
Hühnchen *n* chicken; ***ein ~ zu rupfen haben*** have* a bone to pick
Hühner|auge *med. n* corn; **~brühe** *f* chicken broth; **~ei** *n* hen's egg; **~farm** *f* poultry *od.* chicken farm; **~hof** *m* poultry *od.* chicken yard; **~hund** *m* pointer, setter; **~leiter** *f* chicken ladder; **~stall** *m* henhouse
huldigen *v/i.* pay* homage to; *e-m Laster etc.*: indulge in
Hülle *f* cover(ing), wrap(ping); *Schutz⌒, Buch⌒, Platten⌒*: jacket; *Schirm⌒*: sheath; ***in ~ und Fülle*** in abundance; **⌒n** *v/t.*: ***~ in*** wrap (up) in, cover in
Hülse *f Schote*: pod; *Getreide⌒*: husk; *tech.* case (*a. Patronen⌒*); **~nfrüchte** *pl.* pulse *sg.*
human *adj.* humane; **~itär** *adj.* humanitarian; **⌒ität** *f* humanity
Hummel *zo. f* bumblebee
Hummer *zo. m* lobster
Humor *m* humo(u)r; (***keinen***) ***~ haben*** have* a (no) sense of humo(u)r; **~ist** *m* humorist; **⌒istisch, ⌒voll** *adj.* humorous
humpeln *v/i.* hobble; *hinken*: limp
Hund *m zo.* dog; *Bergbau*: tub
Hunde|hütte *f* kennel, *Am.* doghouse; **~kuchen** *m* dog biscuit; **~leine** *f* lead, leash; **⌒müde** *adj.* dog-tired
hundert *adj.* a *od.* one hundred; ***zu ⌒en*** by the hundreds; **~fach** *adj.* hundredfold; **⌒jahrfeier** *f* centenary, *Am. a.* centennial; **~jährig** *adj.* a hundred years old; *Dauer*: a hundred years of; **~ste** *adj.* hundredth
Hündi|n *zo. f* bitch; **⌒sch** *fig. adj.* doglike, slavish
hunds|miserabel F *adj.* rotten, lousy; **⌒tage** *pl.* dog days *pl.*
Hüne *m* giant; **~ngrab** *n* dolmen
Hunger *m* hunger; ***~ bekommen*** get* hungry; ***~ haben*** be* hungry; ***vor ~ sterben*** die of starvation, starve to death; **~lohn** *m* starvation wages *pl.*; **⌒n** *v/i.* go* hungry, *stärker*: starve; **~snot** *f* famine; **~streik** *m* hunger strike; **~tod** *m* (death from) starvation
hungrig *adj.* hungry (***nach***, ***auf*** for)
Hupe *mot. f* horn; **⌒n** *v/i.* sound one's horn, hoot, honk
hüpfen *v/i.* hop, skip; *Ball etc.*: bounce
Hürde *f* hurdle; *fig. a.* obstacle; *Pferch*: fold, pen; **~nlauf** *m* hurdle race; *Sportart*: hurdles *pl.*; **~nläufer(in)** hurdler
Hure *f* whore, prostitute
huschen *v/i.* flit, dart
hüsteln *v/i.* cough slightly; *iro.* hem
husten *v/i.*, **⌒** *m* cough; **⌒bonbon** *m, n* cough drop; **⌒saft** *m* cough syrup
Hut[1] *m* hat; ***den ~ aufsetzen*** (***abnehmen***) put* on (take* off) one's hat
Hut[2] *f*: ***auf der ~ sein*** be* on one's guard (***vor*** against)
hüten *v/t.* guard, protect, watch over; *Schafe etc.*: herd, mind; *Kind, Haus*: look after; ***das Bett ~*** be* confined to (one's) bed; ***sich ~ vor*** beware of; ***sich ~, et. zu tun*** be* careful not to do s.th.
Hutkrempe *f* (hat) brim
hutschen *östr. v/t. u. v/i.* → ***schaukeln***
Hütte *f* hut; *schäbige*: shack; *Häuschen*: cottage, cabin; *Berg⌒*: mountain hut; *tech.* ironworks
Hyäne *zo. f* hy(a)ena
Hyazinthe *bot. f* hyacinth
Hydrant *m* hydrant
hydraulisch *adj.* hydraulic
Hydrokultur *f* hydroponics *sg.*
Hygien|e *f* hygiene; **⌒isch** *adj.* hygienic
Hymne *f* hymn; → ***Nationalhymne***
Hypno|se *f* hypnosis; **~tiseur** *m* hypnotist; **⌒tisieren** *v/t.* hypnotize
Hypotenuse *math. f* hypotenuse
Hypothek *f* mortgage; ***e-e ~ aufnehmen*** take* out a mortgage
Hypothe|se *f* hypothesis, supposition; **⌒tisch** *adj.* hypothetical
Hysteri|e *f* hysteria; **⌒sch** *adj.* hysterical

i.A. *Abk. für* **im Auftrag** p.p., per procuration

ICE *Abk. für* **Intercity Expreß** intercity express (train)

ich *pers. pron.* I; ~ **selbst** (I) myself; **ich bin's** it's me

ideal *adj.*, **2** *n* ideal; **2ismus** *m* idealism; **2ist** *m* idealist

Idee *f* idea

identi|fizieren *v/t.* identify; **sich ~ mit** identify with; **~sch** *adj.* identical; **2-tätskarte** *östr. f* identity card

Ideolog|e *m* ideologist; **~ie** *f* ideology; **2isch** *adj.* ideological

idiomatisch *ling. adj.* idiomatic; **~er Ausdruck** idiom

Idiot *m* idiot; **~enhügel** F *m* nursery slope, F dope slope; **2ensicher** *adj.* foolproof; **2isch** *adj.* idiotic

Idol *n* idol

Idyll||(e f) *n* idyll(l); **2isch** *adj.* idyllic

Igel *m* hedgehog

ignorieren *v/t.* ignore, disregard

i.H. *Abk. für* **im Hause** on the premises

ihr *poss. pron.* her; *pl.* their; **Ihr** *sg. u. pl.* your; **~erseits** *adv.* on her (*pl.* their) part; **~esgleichen** *indef. pron.* her (*pl.* their) equals *pl.*, people *pl.* like herself (*pl.* themselves); **~etwegen** *adv.* for her (*pl.* their) sake

Ikone *f* icon (*a.* Computer)

illegal *adj.* illegal; **~itim** *adj.* illegitimate

Illus|ion *f* illusion; **2orisch** *adj.* illusory

Illu|stration *f* illustration; **2strieren** *v/t.* illustrate; **~strierte** *f* magazine

im *prep.* in; ~ **Bett** in bed; ~ **Kino etc.** at the cinema *etc.*; ~ **Erdgeschoß** on the ground (*Am.* first) floor; ~ **Mai** in May; ~ **Jahre 1995** in (the year) 1995; ~ **Stehen etc.** (while) standing up *etc.*; → **in**

imaginär *adj.* imaginary

Imbiß *m* snack; **~stube** *f* snack bar

imitieren *v/t.* imitate

Imker *m* beekeeper

immatrikulieren *v/t. u. v/refl.* enrol(l), register

immer *adv.* always, all the time; ~ **mehr** more and more; ~ **wieder** again and again; **für ~** for ever, for good; **2grün** *bot. n* evergreen; **~hin** *adv.* after all; **~zu** *adv.* all the time, constantly

Immigrant(in) immigrant

Immissionen *pl.* (harmful effects *pl.* of) noise, pollutants *pl.*, *etc.*

Immobilien *pl.* real estate *sg.*; **~makler** *m* (*Am.*) real estate agent, *Am. a.* realtor

immun *adj.* immune (**gegen** to, against, from); ~ **machen** → **immunisieren** *v/t.* immunize; **2schein** *m* vaccination certificate; **2stoff** *med. m* vaccine, serum; **2ung** *f* vaccination

Imperativ *gr. m* imperative (mood)

Imperfekt *gr. n* past (tense)

Imperialis|mus *m* imperialism; **~t** *m*, **2tisch** *adj.* imperialist

impf|en *med. v/t.* vaccinate; **2paß** *m* vaccination card; **2schein** *m* vaccination certificate; **2stoff** *med. m* vaccine, serum; **2ung** *f* vaccination

imponieren *v/i.*: **j-m ~** impress s.o.

Import *m* import(ation); **~eur** *m* importer; **2ieren** *v/t.* import

imposant *adj.* impressive, imposing

imprägnier|en *v/t.*, **~t** *adj.* waterproof

improvisieren *v/t. u. v/i.* improvise

Impuls *m* impulse; *Anstoß:* *a.* stimulus; **2iv** *adj.* impulsive

imstande *adj.*: ~ **sein** be* capable of

in *prp.* **1.** *räumlich: wo?* in, at; *innerhalb:* within, inside; *wohin?* into, in; *überall* ~ all over; ~ **der Stadt** in town; ~ **der Schule** at school; ~ **die Schule** to school; **~s Kino** to the cinema; **~s Bett** to bed; **warst du schon mal ~ ...?** have you ever been to ...?; → **im**; **2.** *zeitlich:* in, at, during; ~ **dieser** (**dieser Woche** this (next) week; ~ **diesem Alter** (**Augenblick**) at this age (moment); ~ **der Nacht** at night; **heute ~ acht Tagen** a week from now, *Brt. a.* today week; **heute ~ e-m Jahr** this time next year; → **im**; **3.** *Art u. Weise etc.:* **gut sein ~** be* good at; ~ **Eile** in a hurry; ~ **Behandlung** (**Reparatur**) under treatment (repair); **~s Deutsche** into German; → **im**; **3.** F: ~ **sein** be* in

Inbegriff *m* epitome

inbegriffen *adj.* included

indem *cj. während*: while, as; *dadurch, daß*: by *doing s.th.*

Inder(in) Indian

Indian *östr. m* turkey (cock)

Indianer(in) Native American, (American) Indian

Ind|ien India

Indikativ *gr. m* indicative (mood)

indirekt *adj.* indirect; *gr. a.* reported

indisch *adj.* Indian

indiskret *adj.* indiscreet; **2ion** *f* indiscretion

indiskutabel *adj.* out of the question

individu|ell *adj.*, **2um** *n* individual

Indiz *n* indication, sign; *Indizien pl. jur.* circumstantial evidence *sg.*

industrialisier|en *v/t.* industrialize; **2ung** *f* industrialization

Industrie *f* industry; **~...** *in Zssgn mst* industrial ...; **~abfälle** *pl.* industrial waste *sg.*; **~gebiet** *n* industrial area

industriell *adj.* industrial; **2e** *m* industrialist

Industriestaat *m* industrial nation

ineinander *adv.* into one another; **~verliebt** in love with each other; **~greifen** *tech. v/i.* interlock (*a. fig.*)

Infanter|ie *mil. f* infantry; **~ist** *mil. m* infantryman

Infektion *med.* infection; **~skrankheit** *med. f* infectious disease

Infinitiv *gr. m* infinitive (mood)

infizieren *v/t.* infect

Inflation *f* inflation

infolge *prp.* owing to, due to; **~dessen** *adv.* consequently

Inform|atik *f* computer science; **~atiker(in)** computer scientist; **~ation** *f* information; *die neuesten ~en pl.* the latest information *sg.*; **2ieren** *v/t.* inform; *falsch ~* misinform

infra|rot *phys. adj.* infrared; **2struktur** *f* infrastructure

Ing. *Abk. für Ingenieur* eng., engineer

Ingenieur *m* engineer

Ingwer *m* ginger

Inhaber *m* owner, proprietor; *e-s Amtes etc.*: holder

Inhalt *m* contents *pl.*; *Raum2*: volume, capacity; *fig. Sinn*: meaning

Inhalts|angabe *f* summary; **~verzeichnis** *n Buch*: table of contents

Initiative *f* initiative; *die ~ ergreifen* take* the initiative

inklusive *prp.* including

inkonsequen|t *adj.* inconsistent; **2z** *f* inconsistency

Inkrafttreten *n* coming into force, taking effect

Inland *n* home (country); *Landesinnere*: inland; **~flug** *m* domestic (*od.* internal) flight

inländisch *adj.* domestic, home

Inlett *n* ticking

inmitten *prp.* in the middle of

innen *adv.* inside; *nach ~* inwards

Innen|architekt(in) interior designer; **~architektur** *f* interior design; **~minister** *m* minister of the interior; *Brt.* Home Secretary, *Am.* Secretary of the Interior; **~ministerium** *n* ministry of the interior; *Brt.* Home Office, *Am.* Department of the Interior; **~politik** *f* domestic politics; **2politisch** *adj.* domestic, internal; **~seite** *f*: *auf der ~* (on the) inside; **~stadt** *f* (city *od.* town) cent|re, *Am.* -er, *Am. a.* downtown

inner *adj.* inside; *seelisch*: inner; *med., pol.* internal; **2e** *n* interior, inside

Innereien *pl. gastr.* offal *sg.*; *Fisch*: guts *pl.*

inner|halb *prp.* within; **~lich** *adj.* internal (*a. med.*)

innert *prp. Schweiz*: within

innig *adj.* tender, affectionate

Innung *f* guild

inoffiziell *adj.* unofficial

ins *prep.* → *in*

Insasse *m e-s Autos*: passenger; *e-r Anstalt etc.*: inmate; **~nversicherung** *f* passenger insurance

insbesondere *adv.* particularly, (e)specially

Inschrift *f* inscription, legend

Insekt *n* insect, *bsd. Am.* bug; **~enstich** *m* insect bite

Insel *f* island; **~bewohner** *m* islander

Inser|at *n* advertisement, F ad; **2ieren** *v/t. u. v/i.* advertise

insgeheim *adv.* secretly

insgesamt *adv.* altogether, in all

insofern 1. *adv.* as far as that goes; 2. *cj.*: **~ als** in so far as

Inspek|tion *f* inspection; *mot.* service; **~or(in)** inspector

inspizieren *v/t.* inspect

Install|ateur *m* plumber; (gas *od.* electrical) fitter; **2ieren** *v/t.* put* in, fit, instal(l)

instand adv.: ~ **halten** keep* in good condition od. repair; tech. maintain; ~ **setzen** repair; **Qhaltung** f maintenance; **Qsetzung** f repair

inständig adv.: **j-n ~ bitten** implore s.o.

Instanz f authority; jur. instance

Instinkt m instinct; **Qiv** adv. instinctively

Institut n institute; **~ion** f institution

Instrument n instrument

inszenier|en v/t. (put*) on stage; Film: direct; fig. stage; **Qung** f production

intellektuell adj., **Qe(r)** intellectual, F highbrow

intelligen|t adj. intelligent; **Qz** f intelligence; **Qzquotient** m I.Q.

Intendant thea. m director

intensiv adj. gründlich: intensive; stark: intense; **Qkurs** m crash course

interess|ant adj. interesting; **Qe** n interest (**an, für** in); **~elos** adj. uninterested, indifferent; **Qelosigkeit** f indifference; **Qengebiet** n field of interest; **Qengemeinschaft** f community of interests; econ. combine, pool; **Qent** m interested person; econ. prospective buyer, bsd. Am. prospect; **~ieren** v/t. interest (**für** in); **sich ~ für** take* an interest in; be* interested in

intern adj. internal

Internat n boarding school

international adj. international

Internist med. m internist

Inter|pretation f interpretation; Literatur: a. analysis; **Qpretieren** v/t. interpret, ana/lyse, Am. -lyze; **~punktion** f punctuation; **~vall** n interval; **Qvenieren** v/i. intervene; **~view** n, **Qviewen** v/t. interview

intim adj. intimate (**mit** with) (a. sexuell); **Qität** f intimacy; **Qsphäre** f privacy

intoleran|t adj. intolerant (**gegen** of); **Qz** f intolerance

intransitiv gr. adj. intransitive

Intrig|e f intrigue, scheme, plot; **Qieren** v/i. (plot and) scheme

Invalid|e m invalid; **~enrente** f disability pension; **~ität** f disablement, disability

Inventar n inventory, stock

Inventur econ. f stocktaking; **~ machen** take* stock

invest|ieren v/t. invest (a. fig.); **Qition** f investment

inwie|fern cj. u. adv. in what respect od.

~**weit** cj. u. adv. to what extent

Inzucht f inbreeding

inzwischen adv. meanwhile, in the meantime; jetzt: by now

irdisch adj. earthly, worldly

Ire m Irishman; **die ~n** pl. the Irish pl.

irgend adv. in Zssgn: some...; any... (a. verneint u. fragend); **wenn ~ möglich** if at all possible; **wenn du ~ kannst** if you possibly can; F **so ein** some; **~ et.** something; anything; **~ j.** someone, somebody; anyone, anybody; **~ein(e)** indef. pron. some(one); any(one); **~ein(e)s** indef. pron. some; any; **~wann** adv. unbestimmt: sometime (or other); beliebig: (at) any time; **~wie** adv. somehow (or other); **~wo** adv. somewhere; anywhere

Ir|in f Irishwoman; **Qisch** adj. Irish; **~land** Ireland

Iron|ie f irony; **Qisch** adj. ironic(al)

irre adj. mad, crazy, insane; verwirrt: confused; F sagenhaft: super, terrific

Irre m, f mad|man (-woman), lunatic; **wie ein ~r** like mad od. a madman

irre|führen bsd. fig. v/t. mislead*, lead* astray; **~führend** adj. misleading; **~gehen** v/i. go* astray; fig. a. be* wrong; **~machen** v/t. confuse

irren 1. v/refl. be* wrong od. mistaken; **sich in et. ~** get* s.th. wrong; **2.** v/i. wander, stray, err; **Sie ~** you are wrong

Irrenanstalt f mental hospital

irritieren v/t. ärgern, reizen: irritate; F verwirren: confuse

Irr|licht n will-o'-the-wisp (a. fig.); **~sinn** m madness; **Qsinnig** adj. insane, mad; F Tempo etc.: a. terrific; **~tum** m error, mistake; **im ~ sein** be* mistaken; **Qtümlich** adv. by mistake

Ischias med. m, n, f sciatica

Islam m Islam

Island Iceland

Isländ|er(in) Icelander; **Qisch** adj. Icelandic

Isolier|band n insulating tape; **Qen** v/t. isolate; electr., tech. insulate; **~haft** f solitary confinement; **~station** med. f isolation ward; **~ung** f isolation; electr., tech. insulation

Israel Israel

Israeli m, f, **Qsch** adj. Israeli

Italien Italy; **~er(in)**, **Qisch** adj. Italian

I-Tüpfelchen n: **bis aufs ~** to a T

J

ja *adv.* yes, F *a.* yeah; *naut., parl.* aye, *Am. parl.* yea; **wenn** ~ if so; **da ist er ~!** well, there he is!; **ich sagte es Ihnen ~** I told you so; **ich bin ~ (schließlich)** ... after all, I am ...; **tut es ~!** don't you dare do it!; **sei '~ vorsichtig!** do be careful!; **vergessen Sie es '~ nicht!** be sure not to forget it!; **~, weißt du nicht?** why, don't you know?; **du kommst doch, ~?** you're coming, aren't you?

Jacht *naut. f* yacht

Jacke *f* jacket; *längere, a. Anzug*♀, *Kostüm*♀: coat; **~tt** *n* jacket, coat

Jagd *f* hunt(ing) (*a. fig.*); *mit dem Gewehr*: *a.* shoot(ing); *Verfolgung*: chase; → **Jagdrevier**; **auf (die) ~ gehen** go* hunting *od.* shooting; ~ **machen auf** hunt (for); *j-n: a.* chase; **~aufseher** *m* gamekeeper; **~bomber** *mil. m* fighter bomber; **~flieger** *mil. m* fighter pilot; **~flugzeug** *mil. n* fighter (plane); **~hund** *m* hound; **~hütte** *f* (hunting) lodge; **~revier** *n* hunting ground; **~schein** *m* hunting *od.* shooting licen|ce, *Am.* -se

jagen *v/t. u. v/i.* hunt; *mit dem Gewehr: a.* shoot*; *fig. rasen*: race, dash; *fig. verfolgen*: hunt; chase; **aus dem Haus** *etc.* ~ drive* *od.* chase out of the house *etc.*

Jäger *m* hunter, huntsman

Jaguar *zo. m* jaguar

jäh *adj.* sudden; *steil*: steep

Jahr *n* year; **ein dreiviertel ~** nine months *pl.*; **einmal im ~** once a year; **im ~e 1995** in (the year) 1995; **ein 20 ~e altes Auto** a twenty-year-old car; **mit 18 ~en, im Alter von 18 ~en** at (the age of) eighteen; **heute vor e-m ~** a year ago today; **die 80er ~e** the eighties *pl.*; **♀aus** *adv.*: ~, **jahrein** year in, year out; **year after year**; **~buch** *n* yearbook, annual

jahrelang 1. *adj.* longstanding, (many) years of; **2.** *adv.* for (many) years

Jahres|... in *Zssgn Bericht, Bilanz, Einkommen etc.*: annual ...; **~anfang** *m* beginning of the year; **~ende** *n* end of the year; **~tag** *m* anniversary; **~wechsel** *m* turn of the year; **~zahl** *f* date,

year; **~zeit** *f* season, time of (the) year

Jahrgang *m Personen*: age group; *Schule*: year, *Am. a.* class (**1995** of '95); *Wein*: vintage

Jahrhundert *n* century; **~wende** *f* turn of the century

jährlich 1. *adj.* annual, yearly; **2.** *adv.* every year, yearly, once a year

Jahr|markt *m* fair; **~tausend** *n* millennium; **~zehnt** *n* decade

Jähzorn *m* violent (*Ausbruch*: fit of) temper; **♀ig** *adj.* hot-tempered

Jalousie *f* (venetian) blind

Jammer *m* misery; **es ist ein ~** it is a pity

jämmerlich *adj.* miserable, wretched, *Anblick etc.*: *a.* pitiful, sorry; ~ **versagen** fail miserably

jammer|n *v/i.* moan, lament (*über* over, about); *sich beklagen*: complain (of, about); **~schade** *adj.*: **es ist ~, daß** it's a crying shame that

Janker *m* jacket

Jänner *östr. m*, **Januar** *m* January

Japan Japan; **~er(in)**, **♀isch** *adj.* Japanese

Jargon *m* jargon; slang

Jastimme *parl. f* aye, *Am.* yea

jäten *v/t.* weed (*a. Unkraut ~*)

Jauche *f* liquid manure; F *fig.* muck

jauchzen *v/i.* shout for *od.* with joy; *bsd. lit.* exult, rejoice

Jause *östr. f* snack

jawohl *adv.* (that's) right, (yes,) indeed; *mil.*, F yes, sir!

Jawort *n* consent; **(j-m) sein ~ geben** say* yes (to s.o.'s proposal)

je *adv. u. cj.* ever; each; per; *der beste Film, den ich ~ gesehen habe* the best film I have ever seen; ~ **zwei (Pfund)** two (pounds) each; **drei Mark ~ Kilo** three marks per kilo; ~ **nach Größe (Geschmack)** according to size (taste); ~ **nachdem(, wie)** it depends (on how); ~ **..., desto ...** the ... the ...

Jeans *pl., a. f*: (**e-e ~**) a pair of) jeans; **~jacke** *f* denim jacket

jede(r, -s) *indef. pron.* ~ **insgesamt**: every; ~ **beliebige**: any; ~ **einzelne**: each; *von zweien*: either; *jeder weiß (das)* everybody knows; **du kannst jeden fragen** (you can) ask anyone; **jeder von uns (euch)** each of us (you); **jeder, der** whoever; **jeden zweiten Tag** every other day; **jeden Augenblick** any moment now

jed|enfalls *adv.* in any case, anyhow; **~ermann** *indef. pron.* everyone, everybody; **~erzeit** *adv.* any time, always; **~esmal** *adv.* every time; **~ wenn** whenever

jedoch *cj.* however

jeher *adv.:* **von ~** always

jemals *adv.* ever; → **je**

jemand *indef. pron.* someone, somebody; *fragend, verneint:* anyone, anybody

jene(r, -s) *dem. pron.* that (one); *pl.* those *pl.*; **dies und jenes** this and that

jenseitig *adj.* opposite

jenseits *adv. u. prp.* on the other side (of), beyond (*a. fig.*)

Jenseits *n* next world, hereafter

jetzig *adj.* present; existing

jetzt *adv.* now, at present; **bis ~** up to now, so far; **erst ~** only now; **~ gleich** right now od. away; **für ~** for the present; **von ~ an** from now on

jeweil|ig *adj.* respective; **~s** *adv. je:* each; *gleichzeitig:* at a time

Jh. *Abk. für* **Jahrhundert** cent., century

Jochbein *anat. n* cheekbone

Jockei *m* jockey

Jod *chem. n* iodine

jodeln *v/i.* yodel

Joga *m, n* yoga

jogg|en *v/i.* jog; **2er** *m* jogger; **2ing** *n* jogging; **2inganzug** *m* tracksuit; **2inghose** *f* tracksuit trousers *pl.*

Joghurt *m, n* yog(h)urt, yoghourt

Johannisbeere *f*: **rote ~** redcurrant; **schwarze ~** blackcurrant

johlen *v/i.* howl, yell

Jolle *naut. f* dinghy, jolly boat

Jongl|eur *m* juggler; **2ieren** *v/t. u. v/i.* juggle

Joule *phys. n* joule

Journal|ismus *m* journalism; **~ist(in)** *m* journalist

jr. → **jun.**

Jubel *m* cheering, cheers *pl.*; *Freude:* rejoicing; **2n** *v/i.* cheer, shout for joy; *sich freuen:* rejoice

Jubiläum *n* anniversary; **50jähriges ~** fiftieth anniversary, (golden) jubilee

jucken *v/t. u. v/i.* itch; **es juckt mich am ...** my ... itches

Jude *m* Jewish person; **er ist ~** he is Jewish

Jüd|in *f* Jewish woman od. girl; **sie ist ~** she is Jewish; **2isch** *adj.* Jewish

Judo *n* judo

Jugend *f* youth; **die ~** young people *pl.*; **~amt** *n* youth welfare office; **~arbeitslosigkeit** *f* youth unemployment; **2frei** *adj.:* **~er Film** U (*Am.* G) (-rated) film; **nicht ~** X-rated; **~fürsorge** *f* youth welfare; **~gericht** *n* juvenile court; **~herberge** *f* youth hostel; **~klub** *m* youth club; **~kriminalität** *f* juvenile delinquency; **2lich** *adj.* youthful, young; **~liche(r)** young person, *m. a.* youth, *jur. a.* juvenile; **~stil** *m* Art Nouveau; **~strafanstalt** *f* detention cent|re, *Am.* -er, *Am. a.* reformatory; **~verbot** *n* for adults only; → **jugendfrei**; **~zentrum** *n* youth cent|re, *Am.* -er

Juli *m* July

jun. *Abk. für* **junior** Jun., jun.,Jnr., Jr., junior

jung *adj.* young; **~ verheiratet** newly married

Jumbo-Jet *m* jumbo (jet)

Junge¹ *m* boy; *junger Mann:* lad; *Kartenspiel:* jack, knave

Junge² *zo. n* young; *Hund: a.* puppy; *Katze: a.* kitten; *Raubtier: a.* cub; **~ bekommen** od. **werfen** have* young; **2nhaft** *adj.* boyish; **~nstreich** *m* boyish prank

jünger *adj.* younger

Jünger *rel. m* disciple (*a. fig.*)

Jungfer *f*: **alte ~** old maid

Jungfern|fahrt *naut. f* maiden voyage; **~flug** *aviat. m* maiden flight

Jung|frau *f* virgin; *astr.* Virgo; **er ist ~** he's (a) Virgo; **~geselle** *m* bachelor, single (man); **~gesellin** *f* bachelor girl, single (woman); *bsd. jur.* spinster

Jüngling *lit. iron. m* youth, young man

jüngste *adj.* youngest; *Ereignisse etc.:* latest; **in ~r Zeit** lately, recently; **das 2 Gericht, der 2 Tag** the Last Judg(e)ment, Doomsday

Juni *m* June

junior *adj.,* **2** *m* junior (*a. Sport*)

Jupe *m Schweiz*: skirt
Jura: ~ *studieren* study (the) law
juridisch *östr. adj.* → *juristisch*
Jurist|(in) lawyer; law student; **2isch** *adj.* legal
Jury *f* jury
Jurorenkomitee *östr. n* → *Jury*
justieren *tech. v/t.* adjust, set*
Justiz *f* (administration of) justice, (the) law; **~beamte** *m* judicial officer; **~irrtum** *m* error of justice; **~minister** *m* minister of justice; *Brt.* Lord Chancellor, *Am.* Attorney General; **~ministerium** *n* ministry of justice; *Am.* Department of Justice
Jute *f* jute; **~tasche** *f* jute bag
Juwel *m, n* jewel, gem (*beide a. fig.*); **~en** *pl.* jewel(le)ry; **~ier** *m* jewel(l)er

K

Kabarett *n* (political) revue
Kabel *n* cable; **~fernsehen** *n* cable TV
Kabeljau *zo. m* cod(fish)
Kabelnetz *n* cable network
Kabine *f* cabin; *Umkleide2, Dusch2 etc.*: cubicle; *Sport*: dressing room; *e-r Seilbahn*: car; *tel. etc.*: booth; **~nbahn** *f* cable railway
Kabinett *pol. n* cabinet
Kabis *m Schweiz*: green cabbage
Kabriolett *mot. n* convertible
Kachel *f, 2n v/t.* tile; **~ofen** *m* tiled stove
Kadaver *m* carcass
Kadett *m* cadet
Käfer *m* beetle, *Am. a.* bug
Kaffee *m* coffee (*kochen* make*); ~ *mit (ohne) Milch* white (black) coffee; **~bohne** *f* coffee bean; **~haus** *östr. n* café, coffee house; **~kanne** *f* coffeepot; **~maschine** *f* coffee maker; **~mühle** *f* coffee grinder
Käfig *m* cage (*a. fig.*)
kahl *adj. Mensch*: bald; *Baum, Fels, Wand*: bare; *Landschaft*: barren, bleak
Kahn *m* boat; *Last2*: barge
Kai *m* quay, wharf
Kaiser *m* emperor; **~in** *f* empress; **~reich** *n* empire
Kajüte *naut. f* cabin
Kakao *m* cocoa; *Getränk: a.* (hot) chocolate; *kalter*: chocolate milk
Kakt|ee *f*, **~us** *m* cactus
Kalb *n* calf; **2en** *v/i.* calve; **~fleisch** *n* veal; **~sbraten** *m* roast veal; **~sschnitzel** *n* veal cutlet; *paniertes*: escalope (of veal)

Kalender *m* calendar; **~jahr** *n* calendar year
Kali *chem. n* potash
Kaliber *n* calib|re, *Am.* -er (*a. fig.*)
Kalk *m* lime; *geol.* limestone, chalk; *med.* calcium; **2en** *v/t. Wand etc.*: whitewash; *agr.* lime; **2ig** *adj.* limy; **~stein** *m* limestone
Kalorie *f* calorie; **2arm** *adj.*, **2reduziert** *adj.* low-calorie, low in calories; **2nreich** *adj.* high-calorie, high *od.* rich in calories
kalt *adj.* cold; *mir ist* ~ I'm cold; *es (mir) wird* ~ it's (I'm) getting cold; **~bleiben** *fig. v/i.* keep* (one's) cool; **~blütig 1.** *adj.* cold-blooded (*a. fig.*); **2.** *adv.* in cold blood
Kälte *f* cold; *fig. e-r Person, Farbe*: coldness; *vor* ~ *zittern* shiver with cold; *fünf Grad* ~ five degrees below zero; **~einbruch** *m* cold snap; **~grad** *m* degree below zero; **~periode** *f* cold spell
kalt|lassen *v/t.*: *das läßt mich kalt* that leaves me cold; **~machen** F *v/t.* bump off, *Am. a.* rub out
Kamee *f* cameo
Kamel *n* camel; **~haar** *n* camelhair
Kamera *f* camera
Kamerad *m* companion, F mate, pal, *Am. a.* buddy; *mil. a.* fellow soldier; **~schaft** *f* comradeship; **2schaftlich** *adj. u. adv.* like a good fellow, comradely
Kamera|mann *m* cameraman; **~recorder** *m* camcorder
Kamille *f* camomile (*a. in Zssgn*)

K

Kamin m fireplace; *Schornstein:* chimney (*a. mount.*); **am ~** by the fire(side); **~kehrer** m chimney sweep; **~sims** m, n mantelpiece

Kamm m comb; *zo. a.* crest (*a. fig.*)

kämmen v/t. comb; **sich (die Haare) ~** comb one's hair

Kammer f (small) room; *Abstell♀:* storeroom, *bsd. Am.* closet; *Dach♀:* garret; *pol., econ.* chamber; *jur.* division; **~musik** f chamber music

Kammgarn n worsted (yarn)

Kampagne f campaign

Kampf m fight (*a. fig.*); *schwerer:* struggle (*a. fig.*); *bsd. mil.* combat; *Schlacht:* battle (*a. fig.*); *Wett♀:* contest, match; *Box♀:* fight, bout; *fig.* conflict; **♀bereit** adj. ready for battle (*mil.* combat)

kämpfen v/i. fight* (*gegen* against; *mit* with; *um* for) (*a. fig.*); struggle (*a. fig.*); *fig.* contend, wrestle

Kampfer m camphor

Kämpfer m fighter (*a. fig.*); **♀isch** adj. fighting, aggressive (*a. Sport*)

Kampf|flugzeug n combat aircraft; **~kraft** f fighting strength; **~richter** m judge; → *Schiedsrichter;* **~sportarten** pl. Judo, Karate: martial arts pl.

Kanad|a n Canada; **~ier** m, **~ierin** f, **♀isch** adj. Canadian

Kanal m *künstlicher:* canal; *natürlicher:* channel (*a. TV, tech., fig.*); *Abwasser♀:* sewer, drain; *der ~ (Ärmel♀)* the (English) Channel; **~isation** f sewerage (system); *Fluß:* canalization; **♀isieren** v/t. sewer; canalize; *fig.* channel; **~tunnel** m Channel Tunnel, F Chunnel

Kanarienvogel m canary

Kandid|at m candidate; **~atur** f candidacy, *Brt. a.* candidature; **♀ieren** v/i. stand* *od.* run* for election; **~ für ...** run for the office of ...

Känguruh n kangaroo

Kaninchen n rabbit

Kanister m (fuel) can, *Brt. a.* jerry can

Kanne f *Kaffee♀, Tee♀:* pot; *Milch♀, Öl♀, Gieß♀ etc.:* can

Kannibale m cannibal

Kanon *mus.* m canon, round

Kanone f gun; cannon; *sl. Revolver:* iron, *Am.* rod; F *Könner:* ace, *bsd. Sport: a.* crack

Kant|e f edge; **~en** m crust; **♀en** v/t.

set* on edge, tilt; *Skier:* edge; **♀ig** adj. angular, square(d)

Kantine f canteen

Kanton *pol.* m canton

Kanu n canoe

Kanüle *med.* f cannula, (drain) tube

Kanzel f *rel.* pulpit; *aviat.* cockpit

Kanzlei f office

Kanzler m chancellor

Kap *geogr.* n cape, headland

Kapazität f capacity; *fig.* authority

Kapell|e f *rel.* chapel; *mus.* band; **~meister** m conductor

kapern *naut.* v/t. capture, seize

kapieren F v/t. get*; *kapiert?* got it?

Kapital n capital, funds pl.; **~anlage** f investment; **~ismus** m capitalism; **~ist** m, **♀istisch** adj. capitalist; **~verbrechen** n capital crime

Kapitän m captain (*a. Sport*)

Kapitel n chapter (*a. fig.*); F *fig.* story

Kapitul|ation f capitulation, surrender (*a. fig.*); **♀ieren** v/i. capitulate, surrender (*a. fig.*)

Kaplan *rel.* m curate

Kappe f cap; *tech. a.* top, hood; **♀n** v/t. *Tau:* cut*; *Baum:* lop, top

Kapsel f capsule; *Hülse:* case, box

kaputt adj. broken; *Lift etc.:* out of order; *erschöpft:* dead beat; *Ruf, Gesundheit etc.:* ruined; *Ehe etc.:* broken; **~gehen** v/i. break*; *mot. etc.* break* down; *Ehe etc.:* break* up; **~machen** v/t. break*, wreck (*a. fig.*), ruin (*a. fig.*)

Kapuze f hood; *Mönchs♀:* cowl

Karabiner m *Gewehr:* carbine; **~haken** m karabiner, snaplink

Karaffe f decanter, carafe

Karambolage f collision, crash

Karat n carat

Karate n karate

Karawane f caravan

Kardinal *rel.* m cardinal

Karfiol *östr.* m cauliflower

Karfreitag m *rel.* Good Friday

karg, kärglich adj. meag|re, *Am.* -er, scanty; *Essen, Leben: a.* frugal; *Boden:* poor

kariert adj. checked, chequered, *Am.* checkered; *Papier:* squared; F **~es Zeug reden** talk rot

Karies f *med.* (dental) caries

Karik|atur f *mst* cartoon; *bsd. fig.* caricature; **~aturist(in)** cartoonist; **Qieren** v/t. caricature

Karneval m carnival, Shrovetide

Karo n square, check; *Kartenspiel:* diamonds pl.

Karosserie mot. f body

Karotte f carrot

Karpfen m carp

Karre f, **~n** m cart; *Schub2:* wheelbarrow; F *Auto:* jalopy

Karriere f career; **~ machen** work one's way up, get* to the top

Karte f card; *Land2:* map; *See2:* chart; *Fahr2, Eintritts2:* ticket; *Speise2:* menu; *gute ~* a good hand

Kartei f card index; **~karte** f index od. file card; **~kasten** m card index box

Karten|haus n house of cards (a. fig.); *naut.* chartroom; **~spiel** n card game; *Karten:* pack (*Am.* a. deck) of cards; **~telefon** n cardphone; **~vorverkauf** m advance booking; *Stelle:* box office

Kartoffel f potato; **~brei** m mashed potatoes pl.; **~chips** pl. *Brt.* crisps pl., *Am.* (potato) chips pl.; **~kloß, ~knödel** m potato dumpling; **~puffer** m potato fritter; **~schalen** f potato peelings pl.; **~schäler** m potato peeler

Karton m *Material:* cardboard; *stärker:* pasteboard; *Schachtel:* cardboard box

Karussell n roundabout, merry-go-round, *Am.* a. car(r)ousel

Karwoche rel. f Holy Week

Kaschmir m cashmere (a. in Zssgn)

Käse m cheese; **~kuchen** m cheesecake

Kaserne mil. f barracks sg., pl.; **~nhof** m barrack square

käsig adj. cheesy; *blaß:* pasty

Kasino n casino; *mil.* (officers') mess

Kasperle n, m Punch; **~theater** n Punch and Judy show

Kassa östr. f, **Kasse** f *Laden2:* till; *Registrier2:* cash register; *Supermarkt:* checkout (counter); *Bank:* cash desk; *Bank:* cashier's counter; *thea. etc.:* box office; F *gut (knapp) bei ~ sein* be* flush (a bit hard up)

Kassen|beleg m receipt, *Am.* sales slip; **~erfolg** m *thea. etc.* box-office success; **~patient(in)** *med.* health plan patient; *Brt.* NHS patient, *Am.* medicaid patient; **~schlager** m blockbuster; **~wart** m *Verein etc.:* treasurer

Kassette f *allg.* box, case; *mus., TV,* *phot. etc.* cassette, *Schmuck2:* a. casket; **~n...** in Zssgn Recorder etc.: cassette

kassiere|n v/t. u. v/i. collect, take* (the money); F *verdienen:* make*; **Qr(in)** cashier; *Bank2:* a. teller; *Beiträge etc.:* collector

Kastanie f chestnut

Kasten m box (a. fig. *Fernseher, Tor, Haus etc.*); *Behälter, Geigen2:* case; *Kiste:* chest

kastrieren med., vet. v/t. castrate

Kasus gr. m case

Katalog m catalogue, *Am.* a. catalog

Katalysator m chem. catalyst; *mot.* catalytic converter

Katapult m, n, **Qieren** v/t. catapult

katastroph|al adj. disastrous (a. fig.); **Qe** f catastrophe, disaster (a. fig.); **Qengebiet** n disaster area; **Qenschutz** m disaster control

Katechismus rel. m catechism

Kategorie f category

Kater m zo. male cat, tomcat; *fig.* hangover

kath. Abk. für **katholisch** Cath., Catholic

Kathedrale f cathedral

Katho|lik(in), Qlisch adj. (Roman) Catholic

Kätzchen n kitten, pussy (a. bot.)

Katze zo. f cat; *junge:* kitten

Kauderwelsch n gibberish

kauen v/t. u. v/i. chew

kauern v/i. u. v/refl. crouch, squat

Kauf m purchase (a. econ.), F buy; *purchasing, buying;* *ein guter ~* a bargain, F a good buy; *zum ~ anbieten* offer for sale; **Qen** v/t. buy* (a. fig.), purchase

Käufer m buyer; *Kunde:* customer

Kauf|haus n department store; **~kraft** econ. f purchasing power

käuflich adj. for sale; *fig.* venal

Kauf|mann m *allg.* businessman; *Händler:* dealer, trader, merchant; *Einzelhändler:* shopkeeper, *Am.* mst storekeeper; *bsd. Lebensmittelhändler:* grocer; **Qmännisch** adj. commercial, business; **~er Angestellter** clerk; **~vertrag** m contract of sale

Kaugummi m chewing gum

kaum adv. hardly; **~ zu glauben** hard to believe

Kaution f security; *jur.* bail

Kautschuk m (india) rubber

Kavalier m gentleman
Kavallerie mil. f cavalry
Kaviar m caviar(e)
keck adj. cheeky, saucy, pert
Kegel m für Spiel: skittle, pin; math., tech. cone; **~bahn** f skittle (Brt. bowling) alley; **2förmig** adj. conical; **~kugel** f skittle (bsd. Am. bowling) ball; **2n** v/i. play (at) skittles od. ninepins, bsd. Am. bowl, go* bowling
Kehl|e f throat; **~kopf** m larynx
Kehre f (sharp) bend; **2n** v/t. sweep*; **j-m den Rücken ~** turn one's back on s.o.
Kehricht m sweepings pl.; **~schaufel** f dustpan
Kehrseite f other side, reverse; **die ~ der Medaille** the other side of the coin
kehrtmachen v/i. turn back
keifen v/i. nag, bitch
Keil m wedge; Zwickel: gusset; **~absatz** m wedge heel
Keile f thrashing, hiding
Keiler zo. m wild boar
Keilerei f brawl, fight
keil|förmig adj. wedge-shaped; **2kissen** n wedge-shaped bolster; **2riemen** mot. m fan belt
Keim m biol., med. germ; bot. bud; bot. Trieb: sprout; fig. seed(s pl.); **2en** v/i. Samen: germinate; sprießen: sprout; fig. form, grow*; stir; **2frei** adj. sterile; **2tötend** adj. germicidal; **~zelle** f germ cell
kein indef. pron. **1.** als adj.: **~(e)** no, not any; **~ anderer** no one else; **~(e) ... mehr** not any more ...; **~ Geld (~e Zeit) mehr** no money (time) left; **~ Kind mehr** no longer a child; **2.** als Substantiv: **~er, ~e, ~(e)s** none, no one, nobody; **~er von beiden** neither (of the two); **~er von uns** none of us; **~esfalls** adv. by no means, under no circumstances; **~eswegs** adv. by no means, not in the least; **~mal** adv. not once, not a single time
Keks m, n biscuit, Am. cookie
Kelch m (a. bot., fig.); rel. chalice
Kelle f scoop; Maurer2: trowel
Keller m cellar; bewohnt: basement; **~geschoß** n basement; **~wohnung** f basement (flat, bsd. Am. apartment)
Kellner m waiter; **~in** f waitress
keltern v/t. press

kenn|en v/t. know*, be* acquainted with; **~enlernen** v/t. get* to know, become* acquainted with; j-n: a. meet*; **als ich ihn kennenlernte** when I first met him; **2er** m expert; Kunst2, Wein2: connoisseur; **~tlich** adj. recognizable (an by); **2tnis** f knowledge; ~ nehmen von take* not(ic)e of; **gute ~se in** a good knowledge of; **2wort** n password; **2zeichen** n mark, sign; (distinguishing) feature, characteristic; mot. registration (Am. license) number; **~zeichnen** v/t. mark; fig. characterize
kentern naut. v/i. capsize
Kerbe f notch
Kerker m jail, prison; Verlies: dungeon
Kerl F m fellow, guy, bsd. Brt. bloke; armer ~ poor devil; ein anständiger ~ a decent sort
Kern m Obst: pip, seed; Kirsch2 etc.: stone; Nuß: kernel; tech. core (a. Reaktor2); phys. nucleus (a. Atom2); fig. core, heart, bottom; **~...** in Zssgn Energie, Forschung, Physik, Reaktor, Technik etc.: nuclear ...; **~fach** n basic subject, Brt. appr. set subject; pl. coll. core curriculum; **~gehäuse** bot. n core; **2gesund** adj. F (as) sound as a bell; **2ig** adj. full of pips (Am. seeds); fig.: robust; Satz etc.: pithy; **~kraft** f nuclear power; **~kraftgegner** m anti nuclear activist; **~kraftwerk** n nuclear power station od. plant; **2los** adj. seedless; **~spaltung** f nuclear fission; **~waffe** f nuclear weapon; **2waffenfrei** adj.: **~e Zone** nuclear-free zone; **~waffenversuch** m nuclear test; **~zeit** f core time
Kerze f candle; Turnen: shoulder stand
keß F adj. cheeky, saucy, pert
Kessel m Tee2: kettle; Wasch2, Heiz2, Dampf2: boiler; Behälter: tank
Kette f chain (a. fig.); Hals2: necklace; e-e ~ bilden form a line; **~n...** in Zssgn Antrieb, Raucher, Reaktion etc.: chain ...; **2n** v/t. chain (an to); **~nfahrzeug** n tracked vehicle; **~nladen** m chain (bsd. Brt. multiple) store, F multiple
Ketzer m heretic; **~ei** f heresy
keuch|en v/i. pant, gasp; **2husten** med. m whooping cough
Keule f club; gastr. leg; **chemische ~** chemical mace
keusch adj. chaste; **2heit** f chastity

Kfz *Abk. für* **Kraftfahrzeug** motor vehicle; **~Brief** *m*, **~Schein** *m* vehicle registration document; **~Steuer** *f* road *od.* automobile tax; **~Werkstatt** *f* garage

KG *Abk. für* **Kommanditgesellschaft** limited partnership

kichern *v/i.* giggle

Kiebitz *m zo.* peewit, lapwing; *fig.* kibitzer

Kiefer¹ *m* jaw(bone)

Kiefer² *bot. f* pine(tree)

Kiel *m naut.* keel; **~flosse** *aviat. f* tail fin; **~raum** *m* bilge; **~wasser** *n* wake (*a. fig.*)

Kieme *zo. f* gill

Kies *m* gravel; *sl. Geld:* dough; **~el** *m* pebble; **~weg** *m* gravel path

Kilo|**(gramm)** *n* kilogram(me); **~hertz** *n* kilohertz; **~meter** *m* kilomet|re, *Am.* -er; **~watt** *n* kilowatt

Kimme *f* notch; **~ und Korn** sights *pl.*

Kind *n* child; *Klein*2: baby; **ein ~ erwarten** be* expecting a baby

Kinder|**arzt** *m*, **~ärztin** *f* p(a)ediatrician; **~garten** *m* kindergarten, nursery school; **~gärtnerin** *f* nursery-school *od.* kindergarten teacher; **~geld** *n* child benefit; **~hort** *m* kitsch; *Waren:* trash; *sentimentaler:* slush; 2**ig** *adj.* kitschy; trashy; slushy; **~krippe** *f* day nursery; **~lähmung** *med. f* polio(myelitis); 2**lieb** *adj.* fond of children; 2**los** *adj.* childless; **~mädchen** *n* nanny, nurse(maid); **~spiel** *fig. n:* **ein ~** child's play; **~stube** *fig. f* manners *pl.*, upbringing; **~wagen** *m* pram, *Am.* baby carriage (F buggy); **~zimmer** *n* children's room

Kindes|**alter** *n* childhood; infancy; **~beine** *pl.:* **von ~ an** from early childhood; **~entführung** *f* kidnap(p)ing; **~mißhandlung** *f* child abuse

Kind|**heit** *f* childhood; 2**isch** *adj.* childish; *contp.* babyish; 2**lich** *adj.* childlike

Kinn *n* chin; **~backe** *f*, **~backen** *m* jaw(bone); **~haken** *m Boxen:* hook (to the chin), uppercut

Kino *n* cinema, *bsd. Am.* motion pictures *pl.*, F *the* pictures *pl.*, F *the* movies *pl.*; *Gebäude:* cinema, *bsd. Am.* movie theater; **~besucher(in)**, **~gänger(in)** cinemagoer, filmgoer

Kippe *f* F stub, *bsd. Am.* butt; *Turnen:* upstart; **auf der ~ stehen** be* uncer-

tain; *stärker:* be* touch and go; **er steht auf der ~** it's touch and go with him; 2**n 1.** *v/i.* tip *od.* topple (over); **2.** *v/t.* tilt, tip over *od.* up

Kirche *f* church; **in die ~ gehen** go to church

Kirchen|**buch** *n* parish register; **~diener** *m* sexton; **~gemeinde** *f* parish; **~jahr** *n* Church *od.* ecclesiastical year; **~lied** *n* hymn; **~musik** *f* sacred *od.* church music; **~schiff** *arch. n* nave; **~steuer** *f* church tax; **~tag** *m* church congress; **~stuhl** *m* pew

Kirch|**gang** *m* churchgoing; **~gänger** *m* churchgoer; 2**lich** *adj.* church, ecclesiastical; **~turm** *m* steeple; *Spitze:* spire; *ohne Spitze:* church tower

Kirsche *f* cherry

Kissen *n* pillow; *Sitz*2, *Luft*2: cushion; **~bezug** *m*, **~hülle** *f* pillowcase, pillowslip

Kiste *f* box, chest; *Latten*2: crate

Kitsch *m* kitsch; *Waren:* trash; *sentimentaler:* slush; 2**ig** *adj.* kitschy; trashy; slushy

Kitt *m* cement; *Glaser*2: putty

Kittel *m* smock; *Arbeits*2, *~schürze:* overall; *Arzt*2: (white) coat

kitten *v/t.* cement; *Glaserei:* putty

Kitz|**el** *m* tickle, *fig. a.* thrill, kick; 2**eln** *v/i. u. v/t.* tickle; **~ler** *anat. m* clitoris; 2**lig** *adj.* ticklish (*a. fig.*)

kläffen *v/i.* yap, yelp

klaffend *adj.* gaping; *bsd. Abgrund:* yawning

Klage *f* complaint; *Weh*2: lament; *jur.* action, (law)suit; 2**n** *v/i.* complain (*über* of, about; *bei* to); lament; *jur.* go* to court; *gegen j-n ~* sue s.o

Kläger(in) *jur.* plaintiff

kläglich *adj.* → **jämmerlich**

Klamauk *m* racket; *thea. etc.* slapstick

klamm *adj.* numb; *Raum:* clammy

Klammer *f tech.* cramp, clamp; *Büro*2, *Haar*2: clip; *Wäsche*2: (clothes) peg, *bsd. Am.* clothes pin; *Zahn*2: brace; *math., print.* bracket(s *pl.*); 2**n** *v/t.* fasten *od.* clip together; **sich ~ an** cling* to

Klang *m* sound; *Tonqualität:* tone; *Gläser*2: clink; *Glocken*2: ringing; 2**voll** *adj.* sonorous; *fig.* illustrious

Klappe *f* flap; *Klappdeckel:* hinged lid; *am LKW:* tailboard, *Am.* tailgate;

tech., *bot.*, *anat.* valve; F *Mund*: trap;
2n 1. *v/t.*: *nach oben* ~ lift up, raise;
Sitz etc.: put* *od.* fold up; *nach unten* ~
lower, put* down; *es läßt sich (nach
hinten)* ~ it folds (backward); **2.** *v/i.*
clap, clack; *fig.* work, work out (well)
Klapper f rattle; **2n** *v/i.* clatter, rattle
(*mit et. s.th.*); **~schlange** f rattlesnake
Klapp|fahrrad n folding bicycle; **~fen-
ster** f top-hung window; **~messer** n
jack knife, clasp knife; **2rig** *adj. Auto
etc.*: rattly, ramshackle; *Möbel*: rick-
ety; *Person*: shaky; **~sitz** m folding *od.*
tip-up seat; **~stuhl** m folding chair;
~tisch m folding table
Klaps m slap, pat; *harter*: smack
klar *adj.* clear (*a. fig.*); *ist dir* ~, *daß* ...?
do you realize that ...?; *das ist mir
(nicht ganz)* ~ I (don't quite) understand; *(na)* ~! of course!; *alles* ~?
everything okay?
Klär|anlage f sewage works *sg.*, *pl.*;
2en *v/t. tech.* purify; *Wasser*: a. treat;
fig. clear up; *endgültig*: settle; *Sport*:
clear
Klarheit f clearness; *fig. a.* clarity
Klarinette *mus.* f clarinet
Klarsicht... in *Zssgn* transparent
Klasse f class (*a. pol.*); *Schul2*: *Brt. a.*
form, *Am. a.* grade; **~nzimmer**: classroom; F *großartig*: super, fantastic
Klassen|arbeit f (classroom) test;
~buch n (class) register, *Am.* class-
book; **~kamerad(in)** classmate; **~
lehrer(in)** form teacher, *Brt. a.* form
master (mistress), *Am.* homeroom
teacher; **~sprecher(in)** class representative; **~zimmer** n classroom
klassifizier|en *v/t.* classify; **2ung** f
classification
Klassi|ker m classic; **2sch** *adj.* clas-
sic(al)
Klatsch F *fig. m*, **~base** f gossip; **2en**
v/i. u. v/t. Beifall ~: clap, applaud; F
schlagen, werfen: slap, bang; *ins Wasser*: splash; F *gossip*; *in die Hände* ~
clap one's hands; **2haft** *adj.* gossipy;
~maul F n (old) gossip; **2naß** F *adj.*
soaking wet
klauben *östr. v/t.* pick; gather
Klaue f claw; *fig.* clutches *pl.*
klauen F *v/t.* pinch
Klausel *jur.* f clause; condition
Klausur f test (paper), exam(ination)

Klavier *mus. n* piano; **~ spielen** play the
piano; **~konzert** n *Stück*: piano concerto; *Vortrag*: piano recital
Klebeband n adhesive tape
kleb|en 1. *v/t.* glue, paste (*a. fig. j-m
e-e*); stick*; **2.** *v/i.* stick*, cling* (*an* to)
(*a. fig.*); **~rig** *adj.* sticky; **2stoff** m adhesive; *Leim*: glue; **~streifen** m adhesive tape
kleck|ern F **1.** *v/i.* make* a mess; **2.** *v/t.*
spill*; **2s** F m (ink)blot; *Farb2*: blob;
~sen F *v/i.* blot, make* blots
Klee *bot.* m clover; **~blatt** n cloverleaf
Kleid n dress; **~er** *pl. Kleidung*: clothes
pl.; **2en** *v/t.* dress, clothe; *j-n gut* ~ suit
s.o.; *sich (gut)* ~ dress (well)
Kleider|bügel m (coat) hanger; **~bür-
ste** f clothes brush; **~haken** m coat
hook; **~schrank** m wardrobe; **~stän-
der** m coat stand; **~stoff** m dress material
kleidsam *adj.* becoming
Kleidung f clothes *pl.*, clothing;
~sstück n article of clothing
Kleie f bran
klein *adj.* small, *bsd.* F little (*a. Finger,
Bruder*); *von Wuchs*: short; *von* ~ *auf*
from an early age; *ein* ~ *wenig* a little
bit; **2en** *the young* and old; *die* **2en**
the little ones; **2anzeige** f small ad,
bsd. Am. want ad; **2bildkamera** f 35
mm camera; **2familie** f nuclear family; **2geld** n (small) change; **2holz** n
matchwood; **2igkeit** f little thing,
trifle; *Geschenk*: little something; *e-e* ~
leicht: nothing, child's play; **2kind** n
infant; **2kram** F m odds and ends *pl.*;
~laut *adj.* subdued; **~lich** *adj.* small-
-minded, petty; *geizig*: mean; *pedantisch*: pedantic, fussy; **~schneiden**
v/t. cut* up (into small pieces); **2stadt** f
small town; **~städtisch** *adj.* small-
-town, provincial; **2wagen** m small
od. compact car, *Brt.* F runabout
Kleister m paste; **2n** *v/t.* paste
Klemme f *tech.* clamp; *Haar2*: (hair)
clip; F *in der* ~ *sitzen* be* in a fix *od.*
tight spot; **2n** *v/i. u. v/t.* jam; *stecken*:
stick*; *Tür etc.*: be* stuck *od.* jammed;
sich ~ jam one's finger *od.* hand
Klempner m plumber
Klerus m clergy *pl.*
Klette f *bot.* bur(r); *fig.* leech
klettern *v/i.* climb; *auf e-n Baum* ~

climb (up) a tree; **2pflanze** f climber

Klient(in) f client

Klima n climate; fig. a. atmosphere; **~anlage** f air-conditioning; **2tisch** adj. climatic

klimpern v/i. jingle, chink (**mit et.** s.th.); F strum (away) (**auf** on)

Klinge f blade

Klingel f bell; **~knopf** m bell (push); **2n** v/i. ring* (the bell); **es klingelt** the (door)bell is ringing

klingen v/i. sound; Glocke, Metall etc.: ring*; Gläser etc.: clink

Klini|k f hospital; clinic; Privat2: Brt. nursing home; **2sch** adj. clinical

Klinke f (door) handle

Klippe f cliff, rock(s pl.); fig. obstacle

klirren v/i. Fenster: rattle; Gläser etc.: clink; Scherben: tinkle; Schwerter etc.: clash; Münzen, Schlüssel etc.: jingle

Klischee n cliché

klobig adj. bulky, clumsy (a. fig.)

Klopapier F n loo (Am. toilet) paper

klopfen 1. v/i. Herz, Puls: beat*; heftig: throb; an die Tür etc.: knock; auf die Schulter: tap; tätschelnd: pat; **es klopft** there's a knock at the door; **2.** v/t. beat*; Nagel etc.: knock, drive*

Klops m meat ball

Klosett n lavatory, toilet; **~brille** f toilet seat; **~papier** n toilet paper

Kloß m clod, lump (a. fig. in der Kehle); Speise: dumpling

Kloster n Mönchs2: monastery; Nonnen2: convent

Klotz m block; Holz2: a. log

Klub m club; **~sessel** m lounge chair

Kluft f gap (a. fig.); Abgrund: abyss

klug adj. intelligent, clever, F bright, smart; vernünftig: wise; **daraus (aus ihm) werde ich nicht ~** I don't know what to make of it (him); **2heit** f intelligence, cleverness, F brains pl.; Vernunft: good sense; Wissen: knowledge

Klump|en m allg. lump; Erde etc.: clod; Gold2 etc.: nugget; Haufen: heap; **~fuß** m clubfoot; **2ig** adj. lumpy, cloddish

knabbern v/t. u. v/i. nibble, gnaw

Knabe m boy; **2nhaft** adj. boyish

Knäckebrot n crispbread

knack|en v/t. u. v/i. crack (a. fig. u. F); Zweig: snap; Feuer, Radio: crackle; an et. zu ~ haben have* s.th. to chew on; **2s** F m crack (a. Geräusch); fig. defect

Knall m allg. bang; Schuß: a. crack, report; Peitsche: crack; Korken: pop; F **e-n ~ haben** be* nuts; **~bonbon** m, n cracker; **~effekt** fig. m sensation; **2en** v/i. u. v/t. bang; Tür: slam; crack; pop; F prallen: crash (**gegen** into); F **j-m e-e ~** slap s.o.('s face); **2ig** F adj. loud, flashy; **~körper** m fire cracker; **2rot** F adj. glaring red; Gesicht: scarlet

knapp adj. Vorräte etc.: scarce; Kost, Lohn: scanty, meag(re, Am. -er; Stunde, Meile, Mehrheit: bare; ~ bemessen: limited (a. Zeit); Sieg, Entkommen: narrow, bare; Kleid etc.: tight; Schreiben etc.: brief; ~ an Geld (Zeit etc.) short of money (time etc.); **mit ~er Not** only just, barely

Knappe m Bergbau: miner

knapp|halten v/t. keep* s.o. short; **2heit** f shortage

Knarre f rattle; F Gewehr: gun

knarren v/i. creak

Knast F m jail; **~bruder** F m jailbird

knattern v/i. crackle; mot. roar

Knäuel m, n ball; wirres: tangle

Knauf m knob; Degen2: pommel

knaus(e)rig F adj. stingy

knautsch|en v/t. u. v/i. crumple; **2zone** mot. f crumple zone

Knebel m, **2n** v/t. gag (a. fig.)

Knecht m farmhand; fig. slave; **~schaft** f slavery

kneif|en v/t. u. v/i. pinch (**j-m in den Arm** s.o.'s arm); F fig. chicken out; **2zange** f pincers pl.

Kneipe F f pub, bsd. Am. saloon, bar

knet|en v/t. knead; formen: mo(u)ld; **2masse** f plasticine, Am. pla(y)-dough

Knick m fold, crease; Kurve: bend; **2en** v/t. fold, crease; bend*; Zweig: break*; **nicht ~!** do not bend!

Knicks m curts(e)y; **e-n ~ machen →** **2en** v/i. curts(e)y (**vor** to)

Knie n knee; **~beuge** f knee bend; **~kehle** f hollow of the knee; **2n** v/i. kneel*, be* on one's knees (**vor** before); **~scheibe** f kneecap; **~strumpf** m knee(-length) sock

Kniff m crease, fold; Zwicken: pinch; fig. trick, knack; **2(e)lig** adj. tricky

knipsen v/t. u. v/i. F phot. take* a picture (of); lochen: punch, clip

Knirps m little chap (Am. guy)

knirschen 474

knirschen v/i. crunch; *mit den Zähnen*
~ grind* od. gnash one's teeth
knistern v/i. crackle; *Papier:* rustle
knittern v/t. u. v/i. crumple, crease,
wrinkle
Knoblauch bot. m garlic
Knöchel m ankle; *Finger*2: knuckle
Knoch|en m bone; *Fleisch mit (ohne)*
meat on (off) the bone; **~enbruch** m
fracture; **2ig** adj. bony
Knödel m dumpling
Knolle f bot. 2 tuber; *Zwiebel:* bulb;
~nnase f bulbous nose
Knopf m, **knöpfen** v/t. button
Knopfloch n buttonhole
Knorpel m gristle; *anat.* cartilage
knorrig adj. gnarled, knotted
Knospe f, 2n v/i. bud
knoten v/t. knot, make* a knot in
Knoten m knot (a. fig., naut.); **~punkt**
m rail. junction; *allg.* cent|re, Am. -er
knüllen v/t. u. v/i. crumple
Knüller F m smash (hit); *Presse:* scoop
knüpfen v/t. tie; *Teppich:* weave*
Knüppel m stick, cudgel; *Polizei*2: trun-
cheon, Am. billy (club); **~schal-
tung** mot. f floor shift
knurren v/i. growl, snarl; *fig.* grumble
(*über* at); *Magen:* rumble
knusp(e)rig adj. crisp, crunchy
knutschen F v/i. pet, neck, smooch
k.o. adj. knocked out; *fig.* beat
Kobold m (hob)goblin, imp (a. fig.)
Koch m cook; *im Lokal:* a. chef; **~buch**
n cookery book, *bsd. Am.* cookbook;
2en 1. v/t. cook; *Eier, Wasser, Wäsche:* boil; *Kaffee, Tee:* make*; **2.** v/i.
cook, do* the cooking; *Flüssiges:* boil
(a. fig.); *gut* ~ be* a good cook; *vor Wut*
~ boil with rage; **2endheiß** adj. boiling
hot; **~er** m cooker
Köchin f cook
Koch|löffel m (wooden) spoon; **~ni-
sche** f kitchenette; **~platte** f hotplate;
~salz n common salt; **~topf** m saucepan, pot
Köder m bait (a. fig.), lure; 2n v/t. bait,
decoy (*beide a. fig.*)
Kodex m code
kodier|en v/t. (en)code; **2ung** f
(en)coding
Koffein chem. n caffeine
Koffer m (suit)case; *großer:* trunk; **~ra-
dio** n portable (radio); **~raum** mot.

Brt. boot, *Am.* trunk
Kognak m (French) brandy, cognac
Kohl bot. m cabbage
Kohle f coal; *electr.* carbon; F *Geld:*
dough; **~hydrat** n carbohydrate
Kohlen|... chem. in Zssgn Dioxid etc.:
carbon ...; **~bergwerk** n coalmine,
colliery; **~ofen** m coal-burning stove;
~säure f chem. carbonic acid; *im Getränk:* F fizz; **2säurehaltig** adj. car-
bonated, F fizzy; **~stoff** chem. m carbon; **~wasserstoff** m hydrocarbon
Kohle|papier n carbon paper; **~
zeichnung** f charcoal drawing
Kohl|kopf m (head of) cabbage;
~rabi m bot. kohlrabi
Koje naut. f berth, bunk
Kokain n cocaine
kokett adj. coquettish; **~ieren** v/i. flirt;
fig. mit et.: toy
Kokosnuß bot. f coconut
Koks m coke; F *Geld:* dough; *sl. Kokain:*
coke, snow
Kolben m *Gewehr*2: butt; *tech.* piston;
~stange f piston rod
Kolchose f collective farm, kolkhoz
Kolibri zo. m humming bird
Kolleg n univ. course (of lectures); →
Fachschule; **~e** m, **~in** f colleague;
~ium n teaching staff, Am. a. faculty
Kollekt|e rel. f collection; **~ion** f econ.
collection; *Sortiment:* range; **~iv** n, 2iv
adj. collective (a. in Zssgn)
Koller F f fig. m fit; *Wut:* rage
kolli|dieren v/i. collide (a. fig.); 2sion f
collision; *fig.* a. clash, conflict
Kölnischwasser n (eau de) cologne
Kolonialwaren pl. → **Lebensmittel**
Koloni|e f colony; **2sieren** v/t. colo-
nize; **~sierung** f colonization
Kolonne f column; *mil. Wagen*2: convoy; *Arbeiter*2: gang, crew
Koloß m colossus; *fig. a.* giant (of a
man)
kolossal adj. gigantic
Kombi mot. m estate (car), *bsd. Am.*
station wagon; **~nation** f combination; *Kleidung:* set; *Montur:* overalls
pl., Am. a. coverall(s a. pl.); *Flieger*2: flying suit; *Fußball etc.:* combined move;
2nieren 1. v/t. combine; **2.** v/i. reason
Kombüse naut. f galley
Komet astr. m comet
Komfort m *Ausstattung:* (modern) con-

veniences *pl.*; *Luxus:* luxury; **2abel** *adj.* comfortable; *Hotel etc.: a.* well-appointed; *luxuriös:* luxurious

Komik *f* humo(u)r; *Wirkung:* comic effect; **~er(in)** comedian; *f Beruf:* comedienne

komisch *adj.* comic(al), funny; *fig.* funny, strange, odd

Komitee *n* committee

Komma *n* comma; *sechs ~ vier* six point four

Kommand|ant, ~eur *mil. m* commander, commanding officer; **2ieren** *v/i. u. v/t.* (be* in) command (of); **~o** *n* command; *Befehl: a.* order; *mil. Gruppe:* commando; **~obrücke** *naut. f* (navigating) bridge

kommen *v/i.* come*; *an~:* arrive; *gelangen:* get*; *reichen:* reach; *zu spät ~* be* late; *weit ~* get* far; *zur Schule ~* start school; *ins Gefängnis ~* go* to jail; *~ lassen j-n:* send* for, call; *et.:* order; *~ auf* think* of, hit* upon; remember; *hinter et. ~* find* s.th. out; *um et. ~* lose* s.th.; *verpassen:* miss s.th.; *zu et. ~ come* by s.th.; wieder zu sich ~ come* round od.* to; *wohin kommt ...?* where does ... go?; *daher kommt es, daß* that's why; *woher kommt es, daß ...?* why is it that ...?, F how come ...?

Komment|ar *m* comment(ary); **~ator** *m* commentator; **2ieren** *v/t.* comment (on)

Kommissar *m* commissioner; *Polizei2:* superintendent

Kommission *f* commission (*a. econ. in* on); *Ausschuß: a.* committee

Kommode *f* chest (of drawers), *Am. a.* bureau

Kommun|al... *in Zssgn Politik etc.:* local ...; **~e** *f* commune; **~ikation** *f* communication; **~ion** *rel. f* (Holy) Communion; **~ismus** *m* communism; **~ist(in), 2istisch** *adj.* communist

Komödie *f* comedy; *~ spielen* put* on an act, play-act

kompakt *adj.* compact; **2anlage** *f* music cent|re, *Am.* -er, *Am.* stereo system

Kompanie *mil. f* company

Kompaß *m* compass

kompatibel *adj.* compatible (*a. Computer*)

komplett *adj.* complete

Komplex *m* complex (*a. psych.*)

Kompliment *n* compliment; *j-m ein ~ machen* pay* s.o. a compliment

Komplize *m* accomplice

komplizier|en *v/t.* complicate; **~t** *adj.* complicated, complex; **~er Bruch** *med.* compound fracture

Komplott *n* plot, conspiracy

kompo|nieren *mus. v/t. u. v/i.* compose; *Lied: a.* write*; **2nist** *m* composer; **2sition** *f* composition

Kompott *n* compot(e), stewed fruit

komprimieren *v/t.* compress

Kondens|ator *m electr.* capacitor; *tech.* condenser; **2ieren** *v/t.* condense; **~milch** *f* condensed milk; **~wasser** *n* condensation water

Kondition *f* condition; *Sport: a.* shape, form; *gute ~* (great) stamina

konditional *gr. adj.* conditional

Konditionstraining *n* fitness training

Konditor *m* confectioner, pastrycook; **~ei** *f* cake shop; café, tearoom; **~eiwaren** *pl.* confectionery *sg.*

Kondom *n, m* condom

Kondukteur *m Schweiz:* → *Schaffner*

Konfekt *n* sweets *pl.*, chocolates *pl.*

Konfektion *f* ready-made clothing; **~s...** *in Zssgn* ready-made, off-the-peg

Konferenz *f* conference

Konfession *f* religion, denomination; **2ell** *adj.* confessional, denominational; **~sschule** *f* denominational school

Konfirm|and(in) confirmand; **~ation** *f* confirmation; **2ieren** *v/t.* confirm

konfiszieren *jur. v/t.* confiscate

Konfitüre *f* jam

Konflikt *m* conflict

konfrontieren *v/t.* confront

konfus *adj.* confused, mixed-up

Kongreß *m* congress; *bsd. Am.* convention

König *m* king; **~in** *f* queen; **2lich** *adj.* royal; **~reich** *n* kingdom

Konjug|ation *gr. f* conjugation; **2ieren** *v/t.* conjugate

Konjunkt|iv *gr. m* subjunctive (mood); **~ur** *econ. f* economic situation

konkret *adj.* concrete

Konkurr|ent(in) competitor, rival; **~enz** *f* competition; *die ~* one's competitors *pl.*; *außer ~* not competing; → *konkurrenzlos;* **2enzfähig** *adj.* competitive; **~enzkampf** *m* competition; **2enzlos** *adj.* without competition, un-rival(l)ed; **2ieren** *v/i.* compete

Konkurs *econ., jur. m* bankruptcy; **in ~ gehen** go* bankrupt; **~masse** *jur. f* bankrupt's estate

können *v/aux., v/t. u. v/i.* can*, be* able to; *dürfen:* may*, be* allowed to; *kann ich ...?* can od. may I ...?; *du kannst nicht* you cannot od. can't; *ich kann nicht mehr* I can't go on; *essen:* I can't manage od. eat any more; *es kann sein* it may be; *ich kann nichts dafür* it's not my fault; *e-e Sprache ~* know* od. speak* a language

Könn|en *n* ability, skill; **~er** *m* master, expert; *bsd. Sport:* ace, crack

konsequen|t *adj.* consistent; **2z** *f* consistency; *Folge:* consequence

konservativ *adj.* conservative

Konserven *pl.* canned (*Brt. a.* tinned) foods *pl.;* **~büchse, ~dose** *f* can, *Brt. a.* tin; **~fabrik** *f* cannery

konservier|en *v/t.* preserve; **2ungs-stoff** *m* preservative

Konsonant *m* consonant

konstruieren *v/t.* construct; *entwerfen:* design

Konstruk|teur *tech. m* designer; **~tion** *tech. f* construction

Konsul *m* consul; **~at** *n* consulate; **2ieren** *v/t.* consult

Konsum *m Verbrauch:* consumption; *Genossenschaft:* cooperative (society), F co-op; *Laden:* cooperative (store), F co-op; **~ent** *m* consumer; **~gesell-schaft** *f* consumer society; **2ieren** *v/t.* consume

Kontakt *m* contact (*a. electr.*); **~ aufneh-men** get* in touch; **~ haben** od. **in ~ stehen mit** be* in contact od. touch with; **~ verlieren** lose* touch; **2freudig** *adj.* sociable; **~ sein** be* a good mixer; **~linsen** *opt. pl.* contact lenses *pl.*

Konter *m* counter (*a. in Zssgn*); **2n** *v/i.* counter (*a. fig.*)

Kontinent *m* continent

Konto *econ. n* account; **~auszug** *m* (bank) statement

Kontor *n* (branch) office

Kontrast *m* contrast (*a. phot., TV etc.*)

Kontroll|e *f* control; *Aufsicht: a.* super-vision; *Prüfung: a.* check(up); **~eur** *m*

inspector; *rail. a.* conductor; **2ieren** *v/t.* (*über*)*prüfen:* check; *j-n:* check up on *s.o.; beherrschen, überwachen:* con-trol; **~punkt** *m,* **~stelle** *f* check-point

Kontroverse *f* controversy

konventionell *adj.* conventional

Konversation *f* conversation; **~slexi-kon** *n* encyclop(a)edia

Konzentration *f* concentration; **~sla-ger** *n* concentration camp

konzentrieren *v/t. u. v/refl.* concen-trate; *sich auf et. ~* concentrate on s.th.

Konzept *n* (rough) draft; *Idee:* concep-tion; *j-n aus dem ~ bringen* put* s.o. out

Konzern *econ. m* combine, group

Konzert *mus. n* concert; *Musikstück:* concerto; **~halle** *f,* **~saal** *m* concert hall, auditorium

Konzession *f* concession; *Genehmi-gung:* licen|ce, *Am.* -se

Kopf *m* head (*a. fig.*); **~ende** *n:* top; *Ver-stand: a.* brains *pl.,* mind; **~ hoch!** chin up!; *j-m über den ~ wachsen* out-grow* s.o.; *fig.* be* too much for s.o.; *sich den ~ zerbrechen (über)* rack one's brains (over); *sich et. aus dem ~ schlagen* put* s.th. out of one's mind; **~ an ~** neck and neck; **~arbeit** *f* brain-work; **~ball** *m* header; *Tor:* headed goal; **~bedeckung** *f* headgear; *ohne ~* bareheaded

köpfen *v/t.* behead, decapitate; *Fußball:* head (*ins Tor* home)

Kopf|ende *n* head; **~hörer** *m, pl.* head-phones *pl.;* **~jäger** *m* headhunter; **~kissen** *n* pillow; **2los** *adj.* headless; *fig.* panicky; **~rechnen** *n* mental ar-ithmetic; **~salat** *m* lettuce; **~schmer-zen** *pl.* headache *sg.;* **~sprung** *m* header; **~stand** *m* headstand; **~tuch** *n* scarf, (head)kerchief; **2über** *adv.* headfirst (*a. fig*); **~weh** *n → Kopf-schmerzen; ~zerbrechen n: j-m ~ machen* give* s.o. a headache

Kopie *f,* **2ren** *v/t.* copy; **~rgerät** *n* copier; **~rstift** *m* indelible pencil

Koppel¹ *f Pferde2:* paddock

Koppel² *mil. n* belt

koppeln *v/t.* couple; *Raumfahrt:* dock

Koralle *f* coral

Korb *m* basket; *j-m e-n ~ geben* turn s.o. down; **~möbel** *pl.* wicker furni-ture *sg.*

Kord m corduroy (a. in Zssgn); **~el** f cord; **~hose** f corduroys pl.

Korinthe f currant

Kork bot. m cork; **~eiche** f cork oak

Korken m cork; **~zieher** m corkscrew

Korn¹ n grain; Samen2: seed; Getreide: grain, Brt. a. corn; am Gewehr: front sight

Korn² F m (grain) schnapps

körnig adj. grainy; in Zssgn: ...grained

Körper m body (a. phys., chem.), geom. a. solid; **~bau** m build, physique; 2be-hindert adj. (physically) disabled od. handicapped; **~geruch** m body odo(u)r, BO; **~größe** f height; **~kraft** f physical strength; 2lich adj. physical; **~pflege** f personal hygiene; **~schaft** f corporation, (corporate) body; **~teil** m part of the body; **~verletzung** jur. f bodily injury

korrekt adj. correct; 2ur f correction; Benotung: marking, bsd. Am. grading; 2urzeichen n correction mark

Korrespond|ent(in) correspondent; **~enz** f correspondence; 2ieren v/i. correspond (mit with)

Korridor m corridor; Flur: hall

korrigieren v/t. correct; benoten: mark, bsd. Am. grade

korrupt adj. corrupt(ed); 2ion f corruption

Korsett n corset (a. fig.)

Kosename m pet name

Kosmetik f beauty culture; Mittel: cosmetics pl., toiletries pl.; **~erin** f beautician, cosmetician

Kost f food, diet; Beköstigung: board; 2bar adj. precious, valuable; teuer: costly; **~barkeit** f precious object, treasure (a. fig.)

kosten¹ v/t. cost*, be*; Zeit etc.: take*; was od. wieviel kostet ...? how much is ...?

kosten² v/t. taste, try

Kosten pl. cost(s pl.); price sg.; Un2: expenses pl.; Gebühren: charges pl.; auf j-s ~ at s.o.'s expense; 2los 1. adj. free; 2. adv. free of charge

köstlich adj. delicious; fig. priceless; sich ~ amüsieren have* great fun, I have* a ball

Kost|probe f taste, sample (a. fig.); 2spielig adj. expensive, costly

Kostüm n costume, dress; Damen2:

suit; ~fest n fancy-dress ball

Kot m excrement; Tier: a. droppings pl.

Kotelett n chop, cutlet; **~en** pl. sideburns pl.

Kotflügel mot. m mudguard, Am. fender

kotzen V v/i. puke

Krabbe zo. f shrimp; größere: prawn

krabbeln v/i. crawl

Krach m crash, bang; Lärm: noise; Streit: quarrel, fight; 2en v/i. crack, bang (beide a. Schuß etc.), crash (a. prallen); **~er** m (fire)cracker

krächzen v/t. u. v/i. croak

Kraft f strength, force (a. fig., pol.), power (a. electr., tech., pol.); in ~ sein (setzen, treten) be* in (put* into, come* into) force; 2brühe f consommé, clear soup; **~fahrer** m driver, motorist; **~fahrzeug** n motor vehicle; Zssgn → Auto

kräftig adj. strong (a. fig.), powerful; Essen: substantial; tüchtig: good

kraft|los adj. schwach: weak, feeble; 2probe f test of strength; 2stoff mot. m fuel; 2verschwendung f waste of energy; 2werk n power station

Kragen m collar

Krähe zo. f, 2n v/i. crow*

Krake zo. f octopus

Kralle f claw (a. fig.); 2n v/refl. cling* (an on), clutch (at)

Kram F m stuff, (one's) things pl.

Krampf med. m cramp; stärker: spasm, convulsion; **~ader** med. f varicose vein; 2haft fig. adj. Lachen etc.: forced; Versuch etc.: desperate

Kran tech. m crane

Kranich zo. m crane

krank adj. ill, attr. sick; ~ sein (werden be* (fall*) ill (bsd. Am. sick); 2e m, f sick person, patient; die ~n the sick

kränken v/t. hurt* (s.o.'s feelings), offend

Kranken|bett n sickbed; **~geld** n sickness benefit; **~gymnastik** f physiotherapy; **~haus** n hospital; **~kasse** f health insurance scheme; in e-r ~ sein be* a member of a health insurance scheme od. plan; **~pflege** f nursing; **~pfleger** m male nurse; **~schein** m health insurance certificate; **~schwester** f nurse; **~versicherung** f health insurance; **~wagen** m ambulance; **~zimmer** n sickroom

K

krankhaft adj. morbid (a. fig.)

Krankheit f illness, sickness; bestimmte: disease; **~serreger** med. m germ

kränklich adj. sickly, ailing

Kränkung f insult, offen|ce, Am. -se

Kranz m wreath; fig. ring, circle

kraß adj. crass, gross; Worte: blunt

Krater m crater

kratzen v/t. u. v/refl. scratch (o.s.); ab~: scrape (von off)

kraulen 1. v/t. Tier: stroke; j-s Haar: run* one's fingers through; **2.** v/i. Sport: do the crawl

kraus adj. Haar: curly; Stirn, Stoff: wrinkled; **2e** f Hals2: ruff; Haar2: friz(z)

kräuseln v/t. u. v/refl. Haare: curl, friz(z); Wasser: ripple

Kraut bot. n herb; Rüben2 etc.: tops pl., leaves pl.; Kohl: cabbage; Un2, F Tabak: weed

Krawall m riot; F Lärm: row, racket

Krawatte f tie

kreat|iv adj. creative; **2ivität** f creativity; **2ur** f creature

Krebs m zo. crayfish; med. cancer; astr. Cancer; sie ist (ein) ~ she's (a) Cancer; **2erregend** med. adj. carcinogenic

Kredit econ. m credit; Darlehen: loan; **~hai** m loan shark; **~karte** f credit card; **~n** pl. coll. F plastic money

Kreide f chalk; paint. a. crayon

Kreis m circle (a. fig.); pol. district, Am. a. county; **~bahn** astr. f orbit

kreischen v/i. screech; vor Vergnügen: squeal

Kreisel m (spinning) top; phys. gyro(scope); **2n** v/i. spin* around

kreisen v/i. (move in a) circle, revolve, rotate; Blut: circulate

kreis|förmig adj. circular; **2lauf** m med., Geld etc.: circulation; biol., fig. cycle; tech., electr. a. circuit; **2laufstörungen** med. pl. circulatory trouble sg.; **~rund** adj. circular; **2säge** tech. f circular saw; **2verkehr** m roundabout, Am. traffic circle

Krempe f brim

Kren östr. m horseradish

krepieren v/i. Granate: burst*, explode; sl. Mensch: kick the bucket, peg out; Tier: die, perish

Krepp m crepe (a. in Zssgn Papier etc.)

Kreuz n cross (a. fig.); crucifix; anat. (small of the) back; Kartenspiel: club(s pl.); mus. sharp; **über ~** crosswise; **j-n aufs ~ legen** take* s.o. in

kreuzen 1. v/t. u. v/refl. cross; Pläne etc.: clash; **2.** naut. v/i. cruise

Kreuzer naut. m cruiser

Kreuz|fahrer m crusader; **~fahrt** naut. f cruise; **2igen** v/t. crucify; **~igung** f crucifixion; **~otter** zo. f adder; **~schmerzen** pl. backache sg.; **ins ~ nehmen** cross-examine; **2weise** adv. crosswise, crossways; **~worträtsel** n crossword (puzzle); **~zug** m crusade

kriech|en v/i. creep*, crawl (fig. vor j-m to s.o.); **2r** contp. m toady; **2spur** mot. f slow lane

Krieg m war; **~ führen gegen** be* at war with

kriegen F v/t. get*; fangen: catch*

Krieg|er m warrior; **~erdenkmal** n war memorial; **2erisch** adj. warlike, martial; **2führend** adj. belligerent; **~führung** f warfare

Kriegs|beil fig. n: **das ~ ausgraben** (begraben) dig* up (bury) the hatchet; **~bemalung** f war paint (a. fig.); **~dienstverweigerer** m conscientious objector; **~erklärung** f declaration of war; **~gefangene** m prisoner of war, P.O.W.; **~gefangenschaft** f captivity; **~recht** jur. n martial law; **~schauplatz** m theat|re (Am. -er) of war; **~schiff** n warship; **~teilnehmer** m ehemaliger: ex-serviceman, Am. (war) veteran; **~treiber** pol. m warmonger; **~verbrechen** n war crime; **~verbrecher** m war criminal

Krimi F m (crime) thriller, Buch: a. detective novel

Kriminal|beamte m detective, plainclothesman, Brt. a. C.I.D. officer; **~polizei** f criminal investigation department; **~roman** m → Krimi

kriminell adj.; **2e(r)** criminal

Krippe f crib, manger (a. rel.); Weihnachts2: crib, manger, Am. crèche

Krise f crisis; **~nherd** m trouble spot

Kristall m, **~(glas)** n crystal; **2isieren** v/i. u. v/refl. crystallize

Kriterium n criterion (**für** of)
Krit|ik f criticism; *thea., mus. etc.*: review, critique; **gute ~en** a good press; **~ üben an** criticize; **~iker(in)** critic; **2ik-los** adj. uncritical; **2isch** adj. critical (a. fig.) (**gegenüber** of); **2isieren** v/t. criticize

kritzeln v/t. u. v/i. scrawl, scribble
Krokodil zo. n crocodile
Krone f crown; *Adels2*: coronet
krönen v/t. crown (**j-n zum König** s.o. king)
Kron|leuchter m chandelier; **~prinz** m crown prince; **~prinzessin** f crown princess
Krönung f coronation; *fig.* crowning event, climax, high point
Kropf m med. goit|re, Am. -er; zo. crop
Kröte zo. f toad
Krück|e f crutch; **~stock** m walking stick
Krug m jug, pitcher; *Bier2*: mug, stein; *mit Deckel*: tankard
Krümel m crumb; **2ig** adj. crumbly; **2n** v/t. u. v/i. crumble
krumm adj. crooked (a. fig. Geschäft etc.), bent (a. Rücken); **~beinig** adj. bow-legged
krümmen v/t. bend* (a. tech.), crook (a. Finger); **sich ~** bend*; *vor Schmerz*: writhe (with pain)
Krümmung f bend (a. Straße, Fluß), curve (a. arch.); *geogr., math., med.* curvature
Krüppel m cripple
Kruste f crust
Kto. Abk. für **Konto** a/c, account
Kübel m bucket, pail; *größerer*: tub
Kubik|meter n, m cubic met|re, Am. -er; **~wurzel** math. f cube root
Küche f kitchen; *Kochkunst*: cooking, cuisine; **kalte (warme) ~** cold (hot) meals pl.
Kuchen m cake; *Obst2*: tart, pie
Küchen|geräte pl. kitchen utensils pl. (*Maschinen*: appliances pl.); **~ge-schirr** n kitchen crockery, kitchenware; **~herd** m cooker; **~maschine** f mixer; *weitS.* kitchen appliance; **~schrank** m (kitchen) cupboard, Brt. a. dresser
Kuckuck m cuckoo
Kufe f runner; *aviat.* skid
Kugel f ball; *Gewehr2 etc.*: bullet;

math., geogr. sphere; *Sport*: shot; **2för-mig** adj. ball-shaped; *bsd. astr., math.* spheric(al); **~gelenk** tech., anat. n ball (and socket) joint; **~lager** tech. n ball bearing; **2n** v/i. u. v/t. roll; **~schreiber** m ballpoint (pen); **2sicher** adj. bulletproof; **~stoßen** n shot put(ting); **~stoßer(in)** shot-putter
Kuh f cow
kühl adj. cool (a. fig.); **2box** f coolbox; **2e** f cool(ness); **~en** v/t. cool; *Wein etc.*: chill; *Lebensmittel*: refrigerate; *er-frishen*: refresh; **2er** mot. m radiator; **2erhaube** f bonnet, Am. hood; **2mit-tel** n coolant; **2raum** m cold-storage room; **2schrank** m fridge, refrigerator; **2truhe** f → *Gefriertruhe*
kühn adj. bold; **2heit** f boldness
Kuhstall m cowshed
Küken n chick (a. fig.)
Kukuruz östr. m → **Mais**
Kuli F m ballpoint
Kulisse f *thea.*: **~n** pl. wings pl.; *Dekora-tionsstücke*: scenery; **hinter den ~n** backstage, *bsd. fig.* behind the scenes
Kult m cult; *Akt*: rite, ritual (act)
kultivieren v/t. cultivate
Kultur f culture (a. biol.), civilization; *agr.* cultivation; **~beutel** m toilet bag; **2ell** adj. cultural; **~geschichte** f history of civilization; **~volk** n civilized people; **~zentrum** n cultural cent|re, Am. -er
Kultusminister m minister of education and cultural affairs
Kummer m grief, sorrow; *Verdruß*: trouble, worry; **~ haben mit** have* trouble od. problems with
kümmer|lich adj. miserable; *dürftig*: poor, scanty; **~n** v/refl. u. v/t.: **sich ~ um** j-n od. et.: look after, take* care of, mind; *sich Gedanken machen*: care od. worry about; **be*** interested in; **was kümmert's mich?** what do I care?
Kumpel m *Bergbau*: miner; F mate, *bsd. Am.* buddy
Kunde m customer, client; **~ndienst** m after-sales service; (customer) service; service department; *Wartung*: servicing
Kundgebung f meeting, rally, demonstration
kündig|en v/i. u. v/t. *Vertrag etc.*: cancel; **j-m ~** give* s.o. his (**dem Hausbesit-**

zer od. Arbeitgeber: one's) notice; *entlassen*: dismiss s.o., F sack od. fire s.o.; **2ung** f (*Frist*: period of) notice; cancel(l)ation

Kundschaft f customers pl., clients pl.; **~er** mil. m scout, spy

Kunst f, Fertigkeit: a. skill; **~...** in Zssgn Herz, Leder, Licht etc.: artificial ...; **~akademie** f academy of arts; **~ausstellung** f art exhibition; **~dünger** m artificial fertilizer; **~erziehung** f art (education); **~faser** f man-made od. synthetic fib|re, Am. -er; **~fehler** m professional blunder; **~fliegen** aviat. n stunt flying, aerobatics pl.; **~geschichte** f history of art; **~gewerbe**, **~handwerk** n arts and crafts pl.

Künstler|(in) artist; mus., thea. a. performer; **2isch** adj. artistic

künstlich adj. artificial; unecht: a. false; synthetic; See etc.: man-made

Kunst|schütze m marksman; **~schwimmen** n water ballet; **~seide** f rayon; **~springen** n springboard diving; **~stoff** m plastic (a. in Zssgn); **~stück** n trick, stunt, bsd. fig. feat; **~turnen** n gymnastics sg.; **~turner(in)** gymnast; **2voll** adj. artistic; elaborate; **~werk** n work of art

Kupfer n copper (aus of); **~stich** m copperplate (engraving)

Kupon m coupon

Kuppe f (rounded) hilltop; Nagel2 etc.: head

Kuppel arch. f dome; kleine: cupola; **~ei** jur. f procuring; **2n** mot. v/i. put* the clutch in od. out

Kupplung f mot. clutch

Kur f course of treatment; am Kurort: cure

Kür f Kunstlauf: free skating; Turnen: free exercises pl.

Kurbel tech. f crank, handle; **2n** v/t. crank; wind* (up etc.); **~welle** tech. f crankshaft

Kürbis bot. m pumpkin, gourd, squash

Kurgast m visitor; F tourist

kurieren med. v/t. cure (von of)

kurios adj. curious, odd, strange

Kürlauf m free skating

Kur|ort m health resort, spa; **~pfuscher** m quack (doctor)

Kurs m naut., aviat., fig. course; **~us**: a.

class(es pl.); Wechsel2: (exchange) rate; Börsen2: (stock) price; **~buch** rail. n railway (Am. railroad) guide

Kürschner m furrier

kursieren v/i. circulate (a. fig.)

Kurve f curve (a. math. u. fig.); Straßen2: a. bend, turn; **2nreich** adj. winding, full of bends; fig. Frau: curvaceous

kurz adj. short; zeitlich: a. brief; **~e** Hose shorts pl.; (bis) vor **~em** (until) recently; (erst) seit **~em** (only) for a short time; **~** vorher (darauf) shortly before (after[wards]); **~** vor uns just ahead of us; **~** nacheinander in quick succession; **~** fortgehen etc. go* away for a short time od. a moment; sich **~** fassen be* brief, put* it briefly; **~** gesagt in short; zu **~** kommen go* short; **~** angebunden curt; **2arbeit** econ. f short time; **~arbeiten** v/i. work short time; **~atmig** adj. short of breath

Kürze f shortness; zeitlich: a. brevity; in **~** soon, shortly, before long; **2n** v/t. Kleid etc.: shorten (um by); Buch etc.: abridge; Ausgaben etc.: cut*, reduce (a. math.)

kurz|erhand adv. without hesitation, on the spot; **~fristig 1.** adj. short-term; **2.** adv. at short notice; **2geschichte** f short story; **~lebig** adj. short-lived

kürzlich adv. recently, not long ago

Kurz|nachrichten pl. news summary sg.; **~schluß** electr. m short circuit, F short; **~schrift** f shorthand; **2sichtig** adj. shortsighted, bsd. Am. nearsighted; **~strecke** f short distance

Kürzung f cut, reduction (a. math.)

Kurz|waren pl. haberdashery sg., Am. a. notions pl.; **2weilig** adj. entertaining; **~welle** Radio: f short wave

kuschel|ig F adj. cosy, snug; **~n** v/refl. snuggle, cuddle (an up to; in in)

Kusine f cousin

Kuß m kiss; **2echt** adj. kiss-proof

küssen v/t. kiss

Küste f coast, shore; an der **~** on the coast; an die **~** ashore; **~ngewässer** pl. coastal waters pl.; **~nschiffahrt** f coastal shipping; **~nschutz** m, **~nwache** f coast guard

Küster *rel. m* verger, sexton
Kutsche *f* carriage, coach; **~r** *m* coachman
Kutte *f* (monk's) habit

Kutteln *pl.* tripe *sg.*
Kutter *naut. m* cutter
Kuvert *n* envelope
Kybernetik *f* cybernetics *sg.*

L

labil *adj.* unstable
Labor *n* laboratory, F lab; **~ant(in)** laboratory assistant; **2ieren** *v/i.:* **~ an** suffer from
Labyrinth *n* labyrinth, maze (*beide a. fig.*)
Lache *f* pool, puddle
lächeln *v/i.,* 2 *n* smile; *höhnisch:* sneer
lachen *v/i.* laugh (*über* at)
Lachen *n* laugh(ter); *j-n zum ~ bringen* make* s.o. laugh
lächerlich *adj.* ridiculous; *~ machen* ridicule, make* fun of; *sich ~ machen* make* a fool of o.s.
Lachs *zo. m* salmon
Lack *m* varnish; *Farb2:* lacquer; *mot.* paint(work); **2ieren** *v/t.* varnish; lacquer; *mot., Nägel:* paint; **~schuhe** *pl.* patent-leather shoes *pl.*
Lade|fläche *f* loading space; **~gerät** *electr. n* battery charger; **~hemmung** *mil. f* jam
laden *v/t.* load; *electr.* charge; *Computer:* boot (up); *auf sich ~* burden o.s. with
Laden *m* shop, *bsd. Am.* store; *Fenster2:* shutter; **~dieb(in)** shoplifter; **~diebstahl** *m* shoplifting; **~inhaber** *m* shopkeeper, *bsd. Am.* storekeeper; **~kasse** *f* till; **~schluß** *m* closing time; *nach ~* after hours; **~tisch** *m* counter
Lade|rampe *f* loading platform *od.* ramp; **~raum** *m* loading space; *naut.* hold
Ladung *f* load, freight; *naut., aviat.* cargo; *electr., mil.* charge; *e-e ~ ...* a load of ...
Lage *f* situation, position (*beide a. fig.*); *Platz:* a. location; *Schicht:* layer; *Bier etc.:* round; *in schöner (ruhiger) ~* beautifully (peacefully) situated; *in der*

~ sein zu be* able to, be* in a position to
Lager *n* camp (*a. fig. Partei*); *econ.* stock, store; **~stätte:** bed; *geol.* deposit; *tech.* bearing; *et. auf ~ haben* have* s.th. in store (*a. fig. für j-n*); **~feuer** *n* campfire; **~haus** *n* warehouse; **2n 1.** *v/i.* camp; *econ.* be* stored; **2.** *v/t.* store, keep*; *kühl ~* keep* in a cool place; *Kranken etc.:* lay*, rest; **~raum** *m* storeroom; **~ung** *f* storage
Lagune *f* lagoon
lahm *adj.* lame; **~en** *v/i.* be* lame (*auf* in)
lähmen, lahmlegen *v/t.* paraly|se, *Am.* -ze; *Verkehr:* a. bring* to a standstill
Lähmung *med. f* paralysis
Laib *m* loaf
Laich *m,* 2en *v/i.* spawn
Laie *m* layman; amateur; **2nhaft** *adj.* amateurish; **~nspiel** *n* amateur play
Laken *n* sheet; *Bade2:* bath towel
Lakritze *f* liquorice
lallen *v/i. u. v/t.* speak* drunkenly; *Baby:* babble
lamentieren *v/i.* complain (*über* about)
Lamm *n* lamb; **~fell** *n* lambskin
Lampe *f* lamp, light; *Glüh2:* bulb
Lampen|fieber *n* stage fright; **~schirm** *m* lampshade
Lampion *m* Chinese lantern
Land *n* *Fest2:* land (*a. poet.*); *Staat:* country; *Boden:* ground, soil; **~besitz:** land, property; *an ~ gehen* go* ashore; *auf dem ~e* in the country; *aufs ~ fahren* go* into the country; *außer ~es gehen* go* abroad; **~arbeiter** *m* farmhand; **~bevölkerung** *f* country *od.* rural population

Landebahn *aviat. f* runway
landeinwärts *adv.* up-country, inland
landen *v/i.* land; *fig.* ~ *in* end up in
Landenge *f* neck of land, isthmus
Landeplatz *aviat. m* landing field
Länderspiel *n* international match
Landes|grenze *f* national border; **~innere** *n* interior; **~regierung** *f* Land (östr. Provincial) government; **~sprache** *f* national language; **2üblich** *adj.* customary; **~verrat** *m* treason; **~verräter** *m* traitor (to one's country); **~verteidigung** *f* national defen|ce, *Am.* -se

Land|flucht *f* rural exodus; **~friedensbruch** *jur. m* breach of the public peace; **~gericht** *n appr.* regional superior court; **~gewinnung** *f* reclamation of land; **~haus** *n* countryhouse, cottage; **2karte** *f* map; **~kreis** *m* district; **2läufig** *adj.* customary, current, common

ländlich *adj.* rural; *derb:* rustic
Land|rat *m appr.* District Administrator; **~ratte** *naut.* F *f* landlubber
Landschaft *f* countryside; *bsd. schöne:* scenery; *bsd. paint.* landscape; **2lich** *adj.* scenic
Landsmann *m* (fellow) countryman
Land|straße *f* country road; *nicht Autobahn:* ordinary road; **~streicher** *m* tramp, *Am. a.* hobo; **~streitkräfte** *pl.* land forces *pl.*; **~tag** *m* Land parliament
Landung *f* landing, *aviat. a.* touchdown; **~ssteg** *naut. m* gangway
Land|vermesser *m* land surveyor; **~vermessung** *f* land surveying; **~weg** *m:* **auf dem ~e** by land; **~wirt** *m* farmer; **~wirtschaft** *f* agriculture, farming; **2wirtschaftlich** *adj.* agricultural; **~e Maschinen** *pl.* agricultural machinery *sg.*; **~zunge** *f* promontory, spit

lang *adj. u. adv.* long; F *Person:* tall; *drei Jahre (einige Zeit)* ~ for three years (some time); *den ganzen Tag* ~ all day long; *seit ~em* for a long time; *vor er Zeit* (a) long (time) ago; *über kurz oder* ~ sooner or later; **~atmig** *adj.* long-winded
lange *adv.* (for a) long (time); *es ist schon* ~ *her* (, *seit*) it has been a long time (since); (*noch*) *nicht* ~ *her* not

long ago; *noch* ~ *hin* still a long way off; *es dauert nicht* ~ it won't take long; *ich bleibe nicht* ~ *fort* I won't be long; *wie* ~ *noch?* how much longer?
Länge *f* length; *geogr.* longitude; *der* ~ *nach* (at) full length; (*sich*) *in die* ~ *ziehen* stretch (*a. fig.*)
langen F *v/i.* greifen: reach (*nach* for); genügen: be* enough; *mir langt es* I've had enough; *fig. stärker:* a. I'm sick of it
Längen|grad *m* degree of longitude; **~maß** *n* linear measure
lang|ersehnt *adj.* long-hoped-for; **~erwartet** *adj.* long-awaited
Langeweile *f* boredom; ~ *haben* be* bored; *aus* ~ to pass the time
lang|fristig *adj.* long-term; **~jährig** *adj.* longstanding; **~e Erfahrung** many years *pl.* of experience; **2lauf** *m* cross-country (skiing); **~lebig** *adj.* long-lived (*a. fig.*)
länglich *adj.* longish, oblong
längs 1. *prp.* along(side); **2.** *adv.* lengthwise
lang|sam *adj.* slow; **~er werden** *od.* *fahren* slow down; **2schläfer** *m* late riser, F sleepyhead; **2spielplatte** *f* long-playing record, *mst* LP
längst *adv.* long ago *od.* before; ~ *vorbei* long past; *ich weiß es* ~ I have known it for a long time; **~ens** *adv.* at (the) most
Lang|strecken... *in Zssgn:* long-distance ...; *aviat., mil.* long-range ...; **2weilen** *v/t.* bore; *sich* ~ be* bored; **2weilig** *adj.* boring, dull; **~e Person** bore; **~welle** *f* long wave; **2wierig** *adj.* lengthy, protracted (*a. med.*)
Lanze *f* lance, spear
Lappalie *f* trifle
Lapp|en *m* (piece of) cloth; *Fetzen:* rag (*a. fig.*); *Staub2:* duster; **2ig** *adj.* limp
läppisch *adj.* silly; *Summe etc.:* ridiculous
Lärche *bot. f* larch
Lärm *m* noise; **2en** *v/i.* be* noisy; **2end** *adj.* noisy
Larve *f* mask; *zo.* larva
lasch F *adj.* slack, lax
Lasche *f* flap; *Schuh2:* a. tongue
Laser *phys. m* laser; **~drucker** *m* laser printer; **~strahl** *m* laser beam; **~technik** *f* laser technology

lassen v/t. u. v/aux. let*, leave*; **j-n et. tun** ~ let* s.o. do s.th.; allow s.o. to do s.th.; **veran~**: make* s.o. do s.th.; **j-n (et.) zu Hause** ~ leave* s.o. (s.th.) at home; **j-n allein (in Ruhe)** ~ leave* s.o. alone; **sich die Haare schneiden** ~ have* one's hair cut; **j-n grüßen** ~ send* one's regards (**herzlicher:** love) to s.o.; **sein Leben** ~ (**für**) lose* (give*) one's life (for); **rufen od. kommen** ~ send* for, call in; **es läßt sich machen** it can be done; **laß alles so, wie (wo) es ist** leave everything as (where) it is; **er kann das Rauchen** etc. **nicht** ~ he can't stop smoking etc.; **laß das!** stop it!
lässig adj. casual; **nach~:** careless
Last f load (a. fig.); **Bürde** f: burden (a. fig.); **Gewicht:** weight (a. fig.); **j-m zur ~ fallen** be* a burden to s.o.; **j-n et. zur ~ legen** charge s.o. with s.th.
lasten v/i.: ~ **auf** weigh od. rest (up)on (beide a. fig.); **2aufzug** m goods lift, Am. freight elevator
Laster[1] mot. m → **Lastwagen**
Laster[2] n vice
lästern v/i.: ~ **über** run* down
lästig adj. troublesome, annoying; (**j-m**) ~ **sein** be* a nuisance (to s.o.)
Last|**kahn** m barge; **~tier** n pack animal; **~wagen** m truck; Brt. a. lorry; **~wagenfahrer** m truck (Brt. a. lorry) driver, Am. a. trucker
Latein n Latin
Lateinamerika Latin America; **~ner(in)**, **2nisch** adj. Latin American
lateinisch adj. Latin
Laterne f lantern; **Straßen2:** streetlight; **~npfahl** m lamppost
Latte f lath; **Zaun2:** pale; **Sport:** bar; **~nzaun** m paling, Am. a. picket fence
Lätzchen n bib, Brt. a. feeder
Laub n foliage, leaves pl.; **~baum** m deciduous tree
Laube f arbo(u)r, bower(y)
Laub|**frosch** zo. m tree frog; **~säge** f fretsaw
Lauch bot. m leek
Lauer f: **auf der ~ liegen** od. **sein** lie* in wait; **2n** v/i. lurk; ~ **auf** lie* in wait for
Lauf m run; Bahn: course; Gewehr2: barrel; **im ~(e) der Zeit** in the course of time; **~bahn** f career; **~disziplin** f Sport: track event

laufen v/i. u. v/t. run* (a. tech., mot., econ., fig.); gehen: walk; funktionieren: work; Nase: run; **~d 1.** adj. present, current (a. econ.); ständig: continual; **auf dem ~en sein** be* up to date; **2.** adv. continuously; regelmäßig: regularly; immer: always; **lassen** v/t. j-n: let* go; straffrei: let* off
Läufer m runner (a. Teppich); Schach: bishop
Lauf|**gitter** n playpen; **~masche** f ladder, Am. run; **~paß** F m: den ~ **geben** give* the sack (e-m Freund etc.: the brush-off); **~schritt** m: **im ~** on the double; **~schuhe** pl. walking shoes pl.; Sport: trainers pl.; **~steg** m footbridge; tech., Mode: catwalk; naut. gangway
Lauge f chem. lye; Seifen2: suds pl.
Laun|**e** f mood, temper; **gute (schlechte)** ~ **haben** be* in a good (bad) mood od. temper; **2enhaft**, **2isch** adj. moody; mürrisch: bad-tempered
Laus zo. f louse; **~bub** m (young) rascal od. scamp
Lausch|**angriff** m bugging operation; **2en** v/i. listen (dat. to); heimlich: a. eavesdrop; **2ig** adj. snug, cosy
laut[1] **1.** adj. loud; Straße, Kinder: noisy; **2.** adv. loud(ly); ~ **vorlesen** read* (out) aloud; (**sprich**) ~**er, bitte!** speak up, please!
laut[2] prp. according to
Laut m sound, noise; **2en** v/i. read*; Name: be*
läuten v/i. u. v/t. ring*; **es läutet (an der Tür)** the (door)bell is ringing
lauter adv. Unsinn etc.: sheer; nichts als: nothing but; viele: (so) many
laut|**los** adj. silent, soundless; Stille: hushed; **2schrift** f phonetic transcription; **2sprecher** m (loud)speaker; **2stärke** f loudness; electr. a. (sound) volume; **mit voller ~** (at) full blast; **2stärkeregler** m volume control
lauwarm adj. lukewarm (a. fig.)
Lava geol. f lava
Lavabo n Schweiz: → **Waschbecken**
Lavendel bot. m lavender
Lawine f avalanche (a. fig.)
Lazarett n (military) hospital
leben 1. v/i. live; be* alive; **von et.** ~ live on s.th.; **2.** v/t. live
Leben n life; **am ~ bleiben** stay alive;

überleben: survive; *am ~ sein* be* alive; *ums ~ bringen* kill; *sich das ~ nehmen* take* one's (own) life, commit suicide; *ums ~ kommen* lose* one's life, be* killed; *um sein ~ laufen (kämpfen)* run* (fight*) for one's life; *das tägliche ~* everyday life; *mein ~ lang* all my life; *2d adj.* living; *2dig adj.* living, alive; *fig.* lively

Lebens|abend *m* old age, the last years *pl.* of one's life; *~bedingungen pl.* living conditions *pl.*; *~dauer f* lifespan; *tech.* (service) life; *~erfahrung f* experience of life; *~erwartung f* life expectancy; *2fähig adj. med.* viable (*a. fig.*); *~gefahr f* mortal danger; *in (unter) ~* in danger (at the risk) of one's life; *2gefährlich adj.* dangerous (to life), perilous; *~gefährte m, ~gefährtin f* partner, (lifetime) companion, F lifemate; *2groß adj.* life-size(d); *~größe f: e-e Statue in ~* a life-size(d) statue; *~haltungskosten pl.* cost *sg.* of living; *2länglich 1. adj.* lifelong; *~e Freiheitsstrafe* life sentence; *2. adv.* for life; *~lauf m* personal record, curriculum vitae; *2lustig adj.* fond of life; *~mittel pl.* food(stuffs *pl.*); *Waren: a.* groceries *pl.*; *~mittelgeschäft n* grocery, grocer's (shop); *2müde adj.* tired of life; *~notwendigkeit f* vital necessity; *~retter m* lifesaver, rescuer; *~standard m* standard of living; *~unterhalt m* livelihood; *s-n ~ verdienen* earn one's living (*als* as; *mit* out of, by); *~versicherung f* life insurance; *~weise f* way of life; *2wichtig adj.* vital, essential; *~e Organe* the vitals *pl.*; *~zeichen n* sign of life; *~zeit f* lifetime; *auf ~* for life

Leber *anat. f* liver; *~fleck m* mole; *~tran m* cod-liver oil

Lebewesen *n* living being, creature

leb|haft *adj.* lively; *Verkehr:* heavy; *2kuchen m* gingerbread; *~los adj.* lifeless (*a. fig.*); *2zeiten pl.: zu s-n ~* in his lifetime

lechzen *v/i.: ~ nach* thirst for

leck *adj.* leaking, leaky

Leck *n* leak

lecken¹ *v/t. u. v/i.* lick (*a. ~ an*)

lecken² *v/i.* leak

lecker *adj.* delicious, tasty, F yummy; *2bissen m* delicacy, treat (*a. fig.*)

Leder *n* leather; *2n adj.* leather(n); *~waren pl.* leather goods *pl.*

ledig *adj.* single, unmarried; *~lich adv.* only, merely, solely

Lee *f* lee; *nach ~* leeward

leer 1. adj. empty (*a. fig.*); *unbewohnt: a.* vacant; *Seite etc.:* blank; *Batterie:* flat, *Am.* dead; **2. adv.:** *~ laufen tech.* idle; *2e f* emptiness (*a. fig.*); *~en v/t. u. v/refl.* empty; *2n en* empties *pl.*; *2lauf m tech.* idling; *Gang:* neutral (gear); *fig.* running on the spot; *~stehend adj. Wohnung:* unoccupied, vacant; *2taste f* space bar; *2ung post f* collection

legal *adj.* legal, lawful; *~isieren v/t.* legalize; *2isierung f* legalization

Legasthen|ie *psych. f* dyslexia, F word blindness; *~iker(in)* dyslexic

legen *v/t. u. v/i.* lay* (*a. Eier*); place, put*; *Haare:* set*; *sich ~* lie* down; *fig.* calm down; *Schmerz:* wear* off

Legende *f* legend

leger *adj.* casual, informal

Legislative *f* legislative power

legitim *adj.* legitimate

Lehm *m* loam; *Ton:* clay; *2ig adj.* loamy, F muddy

Lehne *f* back(rest); arm(rest); *2en v/t. u. v/i.* lean* (*a. sich ~*), rest (*an, gegen* against; *auf* on); *sich aus dem Fenster ~* lean* out of the window; *~sessel, ~stuhl m* armchair, easy chair

Lehrbuch *n* textbook

Lehre *f Kunde:* science; *Theorie:* theory; *rel., pol.* teachings *pl.*, doctrine; *e-r Geschichte:* moral; *e-s Lehrlings:* apprenticeship; *in der ~ sein* be* apprenticed (*bei* to); *das wird ihm eine ~ sein* that will teach him a lesson; *2n v/t.* teach*, instruct; *zeigen:* show*

Lehrer *m* teacher, instructor, *Brt. a.* master; *~ausbildung f* teacher training; *~in f* (lady) teacher, *Brt. a.* mistress; *~kollegium n* (teaching) staff; *~zimmer n* staff *od.* teachers' room

Lehr|gang *m* course of instruction *od.* study); *praktischer:* (training) course; *~herr m* master; *~jahr n* year (of apprenticeship); *~ling m* apprentice, trainee; *~meister m* master; *fig.* teacher; *~mittel pl.* teaching aids *pl.*; *~plan m* curriculum, syllabus; *~probe f* demonstration lesson; *2reich adj.* informative, instructive; *~stelle f* apprenticeship; *offene*: vacancy for an apprentice; **~stuhl** *m* professorship; **~schweiz** *f* apprentice; **~vertrag** *m* indenture(s *pl.*); **~zeit** *f* apprenticeship

Leib *m* body; *Bauch*: belly, *anat.* abdomen; *Magen*: stomach; *bei lebendigem* **~e** alive; *mit* **~** *und Seele* (with) heart and soul

Leibes|erziehung *f* physical education, *Abk.* PE; **~kräfte** *pl.*: *aus* **~n** with all one's might; **~übungen** *pl.* → Leibeserziehung

Leib|garde *f* bodyguard; **~gericht** *n* favo(u)rite dish; **2haftig** *adj.*: *der* **~** *Teufel* the devil incarnate; **~es Ebenbild** living image; *ich sehe ihn noch* **~** *vor mir* I can see him (before me) now; **2lich** *adj.* physical; **~rente** *f* life annuity; **~wache** *f*, **~wächter** *m* bodyguard; **~wäsche** *f* underwear

Leiche *f* (dead) body, corpse

leichen|blaß *adj.* deadly pale; **2halle** *f* mortuary; **2schauhaus** *n* morgue; **2verbrennung** *f* cremation; **2wagen** *m* hearse

leicht *adj.* light (*a. fig.*); *einfach*: easy, simple; *geringfügig*: slight, minor; *tech.* light(weight); **~** *möglich* quite possible; **~** *gekränkt* easily offended; *das ist* **~** *gesagt* it's not as easy as that; *es geht* **~** *kaputt* it breaks easily; **2athlet** *m* (track-and-field) athlete; **2athletik** *f* track and field (events *pl.*), athletics *pl.*; **~fallen** *v/i.*: *es fällt mir (nicht) leicht (zu)* I find it easy (difficult) (to); **2gewicht** *n* lightweight; **~gläubig** *adj.* credulous; **2igkeit** *fig. f*: *mit* **~** easily, with ease; **~lebig** *adj.* happy-go-lucky; **2metall** *n* light metal; **~nehmen** *v/t.* not worry (about); *Krankheit etc.*: make* light of; *nimm's leicht!* never mind!, don't worry about it!; △ *nicht take it easy!*; **2sinn** *m* carelessness; *stärker*: recklessness; **~sinnig** *adj.* careless; *stärker*: reckless; **~verständlich** *adj.* easy to understand

Leid *n* sorrow, grief; *Schmerz*: pain **leid** *adj.*: *es tut mir* **~** I'm sorry (*um* for; *wegen* about; *daß ich zu spät komme* for being late?); **~en** *v/t. u. v/i.* suffer (*an, unter* from); *j-n gut* **~** *können* like s.o.; *ich kann od. mag ... nicht* **~** I don't like ...; *stärker*: I can't stand ...

Leiden *n* suffering(s *pl.*); *med.* disease **Leidenschaft** *f* passion; **2lich** *adj.* passionate; *heftig*: vehement

Leidensgenoss|e *m*, **~in** *f* fellow sufferer

leid|er *adv.* unfortunately; **~** *ja (nein)* I'm afraid so (not); **~lich** *adj.* passable, F so-so; **2tragende** *m, f* mourner; *er ist der* **~** *dabei* he is the one who suffers for it; **2wesen** *n*: *zu meinem* **~** to my regret

Leierkasten *m* barrel organ; **~mann** *m* organ grinder

leiern *v/i. u. v/t.* crank (up); *fig.* drone **Leih|bücherei** *f* public library; **2en** *v/t. j-m*: lend*; *vermieten*: hire (*Am.* rent) out; *sich* **~**: borrow (*von* from); *mieten*: rent, hire; **~gebühr** *f* lending fee; **~haus** *n* pawnshop, pawnbroker's (shop); **~mutter** F *f* surrogate mother; **~wagen** *mot. m* hire (*Am.* rented) car; **2weise** *adv.* on loan

Leim *m* glue; **2en** *v/t.* glue

Leine *f* line; *Hund*: lead, leash

Leinen *n* linen; *Segeltuch*: canvas; *in* **~** *gebunden* clothbound; **~schuh** *m* canvas shoe; **~samen** *bot. m* linseed; **~tuch** *n* (linen) sheet; **~wand** *f* linen; *paint., Zelt2 etc.*: canvas; *Kino*: screen

leise *adj.* quiet; *Stimme etc.*: *a.* low, soft (*a. Musik*); *fig.* slight, faint; **~r stellen** turn (the volume) down

Leiste *f* ledge; *anat.* groin

leisten *v/t.* do*, work; *vollbringen*: achieve, accomplish; *Dienst, Hilfe*: render; *Eid*: take*; *gute Arbeit* **~** do* a good job; *sich et.* **~** treat o.s. to s.th.; *ich kann es mir (nicht)* **~** I can('t) afford it

Leistung *f* performance; *besondere*: achievement; *Schule*: a. (piece of) work, result; *tech. a.*: output; *Dienst2*: service; *Sozial2*: benefit; **~sdruck** *m* pressure, stress; **2sfähig** *adj.* efficient; (*physically*) fit; **~sfähigkeit** *f* efficiency (*a. tech., econ.*); fitness; **~skontrolle** *f* (achievement *od.* proficiency) test; **~skurs** *m appr.* special subject; **~ssport** *m* competitive sport(s *pl.*)

Leitartikel *m* editorial, *bsd.* Brt. leader, leading article

leiten *v/t.* lead*, guide (*a. fig.*), conduct (*a. phys., mus.*); *Amt, Geschäft etc.*: run* (*a. Schule*), be* in charge of, manage; *TV etc.* direct; *als Moderator:* host; **~d** *adj.* leading; *phys.* conductive; **~e Stellung** key position; **~er Angestellter** executive

Leiter[1] *f* ladder (*a. fig.*)

Leiter[2] *m* leader; conductor (*a. phys., mus.*); *Amt, Firma etc.:* head, manager; *Versammlung etc.:* chairman; → **Schulleiter**; **~in** *f* leader; head; manageress; *mus.* conductress; chairwoman

Leit|faden *m* manual, guide; **~motiv** *mus. n* leitmotiv; **~planke** *mot. f* crash barrier, *Am.* guardrail; **~spruch** *m* motto

Leitung *f econ.* management; head office; *Verwaltung:* administration; *Vorsitz:* chairmanship; *e-r Veranstaltung:* organization; *künstlerische etc.:* direction; *tech.* Haupt≈: main; *im Haus:* pipe(s *pl.*); *electr., tel.* line; **die ~ haben** be* in charge; **unter der ~ von** *mus.* conducted by; **~srohr** *n* pipe; **~swasser** *n* tap water

Lekt|ion *f* lesson; **~üre** *f* reading (matter); *Schule:* reader

Lende *f* loin; *Rind:* sirloin

lenk|en *v/t.* steer, drive*; *Kind:* guide; *Verkehr, j-s Aufmerksamkeit:* direct; **≈er** *m Fahrrad etc.:* handlebar; **≈rad** *mot. n* steering wheel; **≈ung** *mot. f* steering (system)

Leopard *zo. m* leopard

Lerche *zo. f* lark

lernen *v/t. u. v/i.* learn*; *für die Schule etc.:* study; **er lernt leicht** he is a quick learner; **schwimmen etc. ~** learn* (how) to swim *etc.*

Lernmittelfreiheit *f* free books *pl. etc.*

lesbar *adj.* readable; → **leserlich**

Lesb|ierin *f*, **≈isch** *adj.* lesbian

Lese|buch *n* reader; **~lampe** *f* reading lamp

lesen *v/i. u. v/t.* read*; *Wein:* harvest; **das liest sich wie** it reads like; **~swert** *adj.* worth reading

Lese|r *m* reader; **~ratte** F *f* bookworm; **~rbrief** *m* letter to the editor; **≈rlich** *adj.* legible; **~stoff** *m* reading matter; **~zeichen** *n* bookmark

Lesung *f* reading (*a. parl.*)

Letzt *f:* **zu guter ~** in the end

letzte *adj.* last; *neueste:* latest; **zum ~n Mal(e)** for the last time; **in ~r Zeit** re-

cently; **als ~r ankommen** *etc.* arrive *etc.* last; **≈r sein** be* last (*a. Sport*); **das ist das ≈!** that's the limit!; **~ns** *adv.* finally; **erst ~** just recently; **~re** *adj.:* **der (die, das) ~** the latter

Leucht|anzeige *f* luminous *od.* LED display *f* light; **≈en** *v/i.* shine*; *schwächer:* glow; **~en** *n* shining; glow; **≈end** *adj.* shining (*a. fig.*); *Farbe etc.:* bright; **~er** *m* candlestick; → **Kronleuchter**; **~farbe** *f* luminous paint; **~reklame** *f* neon sign(s *pl.*); **~(stoff)röhre** *electr. f* fluorescent lamp; **~turm** *m* lighthouse; **~ziffer** *f* luminous figure

leugnen *v/t. u. v/i.* deny (*et. getan zu haben* having done s.th.)

Leute *pl.* people *pl.*, F folks *pl.*

Leutnant *mil. m* second lieutenant

Lexikon *n* encyclop(a)edia; *Wörterbuch:* dictionary

Libelle *zo. f* dragonfly

liber|al *adj.* liberal; **≈o** *m* sweeper

licht *adj.* bright; *fig.* lucid

Licht *n* light; *Helle:* brightness; **~ machen** switch *od.* turn on the light(s); **~bild** *n* photo(graph); *Dia:* slide; **~bildervortrag** *m* slide lecture; **~blick** *fig. m* ray of hope; *Idee:* bright moment; **≈empfindlich** *adj.* sensitive to light; *phot.* sensitive; **~empfindlichkeit** *f* (light) sensitivity; *phot.* speed

lichten *v/t. Wald:* clear; **den Anker ~** *naut.* weigh anchor; **sich ~** get* thin(ner); *fig.* be* thinning (out)

Licht|geschwindigkeit *f* speed of light; **~griffel** *m* light pen; **~hupe** *mot. f* (headlight) flash(er); **die ~ betätigen** flash one's lights; **~jahr** *n* light year; **~maschine** *mot. f* generator; **~orgel** *f* colo(u)r organ; **~pause** *f* blueprint; **~schacht** *m* well; **~schalter** *m* (light) switch; **≈scheu** *fig. adj.* shady; **~schutzfaktor** *m* sun protection factor, SPF; **~strahl** *m* ray *od.* beam of light (*a. fig.*)

Lichtung *f* clearing

Lid *n* (eye)lid; **~schatten** *m* eye shadow

lieb *adj.* dear; *liebenswert: a.* sweet; *nett, freundlich:* nice, kind; *Kind:* good; *in Briefen:* **~e Jeanie** dear Jeanie

Liebe *f* love (**zu** of, for); **aus ~ zu** out of love for; **~ auf den ersten Blick** love at first sight; **≈n** *v/t.* love; *j-n: a.* be* in love with; *sexuell:* make* love to

liebens|wert adj. lovable, charming, sweet; **~würdig** adj. kind; **2würdigkeit** f kindness

lieber adv. rather, sooner; **~ haben** prefer, like better; **ich möchte ~ (nicht)** ... I'd rather (not) ...; **du solltest ~ (nicht)** ... you had better (not) ...

Liebes|brief m love letter; **~erklärung** f: **j-m e-e ~ machen** declare one's love to s.o.; **~kummer** m: **~ haben** be* lovesick; **~paar** n lovers pl.

liebevoll adj. loving, affectionate

lieb|gewinnen v/t. get* fond of; **~haben** v/t. love, be* fond of; **2haber** m lover (a. fig.); **2haber...** in Zssgn Preis, Stück etc.: collector's ...; **2haberei** f hobby; **~lich** adj. lovely, charming, sweet (a. Wein)

Liebling m darling; Günstling: favo(u)rite; als Anrede: darling, honey; **~s...** in Zssgn mst favo(u)rite

lieblos adj. unloving, cold; Worte: unkind; nachlässig: careless

Lied n song; Melodie: tune

liederlich adj. slovenly, sloppy

Liedermacher m singer-songwriter

Lieferant econ. m supplier

liefer|bar adj. available; **2frist** f term of delivery; **~n** v/t. deliver; **j-m et. ~** supply s.o. with s.th.; **2ung** f delivery; Versorgung: supply; **2wagen** m (delivery) van

Liege f couch; (camp) bed

liegen v/i. lie*; (gelegen) sein: a. be* (situated); (krank) **im Bett ~** be* (ill) in bed; **nach Osten (der Straße) ~** face east (the street); **daran liegt es(, daß)** that's (the reason) why; **es (er) liegt mir nicht** it (he) is not my cup of tea; **mir liegt viel (wenig) daran** it means a lot (doesn't mean much) to me; **~bleiben** v/i. stay in bed; Tasche etc.: be* left behind; **~lassen** v/t. leave* (behind); **j-n links ~** ignore s.o., give* s.o. the cold shoulder

Liege|sitz m reclining seat; **~stuhl** m deckchair; **~stütz** m bsd. Brt. press-up, bsd. Am. push-up; **~wagen** rail. m couchette

Lift m lift, Am. elevator; ski lift

Liga f league; Sport: a. division

Likör m liqueur

lila adj. purple, violet

Lilie f lily

Liliputaner m dwarf, midget

Limonade f pop; Zitronen2: lemonade, Am. lemon soda

Limousine mot. f saloon car, Am. sedan; Pullman2: limousine

Linde f lime (tree), linden

linder|n v/t. relieve, ease, alleviate; **2ung** f relief, alleviation

Lineal n ruler

Linie f line; **auf s-e ~ achten** watch one's weight; **~nflug** m scheduled flight; **~nrichter(in)** linesman (-woman); **2ntreu** pol. adj.: **~ sein** follow the party line

lin(i)ieren v/t. rule, line

link|e adj. left (a. pol.); **auf der ~n Seite** on the left(-hand side); **2e(r)** pol. leftist, left-winger; **~isch** adj. awkward, clumsy

links adv. on the left (a. pol.); verkehrt: on the wrong side; **nach ~** (to the) left; **~ von** to the left of; **2...** in Zssgn Verkehr etc.: left-hand ...; **2außen** Sport: m outside left, left wing; **2händer(in)** left-hander; **2radikale** m, f left-wing extremist

Linse f bot. lentil; opt. lens

Lippe f lip; **~nstift** m lipstick

liquidieren v/t. liquidate (a. pol.)

lispeln v/i. (have*) a lisp

List f trick; **~igkeit:** cunning

Liste f list; Namens2: a. roll

listig adj. cunning, tricky, sly

Liter n, m lit|re, Am. -er

litera|risch adj. literary; **nach ~** (to the) left; **2tur** f literature; **2tur...** in Zssgn Kritik etc.: mst literary

Litfaßsäule f advertising pillar

Lizenz f licen|ce, Am. -se

LKW, Lkw Abk. für Lastkraftwagen truck, Brt. a. lorry

Lob n, **2en** v/t. praise; **2enswert** adj. praiseworthy, laudable

Loch n hole (a. fig.); im Reifen: puncture; **2en** v/t. Papier, Karte etc.: punch (a. tech.); **~er** m punch; **~karte** f punch(ed) card

Locke f curl; Strähne, Büschel: lock

locken¹ v/t. u. v/refl. curl

locken² v/t. lure, entice; fig. a. attract, tempt (a. reizen)

Locken|kopf m curly head; **~wickler** m curler, roller

locker adj. loose; Seil: a. slack; fig. läs-

sig: relaxed; **~n** *v/t.* loosen, slacken; *Griff*: relax (*a. fig.*); **sich ~** loosen, (be)come* loose; *Sport*: limber up; **~** relax

lockig *adj.* curly, curled

Lock|mittel *n* → *Köder*; **~vogel** *m* decoy, stoolpigeon (*beide a. fig.*)

lodern *v/i.* blaze, flare

Löffel *m* spoon; *Schöpf2*: ladle; **2n** *v/t.* spoon up; **~voll** *m* spoonful

Logbuch *n* log

Loge *f thea.* box; *Bund*: lodge

Log|ik *f* logic; **2isch** *adj.* logical; **2ischerweise** *adv.* logically, obviously

Lohn *m* wages *pl.*, pay(ment); *fig.* reward; **~empfänger(in)** wage earner, *Am.* wageworker; **2en** *v/refl.* be* worth(while), pay*; *es (die Mühe) lohnt sich* it's worth it (the trouble); *das Buch (der Film) lohnt sich* the book (film) is worth reading (seeing); **2end** *adj.* paying; *fig.* rewarding; **~erhöhung** *f* increase in wages, rise, *Am.* raise; **~steuer** *f* income tax; **~stopp** *m* wage freeze; **~tüte** *f* pay packet

Loipe *f* (cross-country) course

Lokal *n* restaurant; *Kneipe*: bar, *bsd.* Brt. pub, *bsd. Am.* saloon; **~... in Zssgn** mst local

Lok|(omotive) *f* engine; **~führer** *m* train driver, *Am.* engineer

Lorbeer *bot. m* laurel; *Gewürz*: bay leaf

Lore *f* Kipp2: tipcart

Los *n* lot; *fig. a.* fate; *Lotterie2*: (lottery) ticket, number

los *adj. u. adv.* ab, fort: off; *Hund etc.*: loose; **~ sein** be* rid of; *was ist ~?* what's the matter?, F what's up?; *ge-schieht*: what's going on (here)?; *hier ist nicht viel ~* there's nothing much going on here; F *da ist was ~!* that's where the action is!; F *also ~!* okay, let's go!; **~binden** *v/t.* untie

Lösch|blatt *n* blotting paper; **2en** *v/t.* extinguish, put* out; *Durst*: quench; *Tinte*: blot; *auf der Tafel*: wipe off; *Zeile, Aufnahme*: erase; *Computer*: erase, delete; *Kalk*: slake; *naut.* unload; **~papier** *n* blotting paper

lose *adj.* loose (*a. fig. Zunge etc.*)

Lösegeld *n* ransom

losen *v/i.* draw* lots (**um** for)

lösen *v/t.* Knoten etc.: undo*; *lockern*: loosen, relax; *Bremse etc.*: release; *ab~*: take* off; *Rätsel, Problem, Aufgabe etc.*: solve; *Konflikt etc.*: settle; *Karte*: buy*, get*; *auf2*: dissolve (*a. chem.*); **sich ~** come* loose *od.* undone; *fig.* free o.s. (**von** from)

los|fahren *v/i.* leave*; *selbst*: drive* off; **~gehen** *v/i.* leave*; *Schuß etc.*: go* off; *auf j-n* go* for s.o.; *ich gehe jetzt los* I'm off now; **~kaufen** *v/t.* ransom; **~ketten** *v/t.* unchain; **~kommen** *v/i.* get* away (**von** from); **~lassen** *v/t.* let* go; *den Hund ~ auf* set* the dog on; **~legen** F *v/i.* get* cracking

löslich *chem. adj.* soluble

los|lösen *v/t* → *lösen*; **~machen** *v/t* → *lösen*; **~reißen** *v/t.* tear* off; *sich ~* break* away; *bsd. fig.* tear* o.s. away (*beide*: **von** from); **~sagen** *v/refl.*: *sich ~ von* break* with; **~schlagen** *v/i.* strike* (*auf j-n* out at s.o.); **~schnallen** *v/t.* unbuckle; *sich ~ mot., aviat.* unfasten one's seatbelt; **~schrauben** *v/t.* unscrew, screw off; **~stürzen** *v/i.*: *~ auf* rush at

Losung *f mil.* password; *fig.* slogan

Lösung *f* solution (*a. fig.*); *e-s Konflikts etc.*: settlement; **~smittel** *n* solvent

los|werden *v/t.* get* rid of; *Geld*: spend*; *lose**; **~ziehen** *v/i.* set* out, take* off, march away

Lot *n* plumbline

löten *v/t.* solder

Lotse *naut. m*, **2n** *v/t.* pilot

Lotterie *f* lottery; **~gewinn** *m* prize; **~los** *n* lottery ticket

Lotto *n allg.* lotto, bingo; *Brt.* national lottery; *deutsches*: Lotto; (*im*) **~spielen** do* Lotto; **~schein** *m* Lotto coupon; **~ziehung** *f* Lotto draw

Löw|e *m zo.* lion; *astr.* Leo; *er ist (ein) ~* he's (a) Leo; **~enzahn** *bot. m* dandelion; **~in** *zo.* f lioness

loyal *adj.* loyal, faithful

Luchs *zo. m* lynx

Lücke *f* gap (*a. fig.*); **~nbüßer** *m* stopgap; **2nhaft** *adj.* full of gaps; *fig.* incomplete; **2nlos** *adj.* without a gap; *fig.* complete; **~ntest** *m* completion *od.* fill-in test

Luft *f* air; *an der frischen ~* (out) in the fresh air; *(frische) ~ schöpfen* get* a breath of fresh air; *die ~ anhalten* catch* (*bsd. fig. a.* hold*) one's breath;

tief ~ *holen* take* a deep breath; *in die* ~ *fliegen* (*sprengen*) blow* up

Luft|angriff *m* air raid; **~aufnahme** *f* → *Luftbild*; **~ballon** *m* balloon; **~bild** *n* aerial photograph *od.* view; **~blase** *f* air bubble; **~brücke** *f* airlift

Lüftchen *n* (gentle) breeze

luft|dicht *adj.* airtight; **2druck** *phys.*, *tech. m* air pressure

lüften *v/t. u. v/i.* air, ventilate; *Geheimnis etc.*: reveal

Luft|fahrt *f* aviation, aeronautics; **~feuchtigkeit** *f* (atmospheric) humidity; **~gewehr** *n* airgun; **2ig** *adj.* airy; *Plätzchen*: breezy; *Kleid etc.*: light; **~kissen** *n* air cushion; **~kissenfahrzeug** *n* hovercraft; **~krankheit** *f* airsickness; **~krieg** *m* air warfare; **~kurort** *m* (climatic) health resort; **~leer** *adj.*: **~er Raum** vacuum; **~linie** *f*: 50 *km* ~ 50 km as the crow flies; **~post** *f* air mail; **~pumpe** *f* air pump; bicycle pump; **~röhre** *anat. f* windpipe, trachea; **~schlange** *f* streamer; **~schloß** *n* castle in the air; **~sprünge** *pl.*: ~ *machen vor Freude* jump for joy

Lüftung *f* airing; *tech.* ventilation

Luft|veränderung *f* change of air; **~verkehr** *m* air traffic; **~verschmutzung** *f* air pollution; **~waffe** *mil. f* air force; **~weg** *m*: *auf dem* ~ by air; **~zug** *m* draught, *Am.* draft

Lüge *f* lie; **2n** *v/i.* lie, tell* a lie *od.* lies; *das ist gelogen* that's a lie

Lügner|(in) liar; **2isch** *adj.* false

Luke *f* hatch; *Dach2*: skylight

Lümmel *m* rascal; **2n** *v/refl.* slouch

lumpen F *v/t.*: *sich nicht* ~ *lassen* be* generous

Lump|en *m* rag; *in* ~ in rags *pl.*; **~en-pack** F *n sl.* bastards *pl.*; **2ig** *fig. adj.*: *für* ~*e zwei Mark* for a paltry two marks

Lunge *anat. f* lungs *pl.*; (*auf*) ~ *rauchen* inhale; **~nentzündung** *med. f* pneumonia; **~nflügel** *anat. m* lung; **~nzug** *m*: *e-n* ~ *machen* inhale

lungern *v/i.* → *herumlungern*

Lupe *f* magnifying glass; *unter die* ~ *nehmen* scrutinize (closely)

Lust *f* desire, interest; *sinnliche*: lust; *Vergnügen*: pleasure, delight; ~ *haben auf et.* (*et. zu tun*) feel* like (doing) s.th.; *hättest du* ~ *auszugehen?* would you like to go out?; *ich habe keine* ~ I don't feel like it, I'm not in the mood for it; *die* ~ *an et. verlieren* (*j-m die* ~ *an et. nehmen*) (make* s.o.) lose* all interest in s.th.

lüstern *adj.* greedy (*nach et.* for s.th.)

lustig *adj.* funny; *fröhlich*: cheerful; *er ist sehr* ~ he is full of fun; *es war sehr* ~ it was great fun; *sich* ~ *machen über* make* fun of

lust|los *adj.* listless, indifferent; **2mord** *m* sex murder; **2spiel** *n* comedy

lutschen *v/i. u. v/t.* suck

Luv *naut. f* windward, weather side

luxuriös *adj.* luxurious

Luxus *m* luxury; **~artikel** *m* luxury (article); **~ausführung** *f* de-luxe (*bsd. Am.* deluxe) version; **~hotel** *n* five-star (*od.* luxury) hotel

Lymphdrüse *anat. f* lymph gland

lynchen *v/t.* lynch

Lyr|ik *f* poetry; **~iker(in)** (lyric) poet(ess); **2isch** *adj.* lyrical (*a. fig.*)

M

M

machbar *adj.* feasible

machen *v/t. tun*: do*; *herstellen, verursachen*: make*; *Essen etc.*: make*, prepare; *in Ordnung bringen, reparieren*: fix (*a. fig.*); *ausmachen, betragen*: be*, come* to, amount to; *Prüfung*: take*, erfolgreich*: pass; *Reise, Ausflug*: make*, go* on; *Hausaufgaben* ~ do* one's homework; *da(gegen) kann man nichts* ~ it can't be helped; *mach, was du willst!* do as you please!; (*nun*) *mach mal od. schon!* hurry up!, come on *od.* along now!; *mach`s gut!* take care (of yourself)!, good luck!; (*das*) *macht nichts* it doesn't matter; *mach dir nichts d(a)raus!* never mind!, don't worry!; *das macht mir nichts aus* I don't mind *od.* care; *was od. wieviel macht das?* how much is it?; *sich ≈ (nichts) ~ aus für (un)wichtig halten:* (not) care about; *(nicht) mögen:* (not) care for

Machenschaften *pl.* machinations *pl.*; *unsaubere ~* sleaze *sg.* (*bsd. pol.*)

Macher *m* man of action, doer

Macho *m* macho

Macht *f* power (*über* of); *an der ~* in power; *mit aller ~* with all one's might; *~haber pol. m* ruler

mächtig *adj.* powerful, mighty (*a. fig.*); *riesig:* enormous, huge; F: *~ klug (stolz)* mighty clever (proud)

Macht|kampf *m* struggle for power; *2los adj.* powerless; *~mißbrauch m* abuse of power; *~politik f* power politics *sg., pl.*; *~übernahme f* takeover; *~wechsel m* transition of power

Mädchen *n* girl; *Dienst2:* maid; *2haft adj.* girlish; *~name m* girl's name; *e-r Frau:* maiden name; *~schule f* girls' school

Made *f* maggot; *Obst2:* worm

Mädel *n* girl, *Brt. a.* lass, *Am.* F chick

madig *adj.* maggoty, *Obst a.:* worm-eaten; F *j-m et. ~ machen* spoil s.th. for s.o.

Magazin *n Zeitschrift, e-r Waffe:* magazine; *Lager:* store(room), warehouse, *bsd. mil.* magazine, depot; *TV, Rundfunk:* magazine, review

Magd *f* (female) farmhand

Magen *m* stomach, F tummy; *~beschwerden pl.* stomach trouble *sg.*; *~Darm-Infektion med. f* gastroenteritis; *~geschwür med. n* (stomach) ulcer; *~schmerzen pl.* stomachache *sg.*

mager *adj. Körper(teil):* lean, thin, skinny; *Käse etc.:* low-fat; *Fleisch:* lean; *Milch:* skim; *fig. Gewinn, Ernte etc.:* meag|re, *Am. a.* -er

Magie *f* magic; *2sch adj.* magic(al)

Magister *m univ.* Master of Arts *od.* Science; *östr.* → **Apotheker**

Magistrat *m* municipal council

Magnet *m* magnet (*a. fig.*); *~... in Zssgn Band, Feld, Nadel etc.:* magnetic ...; *2isch adj.* magnetic (*a. fig.*); *2isieren v/t.* magnetize

Mahagoni *n* mahogany

mäh|en *v/t. Rasen:* mow*; *Gras:* cut*; *bsd. Getreide:* reap; *2drescher agr. m* combine (harvester)

mahlen *v/t.* grind*

Mahlzeit *f meal; Baby:* feed(ing)

Mähne *f* mane

mahn|en *v/t.* remind; *Schuldner:* send* *s.o.* a reminder; → *ermahnen*; *2mal n* memorial; *2gebühr f* reminder fee; *2ung f Brief:* reminder

Mai *m* May; *der Erste ~* May Day; *~baum m* maypole; *~glöckchen n* lily of the valley; *~käfer m* cockchafer

Mais *bot. m* maize, *Am.* corn

Majestät *f: Seine (Ihre, Eure) ~* His (Her, Your) Majesty; *2isch adj.* majestic

Major *mil. m* major

makaber *adj.* macabre

Makel *m* blemish (*a. fig.*)

mäkelig F *adj.* fussy, choos(e)y, *bsd. Am.* picky

makellos *adj.* immaculate (*a. fig.*)

mäkeln F *v/i. carp.* pick, nag (*an* at)

Makler *econ. m Grundstücks2, Wohnungs2: (Am. real)* estate agent; *Börsen2:* broker; *~gebühr econ. f* fee, commission

mal *adv.* math. times, multiplied by; *Maße:* by; F *~ einmal; 12 ~ 5 ist (gleich) 60* 12 times *od.* multiplied by 5 is *od.* equals 60; *ein 7 ~ 4 Meter großes Zimmer* a room 7 metres by 4

Mal¹ *n* time; *zum ersten (letzten) ~(e)* for the first (last) time; *mit e-m ~(e) plötzlich:* all of a sudden; *ein für alle ~(e)* once and for all

Mal² *n Zeichen:* mark; → **Mutter2**

malen *v/t.* paint (*a. streichen*)

Maler *m* painter; *~ei f* painting; *~in f* (woman) painter; *2isch fig. adj.* picturesque

Malkasten *m* paintbox

malnehmen *math. v/t.* multiply (*mit* by)

Malz *n* malt; *~bier n* malt beer

Mama F *f* mum(my), *Am.* mom(my)

Mammut *zo. n* mammoth (*a. in Zssgn*)

man *indef. pron.* you, *förmlicher:* one; they, people; *wie schreibt ~ das?* how do you spell it?; *~ sagt, daß* they *od.* people say (that); *~ hat mir gesagt* I was told

Manager *m* executive; *Sport*: manager

manch|(er, -e, -es) *indef. pron.* (*mst pl.*) *einige*: some; *viele*: quite a few, many; **~mal** *adv.* sometimes

Mandant(in) *jur.* client

Mandarine *bot. f* tangerine

Mandat *bot. n* mandate; *Sitz*: seat

Mandatar *östr. m* → **Abgeordnete(r)**

Mandel *f bot.* almond; *anat.* tonsil; **~entzündung** *med. f* tonsillitis

Manege *f* (circus) ring

Mangel¹ *m Fehlen*: lack (**an** of); *Knappheit*: shortage; *tech.* defect, fault; *e-r Leistung* (*a. Schule*): shortcoming; **aus ~ an** for lack of

Mangel² *f Wäsche²*: mangle

mangelhaft *adj. Qualität*: poor; *Arbeit, Ware*: defective; *Schulleistung, -note*: poor, unsatisfactory, failing

mangeln *v/t. Wäsche*: mangle

mangels *prp.* for lack *od.* want of

Mangelware *f*: **~ sein** be* scarce

Manie *f* mania (*a. fig.*)

Manier|en *pl.* manners *pl.*; **²lich** *adv.*: *sich ~ betragen* behave (decently)

Manifest *n* manifesto

manipulieren *v/t.* manipulate

Mann *m* man; *Ehe²*: husband

Männchen *zo. n* male

Manndeckung *f Sport*: man-to-man marking

Mannequin *n* model

mannig|fach, ~faltig *adj.* many and various *pl.*

männlich *adj. biol.* male; *Aussehen, Eigenschaften, gr.*: masculine (*a. fig.*)

Mannschaft *f Sport*: team (*a. fig.*); *naut., aviat.* crew

Manöv|er *n*, **²rieren** *v/i.* manoeuvre, *Am.* maneuver

Mansarde *f* room in the attic; **~nfenster** *n* dormer (window)

Manschette *f* cuff; *tech. Dichtungs²*: gasket; *Zier²*: frill; **~nknopf** *m* cufflink

Mantel *m* coat; *Reifen*: casing, *Fahrrad*: tyre (*Am.* tire) cover; *tech.* jacket, shell

Manuskript *n* manuscript; *druckreifes*: copy

Mäppchen *n Feder²*: pencil case

Mappe *f Aktentasche*: briefcase; *Schul²*: school bag; *Ranzen*: satchel; *Aktendeckel*: folder; △ *nicht* **map**

Märchen *n* fairytale (*a. fig.*); **~ erzäh-**

len *fig.* tell* (tall) stories *od.* fibs; **~land** *n* fairyland (*a. fig.*)

Marder *zo. m* marten

Margarine *f* margarine

Margerite *bot. f* marguerite

Marienkäfer *zo. m* ladybird, *Am.* lady bug

Marihuana *n* marijuana, *sl.* grass; **~zigarette** *f sl.* reefer, joint

Marille *östr. f* apricot

Marine *mil. f* navy; △ *nicht* **marine**; **²blau** *adj.* navy blue

Marionette *f* puppet (*a. fig.*). **~ntheater** *n* puppet show

Mark¹ *f Währung, Münze*: mark

Mark² *n Knochen²*: marrow; *Frucht²*: pulp

Marke *f Lebensmittel etc.*: brand; *Fahrzeug, Gerät*: make; **~nzeichen**: trademark (*a. fig.*); *Brief² etc.*: stamp; *Erkennungs²*: badge, tag; *Zeichen*: mark

markier|en *v/t.* mark (*a. Sport*); F *fig.* act; **²ung** *f* mark

Markise *f* awning, sun blind

Markt *econ. m* market; *auf den ~ bringen econ.* put* on the market; **~platz** *m* market place; **~wirtschaft** *f freie ~*: free enterprise (economy); *soziale ~*: social (market) economy

Marmelade *f* jam; *Orangen²*: marmalade

Marmor *m* marble (*a. aus ~*)

Marsch¹ *m* march (*a. mus.*)

Marsch² *f* marsh, fen

Marschall *m* marshal

Marsch|befehl *mil. m* marching orders *pl.*; **²ieren** *v/i.* march

Marsmensch *m* Martian

Marter *f* torture; **²n** *v/t.* torture; **~pfahl** *m* stake

Martinshorn *n* (police *etc.*) siren

Märtyrer *m* martyr (*a. fig.*)

Marxis|mus *pol. m* Marxism; **~t(in)** *pol.* Marxist; **²tisch** *pol. adj.* Marxist

März *m* March

Marzipan *n* marzipan

Masche *f Strick²*: stitch; *Netz²*: mesh; F *fig.* trick; *Mode*: fad, craze; **~ndraht** *m* wire netting

Maschine *f* machine; *Motor*: engine; *Flugzeug*: plane; *Motorrad*: motorcycle, machine

Maschinen|bau *tech. m* mechanical engineering; **~gewehr** *n* machinegun;

M

2lesbar adj. Computer: machine-readable; **~öl** n engine oil; **~pistole** f submachine gun, machine pistol; **~schaden** m engine trouble od. failure; **~schlosser** m (engine) fitter

maschineschreiben v/i. type

Masern med. pl. measles pl.

Maserung f Holz etc.: grain

Mask|e f mask (a. Computer u. fig.); **~enball** m fancy-dress ball; **~enbildner(in)** make-up artist; **2ieren** v/t. mask; sich ~ put* on a mask; → verkleiden

maskulin adj. masculine (a. gr.)

Maß¹ n ~einheit: measure (für of); e-s Raumes etc.: dimensions (für), measurements pl., size; fig. extent, degree; ~e und Gewichte weights and measures; nach ~ (gemacht) made to measure; in gewissem (hohem) ~e to a certain (high) degree; in zunehmendem ~e increasingly

Maß² f Bier: lit|re (Am. -er) of beer

Massage f massage

Massaker n massacre

Masse f mass; Substanz: substance; Menschen2: crowd(s pl.); F: e-e ~ Geld etc. loads of; die (breite) ~, pol. die ~n pl. the masses pl.

Maßeinheit f unit of measure(ment)

Massen... in Zssgn Medien, Mörder etc.: mass ...; **~andrang** m crush; **2haft** F adv. masses od. loads of; **~karambolage** mot. f pileup; **~produktion** f mass production

Masseu|r m masseur; **~se** f masseuse

maß|gebend, ~geblich adj. verbindlich: authoritative; beträchtlich: substantial, considerable; **~halten** v/i. be* moderate (in in)

massieren v/t. massage

massig adj. massive, bulky

mäßig adj. moderate; dürftig: poor; **~en** v/t. u. v/refl. moderate; **2ung** f moderation; restraint

massiv adj. solid

Massiv n Berg2: massif

Maß|krug m beer mug, aus Steingut: stein; **2los** adj. Essen, Trinken etc.: immoderate; Übertreibung: gross; **~nahme** f measure, step; **~regel** f rule; **2regeln** v/t. tadeln: reprimand; strafen: discipline; **~stab** m scale; fig. standard; im ~ 1:50000 on the scale of

1:50000; **2stabgetreu** adj. true to scale; **2voll** adj. moderate

Mast¹ naut. m mast

Mast² agr. f Schweine2 etc.: fattening; **~futter**: mast; **~darm** anat. m rectum

mästen v/t. fatten; F j-n: stuff

masturbieren v/i. masturbate

Match östr. n match, Am. game; **~ball** m Tennis: match point

Material n material (a. fig.); Arbeits2: materials pl.; **~ismus** phil. m materialism; **~ist** m materialist; **2istisch** adj. materialistic

Materie f matter (a. fig.); Thema: subject (matter); **2ll** adj. material

Mathemati|k f mathematics sg.; **~ker** m mathematician; **2sch** adj. mathematical

Matinee thea., mus. f morning performance; ⚠ nicht matinee

Matratze f mattress

Matrize f stencil; auf ~ schreiben stencil

Matrose naut. m sailor, seaman

Matsch m mud, bsd. Schnee2: slush; F Brei: mush; **2ig** adj. muddy, slushy; Frucht: squashy, mushy

matt adj. schwach: weak; erschöpft: exhausted, worn out; Farbe: dull, pale; Fotooberfläche: mat(t); Glas, Glühbirne: frosted; Schach: checkmate

Matte f mat

Mattigkeit f exhaustion, weakness

Mattscheibe f phot. focus(s)ing screen; Bildschirm: screen; F Fernseher: Brt. telly, box, Am. (boob) tube

Matura f östr., Schweiz: → Abitur

Mauer f wall; **~blümchen** fig. n wallflower; **~werk** n masonry, brickwork; **2n** v/i. lay* bricks

Maul n mouth; sl.: halt's ~! shut up!; **2en** F v/i. grumble, sulk, pout; **~korb** m muzzle (a. fig.); **~tier** n mule; **~wurf** m mole; **~wurfshaufen, ~wurfshügel** m molehill

Maurer m bricklayer; **~kelle** f trowel; **~meister** m master bricklayer; **~polier** m foreman bricklayer

Maus f mouse (a. Computer); **~efalle** f mousetrap

Mauser f mo(u)lt(ing); in der ~ sein be* mo(u)lting

Maut östr. f toll; **~straße** f toll road, Am. a. turnpike

maxi|mal 1. adj. maximum; **2.** adv. at (the) most; **2mum** n maximum

Mayonnaise f mayonnaise

Mäzen m Kunst: patron; Sport: sponsor

Mechani|k f phys. mechanics mst sg.; tech. mechanism; **~ker** m mechanic; **2sch** adj. mechanical; **2sieren** v/t. mechanize; **~sierung** f mechanization; **~smus** tech. m mechanism; Triebwerk, Uhrwerk: works pl.

meckern v/i. Ziege: bleat; fig. grumble, grouch, Am. a. bitch (**über** at, about)

Medaill|e f medal; **~engewinner(in)** medal(l)ist; **~on** n locket

Medien pl. Massen2: mass media pl.; Unterricht: teaching aids pl.; technische ~: audio-visual aids pl.

Medikament n drug; bsd. zum Einnehmen: medicine

meditieren v/i. meditate (**über** on)

Medizin f (science of) medicine; Arznei: medicine, remedy (**gegen** for); **~er(in)** Arzt: (medical) doctor; Student: medical student; **2isch** adj. medical; **2isch-technische(r) Assistent(in)** (abbr. **MTA**) medical technologist; **~mann** m witchdoctor; Indianer: medicine man

Megabyte n Computer: megabyte

Meer n sea (a. fig.), ocean; **~busen** m gulf, bay; **~enge** f straits pl.; **~esboden** m seabed; **~esfrüchte** pl. seafood sg.; **~esspiegel** m sea level; **~rettich** m horseradish; **~schweinchen** n guinea pig

Mehl n flour; grobes: meal; **2ig** adj. mealy; **~speis(e)** östr. f sweet (dish)

mehr indef. pron. u. adv. more; **immer ~** more and more; **nicht ~** zeitlich: no longer, not any longer (od. more); noch **~** even more; **es ist kein ... ~ da** there isn't any ... left; **~deutig** adj. ambiguous; **~ere** adj. u. indef. pron. several; **2heit** f majority; **2kosten** pl. extra costs pl.; **~mals** adv. several times; **2wegflasche** f returnable (od. deposit) bottle; **2wertsteuer** econ. f value-added tax (abbr. **VAT**); **2zahl** f Mehrheit: majority; gr. plural (form); **2zweck...** in Zssgn Fahrzeug etc.: multi-purpose

meiden v/t. avoid

Meile f mile; **2nweit** adv. (for) miles

mein poss. pron. u. adj. my; **das ist ~er** (-e, -[e]s) gehört mir: that's mine

Meineid jur. m perjury

meinen v/t. glauben, e-r Ansicht sein: think*, believe; sagen wollen, beabsichtigen, sprechen von: mean*; sagen: say*; **~ Sie (wirklich)?** do you (really) think so?; **wie ~ Sie das?** what do you mean by that?; **sie ~ es gut** they mean well; **ich habe es nicht so gemeint** I didn't mean it; **wie ~ Sie?** (I beg your)pardon?

meinetwegen adv. von mir aus: I don't mind od. care!; für mich: for my sake; wegen mir: because of me

Meinung f opinion (**über, von** about, of); △ nicht meaning; **meiner ~ nach** in my opinion; **der ~ sein, daß** be* of the opinion that, feel* od. believe that; **s-e ~ äußern** express one's opinion; **s-e ~ ändern** change one's mind; **ich bin Ihrer (anderer) ~** I (don't) agree with you; **j-m die ~ sagen** give* s.o. a piece of one's mind; **~saustausch** m exchange of views (**über** on); **~sforscher** m pollster; **~sfreiheit** f freedom of speech od. opinion; **~sumfrage** f opinion poll; **~sverschiedenheit** f disagreement (**über** about)

Meise f titmouse

Meißel m chisel; **2n** v/t. u. v/i. chisel, carve

meist 1. adj. most; **das ~e (davon)** most of it; **die ~en (von ihnen)** most of them; **die ~en Leute** most people; **die ~e Zeit** most of the time; **2.** adv.: → **meistens; am ~en** (the) most; gearbeitet etc.: most (of all); **~ens** adv. usually; **die meiste Zeit** most of the time

Meister m Handwerk, Kunst, a. fig.: master; Sport: champion, F champ; **2haft 1.** adj. masterly; **2.** adv.: in a masterly manner od. way; **~in** f → Meister; **2n** v/t. master; **~schaft** f Können: mastery; Sport: championship, cup; Titel: title; **~stück, ~werk** n masterpiece

Melancholi|e f melancholy; **2sch** adj. melancholy; **~ sein** feel* depressed, F have* the blues

Melange f östr. f coffee with milk

meld|en 1. v/t. et. od. j-n: report s.th. od. s.o. (**bei** to); Presse, Funk etc.: announce, report; amtlich: notify s.o. (of *s.th.*); **2.** *v/refl.:* **sich ~** report (*bei* to, **für, zu** for); *polizeilich an~:* register (*bei* with); *Schule etc.:* put* up one's hand; *Telefon:* answer the phone; *Prüfung, Wettbewerb:* enter (**für, zu** for); *freiwillig:* volunteer (**für, zu** for); **~ung** *f Presse, Funk etc.:* report, news, announcement; *Mitteilung:* information, notice; *amtlich:* notification, report; *polizeiliche* **An2:** registration (*bei* with); *Prüfung, Wettbewerb:* entry (**für, zu** for)

melken *v/t.* milk

Melodi|e *mus. f* melody, tune; **2sch** *adj.* melodious, melodic

Melone *f bot.* melon; F *Hut:* bowler(hat), *Am.* derby

Memoiren *pl.* memoirs *pl.*

Menge *f Anzahl:* quantity, amount; *Menschen2:* crowd; *math.* set; F: **e-e ~ Geld** plenty of money, lots *pl.* of money; **2n** *v/t.* → *mischen;* **~nlehre** *math. f* set theory; *Schule:* new math(ematics *sg.*)

Mensa *f* refectory, canteen, *Am.* cafeteria

Mensch *m* human being; *als Gattung:* man; *einzelner:* person, individual; **die ~en** *pl.* people *pl.*; *alle:* mankind *sg.*; **kein ~** nobody; **~! bewundernd:** wow!

Menschen|affe *m* ape; **~fresser** *m* cannibal; *Tier:* man-eater; **~freund** *m* philanthropist; **~handel** *m* slave trade; **~kenntnis** *f:* **~ haben** know* human nature; **~leben** *n* human life; **2leer** *adj.* deserted; **~menge** *f* crowd; **~rechte** *pl.* human rights *pl.*; **~seele** *f:* **keine ~** not a (living) soul; **2unwürdig** *adj.* degrading; *Unterkunft etc.:* unfit for human beings; **~verstand** *m:* **gesunder ~** common sense; **~würde** *f* human dignity

Mensch|heit *f:* **die ~** mankind, the human race; **2lich** *adj. den Menschen betreffend:* human; *human:* humane; **2lichkeit** *f* humanity

Menstruation *med. f* menstruation

Mentalität *f* mentality

Menü *n* set meal, *mittags a.:* set lunch; *Computer:* menu

Meridian *geogr., astr. m* meridian

merk|bar *adj. deutlich:* marked, distinct; *wahrnehmbar:* noticeable; **2blatt** *n* leaflet; **~en** *v/t. wahrnehmen:* notice;

spüren: feel*; *entdecken:* find* (out), discover; **sich et. ~** remember s.th., keep* *od.* bear* s.th. in mind; **~lich** *adj.* → *merkbar;* **2mal** *n sichtbares:* sign; *Eigenart:* feature, trait

merkwürdig *adj.* strange, odd, curious; **~erweise** *adv.* strangely enough

meß|bar *adj.* measurable; **2becher** *m Haushalt:* measuring cup

Messe *f econ.* fair; *rel.* mass; *mil., naut.* mess

messen *v/t.* measure; *Temperatur, Blutdruck etc.:* take*; **sich nicht mit j-m ~ können** be* no match for s.o.; **gemessen an** compared with

Messer *n* knife; **bis aufs ~** to the knife; **auf des ~s Schneide stehen** be* on a razor edge; **~stecherei** *f* knife fight; **~stich** *m* stab (with a knife)

Messing *n* brass

Meßinstrument *n* measuring instrument

Messung *f* measuring; *Ablesung:* reading

Metall *n* metal (*a. aus ~*); **~bearbeitung** *f* metalwork (*a. Schulfach*); **2en, 2isch** *adj.* metallic; **~waren** *pl.* hardware *sg.*

Meta|morphose *f* metamorphosis; **~stase** *med. f* metastasis

Meteor *astr. m* meteor; **~it** *m* meteorite

Meteorolog|e *m* meteorologist; **~ie** *f* meteorology

Meter *n, m* met|re, *Am.* -er; **~maß** *n* tape measure

Method|e *f* method; *tech. a.* technique; **2isch** *adj.* methodical

metrisch *adj.* metric; **~es Maßsystem** metric system

Metropole *f* metropolis

Metzger *m* butcher; **~ei** *f* butcher's (shop)

Meute *f* pack (of hounds); *fig.* mob, pack; **~rei** *f* mutiny; **~rer** *m* mutineer; **2rn** *v/i.* mutiny (**gegen** against)

MEZ *Abk. für Mitteleuropäische Zeit* CET, Central European Time

miau *int.* me(o)w, miaow; **~en** *v/i.* me(o)w

mich *pers. pron.* me; **~ (selbst)** myself

Mieder *n Korsett:* corset(s *pl.*); *an Kleid:* bodice; **~höschen** *n* pantie girdle; **~waren** *pl.* foundation garments *pl.*, corsetry *sg.*

M

Miene f expression, look, air; *gute ~ zum bösen Spiel machen* grin and bear* it

mies F adj. rotten, lousy

Miet|e f rent; *für bewegliche Sachen:* hire charge; *zur ~ wohnen* be* a tenant; lodge (*bei* with); **2en** v/t. rent; *Auto etc.:* hire, bsd. Am. rent; *pachten:* (take* on) lease; *naut., aviat.* charter; **~er** m tenant, Unter2: lodger; **~shaus** n block of flats, F tenement house, Am. apartment building od. house; **~vertrag** m lease (contract); **~wohnung** f (rented) flat, Am. apartment

Migräne med. f migraine

Mikro... in Zssgn Chip, Computer, Elektronik, Film, Prozessor etc.: micro

Mikrophon n microphone, F mike

Mikroskop n microscope, **2isch** adj. microscopic(al)

Mikrowelle F f, **~nherd** m microwave oven

Milbe zo. f mite

Milch f milk; **~geschäft** n dairy, creamery; **~glas** n frosted glass; **2ig** adj. milky; **~kaffee** m white coffee; **~kännchen** n (milk) jug; **~kanne** f milk can; **~mann** m F milkman; **~mixgetränk** n milk shake; **~produkte** pl. dairy products pl.; **~pulver** n powdered milk; **~reis** m rice pudding; **~straße** astr. f Milky Way, Galaxy; **~tüte** f milk carton; **~wirtschaft** f dairy farming; **~zahn** m milk tooth

mild adj. mild, soft; *Lächeln:* gentle

milde adv. mildly; *~ ausgedrückt* to put it mildly

Milde f mildness, gentleness; *Nachsicht:* leniency, mercy; *~ walten lassen* be* merciful

mildern v/t. lessen, soften; **~d** adj.: *~e Umstände* jur. mitigating circumstances

mildtätig adj. charitable

Milieu n Umwelt: environment; Herkunft: social background

Militär n the military, armed forces pl.; Heer: army; **~dienst** m military service; **~diktatur** f military dictatorship; **~gericht** n court martial, **2isch** adj. military; **~regierung** f military government

Milita|rismus m militarism; **~rist** m militarist; **2ristisch** adj. militaristic

Milliarde f billion, Brt. a. a thousand million(s)

Millimeter n, m millimet|re, Am. -er; **~papier** n graph paper

Million f million; **~är(in)** millionaire(ss)

Milz anat. f spleen

Mimik f facial expression; △ nicht **mimic**

minder 1. adj. → geringer, weniger; **2.** adv. less; nicht ~ no less; **2heit** f minority; **~jährig** adj.: ~ sein be* under age od. a minor; **2jährige(r)** minor; **2jährigkeit** f minority

minderwertig adj. inferior, of inferior quality; **2keit** f inferiority; econ. inferior quality; **2keitskomplex** m inferiority complex

mindest adj. least; *das ~e* the (very) least; *nicht im ~en* not in the least, not at all; **2...** in Zssgn Alter, Einkommen, Lohn etc.: minimum ...; **~ens** adv. at least; **2haltbarkeitsdatum** n best-before (od. best-by, sell-by) date, Am. pull date; **2maß** n minimum; *auf ein ~ herabsetzen* reduce to a minimum

Mine f Bergbau:, mil., naut. mine; Bleistift2: lead; Kugelschreiber2: cartridge; Ersatz2: refill

Mineral n mineral; **~ogie** f mineralogy; **~öl** n mineral oil; **~wasser** n mineral water

Miniatur f miniature

Minigolf n crazy (Am. miniature) golf

mini|mal adj., adv. geringfügig: minimal; mindest: minimum (bsd. in Zssgn); wenigstens: at least; **2mum** n minimum

Minirock m miniskirt

Minister m minister, Brt. a. secretary (of state), Am. secretary; **2ium** n ministry, Brt. a. office, Am. department; **~präsident** m e-s Bundeslandes: prime minister

minus adv. math. minus; *bei 10 Grad ~* at 10 degrees below zero

Minute f minute; **~nzeiger** m minute hand

Mio Abk. für Million(en) m, million

mir pers. pron. (to) me

Misch|batterie f Waschbecken etc.: mixer tap, Am. mixing faucet; **~brot** n wheat and rye bread; **2en** v/t. mix; Tabak, Tee etc.: blend; Karten: shuffle;

M

sich unters Volk ~ mingle with the crowd; **~ling** *m bsd. contp.* half-caste; *bot., zo.* hybrid; *Hund:* mongrel; **~masch** F *m* hotchpotch, jumble; **~maschine** *tech.* f mixer; **~pult** *n Rundfunk, TV:* mixer, mixing console; **~ung** f mixture; blend; *Pralinen etc.:* assortment; **~wald** *m* mixed forest

miserabel F *adj.* lousy, rotten

miß|achten *v/t. nicht beachten:* disregard, ignore; *verachten:* despise; **2ach-tung** f disregard; *Verachtung:* contempt; *Vernachlässigung:* neglect; **2bildung** f deformity, malformation; **~billigen** *v/t.* disapprove of; **2brauch** *m* abuse (*a. jur. Frau, Kind*); *falsche Anwendung:* misuse; **~brauchen** *v/t.* abuse; misuse; **~deuten** *v/t.* misinterpret

missen *v/t.* miss; *ich möchte das nicht* ~ I wouldn't (like to) miss it

Miß|erfolg *m* failure; F flop; **~ernte** f bad harvest, crop failure

Misse|tat *iro., poet.* f misdeed; **~täter** *m* wrongdoer, culprit

miß|fallen *v/i.: j-m* ~ displease s.o.; **2fallen** *n* displeasure, dislike; **~gebil-det** *adj.* deformed, malformed; **2ge-burt** f deformed child *od.* animal; *extreme:* freak; **2geschick** *n* Panne etc.: mishap; **2glücken** *v/i.* fail; **~gönnen** *v/t.: j-m et.* ~ envy s.o. s.th.; **~griff** *m* mistake; **~handeln** *v/t.* ill-treat, maltreat (*a. fig.*); *Ehefrau, Kind:* batter; **2handlung** f ill-treatment, maltreatment; *bsd. jur.* assault and battery

Mission f mission (*a. pol. u. fig.*); **~ar(in)** missionary

Miß|klang *m* dissonance, discord (*beide a. fig.*); **~kredit** *m* discredit; **2lingen** *v/i.* fail; *das ist mir mißlungen* I've bungled it; **2mutig** *adj.* bad-tempered, F grumpy; *unzufrieden:* discontented; **2raten 1.** *v/i.* fail; turn out badly; **2.** *adj. Kind:* wayward; **2trauen** *v/i.* distrust; **~trauen** *n* distrust, suspicion (*beide: gegenüber* of); **~trauensan-trag** *parl. m* (*vo:um*) motion (vote) of no confidence; **2trauisch** *adj.* distrustful, suspicious; **~verhält-nis** *n* disproportion; **~verständnis** *n* misunderstanding; **2verstehen** *v/t.* misunderstand*; **~wahl** f beauty contest *od.* competition

Mist *m* dung, manure; F *fig.* trash, rubbish; **~beet** *n* hotbed

Mistel *bot.* f mistletoe

Mist|gabel f dung fork; **~haufen** *m* manure heap

mit *prp. u. adv.* with; ~ *Gewalt* by force; ~ *Absicht* on purpose; ~ *dem Auto* (*der Bahn etc.*) by car (train *etc*); ~ *20 Jah-ren* at (the age of) 20; ~ *100 Stundenki-lometern* at 100 kilometres per hour; ~ *einem Mal plötzlich:* all of a sudden; *gleichzeitig:* (all) at the same time; ~ *lauter Stimme* in a loud voice; ~ *ande-ren Worten* in other words; *ein Mann* ~ *dem Namen* a man by the name of; *j-n* ~ *Namen kennen* know* s.o. by name; ~ *der Grund dafür, daß* one of the reasons why; ~ *der Beste* one of the best

Mit|arbeit f *Zusammen*2: cooperation; *Hilfe:* assistance; *Schule:* activity, class participation; **~arbeiter(in)** *Kollege:* colleague; *Angestellter:* employee; *un-tergeordnet:* assistant; *freier* ~ free-lance; **2bekommen** F *fig. v/t. verste-hen:* get*; *hören:* catch*; **2benutzen** *v/t.* share; **~bestimmungsrecht** *n* (right of) codetermination, *im Betrieb a.* worker participation; **~bewerber** *m* (rival) competitor; *Stelle:* fellow applicant; **~bewohner(in)** *e-r Woh-nung:* flatmate, Am. roommate; **2brin-gen** *v/t.* bring* s.th. *od.* s.o.; *j-m et.* ~ bring* s.o. s.th.; **~bringsel** F *n* little present; *Reise*2: souvenir; **~bür-ger** *m* fellow citizen; **2einander** *adv.* with each other, with one another; *zu-sammen:* together, jointly; **2erleben** *v/t.* live to see; **~esser** *med. m* black-head; **2fahren** *v/i.: mit j-m* ~ drive* *od.* go* with s.o.; *j-n* ~ *lassen* give* s.o. a lift; **~fahrgelegenheit** f lift; **~fahr-zentrale** f car pool(ing) service; **2füh-lend** *adj.* sympathetic; **2geben** *v/t.: j-m et.* ~ give* s.o. s.th. (to take*) along); **~gefühl** *n* sympathy; **2gehen** *v/i.: mit j-m* ~ go* *od.* come* along with s.o.; F *et.* ~ *lassen* walk off with s.th.; **~gift** f dowry

Mitglied *n* member (*bei* of); **~sbeitrag** *m* subscription; **~schaft** f membership

mit|haben *v/t.: ich habe kein Geld mit* I haven't got any money with me *od.* on me; **2hilfe** f assistance, help, coopera-

tion (**bei** in; **von** of); **~hören** v/t. belauschen: listen in to; zufällig: overhear*
Mit|inhaber m joint owner; **2kommen**
v/i. come* along (**mit** with); fig. Schritt
halten: keep* pace (**mit** with), verstehen: follow; Schule: get* on, keep* up
(with the class); **~laut** m consonant
Mitleid n pity (**mit** for); **aus ~** out of
pity; **~ haben mit** feel* sorry for; **2ig**
adj. compassionate, sympathetic; **2s-
los** adj. pitiless
mit|machen 1. v/i. join in; **2.** v/t. take*
part in; die Mode: follow; erleben: go*
through; **2menschen** pl.: **die ~** one's
fellow human beings pl.; people pl.;
~nehmen v/t. take* s.th. od. s.o. with
one; **j-n** (**im Auto**) **~** give* s.o. a lift;
~reden v/i. et. (**nichts**) **mitzureden
haben** (**bei**) have* a say (no say) (in);
~reißen v/t. drag along; fig. begei-
stern: carry away (mst pass.); **~rei-
ßend** adj. Rede, Musik etc.: electri-
fying; **~schneiden** v/t. Rundfunk, TV:
record, tape(-record); **~schreiben 1.**
v/t. take* down; (Prüfungs)Arbeit:
take*, do*; **2.** v/t. take* notes
Mitschuld f partial responsibility; **2ig**
adj.: **~ sein** be* partly to blame (**an** for)
Mitschüler(in) classmate; schoolmate,
fellow student
mitspiele|n v/i. Sport, Orchester etc.:
play; Spiel etc.: join in; **in e-m Film** etc.
~ be* od. appear in a film etc.; **2r(in)**
partner, Sport: a. team-mate
Mittag m noon, midday; **heute 2** at
noon today; **zu ~ essen** have* lunch,
lunch; **~essen** n lunch; **was gibt es
zum ~?** what's for lunch?; **2s** adv. at
noon; **12 Uhr ~** 12 o'clock noon
Mittags|pause f lunch break; **~ruhe** f
midday rest; **~schlaf** m after-dinner
nap; **~zeit** f lunchtime
Mitte f middle; Mittelpunkt: cent|re,
Am. -er (a. pol.); **~ Juli** in the middle of
July; **~ Dreißig** in one's mid thirties
mitteil|en v/t.: **j-m et. ~** inform s.o. of
s.th.; **~sam** adj. communicative; gesprächig: talkative; **2ung** f report, information, message
Mittel n means, way; Maßnahme: measure; Heil: remedy (**gegen** for) (a.
fig.); Durchschnitt: average; math.
mean; phys. medium; **~ pl.** means pl.,
money; **~alter** n Middle Ages pl.; **2al-**

~terlich adj. medi(a)eval; **~ding** n cross
(**zwischen** between); **~feld** n Sport:
midfield; **~feldspieler** m midfield
player, midfielder; **~finger** m middle
finger; **2fristig** adj. medium-term;
~gewicht n Sport: middleweight
(class); **2groß** adj. of medium height;
Sache: medium-sized; **~klasse** f middle class (a. mot.); **2linie** f Sport: halfway line; **~los** adj. without means;
2mäßig adj. average; **~punkt** m
cent|re, Am. -er (a. fig.); **2s** prp. by
(means of), through; **~schule** f → Re-
alschule; **~strecke** f Sport: middle
distance; **~streckenrakete** mil. f me-
dium-range missile; **~streifen** m Autobahn: central reservation, Am. median
strip; **~stufe** f intermediate stage;
Schule: Brt. middle school; Am. junior
highschool; **~stürmer(in)** Sport:
cent|re (Am. -er) forward; **~weg** fig. m
middle course; **~welle** f Radio: medium wave (abbr. AM); **~wort** gr. n participle
mitten adv.: **~ in** (**auf, unter**) in the
midst od. middle of; **~drin** F adv. right
in the middle; **~durch** F adv. right
through (the middle); entzwei: right in
two
Mitternacht f midnight
mittler|e adj. middle, central; durch-
schnittlich: average, medium; **~er Bil-
dungsabschluß** m, **~e Reife** f Brt.
appr. General Certificate of Education
O-Level; **~weile** adv. meanwhile, (in
the) meantime
Mittwoch m Wednesday
mit|unter adv. now and then; **2verant-
wortung** f share of the responsibility
mitwirk|en v/i. take* part (**bei** in); **~en-
de** m, f thea., mus. performer; **die ~n**
pl. thea. the cast sg., pl.; **2ung** f participation
mix|en v/t. mix; **2becher** m shaker;
2er m mixer; **2getränk** n mixed drink,
cocktail, shake
Möbel pl. furniture sg.; **~spedition** f
removal firm; **~stück** n piece of furniture; **~wagen** m furniture (Am.
moving) van
mobil adj. mobile; **~ machen** mil. mo-
bilize; **2telefon** n mobile phone
Mobiliar n furniture
möblieren v/t. furnish

M

Mode f fashion; **in ~** in fashion; **~ sein** be* in fashion, F be* in; **die neueste ~** the latest fashion; **mit der ~ gehen** follow the fashion; **in (aus der) ~ kommen** come* into (go* out of) fashion

Modell n model; **j-m ~ stehen** od. **sitzen** pose od. sit* for s.o.; **~bau** m model construction;; **~baukasten** m model construction kit; **~eisenbahn** f model railway; **2ieren** v/t. model

Modem m, n Computer: modem

Modenschau f fashion show

Moderator(in) TV etc. presenter, host, anchor(wo)man

Modergeruch m musty odo(u)r

moderieren TV etc. v/t. present, host

moderig adj. musty, mo(u)ldy

modern[1] v/i. mo(u)ld, rot, decay

modern[2] adj. modern; **modisch**: modern, fashionable; **~isieren** v/t. modernize, bring* up to date

Mode|schmuck m costume jewel(le)ry; **~schöpfer(in)** fashion designer, couturier(e), stylist; **~waren** pl. fashionwear sg.; **~wort** n vogue word, in word; **~zeichner(in)** fashion designer; **~zeitschrift** f fashion magazine

modisch adj. fashionable, stylish

Modul electr., arch. n module (a. Computer); **~bauweise** f modular design

Mofa n (small) moped, motorized bicycle

mogeln F v/i. cheat; abschreiben: crib

mögen v/t. u. v/aux. like; **er mag sie (nicht)** he likes (doesn't like) her; **lieber ~** like better, prefer; **nicht ~** dislike; **was möchten Sie?** what would you like?; **ich möchte, daß du es weißt** I'd like you to know (it); **ich möchte lieber bleiben** I'd rather stay; **es mag sein, (daß)** it may be (that)

möglich 1. adj. possible; **alle ~en** all sorts of; **sein ~stes tun** do* what one can*; **stärker:** do* one's utmost; **nicht ~!** you don't say (so)!; **so bald (schnell, oft) wie ~** as soon (quickly, often) as possible; **2.** adv.: **~st bald** etc. as soon etc. as possible; **~erweise** adv. possibly; **2keit** f possibility; **Gelegenheit:** opportunity; **Aussicht:** chance; **nach ~** if possible

Mohammedan|er(in) Muslim; **2isch** adj. Muslim

Mohn m poppy

Möhre, Mohrrübe f carrot

Molch zo. m salamander

Mole naut. f mole, jetty

Molekül n molecule

Molkerei f dairy

Moll mus. n minor (key); **a-Moll** A minor

mollig F adj. behaglich, warm: snug, cosy; dicklich: plump, chubby

Molotowcocktail m Molotov cocktail

Moment m moment; **(e-n) ~ bitte!** just a moment please!; **im ~** at the moment

Monarch m monarch; **~ie** f monarchy; **~in** f monarch; **~ist** m monarchist

Monat m month; **zweimal im (pro) ~** twice a month; **2elang** adv. for months; **2lich** adj. u. adv. monthly

Monats|binde f sanitary towel (Am. napkin); **~karte** f (monthly) season ticket, Am. commuter ticket

Mönch m monk; **Bettel2:** friar

Mond m moon; **~finsternis** f lunar eclipse; **2hell** adj. moonlit; **~landefähre** f lunar module; **~landung** f moon landing; **~oberfläche** f moon surface, lunar soil; **~schein** m moonlight; **~sichel** f crescent; **2süchtig** adj.: **~ sein** be* a sleepwalker od. somnambulist; **~umkreisung, ~umlaufbahn** f lunar orbit

Monitor TV etc.: m monitor

Mono|log m monologue, Am. a. monolog; **~pol** econ. m monopoly; **2ton** adj. monotonous; **~tonie** f monotony

Monoxid chem. n monoxide

Monster n monster (a. fig. u. in Zssgn)

Montag m Monday

Montage tech. f Zusammenbau: assembly; e-r Anlage: installation; **auf ~ sein** be* away on a field job; **~band** n assembly line; **~halle** f assembly shop

Mont|eur tech. m fitter; bsd. mot., aviat. mechanic; **2ieren** v/t. zusammensetzen: assemble; anbringen: fit, attach; Anlage: instal(l)

Moor n bog, moor(land); **2ig** adj. boggy

Moos bot. n moss; **2ig** adj. mossy

Moped n moped

Mops zo. m pug(dog)

Moral f Sittlichkeit: morals pl., moral standards pl.; e-r Geschichte etc.: moral; mil. etc.: morale; **2isch** adj. moral; **2isieren** v/i. moralize

Morast m morass; Schlamm: mire, mud

Mord *m* murder (*an* of); **e-n ~ begehen** commit murder; **~anschlag** *m bsd. pol.* assassination attempt

Mörder *m* murderer; △ *nicht* **murder**; *bezahlter:* (hired) killer; *bsd. pol.* assassin

Mord|kommission *f Brt.* murder squad, *Am.* homicide division; **~prozeß** *jur. m* murder trial

Mords|angst *f:* **e-e ~ haben** be* scared stiff; **~glück** F *n* stupendous luck; **~kerl** F *m* devil of a fellow; **~wut** F *f:* **e-e ~ haben** be* in a hell of a rage

Mord|verdacht *m* suspicion of murder; **~versuch** *m* attempted murder

morgen *adv.* tomorrow; **~ abend (früh)** tomorrow night (morning); **~ mittag** at noon tomorrow; **~ in e-r Woche** a week from tomorrow; **~ um diese Zeit** this time tomorrow; **heute ~** this morning

Morgen *m* morning; *Landmaß:* acre; **am (frühen) ~** (early) in the morning; **am nächsten ~** the next morning; **~essen** *n Schweiz:* breakfast; **~grauen** *n* dawn (*im, bei* at); **~gymnastik** *f:* **s-e ~ machen** do* one's morning exercises; **~land** *n* Orient; **~mantel** *m*, **~rock** *m* dressing gown

morgens *adv.* in the morning; **von ~ bis abends** from morning till night

morgig *adj.:* **die ~en Ereignisse** tomorrow's events

Morphium *pharm. n* morphine

morsch *adj.* rotten; **~ werden** rot

Morse|alphabet *tel. n* Morse code; **~zeichen** *n* Morse signal

Mörser *m* mortar (*a. mil.*)

Mörtel *m* mortar

Mosaik *n* mosaic; **~stein** *m* piece

Moschee *f* mosque

Moskito *zo. m* mosquito

Moslem *m*, **2isch** *adj.* Muslim

Most *m* grape juice; *Apfel2:* cider

Motiv *n* motive; *paint., mus.* motif; **~ation** *f* motivation; **2ieren** *v/t.* motivate

Motor *m* motor, engine; **~boot** *n* motor boat; **~haube** *f* bonnet, *Am.* hood; **2isieren** *v/t.* motorize; **~leistung** *f* (engine) performance; **~rad** *n* motorcycle, F motorbike; **~ fahren** ride* a motorcycle; **~radfahrer(in)** *f* motorcyclist, biker; **~roller** *m* (motor) scooter; **~säge** *f* power saw; **~schaden** *m* engine trouble (*od.* failure)

Motte *zo. f* moth; **~nkugel** *f* mothball; **2nzerfressen** *adj.* moth-eaten

Motto *n* motto

motzen F *v/i.* → **meckern** *fig.*

Möwe *zo. f* (sea)gull

Mücke *zo. f* gnat, midge, mosquito; **aus e-r ~ e-n Elefanten machen** make* a mountain out of a molehill; **~nstich** *m* gnat bite

müd|e *adj.* tired; *matt:* weary; *schläfrig:* sleepy; **~ sein (werden)** be* (get*) tired (*fig.* **e-r Sache** of s.th.); **2igkeit** *f* tiredness

Muff *m* muff; **~e** *tech. f* sleeve, socket; **~el** F *m* Griesgram: sourpuss; **2(e)lig**, **2lg** *adj.* Geruch, Luft etc.: musty; *fig.* sulky, sullen

Mühe *f* trouble; *Anstrengung:* effort; *Schwierigkeit(en):* trouble, difficulty (**mit** with s.th.); (**nicht**) **der ~ wert** (not) worth the trouble; **j-m ~ machen** give* s.o. trouble; **sich ~ geben** try hard; **sich die ~ sparen** save o.s. the trouble; **mit ~ und Not** (just) barely; **2los** *adv.* without difficulty; **2n** *v/refl.* struggle, work hard; **2voll** *adj.* laborious

Mühle *f* mill; *Spiel:* morris

Müh|sal *f* toil; **2sam**, **2selig 1.** *adj.* laborious; **2.** *adv.* with difficulty

Mulat|te *m*, **~tin** *f* mulatto

Mulde *f* hollow; *Container:* skip

Muli *n* Maultier: mule

Mull *m bsd. med.* gauze; *Gewebe:* muslin

Müll *m* refuse, rubbish, *Am. a.* garbage, trash; **~abfuhr** *f* refuse (*Am.* garbage) collection; **~beseitigung** *f* waste disposal; **~beutel** *m* dustbin liner, *Am.* garbage bag

Mullbinde *f* gauze bandage

Müll|container *m* rubbish (*Am.* garbage) skip; **deponie** *f* dump; **~eimer** *m* dustbin, *Am.* garbage can; **~fahrer** *m* dustman, *Am.* garbage man; **~halde** *f* dump; **~haufen** *m* rubbish (*Am.* garbage) heap; **~kippe** *f* dump; **~schlukker** *m* refuse (*Am.* garbage) chute; **~tonne** *f* → **Mülleimer**; **~verbrennungsanlage** *f* (waste) incineration plant; **~wagen** *m* dustcart, *Am.* garbage truck

Multipli|kation *math. f* multiplication; **2zieren** *math. v/t.* multiply (**mit** by)

Mumie *f* mummy

Mumps *med. m*, F *f* mumps

Mund m mouth; **den ~ voll nehmen** talk big; **halt den ~!** shut up!; **~art** f dialect; **~dusche** f TM water pic

münden v/i.: **~ in Fluß etc.**: flow into; **Straße etc.**: lead* into

Mund|geruch m bad breath; **~harmonika** mus. f mouthorgan, harmonica

mündig adj. Bürger etc.: emancipated; **~ (werden)** jur. (come*) of age

mündlich adj. Prüfung etc.: oral; Vertrag etc.: verbal

Mundstück n mouthpiece; Zigarette: tip

Mündung f mouth; **e-r Feuerwaffe**: muzzle

Mund|voll m: **ein paar ~** a few mouthfuls (of); **~wasser** n mouthwash; **~werk** F fig. n: **ein gutes ~** the gift of the gab; **ein loses ~** a loose tongue; **~winkel** m corner of the mouth; **~zu-~Beatmung** med. f mouth-to-mouth resuscitation, F kiss of life

Munition f ammunition

munkeln F v/t.: **man munkelt, daß** rumo(u)r has it that

Münster n cathedral, minster

munter adj. wach: awake; lebhaft: lively; fröhlich: merry

Münz|e f coin; Gedenk2: medal; **~einwurf** m Schlitz: (coin) slot; **~ensammler** m collector of coins, numismatist; **~fernsprecher** tel. m pay phone; **~tank(automat)** m coin-operated (petrol, Am. gas) pump; **~wechsler** m change machine

mürb|e adj. zart: tender; Gebäck: crisp; brüchig: brittle; 2teig m short pastry; Kuchen aus ~: shortcake

Murmel f marble; 2n v/t. u. v/i. murmur; **~tier** zo. n marmot

murren v/i. complain (**über** about)

mürrisch adj. sullen; grumpy

Mus n mush; Frucht2: stewed fruit

Muschel f zo. mussel; **~schale**: shell

Museum n museum

Musik f music; 2alisch adj. musical; **~anlage** f hi-fi od. stereo set; **~automat** m, **~box** f juke box; **~er(in)** musician; **~instrument** n musical instrument; **~kapelle** f band; **~kassette** f music cassette; **~lehrer(in)** f music teacher; **~stunde** f music lesson

musisch adv.: **~ interessiert (begabt)** fond of (gifted for) fine arts and music

musizieren v/i. make* music

Muskat m, **~nuß** bot. f nutmeg

Muskel m muscle; **~kater** F m aching muscles pl.; **~zerrung** med. f pulled muscle

muskulös adj. muscular, brawny

Müsli n muesli, Am. granola

Muß n necessity; **es ist ein ~** it is a must

Muße f leisure; Freizeit: spare time

müssen v/i. u. v/aux. must*, have* (got) to; **du mußt den Film sehen!** you must see the film!; **ich muß jetzt (meine) Hausaufgaben machen** I have (got) to do my homework now; **sie muß krank sein** she must be ill; **du mußt es nicht tun** you need not do it; △ nicht must not; **das müßtest du (doch) wissen** you ought to know (that); **sie müßte zu Hause sein** she should (ought to) be (at) home; **das müßte schön sein!** that would be nice!; **du hättest ihm helfen ~** you ought to have helped him

müßig adj. untätig: idle; unnütz: useless

Muster n pattern; Probestück: sample; Vorbild: model; 2gültig, 2haft adj. exemplary; **sich ~ benehmen** behave perfectly; **~haus** arch. n showhouse; 2n v/t. neugierig: eye s.o.; abschätzend: size s.o. up; mil. gemustert werden F have* one's medical; **~ung** mil. f medical (examination for military service)

Mut m courage; **~ machen** encourage s.o.; **den ~ verlieren** lose* courage; 2ig adj. courageous, brave; 2los adj. discouraged

mut|maßen v/t. speculate; **~maßlich** adj. presumed; 2maßung f: bloße ~en mere guesswork

Mutprobe f test of courage

Mutter f mother; tech. Schrauben2: nut; **~boden** agr. m, **~erde** agr. f topsoil

mütterlich adj. motherly; **~erseits** adv.: **Onkel etc. ~** maternal uncle etc.

Mutter|liebe f motherly love; 2los adj. motherless; **~mal** n birthmark, mole; **~milch** f mother's milk; **~schaftsurlaub** m maternity leave; **~schutz** jur. m legal protection of expectant and nursing mothers; **~söhnchen** contp. n sissy; **~sprache** f mother tongue; **~sprachler(in)** native speaker; **~tag** m Mother's Day

Mutti F f mum(my), bsd. Am. mom(my)

mutwillig *adj.* wanton
Mütze *f* cap
MwSt *Abk. für Mehrwertsteuer* VAT, value-added tax

mysteriös *adj.* mysterious
mystisch *adj.* mystic(al)
myth|isch *adj.* mythical; **2ologie** *f* mythology; **2os** *m* myth

N

N *Abk. für Nord(en)* N, north
na *int.* well; ~ **und?** so what?; ~ **gut!** all right then; ~ **ja** (oh) well; ~, (~)! come on!, come now!; ~ **so (et)was!** *bsd. Brt.* I say!, *bsd. Am.* what do you know!; ~, **dann nicht!** oh, forget it!!; ~ **also!** there you are!; ~, **warte!** just you wait!
Nabe *f* hub
Nabel *anat. m* navel; **~schnur** *f* umbilical chord
nach *prp. u. adv. örtlich:* to, toward(s), for; *hinter:* after; *zeitlich:* after, past; *gemäß:* according to, by; ~ *Hause* home; *abfahren* ~ leave* for; ~ *rechts* **(Süden)** to the right (south); ~ *oben* up(stairs); ~ *unten* down(stairs); ~ *vorn* **(hinten)** to the front (back); *der Reihe* ~ one after the other; *s-e Uhr* ~ *dem Radio stellen* set* one's watch by the radio; ~ *m-r Uhr* by my watch; *suchen* **(fragen)** ~ look (ask) for; ~ *Gewicht* **(Zeit)** by weight (the hour); *riechen* **(schmecken)** ~ smell (taste) of; ~ *und* ~ gradually; ~ *wie vor* as before, still
nachäffen *v/t.* j-n u. et.: ape
nachahm|en *v/t.* imitate, copy; *parodieren:* take* off; *fälschen:* counterfeit; **2ung** *f* imitation; counterfeit
Nachbar|(in) neighbo(u)r; **~schaft** *f* neighbo(u)rhood, vicinity
Nachbau *tech. m* reproduction; **2en** *v/t.* copy, reproduce
Nachbildung *f* copy, imitation; *genaue:* replica; *Attrappe:* dummy
nachblicken *v/i.* look after
nachdem *cj.* after, when; *je* ~ *wie* depending on how
nachdenk|en *v/i.* think*; ~ *über* think* about, think* s.th. over; *Zeit zum* 2 time to think (about s.th.); **~lich** *adj.*

thoughtful; *es macht e-n* ~ it makes you think
Nachdruck *m* emphasis, stress; *print.* reprint; **2en** *v/t.* reprint
nachdrücklich *adj.* emphatic; *Forderung etc.:* forceful; ~ *raten* **(empfehlen)** advise (recommend) strongly
nacheifern *v/i.* emulate
nacheinander *adv.* one after the other, in *(abwechselnd:* by) turns
nacherzähl|en *v/t.* retell*; **2ung** *f* *Schule:* reproduction
Nachfolge *f* succession; *j-s* ~ *antreten* succeed s.o.; **2n** *v/i.* follow; *j-m:* succeed; **~r(in)** successor
nachforsch|en *v/i.* investigate; **2ung** *f* investigation, inquiry
Nachfrage *f* inquiry; *econ.* demand; **2n** *v/i.* inquire, ask
nach|fühlen *v/t.:* j-m et. ~ understand* how s.o. feels; **~füllen** *v/t.* refill; **~geben** *v/i.* give* (way); *fig.* give* in; **2gebühr** *post f* surcharge; **~gehen** *v/i.* follow *(a. fig.); Uhr:* be* slow; *e-m Vorfall etc.:* investigate; *s-r Arbeit* ~ go* about one's work; **2geschmack** *m* aftertaste *(a. fig.)*
nachgiebig *adj.* yielding, soft *(beide a. fig.);* **2keit** *f* yieldingness, softness
nachhaltig *adj.* lasting, enduring
nachher *adv.* afterwards; *bis* ~! see you later!, so long!
Nachhilfe *f* help, assistance; **~stunden** *pl.,* **~unterricht** *m* private lesson(s *pl.),* coaching
nachholen *v/t.* make* up for, catch* up on
Nachkomme *m* descendant; **~n** *pl. bsd. jur.* issue *sg.;* **2n** *v/i.* follow, come* later; *e-m Wunsch etc.:* comply with
Nachkriegs... *in Zssgn* postwar ...

Nachlaß m econ. reduction, discount; jur. Erbschaft: estate

nachlassen v/i. decrease, diminish, go* down; Schmerz, Wirkung etc.: wear* off; Schüler etc.: slacken one's effort; leistungsmäßig: go* off

nachlässig adj. careless, negligent

nach|laufen v/i. run* after; **~lesen** v/t. look up; **~machen** v/t. imitate, copy; fälschen: counterfeit, forge

Nachmittag m afternoon; **heute ~** this afternoon; **~s** adv. in the afternoon

Nach|nahme f cash on delivery; **per ~ schicken** send* C.O.D.; **~name** m surname, last (Am. a. family) name; **~porto** n surcharge

nach|prüfen v/t. check (up), make* sure (of); **~rechnen** v/t. check

Nachrede f: **üble ~** malicious gossip; jur. defamation (of character), mündlich a. slander

Nachricht f news sg.; Botschaft: message; Bericht: report; Mitteilung: information, notice; **e-e gute (schlechte) ~** good (bad) news sg.; **~en** pl. news sg., news report sg., newscast sg.; **Sie hören ~** here is the news; **~endienst** m news service; mil. intelligence service; **~ensatellit** m communications satellite; **~ensprecher(in)** newscaster, bsd. Brt. newsreader; **~entechnik** f telecommunications pl.

Nach|ruf m obituary; **2rüsten** pol. mil. v/i. close the armament gap; **2sagen** v/t.: **j-m Schlechtes ~** speak* badly of s.o.; **man sagt ihm nach, daß er** he is said to inf.; **~saison** f off-peak season; **in der ~** out of season

nachschlage|n 1. v/t. look up; **2.** v/i.: **~ in** consult; **2werk** n reference book

Nach|schlüssel m duplicate key; Dietrich: skeleton key; **~schrift** f postscript; Diktat: dictation; **~schub** bsd. mil. m supplies pl.

nach|sehen 1. v/i. follow with one's eyes; (have* a) look; **~ ob** (go* and) see* whether; **2.** v/t. look od. go* over od. through; Hefte a. correct, mark; prüfen: check (a. tech.); **~senden** v/t. send* on, forward; **bitte ~l** post please forward!

Nach|silbe gr. f suffix; **2sitzen** v/i. stay in (after school), be* kept in; **~ lassen** keep* in, detain; **~spiel** fig. n

sequel, consequences pl.; **2spielen** v/i. Sport: **5 Minuten ~ lassen** allow 5 minutes for injury time; **~spielzeit** f bsd. Fußball: injury time; **2spionieren** v/i. spy (up)on; **2sprechen** v/t.: **j-m et. ~** say* od. repeat s.th. after s.o.

nächst|beste adj. beliebige: first, F any old; qualitativ: next-best, second-best; **~e** adj. in der Reihenfolge, zeitlich: next; nächstliegend: nearest (a. Angehörige); **in den ~n Tagen (Jahren)** in the next few days (years); **in ~r Zeit** in the near future; **was kommt als ~s?** what comes next?; **der ~ bitte!** next please!

nachstehen v/i.: **j-m in nichts ~** be* in no way inferior to s.o.

nachstell|en 1. v/t. Uhr: put* back; tech. (re)adjust; **2.** v/i.: **j-m ~** be* after s.o.; **2ung** f persecution

Nächstenliebe f charity

Nacht f night; **Tag und ~** night and day; **die ganze ~** all night (long); **heute ~** letzte: last night; kommende: tonight; **~dienst** m night duty

Nachteil m disadvantage, drawback; **im ~ sein** be* at a disadvantage (**gegenüber** compared with); **2ig** adj. disadvantageous

Nacht|essen n Schweiz: → Abendbrot; **~falter** zo. m moth; **~hemd** n nightdress, bsd. Am. nightgown, F nightie; Männer2: nightshirt

Nachtigall f nightingale

Nachtisch m dessert; sweet

nächtlich adj. all~: nightly; Straßen etc.: at od. by night

Nachtlokal n nightclub

Nachtrag m supplement; **2en** fig. v/t.: **j-m et. ~** bear* s.o. a grudge; **2end** adj. unforgiving

nachträglich adj. zusätzlich: additional; später: later; Wünsche etc.: belated

nachts adv. at night, in the night(time)

Nacht|schicht f night shift; **~ haben** be* on night shift; **2schlafend** adj.: **zu ~er Zeit** in the middle of the night; **~tisch** m bedside table; **~topf** m chamber pot; **~wächter** m night watchman

nach|wachsen v/i. grow* again; **2wahl** parl. f by-election; Am. special election

Nachweis m proof, evidence; **2bar** adj. demonstrable; bsd. chem. etc. detectable; **2en** v/t. prove; *bsd. chem. etc.* detect; **2lich** adv. as can be proved

Nach|welt f posterity; **~wirkung** f aftereffect(s pl.); **~en** pl. a. aftermath sg.; **~wort** n epilog(ue); **~wuchs** m *Beruf, Sport etc.*: young talent, F new blood; **~wuchs...** in *Zssgn* Autor, Schauspieler etc.: talented od. promising young ..., up-and-coming

nach|zahlen v/t. pay* extra; **~zählen** v/t. count over (again), check; **2zahlung** f additional od. extra payment

Nachzügler m straggler, latecomer

Nacken m (back od. nape of the) neck; **~stütze** f headrest

nackt adj. naked; *bsd. paint., phot.* nude; *bloß*: bare (a. *Wand etc.*); *Wahrheit*: plain; *völlig* ~ stark naked; *sich ~ ausziehen* strip; ~ *baden* swim* in the nude; *j-n ~ malen* paint s.o. in the nude

Nadel f needle; *Steck2, Haar2 etc.*: pin; *Brosche*: brooch; **~baum** bot. m conifer(ous tree); **~öhr** n eye of a needle; **~stich** m pinprick (a. *fig*)

Nagel m nail; *an den Nägeln kauen* bite* one's nails; **~lack** m nail varnish od. polish; **2n** v/t. nail (*an, auf* to); **2neu** F adj. brand-new; **~pflege** f manicure

nage|n 1. v/i. gnaw (*an* at); *an e-m Knochen* ~ pick a bone; 2. v/t. gnaw; **2tier** n rodent

nah adj. near, close (*bei* to); ~ *gelegen*: nearby

Nahaufnahme f close-up

Nähe f nearness; *Umgebung*: neighbo(u)rhood, vicinity; *in der* ~ *des Bahnhofs etc.* near the station etc.; *ganz in der* ~ quite near, close by; *in deiner* ~ near you

nahe|gehen v/i. affect deeply; **~kommen** v/i. come* close to; **~legen** v/t. suggest; **~liegen** v/i. seem likely; *stärker*: be* obvious; **~liegend** adj. likely; obvious

nahen v/i. approach

nähen v/t. u. v/i. sew*; *Kleid*: make*

Näheres n details pl., particulars pl.

nähern v/refl. approach, get* near(er) od. close(r) (*dat.* to)

nahezu adv. nearly, almost

Nähgarn n (sewing) cotton

Nahkampf mil. m close combat

Näh|maschine f sewing machine;

~nadel f (sewing) needle

nähren v/t. feed*; *fig.* nurture

nahrhaft adj. nutritious, nourishing

Nährstoff m nutrient

Nahrung f food, nourishment; *Futter*: feed; *Kost*: diet; **~mittel** pl. food sg. (a. in *Zssgn Chemie etc.*), foodstuffs pl.

Nährwert m nutritional value

Naht f seam; *med.* suture

Nahverkehr m local traffic; **~szug** m local od. commuter train

Nähzeug n sewing kit

naiv adj. naive; **2ität** f naivety

Name m; *im ~n von* on behalf of; *nur dem ~n nach* in name only

namen|los adj. nameless (a. *fig.*); *fig. a.* unspeakable; **~s** adv. by (the) name of, named, called

Namens|tag m name day; **~vetter** m namesake; **~zug** m signature

namentlich adj. u. adv. by name

nämlich adv. *das heißt*: that is (to say), namely; *begründend*: you see od. know

Napf m bowl, basin

Narb|e f scar; **2ig** adj. scarred

Narkose f an(a)esthesia; *in* ~ under an an(a)esthetic

Narr m fool; *zum ~en halten* fool

narrensicher adj. foolproof

närrisch adj. foolish; ~ *vor* mad with

Narzisse f daffodil

nasal adj. nasal

nasch|en v/i. u. v/t. nibble (*an* at); *gern* ~ have* a sweet tooth; **2ereien** pl. dainties pl., goodies pl., sweets pl.; **~haft** adj. sweet-toothed

Nase f nose (a. *fig.*); *sich die* ~ *putzen* blow* one's nose; *in der* ~ *bohren* pick one's nose; *die* ~ *voll haben* (*von*) be* fed up (with)

Nasen|bluten n nosebleed; **~loch** n nostril; **~spitze** f tip of the nose

Nashorn zo. n rhinoceros, F rhino

naß adj. wet; *triefend* ~ soaking (wet)

Nässe f wet(ness); **2n 1.** v/t. wet; **2.** v/i. *Wunde*: weep

naßkalt adj. damp and cold, raw

Nation f nation

national adj. national; **2hymne** f national anthem; **2ismus** m nationalism; **2ität** f nationality; **2mannschaft** f national team; **2park** m national park; **2sozialismus** m National Socialism, *contp.* Nazism; **2sozialist** m, **~sozia-**

listisch adj. National Socialist, Nazi
Natter f zo. adder, viper (a. fig.)
Natur f nature; **von ~ (aus)** by nature
Naturalismus m naturalism
Natur|ereignis n, **~erscheinung** f natural phenomenon; **~forscher** m naturalist; **~geschichte** f natural history; **~gesetz** n law of nature; 2**getreu** adj. true to life; lifelike; **~katastrophe** f (natural) catastrophe od. disaster, act of God
natürlich 1. adj. natural; **2.** adv. naturally, of course
Natur|schätze pl. natural resources pl.; **~schutz** m nature conservation; **unter ~** protected; **~schützer** m conservationist; **~schutzgebiet** n nature reserve; großes: national park; **~volk** n primitive race; **~wissenschaft** f (natural) science
n. Chr. Abk. für nach Christus AD, anno domini
Nebel m fog; leichter: mist; Dunst: haze; Künstlicher: smoke; **~horn** n foghorn; **~leuchte** mot. f fog lamp
neben prp. beside, direkt ~: next to; außer: besides, apart from; verglichen mit: compared with; **~ anderem** among other things; **setz dich ~ mich** sit by me od. by my side
neben|an adv. next door; 2**bedeutung** f secondary meaning; ling. connotation; **~bei** adv. in addition, at the same time; **~ (gesagt)** by the way; 2**beruf** m second job, sideline; **~beruflich** adv. as a sideline; 2**buhler(in)** rival; **~einander** adv. side by side; next (wohnen: door) to each other; **~ bestehen** coexist; 2**einkünfte**, 2**einnahmen** pl. extra money sg.; 2**fach** n subsidiary subject, Am. minor (subject); 2**fluß** m tributary; 2**gebäude** n next-door od. adjoining building; Anbau: annex(e); 2**haus** n house next door; 2**kosten** pl. extras pl.; 2**mann** m: **dein ~** the person next to you; 2**produkt** n by-product; 2**rolle** thea. f supporting role, minor part (a. fig.); kleine, für bekannte Schauspieler: cameo (role); 2**sache** f minor matter; **das ist ~** that's of little od. no importance; **~sächlich** adj. unimportant; 2**satz** gr. m subordinate clause; 2**stelle** tel. f extension;

2**straße** f side street; Landstraße: minor road; 2**strecke** rail. f branch line; 2**tisch** m next table; 2**verdienst** m extra earnings pl.; 2**wirkung** f side effect; 2**zimmer** n adjoining room
neblig adj. foggy; misty; hazy
neck|en v/t. tease, F kid; 2**erei** f teasing, F kidding; **~isch** adj. saucy, cheeky
Neffe m nephew
negativ adj. negative
Negativ n negative (a. in Zssgn)
Neger(in) → **Schwarze(r)**
nehmen v/t. take* (a. sich ~); **j-m et. ~** take* s.th. (away) from s.o (a. fig.); et. **zu sich ~** have* s.th. to eat; sich e-n **Tag** etc. **frei ~** take* a day etc. off; **an die Hand ~** take* by the hand
Neid m envy; reiner ~: sheer envy; 2**isch** adj. envious (auf of); → **beneiden**
Neige f: **zur ~ gehen** draw* to its close; Vorräte etc.: run* out; 2**n 1.** v/t. u. refl. bend*, incline; **2.** v/i.: **zu et. ~** tend to (do) s.th
Neigung f inclination (a. fig.), slope, incline; fig. a. tendency
nein adv. no
Nektar m nectar
Nelke bot. f carnation; Gewürz2: clove
nennen v/t. name, call; erwähnen: mention; **sich ~** call o.s., be* called; **man nennt ihn (es)** he (it) is called; **das nenne ich ...!** that's what I call ...!; **~swert** adj. worth mentioning
Nenn|er math. m denominator; **~wert** econ. m nominal od. face value; **zum ~** at par
Neo..., neo... in Zssgn Faschist etc.: neo-
Neon chem. n neon; **~röhre** f neon tube
Nepp F m rip-off; 2**en** v/t. fleece, rip off; **~lokal** n clip joint
Nerv m nerve; **j-m auf die ~en fallen** od. **gehen** get* on s.o.'s nerves; **die ~en behalten (verlieren)** keep* (lose*) one's head; 2**en** F v/t. u. v/i. be* a pain in the neck (to s.o.)
Nerven|arzt m neurologist; 2**aufreibend** adj. nerve-racking; **~belastung** f nervous strain; 2**heilanstalt** f mental hospital; **~kitzel** m thrill, F kick(s pl.); 2**krank** adj. mentally ill; **~säge** F f pain in the neck; **~system** n nervous

system; **~zusammenbruch** m nervous breakdown

nerv|ös adj. nervous; **2osität** f nervousness

Nerz zo. m mink (a. Mantel)

Nessel bot. f nettle

Nest n nest; F Kaff: one-horse town; elendes: dump

nett adj. nice; freundlich: a. kind; **so ~ sein und et.** (od. et. zu) **tun** be* so kind as to do s.th.

netto econ. adv. net (a. in Zssgn)

Netz n net; rail., tel., Computer: network; electr. mains pl.; **am ~ sein** Computer: be* in the network; **~haut** anat. f retina; **~karte** rail. f area season ticket

neu adj new; frisch, erneut: a. fresh; **~zeitlich**: modern; **~ere Sprachen** modern languages; **~este Nachrichten** (Mode) latest news sg. (fashion); **von ~em** anew, afresh; **seit ~(st)em** since (very) recently; **viel 2es** a lot of new things; **was gibt es 2es?** what's the news?, what's new?

neu|artig adj. novel; **2bau** m new building; **2baugebiet** n new housing estate; **~erdings** adv. lately, recently; **2erer** m innovator; **2erung** f innovation; **2gierige** contp. pl. Gaffer: rubbernecks pl.; **2heit** f novelty; **2igkeit** f (piece) of news; **2jahr** n New Year's Day; **Prost ~!** Happy New Year!; **~lich** adv. the other day; **2ling** m newcomer, F greenhorn; **~modisch** contp. adj. newfangled; **2mond** m new moon

neun adj. nine; **~te** adj. ninth; **2tel** n ninth (part); **~tens** adv. ninthly; **~zehn** adj. nineteen; **~zehnte** adj. nineteenth; **~zig** adj. ninety; **~zigste** adj. ninetieth

Neuro|se f neurosis; **2tisch** adj. neurotic

neusprachlich adj. modern-language

neutr|al adj. neutral; **2alität** f neutrality; **2onen...** phys. in Zssgn Bombe etc.: neutron ...; **2um** gr. n neuter

Neu|verfilmung f remake; **2wertig** adj. as good as new; **~zeit** f modern times pl.

nicht adv. not; überhaupt ~ not at all; **~ (ein)mal, gar ~ erst** not even; **~ mehr** not any more od. longer; **sie ist nett (wohnt hier), ~ (wahr)?** she's nice (lives here), isn't (doesn't) she?; **~ so ... wie** not as ... as; **noch ~** not yet; **~ besser** etc. (als) no (od. not any) better etc. (than); **ich (auch) ~** I don't od. I'm not (either); **(bitte) ~!** (please) don't!

Nicht|... in Zssgn Mitglied, Schwimmer etc.: mst non-...; **~beachtung** f disregard; Vorschrift etc.: a. non-observance

Nichte f niece

nichtig adj. trivial; jur. void, invalid

Nichtraucher m non-smoker

nichts indef. pron. nothing, not anything; **~ (anderes) als** nothing but; **gar ~** nothing at all; F: **das ist ~** that's no good

Nichts n nothing(ness); **aus dem ~ erscheinen**: from nowhere; aufbauen: from nothing

nichts|destoweniger adv. nevertheless; **2könner** m bungler, F botcher; **~nutzig** adj. good-for-nothing, worthless; **~sagend** adj. meaningless; **2tuer** m do-nothing, F bum

nicken v/i. nod (one's head)

nie adv. never, at no time; **fast ~** hardly ever; **~ und nimmer** never ever

nieder 1. adj. low; **2.** adv. down

Nieder|gang m decline; **2geschlagen** adj. depressed, (feeling) down; **~kunft** f confinement; **2lage** f defeat, F beating; **2lassen** v/refl. settle (down); econ. set* up (als as); **~lassung** f establishment; Filiale: branch; **2legen** v/t. lay* down (a. Waffen, Amt etc.); **die Arbeit ~** (go* on) strike, down tools, F walk out; **sich ~** lie* down; go* to bed; **2metzeln** v/t. massacre, butcher; **~schlag** m meteor. rain(fall) (nur sg.); radioaktiver: fallout; chem. precipitate; Boxen: knock-down; **2schlagen** v/t. knock down; Augen: cast* down; Aufstand: put* down; jur. Verfahren: quash; **sich ~** chem. precipitate; **2schmettern** fig. v/t. shatter, crush; **2trächtig** adj. base, mean; **~ung** f lowland(s pl.)

niedlich adj. pretty, sweet, cute

niedrig adj. low (a. fig.); Strafe: light; **~ fliegen** fly* low

niemals *adv.* → *nie*

niemand *indef. pron.* nobody, no one, not anybody; ~ *von ihnen* none of them; **2sland** *n* no-man's-land

Niere *f* kidney

nieseln *v/i.* drizzle; **2regen** *m* drizzle

nies|en *v/i.* sneeze; **2pulver** *n* sneezing powder

Niet *tech. m*, **Niete¹** *f* rivet

Niete² *f Los:* blank; *fig.* failure

Nikolaustag *m* St. Nicholas' Day

Nikotin *chem. n* nicotine

Nilpferd *zo. n* hippopotamus, F hippo

Nippel *m* nipple

nippen *v/i.* sip (*an* at)

nirgends *adv.* nowhere

Nische *f* niche, recess

nist|en *v/i.* nest; **2platz** *m* nesting place

Niveau *n* level; *fig. a.* standard

Nixe *f* water nymph, mermaid

noch *adv.* still; ~ *nicht* not yet; ~ *nie* never before; *er hat nur* ~ *5 Mark (Minuten)* he has only 5 marks (minutes) left; *(sonst)* ~ *et.?* anything else?; *ich möchte* ~ *et.* (*Tee*) I'd like some more (tea); ~ *ein(-e, -n)...*, *bitte* another ..., please; ~ *einmal* once more *od.* again; ~ *zwei Stunden* another two hours, two hours to go; ~ *besser (schlimmer)* even better (worse); ~ *gestern* only yesterday; *und wenn es (auch)* ~ *so ... ist* however (*od.* no matter how) ... it may be; **~malig** *adj.* (re)new(ed); **~mals** *adv.* once more *od.* again

Nockerl *östr. n* small dumpling

Nomade *m* nomad

Nominativ *gr. m* nominative (case)

nominieren *v/t.* nominate

Nonne *f* nun; **~nkloster** *n* convent

Norden *m* north; *nach* ~ north(wards); **2isch** *adj.* northern; **~e Kombination** Nordic Combined

nördlich 1. *adj.* north(ern); *Kurs, Wind:* northerly; **2.** *adv.:* ~ *von* north of

Nord|licht *n* northern lights *pl.*; F *Person:* Northerner; **~osten** *m* northeast; **2östlich** *adj.* northeast(ern), *Wind:* northeasterly; **~pol** *m* North Pole; **~westen** *m* northwest; **2westlich** *adj.* northwest(ern); *Wind:* northwesterly; **~wind** *m* north wind

nörg|eln *v/i.* nag (*an* at), carp (at); **2ler(in)** nagger, carper, faultfinder

Norm *f* standard, norm

normal *adj.* normal; F: *nicht ganz* ~ not quite right in the head

Normal|... *bsd. tech. in Zssgn Maß, Zeit etc.:* standard ...; **~benzin** *n* regular (petrol, *Am.* gas); **2erweise** *adv.* normally, usually; **2isieren** *v/refl.* return to normal

normen *v/t.* standardize

Norweg|en Norway; **~er** *m*, **~erin** *f*, **2isch** *adj.* Norwegian

Not *f allg.* need; *Mangel: a.* want; *Armut:* poverty; *Elend:* hardship, misery; *Bedrängnis:* difficulty; **~fall:** emergency; *bsd. seelische:* distress; *in* ~ *sein* be* in trouble; *zur* ~ if need be, if necessary

Notar *m* notary (public)

Not|aufnahme *f* casualty, *Am.* emergency room; **~ausgang** *m* emergency exit; **~behelf** *m* makeshift, expedient; **~bremse** *f* emergency brake; **~dienst** *m* emergency duty; **~durft** *f:* *s-e* ~ *verrichten* relieve o.s.; **2dürftig** *adj.* scanty; *behelfsmäßig:* temporary

Note *f* note (*a. mus. u. pol.*); *Bank2:* (bank)note, *bsd. Am.* bill; *Schule:* mark, *bsd. Am.* grade; **~n** *pl. mus.* (sheet) music *sg.*; **~n lesen** read* music

Notebook *n Computer:* notebook

Noten|durchschnitt *m* average; **~ständer** *m* music stand

Not|fall *m* emergency; **2falls** *adv.* if necessary; **2gedrungen** *adv.:* *et.* ~ *tun* be* forced to do s.th.

notieren *v/t.* make* a note of, note (down); *econ.* quote

nötig *adj.* necessary; ~ *haben* need; ~ *brauchen* need badly; *das* **2ste** the (bare) necessities *pl. od.* essentials *pl.*; **~en** *v/t.* force, compel; *drängen:* press, urge; **~enfalls** *adv.* if necessary; **2ung** *f* coercion; *jur.* intimidation

Notiz *f* note; *keine* ~ *nehmen von* take* no notice of, ignore; *sich* ~ *en machen* take* notes; **~block** *m* notepad; *bsd. Am.* memo pad; **~buch** *n* notebook

Not|lage *f* awkward (*od.* difficult) situation; *finanzielle:* difficulties *pl.*; *plötzlicher Notfall:* emergency; **2landen** *aviat. v/i.* make* an emergency landing; **~landung** *aviat. f* emergency landing; **2leidend** *adj.* needy; **~lösung** *f* expedient; **~lüge** *f* white lie

notorisch *adj.* notorious

Not|ruf *tel. m* emergency call; **~rufsäu-**

oben

le f emergency phone; **~signal** n emergency od. distress signal; **~stand** pol. m state of (national) emergency; **~standsgebiet** n econ. depressed area; bei Katastrophen: disaster area; **~standsgesetze** pl. emergency laws pl.; **~verband** m emergency dressing; **~wehr** f self-defen|ce, Am. -se; 2**wendig** adj. necessary; **~wendigkeit** f necessity; **~zucht** f rape

Novelle f novella; parl. amendment

November m November

Nr. Abk. für **Nummer** No., no., number

Nu m: **im ~** in no time

Nuance f shade

nüchtern adj. sober (a. fig.); sachlich: matter-of-fact; **auf ~en Magen** on an empty stomach; **~ werden (machen)** sober up; 2**heit** f sobriety

Nudel f noodle

nuklear adj. nuclear; Zssgn s. → **Atom**

null adj. nought, bsd. Am. zero; tel. O (Aussprache: əʊ); Sport: nil, nothing; Tennis: love; **~ Grad** zero degrees; **~ Fehler** no mistakes; **gleich** 2 **sein** Chancen etc.: be*nil; 2**diät** f low-calorie (od. F starvation) diet; 2**punkt** m zero (point od. fig. level); **~tarif** m free fare(s pl.); **zum ~** free (of charge)

nume|rieren v/t. number; 2**rus clausus** univ. m restricted admission(s pl.)

Nummer f number; Zeitung etc.: a. issue; Größe: size; **~nschild** mot. n number (Am. license) plate

nun adv. now; also, na: well; → **jetzt, na**

nur adv. only, just; bloß: merely; nichts als: nothing but; **er tut ~ so** he's just pretending; **warte ~!** just you wait!; **mach ~!**, **~ zu!** go ahead!; **~ für Erwachsene** (for) adults only

Nuß f nut; **~baum** m walnut (tree), Holz: walnut; **~knacker** m nutcracker; **~schale** f nutshell

Nüstern pl. nostrils pl.

Nutte F f tart, Am. sl. a. hooker

Nutz|anwendung f practical application; 2**bar** adj. usable; **~ machen** utilize; bsd. Bodenschätze: exploit; bsd. Naturkräfte: harness; 2**bringend** adj. profitable, useful

nütze adj. useful; **zu nichts ~ sein** be* (of) no use; bsd. Person: a. be* good for nothing

Nutzen m use; Gewinn: profit, gain; Vorteil: advantage; **~ ziehen aus** benefit od. profit from od. by; **zum ~ von** for the benefit of

nutzen, nützen 1. v/i.: **j-m** ~ be* of use to s.o.; **es nützt nichts (es zu tun)** it's no use (doing it); **2.** v/t. use, make* use of; Gelegenheit: take* advantage of

nützlich adj. useful, helpful; vorteilhaft: advantageous; **sich ~ machen** make* o.s. useful

nutzlos adj. useless, (of) no use

Nutzung f use (a. Be2), utilization

Nylon n nylon; **~strümpfe** pl. nylons pl., nylon stockings pl.

Nymphe f nymph

O

O Abk. für **Osten** E, east

o int. oh!; **~ weh!** oh dear!

o.ä. Abk. für **oder ähnliche(s)** or the like

Oase f oasis (a. fig.)

ob cj. whether, if; **als** ~ as if, as though; **und ~!** and how!, you bet!

Obacht f: **~ geben auf** pay* attention to; **(gib) ~!** look od. watch out!

Obdach n shelter; 2**los** adj. homeless, without shelter; **~lose** m, f homeless person; **~losenasyl** n shelter for the homeless

Obdu|ktion med. f autopsy; 2**zieren** med. v/t. perform an autopsy on

oben adv. above; in der Höhe: up; auf: on (the) top; an Gegenstand: at the top (a. fig. Stellung); an der Oberfläche: on the surface; im Haus: upstairs; **da** ~ up there; **von ~ bis unten** from top to bottom (*Person:* toe); **links ~** (at the) top left; **siehe ~** see above; F **~ ohne** topless; **von ~ herab** *fig.* patronizing(ly), condescending(ly); **~an** *adv.* at the top; **~auf** *adv.* on the top; *auf der Oberfläche:* on the surface; F **~** *fig.* feeling great; **~drein** *adv.* besides, *nachgestellt:* into the bargain, at that; **~erwähnt, ~genannt** *adj.* abovementioned; **~hin** *adv.* superficially

Ober *m* waiter; **~arm** *m* upper arm; **~arzt** *m*, **~ärztin** *f* assistant medical director; **~befehl** *mil. m* supreme command; **~begriff** *n* generic term; **~bürgermeister** *m* mayor, *Brt.* Lord Mayor

ober|e *adj.* upper, top; *fig. a.* superior; **2fläche** *f* surface (*a. fig.*) (**an** on); **~flächlich** *adj.* superficial; **~halb** *prp.* above; **2hand** *fig. f:* **die ~ gewinnen** (*über*) get* the upper hand (of); **2haupt** *n* head, chief; **2haus** *Brt. parl.* *n* House of Lords; **2hemd** *n* shirt; **2herrschaft** *f* supremacy

Oberin *f rel.* Mother Superior

ober|irdisch *adj.* above ground; *electr.* overhead; **2kellner** *m* head waiter; **2kiefer** *m* upper jaw; **2körper** *m* upper part of the body; **den ~freimachen** strip to the waist; **2leder** *n* uppers *pl.*; **2leitung** *f* chief management; *electr.* overhead contact line; **2lippe** *f* upper lip

Obers *östr. n* cream

Ober|schenkel *m* thigh; **~schule** *f* grammar school, *Am. appr.* highschool

Oberst *mil. m* colonel

oberste *adj.* up(per)most, top(most); *höchste: a.* highest; *wichtigste:* chief, first

Ober|stufe *f Brt. appr.* senior classes *pl.*, *Am. appr.* senior highschool; **~teil** *n* top

obgleich *cj.* (al)though

Obhut *f* care, charge; *in s-e ~ nehmen* take* care *od.* charge of

obig *adj.* above(-mentioned)

Objekt *n* object (*a. gr.*); *Immobilie:* property

objektiv *adj.* objective; *unparteiisch: a.* impartial, unbias(s)ed

Objektiv *phot. n* (object) lens

Objektivität *f* objectivity; impartiality

Oblate *f* wafer; *rel.* host

obligatorisch *adj.* compulsory

Obo|e *mus. f* oboe; **~ist(in)** oboist

Obrigkeit *f* authorities *pl.*; government

Observatorium *astr. n* observatory

Obst *n* fruit; **~garten** *m* orchard; **~konserven** *pl.* canned fruit *sg.*; **~laden** *m bsd. Brt.* fruiterer's (shop), *Am.* fruit store; **~torte** *f* fruit flan (*Am.* pie)

obszön *adj.* obscene, filthy

obwohl *cj.* (al)though

Occasion *f Schweiz:* bargain, good buy

Ochse *m zo.* ox, bullock; *fig.* blockhead; **~nschwanzsuppe** *f* oxtail soup

od. *Abk. für oder* or

öde *adj.* deserted, desolate; *unbebaut:* waste; *fig.* dull, dreary, tedious

oder *cj.* or; **~ aber sonst:** or else, otherwise; **~ vielmehr** or rather; **~ so** or so; *er kommt doch, ~?* he's coming, isn't he?; *du kennst ihn ja nicht, ~ doch?* you don't know him, or do you?

Ofen *m* stove; *Back2:* oven; *tech.* furnace; **~heizung** *f* stove heating; **~rohr** *n* stovepipe

offen 1. *adj.* open (*a. fig.*); *Stelle: a.* vacant; *ehrlich: a.* frank; **2.** *adv.:* **~ gesagt** frankly (speaking); **~s-e Meinung sagen** speak* one's mind (freely)

offenbar *adj.* obvious, evident; *anscheinend:* apparent; **~en** *v/t.* reveal, disclose, show*; **2ung** *f* revelation

Offenheit *fig. f* openness, frankness

offen|herzig *adj.* openhearted, frank, candid; *Kleid etc.:* revealing; **~sichtlich** *adj.* → **offenbar**

offensiv *adj.,* **2e** *f* offensive

offenstehen *v/i.* be* open (*fig.* **j-m** to s.o.); *Rechnung:* be* outstanding; *es steht Ihnen offen zu* you are free to

öffentlich *adj.* public; **~e Verkehrsmittel** *pl.* public transport *sg.*; **~e Schulen** *pl.* state (*Am.* public) schools *pl.*; **~auftreten** appear in public; **2keit** *f* the public; *in aller ~* in public, openly; *an die ~ bringen* make* public

offiziell *adj.* official

Offizier *m* (commissioned) officer

öffn|en *v/t. u. v/refl.* open; **2er** *m* opener; **2ung** *f* opening; **2ungszeiten** *pl.* business hours *pl.*, office hours *pl.*

oft *adv.* often, frequently

oh *int.* o(h)!

ohne *prp. u. cj.* without; **~ mich!** count

me out!; ~ **ein Wort** (**zu sagen**) without (saying) a word; **~gleichen** adv. unequal(l)ed, unparalleled; **~hin** adv. anyhow, anyway

Ohn|macht f unconsciousness; *Hilflosigkeit:* helplessness; **in ~ fallen** faint, F pass out; **Ωmächtig** adj. unconscious; helpless; ~ **werden** faint, F pass out

Ohr n ear; F **j-n ~ übers ~ hauen** cheat s.o.; **bis über die ~en verliebt** (**verschuldet**) head over heels in love (debt)

Öhr n eye

Ohren|arzt m ear specialist; **Ωbetäubend** adj. deafening; **~leiden** n ear trouble; **~schmerzen** pl. earache sg.; **~schützer** pl. earmuffs pl.; **~zeuge** m earwitness

Ohr|feige f slap in the face (a. fig.); **Ωfeigen** v/t.: **j-n ~** slap s.o.'s face; **~läppchen** n earlobe; **~ring** m earring

oje int. oh dear!, dear me!

Öko|loge m ecologist; **~logie** f ecology; **Ωlogisch** adj. ecological; **~nomie** f *Sparsamkeit:* economy; *econ.* economics pl.; **Ωnomisch** adj. *sparsam:* economical; *econ.* economic; **~system** n ecosystem

Oktave mus. f octave

Oktober m October

ökumenisch rel. adj. ecumenical

Öl n oil; *Erdω:* a. petroleum; **nach ~ suchen** (**bohren**) search (drill) for oil; **auf ~ stoßen** strike* oil; **~baum** bot. m olive (tree)

ölen v/t. oil; tech. a. lubricate

oliv adj., **Ωe** bot. f olive

Öl|farbe f oil (paint); **~förderung** f oil production; **~gemälde** n oil painting; **~heizung** f oil heating; **Ωig** adj. oily, greasy (beide a. fig.)

Öl|leitung f (oil) pipeline; **~malerei** f oil painting; **~meßstab** m dipstick; **~pest** f oil pollution; **~quelle** f oil well; **~sardine** f canned (Brt. a. tinned) sardine; **~tanker** m oil tanker; **~teppich** m oil slick; **~stand** m oil level; **~ung** f oiling; tech. a. lubrication; **Letzte ~** rel. extreme unction; **~vorkommen** n oil resources pl.; *Ölfeld:* oilfield; **~wanne** mot. f (oil) sump; **~wechsel** m oil change

Olympia|... in Zssgn *Mannschaft, Me-*

daille etc.: Olympic ...; **~de** f Olympic Games pl., Olympics pl.

Om|a F f grandma; **~i** F f granny

Omnibus m → **Bus**

onanieren v/i. masturbate

Onkel m uncle

Online f *Computer:* online

Opa F m grandpa

Oper f mus. opera; opera (house)

Operation f operation (**vornehmen** perform); **~ssaal** med. m operating theatre (Am. room)

Operette mus. f operetta

operieren 1. v/t. **j-n ~** operate on s.o. (**wegen** for); **operiert werden** be* operated on, have* an operation; **sich ~ lassen** undergo* an operation; **2.** med., mil. v/i. operate; *vorgehen:* proceed

Opernsänger(in) opera singer

Opfer n sacrifice; *Gabe:* a. offering; *Mensch, Tier:* victim; **ein ~ bringen** make* a sacrifice; **zum ~ fallen** fall* victim to; **Ωn** v/t. u. v/i. sacrifice (a. fig.)

Opium n opium

Opposition f opposition (a. parl.)

Optik f optics sg.; *phot.* optical system; **~er** m optician

opti|mal adj. optimum, best; **Ωmismus** m optimism; **Ωmist(in)** optimist; **~mistisch** adj. optimistic

Option f option

optisch adj. optical

Orange f orange (a. Farbe)

Orchester mus. n orchestra

Orchidee bot. f orchid

Orden m *Auszeichnung:* medal, decoration; *bsd. rel.* order; **~sschwester** rel. f sister, nun

ordentlich 1. adj. *Person, Zimmer, Haushalt etc.:* tidy, neat, orderly; *richtig, sorgfältig:* proper; *gründlich:* thorough; *anständig:* decent (a. F fig.); *Leute:* a. respectable; *Mitglied, Professor:* full; *Gericht:* ordinary; *Leistung:* reasonable; F *tüchtig, kräftig:* good, sound; **2.** adv.: **s-e Sache ~ machen** do* a good job; **sich ~ benehmen** (**anziehen**) behave (dress) properly od. decently

ordinär adj. vulgar; *alltäglich:* common

ordn|en v/t. put* in order; *an~:* arrange, sort (out); *Akten:* file; *Angelegenheiten:* settle; **Ωer** m *Akten* etc.: file; *Akten-*

deckel: folder; *Fest*2: attendant, guard; 2*ung f allg.* order; *Ordentlichkeit*: order(liness), tidiness; *Vorschriften*: rules *pl.*, regulations *pl.*; *An*2: arrangement; *System*: system, set-up; *Rang*: class; *in ~* all right; *in ~ bringen* put* right (*a. fig.*); *Zimmer etc.*: tidy up; *reparieren*: repair, F fix (*a. fig.*); (*in*) *~ halten* keep* (in) order; *et. ist nicht in ~* (*mit*) there is s.th. wrong (with)

ordnungs|gemäß, **~mäßig 1.** *adj.* correct, regular; **2.** *adv.* duly, properly; 2*strafe f* fine, penalty; 2*zahl f* ordinal number

Organ *n* organ; **~empfänger** *m* organ recipient; **~handel** *m* sale of (transplant) organs

Organ|isation *f* organization; **~isator** *m* organizer; 2*isatorisch adj.* organizational

organisch *adj.* organic

organisier|en *v/t.* organize; F *beschaffen*: get* (hold of); *sich ~* organize; *gewerkschaftlich*: *a.* unionize; **~t** *adj.* organized; unionized

Organ|ismus *m* organism; **~ist(in)** *mus.* organist; **~spender** *med. m* (organ) donor

Orgasmus *m* orgasm

Orgel *mus. f* organ; **~pfeife** *f* organ pipe

Orgie *f* orgy

Oriental|e *m*, 2*isch adj.* oriental

orientier|en *v/t. j-n*: inform (*über* about), brief (on); *sich ~* orient(ate) o.s. (*nach* by); *erkundigen*: inform o.s.; 2*ung f* orientation; *fig. a.* information; *die ~ verlieren* lose* one's bearings; 2*ungssinn m* sense of direction

original *adj.* original; *echt*: real, genuine; *TV* live

Original *n* original; *fig.* real (*od.* quite a) character; **~...** *in Zssgn Aufnahme*,

Ausgabe etc.: original ...; **~übertragung** *f* live broadcast *od.* program(me)

originell *adj.* original; *einfallsreich*: *a.* ingenious; *komisch*: witty

Orkan *m* hurricane; 2*artig adj. Sturm*: violent; *fig.* thunderous

Ort *m allg.* place; **~schaft**: *a.* village, (small) town; *Stelle, Fleck*: *a.* spot, point; *Schauplatz*: *a.* scene; *vor ~ Bergbau*: at the (pit) face; *fig.* in the field, on the spot; 2*en v/t.* locate, F spot

ortho|dox *adj.* orthodox; 2*graphie f* orthography; 2*päde med. m* orthop(a)edic specialist

örtlich *adj.* local; 2*keiten pl.* scene *sg.*

Ortsbestimmung *f aviat., naut.* location; *gr.* adverb of place

Ortschaft *f → Ort*

Orts|gespräch *tel. n* local call; **~kenntnis** *f*: *~ besitzen* know* a place; **~netz** *tel. n* local exchange; **~zeit** *f* local time

Öse *f* eye; *Schuh*2 *etc.*: eyelet

Ost|block *pol. m* East(ern) Bloc; **~en** *m* east; *pol. der* East; *nach ~* east(wards)

Oster|ei *n* Easter egg; **~hase** *m* Easter bunny *od.* rabbit; **~n** *n* Easter (*zu, an* at); *frohe ~!* Happy Easter!

Österreich|er(in), 2*isch adj.* Austrian

östlich 1. *adj.* east(ern); *Wind etc.*: easterly; **2.** *adv.*: *~ von* (to the) east of

ost|wärts *adv.* east(wards); 2*wind m* east wind

Otter *zo.* **1.** *m* otter; **2.** *f* adder, viper

outen *v/t. Intimes preisgeben*: F out

Ouvertüre *mus. f* overture

oval *adj.*, 2 *n* oval

Oxyd *chem. n* oxide; 2*ieren v/t. u. v/i.* oxidize

Ozean *m* ocean, sea

ozon|freundlich *adj.* ozone-friendly; 2*loch n* ozone hole; 2*schicht f* ozone layer; 2*schild m* ozone shield; 2*werte pl.* ozone levels *pl.*

P

paar indef. pron.: **ein ~** a few, some, F a couple of

Paar n pair; Mann u. Frau: couple; **ein ~ (neue) Schuhe** a (new) pair of shoes; **2en** v/t. u. v/refl. Tiere: mate; fig. combine; **~lauf** m Sport: pair skating; **2mal** adv.: **ein ~** a few times; **~ung** f mating, copulation; Sport: matching; **2weise** adv. in pairs od. twos

Pacht f lease; **~zins** m rent; **2en** v/t. (take* on) lease

Pächter(in) leaseholder; agr. tenant

Pacht|vertrag m lease; **~zins** m rent

Pack¹ m → **Packen**

Pack² contp. n rabble

Päckchen n small parcel; Packung: packet, bsd. Am. pack (a. Zigaretten)

packen v/t. u. v/i. pack; Paket: make* up; ergreifen: grab, seize (**an** by); fig. mitreißen: grip

Pack|en m pack, Haufen: pile (a. fig.); **~er(in)** packer; Möbel2: removal man; **~papier** n packing od. brown paper; **~ung** f package, box; kleinere, a. Zigaretten2 etc.: packet, bsd. Am. pack

Pädagog|e m teacher; education(al)ist; **~ik** f pedagogics g.; **2isch** adj. educational; **~e Hochschule** college of education

Paddel n paddle; **~boot** n canoe; **2n** v/i. paddle, canoe

Page m page(boy)

Paket n package, mail; bsd. post parcel; **~annahme** post f parcel counter; **~karte** post f parcel mailing form, Am. Am. post slip; **~post** f parcel post; **~zustellung** post f parcel delivery

Pakt m pol. pact

Palast m palace

Palm|e bot. f palm (tree); **~sonntag** rel. m Palm Sunday

Pampelmuse bot. f grapefruit

paniert adj. breaded

Pani|k f panic; **2geraten (versetzen)** panic; **in ~** panic-stricken, F panicky; **2sch** adj.: **~e Angst** mortal terror

Panne f breakdown, mot. a. engine trouble; fig. mishap; **~nhilfe** mot. f breakdown service

Panther zo. m panther

Pantoffel m slipper; **unter dem ~ stehen** be* henpecked; **~held** F m henpecked husband

Pantomim|e thea. **1.** f mime, dumb show; **2.** m mime (artist); **2isch** adv.: **~ darstellen** mime

Panzer m armo(u)r (a. fig.); mil. tank; zo. shell; **~glas** n bulletproof glass; **2n** v/t. armo(u)r; **~platte** f armo(u)r plate; **~schrank** m safe; **~ung** f armo(u)r plating; **~wagen** m armo(u)red car

Papa F m dad(dy), pa

Papagei m parrot

Papeterie f Schweiz: stationer('s shop)

Papier n paper; **~e** pl. papers, documents pl.; Ausweis2e: identification (paper); **~...** in Zssgn Geld, Handtuch, Serviette, Tüte usw.: mst paper ...; **~korb** m wastepaper basket; **~krieg** fig. m red tape; **~schnitzel** pl. scraps pl. of paper; **~waren** pl. stationery sg.; **~warenhandlung** f stationer('s shop, Am. store)

Pappe f cardboard, pasteboard

Pappel f poplar

Papp|karton m cardboard box, carton; **~maché** n papier mâché; **~teller** m paper plate

Paprika bot. m ~schote: sweet pepper; Gewürz: paprika; **gefüllter ~** stuffed peppers pl.

Papst m pope

päpstlich adj. papal

Parade f parade; Fußball etc.: save; Boxen, Fechten: parry

Paradeiser östr. m tomato

Paradies n paradise; **2isch** fig. adj. heavenly, delightful

paradox adj. paradoxical

Paragraph m jur. article, section; Absatz: paragraph

parallel adj., **2e** f parallel (a. in Zssgn)

Parasit m parasite

Parfüm n perfume, Brt. a. scent; **~erie** f perfumery; **2ieren** v/t. perfume, scent; **sich ~** put* on perfume

parieren v/t. u. v/i. Schlag etc.: parry; fig. a. counter (**mit** with); Pferd: pull up; gehorchen: obey

Park m park; 2en v/i. u. v/t. park; 2 *verboten!* no parking!

Parkett n parquet (floor); *thea.* stalls pl., Am. orchestra; *Tanz*2: dance floor

Park|gebühr f parking fee; ~(hoch)haus n multi-storey car park, Am. parking garage; ~ieren v/t. u. v/i. Schweiz: → **parken**; ~kralle f wheel clamp; ~lücke f parking space; ~platz m car park, Am. parking lot; → **Parklücke**; e-n ~ suchen (finden) look for (find*) somewhere to park the car; ~scheibe f parking disc (Am. disk); ~sünder m parking offender; ~uhr f parking meter; ~wächter m park keeper; mot. car park (Am. parking lot) attendant

Parlament n parliament; 2arisch adj. parliamentary

Parodie f parody, takeoff (*auf* of); 2ren v/t. parody, take* off

Parole f mil. password; fig. watchword, pol. a. slogan

Partei f party (a. pol.); *j-s ~ ergreifen* take* sides with s.o., side with s.o.; 2isch adj. partial (*für* to); prejudiced (*gegen* against); 2los pol. adj. independent; ~mitglied pol. n party member; ~programm pol. n platform; ~tag pol. m convention; ~zugehörigkeit pol. f party membership

Parterre n ground floor, Am. first floor

Partie f Spiel: game; Sport: a. match; Teil: part, passage (a. mus.); F Heirat: match

Partisan m partisan, guerilla

Partitur f mus. f score

Partizip gr. n participle

Partner|(in) partner; ~schaft f partnership; ~stadt f twin town

paschen östr. v/t. u. v/i. smuggle

Pascher östr. m smuggler

Paß m passport; Sport, Gebirgs2: pass; *langer ~* Sport: long ball

Passage f passage

Passagier m passenger; ~flugzeug n passenger plane; *großes: a.* airliner

Passah, ~fest n Passover

Passant(in) passerby

Paßbild n passport photo(graph)

passen 1. v/i. fit (*j-m* s.o.; *auf od. für od. zu et.* s.th.); zusagen: suit (*j-m* s.o.), be* convenient; Kartenspiel, Sport: pass; ~ zu farblich etc.: go* with, match (with);

sie ~ gut zueinander they are well suited to each other; *paßt es Ihnen morgen?* would tomorrow suit you od. be all right with you?); *das (er) paßt mir gar nicht* I don't like that (him) at all; *das paßt (nicht) zu ihm* that's just like him (not like him, not his style); ~d adj. fitting (a. Kleidung); farblich etc.: matching; geeignet: suitable, right

passier|bar adj. passable; ~en 1. v/i. happen; 2. v/t. pass (through); 2schein m pass, permit

Passion f passion; rel. Passion

passiv adj. passive

Passiv gr. n passive (voice)

Paste f paste

Pastell n pastel

Pastete f pie

Pate m godfather; godchild; ~kind n godchild; ~nschaft f sponsorship

Patent n patent; mil. Offiziers2: commission; ~amt n patent office; ~anwalt m patent agent; 2ieren v/t. patent; *et. ~ lassen* take* out a patent for s.th.; ~inhaber m patentee

Pater rel. m father, padre

pathetisch adj. pompous; △ *nicht pathetic*

Patient(in) patient

Patin f godmother

Patriot(in) patriot; 2isch adj. patriotic; ~ismus m patriotism

Patrone f cartridge

Patrouill|e f, 2ieren v/i. patrol

Patsch|e F f: *in der ~ sitzen* be* in a fix od. jam; 2en F v/i. (s)plash; 2naß adj. soaking wet

patze|n F v/i., 2r m blunder

Pauke mus. f bass drum; Kessel2: kettledrum; 2n F fig. v/i. u. v/t. cram

Pauschal|e f lump sum; ~gebühr f flat rate; ~reise f package tour; ~urteil n sweeping judg(e)ment

Pause[1] f Arbeits2, Schul2: break, Am. recess; bsd. thea., Sport: interval, Am. intermission; Sprech2: pause; Ruhe2: rest (a. mus.)

Pause[2] tech. f tracing; 2n v/t. trace

pausen|los adj. uninterrupted, nonstop; 2zeichen n Radio: interval signal; Schule: bell

pausieren v/i. pause, rest

Pavian m baboon

Pavillon m pavilion

Pazifis|mus m pacifism; **~t(in)**, **2tisch** adj. pacifist

PC m PC (*Abk. für personal computer*); **~-Benutzer** m PC user

Pech n pitch; F *fig.* bad luck; **~strähne** F f run of bad luck; **~vogel** F m unlucky fellow

pedantisch adj. pedantic, fussy

Pegel m level (*a. fig.*)

peilen v/t. *Tiefe*: sound

peinige|n v/t. torment; **2r** m tormentor

peinlich adj. embarrassing; **~ genau** meticulous (**bei**, in in); **es war mir ~** I was od. felt embarrassed

Peitsche f, **2n** v/t. whip; **~nhieb** m lash

Pell|e f skin; *Schale*: peel; **2en** v/t. peel; **~kartoffeln** pl. potatoes pl. (boiled) in their jackets

Pelz m fur; *abgezogener*: skin; **2gefüttert** adj. fur-lined; **~geschäft** n fur(rier's) shop (*Am.* store); **2ig** adj. furry; *med. Zunge*: furred; **~mantel** m fur coat; **~tiere** pl. furred animals pl., furs pl.

Pend|el n pendulum; **2eln** v/i. swing*; *rail. etc.* shuttle; *Person*: commute; **~eltür** f swing door; **~elverkehr** rail. etc. m shuttle service; commuter traffic; **~ler** m commuter

Penis m penis

Penner F m tramp, *Brt. a.* dosser, *Am. a.* hobo, bum

Pension f (old age) pension; boardinghouse, private hotel; **in ~ sein** be* retired; **~är(in)** (old age) pensioner; *Pensionsgast*: boarder; **~at** n boarding school; **2ieren** v/t. pension (off); **sich ~ lassen** retire; **~ierung** f retirement; **~ist(in)** *östr., Schweiz*: (old age) pensioner; **~sgast** m boarder

Pensum n (work) quota, stint

per prp. pro: per; *durch, mit*: by

perfekt adj. perfect; **~ machen** settle

Perfekt gr. n present perfect

Pergament n parchment

Period|e f period; *med. a.* menstruation; **2isch** adj. periodic(al)

Peripherie f periphery, *e-r Stadt a.*: outskirts pl.; **~geräte** pl. *Computer*: peripheral equipment sg.

Perle f pearl; *Glas2 etc.*: bead; **2n** v/i. *Sekt etc.*: sparkle, bubble; **~nkette** f pearl necklace

Perl|muschel zo. f pearl oyster; **~mutt** n mother-of-pearl

Perron m *Schweiz*: platform

Pers|er m Persian; Persian carpet; **~erin** f Persian (woman); **~ien** Persia; **2isch** adj. Persian

Person f person; *thea. etc. a.* character; **ein Tisch für drei ~en** a table for three

Personal n staff, personnel; **zuwenig ~ haben** be* understaffed; **~abbau** m staff reduction; **~abteilung** f personnel department; **~ausweis** m identity card; **~chef** m staff manager; **~ien** pl. particulars pl., personal data pl.; **~pronomen** gr. n personal pronoun

Personen|(kraft)wagen (*abbr.* PKW) m (*Brt. a.* motor)car, *bsd. Am. a.* auto(mobile); **~zug** rail. m passenger train; local od. commuter train

personifizieren v/t. personify

persönlich adj. personal; **2keit** f personality

Perücke f wig

pervers adj. perverted; **ein 2er** a pervert

Pessimis|mus m pessimism; **~t(in)** pessimist; **2tisch** adj. pessimistic

Pest *med.* f plague; △ *nicht* pest

Pestizid n pesticide

Petersilie f parsley

Petroleum n paraffin, *Am.* kerosene; **~lampe** f paraffin (*Am.* kerosene) lamp

petzen F v/i. tell* tales, *Brt. a.* sneak

Pfad m path, track; **~finder** m boyscout; **~finderin** f girl guide, *Am.* girl scout

Pfahl m stake; *Pfosten*: post; *Mast*: pole

Pfand n security; *Gegenstand*: pawn, pledge; *Flaschen2 etc.*: deposit; *im Spiel*: forfeit; **~brief** econ. m mortgage bond

pfänden jur. v/t. et.: seize, distrain (upon)

Pfand|haus n → *Leihhaus*; **~leiher** m pawnbroker; **~schein** m pawn ticket

Pfändung jur. f seizure, distraint

Pfanne f pan; **~kuchen** m pancake

Pfarr|bezirk m parish; **~er** m anglikanisch: vicar; evangelisch: pastor; katholisch: (parish) priest; **~gemeinde** f parish; **~haus** n parsonage; anglikanisch: rectory, vicarage; **~kirche** f parish church

Pfau m peacock

Pfeffer m pepper; **~kuchen** m gingerbread; **~minze** bot. f peppermint; **2n** v/t. pepper; **~streuer** m pepper caster

Pfeife f whistle; Orgel2 etc.: pipe; Tabaks2: pipe; **2n** v/i. u. v/t. whistle (j-m to s.o.); F: **~ auf** not give* a damn about; **~nkopf** m pipe bowl

Pfeil m arrow

Pfeiler m pillar; Brücken2: pier

Pfennig m pfennig; fig. penny

Pferch m fold, pen; **2en** v/t. cram (in into)

Pferd n horse (a. Turnen); **zu ~e** on horseback; **aufs ~ steigen** mount a horse

Pferde|geschirr n harness; **~koppel** f paddock; **~rennen** n horserace; **~stall** m stable; **~stärke** tech. f horsepower; **~wagen** m (horse-drawn) carriage

Pfiff m whistle; **2ig** adj. smart

Pfingst|en n Whitsun (**zu, an** at), Am. Pentecost; **~montag** m Whit Monday; **~rose** bot. f peony; **~sonntag** m Whit Sunday, bsd. Am. Pentecost

Pfirsich m peach

Pflanze f plant; **2en** v/t. plant; **~nfett** n vegetable fat; **2enfressend** adj. herbivorous; **2lich** adj. vegetable; **~ung** f plantation

Pflaster n med. plaster, bsd. Am. Band-Aid (TM); Straßen2: pavement; **2n** v/t. pave; **~stein** m paving stone

Pflaume f plum; Back2: prune

Pflege f care; med. nursing; e-s Gartens, von Beziehungen: cultivation; tech. maintenance; **in ~ nehmen** take* s.o. into one's care; **~...** in Zssgn Eltern, Kind, Sohn etc.: foster ...; Heim, Kosten, Personal etc.: nursing ...; **2bedürftig** adj. needing care; **~fall** m constant-care patient; **~heim** n nursing home; **2leicht** adj. wash-and-wear, easy-care

pflege|n v/t. care for, look after; bsd. Kind, Kranke: a. nurse; tech. maintain; fig. Beziehungen etc.: cultivate; Brauch etc.: keep* up; **sie pflegte zu sagen** she used to od. would say; **2r** m male nurse; **2rin** f nurse; **2stelle** f nursing place

Pflicht f duty (**gegen** to); Sport: compulsory events pl.; **2bewußt** adj. conscientious; **~bewußtsein** n sense of duty; **~erfüllung** f performance of one's duty; **~fach** n compulsory subject; **2gemäß**, **2getreu** adj. dutiful; **2vergessen** adv.: **~ handeln** neglect one's duty; **~versicherung** f compulsory insurance

Pflock m peg, pin; Stöpsel: plug

pflücken v/t. pick, gather

Pflug m, **pflügen** v/t. u. v/i. plough, Am. plow

Pforte f gate, door, entrance

Pförtner m doorman, porter

Pfosten m post (a. Fußball etc.)

Pfote f paw (a. fig.)

Pfropfen m stopper; Kork2: cork; Watte2, Stöpsel: plug; med. clot

pfropfen v/t. stopper; cork; plug; agr. graft; fig. cram, stuff

pfui int. ugh!; Zuschauer: boo!

Pfund n pound; **10 ~** ten pounds; **2weise** adv. by the pound

pfusch|en F v/i. bungle, botch; **2erei** f bungle, botch

Pfütze f puddle, pool

Phänomen n phenomenon; **2al** adj. phenomenal

Phantasie f imagination; Trugbild: fantasy; **2los** adj. unimaginative; **2ren** v/i. daydream*; med. be* delirious; F talk nonsense; **2voll** adj. imaginative

Phantast m dreamer; F **2isch** adj. fantastic; F a. great, terrific

pharmazeutisch adj. pharmaceutic(al)

Phase f phase (a. electr.), stage

Philosoph m philosopher; **~ie** f philosophy; **2ieren** v/i. philosophize (**über** on); **2isch** adj. philosophical

phlegmatisch adj. phlegmatic

Phon|etik f phonetics sg.; **2etisch** adj. phonetic; **~stärke** electr. f decibel level

Phosphor chem. m phosphorus

Photo... → **Foto...**

Phrase contp. f cliché (phrase)

Physik f physics sg.; **2alisch** adj. physical; **~er(in)** physicist

physisch adj. physical

Pian|ist(in) pianist; **~o** n piano

Picke tech. f pick(axe)

Pickel¹ m pick(axe)

Pickel² med. m pimple; **2ig** med. adj. pimpled, pimply

picken v/i. u. v/t. peck, pick

Picknick n picnic; **2en** v/i. (have* a) picnic

piep(s)en v/i. chirp, cheep; *electr.* bleep

Pietät f reverence; *Frömmigkeit:* piety; **2los** adj. irreverent; **2voll** adj. reverent

Pik n *Karten:* spade(s pl.)

pikant adj. piquant, spicy (*beide a. fig.*); *Witz etc.: a.* risqué

Pilger|(in) v/i. chirp, cheep; **~fahrt** f pilgrimage; **2n** v/i. (go* on a) pilgrimage

Pille f pill; F: **die ~ nehmen** be* on the pill

Pilot m pilot (*a. fig. u. in Zssgn*)

Pilz *bot.* m mushroom (*a. fig.*); *giftiger:* toadstool; *med.* fungus; **~e suchen** (*gehen*) go* mushrooming

Pinguin zo. m penguin

pinkeln F v/i. (have* a) pee, piddle

Pinsel m (paint)brush; **~strich** m brushstroke

Pinzette f tweezers pl.; *med.* forceps

Pionier m pioneer; *mil. a.* engineer

Pirat m pirate (*a. in Zssgn*)

Pisse V f, **2n** v/i. piss

Piste f course; *aviat.* runway

Pistole f pistol, gun

Pkw, PKW *Abk. für* **Personenkraftwagen** (motor)car, *bsd. Am.* automobile

Plache *östr.* f awning, tarpaulin

placier|en v/t. place; **sich ~** *Sport:* be* placed; **2ung** f place, placing

plädieren v/i. plead (**für** for)

Plädoyer *jur.* n final speech, pleading

Plage f *Mühsal:* trouble, misery; *Insekten2 etc.:* plague; *Ärgernis:* nuisance, F pest; **2n** v/t. trouble; *belästigen:* bother; *stärker:* pester; **sich ~** toil, drudge

Plakat n poster, placard, bill

Plakette f *Abzeichen:* plaque, badge

Plan m plan; *Absicht: a.* intention

Plane f awning, tarpaulin

planen v/t. plan, make* plans for

Planet m planet

planieren *tech.* v/t. level, plane, grade

Planke f plank, (thick) board

plänkeln v/i. skirmish

plan|los adj. without plan; *ziellos:* aimless; **~mäßig 1.** adj. Ankunft etc.: scheduled; **2.** adv. according to plan

Plansch|becken n paddling pool; **2en** v/i. splash

Plantage f plantation

Plapper|maul F n chatterbox; **2n** F v/i. chatter, prattle, babble

plärren F v/i. u. v/t. blubber; *schreien:* bawl; *Radio:* blare

Plastik[1] f *Skulptur:* sculpture

Plastik|[2] n plastic; **~k...** *in Zssgn Besteck etc.:* plastic ...; **2sch** adj. plastic; *Sehen:* three-dimensional; *fig.* graphic

Platin n platinum

plätschern v/i. ripple (*a. fig.*), splash

platt adj. flat, level, even; *fig.* trite; F *fig.* flabbergasted

Platte f *Metall, Glas:* sheet, plate; *Stein:* slab; *Holz:* board; *Paneel:* panel; *Schall2:* record, disc, *Am.* disk; *Computer:* disk; *Teller:* dish; F *Glatze:* bald pate; **kalte ~** plate of cold meats (*Am.* cuts)

plätten v/t. iron, press

Platten: F **e-n ~ haben** have* a flat tyre (*Am.* tire), F have* a flat

Platten|spieler m record player; **~teller** m turntable

Platt|form f platform; **~fuß** m *med.* flat foot; F *mot.:* → **Platten; ~heit** *fig.* f triviality; *Floskel:* platitude

Plättli *n Schweiz:* tile

Platz m *Ort, Stelle:* place, spot; *Lage, Bau2 etc.:* site; *Raum:* room, space; *öffentlicher:* square; *runder:* circus; *Sitz2:* seat; **es ist (nicht) genug ~** there's (there isn't) enough room; **~ machen** *für* make* room for; *vorbeilassen:* make* way for; **~ nehmen** take* a seat, sit* down; △ *nicht* **take place**; **ist dieser ~ noch frei?** is this seat taken?; *j-n* **vom ~ stellen** send* s.o. off; **auf eigenem ~** at home; **auf die Plätze, fertig, los!** on your marks, get set, go!; **~anweiser(in)** usher(ette)

Plätzchen n (little) place, spot; *Gebäck:* biscuit, *Am.* cookie

platzen v/i. burst* (*a. fig.*); *reißen: a.* crack, split*; *explodieren (a. fig.): a.* explode (**vor** with), blow* up; *fig. scheitern:* come* to grief *od.* nothing, fall* through, blow* up, *sl.* go* phut; *Freundschaft etc.:* break* up

Platzkarte f reservation (ticket)

Plätzli *n Schweiz:* cutlet

Platz|patrone f blank (cartridge); **~regen** m cloudburst, downpour; **~reservierung** f seat reservation; **~verweis** m: *e-n* **~ erhalten** be* sent off; **~wart** m *Sport:* grounds|man, *Am.* -keeper; **~wunde** f cut, laceration

P

Plauder|ei f chat; **2n** v/i. (have* a) chat
plauschen östr. v/i. → **plaudern**
Pleite F f bankruptcy; fig. flop
pleite F adj. broke; **~ gehen** go* broke
Plombe f seal; Zahn2: filling; **2ieren** v/t. seal; fill
plötzlich 1. adj. sudden; **2.** adv. suddenly, all of a sudden
plump adj. clumsy; **~s** int. thud, plop; **~sen** v/i. thud, plop, flop
Plunder F m trash, junk
Plünder|er m looter, plunderer; **2n** v/i. u. v/t. plunder, loot
Plural gr. m plural
plus adv. plus
Plusquamperfekt gr. n past perfect
Pneu m Schweiz: tyre, Am. tire
Po F m bottom, behind
Pöbel m mob, rabble
pochen v/i. knock, rap (beide: **an** at)
Pocke med. f pock; **~n** med. pl. smallpox sg.; **~nimpfung** med. f smallpox vaccination
Podest n, m platform; fig. pedestal
Podium n podium, platform; **~sdiskussion** f panel discussion
Poesie f poetry
Poet m poet; **2isch** adj. poetic(al)
Pointe f point, e-s Witzes a. punch line
Pokal m goblet; Sport: cup; **~endspiel** n cup final; **~spiel** n cup tie
pökeln v/t. salt
Pol m pole; **2ar** adj. polar (a. electr.)
Pol|e m Pole; **~en** Poland; **~in** f Pole, Polish woman
Polemi|k f polemic(s); **2sch** adj. polemic(al); **2sieren** v/i. polemize
Police f policy
Polier tech. m foreman; **2en** v/t. polish
Politi|k f allg. politics sg. u. pl.; bestimmte, fig. Taktik: policy; **~ker(in)** politician; **2sch** adj. political; **2sieren** v/i. talk politics
Polizei f police pl.; **~ auto** n police car; **~beamte** m police officer; **2lich** adj. (of od. by the) police; **~präsidium** n police headquarters pl.; **~revier** n police station; Bezirk: district, Am. a. precinct; **~schutz** m: unter **~** under police guard; **~streife** f police patrol; **~stunde** f closing time; **~wache** f police station
Polizist m policeman; **~in** f policewoman

polnisch adj. Polish
Polster n Sessel2: upholstery; Kissen: cushion; in Kleidung: pad(ding); fig. finanzielles etc.: bolster; **~garnitur** f three-piece suite; **~möbel** pl. upholstered furniture sg.; **2n** v/t. upholster; Kleidung: pad; **~sessel** m easy chair, armchair; **~stuhl** m upholstered chair; **~ung** f upholstery; Kleidung: padding
poltern v/i. rumble; fig. bluster
Pommes frites pl. Brt. chips pl., Am. French fries pl., French fried potatoes pl.
Pomp m pomp; **2ös** adj. showy
Pony[1] zo. n pony
Pony[2] m fringe, bangs pl.
Pop|gruppe f pop group; **~musik** f pop music
popul|är adj. popular; **2arität** f popularity
Pore f pore
Porno|(film) m porn (film), blue movie; **~heft** n porn magazine
porös adj. porous
Portemonnaie n purse
Portier m doorman, porter
Portion f portion, share; bei Tisch: helping, serving
Porto n postage
Porträt n portrait; **2ieren** v/t. portray
Portug|al Portugal; **~iese** m, **~iesin** f, **2iesisch** adj. Portuguese
Porzellan n china (a. Geschirr), porcelain
Posaune f mus. trombone; fig. trumpet
Pose f pose, attitude
Position f position (a. fig.)
positiv adj. positive
possessiv gr. adj. possessive; **2pronomen** n possessive pronoun
possierlich adj. droll, funny
Post f post, bsd. Am. mail; **~sachen**: mail, letters pl.; **mit der ~** by post od. mail; **~amt** n post office; **~anweisung** f money order; **~beamte** m, **~beamtin** f post office clerk; **~bote** m postman, Am. mailman
Posten m post; Anstellung: a. job, position; mil. sentry; Rechnungs2: item; Waren: lot, parcel
Postfach n (PO) box
postieren v/t. post, station, place; **sich ~** station o.s.
Post|karte f postcard; **~kutsche** f

stagecoach; **Қlagernd** adj. poste restante, Am. (in care of) general delivery; **~leitzahl** f post(al) code, Am. zip code; **~minister** m Postmaster General; **~scheck** m postal cheque (Am. check); **~sparbuch** n post-office savings book; **~stempel** m postmark; **Қwendend** adv. by return (of post), Am. by return mail; **~wertzeichen** n (postage) stamp; **~zustellung** f postal od. mail delivery

Potenz f med. potency; math. power

Pracht f splendo(u)r, magnificence

prächtig adj. splendid, magnificent; fig. a. great, super

Prädikat gr. n predicate

prägen v/t. stamp, coin (a. fig.)

prahlen v/i. brag, boast (beide: mit of), talk big, show* off

Prahler m boaster, braggart; **~ei** f boasting, bragging; **Қisch** adj. boastful; prunkend: showy

Prakti|kant(in) trainee; **~ken** pl. practices pl.; **~kum** n practical training; **Қsch 1.** adj. practical; nützlich: a. useful, handy; **~scher Arzt** general practitioner; **2.** adv.practically; so gut wie: a. virtually; **Қzieren** med., jur. v/i. practi|se, Am. -ce medicine od. law

Prälat rel. m prelate

Praline f chocolate

prall adj. tight; Brieftasche, Muskeln etc.: bulging; Busen etc.: well-rounded; Sonne: blazing; **~en** v/i.: **~ gegen** (od. **auf**) crash od. bump into

Prämi|e f premium; Preis: prize; Leistungsқ: bonus; **Қ(i)eren** v/t. award a prize to

Pranke f paw

Präpa|rat n preparation; **Қieren** v/t. prepare; med., bot., zo. dissect

Präposition gr. f preposition

Prärie f prairie

Präsens gr. n present (tense)

präsentieren v/t. present; offer

Präservativ n condom

Präsi|dent m president; Vorsitzender: a. chairman; **Қdieren** v/i. preside (in over); **~dium** n presidency

prasseln v/i. Regen etc.: patter; Feuer: crackle

Präteritum gr. n past (tense)

Praxis f practice (a. med., jur.); med. **~räume**: Brt. surgery, Am. doctor's office

Präzedenzfall m precedent

präzis(e) adj. precise; **Қion** f precision

predig|en v/i. u. v/t. preach; **Қer** m preacher; **Қt** f sermon

Preis m price (a. fig.); im Wettbewerb: prize; Film etc.: award; Belohnung: reward; **um jeden ~** at all costs; **~ausschreiben** n competition

Preiselbeere bot. f cranberry

preisen v/t. praise

Preis|erhöhung f rise od. increase in price(s); **Қgeben** v/t. abandon; Geheimnis: reveal, give* away; **Қgekrönt** adj. prizewinning; Film etc.: award-winning; **~gericht** n jury; **~lage** f price range; **~liste** f price list; **~nachlaß** m discount; **~rätsel** n competition; **~richter** m judge; **~schild** n price tag; **~stopp** m price freeze; **~träger(in)** prizewinner; **Қwert** adj. cheap; **~ sein** a. be* good value

prell|en v/t. fig. cheat (um out of); **sich et. ~** bruise s.th.; **Қung** med. f contusion, bruise

Premiere thea. etc. f first night, première; **~minister** m prime minister

Presse f press; Saftқ: squeezer; **~... in** Zssgn Agentur, Konferenz, Photograph etc.: press ...; **~freiheit** f freedom of the press; **~meldung** f news item; **Қn** v/t. press; squeeze; **~tribüne** f press box; **~vertreter** m reporter

Preßluft f compressed air; **~... in** Zssgn Bohrer, Hammer etc.: pneumatic

Prestige n prestige; **~verlust** m loss of prestige od. face

Preuße m, **Қisch** adj. Prussian

prickeln v/i. prickle; Finger etc.: tingle

Priester|(in) priest(ess); **Қlich** adj. priestly

prim|a F adj. great, super; **~är** adj. primary (a. in Zssgn)

Primar|arzt östr. m → **Oberarzt**; **~schule** f Schweiz: → **Grundschule**

Primel bot. f primrose

primitiv adj. primitive

Prinz m prince; **~essin** f princess; **~gemahl** m prince consort

Prinzip n principle (aus on; im in); **Қiell** adv. as a matter of principle

Prise f: e-e **~ Salz** etc. a pinch of salt etc.

Prisma n prism

Pritsche f plank bed; mot. platform; **~nwagen** m pick-up (truck)

P

privat adj. private; persönlich: personal; ℒ... in Zssgn Leben, Schule, Detektiv etc.: private ...; **ℒangelegenheit** f personal od. private matter od. affair; **das ist m-e ~** that's my own business

Privileg n privilege

pro prp. per; **2 Mark ~ Stück** 2 marks each

Pro n: **das ~ und Kontra** the pros and cons pl.

Probe f Erprobung: trial, test; Muster, Beispiel: sample; thea. rehearsal; math. proof; **auf ~** on probation; **auf die ~ stellen** put* to the test; **~alarm** m test alarm, fire drill; **~aufnahmen** pl. Film: screen test sg.; **~fahrt** f test drive; **~flug** m test flight; **ℒn** thea. v/i. u. v/t. rehearse; **ℒweise** adv. on trial; Person: a. on probation; **~zeit** f (time of) probation

probieren v/t. try; kosten: a. taste

Problem n problem; **ℒatisch** adj. problematic(al)

Produkt n product (a. math.); Ergebnis: result; **~ion** f production; **~smenge**: a. output; **~ionsmittel** pl. means pl. of production; **ℒiv** adj. productive

Produze|nt m producer; **ℒieren** v/t. produce

professionell adj. professional

Profess|or(in) m professor; **~ur** f professorship, chair (**für** et.)

Profi F m pro; **~... in** Zssgn Boxer, Fußballer etc.: professional

Profil n profile; Reifen ℒ: tread; **ℒieren** v/refl. distinguish o.s.

Profit m profit; **ℒieren** v/i. profit (**von** od. **bei** et. from od. by s.th.)

Prognose f prediction; bsd. Wetter: a. forecast; med. prognosis

Programm n program(me); TV Kanal: a. channel; Computer: program; **~fehler** m Computer: program error, bug; **ℒieren** v/t. program; **~ierer(in)** m programmer

Projekt n project; **~ion** f projection; **~or** m projector

proklamieren v/t. proclaim

Prokurist m authorized signatory

Proletari|er m, **ℒsch** adj. proletarian

Prolog m prologue

Promillegrenze f (blood) alcohol limit

prominen|t adj. prominent; **ℒz** f notables pl.; high society

Promo|tion univ. f doctorate; **ℒvieren** v/i. do* one's doctorate

prompt adj. prompt; Antwort: a. quick

Pronomen gr. n pronoun

Propeller m propeller

Prophe|t m prophet; **ℒtisch** adj. prophetic; **ℒzeien** v/t. prophesy, predict; **~zeiung** f prophecy, prediction

Proportion f proportion

Proporz m proportional representation

Prosa f prose

Prospekt m prospectus; Reise ℒ etc.: brochure, pamphlet; △ nicht **prospect**

prost int. cheers!

Prostituierte f prostitute

Protest m protest; **aus ~** in (od. as a) protest

Protestant|(in) m, **ℒisch** adj. Protestant

protestieren v/i. protest

Prothese med. f artificial limb; Zahn ℒ: denture

Protokoll n record, minutes pl.; Diplomatie: protocol; **~führer** m keeper of the minutes; **ℒieren** v/t. u. v/i. take* the minutes (of)

protz|en F v/i. show* off (**mit** et. s.th.); **~ig** adj. showy, flashy

Proviant m provisions pl., food

Provinz f province; fig. country; **ℒiell** adj. provincial (a. fig. contp.)

Provis|ion econ. f commission; **ℒo-risch** adj. provisional, temporary

provozieren v/t. provoke

Prozent n per cent; F **~e** pl. discount sg.; **~satz** m percentage; **ℒual** adj. proportional; **~er Anteil** percentage

Prozeß m Vorgang: process (a. tech., chem. etc.); jur. Klage: action; jur. Rechtsstreit: lawsuit, case; Straf ℒ: trial; **j-m den ~ machen** take* s.o. to court; **e-n ~ gewinnen (verlieren)** win* (lose*) a case

prozessieren v/i. go* to court; **gegen j-n ~** bring* an action against s.o., take* s.o. to court

Prozession f procession

Prozessor m Computer: processor

prüde adj. prudish; **~ sein** be* a prude

prüf|en v/t. Schüler etc.: examine, test; nach ℒ: check; über ℒ: inspect (a. tech.); erproben: test; Vorschlag etc.: consider; **~end** adj. Blick: searching; **ℒer** m examiner; bsd. tech. tester; **ℒling** m candidate; **ℒstein** m touchstone; **ℒung** f examination, F exam; test; check(ing), inspection; *e-e ~ machen* (*bestehen, nicht bestehen*) take* (pass, fail) an exam(ination); **2ungsarbeit** *f* examination *od.* test paper

Prügel F *pl.*: (*e-e Tracht*) *~ bekommen* get* a (good) beating *od.* hiding *od.* thrashing; **~ei** F *f* fight; **2n** F *v/t.* beat*, clobber; *Schüler*: flog, cane; *sich ~* (*have* a) fight*; **~strafe** *f* corporal punishment; *Schule*: *a.* caning

Prunk *m* splendo(u)r, pomp; **2voll** *adj.* splendid, magnificent

PS *Abkürzung für Pferdestärke* horsepower, HP

Psalm *rel. m* psalm

Pseudonym *n* pseudonym

pst *int.* still! sh!, ssh!; *hallo*: psst!

Psych|e *f* mind, psyche; **~iater** *m* psychiatrist; **2iatrisch** *adj.* psychiatric; **2isch** *adj.* mental, *med. a.* psychic

Psycho|analyse *f* psychoanalysis; **~loge** *m* psychologist (*a. fig.*); **~logie** *f* psychology; **2logisch** *adj.* psychological; **~se** *f* psychosis; **2somatisch** *adj.* psychosomatic

Pubertät *f* puberty

Publikum *n* audience; *TV a.* viewers *pl.*; *Radio*: *a.* listeners *pl.*; *Sport*: crowd, spectators *pl.*; *Lokal etc.*: customers *pl.*; *Öffentlichkeit*: public; **~sgeschmack** *m* public taste

publizieren *v/t.* publish

Pudding *m* pudding, *bsd. Brt.* blancmange

Pudel *zo. m* poodle; *Kegeln*: miss

Puder *m* powder; **~dose** *f* powder compact; **2n** *v/t.* powder; *sich ~* powder one's face; **~zucker** *m* icing (*Am.* confectioner's) sugar

Puff¹ F *m Bordell*: brothel

Puff² *Stoß*: thump; *in die Rippen*: poke

Puffer *rail. etc. m* buffer (*a. fig.*)

Puff|mais *m* popcorn; **~reis** *m* puffed rice

Pull|i *m* (light) sweater, *Brt. a.* jumper; **~over** *m* sweater, pullover

Puls *med. m* pulse; **~zahl**: pulse rate; **~ader** *anat. f* artery; **2ieren** *v/i.* pulsate (*a. fig.*)

Pult *n* desk

Pulver *n* powder; F *fig.* cash, *sl.* dough; **2(e)rig** *adj.* powdery; **2erisieren** *v/t.* pulverize; **~erkaffee** *m* instant coffee; **~erschnee** *m* powder snow

pumm(e)lig F *adj.* chubby, plump, tubby

Pumpe *f* pump; **2n** *v/i. u. v/t. tech.* pump; F *verleihen*: lend*; *entleihen*: borrow

Punker F *m* punk

Punkt *m* point (*a. fig.*); *Tupfen*: dot; *Satzzeichen*: full stop, period; *Stelle*: spot, place; *um ~ zehn* (*Uhr*) at ten (o'clock) sharp; *nach ~en gewinnen etc.*: on points; **2ieren** *v/t.* dot; *med.* puncture

pünktlich *adj.* punctual; *~ sein* be* on time; **2keit** *f* punctuality

Punkt|sieger(in) winner on points; **~spiel** *n* league game

Pupille *anat. f* pupil

Puppe *f* doll; F *Mädchen*: *a.* bird, *Am. a.* chick; *thea., fig.* puppet; *für Crashtests*: dummy; *zo.* chrysalis, pupa; **~nspiel** *n* puppet show; **~nstube** *f* doll's house; **~nwagen** *m* doll's pram, *Am.* doll carriage

pur *adj.* pure (*a. fig.*); *Whisky etc.*: neat, *Am.* straight

Purpur *m Farbe*: crimson; **2rot** *adj.* crimson

Purzel|baum *m* somersault; *e-n ~ schlagen* turn a somersault; **2n** *v/i.* tumble

Puste F *f* breath; *aus der ~* puffed; **2n** F *v/i.* blow*; *keuchen*: puff

Pute *zo. f* turkey (hen); **~r** *zo. m* turkey (cock)

Putsch *m* putsch, coup (d'état); **2en** *v/i.* revolt, make* a putsch

Putz *arch. m* plaster(ing); *unter ~* electr. concealed; **2en 1.** *v/t.* clean; *Schuhe, Metall*: *a.* polish; *wischen*: wipe; *sich die Nase* (*Zähne*) *~* blow* one's nose (brush one's teeth); **2.** *v/i.* do* the cleaning; *~ (gehen)* work as a cleaner; **~frau** *f* cleaner, cleaning woman *od.* lady; **2ig** *adj.* droll, funny, *Am. a.* cute; **~lappen** *m* cleaning rag; **~mittel** *n* clean(s)er; polish

Puzzle *n* jigsaw (puzzle)

Pyjama *m* pyjamas *pl.*, *Am.* pajamas *pl.*

Pyramide *f* pyramid (*a. math.*)

Q

Quacksalber *m* quack (doctor)
Quadrat *n* square; **ins ~ erheben** square; **...** *in Zssgn Meile, Meter, Wurzel, Zahl etc.:* square ...; **⊈isch** *adj.* square; *math. Gleichung:* quadratic
quaken *v/i.* Ente: quack; *Frosch:* croak
quäken *v/i.* squeak
Qual *f* pain, torment, agony; *seelische: a.* anguish
quälen *v/t.* torment (*a. fig.*); *foltern:* torture; *fig.* pester, plague; **sich ~ ab-mühen:** struggle (**mit** with)
Qualifi|kation *f* qualification; **~kati-ons...** *in Zssgn* qualifying ...; **⊈zieren** *v/t. u. v/refl.* qualify
Qualit|ät *f* quality; **⊈ativ** *adj. u. adv.* in quality
Qualitäts... *in Zssgn Arbeit, Waren etc.:* high-quality
Qualm *m* (thick) smoke; **⊈en** *v/i.* smoke; F be* a heavy smoker
qualvoll *adj.* very painful; *Schmerz:* agonizing (*a. seelisch*)
Quantit|ät *f* quantity; **⊈ativ** *adj. u. adv.* in quantity
Quantum *n* amount; *fig. a.* share
Quarantäne *f* quarantine; **unter ~ stel-len** put* in quarantine
Quark *m* curd, cottage cheese
Quartal *n* quarter (of a year)
Quartett *mus. n* quartet(te)
Quartier *n* accommodation; *Schweiz Viertel:* quarter
Quarz *min. m* quartz (*a. in Zssgn*)
Quatsch F *m* nonsense, rubbish, *sl.* rot, crap, bullshit; **~ machen** fool around; *scherzen:* joke, F kid; **⊈en** F *v/i.* talk rubbish; *plaudern:* chat
Quecksilber *n* mercury, quicksilver
Quelle *f* spring, source (*a. fig.*); *Öl:* well; *fig. a.* origin; **⊈n** *v/i.* pour (**aus** from); **~nangabe** *f* reference
quengel|n F *v/i.* whine; **~ig** *adj.* pestering
quer *adv.* across; *legen etc.:* a. cross-wise; **kreuz und ~ durcheinander:** all over the place; **kreuz und ~ durch Deutschland etc. fahren** travel all over Germany etc.
Quer|e *f:* F *j-m in die ~ kommen* get* in s.o.'s way; **~feldeinlauf** *m* cross-country race; **~latte** *f Sport:* crossbar; **~schläger** *mil. m* ricochet; **~schnitt** *m* cross-section (*a. fig.*); **⊈schnitt(s)-gelähmt** *med. adj.* paraplegic; **~stra-ße** *f* intersecting road; **zweite ~ rechts** second turning on the right
Querulant *m* querulous person
quetsch|en *v/t. u. v/refl.* squeeze; *med.* bruise (o.s.); **⊈ung** *med. f* bruise
quiek(s)en *v/i.* squeak, squeal
quietschen *v/i.* squeal; *Bremsen, Rei-fen:* a. screech; *Tür, Bett etc.:* squeak, creak
quitt *adj.:* **mit j-m ~ sein** be* quits *od.* even with s.o. (*a. fig.*); **~ieren** *v/t. econ.* give* a receipt for; **den Dienst ~** resign; **⊈ung** *f* receipt; *fig.* answer
Quote *f* quota; *Anteil:* share; *Rate:* rate; **~nregelung** *f* quota system
Quotient *math. m* quotient

R

Rabatt *econ. m* discount, rebate
Rabe *m* raven
rabiat *adj.* rough, tough
Rache *f* revenge
Rachen *anat. m* throat
rächen *v/t. et.:* avenge; *bsd. j-n:* re-venge; **sich an j-m für et. ~** revenge o.s. *od.* take* revenge on s.o. for s.th.
Rächer(in) avenger
rachsüchtig *adj.* revengeful, vindic-tive
Rad *n* wheel; *Fahr⊈:* bicycle, F bike; **ein**

~ schlagen *Pfau:* spread* its tail; *Sport:* turn a (cart)wheel

Radar *m, n* radar; **~falle** *f* speed trap; **~kontrolle** *f* radar speed check; **~schirm** *m* radar screen; **~station** *f* radar station

Radau *F m* row, racket

radeln *F v/i.* → **radfahren**

Rädelsführer *m* ringleader

Räderwerk *tech. n* gearing

rad|fahren *v/i.* cycle, ride* a bicycle, F bike; **2fahrer(in)** cyclist

radier|en *v/t.* erase, rub out; *Kunst:* etch; **2gummi** *m* eraser, *Brt. a.* rubber; **2ung** *f* etching

Radieschen *bot. n* (red) radish

radikal *adj.*, **2e(r)** radical; **2ismus** *m* radicalism

Radio *n* radio; **im ~** on the radio; **~ hören** listen to the radio; **2aktiv** *phys. adj.* radioactive; **~er Niederschlag** fallout; **~aktivität** *f* radioactivity; **~wekker** *m* clock radio

Radius *math. m* radius

Rad|kappe *f* hubcap; **~rennbahn** *f* cycling track; **~rennen** *n* cycle race; **~sport** *m* cycling; **~sportler(in)** cyclist; **~weg** *m* cycle track *od.* path, *Am. a.* bikeway

raffen *v/t.* gather up; **an sich ~** grab

Raffi|nerie *chem. f* refinery; **~nesse** *f* shrewdness; *Ausstattung:* refinement; **2niert** *adj.* refined (*a. fig. verfeinert*); *schlau:* shrewd, clever

ragen *v/i.* tower (up), rise* (high)

Ragout *n* ragout, stew

Rahe *naut. f* yard

Rahm *m* cream

rahmen *v/t.* frame; *Dias:* mount

Rahmen *m* frame; *Gefüge:* framework; *Hintergrund:* setting; *Bereich:* scope; **aus dem ~ fallen** be* out of the ordinary

Rakete *f* rocket, *mil. a.* missile; **ferngelenkte ~** guided missile; **e-e ~ abfeuern (starten)** launch a rocket *od.* missile; **dreistufige ~** three-stage rocket; **~nantrieb** *m* rocket propulsion; **mit ~** rocket-propelled; **~nbasis** *mil. f* rocket *od.* missile base *od.* site

rammen *v/t.* ram; *mot. etc.* hit*, collide with

Rampe *f* (loading) ramp; **~nlicht** *n* footlights *pl.*; *fig.* limelight

Ramsch *m* junk, trash

Rand *m* edge, border; *Abgrund etc.:* brink (*a. fig.*); *Teller, Brille:* rim; *Hut, Glas:* brim; *Seite:* margin; **(e-n) ~ lassen** leave* a margin; **am ~(e) des Ruins (Krieges** *etc.***)** on the brink of ruin (war *etc.*)

randalier|en *v/i.* kick up a racket; **2er** *m* rowdy, hooligan

Rand|bemerkung *f* marginal note; *fig.* comment; **~gruppe** *f* soziale: fringe group; **2los** *adj. Brille:* rimless; **~streifen** *mot. m* shoulder

Rang *m* position, rank (*a. mil.*); *thea.* circle, *Am.* balcony; **Ränge** *pl. Stadion:* terraces *pl.*; **ersten ~es** first-rate

rangieren 1. *rail. v/t.* shunt, *Am.* switch; **2.** *fig. v/i.* rank (**vor j-m** before s.o.)

Rangordnung *f* hierarchy

Ranke *bot. f* tendril; **2n** *v/refl.* creep*, climb

Ranzen *m* knapsack; *Schul2:* satchel

ranzig *adj.* rancid, rank

Rappe *zo. m* black horse

rar *adj.* rare, scarce; **2ität** *f Sache:* curiosity; *Seltenheit:* rarity

rasch *adj.* quick, swift; *sofortig:* prompt

rascheln *v/i.* rustle

Rasen *m* lawn, grass

rasen *v/i.* race, tear*, speed*; *vor Wut, Sturm:* rage; **~ vor Begeisterung** roar with enthusiasm; **~d** *adj. Tempo:* breakneck; *wütend:* raging; *Schmerz:* agonizing; *Kopfschmerz:* splitting; *Beifall:* thunderous; **~ werden (machen)** go* (drive*) mad

Rasen|mäher *m* lawn mower; **~platz** *m* lawn; *Tennis:* grass court

Raserei *f* frenzied rage; *Wahnsinn:* frenzy, madness; *F mot.* reckless driving; **j-n zur ~ bringen** drive* s.o. mad

Rasier|apparat *m* (safety) razor; electric razor *od.* shaver; **~creme** *f* shaving cream; **2en** *v/t. u. v/refl.* shave; **~klinge** *f* razor blade; **~messer** *n* (straight) razor; **~pinsel** *m* shaving brush; **~seife** *f* shaving soap; **~wasser** *n* aftershave (lotion)

Rasse *f* race; *zo.* breed; **~hund** *m* pedigree dog

Rassel *f*, **2n** *v/i.* rattle

Rassen|... in *Zssgn Diskriminierung, Konflikt, Probleme etc.*: **mst** racial ...;

~trennung pol. f (racial) segregation; Südafrika hist.: apartheid; **~unruhen** pl. race riots pl.

rass|ig adj. classy; **~isch** adj. racial; **2ismus** pol. m racism; **2ist** m, **~istisch** adj. racist

Rast f rest, stop; Pause: a. break; **2en** v/i. rest, stop, take* a break; **2los** adj. restless; **~platz** m resting place; mot. lay-by, Am. rest area; **~stätte** mot. f service area

Rasur f shave

Rat m advice; ~schlag: piece of advice; e-r Stadt etc.: council; j-n um ~ fragen (j-s ~ befolgen) ask (take*) s.o.'s advice

Rate f econ. instal(l)ment; Geburten2 etc.: rate; auf ~n by instal(l)ments

raten v/t. u. v/i. advise; er~: guess; Rätsel: solve; j-m zu et. ~ advise s.o. to do s.th.; rate mal! (have a) guess!

Ratenzahlung econ. f → Abzahlung

Ratespiel TV etc. n panel game

Rat|geber m adviser, counsel(l)or; Buch: guide (über to); **~haus** n town (Am. city) hall

ratifizieren v/t. ratify

Ration f ration; **2al** adj. rational; **2ell** adj. efficient; sparsam: economical; **2ieren** v/t. ration

rat|los adj. at a loss; **~sam** adj. advisable, wise; **2schlag** m piece of advice; ein paar gute Ratschläge some good advice sg.

Rätsel n puzzle; ~frage: riddle (beide a. fig.); Geheimnis: mystery; **2haft** adj. puzzling; mysterious

Ratte f rat (a. fig. contp.)

rattern v/i. rattle, clatter

Raub m robbery; Menschen2: kidnap(p)ing; Beute: loot, booty; Opfer: prey; **~bau** m overexploitation (an of); ~ mit s-r Gesundheit treiben ruin one's health; **2en** v/t. rob, steal*; kidnap; j-m et. ~ rob s.o. of s.th. (a. fig.)

Räuber m robber; Straßen2: highwayman

Raub|fisch m predatory fish; **~mord** m murder with robbery; **~mörder** m murderer and robber; **~tier** n beast of prey; **~überfall** m holdup, (armed) robbery; auf der Straße a.: mugging; **~vogel** m bird of prey; **~zug** m raid

Rauch m smoke; chem. etc. fume; **2en**

v/i. u. v/t. smoke; chem. etc. fume; 2 verboten no smoking; Pfeife ~ smoke a pipe; **~er** m smoker (a. rail.); **starker ~** heavy smoker

Räucher|... in Zssgn Aal, Speck etc.: smoked ...; **2n** v/t. smoke; **~stäbchen** n joss stick

Rauch|fahne f trail of smoke; **2ig** adj. smoky; **~waren** pl. tobacco products pl.; Pelze: furs pl.; **~zeichen** n smoke signal

Räud|e vet. f mange, scabies; **2ig** adj. mangy, scabby

rauf|en 1. v/t.: sich die Haare ~ tear* one's hair; **2.** v/i. fight*, scuffle; **2erei** f fight, scuffle

rauh adj. rough, rugged (beide a. fig.); Klima, Stimme: a. harsh; Hände etc.: chapped; Hals: sore; **~fasertapete** f woodchip paper; **2haardackel** m wire-haired dachshund; **2reif** m hoarfrost

Raum m room; Platz: a. space; Gebiet: area; Welt2: (outer) space; **~anzug** m spacesuit; **~deckung** f Sport: zone marking

räumen v/t. Wohnung: leave*, move out of; Hotelzimmer: check out of; Straße, Saal, Lager etc.: clear (von of); bei Gefahr: evacuate (a. mil.); s-e Sachen in ... ~ put* one's things (away)

Raum|fahrt f space travel od. flight; Wissenschaft: astronautics; **~fahrt...** in Zssgn Technik etc.: space ...; **~fähre** f space shuttle; **~flug** m space flight; **~inhalt** m volume; **~kapsel** f space capsule

räumlich adj. three-dimensional

Raum|schiff n spacecraft; bsd. bemanntes: a. spaceship; **~sonde** f space probe; **~station** f space station

Räumung f clearance; bei Gefahr: evacuation (a. mil.); jur. eviction; **~sverkauf** econ. m clearance sale

raunen v/i. whisper, murmur

Raupe f zo., tech. caterpillar, tech. a. track; **~nschlepper** m TM caterpillar tractor

raus int. get out (of here)!

Rausch m drunkenness, intoxication; Drogen2: F high; fig. ecstasy; e-n ~ haben (bekommen) be* (get*) drunk; s-n ~ ausschlafen sleep* it off; **2en** v/i. Wasser: rush; Bach: murmur; Sturm:

roar; *fig. eilen*: sweep*; **₂end** *adj. Applaus*: thunderous; **~es Fest** lavish celebration

Rauschgift *n* drug(*s pl. coll.*), narcotic(*s pl. coll.*), F dope; **~dezernat** *n* narcotics *od.* drugs squad; **~handel** *m* drug traffic(king); **~händler** *m* drug trafficker, *sl.* pusher

räuspern *v/refl.* clear one's throat

Razzia *f* raid, roundup

rd. *Abk. für rund* roughly

Reagenzglas *n* test tube

reagieren *v/i. med., chem.* react (*auf* to); *fig. a.* respond (to)

Reaktion *f chem. , med., phys.* reaction (*auf* to; *a. pol.*); *fig. a.* response (to)

Reaktor *phys. m* (nuclear *od.* atomic) reactor

real *adj.* real; *konkret*: concrete; **~isieren** *v/t.* realize; **₂ismus** *m* realism; **~istisch** *adj.* realistic; **₂ität** *f* reality; **₂schule** *f appr.* Brt. secondary (modern) school, *Am.* (junior) highschool

Rebe *bot. f* vine

Rebell *m* rebel; **~ieren** *v/i.* rebel, revolt, rise* (*alle: gegen* against); **₂isch** *adj.* rebellious

Reb|huhn *zo. n* partridge; **~laus** *zo. f* phylloxera; **~stock** *bot. m* vine

Rechen *m*, **₂** *v/t.* rake

Rechen|aufgabe *f* (arithmetical) problem; *~ lösen* F do* sums; **~fehler** *m* arithmetical error, miscalculation; **~maschine** *f* calculator; computer; **~schaft** *f*: **~ ablegen über** account for; *zur ~ ziehen* call to account (*wegen* for); **~schieber** *math. m* slide rule; **~werk** *n Computer*: arithmetic unit; **~zentrum** *n* computer cent|re, *Am.* -er

Rechnen *n* arithmetic

rechnen *v/i. u. v/t.* calculate, reckon; *Aufgabe etc.*: work out, do*; *zählen*: count; *~ mit* expect; *bauen auf*: count on; *mit mir kannst du nicht ~!* I count me out!

Rechner *m* calculator; computer; **₂abhängig** *adj. Computer*: online; **₂isch** *adj.* arithmetical; **₂unabhängig** *adj. Computer*: offline

Rechnung *f* calculation; *Aufgabe*: problem; sum; *econ.* invoice, *Am. a.* bill; *im Lokal*: bill, *Am. a.* check; *die ~, bitte!* can I have the bill, please?;

das geht auf m-e ~ that's on me

recht **1.** *adj. Hand, Winkel etc.*: right; *richtig*: *a.* correct; *pol.* right-wing; *auf der ~en Seite* on the right(-hand side); *mir ist es ~* I don't mind; *~ haben* be* right; *j-m ~ geben* agree with s.o.; **2.** *adv.* right(ly), correctly; *ziemlich*: rather, quite; *ich weiß nicht ~* I don't really know; *es geschieht ihm ~* it serves him right; *erst ~* all the more; *erst ~ nicht* even less; *du kommst gerade (zu) ~* you're just in time (for)

Recht *n* right; *Anspruch*: *a.* claim (*beide: auf* to); *jur. Gesetz*: law; *Gerechtigkeit*: justice; *gleiches ~* equal rights *pl.*; *im ~ sein* be* in the right; *er hat es mit (vollem) ~ getan* he was (perfectly) right to do so; *ein ~ auf et. haben* be* entitled to s.th.

Rechteck *n* rectangle; **₂ig** *adj.* rectangular

recht|fertigen *v/t.* justify; **₂fertigung** *f* justification; **₂haber** F *m* know-all; **~lich** *adj.* legal; **~los** *adj.* without rights; *ausgestoßen*: outcast; **₂lose(r)** outcast; **~mäßig** *adj.* lawful; *berechtigt*: legitimate; *gesetzmäßig*: legal; **₂mäßigkeit** *f* lawfulness, legitimacy

rechts *adv.* on the right(-hand side); *nach ~* to the right; **₂...** *in Zssgn pol.* right-wing ...

Rechts|anspruch *m* legal claim (*auf* to); **~anwalt** *m*, **~anwältin** *f* lawyer; **~ausleger** *m Boxen*: southpaw; **~außen** *Fußball*: outside right

recht|schaffen *adj.* honest; *gesetzestreu*: law-abiding; **₂schreibfehler** *m* spelling mistake; **₂schreibung** *f* spelling, orthography

rechts|extrem(istisch) *adj.* extreme right; **₂fall** *m* (law) case; **₂händer(in)** right-handed person; *er (sie) ist ~ he (she)* is right-handed

Rechtsprechung *f* jurisdiction

rechts|radikal *pol. adj.* extreme right-wing; **₂schutz** *m* legal protection; *Versicherung*: legal costs insurance; **~widrig** *adj.* illegal, unlawful

recht|wink(e)lig *adj.* rectangular; **~zeitig** **1.** *adj.* punctual; **2.** *adv.* in time (*zu* for)

Reck *n* horizontal bar

recken *v/t.* stretch; *sich ~* stretch o.s.

recyc|eln v/t. recycle; **⌂lingpapier** n recycled paper

Redakt|eur m editor; **~ion** f Tätigkeit: editing; Personen: editorial office (od. department); **⌂ionell** adj. editorial

Rede f speech, address; Geſ.: talk (**von** of); **e-e ~ halten** make* a speech; **direkte (indirekte) ~** gr. direct (reported od. indirect) speech; **zur ~ stellen** take* to task; **nicht der ~ wert** not worth mentioning; **⌂gewandt** adj. eloquent

reden v/i. u. v/t. talk, speak* (beide: **mit** to; **über** about, of); **ich möchte mit dir ~** I'd like to talk to you; **die Leute ~** people talk; **j-n zum ⌂ bringen** make* s.o. talk

Redensart f saying, phrase

redlich adj. upright, honest; **sich ~(e) Mühe geben** do* one's best

Red|ner(in) speaker; **~nerpult** n speaker's desk; **⌂selig** adj. talkative

reduzieren v/t. reduce (**auf** to)

Reeder m shipowner; **~ei** f shipping company

reell adj. Preis etc.: reasonable, fair; Chance: real; Firma: solid

Refer|at n paper; Bericht: report; Vortrag: lecture; **ein ~ halten** read* a paper; **~endar** m Schule: appr. trainee teacher; **~ent(in)** speaker; **~enz** f reference; **⌂ieren** v/i. (give* a) report (Vortrag: lecture) (**über** on)

reflektieren v/t. u. v/i. reflect (fig. **über** [up]on); **~ auf** be* interested in

Reflex m reflex (a. in Zssgn); **⌂iv** gr. adj. reflexive

Reform f reform; **~ator** m, **~er** m reformer; **~haus** n health food shop (Am. store); **⌂ieren** v/t. reform

Refrain m refrain, chorus

Regal n shelf (unit), shelves pl.

rege adj. lively; Verkehr etc.: busy; geistig, körperlich: active

Regel f rule; med. period, menstruation; **in der ~** as a rule; **⌂mäßig** adj. regular; **⌂n** v/t. regulate; tech. a. adjust; Angelegenheit etc.: settle; **⌂recht** adj. regular (a. F fig.); **~technik** f control engineering; **~ung** f regulation; adjustment; settlement; Steuerung: control; **⌂widrig** adj. against the rule(s); Sport: unfair; **~es Spiel** foul play

regen v/t. u. v/refl. move, stir

Regen m rain; **starker ~** heavy rain(fall); **~bogen** m rainbow; **~bogenhaut** anat. f iris; **~guß** m (heavy) shower, downpour; **~mantel** m raincoat; **~schauer** m shower; **~schirm** m umbrella; **~tag** m rainy day; **~tropfen** m raindrop; **~wald** m rain forest; **~wasser** n rainwater; **~wetter** n rainy weather; **~wurm** zo. m earthworm; **~zeit** f rainy season; Tropen a.: the rains pl.

Regie f thea., Film: direction; **unter der ~ von** directed by; **~anweisung** f stage direction

regier|en 1. v/i. reign; **2.** v/t. govern (a. gr.), rule; **⌂ung** f government, Am. a. administration; **~en Monarchen:** reign

Regierungs|bezirk m administrative district; **~chef** m head of government; **~wechsel** m change of government

Regime pol. n regime; **~kritiker** m dissident

Regiment n rule (a. fig.); mil. regiment

Regisseur m director, thea. Brt. a. producer

Regist|er n register (a. mus.), record; in Büchern: index; **⌂rieren** v/t. register, record; fig. note; **~rierkasse** f cash register

Reglement n Schweiz: regulation, order, rule

Regler tech. m control

regne|n v/i. rain (a. fig.); **es regnet in Strömen** it's pouring with rain; **~risch** adj. rainy

regulär adj. regular; üblich: normal

regulier|bar adj. adjustable; steuerbar: controllable; **~en** v/t. regulate, adjust; steuern: control

Regung f movement, motion; Gefühlsⅇ: emotion; Eingebung: impulse; **⌂slos** adj. motionless

Reh n deer, roe; weiblich: doe; gastr. venison

rehabilitieren v/t. rehabilitate

Reh|bock zo. m (roe)buck; **~keule** gastr. f leg of venison; **~kitz** zo. n fawn

Reib|e f, **~eisen** n grater, rasp

reib|en v/i. u. v/t. rub; zerkleinern: grate, grind*; **sich die Augen (Hände) ~** rub one's eyes (hands); **⌂ung** tech. etc. f friction; **~ungslos** adj. frictionless; fig. smooth

reich *adj.* rich (**an** in), wealthy; *Ernte, Vorräte*: rich, abundant

Reich *n* empire, kingdom (*a. rel., bot., zo.*); *fig.* world

reichen 1. *v/t.* reach; *zu~*: a. hand, pass; *s-e Hand*: give*, hold out; **2.** *v/i. aus~*: last, do*; *~ bis* reach *od.* come* up to; *~ nach* reach (out) for; *das reicht* that will do; *mir reicht's!* I've had enough

reich|**haltig** *adj.* rich; **~lich 1.** *adj.* rich, plentiful; *Zeit, Geld etc.*: plenty of; **2.** *adv.* ziemlich: rather; *großzügig*: generously; **Qtum** *m* wealth (**an** of) (*a. fig.*); **Qweite** *f* reach, *aviat., mil., Funk etc.*: range; *in* (**außer**) (*j-s*) *~* within (out of) (s.o.'s) reach

reif *adj.* ripe; *bsd. Mensch*: mature

Reif *m* white frost, hoarfrost

Reife *f* ripeness, *bsd. fig.* maturity

reifen *v/i.* ripen, mature (*beide a. fig.*)

Reifen *m* hoop; *mot. etc.* tyre, *Am.* tire; **~panne** *mot. f* flat tyre (*Am.* tire), puncture, F flat

Reifeprüfung *f* → *Abitur*

reiflich *adj.* careful

Reihe *f* line, row (*a. Sitz*Q); *Anzahl*: number; *Serie*: series; *der ~ nach* in turn; *ich bin an der ~* it's my turn

Reihen|**folge** *f* order; **~haus** *n* Brit. terraced house, *Am.* row house; **Qweise** *adv.* in rows; F *fig.* by the dozen

Reiher *m* zo. *m* heron

Reim *m* rhyme; **Qen** *v/t. u. v/refl.* rhyme (**auf** with)

rein *adj.* pure (*a. fig.*); *sauber*: clean; *Gewissen*: clear; *Wahrheit*: plain; *nichts als*: mere, sheer, nothing but; **Qfall F** *m* flop; *Enttäuschung*: let-down; **Qgewinn** *m* net profit; **Qheit** *f* purity (*a. fig.*)

reinig|**en** *v/t.* clean; *gründlich: a.* cleanse (*a. med.*); *chemisch*: dry-clean; *fig.* purify; **Qung** *f* clean(s)ing; *fig.* purification; **~sanstalt** *f* (dry) cleaners; *chemische ~ Vorgang*: dry cleaning; **Qungsmittel** *n* cleaning agent, household cleaner, detergent

rein|**lich** *adj.* clean; *als Eigenschaft*: cleanly; **Qmachefrau** *f* → *Putzfrau*; **~rassig** *adj.* purebred, *bsd. Hund*: pedigree; *bsd. Pferd*: thoroughbred; **Qschrift** *f* fair copy

Reis *m* rice

Reise *f* allg. trip; *längere*: journey; *naut.*

voyage; *Rund*Q: tour; *auf ~n sein* be* travel(l)ing; *e-e ~ machen* take* a trip; *gute ~!* have a nice trip!; **~andenken** *n* souvenir; **~büro** *n* travel agency *od.* bureau; **~führer** *m* guide(book); **~gesellschaft** *f* tourist party; tour operator; **~kosten** *pl.* travel(l)ing expenses *pl.*; **~krankheit** *f* travel sickness; **~leiter** *m* courier, *Am.* tour guide *od.* manager; **Qn** *v/i.* travel; *durch Frankreich ~* tour France; *ins Ausland ~* go* abroad; **~nde(r)** travel(l)er; tourist; *Fahrgast*: passenger; **~paß** *m* passport; **~scheck** *m* travel(l)er's cheque (*Am.* check); **~tasche** *f* travel(l)ing bag, holdall

Reisig *n* brushwood

Reißbrett *n* drawing board

reißen *v/t. u. v/i.* tear* (*in Stücke* to pieces), rip (up *od.* open); *zerren*: pull, drag; *Kette, Faden*: break*; *töten*: kill; F *Witze*: crack; *Latte etc.*: knock down; *Gewichtheben*: snatch; *an sich ~* seize, snatch, grab; *sich um et. ~* scramble for (*od.* to get) s.th.; **~d** *adj.* torrential; *~en Absatz finden* sell* like hot cakes

Reißer F *m* thriller; *Erfolg*: hit; **Qisch** *adj.* sensational, loud

Reiß|**verschluß** *m* zipper; *den ~ an et. öffnen* (**schließen**) unzip (zip up) s.th.; **~zwecke** *f* drawing pin, *Am.* thumbtack

reiten 1. *v/i.* ride*, go* on horseback; **2.** *v/t.* ride*

Reit|**en** *n* (*bsd. Am.* horseback) riding; **~er(in)** rider, horse|man (-woman); **~pferd** *n* saddle *od.* riding horse

Reiz *m* charm, attraction, appeal; *Kitzel*: thrill; *med., psych.* stimulus; (*für j-n*) *den ~ verlieren* lose* one's appeal (for s.o.); **Qbar** *adj.* irritable, excitable; **Qen 1.** *v/t.* irritate (*a. med.*); *ärgern: a.* annoy; *bsd. Tier*: bait; *herausfordern*: provoke; *anziehen*: appeal to, attract; (*ver*)*locken*: tempt; *Aufgabe etc.*: challenge; **2.** *v/i. Kartenspiel*: bid*; **Qend** *adj.* charming, delightful; *hübsch*: lovely, sweet, *Am.* cute; **Qlos** *adj.* unattractive; **~überflutung** *f* overstimulation; **~ung** *f* irritation; **Qvoll** *adj.* attractive; *Aufgabe etc.*: challenging; **~wäsche** F *f* sexy underwear; **~wort** *n* emotive word

R

rekeln F v/refl. loll, lounge
Reklamation f complaint
Reklame f advertising, publicity; *Anzeige*: advertisement, F ad; ~ *machen für* advertise, promote; → *Werbung*
reklamieren v/i. complain (*wegen* about), protest (against)
Rekord m record; *e-n* ~ *aufstellen* set* od. establish a record
Rekrut mil. m, **2ieren** mil. v/t. recruit
Rektor(in) head|master (-mistress), *Am.* principal; *univ.* rector, *Am.* president
relativ adj. relative (a. in Zssgn)
Relief n relief
Religi|on f religion; *Schulfach*: religious instruction od. education, R.I., R.E.; **2ös** adj. religious
Reling f naut. f rail
Reliquie f relic
Rempel|ei F f, **2n** v/t. jostle
Renn|bahn f racecourse, racetrack; *Rad2*: cycling track; **~boot** n racing boat; *mit Motor*: speedboat
rennen v/i. u. v/t. run*
Rennen n race (a. fig.); *Einzel2*: heat
Renn|fahrer m mot. racing driver; *Rad2*: racing cyclist; **~läufer(in)** ski racer; **~pferd** n racehorse, racer; **~rad** n racing bicycle, racer; **~sport** m racing; **~stall** m racing stable; **~wagen** m racing car, racer
renommiert adj. renowned
renovieren v/t. renovate, F do* up; *Innenraum*: redecorate
rentabel adj. profitable, paying
Rente f (old age) pension; *in ~gehen* retire; **~nalter** n retirement age; **~nversicherung** f pension scheme
Rentier zo. n reindeer
rentieren v/refl. pay*; fig. be* worth it
Rentner(in) (old age) pensioner
Reparatur f repair; **~werkstatt** f repair shop; *mot.* garage
reparieren v/t. repair, mend, F fix
Report|age f report; **~er** m reporter
Repräsent|ant m representative; **~antenhaus** *Am. parl.* n House of Representatives; **2ieren** v/t. represent
Repressalie f reprisal
Reprodu|ktion f reproduction, print; **2zieren** v/t. reproduce
Reptil zo. n reptile
Republik f republic; **~aner(in)** pol., **2anisch** adj. republican

Reserv|at n Wild2: (p)reserve; *Indianer2*: reservation; **~e** f reserve (a. mil.); **2ieren** v/t. reserve (a. → lassen); *j-m e-n Platz* ~ keep* od. save a seat for s.o.; **2iert** adj. reserved (a. fig.)
Residenz f residence
Resign|ation f resignation; **2ieren** v/i. give* up; **2iert** adj. resigned
Resozialisierung f rehabilitation
Respekt m respect (*vor* for); **2ieren** v/t. respect; **2los** adj. irreverent, disrespectful; **2voll** adj. respectful
Ressort n department, province
Rest m rest; *~e pl. Überreste*: remains pl., remnants pl.; *Essen*: leftovers pl.; *das gab ihm den* ~ that finished him (off)
Restaurant n restaurant
restaurieren v/t. restore
Rest|betrag m remainder; **2lich** adj. remaining; **2los** adv. completely
Resultat n result (a. Sport), outcome
Retorte f retort; **~nbaby** n test-tube baby
rett|en v/t. save, rescue (*beide: aus, vor* from); **2er(in)** rescuer
Rettich bot. m radish
Rettung f rescue (*aus, vor* from); *das war s-e* ~ that saved him
Rettungs|boot n lifeboat; **~mannschaft** f rescue party; **~ring** m life belt, life buoy; **~schwimmer** m lifeguard
Reu|e f, **2ig** adj. remorse, repentance (*beide: über* for); **2mütig** adj. repentant
Revanche f revenge
revanchieren v/refl. sich rächen: have* one's revenge (*bei, an* on); et. gutmachen: make* it up (*bei* to)
Revers n, m lapel
revidieren v/t. revise; econ. audit
Revier n allg. district; zo., fig. territory; → *Polizeirevier*
Revision f econ. audit; jur. appeal; *Änderung*: revision
Revolt|e f, **2ieren** v/i. revolt
Revolution f revolution; **2är** adj., **~är(in)** revolutionary
Revolver m revolver, F gun
Revue f thea. (musical) show
Rezept n med. prescription; *Koch2*: recipe (a. fig. Mittel)
Rezession f recession
Rhabarber bot. m rhubarb

rhetorisch adj. rhetorical

Rheuma med. n rheumatism

rhythm|isch adj. rhythmic(al); **♀us** m rhythm

Ribisel östr. f → **Johannesbeere**

richten v/t. allg. fix; (vor)bereiten: a. get* s.th. ready, prepare; Zimmer, Haar etc.: a. do*; (sich) ~ **an** address (o.s.) to; Frage: put* to; ~ **auf (gegen)** direct od. turn to (against); Waffe, Kamera etc.: point od. aim at; **sich ~ nach** go* by, act according to; Mode, Beispiel: follow; abhängen von: depend on; **ich richte mich ganz nach dir** I leave it to you

Richter m judge; **♀lich** adj. judicial

Richtgeschwindigkeit mot. f recommended speed

richtig 1. adj. allg. right; korrekt: a. correct, proper; wahr: true; echt, wirklich, typisch: real; **2.** adv.: ~ **nett (böse)** really nice (angry); et. ~ **machen** do* s.th. right; **m-e Uhr geht ~** my watch is right; **♀keit** f correctness; truth; **~stellen** v/t. put* od. set* straight

Richt|linien pl. guidelines pl.; **~preis** econ. m recommended price; **~schnur** fig. f guiding principle

Richtung f direction; pol. leaning; paint. etc. style; **♀slos** adj. aimless, disorient(at)ed; **♀weisend** fig. adj. pioneering

riechen v/i. u. v/t. smell* (**nach** of; **an** at)

Riegel m bolt, bar (a. Schokolade)

Riemen m strap; Gürtel, tech.: belt; naut. oar

Riese m giant (a. fig.)

rieseln v/i. Wasser, Sand: trickle; Regen: drizzle; Schnee: fall* gently

Riesen|... in Zssgn mst giant ..., gigantic ..., enormous ...; **~erfolg** m huge success; Film etc.: a. smash hit; **♀groß, ♀haft** adj. → **riesig**; **~kräfte** pl. incredible strength sg.; **~rad** n Ferris wheel; **~welle** f Turnen: giant swing

riesig adj. enormous, gigantic, giant

Riff n reef

Rill|e f groove; **♀ig** adj. grooved

Rind zo. n cow; gastr. beef; **~er** pl. cattle pl.

Rinde f bot. bark; Käse♀: rind; Brot♀: crust

Rinder|braten m roast beef; **~herde** f herd of cattle

Rind|fleisch n beef; **~(s)leder** n cowhide; **~vieh** n cattle pl.

Ring m ring (a. fig.); mot. ring road; U-Bahn etc.: circle (line); **~buch** n loose-leaf od. ring binder

ringel|n v/refl. curl, coil (a. Schlange); **♀natter** zo. f grass snake; **♀spiel** östr. n → **Karussell**

ringen 1. v/i. wrestle (**mit** with); fig. a. struggle (against, with; **um** for); **nach Atem ~** gasp (for breath); **2.** v/t. Hände: wring*

Ring|en n wrestling; **~er** m wrestler

ring|förmig adj. circular; **♀kampf** m wrestling match; **♀richter** m referee

rings adv.: ~ **um** around; **~herum, ~um, ~umher** adv. all around; everywhere

Rinn|e f groove, channel; Dach♀: gutter; **♀en** v/i. run* (a. Schweiß etc.); strömen: flow, stream; **~sal** n streamlet; von Blut, Farbe etc.: trickle; **~stein** m gutter

Rippe f rib; **~nfell** anat. n pleura; **~nfellentzündung** med. f pleurisy; **~nstoß** m nudge in the ribs

Risiko n risk; **ein (kein) ~ eingehen** take* a risk (no risks); **auf eigenes ~** at one's own risk

risk|ant adj. risky; **~ieren** v/t. risk

Riß m tear, rip, split (a. fig.); Sprung: crack; in der Haut: chap; **~wunde** f laceration

rissig adj. Haut etc.: chapped; brüchig: cracky, cracked

Rist m instep; back of the hand

Ritt m ride (on horseback)

Ritter m knight; **zum ~ schlagen** knight; **♀lich** fig. adj. chivalrous

Ritz m, **~e** f crack, chink; Schramme: scratch; Lücke: gap; **♀en** v/t. scratch; ein~: carve, cut*

Rival|e m, **~in** f rival; **♀isieren** v/i. compete; **~ität** f rivalry

rk., r.-k. Abk. für römisch-katholisch RC, Roman Catholic

Robbe zo. f seal

Robe f robe, gown

Roboter m robot

robust adj. robust, strong, tough

röcheln 1. v/i. Kranker: moan; **2.** v/t. Worte: gasp

Rock m skirt

Rodel|bahn f toboggan run; **♀n** v/i.

R

sled(ge), *Am. a.* coast; *Sport:* tobog-gan; **~schlitten** *m* sled(ge); toboggan
roden *v/t.* clear; *Wurzeln:* stub
Rogen *zo. m* (hard) roe
Roggen *bot. m* rye
roh *adj.* raw; *unbearbeitet:* rough; *Hand-lung:* brutal; *mit ~er Gewalt* with brute force; **2bau** *m* carcass; **2eisen** *n* pig-iron; **2kost** *f* raw vegetables and fruit, F rabbit food; **2ling** *m* brute; *metall.* blank; **2material** *n* raw material; **2öl** *n* crude (oil)
Rohr *n* pipe, tube; *Kanal2:* duct; *bot. Schilf2:* reed; *Bambus2 etc.:* cane
Röhre *f* pipe, tube (*a. Am. TV*); *TV etc.* valve
Rohr|leitung *f* duct, pipe(s *pl.*); *im Haus:* plumbing; *Fernleitung:* pipeline; **~stock** *m* cane; **~zucker** *m* cane sugar
Rohstoff *m* raw material
Rolladen *m* rolling shutter
Rollbahn *aviat. f* taxiway, taxi strip
Rolle *f* roll (*a. Turnen*); *tech. a.* roller; *Tau2 etc.:* coil; *unter Möbeln:* cast|or, -er; *thea.* part, role (*beide a. fig.*); **~ Garn** reel of cotton, *Am.* spool of thread; *das spielt keine ~* that doesn't matter, that makes no difference; *aus der ~ fallen* forget* o.s.
rollen *v/i. u. v/t.* roll
Roller *m* (*mot.* motor) scooter
Roll|film *phot. m* roll film; **~kragen** *m* polo neck, *bsd. Am.* turtleneck (*a. in Zssgn*)
Rollo *n* (roller) blind, *Am.* shades *pl.*
Rollschuh *m* roller skate; **~ laufen** roller-skate; **~bahn** *f* roller-skating rink; **~läufer(in)** roller skater
Roll|stuhl *m* wheelchair; **~treppe** *f* escalator
Roman *m* novel
Roman|ik *arch. f* Romanesque (style *od.* period); **2isch** *adj. ling.* Romance; *arch.* Romanesque; **~ist(in)** *Stu-dent(in):* student of Romance languages
Romanschriftsteller *m* novelist
Romantik *f* romance; *hist.* Romanti-cism; **2sch** *adj.* romantic
Röm|er *m* Roman; *Glas:* rummer; **2isch** *adj.* Roman
Rommé *n* rummy
röntgen *v/t.* X-ray; **2apparat** *m* X-ray apparatus; **2aufnahme** *f,* **2bild** *n* X-

-ray; **2strahlen** *pl.* X-rays *pl.*
rosa *adj.* pink; *fig.* rose-coloured
Rose *f* rose; **~nkohl** *m* Brussels sprouts *pl.*; **~nkranz** *rel. m* rosary
rosig *adj.* rosy (*a. fig.*)
Rosine *f* raisin
Roß *n* horse; **~haar** *n* horsehair
Rost *m* rust; *tech.* grate; *Brat2:* grid(iron), grill; **2en** *v/i.* rust
rösten *v/t.* roast (*a.* F *fig.*); *Brot:* toast; *Kartoffeln:* fry
Rost|fleck *m* rust stain; **2frei** *adj.* rust-proof, stainless; **2ig** *adj.* rusty (*a. fig.*)
rot *adj.* red (*a. pol.*); *~ werden* blush; *in den ~en Zahlen* in the red
Rot *n* red; *die Ampel steht auf ~* the lights are red; *bei ~* at red; **2blond** *adj.* sandy(-haired)
Röte *f* redness, red (colo[u]r); *Scham2:* blush
Röteln *med. pl.* German measles *pl.*
röten *v/refl.* redden; *Gesicht: a.* flush
rot|glühend *adj.* red-hot; **~haarig** *adj.* red-haired; **2haarige(r)** redhead; **2haut** *f* redskin
rotieren *v/i.* rotate, revolve
Rot|kehlchen *zo. n* robin; **~kohl** *m* red cabbage
rötlich *adj.* reddish
Rot|stift *m* red crayon *od.* pencil; **~wein** *m* red wine; **~wild** *zo. n* (red) deer
Rotz V *m* snot; **~nase** F *f* snotty nose
Route *f* route
Routin|e *f* routine; *Erfahrung:* expe-rience; **~esache** *f* routine (matter); **2iert** *adj.* experienced
Rübe *bot. f* turnip; *Zucker2:* (sugar) beet
Rubin *m* ruby
Rübli *n Schweiz:* carrot
Rubrik *f* heading; *Spalte:* column
Ruck *m* jerk, jolt, start; *fig. pol.* swing
Rückantwortschein *m* reply coupon
ruckartig *adj.* jerky, abrupt
rück|bezüglich *gr. adj.* reflexive; **2-blende** *f* flashback (*auf* to); **2blick** *m* review (*auf* of); *im ~* in retrospect
rücken 1. *v/t.* move, shift, push; **2.** *v/i.* move; *Platz machen:* move over; *näher ~* approach
Rücken *m* back (*a. fig.*); **~deckung** *fig. f* backing, support; **~lehne** *f* back(-rest); **~mark** *n* spinal cord; **~schmer-zen** *pl.* backache *sg.*; **~schwimmen** *n*

backstroke; **~wind** m following wind, tailwind; **~wirbel** m dorsal vertebra

Rück|erstattung f refund; **~fahrkarte** f return (ticket), Am. a. round-trip ticket; **~fahrt** f return trip; *auf der* **~** on the way back; **~fall** m relapse; **2fällig** adj.: **~** *werden* relapse; **~flug** m return flight; **~gabe** f return; **~gang** fig. m drop, fall; *econ.* recession; **2gängig** adj.: **~** *machen* cancel; **~gewinnung** f recovery; **~grat** n anat. spine, backbone (*beide a. fig.*); **~halt** m support; **~hand** f, **~handschlag** m Tennis: backhand; **~kauf** m repurchase; **~kehr** f return; **~kopplung** electr. f feedback (a. fig.); **~lage** f reserve(s pl.); *Ersparnisse:* savings pl.; **~lauf** m Recorder: rewind; **2läufig** adj. falling, downward; **~licht** mot. n rear light, taillight; **2lings** adv. backward(s); *von hinten:* from behind; **~porto** n return postage; **~reise** f → *Rückfahrt*

Rucksack m rucksack, *großer:* Am. a. backpack; **~tourismus** m backpacking; **~tourist(in)** backpacker

Rück|schlag m Sport: return; fig. setback; **~schluß** m conclusion; **~schritt** m step back(ward); **~seite** f back; *Münze:* reverse; *Platte:* flip side; **~sendung** f return; **~sicht** f consideration, regard; *aus (ohne)* **~** *auf* out of (without any) consideration od. regard for; **~** *nehmen auf* show* consideration for; **2sichtslos** adj. inconsiderate (*gegen* of), thoughtless (of); *skrupellos:* ruthless; *Fahren etc.:* reckless; **2sichtsvoll** adj. considerate (*gegen* of), thoughtful; **~sitz** mot. m back seat; **~spiegel** m rear-view mirror; **~spiel** n return match; **2spulen** v/t. rewind*; **~stand** m chem. residue; *mit der Arbeit (e-m Tor) im* **~** *sein* be* behind with one's work (down by one goal); **2ständig** adj. fig. backward; *Land:* a. underdeveloped; **~e** *Miete* arrears pl. of rent; **~stau** mot. m tailback; **~stelltaste** f backspace key; **~tritt** m resignation; *vom Vertrag:* withdrawal; **~trittbremse** f back-pedal (Am. coaster) brake; **2wärts** adv. backward(s); **~** *aus* ... *(in* ...*)* *fahren* back out of ... (into ...); **~wärtsgang** mot. m reverse (gear); **~weg** m way back

ruckweise adv. jerkily, in jerks

rück|wirkend adj. retroactive; **2wirkung** f reaction (*auf* upon); **2zahlung** f repayment; **2zieher** m Fußball: overhead kick; F: *e-n* **~** *machen* back (*aus Angst:* chicken) out (*von* of); **2zug** m retreat

Rüde zo. male (dog etc.)

Rudel n pack; *Rehe:* herd

Ruder n naut. Steuer2, aviat. Seiten2: rudder; *Riemen:* oar; **am** **~** at the helm (a. fig.); **~boot** n rowing boat, rowboat; **~er** m rower, oarsman; **2n** v/i. u. v/t. row; **~regatta** f (rowing) regatta, boat race; **~sport** m rowing

Ruf m call (a. fig.); *Schrei:* cry, shout; *Ansehen:* reputation; **2en** v/i. u. v/t. call (a. Arzt etc.); cry, shout; **~** *nach* call for (a. fig.); **~** *lassen* send* for; *um Hilfe* **~** call od. cry for help

Ruf|nummer f telephone number; **~weite** f: *in (außer)* **~** within (out of) call(ing distance)

Rüge f reproof, reproach (*beide:* *wegen* for); **2n** v/t. reprove, reproach

Ruhe f Stille: quiet, calm; *Schweigen:* silence; *Erholung, Stillstand, a. phys.:* rest; *Frieden:* peace; *Gemüts2:* calm(ness); *zur* **~** *kommen* come* to rest; *j-n in* **~** *lassen* leave* s.o. in peace; *laß mich in* **~**! leave me alone!; *et. in* **~** *tun* take* one's time (doing s.th.); *die* **~** *behalten* F keep* (one's) cool, play it cool; *sich zur* **~** *setzen* retire; **~**, *bitte!* (be) quiet, please!; **2los** adj. restless; **2n** v/i. rest (*auf* on); **~pause** f break; **~stand** m retirement; **~stätte** f: *letzte* **~** last resting place; **~störer** m bsd. jur. disturber of the peace; **~störung** f disturbance (of the peace); **~tag** m a day's rest; *Montag* **~** *haben* be* closed on Mondays

ruhig adj. quiet; *leise, schweigsam:* a. silent; *unbewegt:* calm; *Mensch:* a. cool; *tech.* smooth; **~** *bleiben* F keep* (one's) cool, play it cool

Ruhm m fame; *bsd. mil.* etc. glory

rühm|en v/t. praise (*wegen* for); *sich e-r Sache* **~** boast of s.th.; **~lich** adj. laudable, praiseworthy

ruhm|los adj. inglorious; **~reich**, **~voll** adj. glorious

Ruhr med. f dysentery

Rühr|eier pl. scrambled eggs pl.; **2en** v/t. stir; *(sich) bewegen:* a. move; fig.

innerlich: move, touch, affect; *das rührt mich gar nicht* that leaves me cold; *rührt euch!* mil. (stand) at ease!; ⚥**end** adj. touching, moving; *liebevoll*: very kind; ⚥**ig** adj. active, busy; ⚥**selig** adj. sentimental; **~ung** f emotion

Ruin m ruin

Ruine f ruin

ruinieren v/t. ruin

rülps|en v/i., ⚥**er** m belch

Rumän|e m Romanian; **~ien** romania; **~in** f, ⚥**isch** adj. Romanian

Rummel F m Geschäftigkeit: (hustle and) bustle; Reklame⚥: F ballyhoo: *großen ~ machen um* make* a big fuss od. to-do about; **~platz** F m amusement park, fairground

rumoren v/i. rumble (a. Magen)

Rumpel|kammer F f lumber room; ⚥**n** F v/i. rumble

Rumpf m anat. trunk; naut. hull; aviat. fuselage

rümpfen v/t.: *die Nase ~* turn up one's nose (über at), sneer (at)

rund 1. adj. round (a. fig.); **2.** adv. ungefähr: about; *~ um* (a)round; ⚥**blick** m panorama; ⚥**e** f round (a. fig. u. Sport); Rennsport: lap; *die ~ machen* go* the round(s pl.); ⚥**fahrt** f tour (durch round)

Rundfunk m radio; Gesellschaft: broadcasting corporation; *im ~* on the radio; *im ~ übertragen od. senden* broadcast*; **~hörer** m listener; *~ pl.* a. (radio) audience sg.; **~sender** m broadcasting od. radio station

Rund|gang m tour (durch of); ⚥**heraus** adv. frankly, plainly; ⚥**herum** adv. all around; ⚥**lich** adj. plump, chubby; **~reise** f tour (durch of); **~schau** f review; **~schreiben** n circular (letter); **~spruch** m Schweiz: → Rundfunk; **~ung** f curve; ⚥**weg** adv. flatly, plainly

runter F adv. → *herunter*

Runz|el f wrinkle; ⚥**(e)lig** adj. wrinkled; ⚥**eln** v/t.: *die Stirn ~* frown (über at)

Rüpel m lout; ⚥**haft** adj. rude

rupfen v/t. pluck (a. fig.)

Rüsche f frill, ruffle

Ruß m soot

Russe m Russian

Rüssel m trunk; Schweins⚥: snout

ruß|en v/i. smoke; **~ig** adj. sooty

Russ|in f, ⚥**isch** adj. Russian

Rußland Russia

rüsten 1. v/i. mil. arm; **2.** v/refl. get* ready, prepare (zu, für for); arm o.s. (gegen for)

rüstig adj. vigorous, sprightly

rustikal adj. rustic

Rüstung f mil. armament; Ritter⚥: armo(u)r; **~sindustrie** f armament industry; **~swettlauf** m arms race

Rüstzeug fig. n equipment

Rute f rod (a. fig.), switch

Rutsch|bahn f, **~e** f slide, chute; ⚥**en** v/i. slide*, slip (a. aus~); gleiten: glide; mot. etc. skid; ⚥**ig** adj. slippery; ⚥**sicher** adj. non-skid

rütteln 1. v/t. shake*; **2.** v/i. jolt; *an der Tür ~* rattle at the door

S Abk. für *Süd(en)* S, south

S. Abk. für *Seite* p., page

s. Abk. für *siehe* see

Saal m hall

Saat agr. f Säen: sowing; **~gut**: seed(s pl.) (a. fig.); *junge ~*: crop(s pl.)

Sabbat m sabbath (day)

sabbern F v/i. slobber, slaver

Säbel m sab|re, Am. -er (a. Sport),

sword; ⚥**n** F v/t. cut*, hack

Sabot|age f sabotage; **~eur** m saboteur; ⚥**ieren** v/t. sabotage

Sach|bearbeiter m official in charge; **~beschädigung** f damage to property; **~buch** n specialized book; *pl. coll.* nonfiction sg.; ⚥**dienlich** adj.: *~e Hinweise* relevant information sg.

Sache f thing; Angelegenheit: matter,

business; (*Streit*)*Frage*: issue, problem, question; *Anliegen*: cause; *jur.* matter, case; **~n** *pl. allg.* things *pl.*; *Kleidung*: a. clothes *pl.*; **zur ~ kommen (bei der ~ bleiben)** come* (keep*) to the point; **nicht zur ~ gehören** be* irrelevant

sach|gerecht *adj.* proper; **Ձkenntnis** f expert knowledge; **~kundig** *adj.* expert; **Ձlage** f state of affairs, situation; **~lich** *adj.* nüchtern: matter-of-fact, businesslike; *unparteiisch*: unbias(s)ed, objective; *Gründe etc.*: practical, technical; **~ richtig** factually correct

sächlich *gr. adj.* neuter

Sach|register n (subject) index; **~ schaden** m damage to property

sacht *adj.* soft, gentle; slow; F: (*immer*) **~e!** (take it) easy!

Sach|verhalt m facts *pl.* (of the case); **~verstand** m know-how; **~verständige(r)** *jur.* expert witness; **~wert** m real value; **~zwänge** *pl.* inherent necessities *pl.*

Sack m sack, bag; V *Hoden*: balls *pl.*; **Ձen** F v/i. sink*; **~gasse** f blind alley (*a. fig.*), cul-de-sac, impasse (*a. fig.*), dead end (street) (*a. fig.*); *fig.* a. deadlock; **~hüpfen** n sack race

Sadis|mus m sadism; **~t(in)** sadist; **Ձtisch** *adj.* sadistic

säen v/t. u. v/i. sow* (*a. fig.*)

Safari f safari; **~park** m wildlife reserve, safari park

Saft m juice; *Baum*Ձ: sap (*beide a. fig.*); **Ձig** *adj.* juicy (*a. Witz*); *Wiese*: lush; *Preis*: fancy

Sage f legend, myth (*a. fig.*)

Säge f saw; **~bock** m sawhorse, *Am.* a. sawbuck; **~mehl** n sawdust

sagen v/i. u. v/t. say*; *j-m et.* ~ tell* s.o. s.th.; **die Wahrheit ~** tell* the truth; **er läßt dir ~** he asked me to tell you; **~ wir** (let's) say; **man sagt, er sei** is said to be; **er läßt sich nichts ~** he will not listen to reason; **das hat nichts zu ~** it doesn't matter; **et.** (*nichts*) **zu ~ haben** (*bei*) have* a say (no say) (in); **~ wollen mit** mean* by; **das sagt mir nichts** it doesn't mean anything to me; **unter uns gesagt** between you and me

sägen v/i. u. v/t. saw*

sagenhaft *adj.* legendary; F *fig.* fabulous, incredible, fantastic

Säge|späne *pl.* sawdust *sg.*; **~werk** n sawmill

Sahne f cream; **~torte** f cream gateau

Saison f season; **in der ~** in season; **Ձbedingt** *adj.* seasonal

Saite f string, chord (*a. fig.*); **~ninstrument** n string(ed) instrument

Sakko m, n (sports) jacket, *Am.* a. sport(s) coat

Sakristei f vestry, sacristy

Salat m lettuce; *angemachter*: salad; **~sauce** f salad dressing

Salb|e f ointment; **~ungsvoll** *fig. adj.* unctuous

Saldo *econ.* m balance

Salmiak *chem.* m, n ammonium chloride; **~geist** m liquid ammonia; **~pastillen** *pl.* ammoniac pastilles *pl.*

Salon m *Mode*Ձ, *Friseur*Ձ *etc.*: salon; *mar.* saloon; *bsd. hist.* drawing room

salopp *adj.* casual; *contp.* sloppy

Salpeter *chem.* m saltpet|re, *Am.* -er, nit|re, *Am.* -er

Salto m somersault (*a. fig.*)

Salut m salute; **~ schießen** fire a salute; **Ձieren** v/i. (give*) a salute

Salve f volley (*a. fig.*); *Ehren*Ձ: salute

Salz n salt; **~bergwerk** n salt mine; **Ձen** v/t. salt; **~hering** m pickled herring; **Ձig** *adj.* salty; **~kartoffeln** *pl.* boiled potatoes *pl.*; **~korn** n grain of salt; **~säure** f hydrochloric acid; **~stange** f salt (*Am.* pretzel) stick; **~streuer** m saltcellar, *Am.* salt shaker; **~wasser** n salt water

Same m, **~n** m *bot.* seed (*a. fig.*); *biol.* sperm, semen; **~nbank** f sperm bank; **~nerguß** m ejaculation; **~nfaden** m spermatozoon; **~nflüssigkeit** f semen; **~nkorn** *bot.* n seedcorn; **~nspender** m sperm donor; **~nstrang** m spermatic chord

Sammel|... in *Zssgn Begriff, Bestellung, Konto etc.*: collective ...; **~büchse** f collecting box; **~mappe** f folder, file; **Ձn** v/t. collect; *Pilze etc.*: gather, pick; *anhäufen*: accumulate; **sich ~** assemble; *fig.* compose o.s.; **~platz** m meeting place

Samml|er(in) collector; **~ung** f collection

Samstag m Saturday

samt *prp.* together *od.* along with

Samt m velvet

sämtlich adj.: ~e pl. alle; all the; Werke etc.: the complete

Sanatorium n sanatorium, Am. a. sanitarium

Sand m sand

Sandal|e f sandal; ~ette f high-heeled sandal

Sand|bahn f Sport: dirt track; ~bank f sandbank; ~boden m sandy soil; ~burg f sandcastle; 2ig adj. sandy; ~korn n grain of sand; ~mann m, ~männchen n sandman; ~papier n sandpaper; ~sack m sand bag; ~stein m sandstone; ~strand m sandy beach; ~uhr f hourglass

sanft adj. gentle, soft; mild: mild; Tod: easy; ~mütig adj. gentle, mild

Sänger(in) f singer

sanier|en v/t. redevelop (a. econ.), rehabilitate (a. Haus); 2ung f redevelopment, rehabilitation; 2ungsgebiet n redevelopment area

sani|tär adj. sanitary; 2täter m first-aid man, ambulance man, Am. paramedic; mil. medical orderly, Am. medic; 2tätswagen m ambulance

Sankt Saint, St

Sard|elle f anchovy; ~ine f sardine

Sarg m coffin, Am. a. casket

Sarkas|mus m sarcasm; 2tisch adj. sarcastic

Satan m Satan; fig. devil

Satellit m satellite (a. fig.); über ~ by od. via satellite; ~en... in Zssgn Bild, Staat, Stadt, TV: satellite ...

Satin m satin; Baumwoll2: sateen

Satir|e f satire (auf upon); ~iker m satirist; 2isch adj. satiric(al)

satt adj. F full (up); ich bin ~ I've had enough, F I'm full (up); sich ~ essen eat* one's fill (an of); ~ zu essen haben have* enough to eat; et. od. j-n ~ haben (bekommen) be* (get*) tired od. F sick of, be* (get*) fed up with

Sattel m saddle; ~gurt m girth; 2n v/t. saddle; ~schlepper mot. m articulated lorry, Am. semi-trailer truck

sättig|en 1. v/t. satisfy; ernähren: feed*; chem., phys. saturate; 2. v/i. Essen: be* substantial od. filling; 2ung f satiety; chem., econ., fig. saturation

Sattler m saddler; ~ei f saddlery

Satz m gr. sentence; Sprung: leap; Tennis, zs.-gehörige Dinge: set; econ. rate;

mus. movement; ~aussage gr. f predicate; ~bau gr. m syntax; e-s Satzes: construction; ~gegenstand gr. m subject; ~teil gr. m part of a sentence

Satzung f statute

Satzzeichen n punctuation mark

Sau f zo. sow; hunt. wild sow; V fig. pig; 2... F in Zssgn kalt etc.: damned

sauber adj. clean (a. F fig.); Luft etc.: a. pure; ordentlich: neat (a. fig.), tidy; anständig: decent; iro. fine, nice; ~halten v/t. keep* clean (sich o.s.); 2keit f clean(li)ness; tidiness, neatness; purity; decency; ~machen v/t. u. v/i. clean (up)

säuber|n v/t. clean (up); gründlich: cleanse (a. med.); ~ von clear (pol. fig. a. purge) of; 2ung(saktion) pol. f purge

sauer adj. sour (a. fig. Gesicht), acid (a. chem.); Gurke: pickled; wütend: mad (auf at), cross (with); ~ werden turn sour; fig. get* mad; saurer Regen acid rain; 2kraut n sauerkraut

säuerlich adj. sharp; fig. wry

Sauerstoff chem. m oxygen; ~gerät med. n oxygen apparatus; ~maske f oxygen mask; ~zelt n oxygen tent

Sauerteig m leaven

saufen v/t. u. v/i. drink*; F Mensch: booze

Säufer F m drunkard, F boozer

saugen v/i. u. v/t. suck (an et. [at] s.th.)

säuge|n v/t. suckle (a. Tier), nurse, breastfeed*; 2tier n mammal

saugfähig adj. absorbent

Säugling m baby, infant; ~sheim n (baby) nursery; ~spflege f infant care; ~sschwester f baby nurse; ~sstation f neonatal care unit; ~ssterblichkeit f infant mortality

Säule f column; Pfeiler: pillar (a. fig.); ~ngang m colonnade

Saum m hem(line); Naht: seam

säum|en v/t. hem; umranden: border, edge; die Straßen: line

Sauna f sauna

Säure chem. f, 2haltig adj. acid

sausen v/i. F rush; dash; Ohren: buzz; Wind: howl

Saustall m pigsty (a. fig.)

Saxophon mus. n saxophone, F sax

S-Bahn f suburban train, Am. rapid transit

Schabe zo. f cockroach

schaben v/t. scrape (**von** from)

Schabernack m prank, practical joke

schäbig adj. shabby; fig. a. mean

Schablone f stencil; fig. stereotype

Schach n chess; ~! check!; ~ **und matt!** checkmate!; **in** ~ **halten** keep* s.o. in check; **~brett** n chessboard; **~feld** n square; **~figur** f chessman, piece; **♀matt** adj. fig. all worn out, F dead beat; ~ **setzen** checkmate s.o.; **~spiel** n (game of) chess; chessboard and men

Schacht m shaft; Bergbau: a. pit

Schachtel f box; Papp♀: a. carton; ~ **Zigaretten** packet (bsd. Am. pack) of cigarettes

Schachzug m move (a. fig.)

schade pred. adj.: **es ist** ~ it's a pity; **wie** ~! what a pity od. shame!; **zu** ~ **für** too good for

Schädel m skull, F head; **~bruch** med. m fracture of the skull

schaden v/i. damage, do* damage to, harm, hurt*; **der Gesundheit** ~ be* bad for one's health; **das schadet nichts** it doesn't matter; **es könnte ihm nicht** ~ it wouldn't hurt him

Schaden m damage (**an** to); bsd. tech. trouble, defect (a. med.); Nachteil: disadvantage; econ. loss; **j-m** ~ **zufügen** do* s.o. harm; **~ersatz** m damages pl.; ~ **leisten** pay* damages; **~freude** f: ~ **empfinden über** gloat over; **♀froh** adv. gloatingly

schadhaft adj. damaged; mangelhaft: defective, faulty; Haus etc.: out of repair; Rohr etc.: leaking; Zähne: decayed

schädigen v/t. damage, harm

schädlich adj. harmful, injurious; gesundheits~: a. bad (for your health)

Schädling m pest; **~sbekämpfung** f pest control; **~sbekämpfungsmittel** n pesticide

Schadstoff m harmful substance; bsd. Umwelt: a. pollutant; **♀arm** adj. Treibstoff: low-emission

Schaf n sheep; **~bock** m ram

Schäfer m shepherd; **~hund** m sheepdog; **deutscher** ~ bsd. Brt. Alsatian, bsd. Am. German shepherd

Schaffell n sheepskin; am Schaf: fleece

schaffen 1. v/t. u. er~: create; bewirken, bereiten: cause, bring* about; bewältigen: manage, get* s.th. done; bringen:

take*; **es** ~ make* it; Erfolg haben: a. succeed; **das wäre geschafft** we've done it od. made it; **2.** v/i. work; **j-m zu** ~ **machen** cause s.o. trouble; **sich zu** ~ **machen an** unbefugt: tamper with

Schaffner(in) conduct|or (-ress); Brt. rail. guard

Schafhirt(e) m shepherd

Schafott n scaffold

Schaft m shaft; Gewehr♀: stock; Werkzeug♀, Schlüssel♀: shank; Stiefel♀: leg; **~stiefel** m high boot

Schaf|wolle f sheep's wool; **~zucht** f sheep breeding

schäkern v/i. joke; flirt

schal adj. stale, flat; fig. a. empty

Schal m scarf

Schale f bowl, dish; Eier♀, Nuß♀ etc.: shell; Obst♀, Kartoffel♀: peel, skin; **Kartoffel♀n** pl. peelings pl.

schälen v/t. peel, pare; **sich** ~ Haut: peel od. come* off

Schall m sound; **~dämpfer** m silencer, mot. Am. muffler; **♀dicht** adj. soundproof; **♀en** v/i. sound; klingen, dröhnen: ring* (out); **♀end** adj.: **~es Gelächter** roars pl. of laughter; **~geschwindigkeit** f speed of sound; **~mauer** f sound barrier; **~platte** f record, disc; **~welle** f sound wave

schalten v/i. u. v/t. switch, turn; mot. change (bsd. Am. shift) gear; verstehen: get* it; reagieren: react

Schalter¹ m rail. ticket window; Post♀, Bank♀ etc.: counter; aviat. desk

Schalter² electr. m switch

Schalt|hebel m mot. gear lever; tech., aviat. control lever; electr. switch lever; **♀jahr** n leap year; **♀tafel** electr. f switchboard, control panel; **♀uhr** f time switch; **♀ung** f mot. gearshift; electr. circuit

Scham f shame (**vor** in, for)

schämen v/refl. be* od. feel* ashamed (gen., **wegen** of); **du solltest dich (was)** ~! you ought to be ashamed of yourself!

Scham|gefühl n sense of shame; ~ **haare** pl. pubic hair sg.; **♀haft** adj. bashful; **♀los** adj. shameless; unanständig: indecent; **~losigkeit** f shamelessness; indecency

Schande f shame, disgrace

schänden v/t. disgrace; entweihen: desecrate; vergewaltigen: rape

Schandfleck m stain, taint; *Schande*: disgrace; *Anblick*: eyesore

schändlich adj. disgraceful

Schandtat f atrocity

Schanze f *Sport*: ski jump

Schar f troop, band; F horde; *Menge*: crowd; *Gänse*♀ etc.: flock; *agr. Pflug*♀: ploughshare, *Am.* plowshare; **♀en** v/ refl.: *sich ~ um* gather round

scharf adj. sharp (*a. fig.*); *phot. a.* in focus; *deutlich*: clear; *Hund*: savage, fierce; *Munition*: live; *Bombe* etc.: armed; *~ gewürzt*: hot; *erregt*: hot, *aufreizend*: *a.* sexy; *~ sein auf* be* keen on (*bsd. sexuell*: hot for); *~ (ein)stellen phot.* focus; F *~e Sachen* hard liquor *sg.*

Schärfe f sharpness (*a. phot.*); *Härte*: severity, fierceness; **♀n** v/t. sharpen

Scharf|richter m executioner; **~schütze** m sharpshooter; sniper; **♀sichtig** adj. sharp-sighted; *fig.* clear-sighted; **~sinn** m acumen; **♀sinnig** adj. sharp-witted, shrewd

Scharlach m scarlet; *med.* scarlet fever; **♀rot** adj. scarlet

Scharlatan m charlatan, fraud

Scharnier tech. n hinge

Schärpe f sash

scharren v/i. scrape, scratch

Schart|e f notch, nick; **♀ig** adj. jagged, notchy

Schaschlik m, n shish kebab

Schatten m shadow (*a. fig.*); *nicht Licht od. Sonne*: shade; *im ~* in the shade; **♀haft** adj. shadowy

Schattierung f shade; *fig.* colo(u)r

schattig adj. shady

Schatz m treasure; *fig.* darling; **~amt** *pol.* n Treasury, *Am.* Treasury Department

schätzen v/t. estimate; *Wert*: *a.* value (*beide*: *auf* at); *hoch~*: think* highly of; F *vermuten*: reckon, *Am. a.* guess

Schatz|kammer f treasury (*a. fig.*); **~kanzler** m Chancellor of the Exchequer; **~meister** m treasurer

Schätzung f estimate; valuation

Schau f show, exhibition; *zur ~ stellen* exhibit, display

Schauder m shudder; **♀haft** adj. horrible, dreadful; **♀n** v/i. shudder, shiver (*beide*: *vor* with)

schauen v/i. look (*auf* at); → *sehen*

Schauer m *Regen*♀ etc.: shower; *Schauder*: shudder, shiver; **~geschichte** f horror story (*a. fig.*); **♀lich** adj. dreadful, horrible

Schaufel f shovel; *Kehr*♀: dustpan; **♀n** v/t. shovel; *graben*: dig*

Schaufenster n shop window; **~auslage** f window display; **~bummel** m: *e-n ~ machen* go* window-shopping; **~dekoration** f window dressing

Schaukel f swing; **♀n 1.** v/i. swing*; *Boot* etc.: rock; **2.** v/t. rock; **~pferd** n rocking horse; **~stuhl** m rocking chair, rocker

Schaulustige pl. (curious) onlookers pl., *Am.* F rubbernecks pl.

Schaum m foam; *Bier*♀: froth, head; *Seifen*♀: lather; *Gischt*: spray

schäumen v/i. foam (*a. fig.*), froth; *Seife*: lather; *Gischt*: spray

Schaum|gummi m foam rubber; **♀ig** adj. foamy, frothy; **~löscher** m foam extinguisher

Schau|platz m scene; **~prozeß** *jur.* m show trial

schaurig adj. creepy; horrible

Schau|spiel n *thea.* play; *fig.* spectacle; **~spieler(in)** act|or (-ress); **~spielschule** f drama school; **~steller** m showman

Scheck *econ.* m cheque, *Am.* check; **~heft** n chequebook, *Am.* checkbook

scheckig adj. spotty

Scheckkarte f cheque (*Am.* check cashing) card

scheffeln v/t. *Geld* etc.: rake in

Scheibe f disc, *Am.* disk; *Brot*♀ etc.: slice; *Fenster*♀: pane; *Schieß*♀: target; **~nbremse** *mot.* f disc brake; **~nwischer** *mot.* m windscreen (*Am.* windshield) wiper

Scheide f sheath; *Degen*♀ etc.: *a.* scabbard; *anat.* vagina; **♀n 1.** v/t. separate, part (*beide*: *von* from); *Ehe*: divorce; *sich ~ lassen* get* a divorce; *von j-m*: divorce s.o.; **2.** v/i.: *~ aus Amt* etc.: retire from; *aus dem Leben ~* take* one's life; **~weg** *fig.* m crossroads *sg.*

Scheidung f divorce; **~sklage** *jur.* f divorce suit

Schein¹ m *Bescheinigung*: certificate; *Formular*: form, *Am.* blank; *Geld*♀: note, *Am. a.* bill

Schein² m Licht2: light; fig. appearance; et. (nur) zum ~ tun (only) pretend to do s.th.; 2bar adj. seeming, apparent; 2en v/i. shine*; fig. seem, appear, look; ~**heilig** adj. hypocritical; F ~ **tun** act (the) innocent; ~**welt** f world of illusion; ~**werfer** m Such2: searchlight; mot. headlight; thea. spotlight

Scheiß|... V in Zssgn damn ..., bsd. Brt. bloody ..., bsd. Am. fucking ...; ~**e** V f, 2en V v/i. shit*, crap

Scheit n piece of wood

Scheitel m parting; 2n v/t. Haar: part

Scheiterhaufen m pyre; hist. stake

scheitern fig. v/i. fail, go* wrong

Schelle f (little) bell; tech. clamp, clip

Schellfisch m haddock

Schelm fig. m rascal; 2isch adj. impish

Schema n pattern, system; 2tisch adj. schematic; Arbeit etc.: mechanical

Schemel m stool

schemenhaft adj. shadowy

Schenkel m Ober2: thigh; Unter2: shank; math. leg

schenk|en v/t. give* (as a present) (zu for); 2ung jur. f donation

Scherbe f, ~**n** m (broken) piece, fragment

Schere f scissors pl. (a. fig.); zo. Krebs2 etc.: claw

scheren¹ v/t. Schaf: shear*; Hecke: clip; Haare: cut*

scheren² v/refl.: sich ~ um bother about

scheren³ v/refl.: scher dich zum Teufel! go to hell!

Scherereien pl. trouble sg., bother sg.

Schermaus zo. östr. f mole

Scherz m joke; im (zum) ~ for fun; 2en v/i. joke (über at); 2haft adj. joking; ~ **gemeint** meant as a joke

scheu adj. shy (a. Pferd); schüchtern: bashful; ~ machen frighten

Scheu f shyness; Ehrfurcht: awe

scheuen 1. v/i. shy (vor at), take* fright (at); **2.** v/t. shun, avoid; fürchten: fear; sich ~, et. zu tun be* afraid of doing s.th.

scheuer|n v/t. u. v/i. scrub, scour; wund~: chafe; 2tuch n floor cloth

Scheuklappen pl. blinkers pl., Am. a. blinders pl. (beide a. fig.)

Scheune f barn

Scheusal n monster (a. fig.); F Ekel: beast

scheußlich adj. horrible (a. F Wetter etc.); Verbrechen etc.: a. atrocious

Schicht f layer; Farb2 etc.: coat; dünne ~: film; Arbeits2: shift; Gesellschafts2: class; 2en v/t. arrange in layers, pile up; 2**weise** adv. in layers

schick adj. smart, chic, stylish

Schick m smartness, chic, style

schicken v/t. send* (nach, zu to); das schickt sich nicht that isn't done

Schickeria F f smart set, beautiful people pl., trendies pl.

Schickimicki F contp. m trendy

Schicksal n fate, destiny; Los2: lot

Schiebe|dach mot. n sliding roof, sunroof; ~**fenster** n sliding window; vertikal: sash window

schieben v/t. push

Schieber tech. m slide; Riegel: bolt

Schiebetür f sliding door

Schiebung F f swindle, fix (a. Sport)

Schiedsrichter m Fußball: referee; Tennis: umpire; bei Wettbewerb: judge, bsd. a. jury sg.

schief adj. crooked, not straight; schräg: sloping, oblique (a. math.); Turm etc.: leaning; fig. Bild, Vergleich: false

Schiefer geol. m slate; ~**tafel** f slate

schiefgehen v/i. go* wrong

schielen v/i. squint, be* cross-eyed

Schienbein n shin(bone)

Schiene f rail. etc.: rail; med. splint; 2n med. v/t. splint

Schieß|bude f shooting gallery; 2en v/i. u. v/t. shoot* (a. fig.), fire (beide: auf at); Tor: score; ~**erei** f shooting; Kampf: gunfight; ~**pulver** n gunpowder; ~**scharte** mil. f loophole, embrasure; ~**scheibe** f target; ~**stand** m shooting range

Schiff n ship, boat; arch. Kirchen2: nave; mit dem ~ by boat

Schiffahrt f shipping, navigation

schiff|bar adj. navigable; 2**bau** m shipbuilding; 2**bruch** m shipwreck (a. fig.); ~ **erleiden** be* shipwrecked; 2**er** m sailor; Kapitän: skipper; 2**schaukel** f swing boat(s pl.)

Schiffs|junge m ship's boy; ~**ladung** f shipload; Fracht: cargo; ~**schraube** f (ship's) propeller; ~**werft** f shipyard

Schikan|e f, a. ~**n** pl. harassment; aus reiner ~ out of sheer spite; F mit allen

~n with all the trimmings; **2ieren** v/t. harass; *Mitschüler etc.*: a. bully

Schild[1] n allg. sign (a. mot.); *Namens2, Firmen2 etc.*: plate

Schild[2] mil. etc. m shield

Schilddrüse anat. f thyroid (gland)

schilder|n v/t. describe; *anschaulich*: a. depict, portray; **2ung** f description, portrayal; *sachliche*: account

Schildkröte zo. f *Land2*: tortoise; *See2*: turtle

Schilf bot. ~ reed(s pl.)

schillern v/i. be* iridescent; **~d** adj. iridescent; *fig.* dubious

Schimmel m zo. white horse; *bot.* mo(u)ld; **2eln** v/i. go* mo(u)ldy; **2ig** adj. mo(u)ldy, musty

Schimmer m glimmer (a. fig.), gleam; *fig.* a. trace, touch; **2n** v/i. shimmer, glimmer, gleam

Schimpanse zo. m chimpanzee

schimpf|en v/i. u. v/t. scold (mit j-m s.o.); F tell* s.o. off, bawl s.o. out; **~ über** complain about, grumble at; **2wort** n swearword

Schindel f shingle

schind|en v/t. maltreat; *Arbeiter etc.*: a. slave-drive*; **sich** ~ drudge, slave away; **2er** m fig. slave driver; **2erei** f slavery, drudgery

Schinken m ham

Schippe f, **2n** v/t. shovel

Schirm m *Regen2*: umbrella; *Sonnen2*: sunshade; *Fernseh2, Schutz2 etc.*: screen; *Lampen2*: shade; *Mützen2*: peak, visor; **~herr** m patron, sponsor; **~herrschaft** f patronage, sponsorship; *unter der ~ von* under the auspices of; **~mütze** f peaked cap; **~ständer** m umbrella stand

Schlacht mil. f battle (bei of); **2en** v/t. slaughter, kill, butcher; **~er** m → *Fleischer*

Schlacht|feld mil. n battlefield, battleground; **~haus** n, **~hof** m slaughterhouse; **~plan** m mil. plan of action (a. fig.); **~schiff** n battleship

Schlacke f cinders pl.; *geol., metall.* slag

Schlaf m sleep; *e-n leichten (festen) ~ haben* be* a light (sound) sleeper; F *fig. im ~* blindfold; **~anzug** m pyjamas pl., Am. pajamas pl.

Schläfe f temple

schlafen v/i. sleep* (a. fig.); **~ gehen, sich ~ legen** go* to bed; **fest ~** be* fast asleep; **j-n ~ legen** put* to bed od. sleep

schlaff adj. slack (a. fig.); *Haut, Muskeln etc.*: flabby; *kraftlos*: limp

Schlaf|gelegenheit f sleeping accommodation; **~krankheit** med. f sleeping sickness; **~lied** n lullaby; **2los** adj. sleepless; **~losigkeit** f sleeplessness, med. insomnia; **~mittel** med. n sleeping pill(s pl.); **~mütze** fig. f sleepyhead; slowcoach, Am. slowpoke

schläfrig adj. sleepy, drowsy

Schlaf|saal m dormitory; **~sack** m sleeping bag; **~tablette** f sleeping pill; **2trunken** adj. (very) drowsy; **~wagen** rail. m sleeping car, sleeper; **~wandler** m sleepwalker, somnambulist; **~zimmer** n bedroom

Schlag m allg. blow (a. fig.); *mit der Hand*: slap; *Faust2*: punch; *leichter*: pat, tap; *Uhr2, Blitz2, Tennis*: stroke; *electr.* shock (a. fig.); *Herz, Puls*: beat; *med. ~anfall*: stroke; **Schläge** pl. beating sg.; **~ader** anat. f artery; **~anfall** med. m (apoplectic) stroke; **2artig 1.** adj. sudden, abrupt; **2.** adv. all of a sudden, abruptly; **~baum** m barrier; **~bohrer** m percussion drill

schlagen 1. v/t. hit*, beat* (a. besiegen, Sahne etc.), strike* (a. Uhrzeit), knock; *Baum*: fell, cut* (down); **sich** ~ fight* (um over); **sich geschlagen geben** admit defeat; **2.** v/i. hit*, beat* (a. Herz etc.), strike* (a. Uhr, Blitz), knock; **an od. gegen et.** ~ hit* s.th., bump od. crash into s.th

Schlager m hit (a. fig.), (pop) song

Schläger m *Tennis etc.*: racket; *Tischtennis, Cricket, Baseball*: bat; *Golf*: club; *Hockey*: stick; *Person*: thug; **~ei** f fight, brawl

schlag|fertig fig. adj. quick-witted; **~e Antwort** (witty) repartee; **2instrument** n percussion instrument; **2kraft** f striking power (a. mil.); **2loch** n pothole; **2obers** östr. n → *Schlagsahne*; **2ring** m knuckleduster, Am. a. brass knuckles pl.; **2sahne** f whipped cream; **2seite** naut. f list; **~ haben** naut. be* listing; F *Betrunkener*: be* a bit unsteady on one's feet; **2stock** m baton, truncheon, Am. a. billy (club); **2wort** n catchword, slogan; **2zeile** f headline; **2zeug** *mus. n* drums *pl.*; **2zeuger** *mus. m* drummer

schlaksig *adj.* lanky, gangling

Schlamm *m* mud; **2ig** *adj.* muddy

Schlamp|e *f* slut; **2ig** *adj.* sloppy

Schlange *f zo.* snake, *bsd. große:* serpent (*a. fig.*); *Menschen2, Auto2:* queue, *bsd. Am.* line; ~ **stehen** queue (up), *bsd. Am.* line up, stand* in line (*nach* for)

schlängeln *v/refl.* wind* *od.* snake (one's way); *Person:* worm one's way

Schlangenlinie *f* serpentine line; *in ~n fahren* weave*

schlank *adj.* slim, slender; ~ **machen** *Kleid etc.:* make* *s.o.* look slim; ~e *Unternehmensstruktur econ.* lean management; **2heitskur** *f:* e-e ~ **machen** be* *od.* go* on a diet

schlapp F *adj. worn out; schwach:* weak

Schlappe F *f* setback, *stärker:* beating

schlapp|machen F *v/i.* flake out; **2schwanz** F *m* weakling, wimp

schlau *adj. klug:* clever, smart, bright; *listig:* sly, cunning, crafty

Schlauch *m* tube; *zum Spritzen:* hose; **~boot** *n* (inflatable *od.* rubber) dinghy

Schlaufe *f* loop

schlecht *adj.* bad; *Qualität, Leistung etc.: a.* poor; *mir ist (wird)* ~ I feel (I'm getting) sick (*Am.* to my stomach); ~ (*krank*) *aussehen* look ill; *sich* ~ *fühlen* feel* bad; ~ *werden Fleisch etc.:* go* bad; *es geht ihm sehr* ~ he is in a bad way; **~gelaunt** *adj.* in a bad temper *od.* mood, bad-tempered; **~machen** *v/t. run* *s.o.* down, backbite*

schleich|en *v/i.* creep* (*a. fig.*), sneak; **2weg** *m* secret path; **2werbung** *f* plugging; *für et.* ~ *machen* plug s.th.

Schleier *m* veil (*a. fig.*); *Dunst:* a haze; **2haft** *fig. adj.: es ist mir (völlig)* ~ it's a (complete) mystery to me

Schleife *f* bow; *Zier2:* ribbon; *Fluß2, aviat., Computer, electr.:* loop

schleifen[1] *v/t. u. v/i.* drag (along); *reiben:* rub

schleifen[2] *v/t.* grind* (*a. tech.*), sharpen; *Holz:* sand(paper); *Glas, Edelsteine:* cut*; F *fig. j-n:* drill hard; **2er** *tech. m*, **2maschine** *f* grinder; **2papier** *n* sandpaper; **2stein** *m großer:* grindstone; *bsd. für Messer:* whetstone

Schleim *m* slime; *med.* mucus; **~haut**

anat. f mucous membrane; **2ig** *adj.* slimy (*a. fig.*); mucous

schlemme|n *v/i.* feast; **2r** *m* gourmet; **2rei** *f* feasting

schlendern *v/i.* stroll, saunter, amble

schlenkern *v/i. u. v/t.* dangle, swing* (*mit den Armen* one's arms)

schlepp|en *v/t.* drag (*a. fig.*); *mot., naut.* tow; *sich* ~ drag (on); **~end** *adj.* dragging; *Redeweise:* drawling; **2er** *m naut.* tug; *mot.* tractor; **2lift** *m* T-bar (lift), drag lift, ski tow; **2tau** *n* tow-rope; *im (ins)* ~ in tow (*a. fig.*)

Schleuder *f* catapult (*a. aviat.*), *Am. a.* slingshot; *Trocken2:* spin drier; **2n 1.** *v/t.* fling*, hurl (*beide a. fig.*); *Wäsche:* spin-dry; **2.** *mot. v/i.* skid; **~sitz** *aviat. m* ejector (*bsd. Am.* ejection) seat

schleunigst *adv.* immediately

Schleuse *f* sluice; *Kanal2:* lock

schlicht *adj.* plain, simple; **~en** *v/t.* settle; **2ung** *f* settlement

schließ|en *v/t. u. v/i.* shut*, close (*für immer:* down); *beenden:* close, finish; ~ **aus** conclude from; *nach ... zu* ~ judging by ...; **2fach** *n* rail. etc.: (left luggage) locker; *Bank2:* safe-deposit box; **~lich** *adv.* finally; *am Ende:* eventually, in the end; *immerhin:* after all

Schliff *m von Edelsteinen, Glas:* cut; *Glätte:* polish (*a. fig.*)

schlimm *adj.* bad; *furchtbar:* awful; *das ist nicht od. halb so* ~ it's not as bad as that; *das 2e daran* the bad thing about it; **~stenfalls** *adv.* at (the) worst

Schlinge *f* loop; *zs.-ziehbare:* noose; *hunt.* snare (*a. fig.*); *med.* sling

Schlingel *m* rascal

schlingen *v/t.* wind*, twist; *binden:* tie; *Arme, Schal:* wrap (*um* [a]round); *sich um et.* ~ wind* (a)round

schlingern *bsd. naut. v/i.* roll

Schlingpflanze *bot. f* creeper, climber

Schlips *m* tie, *bsd. Am.* necktie

schlitt|eln *v/i. Schweiz:* go* sledging *od.* tobogganing; **2en** *m* sledge, *Am.* sled; *Pferde2:* sleigh; *Sport:* toboggan; ~ *fahren* go* sledging *od.* tobogganing

Schlittschuh *m* ice-skate (*a.* ~ *laufen*); **~läufer(in)** ice-skater

Schlitz *m* slit; *Hosen2:* fly; *Einwurf2:* slot; **~augen** *pl.:* ~ *haben* be* slit-eyed; **2en** *v/t.* slit*, slash

Schloß *n* lock; *Bau:* castle, palace; *ins* ~

S

fallen Tür: slam shut; *hinter ~ und Riegel* locked up, under lock and key

Schlosser *m* mechanic, fitter; *Schloßmacher:* locksmith; **~ei** *f* metalwork shop

schlottern *v/i.* shake*, tremble (*beide:* *vor* with); F *Hose etc.:* bag

Schlucht *f* gorge, ravine, *Am.* canyon

schluchz|en *v/i.,* **Qer** *m* sob

Schluck *m* draught, swallow; *kleiner:* sip; *großer:* gulp; **~auf** *m* hiccups *pl.;* *(e-n) ~ haben* have* (the) hiccups; **Qen** *v/t. u. v/i.* swallow (*a. fig.*); **~impfung** *f* oral vaccination

Schlummer *m* slumber; **Qn** *v/i.* lie* asleep; *poet., fig.* slumber

schlüpf|en *v/i.* slip, slide*; *zo. Vögel:* hatch (out); *in die (aus der) Kleidung ~* slip on *od.* into (off *od.* out of) one's clothes; **Qer** *m* briefs *pl.,* panties *pl.*

schlüpfrig *adj.* slippery; *fig. Witz:* risqué, off-colo(u)r

Schlupfwinkel *m* hiding place

schlurfen *v/i.* shuffle (along)

schlürfen *v/t. u. v/i.* F slurp

Schluß *m* end; *Ab2, ~folgerung:* conclusion; *e-s Films etc.:* ending; *~ machen* finish; *sich trennen:* break* up; *~ machen mit et.* stop, put* an end to; *zum ~* finally; *(ganz) bis zum ~* to the (very) end; *~ für heute!* that's all for today!

Schlüssel *m* key (*a. fig. u. in Zssgn*) *(für, zu* to); **~bein** *anat. n* collarbone; **~blume** *f* cowslip, primrose; **~bund** *m, n* bunch of keys; **~kind** F *n* latchkey child; **~loch** *n* keyhole; **~wort** *n* keyword; *Computer:* a. password

Schlußfolgerung *f* conclusion

schlüssig *adj. Beweis etc.:* conclusive; *sich ~ werden* make* up one's mind *(über* about)

Schluß|licht *n mot. etc.:* tail-light; **~pfiff** *m* final whistle; **~phase** *f* final stage(s *pl.*); **~verkauf** *econ. m* (end-of-season) sale

Schmach *f* disgrace, shame

schmachten *v/i.* languish (*nach* for), pine (for); *vor Hitze:* swelter

schmächtig *adj.* slight, thin, frail

schmackhaft *adj.* tasty

schmal *adj.* narrow; *Figur:* thin, slender (*a. fig.*)

schmälern *fig. v/t.* detract from

Schmal|film *m* cinefilm; **~spur** *rail. f* narrow ga(u)ge; **~spur...** *fig. in Zssgn* small-time

Schmalz *n* grease; *Schweine2:* lard; *fig.* mush, schmal(t)z; **2ig** *fig. adj.* mushy, soapy

schmarotze|n F *v/i.* sponge (*bei* on); **2r** *m bot., zo.* parasite; *fig. a.* sponger

schmatzen *v/i.* smack (one's lips), eat* noisily

Schmaus *m* feast; **2en** *v/i.* feast

schmecken *v/i. u. v/t.* taste (*nach* of); *gut (schlecht) ~* taste good (bad); *wie schmeckt dir ...?* (how) do you like ...? (*a. fig.*); *es schmeckt süß (nach nichts)* it has a sweet (no) taste

Schmeich|elei *f* flattery; **2elhaft** *adj.* flattering; **2eln** *v/i.* flatter *s.o.;* **~ler(in)** flatterer; **2lerisch** *adj.* flattering

schmeiß|en F *v/t. u. v/i.* throw*, chuck; *Tür etc.:* slam; *mit Geld um sich ~* throw* one's money about; **2fliege** *f* blowfly, bluebottle

schmelz|en *v/i. u. v/t.* melt*; *Schnee:* a. thaw; *metall.* smelt; **2ofen** *m* (s)melting furnace; **2tiegel** *m* melting pot (*a. fig.*)

Schmerz *m* pain (*a. fig.*), anhaltender: ache; *fig.* grief, sorrow; **2en** *v/i. u. v/t.* hurt* (*a. fig.*), ache; *bsd. fig.* pain; **2frei** *adj.* without pain; **2haft** *adj.* painful; **2lich** *adj.* painful, sad; **~mittel** *n* painkiller; **2los** *adj.* painless; **2stillend** *adj.* painkilling

Schmetterling *m* butterfly

schmettern 1. *v/t.* smash (*a. Tennis*) (*in Stücke* to pieces); F *Lied:* belt out **2.** *v/i.* crash, slam; *Trompete etc.:* blare

Schmied *m* (black)smith; **~e** *f* forge, smithy; **~eeisen** *n* wrought iron; **2en** *v/t.* forge; *Pläne etc.:* make*

schmiegen *v/refl.: sich ~ snuggle* up to; *den Körper etc.:* cling* to

Schmier|e *f* grease; **2en** *v/t. tech.* grease, oil, lubricate; *Butter etc.:* spread*; *unsauber schreiben:* scribble, scrawl; **~erei** *f* scrawl; *Wand2:* graffiti *pl.;* **2ig** *adj.* greasy; *schmutzig:* dirty; *unanständig:* filthy; F *kriecherisch:* slimy; **~mittel** *n* lubricant

Schminke *f* make-up (*a. thea.*); **2n** *v/t.* make* *s.o.* up; *sich ~* make* o.s. *od.* one's face up

Schmirgelpapier *n* emery paper

schmollen v/i. sulk, be* sulky, pout

Schmor|braten m pot roast; **2en** v/t. u. v/i. braise, stew (a. fig.), pot-roast

Schmuck m jewel(le)ry, jewels pl.; Zierde: decoration(s pl.), ornament(s pl.)

schmücken v/t. decorate

schmuck|los adj. unadorned; schlicht: plain; **2stück** n piece of jewel(le)ry; fig. gem

Schmuggel m, **~ei** f smuggling; **2n** v/t. u. v/i. smuggle; **~ware** f smuggled goods pl.

Schmuggler m smuggler

schmunzeln v/i. smile (amusedly)

schmusen F v/i. cuddle; Liebespaar: a kiss and cuddle; **~** F smooch

Schmutz m dirt, stärker: filth; fig. a. smut; **~fink** fig. m pig; **~fleck** m smudge, stain; **2ig** adj. dirty (a. fig.); stärker: filthy (a. fig.); **~ werden, sich ~ machen** get* dirty; **~wasser** n waste water, sewage

Schnabel m bill, bsd. Krumm2: beak

Schnalle f buckle; **2n** v/t. buckle; et. **~ an** strap s.th. to

schnalzen v/i. snap one's fingers; click one's tongue

schnapp|en 1. v/i. snap, snatch (beide: nach at); **nach Luft ~** gasp for breath; **2.** F v/t. fangen: catch*; **2schloß** n spring lock; **2schuß** phot. m snapshot

Schnaps m spirits pl., schnapps, F booze

schnarchen v/i. snore

schnarren v/i. rattle; Stimme: rasp

schnattern v/i. cackle; Affen, F fig.: chatter

schnauben v/i. u. v/t. snort; **sich die Nase ~** blow* one's nose

schnaufen v/i. breathe hard, pant, puff

Schnauz|bart m m(o)ustache; **~e** f zo. snout, mouth; bsd. Hunde2: muzzle; F aviat., mot. nose; e-r Kanne: spout; V Mund: trap, kisser; **die ~ halten** keep* one's trap shut; **~er** m zo. m schnauzer

Schnecke f snail; Nackt2: slug; **~nhaus** n snail shell; **~ntempo** n: im **~** at a snail's pace

Schnee m snow; sl. Kokain: snow; **~räumen** remove snow; **~ball** m snowball (a. fig. in Zssgn System etc.); **~ballschlacht** f snowball fight; **2bedeckt** adj. snow-covered, Bergspitze: a. snow-capped; **~fall** m snowfall;

~flocke f snowflake; **~gestöber** n snow flurry; **~glöckchen** bot. n snowdrop; **~grenze** f snow line; **~mann** m snowman; **~matsch** m slush; **~mobil** n snowmobile; **~pflug** m snowplough, Am. snowplow; **~regen** m sleet; **~sturm** m snowstorm, blizzard; **~verwehung** f snowdrift; **2weiß** adj. snow-white

Schneid F m grit, guts pl.

Schneid|brenner tech. m cutting torch; **~e** f edge; **~en** v/t. u. v/i. cut* (a. fig.); Film etc.: a. edit; schnitzen: carve; **~er** m tailor; **~erei** f tailoring, dressmaking; Werkstatt: tailor's od. dressmaker's shop; **~erin** f dressmaker; einfache: seamstress; **2ern** v/i. u. v/t. als Hobby: do* dressmaking; Kleid etc.: make*, sew*; **~ezahn** m incisor; **2ig** adj. dashing; schick: a. smart

schneien v/i. snow

schnell adj. fast, quick; Handeln, Antwort etc.: a. prompt; Puls, Anstieg etc.: a. rapid; **es geht ~** it won't take long; **(mach[t]) ~!** hurry up!; **2... in Zssgn** Dienst, Paket, Zug etc.: mst express ...; **2boot** naut. n speedboat; **~en** v/i. u. v/i. shoot*, spring*; **~gefrieren** v/t. quickfreeze; Am. flashfreeze; **2hefter** m folder; **2igkeit** f speed; im Handeln, Arbeiten etc.: a. quickness, rapidity; **2imbiß** m snack bar; **2straße** mot. f motorway, Am. expressway, thruway

schnetzeln gastr. v/t. bsd. Schweiz: chop up

Schnipp|chen n: F j-m ein **~ schlagen** outwit s.o.; **2isch** adj. pert, saucy, Am. a. sassy

schnipsen v/i. snap one's fingers

Schnitt m cut (a. fig.); Durch2: average; **~blumen** pl. cut flowers pl.; **~e** f slice; belegte: open sandwich; **~fläche** f (surface of) math. intersection od. tech. cut; **2ig** adj. stylish; Boot: a. rakish; **~lauch** m chives pl.; **~muster** n pattern; **~punkt** m (point of) intersection; **~stelle** f Film etc.: cut; Computer: interface; **~wunde** f cut

Schnitzel¹ n cutlet; Wiener **~** schnitzel

Schnitzel² n, m Holz: chip; Papier2: scrap

schnitz|en v/t. carve, cut* (in wood); **2er** m (wood) carver; **2erei** f (wood) carving

S

Schnorchel m, **⹁n** v/i. snorkel

Schnörkel m flourish; arch. scroll

schnorr|en F v/t. cadge; **⹁er** m cadger

schnüff|eln v/i. sniff (**an** at); F fig. snoop (about od. around); **⹁ler** m F fig. snoop(er); Detektiv: sleuth

Schnuller m dummy, Am. pacifier

Schnulz|e F f schmal(t)zy song; Film, Roman etc.: tearjerker; **⹁ensänger** m crooner; **⹁ig** adj. schmal(t)zy, soapy

Schnupf|en m cold; **e-n ⹁ haben** (**bekommen**) have* a (catch* [a]) cold; **⹁tabak** m snuff

schnuppe F adj.: **das ist mir ⹁** I don't care (F a damn)

schnuppern v/i. sniff (**an et.** [at] s.th.)

Schnur f string, cord; electr. flex

Schnür|chen n: **wie am ⹁** like clockwork; **⹁en** v/t. lace (up); **ver⹁:** tie up

schnur|gerade adv. dead straight; **⹁los** adj.: **⹁es Telefon** cordless phone

Schnürlsamt östr. m corduroy

Schnurr|bart m (o)ustache; **⹁en** v/i. Katze, Motor: purr

Schnür|schuh m laced shoe; **⹁senkel** m shoelace, bsd. Am. shoestring

schnurstracks adv. direct(ly), straight; sofort: straight away

Schober m haystack, hayrick; barn

Schock med. m shock; **unter ⹁ stehen** be* in (a state of) shock; **⹁en**, **⹁ieren** v/t. shock

Schokolade f chocolate; **e-e Tafel ⹁** a bar of chocolate

Scholle f Erd⹁: clod; Eis⹁: (ice)floe; zo. plaice, Am. flounder

schon adv. already; jemals: ever; (sogar) **⹁:** even; **⹁ damals** even then; **⹁ 1968** as early as 1968; **⹁ der Gedanke** the very idea; **ist sie ⹁ da** (**zurück**)**?** has she come (is she back) yet?; **habt** (**seid**) **ihr ⹁ ...?** have you ... yet?; **hast** (**bist**) **du ⹁ einmal ...?** have you ever ...?; **ich wohne hier ⹁ seit zwei Jahren** I've been living here for two years now; **ich kenne ihn ⹁, aber** I do know him, but; **er macht das ⹁** he'll do it all right; **⹁ gut!** never mind!; **⹁ gut!** all right!

schön 1. adj. beautiful, lovely; Wetter: a. fine, fair; gut, angenehm, nett: fine, nice (**beide** a. iro.); (**na,**) **⹁** all right; **2.** adv.: **⹁ warm** (**kühl**) nice and warm (cool); **ganz ⹁ teuer** (**schnell**) pretty expensive (fast); **j-n ganz ⹁ erschrek-**

ken (**überraschen**) give* s.o. quite a start (surprise)

schonen v/t. take* care of, go* easy on (a. tech.); j-n, j-s Leben: spare; **sich ⹁** take* it easy; für et.: save o.s. od. one's strength; **⹁d 1.** adj. gentle; Mittel etc.: a. mild; **2.** adv.: **⹁ umgehen mit** take* (good) care of; Glas etc.: handle with care; sparsam: go* easy on

Schönheit f beauty; **⹁spflege** f beauty care

Schonung f (good) care; Ruhe: rest; Erhaltung: preservation; Bäume: tree nursery; **⹁slos** adj. relentless, brutal

schöpf|en v/t. scoop, ladle; aus e-m Brunnen: draw*; → **Luft**, **Verdacht**; **⹁er** m creator; **⹁erisch** adj. creative; **⹁ung** f creation

Schorf med. m scab

Schornstein m chimney; naut., rail. funnel; **⹁feger** m chimneysweep

Schoß m lap; Mutterleib: womb

Schote bot. f pod, husk

Schotte m Scot(sman); **die ⹁n** pl. the Scots pl., the Scottish (people) pl.

Schotter m gravel, road metal

Schott|in f Scotswoman; **⹁isch** adj. Scots, Scottish; typische Produkte: Scotch; **⹁land** Scotland

schräg 1. adj. slanting, sloping, oblique; Linie etc.: diagonal; **2.** adv.: **⹁ gegenüber** diagonally opposite

Schramme f, **⹁n** v/t. u. v/i. scratch

Schrank m cupboard, Am. Wand⹁: closet; Kleider⹁: wardrobe

Schranke f barrier (a. fig.); rail. a. gate; jur. bar; **⹁n** pl. Grenzen: limits pl., bounds pl.; **⹁nlos** fig. adj. boundless; zügellos: unbridled; **⹁nwärter** m gatekeeper

Schrank|koffer m wardrobe trunk; **⹁wand** f wall units pl.

Schraube f, **⹁n** v/t. screw

Schrauben|schlüssel m spanner, wrench; **⹁zieher** m screwdriver

Schraubstock m vice, Am. vise

Schrebergarten m Brt. allotment (garden), Am. garden plot

Schreck m fright, shock; **j-m e-n ⹁ einjagen** give* s.o. a fright, scare s.o.; **⹁en** m terror, fright; Greuel: horror(s pl.); **⹁ensnachricht** f dreadful news sg.; **⹁haft** adj. jumpy; bsd. Pferd: skittish; **⹁lich** adj. awful, terrible; stärker: horrible, dreadful; *Mord etc.*: a. atrocious

Schrei *m* cry; *lauter*: shout, yell; *Angst⚲*: scream (*alle*: **um**, **nach** for)

Schreib|arbeit *f* desk work, *bsd. contp.* paperwork; **~büro** *n* typing pool

schreiben *v/t. u. v/i.* write* (*j-m* to s.o.; *über* about); *tippen*: type; *recht~*: spell*; *groß ~* capitalize; *falsch ~* misspell* *s.th.*; **wie schreibt man ...?** how do you spell ...?

Schreib|en *n* letter; **⚲faul** *adj.*: **~ sein** be* a bad correspondent; **~fehler** *m* spelling mistake; **~heft** *n* exercise book; **~kraft** *f* typist; **~maschine** *f* typewriter; **~material** *n* writing materials *pl.*, stationery; **~schutz** *m* *Computer*: write *od.* file protection; **~tisch** *m* desk; **~ung** *f* spelling; **~unterlage** *f* desk mat, blotter; **~waren** *pl.* stationery *sg.*; **~warengeschäft** *n* stationer's, stationery shop; **~zentrale** *f* typing pool

schreien *v/i. u. v/t.* cry; *lauter*: shout, yell; *kreischend*: scream (*alle*: **um**, **nach** [out] for); **~ vor Schmerz** (**Angst**) cry out with pain (in terror); **es war zum ⚲** it was a scream; **⚲d** *adj. Farben*: loud; *Unrecht etc.*: flagrant

Schreiner *m* → *Tischler*

schreiten *v/i.* stride*

Schrift *f* (hand)writing, hand; *print.* type; *~zeichen*: character, letter; **~en** *pl. Werke*: works *pl.*, writings *pl.*; **die Heilige ~** *rel.* the Scriptures *pl.*; **~art** *f* script; *print.* typeface; **~deutsch** *n* standard German; **⚲lich** *adj.* written; **~ übersetzen** *etc.* translate *etc.* in writing; **~steller(in)** author(ess), writer; **~verkehr**, **~wechsel** *m* correspondence; **~zeichen** *n* character, letter

schrill *adj.* shrill (*a. fig.*), piercing

Schritt *m* step (*a. fig.*); *Einzel⚲*: *a.* pace; **~e unternehmen** take* steps; **~fahren** *mot.* dead slow; **~macher** *m* pacemaker (*a. med.*), *Am. a.* pacesetter; **⚲weise** *adv.* step by step, gradually

schroff *adj.* steep; *zerklüftet*: jagged; *fig.* gruff; *kraß*: sharp, glaring

Schrot *m, n* coarse meal; *hunt.* (small) shot; *~korn*: pellet; **~flinte** *f* shotgun

Schrott *m* scrap (metal); **~haufen** *m* scrap heap (*a. fig.*); **~platz** *m* scrapyard

schrubben *v/t.* scrub, scour

schrumpfen *v/i.* shrink*

Schub *m* → *Schubkraft*; **~fach** *n* drawer; **~karren** *m* wheelbarrow; **~kasten** *m* drawer; **~kraft** *phys., tech.* *f* thrust; **~lade** *f* drawer

Schubs F *m*, **⚲en** F *v/t.* push

schüchtern *adj.* shy, bashful; **⚲heit** *f* shyness, bashfulness

Schuft *m sl.* contp. bastard; *thea. etc.* villain; **⚲en** F *v/i.* work like a dog

Schuh *m* shoe; *j-m et.* **in die ~e schieben** put* the blame for s.th. on s.o.; **~anzieher** *m* shoehorn; **~creme** *f* shoe polish; **~geschäft** *n* shoe shop (*Am.* store); **~löffel** *m* shoehorn; **~macher** *m* shoemaker; **~putzer** *m* shoeshine boy

Schul|abgänger *m* school leaver; *Abbrecher*: dropout; **~amt** *n* education authority, *Am.* school board; **~arbeit** *f* schoolwork; *pl. Hausaufgaben*: homework *sg.*; **~besuch** *m* (school) attendance; **~bildung** *f* education; **~buch** *n* textbook, school book

Schuld *f jur.*, *~gefühl*: guilt; *bsd. rel.* sin; *Geld⚲*: debt; *j-m die* **~ ~** (**an et.**) **geben** blame s.o. (for s.th.); **es ist** (**nicht**) **deine ~** it is(n't) your fault; **~en haben** (**machen**) be* in (run* into) debt; **⚲bewußt** *adj.*: **~e Miene** guilty look; **⚲en** *v/t.*: *j-m et.* **~** owe s.o. s.th.

schuldig *adj. bsd. jur.* guilty (**an** of); *verantwortlich*: responsible *od.* to blame (for); *j-m et.* **~ sein** *od.* **~ sein** owe s.o. s.th.; **⚲e** *m, f* culprit; *jur.* guilty person, offender; **⚲keit** *f* duty

schuld|los *adj.* innocent; **⚲ner** *m* debtor; **⚲schein** *m* promissory note, IOU (= I owe you)

Schule *f* school (*a. fig.*); *höhere* **~** secondary school, *Am. appr.* (senior) high school; *auf od.* **in der ~** at school; *in die* *od.* **zur ~ gehen** (**kommen**) go* to (start) school; *die* **~ fängt an um** school begins at; **⚲n** *v/t.* train, school

Schüler *m jüngerer*: schoolboy, *bsd. Brt. a.* pupil; *älterer, Am. allg.*: student; **~austausch** *m* student exchange (program[me]); **~in** *f* schoolgirl, *bsd. Brt. a.* pupil; *ältere, Am. allg.*: student; **~vertretung** *f etwa* student council (*Am.* government)

Schul|ferien *pl.* holidays *pl.*, *Am.* vacation *sg.*; **~fernsehen** *n* educational

S

TV; **~funk** m schools programmes pl.; **~gebäude** n school (building); **~geld** n school fee(s pl.), tuition; **~heft** n exercise book; **~hof** m school yard, playground; **~kamerad(in)** schoolfellow; **~leiter(in)** head|master (-mistress), head teacher, Am. principal; **~mappe** f schoolbag; Ranzen: a. satchel; **~ordnung** f school regulations pl.; **♀pflichtig** adj.: **~es Kind** school-age child; **~schiff** n training ship; **~schluß** m end of school; vor den Ferien: end of term; nach ~ after school; **~schwänzer** m truant; **~stunde** f lesson, class, period; **~tasche** f schoolbag

Schulter f shoulder; **~blatt** n shoulderblade; **♀frei** adj. strapless; **♀n** v/t. shoulder; **~tasche** f shoulder bag

Schulwesen n education(al system)

schummeln F v/i. cheat

Schund m trash, rubbish, junk

Schuppe f scale; **~n** pl. Kopf♀n: dandruff sg.

Schuppen m shed, bsd. fig. shack

schuppig adj. scaly

schüren v/t. stir up (a. fig.)

schürf|en Bergbau: v/i. prospect (nach for); **♀wunde** f graze, abrasion

Schurke m bsd. thea. etc.: villain

Schurwolle f virgin wool

Schürze f apron

Schuß m shot; Spritzer: dash; Sport: shot, Fußball a. strike; Ski: schuss (a. ~ fahren); sl. Droge: shot, fix; gut in ~ sein be* in good shape

Schüssel f bowl, dish; Wasser♀: basin; Suppen♀: tureen

Schuß|waffe f firearm; **~wunde** f gunshot od. bullet wound

Schuster m shoemaker

Schutt m rubble, debris

Schüttel|frost med. m shivering fit, the shivers pl.; **♀n** v/t. shake*; den Kopf ~ shake* one's head

schütten v/t. pour; werfen: throw*

Schutz m protection (gegen, vor against), defen|ce, Am. -se (against, from); Zuflucht: shelter (from); Vorsichtsmaßnahme: safeguard (against); Deckung: cover; **~blech** n mudguard, Am. fender; **~brille** f goggles pl.

Schütze m mil. rifleman; Jäger: hunter; Tor♀: scorer; astr. Sagittarius; er ist (ein) ~ he's a Sagittarius; ein guter ~ a

good shot; **♀n** v/t. protect (gegen, vor against, from), defend (against, from), guard (against, from); gegen Wetter: shelter (from); sichern: safeguard

Schutzengel m guardian angel

Schützen|graben mil. m trench; **~könig** m champion marksman

Schutzgeld n protection money; **~erpressung** f protection racket

Schutz|haft jur. f protective custody; **~heilige** m, f patron (saint); **~impfung** med. f protective inoculation; Pocken♀: vaccination

Schützling m protégé(e f)

schutz|los adj. unprotected; wehrlos: defen|celess, Am. -seless; **♀maßnahme** f safety measure; **♀patron(in)** patron (saint); **♀umschlag** m dust cover

schwach adj. weak (a. fig.); Leistung, Augen, Gesundheit etc.: a. poor; Ton, Hoffnung, Erinnerung etc.: faint; zart: delicate, frail; **schwächer werden** grow* weak; nachlassen: decline

Schwäch|e f weakness (a. fig.); bsd. Alters♀: infirmity; Nachteil, Mangel: drawback, shortcoming; **e-e ~ haben für** be* partial to; **♀en** v/t. weaken (a. fig.); vermindern: lessen; **♀lich** adj. weakly, feeble; zart: delicate, frail; **~ling** m weakling (a. fig.), softy, sissy

schwach|sinnig adj. feeble-minded; **♀strom** electr. m low-voltage current

Schwager m brother-in-law

Schwägerin f sister-in-law

Schwalbe f zo. swallow; Fußball: dive

Schwall m gush, bsd. fig. a. torrent

Schwamm m sponge; bot. fungus; bot. Haus♀: dry rot; **~erl** bot. östr. n → Pilz; **♀ig** adj. spongy; Gesicht etc.: puffy; vage: hazy, misty

Schwan m swan

schwanger adj. pregnant

Schwangerschaft f pregnancy; **~sabbruch** m abortion

schwank|en v/i. sway, roll (a. Schiff u. Betrunkener); wanken, torkeln: stagger; fig. ~ zwischen ... und ... unschlüssig sein: waver between ... and ...; Preise etc.: range from ... to ...; **♀ung** f change, variation (a. econ.)

Schwanz m tail (a. aviat., astr.); F Penis: cock

schwänzen v/i. u. v/t.: (die Schule) ~ play truant (bsd. Am. F hooky), skip school

Schwarm m swarm; Menschen♀: a. crowd, F bunch; Fisch♀: shoal, school; F Wunsch: dream; Idol: idol; **du bist ihr** ~ she's got a crush on you

schwärmen v/i. Bienen etc.: swarm; **für** be* mad about; sich wünschen: dream* of; j-n: a. adore, worship; verliebt sein: have* a crush on; ~ **von** erzählen: rave about

Schwarte f rind; F fig. (old) tome

schwarz adj. black (a. fig.); ♀**es Brett** notice board, bsd. Am. bulletin board; ~ **auf weiß** in black and white; ♀**arbeit** f illicit work; ♀**brot** n rye bread

Schwarze m, f black (man od. woman); **die** ~**n** pl. the Blacks pl.

schwärzen v/t. blacken

Schwarz|fahrer(in) fare dodger; ~**händler** m black marketeer; ~**markt** m black market; ~**seher** m pessimist; (TV) licen|ce (Am. -se) dodger; ♀**weiß...** in Zssgn Film, Fernseher etc.: black-and-white ...

schwatzen, schwätzen v/i. chatter; Schule: talk; plaudern: chat

Schwätzer m loudmouth, big mouth

schwatzhaft adj. chatty

Schwebe|bahn f cableway, ropeway; ~**balken** m beam; ♀**n** v/i. be* suspended; Vogel, aviat.: hover (a. fig.); gleiten: glide; bsd. jur. be* pending; **in Gefahr** ~ be* in danger

Schwed|e m Swede; ♀**en** Sweden; ~**in** f Swede; ♀**isch** adj. Swedish

Schwefel chem. m sulphur, Am. sulfur; ~**säure** chem. f sulphuric (Am. sulfuric) acid

Schweif m tail (a. astr.); ♀**en** v/i. wander (a. fig.), roam

Schweigen n silence

schweig|en v/i. be* silent; ganz zu ~ **von** let alone; ~**end** adj. silent; ~**sam** adj. quiet, reticent

Schwein n pig, bsd. Am. a. hog; fig. contp. (filthy) pig; F contp. Schuft: swine, bastard; F ~ **haben** be* lucky

Schweine|braten m roast pork; ~**fleisch** n pork; ~**rei** f mess; Gemeinheit: dirty trick; Schande: dirty od. crying shame; Unanständigkeit: filth(y story od. joke); ~**stall** m pigsty (a. fig.)

schweinisch fig. adj. filthy, obscene

Schweinsleder n pigskin

Schweiß m sweat, perspiration; ♀**en** tech. v/t. weld; ~**er** tech. m welder; ♀**gebadet** adj. soaked in sweat; ~**geruch** m body odo(u)r

Schweiz Switzerland; ~**er** m, adj. Swiss; ~**erin** f Swiss woman od. girl; ♀**erisch** adj. Swiss

schwelen v/i. smo(u)lder (a. fig.)

schwelgen v/i.: ~ **in** revel in

Schwelle f Tür♀: threshold (a. fig.); rail. sleeper, Am. tie; ♀**en** v/i. u. v/t. swell*; ~**ung** f swelling

Schwemm|e econ. f glut, oversupply; ♀**en** v/t.: **an Land** ~ wash ashore

Schwengel m Glocken♀: clapper; Pumpen♀: handle

schwenken v/t. u. v/i. swing* (a. tech.); Fahne etc.: wave; tech. a. swivel

schwer 1. adj. heavy; schwierig: difficult, hard (a. Arbeit); Wein, Zigarre etc.: strong; Essen: rich; Krankheit, Fehler, Unfall, Schaden etc.: serious; Strafe etc.: severe; heftig: heavy, violent; ~**e Zeiten** hard times; **es** ~ **haben** have* a bad time; **100 Pfund** ~ **sein** weigh a hundred pounds; 2. adv.: ~ **arbeiten** work hard; → hören; ~**beschädigt** adj. (seriously) disabled; ♀**e** f weight (a. fig.); fig. seriousness; ~**fallen** v/i. be* difficult (dat. for); **es fällt ihm schwer zu** ... he finds it difficult to ...; ~**fällig** adj. awkward, clumsy; ♀**gewicht** n heavyweight; fig. (main) emphasis; ~**hörig** adj. hard of hearing, deaf; ♀**industrie** f heavy industry; ♀**kraft** phys. f gravity; ♀**metall** n heavy metal; ~**mütig** adj. melancholy; ~ **sein** have* the blues; ♀**punkt** m centre (Am. -er) of gravity; fig. (main) emphasis

Schwert n sword

Schwer|verbrecher m dangerous criminal, jur. felon; ♀**verdaulich** adj. indigestible, heavy (beide a. fig.); ♀**verständlich** adj. difficult od. hard to understand; ♀**verwundet** adj. seriously wounded; ♀**wiegend** fig. adj. weighty, serious

Schwester f sister; Ordens♀: a. nun; Kranken♀: nurse

Schwieger... in Zssgn Eltern, Mutter, Sohn etc.: ...-in-law

Schwiel|e f callus; ♀**ig** adj. horny

schwierig adj. difficult, hard; ♀**keit** f difficulty, trouble; **in** ~**en geraten** get* *od.* run* into trouble; **~en haben**, *et.* **zu tun** have* difficulty in doing s.th.

Schwimm|bad *n* (*Hallen*2: indoor) swimming pool; **2en** *v/i.* swim*; *Gegenstand*: float; **~ gehen** go* swimming; **~flosse** *f* flipper, *Am.* swimfin; **~gürtel** *m* swimming belt; **~haut** *f* web; **~lehrer** *m* swimming instructor; **~weste** *f* life jacket

Schwindel *m med.* giddiness, dizziness; *fig.* swindle, fraud; **~anfall** *m* attack of dizziness; **2erregend** *adj.* dizzy; **2n** *v/i.* fib, tell* fibs

schwinden *v/i.* dwindle, decline

Schwindl|er *m* swindler, crook; *Lügner*: liar; **2ig** *med. adj.* dizzy, giddy; *mir ist* **~** I feel dizzy

Schwing|e *f* wing; **2en** *v/i. u. v/t.* swing*; *Fahne etc.*: wave; *tech.* oscillate; vibrate; **~ung** *f* oscillation; vibration

Schwips F *m*: *e-n* **~ haben** be* tipsy

schwirren *v/i.* whirr, whizz; *bsd. Insekt*: buzz (*a. fig.*); *mir schwirrt der Kopf* my head is buzzing

schwitz|en *v/i.* sweat (*stark* profusely; *vor Angst* with fear), perspire; **2kasten** *m*: *j-n in den* **~ nehmen** put* a headlock on s.o.

schwören *v/t. u. v/i.* swear*; *jur.* take* an *od.* the oath; *fig.* **~ auf** swear by

schwul F *adj.* gay; *contp.* queer

schwül *adj.* sultry (*a. fig.*), close

schwülstig *adj.* bombastic, pompous

Schwung *m* swing; *fig.* verve, zest, F vim, pep; *Energie*: drive; *in* **~ kommen** (*bringen*) get* (*s.th.*) going; **2haft** *adj. Handel*: brisk, flourishing; **~rad** *tech. n* flywheel; **2voll** *adj.* full of energy *od.* verve; *Melodie*: swinging, catchy

Schwur *m* oath; **~gericht** *jur. n etwa* jury court

sechs *adj.* six; *Note*: F, *Brt. a.* poor; **2eck** *n* hexagon; **~eckig** *adj.* hexagonal; **~fach** *adj.* sixfold; **~mal** *adv.* six times; **2tagerennen** *n* six-day race; **~tägig** *adj.* lasting *od.* of six days

sechste *adj.* sixth; **2l** *n* sixth (part); **~ns** *adv.* sixthly, in the sixth place

sech|zehn(te) *adj.* sixteen(th); **~zig** *adj.* sixty; **~zigste** *n.o* sixtieth

See[1] *m* lake

See[2] *f* sea, ocean; *auf* **~** at sea; *auf hoher* **~** on the high seas; *an der* **~** at the

seaside; *zur* **~ gehen** (*fahren*) go* to sea (*be* a sailor); *in* **~ stechen** put* to sea; **~bad** *n* seaside resort; **~fahrt** *f* navigation; → **Seereise**; **~gang** *m*: *hoher* **~** heavy sea; **~hafen** *m* seaport; **~hund** *m* seal; **~jungfrau** *myth. f* mermaid; **~karte** *f* nautical chart; **2krank** *adj.* seasick; **~krankheit** *f* seasickness

Seel|e *f* soul (*a. fig.*); **2enlos** *adj.* soulless; **~enruhe** *f* peace of mind; *in aller* **~** as cool as you please; **~enwanderung** *f* reincarnation; **2isch** *adj.* mental; **~ krank** mentally ill; **~sorge** *f* pastoral care; **~sorger** *m* pastor

See|macht *f* sea power; **~mann** *m* seaman, sailor; **~meile** *f* nautical mile; **~not** *f* distress (at sea); **~notkreuzer** *m* rescue cruiser; **~räuber** *m* pirate; **~reise** *f* voyage, cruise; **~rose** *f* water lily; **~sack** *m* kit bag, duffle bag; **~schlacht** *f* naval battle; **~streitkräfte** *pl.* naval forces *pl.*, navy *sg.*; **2tüchtig** *adj. Zustand*: seaworthy; **~warte** *f* naval observatory; **~weg** *m* sea route; *auf dem* **~** by sea; **~zeichen** *naut. n*; **~zunge** *zo. f* sole

Segel *n* sail; **~boot** *n* sailing boat, *Am.* sailboat; **~fliegen** *n* gliding; **~flugzeug** *n* glider; **2n** *v/i.* sail; *Sport: a.* yacht; **~schiff** *n* sailing ship; sailing vessel; **~sport** *m* sailing, yachting; **~tuch** *n* canvas, sailcloth

Segen *m* blessing (*a. fig.*)

Segler(in) *f* yachts|man (-woman)

segn|en *v/t.* bless; **2ung** *f* blessing

Sehbeteiligung *f* (TV) ratings *pl.*

sehen *v/i. u. v/t.* see*; *Sendung*, *Spiel etc.: a.* watch; *bemerken*: notice; **~ nach** *sich kümmern um*: look after; *suchen*: look for; *sich* **~ lassen können**: show* up; *das sieht man* (*kaum*) it (hardly) shows; *siehst du erklärend*: (you) see; *vorwurfsvoll*: I told you; *siehe oben* (*unten, Seite* ...) see above (below, page ...); **~swert** *adj.* worth seeing; **2swürdigkeit** *f* place *etc.* worth seeing, sight; **~en** *pl.* sights *pl.*

Sehkraft *f* eyesight, vision

Sehne *f anat.* sinew; *Bogen*2: string

sehnen *v/refl.* long (*nach* for); *stärker*: yearn (for); *sich danach* **~ zu** *inf.* be* longing to *inf.*

Sehnerv *m* optic nerve

sehnig *adj.* sinewy; *Fleisch: a.* stringy

sehn|lichst adj. Wunsch: dearest; **~sucht** f, **~süchtig**, **~suchtsvoll** adj. longing; stärker: yearning

sehr adv. vor adj. u. adv.: very; mit vb.: very much, greatly

Seh|rohr naut. n periscope; **~schwäche** f weak sight; **~test** m sight test; **~weite** f range of vision

seicht adj. shallow (a. fig.)

Seid|e f, **~en** silk; **~enpapier** n tissue paper; **~enraupe** zo. f silkworm; **~ig** adj. silky

Seif|e f soap; **~enblase** f soap bubble; **~enlauge** f (soap)suds pl.; **~enoper** f TV soap opera; **~enschale** f soap dish; **~enschaum** m lather; **~ig** adj. soapy

seihen v/t. strain, filter

Seil n rope; **~bahn** f cable railway; **~hüpfen** n skipping

Sein n being; existence

sein¹ v/i. be*; bestehen, existieren: a. exist

sein² poss. pron. his; Mädchen: her; Sache: its; **~er**, **~e**, **~(e)s** his; hers;

seiner|seits adv. for his part; **~zeit** adv. then, in those days

seinesgleichen pron. his equals pl.; **j-n wie ~ behandeln** treat s.o. as one's equal

seinetwegen adv. vgl. meinetwegen

seinlassen v/t.: et. ~ stop (bsd. Am. a. quit*) (doing) s.th.

seit prp u. cj. since; ~ 1982 since 1982; ~ **drei Jahren** for three years (now); ~ **langem** (**kurzem**) for a long (short) time; **~dem 1.** adv. since then, since that time, ever since; **2.** cj. since

Seite f side (a. fig.); Buch**~**: page; **auf der linken ~** on the left(-hand side); fig. **auf der e-n** (**anderen**) **~** on the one (other) hand

Seiten|ansicht f side view, profile; **~blick** m sidelong glance; **~hieb** fig. m sideswipe; **~linie** f bsd. Fußball: touchline; **~s** prp. on the part of, by; **~sprung** F m: e-n ~ machen cheat (on one's wife od. husband); **~stechen** n stitches pl.

seither adv. → seitdem 1

seit|lich adj. side ..., at the side(s); **~wärts** adv. sideways, to the side

Sekret|är m secretary; Schreibtisch: bureau; **~ariat** n (secretary's) office; **~ärin** f secretary

Sekt m sparkling wine, champagne

Sekt|e f sect; **~ion** f section; med. dissection; Obduktion: autopsy; **~or** m sector; fig. field

Sekunde f second; **auf die ~** to the second; **~nzeiger** m second(s) hand

selbe adj. same; **~r** pron. → selbst 1

selbst 1. pron.: ich (du etc.) ~ I (you etc.) myself (yourself etc.); **mach es ~** do it yourself; **et. ~** (ohne Hilfe) **tun** do s.th. by oneself; **von ~** by itself; **2.** adv. even

selbständig adj. independent; beruflich: a. self-employed; **2keit** f independence

Selbst|bedienung(sladen m) f self--service (shop, Am. store); **~befriedigung** f masturbation; **~beherrschung** f self-control; **~bestimmung** f self-determination; **2bewußt** adj. self-confident; △ nicht **self-conscious**; **~bewußtsein** n self-confidence; △ nicht **self-consciousness**; **~bildnis** n self-portrait; **~erhaltungstrieb** m survival instinct; **~erkenntnis** f self-knowledge; **2gemacht** adj. homemade; **2gerecht** adj. self-righteous; **~gespräch** n: e-e führen talk to o.s.; **2herrlich** adj. overbearing; unbefugt: unauthorized; **~hilfe** f self-help; **~hilfegruppe** f self-help group; **~kostenpreis** econ. m: **zum ~** at cost (price); **2kritisch** adj. self-critical; **~laut** gr. m vowel; **2los** adj. unselfish; **~mord** m suicide; **~mörder(in)** suicide; **2mörderisch** adj. suicidal; **2sicher** adj. self-confident, self-assured; **2süchtig** adj. selfish, ego(t)istic(al); **2tätig** adj. automatic; **~täuschung** f self-deception; **~unterricht** m self-instruction; **~versorger** m self-supporter; **2verständlich 1.** adj. natural; **das ist ~** that's a matter of course; **2.** adv. of course, naturally; **~! a.** by all means!; **~verständlichkeit** f matter of course; **~verteidigung** f self-defen|ce, Am. -se; **~vertrauen** n self-confidence, self-reliance; **~verwaltung** f self-government, autonomy; **~wähldienst** tel. m automatic long-distance dial(l)ing service; **2zufrieden** adj. self-satisfied; **~zweck** m end in itself

selchen östr. v/t. → räuchern

selig adj. rel. blessed; verstorben: late; fig. overjoyed

Sellerie m, f celeriac; Stauden2: celery

selten 1. adj. rare; ~ sein be* rare od. scarce; **2.** adv. rarely, seldom; 2heit f rarity

seltsam adj. strange, odd, F funny

Semester univ. n term, Am. a. semester

Semikolon n semicolon

Seminar n univ. department; Kurs: seminar; Priester2: seminary; Lehrer2: teacher training college

sen. Abk. für senior sen., Sen.,Sr, Snr, senior

Senat m senate; ~or m senator

sende|n v/t. send* (mit der Post by post, Am. by mail); ausstrahlen: broadcast*, transmit (a. Funk); TV a. televise; 2r m radio od. television station; tech. Anlage: transmitter; 2reihe f TV od. radio series; 2schluß m closedown, sign-off; 2zeichen n call-sign

Sendung f broadcast, program(me); TV a. telecast; Waren2; consignment, shipment; auf ~ sein be* on the air

Senf m mustard (a. bot.)

senil adj. senile; 2ität f senility

Senior 1. m senior (a. Sport); ~en pl. senior citizens pl.; **2.** adj. nach Namen: senior; ~enheim n old people's home

Senk|e geogr. f depression, hollow; 2en v/t. lower (a. Stimme); Kopf: a. bow; Kosten, Preise etc.: a. reduce, cut*; sich ~ drop, go* od. come* down; 2recht adj. vertical; ~ nach oben (unten) straight up (down)

Sensation f sensation; 2ell adj., ~s... in Zssgn Blatt etc.: sensational (...); ~smache contp. f sensationalism

Sense f scythe

sensib|el adj. sensitive; empfindlich: a. touchy; △ nicht sensible; ~ilisieren v/t. sensitize (für to)

sentimental adj. sentimental; 2ität f sentimentality

September m September

Serenade mus. f serenade

Serie f series; TV etc. a. serial; Satz: set; in ~ bauen etc.: in series; 2nmäßig adj. series(-produced); Ausstattung etc.: standard; ~nnummer f serial number; ~nwagen mot. m standard-type car

seriös adj. respectable; ehrlich: honest; Zeitung: serious

Serum n serum

Service[1] n set; Tee2 etc.: a. service

Service[2] m, n service

servier|en v/t. serve; 2erin f waitress; 2tochter f Schweiz: waitress

Serviette f bsd. Brt. serviette, bsd. Am. napkin

Servo|bremse mot. f servo od. power brake; ~lenkung mot. f servo(-assisted) od. power steering

Sessel m armchair, easy chair; ~lift m chair lift

seßhaft adj.: ~ werden settle (down)

Set n, m Platzdeckchen: place mat

setzen v/t. u. v/i. put*, set* (a. print., agr., Segel), place; j-n: a. seat; agr. a. plant; ~ über jump over; Fluß: cross; ~ auf wetten: bet* on, back; sich ~ sit* down; tech. etc. settle; sich ~ auf Pferd, Rad etc.: get* on, mount; sich ~ in Auto etc.: get* into; sich zu j-m ~ sit* beside od. with s.o.; ~ Sie sich bitte! take od. have a seat!

Setz|er print. m compositor, typesetter; ~erei print. f composing room; ~kasten print. typecase

Seuche f epidemic (disease)

seufze|n v/i., 2r m sigh

Sexis|mus m sexism; ~t(in), 2isch adj. sexist

Sexual|... in Zssgn Erziehung, Leben, Trieb etc.: sex(ual) ...; ~verbrechen n sex crime

sex|uell adj. sexual; ~e Belästigung (sexual) harassment; ~y adj. sexy

sezieren v/t. dissect (a. fig.); Leiche: perform an autopsy on

sich refl. pron. oneself; sg. himself, herself, itself; pl. themselves; sg. yourself, pl. yourselves; ~ ansehen im Spiegel etc.: look at o.s.; einander: look at each other

Sichel f sickle; Mond, fig.: crescent

sicher 1. adj. safe (vor from), secure (from); bsd. tech. proof (gegen against); in Zssgn ...proof; gewiß, überzeugt: certain, sure; zuverlässig: reliable; (sich) ~ sein be* sure (e-r Sache of s.th.; daß that); **2.** adv. fahren etc.: safely; natürlich: of course, bsd. Am. a. sure(ly); gewiß: certainly; wahrscheinlich: probably; du hast (bist) ~ ... you must have (be) ...

Sicherheit f security (a. mil., pol.,

econ.); *bsd. körperliche*: safety (*a. tech.*);
Gewißheit: certainty; *Können*: skill;
(**sich**) **~ bringen** get* to safety; **~s...**
bsd. tech. in Zssgn Glas, Schloß *etc.*:
safety ...; **~sgurt** *m* seatbelt, safety belt;
~smaßnahme *f* safety measure; *pol.*
security measure; **~snadel** *f* safety pin
sicher|lich *adv.* → **sicher** 2; **~n** *v/t.*
secure (*a. mil., tech.*); *schützen*: protect,
safeguard; *Computer*: save; **sich ~** secure o.s. (**gegen, vor** against, from);
~stellen *v/t.* secure, guarantee
Sicherung *f* securing; safeguard(ing);
tech. safety device; *electr.* fuse; **~ska-
sten** *electr.* *m* fuse box; **~skopie** *f*
Computer: backup; **e-e ~ machen**
(**von**) back up
Sicht *f* visibility; *Aus~*: view; **in ~ kommen** come* into sight *od.* view; **auf
lange ~** in the long run; **~bar** *adj.* visible; **~en** *v/t.* sight; *fig.* sort (through
od. out); **~karte** *f* season ticket; **~lich**
adv. visibly; **~weite** *f*: **in (außer) ~**
within (out of) sight
sickern *v/i.* trickle, ooze, seep
sie *pers. pron.* she (*a.* Schiff, Staat); *Sache*: it; *pl.* they; **Sie** *sg. u. pl.* you
Sieb *n* sieve; *Tee~ etc.*: strainer
sieben¹ *v/t.* sieve, sift; *fig.* weed out
sieben² *adj.* seven; **~meter** *m* penalty
shot *od.* throw
sieb|te *adj.*, **~tel** *n* seventh; **~zehn(te)**
adj. seventeen(th); **~zig** *adj.* seventy;
~zigste *adj.* seventieth
siedeln *v/i.* settle
siede|n *v/t. u. v/i.* boil, simmer; **~punkt**
m boiling point (*a. fig.*)
Siedl|er *m* settler; **~ung** *f* settlement;
Wohn~: housing development
Sieg *m* victory; *Sport*: *a.* win
Siegel *n* seal (*a. fig.*), *privates*: signet;
~lack *m* sealing wax; **~n** *v/t.* seal;
~ring *m* signet ring
sieg|en *v/i.* win*; **~er(in)** winner;
~reich *adj.* winning; *stärker*: victorious (*a. pol., mil.*)
Signal *n*, **~isieren** *v/t.* signal
signieren *v/t.* sign
Silbe *f* syllable; **~ntrennung** *f* syllabifi-
cation
Silber *n* silver; *Tafel~*: silverware;
~grau *adj.* silver-grey (*Am.* -gray);
~hochzeit *f* silver wedding; **~n** *adj.*
silver

Silhouette *f* silhouette; *e-r Stadt*: *a.*
skyline
Silikon *chem.* *n* silicone
Silizium *chem.* *n* silicon
Silvester *n* New Year's Eve
Sims *m, n* ledge; windowsill
Simul|ant *m* malingerer; **~ieren** *v/t. u.
v/i.* *tech. etc.* simulate; *Krankheit vortäuschen*: sham, malinger
simultan *adj.* simultaneous
Sinfonie *mus.* *f* symphony
singen *v/t. u. v/i.* sing* (**richtig** [**falsch**]
in [out of] tune)
Singular *gr.* *m* singular
Singvogel *m* songbird
sinken *v/i.* sink* (*a. fig.* Person), go*
down (*a. fig.*); *Sonne*: *a.* set*;
Preise etc.: fall*, drop
Sinn *m* sense (**für** of); *Verstand etc.*:
mind; *Bedeutung*: sense, meaning; *e-r
Sache*: point, idea; **im ~ haben** have* in
mind; **es hat keinen ~** (**zu warten** *etc.*)
it's no use *od.* good (waiting *etc.*);
~bild *n* symbol
sinnentstellend *adj.* distorting
Sinnes|organ *n* sense organ; **~täu-
schung** *f* hallucination; **~wandel** *m*
change of mind
sinn|lich *adj.* die Sinne betreffend: sen-
suous; *Wahrnehmung etc.*: sensory; *Begierden etc.*: sensual; **~lichkeit** *f* sen-
suality; **~los** *adj.* senseless; *zwecklos*:
useless; **~losigkeit** *f* senselessness;
uselessness; **~verwandt** *adj.* synonymous; **~voll** *adj.* meaningful; *nützlich*:
useful; *vernünftig*: wise, sensible
Sintflut *f biblisch*: the Flood
Sippe *f* (extended) family, clan
Sirene *f* siren
Sirup *m* Frucht~: syrup, *Am.* sirup;
Zucker~: treacle, molasses
Sitte *f* custom, tradition; **~n** *pl.* morals
pl.; *Benehmen*: manners *pl.*
Sitten|losigkeit *f* immorality; **~poli-
zei** *f* vice squad; **~widrig** *adj.* immoral
Sittlichkeitsverbrechen *n* sex crime
Situation *f* situation; *Lage*: *a.* position
Sitz *m* seat; *e-s Kleides etc.*: fit; **~blok-
kade** *f* sit-down demonstration
sitzen *v/i.* sit* (**an** at; **auf** on); *sich befinden*: be*; *stecken*: be* (stuck); *passen*:
fit; F *im Gefängnis*: do* time; **~ bleiben**
keep* one's seat; **~bleiben** *v/i. Schule*:
have* to repeat a year; F **keinen Mann**

S

kriegen: be* left on the shelf; **~ auf** be* left with; **~lassen** v/t. leave* *s.o.* in the lurch, let* *s.o.* down

Sitz|gelegenheit f seat; **genug ~en** pl. enough seating (room) sg.; **~ordnung** f, **~plan** m seating plan; **~platz** m seat; **~streik** m sit-down strike; **~ung** f session (a. parl.), meeting, conference

Skala f scale; fig. a. range

Skalp m, **Qieren** v/t. scalp

Skandal m scandal; **Qös** adj. scandalous, shocking

Skelett n skeleton (a. tech.)

Skep|sis f scepticism; **~tiker** m sceptic; **Qtisch** adj. sceptical

Ski m ski; **~ laufen** od. **fahren** ski; **~fahrer(in)** m ski flying; **~liſt** m ski lift; **~piste** f ski run; **~schuh** m ski boot; **~sport** m skiing; **~springen** n ski jumping

Skizze f, **Qieren** v/t. sketch

Sklave m slave (a. fig.); **~enhandel** m slave trade; **~erei** f slavery; **Qisch** adj. slavish (a. fig.)

Skonto econ. m, n (cash) discount

Skorpion m zo. scorpion; astr. Scorpio; **er ist (ein) ~** he's a) Scorpio

Skrupel m scruple, qualm; **Qlos** adj. unscrupulous

Skulptur f sculpture

Slalom m slalom

Slaw|e m, **~in** f Slav; **Qisch** adj. Slav(ic)

Slip m briefs pl.; **Damen**Q: a. panties pl.; ⚠ nicht slip; **~per** m slip-on (shoe), bsd. Am. loafer; ⚠ nicht slipper; **~einlage** f panty liner

Slowak|e m Slovak; **~ei** f Slovakia; **~in** f, **Qisch** adj. Slovak

Smaragd m, **Qgrün** adj. emerald

Smoking m dinner jacket, Am. a. tuxedo, F tux

Snob m snob; **~ismus** m snobbery; **Qistisch** adj. snobbish

so 1. adv. so; auf diese Weise: like this od. that, this od. that way; damit, dadurch: a. thus; solch: such; (nicht) ~ groß wie (not) as big as; ~ ein(e) such a; ~ sehr so (F that) much; und ~ weiter and so on; oder ~ et. or s.th. like that; oder ~ or so; ~, fangen wir an! well od. all right, let's begin!; **2.** cj. deshalb: so, therefore; ~ daß so that; **3.** int.: ~! all right!, o.k.!; fertig: that's it!; ach ~! I see; **~bald** cj. as soon as

s.o. Abk. für siehe oben see above

Socke f sock

Sockel m base; Statue: pedestal (a. fig.)

Sodbrennen med. n heartburn

soeben adv. just (now)

Sofa n sofa, Am. a. davenport

sofern cj. if, provided that; ~ nicht unless

sofort adv. at once, immediately, right away; **Qbildkamera** phot. f instant od. Polaroid (TM) camera

Software f Computer: software; **~paket** n software package

Sog m suction, wake (a. fig.)

so|gar adv. even; **~genannt** adj. so-called; **~gleich** adv. → sofort

Sohle f sole; Bergbau: floor

Sohn m son

Sojabohne bot. f soybean (a. in Zssgn)

solange cj. as long as

Solar... in Zssgn Energie etc.: solar ...

solch dem pron. such, like this od. that

Sold mil. m pay

Soldat m soldier

Söldner m mercenary

Sole f brine, salt water

solidarisch adj.: sich ~ erklären mit declare one's solidarity with

solide adj. Material: solid; fig. a. sound; Preise: reasonable; Person: steady

Solist(in) soloist

Soll econ. n debit; PlanQ: target, quota; ~ und Haben debit and credit

sollen v/i. u. v/aux. geplant, bestimmt: be* to; angeblich, verpflichtet: be* supposed to; (was) soll ich ...? (what) shall I ...?; du solltest (nicht) ... you should(n't) ...; stärker: you ought(n't) to; was soll das? what's the idea?

Solo n solo; Sport: solo attempt etc.

somit cj. thus, so, consequently

Sommer m summer; **~ferien** pl. summer holidays pl. (bsd. Am. vacation sg.); **~frische** f summer resort; **Qlich** adj. summery; **~sprosse** f freckle; **Qsprossig** adj. freckled; **~zeit** f summertime; vorverlegte: summer od. Am. daylight saving time

Sonate mus. f sonata

Sonde f probe (a. med.)

Sonder|... in Zssgn Angebot, Ausgabe, Flug, Preis, Wunsch, Zug etc.: special ...; **Qbar** adj. strange, F funny; **Qlich**

adv.: **nicht ~** not particularly; **~ling** *m* eccentric, F crank, weirdo; **~müll** *m* hazardous (*od.* special toxic) waste; **~mülldeponie** *f* special waste dump

sondern *cj.* but; **nicht nur ..., ~ auch** not only ... but also

Sonderschule *f* special school (for the handicapped *etc.*)

Sonnabend *m* Saturday

Sonne *f* sun; **2n** *v/refl.* sunbathe

Sonnen|aufgang *m* sunrise; **~bad** *n*: **ein ~ nehmen** → **2baden** *v/i* sunbathe; **~bank** *f* sunbed; **~blume** *bot.* *f* sunflower; **~brand** *m* sunburn; **~brille** *f* sunglasses *pl.*; **~creme** *f* sun cream; **~energie** *f* solar energy; **~finsternis** *f* solar eclipse; **2klar** *fig. adj.* (as) clear as daylight; **~kollektor** *m* solar panel; **~licht** *n* sunlight; **~öl** *n* suntan oil; **~schein** *m* sunshine; **~schirm** *m* sunshade; **~schutz** *m* Mittel: suntan lotion; **~seite** *f* sunny side (*a. fig.*); **~stich** *m* sunstroke; **~strahl** *m* sunbeam; **~system** *n* solar system; **~uhr** *f* sundial; **~untergang** *m* sunset

sonnig *adj.* sunny (*a. fig.*)

Sonntag *m* Sunday

Sonntags|fahrer *mot. contp. m* Sunday driver; **~rückfahrkarte** *rail. f* weekend ticket

sonst *adv. außerdem*: else; *andernfalls*: otherwise, or (else); *normalerweise*: normally, usually; **~ noch et.** (*jemand*)? anything (anyone) else?; **~ noch Fragen?** any other questions?; **~ nichts** nothing else; **alles wie ~** everything as usual; **nichts ist wie ~** nothing as it used to be; **~ig** *adj.* other

Sopran *mus. m*, **~istin** *mus. f* soprano

Sorge *f* worry; *Kummer*: sorrow; *Ärger*: trouble; *Für2*: care; **sich ~n machen** (**um**) worry *od.* be* worried (about); **keine ~!** don't worry!

sorgen 1. *v/i.*: **~ für** care for, take* care of; **dafür ..., daß** see* (to it) that; **2.** *v/refl.*: **sich ~ um** worry *od.* be* worried about; **2kind** *n* problem child

Sorg|falt *f* care; **2fältig** *adj.* careful; **2los** *adj.* carefree; *nachlässig*: careless; **2losigkeit** *f* carelessness

Sort|e *f* sort, kind, type; **2ieren** *v/t.* sort; *ordnen*: arrange; **~iment** *n* assortment

Soße *f* sauce; *Braten2*: gravy

Souffl|eur *m*, **~euse** *f* prompter; **2ieren** *v/i.* prompt (*j-m* s.o.)

souverän *adj. pol.* sovereign; *fig.* superior; **2ität** *f* sovereignty; *fig.* superior style

so|viel 1. *cj.* as far as; **2.** *adv.*: **doppelt ~** twice as much; **~ wie möglich** as much as possible; **~weit 1.** *cj.* as far as; **2.** *adv. bis jetzt od. hier*: so far; **~ sein** be* ready; **es ist ~** it's time; **~wie** *cj.* as well as, and ...; *zeitlich*: as soon as; **~wieso** *adv.* anyway, anyhow, in any case

Sowjet *m*, **2isch** *adj.* Soviet

sowohl *cj.*: **~ Lehrer als (auch) Schüler** both teachers and students

sozial *adj.* social; **2...** *in Zssgn Arbeiter(in), Demokrat, Versicherung etc.*: social ...; **2hilfe** *f* Social security, Am. welfare; **~ beziehen** be* on social security (Am. on welfare); **~isieren** *v/t. econ.* nationalize; **2ismus** *m* socialism; **2ist(in)**, **~istisch** *adj.* socialist; **2kunde** *f* social studies *pl.*; **2staat** *m* welfare state

Soziolog|e *m* sociologist; **~ie** *f* sociology; **2isch** *adj.* sociological

sozusagen *adv.* so to speak

Spagat *m*: **~ machen** do* the splits

spähen *v/i.* look out (**nach** for)

Spalier *n* espalier; *mil. etc.* lane

Spalt *m* crack, gap; **~e** *f* → **Spalt**; *print.* column; **2en** *v/t.* split* (*a. fig. Haare etc.*); *Staat etc.*: divide; **sich ~** split* (up); **~ung** *f* split(ting); *phys.* fission; *fig.* split; *Staat etc.*: division

Span *m* chip; *tech. pl.* shavings *pl.*

Spange *f* clasp; → **Haarspange**

Spaniel *m* spaniel

Spani|en Spain; **~er(in)** Spaniard; **2sch** *adj.* Spanish

Spann *m* instep

Spanne *f* span

spann|en 1. *v/t.* stretch, tighten; *Leine etc.*: put* up; *Gewehr*: cock; *Bogen*: draw*, bend*; **2.** *v/i.* be* (too) tight; **~end** *adj.* exciting, thrilling, gripping; **2ung** *f* tension (*a. tech., pol., psych.*); *electr.* voltage; *fig.* suspense, excitement; **2weite** *f* span; *fig. a.* range

Spar|buch *n* savings book; **~büchse** *f* money box, F piggy bank; **2en** *v/i. u. v/t.* save; *sich einschränken*: economize;

S

~ **für** od. **auf** save up for; ~**er** m saver;
~**schwein(chen)** n piggy bank

Spargel m asparagus

Spar|kasse f savings bank; ~**konto** n
savings account

spärlich adj. sparse, scant; Lohn, Wissen etc.: scanty; Besuch etc.: poor

sparsam adj. economical (**mit** of); ~
leben lead* a frugal life; ~ **umgehen
mit** use sparingly; 2**keit** f economy

Spaß m fun; Scherz: joke; **aus** (**nur
zum**) ~ (just) for fun; **es macht viel**
(**keinen**) ~ it's great (no) fun; **j-m den ~
verderben** spoil s.o.'s fun; **er macht
nur** (**keinen**) ~ he is only (not) joking (F
kidding); **keinen ~ verstehen** have* no
sense of humo(u)r; 2**en** v/i. joke; 2**ig**
adj. funny; ~**macher**, ~**vogel** m joker

spät adj. u. adv. late; **am ~en Nachmittag** late in the afternoon; **wie ~ ist es?**
what time is it?; **von früh bis ~** from
morning till night; (**fünf Minuten**) **zu ~
kommen** be* (five minutes) late; **bis
~er!** see you (later)!; → **früher**

Spaten m spade

spätestens adv. at the latest

Spatz m sparrow

spazieren|fahren v/i. u. v/t. go* (j-n:
take*) for a drive; Baby: take* out;
~**gehen** v/i. go* for a walk

Spazier|fahrt f drive, ride; ~**gang** m
walk; **e-n ~ machen** go* for a walk;
~**gänger** m walker; ~**weg** m walk

Specht m woodpecker

Speck m bacon; 2**ig** fig. adj. greasy

Spedit|eur m shipping agent; Möbel2:
remover; ~**ion** f shipping agency; removal (Am. moving) firm

Speer m spear; Sport: javelin

Speiche f spoke

Speichel m spittle, saliva, F spit

Speicher m storehouse; Wasser2: tank,
reservoir; Dachboden: attic; Computer:
memory, store; ~**dichte** f Computer:
bit density; ~**kapazität** f Computer:
memory capacity; 2**n** v/t. store (up);
~**ung** f storage

speien v/t. spit*; Wasser: spout; Vulkan etc.: belch

Speise f food; Gericht: dish; ~**eis** n ice
cream; ~**kammer** f larder, pantry;
~**karte** f menu; 2**n 1.** v/i. dine; **2.** v/t.
feed* (a. electr. etc.); ~**röhre** anat. f
gullet; ~**saal** m dining hall; ~**wagen**

rail. m dining car, bsd. Am. diner

Spekul|ant m speculator; ~**ation** f
speculation; econ. a. venture; 2**ieren**
v/i. speculate (**auf** on; **mit** in)

Spende f gift; Beitrag: contribution;
für Hilfswerk etc.: donation; 2**n** v/t.
give* (a. fig. Schatten etc.); Geld, Blut
etc.: donate; ~**r** m giver; donor (a.
Blut2, Organ2)

spendieren v/t.: **j-m et. ~** treat s.o. to
s.th.

Spengler österr. m → **Klempner**

Sperling m sparrow

Sperr|e f barrier; rail. a. gate; fig. allg.
stop; tech. lock(ing device); Straßen2:
barricade; Sport: suspension; psych.
mental block; econ. embargo; 2**en** v/t.
close; econ. embargo; Strom etc.: cut*
off; Scheck: stop; Sport: suspend; behindern: obstruct; ~ **in** lock (up) in;
~**holz** n plywood; ~**müllabfuhr** f removal of bulky refuse; ~**ung** f closing

Spesen pl. expenses pl.

Spezi österr. m pal, Am. buddy

Spezial|ausbildung f special training;
~**gebiet** n special field, special(i)ty;
~**geschäft** n specialized shop od.
store; 2**isieren** v/refl. specialize (**auf**
in); ~**ist(in)** specialist; ~**ität** f speciali(i)ty

speziell adj. specific, particular

spezifisch adj. specific; ~**es Gewicht**
specific gravity

Sphäre f sphere (a. fig.)

spicken 1. v/t. lard (a. fig. Rede etc.); **2.**
F fig. v/i. crib

Spiegel m mirror (a. fig.); ~**bild** n reflection (a. fig.); ~**ei** n fried egg; 2**glatt**
adj. Wasser etc.: glassy; Straße: icy; 2**n**
v/i. u. v/t. reflect (a. fig.); glänzen:
shine*; **sich ~** be* reflected (a. fig.);
~**ung** f reflection

Spiel n game; Wett2: a. match; **das ~en**,
~**weise**: play (a. thea. etc.); Glücks2:
gambling; Spiel, game, gamble; **auf dem
~ stehen** be* at stake; **aufs ~ setzen**
risk; 2**en** v/i. u. v/t. play (a. fig.) (**um**
for); darstellen: a. act; aufführen: perform; Glücksspiel: gamble; Lotto etc.:
do*; Klavier etc. ~ play the piano etc.;
2**end** fig. adv. easily; ~**er** m player;
Glücks2: gambler; ~**feld** n (playing)
field, pitch; ~**film** m feature film; ~**halle** f amusement arcade, game room;

~**hölle** f gambling den; ~**kamerad(in)** playmate; ~**karte** f playing card; ~**kasino** n casino; ~**marke** f counter, chip; ~**plan** m thea. etc.: program(me); ~**platz** m playground; ~**raum** fig. m play, scope; ~**regel** f rule (of the game); ~**sachen** pl. toys pl.; ~**schuld** f gambling debt; ~**stand** m score; ~**uhr** f musical (Am. music) box; ~**verderber(in)** spoilsport; ~**waren** pl. toys pl.; ~**zeit** f thea., Sport: season; Dauer: playing (Film: running) time; ~**zeug** n toy(s pl.); ~**zeug...** in Zssgn Pistole etc.: toy ...

Spieß m spear, pike; Brat2: spit; Fleisch2: skewer; 2en v/t. skewer; ~**er** contp. m petty bourgeois, philistine; 2**ig** adj. petty bourgeois, philistine

Spinat m spinach

Spind n, m locker

Spindel f spindle

Spinn|e f spider; 2**en 1.** v/t. spin* (a. fig.); **2.** F fig. v/i. be* nuts; talk nonsense; ~**er** m spinner; F fig. nut, crackpot; Angeber: braggart, big mouth; ~**rad** n spinning wheel; ~**webe** f cobweb

Spion m informer; F stoolpigeon

Spion|age f espionage; 2**ieren** v/i. spy; F schnüffeln: snoop

Spiral|e f, 2**förmig** adj. spiral

Spirituosen pl. spirits pl.

Spiritus m spirit (a. in Zssgn)

Spital n hospital

spitz adj. pointed (a. fig.); math. Winkel: acute; ~**e Zunge** sharp tongue; 2**bogen** arch. m pointed arch; 2**e** f point; Nasen2, Finger2: tip; Turm2: spire; Baum2, Berg2: top; Pfeil2, Unternehmens2: head; F großartig: super, (the) tops; **an der** ~ at the top (a. fig.)

Spitzel m informer, F stoolpigeon

spitzen v/t. point, sharpen; Lippen: purse; Ohren: prick up

Spitzen... Höchst..., Best... etc. in Zssgn: top ...; ~**technologie** f high tech(nology), hi-tech

spitz|findig adj. quibbling; 2**findigkeit** f subtlety; 2**hacke** f pickax(e), pick; 2**name** m nickname

Splitter m, 2**n** v/i. splinter; 2**nackt** F adj. stark naked

sponsern v/t., **Sponsor(in)** sponsor

spontan adj. spontaneous

Sporen pl. spurs pl. (a. zo.); biol. spores pl.

Sport m sport(s pl. coll.); Fach: physical education; ~ **treiben** do* sports

Sport|... in Zssgn Ereignis, Geschäft, Hemd, Verein, Zentrum etc.: mst sports ...; ~**kleidung** f sportswear; ~**ler(in)** athlete; 2**lich** adj. athletic; Kleidung: casual, sporty; ~**nachrichten** pl. sports news sg.; ~**platz** m sports grounds pl.; ~**tauchen** n scuba diving; ~**wagen** m sports car; für Kinder: pushchair, Am. stroller

Spott m mockery; Hohn: derision; verächtlicher: scorn; 2**billig** F adj. dirt cheap

spotten v/i. mock (über at), scoff (at); sich lustig machen: make* fun (of)

Spött|er m mocker, scoffer; 2**isch** adj. mocking, derisive

Spottpreis m: **für e-n** ~ dirt cheap

Sprache f language (a. fig.); das Sprechen, Sprechweise: speech; **zur** ~ **kommen** come* (bringen: bring* s.th.) up

Sprach|fehler m speech defect; ~**gebrauch** m usage; ~**labor** n language laboratory (F lab); 2**lehre** f grammar; ~**lehrer(in)** language teacher; 2**lich 1.** adj. language (attr.); **2.** adv.: ~ **richtig** grammatically correct; 2**los** adj. speechless; ~**rohr** fig. n mouthpiece; ~**unterricht** m language teaching; ~**wissenschaft** f linguistics sg.

Spraydose f spray can, aerosol (can)

Sprechanlage f intercom

sprechen v/t. u. v/i. speak* (j-n, mit j-m to s.o.); reden, sich unterhalten: talk (to) (beide: über, von about, of); **nicht zu** ~ **sein** be* busy; 2**er** m speaker; Ansager: announcer; Wortführer: spokesman; 2**stunde** f office hours pl.; med. consulting (od. surgery, Am. office) hours pl.; 2**zimmer** n consulting room, Am. a. office

spreizen v/t. spread*

spreng|en v/t. blow* up; Fels: blast; Wasser: sprinkle; Rasen: water; Versammlung: break* up; 2**kopf** mil. m warhead; 2**körper** m explosive; 2**stoff** m explosive; 2**ung** f blasting; blowing up

sprenkeln v/t. speck(le), spot, dot

Spreu f chaff (a. fig.)

Sprich|wort n proverb, saying; 2**wörtlich** adj. proverbial (a. fig.)

sprießen v/i. sprout; fig. burgeon

S

Spring|brunnen *m* fountain; **2en** *v/i.* jump, leap*; *Ball etc.*: bounce; *Schwimmen*: dive*; *Glas etc.*: crack; *zer~*: break*; *platzen*: burst*; *in die Höhe* (*zur Seite*) ~ jump up (aside); **~er** *m* jumper; *Schwimmen*: diver; *Schach*: knight; **~flut** *f* spring tide; **~reiten** *n* show jumping

Spritze *f med.* injection, F jab, *Am.* shot; *Instrument*: syringe; **2n** *v/i. u. v/t.* splash; *sprühen* (*a. tech., agr.*); *med.* inject; *j-m et.*: give* *s.o.* an injection of; *Fett*: spatter; *Blut*: gush (*aus* from); **~r** *m* splash; *kleine Menge*: dash

Spritz|pistole *tech. f* spray gun; **~tour** F *mot. f* spin

spröde *adj.* brittle (*a. fig.*); *Haut*: rough

Sprosse *f* rung

Spruch *m* saying; *Entscheidung*: decision; **~band** *n* banner

Sprudel *m* mineral water; **2n** *v/i.* bubble (*a. fig.*)

Sprüh|dose *f* spray can, aerosol (can); **2en** *v/t. u. v/i.* spray; *Funken*: throw* out; **~regen** *m* drizzle

Sprung *m* jump, leap; *Schwimmen*: dive; *Riß*: crack, fissure; **~brett** *n* diving board; *Turnen*: springboard; *fig.* stepping stone; **~schanze** *f* ski jump

Spucke F *f* spit(tle); **2n** *v/i. u. v/t.* spit*; F *sich übergeben*: throw* up

Spuk *m* apparition, ghost; **2en** *v/i.*: ~ *in* haunt; *hier spukt es* this place is haunted

Spule *f* spool, reel; *Garn2*: bobbin; *electr.* coil; **2n** *v/t.* spool, wind*, reel

spül|en *v/t. u. v/i.* wash up, do* the dishes; *aus~*: rinse; *W.C.*: flush the toilet; **2maschine** *f* dishwasher

Spur *f* Fuß2en, Wagen2en: track(s *pl.*); *Blut2 etc.*: trail; *Abdruck*: print; *Fahr2*: lane; *Tonband2*: track; *kleine Menge*: trace (*a. fig.*); *j-m auf der* ~ *sein* be* on *s.o.*'s trail

spüren *v/t. allg.* feel*; *instinktiv: a.* sense; *wahrnehmen*: notice

spur|los *adv.* without leaving a trace; **2weite** *f* rail. ga(u)ge; *mot.* track

St. *Abk. für Sankt* St, Saint

Staat *m state*; *Regierung*: government; **~enbund** *m* confederacy, confederation; **2enlos** *adj.* stateless; **2lich 1.** *adj.* state; *Einrichtung: a.* public, national; **2.** *adv.*: ~ *geprüft* qualified, re-

gistered

Staats|angehörige(r) national, citizen, *bsd. Brt.* subject; **~angehörigkeit** *f* nationality; **~anwalt** *jur. m* (public) prosecutor, *Am.* district attorney; **~besuch** *m* official *od.* state visit; **~bürger** *m* citizen; **~chef** *m* head of state; **~dienst** *m* civil (*Am. a.* public) service; **2eigen** *adj.* state-owned; **~feind** *m* public enemy; **2feindlich** *adj.* subversive; **~haushalt** *m* budget; **~kasse** *f* treasury; **~mann** *m* statesman; **~oberhaupt** *n* head of (the) state; **~sekretär** *m* undersecretary of state; **~streich** *m* coup d'état; **~vertrag** *m* treaty; **~wissenschaft** *f* political science

Stab *m* staff (*a. fig.*); *Metall2, Holz2*: bar; *Staffel2, mus. Dirigenten2*: baton; *~hochsprung*: pole

Stäbchen *pl. Eß2*: chopsticks *pl.*

Stabhochsprung *m* pole vault

stabil *adj.* stable (*a. econ., pol.*); *robust*: solid, strong; *gesund*: sound; **~isieren** *v/t.* stabilize; **2ität** *f* stability

Stachel *m bot., zo.* spine, prick; *Insekt*: sting; **~beere** *f* gooseberry; **~draht** *m* barbed wire; **2ig** *adj.* prickly; **~schwein** *n* porcupine

Stad(e)l *m östr.* barn

Stadion *n* stadium; **~um** *n* stage, phase

Stadt *f* town; *bsd. Groß2*: city; *die* ~ *Berlin* the city of Berlin; *in die* ~ *fahren* go* (in)to town, *bsd. Am. a.* go* downtown; *Leute*: town; **~bahn** *f* urban railway

Städter *m* city dweller, *Brt.* F townie, city slicker (*oft contp.*)

Stadt|gebiet *n* urban area; **~gespräch** *fig. n* talk of the town

städtisch *adj.* urban; *pol.* municipal

Stadt|mensch *m* → *Städter*; **~plan** *m* city map; **~rand** *m* outskirts *pl.*; **~rat** *m* town council; *Person*: town councill(l)or, *Am.* city council|man (-woman); **~rundfahrt** *f* sightseeing tour; **~streicher(in)** city vagrant; **~teil** *m*, **~viertel** *n* quarter

Staffel *f* relay race *od.* team; *mil. aviat.* squadron; **~ei** *paint. f* easel; **2n** *v/t.* grade, scale

Stahl *m* steel (*a. in Zssgn Helm, Wolle etc.*); **~kammer** *f* strongroom; **~werk** *n* steelworks *pl.*

Stall *m* stable; → *Kuh2, Schweine2*; **~knecht** *m* stableman

Stamm m bot. stem (a. gr.), trunk; Volks2: tribe; Geschlecht: stock; fig. Kern e-r Firma, Mannschaft etc.: regulars pl.; **~...** in Zssgn Gast, Kunde, Spieler etc.: regular ...; **~baum** m family tree; zo. pedigree; **2eln** v/t. stammer; **2en** v/i.: ~ aus (von) allg. come* from; zeitlich: be* from; ~ von Künstler etc.: be* by; **~formen** gr. pl. principal parts pl., mst tenses pl.

stämmig adj. sturdy; dicklich: stout

Stammkneipe F f local

stampfen 1. v/t. mash; **2.** v/i. stamp (mit dem Fuß one's foot)

Stand m stand(ing), standing od. upright position; Halt: footing, foothold; ~platz: stand; Verkaufs2: stand, stall; astr. position; Wasser2 etc.: height, level; des Thermometers: reading; fig. Niveau, Höhe: level; soziale Stellung: social standing, status; Klasse: class; Beruf: profession; Sport: score; Rennen: standings pl.; Lage: state; Zustand: a. condition; auf den neuesten ~ bringen bring* up to date; e-n schweren ~ haben have* a hard time (of it)

Standard m standard (a. in Zssgn)

Standbild n statue

Ständchen n serenade

Ständer m stand; Kleider2 etc.: rack

Standes|amt n registry office, Am. marriage license bureau; **2amtlich** adj.: ~e Trauung civil marriage; **~beamte** m registrar, Am. civil magistrate

standhaft adj. steadfast, firm; ~ bleiben resist temptation

standhalten v/i. withstand*, resist

ständig adj. constant; Adresse etc.: permanent; Einkommen: fixed

Stand|licht mot. n parking light; **~ort** m position; Betrieb etc.: location; mil. garrison, bsd. Am. post; **~pauke** f: j-m e-e ~ halten give s.o. a talking-to; **~photo** n still; **~platz** m stand; **~punkt** fig. m (point of) view, standpoint; **~recht** mil. n martial law; **~spur** mot. hard shoulder, Am. shoulder; **~uhr** f grandfather clock

Stange f pole; Fahnen2: a. staff; Metall2: rod, bar; Zigaretten: carton

Stanniol n tin foil

Stanze tech. f, **2n** v/t. punch

Stapel m pile, stack; Haufen: heap; vom ~ lassen naut. launch (a. fig.); vom ~ laufen naut. be* launched; **~lauf** naut. m launch; **2n** v/t. pile (up), stack

stapfen v/i. trudge, plod

Star m zo. starling; thea. etc.: star; med. cataract

stark 1. adj. strong (a. fig. Kaffee, Bier, Tabak etc.); mächtig, kraftvoll: a. powerful; Raucher, Regen, Erkältung, Verkehr etc.: heavy; F toll: super, great; **2.** adv.: ~ beeindruckt etc. very much od. greatly impressed etc.; ~ beschädigt etc. badly damaged etc.

Stärke f strength, power; Intensität: intensity; Maß: degree; chem. starch; **2n** v/t. strengthen (a. fig.); Wäsche etc.: starch; sich ~ take* some refreshment

Starkstrom electr. m high-voltage (od. heavy) current

Stärkung f strengthening; Imbiß: refreshment; **~smittel** n tonic

starr adj. stiff; unbeweglich: rigid (a. tech.); Gesicht etc.: a. frozen; **~er Blick** (fixed) stare; ~ vor Kälte (Entsetzen) frozen (scared) stiff; **2en** v/i. stare (auf at); **~köpfig** adj. stubborn, obstinate; **2sinn** m stubbornness, obstinacy

Start m start (a. fig.); aviat. take-off; Rakete: lift-off; **~bahn** aviat. f runway; **2bereit** adj. ready to start; aviat. ready for take-off; **2en** v/i. u. v/t. start (a. F fig.); aviat. take* off; Raumfahrt: lift off; e-e Rakete: launch (a. fig. Unternehmen etc.)

Station f station; Kranken2: ward; **2är** med. adj.: ~er Patient in-patient; **2ieren** mil. v/t. station; Raketen: deploy; **~svorsteher** rail. m stationmaster

Statist m thea., Film: extra; **~ik** f statistics pl.; **~iker** m statistician; **2isch** adj. statistical

Stativ n tripod

statt prp. instead of; ~ dessen instead (mst nachgestellt); ~ et. zu tun instead of doing s.th.

Stätte f place; e-s Unglücks etc.: scene

statt|finden v/i. take* place; geschehen: happen; **2lich** adj. imposing; Summe etc.: handsome

Statue f statue

Statur f build, stature; (a. fig.)

Status m state; sozialer: status; **~symbol** n status symbol; **~zeile** f Computer: status line

S

Stau mot. m (traffic) jam, congestion

Staub m dust (a. ~ wischen)

Staubecken n reservoir

staub|en v/i. give* off od. make* dust; ⸗fänger F m dust trap; ~ig adj. dusty; ~saugen v/i. u. v/t. vacuum, F Brt. hoover; ⸗sauger m vacuum cleaner, F Brt. hoover; ⸗tuch n duster

Staudamm m dam

Staude bot. f herbaceous plant

stauen v/t. Fluß etc.: dam up; sich ~ mot. etc.: be* stacked up

staunen v/i. be* astonished od. surprised (über at)

Staunen n astonishment, amazement

Staupe vet. f distemper

Stausee m reservoir

stech|en v/i. u. v/t. Nadel, Dorn etc.: prick; Biene etc.: sting*; Mücke etc.: bite*; mit Messer etc.: stab; durch~: pierce; mit et. ~ in stick* s.th. into(to); sich ~ prick o.s.; ~end adj. Blick: piercing; Schmerz: stabbing; ⸗uhr f time clock

Steck|brief jur. m "wanted" poster; ⸗brieflich jur. adv.: er wird ~ gesucht a warrant is out against him; ~dose electr. f (wall) socket; ⸗en 1. v/t. stick*; wohin tun: put*; bsd. tech. insert (in into); an~: pin (an to, on); agr. set*, plant; 2. v/i. sich befinden: be*; festsitzen: stick*, be* stuck; tief in Schulden ~ be* deeply in debt; ⸗enbleiben (irr.): get* stuck (a. fig.); ~enpferd n Spielzeug: hobby horse; fig. hobby; ~er electr. m plug; ~kontakt electr. m plug (connection); ~nadel f pin; ~platz m Computer: slot

Steg m foot bridge; Brett: plank

Stegreif m: aus dem ~ extempore, F ad lib; aus dem ~ sprechen, spielen etc. extemporize, F ad-lib

stehen v/i. stand*; sich befinden, sein: be*; aufrecht ~: stand* up; es steht ihr it suits (od. looks well on) her; wie steht es (od. das Spiel)? what's the score?; hier steht, daß it says here that; wo steht das? where does it say so od. that?; sich gut (schlecht) ~ be* well (badly) off; sich ~ mit j-m: get* along with; wie steht es mit ...? what about ...?; F: darauf stehe ich it turns me on; ~bleiben v/i. stop; bsd. tech., Entwicklung etc.: come* to a standstill; ~las-

sen v/t. leave* (Essen etc.: untouched); Schirm etc.: leave* behind; alles stehen- und liegenlassen drop everything; sich e-n Bart ~ grow* a beard

Steh|kragen m stand-up collar; ~lampe f standard (Am. floor) lamp; ~leiter f step ladder

stehlen v/t. u. v/i. steal* (a. fig. sich ~)

Stehplatz m standing ticket; pl.: standing room

steif adj. stiff (a. fig.) (vor with)

Steigbügel m stirrup

steigen v/i. sich begeben: go*, step; klettern: climb; hoch~, zunehmen: rise*, go* up, climb (a. aviat.); ~ in (auf) Fahrzeug: get* on; ~ aus (von) get* off (Bett: out of)

steiger|n v/t. raise, increase; verstärken: heighten; verbessern: improve; gr. compare; sich ~ Person: improve, get* better; ⸗ung f rise, increase; heightening; improvement; gr. comparison

Steigung f gradient; Hang: slope

steil adj. steep (a. fig. u. in Zssgn)

Stein m stone (a. bot., med.), Am. a. rock; → Edel⸗; ~bock m zo. rock goat; astr. Capricorn; er ist (ein) ~ he's a(n) Capricorn; ~bruch m quarry; ⸗ern adj. (of) stone; fig. stony; ~gut n earthenware; ⸗ig adj. stony; ⸗igen v/t. stone; ~kohle f (hard) coal; ~metz m stonemason; ~wurf m stone's throw; ~zeit f Stone Age

Stellage östr. f stand, rack, shelf

Stelle f place; genauere: spot; Punkt: point; Arbeits⸗: job; Behörde: authority; math. figure; freie ~ vacancy, opening; auf der (zur) ~ on the spot; an erster ~ stehen (kommen*) be* (come*) first; an j-s ~ in s.o.'s place; ich an deiner ~ if I were you

stellen v/t. allg. put*; Uhr, Aufgabe, Falle etc.: set*; ein, aus, leiser etc.: turn; Frage: ask; zur Verfügung ~: provide; Verbrecher etc.: corner, hunt down; sich ~ give* o.s. up, turn o.s. in; sich ~ gegen (hinter) fig. oppose (back); sich ~ schlafend etc.: pretend to be asleep etc.; stell dich dorthin! (go and) stand over there!

Stellen|angebot n vacancy; ich habe ein ~ I was offered a job; ~anzeige f job ad(vertisement), employment ad; ~gesuch n application for a job;

Ꝗweise adv. partly, in places

Stellung f position; *Arbeitsplatz: a.* post, job; **~ nehmen zu** comment on, give* one's opinion of; **~nahme** f comment, opinion (*beide:* **zu** on); **Ꝗslos** adj. unemployed, jobless

stellvertrete|nd adj. *amtlich:* acting, deputy, vice-...; **Ꝗr** m representative; *amtlich:* deputy

Stelze f stilt; **Ꝗn** v/i. stalk

stemmen v/t. *Gewicht:* lift; **sich ~ gegen** press o.s. against; *fig.* resist *od.* oppose *s.th.*

Stempel m stamp; *Post*Ꝗ*:* postmark; *auf Silber etc.:* hallmark; *bot.* pistil; **~kissen** n ink pad; **Ꝗn 1.** v/t. stamp; *entwerten:* cancel; *Gold, Silber:* hallmark; **2.** v/i. F: **~ gehen** be* on the dole

Stengel m stalk, stem

Steno|gramm n shorthand notes pl.; **~graphie** f shorthand; **Ꝗgraphieren** v/t. take* down in shorthand; **~typistin** f shorthand typist

Stepp|decke f quilt; **Ꝗen 1.** v/t. quilt; *Naht:* stitch; **2.** v/i. tap dance

Steptanz m tap dancing

Sterbe|bett n deathbed; **~klinik** f hospice

sterben v/i. die (**an** of) (a. fig.); **im Ꝗ liegen** be* dying

sterblich adj. mortal; **Ꝗkeit** f mortality

Stereo n stereo (a. in Zssgn)

steril adj. sterile; **Ꝗisation** f sterilization; **~isieren** v/t. sterilize

Stern m star (a. fig.); **~bild** astr. n constellation; *des Tierkreises:* sign of the zodiac; **~chen** print. n asterisk; **~enbanner** n Star-Spangled Banner, Stars and Stripes pl.; **Ꝗenhimmel** m starry sky; **Ꝗklar** adj. starry; **~kunde** f astronomy; **~schnuppe** f shooting *od.* falling star; **~warte** f observatory

stet|(ig) adj. continual, constant; *gleichmäßig:* steady; **~s** adv. always

Steuer[1] n *mot.* (steering) wheel; *naut.* helm, rudder

Steuer[2] f tax (**auf** on); **~beamte** m revenue officer; **~berater** m tax adviser; **~bord** naut. n starboard; **~erklärung** f tax return; **~ermäßigung** f tax allowance; **Ꝗfrei** adj. tax-free; *Waren:* duty-free; **~hinterziehung** f tax-evasion; **~knüppel** aviat. m control column *od.* stick; **~mann** m naut.

helmsman; *Boots*Ꝗ*:* coxswain; **Ꝗn** v/t. u. v/i. allg. steer; *naut., aviat. a.* navigate, pilot; *mot. a.* drive*; *tech.* control; *fig.* direct, control; **Ꝗpflichtig** adj. taxable; *Waren:* dutiable; **~rad** n steering wheel; **~ruder** naut. n helm, rudder; **~senkung** f tax reduction; **~ung** f steering (system); *electr., tech.* control (a. fig); **Ꝗzahler** m taxpayer

Stich m *Nadel*Ꝗ*:* prick; *Bienen*Ꝗ *etc.:* sting; *Mücken*Ꝗ *:* bite; *Messer*Ꝗ*:* stab; *Nähen:* stitch; *Kartenspiel:* trick; *Kupfer*Ꝗ *etc.:* engraving; **im ~ lassen** let* *s.o. verlassen:* abandon, desert

Stichel|ei fig. f dig, gibe; **Ꝗn** fig. v/i. make* digs, gibe (**gegen** at)

Stich|flamme f jet of flame; **Ꝗhaltig** adj. valid, sound; *unwiderlegbar:* watertight; **nicht ~ sein** F not hold* water; **~probe** f spot check; **~n machen** spot-check (**bei et.** s.th.); **~tag** m cutoff date; *letzter Termin:* deadline; **~wahl** f; **~wort** n *thea.* cue; *im Lexikon:* headword; **~e** pl. *Notizen:* notes pl.; **das Wichtigste in ~en** an outline of the main points; **~wortverzeichnis** n index; **~wunde** f stab

stick|en v/t. u. v/i. embroider; **Ꝗerei** f embroidery

stick|ig adj. stuffy; **Ꝗstoff** chem. m nitrogen

Stief... in Zssgn *Mutter etc.:* step ...

Stiefel m boot

Stiefmütterchen n pansy

Stiege östr. f → **Treppe**

Stiel m handle; *Besen*Ꝗ*:* stick; *Glas, Pfeife, Blume etc.:* stem; *bot.* stalk

Stier m zo. bull; *astr.* Taurus; **er ist (ein) ~** he's (a) Taurus; **Ꝗen** v/i. stare (**auf** at); **~kampf** m bullfight

Stift m pen; *Blei*Ꝗ*:* pencil; *Farb*Ꝗ*: a.* crayon; *tech.* pin; *Holz*Ꝗ*:* peg

stift|en v/t. spenden: donate; verursachen: cause; **Ꝗung** f donation

Stil m style (a. fig.); **in großem ~** in (grand) style; *fig.* on a large scale; **Ꝗistisch** adj. stylistic

still adj. quiet, silent; *bsd. unbewegt:* still; **sei(d) ~!** be quiet!; **halt ~!** keep still!; **sich ~ verhalten** keep* quiet (*körperlich:* still); **Ꝗe** f silence (a. Schweigen), quiet(ness); **in aller ~** quietly; *heimlich:* secretly

Stilleben paint. n still life

stillegen v/t. close down

stillen v/t. Baby: nurse, breastfeed*; Schmerz: relieve; Hunger, Neugier etc.: satisfy; Durst: quench

stillhalten v/i. keep* still

stillos adj. lacking style, tasteless

still|schweigend fig. adj. tacit; **~sitzen** v/i. sit* still; **2stand** m standstill, stop; fig. a. stagnation (a. econ.); von Verhandlungen: deadlock; **~stehen** v/i. (have*) stop(ped), (have*) come* to a standstill

Stil|möbel pl. period furniture sg.; **2voll** adj. stylish; **~sein** have* style

Stimm|band n vocal cord; **2berechtigt** adj. entitled to vote

Stimm|e f voice; Pol. vote; sich der ~ enthalten abstain; **2n 1.** v/i. be* right od. true od. correct (a. Rechnung etc.); pol. vote (für for; gegen against); es stimmt et. nicht (damit od. mit ihm) there's s.th. wrong (with it od. him); **2.** v/t. mus. tune; fig. j-n traurig etc.: make*; **~enthaltung** f abstention; **~gabel** mus. f tuning fork; **~recht** n right to vote; **~ung** f mood; Atmosphäre: a. atmosphere; allgemeine: feeling; alle waren in ~ everybody was having fun; **2ungsvoll** adj. atmospheric; **~zettel** m ballot

stinken v/i. stink* (a. fig.) (nach of); F: das (er etc.) stinkt mir I'm sick of (od. fed up with) it (him etc.)

Stipendium n scholarship

stipp|en F v/t. dip; **2visite** F f flying visit

Stirn f forehead; die ~ runzeln frown; **~runzeln** n frown

stöbern F v/i. rummage (about)

stochern v/i.: im Feuer ~ poke the fire; im Essen ~ pick at one's food; in den Zähnen ~ pick one's teeth

Stock m stick; Rohr2: cane; ~werk2: stor(e)y, floor; im ersten ~ on the first floor, Am. on the second floor; **2dunkel** F adj. pitch dark

stocken v/i. stop (short); unsicher werden: falter; Verkehr: be* jammed; **~d 1.** adj. Stimme, Verkehr 2: halting; **2.** adv. ~ lesen stumble through a text; ~ sprechen speak* haltingly

stock|finster F adj. pitch dark; **2fleck** m mo(u)ld stain; **2ung** f holdup, delay (beide a. Verkehr); **2werk** n stor(e)y, floor

Stoff m material, stuff (a. sl. fig.); Gewebe: fabric, textile; Tuch: cloth; chem., phys. etc.: substance; fig. Thema, behandelter ~: subject (matter); **~ sammeln** collect material; **2lich** adj. material; **~tier** n soft toy animal; **~wechsel** physiol. m metabolism

stöhnen v/i. groan, moan (a. fig.)

Stollen m Bergbau: tunnel, gallery

stolpern v/i. stumble (über over), trip (over) (beide a. fig.)

stolz adj. proud (auf of)

Stolz m pride (auf in); **2ieren** v/i. strut, stalk

stopfen v/t. Socken, Loch: darn, mend; pressen, füllen: stuff, fill (a. Pfeife)

Stoppel f stubble; **~bart** F m stubbly beard; **2ig** adj. stubbly; **~zieher** östr. m corkscrew

stopp|en v/i. u. v/t. stop (a. fig.); mit der Uhr: time; **2licht** mot. n stop light; **2schild** n stop sign; **2uhr** f stopwatch

Stöpsel m stopper; Badewanne: plug

Storch m stork

stör|en v/t. u. v/i. disturb; bemühen: trouble; ärgern, belästigen: bother, annoy; im Weg sein: be* in the way; lassen Sie sich nicht ~! don't let me disturb you!; darf ich Sie kurz ~? may I trouble you for a minute?; es (er) stört mich nicht (he) doesn't bother me, I don't mind (him); stört es Sie (wenn ich rauche)? do you mind (my smoking od. if I smoke)?; **2enfried** m troublemaker; Eindringling: intruder; **2fall** m Kernkraftwerk: accident

störrisch adj. stubborn, obstinate

Störung f disturbance; trouble (a. tech.); Betriebs 2: breakdown; mot. holdup, delay; TV, Radio: interference

Stoß m push, shove; mit e-r Waffe: thrust; Fuß 2: kick; Kopf 2: butt; Schlag: blow, knock; Erschütterung: shock; e-s Wagens: jolt; Anprall: bump, bsd. tech., phys. impact; Stapel: pile, stack; **~dämpfer** mot. m shock absorber; **2en** v/t. u. v/i. push, shove; thrust*; kick; butt; knock, strike*; zer~: pound; ~ gegen od. an bump od. run* into od. against; sich den Kopf ~ (an) knock one's head (against); ~ auf fig. zufällig: come* across; Schwierigkeiten etc.: meet* with; Öl etc.: strike*; **2gesichert** adj. shockproof, shock-

-resistant; **~stange** mot. f bumper; **~zahn** m tusk; **~zeit** f rush hour, peak hours pl.

stottern v/i. u. v/t. stutter

Str. Abk. für **Straße** St, Street; Rd, Road

Straf|anstalt f Gefängnis etc.: prison, Am. a. penitentiary; **2bar** adj. punishable, penal; **sich ~ machen** commit an offen ce, Am. -se; **~e** f punishment; jur., econ., Sport, fig.: penalty; Geld2: fine; **20 Mark ~ zahlen müssen** be* fined 20 marks; **zur ~** as a punishment; **2en** v/t. punish

straff adj. tight; fig. strict

straf|frei adj.: **~ ausgehen** go* unpunished; **2gefangene(r)** prisoner, convict; **2gesetz** n criminal law

sträf|lich 1. adj. inexcusable; **2.** adv.: **~ vernachlässigen** neglect badly; **2ling** m convict

Straf|minute f Sport: penalty minute; **~prozeß** m criminal action, trial; **~raum** m Sport: penalty area od. F box; **~stoß** m penalty kick; **~tat** jur. f criminal offen ce, Am. -se; schwere: crime; **~zettel** m ticket

Strahl m ray (a. fig.); Licht2, Funk2 etc.: a. beam; Blitz2 etc.: flash; Wasser2 etc.: jet; **2en** v/i. radiate; Sonne: shine* (brightly); fig. beam (vor with); **~en...** phys. in Zssgn Schutz etc.: radiation ...; **~er** m spotlight; **~ung** f radiation

Strähne f strand; weiße etc.: streak

stramm adj. tight; **~stehen** mil. v/i. stand* to attention

strampeln v/i. kick; F fig. Rad: pedal

Strand m beach; **am ~** on the beach; **2en** v/i. naut. strand; fig. fail; **~gut** n flotsam and jetsam (a. fig.); **~korb** m roofed wicker beach chair

Strang m rope; bsd. anat. cord

Strapaze f strain, exertion, hardship; **2ieren** v/t. wear* s.o. od. s.th. out, be* hard on; **2ierfähig** adj. hardwearing, Am. longwearing; **2iös** adj. exhausting, strenuous

Straße f road; e-r Stadt etc.: street; Meerenge: strait; **auf der ~** on the road; in (Am. a. on) the street

Straßen|arbeiten pl. roadworks pl.; **~bahn** f tram, Am. streetcar; **~café** n pavement (Am. sidewalk) café; **~junge** m street urchin; **~kehrer** m street

sweeper; **~kreuzung** f crossroads sg.; intersection; **~lage** mot. f roadholding; **~rand** m roadside; **~reinigung** f street cleaning; **~sperre** f road block

strategisch adj. strategic

sträuben v/t. u. v/refl. Federn: ruffle (up); Haare: bristle (up); **sich ~ gegen** struggle against

Strauch m shrub, bush

straucheln v/i. stumble; fig. go* astray

Strauß m zo. ostrich; Blumen2: bunch, bouquet

Strebe f prop, stay (a. aviat., naut.)

streben v/i. strive* (nach for, after)

Streben n striving; **~ nach Glück** etc.: pursuit of happiness etc.; **~er(in)** pusher; Schule etc.: Brt. swot, Am. grind; **2sam** adj. ambitious

Strecke f distance (a. Sport, math.), way; Route: route; rail. line; Renn2: course; Abschnitt, Fläche: stretch; **zur ~ bringen** kill; bsd. fig. hunt down; **2n** v/t. stretch (out), extend; in der Schule, Finger, Hand: put* up

Streich fig. m trick, prank, practical joke; **j-m e-n ~ spielen** play a trick od. joke on s.o.; **auf e-n ~** F in one go

streicheln v/t. stroke, caress

streich|en v/t. u. v/i. an~: paint; schmieren: spread*; aus~: cross out; Auftrag etc.: cancel; naut. strike*; mus. bow; **mit der Hand ~ über** run* one's hand over; **~ durch** roam acc.; **2holz** n match; **2instrument** n string instrument; **die ~e** pl. the strings pl.; **2ung** f cancellation; Kürzung: cut; **2orchester** n string orchestra

Streife f patrol (a. Mannschaft); **auf ~ gehen** go* on patrol; Polizist: be* on one's beat

streifen v/t. u. v/i. berühren: touch, brush (against); Auto: scrape against; Kugel: graze; ab~: slip (vor off); Thema: touch on; **~ durch** roam acc., wander through

Streif|en m stripe; Papier2 etc.: strip; **~enwagen** m patrol (Am. squad) car; **~schuß** n graze; **~zug** m tour (durch of)

Streik m strike, walkout; **wilder ~** wildcat strike; **~brecher** m strikebreaker, F blackleg; **2en** v/i. (go* od. be* on) strike*; F fig. refuse (to work etc.); **~ende** m, f striker; **~posten** m picket

Streit m quarrel; Wort2: a. argument; Ehe2: a. fight; pol. etc.: dispute; ~ **anfangen** pick a fight od. quarrel; ~ **suchen** be* looking for trouble; 2en v/i. u. v/refl. quarrel, argue, fight* (alle: **wegen, über** about, over); **sich ~ um** fight* for; ~**frage** f (point at) issue; 2ig adj.: j-m et. ~ **machen** dispute s.o.'s right to s.th.; ~**kräfte** mil. pl. (armed) forces pl.; 2**süchtig** adj. quarrelsome

streng 1. adj. strict; Kälte, Kritik, Strafe etc.: severe; hart: harsh; unnachgiebig: rigid; **2.** adv. ~ **verboten (vertraulich)** strictly prohibited (confidential); 2e f strictness; severity; harshness; rigidity; ~**genommen** adv. strictly speaking; ~**gläubig** adj. orthodox

Streß m stress; **im ~** under stress

Streu f litter; 2en v/t. u. v/i. scatter (a. phys.); Sand etc.: a. spread*; Salz etc.: sprinkle; Gehweg etc.: grit

streunen v/i., ~**d** adj. stray

Strich m Linie: line; Pinsel2: stroke; F red-light district; F **auf den ~ gehen** walk the streets; ~**code** m bar code; ~**junge** F m male prostitute; ~**mädchen** F n streetwalker; 2**weise** adv. in parts; ~ **Regen** scattered showers

Strick m cord; dicker: rope (a. des Henkers); ~... m in Zssgn Nadel etc.: knitting ...; 2en v/t. u. v/i. knit*; ~**jacke** f cardigan; ~**leiter** f rope ladder; ~**waren** pl. knitwear sg.; ~**zeug** n knitting (things pl.)

Striemen m welt, weal

strittig adj. controversial; ~**er Punkt** point at issue

Stroh n straw; Dach2: thatch; ~**dach** n thatch(ed) roof; ~**halm** m straw; ~**hut** m straw hat; ~**witwe(r)** F grass widow(er)

Strom m (large) river; Strömung, electr.: current; **ein ~ von** a stream of (a. fig.); **es gießt in Strömen** it's pouring (with rain); 2**ab(wärts)** adv. downstream; 2**auf(wärts)** adv. upstream; ~**ausfall** electr. m power failure; allgemeiner: blackout

strömen v/i. stream (a. fig.), flow, run*; Regen: pour (a. fig. Menschen etc.)

Strom|kreis electr. m circuit; 2**linienförmig** adj. streamlined; ~**schnelle** f rapid; ~**stärke** electr. f amperage

Strömung f current; fig. a. trend

Strophe f stanza, verse

strotzen v/i.: ~ **von** be* full of, abound with; ~ **vor** be* bursting with

Strudel m whirlpool (a. fig.), eddy

Struktur f structure, pattern

Strumpf m stocking; ~**hose** f tights pl., bsd. Am. pantie hose

struppig adj. shaggy; Bart: bristly

Stück n piece; Teil: a. part; Zucker: lump; Vieh: head (a. pl.); thea. play; **2 Mark das ~** 2 marks each; **im od. am ~** Käse etc.: in one piece; **in ~e schlagen (reißen)** smash (tear*) to pieces; 2**weise** adv. bit by bit (a. fig.); econ. by the piece; ~**werk** fig. n patchwork

Student(in) student

Studie f study (über of); ~**nplatz** univ. m university od. college place; 2**ren** v/t. u. v/i. study, be* a student (of) (**an** at)

Studium n studies pl.; **das ~ der Medizin** etc. the study of medicine etc.

Stufe f step; Niveau: level; Stadium, Raketen2: stage; ~**nbarren** m uneven parallel bars pl.

Stuhl m chair; med. stool; ~**gang** med. m (bowel) movement; ~**lehne** f back of a chair

stülpen v/t. put* (**auf, über** over, on)

stumm adj. dumb, mute; fig. silent

Stummel m stub, stump, butt

Stummfilm m silent film

Stümper F m bungler

Stumpf m stump, stub

stumpf adj. blunt, dull (a. fig.); ~**sinnig** adj. dull; Arbeit: a. monotonous

Stunde f hour; Unterrichts2: class, lesson; erste etc.: period

Stunden|kilometer m kilomet|re (Am. -er) per hour; 2**lang 1.** adj.: **nach ~em Warten** after hours of waiting; **2.** adv. for hours (and hours); ~**lohn** m hourly wage; **im ~** by the hour; ~**plan** m timetable, Am. schedule; 2**weise** adv. by the hour; ~**zeiger** m hour hand

stündlich 1. adj. hourly; **2.** adv. hourly, every hour

Stupsnase F f snub nose

stur F adj. pigheaded

Sturm m storm (a. fig.)

stürm|en v/t. u. v/i. storm; Sport: attack; rennen: rush; 2**er** m Sport: forward; bsd. Fußball: striker; ~**isch** adj. stormy; fig. wild, vehement

Sturz m fall (a. fig.); e-r Regierung etc.: overthrow

stürzen 1. v/i. fall*; laut: crash; rennen: rush, dash; schwer ~ have* a bad fall; **2.** v/t. throw*; Regierung etc.: overthrow*; j-n ins Unglück ~ ruin s.o.; **sich stürzen aus (auf** etc.) throw* o.s. out of (at etc.)

Sturz|flug aviat. m nosedive; **~helm** m crash helmet

Stute f mare

Stütze f support, prop; fig. a. aid

stutzen 1. v/t. trim, clip (a. Flügel); **2.** v/i. stop short; (begin* to) wonder

stützen v/t. support (a. fig.); **sich ~ auf** lean* on; fig. be* based on

stutzig adj.: **j-n ~ machen** make* s.o. wonder (argwöhnisch: suspicious)

Stütz|pfeiler arch. m supporting column; **~punkt** mil. m base (a. fig.)

Styropor TM n polystyrene, Am. Styrofoam (TM)

s.u. Abk. für siehe unten see below

Subjekt n gr. subject; contp. character; **Ջiv** adj. subjective

Sub|stantiv gr. n noun; **~stanz** f substance (a. fig.); **Ջtrahieren** math. v/t. subtract; **Ջtraktion** math. f subtraction; **Ջventionieren** v/t. subsidize

Suche f search (nach for); **auf der ~ nach** in search of; **Ջn** v/t. u. v/i. allg. look for; stärker: search for; **gesucht**: ... wanted: ...; **was hat er hier zu ~?** what's he doing here?; **er hat hier nichts zu ~** he has no business to be here; **~r** m phot. viewfinder

Sucht f addiction (a. in Zssgn) (nach to); Besessenheit: mania (for)

süchtig adj.: ~ **sein** be* addicted to drugs etc., be* a drug etc. addict; **Ջe(r)** addict

Süden m south; **nach ~** south(wards); **~früchte** pl. tropical od. southern fruits pl.; **Ջlich 1.** adj. south(ern); Wind etc.: southerly; **2.** adv.: ~ **von** (to the) south of; **~osten** m southeast; **Ջöstlich** adj. southeast(ern); Wind: southeasterly; **~pol** m South Pole; **Ջwärts** adv. southward(s); **~westen** m southwest; **Ջwestlich** adj. southwest(ern); Wind: southwesterly; **~wind** m south wind

Sühne f atonement (für of); Strafe: punishment (for); **Ջn** v/t. atone for;

Tat etc.: a. pay* for

Sülze f jellied meat

Summe f sum (a. fig.); bsd. Geldჰ: a. amount; Gesamtჰ: (sum) total

summen v/i. u. v/t. buzz, hum (a. Lied etc.)

summieren v/refl. add up (auf to)

Sumpf m swamp, bog; **~...** in Zssgn Pflanze etc.: mst marsh ...; **Ջig** adj. swampy, marshy

Sünd|e f sin (a. fig.); **~enbock** F m scapegoat; **~er(in)** sinner; **Ջig** adj. sinful; **Ջigen** v/i. (commit a) sin

Super|... in Zssgn Macht etc.: mst super...; **~(benzin)** n Brt. four-star (petrol), Am. super od. premium (gasoline); **~lativ** gr. m superlative (a. fig.); **~markt** m supermarket

Suppe f soup; **~n...** in Zssgn Löffel, Tasse, Teller etc.: soup ...

Surf|brett n sail board; Wellenreiten: surfboard; **Ջen** v/i. go* surfing

surren v/i. whirr; Insekten: buzz

süß adj. sweet (a. fig.); **Ջe** f sweetness; **~en** v/t. sweeten; **Ջigkeiten** pl. sweets pl., bsd. Am. a. candy sg.; **~lich** adj. sweetish; fig. mawkish; **~sauer** adj. sweet-and-sour; **Ջstoff** m sweetener; **Ջwasser** n fresh water; in Zssgn: freshwater ...

Symbol n symbol; **~ik** f symbolism; **Ջisch** adj. symbolic(al)

Symmetri|e f symmetry; **Ջsch** adj. symmetric(al)

Sympathi|e f liking (für for); Mitgefühl: sympathy; **~sant** m sympathizer; **Ջsch** adj. nice, likable; △ nicht sympathetic; **er ist mir ~** I like him

Symphonie mus. f symphony; **~orchester** n symphony orchestra

Symptom n symptom

Synagoge f synagogue

synchron tech. adj. synchronous (a. in Zssgn); **~isieren** v/t. synchronize; Film etc.: dub

synonym adj. synonymous

Synonym n synonym

Synthe|se f synthesis; **~tik** tech. f synthetic(s pl.); **Ջtisch** adj. synthetic

System n system; **Ջatisch** adj. systematic, methodical; **~fehler** m Computer: system error

Szene f scene (a. fig.); (j-m) e-e ~ **machen** make* a scene; **~rie** f scenery; Schauplatz: setting

S

T

Tabak m tobacco; **~geschäft** n tobacconist's; **~waren** pl. tobacco products pl., F smokes pl.

Tabelle f table (a. math., Sport); **~nkalkulation** f Computer: spreadsheet; **~nplatz** m position

Tablett n tray

Tablette f tablet

Tabu n, ♀ adj. taboo

Tabulator m tabulator

Tachometer mot. m, n speedometer

Tadel m blame; förmlich: censure, reproof, rebuke; **♀los** adj. faultless; Leben etc.: blameless; ausgezeichnet: excellent; Sitz, Funktionieren etc.: perfect; **♀n** v/t. criticize, blame; förmlich: censure, reprove, rebuke (alle: **wegen** for)

Tafel f Schule etc.: blackboard; Anschlag♀ etc.: (bulletin, bsd. Brt. notice) board; Schild: sign; Gedenk♀ etc.: tablet, plaque; Schokoladen♀: bar; **die ~ putzen** wipe od. clean the board; **an die ~ schreiben** write* on the board; **~dienst** m: **~ haben** be* in charge of the board; **~lappen** m duster

täfel|n v/t. panel; **♀ung** f panel(l)ing

Taft m taffeta

Tag m day; ~eslicht: daylight; **welchen ~ haben wir heute?** what day is it today?; **alle zwei (paar) ~e** every other day (few days); **heute (morgen) in 14 ~en** two weeks from today (tomorrow); **e-s ~es** one day; **den ganzen ~** all day; **am ~e** during the day; **~ und Nacht** night and day; **am hellichten ~** in broad daylight; **ein freier ~** a day off; **guten ~!** hello!, hi!; beim Vorstellen: how do you do?; (j-m) **guten ~ sagen** say* hello (to s.o.); F **sie hat ihre ~e** she has her period; **unter ~e** Bergbau: underground

Tage|bau Bergbau: m opencast mining; **~buch** n diary; **~führen** keep* a diary; **♀lang** adv. for days

tagen v/i. meet*, hold* a meeting; jur. be* in session

Tages|anbruch m: **bei ~** at daybreak od. dawn; **~gespräch** n talk of the day; **~karte** f day ticket; gastr. menu

for the day; **~licht** n daylight; **~mutter** f childminder; **~ordnung** f agenda; **~presse** f daily press; **~rückfahrkarte** f day return (ticket); **~stätte** f day care cent|re, Am. -er; **~tour** f day trip; **~zeit** f time of day; **zu jeder ~** at any hour; **~zeitung** f daily (paper)

tageweise adv. by the day

täglich adj. u. adv. daily

Tagschicht f day shift

tagsüber adv. during the day

Tagung f conference

Taill|e f waist; am Kleid: a. waistline; **♀iert** adj. waisted, Hemd a.: tapered

Takelage naut. f rigging

Takt m mus. time, measure, beat; ein ~: bar; mot. stroke; Feingefühl: tact; **den ~ halten** keep* time; **den ~ schlagen** beat* time; **~ik** f mil. tactics sg., pl. (a. fig.); **♀isch** adj. tactical; **♀los** adj. tactless; **~stock** m baton; **~strich** m bar; **♀voll** adj. tactful

Tal n valley

Talar m robe, gown

Talent n talent (a. Person), gift; **♀iert** adj. talented, gifted

Talg m suet; ausgelassener: tallow

Talisman m talisman, charm

Talk|master m chat-show (bsd. Am. talk-show) host; **~-Show** f chat (Am. talk) show

Talsperre f dam, barrage

Tampon m tampon

Tandler östr. m second-hand dealer

Tang bot. m seaweed

Tank m tank; **♀en** v/t. get* some petrol (Am. gasoline), fill up; **~er** naut. m tanker; **~stelle** f filling (od. petrol, Am. gas) station; **~wart** m petrol pump (Am. gas station) attendant

Tanne f fir (tree); **~nbaum** m Christmas tree; **~nzapfen** m fir cone

Tante f aunt; **~ Lindy** Aunt Lindy; **~-Emma-Laden** F m corner shop, Am. mom-and-pop store

Tantiemen f. royalties pl.

Tanz m, **♀en** v/i. u. v/t. dance

Tänzer(in) dancer

Tanz|fläche f dance floor; **~kurs** m dancing lessons pl.; **~musik** f dance music; **~schule** f dancing school

Tape|te f, **2zieren** v/t. wallpaper

tapfer adj. brave; mutig: courageous; **2keit** f bravery; courage

Tarif m rate(s pl.), tariff; Lohn2: (wage) scale; **~lohn** m standard wage(s pl.); **~verhandlungen** pl. wage negotiations pl., collective bargaining sg.

tarn|en v/t. camouflage; fig. disguise; **2ung** f camouflage

Tasche f bag; Hosen2 etc.: pocket

Taschen|buch n paperback; **~dieb** m pickpocket; **~geld** n pocket money, Am. allowance; **~lampe** f torch, Am. mst flashlight; **~messer** n penknife, großes: jack knife; **~rechner** m pocket calculator; **~schirm** m telescopic umbrella; **~tuch** n handkerchief, F hankie; **~uhr** f pocket watch

Tasse f cup (Tee etc. of tea etc.)

Tastatur f keyboard, keys pl.

Tast|e f key; **2en 1.** v/i. grope (nach for), feel* (for); ungeschickt: fumble (for); **2.** v/t. touch, feel*; sich ~ feel* od. grope (a. fig.) one's way; **~telefon** n push-button phone; **~sinn** m sense of touch

Tat f act, deed (a. Groß2); Handeln: action; Straf2: offen|ce, Am. -se; j-n auf frischer ~ ertappen catch* s.o. in the act; **2enlos** adj. inactive, passive

Täter(in) culprit; jur. offender

tätig adj. active; geschäftig: busy; ~ sein bei m employed with; ~ werden act, take* action; **2keit** f activity; Arbeit: work; Beruf, Beschäftigung: occupation, job; in ~ in action

Tat|kraft f energy; **2kräftig** adj. energetic, active

tätlich adj. violent; ~ werden gegen assault, **2keiten** pl. (acts pl. of) violence; jur. assault (and battery)

Tatort jur. m scene of the crime

tätowier|en v/t., **2ung** f tattoo

Tat|sache f fact; **2sächlich 1.** adj. actual, real; **2.** adv. actually, in fact; wirklich: really

tätscheln v/t. pat, pet

Tatze f paw (a. fig.)

Tau¹ n rope

Tau² m dew

taub adj. deaf (fig.: gegen to) (a. Nuß); Finger etc.: (be)numb(ed)

Taube zo. f pigeon; bsd. poet., fig., pol. dove; **~nschlag** m pigeonhouse

Taub|heit f deafness; numbness; **2stumm** adj. deaf and dumb; **~stumme(r)** deaf mute

tauch|en 1. v/i. dive* (nach for); Sport: skin-dive; U-Boot: a. submerge; unter Wasser bleiben: stay underwater; **2.** v/t. ein~: dip (in into); j-n: duck; **2er(in)** (Sport: skin) diver; **2sport** m skin diving

tauen v/i. u. v/t. thaw, melt*

Taufe f baptism, christening; **2n** v/t. baptize, christen

Tauf|pate m godfather; **~patin** f godmother; **~schein** m certificate of baptism

taug|en v/i. be* good od. fit od. of use od. suited (alle: zu, für for); nichts ~ be* no good; F taugt es was? is it any good?; **2enichts** m good-for-nothing; **~lich** bsd. mil. adj. fit (for service)

Taumel m Schwindel: dizziness; Verzückung: rapture, ecstasy; **2ig** adj. dizzy; **2n** v/i. stagger, reel

Tausch m exchange, F swap; **2en** v/t. exchange, F swap (beide: gegen for); Rollen, Plätze etc.: a. switch; wechseln: change (a. Geld); ich möchte nicht mit ihm ~ I wouldn't like to be in his shoes

täuschen v/t. deceive, fool; delude; betrügen: cheat; Sport etc.: feint; sich ~ deceive o.s.; sich irren: be* mistaken; sich ~ lassen von be* taken in by; **~d** adj. Ähnlichkeit: striking

Täuschung f deception; jur. deceit; Schule etc.: cheating; Selbst2: delusion

tausend adj. a thousand; **~st** adj. thousandth; **2stel** n thousandth (part)

Tau|tropfen m dewdrop; **~wetter** n thaw; **~ziehen** n tug-of-war (a. fig.)

Taxi n taxi(cab), cab

taxieren v/t. rate, estimate (auf at)

Taxistand m taxi rank, bsd. Am. cabstand

Technik f technology; angewandte: a. engineering; Verfahren: technique (a. Sport, Kunst); mus. execution; **~er(in)** engineer; technician (a. Sport, Kunst)

technisch adj. technical (a. Gründe, Daten, Zeichnen etc.); ~wissenschaftlich: technological (a. Fortschritt, Zeitalter etc.); **~e Hochschule** school etc. of technology

T

Technolog|ie f technology; **~isch** adj. technological

Tee m tea; **(e-n) ~ trinken** have* some tea; **(e-n) ~ machen od. kochen** make* some tea; **~beutel** m teabag; **~kanne** f teapot; **~löffel** m teaspoon

Teer m, **~en** v/t. tar

Tee|sieb n tea strainer; **~tasse** f teacup

Teich m pool, pond

Teig m dough, paste; **~ig** adj. doughy, pasty; **~waren** pl. pasta sg.

Teil m, n part; **An~**: portion, share; **Bestand~**: component; **zum ~** partly, in part; **~...** in Zssgn Erfolg etc.: partial ...; **~bar** adj. divisible; **~chen** n particle; **~en** v/t. divide; **mit anderen, sich ~**: share; **~haben** v/i.: **~ an** (have* a) share in; **~haber** econ. m partner; **~nahme** f participation (**an** in); fig. interest (in); **An~**: sympathy (for); **~nahmslos** adj. indifferent; bsd. med. apathetic; **~nahmslosigkeit** f indifference; apathy; **~nehmen** v/i.: **~ an** take* part od. participate in; Freude etc.: share (in); **~nehmer(in)** participant; univ. student; Sport: competitor; **~s** adv. partly; **~strecke** f Reise, Rennen: stage, leg; **~ung** f division; **~weise** adv. partly, in part; **~zahlung** f → **Abzahlung, Rate**

Teint m complexion

Tel. Abk. für **Telefon** tel., telephone

Telefon n telephone, F phone; **am ~** on the (tele)phone; **~ haben** be* on the (Am. have* a) (tele)phone; **ans ~ gehen** answer the (tele)phone; **~anruf** m (tele)phone call; **~anschluß** m telephone connection; **~apparat** m (tele)phone; **~at** n → **~gespräch**; **~buch** n telephone directory, phone book; **~gebühr** f telephone charge; **~gespräch** n (tele)phone call; **~ieren** v/i. (tele)phone; gerade: be* on the phone; **mit j-m ~** talk to s.o. on the phone; **~isch 1.** adj. telephonic, telephone; **2.** adv. by (tele)phone, over the (tele)phone; **~ist(in)** (telephone) operator; **~karte** f phonecard; **~leitung** f telephone line; **~netz** n telephone network; **~nummer** f (tele)phone number; **~zelle** f bsd. Brt. (tele)phone box, Brt. call box, Am. (tele)phone booth; **~zentrale** f im Betrieb: switchboard

telegraf|ieren v/t. u. v/i. telegraph, wire; Übersee: cable; **~isch** adj. u. adv. by telegraph od. wire; by cable

Telegramm n telegram, bsd. Am. a. wire; Übersee: cable(gram)

Teleobjektiv phot. n telephoto lens

Tele|phon n → **Telefon**; **~text** m teletext

Teller m plate; **~voll** m plateful; **~wäscher** m dishwasher

Tempel m temple

Temperament n temper(ament); Schwung: life, F pep; **~los** adj. lifeless, dull; **~voll** adj. full of life od. F pep

Temperatur f temperature; **j-s ~ messen** take* s.o.'s temperature

Tempo n speed; mus. time; **mit ~ ...** at a speed of ... an hour; **in rasendem ~** at breakneck speed

Tendenz f tendency, trend; Neigung: a. leaning; **~iös** adj. tendentious

tendieren v/i. tend (**zu** towards; **dazu, et. zu tun** to do s.th.)

Tennis n tennis; **~platz** m tennis court; **~schläger** m tennis racket; **~spieler(in)** tennis player

Tenor mus. m tenor

Teppich m carpet; **~boden** m fitted carpet, wall-to-wall carpeting

Termin m date; letzter: deadline; Geschäfts~ etc.: engagement; **e-n ~ vereinbaren (einhalten, absagen)** make* (keep*, cancel) an appointment

Terminal aviat. m, Computer: n terminal

Terrasse f terrace; **~nförmig** adj. terraced, in terraces

Terrine f tureen

Territorium n territory

Terror m terror; **~isieren** v/t. terrorize; **~ismus** m terrorism; **~ist(in)**, **~istisch** adj. terrorist

Testament n (last) will; jur. last will and testament; **~arisch** adv. by will; **~svollstrecker** m executor

Test|bild n TV: test card; **~en** v/t. test; **~pilot** m test pilot

Tetanus med. m tetanus

teuer adj. expensive; bsd. Brt. a. dear; **wie ~ ist es?** how much is it?

Teufel m devil (a. fig.); **wer (wo, was) zum ~ ...?** who (where, what) the hell ...?; **~skerl** F m devil of a fellow; **~skreis** m vicious circle

teuflisch adj. devilish, diabolic(al)

Text m text; unter Bild: caption; Lied♀: words pl., lyrics pl.; **~aufgabe** f comprehension test; math. problem; **~er(in)** mus. songwriter

Textil|... in Zssgn textile ...; **~ien** pl. textiles pl.

Textverarbeitung f Computer: word processing; **~sgerät** n word processor

Theater n theat|re, Am. -er; F fig. ~ **machen (um)** make* a fuss (about); **~besucher** m theatregoer; **~karte** f theatre ticket; **~kasse** f box office; **~stück** n play

Thema n subject, topic; bsd. Leitgedanke, mus.: theme; **das ~ wechseln** change the subject

Theolog|e m theologian; **~ie** f theology; **♀isch** adj. theological

Theo|retiker m theorist; **♀retisch** adj. theoretical; **~rie** f theory

Thera|peut m therapist; **~pie** f therapy

Thermometer n thermometer

Thermosflasche TM f thermos flask (Am. bottle) (TM)

These f thesis

Thon m Schweiz: tuna (fish)

Thrombose med. f thrombosis

Thron m throne; **~folger(in)** successor to the throne

Thunfisch m tuna (fish)

Tick F m quirk; **♀en** v/i. tick

Tie-Break m, n Tennis: tiebreak(er)

tief 1. adj. deep (a. fig.); niedrig: low (a. Ausschnitt); **2.** adv.: **~ schlafen** be* fast asleep

Tief n meteor. depression (a. psych.), low (a. econ.); **~e** f depth (a. fig.); **~ebene** f lowland(s pl.); **~flug** m low-level flight; **~gang** m naut. draught, Am. draft; fig. depth; **~garage** f underground car park, Am. parking od. underground garage; **~gekühlt** adj. deep-frozen; **~kühlfach** n freezing compartment; **~kühlschrank** m, **♀kühltruhe** f freezer, deep-freeze; **~kühlkost** f frozen foods pl.

Tier n animal; F hohes ~ bigwig, big shot; **~arzt** m Brt. vet(erinary surgeon), Am. vet(erinarian); **~freund** m animal lover; **~garten** m → Zoo; **~heim** n animal home; **♀isch** adj. animal; fig. bestial, brutish; **~kreis** astr. m zodiac; **~kreiszeichen** n sign of the zodiac; **~medizin** f veterinary medicine; **~quälerei** f cruelty to animals; **~reich** n animal kingdom; **~schutz** m protection of animals; **~schutzverein** m society for the prevention of cruelty to animals; **~versuch** med. m experiment with animals

Tiger m tiger; **~in** zo. f tigress

tilgen v/t. econ. pay* off*; fig. wipe out

Tinte f ink; **~nfisch** m squid; **~nfleck** m ink stain; **~nkiller** m ink killer

Tip m hint, bsd. Wett♀: tip; vertraulich: a. tip-off; **j-m e-n ~ geben** vertraulich: tip s.o. off; **♀pen** v/i. u. v/t. berühren: tap; schreiben: type; raten: guess; im Lotto etc.: do* Lotto etc.

Tisch m table; **am ~ sitzen** sit* at the table; **bei ~** at table; **den ~ decken (abräumen)** lay* (clear) the table; **~decke** f tablecloth; **~gebet** n: **das ~ sprechen** say* grace

Tischler m joiner; Kunst♀: cabinet-maker

Tisch|platte f tabletop; **~rechner** m desktop computer; **~tennis** n table tennis; **~tuch** n tablecloth

Titel m title; **~bild** n cover picture; **~blatt** n, **~seite** f Buch: title page; Zeitung: cover, front page

Toast m, **~en** v/t. toast

tob|en v/i. rasen: rage (a. fig.); Kinder: romp; **~süchtig** adj. raving mad; **♀suchtsanfall** m tantrum

Tochter f daughter; **~gesellschaft** econ. f subsidiary (company)

Tod m death (a. fig.) (durch from); **♀...** in Zssgn ernst, müde, sicher: dead ...

Todes|ängste fig. pl.: **~ ausstehen** be* scared to death; **~anzeige** f obituary (notice); **~fall** m (case of) death; **~kampf** m agony; **~opfer** n casualty; **~strafe** jur. f capital punishment; death penalty; **~ursache** f cause of death; **~urteil** jur. n death sentence

Tod|feind m deadly enemy; **♀krank** adj. mortally ill

tödlich adj. fatal; bsd. todbringend: deadly; bsd. fig. mortal

Todsünde f mortal od. deadly sin

Toilette f toilet, lavatory, Am. bathroom; **~n** pl. ladies' od. men's rooms, Am. rest rooms pl.; **~n...** in Zssgn Papier, Seife etc.: toilet ...

toler|ant adj. tolerant (gegen of, to-

wards); **2anz** f tolerance (a. tech.);
~ieren v/t. tolerate

toll adj. wild: wild; F großartig: great,
fantastic; ein **~er Kerl (Wagen** etc.) a
hell of a fellow (good car etc.); **~kühn**
adj. daredevil; **2wut** vet. f rabies; **~wü-
tig** vet. adj. rabid

Tolpatsch F m clumsy oaf; **2ig** F adj.
clumsy, oafish

Tomate f tomato

Ton¹ m clay

Ton² m tone (a. mus., paint., fig., Stimme);
Klang, Geräusch: sound (a. TV, Film);
Note: note; Betonung: stress; Farb2: a.
shade; **der gute ~** good form; **kein ~**
not a word; **~abnehmer** electr. m pick-
up; **~art** mus. f key; **~band** n (recording) tape; **~bandgerät** n tape recorder

tönen 1. v/i. sound, ring*; **2.** v/t. tinge,
tint (a. Haar); dunkel: shade

Ton|fall m tone (of voice); Akzent: ac-
cent; **~film** m sound film; **~kopf** electr.
m (magnetic) head; **~lage** f pitch;
~leiter mus. f scale

Tonne f Faß: barrel; Gewichtseinheit:
(metric) ton

Tontechniker m sound engineer

Tönung f tint (a. Haar), tinge, shade

Topf m pot; Koch2: a. saucepan

Topfen östr. m curd(s pl.)

Töpfer m potter; **~ei** f pottery; **~schei-
be** f potter's wheel; **~ware** f pottery,
earthenware, crockery

Tor n gate (a. Ski); Fußball etc.: goal; ein
~ **schießen** score (a goal); **im ~ stehen**
keep* goal

Torf m peat; **~mull** m peat dust

Torhüter m → **Torwart**

torkeln v/i. reel, stagger

Tor|latte f Sport: crossbar; **~linie** f goal
line

torpedieren v/t. torpedo (a. fig.)

Tor|pfosten m goalpost; **~raum** m
goalmouth; **~schuß** m shot at goal;
~schütze m scorer

Torte f Obst2: flan, bsd. Am. pie; Sahne2
etc.: cream cake, gateau

Torwart m goalkeeper, F goalie

tosen v/i. roar; stärker: thunder; **~d** adj.
Applaus: thunderous

tot adj. dead (a. fig.); verstorben: late; ~
umfallen drop dead

total adj. total, complete; **~itär** pol. adj.
totalitarian

totarbeiten F v/refl. work o.s. to death

Tote m, f dead man od. woman; Leiche:
(dead) body, corpse; Todesopfer mst
pl.: casualty; **die ~n** pl. the dead pl.

töten v/t. kill

Toten|bett n deathbed; **2blaß** adj.
deadly pale; **~gräber** m grave digger;
~kopf m skull; Symbol: skull and
crossbones; **~maske** f death mask;
~messe rel. f mass for the dead, requi-
em (a. mus.); **~schädel** m skull;
~schein m death certificate; **2still** adj.
deathly still; **~stille** f dead(ly) silence

Tot|geburt f stillbirth; **2lachen** F
v/refl. kill o.s. laughing

Toto m, F n football pools pl.

tot|schießen v/t. shoot* dead, shoot*
and kill; **2schlag** jur. m manslaughter;
~schlagen v/t. kill (fig. **die Zeit** time),
beat* to death; **~schweigen** v/t. hush
up; **~stellen** v/refl. play dead

Toup|et n toupee; **2ieren** v/t. back-
comb

Tour f tour (**durch** of), trip; Ausflug: a.
excursion; tech. turn, revolution; **auf
~en kommen** mot. pick up speed;
krumme ~en underhand methods;
~en... in Zssgn Rad etc.: touring ...

Tourismus m tourism; **~geschäft** n
tourist industry

Touris|t(in) tourist; **2tisch** adj. tour-
istic

Tournee f tour; **auf ~ gehen** go* on
tour

Trab m trot; **auf ~** fig. on the move

Trabant m satellite; **~enstadt** satellite
town

trab|en v/i. trot; **2er** m Pferd: trotter;
2rennen n trotting race

Tracht f costume; Schwestern2 etc.: uniform; Amts2: dress; **e-e gehörige ~
Prügel** a good hiding

trächtig adj. with young, pregnant

Tradition f tradition; **2ell** adj. tradi-
tional

Trafik östr. f → **Tabakgeschäft**; **~ant**
östr. m tobacconist

Trag|bahre f stretcher; **2bar** adj. por-
table; Kleidung: wearable; fig. bearable; Person: acceptable; **~e** f stretcher

träge adj. lazy, indolent; phys. inert

tragen 1. v/t. carry (a. Waffe etc.); Kleidung, Schmuck, Brille, Haar etc.:
wear*; er~, a. Früchte, Folgen, Verant-

wortung, Namen etc.: bear*; **sich gut ~** Stoff etc.: wear* well; **2.** v/i. bear* fruit; **tragfähig sein**: hold*; **~d** adj. arch. supporting; thea. leading

Träger m carrier; Gepäck2: porter; am Kleid: (shoulder) strap; tech. support; arch. girder; fig. eines Namens etc.: bearer; **2los** adj. Kleid etc.: strapless

Tragetasche f carrier bag; für Babys: carrycot

Trag|fähigkeit f load(-carrying) capacity; naut. tonnage; **~fläche** aviat. f wing

Trägheit f laziness, indolence; phys. inertia

Trag|ik f tragedy; **2isch** adj. tragic; **~ödie** thea. f tragedy (a. fig.)

Trag|riemen m strap; am Gewehr: sling; **~weite** f range; fig. significance

Train|er m trainer, coach; **2ieren** v/i. u. v/t. allg. train; j-n, e-e Mannschaft: a. coach; **~ing** n training; **~ingsanzug** m track suit

Traktor tech. m tractor

trällern v/t. u. v/i. warble, trill

Tram östr. f, Schweiz m tram, Am. streetcar

trampel|n v/i. trample, stamp; **2pfad** m beaten track

trampel|n v/i. hitchhike; **2er(in)** hitchhiker

Träne f tear; **in ~n ausbrechen** burst* into tears; **2n** v/i. water; **~ngas** n tear gas

Tränke f watering place; **2n** v/t. water; Material: soak, drench

Trans|fer m transfer (a. Sport); **~formator** electr. m transformer; **~fusion** med. f transfusion

Transistor electr. m transistor (a. in Zssgn)

Transit m transit (a. in Zssgn); **2iv** gr. adj. transitive

transparent adj. transparent

Transparent n banner

Transplant|ation med. f, **2ieren** med. v/t. transplant

Transport m transport (a. in Zssgn); bsd. Sendung: a. shipment; **2abel, 2fähig** adj. transportable; **2ieren** v/t. transport, ship, carry; bsd. mit LKW: a. haul; **~mittel** n (means sg. of) transport(ation); **~unternehmen** n haulier, Am. hauler

Trapez n math. trapezium, Am. trapezoid; Turnen: trapeze

trappeln v/i. clatter; Kind: patter

Traube f bunch of grapes; Beere: grape; fig. cluster; **~n** pl. grapes pl.; **~nsaft** m grape juice; **~nzucker** m glucose, dextrose (a. ~drops)

trauen 1. v/t. marry; **sich ~ lassen** get* married; **2.** v/i. trust (j-m s.o.); **sich ~, et. zu tun** dare (to) do s.th.; **ich traute meinen Ohren (Augen) nicht** I couldn't believe my ears (eyes)

Trauer f grief, sorrow; um j-n: mourning; **in ~** in mourning (a. Kleidung); **~fall** m death; **~feier** f funeral ceremonies pl.; kirchliche: funeral service; **~marsch** m funeral march; **2n** v/i. mourn (um for); **~zug** m funeral procession

träufeln v/t. drip, trickle

Traum m dream (a. fig.); **~...** in Zssgn Beruf, Mann etc.: dream ..., ... of one's dreams; **~deutung** f interpretation of dreams

träum|en v/i. u. v/t. dream* (a. fig.) (von about, of); **schlecht ~** have* bad dreams; **2er** m dreamer (a. fig.); **2erei** fig. f (day)dream(s pl.), reverie (a. mus.); **~erisch** adj. dreamy

traurig adj. sad (über, wegen about); **2keit** f sadness

Trau|ring m wedding ring; **~schein** m marriage certificate; **~ung** f marriage, wedding; **~zeuge** m, **~zeugin** f witness to a marriage

Trecker tech. m tractor

Treff F m meeting place

treffen v/t. u. v/i. hit* (a. fig.); kränken: hurt*; begegnen: meet* (a. Sport); Maßnahmen etc.: take*; nicht ~ miss; **sich ~ (mit j-m)** meet* (s.o.); **gut ~** phot. etc.: capture well

Treffen n meeting; **2d 1.** adj. Bemerkung etc.: apt; **2.** adv.: **~ gesagt** well put

Treff|er m hit (a. fig.); Tor: goal; Gewinn: win; **~punkt** m meeting place

Treibeis n drift ice

treiben 1. v/t. drive* (a. tech. u. fig.); Sport etc.: do*; j-n an~: push, press; Blüten etc.: put* forth; F allg. machen, tun: do*, be* up to; F es (mit j-m) ~ have* sex (with s.o.), make* love (to s.o.); **2.** v/i. drift (a. fig.), float; bot.

shoot* (up); **sich ~ lassen** drift along (*a. fig.*)

Treiben *n* Tun: doings *pl.*; *Vorgänge*: goings-on *pl.*; **geschäftiges ~** bustle; **2d** *adj.*: **~e Kraft** driving force

Treib|haus *n* hothouse; **~hauseffekt** *m* greenhouse effect; **~holz** *n* driftwood; **~jagd** *f* battue; *fig.* hunt; **~riemen** *m* driving belt; **~sand** *m* quicksand; **~stoff** *m* fuel

trenn|en *v/t.* separate; **ab~**: sever; *Kämpfer etc.*: part; *Länder, Gruppen, Wort*: divide; *Rassen*: segregate; *tel.* disconnect; **sich ~** separate (**von** from), auseinandergehen: part (*a. fig.*); **sich ~ von** et.: part with; *j-m*: leave*; **2schärfe** *f* Radio: selectivity; **2ung** *f* separation; *Aufteilung*: division; *Rassen2*: segregation; **2wand** *f* partition.

Treppe *f* staircase, stairs *pl.*

Treppen|absatz *m* landing; **~geländer** *n* banisters *pl.*; **~haus** *n* staircase; *Flur*: hall

Tresor *m* safe; *Bank2*: strongroom, vault

treten *v/i. u. v/t.* kick; *gehen*: step (**aus** out of; **in** into; **auf** on[to]); *radfahren*: pedal (away); **~ auf** step on (*a. Gas, Bremse*); tread on; **~ in** enter (*a. fig.*)

treu *adj.* faithful (*a. fig.*); *Anhänger, Diener etc.*: *a.* loyal; *ergeben*: devoted; **2e** *f* fidelity, faithfulness, loyalty; **2händer** *m* trustee; **2handgesellschaft** *f* trust company; **~herzig** *adj.* innocent, trusting; **~los** *adj.* faithless, disloyal, unfaithful (*alle*: **gegen** to)

Tribüne *f* Redner2: platform; *Zuschauer2*: stand

Trichter *m* funnel; *Erd2*: crater

Trick *m* trick (*a. in Zssgn*); **~aufnahme** *f* trick shot; **~betrüger** *m* confidence trickster

Trieb *m* bot. (young) shoot, sprout; *An2*: impulse, drive; *Geschlechts2*: sex drive; **~feder** *f* mainspring (*a. fig.*); **~kraft** *f* driving force; **~wagen** *m* railcar; **~werk** *m* railcar; **~werk** *tech.* *n* engine

triefen *v/i.* drip, be* dripping (**von** with)

triftig *adj.* weighty; *Grund*: *a.* good

Trikot *n* Sport: shirt, jersey; *Tanz2 etc.*: leotard

Triller *mus.* *m* trill; **2n** *mus. v/i. u. v/t.* trill*; *Vogel*: warble

trimm|en *v/refl.* keep* fit; **2pfad** *m* fitness trail

trink|bar *adj.* drinkable; **~en** *v/t. u. v/i.* drink* (**auf** to); *Tee etc.*: *a.* have*; *et. zu ~* a drink; **2er(in** drinker, alcoholic; **2geld** *n* tip; *j-m* (**e-e Mark**) *~* **geben** tip s.o. (one mark); **2spruch** *m* toast; **2wasser** *n* drinking water

Trio *n* trio

trippeln *v/i.* mince

Tripper *med. m* gonorrh(o)ea

Tritt *m* Fuß2: kick; *Schritt*: step; **~brett** *n* step; *mot.* running board; **~leiter** *f* stepladder

Triumph *m* triumph; **2al** *adj.* triumphant; **2ieren** *v/i.* triumph (**über** over)

trocken *adj.* dry (*a. fig.*); **2...** *in Zssgn*: getrocknet: dried ...; *zum Trocknen*: drying ...; **2haube** *f* hairdryer; **2heit** *f* dryness; *Dürre*: drought; **2legen** *v/t.* drain; *Baby*: change

trockn|en *v/t. u. v/i.* dry; **2er** *m* dryer

Troddel *f* tassel

Tröd|el *m* junk; **2eln** *v/i.* dawdle; **~ler** *m* junk dealer; dawdler

Trog *m* trough

Trommel *f* drum (*a. tech.*); **~fell** *anat.* *n* eardrum; **2n** *v/i. u. v/t.* drum; *fig.* *a.* bang

Trommler *m* drummer

Trompete *f* trumpet; **2n** *v/i. u. v/t.* trumpet (*a. zo.*); **~r** *m* trumpeter

Tropen: **die ~** *pl.* the tropics *pl.*; **~...** *in Zssgn* tropical ...

Tropf *med. m*: **am ~ hängen** be* on a drip

Tröpf|chen *n* droplet; **2eln** *v/i. u. v/t.* drip; **es tröpfelt** it's spitting

tropfen *v/i. u. v/t.* drip (*a. Hahn*), drop

Tropfen *m* drop (*a. fig.*); **ein ~ auf den heißen Stein** a drop in the bucket; **2weise** *adv.* in drops, drop by drop

Trophäe *f* trophy (*a. fig.*)

tropisch *adj.* tropical

Trosse *f* cable; *naut.* *a.* hawser

Trost *m* comfort, consolation; **ein schwacher ~** cold comfort; **du bist wohl nicht (recht) bei ~!** F you must be out of your mind!

tröst|en *v/t.* comfort, console; **sich ~** console o.s. (**mit** with); **~lich** *adj.* comforting

trost|los *adj.* miserable; *Gegend etc.*: desolate; **2losigkeit** *f* misery; desolation; **2preis** *m* consolation prize; **~reich** *adj.* consoling; *Worte etc.*: *a.* of comfort

Trott *m* trot; F: *der alte* ~ the old routine
Trottel F *m* dope **⚥ig** *adj.* F dopey
Trottinett *n Schweiz*: scooter
Trottoir *n Schweiz*: pavement, *Am.* sidewalk
trotten *v/i.* trot
Trotz *m* defiance; *aus reinem* ~ out of sheer spite; *j-m zum* ~ to spite s.o.
trotz *prp.* in spite of, despite; **~dem** *adv.* in spite of it, nevertheless, F anyhow, anyway; **~en** *v/i.* defy; *schmollen*: sulk; **~ig** *adj.* defiant; sulky
trüb(e) *adj.* cloudy; *Wasser*: *a.* muddy; *Licht etc.*: dim; *Himmel, Farben*: dull; *Stimmung, Tag etc.*: *a.* gloomy
Trubel *m* (hustle and) bustle
trüben *v/t. Glück, Freude etc.*: spoil*, mar
Trüb|sal *f*: ~ *blasen* mope; **⚥selig** *adj.* sad, gloomy; *Tag etc.*: *a.* dreary; **~sinn** *m* melancholy, gloom, low spirits *pl.*; **⚥sinnig** *adj.* melancholy, gloomy
Trugbild *n* illusion, hallucination
trüg|en 1. *v/t.* deceive; **2.** *v/i.* be* deceptive; **~erisch** *adj.* deceptive
Trugschluß *m* fallacy
Truhe *f* chest
Trümmer *pl.* ruins *pl.*; *Schutt*: debris *sg.*; *Stücke*: pieces *pl.*, bits *pl.*
Trumpf *m* trump (card) (*a. fig.*); ~ *sein* be* trumps *pl.*; *fig.* ~ *s-n* ~ *ausspielen* play one's trump card
Trunk|enheit *bsd. jur. f*: ~ *am Steuer* drink (*Am.* drunk) driving; **~sucht** *f* alcoholism; **⚥süchtig** *adj.* alcoholic
Trupp *m* band, party; *weitS.* group
Truppe *f mil.* troop; *thea.* company, troupe; **~n** *pl. mil.* troops *pl.*, forces *pl.*; **~ngattung** *mil. f* branch (of service); **~nübungsplatz** *mil. m* training area
Truthahn *m* turkey
Tschech|e *m* Czech; **~ien** Czech Republic; **~in** *f* Czech; **⚥isch** *adj.* Czech; **⚥e Republik** *f* Czech Republic
Tube *f* tube
Tuberkulose *med. f* tuberculosis
Tuch *n* cloth; *Hals⚥, Kopf⚥*: scarf; *Staub⚥*: duster; **~fühlung** *fig. f*: *in* ~ in close contact
tüchtig *adj.* (cap)able, competent; *geschickt*: skil(l)ful; *leistungsfähig*: efficient; F *fig. ordentlich*: good; **⚥keit** *f* (cap)ability, qualities *pl.*; skill; efficiency
tückisch *adj.* malicious; *Krankheit etc.*:

insidious; *gefährlich*: treacherous
tüfteln F *v/i.* puzzle (**an** over)
Tugend *f* virtue (*a. fig.*)
Tulpe *f* tulip
tummeln *v/refl.* romp; *fig.* hurry
Tumor *med. m* tumo(u)r
Tümpel *m* pool
Tumult *m* tumult, uproar
tun *v/t. u. v/i.* do*; *Schritt*: take*; F *legen etc.*: put*; F: *j-m et.* ~ do* s.th. to s.o.; *zu* ~ *haben* have* work to do; *beschäftigt sein*: be* busy; *ich weiß* (*nicht*), *was ich* ~ *soll od. muß* I (don't) know what to do; *so* ~, *als ob* pretend to *be etc.*; *ah, das tut gut!* ah, that's better!
Tünche *f*, **⚥n** *v/t.* whitewash
Tunke *f* sauce; **⚥n** *v/t.* dip
Tunnel *m* tunnel
Tüpfelchen *n fig.*: *das* ~ *auf dem i* the icing on the cake
tupfen *v/t.* dab
Tupf|en *m* dot, spot; **~er** *med. m* swab
Tür *f* door (*a. fig.*); *die* ~(**en**) *knallen* slam the door(s); *vor die* ~ *setzen* throw* out; *Tag der offenen* ~ open day (*Am.* house)
Turban *m* turban
Turb|ine *tech. f* turbine; **~olader** *mot.* turbo(charger)
Tür|griff *m* door handle; → *knauf*
Türk|e *m* Turk; **~ei** *f* Turkey; **~in** *f* Turk(ish woman); **⚥isch** *adj.* Turkish
Tür|klingel *f* doorbell; **~klinke** *f* door handle; **~knauf** *m* doorknob
Turm *m* tower; *Kirch⚥*: *a.* steeple; *Schach*: castle, rook
türmen 1. *v/t.* pile up (*a. sich* ~); **2.** F *v/i.* bolt, do* a bunk
Turm|spitze *f* spire; **~springen** *n* platform diving
turnen *v/i.* do* gymnastics; ~ *an* do* exercises od. work on
Turnen *n* gymnastics *pl.*; *Fach*: physical education, *Abk.* PE
Turn|er(in) *m(f)* gymnast; **~gerät** *n* gymnastic apparatus; **~halle** *f* gym(nasium); **~hemd** *n* gym shirt; **~hose** *f* gym shorts *pl.*
Turnier *n* tournament; **~tanz** *m* ballroom dancing
Turn|lehrer(in) *m(f)* gym(nastics) *od.* PE teacher; **~schuh** *m Brt.* trainer, *Am.* sneaker; **~verein** *m* gym(nastics) club; **~zeug** F *n* gym things *pl.*

Tür|öffner m door opener; **~pfosten** m doorpost; **~rahmen** m door-case od. -frame; **~schild** n doorplate; **~sprechanlage** f entryphone

Tusch|e f Indian ink; *Wasserfarbe*: watercolo(u)r; **~kasten** m paintbox

Tüte f (paper od. plastic) bag; **e-e ~** ... a bag of ...

tuten v/i. toot, honk, blow one's horn

TÜV *Abk. für* **Technischer Überwachungs-Verein** *Brt. etwa* MOT (test), compulsory car inspection; *(nicht)* **durch den ~ kommen** pass (fail) its od. one's MOT

Typ m type; *Modell*: model; F fellow, guy, *Brt. a.* chap; **~e** f tech. type; F *fig.* character

Typhus *med.* m typhoid (fever)

typisch *adj.* typical (*für* of)

Tyrann m tyrant; **~ei** f tyranny; **2isch** *adj.* tyrannical; **2isieren** v/t. tyrannize; *fig. a.* bully

U

u.a. *Abk. für* **unter anderem** among other things; **und andere** and others

U-Bahn f underground; *Londoner*: mst tube; *Am.* subway

übel *adj.* bad; *mir ist (wird)* ~ I feel (I'm getting) sick

Übel n notwendiges, kleineres etc.: evil; **~keit** *med.* f nausea; **2nehmen** v/t. be* offended by, take* offen|ce (*Am.* -se) at; **2riechend** *adj.* foul-smelling; *Atem*: foul; **~täter** m bsd. iro. culprit

üben v/t. u. v/i. practi|se, *Am.* -ce; *Klavier etc.* ~ practise the piano etc.

über *prp.* over; *oberhalb*: a. above (a. *fig.*); *mehr als*: a. more than; *quer* ~: across (a. *Straße, Fluß etc.*); *Thema*: about, of; *Vortrag, Buch etc.*: a. on; *sprechen (nachdenken etc.)* ~ talk (think* *etc.*) about; ~ *Nacht bleiben* stay overnight; ~ *München nach Rom* to Rome via Munich; *froh (traurig)* ~ glad (sad) about; *sich ärgern* ~ be* angry about; *lachen* ~ laugh at

überall *adv.* everywhere; ~ *in* ... a. throughout ..., all over ...

über|anstrengen v/t. u. v/refl. overstrain (o.s.); **~arbeiten** v/t. *Buch etc.*: revise; *sich* ~ overwork o.s.

überaus *adv.* most, extremely

über|belichten *phot.* v/t. overexpose; **~bieten** v/t. *bsd. Auktion*: outbid* (*um* by); *fig.* beat*; *j-n*: a. outdo*; **2bleibsel** n remains *pl.*; *Essen*: a. leftovers *pl.*; **2blick** m view; *fig.* overall view

(*über* of); *Vorstellung*: general idea; **~blicken** v/t. overlook; *fig. Auswirkungen etc.*: be* able to calculate; **~bringen** v/t. deliver; **~brücken** v/t. bridge (a. *fig.*); **~dacht** *adj.* roofed, covered; **~dauern** v/t. outlast, survive; **~denken** v/t. think* s. th. over; **~dies** *adv.* besides, moreover; **2dimensional** *adj.* oversized; **2dosis** *med.* f overdose; **2druck** m tech. overpressure; *post* overprint; **2druß** m weariness; **~drüssig** *adj.* disgusted with, weary od. sick of; **~durchschnittlich** *adj.* above-average; **~eifrig** *adj.* overzealous; **~eilen** v/t. rush; *nichts* ~*!* don't rush things!; **~eilt** *adj.* rash, overhasty

übereinander *adv.* on top of each other; *sprechen etc.*: about one another; **~schlagen** v/t.: *die Beine* ~ cross one's legs

überein|kommen v/i. agree; **2kommen** n, **2kunft** f agreement; **~stimmen** v/i. *Angaben*: tally, correspond (with); *mit j-m* ~ agree with s.o. (*in* on); **2stimmung** f agreement; correspondence; *in* ~ *mit* in accordance with

überfahr|en v/t. run* s.o. over, knock s.o. down; *Ampel etc.*: drive* through; **2fahrt** *naut.* f crossing

Überfall m assault (*auf* on); *Raub2*: hold-up (on, of); *Straßenraub*: a. mugging (of); *mil.* raid (on); invasion (of); **2en** v/t. attack, assault; hold* up; mug; *mil.* raid; invade

überfällig *adj.* overdue

überflieg|en *v/t.* fly* over *od.* across; *fig.* glance over, skim (through)

über|flügeln *v/i.* outstrip, surpass; **2fluß** *m* abundance (**an** of); *Wohlstand:* affluence; *im* ~ **haben** abound in; **2flüssig** *adj.* superfluous; *unnötig:* unnecessary; ~**fluten** *v/t.* flood (*a. fig.*); ~**fordern** *v/t.* Kräfte, Geduld etc.: overtax; *j-n:* expect too much of; ~**fragt** *adj.:* F: *da bin ich* ~ you've got me there

überführ|en *v/t.* transport; *jur.* convict (**e-r Tat** of a crime); **2ung** *f* transfer; *jur.* conviction; *mot.* flyover, *Am.* overpass; *Fußgänger2:* footbridge

Überfüll|e *f* (super)abundance (**an** of); **2t** *adj.* overcrowded, packed

überfüttern *v/t.* overfeed* (*a. fig.*)

Übergang *m* crossing; *fig.* transition (*a. mus.*); ~**sstadium** *n* transition(al) stage

über|geben *v/t.* hand over; *mil.* surrender; *sich* ~ vomit, *bsd. Brt. a.* be* sick; **2gehen 1.** *v/i.* pass (**zu** on to); ~ *in* change *od.* turn (in)to; **2.** *v/t.* pass over; *j-n, Bemerkung:* a. ignore; *auslassen:* a. skip

Übergewicht *n* (~ **haben** be*) overweight; *fig.* predominance

überglücklich *adj.* overjoyed

über|greifen *fig.* ~*v/i.:* **auf** spread* to; *ineinander* ~ overlap; **2griff** *m* infringement (**auf** of); *Gewaltakt:* (act of) violence; **2größe** *f:* *in* ~*n* outsized, oversize(d)

überhandnehmen *v/i.* become* rampant

überhäufen *v/t.* *mit Arbeit etc.:* swamp; *mit Geschenken etc.:* shower

überhaupt *adv.* at all (*nachgestellt*); *sowieso, eigentlich:* anyway; ~ *nicht*(*s*) not(hing) at all

überheblich *adj.* arrogant; **2keit** *f* arrogance

über|hitzen *v/t.* overheat (*a. fig.*); ~**höht** *adj.* excessive; ~**holen** *v/t.* pass, overtake* (*a. Sport*); *tech.* overhaul; service; ~**holt** *adj.* outdated, antiquated; ~**hören** *v/t.* miss, not catch** *od.* get*; *absichtlich:* ignore; △ *nicht* **overhear**

überirdisch *adj.* supernatural

überkleben *v/t.* paste up, cover

überkochen *v/i.* boil over

über|kommen *v/t.:* ... *überkam ihn* he was seized with *od.* overcome by ...; ~**laden** *v/t.* overload (*a. electr.*); *fig.* clutter

über|lassen *v/t.:* *j-m et.* ~ let* s.o. have s.th., leave* s.th. to s.o. (*a. fig.*); *j-n sich selbst* ~ leave* s.o. to himself; *j-n s-m Schicksal* ~ leave* s.o. to his fate; ~**lasten** *v/t.* overload; *fig.* overburden

überlaufen[1] **1.** *v/i.* run** *od.* flow over; *mil.* desert; **2.** *v/t.:* *es überlief mich heiß und kalt* I went hot and cold

über|laufen[2] *adj.* overcrowded; **2läufer** *m mil.* deserter; *pol.* defector

überleben *v/t. u. v/i.* survive (*a. fig.*); *et.:* a. live through; **2de(r)** survivor; ~**sgroß** *adj.* larger than life

überleg|en[1] *v/t. u. v/i.* think* about s.th., think* s.th. over; *erwägen:* a. consider; *lassen Sie mich* ~ let me think; *ich habe es mir* (*anders*) *überlegt* I've made up (changed) my mind

überleg|en[2] *adj.* superior (*j-m* to s.o.); **2enheit** *f* superiority; ~*t* *adj.* deliberate; *klug:* prudent; **2ung** *f* consideration, reflection

über|leiten *v/i.:* ~ *zu* lead* up *od.* over to; **2leitung** *f* transition (*a. mus.*); ~**liefern** *v/t.* hand down, pass on; **2lieferung** *f* tradition; ~**listen** *v/t.* outwit

Über|macht *f* superiority; *bsd. mil.* superior forces *pl.*; *in der* ~ *sein* be* superior in numbers; **2mächtig** *adj.* superior; *fig. Gefühl etc.:* overpowering

Über|maß *n* excess (**an** of); **2mäßig** *adj.* excessive; **2menschlich** *adj.* superhuman

übermittel|n *v/t.* transmit; **2ung** *f* transmission

übermorgen *adv.* the day after tomorrow

übermüd|et *adj.* overtired; **2ung** *f* overtiredness

Über|mut *m* (*aus* out of) overenthusiasm; **2mütig** *adj.* overenthusiastic

übernächst *adj.* the next but one; ~*e* **Woche** the week after next

übernacht|en *v/i.* stay overnight (*bei j-m* at s.o.'s [house], with s.o.), spend* the night (at, with); **2ung** *f* night; *e-e* ~ one overnight stay; ~ *und Frühstück* bed and breakfast

U

Übernahme f takin~ ~ e). e-r Idee etc.: a. adoption

übernatürlich adj. supernatural

übernehmen v/t. take* over; Idee, Brauch, Namen etc.: a. adopt; Führung, Risiko, Verantwortung, Auftrag etc.: take*; erledigen: take* care of

überprüf|en v/t. check, examine; Aussage etc.: verify; bsd. pol. screen; **2ung** f check, examination; verification; screening

über|queren v/t. cross; **~ragen** v/t. tower above (a. fig.); **~ragend** adj. outstanding

überrasch|en v/t. surprise; bsd et. ~ a. catch* s.o. doing s.th.; **2ung** f surprise

überred|en v/t. persuade (et. zu tun to do s.th.); j-n zu etw. ~ talk s.o. into (doing) s.th.; **2ung** f persuasion

überregional adj. Presse etc.: national

überreich|en v/t. present, hand s.th. over (dat. to); **2ung** f presentation

überreiz|en v/t. overexcite; **~t** adj. overwrought, F on edge

Überrest m remains pl.; **~e** pl. e-r Kultur: relics pl.; e-r Mahlzeit: leftovers pl.

überrump|eln v/t. (take* by) surprise

überrunden v/t. Sport: lap; fig. outstrip

übersät adj.: ~ mit Abfall etc.: strewn with; Sternen etc.: studded with

übersättigt adj. oversaturated; Markt: glutted; Person: sated, surfeited

Über|schall... in Zssgn: supersonic ...

über|schatten v/t. overshadow (a. fig.); **~schätzen** v/t. overrate, overestimate

Überschlag m Turnen: somersault; aviat. loop; electr. flashover; Schätzung: estimate, rough calculation

überschlagen 1. v/t. Beine: cross; Kosten: make* a rough estimate of; auslassen: skip; **2.** v/t. v/i.: ~ in turn into; **3.** v/refl. turn (right) over; Person: go* head over heels; Stimme: break*

über|schnappen F v/i. crack up; **~schneiden** v/refl. overlap (a. fig.); Linien: intersect; **~schreiben** v/t. Besitz: make* s.th. over (dat. to); **~schreiten** v/t. cross; fig. go* beyond; Höhepunkt: pass; Höchstgeschwindigkeit: break*

Überschrift f heading, title; Schlagzeile: headline

Über|schuß m, **2schüssig** adj. surplus

überschütt|en v/t.: ~ mit cover with; Geschenken: shower with; Lob etc.: heap s.th. on

überschwemm|en v/t., **2ung** f flood

überschwenglich adj. effusive

Übersee: in (nach) ~ overseas; **~handel** m overseas trade

über|sehen v/t. overlook; absichtlich, bsd. j-n: a. ignore; sich et. ~ get* tired of (seeing) s.th.

übersetzen¹ v/t. translate (in into); tech. transmit

übersetzen² **1.** v/i. cross (über e-n Fluß a river); **2.** v/t. take* over

Übersetz|er(in) translator; **2ung** f translation (aus from; in into); tech. transmission ratio

Übersicht f general idea od. view (über of); Zusammenfassung: outline, summary; **2lich** adj. clear(ly arranged)

über|siedeln v/i. move (nach to); **2sied(e)lung** f move

übersinnlich adj. supernatural

überspann|en v/t. (over)strain; Tal etc.: span; **~t** adj. Person: eccentric; übertrieben: exaggerated

überspielen v/t. record; auf Band: a. tape; fig. cover up

überspitzt adj. exaggerated

überspringen v/t. jump (over); bsd. Sport: a. clear; auslassen: skip

überstehen 1. v/t. get* over; überleben: survive (a. fig.), live through; **2.** v/i. jut out

über|steigen fig. v/t. exceed; **~stimmen** v/t. outvote, vote down

über|streifen v/t. slip s.th. on; **~strömen** v/i. overflow (vor with)

Überstunden pl. overtime sg.; ~ machen work overtime

überstürz|en v/t.: et. ~ rush things; sich ~ Ereignisse: follow in rapid succession; **~t** adj. (over)hasty; Entscheidung etc.: rash

über|teuert adj. overpriced; **~tönen** v/t. drown (out)

übertragbar adj. transferable; med. contagious

übertragen¹ adj. Bedeutung: figurative

übertrag|en² v/t. senden: broadcast*; TV a. televise; übersetzen: translate; Krankheit, tech. Kraft: transmit; Blut: transfuse; Organ etc.: transplant; jur., *econ., Zeichnung etc., Gelerntes:* transfer; **&ung** f *Radio, TV:* broadcast; transmission; translation; transfusion; transfer

übertreffen v/t. outdo*, be* better *etc.* than, surpass, F beat*

übertreib|en v/t. u. v/i. exaggerate; *Tätigkeit:* overdo*; **&ung** f exaggeration

übertret|en 1. v/i. ~ **zu** go* over (*eccl.* convert) to; *Sport:* foul (a jump *od.* throw); **2.** v/t. break*, violate; **&ung** f violation; *jur. a.* offen|ce, *Am.* -se

Übertritt m change (**zu** to); *rel., pol.* conversion (to)

übervölkert adj. overpopulated

überverteilen v/t. cheat, F do*

überwach|en v/t. supervise, oversee*; *leiten:* control; *polizeilich:* keep* under observance *od.* surveillance, shadow; **&ung** f supervision, control; observance, surveillance

überwältigen v/t. overwhelm, overpower; *fig. a.* overcome*; **~d** *fig.* adj. overwhelming, F smashing

überweis|en v/t. *Geld:* transfer (**an j-n** to s.o.'s account); *per Post:* remit; *Patienten:* refer (**an** to); **&ung** f *econ.* transfer; remittance; referral

überwerfen v/t. slip *s.th.* on; *sich* ~ (**mit j-m**) fall* out with each other (with s.o.)

über|wiegen v/i. predominate, **~wiegend** adj. predominant; *Mehrheit:* vast; **~winden** v/t. overcome* (*a. fig.*); *Gegner:* defeat; *sich* ~ **zu** *inf.* bring* o.s. to *inf.*; **~wintern** v/i. spend* the winter (**in** in); **~wuchern** v/t. overgrow*

Über|wurf m wrap; **~zahl** f majority; **in der** ~ **sein** outnumber *s.o.*

überzeug|en v/t. convince (**von** of), persuade; *sich* ~ **von** (**, daß**) make* sure of (that); *sich selbst* ~ (go* and) see* for o.s.; **~t** adj. convinced; ~ **sein** a. be* *od.* feel* (quite) sure; **&ung** f conviction

überziehe|n v/t. put* *s.th.* on; *tech. etc.* cover; *Bett:* change; *Konto:* overdraw*; *sich* ~ *Himmel:* become* overcast

Überzug m cover; *Schicht:* coat(ing)

üblich adj. usual, normal; **es ist** ~ **Brauch:** it's the custom; **wie** ~ as usual

U-Boot n submarine

übrig adj. remaining; **die ~en** pl. the others pl., the rest; ~ **sein** (**haben**) be* (have*) left; **~bleiben** v/i. be* left, remain; **es bleibt mir nichts anderes übrig** (**als zu**) there is nothing else I can do (but *do s.th.*); **~ens** adv. by the way; **~lassen** v/t. leave*

Übung f exercise; *das Üben, Erfahrung:* practice; **in** (**aus der**) ~ in (out of) practice

Ufer n shore; *Fluß&:* bank; **ans** ~ ashore

Uhr f clock; *Armband& etc.:* watch; **um vier** ~ at four o'clock; **~armband** n watchstrap; **~macher** m watchmaker; **~werk** n clockwork; **~zeiger** m hand; **~zeigersinn** m: **im** ~ clockwise; **entgegen dem** ~ anti-clockwise, *Am.* counterclockwise

Uhu zo. m eagle owl

UKW *Abk. für Ultrakurzwelle* VHF, very high frequency

Ulk m joke; hoax; **&ig** adj. funny

Ulme f elm

Ultimatum n ultimatum; **j-m ein** ~ **stellen** deliver an ultimatum to s.o.

um *prp. u. cj. räumlich:* (a)round; *zeitlich:* at; *ungefähr:* about, around; *bitten* ~ ask for; *sich Sorgen machen* ~ worry about; ~ **Geld** for money; ~ **e-e Stunde** (**10 cm**) by an hour (10 cm); **je** ... ~ **so** the ... the; ~ **so besser!** so much the better!; ~ ... **willen** for *s.o.'s* sake, for the sake of ...; ~ **zu** (in order to)

umarm|en v/t. embrace (*a. sich* ~), hug; **&ung** f embrace, hug

Umbau m rebuilding, reconstruction; **&en** v/t. rebuild*, reconstruct

um|binden v/t. put* *s.th.* on; **~blättern** v/t. (turn) over (the page); **~bringen** v/t. kill*; *sich* ~ kill o.s. (*a. fig.*); **~denken** v/i. change one's way of thinking; **~disponieren** v/i. change one's plans

umdrehe|n v/t. turn (round); *sich* ~ turn round; **&ung** f turn; *phys., tech.* rotation, revolution

um|einander adv. *kümmern etc.:* about *od.* for each other; **~fahren** v/t. run* down; drive* (*naut.* sail) round; **~fallen** v/i. fall down (*od.* over); *zs-brechen:* collapse; **tot** ~ drop dead

Umfang m circumference; *Buch etc.:* size; *Ausmaß:* extent; **in großem** ~ on a large scale; **&reich** adj. extensive; *massig:* voluminous

umfassen *fig. v/t.* cover; *enthalten: a.* include; **~d** *adj.* comprehensive; *vollständig:* complete

umform|en *v/t. allg.* turn, change; *electr., gr., math. a.* transform, convert *(alle: in* [in]*to);* **2r** *electr. m* converter

Umfrage *f Meinungs*2: opinion poll

Umgang *m* company; **~ haben mit** associate with; **beim ~ mit** when dealing with

umgänglich *adj.* sociable

Umgangs|formen *pl.* manners *pl.;* **~sprache** *f* colloquial speech; **die englische ~** colloquial English

umgeb|en **1.** *v/t.* surround **(mit** with); **2ung** *f* surroundings *pl.;* Milieu: environment

umgeh|en **1.** *v/i.:* **~ mit** deal* with, handle; **~ können mit** have* a way with, be* good with; **2.** *v/t.* avoid, F get* round; *Stadt etc.: a.* bypass; **~end** *adv.* immediately; **2ungsstraße** *f* bypass; *Ringstraße:* ring road, *Am.* beltway

umgekehrt **1.** *adj.* reverse; opposite; **(genau) ~** (just) the other way round; **2.** *adv.* the other way round; **und ~** and vice versa

umgraben *v/t.* dig* (up), break* up

um|haben F *v/t.* have* *s.th.* on; **2hang** *m* cape; **~hängen** *v/t.* put* around *od.* over *s.o.'s* shoulders *etc.;* Bilder: rehang*; **~hauen** *v/t.* fell, cut* down; F *fig.* knock out

umher *adv.* (a)round, about; **~streifen** *v/i.* roam *od.* wander around

umkehr|en **1.** *v/i.* turn back; **2.** *v/t.* *Reihenfolge etc.:* reverse; **→ umdrehen;** **2ung** *f* reversal *(a. fig.)*

umkippen **1.** *v/t.* tip over, upset; **2.** *v/i.* **→ umfallen**

umklammer|n *v/t.,* **2ung** *f* clasp, clutch, clench

umkleide|n *v/refl.* change (one's clothes); **2kabine** *f* changing cubicle; **2raum** *m bsd. Sport:* changing *od.* locker room; *thea.* dressing room

umkommen *v/i.* be* killed **(bei** in), die (in); F: **~ vor** be* dying with

Umkreis *m:* **im ~ von** within a radius of; **2en** *v/t.* circle; *astr.* revolve around; *Satellit etc.:* orbit

umkrempeln *v/t.* roll up

Umlauf *m* circulation; *phys., tech.* rotation; *Schreiben:* circular; **im (in) ~ sein (bringen)** be* in (put*) into) circulation, circulate; **~bahn** *f* orbit; **2en** *v/i.* circulate

umlegen *v/t. Schal etc.:* put* on; *verlegen:* move; *Kosten:* share; *Hebel etc.:* pull; *sl. töten:* do* *s.o.* in, bump *s.o.* off

umleit|en *v/t.* divert; **2ung** *f* diversion, *Am.* detour

umliegend *adj.* surrounding

umnachtet *adj.:* **geistig ~** mentally deranged

um|packen *v/t.* repack; **~pflanzen** *v/t.* *Topfblumen etc.:* repot

umrahmen *v/t.* frame; *musikalisch* **~** put* into a musical setting

umrand|en *v/t.,* **2ung** *f* edge, border

umräumen *v/t.* rearrange

umrechn|en *v/t.* convert **(in** into); **2ung** *f* conversion; **2ungskurs** *m* exchange rate

um|reißen *v/t.* tear* (*j-n:* knock) down; **~ringen** *v/t.* surround

Um|riß *m* outline *(a. fig.)*, contour; **2rühren** *v/t.* stir; **2rüsten** *tech. v/t.* convert **(auf** to); **2satteln** F *fig. v/i.:* **~ von ... auf** switch from ... to; **~satz** *econ. m* sales *pl.*

umschalt|en *v/t. u. v/i.* switch (over) **(auf** to) *(a. fig.)*

umschauen *v/refl.* **→ umsehen**

Umschlag *m Brief*2: envelope; *Hülle:* cover, wrapper; *Buch*2: jacket; *an der Hose:* turn-up, *Am. a.* cuff; *med.* compress; *econ.* handling; **2en 1.** *v/t. Baum:* cut* down, fell; *Ärmel:* turn up; *Kragen:* turn down; *econ.* handle; **2.** *v/i. Boot etc.:* turn over, (be*) upset*; *sich ändern:* change (suddenly); **~platz** *m* trading cent|re *(Am.* -er)

um|schlungen *adj.:* **eng ~** clasped in a firm embrace; **~schnallen** *v/t.* buckle on

umschreib|en *v/t.* rewrite*; *Begriff etc.:* paraphrase; **2ung** *f* paraphrase

Umschrift *f Lautung:* transcription

um|schulen *v/t.* retrain; *Schüler:* transfer to another school; **~schütten** *v/t.* spill*; **~schwärmt** *adj.* idolized

Um|schweife *pl.:* **ohne ~ sagen:** straight out; *tun:* straight away *od.* off; **~schwung** *m* (drastic) change; *bsd. pol. a.* swing

umseg|eln *v/t.* sail round; *Erde:* circumnavigate; ♀(e)lung *f* sailing round; circumnavigation

um|sehen *v/refl.* look around (**in e-m** *Laden* a shop; **nach** for); *zurückblicken*: look back (**nach** at); *sich ~ nach suchen*: be* looking for; **~sein** F *v/i.* be* over; **die Zeit ist um** time's up; **~setzen** *v/t.* move (*a. Schüler*); *econ.* sell*; **~ in** convert (in)to; **in die Tat ~** put* into action; **sich ~** change places

umsied|eln *v/i. u. v/t.* resettle; → **umziehen**; ♀er *m* resettler; ♀(e)lung *f* resettlement

umsonst *adv.* free (of charge), for nothing; F for free; *vergebens*: in vain

umspanne|n *v/t.* span (*a. fig.*); *electr.* transform; ♀r *electr. m* transformer

umspringen *v/i.* shift, change (suddenly) (*a. fig.*); **~ mit** treat (badly)

Umstand *m* circumstance; *Tatsache*: fact; *Einzelheit*: detail; **unter diesen** (**keinen**) **Umständen** under the (no) circumstances; **unter Umständen** possibly; **keine Umstände machen** *j-m*: not cause any trouble; *sich*: not go* to any trouble, not put* o.s. out; **in anderen Umständen sein** be* expecting

umständlich *adj.* awkward; *kompliziert*: complicated; *Stil etc.*: long-winded; **das ist** (**mir**) **viel zu ~** that's far too much trouble (for me)

Umstands|kleid *n* maternity dress; **~wort** *gr. n* adverb

Umstehenden *pl.* the bystanders *pl.*

umsteigen *v/i.* change (**nach** for); *rail. a.* change trains (for)

umstell|en *v/t. allg.* change (**auf** to), make* a change of. changes in; *bsd. tech. a.* switch (over) (to), convert (to); *anpassen*: adjust (to); *neu ordnen*: rearrange (*a. Möbel*), reorganize; *Uhr*: reset*; *umzingeln*: surround; **sich ~ auf** change od. switch (over) to; *anpassen*: adjust (o.s.) to, get* used to; ♀ung *f* change; switch, conversion; adjustment; rearrangement, reorganization

um|stimmen *v/t.*: *j-n ~* change s.o.'s mind; **~stoßen** *v/t.* knock over: *Dinge*: *a.* upset* (*a. fig. Pläne*)

umstritten *adj.* controversial

Um|sturz *m* overthrow, ♀stürzen *v/i.* overturn, fall* over

Umtausch *m*, ♀en *v/t.* exchange (**gegen** for)

---

umwälz|end *adj.* revolutionary; ♀ung *fig. f* radical change

umwandel|eln *v/t. allg.* turn (**in** into), transform (into); *bsd. chem.*, *electr.*, *phys. a.* convert ([in]to); ♀er *m* converter; ♀ung *f* transformation, conversion

Umweg *m* roundabout route *od.* way (*a. fig.*); *bsd. mot. a.* detour; **ein ~ von 10 Minuten** ten minutes out of the way; *fig.* **auf ~en** in a roundabout way

Umwelt *f* environment; **~...** *in Zssgn mst* environmental ...; **~forscher** *m* ecologist; **~forschung** *f* ecology; ♀freundlich *adj.* environment-friendly, non-polluting; ♀schädlich *adj.* harmful, noxious, polluting; **~schutz** *m* conservation, environmental protection, pollution control; **~schützer** *m* environmentalist, conservationist; **~schutzpapier** *n* recycled paper; **~sünder** *m* (environmental) polluter; **~verschmutzer** *m* polluter; **~verschmutzung** *f* (environmental) pollution; **~zerstörung** *f* ecocide

umwerfen *v/t.* knock over *od.* down (F *fig.* out); *Dinge*: *a.* upset*

umziehen 1. *v/i.* move (**nach** to), **2.** *v/refl.* change (one's clothes)

umzingeln *v/t.* surround, encircle

Umzug *m* move (**nach** to), removal (to); *Festzug*: parade

unab|hängig *adj.* independent (**von** of); **~ davon, ob** (**was**) regardless of whether (what); ♀hängigkeit *f* independence (**von** from); **~sichtlich** *adj.* unintentional; *et.* **~ tun** do* s.th. by mistake; **~wendbar** *adj.* inevitable

unachtsam *adj.* careless, negligent; ♀keit *f* carelessness, negligence

unan|fechtbar *adj.* indisputable; **~gebracht** *adj.* inappropriate; **~ sein** be* out of place; **~gemessen** *adj.* unreasonable; *unzureichend*: inadequate; **~genehm** *adj.* unpleasant; *peinlich*: embarrassing; **~nehmbar** *adj.* unacceptable; ♀nehmlichkeiten *pl.* trouble *sg.*, difficulties *pl.*; **~sehnlich** *adj.* unsightly; **~ständig** *adj.* indecent, *stärker*: obscene; ♀ständigkeit *f* indecency; obscenity; **~tastbar** *adj.* unimpeachable

unappetitlich *adj.* unappetizing, F nasty (*a. fig.*)

U

Unart f bad habit; **2ig** adj. naughty, bad
unauffdringlich adj. unobtrusive;
~fällig adj. inconspicuous, unobtrusive; **~findbar** adj. undiscoverable,
untraceable; **~gefordert** adj. without
being asked, of one's own accord;
~hörlich adj. continuous; **~merksam** adj. inattentive; **2merksamkeit**
f inattention, inattentiveness; **~richtig**
adj. insincere
unaus|löschlich adj. indelible; **~
stehlich** adj. unbearable
unbarmherzig adj. merciless
unbe|absichtigt adj. unintentional;
~achtet adj. unnoticed; **~aufsichtigt**
adj. unattended; **~baut** adj. undeveloped; **~dacht** adj. thoughtless;
~denklich 1. adj. safe; **2.** adv. without
hesitation; **~deutend** adj. insignificant; geringfügig: a. minor; **~dingt 1.**
adj. unconditional, absolute; **2.** adv. by
all means, absolutely; brauchen: badly;
~fahrbar adj. impassable; **~fangen**
adj. unparteiisch: unprejudiced, unbias(s)ed; ohne Hemmung: unembarrassed; **~friedigend** adj. unsatisfactory; enttäuscht: disappointed; **~gabt** adj. untalented; **~greiflich** adj. inconceivable, incomprehensible; **~grenzt** adj.
unlimited, boundless; **~gründet** adj.
unfounded; **2hagen** n uneasiness, discomfort; **~haglich** adj. uneasy, uncomfortable; **~helligt** adj. unmolested; **~herrscht** adj. uncontrolled,
lacking self-control; **~holfen** adj.
clumsy, awkward; **~irrt** adj. unwavering; **~kannt** adj. unknown; **2kannte**
math. f unknown quantity; **~kümmert**
adj. light-hearted, cheerful; **~lehrbar**
adj.: er ist ~ he'll never learn; **~liebt**
adj. unpopular; er ist überall ~ nobody
likes him; **~mannt** adj. unmanned;
~merkt adj. unnoticed; **~nutzt** adj.
unused; **~quem** adj. uncomfortable;
lästig: inconvenient; **2rechenbar** adj.
unpredictable; **~rechtigt** adj. unauthorized; ungerechtfertigt: unjustified;
~schädigt adj. undamaged; **~scheiden** adj. immodest; **~schränkt** adj.
unlimited; Macht etc.: a. absolute;
~schreiblich adj. indescribable; **~sehen** adv. unseen; **~siegbar** adj. invincible; **~sonnen** adj. thoughtless, im-

prudent; überstürzt: rash; **~ständig**
adj. unstable; Wetter: changeable, unsettled; **~stätigt** adj. unconfirmed;
~stechlich adj. incorruptible; fig. unerring; **~stimmt** adj. indefinite (a. gr.);
unsicher: uncertain; Gefühl etc.: vague;
~streitbar adj. indisputable; **~stritten** adj. undisputed; **~teiligt** adj. nicht
verwickelt: not involved; gleichgültig:
indifferent; **~tont** adj. unstressed
unbeugsam adj. inflexible
unbe|wacht adj. unwatched, unguarded (a. fig.); **~waffnet** adj. unarmed;
~weglich adj. immovable; bewegungslos: motionless; **~wohnbar** adj. uninhabitable; **~wohnt** adj. uninhabited;
Gebäude: unoccupied, vacant; **~wußt**
adj. unconscious; **~zahlbar** fig. adj.
invaluable, priceless (a. komisch)
un|blutig 1. adj. bloodless; **2.** adv. without bloodshed; **~brauchbar** adj. useless
und cj. and; F: na ~? so what?
undankbar adj. ungrateful (gegen to);
Aufgabe: thankless; **2keit** f ingratitude, ungratefulness
un|denkbar adj. unthinkable; **~definierbar** adj. nondescript; **~deutlich**
adj. indistinct; Sprache: a. inarticulate;
fig. vague; **~dicht** adj. leaky
unduldsam adj. intolerant; **2keit** f intolerance
undurch|dringlich adj. impenetrable;
~führbar adj. impracticable; **~lässig**
adj. impervious, impermeable; **~sichtig** adj. opaque; fig. mysterious
uneben adj. uneven; **2heit** f unevenness; Stelle: bump
un|echt adj. false; künstlich: artificial;
imitiert: imitation; F contp. vorgetäuscht: fake, phon(e)y; **~ehelich** adj.
illegitimate; **~ehrenhaft** adj. dishono(u)rable; **~ehrlich** adj. dishonest;
~eigennützig adj. unselfish
uneinig adj.: (sich) ~ sein disagree
(über on); **2keit** f disagreement
un|einnehmbar adj. impregnable;
~empfänglich adj. insusceptible (für
to); **~empfindlich** adj. insensitive (gegen to); haltbar: durable
unendlich adj. infinite; endlos: endless,
never-ending; **2keit** f infinity (a. fig.)
unent|behrlich adj. indispensable; **~geltlich** adj. u. adv. free (of charge);

~**schieden** adj. undecided; ~ **enden** end in a draw od. tie; **es steht** ~ the score is even; 2**schieden** n draw, tie; ~**schlossen** adj. irresolute; ~**schuldbar** adj. inexcusable; ~**wegt** adv. untiringly; *unaufhörlich:* continuously

uner|fahren adj. inexperienced; ~**freulich** adj. unpleasant; ~**füllt** adj. unfulfilled; ~**giebig** adj. unproductive; ~**heblich** adj. irrelevant (**für** to); *geringfügig:* insignificant; ~**hört** adj. outrageous; ~**kannt** adj. unrecognized; ~**klärlich** adj. inexplicable; ~**läßlich** adj. essential; ~**laubt** adj. unallowed; *unbefugt:* unauthorized; ~**ledigt** adj. unsettled (*a. econ.*); ~**meßlich** adj. immeasurable, immense; ~**müdlich** adj. *Person:* indefatigable; *Anstrengungen:* untiring; ~**reichbar** adj. inaccessible; *bsd. fig.* unattainable; ~**reicht** adj. unequal(l)ed; ~**sättlich** adj. insatiable; ~**schlossen** adj. undeveloped; ~**schöpflich** adj. inexhaustible; ~**schütterlich** adj. unshakable; ~**schwinglich** adj. *Preise:* exorbitant; **für j-n** ~ **sein** be* beyond s.o.'s means; ~**setzlich** adj. irreplaceable; *Schaden etc.:* irreparable; ~**träglich** adj. unbearable; ~**wartet** adj. unexpected; ~**wünscht** adj. unwanted

unfähig adj. incapable (**zu tun** of doing), incompetent (*a. beruflich*); *außerstande:* unable (to *inf.*); 2**keit** f incapacity, incompetence; inability

Unfall m accident; *Verkehrs*2: *a.* crash; ~**stelle** f scene of the accident

un|fehlbar adj. infallible (*a. rel.*); *Instinkt etc.:* unfailing; ~**förmig** adj. shapeless; *mißgestaltet:* misshapen; *stärker:* monstrous; ~**frankiert** adj. unstamped; ~**frei** adj. unfree; *post* unpaid; ~**freiwillig** adj. involuntary; *Humor:* unconscious; ~**freundlich** adj. unfriendly (**zu** to), unkind (to); *Zimmer, Tag:* cheerless; 2**frieden** m discord; ~ **stiften** make* mischief

unfruchtbar adj. infertile; 2**keit** f infertility

Unfug m nonsense; ~ **treiben** be* up to mischief, fool around

Ungar|(in), 2**isch** adj. Hungarian; ~**n** Hungary

ungastlich adj. inhospitable

unge|achtet prp. regardless of; *trotz:* despite; ~**ahnt** adj. unthought-of; ~**beten** adj. uninvited, unasked; ~**er Gast** intruder; ~**bildet** adj. uneducated; ~**boren** adj. unborn; ~**bräuchlich** adj. uncommon, unusual; ~**bührlich** adj. unseemly; ~**bunden** *fig.* adj. free, independent; **frei und** ~ footloose and fancy-free; ~**deckt** adj. *Schech:* uncovered; *Sport:* unmarked

Ungeduld f impatience; 2**ig** adj. impatient

ungeeignet adj. unfit; *Person: a.* unqualified

ungefähr 1. adj. approximate; *Vorstellung etc.:* a. rough; **2.** adv. approximately, roughly, about, around, ... or so; **so** ~ something like that

ungefährlich adj. harmless; *sicher:* safe

Ungeheuer n monster (*a. fig.*)

ungeheuer 1. adj. enormous (*a. fig.*), huge, vast; **2.** adv.: ~ **reich** etc. enormously rich etc.; ~**lich** adj. monstrous

unge|hindert adj. u. adv. unhindered; ~**hobelt** *fig.* adj. uncouth, rough; ~**hörig** adj. improper, unseemly

ungehorsam adj. disobedient

Ungehorsam m disobedience

unge|kocht adj. uncooked; **künstelt** adj. unaffected; ~**kürzt** adj. unabridged

ungelegen adj. inconvenient; **j-m** ~ **kommen** be* inconvenient for s.o.

unge|lenk adj. awkward, clumsy; ~**lernt** adj. unskilled; ~**mütlich** adj. uncomfortable; F: ~ **werden** get* nasty

ungenau adj. inaccurate; *fig.* vague; 2**igkeit** f inaccuracy

ungeniert adj. uninhibited

unge|nießbar adj. uneatable; undrinkable; F *Person:* unbearable; ~**nügend** adj. insufficient; *Leistung:* a. poor, unsatisfactory; *Note:* a. F; ~**pflegt** adj. neglected; *Person:* untidy, unkempt; ~**rade** adj. uneven; *Zahl:* odd

ungerecht adj. unfair, unjust; 2**igkeit** f injustice, unfairness

un|gern adv. *widerwillig:* unwillingly; **et.** ~ **tun** hate od. not like to do s.th.; ~**geschehen** adj.: ~ **machen** undo*

unge|schickt adj. awkward, clumsy; ~**schliffen** adj. *Diamant etc.:* uncut; *Marmor etc., Benehmen etc.:* unpolished; ~**schminkt** adj. without make-

U

-up; *fig.* unvarnished, plain; **~setzlich** *adj.* illegal, unlawful; **~stört** *adj.* undisturbed, uninterrupted; **~straft** *adj.*: ~ *davonkommen* get* off unpunished (F *scot-free*); **~sund** *adj.* unhealthy (*a. fig.*); **~teilt** *adj.* undivided (*a. fig.*); **2tüm** *n* monster; *fig. a.* monstrosity

ungewiß *adj.* uncertain; *j-n im ungewissen lassen* keep* s.o. in the dark (*über* about); **2heit** *f* uncertainty

unge|wöhnlich *adj.* unusual; **~wohnt** *adj.* strange, unfamiliar; *unüblich*: unusual; **2ziefer** *n* vermin; **~zogen** *adj.* naughty, bad; *verzogen*: spoilt; **~zwungen** *adj.* relaxed, informal; *Person*: *a.* easygoing

ungläubig *adj.* incredulous, unbelieving (*a. rel.*)

unglaub|lich *adj.* incredible, unbelievable; **~würdig** *adj.* untrustworthy; *bsd. pol. a.* not credible; *Geschichte, Entschuldigung*: incredible

ungleich *adj.* unequal, different; *unähnlich*: unlike; **~mäßig** *adj.* uneven; *unregelmäßig*: irregular

Unglück *n* bad luck, misfortune; *Unfall*: accident; *stärker*: disaster; *Elend*: misery; **2lich** *adj.* unhappy; *bedauernswert*: unfortunate (*a. Umstände etc.*); **2licherweise** *adv.* unfortunately

ungültig *adj.* invalid, F no good; *für ~ erklären* invalidate; *bsd. jur.* nullify

Un|gunst *f*: *zu j-s ~en* to s.o.'s disadvantage; **2günstig** *adj.* unfavo(u)rable; *nachteilig*: disadvantageous

un|gut *adj.*: *~es Gefühl* misgivings *pl.* (*bei et.* about s.th.); *nichts für ~!* no offen|ce (*Am.* -se) meant!; **~haltbar** *fig. adj. Argument etc*: untenable; *Zustände*: intolerable; *Torschuß*: unstoppable; **~handlich** *adj.* unwieldy

Unheil *n* mischief; *Übel*: evil; *Unglück*: disaster; **2bar** *adj.* incurable; **2voll** *adj.* disastrous; *Blick etc.*: sinister

unheimlich 1. *adj.* creepy, spooky, eerie; F *fig.* tremendous; **2.** F *adv.*: *~ gut* terrific, fantastic

unhöflich *adj.* impolite; *stärker*: rude; **2keit** *f* impoliteness; rudeness

un|hörbar *adj.* inaudible; **~hygienisch** *adj.* insanitary

Uniform *f* uniform

uninteress|ant *adj.* uninteresting; **~iert** *adj.* uninterested (*an* in)

Universität *f* university

Universum *n* universe

Unke *f zo.* toad; F *fig.* croaker; **2n** F *v/i.* croak

unklar *adj.* unclear; *ungewiss*: uncertain; *verworren*: confused, muddled; *im ~en sein (lassen)* be* (leave* *s.o.*) in the dark; **2heit** *f* unclarity; uncertainty

unklug *adj.* imprudent, unwise

Unkosten *pl.* expenses *pl.*, costs *pl.*

Unkraut *n* weed; *coll.* weeds *pl.*; ~ *jäten* weed (the garden)

un|kündbar *adj. Stellung*: permanent; **~längst** *adv.* lately, recently; **~leserlich** *adj.* illegible; **~logisch** *adj.* illogical; **~lösbar** *adj.* insoluble; **~männlich** *adj.* unmanly, effeminate; **~mäßig** *adj.* excessive; **2menge** *f* vast quantity *od.* number(s *pl.*) (*von* of), F loads *pl.* (of), tons *pl.* (of)

Unmensch *m* monster, brute; **2lich** *adj.* inhuman, cruel; **~lichkeit** *f* inhumanity, cruelty

un|merklich *adj.* imperceptible; **~mißverständlich** *adj.* unmistakable; **~mittelbar 1.** *adj.* immediate, direct; **2.** *adv.*: ~ *nach* (*hinter*) right after (behind); **~möbliert** *adj.* unfurnished; **~modern** *adj.* out of fashion *od.* style; **~möglich 1.** *adj.* impossible; **2.** *adv.*: *ich kann es ~ tun* I can't possibly do it; **~moralisch** *adj.* immoral; **~mündig** *adj.* under age; **~musikalisch** *adj.* unmusical; **~nachahmlich** *adj.* inimitable; **~nachgiebig** *adj.* unyielding; **~nachsichtig** *adj.* strict, severe; **~nahbar** *adj.* standoffish, cold; **~natürlich** *adj.* unnatural (*a. fig.*); *geziert*: affected; *unnötig*: unnecessary, needless; **~nütz** *adj.* useless; **~ordentlich** *adj.* untidy; ~ *sein Zimmer etc.*: be* (in) a mess; **2ordnung** *f* disorder, mess; **~parteiisch** *adj.* impartial, unbias(s)ed; **2parteiische** *m Sport*: referee; **~passend** *adj.* unsuitable; *unschicklich*: improper; *unangebracht*: inappropriate; **~passierbar** *adj.* impassable; **~päßlich** *adj.* indisposed, unwell; **~persönlich** *adj.* impersonal (*a. gr.*); **~politisch** *adj.* unpolitical; **~praktisch** *adj.* impractical; **~pünktlich** *adj.* unpunctual

unrecht *adj.* wrong; ~ **haben (tun)** be* (do* *s.o.*) wrong

Unrecht *n* injustice, wrong; **zu ~** wrong(ful)ly; **2mäßig** *adj.* unlawful

unregelmäßig *adj.* irregular (*a. gr.*); **2keit** *f* irregularity

unreif *adj.* unripe; *fig.* immature; **2e** *fig. f* immaturity

unrein *adj.* unclean; *bsd. Wasser etc.*: *a.* impure (*a. rel.*); **2heit** *f* impurity

unrichtig *adj.* incorrect, wrong

Unruh|e *f* restlessness, unrest (*a. pol.*); *Besorgnis*: anxiety, alarm; **~n** *pl.* disturbances *pl.*; *stärker*: riots *pl.*; **2ig** *adj.* restless; *innerlich*: *a.* uneasy; *besorgt*: worried, alarmed; *See*: rough

uns *pers. pron.* (to) us; *einander*: each other; ~ (**selbst**) (to) ourselves; **ein Freund von ~** a friend of ours

un|sachgemäß *adj.* improper; **~sachlich** *adj.* unobjective; **~sanft** *adj.* ungentle; *grob*: rude, rough; **~sauber** *adj.* unclean; *bsd. fig. a.* impure; *Sport*: unfair; *Methoden*: underhand; **~schädlich** *adj.* harmless; ~ **machen** *fig.* eliminate; **~scharf** *adj. Foto*: blurred, out of focus; **~schätzbar** *adj.* inestimable, invaluable; **~scheinbar** *adj.* inconspicuous; *einfach*: plain; **~schicklich** *adj.* indecent; **~schlüssig** *adj.* undecided; **~schön** *adj.* unsightly; *fig.* unpleasant

Unschuld *f* innocence; *fig.* virginity; **2ig** *adj.* innocent (**an** of); (**noch**) ~ **sein** be* (still) a virgin

unselbständig *adj.* dependent on others; **2keit** *f* lack of independence, dependence on others

unser *poss. pron.* our; **~er**, **~e**, **~es** ours

unsicher *adj.* unsafe, insecure (*a. psych.*); *gehemmt*: self-conscious; *ungewiß*: uncertain; **2heit** *f* insecurity, unsafeness; self-consciousness; uncertainty

unsichtbar *adj.* invisible

Unsinn *m* nonsense; **2ig** *adj.* nonsensical, stupid; *absurd*: absurd

Unsitt|e *f* bad habit; *Mißbrauch*: abuse; **2lich** *adj.* immoral, indecent

un|sozial *adj.* unsocial; **~sportlich** *adj.* unfair; *Mensch*: unathletic

unsterblich 1. *adj.* immortal (*a. fig.*); **2.** *adv.*: ~ **verliebt** madly in love (**in** with); **2keit** *f* immortality

Un|stimmigkeit *f* discrepancy; **~en** *pl.* disagreements *pl.*; **2sympathisch** *adj.* disagreeable; **er** (**es**) **ist mir ~** I don't like him (it); **2tätig** *adj.* inactive; *müßig*: idle; **~tätigkeit** *f* inactivity; **2-tauglich** *adj.* unfit (*a. mil.*); *Person*: *a.* incompetent; **2teilbar** *adj.* indivisible

unten *adv.* (down) below, down (*a.* **nach** ~); *im Hause*: downstairs; ~ **auf der Seite etc.*: at the bottom of; *siehe* ~ see below; **von oben bis** ~ from top to bottom

unter *prp.* under; *örtlich, rangmäßig*: *a.* below; *weniger als*: *a.* less than; *zwischen*: among; ~ **anderem** among other things; ~ **uns** (**gesagt**) between you and me; ~ **Wasser** underwater

Unter|arm *m* forearm; **2belichtet** *phot. adj.* underexposed; **2besetzt** *adj.* understaffed; **~bewußtsein** *n* subconscious; **im** ~ subconsciously

unter|bieten *v/t.* underbid*; *Preis*: undercut; *Rekord*: beat*; **~binden** *fig. v/t.* put* a stop to; *verhindern*: prevent

unterbrech|en *v/t.* interrupt; **2ung** *f* interruption

unterbring|en *v/t. beherbergen*: accommodate, put* *s.o.* up; *Platz finden für*: find* a place for, put* (**in** into); **2ung** *f* accommodation

unterdessen *adv.* in the meantime, meanwhile

unterdrück|en *v/t. Volk etc.*: oppress; *Gefühl etc.*: suppress; **2er** *m* oppressor; **2ung** *f* oppression; suppression

untere *adj.* lower (*a. fig.*)

unter|entwickelt *adj.* underdeveloped; **~ernährt** *adj.* undernourished, underfed; **2ernährung** *f* undernourishment, malnutrition

Unter|führung *f* underpass, *Brt. a.* subway; **~gang** *m Sonne etc.*: setting; *naut.* sinking; *fig.* downfall; *allmählicher*: decline; *e-s Reiches etc.*: fall; **2gehen** *v/i.* go* down (*a. fig.*); *Sonne etc.*: *a.* set*; *naut. a.* sink*

unterge|ordnet *adj.* subordinate, inferior; *zweitrangig*: secondary; **2wicht** *n*, **~wichtig** *adj.* underweight

untergraben *fig. v/t.* undermine

Untergrund *m* subsoil; *pol.* underground (*a. in Zssgn*); **in den ~ gehen** go underground; **~bahn** *f* → **U-Bahn**

unterhalb *prp.* below, under

Unterhalt m support, maintenance (a.jur.); **2en** v/t. Publikum etc.: entertain; Familie etc.: support; **sich ~ (mit)** talk (to, with); **sich (gut) ~** enjoy o.s., have* a good time; **2sam** adj. entertaining; **~ung** f talk, conversation; Vergnügen: entertainment (a. TV etc.); **~ungsbranche** f show business

Unter|händler m negotiator; **~haus** Brt. parl. n House of Commons; **~hemd** n vest, Am. undershirt; **~holz** n undergrowth; **~hose** f underpants pl., bsd. Am. shorts pl.; Damen2: pants pl., Am. panties pl.; **(e-e) lange ~** (a pair of) longjohns pl.; **2irdisch** adj. underground; **~kiefer** m lower jaw; **~kleid** n slip

unterkommen v/i. find* accommodation; find* work od. a job (**bei** with)

Unter|kunft f accommodation, lodging(s pl.); mil. quarters pl.; **~ und Verpflegung** board and lodging; **~lage** f tech. base; Schreib2: pad; **~n** pl. documents pl.; Angaben: data pl.

unterlass|en v/t. fail to do s.th.: aufhören mit: stop od. quit* doing s.th.; **2ung** f omission (a. jur.)

unterlegen[1] v/t. underlay*

unterlegen[2] adj. inferior (dat. to); **2e** m, f loser; Schwächere: underdog; **2heit** f inferiority

Unter|leib m abdomen, belly; **2liegen** v/i. be* defeated (j-m by s.o.), lose* (to s.o.); fig. be* subject to; **~lippe** f lower lip; **~mieter(in)** lodger, subtenant, Am. a. roomer

unternehmen v/t. Reise etc.: make*, take*, go* on; et. ~ do* s.th. (**gegen** about s.th.), take* action (against s.o.)

Unternehm|en n firm, business; Vorhaben: undertaking, enterprise; mil. operation; gewagtes ~ venture, risky undertaking; **~ensberater** m management consultant; **~er** m businessman, entrepreneur; Arbeitgeber: employer; **2ungslustig** adj. active, dynamic; abenteuerlustig: adventurous

Unter|offizier mil. m non-commissioned officer; **2ordnen** v/t. u. v/refl. subordinate (o.s.) (dat. to)

Unterredung f talk(s pl.)

Unterricht m instruction, teaching; Schul2: school, classes pl., lessons pl.; **2en** v/i. u. v/t. teach*; Stunden geben: give* lessons; informieren: inform (**über** of); a. class, period

Unterrock m slip

untersagen v/t. prohibit

Untersatz m → **Untersetzer**

unter|schätzen v/t. underestimate; Können etc.: a. underrate; **~scheiden** v/t. u. v/i. distinguish (**zwischen** between; **von** from); auseinanderhalten: a. tell* apart; **sich ~** differ (**von** from; **in** in; **durch** by); **2scheidung** f distinction

Unterschied m difference; **im ~ zu** unlike, as opposed to; **2lich** adj. different; schwankend: varying

unterschlag|en v/t. Geld: embezzle; fig. hold* back; **2ung** f embezzlement

Unterschlupf m hiding place

unter|schreiben v/t. u. v/i. sign; **2schrift** f signature; Bild2: caption

Unterseeboot n → **U-Boot**

Untersetzer m für Gläser: coaster; für Blumentopf: saucer

untersetzt adj. thickset, stocky

Unterstand m shelter, mil. a. dugout

unter|stehen 1. v/i. be* under (the control of); **2.** v/refl. dare; **~ Sie sich (et. zu tun)!** I don't you dare ([to] do s.th.)!; **~stellen** v/t. put* s.th. in; lagern: store; annehmen: assume; **sich ~** take* shelter; j-m ~, daß er ... insinuate that s.o. ...; **2stellung** f insinuation; **~streichen** v/t. underline (a. fig.)

unterstütz|en v/t. support; bsd. ideell: a. back (up); **2ung** f support; bsd. soziale, staatliche: a. aid; Fürsorge: welfare (payments pl.)

untersuch|en v/t. examine (a. med.), investigate (a. jur.); Gepäck etc.: search (a. jur.); chem. analyze; **2ung** f examination (a. med.), investigation (a. jur.); med. a. (medical) checkup; chem. analysis

Untersuchungs|gefangene m prisoner on remand; **~gefängnis** n remand prison; **~haft** f: **in ~ sein** be* on remand; **~richter** m examining magistrate

Unter|tan m subject; **~tasse** f saucer; **2tauchen** v/i. u. v/t. dive*, submerge (a. U-Boot); in: duck; fig. disappear; bsd. pol. go* underground; **~teil** n, m lower part, bottom

unterteil|en v/t. subdivide; **2ung** f subdivision

Unter|titel m subtitle; **~ton** m undertone; **~treibung** f understatement; **2vermieten** v/t. sublet*; **2wandern** v/t. infiltrate; **~wäsche** f underwear; **~wasser...** in Zssgn underwater ...; **2wegs** adv. on the od. one's way (**nach** to); **viel ~ sein** be* away a lot

unterweis|en v/t. instruct; **2ung** f instruction

Unterwelt f underworld (a. fig.)

unterwerf|en v/t. subject (dat. to); **sich ~** submit (to); **2ung** f subjection; submission (**unter** to)

unterwürfig adj. servile; **2keit** f servility

unterzeichn|en v/t. sign; **2ete(r)** the undersigned; **2ung** f signing

unterziehen v/t. Kleidung: put* s.th. on underneath; **sich ~** e-r Behandlung etc.: undergo*; e-r Prüfung: take*

Untiefe f shallow, shoal

un|tragbar adj. unbearable, intolerable; **~trennbar** adj. inseparable; **~treu** adj. unfaithful (dat. to); **~tröstlich** adj. inconsolable; **~trüglich** adj. unmistakable

Untugend f vice, bad habit

un|überlegt adj. thoughtless; **~sichtlich** adj. Kurve etc.: blind; komplex: intricate; **~trefflich** adj. unsurpassable, matchless; **~windlich** adj. Schwierigkeiten etc.: insuperable

unum|gänglich adj. inevitable; **~schränkt** adj. unlimited; pol. absolute; **~stritten** adj. undisputed; **~wunden** adv. straight out, frankly

ununterbrochen adj. uninterrupted; ständig: continuous

unver|änderlich adj. unchanging; **~antwortlich** adj. irresponsible; **~besserlich** adj. incorrigible; **~bindlich** adj. Angebot etc.: not binding; Art etc.: noncommittal; **~daulich** adj. indigestible (a. fig.); **~dient** adj. undeserved; **~dorben** adj. unspoiled; fig. a. uncorrupted; rein: pure, innocent; **~dünnt** adj. undiluted; Drink: neat, Am. straight; **~einbar** adj. incompatible; **~fälscht** adj. unadulterated; fig. genuine; **~fänglich** adj. harmless; **~froren** adj. brazen, impertinent; **~gänglich** adj. immortal, eternal;

~geßlich adj. unforgettable; **~gleichlich** adj. incomparable; **~hältnismäßig** adv. disproportionately; **~hoch** excessive; **~heiratet** adj. unmarried, single; **~hofft** adj. unhoped-for; unerwartet: unexpected; **~hohlen** adj. unconcealed; **~käuflich** adj. not for sale; nicht gefragt: unsal(e)able; **~kennbar** adj. unmistakable; **~letzt** adj. unhurt; **~meidlich** adj. inevitable; **~mindert** adj. undiminished; **~mittelt** adj. abrupt

Unvermögen n inability, incapacity; **2d** adj. without means

unver|mutet adj. unexpected; **~nünftig** adj. unreasonable; töricht: foolish; **~richteterdinge** adv. unsuccessfully, without having achieved anything

unverschämt adj. rude, impertinent; Preis etc.: outrageous; **~ werden** a. zudringlich: get* fresh; **2heit** f impertinence (a. Bemerkung); **die ~ haben zu** have* the nerve to

unver|schuldet adj. through no fault of one's own; **~sehens** adv. unexpectedly, all of a sudden; **~sehrt** adj. unhurt; Sache: undamaged; **~söhnlich** adj. irreconcilable (a. fig.); **~sorgt** adj. unprovided for; **~standen** adj. (sich fühlen feel*) misunderstood; **~ständlich** adj. unintelligible; **es ist mir ~** I can't see how od. why, F it beats me; **~sucht** adj.: **nichts ~ lassen** leave* nothing undone; **~wundbar** adj. invulnerable; **~wüstlich** adj. indestructible; **~zeihlich** adj. inexcusable; **~züglich 1.** adj. immediate, prompt; **2.** adv. immediately, without delay

unvollendet adj. unfinished

unvollkommen adj. imperfect; **2heit** f imperfection

unvollständig adj. incomplete

unvor|bereitet adj. unprepared; **~eingenommen** adj. unbias(s)ed, unprejudiced; **~hergesehen** adj. unforeseen; **~hersehbar** adj. unforeseeable; **~sichtig** adj. careless; **2sichtigkeit** f carelessness; **~stellbar** adj. inconceivable; undenkbar: unthinkable; **~teilhaft** adj. unprofitable; Kleid etc.: unbecoming

unwahr adj. untrue; **2heit** f untruth; **~scheinlich** adj. improbable, unlikely; F toll: fantastic

un|wegsam adj. Gelände: difficult, rough; **~weigerlich** adv. inevitably; **~weit** prp. not far from; **~wesentlich** adj. irrelevant; geringfügig: negligible; **2wetter** n disastrous (thunder)storm; **~wichtig** adj. unimportant

unwider|legbar adj. irrefutable; **~ruflich** adj. irrevocable; **~stehlich** adj. irresistible

Unwill|e(n) m indignation (**über** at); **2ig** adj. indignant (**über** at); widerwillig: unwilling, reluctant

unwillkürlich adv. involuntarily

unwirk|lich adj. unreal; **~sam** adj. ineffective; jur. etc. inoperative

unwirsch adj. surly, gruff, unfriendly

unwirt|lich adj. inhospitable; **~schaftlich** adj. uneconomic(al)

unwissen|d adj. ignorant; **2heit** f ignorance

un|wohl adj. unwell; unbehaglich: uneasy; **~würdig** adj. unworthy (gen. of); **~zählig** adj. innumerable, countless; **~zeitgemäß** adj. old-fashioned

unzer|brechlich adj. unbreakable; **~reißbar** adj. untearable; **~störbar** adj. indestructible; **~trennlich** adj. inseparable

Un|zucht f jur. sexual offen|ce, Am. -se; **2züchtig** adj. indecent; Literatur etc.: obscene

unzufrieden adj. discontent(ed) (**mit** with), dissatisfied (with); **2heit** f discontent, dissatisfaction

unzu|gänglich adj. inaccessible; **~länglich** adj. inadequate; **~lässig** adj. inadmissible; **~mutbar** adj. unacceptable

unzurechnungsfähig adj. irresponsible; **2keit** f irresponsibility

unzu|reichend adj. insufficient; **~sammenhängend** adj. incoherent; **~verlässig** adj. unreliable; Methode etc.: uncertain

üppig adj. luxuriant, lush (beide a. fig. Leben etc.); Figur: a. voluptuous, luscious; Mahl: opulent; gehaltvoll: rich

uralt adj. ancient (a. fig. iro.)

Uran n uranium

Ur|aufführung f première, first performance (Film: showing); **2bar** adj. arable; **~machen** cultivate; Wüste etc.: reclaim; **~bevölkerung** f, **~einwohner** pl. aboriginal inhabitants pl.; Australiens: Aborigines pl.; **~enkel(in)** great-grand|son (-daughter); **~groß...** in Zssgn Eltern, Mutter, Vater: great-grand...; **~heberrechte** pl. copyright sg. (**an** on, for)

Urin n urine; **2ieren** v/i. urinate

Urkunde f document; Zeugnis, Ehren2: diploma; **~nfälschung** f forgery of documents

Urlaub m Ferien: holiday(s pl.), bsd. Am. vacation; bsd. amtlich, mil.: leave; **in** od. **im ~ sein** (**auf ~ gehen**) be* (go*) on holiday (Am. a. vacation); **e-n Tag** (**ein paar Tage**) **~ nehmen** take* a day (a few days) off; **~er** m holidaymaker, bsd. Am. vacationist, vacationer

Urne f urn; Wahl2: ballot box

Ur|sache f cause; Grund: reason; **keine ~!** not at all, you're welcome; **~sprung** m origin; germanischen **~s** of Germanic origin; **2sprünglich** adj. original; natürlich: natural, unspoilt

Urteil n judg(e)ment (a. **~svermögen**); jur. Strafmaß: sentence; **sich ein ~ bilden** form a judg(e)ment (**über** about); **2en** v/i. judge (**über** j-n, et. s.o., s.th.; **nach** by)

Ur|wald m primeval forest; Dschungel: jungle; **2wüchsig** adj. coarse, earthy; **~zeit** f prehistoric times pl.

usw. Abk. für **und so weiter** etc., and so on

Utensilien pl. utensils pl.

Utop|ie f illusion; **2isch** adj. utopian; Plan etc.: fantastic

V

Vagabund m vagabond, tramp, *Am. sl.* hobo, bum

vage *adj.* vague

Vakuum n vacuum (*a. in Zssgn*)

Vampir zo. m vampire (*a. fig.*)

Vanille f vanilla (*a. in Zssgn*)

variabel *adj.* variable

Varia|nte f variant; **~tion** f variation

Varieté n variety theatre, music hall, *Am.* vaudeville theater

variieren *v/i. u. v/t.* vary

Vase f vase

Vater m father; **~land** n native country; **~landsliebe** f patriotism

väterlich *adj.* fatherly, paternal

Vaterunser *rel.* n Lord's Prayer

v. Chr. *Abk. für* **vor Christus** BC, before Christ

V-Ausschnitt m V-neck

Veget|arier(in), **2arisch** *adj.* vegetarian; **~ation** f vegetation; **2ieren** *v/i.* vegetate

Veilchen n violet

Velo n *Schweiz:* bicycle, F bike

Ventil n valve; *fig.* vent, outlet; **~ation** f ventilation; **~ator** m fan

verab|reden *v/t.* agree (up)on, arrange; *Ort, Zeit: a.* appoint, fix; **sich ~** make* a date (*bsd. geschäftlich:* an appointment) (*mit* with); **2redung** f appointment; *bsd. private:* date; **~reichen** *v/t.* give*; *med.* administer; **~scheuen** *v/t.* loathe, detest; **~schieden** *v/t.* say* goodbye to (*sich ~ von*); *entlassen:* dismiss; *Gesetz:* pass; **2schiedung** f dismissal; passing

ver|achten *v/t.* despise; **~ächtlich** *adj.* contemptuous; **~achtung** f contempt; **~allgemeinern** *v/t.* generalize; **~altet** *adj.* antiquated, out of date

Veranda f veranda(h), *Am.* porch

veränder|lich *adj.* changeable (*a. Wetter*), variable (*a. math., gr.*); **~n** *v/t. u. v/refl.*, **2ung** f change

verängstigt *adj.* frightened, scared

veranlag|en *v/t.* assess; **~t** *adj.* inclined (*zu, für* to); *künstlerisch (musikalisch) ~ sein* have* a gift *od.* bent for art (music); **2ung** f (pre)disposition (*a.*

med.); talent, gift; *steuerliche:* assessment

veranlass|en *v/t. et.:* make* arrangements (*od.* arrange) for; *j-n zu et. ~* make* s.o. do s.th.; **2ung** f cause (*zu* for)

ver|anschaulichen *v/t.* illustrate; **~anschlagen** *v/t.* estimate (*auf* at)

veranstalt|en *v/t.* arrange, organize; *Konzert etc.:* give*; **2ung** f event; *Sport: a.* meeting, *Am.* meet

verantwort|en *v/t.* take* the responsibility for; **~lich** *adj.* responsible; *j-n ~ machen für* hold* s.o. responsible for

Verantwortung f responsibility; *auf eigene ~* at one's own risk; *zur ~ ziehen* call to account; **~sbewußtsein**, **~sgefühl** n sense of responsibility; **2slos** *adj.* irresponsible

ver|arbeiten *v/t.* process; *fig.* digest; *et. ~ zu* manufacture (*od.* make*) s.th. into; **~ärgern** *v/t.* make* s.o. angry, annoy; **~armt** *adj.* impoverished; **~arschen** *sl. v/t.: j-n ~* take the mickey out of s.o.; **~ausgaben** *v/refl.* overspend*; *fig.* exhaust o.s.

Verb *gr.* n verb

Verband m *med.* dressing, bandage; *Vereinigung:* association; *mil.* formation, unit; **~(s)kasten** m first-aid kit *od.* box; **~(s)zeug** n dressing material

verbann|en *v/t.* banish (*a. fig.*), exile; **2ung** f banishment, exile

ver|barrikadieren *v/t.* barricade; *Straße etc.:* block; **~bergen** *v/t.* hide* (*a. sich ~*), conceal

verbesser|n *v/t.* improve; *berichtigen:* correct; **2ung** f improvement; correction

verbeug|en *v/refl.*, **2ung** f bow (*vor* to)

ver|biegen *v/t.* twist; **~bieten** *v/t.* forbid*; *amtlich:* prohibit; **~billigen** *v/t.* reduce in price; **~billigt** *adj.* reduced, at reduced prices

verbind|en *v/t. med. Wunde:* dress, bandage; *j-n:* bandage *s.o.* up; *mit et., a. tech.:* connect, join, link (up); *tel.* put* s.o. through (*mit* to); *kombinieren:* combine (*a. chem. sich ~*); *vereinen:* unite; *Vorstellung etc.:* associ-

verbindlich 582

ate; *j-m die Augen ~* blindfold s.o.; *damit sind beträchtliche Kosten verbunden* that involves considerable cost; *falsch verbunden!* wrong number!; **~lich** adj. obligatory, compulsory (a. *Schulfach*); *gefällig:* obliging; **2lichkeit** f obligingness; *pl.* econ. liabilities *pl.*

Verbindung f allg. connection; *Kombination:* combination; chem. compound; univ. society, Am. fraternity; *sich in ~ setzen mit* get* in touch with; *in ~ stehen (bleiben)* be* (keep*) in touch

ver|bitten adj. dogged; **~bitten** v/t.: *das verbitte ich mir!* I won't stand for that!

verbitter|t adj. bitter, embittered; **2ung** f embitterment, bitterness

verblassen v/i. fade (a. fig.)

Verbleib m whereabouts *pl.*; **2en** v/i. remain

verbleit adj. *Benzin:* leaded

verblend|et fig. adj. blind; **2ung** fig. f blindness

verblichen adj. *Farbe:* faded

verblüff|en v/t. amaze, baffle, F flabbergast; **2ung** f amazement, bafflement

ver|blühen v/i. fade, wither (beide a. fig.); **~bluten** v/i. bleed* to death

verborgen adj. hidden, concealed; *im ~en* in secret

Verbot n prohibition, ban (on *s.th.*); **2en** adj.: *Rauchen ~* no smoking

Verbrauch m consumption (an of); **2en** v/t. consume, use up; **~er** m consumer; **~erschutz** m consumer protection; **2t** adj. used up (a. fig.)

Verbrech|en n crime; *ein ~ begehen* commit a crime; **~er(in)**, **2erisch** adj. criminal

verbreit|en v/t. u. v/refl. spread* (in, über over, through); *Nachricht etc.: a.* circulate; **~ern** v/t. u. v/refl. widen, broaden; **2ung** f spread(ing); circulation

verbrenn|en v/i. u. v/t. burn* (up); *Leiche:* cremate; **2ung** f burning; bsd. tech. combustion; cremation; *Wunde:* burn

verbringen v/t. spend*, pass

verbrüder|n v/refl. fraternize; **2ung** f fraternization

ver|brühen v/t. scald; *sich ~* scald o.s.; **~buchen** v/t. book

verbünde|n v/refl. ally o.s. (mit to, with); **2te** m, f ally (a. fig.)

ver|bürgen v/refl.: *sich ~ für* vouch for, guarantee; **~büßen** v/t.: *e-e Strafe ~* serve a sentence, serve time; **~chromt** adj. chromium-plated

Verdacht m suspicion; *~ schöpfen* become* suspicious; *im ~ stehen, et. zu tun* be* under suspicion of doing s.th.

verdächtig adj. suspicious, suspect; **2e** m, f suspect; **~en** v/t. suspect (*j-n e-r Tat* s.o. of [doing] s.th.); **2ung** f suspicion; *Unterstellung:* insinuation

verdamm|en v/t. condemn (zu to), damn (a. rel.); **2nis** f damnation; **~t 1.** adj. damned, F a. damn, darn(ed), Brt. sl. a. bloody; F: *~ (noch mal)!* damn (it)!; **2.** adv.: *~ gut etc.* damn (Brt. sl. a. bloody) good etc.; **2ung** f condemnation, damnation

ver|dampfen v/t. u. v/i. evaporate; **~danken** v/t.: *j-m ~ (e-m Umstand etc.)* et. *~* owe s.th. to s.o. (s.th.)

verdau|en v/t. digest (a. fig.); **~lich** adj. digestible; *leicht (schwer) ~* easy (hard) to digest; **2ung** f digestion; **2ungsstörungen** pl. *Verstopfung:* constipation *sg.*

Verdeck n top; **2en** v/t. cover (up) (a. fig.)

verdenken v/t.: *ich kann es ihm nicht ~(, daß er ...)* I can't blame him (for ...ing)

verderb|en 1. v/i. spoil* (a. fig.); *Fleisch etc.:* go* bad; **2.** v/t. spoil* (a. *Spaß, Appetit etc.*), ruin; *sich den Magen ~* upset* one's stomach; **2en** n ruin; **~lich** adj. perishable; fig. pernicious; *~e Waren* perishables *pl.*

ver|deutlichen v/t. make* s.th. clear; **~dichten** v/t. compress, condense; *sich ~* condense; fig. grow* stronger; **~dienen** v/t. Geld: earn, make*; *Lob, Strafe etc.:* deserve

Verdienst¹ m earnings *pl.*; *Lohn:* wages *pl.*; *Gehalt:* salary; *Gewinn:* gain, profit

Verdienst² n merit; *es ist sein ~, daß* it is thanks to him that

ver|dient adj. *Strafe etc.:* (well-)deserved; **~doppeln** v/t. double

verdorben adj. spoilt (a. fig.); *Charakter, Lebensmittel: a.* bad; *Magen:* upset

ver|dorren *v/i.* wither , dry up; **~drängen** *v/t. j-n:* supplant, supersede (*a. Methode etc.*); *ersetzen:* replace; *phys.* displace; *psych.* repress; *bewußt:* suppress; **~drehen** *v/t.* twist; *fig. a.* distort; *Augen:* roll; **j-m den Kopf ~** turn s.o.'s head; **~dreht** F *fig. adj.* mixed up; **~dreifachen** *v/t. u. v/refl.* treble, triple

ver|drießlich, **~drossen** *adj.* glum, morose, sullen

Verdruß *m* displeasure; *Ärger:* trouble

verdummen 1. *v/t.* make* stupid, stultify; 2. *v/i.* become* stultified

verdunk|eln *v/t. u. v/refl.* darken; *völlig:* black out; *fig.* obscure; **2(e)lung** *f* darkening; black-out; *jur.* collusion; **2(e)lungsgefahr** *jur. f* danger of collusion

ver|dünnen *v/t.* thin (down), dilute (*a. chem.*); **~dunsten** *v/i.* evaporate; **~dursten** *v/i.* die of thirst; **~dutzt** *adj.* puzzled

vered|eln *v/t. bot.* graft; *tech.* process; *Öl, Stahl:* refine; **2(e)lung** *f bot.* grafting; *tech.* processing, refinement

verehr|en *v/t. bewundern:* admire; *anbeten, a. fig.:* adore, worship; *bsd. rel. a.* revere, venerate; **2er(in)** *f* admirer (*a. e-r Frau etc.*); *bsd. e-s Stars:* a. fan; **2ung** *f* admiration; adoration, worship; reverence, veneration

vereidigen *v/t.* swear* *s.o.* in; *jur. Zeugen:* put* *s.o.* under an oath

Verein *m* club (*a. Sport*2); *bsd. eingetragener:* a. society, association

vereinbar *adj.* compatible (*mit* with); **~en** *v/t.* agree (up)on, arrange; **2ung** *f* agreement, arrangement

vereinen *v/t.* → *vereinigen*

vereinfach|en *v/t.* simplify; **2ung** *f* simplification

vereinheitlichen *v/t.* standardize

vereinig|en *v/t. u. v/refl.* unite (**zu** into); (*sich*) *verbinden:* a. combine, join; **2ung** *f* union; combination; *Bündnis:* alliance

verein|samen *v/i.* become* lonely *od.* isolated; **~zelt** *adj.* occasional, odd; **~ Regen** scattered showers

ver|eiteln *v/t.* prevent; *Plan etc.:* a. frustrate; **~enden** *v/i.* die, perish; **~enge(r)n** *v/t. u. v/refl.* narrow

vererb|en *v/t.:* **j-m et. ~** leave* (*med.*

transmit) *s.th.* to *s.o.*; *sich ~ (auf)* be* passed on *od.* down (to) (*a. med. u. fig.*); **2ung** *biol. f* heredity; **2ungslehre** *f* genetics *sg.*

verewigen *v/t.* immortalize

verfahren 1. *v/i.* proceed; **~ mit** deal* with; 2. *v/refl.* get* lost

Verfahren *n* procedure, method; *bsd. tech. a.* technique, way; *jur.* (legal) proceedings *pl.* (**gegen** against)

Verfall *m* decay (*a. fig.*); *e-s Hauses etc.:* a. dilapidation; *Niedergang:* decline; *econ. etc.* expiry

verfall|en 1. *v/i.* decay (*a. fig.*); *bsd. fig. a.* decline; *Haus etc.:* a. dilapidate; *ablaufen:* expire; *Kranker:* waste away; *e-m Laster etc.:* become* addicted to; **(wieder) ~ in** fall* (back) into; **~ auf** hit* (up)on; 2. *adj.* decayed; *Haus:* a. dilapidated; **j-m ~ sein** be* s.o.'s slave; **2sdatum** *n* expiry date; *Lebensmittel:* best-before (*od.* best-by) date, *Am.* pull date; *Medikamente:* sell-by date

ver|fälschen *v/t.* falsify; *Bericht etc.:* a. distort; *Speisen etc.:* adulterate; **~fänglich** *adj.* delicate, tricky; *peinlich:* embarrassing, compromising; **~färben** *v/refl.* discolo(u)r

verfass|en *v/t.* write*; **2er(in)** author(ess)

Verfassung *f* state (*gesundheitlich:* of health; *seelisch:* of mind), condition; *pol.* constitution; **2smäßig** *adj.* constitutional; **2swidrig** *adj.* unconstitutional

ver|faulen *v/i.* rot, decay; **~fechten** *v/t.*, **~fechter(in)** advocate

verfehl|en *v/t.* miss (*sich* each other); **2ung** *f* offen|ce, *Am.* -se

ver|feinden *v/refl.* become* enemies; **~feindet** *adj.* hostile; **~feinern** *v/t. u. v/refl.* refine

verfilm|en *v/t.* film; **2ung** *f* filming; *Film:* film version

ver|flechten *v/t.* intertwine (*a. sich ~*); *econ.* interlock; **2flechtung** *f* intertwinement; *econ.* interlocking; **~ in** involvement in; **~flossen** *adj. Zeit:* past; F: **mein 2er** my ex-husband

verfluch|en *v/t.* curse; **~t** *adj.* → *verdammt*

verfolg|en *v/t.* pursue (*a. fig.*); *jagen, a. fig.:* chase, hunt; *pol., rel.* persecute; *Spuren:* follow; *Gedanken, Traum:*

haunt; **gerichtlich** ~ prosecute; **2er** *m* pursuer; persecutor; **2ung** *f* pursuit (*a. Radsport*); chase, hunt; persecution; **gerichtliche** ~ prosecution; **2ungswahn** *psych. m* persecution mania

ver|frachten *v/t.* freight, ship; F *j-n. etw.:* bundle (*in* into); **~fremden** *v/t. Kunst etc.:* alienate; **2fremdungseffekt** *bsd. thea. m* alienation effect; **~früht** *adj.* premature

verfüg|bar *adj.* available; **~en 1.** *v/t.* decree, order; **2.** *v/i.:* ~ **über** have* at one's disposal; **2ung** *f* decreee, order; disposal; *j-m zur* ~ **stehen** (**stellen**) be* (place) at s.o.'s disposal

verführ|en *v/t.* seduce (*et. zu tun* into doing s.th.); **2er** *m* seducer; **2erin** *f* seductress; **~erisch** *adj.* seductive; *verlockend:* tempting; **2ung** *f* seduction

vergangen *adj.* gone, past; *im* ~*en Jahr* last year; **2heit** *f* past; *gr.* past tense

vergänglich *adj.* transitory

vergas|en *v/t. chem.* gasify; *töten:* gas; **2er** *mot. m* carburet(t)or

vergeben *v/t.* give* away (*a. Chance*); *Preis etc.: a.* award; *verzeihen:* forgive*; **~ens** *adv.* in vain; **~lich 1.** *adj.* futile; **2.** *adv.* in vain; **2ung** *f* forgiveness, pardon

vergegenwärtigen *v/t.* visualize

vergehen 1. *v/i. Zeit etc.:* go* by, pass; *nachlassen:* wear* off; ~ *vor* be* dying with; *wie die Zeit vergeht!* how time flies!; **2.** *v/refl.:* **sich** ~ **an** violate; *vergewaltigen: a.* rape

Vergehen *jur. n* offen|ce, *Am.* -se

vergelt|en *v/t.* repay*; *belohnen: a.* reward; **2ung** *f Rache:* retaliation (*a. mil.*); **2ungsmaßnahme** *f* retaliatory measure

vergessen *v/t.* forget*; *liegenlassen:* leave*; **2heit** *f: in* ~ *geraten* fall* into oblivion

vergeßlich *adj.* forgetful

vergeud|en *v/t.* waste, **2ung** *f* waste

vergewaltig|en *v/t.* rape, violate (*a. fig.*); **2ung** *f* rape, violation

ver|gewissern *v/refl.* make* sure (*e-r Sache* of s.th.; *ob* whether; *daß* that); **~gießen** *v/t.* shed*; *verschütten:* spill*

vergift|en *v/t.* poison (*a. fig.*); *Umwelt:* contaminate; **2ung** *f* poisoning; contamination

vergittert *adj. Fenster etc.:* barred

Vergleich *m* comparison; *jur.* compromise; **2bar** *adj.* comparable (*mit* to, with); **2en** *v/t.* compare (*mit* with; *gleichstellend:* to); *ist nicht zu* ~ *mit* cannot be compared to; *an Wert etc.:* cannot compare with; *vergleichen mit* compared to *od.* with; **2sweise** *adv.* comparatively

verglühen *v/i.* burn* out (*Rakete etc.:* up)

Vergnüg|en *n* pleasure, enjoyment, *Spaß:* fun; *mit* ~ with pleasure; *viel* ~*!* have fun! have a good time!

vergnüg|en *v/refl.* enjoy o.s. (*mit et.* doing s.th.); **~t** *adj.* cheerful; **2ung** *f* pleasure, amusement, entertainment; **2ungspark** *m* amusement park, *bsd. Brt. a.* fun fair; **~ungssüchtig** *adj.* pleasure-seeking; **2ungsviertel** *n* night-life district

ver|golden *v/t.* gild*; **~göttern** *v/t.* idolize, adore; **~graben** *v/t.* bury (*a. fig.*); *fig.* **sich** ~ *in* bury o.s. in (*one's work etc.*); **~greifen** *v/refl.:* **sich** ~ **an** lay* hands on; **~griffen** *adj. Buch:* out of print

vergrößer|n *v/t.* enlarge (*a. phot.*); *vermehren:* increase; *opt.* magnify; **sich** ~ increase, grow*, expand; **2ung** *f phot.* enlargement; *opt.* magnification; *increase;* **2ungsglas** *n* magnifying glass

Vergünstigung *f* privilege

vergüt|en *v/t.* reimburse, pay* (for); **2ung** *f* reimbursement

verhaft|en *v/t.,* **2ung** *f* arrest

verhalten¹ *v/refl.* behave; *Person: a.* conduct o.s., act; *sich ruhig* ~ keep* quiet

verhalten² *adj.* restrained; *Ton:* subdued

Verhalten *n* behavio(u)r, conduct; **~sforschung** *f* behavio(u)ral science; **2sgestört** *adj.* disturbed, maladjusted

Verhältnis *n Beziehung, a. pol. etc.:* relationship, relations *pl.*; *Einstellung:* attitude; *zahlenmäßig etc.:* proportion, relation, *bsd. math.* ratio; F *Liebes-:* affair; **~se** *pl.* circumstances *pl.*, conditions *pl.* (*a. soziale*); *über j-s* ~*se* beyond s.o.'s means; **2mäßig** *adv.* comparatively, relatively; **~wort** *gr. n* preposition

verhand|eln 1. v/i. negotiate; **2.** v/t. jur. Fall: hear*; **♀ung** f negotiation, talk; jur. hearing; Strafrecht: trial; **~lungsbasis** econ. f asking price

verhäng|en v/t. cover (mit with); Strafe etc.: impose (über on); **♀nis** n fate; Unheil: disaster; **~nisvoll** adj. fatal, disastrous

ver|heerend adj. disastrous

ver|hehlen v/t. → **verheimlichen**; **~heilen** v/i. heal (up)

verheimlich|en v/t. hide*, conceal; **♀ung** f concealment

verheirat|en v/t. marry (s.o. off) (mit to); **sich ~** get* married; **~et** adj. married; F: frisch ~ just married

verheißungsvoll adj. promising

verhelfen v/i.: j-m zu et. ~ help s.o. to get s.th.

verherrlich|en v/t. glorify; contp. a. idolize; **♀ung** f glorification

verhexen v/t. bewitch; es ist wie verhext there's a jinx on it

verhinder|n v/t. prevent (daß j. et. tut s.o. from doing s.th.); **~t** adj. unable to come; ein **~er Künstler** a would-be artist; **♀ung** f prevention

verhöhn|en v/t. deride, mock (at), jeer (at); **♀ung** f derision

Verhör jur. n interrogation; **♀en 1.** v/t. interrogate, question; **2.** v/refl. get* it wrong

ver|hüllen v/t. cover, veil (a. fig.); **~hungern** v/i. die of hunger, starve (to death); **♀hungern** n starvation

verhüt|en v/t. prevent; **♀ungsmittel** n contraceptive

verirr|en v/refl. get* lost, lose* one's way, go* astray (a. fig.); **♀ung** fig. f aberration

verjagen v/t. chase od. drive* away

verjähr|en jur. v/i. come* under the statute of limitation; **~t** jur. adj. statute-barred

verjüngen v/t. make* s.o. (look) younger, rejuvenate; **sich ~** arch. etc.: taper (off)

verkabeln electr. v/t. cable

Verkauf m sale; **♀en** v/t. sell*; zu **~** for

sale; **sich gut ~** sell* well

Verkäuf|er m shop assistant, Am. (sales)clerk; econ. seller; Auto♀ etc.: salesman; **~erin** f shop assistant, saleslady, Am. (sales)clerk; **♀lich** adj. for sale; **schwer ~** hard to sell

Verkehr m traffic; öffentlicher: transport(ation Am.); Umgang: contact, dealings pl.; Geschlechts♀: intercourse; Umlauf: circulation; starker (schwacher) ~ heavy (light) traffic; **♀en 1.** v/i. Bus etc.: run*; ~ in Lokal etc.: frequent; ~ mit associate od. mix with; sexuell: have* intercourse with; **2.** v/t. turn (in into); ins Gegenteil ~ reverse

Verkehrs|ader f arterial road; **~ampel** f traffic light(s pl.); **~behinderung** f holdup, delay; jur. obstruction of traffic; **~delikt** n traffic offen|ce, Am. -se; **~flugzeug** n airliner; **~funk** m traffic bulletin; **~insel** f traffic island; **~meldung** f traffic announcement, flash; **~minister** m minister of transport; **~ministerium** n ministry of transport; **~mittel** n means of transport; öffentliche ~ pl. public transport(ation Am.) sg.; **~opfer** n road casualty; **~polizei** f traffic police pl.; **~rowdy** m F road hog; **♀sicher** mot. adj. roadworthy; **~sicherheit** f road safety; e-s Autos etc.: roadworthiness; **~stau** m traffic jam; **~sünder** F m traffic offender; **~teilnehmer** m road user; **~unfall** m traffic accident; schwerer: (car) crash; **~unterricht** m traffic instruction; **~zeichen** n traffic sign

ver|kehrt adj. u. adv. falsch: wrong; ~ herum: upside down; Pulli etc.: inside out; **~kennen** v/t. mistake*, misjudge

Verkettung f: ~ unglücklicher Umstände concatenation of misfortunes

ver|klagen jur. v/t. sue (auf, wegen for); **~klappen** v/t. dump (into the sea); **~kleben** v/t. glue (together)

verkleid|en v/t. disguise (als as), dress s.o. up (as); tech. cover, (en)case; täfeln: panel; **sich ~** disguise o.s., dress (o.s.) up; **♀ung** f disguise; tech. cover, encasement; panel(l)ing; mot. fairing

verkleiner|n v/t. make* smaller, reduce, diminish; **♀ung** f reduction, diminution

ver|klingen v/i. die away; **~knallt** F

adj.: ~ **sein in** be* madly in love with, have* a crush on; **⚫knappung** *f* shortage (**an** of); **~knoten** *v/t.* knot; **~knüpfen** *v/t.* knot together; *fig.* connect, combine; **~kohlen 1.** *v/t.* carbonize, char; *f: j-n* ~ pull s.o.'s leg; **2.** *v/i.* char; **~kommen 1.** *v/i. Haus etc.*: become* run-down *od.* dilapidated; *Person*: go* to the dogs; *Speisen etc.*: go* bad; **2.** *adj.* run-down, dilapidated; *verwahrlost*: neglected; *Person*: depraved, rotten (to the core); **~korken** *v/t.* cork (up)

verkörper|n *v/t.* personify; *bsd. Sache*: embody; *bsd. thea.* impersonate; **⚫ung** *f* personification, embodiment; *thea.* impersonation

ver|krachen *F v/refl.* fall* out (**mit** with); **~kriechen** *v/refl.* hide*; **~krümmt** *adj.* crooked, curved (*a. med.*); **~krüppelt** *adj.* crippled; **~kühlen** *v/refl.* catch* a chill

verkümmer|n *v/i.* become* stunted; **~t** *adj.* stunted

verkünd|en *v/t.* announce; *bsd. öffentlich*: proclaim; *Urteil*: pronounce; *rel. predigen*: preach; **⚫ung** *f* announcement; proclamation; pronouncement; *rel.* preaching

ver|kürzen *v/t.* shorten; (*Arbeits*)*Zeit*: *a.* reduce; **~laden** *v/t.* load (**auf** onto; **in** into)

Verlag *m* publishing house *od.* company, publisher(s *pl.*)

verlagern *v/t. u. v/refl.* shift (**auf** to)

verlangen *v/t.* ask for; *fordern*: demand; *beanspruchen*: claim; *Preis*: charge; *erfordern*: take*, call for

Verlangen *n* desire (**nach** for); *Sehnen*: longing (for), yearning (for); **auf** ~ by request; *econ.* on demand

verlänger|n *v/t.* lengthen, make* longer; *zeitlich*: prolong (*a. Leben*), extend (*a. econ.*); **⚫ung** *f* lengthening; prolongation, extension; *Sport*: extra time, *Am.* overtime

verlangsamen *v/t. u. v/refl.* slacken, slow down (*beide a. fig.*)

verlassen 1. *v/t.* leave*; *im Stich lassen*: *a.* abandon, desert; **2.** *v/refl.*: **sich** ~ **auf** rely *od.* depend on

verläßlich *adj.* reliable, dependable

Verlauf *m* course; **⚫en 1.** *v/i.* run*; *ablaufen*: go*; *enden*: end (up); **2.**

v/refl. get* lost, lose* one's way

verlauten *v/i.*: ~ **lassen** give* to understand; *wie verlautet* as reported

verleben *v/t.* spend*; *Zeit etc.*: a. have*

verleg|en¹ *v/t. Ort etc.*: move; *Brille etc.*: mislay*; *tech.* lay*; *zeitlich*: put* off, postpone; *Buch*: publish

verlegen² *adj.* embarrassed; **⚫heit** *f* embarrassment; *Lage*: embarrassing situation, *F* fix

Verleger *m* publisher

verleiden *v/t.* spoil* (*j-m et.* s.th. for s.o.)

Verleih *m* hire, rental; *Film*⚫: distributor(s *pl.*); **⚫en** *v/t.* lend*, *Am. a.* loan; *Autos etc.*: hire (*Am.* rent) out; *Preis etc.*: award; *Recht etc.*: grant; **~ung** *f* award(ing), presentation; grant(ing)

ver|leiten *v/t.*: *j-n zu et.* ~ make* s.o. do s.th., lead* s.o. to do s.th.; **~lernen** *v/t.* forget*; **~lesen 1.** *v/t.* read* (*Namen*: *a.* call) out; **2.** *v/refl.* make* a slip (in reading); *in, bei et.*: misread* *s.th.*

verletz|en *v/t.* hurt*, injure; *fig. a.* offend; *sich* ~ hurt* o.s., get* hurt; **~end** *adj.* offensive; **⚫te** *m, f* injured person; *die* ~*n pl.* the injured *pl.*; **⚫ung** *f* injury, *bsd. pl. a.* hurt; *fig., jur.* violation

verleugnen *v/t.* deny; *Glauben etc.*: *a.* renounce

verleumd|en *v/t.* defame; *jur. mündlich*: slander; *schriftlich*: libel; **~erisch** *adj.* slanderous, libel(l)ous; **⚫ung** *jur. f* slander; libel

verlieb|en *v/refl.* fall* in love (**in** with); **~t** *adj.* in love (**in** with); *Blick etc.*: amorous; **⚫te** *m, f* lovers *pl.*

verlier|en *v/t. u. v/refl.* lose*; **⚫er(in)** loser

verlob|en *v/refl.* get* engaged (**mit** to); **⚫te(r)** fiancé(e *f*); **⚫ung** *f* engagement

verlock|en *v/t.* tempt; **~end** *adj.* tempting; **⚫ung** *f* temptation

verlogen *adj.* untruthful, lying; **⚫heit** *f* untruthfulness, dishonesty

verloren *adj.* lost; *Zeit etc.*: *a.* wasted; **~gehen** *v/i.* be* *od.* get* lost

verlos|en *v/t.* raffle (off); **⚫ung** *f* raffle

Verlust *m* loss (*a. fig.*); **~e** *pl. bsd. mil.* casualties *pl.*

vermachen *v/t.* leave*, will

Vermächtnis *n* legacy (*a. fig.*)

vermarkt|en *v/t.* market; *bsd. contp.* commercialize; **⚫ung** *f* marketing; commercialization

vermehr|en v/t. u. v/refl. increase (**um** by), multiply (by) (a. biol.); biol. reproduce, bsd. zo. a. breed*; **Ωung** f increase; biol. reproduction

vermeid|bar adj. avoidable; **∼en** v/t. avoid

ver|meintlich adj. supposed; **∼mengen** v/t. mix, mingle, blend

Vermerk m note; **Ωen** v/t. make* a note of

vermess|en¹ v/t. measure; Land: survey

vermessen² adj. presumptuous; **Ωenheit** f presumption

Vermessung f measuring; survey(ing)

vermiete|n v/t. let*, rent, lease (out); Autos etc.: hire (Am. rent) out; **zu ∼** to let; Autos etc.: for hire; beide: bsd. Am. for rent; **Ωr(in)** land|lord (-lady); **Ωung** f letting, renting; → **Verleih**

vermindern → **verringern**

vermisch|en v/t. u. v/refl. mix, mingle, blend (**with**); **∼t** adj. mixed; **Ωes** Überschrift: miscellaneous

vermi|ssen v/t. miss; **∼ßt** adj. missing; **die Ωen** pl. the missing pl.

vermitt|eln 1. v/t. arrange; Eindruck etc.: give*, convey; **j-m et. ∼** get* od. find* s.o. s.th.; 2. v/i. mediate (**zwischen** between); **Ωler** m mediator, go--between; econ. agent, broker; **Ωlung** f mediation; Herbeiführung: arrangement; Stelle: agency, office; tel. (telephone) exchange; Mensch: operator

vermodern v/i. mo(u)lder, rot

Vermögen n fortune (a. F fig.); Besitz: property, possessions pl.; econ. assets pl.; **Ωd** adj. well-to-do, well-off

vermummen v/refl. mask o.s., disguise o.s.

vermut|en v/t. suppose, expect, think*, Am. a. guess; **∼lich** adv. probably; **Ωung** f supposition; bloße: speculation

vernachlässig|en v/t., **Ωung** f neglect

vernarben v/i. scar over; fig. heal

vernarrt adj.: **∼ in** mad od. crazy about; → **verknallt**

vernehm|en v/t. hear*; jur. question, interrogate; **∼lich** adj. clear, distinct; **Ωung** jur. f interrogation, examination

verneig|en v/refl., **Ωung** f bow (**vor** to) (a. fig.)

verlein|en 1. v/t. deny; 2. v/i. say* no, answer in the negative; **∼end** adj. nega-

tive; **Ωung** f denial, negative (a. gr.)

vernicht|en v/t. destroy; **∼end** adj. devastating (a. fig.); Antwort, Niederlage: crushing; **Ωung** f destruction; bsd. mil. a. annihilation; Ausrottung: extermination

Vernunft f reason; **∼ annehmen** listen to reason; **j-n zur ∼ bringen** bring* s.o. to reason

vernünftig adj. sensible, reasonable (a. Preis etc.); F ordentlich: decent

veröden v/i. become* deserted

veröffentlich|en v/t. publish; **Ωung** f publication

verordn|en v/t. order; med. a. prescribe (**gegen** for); **Ωung** f order; Rezept: prescription

ver|pachten v/t. lease; **Ωpächter** m lessor

verpack|en v/t. pack (up); tech. package; einwickeln: wrap up; **Ωung** f pack(ag)ing; PapierΩ: wrapping; **Ωungsmüll** m superfluous packaging

ver|passen v/t. miss; **∼patzen** F v/t. mess up, spoil*; **∼pesten** v/t. pollute, foul, contaminate; F stink* out; **∼petzen** F v/t.: **j-n ∼** tell* on s.o. (**bei** to); **∼pfänden** v/t. pawn; fig. pledge

verpflanz|en v/t., **Ωung** f transplant (a. med.)

verpfleg|en v/t. feed*; **Ωung** f food

verpflicht|en v/t. oblige; engagieren: engage; **sich ∼, et. zu tun** undertake* (econ. agree) to do s.th.; **∼et adj.: ∼ sein** (**sich ∼ fühlen**) **zu et.** be* (feel*) obliged to do s.th.; **Ωung** f obligation; Pflicht: duty; econ. jur. liability; übernommene: engagement; commitment

ver|pfuschen F v/t. bungle, botch; **∼plappern** v/refl. blab; **∼pönt** adj. taboo; **∼prügeln** F v/t. beat* s.o. up; **∼puffen** fig. v/i. fizzle out

Verputz arch. m, **Ωen** v/t. plaster

ver|quollen adj. Holz: warped; Gesicht etc.: puffy, swollen; **∼rammeln** v/t. barricade, block

Verrat m betrayal (**an** of); Treulosigkeit: treachery (to); jur. Landes∼: treason (to); **Ωen** v/t. betray, give* away (beide a. fig.); **sich ∼** betray o.s., give* o.s. away

Verräter m traitor; **Ωisch** adj. treacherous; fig. revealing, telltale

verrechn|en 1. v/t. set* off (**mit**

V

against); **2.** v/refl. miscalculate, make* a mistake (a. fig.); **sich um e-e Mark ~** be* one mark out; **♀ung** f setting off; **♀ungsscheck** m crossed cheque, Am. voucher check

verregnet adj. rainy

verreis|en v/i. go* away (geschäftlich: on business); **~t** adj. away (geschäftlich on business)

verrenk|en v/t. med. dislocate, luxate; **sich et. ~** med. dislocate s.th.; **sich den Hals ~** crane one's neck; **♀ung** med. f dislocation, luxation

ver|richten v/t. do*, perform, carry out; **~riegeln** v/t. bolt, bar

verringer|n v/t. decrease, lessen (beide a. sich ~), reduce, cut* down; **♀ung** f reduction, decrease

ver|rosten v/t. rust, get* rusty (a. fig.); **~rotten** v/i. rot; **~rottet** adj. rotten

verrück|en v/t. move, shift; **~t** adj. mad, crazy (beide a. fig.: **nach** about); **wie ~** like mad; **~ werden** go* mad od. crazy; **j-n ~ machen** drive* s.o. mad; **♀te(r)** mad|man (-woman), lunatic, maniac (alle a. F fig.); **♀theit** f madness, craziness; Tat etc.: crazy thing

Verruf m: **in ~ bringen** bring* discredit (up)on; **in ~ kommen** get* into discredit; **♀en** adj. notorious

verrutschen v/i. slip, get* out of place

Vers m verse; Zeile: a. line

versagen 1. v/i. allg. fail (a. med.); mot. etc. a. break* down; Waffe: misfire; **2.** v/t. deny, refuse

Versag|en n failure; **~er** m failure

versalzen v/t. oversalt; F fig. spoil

versamm|eln v/t. gather, assemble; **sich ~** a. meet*; **♀lung** f assembly, meeting

Versand m dispatch, shipment; **~... in** Zssgn Haus, Katalog etc.: mail-order ...

versäum|en v/t. miss; **et. zu tun ~** fail to do s.th.; **♀nis** n Unterlassung: omission; Schule, Arbeit: absence (from school od. work)

ver|schaffen v/t. get*, find*; **sich ~** a. obtain; **~schämt** adj. bashful; **~schanzen** v/refl. entrench o.s. (a. fig. **hinter** behind); **~schärfen** v/t. verschlimmern: aggravate; Kontrollen etc.: tighten up; erhöhen: increase; **sich ~** schlimmer werden: get* worse; **~schenken** v/t. give* away (a. fig.);

~scherzen v/t. forfeit; **~scheuchen** v/t. scare off, chase away (a. fig.); **~schicken** v/t. send* off; bsd. econ. a. dispatch

verschieb|en v/t. move, shift (a. **sich ~**); zeitlich: postpone, put* off; **♀ung** f shift(ing); postponement

verschieden adj. different (**von** from); **~e** pl. mehrere: various, several; **~artig** adj. different; mannigfaltig: various; **♀heit** f difference; **~tlich** adv. repeatedly

verschiff|en v/t. ship; **♀ung** f shipment

verschimmeln v/i. get* mo(u)ldy

verschlafen 1. v/i. oversleep*; **2.** v/t. et.: sleep* through; **2.** adj. sleepy (a. fig.)

Verschlag m shed

verschlagen¹ v/t. **j-m den Atem ~** take* s.o.'s breath away; **j-m die Sprache ~** leave* s.o. speechless; **es hat ihn nach X ~** he ended up in X

verschlagen² adj. sly, cunning

verschlechter|n v/t. u. v/refl. make* (refl. get*) worse, worsen, deteriorate; **♀ung** f deterioration; e-s Zustands: a. change for the worse

verschleiern v/t. veil; fig. a. cover up

Verschleiß m wear (and tear); **♀en** v/t. wear* out

ver|schleppen v/t. carry off; pol. displace; in die Länge ziehen: draw* out, delay; Krankheit: neglect; **~schleudern** v/t. waste; econ. sell* dirt cheap; **~schließen** v/t. close (a. fig. die Augen); absperren: lock (up)

verschlimmern v/t. u. v/refl. → verschlechtern

verschlingen v/t. devour (a. fig.); bsd. Essen: gulp (down)

verschlossen adj. closed; fig. aloof, reserved; **♀heit** f aloofness

verschlucken 1. v/t. swallow (fig. up); **2.** v/refl. choke; **ich habe mich verschluckt** it went down the wrong way

Verschluß m fastener; aus Metall: a. clasp; Schnapp♀: catch; Schloß: lock; Deckel: cover, lid; a. Schraub♀: cap, top; phot. shutter; **unter ~** under lock and key

ver|schlüsseln v/t. (en)code, (en)cipher; **♀schlußzeit** phot. f shutter speed; **~schmähen** v/t. disdain, scorn

verschmelz|en v/i. u. v/t. merge, fuse

(*beide a. econ., pol. etc.*), melt*; **ung** *f* fusion (*a. fig.*)

ver|schmerzen *v/t.* get* over *s.th.*; **~schmieren** *v/t.* smear, smudge; **~schmitzt** *adj.* mischievous; **~schmutzen 1.** *v/t.* soil, dirty; *Umwelt:* pollute; **2.** *v/i.* get* dirty; get* polluted; **~schnaufen** F *v/i. u. v/refl.* stop for breath; **~schneit** *adj.* snow-covered, snowy

Verschnitt *m* blend; *Abfall:* waste

verschnupft *adj.:* **~ sein** *med.* have* a cold; F *fig.* be* peeved

ver|schnüren *v/t.* tie up; **~schollen** *adj.* missing; *jur.* presumed dead; **~schonen** *v/t.* spare; **j-n mit et. ~** spare *s.o. s.th.*

verschöne|(r)n *v/t.* embellish; **rung** *f* embellishment

ver|schossen *adj.* Farbe: faded; F: **~ sein** *in* have* a crush on; **~schränken** *v/t.* fold; *Beine:* cross

verschreib|en 1. *v/t. med.* prescribe (**gegen** for); **2.** *v/refl.* make* a slip of the pen; **sich e-r Sache ~** devote *o.s.* to *s.th.;* **~ungspflichtig** *pharm. adj.* available on prescription only

ver|schroben *adj.* eccentric, odd; **~schrotten** *v/t.* scrap; **~schüchtert** *adj.* intimidated

verschulde|n *v/t.* be* responsible for, cause, be* the cause of; **sich ~** get* into debt; **~t** *adj.* in debt

ver|schütten *v/t. Flüssigkeit:* spill*; *j-n:* bury (alive); **~schwägert** *adj.* related by marriage; **~schweigen** *v/t.* keep* *s.th.* a secret, hide*

verschwend|en 1. *v/t.* waste; **~er(in)** spendthrift; **~erisch** *adj.* wasteful, extravagant; *üppig:* lavish; **ung** *f* waste

verschwiegen *adj.* discreet; *verborgen:* hidden, secret; **heit** *f* secrecy, discretion

ver|schwimmen *v/i.* become* blurred; **~schwinden** *v/i.* disappear, vanish; F: **verschwinde!** beat it!; **ung** *f* disappearance; **~schwommen** *adj.* blurred (*a. phot.*); *fig. a.* vague, hazy

verschwör|en *v/refl.* conspire, plot; **er** *m* conspirator; **ung** *f* conspiracy, plot

verschwunden *adj.* missing

versehen 1. *v/t. Haushalt etc.:* take* care of; **~ mit** provide with; **2.** *v/refl.* make* a mistake

Versehen *n* mistake, error; **aus ~, tlich** *adv.* by mistake, unintentionally

Versehrte(r) disabled person

versenden *v/t.* → *verschicken*

ver|sengen *v/t.* singe, scorch; **~senken** *v/t.* sink*; **sich ~ in** become* absorbed in; **~sessen** *adj.:* **~ auf** mad *od.* crazy about

versetz|en *v/t.* move, shift; *dienstlich:* transfer; *Schüler:* move *s.o.* up, *Am.* promote; *Schlag etc.:* give*; *verpfänden:* pawn; *agr.* transplant; **j-n ~** stand* *s.o.* up; **in die Lage ~, zu** put* in a position to, enable to; **jdn in j-s Lage ~** put* *o.s.* in *s.o.'s* place; **ung** *f* transfer; *Schule:* remove, *Am.* promotion

verseuch|en *v/t.* contaminate; **ung** *f* contamination

versicher|n *v/t. econ.* insure (**bei** with); *behaupten:* assure (**j-m et.** *s.o.* of *s.th.*), assert; **sich ~** insure *o.s.;* *sichergehen:* make* sure (**daß** that); **te(r)** *the* insured; **ung** *f* insurance; assurance, assertion

Versicherungs|gesellschaft *f* insurance company; **~police** *f*, **~schein** *m* insurance policy

ver|sickern *v/i.* trickle away; **~siegeln** *v/t.* seal; **~siegen** *v/i.* dry up, run* dry; **~silbern** *v/t.* silver-plate; F *fig.* turn into cash; **~sinken** *v/i.* sink*; → *versunken*; **~sinnbildlichen** *v/t.* symbolize

Version *f* version

versklaven *v/t.* enslave (*a. fig.*)

Versmaß *n* met|re, *Am.* -er

versöhn|en *v/t.* reconcile; **sich (wieder) ~** make* it up (**mit** with); **~lich** *adj.* conciliatory; **ung** *f* reconciliation; *bsd. pol.* appeasement

versorg|en *v/t.* provide (**mit** with), supply (with); *Familie etc.:* support; **sich kümmern um:** take* care of, look after; **ung** *f* supply (**mit** with); *Unterhalt:* support; *Betreuung:* care

verspät|en *v/refl.* be* late; **~et** *adj.* belated, late, *Am. a.* tardy; *Zug etc.: a.* delayed; **ung** *f* being late *od.* coming late; *Am. a.* tardiness; *Schule: Am.* tardy; *Zug etc.:* delay; **20 Minuten ~ haben** be* 20 minutes late

ver|speisen *v/t.* eat* (up); **~sperren** *v/t.* bar, block (up), obstruct (*a. Sicht*);

zuschließen: lock; **~spielen** *v/t.* lose*; **~spielt** *adj.* playful; **~spotten** *v/t.* make* fun of, ridicule; **~sprechen 1.** *v/t.* promise (*a. fig.*); *sich zuviel ~* (*von*) expect too much (of); **2.** *v/refl.* make* a mistake *od.* slip; **2sprechen** *n* promise; *ein ~ geben* (*halten, brechen*) make* (keep*, break*) a promise; **~sprecher** F *m* slip (of the tongue) **verstaatlich|en** *v/t.* nationalize; **2ung** *f* nationalization

Verstädterung *f* urbanization

Verstand *m* mind, intellect; *Vernunft*: reason, (common) sense; *Intelligenz*: intelligence, brains *pl.*; *nicht bei ~ sein*: out of one's mind, not in one's right mind; *den ~ verlieren* go* out of one's mind; **2esmäßig** *adj.* rational

verständ|ig *adj.* reasonable, sensible; **~igen** *v/t.* inform (*von* of), notify (of); *Arzt, Polizei*: *a.* call; *sich ~* communicate; *sich einigen*: come* to an agreement (*über* on); **2igung** *f* communication (*a. tel.*); *Einigung*: agreement; **~lich** *adj.* intelligible; *begreiflich*: comprehensible; *Verhalten*: understandable; *hörbar*: audible; *schwer* (*leicht*) *~*: difficult (easy) to understand; *j-m et. ~ machen* make* s.th. clear to s.o.; *sich ~ machen* make* o.s. understood

Verständnis *n* comprehension, understanding (*a. menschliches*); *Mitgefühl*: *a.* sympathy; (*viel*) *~ haben* be* (very) understanding; *~ haben für* understand*; *appreciate*; **2los** *adj.* unappreciative; *Blick etc.*: blank; **2voll** *adj.* understanding, sympathetic; *Blick etc.*: knowing

verstärk|en *v/t.* reinforce (*a. tech., mil.*); *zahlenmäßig*: strengthen (*a. tech.*); *Radio, phys.*: amplify; *steigern*: intensify; **2er** *m* amplifier; **2ung** *f* strengthening; reinforcement(s *pl. mil.*); amplification; intensification

verstauben *v/i.* get* dusty

verstauch|en *med.* *v/t.*, **2ung** *med.* *f* sprain

verstauen *v/t.* stow away

Versteck *n* hiding place, F hideout, hideaway; **2en** *v/t. u. v/refl.* hide* (*a. fig.*); **~en** *n*: *~ spielen* play (at) hide-and-seek

verstehen *v/t.* understand*, F get*; *akustisch*: *a.* catch*; *einsehen*: see*; *sich im klaren sein*: realize; *können*: know*; *es ~ zu* know* how to; *zu ~ geben* give* *s.o.* to understand, suggest; *~ Sie* (*?*) *erklärend*: you know *od.* see; *fragend*: you see?; *ich verstehe!* I see!; *falsch ~* misunderstand*; *was ~ Sie unter* ...? what do you mean *od.* understand by ...?; *sich* (*gut*) *~* get* along (well) (*mit* with); *es versteht sich von selbst* it goes without saying

versteifen 1. *v/t.* stiffen (*a. sich ~*); *tech.* strut, brace; **2.** *v/refl.*: *sich auf et. ~* insist on (doing) s.th.

versteiger|n *v/t.* (sell* by) auction; **2ung** *f* auction (sale)

versteinern *v/i.* petrify (*a. fig.*)

verstell|bar *adj.* adjustable; **~en** *v/t.* *versperren*: block; *umstellen*: move; *falsch einstellen*: set* *s.th.* wrong *od.* the wrong way; *tech.* adjust, regulate; *Stimme etc.*: disguise; *sich ~* pretend, put* on an act; *s-e Gefühle verbergen*: hide* one's feelings; **2ung** *fig.* f disguise, make-believe, (false) show

ver|steuern *v/t.* pay* duty *od.* tax on; **~stiegen** *fig. adj.* high-flown

verstimm|en *v/t.* put* out of tune; *fig.* annoy; **~t** *adj.* out of tune; *Magen*: upset; *verärgert*: annoyed, F cross; **2ung** *f* annoyance

verstockt *adj.* stubborn, obstinate

verstohlen *adj.* furtive, stealthy

verstopf|en *v/t.* plug (up); *versperren*: block, jam; *med.* constipate; **~t** *adj.* *Nase*: stuffed; *med.* constipated; **2ung** *f* block(age); *med.* constipation

verstorben *adj.* late, deceased; **2e** *m, f* *the* deceased; *die ~n pl.* the deceased *pl.*

verstört *adj.* upset; *erschreckt*: dismayed; *Blick etc.*: *a.* wild

Verstoß *m* offen|ce, *Am.* -se (*gegen* against), violation (of); **2en 1.** *v/t.* expel (*aus* from); *Frau, Kind etc.*: repudiate, disown; **2.** *v/i.*: *~ gegen* offend against, violate

verstrahlt *adj.* (radioactively) contaminated

ver|streichen 1. *v/i. Zeit*: pass, go* by; *Frist*: expire; **2.** *v/t.* spread~; **~streuen** *v/t.* scatter

verstümmel|n *v/t.* mutilate; *Text etc.*: *a.* garble; **2ung** *f* mutilation

verstummen *v/i.* grow* silent; *Gespräch etc.*: stop; *langsam*: die down

Versuch m attempt, try; *Probe:* trial, test; *phys.* experiment; *mit et. (j-m) e-n ~ machen* give* s.th. (s.o.) a trial; **2en** *v/t.* try, attempt; *kosten:* try, taste; *rel. j-n:* tempt; *es ~ haben* have* a try (at it)

Versuchs|... *in Zssgn Bohrung etc.:* test *od.* trial ...; **~kaninchen** *fig. n* guinea pig; **~stadium** *n* experimental stage; **~tier** *n* laboratory *od.* test animal; **2weise** *adv.* by way of trial; *auf Probe:* on a trial basis

Versuchung f temptation; *j-n in ~ führen* tempt s.o.

ver|sunken *fig. adj.:* **~ in** absorbed *od.* lost in; **~süßen** *v/t.* sweeten

vertagen *v/t. u. v/refl.* adjourn; **2ung** f adjournment

vertauschen *v/t.* exchange (*mit* for)

verteidig|en *v/t.* defend (*sich* o.s.); **2er** m defender; *Sport:* a. back; *fig.* advocate; **2ung** f defen[c]e, *Am.* -se

Verteidigungs|... *in Zssgn Politik etc.:* *mst* defen[c]e, *Am.* -se ...; **~minister** m Minister of Defence, *Am.* Secretary of Defense; **~ministerium** n Ministry of Defence, *Am.* Department of Defense

verteil|en *v/t.* distribute; *austeilen:* hand out; **2er** m distributor; **2ung** f distribution

vertief|en *v/t. u. v/refl.* deepen (a. *fig.*); *sich ~ in* become* absorbed in; **2ung** f hollow, depression, *kleine:* dent; *fig. von Wissen etc.:* reinforcement

vertikal *adj.,* **2e** f vertical

vertilg|en *v/t.* exterminate; F consume; **2ung** f extermination

vertonen *mus. v/t.* set* to music

Vertrag m contract; *pol.* treaty; **2en** *v/t.* endure, bear*, stand*; *ich kann ... nicht ~ Essen, Alkohol etc.:* ... doesn't agree with me; *j-n, Lärm etc.:* I can't stand ...; *er kann viel ~* he can take a lot (*Spaß* a joke); *Alkohol:* a. he can hold his drink; F: *ich (es) könnte ... ~* I (it) could do with ...; *sich (gut) ~* get* along (well) (*mit* with); *sich wieder ~* make* it up; **2lich** *adv.* by contract

verträglich *adj.* easy to get on with; *Essen:* (easily) digestible

vertrauen *v/i.* trust (*auf* on)

Vertrauen n confidence, trust, faith; *im ~ (gesagt)* between you and me; **2er-weckend** *adj.:* (*wenig*) ~ *sein od.* *aussehen* inspire (little) confidence

Vertrauens|frage *parl. f:* *die ~ stellen* ask for a vote of confidence; **~sache** f: *das ist ~* that is a matter of confidence; **~stellung** f position of trust; **2voll** *adj.* trustful, trusting; **~votum** *parl. n* vote of confidence; **2würdig** *adj.* trustworthy

vertraulich *adj.* confidential; *plump~:* familiar

vertraut *adj.* familiar; *Freund etc.:* close; **2e(r)** intimate; **2heit** f familiarity

vertreib|en *v/t.* drive* *od.* chase away (a. *fig.*); *Zeit:* pass; *econ.* sell*; *~ aus* drive* out of; **2ung** f expulsion (*aus* from)

vertret|en *v/t.* substitute for, replace, stand* in for (*alle a. Schule*); *pol., econ.* represent; *parl. a.* sit* for; *jur. j-n:* act for; *j-s Sache ~* plead s.o.'s cause; *die Ansicht ~, daß* argue that; *sich den Fuß ~* sprain one's ankle; F: *sich die Beine ~* stretch one's legs; **2er** m substitute, deputy; *pol., econ.* representative; *econ. a.* agent; *Handels2:* sales representative, *bsd. Am.* (travel[l]ing) salesman; *e-s Arztes:* locum; **2ung** f substitution, replacement; *Person:* substitute, stand-in (*alle a. Schule*); *Lehrer: a.* supply teacher; *econ., pol.* representation

Vertrieb *econ.* m sale, distribution; **~ene(r)** expellee, refugee

ver|trocknen *v/i.* dry up; **~trödeln** F *v/t.* dawdle away, waste; **~trösten** *v/t.* put* off; **~tuschen** F *v/t.* cover up; **~übeln** *v/t.* take* amiss; *ich kann es ihr nicht ~* I can't blame her for it; **~üben** *v/t.* commit

verunglücken *v/i.* have* (*tödlich:* die in) an accident; *fig.* go* wrong

verun|reinigen *v/t.* → *verschmutzen* 1; **~stalten** *v/t.* disfigure

veruntreuen *v/t.* embezzle

verursachen *v/t.* cause, bring* about

verurteil|en *v/t.* condemn (*zu* to) (a. *fig.*), sentence (to), convict (*wegen* of); **2ung** f condemnation (a. *fig.*)

verviel|fachen *v/t.* multiply; **~fältigen** *v/t.* copy, duplicate; **2fältigung** f duplication; *Abzug:* copy

vervoll|kommnen *v/t.* perfect; *verbessern:* improve; **~ständigen** *v/t.* complete

ver|wachsen adj. deformed, crippled; fig. ~ mit deeply rooted in, bound up with; ~wackelt adj. Foto: blurred

verwahr|en v/t. keep* (in a safe place); sich ~ gegen protest against; ~lost adj. uncared-for, neglected; 2ung f custody (a. jur.)

verwaist adj. orphan(ed); fig. deserted

verwalt|en v/t. manage; bsd. pol. a. administer; 2er m manager; administrator; 2ung f administration (a. öffentliche), management; 2ungs... in Zssgn Gericht, Kosten etc.: administrative ...

verwand|eln v/t. change, turn (beide a. sich ~); bsd. phys., chem. a. transform, convert (alle: in into); 2lung f change, transformation; Umwandlung: a. conversion

verwandt adj. related (mit to); 2e m, f relative; (alle) m-e ~n (all) my relatives od. relations od. F folks; der nächste ~ the next of kin; 2schaft f relationship; Verwandte: relations pl., F folks pl.

verwarn|en v/t. caution; Sport: F book; 2ung f caution; Sport: F booking

ver|waschen adj. washed-out; ~wässern v/t. water down (a. fig.)

verwechs|eln v/t. confuse (mit with), mix up (with), mistake* (for); 2(e)lung f mistake; confusion

verwegen adj. daring, bold; 2heit f boldness, daring, audacity

ver|wehren v/t. u. refl.: refuse; et. zu tun: keep* from doing s.th.; ~weichlicht adj. soft

verweiger|n v/t. refuse; Befehl: disobey; 2ung f denial, refusal

verweilen v/i. stay; fig. Blick: rest

Verweis m reprimand, reproof; reference (auf to); 2en v/t. refer (auf, an to); hinauswerfen: expel (gen. from)

verwelken v/i. wither; fig. a. fade

verwend|en v/t. use; Zeit etc.: spend* (auf on); 2ung f use; keine ~ haben für have* no use for

verwerf|en v/t. drop, give* up; ablehnen: reject; ~lich adj. abject

verwerten v/t. use, make* use of

verwes|en v/i. rot, decay; 2ung f decay

verwick|eln fig. v/t. involve; sich ~ in get* caught in; ~elt fig. adj. complicated; ~ sein (werden) in be* (get*) involved in; 2lung fig. f involvement; complication

verwilder|n v/i. grow* (Kinder: run*) wild; ~t adj. Garten etc.: wild (a. fig.), overgrown

verwinden v/t. get* over s.th.

verwirklich|en v/t. realize; sich ~ come* true; sich selbst ~ fulfil(l) o.s.; 2ung f realization

verwirr|en v/t. confuse; ~t fig. adj. confused; 2ung fig. f confusion

verwischen v/t. blur (a. fig.); Spuren: cover

verwitter|n geol. v/i. weather; ~t adj. geol. weather-beaten (a. fig.)

verwitwet adj. widowed

verwöhn|en v/t. spoil*; ~t adj. spoilt

verworren adj. confused, muddled; Situation: complicated

verwund|bar adj. vulnerable (a. fig.); ~en v/t. wound

verwunder|lich adj. surprising; 2ung f surprise

Verwund|ete(r) wounded (person), casualty; ~ung f wound, injury

verwünsch|en v/t., 2ung f curse

verwüst|en v/t. lay* waste, devastate, ravage; 2ung f devastation, ravage

ver|zählen v/refl. count wrong; ~zärteln v/t. coddle, pamper; ~zaubern v/t. enchant; fig. a. charm; ~ in turn into; ~zehren v/t. consume (a. fig.)

verzeichn|en v/t. record, keep* a record of, list; fig. erzielen: achieve; erleiden: suffer; 2is n list, catalog(ue); record, register; Stichwort2: index

verzeih|en v/t. u. v/i. bsd. j-m: forgive*; bsd. et.: pardon, excuse; ~lich adj. pardonable; 2ung f pardon; (j-n) um ~ bitten apologize (to s.o.); ~! (I'm) sorry!; vor Bitten etc.: excuse me!

verzerr|en v/t. distort (a. fig.); sich ~ become* distorted; 2ung f distortion

verzetteln v/refl. fritter away one's time

Verzicht m förmlich: renunciation (auf of); mst giving up, doing without etc.; 2en v/i.: ~ auf do* without; aufgeben: give* up; förmlich: renounce (a. jur.)

verziehen 1. v/i. move (nach to); **2.** v/t. Kind: spoil*; das Gesicht ~ make* a face; sich ~ Holz: warp; Gewitter etc.: pass (over); F verschwinden: disappear

verzier|en v/t. decorate; 2ung f decoration, ornament

verzins|en v/t. pay* interest on; sich ~ yield interest; 2ung f interest

verzöger|n v/t. delay; **sich ~** be* delayed; **♀ung** f delay

verzollen v/t. pay* duty on; **et. (nichts) zu ~** s.th. (nothing) to declare

verzück|t adj. ecstatic; **♀ung** f ecstasy; **in ~ geraten** go* into ecstasies od. raptures (**wegen, über** over)

Verzug m delay; **im ~ sein** (**in ~ geraten**) econ. be* (**come***) in default

verzweif|eln v/i. despair (**an** of); **~elt** adj. desperate; **♀lung** f despair; **j-n zur ~ bringen** drive* s.o. to despair

verzweig|en v/refl. branch (out); **♀ung** f ramification (a. fig.)

verzwickt adj. intricate, tricky

Veteran m mil. veteran (a. fig.)

Veterinär m veterinary surgeon, Am. veterinarian, F vet

Veto n veto (a. ~ **einlegen gegen**)

Vetter m cousin; **~nwirtschaft** f nepotism

vgl. Abk. für **vergleiche** cf., confer

VHS Abk. für **Volkshochschule** Institution: adult education program(me); Kurse: adult evening classes pl.

Vibr|ation f vibration; **♀ieren** v/i. vibrate

Video n video (a. in Zssgn Aufnahme, Clip, Kamera, Kassette, Recorder etc.); **auf ~ aufnehmen** video(tape), bsd. Am. tape; **~band** n videotape; **~text** m teletext; **~thek** f video(tape) library, video shop (Am. store)

Vieh n cattle pl.; **20 Stück ~** 20 head of cattle; **~bestand** m livestock; **~händler** m cattle dealer; **♀isch** adj. bestial, brutal; **~zucht** f cattle breeding, stockbreeding; **~züchter** m cattle breeder, stockbreeder

viel adj. u. adv. a lot (of), plenty (of), F lots of; **~e** many; **nicht ~** not much; **nicht ~e** not many; **sehr ~** a great deal (of); **sehr ~e** very many, a lot (of); **das ~e Geld** all that money; **ziemlich ~** quite a lot (of); **ziemlich ~e** quite a few; **~ besser** much better; **~ teurer** much more expensive; **~zuviel** far too much; **~ zuwenig** not nearly enough; **~ lieber** much rather

viel|beschäftigt adj. very busy; **~deutig** adj. ambiguous; **~erlei** adj. all kinds od. sorts of; **~fach 1.** adj. multiple; **2.** adv. in many cases, (very) often; **♀falt** f (great) variety (gen. of); **~farbig** adj. multicolo(u)red; **~leicht** adv. perhaps, maybe; **~ ist er ...** he may od. might be ...; **~mals** adv.: **(ich) danke (Ihnen) ~** thank you very much; **entschuldigen Sie ~** I'm very sorry, I do apologize; **~mehr** cj. rather; **~sagend** adj. meaningful; **~seitig** adj. versatile; **♀seitigkeit** f versatility; **~versprechend** adj. promising

vier adj. four; **zu ~t sein** be* four; **auf allen ~en** on all fours; **unter ~ Augen** in private, privately; **♀beiner** m quadruped, four-legged animal; **~beinig** adj. four-legged; **♀eck** n quadrangle; **~eckig** adj. quadrangular; rechteckig: rectangular; quadratisch: square; **♀er** m Rudern: four; **~erlei** adj. four (different) kinds od. sorts of; **~fach** adj. fourfold; **~e Ausfertigung** four copies pl.; **~füßig** adj. four-footed; **♀füßler** zo. m quadruped; **~händig** mus. adj. four-handed; **~jährig** adj. four-year-old, of four; **♀linge** pl. quadruplets pl.; **~mal** adv. four times; **♀radantrieb** mot. m four-wheel drive; **~seitig** adj. four-sided; math. quadrilateral; **♀sitzer** mot. m four-seater; **~spurig** adj. four-lane; **~stöckig** adj. foursto(re)yed, Am. -ried; **♀taktmotor** mot. m four-stroke engine; **~te** adj. fourth

Viertel n fourth (part); Stadt♀: quarter; **(ein) ~ vor (nach)** (a) quarter to (past); **~finale** n Sport: quarter finals pl.; **~jahr** n three months pl.; **♀jährlich 1.** adj. quarterly; **2.** adv. every three months, quarterly; **♀n** v/t. quarter; **~note** mus. f crotchet, Am. a. quarter note; **~pfund** n quarter of a pound; **~stunde** f quarter of an hour

vier|tens adv. fourthly; **♀vierteltakt** mus. m four-four od. common time

vierzehn adj. fourteen; **~ Tage** pl. two weeks pl., bsd. Brt. a. a fortnight sg.; **~te** adj. fourteenth

vierzig adj. forty; **~ste** adj. fortieth

Villa f villa

violett adj. violet, purple

Violine mus. f violin

Virtuelle Realität f Computer: virtual reality, Cyberspace

virtuos adj. masterly; **♀e** m, **♀in** f virtuoso; **♀ität** f virtuosity

Virus med. n, m virus

Visier n am Gewehr: sights pl.; am Helm: visor

Vision f vision
Visite med. f round; **~nkarte** f (visiting) card
Visum n visa (a. **mit e-m ~ versehen**)
vital adj. vigorous; **2ität** f vigo(u)r
Vitamin n vitamin
Vitrine f (glass) cabinet; Schaukasten: showcase
Vize... in Zssgn Präsident etc.: vice(-)...
Vogel m bird (a. F Flugzeug); F **e-n ~ haben** be* off one's rocker; **den ~ abschießen** take* the cake; **~bauer** n birdcage; **2frei** adj. outlawed; **~futter** n birdseed; **~kunde** f ornithology; **~käfig** m birdcage
vögeln V v/t. u. v/i. screw
Vogel|nest n bird's nest; **~perspektive** f bird's-eye view; **~scheuche** f scarecrow (a. fig.); **~schutzgebiet** n bird sanctuary; **~warte** f ornithological station; **~zug** m bird migration
Vokabel f word; **~n** pl. → **~ular** n vocabulary sg.
Vokal ling. m vowel
Volant östr. m → **Lenkrad**
Volk n people, nation; Leute: the people pl.; Bienen2: swarm; **ein Mann aus dem ~e** a man of the people
Völker|kunde f ethnology; **~mord** m genocide; **~recht** n international law; **~wanderung** f migration of peoples; fig. exodus
Volks|abstimmung f referendum; **~fest** n funfair; **~hochschule** f adult evening classes pl.; **~lied** n folk song; **~mund** m: im **~** in the vernacular; **~musik** f folk music; **~republik** f people's republic; **~schule** hist. f → Grundschule; **~sport** m popular sport; **~sprache** f vernacular; **~stamm** m tribe, race; **~tanz** m folk dance; **~tracht** f national costume; **2tümlich** adj. popular, folk ...; herkömmlich: traditional; **~versammlung** f public meeting; **~wirt** m economist; **~wirtschaft** f (national) economy; → **~wirtschaftslehre** f economics sg.; **~zählung** f census
voll 1. adj. full (a. fig.); besetzt, F satt: a. full up; F betrunken: a. plastered; Haar: thick, rich; **~er** full of, filled with; Schmutz, Flecken etc.: a. covered with; **2.** adv. fully; vollkommen, **~ und ganz**: a. completely, totally, wholly;

zahlen etc.: in full, the full price; direkt, genau: full, straight, right; **(nicht) für ~ nehmen** (not) take* seriously
voll|auf adv. perfectly, quite; **~automatisch** adj. fully automatic; **2bart** m (full) beard; **2beschäftigung** f full employment; **2blut...** in Zssgn full-blooded (a. fig.); **2blut(pferd)** n thoroughbred (horse); **~bringen** v/t. accomplish, achieve; Wunder: perform; **2dampf** m full steam; F: **mit ~** (at) full blast; **~enden** v/t. finish, complete; **~endet** adj. completed; fig. perfect; **~ends** adv. completely; **2endung** f finishing, completion; fig. perfection; **~entwickelt** adj. fully developed
Völlerei f gluttony
voll|führen v/t. perform; **~füllen** v/t. fill (up); **2gas** mot. n full throttle; **~ geben** F step on it; **~gießen** v/t. fill (up)
völlig 1. adj. complete, absolute, total; **2.** adv. completely; **~ unmöglich** absolutely impossible
volljährig adj.: **~ sein (werden)** be* (come*) of age; **noch nicht ~** under age; **2keit** f majority
vollkommen adj. perfect; fig. → völlig; **2heit** f perfection
Voll|kornbrot n wholemeal bread; **2machen** v/t. fill (up); F soil, dirty; **um das Unglück vollzumachen** to crown it all; **~macht** f full power(s pl.), authority; jur. power of attorney; **~haben** be* authorized; **~milch** f full-cream milk; **~mond** m full moon; **2packen** v/t. load (mit with) (a. fig.); **~pension** f full board; **2schlank** adj. plump, on the plump side; **2ständig** adj. complete; fig. → völlig; **2stopfen** v/t. stuff; fig. a. cram, pack (alle: mit with); **2strecken** v/t. execute; **~streckung** f execution; **2tanken** v/t.: **bitte ~!** fill her up, please!; **2transistoriert** electr. adj. solid-state; **~treffer** m direct hit; Schießen: bull's eye (a. fig.); **~versammlung** f plenary session; **2wertig** adj. full; **~wertkost** f wholefoods pl.; **2zählig** adj. complete; **2ziehen** v/t. execute; Trauung: perform; **sich ~** take* place; **~ziehung** f, **~zug** m execution
Volontär(in) unpaid trainee
Volt electr. n volt; **~zahl** f voltage

Volumen *n* volume; *Größe: a.* size
von *prp. räumlich, zeitlich:* from; *für Genitiv:* of; *Urheberschaft, a. beim Passiv:* by; *über j-n od. et.:* about; **südlich ~** south of; **weit ~** far from; **~ Hamburg** from Hamburg; **~ nun an** from now on; **ein Freund ~ mir** a friend of mine; **die Freunde ~ Alice** Alice's friends; **ein Brief (Geschenk) ~ Tom** a letter (gift) from Tom; **ein Buch (Bild) ~ Orwell (Picasso)** a book (painting) by Orwell (Picasso); **~ the King (Mayor etc.)** of; **ein Kind ~ 10 Jahren** a child of ten; **müde ~ der Arbeit** tired from work; **es war nett (gemein) ~ dir** it was nice (mean) of you; **reden (hören) ~** talk (hear*) about *od.* of; **~ Beruf (Geburt)** by profession (birth); **~ selbst** by itself; **von mir aus!** I don't mind *od.* care; **~statten** *adv.:* **~ gehen** go*, come* off
vor *prp. räumlich:* in front of; *außerhalb:* outside (*a. der Tür, dem Haus etc.*); *zeitlich, Reihenfolge:* before; *e-m Jahr etc.:* ago (*nachgestellt*); *infolge:* with, for; **~ der Klasse** in front of the class; **~ der Schule** in front of *od.* outside the school; *zeitlich:* before school; **~ kurzem (e-r Stunde)** a short time (an hour) ago; **5 Minuten ~ 12** five (minutes) to twelve; **~ j-m liegen** be* *od.* lie* ahead of s.o. (*a. fig. u. Sport*); **~ sich hin lächeln** etc.: to o.s.; **sicher ~** safe from; **~ Kälte (Angst)** with cold (for fear); **~ allem** above all; **~ sich gehen** go* on, happen
Vor|abend *m* eve (*a. fig.*); **~ahnung** *f* presentiment, foreboding
voran *adv.* at the head (*dat.* of), in front (of), before; *Kopf ~* head first; **~gehen** *v/i.* go* in front *od.* first; *bsd. fig.* lead* the way; **~kommen** *v/i.* get* on *od.* along (*a. fig.*)
Voranzeige *f* preannouncement; *Film:* trailer
vorarbeite|n *v/i.* work in advance; *fig.* pave the way; **~r** *m* foreman
voraus *adv.* ahead (*dat.* of); **im ~** in advance; **~gehen** *v/i. zeitlich:* precede; → **vorangehen**; **~gesetzt** *cj.:* **~, daß** provided that; **~sage** *f* prediction; *Wetter:* forecast; **~sagen** *v/t.* predict; forecast; **~schicken** *v/t.* send* on ahead; **lassen Sie mich ~, daß** let me

begin by mentioning that; **~sehen** *v/t.* foresee*, see* *s.th.* coming; **~setzen** *v/t.* assume; *selbstverständlich:* take* *s.th.* for granted; **~setzung** *f* *Vorbedingung:* condition, prerequisite; *Annahme:* assumption; **die ~en erfüllen** meet* the requirements; **~sicht** *f* foresight; **aller ~ nach** in all probability; **~sichtlich** *adv.* probably; **er kommt ~ morgen** he is expected to arrive tomorrow; **~zahlung** *f* advance payment
Vorbe|deutung *f* omen; **~dingung** *f* prerequisite; **~halt** *m* reservation; **~halten** *v/t.:* **sich (das Recht) ~, zu** reserve the right to; **1.** 2. *adj.* reserved; **~haltlos 1.** *adj.* unconditional; **2.** *adv.* without reservation
vorbei *adv. zeitlich:* over; *Winter, Woche etc.: a.* past; *aus, beendet:* finished; *vergangen:* gone; *räumlich:* past, by; **jetzt ist alles ~** it's all over now; **~!** *daneben:* missed!; **~fahren** *v/i.* go* (*mot. drive*) past (**an** *s.o. od. s.th.*), pass (*s.o. od. s.th.*); **~gehen** *v/i.* walk past; *a. fig.* go* by, pass; *nicht treffen:* miss; **~kommen** *v/i.* pass (**an** *et. s.th.*); *an e-m Hindernis:* get* past; *F besuchen:* drop in (**bei** *j-m* on s.o.); *fig. an et.:* avoid; **~lassen** *v/t.* let* *s.o.* pass
Vorbemerkung *f* preliminary remark
vorbereit|en *v/t. u. v/refl.* prepare (**auf** for); **~ung** *f* preparation (**auf** for)
vorbestell|en *v/t.* book (*Waren:* order) in advance; *Tisch, Platz, Zimmer etc.: a.* reserve; **~ung** *f* advance booking, reservation
vorbestraft *adj.:* **~ sein** have* a police record
vorbeug|en 1. *v/i.* prevent (**e-r Sache** s.th.); **2.** *v/refl.* bend* forward; **~end** *adj.* preventive; *med. a.* prophylactic; **~ung** *f* prevention
Vorbild *n* model, pattern; *(j-m) ein ~ sein* set* an example (to s.o.); *sich j-n zum ~ nehmen* follow s.o.'s example; **~lich** *adj.* exemplary; **~ung** *f* education(al background)
vor|bringen *v/t. Angelegenheit, Beweis etc.:* bring* forward; *sagen:* say*, state; **~datieren** *v/t. zurück:* antedate; *voraus:* postdate
Vorder|... *in Zssgn Achse, Ansicht, Rad, Sitz, Tür, Zahn etc.:* front ...; **~e** *adj.* front; **~grund** *m* foreground (*a. fig.*);

~lader m muzzle-loader; **~mann** m: **mein ~** the man od. boy in front of me; **~seite** f front (side); *Münze:* head

vor|dräng(l)en v/refl. *Brt.* jump the queue, *Am.* cut* into line, butt in; **~drängen** v/i. advance; **~ (bis) zu** work one's way through to (a. *fig.*); **~dringlich 1.** adj. (most) urgent; **2.** adv. **~ behandeln** give* s.th. priority; **2druck** m form, *Am.* a. blank

voreilig adj. hasty, rash, precipitate; **~e Schlüsse ziehen** jump to conclusions

voreingenommen adj. prejudiced, bias(s)ed; **2heit** f prejudice, bias

vor|enthalten v/t. keep* back, withhold* (*beide: j-m et.* s.th. from s.o.); **2entscheidung** f preliminary decision; **~erst** adv. for the present, for the time being

Vorfahr m ancestor

vorfahr|en v/i. drive* up (*weiter:* on); **2t(srecht** n) f right of way, priority

Vorfall m incident, occurrence, event; **2en** v/i. happen, occur

vorfinden v/t. find*

Vorfreude f anticipation

vorführ|en v/t. show*, present; *Kunststück etc.:* demonstrate; *Gerät etc.:* demonstrate; *jur.* bring* (*j-m* before s.o.); **2er** m *Kino:* projectionist; **2ung** f presentation, show(ing); performance (a. *Vorstellung*); demonstration; *jur.* production; **2wagen** *mot.* m demonstration car, *Am.* demonstrator

Vor|gabe f handicap; **~gang** m event, occurrence, happening; *Akte:* file, record(s pl.); *biol., tech.* process; **e-n ~ schildern** give* an account of what happened; **~gänger(in)** predecessor; **~garten** m front garden (*Am. a.* yard)

vorgeben v/t. *Sport:* give*; *fig.* use s.th. as a pretext

Vorgebirge n foothills pl.

vorgefertigt adj. prefabricated; *Meinung:* preconceived

Vorgefühl n presentiment

vorgehen v/i. *geschehen:* go* on; *wichtiger sein:* come* first; *handeln:* act; *gerichtlich:* sue (*gegen j-n* s.o.); *verfahren:* proceed; *Uhr:* be* fast

Vorgehen n procedure

vorgeschichtlich adj. prehistoric

Vorgeschmack m foretaste (*auf* of)

Vorgesetzte(r) superior, F boss

vorgestern adv. the day before yesterday

vorgreifen v/i. anticipate *s.o. od. s.th.*

vorhaben v/t. plan, intend; **haben Sie heute abend et. vor?** have you anything on tonight?; **was hat er jetzt wieder vor?** what is he up to now?

Vorhaben n plan(s pl.), intention; *tech., econ.* a. project

Vorhalle f (entrance) hall, lobby

vorhalt|en 1. v/t.: *j-m et.* ~ hold* s.th. in front of s.o.; *fig.* blame s.o. for (doing) s.th.; **2.** v/i. last; **2ungen** pl. reproaches pl.; *j-m* ~ **machen (für et.)** reproach s.o. (with s.th., for being ...)

Vorhand f *Tennis:* forehand

vorhanden adj. verfügbar: available; *bestehend:* in existence; **~ sein** exist; **es ist nichts mehr ~** there's nothing left; **2sein** n existence

Vor|hang m curtain; **~hängeschloß** n padlock

vorher adv. before, earlier; *im voraus:* in advance, beforehand

vorher|bestimmen v/t. predetermine; **2bestimmung** f predetermination; **~gehen** v/i. precede; **~ig** adj. preceding, previous

Vorherr|schaft f predominance; **2schen** v/i. predominate, prevail; **2schend** adj. predominant, prevailing

Vorher|sage f → *Voraussage*; **2sagen** v/t. → *voraussagen*; **2sehbar** adj. foreseeable

vorhin adv. a (little) while ago; **~ein** adv.: **im ~** beforehand

Vorhut f *mil.* f vanguard

vor|ig adj. last; *früher:* former, previous; **~jährig** adj. of last year, last year's

Vor|kämpfer(in) champion, pioneer; **~kehrungen** pl.: ~ **treffen** take* precautions; **~kenntnisse** pl. previous knowledge sg. od. experience sg. (*of* in)

vorkommen v/i. be* found; *geschehen:* happen; **es kommt mir ... vor** it seems ... to me

Vorkomm|en n *Bergbau:* deposit(s pl.); *Ereignis:* → **~nis** n occurrence, incident, event

Vorkriegs... in *Zssgn* prewar ...

vorlad|en *jur.* v/t. summon; **2ung** *jur.* f summons

Vorlage f model; *Muster:* pattern; *Zei-*

*chen*2 *etc.*: copy; *Unterbreitung*: presentation; *parl.* bill; *Fußball etc.*: pass

vorlassen *v/t.* 2 go* first; *vorbei*: let* *s.o.* pass; **vorgelassen werden** be* admitted (*bei* to)

Vorlauf *m* Recorder: fast-forward; *Sport*: (preliminary) heat

Vorläuf|er(in) forerunner, precursor; **2ig 1.** *adj.* provisional, temporary; **2.** *adv.* for the present, for the time being

vorlaut *adj.* pert, cheeky

Vorleben *n* former life, past

vorlege|n *v/t.* present; *Dokument etc.*: produce; *zeigen*: show*; *j-m e-e Frage* ~ put* a question to s.o.; **2r** *m* rug; *Matte*: mat

vorles|en *v/t.* read* out (aloud); *j-m et.* ~ read* s.th. to s.o.; **2ung** *f* lecture (*über* on; *vor* to); *e-e* ~ *halten* (give* a) lecture

vorletzte *adj.* last but one; ~ *Nacht* (*Woche*) the night (week) before last

Vorlieb|e *f* preference, special liking; **2nehmen** *v/i.*: ~ *mit* make* do with

vorliegen *v/i.*: *es liegen* (*keine*) ... *vor* there are (no) ...; *was liegt gegen ihn vor?* what is he charged with?; **~d** *adj.* present, in question

vor|lügen *v/t.*: *j-m et.* ~ tell* s.o. lies; **~machen** *v/t.*: *j-m et.* ~ show* s.th. to s.o., show* s.o. how to do s.th.; *fig.* fool s.o.; **2machtstellung** *f* supremacy; **2marsch** *mil. m* advance (*a. fig.*); **~merken** *v/t.* put* (*j-n*: s.o.'s name) down

Vormittag *m* morning; *heute* 2 this morning; **2s** *adv.* in the morning; *sonntags* ~ on Sunday mornings

Vormund *m* guardian; **~schaft** *f* guardianship

vorn *adv.* in front; *nach* ~ forward; *von* ~ from the front; *zeitlich*: from the beginning; *j-n von* ~(*e*) *sehen* see* s.o.'s face; *noch einmal von* ~(*e*) (*anfangen*) (start) all over again

Vorname *m* first od. Christian name, *bsd. amtlich*: *a.* forename

vornehm *adj.* distinguished; *edel, adlig*: noble; F *fein, teuer etc.*: smart, fashionable, exclusive, F posh; *die* ~*e Gesellschaft* (high) society, the upper crust; **~tun** *v/t.* put* on airs; **~en** *v/t.* carry out, do*; *Änderungen etc.*: make*; *sich et.* ~ decide *od.* resolve to do s.th.; *planen*: make* plans for s.th.; *sich fest*

vorgenommen haben, zu have* the firm intention to, be* determined to; *sich j-n* ~ take* s.o. to task (*wegen* about, for)

vornherein *adv.*: *von* ~ from the start *od.* beginning

Vorort *m* suburb; **~(s)zug** *m* suburban *od.* local *od.* commuter train

Vor|posten *m* outpost (*a. mil.*); **2programmieren** *v/t.* (pre)program(me); *fig.* *das war vorprogrammiert* that was bound to happen; **~rang** *m* precedence (*vor* over), priority (over); **~rat** *m* store, stock, supply (*alle*: an of); *Lebensmittel*: *a.* provisions *pl.*; *bsd. Rohstoffe etc.*: resources *pl.*, reserves *pl.*; *e-n* ~ *anlegen* an stockpile; **2rätig** *adj.* available; *econ.* in stock; **~recht** *n* privilege; **~redner** *m* previous speaker; **~richtung** *tech. f* device; **~rükken 1.** *v/t.* move forward; **2.** *v/i.* advance; **~runde** *f Sport*: preliminary round; **2sagen** *v/i.*: ~ prompt s.o.; **~saison** *f* off-peak season; **~satz** *m* resolution; *Absicht*: intention; *jur.* intent; **2sätzlich** *adj.* intentional; *bsd. jur.* will(l)ful; **~schau** *f* preview (*auf* of); *Film, TV*: *a.* trailer; **~schein** *m*: *zum* ~ *bringen* produce; *fig.* bring* out; *zum* ~ *kommen* appear, come* out; **2schieben** *v/t.* push forward; *Riegel*: slip; *fig.* use as a pretext; **2schießen** *v/t. Geldbetrag*: advance

Vorschlag *m* suggestion, proposal (*a. parl. etc.*); *den* ~ *machen* → **2en** *v/t.* suggest, propose

Vor|schlußrunde *f Sport*: semifinal; **2schnell** *adj.* hasty, rash; **2schreiben** *fig. v/t.* prescribe; *anordnen*: tell*; *ich lasse mir nichts* ~ I won't be dictated to

Vorschrift *f* rule, regulation; *Anweisung*: instruction; direction; *Dienst nach* ~ *machen* work to rule; **2smäßig** *adj.* correct, proper; **2swidrig** *adj. u. adv.* contrary to regulations

Vor|schub *m*: ~ *leisten* encourage; *jur.* aid and abet; **~schul...** in *Zssgn* pre-school ...; **~schule** *f* Brt. nursery (*od.* infant) school, *Am.* preschool, kindergarten; **~schuß** *m* advance; **2schützen** *v/t.* use *s.th.* as a pretext; **2schweben** *v/i.*: *mir schwebt et. vor* I have s.th. in mind

vorseh|en 1. v/t. plan; jur. provide; ~ **für** intend (ein Amt: designate) for; **2.** v/refl. be* careful, take* care, watch out (vor for); **2ung** f providence

vorsetzen v/t.: j-m et. ~ put* s.th. before s.o.; anbieten: offer s.o. s.th.; fig. dish up s.th. to s.o.

Vorsicht f caution, care; ~! look od. watch out!, (be) careful!; ~, Glas! Glass, with care!; ~, Stufe! mind the step!; **2ig** adj. careful, cautious; ~! careful!

vorsichts|halber adv. to be on the safe side; **2maßnahme** f precaution(ary measure); ~n treffen take* precautions

Vorsilbe gr. f prefix

vorsingen v/t. u. v/i.: j-m et. ~ sing* s.th. to s.o.; zur Probe: (have*) an) audition

Vorsitz m chair(manship), presidency; den ~ haben (übernehmen) be* in (take*) the chair, preside (bei over, at); ~ende m, f chairman (chairwoman), president

Vorsorge f precaution; ~ treffen take* precautions; ~untersuchung f preventive checkup

vorsorglich 1. adj. precautionary; **2.** adv. as a precaution

Vor|spann m Film etc.: credits pl.; ~speise f hors d'œuvre; F starter; als ~ for starters

vorspiegeln v/t. pretend; **2(e)lung** f pretence, Am. -se

Vorspiel n mus. prelude (a. fig.); sexuelles: foreplay; **2en** v/t.: j-m et. ~ play s.th. to s.o.

vor|sprechen 1. v/t. pronounce (j-m for s.o.); **2.** v/i. call (bei at); thea. (have*) an) audition; ~springen fig. v/i. project, protrude (beide a. arch.); **2sprung** m arch. projection; Sport: lead; e-n ~ haben be* leading (von by); bsd. fig. a. be* (von 2 Jahren two years) ahead; **2stadt** f suburb; **2stand** m board (of directors); e-s Clubs etc.: managing committee

vorsteh|en v/i. project, protrude; fig. leiten: manage, be* the head of, be* in charge of

vorstell|en v/t. introduce (sich o.s.; j-n j-m s.o. to s.o.); Uhr: put* forward (um by); bedeuten: mean*; sich et. (j-n als ...) ~ imagine s.th. (s.o. as ...); so stelle ich mir ... vor that's my idea of ...; sich

~ bei Firma etc.: have* an interview with; **2ung** f thea. performance; Kino2 etc.: a. show; Gedanke etc.: idea; Erwartung: expectation; von j-m od. et.: introduction; ~sgespräch: interview; **2ungsvermögen** n imagination

Vor|stopper m cent|re (Am. -er) back; ~stoß m mil. advance; Versuch: attempt; ~strafe f previous conviction; **2strecken** v/t. Geld: advance; ~stufe f preliminary stage; **2täuschen** v/t. feign, fake

Vorteil m advantage (a. Sport); Nutzen: benefit, profit; die ~e und Nachteile the pros and cons; **2haft** adj. advantageous, profitable; ~sregel f Sport: advantage rule

Vortrag m talk; bsd. akademischer: lecture; mus., Gedicht2: recital; e-n ~ halten give* a talk od. lecture (vor to); **2en** v/t. äußern: express, state; mus. etc.: perform, play; Gedicht etc.: recite

vor|trefflich adj. splendid; ~treten v/i. step forward, fig. protrude (a. Augen etc.), stick* out; **2tritt** m precedence; j-m den ~ lassen let* s.o. go first

vorüber adv.: ~ sein be* over; ~gehen v/i. pass, go* by; ~gehend adj. temporary

Vor|übung f preparatory exercise; ~untersuchung jur., med. f preliminary examination

Vorurteil n prejudice; **2slos** adj. unprejudiced, unbias(s)ed

Vor|verkauf thea. m advance booking; **2verlegen** v/t. advance; ~wahl f tel. STD (od. dial[l]ing, Am. area) code; pol. preliminary election, Am. primary; ~wand m pretext, excuse

vorwärts adv. forward, on(ward), ahead; ~! come on!, let's go!; ~kommen v/i. make* headway (a. fig.); fig. get* on (Am. along)

vorweg adv. beforehand; ~nehmen v/t. anticipate

vor|weisen v/t. produce, show*; et. ~ können boast s.th.; ~werfen fig. v/t.: j-m et. ~ reproach s.o. with s.th.; ~wiegend adv. predominantly, chiefly, mainly, mostly; ~witzig adj. cheeky, pert

Vor|wort n foreword; bsd. des Autors: preface; ~wurf m reproach; j-m Vorwürfe machen (wegen) reproach s.o.

(for); ⚲**wurfsvoll** adj. reproachful;
~**zeichen** n omen, sign (a. math.);
⚲**zeigen** v/t. show*; Karte etc.: a.
produce

vorzeitig adj. premature, early
vor|ziehen v/t. Vorhänge: draw*; fig.
prefer; ⚲**zimmer** n anteroom; Büro:
outer office; östr. → Hausflur; ⚲**zug** m
Vorteil: advantage; gute Eigenschaft:

merit; **den ~ geben** give preference to;
~**züglich** adj. excellent, exquisite;
~**zugsweise** adv. preferably
Votum n vote
VP Abk. für **Vollpension** full board;
(full) board and lodging
vulgär adj. vulgar
Vulkan m volcano; ~**ausbruch** m volcanic eruption; ⚲**isch** adj. volcanic

W

W Abk. für: **West(en)** W, west; **Watt** W,
watt(s)
Waag|e f scale(s pl. Brt.); Fein⚲: balance; astr. Libra; **sich die ~ halten** balance each other; **er ist (e-e)** ~ he's (a)
Libra; ⚲**(e)recht** adj. horizontal;
~**schale** f scale
Wabe f honeycomb (a. fig. tech.)
wach adj. awake; **~ werden** wake* (up);
bsd. fig. awake*; ⚲**e** f guard (a.
mil.); Posten: a. sentry; naut., Kranken⚲ etc.: watch; Polizei⚲: police station; **~ haben** be* on guard (naut.
watch); **~ halten** keep* watch; ~**en** v/i.
(keep*) watch (über over); ⚲**hund** m
watch-dog (a. fig.); ⚲**mann** m watchman; östr. → Polizist
Wacholder bot. m juniper
wach|rufen v/t. call up, evoke; ~**rütteln** v/t. rouse; fig. a. shake* up
Wachs n wax (a. in Zssgn: Kerze etc.)
wachsam adj. watchful, on one's
guard, vigilant; ⚲**keit** f watchfulness,
vigilance
wachsen[1] v/i. grow* (a. sich ~ lassen);
fig. a. increase
wachsen[2] v/t. wax
Wachs|figurenkabinett n waxworks
pl.; ⚲**tuch** n oilcloth
Wachstum n growth; fig. a. increase
Wachtel zo. f quail
Wächter m guard
Wachtmeister m (police) constable,
Am. patrolman; Anrede: officer
Wach(t)turm m watchtower

wackel|ig adj. shaky (a. fig.); Zahn:
loose; ⚲**kontakt** electr. m loose contact; ~**n** v/i. shake*; Tisch etc.: wobble;
Zahn: be* loose; phot. move; ~ **mit** bsd.
Körperteil: wag; **mit den Hüften** ~ wiggle
Wade f calf
Waffe f weapon (a. fig.); ~**n** pl. a. arms
pl.
Waffel f waffle; bsd. Eis⚲: wafer
Waffen|gattung f arm; ~**gewalt** f: **mit**
~ by force of arms; ~**schein** m gun
licen|ce, Am. -se; ~**stillstand** m armistice (a. fig.); zeitweiliger: truce
wagen v/t. dare; riskieren: risk; **sich**
aus dem Haus etc. ~ venture out of
doors etc.
Wagen m Auto: car; rail. Brt. carriage,
Am. car; ~**heber** m jack; ~**ladung** f
carload; fig. cartload; ~**rad** n cartwheel; ~**spur** f (wheel) track
Waggon rail. m Brt. (railway) carriage,
Am. (railroad) car; Güter⚲: Brt. goods
waggon, Am. freight car
wag|halsig adj. daring; ⚲**nis** n venture,
risk
Wahl f choice; andere: alternative; Auslese: selection; pol. election; ~**vorgang**:
voting, poll; Abstimmung: vote; **die** ~
haben (s-e ~ **treffen)** have* the (make*
one's) choice; **keine (andere)** ~ **haben**
have* no choice od. alternative; ⚲**berechtigt** adj. entitled to vote; ~**beteiligung** f (voter) turnout; **hohe (niedrige)** ~ heavy (light) poll; ~**bezirk** m →
Wahlkreis

wählen v/t. u. v/i. choose*, aus~: a. pick, select; pol. Stimme abgeben: vote (j-n, et.: for); in ein Amt etc.: elect; tel. dial

Wähler m voter

Wahlergebnis n election returns pl.

wähler|isch adj. choos(e)y, F picky (in about); **Sschaft** f electorate, voters pl.

Wahl|fach n optional subject, elective; **kabine** f polling (od. voting) booth; **kampf** m election campaign; **kreis** m constituency, Am. electoral district; **lokal** n polling station (Am. place); **Slos** adj. indiscriminate; **programm** n election platform; **recht** n (right to) vote, suffrage, franchise; **rede** f election speech

Wählscheibe tel. f dial

Wahl|spruch m motto; **urne** f ballot box; **versammlung** f election rally; **zettel** m ballot, voting paper

Wahn m delusion; Besessenheit: mania; **sinn** m madness (a. fig.), insanity; **Ssinnig 1.** adj. mad (a. fig.), insane; F fig. a. crazy; Angst, Schmerz etc.: awful, terrible; **2.** F fig. adv. sehr: terribly, awfully; verliebt: madly; **sinnige(r)** mad|man (-woman), lunatic; **wie ein** ~ like a maniac; **vorstellung** f delusion, hallucination

wahr adj. true; wirklich: a. real; echt: genuine; **en** v/t. Interessen, Rechte: protect; **den Schein** ~ keep* up appearances

während 1. prp. during; **2.** cj. while; Gegensatz: a. whereas

wahrhaft(ig) adv. really, truly

Wahrheit f truth; **Sgemäß**, **Ssgetreu** adj. true, truthful; **sliebe** f truthfulness, love of truth; **Ssliebend** adj. truthful

wahr|nehmbar adj. noticeable, perceptible; **nehmen** v/t. perceive, notice; Gelegenheit, Vorteil: seize, take*; Interessen: look after; **nehmung** f perception; **sagen** v/i.: j-m ~ tell* s.o. his fortune; **sich ~ lassen** have* one's fortune told; **sager(in)** fortune-teller; **scheinlich 1.** adj. probable, likely; **2.** adv. probably, (very od. most) likely; ~ **gewinnt er (nicht)** he is (not) likely to win; **Sscheinlichkeit** f probability, likelihood; **aller ~ nach** in all probability od. likelihood

Währung f currency; **~s...** in Zssgn Politik, Reform etc.: monetary ...

Wahrzeichen n landmark

Waise f orphan; **nhaus** n orphanage

Wal zo. m whale

Wald m wood(s pl.), forest; **brand** m forest fire; **Sreich** adj. wooded; **sterben** n dying of forests, forest deaths pl. (od. dieback)

Wal|fang m whaling; **fänger** m whaler

Walkman (TM) m personal stereo, Walkman (TM)

Wall m mound; mil. rampart

Wallach m gelding

wallen v/i. Haar, Gewand: flow

Wallfahr|er(in) m pilgrim; **t** f pilgrimage

Wal|nuß f walnut; **roß** zo. n walrus

walten v/i.: **lassen** Gnade etc.: show*

Walze f roller (a. Straßen2, print.); cylinder (a. print.); tech., mus. barrel; **Sn** v/t. roll (a. tech.)

wälzen v/t. roll (a. **sich** ~); Problem: turn over in one's mind

Walzer mus. m waltz (a. ~ **tanzen**)

Wand f wall; fig. a. barrier

Wandale m vandal; **sismus** m vandalism

Wandel m, **Sn** v/t. u. v/refl. change

Wander|er m hiker; **Sn** v/i. hike; umherstreifen: ramble (about); fig. Blick etc.: roam, wander; **pokal** m challenge cup; **preis** m challenge trophy; **schuhe** pl. walking shoes pl.; **tag** m (school) outing od. excursion; **ung** f walking tour, hike; von Tieren, Völkern etc.: migration

Wand|gemälde n mural (painting); **kalender** m wall calendar; **karte** f wallchart

Wandlung f change, transformation; rel. transubstantiation

Wand|schrank m built-in cupboard, Am. closet; **tafel** f blackboard; **teppich** m tapestry; **uhr** f wall clock

Wange f cheek

Wankelmotor m rotary piston od. Wankel engine

wankelmütig adj. fickle, inconstant

wanken v/i. stagger, reel; fig. rock

wann interr. adv. when, (at) what time; **seit ~?** (for) how long?, since when?

Wanne f tub; bath(tub), F tub

Wanze zo. f bug (a. F fig. Abhörgerät)
Wapitihirsch m elk
Wappen n (coat of) arms pl.; **~kunde** f heraldry; **~tier** n heraldic animal
wappnen fig. v/refl. arm o.s.
Ware f coll. mst goods pl.; Artikel: article; Produkt: product
Waren|haus n department store; △ nicht warehouse; **~lager** n stock; **~probe** f sample; **~zeichen** n trade mark
warm adj. warm (a. fig.); Essen: hot; schön ~ nice and warm; ~ halten (stellen) keep* warm; ~ machen (up)
Wärm|e f warmth; phys. heat; **~e-isolierung** f heat insulation; **2en** v/t. warm; sich die Füße ~ warm one's feet; **~flasche** f hot-water bottle
warmherzig adj. warmhearted
Warmwasser|bereiter m water heater; **~versorgung** f hot-water supply
Warn|blinkanlage mot. f warning flasher; **~dreieck** mot. n warning triangle; **2en** v/t. warn (vor of, against); j-n davor ~, et. zu tun warn s.o. not to do s.th.; **~schild** n danger sign; **~signal** n warning signal; **~streik** m token strike; **~ung** f warning
warten¹ v/i. wait (auf for); ~ auf a. await (beide a. fig. bevorstehen); j-n ~ lassen keep* s.o. waiting
warten² tech. v/t. service, maintain
Wärter(in) Museum etc.: attendant; Zoo etc.: keeper; → Gefängniswärter
Warte|liste f waiting list; **~saal** m, **~zimmer** n waiting room
Wartung tech. f maintenance
warum adv. why
Warze f wart
was 1. interr. pron. what; ~? überrascht etc.: what?; wie bitte?: pardon?, F what?; ~ gibt's? what is it?, F what's up?; zu essen: what's for lunch etc.?; ~ soll's? so what?; ~ machen Sie? gerade: what are you doing?; beruflich: what do you do?; ~ kostet ...? how much is ...?; ~ für ...? what kind od. sort of ...?; ~ für eine Farbe (Größe)?, what colo(u)r (size)?; ~ für ein Unsinn (e-e gute Idee)! what nonsense (a good idea)!; **2.** rel. pron. what; ~ (auch) immer whatever; alles, ~ ich habe (brauche) all I have (need); ich weiß nicht, ~ ich tun (sagen) soll I don't know what

to do (say); ..., ~ mich ärgerte ..., which made me angry; **3.** F indef. pron. → etwas
wasch|bar adj. washable; **2becken** n washbasin, bsd. Am. washbowl
Wäsche f washing, laundry; Bett2, Tisch2: linen; Unter2: underwear; in der ~ in the wash; fig. schmutzige ~ waschen wash one's dirty linen in public
waschecht adj. washable; Farben: fast; fig. trueborn, genuine
Wäsche|klammer f clothes peg, Am. clothespin; **~leine** f clothesline
waschen v/t. u. v/refl. wash (sich die Haare [Hände] one's hair [hands])
Wäscherei f laundry; → Waschsalon
Wasch|küche f washing room; fig. Nebel: pea souper; **~lappen** m flannel, facecloth, Am. washcloth; **~maschine** f washing machine, Am. washer; **2maschinenfest** adj. machine-washable; **~mittel**, **~pulver** n washing powder; **~raum** m lavatory, Am. a. washroom; **~salon** m Brt. launderette, Am. laundromat; **~straße** mot. f car wash
Wasser n water; **~ball** m beach ball; Sport: water polo; **~bett** n water bed; **~dampf** m steam; **2dicht** adj. waterproof; bsd. naut. watertight (a. fig.); **~fall** m waterfall; großer: falls pl.; **~farbe** f water colo(u)r; **~flugzeug** n seaplane; **~graben** m ditch; **~hahn** m tap, Am. a. faucet
wässerig adj. watery; j-m den Mund ~ machen make* s.o.'s mouth water
Wasser|kessel m kettle; **~klosett** n water closet, W.C.; **~kraft** f water power; **~kraftwerk** n hydroelectric power station od. plant; **~lauf** m watercourse; **~leitung** f waterpipe(s pl.); **~mangel** m water shortage; **~mann** astr. m Aquarius; er ist (ein) ~ he's (an) Aquarius; **2n** v/i. touch down on water; Raumfahrzeug: splash down
wässern v/t. water; Felder etc.: irrigate; gastr. soak; phot. rinse
Wasser|pflanze f aquatic plant; **~rohr** n water pipe; **2scheu** adj. afraid of water; **~ski 1.** m water ski; **2.** n water skiing; ~ fahren water-ski; **~spiegel** m water level; **~sport** m water (od. aquatic) sports pl., aquatics pl.;

W

~**spülung** f tech. flushing cistern; **Toilette mit ~** (flush) toilet, W.C.; ~**stand** m water level; ~**standsanzeiger** m water ga(u)ge; ~**stiefel** pl. waders pl.; ~**stoff** chem. m hydrogen; ~**stoffbombe** f hydrogen bomb, H-bomb; ~**strahl** m jet of water; ~**straße** f waterway; ~**tier** n aquatic animal; ~**verdrängung** f displacement; ~**verschmutzung** f water pollution; ~**versorgung** f water supply; ~**waage** f spirit level, Am. level; ~**weg** m waterway; **auf dem ~** by water; ~**welle** f water wave; ~**werk(e** pl) n waterworks sg., pl.; ~**zeichen** n watermark

waten v/i. wade

watscheln v/i. waddle

Watt[1] electr. n watt

Watt[2] geogr. n mud flats pl.

Watt|**e** f cotton wool; ~**ebausch** m cotton-wool pad; **Ωiert** adj. padded; Jacke etc.: quilted

web|**en** v/t. u. v/i. weave; **Ωer** m weaver; **Ωerei** f weaving mill; **Ωstuhl** m loom

Wechsel m change; Geld**Ω**: exchange; Bank**Ω**: bill of exchange; Monats**Ω**: allowance; ~**beziehung** f correlation; ~**geld** n (small) change; **Ωhaft** adj. changeable; ~**jahre** pl. menopause sg.; ~**kurs** m exchange rate; **Ωn** v/t. u. v/i. allg. change; austauschen: exchange; variieren: vary; ab~: alternate; **Ωnd** adj. varying; **Ωseitig** adj. mutual, reciprocal; ~**strom** electr. m alternating current, Abk. A.C.; ~**stube** f exchange office; **Ωweise** adv. alternately; ~**wirkung** f interaction

wecke|**n** v/t. wake (up), F call; fig. Erinnerung etc.: awaken; fig. Neugier etc.: rouse; **Ωr** m alarm (clock)

wedeln v/i. wave (mit et. s.th.); Ski wedel; **mit dem Schwanz ~** Hund: wag its tail

weder cj.: ~ ... noch neither ... nor

Weg m way (a. fig.); Straße: road (a. fig.); Pfad: path; Reise**Ω**: route; Fuß**Ω**: walk; **auf friedlichem (legalem) ~e** by peaceful (legal) means; **j-m aus dem ~ gehen** get* (fig. keep*) out of s.o.'s way; **aus dem ~ räumen** get* s.o. out of the way; **vom ~ abkommen** lose* one's way; → **halb**

weg adv. entfernt, fort, verreist etc.:

away; verschwunden, verloren etc.: gone; los, ab: off; F begeistert: in raptures (**von** over, about); **Finger ~!** (keep your) hands off!; **nichts wie ~** let's get out of here!; F **sein bewußtlos**: be out; ~**bleiben** F v/i. stay away; ausgelassen werden: be* left out; ~**bringen** v/t. take* away; ~ **von** get* s.o. away from

wegen prp. because of; um ... willen: for s.o.'s od. s.th.'s sake, for the sake of; infolge: due od. owing to; ~ **Mordes** etc.: for

weg|**fahren 1.** v/i. leave*; **2.** v/t. take* away, remove; ~**fallen** v/i. be* dropped; aufhören: stop, be* stopped; **die ... werden** ~ there will be no more ...; **Ωgang** m leaving; ~**gehen** v/i. go* away (a. fig. Schmerz etc.), leave*; Fleck etc.: come* off; Ware: sell*; ~**jagen** v/t. drive* od. chase away; ~**kommen** F v/i. get* away; verlorengehen: get* lost; **gut ~** come* off well; **mach, daß du wegkommst!** get out of here!, sl. get lost!; ~**lassen** v/t. let* s.o. go; bsd. et.: leave* out; ~**laufen** v/i. run* away (**[vor] j-m** from s.o.) (a. fig.); ~**legen** v/t. put* away; ~**machen** F v/t. get* off; Kind: get* rid of; ~**müssen** F v/i. have* to go; **ich muß weg** I must be off od. going; ~**nehmen** v/t. take* away (**von** from); Platz, Zeit: take* up; stehlen (a. fig. Frau etc.): steal*; **j-m et. ~** take* s.th. (away) from s.o.

Wegrand m (am by the) wayside

weg|**räumen** v/t. clear away, remove; ~**schaffen** v/t. remove; ~**schicken** v/t. send* away od. off; ~**sehen** v/t. look away; ~**setzen** v/t. move (a. j-n); ~**tun** F v/t. put* away

Wegweiser m signpost; fig. guide

Wegwerf|... in Zssgn Geschirr, Besteck, Rasierer etc.: throwaway ..., disposable ...; Flasche etc.: non-returnable ...; **Ωen** v/t. throw* away (a. fig.)

weg|**wischen** v/t. wipe off; fig. Einwand etc.: brush aside; ~**ziehen 1.** v/i. move away; **2.** v/t. pull away

weh adv.: ~ **tun** hurt* (**j-m** s.o.; fig. a. s.o.'s feelings); Kopf etc.: a. be* aching; **sich (am Finger)** ~ **tun** hurt* o.s. (hurt* one's finger)

Wehen med. pl. labo(u)r sg.

wehen v/i. blow*; Haare, Fahne etc.: wave

W

weh|leidig adj. hypochondriac; *Stimme*: whining; **2mut** f melancholy; **~mütig** adj. *Gefühl*: melancholy; *Lächeln etc.*: wistful

Wehr¹ n weir

Wehr² f: *sich zur* ~ *setzen* → *wehren*; **~dienst** mil. m military service; **~dienstverweigerer** mil. m conscientious objector; **2en** v/refl. defend o.s. (*gegen* against), fight* (a. fig. *gegen et.* s.th.); **~los** adj. defenceless, Am. defenseless; fig. helpless; **~pflicht** mil. f compulsory military service; **2pflichtig** mil. adj. liable to military service; **~pflichtiger** m *Soldat*: conscript, Am. draftee

Weib n bsd. iro., contp. woman; *böses*: bitch; **~chen** zo. n female; **2isch** adj. effeminate, F sissy (a. **~er Junge**); **2lich** adj. female; gr., *Art*, *Stimme etc.*: feminine

weich adj. soft (a. fig.) *zart*: tender; *gar*: done; *Ei*: soft-boiled; ~ *werden* soften; fig. give in*

Weiche rail. f switch, points pl.

weichen v/i. way* way (dat. to), yield (to); *verschwinden*: go* (away)

weich|lich adj. soft, effeminate, F sissy; **2ling** m weakling, F softy, sissy; **~machen** F v/t. soften s.o. up; **2macher** tech. m softener, softening agent; **2spüler** m fabric softener; **2tier** zo. n mollus|c, Am. -k

Weide¹ bot. f willow

Weide² agr. f pasture; *auf die (der)* ~ to (at) pasture; **~land** n pasture(land), Am. a. range; **2n** v/t. u. v/i. graze, pasture; *sich* ~ *an* feast on; contp. gloat over

Weidenkorb m wicker basket

weiger|n v/refl. refuse; **2ung** f refusal

Weihe rel. f consecration; *Priester*2: ordination; **2n** rel. v/t. consecrate; *j-n zum Priester* ~ ordain s.o. priest

Weiher m pond

Weihnachten n Christmas, F Xmas

Weihnachts|abend m Christmas Eve; **~baum** m Christmas tree; **~einkäufe** pl. Christmas shopping sg.; **~geschenk** n Christmas present; **~lied** n (Christmas) carol; **~mann** m Father Christmas, Santa Claus; **~markt** m Christmas fair; **~tag** m Christmas Day; *zweiter* ~ day after Christmas,

bsd. Brt. Boxing Day; **~zeit** f Christmas season

Weih|rauch m incense; **~wasser** rel. n holy water

weil cj. because; *da*: since, as

Weil|chen n: *ein* ~ a little while; **~e** f: *e-e* ~ a while

Wein m wine; *Rebe*: vine; **~(an)bau** m wine growing; **~beere** f grape; **~berg** m vineyard; **~brand** m brandy

weine|n v/i. cry (*vor* with; *nach* for; *wegen* about, over); bsd. lit. weep* (*um* for, over; *über* at; *vor* for, with); **~rlich** adj. tearful; *Stimme*: whining

Wein|ernte f vintage; **~faß** n wine cask od. barrel; **~flasche** f wine bottle; **~gut** n wine-growing estate, bsd. Am. winery; **~händler** m wine merchant; **~hauer** östr. m → *Winzer*; **~karte** f wine list; **~keller** m wine cellar od. vault, vaults pl.; **~kellerei** f winery; **~kenner** m wine connoisseur; **~lese** f vintage; **~presse** f wine press; **~probe** f wine tasting; **~rebe** f vine; **2rot** adj. claret; **~stock** m vine; **~traube** f → *Traube*

weise adj. wise

Weise f *Art u.* ~: way; mus. tune; *auf diese (die gleiche)* ~ this (the same) way; *auf m-e (s-e)* ~ my (his) way

weisen v/t. u. v/i. zeigen: show*; *j-n von der Schule etc. od. aus dem Lande etc.* ~ expel s.o. from, F kick s.o. out of; ~ *auf* point to od. at; *von sich* ~ reject; *Verdacht etc.*: repudiate

Weis|heit f wisdom; *mit s-r* ~ *am Ende* at one's wit's end; **~heitszahn** m wisdom tooth; **2machen** F v/t.: *j-m daß* make* s.o. believe that; *du kannst mir nichts* ~ you can't fool me

weiß adj. white; **2brot** n white bread; **2e** m, f white, white man (woman); *die* **~n** pl. the whites pl.; **~en** v/t. whitewash; **~glühend** adj. white-hot; **2glut** f white heat; **2kraut** n white (Am. green) cabbage; **~lich** adj. whitish; **2wein** m white wine

Weisung f instruction, directive

weit 1. adj. wide; *Kleidung*: a. big; *Reise*, *Weg*: long; **2.** adv. far, a long way (a. *zeitlich u. fig.*); ~ *weg* far away (*von* from); *von* **~em** from a distance; *~ und breit* far and wide; *bei* **~em** by far; *bei* **~em nicht so** not nearly as; ~ *über* well over; ~ **besser** far od. much better; **zu ~ gehen** go* too far; **es ~ bringen** go* far, F go* places; **wir haben es ~ gebracht** we have come a long way

weit|ab adv. far away (**von** from); **~aus** adv. (by) far, much; **Qblick** m farsightedness; **Qe** f width; **weite Fläche**: vastness, expanse; bsd. Sport: distance; **~en** v/t. u. v/refl. widen

weiter adv. on, further; (**mach**) **~!** go on!; (**geh**) **~!** move on!; **und so ~** and so on od. forth, et cetera; **nichts ~** nothing else; **~arbeiten** v/i. go* on working; **~bilden** v/refl. improve one's knowledge; schulisch, beruflich: continue one's education od. training; **Qbildung** f further education od. training

weitere adj. further, additional; **alles ~** the rest; **bis auf ~s** until further notice; **ohne ~s** easily; **Qs** n more, (further) details pl.

weiter|geben v/t. pass (dat., **an** to) (a. fig.); **~gehen** v/i. continue, go* on; **~hin** adv. ferner: further(more); et. ~ tun go* on doing s.th., continue to do s.th.; **~kommen** v/i. get* on (fig. in life); **~können** v/i. be* able to go on; **~leben** v/i. live on; fig. a. survive; **Qleben** n life after death; **~machen** v/t. u. v/i. go* od. carry on, continue; **Qverkauf** m resale

weit|gehend 1. adj. considerable; **2.** adv. largely; **~läufig** adj. Haus etc.: spacious; Verwandter: distant; **~reichend** adj. far-reaching; **~sichtig** med. adj. longsighted, bsd. Am. u. fig. farsighted; **Qsprung** m long jump, Am. broad jump; **~verbreitet** adj. widespread; **Qwinkelobjektiv** phot. n wide-angle lens

Weizen m wheat

welche(r), ~s 1. interr. pron. what, auswählend: which; **welcher?** which one?; **welcher von beiden?** which of the two?; **2.** rel. pron. who, that; bei Sachen: which, that; **3.** F indef. pron. some, any

welk adj. faded, withered; Haut: flabby; **~en** v/i. fade, wither

Wellblech n corrugated iron

Welle f wave (a. phys., fig.); tech. shaft

wellen v/t. u. v/refl. wave; **Qbereich** electr. m wave range; **Qlänge** electr. f wavelength; **Qlinie** f wavy line

Wellensittich m budgerigar, F budgie

wellig adj. wavy

Wellpappe f corrugated cardboard

Welt f world; **die ~** the whole world; **auf der ganzen ~** all over od. throughout the world; **das beste etc. ... der ~** the best etc. ... in the world, the world's best etc. ...; **zur ~ kommen** be* born; **zur ~ bringen** give* birth to

Welt|all n universe; **~anschauung** f philosophy (of life); **~ausstellung** f world fair; **Qberühmt** adj. world-famous

Weltgewicht n, der m welterweight

welt|fremd adj. naive, unrealistic; **Qfriede(n)** m world peace; **Qgeschichte** f world history; **Qkrieg** m world war; **der Zweite ~** World War II; **Qkugel** f globe; **Qlage** f international situation; **~lich** adj. worldly; **Qliteratur** f world literature; **Qmacht** f world power; **Qmarkt** m world market; **Qmeer** n ocean; **Qmeister(in)** f world champion; **Qmeisterschaft** f world championship; bsd. FußballQ: World Cup; **Qraum** m (outer) space; **Qraum...** in Zssgn → **Raum**...; **Qreich** n empire; **Qreise** f world trip; **Qrekord** m world record; **Qruf** m worldwide reputation; **Qstadt** f metropolis; **Quntergang** m end of the world; **~weit** adv. worldwide; **Qwirtschaft** f world economy; **Qwirtschaftskrise** f worldwide economic crisis; **Qwunder** n wonder of the world

Wende f turn (a. Schwimmen); Änderung: change; **~hals** F pol. m (political) turncoat; **~kreis** n astr., geogr. tropic; mot. turning circle; **der ~ des Krebses** the tropic of Cancer

Wendeltreppe f spiral staircase

wende|n v/t. u. v/i. u. v/refl. turn (**nach** to; **gegen** against; **an j-n um Hilfe** for s.o. for help); Auto etc.: turn (round); Braten etc.: turn over; **bitte ~** please turn over, pto; **Qpunkt** m turning point

wend|ig adj. mot., naut. manoeuvrable, Am. maneuverable; fig. nimble; **Qung** f turn (a. fig.); fig. a. change; Ausdruck: expression, phrase

wenig indef. pron. u. adv. little; **~(e)** pl. few; **nur ~e** only few; **ein paar**: only a few; **(in) ~er als** (in) less than; **am ~sten** least of all; **er spricht ~** he doesn't talk much; *(nur) ein (klein)* ~ (just) a little (bit); → *bißchen*; ~**stens** *adv.* at least

wenn *cj.* when; *falls*: if; ~ ... *nicht* if ... not, unless; ~ *auch* (al)though, even though; *wie od. als* ~ as though, as if; ~ *ich nur ... wäre!* if only I were ...!; ~ *auch noch so* ... no matter how ...; *und* ~ *nun* ...? what if ...?

wer 1. *interr. pron.* who, *auswählend*: which; ~ *von euch?* which of you?; **2.** *rel. pron.* who; ~ *auch (immer)* who(so)ever; **3.** F *indef. pron.* somebody, anybody

Werbe|abteilung *f* publicity department; ~**agentur** *f* advertising agency; ~**feldzug** *m* advertising campaign; ~**fernsehen** *n* commercial television; *Werbung*: TV adverts *pl.*, *Am.* (TV) commercials *pl.*; ~**film** *m* promotion(al) film; ~**funk** *m* radio adverts *pl.* (*Am.* commercials *pl.*); 2**n 1.** *v/i.* advertise (*für et.* s.th.), promote (s.th.), give* s.th. *od. s.o.* publicity; *bsd. pol.* make* propaganda (*für* for), canvass (for); ~ *um Frau, Beliebtheit etc.*: court; **2.** *v/t. an*~: recruit; *Stimmen, Kunden*: canvass, solicit; ~**sendung** *f*, ~**spot** *m* TV advert, *Am.* (TV) commercial

Werbung *f* advertising, (sales) promotion; *a. pol. etc.*: publicity, propaganda; *An*2: recruitment; ~ *machen für et.* advertise s.th

Werdegang *m* beruflicher: career

werden *v/i. u. v/aux.* become*, get*; *sich wandeln*: turn, go*; *bsd. allmählich*: grow*; *ausfallen*: turn out; *Futur*: *wir* ~ we will (*lit.* shall), we are going to; *Passiv*: *geliebt* ~ be* loved (*von* by); *was willst du* ~? what do you want to be?; *mir wird schlecht* I'm going to be sick; F: *es wird schon wieder* (~) it'll be all right

werfen *v/i. u. v/t.* throw* (*a. zo.*) ([*mit*] *et. nach* s.th. at); *aviat. Bomben*: drop; *Schatten*: cast*; *sich* ~ throw* o.s.; *Torwart*: dive* (*nach* for)

Werft *naut.* shipyard, dockyard

Werk *n* work; *gutes*: *a.* deed; *tech.* mechanism; *Fabrik*: works *sg. od. pl.*, factory; *ans* ~ *gehen* set* *od.* go* to work; ~**bank** *tech. f* workbench; ~**meister** *m* foreman; ~**statt** *f* workshop; *Auto*2: garage; ~**tag** *m* workday;

2**tätig** *adj.* working; ~**zeug** *n* tool (*a. fig.*); *coll.* tools *pl.*; *feines*: instrument; ~**zeugmacher** *m* toolmaker

wert *adj.* worth; *in Zssgn sehens*~ *etc.*: worth *seeing etc.*; *die Mühe* (*e-n Versuch*) ~ worth the trouble (a try); *fig. nichts* ~ no good

Wert *m allg.* value; *bsd. fig. u. in Zssgn*: *a.* worth; *Sinn, Nutzen*: use; ~**e** *pl. Daten*: data *sg. od. pl.*, figures *pl.*; ... *im* ~(*e*) *von e-m Pfund* a pound's worth of ...; *großen* (*wenig, keinen, nicht viel*) ~ *legen auf* set* great (little, no, not much) store by

wert|en *v/t.* value; *beurteilen, a. Sport*: rate, judge; 2**gegenstand** *m* article of value; ~**los** *adj.* worthless; 2**papiere** *pl.* securities *pl.*; 2**sachen** *pl.* valuables *pl.*; 2**ung** *f* valuation; *a. Sport*: rating, judging; *Punktzahl etc.*: score, points *pl.*; ~**voll** *adj.* valuable

Wesen *n Lebe*2: being, creature; ~**skern**: essence; *Natur*: nature, character; *viel* ~*s machen um* make* a fuss about

wesentlich *adj.* essential; *beträchtlich*: considerable; *im* ~*en* on the whole

weshalb *interr. adv.* → *warum*

Wespe *f* wasp

Weste *f* waistcoat, *Am.* vest

West|en *m* west; *pol.* West; *der Wilde* ~ the Wild West; 2**lich 1.** *adj.* western; *Kurs, Wind*: westerly; *pol.* West(ern); **2.** *adv.*: ~ *von* (to the) west of; ~**wind** *m* west(erly) wind

Wett|bewerb *m* competition (*a. econ.*), contest; 2**büro** *n* betting office; ~**e** *f* bet; *e-e* ~ *schließen* make* a bet; *um die* ~ *laufen etc.* race (*mit j-m* s.o.); 2**eifern** *v/i.* compete (*mit* with; *um* for); 2**en** *v/i. u. v/t.* bet*; *mit j-m um 10 Pfund* ~ bet* s.o. ten pounds; ~ *auf* bet* on, back

Wetter *n* weather; ~**bericht** *m* weather report; 2**fest** *adj.* weatherproof; ~**karte** *f* weather chart; ~**lage** *f* weather situation; ~**leuchten** *n* sheet lightning; ~**vorhersage** *f* weather forecast; ~**warte** *f* weather station

Wett|kampf *m* competition, contest; ~**kämpfer(in)** contestant, competitor; ~**lauf** *m* race (*a. fig. mit* against); ~**läufer(in)** runner; 2**machen** *v/t.* make* up for; ~**rennen** *n* race; ~**rü-**

W

sten n arms race; **~streit** m contest, competition

wetzen v/t. whet, sharpen

wichtig adj. important; et. **~ nehmen** take* s.th. seriously; **♀keit** f importance; **♀tuer** m pompous ass

Wickel med. m compress; **~kommode** f changing unit; **♀n** v/t. Baby: change; **~ in (um)** wrap in ([a]round)

Widder m zo. ram; astr. Aries; **er ist (ein) ~** he's (an) Aries

wider prp.: **~ Willen** against one's will; **~ Erwarten** contrary to expectation; **♀haken** m barb; **~hallen** v/i. resound (**von** with); **~legen** v/t. refute, disprove; **~lich** adj. sickening, disgusting; **~rechtlich** adj. illegal, unlawful; **♀rede** f contradiction; **keine ~!** no arguing!, don't talk back!; **♀ruf** m jur. revocation; e-r Erklärung: withdrawal; **~rufen** v/t. revoke; withdraw*; **♀sacher(in)** adversary, rival; **♀schein** m reflection; **~setzen** v/refl. oppose, resist (e-r Sache s.th.); **~sinnig** adj. absurd; **~spenstig** adj. unruly (a. Haar etc.), stubborn; **~spiegeln** v/t. reflect (a. fig.); **sich ~ in** be* reflected in; **~sprechen** v/i. contradict; **♀spruch** m contradiction; **~sprüchlich** adj. contradictory; **~spruchslos** adv. without contradiction; **♀stand** m resistance (a. electr.), opposition; **~ leisten** offer resistance (dat. to); **~standsfähig** adj. resistant (a. tech.); **~stehen** v/i. resist; **~streben** v/i.: **es widerstrebt mir, dies zu tun** I hate doing od. to do that; **~strebend** adv. reluctantly; **~wärtig** adj. disgusting; **♀wille** m aversion (**gegen** to), dislike (of, for); Ekel: disgust (at); **~willig** adj. reluctant, unwilling

widm|en v/t. dedicate; **♀ung** f dedication

wie 1. interr. adv. how; **~ geht es Gordon?** how is Gordon?; **~ ist er?** what's he like?; **~ ist das Wetter?** what's the weather like?; **~ heißen Sie?** what's your name?; **~ nennt man ...?** what do you call ...?; **~ wäre (ist, steht) es mit ...?** what od. how about ...?; **~ viele ...?** how many ...?; **2.** cj. like; as; **~ neu (verrückt)** like new (mad); **doppelt so ... ~** twice as ... as; **~ (zum Beispiel)** such as, like; **~ üblich** as usual; **~ er**

sagte as he said; **ich zeige (sage) dir, ~ (...)** I'll show (tell) you how (...)

wieder adv. again; **~... in** Zssgn oft re...; **immer ~** again and again; **♀aufbau** m reconstruction, rebuilding; **~aufbauen** v/t. reconstruct; **♀aufbereitung** tech. f recycling, reprocessing (a. nukleare); **♀aufbereitungsanlage** f reprocessing plant; **♀aufleben** n revival; **♀aufnahme** f resumption; **~aufnehmen** v/t. resume; **~bekommen** v/t. get* back; **~beleben** v/t. resuscitate, revive (a. fig.); **♀belebung** f resuscitation; **♀belebungsversuch** m attempt at resuscitation; **♀bewaffnung** f rearmament; **~bringen** v/t. bring* back; zurückgeben: return; **♀einführung** f reintroduction; **♀entdeckung** f rediscovery; **~erkennen** v/t. recognize (an by); **~finden** v/t. find* (what one has lost); fig. regain; **♀gabe** tech. f reproduction, play-back; **~geben** v/t. give* back, return; schildern: describe; tech. play back, reproduce; **~gutmachen** v/t. make* up for; **♀gutmachung** f reparation; **~herstellen** v/t. restore; **~holen** v/t. repeat; Lernstoff: revise, review; Szene etc.: replay; zurückholen: (go* and) get* s.th. od. s.o. back; **sich ~** repeat o.s. (a. fig Geschichte etc.); **~holt** adv. repeatedly, several times; **♀holung** f repetition; von Lernstoff: revision, review; TV etc.: rerun; e-r Szene: replay; **♀kehr** f return; periodische: a. recurrence; **~kehren** v/i. return; recur; **~kommen** v/i. come* back, return; **~sehen** v/t. see* again od. meet* again; **♀sehen** n seeing s.o. again; Treffen: reunion; **auf ~!** goodbye!; **~um** adv. again; on the other hand; **♀vereinigung** f reunion; bsd. pol. a. reunification; **~verwendbar** adj. reusable; **♀verwendung** f re-use; **~verwerten** v/t. tech. recycle; **♀verwertung** tech. f recycling; **♀wahl** f re-election

Wiege f cradle

wiegen[1] v/t. u. v/i. weigh

wiegen[2] v/t. rock (**in den Schlaf** to sleep); **♀lied** n lullaby

wiehern v/i. neigh; F fig. guffaw

Wiese f meadow

Wiesel zo. n weasel

wieso interr. adv. → warum

wieviel *adv.* how much; *pl.* how many; **~te** *adv.*: **den ~n haben wir heute?** what's the date today?

wild *adj.* wild (*a. fig.*) (F **auf** about); *heftig*: violent; **~er Streik** wildcat strike

Wild *n hunt.* game; *Braten*: *mst* venison; **~bach** *m* torrent; **~e(r)** savage; F: **wie ein Wilder** like mad; **~erer** *m* poacher; **~ern** *v/i.* poach; **~hüter** *m* gamekeeper; **~leder** *n* suede; **~nis** *f* wilderness; **~park** *m*, **~reservat** *n* game park *od.* reserve; **~schwein** *n* wild boar; **~wasserfahren** *n* white-water canoeing; **~westfilm** *m*, **~westroman** *m* western

Wille *m* will; *Absicht*: *a.* intention; **s-n ~n durchsetzen** have* *od.* get* one's own way; **j-m s-n ~n lassen** let* s.o. have his (own) way

willen *prp.*: **um B.'s ~** for B.'s sake, for the sake of B.

willenlos *adj.* weak(-willed)

Willens|freiheit *f* freedom of will; **~kraft** *f* willpower; **2stark** *adj.* strong-willed

will|ig *adj.* willing; **~kommen** *adj.* welcome (*a.* **~ heißen**) (**in** to); **~kürlich** *adj.* arbitrary; *Auswahl etc.*: *a.* random

wimm|eln *v/i.*: **~ von** be* teeming (with); **~ern** *v/i.* whimper

Wimpel *m* pennant

Wimper *f* eyelash; **~ntusche** *f* mascara

Wind *m* wind

Winde *f* winch, windlass, hoist

Windel *f* nappy, *Am.* diaper

winden *v/t.* wind*; *tech. a.* hoist; **sich ~** wind* (one's way); *vor Schmerz*: writhe

Windhund *zo. m* greyhound

wind|ig *adj.* windy; **~mühle** *f* windmill; **2pocken** *med. pl.* chickenpox *sg.*; **2richtung** *f* direction of the wind; **2schutzscheibe** *f* windscreen, *Am.* windshield; **2stärke** *f* wind force; **~still** *adj.*, **2stille** *f* calm; **2stoß** *m* gust; **2surfen** *n* windsurfing

Windung *f* bend, turn (*a. tech.*)

Wink *m* sign; *fig.* hint

Winkel *m math.* angle; *Ecke*: corner; **2ig** *adj.* angular; *Straße*: crooked

winken *v/i.* wave (one's hand *etc.*), signal; *Taxi*: hail; *her~* beckon

winseln *v/i.* whimper, whine

Winter *m* winter; **~ausrüstung** *mot. f* winter equipment; **2lich** *adj.* wintry;

~reifen *mot. m* snow tyre (*Am.* tire); **~schlaf** *m* hibernation; **~spiele** *pl.*: *Olympische* **~** Winter Olympics *pl.*; **~sport** *m* winter sports *pl.*

Winzer *m* winegrower

winzig *adj.* tiny, diminutive

Wipfel *m* (tree)top

Wippe *f*, **2n** *v/i.* seesaw

wir *pers. pron.* we; **~ drei** the three of us; F: **~ sind's!** it's us!

Wirbel *m* whirl (*a. fig.*); *anat.* vertebra; *im Haar*: crown, *bsd. Am.* cowlick; **2n** *v/i.* whirl; **~säule** *anat. f* spinal column, spine; **~sturm** *m* cyclone, tornado; **~tier** *n* vertebrate; **~wind** *m* whirlwind (*a. fig.*)

wirk|en 1. *v/i.* work; be* effective (*gegen* against); (*er*)*scheinen, aussehen*: look; *anregend etc.*: have* a stimulating *etc.* effect (**auf** [up]on); **~ als** act as; 2. *v/t.* weave*; *Wunder*: work; **~lich** *adj.* real, actual; *echt*: true, genuine; **2lichkeit** *f* reality; **in ~** in reality, actually; **~sam** *adj.* effective; **2ung** *f* effect

Wirkungs|grad *tech. m* efficiency; **2los** *adj.* ineffective; **2voll** *adj.* effective

wirr *adj.* confused, mixed-up; *Haar*: tousled; **2en** *pl.* disorder *sg.*, confusion *sg.*; **2warr** *m* confusion, mess, chaos

Wirt(in) *m* land(-lady)

Wirtschaft *f econ. pol.* economy; *Geschäftswelt*: business; **~** Gastwirtschaft; **2en** *v/i.* keep* house; *bsd. finanziell*: manage one's money *od.* affairs *od.* business; *sparen*: economize; **gut** (**schlecht**) **~** be* a good (bad) manager; **~erin** *f* housekeeper; **2lich** *adj.* economic; *sparsam*: economical; **~s...** *econ.* in *Zssgn* Gemeinschaft, Krise, System, Wunder *etc.*: economic ...

Wirtshaus *n* **~** Gastwirtschaft

wischen *v/t.* wipe; *Staub*: dust

wispern *v/t. u. v/i.* whisper

wißbegierig *adj.* curious

wissen *v/t. u. v/i.* know*; *ich möchte* **~** I'd like to know, I wonder; *ich weiß* **~** as far as I know; *weißt du* you know; *weißt du noch?* (do you) remember?; *woher weißt du das?* how do you know?; *man kann nie* **~** you never know; *ich will davon* (*von ihm*) *nichts* **~** I don't want anything to do with it (him)

Wissen n knowledge; *praktisches: a.* know-how; *m-s ~s* as far as I know

Wissenschaft f science; **~ler(in)** scientist; **2lich** adj. scientific

wissenswert adj. worth knowing; **2es** useful facts pl.; **2e (über)** all you need to know (about)

wittern v/t. scent, smell* (beide a. fig.)

Witwe f widow; **~r** m widower

Witz m joke; **~e reißen** crack jokes; **2ig** adj. funny; geistreich: witty

wo adv. where; **~ ... doch** when, although; **~bei** adv.: **~ bist du?** what are you at?; **~ mir einfällt** which reminds me

Woche f week; **~n...** in Zssgn Lohn, Markt, Zeitung etc.: weekly ...; **~nende** n weekend; **am ~** at (Am. on) the weekend; **2nlang 1.** adj.: **~es Warten** (many) weeks of waiting; **2.** adv. for weeks; **~nschau** f newsreel; **~ntag** m weekday

wöchentlich 1. adj. weekly; **2.** adv. weekly, every week; **einmal ~** once a week

wo|durch adv. how; durch was: through which; **~für** adv. für was: for which; **~?** what (...) for?

Woge f wave; bsd. fig. a. surge; Brecher: breaker; **2n** v/i. surge (a. fig.), heave (a. fig. Busen)

wo|her adv. where ... from; **~ weißt du (das)?** how do you know?; **~hin** adv. where (... to)

wohl adv. u. cj. well; vermutlich: probably, I suppose; **sich ~ fühlen** be* well; seelisch: feel* good; in e-m Haus, bei j-m etc.: feel* at home (bei with); **ich fühle mich nicht ~** I don't feel well; od. übel: willy-nilly, whether I etc. like it or not; **~ kaum** hardly

Wohl n **~befinden:** well-being; **auf j-s ~ trinken** drink* to s.o.'s health); **zum ~!** to your health!; F cheers!; **2behalten** adv. safely; **~fahrts...** in Zssgn Staat etc.: welfare ...; **2gemerkt** adv. mind you; **2genährt** adj. well-fed; **2gesinnt** adj.: **j-m ~ sein** be* well-disposed towards s.o.; **2habend** adj. well-off, well-to-do; **2ig** adj. cosy, snug; **~stand** m prosperity, affluence; **~standsgesellschaft** f affluent society; **~tat** fig. f pleasure; Erleichterung: relief; Segen: blessing; **~täter** m benefactor; **2tätig** adj. charitable; **für ~e Zwecke** for

charity; **~tätigkeits...** in Zssgn Ball, Konzert etc.: charity ...; **2tun** v/i. do* good; **2verdient** adj. well-deserved; **2wollend** adj. benevolent

wohn|en v/i. live (in in; bei j-m with s.o.); vorübergehend: stay (in at; bei with); **2gebiet** n residential area; **2gemeinschaft** f: (mit j-m) in e-r ~ leben share a flat (Am. an apartment) od. a house (with s.o.); **~lich** adj. comfortable, cosy, snug; **2mobil** n camper, Brt. a. motor caravan, Am. a. motor home; **2siedlung** f housing estate (Am. development); **2sitz** m residence; **ohne festen ~** of no fixed abode; **2ung** f flat, Am. apartment; **m-e** etc. **~** my etc. place

Wohnungs|amt n housing office; **~bau** m house building; **~not** f housing shortage

Wohn|wagen m caravan, Am. trailer; großer: mobile home; **~zimmer** n sitting od. living room

wölb|en v/refl., **2ung** f vault, arch

Wolf m wolf

Wolk|e f cloud; **~enbruch** m cloudburst; **~enkratzer** m skyscraper; **2enlos** adj. cloudless; **2ig** adj. cloudy, clouded

Woll|... in Zssgn Schal, Socken etc.: wool(l)en ...; **~decke** f (wool[l]en) blanket; **~e** f wool

wollen v/t. u. v/i. u. v/aux. want (to); lieber ~ prefer; ~ wir (gehen etc.)? shall we (go etc.)?; **~ Sie bitte ...** will od. would you please ...; **wie (was, wann) du willst** as (whatever, whenever) you like; **sie will, daß ich komme** she wants me to come; **ich wollte, ich wäre (hätte)** ... I wish I were (had) ...

Wolljacke f cardigan

wo|mit adv. mit dem: with which; **~?** what ... with?

Wonne f joy, delight

wor|an adv. **~ denkst du?** what are you thinking of?; **~ liegt es, daß ...?** how is it that ...?; **~ sieht man, welche (ob)** ...? how can you tell which (if) ...?; **~auf** adv. zeitlich: after which; örtlich: on which; **~?** what ... on?; **~ wartest du?** what are you waiting for?; **~aus** adv. von dem: from which; **~ ist es?** what's it made of?; **~in** adv. in dem: in which; **~?** where?

Wort n word; *mit anderen ~en* in other words; *sein ~ geben (halten, brechen)* give* (keep*, break*) one's word; *j-n beim ~ nehmen* take* s.o. at his word; *ein gutes ~ einlegen für* put* in a good word for; *j-m ins ~ fallen* cut* s.o. short; **~art** gr. f part of speech

Wörter|buch n dictionary; **~verzeichnis** n vocabulary, list of words

Wort|führer m spokesman; **2karg** adj. taciturn

wörtlich adj. literal; **~e Rede** direct speech

Wort|schatz m vocabulary; **~spiel** n play on words; *witziges:* pun; **~stellung** gr. f word order

wo|rüber adv. *über was:* about which; *~ lachen Sie?* what are you laughing at od. about?; **~rum** adv. *um was:* about which; *~ handelt es sich?* what is it about?; **~runter** adv. *unter denen:* among which; *~?* what ... under?; **~von** adv. about which; *~ redest du?* what are you talking about?; **~vor** adv. of which; *~ hast du Angst?* what are you afraid of?; **~zu** adv.: *~ er mir rät* what he advised me to do; *~?* what (...) for?; *warum?:* a. why?

Wrack n naut. wreck (a. fig.)

wringen v/t. wring*

Wucher m usury; **~er** m usurer; **2n** v/i. grow* (fig. be*) rampant; **~ung** med. f growth

Wuchs m growth; *Gestalt:* build

Wucht f force; *e-s Aufpralls etc.:* impact; **2ig** adj. massive; *kraftvoll:* powerful

wühlen v/i. dig*; *Schwein:* root; *suchen:* rummage (*in* in, through)

Wulst m, f bulge; *von Fett:* roll; **2ig** adj. bulging; *Lippen:* thick

wund adj. sore; **~e Stelle** sore; **~er Punkt** sore point; **2e** f wound

Wunder n miracle; *fig. a.* wonder, marvel (*beide:* an of); *~ wirken* work wonders; (*es ist*) *kein ~, daß du müde bist* no wonder you are tired; **2bar** adj. fig. wonderful, marvel(l)ous; *wie ein Wunder:* miraculous; **~kind** n infant prodigy; **2lich** adj. funny, odd; *alter Mensch:* a. senile; **2n** v/refl. be* surprised od. astonished (*über* at);

2schön adj. lovely; **2voll** adj. wonderful; **~werk** n marvel, wonder

Wundstarrkrampf med. m tetanus

Wunsch m wish (a. Glück2); *Bitte:* request; *auf j-s (eigenen) ~* at s.o.'s (own) request; (*je*) *nach ~* as desired

wünschen v/t. wish; *sich et. (zu Weihnachten etc.) ~* want s.th. (for Christmas etc.); *das habe ich mir (schon immer) gewünscht* that's what I (always) wanted; *alles, was man sich nur ~ kann* everything one could wish for; *ich wünschte, ich wäre (hätte)* I wish I were (had); **~swert** adj. desirable

Würde f dignity; **2los** adj. undignified; **~nträger** m dignitary; **2voll** adj. dignified

würdig adj. worthy (gen. of); *würdevoll:* dignified; **~en** v/t. appreciate; *j-n keines Blickes ~* ignore s.o. completely; **2ung** f appreciation

Wurf m throw; zo. litter

Würfel m cube (a. math.); *Spiel2:* dice; **2n** v/i. throw dice (*um* for); *spielen:* play dice; *e-e Sechs ~* throw* a six; **~spiel** n dice game; *einzelne Partie:* game of dice; **~zucker** m lump sugar

Wurfgeschoß n missile (a. Flasche etc.)

würgen v/i. u. v/t. choke; *j-n:* a. throttle

Wurm m worm; **2en** F v/t. gall; **2stichig** adj. worm-eaten

Wurst f sausage

Würstchen n small sausage, frankfurter, wiener; *im Brötchen:* hot dog; **~bude** f sausage stand

Würze f spice (a. fig.)

Wurzel f root (a. math.); *zweite (dritte) ~* square (cubic) root; **~n schlagen** take* root (a. fig.); **2n** v/i.: *~ in* be* rooted in (a. fig.)

würz|en v/t. spice, season, flavo(u)r; **~ig** adj. spicy, well-seasoned

Wust F m tangled mass

wüst adj. waste; *wirr:* confused; *liederlich:* wild, dissolute

Wüste f desert

Wut f rage, fury; *e-e ~ haben* be* furious (*auf* with); **~anfall** m fit of rage

wüten v/i. rage (a. fig.); **~d** adj. furious (*auf* with; *über* at), F mad (at)

wutschnaubend adj. fuming

W

X, Y

X-Beine pl. knock-knees pl.; **X-beinig** adj. knock-kneed
x-beliebig adj.: jede(r, -s) ~e ... any ... you like, F any old ...
x-mal F adv. umpteen times

x-te adj.: zum ~n Male for the umpteenth time
Xylophon mus. n xylophone
Yacht naut. f yacht
Yoga m, n yoga

Z

Zack|e f, **~en** m (sharp) point; Säge, Kamm, Briefmarke: tooth; **2ig** adj. pointed; gezahnt: serrated; Linie, Blitz, Felsen: jagged; fig. smart
zaghaft adj. timid; **2igkeit** f timidity
zäh adj. tough (a. fig.); **~fließend** adj.: ~er Verkehr slow-moving traffic; **~flüssig** adj. thick, viscous; Verkehr: slow-moving; **2igkeit** f toughness; fig. a. stamina
Zahl f number; Ziffer: figure; **2bar** adj. payable (an to; bei at)
zahlbar adj. countable
zahlen v/i. u. v/t. pay*; ~, bitte! the bill (Am. a. check), please!
zählen v/t. u. v/i. count (bis up to; fig. auf on); ~ zu den Besten etc.: rank with
zahlenmäßig 1. adj. numerical; **2.** adv.: j-m ~ überlegen sein outnumber s.o.
Zähler m counter (a. tech.); math. numerator; Gas2, electr. etc.: meter
Zahl|karte post f paying-in (Am. deposit) slip; **2los** adj. countless; **~meister** m mil. paymaster; naut. purser; **2reich 1.** adj. numerous; **2.** adv. in great number; **~tag** m payday; **~ung** f payment
Zählung f count; Volks2: census
Zahlungs|aufforderung f request for payment; **~bedingungen** pl. terms pl. of payment; **~befehl** m order to pay; **~bilanz** f balance of payments; **2fähig** adj. solvent; **~frist** f term of payment; **~mittel** n currency; gesetzliches ~ legal tender; **~schwierigkei-**

ten pl. financial difficulties pl.; **~termin** m date of payment; **2unfähig** adj. insolvent
Zählwerk tech. n counter
Zahlwort gr. n numeral
zahm adj. tame (a. fig.)
zähm|en v/t. tame (a. fig.); **2ung** f taming (a. fig.)
Zahn m tooth; tech. a. cog; **~arzt** m, **~ärztin** f dentist, dental surgeon; **~bürste** f toothbrush; **~creme** f toothpaste; **2en** v/i. cut* one's teeth; teethe; **~fleisch** n gums pl.; **2los** adj. toothless; **~lücke** f gap between the teeth; **~medizin** f dentistry; **~pasta, ~paste** f toothpaste; **~rad** tech. n gearwheel, cogwheel; **~radbahn** f rack (od. cog) railway; **~schmerzen** pl. toothache sg.; **~spange** f brace; **~stein** m tartar; **~stocher** m toothpick
Zange f tech. pliers pl.; Kneif2: pincers pl.; Greif2, Zucker2 etc.: tongs pl.; med. forceps pl.; zo. pincer
zanken v/refl. quarrel (wegen about; um over), fight*, argue (about; over)
zänkisch adj. quarrelsome
Zäpfchen n anat. uvula; pharm. suppository
Zapf|en m am Faß: tap, Am. faucet; Pflock: peg, pin; Spund: bung; Verbindungs2: tenon; Dreh2: pivot; bot. cone; **2en** v/t. Bier etc.: tap; **~enstreich** mil. m tattoo, Am. a. taps; **~hahn** m tap, Am. faucet; mot. nozzle; **~säule** mot. f petrol (Am. gasoline) pump

zappel|ig *adj.* fidgety; **~n** *v/i.* fidget, wriggle (*a.* Fisch *etc.*)

zappen *TV v/i.* zap

zart *adj.* tender; *sanft:* gentle; **~fühlend** *adj.* sensitive; **&gefühl** *n* delicacy (of feeling), sensitivity

zärtlich *adj.* tender, affectionate (**zu** with); **&keit** *f* tenderness, affection; *Liebkosung:* caress

Zauber *m* magic, spell, charm (*alle a. fig.*); **~ei** *f* magic, witchcraft; **~er** *m* magician, sorcerer, wizard (*a. fig.*); → **~künstler;** **~formel** *f* spell; *fig.* magic formula; **&haft** *fig. adj.* enchanting, charming; **~in** *f* sorceress; **~kraft** *f* magic power; **~künstler** *m* magician, conjurer; **~kunststück** *n* conjuring trick; **1.** *v/i.* practise magic; *im Zirkus etc.:* do* conjuring tricks; **2.** *v/t.* conjure (up); **~spruch** *m* spell; **~stab** *m* (magic) wand; **~wort** *n* magic word, spell

zaudern *v/i.* hesitate

Zaum *m* bridle; *im ~ halten* control (*sich* o.s.), keep* in check

zäumen *v/t.* bridle

Zaumzeug *n* bridle

Zaun *m* fence; **~gast** *m* onlooker; **~pfahl** *m* pale

z.B. *Abk. für* **zum Beispiel** e.g., for example, for instance

Zebrastreifen *m* zebra crossing

Zeche *f* bill, *Am.* check; *Bergbau:* (coal) mine, pit; *die ~ zahlen* pay* (*F u. fig.* foot) the bill

Zeh *m,* **~e** *f* toe; *große (kleine) ~* big (little) toe; **~ennagel** *m* toenail; **~enspitze** *f* tip of the toe; *auf ~en gehen* (walk on) tiptoe

zehn *adj.* ten; **~fach** *adj.* tenfold; **~jährig** *adj.* Kind: ten-year-old; *Jubiläum etc.:* ten-year ...; *Abwesenheit etc.:* of ten years; **~kampf** *m* decathlon; **~mal** *adv.* ten times; **~te** *adj.* tenth; **&tel** *n* tenth; **~tens** *adv.* tenthly

Zeichen *n* sign; *Merk&:* a. mark; *Signal:* signal; *zum ~ gen.* as a token of; **~block** *m* sketch pad; **~brett** *n* drawing board; **~dreieck** *math. n* set square; **~folge** *f* Computer: string; **~lehrer(in)** art teacher; **~papier** *n* drawing paper; **~setzung** *gr. f* punctuation; **~sprache** *f* sign language; **~trickfilm** *m* (animated) cartoon

zeichnen *v/i. u. v/t.* draw*; *kenn~:* mark; *unter~:* sign; *fig.* mark, leave* its mark on *s.o.*

Zeichn|en *n* drawing; *Schulfach:* art; **~er(in)** *mst* graphic artist; *genauer:* draughts|man (-woman), *Am.* drafts|man (-woman); **~ung** *f* drawing; *Graphik:* diagram; *zo.* marking

Zeige|finger *m* forefinger, index finger; **&n 1.** *v/t.* show* (*a. sich ~*); **2.** *v/i.: ~ auf (nach)* point to; (*mit dem Finger*) *~ auf* point (one's finger) at; **~r** *m Uhr&:* hand; *tech.* pointer, needle; **~stock** *m* pointer

Zeile *f* line (*a. TV*); *j-m ein paar ~n schreiben* drop *s.o.* a line

Zeit *f* time; *~alter: a.* age, era; *gr.* tense; *vor einiger ~* some time (*od.* a while) ago; *zur ~* at the moment, at present; *in letzter ~* lately, recently; *in der (od. zur) ~ gen.* in the days of; ... *aller ~en* of all time; *die ~ ist um* time's up; *sich ~ lassen* take* one's time; *es wird ~, daß ...* it's time to *inf.;* *das waren noch ~en* those were the days

Zeit|abschnitt *m* period (of time); **~alter** *n* age; **~bombe** *f* time bomb (*a. fig.*); **~druck** *m: unter ~ stehen* be* pressed for time; **~fahren** *n* time trials *pl.;* **&gemäß** *adj.* modern, up-to-date; **~genosse** *m,* **&genössisch** *adj.* contemporary; **~geschichte** *f* contemporary history; **~gewinn** *m* gain of time; **~karte** *f* season ticket; **~lang** *f: e-e ~* for some time, for a while; **&lebens** *adv.* all one's life; **&lich 1.** *adj.* time ...; **2.** *adv.: et. ~ planen od. abstimmen* time s.th.; **&los** *adj.* timeless; *a.* Stil, Kleidung *etc.:* classic; **~lupe** *f* (*in*) slow motion; **~not** *f: in ~ sein* → **Zeitdruck;** **~punkt** *m* moment; **~raffer** *m: im ~* in quick motion; **&raubend** *adj.* time-consuming; **~raum** *m* period of time; **~rechnung** *f: unsere ~* our time; **~schrift** *f* magazine

Zeitung *f* (news)paper

Zeitungs|abonnement *n* subscription to a paper; **~artikel** *m* newspaper article; **~ausschnitt** *m* (newspaper) cutting (*Am.* clipping); **~junge** *m* paper boy; **~kiosk** *m* newspaper kiosk; **~notiz** *f* press item; **~papier** *n* newspaper; **~stand** *m* newsstand; **~verkäufer** *m* news vendor, *Am.* newsdealer

Zeit|verlust m loss of time; **~verschiebung** f aviat. time lag; **~verschwendung** f waste of time; **~vertreib** m pastime; **zum ~** to pass the time; **2weilig** adj. temporary; **2weise** adv. at times, occasionally; **~wort** gr. n verb; **~zeichen** n Radio: time signal; **~zünder** m time fuse

Zelle f cell

Zell|stoff m, **~ulose** tech. f cellulose

Zelt n tent; **2en** v/i. camp; **~lager** n camp; **~platz** m campsite

Zement m, **2ieren** v/t. cement

Zenit m zenith (a. fig.)

zens|ieren v/t. censor; Schule: mark, grade; **2or** m censor; **2ur** f censorship; mark, grade

Zentimeter m, n centimet|re, Am. -er

Zentner m 50 kilograms, metric hundredweight

zentral adj. central; **2e** f head office; Polizei etc.: headquarters pl. (a. Taxi2); tel. in Firma: switchboard; tech. control room; **2heizung** f central heating; **2verriegelung** mot. f central locking

Zentrum n cent|re, Am. -er

Zepter n scept|re, Am. -er

zerbeißen v/t. bite* to pieces

zerbrech|en v/i. u. v/t. break* ; → Kopf; **~lich** adj. fragile

zer|bröckeln v/t. u. v/i. crumble; **~drücken** v/t. crush

Zeremon|ie f ceremony; **2iell** adj., **~iell** n ceremonial

Zerfall m disintegration, decay; **2en** v/i. disintegrate, decay; **~ in** break* up into

zer|fetzen, **~fleischen** v/t. tear* to pieces; **~fressen** v/t. eat* (holes in); chem. corrode; **~gehen** v/i. melt*, dissolve; **~hacken** v/t. cut* od. chop up; electr. chop; **~kauen** v/t. chew; **~kleinern** v/t. cut* od. chop up; zermahlen: grind*

zerknirsch|t adj. remorseful; **2ung** f remorse

zer|knittern v/t. (c)rumple, crease; **~knüllen** v/t. crumple up; **~kratzen** v/t. scratch; **~krümeln** v/t. crumble; **~lassen** v/t. melt*; **~legen** v/t. take* apart od. to pieces; tech. dismantle; Fleisch: carve; chem., gr., fig. analy|se, Am. -ze; **~lumpt** adj. ragged, tattered; **~mahlen** v/t. grind*; **~malmen** v/t.

crush; **~mürben** v/t. wear* down; **~platzen** v/i. burst*; explode; **~quetschen** v/t. crush

Zerrbild n caricature

zer|reiben v/t. rub to powder, pulverize; **~reißen 1.** v/t. tear* up od. to pieces; **sich die Hose** etc.: **~** tear* od. rip one's trousers etc.; **2.** v/i. tear*; Seil etc.: break*

zerren 1. v/t. drag, pull (a. Muskel etc.); **2.** v/i.: **~ an** tug (stärker: strain) at

zerrinnen v/i. melt* away (a. fig.)

Zerrung med. f pulled muscle

zer|rütten v/t. ruin; **~rüttet** adj.: **~e Ehe (Verhältnisse)** broken marriage (home); **~sägen** v/t. saw* up; **~schellen** v/i. be* smashed; aviat. a. crash; **~schlagen 1.** v/t. smash (to pieces); fig. Spionagering etc.: smash; **sich ~** come* to nothing; **2.** adj. **sich ~ fühlen** be* (all) worn out od. F dead beat; **~schmettern** v/t. smash (to pieces), shatter (a. fig.); **~schneiden** v/t. cut* (up)

zersetz|en v/t. chem. decompose (a. sich); fig. corrupt, undermine; **2ung** f decomposition; corruption

zer|splittern v/t. u. v/i. split* (up), splinter; Glas: shatter; **~springen** v/i. Glas: crack; völlig: shatter; **~stampfen** v/t. pound; Kartoffeln: mash

zerstäub|en v/t. spray; **2er** m atomizer, sprayer

zerstör|en v/t. destroy, ruin (beide a. fig.); **2er** m destroyer (a. naut.); **~erisch** adj. destructive; **2ung** f destruction

zerstreu|en v/t. u. v/refl. scatter, disperse; Menge: a. break* up; fig. take* s.o.'s (refl. one's) mind off things; **~t** fig. adj. absent-minded; **2theit** f absent-mindedness; **2ung** fig. f diversion, distraction

zer|stückeln v/t. cut* up od. (in)to pieces; Leiche etc.: dismember; **~teilen** v/t. u. v/refl. divide (in into)

Zertifikat n certificate

zer|treten v/t. crush (a. fig.); **~trümmern** v/t. smash; **~zaust** adj. tousled, dishevel(l)ed

Zettel m slip (of paper); Nachricht: note; Klebe2: label, sticker

Zeug n stuff (a. fig. contp.); Sachen: things pl. (a. in Zssgn Schwimm2 etc.);

er hat das ~ dazu he's got what it takes; **dummes ~** nonsense, *sl.* bullshit

Zeuge *m* witness; **2n**[1] *v/i. jur.* give* evidence (**für** for); *fig.* **~ von** testify to; **2n**[2] *v/t. biol.* procreate; *Kinder:* father

Zeugen|aussage *jur. f* evidence, testimony; **~bank** *f* witness box (*Am.* stand)

Zeugin *f* (female) witness

Zeugnis *n* (school) report, *Am.* report card; *Prüfungs2:* certificate, diploma; *vom Arbeitgeber:* reference; **~se** *pl.* credentials *pl.*

Zeugung *biol. f* procreation

z. H(d). *Abk. für zu Händen* attn, attention

Zickzack *m* zigzag; **im ~ fahren** *etc.* (go* in a) zigzag

Ziege *f zo.* (nanny) goat; F *contp.:* (**blöde**) **~** (silly old) cow

Ziegel *m* brick; *Dach2:* tile; **~dach** *n* tiled roof; **~ei** *f* brickyard; **~stein** *m* brick

Ziegen|bock *zo. m* billy goat; **~leder** *n* kid (leather); **~peter** *med. m* mumps

ziehen 1. *v/t.* pull (a. Bremse *etc.*), draw* (a. Waffe, Karte, Lose, Linie); *Hut:* take* off (**vor** to) (a. *fig.*); *Blumen:* grow*; *heraus:* pull *od.* take* out (**aus** of); **j-n ~** an pull s.o. by; **auf sich ~** Aufmerksamkeit, Augen: attract; **sich ~** run* (*an* along); → *Länge, Erwägung;* **2.** *v/i.* pull (*an* at); *sich bewegen, um~:* move; *Vögel, Volk:* migrate; *gehen: reisen:* travel; *ziellos:* wander, roam; **es zieht** there's a draught (*Am.* draft)

Zieh|harmonika *mus. f* accordion; **~ung** *f Lotto etc.:* draw

Ziel *n* aim, **~scheibe:** target, mark (*alle a. fig.*); *fig. a.* goal, objective; *Reise2:* destination: *Sport:* finish; **sich ein ~ setzen** (**sein ~ erreichen**) set* o.s. a (reach one's) goal; **sich zum ~ gesetzt haben, et. zu tun** aim to do *od.* at doing s.th.; **~band** *n* tape; **2en** *v/i.* (take*) aim (**auf** at); **~fernrohr** *n* telescopic sight; **~linie** *f* finishing line; **2los** *adj.* aimless; **~scheibe** *f* target; *fig. a.* object; **2strebig** *adj.* purposeful, determined

ziemlich 1. *adj.* quite a; **2.** *adv.* rather, fairly, quite, F pretty; **~ viele** quite a few

Zier|de *f* (**zur** as a) decoration; **2en** *v/t.* decorate; **sich ~** be* coy; make* a fuss; **2lich** *adj.* dainty; *Frau: a.* petite; **~pflanze** *f* ornamental plant

Ziffer *f* figure; **~blatt** *n* dial, face

Zigarette *f* cigarette; **~nautomat** *m* cigarette machine; **~nstummel** *m* cigarette end, stub, butt

Zigarre *f* cigar

Zigeuner(in) gipsy, *bsd. Am.* gypsy

Zimmer *n* room; apartment; **~einrichtung** *f* furniture; **~mädchen** *n* (chamber)maid; **~mann** *m* carpenter; **2n** *v/t. allg.* build*, make*; *Dach etc.:* carpenter; **~nachweis** *m* accommodation office; **~pflanze** *f* indoor plant; **~service** *m* room service; **~suche** *f:* **auf ~ sein** be* looking (*od.* hunting) for a room; **~vermittlung** *f* accommodation agency *od.* service

zimperlich *adj.* prudish; *weichlich:* soft, F sissy; **nicht gerade ~ behandeln** *etc.:* none too gently

Zimt *m* cinnamon

Zink *chem. n* zinc

Zinke *f* tooth; *Gabel:* prong

Zinn *n chem.* tin; *legiertes:* pewter (a. **~geschirr**)

Zins *econ. m* interest (a. **~en** *pl.*); **3% ~en bringen** bear* interest at 3%; **2los** *adj.* interest-free; **~satz** *m* interest rate

Zipfel *m Tuch etc.:* corner; *Mütze:* point; *Hemd:* tail; *Wurst:* end; **~mütze** *f* pointed cap

zirka *adv.* about, approximately

Zirkel *m math.* compasses *pl.*, dividers *pl.*; *Kreis:* circle (a. *fig.*)

zirkulieren *v/i.* circulate

Zirkus *m* circus

zirpen *v/i.* chirp

zischen *v/i. u. v/t.* hiss; *Fett etc.:* sizzle; *fig. durch die Luft etc.:* whiz(z)

ziselieren *v/t.* chase

Zit|at *n* quotation, F quote; **2ieren** *v/t.* quote, cite; *vorladen:* summon, cite

Zitrone *f* lemon; **~nlimonade** *f* (fizzy) lemonade, *Am.* lemon soda *od.* pop; **~nsaft** *m* lemon juice; **~npresse** *f* lemon squeezer; **~nschale** *f* lemon peel

zitt|erig *adj.* shaky; **~ern** *v/i.* tremble, shake* (*beide:* **vor** with)

zivil *adj.* civil, civilian; *Preis:* reasonable

Zivil *n* civilian clothes *pl.*; **Polizist in ~**

Z

plainclothes policeman; **~bevölkerung** f civilians pl.; **~dienst** m → **Ersatzdienst**; **~isation** f civilization; **2isieren** v/t. civilize; **~ist** m civilian; **~recht** jur. n civil law; **~schutz** m civil defen|ce, Am. -se

Znüni m, n Schweiz: mid-morning snack, tea (od. coffee) break

zögern v/i. hesitate

Zögern n hesitation

Zoll m Behörde: customs sg.; Abgabe: duty; Maß: inch; **~abfertigung** f customs clearance; **~beamter** m customs officer; **~erklärung** f customs declaration; **~frei** adj. duty-free; **~kontrolle** f customs examination; **2pflichtig** adj. liable to duty; **~stock** m (folding) rule

Zone f zone

Zoo m zoo; **~handlung** f pet shop

Zoologe m zoologist; **~ie** f zoology; **2isch** adj. zoological

Zopf m plait; bsd. Kind: pigtail

Zorn m anger; **2ig** adj. angry

Zote f filthy joke, obscenity

zott(el)ig adj. shaggy

z.T. Abk. für **zum Teil** partly

zu prp. Richtung: to, toward(s); Ort, Zeit: at, Zweck, Anlaß: for; ~ **Fuß** (Pferd) on foot (horseback); ~ **Hause** (Ostern etc.) at home (Easter etc.); ~ **Weihnachten** schenken etc.: for Christmas; **Tür** (Schlüssel) ~ ...door (key) to ...; ~ **m-r Überraschung** to my surprise; **wir sind** ~ **dritt** there are three of us; ~ **zweien** two by two; ~ **e-r Mark** at od. for one mark; Sport: **1** ~ **1** one all; **2** ~ **1 gewinnen** win* two one, win by two goals etc. to one; → **zum, zur**; **2.** adv. too; F geschlossen: closed, shut; **ein** ~ **großes Risiko** too much of a risk; **3.** cj. to; **es ist** ~ **erwarten** it is to be expected

Zubehör n accessories pl.

zubereit|en v/t. prepare; **2ung** f preparation

zu|binden v/t. tie (up); **~bleiben** v/i. stay shut; **~blinzeln** v/i. wink at; **~bringen** v/t. spend*; **2bringer** mot. m, **2bringerstraße** f feeder (road), access road

Zucht f zo. breeding; bot. cultivation; Rasse: breed

züchten v/t. zo. breed*; bot. grow*,

cultivate; **2er** m breeder; grower

Zucht|haus n prison, Am. a. penitentiary; Strafe: imprisonment, confinement; **~perle** f culture(d) pearl

zucken v/i. jerk; krampfhaft: twitch (**mit et.** s.th.); vor Schmerz: wince; Blitz: flash

zücken v/t. Waffe: draw*; F fig. pull out

Zucker m sugar; **~dose** f sugar bowl; **~guß** m icing, frosting; **2krank** adj., **~kranke(r)** diabetic; **~krankheit** f diabetes; **~mais** m sweet corn; **2n** v/t. sugar; **~rohr** bot. n sugarcane; **~rübe** bot. f sugar beet; **2süß** adj. (as) sweet as sugar; **~wasser** n sugared water; **~watte** f candy floss; **~zange** f sugar tongs pl.

zuckrig adj. sugary

Zuckung f twitch(ing); Tick: tic; Krampf: convulsion, spasm

zudecken v/t. cover (up)

zudem adv. besides, moreover

zu|drehen v/t. turn off; **j-m den Rücken** ~ turn one's back on s.o.; **~dringlich** adj.: ~ **werden** F get* fresh (**zu** with); **~drücken** v/t. close, push s.th. shut; → **Auge**

zuerst adv. first; anfangs: at first; zunächst: first (of all), to begin with

zufahr|en v/i. drive* on; ~ **auf** drive* toward(s), head for; **2t** f approach; zum Haus: drive(way); **2tsstraße** f access road

Zufall m chance; **durch** ~ by chance, by accident; **zufallen** v/i. Tür etc.: slam (shut); j-m: fall* to; **mir fallen die Augen zu** I can't keep my eyes open

zufällig 1. adj. accidental; attr. a. chance; Begegnung: by accident, by chance; ~ **et. tun** happen to do s.th.

Zuflucht f: ~ **suchen** (**finden**) look for (find*) refuge od. shelter (**vor** from; **bei** with); (**s-e**) ~ **nehmen zu** resort to

zufolge prp. according to

zufrieden adj. content(ed), satisfied; **~geben** v/refl.: **sich** ~ **mit** content o.s. with; **2heit** f contentment, satisfaction; **~lassen** v/t. leave* s.o. alone; **~stellen** v/t. satisfy; **~stellend** adj. satisfactory

zu|frieren v/i. freeze* up od. over; **~fügen** v/t. do*, cause; **j-m Schaden** ~ a. harm s.o.; **2fuhr** f supply

Zug m rail. train; Menschen, Wagen etc.: procession, line; Fest2: parade; Gesichts2: feature; Charakter2: trait; Hang: tendency; Schach etc.: move (a. fig.); Schwimm2: stroke; Ziehen: pull (a. tech. Griff etc.); phys. a. tension; Rauchen: a. puff; Schluck: a. draught, Am. draft; Luft: draught, Am. draft; Schule: stream; im ~e gen. in the course of; in e-m ~ at one go; ~ um ~ step by step; in groben Zügen in broad outlines

Zu|gabe f addition; thea. encore; ~gang m access (a. fig.); 2gänglich adj. accessible (für to) (a. fig.)

Zugbrücke f drawbridge

zugeben v/t. add; fig. admit

zugehen v/i. Tür etc.: close, shut*; geschehen: happen; ~ auf walk up to, approach (a. fig.); es geht auf 8 zu it's getting on for 8; es ging lustig zu we had a lot of fun

Zugehörigkeit f membership

Zügel m rein (a. fig.); 2n 1. v/t. fig. curb, control, bridle; 2. v/i. Schweiz: move

Zuge|ständnis n concession; 2stehen v/t. concede, grant

zugetan adj. attached (dat. to)

Zugführer rail. m guard, Am. conductor

zug|ig adj. draughty, Am. drafty; 2kraft f tech. traction; fig. attraction, draw, appeal; ~kräftig adj.: ~ sein be* a draw

zugleich adv. at the same time

Zug|luft f draught, Am. draft; ~maschine f tractor

zugreifen v/i. grab (at) it; fig. grab the opportunity; greifen Sie zu! bei Tisch: help yourself!; Werbung: buy now!; mit ~ lend a hand; F chip in

Zugriffszeit f Computer: access time

Zugriffscode m Computer: access code

zugrunde adv.: ~ gehen (an) perish (of); e-r Sache et. ~ legen base s.th. on s.th.; ~ richten ruin

Zu|gunsten prp. in favo(u)r of; ~gute adv.: j-m et. ~ halten give* s.o. credit for s.th.; make* allowances for s.o.'s ...; j-m ~ kommen be* for the benefit of s.o.

Zugvogel m bird of passage

zu|halten v/t. keep* shut; sich die Ohren (Augen) ~ cover one's ears (eyes) with one's hands; sich die Nase ~ hold* one's nose; 2hälter m pimp

Zuhause n home

zuhör|en v/i. listen (dat. to s.o. od. s.th.); ~er(in) listener; die ~ pl. a. the audience sg., pl.

zu|jubeln v/i. cheer; ~kleben v/t. Umschlag: seal; ~knallen v/t. slam (shut); ~knöpfen v/t. button (up); ~kommen v/i.: ~ auf come* up to; fig. be* ahead of; die Dinge auf sich ~ lassen wait and see*

Zu|kunft f future (a. gr.); 2künftig 1. adj. future; 2. adv. in future; ~kunftsforschung f futurology

zu|lächeln v/i. smile at; ~lage f bonus; ~lassen v/t. keep* s.th. closed; erlauben: allow; beruflich, mot.: licen|se, Brt. a. -ce, register; j-n zu et. ~ admit s.o. to s.th.; ~lässig adj. admissible (a. jur.); ~ sein be* allowed; 2lassung f admission; mot. etc.: licen|ce, Am. -se

zulegen v/t. add; F: sich ~ get* o.s. s.th.; Namen: adopt

zu|letzt adv. in the end; kommen etc.: last; schließlich: finally; wann hast du ihn ~ gesehen? when did you last see him?; ~liebe adv.: j-m ~ for s.o.'s sake

zum prp. zu dem: → zu; ~ ersten Mal for the first time; et. ~ Kaffee s.th. with one's coffee; ~ Schwimmen etc. gehen go* swimming etc.

zumachen 1. v/t. close, shut*; zuknöpfen: button (up); 2. v/i. Geschäft: close; für immer: close down

zumal cj. especially since

zumauern v/t. brick od. wall up

zumut|bar adj. reasonable; ~e adv.: mir ist ... ~ I feel ...; ~en v/t.: j-m et. ~ expect s.th. of s.o.; sich zuviel ~ overtax o.s.; 2ung f: das ist e-e ~ that's asking od. expecting a bit much

zunächst adv. → zuerst

zu|nageln v/t. nail up; ~nähen v/t. sew* up; 2nahme f increase; 2name m surname

zünd|en v/i. kindle; electr., mot. ignite, fire; ~end fig. adj. stirring; 2er m mil. fuse; pl. östr. matches pl.; ~holz n match; 2kerze mot. f spark plug; 2schlüssel mot. m ignition key; 2schnur f fuse; 2ung f ignition

Z

zunehmen v/i. increase (**an** in); *Person:* put* on weight; *Mond:* wax; *Tage:* grow* longer

zuneig|en v/refl.: *sich dem Ende* ~ draw* to a close; **2ung** f affection

Zunft hist. f guild

Zunge f tongue; *es liegt mir auf der* ~ it's on the tip of my tongue

züngeln v/i. *Flamme:* lick, flicker

Zungen|brecher m tongue twister; **~spitze** f tip of the tongue

zunicken v/i. nod at

zunutze adv.: *sich et.* ~ *machen* make* (good) use of s.th.; *ausnutzen:* take* advantage of s.th.

zupfen v/t. u. v/i. pull (**an** at), pick, pluck (at) (a. mus.)

zur prp. zu der: → **zu**; ~ *Schule (Kirche) gehen* go* to school (church); ~ *Hälfte* half (of it od. them); ~ *Belohnung etc.* as a reward etc.

zurechnungsfähig jur. adj. responsible; **2keit** f jur. f responsibility

zurecht|finden v/refl. find* one's way; *fig.* cope, manage; **~kommen** v/i. get* along (**mit** with); *bsd. mit et.:* a. cope (with); **~legen** v/t. arrange; *fig. sich et.* ~ think* s.th. out; *nicht mithalten:* fall* behind (a. schulisch etc.); **~blik-ken** v/i. look back (**auf** at; *fig.* on); **~bringen** v/t. bring* od. take* back, return; **~datieren** v/t. backdate (**auf** to); **~fallen** *fig.* v/i. fall* behind; *Sport:* a. drop back; **~finden** v/i. find* one's way back (**nach**, **zu** to); *fig.* return (to); **~fordern** v/t. reclaim; **~füh-ren** v/t. lead* back; ~ *auf* attribute to; **~geben** v/t. give* back, return; **~ge-blieben** *fig.* adj. backward; *geistig:* retarded; **~gehen** v/i. go* back, return;

fig. decrease; *fallen:* a. go* down, drop; **~gezogen** adj. secluded; **~greifen** *fig.* v/i.: ~ *auf* fall* back (up)on; **~hal-ten 1.** v/t. hold* back; **2.** v/refl. control o.s.; *im Essen, Reden etc.:* be* careful; **~haltend** adj. reserved; **2haltung** f reserve; **~kehren** v/i. return; **~kom-men** v/i. come* back, return (*beide fig. auf* to); **~lassen** v/t. leave* (behind); **~legen** v/t. put* back; *Geld:* put* aside, save; *Strecke:* cover, do*; **~nehmen** v/t. take* back (a. fig. *Wor-te etc.*); **~rufen 1.** v/t. call back (a. *teleph.*); *Autos in die Werkstatt etc.:* recall; *ins Gedächtnis* ~ recall; **2.** v/i. *tel.* call back; **~schlagen 1.** v/t. *An-griff etc.:* beat* off; *Tennisball:* return; *Decke, Verdeck etc.:* fold back; **2.** v/i. hit* back; *fig., mil.* retaliate; **~schrek-ken** v/i.: ~ *vor* shrink* from; *vor nichts* ~ stop at nothing; **~setzen** v/t. Auto: back (up); *fig. j-n:* neglect; **~stehen** *fig.* v/i. stand* aside; **~stellen** v/t. put* back (a. *Uhr*); *fig.* put* aside; *mil.* defer; **~strahlen** v/t. reflect; **~treten** v/i. step od. stand* back; resign (*von e-m Amt* [*Posten*] one's office [post]); *econ., jur.* withdraw* (*von* from); **~weichen** v/i. fall* back (a. mil.); **~weisen** v/t. turn down; *jur.* dismiss; **~zahlen** v/t. pay* back (a. fig.); **~ziehen** v/t. draw* back; *fig.* withdraw*; *sich* ~ retire, withdraw* (a. mil.); *mil.* a. retreat

Zuruf m shout; **2en** v/t.: *j-m et.* ~ shout s.th. to s.o.

Zusage f promise, *Einwilligung:* assent; **2n** v/i. u. v/t. accept (an invitation); *einwilligen:* agree; *passen:* suit; *gefal-len:* appeal to; *s-e Hilfe* ~ promise to help

zusammen adv. together; *alles* ~ (all) in all; *das macht* ~ ... that makes ... altogether; **2arbeit** f cooperation; *in* ~ *mit* in collaboration with; **~arbeiten** v/i. cooperate, collaborate; **~beißen** v/t.: *die Zähne* ~ clench one's teeth; **~brechen** v/i. break* down, collapse (*beide a. fig.*); **2bruch** m breakdown, collapse; **~fallen** v/i. collapse; *zeitlich:* coincide; **~falten** v/t. fold up; **~fas-sen** v/t. summarize, sum up; **2fas-sung** f summary; **~fügen** v/t. join (together); **~gesetzt** adj. compound; **~halten** v/i. u. v/t. hold* together (a.

fig.); F *fig.* stick* together; **Ձhang** *m* *Beziehung*: connection; *e-s Textes etc.*: context; **im ~ stehen** (*mit*) be* connected (with); **~hängen** *v/i.* be* connected; **~hängend** *adj.* coherent; **~hang(s)los** *adj.* incoherent, disconnected; **~klappen** *v/i. u. v/t. tech.* fold up; F *fig.* break* down; **~kommen** *v/i.* meet*; **Ձkunft** *f* meeting; **~legen 1.** *v/t. vereinigen:* combine; *falten:* fold up; **2.** *v/i. Geld:* club together; **~nehmen** *fig. v/t. Mut, Kraft:* muster (up); *sich* ~ pull o.s. together; **~packen** *v/t.* pack up; **~passen** *v/i. allg.* harmonize; *Dinge, Farben: a.* match; **~rechnen** *v/t.* add up; **~reißen** F *v/refl.* pull o.s. together; **~rollen** *v/t.* roll up; *sich* ~ coil up; **~rotten** *v/refl.* band together; **~rücken 1.** *v/t.* move closer together; **2.** *v/i.* move up; **~schlagen** *v/t. Hände:* clap; *Hacken:* click; *j-n:* beat* up; *et.:* smash (up); **~schließen** *v/refl.* join, unite; **Ձschluß** *m* union; **~schreiben** *v/t.* write* in one word; **~schrumpfen** *v/i.* shrivel (up), shrink*; **~setzen** *v/t. tech.* put* together; *tech.* assemble; *sich* ~ *aus* consist of, be* composed of; **Ձsetzung** *f* composition; *chem., ling.* compound; *tech.* assembly; **~stellen** *v/t.* put* together; *anordnen:* arrange; **Ձstoß** *m* collision (*a. fig.*), crash; *Aufprall:* impact; *fig.* clash; **~stoßen** *v/i.* collide (*a.fig.*); *fig.* clash; ~ *mit* run* *od.* bump into; *fig.* have* a clash with; **~stürzen** *v/i.* collapse, fall* in; **~tragen** *v/t.* collect; **~treffen** *v/i.* meet*; *zeitlich:* coincide; **Ձtreffen** *n* meeting; coincidence; *besonderes:* encounter; **~treten** *v/i.* meet*; **~tun** *v/refl.* join (forces), F team up; **~wirken** *v/i.* combine; **Ձwirken** *n* combination; **~zählen** *v/t.* add up; **~ziehen** *v/t. u. v/refl.* contract; **~zuk-ken** *v/i.* wince, flinch

Zusatz *m* addition; *chemischer etc.:* additive; **~... in Zssgn** *mst* additional ..., supplementary ...; *Hilfs...:* auxiliary ...

zusätzlich *adj.* additional, extra

zuschau|en *v/i.* look on (**bei et.** at s.th.); *j-m* ~ watch s.o. (**bei** doing s.th.); **Ձer(in)** spectator; *TV* viewer; **die ~** *pl. a.* the audience *sg., pl.;* **Ձerraum** *m* auditorium

Zuschlag *m* extra charge; *rail. etc.:* ex-

cess fare; *Gehalts* Ձ: bonus; *Auktion:* knocking down; **Ձen** *v/i. u. v/t. Tür etc.:* slam *od.* bang shut; *Boxer etc.:* hit*, strike* (a blow); *fig.* act; *j-m et.* ~ knock s.th. down to s.o.

zu|schließen *v/t.* lock (up); **~schnal-len** *v/t.* buckle (up); **~schnappen** *v/i. Hund:* snap; *Tür etc.:* snap shut; **~schneiden** *v/t. Kleid etc.:* cut* out; *Holz etc.:* cut* (to size); **~schnüren** *v/t.* tie (*Schuh a.* lace) up; **~schrauben** *v/t.* screw shut; **~schreiben** *v/t.* ascribe *od.* attribute (*dat.* to); **Ձschrift** *f* letter

zuschulden *adv.:* *sich et.* (*nichts*) ~ *kommen lassen* do* s.th. (nothing) wrong

Zu|schuß *m* allowance; *staatlich:* subsidy; **Ձschütten** *v/t.* fill up; F add; **Ձsehen** *v/i.* ~ *zuschauen*; **~daß** see* (to it) that, take* care to *inf.*; **Ձsehends** *adv.* noticeably; *schnell:* rapidly; **Ձsetzen 1.** *v/t.* add; *Geld:* lose*; **2.** *v/i.* lose* money; *j-m* ~ press s.o. (hard)

zusicher|n *v/t.,* **Ձung** *f* promise

zu|spielen *v/t. Ball:* pass; **~spitzen** *v/t.* point; *sich* ~ become* critical; **Ձspruch** *m* encouragement; *Trost:* words *pl.* of comfort; **Ձstand** *m* condition, state, form

zustande *adv.:* ~ *bringen* bring* about, manage (to do); ~ *kommen* come* about; *es kam nicht* ~ it didn't come off

zuständig *adj.* responsible (*für* for), in charge (of)

zustehen *v/i.: j-m steht es* (*zu tun*) *zu* s.o. is entitled to (do) s.th.

zustell|en *v/t.* deliver; **Ձung** *f* delivery

zustimm|en *v/i.* agree (*dat.* to s.th.; *with s.o.*); **Ձung** *f* approval, consent; (*j-s*) ~ *finden* meet* with (s.o.'s) approval

zustoßen *v/i.: j-m* ~ happen to s.o.

zutage *adv.:* ~ *bringen* (*kommen*) bring* (come*) to light

Zutaten *pl.* ingredients *pl.*

zuteil|en *v/t.* assign, allot; **Ձung** *f* allotment; *Ration:* ration

zutragen *v/t.: j-m et.* ~ inform s.o. of s.th.; *sich* ~ happen

zutrauen *v/t.: j-m et.* ~ credit s.o. with s.th.; *sich zuviel* ~ overrate o.s.

Zutrauen *n* confidence (*zu* in)

Z

zutraulich adj. trusting; Tier: friendly
zutreffen v/i. be* true; ~ auf apply to, go* for; ~d adj. true, correct
zutrinken v/i.: j-m ~ drink* to s.o.
Zutritt m admission; Zugang: access; ~ verboten! no admittance!
zuverlässig adj. reliable, dependable; sicher: safe; 2keit f reliability, dependability
Zuversicht f confidence; 2lich adj. confident, optimistic
zuviel too much; vor pl.: too many; e-r ~ one too many
zuvor adv. before, previously; zunächst: first; ~kommen v/i. anticipate; verhindern: prevent; j-m ~ a. F beat* s.o. to it; ~kommend adj. obliging; höflich: polite
Zuwachs m increase, growth; 2en v/i. become* overgrown; Wunde: close
zu|wege adv.: et. ~ bringen manage to do s.th., succeed in doing s.th.; ~weilen adv. occasionally, now and then; ~weisen v/t. assign
zuwend|en v/t. u. v/refl. turn to (a. fig. e-m Thema etc.); 2ung f payment; fig. attention; Kind etc.: a. (loving) care, love, affection
zuwenig adv. too little; vor pl.: too few
zuwerfen v/t. Tür: slam (shut); j-m et.: throw* s.o. s.th.; j-m e-n Blick ~ cast* a glance at s.o.
zuwider adj.: ... ist mir ~ I hate od. detest ...; ~handeln v/i. act contrary to; Vorschriften etc.: violate
zu|winken v/i. wave to; signal to; ~zahlen v/t. pay* extra; ~ziehen 1. v/t. Vorhänge: draw*; Schlinge etc.: pull tight; Arzt etc.: consult; sich ~ med. catch*; 2. v/i. move in; ~züglich prp. plus
Zvieri m, n Schweiz: afternoon snack, tea od. coffee break
Zwang m compulsion (a. innerer), constraint (a. moralischer); sozialer: restraint; Nötigung, Unterdrückung: coercion; Gewalt: force; ~ sein be* compulsory
zwängen v/t. press, squeeze, force
zwanglos adj. informal; bsd. Kleidung: a. casual; 2igkeit f informality
Zwangs|arbeit jur. f hard labo(u)r; 2ernähren v/t. force-feed*; ~herrschaft f despotism, tyranny; ~jacke f

straitjacket (a. fig.); ~lage f predicament; 2läufig adv. inevitably; ~maßnahme f sanction; ~vollstreckung jur. f compulsory execution; ~vorstellung psych. f obsession; 2weise adv. by force
zwanzig adj. twenty; ~ste adj. twentieth
zwar adv.: ich kenne ihn ~, aber ... I do know him, but ..., I (know him all right, but ...; und ~ that is (to say), namely
Zweck m purpose, aim; s-n ~ erfüllen serve its purpose; es hat keinen ~ (zu warten etc.) it's no use (waiting etc.); 2los adj. useless; 2mäßig adj. practical; angebracht: wise; tech., arch. functional; ~mäßigkeit f practicality, functionality; 2s prp. for the purpose of
zwei adj. two; ~beinig adj. two-legged; 2bettzimmer n twin-bedded room; 2deutig adj. ambiguous; Witz: off-colo(u)r; 2er m Rudern: (mit coxed) pair; ~erlei adj. two kinds of; ~fach adj. double, twofold; 2familienhaus n two-family-house, Am. duplex (house)
Zweifel m doubt; 2haft adj. doubtful, dubious; 2los adv. undoubtedly, no od. without doubt; 2n v/i.: ~ an doubt s.th., have* one's doubts about
Zweig m branch (a. fig.); kleiner: twig; ~geschäft n, ~niederlassung f, ~stelle f branch
zwei|jährig adj. two-year-old, of two (years); 2kampf m duel; ~mal adv. twice; ~malig adj. (twice) repeated; ~motorig adj. twin-engined; ~reihig adj. Anzug: double-breasted; ~schneidig adj. double-edged. two-edged (beide a. fig.); ~seitig adj. two-sided; Vertrag etc.: bilateral; Stoff: reversible; beschriebene Diskette: double-sided; 2sitzer bsd. mot. m two-seater; ~sprachig adj. bilingual; ~stimmig adj. for two voices; ~stöckig adj. two-stor(e)yed, Am. -ied; ~stufig tech. adj. two-stage; ~stündig adj. two-hour
zweit adj. second; ein ~er another; jede(r, -s) ~e ... every other ...; aus ~er Hand second-hand; wir sind zu ~ there are two of us
zweitbeste adj. second-best
zweiteilig adj. Anzug etc.: two-piece

zweit|ens *adv.* secondly; **~klassig** *adj.*, **~rangig** *adj.* second-class *od.* -rate

Zwerchfell *anat. n* diaphragm

Zwerg *m* dwarf; *myth. a.* gnome (*a. Figur*); *Mensch*: midget; **~...** *in Zssgn bot.* dwarf ...; *zo.* pygmy ...

Zwetsch(g)e *f* plum

Zwick|el *m* gusset; **2en** *v/t. u. v/i.* pinch, nip; **~mühle** *fig. f* fix

Zwieback *m* rusk, *Am. a.* zwieback

Zwiebel *f* onion; *Blumen2*: bulb

Zwie|gespräch *n* dialog(ue); **2licht** *n* twilight; **~spalt** *m* conflict; **2spältig** *adj.* conflicting; **~tracht** *f* discord

Zwilling *m* twin; *pl. astr.* Gemini *pl.*; **er ist (ein) ~** he's a (a) Gemini; **~sbruder** *m* twin brother; **~sschwester** *f* twin sister

Zwinge *tech. f* clamp, vi|ce, *Am.* -se

zwingen *v/t.* force; **2d** *adj.* cogent, compelling

Zwinger *m Hunde2*: kennels *sg.*

zwinkern *v/i.* wink, blink

Zwirn *m* thread, yarn, twist

zwischen *prp.* between; *unter*: among; **2deck** *naut. n* 'tween deck; **~durch** F *adv.* in between; **2ergebnis** *n* intermediate result; **2fall** *m* incident; **2händler** *econ. m* middleman; **2landung**

aviat. f stopover; (*Flug*) **ohne ~** nonstop (flight); **~menschlich** *adj.* interpersonal, interhuman; **2pause** *f* break, intermission; **2raum** *m* space, interval; **2ruf** *m* (loud) interruption; **~e** *pl.* heckling *sg.*; **2rufer** *m* heckler; **2spiel** *n* interlude; **2station** *f* stop(over); **~ machen (in)** stop over (in); **2stecker** *electr. m* adapter; **2stück** *n* connection; **2stufe** *f* intermediate stage; **2wand** *f* partition (wall); **2zeit** *f*: **in der ~** in the meantime, meanwhile

Zwist *m*, **~igkeiten** *pl.* discord *sg.*

zwitschern *v/i.* twitter, chirp

Zwitter *biol. m* hermaphrodite

zwölf *adj.* twelve; **um ~** (*Uhr*) at twelve (o'clock); *mittags: a.* at noon; *nachts: a.* at midnight; **~te** *adj.* twelfth

Zyankali *n* potassium cyanide

Zyklus *m* cycle; *Reihe*: series, course

Zylind|er *m* top hat; *math., tech.* cylinder; **2risch** *adj.* cylindrical

Zyni|ker *m* cynic; **2sch** *adj.* cynical; **~smus** *m* cynicism

Zypresse *bot. f* cypress

Zyste *med. f* cyst

z.Z(t). *Abk. für* **zur Zeit** at the moment, at present

Z

Unregelmäßige Verben

Die an erster Stelle stehende Form bezeichnet das Präsens (present tense), nach dem ersten Gedankenstrich steht das Präteritum (past tense), nach dem zweiten das Partizip Perfekt (past participle).

alight – alighted, alit – alighted, alit
arise – arose – arisen
awake – awoke, awaked – awoke, awaked, awoken
be (am, is, are) – was (were) – been
bear – bore – borne *getragen*, born *geboren*
beat – beat – beaten, beat
become – became – become
beget – begot – begotten
begin – began – begun
bend – bent – bent
bereave – bereaved, bereft – bereaved, bereft
beseech – besought, beseeched – besought, beseeched
bet – bet, betted – bet, betted
bid – bade, bid – bidden, bid, *a.* bade
bind – bound – bound
bite – bit – bitten
bleed – bled – bled
bless – blessed, *a.* blest – blessed, *a.* blest
blow – blew – blown
break – broke – broken
breed – bred – bred
bring – brought – brought
broadcast – broadcast(ed) – broadcast(ed)
build – built – built
burn – burnt, burned – burnt, burned
burst – burst – burst
bust – bust(ed) – bust(ed)
buy – bought – bought
can – could
cast – cast – cast
catch – caught – caught
choose – chose – chosen
cleave – cleft, cleaved, clove – cleft, cleaved, cloven
cling – clung – clung
clothe – clothed, clad – clothed, clad
come – came – come
cost – cost – cost
creep – crept – crept
crow – crowed, crew – crowed
cut – cut – cut

deal – dealt – dealt
dig – dug – dug
do – did – done
draw – drew – drawn
dream – dreamt, dreamed – dreamt, [dreamed}
drink – drank – drunk
drive – drove – driven
dwell – dwelt, dwelled – dwelt, dwelled
eat – ate – eaten
fall – fell – fallen
feed – fed – fed
feel – felt – felt
fight – fought – fought
find – found – found
flee – fled – fled
fling – flung – flung
fly – flew – flown
forbid – forbad(e) – forbid(den)
forecast – forecast(ed) – forecast(ed)
forget – forgot – forgotten
forsake – forsook – forsaken
freeze – froze – frozen
geld – gelded, gelt – gelded, gelt
get – got – got, *Am. a.* gotten
give – gave – given
gnaw – gnawed – gnawed, gnawn
go – went – gone
grind – ground – ground
grip – gripped, *Am. a.* gript – gripped, *Am. a.* gript
grow – grew – grown
hang – hung – hung
have (has) – had – had
hear – heard – heard
heave – heaved, *bsd. naut.* hove – heaved, *bsd. naut.* hove
hew – hewed – hewed, hewn
hide – hid – hidden, hid
hit – hit – hit
hold – held – held
hurt – hurt – hurt
keep – kept – kept
kneel – knelt, kneeled – knelt, kneeled
knit – knitted, knit – knitted, knit
know – knew – known
lay – laid – laid
lead – led – led

lean – leaned, *bsd. Br.* leant – leaned, *bsd. Br.* leant
leap – leaped, leapt – leaped, leapt
learn – learned, learnt – learned, learnt
leave – left – left
lend – lent – lent
let – let – let
lie – lay – lain
light – lighted, lit – lighted, lit
lose – lost – lost
make – made – made
may – might
mean – meant – meant
meet – met – met
melt – melted – melted, molten
mow – mowed – mowed, mown
pay – paid – paid
pen – penned, pent – penned, pent
plead – pleaded, *bsd. schott. u. Am.* pled – pleaded, *bsd. schott. u. Am.* pled
prove – proved – proved, *a.* proven
put – put – put
quit – quit(ted) – quit(ted)
read – read – read
rid – rid, *a.* ridded – rid, *a.* ridded
ride – rode – ridden
ring – rang – rung
rise – rose – risen
run – ran – run
saw – sawed – sawn, sawed
say – said – said
see – saw – seen
seek – sought – sought
sell – sold – sold
send – sent – sent
set – set – set
sew – sewed – sewed, sewn
shake – shook – shaken
shall – should
shear – sheared – sheared, shorn
shed – shed – shed
shine – shone – shone
shit – shit(ted), shat – shit(ted), shat
shoe – shod, *a.* shoed – shod, *a.* shoed
shoot – shot – shot
show – showed – shown, showed
shred – shredded, *a.* shred – shredded, *a.* shred
shrink – shrank, shrunk – shrunk
shut – shut – shut
sing – sang – sung
sink – sank, sunk – sunk
sit – sat – sat
slay – slew – slain

sleep – slept – slept
slide – slid – slid
sling – slung – slung
slink – slunk – slunk
slit – slit – slit
smell – smelt, smelled – smelt, smelled
smite – smote – smitten
sow – sowed – sown, sowed
speak – spoke – spoken
speed – sped, speeded – sped, speeded
spell – spelt, spelled – spelt, spelled
spend – spent – spent
spill – spilt, spilled – spilt, spilled
spin – spun – spun
spit – spat – spat
split – split – split
spoil – spoiled, spoilt – spoiled, spoilt
spread – spread – spread
spring – sprang, *Am. a.* sprung – sprung
stand – stood – stood
steal – stole – stolen
stick – stuck – stuck
sting – stung – stung
stink – stank, stunk – stunk
stride – strode – stridden
strike – struck – struck
string – strung – strung
swear – swore – sworn
sweat – sweated, *Am. a.* sweat – sweated, *Am. a.* sweat
sweep – swept – swept
swell – swelled – swollen, swelled
swim – swam – swum
swing – swung – swung
take – took – taken
teach – taught – taught
tear – tore – torn
telecast – telecast(ed) – telecast(ed)
tell – told – told
think – thought – thought
thrive – thrived, throve – thrived
throw – threw – thrown
thrust – thrust – thrust
tread – trod – trodden
wake – woke, waked – waked, woken
wear – wore – worn
weave – wove, weaved – woven, weaved
wed – wed(ded) – wed(ded)
weep – wept – wept
wet – wetted, wet – wetted, wet
win – won – won
wind – wound – wound
wring – wrung – wrung
write – wrote – written

Zahlwörter
Grundzahlen

0 zero, nought [nɔːt]	**18** eighteen *achtzehn*
1 one *eins*	**19** nineteen *neunzehn*
2 two *zwei*	**20** twenty *zwanzig*
3 three *drei*	**21** twenty-one *einundzwanzig*
4 four *vier*	**22** twenty-two *zweiundzwanzig* etc.
5 five *fünf*	**100** a od. one hundred *(ein)hundert*
6 six *sechs*	**200** two hundred *zweihundert*
7 seven *sieben*	**572** five hundred and seventy-two
8 eight *acht*	*fünfhundert(und)zweiundsiebzig*
9 nine *neun*	**1000** a od. one thousand *(ein)tausend*
10 ten *zehn*	**1998** nineteen (hundred and) ninety-
11 eleven *elf*	-eight *neunzehnhundertachtund-*
12 twelve *zwölf*	*neunzig*
13 thirteen *dreizehn*	**2000** two thousand *zweitausend*
14 fourteen *vierzehn*	**5044** *tel.* five 0 [əʊ] (*Am. a.* zero) dou-
15 fifteen *fünfzehn*	ble four *fünfzig vierundvierzig*
16 sixteen *sechzehn*	**1,000,000** one million *eine Million*
17 seventeen *siebzehn*	**2,000,000** two million *zwei Millionen*

Ordnungszahlen

1st first *erste*	**13th** thirteenth *dreizehnte*
2nd second *zweite*	**14th** fourteenth *vierzehnte*
3rd third *dritte*	**15th** fifteenth *fünfzehnte*
4th fourth *vierte*	**16th** sixteenth *sechzehnte*
5th fifth *fünfte*	**17th** seventeenth *siebzehnte*
6th sixth *sechste*	**18th** eighteenth *achtzehnte*
7th seventh *siebente*	**19th** nineteenth *neunzehnte*
8th eighth *achte*	**20th** twentieth *zwanzigste*
9th ninth *neunte*	**21st** twenty-first *einundzwanzigste*
10th tenth *zehnte*	**22nd** twenty-second *zweiundzwanzigste*
11th eleventh *elfte*	**23rd** twenty-third *dreiundzwanzigste*
12th twelfth *zwölfte*	**100th** (one) hundredth *hundertste* etc.

Bruchzahlen und andere Zahlenwerte

$^1/_2$ one *od.* a half *ein halb*	$^5/_8$ five eighths *fünf Achtel*
$1^1/_2$ one and a half *anderthalb*	0.45 (nought [nɔːt]) point four five *null*
$^1/_3$ one *od.* a third *ein Drittel*	*Komma vier fünf*
$^2/_3$ two thirds *zwei Drittel*	2.5 two point five *zwei Komma fünf*
$^1/_4$ one *od.* a quarter, one *od.* a fourth	once *einmal* – twice *zweimal*
ein Viertel	three (four) times *drei-(vier)mal*
$^3/_4$ three quarters, three fourths	2 x 3 = 6 twice three is six *zweimal drei*
drei Viertel	*ist sechs*

Maße und Gewichte

1. Längenmaße

1 inch (in)
= 2,54 cm

1 foot (ft)
= 12 inches = 30,48 cm

1 yard (yd)
= 3 feet = 91,44 cm

2. Wege- und Vermessungsmaße

1 link (li, l)
= 7.92 inches = 20,12 cm

1 rod (rd), pole *od.* **perch (p)**
= 25 links = 5,03 m

1 chain (ch)
= 4 rods = 20,12 m

1 furlong (fur)
= 10 chains = 201,17 m

1 (statute) mile (ml, *Am.* **mi)**
= 8 furlongs = 1609,34 m

3. Nautische Maße

1 fathom (fm)
= 6 feet = 1,83 m

1 cable('s) length
= 100 fathoms = 183 m
naut., mil. Brt. = 608 feet
= 185,3 m
naut., mil. Am. = 720 feet
= 219,5 m

1 nautical mile (n m)
international = 6076.1 feet
= 1,852 km
naut. Brt. = 10 cable('s) lengths
= 1,853 km

4. Flächenmaße

1 square inch (sq in)
= 6,45 cm²

1 square foot (sq ft)
= 144 square inches
= 929,03 cm²

1 square yard (sq yd)
= 9 square feet = 0,836 m²

1 square rod (sq rd)
= 30.25 square yards = 25,29 m²

1 rood (ro)
= 40 square rods = 10,12 a

1 acre (a)
= 4 roods = 40,47 a

1 square mile (sq ml, *Am.* **sq mi)**
= 640 acres = 2,59 km²

5. Raummaße

1 cubic inch (cu in)
= 16,387 cm³

1 cubic foot (cu ft)
= 1728 cubic inches
= 0,028 m³

1 cubic yard (cu yd)
= 27 cubic feet = 0,765 m³

1 register ton (reg tn)
= 100 cubic feet = 2,832 m³

6. Britische Hohlmaße

Trocken- und Flüssigkeitsmaße

1 imperial gill (gi, gl)
= 0,142 l

1 imperial pint (pt)
= 4 gills = 0,568 l

1 imperial quart (qt)
= 2 imperial pints = 1,136 l

1 imperial gallon (imp gal)
= 4 imperial quarts = 4,546 l

Trockenmaße

1 imperial peck (pk)
= 2 imperial gallons = 9,092 l

1 imperial bushel (bu, bsh)
= 4 imperial pecks = 36,36 l

1 imperial quarter (qr)
= 8 imperial bushels = 290,94 l

Flüssigkeitsmaß

1 imperial barrel (bbl, bl)
= 36 imperial gallons = 1,636 hl

7. Hohlmaße der USA

Trockenmaße

1 US dry pint
= 0,551 l

1 US dry quart
= 2 dry pints = 1,11

1 US peck
= 8 dry quarts = 8,81 l

1 US bushel (*Getreidemaß*)
= 4 pecks = 35,24 l

Flüssigkeitsmaße

1 US liquid gill
= 0,118 l

1 US liquid pint
= 4 gills = 0,473 l

1 US liquid quart
= 2 liquid pints = 0,946 l

1 US gallon
= 4 liquid quarts = 3,785 l

1 US barrel
= 31.5 gallons = 119,2 l

1 US barrel petroleum
= 42 gallons = 158,97 l
(*internationales Standardmaß für Erdöl*)

8. Handelsgewichte

1 grain (gr)
= 0,0648 g

1 dram (dr av)
= 27.34 grains = 1,77 g

1 ounce (oz av)
= 16 drams = 28,35 g

1 pound (lb av)
= 16 ounces = 0,453 kg

1 stone (st)
= 14 pounds = 6,35 kg

1 quarter (qr)
Brt. = 28 pounds = 12,7 kg
Am. = 25 pounds = 11,34 kg

1 hundredweight (cwt)
Brt. = 112 pounds = 50,8 kg
(a. long hundredweight: cwt l)
Am. = 100 pounds = 45,36 kg
(a. short hundredweight: cwt sh)

1 ton (t, tn)
Brt. = 2240 pounds (= 20 cwt l) = 1016 kg (a. long ton: tn l)
Am. = 2000 pounds (= 20 cwt sh) = 907,18 kg (a. short ton: tn sh)

Am 1. Oktober 1995 hat Großbritannien auf das metrische System umgestellt. Das **pint** für Bier und Milch und die Entfernungsangaben in **Meilen** auf den Verkehrsschildern sollen aber, wenigstens vorerst, noch bleiben. Die Angaben für lose und offen gehandelte Lebensmittel sollen erst im Jahre 2000 auf das metrische System umgestellt werden.

Temperaturumrechnung

$$°\text{Fahrenheit} = (\tfrac{9}{5} °C) + 32$$
$$°\text{Celsius} = (°F - 32) \cdot \tfrac{5}{9}$$

Abkürzungen

a.	*also*, auch
Abk.	Abkürzung, *abbreviation*
acc.	*accusative (case)*, Akkusativ
adj.	*adjective*, Adjektiv
adv.	*adverb*, Adverb
agr.	*agriculture*, Landwirtschaft
allg.	allgemein, *commonly*
Am.	*American English*, amerikanisches Englisch
amer.	amerikanisch, *American*
anat.	*anatomy*, Anatomie
arch.	*architecture*, Architektur
art.	*article*, Artikel
astr.	*astrology*, Astrologie
	astronomy, Astronomie
attr.	*attributive*, attributiv
aviat.	*aviation*, Luftfahrt
biol.	*biology*, Biologie
bot.	*botany*, Botanik
brit.	britisch, *British*
Brt.	*British English*, britisches Englisch
bsd.	besonders, *especially*
chem.	*chemistry*, Chemie
cj.	*conjunction*, Konjunktion
coll.	*collectively*, als Sammelwort
comp.	*comparative*, Komparativ
contp.	*contemptuously*, verächtlich
dat.	*dative (case)*, Dativ
dem.	*demonstrative*, hinweisend
econ.	*economics*, Volkswirtschaft
electr.	*electrical engineering*, Elektrotechnik
et., et.	etwas, *something*
etc.	*et cetera, and so on*, und so weiter
euphem.	*euphemistic*, euphemistisch, verhüllend
F	umgangssprachlich, *colloquial*
f	*feminine*, weiblich
fig.	*figuratively*, übertragen
gastr.	*gastronomy*, Kochkunst
gen.	*genitive (case)*, Genitiv
geogr.	*geography*, Geographie
geol.	*geology*, Geologie
geom.	*geometry*, Geometrie
ger.	*gerund*, Gerundium
geschr.	geschrieben, *written*
gr.	*grammar*, Grammatik